The Norton Anthology
of American Literature

SHORTER SEVENTH EDITION

VOLUME 2

1865 to the Present

The Norton Anthology
of American Literature

SHORTER SEVENTH EDITION

Nina Baym, *General Editor*

SWANLUND CHAIR AND CENTER FOR
ADVANCED STUDY PROFESSOR EMERITA OF ENGLISH
JUBILEE PROFESSOR OF LIBERAL ARTS AND SCIENCES
UNIVERSITY OF ILLINOIS AT URBANA-CHAMPAIGN

VOLUME 2

1865 to the Present

W • W • NORTON & COMPANY • *New York* • *London*

W. W. Norton & Company has been independent since its founding in 1923, when William Warder Norton and Mary D. Herter Norton first published lectures delivered at the People's Institute, the adult education division of New York City's Cooper Union. The Nortons soon expanded their program beyond the Institute, publishing books by celebrated academics from America and abroad. By mid-century, the two major pillars of Norton's publishing program—trade books and college texts—were firmly established. In the 1950s, the Norton family transferred control of the company to its employees, and today—with a staff of four hundred and a comparable number of trade, college, and professional titles published each year—W. W. Norton & Company stands as the largest and oldest publishing house owned wholly by its employees.

Editor: Julia Reidhead
Manuscript Editors: Kurt Wildermuth, Michael Fleming,
Katharine Ings, Candace Levy, Pam Lawson
Electronic Media Editor: Eileen Connell
Production Manager: Diane O'Connor
Permissions Manager: Nancy Rodwan
Permissions Clearing: Margaret Gorenstein
Text Design: Antonina Krass
Art Research: Neil Ryder Hoos
Managing Editor, College: Marian Johnson

Composition: Binghamton Valley Composition
Manufacturing: RR Donnelley

ISBN: 978-0-393-93055-9

W. W. Norton & Company, Inc., 500 Fifth Avenue, New York, NY 10110
www.wwnorton.com

W. W. Norton & Company Ltd., Castle House, 75/76 Wells Street, London W1T 3QT

Contents

American Literature 1914–1945

American Literature since 1945

Preface to the Shorter Seventh Edition

In this Shorter Seventh Edition of *The Norton Anthology of American Literature*, we offer the most extensive revision in our long publishing history. Three new section editors have joined the team, working with each other and the General Editor to look again at each selection and rethink the entire apparatus from headnotes to footnotes to section introductions to bibliographies. These editors are Robert S. Levine, Professor of English at the University of Maryland, College Park, who succeeds Hershel Parker as editor of "American Literature 1820–1865"; Jeanne Campbell Reesman, Ashbel Smith Professor of English at the University of Texas at San Antonio, who succeeds Ronald Gottesman as editor of "American Literature 1865–1914"; and Mary Loeffelholz, Professor of English at Northeastern University, who succeeds Nina Baym as editor of "American Literature 1914–1945." Each editor, new or continuing, is a well-known expert in the relevant field or period and had ultimate responsibility for his or her section of the anthology, but we have all worked together closely from first to last. We are all excited about the outcome of our collaboration and anticipate that this edition of *The Norton Anthology of American Literature* will continue to lead the field among American literature anthologies.

The Shorter Seventh Edition also offers new format options to increase the anthology's flexibility. Along with the familiar one-volume format there is now—at the same cost to students—a two-volume version as well. Either of these two volumes can be ordered individually for appropriate courses. All format options draw on the resources of the five-volume parent edition and aim for a selection sufficiently rich, diverse, and complete to enable the book either to stand alone or to serve as a flexible core for teachers who wish to assign additional works.

From the anthology's inception in 1979, the editors have aimed, first, to present a rich and substantial enough variety of works for teachers to build courses according to their own ideals (thus, there are more authors and more selections than an instructor will use in any one course); second, to make the anthology self-sufficient by featuring many works in their entirety along with extensive selections for individual authors; and third, to balance traditional interests with developing critical concerns in a way that points to a coherent literary history. As early as 1979, we anthologized work by Anne Bradstreet, Sarah Kemble Knight, Phillis Wheatley, Margaret Fuller, Frederick Douglass, Kate Chopin, and other writers who were not yet part of a standard canon. Yet we never shortchanged writers like Franklin, Emerson, Whitman, Hawthorne,

Melville, Dickinson, Hemingway, Fitzgerald, or Faulkner, whose work students expected to read in their American literature courses and whom teachers then and now would not think of doing without.

Although the so-called "canon wars" of the 1980s and 1990s have subsided, the number and diversity of authors who are now recognized as contributors to American literature has expanded dramatically since 1979. The traditional writers look different in this expanded context; they also change according to which of their works are selected. Teachers and students remain committed to the idea of the literary—that writers strive to produce artifacts that are both intellectually serious and formally skillful—but believe more than ever that writers should be understood in relation to their cultural and historical situations. In endeavoring to do justice to these complex realities, we have worked, as in previous editions, with detailed suggestions from many teachers and, through those teachers, from the students who use the anthology. Thanks to questionnaires, comment cards, face-to-face discussions, letters, and email communications, we have been able to hear and listen to those for whom this book is intended. For this Shorter Seventh Edition, we have drawn on the careful commentary of fifty reviewers.

To this Shorter Edition we have added twenty-three writers in depth, without sacrificing widely assigned writers, many of whose selections have been reconsidered, reselected, and expanded. Our aim is always to provide extensive enough selections to do the writers justice, including complete works wherever possible. Two new major works—Frederick Douglass's *Narrative of the Life* and Arthur Miller's *Death of a Salesman*—join such widely assigned works as Melville's *Benito Cereno* and *Bartleby, the Scrivener*, Davis's *Life in the Iron-Mills*, Twain's *Adventures of Huckleberry Finn*, James's *Daisy Miller: A Study*, and—both exclusive to the Norton Anthology—O'Neill's *Long Day's Journey into Night* and Williams's *A Streetcar Named Desire*. The Shorter Seventh Edition has expanded and in some cases reconfigured such central figures as Emerson, Hawthorne, Melville, Dickinson, and Twain, emphasizing new approaches in the headnotes and section introductions. There are more women writers and writers of diverse ethnic, racial, and regional origins—African Americans, Native Americans, Latina/os, and Asian Americans—whose critically acclaimed works have contributed to the American literary record. Under Arnold Krupat's editorship, Native American materials throughout have been rethought. Two new clusters (described below) enable teachers to mesh early Native American writing and oratory with a course syllabus or, should they prefer, to focus on these selections as a free-standing unit leading toward the moment after 1945 when Native writers fully entered the mainstream of literary activity.

New to the Shorter Seventh Edition are clusters that gather short texts to illuminate important cultural, historical, intellectual, and literary concerns of the period. Each cluster brings together markedly diverse voices—thirty-two new to the anthology overall—to highlight the range of views on a key topic. For example, in "Slavery, Race, and the Making of American Literature," texts by David Walker, William Lloyd Garrison, Angelina Grimke, Sojourner Truth, and Martin R. Delany speak to the pre–Civil War rupture between the reality of slavery and the ideals of freedom. Each of the six clusters, consisting of brief, carefully excerpted primary texts (about 6 to 10 per cluster), may be taught in a class period or two or used for context. Introductions to the clusters suggest how the selections might be taught as units.

Visual media, so central in contemporary American culture as well as in the classroom, now has a prominent place in the Shorter Seventh Edition, which features forty pages of color plates. In selecting the color images—from Charles Wilson Peale's *Exhuming the Mastodon* at the beginning of the nineteenth century to "The Gates" by Christo and Jeanne-Claude at the beginning of the twenty-first—the editors looked for images relevant to literary works in the anthology while depicting arts and artifacts typical of the era. The visually striking images can provoke discussion, and the captions draw attention to important details and cross-reference related literary texts.

Period-by-Period Revisions

"Beginnings to 1700," edited by Wayne Franklin, continues to feature narratives by a range of early European explorers of the North American continent and adds Thomas Harriot, Roger Williams, Edward Taylor's (much-requested) "Meditation 150," and Cotton Mather (new selections from *Wonders of the Invisible World*). The selections not only point to the religious and territorial aspirations of the Anglo settlers, but show how deeply these aspirations were combined, giving students a fuller sense of the conflicts that were to ensue when Europeans, who saw the North American continent as a "New World" waiting for their activities, encountered indigenous peoples with their long-standing ways of life.

In "American Literature 1700–1820," edited by Philip Gura, we distinguish the eighteenth century as a period of literary consolidation and development that parallels the establishment of the United States as a nation and manifests the influence of secular Enlightenment ideals. We also point to the emergence, in this atmosphere, of women writers energized by patriotic ideals and a belief in gender equality. Newly added are selections by Sarah Kemble Knight, John Woolman, John and Abigail Adams, and Judith Sargent Murray, as well as two *Federalist Papers*. The cluster "Women's Poetry: From Manuscript to Print" features six poets—among them Mercy Otis Warren, Sarah Wentworth Morton, and Annis Boudinot Stockton—whose work contributed to the civil and political discourse of the early republic. A cluster, prepared by Arnold Krupat, "Native Americans: Contact and Conflict," highlights speeches and accounts by Pontiac, Samson Occom, Chief Logan (as cited by Thomas Jefferson), Red Jacket, and Tecumseh that underscore the pattern of initial friendly contact mutating into violent conflict between Native Americans and whites.

In "American Literature 1820–1865," under the editorship of Robert S. Levine, teachers will still find Emerson's *Nature* and Whitman's *Song of Myself* complete, as well as novellas by Melville, Davis's *Life in the Iron Mills*, and other indispensable works. But, cognizant of the important role played by African American writers in the period and the omnipresence of race and slavery as literary and political themes, we have not only added the cluster mentioned above ("Slavery, Race, and the Making of American Literature") but also expanded Douglass's selections with the complete *Narrative of the Life* and the powerful speech "What to the Slave Is the Fourth of July?" and added the major African American writer Frances E. W. Harper. A second new cluster, "Native Americans: Resistance and Removal," prepared by Arnold Krupat, gathers oratory and writings—by Native Americans such as Black

Hawk, Petalesharo, Elias Boudinot, and the authors of the Cherokee Memorials as well as by whites such as Ralph Waldo Emerson—protesting Andrew Jackson's tragic national policy of Indian removal.

New prose fiction includes chapters from Cooper's *Last of the Mohicans*, Poe's "The Black Cat," and Elizabeth Drew Stoddard's "Lemorne *versus* Huell." At instructors' request, we have increased the representation of poems by Emerson, Longfellow, and Melville. Poetry by Emily Dickinson has been reselected, using the newly established texts by Franklin (we retain the Johnson numbers in brackets for reference), and now includes a facsimile page from Fascicle 10. Finally, the section introduction has been entirely recast; author headnotes have been updated to reflect the latest biographies and critical discussions; and the selected bibliographies have been completely revised and updated.

"American Literature 1865–1914," edited by Jeanne Campbell Reesman, also has a striking new look. We have retained Twain's *Adventures of Huckleberry Finn* and James's *Daisy Miller* while adding new short fiction: Bret Harte's "The Luck of Roaring Camp"; a second story by Charles Chesnutt, "The Passing of Grandison"; Edith Wharton's "The Other Two" and "Roman Fever"; Sui Sin Far's "In the Land of the Free"; and Zitkala-Ša's "The Soft-Hearted Sioux." Theodore Dreiser is newly represented by chapters from *Sister Carrie*. New poets Paul Laurence Dunbar and Emma Lazarus (moved from the preceding section to this one, where she belongs chronologically) and new prose writers Sarah Winnemucca and Pauline Hopkins underscore that writers—male and female—from diverse ethnic, racial, and regional origins entered the literary field to represent the American scene in the late nineteenth century. Finally, two clusters take up important political and literary disputes from the era. "Debates over 'Americanization'" explores the increasingly multicultural character of the American people, with writers across the ethnic range asking whether there was or should be a single national identity attainable by immigrants from all over Europe, Native Americans in the path of "manifest destiny," African Americans after the Civil War, and even those from neighboring countries on the continent. There are texts by Frederick Jackson Turner, Theodore Roosevelt, Jose Martí, Charles W. Chesnutt, Jane Addams, and Anna Julia Cooper. Literary movements attuned to the new diversity of the American population are considered in the cluster "Realism and Naturalism," where selected critical writings by William Dean Howells, Henry James, Frank Norris, Theodore Dreiser, and Jack London illuminate the turn to realism and naturalism as styles developed to represent the complicated social and occupational scene of late nineteenth-century America.

In "American Literature 1914–1945," Mary Loeffelholz expands the offering of complete longer works—among them O'Neill's *Long Day's Journey into Night* and Hemingway's "The Snows of Kilimanjaro"—with "Hands" from Sherwood Anderson's *Winesburg, Ohio*, and "The Leader of the People" by John Steinbeck, restored by instructors' request. The poets Mina Loy and Sterling A. Brown appear for the first time, and selections by Ezra Pound, H. D., Marianne Moore, Hart Crane, E. E. Cummings, and Langston Hughes are reconsidered, encouraging students and teachers to contemplate the interrelation of modernist aesthetics with ethnic, regional, and popular writing.

Newly titled "American Literature since 1945," this section, previously separately edited by Jerome Klinkowitz (prose) and Patricia B. Wallace (poetry), has been unified, producing a richer representation of the period's literary activity and a more accurate presentation of the writers themselves, many of whom write in multiple genres. The collaboratively rewritten period introduction and headnotes provide a more nuanced, vital picture of the post-war literary scene and individual writers' contributions to it. The section continues to feature the complete texts of Tennessee Williams's *A Streetcar Named Desire* (exclusive to this anthology) and Allen Ginsberg's *Howl* and adds Arthur Miller's *Death of a Salesman*. Poets Lucille Clifton and Yusef Komunyakaa are new to this edition, as are several poems by Theodore Roethke, John Berryman, Adrienne Rich, Rita Dove, and Louise Erdrich. Prose fiction has been enriched with short stories by newly added authors Julia Alvarez, Sherman Alexie, and Jhumpa Lahiri and new selections by Sandra Cisneros. We also introduce teachable stand-alone segments from important novels by Saul Bellow (*The Adventures of Augie March*) and Jack Kerouac (*Big Sur*).

Additional Resources from the Publisher

To give instructors even more flexibility, the publisher is offering a Norton Critical Edition—any one from the full list of 180—to be packaged with any volume of the Shorter Seventh Edition for free. This includes such frequently assigned novels as Harriet Beecher Stowe's *Uncle Tom's Cabin*, Herman Melville's *Moby-Dick*, Edith Wharton's *The House of Mirth*, and William Faulkner's *The Sound and the Fury*. Each Norton Critical Edition contains an authoritative, annotated text accompanied by rich contextual and critical materials, prepared by an expert.

For the Shorter Seventh Edition, the publisher has expanded its extensive online resource, Norton Literature Online (wwnorton.com/literature). Students who activate the free password in each new copy of the Norton Anthology gain access to such resources as a glossary of literary terms, advice on writing about literature and using MLA documentation style, study aids and quizzes, an author portrait gallery, maps, and over 90 minutes of recorded readings and musical selections. With their passwords, students also gain access to a site specifically developed to support *The Norton Anthology of American Literature*. Redesigned for easier navigation, this student website (wwnorton.com/naal), prepared by Bruce Michelson, offers timelines, outlines of the period introductions, over 400 annotated links, author resource pages for 160 writers in the anthology, searchable "Explorations" that provide questions and research projects, as well as self-grading quizzes, prepared by Jason Coats, on 30 of the most widely taught works in the anthology.

Teaching with The Norton Anthology of American Literature: *A Guide for Instructors* has been expanded and updated by Bruce Michelson. This much-praised guide offers extensive suggestions for all aspects of a course, from planning the syllabus to preparing exams. The Guide entries suggest approaches to each author and feature questions for starting class discussion. Finally, the Norton Resource Library (wwnorton.com/nrl) offers PDF files of the Guide and student website content as well as a WebCT/BlackBoard Coursepack featuring tests and quizzes on the period introductions and individual works, lecture outlines, maps, and timelines, among other resources.

Instructors who adopt *The Norton Anthology of American Literature* have access to an extensive array of films and videos. In addition to videos of the plays by O'Neill, Williams, and Miller included in the anthology, segments of the award-winning video series *American Passages: A Literary Survey* are available without charge on orders of specified quantities of the Norton Anthology. Funded by Annenberg/CPB, produced by Oregon Public Broadcasting, and developed with the Norton Anthology as its exclusive companion anthology, the *American Passages* series covers one literary movement or period by exploring two or three authors in depth. A website (learner.org/amerpass), instructor's guide, and student guide are also available. For information about the videos, contact your Norton representative.

Editorial Procedures

As in past editions, editorial features—period introductions, headnotes, and annotations—are designed to be concise yet full and to give students useful information without imposing an interpretation. All apparatus has been updated in response to new scholarship and new ways of thinking about the literature of the United States: period introductions have been entirely or substantially rewritten, as have dozens of headnotes; the Selected Bibliographies have been updated and augmented with new general-resources bibliographies, categorized by Reference Works, Histories, and Literary Criticism, for each period. The Shorter Seventh Edition retains two editorial features that help students place their reading in historical and cultural context—a Texts/Contexts timeline following each period introduction and maps on the front and back endpapers of each volume.

Our policy has been to reprint each text in the form that accords, as far as it is possible to determine, to the author's own preferences. We have, however, modernized most spellings and (very sparingly) the punctuation in the two earliest sections on the principle that archaic spellings and typography are unnecessarily intimidating for beginning students. We have used square brackets to indicate titles supplied by the editors for the convenience of students. Whenever a portion of a text has been omitted, we have indicated that omission with three asterisks. If the omitted portion is important for following the plot or argument, we summarize the needed information. After each work, we cite (when known) the date of composition on the left and the date of first publication on the right; in some instances, the latter is followed by the date of a revised edition for which the author was responsible.

Our editors, new or continuing, are experienced, active, expert classroom teachers and scholars. We have all benefited from commentary offered by hundreds of teachers throughout the country. Those teachers who prepared detailed critiques, or who offered special help in preparing texts, are listed under Acknowledgments, on a separate page. The editors would like to express appreciation for their assistance to Kenneth L. Baughman, John Bryant, Lawrence I. Berkove, Kirby Brown, Lawrence Buell, Brad Campbell, Russ Castronovo, Granville Ganter, Samuel L. Gladden, Ivy Goodman, Vince Gotera, Ezra Greenspan, Tim Gustafson, Katrina Huffman, Julie Huffman-Klinkowitz, Julie Husband, Daniel Heath Justice, Carolyn Karcher, Virginia Kennedy, Judith Kicinski, Maurice Lee, David Wei Li, Joseph R. McElrath Jr., Anne Myles, James O'Laughlin, Samuel Otter, Kenneth Price, Sally Promey, Julian Rice, Alan Shucard, Martha Nell Smith, Paul Sorrentino, Julia Stern,

Jesse Swan, John Swope, Heidi Shira Tannenbaum, Karen Tracey, Jennie Wang, Edward Whitley, Thomas Wolfe, and Christina Zwarg. We also thank the many people at Norton who contributed to the Seventh Edition: Julia Reidhead, who supervised the Seventh Edition; Marian Johnson, Managing Editor, College; Kurt Wildermuth, developmental and project editor; Mike Fleming, Katharine Ings, Candace Levy, manuscript editors; Catherine Spencer and Ann Abrams, editorial assistants; Eileen Connell, electronic media editor; Diane O'Connor, production manager; Toni Krass, designer; Neil Ryder Hoos, art researcher; Debra Morton Hoyt, art director; Nancy Rodwan, permissions manager; and Margaret Gorenstein, who cleared permissions. We also wish to acknowledge our debt to the late George P. Brockway, former president and chairman at Norton, who invented this anthology, and to M. H. Abrams, Norton's advisor on English texts. All have helped us to create an anthology that, more than ever, is testimony to the continuing richness of American literary traditions.

NINA BAYM

Acknowledgments

Among our many critics, advisors, and friends, the following were of especial help toward the preparation of the Shorter Seventh Edition, either with advice or by providing critiques of particular periods of the anthology: David Anderson (University of North Texas), George Bagby (Hampden-Sydney College), Barbara J. Bass (Towson University), Roy K. Bird (University of Alaska, Fairbanks), Jennifer Brezina (College of the Canyons), Charles W. Carter (Shepherd University), George Chambers (Bradley University), John Cox (Georgia College & State University), Barbara Cummings (Shepherd University), Ed Cutler (Brigham Young University), Corinne Dale (Belmont University), Julia Eichelberger (College of Charleston), Daniel Fineman (Occidental College), Evelyn I. Funda (Utah State University), Pat Garrett (Louisiana Tech University), Hilary Hawley (Washington State University), Trenton Hickman (Brigham Young University), Jane Hill (University of West Georgia), Clayton G. Holloway (Hampton University), Paul C. Jones (Ohio University), Mabel Khawaja (Hampton University), Peter Kvidera (John Carroll University), Jill LeRoy-Frazier (Milligan College), Michael J. Martin (Stephen F. Austin State University), Lowery McClendon (Bronx Community College), Michael McDonough (Alfred University), Philip Metres (John Carroll University), Clay Motley (Charleston Southern University), Lily Phillips (North Carolina State University), Roxanna Pisiak (Morrisville State College), Scott Pound (Lakehead University), Paula Reif (Carl Albert State College), Susan Roberson (Texas A&M University, Kingsville), Arthur Rogers (Rogers State University), Debby Rosenthal (John Carroll University), Derek Parker Royal (Texas A&M University, Commerce), Richard Ruland (Washington University), Alice Rutkowski (State University of New York, Geneseo), Melissa Ryan (Alfred University), Bill Schlientz (Philander Smith College), Larry W. Severeid (College of Eastern Utah), Cristobal Silva (Texas Tech University), Gerald F. Snelson (Frostburg State University), Mark Walhout (Seattle Pacific University), Rebecca A. Wall (Winston-Salem State University), Lloyd Willis (University of Florida), Scott D. Yarbrough (Charleston Southern University), Todd Young (Shepherd University), and Dede Yow (Kennesaw State University).

The Norton Anthology
of American Literature

SHORTER SEVENTH EDITION

VOLUME 2

1865 to the Present

American Literature
1865–1914

THE TRANSFORMATION OF A NATION

From the earliest moment in their nation's history, Americans had been pushing westward. Thomas Jefferson's Louisiana Purchase (1803) had added a huge swath of territory west of the Alleghenies; the outcome of the Mexican War (1846–48) brought the entire Southwest, including California, into the nation; and the discovery of gold in California late in 1848 increased the pace of westward movement beyond anything that could have been imagined even one year earlier. The westward settlement by Americans—most of them of Northern European ancestry—from the older parts of the country displaced Native American cultures and Spanish settlements, and the process became more intense and systematic as these whites settled on more and more terrain west of the Mississippi River.

The Civil War, which began in 1861 and lasted for four years, was the ultimate result of economic, political, social, and cultural divisions between North and South—above all, the division between an economy and way of life based on wage labor and one based on slavery. The war cost 8 billion dollars and claimed over six hundred thousand American lives, more than any other war in U.S. history. Nevertheless, the country prospered materially over the following five decades. The war effort had stimulated innovations in methods of efficiently moving large numbers of people, raw materials, and goods. The first transcontinental railroad, completed in 1869, made it possible to cross the country cheaply in just a few days, whereas covered wagon processions on the overland trail (expensive to outfit and difficult to organize) required two or three months. The railroad took settlers west from the eastern seaports, and also allowed for rapid, inexpensive shipments of goods, thereby transporting the American economy itself into the industrial age, once and for all. But the railroad also disrupted the migration of the buffalo herds on which Native peoples of the Plains depended. The telegraph, introduced in the 1840s, now ran into small towns (many of them newly settled) everywhere; electricity was introduced on a large scale; the telephone began to revolutionize daily life; coal, oil, iron, gold, silver, and other kinds of mineral wealth were discovered and extracted, producing many individual fortunes that allowed the nation for the first time to capitalize its own further development. All this development required more people, preferably (from the point of view of employers) in numbers sufficient to keep the cost of labor cheap. Often lured by advertisements from railroad and land companies, immigrants arrived in the United States from the Scandinavian countries and from Italy, Poland, Czechoslovakia, Lithuania, Russia, and more. Many European newcomers, taking advantage of the railroad's cheap passenger fares, went on to the plains to farm; but most became urban dwellers, causing enormous population growth in such cities as New York, Boston, and Chicago at the same time that Chinese and then Japanese immigrants hastened the growth of San Francisco and other western cities.

The historian Frederick Jackson Turner declared in 1893 that the frontier in which many Americans had believed for so long was now closed, basing his analysis on the census of 1890, which found no place in the United States with fewer than two people per square mile. Now the United States, eager to join the European imperialist nations, turned to imperialist ventures of its own, including expansion into the former Spanish possessions of Cuba, Puerto Rico, and the Philippines following the Spanish-American War in 1898. U.S. colonization also included Hawai'i. The expanding power of American capitalism and imperialism had long been experienced by indigenous peoples, whose populations suffered enormous declines in the last few decades of the nineteenth century, especially when tribes were assigned to reservations. Along with Native American reservations came a new desire to "study" the tribes—always with the expectation that their members would "vanish." Anthropologists—most of them originally students of Franz Boas—began to study Native American oral productions, even as Euro-American authors such as Helen Hunt Jackson (1830–1885) wrote book-length denunciations of the treatment of Native Americans. While the Lakota writer Zitkala-Ša (Gertrude Simmons Bonnin) (1876–1938) published prose accounts of her life toward the end of the nineteenth century, it was not until the twentieth century, with the work of Native writers such as Charles Alexander Eastman (Ohiyesa) (1858–1939), also a Lakota, among others, that a "modern" Indian literature began to be produced.

With the end of the frontier era, industrialization on a scale unprecedented in Great Britain and Europe came to the fore in the United States. Between 1850 and 1880, capital invested in manufacturing industries more than quadrupled and factory employment nearly doubled. By 1885 four transcontinental railroad lines had been completed, using in their own construction and carrying to manufacturing centers in Cleveland and Detroit the nation's quintupled output of steel from Pittsburgh and Chicago. As major industries were consolidated into monopolies, a small number of men came to control such enormously profitable enterprises as steel, oil, railroads, meat packing, banking, and finance, among them Jay Gould, Jim Hill, Leland Stanford, Cornelius Vanderbilt, Andrew Carnegie, J. P. Morgan, and John D. Rockefeller. Robber barons to some, captains of industry to others, these men successfully squeezed out competitors and accumulated vast wealth and power, social, political, and economic; whereas there had been only a handful of millionaires before the Civil War, now there were hundreds, and they formed a class whose wealth and the styles of life associated with what the sociologist Thorstein Veblen called "conspicuous consumption" had not been seen before in American life.

In 1865 the United States, except for the manufacturing centers of the northeastern seaboard, was a country of farms, villages, and small towns. Manufacturing was more a matter of workshops than factories. In 1870 the U.S. population was 38.5 million; by 1910, 92 million; by 1920, 123 million.

This increase in population was due almost entirely to immigration, as was the shift in the percentages of dwellers in the country and the city. For example, the population of New York City grew sevenfold, from half a million to nearly 3.5 million between 1865 and the turn of the twentieth century, while Chicago, with a population of only 29,000 in 1850, had more than 2 million inhabitants by 1910. These immigrants and their descendants enabled the United States to become an urban, industrial, international, capitalist power while altering the ethnic composition of the still mostly white population and contributing immeasurably to the democratization of the nation's cultural life. By 1890, New Englanders and their descendents were no longer numerically dominant. Long-settled white Americans faced newly arrived white people across divides of power, income, and privilege—worker against owner, farm against city, immigrant against native-born, leading to suspicion and social turbulence on a scale that the nation had not seen.

The transformation of an entire continent involved suffering for millions even as others prospered. Farmers in the Midwest and high plains depended on the railroads for transport of their crops but were squeezed off the land by the pricing policies of these very same railroads—what the novelist Frank Norris characterized as the giant "octopus" of corporate power, especially the Southern Pacific Railroad. Though the Homestead Act of 1862 promised free or cheap acreage to every individual or family who would settle and "improve" land according to a set formula, much available land was donated to railroads to encourage their growth, while speculators bought up much land as well by various subterfuges. It is estimated that only 10 percent of the land opened by the Homestead Act actually went to would-be independent farmers. Buying at high prices, or forced to rent, everywhere such farmers were "under the lion's paw," as the midwestern writer Hamlin Garland put it, of land speculators and absentee landlords, or faced with mortgage payments they could not make. Large-scale farming quickly began to squeeze out such small family farms as had been able to develop—even as it increased agricultural yields. And for many, the great cities were also, as the socialist novelists Jack London and Upton Sinclair argued, jungles where only the strongest, most ruthless, and luckiest survived. An oversupply of labor brought about by immigration campaigns kept wages low, and—in the absence of laws regulating factory conditions and working hours—workers faced inhumane and dangerous working conditions.

Neither farmers nor urban laborers organized effectively to pursue their own interests. Legislators usually served the interests of business and industry—sometimes in the honest belief that a healthy economy required capitalism, sometimes via bribery and kickbacks, as in President Ulysses S. Grant's administration, or the looting of the New York City treasury by William Marcy ("Boss") Tweed in the 1870s, or municipal corruption cases exposed by the journalist Lincoln Steffens and other "muckrakers," including the writers Stephen Crane and Frank Norris. Early attempts by labor to organize were often violent, and such groups as the terroristic "Molly Maguires," active in the 1870s and 1880s in the coal-mining area of northeastern Pennsylvania, bolstered the conviction of those who believed in open markets and free enterprise that labor organizations were un-American. Industrial workers had little significant political leverage until the 1880s, when the American Federation of Labor emerged as the first unified national voice of workers. But not until collective bargaining legislation was enacted in the 1930s did labor acquire the right to strike. As for farmers, their organizing efforts involved experiments in cooperative farming and storage, which usually failed—partly for lack of funds but also because of the long tradition of independence among agricultural people. It was exactly to own one's own land that immigrants and native-born white people had moved to the prairies in the first place. On the other hand, individual ownership of land parcels was forced on the Native people through the Dawes Allotment Act of 1887, fragmenting the collectively held Native land base and resulting in the loss of some 60 million acres from Native possession.

THE LITERARY MARKETPLACE

Rapid transcontinental settlement and new urban industrial conditions were accompanied by the development of a national literature of great abundance and variety. New themes, new forms, new subjects, new regions, new authors, new audiences—all emerged in the literature of this half century. Inevitably, Americans new and old were drawn into more complex social and cultural engagements as citizens of a nation still largely composed of dispossessed and otherwise "marginalized" people. In literature, realism, naturalism, and regionalism strove to express the challenges and rewards of what President Theodore Roosevelt called—from his perspective as a wealthy and entitled New Yorker—"the winning of the west." The notion of what makes one an American was defined from diverse points of view. Fictionalized representations of characters rarely encountered before the Civil War became familiar: industrial workers, the rural poor, ambitious business leaders and downcast vagrants, prostitutes and unheroic soldiers, as described by Ambrose Bierce, Bret Harte, Jack London, and Stephen Crane. Women from many social groups, African Americans, Native Americans, Mexican Americans, Asian Americans, and immigrants began to write for publication, and a rapidly growing market for their work helped confirm authorship as a possible career.

Literature in the sense of fine writing figured at the top of a market that began with newspapers, which had been important to the political, social, and cultural life of America since colonial times. After the Civil War their numbers and influence grew. Joseph Pulitzer established the *St. Louis Post-Dispatch* in 1878, and in 1883 he bought the *New York World*; both papers were hugely successful. William Randolph Hearst, a Californian who inherited a fortune from his mining entrepreneur father, made the *San Francisco Examiner* the dominant newspaper in the Far West, then bought the *New York Journal* in 1895 to compete with Pulitzer's *World,* and gradually acquired newspapers across the country. In 1897 the *Jewish Daily Forward*, in Yiddish, was founded by Abraham Cahan; its circulation eventually reached 250,000, and it was read by three or four times that number. Many "writers" who went on to become "authors" started as newspaper journalists: Ambrose Bierce, Abraham Cahan, Stephen Crane, Theodore Dreiser, Jack London, Sui Sin Far, Joel Chandler Harris, William Dean Howells, Frank Norris, and Mark Twain among them. Perhaps of equal importance to the development of literary careers and literature as an American institution was the establishment of newspaper syndicates in the 1880s by Irving Bachellor and S. S. McClure. These syndicates, which distributed material to newspapers and magazines in all sections of the country, published humor, news, and novels—Crane's *The Red Badge of Courage*, for example—in installments.

Magazines became another feature of American life as early as the mid-eighteenth century. After the Civil War, East Coast magazines such as *Harper's New Monthly Magazine* (1850), *Scribner's Monthly* (1870), *Century Illustrated Monthly Magazine* (1881), the *Atlantic Monthly* (1857), and the *Galaxy* (1866) provided outlets for such figures as Kate Chopin, Sarah Orne Jewett, Henry James, William Dean Howells, Sui Sin Far, and Mark Twain. On the West Coast, the *Overland Monthly* (1868) emerged as the leading literary periodical; designed to showcase western-themed writing, it published Bret Harte, Ambrose Bierce, London, Mary Austin, Sui Sin Far, and Twain among others. Without the periodicals, many writers would not have been able to support themselves; the income and audiences these magazines provided were crucial to the further formation of the complex literary tradition of a vast nation undergoing modernization.

Periodicals also contributed to the emergence toward the end of the nineteenth century of what the critic Warner Berthoff calls "the literature of argument"—powerful works in sociology, philosophy, and psychology, many of them impelled by the spirit of exposure and reform. It would be hard to exaggerate the influence—on other writers as well as on the educated public—of works such as Henry George's *Progress and Poverty* (1879), Henry Demarest Lloyd's *Wealth against Commonwealth* (1894), Charlotte Perkins Gilman's *Women and Economics* (1898), Thorstein Veblen's *The Theory of the Leisure Class* (1899), and William James's *The Varieties of Religious Experience* (1902). For many women writers, magazines provided an important public forum in which to explore new views of women and women's rights.

In short, as the United States became an international political, economic, and military power during this half century, its literary production kept pace, and it welcomed (in translation) works by the leading European figures of the time, such as Leo Tolstoy, Henrik Ibsen, Anton Chekhov, and Émile Zola. American writers in this period, like most writers of other times and places, wrote to earn money, gain fame, change the world, and express themselves in a permanent art form. The nature of that form—what might be called the "realistic international art story"—was itself a product of the interplay of historical forces and aesthetic developments apparent, in retrospect, since the publication of the French writer Gustave Flaubert's *Madame Bovary* (1856). Among the most critically praised American writers of the period were Mark Twain, Henry James, Edith Wharton, and William Dean Howells, two of them from the Midwest and two of them easterners, whose literary styles encompassed the comic vernacular, ordinary discourse, and impressionistic subjectivity. These writers recorded life on the vanishing frontier, in the village, small town, and turbulent metropolis, as well as in European resorts and capitals. They established the literary identity of distinctively American protagonists, specifically the vernacular boy hero and the "American Girl," the baffled and strained middle-class family, the businessman, the psychologically complicated citizens of a new international culture. They set the example and charted the future course for the subjects, themes, techniques, and styles of fiction we still call modern.

FORMS OF REALISM

The term *realism* labels a movement in English, European, and American literature that gathered force from the 1830s to the end of the century. Realists attempted to record life as it was lived rather than life as it ought to be lived (the term used for this at the time was *idealism*) or had been lived in times past (the term used for this at the time was *romance*). As defined by William Dean Howells (1837–1920), the magazine editor who was for some decades the chief American advocate of realist aesthetics as well as author of over thirty novels, realism "is nothing more and nothing less than the truthful treatment of material." Henry James spoke of the "documentary" value of Howells's work, thereby calling attention to realism's preoccupation with the physical surfaces, the particularities of the sensate world in which fictional characters lived. Characters in Howell's novels were "representative" or ordinary characters—people much like the readers themselves, without fame or huge fortunes, without startling accomplishments or immense abilities. Realism, as practiced by Howells, particularly in *The Rise of Silas Lapham* (1885), the novel many literary historians have identified as the epitome of American realism, seeks to convince readers that the life in the book's pages is true to ordinary people in familiar surroundings.

Edith Wharton's realism, like Henry James's, is less about middle-class people than about characters' psychological and moral interiors. Wharton (1862–1937) holds a mirror up to New York high society, especially as its dramas of human consciousness play out; the achievement of what might be called upper-class realism is to convince readers that the inner lives of these wealthy people accord with the truth of human nature. In novels such as *The House of Mirth* (1905), *The Custom of the Country* (1913), and *The Age of Innocence* (1920), Wharton's primary concerns are with the intangible—thwarted desire, self-betrayal, murderous emotion, repressed voices. In this sense, her depiction of the struggles of individuals such as Lily Bart of *The House of Mirth* to survive in a seemingly pleasant but actually hostile society goes beyond realism to reflect an almost Darwinian view of upper-class life.

In fact, it proved impossible for any realist to represent things exactly as they were. Present-day literary theorists are probably more aware of what may be called "the crisis of representation"—the difference between the representation and the thing represented—than were these realists of the late nineteenth and early twentieth centuries. But whether they could actually duplicate "reality" or not, these writers insisted that their work called attention to areas of experience that literature had not dealt with before and made such areas legitimate subjects for serious writing. The two most acclaimed artists of the era—Mark Twain and Henry James—understood that language was an interpretation of the real rather than the real thing itself. Twain's work was realistic in its use of colloquial and vernacular speech and its parade of characters from ordinary walks of life. For many later writers, the simple language of *Adventures of Huckleberry Finn* (1884) signified the beginning of a truly American style. But Twain (1835–1910) is also a comic genius whose language goes well beyond the demands of realism. The author of *Huckleberry Finn* is funny in ways that Huck could never be—Twain's writing resembles performance art, and, indeed, he achieved enormous success as a public reader of his own work. (At the same time, readers misinterpret Twain if they read him only for his jokes and do not sense the pessimism about humankind that lies not far beneath the surface.) He was, as a western writer, ambiguously attached to an oral tradition of vernacular speech. At the other extreme, Henry James (1843–1916) worked his way from recognizably realistic fiction, with a large cast of socially specified (typically upper-class) characters described by an all-knowing narrator, as in *The American* (1876), toward increasingly subtle metaphorical representations of the flow of a character's inner thought, as in *The Golden Bowl* (1904). All strong realist writers believed in the power of language to represent reality in ways that were aesthetically satisfying and thus demanded the skill of a literary artist as well as the observational precision of a journalist.

Naturalism is understood by some as an extension or intensification of realism; it introduces characters from the fringes and depths of society whose fates are determined by degenerate heredity, a sordid environment, and/or a good deal of bad luck. Stephen Crane, Theodore Dreiser, Jack London, and Frank Norris are usually identified as the leading American naturalists of this period, but before we turn to their work, the philosophic and scientific backgrounds of naturalism require some attention.

One of the most far-reaching intellectual events of the last half of the nineteenth century was the publication in 1859 of Charles Darwin's *Origin of Species*. This book, together with his *Descent of Man* (1870), hypothesized on the basis of massive physical evidence that over the millennia humans had evolved from "lower" forms of life. Humans were special, not—as the Bible taught—because God had created them in his image, but because as a species they had successfully adapted to changing environmental conditions and had passed on their survival-making characteristics. Indigenous Native traditions were consistent with Darwinism in their sense that humans were, indeed, the last creatures to develop, but Native traditions also saw the last formed as handicapped by their belatedness, needing the wisdom derived from their winged and four-legged brothers and sisters, beings that had been on this earth for a great deal longer. In the 1870s, the English philosopher Herbert Spencer's application of Darwin's theory of evolution to social relations, applying the concept of "survival of the fittest" to human groups, was enthusiastically welcomed by many leading American businessmen. Andrew Carnegie was only one of the successful industrialists who argued that unrestrained competition was the equivalent of a law of nature designed to eliminate those unfit for the new economic order.

Another response to Darwin was to accept the deterministic implications of evolutionary theory and to use them to explain the behavior of characters in literary works. As Émile Zola (1840–1902), the influential French theorist and novelist, put the matter in his essay "The Experimental Novel" (1880):

> [W]e must operate with characters, passions, human and social data as the chemist and the physicist work on inert bodies, as the physiologist works on living bodies. Determinism governs everything. It is scientific investigation . . . and will replace novels of pure imagination by novels of observation and experiment.

A number of American writers adopted aspects of this form of naturalism, though each brought naturalism into his or her work in individual ways. For Frank Norris, naturalism was not a "realistic" genre or "an inner circle of realism." To be a naturalist, Norris believed, was to enter the zone of romance:

> [W]e must leave the rank and file . . . [and] separate ourselves; we must become individual, unique. The naturalist takes no note of common people, common as far as their interests, their lives, and the things that occur in them are common, are ordinary. Terrible things must happen to the characters of the naturalistic tale. They must be twisted from the ordinary, wrenched out from the quiet, uneventful round of every-day life, and flung into the throes of a vast and terrible drama that works itself out in unleashed passions, in blood, and in sudden death.

Characters may be "common," but what happens to them cannot be: "These great, terrible dramas no longer happen among the personnel of a feudal and Renaissance nobility . . . but among the lower—almost the lowest—classes; those who have been thrust or wrenched from the ranks who are falling by the roadway." Certainly the slum families in Norris's "Fantaisie Printanière" and Stephen Crane's *Maggie: A Girl of the Streets* (1893) experience "terrible things" and react in predictable "terrible" ways. Though American naturalists were concerned on the one hand to explore the new territories opened up by Darwin, Spencer, and Zola—the pressures of biology, environment, and other material forces—in depicting people, particularly lower-class people, they allowed in different degrees for the value of human beings, for their potential to make some sense out of their experience, and for their capacity to act compassionately—even altruistically—under the most adverse circumstances. Even though these writers were challenging conventional wisdom about human motivation and causality in the natural world, the bleakness and pessimism sometimes found in their fiction are not the same as despair and cynicism.

Stephen Crane (1871–1900) believed, as he said of his pitiful protagonist in *Maggie*, that environments such as slums count for a great deal in determining human fate. In the wild, nature is not hostile, he observes in "The Open Boat," only "indifferent, flatly indifferent." Crane, like most naturalists, is ambiguous, accepting of paradoxes. In his *Red Badge of Courage* (1895), the soldier Henry Fleming responds to the chaos and violence that surround him with alternating surges of panic and self-congratulation, never fully understanding himself and his place in the world. After granting an apparently naturalistic perspective to Crane, we are left with his distinctiveness, especially his use of impressionistic literary techniques to present incomplete characters in a broken world—a world more random than scientifically predictable. We are also left, however, with the hardly pessimistic implication of "The Open Boat": that precisely because human beings are exposed to a world of chance where death is always imminent, they would do well to learn the arts of sympathetic identification and solidarity, arts often learned at the price of death. Jack London's "To Build a Fire" (1908) illustrates the fate of those who decide to do without trail mates.

Theodore Dreiser (1871–1945) did not share Crane's tendency to use words and images as if he were a composer or a painter; his sense of the solidity of the real world called out a heavily solid prose. But he did share, at least early in his career, Crane's skepticism; like Crane, he was inclined to see men and women as moths drawn to flame rather than as lords of creation. Still, it is not Dreiser's beliefs that make him significant in American letters: it is what his imagination and literary technique do with a rich set of ideas, experiences, and emotions to create the "color of life" in his fiction. If Crane gave American readers a new sense of human consciousness under conditions of extreme pressure, Dreiser gave them in novels such as *Sister Carrie* (1900) and *Jennie Gerhardt* (1911) a sense of the fumbling, yearning, confused response to the simultaneously enchanting, exciting, ugly, and dangerous metropolis that had become home to such large numbers of Americans by the turn of the century.

Jack London (1876–1916) is also far from a "pure" naturalist or determinist; a powerful current of myth and romance underlies his most successful works, such as *The Call of the Wild* (1903) and *The Sea-Wolf* (1904), and most of his nearly two hundred short stories. London is a writer notorious for his contradictions, at once a socialist and an individualist, a believer in Anglo-Saxon superiority who attacked white racism and colonialism. As the critic Earle Labor has noted, "[T]he essential creative tension for [London's] literary artistry is the opposition of materialism versus spiritualism—that is, the tension between the logical and the scientific on the one hand and the irrational and mystical on the other." In "The Law of Life" (1901) Old Koskoosh—an imagined not a realistic representation of an indigenous person—when about to be left to die by his tribe, thinks: "Nature did not care. To life she set one task, gave one law. To perpetuate was the task of life, its law is death." This thought suggests a deterministic view of life—that nothing individuals do is of real significance. Yet the bulk of the story is given over to Old Koskoosh's memories, particularly to the re-creation of a formative moment from his youth when he and a companion came upon an old moose struggling against the wolves that have wounded and will soon devour him. In re-creating this extraordinary moment in all of its vivid, dramatic power, and in identifying with the totemic figure of the moose, Koskoosh, it might be argued, has erased his earlier generalization about evolutionary necessity and the meaninglessness of the individual.

In sum, despite a residual insistence on humanity's elevated place in the universe and a middle-class readership that disliked ugliness and "immorality," urban America and the sparsely populated hinterlands offered much material for realistic and naturalistic literary techniques and ideas. The "Realism and Naturalism" cluster in this volume brings together diverse voices to debate these important terms of late-nineteenth- and early-twentieth-century American literature.

REGIONAL WRITING

Regional writing, another expression of the realist impulse, resulted from the desire both to preserve a record of distinctive ways of life before industrialization dispersed or homogenized them and to come to terms with the harsh realities that seemed to be replacing these early and allegedly happier times. At a more practical level, much of the regional writing was a response to the rapid growth of magazines, which created a new, largely female market for short fiction along with opportunities for women writers. By the end of the nineteenth century, virtually every region of the country, from Maine to California, from the northern plains to the Louisiana bayous, had a "local colorist" (the implied comparison is to painters of so-called genre scenes) to immortalize its natural, social, and linguistic features. Though often suffused with nostalgia, the best work of the regionalists both renders a convincing surface of a particular time and location and investigates psychological character traits from a more universal perspective. This mélange may be seen in such an early example of regional writing as Bret Harte's "The Luck of Roaring Camp," which, when it was published in 1868, made Harte a national celebrity. The story is locally specific as well as entertaining, and it created mythic types as well as offered realistic depictions of frontier characters, though these depictions were later called into question by Ambrose Bierce, among others.

One school of regionalist writing that developed quickly, once the "West" was "won," was the "Western." Although the origins of this type go back to James Fenimore Cooper's tales of the frontier when it was located in western New York State, the addition of gold mines and cowboys to the formula identified the genre with the Far West. Diverse writers such as Owen Wister, author of the popular novel *The Virginian* (1902), Mark Twain, Bret Harte, Ambrose Bierce, Mary Austin, and Jack London all contributed to the work of depicting the West as a legendary region—or (as in the case of Twain and Bierce) to the work of debunking the legends. Native Americans also described their lives and traditions—especially as these were imperiled by white advances into their territories. Navajo chants and Chippewa songs; the native oratory of Cochise, Charlot, and Wovoka; and the writings of Zitkala-Ša, Sarah Winnemucca, and Charles Alexander Eastman (Ohiyesa) have not only been increasingly added to the discourse of the West but have challenged the Euro-American identification of the West with the moving line of the frontier as it incorporated territory for that particular ethnic group. One of the great themes of Native American literary work is the land and the people's relation to it, whether in oratorical performances that dramatize this relation or in chants and tales about its sacredness. But Native American conceptions about land were radically at odds with the profit-oriented conceptions of the settlers and the railroads. "With beauty all around me, may I walk" is the prayer of the Navajo Night Chant, but though these traditional songs and other communal and artistic practices are kept alive today, a new theme emerged in Native American cultures in general: loss of the beloved land. Zitkala-Ša writes as a citizen of the modern age, educated in eastern schools by missionaries, but she still laments the vision of "my mother far away on the Western plains." Similarly, the voices of Mexican Americans, as in the "corridos," or border ballads of the Mexican Revolution, are now understood as important to an enlarged understanding of the U.S. literary West.

Hamlin Garland (1860–1940), rather than creating a myth, set out to destroy one. Like many writers of the time, Garland was encouraged by William Dean Howells to write about what he knew best—in his case the farmers of the upper Midwest. As he later said, his purpose in his early stories was to show that the "mystic quality connected with free land . . . was a myth." Garland's farmers are not the vigorous, sensuous, and thoughtful yeomen of Crèvecoeur's *Letters from an American Farmer* (1782) but bent, drab figures. In Garland's "Under the Lion's Paw," from the collection *Main-*

Travelled Roads (1891), local color is not nostalgia but realism deployed for social protest—another way in which realism could never be only "realistic" but was always something more.

Regional writers created not only places but also themes that assumed increasing importance in the twentieth century. The work of Harriet Beecher Stowe, Sarah Orne Jewett, Mary E. Wilkins Freeman, Sui Sin Far, Charlotte Perkins Gilman, Winnemucca, and others may be seen as considering the world from the perspective of women awakening to, protesting against, and offering alternatives to a world dominated by men and male interests and values. Mary Austin was a feminist, and much of her writing, including her classic *Land of Little Rain* (1903), invites readers to see the world from a woman's perspective. But Austin's larger claim on literary history is to have made the deserts of southern California palpable for the first time in literature, as in "The Walking Woman" and other sketches. The marginal characters that people this inhospitable terrain cannot be imagined as existing anywhere else. Stowe, Jewett, and Freeman do more than lament the postwar economic and spiritual decline of New England; their female characters suggest the capacity of human beings to live independently and with dignity in the face of community pressures, patriarchal power over women, including women artists and writers, and material deprivation.

Kate Chopin (1850–1904) may be thought of as a regional writer interested in the customs, language, and landscapes of the northern Louisiana countryside and, downriver, New Orleans. But in addition to preserving local color, Chopin wrote probing psychological fiction. Edna Pontellier of *The Awakening* (1899) looks back to Flaubert's Madame Bovary and forward to Virginia Woolf's Mrs. Dalloway. Chopin began her writing career only after she returned to her native St. Louis from a long sojourn in Louisiana, and in her narratives she memorializes the relaxed and sensuous way of life of the Creole population. As an urban outsider, Chopin was perhaps all the more sensitive to the nuances of Louisiana country life. Perhaps, too, as a woman, she was attracted to a way of life that centered on families and small communities. In any case, her treatment of New Orleans and of Natchitoches Parish provides a fine example of the literary portrayal of a distinctive region—one less severe and less repressed than the towns and villages portrayed by the New England regionalists. Yet Chopin, especially in *The Awakening*, with its portrayal of the interior life of a Protestant woman in a conservative Catholic community, gives the ugly side as well. That *The Awakening* has served to crystallize many women's issues of the turn of the nineteenth century, and since, shows that regional realism, even if its settings and characters are marginal to modern life, is by no means a marginal genre.

REALISM AS SOCIAL ARGUMENT

Between the end of the Civil War and the outbreak of World War I, a vast body of nonfiction prose was devoted to the description, analysis, and critique of social, economic, and political institutions and to the unsolved social problems that were one consequence of rapid growth and change. Women's rights, political corruption, the degradation of the natural world, economic inequity, business deceptions, the exploitation of labor—these became the subjects of articles and books by numerous journalists, historians, social critics, and economists. Much of this writing had literary ambitions, survives as literature, and continues to have genuine power. In his ambitious work of moral exhortation, *The Education of Henry Adams* (1918), Henry Adams registers through a literary sensibility a historian's sense of the disorientation that accompanies rapid and continuous change. Among the most significant and influential voices of the period were those of African Americans speaking out against racism, including W. E. B. Du Bois, Booker T. Washington, Ida B. Wells-Barnett, and Anna Julia Cooper.

Several selections in this volume address the long, shameful history of white injustices against black Americans, as the shift from Reconstruction to Jim Crow laws and the "separate but equal" decision in *Plessy v. Ferguson* (1896) defined and redefined racial inequalities in America. Two works by black writers and leaders from the turn of the century have a special claim on our attention: the widely admired autobiography of Washington, *Up from Slavery* (1900) and the richly imagined *The Souls of Black Folk* (1903) by Du Bois, with its brilliantly argued rejection of Washington's philosophy. The Washington–Du Bois controversy set the major terms of the continuing debate between black leaders and in the black community: which strategies will most effectively hasten equality for blacks educationally, socially, politically, and economically? It is fair to say that in very different ways *Up from Slavery* and *The Souls of Black Folk*—admirable literary achievements in themselves—carried forward the antebellum traditions of such writers as Frederick Douglass and Harriet Jacobs and helped encourage other African American writers of the era such as Wells-Barnett and Cooper, leading eventually to the powerful statements of Harlem Renaissance modernism. In fiction, characters in Pauline Hopkins's novel *Contending Forces* take opposite sides of this argument, while its various implications are also addressed by Charles Chesnutt and James Weldon Johnson in their work. In poetry, authors such as Paul Laurence Dunbar gave voice to African American identities. Their interrelated perspectives on race and national identity are among those in our cluster on "Americanization."

This volume begins with perhaps the two most fundamental American writers of their time and subsequent decades, Walt Whitman and Emily Dickinson. These poets, whose roots are in the antebellum period, continued their work into the 1880s. Though their influence would be felt most strongly after World War II, in hindsight they can be seen as the fountainheads of two major strains in modern poetry: the expansive, gregarious open form of the self-celebratory Whitman and the concise, compact idiosyncratic verse of the radically private Dickinson. Whitman especially, with his interest in the city, prefigures realism and naturalism in surprising ways, while Dickinson focuses on the inner life of the psyche.

In the half century from 1865 to 1914, material, intellectual, social, and psychological changes in the lives of many Americans went forward at such extreme speed and on such a massive scale that the diverse writing of the time registers, at its core, shocked recognition of the human consequences of these radical transformations. Sometimes the shock is expressed in recoil and denial—thus the persistence, in the face of the apparent triumph of realism, of the literature of diversion: nostalgic poetry, sentimental and melodramatic drama, and swashbuckling historical novels. The more enduring fictional and nonfictional prose forms of the era, however, try to come to terms imaginatively with the individual and collective dislocations and discontinuities associated with the closing of the frontier, urbanization, unprecedented immigration, the surge of national wealth unequally distributed, revised conceptions of human nature and destiny, the increasing assertion of the full rights of humanity and citizenship by marginalized minorities, the reordering of family and civil life, and the pervasive spread of mechanical and organizational technologies.

AMERICAN LITERATURE 1865–1914

TEXTS	CONTEXTS
1855 Walt Whitman, *Leaves of Grass*	
1860–65 Emily Dickinson writes several hundred poems	**1860** Short-lived Pony Express runs from Missouri to California
	1861 South Carolina batteries fire on Fort Sumter, initiating the Civil War • Southern states secede from the Union and found the Confederate States of America
	1865 Civil War ends • Reconstruction begins • Lincoln assassinated • Thirteenth Amendment ratified, prohibiting slavery
	1867 United States purchases Alaska from Russia • Jesse Chisholm maps out the Chisholm Trail, connecting Texas cattle ranches to railheads in Kansas City, Cheyenne, Dodge City, and Abilene
	1868 Fourteenth Amendment passed, guaranteeing citizenship to all peoples born in the United States (exclusive of Native peoples) • Congress institutes eight-hour workday for federal employees • sweatshops, using mostly immigrant labor, begin to proliferate in cities
	1869 First transcontinental railroad completed by construction crews composed largely of Chinese laborers • Susan B. Anthony elected president of American Equal Rights Association; Elizabeth Cady Stanton elected president of National Women's Suffrage Association
1870 Bret Harte, *The Luck of Roaring Camp* and Other Sketches	**1870** Fifteenth Amendment, giving African American men the right to vote, ratified
	1871 Indian Appropriation Act deems Native peoples wards of the state
1872 Mark Twain, *Roughing It*	**1872** Yellowstone, first U.S. national park, established
	1874 Women's Christian Temperance Union founded in Cleveland • invention of barbed wire effectively ends the open range
	1876 Custer's regiment defeated by the Sioux and Cheyenne at Little Big Horn River, Montana • Alexander Graham Bell invents the telephone
	1877 Reconstruction ends • segregationist Jim Crow laws begin

Boldface titles indicate works in the anthology.

TEXTS	CONTEXTS
1878 Henry James, "**Daisy Miller**"	
	1879 Thomas Edison invents the electric light bulb • female lawyers permitted to argue before Supreme Court
1880 Joel Chandler Harris, *Uncle Remus: His Songs and Sayings*	1880–1910 Massive immigration from Europe
1881 Helen Hunt Jackson, *A Century of Dishonor*	1881 Tuskegee Institute founded
	1882 J. D. Rockefeller organizes Standard Oil Trust • Chinese Exclusion Act instituted
1883 Emma Lazarus, "**The New Colossus**"	
1884 Twain, *Adventures of Huckleberry Finn*	1884 Tailor's strike in New York City brings national attention to sweatshops
1885 María Amparo Ruiz de Burton, *The Squatter and the Don*	
	1886 Statue of Liberty dedicated • Haymarket Square labor riot leaves eleven dead • American Federation of Labor organized
	1887 General Allotment Act (Dawes Act) passed, limiting the amount of tribally held land
1889 Theodore Roosevelt, *The Winning of the West* • Hamlin Garland, "Under the Lion's Paw"	1889 Violating treaties with Native peoples, Congress opens Indian Territory to settlement, giving rise to the "Oklahoma Land Rush"
1890 Ambrose Bierce, "**An Occurrence at Owl Creek Bridge**"	1890 Census Bureau declares frontier "closed" • Seventh Cavalry massacre at Wounded Knee ends Native American armed resistance to U.S. government • Ellis Island Immigration Station opens
1891 José Martí, "**Our America**" • Mary E. Wilkins Freeman, "**A New England Nun**"	
1892 Anna Julia Cooper, *A Voice from the South* • Charlotte Perkins Gilman, "**The Yellow Wall-Paper**"	
1893 Stephen Crane, *Maggie: A Girl of the Streets* • Frederick Jackson Turner, *The Significance of the Frontier*	1893 World's Columbian Exposition held in Chicago
1895 Crane, **Black Riders** and *The Red Badge of Courage*	
1896 Paul Laurence Dunbar, *Lyrics of a Lowly Life*	1896 *Plessy v. Ferguson* upholds segregated transportation

TEXTS	CONTEXTS
1897 Crane, *The Open Boat and Other Tales of Adventure*	
1898 Abraham Cahan, "The Imported Bridegroom" *and Other Stories*	**1898** United States annexes Hawai'i
	1898–99 Spanish-American War
1899 Charles Chesnutt, *The Conjure Woman* and *The Life of His Youth and Other Stories of the Color Line* • Kate Chopin, *The Awakening* • Frank Norris, *McTeague*	
1900 Theodore Dreiser, *Sister Carrie* • Ida B. Wells-Barnett, *Mob-Rule in New Orleans* • Pauline Hopkins, *Contending Forces*	**1900** U.S. population exceeds seventy-five million
1901 Zitkala-Ša, *Impressions of an Indian Childhood,* The School Days of an Indian Girl, and An Indian Teacher Among Indians • Norris, *The Octopus* • Booker T. Washington, *Up From Slavery*	**1901** J. P. Morgan founds U.S. Steel Corporation • first transatlantic radio • oil discovered in Spindletop, Texas
1903 W. E. B. Du Bois, *The Souls of Black Folks* • London, *The Call of the Wild* • Washington Matthews edits *The Night Chant: A Navajo Ceremony*	**1903** Henry Ford founds Ford Motor Co. • Wright brothers make the first successful airplane flight • *The Great Train Robbery* is first U.S. cinematic narrative
1904 Edith Wharton, "The Other Two"	**1904** National Child Labor Committee formed
	1905 Industrial Workers of the World (the Wobblies) founded
	1906 April 18: San Francisco earthquake and fire
1907 Henry Adams, *The Education of Henry Adams,* privately printed	
1909 Mary Austin, *Lost Borders*	**1909** National Association for the Advancement of Colored People (NAACP) founded
1910 Jane Addams, *Twenty Years at Hull-House* • Sui Sin Far, *Mrs. Spring Fragrance* • Francis Densmore publishes *Chippewa Songs*	**1910** Mexican Revolution
1912 James Weldon Johnson • *The Autobiography of an Ex-Coloured Man*	
	1914 U.S. Marines invade and occupy Vera Cruz, Mexico • Panama Canal opens

16

WALT WHITMAN
1819–1892

Walt Whitman revolutionized American poetry. Responding to Emerson's call in "The Poet" (1842) for an American bard who would address all "the facts of the animal economy, sex, nutriment, gestation, birth," he put the living, breathing, sexual body at the center of much of his poetry, challenging conventions of the day. Responding also to Emerson's call for a "metre-making argument" rather than mere meters, he rejected traditions of poetic scansion and elevated diction, improvising the form that has came to be known as free verse, while adopting a wide-ranging vocabulary opening new possibilities for poetic expression. A poet of democracy, Whitman celebrated the mystical, divine potential of the individual; a poet of the urban, he wrote about the sights, sounds, and energies of the modern metropolis. In his 1855 preface to *Leaves of Grass*, he declared that "the proof of a poet is that his country absorbs him as affectionately as he has absorbed it." On the evidence of his enormous influence on later poets—Hart Crane, Langston Hughes, Robert Lowell, Allen Ginsberg, Cherrie Moraga, and countless others, including Spain's Federico García Lorca and Chile's Pablo Neruda—Whitman not only was affectionately absorbed by his own country but remains a persistent presence who continues to influence poetic traditions throughout the world.

Whitman was born on May 31, 1819, in West Hills, Long Island (New York), the second of eight surviving children of the Quakers Louisa Van Velsor and Walter Whitman. In 1823, Whitman's father, a farmer turned carpenter, sought to take advantage of a building boom by moving the family to Brooklyn—then a town at the western and most urbanized part of Long Island. The Whitmans' ancestors were early settlers of Long Island, and stories survived of some forceful characters among them. Whitman left school at eleven to become an office boy in a law firm, and then briefly worked for a doctor. By the age of twelve he was employed in the printing office of a newspaper, reading the novels of Sir Walter Scott and contributing short items; and when his family moved east on Long Island in 1833, he remained in Brooklyn on his own. In his midteens he contributed pieces to one of the best Manhattan papers, the *Mirror*, and often crossed the East River on the ferry from Brooklyn to Manhattan to attend debating societies and the theater. He was hired as a compositor in Manhattan in 1835, but two fires later that year disrupted the printing industry, and he rejoined his family. For five years Whitman taught at country and small-town schools at East Norwich, Long Swamp, and other towns on Long Island, interrupting his teaching to start a newspaper of his own in 1838 and to work briefly on another Long Island paper. By early 1840 he had started the series "Sun-Down Papers from the Desk of a School-Master" for the Jamaica, New York, *Democrat* and was writing poems and fiction. One of his stories prophetically culminated with the dream of writing "a wonderful and ponderous book."

Just before he turned twenty-one Whitman stopped teaching, went back to Manhattan, and began work at Park Benjamin's *New World*, a literary weekly that pirated British novels; he also began a political career by speaking at Democratic rallies. Simultaneously, he published stories in the *Democratic Review*, the foremost magazine of the Democratic Party, which was also Hawthorne's main publishing venue during the 1840s. Before he was twenty-three, Whitman became editor of a Manhattan daily, the *Aurora*. He exulted in the extremes of the city, where street-gang violence was countered by the lectures of Emerson and where even a young editor could get to know the poet William Cullen Bryant, editor of the *Evening Post*. Fired from the *Aurora*, which publicly charged him with laziness, he wrote a temperance novel, *Franklin Evans, or the Inebriate*, for a one-issue extra of the *New World* late in 1842. After three years of various literary and political jobs, he returned to Brooklyn in 1845, becoming a special contributor to the Long Island *Star*, assigned to Manhattan events, including theatrical and musical performances. All through the 1840s he attended operas on his journalist's passes, hearing the greatest singers of the time, and he would later say that without the "emotions, raptures, uplifts" of opera he could never have written *Leaves of Grass*. Just before he was twenty-seven he took over the editorship of the Brooklyn *Eagle*, writing most of the literary reviews, which included books by Carlyle, Emerson, Melville, Fuller, and Goethe, among others. Like most Democrats, he was able to justify the Mexican War (1846–48) by linking territorial acquisition to personal and civic betterment, and by hailing the great American mission of "peopling the New World with a noble race." Yet at the beginning of 1848 he was fired from the *Eagle* because, like Bryant, he had become a Free-Soiler, opposed to the acquisition of more territory for slavery. Taking a chance offer of newspaper work, he traveled to New Orleans, his only extensive journey until late in life, when in 1879 and 1880 he made trips as far west as Colorado and north to Canada.

By the summer of 1848, Whitman was back in Brooklyn, serving as a delegate to the Buffalo Free-Soil convention and helping to found the Free-Soil newspaper the *Brooklyn Freeman*. Around this time he began writing poetry in a serious way, experimenting with form and prosody; he published several topical poems in 1850, including "Europe," which would appear in *Leaves of Grass*. He also started a house-building business in Brooklyn, acting as a contractor and sometimes hiring himself out as a carpenter, while continuing to read, study, and write. He became a student of astronomy, attending lectures and reading recent books; some of this material, along with other scientific information, appears in the poetry. Cutting articles out of the great British quarterlies and monthlies, he annotated them and argued with them in the margins, developing in the process clear ideas about aesthetics, such as his distrust of "fine" or what he termed "artificial" poetry. Around the end of 1854 he gave up carpentry and committed himself to writing. He also enjoyed sessions with literary, publishing, and theatrical people in such bohemian spots as the famous Pfaff's saloon on lower Broadway.

Whitman's notebook fragments suggest that he envisioned the overall shape for his first volume of poetry in 1853 and 1854. On May 15, 1855, he took out a copyright for *Leaves of Grass*, and he spent the spring and early summer seeing his book through the press, probably setting some of the type himself. Published in Brooklyn, New York, during the first week of July, the volume, bound in dark green cloth with a sprig of grass in gilt on the cover, contained twelve untitled poems (including the initial version of "Song of Myself") along with an exuberant preface declaring his ambition to be *the* American bard. In the image of Whitman on the book's frontispiece, which was based on an 1854 daguerreotype, the bearded Whitman—rejecting the conventional suit jacket, buttoned-up shirt, and high collar of the formal studio portrait—stands with one arm akimbo, one hand in a pocket, workingman's hat on slightly cocked head, shirt unbuttoned at the collar, looking directly at the reader. The image, like the poetry itself, defied convention by aligning the poet with working people rather than the educated classes. The poems, with their absence of standard verse and stanza patterns (although strongly rhythmic and controlled by numerous poetic devices of repetition and variation), also introduced his use of "catalogs"—journalistic and encyclopedic listings—that were to become a hallmark of his style, turning poetry toward realism. In "The Poet," Emerson had called for a poetry of logrolling, political stump speeches, northern trade, southern planting, and western clearing; "America is a poem in our eyes," he said. This was the challenge that Whitman initially sought to answer by producing national, and nationalistic, poetry from a democratic perspective. Appearing in 1855 during a time of increasing sectional conflict, the volume was offered as a statement of "union." But ordinary people were less drawn to Whitman's poetry than to that of the Harvard professor Longfellow, the era's most popular poet by far; in his lifetime, Whitman fell short of achieving his goal of being regarded as the writer for (or representative of) the masses.

Whitman's father died just after *Leaves of Grass* appeared, and Whitman became mostly responsible for support of his mother and a mentally slow younger brother. He sent out numerous presentation and review copies of his book, receiving an immediate response from Emerson, who greeted him "at the beginning of a great career," but met mostly silence. As weeks passed with few reviews, Whitman chose to write a few himself to be published anonymously, praising *Leaves of Grass* in the *American Phrenological Journal*, for instance, as one of "the most glorious triumphs, in the known history of literature." In October he let Horace Greeley's *New York Tribune* print Emerson's private letter of praise, and he put clippings of the letter in presentation copies to Longfellow, among others. Emerson termed Whitman's appropriation of the letter "a strange, rude thing," but he remained interested in meeting the poet. While Whitman was angling for reviews in England and working on expanding his book, Emerson visited him in December of 1855. Thoreau, who admired *Leaves of Grass* but found several of its poems "simply sensual," visited him later in 1856. That year also saw the appearance of the second edition of *Leaves of Grass*, now with thirty-three poems, including "Crossing Brooklyn Ferry" under the title "Sundown Poem." Returning to miscellaneous journalism, Whitman edited the Brooklyn *Times* from 1857 to 1859 and published several pieces in the *Times* affirming his Free-Soiler hopes for a continued national expansion into the western territories that would not entail the expansion of slavery.

During the late 1850s Whitman wrote a group of twelve poems, "Live Oak, with Moss," that seems to recount his passionate love for another man. Had he printed it, the sequence would have constituted a public declaration of the pleasures, but also the ordinariness, of same-sex love—a stunning challenge to the conventional norms of the time. He chose instead to disperse these poems among others treating bodily and romantic attractions, and including in the third (1860) edition of *Leaves of Grass* a cluster (he had begun to break his poems into clusters) called "Enfans d'Adam," for which he wrote fifteen poems focused on what he termed the "amative" love of man for woman in contrast to the "adhesive" love of man for man. Adhesive love figured in forty-five poems under the heading "Calamus," among which he distributed (or concealed) his "Live Oak" poems. The two clusters as printed in 1860 differ from the poems in the now-familiar 1891–92 "Children of Adam" (as "Enfans d'Adam" was retitled in 1867) and "Calamus" sections, for in the intervening editions (1867, 1871, 1881) Whitman revised poems and moved some poems out of and into the clusters, as he did with all the poems in the expanded editions he published. For him, *Leaves of Grass* was an organic creation responsive to the fluctuations of his life, so that really to read him would require comprehending all the editions at once. Inevitably, editors and anthologists have been forced to make choices, as we do here.

With the outbreak of the Civil War, Whitman turned his attention to the wounded. Having visited prisoners and the sick for years, this role merged almost imperceptibly into Civil War service as a hospital attendant. He started at New-York Hospital; but in early 1863, after visiting with his wounded brother George in an army camp in Virginia, he moved to Washington, D.C., and began to work at the huge open-air military hospitals there. Nursing gave Whitman a profound sense of vocation. As he wrote a friend in 1863: "I am very happy . . . I was never so beloved. I am running over with health, fat, red & sunburnt in face. I tell thee I am just the one to go to our sick boys." But ministering to tens of thousands of maimed and dying young men took its toll, and eventually contributed to undercutting his previously buoyant physical health. He succinctly voiced his despair in a notebook entry of 1864: "the dead, the dead, the dead, *our* dead." At the same time, he worked on a series of war poems, tracing his changed attitudes toward the conflict, from his early jingoistic celebrations of impending battles to starkly realistic depictions of the ravages of warfare. He later wrote a section in his prose work *Specimen Days* (1882) titled "The Real War Will Never Get in the Books"; but to incorporate the "real war" into a book of poetry became one of the dominant impulses of the *Drum-Taps* collection, which he published in 1865. After Lincoln's assassination, Whitman reissued the volume with a sequel including "O Captain! My Captain!" and "When Lilacs Last in the Dooryard Bloom'd," his famous elegy for the murdered president.

As he prepared *Drum-Taps and Sequel* for publication in late 1865, Whitman was also revising a copy of the Boston edition (1860) of *Leaves of Grass* at his desk in the Department of the Interior, where he had obtained a position as clerk to support himself while doing his hospital work. The new secretary of the interior, James Harlan, read the annotated copy and abruptly fired Whitman on the grounds that he was writing an obscene book, objecting to Whitman's frankness about bodily functions and heterosexual love; the erotic same-sex implications of some of the poems remained uncommented upon. Whitman's friend William O'Connor quickly got him a new position as clerk in the attorney general's office; and in his rage at the firing (and with significant help from Whitman), he wrote *The Good Gray Poet* (1866), a piece of pure hero worship in which Whitman was identified with Jesus and Harlan with the forces of evil. O'Connor's book appeared shortly after the publication of *Drum-Taps*, and only strengthened Whitman's determination not to yield to censorship or to apologize for his earlier poems. He continued to rework *Leaves of Grass*, incorporating *Drum-Taps* into it in 1867, and with his friends' help continued to propagandize for its recognition as a landmark in the history of poetry. Ruminations that in earlier years might have gone into editorials went into essays in 1867 and 1868 numbers of the New York periodical *Galaxy*, and then (in expanded form) into his book *Democratic Vistas* (1870), a disquisition on democracy and democratic literature in the United States, based on his sometimes condemnatory but always hopeful appraisal of the possibilities of postwar culture.

The Washington years ended early in 1873 when Whitman suffered a paralytic stroke. His mother died a few months later, and Whitman joined his brother George's household in Camden, New Jersey, to recuperate. During the second year of his illness, the government ceased to hold his clerk job open for him, and he became dependent for a living on occasional publication in newspapers and magazines. The 1867 edition of *Leaves of Grass* had involved much reworking and rearrangement, and the fifth edition (1871) continued that process, with many of the original *Drum-Taps* poems distributed throughout the book and with an assemblage of old and new poems in a large new section, "Passage to India." In 1876 he privately published a prose work, *Memoranda during the War*, and six years later he brought out *Specimen Days*, which has affinities with his early editorial accounts of strolls through the city but is even more intensely personal, the record of representative days in the life of a poet who had lived in the midst of great national events.

Throughout the 1870s and early 1880s, Whitman was increasingly noticed by the leading writers of the time, especially in England. The English poet Algernon Swinburne sent him a poem, the Poet Laureate Alfred, Lord Tennyson sent him an admiring letter, and both Longfellow and Oscar Wilde visited him in Camden. Despite his frail health, he lectured on Thomas Paine in Philadelphia in 1877 and on Abraham Lincoln in New York in 1879 (he would continue to deliver occasional public lectures on Lincoln until 1890). Opposition to his poetry because of its supposed immorality began to dissipate, and readers, having become accustomed over time to Whitman's poetic devices, began to recognize the poet as an artist. Still, in 1881, when the reputable Boston firm of James R. Osgood & Co. printed the sixth edition of *Leaves of Grass*, the Boston district attorney threatened to prosecute on the grounds of obscenity. Ironically, when the Philadelphia firm of Rees Welsh and Co. reprinted this edition in 1882, the publicity contributed to Whitman's greatest sales in his lifetime: he earned nearly $1,500 in royalties from that edition (around $50,000 in today's value), compared to the $25 he had earned from the Osgood edition before the publisher withdrew it.

In 1884, the still infirm Whitman moved to a cottage at 328 Mickle Street in Camden, which he purchased for $1,750. A year later friends and admirers, including Mark

Twain and John Greenleaf Whittier, presented him with a horse and buggy for local travel. He had another stroke in 1888 and in 1890 made preparations for his death by signing a $4,000 contract for the construction in Camden's Harleigh Cemetery of a granite mausoleum, or what he termed a "burial house," suitable for a national bard. In 1891 he did the final editing of *Complete Prose Works* (1892) and oversaw the preparations of the "deathbed" edition of the now more than three hundred poems in *Leaves of Grass* (1891–92), which was in fact a reissue of the 1881 edition with the addition of two later groups of poems, "Sands at Seventy" (from *November Boughs* [1888]) and *Good-bye My Fancy* (1891). Whitman died at Camden on March 26, 1892, and was buried in Harleigh Cemetery in the mausoleum he had helped design.

The Whitman poems reprinted here, regardless of when they were first composed and printed, are given in their final form: that of the 1891–92 edition of *Leaves of Grass*.

[handwritten margin note: Id- personal pleasure. Still has community and unpleasant emotions]

[handwritten margin note: Bodies: live —female —male; dead—; Slaves no free will]

Song of Myself[1]

1

I celebrate myself, and sing myself,
And what I assume you shall assume,
For every atom belonging to me as good belongs to you.

[handwritten margin note: Who is "I"? ambiguity of "I" or "myself" everyone is one]

I loafe and invite my soul,
I lean and loafe at my ease observing a spear of summer grass.   5

My tongue, every atom of my blood, form'd from this soil, this air,
Born here of parents born here from parents the same, and their parents the same,
I, now thirty-seven years old in perfect health begin,
Hoping to cease not till death.

Creeds and schools in abeyance,   10
Retiring back a while sufficed at what they are, but never forgotten,
I harbor for good or bad, I permit to speak at every hazard,
Nature without check with original energy.

2

Houses and rooms are full of perfumes, the shelves are crowded with perfumes,
I breathe the fragrance myself and know it and like it,
The distillation would intoxicate me also, but I shall not let it.   15

---

1. In the 1855 first edition of *Leaves of Grass*, the poem that has come to be known as "Song of Myself" appeared without a title and without numbered subdivisions or stanzas. For the 1856 edition, Whitman titled it "Poem of Walt Whitman, an American," and in the 1860 edition he titled it "Walt Whitman"; it retained that title in the 1867 and 1871 editions. Whitman first gave the title "Song of Myself" to this, his most famous and influential poem, in the 1881 edition of *Leaves of Grass*. In addition to the change of title and use of numbered subdivisions, Whitman made numerous other changes in the poem from the first 1855 printing to the 1881 final version.

The atmosphere is not a perfume, it has no taste of the distillation, it is
  odorless,
It is for my mouth forever, I am in love with it,
I will go to the bank by the wood and become undisguised and naked,
I am mad for it to be in contact with me.   20

The smoke of my own breath,
Echoes, ripples, buzz'd whispers, love-root, silk-thread, crotch and vine,
My respiration and inspiration, the beating of my heart, the passing of
  blood and air through my lungs,
The sniff of green leaves and dry leaves, and of the shore and dark-color'd
  sea-rocks, and of hay in the barn,
The sound of the belch'd words of my voice loos'd to the eddies of the
  wind,   25
A few light kisses, a few embraces, a reaching around of arms,
The play of shine and shade on the trees as the supple boughs wag,
The delight alone or in the rush of the streets, or along the fields and
  hill-sides,
The feeling of health, the full-noon trill, the song of me rising from bed and
  meeting the sun.

Have you reckon'd a thousand acres much? have you reckon'd the earth
  much?   30
Have you practis'd so long to learn to read?
Have you felt so proud to get at the meaning of poems?

Stop this day and night with me and you shall possess the origin of all
  poems,
You shall possess the good of the earth and sun, (there are millions of suns
  left,)
You shall no longer take things at second or third hand, nor look through
  the eyes of the dead, nor feed on the spectres in books,   35
You shall not look through my eyes either, nor take things from me,
You shall listen to all sides and filter them from your self.

3

I have heard what the talkers were talking, the talk of the beginning and
  the end,
But I do not talk of the beginning or the end.

There was never any more inception than there is now,   40
Nor any more youth or age than there is now,
And will never be any more perfection than there is now,
Nor any more heaven or hell than there is now.
Urge and urge and urge,
Always the procreant urge of the world.   45

Out of the dimness opposite equals advance, always substance and
  increase, always sex,
Always a knit of identity, always distinction, always a breed of life.

To elaborate is no avail, learn'd and unlearn'd feel that it is so.

Sure as the most certain sure, plumb in the uprights, well entretied,[2]
    braced in the beams,
Stout as a horse, affectionate, haughty, electrical,   50
I and this mystery here we stand.

Clear and sweet is my soul, and clear and sweet is all that is not my soul.

Lack one lacks both, and the unseen is proved by the seen,
Till that becomes unseen and receives proof in its turn.

Showing the best and dividing it from the worst age vexes age,   55
Knowing the perfect fitness and equanimity of things, while they discuss I
    am silent, and go bathe and admire myself.

Welcome is every organ and attribute of me, and of any man hearty and
    clean,
Not an inch nor a particle of an inch is vile, and none shall be less familiar
    than the rest.

I am satisfied—I see, dance, laugh, sing;
As the hugging and loving bed-fellow sleeps at my side through the night,
    and withdraws at the peep of the day with stealthy tread,   60
Leaving me baskets cover'd with white towels swelling the house with their
    plenty,
Shall I postpone my acceptation and realization and scream at my eyes,
That they turn from gazing after and down the road,
And forthwith cipher[3] and show me to a cent,
Exactly the value of one and exactly the value of two, and which is
    ahead?
                                          65

4

Trippers and askers surround me,
People I meet, the effect upon me of my early life or the ward and city I live
    in, or the nation,
The latest dates, discoveries, inventions, societies, authors old and new,
My dinner, dress, associates, looks, compliments, dues,
The real or fancied indifference of some man or woman I love,   70
The sickness of one of my folks or of myself, or ill-doing or loss or lack of
    money, or depressions or exaltations,
Battles, the horrors of fratricidal war, the fever of doubtful news, the fitful
    events;
These come to me days and nights and go from me again,
But they are not the Me myself.

Apart from the pulling and hauling stands what I am,   75
Stands amused, complacent, compassionating, idle, unitary,
Looks down, is erect, or bends an arm on an impalpable certain rest,
Looking with side-curved head curious what will come next,
Both in and out of the game and watching and wondering at it.

---

2. Cross-braced.   3. Calculate.

Backward I see in my own days where I sweated through fog with linguists
    and contenders,   80
I have no mockings or arguments, I witness and wait.

5

I believe in you my soul, the other I am must not abase itself to you,
And you must not be abased to the other.

Loafe with me on the grass, loose the stop from your throat,
Not words, not music or rhyme I want, not custom or lecture, not even the
    best,   85
Only the lull I like, the hum of your valvèd voice.

I mind how once we lay such a transparent summer morning,
How you settled your head athwart my hips and gently turn'd over upon me,
And parted the shirt from my bosom-bone, and plunged your tongue to my
    bare-stript heart,
And reach'd till you felt my beard, and reach'd till you held my feet.   90

Swiftly arose and spread around me the peace and knowledge that pass all
    the argument of the earth,
And I know that the hand of God is the promise of my own,
And I know that the spirit of God is the brother of my own,
And that all the men ever born are also my brothers, and the women my
    sisters and lovers,
And that a kelson[4] of the creation is love,   95
And limitless are leaves stiff or drooping in the fields,
And brown ants in the little wells beneath them,
And mossy scabs of the worm fence,[5] heap'd stones, elder, mullein and
    poke-weed.

6

A child said *What is the grass?* fetching it to me with full hands;
How could I answer the child? I do not know what it is any more than
    he.   100

I guess it must be the flag of my disposition, out of hopeful green stuff
    woven.

Or I guess it is the handkerchief of the Lord,
A scented gift and remembrancer designedly dropt,
Bearing the owner's name someway in the corners, that we may see and
    remark, and say *Whose?*

Or I guess the grass is itself a child, the produced babe of the vegetation. 105

Or I guess it is a uniform hieroglyphic,
And it means, Sprouting alike in broad zones and narrow zones,

---

4. A basic structural unit; a reinforcing timber   5. Zigzag fence of split rails.
bolted to the keel (backbone) of a ship.

Growing among black folks as among white,
Kanuck, Tuckahoe, Congressman, Cuff,[6] I give them the same, I receive
    them the same.

And now it seems to me the beautiful uncut hair of graves.   110

Tenderly will I use you curling grass,
It may be you transpire from the breasts of young men,
It may be if I had known them I would have loved them,
It may be you are from old people, or from offspring taken soon out of their
    mothers' laps,
And here you are the mothers' laps.   115

This grass is very dark to be from the white heads of old mothers,
Darker than the colorless beards of old men,
Dark to come from under the faint red roofs of mouths.

O I perceive after all so many uttering tongues,
And I perceive they do not come from the roofs of mouths for nothing.   120

I wish I could translate the hints about the dead young men and women,
And the hints about old men and mothers, and the offspring taken soon out
    of their laps.

What do you think has become of the young and old men?
And what do you think has become of the women and children?

They are alive and well somewhere,   125
The smallest sprout shows there is really no death,
And if ever there was it led forward life, and does not wait at the end to
    arrest it,
And ceas'd the moment life appear'd.

All goes onward and outward, nothing collapses,
And to die is different from what any one supposed, and luckier.   130

7

Has any one supposed it lucky to be born?
I hasten to inform him or her it is just as lucky to die, and I know it.

I pass death with the dying and birth with the new-wash'd babe, and am
    not contain'd between my hat and boots,
And peruse manifold objects, no two alike and every one good,
The earth good and the stars good, and their adjuncts all good.   135

I am not an earth nor an adjunct of an earth,
I am the mate and companion of people, all just as immortal and
    fathomless as myself,
(They do not know how immortal, but I know.)

---

6. Black, from the African word *cuffee* (name for a
black male born on a Friday). "Kanuck": French
Canadian (now considered pejorative). "Tuckahoe": Virginian, from eaters of the American Indian food
plant Tuckahoe.

Every kind for itself and its own, for me mine male and female,
For me those that have been boys and that love women,   140
For me the man that is proud and feels how it stings to be slighted,
For me the sweet-heart and the old maid, for me mothers and the mothers
    of mothers,
For me lips that have smiled, eyes that have shed tears,
For me children and the begetters of children.

Undrape! you are not guilty to me, nor stale nor discarded,   145
I see through the broadcloth and gingham whether or no,
And am around, tenacious, acquisitive, tireless, and cannot be shaken
    away.

                                    8

The little one sleeps in its cradle,
I lift the gauze and look a long time, and silently brush away flies with my
    hand.

The youngster and the red-faced girl turn aside up the bushy hill,   150
I peeringly view them from the top.

The suicide sprawls on the bloody floor of the bedroom,
I witness the corpse with its dabbled hair, I note where the pistol has fallen.

The blab of the pave, tires of carts, sluff of boot-soles, talk of the
    promenaders,
The heavy omnibus, the driver with his interrogating thumb, the clank of
    the shod horses on the granite floor,   155
The snow-sleighs, clinking, shouted jokes, pelts of snow-balls,
The hurrahs for popular favorites, the fury of rous'd mobs,
The flap of the curtain'd litter, a sick man inside borne to the hospital,
The meeting of enemies, the sudden oath, the blows and fall,
The excited crowd, the policeman with his star quickly working his passage
    to the centre of the crowd,   160
The impassive stones that receive and return so many echoes,
What groans of over-fed or half-starv'd who fall sunstruck or in fits,
What exclamations of women taken suddenly who hurry home and give
    birth to babes,
What living and buried speech is always vibrating here, what howls
    restrain'd by decorum,
Arrests of criminals, slights, adulterous offers made, acceptances,
    rejections with convex lips,   165
I mind them or the show or resonance of them—I come and I depart.

                                    9

The big doors of the country barn stand open and ready,
The dried grass of the harvest-time loads the slow-drawn wagon,
The clear light plays on the brown gray and green intertinged,
The armfuls are pack'd to the sagging mow.   170

I am there, I help, I came stretch'd atop of the load,
I felt its soft jolts, one leg reclined on the other,
I jump from the cross-beams and sieze the clover and timothy,
And roll head over heels and tangle my hair full of wisps.

10

Alone far in the wilds and mountains I hunt,   175
Wandering amazed at my own lightness and glee,
In the late afternoon choosing a safe spot to pass the night,
Kindling a fire and broiling the fresh-kill'd game,
Falling asleep on the gather'd leaves with my dog and gun by my side.

The Yankee clipper is under her sky-sails, she cuts the sparkle and scud,   180
My eyes settle the land, I bend at her prow or shout joyously from the deck.

The boatmen and clam-diggers arose early and stopt for me,
I tuck'd my trowser-ends in my boots and went and had a good time;
You should have been with us that day round the chowder-kettle.

I saw the marriage of the trapper in the open air in the far west, the bride
        was a red girl,   185
Her father and his friends sat near cross-legged and dumbly smoking, they
        had moccasins to their feet and large thick blankets hanging from their
        shoulders,
On a bank lounged the trapper, he was drest mostly in skins, his luxuriant
        beard and curls protected his neck, he held his bride by the hand,
She had long eyelashes, her head was bare, her coarse straight locks
        descended upon her voluptuous limbs and reach'd to her feet.

The runaway slave came to my house and stopt outside,
I heard his motions crackling the twigs of the woodpile,   190
Through the swung half-door of the kitchen I saw him limpsy[7] and weak,
And went where he sat on a log and led him in and assured him,
And brought water and fill'd a tub for his sweated body and bruis'd feet,
And gave him a room that enter'd from my own, and gave him some coarse
        clean clothes,
And remember perfectly well his revolving eyes and his awkwardness,   195
And remember putting plasters on the galls of his neck and ankles;
He staid with me a week before he was recuperated and pass'd north,
I had him sit next me at table, my fire-lock lean'd in the corner.

11

Twenty-eight young men bathe by the shore,
Twenty-eight young men and all so friendly;   200
Twenty-eight years of womanly life and all so lonesome.

She owns the fine house by the rise of the bank,
She hides handsome and richly drest aft the blinds of the window.

7. Limping or swaying.

Which of the young men does she like the best?
Ah the homeliest of them is beautiful to her.   205

Where are you off to, lady? for I see you,
You splash in the water there, yet stay stock still in your room.

Dancing and laughing along the beach came the twenty-ninth bather,
The rest did not see her, but she saw them and loved them.

The beards of the young men glisten'd with wet, it ran from their long
    hair,   210
Little streams pass'd over their bodies.

An unseen hand also pass'd over their bodies,
It descended tremblingly from their temples and ribs.

The young men float on their backs, their white bellies bulge to the sun,
    they do not ask who seizes fast to them,
They do not know who puffs and declines with pendant and
    bending arch,   215
They do not think whom they souse with spray.

12

The butcher-boy puts off his killing-clothes, or sharpens his knife at the
    stall in the market,
I loiter enjoying his repartee and his shuffle and break-down.[8]

Blacksmiths with grimed and hairy chests environ the anvil,
Each has his main-sledge, they are all out, there is a great heat in the
    fire.   220

From the cinder-strew'd threshold I follow their movements,
The lithe sheer of their waists plays even with their massive arms,
Overhand the hammers swing, overhand so slow, overhand so sure,
They do not hasten, each man hits in his place.

13

The negro holds firmly the reins of his four horses, the block swags
    underneath on its tied-over chain,   225
The negro that drives the long dray of the stone-yard, steady and tall he
    stands pois'd on one leg on the string-piece,[9]
His blue shirt exposes his ample neck and breast and loosens over his
    hip-band,
His glance is calm and commanding, he tosses the slouch of his hat away
    from his forehead,
The sun falls on his crispy hair and mustache, falls on the black of his
    polish'd and perfect limbs.

8. Dances familiar in popular entertainment and minstrelsy. The "shuffle" involves the sliding of feet across the floor, and the "break-down" is faster and noisier.
9. Long, heavy timber used to keep a load in place.

I behold the picturesque giant and love him, and I do not stop there,   230
I go with the team also.

In me the caresser of life wherever moving, backward as well as forward
     sluing,[1]
To niches aside and junior[2] bending, not a person or object missing,
Absorbing all to myself and for this song.

Oxen that rattle the yoke and chain or halt in the leafy shade, what is that
     you express in your eyes?
   235
It seems to me more than all the print I have read in my life.

My tread scares the wood-drake and wood-duck on my distant and day-long
     ramble.
They rise together, they slowly circle around.

I believe in those wing'd purposes,
And acknowledge red, yellow, white, playing within me,   240
And consider green and violet and the tufted crown[3] intentional,
And do not call the tortoise unworthy because she is not something else,
And the jay in the woods never studied the gamut,[4] yet trills pretty well to
     me,
And the look of the bay mare shames silliness out of me.

14

The wild gander leads his flock through the cool night,   245
Ya-honk he says, and sounds it down to me like an invitation,
The pert may suppose it meaningless, but I listening close,
Find its purpose and place up there toward the wintry sky.

The sharp-hoof'd moose of the north, the cat on the house-sill, the
     chickadee, the prairie-dog,
The litter of the grunting sow as they tug at her teats,   250
The brood of the turkey-hen and she with her half-spread wings,
I see in them and myself the same old law.
The press of my foot to the earth springs a hundred affections,
They scorn the best I can do to relate them.

I am enamour'd of growing out-doors,
Of men that live among cattle or taste of the ocean or woods,   255
Of the builders and steerers of ships and the wielders of axes and mauls,
     and the drivers of horses,
I can eat and sleep with them week in and week out.

What is commonest, cheapest, nearest, easiest, is Me,
Me going in for my chances, spending for vast returns,   260
Adorning myself to bestow myself on the first that will take me,
Not asking the sky to come down to my good will,
Scattering it freely forever.

1. Twisting.   3. Of the wood drake.
2. Smaller.   4. Here, the series of recognized musical notes.

15

The pure contralto sings in the organ loft,
The carpenter dresses his plank, the tongue of his foreplane whistles its
    wild ascending lisp,   265
The married and unmarried children ride home to their Thanksgiving
    dinner,
The pilot seizes the king-pin,[5] he heaves down with a strong arm,
The mate stands braced in the whale-boat, lance and harpoon are ready,
The duck-shooter walks by silent and cautious stretches,
The deacons are ordain'd with cross'd hands at the altar,   270
The spinning-girl retreats and advances to the hum of the big wheel,
The farmer stops by the bars as he walks on a First-day[6] loafe and looks at
    the oats and rye,
The lunatic is carried at last to the asylum a confirm'd case,
(He will never sleep any more as he did in the cot in his mother's
    bed-room;)
The jour printer[7] with gray head and gaunt jaws works at his case,   275
He turns his quid of tobacco while his eyes blurr with the manuscript;
The malform'd limbs are tied to the surgeon's table,
What is removed drops horribly in a pail;
The quadroon[8] girl is sold at the auction-stand, the drunkard nods by the
    bar-room stove,
The machinist rolls up his sleeves, the policeman travels his beat, the gate-
    keeper marks who pass,   280
The young fellow drives the express-wagon, (I love him, though I do not
    know him;)
The half-breed straps on his light boots to compete in the race,
The western turkey-shooting draws old and young, some lean on their
    rifles, some sit on logs,
Out from the crowd steps the marksman, takes his position, levels his
    piece;
The groups of newly-come immigrants cover the wharf or levee,   285
As the woolly-pates[9] hoe in the sugar-field, the overseer views them from
    his saddle,
The bugle calls in the ball-room, the gentlemen run for their partners, the
    dancers bow to each other,
The youth lies awake in the cedar-roof'd garret and harks to the musical
    rain,
The Wolverine[1] sets traps on the creek that helps fill the Huron,
The squaw wrapt in her yellow-hemm'd cloth is offering moccasins and
    bead-bags for sale,   290
The connoisseur peers along the exhibition-gallery with half-shut eyes bent
    sideways,
As the deck-hands make fast the steamboat the plank is thrown for the
    shore-going passengers,

---

5. The extended spoke of the pilot wheel, used to maintain leverage during storms.
6. Sunday. Whitman frequently uses the numerical Quaker designations for the names of days and months. "Bars": i.e., of a rail fence.
7. I.e., a journeyman printer, or one who has passed an apprenticeship and is fully qualified for all professional work.
8. One quarter black.
9. Black slaves (with stereotypical emphasis on the "woolly" hair on their heads).
1. Inhabitant of Michigan.

The young sister holds out the skein while the elder sister winds it off in a
    ball, and stops now and then for the knots,
The one-year wife is recovering and happy having a week ago borne her
    first child,
The clean-hair'd Yankee girl works with her sewing-machine or in the
    factory or mill,   295
The paving-man[2] leans on his two-handed rammer, the reporter's lead flies
    swiftly over the note-book, the sign-painter is lettering with blue and
    gold,
The canal boy trots on the tow-path, the book-keeper counts at his desk,
    the shoemaker waxes his thread,
The conductor beats time for the band and all the performers follow him,
The child is baptized, the convert is making his first professions,
The regatta is spread on the bay, the race is begun, (how the white sails
    sparkle!)   300
The drover watching his drove sings out to them that would stray,
The pedler sweats with his pack on his back, (the purchaser higgling about
    the odd cent;)
The bride unrumples her white dress, the minute-hand of the clock moves
    slowly,
The opium-eater reclines with rigid head and just-open'd lips,
The prostitute draggles her shawl, her bonnet bobs on her tipsy and
    pimpled neck,   305
The crowd laugh at her blackguard oaths, the men jeer and wink to each
    other,
(Miserable! I do not laugh at your oaths nor jeer you;)
The President holding a cabinet council is surrounded by the great
    Secretaries,
On the piazza walk three matrons stately and friendly with twined arms,
The crew of the fish-smack pack repeated layers of halibut in the hold,   310
The Missourian crosses the plains toting his wares and his cattle,
As the fare-collector goes through the train he gives notice by the jingling
    of loose change,
The floor-men are laying the floor, the tinners are tinning the roof, the
    masons are calling for mortar,
In single file each shouldering his hod pass onward the laborers;
Seasons pursuing each other the indescribable crowd is gather'd, it is the
    fourth of Seventh-month,[3] (what salutes of cannon and small arms!) 315
Seasons pursuing each other the plougher ploughs, the mower mows, and
    the winter-grain falls in the ground;
Off on the lakes the pike-fisher watches and waits by the hole in the frozen
    surface,
The stumps stand thick round the clearing, the squatter strikes deep with
    his axe,
Flatboatmen make fast towards dusk near the cotton-wood or pecan-trees,
Coon-seekers go through the regions of the Red river or through those
    drain'd by the Tennessee, or through those of the Arkansas,   320
Torches shine in the dark that hangs on the Chattahooch or Altamahaw,[4]

2. Man building or repairing streets.   4. Georgia rivers.
3. I.e., the Fourth of July.

Patriarchs sit at supper with sons and grandsons and great-grandsons
    around them,
In walls of adobie, in canvas tents, rest hunters and trappers after their
    day's sport,
The city sleeps and the country sleeps,
The living sleep for their time, the dead sleep for their time,   325
The old husband sleeps by his wife and the young husband sleeps by his
    wife;
And these tend inward to me, and I tend outward to them,
And such as it is to be of these more or less I am,
And of these one and all I weave the song of myself.

16

I am of old and young, of the foolish as much as the wise,   330
Regardless of others, ever regardful of others,
Maternal as well as paternal, a child as well as a man,
Stuff'd with the stuff that is coarse and stuff'd with the stuff that is fine,
One of the Nation of many nations, the smallest the same and the largest
    the same,
A Southerner soon as a Northerner, a planter nonchalant and hospitable
    down by the Oconee[5] I live,   335
A Yankee bound my own way ready for trade, my joints the limberest joints
    on earth and the sternest joints on earth,
A Kentuckian walking the vale of the Elkhorn[6] in my deer-skin leggings, a
    Louisianian or Georgian,
A boatman over lakes or bays or along coasts, a Hoosier, Badger, Buckeye;[7]
At home on Kanadian[8] snow-shoes or up in the bush, or with fishermen off
    Newfoundland,
At home in the fleet of ice-boats, sailing with the rest and tacking,   340
At home on the hills of Vermont or in the woods of Maine, or the Texan
    ranch,
Comrade of Californians, comrade of free North-Westerners, (loving their
    big proportions,)
Comrade of raftsmen and coalmen, comrade of all who shake hands and
    welcome to drink and meat,
A learner with the simplest, a teacher of the thoughtfullest,
A novice beginning yet experient of myriads of seasons,   345
Of every hue and caste am I, of every rank and religion,
A farmer, mechanic, artist, gentleman, sailor, quaker,
Prisoner, fancy-man, rowdy, lawyer, physician, priest.

I resist any thing better than my own diversity,
Breathe the air but leave plenty after me,   350
And am not stuck up, and am in my place.

(The moth and the fish-eggs are in their place,
The bright suns I see and the dark suns I cannot see are in their place,
The palpable is in its place and the impalpable is in its place.)

---

5. River in central Georgia.
6. River in Nebraska.
7. Inhabitants of Indiana, Wisconsin, and Ohio, respectively.
8. Canadian.

17

These are really the thoughts of all men in all ages and lands, they are not
    original with me,   355
If they are not yours as much as mine they are nothing, or next to nothing,
If they are not the riddle and the untying of the riddle they are nothing,
If they are not just as close as they are distant they are nothing.

This is the grass that grows wherever the land is and the water is,
This the common air that bathes the globe.   360

18

With music strong I come, with my cornets and my drums,
I play not marches for accepted victors only, I play marches for conquer'd
    and slain persons.

Have you heard that it was good to gain the day?
I also say it is good to fall, battles are lost in the same spirit in which they
    are won.

I beat and pound for the dead,   365
I blow through my embouchures[9] my loudest and gayest for them.

Vivas to those who have fail'd!
And to those whose war-vessels sank in the sea!
And to those themselves who sank in the sea!
And to all generals that lost engagements, and all overcome heroes!   370
And the numberless unknown heroes equal to the greatest heroes known!

19

This is the meal equally set, this the meat for natural hunger,
It is for the wicked just the same as the righteous, I make appointments
    with all,
I will not have a single person slighted or left away,
The kept-woman, sponger, thief, are hereby invited,   375
The heavy-lipp'd slave is invited, the venerealee[1] is invited;
There shall be no difference between them and the rest.

This is the press of a bashful hand, this the float and odor of hair,
This is the touch of my lips to yours, this the murmur of yearning,
This the far-off depth and height reflecting my own face,   380
This the thoughtful merge of myself, and the outlet again.

Do you guess I have some intricate purpose?
Well I have, for the Fourth-month showers have, and the mica on the side
    of a rock has.

9. Mouthpieces of musical instruments such as
the cornet.

1. Someone afflicted with a venereal (sexually
transmitted) disease.

Do you take it I would astonish?
Does the daylight astonish? does the early redstart twittering through the
    woods? 385
Do I astonish more than they?

This hour I tell things in confidence,
I might not tell everybody, but I will tell you.

20

Who goes there? hankering, gross, mystical, nude;
How is it I extract strength from the beef I eat? 390

What is a man anyhow? what am I? what are you?

All I mark as my own you shall offset it with your own,
Else it were time lost listening to me.

I do not snivel that snivel the world over,
That months are vacuums and the ground but wallow and filth. 395

Whimpering and truckling fold with powders for invalids, conformity goes
    to the fourth-remov'd,[2]
I wear my hat as I please indoors or out.

Why should I pray? why should I venerate and be ceremonious?

Having pried through the strata, analyzed to a hair, counsel'd with doctors
    and calculated close,
I find no sweeter fat than sticks to my bones. 400

In all people I see myself, none more and not one a barley-corn[3] less,
And the good or bad I say of myself I say of them.

I know I am solid and sound,
To me the converging objects of the universe perpetually flow,
All are written to me, and I must get what the writing means. 405

I know I am deathless,
I know this orbit of mine cannot be swept by a carpenter's compass,
I know I shall not pass like a child's carlacue[4] cut with a burnt stick at
    night.

I know I am august,
I do not trouble my spirit to vindicate itself or be understood, 410
I see that the elementary laws never apologize,
(I reckon I behave no prouder than the level I plant my house by, after all.)

---

2. Those very remote in relationship; from the genealogical use such as "third cousin, fourth removed." "Fold with powders": a reference to the custom of a physician's wrapping up a dose of medicine in a piece of paper.

3. The seed or grain of barley, but also a unit of measure equal to about one-third inch.
4. Or *curlicue*, a fancy flourish made with a writing implement, here made in the dark with a lighted stick.

I exist as I am, that is enough,
If no other in the world be aware I sit content,
And if each and all be aware I sit content.   415

One world is aware and by far the largest to me, and that is myself,
And whether I come to my own to-day or in ten thousand or ten million
      years,
I can cheerfully take it now, or with equal cheerfulness I can wait.

My foothold is tenon'd and mortis'd[5] in granite,
I laugh at what you call dissolution,   420
And I know the amplitude of time.

                                  21

I am the poet of the Body and I am the poet of the Soul,
The pleasures of heaven are with me and the pains of hell are with me,
The first I graft and increase upon myself, the latter I translate into a new
      tongue.

I am the poet of the woman the same as the man,   425
And I say it is as great to be a woman as to be a man,
And I say there is nothing greater than the mother of men.

I chant the chant of dilation or pride,
We have had ducking and deprecating about enough,
I show that size is only development.   430

Have you outstript the rest? are you the President?
It is a trifle, they will more than arrive there every one, and still pass on.

I am he that walks with the tender and growing night,
I call to the earth and sea half-held by the night.

Press close bare-bosom'd night—press close magnetic nourishing night! 435
Night of south winds—night of the large few stars!
Still nodding night—mad naked summer night.

Smile O voluptuous cool-breath'd earth!
Earth of the slumbering and liquid trees!
Earth of departed sunset—earth of the mountains misty-topt!   440
Earth of the vitreous pour of the full moon just tinged with blue!
Earth of shine and dark mottling the tide of the river!
Earth of the limpid gray of clouds brighter and clearer for my sake!
Far-swooping elbow'd earth—rich apple-blossom'd earth!
Smile, for your lover comes.   445

Prodigal, you have given me love—therefore I to you give love!
O unspeakable passionate love.

5. Carpenter's terms for a particular way of joining two boards together. A mortise is a cavity in a piece of
wood into which is placed the projection (tenon) from another piece of wood.

22

You sea! I resign myself to you also—I guess what you mean,
I behold from the beach your crooked inviting fingers,
I believe you refuse to go back without feeling of me,   450
We must have a turn together, I undress, hurry me out of sight of the land,
Cushion me soft, rock me in billowy drowse,
Dash me with amorous wet, I can repay you.

Sea of stretch'd ground-swells,
Sea breathing broad and convulsive breaths,   455
Sea of the brine of life and of unshovell'd yet always-ready graves,
Howler and scooper of storms, capricious and dainty sea,
I am integral with you, I too am of one phase and of all phases.

Partaker of influx and efflux I, extoller of hate and conciliation,
Extoller of amies[6] and those that sleep in each others' arms.   460

I am he attesting sympathy,
(Shall I make my list of things in the house and skip the house that
    supports them?)

I am not the poet of goodness only, I do not decline to be the poet of
    wickedness also.

What blurt is this about virtue and about vice?
Evil propels me and reform of evil propels me, I stand indifferent,   465
My gait is no fault-finder's or rejecter's gait,
I moisten the roots of all that has grown.

Did you fear some scrofula[7] out of the unflagging pregnancy?
Did you guess the celestial laws are yet to be work'd over and rectified?

I find one side a balance and the antipodal side a balance,   470
Soft doctrine as steady help as stable doctrine,
Thoughts and deeds of the present our rouse and early start.

This minute that comes to me over the past decillions,[8]
There is no better than it and now.
What behaved well in the past or behaves well to-day is not such a
    wonder,   475
The wonder is always and always how there can be a mean man or an
    infidel.

23

Endless unfolding of words of ages!
And mine a word of the modern, the word En-Masse.

6. Friends (French).   of the lymph glands.
7. Form of tuberculosis characterized by swelling   8. The number 1 followed by thirty-three zeroes.

A word of the faith that never balks,
Here or henceforward it is all the same to me, I accept Time absolutely.   480

It alone is without flaw, it alone rounds and completes all,
That mystic baffling wonder alone completes all.

I accept Reality and dare not question it.
Materialism first and last imbuing.

Hurrah for positive science! long live exact demonstration!   485
Fetch stonecrop mixt with cedar and branches of lilac,
This is the lexicographer, this the chemist, this made a grammar of the old
      cartouches,[9]
These mariners put the ship through dangerous unknown seas,
This is the geologist, this works with the scalpel, and this is a
      mathematician.

Gentlemen, to you the first honors always!   490
Your facts are useful, and yet they are not my dwelling,
I but enter by them to an area of my dwelling.

Less the reminders of properties told my words,
And more the reminders they of life untold, and of freedom and extrication,
And make short account of neuters and geldings, and favor men and
      women fully equipt,   495
And beat the gong of revolt, and stop with fugitives and them that plot and
      conspire.

24

Walt Whitman, a kosmos, of Manhattan the son,
Turbulent, fleshy, sensual, eating, drinking and breeding,
No sentimentalist, no stander above men and women or apart from them,
No more modest than immodest.   500

Unscrew the locks from the doors!
Unscrew the doors themselves from their jambs!

Whoever degrades another degrades me,
And whatever is done or said returns at last to me.

Through me the afflatus[1] surging and surging, through me the current and
      index.   505

I speak the pass-word primeval, I give the sign of democracy,
By God! I will accept nothing which all cannot have their counterpart of on
      the same terms.

9. Scroll-like tablet with space for an inscription.
Whitman knew the Egyptian cartouches with
hieroglyphics, the deciphering of which contributed to knowledge of ancient life. "Stonecrop":
a fleshy-leafed plant.
1. Divine wind or spirit.

Through me many long dumb voices,
Voices of the interminable generations of prisoners and slaves,
Voices of the diseas'd and despairing and of thieves and dwarfs,   510

Voices of cycles of preparation and accretion,
And of the threads that connect the stars, and of wombs and of the
    fatherstuff,
And of the rights of them the others are down upon,
Of the deform'd, trivial, flat, foolish, despised,
Fog in the air, beetles rolling balls of dung.   515

Through me forbidden voices,
Voices of sexes and lusts, voices veil'd and I remove the veil,
Voices indecent by me clarified and transfigur'd.

I do not press my fingers across my mouth,
I keep as delicate around the bowels as around the head and heart,   520
Copulation is no more rank to me than death is.

I believe in the flesh and the appetites,
Seeing, hearing, feeling, are miracles, and each part and tag of me is a
    miracle.

Divine am I inside and out, and I make holy whatever I touch or am
    touch'd from,
The scent of these arm-pits aroma finer than prayer,   525
This head more than churches, bibles, and all the creeds.

If I worship one thing more than another it shall be the spread of my own
    body, or any part of it,
Translucent mould of me it shall be you!
Shaded ledges and rests it shall be you!
Firm masculine colter[2] it shall be you!   530
Whatever goes to the tilth[3] of me it shall be you!
You my rich blood! your milky stream pale strippings of my life!
Breast that presses against other breasts it shall be you!
My brain it shall be your occult convolutions!
Root of wash'd sweet-flag! timorous pond-snipe! nest of guarded duplicate
    eggs! it shall be you!   535
Mix'd tussled hay of head, beard, brawn, it shall be you!
Trickling sap of maple, fibre of manly wheat, it shall be you!
Sun so generous it shall be you!
Vapors lighting and shading my face it shall be you!
You sweaty brooks and dews it shall be you!   540
Winds whose soft-tickling genitals rub against me it shall be you!
Broad muscular fields, branches of live oak, loving lounger in my winding
    paths, it shall be you!
Hands I have taken, face I have kiss'd, mortal I have ever touch'd, it shall
    be you.

---

2. This phallic passage begins with reference to   3. Cultivation or tillage of the soil.
the blade at the front of a plow.

I dote on myself, there is that lot of me and all so luscious,
Each moment and whatever happens thrills me with joy,   545
I cannot tell how my ankles bend, nor whence the cause of my faintest
    wish,
Nor the cause of the friendship I emit, nor the cause of the friendship I
    take again.

That I walk up my stoop, I pause to consider if it really be,
A morning-glory at my window satisfies me more than the metaphysics of
    books.

To behold the day-break!   550
The little light fades the immense and diaphanous shadows,
The air tastes good to my palate.

Hefts⁴ of the moving world at innocent gambols silently rising freshly
    exuding,
Scooting obliquely high and low.

Something I cannot see puts upward libidinous prongs,   555
Seas of bright juice suffuse heaven.

The earth by the sky staid with, the daily close of their junction,
The heav'd challenge from the east that moment over my head,
The mocking taunt, See then whether you shall be master!

                              25

Dazzling and tremendous how quick the sun-rise would kill me,   560
If I could not now and always send sun-rise out of me.

We also ascend dazzling and tremendous as the sun,
We found our own O my soul in the calm and cool of the day-break.

My voice goes after what my eyes cannot reach,
With the twirl of my tongue I encompass worlds and volumes of worlds. 565

Speech is the twin of my vision, it is unequal to measure itself,
It provokes me forever, it says sarcastically,
Walt you contain enough, why don't you let it out then?

Come now I will not be tantalized, you conceive too much of articulation,
Do you not know O speech how the buds beneath you are folded?   570
Waiting in gloom, protected by frost,
The dirt receding before my prophetical screams,
I underlying causes to balance them at last,
My knowledge my live parts, it keeping tally with the meaning of all things,
Happiness, (which whoever hears me let him or her set out in search of
    this day.)   575

---

4. Something being heaved or raised upward.

My final merit I refuse you, I refuse putting from me what I really am,
Encompass worlds, but never try to encompass me.
I crowd your sleekest and best by simply looking toward you.

Writing and talk do not prove me,
I carry the plenum[5] of proof and every thing else in my face,   580
With the hush of my lips I wholly confound the skeptic.

26

Now I will do nothing but listen,
To accrue what I hear into this song, to let sounds contribute toward it.

I hear bravuras of birds, bustle of growing wheat, gossip of flames, clack of
          sticks cooking my meals,
I hear the sound I love, the sound of the human voice,   585
I hear all sounds running together, combined, fused or following,
Sounds of the city and sounds out of the city, sounds of the day and night,
Talkative young ones to those that like them, the loud laugh of work-people
          at their meals,
The angry base of disjointed friendship, the faint tones of the sick,
The judge with hands tight to the desk, his pallid lips pronouncing a
          death-sentence,   590
The heave'e'yo of stevedores unlading ships by the wharves, the refrain of
          the anchor-lifters,
The ring of alarm-bells, the cry of fire, the whirr of swift-streaking engines
          and hose-carts with premonitory tinkles and color'd lights,
The steam-whistle, the solid roll of the train of approaching cars,
The slow march play'd at the head of the association marching two and
          two,
(They go to guard some corpse, the flag-tops are draped with black muslin.)   595

I hear the violoncello ('tis the young man's heart's complaint,)
I hear the key'd cornet, it glides quickly in through my ears,
It shakes mad-sweet pangs through my belly and breast.

I hear the chorus, it is a grand opera,
Ah this indeed is music—this suits me.   600

A tenor large and fresh as the creation fills me,
The orbic flex of his mouth is pouring and filling me full.

I hear the train'd soprano (what work with hers is this?)
The orchestra whirls me wider than Uranus[6] flies,
It wrenches such ardors from me I did not know I possess'd them,   605
It sails me, I dab with bare feet, they are lick'd by the indolent waves,
I am cut by bitter and angry hail, I lose my breath,
Steep'd amid honey'd morphine, my windpipe throttled in fakes[7] of death,
At length let up again to feel the puzzle of puzzles,
And that we call Being.   610

5. Fullness.
6. The seventh planet from the sun; at that time it was thought to be the most remote planet in the solar system.
7. Coils of rope.

27

To be in any form, what is that?
(Round and round we go, all of us, and ever come back thither,)
If nothing lay more develop'd the quahaug[8] in its callous shell were
    enough.

Mine is no callous shell,
I have instant conductors all over me whether I pass or stop,   615
They seize every object and lead it harmlessly through me.

I merely stir, press, feel with my fingers, and am happy,
To touch my person to some one else's is about as much as I can stand.

28

Is this then a touch? quivering me to a new identity,
Flames and ether making a rush for my veins,   620
Treacherous tip of me reaching and crowding to help them,
My flesh and blood playing out lightning to strike what is hardly different
    from myself,
On all sides prurient provokers stiffening my limbs,
Straining the udder of my heart for its withheld drip,
Behaving licentious toward me, taking no denial,   625
Depriving me of my best as for a purpose,
Unbuttoning my clothes, holding me by the bare waist,
Deluding my confusion with the calm of the sunlight and pasture-fields,
Immodestly sliding the fellow-senses away,
They bribed to swap off with touch and go and graze at the edges of me, 630
No consideration, no regard for my draining strength or my anger,
Fetching the rest of the herd around to enjoy them a while,
Then all uniting to stand on a headland and worry me.

The sentries desert every other part of me,
They have left me helpless to a red marauder,   635
They all come to the headland to witness and assist against me.

I am given up by traitors,
I talk wildly, I have lost my wits, I and nobody else am the greatest traitor,
I went myself first to the headland, my own hands carried me there.

You villain touch! what are you doing? my breath is tight in its throat, 640
Unclench your floodgates, you are too much for me.

29

Blind loving wrestling touch, sheath'd hooded sharp-tooth'd touch!
Did it make you ache so, leaving me?

Parting track'd by arriving, perpetual payment of perpetual loan,
Rich showering rain, and recompense richer afterward.   645

Sprouts take and accumulate, stand by the curb prolific and vital,
Landscapes projected masculine, full-sized and golden.

8. Edible clam of the Atlantic coast.

30

All truths wait in all things,
They neither hasten their own delivery nor resist it,
They do not need the obstetric forceps of the surgeon,   650
The insignificant is as big to me as any,
(What is less or more than a touch?)

Logic and sermons never convince,
The damp of the night drives deeper into my soul.

(Only what proves itself to every man and woman is so,   655
Only what nobody denies is so.)

A minute and a drop of me settle my brain,
I believe the soggy clods shall become lovers and lamps,
And a compend⁹ of compends is the meat of a man or woman,
And a summit and flower there is the feeling they have for each other,   660
And they are to branch boundlessly out of that lesson until it becomes
     omnific,¹
And until one and all shall delight us, and we them.

31

I believe a leaf of grass is no less than the journey-work of the stars,
And the pismire² is equally perfect, and a grain of sand, and the egg of the
     wren,
And the tree-toad is a chief-d'œuvre for the highest,   665
And the running blackberry would adorn the parlors of heaven,
And the narrowest hinge in my hand puts to scorn all machinery,
And the cow crunching with depress'd head surpasses any statue,
And a mouse is miracle enough to stagger sextillions of infidels.

I find I incorporate gneiss,³ coal, long-threaded moss, fruits, grains,
     esculent roots,   670
And am stucco'd with quadrupeds and birds all over,
And have distanced what is behind me for good reasons,
But call any thing back again when I desire it.
In vain the speeding or shyness,
In vain the plutonic rocks⁴ send their old heat against my approach,   675
In vain the mastodon retreats beneath its own powder'd bones,
In vain objects stand leagues off and assume manifold shapes,
In vain the ocean settling in hollows and the great monsters lying low,
In vain the buzzard houses herself with the sky,
In vain the snake slides through the creepers and logs,   680
In vain the elk takes to the inner passes of the woods,
In vain the razor-bill'd auk sails far north to Labrador,
I follow quickly, I ascend to the nest in the fissure of the cliff.

9. I.e., a compendium, in which something is
reduced to a short, essential summary.
1. All-encompassing.
2. Ant.
3. Metamorphic rock in which minerals are
arranged in layers.
4. Rock of igneus (fire created) or magmatic
(molten) origin; from Pluto, ruler of infernal
regions.

32

I think I could turn and live with animals, they are so placid and self-
    contain'd,
I stand and look at them long and long.   685

They do not sweat and whine about their condition,
They do not lie awake in the dark and weep for their sins,
They do not make me sick discussing their duty to God,
Not one is dissatisfied, not one is demented with the mania of owning
    things,
Not one kneels to another, nor to his kind that lived thousands of years
    ago,   690
Not one is respectable or unhappy over the whole earth.

So they show their relations to me and I accept them,
They bring me tokens of myself, they evince them plainly in their
    possession.

I wonder where they get those tokens,
Did I pass that way huge times ago and negligently drop them?   695

Myself moving forward then and now and forever,
Gathering and showing more always and with velocity,
Infinite and omnigenous,[5] and the like of these among them,
Not too exclusive toward the reachers of my remembrancers,
Picking out here one that I love, and now go with him on brotherly
    terms.   700

A gigantic beauty of a stallion, fresh and responsive to my caresses,
Head high in the forehead, wide between the ears,
Limbs glossy and supple, tail dusting the ground,
Eyes full of sparkling wickedness, ears finely cut, flexibly moving.

His nostrils dilate as my heels embrace him,   705
His well-built limbs tremble with pleasure as we race around and return.

I but use you a minute, then I resign you, stallion,
Why do I need your paces when I myself out-gallop them?
Even as I stand or sit passing faster than you.

33

Space and Time! now I see it is true, what I guess'd at,   710
What I guess'd when I loaf'd on the grass,
What I guess'd while I lay alone in my bed,
And again as I walk'd the beach under the paling stars of the morning.

My ties and ballasts leave me, my elbows rest in sea-gaps,[6]
I skirt sierras, my palms cover continents,
I am afoot with my vision.   715

5. Belonging to every form of life.   6. Estuaries or bays.

By the city's quadrangular houses—in log huts, camping with lumbermen,
Along the ruts of the turnpike, along the dry gulch and rivulet bed,
Weeding my onion-patch or hoeing rows of carrots and parsnips, crossing
    savannas,⁷ trailing in forests,
Prospecting, gold-digging, girdling the trees of a new purchase,   720
Scorch'd ankle-deep by the hot sand, hauling my boat down the shallow
    river,
Where the panther walks to and fro on a limb overhead, where the buck
    turns furiously at the hunter,
Where the rattlesnake suns his flabby length on a rock, where the otter is
    feeding on fish,
Where the alligator in his tough pimples sleeps by the bayou,
Where the black bear is searching for roots or honey, where the beaver pats
    the mud with his paddle-shaped tail;   725
Over the growing sugar, over the yellow-flower'd cotton plant, over the rice
    in its low moist field,
Over the sharp-peak'd farm house, with its scallop'd scum and slender
    shoots from the gutters,⁸

Over the western persimmon, over the long-leav'd corn, over the delicate
    blue-flower flax,
Over the white and brown buckwheat, a hummer and buzzer there with the
    rest,
Over the dusky green of the rye as it ripples and shades in the breeze;   730
Scaling mountains, pulling myself cautiously up, holding on by low
    scragged limbs,
Walking the path worn in the grass and beat through the leaves of the
    brush,
Where the quail is whistling betwixt the woods and the wheat-lot,
Where the bat flies in the Seventh-month eve, where the great gold-bug⁹
    drops through the dark,
Where the brook puts out of the roots of the old tree and flows to the
    meadow,   735
Where cattle stand and shake away flies with the tremulous shuddering of
    their hides,
Where the cheese-cloth hangs in the kitchen, where andirons straddle the
    hearth-slab, where cobwebs fall in festoons from the rafters;
Where trip-hammers crash, where the press is whirling its cylinders,
Wherever the human heart beats with terrible throes under its ribs,
Where the pear-shaped balloon is floating aloft, (floating in it myself and
    looking composedly down,)   740
Where the life-car¹ is drawn on the slip-noose, where the heat hatches
    pale-green eggs in the dented sand,
Where the she-whale swims with her calf and never forsakes it,
Where the steam-ship trails hind-ways its long pennant of smoke,
Where the fin of the shark cuts like a black chip out of the water,

---

7. Flat, treeless, tropical grasslands.
8. Presumably debris washed or blown down roofs, settling into scalloplike shapes in the gutter and providing nutrients for grasses or weeds.
9. Beetle.
1. Watertight compartment for lowering passengers from a ship when emergency evacuation is required.

Where the half-burn'd brig is riding on unknown currents,   745
Where shells grow to her slimy deck, where the dead are corrupting below;
Where the dense-star'd flag is borne at the head of the regiments,
Approaching Manhattan up by the long-stretching island,
Under Niagara, the cataract falling like a veil over my countenance,
Upon a door-step, upon the horse-block of hard wood outside,   750
Upon the race-course, or enjoying picnics or jigs or a good game of
     baseball,
At he-festivals, with blackguard gibes, ironical license, bull-dances,[2]
     drinking, laughter,
At the cider-mill tasting the sweets of the brown mash, sucking the juice
     through a straw,
At apple-peelings wanting kisses for all the red fruit I find,
At musters, beach-parties, friendly bees,[3] huskings, house-raisings;   755
Where the mocking-bird sounds his delicious gurgles, cackles, screams,
     weeps,
Where the hay-rick[4] stands in the barn-yard, where the dry-stalks are
     scatter'd, where the brood-cow waits in the hovel,
Where the bull advances to do his masculine work, where the stud to the
     mare, where the cock is treading the hen,
Where the heifers browse, where geese nip their food with short jerks,
Where sun-down shadows lengthen over the limitless and lonesome prairie, 760
Where herds of buffalo make a crawling spread of the square miles far and
     near,
Where the humming-bird shimmers, where the neck of the long-lived swan
     is curving and winding,
Where the laughing-gull scoots by the shore, where she laughs her near-
     human laugh,
Where bee-hives range on a gray bench in the garden half hid by the high
     weeds,
Where band-neck'd partridges roost in a ring on the ground with their
     heads out,   765
Where burial coaches enter the arch'd gates of a cemetery,
Where winter wolves bark amid wastes of snow and icicled trees,
Where the yellow-crown'd heron comes to the edge of the marsh at night
     and feeds upon small crabs,
Where the splash of swimmers and divers cools the warm noon,
Where the katy-did works her chromatic[5] reed on the walnut-tree over the
     well,   770
Through patches of citrons[6] and cucumbers with silver-wired leaves,
Through the salt-lick or orange glade, or under conical firs,
Through the gymnasium, through the curtain'd saloon, through the office
     or public hall;
Pleas'd with the native and pleas'd with the foreign, pleas'd with the new
     and old,
Pleas'd with the homely woman as well as the handsome,   775

2. Rowdy backwoods dances for which, in the
absence of women, men took male partners.
3. Gatherings where people work while socializing
with their neighbors. "Musters": assemblages of
people, particularly gatherings of military troops

for drill.
4. Hayracks, from which livestock eat hay.
5. Consisting of chords or harmonies based on
nonharmonic tones.
6. Here, small, hard-skinned watermelons.

Pleas'd with the quakeress as she puts off her bonnet and talks melodiously,
Pleas'd with the tune of the choir of the whitewash'd church,
Pleas'd with the earnest words of the sweating Methodist preacher, impress'd seriously at the camp-meeting;
Looking in at the shop-windows of Broadway the whole forenoon, flatting the flesh of my nose on the thick plate glass,
Wandering the same afternoon with my face turn'd up to the clouds, or down a lane or along the beach,   780
My right and left arms round the sides of two friends, and I in the middle;
Coming home with the silent and dark-cheek'd bush-boy, (behind me he rides at the drape of the day,)
Far from the settlements studying the print of animals' feet, or the moccasin print,
By the cot in the hospital reaching lemonade to a feverish patient,
Nigh the coffin'd corpse when all is still, examining with a candle;   785
Voyaging to every port to dicker and adventure,
Hurrying with the modern crowd as eager and fickle as any,
Hot toward one I hate, ready in my madness to knife him,
Solitary at midnight in my back yard, my thoughts gone from me a long while,
Walking the old hills of Judæa with the beautiful gentle God by my side, 790
Speeding through space, speeding through heaven and the stars,
Speeding amid the seven satellites[7] and the broad ring, and the diameter of eighty thousand miles,
Speeding with tail'd meteors, throwing fire-balls like the rest,
Carrying the crescent child that carries its own full mother in its belly,[8]
Storming, enjoying, planning, loving, cautioning,   795
Backing and filling, appearing and disappearing,
I tread day and night such roads.

I visit the orchards of spheres and look at the product,
And look at quintillions ripen'd and look at quintillions green.

I fly those flights of a fluid and swallowing soul,   800
My course runs below the soundings of plummets.

I help myself to material and immaterial,
No guard can shut me off, no law prevent me.

I anchor my ship for a little while only,
My messengers continually cruise away or bring their returns to me.   805

I go hunting polar furs and the seal, leaping chasms with a pike-pointed staff, clinging to topples of brittle and blue.[9]

I ascend to the foretruck,[1]
I take my place late at night in the crow's-nest,
We sail the arctic sea, it is plenty light enough,
Through the clear atmosphere I stretch around on the wonderful beauty,   810

---

7. The then-known moons of Saturn.
8. Image of a crescent moon, with the full moon also palely visible.
9. Toppled pieces of ice.
1. Platform of a foremast.

The enormous masses of ice pass me and I pass them, the scenery is plain
    in all directions,
The white-topt mountains show in the distance, I fling out my fancies
    toward them,
We are approaching some great battle-field in which we are soon to be
    engaged,
We pass the colossal outposts of the encampment, we pass with still feet
    and caution,
Or we are entering by the suburbs some vast and ruin'd city,   815
The blocks and fallen architecture more than all the living cities of the
    globe.

I am a free companion, I bivouac by invading watchfires,
I turn the bridegroom out of bed and stay with the bride myself,
I tighten her all night to my thighs and lips.

My voice is the wife's voice, the screech by the rail of the stairs,   820
They fetch my man's body up dripping and drown'd.

I understand the large hearts of heroes,
The courage of present times and all times,
How the skipper saw the crowded and rudderless wreck of the steam-ship,
    and Death chasing it up and down the storm,
How he knuckled tight and gave not back an inch, and was faithful of days
    and faithful of nights,   825
And chalk'd in large letters on a board, *Be of good cheer, we will not desert
    you;*
How he follow'd with them and tack'd with them three days and would not
    give it up,
How he saved the drifting company at last,
How the lank loose-gown'd women look'd when boated from the side of
    their prepared graves,
How the silent old-faced infants and the lifted sick, and the sharp-lipp'd
    unshaved men;   830
All this I swallow, it tastes good, I like it well, it becomes mine,
I am the man, I suffer'd, I was there.[2]

The disdain and calmness of martyrs,
The mother of old, condemn'd for a witch, burnt with dry wood, her
    children gazing on,
The hounded slave that flags in the race, leans by the fence, blowing,
    cover'd with sweat,
The twinges that sting like needles his legs and neck, the murderous   835
    buckshot and the bullets,
All these I feel or am.

I am the hounded slave, I wince at the bite of the dogs,
Hell and despair are upon me, crack and again crack the marksmen,
I clutch the rails of the fence, my gore dribs, thinn'd with the ooze of my
    skin,[3]   840

2. Whitman describes the wreck of the *San Francisco*, which sailed from New York on December
22, 1853, bound for South America, and was
caught in a storm a day later. The ship drifted helplessly until early January. Over 150 died in the disaster, which was reported widely in the New York
papers.
3. Dribbles down, diluted with sweat.

I fall on the weeds and stones,
The riders spur their unwilling horses, haul close,
Taunt my dizzy ears and beat me violently over the head with whip-stocks.

Agonies are one of my changes of garments,
I do not ask the wounded person how he feels, I myself become the
    wounded person,   845
My hurts turn livid upon me as I lean on a cane and observe.

I am the mash'd fireman with breast-bone broken,
Tumbling walls buried me in their debris,
Heat and smoke I inspired, I heard the yelling shouts of my comrades,
I heard the distant click of their picks and shovels,   850
They have clear'd the beams away, they tenderly lift me forth.

I lie in the night air in my red shirt, the pervading hush is for my sake,
Painless after all I lie exhausted but not so unhappy,
White and beautiful are the faces around me, the heads are bared of their
    fire-caps,
The kneeling crowd fades with the light of the torches.   855

Distant and dead resuscitate,
They show as the dial or move as the hands of me, I am the clock myself.

I am an old artillerist, I tell of my fort's bombardment,
I am there again.

Again the long roll of the drummers,   860
Again the attacking cannon, mortars,
Again to my listening ears the cannon responsive.

I take part, I see and hear the whole,
The cries, curses, roar, the plaudits of well-aim'd shots,
The ambulanza slowly passing trailing its red drip,   865
Workmen searching after damages, making indispensable repairs,
The fall of grenades through the rent roof, the fan-shaped explosion,
The whizz of limbs, heads, stone, wood, iron, high in the air.

Again gurgles the mouth of my dying general, he furiously waves with his
    hand,
He gasps through the clot *Mind not me—mind—the entrenchments.*   870

34

Now I tell what I knew in Texas in my early youth,
(I tell not the fall of Alamo,[4]
Not one escaped to tell the fall of Alamo,

---

4. During the Texan Revolution of 1835–36, emigrants from the United States to Texas—at the time part of Mexico—attempted to make Texas into a separate republic. Among battles fought in what is now the state of Texas were the defense of the Alamo, which fell on March 6, 1836, after a siege by Mexican forces beginning on February 23, when around two hundred men were killed, and the battle of Goliad, when some four hundred secessionist troops were killed after surrendering to the Mexicans on March 19 of the same year.

The hundred and fifty are dumb yet at Alamo,)
'Tis the tale of the murder in cold blood of four hundred and twelve young
    men. 875

Retreating they had form'd in a hollow square with their baggage for
    breastworks,
Nine hundred lives out of the surrounding enemy's, nine times their
    number, was the price they took in advance,
Their colonel was wounded and their ammunition gone,
They treated for an honorable capitulation, receiv'd writing and seal, gave
    up their arms and march'd back prisoners of war.

They were the glory of the race of rangers, 880
Matchless with horse, rifle, song, supper, courtship,
Large, turbulent, generous, handsome, proud, and affectionate,
Bearded, sunburnt, drest in the free costume of hunters,
Not a single one over thirty years of age.

The second First-day morning they were brought out in squads and
    massacred, it was beautiful early summer,
The work commenced about five o'clock and was over by eight. 885

None obey'd the command to kneel,
Some made a mad and helpless rush, some stood stark and straight,
A few fell at once, shot in the temple or heart, the living and dead lay
    together,
The maim'd and mangled dug in the dirt, the new-comers saw
    them there, 890
Some half-kill'd attempted to crawl away,
These were despatch'd with bayonets or batter'd with the blunts of
    muskets,
A youth not seventeen years old seiz'd his assassin till two more came to
    release him,
The three were all torn and cover'd with the boy's blood.

At eleven o'clock began the burning of the bodies; 895
That is the tale of the murder of the four hundred and twelve young men.

35

Would you hear of an old-time sea-fight?[5]
Would you learn who won by the light of the moon and stars?
List to the yarn, as my grandmother's father the sailor told it to me.

Our foe was no skulk in his ship I tell you, (said he,) 900
His was the surly English pluck, and there is no tougher or truer, and never
    was, and never will be;
Along the lower'd eve he came horribly raking us.

5. The famous Revolutionary sea battle on September 23, 1779, between the American *Bon-
Homme Richard,* commanded by John Paul Jones,
and the British *Serapis* off the coast of Yorkshire.

When Jones was asked to surrender, he famously
declared, "I have not yet begun to fight." He eventually defeated the *Serapis*.

We closed with him, the yards entangled, the cannon touch'd,
My captain lash'd fast with his own hands.

We had receiv'd some eighteen pound shots under the water,   905
On our lower-gun-deck two large pieces had burst at the first fire, killing all
    around and blowing up overhead.

Fighting at sun-down, fighting at dark,
Ten o'clock at night, the full moon well up, our leaks on the gain, and five
    feet of water reported,
The master-at-arms loosing the prisoners confined in the after-hold to give
    them a chance for themselves.

The transit to and from the magazine⁶ is now stopt by the sentinels,   910
They see so many strange faces they do not know whom to trust.

Our frigate takes fire,
The other asks if we demand quarter?
If our colors are struck and the fighting done?

Now I laugh content, for I hear the voice of my little captain,   915
We have not struck, he composedly cries, *we have just begun our part of the
    fighting.*

Only three guns are in use,
One is directed by the captain himself against the enemy's mainmast,
Two well serv'd with grape and canister⁷ silence his musketry and clear his
    decks.

The tops⁸ alone second the fire of this little battery, especially the
    main-top,   920
They hold out bravely during the whole of the action.

Not a moment's cease,
The leaks gain fast on the pumps, the fire eats toward the powder-
    magazine.

One of the pumps has been shot away, it is generally thought we are
    sinking.

Serene stands the little captain,   925
He is not hurried, his voice is neither high nor low,
His eyes give more light to us than our battle-lanterns.

Toward twelve there in the beams of the moon they surrender to us.

36

Stretch'd and still lies the midnight,
Two great hulls motionless on the breast of the darkness,   930

6. Storeroom for ammunition.
7. Grapeshot ("grape"), clusters of small iron
balls, was packed inside a metal cylinder ("canis-
ter") and used to charge a cannon.
8. Platforms enclosing the heads of each mast;
here, the sailors manning the tops.

Our vessel riddled and slowly sinking, preparations to pass to the one we
    have conquer'd,
The captain on the quarter-deck coldly giving his orders through a
    countenance white as a sheet,
Near by the corpse of the child that serv'd in the cabin,
The dead face of an old salt with long white hair and carefully curl'd
    whiskers,
The flames spite of all that can be done flickering aloft and below,   935
The husky voices of the two or three officers yet fit for duty,
Formless stacks of bodies and bodies by themselves, dabs of flesh upon the
    masts and spars,
Cut of cordage, dangle of rigging, slight shock of the soothe of waves,
Black and impassive guns, litter of powder-parcels, strong scent,
A few large stars overhead, silent and mournful shining,   940
Delicate sniffs of sea-breeze, smells of sedgy grass and fields by the shore,
    death-messages given in charge to survivors,
The hiss of the surgeon's knife, the gnawing teeth of his saw,
Wheeze, cluck, swash of falling blood, short wild scream, and long, dull,
    tapering groan,
These so, these irretrievable.

37

You laggards there on guard! look to your arms!   945
In at the conquer'd doors they crowd! I am possess'd!
Embody all presences outlaw'd or suffering,
See myself in prison shaped like another man,
And feel the dull unintermitted pain.

For me the keepers of convicts shoulder their carbines and keep watch,   950
It is I let out in the morning and barr'd at night.

Not a mutineer walks handcuff'd to jail but I am handcuff'd to him and
    walk by his side,
(I am less the jolly one there, and more the silent one with sweat on my
    twitching lips.)

Not a youngster is taken for larceny but I go up too, and am tried and
    sentenced.

Not a cholera patient lies at the last gasp but I also lie at the last gasp,   955
My face is ash-color'd, my sinews gnarl, away from me people retreat.

Askers embody themselves in me and I am embodied in them,
I project my hat, sit shame-faced, and beg.

38

Enough! enough! enough!
Somehow I have been stunn'd. Stand back!   960
Give me a little time beyond my cuff'd head, slumbers, dreams, gaping,
I discover myself on the verge of a usual mistake.

That I could forget the mockers and insults!
That I could forget the trickling tears and the blows of the bludgeons and
    hammers!
That I could look with a separate look on my own crucifixion and bloody
    crowning.   965

I remember now,
I resume the overstaid fraction,
The grave of rock multiplies what has been confided to it, or to any graves,
Corpses rise, gashes heal, fastenings roll from me.

I troop forth replenish'd with supreme power, one of an average unending
    procession,   970
Inland and sea-coast we go, and pass all boundary lines,
Our swift ordinances on their way over the whole earth,
The blossoms we wear in our hats the growth of thousands of years.

Eleves,[9] I salute you! come forward!
Continue your annotations, continue your questionings.   975

39

The friendly and flowing savage, who is he?
Is he waiting for civilization, or past it and mastering it?

Is he some Southwesterner rais'd out-doors? is he Kanadian?
Is he from the Mississippi country? Iowa, Oregon, California?
The mountains? prairie-life, bush-life? or sailor from the sea?   980

Wherever he goes men and women accept and desire him,
They desire he should like them, touch them, speak to them, stay with
    them.

Behavior lawless as snow-flakes, words simple as grass, uncomb'd head,
    laughter, and naivetè,
Slow-stepping feet, common features, common modes and emanations,
They descend in new forms from the tips of his fingers,   985
They are wafted with the odor of his body or breath, they fly out of the
    glance of his eyes.

40

Flaunt of the sunshine I need not your bask—lie over!
You light surfaces only, I force surfaces and depths also.

Earth! you seem to look for something at my hands,
Say, old top-knot,[1] what do you want?   990

---

9. Students (French).
1. An epithet common in frontier humor, deriving from the fact that some Native Americans gathered their hair into tufts at the top of the head. The poet seems to be addressing an older Indian, perhaps picking up on the reference to "the friendly and flowing savage" of the previous stanza.

Man or woman, I might tell how I like you, but cannot,
And might tell what it is in me and what it is in you, but cannot,
And might tell that pining I have, that pulse of my nights and days.

Behold, I do not give lectures or a little charity,
When I give I give myself.   995

You there, impotent, loose in the knees,
Open your scarf'd chops till I blow grit[2] within you,
Spread your palms and lift the flaps of your pockets,
I am not to be denied, I compel, I have stores plenty and to spare,
And any thing I have I bestow.   1000

I do not ask who you are, that is not important to me,
You can do nothing and be nothing but what I will infold you.

To cotton-field drudge or cleaner of privies I lean,
On his right cheek I put the family kiss,
And in my soul I swear I never will deny him.   1005

On women fit for conception I start bigger and nimbler babes,
(This day I am jetting the stuff of far more arrogant republics.)

To any one dying, thither I speed and twist the knob of the door,
Turn the bed-clothes toward the foot of the bed,
Let the physician and the priest go home.   1010

I seize the descending man and raise him with resistless will,
O despairer, here is my neck,
By God, you shall not go down! hang your whole weight upon me.

I dilate you with tremendous breath, I buoy you up,
Every room of the house do I fill with an arm'd force,   1015
Lovers of me, bafflers of graves.

Sleep—I and they keep guard all night,
Not doubt, not decease shall dare to lay finger upon you,
I have embraced you, and henceforth possess you to myself,
And when you rise in the morning you will find what I tell you is so. 1020

41

I am he bringing help for the sick as they pant on their backs,
And for strong upright men I bring yet more needed help.

I heard what was said of the universe,
Heard it and heard it of several thousand years;
It is middling well as far as it goes—but is that all?   1025

---

2. Courage. "Scarf'd chops": lined, worn-down jaw or face.

Magnifying and applying come I,
Outbidding at the start the old cautious hucksters,
Taking myself the exact dimensions of Jehovah,[3]
Lithographing Kronos, Zeus his son, and Hercules[4] his grandson,
Buying drafts of Osiris, Isis, Belus, Brahma, Buddha,[5]   1030
In my portfolio placing Manito loose, Allah[6] on a leaf, the crucifix
    engraved,
With Odin and the hideous-faced Mexitli[7] and every idol and image,
Taking them all for what they are worth and not a cent more,
Admitting they were alive and did the work of their days,
(They bore mites as for unfledg'd birds who have now to rise and fly and
    sing for themselves,)   1035
Accepting the rough deific sketches to fill out better in myself, bestowing
    them freely on each man and woman I see,
Discovering as much or more in a framer framing a house,
Putting higher claims for him there with his roll'd-up sleeves driving the
    mallet and chisel,
Not objecting to special revelations, considering a curl of smoke or a hair
    on the back of my hand just as curious as any revelation,
Lads ahold of fire-engines and hook-and-ladder ropes no less to me than
    the gods of the antique wars,   1040
Minding their voices peal through the crash of destruction,
Their brawny limbs passing safe over charr'd laths, their white foreheads
    whole and unhurt out of the flames;
By the mechanic's wife with her babe at her nipple interceding for every
    person born,
Three scythes at harvest whizzing in a row from three lusty angels with
    shirts bagg'd out at their waists,
The snag-tooth'd hostler with red hair redeeming sins past and to come, 1045
Selling all he possesses, traveling on foot to fee lawyers for his brother and
    sit by him while he is tried for forgery;
What was strewn in the amplest strewing the square rod about me, and not
    filling the square rod then,
The bull and the bug never worshipp'd half enough,[8]
Dung and dirt more admirable than was dream'd,
The supernatural of no account, myself waiting my time to be one of the
    supremes,   1050
The day getting ready for me when I shall do as much good as the best, and
    be as prodigious;
By my life-lumps![9] becoming already a creator,
Putting myself here and now to the ambush'd womb of the shadows.

---

3. God of the Jews and Christians.
4. Kronos (or Cronus), in Greek mythology, was the Titan who ruled the universe until dethroned by Zeus, his son, the chief of the Olympian gods. Hercules was the son of Zeus and the mortal Alcmene, won immortality by performing twelve supposedly impossible feats.
5. The Indian philosopher Gautama Siddhartha, founder of Buddhism. Osiris was the Egyptian god who annually died and was reborn, symbolizing the fertility of nature. Isis was the Egyptian goddess of fertility and the sister and wife of Osiris. Belus was a legendary god-king of Assyria. Brahma, in Hinduism, was the divine reality in the role of creator.
6. The supreme being in Islam. Manito was the nature god of the Algonquian Indians.
7. An Aztec war god. Odin was the chief Norse god.
8. As Whitman implies, the bull and the bug had in fact been worshiped in earlier religions, the bull in several, the scarab beetle as an Egyptian symbol of the soul; but they had been worshiped wrongly, as supernatural objects.
9. Testicles.

42

A call in the midst of the crowd,
My own voice, orotund sweeping and final.   1055

Come my children,
Come my boys and girls, my women, household and intimates,
Now the performer launches his nerve, he has pass'd his prelude on the
    reeds within.

Easily written loose-finger'd chords—I feel the thrum of your climax and
    close.

My head slues round on my neck,   1060
Music rolls, but not from the organ,
Folks are around me, but they are no household of mine.

Ever the hard unsunk ground,
Ever the eaters and drinkers, ever the upward and downward sun, ever the
    air and the ceaseless tides,
Ever myself and my neighbors, refreshing, wicked, real,   1065
Ever the old inexplicable query, ever that thorn'd thumb, that breath of
    itches and thirsts,
Ever the vexer's *hoot! hoot!* till we find where the sly one hides and bring
    him forth,
Ever love, ever the sobbing liquid of life,
Ever the bandage under the chin, ever the trestles[1] of death.

Here and there with dimes on the eyes[2] walking,   1070
To feed the greed of the belly the brains liberally spooning,
Tickets buying, taking, selling, but in to the feast never once going,
Many sweating, ploughing, thrashing, and then the chaff for payment
    receiving,
A few idly owning, and they the wheat continually claiming.

This is the city and I am one of the citizens,   1075
Whatever interests the rest interests me, politics, wars, markets,
    newspapers, schools,
The mayor and councils, banks, tariffs, steamships, factories, stocks, stores,
    real estate and personal estate.

The little plentiful manikins skipping around in collars and tail'd coats,
I am aware who they are, (they are positively not worms or fleas,)
I acknowledge the duplicates of myself, the weakest and shallowest is
    deathless with me,   1080
What I do and say the same waits for them,
Every thought that flounders in me the same flounders in them.

---

1. Sawhorses or similar supports holding up a coffin.

2. Coins were placed on eyelids to hold them closed until burial.

I know perfectly well my own egotism,
Know my omnivorous lines and must not write any less,
And would fetch you whoever you are flush with myself.   1085
Not words of routine this song of mine,
But abruptly to question, to leap beyond yet nearer bring;
This printed and bound book—but the printer and the printing-office boy?
The well-taken photographs—but your wife or friend close and solid in
     your arms?
The black ship mail'd with iron, her mighty guns in her turrets—but the
     pluck of the captain and engineers?   1090
In the houses the dishes and fare and furniture—but the host and hostess,
     and the look out of their eyes?
The sky up there—yet here or next door, or across the way?
The saints and sages in history—but you yourself?
Sermons, creeds, theology—but the fathomless human brain,
And what is reason? and what is love? and what is life?   1095

43

I do not despise you priests, all time, the world over,
My faith is the greatest of faiths and the least of faiths,
Enclosing worship ancient and modern and all between ancient and
     modern,
Believing I shall come again upon the earth after five thousand years,
Waiting responses from oracles, honoring the gods, saluting the sun,   1100
Making a fetich of the first rock or stump, powowing with sticks in the
     circle of obis.[3]
Helping the llama or brahmin[4] as he trims the lamps of the idols,
Dancing yet through the streets in a phallic procession, rapt and austere in
     the woods a gymnosophist,[5]
Drinking mead from the skull-cup, to Shastas and Vedas admirant, minding
     the Koran,[6]
Walking the teokallis,[7] spotted with gore from the stone and knife, beating
     the serpent-skin drum,   1105
Accepting the Gospels,[8] accepting him that was crucified, knowing
     assuredly that he is divine,
To the mass kneeling or the puritan's prayer rising, or sitting patiently in a
     pew,
Ranting and frothing in my insane crisis, or waiting dead-like till my spirit
     arouses me,
Looking forth on pavement and land, or outside of pavement and land,
Belonging to the winders of the circuit of circuits.   1110

---

3. Magical charms, such as shells, used in African and West Indian religious practices. "Fetich": i.e., fetish; object of worship.
4. Here, also a Buddhist priest. "Llama": i.e., lama; a Buddhist monk of Tibet or Mongolia.
5. Members of an ancient Hindu ascetic sect.
6. The other worshipers include old Teutonic drinkers of mead (an alcoholic beverage made of fermented honey), admiring or wondering readers of the sastras (or shastras or shasters, books of Hindu law) or of the Vedas (the oldest sacred writings of Hinduism), those attentive to the Koran (the sacred book of Islam, containing Allah's revelations to Muhammad).
7. An ancient Central American temple built on a pyramidal mound.
8. Of the New Testament of the Bible.

One of that centripetal and centrifugal gang I turn and talk like a man
    leaving charges before a journey.

Down-hearted doubters dull and excluded,
Frivolous, sullen, moping, angry, affected, dishearten'd, atheistical,
I know every one of you, I know the sea of torment, doubt, despair and
    unbelief.

How the flukes[9] splash!
How they contort rapid as lightning, with spasms and spouts of blood!   1115

Be at peace bloody flukes of doubters and sullen mopers,
I take my place among you as much as among any,
The past is the push of you, me, all, precisely the same,
And what is yet untried and afterward is for you, me, all, precisely the
    same.   1120

I do not know what is untried and afterward,
But I know it will in its turn prove sufficient, and cannot fail.

Each who passes is consider'd, each who stops is consider'd, not a single
    one can it fail.

It cannot fail the young man who died and was buried,
Nor the young woman who died and was put by his side,   1125
Nor the little child that peep'd in at the door, and then drew back and was
    never seen again,
Nor the old man who has lived without purpose, and feels it with bitterness
    worse than gall,
Nor him in the poor house tubercled by rum and the bad disorder,[1]

Nor the numberless slaughter'd and wreck'd, nor the brutish koboo[2] call'd
    the ordure of humanity,
Nor the sacs merely floating with open mouths for food to slip in,   1130
Nor any thing in the earth, or down in the oldest graves of the earth,
Nor any thing in the myriads of spheres, nor the myriads of myriads that
    inhabit them,
Nor the present, nor the least wisp that is known.

44

It is time to explain myself—let us stand up.

What is known I strip away,   1135
I launch all men and women forward with me into the Unknown.

The clock indicates the moment—but what does eternity indicate?

We have thus far exhausted trillions of winters and summers,
There are trillions ahead, and trillions ahead of them.

9. The flat parts on either side of a whale's tail;
here used figuratively.
1. Syphilis.
2. Native of Sumatra.

Births have brought us richness and variety, 1140
And other births will bring us richness and variety.

I do not call one greater and one smaller,
That which fills its period and place is equal to any.

Were mankind murderous or jealous upon you, my brother, my sister?
I am sorry for you, they are not murderous or jealous upon me, 1145
All has been gentle with me, I keep no account with lamentation,
(What have I to do with lamentation?)

I am an acme of things accomplish'd, and I an encloser of things to be.

My feet strike an apex of the apices[3] of the stairs,
On every step bunches of ages, and larger bunches between the steps, 1150
All below duly travel'd, and still I mount and mount.

Rise after rise bow the phantoms behind me,
Afar down I see the huge first Nothing, I know I was even there,
I waited unseen and always, and slept through the lethargic mist,
And took my time, and took no hurt from the fetid carbon.[4] 1155

Long I was hugg'd close—long and long.

Immense have been the preparations for me,
Faithful and friendly the arms that have help'd me.

Cycles[5] ferried my cradle, rowing and rowing like cheerful boatmen,
For room to me stars kept aside in their own rings, 1160
They sent influences to look after what was to hold me.

Before I was born out of my mother generations guided me,
My embryo has never been torpid, nothing could overlay it.

For it the nebula cohered to an orb,
The long slow strata piled to rest it on, 1165
Vast vegetables gave it sustenance,
Monstrous sauroids[6] transported it in their mouths and deposited it with
     care.

All forces have been steadily employ'd to complete and delight me,
Now on this spot I stand with my robust soul.

45

O span of youth! ever-push'd elasticity! 1170
O manhood, balanced, florid and full.

---

3. The highest points (variant plural of *apex*).
4. The "lethargic mist" (line 1154) and "fetid carbon" suggest a time before the appearance of
human beings on earth.

5. Centuries.
6. Prehistoric mammoth reptiles or dinosaurs,
thought to have carried their eggs in their mouths.

My lovers suffocate me,
Crowding my lips, thick in the pores of my skin,
Jostling me through streets and public halls, coming naked to me at night,
Crying by day *Ahoy!* from the rocks of the river, swinging and chirping over
 my head, 1175
Calling my name from flower-beds, vines, tangled underbrush,
Lighting on every moment of my life,
Bussing[7] my body with soft balsamic busses,
Noiselessly passing handfuls out of their hearts and giving them to be
 mine.

Old age superbly rising! O welcome, ineffable grace of dying days! 1180

Every condition promulges[8] not only itself, it promulges what grows after
 and out of itself,
And the dark hush promulges as much as any.

I open my scuttle[9] at night and see the far-sprinkled systems,
And all I see multiplied as high as I can cipher edge but the rim of the
 farther systems.

Wider and wider they spread, expanding, always expanding, 1185
Outward and outward and forever outward.

My sun has his sun and round him obediently wheels,
He joins with his partners a group of superior circuit,
And greater sets follow, making specks of the greatest inside them.

There is no stoppage and never can be stoppage, 1190
If I, you, and the worlds, and all beneath or upon their surfaces, were this
 moment reduced back to a pallid float,[1] it would not avail in the long
 run,
We should surely bring up again where we now stand,
And surely go as much farther, and then farther and farther.

A few quadrillions of eras, a few octillions of cubic leagues, do not hazard[2]
 the span or make it impatient,
They are but parts, any thing is but a part. 1195

See ever so far, there is limitless space outside of that,
Count ever so much, there is limitless time around that.

My rendezvous is appointed, it is certain,
The Lord will be there and wait till I come on perfect terms,
The great Camerado, the lover true for whom I pine will be there. 1200

46

I know I have the best of time and space, and was never measured and
 never will be measured.

7. Kissing.
8. Promulgates, officially announces.
9. Roof hatch.

1. That period before the solar system had defined
itself.
2. Imperil, make hazardous.

I tramp a perpetual journey, (come listen all!)
My signs are a rain-proof coat, good shoes, and a staff cut from the woods,
No friend of mine takes his ease in my chair,
I have no chair, no church, no philosophy,   1205
I lead no man to a dinner-table, library, exchange,[3]
But each man and each woman of you I lead upon a knoll,
My left hand hooking you round the waist,
My right hand pointing to landscapes of continents and the public road.

Not I, not any one else can travel that road for you,   1210
You must travel it for yourself.

It is not far, it is within reach,
Perhaps you have been on it since you were born and did not know,
Perhaps it is everywhere on water and on land.

Shoulder your duds dear son, and I will mine, and let us hasten forth,   1215
Wonderful cities and free nations we shall fetch as we go.

If you tire, give me both burdens, and rest the chuff[4] of your hand on my
    hip,
And in due time you shall repay the same service to me,
For after we start we never lie by again.

This day before dawn I ascended a hill and look'd at the crowded
    heaven,   1220
And I said to my spirit *When we become the enfolders of those orbs,
    and the pleasure and knowledge of every thing in them, shall we be
    fill'd and satisfied then?*
And my spirit said *No, we but level that lift to pass and continue beyond.*

You are also asking me questions and I hear you,
I answer that I cannot answer, you must find out for yourself.

Sit a while dear son,   1225
Here are biscuits to eat and here is milk to drink,
But as soon as you sleep and renew yourself in sweet clothes, I kiss you
    with a good-by kiss and open the gate for your egress hence.

Long enough have you dream'd contemptible dreams,
Now I wash the gum from your eyes,
You must habit yourself to the dazzle of the light and of every moment of
    your life.   1230

Long have you timidly waded holding a plank by the shore,
Now I will you to be a bold swimmer,
To jump off in the midst of the sea, rise again, nod to me, shout, and
    laughingly dash with your hair.

---

3. Stock exchange.   4. The fleshy part of the palm.

47

I am the teacher of athletes,
He that by me spreads a wider breast than my own proves the width of my
    own,   1235
He most honors my style who learns under it to destroy the teacher.

The boy I love, the same becomes a man not through derived power, but in
    his own right,
Wicked rather than virtuous out of conformity or fear,
Fond of his sweetheart, relishing well his steak,
Unrequited love or a slight cutting him worse than sharp steel cuts,   1240
First-rate to ride, to fight, to hit the bull's eye, to sail a skiff, to sing a song
    or play on the banjo,
Preferring scars and the beard and faces pitted with small-pox over all
    latherers,
And those well-tann'd to those that keep out of the sun.

I teach straying from me, yet who can stray from me?
I follow you whoever you are from the present hour,   1245
My words itch at your ears till you understand them.

I do not say these things for a dollar or to fill up the time while I wait for a
    boat,
(It is you talking just as much as myself, I act as the tongue of you,
Tied in your mouth, in mine it begins to be loosen'd.)

I swear I will never again mention love or death inside a house,   1250
And I swear I will never translate myself at all, only to him or her who
    privately stays with me in the open air.

If you would understand me go to the heights or water-shore,
The nearest gnat is an explanation, and a drop or motion of waves a key,
The maul, the oar, the hand-saw, second my words.

No shutter'd room or school can commune with me,   1255
But roughs and little children better than they.

The young mechanic is closest to me, he knows me well,
The woodman that takes his axe and jug with him shall take me with him
    all day,
The farm-boy ploughing in the field feels good at the sound of my voice,
In vessels that sail my words sail, I go with fishermen and seamen and love
    them.   1260

The soldier camp'd or upon the march is mine,
On the night ere the pending battle many seek me, and I do not fail them,
On that solemn night (it may be their last) those that know me seek me.

My face rubs to the hunter's face when he lies down alone in his blanket,
The driver thinking of me does not mind the jolt of his wagon,   1265
The young mother and old mother comprehend me,

The girl and the wife rest the needle a moment and forget where they are,
They and all would resume what I have told them.

48

I have said that the soul is not more than the body,
And I have said that the body is not more than the soul,   1270
And nothing, not God, is greater to one than one's self is,
And whoever walks a furlong without sympathy walks to his own funeral
    drest in his shroud,
And I or you pocketless of a dime may purchase the pick of the earth,
And to glance with an eye or show a bean in its pod confounds the learning
    of all times,
And there is no trade or employment but the young man following it may
    become a hero,   1275
And there is no object so soft but it makes a hub for the wheel'd universe,
And I say to any man or woman, Let your soul stand cool and composed
    before a million universes.

And I say to mankind, Be not curious about God,
For I who am curious about each am not curious about God,
(No array of terms can say how much I am at peace about God and about
    death.)   1280

I hear and behold God in every object, yet understand God not in the least,
Nor do I understand who there can be more wonderful than myself.

Why should I wish to see God better than this day?
I see something of God each hour of the twenty-four, and each moment
    then,
In the faces of men and women I see God, and in my own face in
    the glass,   1285
I find letters from God dropt in the street, and every one is sign'd by God's
    name,
And I leave them where they are, for I know that wheresoe'er I go,
Others will punctually come for ever and ever.

49

And as to you Death, and you bitter hug of mortality, it is idle to try to
    alarm me.

To his work without flinching the accoucheur⁵ comes,   1290
I see the elder-hand pressing receiving supporting,
I recline by the sills of the exquisite flexible doors,
And mark the outlet, and mark the relief and escape.

And as to you Corpse I think you are good manure, but that does not
    offend me,
I smell the white roses sweet-scented and growing,   1295
I reach to the leafy lips, I reach to the polish'd breasts of melons.

5. Midwife.

And as to you Life I reckon you are the leavings of many deaths,
(No doubt I have died myself ten thousand times before.)

I hear you whispering there O stars of heaven,
O suns—O grass of graves—O perpetual transfers and promotions,   1300
If you do not say any thing how can I say any thing?
Of the turbid pool that lies in the autumn forest,
Of the moon that descends the steeps of the soughing twilight,
Toss, sparkles of day and dusk—toss on the black stems that decay in the
    muck,
Toss to the moaning gibberish of the dry limbs.   1305

I ascend from the moon, I ascend from the night,
I perceive that the ghastly glimmer is noonday sunbeams reflected,
And debouch⁶ to the steady and central from the offspring great or small.

50

There is that in me—I do not know what it is—but I know it is in me.

Wrench'd and sweaty—calm and cool then my body becomes, I sleep—I
    sleep long.   1310

I do not know it—it is without name—it is a word unsaid,
It is not in any dictionary, utterance, symbol.

Something it swings on more than the earth I swing on,
To it the creation is the friend whose embracing awakes me.

Perhaps I might tell more. Outlines! I plead for my brothers and sisters. 1315
Do you see O my brothers and sisters?
It is not chaos or death—it is form, union, plan—it is eternal life—it is
    Happiness.

51

The past and present wilt—I have fill'd them, emptied them,
And proceed to fill my next fold of the future.

Listener up there! what have you to confide to me?   1320
Look in my face while I snuff the sidle⁷ of evening,
(Talk honestly, no one else hears you, and I stay only a minute longer.)

Do I contradict myself?
Very well then I contradict myself,
(I am large, I contain multitudes.)   1325

I concentrate toward them that are nigh, I wait on the door-slab.

---

6. Pour forth.
7. To snuff is to put out, as in extinguishing a candle; here the light is the hesitant last light of day,
sidling or moving along sideways.

Who has done his day's work? who will soonest be through with his supper?
Who wishes to walk with me?

Will you speak before I am gone? will you prove already too late?

52

The spotted hawk swoops by and accuses me, he complains of my gab and
    my loitering.   1330

I too am not a bit tamed, I too am untranslatable.
I sound my barbaric yawp over the roofs of the world.

The last scud of day[8] holds back for me,
It flings my likeness after the rest and true as any on the shadow'd wilds,
It coaxes me to the vapor and the dusk.   1335

I depart as air, I shake my white locks at the runaway sun,
I effuse my flesh in eddies,[9] and drift it in lacy jags.

I bequeath myself to the dirt to grow from the grass I love,
If you want me again look for me under your boot-soles.

You will hardly know who I am or what I mean,   1340
But I shall be good health to you nevertheless,
And filter and fibre your blood.

Failing to fetch me at first keep encouraged,
Missing me one place search another,
I stop somewhere waiting for you.   1345

The poem will make sense once you go out into the world

1855, 1881

Crossing Brooklyn Ferry[1]

1

Flood-tide below me! I see you face to face!
Clouds of the west—sun there half an hour high—I see you also face to
    face.

Crowds of men and women attired in the usual costumes, how curious you
    are to me!
On the ferry-boats the hundreds and hundreds that cross, returning home,
    are more curious to me than you suppose,
And you that shall cross from shore to shore years hence are more to me,
    and more in my meditations, than you might suppose.   5

---

8. Wind-driven clouds, or merely the last rays of the sun.
9. Air currents. "Effuse": pour forth.

1. First published as "Sun-Down Poem" in the 2nd edition of *Leaves of Grass* (1856), "Crossing Brooklyn Ferry" was given its final title in 1860.

2

The impalpable sustenance of me from all things at all hours of the day,
The simple, compact, well-join'd scheme, myself disintegrated, every one
    disintegrated yet part of the scheme,
The similitudes of the past and those of the future,
The glories strung like beads on my smallest sights and hearings, on the
    walk in the street and the passage over the river,
The current rushing so swiftly and swimming with me far away,   10
The others that are to follow me, the ties between me and them,
The certainty of others, the life, love, sight, hearing of others.

Others will enter the gates of the ferry and cross from shore to shore,
Others will watch the run of the flood-tide,
Others will see the shipping of Manhattan north and west, and the heights
    of Brooklyn to the south and east,   15
Others will see the islands large and small;
Fifty years hence, others will see them as they cross, the sun half an hour
    high,
A hundred years hence, or ever so many hundred years hence, others will
    see them,
Will enjoy the sunset, the pouring-in of the flood-tide, the falling-back to
    the sea of the ebb-tide.

3

It avails not, time nor place—distance avails not,   20
I am with you, you men and women of a generation, or ever so many
    generations hence,
Just as you feel when you look on the river and sky, so I felt,
Just as any of you is one of a living crowd, I was one of a crowd,
Just as you are refresh'd by the gladness of the river and the bright flow, I
    was refresh'd,
Just as you stand and lean on the rail, yet hurry with the swift current, I
    stood yet was hurried,   25
Just as you look on the numberless masts of ships and the thick-stemm'd
    pipes of steamboats, I look'd.

I too many and many a time cross'd the river of old,
Watched the Twelfth-month[2] sea-gulls, saw them high in the air floating
    with motionless wings, oscillating their bodies,
Saw how the glistening yellow lit up parts of their bodies and left the rest in
    strong shadow,
Saw the slow-wheeling circles and the gradual edging toward the south,   30
Saw the reflection of the summer sky in the water,
Had my eyes dazzled by the shimmering track of beams,
Look'd at the fine centrifugal spokes of light round the shape of my head in
    the sunlit water,
Look'd on the haze on the hills southward and south-westward,

2. December.

Look'd on the vapor as it flew in fleeces tinged with violet,   35
Look'd toward the lower bay to notice the vessels arriving,
Saw their approach, saw aboard those that were near me,
Saw the white sails of schooners and sloops, saw the ships at anchor,
The sailors at work in the rigging or out astride the spars,
The round masts, the swinging motion of the hulls, the slender serpentine
    pennants,   40
The large and small steamers in motion, the pilots in their pilot-houses,
The white wake left by the passage, the quick tremulous whirl of the
    wheels,
The flags of all nations, the falling of them at sunset.
The scallop-edged waves in the twilight, the ladled cups, the frolicsome
    crests and glistening,
The stretch afar growing dimmer and dimmer, the gray walls of the granite
    storehouses by the docks,   45
On the river the shadowy group, the big steam-tug closely flank'd on each
    side by the barges, the hay-boat, the belated lighter,[3]
On the neighboring shore the fires from the foundry chimneys burning
    high and glaringly into the night,
Casting their flicker of black contrasted with wild red and yellow light over
    the tops of houses, and down into the clefts of streets.

4

These and all else were to me the same as they are to you,
I loved well those cities, loved well the stately and rapid river,   50
The men and women I saw were all near to me,
Others the same—others who looked back on me because I look'd forward
    to them,
(The time will come, though I stop here to-day and to-night.)

5

What is it then between us?
What is the count of the scores or hundreds of years between us?   55

Whatever it is, it avails not—distance avails not, and place avails not,
I too lived, Brooklyn of ample hills was mine,
I too walk'd the streets of Manhattan island, and bathed in the waters
    around it,
I too felt the curious abrupt questionings stir within me,
In the day among crowds of people sometimes they came upon me,   60
In my walks home late at night or as I lay in my bed they came upon me,
I too had been struck from the float forever held in solution,
I too had receiv'd identity by my body,
That I was I knew was of my body, and what I should be I knew I should be
    of my body.

_____

3. Barge used to load or unload a cargo ship.

6

It is not upon you alone the dark patches fall, 65
The dark threw its patches down upon me also,
The best I had done seem'd to me blank and suspicious,
My great thoughts as I supposed them, were they not in reality meagre?
Nor is it you alone who know what it is to be evil,
I am he who knew what it was to be evil, 70
I too knitted the old knot of contrariety,
Blabb'd, blush'd, resented, lied, stole, grudg'd,
Had guile, anger, lust, hot wishes I dared not speak,
Was wayward, vain, greedy, shallow, sly, cowardly, malignant,
The wolf, the snake, the hog, not wanting in me, 75
The cheating look, the frivolous word, the adulterous wish, not wanting,
Refusals, hates, postponements, meanness, laziness, none of these
     wanting,
Was one with the rest, the days and haps of the rest,
Was call'd by my nighest name by clear loud voices of young men as they
     saw me approaching or passing,
Felt their arms on my neck as I stood, or the negligent leaning of their flesh
     against me as I sat, 80
Saw many I loved in the street or ferry-boat or public assembly, yet never
     told them a word,
Lived the same life with the rest, the same old laughing, gnawing, leeping,
Play'd the part that still looks back on the actor or actress,
The same old role, the role that is what we make it, as great as we like,
Or as small as we like, or both great and small. 85

7

Closer yet I approach you,
What thought you have of me now, I had as much of you—I laid in my
     stores in advance,
I consider'd long and seriously of you before you were born.

Who was to know what should come home to me?
Who knows but I am enjoying this?
Who knows, for all the distance, but I am as good as looking at you now, for 90
     all you cannot see me?

8

Ah, what can ever be more stately and admirable to me than mast-hemm'd
     Manhattan?
River and sunset and scallop-edg'd waves of flood-tide?
The sea-gulls oscillating their bodies, the hay-boat in the twilight, and the
     belated lighter?
What gods can exceed these that clasp me by the hand, and with voices I
     love call me promptly and loudly by my nighest name as I approach? 95
What is more subtle than this which ties me to the woman or man that
     looks in my face?
Which fuses me into you now, and pours my meaning into you?

We understand then do we not?
What I promis'd without mentioning it, have you not accepted?
What the study could not teach—what the preaching could not accomplish
    is accomplish'd, is it not?   100

9

Flow on, river! flow with the flood-tide, and ebb with the ebb-tide!
Frolic on, crested and scallop-edg'd waves!
Gorgeous clouds of the sunset! drench with your splendor me, or the men
    and women generations after me!
Cross from shore to shore, countless crowds of passengers!
Stand up, tall masts of Mannahatta![4] stand up, beautiful hills
    of Brooklyn!   105
Throb, baffled and curious brain! throw out questions and answers!
Suspend here and everywhere, eternal float of solution!
Gaze, loving and thirsting eyes, in the house or street or public assembly!
Sound out, voices of young men! loudly and musically call me by my
    nighest name!
Live, old life! play the part that looks back on the actor or actress!   110
Play the old role, the role that is great or small according as one makes it!
Consider, you who peruse me, whether I may not in unknown ways be
    looking upon you;
Be firm, rail over the river, to support those who lean idly, yet haste with
    the hasting current;
Fly on, sea-birds! fly sideways, or wheel in large circles high in the air;
Receive the summer sky, you water, and faithfully hold it till all downcast
    eyes have time to take it from you!   115
Diverge, fine spokes of light, from the shape of my head, or any one's head,
    in the sunlit water!
Come on, ships from the lower bay! pass up or down, white-sail'd
    schooners, sloops, lighters!
Flaunt away, flags of all nations! be duly lower'd at sunset!
Burn high your fires, foundry chimneys! cast black shadows at nightfall!
    cast red and yellow light over the tops of the houses!
Appearances, now or henceforth, indicate what you are,   120
You necessary film, continue to envelop the soul,
About my body for me, and your body for you, be hung our divinest aromas,
Thrive, cities—bring your freight, bring your shows, ample and sufficient
    rivers,
Expand, being than which none else is perhaps more spiritual,
Keep your places, objects than which none else is more lasting.   125

You have waited, you always wait, you dumb, beautiful ministers,
We receive you with free sense at last, and are insatiate henceforward,
Not you any more shall be able to foil us, or withhold yourselves from us,
We use you, and do not cast you aside—we plant you permanently within
    us,
We fathom you not—we love you—there is perfection in you also,   130

---

4. Variant of the American Indian word normally spelled "Manhattan."

You furnish your parts toward eternity,
Great or small, you furnish your parts toward the soul.

                                                              1856, 1881

The Wound-Dresser

1

An old man bending I come among new faces,
Years looking backward resuming in answer to children,
Come tell us old man, as from young men and maidens that love me,
(Arous'd and angry, I'd thought to beat the alarum, and urge relentless war,
But soon my fingers fail'd me, my face droop'd and I resign'd myself,   5
To sit by the wounded and soothe them, or silently watch the dead;)
Years hence of these scenes, of these furious passions, these chances,
Of unsurpass'd heroes, (was one side so brave? the other was equally
    brave;)
Now be witness again, paint the mightiest armies of earth,
Of those armies so rapid so wondrous what saw you to tell us?   10
What stays with you latest and deepest? of curious panics,
Of hard-fought engagements or sieges tremendous what deepest remains?

2

O maidens and young men I love and that love me,
What you ask of my days those the strangest and sudden your talking
    recalls,
Soldier alert I arrive after a long march cover'd with sweat and dust,   15
In the nick of time I come, plunge in the fight, loudly shout in the rush
    of successful charge,
Enter the captur'd works[1]—yet lo, like a swift-running river they fade,
Pass and are gone they fade—I dwell not on soldiers' perils or soldiers' joys,
(Both I remember well—many the hardships, few the joys, yet I was
    content.)

But in silence in dreams' projections,   20
While the world of gain and appearance and mirth goes on,
So soon what is over forgotten, and waves wash the imprints off the sand,
With hinged knees returning I enter the doors, (while for you up there,
Whoever you are, follow without noise and be of strong heart.)

Bearing the bandages, water and sponge,   25
Straight and swift to my wounded I go,
Where they lie on the ground after the battle brought in,
Where their priceless blood reddens the grass the ground,
Or to the rows of the hospital tent, or under the roof'd hospital,
To the long rows of cots up and down each side I return,   30

---

1. Fortifications.

To each and all one after another I draw near, not one do I miss,
An attendant follows holding a tray, he carries a refuse pail,
Soon to be fill'd with clotted rags and blood, emptied, and fill'd again.

I onward go, I stop,
With hinged knees and steady hand to dress wounds,   35
I am firm with each, the pangs are sharp yet unavoidable,
One turns to me his appealing eyes—poor boy! I never knew you,
Yet I think I could not refuse this moment to die for you, if that would
    save you.

3

On, on I go, (open doors of time! open hospital doors!)
The crush'd head I dress, (poor crazed hand tear not the bandage away,)   40
The neck of the cavalry-man with the bullet through and through I
    examine,
Hard the breathing rattles, quite glazed already the eye, yet life struggles
    hard,
(Come sweet death! be persuaded O beautiful death!
In mercy come quickly.)

From the stump of the arm, the amputated hand,   45
I undo the clotted lint, remove the slough, wash off the matter and blood,
Back on his pillow the soldier bends with curv'd neck and side-falling head,
His eyes are closed, his face is pale, he dares not look on the bloody stump,
And has not yet look'd on it.

I dress a wound in the side, deep, deep,   50
But a day or two more, for see the frame all wasted and sinking,
And the yellow-blue countenance see.

I dress the perforated shoulder, the foot with the bullet-wound,
Cleanse the one with a gnawing and putrid gangrene, so sickening, so
    offensive,
While the attendant stands behind aside me holding the tray and pail.   55

I am faithful, I do not give out,
The fractur'd thigh, the knee, the wound in the abdomen,
These and more I dress with impassive hand, (yet deep in my breast a fire,
    a burning flame.)

4

Thus in silence in dreams' projections,
Returning, resuming, I thread my way through the hospitals,   60
The hurt and wounded I pacify with soothing hand,
I sit by the restless all the dark night, some are so young,
Some suffer so much, I recall the experience sweet and sad,
(Many a soldier's loving arms about this neck have cross'd and rested,
Many a soldier's kiss dwells on these bearded lips.)   65

1865, 1881

When Lilacs Last in the Dooryard Bloom'd[1]

1

When lilacs last in the dooryard bloom'd,
And the great star[2] early droop'd in the western sky in the night,
I mourn'd, and yet shall mourn with ever-returning spring.

Ever-returning spring, trinity sure to me you bring,
Lilac blooming perennial and drooping star in the west,   5
And thought of him I love.

2

O powerful western fallen star!
O shades of night—O moody, tearful night!
O great star disappear'd—O the black murk that hides the star!
O cruel hands that hold me powerless—O helpless soul of me!   10
O harsh surrounding cloud that will not free my soul.

3

In the dooryard fronting an old farm-house near the white-wash'd palings,
Stands the lilac-bush tall-growing with heart-shaped leaves of rich green,
With many a pointed blossom rising delicate, with the perfume strong I
    love,
With every leaf a miracle—and from this bush in the dooryard,   15
With delicate-color'd blossoms and heart-shaped leaves of rich green,
A sprig with its flower I break.

4

In the swamp in secluded recesses,
A shy and hidden bird is warbling a song.

Solitary the thrush,   20
The hermit withdrawn to himself, avoiding the settlements,
Sings by himself a song.
Song of the bleeding throat,
Death's outlet song of life, (for well dear brother I know,
If thou wast not granted to sing thou would'st surely die.)   25

5

Over the breast of the spring, the land, amid cities,
Amid lanes and through old woods, where lately the violets peep'd from
    the ground, spotting the gray debris,

---

1. Composed in the months following Lincoln's assassination on April 14, 1865, this elegy was printed in the fall of that year as an appendix to the recently published *Drum-Taps* volume. In the 1881 edition of *Leaves of Grass* it and three lesser poems were joined to make up the section *Memories of President Lincoln*.
2. Literally Venus, although it becomes associated with Lincoln himself.

Amid the grass in the fields each side of the lanes, passing the endless
  grass,
Passing the yellow-spear'd wheat, every grain from its shroud in the dark-
  brown fields uprisen,
Passing the apple-tree blows[3] of white and pink in the orchards,   30
Carrying a corpse to where it shall rest in the grave,
Night and day journeys a coffin.[4]

6

Coffin that passes through lanes and streets,
Through day and night with the great cloud darkening the land,
With the pomp of the inloop'd flags with the cities draped in black,   35
With the show of the States themselves as of crape-veil'd women standing,
With processions long and winding and the flambeaus[5] of the night,
With the countless torches lit, with the silent sea of faces and the
  unbared heads,
With the waiting depot, the arriving coffin, and the sombre faces,
With dirges through the night, with the thousand voices rising strong
  and solemn,   40
With all the mournful voices of the dirges pour'd around the coffin,
The dim-lit churches and the shuddering organs—where amid these you
  journey,
With the tolling tolling bells' perpetual clang,
Here, coffin that slowly passes,
I give you my sprig of lilac.   45

7

(Nor for you, for one alone,
Blossoms and branches green to coffins all I bring,
For fresh as the morning, thus would I chant a song for you O sane and
  sacred death.

All over bouquets of roses,
O death, I cover you over with roses and early lilies,   50
But mostly and now the lilac that blooms the first,
Copious I break, I break the sprigs from the bushes,
With loaded arms I come, pouring for you,
For you and the coffins all of you O death.)

8

O western orb sailing the heaven,   55
Now I know what you must have meant as a month since I walk'd,
As I walk'd in silence the transparent shadowy night,
As I saw you had something to tell as you bent to me night after night,

3. Blossoms.
4. Shortly after the assassination, a train carrying
Lincoln's body for burial traveled from Washington, D.C., to Springfield, Illinois.
5. Torches.

As you droop'd from the sky low down as if to my side, (while the other
    stars all look'd on,)
As we wander'd together the solemn night, (for something I know not
    what kept me from sleep,)   60
As the night advanced, and I saw on the rim of the west how full you
    were of woe,
As I stood on the rising ground in the breeze in the cool transparent night,
As I watch'd where you pass'd and was lost in the netherward black of the
    night,
As my soul in its trouble dissatisfied sank, as where you sad orb,
Concluded, dropt in the night, and was gone.   65

9

Sing on there in the swamp,
O singer bashful and tender, I hear your notes, I hear your call,
I hear, I come presently, I understand you,
But a moment I linger, for the lustrous star has detain'd me,
The star my departing comrade holds and detains me.   70

10

O how shall I warble myself for the dead one there I loved?
And how shall I deck my song for the large sweet soul that has gone?
And what shall my perfume be for the grave of him I love?

Sea-winds blown from east and west,
Blown from the Eastern sea and blown from the Western sea, till there
    on the prairies meeting,   75
These and with these and the breath of my chant,
I'll perfume the grave of him I love.

11

O what shall I hang on the chamber walls?
And what shall the pictures be that I hang on the walls,
To adorn the burial-house of him I love?   80

Pictures of growing spring and farms and homes,
With the Fourth-month[6] eve at sundown, and the gray smoke lucid and
    bright,
With floods of the yellow gold of the gorgeous, indolent, sinking sun,
    burning, expanding the air,
With the fresh sweet herbage under foot, and the pale green leaves of the
    trees prolific,
In the distance the flowing glaze, the breast of the river, with a
    wind-dapple here and there,   85

---

6. April.

With ranging hills on the banks, with many a line against the sky, and
    shadows,
And the city at hand with dwellings so dense, and stacks of chimneys,
And all the scenes of life and the workshops, and the workmen homeward
    returning.

12

Lo, body and soul—this land,
My own Manhattan with spires, and the sparkling and hurrying tides,
    and the ships,   90
The varied and ample land, the South and the North in the light, Ohio's
    shores and flashing Missouri,
And ever the far-spreading prairies cover'd with grass and corn.

Lo, the most excellent sun so calm and haughty,
The violet and purple morn with just-felt breezes,
The gentle soft-born measureless light,   95
The miracle spreading bathing all, the fulfill'd noon,
The coming eve delicious, the welcome night and the stars,
Over my cities shining all, enveloping man and land.

13

Sing on, sing on you gray-brown bird,
Sing from the swamps, the recesses, pour your chant from the bushes, 100
Limitless out of the dusk, out of the cedars and pines.

Sing on dearest brother, warble your reedy song,
Loud human song, with voice of uttermost woe.

O liquid and free and tender!
O wild and loose to my soul!—O wondrous singer!   105
You only I hear—yet the star holds me, (but will soon depart,)
Yet the lilac with mastering odor holds me.

14

Now while I sat in the day and look'd forth,
In the close of the day with its light and the fields of spring, and the
    farmers preparing their crops,
In the large unconscious scenery of my land with its lakes and forests, 110
In the heavenly aerial beauty, (after the perturb'd winds and the storms,)
Under the arching heavens of the afternoon swift passing, and the voices
    of children and women,
The many-moving sea-tides, and I saw the ships how they sail'd,
And the summer approaching with richness, and the fields all busy with
    labor,
And the infinite separate houses, how they all went on, each with its
    meals and minutia of daily usages,   115
And the streets how their throbbings throbb'd, and the cities pent—lo,
    then and there,

Falling upon them all and among them all, enveloping me with the rest,
Appear'd the cloud, appear'd the long black trail,
And I knew death, its thought, and the sacred knowledge of death.

Then with the knowledge of death as walking one side of me,   120
And the thought of death close-walking the other side of me,
And I in the middle as with companions, and as holding the hands of
  companions,
I fled forth to the hiding receiving night that talks not,
Down to the shores of the water, the path by the swamp in the dimness,
To the solemn shadowy cedars and ghostly pines so still.   125

And the singer so shy to the rest receiv'd me,
The gray-brown bird I know receiv'd us comrades three,
And he sang the carol of death, and a verse for him I love.

From deep secluded recesses,
From the fragrant cedars and the ghostly pines so still,   130
Came the carol of the bird.

And the charm of the carol rapt me,
As I held as if by their hands my comrades in the night,
And the voice of my spirit tallied the song of the bird.

Come lovely and soothing death,   135
Undulate round the world, serenely arriving, arriving,
In the day, in the night, to all, to each,
Sooner or later delicate death.

Prais'd be the fathomless universe,
For life and joy, and for objects and knowledge curious,   140
And for love, sweet love—but praise! praise! praise!
For the sure-enwinding arms of cool-enfolding death.

Dark mother always gliding near with soft feet,
Have none chanted for thee a chant of fullest welcome?
Then I chant it for thee, I glorify thee above all,   145
I bring thee a song that when thou must indeed come, come unfalteringly.

Approach strong deliveress,
When it is so, when thou hast taken them I joyously sing the dead,
Lost in the loving floating ocean of thee,
Laved in the flood of thy bliss O death.   150

From me to thee glad serenades,
Dances for thee I propose saluting thee, adornments and feastings for thee,
And the sights of the open landscape and the high-spread sky are fitting,
And life and the fields, and the huge and thoughtful night.

The night in silence under many a star,   155
The ocean shore and the husky whispering wave whose voice I know,
And the soul turning to thee O vast and well-veil'd death,
And the body gratefully nestling close to thee.

Over the tree-tops I float thee a song,
Over the rising and sinking waves, over the myriad fields and the prairies
    wide,   160
Over the dense-pack'd cities all and the teeming wharves and ways,
I float this carol with joy, with joy to thee O death.

15

To the tally of my soul,
Loud and strong kept up the gray-brown bird,
With pure deliberate notes spreading filling the night.   165

Loud in the pines and cedars dim,
Clear in the freshness moist and the swamp-perfume,
And I with my comrades there in the night.

While my sight that was bound in my eyes unclosed,
As to long panoramas of visions.   170

And I saw askant[7] the armies,
I saw as in noiseless dreams hundreds of battle-flags,
Borne through the smoke of the battles and pierc'd with missiles I saw
    them,
And carried hither and yon through the smoke, and torn and bloody,
And at last but a few shreds left on the staffs, (and all in silence,)   175
And the staffs all splinter'd and broken.

I saw battle-corpses, myriads of them,
And the white skeletons of young men, I saw them,
I saw the debris and debris of all the slain soldiers of the war,
But I saw they were not as was thought,   180
They themselves were fully at rest, they suffer'd not,
The living remain'd and suffer'd, the mother suffer'd,
And the wife and the child and the musing comrade suffer'd,
And the armies that remain'd suffer'd.

16

Passing the visions, passing the night,   185
Passing, unloosing the hold of my comrades' hands,
Passing the song of the hermit bird and the tallying song of my soul,
Victorious song, death's outlet song, yet varying ever-altering song,
As low and wailing, yet clear the notes, rising and falling, flooding the
    night,
Sadly sinking and fainting, as warning and warning, and yet again
    bursting with joy,   190
Covering the earth and filling the spread of the heaven,
As that powerful psalm in the night I heard from recesses,
Passing, I leave thee lilac with heart-shaped leaves,
I leave thee there in the door-yard, blooming, returning with spring.

7. Sideways, aslant.

I cease from my song for thee,   195
From my gaze on thee in the west, fronting the west, communing with
    thee,
O comrade lustrous with silver face in the night.

Yet each to keep and all, retrievements out of the night,
The song, the wondrous chant of the gray-brown bird,
And the tallying chant, the echo arous'd in my soul,   200
With the lustrous and drooping star with the countenance full of woe,
With the holders holding my hand nearing the call of the bird,
Comrades mine and I in the midst, and their memory ever to keep, for
    the dead I loved so well,
For the sweetest, wisest soul of all my days and lands—and this for his
    dear sake,
Lilac and star and bird twined with the chant of my soul,   205
There in the fragrant pines and the cedars dusk and dim.

1865–66, 1881

EMILY DICKINSON
1830–1886

With her formal experimentation and bold thematic ambitions, Emily Dickinson is recognized as one of the greatest American poets, a poet who continues to exert an enormous influence on the way writers think about the possibilities of poetic craft and vocation. Little known in her own lifetime, she was first publicized in almost mythic terms as a reclusive, eccentric, death-obsessed spinster who wrote in fits and starts as the spirit moved her—the image of the woman poet at her oddest. As with all myths, this one has some truth in it, but the reality is more interesting and complicated. Though she lived in her parents' homes for all but a year of her life, she was acutely aware of current events and drew on them for some of her poetry. Her dazzlingly complex lyrics—compressed statements abounding in startling imagery and marked by an extraordinary vocabulary—explore a wide range of subjects: psychic pain and joy, the relationship of self to nature, the intensely spiritual, and the intensely ordinary. Her poems about death confront its grim reality with honesty, humor, curiosity, and above all a refusal to be comforted. In her poems about religion, she expressed piety and hostility, and she was fully capable of moving within the same poem from religious consolation to a rejection of doctrinal piety and a querying of God's plans for the universe. Her many love poems seem to have emerged in part from close relationships with at least one woman and several men. It is sometimes possible to extract autobiography from her poems, but she was not a confessional poet; rather, she used personae— invented first-person speakers—to dramatize the various situations, moods, and perspectives she explored in her lyrics. Though each of her poems is individually short, when collected in one volume, her nearly eighteen hundred surviving poems (she probably wrote hundreds more that were lost) have the feel of an epic produced by a person who devoted much of her life to her art.

Emily Elizabeth Dickinson was born on December 10, 1830, in Amherst, Massachusetts, the second child of Emily Norcross Dickinson and Edward Dickinson. Economically, politically, and intellectually, the Dickinsons were among Amherst's most prominent families. Edward Dickinson, a lawyer, served as a state representative and a state senator. He helped found Amherst College as a Calvinist alternative to the more liberal Harvard and Yale, and was its treasurer for thirty-six years. During his term in the national House of Representatives (1853–54), Emily visited him in Washington and stayed briefly in Philadelphia on her way home, but travel of any kind was unusual for her. She lived most of her life in the spacious Dickinson family house in Amherst called the Homestead. Among her closest friends and lifelong allies were her brother, Austin, a year and a half older than she, and her younger sister, Lavinia. In 1856, when her brother married Emily's close friend Susan Gilbert, the couple moved into what was called the Evergreens, a house next door to the Homestead, built for the newlyweds by Edward Dickinson. Neither Emily nor Lavinia married. The two women stayed with their parents, as was typical of unmarried middle- and upper-class women of the time. New England in this period had many more women than men in these groups, owing to the male population exodus during the gold rush years (1849 and after) and the carnage of the Civil War. For Dickinson, home was a place of "Infinite power."

Dickinson attended Amherst Academy from 1840 through 1846, and then boarded for less than a year at the Mount Holyoke Female Seminary in South Hadley, ten miles from Amherst. She quickly became intensely homesick for her "*own* DEAR HOME" and never completed the three-year course of study, dropping out in less than a year. Her stay at Mount Holyoke was not just a time of homesickness but of religious crisis. The school, presided over by the energetic Mary Lyon, sought to develop women intellectually and spiritually so that some might one day serve as Christian missionaries. In line with the Seminary's Calvinist expectations that individuals would experience a religious awakening as a sign of divine favor, students were regularly queried as to whether they "professed faith," had "hope," or were resigned to "no hope." Dickinson remained adamantly among the small group of "no hopes." Arguably, her assertion of no hope was a matter of defiance, a refusal to capitulate to the demands of orthodoxy. A year after leaving Mount Holyoke, Dickinson, in a letter to a friend, described her failure to convert with darkly comic glee: "*I am one of the lingering bad ones,*" she said. But she went on to assert that it was her very "failure" to conform to the conventional expectations of her evangelical culture that helped to liberate her to think on her own—to "pause," as she put it, "and ponder, and ponder."

Once back at home, Dickinson embarked on a lifelong course of reading. Her deepest literary debts were to the Bible and classic English authors, such as Shakespeare and Milton. Through the national magazines the family subscribed to and books ordered from Boston, she encountered the full range of the English and American literature of her time, including among Americans Longfellow, Holmes, Lowell, Hawthorne, and Emerson. Characteristically, however, she did not go next door to meet Emerson in 1857 when he stayed at the Evergreens during a lecture tour—preferring the Emerson she could imagine to the actual presence. She read the novels of Charles Dickens as they appeared and knew the poems of Robert Browning and the poet laureate Tennyson. But the English contemporaries who mattered most to her were the Brontë sisters, George Eliot, and above all, as an example of a successful contemporary woman poet, Elizabeth Barrett Browning.

No one has persuasively traced the precise stages of Dickinson's artistic growth from this supposedly "somber Girl" to the young woman who, within a few years of her return from Mount Holyoke, began writing a new kind of poetry, with its distinctive voice, style, and transformation of traditional form. She found a paradoxical poetic freedom within the confines of the meter of the "fourteener"—seven-beat lines usually broken into stanzas alternating four and three beats—familiar to her from earliest childhood. This is the form of nursery rhymes, ballads, church hymns, and some classic English poetry—strongly rhythmical, easy to memorize and recite. But Dickinson veered sharply from this form's expectations. If Walt Whitman at this time was heeding Emerson's call for a "metre-making argument" by turning to an open form— as though rules did not exist—Dickinson made use of this and other familiar forms only to break their rules. She used dashes and syntactical fragments to convey her pursuit of a truth that could best be communicated indirectly; these fragments dispensed with prosy verbiage and went directly to the core. Her use of enjambment (the syntactical technique of running past the conventional stopping place of a line or a stanza break) forced her reader to learn where to pause to collect the sense before reading on, often creating dizzying ambiguities. She multiplied aural possibilities by making use of what later critics termed "off" or "slant" rhymes that, as with her metrical and syntactical experimentations, contributed to the expressive power of her poetry. In short, poetic forms thought to be simple, predictable, and safe were altered irrevocably by Dickinson's language experiments with the lyric. Along with its opposite, free verse, the compressed lyric flaunting its refusal to conform became a hallmark of modernist poetry in the twentieth century.

Writing about religion, science, music, nature, books, and contemporary events both national and local, Dickinson often presented her poetic ideas as terse, striking definitions or propositions, or dramatic narrative scenes, in a highly abstracted moment, or setting, often at the boundaries between life and death. The result was a poetry that, as is typical of the lyric tradition, focused on the speaker's response to a situation rather than the details of the situation itself. Her "nature" poems offer sharp, precise observations but, infused with mingled ecstasy and pain, are often as much about psychological and spiritual matters as about the specifics of nature. The sight of a familiar bird—the robin—in the poem beginning "A bird came down the walk" leads to a statement about nature's strangeness rather than the expected statement about friendly animals. Whitman generally seems intoxicated by his ability to appropriate nature for his own purposes; Dickinson's nature is much more resistant to human schemes, and the poet's experiences of nature range from a sense of its hostility to an ability to become an "Inebriate of Air" and "Debauchee of Dew." Openly expressive of sexual and romantic longings, her personae reject conventional gender roles. In one of her most famous poems, for instance, she imagines herself as a "Loaded Gun" with "the power to kill."

Dickinson's private letters, in particular three drafts of letters to an unidentified "Master," and dozens of love poems have convinced biographers that she fell in love a number of times; candidates include Benjamin Newton, a law clerk in her father's office; one or more married men; and above all, Susan Gilbert Dickinson, the friend who became her sister-in-law. The exact nature of any of these relationships is hard to determine, in part because Dickinson's letters and poems could just as easily be taken as poetic meditations on desire as writings directed to specific people. On the evidence of the approximately five hundred letters that Dickinson wrote Susan, many of which contained drafts or copies of her latest poems, that relationship would appear to have been the most passionate (and long-lived) of Dickinson's life. Whatever the nature of their relationship, it melded love, friendship, intellectual exchange, and art. One of the men she was involved with was Samuel Bowles, editor of the Springfield *Republican*, whom Dickinson described (in a letter to Bowles himself) as having "the most triumphant face out of paradise"; another was the Reverend Charles Wadsworth, whom she met in Philadelphia in 1855 and who visited her in Amherst in 1860. Evidence suggests that she was upset by his decision to move to San Francisco in 1862, but none of her letters to Wadsworth survive.

Knowing her powers as a poet, Dickinson wanted to be published, but only around a dozen poems appeared during her lifetime. She sent many poems to Bowles, perhaps hoping he would publish them in the *Republican*. Although he did publish a few, he also edited them into more conventional shape. She also sent poems to editor Josiah Holland at *Scribner's*, who chose not to publish her. She sent a few poems to Thomas Wentworth Higginson, editor at the *Atlantic Monthly*, after he printed "Letter to a Young Contributor" in the April 1862 issue. Her cover letter of April 15, 1862, asked him, "Are you too deeply occupied to say if my Verse is alive?" Higginson, like other editors, saw her formal innovations as imperfections. But he remained intrigued by Dickinson and in 1869 invited her to visit him in Boston. When she refused, he visited

her in 1870. He would eventually become one of the editors of her posthumously published poetry.

But if Dickinson sought publication, she also regarded it as "the Auction / Of the
Mind of Man," as she put it in poem 788; at the very least, she was unwilling to submit to the touching-up operations editors performed on her poems. Some critics have
argued that Dickinson's letters constituted a form of publication, for Dickinson
included poems in many of her letters. Even more intriguing, beginning around 1858
Dickinson began to record her poems on white, unlined paper, in some cases marking moments of textual revision, and then folded and stacked the sheets and sewed
groups of them together in what are called fascicles. She created thirty such fascicles,
ranging in length from sixteen to twenty-four pages; and there is considerable evidence that she worked diligently at the groupings, thinking about chronology, subject
matter, and specific thematic orderings within each. These fascicles were left for others to discover after her death, neatly stacked in a drawer. It can be speculated that
Dickinson, realizing that her unconventional poetry would not be published in her
own lifetime as written, became a sort of self-publisher. Critics remain uncertain,
however, about just how self-conscious her arrangements were and argue over what
is lost and gained by considering individual poems in the context of their fascicle
placement. There is also debate about whether the posthumous publication of Dickinson's manuscript poetry violates the visual look of the poems—their inconsistent
dashes and even some of the designs that Dickinson added to particular poems. The
selections printed here include a photographic reproduction of poem 269, which can
be compared to the now-standard printed version, also included.

Dickinson's final decades were marked by health problems and a succession of
losses. Beginning in the early 1860s she suffered from eye pain. She consulted with
an ophthalmologist in Boston in 1864 and remained concerned about losing her
vision. In 1874 her father died in a Boston hotel room after taking an injection of morphine for his pain, and one year later her mother had a stroke and would remain
bedridden until her death in 1882. Her beloved eight-year-old nephew Gilbert died of
typhoid fever in 1883, next door at the Evergreens; and in 1885, her close friend from
childhood, Helen Hunt Jackson, who had asked to be Dickinson's literary executor,
died suddenly in San Francisco. Dickinson's seclusion late in life may have been a
response to her grief at these losses or a concern for her own health, but ultimately a
focus on the supposed eccentricity of her desire for privacy draws attention away from
the huge number of poems she wrote—she may well have secluded herself so that she
could follow her vocation. Emily Dickinson died on May 15, 1886, perhaps from a kidney disorder called "Bright's Disease," the official diagnosis, but just as likely from
hypertension.

In 1881 the astronomer David Todd, with his young wife, Mabel Loomis Todd,
arrived in Amherst to direct the Amherst College Observatory. The next year, Austin
Dickinson and Mabel Todd began an affair that lasted until Austin's death in 1895.
Despite this turn of events Mabel Todd and Emily Dickinson established a friendship
without actually meeting (Todd saw Dickinson once, in her coffin), and Todd decided
that the poet was "in many respects a genius." Soon after Dickinson's death, Mabel
Todd (at Emily's sister Lavinia's invitation) painstakingly transcribed many of her
poems. The subsequent preservation and publication of her poetry and letters were
initiated and carried forth by Todd. She persuaded Higginson to help her see a posthumous collection of poems into print in 1890 and a second volume of poems in 1891;
she went on to publish a collection of Dickinson's letters in 1894 and a third volume
of poems in 1896. In the 1890s some critics reacted patronizingly toward what they
saw as verse that violated the laws of meter, and even Todd and Higginson edited some
of the poems to make them more conventional. The three volumes were popular, going
through several printings and selling over ten thousand copies. During the 1890s,
Susan Dickinson and her daughter, Martha Dickinson Bianchi, also published a few
of Dickinson's poems in journals such as *The Century*. By 1900 or so, however, Dick-

inson's work had fallen out of favor, and had Martha Dickinson Bianchi not resumed publication of her aunt's poetry in 1914 (she published eight volumes of Dickinson's work between 1914 and 1937), Dickinson's writings might never have achieved the audience they have today. Taken together, the editorial labors of Todd, Susan Dickinson, and Bianchi set in motion the critical and textual work that would help establish Dickinson as one of the great American poets. They also made her poetry available to the American modernists, poets such as Hart Crane and Marianne Moore; Dickinson and Whitman are the nineteenth-century poets who exerted the greatest influence on American poetry to come.

The texts of the poems, and the numbering, are from R. W. Franklin's one-volume edition, *The Poems of Emily Dickinson: Reading Edition* (1999), which draws on his three-volume variorum, *The Poems of Emily Dickinson* (1998). Bracketed numbers refer to the numbering of Thomas Johnson's *The Poems of Emily Dickinson* (1955), for many years the standard edition. The dating of Dickinson's poetry remains uncertain, though Franklin is more accurate than Johnson. The date following each poem corresponds to Franklin's estimate of Dickinson's first finished draft; if the poem was published in Dickinson's lifetime, that date is supplied as well.

122[1]

[130]

These are the days when Birds come back -
A very few - a Bird or two -
To take a backward look.

These are the days when skies resume
The old - old sophistries[2] of June -   5
A blue and gold mistake.

Oh fraud that cannot cheat the Bee.
Almost thy plausibility
Induces my belief,

Till ranks of seeds their witness bear -   10
And softly thro' the altered air
Hurries a timid leaf.

Oh sacrament of summer days,
Oh Last Communion[3] in the Haze -
Permit a child to join -   15

Thy sacred emblems to partake -
Thy consecrated bread to take
And thine immortal wine!

1859, 1864

---

1. Dickinson published a version of this poem in the *Drum Beat*, March 11, 1864.
2. Deceptively subtle reasonings.

3. I.e., the end of summer is compared to the death of Christ commemorated by the Christian sacrament of Communion.

207

[214]

I taste a liquor never brewed -
From Tankards scooped in Pearl -
Not all the Frankfort Berries
Yield such an Alcohol!

Inebriate of air - am I -   5
And Debauchee of Dew -
Reeling - thro' endless summer days -
From inns of molten Blue -

When "Landlords" turn the drunken Bee
Out of the Foxglove's door -   10
When Butterflies - renounce their "drams" -
I shall but drink the more!

Till Seraphs[1] swing their snowy Hats -
And Saints - to windows run -
To see the little Tippler   15
Leaning against the - Sun!

                                                                      1861

236

[324]

Some keep the Sabbath going to Church -
I keep it, staying at Home -
With a Bobolink for a Chorister -
And an Orchard, for a Dome -

Some keep the Sabbath in Surplice[1]   5
I, just wear my Wings -
And instead of tolling the Bell, for Church,
Our little Sexton[2] - sings.

God preaches, a noted Clergyman -
And the sermon is never long,   10
So instead of getting to Heaven, at last -
I'm going, all along.

                                                                      1861

---

1. Angels.   2. Church custodian.
1. Open-sleeved gown worn by clergymen.

260

[288]

I'm Nobody! Who are you?
Are you - Nobody - too?
Then there's a pair of us!
Dont tell! they'd advertise - you know!

How dreary - to be - Somebody!   5
How public - like a Frog ——— *general, "frog-king"*
To tell one's name - the livelong June -
To an admiring Bog!

1861

269

[249]

Wild nights - Wild nights!
Were I with thee
Wild nights should be
Our luxury!

Futile - the winds -   5
To a Heart in port -
Done with the Compass -
Done with the Chart!

Rowing in Eden -
Ah - the Sea!   10
Might I but moor - tonight -
In thee!

1861

320

[258]

There's a certain Slant of light,
Winter Afternoons -
That oppresses, like the Heft
Of Cathedral Tunes -

Heavenly Hurt, it gives us -   5
We can find no scar,
But internal difference -
Where the Meanings, are -

None may teach it - Any -
'Tis the Seal Despair -   10

Poem 269 [249] of Fascicle 11, from vol. 1 of *The Manuscript Books of Emily Dickinson* (1981), ed. R. W. Franklin, reproduced with the permission of Harvard University Press. Dickinson's handwriting, which changed over the years, can be dated by comparison with her letters. Ambiguities of punctuation are typical. Line 1, for instance, may or may not end with a dash and an exclamation point; Dickinson's modern editors use the exclamation point only.

An imperial affliction
Sent us of the Air -

When it comes, the Landscape listens -
Shadows - hold their breath -
When it goes, 'tis like the Distance   15
On the look of Death -

1862

339

[241]

I like a look of Agony,
Because I know it's true -
Men do not sham Convulsion,
Nor simulate, a Throe -

The eyes glaze once - and that is Death -   5
Impossible to feign
The Beads opon the Forehead
By homely Anguish strung.

1862

340

[280]

I felt a Funeral, in my Brain,
And Mourners to and fro
Kept treading - treading - till it seemed
That Sense was breaking through -

And when they all were seated,   5
A Service, like a Drum -
Kept beating - beating - till I thought
My mind was going numb -

And then I heard them lift a Box
And creak across my Soul   10
With those same Boots of Lead, again,
Then Space - began to toll,

As all the Heavens were a Bell,
And Being, but an Ear,
And I, and Silence, some strange Race   15
Wrecked, solitary, here -

And then a Plank in Reason, broke,
And I dropped down, and down -

And hit a World, at every plunge,
And Finished knowing - then -   20

                                                              1862

359

[328]

A Bird, came down the Walk -
He did not know I saw -
He bit an Angle Worm in halves
And ate the fellow, raw,

And then, he drank a Dew
From a convenient Grass -   5
And then hopped sidewise to the Wall
To let a Beetle pass -

He glanced with rapid eyes,
That hurried all abroad -   10
They looked like frightened Beads, I thought,
He stirred his Velvet Head. -

Like one in danger, Cautious,
I offered him a Crumb,
And he unrolled his feathers,   15
And rowed him softer Home -

Than Oars divide the Ocean,
Too silver for a seam,
Or Butterflies, off Banks of Noon,
Leap, plashless¹ as they swim.   20

                                                              1862

365

[338]

I know that He exists.
Somewhere - in silence -
He has hid his rare life
From our gross eyes.

'Tis an instant's play-   5
'Tis a fond Ambush -
Just to make Bliss
Earn her own surprise!

_____
1. I.e., splashless.

But - should the play
Prove piercing earnest -   10
Should the glee - glaze -
In Death's - stiff - stare -

Would not the fun
Look too expensive!
Would not the jest -   15
Have crawled too far!

                                         1862

409
[303]

The Soul selects her own Society -
Then - shuts the Door -
To her divine Majority -
Present no more -

Unmoved - she notes the Chariots - pausing -   5
At her low Gate -
Unmoved - an Emperor be kneeling
Opon her Mat -

I've known her - from an ample nation -
Choose One -
Then - close the Valves of her attention -   10
Like Stone -

                                         1862

411
[528]

Mine - by the Right of the White Election!
Mine - by the Royal Seal!
Mine - by the sign in the Scarlet prison -
Bars - cannot conceal!

Mine - here - in Vision - and in Veto!   5
Mine - by the Grave's Repeal -
Titled - Confirmed -
Delirious Charter!
Mine - long as Ages steal!

                                         1862

446

[448]

This was a Poet -
It is That
Distills amazing sense
From Ordinary Meanings -
And Attar[1] so immense   5

From the familiar species
That perished by the Door -
We wonder it was not Ourselves
Arrested it - before -

Of Pictures, the Discloser -   10
The Poet - it is He -
Entitles Us - by Contrast -
To ceaseless Poverty -

Of Portion - so unconscious -
The Robbing - could not harm -   15
Himself - to Him - a Fortune -
Exterior - to Time -

                                                              1862

479

[712]

Because I could not stop for Death -
He kindly stopped for me -
The Carriage held but just Ourselves -
And Immortality.

We slowly drove - He knew no haste   5
And I had put away
My labor and my leisure too,
For His Civility -

We passed the School, where Children strove
At Recess - in the Ring -   10
We passed the Fields of Gazing Grain -
We passed the Setting Sun -

Or rather - He passed Us -
The Dews drew quivering and Chill -
For only Gossamer,[1] my Gown -   15
My Tippet - only Tulle[2] -

---

1. Perfume obtained from flowers.   2. Thin silk. "Tippet": scarf for covering neck and
1. Delicate, light fabric.   shoulders.

We paused before a House that seemed
A Swelling of the Ground -
The Roof was scarcely visible -
The Cornice[3] - in the Ground -   20

Since then - 'tis Centuries - and yet
Feels shorter than the Day
I first surmised the Horses' Heads
Were toward Eternity -

                                                                1862

519

[441]

This is my letter to the World
That never wrote to Me -
The simple News that Nature told -
With tender Majesty

Her Message is committed   5
To Hands I cannot see -
For love of Her - Sweet - countrymen -
Judge tenderly - of Me

                                                                1863

591

[465]

I heard a Fly buzz - when I died -
The Stillness in the Room
Was like the Stillness in the Air -
Between the Heaves of Storm -

The Eyes around - had wrung them dry -   5
And Breaths were gathering firm
For that last Onset - when the King
Be witnessed - in the Room -

I willed my Keepsakes - Signed away
What portion of me be   10
Assignable - and then it was
There interposed a Fly -

3. Decorative molding beneath a roof.

With Blue - uncertain - stumbling Buzz -
Between the light - and me -
And then the Windows failed - and then   15
I could not see to see -

                                                          1863

620

[435]

Much Madness is divinest Sense -
To a discerning Eye -
Much Sense - the starkest Madness -
'Tis the Majority
In this, as all, prevail -   5
Assent - and you are sane -
Demur - you're straightway dangerous -
And handled with a Chain -

                                                          1863

656

[520]

I started Early - Took my Dog -
And visited the Sea -
The Mermaids in the Basement
Came out to look at me -

And Frigates - in the Upper Floor   5
Extended Hempen Hands -
Presuming Me to be a Mouse -
Aground - opon the Sands -

But no Man moved Me - till the Tide
Went past my simple Shoe -   10
And past my Apron - and my Belt
And past my Boddice - too -

And made as He would eat me up -
As wholly as a Dew
Opon a Dandelion's Sleeve -   15
And then - I started - too -

And He - He followed - close behind -
I felt His Silver Heel
Opon my Ancle - Then My Shoes
Would overflow with Pearl -   20

Until We met the Solid Town -
No One He seemed to know -

And bowing - with a Mighty look -
At me - The Sea withdrew -

1863

764

[754]

My Life had stood - a Loaded Gun -
In Corners - till a Day
The Owner passed - identified -
And carried Me away -

And now We roam in Sovreign Woods -   5
And now We hunt the Doe -
And every time I speak for Him
The Mountains straight reply -

And do I smile, such cordial light
Opon the Valley glow -   10
It is as a Vesuvian[1] face
Had let it's pleasure through

And when at Night - Our good Day done -
I guard My Master's Head -
'Tis better than the Eider Duck's   15
Deep Pillow - to have shared -

To foe of His - I'm deadly foe -
None stir the second time -
On whom I lay a Yellow Eye -
Or an emphatic Thumb -   20

Though I than He - may longer live
He longer must - than I -
For I have but the power to kill,
Without - the power to die -

1863

788

[709]

Publication - is the Auction
Of the Mind of Man -
Poverty - be justifying
For so foul a thing

1. Reference to Mount Vesuvius, the active volcano in southern Italy that destroyed Pompeii (79 C.E.).

Possibly - but We - would rather   5
From Our Garret go
White - unto the White Creator -
Than invest - Our Snow -

Thought belong to Him who gave it -
Then - to Him Who bear   10
It's Corporeal illustration - sell
The Royal Air -

In the Parcel - Be the Merchant
Of the Heavenly Grace -
But reduce no Human Spirit
To Disgrace of Price -

1863

1096

[986]

A narrow Fellow in the Grass
Occasionally rides -
You may have met him? Did you not
His notice instant is -

The Grass divides as with a Comb -   5
A spotted Shaft is seen,
And then it closes at your Feet
And opens further on -

He likes a Boggy Acre -
A Floor too cool for Corn -   10
But when a Boy and Barefoot
I more than once at Noon

Have passed I thought a Whip Lash
Unbraiding in the Sun
When stooping to secure it   15
It wrinkled And was gone -

Several of Nature's People
I know and they know me
I feel for them a transport
Of Cordiality   20

But never met this Fellow
Attended or alone
Without a tighter Breathing
And Zero at the Bone.

1865

1263

[*1129*]

Tell all the truth but tell it slant -
Success in Circuit lies
Too bright for our infirm Delight
The Truth's superb surprise
As Lightning to the Children eased   5
With explanation kind
The Truth must dazzle gradually
Or every man be blind -

1872

1577

[*1545*]

The Bible is an antique Volume -
Written by faded Men
At the suggestion of Holy Spectres -
Subjects - Bethlehem -
Eden - the ancient Homestead -   5
Satan - the Brigadier -
Judas - the Great Defaulter -
David - the Troubadour -
Sin - a distinguished Precipice
Others must resist -   10
Boys that "believe" are very lonesome -
Other Boys are "lost" -
Had but the Tale a warbling Teller -
All the Boys would come -
Orpheu's Sermon[1] captivated -   15
It did not condemn -

1882

MARK TWAIN (SAMUEL L. CLEMENS)
1835–1910

Samuel Langhorne Clemens, the third of five children, was born on November 30, 1835, in the village of Florida, Missouri, and grew up in the somewhat larger river town of Hannibal, Missouri, that place of idylls and also dangers he called St. Petersburg in his writings, home to his two most famous characters, Tom Sawyer and Huck Finn. Twain's father, a justice of the peace who had unsuccessfully tried to become a storekeeper and clerk, died when Twain was twelve, and from that time on Twain worked to support himself and the rest of the family. He seems to have acquired his dry sense of humor and love for literature from his mother, Jane Lampton Clemens, to whom he was very close. After his father's death, Twain was apprenticed to a printer, and in 1851, when his brother Orion became a publisher in Hannibal, Twain went to work for him. In 1853 he began three years of travel, stopping in St. Louis, New York, Philadelphia, Keokuk (Iowa), and Cincinnati, in each place earning his living as printer hired by the day. In 1856 he left Cincinnati for New Orleans by steamboat, intending to go to the Amazon. He changed his plans, however, and instead apprenticed himself to Horace Bixby, a Mississippi riverboat pilot. After training for eighteen months, Twain satisfied a boyhood ambition by becoming a pilot himself, and he practiced this lucrative and prestigious trade until 1861, when the Civil War virtually ended commercial river traffic. During this time he began to write humorous accounts of his activities for the *Keokuk Saturday Post*; though only three of these articles were published (under the pseudonym Thomas Jefferson Snodgrass), they introduced him to journalism, his occupation for much of the next ten years. Twain never forgot the inspiration of his time on the Mississippi; as he remarked, "When I find a well-drawn character in fiction or biography I generally take a warm personal interest in him, for the reason that I have known him before—met him on the river."

Slavery was legal in Missouri, though the state did not join the Confederacy, and Twain may have seen brief service in a woefully unorganized Confederate militia, an experience that he later fictionalized in "The Private History of a Campaign That Failed" (1885). In 1861 he went west with his brother Orion, who had been appointed secretary of the Nevada Territorial government. This move started him on the path toward his life as a humorist, lecturer, journalist, and author. In *Roughing It* (1872), written a decade later, Twain fictionally elaborated the brothers' stagecoach adventures on the way to Carson City and recounted his unsuccessful schemes for making money (including mining the Comstock lode in Virginia City) once he got there. Throughout *Roughing It,* which also covers his stint in San Francisco as a reporter and his half-hearted gold-mining in the Sierras, as well as his trip to Hawai'i, Twain's project is to debunk the sentimental idea of the West as a place where fortunes could be easily made and show its disappointing and even brutal side.

In the West, Twain began writing for newspapers, first the *Territorial Enterprise* in Virginia City and then, after 1864, the *Californian.* The fashion of the time called for a pen name, and so from a columnist for the New Orleans *Times-Picayune,* he borrowed "Mark Twain," which means in riverboat terms "two fathoms deep," or "safe water." His early writing was modeled on the humorous journalism of the day, especially that practiced by his friend and roommate in Nevada, who wrote under the penname Dan De Quille. Also important to his development during these years were friendships with the western writer Bret Harte, the famous professional lecturer and comic Artemus Ward, and the obscure amateur raconteur Jim Gillis. Twain's reputation as a lecturer and his first success as a writer lay in his skillful retelling of a well-known tall tale, "The Notorious Jumping Frog of Calaveras County," first published in 1865.

In this same year Twain signed with the *Sacramento Union* to write a series of letters covering the newly opened steamboat passenger service between San Francisco and Honolulu. In these letters he used a fictitious character, Mr. Brown, to present inelegant ideas and unorthodox views, attitudes, and information, often in impolite language. This device allowed him to say just about anything he wanted, provided he could convincingly claim he was simply reporting what others said and did. The refinement of this deadpan technique made it a staple of his lectures. Twain's first book of this period, and still one of his most popular, was *Innocents Abroad* (1869), consisting of a revised form of the letters he wrote for the *Alta California* and *New York Tribune* during his 1867 excursion on the *Quaker City* to the Mediterranean and Holy Land. Led by the pious Henry Ward Beecher, the passengers were a group of largely New England and Midwestern Protestants, and at the last moment Twain was hired to entertain them. What a mismatch it was! Twain wrote hilarious satires of his fellow passengers as well as the pretentious, decadent, and undemocratic Old World as viewed by a citizen of a young country on the rise. A characteristically impertinent note was sounded in a remark upon disembarking in New York: When Twain was asked for his impressions of the Holy Land, he said he knew for a fact there would be no Second Coming, for if Jesus had been there once he certainly wouldn't go back. Such scoffing drew angry editorials and speeches, publicity that helped make *Innocents Abroad* successful.

Twain's many travels, including lecture tours around the globe, did not erase the rich material of his Missouri boyhood, which ran deep in his memory and imagination. To get to it, he had, in effect, to work chronologically backward and psychically inward. He tentatively probed this material as early as 1870 in an early version of *The Adventures of Tom Sawyer* called *A Boy's Manuscript*. In 1875 he wrote *Old Times on the Mississippi* in seven installments for the *Atlantic Monthly* (edited by his friend William Dean Howells, who tirelessly promoted Twain's career), arriving at the place that many critics see as his imaginative home. In this work, an account of Twain's adventures as an apprentice to the pilot Horace Bixby, he evokes not only "the great Mississippi, the majestic, the magnificent Mississippi, rolling its mile-wide tide along, shining in the sun," but also his sense of the inner life of what took place on the river's surface and shores. These sketches were later incorporated into *Life on the Mississippi* (1883), written after Twain took a monthlong steamboat trip on the Mississippi, stopping along the way to visit Hannibal. The added material—part history, part memoir, part travelogue—offers, among other things, a scathing critique of the southern romanticism Twain believed had made the Civil War inevitable, a theme that would reappear in his masterpiece, *Adventures of Huckleberry Finn*.

Twain had married Olivia Langdon, genteel and devout daughter of a wealthy coal dealer from Buffalo, New York, in 1870. This entry into a higher stratum of society than he had previously known, along with his increasing fascination with wealth, created a constant struggle in his work between the conventional and the disruptive, which is typical of much of the best American humor. In the perennially popular *The Adventures of Tom Sawyer* (1876), the struggle emerges in the contrast between the entrepreneurial but entirely respectable Tom and his disreputable friend Huck. In this narrative, Twain also mingles childhood pleasures with childhood fears of the violence, terror, and death lurking at the edges of the village. This book has long been recognized as an adult classic as well as a children's book, and its publication established Twain as a popular writer of fiction.

Twain's marriage was a happy one. He went to such lengths as (for a time) attending church and quitting smoking and drinking. His wife read his manuscripts, occasionally noting unseemly material; though she has been criticized for censoring him, this is what Twain wanted her to do. Her unquestioned love and respect for him gave him the security he needed, especially when his fiery personality caused him to become frustrated or depressed.

Twain began *Adventures of Huckleberry Finn* in 1876 and, after several stops and starts, published it in 1884 and 1885. In recent years the racial (and racist) implications of every aspect of the novel have been the subjects of critical debate, as have questions about the racial beliefs of the author. Similar questions have been raised about gender and sexuality in Twain's life and work. In Twain's own day *Huck* was banned in many libraries and schools around the country and denounced in pulpits not for its racial content but for its supposedly encouraging boys to swear, smoke, and run away. Nevertheless, *Huck Finn* has enjoyed extraordinary popularity since its publication. It broke literary ground as a novel written entirely in the vernacular and established the vernacular's capacity to result in high art. Its unpretentious, colloquial, yet poetic style, its wide-ranging humor, its embodiment of the enduring and widely shared dream of innocence and freedom, and its recording of a vanished way of life in the pre–Civil War Mississippi Valley have instructed and moved people of all ages and conditions all over the world. *Huck* sold 51,000 copies in its first fourteen months, compared to *Tom Sawyer's* 25,000 in the same period. Ernest Hemingway once called it the source of "all modern American literature."

Twain wrote another successful and memorable book in this period, the bitter *A Connecticut Yankee in King Arthur's Court* (1889). The novel seems to be a satire on sixth-century Arthurian England seen through the eyes of a crafty "Yankee," Hank Morgan, who is transported back thirteen centuries and tries to "introduce," in Twain's words, the "great and beneficent civilization of the nineteenth century" into the chivalric and decidedly undemocratic world of Camelot. But Hank's "Gilded Age" schemes end in their own destruction and the massacre of thousands of knights. *The Tragedy of Pudd'nhead Wilson* (1894), though a confusing mishmash of separate storylines, is also a dark and troubling view of nineteenth-century American values, set in a Mississippi river town of the 1830s and centered on the switching of two babies born the same day—one the result of miscegenation, the other the legitimate son of a white slave owner. The book painfully reveals the absurdities of slavery and its terrible effects on victims and victimizers alike—the undeserved self-hate of slaves and the unearned pride of whites. The way in which Twain portrays the twinning of law and custom in sustaining the institution of slavery (the book is full of such doublings) indicates his despair over prospects for true racial equality, a despair supported by the realities of Jim Crow laws and the escalation of lynchings in the post-Reconstruction period.

In the decade after *Pudd'nhead Wilson* was published, Twain experienced a series of calamities. Suddenly, his health became bad; poor investments led to bankruptcy in the panic of 1893; his youngest daughter, Jean, was diagnosed as epileptic; his oldest daughter, Susy, died of meningitis while he was away; and his wife, Livy, began to decline into permanent invalidism. Twain's grief for a time threatened his sanity; for several years writing was both agonized labor and necessary therapy. The results of these circumstances were a travel book, *Following the Equator* (1897), which records the round-the-world lecture tour that Twain undertook to pay off debts; a sardonically brilliant interrogation of middle-class American morality, "The Man That Corrupted Hadleyburg" (1900); an embittered treatise on humanity's foibles, follies, and venality, *What Is Man?* (1906); and the bleakly despairing *The Mysterious Stranger*, first published in an inaccurate and unauthorized version by Albert Bigelow Paine, Twain's first biographer, in 1916. Scholars continue to study the large bulk of Twain's unfinished or (until recently) unpublished writings and have called for reevaluation of his work from the decade after 1895. But Lawrence I. Berkove, among others, has emphasized that the notion of a sudden turn to bleak pessimism in his later work, especially the pieces included by Bernard De Voto in the posthumously published *Letters from the Earth* (1961), is incorrect. Twain, argues Berkove, was from the beginning a pessimist, an unorthodox Calvinist who hated God for his malice toward humanity, especially his duplicity in commanding humans to be moral, when he had predestined them to be as they were, and in urging humans to seek salvation, when he had predestined most of them to Hell. Twain was also disgusted with his fellow humans and found the world intolerable. He did not believe that things were meant to turn out right. This can be clearly seen even in such seemingly upbeat earlier works as *Roughing It* and *Huck Finn*. Many humorists have been deeply pessimistic, and Twain fits this mold.

Twain became a revered public institution in his last years, his opinions sought by the press on every subject of general interest. Though his views on political, military, and social subjects were often acerbic, it was only to his best friends that he confessed the depth of his disillusionment. Much of this bitterness informs such published works as "To a Person Sitting in Darkness" (1901), "The United States of Lyncherdom" (1901), and "King Leopold's Soliloquy" (1905), as well as other writings unpublished in his lifetime, such as *Letters from the Earth,* in which he skewers religion from the skeptical and irreverent perspective of Satan, who was punished by being cast down to earth, and who writes letters back to his friend Gabriel.

Twain maintained his magical power with language throughout his career. What he said of one of his characters explains a large part of his permanent appeal: "He could curl his tongue around the bulliest words in the language when he was a mind to, and lay them before you without a jint started, anywheres" (*Life on the Mississippi* [1883], Chapter 3). His love of language informs his hilarious attack on the novels of James Fenimore Cooper, "Fenimore Cooper's Literary Offences" (printed here). As his friend Howells observed, Twain was unlike any of his contemporaries in American letters: "Emerson, Longfellow, Lowell, Holmes—I knew them all and all the rest of our sages, poets, seers, critics, humorists; they were like one another and like other literary men; but Clemens was sole, incomparable, the Lincoln of our literature."

The Notorious Jumping Frog of Calaveras County[1]

In compliance with the request of a friend of mine, who wrote me from the East, I called on good-natured, garrulous old Simon Wheeler, and inquired after my friend's friend, Leonidas W. Smiley, as requested to do, and I hereunto append the result. I have a lurking suspicion that *Leonidas W.* Smiley is a myth; that my friend never knew such a personage; and that he only conjectured that if I asked old Wheeler about him, it would remind him of his infamous *Jim* Smiley, and he would go to work and bore me to death with some exasperating reminiscence of him as long and as tedious as it should be useless to me. If that was the design, it succeeded.

I found Simon Wheeler dozing comfortably by the barroom stove of the dilapidated tavern in the decayed mining camp of Angel's, and I noticed that he was fat and bald-headed, and had an expression of winning gentleness and simplicity upon his tranquil countenance. He roused up, and gave me good-day. I told him a friend of mine had commissioned me to make some inquiries about a cherished companion of his boyhood named *Leonidas W.* Smiley—*Rev. Leonidas W.* Smiley, a young minister of the Gospel, who he had heard was at one time a resident of Angel's Camp. I added that if Mr. Wheeler could tell me anything about this Rev. Leonidas W. Smiley, I would feel under many obligations to him.

Simon Wheeler backed me into a corner and blockaded me there with his chair, and then sat down and reeled off the monotonous narrative which follows this paragraph. He never smiled, he never frowned, he never changed his voice from the gentle-flowing key to which he tuned his initial sentence, he never betrayed the slightest suspicion of enthusiasm; but all through the interminable narrative there ran a vein of impressive earnestness and sincerity, which showed me plainly that, so far from his imagining that there was anything ridiculous or funny about his story, he regarded it as a really important matter, and admired its two heroes as men of transcendent genius in *finesse*. I let him go on in his own way, and never interrupted him once.

Rev. Leonidas W. H'm, Reverend Le—well, there was a feller here once by the name of *Jim* Smiley, in the winter of '49—or may be it was the spring of '50—I don't recollect exactly, somehow, though what makes me think it was one or the other is because I remember the big flume warn't finished when he first come to the camp; but any way, he was the curiosest man about

---

1. The story first appeared in the *New York Saturday Press* of November 18, 1865, and was subsequently revised several times. The source of the text is the version published in *Mark Twain's* *Sketches, New and Old* (1875). In a note, Twain instructs his readers that "Calaveras" is pronounced *Cal-e-va'-ras*.

always betting on anything that turned up you ever see, if he could get any-body to bet on the other side; and if he couldn't he'd change sides. Any way that suited the other man would suit *him*—any way just so's he got a bet, *he* was satisfied. But still he was lucky, uncommon lucky; he most always come out winner. He was always ready and laying for a chance; there couldn't be no solit'ry thing mentioned but that feller'd offer to bet on it, and take ary side you please, as I was just telling you. If there was a horse-race, you'd find him flush or you'd find him busted at the end of it; if there was a dog-fight, he'd bet on it; if there was a cat-fight, he'd bet on it; if there was a chicken-fight, he'd bet on it; why, if there was two birds setting on a fence, he would bet you which one would fly first; or if there was a camp-meeting, he would be there reg'lar to bet on Parson Walker, which he judged to be the best exhorter about here, and so he was too, and a good man. If he even see a straddle-bug start to go anywheres, he would bet you how long it would take him to get to—to wherever he was going to, and if you took him up, he would foller that straddle-bug to Mexico but what he would find out where he was bound for and how long he was on the road. Lots of the boys here has seen that Smiley, and can tell you about him. Why, it never made no difference to *him*—he'd bet on *any* thing—the dangdest feller. Parson Walker's wife laid very sick once, for a good while, and it seemed as if they warn't going to save her; but one morning he come in, and Smiley up and asked him how she was, and he said she was considable better—thank the Lord for his inf'nite mercy—and coming on so smart that with the blessing of Prov'dence she'd get well yet; and Smiley, before he thought says, "Well, I'll resk two-and-a-half she don't anyway."

Thish-yer Smiley had a mare—the boys called her the fifteen-minute nag, but that was only in fun, you know, because of course she was faster than that—and he used to win money on that horse, for all she was so slow and always had the asthma, or the distemper, or the consumption, or something of that kind. They used to give her two or three hundred yards start, and then pass her under way; but always at the fag end of the race she'd get excited and desperate-like, and come cavorting and straddling up, and scattering her legs around limber, sometimes in the air, and sometimes out to one side among the fences, and kicking up m-o-r-e dust and raising m-o-r-e racket with her coughing and sneezing and blowing her nose—and *always* fetch up at the stand just about a neck ahead, as near as you could cipher it down.

And he had a little small bull-pup, that to look at him you'd think he warn't worth a cent but to set around and look ornery and lay for a chance to steal something. But as soon as money was up on him he was a different dog; his under-jaw'd begin to stick out like the fo'castle of a steamboat, and his teeth would uncover and shine like the furnaces. And a dog might tackle him and bully-rag him, and bite him, and throw him over his shoulder two or three times, and Andrew Jackson—which was the name of the pup—Andrew Jackson would never let on but what *he* was satisfied, and hadn't expected noth-ing else—and the bets being doubled and doubled on the other side all the time, till the money was all up; and then all of a sudden he would grab that other dog jest by the j'int of his hind leg and freeze to it—not chaw, you understand, but only just grip and hang on till they throwed up the sponge, if it was a year. Smiley always come out winner on that pup, till he harnessed a dog once that didn't have no hind legs, because they'd been sawed off in a circular saw, and when the thing had gone along far enough, and the money was all up, and he come to make a snatch for his pet holt, he see in a minute how he's been imposed on, and how the other dog had him in the door, so to speak, and he 'peared surprised, and then he looked sorter discouraged-like, and didn't try no more to win the fight, and so he got shucked out bad. He give Smiley a look, as much as to say his heart was broke, and it was *his* fault, for putting up a dog that hadn't no hind legs for him to take holt of, which was his main dependence in a fight, and then he limped off a piece and laid down and died. It was a good pup, was that Andrew Jackson, and would have made a name for hisself if he'd lived, for the stuff was in him and he had genius—I know it, because he hadn't no opportunities to speak of, and it don't stand to reason that a dog could make such a fight as he could under them circumstances if he hadn't no talent. It always makes me feel sorry when I think of that last fight of his'n, and the way it turned out.

Well, thish-yer Smiley had rat-tarriers, and chicken cocks, and tomcats and all them kind of things, till you couldn't rest, and you couldn't fetch nothing for him to bet on but he'd match you. He ketched a frog one day, and took him home, and said he cal'lated to educate him; and so he never done nothing for three months but set in his back yard and learn that frog to jump. And you bet you he *did* learn him, too. He'd give him a little punch behind, and the next minute you'd see that frog whirling in the air like a doughnut—see him turn one summerset, or may be a couple, if he got a good start, and come down flat-footed and all right, like a cat. He got him up so in the matter of ketching flies, and kep' him in practice so constant, that he'd nail a fly every time as fur as he could see him. Smiley said all a frog wanted was education, and he could do 'most anything—and I believe him. Why, I've seen him set Dan'l Webster down here on this floor—Dan'l Webster was the name of the frog—and sing out, "Flies, Dan'l, flies!" and quicker'n you could wink he'd spring straight up and snake a fly off'n the counter there, and flop down on the floor ag'in as solid as a gob of mud, and fall to scratching the side of his head with his hind foot as indifferent as if he hadn't no idea he'd been doin' any more'n any frog might do. You never see a frog so modest and straight-for'ard as he was, for all he was so gifted. And when it come to fair and square jumping on a dead level, he could get over more ground at one straddle than any animal of his breed you ever see. Jumping on a dead level was his strong suit, you understand; and when it come to that, Smiley would ante up money on him as long as he had a red. Smiley was monstrous proud of his frog, and well he might be, for fellers that had traveled and been everywheres all said he laid over any frog that ever *they* see.

Well, Smiley kep' the beast in a little lattice box, and he used to fetch him down town sometimes and lay for a bet. One day a feller—a stranger in the camp, he was—come acrost him with his box, and says:

"What might it be that you've got in the box?"

And Smiley says, sorter indifferent-like, "It might be a parrot, or it might be a canary, maybe, but it ain't—it's only just a frog."

And the feller took it, and looked at it careful, and turned it round this way and that, and says, "H'm—so 'tis. Well, what's *he* good for?"

"Well," Smiley says, easy and careless, "he's good enough for *one* thing, I should judge—he can outjump any frog in Calaveras county."

The feller took the box again, and took another long, particular look, and give it back to Smiley, and says, very deliberate, "Well," he says, "I don't see no p'ints about that frog that's any better'n any other frog."

"Maybe you don't," Smiley says. "Maybe you understand frogs and maybe you don't understand 'em; maybe you've had experience, and maybe you ain't only an amature, as it were. Anyways, I've got *my* opinion and I'll resk forty dollars that he can outjump any frog in Calaveras county."

And the feller studied a minute, and then says, kinder sad like, "Well, I'm only a stranger here, and I ain't got no frog; but if I had a frog, I'd bet you."

And then Smiley says, "That's all right—that's all right—if you'll hold my box a minute, I'll go and get you a frog." And so the feller took the box, and put up his forty dollars along with Smiley's, and set down to wait.

So he set there a good while thinking and thinking to hisself, and then he got the frog out and prized his mouth open and took a teaspoon and filled him full of quail shot—filled him pretty near up to his chin—and set him on the floor. Smiley he went to the swamp and slopped around in the mud for a long time, and finally he ketched a frog, and fetched him in, and give him to this feller, and says:

"Now, if you're ready, set him alongside of Dan'l, with his forepaws just even with Dan'l's, and I'll give the word." Then he says, "One—two—three—*git!*" and him and the feller touched up the frogs from behind, and the new frog hopped off lively, but Dan'l give a heave, and hysted up his shoulders—so—like a Frenchman, but it warn't no use—he couldn't budge; he was planted as solid as a church, and he couldn't no more stir than if he was anchored out. Smiley was a good deal surprised, and he was disgusted too, but he didn't have no idea what the matter was, of course.

The feller took the money and started away; and when he was going out at the door, he sorter jerked his thumb over his shoulder—so—at Dan'l, and says again, very deliberate, "Well," he says, "*I* don't see no p'ints about that frog that's any better'n any other frog."

Smiley he stood scratching his head and looking down at Dan'l a long time, and at last he says, "I do wonder what in the nation that frog throw'd off for—I wonder if there ain't something the matter with him—he 'pears to look mighty baggy, somehow." And he ketched Dan'l by the nap of the neck, and hefted him, and says, "Why blame my cats if he don't weigh five pound!" and turned him upside down and he belched out a double handful of shot. And then he see how it was, and he was the maddest man—he set the frog down and took out after that feller, but he never ketched him. And——"

[Here Simon Wheeler heard his name called from the front yard, and got up to see what was wanted.] And turning to me as he moved away, he said: "Just set where you are, stranger, and rest easy—I ain't going to be gone a second."

But, by your leave, I did not think that a continuation of the history of the enterprising vagabond *Jim* Smiley would be likely to afford me much information concerning the *Rev. Leonidas W.* Smiley, and so I started away.

At the door I met the sociable Wheeler returning, and he button-holed me and recommenced:

"Well, thish-yer Smiley had a yaller one-eyed cow that didn't have no tail, only jest a short stump like a bannanner, and——"

However, lacking both time and inclination, I did not wait to hear about the afflicted cow, but took my leave.

1865, 1867

Adventures of Huckleberry Finn[1]

(Tom Sawyer's Comrade)

Scene: The Mississippi Valley

Time: Forty to Fifty Years Ago[2]

NOTICE

Persons attempting to find a motive in this narrative will be prosecuted; persons attempting to find a moral in it will be banished; persons attempting to find a plot in it will be shot.

BY ORDER OF THE AUTHOR
PER G. G., CHIEF OF ORDNANCE.

Explanatory

In this book a number of dialects are used, to wit: the Missouri negro dialect; the extremest form of the backwoods South-Western dialect; the ordinary "Pike-County"[3] dialect; and four modified varieties of this last. The shadings have not been done in a hap-hazard fashion, or by guess-work; but pains-takingly, and with the trustworthy guidance and support of personal familiarity with these several forms of speech.

I make this explanation for the reason that without it many readers would suppose that all these characters were trying to talk alike and not succeeding.

THE AUTHOR

Chapter I

You don't know about me, without you have read a book by the name of "The Adventures of Tom Sawyer,"[4] but that ain't no matter. That book was made by Mr. Mark Twain, and he told the truth, mainly. There was things which he stretched, but mainly he told the truth. That is nothing. I never seen anybody but lied, one time or another, without it was Aunt Polly, or the widow, or maybe Mary. Aunt Polly—Tom's Aunt Polly, she is—and Mary, and the Widow Douglas, is all told about in that book—which is mostly a true book; with some stretchers, as I said before.

---

1. *Adventures of Huckleberry Finn* was first published in England in December 1884. The text printed here is a corrected version of the first American edition of 1885.

2. I.e., in 1835 or 1845—well before the Civil War.

3. Pike County, Missouri.

4. Published in 1876.

Now the way that the book winds up, is this: Tom and me found the money that the robbers hid in the cave, and it made us rich. We got six thousand dollars apiece—all gold. It was an awful sight of money when it was piled up. Well, Judge Thatcher, he took it and put it out at interest, and it fetched us a dollar a day apiece, all the year round—more than a body could tell what to do with. The Widow Douglas, she took me for her son, and allowed she would sivilize me; but it was rough living in the house all the time, considering how dismal regular and decent the widow was in all her ways; and so when I couldn't stand it no longer, I lit out. I got into my old rags, and my sugar-hogshead[5] again, and was free and satisfied. But Tom Sawyer, he hunted me up and said he was going to start a band of robbers, and I might join if I would go back to the widow and be respectable. So I went back.

The widow she cried over me, and called me a poor lost lamb, and she called me a lot of other names, too, but she never meant no harm by it. She put me in them new clothes again, and I couldn't do nothing but sweat and sweat, and feel all cramped up. Well, then, the old thing commenced again. The widow rung a bell for supper, and you had to come to time. When you got to the table you couldn't go right to eating, but you had to wait for the widow to tuck down her head and grumble a little over the victuals, though there warn't really anything the matter with them. That is, nothing only everything was cooked by itself. In a barrel of odds and ends it is different; things get mixed up, and the juice kind of swaps around, and the things go better.

After supper she got out her book and learned me about Moses and the Bulrushers;[6] and I was in a sweat to find out all about him; but by-and-by she let it out that Moses had been dead a considerable long time; so then I didn't care no more about him; because I don't take no stock in dead people.

Pretty soon I wanted to smoke, and asked the widow to let me. But she wouldn't. She said it was a mean practice and wasn't clean, and I must try to not do it any more. That is just the way with some people. They get down on a thing when they don't know nothing about it. Here she was a bothering about Moses, which was no kin to her, and no use to anybody, being gone, you see, yet finding a power of fault with me for doing a thing that had some good in it. And she took snuff too; of course that was all right, because she done it herself.

Her sister, Miss Watson, a tolerable slim old maid, with goggles on, had just come to live with her, and took a set at me now, with a spelling-book. She worked me middling hard for about an hour, and then the widow made her ease up. I couldn't stood it much longer. Then for an hour it was deadly dull, and I was fidgety. Miss Watson would say, "Don't put your feet up there, Huckleberry"; and "don't scrunch up like that, Huckleberry—set up straight"; and pretty soon she would say, "Don't gap and stretch like that, Huckleberry—why don't you try to behave?" Then she told me all about the bad place, and I said I wished I was there. She got mad, then, but I didn't mean no harm. All I wanted was to go somewheres; all I wanted was a change, I warn't particular. She said it was wicked to say what I said; said she wouldn't say it for the whole world; *she* was going to live so as to go to the good place. Well, I couldn't see no advantage in going where she was going, so I made up

5. A large barrel.
6. Pharaoh's daughter discovered the infant Moses floating in the Nile in a basket woven from bulrushes (Exodus 2). She adopted him into the royal family just as the widow has adopted Huck.

my mind I wouldn't try for it. But I never said so, because it would only make trouble, and wouldn't do no good.

Now she had got a start, and she went on and told me all about the good place. She said all a body would have to do there was to go around all day long with a harp and sing, forever and ever.[7] So I didn't think much of it. But I never said so. I asked her if she reckoned Tom Sawyer would go there, and, she said, not by a considerable sight. I was glad about that, because I wanted him and me to be together.

Miss Watson she kept pecking at me, and it got tiresome and lonesome. By-and-by they fetched the niggers[8] in and had prayers, and then everybody was off to bed. I went up to my room with a piece of candle and put it on the table. Then I set down in a chair by the window and tried to think of something cheerful, but it warn't no use. I felt so lonesome I most wished I was dead. The stars was shining, and the leaves rustled in the woods ever so mournful; and I heard an owl, away off, who-whooing about somebody that was dead, and a whippowill and a dog crying about somebody that was going to die; and the wind was trying to whisper something to me and I couldn't make out what it was, and so it made the cold shivers run over me. Then away out in the woods I heard that kind of a sound that a ghost makes when it wants to tell about something that's on its mind and can't make itself understood, and so can't rest easy in its grave and has to go about that way every night grieving. I got so down-hearted and scared, I did wish I had some company. Pretty soon a spider went crawling up my shoulder, and I flipped it off and it lit in the candle; and before I could budge it was all shriveled up. I didn't need anybody to tell me that that was an awful bad sign and would fetch me some bad luck, so I was scared and most shook the clothes off of me. I got up and turned around in my tracks three times and crossed my breast every time; and then I tied up a little lock of my hair with a thread to keep witches away. But I hadn't no confidence. You do that when you've lost a horse-shoe that you've found, instead of nailing it up over the door, but I hadn't ever heard anybody say it was any way to keep off bad luck when you'd killed a spider.

I set down again, a shaking all over, and got out my pipe for a smoke; for the house was all as still as death, now, and so the widow wouldn't know. Well, after a long time I heard the clock away off in the town go boom—boom—boom—twelve licks—and all still again—stiller than ever. Pretty soon I heard a twig snap, down in the dark amongst the trees—something was a stirring. I set still and listened. Directly I could just barely hear a *"me-yow! me-yow!"* down there. That was good! Says I, *"me-yow! me-yow!"* as soft as I could, and then I put out the light and scrambled out of the window onto the shed. Then I slipped down to the ground and crawled in amongst the trees, and sure enough there was Tom Sawyer waiting for me.

Chapter II

We went tip-toeing along a path amongst the trees back towards the end of the widow's garden, stooping down so as the branches wouldn't scrape our

7. Conventional conceptions of the Christian heaven were satirized early and late in Twain's writings.
8. Huck appropriately speaks the colloquial word used in the South to describe black slaves; it is not used derisively or contemptuously by him, though for much of the narrative Huck expresses the racial prejudices of his time and place.

the fakeness of Christians

heads. When we was passing by the kitchen I fell over a root and made a noise. We scrouched down and laid still. Miss Watson's big nigger, named Jim, was setting in the kitchen door; we could see him pretty clear, because there was a light behind him. He got up and stretched his neck out about a minute, listening. Then he says,

"Who dah?"

humour

He listened some more; then he come tip-toeing down and stood right between us; we could a touched him, nearly. Well, likely it was minutes and minutes that there warn't a sound, and we all there so close together. There was a place on my ankle that got to itching; but I dasn't scratch it; and then my ear begun to itch; and next my back, right between my shoulders. Seemed like I'd die if I couldn't scratch. Well, I've noticed that thing plenty of times since. If you are with the quality, or at a funeral, or trying to go to sleep when you ain't sleepy—if you are anywhere where it won't do for you to scratch, why you will itch all over in upwards of a thousand places. Pretty soon Jim says:

"Say—who is you? Whar is you? Dog my cats ef I didn' hear sumf'n. Well, I knows what I's gwyne to do. I's gwyne to set down here and listen tell I hears it agin."

So he set down on the ground betwixt me and Tom. He leaned his back up against a tree, and stretched his legs out till one of them most touched one of mine. My nose begun to itch. It itched till the tears come into my eyes. But I dasn't scratch. Then it begun to itch on the inside. Next I got to itching underneath. I didn't know how I was going to set still. This miserableness went on as much as six or seven minutes; but it seemed a sight longer than that. I was itching in eleven different places now. I reckoned I couldn't stand it more'n a minute longer, but I set my teeth hard and got ready to try. Just then Jim begun to breathe heavy; next he begun to snore—and then I was pretty soon comfortable again.

Tom he made a sign to me—kind of a little noise with his mouth—and we went creeping away on our hands and knees. When we was ten foot off, Tom whispered to me and wanted to tie Jim to the tree for fun; but I said no; he might wake and make a disturbance, and then they'd find out I warn't in. Then Tom said he hadn't got candles enough, and he would slip in the kitchen and get some more. I didn't want him to try. I said Jim might wake up and come. But Tom wanted to resk it; so we slid in there and got three candles, and Tom laid five cents on the table for pay. Then we got out, and I was in a sweat to get away; but nothing would do Tom but he must crawl to where Jim was, on his hands and knees, and play something on him. I waited, and it seemed a good while, everything was so still and lonesome.

strong sense of morality

As soon as Tom was back, we cut along the path, around the garden fence, and by-and-by fetched up on the steep top of the hill the other side of the house. Tom said he slipped Jim's hat off of his head and hung it on a limb right over him, and Jim stirred a little, but he didn't wake. Afterwards Jim said the witches bewitched him and put him in a trance, and rode him all over the State, and then set him under the trees again and hung his hat on a limb to show who done it. And next time Jim told it he said they rode him down to New Orleans; and after that, every time he told it he spread it more and more, till by-and-by he said they rode him all over the world, and tired him most to death, and his back was all over saddle-boils. Jim was monstrous proud about it, and he got so he wouldn't hardly notice the other niggers. Niggers would come miles to hear Jim tell about it, and he was more looked up to than any nigger in that country. Strange niggers[9] would stand with their mouths open and look him all over, same as if he was a wonder. Niggers is always talking about witches in the dark by the kitchen fire; but whenever one was talking and letting on to know all about such things, Jim would happen in and say, "Hm! What you know 'bout witches?" and that nigger was corked up and had to take a back seat. Jim always kept that five-center piece around his neck with a string and said it was a charm the devil give to him with his own hands and told him he could cure anybody with it and fetch witches whenever he wanted to, just by saying something to it; but he never told what it was he said to it. Niggers would come from all around there and give Jim anything they had, just for a sight of the five-center piece; but they wouldn't touch it, because the devil had had his hands on it. Jim was most ruined, for a servant, because he got so stuck up on account of having seen the devil and been rode by witches.

Well, when Tom and me got to the edge of the hill-top, we looked away down into the village[1] and could see three or four lights twinkling, where there was sick folks, may be; and the stars over us was sparkling ever so fine; and down by the village was the river, a whole mile broad, and awful still and grand. We went down the hill and found Jo Harper, and Ben Rogers, and two or three more of the boys, hid in the old tanyard. So we unhitched a skiff and pulled down the river two mile and a half, to the big scar on the hillside, and went ashore.

We went to a clump of bushes, and Tom made everybody swear to keep the secret, and then showed them a hole in the hill, right in the thickest part of the bushes. Then we lit the candles and crawled in on our hands and knees. We went about two hundred yards, and then the cave opened up. Tom poked about amongst the passages and pretty soon ducked under a wall where you wouldn't a noticed that there was a hole. We went along a narrow place and got into a kind of room, all damp and sweaty and cold, and there we stopped. Tom says:

"Now we'll start this band of robbers and call it Tom Sawyer's Gang. Everybody that wants to join has got to take an oath, and write his name in blood."

Everybody was willing. So Tom got out a sheet of paper that he had wrote the oath on, and read it. It swore every boy to stick to the band, and never tell any of the secrets; and if anybody done anything to any boy in the band, whichever boy was ordered to kill that person and his family must do it, and he mustn't eat and he mustn't sleep till he had killed them and hacked a cross in their breasts, which was the sign of the band. And nobody that didn't belong to the band could use that mark, and if he did he must be sued; and if he done it again he must be killed. And if anybody that belonged to the band told the secrets, he must have his throat cut, and then have his carcass burnt up and the ashes scattered all around, and his name blotted off of the list with blood and never mentioned again by the gang, but have a curse put on it and be forgot, forever.

9. Those who did not live in the immediate area.
1. The village, called St. Petersburg here and in *Tom Sawyer*, is modeled on Hannibal, Missouri.

Everybody said it was a real beautiful oath, and asked Tom if he got it out of his own head. He said, some of it, but the rest was out of pirate books, and robber books, and every gang that was high-toned had it.

Some thought it would be good to kill the *families* of boys that told the secrets. Tom said it was a good idea, so he took a pencil and wrote it in. Then Ben Rogers says:

"Here's Huck Finn, he hain't got no family—what you going to do 'bout him?"

"Well, hain't he got a father?" says Tom Sawyer.

"Yes, he's got a father, but you can't never find him, these days. He used to lay drunk with the hogs in the tanyard, but he hain't been seen in these parts for a year or more."

They talked it over, and they was going to rule me out, because they said every boy must have a family or somebody to kill, or else it wouldn't be fair and square for the others. Well, nobody could think of anything to do—everybody was stumped, and set still. I was most ready to cry; but all at once I thought of a way, and so I offered them Miss Watson—they could kill her. Everybody said:

"Oh, she'll do, she'll do. That's all right. Huck can come in."

Then they all stuck a pin in their fingers to get blood to sign with, and I made my mark on the paper.

"Now," says Ben Rogers, "what's the line of business of this Gang?"

"Nothing only robbery and murder," Tom said.

"But who are we going to rob? houses—or cattle—or—"

"Stuff! stealing cattle and such things ain't robbery, it's burglary," says Tom Sawyer. "We ain't burglars. That ain't no sort of style. We are highwaymen. We stop stages and carriages on the road, with masks on, and kill the people and take their watches and money."

"Must we always kill the people?"

"Oh, certainly. It's best. Some authorities think different, but mostly it's considered best to kill them. Except some that you bring to the cave here and keep them till they're ransomed."

"Ransomed? What's that?"

"I don't know. But that's what they do. I've seen it in books; and so of course that's what we've got to do."

"But how can we do it if we don't know what it is?"

"Why blame it all, we've *got* to do it. Don't I tell you it's in the books? Do you want to go to doing different from what's in the books, and get things all muddled up?"

"Oh, that's all very fine to *say*, Tom Sawyer, but how in the nation[2] are these fellows going to be ransomed if we don't know how to do it to them? that's the thing *I* want to get at. Now what do you *reckon* it is?"

"Well I don't know. But per'aps if we keep them till they're ransomed, it means that we keep them till they're dead."

"Now, that's something *like*. That'll answer. Why couldn't you said that before? We'll keep them till they're ransomed to death—and a bothersome lot they'll be, too, eating up everything and always trying to get loose."

---

2. Damnation.

"How you talk, Ben Rogers. How can they get loose when there's a guard over them, ready to shoot them down if they move a peg?"

"A guard. Well, that *is* good. So somebody's got to set up all night and never get any sleep, just so as to watch them. I think that's foolishness. Why can't a body take a club and ransom them as soon as they get here?"

"Because it ain't in the books so—that's why. Now Ben Rogers, do you want to do things regular, or don't you?—that's the idea. Don't you reckon that the people that made the books knows what's the correct thing to do? Do you reckon *you* can learn 'em anything? Not by a good deal. No, sir, we'll just go on and ransom them in the regular way."

"All right. I don't mind; but I say it's a fool way, anyhow. Say—do we kill the women, too?"

"Well, Ben Rogers, if I was as ignorant as you I wouldn't let on. Kill the women? No—nobody ever saw anything in the books like that. You fetch them to the cave, and you're always as polite as pie to them; and by-and-by they fall in love with you and never want to go home any more."

"Well, if that's the way, I'm agreed, but I don't take no stock in it. Mighty soon we'll have the cave so cluttered up with women, and fellows waiting to be ransomed, that there won't be no place for the robbers. But go ahead, I ain't got nothing to say."

Little Tommy Barnes was asleep, now, and when they waked him up he was scared, and cried, and said he wanted to go home to his ma, and didn't want to be a robber any more.

So they all made fun of him, and called him cry-baby, and that made him mad, and he said he would go straight and tell all the secrets. But Tom give him five cents to keep quiet, and said we would all go home and meet next week and rob somebody and kill some people.

Ben Rogers said he couldn't get out much, only Sundays, and so he wanted to begin next Sunday; but all the boys said it would be wicked to do it on Sunday, and that settled the thing. They agreed to get together and fix a day as soon as they could, and then we elected Tom Sawyer first captain and Jo Harper second captain of the Gang, and so started home.

I clumb up the shed and crept into my window just before day was breaking. My new clothes was all greased up and clayey, and I was dog-tired.

Chapter III

Well, I got a good going-over in the morning, from old Miss Watson, on account of my clothes; but the widow she didn't scold, but only cleaned off the grease and clay and looked so sorry that I thought I would behave a while if I could. Then Miss Watson she took me in the closet[3] and prayed, but nothing come of it. She told me to pray every day, and whatever I asked for I would get it. But it warn't so. I tried it. Once I got a fish-line, but no hooks. It warn't any good to me without hooks. I tried for the hooks three or four times, but somehow I couldn't make it work. By-and-by, one day, I asked Miss Watson to try for me, but she said I was a fool. She never told me why, and I couldn't make it out no way.

---

3. "But thou, when thou prayest, enter into thy closet" (Matthew 6.6) is apparently the admonition Miss Watson has in mind.

criticism of religion

a spiritual place

I set down, one time, back in the woods, and had a long think about it. I says to myself, if a body can get anything they pray for, why don't Deacon Winn get back the money he lost on pork? Why can't the widow get back her silver snuff-box that was stole? Why can't Miss Watson fat up? No, says I to myself, there ain't nothing in it. I went and told the widow about it, and she said the thing a body could get by praying for it was "spiritual gifts." This was too many for me, but she told me what she meant—I must help other people, and do everything I could for other people, and look out for them all the time, and never think about myself. This was including Miss Watson, as I took it. I went out in the woods and turned it over in my mind a long time, but I couldn't see no advantage about it—except for the other people—so at last I reckoned I wouldn't worry about it any more, but just let it go. Sometimes the widow would take me one side and talk about Providence in a way to make a boy's mouth water; but maybe next day Miss Watson would take hold and knock it all down again. I judged I could see that there was two Providences, and a poor chap would stand considerable show with the widow's Providence, but if Miss Watson's got him there warn't no help for him any more. I thought it all out, and reckoned I would belong to the widow's, if he wanted me, though I couldn't make out how he was agoing to be any better off then than what he was before, seeing I was so ignorant and so kind of low-down and ornery.

Pap he hadn't been seen for more than a year, and that was comfortable for me; I didn't want to see him no more. He used to always whale me when he was sober and could get his hands on me; though I used to take to the woods most of the time when he was around. Well, about this time he was found in the river drowned, about twelve mile above town, so people said. They judged it was him, anyway; said this drowned man was just his size, and was ragged, and had uncommon long hair—which was all like pap—but they couldn't make nothing out of the face, because it had been in the water so long it warn't much like a face at all. They said he was floating on his back in the water. They took him and buried him on the bank. But I warn't comfortable long, because I happened to think of something. I knowed mighty well that a drownded man don't float on his back, but on his face. So I knowed, then, that this warn't pap, but a woman dressed up in a man's clothes. So I was uncomfortable again. I judged the old man would turn up again by-and-by, though I wished he wouldn't.

We played robber now and then about a month, and then I resigned. All the boys did. We hadn't robbed nobody, we hadn't killed any people, but only just pretended. We used to hop out of the woods and go charging down on hog-drovers and women in carts taking garden stuff to market, but we never hived[4] any of them. Tom Sawyer called the hogs "ingots," and he called the turnips and stuff "julery" and we would go to the cave and pow-wow over what we had done and how many people we had killed and marked. But I couldn't see no profit in it. One time Tom sent a boy to run about town with a blazing stick, which he called a slogan (which was the sign for the Gang to get together), and then he said he had got secret news by his spies that next day a whole parcel of Spanish merchants and rich A-rabs was going to camp in Cave Hol-

a realist

---

4. Captured, secured.

low with two hundred elephants, and six hundred camels, and over a thousand "sumter" mules,[5] all loaded with di'monds, and they didn't have only a guard of four hundred soldiers, and so we would lay in ambuscade, as he called it, and kill the lot and scoop the things. He said we must slick up our swords and guns, and get ready. He never could go after even a turnip-cart but he must have the swords and guns all scoured up for it; though they was only lath and broom-sticks, and you might scour at them till you rotted and then they warn't worth a mouthful of ashes more than what they was before. I didn't believe we could lick such a crowd of Spaniards and A-rabs, but I wanted to see the camels and elephants, so I was on hand next day, Saturday, in the ambuscade; and when we got the word, we rushed out of the woods and down the hill. But there warn't no Spaniards and A-rabs, and there warn't no camels nor no elephants. It warn't anything but a Sunday-school picnic, and only a primer-class at that. We busted it up, and chased the children up the hollow; but we never got anything but some doughnuts and jam, though Ben Rogers got a rag doll, and Jo Harper got a hymn-book and a tract; and then the teacher charged in and made us drop everything and cut. I didn't see no di'monds, and I told Tom Sawyer so. He said there was loads of them there, anyway; and he said there was A-rabs there, too, and elephants and things. I said, why couldn't we see them, then? He said if I warn't so ignorant, but had read a book called "Don Quixote,"[6] I would know without asking. He said it was all done by enchantment. He said there was hundreds of soldiers there, and elephants and treasure, and so on, but we had enemies which he called magicians, and they had turned the whole thing into an infant Sunday school, just out of spite. I said, all right, then the thing for us to do was to go for the magicians. Tom Sawyer said I was a numskull.

"Why," says he, "a magician could call up a lot of genies, and they would hash you up like nothing before you could say Jack Robinson. They are as tall as a tree and as big around as a church."

"Well," I says, "s'pose we got some genies to help *us*—can't we lick the other crowd then?"

"How you going to get them?"

"I don't know. How do *they* get them?"

"Why they rub an old tin lamp or an iron ring, and then the genies come tearing in, with the thunder and lightning a-ripping around and the smoke a-rolling, and everything they're told to do they up and do it. They don't think nothing of pulling a shot tower[7] up by the roots, and belting a Sunday-school superintendent over the head with it—or any other man."

"Who makes them tear around so?"

"Why, whoever rubs the lamp or the ring. They belong to whoever rubs the lamp or the ring, and they've got to do whatever he says. If he tells them to build a palace forty miles long, out of di'monds, and fill it full of chewing gum, or whatever you want, and fetch an emperor's daughter from China for you to marry, they've got to do it—and they've got to do it before sun-up next morning, too. And more—they've got to waltz that palace around over the country whenever you want it, you understand."

---

5. Pack mules.
6. Tom is here alluding to stories in *The Arabian Nights Entertainments* (1838–41) and to the hero in Cervantes' *Don Quixote* (1605).
7. A device in which gunshot was formed by dripping molten lead into water.

"Well," says I, "I think they are a pack of flatheads for not keeping the palace themselves 'stead of fooling them away like that. And what's more—if I was one of them I would see a man in Jericho before I would drop my business and come to him for the rubbing of an old tin lamp."

"How you talk, Huck Finn. Why, you'd *have* to come when he rubbed it, whether you wanted to or not."

"What, and I as high as a tree and as big as a church? All right, then; I *would* come; but I lay I'd make that man climb the highest tree there was in the country."

"Shucks, it ain't no use to talk to you, Huck Finn. You don't seem to know anything, somehow—perfect sap-head."

I thought all this over for two or three days, and then I reckoned I would see if there was anything in it. I got an old tin lamp and an iron ring and went out in the woods and rubbed and rubbed till I sweat like an Injun, calculating to build a palace and sell it; but it warn't no use, none of the genies come. So then I judged that all that stuff was only just one of Tom Sawyer's lies. I reckoned he believed in the A-rabs and the elephants, but as for me I think different. It had all the marks of a Sunday school.

Chapter IV

Well, three or four months run along, and it was well into the winter, now. I had been to school most all the time, and could spell, and read, and write just a little, and could say the multiplication table up to six times seven is thirty-five, and I don't reckon I could ever get any further than that if I was to live forever. I don't take no stock in mathematics, anyway.

At first I hated the school, but by-and-by I got so I could stand it. Whenever I got uncommon tired I played hookey, and the hiding I got next day done me good and cheered me up. So the longer I went to school the easier it got to be. I was getting sort of used to the widow's ways, too, and they warn't so raspy on me. Living in a house, and sleeping in a bed, pulled on me pretty tight, mostly, but before the cold weather I used to slide out and sleep in the woods, sometimes, and so that was a rest to me. I liked the old ways best, but I was getting so I liked the new ones, too, a little bit. The widow said I was coming along slow but sure, and doing very satisfactory. She said she warn't ashamed of me.

One morning I happened to turn over the salt-cellar at breakfast. I reached for some of it as quick as I could, to throw over my left shoulder and keep off the bad luck, but Miss Watson was in ahead of me, and crossed me off. She says, "Take your hands away, Huckleberry—what a mess you are always making." The widow put in a good word for me, but that warn't going to keep off the bad luck, I knowed that well enough. I started out, after breakfast, feeling worried and shaky, and wondering where it was going to fall on me, and what it was going to be. There is ways to keep off some kinds of bad luck, but this wasn't one of them kind; so I never tried to do anything, but just poked along low-spirited and on the watch-out.

I went down the front garden and clumb over the stile,[8] where you go through the high board fence. There was an inch of new snow on the ground,

8. Steps that flank and straddle a fence.

and I seen somebody's tracks. They had come up from the quarry and stood around the stile a while, and then went on around the garden fence. It was funny they hadn't come in, after standing around so. I couldn't make it out. It was very curious, somehow. I was going to follow around, but I stooped down to look at the tracks first. I didn't notice anything at first, but next I did. There was a cross in the left boot-heel made with big nails, to keep off the devil.

I was up in a second and shinning down the hill. I looked over my shoulder every now and then, but I didn't see nobody. I was at Judge Thatcher's as quick as I could get there. He said:

"Why, my boy, you are all out of breath. Did you come for your interest?"

"No sir," I says; "is there some for me?"

"Oh, yes, a half-yearly is in, last night. Over a hundred and fifty dollars. Quite a fortune for you. You better let me invest it along with your six thousand, because if you take it you'll spend it."

"No sir," I says, "I don't want to spend it. I don't want it at all—nor the six thousand, nuther. I want you to take it; I want to give it to you—the six thousand and all."

He looked surprised. He couldn't seem to make it out. He says:

"Why, what can you mean, my boy?"

I says, "Don't you ask me no questions about it, please. You'll take it—won't you?"

He says:

"Well I'm puzzled. Is something the matter?"

"Please take it," says I, "and don't ask me nothing—then I won't have to tell no lies."

He studied a while, and then he says:

"Oho-o. I think I see. You want to *sell* all your property to me—not give it. That's the correct idea."

Then he wrote something on a paper and read it over, and says:

"There—you see it says 'for a consideration.' That means I have bought it of you and paid you for it. Here's a dollar for you. Now, you sign it."

So I signed it, and left.

Miss Watson's nigger, Jim, had a hair-ball as big as your fist, which had been took out of the fourth stomach of an ox, and he used to do magic with it.[9] He said there was a spirit inside of it, and it knowed everything. So I went to him that night and told him pap was here again, for I found his tracks in the snow. What I wanted to know, was, what he was going to do, and was he going to stay? Jim got out his hair-ball, and said something over it, and then he held it up and dropped it on the floor. It fell pretty solid, and only rolled about an inch. Jim tried it again, and then another time, and it acted just the same. Jim got down on his knees and put his ear against it and listened. But it warn't no use; he said it wouldn't talk. He said sometimes it wouldn't talk without money. I told him I had an old slick counterfeit quarter that warn't no good because the brass showed through the silver a little, and it wouldn't pass nohow, even if the brass didn't show, because it was so slick it felt greasy, and so that would tell on it every time. (I reckoned I wouldn't say nothing about the dollar I got from the judge.) I said it was pretty bad money, but

---

9. Though most of the superstitions in *Tom Sawyer* and *Huck Finn* have been traced to European sources, belief in the magical powers of hair balls found in the stomachs of oxen seems to be African American in origin.

maybe the hair-ball would take it, because maybe it wouldn't know the difference. Jim smelt it, and bit it, and rubbed it, and said he would manage so the hair-ball would think it was good. He said he would split open a raw Irish potato and stick the quarter in between and keep it there all night, and next morning you couldn't see no brass, and it wouldn't feel greasy no more, and so anybody in town would take it in a minute, let alone a hair-ball. Well, I knowed a potato would do that, before, but I had forgot it.

Jim put the quarter under the hair-ball and got down and listened again. This time he said the hair-ball was all right. He said it would tell my whole fortune if I wanted it to. I says, go on. So the hair-ball talked to Jim, and Jim told it to me. He says:

"Yo' ole father doan' know, yit, what he's a-gwyne to do. Sometimes he spec he'll go 'way, en den agin he spec he'll stay. De bes' way is to res' easy en let de ole man take his own way. Dey's two angels hoverin' roun' 'bout him. One uv 'em is white en shiny, en 'tother one is black. De white one gits him to go right, a little while, den de black one sail in en bust it all up. A body can't tell, yit, which one gwyne to fetch him at de las'. But you is all right. You gwyne to have considable trouble in yo' life, en considable joy. Sometimes you gwyne to git hurt, en sometimes you gwyne to git sick; but every time you's gwyne to git well agin. Dey's two gals flyin' 'bout you in yo' life. One uv 'em's light en 'tother one is dark. One is rich en 'tother is po'. You's gwyne to marry de po' one fust en de rich one by-en-by. You wants to keep 'way fum de water as much as you kin, en don't run no resk, 'kase it's down in de bills dat you's gwyne to git hung."

When I lit my candle and went up to my room that night, there set pap, his own self!

Chapter V

I had shut the door to. Then I turned around, and there he was. I used to be scared of him all the time, he tanned me so much. I reckoned I was scared now, too; but in a minute I see I was mistaken. That is, after the first jolt, as you may say, when my breath sort of hitched—he being so unexpected; but right away after, I see I warn't scared of him worth bothering about.

He was most fifty, and he looked it. His hair was long and tangled and greasy, and hung down, and you could see his eyes shining through like he was behind vines. It was all black, no gray; so was his long, mixed-up whiskers. There warn't no color in his face, where his face showed; it was white; not like another man's white, but a white to make a body sick, a white to make a body's flesh crawl—a tree-toad white, a fish-belly white. As for his clothes—just rags, that was all. He had one ankle resting on 'tother knee; the boot on that foot was busted, and two of his toes stuck through, and he worked them now and then. His hat was laying on the floor; an old black slouch with the top caved in, like a lid.

I stood a-looking at him; he set there a-looking at me, with his chair tilted back a little. I set the candle down. I noticed the window was up; so he had clumb in by the shed. He kept a-looking me all over. By-and-by he says:

"Starchy clothes—very. You think you're a good deal of a big-bug, *don't* you?"

"Maybe I am, maybe I ain't," I says.

father

"Don't you give me none o' your lip," says he. "You've put on considerble many frills since I been away. I'll take you down a peg before I get done with you. You're educated, too, they say; can read and write. You think you're better'n your father, now, don't you, because he can't? *I'll* take it out of you. Who told you you might meddle with such hifalut'n foolishness, hey?—who told you you could?"

"The widow. She told me."

"The widow, hey?—and who told the widow she could put in her shovel about a thing that ain't none of her business?"

"Nobody never told her."

"Well, I'll learn her how to meddle. And looky here—you drop that school, you hear? I'll learn people to bring up a boy to put on airs over his own father and let on to be better'n what *he* is. You lemme catch you fooling around that school again, you hear? Your mother couldn't read, and she couldn't write, nuther, before she died. None of the family couldn't, before *they* died. *I* can't; and here you're a-swelling yourself up like this. I ain't the man to stand it— you hear? Say—lemme hear you read."

I took up a book and begun something about General Washington and the wars. When I'd read about a half a minute, he fetched the book a whack with his hand and knocked it across the house. He says:

"It's so. You can do it. I had my doubts when you told me. Now looky here; you stop that putting on frills. I won't have it. I'll lay for you, my smarty; and if I catch you about that school I'll tan you good. First you know you'll get religion, too. I never see such a son."

He took up a little blue and yaller picture of some cows and a boy, and says:

"What's this?"

"It's something they give me for learning my lessons good."

He tore it up, and says—

"I'll give you something better—I'll give you a cowhide."[1]

He set there a-mumbling and a-growling a minute, and then he says—

"*Ain't* you a sweet-scented dandy, though? A bed; and bedclothes; and a look'n-glass; and a piece of carpet on the floor—and your own father got to sleep with the hogs in the tanyard. I never see such a son. I bet I'll take some o' these frills out o' you before I'm done with you. Why there ain't no end to your airs—they say you're rich. Hey?—how's that?"

money!

"They lie—that's how."

"Looky here—mind how you talk to me; I'm a-standing about all I can stand, now—so don't gimme no sass. I've been in town two days, and I hain't heard nothing but about you bein' rich. I heard about it away down the river, too. That's why I come. You git me that money to-morrow—I want it."

"I hain't got no money."

"It's a lie. Judge Thatcher's got it. You git it. I want it."

"I hain't got no money, I tell you. You ask Judge Thatcher; he'll tell you the same."

"All right. I'll ask him; and I'll make him pungle,[2] too, or I'll know the reason why. Say—how much you got in your pocket? I want it."

"I hain't got only a dollar, and I want that to—"

"It don't make no difference what you want it for—you just shell it out."

---

1. A beating with a cowhide whip.   2. Turn over the money.

He took it and bit it to see if it was good, and then he said he was going down town to get some whiskey; said he hadn't had a drink all day. When he had got out on the shed, he put his head in again, and cussed me for putting on frills and trying to be better than him; and when I reckoned he was gone, he come back and put his head in again, and told me to mind about that school, because he was going to lay for me and lick me if I didn't drop that.

Next day he was drunk, and he went to Judge Thatcher's and bullyragged him and tried to make him give up the money, but he couldn't, and then he swore he'd make the law force him.

The judge and the widow went to law to get the court to take me away from him and let one of them be my guardian; but it was a new judge that had just come, and he didn't know the old man; so he said courts mustn't interfere and separate families if they could help it; said he'd druther not take a child away from its father. So Judge Thatcher and the widow had to quit on the business.

That pleased the old man till he couldn't rest. He said he'd cowhide me till I was black and blue if I didn't raise some money for him. I borrowed three dollars from Judge Thatcher, and pap took it and got drunk and went a-blowing around and cussing and whooping and carrying on; and he kept it up all over town, with a tin pan, till most midnight; then they jailed him, and next day they had him before court, and jailed him again for a week. But he said *he* was satisfied; said he was boss of his son, and he'd make it warm for *him*.

When he got out the new judge said he was agoing to make a man of him. So he took him to his own house, and dressed him up clean and nice, and had him to breakfast and dinner and supper with the family, and was just old pie to him, so to speak. And after supper he talked to him about temperance and such things till the old man cried, and said he'd been a fool, and fooled away his life; but now he was agoing to turn over a new leaf and be a man nobody wouldn't be ashamed of, and he hoped the judge would help him and not look down on him. The judge said he could hug him for them words; so *he* cried, and his wife she cried again; pap said he'd been a man that had always been misunderstood before, and the judge said he believed it. The old man said that what a man wanted that was down, was sympathy; and the judge said it was so; so they cried again. And when it was bedtime, the old man rose up and held out his hand, and says:

"Look at it gentlemen, and ladies all; take ahold of it; shake it. There's a hand that was the hand of a hog; but it ain't so no more; it's the hand of a man that's started in on a new life, and 'll die before he'll go back. You mark them words—don't forget I said them. It's a clean hand now; shake it—don't be afeard."

So they shook it, one after the other, all around, and cried. The judge's wife she kissed it. Then the old man he signed a pledge—made his mark. The judge said it was the holiest time on record, or something like that. Then they tucked the old man into a beautiful room, which was the spare room, and in the night sometime he got powerful thirsty and clumb out onto the porch-roof and slid down a stanchion and traded his new coat for a jug of forty-rod,[3] and clumb back again and had a good old time; and towards daylight he crawled out again, drunk as a fiddler, and rolled off the porch and broke his left arm in two places and was almost froze to death when somebody found

---

3. Home-distilled whiskey strong enough to knock a person forty rods, or 220 yards.

him after sun-up. And when they come to look at that spare room, they ha
to take soundings before they could navigate it.

The judge he felt kind of sore. He said he reckoned a body could reform
the ole man with a shot-gun, maybe, but he didn't know no other way.

Chapter VI

Well, pretty soon the old man was up and around again, and then he went
for Judge Thatcher in the courts to make him give up that money, and he went
for me, too, for not stopping school. He catched me a couple of times and
thrashed me, but I went to school just the same, and dodged him or out-run
him most of the time. I didn't want to go to school much, before, but I reckoned I'd go now to spite pap. That law trial was a slow business; appeared like
they warn't ever going to get started on it; so every now and then I'd borrow
two or three dollars off of the judge for him, to keep from getting a cowhid-
ing. Every time he got money he got drunk; and every time he got drunk he
raised Cain around town; and every time he raised Cain he got jailed. He was
just suited—this kind of thing was right in his line.

He got to hanging around the widow's too much, and so she told him at last,
that if he didn't quit using around there she would make trouble for him. Well,
wasn't he mad? He said he would show who was Huck Finn's boss. So he
watched out for me one day in the spring, and catched me, and took me up the
river about three mile, in a skiff, and crossed over to the Illinois shore where it
was woody and there warn't no houses but an old log hut in a place where the
timber was so thick you couldn't find it if you didn't know where it was.

He kept me with him all the time, and I never got a chance to run off. We
lived in that old cabin, and he always locked the door and put the key under
his head, nights. He had a gun which he had stole, I reckon, and we fished
and hunted, and that was what we lived on. Every little while he locked me
in and went down to the store, three miles, to the ferry, and traded fish and
game for whisky and fetched it home and got drunk and had a good time, and
licked me. The widow she found out where I was, by-and-by, and she sent a
man over to try to get hold of me, but pap drove him off with the gun, and it
warn't long after that till I was used to being where I was, and liked it, all but
the cowhide part.

It was kind of lazy and jolly, laying off comfortable all day, smoking and fishing, and no books nor study. Two months or more run along, and my clothes
got to be all rags and dirt, and I didn't see how I'd ever got to like it so well at
the widow's, where you had to wash, and eat on a plate, and comb up, and go
to bed and get up regular, and be forever bothering over a book and have old
Miss Watson pecking at you all the time. I didn't want to go back no more. I
had stopped cussing, because the widow didn't like it; but now I took to it
again because pap hadn't no objections. It was pretty good times up in the
woods there, take it all around.

But by-and-by pap got too handy with his hick'ry, and I couldn't stand it. I
was all over welts. He got to going away so much, too, and locking me in. Once
he locked me in and was gone three days. It was dreadful lonesome. I judged
he had got drowned and I wasn't ever going to get out any more. I was scared.
I made up my mind I would fix up some way to leave there. I had tried to get
out of that cabin many a time, but I couldn't find no way. There warn't a win-

dow to it big enough for a dog to get through. I couldn't get up the chimbly, it was too narrow. The door was thick solid oak slabs. Pap was pretty careful not to leave a knife or anything in the cabin when he was away; I reckon I had hunted the place over as much as a hundred times; well, I was 'most all the time at it, because it was about the only way to put in the time. But this time I found something at last; I found an old rusty wood-saw without any handle; it was laid in between a rafter and the clapboards of the roof. I greased it up and went to work. There was an old horse-blanket nailed against the logs at the far end of the cabin behind the table, to keep the wind from blowing through the chinks and putting the candle out. I got under the table and raised the blanket and went to work to saw a section of the big bottom log out, big enough to let me through. Well, it was a good long job, but I was getting towards the end of it when I heard pap's gun in the woods. I got rid of the signs of my work, and dropped the blanket and hid my saw, and pretty soon pap come in.

Pap warn't in a good humor—so he was his natural self. He said he was down to town, and everything was going wrong. His lawyer said he reckoned he would win his lawsuit and get the money, if they ever got started on the trial; but then there was ways to put it off a long time, and Judge Thatcher knowed how to do it. And he said people allowed there'd be another trial to get me away from him and give me to the widow for my guardian, and they guessed it would win, this time. This shook me up considerable, because I didn't want to go back to the widow's any more and be so cramped up and siv-ilized, as they called it. Then the old man got to cussing, and cussed every-thing and everybody he could think of, and then cussed them all over again to make sure he hadn't skipped any, and after that he polished off with a kind of general cuss all round, including a considerable parcel of people which he didn't know the names of, and so called them what's-his-name, when he got to them, and went right along with his cussing.

He said he would like to see the widow get me. He said he would watch out, and if they tried to come any such game on him he knowed of a place six or seven mile off, to stow me in, where they might hunt till they dropped and they couldn't find me. That made me pretty uneasy again, but only for a minute; I reckoned I wouldn't stay on hand till he got that chance.

The old man made me go to the skiff and fetch the things he had got. There was a fifty-pound sack of corn meal, and a side of bacon, ammunition, and a four-gallon jug of whisky, and an old book and two newspapers for wadding, besides some tow.[4] I toted up a load, and went back and set down on the bow of the skiff to rest. I thought it all over, and I reckoned I would walk off with the gun and some lines, and take to the woods when I run away. I guessed I wouldn't stay in one place, but just tramp right across the country, mostly night times, and hunt and fish to keep alive, and so get so far away that the old man nor the widow couldn't ever find me any more. I judged I would saw out and leave that night if pap got drunk enough, and I reckoned he would. I got so full of it I didn't notice how long I was staying, till the old man hollered and asked me whether I was asleep or drownded.

I got the things all up to the cabin, and then it was about dark. While I was cooking supper the old man took a swig or two and got sort of warmed up, and went to ripping again. He had been drunk over in town, and laid in the

---

4. Cheap rope. "Wadding": material (here paper) used to pack the gunpowder in a rifle.

gutter all night, and he was a sight to look at. A body would a thought he was Adam, he was just all mud.[5] Whenever his liquor begun to work, he most always went for the govment. This time he says:

"Call this a govment! why, just look at it and see what it's like. Here's the law a-standing ready to take a man's son away from him—a man's own son, which he has had all the trouble and all the anxiety and all the expense of rais-ing. Yes, just as that man has got that son raised at last, and ready to go to work and begin to do suthin' for *him* and give him a rest, the law up and goes for him. And they call *that* govment! That ain't all, nuther. The law backs that old Judge Thatcher up and helps him to keep me out o' my property. Here's what the law does. The law takes a man worth six thousand dollars and upards, and jams him into an old trap of a cabin like this, and lets him go round in clothes that ain't fitten for a hog. They call that govment! A man can't get his rights in a govment like this. Sometimes I've a mighty notion to just leave the country for good and all. Yes, and I *told* 'em so: I told old Thatcher so to his face. Lots of 'em heard me, and can tell what I said. Says I, for two cents I'd leave the blamed country and never come anear it agin. Them's the very words. I says, look at my hat—if you call it a hat—but the lid raises up and the rest of it goes down till it's below my chin, and then it ain't rightly a hat at all, but more like my head was shoved up through a jint o' stove-pipe. Look at it, says I—such a hat for me to wear—one of the wealth-iest men in this town, if I could git my rights.

"Oh, yes, this is a wonderful govment, wonderful. Why, looky here. There was a free nigger there, from Ohio; a mulatter,[6] most as white as a white man. He had the whitest shirt on you ever see, too, and the shiniest hat; and there ain't a man in that town that's got as fine clothes as what he had; and he had a gold watch and chain and a silver-headed cane—the awfulest old gray-headed nabob in the State. And what do you think? they said he was a p'fes-sor in a college, and could talk all kinds of languages, and knowed every thing. And that ain't the wust. They said he could *vote,* when he was at home. Well, that let me out. Thinks I, what is the country a-coming to? It was 'lection day, and I was just about to go and vote, myself, if I warn't too drunk to get there; but when they told me there was a State in this country where they'd let that nigger vote, I drawed out. I says I'll never vote agin. Them's the very words I said; they all heard me; and the country may rot for all me—I'll never vote agin as long as I live. And to see the cool way of that nigger—why, he wouldn't a give me the road if I hadn't shoved him out o' the way. I says to the people, why ain't this nigger put up at auction and sold?—that's what I want to know. And what do you reckon they said? Why, they said he couldn't be sold till he'd been in the State six months, and he hadn't been there that long yet. There, now— that's a specimen. They call that a govment that can't sell a free nigger till he's been in the State six months. Here's a govment that calls itself a govment, and lets on to be a govment, and thinks it is a govment, and yet's got to set stock-still for six whole months before it can take ahold of a prowling, thieving, infernal, white-shirted free nigger, and[7]—"

5. God created Adam from earth in Genesis 2.7.
6. Mulatto, a person of mixed white and black ancestry.
7. Missouri's original constitution prohibited the entrance of freed slaves and mulattoes into the state, but the "second Missouri Compromise" of

1820 deleted the provision. In the 1830s and 1840s, however, increasingly strict antiblack laws were passed, and by 1850 a black person without freedom papers could be sold downriver with a mere sworn statement of ownership from a white man.

Pap was agoing on so, he never noticed where his old limber legs was taking him to, so he went head over heels over the tub of salt pork, and barked both shins, and the rest of his speech was all the hottest kind of language—mostly hove at the nigger and the govment, though he give the tub some, too, all along, here and there. He hopped around the cabin considerble, first on one leg and then on the other, holding first one shin and then the other one, and at last he let out with his left foot all of a sudden and fetched the tub a rattling kick. But it warn't good judgment, because that was the boot that had a couple of his toes leaking out of the front end of it; so now he raised a howl that fairly made a body's hair raise, and down he went in the dirt, and rolled there, and held his toes; and the cussing he done then laid over anything he had ever done previous. He said so his own self, afterwards. He had heard old Sowberry Hagan in his best days, and he said it laid over him, too; but I reckon that was sort of piling it on, maybe.

After supper pap took the jug, and said he had enough whiskey there for two drunks and one delirium tremens. That was always his word. I judged he would be blind drunk in about an hour, an then I would steal the key, or saw myself out, one or 'tother. He drank, and drank, and tumbled down on his blankets, by-and-by; but luck didn't run my way. He didn't go sound asleep, but was uneasy. He groaned, and moaned, and thrashed around this way and that, for a long time. At last I got so sleepy I couldn't keep my eyes open, all I could do, and so before I knowed what I was about I was sound asleep, and the candle burning.

I don't know how long I was asleep, but all of a sudden there was an awful scream and I was up. There was pap, looking wild and skipping around every which way and yelling about snakes. He said they was crawling up his legs; and then he would give a jump and scream, and say one had bit him on the cheek—but I couldn't see no snakes. He started to run round and round the cabin, hollering "take him off! take him off! he's biting me on the neck!" I never see a man look so wild in the eyes. Pretty soon he was all fagged out, and fell down panting; then he rolled over and over, wonderful fast, kicking things every which way, and striking and grabbing at the air with his hands, and screaming, and saying there was devils ahold of him. He wore out, by-and-by, and laid still a while, moaning. Then he laid stiller, and didn't make a sound. I could hear the owls and the wolves, away off in the woods, and it seemed terrible still. He was laying over by the corner. By-and-by he raised up, part way, and listened, with his head to one side. He says very low:

"Tramp—tramp—tramp; that's the dead; tramp—tramp—tramp; they're coming after me; but I won't go—Oh, they're here! don't touch me—don't! hands off—they're cold; let go—Oh, let a poor devil alone!"

Then he went down on all fours and crawled off begging them to let him alone, and he rolled himself up in his blanket and wallowed in under the old pine table, still a-begging; and then he went to crying. I could hear him through the blanket.

By-and-by he rolled out and jumped up on his feet looking wild, and he see me and went for me. He chased me round and round the place, with a clasp-knife, calling me the Angel of Death and saying he would kill me and then I couldn't come for him no more. I begged, and told him I was only Huck, but he laughed *such* a screechy laugh, and roared and cussed, and kept on chasing me up. Once when I turned short and dodged under his arm he made a grab and got me by the jacket between my shoulders, and I thought I was gone; but I skid out of the jacket quick as lightning, and saved myself. Pretty soon he was all tired out, and dropped down with his back against the door, and said he would rest a minute and then kill me. He put his knife under him, and said he would sleep and get strong, and then he would see who was who.

So he dozed off, pretty soon. By-and-by I got the old split bottom[8] chair and clumb up, as easy as I could, not to make any noise, and got down the gun. I slipped the ramrod down it to make sure it was loaded, and then I laid it across the turnip barrel, pointing towards pap, and set down behind it to wait for him to stir. And how slow and still the time did drag along.

Chapter VII

"Git up! what you 'bout!"

I opened my eyes and looked around, trying to make out where I was. It was after sun-up, and I had been sound asleep. Pap was standing over me, looking sour—and sick, too. He says—

"What you doin' with this gun?"

I judged he didn't know nothing about what he had been doing, so I says:

"Somebody tried to get in, so I was laying for him."

"Why didn't you rouse me out?"

"Well I tried to, but I couldn't; I couldn't budge you."

"Well, all right. Don't stand there palavering all day, but out with you and see if there's a fish on the lines for breakfast. I'll be along in a minute."

He unlocked the door and I cleared out, up the river bank. I noticed some pieces of limbs and such things floating down, and a sprinkling of bark; so I knowed the river had begun to rise. I reckoned I would have great times, now, if I was over at the town. The June rise used to be always luck for me; because as soon as that rise begins, here comes cord-wood floating down, and pieces of log rafts—sometimes a dozen logs together; so all you have to do is to catch them and sell them to the wood yards and the sawmill.

I went along up the bank with one eye out for pap and 'tother one out for what the rise might fetch along. Well, all at once, here comes a canoe; just a beauty, too, about thirteen or fourteen foot long, riding high like a duck. I shot head first off of the bank, like a frog, clothes and all on, and struck out for the canoe. I just expected there'd be somebody laying down in it, because people often done that to fool folks, and when a chap had pulled a skiff out most to it they'd raise up and laugh at him. But it warn't so this time. It was a drift-canoe, sure enough, and I clumb in and paddled her ashore. Thinks I, the old man will be glad when he sees this—she's worth ten dollars. But when I got to shore pap wasn't in sight yet, and as I was running her into a little creek like a gully, all hung over with vines and willows, I struck another idea; I judged I'd hide her good, and then, stead of taking to the woods when I run off, I'd go down the river about fifty mile and camp in one place for good, and not have such a rough time tramping on foot.

It was pretty close to the shanty, and I thought I heard the old man coming, all the time; but I got her hid; and then I out and looked around a bunch

---

8. I.e., splint-bottom, made by weaving thin strips of wood.

of willows, and there was the old man down the path apiece just drawing a bead on a bird with his gun. So he hadn't seen anything.

When he got along, I was hard at it taking up a "trot" line.[9] He abused me a little for being so slow, but I told him I fell in the river and that was what made me so long. I knowed he would see I was wet, and then he would be asking questions. We got five catfish off of the lines and went home.

While we laid off, after breakfast, to sleep up, both of us being about wore out, I got to thinking that if I could fix up some way to keep pap and the widow from trying to follow me, it would be a certainer thing than trusting to luck to get far enough off before they missed me; you see, all kinds of things might happen. Well, I didn't see no way for a while, but by-and-by pap raised up a minute, to drink another barrel of water, and he says:

"Another time a man comes a-prowling round here, you roust me out, you hear? That man warn't here for no good. I'd a shot him. Next time, you roust me out, you hear?"

Then he dropped down and went to sleep again—but what he had been saying give me the very idea I wanted. I says to myself, I can fix it now so nobody won't think of following me.

About twelve o'clock we turned out and went along up the bank. The river was coming up pretty fast, and lots of drift-wood going by on the rise. By-and-by, along comes part of a log raft—nine logs fast together. We went out with the skiff and towed it ashore. Then we had dinner. Anybody but pap would a waited and seen the day through, so as to catch more stuff; but that warn't pap's style. Nine logs was enough for one time; he must shove right over to town and sell. So he locked me in and took the skiff and started off towing the raft about half-past three. I judged he wouldn't come back that night. I waited till I reckoned he had got a good start, then I out with my saw and went to work on that log again. Before he was 'tother side of the river I was out of the hole; him and his raft was just a speck on the water away off yonder.

I took the sack of corn meal and took it to where the canoe was hid, and shoved the vines and branches apart and put it in; then I done the same with the side of bacon; then the whiskey jug; I took all the coffee and sugar there was, and all the ammunition; I took the wadding; I took the bucket and gourd, I took a dipper and a tin cup, and my old saw and two blankets, and the skillet and the coffee-pot. I took fish-lines and matches and other things—everything that was worth a cent. I cleaned out the place. I wanted an axe, but there wasn't any, only the one out at the wood pile, and I knowed why I was going to leave that. I fetched out the gun, and now I was done.

I had wore the ground a good deal, crawling out of the hole and dragging out so many things. So I fixed that as good as I could from the outside by scattering dust on the place, which covered up the smoothness and the sawdust. Then I fixed the piece of log back into its place, and put two rocks under it and one against it to hold it there,—for it was bent up at the place, and didn't quite touch ground. If you stood four or five foot away and didn't know it was sawed, you wouldn't ever notice it; and besides, this was the back of the cabin and it warn't likely anybody would go fooling around there.

It was all grass clear to the canoe; so I hadn't left a track. I followed around

9. A long fishing line fastened across a stream; to this line several shorter baited lines are attached.

to see. I stood on the bank and looked out over the river. All safe. So I took the gun and went up a piece into the woods and was hunting around for some birds, when I see a wild pig; hogs soon went wild in them bottoms after they had got away from the prairie farms. I shot this fellow and took him into camp.

I took the axe and smashed in the door—I beat it and hacked it considerable, a-doing it. I fetched the pig in and took him back nearly to the table and hacked into his throat with the ax, and laid him down on the ground to bleed—I say ground, because it *was* ground—hard packed, and no boards. Well, next I took an old sack and put a lot of big rocks in it,—all I could drag—and I started it from the pig and dragged it to the door and through the woods down to the river and dumped it in, and down it sunk, out of sight. You could easy see that something had been dragged over the ground. I did wish Tom Sawyer was there, I knowed he would take an interest in this kind of business, and throw in the fancy touches. Nobody could spread himself like Tom Sawyer in such a thing as that.

Well, last I pulled out some of my hair, and bloodied the ax good, and stuck it on the back side, and slung the ax in the corner. Then I took up the pig and held him to my breast with my jacket (so he couldn't drip) till I got a good piece below the house and then dumped him into the river. Now I thought of something else. So I went and got the bag of meal and my old saw out of the canoe and fetched them to the house. I took the bag to where it used to stand, and ripped a hole in the bottom of it with the saw, for there warn't no knives and forks on the place—pap done everything with his clasp-knife, about the cooking. Then I carried the sack about a hundred yards across the grass and through the willows east of the house, to a shallow lake that was five mile wide and full of rushes—and ducks too, you might say, in the season. There was a slough or a creek leading out of it on the other side, that went miles away, I don't know where, but it didn't go to the river. The meal sifted out and made a little track all the way to the lake. I dropped pap's whetstone there too, so as to look like it had been done by accident. Then I tied up the rip in the meal sack with a string, so it wouldn't leak no more, and took it and my saw to the canoe again.

It was about dark, now; so I dropped the canoe down the river under some willows that hung over the bank, and waited for the moon to rise. I made fast to a willow; then I took a bite to eat, and by-and-by laid down in the canoe to smoke a pipe and lay out a plan. I says to myself, they'll follow the track of that sackful of rocks to the shore and then drag the river for me. And they'll follow that meal track to the lake and go browsing down the creek that leads out of it to find the robbers that killed me and took the things. They won't ever hunt the river for anything but my dead carcass. They'll soon get tired of that, and won't bother no more about me. All right; I can stop anywhere I want to. Jackson's Island[1] is good enough for me; I know that island pretty well, and nobody ever comes there. And then I can paddle over to town, nights, and slink around and pick up things I want. Jackson's Island's the place.

I was pretty tired, and the first thing I knowed, I was asleep. When I woke

---

1. The same island that serves for an adventure in *Tom Sawyer* (Ch. 13); actually known as Glasscock's Island, it has been washed away.

up I didn't know where I was, for a minute. I set up and looked around, a little scared. Then I remembered. The river looked miles and miles across. The moon was so bright I could a counted the drift logs that went a slipping along, black and still, hundreds of yards out from shore. Everything was dead quiet, and it looked late, and *smelt* late. You know what I mean—I don't know the words to put it in.

I took a good gap and a stretch, and was just going to unhitch and start, when I heard a sound away over the water. I listened. Pretty soon I made it out. It was that dull kind of a regular sound that comes from oars working in rowlocks when it's a still night. I peeped out through the willow branches, and there it was—a skiff, away across the water. I couldn't tell how many was in it. It kept a-coming, and when it was abreast of me I see there warn't but one man in it. Thinks I, maybe it's pap, though I warn't expecting him. He dropped below me, with the current, and by-and-by he come a-swinging up shore in the easy water, and he went by so close I could a reached out the gun and touched him. Well, it *was* pap, sure enough—and sober, too, by the way he laid to his oars.

I didn't lose no time. The next minute I was a-spinning down stream soft but quick in the shade of the bank. I made two mile and a half, and then struck out a quarter of a mile or more towards the middle of the river, because pretty soon I would be passing the ferry landing and people might see me and hail me. I got out amongst the drift-wood and then laid down in the bottom of the canoe and let her float. I laid there and had a good rest and a smoke out of my pipe, looking away into the sky, not a cloud in it. The sky looks ever so deep when you lay down on your back in the moonshine; I never knowed it before. And how far a body can hear on the water such nights! I heard people talking at the ferry landing. I heard what they said, too, every word of it. One man said it was getting towards the long days and the short nights, now. 'Tother one said *this* warn't one of the short ones, he reckoned—and then they laughed, and he said it over again and they laughed again; then they waked up another fellow and told him, and laughed, but he didn't laugh; he ripped out something brisk and said let him alone. The first fellow said he 'lowed to tell it to his old woman—she would think it was pretty good; but he said that warn't nothing to some things he had said in his time. I heard one man say it was nearly three o'clock, and he hoped daylight wouldn't wait more than about a week longer. After that, the talk got further and further away, and I couldn't make out the words any more, but I could hear the mumble; and now and then a laugh, too, but it seemed a long ways off.

I was away below the ferry now. I rose up and there was Jackson's Island, about two mile and a half down stream, heavy-timbered and standing up out of the middle of the river, big and dark and solid, like a steamboat without any lights. There warn't any signs of the bar at the head—it was all under water, now.

It didn't take me long to get there. I shot past the head at a ripping rate, the current was so swift, and then I got into the dead water and landed on the side towards the Illinois shore. I run the canoe into a deep dent in the bank that I knowed about; I had to part the willow branches to get in; and when I made fast nobody could a seen the canoe from the outside.

I went up and set down on a log at the head of the island and looked out on the big river and the black driftwood, and away over to the town, three mile away, where there was three or four lights twinkling. A monstrous big lumber raft was about a mile up stream, coming along down, with a lantern in the middle of it. I watched it come creeping down, and when it was most abreast of where I stood I heard a man say, "Stern oars, there! heave her head to stab-board!"[2] I heard that just as plain as if the man was by my side.

There was a little gray in the sky, now; so I stepped into the woods and laid down for a nap before breakfast.

Chapter VIII

The sun was up so high when I waked, that I judged it was after eight o'clock. I laid there in the grass and the cool shade, thinking about things and feeling rested and ruther comfortable and satisfied. I could see the sun out at one or two holes, but mostly it was big trees all about, and gloomy in there amongst them. There was freckled places on the ground where the light sifted down through the leaves, and the freckled places swapped about a little, showing there was a little breeze up there. A couple of squirrels set on a limb and jabbered at me very friendly.

I was powerful lazy and comfortable—didn't want to get up and cook break-fast. Well, I was dozing off again, when I thinks I hears a deep sound of "boom!" away up the river. I rouses up and rests on my elbow and listens; pretty soon I hears it again. I hopped up and went and looked out at a hole in the leaves, and I see a bunch of smoke laying on the water a long ways up— about abreast the ferry. And there was the ferry-boat full of people, floating along down. I knowed what was the matter, now. "Boom!" I see the white smoke squirt out of the ferry-boat's side. You see, they was firing cannon over the water, trying to make my carcass come to the top.

I was pretty hungry, but it warn't going to do for me to start a fire, because they might see the smoke. So I set there and watched the cannon-smoke and listened to the boom. The river was a mile wide, there, and it always looks pretty on a summer morning—so I was having a good enough time seeing them hunt for my remainders, if I only had a bite to eat. Well, then I hap-pened to think how they always put quicksilver in loaves of bread and float them off because they always go right to the drownded carcass and stop there. So says I, I'll keep a lookout, and if any of them's floating around after me, I'll give them a show. I changed to the Illinois edge of the island to see what luck I could have, and I warn't disappointed. A big double loaf come along, and I most got it, with a long stick, but my foot slipped and she floated out further. Of course I was where the current set in the closest to the shore—I knowed enough for that. But by-and-by along comes another one, and this time I won. I took out the plug and shook out the little dab of quicksilver, and set my teeth in. It was "baker's bread"—what the quality eat—none of your low-down corn-pone.[3]

I got a good place amongst the leaves, and set there on a log, munching the bread and watching the ferry-boat, and very well satisfied. And then some-thing struck me. I says, now I reckon the widow or the parson or somebody prayed that this bread would find me, and here it has gone and done it. So

Superstition

---

2. Starboard, the right-hand side of a boat, facing forward.   3. A simple corn bread.

're ain't no doubt but there is something in that thing. That is, there's
nething in it when a body like the widow or the parson prays, but it don't
work for me, and I reckon it don't work for only just the right kind.

I lit a pipe and had a good long smoke and went on watching. The ferry-
boat was floating with the current, and I allowed I'd have a chance to see
who was aboard when she come along, because she would come in close,
where the bread did. When she'd got pretty well along down towards me, I
put out my pipe and went to where I fished out the bread, and laid down
behind a log on the bank in a little open place. Where the log forked I could
peep through.

By-and-by she came along, and she drifted in so close that they could a run
out a plank and walked ashore. Most everybody was on the boat. Pap, and
Judge Thatcher, and Bessie Thatcher, and Jo Harper, and Tom Sawyer, and
his old Aunt Polly, and Sid and Mary, and plenty more. Everybody was talking about the murder, but the captain broke in and says:

"Look sharp, now; the current sets in the closest here, and maybe he's
washed ashore and got tangled amongst the brush at the water's edge. I hope
so, anyway."

I didn't hope so. They all crowded up and leaned over the rails, nearly in
my face, and kept still, watching with all their might. I could see them first-
rate, but they couldn't see me. Then the captain sung out:

"Stand away!" and the cannon let off such a blast right before me that it
made me deef with the noise and pretty near blind with the smoke, and I
judged I was gone. If they'd a had some bullets in, I reckon they'd a got the
corpse they was after. Well, I see I warn't hurt, thanks to goodness. The boat
floated on and went out of sight around the shoulder of the island. I could
hear the booming, now and then, further and further off, and by-and-by after
an hour, I didn't hear it no more. The island was three mile long. I judged they
had got to the foot, and was giving it up. But they didn't yet a while. They
turned around the foot of the island and started up the channel on the Missouri side, under steam, and booming once in a while as they went. I crossed
over to that side and watched them. When they got abreast the head of the
island they quit shooting and dropped over to the Missouri shore and went
home to the town.

I knowed I was all right now. Nobody else would come a-hunting after me.
I got my traps out of the canoe and made me a nice camp in the thick woods.
I made a kind of a tent out of my blankets to put my things under so the rain
couldn't get at them. I catched a cat fish and haggled him open with my saw,
and towards sundown I started my camp fire and had supper. Then I set out
a line to catch some fish for breakfast.

When it was dark I set by my camp fire smoking, and feeling pretty satisfied; but by-and-by it got sort of lonesome, and so I went and set on the bank
and listened to the currents washing along, and counted the stars and drift-
logs and rafts that come down, and then went to bed; there ain't no better way
to put in time when you are lonesome; you can't stay so, you soon get over it.

And so for three days and nights. No difference—just the same thing. But
the next day I went exploring around down through the island. I was boss of
it; it all belonged to me, so to say, and I wanted to know all about it; but
mainly I wanted to put in the time. I found plenty strawberries, ripe and
prime; and green summer-grapes, and green razberries; and the green black-

berries was just beginning to show. They would all come handy by-and-by, I judged.

Well, I went fooling along in the deep woods till I judged I warn't far from the foot of the island. I had my gun along, but I hadn't shot nothing; it was for protection; thought I would kill some game nigh home. About this time I mighty near stepped on a good sized snake, and it went sliding off through the grass and flowers, and I after it, trying to get a shot at it. I clipped along, and all of sudden I bounded right on to the ashes of a camp fire that was still smoking.

My heart jumped up amongst my lungs. I never waited for to look further, but uncocked my gun and went sneaking back on my tip-toes as fast as ever I could. Every now and then I stopped a second, amongst the thick leaves, and listened; but my breath come so hard I couldn't hear nothing else. I slunk along another piece further, then listened again; and so on, and so on; if I see a stump, I took it for a man; if I trod on a stick and broke it, it made me feel like a person had cut one of my breaths in two and I only got half, and the short half, too.

When I got to camp I warn't feeling very brash, there warn't much sand in my craw;[4] but I says, this ain't no time to be fooling around. So I got all my traps into my canoe again so as to have them out of sight, and I put out the fire and scattered the ashes around to look like an old last year's camp, and then clumb a tree.

I reckon I was up in the tree two hours; but I didn't see nothing, I didn't hear nothing—I only *thought* I heard and seen as much as a thousand things. Well, I couldn't stay up there forever; so at last I got down, but I kept in the thick woods and on the lookout all the time. All I could get to eat was berries and what was left over from breakfast.

By the time it was night I was pretty hungry. So when it was good and dark, I slid out from shore before moonrise and paddled over to the Illinois bank— about a quarter of a mile. I went out in the woods and cooked a supper, and I had about made up my mind I would stay there all night, when I hear a *plun-kety-plunk, plunkety-plunk,* and says to myself, horses coming; and next I hear people's voices. I got everything into the canoe as quick as I could, and then went creeping through the woods to see what I could find out. I hadn't got far when I hear a man say:

"We'd better camp here, if we can find a good place; the horses is about beat out. Let's look around."[5]

I didn't wait, but shoved out and paddled away easy. I tied up in the old place, and reckoned I would sleep in the canoe.

I didn't sleep much. I couldn't, somehow, for thinking. And every time I waked up I thought somebody had me by the neck. So the sleep didn't do me no good. By-and-by I says to myself, I can't live this way; I'm agoing to find out who it is that's here on the island with me; I'll find it out or bust. Well, I felt better, right off.

So I took my paddle and slid out from shore just a step or two, and then let the canoe drop along down amongst the shadows. The moon was shining, and outside of the shadows it made it most as light as day. I poked along well onto

4. Slang for not feeling very brave.
5. Apparently this episode is a vestige of an early conception of the novel involving Pap in a murder plot and court trial.

an hour, everything still as rocks and sound asleep. Well by this time I was most down to the foot of the island. A little ripply, cool breeze begun to blow, and that was as good as saying the night was about done. I give her a turn with the paddle and brung her nose to shore; then I got my gun and slipped out and into the edge of the woods. I set down there on a log and looked out through the leaves. I see the moon go off watch and the darkness begin to blanket the river. But in a little while I see a pale streak over the tree-tops, and knowed the day was coming. So I took my gun and slipped off towards where I had run across that camp fire, stopping every minute or two to listen. But I hadn't no luck, somehow; I couldn't seem to find the place. But by-and-by, sure enough, I catched a glimpse of fire, away through the trees. I went for it, cautious and slow. By-and-by I was close enough to have a look, and there laid a man on the ground. It most give me the fan-tods.[6] He had a blanket around his head, and his head was nearly in the fire. I set there behind a clump of bushes, in about six foot of him, and kept my eyes on him steady. It was getting gray daylight, now. Pretty soon he gapped, and stretched himself, and hove off the blanket, and it was Miss Watson's Jim! I bet I was glad to see him. I says:

"Hello, Jim!" and skipped out.

He bounced up and stared at me wild. Then he drops down on his knees, and puts his hands together and says:

"Doan' hurt me—don't! I hain't ever done no harm to a ghos'. I awluz liked dead people, en done all I could for 'em. You go en git in de river agin, whah you b'longs, en doan' do nuffn to Ole Jim, 'at 'uz awluz yo' fren'."

Well, I warn't long making him understand I warn't dead. I was ever so glad to see Jim. I warn't lonesome, now. I told him I warn't afraid of *him* telling the people where I was. I talked along, but he only set there and looked at me; never said nothing. Then I says:

"It's good daylight. Let's get breakfast. Make up your camp fire good."

"What's de use er makin' up de camp fire to cook strawbries en sich truck? But you got a gun, hain't you? Den we kin git sumfn better den strawbries."

"Strawberries and such truck," I says. "Is that what you live on?"

"I couldn' git nuffn else," he says.

"Why, how long you been on the island, Jim?"

"I come heah de night arter you's killed."

"What, all that time?"

"Yes-indeedy."

"And ain't you had nothing but that kind of rubbage to eat?"

"No, sah—nuffn else."

"Well, you must be most starved, ain't you?"

"I reck'n I could eat a hoss. I think I could. How long you ben on de islan'?"

"Since the night I got killed."

"No! W'y, what has you lived on? But you got a gun. Oh, yes, you got a gun. Dat's good. Now you kill sumfn en I'll make up de fire."

So we went over to where the canoe was, and while he built a fire in a grassy open place amongst the trees, I fetched meal and bacon and coffee, and coffee-pot and frying-pan, and sugar and tin cups, and the nigger was set back considerable, because he reckoned it was all done with witchcraft. I

ghost

Jim's food

6. Slang for the hallucinatory state associated with delirium tremens, a condition that afflicts alcoholics.

catched a good big cat-fish, too, and Jim cleaned him with his knife, and fried him.

When breakfast was ready, we lolled on the grass and eat it smoking hot. Jim laid it in with all his might, for he was most about starved. Then when we had got pretty well stuffed, we laid off and lazied.

By-and-by Jim says:

"But looky here, Huck, who wuz it dat 'uz killed in dat shanty, ef it warn't you?"

Then I told him the whole thing, and he said it was smart. He said Tom Sawyer couldn't get up no better plan than what I had. Then I says:

"How do you come to be here, Jim, and how'd you get here?"

He looked pretty uneasy, and didn't say nothing for a minute. Then he says:

"Maybe I better not tell."

"Why, Jim?"

"Well, dey's reasons. But you wouldn' tell on me ef I 'uz to tell you, would you, Huck?"

"Blamed if I would, Jim."

"Well, I b'lieve you, Huck. I—*I run off.*"

"Jim!"

"But mind, you said you wouldn't tell—you know you said you wouldn't tell, Huck."

"Well, I did. I said I wouldn't, and I'll stick to it. Honest *injun* I will. People would call me a low down Ablitionist and despise me for keeping mum—but that don't make no difference. I ain't agoing to tell, and I ain't agoing back there anyways. So now, le's know all about it."

"Well, you see, it 'uz dis way. Ole Missus—dat's Miss Watson—she pecks on me all de time, en treats me pooty rough, but she awluz said she wouldn' sell me down to Orleans. But I noticed dey wuz a nigger trader roun' de place considable, lately, en I begin to git oneasy. Well, one night I creeps to de do', pooty late, en de do' warn't quite shet, en I hear ole missus tell de widder she gwyne to sell me down to Orleans, but she didn' want to, but she could git eight hund'd dollars for me,[7] en it 'uz sich a big stack o' money she couldn' resis'. De widder she try to git her to say she wouldn' do it, but I never waited to hear de res'. I lit out mighty quick, I tell you.

"I tuck out en shin down de hill en 'spec to steal a skift 'long de sho' som'ers 'bove de town, but dey wuz people a-stirrin' yit, so I hid in de ole tumble-down cooper shop on de bank to wait for everybody to go 'way. Well, I wuz dah all night. Dey wuz somebody roun' all de time. 'Long 'bout six in de mawnin', skifts begin to go by, en 'bout eight or nine every skift dat went 'long wuz talkin' 'bout how yo' pap come over to de town en say you's killed. Dese las' skifts wuz full o' ladies en genlmen agoin' over for to see de place. Sometimes dey'd pull up at de sho' en take a res' b'fo' dey started acrost, so by de talk I got to know all 'bout de killin'. I 'uz powerful sorry you's killed, Huck, but I ain't no mo', now.

"I laid dah under de shavins all day. I 'uz hungry, but I warn't afeared; bekase I knowed ole missus en de widder wuz goin' to start to de camp-meetn' right arter breakfas' en be gone all day, en dey knows I goes off wid de cattle 'bout daylight, so dey wouldn' 'spec to see me roun' de place, en so dey

---

7. A realistic price for a healthy male slave in the 1840s.

wouldn' miss me tell arter dark in de evenin'. De yuther servants wouldn' miss me, kase dey'd shin out en take holiday, soon as de ole folks 'uz out'n de way.

"Well, when it come dark I tuck out up de river road, en went 'bout two mile er more to whah dey warn't no houses. I'd made up my mind 'bout what I's agwyne to do. You see ef I kep' on tryin' to git away afoot, de dogs 'ud track me; ef I stole a skift to cross over, dey'd miss dat skift, you see, en dey'd know 'bout whah I'd lan' on de yuther side en whah to pick up my track. So I says, a raff is what I's arter; it doan' *make* no track.

"I see a light a-comin' roun' de p'int, bymeby, so I wade' in en shove' a log ahead o' me, en swum more'n half-way acrost de river, en got in 'mongst de drift-wood, en kep' my head down low, en kinder swum agin de current tell de raff come along. Den I swum to de stern uv it, en tuck aholt. It clouded up en 'uz pooty dark for a little while. So I clumb up en laid down on de planks. De men 'uz all 'way yonder in de middle,[8] whah de lantern wuz. De river wuz arisin' en dey wuz a good current; so I reck'n'd 'at by fo' in de mawnin' I'd be twenty-five mile down de river, en den I'd slip in, jis' b'fo' daylight, en swim asho' en take to de woods on de Illinoi side.[9]

"But I didn' have no luck. When we 'uz mos' down to de head er de islan', a man begin to come aft wid de lantern. I see it warn't no use fer to wait, so I slid overboad, en struck out fer de islan'. Well, I had a notion I could lan' mos' anywhers, but I couldn'—bank too bluff. I 'uz mos' to de foot er de islan' b'fo' I foun' a good place. I went into de woods en jedged I wouldn' fool wid raffs no mo', long as dey move de lantern roun' so. I had my pipe en a plug er dog-leg,[1] en some matches in my cap, en dey warn't wet, so I 'uz all right."

"And so you ain't had no meat nor bread to eat all this time? Why didn't you get mud-turkles?"

"How you gwyne to git'm? You can't slip up on um en grab um; en how's a body gwyne to hit um wid a rock? How could a body do it in de night? en I warn't gwyne to show myself on de bank in de daytime."

"Well, that's so. You've had to keep in the woods all the time, of course. Did you hear 'em shooting the cannon?"

"Oh, yes. I knowed dey was arter you. I see um go by heah; watched um thoo de bushes."

Some young birds come along, flying a yard or two at a time and lighting. Jim said it was a sign it was going to rain. He said it was a sign when young chickens flew that way, and so he reckoned it was the same way when young birds done it. I was going to catch some of them, but Jim wouldn't let me. He said it was death. He said his father laid mighty sick once, and some of them catched a bird, and his old granny said his father would die, and he did.

And Jim said you mustn't count the things you are going to cook for dinner, because that would bring bad luck. The same if you shook the table-cloth after sundown. And he said if a man owned a bee-hive, and that man died, the bees must be told about it before sun-up next morning, or else the bees would all weaken down and quit work and die. Jim said bees wouldn't sting idiots; but I didn't believe that, because I had tried them lots of times myself, and they wouldn't sting me.

---

8. A river raft would be large enough to make this easily possible.

9. Though Illinois was not a slave state, by state law any black person without freedom papers could be arrested and subjected to forced labor. Jim's chances for escape would be improved if he went down the Mississippi and then up the Ohio.

1. Cheap tobacco.

I had heard about some of these things before, but not all of them. Jim knowed all kinds of signs. He said he knowed most everything. I said it looked to me like all the signs was about bad luck, and so I asked him if there warn't any good-luck signs. He says:

"Mighty few—an' *dey* ain' no use to a body. What you want to know when good luck's a-comin' for? want to keep it off?" And he said: "Ef you's got hairy arms en a hairy breas', it's a sign dat you's agwyne to be rich. Well, dey's some use in a sign like dat, 'kase it's so fur ahead. You see, maybe you's got to be po' a long time fust, en so you might git discourage' en kill yo'sef 'f you didn' know by de sign dat you gwyne to be rich bymeby."

"Have you got hairy arms and a hairy breast, Jim?"

"What's de use to ax dat question? don' you see I has?"

"Well, are you rich?"

"No, but I ben rich wunst, and gwyne to be rich agin. Wunst I had foteen dollars, but I tuck to specalat'n', en got busted out."

"What did you speculate in, Jim?"

"Well, fust I tackled stock."

"What kind of stock?"

"Why, live stock. Cattle, you know. I put ten dollars in a cow. But I ain't gwyne to resk no mo' money in stock. De cow up 'n' died on my han's."

"So you lost the ten dollars."

"No, I didn' lose it all. I on'y los' 'bout nine of it. I sole de hide en taller for a dollar en ten cents."

"You had five dollars and ten cents left. Did you speculate any more?"

"Yes. You know dat one-laigged nigger dat b'longs to old Misto Bradish? well, he sot up a bank, en say anybody dat put in a dollar would git fo' dollars mo' at de en' er de year. Well, all de niggers went in, but dey didn' have much. I wuz de on'y one dat had much. So I stuck out for mo' dan fo' dollars, en I said 'f I didn' git it I'd start a bank myself. Well o' course dat nigger want' to keep me out er de business, bekase he say dey warn't business 'nough for two banks, so he say I could put in my five dollars en he pay me thirty-five at de en' er de year.

"So I done it. Den I reck'n'd I'd inves' de thirty-five dollars right off en keep things a-movin'. Dey wuz a nigger name' Bob, dat had ketched a wood-flat,[2] en his marster didn' know it; en I bought it off'n him en told him to take de thirty-five dollars when de en' er de year come; but somebody stole de wood-flat dat night, en nex' day de one-laigged nigger say de bank 's busted. So dey didn' none uv us git no money."

"What did you do with the ten cents, Jim?"

"Well, I 'uz gwyne to spen' it, but I had a dream, en de dream tole me to give it to a nigger name' Balum—Balum's Ass[3] dey call him for short, he's one er dem chuckle-heads, you know. But he's lucky, dey say, en I see I warn't lucky. De dream say let Balum inves' de ten cents en he'd make a raise for me. Well, Balum he tuck de money, en when he wuz in church he hear de preacher say dat whoever give to de po' len' to de Lord, en boun' to git his

2. A flat-bottomed boat used to transport timber.
3. Balaam, Old Testament prophet. God's aveng-ing angel interrupted this prophet's journey to curse the Israelites by standing in the path of his progress. Balaam was blind to the angel's presence, but his ass saw the angel clearly and swerved off the road, much to Balaam's chagrin (Numbers 22).

money back a hund'd times. So Balum he tuck en give de ten cents to de po', en laid low to see what wuz gwyne to come of it."

"Well, what did come of it, Jim?"

"Nuffn never come of it. I couldn' manage to k'leck dat money no way; en Balum he couldn'. I ain' gwyne to len' no mo' money 'dout I see de security. Boun' to git yo' money back a hund'd times, de preacher says! Ef I could git de ten *cents* back, I'd call it squah, en be glad er de chanst."

"Well, it's all right anyway, Jim, long as you're going to be rich again some time or other."

"Yes—en I's rich now, come to look at it. I owns mysef, en I's wuth eight hund'd dollars. I wisht I had de money, I wouldn' want no mo'."

Chapter IX

I wanted to go and look at a place right about the middle of the island, that I'd found when I was exploring; so we started, and soon got to it, because the island was only three miles long and a quarter of a mile wide.

This place was a tolerable long steep hill or ridge, about forty foot high. We had a rough time getting to the top, the sides was so steep and the bushes so thick. We tramped and clumb around all over it, and by-and-by found a good big cavern in the rock, most up to the top on the side towards Illinois. The cavern was as big as two or three rooms bunched together, and Jim could stand up straight in it. It was cool in there. Jim was for putting our traps in there, right away, but I said we didn't want to be climbing up and down there all the time.

Jim said if we had the canoe hid in a good place, and had all the traps in the cavern, we could rush there if anybody was to come to the island, and they would never find us without dogs. And besides, he said them little birds had said it was going to rain, and did I want the things to get wet?

So we went back and got the canoe and paddled up abreast the cavern, and lugged all the traps up there. Then we hunted up a place close by to hide the canoe in, amongst the thick willows. We took some fish off of the lines and set them again, and begun to get ready for dinner.

The door of the cavern was big enough to roll a hogshead in, and on one side of the door the floor stuck out a little bit and was flat and a good place to build a fire on. So we built it there and cooked dinner.

We spread the blankets inside for a carpet, and eat our dinner in there. We put all the other things handy at the back of the cavern. Pretty soon it darkened up and begun to thunder and lighten; so the birds was right about it. Directly it begun to rain, and it rained like all fury, too, and I never see the wind blow so. It was one of these regular summer storms. It would get so dark that it looked all blue-black outside, and lovely; and the rain would thrash along by so thick that the trees off a little ways looked dim and spider-webby; and here would come a blast of wind that would bend the trees down and turn up the pale underside of the leaves; and then a perfect ripper of a gust would follow along and set the branches to tossing their arms as if they was just wild; and next, when it was just about the bluest and blackest—*fst!* it was as bright as glory and you'd have a little glimpse of tree-tops a-plunging about, away off yonder in the storm, hundreds of yards further than you could see before;

dark as sin again in a second, and now you'd hear the thunder let go with an awful crash and then go rumbling, grumbling, tumbling down the sky towards the under side of the world, like rolling empty barrels down stairs, where it's long stairs and they bounce a good deal, you know.

"Jim, this is nice," I says. "I wouldn't want to be nowhere else but here. Pass me along another hunk of fish and some hot cornbread."

"Well, you wouldn' a ben here, 'f it hadn' a ben for Jim. You'd a ben down dah in de woods widout any dinner, en gittn' mos' drownded, too, dat you would, honey. Chickens knows when its gwyne to rain, en so do de birds, chile."

The river went on raising and raising for ten or twelve days, till at last it was over the banks. The water was three or four foot deep on the island in the low places and on the Illinois bottom. On that side it was a good many miles wide; but on the Missouri side it was the same old distance across—a half a mile— because the Missouri shore was just a wall of high bluffs.

Daytimes we paddled all over the island in the canoe. It was mighty cool and shady in the deep woods even if the sun was blazing outside. We went winding in and out amongst the trees; and sometimes the vines hung so thick we had to back away and go some other way. Well, on every old broken-down tree, you could see rabbits, and snakes, and such things; and when the island had been overflowed a day or two, they got so tame, on account of being hungry, that you could paddle right up and put your hand on them if you wanted to; but not the snakes and turtles—they would slide off in the water. The ridge our cavern was in, was full of them. We could a had pets enough if we'd wanted them.

One night we catched a little section of a lumber raft—nice pine planks. It was twelve foot wide and about fifteen or sixteen foot long, and the top stood above water six or seven inches, a solid level floor. We could see saw-logs go by in the daylight, sometimes, but we let them go; we didn't show ourselves in daylight.

Another night, when we was up at the head of the island, just before daylight, here comes a frame house down, on the west side. She was a two-story, and tilted over, considerable. We paddled out and got aboard—clumb in at an up-stairs window. But it was too dark to see yet, so we made the canoe fast and set in her to wait for daylight.

The light begun to come before we got to the foot of the island. Then we looked in at the window. We could make out a bed, and a table, and two old chairs, and lots of things around about on the floor; and there was clothes hanging against the wall. There was something laying on the floor in the far corner that looked like a man. So Jim says.

"Hello, you!"

But it didn't budge. So I hollered again, and then Jim says:

"De man ain' asleep—he's dead. You hold still—I'll go en see."

He went and bent down and looked, and says:

"It's a dead man. Yes, indeedy; naked, too. He's ben shot in de back. I reck'n he's ben dead two er three days. Come in, Huck, but doan' look at his face— it's too gashly."

I didn't look at him at all. Jim throwed some old rags over him, but he needn't done it; I didn't want to see him. There was heaps of old greasy cards scattered around over the floor, and old whisky bottles, and a couple of masks made out of black cloth; and all over the walls was the ignorantest kind of words and pictures, made with charcoal. There was two old dirty calico dresses, and a sun-bonnet, and some women's under-clothes, hanging against the wall, and some men's clothing, too. We put the lot into the canoe; it might come good. There was a boy's old speckled straw hat on the floor; I took that too. And there was a bottle that had had milk in it; and it had a rag stopper for a baby to suck. We would a took the bottle, but it was broke. There was a seedy old chest, and an old hair trunk with the hinges broke. They stood open, but there warn't nothing left in them that was any account. The way things was scattered about, we reckoned the people left in a hurry and warn't fixed so as to carry off most of their stuff.

We got an old tin lantern, and a butcher-knife without any handle, and a bran-new Barlow knife[4] worth two bits in any store, and a lot of tallow candles, and a tin candlestick, and a gourd, and a tin cup, and a ratty old bed-quilt off the bed, and a reticule with needles and pins and beeswax and buttons and thread and all such truck in it, and a hatchet and some nails, and a fish-line as thick as my little finger, with some monstrous hooks on it, and a roll of buckskin, and a leather dog-collar, and a horse-shoe, and some vials of medicine that didn't have no label on them; and just as we was leaving I found a tolerable good curry-comb, and Jim he found a ratty old fiddle-bow, and a wooden leg. The straps was broke off of it, but barring that, it was a good enough leg, though it was too long for me and not long enough for Jim, and we couldn't find the other one, though we hunted all around.

And so, take it all around, we made a good haul. When we was ready to shove off, we was a quarter of a mile below the island, and it was pretty broad day; so I made Jim lay down in the canoe and cover up with the quilt, because if he set up, people could tell he was a nigger a good ways off. I paddled over to the Illinois shore, and drifted down most a half a mile doing it. I crept up the dead water under the bank, and hadn't no accidents and didn't see nobody. We got home all safe.

Chapter X

After breakfast I wanted to talk about the dead man and guess out how he come to be killed, but Jim didn't want to. He said it would fetch bad luck; and besides, he said, he might come and ha'nt us; he said a man that warn't buried was more likely to go a-ha'nting around than one that was planted and comfortable. That sounded pretty reasonable, so I didn't say no more; but I couldn't keep from studying over it and wishing I knowed who shot the man, and what they done it for.

We rummaged the clothes we'd got, and found eight dollars in silver sewed up in the lining of an old blanket overcoat. Jim said he reckoned the people in that house stole the coat, because if they'd a knowed the money was there they wouldn't a left it. I said I reckoned they killed him, too; but Jim didn't want to talk about that. I says:

"Now, you think it's bad luck; but what did you say when I fetched in the snake-skin that I found on the top of the ridge day before yesterday? You said it was the worst bad luck in the world to touch a snake-skin with my hands.

4. Pocketknife with one blade, named for the inventor.

Well, here's your bad luck! We've raked in all this truck and eight dollars besides. I wish we could have some bad luck like this every day, Jim."

"Never you mind, honey, never you mind. Don't you git too peart. It's a-comin'. Mind I tell you, it's a-comin'.""

It did come, too. It was Tuesday that we had that talk. Well, after dinner Friday, we was laying around in the grass at the upper end of the ridge, and got out of tobacco. I went to the cavern to get some, and found a rattlesnake in there. I killed him, and curled him up on the foot of Jim's blanket, ever so natural, thinking there'd be some fun when Jim found him there. Well, by night I forgot all about the snake, and when Jim flung himself down on the blanket while I struck a light, the snake's mate was there, and bit him.

He jumped up yelling, and the first thing the light showed was the varmint curled up and ready for another spring. I laid him out in a second with a stick, and Jim grabbed pap's whiskey jug and began to pour it down.

He was barefooted, and the snake bit him right on the heel. That all comes of my being such a fool as to not remember that whenever you leave a dead snake its mate always comes there and curls around it. Jim told me to chop off the snake's head and throw it away, and then skin the body and roast a piece of it. I done it, and he eat it and said it would help cure him.[5] He made me take off the rattles and tie them around his wrist, too. He said that that would help. Then I slid out quiet and throwed the snakes clear away amongst the bushes; for I warn't going to let Jim find out it was all my fault, not if I could help it.

Jim sucked and sucked at the jug, and now and then he got out of his head and pitched around and yelled; but every time he come to himself he went to sucking at the jug again. His foot swelled up pretty big, and so did his leg; but by-and-by the drunk begun to come, and so I judged he was all right; but I'd druther been bit with a snake than pap's whiskey.

Jim was laid up for four days and nights. Then the swelling was all gone and he was around again. I made up my mind I wouldn't ever take aholt of a snake-skin again with my hands, now that I see what had come of it. Jim said he reckoned I would believe him next time. And he said that handling a snake-skin was such awful bad luck that maybe we hadn't got to the end of it yet. He said he druther see the new moon over his left shoulder as much as a thousand times than take up a snake-skin in his hand. Well, I was getting to feel that way myself, though I've always reckoned that looking at the new moon over your left shoulder is one of the carelessest and foolishest things a body can do. Old Hank Bunker done it once, and bragged about it; and in less than two years he got drunk and fell off of the shot tower and spread himself out so that he was just a kind of layer, as you may say; and they slid him edge-ways between two barn doors for a coffin, and buried him so, so they say, but I didn't see it. Pap told me. But anyway, it all come of looking at the moon that way, like a fool.

Well, the days went along, and the river went down between its banks again; and about the first thing we done was to bait one of the big hooks with a skinned rabbit and set it and catch a cat-fish that was as big as a man, being six foot two inches long, and weighed over two hundred pounds. We couldn't handle him, of course; he would a flung us into Illinois. We just set there and

5. Jim's homeopathic remedy is a common folk-medical practice.

watched him rip and tear around till he drowned. We found a brass button in his stomach, and a round ball, and lots of rubbage. We split the ball open with the hatchet, and there was a spool in it. Jim said he'd had it there a long time, to coat it over so and make a ball of it. It was as big a fish as was ever catched in the Mississippi, I reckon. Jim said he hadn't ever seen a bigger one. He would a been worth a good deal over at the village. They peddle out such a fish as that by the pound in the market house there; everybody buys some of him; his meat's as white as snow and makes a good fry.

Next morning I said it was getting slow and dull, and I wanted to get a stirring up, some way. I said I reckoned I would slip over the river and find out what was going on. Jim liked that notion; but he said I must go in the dark and look sharp. Then he studied it over and said, couldn't I put on some of them old things and dress up like a girl? That was a good notion, too. So we shortened up one of the calico gowns and I turned up my trowser-legs to my knees and got into it. Jim hitched it behind with the hooks, and it was a fair fit. I put on the sun-bonnet and tied it under my chin, and then for a body to look in and see my face was like looking down a joint of stove-pipe. Jim said nobody would know me, even in the daytime, hardly. I practiced around all day to get the hang of the things, and by-and-by I could do pretty well in them, only Jim said I didn't walk like a girl; and he said I must quit pulling up my gown to get at my britches pocket. I took notice, and done better.

I started up the Illinois shore in the canoe just after dark.

I started across to the town from a little below the ferry landing, and the drift of the current fetched me in at the bottom of the town. I tied up and started along the bank. There was a light burning in a little shanty that hadn't been lived in for a long time, and I wondered who had took up quarters there. I slipped up and peeped in at the window. There was a woman about forty year old in there, knitting by a candle that was on a pine table. I didn't know her face; she was a stranger, for you couldn't start a face in that town that I didn't know. Now this was lucky, because I was weakening; I was getting afraid I had come; people might know my voice and find me out. But if this woman had been in such a little town two days she could tell me all I wanted to know; so I knocked at the door, and made up my mind I wouldn't forget I was a girl.

Chapter XI

"Come in," says the woman, and I did. She says:

"Take a cheer."

I done it. She looked me all over with her little shiny eyes, and says:

"What might your name be?"

"Sarah Williams."

"Where 'bouts do you live? In this neighborhood?"

"No'm. In Hookerville, seven mile below. I've walked all the way and I'm all tired out."

"Hungry, too, I reckon. I'll find you something."

"No'm, I ain't hungry. I was so hungry I had to stop two mile below here at a farm; so I ain't hungry no more. It's what makes me so late. My mother's down sick, and out of money and everything, and I come to tell my uncle

Abner Moore. He lives at the upper end of the town, she says. I hain't ever been here before. Do you know him?"

"No; but I don't know everybody yet. I haven't lived here quite two weeks. It's a considerable ways to the upper end of the town. You better stay here all night. Take off your bonnet."

"No," I says, "I'll rest a while, I reckon, and go on. I ain't afeard of the dark."

She said she wouldn't let me go by myself, but her husband would be in by-and-by, maybe in a hour and a half, and she'd send him along with me. Then she got to talking about her husband, and about her relations up the river, and her relations down the river, and how much better off they used to was, and how they didn't know but they'd made a mistake coming to our town, instead of letting well alone—and so on and so on, till I was afeard I had made a mistake coming to her to find out what was going on in the town; but by-and-by she dropped onto pap and the murder, and then I was pretty willing to let her clatter right along. She told about me and Tom Sawyer finding the six thousand dollars (only she got it ten) and all about pap and what a hard lot he was, and what a hard lot I was, and at last she got down to where I was murdered. I says:

"Who done it? We've heard considerable about these goings on, down in Hookerville, but we don't know who 'twas that killed Huck Finn."

"Well, I reckon there's a right smart chance of people *here* that'd like to know who killed him. Some thinks old Finn done it himself."

"No—is that so?"

"Most everybody thought it at first. He'll never know how nigh he come to getting lynched. But before night they changed around and judged it was done by a runaway nigger named Jim."

"Why *he*—"

I stopped. I reckoned I better keep still. She run on, and never noticed I had put in at all.

"The nigger run off the very night Huck Finn was killed. So there's a reward out for him—three hundred dollars. And there's a reward out for old Finn too—two hundred dollars. You see, he come to town the morning after the murder, and told about it, and was out with 'em on the ferry-boat hunt, and right away after he up and left. Before night they wanted to lynch him, but he was gone, you see. Well, next day they found out the nigger was gone; they found out he hadn't ben seen sence ten o'clock the night the murder was done. So then they put it on him, you see, and while they was full of it, next day back comes old Finn and went boohooing to Judge Thatcher to get money to hunt for the nigger all over Illinois with. The judge give him some, and that evening he got drunk and was around till after midnight with a couple of mighty hard looking strangers, and then went off with them. Well, he hain't come back sence, and they ain't looking for him back till this thing blows over a little, for people thinks now that he killed his boy and fixed things so folks would think robbers done it, and then he'd get Huck's money without having to bother a long time with a lawsuit. People do say he warn't any too good to do it. Oh, he's sly, I reckon. If he don't come back for a year, he'll be all right. You can't prove anything on him, you know; everything will be quieted down then, and he'll walk into Huck's money as easy as nothing."

"Yes, I reckon so, 'm. I don't see nothing in the way of it. Has everybody quit thinking the nigger done it?"

"Oh no, not everybody. A good many thinks he done it. But they'll get the nigger pretty soon, now, and maybe they can scare it out of him."

"Why, are they after him yet?"

"Well, you're innocent, ain't you! Does three hundred dollars lay round every day for people to pick up? Some folks thinks the nigger ain't far from here. I'm one of them—but I hain't talked it around. A few days ago I was talking with an old couple that lives next door in the log shanty, and they happened to say hardly anybody ever goes to that island over yonder that they call Jackson's Island. Don't anybody live there? says I. No, nobody, says they. I didn't say any more, but I done some thinking. I was pretty near certain I'd seen smoke over there, about the head of the island, a day or two before that, so I says to myself, like as not that nigger's hiding over there; anyway, says I, it's worth the trouble to give the place a hunt. I hain't seen any smoke sence, so I reckon maybe he's gone, if it was him; but husband's going over to see—him and another man. He was gone up the river; but he got back to-day and I told him as soon as he got here two hours ago."

I had got so uneasy I couldn't set still. I had to do something with my hands; so I took up a needle off of the table and went to threading it. My hands shook and I was making a bad job of it. When the woman stopped talking, I looked up, and she was looking at me pretty curious, and smiling a little. I put down the needle and thread and let on to be interested—and I was, too—and says:

"Three hundred dollars is a power of money. I wish my mother could get it. Is your husband going over there to-night?"

"Oh, yes. He went up town with the man I was telling you of, to get a boat and see if they could borrow another gun. They'll go over after midnight."

"Couldn't they see better if they was to wait till daytime?"

"Yes. And couldn't the nigger see better too? After midnight he'll likely be asleep, and they can slip around through the woods and hunt up his camp fire all the better for the dark, if he's got one."

"I didn't think of that."

The woman kept looking at me pretty curious, and I didn't feel a bit comfortable. Pretty soon she says:

"What did you say your name was, honey?"

"M—Mary Williams."

Somehow it didn't seem to me that I said it was Mary before, so I didn't look up; seemed to me I said it was Sarah; so I felt sort of cornered, and was afeared maybe I was looking it, too. I wished the woman would say something more; the longer she set still, the uneasier I was. But now she says:

"Honey, I thought you said it was Sarah when you first come in?"

"Oh, yes'm, I did. Sarah Mary Williams. Sarah's my first name. Some calls me Sarah, some calls me Mary."

"Oh, that's the way of it?"

"Yes'm."

I was feeling better, then, but I wished I was out of there, anyway. I couldn't look up yet.

Well, the woman fell to talking about how hard times was, and how poor they had to live, and how the rats was as free as if they owned the place, and so forth, and so on, and then I got easy again. She was right about the rats. You'd see one stick his nose out of a hole in the corner every little while. She said she had to have things handy to throw at them when she was alone, or they wouldn't give her no peace. She showed me a bar of lead, twisted up into a knot, and she said she was a good shot with it generly, but she'd wrenched her arm a day or two ago, and didn't know whether she could throw true, now. But she watched for a chance, and directly she banged away at a rat, but she missed him wide, and said "Ouch!" it hurt her arm so. Then she told me to try for the next one. I wanted to be getting away before the old man got back, but of course I didn't let on. I got the thing, and the first rat that showed his nose I let drive, and if he'd a stayed where he was he'd a been a tolerable sick rat. She said that that was first-rate, and she reckoned I would hive[6] the next one. She went and got the lump of lead and fetched it back and brought along a hank of yarn, which she wanted me to help her with. I held up my two hands and she put the hank over them and went on talking about her and her husband's matters. But she broke off to say:

"Keep your eye on the rats. You better have the lead in your lap, handy."

So she dropped the lump into my lap, just at that moment, and I clapped my legs together on it and she went on talking. But only about a minute. Then she took off the hank and looked me straight in the face, but very pleasant, and says:

"Come, now—what's your real name?"

"Wh-what, mum?"

"What's your real name? Is it Bill, or Tom, or Bob?—or what is it?"

I reckon I shook like a leaf, and I didn't know hardly what to do. But I says:

"Please to don't poke fun at a poor girl like me, mum. If I'm in the way, here I'll—"

"No, you won't. Set down and stay where you are. I ain't going to hurt you, and I ain't going to tell on you, nuther. You just tell me your secret, and trust me. I'll keep it; and what's more, I'll help you. So'll my old man, if you want him to. You see, you're a run-away 'prentice—that's all. It ain't anything. There ain't any harm in it. You've been treated bad, and you made up your mind to cut. Bless you, child, I wouldn't tell on you. Tell me all about it, now—that's a good boy.

So I said it wouldn't be no use to try to play it any longer, and I would just make a clean breast and tell her everything, but she mustn't go back on her promise. Then I told her my father and mother was dead, and the law had bound me out to a mean old farmer in the country thirty mile back from the river, and he treated me so bad I couldn't stand it no longer; he went away to be gone a couple of days, and so I took my chance and stole some of his daughter's old clothes, and cleared out, and I had been three nights coming the thirty miles; I traveled nights, and hid daytimes and slept, and the bag of bread and meat I carried from home lasted me all the way and I had a plenty. I said I believed my uncle Abner Moore would take care of me, and so that was why I struck out for this town of Goshen.

"Goshen, child? This ain't Goshen. This is St. Petersburg. Goshen's ten mile further up the river. Who told you this was Goshen?"

"Why, a man I met at day-break this morning, just as I was going to turn into the woods for my regular sleep. He told me when the roads forked I must take the right hand, and five mile would fetch me to Goshen."

"He was drunk I reckon. He told you just exactly wrong."

6. Get, in the sense of hit and kill.

"Well, he did act like he was drunk, but it ain't no matter now. I got to be moving along. I'll fetch Goshen before day-light."

"Hold on a minute. I'll put you up a snack to eat. You might want it."

So she put me up a snack, and says:

"Say—when a cow's laying down, which end of her gets up first? Answer up prompt, now—don't stop to study over it. Which end gets up first?"

"The hind end, mum."

"Well, then, a horse?"

"The for'rard end, mum."

"Which side of a tree does the most moss grow on?"

"North side."

"If fifteen cows is browsing on a hillside, how many of them eats with their heads pointed the same direction?"

"The whole fifteen, mum."

"Well, I reckon you *have* lived in the country. I thought maybe you was trying to hocus me again. What's your real name, now?"

"George Peters, mum."

"Well, try to remember it, George. Don't forget and tell me it's Elexander before you go, and then get out by saying it's George Elexander when I catch you. And don't go about women in that old calico. You do a girl tolerable poor, but you might fool men, maybe. Bless you, child, when you set out to thread a needle, don't hold the thread still and fetch the needle up to it; hold the needle still and poke the thread at it—that's the way a woman most always does; but a man always does 'tother way. And when you throw at a rat or anything, hitch yourself up a tip-toe, and fetch your hand up over your head as awkard as you can, and miss your rat about six or seven foot. Throw stiff-armed from the shoulder, like there was a pivot there for it to turn on— like a girl; not from the wrist and elbow, with your arm out to one side, like a boy. And mind you, when a girl tries to catch anything in her lap, she throws her knees apart; she don't clap them together, the way you did when you catched the lump of lead. Why, I spotted you for a boy when you was threading the needle; and I contrived the other things just to make certain. Now trot along to your uncle, Sarah Mary Williams George Elexander Peters, and if you get into trouble you send word to Mrs. Judith Loftus, which is me, and I'll do what I can to get you out of it. Keep the river road, all the way, and next time you tramp, take shoes and socks with you. The river road's a rocky one, and your feet 'll be in a condition when you get to Goshen, I reckon."

I went up the bank about fifty yards, and then I doubled on my tracks and slipped back to where my canoe was, a good piece below the house. I jumped in and was off in a hurry. I went up stream far enough to make the head of the island, and then started across. I took off the sun-bonnet, for I didn't want no blinders on, then. When I was about the middle, I hear the clock begin to strike; so I stops and listens; the sound come faint over the water, but clear— eleven. When I struck the head of the island I never waited to blow, though I was most winded, but I shoved right into the timber where my old camp used to be, and started a good fire there on a high-and-dry spot.

Then I jumped in the canoe and dug out for our place a mile and a half below, as hard as I could go. I landed, and slopped through the timber and up the ridge and into the cavern. There Jim laid, sound asleep on the ground. I roused him out and says.

"Git up and hump yourself, Jim! There ain't a minute to lose. They're after us!"

Jim never asked no questions, he never said a word; but the way he worked for the next half an hour showed about how he was scared. By that time everything we had in the world was on our raft and she was ready to be shoved out from the willow cove where she was hid. We put out the camp fire at the cavern the first thing, and didn't show a candle outside after that.

I took the canoe out from shore a little piece and took a look, but if there was a boat around I couldn't see it, for stars and shadows ain't good to see by. Then we got out the raft and slipped along down in the shade, past the foot of the island dead still, never saying a word.

Chapter XII

It must a been close onto one o'clock when we got below the island at last, and the raft did seem to go mighty slow. If a boat was to come along, we was going to take to the canoe and break for the Illinois shore; and it was well a boat didn't come, for we hadn't ever thought to put the gun into the canoe, or a fishing-line or anything to eat. We was in ruther too much of a sweat to think of so many things. It warn't good judgment to put *everything* on the raft.

If the men went to the island, I just expect they found the camp fire I built, and watched it all night for Jim to come. Anyways, they stayed away from us, and if my building the fire never fooled them it warn't no fault of mine. I played it as low-down on them as I could.

When the first streak of day begun to show, we tied up to a tow-head in a big bend on the Illinois side, and hacked off cotton-wood branches with the hatchet and covered up the raft with them so she looked like there had been a cave-in in the bank there. A tow-head is a sand-bar that has cotton-woods on it as thick as harrow-teeth.

We had mountains on the Missouri shore and heavy timber on the Illinois side, and the channel was down the Missouri shore at that place, so we warn't afraid of anybody running across us. We laid there all day and watched the rafts and steamboats spin down the Missouri shore, and up-bound steamboats fight the big river in the middle. I told Jim all about the time I had jabbering with that woman; and Jim said she was a smart one, and if she was to start after us herself *she* wouldn't set down and watch a camp fire—no, sir, she'd fetch a dog. Well, then, I said, why couldn't she tell her husband to fetch a dog? Jim said he bet she did think of it by the time the men was ready to start, and he believed they must a gone up town to get a dog and so they lost all that time, or else we wouldn't be here on a tow-head sixteen or seventeen mile below the village—no, indeedy, we would be in that same old town again. So I said I didn't care what was the reason they didn't get us, as long as they didn't.

When it was beginning to come on dark, we poked our heads out of the cottonwood thicket and looked up, and down, and across; nothing in sight; so Jim took up some of the top planks of the raft and built a snug wigwam to get under in blazing weather and rainy, and to keep the things dry. Jim made a floor for the wigwam, and raised it a foot or more above the level of the raft, so now the blankets and all the traps was out of the reach of steamboat waves. Right in the middle of the wigwam we made a layer of dirt about five or six inches deep with a frame around it for to hold it to its place; this was to build a fire on in sloppy weather or chilly; the wigwam would keep it from being seen. We made an extra steering oar, too, because one of the others might get broke, on a snag or something. We fixed up a short forked stick to hang the old lantern on; because we must always light the lantern whenever we see a steamboat coming down stream, to keep from getting run over; but we wouldn't have to light it up for upstream boats unless we see we was in what they call "crossing;" for the river was pretty high yet, very low banks being still a little under water; so up-bound boats didn't always run the channel, but hunted easy water.

This second night we run between seven and eight hours, with a current that was making over four mile an hour. We catched fish, and talked, and we took a swim now and then to keep off sleepiness. It was kind of solemn, drifting down the big still river, laying on our backs looking up at the stars, and we didn't ever feel like talking loud, and it warn't often that we laughed, only a little kind of a low chuckle. We had mighty good weather, as a general thing, and nothing ever happened to us at all, that night, nor the next, nor the next.

Every night we passed towns, some of them away up on black hillsides, nothing but just a shiny bed of lights, not a house could you see. The fifth night we passed St. Louis, and it was like the whole world lit up. In St. Petersburg they used to say there was twenty or thirty thousand people in St. Louis,[7] but I never believed it till I see that wonderful spread of lights at two o'clock that still night. There warn't a sound there; everybody was asleep.

Every night now, I used to slip ashore, towards ten o'clock, at some little village, and buy ten or fifteen cents' worth of meal or bacon or other stuff to eat; and sometimes I lifted a chicken that warn't roosting comfortable, and took him along. Pap always said, take a chicken when you get a chance, because if you don't want him yourself you can easy find somebody that does, and a good deed ain't ever forgot. I never see pap when he didn't want the chicken himself, but that is what he used to say, anyway.

Mornings, before daylight, I slipped into corn fields and borrowed a watermelon, or a mushmelon, or a punkin, or some new corn, or things of that kind. Pap always said it warn't no harm to borrow things, if you was meaning to pay them back, sometime; but the widow said it warn't anything but a soft name for stealing, and no decent body would do it. Jim said he reckoned the widow was partly right and pap was partly right; so the best way would be for us to pick out two or three things from the list and say we wouldn't borrow them any more—then he reckoned it wouldn't be no harm to borrow the others. So we talked it over all one night, drifting along down the river, trying to make up our minds whether to drop the watermelons, or the cantelopes, or the mushmelons, or what. But towards daylight we got it all settled satisfactory, and concluded to drop crabapples and p'simmons. We warn't feeling just right, before that, but it was all comfortable now. I was glad the way it come out, too, because crabapples ain't ever good, and the p'simmons wouldn't be ripe for two or three months yet.

We shot a water-fowl, now and then, that got up too early in the morning or didn't go to bed early enough in the evening. Take it all around, we lived pretty high.

7. St. Louis is 170 miles down the Mississippi from Hannibal.

The fifth night below St. Louis we had a big storm after midnight, with a power of thunder and lightning, and the rain poured down in a solid sheet. We stayed in the wigwam and let the raft take care of itself. When the lightning glared out we could see a big straight river ahead, and high rocky bluffs on both sides. By-and-by says I, "Hel-*lo* Jim, looky yonder!" It was a steamboat that had killed herself on a rock. We was drifting straight down for her. The lightning showed her very distinct. She was leaning over, with part of her upper deck above water, and you could see every little chimbly-guy[8] clean and clear, and a chair by the big bell, with an old slouch hat hanging on the back of it when the flashes come.

Well, it being away in the night, and stormy, and all so mysterious-like, I felt just the way any other boy would a felt when I see that wreck laying there so mournful and lonesome in the middle of the river. I wanted to get aboard of her and slink around a little, and see what there was there. So I says:

"Le's land on her, Jim."

But Jim was dead against it, at first. He says:

"I doan' want to go fool'n 'long er no wrack. We's doin' blame' well, en we better let blame' well alone, as de good book says. Like as not dey's a watchman on dat wrack."

"Watchman your grandmother," I says; "there ain't nothing to watch but the texas[9] and the pilot-house; and do you reckon anybody's going to resk his life for a texas and a pilot-house such a night as this, when it's likely to break up and wash off down the river any minute?" Jim couldn't say nothing to that, so he didn't try. "And besides," I says, "we might borrow something worth having, out of the captain's stateroom. Seegars, *I* bet you—and cost five cents apiece, solid cash. Steamboat captains is always rich, and get sixty dollars a month, and *they* don't care a cent what a thing costs, you know, long as they want it. Stick a candle in your pocket; I can't rest, Jim, till we give her a rummaging. Do you reckon Tom Sawyer would ever go by this thing? Not for pie, he wouldn't. He'd call it an adventure—that's what he'd call it; and he'd land on that wreck if it was his last act. And wouldn't he throw style into it?—wouldn't he spread himself, nor nothing? Why, you'd think it was Christopher C'lumbus discovering Kingdom-Come. I wish Tom Sawyer *was* here."

Jim he grumbled a little, but give in. He said we mustn't talk any more than we could help, and then talk mighty low. The lightning showed us the wreck again, just in time, and we fetched the starboard derrick,[1] and made fast there.

The deck was high out, here. We went sneaking down the slope of it to labboard, in the dark, towards the texas, feeling our way slow with our feet, and spreading our hands out to fend off the guys, for it was so dark we couldn't see no sign of them. Pretty soon we struck the forward end of the skylight, and clumb onto it; and the next step fetched us in front of the captain's door, which was open, and by Jimminy, away down through the texas-hall we see a light! and all in the same second we seem to hear low voices in yonder!

Jim whispered and said he was feeling powerful sick, and told me to come along. I says, all right; and was going to start for the raft; but just then I heard a voice wail out and say:

"Oh, please don't, boys; I swear I won't ever tell!"

8. Wires used to steady the chimney stacks.
9. The large cabin on the top deck located just behind or beneath the pilothouse; it serves as officers' quarters.
1. Boom for lifting cargo.

Another voice said, pretty loud:

"It's a lie, Jim Turner. You've acted this way before. You always want more'n your share of the truck and you've always got it, too, because you've swore 't if you didn't you'd tell. But this time you've said it jest one time too many. You're the meanest, treacherousest hound in this country."

By this time Jim was gone for the raft. I was just a-biling with curiosity; and I says to myself, Tom Sawyer wouldn't back out now, and so I won't either; I'm agoing to see what's going on here. So I dropped on my hands and knees, in the little passage, and crept aft in the dark, till there warn't but about one stateroom betwixt me and the cross-hall of the texas. Then, in there I see a man stretched on the floor and tied hand and foot, and two men standing over him, and one of them had a dim lantern in his hand, and the other one had a pistol. This one kept pointing the pistol at the man's head on the floor and saying—

"I'd *like* to! And I orter, too, a mean skunk!"

The man on the floor would shrivel up, and say: "Oh, please don't, Bill—I hain't ever goin' to tell."

And every time he said that, the man with the lantern would laugh and say:

" 'Deed you *ain't*! You never said no truer thing 'n that, you bet you." And once he said, "Hear him beg! and yit if we hadn't got the best of him and tied him, he'd a killed us both. And what *for*? Jist for noth'n. Jist because we stood on our *rights*—that's what for. But I lay you ain't agoin' to threaten nobody any more, Jim Turner. Put *up* that pistol, Bill."

Bill says:

"I don't want to, Jake Packard. I'm for killin' him—and didn't he kill old Hatfield jist the same way—and don't he deserve it?"

"But I don't *want* him killed, and I've got my reasons for it."

"Bless yo' heart for them words, Jake Packard! I'll never forget you, long's I live!" says the man on the floor, sort of blubbering.

Packard didn't take no notice of that, but hung up his lantern on a nail, and started towards where I was, there in the dark, and motioned Bill to come. I crawfished[2] as fast as I could, about two yards, but the boat slanted so that I couldn't make very good time; so to keep from getting run over and catched I crawled into a stateroom on the upper side. The man come a-pawing along in the dark, and when Packard got to my stateroom, he says:

"Here—come in here."

And in he come, and Bill after him. But before they got in, I was up in the upper berth, cornered, and sorry I come. Then they stood there, with their hands on the ledge of the berth, and talked. I couldn't see them, but I could tell where they was, by the whisky they'd been having. I was glad I didn't drink whisky; but it wouldn't made much difference, anyway, because most of the time they couldn't a treed me because I didn't breathe. I was too scared. And besides, a body *couldn't* breathe, and hear such talk. They talked low and earnest. Bill wanted to kill Turner. He says:

"He's said he'll tell, and he will. If we was to give both our shares to him *now*, it wouldn't make no difference after the row, and the way we've served him. Shore's you're born, he'll turn State's evidence; now you hear *me*. I'm for putting him out of his troubles."

2. Crept backward on all fours.

"So'm I," says Packard, very quiet.

"Blame it, I'd sorter begun to think you wasn't. Well, then, that's all right. Les' go and do it."

"Hold on a minute; I hain't had my say yit. You listen to me. Shooting's good, but there's quieter ways if the thing's *got* to be done. But what I say, is this; it ain't good sense to go court'n around after a halter,[3] if you can git at what you're up to in some way that's jist as good and at the same time don't bring you into no resks. Ain't that so?"

"You bet it is. But how you goin' to manage it this time?"

"Well, my idea is this: we'll rustle around and gether up whatever pickins we've overlooked in the staterooms, and shove for shore and hide the truck. Then we'll wait. Now I say it ain't agoin' to be more 'n two hours befo' this wrack breaks up and washes off down the river. See? He'll be drownded, and won't have nobody to blame for it but his own self. I reckon that's a considerble sight better'n killin' of him. I'm unfavorable to killin' a man as long as you can git around it; it ain't good sense, it ain't good morals. Ain't I right?"

"Yes—I reck'n you are. But s'pose she *don't* break up and wash off?"

"Well, we can wait the two hours, anyway, and see, can't we?"

"All right, then; come along."

So they started, and I lit out, all in a cold sweat, and scrambled forward. It was dark as pitch there; but I said in a kind of a coarse whisper, "Jim!" and he answered up, right at my elbow, with a sort of a moan, and I says:

"Quick, Jim, it ain't no time for fooling around and moaning; there's a gang of murderers in yonder, and if we don't hunt up their boat and set her drifting down the river so these fellows can't get away from the wreck, there's one of 'em going to be in a bad fix. But if we find their boat we can put *all* of 'em in a bad fix—for the Sheriff 'll get 'em. Quick—hurry! I'll hunt the labboard side, you hunt the stabboard. You start at the raft, and—"

"Oh, my lordy, lordy! *Raf*'? Dey ain' no raf' no mo', she done broke loose en gone!—'en here we is!"

Chapter XIII

Well, I catched my breath and most fainted. Shut up on a wreck with such a gang as that! But it warn't no time to be sentimentering. We'd *got* to find that boat, now—had to have it for ourselves. So we went a-quaking and down the stabboard side, and slow work it was, too—seemed a week before we got to the stern. No sign of a boat. Jim said he didn't believe he could go any further—so scared he hadn't hardly any strength left, he said. But I said come on, if we get left on this wreck, we are in a fix, sure. So on we prowled, again. We struck for the stern of the texas, and found it, and then scrabbled along forwards on the skylight, hanging on from shutter to shutter, for the edge of the skylight was in the water. When we got pretty close to the cross-hall door there was the skiff, sure enough! I could just barely see her. I felt ever so thankful. In another second I would a been aboard of her; but just then the door opened. One of the men stuck his head out, only about a couple of foot from me, and I thought I was gone; but he jerked it in again, and says:

---

3. Hangman's noose.

"Heave that blame lantern out o' sight, Bill!"

He flung a bag of something into the boat, and then got in himself, and set down. It was Packard. Then Bill *he* come out and got in. Packard says, in a low voice:

"All ready—shove off!"

I couldn't hardly hang onto the shutters, I was so weak. But Bill says:

"Hold on—'d you go through him?"

"No. Didn't you?"

"No. So he's got his share o' the cash, yet."

"Well, then, come along—no use to take truck and leave money."

"Say—won't he suspicion what we're up to?"

"Maybe he won't. But we got to have it anyway. Come along." So they got out and went in.

The door slammed to, because it was on the careened side; and in a half second I was in the boat, and Jim come a tumbling after me. I out with my knife and cut the rope, and away we went!

We didn't touch an oar, and we didn't speak nor whisper, nor hardly even breathe. We went gliding swift along, dead silent, past the tip of the paddle-box, and past the stern; then in a second or two more we was a hundred yards below the wreck, and the darkness soaked her up, every last sign of her, and we was safe, and knowed it.

When we was three or four hundred yards down stream, we see the lantern show like a little spark at the texas door, for a second, and we knowed by that that the rascals had missed their boat, and was beginning to understand that they was in just as much trouble, now, as Jim Turner was.

Then Jim manned the oars, and we took out after our raft. Now was the first time that I begun to worry about the men—I reckon I hadn't had time to before. I begun to think how dreadful it was, even for murderers, to be in such a fix. I says to myself, there ain't no telling but I might come to be a murderer myself, yet, and then how would I like it? So says I to Jim:

"The first light we see, we'll land a hundred yards below it or above it, in a place where it's a good hiding-place for you and the skiff, and then I'll go and fix up some kind of a yarn, and get somebody to go for that gang and get them out of their scrape, so they can be hung when their time comes."

But that idea was a failure; for pretty soon it begun to storm again, and this time worse than ever. The rain poured down, and never a light showed; everybody in bed, I reckon. We boomed along down the river, watching for lights and watching for our raft. After a long time the rain let up, but the clouds staid, and the lightning kept whimpering, and by-and-by a flash showed us a black thing ahead, floating, and we made for it.

It was the raft, and mighty glad was we to get aboard of it again. We seen a light, now, away down to the right, on shore. So I said I would go for it. The skiff was half full of plunder which that gang had stole, there on the wreck. We hustled it onto the raft in a pile, and I told Jim to float along down, and show a light when he judged he had gone about two mile, and keep it burning till I come; then I manned my oars and shoved for the light. As I got down towards it, three or four more showed—up on a hillside. It was a village. I closed in above the shore-light, and laid on my oars and floated. As I went by, I see it was a lantern hanging on the jackstaff of a double-hull ferry-boat. I skimmed around for the watchman, a-wondering whereabouts he slept; and by-and-by I found him roosting on the bitts,[4] forward, with his head down between his knees. I give his shoulder two or three little shoves, and begun to cry.

He stirred up, in a kind of startlish way; but when he see it was only me, he took a good gap and stretch, and then he says:

"Hello, what's up? Don't cry, bub. What's the trouble?"

I says:

"Pap, and mam, and sis, and—"

Then I broke down. He says:

"Oh, dang it, now, *don't* take on so, we all has to have our troubles and this'n 'll come out all right. What's the matter with 'em?"

"They're—they're—are you the watchman of the boat?"

"Yes," he says, kind of pretty-well-satisfied like. "I'm the captain and the owner, and the mate, and the pilot, and watchman, and head deck-hand; and sometimes I'm the freight and passengers. I ain't as rich as old Jim Hornback, and I can't be so blame' generous and good to Tom, Dick and Harry as what he is, and slam around money the way he does; but I've told him a many a time 't I wouldn't trade places with him; for, says I, a sailor's life's the life for me, and I'm derned if *I'd* live two mile out o' town, where there ain't nothing ever goin' on, not for all his spondulicks and as much more on top of it. Says I—"

I broke in and says:

"They're in an awful peck of trouble, and—"

"*Who* is?"

"Why, pap, and mam, and sis, and Miss Hooker; and if you'd take your ferry-boat and go up there—"

"Up where? Where are they?"

"On the wreck."

"What wreck?"

"Why, there ain't but one."

"What, you don't mean the *Walter Scott?*"[5]

"Yes."

"Good land! what are they doin' *there*, for gracious sakes?"

"Well, they didn't go there a-purpose."

"I bet they didn't! Why, great goodness, there ain't no chance for 'em if they don't git off mighty quick! Why, how in the nation did they ever git into such a scrape?"

"Easy enough. Miss Hooker was a-visiting, up there to the town—"

"Yes, Booth's Landing—go on."

"She was a-visiting, there at Booth's Landing, and just in the edge of the evening she started over with her nigger woman in the horse-ferry,[6] to stay all night at her friend's house, Miss What-you-may-call her, I disremember her name, and they lost their steering-oar, and swung around and went a-floating

---

4. Vertical wooden posts to which cables can be secured.
5. Twain held Sir Walter Scott's romantic adventure novels set in feudal England responsible for the distorted antidemocratic notions held by so many Southerners and thus for the false ideology they were willing to fight and die for in the Civil

War. Twain expressed himself most vividly on this subject in *Life on the Mississippi* (Ch. 46), where he observes: "Sir Walter had so large a hand in making Southern character, as it existed before the war, that he is in great measure responsible for the war."
6. A ferry large enough to take horses and wagons.

down, stern-first, about two mile, and saddle-baggsed[7] on the wreck, and the ferry man and the nigger woman and the horses was all lost, but Miss Hooker she made a grab and got aboard the wreck. Well, about an hour after dark, we come along down in our trading-scow, and it was so dark we didn't notice the wreck till we was right on it; and so we saddle-baggsed; but all of us was saved but Bill Whipple—and oh, he was the best cretur!—I most wish't it had been me, I do."

"My George! It's the beatenest thing I ever struck. And then what did you all do?"

"Well, we hollered and took on, but it's so wide there, we couldn't make nobody hear. So pap said somebody got to get ashore and get help somehow. I was the only one that could swim, so I made a dash for it, and Miss Hooker she said if I didn't strike help sooner, come here and hunt up her uncle, and he'd fix the thing. I made the land about a mile below, and been fooling along ever since, trying to get people to do something, but they said, 'What, in such a night and such a current? there ain't no sense in it; go for the steam-ferry.' Now if you'll go, and—"

"By Jackson, I'd like to, and blame it I don't know but I will; but who in the dingnation's agoin' to pay for it? Do you reckon your pap—"

"Why that's all right. Miss Hooker she told me, particular, that her uncle Hornback—"

"Great guns! is he her uncle? Look here, you break for that light over yonder-way, and turn out west when you git there, and about a quarter of a mile out you'll come to the tavern; tell 'em to dart you out to Jim Hornback's and he'll foot the bill. And don't you fool around any, because he'll want to know the news. Tell him I'll have his niece all safe before he can get to town. Hump your-self, now; I'm agoing up around the corner here, to roust out my engineer."

I struck for the light, but as soon as he turned the corner I went back and got into my skiff and bailed her out and then pulled up shore in the easy water about six hundred yards, and tucked myself in among some woodboats; for I couldn't rest easy till I could see the ferry-boat start. But take it all around, I was feeling ruther comfortable on accounts of taking all this trouble for that gang, for not many would a done it. I wished the widow knowed about it. I judged she would be proud of me for helping these rapscallions, because rap-scallions and dead beats is the kind the widow and good people takes the most interest in.

Well, before long, here comes the wreck, dim and dusky, sliding along down! A kind of cold shiver went through me, and then I struck out for her. She was very deep, and I see in a minute there warn't much chance for any-body being alive in her. I pulled all around her and hollered a little, but there wasn't any answer; all dead still. I felt a little bit heavy-hearted about the gang, but not much, for I reckoned if they could stand it, I could.

Then here comes the ferry-boat; so I shoved for the middle of the river on a long down-stream slant; and when I judged I was out of eye-reach, I laid on my oars, and looked back and see her go and smell around the wreck for Miss Hooker's remainders, because the captain would know her uncle Hornback would want them; and then pretty soon the ferry-boat give it up and went for shore, and I laid into my work and went a-booming down the river.

7. Broken and doubled around the wreck.

It did seem a powerful long time before Jim's light showed up; and when it did show, it looked like it was a thousand mile off. By the time I got there the sky was beginning to get a little gray in the east; so we struck for an island, and hid the raft, and sunk the skiff, and turned in and slept like dead people.

Chapter XIV

By-and-by, when we got up, we turned over the truck the gang had stole off of the wreck, and found boots, and blankets, and clothes, and all sorts of other things, and a lot of books, and a spyglass, and three boxes of seegars. We hadn't ever been this rich before, in neither of our lives. The seegars was prime. We laid off all the afternoon in the woods talking, and me reading the books, and having a general good time. I told Jim all about what happened inside the wreck, and at the ferry-boat; and I said these kinds of things was adventures; but he said he didn't want no more adventures. He said that when I went in the texas and he crawled back to get on the raft and found her gone, he nearly died; because he judged it was all up with *him*, anyway it could be fixed; for if he didn't get saved he would get drownded; and if he did get saved, whoever saved him would send him back home so as to get the reward, and then Miss Watson would sell him South, sure. Well, he was right; he was most always right; he had an uncommon level head, for a nigger.

I read considerable to Jim about kings, and dukes, and earls, and such, and how gaudy they dressed, and how much style they put on, and called each other your majesty, and your grace, and your lordship, and so on, 'stead of mister; and Jim's eyes bugged out, and he was interested. He says:

"I didn't know dey was so many un um. I hain't hearn 'bout none un um, skasely, but ole King Sollermun, onless you counts dem kings dat's in a pack er k'yards. How much do a king git?"

"Get?" I says; "why, they get a thousand dollars a month if they want it; they can have just as much as they want; everything belongs to them."

"*Ain'* dat gay? En what dey got to do, Huck?"

"*They* don't do nothing! Why how you talk. They just set around."

"No—is dat so?"

"Of course it is. They just set around. Except maybe when there 's a war; then they go to the war. But other times they just lazy around; or go hawking—just hawking and sp—Sh!—d' you hear a noise?"

We skipped out and looked; but it warn't nothing but the flutter of a steamboat's wheel, away down coming around the point; so we come back.

"Yes," says I, "and other times, when things is dull, they fuss with the parlyment; and if everybody don't go just so he whacks their heads off. But mostly they hang round the harem."

"Roun' de which?"

"Harem."

"What's de harem?"

"The place where he keep his wives. Don't you know about the harem? Solomon had one; he had about a million wives."

"Why, yes, dat's so; I—I'd done forgot it. A harem's a bo'd'n-house, I reck'n. Mos' likely dey has rackety times in de nussery. En I reck'n de wives quarrels considable; en dat 'crease de racket. Yit dey say Sollermun de wises' man dat ever live.' I doan' take no stock in dat. Bekase why: would a wise man want to live in de mids' er sich a blimblammin' all de time? No—'deed he wouldn't. A wise man 'ud take en buil' a biler-factry; en den he could shet *down* de biler-factry when he want to res'."

"Well, but he *was* the wisest man, anyway; because the widow she told me so, her own self."

"I doan k'yer what de widder say, he *warn'* no wise man, nuther. He had some er de dad-fetchedes' ways I ever see. Does you know 'bout dat chile dat he 'uz gwyne to chop in two?"[8]

"Yes, the widow told me all about it."

"*Well,* den! Warn' dat de beatenes' notion in de worl'? You jes' take en look at it a minute. Dah's de stump, dah—dat's one er de women; heah's you—dat's de yuther one; I's Sollermun; en dish-yer dollar bill's de chile. Bofe un you claims it. What does I do? Does I shin aroun' mongs' de neighbors en fine out which un you de bill do b'long to, en han' it over to de right one, all safe en soun', de way dat anybody dat had any gumption would? No—I take en whack de bill in *two,* en give half un it to you, en de yuther half to de yuther woman. Dat's de way Sollermun was gwyne to do wid de chile. Now I want to ask you: what's de use er dat half a bill?—can't buy noth'n wid it. En what use is a half a chile? I wouldn' give a dern for a million un um."

"But hang it, Jim, you've clean missed the point—blame it, you've missed it a thousand mile."

"Who? Me? Go 'long. Doan' talk to *me* 'bout yo' pints. I reck'n I knows sense when I sees it; en dey ain' no sense in sich doin's as dat. De 'spute warn' 'bout a half a chile, de 'spute was 'bout a whole chile; en de man dat think he kin settle a 'spute 'bout a whole chile wid a half a chile, doan' know enough to come in out'n de rain. Doan' talk to me 'bout Sollermun, Huck, I knows him by de back."

"But I tell you you don't get the point."

"Blame de pint! I reck'n I knows what I knows. En mine you, de *real* pint is down furder—it's down deeper. It lays in de way Sollermun was raised. You take a man dat's got on'y one er two children; is dat man gwyne to be wase-ful o' chillen? No, he ain't; he can't 'ford it. *He* know how to value 'em. But you take a man dat's got 'bout five million chillen runnin' roun' de house, en it's diffunt. *He* as soon chop a chile in two as a cat. Dey's plenty mo'. A chile er two, mo' er less, warn't no consekens to Sollermun, dad fetch him!"

I never see such a nigger. If he got a notion in his head once, there warn't no getting it out again. He was the most down on Solomon of any nigger I ever see. So I went to talking about other kings, and let Solomon slide. I told about Louis Sixteenth that got his head cut off in France long time ago; and about his little boy the dolphin,[9] that would a been a king, but they took and shut him up in jail, and some say he died there.

"Po' little chap."

"But some says he got out and got away, and come to America."

"Dat's good! But he'll be pooty lonesome—dey ain' no kings here, is dey, Huck?"

8. In 1 Kings 3.16–28. When two women appeared before him claiming to be the mother of the same infant, Solomon ordered the child cut in two. The real mother pleaded with him to save the baby and to give it to the other woman, who maliciously agreed to Solomon's original plan.
9. The Dauphin, Louis Charles, next in line of the succession to the throne, was eight years old when his father, Louis XVI, was beheaded (1793). Though the boy died in prison, probably in 1795, legends of his escape to America (and elsewhere) persisted, and Twain owned a book on the subject by Horace W. Fuller: *Imposters and Adventurers, Noted French Trials* (1882).

"No."

"Den he cain't git no situation. What he gwyne to do?"

"Well, I don't know. Some of them gets on the police, and some of them learns people how to talk French."

"Why, Huck, doan' de French people talk de same way we does?"

"No, Jim; you couldn't understand a word they said—not a single word."

"Well now, I be ding-busted! How do dat come?"

"I don't know; but it's so. I got some of their jabber out of a book. Spose a man was to come to you and say *Polly-voo-franzy*—what would you think?"

"I wouldn' think nuff'n; I'd take en bust him over de head. Dat is, if he warn't white. I wouldn't 'low no nigger to call me dat."

"Shucks, it ain't calling you anything. It's only saying do you know how to talk French?"

"Well, den, why couldn't he *say* it?"

"Why, he *is* a-saying it. That's a Frenchman's *way* of saying it."

"Well, it's a blame' ridicklous way, en I doan' want to hear no mo' 'bout it. Dey ain' no sense in it."

"Looky here, Jim; does a cat talk like we do?"

"No, a cat don't."

"Well, does a cow?"

"No, a cow don't, nuther."

"Does a cat talk like a cow, or a cow talk like a cat?"

"No, dey don't."

"It's natural and right for 'em to talk different from each other, ain't it?"

" 'Course."

"And ain't it natural and right for a cat and a cow to talk different from *us*?"

"Why, mos' sholy it is."

"Well, then, why ain't it natural and right for a *Frenchman* to talk different from us? You answer me that."

"Is a cat a man, Huck?"

"No."

"Well, den, dey ain't no sense in a cat talkin' like a man. Is a cow a man?—er is a cow a cat?"

"No, she ain't either of them."

"Well, den, she ain' got no business to talk like either one er the yuther of 'em. Is a Frenchman a man?"

"Yes."

"*Well*, den! Dad blame it, why doan' he *talk* like a man? You answer me *dat*!"

I see it warn't no use wasting words—you can't learn a nigger to argue. So I quit.

racism

Chapter XV

We judged that three nights more would fetch us to Cairo,[1] at the bottom of Illinois, where the Ohio River comes in, and that was what we was after. We would sell the raft and get on a steamboat and go way up the Ohio amongst the free States, and then be out of trouble.[2]

1. Pronounced *Cair-ō*, the town is 364 miles from Hannibal, 194 miles from St. Louis.
2. Southern Illinois was proslavery in sentiment. The state, moreover, had a system of indentured labor, not unlike slavery, to which a black person without proof of free status might be subjected. Although even in the "free" states there were similar dangers for Jim, the chances of his making his way to freedom and safety in Canada from Ohio or Pennsylvania would be much greater.

Well, the second night a fog begun to come on, and we made for a tow-head to tie to, for it wouldn't do to try to run in fog; but when I paddled ahead in the canoe, with the line, to make fast, there warn't anything but little saplings to tie to. I passed the line around one of them right on the edge of the cut bank, but there was a stiff current, and the raft come booming down so lively she tore it out by the roots and away she went. I see the fog closing down, and it made me so sick and scared I couldn't budge for most a half a minute it seemed to me—and then there warn't no raft in sight; you couldn't see twenty yards. I jumped into the canoe and run back to the stern and grabbed the paddle and set her back a stroke. But she didn't come. I was in such a hurry I hadn't untied her. I got up and tried to untie her, but I was so excited my hands shook so I couldn't hardly do anything with them.

As soon as I got started I took out after the raft, hot and heavy, right down the tow-head. That was all right as far as it went, but the tow-head warn't sixty yards long, and the minute I flew by the foot of it I shot out into the solid white fog, and hadn't no more idea which way I was going than a dead man.

Thinks I, it won't do to paddle; first I know I'll run into the bank or a tow-head or something; I got to set still and float, and yet it's mighty fidgety business to have to hold your hands still at such a time. I whooped and listened. Away down there, somewheres, I hears a small whoop, and up comes my spirits. I went tearing after it, listening sharp to hear it again. The next time it come, I see I warn't heading for it but heading away to the right of it. And the next time, I was heading away to the left of it—and not gaining on it much, either, for I was flying around, this way and that and 'tother, but it was going straight ahead all the time.

I did wish the fool would think to beat a tin pan, and beat it all the time, but he never did, and it was the still places between the whoops that was making the trouble for me. Well, I fought along, and directly I hears the whoops *behind* me. I was tangled good, now. That was somebody's else's whoop, or else I was turned around.

I throwed the paddle down. I heard the whoop again; it was behind me yet, but in a different place; it kept coming, and kept changing its place, and I kept answering, till by-and-by it was in front of me again and I knowed the current had swung the canoe's head down stream and I was all right, if that was Jim and not some other raftsman hollering. I couldn't tell nothing about voices in a fog, for nothing don't look natural nor sound natural in a fog.

The whooping went on, and in about a minute I come a booming down on a cut bank[3] with smoky ghosts of big trees on it, and the current throwed me off to the left and shot by, amongst a lot of snags that fairly roared, the current was tearing by them so swift.

In another second or two it was solid white and still again. I set perfectly still, then, listening to my heart thump, and I reckon I didn't draw a breath while it thumped a hundred.

I just give up, then. I knowed what the matter was. That cut bank was an island, and Jim had gone down 'tother side of it. It warn't no tow-head, that you could float by in ten minutes. It had the big timber of a regular island; it might be five or six mile long and more than a half a mile wide.

I kept quiet, with my ears cocked, about fifteen minutes, I reckon. I was

---

3. Steep bank carved out by the force of the current.

floating along, of course, four or five mile an hour; but you don't ever think of that. No, you *feel* like you are laying dead still on the water; and if a little glimpse of a snag slips by, you don't think to yourself how fast *you're* going, but you catch your breath and think, my! how that snag's tearing along. If you think it ain't dismal and lonesome out in a fog that way, by yourself, in the night, you try it once—you'll see.

Next, for about a half an hour, I whoops now and then; at last I hears the answer a long ways off, and tries to follow it, but I couldn't do it, and directly I judged I'd got into a nest of tow-heads, for I had little dim glimpses of them on both sides of me, sometimes just a narrow channel between; and some that I couldn't see, I knowed was there, because I'd hear the wash of the current against the old dead brush and trash that hung over the banks. Well, I warn't long losing the whoops, down amongst the tow-heads; and I only tried to chase them a little while, anyway, because it was worse than chasing a Jack-o-lantern. You never knowed a sound dodge around so, and swap places so quick and so much.

I had to claw away from the bank pretty lively, four or five times, to keep from knocking the islands out of the river; and so I judged the raft must be butting into the bank every now and then, or else it would get further ahead and clear out of hearing—it was floating a little faster than what I was.

Well, I seemed to be in the open river again, by-and-by, but I couldn't hear no sign of a whoop nowheres. I reckoned Jim had fetched up on a snag, maybe, and it was all up with him. I was good and tired, so I laid down in the canoe and said I wouldn't bother no more. I didn't want to go to sleep, of course; but I was so sleepy I couldn't help it; so I thought I would take just one little cat-nap.

But I reckon it was more than a cat-nap, for when I waked up the stars was shining bright, the fog was all gone, and I was spinning down a big bend stern first. First I didn't know where I was; I thought I was dreaming; and when things begun to come back to me, they seemed to come up dim out of last week.

It was a monstrous big river here, with the tallest and the thickest kind of timber on both banks; just a solid wall, as well as I could see, by the stars. I looked away down stream, and seen a black speck on the water. I took out after it; but when I got to it it warn't nothing but a couple of saw-logs made fast together. Then I see another speck, and chased that; then another, and this time I was right. It was the raft.

When I got to it Jim was setting there with his head down between his knees, asleep, with his right arm hanging over the steering oar. The other oar was smashed off, and the raft was littered up with leaves and branches and dirt. So she'd had a rough time.

I made fast and laid down under Jim's nose on the raft, and begun to gap, and stretch my fists out against Jim, and says:

"Hello, Jim, have I been asleep? Why didn't you stir me up?"

"Goodness gracious, is dat you, Huck? En you ain' dead—you ain' drownded—you's back agin? It's too good for true, honey, it's too good for true. Lemme look at you, chile, lemme feel o' you. No, you ain' dead? you's back agin, 'live en soun', jis de same ole Huck—de same ole Huck, thanks to goodness!"

"What's the matter with you, Jim? You been a drinking?"

"Drinkin'? Has I ben a drinkin'? Has I had a chance to be a drinkin'?"

"Well, then, what makes you talk so wild?"

"How does I talk wild?"

"*How?* why, haint you been talking about my coming back, and all that stuff, as if I'd been gone away?"

"Huck—Huck Finn, you look me in de eye; look me in de eye. *Hain't* you ben gone away?"

"Gone away? Why, what in the nation do you mean? *I* hain't been gone anywhere. Where would I go to?"

"Well, looky here, boss, dey's sumf'n wrong, dey is. Is I *me,* or who *is* I? Is I heah, or whah *is* I? Now dat's what I wants to know?"

"Well, I think you're here, plain enough, but I think you're a tangle-headed old fool, Jim."

"I is, is I? Well you answer me dis. Didn't you tote out de line in de canoe, fer to make fas' to de tow-head?"

"No, I didn't. What tow-head? I hain't seen no tow-head."

"You hain't seen no tow-head? Looky here—didn't de line pull loose en de raf' go a hummin' down de river, en leave you en de canoe behine in de fog?"

"What fog?"

"Why *de* fog. De fog dat's ben aroun' all night. En didn't you whoop, en didn't I whoop, tell we got mix' up in de islands en one un us got 'los' en 'tother one was jis' as good as los', 'kase he didn' know whah he wuz? En didn't I bust up agin a lot er dem islands en have a turrible time en mos' git drownded? Now ain' dat so, boss—ain' it so? You answer me dat."

"Well, this is too many for me, Jim. I hain't seen no fog, nor no islands, nor no troubles, nor nothing. I been setting here talking with you all night till you went to sleep about ten minutes ago, and I reckon I done the same. You couldn't a got drunk in that time, so of course you've been dreaming."

"Dad fetch it, how is I gwyne to dream all dat in ten minutes?"

"Well, hang it all, you did dream it, because there didn't any of it happen."

"But Huck, it's all jis' as plain to me as—"

"It don't make no difference how plain it is, there ain't nothing in it. I know, because I've been here all the time."

Jim didn't say nothing for about five minutes, but set there studying over it. Then he says:

"Well, den, I reck'n I did dream it, Huck; but dog my cats ef it ain't de powerfullest dream I ever see. En I hain't ever had no dream b'fo' dat's tired me like dis one."

"Oh, well, that's all right, because a dream does tire a body like everything, sometimes. But this one was a staving[4] dream—tell me all about it, Jim."

So Jim went to work and told me the whole thing right through, just as it happened, only he painted it up considerable. Then he said he must start in and " 'terpret" it, because it was sent for a warning. He said the first tow-head stood for a man that would try to do us some good, but the current was another man that would get us away from him. The whoops was warnings that would come to us every now and then, and if we didn't try hard to make out to understand them they'd just take us into bad luck, 'stead of keeping us out of it. The lot of tow-heads was troubles we was going to get into with quar-

---

4. Vivid, compelling.

relsome people and all kinds of mean folks, but if we minded our business and didn't talk back and aggravate them, we would pull through and get out of the fog and into the big clear river, which was the free States, and wouldn't have no more trouble.

It had clouded up pretty dark just after I got onto the raft, but it was clearing up again, now.

"Oh, well, that's all interpreted well enough, as far as it goes, Jim," I says; "but what does *these* things stand for?"

It was the leaves and rubbish on the raft, and the smashed oar. You could see them first rate, now.

Jim looked at the trash, and then looked at me, and back at the trash again. He had got the dream fixed so strong in his head that he couldn't seem to shake it loose and get the facts back into its place again, right away. But when he did get the thing straightened around, he looked at me steady, without ever smiling, and says:

"What do dey stan' for? I's gwyne to tell you. When I got all wore out wid work, en wid de callin' for you, en went to sleep, my heart wuz mos' broke bekase you wuz los', en I didn' k'yer no mo' what become er me en de raf'. En when I wake up en fine you back agin', all safe en soun', de tears come en I could a got down on my knees en kiss' yo' foot I's so thankful. En all you wuz thinkin' 'bout wuz how you could make a fool uv ole Jim wid a lie. Dat truck dah is *trash;* en trash is what people is dat puts dirt on de head er dey fren's en makes 'em ashamed."

Then he got up slow, and walked to the wigwam, and went in there, without saying anything but that. But that was enough. It made me feel so mean I could almost kissed *his* foot to get him to take it back.

It was fifteen minutes before I could work myself up to go and humble myself to a nigger—but I done it, and I warn't ever sorry for it afterwards, neither. I didn't do him no more mean tricks, and I wouldn't done that one if I'd a knowed it would make him feel that way.

Chapter XVI

We slept most all day, and started out at night, a little ways behind a monstrous long raft that was as long going by as a procession. She had four long sweeps[5] at each end, so we judged she carried as many as thirty men, likely. She had five big wigwams aboard, wide apart, and an open camp fire in the middle, and a tall flagpole at each end. There was a power of style about her. It *amounted* to something being a raftsman on such a craft as that.

We went drifting down into a big bend, and the night clouded up and got hot. The river was very wide, and was walled with solid timber on both sides; you couldn't see a break in it hardly ever, or a light. We talked about Cairo, and wondered whether we would know it when we got to it. I said likely we wouldn't, because I had heard say there warn't but about a dozen houses there, and if they didn't happen to have them lit up, how was we going to know we was passing a town? Jim said if the two big rivers joined together there, that would show. But I said maybe we might think we was passing the foot of an island and coming into the same old river again. That disturbed

---

5. Long oars used chiefly for steering.

Jim—and me too. So the question was, what to do? I said, paddle ashore the first time a light showed, and tell them pap was behind, coming along with a trading-scow, and was a green hand at the business, and wanted to know how far it was to Cairo. Jim thought it was a good idea, so we took a smoke on it and waited.[6]

But you know a young person can't wait very well when he is impatient to find a thing out. We talked it over, and by and by Jim said it was such a black night, now, that it wouldn't be no risk to swim down to the big raft and crawl aboard and listen—they would talk about Cairo, because they would be calculating to go ashore there for a spree, maybe; or anyway they would send boats ashore to buy whisky or fresh meat or something. Jim had a wonderful level head, for a nigger: he could most always start a good plan when you wanted one.

I stood up and shook my rags off and jumped into the river, and struck out for the raft's light. By and by, when I got down nearly to her, I eased up and went slow and cautious. But everything was all right—nobody at the sweeps. So I swum down along the raft till I was most abreast the camp fire in the middle, then I crawled aboard and inched along and got in among some bundles of shingles on the weather side of the fire. There was thirteen men there— they was the watch on deck of course. And a mighty rough-looking lot, too. They had a jug, and tin cups, and they kept the jug moving. One man was singing—roaring, you may say; and it wasn't a nice song—for a parlor, anyway. He roared through his nose, and strung out the last word of every line very long. When he was done they all fetched a kind of Injun war-whoop, and then another was sung. It begun:

> "There was a woman in our towdn,
>   In our towdn did dwed'l [dwell],
> She loved her husband dear-i-lee,
>   But another man twyste as wed'l.

> "Singing too, riloo, riloo, riloo,
>   Ri-too, riloo, rilay—e,
> She loved her husband dear-i-lee,
>   But another man twyste as wed'l."

And so on—fourteen verses. It was kind of poor, and when he was going to start on the next verse one of them said it was the tune the old cow died on; and another one said: "Oh, give us a rest!" And another one told him to take a walk. They made fun of him till he got mad and jumped up and begun to cuss the crowd, and said he could lam any thief in the lot.

They was all about to make a break for him, but the biggest man there jumped up and says:

"Set whar you are, gentlemen. Leave him to me; he's my meat."

Then he jumped up in the air three times, and cracked his heels together

6. The passage that follows was part of the final autograph manuscript for *Huck Finn* that Twain sent to his nephew-publisher Charles L. Webster in April 1884. Though Twain acquiesced to the cutting of this "Raft Passage" (on a suggestion made initially by W. D. Howells), the cut was made to save space and not on literary or aesthetic grounds, and the passage is, therefore, reinstated in this text. The raft material had already appeared—with an introductory note explaining that it was part of a book in progress—as part of Ch. 3 of *Life on the Mississippi* (1883). For a further discussion of this textual crux see Walter Blair, *Mark Twain and "Huck Finn"* (1960), and Peter G. Beidler, "The Raft Episode in *Huckleberry Finn*," *Modern Fiction Studies* 14 (Spring 1965): 11–20. See also Victor Doyno's *Writing "Huck Finn": Mark Twain's Creative Process* (1991).

every time. He flung off a buckskin coat that was all hung with fringes, and says, "You lay thar tell the chawin-up's done"; and flung his hat down, which was all over ribbons, and says, "You lay thar tell his sufferin's is over."

Then he jumped up in the air and cracked his heels together again, and shouted out:

"Whoo-oop! I'm the old original iron-jawed, brass-mounted, copper-bellied corpse-maker from the wilds of Arkansaw. Look at me! I'm the man they call Sudden Death and General Desolation! Sired by a hurricane, dam'd by an earthquake, half-brother to the cholera, nearly related to the smallpox on the mother's side! Look at me! I take nineteen alligators and a bar'l of whisky for breakfast when I'm in robust health, and a bushel of rattlesnakes and a dead body when I'm ailing. I split the everlasting rocks with my glance, and I squench[7] the thunder when I speak! Whoo-oop! Stand back and give me room according to my strength! Blood's my natural drink, and the wails of the dying is music to my ear. Cast your eye on me, gentlemen! and lay low and hold your breath, for I'm 'bout to turn myself loose![8]

All the time he was getting this off, he was shaking his head and looking fierce, and kind of swelling around in a little circle, tucking up his wristbands, and now and then straightening up and beating his breast with his fist, saying, "Look at me, gentlemen!" When he got through, he jumped up and cracked his heels together three times, and let off a roaring "Whoo-oop! I'm the bloodiest son of a wildcat that lives!"

Then the man that had started the row tilted his old slouch hat down over his right eye; then he bent stooping forward, with his back sagged and his south end sticking out far, and his fists a-shoving out and drawing in in front of him, and so went around in a little circle about three times, swelling himself up and breathing hard. Then he straightened, and jumped up and cracked his heels together three times before he lit again (that made them cheer), and he began to shout like this:

"Whoo-oop! bow you neck and spread, for the kingdom of sorrow's a-coming! Hold me down to the earth, for I feel my powers a-working! whoo-oop! I'm a child of sin, *don't* let me get a start! Smoked glass, here, for all! Don't attempt to look at me with the naked eye, gentlemen! When I'm play-ful I use the meridians of longitude and parallels of latitude for a seine, and drag the Atlantic Ocean for whales! I scratch my head with the lightning and purr myself to sleep with the thunder! When I'm cold, I bile the Gulf of Mex-ico and bathe in it; when I'm hot I fan myself with an equinoctial storm; when I'm thirsty I reach up and suck a cloud dry like a sponge; when I range the earth hungry, famine follows in my tracks! Whoo-oop! Bow your neck and spread! I put my hand on the sun's face and make it night in the earth; I bite a piece out of the moon and hurry the seasons; I shake myself and crumble the mountains! Contemplate me through leather—*don't* use the naked eye! I'm the man with a petrified heart and biler-iron bowels! The massacre of iso-lated communities is the pastime of my idle moments, the destruction of nationalities the serious business of my life! The boundless vastness of the great American desert is my inclosed property, and I bury my dead on my own premises!" He jumped up and cracked his heels together three times before

7. Outdo, overpower.
8. Twain here immortalizes the ritual boasting of the "ring-tailed roarers," chiefly associated with Kentucky but familiar both in the oral traditions of the frontier and in the writings of the southwestern humorists, in whose tradition Twain follows.

he lit (they cheered him again), and as he come down he shouted out: "Whoo-oop! bow your neck and spread, for the Pet Child of Calamity's a-coming!"

Then the other one went to swelling around and blowing again—the first one—the one they called Bob; next, the Child of Calamity chipped in again, bigger than ever; then they both got at it at the same time, swelling round and round each other and punching their fists most into each other's faces, and whooping and jawing like Injuns; then Bob called the Child names, and the Child called him names back again; next, Bob called him a heap rougher names, and the Child come back at him with the very worst kind of language; next, Bob knocked the Child's hat off, and the Child picked it up and kicked Bob's ribbony hat about six foot; Bob went and got it and said never mind, this warn't going to be the last of this thing, because he was a man that never forgot and never forgive, and so the Child better look out, for there was a time a-coming, just as sure as he was a living man, that he would have to answer to him with the best blood in his body. The Child said no man was willinger than he for that time to come, and he would give Bob fair warning, *now*, never to cross his path again, for he could never rest till he had waded in his blood, for such was his nature, though he was sparing him now on account of his family, if he had one.

Both of them was edging away in different directions, growling and shaking their heads and going on about what they was going to do; but a little black-whiskered chap skipped up and says:

"Come back here, you couple of chicken-livered cowards, and I'll thrash the two of ye!"

And he done it, too. He snatched them, he jerked them his way and that, he booted them around, he knocked them sprawling faster than they could get up. Why, it warn't two minutes till they begged like dogs—and how the other lot did yell and laugh and clap their hands all the way through, and shout "Sail in, Corpse-Maker!" "Hit at him again, Child of Calamity!" "Bully for you, little Davy!" Well, it was a perfect pow-wow for a while. Bob and the Child had red noses and black eyes when they got through. Little Davy made them own up that they were sneaks and cowards and not fit to eat with a dog or drink with a nigger; then Bob and the Child shook hands with each other, very solemn, and said they had always respected each other and was willing to let bygones be bygones. So then they washed their faces in the river; and just then there was a loud order to stand by for a crossing, and some of them went forward to man the sweeps there, and the rest went aft to handle the after sweeps.

I laid still and waited for fifteen minutes, and had a smoke out of a pipe that one of them left in reach; then the crossing was finished, and they stumped back and had a drink around and went to talking and singing again. Next they got out an old fiddle, and one played, and another patted juba, and the rest turned themselves loose on a regular old-fashioned keelboat break-down.[9] They couldn't keep that up very long without getting winded, so by and by they settled around the jug again.

They sung "Jolly, Jolly Raftsman's the Life for Me," with a rousing chorus, and then they got to talking about differences betwixt hogs, and their differ-

9. As the name suggests, a wild dance with a rapid rhythm. The "juba" is a strongly rhythmical dance that originated among southern blacks about 1830; to "pat a juba" would be to clap the hands or tap the feet to make the rhythm.

ent kind of habits, and next about women and their different ways; and next about the best ways to put out houses that was afire; and next about what ought to be done with the Injuns; and next about what a king had to do, and how much he got; and next about how to make cats fight; and next about what to do when a man has fits; and next about differences betwixt clear-water rivers and muddy-water ones. The man they called Ed said the muddy Mississippi water was wholesomer to drink than the clear water of the Ohio; he said if you let a pint of this yaller Mississippi water settle, you would have about a half to three-quarters of an inch of mud in the bottom, according to the stage of the river, and then it warn't no better than Ohio water—what you wanted to do was to keep it stirred up—and when the river was low, keep mud on hand to put in and thicken the water up the way it ought to be.

The Child of Calamity said that was so; he said there was nutritiousness in the mud, and a man that drunk Mississippi water could grow corn in his stomach if he wanted to. He says:

"You look at the graveyards; that tells the tale. Trees won't grow worth shucks in a Cincinnati graveyard, but in a Sent Louis graveyard they grow upwards of eight hundred foot high. It's all on account of the water the people drunk before they laid up. A Cincinnati corpse don't richen a soil any."

And they talked about how Ohio water didn't like to mix with Mississippi water. Ed said if you take the Mississippi on a rise when the Ohio is low, you'll find a wide band of clear water all the way down the east side of the Mississippi for a hundred miles or more, and the minute you get out a quarter of a mile from shore and pass the line, it is all thick and yaller the rest of the way across. Then they talked about how to keep tobacco from getting moldy, and from that they went into ghosts and told about a lot that other folks had seen; but Ed says:

"Why don't you tell something that you've seen yourselves? Now let me have a say. Five years ago I was on a raft as big as this, and right along here it was a bright moonshiny night, and I was on watch and boss of the stabboard oar forrard, and one of my pards was a man named Dick Allbright, and he come along to where I was sitting, forrard—gaping and stretching, he was—and stooped down on the edge of the raft and washed his face in the river, and come and set down by me and got out his pipe, and had just got it filled, when he looks up and says:

" 'Why looky-here,' he says, 'ain't that Buck Miller's place, over yander in the bend?'

" 'Yes,' says I, 'it is—why?' He laid his pipe down and leaned his head on his hand, and says:

" 'I thought we'd be furder down.' I says:

" 'I thought it, too, when I went off watch'—we was standing six hours on and six off—'but the boys told me,' I says, 'that the raft didn't seem to hardly move, for the last hour,' says I, 'though she's a-slipping along all right now,' says I. He give a kind of a groan, and says:

" 'I've seed a raft act so before, along here,' he says. 'Pears to me the current has most quit above the head of this bend durin' the last two years,' he says.

"Well, he raised up two or three times, and looked away off and around on the water. That started me at it, too. A body is always doing what he sees somebody else doing, though there mayn't be no sense in it. Pretty soon I see a black something floating on the water away off to stabboard and quartering behind us. I see he was looking at it, too. I says:

" 'What's that?' He says, sort of pettish:

" ' 'Tain't nothing but an old empty bar'l.'

" 'An empty bar'l!' says I, 'why,' says I, 'a spy-glass is a fool to *your* eyes. How can you tell it's an empty bar'l?' He says:

" 'I don't know; I reckon it ain't a bar'l, but I thought it might be,' says he.

" 'Yes,' I says, 'so it might be, and it might be anything else too; a body can't tell nothing about it, such a distance as that,' I says.

"We hadn't nothing else to do, so we kept on watching it. By and by I says:

" 'Why, looky-here, Dick Allbright, that thing's a-gaining on us, I believe.'

"He never said nothing. The thing gained and gained, and I judged it must be a dog that was about tired out. Well, we swung down into the crossing, and the thing floated across the bright streak of the moonshine, and by George, it *was* a bar'l. Says I:

" 'Dick Allbright, what made you think that thing was a bar'l, when it was half a mile off?' says I. Says he:

" 'I don't know.' Says I:

" 'You tell me, Dick Allbright.' Says he:

" 'Well, I knowed it was a bar'l; I've seen it before; lots has seen it; they says it's a ha'nted bar'l.'

"I called the rest of the watch, and they come and stood there, and I told them what Dick said. It floated right along abreast, now, and didn't gain any more. It was about twenty foot off. Some was for having it aboard, but the rest didn't want to. Dick Allbright said rafts that had fooled with it had got bad luck by it. The captain of the watch said he didn't believe in it. He said he reckoned the bar'l gained on us because it was in a little better current than what we was. He said it would leave by and by.

"So then we went to talking about other things, and we had a song, and then a breakdown; and after that the captain of the watch called for another song; but it was clouding up now, and the bar'l stuck right thar in the same place, and the song didn't seem to have much warm-up to it, somehow, and so they didn't finish it, and there warn't any cheers, but it sort of dropped flat, and nobody said anything for a minute. Then everybody tried to talk at once, and one chap got off a joke, but it warn't no use, they didn't laugh, and even the chap that made the joke didn't laugh at it, which ain't usual. We all just settled down glum, and watched the bar'l, and was oneasy and oncomfortable. Well, sir, it shut down black and still, and then the wind began to moan around, and next the lightning began to play and the thunder to grumble. And pretty soon there was a regular storm, and in the middle of it a man that was running aft stumbled and fell and sprained his ankle so that he had to lay up. This made the boys shake their heads. And every time the lightning come, there was that bar'l, with the blue lights winking around it. We was always on the lookout for it. But by and by, toward dawn, she was gone. When the day come we couldn't see her anywhere, and we warn't sorry, either.

"But next night about half-past nine, when there was songs and high jinks going on, here she comes again, and took her old roost on the stabboard side. There warn't no more high jinks. Everybody got solemn; nobody talked; you couldn't get anybody to do anything but set around moody and look at the bar'l. It begun to cloud up again. When the watch changed, the off watch stayed up, 'stead of turning in. The storm ripped and roared around all night, and in the middle of it another man tripped and sprained his ankle, and had to knock off. The bar'l left toward day, and nobody see it go.

"Everybody was sober and down in the mouth all day. I don't mean the kind of sober that comes of leaving liquor alone—not that. They was quiet, but they all drunk more than usual—not together, but each man sidled off and took it private, by himself.

"After dark the off watch didn't turn in; nobody sung, nobody talked; the boys didn't scatter around, neither; they sort of huddled together, forrard; and for two hours they set there, perfectly still, looking steady in the one direction, and heaving a sigh once in a while. And then, here comes the bar'l again. She took up her old place. She stayed there all night; nobody turned in. The storm come on again, after midnight. It got awful dark; the rain poured down; hail, too; the thunder boomed and roared and bellowed; the wind blowed a hurricane; and the lightning spread over everything in big sheets of glare, and showed the whole raft as plain as day; and the river lashed up white as milk as far as you could see for miles, and there was that bar'l jiggering along, same as ever. The captain ordered the watch to man the after sweeps for a crossing, and nobody would go—no more sprained ankles for them, they said. They wouldn't even *walk* aft. Well, then, just then the sky split wide open, with a crash, and the lightning killed two men of the after watch, and crippled two more. Crippled them how, say you? Why, *sprained their ankles!*

"The bar'l left in the dark betwixt lightnings, toward dawn. Well, not a body eat a bite at breakfast that morning. After that the men loafed around, in twos and threes, and talked low together. But none of them herded with Dick Allbright. They all give him the cold shake. If he come around where any of the men was, they split up and sidled away. They wouldn't man the sweeps with him. The captain had all the skiffs hauled up on the raft, alongside of his wigwam, and wouldn't let the dead men be took ashore to be planted; he didn't believe a man that got ashore would come back: and he was right.

"After night come, you could see pretty plain that there was going to be trouble if that bar'l come again; there was such a muttering going on. A good many wanted to kill Dick Allbright, because he'd seen the bar'l on other trips, and that had an ugly look. Some wanted to put him ashore. Some said: 'Let's all go ashore in a pile, if the bar'l comes again.'

"This kind of whispers was still going on, the men being bunched together forrard watching for the bar'l, when lo and behold you! here she comes again. Down she comes, slow and steady, and settles into her old tracks. You could 'a' heard a pin drop. Then up comes the captain, and says:

" 'Boys, don't be a pack of children and fools; I don't want this bar'l to be dogging us all the way to Orleans, and *you* don't: Well, then, how's the best way to stop it? Burn it up—that's the way. I'm going to fetch it aboard,' he says. And before anybody could say a word, in he went.

"He swum to it, and as he come pushing it to the raft, the men spread to one side. But the old man got it aboard and busted in the head, and there was a baby in it! Yes, sir; a stark-naked baby. It was Dick Allbright's baby; he owned up and said so.

" 'Yes,' he says, a-leaning over it, 'yes, it is my own lamented darling, my poor lost Charles William Allbright deceased,' says he—for he could curl his tongue around the bulliest words in the language when he was a mind to, and lay them before you without a jint started anywheres.[1] Yes, he said, he used to live up at the head of this bend, and one night he choked his child, which was crying, not intending to kill it—which was prob'ly a lie—and then he was scared, and buried it in a bar'l, before his wife got home, and off he went, and struck the northern trail and went to rafting; and this was the third year that the bar'l had chased him. He said the bad luck always begun light, and lasted till four men was killed, and then the bar'l didn't come any more after that. He said if the men would stand it one more night—and was a-going on like that—but the men had got enough. They started to get out a boat to take him ashore and lynch him, but he grabbed the little child all of a sudden and jumped overboard with it, hugged up to his breast and shedding tears, and we never see him again in this life, poor old suffering soul, nor Charles William neither."

"*Who* was shedding tears?" says Bob; "was it Allbright or the baby?"

"Why, Allbright, of course; didn't I tell you the baby was dead? Been dead three years—how could it cry?"

"Well, never mind how it could cry—how could it *keep* all that time?" says Davy. "You answer me that."

"I don't know how it done it," says Ed. "It done it, though—that's all I know about it."

"Say—what did they do with the bar'l?" says the Child of Calamity.

"Why, they hove it overboard, and it sunk like a chunk of lead."

"Edward, did the child look like it was choked?" says one.

"Did it have its hair parted?" says another.

"What was the brand on that bar'l, Eddy?" says a fellow they called Bill.

"Have you got the papers for them statistics, Edmund?" says Jimmy.

"Say, Edwin, was you one of the men that was killed by the lightning?" says Davy.

"Hm? Oh, no! he was both of 'em," says Bob. Then they all haw-hawed.

"Say, Edward, don't you reckon you'd better take a pill? You look bad—don't you feel pale?" says the Child of Calamity.

"Oh, come now, Eddy," says Jimmy, "show up; you must 'a' kept part of that bar'l to prove the thing by. Show us the bung-hole—*do*—and we'll all believe you."

"Say, boys," says Bill, "less divide it up. Thar's thirteen of us. I can swaller a thirteenth of the yarn, if you can worry down the rest."

Ed got up mad and said they could all go to some place which he ripped out pretty savage, and then walked off aft, cussing to himself, and they yelling and jeering at him, and roaring and laughing so you could hear them a mile.

"Boys, we'll split a watermelon on that," says the Child of Calamity; and he came rummaging around in the dark amongst the shingle bundles where I was, and put his hand on me. I was warm and soft and naked; so he says "Ouch!" and jumped back.

"Fetch a lantern or a chunk of fire here, boys—there's a snake here as big as a cow!"

So they run there with a lantern, and crowded up and looked in on me.

"Come out of that, you beggar!" says one.

---

1. Without cracking open joints; i.e., perfectly smoothly and eloquently.

"Who are you?" says another.

"What are you after here? Speak up prompt, or overboard you go."

"Snake him out, boys. Snatch him out by the heels."

I began to beg, and crept out amongst them trembling. They looked me over, wondering, and the Child of Calamity says:

"A cussed thief! Lend a hand and less heave him overboard!"

"No," says Big Bob, "less get out the paint-pot and paint him a sky-blue all over from head to heel, and *then* heave him over."

"Good! that's it. Go for the paint, Jimmy."

When the paint come, and Bob took the brush and was just going to begin, the others laughing and rubbing their hands. I begun to cry, and that sort of worked on Davy, and he says:

" 'Vast there. He's nothing but a cub. I'll paint the man that teches him!"

So I looked around on them, and some of them grumbled and growled, and Bob put down the paint, and the others didn't take it up.

"Come here to the fire, and less see what you're up to here," says Davy. "Now set down there and give an account of yourself. How long have you been aboard here?"

"Not over a quarter of a minute, sir," says I.

"How did you get dry so quick?"

"I don't know, sir. I'm always that way, mostly."

"Oh, you are, are you? What's your name?"

I warn't going to tell my name. I didn't know what to say, so I just says:

"Charles William Allbright, sir."

Then they roared—the whole crowd; and I was mighty glad I said that, because, maybe, laughing would get them in a better humor.

When they got done laughing, Davy says:

"It won't hardly do, Charles William. You couldn't have growed this much in five year, and you was a baby when you come out of the bar'l, you know, and dead at that. Come, now, tell a straight story, and nobody'll hurt you, if you ain't up to anything wrong. What is your name?"

"Aleck Hopkins, sir. Aleck James Hopkins."

"Well, Aleck, where did you come from, here?"

"From a trading-scow. She lays up the bend yonder. I was born on her. Pap has traded up and down here all his life; and he told me to swim off here, because when you went by he said he would like to get some of you to speak to a Mr. Jonas Turner, in Cairo, and tell him—"

"Oh, come!"

"Yes, sir, it's as true as the world. Pap he says—"

"Oh, your grandmother!"

They all laughed, and I tried again to talk, but they broke in on me and stopped me.

"Now, looky-here," says Davy; "you're scared, and so you talk wild. Honest, now, do you live in a scow, or is it a lie?"

"Yes, sir, in a trading-scow. She lays up at the head of the bend. But I warn't born in her. It's our first trip."

"Now you're talking! What did you come aboard here for? To steal?"

"No sir, I didn't. It was only to get a ride on the raft. All boys does that."

"Well, I know that. But what did you hide for?"

"Sometimes they drive the boys off."

"So they do. They might steal. Looky-here; if we let you off this time, will you keep out of these kind of scrapes hereafter?"

" 'Deed I will, boss. You try me."

"All right, then. You ain't but little ways from shore. Overboard with you, and don't you make a fool of yourself another time this way. Blast it, boy, some raftsmen would rawhide you till you were black and blue!"

I didn't wait to kiss good-by, but went overboard and broke for shore. When Jim come along by and by, the big raft was away out of sight around the point. I swum out and got aboard, and was mighty glad to see home again.[2]

There warn't nothing to do, now, but to look out sharp for the town, and not pass it without seeing it. He said he'd be mighty sure to see it, because he'd be a free man the minute he seen it, but if he missed it he'd be in the slave country again and no more show for freedom. Every little while he jumps up and says:

"Dah she is!"

But it warn't. It was Jack-o-lanterns, or lightning-bugs; so he set down again, and went to watching, same as before. Jim said it made him all over trembly and feverish to be so close to freedom. Well, I can tell you it made me all over trembly and feverish, too, to hear him, because I begun to get it through my head that he *was* most free—and who was to blame for it? Why, *me*. I couldn't get that out of my conscience, no how nor no way. It got to troubling me so I couldn't rest; I couldn't stay still in one place. It hadn't ever come home to me before, what this thing was that I was doing. But now it did; and it staid with me, and scorched me more and more. I tried to make out to myself that *I* warn't to blame, because I didn't run Jim off from his rightful owner; but it warn't no use, conscience up and says, every time, "But you knowed he was running for his freedom, and you could a paddled ashore and told somebody." That was so—I couldn't get around that, noway. That was where it pinched. Conscience says to me, "What had poor Miss Watson done to you, that you could see her nigger go off right under your eyes and never say one single word? What did that poor old woman do to you, that you could treat her so mean? Why, she tried to learn you your book, she tried to learn you your manners, she tried to be good to you every way she knowed how. *That's* what she done."

I got to feeling so mean and so miserable I most wished I was dead. I fidgeted up and down the raft, abusing myself to myself, and Jim was fidgeting up and down past me. We neither of us could keep still. Every time he danced around and says, "Dah's Cairo!" it went through me like a shot, and I thought if it *was* Cairo I reckoned I would die of miserableness.

Jim talked out loud all the time while I was talking to myself. He was saying how the first thing he would do when he got to a free State he would go to saving up money and never spend a single cent, and when he got enough he would buy his wife, which was owned on a farm close to where Miss Watson lived; and then they would both work to buy the two children, and if their master wouldn't sell them, they'd get an Ab'litionist to go and steal them.

It most froze me to hear such talk. He wouldn't ever dared to talk such talk in his life before. Just see what a difference it made in him the minute he

2. End of the interpolated passage.

judged he was about free. It was according to the old saying, "give a nigger an inch and he'll take an ell." Thinks I, this is what comes of my not thinking. Here was this nigger which I had as good as helped to run away, coming right out flat-footed and saying he would steal his children—children that belonged to a man I didn't even know; a man that hadn't ever done me no harm.

I was sorry to hear Jim say that, it was such a lowering of him. My conscience got to stirring me up hotter than ever, until at last I says to it, "Let up on me—it ain't too late, yet—I'll paddle ashore at the first light, and tell." I felt easy, and happy, and light as a feather, right off. All my troubles was gone. I went to looking out sharp for a light, and sort of singing to myself. By-and-by one showed. Jim sings out:

"We's safe, Huck, we's safe! Jump up and crack yo' heels, dat's de good ole Cairo at las', I jis knows it!"

I says:

"I'll take the canoe and go see, Jim. It mightn't be, you know."

He jumped and got the canoe ready, and put his old coat in the bottom for me to set on, and give me the paddle; and as I shoved off, he says:

"Pooty soon I'll be a-shout'n for joy, en I'll say, it's all on accounts o' Huck; I's a free man, en I couldn't ever ben free ef it hadn' ben for Huck; Huck done it. Jim won't ever forgit you, Huck; you's de bes' fren' Jim's ever had; en you's de *only* fren' ole Jim's got now."

I was paddling off, all in a sweat to tell on him; but when he says this, it seemed to kind of take the tuck all out of me. I went along slow then, and I warn't right down certain whether I was glad I started or whether I warn't. When I was fifty yards off, Jim says:

"Dah you goes, de ole true Huck; de on'y white genlman dat ever kep' his promise to ole Jim."

Well, I just felt sick. But I says, I *got* to do it—I can't get *out* of it. Right then, along comes a skiff with two men in it, with guns, and they stopped and I stopped. One of them says:

"What's that, yonder?"

"A piece of raft," I says.

"Do you belong on it?"

"Yes, sir."

"Any men on it?"

"Only one, sir."

"Well, there's five niggers run off to-night, up yonder above the head of the bend. Is your man white or black?"

I didn't answer up prompt. I tried to, but the words wouldn't come. I tried, for a second or two, to brace up and out with it, but I warn't man enough—hadn't the spunk of a rabbit. I see I was weakening; so I just give up trying, and up and says—

"He's white."

"I reckon we'll go and see for ourselves."

"I wish you would," says I, "because it's pap that's there, and maybe you'd help me tow the raft ashore where the light is. He's sick—and so is mam and Mary Ann."

"Oh, the devil! we're in a hurry, boy. But I s'pose we've got to. Come—buckle to your paddle, and let's get along."

I buckled to my paddle and they laid to their oars. When we had made a stroke or two, I says:

"Pap'll be mighty much obleeged to you, I can tell you. Everybody goes away when I want them to help me tow the raft ashore, and I can't do it myself."

"Well, that's infernal mean. Odd, too. Say, boy, what's the matter with your father?"

"It's the—a—the—well, it ain't anything, much."

They stopped pulling. It warn't but a mighty little ways to the raft, now. One says:

"Boy, that's a lie. What *is* the matter with your pap? Answer up square, now, and it'll be the better for you."

"I will, sir, I will, honest—but don't leave us, please. It's the—the—gentlemen, if you'll only pull ahead, and let me heave you the head-line you won't have to come a-near the raft—please do."

"Set her back, John, set her back!" says one. They backed water. "Keep away, boy—keep to looard.[3] Confound it, I just expect the wind has blowed it to us. Your pap's got the small-pox,[4] and you know it precious well. Why didn't you come out and say so? Do you want to spread it all over?"

"Well," says I, a-blubbering, "I've told everybody before, and then they just went away and left us."

"Poor devil, there's something in that. We are right down sorry for you, but we—well, hang it, we don't want the small-pox, you see. Look here, I'll tell you what to do. Don't you try to land by yourself, or you'll smash everything to pieces. You float along down about twenty miles and you'll come to a town on the left-hand side of the river. It will be long after sun-up, then, and when you ask for help, you tell them your folks are all down with chills and fever. Don't be a fool again, and let people guess what is the matter. Now we're trying to do you a kindness; so you just put twenty miles between us, that's a good boy. It wouldn't do any good to land yonder where the light is—it's only a wood-yard. Say—I reckon your father's poor, and I'm bound to say he's in pretty hard luck. Here—I'll put a twenty dollar gold piece on this board, and you get it when it floats by. I feel mighty mean to leave you, but my kingdom! it won't do to fool with small-pox, don't you see?"

"Hold on, Parker," says the other man, "here's a twenty to put on the board for me. Good-bye boy, you do as Mr. Parker told you, and you'll be all right."

"That's so, my boy—good-bye, good-bye. If you see any runaway niggers, you get help and nab them, and you can make some money by it."

"Good-bye, sir," says I, "I won't let no runaway niggers get by me if I can help it."

They went off, and I got aboard the raft, feeling bad and low, because I knowed very well I had done wrong, and I see it warn't no use for me to try to learn to do right; a body that don't get *started* right when he's little, ain't got no show—when the pinch comes there ain't nothing to back him up and keep him to his work, and so he gets beat. Then I thought a minute, and says to myself, hold on,—s'pose you'd a done right and give Jim up; would you felt better than what you do now? No, says I, I'd feel bad—I'd feel just the same way I do now. Well, then, says I, what's the use you learning to do right, when it's

<hr />

3. I.e., leeward.   4. A highly infectious, often fatal disease.

troublesome to do right and ain't no trouble to do wrong, and the wages is just the same? I was stuck. I couldn't answer that. So I reckoned I wouldn't bother no more about it, but after this always do whichever come handiest at the time.

I went into the wigwam; Jim warn't there. I looked all around; he warn't anywhere. I says:

"Jim!"

"Here I is, Huck. Is dey out o' sight yit? Don't talk loud."

He was in the river, under the stern oar, with just his nose out. I told him they was out of sight, so he come aboard. He says:

"I was a-listenin' to all de talk, en I slips into de river en was gwyne to shove for sho' if dey come aboard. Den I was gwyne to swim to de raf' agin when dey was gone. But lawsy, how you did fool 'em, Huck! Dat *wuz* de smartes' dodge! I tell you, chile, I 'speck it save' ole Jim—ole Jim ain' gwyne to forgit you for dat, honey."

Then we talked about the money. It was a pretty good raise, twenty dollars apiece. Jim said we could take deck passage on a steamboat now, and the money would last us as far as we wanted to go in the free States. He said twenty mile more warn't far for the raft to go, but he wished we was already there.

Towards daybreak we tied up, and Jim was mighty particular about hiding the raft good. Then he worked all day fixing things in bundles, and getting all ready to quit rafting.

That night about ten we hove in sight of the lights of a town away down in a left-hand bend.

I went off in the canoe, to ask about it. Pretty soon I found a man out in the river with a skiff, setting a trot-line. I ranged up and says:

"Mister, is that town Cairo?"

"Cairo? no. You must be a blame' fool."

"What town is it, mister?"

"If you want to know, go and find out. If you stay here botherin' around me for about a half a minute longer, you'll get something you won't want."

I paddled to the raft. Jim was awful disappointed, but I said never mind, Cairo would be the next place, I reckoned.

We passed another town before daylight, and I was going out again; but it was high ground, so I didn't go. No high ground about Cairo, Jim said. I had forgot it. We laid up for the day, on a tow-head tolerable close to the left-hand bank. I begun to suspicion something. So did Jim. I says:

"Maybe we went by Cairo in the fog that night."

He says:

"Doan' less' talk about it, Huck. Po' niggers can't have no luck. I awluz 'spected dat rattle-snake skin warn't done wid it's work."

"I wish I'd never seen that snake-skin, Jim—I do wish I'd never laid eyes on it."

"It ain't yo' fault, Huck; you didn't know. Don't you blame yo'sef 'bout it."

When it was daylight, here was the clear Ohio water in shore, sure enough, and outside was the old regular Muddy! So it was all up with Cairo.[5]

5. Because Cairo is located at the confluence of the Ohio and Mississippi rivers, which in turn lies below the confluence of the Missouri (Big Muddy) and Mississippi, they know that they have passed Cairo and lost the opportunity to sell the raft and travel up the Ohio by steamboat to freedom.

We talked it all over. It wouldn't do to take to the shore; we couldn't take the raft up the stream, of course. There warn't no way but to wait for dark, and start back in the canoe and take the chances. So we slept all day amongst the cotton-wood thicket, so as to be fresh for the work, and when we went back to the raft about dark the canoe was gone!

We didn't say a word for a good while. There warn't anything to say. We both knowed well enough it was some more work of the rattle-snake skin; so what was the use to talk about it? It would only look like we was finding fault, and that would be bound to fetch more bad luck—and keep on fetching it, too, till we knowed enough to keep still.

By-and-by we talked about what we better do, and found there warn't no way but just to go along down with the raft till we got a chance to buy a canoe to go back in. We warn't going to borrow it when there warn't anybody around, the way pap would do, for that might set people after us.

So we shoved out, after dark, on the raft.[6]

Anybody that don't believe yet, that it's foolishness to handle a snake-skin, after all that that snake-skin done for us, will believe it now, if they read on and see what more it done for us.

The place to buy canoes is off of rafts laying up at shore. But we didn't see no rafts laying up; so we went along during three hours and more. Well, the night got gray, and ruther thick, which is the next meanest thing to fog. You can't tell the shape of the river, and you can't see no distance. It got to be very late and still, and then along comes a steamboat up the river. We lit the lantern, and judged she would see it. Up-stream boats didn't generly come close to us; they go out and follow the bars and hunt for easy water under the reefs; but nights like this they bull right up the channel against the whole river.

We could hear her pounding along, but we didn't see her good till she was close. She aimed right for us. Often they do that and try to see how close they can come without touching; sometimes the wheel bites off a sweep, and then the pilot sticks his head out and laughs, and thinks he's mighty smart. Well, here she comes, and we said she was going to try to shave us; but she didn't seem to be sheering off a bit. She was a big one, and she was coming in a hurry, too, looking like a black cloud with rows of glow-worms around it; but all of a sudden she bulged out, big and scary, with a long row of wide-open furnace doors shining like red-hot teeth, and her monstrous bows and guards hanging right over us. There was a yell at us, and a jingling of bells to stop the engines, a pow-wow of cussing, and whistling of steam—and as Jim went overboard on one side and I on the other, she come smashing straight through the raft.

I dived—and I aimed to find the bottom, too, for a thirty-foot wheel had got to go over me, and I wanted it to have plenty of room. I could always stay under water a minute; this time I reckon I staid under water a minute and a

---

6. Twain was "stuck" at this point in the writing of the novel and put the 400-page manuscript aside for approximately three years. In the winter of 1879–80 he added the two chapters dealing with the feud (XVII and XVIII) and then the three chapters (XIX–XXI) in which the king and duke enter the story and for a time dominate the action. The novel was not completed until 1883, when Twain wrote the last half of it in a few months of concentrated work. As late as 1882, he was not confident he would ever complete the book. See Walter Blair, *Mark Twain and "Huck Finn"* (1960); Victor Doyno, *Writing "Huck Finn": Mark Twain's Creative Process* (1991); and Doyno's Foreword and Textual Addendum to the 1996 Random House edition of *Adventures of Huckleberry Finn*.

half. Then I bounced for the top in a hurry, for I was nearly busting. I popped out to my arm-pits and blowed the water out of my nose, and puffed a bit. Of course there was a booming current; and of course that boat started her engines again ten seconds after she stopped them, for they never cared much for raftsmen; so now she was churning along up the river, out of sight in the thick weather, though I could hear her.

I sung out for Jim about a dozen times, but I didn't get any answer; so I grabbed a plank that touched me while I was "treading water," and struck out for shore, shoving it ahead of me. But I made out to see that the drift of the current was towards the left-hand shore,[7] which meant that I was in a crossing; so I changed off and went that way.

It was one of these long, slanting, two-mile crossings; so I was a good long time in getting over. I made a safe landing, and clum up the bank. I couldn't see but a little ways, but I went poking along over rough ground for a quarter of a mile or more, and then I run across a big old-fashioned double log house before I noticed it. I was going to rush by and get away, but a lot of dogs jumped out and went to howling and barking at me, and I knowed better than to move another peg.

Chapter XVII

In about half a minute somebody spoke out of a window, without putting his head out, and says:

"Be done, boys! Who's there?"

I says:

"It's me."

"Who's me?"

"George Jackson, sir."

"What do you want?"

"I don't want nothing, sir. I only want to go along by, but the dogs won't let me."

"What are you prowling around here this time of night, for—hey?"

"I warn't prowling around, sir; I fell overboard off of the steamboat."

"Oh, you did, did you? Strike a light there, somebody. What did you say your name was?"

"George Jackson, sir. I'm only a boy."

"Look here; if you're telling the truth, you needn't be afraid—nobody'll hurt you. But don't try to budge; stand right where you are. Rouse our Bob and Tom, some of you, and fetch the guns. George Jackson, is there anybody with you?"

"No, sir, nobody."

I heard the people stirring around in the house, now, and see a light. The man sung out:

"Snatch that light away, Betsy, you old fool—ain't you got any sense? Put it on the floor behind the front door. Bob, if you and Tom are ready, take your places."

"All ready."

"Now, George Jackson, do you know the Shepherdsons?"

7. Kentucky, where the feud in Chs. XVII and XVIII is set.

"No, sir—I never heard of them."

"Well, that may be so, and it mayn't. Now, all ready. Step forward, George Jackson. And mind, don't you hurry—come mighty slow. If there's anybody with you, let him keep back—if he shows himself he'll be shot. Come along, now. Come slow; push the door open, yourself—just enough to squeeze in, d' you hear?"

I didn't hurry, I couldn't if I'd a wanted to. I took one slow step at a time, and there warn't a sound, only I thought I could hear my heart. The dogs were as still as the humans, but they followed a little behind me. When I got to the three log door-steps, I heard them unlocking and unbarring and unbolting. I put my hand on the door and pushed it a little and a little more, till somebody said, "There, that's enough—put your head in." I done it, but I judged they would take it off.

The candle was on the floor, and there they all was, looking at me, and me at them, for about a quarter of a minute. Three big men with guns pointed at me, which made me wince, I tell you; the oldest, gray and about sixty, the other two thirty or more—all of them fine and handsome—and the sweetest old gray-headed lady, and back of her two young women which I couldn't see right well. The old gentleman says:

"There—I reckon it's all right. Come in."

As soon as I was in, the old gentleman he locked the door and barred it and bolted it, and told the young men to come in with their guns, and they all went in a big parlor that had a new rag carpet on the floor, and got together in a corner that was out of range of the front windows—there warn't none on the side. They held the candle, and took a good look at me, and all said, "Why *he* ain't a Shepherdson—no, there ain't any Shepherdson about him." Then the old man said he hoped I wouldn't mind being searched for arms, because he didn't mean no harm by it—it was only to make sure. So he didn't pry into my pockets, but only felt outside with his hands, and said it was all right. He told me to make myself easy and at home, and tell all about myself; but the old lady says:

"Why bless you, Saul, the poor thing's as wet as he can be; and don't you reckon it may be he's hungry?"

"True for you, Rachel—I forgot."

So the old lady says:

"Betsy" (this was a nigger woman), "you fly around and get him something to eat, as quick as you can, poor thing; and one of you girls go and wake up Buck and tell him—Oh, here he is himself. Buck, take this little stranger and get the wet clothes off from him and dress him up in some of yours that's dry."

Buck looked about as old as me—thirteen or fourteen[8] or along there, though he was a little bigger than me. He hadn't on anything but a shirt, and he was very frowsy-headed. He come in gaping and digging one fist into his eyes, and he was dragging a gun along with the other one. He says:

"Ain't they no Shepherdsons around?"

They said, no, 'twas a false alarm.

"Well," he says, "if they'd a ben some, I reckon I'd a got one."

They all laughed, and Bob says:

"Why, Buck, they might have scalped us all, you've been so slow in coming."

---

8. Twain identifies Huck as "a boy of 14" in a notebook.

"Well, nobody come after me, and it ain't right. I'm always kep' down; I don't get no show."

"Never mind, Buck, my boy," says the old man, "you'll have show enough, all in good time, don't you fret about that. Go 'long with you now, and do as your mother told you."

When we got up stairs to his room, he got me a coarse shirt and a round-about[9] and pants of his, and I put them on. While I was at it he asked me what my name was, but before I could tell him, he started to telling me about a blue jay and a young rabbit he had catched in the woods day before yesterday, and he asked me where Moses was when the candle went out. I said I didn't know; I hadn't heard about it before, no way.

"Well, guess," he says.

"How'm I going to guess," says I, "when I never heard tell about it before?"

"But you can guess, can't you? It's just as easy."

"*Which* candle?" I says.

"Why, any candle," he says.

"I don't know where he was," says I; "where was he?"

"Why he was in the *dark!* That's where he was!"

"Well, if you knowed where he was, what did you ask me for?"

"Why, blame it, it's a riddle, don't you see? Say, how long are you going to stay here? You got to stay always. We can just have booming times—they don't have no school now. Do you own a dog? I've got a dog—and he'll go in the river and bring out chips that you throw in. Do you like to comb up, Sundays, and all that kind of foolishness? You bet I don't, but ma she makes me. Confound these ole britches, I reckon I'd better put 'em on, but I'd ruther not, it's so warm. Are you all ready? All right—come along, old hoss."

Cold corn-pone, cold corn-beef, butter and butter-milk—that is what they had for me down there, and there ain't nothing better that ever I've come across yet. Buck and his ma and all of them smoked cob pipes, except the nigger woman, which was gone, and the two young women. They all smoked and talked, and I eat and talked. The young women had quilts around them, and their hair down their backs. They all asked me questions, and I told them how pap and me and all the family was living on a little farm down at the bottom of Arkansaw, and my sister Mary Ann run off and got married and never was heard of no more, and Bill went to hunt them and he warn't heard of no more, and Tom and Mort died, and then there warn't nobody but just me and pap left, and he was just trimmed down to nothing, on account of his troubles; so when he died I took what there was left, because the farm didn't belong to us, and started up the river, deck passage, and fell overboard; and that was how I come to be here. So they said I could have a home there as long as I wanted it. Then it was most daylight, and everybody went to bed, and I went to bed with Buck, and when I waked up in the morning, drat it all, I had forgot what my name was. So I laid there about an hour trying to think and when Buck waked up, I says:

"Can you spell, Buck?"

"Yes," he says.

"I bet you can't spell my name," says I.

"I bet you what you dare I can," says he.

"All right," says I, "go ahead."

9. Short, close-fitting jacket.

"G-o-r-g-e J-a-x-o-n—there now," he says.

"Well," says I, "you done it, but I didn't think you could. It ain't no slouch of a name to spell—right off without studying."

I set it down, private, because somebody might want *me* to spell it, next, and so I wanted to be handy with it and rattle it off like I was used to it.

It was a mighty nice family, and a mighty nice house, too. I hadn't seen no house out in the country before that was so nice and had so much style.[1] It didn't have an iron latch on the front door, nor a wooden one with a buckskin string, but a brass knob to turn, the same as houses in a town. There warn't no bed in the parlor, not a sign of a bed; but heaps of parlors in towns has beds in them. There was a big fireplace that was bricked on the bottom, and the bricks was kept clean and red by pouring water on them and scrubbing them with another brick; sometimes they washed them over with red water-paint that they call Spanish-brown, same as they do in town. They had big brass dog-irons that could hold up a saw-log.[2] There was a clock on the middle of the mantel-piece, with a picture of a town painted on the bottom half of the glass front, and a round place in the middle of it for the sun, and you could see the pendulum swing behind it. It was beautiful to hear that clock tick; and sometimes when one of these peddlers had been along and scoured her up and got her in good shape, she would start in and strike a hundred and fifty before she got tuckered out. They wouldn't took any money for her.

Well, there was a big outlandish parrot on each side of the clock, made out of something like chalk, and painted up gaudy. By one of the parrots was a cat made of crockery, and a crockery dog by the other; and when you pressed down on them they squeaked, but didn't open their mouths nor look different nor interested. They squeaked through underneath. There was a couple of big wild-turkey-wing fans spread out behind those things. On a table in the middle of the room was a kind of a lovely crockery basket that had apples and oranges and peaches and grapes piled up in it which was much redder and yellower and prettier than real ones is, but they warn't real because you could see where pieces had got chipped off and showed the white chalk or whatever it was, underneath.

This table had a cover made out of beautiful oil-cloth, with a red and blue spread-eagle painted on it, and a painted border all around. It come all the way from Philadelphia, they said. There was some books too, piled up perfectly exact, on each corner of the table. One was a big family Bible, full of pictures. One was "Pilgrim's Progress," about a man that left his family it didn't say why. I read considerable in it now and then. The statements was interesting, but tough. Another was "Friendship's Offering," full of beautiful stuff and poetry; but I didn't read the poetry. Another was Henry Clay's Speeches, and another was Dr. Gunn's Family Medicine, which told you all about what to do if a body was sick or dead. There was a Hymn Book, and a lot of other books.[3] And there was nice split-bottom chairs, and perfectly sound, too—not bagged down in the middle and busted, like an old basket.

They had pictures hung on the walls—mainly Washingtons and Lafayettes,

---

1. Every detail of the furniture, furnishing, and decorations as well as the dress, speech, manners, and mores of the Grangerford household is carefully selected to satirically epitomize pre–Civil War culture of the lower Mississippi Valley.
2. A log large enough to be sawed into planks.
3. The neatly stacked, unread books are meant to define the values and tastes of the time and place. The Bible, Bunyan's *Pilgrim's Progress*, and the hymn book establish Calvinistic piety. Clay's speeches suggest political orthodoxy. Gunn's *Domestic Medicine* suggests popular notions of science and medical practice. *Friendship's Offering* was a popular gift book.

and battles, and Highland Marys,[4] and one called "Signing the Declaration." There was some that they called crayons, which one of the daughters which was dead made her own self when she was only fifteen years old. They was different from any pictures I ever see before; blacker, mostly, than is common. One was a woman in a slim black dress, belted small under the armpits, with bulges like a cabbage in the middle of the sleeves, and a large black scoop-shovel bonnet with a black veil, and white slim ankles crossed about with black tape, and very wee black slippers, like a chisel, and she was leaning pensive on a tombstone on her right elbow, under a weeping willow, and her other hand hanging down her side holding a white handkerchief and a reticule, and underneath the picture it said "Shall I Never See Thee More Alas." Another one was a young lady with her hair all combed up straight to the top of her head, and knotted there in front of a comb like a chair-back, and she was crying into a handkerchief and had a dead bird laying on its back in her other hand with its heels up, and underneath the picture it said "I Shall Never Hear Thy Sweet Chirrup More Alas." There was one where a young lady was at a window looking up at the moon, and tears running down her cheeks; and she had an open letter in one hand with black sealing-wax showing on one edge of it, and she was mashing a locket with a chain to it against her mouth, and underneath the picture it said "And Art Thou Gone Yes Thou Art Gone Alas." These was all nice pictures, I reckon, but I didn't somehow seem to take to them, because if ever I was down a little, they always give me the fan-tods. Everybody was sorry she died, because she had laid out a lot more of these pictures to do, and a body could see by what she had done what they had lost. But I reckoned, that with her disposition, she was having a better time in the graveyard. She was at work on what they said was her greatest picture when she took sick, and every day and every night it was her prayer to be allowed to live till she got it done, but she never got the chance. It was a picture of a young woman in a long white gown, standing on the rail of a bridge all ready to jump off, with her hair all down her back, and looking up to the moon, with the tears running down her face, and she had two arms folded across her breast, and two arms stretched out in front, and two more reaching up towards the moon—and the idea was, to see which pair would look best and then scratch out all the other arms; but, as I was saying, she died before she got her mind made up, and now they kept this picture over the head of the bed in her room, and every time her birthday come they hung flowers on it. Other times it was hid with a little curtain. The young woman in the picture had a kind of a nice sweet face, but there was so many arms it made her look too spidery, seemed to me.

This young girl kept a scrap-book when she was alive, and used to paste obituaries and accidents and cases of patient suffering in it out of the *Presbyterian Observer*, and write poetry after them out of her own head. It was very good poetry.[5] This is what she wrote about a boy by the name of Stephen Dowling Bots that fell down a well and was drownded:

4. The pictures similarly typify the culture of the region in the 1840s and 1850s. "Highland Mary" depicts poet Robert Burns's first love, who died a few months after they met. He memorialized her in several poems, especially "To Mary in Heaven."
5. This parody derives in particular from two poems by "The Sweet Singer of Michigan," Julia A. Moore (1847–1920), whose sentimental poetry

was popular at the time Twain was writing *Huck Finn*. In one of the two poems, "Little Libbie," the heroine "was choken on a piece of beef." The graveyard and obituary (or "sadful") schools of popular poetry are much older and more widespread. See Walter Blair, *Mark Twain and "Huck Finn"* (1960).

ODE TO STEPHEN DOWLING BOTS, DEC'D

And did young Stephen sicken,
    And did young Stephen die?
And did the sad hearts thicken,
    And did the mourners cry?

No; such was not the fate of
    Young Stephen Dowling Bots;
Though sad hearts round him thickened,
    'Twas not from sickness' shots.

No whooping-cough did rack his frame,
    Nor measles drear, with spots;
Not these impaired the sacred name
    Of Stephen Dowling Bots.

Despised love struck not with woe
    That head of curly knots,
Nor stomach troubles laid him low,
    Young Stephen Dowling Bots.

O no. Then list with tearful eye,
    Whilst I his fate do tell.
His soul did from this cold world fly,
    By falling down a well.

They got him out and emptied him;
    Alas it was too late;
His spirit was gone for to sport aloft
    In the realms of the good and great.

If Emmeline Grangerford could make poetry like that before she was four-teen, there ain't no telling what she could a done by-and-by. Buck said she could rattle off poetry like nothing. She didn't ever have to stop to think. He said she would slap down a line, and if she couldn't find anything to rhyme with it she would just scratch it out and slap down another one, and go ahead. She warn't particular, she could write about anything you choose to give her to write about, just so it was sadful. Every time a man died, or a woman died, or a child died, she would be on hand with her "tribute" before he was cold. She called them tributes. The neighbors said it was the doctor first, then Emmeline, then the undertaker—the undertaker never got in ahead of Emmeline but once, and then she hung fire on a rhyme for the dead person's name, which was Whistler. She warn't ever the same, after that; she never complained, but she kind of pined away and did not live long. Poor thing, many's the time I made myself go up to the little room that used to be hers and get out her poor old scrapbook and read in it when her pictures had been aggravating me and I had soured on her a little. I liked all the family, dead ones and all, and warn't going to let anything come between us. Poor Emme-line made poetry about all the dead people when she was alive, and it didn't seem right that there warn't nobody to make some about her, now she was gone; so I tried to sweat out a verse or two myself, but I couldn't seem to make it go, somehow. They kept Emmeline's room trim and nice and all the things fixed in it just the way she liked to have them when she was alive, and nobody ever slept there. The old lady took care of the room herself, though there was plenty of niggers, and she sewed there a good deal and read her Bible there, mostly.

Well, as I was saying about the parlor, there was beautiful curtains on the windows: white, with pictures painted on them, of castles with vines all down the walls, and cattle coming down to drink. There was a little old piano, too, that had tin pans in it, I reckon, and nothing was ever so lovely as to hear the young ladies sing, "The Last Link is Broken" and play "The Battle of Prague"[6] on it. The walls of all the rooms was plastered, and most had carpets on the floors, and the whole house was whitewashed on the outside.

It was a double house, and the big open place betwixt them was roofed and floored, and sometimes the table was set there in the middle of the day, and it was a cool, comfortable place. Nothing couldn't be better. And warn't the cooking good, and just bushels of it too!

Chapter XVIII

Col. Grangerford was a gentleman, you see. He was a gentleman all over; and so was his family. He was well born, as the saying is, and that's worth as much in a man as it is in a horse, so the Widow Douglas said, and nobody ever denied that she was of the first aristocracy in our town; and pap he always said it, too, though he warn't no more quality than a mudcat,[7] himself. Col. Grangerford was very tall and very slim, and had a darkish-paly complexion, not a sign of red in it anywheres; he was clean-shaved every morning, all over his thin face, and he had the thinnest kind of lips, and the thinnest kind of nostrils, and a high nose, and heavy eyebrows, and the blackest kind of eyes, sunk so deep back that they seemed like they was looking out of caverns at you, as you may say. His forehead was high, and his hair was black and straight, and hung to his shoulders. His hands was long and thin, and every day of his life he put on a clean shirt and a full suit from head to foot made out of linen so white it hurt your eyes to look at it; and on Sundays he wore a blue tail-coat with brass buttons on it. He carried a mahogany cane with a silver head to it. There warn't no frivolishness about him, not a bit, and he warn't ever loud. He was as kind as he could be—you could feel that, you know, and so you had confidence. Sometimes he smiled, and it was good to see; but when he straightened himself up like a liberty-pole,[8] and the lightning begun to flicker out from under his eyebrows you wanted to climb a tree first, and find out what the matter was afterwards. He didn't ever have to tell anybody to mind their manners— everybody was always good mannered where he was. Everybody loved to have him around, too; he was sunshine most always—I mean he made it seem like good weather. When he turned into a cloud-bank it was awful dark for a half a minute and that was enough; there wouldn't nothing go wrong again for a week.

When him and the old lady come down in the morning, all the family got up out of their chairs and give them good-day, and didn't set down again till they had set down. Then Tom and Bob went to the sideboard where the

---

6. A bloody story told in clichéd style, written by the Czech composer Franz Kotswara in about 1788; Twain first heard it in 1878. William Clifton's *The Last Link Is Broken* was published about 1840; it is the musical equivalent of Moore's poetry.
7. General term for a number of species of catfish; in this context the lowliest and least esteemed.
8. Flagpole.

decanters was, and mixed a glass of bitters and handed it to him, and he held it in his hand and waited till Tom's and Bob's was mixed, and then they bowed and said "Our duty to you, sir, and madam;" and *they* bowed the least bit in the world and said thank you, and so they drank, all three, and Bob and Tom poured a spoonful of water on the sugar and the mite of whisky or apple brandy in the bottom of their tumblers, and give it to me and Buck, and we drank to the old people too.

Bob was the oldest, and Tom next. Tall, beautiful men with very broad shoulders and brown faces, and long black hair and black eyes. They dressed in white linen from head to foot, like the old gentleman, and wore broad Panama hats.

Then there was Miss Charlotte, she was twenty-five, and tall and proud and grand, but as good as she could be, when she warn't stirred up; but when she was, she had a look that would make you wilt in your tracks, like her father. She was beautiful.

So was her sister, Miss Sophia, but it was a different kind. She was gentle and sweet, like a dove, and she was only twenty.

Each person had their own nigger to wait on them—Buck, too. My nigger had a monstrous easy time, because I warn't used to having anybody do anything for me, but Buck's was on the jump most of the time.

This was all there was of the family, now; but there used to be more—three sons; they got killed; and Emmeline that died.

The old gentleman owned a lot of farms, and over a hundred niggers. Sometimes a stack of people would come there, horseback, from ten or fifteen miles around, and stay five or six days, and have such junketings round about and on the river, and dances and picnics in the woods, day-times, and balls at the house, nights. These people was mostly kin-folks of the family. The men brought their guns with them. It was a handsome lot of quality, I tell you.

There was another clan of aristocracy around there—five or six families—mostly of the name of Shepherdson. They was as high-toned, and well born, and rich and grand, as the tribe of Grangerfords. The Shepherdsons and the Grangerfords used the same steamboat landing, which was about two mile above our house; so sometimes when I went up there with a lot of our folks I used to see a lot of Shepherdsons there, on their fine horses.

One day Buck and me was away out in the woods, hunting, and heard a horse coming. We was crossing the road. Buck says:

"Quick! Jump for the woods!"

We done it, and then peeped down the woods through the leaves. Pretty soon a splendid young man come galloping down the road, setting his horse easy and looking like a soldier. He had his gun across his pommel. I had seen him before. It was young Harney Shepherdson. I heard Buck's gun go off at my ear, and Harney's hat tumbled off from his head. He grabbed his gun and rode straight to the place where we was hid. But we didn't wait. We started through the woods on a run. The woods warn't thick, so I looked over my shoulder, to dodge the bullet, and twice I seen Harney cover Buck with his gun; and then he rode away the way he come—to get his hat, I reckon, but I couldn't see. We never stopped running till we got home. The old gentleman's eyes blazed a minute—'twas pleasure, mainly, I judged—then his face sort of smoothed down, and he says, kind of gentle:

"I don't like that shooting from behind a bush. Why didn't you step into the road, my boy?"

"The Shepherdsons don't, father. They always take advantage."

Miss Charlotte she held her head up like a queen while Buck was telling his tale, and her nostrils spread and her eyes snapped. The two young men looked dark, but never said nothing. Miss Sophia she turned pale, but the color come back when she found the man warn't hurt.

Soon as I could get Buck down by the corn-cribs under the trees by ourselves, I says:

"Did you want to kill him, Buck?"

"Well, I bet I did."

"What did he do to you?"

"Him? He never done nothing to me."

"Well, then, what did you want to kill him for?"

"Why nothing—only it's on account of the feud."

"What's a feud?"

"Why, where was you raised? Don't you know what a feud is?"

"Never heard of it before—tell me about it."

"Well," says Buck, "a feud is this way. A man has a quarrel with another man, and kills him; then that other man's brother kills *him*; then the other brothers, on both sides, goes for one another; then the *cousins* chip in—and by-and-by everybody's killed off, and there ain't no more feud. But it's kind of slow, and takes a long time."

"Has this one been going on long, Buck?"

"Well I should *reckon!* it started thirty year ago, or som'ers along there. There was trouble 'bout something and then a lawsuit to settle it; and the suit went agin one of the men, and so he up and shot the man that won the suit—which he would naturally do, of course. Anybody would."

"What was the trouble about, Buck?—land?"

"I reckon maybe—I don't know."

"Well, who done the shooting?—was it a Grangerford or a Shepherdson?"

"Laws, how do *I* know? it was so long ago."

"Don't anybody know?"

"Oh, yes, pa knows, I reckon, and some of the other old folks; but they don't know, now, what the row was about in the first place."

"Has there been many killed, Buck?"

"Yes—right smart chance of funerals. But they don't always kill. Pa's got a few buck-shot in him; but he don't mind it 'cuz he don't weigh much anyway. Bob's been carved up some with a bowie, and Tom's been hurt once or twice."

"Has anybody been killed this year, Buck?"

"Yes, we got one and they got one. 'Bout three months ago, my cousin Bud, fourteen year old, was riding through the woods, on t'other side of the river, and didn't have no weapon with him, which was blame' foolishness, and in a lonesome place he hears a horse a-coming behind him, and sees old Baldy Shepherdson a-linkin' after him with his gun in his hand and his white hair a-flying in the wind; and 'stead of jumping off and taking to the brush, Bud 'lowed he could outrun him; so they had it, nip and tuck, for five mile or more, the old man a-gaining all the time; so at last Bud seen it warn't any use, so he stopped and faced around so as to have the bullet holes in front, you know, and the old man he rode up and shot him down. But he didn't git much chance to enjoy his luck, for inside of a week our folks laid *him* out."

"I reckon that old man was a coward, Buck."

"I reckon he *warn't* a coward. Not by a blame' sight. There ain't a coward amongst them Shepherdsons—not a one. And there ain't no cowards amongst the Grangerfords, either. Why, that old man kep' up his end in a fight one day, for a half an hour, against three Grangerfords, and come out winner. They was all a-horseback; he lit off of his horse and got behind a little wood-pile, and kep' his horse before him to stop the bullets; but the Grangerfords staid on their horses and capered around the old man, and peppered away at him, and he peppered away at them. Him and his horse both went home pretty leaky and crippled, but the Grangerfords had to be *fetched* home—and one of 'em was dead, and another died the next day. No, sir, if a body's out hunting for cowards, he don't want to fool away any time amongst them Shepherdsons, becuz they don't breed any of that *kind*."

Next Sunday we all went to church, about three mile, everybody a-horseback. The men took their guns along, so did Buck, and kept them between their knees or stood them handy against the wall. The Shepherdsons done the same. It was pretty ornery preaching—all about brotherly love, and such-like tiresomeness; but everybody said it was a good sermon, and they all talked it over going home, and had such a powerful lot to say about faith, and good works, and free grace, and preforeordestination,[9] and I don't know what all, that it did seem to me to be one of the roughest Sundays I had run across yet.

About an hour after dinner everybody was dozing around, some in their chairs and some in their rooms, and it got to be pretty dull. Buck and a dog was stretched out on the grass in the sun, sound asleep. I went up to our room, and judged I would take a nap myself. I found that sweet Miss Sophia standing in her door, which was next to ours, and she took me in her room and shut the door very soft, and asked me if I liked her, and I said I did; and she asked me if I would do something for her and not tell anybody, and I said I would. Then she said she'd forgot her Testament, and left it in the seat at church, between two other books and would I slip out quiet and go there and fetch it to her, and not say nothing to nobody. I said I would. So I slid out and slipped off up the road, and there warn't anybody at the church, except maybe a hog or two, for there warn't any lock on the door, and hogs like a puncheon floor[1] in summer-time because it's cool. If you notice, most folks don't go to church only when they've got to; but a hog is different.

Says I to myself something's up—it ain't natural for a girl to be in such a sweat about a Testament; so I give it a shake, and out drops a little piece of paper with "*Half-past two*" wrote on it with a pencil. I ransacked it, but couldn't find anything else. I couldn't make anything out of that, so I put the paper in the book again, and when I got home and up stairs, there was Miss Sophia in her door waiting for me. She pulled me in and shut the door; then she looked in the Testament till she found the paper, and as soon as she read it she looked glad; and before a body could think, she grabbed me and give me a squeeze, and said I was the best boy in the world, and not to tell anybody. She was mighty red in the face, for a minute, and her eyes lighted up and it made her powerful pretty. I was a good deal astonished, but when I got my breath I asked her what the paper was about, and she asked me if I had read it, and I said no, and she asked me if I could read writing, and I told her "no, only coarse-hand,"[2] and then she said the paper warn't anything but a book-mark to keep her place, and I might go and play now.

I went off down to the river, studying over this thing, and pretty soon I noticed that my nigger was following along behind. When we was out of sight of the house, he looked back and around a second, and then comes a-running, and says:

"Mars Jawge, if you'll come down into de swamp, I'll show you a whole stack o' water-moccasins."

Thinks I, that's mighty curious; he said that yesterday. He oughter know a body don't love water-moccasins enough to go around hunting for them. What is he up to anyway? So I says—

"All right, trot ahead."

I followed a half a mile, then he struck out over the swamp and waded ankle deep as much as another half mile. We come to a little flat piece of land which was dry and very thick with trees and bushes and vines, and he says—

"You shove right in dah, jist a few steps, Mars Jawge, dah's whah dey is. I's seed 'm befo', I don't k'yer to see 'em no mo'."

Then he slopped right along and went away, and pretty soon the trees hid him. I poked into the place a-ways, and come to a little open patch as big as a bedroom, all hung around with vines, and found a man laying there asleep—and by jings it was my old Jim!

I waked him up, and I reckoned it was going to be a grand surprise to him to see me again, but it warn't. He nearly cried, he was so glad, but he warn't surprised. Said he swum along behind me, that night, and heard me yell every time, but dasn't answer, because he didn't want nobody to pick *him* up, and take him into slavery again. Says he—

"I got hurt a little, en couldn't swim fas', so I wuz a considerable ways behine you, towards de las'; when you landed I reck'ned I could ketch up wid you on de lan' 'dout havin' to shout at you, but when I see dat house I begin to go slow. I 'uz off too fur to hear what dey say to you—I wuz 'fraid o' de dogs—but when it 'uz all quiet again, I knowed you's in de house, so I struck out for de woods to wait for day. Early in de mawnin' some er de niggers come along, gwyne to de fields, en dey tuck me en showed me dis place, whah de dogs can't track me on accounts o' de water, en dey brings me truck to eat every night, en tells me how you's a gitt'n along."

"Why didn't you tell my Jack to fetch me here sooner, Jim?"

"Well, 'twarn't no use to 'sturb you, Huck, tell we could do sumfn—but we's all right, now. I ben a-buyin' pots en pans en vittles, as I got a chanst, en a patchin' up de raf', nights, when—"

"*What* raft, Jim?"

"Our ole raf'."

"You mean to say our old raft warn't smashed all to flinders?"

2. Block printing.

"No, she warn't. She was tore up a good deal—one en' of her was—but dey warn't no great harm done, on'y our traps was mos' all los'. Ef we hadn' dive' so deep en swum so fur under water, en de night hadn' ben so dark, en we warn't so sk'yerd, en ben sich punkin-heads, as de sayin' is, we'd a seed de raf'. But it's jis' as well we didn't, 'kase now she's all fixed up agin mos' as good as new, en we's got a new lot o' stuff, too, in de place o' what 'uz los'."

"Why, how did you get hold of the raft again, Jim—did you catch her?"

"How I gwyne to ketch her, en I out in de woods? No, some er de niggers foun' her ketched on a snag, along heah in de ben', en dey hid her in a crick, 'mongst de willows, en dey wuz so much jawin' 'bout which un 'um she b'long to de mos', dat I come to heah 'bout it pooty soon, so I ups en settles de trouble by tellin' um she don't b'long to none uv um, but to you en me; en I ast 'm if dey gwyne to grab a young white genlman's propaty, en git a hid'n for it? Den I gin 'm ten cents apiece, en dey 'uz mighty well satisfied, en wisht some mo' raf's 'ud come along en make 'm rich agin. Dey's mighty good to me, dese niggers is, en whatever I wants 'm to do fur me, I doan' have to ast 'm twice, honey. Dat Jack's a good nigger, en pooty smart."

"Yes, he is. He ain't ever told me you was here; told me to come, and he'd show me a lot of water-moccasins. If anything happens, *he* ain't mixed up in it. He can say he never seen us together, and it'll be the truth."

I don't want to talk much about the next day. I reckon I'll cut it pretty short. I waked up about dawn, and was agoing to turn over and go to sleep again, when I noticed how still it was—didn't seem to be anybody stirring. That warn't usual. Next I noticed that Buck was up and gone. Well, I gets up, a-wondering, and goes down stairs—nobody around; everything as still as a mouse. Just the same outside; thinks I, what does it mean? Down by the wood-pile I comes across my Jack, and says:

"What's it all about?"

Says he:

"Don't you know, Mars Jawge?"

"No," says I, "I don't."

"Well, den, Miss Sophia's run off! 'deed she has. She run off in de night, sometime—nobody don't know jis' when—run off to git married to dat young Harney Shepherdson, you know—leastways, so dey 'spec. De fambly foun' it out, 'bout half an hour ago—maybe a little mo'—en' I *tell* you dey warn't no time los'. Sich another hurryin' up guns en hosses *you* never see! De women folks has gone for to stir up de relations, en ole Mars Saul en de boys tuck dey guns en rode up de river road for to try to ketch dat young man en kill him 'fo' he kin git acrost de river wid Miss Sophia. I reck'n dey's gwyne to be mighty rough times."

"Buck went off 'thout waking me up."

"Well I reck'n he *did*! Dey warn't gwyne to mix you up in it. Mars Buck he loaded up his gun en 'lowed he's gwyne to fetch home a Shepherdson or bust. Well, dey'll be plenty un 'm dah, I reck'n, en you bet you he'll fetch one ef he gits a chanst."

I took up the river road as hard as I could put. By-and-by I begin to hear guns a good ways off. When I come in sight of the log store and the wood-pile where the steamboats lands, I worked along under the trees and brush till I got to a good place, and then I clumb up into the forks of a cotton-wood that was out of reach, and watched. There was a wood-rank four foot high,[3] a little ways in front of the tree, and first I was going to hide behind that; but maybe it was luckier I didn't.

There was four or five men cavorting around on their horses in the open place before the log store, cussing and yelling, and trying to get at a couple of young chaps that was behind the wood-rank alongside of the steamboat landing—but they couldn't come it. Every time one of them showed himself on the river side of the wood-pile he got shot at. The two boys was squatting back to back behind the pile, so they could watch both ways.

By-and-by the men stopped cavorting around and yelling. They started riding towards the store; then up gets one of the boys, draws a steady bead over the wood-rank, and drops one of them out of his saddle. All the men jumped off of their horses and grabbed the hurt one and started to carry him to the store; and that minute the two boys started on the run. They got half-way to the tree I was in before the men noticed. Then the men see them, and jumped on their horses and took out after them. They gained on the boys, but it didn't do no good, the boys had too good a start; they got to the wood-pile that was in front of my tree, and slipped in behind it, and so they had the bulge[4] on the men again. One of the boys was Buck, and the other was a slim young chap about nineteen years old.

The men ripped around awhile, and then rode away. As soon as they was out of sight, I sung out to Buck and told him. He didn't know what to make of my voice coming out of the tree, at first. He was awful surprised. He told me to watch out sharp and let him know when the men come in sight again; said they was up to some devilment or other—wouldn't be gone long. I wished I was out of that tree, but I dasn't come down. Buck began to cry and rip, and 'lowed that him and his cousin Joe (that was the other young chap) would make up for this day, yet. He said his father and his two brothers was killed, and two or three of the enemy. Said the Shepherdsons laid for them, in ambush. Buck said his father and brothers ought to waited for their relations—the Shepherdsons was too strong for them. I asked him what was become of young Harney and Miss Sophia. He said they'd got across the river and was safe. I was glad of that; but the way Buck did take on because he didn't manage to kill Harney that day he shot at him—I hain't ever heard anything like it.

All of a sudden, bang! bang! bang! goes three or four guns—the men had slipped around through the woods and come in from behind without their horses! The boys jumped for the river—both of them hurt—and as they swum down the current the men run along the bank shooting at them and singing out, "Kill them, kill them!" It made me so sick I most fell out of the tree. I ain't agoing to tell *all* that happened!—it would make me sick again if I was to do that. I wished I hadn't ever come ashore that night, to see such things. I ain't ever going to get shut of them—lots of times I dream about them.

I staid in the tree till it begun to get dark, afraid to come down. Sometimes I heard guns away off in the woods; and twice I seen little gangs of men gallop past the log store with guns; so I reckoned the trouble was still agoing on. I was mighty downhearted; so I made up my mind I wouldn't ever go anear that house again, because I reckoned I was to blame, somehow. I judged that

---

3. Half a cord of stacked firewood.   4. Upper hand.

that piece of paper meant that Miss Sophia was to meet Harney somewheres at half-past two and run off; and I judged I ought to told her father about that paper and the curious way she acted, and then maybe he would a locked her up and this awful mess wouldn't ever happened.

When I got down out of the tree, I crept along down the river bank a piece, and found the two bodies laying in the edge of the water, and tugged at them till I got them ashore; then I covered up their faces, and got away as quick as I could. I cried a little when I was covering up Buck's face, for he was mighty good to me.

It was just dark, now. I never went near the house, but struck through the woods and made for the swamp. Jim warn't on his island, so I tramped off in a hurry for the crick, and crowded through the willows, red-hot to jump aboard and get out of that awful country—the raft was gone! My souls, but I was scared! I couldn't get my breath for most a minute. Then I raised a yell. A voice not twenty-five foot from me, says—

"Good lan'! is dat you, honey? Doan' make no noise."

It was Jim's voice—nothing ever sounded so good before. I run along the bank a piece and got aboard, and Jim he grabbed me and hugged me, he was so glad to see me. He says—

"Laws bless you, chile, I 'uz right down sho' you's dead agin. Jack's been heah, he say he reck'n you's ben shot, kase you didn' come home no mo'; so I's jes' dis minute a startin' de raf' down towards de mouf er de crick, so's to be all ready for to shove out en leave soon as Jack comes agin en tells me for certain you *is* dead. Lawsy, I's mighty glad to git you back agin, honey."

I says—

"All right—that's mighty good; they won't find me, and they'll think I've been killed, and floated down the river—there's something up there that'll help them to think so—so don't you lose no time, Jim, but just shove off for the big water as fast as ever you can."

I never felt easy till the raft was two mile below there and out in the middle of the Mississippi. Then we hung up our signal lantern, and judged that we was free and safe once more. I hadn't had a bite to eat since yesterday; so Jim he got out some corn-dodgers[5] and buttermilk, and pork and cabbage, and greens—there ain't nothing in the world so good, when it's cooked right—and whilst I eat my supper we talked, and had a good time. I was powerful glad to get away from the feuds, and so was Jim to get away from the swamp. We said there warn't no home like a raft, after all. Other places do seem so cramped up and smothery, but a raft don't. You feel mighty free and easy and comfortable on a raft.

Chapter XIX

Two or three days and nights went by; I reckon I might say they swum by, they slid along so quiet and smooth and lovely. Here is the way we put in the time. It was a monstrous big river down there—sometimes a mile and a half wide; we run nights, and laid up and hid day-times; soon as night was most gone, we stopped navigating and tied up—nearly always in the dead water under a tow-head; and then cut young cottonwoods and willows and hid the

5. Hard cornmeal rolls or cakes.

raft with them. Then we set out the lines. Next we slid into the river and had a swim, so as to freshen up and cool off; then we set down on the sandy bottom where the water was about knee deep, and watched the daylight come. Not a sound, anywheres—perfectly still—just like the whole world was asleep, only sometimes the bull-frogs a-cluttering, maybe. The first thing to see, looking away over the water, was a kind of dull line—that was the woods on t'other side—you couldn't make nothing else out; then a pale place in the sky; then more paleness, spreading around; then the river softened up, away off, and warn't black any more, but gray; you could see little dark spots drifting along, ever so far away—trading scows, and such things; and long black streaks—rafts; sometimes you could hear a sweep screaking; or jumbled up voices, it was so still, and sounds come so far; and by-and-by you could see a streak on the water which you know by the look of the streak that there's a snag there in a swift current which breaks on it and makes that streak look that way; and you see the mist curl up off of the water, and the east reddens up, and the river, and you make out a log cabin in the edge of the woods, away on the bank on t'other side of the river, being a wood-yard, likely, and piled by them cheats so you can throw a dog through it anywheres;[6] then the nice breeze springs up, and comes fanning you from over there, so cool and fresh, and sweet to smell, on account of the woods and the flowers; but sometimes not that way, because they've left dead fish laying around, gars, and such, and they do get pretty rank; and next you've got the full day, and everything smiling in the sun, and the song-birds just going it!

A little smoke couldn't be noticed, now, so we would take some fish off of the lines, and cook up a hot breakfast. And afterwards we would watch the lonesomeness of the river, and kind of lazy along, and by-and-by lazy off to sleep. Wake up, by-and-by, and look to see what done it, and maybe see a steamboat coughing along up stream, so far off towards the other side you couldn't tell nothing about her only whether she was stern-wheel or side-wheel; then for about an hour there wouldn't be nothing to hear nor nothing to see—just solid lonesomeness. Next you'd see a raft sliding by, away off yonder, and maybe a galoot on it chopping, because they're almost always doing it on a raft; you'd see the ax flash, and come down—you don't hear nothing; you see that ax go up again, and by the time it's above the man's head, then you hear the *k'chunk!*—it had took all that time to come over the water. So we would put in the day, lazying around, listening to the stillness. Once there was a thick fog, and the rafts and things that went by was beating tin pans so the steamboats wouldn't run over them. A scow or a raft went by so close we could hear them talking and cussing and laughing—heard them plain; but we couldn't see no sign of them; it made you feel crawly, it was like spirits carrying on that way in the air. Jim said he believed it was spirits; but I says:

"No, spirits wouldn't say, 'dern the dern fog.' "

Soon as it was night, out we shoved; when we got her out to about the middle, we let her alone, and let her float wherever the current wanted her to; then we lit the pipes, and dangled our legs in the water and talked about all kinds of things—we was always naked, day and night, whenever the mosquitoes would let us—the new clothes Buck's folks made for me was too good to be comfortable, and besides I didn't go much on clothes, nohow.

6. Stacks of wood in this yard were sold by their volume, gappage included.

Sometimes we'd have that whole river all to ourselves for the longest time. Yonder was the banks and the islands, across the water; and maybe a spark—which was a candle in a cabin window—and sometimes on the water you could see a spark or two—on a raft or a scow, you know; and maybe you could hear a fiddle or a song coming over from one of them crafts. It's lovely to live on a raft. We had the sky, up there, all speckled with stars, and we used to lay on our backs and look up at them, and discuss about whether they was made, or only just happened—Jim he allowed they was made, but I allowed they happened; I judged it would have took too long to *make* so many. Jim said the moon could a *laid* them; well, that looked kind of reasonable, so I didn't say nothing against it, because I've seen a frog lay most as many, so of course it could be done. We used to watch the stars that fell, too, and see them streak down. Jim allowed they'd got spoiled and was hove out of the nest.

Once or twice of a night we would see a steamboat slipping along in the dark, and now and then she would belch a whole world of sparks up out of her chimbleys, and they would rain down in the river and look awful pretty; then she would turn a corner and her lights would wink out and her pow-wow shut off and leave the river still again; and by-and-by her waves would get to us, a long time after she was gone, and joggle the raft a bit, and after that you wouldn't hear nothing for you couldn't tell how long, except maybe frogs or something.

After midnight the people on shore went to bed, and then for two or three hours the shores was black—no more sparks in the cabin windows. These sparks was our clock—the first one that showed again meant morning was coming, so we hunted a place to hide and tie up, right away.

One morning about day-break, I found a canoe and crossed over a chute[7] to the main shore—it was only two hundred yards—and paddled about a mile up a crick amongst the cypress woods, to see if I couldn't get some berries. Just as I was passing a place where a kind of a cow-path crossed the crick, here comes a couple of men tearing up the path as tight as they could foot it. I thought I was a goner, for whenever anybody was after anybody I judged it was *me*—or maybe Jim. I was about to dig out from there in a hurry, but they was pretty close to me then, and sung out and begged me to save their lives—said they hadn't been doing nothing, and was being chased for it—said there was men and dogs a-coming. They wanted to jump right in, but I says—

"Don't you do it. I don't hear the dogs and horses yet; you've got time to crowd through the brush and get up the crick a little ways; then you take to the water and wade down to me and get in—that'll throw the dogs off the scent."

They done it, and soon as they was aboard I lit out for our tow-head, and in about five or ten minutes we heard the dogs and the men away off, shouting. We heard them come along towards the crick, but couldn't see them; they seemed to stop and fool around a while; then, as we got further and further away all the time, we couldn't hardly hear them at all; by the time we had left a mile of woods behind us and struck the river, everything was quiet, and we paddled over to the tow-head and hid in the cotton-woods and was safe.

One of these fellows was about seventy, or upwards, and had a bald head and very gray whiskers. He had an old battered-up slouch hat on, and a greasy

7. A narrow channel with swift-flowing water.

blue woolen shirt, and ragged old blue jeans britches stuffed into his boot tops, and home-knit galluses[8]—no, he only had one. He had an old long-tailed blue jeans coat with slick brass buttons, flung over his arm, and both of them had big fat ratty-looking carpet-bags.

The other fellow was about thirty and dressed about as ornery. After breakfast we all laid off and talked, and the first thing that come out was that these chaps didn't know one another.

"What got you into trouble?" says the baldhead to t'other chap.

"Well, I'd been selling an article to take the tartar off the teeth—and it does take it off, too, and generly the enamel along with it—but I staid about one night longer than I ought to, and was just in the act of sliding out when I ran across you on the trail this side of town, and you told me they were coming, and begged me to help you to get off. So I told you I was expecting trouble myself and would scatter out *with* you. That's the whole yarn—what's yourn?"

"Well, I'd ben a-runnin' a little temperance revival thar, 'bout a week, and was the pet of the women-folks, big and little, for I was makin' it mighty warm for the rummies, I *tell* you, and takin' as much as five or six dollars a night— ten cents a head, children and niggers free—and business a growin' all the time; when somehow or another a little report got around, last night, that I had a way of puttin' in my time with a private jug, on the sly. A nigger rousted me out this mornin', and told me the people was getherin' on the quiet, with their dogs and horses, and they'd be along pretty soon and give me 'bout half an hour's start, and then run me down, if they could; and if they got me they'd tar and feather me and ride me on a rail, sure. I didn't wait for no breakfast— I warn't hungry."

"Old man," says the young one, "I reckon we might double-team it together; what do you think?"

"I ain't undisposed. What's your line—mainly?"

"Jour printer,[9] by trade; do a little in patent medicines; theatre-actor— tragedy, you know; take a turn at mesmerism and phrenology,[1] when there's a chance; teach singing-geography school for a change; sling a lecture, some-times—oh, I do lots of things—most anything that comes handy, so it ain't work. What's your lay?"[2]

"I've done considerable in the doctoring way in my time. Layin' on o' hands is my best holt—for cancer, and paralysis, and sich things; and I k'n tell a for-tune pretty good, when I've got somebody along to find out the facts for me. Preachin's my line, too; and workin' camp-meetin's; and missionaryin' around."

Nobody never said anything for a while; then the young man hove a sigh and says—

"Alas!"

"What 're you alassin' about?" says the baldhead.

"To think I should have lived to be leading such a life, and be degraded down into such company." And he begun to wipe the corner of his eye with a rag.

"Dern your skin, ain't the company good enough for you?" says the bald-head, pretty pert and uppish.

8. Suspenders.
9. A journeyman printer, not yet a salaried master-printer, who worked by the day.
1. The study of the shape of the skull as an indi-

cator of intelligence and character. "Mesmerism": hypnotic induction involving animal magnetism— broadly, hypnotism.
2. Work, in the sense here of hustle or scheme.

"Yes, it *is* good enough for me; it's as good as I deserve; for who fetched me so low, when I was so high? *I* did myself. I don't blame *you*, gentlemen—far from it; I don't blame anybody. I deserve it all. Let the cold world do its worst; one thing I know—there's a grave somewhere for me. The world may go on just as its always done, and take everything from me—loved ones, property, everything—but it can't take that. Some day I'll lie down in it and forget it all, and my poor broken heart will be at rest." He went on a-wiping.

"Drot your pore broken heart," says the baldhead; "what are you heaving your pore broken heart at *us* f'r? *We* hain't done nothing."

"No, I know you haven't. I ain't blaming you, gentlemen. I brought myself down—yes, I did it myself. It's right I should suffer—perfectly right—I don't make any moan."

"Brought you down from whar? Whar was you brought down from?"

"Ah, you would not believe me; the world never believes—let it pass—'tis no matter. The secret of my birth—"

"The secret of your birth? Do you mean to say—"

"Gentlemen," says the young man, very solemn, "I will reveal it to you, for I feel I may have confidence in you. By rights I am a duke!"

Jim's eyes bugged out when he heard that; and I reckon mine did, too. Then the baldhead says: "No! you can't mean it?"

"Yes. My great-grandfather, eldest son of the Duke of Bridgewater, fled to this country about the end of the last century, to breathe the pure air of freedom; married here, and died, leaving a son, his own father dying about the same time. The second son of the late duke seized the title and estates—the infant real duke was ignored. I am the lineal descendant of that infant—I am the rightful Duke of Bridgewater; and here am I, forlorn, torn from my high estate, hunted of men, despised by the cold world, ragged, worn, heart-broken, and degraded to the companionship of felons on a raft!"

Jim pitied him ever so much, and so did I. We tried to comfort him, but he said it warn't much use, he couldn't be much comforted; said if we was a mind to acknowledge him, that would do him more good than most anything else; so we said we would, if he would tell us how. He said we ought to bow, when we spoke to him, and say "Your Grace," or "My Lord," or "Your Lordship"—and he wouldn't mind it if we called him plain "Bridgewater," which he said was a title, anyway, and not a name; and one of us ought to wait on him at dinner, and do any little thing for him he wanted done.

Well, that was all easy, so we done it. All through dinner Jim stood around and waited on him, and says, "Will yo' Grace have some o' dis, or some o' dat?" and so on, and a body could see it was mighty pleasing to him.

But the old man got pretty silent, by-and-by—didn't have much to say, and didn't look pretty comfortable over all that petting that was going on around that duke. He seemed to have something on his mind. So, along in the afternoon, he says:

"Looky here, Bilgewater," he says, "I'm nation sorry for you, but you ain't the only person that's had troubles like that."

"No?"

"No, you ain't. You ain't the only person that's ben snaked down wrongfully out'n a high place."

"Alas!"

"No, you ain't the only person that's had a secret of his birth." And by jings, *he* begins to cry.

"Hold! What do you mean?"

"Bilgewater, kin I trust you?" says the old man, still sort of sobbing.

"To the bitter death!" He took the old man by the hand and squeezed it, and says, "The secret of your being: speak!"

"Bilgewater, I am the late Dauphin!"[3]

You bet you Jim and me stared, this time. Then the duke says:

"You are what?"

"Yes, my friend, it is too true—your eyes is lookin' at this very moment on the pore disappeared Dauphin, Looy the Seventeen, son of Looy the Sixteen and Marry Antonette."

"You! At your age! No! You mean you're the late Charlemagne;[4] you must be six or seven hundred years old, at the very least."

"Trouble has done it, Bilgewater, trouble has done it; trouble has brung these gray hairs and this premature balditude. Yes, gentlemen, you see before you, in blue jeans and misery, the wanderin', exiled, trampled-on and sufferin' rightful King of France."

Well, he cried and took on so, that me and Jim didn't know hardly what to do, we was so sorry—and so glad and proud we'd got him with us, too. So we set in, like we done before with the duke, and tried to comfort *him*. But he said it warn't no use, nothing but to be dead and done with it all could do him any good; though he said it often made him feel easier and better for a while if people treated him according to his rights, and got down on one knee to speak to him, and always called him "Your Majesty," and waited on him first at meals, and didn't set down in his presence till he asked them. So Jim and me set to majestying him, and doing this and that and t'other for him, and standing up till he told us we might set down. This done him heaps of good, and so he got cheerful and comfortable. But the duke kind of soured on him, and didn't look a bit satisfied with the way things was going; still, the king acted real friendly towards him, and said the duke's great-grandfather and all the other Dukes of Bilgewater was a good deal thought of by *his* father and was allowed to come to the palace considerable; but the duke staid huffy a good while, till by-and-by the king says:

"Like as not we got to be together a blamed long time, on this h-yer raft, Bilgewater, and so what's the use o' your bein' sour? It'll only make things oncomfortable. It ain't my fault I warn't born a duke, it ain't your fault you warn't born a king—so what's the use to worry? Make the best o' things the way you find 'em, says I—that's my motto. This ain't no bad thing that we've struck here—plenty grub and an easy life—come, give us your hand, Duke, and less all be friends."

The duke done it, and Jim and me was pretty glad to see it. It took away all the uncomfortableness, and we felt mighty good over it, because it would a been a miserable business to have any unfriendliness on the raft; for what you want, above all things, on a raft, is for everybody to be satisfied, and feel right and kind towards the others.

It didn't take me long to make up my mind that these liars warn't no kings nor dukes, at all, but just low-down humbugs and frauds. But I never said nothing, never let on; kept it to myself; it's the best way; then you don't have no quarrels, and don't get into no trouble. If they wanted us to call them kings

---

3. The Dauphin, born in 1785, would have been in his mid-fifties or sixties had he survived.

4. Charlemagne (742–814), emperor of the West (800–814).

and dukes, I hadn't no objections, 'long as it would keep peace in the family; and it warn't no use to tell Jim, so I didn't tell him. If I never learnt nothing else out of pap, I learnt that the best way to get along with his kind of people is to let them have their own way.

Chapter XX

They asked us considerable many questions; wanted to know what we covered up the raft that way for, and laid by in the daytime instead of running— was Jim a runaway nigger? Says I—

"Goodness sakes, would a runaway nigger run *south?*"

No, they allowed he wouldn't. I had to account for things some way, so I says:

"My folks was living in Pike County, in Missouri, where I was born, and they all died off but me and pa and my brother Ike. Pa, he 'lowed he'd break up and go down and live with Uncle Ben, who's got a little one-horse place on the river, forty-four mile below Orleans. Pa was pretty poor, and had some debts; so when he'd squared up there warn't nothing left but sixteen dollars and our nigger, Jim. That warn't enough to take us fourteen hundred mile, deck passage nor no other way. Well, when the river rose, pa had a streak of luck one day; he ketched this piece of a raft; so we reckoned we'd go down to Orleans on it. Pa's luck didn't hold out; a steamboat run over the forrard corner of the raft, one night, and we all went overboard and dove under the wheel; Jim and me come up, all right, but pa was drunk, and Ike was only four years old, so they never come up no more. Well, for the next day or two we had considerable trouble, because people was always coming out in skiffs and trying to take Jim away from me, saying they believed he was a runaway nigger. We don't run day-times no more, now; nights they don't bother us."

The duke says—

"Leave me alone to cipher out a way so we can run in the daytime if we want to. I'll think the thing over—I'll invent a plan that'll fix it. We'll let it alone for to-day, because of course we don't want to go by that town yonder in daylight—it mightn't be healthy."

Towards night it begun to darken up and look like rain; the heat lightning was squirting around, low down in the sky, and the leaves was beginning to shiver—it was going to be pretty ugly, it was easy to see that. So the duke and the king went to overhauling our wigwam, to see what the beds was like. My bed was a straw tick[5]—better than Jim's, which was a corn-shuck tick; there's always cobs around about in a shuck tick, and they poke into you and hurt; and when you roll over, the dry shucks sound like you was rolling over in a pile of dead leaves; it makes such a rustling that you wake up. Well, the duke allowed he would take my bed; but the king allowed he wouldn't. He says—

"I should a reckoned the difference in rank would a sejested to you that a corn-shuck bed warn't just fitten for me to sleep on. Your Grace'll take the shuck bed yourself."

Jim and me was in a sweat again, for a minute, being afraid there was going

---

5. Mattress.

to be some more trouble amongst them; so we was pretty glad when the duke says—

" 'Tis my fate to be always ground into the mire under the iron heel of oppression. Misfortune has broken my once haughty spirit; I yield, I submit; 'tis my fate. I am alone in the world—let me suffer; I can bear it."

We got away as soon as it was good and dark. The king told us to stand well out towards the middle of the river, and not show a light till we got a long ways below the town. We come in sight of the little bunch of lights by-and-by— that was the town, you know—and slid by, about a half a mile out, all right. When we was three-quarters of a mile below, we hoisted up our signal lantern; and about ten o'clock it come on to rain and blow and thunder and lighten like everything; so the king told us to both stay on watch till the weather got better; then him and the duke crawled into the wigwam and turned in for the night. It was my watch below, till twelve, but I wouldn't a turned in, anyway, if I'd had a bed; because a body don't see such a storm as that every day in the week, not by a long sight. My souls, how the wind did scream along! And every second or two there'd come a glare that lit up the white-caps for a half a mile around, and you'd see the islands looking dusty through the rain, and the trees thrashing around in the wind; then comes a *h-wack!*—bum! bum! bumble-umble-um-bum-bum-bum-bum—and the thunder would go rumbling and grumbling away, and quit—and then *rip* comes another flash and another sock-dolager.[6] The waves most washed me off the raft, sometimes, but I hadn't any clothes on, and didn't mind. We did-n't have no trouble about snags; the lightning was glaring and flittering around so constant that we could see them plenty soon enough to throw her head this way or that and miss them.

I had the middle watch, you know, but I was pretty sleepy by that time, so Jim he said he would stand the first half of it for me; he was always mighty good, that way, Jim was. I crawled into the wigwam, but the king and the duke had their legs sprawled around so there warn't no show for me; so I laid out-side—I didn't mind the rain, because it was warm, and the waves warn't run-ning so high, now. About two they come up again, though, and Jim was going to call me, but he changed his mind because he reckoned they warn't high enough yet to do any harm; but he was mistaken about that, for pretty soon all of a sudden along comes a regular ripper, and washed me overboard. It most killed Jim a-laughing. He was the easiest nigger to laugh that ever was, anyway.

I took the watch, and Jim he laid down and snored away; and by-and-by the storm let up for good and all; and the first cabin-light that showed, I rousted him out and we slid the raft into hiding-quarters for the day.

The king got out an old ratty deck of cards, after breakfast, and him and the duke played seven-up a while, five cents a game. Then they got tired of it, and allowed they would "lay out a campaign," as they called it. The duke went down into his carpet-bag and fetched up a lot of little printed bills, and read them out loud. One bill said "The celebrated Dr. Armand de Montalban of Paris," would "lecture on the Science of Phrenology" at such and such a place, on the blank day of blank, at ten cents admission, and "furnish charts of character at twenty-five cents apiece." The duke said that was *him*. In

6. Something exceptionally strong or climactic.

another bill he was the "world renowned Shaksperean tragedian, Garrick the Younger,[7] of Drury Lane, London." In other bills he had a lot of other names and done other wonderful things, like finding water and gold with a "divining rod," "dissipating witch-spells," and so on. By-and-by he says—

"But the histrionic muse is the darling. Have you ever trod the boards, Royalty?"

"No," says the king.

"You shall, then, before you're three days older, Fallen Grandeur," says the duke. "The first good town we come to, we'll hire a hall and do the sword-fight in Richard III. and the balcony scene in Romeo and Juliet. How does that strike you?"

"I'm in, up to the hub, for anything that will pay, Bilgewater, but you see I don't know nothing about play-actn', and hain't ever seen much of it. I was too small when pap used to have 'em at the palace. Do you reckon you can learn me?"

"Easy!"

"All right. I'm jist a-freezn' for something fresh, anyway. Less commence, right away."

So the duke he told him all about who Romeo was, and who Juliet was, and said he was used to being Romeo, so the king could be Juliet.

"But if Juliet's such a young gal, Duke, my peeled head and my white whiskers is goin' to look oncommon odd on her, maybe."

"No, don't you worry—these country jakes won't ever think of that. Besides, you know, you'll be in costume, and that makes all the difference in the world; Juliet's in a balcony, enjoying the moonlight before she goes to bed, and she's got on her night-gown and her ruffled night-cap. Here are the costumes for the parts."

He got out two or three curtain-calico suits, which he said was meedyevil armor for Richard III. and t'other chap, and a long white cotton night-shirt and a ruffled night-cap to match. The king was satisfied; so the duke got out his book and read the parts over in the most splendid spread-eagle way, prancing around and acting at the same time, to show how it had got to be done; then he give the book to the king and told him to get his part by heart.

There was a little one-horse town about three mile down the bend, and after dinner the duke said he had ciphered out his idea about how to run in daylight without it being dangersome for Jim; so he allowed he would go down to the town and fix that thing. The king allowed he would go too, and see if he couldn't strike something. We was out of coffee, so Jim said I better go along with them in the canoe and get some.

When we got there, there warn't nobody stirring; streets empty, and perfectly dead and still, like Sunday. We found a sick nigger sunning himself in a back yard, and he said everybody that warn't too young or too sick or too old, was gone to camp-meeting, about two mile back in the woods. The king got the directions, and allowed he'd go and work that camp-meeting for all it was worth, and I might go, too.[8]

---

7. David Garrick (1717–1779) was a famous tragedian at the Theatre Royal in Drury Lane, London.
8. Notoriously easy pickings for confidence men, camp meetings are extended outdoor evangelical meetings. Families camp nearby for the duration of the event. One of the best-known literary renderings of this stock situation is Johnson J. Hooper's "The Captain Attends a Camp-Meeting."

The duke said what he was after was a printing office. We found it; a little bit of a concern, up over a carpenter shop—carpenters and printers all gone to the meeting, and no doors locked. It was a dirty, littered-up place, and had ink marks, and handbills with pictures of horses and runaway niggers on them, all over the walls. The duke shed his coat and said he was all right, now. So me and the king lit out for the camp-meeting.

We got there in about a half an hour, fairly dripping, for it was a most awful hot day. There was as much as a thousand people there, from twenty mile around. The woods was full of teams and wagons, hitched everywheres, feeding out of the wagon troughs and stomping to keep off the flies. There was sheds made out of poles and roofed over with branches, where they had lemonade and gingerbread to sell, and piles of watermelons and green corn and such-like truck.

The preaching was going on under the same kinds of sheds, only they was bigger and held crowds of people. The benches was made out of outside slabs of logs, with holes bored in the round side to drive sticks into for legs. They didn't have no backs. The preachers had high platforms to stand on, at one end of the sheds. The women had on sunbonnets; and some had linsey-woolsey frocks, some gingham ones, and a few of the young ones had on calico. Some of the young men was barefooted, and some of the children didn't have on any clothes but just a tow-linen[9] shirt. Some of the old women was knitting, and some of the young folks was courting on the sly.

The first shed we come to, the preacher was lining out a hymn. He lined out two lines, everybody sung it, and it was kind of grand to hear it, there was so many of them and they done it in such a rousing way; then he lined out two more for them to sing—and so on. The people woke up more and more, and sung louder and louder; and towards the end, some begun to groan, and some begun to shout. Then the preacher begun to preach; and begun in earnest, too; and went weaving first to one side of the platform and then the other, and then a leaning down over the front of it, with his arms and his body going all the time, and shouting his words out with all his might; and every now and then he would hold up his Bible and spread it open, and kind of pass it around this way and that, shouting, "It's the brazen serpent in the wilderness! Look upon it and live!" And people would shout out, "Glory!—A-*a-men!*" And so he went on, and the people groaning and crying and saying amen:

"Oh, come to the mourners' bench![1] come, black with sin! (*amen!*) come, sick and sore! (*amen!*) come, lame and halt, and blind! (*amen!*) come, pore and needy, sunk in shame! (*a-a-men!*) come all that's worn, and soiled, and suffering!—come with a broken spirit! come with a contrite heart! come in your rags and sin and dirt! the waters that cleanse is free, the door of heaven stands open—oh, enter in and be at rest!" (*a-a-men! glory, glory hallelujah!*)

And so on. You couldn't make out what the preacher said, any more, on account of the shouting and crying. Folks got up, everywheres in the crowd, and worked their way, just by main strength, to the mourners' bench, with the tears running down their faces; and when all the mourners had got up there to the front benches in a crowd, they sung, and shouted, and flung themselves down on the straw, just crazy and wild.

9. Coarse linen cloth. "Linsey-woolsey": cheap, often homespun, unpatterned cloth composed of wool and flax. "Gingham" and "calico" are inex-pensive, store-bought printed cotton.
1. Front-row pews filled by penitents.

Well, the first I knowed, the king got agoing; and you could hear him over everybody; and next he went a-charging up on to the platform and the preacher he begged him to speak to the people, and he done it. He told them he was a pirate—been a pirate for thirty years, out in the Indian Ocean, and his crew was thinned out considerable, last spring, in a fight, and he was home now, to take out some fresh men, and thanks to goodness he'd been robbed last night, and put ashore off of a steamboat without a cent, and he was glad of it, it was the blessedest thing that ever happened to him, because he was a changed man now, and happy for the first time in his life; and poor as he was, he was going to start right off and work his way back to the Indian Ocean and put in the rest of his life trying to turn the pirates into the true path; for he could do it better than anybody else, being acquainted with all the pirate crews in that ocean; and though it would take him a long time to get there, without money, he would get there anyway, and every time he convinced a pirate he would say to him, "Don't you thank me, don't you give me no credit, it all belongs to them dear people in Pokeville camp-meeting, natural brothers and benefactors of the race—and that dear preacher there, the truest friend a pirate ever had!"

And then he busted into tears, and so did everybody. Then somebody sings out, "Take up a collection for him, take up a collection!" Well, a half a dozen made a jump to do it, but somebody sings out, "Let *him* pass the hat around!" Then everybody said it, the preacher too.

So the king went all through the crowd with his hat, swabbing his eyes, and blessing the people and praising them and thanking them for being so good to the poor pirates away off there; and every little while the prettiest kind of girls, with the tears running down their cheeks, would up and ask him would he let them kiss him, for to remember him by; and he always done it; and some of them he hugged and kissed as many as five or six times—and he was invited to stay a week; and everybody wanted him to live in their houses, and said they'd think it was an honor; but he said as this was the last day of the camp-meeting he couldn't do no good, and besides he was in a sweat to get to the Indian Ocean right off and go to work on the pirates.

When we got back to the raft and he come to count up, he found he had collected eighty-seven dollars and seventy-five cents. And then he had fetched away a three-gallon jug of whisky, too, that he found under a wagon when we was starting home through the woods. The king said, take it all around, it laid over any day he'd ever put in in the missionarying line. He said it warn't no use talking, heathens don't amount to shucks, alongside of pirates, to work a camp-meeting with.

The duke was thinking *he'd* been doing pretty well, till the king come to show up, but after that he didn't think so so much. He had set up and printed off two little jobs for farmers, in that printing office—horse bills—and took the money, four dollars. And he had got in ten dollars worth of advertisements for the paper, which he said he would put in for four dollars if they would pay in advance—so they done it. The price of the paper was two dollars a year, but he took in three subscriptions for half a dollar apiece on condition of them paying him in advance; they were going to pay in cord-wood and onions, as usual, but he said he had just bought the concern and knocked down the price as low as he could afford it, and was going to run it for cash. He set up a little piece of poetry, which he made, himself, out of his own head—three verses—kind of sweet and saddish—the name of it was, "Yes, crush, cold world, this breaking heart"—and he left that all set up and ready to print in the paper and didn't charge nothing for it. Well, he took in nine dollars and a half, and said he'd done a pretty square day's work for it.

Then he showed us another little job he'd printed and hadn't charged for, because it was for us. It had a picture of a runaway nigger, with a bundle on a stick, over his shoulder, and "$200 reward" under it. The reading was all about Jim, and just described him to a dot. It said he run away from St. Jacques' plantation, forty mile below New Orleans, last winter, and likely went north, and whoever would catch him and send him back, he could have the reward and expenses.

"Now," says the duke, "after to-night we can run in the daytime if we want to. Whenever we see anybody coming, we can tie Jim hand and foot with a rope, and lay him in the wigwam and show this handbill and say we captured him up the river, and were too poor to travel on a steamboat, so we got this little raft on credit from our friends and are going down to get the reward. Handcuffs and chains would look still better on Jim, but it wouldn't go well with the story of us being so poor. Too much like jewelry. Ropes are the correct thing—we must preserve the unities,[2] as we say on the boards."

We all said the duke was pretty smart, and there couldn't be no trouble about running daytimes. We judged we could make miles enough that night to get out of the reach of the pow-wow we reckoned the duke's work in the printing office was going to make in that little town—then we could boom right along, if we wanted to.

We laid low and kept still, and never shoved out till nearly ten o'clock; then we slid by, pretty wide away from the town, and didn't hoist our lantern till we was clear out of sight of it.

When Jim called me to take the watch at four in the morning, he says—

"Huck, does you reck'n we gwyne to run acrost any mo' kings on dis trip?"

"No," I says, "I reckon not."

"Well," says he, "dat's all right, den. I doan' mine one er two kings, but dat's enough. Dis one's powerful drunk, en de duke ain' much better."

I found Jim had been trying to get him to talk French, so he could hear what it was like; but he said he had been in this country so long, and had so much trouble, he'd forgot it.

Chapter XXI

It was after sun-up, now, but we went right on, and didn't tie up. The king and the duke turned out, by-and-by, looking pretty rusty; but after they'd jumped overboard and took a swim, it chippered them up a good deal. After breakfast the king he took a seat on a corner of the raft, and pulled off his boots and rolled up his britches, and let his legs dangle in the water, so as to be comfortable, and lit his pipe, and went to getting his Romeo and Juliet by heart. When he had got it pretty good, him and the duke begun to practice it together. The duke had to learn him over and over again, how to say every speech; and he made him sigh, and put his hand on his heart, and after while he said he done it pretty well; "only," he says, "you mustn't bellow out *Romeo!*

---

2. Of time, place, and action in classical drama; here the duke is using the term to mean "consistent with the rest of our story."

that way, like a bull—you must say it soft, and sick, and languishy, so—R-o-o-meo! that is the idea; for Juliet's a dear sweet mere child of a girl, you know, and she don't bray like a jackass."

Well, next they got out a couple of long swords that the duke made out of oak laths, and begun to practice the sword-fight—the duke called himself Richard III.; and the way they laid on, and pranced around the raft was grand to see. But by-and-by the king tripped and fell overboard, and after that they took a rest, and had a talk about all kinds of adventures they'd had in other times along the river.

After dinner, the duke says:

"Well, Capet,[3] we'll want to make this a first-class show, you know, so I guess we'll add a little more to it. We want a little something to answer encores with, anyway."

"What's onkores, Bilgewater?"

The duke told him, and then says:

"I'll answer by doing the Highland fling or the sailor's hornpipe; and you—well, let me see—oh, I've got it—you can do Hamlet's soliloquy."

"Hamlet's which?"

"Hamlet's soliloquy, you know; the most celebrated thing in Shakespeare. Ah, it's sublime, sublime! Always fetches the house. I haven't got it in the book—I've only got one volume—but I reckon I can piece it out from memory. I'll just walk up and down a minute, and see if I can call it back from recollection's vaults."

So he went to marching up and down, thinking, and frowning horrible every now and then; then he would hoist up his eyebrows; next he would squeeze his hand on his forehead and stagger back and kind of moan; next he would sigh, and next he'd let on to drop a tear. It was beautiful to see him. By-and-by he got it. He told us to give attention. Then he strikes a most noble attitude, with one leg shoved forwards, and his arms stretched away up, and his head tilted back, looking up at the sky; and then he begins to rip and rave and grit his teeth; and after that, all through his speech he howled, and spread around, and swelled up his chest, and just knocked the spots out of any acting ever I see before. This is the speech—I learned it, easy enough, while he was learning it to the king:[4]

To be, or not to be; that is the bare bodkin
That makes calamity of so long life;
For who would fardels bear, till Birnam Wood do come to Dunsinane,
But that the fear of something after death
Murders the innocent sleep,
Great nature's second course,
And makes us rather sling the arrows of outrageous fortune
Than fly to others that we know not of.
There's the respect must give us pause:
Wake Duncan with thy knocking! I would thou couldst;
For who would bear the whips and scorns of time,
The oppressor's wrong, the proud man's contumely,

3. The family name of Louis VI–X.
4. The comical garbling of Shakespeare was another stock-in-trade of the southwestern humorists in whose tradition Twain follows. The soliloquy is composed chiefly of phrases from *Hamlet* and *Macbeth*, but Twain also draws on several other plays.

The law's delay, and the quietus which his pangs might take,
In the dead waste and middle of the night, when churchyards yawn
In customary suits of solemn black,
But that the undiscovered country from whose bourne no traveler returns,
Breathes forth contagion on the world,
And thus the native hue of resolution, like the poor cat i' the adage,
Is sicklied o'er with care,
And all the clouds that lowered o'er our housetops,
With this regard their currents turn awry,
And lose the name of action.
'Tis a consummation devoutly to be wished. But soft you, the fair Ophelia:
Ope not thy ponderous and marble jaws,
But get thee to a nunnery—go!

Well, the old man he liked that speech, and he mighty soon got it so he could do it first rate. It seemed like he was just born for it; and when he had his hand in and was excited, it was perfectly lovely the way he would rip and tear and rair up behind when he was getting it off.

The first chance we got, the duke he had some show bills printed; and after that, for two or three days as we floated along, the raft was a most uncommon lively place, for there warn't nothing but sword-fighting and rehearsing—as the duke called it—going on all the time. One morning, when we was pretty well down the State of Arkansaw, we come in sight of a little one-horse town[5] in a big bend; so we tied up about three-quarters of a mile above it, in the mouth of a crick which was shut in like a tunnel by the cypress trees, and all of us but Jim took the canoe and went down there to see if there was any chance in that place for our show.

We struck it mighty lucky; there was going to be a circus there that afternoon, and the country people was already beginning to come in, in all kinds of old shackly wagons, and on horses. The circus would leave before night, so our show would have a pretty good chance. The duke he hired the court house, and we went around and stuck up our bills. They read like this:

Shaksperean Revival! ! !
Wonderful Attraction!
For One Night Only!
The world renowned tragedians,
David Garrick the younger, of Drury Lane Theatre, London,
and
Edmund Kean the elder,[6] of the Royal Haymarket Theatre, White-
chapel, Pudding Lane, Piccadilly, London, and the
Royal Continental Theatres, in their sublime
Shaksperean Spectacle entitled
The Balcony Scene
in
Romeo and Juliet! ! !

Romeo . . . . Mr. Garrick.
Juliet . . . . Mr. Kean.

5. Twain's Bricksville is apparently modeled after Napoleon, Arkansas, although certain unattractive elements of Bricksville and its inhabitants were common to most river towns—including Hannibal.

6. Here, as elsewhere, the duke garbles the facts. Garrick, Edmund Kean (1787–1833), and Charles John Kean (1811–1868) were all famous tragedians at the Theatre Royal in Drury Lane, London.

Assisted by the whole strength of the company!
New costumes, new scenery, new appointments!
Also:
The thrilling, masterly, and blood-curdling
Broad-sword conflict
In Richard III.!!!

Richard III . . . . Mr. Garrick.
Richmond . . . . Mr. Kean.
also:
(by special request,)
Hamlet's Immortal Soliloquy! !
By the Illustrious Kean!
Done by him 300 consecutive nights in Paris!
For One Night Only,
On account of imperative European engagements!
Admission 25 cents; children and servants, 10 cents.

Then we went loafing around the town. The stores and houses was most all old shackly dried-up frame concerns that hadn't ever been painted; they was set up three or four foot above ground on stilts, so as to be out of reach of the water when the river was overflowed. The houses had little gardens around them, but they didn't seem to raise hardly anything in them but jimpson weeds, and sunflowers, and ash-piles, and old curled-up boots and shoes, and pieces of bottles, and rags, and played-out tin-ware. The fences was made of different kinds of boards, nailed on at different times; and they leaned every which-way, and had gates that didn't generly have but one hinge—a leather one. Some of the fences had been whitewashed, some time or another, but the duke said it was in Clumbus's time, like enough. There was generly hogs in the garden, and people driving them out.

All the stores was along one street. They had white-domestic awnings[7] in front, and the country people hitched their horses to the awning-posts. There was empty dry-goods boxes under the awnings, and loafers roosting on them all day long, whittling them with their Barlow knives; and chawing tobacco, and gaping and yawning and stretching—a mighty ornery lot. They generly had on yellow straw hats most as wide as an umbrella, but didn't wear no coats nor waistcoats; they called one another Bill, and Buck, and Hank, and Joe, and Andy, and talked lazy and drawly, and used considerable many cuss-words. There was as many as one loafer leaning up against every awning-post, and he most always had his hands in his britches pockets, except when he fetched them out to lend a chaw of tobacco or scratch. What a body was hearing amongst them, all the time was—

"Gimme a chaw 'v tobacker, Hank."

"Cain't—I hain't got but one chaw left. Ask Bill."

Maybe Bill he gives him a chaw; maybe he lies and says he ain't got none. Some of them kinds of loafers never has a cent in the world, nor a chaw of tobacco of their own. They get all their chawing by borrowing—they say to a fellow, "I wisht you'd len' me a chaw, Jack, I jist this minute give Ben Thompson the last chaw I had"—which is a lie, pretty much every time; it don't fool anybody but a stranger; but Jack ain't no stranger, so he says—

---

7. Awnings made from crude canvas.

"You give him a chaw, did you? so did your sister's cat's grandmother. You pay me back the chaws you've awready borry'd off'n me, Lafe Buckner, then I'll loan you one or two ton of it, and won't charge you no back intrust, nuther."

"Well, I *did* pay you back some of it wunst."

"Yes, you did—'bout six chaws. You borry'd store tobacker and paid back nigger-head."

Store tobacco is flat black plug, but these fellows mostly chaws the natural leaf twisted. When they borrow a chaw, they don't generly cut it off with a knife, but they set the plug in between their teeth, and gnaw with their teeth and tug at the plug with their hands till they get it in two—then sometimes the one that owns the tobacco looks mournful at it when it's handed back, and says, sarcastic—

"Here, gimme the *chaw,* and you take the *plug."*

All the streets and lanes was just mud, they warn't nothing else *but* mud—as black as tar, and nigh about a foot deep in some places; and two or three inches deep in *all* the places. The hogs loafed and grunted around, everywheres. You'd see a muddy sow and a litter of pigs come lazying along the street and whollop herself right down in the way, where folks had to walk around her, and she'd stretch out, and shut her eyes, and wave her ears, whilst the pigs was milking her, and look as happy as if she was on salary. And pretty soon you'd hear a loafer sing out, "Hi! *so* boy! sick him, Tige!" and away the sow would go, squealing most horrible, with a dog or two swinging to each ear, and three or four dozen more a-coming; and then you would see all the loafers get up and watch the thing out of sight, and laugh at the fun and look grateful for the noise. Then they'd settle back again till there was a dog-fight. There couldn't anything wake them up all over, and make them happy all over, like a dog-fight—unless it might be putting turpentine on a stray dog and setting fire to him, or tying a tin pan to his tail and see him run himself to death.

On the river front some of the houses was sticking out over the bank, and they was bowed and bent, and about ready to tumble in. The people had moved out of them. The bank was caved away under one corner of some others, and that corner was hanging over. People lived in them yet, but it was dangersome, because sometimes a strip of land as wide as a house caves in at a time. Sometimes a belt of land a quarter of a mile deep will start in and cave along and cave along till it all caves into the river in one summer. Such a town as that has to be always moving back, and back, and back, because the river's always gnawing at it.

The nearer it got to noon that day, the thicker and thicker was the wagons and horses in the streets, and more coming all the time. Families fetched their dinners with them, from the country, and eat them in the wagons. There was considerable whiskey drinking going on, and I seen three fights. By-and-by somebody sings out—

"Here comes old Boggs!—in from the country for his little old monthly drunk—here he comes, boys!"

All the loafers looked glad—I reckoned they was used to having fun out of Boggs. One of them says—

"Wonder who he's a gwyne to chaw up this time. If he'd a chawed up all the men he's ben a gwyne to chaw up in the last twenty year, he'd have considerable ruputation, now."

Another one says, "I wisht old Boggs'd threaten me, 'cuz then I'd know I warn't gwyne to die for a thousan' year."

Boggs comes a-tearing along on his horse, whooping and yelling like an Injun, and singing out—

"Cler the track, thar. I'm on the war-path, and the price uv coffins is a gwyne to raise."

He was drunk, and weaving about in his saddle; he was over fifty year old, and had a very red face. Everybody yelled at him, and laughed at him, and sassed him, and he sassed back, and said he'd attend to them and lay them out in their regular turns, but he couldn't wait now, because he'd come to town to kill old Colonel Sherburn, and his motto was, "meat first, and spoon vittles to top off on."

He see me, and rode up and says—

"Whar'd you come f'm, boy? You prepared to die?"

Then he rode on. I was scared; but a man says—

"He don't mean nothing; he's always a carryin' on like that, when he's drunk. He's the best-naturedest old fool in Arkansaw—never hurt nobody, drunk nor sober."

Boggs rode up before the biggest store in town and bent his head down so he could see under the curtain of the awning, and yells—

"Come out here, Sherburn! Come out and meet the man you've swindled. You're the houn' I'm after, and I'm a gwyne to have you, too!"

And so he went on, calling Sherburn everything he could lay his tongue to, and the whole street packed with people listening and laughing and going on. By-and-by a proud-looking man about fifty-five—and he was a heap the best dressed man in that town, too—steps out of the store, and the crowd drops back on each side to let him come. He says to Boggs, mighty ca'm and slow—he says:

"I'm tired of this; but I'll endure it till one o'clock. Till one o'clock, mind—no longer. If you open your mouth against me only once, after that time, you can't travel so far but I will find you."

Then he turns and goes in. The crowd looked mighty sober; nobody stirred, and there warn't no more laughing. Boggs rode off blackguarding Sherburn as loud as he could yell, all down the street; and pretty soon back he comes and stops before the store, still keeping it up. Some men crowded around him and tried to get him to shut up, but he wouldn't; they told him it would be one o'clock in about fifteen minutes, and so he *must* go home—he must go right away. But it didn't do no good. He cussed away, with all his might, and throwed his hat down in the mud and rode over it, and pretty soon away he went a-raging down the street again, with his gray hair a-flying. Everybody that could get a chance at him tried their best to coax him off of his horse so they could lock him up and get him sober; but it warn't no use—up the street he would tear again, and give Sherburn another cussing. By-and-by somebody says—

"Go for his daughter!—quick, go for his daughter; sometimes he'll listen to her. If anybody can persuade him, she can."

So somebody started on a run. I walked down street a ways, and stopped. In about five or ten minutes, here comes Boggs again—but not on his horse. He was a-reeling across the street towards me, bareheaded, with a friend on both sides of him aholt of his arms and hurrying him along. He was quiet, and looked uneasy; and he warn't hanging back any, but was doing some of the hurrying himself. Somebody sings out—

"Boggs!"

I looked over there to see who said it, and it was that Colonel Sherburn. He was standing perfectly still, in the street, and had a pistol raised in his right hand—not aiming it, but holding it out with the barrel tilted up towards the sky. The same second I see a young girl coming on the run, and two men with her. Boggs and the men turned round, to see who called him, and when they see the pistol the men jumped to one side, and the pistol barrel come down slow and steady to a level—both barrels cocked. Boggs throws up both of his hands, and says, "O Lord, don't shoot!" Bang! goes the first shot, and he staggers back clawing at the air—bang! goes the second one, and he tumbles backwards onto the ground, heavy and solid, with his arms spread out. That young girl screamed out, and comes rushing, and down she throws herself on her father, crying, and saying, "Oh, he's killed him, he's killed him!" The crowd closed up around them, and shouldered and jammed one another, with their necks stretched, trying to see, and people on the inside trying to shove them back, and shouting, "Back, back! give him air, give him air!"

Colonel Sherburn he tossed his pistol onto the ground, and turned around on his heels and walked off.

They took Boggs to a little drug store, the crowd pressing around, just the same, and the whole town following, and I rushed and got a good place at the window, where I was close to him and could see in. They laid him on the floor, and put one large Bible under his head, and opened another one and spread it on his breast—but they tore open his shirt first, and I seen where one of the bullets went in. He made about a dozen long gasps, his breast lifting the Bible up when he drawed in his breath, and letting it down again when he breathed it out—and after that he laid still; he was dead.[8] Then they pulled his daughter away from him, screaming and crying, and took her off. She was about sixteen, and very sweet and gentle-looking, but awful pale and scared.

Well, pretty soon the whole town was there, squirming and scrouging and pushing and shoving to get at the window and have a look, but people that had the places wouldn't give them up, and folks behind them was saying all the time, "Say, now, you've looked enough, you fellows; 'taint right and 'taint fair, for you to stay thar all the time, and never give nobody a chance; other folks has their rights as well as you."

There was considerable jawing back, so I slid out, thinking maybe there was going to be trouble. The streets was full, and everybody was excited. Everybody that seen the shooting was telling how it happened, and there was a big crowd packed around each one of these fellows, stretching their necks and listening. One long lanky man, with long hair and a big white fur stovepipe hat on the back of his head, and a crooked-handled cane, marked out the places on the ground where Boggs stood, and where Sherburn stood, and the people following him around from one place to t'other and watching everything he done, and bobbing their heads to show they understood, and stooping a little and resting their hands on their thighs to watch him mark the places on the ground with his cane; and then he stood up straight and stiff

8. Twain had witnessed a shooting very much like this one when he was ten years old. His father was the presiding judge at the trial, which ended in acquittal. Only the Bibles under the victim's head and on his chest seem to have been added by Twain, who seldom could resist ironies at the expense of institutionalized religion.

where Sherburn had stood, frowning and having his hat-brim down over his eyes, and sung out, "Boggs!" and then fetched his cane down slow to a level, and says "Bang!" staggered backwards, says "Bang!" again, and fell down flat on his back. The people that had seen the thing said he done it perfect; said it was just exactly the way it all happened. Then as much as a dozen people got out their bottles and treated him.

Well, by-and-by somebody said Sherburn ought to be lynched. In about a minute everybody was saying it; so away they went, mad and yelling, and snatching down every clothes-line they come to, to do the hanging with.

Chapter XXII

They swarmed up the street towards Sherburn's house, a-whooping and yelling and raging like Injuns, and everything had to clear the way or get run over and tromped to mush, and it was awful to see. Children was heeling it ahead of the mob, screaming and trying to get out of the way; and every window along the road was full of women's heads, and there was nigger boys in every tree, and bucks and wenches looking over every fence; and as soon as the mob would get nearly to them they would break and skaddle back out of reach. Lots of the women and girls was crying and taking on, scared most to death.

They swarmed up in front of Sherburn's palings as thick as they could jam together, and you couldn't hear yourself think for the noise. It was a little twenty-foot yard. Some sung out "Tear down the fence! tear down the fence!" Then there was a racket of ripping and tearing and smashing, and down she goes, and the front wall of the crowd begins to roll in like a wave.

Just then Sherburn steps out on to the roof of his little front porch, with a double-barrel gun in his hand, and takes his stand, perfectly ca'm and deliberate, not saying a word. The racket stopped, and the wave sucked back.

Sherburn never said a word—just stood there, looking down. The stillness was awful creepy and uncomfortable. Sherburn run his eye slow along the crowd; and wherever it struck, the people tried a little to outgaze him, but they couldn't; they dropped their eyes and looked sneaky. Then pretty soon Sherburn sort of laughed; not the pleasant kind, but the kind that makes you feel like when you are eating bread that's got sand in it.

Then he says, slow and scornful:

"The idea of *you* lynching anybody! It's amusing. The idea of you thinking you had pluck enough to lynch a *man!* Because you're brave enough to tar and feather poor friendless cast-out women that come along here, did that make you think you had grit enough to lay your hands on a *man?* Why, a *man's* safe in the hands of ten thousand of your kind—as long as it's day-time and you're not behind him.

"Do I know you? I know you clear through. I was born and raised in the South, and I've lived in the North; so I know the average all around. The average man's a coward. In the North he lets anybody walk over him that wants to, and goes home and prays for a humble spirit to bear it. In the South one man, all by himself, has stopped a stage full of men, in the day-time, and robbed the lot. Your newspapers call you a brave people so much that you think you *are* braver than any other people—whereas you're just *as* brave, and no braver. Why don't your juries hang murderers? Because they're afraid the man's friends will shoot them in the back, in the dark—and it's just what they *would* do.

"So they always acquit; and then a *man* goes in the night, with a hundred masked cowards at his back, and lynches the rascal. Your mistake is, that you didn't bring a man with you; that's one mistake, and the other is that you didn't come in the dark, and fetch your masks. You brought *part* of a man—Buck Harkness, there—and if you hadn't had him to start you, you'd a taken it out in blowing.

"You didn't want to come. The average man don't like trouble and danger. *You* don't like trouble and danger. But if only *half* a man—like Buck Harkness, there—shouts 'Lynch him, lynch him!' you're afraid to back down—afraid you'll be found out to be what you are—*cowards*—and so you raise a yell, and hang yourselves onto that half-a-man's coat tail, and come raging up here, swearing what big things you're going to do. The pitifulest thing out is a mob; that's what an army is—a mob; they don't fight with courage that's born in them, but with courage that's borrowed from their mass, and from their officers. But a mob without any *man* at the head of it, is *beneath* pitifulness. Now the thing for *you* to do, is to droop your tails and go home and crawl in a hole. If any real lynching's going to be done, it will be done in the dark, Southern fashion; and when they come they'll bring their masks, and fetch a *man* along. Now *leave*—and take your half-a-man with you"—tossing his gun up across his left arm and cocking it, when he says this.

The crowd washed back sudden, and then broke all apart and went tearing off every which way, and Buck Harkness he heeled it after them, looking tolerable cheap. I could a staid, if I'd a wanted to, but I didn't want to.

I went to the circus, and loafed around the back side till the watchman went by, and then dived in under the tent. I had my twenty-dollar gold piece and some other money, but I reckoned I better save it, because there ain't no telling how soon you are going to need it, away from home and amongst strangers, that way. You can't be too careful. I ain't opposed to spending money on circuses, when there ain't no other way, but there ain't no use in *wasting* it on them.

It was a real bully circus. It was the splendidest sight that ever was, when they all come riding in, two and two, a gentleman and lady, side by side, the men just in their drawers and under-shirts, and no shoes nor stirrups, and resting their hands on their thighs, easy and comfortable—there must a' been twenty of them—and every lady with a lovely complexion, and perfectly beautiful, and looking just like a gang of real sure-enough queens, and dressed in clothes that cost millions of dollars, and just littered with diamonds. It was a powerful fine sight; I never see anything so lovely. And then one by one they got up and stood, and went a-weaving around the ring so gentle and wavy and graceful, the men looking ever so tall and airy and straight, with their heads bobbing and skimming along, away up there under the tent-roof, and every lady's rose-leafy dress flapping soft and silky around her hips, and she looking like the most loveliest parasol.

And then faster and faster they went, all of them dancing, first one foot stuck out in the air and then the other, the horses leaning more and more, and the ring-master going round and round the centre-pole, cracking his whip and shouting "hi!—hi!" and the clown cracking jokes behind him; and by-and-by all hands dropped the reins, and every lady put her knuckles on her hips and every gentlemen folded his arms, and then how the horses did lean over and hump themselves! And so, one after the other they all skipped off into the ring, and made the sweetest bow I ever see, and then scampered out, and everybody clapped their hands and went just about wild.

Well, all through the circus they done the most astonishing things; and all the time that clown carried on so it most killed the people. The ring-master couldn't ever say a word to him but he was back at him quick as a wink with the funniest things a body ever said; and how he ever *could* think of so many of them, and so sudden and so pat, was what I couldn't noway understand. Why, I couldn't a thought of them in a year. And by-and-by a drunk man tried to get into the ring—said he wanted to ride; said he could ride as well as anybody that ever was. They argued and tried to keep him out, but he wouldn't listen, and the whole show come to a standstill. Then the people begun to holler at him and make fun of him, and that made him mad, and be begun to rip and tear; so that stirred up the people, and a lot of men began to pile down off of the benches and swarm towards the ring, saying "Knock him down! throw him out!" and one or two women begun to scream. So, then, the ring-master he made a little speech, and said he hoped there wouldn't be no disturbance, and if the man would promise he wouldn't make no more trouble, he would let him ride, if he thought he could stay on the horse. So everybody laughed and said all right, and the man got on. The minute he was on, the horse begun to rip and tear and jump and cavort around, with two circus men hanging onto his bridle trying to hold him, and the drunk man hanging onto his neck, and his heels flying in the air every jump, and the whole crowd of people standing up shouting and laughing till the tears rolled down. And at last, sure enough, all the circus men could do, the horse broke loose, and away he went like the very nation, round and round the ring, with that sot laying down on him and hanging to his neck, with first one leg hanging most to the ground on one side, and then t'other one on t'other side, and the people just crazy. It warn't funny to me, though; I was all of a tremble to see his danger. But pretty soon he struggled up astraddle and grabbed the bridle, a-reeling this way and that; and the next minute he sprung up and dropped the bridle and stood! and the horse agoing like a house afire too. He just stood up there, a-sailing around as easy and comfortable as if he warn't ever drunk in his life—and then he begun to pull off his clothes and sling them. He shed them so thick they kind of clogged up the air, and altogether he shed seventeen suits. And then, there he was, slim and handsome, and dressed the gaudiest and prettiest you ever saw, and he lit into that horse with his whip and made him fairly hum—and finally skipped off, and made his bow and danced off to the dressing-room, and everybody just a-howling with pleasure and astonishment.

Then the ring-master he see how he had been fooled, and he *was* the sickest ring-master you ever see, I reckon. Why, it was one of his own men! He had got up that joke all out of his own head, and never let on to nobody. Well, I felt sheepish enough, to be took in so, but I wouldn't a been in that ring-master's place, not for a thousand dollars. I don't know; there may be bullier circuses than what that one was, but I never struck them yet. Anyways it was plenty good enough for *me*; and wherever I run across it, it can have all of *my* custom, everytime.

Well, that night we had *our* show; but there warn't only about twelve people there; just enough to pay expenses. And they laughed all the time, and that made the duke mad; and everybody left, anyway, before the show was over, but one boy which was asleep. So the duke said these Arkansaw lunkheads couldn't come up to Shakspeare; what they wanted was low comedy—and may be something ruther worse than low comedy, he reckoned. He said he could size their style. So next morning he got some big sheets of wrapping-paper and some black paint, and drawed off some handbills and stuck them up all over the village. The bills said:

AT THE COURT HOUSE!
FOR 3 NIGHTS ONLY!
The World-Renowned Tragedians
DAVID GARRICK THE YOUNGER
AND
EDMUND KEAN THE ELDER!
Of the London and Continental
Theatres,
In their Thrilling Tragedy of
THE KING'S CAMELOPARD[9]
OR
THE ROYAL NONESUCH! ! !
Admission 50 cents.

Then at the bottom was the biggest line of all—which said:

LADIES AND CHILDREN NOT ADMITTED.

"There," says he, "if that line don't fetch them, I don't know Arkansaw!"

Chapter XXIII

Well, all day him and the king was hard at it, rigging up a stage, and a curtain, and a row of candles for footlights; and that night the house was jam full of men in no time. When the place couldn't hold no more, the duke he quit tending door and went around the back way and come onto the stage and stood up before the curtain, and made a little speech, and praised up this tragedy, and said it was the most thrillingest one that ever was; and so he went on a-bragging about the tragedy and about Edmund Kean the Elder, which was to play the main principal part in it; and at last when he'd got everybody's expectations up high enough, he rolled up the curtain, and the next minute the king come a-prancing out on all fours, naked; and he was painted all over, ring-streaked-and-striped, all sorts of colors, as splendid as a rainbow. And—but never mind the rest of his outfit, it was just wild, but it was awful funny. The people most killed themselves laughing; and when the king got done capering, and capered off behind the scenes, they roared and clapped and stormed and haw-hawed till he come back and done it over again; and after that, they made him do it another time. Well, it would a made a cow laugh to see the shines that old idiot cut.

Then the duke he lets the curtain down, and bows to the people, and says the great tragedy will be performed only two nights more, on accounts of pressing London engagements, where the seats is all sold aready for it in Drury Lane; and then he makes them another bow, and says if he has succeeded in pleasing them and instructing them, he will be deeply obleeged if they will mention it to their friends and get them to come and see it.

9. An archaic name for a giraffe, but also describes a legendary spotted beast the size of a camel. This hoax performance was a popular subject of comic stories, and Twain had heard a version he referred to as "The Burning Shame" from his friend Jim Gillis in his California newspaper days.

Twenty people sings out:

"What, is it over? Is that *all?*"

The duke says yes. Then there was a fine time. Everybody sings out "sold," and rose up mad, and was agoing for that stage and them tragedians. But a big fine-looking man jumps up on a bench, and shouts:

"Hold on! Just a word, gentlemen." They stopped to listen. "We are sold— mighty badly sold. But we don't want to be the laughing-stock of this whole town, I reckon, and never hear the last of this thing as long as we live. *No.* What we want, is to go out of here quiet, and talk this show up, and sell the *rest* of the town! Then we'll all be in the same boat. Ain't that sensible?" ("You bet it is!—the jedge is right!" everybody sings out.) "All right, then—not a word about any sell. Go along home, and advise everybody to come and see the tragedy."

Next day you couldn't hear nothing around that town but how splendid that show was. House was jammed again, that night, and we sold this crowd the same way. When me and the king and the duke got home to the raft, we all had a supper; and by-and-by, about midnight, they made Jim and me back her out and float her down the middle of the river and fetch her in and hide her about two mile below town.

The third night the house was crammed again—and they warn't new-comers, this time, but people that was at the show the other two nights. I stood by the duke at the door, and I see that every man that went in had his pockets bulging, or something muffled up under his coat—and I see it warn't no perfumery nei- ther, not by a long sight. I smelt sickly eggs by the barrel, and rotten cabbages, and such things; and if I know the signs of a dead cat being around, and I bet I do, there was sixty-four of them went in. I shoved in there for a minute, but it was too various for me, I couldn't stand it. Well, when the place couldn't hold no more people, the duke he give a fellow a quarter and told him to tend door for him a minute, and then he started around for the stage door, I after him; but the minute we turned the corner and was in the dark, he says:

"Walk fast, now, till you get away from the houses, and then shin for the raft like the dickens was after you!"

I done it, and he done the same. We struck the raft at the same time, and in less than two seconds we was gliding down stream, all dark and still, and edging towards the middle of the river, nobody saying a word. I reckoned the poor king was in for a gaudy time of it with the audience; but nothing of the sort; pretty soon he crawls out from under the wigwam, and says:

"Well, how'd the old thing pan out this time, Duke?"

He hadn't been up town at all.

We never showed a light till we was about ten mile below that village. Then we lit up and had a supper, and the king and the duke fairly laughed their bones loose over the way they'd served them people. The duke says:

"Greenhorns, flatheads! *I* knew the first house would keep mum and let the rest of the town get roped in; and I knew they'd lay for us the third night, and consider it was *their* turn now. Well, it *is* their turn, and I'd give something to know how much they'd take for it. I *would* just like to know how they're put- ting in their opportunity. They can turn it into a picnic, if they want to—they brought plenty provisions."

Them rapscallions took in four hundred and sixty-five dollars in that three nights. I never see money hauled in by the wagon-load like that, before.

By-and-by, when they was asleep and snoring, Jim says:

"Don't it 'sprise you, de way dem kings carries on, Huck?"

"No," I says, "it don't."

"Why don't it, Huck?"

"Well, it don't, because it's in the breed. I reckon they're all alike."

"But, Huck, dese kings o' ourn is reglar rapscallions; dat's jist what dey is; dey's reglar rapscallions."

"Well, that's what I'm a-saying; all kings is mostly rapscallions, as fur as I can make out."

"Is dat so?"

"You read about them once—you'll see. Look at Henry the Eight; this'n 's a Sunday-School Superintendent to *him.* And look at Charles Second, and LouisFourteen, and Louis Fifteen, and James Second, and Edward Second, and Richard Third, and forty more; besides all them Saxon heptarchies that used to rip around so in old times and raise Cain. My, you ought to seen old Henry the Eight when he was in bloom. He *was* a blossom. He used to marry a new wife every day, and chop off her head next morning. And he would do it just as indifferent as if he was ordering up eggs. 'Fetch up Nell Gwynn,' he says. They fetch her up. Next morning, 'Chop off her head!' And they chop it off. 'Fetch up Jane Shore,' he says; and up she comes. Next morning 'Chop off her head'—and they chop it off. 'Ring up Fair Rosamun.' Fair Rosamun answers the bell. Next morning, 'Chop off her head.' And he made every one of them tell him a tale every night; and he kept that up till he had hogged a thousand and one tales that way, and then he put them all in a book, and called it Domesday Book—which was a good name and stated the case. You don't know kings, Jim, but I know them; and this old rip of ourn is one of the cleanest I've struck in history. Well, Henry he takes a notion he wants to get up some trouble with this country. How does he go at it—give notice?—give the country a show? No. All of sudden he heaves all the tea in Boston Harbor overboard, and whacks out a declaration of independence, and dares them to come on. That was *his* style—he never give anybody a chance. He had suspicions of his father, the Duke of Wellington. Well, what did he do?—ask him to show up? No—drownded him in a butt of mamsey, like a cat. Spose people left money laying around where he was—what did he do? He collared it. Spose he contracted to do a thing; and you paid him, and didn't set down there and see that he done it—what did he do? He always done the other thing. Spose he opened his mouth—what then? If he didn't shut it up powerful quick, he'd lose a lie, every time. That's the kind of a bug Henry was; and if we'd a had him along 'stead of our kings, he'd a fooled that town a heap worse than ourn done.[1] I don't say that ourn is lambs, because they ain't, when you come right down to the cold facts; but they ain't nothing to *that* old ram, anyway. All I say is, kings is kings, and you

1. Huck's "history" of kingly behavior is a hodge-podge of fact and fiction. Henry VIII, king of England from 1509 to 1547, did execute two of his wives and divorced two others. Nell Gwynn, however, was the mistress of Charles II (r. 1660–85). Jane Shore was mistress to Edward IV (r. 15th century). Rosamund Clifford was mistress to Henry II in the 12th century. The Anglo-Saxon heptarchy (seven friendly kingdoms) ruled England from 449 to 829. The Domesday Book, in which William the Conqueror of England recorded all landowners and the value of their holdings, was completed in 1086; Huck confuses it with *The Arabian Nights.* The duke of Wellington is a 19th-century personage. The duke of Clarence was reportedly drowned in a cask of wine in the late 15th century. The Boston Tea Party took place in 1773, and the Declaration of Independence was adopted in 1776; neither event, of course, has any connection with Henry VIII.

got to make allowances. Take them all around, they're a mighty ornery lot. It's the way they're raised."

"But dis one do *smell* so like de nation, Huck."

"Well, they all do, Jim. *We* can't help the way a king smells; history don't tell no way."

"Now de duke, he's a tolerable likely man, in some ways."

"Yes, a duke's different. But not very different. This one's a middling hard lot, for a duke. When he's drunk, there ain't no near-sighted man could tell him from a king."

"Well, anyways, I doan' hanker for no mo' un um, Huck. Dese is all I kin stan'."

"It's the way I feel, too, Jim. But we've got them on our hands, and we got to remember what they are, and make allowances. Sometimes I wish we could hear of a country that's out of kings."

What was the use to tell Jim these warn't real kings and dukes? It wouldn't a done no good; and besides, it was just as I said; you couldn't tell them from the real kind.

I went to sleep, and Jim didn't call me when it was my turn. He often done that. When I waked up, just at day-break, he was setting there with his head down betwixt his knees, moaning and mourning to himself. I didn't take notice, nor let on. I knowed what it was about. He was thinking about his wife and his children, away up yonder, and he was low and homesick; because he hadn't ever been away from home before in his life; and I do believe he cared just as much for his people as white folks does for their'n. It don't seem natural, but I reckon it's so. He was often moaning and mourning that way, nights, when he judged I was asleep, and saying "Po' little 'Lizabeth! po' little Johnny! its mighty hard; I spec' I ain't ever gwyne to see you no mo', no mo'!" He was a mighty good nigger, Jim was.

But this time I somehow got to talking to him about his wife and young ones; and by-and-by he says:

"What makes me feel so bad dis time, 'uz bekase I hear sumpn over yonder on de bank like a whack, er a slam, while ago, en it mine me er de time I treat my little 'Lizabeth so ornery. She warn't on'y 'bout fo' year ole, en she tuck de sk'yarlet-fever, en had a powful rough spell; but she got well, en one day she was a-stannin' aroun', en I says to her, I says:

" 'Shet de do'.'

"She never done it; jis' stood dar, kiner smilin' up at me. It make me mad; en I says agin, mighty loud, I says:

" 'Doan' you hear me?—shet de do'!'

"She jis' stood de same way, kiner smilin' up. I was a-bilin'! I says:

" 'I lay I *make* you mine!'

"En wid dat I fetch' her a slap side de head dat sont her a-sprawlin'. Den I went into de yuther room, en 'uz gone 'bout ten minutes; en when I come back, dah was dat do' a-stannin' open *yit*, en dat chile stannin' mos' right in it, a-lookin' down and mournin', en de tears runnin' down. My, but I *wuz* mad, I was agwyne for de chile, but jis' den—it was a do' dat open innerds—jis' den, 'long come de wind en slam it to, behine de chile, *ker-blam!*—en my lan', de chile never move'! My breff mos' hop outer me; en I feel so—so—I doan' know *how* I feel. I crope out, all a-tremblin', en crope aroun' en open de do' easy en slow, en poke my head in behine de chile, sof' en still, en all uv a sudden, I says *pow!* jis' as loud as I could yell. *She never budge!* Oh, Huck, I bust out a-cryin' en grab her up in my arms, en say, 'Oh, de po' little thing! de Lord God Amighty fogive po' ole Jim, kaze he never gwyne to fogive hisself as long's he live!' Oh, she was plumb deef en dumb, Huck, plumb deef en dumb—en I'd ben a'treat'n her so!"

Chapter XXIV

Next day, towards night, we laid up under a little willow tow-head out in the middle, where there was a village on each side of the river, and the duke and the king begun to lay out a plan for working them towns. Jim he spoke to the duke, and said he hoped it wouldn't take but a few hours, because it got mighty heavy and tiresome to him when he had to lay all day in the wigwam tied with the rope. You see, when we left him all alone we had to tie him, because if anybody happened on him all by himself and not tied, it wouldn't look much like he was a runaway nigger, you know. So the duke said it *was* kind of hard to have to lay roped all day, and he'd cipher out some way to get around it.

He was uncommon bright, the duke was, and he soon struck it. He dressed Jim up in King Lear's outfit—it was a long curtain-calico gown, and a white horse-hair wig and whiskers; and then he took his theatre-paint and painted Jim's face and hands and ears and neck all over a dead bull solid blue, like a man that's been drownded nine days. Blamed if he warn't the horriblest looking outrage I ever see. Then the duke took and wrote out a sign on a shingle so—

Sick Arab—but harmless when not out of his head.

And he nailed that shingle to a lath, and stood the lath up four or five foot in front of the wigwam. Jim was satisfied. He said it was a sight better than laying tied a couple of years every day and trembling all over every time there was a sound. The duke told him to make himself free and easy, and if anybody ever come meddling around, he must hop out of the wigwam, and carry on a little, and fetch a howl or two like a wild beast, and he reckoned they would light out and leave him alone. Which was sound enough judgment; but you take the average man, and he wouldn't wait for him to howl. Why, he didn't only look like he was dead, he looked considerable more than that.

These rapscallions wanted to try the Nonesuch again, because there was so much money in it, but they judged it wouldn't be safe, because maybe the news might a worked along down by this time. They couldn't hit no project that suited, exactly; so at last the duke said he reckoned he'd lay off and work his brains an hour or two and see if he couldn't put up something on the Arkansaw village; and the king he allowed he would drop over to t'other village, without any plan, but just trust in Providence to lead him the profitable way—meaning the devil, I reckon. We had all bought store clothes where we stopped last; and now the king put his'n on, and he told me to put mine on. I done it, of course. The king's duds was all black, and he did look real swell and starchy. I never knowed how clothes could change a body before. Why, before, he looked like the orneriest old rip that ever was; but now, when he'd take off his new white beaver and make a bow and do a smile, he looked that grand and good and pious that you'd say he had walked right out of the ark, and maybe was old Leviticus[2] himself. Jim cleaned up the canoe, and I got my paddle ready. There was a big steamboat laying at the shore away up under the point, about three mile above town—been there a couple of hours, taking on freight. Says the king:

"Seein' how I'm dressed, I reckon maybe I better arrive down from St. Louis or Cincinnati, or some other big place. Go for the steamboat, Huckleberry; we'll come down to the village on her."

I didn't have to be ordered twice, to go and take a steamboat ride. I fetched the shore a half a mile above the village, and then went scooting along the bluff bank in the easy water. Pretty soon we come to a nice innocent-looking young country jake setting on a log swabbing the sweat off of his face, for it was powerful warm weather; and he had a couple of big carpet-bags by him.

"Run her nose in shore," says the king. I done it. "Wher' you bound for, young man?"

"For the steamboat; going to Orleans."

"Git aboard," says the king. "Hold on a minute, my servant 'll he'p you with them bags. Jump out and he'p the gentleman, Adolphus"—meaning me, I see.

I done so, and then we all three started on again. The young chap was mighty thankful; said it was tough work toting his baggage such weather. He asked the king where he was going, and the king told him he'd come down the river and landed at the other village this morning, and now he was going up a few mile to see an old friend on a farm up there. The young fellow says:

"When I first see you, I says to myself, 'It's Mr. Wilks, sure, and he come mighty near getting here in time.' But then I says again, 'No, I reckon it ain't him, or else he wouldn't be paddling up the river.' You *ain't* him, are you?"

"No, my name's Blodgett—Elexander Blodgett—*Reverend* Elexander Blodgett, I spose I must say, as I'm one o' the Lord's poor servants. But still I'm jist as able to be sorry for Mr. Wilks for not arriving in time, all the same, if he's missed anything by it—which I hope he hasn't."

"Well, he don't miss any property by it, because he'll get that all right; but he's missed seeing his brother Peter die—which he mayn't mind, nobody can tell as to that—but his brother would a give anything in this world to see *him* before he died; never talked about nothing else all these three weeks; hadn't seen him since they was boys together—and hadn't ever seen his brother William at all—that's the deef and dumb one—William ain't more than thirty or thirty-five. Peter and George was the only ones that come out here; George was the married brother; him and his wife both died last year. Harvey and William's the only ones that's left now; and, as I was saying, they haven't got here in time."

"Did anybody send 'em word?"

"Oh, yes; a month or two ago, when Peter was first took; because Peter said then that he sorter felt like he warn't going to get well this time. You see, he was pretty old, and George's g'yirls was too young to be much company for him, except Mary Jane the red-headed one; and so he was kinder lonesome after George and his wife died, and didn't seem to care much to live. He most desperately wanted to see Harvey—and William too, for that matter—because he was one of them kind that can't bear to make a will. He left a letter behind for Harvey, and said he'd told in it where his money was hid, and

2. The third book of the Old Testament is here confused with Noah.

how he wanted the rest of the property divided up so George's g'yirls would be all right—for George didn't leave nothing. And that letter was all they could get him to put a pen to."

"Why do you reckon Harvey don't come? Wher' does he live?"

"Oh, he lives in England—Sheffield—preaches there—hasn't ever been in this country. He hasn't had any too much time—and besides he mightn't a got the letter at all, you know."

"Too bad, too bad he couldn't a lived to see his brothers, poor soul. You going to Orleans, you say?"

"Yes, but that ain't only a part of it. I'm going in a ship, next Wednesday, for Ryo Janeero, where my uncle lives."

"It's a pretty long journey. But it'll be lovely; I wisht I was agoing. Is Mary Jane the oldest? How old is the others?"

"Mary Jane's nineteen, Susan's fifteen, and Joanna's about fourteen—that's the one that gives herself to good works and has a hare-lip."

"Poor things! to be left alone in the cold world so."

"Well, they could be worse off. Old Peter had friends, and they ain't going to let them come to no harm. There's Hobson, the Babtis' preacher; and Deacon Lot Hovey, and Ben Rucker, and Abner Shackleford, and Levi Bell, the lawyer; and Dr. Robinson, and their wives, and the widow Bartley, and—well, there's a lot of them; but these are the ones that Peter was thickest with, and used to write about sometimes, when he wrote home; so Harvey'll know where to look for friends when he gets here."

Well, the old man he went on asking questions till he just fairly emptied that young fellow. Blamed if he didn't inquire about everybody and everything in that blessed town, and all about all the Wilkses; and about Peter's business—which was a tanner; and about George's—which was a carpenter; and about Harvey's—which was a dissentering[3] minister, and so on, and so on. Then he says:

"What did you want to walk all the way up to the steamboat for?"

"Because she's a big Orleans boat, and I was afeard she mightn't stop there. When they're deep they won't stop for a hail. A Cincinnati boat will, but this is a St. Louis one."

"Was Peter Wilks well off?"

"Oh, yes, pretty well off. He had houses and land, and it's reckoned he left three or four thousand in cash hid up som'ers."

"When did you say he died?"

"I didn't say, but it was last night."

"Funeral to-morrow, likely?"

"Yes, 'bout the middle of the day."

"Well, it's all terrible sad; but we've all got to go, one time or another. So what we want to do is to be prepared; then we're all right."

"Yes, sir, it's the best way. Ma used to always say that."

When we struck the boat, she was about done loading, and pretty soon she got off. The king never said nothing about going aboard, so I lost my ride, after all. When the boat was gone, the king made me paddle up another mile to a lonesome place, and then he got ashore, and says:

3. Dissenting.

"Now hustle back, right off, and fetch the duke up here, and the new carpet-bags. And if he's gone over to t'other side, go over there and git him. And tell him to git himself up regardless. Shove along, now."

I see what *he* was up to; but I never said nothing, of course. When I got back with the duke, we hid the canoe and then they set down on a log, and the king told him everything, just like the young fellow had said it—every last word of it. And all the time he was a doing it, he tried to talk like an Englishman; and he done it pretty well too, for a slouch. I can't imitate him, and so I ain't agoing to try to; but he really done it pretty good. Then he says:

"How are you on the deef and dumb, Bilgewater?"

The duke said, leave him alone for that; said he had played a deef and dumb person on the histrionic boards. So then they waited for a steamboat.

About the middle of the afternoon a couple of little boats come along, but they didn't come from high enough up the river; but at last there was a big one, and they hailed her. She sent out her yawl, and we went aboard, and she was from Cincinnati; and when they found we only wanted to go four or five mile, they was booming mad, and give us a cussing, and said they wouldn't land us. But the king was ca'm. He says:

"If gentlemen kin afford to pay a dollar a mile apiece, to be took on and put off in a yawl, a steamboat kin afford to carry 'em, can't it?"

So they softened down and said it was all right; and when we got to the village, they yawled us ashore. About two dozen men flocked down, when they see the yawl a coming; and when the king says—

"Kin any of you gentlemen tell me wher' Mr. Peter Wilks lives?" they give a glance at one another, and nodded their heads, as much as to say, "What d' I tell you?" Then one of them says, kind of soft and gentle:

"I'm sorry, sir, but the best we can do is to tell you where he *did* live yesterday evening."

Sudden as winking, the ornery old cretur went all to smash, and fell up against the man, and put his chin on his shoulder, and cried down his back, and says:

"Alas, alas, our poor brother—gone, and we never got to see him; oh, it's too, *too* hard!"

Then he turns around, blubbering, and makes a lot of idiotic signs to the duke on his hands, and blamed if *he* didn't drop a carpet-bag and bust out a-crying. If they warn't the beatenest lot, them two frauds, that ever I struck.

Well, the men gethered around, and sympathized with them, and said all sorts of kind things to them, and carried their carpet-bags up the hill for them, and let them lean on them and cry, and told the king all about his brother's last moments, and the king he told it all over again on his hands to the duke, and both of them took on about that dead tanner like they'd lost the twelve disciples. Well, if ever I struck anything like it, I'm a nigger. It was enough to make a body ashamed of the human race.

Chapter XXV

The news was all over town in two minutes, and you could see the people tearing down on the run, from every which way, some of them putting on their coats as they come. Pretty soon we was in the middle of a crowd, and the noise of the tramping was like a soldier-march. The windows and dooryards was full; and every minute somebody would say, over a fence:

"Is it *them!*"

And somebody trotting along with the gang would answer back and say. "You bet it is."

When we got to the house, the street in front of it was packed, and the three girls was standing in the door. Mary Jane *was* red-headed, and that don't make no difference, she was most awful beautiful, and her face and her eyes was all lit up like glory, she was so glad her uncles was come. The king he spread his arms, and Mary Jane she jumped for them, and the hare-lip jumped for the duke, and there they *had* it! Everybody most, leastways women, cried for joy to see them meet again at last and have such good times.

Then the king he hunched the duke, private—I see him do it—and then he looked around and see the coffin, over in the corner on two chairs; so then, him and the duke, with a hand across each other's shoulder, and t'other hand to their eyes, walked slow and solemn over there, everybody dropping back to give them room, and all the talk and noise stopping, people saying "Sh!" and all the men taking their hats off and drooping their heads, so you could a heard a pin fall. And when they got there, they bent over and looked in the coffin, and took one sight, and then they bust out a crying so you could a heard them to Orleans, most; and then they put their arms around each other's necks, and hung their chins over each other's shoulders; and then for three minutes, or maybe four, I never see two men leak the way they done. And mind you, everybody was doing the same; and the place was that damp I never see anything like it. Then one of them got on one side of the coffin, and t'other on t'other side, and they kneeled down and rested their foreheads on the coffin, and let on to pray all to theirselves. Well, when it come to that, it worked the crowd like you never see anything like it, and so everybody broke down and went to sobbing right out loud—the poor girls, too; and every woman, nearly, went up to the girls, without saying a word, and kissed them, solemn, on the forehead, and then put their hand on their head, and looked up towards the sky, with the tears running down, and then busted out and went off sobbing and swabbing, and give the next woman a show. I never see anything so disgusting.

Well, by-and-by the king he gets up and comes forward a little, and works himself up and slobbers out a speech, all full of tears and flapdoodle about its being a sore trial for him and his poor brother to lose the diseased, and to miss seeing diseased alive, after the long journey of four thousand mile, but it's a trial that's sweetened and sanctified to us by this dear sympathy and these holy tears, and so he thanks them out of his heart and out of his brother's heart, because out of their mouths they can't, words being too weak and cold, and all that kind of rot and slush, till it was just sickening; and then he blubbers out a pious goody-goody Amen, and turns himself loose and goes to crying fit to bust.

And the minute the words was out of his mouth somebody over in the crowd struck up the doxolojer,[4] and everybody joined in with all their might, and it just warmed you up and made you feel as good as church letting out.

---

4. I.e., doxology, or hymn of praise to God. The particular doxology referred to here begins "Praise God, from whom all blessings flow."

Music *is* a good thing; and after all that soul-butter and hogwash, I never see it freshen up things so, and sound so honest and bully.

Then the king begins to work his jaw again, and says how him and his nieces would be glad if a few of the main principal friends of the family would take supper here with them this evening, and help set up with the ashes of the diseased; and says if his poor brother laying yonder could speak, he knows who he would name, for they was names that was very dear to him, and mentioned often in his letters; and so he will name the same, to-wit, as follows, vizz:—Rev. Mr. Hobson, and Deacon Lot Hovey, and Mr. Ben Rucker, and Abner Shackleford, and Levi Bell, and Dr. Robinson, and their wives, and the widow Bartley.

Rev. Hobson and Dr. Robinson was down to the end of the town, a-hunting together; that is, I mean the doctor was shipping a sick man to t'other world, and the preacher was pinting him right. Lawyer Bell was away up to Louisville on some business. But the rest was on hand, and so they all come and shook hands with the king and thanked him and talked to him; and then they shook hands with the duke, and didn't say nothing but just kept a-smiling and bobbing their heads like a passel of sapheads whilst he made all sorts of signs with his hands and said "Goo-goo—goo-goo-goo," all the time, like a baby that can't talk.

So the king he blatted along, and managed to inquire about pretty much everybody and dog in town, by his name, and mentioned all sorts of little things that happened one time or another in the town, or to George's family, or to Peter; and he always let on that Peter wrote him the things, but that was a lie, he got every blessed one of them out of that young flathead that we canoed up to the steamboat.

Then Mary Jane she fetched the letter her father left behind, and the king he read it out loud and cried over it. It give the dwelling-house and three thousand dollars, gold, to the girls; and it give the tanyard (which was doing a good business), along with some other houses and land (worth about seven thousand), and three thousand dollars in gold to Harvey and William, and told where the six thousand cash was hid, down cellar. So these two frauds said they'd go and fetch it up, and have everything square and above-board; and told me to come with a candle. We shut the cellar door behind us, and when they found the bag they spilt it out on the floor, and it was a lovely sight, all them yallerboys.[5] My, the way the king's eyes did shine! He slaps the duke on the shoulder, and says:

"Oh, *this* ain't bully, nor noth'n! Oh, no, I reckon not! Why, Biljy, it beats the Nonesuch, *don't* it!"

The duke allowed it did. They pawed the yaller-boys, and sifted them through their fingers and let them jingle down on the floor; and the king says:

"It ain't no use talkin'; bein' brothers to a rich dead man, and representatives of furrin heirs that's got left, is the line for you and me, Bilge. Thish-yer comes of trust'n to Providence. It's the best way, in the long run. I've tried 'em all, and ther' ain't no better way."

Most everybody would a been satisfied with the pile, and took it on trust; but no, they must count it. So they counts it, and it comes out four hundred and fifteen dollars short. Says the king:

5. Gold coins.

"Dern him, I wonder what he done with that four hundred and fifteen dollars?"

They worried over that a while, and ransacked all around for it. Then the duke says:

"Well, he was a pretty sick man, and likely he made a mistake—I reckon that's the way of it. The best way's to let it go, and keep still about it. We can spare it."

"Oh, shucks, yes, we can *spare* it. I don't k'yer noth'n 'bout that—it's the *count* I'm thinkin' about. We want to be awful square and open and aboveboard, here, you know. We want to lug this h'yer money up stairs and count it before everybody—then ther' ain't noth'n suspicious. But when the dead man says ther's six thous'n dollars, you know, we don't want to—"

"Hold on," says the duke. "Less make up the deffisit"—and he begun to haul out yallerboys out of his pocket.

"It's a most amaz'n good idea, duke—you *have* got a rattlin' clever head on you," says the king. "Blest if the old Nonesuch ain't a heppin' us out agin"—and *he* begun to haul out yallerjackets and stack them up.

It most busted them, but they made up the six thousand clean and clear.

"Say," says the duke, "I got another idea. Le's go up stairs and count this money, and then take and *give it to the girls.*"

"Good land, duke, lemme hug you! It's the most dazzling idea 'at ever a man struck. You have cert'nly got the most astonishin' head I ever see. Oh, this is the boss dodge,[6] ther' ain't no mistake 'bout it. Let 'em fetch along their suspicions now, if they want to—this'll lay 'em out."

When we got up stairs, everybody gathered around the table, and the king he counted it and stacked it up, three hundred dollars in a pile—twenty elegant little piles. Everybody looked hungry at it, and licked their chops. Then they raked it into the bag again, and I see the king begin to swell himself up for another speech. He says:

"Friends all, my poor brother that lays yonder, has done generous by them that's left behind in the vale of sorrers. He has done generous by these-yer poor little lambs that he loved and sheltered, and that's left fatherless and motherless. Yes, and we that knowed him, knows that he would a done *more* generous by 'em if he hadn't been afeard o' woundin' his dear William and me. Now, *wouldn't* he? Ther' ain't no question 'bout it, in *my* mind. Well, then— what kind o' brothers would it be, that 'd stand in his way at sech a time? And what kind o' uncles would it be that 'd rob—yes, *rob*—sech poor sweet lambs as these 'at he loved so, at sech a time? If I know William—and I *think* I do— he—well, I'll jest ask him." He turns around and begins to make a lot of signs to the duke with his hands; and the duke he looks at him stupid and leatherheaded a while, then all of sudden he seems to catch his meaning, and jumps for the king, goo-gooing with all his might for joy, and hugs him about fifteen times before he lets up. Then the king says, "I knowed it; I reckon *that* 'll convince anybody the way *he* feels about it. Here, Mary Jane, Susan, Joanner, take the money—take it *all.* It's the gift of him that lays yonder, cold but joyful."

Mary Jane she went for him, Susan and the hare-lip went for the duke, and then such another hugging and kissing I never see yet. And everybody

6. Best confidence trick.

212 / Mark Twain

crowded up with the tears in their eyes, and most shook the hands off of them frauds, saying all the time:

"You *dear* good souls!—how *lovely!*—how *could* you!"

Well, then, pretty soon all hands got to talking about the diseased again, and how good he was, and what a loss he was, and all that; and before long a big iron-jawed man worked himself in there from outside, and stood a listening and looking, and not saying anything; and nobody saying anything to him either, because the king was talking and they was all busy listening. The king was saying—in the middle of something he'd started in on—

"—they bein' partickler friends o' the diseased. That's why they're invited here this evenin'; but to-morrow we want *all* to come—everybody; for he respected everybody, he liked everybody, and so it's fitten that his funeral orgies sh'd be public."

And so he went a-mooning on and on, liking to hear himself talk, and every little while he fetched in his funeral orgies again, till the duke he couldn't stand it no more; so he writes on a little scrap of paper, *"obsequies,* you old fool," and folds it up and goes to goo-gooing and reaching it over people's heads to him. The king he reads it, and puts it in his pocket, and says:

"Poor William, afflicted as he is, his *heart's* aluz right. Asks me to invite everybody to come to the funeral—wants me to make 'em all welcome. But he needn't a worried—it was jest what I was at."

Then he weaves along again, perfectly ca'm, and goes to dropping in his funeral orgies again every now and then, just like he done before. And when he done it the third time, he says:

"I say orgies, not because it's the common term, because it ain't—obsequies bein' the common term—but because orgies is the right term. Obsequies ain't used in England no more, now—it's gone out. We say orgies now, in England. Orgies is better, because it means the thing you're after, more exact. It's a word that's made up out'n the Greek *orgo,* outside, open, abroad; and the Hebrew *jeesum,* to plant, cover up; hence in*ter.* So, you see, funeral orgies is an open er public funeral."[7]

He was the *worst* I ever struck. Well, the iron-jawed man he laughed right in his face. Everybody was shocked. Everybody says, "Why *doctor!*" and Abner Shackleford says:

"Why, Robinson, hain't you heard the news? This is Harvey Wilks."

The king he smiled eager, and shoved out his flapper, and says:

"Is it my poor brother's dear good friend and physician? I—"

"Keep your hands off of me!" says the doctor. *"You* talk like an Englishman—*don't* you? It's the worse imitation I ever heard. *You* Peter Wilks's brother. You're a fraud, that's what you are!"

Well, how they all took on! They crowded around the doctor, and tried to quiet him down, and tried to explain to him, and tell him how Harvey'd showed in forty ways that he *was* Harvey, and knowed everybody by name, and the names of the very dogs, and begged and *begged* him not to hurt Harvey's feelings and the poor girls' feelings, and all that; but it warn't no use, he stormed right along, and said any man that pretended to be an Englishman and couldn't imitate the lingo no better than what he did, was a fraud and a

---

7. The comic etymology was a stock-in-trade of the southwestern humorists and is still popular in comedy routines.

liar. The poor girls was hanging to the king and crying; and all of a sudden the doctor ups and turns on *them*. He says:

"I was your father's friend, and I'm your friend; and I warn you *as* a friend, and an honest one, that wants to protect you and keep you out of harm and trouble, to turn your backs on that scoundrel, and have nothing to do with him, the ignorant tramp, with his idiotic Greek and Hebrew as he calls it. He is the thinnest kind of an impostor—has come here with a lot of empty names and facts which he has picked up somewheres, and you take them for *proofs*, and are helped to fool yourselves by these foolish friends here, who ought to know better. Mary Jane Wilks, you know me for your friend, and for your unselfish friend, too. Now listen to me; turn this pitiful rascal out—I *beg* you to do it. Will you?"

Mary Jane straightened herself up, and my, but she was handsome! She says:

"*Here* is my answer." She hove up the bag of money and put it in the king's hands, and says, "Take this six thousand dollars, and invest it for me and my sisters any way you want to, and don't give us no receipt for it."

Then she put her arm around the king on one side, and Susan and the hare-lip done the same on the other. Everybody clapped their hands and stomped on the floor like a perfect storm, whilst the king held up his head and smiled proud. The doctor says:

"All right, I wash *my* hands of the matter. But I warn you all that a time's coming when you're going to feel sick whenever you think of this day"—and away he went.

"All right, doctor," says the king, kinder mocking him, "we'll try and get 'em to send for you"—which made them all laugh, and they said it was a prime good hit.

Chapter XXVI

Well, when they was all gone, the king he asks Mary Jane how they was off for spare rooms, and she said she had one spare room, which would do for Uncle William, and she'd give her own room to Uncle Harvey, which was a little bigger, and she would turn into the room with her sisters and sleep on a cot; and up garret was a little cubby, with a pallet in it. The king said the cubby would do for his valley—meaning me.

So Mary Jane took us up, and she showed them their rooms, which was plain but nice. She said she'd have her frocks and a lot of other traps took out of her room if they was in Uncle Harvey's way, but he said they warn't. The frocks was hung along the wall, and before them was a curtain made out of calico that hung down to the floor. There was an old hair trunk in one corner, and a guitar box in another, and all sorts of little knickknacks and jim-cracks around, like girls brisken up a room with. The king said it was all the more homely and more pleasanter for these fixings, and so don't disturb them. The duke's room was pretty small, but plenty good enough, and so was my cubby.

That night they had a big supper, and all them men and women was there, and I stood behind the king and the duke's chairs and waited on them, and the niggers waited on the rest. Mary Jane she set at the head of the table, with Susan along side of her, and said how bad the biscuits was, and how mean the preserves was, and how ornery and tough the fried chickens was—and all that kind of rot, the way women always do for to force out compliments; and the people all knowed everything was tip-top, and said so—said "How *do* you get biscuits to brown so nice?" and "Where, for the land's sake *did* you get these amaz'n pickles?" and all that kind of humbug talky-talk, just the way people always does at a supper, you know.

And when it was all done, me and the hare-lip had supper in the kitchen off of the leavings, whilst the others was helping the niggers clean up the things. The hare-lip she got to pumping me about England, and blest if I didn't think the ice was getting mighty thin, sometimes. She says:

"Did you ever see the king?"

"Who? William Fourth? Well, I bet I have—he goes to our church." I knowed he was dead years ago, but I never let on. So when I says he goes to our church, she says:

"What—regular?"

"Yes—regular. His pew's right over opposite ourn—on 'tother side the pulpit."

"I thought he lived in London?"

"Well, he does. Where *would* he live?"

"But I thought *you* lived in Sheffield?"

I see I was up a stump. I had to let on to get choked with a chicken bone, so as to get time to think how to get down again. Then I says:

"I mean he goes to our church regular when he's in Sheffield. That's only in the summer-time, when he comes there to take the sea baths."

"Why, how you talk—Sheffield ain't on the sea."

"Well, who said it was?"

"Why, you did."

"I *didn't*, nuther."

"You did!"

"I didn't."

"You did."

"I never said nothing of the kind."

"Well, what *did* you say, then?"

"Said he come to take the sea *baths*—that's what I said."

"Well, then! how's he going to take the sea baths if it ain't on the sea?"

"Looky here," I says, "did you ever see any Congress water?"[8]

"Yes."

"Well, did you have to go to Congress to get it?"

"Why, no."

"Well, neither does William Fourth have to go to the sea to get a sea bath."

"How does he get it, then?"

"Gets it the way people down here gets Congress water—in barrels. There in the palace at Sheffield they've got furnaces, and he wants his water hot. They can't bile that amount of water away off there at the sea. They haven't got no conveniences for it."

"Oh, I see, now. You might a said that in the first place and saved time."

When she said that, I see I was out of the woods again, and so I was comfortable and glad. Next, she says:

"Do you go to church, too?"

_____

8. Famous mineral water from the Congress Spring in Saratoga Springs, New York.

"Yes—regular."

"Where do you set?"

"Why, in our pew."

"*Whose* pew?"

"Why, *ourn*—your Uncle Harvey's."

"His'n? What does *he* want with a pew?"

"Wants it to set in. What did you *reckon* he wanted with it?"

"Why, I thought he'd be in the pulpit."

Rot him, I forgot he was a preacher. I see I was up a stump again, so I played another chicken bone and got another think. Then I says:

"Blame it, do you suppose there ain't but one preacher to a church?"

"Why, what do they want with more?"

"What!—to preach before a king? I never see such a girl as you. They don't have no less than seventeen."

"Seventeen! My land! Why, I wouldn't set out such a string as that, not if I *never* got to glory. It must take 'em a week."

"Shucks, they don't *all* of 'em preach the same day—only *one* of 'em."

"Well, then, what does the rest of 'em do?"

"Oh, nothing much. Loll around, pass the plate—and one thing or another. But mainly they don't do nothing."

"Well, then, what are they *for?*"

"Why, they're for *style*. Don't you know nothing?"

"Well, I don't *want* to know no such foolishness as that. How is servants treated in England? Do they treat 'em better 'n we treat our niggers?"

"*No!* A servant ain't nobody there. They treat them worse than dogs."

"Don't they give 'em holidays, the way we do, Christmas and New Year's week, and Fourth of July?"

"Oh, just listen! A body could tell *you* hain't ever been to England, by that. Why, Hare-l—why, Joanna, they never see a holiday from year's end to year's end; never go to the circus, nor theatre, nor nigger shows, nor nowheres."

"Nor church?"

"Nor church."

"But *you* always went to church."

Well, I was gone up again. I forgot I was the old man's servant. But next minute I whirled in on a kind of an explanation how a valley was different from a common servant, and *had* to go to church whether he wanted to or not, and set with the family, on account of it's being the law. But I didn't do it pretty good, and when I got done I see she warn't satisfied. She says:

"Honest injun, now, hain't you been telling me a lot of lies?"

"Honest injun," says I.

"None of it at all?"

"None of it at all. Not a lie in it," says I.

"Lay your hand on this book and say it."

I see it warn't nothing but a dictionary, so I laid my hand on it and said it. So then she looked a little better satisfied, and says:

"Well, then, I'll believe some of it; but I hope to gracious if I'll believe the rest."

"What is it you won't believe, Joe?" says Mary Jane, stepping in with Susan behind her. "It ain't right nor kind for you to talk so to him, and him a stranger and so far from his people. How would you like to be treated so?"

"That's always your way, Maim—always sailing in to help somebody before they're hurt. I hain't done nothing to him. He's told some stretchers, I reckon; and I said I wouldn't swallow it all; and that's every bit and grain I *did* say. I reckon he can stand a little thing like that, can't he?"

"I don't care whether 'twas little or whether 'twas big, he's here in our house and a stranger, and it wasn't good of you to say it. If you was in his place, it would make you feel ashamed; and so you ought'nt to say a thing to another person that will make *them* feel ashamed."

"Why, Maim, he said—"

"It don't make no difference what he *said*—that ain't the thing. The thing is for you to treat him *kind,* and not be saying things to make him remember he ain't in his own country and amongst his own folks."

I says to myself, *this* is a girl that I'm letting that old reptle rob her of her money!

Then Susan *she* waltzed in; and if you'll believe me, she did give Hare-lip hark from the tomb![9]

Says I to myself, And this is *another* one that I'm letting him rob her of her money!

Then Mary Jane she took another inning, and went in sweet and lovely again—which was her way—but when she got done there warn't hardly anything left o' poor Hare-lip. So she hollered.

"All right, then," says the other girls, "you just ask his pardon."

She done it, too. And she done it beautiful. She done it so beautiful it was good to hear; and I wished I could tell her a thousand lies, so she could do it again.

I says to myself, this is *another* one that I'm letting him rob her of her money. And when she got through, they all jest laid theirselves out to make me feel at home and know I was amongst friends. I felt so ornery and low down and mean, that I says to myself, My mind's made up; I'll hive that money for them or bust.

So then I lit out—for bed, I said, meaning some time or another. When I got by myself, I went to thinking the thing over. I says to myself, shall I go to that doctor, private, and blow on these frauds? No—that won't do. He might tell who told him; then the king and the duke would make it warm for me. Shall I go, private, and tell Mary Jane? No—I dasn't do it. Her face would give them a hint, sure; they've got the money, and they'd slide right out and get away with it. If she was to fetch in help, I'd get mixed up in the business, before it was done with, I judge. No, there ain't no good way but one. I got to steal that money, somehow; and I got to steal it some way that they won't suspicion that I done it. They've got a good thing, here; and they ain't agoing to leave till they've played this family and this town for all they're worth, so I'll find a chance time enough. I'll steal it, and hide it; and by-and-by, when I'm away down the river, I'll write a letter and tell Mary Jane where it's hid. But I better hive it to-night, if I can, because the doctor maybe hasn't let up as much as he lets on he has; he might scare them out of here, yet.

So, thinks I, I'll go and search them rooms. Up stairs the hall was dark, but I found the duke's room, and started to paw around it with my hands; but I recollected it wouldn't be much like the king to let anybody else take care of that money but his own self; so then I went to his room and begun to paw

9. A chewing out.

around there. But I see I couldn't do nothing without a candle, and I dasn't light one, of course. So I judged I'd got to do the other thing—lay for them, and eavesdrop. About that time, I hears their footsteps coming, and was going to skip under the bed; I reached for it, but it wasn't where I thought it would be; but I touched the curtain that hid Mary Jane's frocks, so I jumped in behind that and snuggled in amongst the gowns, and stood there perfectly still.

They come in and shut the door; and the first thing the duke done was to get down and look under the bed. Then I was glad I hadn't found the bed when I wanted it. And yet, you know, it's kind of natural to hide under the bed when you are up to anything private. They sets down, then, and the king says:

"Well, what is it? and cut it middlin' short, because it's better for us to be down there a whoopin'-up the mournin', than up here givin' 'em a chance to talk us over."

"Well, this is it, Capet. I ain't easy; I ain't comfortable. That doctor lays on my mind. I wanted to know your plans. I've got a notion, and I think it's a sound one."

"What is it, duke?"

"That we better glide out of this, before three in the morning, and clip it down the river with what we've got. Specially, seeing we got it so easy—*given* back to us, flung at our heads, as you may say, when of course we allowed to have to steal it back. I'm for knocking off and lighting out."

That made me feel pretty bad. About an hour or two ago, it would a been a little different, but now it made me feel bad and disappointed. The king rips out and says:

"What! And not sell out the rest o' the property? March off like a passel o' fools and leave eight or nine thous'n dollars' worth o' property layin' around jest sufferin' to be scooped in?—and all good salable stuff, too."

The duke he grumbled; said the bag of gold was enough, and he didn't want to go no deeper—didn't want to rob a lot of orphans of *everything* they had.

"Why, how you talk!" says the king. "We shan't rob 'em of nothing at all but jest this money. The people that *buys* the property is the suff'rers; because as soon's it's found out 'at we didn't own it—which won't be long after we've slid—the sale won't be valid, and it'll all go back to the estate. These-yer orphans 'll git their house back agin, and that's enough for *them;* they're young and spry, and k'n easy earn a livin'. *They* ain't agoing to suffer. Why, jest think—there's thous'n's and thous'n's that ain't nigh so well off. Bless you, *they* ain't got noth'n to complain of."

Well, the king he talked him blind; so at last he give in, and said all right, but said he believed it was blame foolishness to stay, and that doctor hanging over them. But the king says:

"Cuss the doctor! What do we k'yer for *him?* Hain't we got all the fools in town on our side? and ain't that a big enough majority in any town?"

So they got ready to go down stairs again. The duke says:

"I don't think we put that money in a good place."

That cheered me up. I'd begun to think I warn't going to get a hint of no kind to help me. The king says:

"Why?"

"Because Mary Jane 'll be in mourning from this out; and first you know the nigger that does up the rooms will get an order to box these duds up and

put 'em away; and do you reckon a nigger can run across money and not borrow some of it?"

"Your head's level, agin, duke," says the king; and he come a fumbling
under the curtain two or three foot from where I was. I stuck tight to the wall,
and kept mighty still, though quivery; and I wondered what them fellows
would say to me if they catched me; and I tried to think what I'd better do if
they did catch me. But the king he got the bag before I could think more than
about a half a thought, and he never suspicioned I was around. They took and
shoved the bag through a rip in the straw tick that was under the feather bed,
and crammed it in a foot or two amongst the straw and said it was all right,
now, because a nigger only makes up the feather bed, and don't turn over the
straw tick only about twice a year, and so it warn't in no danger of getting
stole, now.

But I knowed better. I had it out of there before they was halfway down
stairs. I groped along up to my cubby, and hid it there till I could get a chance
to do better. I judged I better hide it outside of the house somewheres, because
if they missed it they would give the house a good ransacking. I knowed that
very well. Then I turned in, with my clothes all on; but I couldn't a gone to
sleep, if I'd a wanted to, I was in such a sweat to get through with the business. By-and-by I heard the king and the duke come up; so I rolled off of my
pallet and laid with my chin at the top of my ladder and waited to see if anything was going to happen. But nothing did.

So I held on till all the late sounds had quit and the early ones hadn't
begun, yet; and then I slipped down the ladder.

Chapter XXVII

I crept to their doors and listened; they was snoring, so I tip-toed along, and
got down stairs all right. There warn't a sound anywheres. I peeped through
a crack of the dining-room door, and see the men that was watching the
corpse all sound asleep on their chairs. The door was open into the parlor,
where the corpse was laying, and there was a candle in both rooms. I passed
along, and the parlor door was open; but I see there warn't nobody in there
but the remainders of Peter; so I shoved on by; but the front door was locked,
and the key wasn't there. Just then I heard somebody coming down the stairs,
back behind me. I run in the parlor, and took a swift look around, and the only
place I see to hide the bag was in the coffin. The lid was shoved along about
a foot, showing the dead man's face down in there, with a wet cloth over it,
and his shroud on. I tucked the money-bag in under the lid, just down beyond
where his hands was crossed, which made me creep, they was so cold, and
then I run back across the room and in behind the door.

The person coming was Mary Jane. She went to the coffin, very soft, and
kneeled down and looked in; then she put up her handkerchief and I see she
begun to cry, though I couldn't hear her, and her back was to me. I slid out, and
as I passed the dining-room I thought I'd make sure them watchers hadn't seen
me; so I looked through the crack and everything was all right. They hadn't
stirred.

I slipped up to bed, feeling ruther blue, on accounts of the thing playing
out that way after I had took so much trouble and run so much resk about it.
Says I, if it could stay where it is, all right; because when we get down the

river a hundred mile or two, I could write back to Mary Jane, and she could dig him up again and get it; but that ain't the thing that's going to happen; the thing that's going to happen is, the money 'll be found when they come to screw on the lid. Then the king 'll get it again, and it 'll be a long day before he gives anybody another chance to smouch it from him. Of course I *wanted* to slide down and get it out of there, but I dasn't try it. Every minute it was getting earlier, now, and pretty soon some of them watchers would begin to stir, and I might get catched—catched with six thousand dollars in my hands that nobody hadn't hired me to take care of. I don't wish to be mixed up in no such business as that, I says to myself.

When I got down stairs in the morning, the parlor was shut up, and the watchers was gone. There warn't nobody around but the family and the widow Bartley and our tribe. I watched their faces to see if anything had been happening, but I couldn't tell.

Towards the middle of the day the undertaker come, with his man, and they set the coffin in the middle of the room on a couple of chairs, and then set all our chairs in rows, and borrowed more from the neighbors till the hall and the parlor and the dining-room was full. I see the coffin lid was the way it was before, but I dasn't go to look in under it, with folks around.

Then the people begun to flock in, and the beats and the girls took seats in the front row at the head of the coffin, and for a half an hour the people filed around slow, in single rank, and looked down at the dead man's face a minute, and some dropped in a tear, and it was all very still and solemn, only the girls and the beats holding handkerchiefs to their eyes and keeping their heads bent, and sobbing a little. There warn't no other sound but the scraping of the feet on the floor, and blowing noses—because people always blows them more at a funeral than they do at other places except church.

When the place was packed full, the undertaker he slid around in his black gloves with his softy soothering ways, putting on the last touches, and getting people and things all shipshape and comfortable, and making no more sound than a cat. He never spoke; he moved people around, he squeezed in late ones, he opened up passage-ways, and done it all with nods, and signs with his hands. Then he took his place over against the wall. He was the softest, glidingest, stealthiest man I ever see; and there warn't no more smile to him than there is to a ham.

They had borrowed a melodeum[1]—a sick one; and when everything was ready, a young woman set down and worked it, and it was pretty skreeky and colicky, and everybody joined in and sung, and Peter was the only one that had a good thing, according to my notion. Then the Reverend Hobson opened up, slow and solemn, and begun to talk; and straight off the most outrageous row busted out in the cellar a body ever heard; it was only one dog, but he made a most powerful racket, and he kept it up, right along; the parson he had to stand there, over the coffin, and wait—you couldn't hear yourself think. It was right down awkward, and nobody didn't seem to know what to do. But pretty soon they see that long-legged undertaker make a sign to the preacher as much as to say, "Don't you worry—just depend on me." Then he stooped down and begun to glide along the wall, just his shoulders showing

---

1. A melodeon, small keyboard organ.

over the people's heads. So he glided along, and the pow-wow and racket getting more and more outrageous all the time; and at last, when he had gone
around two sides of the room, he disappears down cellar. Then, in about two
seconds we heard a whack, and the dog he finished up with a most amazing
howl or two, and then everything was dead still, and the parson begun his
solemn talk where he left off. In a minute or two here comes this undertaker's
back and shoulders gliding along the wall again; and so he glided, and glided,
around three sides of the room, and then rose up, and shaded his mouth with
his hands, and stretched his neck out towards the preacher, over the people's
heads, and says, in a kind of a coarse whisper, *"He had a rat!"* Then he
drooped down and glided along the wall again to his place. You could see it
was a great satisfaction to the people, because naturally they wanted to know.
A little thing like that don't cost nothing, and it's just the little things that
makes a man to be looked up to and liked. There warn't no more popular man
in town than what that undertaker was.

Well, the funeral sermon was very good, but pison long and tiresome; and
then the king he shoved in and got off some of his usual rubbage, and at last
the job was through, and the undertaker begun to sneak up on the coffin with
his screw-driver. I was in a sweat then, and watched him pretty keen. But he
never meddled at all; just slid the lid along, as soft as mush, and screwed it
down tight and fast. So there I was! I didn't know whether the money was in
there, or not. So, says I, spose somebody has hogged that bag on the sly?—
now how do I know whether to write to Mary Jane or not? 'Spose she dug him
up and didn't find nothing—what would she think of me? Blame it, I says, I
might get hunted up and jailed; I'd better lay low and keep dark, and not write
at all; the thing's awful mixed, now; trying to better it, I've worsened it a hundred times, and I wish to goodness I'd just let it alone, dad fetch the whole
business!

They buried him, and we come back home, and I went to watching faces
again—I couldn't help it, and I couldn't rest easy. But nothing come of it; the
faces didn't tell me nothing.

The king he visited around, in the evening, and sweetened every body up,
and made himself ever so friendly; and he give out the idea that his congregation over in England would be in a sweat about him, so he must hurry and
settle up the estate right away, and leave for home. He was very sorry he was
so pushed, and so was everybody; they wished he could stay longer, but they
said they could see it couldn't be done. And he said of course him and William
would take the girls home with them; and that pleased everybody too, because
then the girls would be well fixed, and amongst their own relations; and it
pleased the girls, too—tickled them so they clean forgot they ever had a trouble in the world; and told him to sell out as quick as he wanted to, they would
be ready. Them poor things was that glad and happy it made my heart ache
to see them getting fooled and lied to so, but I didn't see no safe way for me
to chip in and change the general tune.

Well, blamed if the king didn't bill the house and the niggers and all the
property for auction straight off—sale two days after the funeral; but anybody
could buy private beforehand if they wanted to.

So the next day after the funeral, along about noontime, the girls' joy got
the first jolt; a couple of nigger traders come along, and the king sold them

the niggers reasonable, for three-day drafts[2] as they called it, and away they went, the two sons up the river to Memphis, and their mother down the river to Orleans. I thought them poor girls and them niggers would break their hearts for grief; they cried around each other, and took on so it most made me down sick to see it. The girls said they hadn't ever dreamed of seeing the family separated or sold away from the town. I can't ever get it out of my memory, the sight of them poor miserable girls and niggers hanging around each other's necks and crying; and I reckon I couldn't a stood it all but would a had to bust out and tell on our gang if I hadn't knowed the sale warn't no account and the niggers would be back home in a week or two.

The thing made a big stir in the town, too, and a good many come out flat-footed and said it was scandalous to separate the mother and the children that way. It injured the frauds some; but the old fool he bulled right along, spite of all the duke could say or do, and I tell you the duke was powerful uneasy.

Next day was auction day. About broad-day in the morning, the king and the duke come up in the garret and woke me up, and I see by their look that there was trouble. The king says:

"Was you in my room night before last?"

"No, your majesty"—which was the way I always called him when nobody but our gang warn't around.

"Was you in there yesterday er last night?"

"No, your majesty."

"Honor bright, now—no lies."

"Honor bright, your majesty, I'm telling you the truth. I hain't been anear your room since Miss Mary Jane took you and the duke and showed it to you."

The duke says:

"Have you seen anybody else go in there?"

"No, your grace, not as I remember, I believe."

"Stop and think."

I studied a while, and see my chance, then I says:

"Well, I see the niggers go in there several times."

Both of them give a little jump; and looked like they hadn't ever expected it, and then like they *had*. Then the duke says:

"What, *all* of them?"

"No—leastways not all at once. That is, I don't think I ever see them all come *out* at once but just one time."

"Hello—when was that?"

"It was the day we had the funeral. In the morning. It warn't early, because I overslept. I was just starting down the ladder, and I see them."

"Well, go on, *go on*—what did they do? How'd they act?"

"They didn't do nothing. And they didn't act anyway, much, as fur as I see. They tip-toed away; so I seen, easy enough, that they'd shoved in there to do up your majesty's room, or something, sposing you was up; and found you *warn't* up, and so they was hoping to slide out of the way of trouble without waking you up, if they hadn't already waked you up."

"Great guns, *this* is a go!" says the king; and both of them looked pretty sick,

2. Bank drafts or checks payable three days later.

and tolerable silly. They stood there a thinking and scratching their heads, a minute, and then the duke he bust into a kind of a little raspy chuckle, and says:

"It does beat all, how neat the niggers played their hand. They let on to be *sorry* they was going out of this region! and I believed they *was* sorry. And so did you, and so did everybody. Don't ever tell *me* any more that a nigger ain't got any histrionic talent. Why, the way they played that thing, it would fool *anybody*. In my opinion there's a fortune in 'em. If I had capital and a theatre, I wouldn't want a better lay out than that—and here we've gone and sold 'em for a song. Yes, and ain't privileged to sing the song, yet. Say, where *is* that song?—that draft."

"In the bank for to be collected. Where *would* it be?"

"Well, *that's* all right then, thank goodness."

Says I, kind of timid-like:

"Is something gone wrong?"

The king whirls on me and rips out:

"None o' your business! You keep your head shet, and mind y'r own affairs—if you got any. Long as you're in this town, don't you forgit *that,* you hear?" Then he says to the duke, "We got to jest swaller it, and say noth'n: mum's the word for *us*."

As they was starting down the ladder, the duke he chuckles again, and says:

"Quick sales *and* small profits! It's a good business—yes."

The king snarls around on him and says,

"I was trying to do for the best, in sellin' 'm out so quick. If the profits has turned out to be none, lackin' considable, and none to carry, is it my fault any more'n it's yourn?"

"Well, *they'd* be in this house yet, and we *wouldn't* if I could a got my advice listened to."

The king sassed back, as much as was safe for him, and then swapped around and lit into *me* again. He give me down the banks[3] for not coming and *telling* him I see the niggers come out of his room acting that way—said any fool would a *knowed* something was up. And then waltzed in and cussed *himself* a while; and said it all come of him not laying late and taking his natural rest that morning, and he'd be blamed if he'd ever do it again. So they went off a jawing; and I felt dreadful glad I'd worked it all off onto the niggers and yet hadn't done the niggers no harm by it.

Chapter XXVIII

By-and-by it was getting-up time; so I come down the ladder and started for down stairs, but as I come to the girls' room, the door was open, and I see Mary Jane setting by her old hair trunk, which was open and she'd been packing things in it—getting ready to go to England. But she had stopped now, with a folded gown in her lap, and had her face in her hands, crying. I felt awful bad to see it; of course anybody would. I went in there, and says:

"Miss Mary Jane, you can't abear to see people in trouble, and *I* can't—most always. Tell me about it."

So she done it. And it was the niggers—I just expected it. She said the beautiful trip to England was most about spoiled for her; she didn't know *how*

---

3. A cussing out.

she was ever going to be happy there, knowing the mother and the children warn't ever going to see each other no more—and then busted out bitterer than ever, and flung up her hands, and says

"Oh, dear, dear, to think they ain't *ever* going to see each other any more!"

"But they *will*—and inside of two weeks—and I *know* it!" says I.

Laws it was out before I could think!—and before I could budge, she throws her arms around my neck, and told me to say it *again*, say it *again*, say it *again!*

I see I had spoke too sudden, and said too much, and was in a close place. I asked her to let me think a minute; and she set there, very impatient and excited, and handsome, but looking kind of happy and eased-up, like a person that's had a tooth pulled out. So I went to studying it out. I says to myself, I reckon a body that ups and tells the truth when he is in a tight place, is taking considerable many resks, though I ain't had no experience, and can't say for certain; but it looks so to me, anyway; and yet here's a case where I'm blest if it don't look to me like the truth is better, and actuly *safer,* than pa lie. I must lay it by in my mind, and think it over some time or other, it's so kind of strange and unregular. I never see nothing like it. Well, I says to myself at last, I'm agoing to chance it; I'll up and tell the truth this time, though it does seem most like setting down on a kag of powder and touching it off just to see where you'll go to. Then I says:

"Miss Mary Jane, is there any place out of town a little ways, where you could go and stay three or four days?"

"Yes—Mr. Lothrop's. Why?"

"Never mind why, yet. If I'll tell you how I know the niggers will see each other again—inside of two weeks—here in this house—and *prove* how I know it—will you go to Mr. Lothrop's and stay four days?"

"Four days!" she says; "I'll stay a year!"

"All right," I says, "I don't want nothing more out of *you* than just your word—I druther have it than another man's kiss-the-Bible." She smiled, and reddened up very sweet, and I says, "If you don't mind it, I'll shut the door—and bolt it."

Then I come back and set down again, and says:

"Don't you holler. Just set still, and take it like a man. I got to tell the truth, and you want to brace up, Miss Mary, because it's a bad kind, and going to be hard to take, but there ain't no help for it. These uncles of yourn ain't no uncles at all—they're a couple of frauds—regular dead-beats. There, now we're over the worst of it—you can stand the rest middling easy."

It jolted her up like everything, of course; but I was over the shoal water now, so I went right along, her eyes a blazing higher and higher all the time, and told her every blame thing, from where we first struck that young fool going up to the steamboat, clear through to where she flung herself onto the king's breast at the front door and he kissed her sixteen or seventeen times—and then up she jumps, with her face afire like sunset, and says:

"The brute! Come—don't waste a minute—not a *second*—we'll have them tarred and feathered, and flung in the river!"[4]

4. The victim of this fairly commonplace mob punishment was tied to a rail, smeared with hot tar, and covered with feathers. Then the victim would be ridden out of town on the rail to the jeers of the mob.

Says I;

"Cert'nly. But do you mean, *before* you go to Mr. Lothrop's, or—"

"Oh," she says, "what am I *thinking* about!" she says, and set right down again. "Don't mind what I said—please don't—you *won't*, now, *will* you?" Laying her silky hand on mine in that kind of a way that I said I would die first. "I never thought, I was so stirred up," she says; "now go on, and I won't do so any more. You tell me what to do, and whatever you say, I'll do it."

"Well," I says, "it's a rough gang, them two frauds, and I'm fixed so I got to travel with them a while longer, whether I want to or not—I druther not tell you why—and if you was to blow on them this town would get me out of their claws, and *I'd* be all right, but there'd be another person that you don't know about who'd be in big trouble. Well, we got to save *him*, hain't we? Of course. Well, then, we won't blow on them."

Saying them words put a good idea in my head. I see how maybe I could get me and Jim rid of the frauds; get them jailed here, and then leave. But I didn't want to run the raft in day-time, without anybody aboard to answer questions but me; so I didn't want the plan to begin working till pretty late to-night. I says:

"Miss Mary Jane, I'll tell you what we'll do—and you won't have to stay at Mr. Lothrop's so long, nuther. How fur is it?"

"A little short of four miles—right out in the country, back here."

"Well, that'll answer. Now you go along out there, and lay low till nine or half-past, to-night, and then get them to fetch you home again—tell them you've thought of something. If you get here before eleven, put a candle in this window, and if I don't turn up, wait *till* eleven, and *then* if I don't turn up it means I'm gone, and out of the way, and safe. Then you come out and spread the news around, and get these beats jailed."

"Good," she says, "I'll do it."

"And if it just happens so that I don't get away, but get took up along with them, you must up and say I told you the whole thing beforehand, and you must stand by me all you can."

"Stand by you, indeed I will. They sha'n't touch a hair of your head!" she says, and I see her nostrils spread and her eyes snap when she said it, too.

"If I get away, I sha'n't be here," I says, "to prove these rapscallions ain't your uncles, and I couldn't do it if I *was* here. I could swear they was beats and bummers, that's all; though that's worth something. Well, there's others can do that better than what I can—and they're people that ain't going to be doubted as quick as I'd be. I'll tell you how to find them. Gimme a pencil and a piece of paper. There—'Royal Nonesuch, Bricksville.' Put it away, and don't lose it. When the court wants to find out something about these two, let them send up to Bricksville and say they've got the men that played the Royal Nonesuch, and ask for some witnesses—why, you'll have that entire town down here before you can hardly wink, Miss Mary. And they'll come a-biling, too."

I judged we had got everything fixed about right, now. So I says:

"Just let the auction go right along, and don't worry. Nobody don't have to pay for the things they buy till a whole day after the auction, on accounts of the short notice, and they ain't going out of this till they get that money—and the way we've fixed it the sale ain't going to count, and they ain't going to *get* no money. It's just like the way it was with the niggers—it warn't no sale, and the niggers will be back before long. Why, they can't collect the money for the *niggers,* yet—they're in the worst kind of a fix, Miss Mary."

"Well," she says, "I'll run down to breakfast now, and then I'll start straight for Mr. Lothrop's."

" 'Deed, *that* ain't the ticket, Miss Mary Jane," I says, "by no manner of means; go *before* breakfast."

"Why?"

"What did you reckon I wanted you to go at all for, Miss Mary?"

"Well, I never thought—and come to think, I don't know. What was it?"

"Why, it's because you ain't one of these leather-face people. I don't want no better book than what your face is. A body can set down and read it off like coarse paint. Do you reckon you can go and face your uncles, when they come to kiss you good-morning, and never—"

"There, there, don't! Yes, I'll go before breakfast—I'll be glad to. And leave my sisters with them?"

"Yes—never mind about them. They've got to stand it yet a while. They might suspicion something if all of you was to go. I don't want you to see them, nor your sisters, nor nobody in this town—if a neighbor was to ask how is your uncles this morning, your face would tell something. No, you go right along, Miss Mary Jane, and I'll fix it with all of them. I'll tell Miss Susan to give your love to your uncles and say you've went away for a few hours for to get a little rest and change, or to see a friend, and you'll be back to-night or early in the morning."

"Gone to see a friend is all right, but I won't have my love given to them."

"Well, then, it sha'n't be." It was well enough to tell *her* so—no harm in it. It was only a little thing to do, and no trouble; and it's the little things that smoothes people's roads the most, down here below; it would make Mary Jane comfortable, and it wouldn't cost nothing. Then I says: "There's one more thing—that bag of money."

"Well, they've got that; and it makes me feel pretty silly to think *how* they got it."

"No, you're out, there. They hain't got it."

"Why, who's got it?"

"I wish I knowed, but I don't. I *had* it, because I stole it from them: and I stole it to give to you; and I know where I hid it, but I'm afraid it ain't there no more. I'm awful sorry, Miss Mary Jane, I'm just as sorry as I can be; but I done the best I could; I did, honest. I come nigh getting caught, and I had to shove it into the first place I come to, and run—and it warn't a good place."

"Oh, stop blaming yourself—it's too bad to do it, and I won't allow it—you couldn't help it; it wasn't your fault. Where did you hide it?"

I didn't want to set her to thinking about her troubles again; and I couldn't seem to get my mouth to tell her what would make her see that corpse laying in the coffin with that bag of money on his stomach. So for a minute I didn't say nothing—then I says:

"I'd ruther not *tell* you where I put it, Miss Mary Jane, if you don't mind letting me off; but I'll write it for you on a piece of paper, and you can read it along the road to Mr. Lothrop's; if you want to. Do you reckon that'll do?"

"Oh, yes."

So I wrote: "I put it in the coffin. It was in there when you was crying there, away in the night. I was behind the door, and I was mighty sorry for you, Miss Mary Jane."

It made my eyes water a little, to remember her crying there all by herself in the night, and them devils laying there right under her own roof, shaming her and robbing her; and when I folded it up and give it to her, I see the water come into her eyes, too; and she shook me by the hand, hard, and says:

"*Good*-bye—I'm going to do everything just as you've told me; and if I don't ever see you again, I sha'n't ever forget you, and I'll think of you a many and a many a time, and I'll *pray* for you, too!"—and she was gone.

Pray for me! I reckoned if she knowed me she'd take a job that was more nearer her size. But I bet she done it, just the same—she was just that kind. She had the grit to pray for Judus if she took the notion—there warn't no backdown to her, I judge. You may say what you want to, but in my opinion she had more sand in her than any girl I ever see; in my opinion she was just full of sand.[5] It sounds like flattery, but it ain't no flattery. And when it comes to beauty—and goodness too—she lays over them all. I hain't ever seen her since that time that I see her go out of that door; no, I hain't ever seen her since, but I reckon I've thought of her a many and a many a million times, and of her saying she would pray for me; and if ever I'd a thought it would do any good for me to pray for *her*, blamed if I wouldn't a done it or bust.

Well, Mary Jane she lit out the back way, I reckon; because nobody see her go. When I struck Susan and the hare-lip, I says:

"What's the name of them people over on t'other side of the river that you all goes to see sometimes?"

They says:

"There's several; but it's the Proctors, mainly."

"That's the name," I says; "I most forgot it. Well, Miss Mary Jane she told me to tell you she's gone over there in a dreadful hurry—one of them's sick."

"Which one?"

"I don't know; leastways I kinder forget; but I think it's—"

"Sakes alive, I hope it ain't *Hanner*?"

"I'm sorry to say it," I says, "but Hanner's the very one."

"My goodness—and she so well only last week! Is she took bad?"

"It ain't no name for it. They set up with her all night, Miss Mary Jane said, and they don't think she'll last many hours."

"Only think of that, now! What's the matter with her!"

I couldn't think of anything reasonable, right off that way, so I says:

"Mumps."

"Mumps your granny! They don't set up with people that's got the mumps."

"They don't, don't they? You better bet they do with *these* mumps. These mumps is different. It's a new kind, Miss Mary Jane said."

"How's it a new kind?"

"Because it's mixed up with other things."

"What other things?"

"Well, measles, and whooping-cough, and erysiplas, and consumption, and yaller janders, and brain fever, and I don't know what all."

"My land! And they call it the *mumps*?"

"That's what Miss Mary Jane said."

5. Courage, guts.

"Well, what in the nation do they call it the *mumps* for?"

"Why, because it *is* the mumps. That's what it starts with."

"Well, ther' ain't no sense in it. A body might stump his toe, and take pison, and fall down the well, and break his neck, and bust his brains out, and somebody come along and ask what killed him, and some numskull up and say, 'Why, he stumped his *toe*.' Would ther' be any sense in that? *No*. And ther' ain't no sense in *this*, nuther. Is it ketching?"

"Is it *ketching*? Why, how you talk. Is a *harrow* catching?—in the dark? If you don't hitch onto one tooth, you're bound to on another, ain't you? And you can't get away with that tooth without fetching the whole harrow along, can you? Well, these kind of mumps is a kind of a harrow, as you may say— and it ain't no slouch of a harrow, nuther, you come to get it hitched on good."

"Well, it's awful, *I* think," says the hare-lip. "I'll go to Uncle Harvey and—"

"Oh, yes," I says, "I *would*. Of *course* I would. I wouldn't lose no time."

"Well, why wouldn't you?"

"Just look at it a minute, and maybe you can see. Hain't your uncles obleeged to get along home to England as fast as they can? And do you reckon they'd be mean enough to go off and leave you to go all that journey by yourselves? *You* know they'll wait for you. So fur, so good. Your uncle Harvey's a preacher, ain't he? Very well, then; is a *preacher* going to deceive a steamboat clerk? is he going to deceive a *ship clerk*?—so as to get them to let Miss Mary Jane go aboard? Now *you* know he ain't. What *will* he do, then? Why, he'll say, 'It's a great pity, but my church matters has got to get along the best way they can; for my niece has been exposed to the dreadful pluribus-unum[6] mumps, and so it's my bounden duty to set down here and wait the three months it takes to show on her if she's got it.' But never mind, if you think it's best to tell your uncle Harvey—"

"Shucks, and stay fooling around here when we could all be having good times in England whilst we was waiting to find out whether Mary Jane's got it or not? Why, you talk like a muggins."[7]

"Well, anyway, maybe you better tell some of the neighbors."

"Listen at that, now. You do beat all, for natural stupidity. Can't you *see* that *they'd* go and tell? Ther' ain't no way but just to not tell anybody at *all*."

"Well, maybe you're right—yes, I judge you *are* right."

"But I reckon we ought to tell Uncle Harvey she's gone out a while, anyway, so he wont be uneasy about her?"

"Yes, Miss Mary Jane she wanted you to do that. She says, 'Tell them to give Uncle Harvey and William my love and a kiss, and say I've run over the river to see Mr.—Mr.—what *is* the name of that rich family your uncle Peter used to think so much of?—I mean the one that—"

"Why, you must mean the Apthorps, ain't it?"

"Of course; bother them kind of names, a body can't ever seem to remember them, half the time, somehow. Yes, she said, say she has run over for to ask the Apthorps to be sure and come to the auction and buy this house, because she allowed her uncle Peter would ruther they had it than anybody else; and she's going to stick to them till they say they'll come, and then, if she ain't too tired, she's coming home; and if she is, she'll be home in the

---

6. Huck reaches for the handiest Latin phrase he could be expected to know; meaning "out of many, one," the phrase is appropriate.

7. A fool.

morning anyway. She said, don't say nothing about the Proctors, but only about the Apthorps—which'll be perfectly true, because she *is* going there to speak about their buying the house; I know it, because she told me so, her-self."

"All right," they said, and cleared out to lay for their uncles, and give them the love and the kisses, and tell them the message.

Everything was all right now. The girls wouldn't say nothing because they wanted to go to England; and the king and the duke would ruther Mary Jane was off working for the auction than around in reach of Doctor Robinson. I felt very good; I judged I had done it pretty neat—I reckoned Tom Sawyer couldn't a done it no neater himself. Of course he would a throwed more style into it, but I can't do that very handy, not being brung up to it.

Well, they held the auction in the public square, along towards the end of the afternoon, and it strung along, and strung along, and the old man he was on hand and looking his level piousest, up there longside of the auctioneer, and chipping in a little Scripture, now and then, or a little goody-goody say-ing, of some kind, and the duke he was around goo-gooing for sympathy all he knowed how, and just spreading himself generly.

But by-and-by the thing dragged through, and everything was sold. Every-thing but a little old trifling lot in the graveyard. So they'd got to work *that* off—I never see such a girafft as the king was for wanting to swallow *every-thing*. Well, whilst they was at it, a steamboat landed, and in about two min-utes up comes a crowd a whooping and yelling and laughing and carrying on, and singing out:

"*Here's* your opposition line! here's your two sets o' heirs to old Peter Wilks—and you pays your money and you takes your choice!"

Chapter XXIX

They was fetching a very nice looking old gentleman along, and a nice look-ing younger one, with his right arm in a sling. And my souls, how the people yelled, and laughed, and kept it up. But I didn't see no joke about it, and I judged it would strain the duke and the king some to see any. I reckoned they'd turn pale. But no, nary a pale did *they* turn. The duke he never let on he suspicioned what was up, but just went a goo-gooing around, happy and satisfied, like a jug that's googling out buttermilk; and as for the king, he just gazed and gazed down sorrowful on them newcomers like it give him the stomach-ache in his very heart to think there could be such frauds and ras-cals in the world. Oh, he done it admirable. Lots of the principal people geth-ered around the king, to let him see they was on his side. That old gentleman that had just come looked all puzzled to death. Pretty soon he begun to speak, and I see, straight off, he pronounced *like* an Englishman, not the king's way, though the king's *was* pretty good, for an imitation. I can't give the old gent's words, nor I can't imitate him; but he turned around to the crowd, and says, about like this:

"This is a surprise to me which I wasn't looking for; and I'll acknowledge, candid and frank, I ain't very well fixed to meet it and answer it; for my brother and me has had misfortunes, he's broke his arm, and our baggage got put off at a town above here, last night in the night by a mistake. I am Peter Wilks's brother Harvey, and this is his brother William, which can't hear nor speak—and can't even make signs to amount to much, now 't he's only got one hand to work them with. We are who we say we are; and in a day or two, when I get the baggage, I can prove it. But, up till then, I won't say nothing more, but go to the hotel and wait."

So him and the new dummy started off; and the king he laughs, and blethers out:

"Broke his arm—*very* likely *ain't* it?—and very convenient, too, for a fraud that's got to make signs, and hain't learnt how. Lost their baggage! That's *mighty* good!—and mighty ingenious—under the *circumstances!*"

So he laughed again; and so did everybody else, except three or four, or maybe half a dozen. One of these was that doctor; another one was a sharp looking gentleman, with a carpet-bag of the old-fashioned kind made out of carpet-stuff, that had just come off of the steamboat and was talking to him in a low voice, and glancing towards the king now and then and nodding their heads—it was Levi Bell, the lawyer that was gone up to Louisville; and another one was a big rough husky that come along and listened to all the old gentleman said, and was listening to the king now. And when the king got done, this husky up and says:

"Say, looky here; if you are Harvey Wilks, when'd you come to this town?"

"The day before the funeral, friend," says the king.

"But what time o' day?"

"In the evenin'—'bout an hour er two before sundown."

"*How'd* you come?"

"I come down on the *Susan Powell,* from Cincinnati."

"Well, then, how'd you come to be up at the Pint in the *mornin'*—in a canoe?"

"I warn't up at the Pint in the mornin'."

"It's a lie."

Several of them jumped for him and begged him not to talk that way to an old man and a preacher.

"Preacher be hanged, he's a fraud and a lair. He was up at the Pint that mornin'. I live up there, don't I? Well, I was up there, and he was up there. I *see* him there. He come in a canoe, along with Tim Collins and a boy."

The doctor he up and says:

"Would you know the boy again if you was to see him, Hines?"

"I reckon I would, but I don't know. Why, yonder he is, now. I know him perfectly easy."

It was me he pointed at. The doctor says:

"Neighbors. I don't know whether the new couple is frauds or not; but if *these* two ain't frauds, I am an idiot, that's all. I think it's our duty to see that they don't get away from here till we've looked into this thing. Come along, Hines; come along, the rest of you. We'll take these fellows to the tavern and affront them with t'other couple, and I reckon we'll find out *something* before we get through."

It was nuts for the crowd, though maybe not for the king's friends; so we all started. It was about sundown. The doctor he led me along by the hand, and was plenty kind enough, but he never let *go* my hand.

We all got in a big room in the hotel, and lit up some candles, and fetched in the new couple. First, the doctor says:

"I don't wish to be too hard on these two men, but *I* think they're frauds, and they may have complices that we don't know nothing about. If they have, won't the complices get away with that bag of gold Peter Wilks left? It ain't unlikely. If these men ain't frauds, they won't object to sending for that money and letting us keep it till they prove they're all right—ain't that so?"

Everybody agreed to that. So I judged they had our gang in a pretty tight place, right at the outstart. But the king he only looked sorrowful, and says:

"Gentlemen, I wish the money was there, for I ain't got no disposition to throw anything in the way of a fair, open, out-and-out investigation o' this misable business; but alas, the money ain't there; you k'n send and see, if you want to."

"Where is it, then?"

"Well, when my niece give it to me to keep for her, I took and hid it inside o' the straw tick o' my bed, not wishin' to bank it for the few days we'd be here, and considerin' the bed a safe place, we not bein' used to niggers, and sup-pos'n' 'em honest, like servants in England. The niggers stole it the very next mornin' after I had went down stairs; and when I sold 'em, I hadn't missed the money yit, so they got clean away with it. My servant here k'n tell you 'bout it gentlemen."

The doctor and several said "Shucks!" and I see nobody didn't altogether believe him. One man asked me if I see the niggers steal it. I said no, but I see them sneaking out of the room and hustling away, and I never thought nothing, only I reckoned they was afraid they had waked up my master and was trying to get away before he made trouble with them. That was all they asked me. Then the doctor whirls on me and says:

"Are *you* English too?"

I says yes; and him and some others laughed, and said, "Stuff!"

Well, then they sailed in on the general investigation, and there we had it, up and down, hour in, hour out, and nobody never said a word about supper, nor ever seemed to think about it—and so they kept it up, and kept it up; and it *was* the worst mixed-up thing you ever see. They made the king tell his yarn, and they made the old gentleman tell his'n; and anybody but a lot of prejudiced chuckleheads would a *seen* that the old gentleman was spinning truth and t'other one lies. And by-and-by they had me up to tell what I knowed. The king he give me a left-handed look out of the corner of his eye, and so I knowed enough to talk on the right side. I begun to tell about Sheffield, and how we lived there, and all about the English Wilkses, and so on; but I didn't get pretty fur till the doctor begun to laugh; and Levi Bell, the lawyer says:

"Set down, my boy, I wouldn't strain myself, if I was you. I reckon you ain't used to lying, it don't seem to come handy; what you want is practice. You do it pretty awkward."

I didn't care nothing for the compliment, but I was glad to be let off, any-way.

The doctor he started to say something, and turns and says:

"If you'd been in town at first, Levi Bell—"

The king broke in and reached out his hand, and says:

"Why, is this my poor dead brother's old friend that he's wrote so often about?"

The lawyer and him shook hands, and the lawyer smiled and looked pleased, and they talked right along a while, and then got to one side and talked low; and at last the lawyer speaks up and says:

"That'll fix it. I'll take the order and send it, along with your brother's, and then they'll know it's all right."

So they got some paper and a pen, and the king he set down and twisted his head to one side, and chawed his tongue, and scrawled off something; and then they give the pen to the duke—and then for the first time, the duke looked sick. But he took the pen and wrote. So then the lawyer turns to the new old gentleman and says:

"You and your brother please write a line or two and sign your names."

The old gentleman wrote, but nobody couldn't read it. The lawyer looked powerful astonished, and says:

"Well, it beats *me*"—and snaked a lot of old letters out of his pocket, and examined them, and then examined the old man's writing, and then *them* again; and then says: "These old letters is from Harvey Wilks; and here's *these* two's handwritings, and anybody can see *they* didn't write them" (the king and the duke looked sold and foolish, I tell you, to see how the lawyer had took them in), "and here's *this* old gentleman's handwriting, and anybody can tell, easy enough, *he* didn't write them—fact is, the scratches he makes ain't properly *writing,* at all. Now here's some letters from—"

The new old gentleman says:

"If you please, let me explain. Nobody can read my hand but my brother there—so he copies for me. It's *his* hand you've got there, not mine."

"*Well!*" says the lawyer, "this *is* a state of things. I've got some of William's letters too; so if you'll get him to write a line or so we can com—"

"He *can't* write with his left hand," says the old gentleman. "If he could use his right hand, you would see that he wrote his own letters and mine too. Look at both, please—they're by the same hand."

The lawyer done it, and says:

"I believe it's so—and if it ain't so, there's a heap stronger resemblance than I'd noticed before, anyway. Well, well, well! I thought we was right on the track of a slution, but it's gone to grass, partly. But anyway, *one* thing is proved—*these* two ain't either of 'em Wilkses"—and he wagged his head towards the king and the duke.

Well, what do you think?—that muleheaded old fool wouldn't give in *then!* Indeed he wouldn't. Said it warn't no fair test. Said his brother William was the cussedest joker in the world, and hadn't *tried* to write—*he* see William was going to play one of his jokes the minute he put the pen to paper. And so he warmed up and went warbling and warbling right along, till he was actuly beginning to believe what he was saying, *himself*—but pretty soon the new old gentleman broke in, and says:

"I've thought of something. Is there anybody here that helped to lay out my br—helped to lay out the late Peter Wilks for burying?"

"Yes," says somebody, "me and Ab Turner done it. We're both here."

Then the old man turns towards the king, and says:

"Peraps this gentleman can tell me what was tatooed on his breast?"

Blamed if the king didn't have to brace up mighty quick, or he'd a squshed down like a bluff bank that the river has cut under, it took him so sudden—and mind you, it was a thing that was calculated to make most *anybody* sqush to get fetched such a solid one as that without any notice—because how was *he* going to know what was tatooed on the man? He whitened a little; he couldn't help it; and it was mighty still in there, and everybody bending a little forwards and gazing at him. Says I to myself, *Now* he'll throw up the sponge—there ain't no more use. Well, did he? A body can't hardly believe it, but he didn't. I reckon he thought he'd keep the thing up till he tired them people out, so they'd thin out, and him and the duke could break loose and get away. Anyway, he set there, and pretty soon he begun to smile, and says:

"Mf! It's a *very* tough question, *ain't* it! *Yes,* sir, I k'n tell you what's tatooed on his breast. It's jest a small, thin, blue arrow—that's what it is; and if you don't look clost, you can't see it. *Now* what do you say—hey?"

Well, *I* never see anything like that old blister for clean out-and-out cheek.

The new old gentleman turns brisk towards Ab Turner and his pard, and his eye lights up like he judged he'd got the king *this* time, and says:

"There—you've heard what he said! Was there any such mark on Peter Wilks's breast?"

Both of them spoke up and says:

"We didn't see no such mark."

"Good!" says the old gentleman. "Now, what you *did* see on his breast was a small dim P, and a B (which is an initial he dropped when he was young), and a W, with dashes between them, so: P—B—W"—and he marked them that way on a piece of paper. "Come—ain't that what you saw?"

Both of them spoke up again, and says:

"No, we *didn't.* We never seen any marks at all."

Well, everybody *was* in a state of mind, now; and they sings out:

"The whole *bilin'* of 'm 's frauds! Le's duck 'em! le's drown 'em! le's ride 'em on a rail!" and everybody was whooping at once, and there was a rattling powwow. But the lawyer he jumps on the table and yells, and says:

"Gentlemen—gentle*men!* Hear me just a word—just a *single* word—if you PLEASE! There's one way yet—let's go and dig up the corpse and look."

That took them.

"Hooray!" they all shouted, and was starting right off; but the lawyer and the doctor sung out:

"Hold on, hold on! Collar all these four men and the boy, and fetch *them* along, too!"

"We'll do it!" they all shouted: "and if we don't find them marks we'll lynch the whole gang!"

I *was* scared, now, I tell you. But there warn't no getting away, you know. They gripped us all, and marched us right along, straight for the graveyard, which was a mile and a half down the river, and the whole town at our heels, for we made noise enough, and it was only nine in the evening.

As we went by our house I wished I hadn't sent Mary Jane out of town; because now if I could tip her the wink, she'd light out and save me, and blow on our dead-beats.

Well, we swarmed along down the river road, just carrying on like wild-cats; and to make it more scary, the sky was darking up, and the lightning beginning to wink and flitter, and the wind to shiver amongst the leaves. This was the most awful trouble and most dangersome I ever was in; and I was kinder stunned; everything was going so different from what I had allowed for; stead of being fixed so I could take my own time, if I wanted to, and see all the fun, and have Mary Jane at my back to save me and set me free when the close-fit come, here was nothing in the world betwixt me and sudden death but just them tatoo-marks. If they didn't find them—

I couldn't bear to think about it; and yet, somehow, I couldn't think about nothing else. It got darker and darker, and it was a beautiful time to give the crowd the slip; but that big husky had me by the wrist—Hines—and a body might as well try to give Goliar[8] the slip. He dragged me right along, he was so excited; and I had to run to keep up.

When they got there they swarmed into the graveyard and washed over it like an overflow. And when they got to the grave, they found they had about a hundred times as many shovels as they wanted, but nobody hadn't thought to fetch a lantern. But they sailed into digging, anyway, by the flicker of the lightning, and sent a man to the nearest house a half a mile off, to borrow one.

So they dug and dug, like everything; and it got awful dark, and the rain started, and the wind swished and swushed along, and the lightning come brisker and brisker, and the thunder boomed; but them people never took no notice of it, they was so full of this business; and one minute you could see everything and every face in that big crowd, and the shovelfuls of dirt sailing up out of the grave, and the next second the dark wiped it all out, and you couldn't see nothing at all.

At last they got out the coffin, and begun to unscrew the lid, and then such another crowding, and shouldering, and shoving as there was, to scrouge in and get a sight, you never see; and in the dark, that way, it was awful. Hines he hurt my wrist dreadful, pulling and tugging so, and I reckon he clean forgot I was in the world, he was so excited and panting.

All of a sudden the lightning let go a perfect sluice of white glare, and somebody sings out:

"By the living jingo, here's the bag of gold on his breast!"

Hines let out a whoop, like everybody else, and dropped my wrist and give a big surge to bust his way in and get a look, and the way I lit out and shinned for the road in the dark, there ain't nobody can tell.

I had the road all to myself, and I fairly flew—leastways I had it all to myself except the solid dark, and the now-and-then glares, and the buzzing of the rain, and the thrashing of the wind, and the splitting of the thunder; and sure as you are born I did clip it along!

When I struck the town, I see there warn't nobody out in the storm, so I never hunted for no back streets, but humped it straight through the main one; and when I begun to get towards our house I aimed my eye and set it. No light there; the house all dark—which made me feel sorry and disappointed, I didn't know why. But at last, just as I was sailing by, *flash* comes the light in Mary Jane's window! and my heart swelled up sudden, like to bust; and the same second the house and all was behind me in the dark, and wasn't ever going to be before me no more in this world. She *was* the best girl I ever see, and had the most sand.

The minute I was far enough above the town to see I could make the towhead, I begun to look sharp for a boat to borrow; and the first time the lightning showed me one that wasn't chained, I snatched it and shoved. It was a canoe, and warn't fastened with nothing but a rope. The tow-head was a rattling big distance off, away out there in the middle of the river, but I didn't

---

8. Goliath, a Philistine giant who challenged the Israelites. David, a young shepherd, accepted his challenge and killed him with a stone thrown from a sling.

lose no time; and when I struck the raft at last, I was so fagged I would a just laid down to blow and gasp if I could afforded it. But I didn't. As I sprung aboard I sung out:

"Out with you Jim, and set her loose! Glory be to goodness, we're shut of them!"

Jim lit out, and was a coming for me with both arms spread, he was so full of joy; but when I glimpsed him in the lightning, my heart shot up in my mouth, and I went overboard backwards; for I forgot he was old King Lear and a drownded A-rab all in one, and it most scared the livers and lights out of me. But Jim fished me out, and was going to hug me and bless me, and so on, he was so glad I was back and we was shut of the king and the duke, but I says:

"Not now—have it for breakfast, have it for breakfast! Cut loose and let her slide!"

So, in two seconds, away we went, a sliding down the river, and it *did* seem so good to be free again and all by ourselves on the big river and nobody to bother us. I had to skip around a bit, and jump up and crack my heels a few times, I couldn't help it; but about the third crack, I noticed a sound that I knowed mighty well—and held my breath and listened and waited—and sure enough, when the next flash busted out over the water, here they come!—and just a laying to their oars and making their skiff hum! It was the king and the duke.

So I wilted right down onto the planks, then, and give up; and it was all I could do to keep from crying.

Chapter XXX

When they got aboard, the king went for me, and shook me by the collar, and says:

"Tryin' to give us the slip, was ye, you pup! Tired of our company—hey!"

I says:

"No, your majesty, we warn't—*please* don't, your majesty!"

"Quick, then, and tell us what *was* your idea, or I'll shake the insides out o' you!"

"Honest, I'll tell you everything, just as it happened, your majesty. The man that had aholt of me was very good to me, and kept saying he had a boy about as big as me that died last year, and he was sorry to see a boy in such a dangerous fix; and when they was all took by surprise by finding the gold, and made a rush for the coffin, he lets go of me and whispers, 'Heel it, now, or they'll hang ye, sure!' and I lit out. It didn't seem no good for *me* to stay—I couldn't do nothing, and I didn't want to be hung if I could get away. So I never stopped running till I found the canoe; and when I got here I told Jim to hurry, or they'd catch me and hang me yet, and said I was afeard you and the duke wasn't alive, now, and I was awful sorry, and so was Jim, and was awful glad when we see you coming, you may ask Jim if I didn't."

Jim said it was so; and the king told him to shut up, and said, "Oh, yes, it's *mighty* likely!" and shook me up again, and said he reckoned he'd drownded me. But the duke says:

"Leggo the boy, you old idiot! Would *you* a done any different? Did you inquire around for *him,* when you got loose? *I* don't remember it."

So the king let go of me, and begun to cuss that town and everybody in it. But the duke says:

"You better a blame sight give *yourself* a good cussing, for you're the one that's entitled to it most. You hain't done a thing, from the start, that had any sense in it, except coming out so cool and cheeky with that imaginary blue-arrow mark. That *was* bright—it was right down bully; and it was the thing that saved us. For if it hadn't been for that, they'd a jailed us till them Englishmen's baggage come—and then—the penitentiary, you bet! But that trick took 'em to the graveyard, and the gold done us a still bigger kindness; for if the excited fools hadn't let go all holts and made that rush to get a look, we'd a slept in our cravats to-night—cravats warranted to *wear,* too—longer than *we'd* need 'em."

They was still a minute—thinking—then the king says, kind of absent-minded like:

"Mf! And we reckoned the *niggers* stole it!"

That made me squirm!

"Yes," says the duke, kinder slow, and deliberate, and sarcastic, "*We* did."

After about a half a minute, the king drawls out:

"Leastways—*I* did."

The duke says, the same way:

"On the contrary—*I* did."

The king kind of ruffles up, and says:

"Looky here, Bilgewater, what'r you referrin' to?"

The duke says, pretty brisk:

"When it comes to that, maybe you'll let me ask, what was *you* referring to?"

"Shucks!" says the king, very sarcastic; "but *I* don't know—maybe you was asleep, and didn't know what you was about."

The duke bristles right up, now, and says:

"Oh, let *up* on this cussed nonsense—do you take me for a blame' fool? Don't you reckon *I* know who hid that money in that coffin?"

"*Yes,* sir! I know you *do* know—because you done it yourself!"

"It's a lie!"—and the duke went for him. The king sings out:

"Take y'r hands off!—leggo my throat!—I take it all back!"

The duke says:

"Well, you just own up, first, that you *did* hide that money there, intending to give me the slip one of these days, and come back and dig it up, and have it all to yourself."

"Wait jest a minute, duke—answer me this one question, honest and fair; if you didn't put the money there, say it, and I'll b'lieve you, and take back everything I said."

"You old scoundrel, I didn't, and you know I didn't. There, now!"

"Well, then, I b'lieve you. But answer me only jest this one more—now *don't* git mad; didn't you have it in your *mind* to hook the money and hide it?"

The duke never said nothing for a little bit; then he says:

"Well—I don't care if I *did,* I didn't *do* it, anyway. But you not only had it in mind to do it, but you *done* it."

"I wisht I may never die if I done it, duke, and that's honest. I won't say I warn't *goin'* to do it, because I *was;* but you—I mean somebody—got in ahead o' me."

"It's a lie! You done it, and you got to *say* you done it, or—"

The king begun to gurgle, and then he gasps out:

" 'Nough!—I *own up!*"

I was very glad to hear him say that, it made me feel much more easier than what I was feeling before. So the duke took his hands off, and says:

"If you ever deny it again, I'll drown you. It's *well* for you to set there and blubber like a baby—it's fitten for you, after the way you've acted. I never see such an old ostrich for wanting to gobble everything—and I a trusting you all the time, like you was my own father. You ought to be ashamed of yourself to stand by and hear it saddled onto a lot of poor niggers and you never say a word for 'em. It makes me feel ridiculous to think I was soft enough to *believe* that rubbage. Cuss you, I can see, now, why you was so anxious to make up the deffesit—you wanted to get what money I'd got out of the Nonesuch and one thing or another, and scoop it *all!*"

The king says, timid, and still a snuffling:

"Why, duke, it was you that said make up the deffersit, it warn't me."

"Dry up! I don't want to hear no more *out* of you!" says the duke. "And *now* you see what you *got* by it. They've got all their own money back, and all of *ourn* but a shekel or two, *besides.* G'long to bed—and don't you deffersit *me* no more deffersits, long 's *you* live!"

So the king sneaked into the wigwam, and took to his bottle for comfort; and before long the duke tackled *his* bottle; and so in about a half an hour they was as thick as thieves again, and the tighter they got, the lovinger they got; and went off a snoring in each other's arms. They both got powerful mellow, but I noticed the king didn't get mellow enough to forget to remember to not deny about hiding the money-bag again. That made me feel easy and satisfied. Of course when they got to snoring, we had a long gabble, and I told Jim everything.

Chapter XXXI

We dasn't stop again at any town, for days and days; kept right along down the river. We was down south in the warm weather, now, and a mighty long ways from home. We begun to come to trees with Spanish moss on them, hanging down from the limbs like long gray beards. It was the first I ever see it growing, and it made the woods look solemn and dismal. So now the frauds reckoned they was out of danger, and they begun to work the villages again.

First they done a lecture on temperance; but they didn't make enough for them both to get drunk on. Then in another village they started a dancing school; but they didn't know no more how to dance than a kangaroo does; so the first prance they made, the general public jumped in and pranced them out of town. Another time they tried a go at yellocution; but they didn't yellocute long till the audience got up and give them a solid good cussing and made them skip out. They tackled missionarying, and mesmerizering, and doctoring, and telling fortunes, and a little of everything; but they couldn't seem to have no luck. So at last they got just about dead broke, and laid around the raft, as she floated along, thinking, and thinking, and never saying nothing, by the half a day at a time, and dreadful blue and desperate.

And at last they took a change, and begun to lay their heads together in the wigwam and talk low and confidential two or three hours at a time. Jim and me got uneasy. We didn't like the look of it. We judged they was studying up some kind of worse deviltry than ever. We turned it over and over, and at last we made up our minds they was going to break into somebody's house or store, or was going into the counterfeit-money business, or something. So then we was pretty scared, and made up an agreement that we wouldn't have nothing in the world to do with such actions, and if we ever got the least show we would give them the cold shake, and clear out and leave them behind. Well, early one morning we hid the raft in a good safe place about two mile below a little bit of a shabby village, named Pikesville, and the king he went ashore, and told us all to stay hid whilst he went up to town and smelt around to see if anybody had got any wind of the Royal Nonesuch there yet. ("House to rob, you *mean*," says I to myself; "and when you get through robbing it you'll come back here and wonder what's become of me and Jim and the raft—and you'll have to take it out in wondering.") And he said if he warn't back by midday, the duke and me would know it was all right, and we was to come along.

So we staid where we was. The duke he fretted and sweated around, and was in a mighty sour way. He scolded us for everything, and we couldn't seem to do nothing right; he found fault with every little thing. Something was a-brewing, sure. I was good and glad when midday come and no king; we could have a change, anyway—and maybe a chance for *the* change, on top of it. So me and the duke went up to the village, and hunted around there for the king, and by-and-by we found him in the back room of a little low doggery,[9] very tight, and a lot of loafers bullyragging him for sport, and he a cussing and threatening with all his might, and so tight he couldn't walk, and couldn't do nothing to them. The duke he begun to abuse him for an old fool, and the king begun to sass back; and the minute they was fairly at it, I lit out, and shook the reefs out of my hind legs, and spun down the river road like a deer—for I see our chance; and I made up my mind that it would be a long day before they ever see me and Jim again. I got down there all out of breath but loaded up with joy, and sung out—

"Set her loose, Jim, we're all right, now!"

But there warn't no answer, and nobody come out of the wigwam. Jim was gone! I set up a shout—and then another—and then another one; and run this way and that in the woods, whooping and screeching; but it warn't no use—old Jim was gone. Then I set down and cried; I couldn't help it. But I couldn't set still long. Pretty soon I went out on the road, trying to think what I better do, and I run across a boy walking, and asked him if he'd seen a strange nigger, dressed so and so, and he says:

"Yes."

"Whereabouts?" says I.

"Down to Silas Phelps's place, two mile below here. He's a runaway nigger, and they've got him. Was you looking for him?"

"You bet I ain't! I run across him in the woods about an hour or two ago,

9. Cheap barroom.

and he said if I hollered he'd cut my livers out—and told me to lay down and stay where I was; and I done it. Been there ever since; afeard to come out."

"Well," he says, "you needn't be afraid no more, becuz they've got him. He run off f'm down South, som'ers."

"It's a good job they got him."

"Well, I *reckon!* There's two hundred dollars reward on him. It's like picking up money out'n the road."

"Yes, it is—and *I* could a had it if I'd been big enough; I see him *first.* Who nailed him?"

"It was an old fellow—a stranger—and he sold out his chance in him for forty dollars, becuz he's got to go up the river and can't wait. Think o' that, now! You bet *I'd* wait, if it was seven year."

"That's me, every time," says I. "But maybe his chance ain't worth no more than that, if he'll sell it so cheap. Maybe there's something ain't straight about it."

"But it *is*, though—straight as a string. I see the handbill myself. It tells all about him, to a dot—paints him like a picture, and tells the plantation he's frum, below New*rleans.* No-siree-*bob*, they ain't no trouble 'bout *that* speculation, you bet you. Say, gimme a chaw tobacker, won't ye?"

I didn't have none, so he left. I went to the raft, and set down in the wigwam to think. But I couldn't come to nothing. I thought till I wore my head sore, but I couldn't see no way out of the trouble. After all this long journey, and after all we'd done for them scoundrels, here was it all come to nothing, everything all busted up and ruined, because they could have the heart to serve Jim such a trick as that, and make him a slave again all his life, and amongst strangers, too, for forty dirty dollars.

Once I said to myself it would be a thousand times better for Jim to be a slave at home where his family was, as long as he'd *got* to be a slave, and so I'd better write a letter to Tom Sawyer and tell him to tell Miss Watson where he was. But I soon give up that notion, for two things: she'd be mad and disgusted at his rascality and ungratefulness for leaving her, and so she'd sell him straight down the river again; and if she didn't, everybody naturally despises an ungrateful nigger, and they'd make Jim feel it all the time, and so he'd feel ornery and disgraced. And then think of *me!* It would get all around, that Huck Finn helped a nigger to get his freedom; and if I was to ever see anybody from that town again, I'd be ready to get down and lick his boots for shame. That's just the way: a person does a low-down thing, and then he don't want to take no consequences of it. Thinks as long as he can hide it, it ain't no disgrace. That was my fix exactly. The more I studied about this, the more my conscience went to grinding me, and the more wicked and low-down and ornery I got to feeling. And at last, when it hit me all of a sudden that here was the plain hand of Providence slapping me in the face and letting me know my wickedness was being watched all the time from up there in heaven, whilst I was stealing a poor old woman's nigger that hadn't ever done me no harm, and now was showing me there's One that's always on the lookout, and ain't agoing to allow no such miserable doings to go only just so fur and no further, I most dropped in my tracks I was so scared. Well, I tried the best I could to kinder soften it up somehow for myself, by saying I was brung up wicked, and so I warn't so much to blame; but something inside of me kept saying, "There was the Sunday school, you could a gone to it; and if you'd a done it they'd a learnt you, there, that people that acts as I'd been acting about the nigger goes to everlasting fire."

It made me shiver. And I about made up my mind to pray; and see if I couldn't try to quit being the kind of a boy I was, and be better. So I kneeled down. But the words wouldn't come. Why wouldn't they? It warn't no use to try and hide it from Him. Nor from *me*, neither. I knowed very well why they wouldn't come. It was because my heart warn't right; it was because I warn't square; it was because I was playing double. I was letting *on* to give up sin, but away inside of me I was holding on to the biggest one of all. I was trying to make my mouth *say* I would do the right thing and the clean thing, and go and write to that nigger's owner and tell where he was; but deep down in me I knowed it was a lie—and He knowed it. You can't pray a lie—I found that out.

So I was full of trouble, full as I could be; and didn't know what to do. At last I had an idea; and I says, I'll go and write the letter—and *then* see if I can pray. Why, it was astonishing, the way I felt as light as a feather, right straight off, and my troubles all gone. So I got a piece of paper and a pencil, all glad and excited, and set down and wrote:

> Miss Watson your runaway nigger Jim is down here two mile below Pikesville and Mr. Phelps has got him and he will give him up for the reward if you send.
>
> Huck Finn.

I felt good and all washed clean of sin for the first time I had ever felt so in my life, and I knowed I could pray now. But I didn't do it straight off, but laid the paper down and set there thinking—thinking how good it was all this happened so, and how near I come to being lost and going to hell. And went on thinking. And got to thinking over our trip down the river; and I see Jim before me, all the time, in the day, and in the night-time, sometimes moonlight, sometimes storms, and we a floating along, talking, and singing, and laughing. But somehow I couldn't seem to strike no places to harden me against him, but only the other kind. I'd see him standing my watch on top of his'n, stead of calling me, so I could go on sleeping; and see him how glad he was when I come back out of the fog; and when I come to him again in the swamp, up there where the feud was; and such-like times; and would always call me honey, and pet me, and do everything he could think of for me, and how good he always was; and at last I struck the time I saved him by telling the men we had small-pox aboard, and he was so grateful, and said I was the best friend old Jim ever had in the world, and the *only* one he's got now; and then I happened to look around, and see that paper.

It was a close place. I took it up, and held it in my hand. I was a trembling, because I'd got to decide, forever, betwixt two things, and I knowed it. I studied a minute, sort of holding my breath, and then says to myself:

"All right, then, I'll *go* to hell"—and tore it up.

It was awful thoughts, and awful words, but they was said. And I let them stay said; and never thought no more about reforming. I shoved the whole thing out of my head; and said I would take up wickedness again, which was in my line, being brung up to it, and the other warn't. And for a starter, I would go to work and steal Jim out of slavery again; and if I could think up anything worse, I would do that, too; because as long as I was in, and in for good, I might as well go the whole hog.

Then I set to thinking over how to get at it, and turned over considerable many ways in my mind; and at last fixed up a plan that suited me. So then I took the bearings of a woody island that was down the river a piece, and as soon as it was fairly dark I crept out with my raft and went for it, and hid it there, and then turned in. I slept the night through, and got up before it was light, and had my breakfast, and put on my store clothes, and tied up some others and one thing or another in a bundle, and took the canoe and cleared for shore. I landed below where I judged was Phelps's place, and hid my bundle in the woods, and then filled up the canoe with water, and loaded rocks into her and sunk her where I could find her again when I wanted her, about a quarter of a mile below a little steam sawmill that was on the bank.

Then I struck up the road, and when I passed the mill I see a sign on it, "Phelps's Sawmill," and when I come to the farmhouses, two or three hundred yards further along, I kept my eyes peeled, but didn't see nobody around, though it was good daylight, now. But I didn't mind, because I didn't want to see nobody just yet—I only wanted to get the lay of the land. According to my plan, I was going to turn up there from the village, not from below. So I just took a look, and shoved along, straight for town. Well, the very first man I see, when I got there, was the duke. He was sticking up a bill for the Royal None-such—three-night performance—like that other time. *They* had the cheek, them frauds! I was right on him, before I could shirk. He looked astonished, and says:

"Hel-*lo!* Where'd *you* come from?" Then he says, kind of glad and eager, "Where's the raft?—got her in a good place?"

I says:

"Why, that's just what I was agoing to ask your grace."

Then he didn't look so joyful—and says:

"What was your idea for asking *me?*" he says.

"Well," I says, "when I see the king in that doggery yesterday, I says to myself, we can't get him home for hours, till he's soberer; so I went a loafing around town to put in the time, and wait. A man up and offered me ten cents to help him pull a skiff over the river and back to fetch a sheep, and so I went along; but when we was dragging him to the boat, and the man left me aholt of the rope and went behind him to shove him along, he was too strong for me, and jerked loose and run, and we after him. We didn't have no dog, and so we had to chase him all over the country till we tired him out. We never got him till dark, then we fetched him over, and I started down for the raft. When I got there and see it was gone, I says to myself, 'they've got into trouble and had to leave; and they've took my nigger, which is the only nigger I've got in the world, and now I'm in a strange country, and ain't got no property no more, nor nothing, and no way to make my living;' so I set down and cried. I slept in the woods all night. But what *did* become of the raft then?—and Jim, poor Jim!"

"Blamed if *I* know—that is, what's become of the raft. That old fool had made a trade and got forty dollars, and when we found him in the doggery the loafers had matched half dollars with him and got every cent but what he'd spent for whisky; and when I got him home late last night and found the raft gone, we said, 'That little rascal has stole our raft and shook us, and run off down the river.'"

"I wouldn't shake my *nigger*, would I?—the only nigger I had in the world, and the only property."

"We never thought of that. Fact is, I reckon we'd come to consider him *our* nigger; yes, we did consider him so—goodness knows we had trouble enough for him. So when we see the raft was gone, and we flat broke, there warn't anything for it but to try the Royal Nonesuch another shake. And I've pegged along ever since, dry as a powderhorn. Where's that ten cents? Give it here."

I had considerable money, so I give him ten cents, but begged him to spend it for something to eat, and give me some, because it was all the money I had, and I hadn't had nothing to eat since yesterday. He never said nothing. The next minute he whirls on me and says:

"Do you reckon that nigger would blow on us? We'd skin him if he done that!"

"How can he blow? Hain't he run off?"

"No! That old fool sold him, and never divided with me, and the money's gone."

"*Sold* him?" I says, and begun to cry; "why, he was *my* nigger, and that was my money. Where is he?—I want my nigger."

"Well, you can't *get* your nigger, that's all—so dry up your blubbering. Looky here—do you think *you'd* venture to blow on us? Blamed if I think I'd trust you. Why, if you *was* to blow on us—"

He stopped, but I never see the duke look so ugly out of his eyes before. I went on a-whimpering, and says:

"I don't want to blow on nobody; and I ain't got no time to blow, nohow. I got to turn out and find my nigger."

He looked kinder bothered, and stood there with his bills fluttering on his arm, thinking, and wrinkling up his forehead. At last he says:

"I'll tell you something. We got to be here three days. If you'll promise you won't blow, and won't let the nigger blow, I'll tell you where to find him."

So I promised, and he says:

"A farmer by the name of Silas Ph—" and then he stopped. You see he started to tell me the truth; but when he stopped, that way, and begun to study and think again, I reckoned he was changing his mind. And so he was. He wouldn't trust me; he wanted to make sure of having me out of the way the whole three days. So pretty soon he says: "The man that bought him is named Abram Foster—Abram G. Foster—and he lives forty mile back here in the country, on the road to Lafayette."

"All right," I says, "I can walk it in three days. And I'll start this very afternoon."

"No you won't, you'll start *now*; and don't you lose any time about it, neither, nor do any gabbling by the way. Just keep a tight tongue in your head and move right along, and then you won't get into trouble with *us*, d'ye hear?"

That was the order I wanted, and that was the one I played for. I wanted to be left free to work my plans.

"So clear out," he says; "and you can tell Mr. Foster whatever you want to. Maybe you can get him to believe that Jim *is* your nigger—some idiots don't require documents—leastways I've heard there's such down South here. And when you tell him the handbill and the reward's bogus, maybe he'll believe you when you explain to him what the idea was for getting 'em out. Go 'long, now, and tell him anything you want to; but mind you don't work your jaw any *between* here and there."

So I left, and struck for the back country. I didn't look around, but I kinder felt like he was watching me. But I knowed I could tire him out at that. I went straight out in the country as much as a mile, before I stopped; then I doubled back through the woods towards Phelps's. I reckoned I better start in on my plan straight off, without fooling around, because I wanted to stop Jim's mouth till these fellows could get away. I didn't want no trouble with their kind. I'd seen all I wanted to of them, and wanted to get entirely shut of them.

Chapter XXXII

When I got there it was all still and Sunday-like, and hot and sunshiny—the hands was gone to the fields; and there was them kind of faint dronings of bugs and flies in the air that makes it seem so lonesome and like everybody's dead and gone; and if a breeze fans along and quivers the leaves, it makes you feel mournful, because you feel like it's spirits whispering—spirits that's been dead ever so many years—and you always think they're talking about *you*. As a general thing it makes a body wish *he* was dead, too, and done with it all.

Phelps's was one of these little one-horse cotton plantations; and they all look alike. A rail fence round a two-acre yard; a stile, made out of logs sawed off and up-ended, in steps, like barrels of a different length, to climb over the fence with, and for the women to stand on when they are going to jump onto a horse; some sickly grass-patches in the big yard, but mostly it was bare and smooth, like an old hat with the nap rubbed off; big double log house for the white folks—hewed logs, with the chinks stopped up with mud or mortar, and these mud-stripes been whitewashed some time or another; round-log kitchen, with a big broad, open but roofed passage joining it to the house; log smoke-house back of the kitchen; three little log nigger-cabins in a row t'other side the smokehouse; one little hut all by itself away down against the back fence, and some outbuildings down a piece the other side; ash-hopper,[1] and big kettle to bile soap in, by the little hut; bench by the kitchen door, with bucket of water and a gourd; hound asleep there, in the sun; more hounds asleep, round about; about three shade-trees away off in a corner; some currant bushes and gooseberry bushes in one place by the fence; outside of the fence a garden and a water-melon patch; then the cotton fields begins; and after the fields, the woods.

I went around and clumb over the back stile by the ash-hopper, and started for the kitchen. When I got a little ways, I heard the dim hum of a spinning-wheel wailing along up and sinking along down again; and then I knowed for certain I wished I was dead—for that *is* the lonesomest sound in the whole world.[2]

I went right along, not fixing up any particular plan, but just trusting to Providence to put the right words in my mouth when the time come; for I'd noticed that Providence always did put the right words in my mouth, if I left it alone.

1. A container for lye used in making soap.
2. For the details of the Phelps plantation, Twain drew on memories of vacations at his uncle John

Quarles's farm near Hannibal. See Twain's *Autobiography* for his vivid evocation of the farm.

When I got half-way, first one hound and then another got up and went for me, and of course I stopped and faced them, and kept still. And such another pow-wow as they made! In a quarter of a minute I was a kind of a hub of a wheel, as you may say—spokes made out of dogs—circle of fifteen of them packed together around me, with their necks and noses stretched up towards me, a barking and howling; and more a coming; you could see them sailing over fences and around corners from everywheres.

A nigger woman come tearing out of the kitchen with a rolling-pin in her hand, singing out, "Begone! *you* Tige! you Spot! begone, sah!" and she fetched first one and then another of them a clip and sent him howling, and then the rest followed; and the next second, half of them come back, wagging their tails around me and making friends with me. There ain't no harm in a hound, nohow.

And behind the woman comes a little nigger girl and two little nigger boys, without anything on but tow-linen shirts, and they hung onto their mother's gown, and peeped out from behind her at me, bashful, the way they always do. And here comes the white woman running from the house, about forty-five or fifty year old, bare-headed, and her spinning-stick in her hand; and behind her comes her little white children, acting the same way the little niggers was doing. She was smiling all over so she could hardly stand—and says:

"It's *you*, at last!—*ain't* it?"

I out with a "Yes'm," before I thought.

She grabbed me and hugged me tight; and then gripped me by both hands and shook and shook; and the tears come in her eyes, and run down over; and she couldn't seem to hug and shake enough, and kept saying, "You don't look as much like your mother as I reckoned you would, but law sakes, I don't care for that, I'm *so* glad to see you! Dear, dear, it does seem like I could eat you up! Children, it's your cousin Tom!—tell him howdy."

But they ducked their heads, and put their fingers in their mouths, and hid behind her. So she run on:

"Lize, hurry up and get him a hot breakfast, right away—or did you get your breakfast on the boat?"

I said I had got it on the boat. So then she started for the house, leading me by the hand, and the children tagging after. When we got there, she set me down in a split-bottomed chair, and set herself down on a little low stool in front of me, holding both of my hands, and says:

"Now I can have a *good* look at you; and laws-a-me, I've been hungry for it a many and a many a time, all these long years, and it's come at last! We been expecting you a couple of days and more. What's kep' you?—boat get aground?"

"Yes'm—she—"

"Don't say yes'm—say Aunt Sally. Where'd she get aground?"

I didn't rightly know what to say, because I didn't know whether the boat would be coming up the river or down. But I go a good deal on instinct; and my instinct said she would be coming up—from down toward Orleans. That didn't help me much, though; for I didn't know the names of bars down that way. I see I'd got to invent a bar, or forget the name of the one we got aground on—or—Now I struck an idea, and fetched it out:

"It warn't the grounding—that didn't keep us back but a little. We blowed out a cylinder-head."

"Good gracious! anybody hurt?"

"No'm. Killed a nigger."

"Well, it's lucky; because sometimes people do get hurt. Two years ago last Christmas, your uncle Silas was coming up from Newrleans on the old *Lally Rook*,[3] and she blowed out a cylinder-head and crippled a man. And I think he died afterwards. He was a Babtist. Your uncle Silas knowed a family in Baton Rouge that knowed his people very well. Yes, I remember, now he *did* die. Mortification[4] set in, and they had to amputate him. But it didn't save him. Yes, it was mortification—that was it. He turned blue all over, and died in the hope of a glorious resurrection. They say he was a sight to look at. Your uncle's been up to the town every day to fetch you. And he's gone again, not more'n an hour ago; he'll be back any minute, now. You must a met him on the road, didn't you?—oldish man, with a—"

"No, I didn't see nobody, Aunt Sally. The boat landed just at daylight, and I left my baggage on the wharf-boat and went looking around the town and out a piece in the country, to put in the time and not get here too soon; and so I come down the back way."

"Who'd you give the baggage to?"

"Nobody."

"Why, child, it'll be stole!"

"Not where *I* hid it I reckon it won't," I says.

"How'd you get your breakfast so early on the boat?"

It was kinder thin ice, but I says:

"The captain see me standing around, and told me I better have something to eat before I went ashore; so he took me in the texas to the officers' lunch, and give me all I wanted."

I was getting so uneasy I couldn't listen good. I had my mind on the children all the time; I wanted to get them out to one side, and pump them a little, and find out who I was. But I couldn't get no show, Mrs. Phelps kept it up and run on so. Pretty soon she made the cold chills streak all down my back, because she says:

"But here we're a running on this way, and you hain't told me a word about Sis, nor any of them. Now I'll rest my works a little, and you start up yourn; just tell me *everything*—tell me all about 'm all—every one of 'm; and how they are, and what they're doing, and what they told you to tell me; and every last thing you can think of."

Well, I see I was up a stump—and up it good. Providence had stood by me this fur, all right, but I was hard and tight aground, now. I see it warn't a bit of use to try to go ahead—I'd *got* to throw up my hand. So I says to myself, here's another place where I got to resk the truth. I opened my mouth to begin; but she grabbed me and hustled me in behind the bed, and says:

"Here he comes! stick your head down lower—there, that'll do; you can't be seen, now. Don't you let on you're here. I'll play a joke on him. Children, don't you say a word."

I see I was in a fix, now. But it warn't no use to worry; there warn't nothing to do but just hold still, and try to be ready to stand from under when the lightning struck.

---

3. "Lalla Rookh" (1817), a popular Romantic poem by Thomas Moore.

4. Gangrene.

I had just one little glimpse of the old gentleman when he come in, then the bed hid him. Mrs. Phelps she jumps for him and says:

"Has he come?"

"No," says her husband.

"Good-*ness* gracious!" she says, "what in the world *can* have become of him?"

"I can't imagine," says the old gentleman; "and I must say, it makes me dreadful uneasy."

"Uneasy!" she says, "I'm ready to go distracted! He *must* a come; and you've missed him along the road. I *know* it's so—something *tells* me so."

"Why Sally, I *couldn't* miss him along the road—*you* know that."

"But oh, dear, dear, what *will* Sis say! He must a come! You must a missed him. He—"

"Oh, don't distress me any more'n I'm already distressed. I don't know what in the world to make of it. I'm at my wit's end, and I don't mind acknowledging 't I'm right down scared. But there's no hope that he's come; for he *couldn't* come and me miss him. Sally, it's terrible—just terrible—something's happened to the boat, sure!"

"Why, Silas! Look yonder!—up the road!—ain't that somebody coming?"

He sprung to the window at the head of the bed, and that give Mrs. Phelps the chance she wanted. She stooped down quick, at the foot of the bed, and give me a pull, and out I come; and when he turned back from the window, there she stood, a-beaming and a-smiling like a house afire, and I standing pretty meek and sweaty alongside. The old gentleman stared, and says:

"Why, who's that?"

"Who do you reckon 't is?"

"I hain't no idea. Who *is* it?"

"It's *Tom Sawyer!*"[5]

By jings, I most slumped through the floor. But there warn't no time to swap knives;[6] the old man grabbed me by the hand and shook, and kept on shaking; and all the time, how the woman did dance around and laugh and cry; and then how they both did fire off questions about Sid, and Mary, and the rest of the tribe.

But if they was joyful, it warn't nothing to what I was; for it was like being born again, I was so glad to find out who I was. Well, they froze to me for two hours; and at last when my chin was so tired it couldn't hardly go, any more, I had told them more about my family—I mean the Sawyer family—than ever happened to any six Sawyer families. And I explained all about how we blowed out a cylinder-head at the mouth of the White River and it took us three days to fix it. Which was all right, and worked first rate; because *they* didn't know but what it would take three days to fix it. If I'd a called it a bolt-head it would a done just as well.

Now I was feeling pretty comfortable all down one side, and pretty uncomfortable all up the other. Being Tom Sawyer was easy and comfortable; and it stayed easy and comfortable till by-and-by I hear a steamboat coughing along down the river—then I says to myself, spose Tom Sawyer come down on that

---

5. Huck's being mistaken for Tom is seen by many critics as a sardonic comment on Huck's seeming to forget his loyalty to Jim and once again falling under Tom's sway in tormenting Jim at the Phelps farm.
6. Change plans.

boat?—and spose he steps in here, any minute, and sings out my name before I can throw him a wink to keep quiet? Well, I couldn't *have* it that way—it wouldn't do at all. I must go up the road and waylay him. So I told the folks I reckoned I would go up to the town and fetch down my baggage. The old gentleman was for going along with me, but I said no, I could drive the horse myself, and I druther he wouldn't take no trouble about me.

Chapter XXXIII

So I started for town, in the wagon, and when I was half-way I see a wagon coming, and sure enough it was Tom Sawyer, and I stopped and waited till he come along. I says "Hold on!" and it stopped alongside, and his mouth opened up like a trunk, and staid so; and he swallowed two or three times like a person that's got a dry throat, and then says:

"I hain't ever done you no harm. You know that. So then, what you want to come back and ha'nt *me* for?"

I says:

"I hain't come back—I hain't been *gone.*"

When he heard my voice, it righted him up some, but he warn't quite satisfied yet. He says:

"Don't you play nothing on me, because I wouldn't on you. Honest injun, now, you ain't a ghost?"

"Honest injun, I ain't," I says.

"Well—I—I—well, that ought to settle it, of course; but I can't somehow seem to understand it, no way. Looky here, warn't you ever murdered *at all?*"

"No. I warn't ever murdered at all—I played it on them. You come in here and feel of me if you don't believe me."

So he done it; and it satisfied him; and he was that glad to see me again, he didn't know what to do. And he wanted to know all about it right off; because it was a grand adventure, and mysterious, and so it hit him where he lived. But I said, leave it along till by-and-by; and told his driver to wait, and we drove off a little piece, and I told him the kind of a fix I was in, and what did he reckon we better do? He said, let him alone a minute, and don't disturb him. So he thought and thought, and pretty soon he says:

"It's all right, I've got it. Take my trunk in your wagon, and let on it's your'n; and you turn back and fool along slow, so as to get to the house about the time you ought to; and I'll go towards town a piece, and take a fresh start, and get there a quarter or a half an hour after you; and you needn't let on to know me, at first."

I says:

"All right; but wait a minute. There's one more thing—a thing that *nobody* don't know but me. And that is, there's a nigger here that I'm trying to steal out of slavery—and his name is *Jim*—old Miss Watson's Jim."

He says:

"What! Why Jim is—"

He stopped and went to studying. I says:

"*I* know what you'll say. You'll say it's dirty low-down business; but what if it is?—*I'm* low down; and I'm agoing to steal him, and I want you to keep mum and not let on. Will you?"

His eye lit up, and he says:

"I'll *help* you steal him!"

Well, I let go all holts then, like I was shot. It was the most astonishing speech I ever heard—and I'm bound to say Tom Sawyer fell, considerable, in my estimation. Only I couldn't believe it. Tom Sawyer a *nigger stealer!*

"Oh, shucks," I says, "you're joking."

"I ain't joking, either."

"Well, then," I says, "joking or no joking, if you hear anything said about a runaway nigger, don't forget to remember that *you* don't know nothing about him, and *I* don't know nothing about him."

Then we took the trunk and put it in my wagon, and he drove off his way, and I drove mine. But of course I forgot all about driving slow, on accounts of being glad and full of thinking; so I got home a heap too quick for that length of trip. The old gentleman was at the door, and he says.

"Why, this is wonderful. Who ever would a thought it was in that mare to do it. I wish we'd a timed her. And she hain't sweated a hair—not a hair. It's wonderful. Why, I wouldn't take a hundred dollars for that horse now; I wouldn't, honest; and yet I'd a sold her for fifteen before, and thought 'twas all she was worth."

That's all he said. He was the innocentest, best old soul I ever see. But it warn't surprising; because he warn't only just a farmer, he was a preacher, too, and had a little one-horse log church down back of the plantation, which he built it himself at his own expense, for a church and school-house, and never charged nothing for his preaching, and it was worth it, too. There was plenty other farmer-preachers like that, and done the same way, down South.

In about half an hour Tom's wagon drove up to the front stile, and Aunt Sally she see it through the window because it was only about fifty yards, and says:

"Why, there's somebody come! I wonder who 'tis? Why, I do believe it's a stranger. Jimmy" (that's one of the children), "run and tell Lize to put on another plate for dinner."

Everybody made a rush for the front door, because, of course, a stranger don't come *every* year, and so he lays over the yaller fever, for interest, when he does come. Tom was over the stile and starting for the house; the wagon was spinning up the road for the village, and we was all bunched in the front door. Tom had his store clothes on, and an audience—and that was always nuts for Tom Sawyer. In them circumstances it warn't no trouble to him to throw in an amount of style that was suitable. He warn't a boy to meeky along up that yard like a sheep; no, he come ca'm and important, like the ram. When he got afront of us, he lifts his hat ever so gracious and dainty, like it was the lid of a box that had butterflies asleep in it and he didn't want to disturb them, and says:

"Mr. Archibald Nichols, I presume?"

"No, my boy," says the old gentleman, "I'm sorry to say 't your driver has deceived you; Nichols's place is down a matter of three mile more. Come in, come in."

Tom he took a look back over his shoulder, and says, "Too late—he's out of sight."

"Yes, he's gone, my son, and you must come in and eat your dinner with us; and then we'll hitch up and take you down to Nichols's."

"Oh, I *can't* make you so much trouble; I couldn't think of it. I'll walk—I don't mind the distance."

"But we won't *let* you walk—it wouldn't be Southern hospitality to do it. Come right in."

"Oh, *do*," says Aunt Sally; "it ain't a bit of trouble to us, not a bit in the world. You *must* stay. It's a long, dusty three mile, and we *can't* let you walk. And besides, I've already told 'em to put on another plate, when I see you coming; so you mustn't disappoint us. Come right in, and make yourself at home."

So Tom he thanked them very hearty and handsome, and let himself be persuaded, and come in; and when he was in, he said he was a stranger from Hicksville, Ohio, and his name was William Thompson—and he made another bow.

Well, he run on, and on, and on, making up stuff about Hicksville and everybody in it he could invent, and I getting a little nervous, and wondering how this was going to help me out of my scrape; and at last, still talking along, he reached over and kissed Aunt Sally right on the mouth, and then settled back again in his chair, comfortable, and was going on talking; but she jumped up and wiped it off with the back of her hand, and says:

"You owdacious puppy!"

He looked kind of hurt, and says:

"I'm surprised at you, m'am."

"You're s'rp—Why, what do you reckon I am? I've a good notion to take and—say, what do you mean by kissing me?"

He looked kind of humble, and says:

"I didn't mean nothing, m'am. I didn't mean no harm. I—I—thought you'd like it."

"Why, you born fool!" She took up the spinning-stick, and it looked like it was all she could do to keep from giving him a crack with it. "What made you think I'd like it?"

"Well, I don't know. Only, they—they—told me you would."

"*They* told you I would. Whoever told you's *another* lunatic. I never heard the beat of it. Who's *they*?"

"Why—everybody. They all said so, m'am."

It was all she could do to hold in; and her eyes snapped, and her fingers worked like she wanted to scratch him; and she says:

"Who's everybody?' Out with their names—or ther'll be an idiot short."

He got up and looked distressed, and fumbled his hat, and says:

"I'm sorry, and I warn't expecting it. They told me to. They all told me to. They all said kiss her; and said she'll like it. They all said it—every one of them. But I'm sorry, m'am, and I won't do it no more—I won't, honest."

"You won't, won't you? Well, I sh'd *reckon* you won't!"

"No'm, I'm honest about it; I won't ever do it again. Till you ask me."

"Till I *ask* you! Well, I never see the beat of it in my born days! I lay you'll be the Methusalem-numskull[7] of creation before ever *I* ask you—or the likes of you."

"Well," he says, "it does surprise me so. I can't make it out, somehow. They said you would, and I thought you would. But—" He stopped and looked

---

7. Methuselah was a biblical patriarch said to have lived 969 years.

around slow, like he wished he could run across a friendly eye, somewhere's; and fetched up on the old gentleman's, and says, "Didn't *you* think she'd like me to kiss her, sir?"

"Why, no, I—I—well, no, I b'lieve I didn't."

Then he looks on around, the same way, to me—and says:

"Tom, didn't *you* think Aunt Sally 'd open out her arms and say, 'Sid Sawyer—' "

"My land!" she says, breaking in and jumping for him, "you impudent young rascal, to fool a body so—" and was going to hug him, but he fended her off, and says:

"No, not till you've asked me, first."

So she didn't lose no time, but asked him; and hugged him and kissed him, over and over again, and then turned him over to the old man, and he took what was left. And after they got a little quiet again, she says:

"Why, dear me, I never see such a surprise. We warn't looking for *you,* at all, but only Tom. Sis never wrote to me about anybody coming but him."

"It's because it warn't *intended* for any of us to come but Tom," he says; "but I begged and begged, and at the last minute she let me come, too; so, coming down the river, me and Tom thought it would be a first-rate surprise for him to come here to the house first, and for me to by-and-by tag along and drop in and let on to be a stranger. But it was a mistake, Aunt Sally. This ain't no healthy place for a stranger to come."

"No—not impudent whelps, Sid. You ought to had your jaws boxed; I hain't been so put out since I don't know when. But I don't care, I don't mind the terms—I'd be willing to stand a thousand such jokes to have you here. Well, to think of that performance! I don't deny it, I was most putrified[8] with astonishment when you give me that smack."

We had dinner out in that broad open passage betwixt the house and the kitchen; and there was things enough on that table for seven families—and all hot, too; none of your flabby tough meat that's laid in a cupboard in a damp cellar all night and tastes like a hunk of old cold cannibal in the morning. Uncle Silas he asked a pretty long blessing over it, but it was worth it; and it didn't cool it a bit, neither, the way I've seen them kind of interruptions do, lots of times.

There was a considerable good deal of talk, all the afternoon, and me and Tom was on the lookout all the time, but it warn't no use, they didn't happen to say nothing about any runaway nigger, and we was afraid to try to work up to it. But at supper, at night, one of the little boys says:

"Pa, mayn't Tom and Sid and me go to the show?"

"No," says the old man, "I reckon there ain't going to be any; and you couldn't go if there was; because the runaway nigger told Burton and me all about that scandalous show, and Burton said he would tell the people; so I reckon they've drove the owdacious loafers out of town before this time."

So there it was!—but *I* couldn't help it. Tom and me was to sleep in the same room and bed; so, being tired, we bid good-night and went up to bed, right after supper, and clumb out of the window and down the lightning-rod, and shoved for the town; for I didn't believe anybody was going to give the

8. Petrified or stunned.

king and the duke a hint, and so, if I didn't hurry up and give them one they'd get into trouble sure.

On the road Tom he told me all about how it was reckoned I was murdered, and how pap disappeared, pretty soon, and didn't come back no more, and what a stir there was when Jim run away; and I told Tom all about our Royal Nonesuch rapscallions, and as much of the raft-voyage as I had time to; and as we struck into the town and up through the middle of it—it was as much as half-after eight, then—here comes a raging rush of people, with torches, and an awful whooping and yelling, and banging tin pans and blowing horns; and we jumped to one side to let them go by; and as they went by, I see they had the king and the duke astraddle of a rail—that is, I knowed it *was* the king and the duke, though they was all over tar and feathers, and didn't look like nothing in the world that was human—just looked like a couple of monstrous big soldier-plumes. Well, it made me sick to see it; and I was sorry for them poor pitiful rascals, it seemed like I couldn't ever feel any hardness against them any more in the world. It was a dreadful thing to see. Human beings *can* be awful cruel to one another.

We see we was too late—couldn't do no good. We asked some stragglers about it, and they said everybody went to the show looking very innocent; and laid low and kept dark till the poor old king was in the middle of his cavortings on the stage; then somebody give a signal, and the house rose up and went for them.

So we poked along back home, and I warn't feeling so brash as I was before, but kind of ornery, and humble, and to blame, somehow—though *I* hadn't done anything. But that's always the way; it don't make no difference whether you do right or wrong, a person's conscience ain't got no sense, and just goes for him *anyway*. If I had a yaller dog that didn't know no more than a person's conscience does, I would pison him. It takes up more room than all the rest of a person's insides, and yet ain't no good, nohow. Tom Sawyer he says the same.

Chapter XXXIV

We stopped talking, and got to thinking. By-and-by Tom says:

"Looky here, Huck, what fools we are, to not think of it before! I bet I know where Jim is."

"No! Where?"

"In that hut down by the ash-hopper. Why, looky here. When we was at dinner, didn't you see a nigger man go in there with some vittles?"

"Yes."

"What did you think the vittles was for?"

"For a dog."

"So'd I. Well, it wasn't for a dog."

"Why?"

"Because part of it was watermelon."

"So it was—I noticed it. Well, it does beat all, that I never thought about a dog not eating watermelon. It shows how a body can see and don't see at the same time."

"Well, the nigger unlocked the padlock when he went in, and he locked it again when he come out. He fetched uncle a key, about the time we got up from table—same key, I bet. Watermelon shows man, lock shows prisoner; and it ain't likely there's two prisoners on such a little plantation, and where the people's all so kind and good. Jim's the prisoner. All right—I'm glad we found it out detective fashion; I wouldn't give shucks for any other way. Now you work your mind and study out a plan to steal Jim, and I will study out one, too; and we'll take the one we like the best."

What a head for just a boy to have! If I had Tom Sawyer's head, I wouldn't trade it off to be a duke, nor mate of a steamboat, nor clown in a circus, nor nothing I can think of. I went to thinking out a plan, but only just to be doing something; I knowed very well where the right plan was going to come from. Pretty soon, Tom says:

"Ready?"

"Yes," I says.

"All right—bring it out."

"My plan is this," I says. "We can easy find out if it's Jim in there. Then get up my canoe to-morrow night, and fetch my raft over from the island. Then the first dark night that comes, steal the key out of the old man's britches, after he goes to bed, and shove off down the river on the raft, with Jim, hiding daytimes and running nights, the way me and Jim used to do before. Wouldn't that plan work?"

"*Work?* Why cert'nly, it would work, like rats a fighting. But it's too blame' simple; there ain't nothing *to* it. What's the good of a plan that ain't no more trouble than that? It's as mild as goose-milk. Why, Huck, it wouldn't make no more talk than breaking into a soap factory."

I never said nothing, because I warn't expecting nothing different; but I knowed mighty well that whenever he got *his* plan ready it wouldn't have none of them objections to it.

And it didn't. He told me what it was, and I see in a minute it was worth fifteen of mine, for style, and would make Jim just as free a man as mine would, and maybe get us all killed besides. So I was satisfied, and said we would waltz in on it. I needn't tell what it was, here, because I knowed it wouldn't stay the way it was. I knowed he would be changing it around, every which way, as we went along, and heaving in new bullinesses wherever he got a chance. And that is what he done.

Well, one thing was dead sure; and that was, that Tom Sawyer was in earnest and was actly going to help steal that nigger out of slavery. That was the thing that was too many for me. Here was a boy that was respectable, and well brung up; and had a character to lose; and folks at home that had characters; and he was bright and not leather-headed; and knowing and not ignorant; and not mean, but kind; and yet here he was, without any more pride, or rightness, or feeling, than to stoop to this business, and make himself a shame, and his family a shame, before everybody. I *couldn't* understand it, no way at all. It was outrageous, and I knowed I ought to just up and tell him so; and so be his true friend, and let him quit the thing right where he was, and save himself. And I *did* start to tell him; but he shut me up, and says:

"Don't you reckon I know what I'm about? Don't I generly know what I'm about?"

"Yes."

"Didn't I *say* I was going to help steal the nigger?"

"Yes."

"*Well* then."

That's all he said, and that's all I said. It warn't no use to say any more; because when he said he'd do a thing, he always done it. But *I* couldn't make out how he was willing to go into this thing; so I just let it go, and never bothered no more about it. If he was bound to have it so, I couldn't help it.

When we got home, the house was all dark and still; so we went on down to the hut by the ash-hopper, for to examine it. We went through the yard, so as to see what the hounds would do. They knowed us, and didn't make no more noise than country dogs is always doing when anything comes by in the night. When we got to the cabin, we took a look at the front and the two sides; and on the side I warn't acquainted with—which was the north side—we found a square window-hole, up tolerable high, with just one stout board nailed across it. I says:

"Here's the ticket. This hole's big enough for Jim to get through, if we wrench off the board."

Tom says:

"It's as simple as tit-tat-toe, three-in-a-row, and as easy as playing hooky. I should *hope* we can find a way that's a little more complicated than *that*, Huck Finn."

"Well, then," I says, "how'll it do to saw him out, the way I done before I was murdered, that time?"

"That's more *like*," he says, "It's real mysterious, and troublesome, and good," he says; "but I bet we can find a way that's twice as long. There ain't no hurry; le's keep on looking around."

Betwixt the hut and the fence, on the back side, was a lean-to, that joined the hut at the eaves, and was made out of plank. It was as long as the hut, but narrow—only about six foot wide. The door to it was at the south end, and was padlocked. Tom he went to the soap kettle, and searched around and fetched back the iron thing they lift the lid with; so he took it and prized out one of the staples. The chain fell down, and we opened the door and went in, and shut it, and struck a match, and see the shed was only built against the cabin and hadn't no connection with it; and there warn't no floor to the shed, nor nothing in it but some old rusty played-out hoes, and spades, and picks, and a crippled plow. The match went out, and so did we, and shoved in the staple again, and the door was locked as good as ever. Tom was joyful. He says:

"Now we're all right. We'll *dig* him out. It'll take about a week!"

Then we started for the house, and I went in the back door—you only have to pull a buckskin latch-string, they don't fasten the doors—but that warn't romantical enough for Tom Sawyer: no way would do him but he must climb up the lightning-rod. But after he got up half-way about three times, and missed fire and fell every time, and the last time most busted his brains out, he thought he'd got to give it up; but after he rested, he allowed he would give her one more turn for luck, and this time he made the trip.

In the morning we was up at break of day, and down to the nigger cabins to pet the dogs and make friends with the nigger that fed Jim—if it *was* Jim that was being fed. The niggers was just getting through breakfast and starting for the fields; and Jim's nigger was piling up a tin pan with bread and meat and things; and whilst the other was leaving, the key come from the house.

This nigger had a good-natured, chuckle-headed face, and his wool was all tied up in little bunches with thread. That was to keep witches off. He said the witches was pestering him awful, these nights, and making him see all kinds of strange things, and hear all kinds of strange words and noises, and he didn't believe he was ever witched so long, before, in his life. He got so worked up, and got to running on so about his troubles, he forgot all about what he'd been agoing to do. So Tom says:

"What's the vittles for? Going to feed the dogs?"

The nigger kind of smiled around graduly over his face, like when you heave a brickbat in a mud puddle, and he says:

"Yes, Mars Sid, *a* dog. Cur'us dog too. Does you want to go en look at 'im?"

"Yes."

I hunched Tom, and whispers:

"You going, right here in the day-break? *That* warn't the plan."

"No, it warn't—but it's the plan *now*."

So, drat him, we went along, but I didn't like it much. When we got in, we couldn't hardly see anything, it was so dark; but Jim was there, sure enough, and could see us; and he sings out:

"Why, *Huck!* En good *lan'!* ain' dat Misto Tom?"

I just knowed how it would be; I just expected it. *I* didn't know nothing to do; and if I had, I couldn't done it; because that nigger busted in and says:

"Why, de gracious sakes! do he know you genlmen?"

We could see pretty well, now. Tom he looked at the nigger, steady and kind of wondering, and says:

"Does *who* know us?"

"Why, dish-yer runaway nigger."

"I don't reckon he does; but what put that into your head?"

"What *put* it dar? Didn' he jis' dis minute sing out like he knowed you?"

Tom says, in a puzzled-up kind of way:

"Well, that's mighty curious. *Who* sung out? *When* did he sing out? *What* did he sing out?" And turns to me, perfectly ca'm, and says, "Did *you* hear anybody sing out?"

Of course there warn't nothing to be said but the one thing; so I says:

"No; *I* ain't heard nobody say nothing."

Then he turns to Jim, and looks him over like he never see him before; and says:

"Did you sing out?"

"No, sah," says Jim; "I hain't said nothing, sah."

"Not a word?"

"No, sah, I hain't said a word."

"Did you ever see us before?"

"No, sah; not as *I* knows on."

So Tom turns to the nigger, which was looking wild and distressed, and says, kind of severe:

"What do you reckon's the matter with you, anyway? What made you think somebody sung out?"

"Oh, it's de dad-blame' witches, sah, en I wisht I was dead, I do. Dey's awluz at it, sah, en dey do mos' kill me, dey sk'yers me so. Please to don't tell nobody 'bout it sah, er old Mars Silas he'll scole me; 'kase he say dey *ain't* no witches. I jis' wish to goodness he was heah now—*den* what would he say! I jis' bet he couldn' fine no way to git aroun' it *dis* time. But it's awluz jis' so; people dat's *sot,* stays sot; dey won't look into nothn' en fine it out f'r deyselves, en when *you* fine it out en tell um 'bout it, dey doan' b'lieve you."

Tom give him a dime, and said we wouldn't tell nobody; and told him to buy some more thread to tie up his wool with; and then looks at Jim, and says:

"I wonder if Uncle Silas is going to hang this nigger. If I was to catch a nigger that was ungrateful enough to run away, *I* wouldn't give him up, I'd hang him." And whilst the nigger stepped to the door to look at the dime and bite it to see if it was good, he whispers to Jim and says:

"Don't ever let on to know us. And if you hear any digging going on nights, it's us: we're going to set you free."

Jim only had time to grab us by the hand and squeeze it, then the nigger come back, and we said we'd come again some time if the nigger wanted us to; and he said he would, more particular if it was dark, because the witches went for him mostly in the dark, and it was good to have folks around then.

Chapter XXXV

It would be most an hour, yet, till breakfast, so we left, and struck down into the woods; because Tom said we got to have *some* light to see how to dig by, and a lantern makes too much, and might get us into trouble; what we must have was a lot of them rotten chunks that's called fox-fire[9] and just makes a soft kind of a glow when you lay them in a dark place. We fetched an armful and hid it in the weeds, and set down to rest, and Tom says, kind of dissatisfied:

"Blame it, this whole thing is just as easy and awkard as it can be. And so it makes it so rotten difficult to get up a difficult plan. There ain't no watchman to be drugged—now there *ought* to be a watchman. There ain't even a dog to give a sleeping-mixture to. And there's Jim chained by one leg, with a ten-foot chain, to the leg of his bed; why, all you got to do is to lift up the bedstead and slip off the chain. And Uncle Silas he trusts everybody; sends the key to the punkin-headed nigger, and don't send nobody to watch the nigger. Jim could a got out of that window hole before this, only there wouldn't be no use trying to travel with a ten-foot chain on his leg. Why, drat it, Huck, it's the stupidest arrangement I ever see. You got to invent *all* the difficulties. Well, we can't help it, we got to do the best we can with the materials we've got. Anyhow, there's one thing—there's more honor in getting him out through a lot of difficulties and dangers, where there warn't one of them furnished to you by the people who it was their duty to furnish them, and you had to contrive them all out of your own head. Now look at just that one thing of the lantern. When you come down to the cold facts, we simply got to *let on* that a lantern's resky. Why, we could work with a torchlight procession if we wanted to, I believe. Now, whilst I think of it, we got to hunt up something to make a saw out of, the first chance we get."

"What do we want of a saw?"

"What do we *want* of it? Hain't we got to saw the leg of Jim's bed off, so as to get the chain loose?"

---

9. Phosphorescent glow of fungus on rotting wood.

"Why, you just said a body could lift up the bedstead and slip the chain off."

"Well, if that ain't just like you, Huck Finn. You *can* get up the infant-schooliest ways of going at a thing. Why, hain't you ever read any books at all?—Baron Trenck, nor Casanova, nor Benvenuto Chelleeny, nor Henri IV.,[1] nor none of them heroes? Whoever heard of getting a prisoner loose in such an old-maidy way as that? No; the way all the best authorities does, is to saw the bedleg in two, and leave it just so, and swallow the sawdust, so it can't be found, and put some dirt and grease around the sawed place so the very keen-est seneskal[2] can't see no sign of it's being sawed, and thinks the bed-leg is perfectly sound. Then, the night you're ready, fetch the leg a kick, down she goes; slip off your chain, and there you are. Nothing to do but hitch your rope-ladder to the battlements, shin down it, break your leg in the moat—because a rope-ladder is nineteen foot too short, you know—and there's your horses and your trusty vassles, and they scoop you up and fling you across a saddle and away you go, to your native Langudoc, or Navarre,[3] or wherever it is. It's gaudy, Huck. I wish there was a moat to this cabin. If we get time, the night of the escape, we'll dig one."

I says:

"What do we want of a moat, when we're going to snake him out from under the cabin?"

But he never heard me. He had forgot me and everything else. He had his chin in his hand, thinking. Pretty soon, he sighs, and shakes his head; then sighs again, and says:

"No, it wouldn't do—there ain't necessity enough for it."

"For what?" I says.

"Why, to saw Jim's leg off," he says.

"Good land!" I says, "why, there ain't *no* necessity for it. And what would you want to saw his leg off for, anyway?"

"Well, some of the best authorities has done it. They couldn't get the chain off, so they just cut their hand off, and shoved. And a leg would be better still. But we got to let that go. There ain't necessity enough in this case; and besides, Jim's a nigger and wouldn't understand the reasons for it, and how it's the custom in Europe, so we'll let it go. But there's one thing—he can have a rope-ladder; we can tear up our sheets and make him a rope-ladder easy enough. And we can send it to him in a pie; it's mostly done that way. And I've et worse pies."

"Why, Tom Sawyer, how you talk," I says; "Jim ain't got no use for a rope-ladder."

"He *has* got use for it. How *you* talk, you better say; you don't know noth-ing about it. He's *got* to have a rope ladder; they all do."

"What in the nation can he *do* with it?"

"*Do* with it? He can hide it in his bed, can't he? That's what they all do; and he's got to, too. Huck, you don't ever seem to want to do anything that's reg-ular; you want to be starting something fresh all the time. Spose he *don't* do

1. Baron Friedrich von der Trenck (1726–1794), an Austrian soldier, and Henry IV of France (1553–1610), military heroes. Benvenuto Cellini (1500–1571), an artist, and Giovanni Jacopo Casanova (1725–1798) were both famous lovers. All four were involved in daring escape attempts.
2. Seneschal, powerful official in the service of medieval nobles.
3. Provinces in France and Spain, respectively.

nothing with it? ain't it there in his bed, for a clew, after he's gone? and don't you reckon they'll want clews? Of course they will. And you wouldn't leave them any? That would be a *pretty* howdy-do *wouldn't* it! I never heard of such a thing."

"Well," I says, "if it's in the regulations, and he's got to have it, all right, let him have it; because I don't wish to go back on no regulations; but there's one thing, Tom Sawyer—if we go tearing up our sheets to make Jim a rope-ladder, we're going to get into trouble with Aunt Sally, just as sure as you're born. Now, the way I look at it, a hickry-bark ladder don't cost nothing, and don't waste nothing, and is just as good to load up a pie with, and hide in a straw tick, as any rag ladder you can start; and as for Jim, he hain't had no experience, and so *he* don't care what kind of a—"

"Oh, shucks, Huck Finn, if I was as ignorant as you, I'd keep still—that's what *I'd* do. Who ever heard of a state prisoner escaping by a hickry-bark ladder? Why, it's perfectly ridiculous."

"Well, all right, Tom, fix it your own way; but if you'll take my advice, you'll let me borrow a sheet off of the clothes-line."

He said that would do. And that give him another idea, and he says:

"Borrow a shirt, too."

"What do we want of a shirt, Tom?"

"Want it for Jim to keep a journal on."

"Journal your granny—*Jim* can't write."

"Spose he *can't* write—he can make marks on the shirt, can't he, if we make him a pen out of an old pewter spoon or a piece of an old iron barrel-hoop?"

"Why, Tom, we can pull a feather out of a goose and make him a better one; and quicker, too."

"*Prisoners* don't have geese running around the donjon-keep to pull pens out of, you muggins. They *always* make their pens out of the hardest, toughest, troublesomest piece of old brass candlestick or something like that they can get their hands on; and it takes them weeks and weeks, and months and months to file it out, too, because they've got to do it by rubbing it on the wall. *They* wouldn't use a goose-quill if they had it. It ain't regular."

"Well, then, what'll we make him the ink out of?"

"Many makes it out of iron-rust and tears; but that's the common sort and women; the best authorities uses their own blood. Jim can do that; and when he wants to send any little common ordinary mysterious message to let the world know where he's captivated, he can write it on the bottom of a tin plate with a fork and throw it out of the window. The Iron Mask[4] always done that, and it's a blame' good way, too."

"Jim ain't got no tin plates. They feed him in a pan."

"That ain't anything; we can get him some."

"Can't nobody *read* his plates."

"That ain't got nothing to *do* with it, Huck Finn. All *he's* got to do is to write on the plate and throw it out. You don't *have* to be able to read it. Why, half the time you can't read anything a prisoner writes on a tin plate, or anywhere else."

"Well, then, what's the sense in wasting the plates?"

4. The chief character in Alexandre Dumas's novel *Le Vicomte de Bragelonne* (1848–50), part of which was translated into English as *The Man in the Iron Mask*.

"Why, blame it all, it ain't the *prisoner's* plates."

"But it's *somebody's* plates, ain't it?"

"Well, spos'n it is? What does the *prisoner* care whose—"

He broke off there, because we heard the breakfast-horn blowing. So we cleared out for the house.

Along during that morning I borrowed a sheet and a white shirt off of the clothes-line; and I found an old sack and put them in it, and we went down and got the fox-fire, and put that in too. I called it borrowing, because that was what pap always called it; but Tom said it warn't borrowing, it was stealing. He said we was representing prisoners; and prisoners don't care how they get a thing so they get it, and nobody don't blame them for it, either. It ain't no crime in a prisoner to steal the thing he needs to get away with, Tom said; it's his right; and so, as long as we was representing a prisoner, we had a perfect right to steal anything on this place we had the least use for, to get ourselves out of prison with. He said if we warn't prisoners it would be a very different thing, and nobody but a mean ornery person would steal when he warn't a prisoner. So we allowed we would steal everything there was that come handy. And yet he made a mighty fuss, one day, after that, when I stole a watermelon out of the nigger patch and eat it; and he made me go and give the niggers a dime, without telling them what it was for. Tom said that what he meant was, we could steal anything we *needed*. Well, I says, I needed the watermelon. But he said I didn't need it to get out of prison with, there's where the difference was. He said if I'd a wanted it to hide a knife in, and smuggle it to Jim to kill the seneskal with, it would a been all right. So I let it go at that, though I couldn't see no advantage in my representing a prisoner, if I got to set down and chaw over a lot of gold-leaf distinctions like that, every time I see a chance to hog a watermelon.

Well, as I was saying, we waited that morning till everybody was settled down to business, and nobody in sight around the yard; then Tom he carried the sack into the lean-to whilst I stood off a piece to keep watch. By-and-by he come out, and we went and set down on the wood-pile, to talk. He says:

"Everything's all right, now, except tools; and that's easy fixed."

"Tools?" I says.

"Yes."

"Tools for what?"

"Why, to dig with. We ain't agoing to *gnaw* him out, are we?"

"Ain't them old crippled picks and things in there good enough to dig a nigger out with?" I says.

He turns on me looking pitying enough to make a body cry, and says:

"Huck Finn, did you *ever* hear of a prisoner having picks and shovels, and all the modern conveniences in his wardrobe to dig himself out with? Now I want to ask you—if you got any reasonableness in you at all—what kind of a show would *that* give him to be a hero? Why, they might as well lend him the key, and done with it. Picks and shovels—why they wouldn't furnish 'em to a king."

"Well, then," I says, "if we don't want the picks and shovels, what do we want?"

"A couple of case-knives."[5]

---

5. Ordinary kitchen knives.

"To dig the foundations out from under that cabin with?"

"Yes."

"Confound it, it's foolish, Tom."

"It don't make no difference how foolish it is, it's the *right* way—and it's the regular way. And there ain't no *other* way, that ever *I* heard of, and I've read all the books that gives any information about these things. They always dig out with a case-knife—and not through dirt, mind you; generly it's through solid rock. And it takes them weeks and weeks and weeks, and for ever and ever. Why, look at one of them prisoners in the bottom dungeon of the Castle Deef,[6] in the harbor of Marseilles, that dug himself out that way; how long was *he* at it, you reckon?"

"I don't know."

"Well, guess."

"I don't know. A month and a half?"

"*Thirty-seven year*—and he come out in China. *That's* the kind. I wish the bottom of *this* fortress was solid rock."

"*Jim* don't know nobody in China."

"What's *that* got to do with it? Neither did that other fellow. But you're always a-wandering off on a side issue. Why can't you stick to the main point?"

"All right—*I* don't care where he comes out, so he *comes* out; and Jim don't, either, I reckon. But there's one thing, anyway—Jim's too old to be dug out with a case-knife. He won't last."

"Yes he will *last*, too. You don't reckon it's going to take thirty-seven years to dig out through a *dirt* foundation, do you?"

"How long will it take, Tom?"

"Well, we can't resk being as long as we ought to, because it mayn't take very long for Uncle Silas to hear from down there by New Orleans. He'll hear Jim ain't from there. Then his next move will be to advertise Jim, or something like that. So we can't resk being as long digging him out as we ought to. By rights I reckon we ought to be a couple of years; but we can't. Things being so uncertain, what I recommend is this: that we really dig right in, as quick as we can; and after that, we can *let on*, to ourselves, that we was at it thirty-seven years. Then we can snatch him out and rush him away the first time there's an alarm. Yes, I reckon that'll be the best way."

"Now, there's *sense* in that," I says. "Letting on don't cost nothing; letting on ain't no trouble; and if it's any object, I don't mind letting on we was at it a hundred and fifty year. It wouldn't strain me none, after I got my hand in. So I'll mosey along now, and smouch a couple of case-knives."

"Smouch three," he says; "we want one to make a saw out of."

"Tom, if it ain't unregular and irreligious to sejest it," I says, "there's an old rusty saw-blade around yonder sticking under the weatherboarding behind the smoke-house."

He looked kind of weary and discouraged-like, and says:

"It ain't no use to try to learn you nothing, Huck. Run along and smouch the knives—three of them." So I done it.

---

6. The hero of Alexandre Dumas's popular Romantic novel *The Count Château of Monte Cristo* (1844) was held prisoner at the Chateau d'If, a castle built by Francis I in 1524 on a small island in Marseilles harbor and used for many years as a state prison.

Chapter XXXVI

As soon as we reckoned everybody was asleep, that night, we went down the lightning-rod, and shut ourselves up in the lean-to, and got out our pile of fox-fire, and went to work. We cleared everything out of the way, about four or five foot along the middle of the bottom log. Tom said he was right behind Jim's bed now, and we'd dig in under it, and when we got through there couldn't nobody in the cabin ever know there was any hole there, because Jim's counterpin[7] hung down most to the ground, and you'd have to raise it up and look under to see the hole. So we dug and dug, with case-knives, till most midnight; and then we was dog-tired, and our hands was blistered, and yet you couldn't see we'd done anything, hardly. At last I says:

"This ain't no thirty-seven year job, this is a thirty-eight year job, Tom Sawyer."

He never said nothing. But he sighed, and pretty soon he stopped digging, and then for a good little while I knowed he was thinking. Then he says:

"It ain't no use, Huck, it ain't agoing to work. If we was prisoners it would, because then we'd have as many years as we wanted, and no hurry; and we wouldn't get but a few minutes to dig, every day, while they was changing watches, and so our hands wouldn't get blistered, and we could keep it up right along, year in and year out, and do it right, and the way it ought to be done. But *we* can't fool along, we got to rush; we ain't got no time to spare. If we was to put in another night this way, we'd have to knock off for a week to let our hands get well—couldn't touch a case-knife with them sooner."

"Well, then, what we going to do, Tom?"

"I'll tell you. It ain't right, and it ain't moral, and I wouldn't like it to get out—but there ain't only just the one way; we got to dig him out with the picks, and *let on* it's case-knives."

"*Now* you're *talking!*" I says; "your head gets leveler and leveler all the time, Tom Sawyer," I says. "Picks is the thing, moral or no moral; and as for me, I don't care shucks for the morality of it, nohow. When I start in to steal a nigger, or a watermelon, or a Sunday-school book, I ain't no ways particular how it's done so it's done. What I want is my nigger; or what I want is my watermelon; or what I want is my Sunday-school book; and if a pick's the handiest thing, that's the thing I'm agoing to dig that nigger or that watermelon or that Sunday-school book out with; and I don't give a dead rat what the authorities thinks about it nuther."

"Well," he says, "there's excuse for picks and letting-on in a case like this; if it warn't so, I wouldn't approve of it, nor I wouldn't stand by and see the rules broke—because right is right, and wrong is wrong, and a body ain't got no business doing wrong when he ain't ignorant and knows better. It might answer for *you* to dig Jim out with a pick, *without* any letting-on, because you don't know no better; but it wouldn't for me, because I do know better. Gimme a case-knife."

He had his own by him, but I handed him mine. He flung it down, and says:

"Gimme a *case-knife.*"

I didn't know just what to do—but then I thought. I scratched around

7. Counterpane or bedspread.

amongst the old tools, and got a pick-ax and give it to him, and he took it and went to work, and never said a word.

He was always just that particular. Full of principle.

So then I got a shovel, and then we picked and shoveled, turn about, and made the fur fly. We stuck to it about a half an hour, which was as long as we could stand up; but we had a good deal of a hole to show for it. When I got up stairs, I looked out at the window and see Tom doing his level best with the lightning-rod, but he couldn't come it, his hands was so sore. At last he says:

"It ain't no use, it can't be done. What you reckon I better do? Can't you think up no way?"

"Yes," I says, "but I reckon it ain't regular. Come up the stairs, and let on it's a lightning-rod."

So he done it.

Next day Tom stole a pewter spoon and a brass candlestick in the house, for to make some pens for Jim out of, and six tallow candles; and I hung around the nigger cabins, and laid for a chance, and stole three tin plates. Tom said it wasn't enough; but I said nobody wouldn't ever see the plates that Jim throwed out, because they'd fall in the dog-fennel and jimpson weeds under the window-hole—then we could tote them back and he could use them over again. So Tom was satisfied. Then he says:

"Now, the thing to study out is, how to get the things to Jim."

"Take them in through the hole," I says, "when we get it done."

He only just looked scornful, and said something about nobody ever heard of such an idiotic idea, and then he went to studying. By-and-by he said he had ciphered out two or three ways, but there warn't no need to decide on any of them yet. Said we'd got to post Jim first.

That night we went down the lightning-rod a little after ten, and took one of the candles along, and listened under the window-hole, and heard Jim snoring; so we pitched it in, and it didn't wake him. Then we whirled in with the pick and shovel, and in about two hours and a half the job was done. We crept in under Jim's bed and into the cabin, and pawed around and found the candle and lit it, and stood over Jim a while, and found him looking hearty and healthy, and then we woke him up gentle and gradual. He was so glad to see us he most cried; and called us honey, and all the pet names he could think of; and was for having us hunt up a cold chisel to cut the chain off of his leg with, right away, and clearing out without losing any time. But Tom he showed him how unregular it would be, and set down and told him all about our plans, and how we could alter them in a minute any time there was an alarm; and not to be the least afraid, because we would see he got away, *sure*. So Jim he said it was all right, and we set there and talked over old times a while, and then Tom asked a lot of questions, and when Jim told him Uncle Silas come in every day or two to pray with him, and Aunt Sally come in to see if he was comfortable and had plenty to eat, and both of them was kind as they could be, Tom says:

"*Now* I know how to fix it. We'll send you some things by them."

I said, "Don't do nothing of the kind; it's one of the most jackass ideas I ever struck;" but he never paid no attention to me; went right on. It was his way when he'd got his plans set.

So he told Jim how we'd have to smuggle in the rope-ladder pie, and other large things, by Nat, the nigger that fed him, and he must be on the lookout, and not be surprised, and not let Nat see him open them; and we would put small things in uncle's coat pockets and he must steal them out; and we would tie things to aunt's apron strings or put them in her apron pocket, if we got a chance; and told him what they would be and what they was for. And told him how to keep a journal on the shirt with his blood, and all that. He told him everything. Jim he couldn't see no sense in the most of it, but he allowed we was white folks and knowed better than him; so he was satisfied, and said he would do it all just as Tom said.

Jim had plenty corn-cob pipes and tobacco; so we had a right down good sociable time; then we crawled out through the hole, and so home to bed, with hands that looked like they'd been chawed. Tom was in high spirits. He said it was the best fun he ever had in his life, and the most intellectural; and said if he only could see his way to it we would keep it up all the rest of our lives and leave Jim to our children to get out; for he believed Jim would come to like it better and better the more he got used to it. He said that in that way it could be strung out to as much as eighty year, and would be the best time on record. And he said it would make us all celebrated that had a hand in it.

In the morning we went out to the wood-pile and chopped up the brass candlestick into handy sizes, and Tom put them and the pewter spoon in his pocket. Then we went to the nigger cabins, and while I got Nat's notice off, Tom shoved a piece of candlestick into the middle of a corn-pone that was in Jim's pan, and we went along with Nat to see how it would work, and it just worked noble; when Jim bit into it it most mashed all his teeth out; and there warn't ever anything could a worked better. Tom said so himself. Jim he never let on but what it was only just a piece of rock or something like that that's always getting into bread, you know; but after that he never bit into nothing but what he jabbed his fork into it in three or four places, first.

And whilst we was a standing there in the dimmish light, here comes a couple of the hounds bulging in, from under Jim's bed; and they kept on piling in till there was eleven of them, and there warn't hardly room in there to get your breath. By jings, we forgot to fasten that lean-to door. The nigger Nat he only just hollered "witches!" once, and kneeled over onto the floor amongst the dogs, and begun to groan like he was dying. Tom jerked the door open and flung out a slab of Jim's meat, and the dogs went for it, and in two seconds he was out himself and back again and shut the door, and I knowed he'd fixed the other door too. Then he went to work on the nigger, coaxing him and petting him, and asking him if he'd been imagining he saw something again. He raised up, and blinked his eyes around, and says:

"Mars Sid, you'll say I's a fool, but if I didn't b'lieve I see most a million dogs, er devils, er some'n, I wisht I may die right heah in dese tracks. I did, mos' sholy. Mars Sid, I *felt* um—I *felt* um, sah; dey was all over me. Dad fetch it, I jis' wisht I could git my han's on one er dem witches jis' wunst—on'y jis' wunst—it's all *I*'d ast. But mos'ly I wisht dey'd lemme 'lone, I does."

Tom says:

"Well, I tell you what *I* think. What makes them come here just at this runaway nigger's breakfast-time? It's because they're hungry; that's the reason. You make them a witch pie; that's the thing for *you* to do."

"But my lan', Mars Sid, how's I gwyne to make 'm a witch pie? I doan' know how to make it. I hain't ever hearn er sich a thing b'fo.' "

"Well, then, I'll have to make it myself."

"Will you do it, honey?—will you? I'll wusshup de groun' und' yo' foot, I will!"

"All right, I'll do it, seeing it's you, and you've been good to us and showed us the runaway nigger. But you got to be mighty careful. When we come around, you turn your back; and then whatever we've put in the pan, don't you let on you see it at all. And don't you look, when Jim unloads the pan— something might happen, I don't know what. And above all, don't you *handle* the witch-things."

"*Hannel* 'm Mars Sid? What *is* you a talkin' 'bout? I wouldn' lay de weight er my finger on um, not f'r ten hund'd thous'n' billion dollars, I wouldn't."

Chapter XXXVII

That was all fixed. So then we went away and went to the rubbage-pile in the back yard where they keep the old boots, and rags, and pieces of bottles, and wore-out tin things, and all such truck, and scratched around and found an old tin washpan and stopped up the holes as well as we could, to bake the pie in, and took it down cellar and stole it full of flour, and started for breakfast and found a couple of shingle-nails that Tom said would be handy for a prisoner to scrabble his name and sorrows on the dungeon walls with, and dropped one of them in Aunt Sally's apron pocket which was hanging on a chair, and t'other we stuck in the band of Uncle Silas's hat, which was on the bureau, because we heard the children say their pa and ma was going to the runaway nigger's house this morning, and then went to breakfast, and Tom dropped the pewter spoon in Uncle Silas's coat pocket, and Aunt Sally wasn't come yet, so we had to wait a little while.

And when she come she was hot, and red, and cross, and couldn't hardly wait for the blessing; and then she went to sluicing out coffee with one hand and cracking the handiest child's head with her thimble with the other, and says:

"I've hunted high, and I've hunted low, and it does beat all, what *has* become of your other shirt."

My heart fell down amongst my lungs and livers and things, and a hard piece of corn-crust started down my throat after it and got met on the road with a cough and was shot across the table and took one of the children in the eye and curled him up like a fishing-worm, and let a cry out of him the size of a war-whoop, and Tom he turned kinder blue around the gills, and it all amounted to a considerable state of things for about a quarter of a minute or as much as that, and I would a sold out for half price if there was a bidder. But after that we was all right again—it was the sudden surprise of it that knocked us so kind of cold. Uncle Silas he says:

"It's most uncommon curious, I can't understand it. I know perfectly well I took it *off*, because——"

"Because you hain't got but one on. Just *listen* at the man! *I* know you took it off, and know it by a better way than your wool-gethering memory, too, because it was on the clo'es-line yesterday—I see it there myself. But it's gone—that's the long and the short of it, and you'll just have to change to a red flann'l one till I can get time to make a new one. And it'll be the third I've made in two years; it just keeps a body on the jump to keep you in shirts; and whatever you do manage to *do* with 'm all, is more'n *I* can make out. A body'd think you *would* learn to take some sort of care of 'em, at your time of life."

"I know it, Sally, and I do try all I can. But it oughtn't to be altogether my fault, because you know I don't see them nor have nothing to do with them except when they're on me; and I don't believe I've ever lost one of them *off* of me."

"Well, it ain't *your* fault if you haven't, Silas—you'd a done it if you could, I reckon. And the shirt ain't all that's gone, nuther. Ther's a spoon gone; and *that* ain't all. There was ten, and now ther's only nine. The calf got the shirt I reckon, but the calf never took the spoon, *that's* certain."

"Why, what else is gone, Sally?"

"Ther's six *candles* gone—that's what. The rats could a got the candles, and I reckon they did; I wonder they don't walk off with the whole place, the way you're always going to stop their holes and don't do it; and if they warn't fools they'd sleep in your hair, Silas—*you'd* never find it out; but you can't lay the *spoon* on the rats, and that I *know*."

"Well, Sally, I'm in fault, and I acknowledge it; I've been remiss; but I won't let to-morrow go by without stopping up them holes."

"Oh, I wouldn't hurry, next year'll do. Matilda Angelina Araminta *Phelps!*"

Whack comes the thimble, and the child snatches her claws out of the sugar-bowl without fooling around any. Just then, the nigger woman steps onto the passage, and says:

"Missus, dey's a sheet gone."

"A *sheet* gone! Well, for land's sake!"

"I'll stop up them holes *to-day*," says Uncle Silas, looking sorrowful.

"Oh, *do* shet up!—spose the rats took the *sheet? Where's* it gone, Lize?"

"Clah to goodness I hain't no notion, Miss Sally. She wuz on de clo's-line yistiddy, but she done gone; she ain' dah no mo', now."

"I reckon the world *is* coming to an end. I *never* see the beat of it, in all my born days. A shirt, and a sheet, and a spoon, and six can—"

"Missus," comes a young yaller wench, "dey's a brass candlestick miss'n."

"Cler out from here, you hussy, er I'll take a skillet to ye!"

Well, she was just a biling. I begun to lay for a chance; I reckoned I would sneak out and go for the woods till the weather moderated. She kept a raging right along, running her insurrection all by herself, and everybody else mighty meek and quiet; and at last Uncle Silas, looking kind of foolish, fishes up that spoon out of his pocket. She stopped, with her mouth open and her hands up, and as for me, I wished I was in Jeruslem or somewheres. But not long; because she says:

"It's *just* as I expected. So you had it in your pocket all the time; and like as not you've got the other things there, too. How'd it get there?"

"I reely don't know, Sally," he says, kind of apologizing, "or you know I would tell. I was a-studying over my text in Acts Seventeen, before breakfast, and I reckon I put it in there, not noticing, meaning to put my Testament in, and it must be so, because my Testament ain't in, but I'll go and see, and if the Testament is where I had it, I'll know I didn't put it in, and that will show that I laid the Testament down and took up the spoon, and——"

"Oh, for the land's sake! Give a body a rest! Go 'long now, the whole kit and biling of ye; and don't come nigh me again till I've got back my peace of mind."

I'd a heard her, if she'd a said it to herself, let alone speaking it out; and I'd a got up and obeyed her, if I'd a been dead. As we was passing through the setting-room, the old man he took up his hat, and the shingle-nail fell out on the floor, and he just merely picked it up and laid it on the mantel-shelf, and never said nothing, and went out. Tom see him do it, and remembered about the spoon, and says:

"Well, it ain't no use to send things by *him* no more, he ain't reliable." Then he says: "But he done us a good turn with the spoon, anyway, without knowing it, and so we'll go and do him one without *him* knowing it—stop up his rat-holes."

There was a noble good lot of them, down cellar, and it took us a whole hour, but we done the job tight and good, and ship-shape. Then we heard steps on the stairs, and blowed out our light, and hid; and here comes the old man, with a candle in one hand and a bundle of stuff in t'other, looking as absent-minded as year before last. He went a mooning around, first to one rat-hole and then another, till he'd been to them all. Then he stood about five minutes, picking tallow-drip off of his candle and thinking. Then he turns off slow and dreamy towards the stairs, saying:

"Well, for the life of me I can't remember when I done it. I could show her now that I warn't to blame on account of the rats. But never mind—let it go. I reckon it wouldn't do no good."

And so he went on a mumbling up stairs, and then we left. He was a mighty nice old man. And always is.

Tom was a good deal bothered about what to do for a spoon, but he said we'd got to have it; so he took a think. When he had ciphered it out, he told me how we was to do; then we went and waited around the spoon-basket till we see Aunt Sally coming, and then Tom went to counting the spoons and laying them out to one side, and I slip one of them up my sleeve, and Tom says:

"Why, Aunt Sally, there ain't but nine spoons, *yet*."

She says:

"Go 'long to your play, and don't bother me. I know better, I counted 'm myself."

"Well, I've counted them twice, Aunty, and I can't make but nine."

She looked out of all patience, but of course she come to count—anybody would.

"I declare to gracious ther' *ain't* but nine!" she says. "Why, what in the world—plague *take* the things, I'll count 'm again."

So I slipped back the one I had, and when she got done counting, she says:

"Hang the troublesome rubbage, ther's *ten* now!" and she looked huffy and bothered both. But Tom says:

"Why, Aunty *I* don't think there's ten."

"You numskull, didn't you see me *count* 'm?"

"I know, but—"

"Well, I'll count 'm *again*."

So I smouched one, and they come out nine same as the other time. Well, she *was* in a tearing way—just a trembling all over, she was so mad. But she counted and counted, till she got that addled she'd start to count-in the *basket* for a spoon, sometimes; and so, three times they come out right, and three times they come out wrong. Then she grabbed up the basket and slammed it across the house and knocked the cat galley-west;[8] and she said cle'r out and let her have some peace, and if we come bothering around her again betwixt

8. Knocked the cat out completely.

that and dinner, she'd skin us. So we had the odd spoon; and dropped it in her apron pocket whilst she was giving us our sailing-orders, and Jim got it all right, along with her shingle-nail, before noon. We was very well satisfied with the business, and Tom allowed it was worth twice the trouble it took, because he said *now* she couldn't ever count them spoons twice alike again to save her life; and wouldn't believe she'd counted them right, if she *did;* and said that after she'd about counted her head off, for the last three days, he judged she'd give it up and offer to kill anybody that wanted her to ever count them any more.

So we put the sheet back on the line, that night, and stole one out of her closet; and kept on putting it back and stealing it again, for a couple of days, till she didn't know how many sheets she had, any more, and said she didn't *care,* and warn't agoing to bullyrag[9] the rest of her soul out about it, and wouldn't count them again not to save her life, she druther die first.

So we was all right now, as to the shirt and the sheet and the spoon and the candles, by the help of the calf and the rats and the mixed-up counting; and as to the candlestick, it warn't no consequence, it would blow over by-and-by.

But that pie was a job; we had no end of trouble with that pie. We fixed it up away down in the woods, and cooked it there; and we got it done at last, and very satisfactory, too; but not all in one day; and we had to use up three wash-pans full of flour, before we got through, and we got burnt pretty much all over, in places, and eyes put out with the smoke; because, you see, we didn't want nothing but a crust, and we couldn't prop it up right, and she would always cave in. But of course we thought of the right way at last; which was to cook the ladder, too, in the pie. So then we laid in with Jim, the second night, and tore up the sheet all in little strings, and twisted them together, and long before daylight we had a lovely rope, that you could a hung a person with. We let on it took nine months to make it.

And in the forenoon we took it down to the woods, but it wouldn't go in the pie. Being made of a whole sheet, that way, there was rope enough for forty pies, if we'd a wanted them, and plenty left over for soup, or sausage, or anything you choose. We could a had a whole dinner.

But we didn't need it. All we needed was just enough for the pie, and so we throwed the rest away. We didn't cook none of the pies in the washpan, afraid the solder would melt; but Uncle Silas he had a noble brass warming-pan which he thought considerable of, because it belonged to one of his ancestors with a long wooden handle that come over from England with William the Conqueror in the *Mayflower*[1] or one of them early ships and was hid away up garret with a lot of other old pots and things that was valuable, not on account of being any account because they warn't, but on account of them being relicts, you know, and we snaked her out, private, and took her down there, but she failed on the first pies, because we didn't know how, but she come up smiling on the last one. We took and lined her with dough, and set her in the coals, and loaded her up with rag-rope, and put on a dough roof, and shut down the lid, and put hot embers on top, and stood off five foot, with the long handle, cool and comfortable, and in fifteen minutes she

---

9. To nag mercilessly.
1. William the Conqueror lived in the 11th century. The *Mayflower* made its crossing in 1620.

turned out a pie that was a satisfaction to look at. But the person that et it would want to fetch a couple of kags of toothpicks along, for if that rope-ladder wouldn't cramp him down to business, I don't know nothing what I'm talking about, and lay him in enough stomach-ache to last him till next time, too.

Nat didn't look, when we put the witch-pie in Jim's pan; and we put the three tin plates in the bottom of the pan under the vittles; and so Jim got everything all right, and as soon as he was by himself he busted into the pie and hid the rope-ladder inside of his straw tick, and scratched some marks on a tin plate and throwed it out of the window-hole.

Chapter XXXVIII

Making them pens was a distressid-tough job, and so was the saw; and Jim allowed the inscription was going to be the toughest of all. That's the one which the prisoner has to scrabble on the wall. But we had to have it; Tom said we'd *got* to; there warn't no case of a state prisoner not scrabbling his inscription to leave behind, and his coat of arms.

"Look at Lady Jane Grey," he says; "look at Gilford Dudley; look at old Northumberland![2] Why, Huck, spose it *is* considerable trouble?—what you going to do?—how you going to get around it? Jim's *got* to do his inscription and coat of arms. They all do."

Jim says:

"Why, Mars Tom, I hain't got no coat o' arms; I hain't got nuffn but dish-yer old shirt, en you knows I got to keep de journal on dat."

"Oh, you don't understand, Jim; a coat of arms is very different."

"Well," I says, "Jim's right, anyway, when he says he hain't got no coat of arms, because he hain't."

"I reckon *I* knowed that," Tom says, "but you bet he'll have one before he goes out of this—because he's going out *right,* and there ain't going to be no flaws in his record."

So whilst me and Jim filed away at the pens on a brickbat[3] apiece, Jim a making his'n out of the brass and I making mine out of the spoon, Tom set to work to think out the coat of arms. By-and-by he said he'd struck so many good ones he didn't hardly know which to take, but there was one which he reckoned he'd decide on. He says:

"On the scutcheon[4] we'll have a bend *or* in the dexter base, a saltire *murrey* in the fess, with a dog, couchant, for common charge, and under his foot a chain embattled, for slavery, with a chevron *vert* in a chief engrailed, and three invected lines on a field *azure,* with the nombril points rampant on a dancette indented; crest, a runaway nigger, *sable,* with his bundle over his shoulder on a bar sinister: and a couple of gules for supporters, which is you and me; motto, *Maggiore fretta, minore atto.* Got it out of a book—means, the more haste, the less speed."

"Geewhillikins," I says, "but what does the rest of it mean?"

---

2. The story of Lady Jane Grey (1537–1554), her husband, Guildford Dudley, and his father, the duke of Northumberland, was told in W. H. Ainsworth's romance *The Tower of London* (1840). The duke was at work carving a poem on the wall of his cell when the executioners came for him.
3. A fragment of brick.
4. An escutcheon is the shield-shaped surface on which a coat of arms is inscribed. The details are expressed in the technical terminology of heraldry.

"We ain't got no time to bother over that," he says, "we got to dig in like all git-out."

"Well, anyway," I says, "what's *some* of it? What's a fess?"

"A fess—a fess is—*you* don't need to know what a fess is. I'll show him how to make it when he gets to it."

"Shucks, Tom," I says, "I think you might tell a person. What's a bar sinister?"

"Oh, *I* don't know. But he's got to have it. All the nobility does."

That was just his way. If it didn't suit him to explain a thing to you, he wouldn't do it. You might pump at him a week, it wouldn't make no difference.

He'd got all that coat of arms business fixed, so now he started in to finish up the rest of that part of the work, which was to plan out a mournful inscription—said Jim got to have one, like they all done. He made up a lot, and wrote them out on a paper, and read them off, so:

1. *Here a captive heart busted.*

2. *Here a poor prisoner, forsook by the world and friends, fretted out his sorrowful life.*

3. *Here a lonely heart broke, and a worn spirit went to its rest, after thirty-seven years of solitary captivity.*

4. *Here, homeless and friendless, after thirty-seven years of bitter captivity, perished a noble stranger, natural son of Louis XIV.*

Tom's voice trembled, whilst he was reading them, and he most broke down. When he got done, he couldn't no way make up his mind which one for Jim to scrabble onto the wall, they was all so good; but at last he allowed he would let him scrabble them all on. Jim said it would take him a year to scrabble such a lot of truck onto the logs with a nail, and he didn't know how to make letters, besides; but Tom said he would block them out for him, and then he wouldn't have nothing to do but just follow the lines. Then pretty soon he says:

"Come to think, the logs ain't agoing to do; they don't have log walls in a dungeon: we got to dig the inscriptions into a rock. We'll fetch a rock."

Jim said the rock was worse than the logs; he said it would take him such a pison long time to dig them into a rock, he wouldn't ever get out. But Tom said he would let me help him do it. Then he took a look to see how me and Jim was getting along with the pens. It was most pesky tedious hard work and slow, and didn't give my hands no show to get well of the sores, and we didn't seem to make no headway, hardly. So Tom says:

"I know how to fix it. We got to have a rock for the coat of arms and mournful inscriptions, and we can kill two birds with that same rock. There's a gaudy big grindstone down at the mill, and we'll smouch it, and carve the things on it, and file out the pens and the saw on it, too."

It warn't no slouch of an idea; and it warn't no slouch of a grindstone nuther; but we allowed we'd tackle it. It warn't quite midnight, yet, so we cleared out for the mill, leaving Jim at work. We smouched the grindstone, and set out to roll her home, but it was a most nation tough job. Sometimes, do what we could, we couldn't keep her from falling over, and she come mighty near mashing us, every time. Tom said she was going to get one of us, sure, before we got through. We got her half way; and then we was plumb played out, and most drownded with sweat. We see it warn't no use, we got to go and fetch Jim. So he raised up his bed and slid the chain off of the bed-leg, and wrapt it round and round his neck, and we crawled out through our hole and down there, and Jim and me laid into that grindstone and walked her along like nothing; and Tom superintended. He could out-superintend any boy I ever see. He knowed how to do everything.

Our hole was pretty big, but it warn't big enough to get the grindstone through; but Jim he took the pick and soon made it big enough. Then Tom marked out them things on it with the nail, and set Jim to work on them, with the nail for a chisel and an iron bolt from the rubbage in the lean-to for a hammer, and told him to work till the rest of his candle quit on him, and then he could go to bed, and hide the grindstone under his straw tick and sleep on it. Then we helped him fix his chain back on the bed-leg, and was ready for bed ourselves. But Tom thought of something, and says:

"You got any spiders in here, Jim?"

"No, sah, thanks to goodness I hain't, Mars Tom."

"All right, we'll get you some."

"But bless you, honey, I doan' *want* none. I's afeard un um. I jis' 's soon have rattlesnakes aroun'."

Tom thought a minute or two, and says:

"It's a good idea. And I reckon it's been done. It *must* a been done; it stands to reason. Yes, it's a prime good idea. Where could you keep it?"

"Keep what, Mars Tom?"

"Why, a rattlesnake."

"De goodness gracious alive, Mars Tom! Why, if dey was a rattlesnake to come in heah, I'd take en bust right out thoo dat log wall, I would, wid my head."

"Why, Jim, you wouldn't be afraid of it, after a little. You could tame it."

"*Tame* it!"

"Yes—easy enough. Every animal is grateful for kindness and petting, and they wouldn't *think* of hurting a person that pets them. Any book will tell you that. You try—that's all I ask; just try for two or three days. Why, you can get him so, in a little while, that he'll love you; and sleep with you; and won't stay away from you a minute; and will let you wrap him round your neck and put his head in your mouth."

"*Please*, Mars Tom—*doan'* talk so! I can't *stan'* it! He'd *let* me shove his head in my mouf—fer a favor, hain't it? I lay he'd wait a pow'ful long time 'fo' I *ast* him. En mo' en dat, I doan' *want* him to sleep wid me."

"Jim, don't act so foolish. A prisoner's *got* to have some kind of a dumb pet, and if a rattlesnake hain't ever been tried, why, there's more glory to be gained in your being the first to ever try it than any other way you could ever think of to save your life."

"Why, Mars Tom, I doan' *want* no sich glory. Snake take 'n bite Jim's chin off, den *whah* is de glory? No, sah, I doan' want no sich doin's."

"Blame it, can't you *try*? I only *want* you to try—you needn't keep it up if it don't work."

"But de trouble all *done*, ef de snake bite me while I's a tryin' him. Mars Tom, I's willin' to tackle mos' anything 'at ain't onreasonable, but ef you en Huck fetches a rattlesnake in heah for me to tame, I's gwyne to *leave*, dat's *shore*."

"Well, then, let it go, let it go, if you're so bullheaded about it. We can get you some garter-snakes and you can tie some buttons on their tails, and let on they're rattlesnakes, and I reckon that'll have to do."

"I k'n stan' *dem*, Mars Tom, but blame' 'f I couldn't get along widout um, I tell you dat. I never knowed b'fo', 't was so much bother and trouble to be a prisoner."

"Well, it *always* is, when it's done right. You got any rats around here?"

"No, sah, I hain't seed none."

"Well, we'll get you some rats."

"Why, Mars Tom, I doan' *want* no rats. Dey's de dad-blamedest creturs to sturb a body, en rustle roun' over 'im, en bite his feet, when he's tryin' to sleep, I ever see. So, sah, gimme g'yarter-snakes, 'f I's got to have 'm, but doan' gimme no rats. I ain' got not use f'r um, skasely."

"But Jim, you *got* to have 'em—they all do. So don't make no more fuss about it. Prisoners ain't ever without rats. There ain't no instance of it. And they train them, and pet them, and learn them tricks, and they get to be as sociable as flies. But you got to play music to them. You got anything to play music on?"

"I ain't got nuffn but a coase comb en a piece o' paper, en a juice-harp; but I reck'n dey wouldn't take no stock in a juice-harp."

"Yes, they would. *They* don't care what kind of music 'tis. A jews-harp's plenty good enough for a rat. All animals likes music—in a prison they dote on it. Specially, painful music; and you can't get no other kind out of a jews-harp. It always interests them; they come out to see what's the matter with you. Yes, you're all right; you're fixed very well. You want to set on your bed, nights, before you go to sleep, and early in the mornings, and play your jews-harp; play The Last Link is Broken—that's the thing that'll scoop a rat, quicker'n anything else: and when you've played about two minutes, you'll see all the rats, and the snakes, and spiders, and things begin to feel worried about you, and come. And they'll just fairly swarm over you, and have a noble good time."

"Yes, *dey* will, I reck'n, Mars Tom, but what kine er time is *Jim* havin'? Blest if I kin see de pint. But I'll do it ef I got to. I reck'n I better keep de animals satisfied, en not have no trouble in de house."

Tom waited to think over, and see if there wasn't nothing else; and pretty soon he says:

"Oh—there's one thing I forgot. Could you raise a flower here, do you reckon?"

"I doan' know but maybe I could, Mars Tom; but it's tolable dark in heah, en I ain' got no use f'r no flower, nohow, en she'd be a pow'ful sight o' trouble."

"Well, you try it, anyway. Some other prisoners has done it."

"One er dem big cat-tail-lookin' mullen-stalks would grow in heah, Mars Tom, I reck'n, but she wouldn' be wuth half de trouble she'd coss."

"Don't you believe it. We'll fetch you a little one, and you plant it in the corner, over there, and raise it. And don't call it mullen, call it Pitchiola—that's its right name, when it's in a prison.[5] And you want to water it with your tears."

---

5. *Picciola* (1836) was a popular romantic story by Xavier Saintine (pseudonym for Joseph Xavier Boniface, 1798–1865), in which a plant helps a prisoner survive.

"Why, I got plenty spring water, Mars Tom."

"You don't *want* spring water; you want to water it with your tears. It's the way they always do."

"Why, Mars Tom, I lay I kin raise one er dem mullen-stalks twyste wid spring water whiles another man's a *start'n* one wid tears."

"That ain't the idea. You *got* to do it with tears."

"She'll die on my han's, Mars Tom, she sholy will; kase I doan' skasely ever cry."

So Tom was stumped. But he studied it over, and then said Jim would have to worry along the best he could with an onion. He promised he would go to the nigger cabins and drop one, private, in Jim's coffee-pot, in the morning. Jim said he would "jis' 's soon have tobacker in his coffee;" and found so much fault with it, and with the work and bother of raising the mullen, and jews-harping the rats, and petting and flattering up the snakes and spiders and things, on top of all the other work he had to do on pens, and inscriptions, and journals, and things, which made it more trouble and worry and respon-sibility to be a prisoner than anything he ever undertook, that Tom most lost all patience with him; and said he was just loadened down with more gaudier chances than a prisoner ever had in the world to make a name for himself, and yet he didn't know enough to appreciate them, and they was just about wasted on him. So Jim he was sorry, and said he wouldn't behave so no more, and then me and Tom shoved for bed.

Chapter XXXIX

In the morning we went up to the village and bought a wire rat trap and fetched it down, and unstopped the best rat hole, and in about an hour we had fifteen of the bulliest kind of ones; and then we took it and put it in a safe place under Aunt Sally's bed. But while we was gone for spiders, little Thomas Franklin Benjamin Jefferson Elexander Phelps found it there, and opened the door of it to see if the rats would come out, and they did; and Aunt Sally she come in, and when we got back she was standing on top of the bed raising Cain, and the rats was doing what they could to keep off the dull times for her. So she took and dusted us both with the hickry, and we was as much as two hours catching another fifteen or sixteen, drat that meddlesome cub, and they warn't the likeliest, nuther, because the first haul was the pick of the flock. I never see a likelier lot of rats than what that first haul was.

We got a splendid stock of sorted spiders, and bugs, and frogs, and cater-pillars, and one thing or another; and we like-to got a hornet's nest, but we didn't. The family was at home. We didn't give it right up, but staid with them as long as we could; because we allowed we'd tire them out or they'd got to tire us out, and they done it. Then we got allycumpain[6] and rubbed on the places, and was pretty near all right again, but couldn't set down convenient. And so we went for the snakes, and grabbed a couple of dozen garters and house-snakes, and put them in a bag, and put it in our room, and by that time it was supper time, and a rattling good honest day's work; and hungry?—oh, no I reckon not! And there warn't a blessed snake up there, when we went back—we didn't half tie the sack, and they worked out, somehow, and left. But it didn't matter much, because they was still on the premises some-

---

6. Elecampane is an herb that Tom and Huck are using to relieve the pain of the hornet stings.

wheres. So we judged we could get some of them again. No, there warn't no real scarcity of snakes about the house for a considerble spell. You'd see them dripping from the rafters and places, every now and then; and they generly landed in your plate, or down the back of your neck, and most of the time where you didn't want them. Well, they was handsome, and striped, and there warn't no harm in a million of them; but that never made no difference to Aunt Sally, she despised snakes, be the breed what they might, and she couldn't stand them no way you could fix it; and every time one of them flopped down on her, it didn't make no difference what she was doing, she would just lay that work down and light out. I never see such a woman. And you could hear her whoop to Jericho. You couldn't get her to take aholt of one of them with the tongs. And if she turned over and found one in bed, she would scramble out and lift a howl that you would think the house was afire. She disturbed the old man so, that he said he could most wish there hadn't ever been no snakes created. Why, after every last snake had been gone clear out of the house for as much as a week, Aunt Sally warn't over it yet; she warn't near over it; when she was setting thinking about something, you could touch her on the back of her neck with a feather and she would jump right out of her stockings. It was very curious. But Tom said all women was just so. He said they was made that way; for some reason or other.

We got a licking every time one of our snakes come in her way; and she allowed these lickings warn't nothing to what she would do if we ever loaded up the place again with them. I didn't mind the lickings, because they didn't amount to nothing; but I minded the trouble we had, to lay in another lot. But we got them laid in, and all the other things; and you never see a cabin as blithesome as Jim's was when they'd all swarm out for music and go for him. Jim didn't like the spiders, and the spiders didn't like Jim; and so they'd lay for him and make it mighty warm for him. And he said that between the rats, and the snakes, and the grindstone, there warn't no room in bed for him, skasely; and when there was, a body couldn't sleep, it was so lively, and it was always lively, he said, because *they* never all slept at one time, but took turn about, so when the snakes was asleep the rats was on deck, and when the rats turned in the snakes come on watch, so he always had one gang under him, in his way, and t'other gang having a circus over him, and if he got up to hunt a new place, the spiders would take a chance at him as he crossed over. He said if he ever got out, this time, he wouldn't ever be a prisoner again, not for a salary.

Well, by the end of three weeks, everything was in pretty good shape. The shirt was sent in early, in a pie, and every time a rat bit Jim he would get up and write a little in his journal whilst the ink was fresh; the pens was made, the inscriptions and so on was all carved on the grindstone; the bed-leg was sawed in two, and we had et up the sawdust, and it give us a most amazing stomach-ache. We reckoned we was all going to die, but didn't. It was the most undigestible sawdust I ever see; and Tom said the same. But as I was saying, we'd got all the work done, now, at last; and we was all pretty much fagged out, too, but mainly Jim. The old man had wrote a couple of times to the plantation below Orleans to come and get their runaway nigger, but hadn't got no answer, because there warn't no such plantation; so he allowed he would advertise Jim in the St. Louis and New Orleans papers; and when he mentioned the St. Louis ones, it give me the cold shivers, and I see we hadn't no time to lose. So Tom said, now for the nonnamous letters.

"What's them?" I says.

"Warnings to the people that something is up. Sometimes it's done one way, sometimes another. But there's always somebody spying around, that gives notice to the governor of the castle. When Louis XVI was going to light out of the Tooleries,[7] a servant girl done it. It's a very good way, and so is the nonnamous letters. We'll use them both. And it's usual for the prisoner's mother to change clothes with him, and she stays in, and he slides out in her clothes. We'll do that too."

"But looky here, Tom, what do we want to *warn* anybody for, that something's up? Let them find it out for themselves—it's their lookout."

"Yes, I know; but you can't depend on them. It's the way they've acted from the very start—left us to do *everything*. They're so confiding and mulletheaded they don't take notice of nothing at all. So if we don't *give* them notice, there won't be nobody nor nothing to interfere with us, and so after all our hard work and trouble this escape 'll go off perfectly flat: won't amount to nothing—won't be nothing *to* it."

"Well, as for me, Tom, that's the way I'd like."

"Shucks," he says, and looked disgusted. So I says:

"But I ain't going to make no complaint. Anyway that suits you suits me. What you going to do about the servant-girl?"

"You'll be her. You slide in, in the middle of the night, and hook that yaller girl's frock."

"Why, Tom, that'll make trouble next morning; because of course she prob'bly hain't got any but that one."

"I know; but you don't want it but fifteen minutes, to carry the nonnamous letter and shove it under the front door."

"All right, then, I'll do it; but I could carry it just as handy in my own togs."

"You wouldn't look like a servant-girl *then*, would you?"

"No, but there won't be nobody to see what I look like, *anyway.*"

"That ain't got nothing to do with it. The thing for us to do, is just to do our *duty*, and not worry about whether anybody *sees* us do it or not. Hain't you got no principle at all?"

"All right, I ain't saying nothing; I'm the servant-girl. Who's Jim's mother?"

"I'm his mother. I'll hook a gown from Aunt Sally."

"Well, then, you'll have to stay in the cabin when me and Jim leaves."

"Not much. I'll stuff Jim's clothes full of straw and lay it on his bed to represent his mother in disguise: and Jim 'll take Aunt Sally's gown off of me and wear it, and we'll all evade together. When a prisoner of style escapes, it's called an evasion. It's always called so when a king escapes, f'rinstance. And the same with a king's son; it don't make no difference whether he's a natural one or an unnatural one."

So Tom he wrote the nonnamous letter, and I smouched the yaller wench's frock, that night, and put it on, and shoved it under the front door, the way Tom told me to. It said:

> *Beware, Trouble is brewing. Keep a sharp lookout.*
> UNKNOWN FRIEND.

Next night we stuck a picture which Tom drawed in blood, of a skull and crossbones, on the front door; and next night another one of a coffin, on the

---

7. Twain probably read this episode of the Tuileries, a palace in Paris, in Thomas Carlyle's *French Revolution* (1837).

back door. I never see a family in such a sweat. They couldn't a been worse scared if the place had a been full of ghosts laying for them behind everything and under the beds and shivering through the air. If a door banged, Aunt Sally she jumped, and said "ouch!" if anything fell, she jumped and said "ouch!" if you happened to touch her, when she warn't noticing, she done the same; she couldn't face noway and be satisfied, because she allowed there was something behind her every time—so she was always a whirling around, sudden, and saying "ouch," and before she'd get two-thirds around, she'd whirl back again, and say it again; and she was afraid to go to bed, but she dasn't set up. So the thing was working very well, Tom said; he said he never see a thing work more satisfactory. He said it showed it was done right.

So he said, now for the grand bulge! So the very next morning at the streak of dawn we got another letter ready, and was wondering what we better do with it, because we heard them say at supper they was going to have a nigger on watch at both doors all night. Tom he went down the lightning-rod to spy around; and the nigger at the back door was asleep, and he stuck it in the back of his neck and come back. This letter said:

> Don't betray me, I wish to be your friend. There is a desprate gang of cut-throats from over in the Ingean Territory[8] going to steal your runaway nigger to-night, and they have been trying to scare you so as you will stay in the house and not bother them. I am one of the gang, but have got relig-gion and wish to quit it and lead a honest life again, and will betray the hel-ish design. They will sneak down from northards, along the fence, at midnight exact, with a false key, and go in the nigger's cabin to get him. I am to be off a piece and blow a tin horn if I see any danger; but stead of that, I will BA like a sheep soon as they get in and not blow at all; then whilst they are getting his chains loose, you slip there and lock them in, and can kill them at your leasure. Don't do anything but just the way I am telling you, if you do they will suspicion something and raise whoopjam-boreehoo. I do not wish any reward but to know I have done the right thing.
>
> UNKNOWN FRIEND.

Chapter XL

We was feeling pretty good, after breakfast, and took my canoe and went over the river a fishing, with a lunch, and had a good time, and took a look at the raft and found her all right, and got home late to supper, and found them in such a sweat and worry they didn't know which end they was standing on, and made us go right off to bed the minute we was done supper, and wouldn't tell us what the trouble was, and never let on a word about the new letter, but didn't need to, because we knowed as much about it as anybody did, and as soon as we was half up stairs and her back was turned, we slid for the cellar cupboard and loaded up a good lunch and took it up to our room and went to bed, and got up about half-past eleven, and Tom put on Aunt Sally's dress that he stole and was going to start with the lunch, but says:

"Where's the butter?"

"I laid out a hunk of it," I says, "on a piece of a corn-pone."

"Well, you *left* it laid out, then—it ain't here."

---

8. The area now the state of Oklahoma was granted to displaced Native Americans in the 1830s and was a base of operations for outlaws for most of the 19th century.

"We can get along without it," I says.

"We can get along *with* it, too," he says; "just you slide down cellar and fetch it. And then mosey right down the lightning-rod and come along. I'll go and stuff the straw into Jim's clothes to represent his mother in disguise, and be ready to *ba* like a sheep and shove soon as you get there."

So out he went, and down cellar went I. The hunk of butter, big as a person's fist, was where I had left it, so I took up the slab of corn-pone with it on, and blowed out my light, and started up stairs, very stealthy, and got up to the main floor all right, but here comes Aunt Sally with a candle, and I clapped the truck in my hat, and clapped my hat on my head, and the next second she see me; and she says:

"You been down cellar?"

"Yes'm."

"What you been doing down there?"

"Noth'n."

"*Noth'n!*"

"No'm."

"Well, then, what possessed you to go down there, this time of night?"

"I don't know'm."

"You don't *know?* Don't answer me that way, Tom, I want to know what you been *doing* down there?"

"I hain't been doing a single thing, Aunt Sally, I hope to gracious if I have."

I reckoned she'd let me go, now, and as a generl thing she would; but I spose there was so many strange things going on she was just in a sweat about every little thing that warn't yard-stick straight; so she says, very decided:

"You just march into that setting-room and stay there till I come. You been up to something you no business to, and I lay I'll find out what it is before *I'm* done with you."

So she went away as I opened the door and walked into the setting-room. My, but there was a crowd there! Fifteen farmers, and every one of them had a gun. I was most powerful sick, and slunk to a chair and set down. They was setting around, some of them talking a little, in a low voice, and all of them fidgety and uneasy, but trying to look like they warn't; but I knowed they was, because they was always taking off their hats, and putting them on, and scratching their heads, and changing their seats, and fumbling with their buttons. I warn't easy myself, but I didn't take my hat off, all the same.

I did wish Aunt Sally would come, and get done with me, and lick me, if she wanted to, and let me get away and tell Tom how we'd overdone this thing, and what a thundering hornet's nest we'd got ourselves into, so we could stop fooling around, straight off, and clear out with Jim before these rips got out of patience and come for us.

At last she come, and begun to ask me questions, but I *couldn't* answer them straight, I didn't know which end of me was up; because these men was in such a fidget now, that some was wanting to start right *now* and lay for them desperadoes, and saying it warn't but a few minutes to midnight; and others was trying to get them to hold on and wait for the sheep-signal; and here was aunty pegging away at the questions, and me a shaking all over and ready to sink down in my tracks I was that scared; and the place getting hotter and hotter, and the butter beginning to melt and run down my neck and behind my ears: and pretty soon, when one of them says, "*I'm* for going and getting in the cabin *first,* and right *now,* and catching them when they come," I most dropped; and a streak of butter came a trickling down my forehead, and Aunt Sally she see it, and turns white as a sheet, and says:

"For the land's sake what *is* the matter with the child!—he's got the brain fever as shore as you're born, and they're oozing out!"

And everybody runs to see, and she snatches off my hat, and out comes the bread, and what was left of the butter, and she grabbed me, and hugged me, and says:

"Oh, what a turn you did give me! and how glad and grateful I am it ain't no worse; for luck's against us, and it never rains but it pours, and when I see that truck I thought we'd lost you, for I knowed by the color and all, it was just like your brains would be if—Dear, dear, whyd'nt you *tell* me that was what you'd been down there for, *I* wouldn't a cared. Now cler out to bed, and don't lemme see no more of you till morning!"

I was up stairs in a second, and down the lightning-rod in another one, and shinning through the dark for the lean-to. I couldn't hardly get my words out, I was so anxious; but I told Tom as quick as I could, we must jump for it, now, and not a minute to lose—the house full of men, yonder, with guns!

His eyes just blazed; and he says:

"No!—is that so? *Ain't* it bully! Why, Huck, if it was to do over again, I bet I could fetch two hundred! If we could put it off till—"

"Hurry! *hurry!*" I says. "Where's Jim?"

"Right at your elbow; if you reach out your arm you can touch him. He's dressed, and everything's ready. Now we'll slide out and give the sheep-signal."

But then we heard the tramp of men, coming to the door, and heard them begin to fumble with the padlock; and heard a man say:

"I *told* you we'd be too soon; they haven't come—the door is locked. Here, I'll lock some of you into the cabin and you lay for 'em in the dark and kill 'em when they come; and the rest scatter around a piece, and listen if you can hear 'em coming."

So in they come, but couldn't see us in the dark, and most trod on us whilst we was hustling to get under the bed. But we got under all right, and out through the hole, swift but soft—Jim first, me next, and Tom last, which was according to Tom's orders. Now we was in the lean-to, and heard trampings close by outside. So we crept to the door, and Tom stopped us there and put his eye to the crack, but couldn't make out nothing, it was so dark; and whispered and said he would listen for the steps to get further, and when he nudged us Jim must glide out first, and him last. So he set his ear to the crack and listened, and listened, and listened, and the steps a scraping around, out there, all the time; and at last he nudged us, and we slid out, and stooped down, not breathing, and not making the least noise, and slipped stealthy towards the fence, in Injun file, and got to it, all right, and me and Jim over it; but Tom's britches catched fast on a splinter on the top rail, and then he hear the steps coming, so he had to pull loose, which snapped the splinter and made a noise; and as he dropped in our tracks and started, somebody sings out:

"Who's that? Answer, or I'll shoot!"

But we didn't answer; we just unfurled our heels and shoved. Then there was a rush, and a *bang, bang, bang!* and the bullets fairly whizzed around us! We heard them sing out:

"Here they are! They've broke for the river! after 'em, boys! And turn loose the dogs!"

So here they come, full tilt. We could hear them, because they wore boots, and yelled, but we didn't wear no boots, and didn't yell. We was in the path to the mill; and when they got pretty close onto us, we dodged into the bush and let them go by, and then dropped in behind them. They'd had all the dogs shut up, so they wouldn't scare off the robbers; but by this time somebody had let them loose, and here they come, making pow-wow enough for a million; but they was our dogs; so we stopped in our tracks till they catched up; and when they see it warn't nobody but us, and no excitement to offer them, they only just said howdy, and tore right ahead towards the shouting and clatter-ing; and then we up steam again and whizzed along after them till we was nearly to the mill, and then struck up through the bush to where my canoe was tied, and hopped in and pulled for dear life towards the middle of the river, but didn't make no more noise than we was obleeged to. Then we struck out, easy and comfortable, for the island where my raft was; and we could hear them yelling and barking at each other all up and down the bank, till we was so far away the sounds got dim and died out. And when we stepped onto the raft, I says:

"*Now*, old Jim, you're a free man *again*, and I bet you won't ever be a slave no more."

"En a mighty good job it wuz, too, Huck. It 'uz planned beautiful, en it 'uz *done* beautiful; en dey aint' *nobody* kin git up a plan dat's mo' mixed-up en splendid den what dat one wuz."

We was all as glad as we could be, but Tom was the gladdest of all, because he had a bullet in the calf of his leg.

When me and Jim heard that, we didn't feel so brash as what we did before. It was hurting him considerble, and bleeding; so we laid him in the wigwam and tore up one of the duke's shirts for to bandage him, but he says:

"Gimme the rags, I can do it myself. Don't stop, now; don't fool around here, and the evasion booming along so handsome; man the sweeps, and set her loose! Boys, we done it elegant!—'deed we did. I wish *we'd* a had the han-dling of Louis XVI, there wouldn't a been no 'Son of Saint Louis, ascend to heaven!'[9] wrote down in *his* biography: no, sir, we'd a whooped him over the *border*—that's what we'd a done with *him*—and done it just as slick as noth-ing at all, too. Man the sweeps—man the sweeps!"

But me and Jim was consulting—and thinking. And after we'd thought a minute, I says:

"Say it, Jim."

So he says:

"Well, den, dis is de way it look to me, Huck. Ef it wuz *him* dat 'uz bein' sot free, en one er de boys wuz to git shot, would he say, 'Go on en save me, nem-mine 'bout a doctor f'r to save dis one?' Is dat like Mars Tom Sawyer? Would he say dat? You *bet* he wouldn't! *Well*, den, is *Jim* gwyne to say it? No, sah—I doan' budge a step out'n dis place, 'dout a *doctor*; not if its forty year!"

I knowed he was white inside, and I reckoned he'd say what he did say—so it was all right, now, and I told Tom I was agoing for a doctor. He raised considerble row about it, but me and Jim stuck to it and wouldn't budge; so

9. Taken from Carlyle's rendering of the king's execution in *The French Revolution* (1837).

he was for crawling out and setting the raft loose himself; but we wouldn't let him. Then he give us a piece of his mind—but it didn't do no good.

So when he see me getting the canoe ready, he says:

"Well, then, if you're bound to go, I'll tell you the way to do, when you get to the village. Shut the door, and blindfold the doctor tight and fast, and make him swear to be silent as the grave, and put a purse full of gold in his hand, and then take and lead him all around the back alleys and everywheres, in the dark, and then fetch him here in the canoe, in a roundabout way amongst the islands, and search him and take his chalk away from him, and don't give it back to him till you get him back to the village, or else he will chalk this raft so he can find it again. It's the way they all do."

So I said I would, and left, and Jim was to hide in the woods when he see the doctor coming, till he was gone again.

Chapter XLI

The doctor was an old man; a very nice, kind-looking old man, when I got him up. I told him me and my brother was over on Spanish Island hunting, yesterday afternoon, and camped on a piece of a raft we found, and about midnight he must a kicked his gun in his dreams, for it went off and shot him in the leg, and we wanted him to go over there and fix it and not say nothing about it, nor let anybody know, because we wanted to come home this evening, and surprise the folks.

"Who is your folks?" he says.

"The Phelpses, down yonder."

"Oh," he says. And after a minute, he says: "How'd you say he got shot?"

"He had a dream," I says, "and it shot him."

"Singular dream," he says.

So he lit up his lantern, and got his saddle-bags, and we started. But when he see the canoe, he didn't like the look of her—said she was big enough for one, but didn't look pretty safe for two. I says:

"Oh, you needn't be afeard, sir, she carried the three of us, easy enough."

"What three?"

"Why, me and Sid, and—and—and *the guns;* that's what I mean."

"Oh," he says.

But he put his foot on the gunnel, and rocked her; and shook his head, and said he reckoned he'd look around for a bigger one. But they was all locked and chained; so he took my canoe, and said for me to wait till he come back, or I could hunt around further, or maybe I better go down home and get them ready for the surprise, if I wanted to. But I said I didn't; so I told him just how to find the raft, and then he started.

I struck an idea, pretty soon. I says to myself, spos'n he can't fix that leg just in three shakes of a sheep's tail, as the saying is? spos'n it takes him three or four days? What are we going to do?—lay around there till he lets the cat out of the bag? No, sir, I know what *I'll* do. I'll wait, and when he comes back, if he says he's got to go any more, I'll get him down there, too, if I swim; and we'll take and tie him, and keep him, and shove out down the river; and when Tom's done with him, we'll give him what it's worth, or all we got, and then let him get shore.

So then I crept into a lumber pile to get some sleep; and next time I waked up the sun was away up over my head! I shot out and went for the doctor's house, but they told me he'd gone away in the night, some time or other, and warn't back yet. Well, thinks I, that looks powerful bad for *Tom,* and I'll dig out for the island, right off. So away I shoved, and turned the corner, and nearly rammed my head into Uncle Silas's stomach! He says:

"Why, Tom! Where you been, all this time, you rascal?"

"*I* hain't been nowheres," I says, "only just hunting for the runaway nigger—me and Sid."

"Why, where ever did you go?" he says. "Your aunt's been mighty uneasy."

"She needn't," I says, "because we was all right. We followed the men and the dogs, but they out-run us, and we lost them; but we thought we heard them on the water, so we got a canoe and took out after them, and crossed over but couldn't find nothing of them; so we cruised along up-shore till we got kind of tired and beat out; and tied up the canoe and went to sleep, and never waked up till about an hour ago, then we paddled over here to hear the news, and Sid's at the post-office to see what he can hear, and I'm a-branching out to get something to eat for us, and then we're going home."

So then we went to the post-office to get "Sid"; but just as I suspicioned, he warn't there; so the old man he got a letter out of the office, and we waited a while longer but Sid didn't come; so the old man said come along, let Sid foot it home, or canoe-it, when he got done fooling around—but we would ride. I couldn't get him to let me stay and wait for Sid; and he said there warn't no use in it, and I must come along, and let Aunt Sally see we was all right.

When we got home, Aunt Sally was that glad to see me she laughed and cried both, and hugged me, and give me one of them lickings of hern that don't amount to shucks, and said she'd serve Sid the same when he come.

And the place was plumb full of farmers and farmers' wives, to dinner; and such another clack a body never heard. Old Mrs. Hotchkiss was the worst; her tongue was a-going all the time. She says:

"Well, Sister Phelps, I've ransacked that-air cabin over an' I b'lieve the nigger was crazy. I says so to Sister Damrell—didn't I, Sister Damrell?—s'I, he's crazy, s'I—them's the very words I said. You all hearn me: he's crazy, s'I; everything shows it, s'I. Look at that-air grindstone, s'I; want to tell *me*'t any cretur 'ts in his right mind 's a-goin' to scrabble all them crazy things onto a grindstone, s'I? Here sich 'n' sich a person busted his heart; 'n' here so 'n' so pegged along for thirty-seven year, 'n' all that—natcherl son o' Louis somebody, 'n' sich everlast'n rubbage. He's plumb crazy, s'I; it's what I says in the fust place, it's what I says in the middle, 'n' it's what I says last 'n' all the time—the nigger's crazy—crazy's Nebokoodneezer,[1] s'I."

"An' look at that-air ladder made out'n rags, Sister Hotchkiss," says old Mrs. Damrell, "what in the name o'goodness *could* he ever want of—"

"The very words I was a-sayin' no longer ago th'n this minute to Sister Utterback, 'n' she'll tell you so herself. Sh-she, look at that-air rag ladder, sh-she; 'n' s'I, yes, *look* at it, s'I—what *could* he a wanted of it, s'I. Sh-she, Sister Hotchkiss, sh-she—"

"But how in the nation'd they ever *git* that grindstone *in* there, *anyway?* 'n' who dug that-air *hole?* 'n' who—"

---

1. Nebuchadnezzar (605–562 B.C.E.), king of Babylon, is described in Daniel 4.33 as going mad and eating grass.

"My very *words*, Brer Penrod! I was a-sayin'—pass that-air sasser o' m'lasses, won't ye?—I was a-sayin' to Sister Dunlap, jist this minute, how *did* they git that grindstone in there, s'I. Without *help,* mind you—'thout *help!* *Thar's* wher' 'tis. Don't tell *me*, s'I; there *wuz* help, s'I; 'n' ther' wuz a *plenty* help, too, s'I; ther's ben a *dozen* a-helpin' that nigger, 'n' I lay I'd skin every last nigger on this place, but *I'd* find out who done it, s'I; 'n' moreover, s'I—"

"A *dozen* says you!—*forty* couldn't a done everything that's been done. Look at them case-knife saws and things, how tedious they've been made; look at that bed-leg sawed off with 'em, a week's work for six men; look at that nigger made out'n straw on the bed; and look at—"

"You may *well* say it, Brer Hightower! It's jist as I was a-sayin' to Brer Phelps, his own self. S'e, what do *you* think of it, Sister Hotchkiss, s'e? think o' what, Brer Phelps, s'I? think o' that bed-leg sawed off that a way, s'e? *think* of it, s'I? I lay it never sawed *itself* off, s'I—somebody sawed it, s'I; that's my opinion, take it or leave it, it mayn't be no 'count, s'I, but sich as 't is, it's my opinion, s'I, 'n' if anybody k'n start a better one, s'I, let him *do* it, s'I, that's all. I says to Sister Dunlap, s'I—"

"Why, dog my cats, they must a ben a house-full o' niggers in there every night for four weeks, to a done all that work, Sister Phelps. Look at that shirt—every last inch of it kivered over with secret African writ'n done with blood! Must a ben a raft uv 'm at it right along, all the time, amost. Why, I'd give two dollars to have it read to me; 'n' as for the niggers that wrote it, I 'low I'd take 'n' lash 'm t'll—"

"People to *help* him, Brother Marples! Well, I reckon you'd *think* so, if you'd a been in this house for a while back. Why, they've stole everything they could lay their hands on—and we a watching, all the time, mind you. They stole that shirt right off o' the line! and as for that sheet they made the rag ladder out of ther' ain't no telling how many times they *didn't* steal that; and flour, and candles, and candlesticks, and spoons, and the old-warming-pan, and most a thousand things that I disremember, now, and my new calico dress; and me, and Silas, and my Sid and Tom on the constant watch day *and* night, as I was a telling you, and not a one of us could catch hide nor hair, nor sight nor sound of them; and here at the last minute, lo and behold you, they slides right in under our noses, and fools us, and not only fools *us* but the Injun Territory robbers too, and actuly gets *away* with that nigger, safe and sound, and that with sixteen men and twenty-two dogs right on their very heels at that very time! I tell you, it just bangs anything I ever *heard* of. Why, *sperits* couldn't a done better, and been no smarter. And I reckon they must a *been* sperits—because, *you* know our dogs, and ther' ain't no better; well, them dogs never even got on the *track* of 'm, once! You explain *that* to me, if you can!—*any* of you!"

"Well, it does beat—"

"Laws alive, I never—"

"So help me, I wouldn't a be—"

"*House* thieves as well as—"

"Goodnessgracioussakes, I'd a ben afeard to *live* in sich a—"

" 'Fraid to *live!*—why, I was that scared I dasn't hardly go to bed, or get up, or lay down, or *set* down, Sister Ridgeway. Why, they'd steal the very—why, goodness sakes, you can guess what kind of a fluster *I* was in by the time midnight come, last night. I hope to gracious if I warn't afraid they'd steal some o' the family! I was just to that pass, I didn't have no reasoning faculties no more. It looks foolish enough, *now*, in the day-time; but I says to myself, there's my two poor boys asleep, 'way up stairs in that lonesome room, and I declare to goodness I was that uneasy 't I crep' up there and locked 'em in! I *did*. And anybody would. Because, you know, when you get scared, that way, and it keeps running on, and getting worse and worse, all the time, and your wits gets to addling, and you get to doing all sorts o' wild things, and by-and-by you think to yourself, spos'n *I* was a boy, and was away up there, and the door ain't locked, and you—" She stopped, looking kind of wondering, and then she turned her head around slow, and when her eye lit on me—I got up and took a walk.

Says I to myself, I can explain better how we come to not be in that room this morning, if I go out to one side and study over it a little. So I done it. But I dasn't go fur, or she'd a sent for me. And when it was late in the day, the people all went, and then I come in and told her the noise and shooting waked up me and "Sid," and the door was locked, and we wanted to see the fun, so we went down the lightning-rod, and both of us got hurt a little, and we didn't never want to try *that* no more. And then I went on and told her all what I told Uncle Silas before; and then she said she'd forgive us, and maybe it was all right enough anyway, and about what a body might expect of boys, for all boys was a pretty harum-scarum lot, as fur as she could see; and so, as long as no harm hadn't come of it, she judged she better put in her time being grateful we was alive and well and she had us still, stead of fretting over what was past and done. So then she kissed me, and patted me on the head, and dropped into a kind of a brown study; and pretty soon jumps up, and says:

"Why, lawsamercy, it's most night, and Sid not come yet! What *has* become of that boy?"

I see my chance; so I skips up and says:

"I'll run right up to town and get him," I says.

"No, you won't," she says. "You'll stay right wher' you are; *one's* enough to be lost at a time. If he ain't here to supper, your uncle 'll go."

Well, he warn't there to supper; so right after supper uncle went.

He come back about ten, a little bit uneasy; hadn't run across Tom's track. Aunt Sally was a good *deal* uneasy; but Uncle Silas he said there warn't no occasion to be—boys will be boys, he said, and you'll see this one turn up in the morning, all sound and right. So she had to be satisfied. But she said she'd set up for him a while, anyway, and keep a light burning, so he could see it.

And then when I went up to bed she come up with me and fetched her candle, and tucked me in, and mothered me so good I felt mean, and like I couldn't look her in the face; and she set down on the bed and talked with me a long time, and said what a splendid boy Sid was, and didn't seem to want to ever stop talking about him; and kept asking me every now and then, if I reckoned he could a got lost, or hurt, or maybe drownded, and might be laying at this minute, somewheres, suffering or dead, and she not by him to help him, and so the tears would drip down, silent, and I would tell her that Sid was all right, and would be home in the morning, sure; and she would squeeze my hand, or maybe kiss me, and tell me to say it again, and keep on saying it, because it done her good, and she was in so much trouble. And when she was going away, she looked down in my eyes, so steady and gentle, and says:

"The door ain't going to be locked, Tom; and there's the window and the rod; but you'll be good, *won't* you? And you won't go? For *my* sake."

Laws knows I *wanted* to go, bad enough, to see about Tom, and was all intending to go; but after that, I wouldn't a went, not for kingdoms.

But she was on my mind, and Tom was on my mind; so I slept very restless. And twice I went down the rod, away in the night, and slipped around front, and see her setting there by her candle in the window with her eyes towards the road and the tears in them; and I wished I could do something for her, but I couldn't, only to swear that I wouldn't never do nothing to grieve her any more. And the third time, I waked up at dawn, and slid down, and she was there yet, and her candle was most out, and her old gray head was resting on her hand, and she was asleep.

Chapter XLII

The old man was up town again, before breakfast, but couldn't get no track of Tom; and both of them set at the table, thinking, and not saying nothing, and looking mournful, and their coffee getting cold, and not eating anything. And by-and-by the old man says:

"Did I give you the letter?"

"What letter?"

"The one I got yesterday out of the post-office."

"No, you didn't give me no letter."

"Well, I must a forgot it."

So he rummaged his pockets, and then went off somewheres where he had laid it down, and fetched it, and give it to her. She says:

"Why, it's from St. Petersburg—it's from Sis."

I allowed another walk would do me good; but I couldn't stir. But before she could break it open, she dropped it and run—for she see something. And so did I. It was Tom Sawyer on a mattress; and that old doctor; and Jim, in *her* calico dress, with his hands tied behind him; and a lot of people. I hid the letter behind the first thing that come handy, and rushed. She flung herself at Tom, crying, and says:

"Oh, he's dead, he's dead, I know he's dead!"

And Tom he turned his head a little, and muttered something or other, which showed he warn't in his right mind; then she flung up her hands and says:

"He's alive, thank God! And that's enough!" and she snatched a kiss of him, and flew for the house to get the bed ready, and scattering orders right and left at the niggers and everybody else, as fast as her tongue could go, every jump of the way.

I followed the men to see what they was going to do with Jim; and the old doctor and Uncle Silas followed after Tom into the house. The men was very huffy, and some of them wanted to hang Jim, for an example to all the other niggers around there, so they wouldn't be trying to run away, like Jim done, and making such a raft of trouble, and keeping a whole family scared most to death for days and nights. But the others said, don't do it, it wouldn't answer at all, he ain't our nigger, and his owner would turn up and make us pay for him, sure. So that cooled them down a little, because the people that's always the most anxious for to hang a nigger that hain't done just right, is always the very ones that ain't the most anxious to pay for him when they've got their satisfaction out of him.

They cussed Jim considerble, though, and give him a cuff or two, side the head, once in a while, but Jim never said nothing, and he never let on to know me, and they took him to the same cabin, and put his own clothes on him, and chained him again, and not to no bed-leg, this time, but to a big staple drove into the bottom log, and chained his hands, too, and both legs, and said he warn't to have nothing but bread and water to eat, after this, till his owner come or he was sold at auction, because he didn't come in a certain length of time, and filled up our hole, and said a couple of farmers with guns must stand watch around about the cabin every night, and a bull-dog tied to the door in the day time; and about this time they was through with the job and was tapering off with a kind of generl good-bye cussing, and then the old doctor comes and takes a look and says:

"Don't be no rougher on him than you're obleeged to, because he ain't a bad nigger. When I got to where I found the boy, I see I couldn't cut the bullet out without some help, and he warn't in no condition for me to leave, to go and get help; and he got a little worse and a little worse, and after a long time he went out of his head, and wouldn't let me come anigh him, any more, and said if I chalked his raft he'd kill me, and no end of wild foolishness like that, and I see I couldn't do anything at all with him; so I says, I got to have *help*, somehow; and the minute I says it, out crawls this nigger from somewheres, and says he'll help, and he done it, too, and done it very well. Of course I judged he must be a runaway nigger, and there I *was*! and there I had to stick, right straight along all the rest of the day, and all night. It was a fix, I tell you! I had a couple of patients with the chills, and of course I'd of liked to run up to town and see them, but I dasn't, because the nigger might get away, and then I'd be to blame; and yet never a skiff come close enough for me to hail. So there I had to stick, plumb till daylight this morning; and I never see a nigger that was a better nuss or faithfuller, and yet he was resking his freedom to do it, and was all tired out, too, and I see plain enough he'd been worked main hard, lately. I liked the nigger for that; I tell you, gentlemen, a nigger like that is worth a thousand dollars—and kind treatment, too. I had everything I needed, and the boy was doing as well there as he would a done at home—better, maybe, because it was so quiet; but there I *was*, with both of 'm on my hands; and there I had to stick, till about dawn this morning; then some men in a skiff come by, and as good luck would have it, the nigger was setting by the pallet with his head propped on his knees, sound asleep; so I motioned them in, quiet, and they slipped up on him and grabbed him and tied him before he knowed what he was about, and we never had no trouble. And the boy being in a kind of a flighty sleep, too, we muffled the oars and hitched the raft on, and towed her over very nice and quiet, and the nigger never made the least row nor said a word, from the start. He ain't no bad nigger, gentlemen; that's what I think about him."

Somebody says:

"Well, it sounds very good, doctor, I'm obleeged to say."

Then the others softened up a little, too, and I was mighty thankful to that old doctor for doing Jim that good turn; and I was glad it was according to my judgment of him, too; because I thought he had a good heart in him and was a good man, the first time I see him. Then they all agreed that Jim had acted very well, and was deserving to have some notice took of it, and reward. So every one of them promised, right out and hearty, that they wouldn't cuss him no more.

Then they come out and locked him up. I hoped they was going to say he could have one or two of the chains took off, because they was rotten heavy, or could have meat and greens with his bread and water, but they didn't think of it, and I reckoned it warn't best for me to mix in, but I judged I'd get the doctor's yarn to Aunt Sally, somehow or other, as soon as I'd got through the breakers that was laying just ahead of me. Explanations, I mean, of how I forgot to mention about Sid being shot, when I was telling how him and me put in that dratted night paddling around hunting the runaway nigger.

But I had plenty time. Aunt Sally she stuck to the sick-room all day and all night; and every time I see Uncle Silas mooning around, I dodged him.

Next morning I heard Tom was a good deal better, and they said Aunt Sally was gone to get a nap. So I slips to the sick-room, and if I found him awake I reckoned we could put up a yarn for the family that would wash. But he was sleeping, and sleeping very peaceful, too; and pale, not fire-faced the way he was when he come. So I set down and laid for him to wake. In about a half an hour, Aunt Sally comes gliding in, and there I was, up a stump again! She motioned me to be still, and set down by me, and begun to whisper, and said we could all be joyful now, because all the symptoms was first rate, and he'd been sleeping like that for ever so long, and looking better and peacefuller all the time, and ten to one he'd wake up in his right mind.

So we set there watching, and by-and-by he stirs a bit, and opened his eyes very natural, and takes a look, and says:

"Hello, why I'm at *home*! How's that? Where's the raft?"

"It's all right," I says.

"And *Jim*?"

"The same," I says, but couldn't say it pretty brash. But he never noticed, but says:

"Good! Splendid! *Now* we're all right and safe! Did you tell Aunty?"

I was about to say yes; but she chipped in and says:

"About what, Sid?"

"Why, about the way the whole thing was done."

"What whole thing?"

"Why, *the* whole thing. There ain't but one; how we set the runaway nigger free—me and Tom."

"Good land! Set the run—What *is* the child talking about! Dear, dear, out of his head again!"

"*No,* I ain't out of my HEAD; I know all what I'm talking about. We *did* set him free—me and Tom. We laid out to do it, and we *done* it. And we done it elegant, too." He'd got a start, and she never checked him up, just set and stared and stared, and let him clip along, and I see it warn't no use for *me* to put in. "Why, Aunty, it cost us a power of work—weeks of it—hours and hours, every night, whilst you was all asleep. And we had to steal candles, and the sheet, and the shirt, and your dress, and spoons, and tin plates, and case-knives, and the warming-pan, and the grindstone, and flour, and just no end of things, and you can't think what work it was to make the saws, and pens, and inscriptions, and one thing or another, and you can't think *half* the fun it was. And we had to make up the pictures of coffins and things, and nonnamous letters from the robbers, and get up and down the lightning-rod, and dig the hole into the cabin, and make the rope-ladder and send it in cooked up in a pie, and send in spoons and things to work with, in your apron pocket"—

"Mercy sakes!"

—"and load up the cabin with rats and snakes and so on, for company for

Jim; and then you kept Tom here so long with the butter in his hat that you come near spiling the whole business, because the men come before we was out of the cabin, and we had to rush, and they heard us and let drive at us, and I got my share, and we dodged out of the path and let them go by, and when the dogs come they warn't interested in us, but went for the most noise, and we got our canoe, and made for the raft, and was all safe, and Jim was a free man, and we done it all by ourselves, and *wasn't* it bully, Aunty!"

"Well, I never heard the likes of it in all my born days! So it was *you*, you little rapscallions, that's been making all this trouble, and turn everybody's wits clean inside out and scared us all most to death. I've as good a notion as ever I had in my life, to take it out o' you this very minute. To think, here I've been, night after night, a—*you* just get well once, you young scamp, and I lay I'll tan the Old Harry out o' both o' ye!"

But Tom, he *was* so proud and joyful, he just *couldn't* hold in, and his tongue just *went* it—she a-chipping in, and spitting fire all along, and both of them going it at once, like a cat-convention; and she says:

"*Well*, you get all the enjoyment you can out of it *now*, for mind I tell you if I catch you meddling with him again—"

"Meddling with *who?*" Tom says, dropping his smile and looking surprised.

"With *who?* Why, the runaway nigger, of course. Who'd you reckon?"

Tom looks at me very grave, and says:

"Tom, didn't you just tell me he was all right? Hasn't he got away?"

"*Him?*" says Aunt Sally; "the runaway nigger? 'Deed he hasn't. They've got him back, safe and sound, and he's in that cabin again, on bread and water, and loaded down with chains, till he's claimed or sold!"

Tom rose square up in bed, with his eye hot, and his nostrils opening and shutting like gills, and sings out to me:

"They hain't no *right* to shut him up! *Shove!*—and don't you lose a minute. Turn him loose! he ain't no slave; he's as free as any cretur that walks this earth!"

"What *does* the child mean?"

"I mean every word I *say*, Aunt Sally, and if somebody don't go, *I'll* go. I've knowed him all his life, and so has Tom, there. Old Miss Watson died two months ago, and she was ashamed she ever was going to sell him down the river, and *said* so; and she set him free in her will."

"Then what on earth did *you* want to set him free for, seeing he was already free?"

"Well, that *is* a question, I must say; and *just* like women! Why, I wanted the *adventure* of it; and I'd a waded neck-deep in blood to—goodness alive, AUNT POLLY!"[2]

If she warn't standing right there, just inside the door, looking as sweet and contented as an angel half-full of pie, I wish I may never!

Aunt Sally jumped for her, and most hugged the head off of her, and cried over her, and I found a good enough place for me under the bed, for it was getting pretty sultry for *us*, seemed to me. And I peeped out, and in a little while Tom's Aunt Polly shook herself loose and stood there looking across at Tom over her spectacles—kind of grinding him into the earth, you know. And then she says:

2. Tom Sawyer's aunt and guardian.

"Yes, you *better* turn y'r head away—I would if I was you, Tom."

"Oh, deary me!" says Aunt Sally; "*is* he changed so? Why, that ain't *Tom* it's Sid; Tom's—Tom's—why, where is Tom? He was here a minute ago."

"You mean where's Huck *Finn*—that's what you mean! I reckon I hain't raised such a scamp as my Tom all these years, not to know him when I *see* him. That *would* be a pretty howdy-do. Come out from under the bed, Huck Finn."

So I done it. But not feeling brash.

Aunt Sally she was one of the mixed-upest looking persons I ever see; except one, and that was Uncle Silas, when he come in, and they told it all to him. It kind of made him drunk, as you may say, and he didn't know nothing at all the rest of the day, and preached a prayer-meeting sermon that night that give him a rattling ruputation, because the oldest man in the world couldn't a understood it. So Tom's Aunt Polly, she told all about who I was, and what; and I had to up and tell how I was in such a tight place that when Mrs. Phelps took me for Tom Sawyer—she chipped in and says, "Oh, go on and call me Aunt Sally, I'm used to it, now, and 'tain't no need to change"— that when Aunt Sally took me for Tom Sawyer, I had to stand it—that warn't no other way, and I knowed he wouldn't mind, because it would be nuts for him, being a mystery, and he'd make an adventure out of it and be perfectly satisfied. And so it turned out, and he let on to be Sid, and made things as soft as he could for me.

And his Aunt Polly she said Tom was right about old Miss Watson setting Jim free in her will; and so, sure enough, Tom Sawyer had gone and took all that trouble and bother to set a free nigger free! and I couldn't ever understand, before, until that minute and that talk, how he *could* help a body set a nigger free, with his bringing-up.

Well, Aunt Polly she said that when Aunt Sally wrote to her that Tom and *Sid* had come, all right and safe, she says to herself:

"Look at that, now! I might have expected it, letting him go off that way without anybody to watch him. So now I got to go and trapse all the way down the river, eleven hundred mile,[3] and find out what that creetur's up to, *this* time; as long as I couldn't seem to get any answer out of you about it."

"Why, I never heard nothing from you," says Aunt Sally.

"Well, I wonder! Why, I wrote to you twice, to ask you what you could mean by Sid being here."

"Well, I never got 'em, Sis."

Aunt Polly, she turns around slow and severe, and says:

"You, Tom!"

"Well—*what?*" he says, kind of pettish.

"Don't you what *me*, you impudent thing—hand out them letters."

"What letters?"

"*Them* letters. I be bound, if I have to take aholt of you I'll—"

"They're in the trunk. There, now. And they're just the same as they was when I got them out of the office. I hain't looked into them, I hain't touched them. But I knowed they'd make trouble, and I thought if you warn't in no hurry, I'd—"

---

3. This distance from Hannibal would place the Phelps plantation in northern Louisiana.

"Well, you *do* need skinning, there ain't no mistake about it. And I wrote another one to tell you I was coming; and I spose he—"

"No, it come yesterday; I hain't read it yet, but *it's* all right, I've got that one."

I wanted to offer to bet two dollars she hadn't, but I reckoned maybe it was just as safe to not to. So I never said nothing.

Chapter the Last

The first time I catched Tom, private, I asked him what was his idea, time of the evasion?—what it was he'd planned to do if the evasion worked all right and he managed to set a nigger free that was already free before? And he said, what he had planned in his head, from the start, if we got Jim out all safe, was for us to run him down the river, on the raft, and have adventures plumb to the mouth of the river, and then tell him about his being free, and take him back up home on a steamboat, in style, and pay him for his lost time, and write word ahead and get out all the niggers around, and have them waltz him into town with a torchlight procession and a brass band, and then he would be a hero, and so would we. But I reckoned it was about as well the way it was.

We had Jim out of the chains in no time, and when Aunt Polly and Uncle Silas and Aunt Sally found out how good he helped the doctor nurse Tom, they made a heap of fuss over him, and fixed him up prime, and give him all he wanted to eat, and a good time, and nothing to do. And we had him up to the sickroom; and had a high talk; and Tom give Jim forty dollars for being prisoner for us so patient, and doing it up so good, and Jim was pleased most to death, and busted out, and says:

"*Dah,* now, Huck, what I tell you?—what I tell you up dah on Jackson islan'? I *tole* you I got a hairy breas', en what's de sign un it; en I *tole* you I ben rich wunst, en gwineter to be rich *agin*; en it's come true; en heah she *is*! *Dah,* now! doan' talk to *me*—signs is *signs,* mine I tell you; en I knowed jis' 's well 'at I 'uz gwineter be rich agin as I's a stannin' heah dis minute!"

And then Tom he talked along, and talked along, and says, le's all three slide out of here, one of these nights, and get an outfit, and go for howling adventures amongst the Injuns, over in the Territory, for a couple of weeks or two; and I says, all right, that suits me, but I ain't got no money for to buy the outfit, and I reckon I couldn't get none from home, because it's likely pap's been back before now, and got it all away from Judge Thatcher and drunk it up.

"No he hain't," Tom says; "it's all there, yet—six thousand dollars and more; and your pap hain't ever been back since. Hadn't when I come away, anyhow."

Jim says, kind of solemn:

"He ain't a comin' back no mo', Huck."

I says:

"Why, Jim?"

"Nemmine why, Huck—but he ain't comin' back no mo'."

But I kept at him; so at last he says:

"Doan' you 'member de house dat was float'n down de river, en dey wuz a man in dah, kivered up, en I went in en unkivered him and didn' let you come in? Well, den, you k'n git yo' money when you wants it; kase dat wuz him."

Tom's most well, now, and got his bullet around his neck on a watch-guard for a watch, and is always seeing what time it is, and so there ain't nothing more to write about, and I am rotten glad of it, because if I'd a knowed what a trouble it was to make a book I wouldn't a tackled it and ain't agoing to no more. But I reckon I got to light out for the Territory ahead of the rest, because Aunt Sally she's going to adopt me and sivilize me and I can't stand it. I been there before.

THE END. YOURS TRULY, HUCK FINN.

1876–83   1884

W. D. HOWELLS
1837–1920

As a steadily productive novelist, playwright, critic, essayist, reviewer, and editor, W. D. Howells was always in the public eye, and his influence during the 1880s and 1890s on a growing, serious, middle-class readership was incalculable. In his writings an entire generation discovered, through his faithful description of familiar places, his dramatizations of ordinary lives, and his shrewd analyses of shared moral issues, its tastes, its social behavior, its values, and its problems. Howells was by temperament genial and modest, but he was also forthright and tough-minded. He was, as critic Lionel Trilling has observed, a deeply civil man with a balanced sense of life. Perhaps that is why when he died, in 1920, the spontaneous outpouring of sorrow and admiration was the kind reserved for national heroes.

Howells was born, one of eight children, in the postfrontier village of Martin's Ferry, Ohio, on March 1, 1837, to a poor, respectable, proud, and culturally informed family. Like his contemporary Samuel L. Clemens and his predecessor Ben Franklin, Howells went to school at the printer's office, setting type for the series of unsuccessful newspapers that his good-natured, somewhat impractical father owned. Though the family moved around a good deal in Ohio, Howells's youth was emotionally secure and, on the whole, happy. His mother, he observed, had the gift of making each child feel that he or she was the center of the world.

From his earliest years Howells had both literary passions and literary ambitions. When he was not setting type or reading Oliver Goldsmith, Washington Irving, William Shakespeare, Charles Dickens, William Makepeace Thackeray, or other favorites, he was teaching himself several foreign languages. Howells tried his hand at a number of literary forms in his teens, but his first regular jobs involved reporting for newspapers in Columbus and Cincinnati. It was as a journalist that he made his first pilgrimage to New England in 1860, where he was welcomed by such literary leaders as James Russell Lowell, Oliver Wendell Holmes, Ralph Waldo Emerson, and Nathaniel Hawthorne, who must have recognized that he possessed talent and the will to succeed as well as courtesy and deference.

A campaign biography of Lincoln, his first significant book, won for Howells the consulship at Venice in 1861. There he wrote a series of travel letters, eventually published as *Venetian Life* (1866), that made his name known in eastern literary circles. After returning to America in 1866, he worked briefly for the *Nation* in New York until James T. Fields offered him the assistant editorship of the *Atlantic Monthly*, to which he had contributed some of his earliest verse before the war. (Like a good many American authors, Howells published little poetry once he committed himself to other forms.) In effect, Howells assumed control of the magazine from the very beginning, and he succeeded officially to the editorship in 1871, a position he held until resigning in 1881 to have more time to write fiction. Because the *Atlantic* was the preeminent literary magazine of the day, Howells had, as a young man, the power to make or break careers, a power he exercised both generously and responsibly. No American editor introduced and promoted the careers of a wider variety of writers than did Howells.

Howells had been finding his way as a novelist during his ten years as editor, publishing seven novels in this period, beginning with *Their Wedding Journey* (1872) and concluding with *The Undiscovered Country* (1880). These first novels are short, uncomplicated linear narratives that deliberately eschew passionate, heroic, action-packed, and exciting adventures in favor of a more mundane realism. In the 1880s Howells came into his own as novelist and critic. *A Modern Instance* (1882) examines psychic, familial, and social disintegration under the pressure of the secularization and urbanization of post-Civil War America, the disintegration that is Howells's central and deepest subject. His treatment in this novel of journalism as a profession and the issue of divorce, just beginning to emerge as a significant social fact, opened new territories for American novelists.

Three years later Howells published his most famous novel, *The Rise of Silas Lapham* (1885). This novel traces the moral rise of Silas Lapham, a prototypical American entrepreneur, at the same time that it charts the collapse of the paint manufacturing company that he had built out of a combination of sheer luck, hard work, and shady business dealings. Within a year of its publication, Howells was profoundly affected by Russian novelist and philosopher Count Leo Tolstoy's ideas of nonviolence, spartan living, and economic equality and publicly defended the "Haymarket Anarchists," a group of Chicago workers, several of whom were executed without clear proof of their complicity in a dynamiting at a public demonstration in May of 1886. Thereafter, Howells offered more direct, ethical criticism of social and economic injustice in such succeeding novels as the popular, large-canvassed *A Hazard of New Fortunes* (1890) and the utopian romance *A Traveller from Altruria* (1894). In these same years Howells also penetrated more deeply into individual consciousness, particularly in two short novels, *The Shadow of a Dream* (1890) and *An Imperative Duty* (1892). In the short story *Editha* (1905), Howells characteristically explores the double moral failure of a society and of an individual who has been corrupted by its worst values.

In his later years, Howells sustained and deepened his varied literary output. Among his novels of consequence in this period are the naturalistic *The Landlord at Lion's Head* (1897) and the elegiac *The Vacation of the Kelwyns* (published posthumously, 1920). He also wrote charming and vivid autobiography and reminiscence in *A Boy's Town* (1890) and *Years of My Youth* (1916), and as he had since the 1870s, Howells continued to produce plays and farces, which served, as one critic has remarked, as "finger exercises for his novels."

In the mid-1880s Howells had aggressively argued the case for realism and against "romanticistic" fiction, promoting Henry James in particular at the expense of such English novelists as Sir Walter Scott, Dickens, and Thackeray. In *The Editor's Study* essays he wrote for *Harper's Monthly* starting in 1886 (some of which in 1891 he made into *Criticism and Fiction*), Howells attacked sentimentality of thought and feeling and the falsification of moral nature and ethical options wherever he found them in fiction. He believed that realism "was nothing more or less than the truthful treatment of material," especially the motives and actions of *ordinary* men and women. He insisted, sooner and more vigorously than any other American critic, that the novel be objective or dramatic in point of view, solidly based in convincingly motivated characters speaking the language of actual men and women, free of contrived events or melodramatic effects, true to the particulars of a recent time and specific place, and ethically and aesthetically seamless. Indeed, perhaps the polemical nature of his critical stance in the 1880s did as much as anything to obscure until recently the flexibility and range of his sensibility. Certainly *Novel-Writing and Novel-Reading,* first delivered as a lecture in 1899, suggests more accurately than *Criticism and Fiction* (1891) the shrewdness, common sense, and penetrating thoughtfulness that characterize his criticism at its best. He ranks with James at the top of the short list of important American critics of the late nineteenth century.

In the course of his lifelong career as literary arbiter, Howells was remarkably international in outlook and promoted in his diverse critical writings such non-American contemporaries as Ivan Turgenev, Benito Perez Caldós, Björnstierne Björnson, Leo Tolstoy, Henrik Ibsen, Émile Zola, George Eliot, and Thomas Hardy. Howells also championed many younger American writers and early recognized many talented women writers in the relentless stream of reviews he wrote over six decades— among them Sarah Orne Jewett, Mary E. Wilkins Freeman, Edith Wharton, and Emily Dickinson. He is even better known for actively promoting the careers of such emerging realists and naturalists as Stephen Crane, Hamlin Garland, and Frank Norris.

The two contemporaries in whom Howells had the greatest critical confidence, however, were Henry James and Samuel L. Clemens, both of whom he served from the 1860s on as editor and with both of whom he also sustained personal friendships. In the late 1860s, Howells had walked the Cambridge streets with James, discussing the present state and future prospects for the substance and techniques of fiction. As editor of *Atlantic Monthly,* Howells had accepted a number of James's early tales. Throughout his career he wrote essays and reviews in praise of James's work; on his deathbed Howells was working on an essay, *The American James.* He genuinely admired and was friendly with the patrician James, but he clearly loved and was more intimate with the rough-textured Clemens, whose childhood background was much like his. *My Mark Twain,* written immediately after his friend's death in 1910, records that affection in one of the enduring memoirs of our literary history.

By the time Howells died, he had served for thirteen years as first president of the American Academy of Arts and Letters, the organization that seeks to identify and honor the most distinguished work in these fields, and was himself a national institution. For rebels and iconoclasts of the 1930s such as H. L. Mencken, Sinclair Lewis, and the young Van Wyck Brooks, he epitomized the dead hand of the past, the genteel, Victorian enemy. Howells's reputation has slowly recovered from these charges. Without denying his intelligent and diplomatic civility, critics have come to recognize his steady, masterful style and the courage of his liberal—at times radical—perspective in his own time

Editha[1]

The air was thick with the war feeling,[2] like the electricity of a storm which has not yet burst. Editha sat looking out into the hot spring afternoon, with her lips parted, and panting with the intensity of the question whether she could let him go. She had decided that she could not let him stay, when she saw him at the end of the still leafless avenue, making slowly up towards the house, with his head down and his figure relaxed. She ran impatiently out on the veranda, to the edge of the steps, and imperatively demanded greater haste of him with her will before she called aloud to him: "George!"

1. First printed in *Harper's Monthly* for January 1905, the source of the present text. Published first in book form in *Between the Dark and the Daylight: Romances* (1907).

2. I.e., "war fever," the excessive patriotism or "jingoism" preceding the Spanish-American War (1898).

He had quickened his pace in mystical response to her mystical urgence, before he could have heard her; now he looked up and answered, "Well?"

"Oh, how united we are!" she exulted, and then she swooped down the steps to him. "What is it?" she cried.

"It's war," he said, and he pulled her up to him and kissed her.

She kissed him back intensely, but irrelevantly, as to their passion, and uttered from deep in her throat. "How glorious!"

"It's war," he repeated, without consenting to her sense of it; and she did not know just what to think at first. She never knew what to think of him; that made his mystery, his charm. All through their courtship, which was contemporaneous with the growth of the war feeling, she had been puzzled by his want of seriousness about it. He seemed to despise it even more than he abhorred it. She could have understood his abhorring any sort of blood-shed; that would have been a survival of his old life when he thought he would be a minister, and before he changed and took up the law. But making light of a cause so high and noble seemed to show a want of earnestness at the core of his being. Not but that she felt herself able to cope with a con-genital defect of that sort, and make his love for her save him from himself. Now perhaps the miracle was already wrought in him. In the presence of the tremendous fact that he announced, all triviality seemed to have gone out of him; she began to feel that. He sank down on the top step, and wiped his forehead with his handkerchief, while she poured out upon him her question of the origin and authenticity of his news.

All the while, in her duplex emotioning, she was aware that now at the very beginning she must put a guard upon herself against urging him, by any word or act, to take the part that her whole soul willed him to take, for the completion of her ideal of him. He was very nearly perfect as he was, and he must be allowed to perfect himself. But he was peculiar, and he might very well be reasoned out of his peculiarity. Before her reasoning went her emotioning: her nature pulling upon his nature, her womanhood upon his manhood, without her knowing the means she was using to the end she was willing. She had always supposed that the man who won her would have done something to win her; she did not know what, but something. George Gearson had simply asked her for her love, on the way home from a concert, and she gave her love to him, without, as it were, thinking. But now, it flashed upon her, if he could do something worthy to *have* won her—be a hero, *her* hero—it would be even better than if he had done it before asking her; it would be grander. Besides, she had believed in the war from the beginning.

"But don't you see, dearest," she said, "that it wouldn't have come to this, if it hadn't been in the order of Providence? And I call any war glorious that is for the liberation of people who have been struggling for years against the cruelest oppression. Don't you think so, too?"

"I suppose so," he returned, languidly. "But war! Is it glorious to break the peace of the world?"

"That ignoble peace! It was no peace at all, with that crime and shame at our very gates." She was conscious of parroting the current phrases of the newspapers, but it was no time to pick and choose her words. She must sacrifice anything to the high ideal she had for him, and after a good deal of rapid argument she ended with the climax: "But now it doesn't matter about the how or why. Since the war has come, all that is gone. There are no two sides, any more. There is nothing now but our country."

He sat with his eyes closed and his head leant back against the veranda, and he said with a vague smile, as if musing aloud, "Our country—right or wrong."[3]

"Yes, right or wrong!" she returned, fervidly. "I'll go and get you some lemonade." She rose rustling, and whisked away; when she came back with two tall glasses of clouded liquid, on a tray, and the ice clucking in them, he still sat as she had left him, and she said as if there had been no interruption: "But there is no question of wrong in this case. I call it a sacred war. A war for liberty, and humanity, if ever there was one. And I know you will see it just as I do, yet."

He took half the lemonade at a gulp, and he answered as he set the glass down: "I know you always have the highest ideal. When I differ from you, I ought to doubt myself."

A generous sob rose in Editha's throat for the humility of a man, so very nearly perfect, who was willing to put himself below her.

Besides, she felt, more subliminally, that he was never so near slipping through her fingers as when he took that meek way.

"You shall not say that! Only, for once I happen to be right." She seized his hand in her two hands, and poured her soul from her eyes into his. "Don't you think so?" she entreated him.

He released his hand and drank the rest of his lemonade, and she added, "Have mine, too," but he shook his head in answering, "I've no business to think so, unless I act so, too."

Her heart stopped a beat before it pulsed on with leaps that she felt in her neck. She had noticed that strange thing in men: they seemed to feel bound to do what they believed, and not think a thing was finished when they said it, as girls did. She knew what was in his mind, but she pretended not, and she said, "Oh, I am not sure," and then faltered.

He went on as if to himself without apparently heeding her. "There's only one way of proving one's faith in a thing like this."

She could not say that she understood, but she did understand.

He went on again. "If I believed—if I felt as you do about this war—Do you wish me to feel as you do?"

Now she was really not sure; so she said, "George, I don't know what you mean."

He seemed to muse away from her as before. "There is a sort of fascination in it. I suppose that at the bottom of his heart every man would like at times to have his courage tested, to see how he would act."

"How can you talk in that ghastly way?"

"It *is* rather morbid. Still, that's what it comes to, unless you're swept away by ambition, or driven by conviction. I haven't the conviction or the ambition, and the other thing is what it comes to with me. I ought to have been a preacher, after all; then I couldn't have asked it of myself, as I must, now I'm

3. "Our country! In her intercourse with foreign nations may she always be in the right; but our country right or wrong." Part of a toast given by American naval officer Stephen Decatur (1779–1820).

a lawyer. And you believe it's a holy war, Editha?" he suddenly addressed her. "Oh, I know you do! But you wish me to believe so, too?"

She hardly knew whether he was mocking or not, in the ironical way he always had with her plainer mind. But the only thing was to be outspoken with him.

"George, I wish you to believe whatever you think is true, at any and every cost. If I've tried to talk you into anything, I take it all back."

"Oh, I know that, Editha. I know how sincere you are, and how—I wish I had your undoubting spirit! I'll think it over; I'd like to believe as you do. But I don't, now; I don't, indeed. It isn't this war alone; though this seems peculiarly wanton and needless; but it's every war—so stupid; it makes me sick. Why shouldn't this thing have been settled reasonably?"

"Because," she said, very throatily again, "God meant it to be war."

"You think it was God? Yes, I suppose that is what people will say."

"Do you suppose it would have been war if God hadn't meant it?"

"I don't know. Sometimes it seems as if God had put this world into men's keeping to work it as they pleased."

"Now, George, that is blasphemy."

"Well, I won't blaspheme. I'll try to believe in your pocket Providence," he said, and then he rose to go.

"Why don't you stay to dinner?" Dinner at Balcom's Works was at one o'clock.

"I'll come back to supper, if you'll let me. Perhaps I shall bring you a convert."

"Well, you may come back, on that condition."

"All right. If I don't come, you'll understand."

He went away without kissing her, and she felt it a suspension of their engagement. It all interested her intensely; she was undergoing a tremendous experience, and she was being equal to it. While she stood looking after him, her mother came out through one of the long windows, on to the veranda, with a catlike softness and vagueness.

"Why didn't he stay to dinner?"

"Because—because—war has been declared," Editha pronounced, without turning.

Her mother said, "Oh, my!" and then said nothing more until she had sat down in one of the large Shaker chairs[4] and rocked herself for some time. Then she closed whatever tacit passage of thought there had been in her mind with the spoken words: "Well, I hope *he* won't go."

"And *I* hope he *will*," the girl said, and confronted her mother with a stormy exaltation that would have frightened any creature less unimpressionable than a cat.

Her mother rocked herself again for an interval of cogitation. What she arrived at in speech was: "Well, I guess you've done a wicked thing, Editha Balcom."

The girl said, as she passed indoors through the same window her mother had come out by: "I haven't done anything—yet."

In her room, she put together all her letters and gifts from Gearson, down to the withered petals of the first flower he had offered, with that timidity of

---

4. Sturdy, simple, unadorned chairs made by the Shaker sect.

his veiled in that irony of his. In the heart of the packet she enshrined her engagement ring which she had restored to the pretty box he had brought it her in. Then she sat down, if not calmly yet strongly, and wrote:

"GEORGE:—I understood—when you left me. But I think we had better emphasize your meaning that if we cannot be one in everything we had better be one in nothing. So I am sending these things for your keeping till you have made up your mind.

"I shall always love you, and therefore I shall never marry any one else. But the man I marry must love his country first of all, and be able to say to me,

"'I could not love thee, dear, so much,
Loved I not honor more.'[5]

"There is no honor above America with me. In this great hour there is no other honor.

"Your heart will make my words clear to you. I had never expected to say so much, but it has come upon me that I must say the utmost.

EDITHA

She thought she had worded her letter well, worded it in a way that could not be bettered; all had been implied and nothing expressed.

She had it ready to send with the packet she had tied with red, white, and blue ribbon, when it occurred to her that she was not just to him, that she was not giving him a fair chance. He had said he would go and think it over, and she was not waiting. She was pushing, threatening, compelling. That was not a woman's part. She must leave him free, free, free. She could not accept for her country or herself a forced sacrifice.

In writing her letter she had satisfied the impulse from which it sprang; she could well afford to wait till he had thought it over. She put the packet and the letter by, and rested serene in the consciousness of having done what was laid upon her by her love itself to do, and yet used patience, mercy, justice.

She had her reward. Gearson did not come to tea, but she had given him till morning, when, late at night there came up from the village the sound of a fife and drum with a tumult of voices, in shouting, singing, and laughing. The noise drew nearer and nearer; it reached the street end of the avenue; there it silenced itself, and one voice, the voice she knew best, rose over the silence. It fell; the air was filled with cheers; the fife and drum struck up, with the shouting, singing, and laughing again, but now retreating; and a single figure came hurrying up the avenue.

She ran down to meet her lover and clung to him. He was very gay, and he put his arm round her with a boisterous laugh. "Well, you must call me Captain, now; or Cap, if you prefer; that's what the boys call me. Yes, we've had a meeting at the town hall, and everybody has volunteered; and they selected me for captain, and I'm going to the war, the big war, the glorious war, the holy war ordained by the pocket Providence that blesses butchery.

---

5. Lines from Richard Lovelace's (1618–1658) "To Lucasta, on Going to the Wars."

Come along; let's tell the whole family about it. Call them from their downy beds, father, mother, Aunt Hitty, and all the folks!"

But when they mounted the veranda steps he did not wait for a larger audience; he poured the story out upon Editha alone.

"There was a lot of speaking, and then some of the fools set up a shout for me. It was all going one way, and I thought it would be a good joke to sprinkle a little cold water on them. But you can't do that with a crowd that adores you. The first thing I knew I was sprinkling hell-fire on them. 'Cry havoc, and let slip the dogs of war.'[6] That was the style. Now that it had come to the fight, there were no two parties; there was one country, and the thing was to fight the fight to a finish as quick as possible. I suggested volunteering then and there, and I wrote my name first of all on the roster. Then they elected me—that's all. I wish I had some ice-water!"

She left him walking up and down the veranda, while she ran for the ice-pitcher and a goblet, and when she came back he was still walking up and down, shouting the story he had told her to her father and mother, who had come out more sketchily dressed than they commonly were by day. He drank goblet after goblet of the ice-water without noticing who was giving it, and kept on talking, and laughing through his talk wildly. "It's astonishing," he said, "how well the worse reason looks when you try to make it appear the better. Why, I believe I was the first convert to the war in that crowd to-night! I never thought I should like to kill a man; but now, I shouldn't care; and the smokeless powder lets you see the man drop that you kill. It's all for the country! What a thing it is to have a country that *can't* be wrong, but if it is, is right, anyway!"

Editha had a great, vital thought, an inspiration. She set down the ice-pitcher on the veranda floor, and ran up-stairs and got the letter she had written him. When at last he noisily bade her father and mother, "Well, good night. I forgot I woke you up; I sha'n't want any sleep myself," she followed him down the avenue to the gate. There, after the whirling words that seemed to fly away from her thoughts and refuse to serve them, she made a last effort to solemnize the moment that seemed so crazy, and pressed the letter she had written upon him.

"What's this?" he said. "Want me to mail it?"

"No, no. It's for you. I wrote it after you went this morning. Keep it—keep it—and read it sometime—" She thought, and then her inspiration came: "Read it if ever you doubt what you've done, or fear that I regret your having done it. Read it after you've started."

They strained each other in embraces that seemed as ineffective as their words, and he kissed her face with quick, hot breaths that were so unlike him, that made her feel as if she had lost her old lover and found a stranger in his place. The stranger said: "What a gorgeous flower you are, with your red hair, and your blue eyes that look black now, and your face with the color painted out by the white moonshine! Let me hold you under my chin, to see whether I love blood, you tiger-lily!" Then he laughed Gearson's laugh, and released her, scared and giddy. Within her wilfulness she had been fright-

---

6. From Antony's soliloquy after the murder of Caesar, in Shakespeare's *Julius Caesar* (3.1.274).

ened by a sense of subtler force in him, and mystically mastered as she had never been before.

She ran all the way back to the house, and mounted the steps panting. Her mother and father were talking of the great affair. Her mother said: "Wa'n't Mr. Gearson in rather of an excited state of mind? Didn't you think he acted curious?"

"Well, not for a man who'd just been elected captain and had to set 'em up for the whole of Company A," her father chuckled back.

"What in the world do you mean, Mr. Balcom? Oh! There's Editha!" She offered to follow the girl indoors.

"Don't come, mother!" Editha called, vanishing.

Mrs. Balcom remained to reproach her husband. "I don't see much of anything to laugh at."

"Well, it's catching. Caught it from Gearson. I guess it won't be much of a war, and I guess Gearson don't think so, either. The other fellows will back down as soon as they see we mean it. I wouldn't lose any sleep over it. I'm going back to bed, myself."

Gearson came again next afternoon, looking pale, and rather sick, but quite himself, even to his languid irony. "I guess I'd better tell you, Editha, that I consecrated myself to your god of battles last night by pouring too many libations to him down my own throat. But I'm all right now. One has to carry off the excitement, somehow."

"Promise me," she commanded, "that you'll never touch it again!"

"What! Not let the cannikin clink? Not let the soldier drink?[7] Well, I promise."

"You don't belong to yourself now; you don't even belong to *me.* You belong to your country, and you have a sacred charge to keep yourself strong and well for your country's sake. I have been thinking, thinking all night and all day long."

"You look as if you had been crying a little, too," he said with his queer smile.

"That's all past. I've been thinking, and worshipping *you.* Don't you suppose I know all that you've been through, to come to this? I've followed you every step from your old theories and opinions."

"Well, you've had a long row to hoe."

"And I know you've done this from the highest motives—"

" 'Oh, there won't be much pettifogging to do till this cruel war is—"

"And you haven't simply done it for my sake. I couldn't respect you if you had."

"Well, then we'll say I haven't. A man that hasn't got his own respect intact wants the respect of all the other people he can corner. But we won't go into that. I'm in for the thing now, and we've got to face our future. My idea is that this isn't going to be a very protracted struggle; we shall just scare the enemy to death before it comes to a fight at all. But we must provide for contingencies, Editha. If anything happens to me—"

"Oh, George!" She clung to him sobbing.

7. Allusion to Shakespeare's *Othello* (2.3.64–68), in which Iago sings a soldier's drinking song.

"I don't want you to feel foolishly bound to my memory. I should hate that, wherever I happened to be."

"I am yours, for time and eternity—time and eternity." She liked the words; they satisfied her famine for phrases.

"Well, say eternity; that's all right; but time's another thing; and I'm talking about time. But there is something! My mother! If anything happens—"

She winced, and he laughed. "You're not the bold soldier-girl of yesterday!" Then he sobered. "If anything happens, I want you to help my mother out. She won't like my doing this thing. She brought me up to think war a fool thing as well as a bad thing. My father was in the civil war, all through it; lost his arm in it." She thrilled with the sense of the arm round her; what if that should be lost? He laughed as if divining her: "Oh, it doesn't run in the family, as far as I know!" Then he added, gravely: "He came home with misgivings about war, and they grew on him. I guess he and mother agreed between them that I was to be brought up in his final mind about it; but that was before my time. I only knew him from my mother's report of him and his opinions; I don't know whether they were hers first; but they were hers last. This will be a blow to her. I shall have to write and tell her—"

He stopped, and she asked: "Would you like me to write too, George?"

"I don't believe that would do. No, I'll do the writing. She'll understand a little if I say that I thought the way to minimize it was to make war on the largest possible scale at once—that I felt I must have been helping on the war somehow if I hadn't helped keep it from coming, and I knew I hadn't; when it came, I had no right to stay out of it."

Whether his sophistries satisfied him or not, they satisfied her. She clung to his breast, and whispered, with closed eyes and quivering lips: "Yes, yes, yes!"

"But if anything should happen, you might go to her, and see what you could do for her. You know? It's rather far off; she can't leave her chair—"

"Oh, I'll go, if it's the ends of the earth! But nothing will happen! Nothing can! I—"

She felt herself lifted with his rising, and Gearson was saying, with his arm still round her, to her father: "Well, we're off at once, Mr. Balcom. We're to be formally accepted at the capital, and then bunched up with the rest somehow, and sent into camp somewhere, and got to the front as soon as possible. We all want to be in the van,[8] of course; we're the first company to report to the Governor. I came to tell Editha, but I hadn't got round to it."

She saw him again for a moment at the capital, in the station, just before the train started southward with his regiment. He looked well, in his uniform, and very soldierly, but somehow girlish, too, with his clean-shaven face and slim figure. The manly eyes and the strong voice satisfied her, and his preoccupation with some unexpected details of duty flattered her. Other girls were weeping and bemoaning themselves, but she felt a sort of noble distinction in the abstraction, the almost unconsciousness, with which they parted. Only at the last moment he said: "Don't forget my mother. It mayn't be such a walk-over as I supposed," and he laughed at the notion.

8. Short for vanguard, the foremost division of an army.

He waved his hand to her as the train moved off—she knew it among a score of hands that were waved to other girls from the platform of the car, for it held a letter which she knew was hers. Then he went inside the car to read it, doubtless, and she did not see him again. But she felt safe for him through the strength of what she called her love. What she called her God, always speaking the name in a deep voice and with the implication of a mutual understanding, would watch over him and keep him and bring him back to her. If with an empty sleeve, then he should have three arms instead of two, for both of hers should be his for life. She did not see, though, why she should always be thinking of the arm his father had lost.

There were not many letters from him, but they were such as she could have wished, and she put her whole strength into making hers such as she imagined he could have wished, glorifying and supporting him. She wrote to his mother glorifying him as their hero, but the brief answer she got was merely to the effect that Mrs. Gearson was not well enough to write herself, and thanking her for her letter by the hand of someone who called herself "Yrs truly, Mrs. W. J. Andrews."

Editha determined not to be hurt, but to write again quite as if the answer had been all she expected. But before it seemed as if she could have written, there came news of the first skirmish, and in the list of the killed, which was telegraphed as a trifling loss on our side, was Gearson's name. There was a frantic time of trying to make out that it might be, must be, some other Gearson; but the name and the company and the regiment, and the State were too definitely given.

Then there was a lapse into depths out of which it seemed as if she never could rise again; then a lift into clouds far above all grief, black clouds, that blotted out the sun, but where she soared with him, with George, George! She had the fever that she expected of herself, but she did not die in it; she was not even delirious, and it did not last long. When she was well enough to leave her bed, her one thought was of George's mother, of his strangely worded wish that she should go to her and see what she could do for her. In the exaltation of the duty laid upon her—it buoyed her up instead of burdening her—she rapidly recovered.

Her father went with her on the long railroad journey from northern New York to western Iowa; he had business out at Davenport, and he said he could just as well go then as any other time; and he went with her to the little country town where George's mother lived in a little house on the edge of illimitable corn-fields, under trees pushed to a top of the rolling prairie. George's father had settled there after the civil war, as so many other old soldiers had done; but they were Eastern people, and Editha fancied touches of the East in the June rose overhanging the front door, and the garden with early summer flowers stretching from the gate of the paling fence.

It was very low inside the house, and so dim, with the closed blinds, that they could scarcely see one another: Editha tall and black in her crapes which filled the air with the smell of their dyes; her father standing decorously apart with his hat on his forearm, as at funerals; a woman rested in a deep armchair, and the woman who had let the strangers in stood behind the chair.

The seated woman turned her head round and up, and asked the woman behind her chair: "*Who* did you say?"

Editha, if she had done what she expected of herself, would have gone down on her knees at the feet of the seated figure and said, "I am George's Editha," for answer.

But instead of her own voice she heard that other woman's voice, saying: "Well, I don't know as I *did* get the name just right. I guess I'll have to make a little more light in here," and she went and pushed two of the shutters ajar.

Then Editha's father said, in his public will-now-address-a-few-remarks tone: "My name is Balcom, ma'am—Junius H. Balcom, of Balcom's Works, New York; my daughter—"

"Oh!" the seated woman broke in, with a powerful voice, the voice that always surprised Editha from Gearson's slender frame. "Let me see you! Stand round where the light can strike on your face," and Editha dumbly obeyed. "So, you're Editha Balcom," she sighed.

"Yes," Editha said, more like a culprit than a comforter.

"What did you come for?" Mrs. Gearson asked.

Editha's face quivered and her knees shook. "I came—because—because George—" She could go no further.

"Yes," the mother said, "he told me he had asked you to come if he got killed. You didn't expect that, I suppose, when you sent him."

"I would rather have died myself than done it!" Editha said with more truth in her deep voice than she ordinarily found in it. "I tried to leave him free—"

"Yes, that letter of yours, that came back with his other things, left him free."

Editha saw now where George's irony came from.

"It was not to be read before—unless—until—I told him so," she faltered.

"Of course, he wouldn't read a letter of yours, under the circumstances, till he thought you wanted him to. Been sick?" the woman abruptly demanded.

"Very sick," Editha said, with self-pity.

"Daughter's life," her father interposed, "was almost despaired of, at one time."

Mrs. Gearson gave him no heed. "I suppose you would have been glad to die, such a brave person as you! I don't believe *he* was glad to die. He was always a timid boy, that way; he was afraid of a good many things; but if he was afraid he did what he made up his mind to. I suppose he made up his mind to go, but I knew what it cost him, by what it cost me when I heard of it. I had been through *one* war before. When you sent him you didn't expect he would get killed."

The voice seemed to compassionate Editha, and it was time. "No," she huskily murmured.

"No, girls don't; women don't, when they give their men up to their country. They think they'll come marching back, somehow, just as gay as they went, or if it's an empty sleeve, or even an empty pantaloon, it's all the more glory, and they're so much the prouder of them, poor things!"

The tears began to run down Editha's face; she had not wept till then; but it was now such a relief to be understood that the tears came.

"No, you didn't expect him to get killed," Mrs. Gearson repeated in a voice which was startlingly like George's again. "You just expected him to kill some one else, some of those foreigners, that weren't there because they had any say about it, but because they had to be there, poor wretches—conscripts, or whatever they call 'em. You thought it would be all right for my George, *your* George, to kill the sons of those miserable mothers and the husbands of those girls that you would never see the faces of." The woman lifted her powerful voice in a psalmlike note. "I thank my God he didn't live to do it! I thank my God they killed him first, and that he ain't livin' with their blood on his hands!" She dropped her eyes, which she had raised with her voice, and glared at Editha. "What you got that black on for?" She lifted herself by her powerful arms so high that her helpless body seemed to hang limp its full length. "Take it off, take it off, before I tear it from your back!"

The lady who was passing the summer near Balcom's Works was sketching Editha's beauty, which lent itself wonderfully to the effects of a colorist. It had come to that confidence which is rather apt to grow between artist and sitter, and Editha told her everything.

"To think of your having such a tragedy in your life!" the lady said. She added: "I suppose there are people who feel that way about war. But when you consider the good this war has done—how much it has done for the country I can't understand such people, for my part. And when you had come all the way out there to console her—got up out of a sick-bed! Well!"

"I think," Editha said, magnanimously, "she wasn't quite in her right mind; and so did papa."

"Yes," the lady said, looking at Editha's lips in nature and then at her lips in art, and giving an empirical touch to them in the picture. "But how dreadful of her! How perfectly—excuse me—how *vulgar!*"

A light broke upon Editha in the darkness which she felt had been without a gleam of brightness for weeks and months. The mystery that had bewildered her was solved by the word; and from that moment she rose from grovelling in shame and self-pity, and began to live again in the ideal.

1905

AMBROSE BIERCE
1842–1914?

Ambrose Gwinnett Bierce was born on June 24, 1842, in Meigs County, Ohio, the last of nine children of strongly religious parents. Bierce's childhood was unhappy, and as an adult he cut himself off from his parents and all but one of his siblings. Perhaps the fascination with the supernatural that he displays in his fiction is similarly an attempt to escape the ordinary society of humanity he claimed to detest. In any case, from his earliest days "Bitter Bierce," as he came to be called, seemed disappointed with what had been, displeased with his present condition, and pessimistic about what lay ahead.

Not long after he spent one year at a military academy in Kentucky—his only formal schooling—the Civil War broke out and Bierce volunteered for the Union Army. After being involved in several battles, he was mustered out a lieutenant. Bierce later defined war (in his *Devil's Dictionary*) as a "by-product of the arts of peace" and peace as "a period of cheating between two periods of fighting," and it is hard to accept his own testimony that he was a zealous soldier. The Civil War, however, was an important source of some of his best fiction, including the suspenseful "An Occurrence at Owl Creek Bridge" (1890) and the equally bitter war narrative "Chickamauga" (1889).

After the war, Bierce moved to San Francisco. By 1866 he was working as a journalist, the career he pursued for the rest of his life. He began as a columnist for the *News Letter* and in 1868 became its editor. Among his writer friends in San Francisco were Mark Twain, Bret Harte, Joaquin Miller, Jack London, and George Sterling, all of whom were involved as journalists, lecturers, and writers in establishing San Francisco as a literary center. Bierce married in 1872 and with his wife traveled to England, where they lived until 1876. There, under the influence of literary sophisticates such as George Augustus Sala and Thomas Hood, he developed from a crude western humorist into a satirist of elegance and bite. His best early work appeared in his "Prattler" columns written first for the *Argonaut* (1877–79) and then for the *Wasp* (1880–86). In that year the popular column was picked up by William Randolph Hearst's *San Francisco Sunday Examiner*, where it continued until 1896. A mixture of reviews, gossip, and political and social commentary, the "Prattler" also served as an outlet for a number of Bierce's best short stories.

Bierce's personal life was a series of disasters. His definition of marriage—"the state or condition of a community consisting of a master, a mistress, and two slaves, making in all, two"—reflected his views on his own marriage (which ended in divorce in 1891). In 1889 his elder son was shot to death during a fight over a girl; in 1901 his younger son died of alcoholism. In 1913, Bierce went to Mexico and disappeared without a trace, although there is a story that he was killed in the Mexican Revolution, which pitted Pancho Villa, whom Bierce had planned to join, and Venustiano Carranza against General Victoriano Huerta, the dictator of Mexico. His time in Mexico was retold in Carlos Fuentes's novel *The Old Gringo* (1985), which was made into a film starring Gregory Peck.

Bierce's pessimism, cynicism, nihilism, and gallows humor, as well as his publicized spats with fellow writers, are in the American tradition of naysaying, which runs from Herman Melville to Thomas Pynchon. It is not the mordant wit of the *Devil's Dictionary* (first published in 1906 as *The Cynic's Word Book*) or Bierce's penchant for the grotesque, however, that finally makes him significant. In his best work, such as *Tales of Soldiers and Civilians* (1891; later retitled *In the Midst of Life*), Bierce, like Stephen Crane and Ernest Hemingway after him, converted the disordered experience of war into resonant and dramatic fictional revelations with strong moral and ethical messages.

An Occurrence at Owl Creek Bridge[1]

I

A man stood upon a railroad bridge in northern Alabama, looking down into the swift water twenty feet below. The man's hands were behind his back, the wrists bound with a cord. A rope closely encircled his neck. It was attached to a stout cross-timber above his head and the slack fell to the level of his knees. Some loose boards laid upon the sleepers[2] supporting the metals of the railway supplied a footing for him and his executioners—two private soldiers of the Federal army, directed by a sergeant who in civil life may have been a deputy sheriff. At a short remove upon the same temporary platform was an

1. First published in the *San Francisco Examiner* on July 13, 1890, this story was subsequently reprinted as part of the collection *Tales of Soldiers and Civilians* (1891; retitled *In the Midst of Life* in 1898) and in Volume II of *The Collected Works of* Ambrose Bierce (1909–12), the basis of the text printed here.
2. Pieces of timber, stone, or steel on or near the ground to keep railroad rails in place.

officer in the uniform of his rank, armed. He was a captain. A sentinel at each end of the bridge stood with his rifle in the position known as "support," that is to say, vertical in front of the left shoulder, the hammer resting on the forearm thrown straight across the chest—a formal and unnatural position, enforcing an erect carriage of the body. It did not appear to be the duty of these two men to know what was occurring at the centre of the bridge; they merely blockaded the two ends of the foot planking that traversed it.

Beyond one of the sentinels nobody was in sight; the railroad ran straight away into a forest for a hundred yards, then, curving, was lost to view. Doubtless there was an outpost farther along. The other bank of the stream was open ground—a gentle acclivity topped with a stockade of vertical tree trunks, loopholed for rifles, with a single embrasure through which protruded the muzzle of a brass cannon commanding the bridge. Midway of the slope between bridge and fort were the spectators—a single company of infantry in line, at "parade rest," the butts of the rifles on the ground, the barrels inclining slightly backward against the right shoulder, the hands crossed upon the stock. A lieutenant stood at the right of the line, the point of his sword upon the ground, his left hand resting upon his right. Excepting the group of four at the centre of the bridge, not a man moved. The company faced the bridge, staring stonily, motionless. The sentinels, facing the banks of the stream, might have been statues to adorn the bridge. The captain stood with folded arms, silent, observing the work of his subordinates, but making no sign. Death is a dignitary who when he comes announced is to be received with formal manifestations of respect, even by those most familiar with him. In the code of military etiquette silence and fixity are forms of deference.

The man who was engaged in being hanged was apparently about thirty-five years of age. He was a civilian, if one might judge from his habit, which was that of a planter. His features were good—a straight nose, firm mouth, broad forehead, from which his long, dark hair was combed straight back, falling behind his ears to the collar of his well-fitting frock-coat. He wore a mustache and pointed beard, but no whiskers; his eyes were large and dark gray, and had a kindly expression which one would hardly have expected in one whose neck was in the hemp. Evidently this was no vulgar assassin. The liberal military code makes provision for hanging many kinds of persons, and gentlemen are not excluded.

The preparations being complete, the two private soldiers stepped aside and each drew away the plank upon which he had been standing. The sergeant turned to the captain, saluted and placed himself immediately behind that officer, who in turn moved apart one pace. These movements left the condemned man and the sergeant standing on the two ends of the same plank, which spanned three of the cross-ties of the bridge. The end upon which the civilian stood almost, but not quite, reached a fourth. This plank had been held in place by the weight of the captain; it was now held by that of the sergeant. At a signal from the former the latter would step aside, the plank would tilt and the condemned man go down between two ties. The arrangement commended itself to his judgment as simple and effective. His face had not been covered nor his eyes bandaged. He looked a moment at his "unsteadfast footing," then let his gaze wander to the swirling water of the stream racing madly beneath his feet. A piece of dancing driftwood caught his attention and his eyes followed it down the current. How slowly it appeared to move! What a sluggish stream!

He closed his eyes in order to fix his last thoughts upon his wife and children. The water, touched to gold by the early sun, the brooding mists under the banks at some distance down the stream, the fort, the soldiers, the piece of drift—all had distracted him. And now he became conscious of a new disturbance. Striking through the thought of his dear ones was a sound which he could neither ignore nor understand, a sharp, distinct, metallic percussion like the stroke of a blacksmith's hammer upon the anvil; it had the same ringing quality. He wondered what it was, and whether immeasurably distant or near by—it seemed both. Its recurrence was regular, but as slow as the tolling of a death knell. He awaited each stroke with impatience and—he knew not why—apprehension. The intervals of silence grew progressively longer; the delays became maddening. With their greater infrequency the sounds increased in strength and sharpness. They hurt his ear like the thrust of a knife; he feared he would shriek. What he heard was the ticking of his watch.

He unclosed his eyes and saw again the water below him. "If I could free my hands," he thought, "I might throw off the noose and spring into the stream. By diving I could evade the bullets and, swimming vigorously, reach the bank, take to the woods and get away home. My home, thank God, is as yet outside their lines; my wife and little ones are still beyond the invader's farthest advance."

As these thoughts, which have here to be set down in words, were flashed into the doomed man's brain rather than evolved from it the captain nodded to the sergeant. The sergeant stepped aside.

II

Peyton Farquhar was a well-to-do planter, of an old and highly respected Alabama family. Being a slave owner and like other slave owners a politician he was naturally an original secessionist and ardently devoted to the Southern cause. Circumstances of an imperious nature, which it is unnecessary to relate here, had prevented him from taking service with the gallant army that had fought the disastrous campaigns ending with the fall of Corinth,[3] and he chafed under the inglorious restraint, longing for the release of his energies, the larger life of the soldier, the opportunity for distinction. That opportunity, he felt, would come, as it comes to all in war time. Meanwhile he did what he could. No service was too humble for him to perform in aid of the South, no adventure too perilous for him to undertake if consistent with the character of a civilian who was at heart a soldier, and who in good faith and without too much qualification assented to at least a part of the frankly villainous dictum that all is fair in love and war.

One evening while Farquhar and his wife were sitting on a rustic bench near the entrance to his grounds, a gray-clad soldier rode up to the gate and asked for a drink of water. Mrs. Farquhar was only too happy to serve him with her own white hands. While she was fetching the water her husband approached the dusty horseman and inquired eagerly for news from the front.

"The Yanks are repairing the railroads," said the man, "and are getting ready for another advance. They have reached the Owl Creek bridge, put it in order

3. Corinth, Mississippi, fell to the Union forces on April 6 and 7, 1862, under General Ulysses S. Grant in the Battle of Shiloh.

and built a stockade on the north bank. The commandant has issued an order, which is posted everywhere, declaring that any civilian caught interfering with the railroad, its bridges, tunnels or trains will be summarily hanged. I saw the order."

"How far is it to the Owl Creek bridge?" Farquhar asked.

"About thirty miles."

"Is there no force on this side the creek?"

"Only a picket post[4] half a mile out, on the railroad, and a single sentinel at this end of the bridge."

"Suppose a man—a civilian and student of hanging—should elude the picket post and perhaps get the better of the sentinel," said Farquhar, smiling, "what could he accomplish?"

The soldier reflected. "I was there a month ago," he replied. "I observed that the flood of last winter had lodged a great quantity of driftwood against the wooden pier at this end of the bridge. It is now dry and would burn like tow."

The lady had now brought the water, which the soldier drank. He thanked her ceremoniously, bowed to her husband and rode away. An hour later, after nightfall, he repassed the plantation, going northward in the direction from which he had come. He was a Federal scout.

III

As Peyton Farquhar fell straight downward through the bridge he lost consciousness and was as one already dead. From this state he was awakened—ages later, it seemed to him—by the pain of a sharp pressure upon his throat, followed by a sense of suffocation. Keen, poignant agonies seemed to shoot from his neck downward through every fibre of his body and limbs. These pains appeared to flash along well-defined lines of ramification and to beat with an inconceivably rapid periodicity. They seemed like streams of pulsating fire heating him to an intolerable temperature. As to his head, he was conscious of nothing but a feeling of fulness—of congestion. These sensations were unaccompanied by thought. The intellectual part of his nature was already effaced; he had power only to feel, and feeling was torment. He was conscious of motion. Encompassed in a luminous cloud, of which he was now merely the fiery heart, without material substance, he swung through unthinkable arcs of oscillation, like a vast pendulum. Then all at once, with terrible suddenness, the light about him shot upward with the noise of a loud plash; a frightful roaring was in his ears, and all was cold and dark. The power of thought was restored; he knew that the rope had broken and he had fallen into the stream. There was no additional strangulation; the noose about his neck was already suffocating him and kept the water from his lungs. To die of hanging at the bottom of a river!—the idea seemed to him ludicrous. He opened his eyes in the darkness and saw above him a gleam of light, but how distant, how inaccessible! He was still sinking, for the light became fainter and fainter until it was a mere glimmer. Then it began to grow and brighten, and he knew that he was rising toward the surface—knew it with reluctance, for he was now very comfortable. "To be hanged and drowned," he thought, "that is not so bad; but I do not wish to be shot. No; I will not be shot; that is not fair."

4. Guard post.

He was not conscious of an effort, but a sharp pain in his wrist apprised him that he was trying to free his hands. He gave the struggle his attention, as an idler might observe the feat of a juggler, without interest in the outcome. What splendid effort!—what magnificent, what superhuman strength! Ah, that was a fine endeavor! Bravo! The cord fell away; his arms parted and floated upward, the hands dimly seen on each side in the growing light. He watched them with a new interest as first one and then the other pounced upon the noose at his neck. They tore it away and thrust it fiercely aside, its undulations resembling those of a water-snake. "Put it back, put it back!" He thought he shouted these words to his hands, for the undoing of the noose had been succeeded by the direst pang that he had yet experienced. His neck ached horribly; his brain was on fire; his heart, which had been fluttering faintly, gave a great leap, trying to force itself out at his mouth. His whole body was racked and wrenched with an insupportable anguish! But his disobedient hands gave no heed to the command. They beat the water vigorously with quick, downward strokes, forcing him to the surface. He felt his head emerge; his eyes were blinded by the sunlight; his chest expanded convulsively, and with a supreme and crowning agony his lungs engulfed a great draught of air, which instantly he expelled in a shriek!

He was now in full possession of his physical senses. They were, indeed, preternaturally keen and alert. Something in the awful disturbance of his organic system had so exalted and refined them that they made record of things never before perceived. He felt the ripples upon his face and heard their separate sounds as they struck. He looked at the forest on the bank of the stream, saw the individual trees, the leaves and the veining of each leaf— saw the very insects upon them: the locusts, the brilliant-bodied flies, the gray spiders stretching their webs from twig to twig. He noted the prismatic colors in all the dewdrops upon a million blades of grass. The humming of the gnats that danced above the eddies of the stream, the beating of the dragon-flies' wings, the strokes of the water-spiders' legs, like oars which had lifted their boat—all these made audible music. A fish slid along beneath his eyes and he heard the rush of its body parting the water.

He had come to the surface facing down the stream; in a moment the visible world seemed to wheel slowly round, himself the pivotal point, and he saw the bridge, the fort, the soldiers upon the bridge, the captain, the sergeant, the two privates, his executioners. They were in silhouette against the blue sky. They shouted and gesticulated, pointing at him. The captain had drawn his pistol, but did not fire; the others were unarmed. Their movements were grotesque and horrible, their forms gigantic.

Suddenly he heard a sharp report and something struck the water smartly within a few inches of his head, spattering his face with spray. He heard a second report, and saw one of the sentinels with his rifle at his shoulder, a light cloud of blue smoke rising from the muzzle. The man in the water saw the eye of the man on the bridge gazing into his own through the sights of the rifle. He observed that it was a gray eye and remembered having read that gray eyes were keenest, and that all famous marksmen had them. Nevertheless, this one had missed.

A counter-swirl had caught Farquhar and turned him half round; he was again looking into the forest on the bank opposite the fort. The sound of a clear, high voice in a monotonous singsong now rang out behind him and came across the water with a distinctness that pierced and subdued all other sounds, even the beating of the ripples in his ears. Although no soldier, he had frequented camps enough to know the dread significance of that deliberate, drawling, aspirated chant; the lieutenant on shore was taking a part in the morning's work. How coldly and pitilessly—with what an even, calm intonation, presaging, and enforcing tranquillity in the men—with what accurately measured intervals fell those cruel words:

"Attention, company! . . . Shoulder arms! . . . Ready! . . . Aim! . . . Fire!"

Farquhar dived—dived as deeply as he could. The water roared in his ears like the voice of Niagara, yet he heard the dulled thunder of the volley and, rising again toward the surface, met shining bits of metal, singularly flattened, oscillating slowly downward. Some of them touched him on the face and hands, then fell away, continuing their descent. One lodged between his collar and neck; it was uncomfortably warm and he snatched it out.

As he rose to the surface, gasping for breath, he saw that he had been a long time under water; he was perceptibly farther down stream—nearer to safety. The soldiers had almost finished reloading; the metal ramrods flashed all at once in the sunshine as they were drawn from the barrels, turned in the air, and thrust into their sockets. The two sentinels fired again, independently and ineffectually.

The hunted man saw all this over his shoulder; he was now swimming vigorously with the current. His brain was as energetic as his arms and legs; he thought with the rapidity of lightning.

"The officer," he reasoned, "will not make that martinet's error a second time. It is as easy to dodge a volley as a single shot. He has probably already given the command to fire at will. God help me, I cannot dodge them all!"

An appalling plash within two yards of him was followed by a loud, rushing sound, *diminuendo*,[5] which seemed to travel back through the air to the fort and died in an explosion which stirred the very river to its deeps! A rising sheet of water curved over him, fell down upon him, blinded him, strangled him! The cannon had taken a hand in the game. As he shook his head free from the commotion of the smitten water he heard the deflected shot humming through the air ahead, and in an instant it was cracking and smashing the branches in the forest beyond.

"They will not do that again," he thought; "the next time they will use a charge of grape.[6] I must keep my eye upon the gun; the smoke will apprise me—the report arrives too late; it lags behind the missile. That is a good gun."

Suddenly he felt himself whirled round and round—spinning like a top. The water, the banks, the forests, the now distant bridge, fort and men—all were commingled and blurred. Objects were represented by their colors only; circular horizontal streaks of color—that was all he saw. He had been caught in a vortex and was being whirled on with a velocity of advance and gyration that made him giddy and sick. In a few moments he was flung upon the gravel at the foot of the left bank of the stream—the southern bank—and behind a projecting point which concealed him from his enemies. The sudden arrest of his motion, the abrasion of one of his hands on the gravel, restored him, and he wept with delight. He dug his fingers into the sand, threw it over himself in handfuls and audibly blessed it. It looked like diamonds, rubies, emeralds; he could think of nothing beautiful which it did not resemble. The trees

5. Diminishing.
6. Grapeshot, a cluster of small iron balls used as a cannon charge.

upon the bank were giant garden plants; he noted a definite order in their arrangement, inhaled the fragrance of their blooms. A strange, roseate light shone through the spaces among their trunks and the wind made in their branches the music of aeolian harps.[7] He had no wish to perfect his escape— was content to remain in that enchanting spot until retaken.

A whiz and rattle of grapeshot among the branches high above his head roused him from his dream. The baffled cannoneer had fired him a random farewell. He sprang to his feet, rushed up the sloping bank, and plunged into the forest.

All that day he traveled, laying his course by the rounding sun. The forest seemed interminable; nowhere did he discover a break in it, not even a wood-man's road. He had not known that he lived in so wild a region. There was something uncanny in the revelation.

By nightfall he was fatigued, footsore, famishing. The thought of his wife and children urged him on. At last he found a road which led him in what he knew to be the right direction. It was as wide and straight as a city street, yet it seemed untraveled. No fields bordered it, no dwelling anywhere. Not so much as the barking of a dog suggested human habitation. The black bodies of the trees formed a straight wall on both sides, terminating on the horizon in a point, like a diagram in a lesson in perspective. Overhead, as he looked up through this rift in the wood, shone great golden stars looking unfamiliar and grouped in strange constellations. He was sure they were arranged in some order which had a secret and malign significance. The wood on either side was full of singular noises, among which—once, twice, and again—he distinctly heard whispers in an unknown tongue.

His neck was in pain and lifting his hand to it he found it horribly swollen. He knew that it had a circle of black where the rope had bruised it. His eyes felt congested; he could no longer close them. His tongue was swollen with thirst; he relieved its fever by thrusting it forward from between his teeth into the cold air. How softly the turf had carpeted the untraveled avenue—he could no longer feel the roadway beneath his feet!

Doubtless, despite his suffering, he had fallen asleep while walking, for now he sees another scene—perhaps he has merely recovered from a delir-ium. He stands at the gate of his own home. All is as he left it, and all bright and beautiful in the morning sunshine. He must have traveled the entire night. As he pushes open the gate and passes up the wide white walk, he sees a flutter of female garments; his wife, looking fresh and cool and sweet, steps down from the veranda to meet him. At the bottom of the steps she stands waiting, with a smile of ineffable joy, an attitude of match less grace and dig-nity. Ah, how beautiful she is! He springs forward with extended arms. As he is about to clasp her he feels a stunning blow upon the back of the neck; a blinding white light blazes all about him with a sound like the shock of a can-non—then all is darkness and silence!

Peyton Farquhar was dead; his body, with a broken neck, swung gently from side to side beneath the timbers of the Owl Creek bridge.

1890, 1891

---

7. Stringed instruments activated by the wind (Aeolus was the keeper of the winds in classical mythology).

BRET HARTE
1836–1902

Francis Bret[t] Harte was born August 25, 1836, in Albany, New York, of English, Dutch, and Jewish descent. His father, Henry, a schoolteacher, died in 1845, and four years later Harte left school to work in a lawyer's office and then in the counting room of a merchant. In 1854 he followed his mother, Elizabeth Rebecca, and his elder sister and brother to Oakland, California, and for a year lived with his mother and stepfather, Colonel Andrew Williams, the first mayor of Oakland. When he turned twenty-one, he left to seek employment further north in California, where he worked for a time for Wells Fargo (he claimed that he "rode shotgun") and also as a miner, teacher, tutor, pharmacist's clerk, and in the printing room of the *Humboldt Times*. From 1858 to 1860 he set type and served as an editorial assistant on the staff of the Uniontown *Northern Californian*. In late February 1860, while the editor-in-chief was out of town, Harte wrote an editorial expressing outrage over the massacre in nearby Eureka of sixty Native Americans, mostly women and children, by a small gang of white vigilantes. After the appearance of the editorial, his life was apparently threatened, and within a month he left for San Francisco.

Harte quickly found a job setting type for *The Golden Era* and soon began contributing poems, stories, and sketches to the paper, many under the pseudonym "The Bohemian." Several of these pieces became part of the collection *"The Luck of Roaring Camp" and Other Sketches* (1870), his best-known book, which Kate Chopin called "the first resounding note" in the development of a distinctive western American literature; in it Harte "reached across the continent and startled the Academists on the Atlantic Coast. . . . They opened their eyes and ears at the sound and awoke to the fact that there might some day be a literary West." Like his fellow westerners Mark Twain, Joaquin Miller, Ambrose Bierce, Ina Coolbrith, and later, Jack London, Harte challenged genteel assumptions about the West and presented a first-hand view of its variety, both romantic and realistic.

Jessie Benton Frémont, daughter of John C. Frémont, a former presidential candidate, befriended Harte and helped him obtain a series of government appointments that culminated in 1863 in his being named secretary to the superintendent in the U.S. Branch Mint in San Francisco, a position that left him free to write nearly full time. Harte's career as a writer was confirmed in 1868 when he became the first editor of the newly established and quickly influential *Overland Monthly*, for which he wrote the works that made him and other western writers famous. In the second issue appeared "The Luck of Roaring Camp," which made him a national celebrity. In this story, as elsewhere, Harte's success rested on his ability to combine features of regional writing—distinctive characters and realistically described settings—with romantic and sentimentalized settings and characters. But perhaps what most distinguishes him from other writers who exploited the myths of the Wild West is an ironic perspective that often went undetected by readers unfamiliar with California, who wished to believe in noble gamblers and prostitutes with hearts of gold. The strange tale "Miggles," for its time quite a challenge to American sexual and gender mores, takes this ironic perspective on the "mystery" of the title character.

Harte focused on character types, such as schoolmarms, stagedrivers, and whores, to give readers a feel for what he called "a heterogeneous and remarkable population" drawn to the Pacific coast by the discovery of gold and remaining there to make their fortunes. There, "men were accepted for what they actually were" and what they could contribute to camp or settlement, and "distinction of previous position or advantages were unknown." If he condescended to these subjects in order to appeal to eastern readers, he also immortalized them. As the critic Gary Scharnhorst has noted, "[I]n his best Western writing Harte challenged the dime-novelized treatment of the frontier. His gamblers may be libertines, but they are also chivalrous; his redshirt miners may be coarse, but they are also charitable; and his fallen women may be 'easy,' but they are also self-sacrificial."

Harte often parodied biblical texts in order to challenge accepted beliefs and ridicule religious hypocrisy. If, as Scharnhorst has also pointed out, "The Luck of Roaring Camp" is a retelling of the gospel story of the Nativity, the Madonna is a mixed-blood prostitute named Cherokee Sal, and her son Tommy (the name of the doubting Apostle) is a false Messiah. The name "Luck" denotes merely chance, not faith; in the end all is swept away by a flood of biblical proportions. "The Luck of Roaring Camp," turns out to be all bad.

Harte, who had married Anna Griswold in 1862, left San Francisco early in 1871 at the height of his fame in hopes that in the East his literary reputation would grow even more. After a journey cross-country that was covered by the daily press, the Hartes were entertained in Boston by the new editor of the *Atlantic Monthly*, William Dean Howells. James T. Fields, who owned the *Atlantic Monthly* and the firm of J. R. Osgood and Company, Harte's publisher, offered Harte the unheard-of sum of ten thousand dollars to write twelve or more poems and sketches to be published in the *Atlantic* and *Every Saturday* during the course of the year. Unfortunately, Harte did not produce much writing in the twelve months following, and his contract was not renewed. At the same time, his drinking was harming his lecturing career, which was already shaky due to performances that some saw as "dandified" and not at all those of a rugged western character. Whenever Harte departed from his standard western stories, he was castigated by critics, and so remained trapped in formula and self-parody. During the winter of 1877–78, his contract with Osgood having ended, Harte became nearly penniless.

The last three decades of Harte's life constitute a decline in his personal and literary fortunes. His novel *Gabriel Conroy* (1876) sold well but was slammed by the critics, and though his two plays, *Two Men of Sandy Bar* (1876) and (with Mark Twain) *Ah Sin* (1877), were produced, neither was successful. Harte was appointed consul to Crefield, Prussia, in 1878 and to Glasgow, Scotland, in 1880, and moved to Europe. But when Grover Cleveland became president in 1885, Harte lost his consulship. Though his American audience waned, Harte's English readers continued to receive his work favorably until his death, from throat cancer, in May 1902.

Harte should be remembered as a literary pioneer for his use of local color, his bringing of California and western subjects to readers in the East, and his encouragement of western writers. He spawned a host of imitators, including Damon Runyon and O. Henry. Like his friend Buffalo Bill Cody, Harte helped create the West as a place of adventure and romance, injecting a characteristic note of gritty realism and irony. On the side of the San Francisco Bohemian Club is a bronze memorial commemorating Harte's life and featuring Cherokee Sal, Colonel Starbottle, and Miggles, among other of his most memorable characters.

The Luck of Roaring Camp[1]

There was commotion in Roaring Camp. It could not have been a fight, for in 1850 that was not novel enough to have called together the entire settlement. The ditches and claims were not only deserted, but "Tuttle's grocery" had contributed its gamblers, who, it will be remembered, calmly continued their game the day that French Pete and Kanaka Joe[2] shot each other to death

1. First appearing in 1868 in *Overland Monthly*, the tale was reprinted by Osgood of Boston in 1870 in *"The Luck of Roaring Camp" and Other Sketches* and by Houghton Mifflin in 1878 in *"The Luck of Roaring Camp" and Other Tales*; the present text is taken from the 1878 revision.
2. Hawai'ian word for adult man, used (nonpejoratively) by both Hawaiians and Americans at the time.

over the bar in the front room. The whole camp was collected before a rude cabin on the outer edge of the clearing. Conversation was carried on in a low tone, but the name of a woman was frequently repeated. It was a name familiar enough in the camp,—"Cherokee Sal."

Perhaps the less said of her the better. She was a coarse and, it is to be feared, a very sinful woman. But at that time she was the only woman in Roaring Camp, and was just then lying in sore extremity, when she most needed the ministration of her own sex. Dissolute, abandoned, and irreclaimable, she was yet suffering a martyrdom hard enough to bear even when veiled by sympathizing womanhood, but now terrible in her loneliness. The primal curse had come to her in that original isolation which must have made the punishment of the first transgression so dreadful. It was, perhaps, part of the expiation of her sin that, at a moment when she most lacked her sex's intuitive tenderness and care, she met only the half-contemptuous faces of her masculine associates. Yet a few of the spectators were, I think, touched by her sufferings. Sandy Tipton thought it was "rough on Sal," and, in the contemplation of her condition, for a moment rose superior to the fact that he had an ace and two bowers[3] in his sleeve.

It will be seen also that the situation was novel. Deaths were by no means uncommon in Roaring Camp, but a birth was a new thing. People had been dismissed the camp effectively, finally, and with no possibility of return; but this was the first time that anybody had been introduced *ab initio*.[4] Hence the excitement.

"You go in there, Stumpy," said a prominent citizen known as "Kentuck," addressing one of the loungers. "Go in there, and see what you kin do. You've had experience in them things."

Perhaps there was a fitness in the selection. Stumpy, in other climes, had been the putative head of two families; in fact, it was owing to some legal informality in these proceedings that Roaring Camp—a city of refuge—was indebted to his company. The crowd approved the choice, and Stumpy was wise enough to bow to the majority. The door closed on the extempore surgeon and midwife, and Roaring Camp sat down outside, smoked its pipe, and awaited the issue.

The assemblage numbered about a hundred men. One or two of these were actual fugitives from justice, some were criminal, and all were reckless. Physically they exhibited no indication of their past lives and character. The greatest scamp had a Raphael[5] face, with a profusion of blonde hair; Oakhurst, a gambler, had the melancholy air and intellectual abstraction of a Hamlet; the coolest and most courageous man was scarcely over five feet in height, with a soft voice and an embarrassed, timid manner. The term "roughs" applied to them was a distinction rather than a definition. Perhaps in the minor details of fingers, toes, ears, etc., the camp may have been deficient, but these slight omissions did not detract from their aggregate force. The strongest man had but three fingers on his right hand; the best shot had but one eye.

Such was the physical aspect of the men that were dispersed around the cabin. The camp lay in a triangular valley between two hills and a river. The only outlet was a steep trail over the summit of a hill that faced the cabin, now illuminated by the rising moon. The suffering woman might have seen it from

3. In the card game euchre, jacks of the trump suit or the other suit of the same color.
4. From the beginning (Latin).

5. Raffaello Sanzio (1483–1520), painter and architect of the Italian High Renaissance, best known for his Madonnas.

the rude bunk whereon she lay,—seen it winding like a silver thread until it was lost in the stars above.

A fire of withered pine boughs added sociability to the gathering. By degrees the natural levity of Roaring Camp returned. Bets were freely offered and taken regarding the result. Three to five that "Sal would get through with it;" even that the child would survive; side bets as to the sex and complexion of the coming stranger. In the midst of an excited discussion an exclamation came from those nearest the door, and the camp stopped to listen. Above the swaying and moaning of the pines, the swift rush of the river, and the crackling of the fire rose a sharp, querulous cry,—a cry unlike anything heard before in the camp. The pines stopped moaning, the river ceased to rush, and the fire to crackle. It seemed as if Nature had stopped to listen too.

The camp rose to its feet as one man! It was proposed to explode a barrel of gunpowder; but in consideration of the situation of the mother, better counsels prevailed, and only a few revolvers were discharged; for whether owing to the rude surgery of the camp, or some other reason, Cherokee Sal was sinking fast. Within an hour she had climbed, as it were, that rugged road that led to the stars, and so passed out of Roaring Camp, its sin and shame, forever. I do not think that the announcement disturbed them much, except in speculation as to the fate of the child. "Can he live now?" was asked of Stumpy. The answer was doubtful. The only other being of Cherokee Sal's sex and maternal condition in the settlement was an ass. There was some conjecture as to fitness, but the experiment was tried. It was less problematical than the ancient treatment of Romulus and Remus,[6] and apparently as successful.

When these details were completed, which exhausted another hour, the door was opened, and the anxious crowd of men, who had already formed themselves into a queue, entered in single file. Beside the low bunk or shelf, on which the figure of the mother was starkly outlined below the blankets, stood a pine table. On this a candle-box was placed, and within it, swathed in staring red flannel, lay the last arrival at Roaring Camp. Beside the candle-box was placed a hat. Its use was soon indicated. "Gentlemen," said Stumpy, with a singular mixture of authority and *ex officio*[7] complacency,—"gentlemen will please pass in at the front door, round the table, and out at the back door. Them as wishes to contribute anything toward the orphan will find a hat handy." The first man entered with his hat on; he uncovered, however, as he looked about him, and so unconsciously set an example to the next. In such communities good and bad actions are catching. As the procession filed in comments were audible,—criticisms addressed perhaps rather to Stumpy in the character of showman: "Is that him?" "Mighty small specimen;" "Hasn't more'n got the color;" "Ain't bigger nor a derringer." The contributions were as characteristic: A silver tobacco box; a doubloon; a navy revolver, silver mounted; a gold specimen; a very beautifully embroidered lady's handkerchief (from Oakhurst the gambler); a diamond breastpin; a diamond ring (suggested by the pin, with the remark from the giver that he "saw that pin

---

6. Twin brothers Romulus and Remus, traditional founders of Rome, were sons of Mars and Rhea, daughter of King Numitor of Alba Longa. When Numitor's brother Amulius deposed him, he made Rhea a Vestal Virgin (and thus forbidden to marry). But when Mars fell in love with her and she bore him the twins, Amulius, fearing they would grow up to overthrow him, left them by the banks of the River Tiber to fend for themselves; they were found by a she-wolf who took pity on them and fed them with her milk.

7. By virtue of one's office, or position (Latin).

and went two diamonds better"); a slung-shot; a Bible (contributor not detected); a golden spur; a silver teaspoon (the initials: I regret to a say, were not the giver's); a pair of surgeon's shears; a lancet;[8] Bank of England note for £5; and about $200 in loose gold and silver coin. During these proceedings Stumpy maintained a silence as impassive as the dead on his left, a gravity as inscrutable as that of the newly born on his right. Only one incident occurred to break the monotony of the curious procession. As Kentuck bent over the candle-box half curiously, the child turned, and, in a spasm of pain, caught at his groping finger, and held it fast for a moment. Kentuck looked foolish and embarrassed. Something like a blush tried to assert itself in his weather-beaten cheek. "The d—d little cuss!" he said, as he extricated his finger, with perhaps more tenderness and care than he might have been deemed capable of showing. He held that finger a little apart from its fellows as he went out, and examined it curiously. The examination provoked the same original remark in regard to the child. In fact, he seemed to enjoy repeating it. "He rastled with my finger," he remarked to Tipton, holding up the member, "the d—d little cuss!"

It was four o'clock before the camp sought repose. A light burnt in the cabin where the watchers sat, for Stumpy did not go to bed that night. Nor did Kentuck. He drank quite freely, and related with great gusto his experience, invariably ending with his characteristic condemnation of the newcomer. It seemed to relieve him of any unjust implication of sentiment, and Kentuck had the weaknesses of the nobler sex. When everybody else had gone to bed, he walked down to the river and whistled reflectingly. Then he walked up the gulch past the cabin, still whistling with demonstrative unconcern. At a large redwood-tree he paused and retraced his steps, and again passed the cabin. Halfway down to the river's bank he again paused, and then returned and knocked at the door. It was opened by Stumpy. "How goes it?" said Kentuck, looking past Stumpy toward the candle-box. "All serene!" replied Stumpy. "Anything up?" "Nothing." There was a pause—an embarrassing one—Stumpy still holding the door. Then Kentuck had recourse to his finger, which he held up to Stumpy. "Rastled with it,—the d—d little cuss," he said, and retired.

The next day Cherokee Sal had such rude sepulture as Roaring Camp afforded. After her body had been committed to the hillside, there was a formal meeting of the camp to discuss what should be done with her infant. A resolution to adopt it was unanimous and enthusiastic. But an animated discussion in regard to the manner and feasibility of providing for its wants at once sprang up. It was remarkable that the argument partook of none of those fierce personalities with which discussions were usually conducted at Roaring Camp. Tipton proposed that they should send the child to Red Dog,—a distance of forty miles,—where female attention could be procured. But the unlucky suggestion met with fierce and unanimous opposition. It was evident that no plan which entailed parting from their new acquisition would for a moment be entertained. "Besides," said Tom Ryder, "them fellows at Red Dog would swap it, and ring in somebody else on us."[9] A disbelief in the honesty of other camps prevailed at Roaring Camp, as in other places.

The introduction of a female nurse in the camp also met with objection. It was argued that no decent woman could be prevailed to accept Roaring Camp

8. A small surgical knife.
9. Tom fears that the men of Red Dog might substitute another baby for theirs.

as her home, and the speaker urged that "they did n't want any more of the other kind." This unkind allusion to the defunct mother, harsh as it may seem, was the first spasm of propriety,—the first symptom of the camp's regeneration. Stumpy advanced nothing. Perhaps he felt a certain delicacy in interfering with the selection of a possible successor in office. But when questioned, he averred stoutly that he and "Jinny"—the mammal before alluded to—could manage to rear the child. There was something original, independent, and heroic about the plan that pleased the camp. Stumpy was retained. Certain articles were sent for to Sacramento. "Mind," said the treasurer, as he pressed a bag of gold-dust into the expressman's hand, "the best that can be got,—lace, you know, and filigree-work and frills,—d—n the cost!"

Strange to say, the child thrived. Perhaps the invigorating climate of the mountain camp was compensation for material deficiencies. Nature took the foundling to her broader breast. In that rare atmosphere of the Sierra foothills,—that air pungent with balsamic odor, that ethereal cordial at once bracing and exhilarating,—he may have found food and nourishment, or a subtle chemistry that transmuted ass's milk to lime and phosphorus.[1] Stumpy inclined to the belief that it was the latter and good nursing. "Me and that ass," he would say, "has been father and mother to him! Don't you," he would add, apostrophizing the helpless bundle before him, "never go back on us."

By the time he was a month old the necessity of giving him a name became apparent. He had generally been known as "The Kid," "Stumpy's Boy," "The Coyote" (an allusion to his vocal powers), and even by Kentuck's endearing diminutive of "The d—d little cuss." But these were felt to be vague and unsatisfactory, and were at last dismissed under another influence. Gamblers and adventurers are generally superstitious, and Oakhurst one day declared that the baby had brought "the luck" to Roaring Camp. It was certain that of late they had been successful. "Luck" was the name agreed upon, with the prefix of Tommy for greater convenience. No allusion was made to the mother, and the father was unknown. "It's better," said the philosophical Oakhurst, "to take a fresh deal all round. Call him Luck, and start him fair." A day was accordingly set apart for the christening. What was meant by this ceremony the reader may imagine who has already gathered some idea of the reckless irreverence of Roaring Camp. The master of ceremonies was one "Boston," a noted wag, and the occasion seemed to promise the greatest facetiousness. This ingenious satirist had spent two days in preparing a burlesque of the Church service, with pointed local allusions. The choir was properly trained, and Sandy Tipton was to stand godfather. But after the procession had marched to the grove with music and banners, and the child had been deposited before a mock altar, Stumpy stepped before the expectant crowd. "It ain't my style to spoil fun, boys," said the little man, stoutly eying the faces around him, "but it strikes me that this thing ain't exactly on the squar. It's playing it pretty low down on this yer baby to ring in fun on him that he ain't goin' to understand. And ef there's goin' to be any godfathers round, I'd like to see who's got any better rights than me." A silence followed Stumpy's speech. To the credit of all humorists be it said that the first man to acknowledge its justice was the satirist thus stopped of his fun. "But," said Stumpy, quickly following up his advantage, "we're here for a christening, and we'll

1. Both lime and phosphorus are used as fertilizer and both are generally white; the suggestion is that the ass's milk would help the child's bones grow strong.

have it. I proclaim you Thomas Luck, according to the laws of the United States and the State of California, so help me God." It was the first time that the name of the Deity had been otherwise uttered than profanely in the camp. The form of christening was perhaps even more ludicrous than the satirist had conceived; but strangely enough, nobody saw it and nobody laughed. "Tommy" was christened as seriously as he would have been under a Christian roof, and cried and was comforted in as orthodox fashion.

And so the work of regeneration began in Roaring Camp. Almost imperceptibly a change came over the settlement. The cabin assigned to "Tommy Luck"—or "The Luck," as he was more frequently called—first showed signs of improvement. It was kept scrupulously clean and whitewashed. Then it was boarded, clothed, and papered. The rosewood cradle, packed eighty miles by mule, had, in Stumpy's way of putting it, "sorter killed the rest of the furniture." So the rehabilitation of the cabin became a necessity. The men who were in the habit of lounging in at Stumpy's to see "how 'The Luck' got on" seemed to appreciate the change, and in self-defense the rival establishment of "Tuttle's grocery" bestirred itself and imported a carpet and mirrors. The reflections of the latter on the appearance of Roaring Camp tended to produce stricter habits of personal cleanliness. Again Stumpy imposed a kind of quarantine upon those who aspired to the honor and privilege of holding The Luck. It was a cruel mortification to Kentuck—who, in the carelessness of a large nature and the habits of frontier life, had begun to regard all garments as a second cuticle, which, like a snake's, only sloughed off through decay—to be debarred this privilege from certain prudential reasons. Yet such was the subtle influence of innovation that he thereafter appeared regularly every afternoon in a clean shirt and face still shining from his ablutions. Nor were moral and social sanitary laws neglected. "Tommy," who was supposed to spend his whole existence in a persistent attempt to repose, must not be disturbed by noise. The shouting and yelling, which had gained the camp its infelicitous title, were not permitted within hearing distance of Stumpy's. The men conversed in whispers or smoked with Indian gravity. Profanity was tacitly given up in these sacred precincts, and throughout the camp a popular form of expletive, known as "D—n the luck!" and "Curse the luck!" was abandoned, as having a new personal bearing. Vocal music was not interdicted, being supposed to have a soothing, tranquilizing quality; and one song, sung by "Man-o'-War Jack," an English sailor from her Majesty's Australian colonies, was quite popular as a lullaby. It was a lugubrious recital of the exploits of "the Arethusa, Seventy-four," in a muffled minor, ending with a prolonged dying fall at the burden of each verse, "On b-oo-o-ard of the Arethusa." It was a fine sight to see Jack holding The Luck, rocking from side to side as if with the motion of a ship, and crooning forth this naval ditty. Either through the peculiar rocking of Jack or the length of his song,—it contained ninety stanzas, and was continued with conscientious deliberation to the bitter end,—the lullaby generally had the desired effect. At such times the men would lie at full length under the trees in the soft summer twilight, smoking their pipes and drinking in the melodious utterances. An indistinct idea that this was pastoral happiness pervaded the camp. "This 'ere kind o' think," said the Cockney Simmons, meditatively reclining on his elbow, "is 'evingly." It reminded him of Greenwich.[2]

2. A town on the Thames River in England, birthplace of Henry VIII and site of the Royal Naval College, venerated by seafarers for its keeping of official, or Greenwich Mean, time.

On the long summer days The Luck was usually carried to the gulch from whence the golden store of Roaring Camp was taken. There, on a blanket spread over pine boughs, he would lie while the men were working in the ditches below. Latterly there was a rude attempt to decorate this bower with flowers and sweet-smelling shrubs, and generally some one would bring him a cluster of wild honeysuckles, azaleas, or the painted blossoms of Las Mariposas. The men had suddenly awakened to the fact that there were beauty and significance in these trifles, which they had so long trodden carelessly beneath their feet. A flake of glittering mica, a fragment of variegated quartz, a bright pebble from the bed of the creek, became beautiful to eyes thus cleared and strengthened, and were invariably put aside for The Luck. It was wonderful how many treasures the woods and hillsides yielded that "would do for Tommy." Surrounded by playthings such as never child out of fairyland had before, it is to be hoped that Tommy was content. He appeared to be serenely happy, albeit there was an infantine gravity about him, a contemplative light in his round gray eyes, that sometimes worried Stumpy. He was always tractable and quiet, and it is recorded that once, having crept beyond his "corral,"—a hedge of tessellated pine boughs, which surrounded his bed,—he dropped over the bank on his head in the soft earth, and remained with his mottled legs in the air in that position for at least five minutes with unflinching gravity. He was extricated without a murmur. I hesitate to record the many other instances of his sagacity, which rest, unfortunately, upon the statements of prejudiced friends. Some of them were not without a tinge of superstition. "I crep' up the bank just now," said Kentuck one day, in a breathless state of excitement, "and dern my skin if he wasn't a-talking to a jaybird as was a-sittin' on his lap. There they was, just as free and sociable as anything you please, a-jawin' at each other just like two cherrybums." Howbeit, whether creeping over the pine boughs or lying lazily on his back blinking at the leaves above him, to him the birds sang, the squirrels chattered, and the flowers bloomed. Nature was his nurse and playfellow. For him she would let slip between the leaves golden shafts of sunlight that fell just within his grasp; she would send wandering breezes to visit him with the balm of bay and resinous gum; to him the tall redwoods nodded familiarly and sleepily, the bumblebees buzzed, and the rooks cawed a slumbrous accompaniment.

Such was the golden summer of Roaring Camp. They were "flush times," and the luck was with them. The claims had yielded enormously. The camp was jealous of its privileges and looked suspiciously on strangers. No encouragement was given to immigration, and, to make their seclusion more perfect, the land on either side of the mountain wall that surrounded the camp they duly preëmpted. This, and a reputation for singular proficiency with the revolver, kept the reserve of Roaring Camp inviolate. The expressman—their only connecting link with the surrounding world—sometimes told wonderful stories of the camp. He would say, "They've a street up there in 'Roaring' that would lay over any street in Red Dog. They've got vines and flowers round their houses, and they wash themselves twice a day. But they're mighty rough on strangers, and they worship an Ingin baby."

With the prosperity of the camp came a desire for further improvement. It was proposed to build a hotel in the following spring, and to invite one or two decent families to reside there for the sake of The Luck, who might perhaps profit by female companionship. The sacrifice that this concession to the sex cost these men, who were fiercely skeptical in regard to its general virtue and usefulness, can only be accounted for by their affection for Tommy. A few still held out. But the resolve could not be carried into effect for three months, and the minority meekly yielded in the hope that something might turn up to prevent it. And it did.

The winter of 1851 will long be remembered in the foothills. The snow lay deep on the Sierras, and every mountain creek became a river, and every river a lake. Each gorge and gulch was transformed into a tumultuous watercourse that descended the hillsides, tearing down giant trees and scattering its drift and débris along the plain. Red Dog had been twice under water, and Roaring Camp had been forewarned. "Water put the gold into them gulches," said Stumpy. "It's been here once and will be here again!" And that night the North Fork suddenly leaped over its banks and swept up the triangular valley of Roaring Camp.

In the confusion of rushing water, crashing trees, and crackling timber, and the darkness which seemed to flow with the water and blot out the fair valley, but little could be done to collect the scattered camp. When the morning broke, the cabin of Stumpy, nearest the river-bank, was gone. Higher up the gulch they found the body of its unlucky owner; but the pride, the hope, the joy, The Luck, of Roaring Camp had disappeared. They were returning with sad hearts when a shout from the bank recalled them.

It was a relief-boat from down the river. They had picked up, they said, a man and an infant, nearly exhausted, about two miles below. Did anybody know them, and did they belong here?

It needed but a glance to show them Kentuck lying there, cruelly crushed and bruised, but still holding The Luck of Roaring Camp in his arms. As they bent over the strangely assorted pair, they saw that the child was cold and pulseless. "He is dead," said one. Kentuck opened his eyes. "Dead?" he repeated feebly. "Yes, my man, and you are dying too." A smile lit the eyes of the expiring Kentuck. "Dying!" he repeated; "he's a-taking me with him. Tell the boys I've got The Luck with me now;" and the strong man, clinging to the frail babe as a drowning man is said to cling to a straw, drifted away into the shadowy river that flows forever to the unknown sea.

1868   1870, 1878

HENRY JAMES
1843–1916

As a young man Henry James set out to be a "literary master" in the European sense. Even though the highly cultivated characters in his fiction ran counter to the vernacular tradition popularized by Mark Twain, James attracted, in his own lifetime, a select company of admirers and made a good living from his writings. His writings, the product of more than half a century as a publishing author, include tales, novellas, novels, plays, autobiographies, criticism, travel pieces, letters, reviews, and biographies—altogether perhaps as many as one hundred volumes, a prodigious output even by late-nineteenth-century standards. The recognition of his importance as well as his wide influence as novelist and critic increased in the years between the world wars, when American literary taste reached a new level of sophistication. Since that time James has been firmly established as one of America's greatest novelists and critics, a subtle psychological realist and an unsurpassed literary stylist and craftsman.

Henry James was born in New York City on April 15, 1843. His father was an eccentric, independently wealthy philosopher and religious visionary; his mother, Mary Robertson Walsh James, had enormous influence on her children—James once said of her, "She was our life, she was the house, she was the keystone of the arch." His slightly older brother, William, was America's first notable psychologist and perhaps its most influential philosopher. There were also two younger brothers and a sister, Alice, herself a perceptive observer and diarist, to complete this remarkable American family. First taken to Europe as an infant, James spent his boyhood in a then almost bucolic Washington Square in New York City before the family once again left for the Continent when he was twelve. His father wanted the children to have a rich, "sensuous education," and during the next four years, with stays in England, Switzerland, and France, they were taken to galleries, libraries, museums, and (of special interest to Henry) theaters. Henry's formal schooling was unsystematic, but he mastered French well enough to begin a lifelong study of its literature, and from childhood on he was aware of the intricate network of institutions and traditions in Europe that he later lamented (in *Hawthorne* [1879], his first book and the first book-length critical study of an American author) American novelists had to do without. Two of his earliest memories were of the Place Vendome in Paris, with its huge monument to Napoleonic grandeur, and the Louvre's Galerie d'Apollon.

James early developed what he described in *A Small Boy and Others* (1913) as the "practice of wondering and dawdling and gaping." This memoir also tells about an "obscure hurt" to his back that, disqualifying him from service in the Civil War, must have reinforced his inclination to observe rather than participate. In his later teens, his interest in literature and in writing intensified, and by the time he was twenty-one he was publishing reviews and stories in some of the leading American journals— *Atlantic Monthly, North American Review, Galaxy,* and *Nation.* He settled permanently in England in 1876 (after much shuttling back and forth between America and Europe and after trial residences in France and Italy). James never married. He maintained close ties with his family, including William's children. He kept up a large correspondence, was extremely sociable, and knew most of his great contemporaries in the arts, many intimately. Still, James lived and worked alone. His emotional life and prodigious creative energy were invested for more than fifty years in what he called the "sacred rage" of his art.

Leon Edel, James's biographer, divides the writer's mature career into three parts. In the first, which culminated with *The Portrait of a Lady* (1881), he felt his way toward and appropriated the so-called international theme—the drama, comic and tragic, of Americans in Europe and occasionally of Europeans in America. In the tripartite second period, he experimented with diverse themes and forms—initially in novels dealing explicitly with the social and political currents of the 1870s and 1880s, then in writing for the theater, and finally in shorter fictions exploring the relationship of artists to society and the troubled psyches of oppressed children, as in *What Maisie Knew* (1908), and haunted or obsessed adults, as in "The Beast in the Jungle" (1903, 1909). Surprisingly, James the bachelor wrote some of the finest characterizations of the child or adolescent mind in American literature. In his last period, the so-called major phase, which culminated with *The Golden Bowl* (1904), he returned to international and cosmopolitan subjects in elaborately complex narratives of great epistemological and moral challenge to readers.

Three of his earliest books, *A Passionate Pilgrim* (stories), *Transatlantic Sketches* (travel pieces), and *Roderick Hudson* (a novel), were published in 1875. *The American* (1877) was his first successful extended treatment of the naïve young American in conflict with the traditions, customs, and values of the Old World. "Daisy Miller"

(1878), with its portrayal of the "new" American girl, brought him widespread popularity. In this "study," as it was originally subtitled, a dangerously naïve American girl willfully resists European (and American) social mores. These works show James as neither a chauvinist for America nor a resentful émigré but a true cosmopolitan concerned with exploring American national character as it is tested by cultural displacement.

Despite their appeal, the relatively simple characters of Christopher Newman (*The American*) and Daisy Miller present romance, melodrama, and pathos more than psychological complexity and genuine tragedy, which required for James a broader canvas. In the character and career of Isabel Archer he found the focus for his first masterpiece of the international theme, *The Portrait of a Lady*. Here, the complex inner lives of his American characters are fully and realistically projected. Yet in "Daisy Miller" these complexities are already hinted at. In this work James's skillful use of the limited point of view, which seems to be largely from Winterbourne's perspective but actually is not, projects a character who is himself limited by self-absorption and class position and who is thus unable to see Daisy for who she is. This device, described by Percy Lubbock as the use of a "focal character" somewhere over the protagonist's left shoulder, became an increasingly important part of James's technique. In these early works James was already developing the hallmarks of his later greatness. He was also beginning to make problems of knowledge, whether characters' knowledge of each other or readers' struggles with deliberately limited information, the central problems of his texts.

From 1885 to 1890 James was largely occupied by writing three novels in the naturalistic mode—*The Bostonians* (1886), *The Princess Casamassima* (1886), and *The Tragic Muse* (1889). These stories of reformers, radicals, and revolutionaries are better appreciated, perhaps, in our time than they were in his. Out of a sense of artistic challenge as well as financial need, James attempted to regain the popularity of "Daisy Miller" and earn money by turning dramatist. Between 1890 and 1895 he wrote seven plays; two were produced, and both were painful public failures for their author, leading him into a period of intense self-doubt. Between 1895 and 1900 he returned to fiction, especially to experimental works with three dominant subjects, which he often combined: misunderstood or troubled writers and artists, ghosts and apparitions, and doomed or threatened children and adolescents. Emotionally close to home, "The Beast in the Jungle" projects the life of an egocentric man whose obsessive concern over the vague prospect of personal disaster destroys his chances for love and life in the present. James's biographers trace the guilt in this tale to the suicide of Constance Fenimore Woolson in 1894, which she may have resorted to partly out of unrequited (and entirely unrecognized) love for James.

Following his own advice to other novelists to "dramatize, dramatize, dramatize," James increasingly removed himself as controlling narrator; in T. S. Eliot's phrase, he became invisible in his work. The benefits of this heightened emphasis on showing rather than telling were compression or intensification and enhanced opportunity for ambiguity. The more the author withdrew—not telling what was said, not analyzing a character's responses—the more the reader was forced to enter the process of creating meaning. Though we are accustomed today to having our fiction thus "objectified," it is James who was largely responsible for the development of this narrative technique. The major works in which he developed such realism were his last three great novels, *The Wings of the Dove* (1902), *The Ambassadors* (1903), and *The Golden Bowl* (1904). All three return to the international theme, but with a new and remorseless insight into how people make their own realities through their perceptions, impressions, and inner motivations. American innocence, at this point, becomes only a willful refusal to see, while awareness of one's own character as well as others' provides the wisdom to escape the designs that lead to disaster—though disaster is rarely thwarted in time and we are usually left both with insight and with the knowledge that it has come "too late." James's remedy for unhappiness is sometimes more unhappiness, but more importantly the willingness to entertain diverse points of view on moral struggles. His treatment of such an extraordinarily complex theme allows him an unparalleled richness of syntax, sentence structure, metaphoric webs, symbols, characterization, point of view, and organizing rhythms. The world of these novels is the one James defined in "The Art of Fiction" (1884) as representing "the very atmosphere of the mind." These late dramas of perception are widely considered to be James's most influential contribution to the craft of fiction.

When James was not writing fiction, he often wrote about it—either his own or others'. He was, as he noted in a letter, "a critical, a *non-naif*, a questioning, worrying reader." If he was somewhat narrow in his reading—restricting himself chiefly to nineteenth-century fiction—he made his limited experience count for as much in criticism as it did in fiction. His inquiries into the achievement of other writers—preserved in such volumes as *French Poets and Novelists* (1878), *Partial Portraits* (1888), and *Notes on Novelists* (1914)—are remarkable for their breadth, balance, and acuteness. More broadly theoretical than his reviews or essays on individual writers, "The Art of Fiction" (an excerpt from which appears later in this volume, fairly represents James's central aesthetic conceptions. Calling attention to the unparalleled opportunities open to the artist of fiction and the beauty of the novel form, James also insists that "the deepest quality of a work of art will always be the quality of the mind of the producer" and that "no good novel will ever proceed from a superficial mind." James left no better record than this essay of his always twinned concerns over the moral and formal qualities of fiction, of the relationship between aesthetic and moral perception.

James was an extremely self-conscious writer, and his *Complete Notebooks*, edited and published in 1987 with an introduction by Leon Edel and Lyall Powers, reveal a subtle, intense mind in the act of discovering subjects, methods, and principles. The prefaces he wrote for Scribner's lavish twenty-four-volume New York Edition (1907–09) of his extensively revised novels and tales, gathered and published in 1934 with an introduction by R. P. Blackmur as *The Art of the Novel*, contain James's final analyses of the works he considered to best represent his achievement—not to mention the extensive revisions themselves. As the culmination of a lifetime of reflection on the craft of fiction, they provide extraordinary accounts of the origins and growth of his major writings and exquisite analyses of the fictional problems each work posed. These prefaces lent both vocabulary and example for the close textual analysis of prose fiction dominant in English departments following World War II.

During his 1904–05 visit to the United States, the first after nearly twenty years, James traveled extensively and lectured in his native land and in Canada. The chief result of this visit was *The American Scene* (1907). This "absolutely personal" book is a vivid account of the profound changes that occurred in America between the Civil War and World War I, the period James characterized as the "Age of the Mistake." His views of turn-of-the-century America seem quite inadequate, however, when he deals with race and immigration in prejudicial terms. The same richness of personal rumination is found in three other autobiographical reminiscences he wrote later in life: *A Small Boy and Others* (1913), *Notes of a Son and Brother* (1914), and the fragmentary and posthumously published *The Middle Years* (1917).

Henry James became a naturalized British subject out of impatience with America's reluctance to enter World War I. He had involved himself in war-relief work starting in 1915. In 1916, he was awarded the British Order of Merit. Despite their considerable difficulty, most of James's novels and tales have remained in print. The rich depth of his work—especially his incisive psychological renderings of *why* people do the things they do—has continued to attract literary scholars and critics, as well as millions of readers around the world.

Daisy Miller: A Study[1]

I

At the little town of Vevey, in Switzerland, there is a particularly comfortable hotel. There are, indeed, many hotels; for the entertainment of tourists is the business of the place, which, as many travelers will remember, is seated upon the edge of a remarkably blue lake[2]—a lake that it behoves every tourist to visit. The shore of the lake presents an unbroken array of establishments of this order, of every category, from the "grand hotel" of the newest fashion, with a chalk-white front, a hundred balconies, and a dozen flags flying from its roof, to the little Swiss *pension* of an elder day, with its name inscribed in German-looking lettering upon a pink or yellow wall, and an awkward summer-house in the angle of the garden. One of the hotels at Vevey, however, is famous, even classical, being distinguished from many of its upstart neighbors by an air both of luxury and of maturity. In this region, in the month of June, American travelers are extremely numerous; it may be said, indeed, that Vevey assumes at this period some of the characteristics of an American watering-place. There are sights and sounds which evoke a vision, an echo, of Newport and Saratoga.[3] There is a flitting hither and thither of "stylish" young girls, a rustling of muslin flounces, a rattle of dance-music in the morning hours, a sound of high-pitched voices at all times. You receive an impression of these things at the excellent inn of the "Trois Couronnes,"[4] and are transported in fancy to the Ocean House or to Congress Hall. But at the "Trois Couronnes," it must be added, there are other features that are much at variance with these suggestions: neat German waiters, who look like secretaries of legation; Russian princesses sitting in the garden; little Polish boys walking about, held by the hand, with their governors; a view of the snowy crest of the Dent du Midi and the picturesque towers of the Castle of Chillon.[5]

I hardly know whether it was the analogies or the differences that were uppermost in the mind of a young American, who, two or three years ago, sat in the garden of the "Trois Couronnes," looking about him, rather idly, at some of the graceful objects I have mentioned. It was a beautiful summer morning, and in whatever fashion the young American looked at things, they must have seemed to him charming. He had come from Geneva the day before, by the little steamer, to see his aunt, who was staying at the hotel— Geneva having been for a long time his place of residence. But his aunt had a headache—his aunt had almost always a headache—and now she was shut up in her room, smelling camphor,[6] so that he was at liberty to wander about. He was some seven-and-twenty years of age; when his friends spoke of him, they usually said that he was at Geneva, "studying." When his enemies spoke of him they said—but, after all, he had no enemies; he was an extremely ami-

1. First published in the *Cornhill Magazine* 37 (June–July 1878). The text reprinted here follows the first British book edition, published by Macmillan in 1879. Punctuation and spelling have been Americanized. The editor was Sir Leslie Stephen, Virginia Woolf's father, an editor willing to take on this then-scandalous story, vilified in America as slandering American womanhood. Of course, the "scandal," once the story was published at home, made for James's rapid fame.
2. Lac Léman, or Lake of Geneva.
3. Newport, Rhode Island, and Saratoga, New

York, resort areas for the rich, where the Ocean House and Congress Hall (below) are located.
4. Three Crowns (French).
5. The romantic setting for Byron's poem "The Prisoner of Chillon" (1816). "Dent du Midi": the highest peak in the Dents du Midi, a mountain group in the Alps in southwest Switzerland.
6. An aromatic substance from the bark and wood of the camphor laurel; made into oils and liniments, it was used as a light topical anesthetic and also administered in small amounts for minor heart symptoms and fatigue.

able fellow, and universally liked. What I should say is, simply, that when certain persons spoke of him they affirmed that the reason of his spending so
much time at Geneva was that he was extremely devoted to a lady who lived
there—a foreign lady—a person older than himself. Very few Americans—
indeed I think none—had ever seen this lady, about whom there were some
singular stories. But Winterbourne had an old attachment for the little
metropolis of Calvinism;[7] he had been put to school there as a boy, and he
had afterwards gone to college there—circumstances which had led to his
forming a great many youthful friendships. Many of these he had kept, and
they were a source of great satisfaction to him.

After knocking at his aunt's door and learning that she was indisposed, he
had taken a walk about the town, and then he had come in to his breakfast.
He had now finished his breakfast, but he was drinking a small cup of coffee,
which had been served to him on a little table in the garden by one of the
waiters who looked like an *attaché*.[8] At last he finished his coffee and lit a cigarette. Presently a small boy came walking along the path—an urchin of nine
or ten. The child, who was diminutive for his years, had an aged expression
of countenance, a pale complexion, and sharp little features. He was dressed
in knickerbockers, with red stockings, which displayed his poor little spindle-
shanks; he also wore a brilliant red cravat. He carried in his hand a long
alpenstock, the sharp point of which he thrust into everything that he
approached—the flower-beds, the garden-benches, the trains of the ladies'
dresses. In front of Winterbourne he paused, looking at him with a pair of
bright, penetrating little eyes.

"Will you give me a lump of sugar?" he asked, in a sharp, hard little voice—
a voice immature, and yet, somehow, not young.

Winterbourne glanced at the small table near him, on which his coffee-
service rested, and saw that several morsels of sugar remained. "Yes, you may
take one," he answered; "but I don't think sugar is good for little boys."

This little boy stepped forward and carefully selected three of the coveted
fragments, two of which he buried in the pocket to his knickerbockers,
depositing the other as promptly in another place. He poked his alpenstock,
lance-fashion, into Winterbourne's bench, and tried to crack the lump of
sugar with his teeth.

"Oh, blazes; it's har-r-d!" he exclaimed, pronouncing the adjective in a
peculiar manner.

Winterbourne had immediately perceived that he might have the honor of
claiming him as a fellow-countryman. "Take care you don't hurt your teeth,"
he said, paternally.

"I haven't got any teeth to hurt. They have all come out. I have only got
seven teeth. My mother counted them last night, and one came out right
afterwards. She said she'd slap me if any more came out. I can't help it. It's
this old Europe. It's the climate that makes them come out. In America they
didn't come out. It's these hotels."

Winterbourne was much amused. "If you eat three lumps of sugar, your
mother will certainly slap you," he said.

"She's got to give me some candy, then," rejoined his young interlocutor. "I
can't get any candy here—any American candy. American candy's the best
candy."

7. Geneva, where John Calvin (1509–1564) cen-   8. I.e., like a member of the diplomatic corps.
tered his Protestant regime.

"And are American little boys the best little boys?" asked Winterbourne.

"I don't know. I'm an American boy," said the child.

"I see you are one of the best!" laughed Winterbourne.

"Are you an American man?" pursued this vivacious infant. And then, on Winterbourne's affirmative reply—"American men are the best," he declared.

His companion thanked him for the compliment; and the child, who had now got astride of his alpenstock, stood looking about him, while he attacked a second lump of sugar. Winterbourne wondered if he himself had been like this in his infancy, for he had been brought to Europe at about this age.

"Here comes my sister!" cried the child, in a moment. "She's an American girl."

Winterbourne looked along the path and saw a beautiful young lady advancing. "American girls are the best girls," he said, cheerfully, to his young companion.

"My sister ain't the best!" the child declared. "She's always blowing at me."

"I imagine that is your fault, not hers," said Winterbourne. The young lady meanwhile had drawn near. She was dressed in white muslin, with a hundred frills and flounces, and knots of pale-colored ribbon. She was bare-headed; but she balanced in her hand a large parasol, with a deep border of embroidery; and she was strikingly, admirably pretty. "How pretty they are!" thought Winterbourne, straightening himself in his seat, as if he were prepared to rise.

The young lady paused in front of his bench, near the parapet of the garden, which overlooked the lake. The little boy had now converted his alpenstock into a vaulting-pole, by the aid of which he was springing about in the gravel, and kicking it up not a little.

"Randolph," said the young lady, "what *are* you doing?"

"I'm going up the Alps," replied Randolph. "This is the way!" And he gave another little jump, scattering the pebbles about Winterbourne's ears.

"That's the way they come down," said Winterbourne.

"He's an American man!" cried Randolph, in his little hard voice.

The young lady gave no heed to this announcement, but looked straight at her brother. "Well, I guess you had better be quiet," she simply observed.

It seemed to Winterbourne that he had been in a manner presented. He got up and stepped slowly towards the young girl, throwing away his cigarette. "This little boy and I have made acquaintance," he said, with great civility. In Geneva, as he had been perfectly aware, a young man was not at liberty to speak to a young unmarried lady except under certain rarely-occurring conditions; but here at Vevey, what conditions could be better than these?—a pretty American girl coming and standing in front of you in a garden. This pretty American girl, however, on hearing Winterbourne's observation, simply glanced at him; she then turned her head and looked over the parapet, at the lake and the opposite mountains. He wondered whether he had gone too far; but he decided that he must advance farther, rather than retreat. While he was thinking of something else to say, the young lady turned to the little boy again.

"I should like to know where you got that pole," she said.

"I bought it!" responded Randolph.

"You don't mean to say you're going to take it to Italy!"

"Yes, I am going to take it to Italy!" the child declared.

The young girl glanced over the front of her dress, and smoothed out a knot or two of ribbon. Then she rested her eyes upon the prospect again. "Well, I guess you had better leave it somewhere," she said, after a moment.

"Are you going to Italy?" Winterbourne inquired, in a tone of great respect.

The young lady glanced at him again.

"Yes, sir," she replied. And she said nothing more.

"Are you—a—going over the Simplon?"[9] Winterbourne pursued, a little embarrassed.

"I don't know," she said, "I suppose it's some mountain. Randolph, what mountain are we going over?"

"Going where?" the child demanded.

"To Italy," Winterbourne explained.

"I don't know," said Randolph. "I don't want to go to Italy. I want to go to America."

"Oh, Italy is a beautiful place!" rejoined the young man.

"Can you get candy there?" Randolph loudly inquired.

"I hope not," said his sister. "I guess you have had enough candy, and mother thinks so too."

"I haven't had any for ever so long—for a hundred weeks!" cried the boy, still jumping about.

The young lady inspected her flounces and smoothed her ribbons again; and Winterbourne presently risked an observation upon the beauty of the view. He was ceasing to be embarrassed, for he had begun to perceive that she was not in the least embarrassed herself. There had not been the slightest alteration in her charming complexion; she was evidently neither offended nor fluttered. If she looked another way when he spoke to her, and seemed not particularly to hear him, this was simply her habit, her manner. Yet, as he talked a little more, and pointed out some of the objects of interest in the view, with which she appeared quite unacquainted, she gradually gave him more of the benefit of her glance; and then he saw that this glance was perfectly direct and unshrinking. It was not, however, what would have been called an immodest glance, for the young girl's eyes were singularly honest and fresh. They were wonderfully pretty eyes; and, indeed, Winterbourne had not seen for a long time anything prettier than his fair countrywoman's various features—her complexion, her nose, her ears, her teeth. He had a great relish for feminine beauty; he was addicted to observing and analyzing it; and as regards this young lady's face he made several observations. It was not at all insipid, but it was not exactly expressive; and though it was eminently delicate, Winterbourne mentally accused it—very forgivingly—of a want of finish. He thought it very possible that Master Randolph's sister was a coquette; he was sure she had a spirit of her own; but in her bright, sweet, superficial little visage there was no mockery, no irony. Before long it became obvious that she was much disposed towards conversation. She told him that they were going to Rome for the winter—she and her mother and Randolph. She asked him if he was a "real American"; she wouldn't have taken him for one; he seemed more like a German—this was said after a little hesitation, especially when he spoke. Winterbourne, laughing, answered that he had met Germans who spoke like Americans; but that he had not, so far as he remembered, met an American who spoke like a German. Then he asked her if she would not be more comfortable in sitting upon the bench which he had just quitted. She answered that she liked standing up and walking about; but she presently sat down. She told him she was from New York State—"if you know

9. A pass in the Alps between Switzerland and Italy.

where that is." Winterbourne learned more about her by catching hold of her small, slippery brother and making him stand a few minutes by his side.

"Tell me your name, my boy," he said.

"Randolph C. Miller," said the boy, sharply. "And I'll tell you her name"; and he leveled his alpenstock at his sister.

"You had better wait till you are asked!" said this young lady, calmly.

"I should like very much to know your name," said Winterbourne.

"Her name is Daisy Miller!" cried the child. "But that isn't her real name; that isn't her name on her cards."

"It's a pity you haven't got one of my cards!" said Miss Miller.

"Her real name is Annie P. Miller," the boy went on.

"Ask him *his* name," said his sister, indicating Winterbourne.

But on this point Randolph seemed perfectly indifferent; he continued to supply information with regard to his own family. "My father's name is Ezra B. Miller," he announced. "My father ain't in Europe; my father's in a better place than Europe."

Winterbourne imagined for a moment that this was the manner in which the child had been taught to intimate that Mr. Miller had been removed to the sphere of celestial rewards. But Randolph immediately added, "My father's in Schenectady. He's got a big business. My father's rich, you bet."

"Well!" ejaculated Miss Miller, lowering her parasol and looking at the embroidered border. Winterbourne presently released the child, who departed, dragging his alpenstock along the path. "He doesn't like Europe," said the young girl. "He wants to go back."

"To Schenectady, you mean?"

"Yes; he wants to go right home. He hasn't got any boys here. There is one boy here, but he always goes round with a teacher; they won't let him play."

"And your brother hasn't any teacher?" Winterbourne inquired.

"Mother thought of getting him one, to travel round with us. There was a lady told her of a very good teacher; an American lady—perhaps you know her—Mrs. Sanders. I think she came from Boston. She told her of this teacher, and we thought of getting him to travel round with us. But Randolph said he didn't want a teacher traveling round with us. He said he wouldn't have lessons when he was in the cars.[1] And we *are* in the cars about half the time. There was an English lady we met in the cars—I think her name was Miss Featherstone; perhaps you know her. She wanted to know why I didn't give Randolph lessons—give him 'instruction,' she called it. I guess he could give me more instruction than I could give him. He's very smart."

"Yes," said Winterbourne; "he seems very smart."

"Mother's going to get a teacher for him as soon as we get to Italy. Can you get good teachers in Italy?"

"Very good, I should think," said Winterbourne.

"Or else she's going to find some school. He ought to learn some more. He's only nine. He's going to college." And in this way Miss Miller continued to converse upon the affairs of her family, and upon other topics. She sat there with her extremely pretty hands, ornamented with very brilliant rings, folded in her lap, and with her pretty eyes now resting upon those of Winterbourne, now wandering over the garden, the people who passed by, and the beautiful view. She talked to Winterbourne as if she had known him a long time. He

---

1. Railway cars.

found it very pleasant. It was many years since he heard a young girl talk so much. It might have been said of this unknown young lady, who had come and sat down beside him upon a bench, that she chattered. She was very quiet, she sat in a charming tranquil attitude; but her lips and her eyes were constantly moving. She had a soft, slender, agreeable voice, and her tone was decidedly sociable. She gave Winterbourne a history of her movements and intentions, and those of her mother and brother, in Europe, and enumerated, in particular, the various hotels at which they had stopped. "That English lady in the cars," she said—"Miss Featherstone—asked me if we didn't all live in hotels in America. I told her I had never been in so many hotels in my life as since I came to Europe. I have never seen so many—it's nothing but hotels." But Miss Miller did not make this remark with a querulous accent; she appeared to be in the best humor with everything. She declared that the hotels were very good, when once you got used to their ways, and that Europe was perfectly sweet. She was not disappointed—not a bit. Perhaps it was because she had heard so much about it before. She had ever so many intimate friends that had been there ever so many times. And then she had had ever so many dresses and things from Paris. Whenever she put on a Paris dress she felt as if she were in Europe.

"It was a kind of wishing-cap," said Winterbourne.

"Yes," said Miss Miller, without examining this analogy; "it always made me wish I was here. But I needn't have done that for dresses. I am sure they send all the pretty ones to America; you see the most frightful things here. The only thing I don't like," she proceeded, "is the society. There isn't any society; or, if there is, I don't know where it keeps itself. Do you? I suppose there is some society somewhere, but I haven't seen anything of it. I'm very fond of society, and I have always had a great deal of it. I don't mean only in Schenectady, but in New York. I used to go to New York every winter. In New York I had lots of society. Last winter I had seventeen dinners given me; and three of them were by gentlemen," added Daisy Miller. "I have more friends in New York than in Schenectady—more gentlemen friends; and more young lady friends too," she resumed in a moment. She paused again for an instant; she was looking at Winterbourne with all her prettiness in her lively eyes and in her light, slightly monotonous smile. "I have always had," she said, "a great deal of gentlemen's society."

Poor Winterbourne was amused, perplexed, and decidedly charmed. He had never yet heard a young girl express herself in just this fashion; never, at least, save in cases where to say such things seemed a kind of demonstrative evidence of a certain laxity of deportment. And yet was he to accuse Miss Daisy Miller of actual or potential *inconduite*,[2] as they said at Geneva? He felt that he had lived at Geneva so long that he had lost a good deal; he had become dishabituated to the American tone. Never, indeed, since he had grown old enough to appreciate things, had he encountered a young American girl of so pronounced a type as this. Certainly she was very charming; but how deucedly sociable! Was she simply a pretty girl from New York State— were they all like that, the pretty girls who had a good deal of gentlemen's society? Or was she also a designing, an audacious, an unscrupulous young person? Winterbourne had lost his instinct in this matter, and his reason

2. Misconduct (French).

could not help him. Miss Daisy Miller looked extremely innocent. Some people had told him that, after all, American girls were exceedingly innocent; and others had told him that, after all, they were not. He was inclined to think Miss Daisy Miller was a flirt—a pretty American flirt. He had never, as yet, had any relations with young ladies of this category. He had known, here in Europe, two or three women—persons older than Miss Daisy Miller, and provided, for respectability's sake, with husbands—who were great coquettes—dangerous, terrible women, with whom one's relations were liable to take a serious turn. But this young girl was not a coquette in that sense; she was very unsophisticated; she was only a pretty American flirt. Winterbourne was almost grateful for having found the formula that applied to Miss Daisy Miller. He leaned back in his seat; he remarked to himself that she had the most charming nose he had ever seen; he wondered what were the regular conditions and limitations of one's intercourse with a pretty American flirt. It presently became apparent that he was on the way to learn.

"Have you been to that old castle?" asked the young girl, pointing with her parasol to the far-gleaming walls of the Château de Chillon.

"Yes, formerly, more than once," said Winterbourne. "You too, I suppose, have seen it?"

"No; we haven't been there. I want to go there dreadfully. Of course I mean to go there. I wouldn't go away from here without having seen that old castle."

"It's a very pretty excursion," said Winterbourne, "and very easy to make. You can drive, you know, or you can go by the little steamer."

"You can go in the cars," said Miss Miller.

"Yes; you can go in the cars," Winterbourne assented.

"Our courier[3] says they take you right up to the castle," the young girl continued. "We were going last week; but my mother gave out. She suffers dreadfully from dyspepsia. She said she couldn't go. Randolph wouldn't go either; he says he doesn't think much of old castles. But I guess we'll go this week, if we can get Randolph."

"Your brother is not interested in ancient monuments?" Winterbourne inquired, smiling.

"He says he don't care much about old castles. He's only nine. He wants to stay at the hotel. Mother's afraid to leave him alone, and the courier won't stay with him; so we haven't been to many places. But it will be too bad if we don't go up there." And Miss Miller pointed again at the Château de Chillon.

"I should think it might be arranged," said Winterbourne. "Couldn't you get some one to stay—for the afternoon—with Randolph?"

Miss Miller looked at him a moment; and then, very placidly—"I wish *you* would stay with him!" she said.

Winterbourne hesitated a moment. "I would much rather go to Chillon with you."

"With me?" asked the young girl, with the same placidity.

She didn't rise, blushing, as a young girl at Geneva would have done; and yet Winterbourne, conscious that he had been very bold, thought it possible she was offended. "With your mother," he answered very respectfully.

But it seemed that both his audacity and his respect were lost upon Miss

3. Social guide.

Daisy Miller. "I guess my mother won't go, after all," she said. "She don't like to ride round in the afternoon. But did you really mean what you said just now; that you would like to go up there?"

"Most earnestly," Winterbourne declared.

"Then we may arrange it. If mother will stay with Randolph, I guess Eugenio will."

"Eugenio?" the young man inquired.

"Eugenio's our courier. He doesn't like to stay with Randolph; he's the most fastidious man I ever saw. But he's a splendid courier. I guess he'll stay at home with Randolph if mother does, and then we can go to the castle."

Winterbourne reflected for an instant as lucidly as possible—"we" could only mean Miss Daisy Miller and himself. This programme seemed almost too agreeable for credence; he felt as if he ought to kiss the young lady's hand. Possibly he would have done so—and quite spoiled the project; but at this moment another person—presumably Eugenio—appeared. A tall, handsome man, with superb whiskers, wearing a velvet morning-coat and a brilliant watch-chain, approached Miss Miller, looking sharply at her companion. "Oh, Eugenio!" said Miss Miller, with the friendliest accent.

Eugenio had looked at Winterbourne from head to foot; he now bowed gravely to the young lady. "I have the honor to inform mademoiselle that luncheon is upon the table."

Miss Miller slowly rose. "See here, Eugenio," she said. "I'm going to that old castle, any way."

"To the Château de Chillon, mademoiselle?" the courier inquired. "Mademoiselle had made arrangements?" he added, in a tone which struck Winterbourne as very impertinent.

Eugenio's tone apparently threw, even to Miss Miller's own apprehension, a slightly ironical light upon the young girl's situation. She turned to Winterbourne, blushing a little—a very little. "You won't back out?" she said.

"I shall not be happy till we go!" he protested.

"And you are staying in this hotel?" she went on. "And you are really an American?"

The courier stood looking at Winterbourne, offensively. The young man, at least, thought his manner of looking an offence to Miss Miller; it conveyed an imputation that she "picked up" acquaintances. "I shall have the honor of presenting to you a person who will tell you all about me," he said smiling, and referring to his aunt.

"Oh well, we'll go some day," said Miss Miller. And she gave him a smile and turned away. She put up her parasol and walked back to the inn beside Eugenio. Winterbourne stood looking after her; and as she moved away, drawing her muslin furbelows over the gravel, said to himself that she had the *tournure*[4] of a princess.

II

He had, however, engaged to do more than proved feasible, in promising to present his aunt, Mrs. Costello, to Miss Daisy Miller. As soon as the former lady had got better of her headache he waited upon her in her apartment; and, after the proper inquiries in regard to her health, he asked her if she had observed, in the hotel, an American family—a mamma, a daughter, and a little boy.

4. Grace, poise, expression (French).

"And a courier?" said Mrs. Costello. "Oh, yes, I have observed them. Seen them—heard them—and kept out of their way." Mrs. Costello was a widow with a fortune; a person of much distinction, who frequently intimated that, if she were not so dreadfully liable to sick-headaches, she would probably have left a deeper impress upon her time. She had a long pale face, a high nose, and a great deal of very striking white hair, which she wore in large puffs and *rouleaux*[5] over the top of her head. She had two sons married in New York, and another who was now in Europe. This young man was amusing himself at Homburg,[6] and, though he was on his travels, was rarely perceived to visit any particular city at the moment selected by his mother for her own appearance there. Her nephew, who had come up to Vevey expressly to see her, was therefore more attentive than those who, as she said, were nearer to her. He had imbibed at Geneva the idea that one must always be attentive to one's aunt. Mrs. Costello had not seen him for many years, and she was greatly pleased with him, manifesting her approbation by initiating him into many of the secrets of that social sway which, as she gave him to understand, she exerted in the American capital. She admitted that she was very exclusive; but, if he were acquainted with New York, he would see that one had to be. And her picture of the minutely hierarchical constitution of the society of that city, which she presented to him in many different lights, was, to Winterbourne's imagination, almost oppressively striking.

He immediately perceived, from her tone, that Miss Daisy Miller's place in the social scale was low. "I am afraid you don't approve of them," he said.

"They are very common," Mrs. Costello declared. "They are the sort of Americans that one does one's duty by not—not accepting."

"Ah, you don't accept them?" said the young man.

"I can't, my dear Frederick. I would if I could, but I can't."

"The young girl is very pretty," said Winterbourne, in a moment.

"Of course she's pretty. But she is very common."

"I see what you mean, of course," said Winterbourne, after another pause.

"She has that charming look that they all have," his aunt resumed. "I can't think where they pick it up; and she dresses in perfection—no, you don't know how well she dresses. I can't think where they get their taste."

"But, my dear aunt, she is not, after all, a Comanche savage."

"She is a young lady," said Mrs. Costello, "who has an intimacy with her mamma's courier?"

"An intimacy with the courier?" the young man demanded.

"Oh, the mother is just as bad! They treat the courier like a familiar friend—like a gentleman. I shouldn't wonder if he dines with them. Very likely they have never seen a man with such good manners, such fine clothes, so like a gentleman. He probably corresponds to the young lady's idea of a Count. He sits with them in the garden, in the evening. I think he smokes."

Winterbourne listened with interest to these disclosures; they helped him to make up his mind about Miss Daisy. Evidently she was rather wild. "Well," he said, "I am not a courier, and yet she was very charming to me."

"You had better have said at first," said Mrs. Costello with dignity, "that you had made her acquaintance."

"We simply met in the garden, and we talked a bit."

"*Tout bonnement!*[7] And pray what did you say?"

---

5. Small rolls, especially of coins wrapped in paper, but in this case of hair.

6. A resort in Germany.

7. Quite simply the best! (French).

"I said I should take the liberty of introducing her to my admirable aunt."

"I am much obliged to you."

"It was to guarantee my respectability," said Winterbourne.

"And pray who is to guarantee hers?"

"Ah, you are cruel!" said the young man. "She's a very nice girl."

"You don't say that as if you believed it," Mrs. Costello observed.

"She is completely uncultivated," Winterbourne went on. "But she is wonderfully pretty, and, in short, she is very nice. To prove that I believe it, I am going to take her to the Château de Chillon."

"You two are going off there together? I should say it proved just the contrary. How long had you known her, may I ask, when this interesting project was formed. You haven't been twenty-four hours in the house."

"I had known her half-an-hour!" said Winterbourne, smiling.

"Dear me!" cried Mrs. Costello. "What a dreadful girl!"

Her nephew was silent for some moments.

"You really think, then," he began earnestly, and with a desire for trustworthy information—"you really think that—" But he paused again.

"Think what, sir," said his aunt.

"That she is the sort of young lady who expects a man—sooner or later—to carry her off?"

"I haven't the least idea what such young ladies expect a man to do. But I really think that you had better not meddle with little American girls that are uncultivated, as you call them. You have lived too long out of the country. You will be sure to make some great mistake. You are too innocent."

"My dear aunt, I am not so innocent," said Winterbourne, smiling and curling his moustache.

"You are too guilty, then?"

Winterbourne continued to curl his moustache, meditatively. "You won't let the poor girl know you then?" he asked at last.

"Is it literally true that she is going to the Château de Chillon with you?"

"I think that she fully intends it."

"Then, my dear Frederick," said Mrs. Costello, "I must decline the honor of her acquaintance. I am an old woman, but I am not too old—thank Heaven—to be shocked!"

"But don't they all do these things—the young girls in America?" Winterbourne inquired.

Mrs. Costello stared a moment. "I should like to see my granddaughters do them!" she declared, grimly.

This seemed to throw some light upon the matter, for Winterbourne remembered to have heard that his pretty cousins in New York were "tremendous flirts." If, therefore, Miss Daisy Miller exceeded the liberal license allowed to these young ladies, it was probable that anything might be expected of her. Winterbourne was impatient to see her again, and he was vexed with himself that, by instinct, he should not appreciate her justly.

Though he was impatient to see her, he hardly knew what he should say to her about his aunt's refusal to become acquainted with her; but he discovered, promptly enough, that with Miss Daisy Miller there was no great need of walking on tiptoe. He found her that evening in the garden, wandering about in the warm starlight, like an indolent sylph, and swinging to and fro the largest fan he had ever beheld. It was ten o'clock. He had dined with his aunt, had been sitting with her since dinner, and had just taken leave of her till the morrow. Miss Daisy Miller seemed very glad to see him; she declared it was the longest evening she had ever passed.

"Have you been all alone?" he asked.

"I have been walking round with mother. But mother gets tired walking round," she answered.

"Has she gone to bed?"

"No; she doesn't like to go to bed," said the young girl. "She doesn't sleep—not three hours. She says she doesn't know how she lives. She's dreadfully nervous. I guess she sleeps more than she thinks. She's gone somewhere after Randolph; she wants to try to get him to go to bed. He doesn't like to go to bed."

"Let us hope she will persuade him," observed Winterbourne.

"She will talk to him all she can; but he doesn't like her to talk to him," said Miss Daisy, opening her fan. "She's going to try to get Eugenio to talk to him. But he isn't afraid of Eugenio. Eugenio's a splendid courier, but he can't make much impression on Randolph! I don't believe he'll go to bed before eleven." It appeared that Randolph's vigil was in fact triumphantly prolonged, for Winterbourne strolled about with the young girl for some time without meeting her mother. "I have been looking round for that lady you want to introduce me to," his companion resumed. "She's your aunt." Then, on Winterbourne's admitting the fact, and expressing some curiosity as to how she had learned it, she said she had heard all about Mrs. Costello from the chambermaid. She was very quiet and very *comme il faut*; she wore white puffs; she spoke to no one, and she never dined at the *table d'hôte*.[8] Every two days she had a headache. "I think that's a lovely description, headache and all!" said Miss Daisy, chattering along in her thin, gay voice. "I want to know her ever so much. I know just what *your* aunt would be; I know I should like her. She would be very exclusive. I like a lady to be exclusive; I'm dying to be exclusive myself. Well, we *are* exclusive, mother and I. We don't speak to every one—or they don't speak to us. I suppose it's about the same thing. Any way, I shall be ever so glad to know your aunt."

Winterbourne was embarrassed. "She would be most happy," he said, "but I am afraid those headaches will interfere."

The young girl looked at him through the dusk. "But I suppose she doesn't have a headache every day," she said, sympathetically.

Winterbourne was silent a moment. "She tells me she does," he answered at last—not knowing what to say.

Miss Daisy Miller stopped and stood looking at him. Her prettiness was still visible in the darkness; she was opening and closing her enormous fan. "She doesn't want to know me!" she said suddenly. "Why don't you say so? You needn't be afraid. I'm not afraid!" And she gave a little laugh.

Winterbourne fancied there was a tremor in her voice; he was touched, shocked, mortified by it. "My dear young lady," he protested, "she knows no one. It's her wretched health."

The young girl walked on a few steps, laughing still. "You needn't be afraid," she repeated. "Why should she want to know me?" Then she paused again; she was close to the parapet of the garden, and in front of her was the starlit lake. There was a vague sheen upon its surface, and in the distance were dimly-seen mountain forms. Daisy Miller looked out upon the mysterious

8. A common table for guests in a restaurant or hotel (French). "*Comme il faut*": well mannered (French).

prospect, and then she gave another little laugh. "Gracious! she *is* exclusive!" she said. Winterbourne wondered whether she was seriously wounded, and for a moment almost wished that her sense of injury might be such as to make it becoming in him to attempt to reassure and comfort her. He had a pleasant sense that she would be very approachable for consolatory purposes. He felt then, for the instant, quite ready to sacrifice his aunt, conversationally; to admit that she was a proud, rude woman, and to declare that they needn't mind her. But before he had time to commit himself to this perilous mixture of gallantry and impiety, the young lady, resuming her walk, gave an exclamation in quite another tone. "Well; here's mother! I guess she hasn't got Randolph to go to bed." The figure of a lady appeared, at a distance, very indistinct in the darkness, and advancing with a slow and wavering movement. Suddenly it seemed to pause.

"Are you sure it is your mother? Can you distinguish her in this thick dusk?" Winterbourne asked.

"Well!" cried Miss Daisy Miller, with a laugh, "I guess I know my own mother. And when she has got on my shawl, too! She is always wearing my things."

The lady in question, ceasing to advance, hovered vaguely about the spot at which she had checked her steps.

"I am afraid your mother doesn't see you," said Winterbourne. "Or perhaps," he added—thinking, with Miss Miller, the joke permissible—"perhaps she feels guilty about your shawl."

"Oh, it's a fearful old thing!" the young girl replied, serenely. "I told her she could wear it. She won't come here, because she sees you."

"Ah, then," said Winterbourne, "I had better leave you."

"Oh, no; come on!" urged Miss Daisy Miller.

"I'm afraid your mother doesn't approve of my walking with you."

Miss Miller gave him a serious glance. "It isn't for me; it's for you—that is, it's for *her*. Well; I don't know who it's for! But mother doesn't like any of my gentlemen friends. She's right down timid. She always makes a fuss if I introduce a gentleman. But I *do* introduce them—almost always. If I didn't introduce my gentlemen friends to mother," the young girl added, in her little soft, flat monotone, "I shouldn't think I was natural."

"To introduce me," said Winterbourne, "you must know my name." And he proceeded to pronounce it.

"Oh, dear; I can't say all that!" said his companion, with a laugh. But by this time they had come up to Mrs. Miller, who, as they drew near, walked to the parapet of the garden and leaned upon it, looking intently at the lake and turning her back upon them. "Mother!" said the young girl, in a tone of decision. Upon this the elderly lady turned round. "Mr. Winterbourne," said Miss Daisy Miller, introducing the young man very frankly and prettily. "Common" she was, as Mrs. Costello had pronounced her; yet it was a wonder to Winterbourne that, with her commonness, she had a singularly delicate grace.

Her mother was a small, spare, light person, with a wandering eye, a very exiguous nose, and a large forehead, decorated with a certain amount of thin, much-frizzled hair. Like her daughter, Mrs. Miller was dressed with extreme elegance; she had enormous diamonds in her ears. So far as Winterbourne could observe, she gave him no greeting—she certainly was not looking at him. Daisy was near her, pulling her shawl straight. "What are you doing, poking round here?" this young lady inquired; but by no means with that harshness of accent which her choice of words may imply.

"I don't know," said her mother, turning towards the lake again.

"I shouldn't think you'd want that shawl!" Daisy exclaimed.

"Well—I do!" her mother answered, with a little laugh.

"Did you get Randolph to go to bed?" asked the young girl.

"No; I couldn't induce him," said Mrs. Miller, very gently. "He wants to talk to the waiter. He likes to talk to that waiter."

"I was telling Mr. Winterbourne," the young girl went on; and to the young man's ear her tone might have indicated that she had been uttering his name all her life.

"Oh, yes!" said Winterbourne; "I have the pleasure of knowing your son."

Randolph's mamma was silent; she turned her attention to the lake. But at last she spoke. "Well, I don't see how he lives!"

"Anyhow, it isn't so bad as it was at Dover," said Daisy Miller.

"And what occurred at Dover?" Winterbourne asked.

"He wouldn't go to bed at all. I guess he sat up all night—in the public parlour. He wasn't in bed at twelve o'clock: I know that."

"It was half-past twelve," declared Mrs. Miller, with mild emphasis.

"Does he sleep much during the day?" Winterbourne demanded.

"I guess he doesn't sleep much," Daisy rejoined.

"I wish he would!" said her mother. "It seems as if he couldn't."

"I think he's real tiresome," Daisy pursued.

Then, for some moments, there was silence. "Well, Daisy Miller," said the elder lady, presently, "I shouldn't think you'd want to talk against your own brother!"

"Well, he is tiresome, mother," said Daisy, quite without the asperity of a retort.

"He's only nine," urged Mrs. Miller.

"Well, he wouldn't go to that castle," said the young girl. "I'm going there with Mr. Winterbourne."

To this announcement, very placidly made, Daisy's mamma offered no response. Winterbourne took for granted that she deeply disapproved of the projected excursion; but he said to himself that she was a simple, easily managed person, and that a few deferential protestations would take the edge from her displeasure. "Yes," he began; "your daughter has kindly allowed me the honor of being her guide."

Mrs. Miller's wandering eyes attached themselves, with a sort of appealing air, to Daisy, who, however, strolled a few steps farther, gently humming to herself. "I presume you will go in the cars," said her mother.

"Yes; or in the boat," said Winterbourne.

"Well, of course, I don't know," Mrs. Miller rejoined. "I have never been to that castle."

"It is a pity you shouldn't go," said Winterbourne, beginning to feel reassured as to her opposition. And yet he was quite prepared to find that, as a matter of course, she meant to accompany her daughter.

"We've been thinking ever so much about going," she pursued; "but it seems as if we couldn't. Of course Daisy—she wants to go round. But there's a lady here—I don't know her name—she says she shouldn't think we'd want to go to see castles here; she should think we'd want to wait till we got to Italy. It seems as if there would be so many there," continued Mrs. Miller, with an air of increasing confidence. "Of course, we only want to see the principal ones. We visited several in England," she presently added.

"Ah, yes! in England there are beautiful castles," said Winterbourne. "But Chillon, here, is very well worth seeing."

"Well, if Daisy feels up to it—," said Mrs. Miller, in a tone impregnated with a sense of the magnitude of the enterprise. "It seems as if there was nothing she wouldn't undertake."

"Oh, I think she'll enjoy it!" Winterbourne declared. And he desired more and more to make it a certainty that he was to have the privilege of a *tête-à-tête* with the young lady, who was still strolling along in front of them, softly vocalizing. "You are not disposed, madam," he inquired, "to undertake it yourself?"

Daisy's mother looked at him, an instant, askance, and then walked forward in silence. Then—"I guess she had better go alone," she said, simply.

Winterbourne observed to himself that this was a very different type of maternity from that of the vigilant matrons who massed themselves in the forefront of social intercourse in the dark old city at the other end of the lake. But his meditations were interrupted by hearing his name very distinctly pronounced by Mrs. Miller's unprotected daughter.

"Mr. Winterbourne!" murmured Daisy.

"Mademoiselle!" said the young man.

"Don't you want to take me out in a boat?"

"At present?" he asked.

"Of course!" said Daisy.

"Well, Annie Miller!" exclaimed her mother.

"I beg you, madam, to let her go," said Winterbourne, ardently; for he had never yet enjoyed the sensation of guiding through the summer starlight a skiff freighted with a fresh and beautiful young girl.

"I shouldn't think she'd want to," said her mother. "I should think she'd rather go indoors."

"I'm sure Mr. Winterbourne wants to take me," Daisy declared. "He's so awfully devoted!"

"I will row you over to Chillon, in the starlight."

"I don't believe it!" said Daisy.

"Well!" ejaculated the elderly lady again.

"You haven't spoken to me for half-an-hour," her daughter went on.

"I have been having some very pleasant conversation with your mother," said Winterbourne.

"Well; I want you to take me out in a boat!" Daisy repeated. They had all stopped, and she had turned round and was looking at Winterbourne. Her face wore a charming smile, her pretty eyes were gleaming, she was swinging her great fan about. No; it's impossible to be prettier than that, thought Winterbourne.

"There are half-a-dozen boats moored at that landing-place," he said, pointing to certain steps which descended from the garden to the lake. "If you will do me the honor to accept my arm, we will go and select one of them."

Daisy stood there smiling; she threw back her head and gave a little light laugh. "I like a gentleman to be formal!" she declared.

"I assure you it's a formal offer."

"I was bound I would make you say something," Daisy went on.

"You see it's not very difficult," said Winterbourne. "But I am afraid you are chaffing me."

"I think not, sir," remarked Mrs. Miller, very gently.

"Do, then, let me give you a row," he said to the young girl.

"It's quite lovely, the way you say that!" said Daisy.

"It will be still more lovely to do it."

"Yes, it would be lovely!" said Daisy. But she made no movement to accompany him; she only stood there laughing.

"I should think you had better find out what time it is," interposed her mother.

"It is eleven o'clock, madam," said a voice, with a foreign accent, out of the neighboring darkness; and Winterbourne, turning, perceived the florid personage who was in attendance upon the two ladies. He had apparently just approached.

"Oh, Eugenio," said Daisy, "I am going out in a boat!"

Eugenio bowed. "At eleven o'clock, mademoiselle?"

"I am going with Mr. Winterbourne. This very minute."

"Do tell her she can't," said Mrs. Miller to the courier.

"I think you had better not go out in a boat, mademoiselle," Eugenio declared.

Winterbourne wished to Heaven this pretty girl were not so familiar with her courier; but he said nothing.

"I suppose you don't think it's proper!" Daisy exclaimed, "Eugenio doesn't think anything's proper."

"I am at your service," said Winterbourne.

"Does mademoiselle propose to go alone?" asked Eugenio of Mrs. Miller.

"Oh, no; with this gentleman!" answered Daisy's mamma.

The courier looked for a moment at Winterbourne—the latter thought he was smiling—and then, solemnly, with a bow, "As mademoiselle pleases!" he said.

"Oh, I hoped you would make a fuss!" said Daisy. "I don't care to go now."

"I myself shall make a fuss if you don't go," said Winterbourne.

"That's all I want—a little fuss!" And the young girl began to laugh again.

"Mr. Randolph has gone to bed!" the courier announced, frigidly.

"Oh, Daisy; now we can go!" said Mrs. Miller.

Daisy turned away from Winterbourne, looking at him, smiling and fanning herself. "Good night," she said; "I hope you are disappointed, or disgusted, or something!"

He looked at her, taking the hand she offered him. "I am puzzled," he answered.

"Well; I hope it won't keep you awake!" she said, very smartly; and, under the escort of the privileged Eugenio, the two ladies passed towards the house.

Winterbourne stood looking after them; he was indeed puzzled. He lingered beside the lake for a quarter of an hour, turning over the mystery of the young girl's sudden familiarities and caprices. But the only very definite conclusion he came to was that he should enjoy deucedly "going off" with her somewhere.

Two days afterwards he went off with her to the Castle of Chillon. He waited for her in the large hall of the hotel, where the couriers, the servants, the foreign tourists were lounging about and staring. It was not the place he would have chosen, but she had appointed it. She came tripping downstairs, buttoning her long gloves, squeezing her folded parasol against her pretty figure, dressed in the perfection of a soberly elegant travelling-costume.

Winterbourne was a man of imagination and, as our ancestors used to say, of sensibility; as he looked at her dress and, on the great staircase, her little rapid, confiding step, he felt as if there were something romantic going forward. He could have believed he was going to elope with her. He passed out with her among all the idle people that were assembled there; they were all looking at her very hard; she had begun to chatter as soon as she joined him. Winterbourne's preference had been that they should be conveyed to Chillon in a carriage; but she expressed a lively wish to go in the little steamer; she declared that she had a passion for steamboats. There was always such a lovely breeze upon the water, and you saw such lots of people. The sail was not long, but Winterbourne's companion found time to say a great many things. To the young man himself their little excursion was so much of an escapade—an adventure—that, even allowing for her habitual sense of freedom, he had some expectation of seeing her regard it in the same way. But it must be confessed that, in this particular, he was disappointed. Daisy Miller was extremely animated, she was in charming spirits; but she was apparently not at all excited; she was not fluttered; she avoided neither his eyes nor those of any one else; she blushed neither when she looked at him nor when she saw that people were looking at her. People continued to look at her a great deal, and Winterbourne took much satisfaction in his pretty companion's distinguished air. He had been a little afraid that she would talk loud, laugh overmuch, and even, perhaps, desire to move about the boat a good deal. But he quite forgot his fears; he sat smiling, with his eyes upon her face, while, without moving from her place, she delivered herself of a great number of original reflections. It was the most charming garrulity he had ever heard. He had assented to the idea that she was "common"; but was she so, after all, or was he simply getting used to her commonness? Her conversation was chiefly of what metaphysicians term the objective cast; but every now and then it took a subjective turn.

"What on *earth* are you so grave about?" she suddenly demanded, fixing her agreeable eyes upon Winterbourne's.

"Am I grave?" he asked. "I had an idea I was grinning from ear to ear."

"You look as if you were taking me to a funeral. If that's a grin, your ears are very near together."

"Should you like me to dance a hornpipe[9] on the deck?"

"Pray do, and I'll carry round your hat. It will pay the expenses of our journey."

"I never was better pleased in my life," murmured Winterbourne.

She looked at him a moment, and then burst into a little laugh. "I like to make you say those things! You're a queer mixture!"

In the castle, after they had landed, the subjective element decidedly prevailed. Daisy tripped about the vaulted chambers, rustled her skirts in the corkscrew staircases, flirted back with a pretty little cry and a shudder from the edge of the *oubliettes*,[1] and turned a singularly well-shaped ear to everything that Winterbourne told her about the place. But he saw that she cared very little for feudal antiquities, and that the dusky traditions of Chillon made but a slight impression upon her. They had the good fortune to have been able to walk about without other companionship than that of the custodian;

9. An English dance similar to the jig, popular with sailors from the 16th through the 19th centuries.

1. Secret pitlike dungeons with an opening only at the top; places where one is forgotten (French).

and Winterbourne arranged with this functionary that they should not be hurried—that they should linger and pause wherever they chose. The custodian interpreted the bargain generously—Winterbourne, on his side, had been generous—and ended by leaving them quite to themselves. Miss Miller's observations were not remarkable for logical consistency; for anything she wanted to say she was sure to find a pretext. She found a great many pretexts in the rugged embrasures of Chillon for asking Winterbourne sudden questions about himself—his family, his previous history, his tastes, his habits, his intentions—and for supplying information upon corresponding points in her own personality. Of her own tastes, habits, and intentions Miss Miller was prepared to give the most definite, and indeed the most favourable, account.

"Well; I hope you know enough!" she said to her companion, after he had told her the history of the unhappy Bonivard.[2] "I never saw a man that knew so much!" The history of Bonivard had evidently, as they say, gone into one ear and out of the other. But Daisy went on to say that she wished Winterbourne would travel with them and "go round" with them; they might know something, in that case. "Don't you want to come and teach Randolph?" she asked. Winterbourne said that nothing could possibly please him so much; but that he had unfortunately other occupations. "Other occupations? I don't believe it!" said Miss Daisy. "What do you mean? You are not in business." The young man admitted that he was not in business; but he had engagements which, even within a day or two, would force him to go back to Geneva. "Oh, bother!" she said. "I don't believe it!" and she began to talk about something else. But a few moments later, when he was pointing out to her the pretty design of an antique fireplace, she broke out irrelevantly, "You don't mean to say you are going back to Geneva?"

"It is a melancholy fact that I shall have to return to Geneva to-morrow."

"Well, Mr. Winterbourne," said Daisy; "I think you're horrid!"

"Oh, don't say such dreadful things!" said Winterbourne—"just at the last."

"The last!" cried the young girl; "I call it the first. I have half a mind to leave you here and go straight back to the hotel alone." And for the next ten minutes she did nothing but call him horrid. Poor Winterbourne was fairly bewildered; no young lady had as yet done him the honor to be so agitated by the announcement of his movements. His companion, after this, ceased to pay any attention to the curiosities of Chillon or the beauties of the lake; she opened fire upon the mysterious charmer in Geneva, whom she appeared to have instantly taken it for granted that he was hurrying back to see. How did Miss Daisy Miller know that there was a charmer in Geneva? Winterbourne, who denied the existence of such a person, was quite unable to discover; and he was divided between amazement at the rapidity of her induction and amusement at the frankness of her *persiflage*.[3] She seemed to him, in all this, an extraordinary mixture of innocence and crudity. "Does she never allow you more than three days at a time?" asked Daisy, ironically. "Doesn't she give you a vacation in summer? There's no one so hard worked but they can get leave to go off somewhere at this season. I suppose, if you stay another day, she'll come after you in the boat. Do wait over till Friday, and I will go down to the landing to see her arrive!" Winterbourne began to think he had been wrong

---

2. Hero of Byron's poem "The Prisoner of Chillon"; François de Bonivard (1496–1570), Swiss patriot and martyr, was confined for seven years in the Castle of Chillon.
3. Frivolous or bantering talk.

to feel disappointed in the temper in which the young lady had embarked. If he had missed the personal accent, the personal accent was now making its appearance. It sounded very distinctly, at last, in her telling him she would stop "teasing" him if he would promise her solemnly to come down to Rome in the winter.

"That's not a difficult promise to make," said Winterbourne. "My aunt has taken an apartment in Rome for the winter, and has already asked me to come and see her."

"I don't want you to come for your aunt," said Daisy; "I want you to come for me." And this was the only allusion that the young man was ever to hear her make to his invidious kinswoman. He declared that, at any rate, he would certainly come. After this Daisy stopped teasing. Winterbourne took a carriage, and they drove back to Vevey in the dusk; the young girl was very quiet.

In the evening Winterbourne mentioned to Mrs. Costello that he had spent the afternoon at Chillon, with Miss Daisy Miller.

"The Americans—of the courier?" asked this lady.

"Ah, happily," said Winterbourne, "the courier stayed at home."

"She went with you all alone?"

"All alone."

Mrs. Costello sniffed a little at her smelling-bottle. "And that," she exclaimed, "is the young person you wanted me to know!"

III

Winterbourne, who had returned to Geneva the day after his excursion to Chillon, went to Rome towards the end of January. His aunt had been established there for several weeks, and he had received a couple of letters from her. "Those people you were so devoted to last summer at Vevey have turned up here, courier and all," she wrote. "They seem to have made several acquaintances, but the courier continues to be the most *intime*. The young lady, however, is also very intimate with some third-rate Italians, with whom she rackets about in a way that makes much talk. Bring me that pretty novel of Cherbuliez's[4]—'Paule Méré'—and don't come later than the 23rd."

In the natural course of events, Winterbourne, on arriving in Rome, would presently have ascertained Mrs. Miller's address at the American banker's and have gone to pay his compliments to Miss Daisy. "After what happened at Vevey I certainly think I may call upon them," he said to Mrs. Costello.

"If, after what happens—at Vevey and everywhere—you desire to keep up the acquaintance, you are very welcome. Of course a man may know every one. Men are welcome to the privilege!"

"Pray what is it that happens—here, for instance?" Winterbourne demanded.

"The girl goes about alone with her foreigners. As to what happens farther, you must apply elsewhere for information. She has picked up half-a-dozen of the regular Roman fortune-hunters, and she takes them about to people's houses. When she comes to a party she brings with her a gentleman with a good deal of manner and a wonderful moustache."

"And where is the mother?"

"I haven't the least idea. They are very dreadful people."

---

4. Victor Cherbuliez (1829–1899), which James spelled "Cherbuliex," a minor French novelist of Swiss origin.

Winterbourne meditated a moment. "They are very ignorant—very innocent only. Depend upon it they are not bad."

"They are hopelessly vulgar," said Mrs. Costello. "Whether or no being hopelessly vulgar is being 'bad' is a question for the metaphysicians. They are bad enough to dislike, at any rate; and for this short life that is quite enough."

The news that Daisy Miller was surrounded by half-a-dozen wonderful moustaches checked Winterbourne's impulse to go straightway to see her. He had perhaps not definitely flattered himself that he had made an ineffaceable impression upon her heart, but he was annoyed at hearing of a state of affairs so little in harmony with an image that had lately flitted in and out of his own meditations; the image of a very pretty girl looking out of an old Roman window and asking herself urgently when Mr. Winterbourne would arrive. If, however, he determined to wait a little before reminding Miss Miller of his claims to her consideration, he went very soon to call upon two or three other friends. One of these friends was an American lady who had spent several winters at Geneva, when she had placed her children at school. She was a very accomplished woman and she lived in the Via Gregoriana. Winterbourne found her in a little crimson drawing-room, on a third floor; the room was filled with southern sunshine. He had not been there ten minutes when the servant came in, announcing "Madame Mila!" This announcement was presently followed by the entrance of little Randolph Miller, who stopped in the middle of the room and stood staring at Winterbourne. An instant later his pretty sister crossed the threshold; and then, after a considerable interval, Mrs. Miller slowly advanced.

"I know you!" said Randolph.

"I'm sure you know a great many things," exclaimed Winterbourne, taking him by the hand. "How is your education coming on?"

Daisy was exchanging greetings very prettily with her hostess; but when she heard Winterbourne's voice she quickly turned her head. "Well, I declare!" she said.

"I told you I should come, you know," Winterbourne rejoined smiling.

"Well—I didn't believe it," said Miss Daisy.

"I am much obliged to you," laughed the young man.

"You might have come to see me!" said Daisy.

"I arrived only yesterday."

"I don't believe that!" the young girl declared.

Winterbourne turned with a protesting smile to her mother; but this lady evaded his glance, and seating herself, fixed her eyes upon her son. "We've got a bigger place than this," said Randolph. "It's all gold on the walls."

Mrs. Miller turned uneasily in her chair. "I told you if I were to bring you, you would say something!" she murmured.

"I told *you!*" Randolph exclaimed. "I tell *you,* sir!" he added jocosely, giving Winterbourne a thump on the knee. "It *is* bigger, too!"

Daisy had entered upon a lively conversation with her hostess; Winterbourne judged it becoming to address a few words to her mother. "I hope you have been well since we parted at Vevey," he said.

Mrs. Miller now certainly looked at him—at his chin. "Not very well, sir," she answered.

"She's got the dyspepsia," said Randolph. "I've got it too. Father's got it. I've got it worst!"

This announcement, instead of embarrassing Mrs. Miller, seemed to relieve her. "I suffer from the liver," she said. "I think it's the climate; it's less bracing than Schenectady, especially in the winter season. I don't know whether you know we reside at Schenectady. I was saying to Daisy that I certainly hadn't found any one like Dr. Davis, and I didn't believe I should. Oh, at Schenectady, he stands first; they think everything of him. He has so much to do, and yet there was nothing he wouldn't do for me. He said he never saw anything like my dyspepsia, but he was bound to cure it. I'm sure there was nothing he wouldn't try. He was just going to try something new when we came off. Mr. Miller wanted Daisy to see Europe for herself. But I wrote to Mr. Miller that it seems as if I couldn't get on without Dr. Davis. At Schenectady he stands at the very top; and there's a great deal of sickness there, too. It affects my sleep."

Winterbourne had a good deal of pathological gossip with Dr. Davis's patient, during which Daisy chattered unremittingly to her own companion. The young man asked Mrs. Miller how she was pleased with Rome. "Well, I must say I am disappointed," she answered. "We had heard so much about it; I suppose we had heard too much. But we couldn't help that. We had been led to expect something different."

"Ah, wait a little, and you will become very fond of it," said Winterbourne.

"I hate it worse and worse every day!" cried Randolph.

"You are like the infant Hannibal,"[5] said Winterbourne.

"No, I ain't!" Randolph declared, at a venture.

"You are not much like an infant," said his mother. "But we have seen places," she resumed, "that I should put a long way before Rome." And in reply to Winterbourne's interrogation, "There's Zurich," she observed; "I think Zurich is lovely; and we hadn't heard half so much about it."

"The best place we've seen is the City of Richmond!" said Randolph.

"He means the ship," his mother explained. "We crossed in that ship. Randolph had a good time on the City of Richmond."

"It's the best place I've seen," the child repeated. "Only it was turned the wrong way."

"Well, we've got to turn the right way some time," said Mrs. Miller, with a little laugh. Winterbourne expressed the hope that her daughter at least found some gratification in Rome, and she declared that Daisy was quite carried away. "It's on account of the society—the society's splendid. She goes round everywhere; she has made a great number of acquaintances. Of course she goes round more than I do. I must say they have been very sociable; they have taken her right in. And then she knows a great many gentlemen. Oh, she thinks there's nothing like Rome. Of course, it's a great deal pleasanter for a young lady if she knows plenty of gentlemen."

By this time Daisy had turned her attention again to Winterbourne. "I've been telling Mrs. Walker how mean you were!" the young girl announced.

"And what is the evidence you have offered?" asked Winterbourne, rather annoyed at Miss Miller's want of appreciation of the zeal of an admirer who on his way down to Rome had stopped neither at Bologna nor at Florence, simply because of a certain sentimental impatience. He remembered that a cynical compatriot had once told him that American women—the pretty

---

5. The Carthaginian general (247–183 B.C.E.) was sworn at his birth to an eternal hatred of Rome.

ones, and this gave a largeness to the axiom—were at once the most exacting in the world and the least endowed with a sense of indebtedness.

"Why, you were awfully mean at Vevey," said Daisy. "You wouldn't do anything. You wouldn't stay there when I asked you."

"My dearest young lady," cried Winterbourne, with eloquence, "have I come all the way to Rome to encounter your reproaches?"

"Just hear him say that!" said Daisy to her hostess, giving a twist to a bow on this lady's dress. "Did you ever hear anything so quaint?"

"So quaint, my dear?" murmured Mrs. Walker, in the tone of a partisan of Winterbourne.

"Well, I don't know," said Daisy, fingering Mrs. Walker's ribbons. "Mrs. Walker, I want to tell you something."

"Motherr," interposed Randolph, with his rough ends to his words, "I tell you you've got to go. Eugenio'll raise something!"

"I'm not afraid of Eugenio," said Daisy, with a toss of her head. "Look here, Mrs. Walker," she went on, "you know I'm coming to your party."

"I am delighted to hear it."

"I've got a lovely dress."

"I am very sure of that."

"But I want to ask a favor—permission to bring a friend."

"I shall be happy to see any of your friends," said Mrs. Walker, turning with a smile to Mrs. Miller.

"Oh, they are not my friends," answered Daisy's mamma, smiling shyly, in her own fashion. "I never spoke to them!"

"It's an intimate friend of mine—Mr. Giovanelli," said Daisy, without a tremor in her clear little voice or a shadow on her brilliant little face.

Mrs. Walker was silent a moment, she gave a rapid glance at Winterbourne. "I shall be glad to see Mr. Giovanelli," she then said.

"He's an Italian," Daisy pursued, with the prettiest serenity. "He's a great friend of mine—he's the handsomest man in the world—except Mr. Winterbourne! He knows plenty of Italians, but he wants to know some Americans. He thinks ever so much of Americans. He's tremendously clever. He's perfectly lovely!"

It was settled that this brilliant personage should be brought to Mrs. Walker's party, and then Mrs. Miller prepared to take her leave. "I guess we'll go back to the hotel," she said.

"You may go back to the hotel, mother, but I'm going to take a walk," said Daisy.

"She's going to walk with Mr. Giovanelli," Randolph proclaimed.

"I am going to the Pincio," said Daisy, smiling.

"Alone, my dear at this hour?" Mrs. Walker asked. The afternoon was drawing to a close—it was the hour for the throng of carriages and of contemplative pedestrians. "I don't think it's safe, my dear," said Mrs. Walker.

"Neither do I," subjoined Mrs. Miller. "You'll get the fever[6] as sure as you live. Remember what Dr. Davis told you!"

"Give her some medicine before she goes," said Randolph.

The company had risen to its feet; Daisy, still showing her pretty teeth, bent

---

6. What is meant is malaria, whose means of transmission (the mosquito) was unknown in James's day, but which was associated with damp, dark places.

over and kissed her hostess. "Mrs. Walker, you are too perfect," she said. "I'm not going alone; I am going to meet a friend."

"Your friend won't keep you from getting the fever," Mrs. Miller observed.

"Is it Mr. Giovanelli?" asked the hostess.

Winterbourne was watching the girl; at this question his attention quickened. She stood there smiling and smoothing her bonnet-ribbons; she glanced at Winterbourne. Then, while she glanced and smiled, she answered without a shade of hesitation, "Mr. Giovanelli—the beautiful Giovanelli."

"My dear young friend," said Mrs. Walker, taking her hand, pleadingly, "don't walk off to the Pincio at this hour to meet a beautiful Italian."

"Well, he speaks English," said Mrs. Miller.

"Gracious me!" Daisy exclaimed, "I don't want to do anything improper. There's an easy way to settle it." She continued to glance at Winterbourne. "The Pincio is only a hundred yards distant, and if Mr. Winterbourne were as polite as he pretends he would offer to walk with me!"

Winterbourne's politeness hastened to affirm itself, and the young girl gave him gracious leave to accompany her. They passed downstairs before her mother, and at the door Winterbourne perceived Mrs. Miller's carriage drawn up, with the ornamental courier whose acquaintance he had made at Vevey seated within. "Good-bye, Eugenio!" cried Daisy, "I'm going to take a walk." The distance from the Via Gregoriana to the beautiful garden at the other end of the Pincian Hill is, in fact, rapidly traversed. As the day was splendid, however, and the concourse of vehicles, walkers, and loungers numerous, the young Americans found their progress much delayed. This fact was highly agreeable to Winterbourne, in spite of his consciousness of his singular situation. The slow-moving, idly-gazing Roman crowd bestowed much attention upon the extremely pretty young foreign lady who was passing through it upon his arm; and he wondered what on earth had been in Daisy's mind when she proposed to expose herself, unattended, to its appreciation. His own mission, to her sense, apparently, was to consign her to the hands of Mr. Giovanelli; but Winterbourne, at once annoyed and gratified, resolved that he would do no such thing.

"Why haven't you been to see me?" asked Daisy. "You can't get out of that."

"I have had the honor of telling you that I have only just stepped out of the train."

"You must have stayed in the train a good while after it stopped!" cried the young girl, with her little laugh. "I suppose you were asleep. You have had time to go to see Mrs. Walker."

"I knew Mrs. Walker—" Winterbourne began to explain.

"I knew where you knew her. You knew her at Geneva. She told me so. Well, you knew me at Vevey. That's just as good. So you ought to have come." She asked him no other question than this; she began to prattle about her own affairs. "We've got splendid rooms at the hotel; Eugenio says they're the best rooms in Rome. We are going to stay all winter—if we don't die of the fever; and I guess we'll stay then. It's a great deal nicer than I thought; I thought it would be fearfully quiet; I was sure it would be awfully poky. I was sure we should be going round all the time with one of those dreadful old men that explain about the pictures and things. But we only had about a week of that, and now I'm enjoying myself. I know ever so many people, and they are all so charming. The society's extremely select. There are all kinds—English, and Germans, and Italians. I think I like the English best. I like their style of conversation. But there are some lovely Americans. I never saw anything so hospitable. There's something or other every day. There's not much dancing; but I must say I never thought dancing was everything. I was always fond of conversation. I guess I shall have plenty at Mrs. Walker's—her rooms are so small." When they had passed the gate of the Pincian Gardens, Miss Miller began to wonder where Mr. Giovanelli might be. "We had better go straight to that place in front," she said, "where you look at the view."

"I certainly shall not help you to find him," Winterbourne declared.

"Then I shall find him without you," said Miss Daisy.

"You certainly won't leave me!" cried Winterbourne.

She burst into her little laugh. "Are you afraid you'll get lost—or run over? But there's Giovanelli, leaning against that tree. He's staring at the women in the carriages: did you ever see anything so cool?"

Winterbourne perceived at some distance a little man standing with folded arms, nursing his cane. He had a handsome face, an artfully poised hat, a glass in one eye, and a nosegay in his button-hole. Winterbourne looked at him a moment and then said, "Do you mean to speak to that man?"

"Do I mean to speak to him? Why, you don't suppose I mean to communicate by signs?"

"Pray understand, then," said Winterbourne, "that I intend to remain with you."

Daisy stopped and looked at him, without a sign of troubled consciousness in her face; with nothing but the presence of her charming eyes and her happy dimples. "Well, she's a cool one!" thought the young man.

"I don't like the way you say that," said Daisy. "It's too imperious."

"I beg your pardon if I say it wrong. The main point is to give you an idea of my meaning."

The young girl looked at him more gravely, but with eyes that were prettier than ever. "I have never allowed a gentleman to dictate to me, or to interfere with anything I do."

"I think you have made a mistake," said Winterbourne. "You should sometimes listen to a gentleman—the right one?"

Daisy began to laugh again, "I do nothing but listen to gentlemen!" she exclaimed. "Tell me if Mr. Giovanelli is the right one?"

The gentleman with the nosegay in his bosom had now perceived our two friends, and was approaching the young girl with obsequious rapidity. He bowed to Winterbourne as well as to the latter's companion; he had a brilliant smile, an intelligent eye; Winterbourne thought him not a bad-looking fellow. But he nevertheless said to Daisy—"No, he's not the right one."

Daisy evidently had a natural talent for performing introductions; she mentioned the name of each of her companions to the other. She strolled along with one of them on each side of her; Mr. Giovanelli, who spoke English very cleverly—Winterbourne afterwards learned that he had practiced the idiom upon a great many American heiresses—addressed her a great deal of very polite nonsense; he was extremely urbane, and the young American, who said nothing, reflected upon that profundity of Italian cleverness which enables people to appear more gracious in proportion as they are more acutely disappointed. Giovanelli, of course, had counted upon something more intimate; he had not bargained for a party of three. But he kept his temper in a manner which suggested far-stretching intentions. Winterbourne flattered himself that he had taken his measure. "He is not a gentleman," said the young American; "he is only a clever imitation of one. He is a music-master, or a penny-a-liner, or a third-rate artist. Damn his good looks!" Mr. Giovanelli had certainly a very pretty face; but Winterbourne felt a superior indignation at his own lovely fellow-countrywoman's not knowing the difference between a spurious gentleman and a real one. Giovanelli chattered and jested and made himself wonderfully agreeable. It was true that if he was an imitation the imitation was very skillful. "Nevertheless," Winterbourne said to himself, "a nice girl ought to know!" And then he came back to the question whether this was in fact a nice girl. Would a nice girl—even allowing for her being a little American flirt—make a rendezvous with a presumably low-lived foreigner? The rendezvous in this case, indeed, had been in broad daylight, and in the most crowded corner of Rome; but was it not impossible to regard the choice of these circumstances as a proof of extreme cynicism? Singular though it may seem, Winterbourne was vexed that the young girl, in joining her *amoroso*,[7] should not appear more impatient of his own company, and he was vexed because of his inclination. It was impossible to regard her as a perfectly well-conducted young lady; she was wanting in a certain indispensable delicacy. It would therefore simplify matters greatly to be able to treat her as the object of one of those sentiments which are called by romancers "lawless passions." That she should seem to wish to get rid of him would help him to think more lightly of her, and to be able to think more lightly of her would make her much less perplexing. But Daisy, on this occasion, continued to present herself as an inscrutable combination of audacity and innocence.

She had been walking some quarter of an hour, attended by her two cavaliers, and responding in a tone of very childish gaiety, as it seemed to Winterbourne, to the pretty speeches of Mr. Giovanelli, when a carriage that had detached itself from the revolving train drew up beside the path. At the same moment Winterbourne perceived that his friend Mrs. Walker—the lady whose house he had lately left—was seated in the vehicle and was beckoning to him. Leaving Miss Miller's side, he hastened to obey her summons. Mrs. Walker was flushed; she wore an excited air. "It is really too dreadful," she said. "That girl must not do this sort of thing. She must not walk here with you two men. Fifty people have noticed her."

Winterbourne raised his eyebrows. "I think it's a pity to make too much fuss about it."

"It's a pity to let the girl ruin herself!"

"She is very innocent," said Winterbourne.

"She's very crazy!" cried Mrs. Walker. "Did you ever see anything so imbecile as her mother? After you had all left me, just now, I could not sit still for thinking of it. It seemed too pitiful, not even to attempt to save her. I ordered the carriage and put on my bonnet, and came here as quickly as possible. Thank heaven I have found you!"

"What do you propose to do with us?" asked Winterbourne, smiling.

"To ask her to get in, to drive her about here for half-an-hour, so that the world may see she is not running absolutely wild, and then to take her safely home."

"I don't think it's a very happy thought," said Winterbourne; "but you can try."

Mrs. Walker tried. The young man went in pursuit of Miss Miller, who had simply nodded and smiled at his interlocutrix in the carriage and had gone

7. Lover (Italian).

her way with her own companion. Daisy, on learning that Mrs. Walker wished to speak to her, retraced her steps with a perfect good grace and with Mr. Giovanelli at her side. She declared that she was delighted to have a chance to present this gentleman to Mrs. Walker. She immediately achieved the introduction, and declared that she had never in her life seen anything so lovely as Mrs. Walker's carriage-rug.

"I am glad you admire it," said this lady, smiling sweetly. "Will you get in and let me put it over you?"

"Oh, no, thank you," said Daisy. "I shall admire it much more as I see you driving round with it."

"Do get in and drive with me," said Mrs. Walker.

"That would be charming, but it's so enchanting just as I am!" and Daisy gave a brilliant glance at the gentlemen on either side of her.

"It may be enchanting, dear child, but it is not the custom here," urged Mrs. Walker, leaning forward in her victoria[8] with her hands devoutly clasped.

"Well, it ought to be, then!" said Daisy. "If I didn't walk I should expire."

"You should walk with your mother, dear," cried the lady from Geneva, losing patience.

"With my mother dear!" exclaimed the young girl. Winterbourne saw that she scented interference. "My mother never walked ten steps in her life. And then, you know," she added with a laugh, "I am more than five years old."

"You are old enough to be more reasonable. You are old enough, dear Miss Miller, to be talked about."

Daisy looked at Mrs. Walker, smiling intensely. "Talked about? What do you mean?"

"Come into my carriage and I will tell you."

Daisy turned her quickened glance again from one of the gentlemen beside her to the other. Mr. Giovanelli was bowing to and fro, rubbing down his gloves and laughing very agreeably; Winterbourne thought it a most unpleasant scene. "I don't think I want to know what you mean," said Daisy presently. "I don't think I should like it."

Winterbourne wished that Mrs. Walker would tuck in her carriage-rug and drive away; but this lady did not enjoy being defied, as she afterwards told him. "Should you prefer being thought a very reckless girl?" she demanded.

"Gracious me!" exclaimed Daisy. She looked again at Mr. Giovanelli, then she turned to Winterbourne. There was a little pink flush in her check; she was tremendously pretty. "Does Mr. Winterbourne think," she asked slowly, smiling, throwing back her head and glancing at him from head to foot, "that—to save my reputation—I ought to get into the carriage?"

Winterbourne colored; for an instant he hesitated greatly. It seemed so strange to hear her speak that way of her "reputation." But he himself, in fact, must speak in accordance with gallantry. The finest gallantry, here, was simply to tell her the truth; and the truth, for Winterbourne, as the few indications I have been able to give have made him known to the reader, was that Daisy Miller should take Mrs. Walker's advice. He looked at her exquisite prettiness; and then he said very gently, "I think you should get into the carriage."

Daisy gave a violent laugh. "I never heard anything so stiff! If this is improper, Mrs. Walker," she pursued, "then I am all improper, and you must

8. A horse-drawn carriage for two with a raised seat in front for the driver.

give me up. Good-bye; I hope you'll have a lovely ride!" and, with Mr. Giovanelli, who made a triumphantly obsequious salute, she turned away.

Mrs. Walker sat looking after her, and there were tears in Mrs. Walker's eyes. "Get in here, sir," she said to Winterbourne, indicating the place beside her. The young man answered that he felt bound to accompany Miss Miller; whereupon Mrs. Walker declared that if he refused her this favor she would never speak to him again. She was evidently in earnest. Winterbourne overtook Daisy and her companion and, offering the young girl his hand, told her that Mrs. Walker had made an imperious claim upon his society. He expected that in answer she would say something rather free, something to commit herself still farther to that "recklessness" from which Mrs. Walker had so charitably endeavored to dissuade her. But she only shook his hand, hardly looking at him, while Mr. Giovanelli bade him farewell with a too emphatic flourish of the hat.

Winterbourne was not in the best possible humor as he took his seat in Mrs. Walker's victoria. "That was not clever of you," he said candidly, while the vehicle mingled again with the throng of carriages.

"In such a case," his companion answered, "I don't wish to be clever, I wish to be *earnest!*"

"Well, your earnestness has only offended her and put her off."

"It has happened very well," said Mrs. Walker. "If she is so perfectly determined to compromise herself, the sooner one knows it the better; one can act accordingly."

"I suspect she meant no harm," Winterbourne rejoined.

"So I thought a month ago. But she has been going too far."

"What has she been doing?"

"Everything that is not done here. Flirting with any man she could pick up; sitting in corners with mysterious Italians; dancing all the evening with the same partners; receiving visits at eleven o'clock at night. Her mother goes away when visitors come."

"But her brother," said Winterbourne, laughing, "sits up till midnight."

"He must be edified by what he sees. I'm told that at their hotel every one is talking about her, and that a smile goes round among the servants when a gentleman comes and asks for Miss Miller."

"The servants be hanged!" said Winterbourne angrily. "The poor girl's only fault," he presently added, "is that she is very uncultivated."

"She is naturally indelicate," Mrs. Walker declared. "Take that example this morning. How long had you known her at Vevey?"

"A couple of days."

"Fancy, then, her making it a personal matter that you should have left the place!"

Winterbourne was silent for some moments; then he said, "I suspect, Mrs. Walker, that you and I have lived too long at Geneva!" And he added a request that she should inform him with what particular design she had made him enter her carriage.

"I wished to beg you to cease your relations with Miss Miller—not to flirt with her—to give her no farther opportunity to expose herself—to let her alone, in short."

"I'm afraid I can't do that," said Winterbourne. "I like her extremely."

"All the more reason that you shouldn't help her to make a scandal."

"There shall be nothing scandalous in my attentions to her."

"There certainly will be in the way she takes them. But I have said what I had on my conscience," Mrs. Walker pursued. "If you wish to rejoin the young lady I will put you down. Here, by-the-way, you have a chance."

The carriage was traversing that part of the Pincian Garden which overhangs the wall of Rome and overlooks the beautiful Villa Borghese. It is bordered by a large parapet, near which there are several seats. One of the seats, at a distance, was occupied by a gentleman and a lady, towards whom Mrs. Walker gave a toss of her head. At the same moment these persons rose and walked towards the parapet. Winterbourne had asked the coachman to stop; he now descended from the carriage. His companion looked at him a moment in silence; then, while he raised his hat, she drove majestically away. Winterbourne stood there; he had turned his eyes towards Daisy and her cavalier. They evidently saw no one; they were too deeply occupied with each other. When they reached the low garden-wall they stood a moment looking off at the great flat-topped pine-clusters of the Villa Borghese; then Giovanelli seated himself familiarly upon the broad ledge of the wall. The western sun in the opposite sky sent out a brilliant shaft through a couple of cloud-bars; whereupon Daisy's companion took her parasol out of her hands and opened it. She came a little nearer and he held the parasol over her; then, still holding it, he let it rest upon her shoulder, so that both of their heads were hidden from Winterbourne. This young man lingered a moment, then he began to walk. But he walked—not towards the couple with the parasol; towards the residence of his aunt, Mrs. Costello.

IV

He flattered himself on the following day that there was no smiling among the servants when he, at least, asked for Mrs. Miller at her hotel. This lady and her daughter, however, were not at home; and on the next day, after repeating his visit, Winterbourne again had the misfortune not to find them. Mrs. Walker's party took place on the evening of the third day, and in spite of the frigidity of his last interview with the hostess, Winterbourne was among the guests. Mrs. Walker was one of those American ladies who, while residing abroad, make a point, in their own phrase, of studying European society; and she had on this occasion collected several specimens of her diversely-born fellow-mortals to serve, as it were, as text-books. When Winterbourne arrived Daisy Miller was not there; but in a few moments he saw her mother come in alone, very shyly and ruefully. Mrs. Miller's hair, above her exposed-looking temples, was more frizzled than ever. As she approached Mrs. Walker, Winterbourne also drew near.

"You see I've come all alone," said poor Mrs. Miller. "I'm so frightened; I don't know what to do; it's the first time I've ever been to a party alone—especially in this country. I wanted to bring Randolph or Eugenio, or someone, but Daisy just pushed me off by myself. I ain't used to going round alone."

"And does not your daughter intend to favor us with her society?" demanded Mrs. Walker, impressively.

"Well, Daisy's all dressed," said Mrs. Miller, with that accent of the dispassionate, if not of the philosophic, historian with which she always recorded the current incidents of her daughter's career. "She's got dressed on purpose before dinner. But she's got a friend of hers there; that gentleman—the Italian—that she wanted to bring. They've got going at the piano; it seems as if they couldn't leave off. Mr. Giovanelli sings splendidly. But I guess they'll come before very long," concluded Mrs. Miller hopefully.

"I'm sorry she should come—in that way," said Mrs. Walker.

"Well, I told her that there was no use in her getting dressed before dinner if she was going to wait three hours," responded Daisy's mamma. "I didn't see the use of her putting on such a dress as that to sit round with Mr. Giovanelli."

"This is most horrible!" said Mrs. Walker, turning away and addressing herself to Winterbourne. "*Elle s'affiche.*[9] It's her revenge for my having ventured to remonstrate with her. When she comes I shall not speak to her."

Daisy came after eleven o'clock, but she was not, on such an occasion, a young lady to wait to be spoken to. She rustled forward in radiant loveliness, smiling and chattering, carrying a large bouquet and attended by Mr. Giovanelli. Every one stopped talking, and turned and looked at her. She came straight to Mrs. Walker. "I'm afraid you thought I never was coming, so I sent mother off to tell you. I wanted to make Mr. Giovanelli practice some things before he came; you know he sings beautifully, and I want you to ask him to sing. This is Mr. Giovanelli; you know I introduced him to you; he's got the most lovely voice and he knows the most charming set of songs. I made him go over them this evening, on purpose; we had the greatest time at the hotel." Of all this Daisy delivered herself with the sweetest, brightest audibleness, looking now at her hostess and now round the room, while she gave a series of little pats, round her shoulders, to the edges of her dress. "Is there anyone I know?" she asked.

"I think every one knows you!" said Mrs. Walker pregnantly, and she gave a very cursory greeting to Mr. Giovanelli. This gentleman bore himself gallantly. He smiled and bowed and showed his white teeth, he curled his moustaches and rolled his eyes, and performed all the proper functions of a handsome Italian at an evening party. He sang, very prettily, half-a-dozen songs, though Mrs. Walker afterwards declared that she had been quite unable to find out who asked him. It was apparently not Daisy who had given him his orders. Daisy sat at a distance from the piano, and though she had publicly, as it were, professed a high admiration for his singing, talked, not inaudibly, while it was going on.

"It's a pity these rooms are so small; we can't dance," she said to Winterbourne, as if she had seen him five minutes before.

"I am not sorry we can't dance," Winterbourne answered; "I don't dance."

"Of course you don't dance; you're too stiff," said Miss Daisy. "I hope you enjoyed your drive with Mrs. Walker."

"No, I didn't enjoy it; I preferred walking with you."

"We paired off, that was much better," said Daisy. "But did you ever hear anything so cool as Mrs. Walker's wanting me to get into her carriage and drop poor Mr. Giovanelli; and under the pretext that it was proper? People have different ideas! It would have been most unkind; he had been talking about that walk for ten days."

9. She's making a spectacle of herself (French).

"He should not have talked about it at all," said Winterbourne; "he would never have proposed to a young lady of this country to walk about the streets with him."

"About the streets?" cried Daisy, with her pretty stare. "Where then would he have proposed to her to walk? The Pincio is not the streets, either; and I, thank goodness, am not a young lady of this country. The young ladies of this country have a dreadfully pokey time of it, so far as I can learn; I don't see why I should change my habits for *them*."

"I am afraid your habits are those of a flirt," said Winterbourne gravely.

"Of course they are," she cried, giving him her little smiling stare again. "I'm a fearful, frightful flirt! Did you ever hear of a nice girl that was not? But I suppose you will tell me now that I am not a nice girl."

"You're a very nice girl, but I wish you would flirt with me, and me only," said Winterbourne.

"Ah! thank you, thank you very much; you are the last man I should think of flirting with. As I have had the pleasure of informing you, you are too stiff."

"You say that too often," said Winterbourne.

Daisy gave a delighted laugh. "If I could have the sweet hope of making you angry, I would say it again."

"Don't do that; when I am angry I'm stiffer than ever. But if you won't flirt with me, do cease at least to flirt with your friend at the piano; they don't understand that sort of thing here."

"I thought they understood nothing else!" exclaimed Daisy.

"Not in young unmarried women."

"It seems to me much more proper in young unmarried women than in old married ones," Daisy declared.

"Well," said Winterbourne, "when you deal with natives you must go by the custom of the place. Flirting is a purely American custom; it doesn't exist here. So when you show yourself in public with Mr. Giovanelli and without your mother—"

"Gracious! Poor mother!" interposed Daisy.

"Though you may be flirting, Mr. Giovanelli is not; he means something else."

"He isn't preaching, at any rate," said Daisy with vivacity. "And if you want very much to know, we are neither of us flirting; we are too good friends for that; we are very intimate friends."

"Ah," rejoined Winterbourne, "if you are in love with each other it is another affair."

She had allowed him up to this point to talk so frankly that he had no expectation of shocking her by this ejaculation; but she immediately got up, blushing visibly, and leaving him to exclaim mentally that little American flirts were the queerest creatures in the world. "Mr. Giovanelli, at least," she said, giving her interlocutor a single glance, "never says such very disagreeable things to me."

Winterbourne was bewildered; he stood staring. Mr. Giovanelli had finished singing; he left the piano and came over to Daisy. "Won't you come into the other room and have some tea?" he asked, bending before her with his decorative smile.

Daisy turned to Winterbourne, beginning to smile again. He was still more perplexed, for this inconsequent smile made nothing clear, though it seemed to prove, indeed, that she had a sweetness and softness that reverted instinctively to the pardon of offences. "It has never occurred to Mr. Winterbourne to offer me any tea," she said, with her little tormenting manner.

"I have offered you advice," Winterbourne rejoined.

"I prefer weak tea!" cried Daisy, and she went off with the brilliant Giovanelli. She sat with him in the adjoining room, in the embrasure of the window, for the rest of the evening. There was an interesting performance at the piano, but neither of these young people gave heed to it. When Daisy came to take leave of Mrs. Walker, this lady conscientiously repaired the weakness of which she had been guilty at the moment of the young girl's arrival. She turned her back straight upon Miss Miller and left her to depart with what grace she might. Winterbourne was standing near the door; he saw it all. Daisy turned very pale and looked at her mother, but Mrs. Miller was humbly unconscious of any violation of the usual social forms. She appeared, indeed, to have felt an incongruous impulse to draw attention to her own striking observance of them. "Good night, Mrs. Walker," she said; "we've had a beautiful evening. You see if I let Daisy come to parties without me, I don't want her to go away without me." Daisy turned away, looking with a pale, grave face at the circle near the door; Winterbourne saw that, for the first moment, she was too much shocked and puzzled even for indignation. He on his side was greatly touched.

"That was very cruel," he said to Mrs. Walker.

"She never enters my drawing-room again," replied his hostess.

Since Winterbourne was not to meet her in Mrs. Walker's drawing-room, he went as often as possible to Mrs. Miller's hotel. The ladies were rarely at home, but when he found them the devoted Giovanelli was always present. Very often the polished little Roman was in the drawing-room with Daisy alone, Mrs. Miller being apparently constantly of the opinion that discretion is the better part of surveillance. Winterbourne noted, at first with surprise, that Daisy on these occasions was never embarrassed or annoyed by his own entrance; but he very presently began to feel that she had no more surprises for him; the unexpected in her behavior was the only thing to expect. She showed no displeasure at her tête-à-tête with Giovanelli being interrupted; she could chatter as freshly and freely with two gentlemen as with one; there was always, in her conversation, the same odd mixture of audacity and puerility. Winterbourne remarked to himself that if she was seriously interested in Giovanelli it was very singular that she should not take more trouble to preserve the sanctity of their interviews, and he liked her the more for her innocent-looking indifference and her apparently inexhaustible good humor. He could hardly have said why, but she seemed to him a girl who would never be jealous. At the risk of exciting a somewhat derisive smile on the reader's part, I may affirm that with regard to the women who had hitherto interested him it very often seemed to Winterbourne among the possibilities that, given certain contingencies, he should be afraid—literally afraid—of these ladies. He had a pleasant sense that he should never be afraid of Daisy Miller. It must be added that this sentiment was not altogether flattering to Daisy; it was part of his conviction, or rather of his apprehension, that she would prove a very light young person.

But she was evidently very much interested in Giovanelli. She looked at him whenever he spoke; she was perpetually telling him to do this and to do that; she was constantly "chaffing" and abusing him. She appeared completely to have forgotten that Winterbourne had said anything to displease her at Mrs. Walker's little party. One Sunday afternoon, having gone to St. Peter's with his aunt, Winterbourne perceived Daisy strolling about the great church in company with the inevitable Giovanelli. Presently he pointed out the young girl and her cavalier to Mrs. Costello. This lady looked at them a moment through her eyeglasses, and then she said:

"That's what makes you so pensive in these days, eh?"

"I had not the least idea I was pensive," said the young man.

"You are very much preoccupied, you are thinking of something."

"And what is it," he asked, "that you accuse me of thinking of?"

"Of that young lady's, Miss Baker's, Miss Chandler's—what's her name?— Miss Miller's intrigue with that little barber's block."

"Do you call it an intrigue," Winterbourne asked—"an affair that goes on with such peculiar publicity?"

"That's their folly," said Mrs. Costello, "it's not their merit."

"No," rejoined Winterbourne, with something of that pensiveness to which his aunt had alluded. "I don't believe that there is anything to be called an intrigue."

"I have heard a dozen people speak of it; they say she is quite carried away by him."

"They are certainly very intimate," said Winterbourne.

Mrs. Costello inspected the young couple again with her optical instrument. "He is very handsome. One easily sees how it is. She thinks him the most elegant man in the world, the finest gentleman. She has never seen anything like him; he is better even than the courier. It was the courier probably who introduced him, and if he succeeds in marrying the young lady, the courier will come in for a magnificent commission."

"I don't believe she thinks of marrying him," said Winterbourne, "and I don't believe he hopes to marry her."

"You may be very sure she thinks of nothing. She goes on from day to day, from hour to hour, as they did in the Golden Age. I can imagine nothing more vulgar. And at the same time," added Mrs. Costello, "depend upon it that she may tell you any moment that she is 'engaged.'"

"I think that is more than Giovanelli expects," said Winterbourne.

"Who is Giovanelli?"

"The little Italian. I have asked questions about him and learned something. He is apparently a perfectly respectable little man. I believe he is in a small way a *cavaliere avvocato*.[1] But he doesn't move in what are called the first circles. I think it is really not absolutely impossible that the courier introduced him. He is evidently immensely charmed with Miss Miller. If she thinks him the finest gentleman in the world, he, on his side, has never found himself in personal contact with such splendor, such opulence, such expensiveness, as this young lady's. And then she must seem to him wonderfully pretty and interesting. I rather doubt whether he dreams of marrying her. That must appear to him too impossible a piece of luck. He has nothing but his handsome face to offer, and there is a substantial Mr. Miller in that mysterious land of dollars. Giovanelli knows that he hasn't a title to offer. If he

---

1. Lawyer (Italian). *"Cavaliere"*: an honorific.

were only a count or a *marchese*![2] He must wonder at his luck at the way they have taken him up."

"He accounts for it by his handsome face, and thinks Miss Miller a young lady *qui se passe ses fantaisies*!"[3] said Mrs. Costello.

"It is very true," Winterbourne pursued, "that Daisy and her mamma have not yet risen to that stage of—what shall I call it?—of culture, at which the idea of catching a count or a *marchese* begins. I believe that they are intellectually incapable of that conception."

"Ah! but the *cavalier* can't believe it," said Mrs. Costello.

Of the observation excited by Daisy's "intrigue," Winterbourne gathered that day at St. Peter's sufficient evidence. A dozen of the American colonists in Rome came to talk with Mrs. Costello, who sat on a little portable stool at the base of one of the great pilasters. The vesper-service was going forward in splendid chants and organ-tones in the adjacent choir, and meanwhile, between Mrs. Costello and her friends, there was a great deal said about poor little Miss Miller's going really "too far." Winterbourne was not pleased with what he heard; but when, coming out upon the great steps of the church, he saw Daisy, who had emerged before him, get into an open cab with her accomplice and roll away through the cynical streets of Rome, he could not deny to himself that she was going very far indeed. He felt very sorry for her— not exactly that he believed that she had completely lost her head, but because it was painful to hear so much that was pretty and undefended and natural assigned to a vulgar place among the categories of disorder. He made an attempt after this to give a hint to Mrs. Miller. He met one day in the Corso a friend—a tourist like himself—who had just come out of the Doria Palace, where he had been walking through the beautiful gallery. His friend talked for a moment about the superb portrait of Innocent X. by Velasquez,[4] which hangs in one of the cabinets of the palace, and then said, "And in the same cabinet, by-the-way, I had the pleasure of contemplating a picture of a different kind—that pretty American girl whom you pointed out to me last week." In answer to Winterbourne's inquiries, his friend narrated that the pretty American girl—prettier than ever—was seated with a companion in the secluded nook in which the great papal portrait is enshrined.

"Who was her companion?" asked Winterbourne.

"A little Italian with a bouquet in his button-hole. The girl is delightfully pretty, but I thought I understood from you the other day that she was a young lady *du meilleur monde*."[5]

"So she is!" answered Winterbourne; and having assured himself that his informant had seen Daisy and her companion but five minutes before, he jumped into a cab and went to call on Mrs. Miller. She was at home; but she apologized to him for receiving him in Daisy's absence.

"She's gone out somewhere with Mr. Giovanelli," said Mrs. Miller. "She's always going round with Mr. Giovanelli."

"I have noticed that they are very intimate," Winterbourne observed.

"Oh! it seems as if they couldn't live without each other!" said Mrs. Miller. "Well, he's a real gentleman, anyhow. I keep telling Daisy she's engaged!"

"And what does Daisy say?"

---

2. Marquis (Italian).
3. Who is indulging her whims (French).
4. Diego Rodríguez de Silva y Velázque (1599–

1660), Spanish painter.
5. Of the better society (French).

"Oh, she says she isn't engaged. But she might as well be!" this impartial parent resumed. "She goes on as if she was. But I've made Mr. Giovanelli promise to tell me, if *she* doesn't. I should want to write to Mr. Miller about it—shouldn't you?"

Winterbourne replied that he certainly should; and the state of mind of Daisy's mamma struck him as so unprecedented in the annals of parental vigilance that he gave up as utterly irrelevant the attempt to place her upon her guard.

After this Daisy was never at home, and Winterbourne ceased to meet her at the houses of their common acquaintances, because, as he perceived, these shrewd people had quite made up their minds that she was going too far. They ceased to invite her, and they intimated that they desired to express to observant Europeans the great truth that, though Miss Daisy Miller was a young American lady, her behavior was not representative—was regarded by her compatriots as abnormal. Winterbourne wondered how she felt about all the cold shoulders that were turned towards her, and sometimes it annoyed him to suspect that she did not feel at all. He said to himself that she was too light and childish, too uncultivated and unreasoning, too provincial, to have reflected upon her ostracism or even to have perceived it. Then at other moments he believed that she carried about in her elegant and irresponsible little organism a defiant, passionate, perfectly observant consciousness of the impression she produced. He asked himself whether Daisy's defiance came from the consciousness of innocence or from her being, essentially, a young person of the reckless class. It must be admitted that holding oneself to a belief in Daisy's "innocence" came to seem to Winterbourne more and more a matter of fine-spun gallantry. As I have already had occasion to relate, he was angry at finding himself reduced to chopping logic about this young lady; he was vexed at his want of instinctive certitude as to how far her eccentricities were generic, national, and how far they were personal. From either view of them he had somehow missed her, and now it was too late. She was "carried away" by Mr. Giovanelli.

A few days after his brief interview with her mother, he encountered her in that beautiful abode of flowering desolation known as the Palace of the Cæsars. The early Roman spring had filled the air with bloom and perfume, and the rugged surface of the Palatine was muffled with tender verdure. Daisy was strolling along the top of one of those great mounds of ruin that are embanked with mossy marble and paved with monumental inscriptions. It seemed to him that Rome had never been so lovely as just then. He stood looking off at the enchanting harmony of line and color that remotely encircles the city, inhaling the softly humid odors and feeling the freshness of the year and the antiquity of the place reaffirm themselves in mysterious interfusion. It seemed to him also that Daisy had never looked so pretty; but this had been an observation of his whenever he met her. Giovanelli was at her side, and Giovanelli, too, wore an aspect of even unwonted brilliancy.

"Well," said Daisy, "I should think you would be lonesome!"

"Lonesome?" asked Winterbourne.

"You are always going round by yourself. Can't you get any one to walk with you?"

"I am not so fortunate," said Winterbourne, "as your companion."

Giovanelli, from the first, had treated Winterbourne with distinguished

politeness; he listened with a deferential air to his remarks; he laughed, punc-
tiliously, at his pleasantries; he seemed disposed to testify to his belief that
Winterbourne was a superior young man. He carried himself in no degree like
a jealous wooer; he had obviously a great deal of tact; he had no objection to
your expecting a little humility of him. It even seemed to Winterbourne at
times that Giovanelli would find a certain mental relief in being able to have
a private understanding with him—to say to him, as an intelligent man, that,
bless you, *he* knew how extraordinary was this young lady, and didn't flatter
himself with delusive—or at least *too* delusive—hopes of matrimony and dollars. On this occasion he strolled away from his companion to pluck a sprig
of almond blossom, which he carefully arranged in his button-hole.

"I know why you say that," said Daisy, watching Giovanelli. "Because you
think I go round too much with *him*!" And she nodded at her attendant.

"Everyone thinks so—if you care to know," said Winterbourne.

"Of course I care to know!" Daisy exclaimed seriously. "But I don't believe
it. They are only pretending to be shocked. They don't really care a straw what
I do. Besides, I don't go round so much."

"I think you will find they do care. They will show it—disagreeably."

Daisy looked at him a moment. "How—disagreeably?"

"Haven't you noticed anything?" Winterbourne asked.

"I have noticed you. But I noticed you were as stiff as an umbrella the first
time I saw you."

"You will find I am not so stiff as several others," said Winterbourne, smiling.

"How shall I find it?"

"By going to see the others."

"What will they do to me?"

"They will give you the cold shoulder. Do you know what that means?"

Daisy was looking at him intently; she began to color. "Do you mean as
Mrs. Walker did the other night?"

"Exactly!" said Winterbourne.

She looked away at Giovanelli, who was decorating himself with his
almond-blossom. Then looking back at Winterbourne—"I shouldn't think you
would let people be so unkind!" she said.

"How can I help it?" he asked.

"I should think you would say something."

"I do say something"; and he paused a moment. "I say that your mother
tells me that she believes you are engaged."

"Well, she does," said Daisy very simply.

Winterbourne began to laugh. "And does Randolph believe it?" he asked.

"I guess Randolph doesn't believe anything," said Daisy. Randolph's scep-
ticism excited Winterbourne to farther hilarity, and he observed that Giovanelli was coming back to them. Daisy, observing it too, addressed herself
again to her countryman. "Since you have mentioned it," she said, "I *am*
engaged." . . . Winterbourne looked at her; he had stopped laughing. "You
don't believe it!" she added.

He was silent a moment; and then, "Yes, I believe it!" he said.

"Oh, no, you don't," she answered. "Well, then—I am not!"

The young girl and her cicerone[6] were on their way to the gate of the enclosure, so that Winterbourne, who had but lately entered, presently took leave

<hr>

6. Chaperone (Italian).

of them. A week afterwards he went to dine at a beautiful villa on the Cælian Hill, and, on arriving, dismissed his hired vehicle. The evening was charming, and he promised himself the satisfaction of walking home beneath the Arch of Constantine and past the vaguely-lighted monuments of the Forum. There was a waning moon in the sky, and her radiance was not brilliant, but she was veiled in a thin cloud-curtain which seemed to diffuse and equalize it. When, on his return from the villa (it was eleven o'clock), Winterbourne approached the dusky circle of the Colosseum, it occurred to him, as a lover of the picturesque, that the interior, in the pale moonshine, would be well worth a glance. He turned aside and walked to one of the empty arches, near which, as he observed, an open carriage—one of the little Roman street-cabs—was stationed. Then he passed in among the cavernous shadows of the great structure, and emerged upon the clear and silent arena. The place had never seemed to him more impressive. One-half of the gigantic circus was in deep shade; the other was sleeping in the luminous dusk. As he stood there he began to murmur Byron's famous lines, out of "Manfred";[7] but before he had finished his quotation he remembered that if nocturnal meditations in the Colosseum are recommended by the poets, they are deprecated by the doctors. The historic atmosphere was there, certainly; but the historic atmosphere, scientifically considered, was not better than a villainous miasma. Winterbourne walked to the middle of the arena, to take a more general glance, intending thereafter to make a hasty retreat. The great cross in the center was covered with shadow; it was only as he drew near it that he made it out distinctly. Then he saw that two persons were stationed upon the low steps which formed its base. One of these was a woman, seated; her companion was standing in front of her.

Presently the sound of the woman's voice came to him distinctly in the warm night air. "Well, he looks at us as one of the old lions or tigers may have looked at the Christian martyrs!" These were the words he heard, in the familiar accent of Miss Daisy Miller.

"Let us hope he is not very hungry," responded the ingenious Giovanelli. "He will have to take me first; you will serve for dessert!"

Winterbourne stopped, with a sort of horror; and, it must be added, with a sort of relief. It was as if a sudden illumination had been flashed upon the ambiguity of Daisy's behavior and the riddle had become easy to read. She was a young lady whom a gentleman need no longer be at pains to respect. He stood there looking at her—looking at her companion, and not reflecting that though he saw them vaguely, he himself must have been more brightly visible. He felt angry with himself that he had bothered so much about the right way of regarding Miss Daisy Miller. Then, as he was going to advance again, he checked himself; not from the fear that he was doing her injustice, but from a sense of the danger of appearing unbecomingly exhilarated by this sudden revulsion from cautious criticism. He turned away towards the entrance of the place; but as he did so he heard Daisy speak again.

"Why, it was Mr. Winterbourne! He saw me—and he cuts me!"

7. Byron's 1817 dramatic poem contains the following lines: ". . . the night / Hath been to me a more familiar face / Than that of man; and in her starry shade / Of dim and solitary loveliness, / I learn'd the language of another world. / I do remember me, that in my youth, / When I was wan-dering,—upon such a night / I stood within the Colosseum's wall, / 'Midst the chief relics of almighty Rome; / The trees which grew along the broken arches / Waved dark in the blue midnight, and the stars / Shone through the rents of ruin. . . ."

What a clever little reprobate she was, and how smartly she played an injured innocence! But he wouldn't cut her. Winterbourne came forward again, and went towards the great cross. Daisy had got up; Giovanelli lifted his hat. Winterbourne had now begun to think simply of the craziness, from a sanitary point of view, of a delicate young girl lounging away the evening in this nest of malaria. What if she *were* a clever little reprobate? that was no reason for her dying of the *perniciosa*.[8] "How long have you been there?" he asked, almost brutally.

Daisy, lovely in the flattering moonlight, looked at him a moment. Then— "All the evening," she answered gently. . . . . "I never saw anything so pretty."

"I am afraid," said Winterbourne, "that you will not think Roman fever very pretty. This is the way people catch it. I wonder," he added, turning to Giovanelli, "that you, a native Roman, should countenance such a terrible indiscretion."

"Ah," said the handsome native, "for myself, I am not afraid."

"Neither am I—for you! I am speaking for this young lady."

Giovanelli lifted his well-shaped eyebrows and showed his brilliant teeth. But he took Winterbourne's rebuke with docility. "I told the Signorina it was a grave indiscretion; but when was the Signorina ever prudent?"

"I never was sick, and I don't mean to be!" the Signorina declared. "I don't look like much, but I'm healthy! I was bound to see the Colosseum by moonlight; I shouldn't have wanted to go home without that; and we have had the most beautiful time, haven't we, Mr. Giovanelli! If there has been any danger, Eugenio can give me some pills. He has got some splendid pills."

"I should advise you," said Winterbourne, "to drive home as fast as possible and take one!"

"What you say is very wise," Giovanelli rejoined. "I will go and make sure the carriage is at hand." And he went forward rapidly.

Daisy followed with Winterbourne. He kept looking at her; she seemed not in the least embarrassed. Winterbourne said nothing; Daisy chattered about the beauty of the place. "Well, I *have* seen the Colosseum by moonlight!" she exclaimed. "That's one good thing." Then, noticing Winterbourne's silence, she asked him why he didn't speak. He made no answer; he only began to laugh. They passed under one of the dark archways; Giovanelli was in front with the carriage. Here Daisy stopped a moment, looking at the young American. "*Did* you believe I was engaged the other day?" she asked.

"It doesn't matter what I believed the other day," said Winterbourne, still laughing.

"Well, what do you believe now?"

"I believe that it makes very little difference whether you are engaged or not!"

He felt the young girl's pretty eyes fixed upon him through the thick gloom of the archway; she was apparently going to answer. But Giovanelli hurried her forward. "Quick, quick," he said; "if we get in by midnight we are quite safe."

Daisy took her seat in the carriage, and the fortunate Italian placed himself beside her. "Don't forget Eugenio's pills!" said Winterbourne, as he lifted his hat.

"I don't care," said Daisy, in a little strange tone, "whether I have Roman

---

8. Malaria (Italian).

fever or not!" Upon this the cab-driver cracked his whip, and they rolled away over the desultory patches of the antique pavement.

Winterbourne—to do him justice, as it were—mentioned to no one that he had encountered Miss Miller, at midnight, in the Colosseum with a gentleman; but nevertheless, a couple of days later, the fact of her having been there under these circumstances was known to every member of the little American circle, and commented accordingly. Winterbourne reflected that they had of course known it at the hotel, and that, after Daisy's return, there had been an exchange of jokes between the porter and the cab-driver. But the young man was conscious at the same moment that it had ceased to be a matter of serious regret to him that the little American flirt should be "talked about" by low-minded menials. These people, a day or two later, had serious information to give: the little American flirt was alarmingly ill. Winterbourne, when the rumor came to him, immediately went to the hotel for more news. He found that two or three charitable friends had preceded him, and that they were being entertained in Mrs. Miller's salon by Randolph.

"It's going round at night," said Randolph—"that's what made her sick. She's always going round at midnight. I shouldn't think she'd want to—it's so plaguey dark. You can't see anything here at night, except when there's a moon. In America there's always a moon!" Mrs. Miller was invisible; she was now, at least, giving her daughter the advantage of her society. It was evident that Daisy was dangerously ill.

Winterbourne went often to ask for news of her, and once he saw Mrs. Miller, who, though deeply alarmed, was—rather to his surprise—perfectly composed, and, as it appeared, a most efficient and judicious nurse. She talked a good deal about Dr. Davis, but Winterbourne paid her the compliment of saying to himself that she was not, after all, such a monstrous goose. "Daisy spoke of you the other day," she said to him. "Half the time she doesn't know what she's saying, but that time I think she did. She gave me a message: she told me to tell you. She told me to tell you that she never was engaged to that handsome Italian. I am sure I am very glad; Mr. Giovanelli hasn't been near us since she was taken ill. I thought he was so much of a gentleman; but I don't call that very polite! A lady told me that he was afraid I was angry with him for taking Daisy round at night. Well, so I am; but I suppose he knows I'm a lady. I would scorn to scold him. Any way, she says she's not engaged. I don't know why she wanted you to know; but she said to me three times—'Mind you tell Mr. Winterbourne.' And then she told me to ask if you remembered the time you went to that castle, in Switzerland. But I said I wouldn't give any such messages as that. Only, if she is not engaged, I'm sure I'm glad to know it."

But, as Winterbourne had said, it mattered very little. A week after this the poor girl died; it had been a terrible case of the fever. Daisy's grave was in the little Protestant cemetery, in an angle of the wall of imperial Rome, beneath the cypresses and the thick spring-flowers. Winterbourne stood there beside it, with a number of other mourners; a number larger than the scandal excited by the young lady's career would have led you to expect. Near him stood Giovanelli, who came nearer still before Winterbourne turned away. Giovanelli was very pale; on this occasion he had no flower in his button-hole; he seemed to wish to say something. At last he said, "She was the most beautiful young lady I ever saw, and the most amiable." And then he added in a moment, "And she was the most innocent."

Winterbourne looked at him, and presently repeated his words, "And the most innocent?"

"The most innocent!"

Winterbourne felt sore and angry. "Why the devil," he asked, "did you take her to that fatal place?"

Mr. Giovanelli's urbanity was apparently imperturbable. He looked on the ground a moment, and then he said, "For myself, I had no fear; and she wanted to go."

"That was no reason!" Winterbourne declared.

The subtle Roman again dropped his eyes. "If she had lived, I should have got nothing. She would never have married me, I am sure."

"She would never have married you?"

"For a moment I hoped so. But no, I am sure."

Winterbourne listened to him; he stood staring at the raw protuberance among the April daisies. When he turned away again Mr. Giovanelli, with his light slow step, had retired.

Winterbourne almost immediately left Rome; but the following summer he again met his aunt, Mrs. Costello, at Vevey. Mrs. Costello was fond of Vevey. In the interval Winterbourne had often thought of Daisy Miller and her mystifying manners. One day he spoke of her to his aunt—said it was on his conscience that he had done her injustice.

"I am sure I don't know," said Mrs. Costello. "How did your injustice affect her?"

"She sent me a message before her death which I didn't understand at the time. But I have understood it since. She would have appreciated one's esteem."

"Is that a modest way," asked Mrs. Costello, "of saying that she would have reciprocated one's affection?"

Winterbourne offered no answer to this question; but he presently said, "You were right in that remark that you made last summer. I was booked to make a mistake. I have lived too long in foreign parts."

Nevertheless, he went back to live at Geneva, whence there continue to come the most contradictory accounts of his motives of sojourn: a report that he is "studying" hard—an intimation that he is much interested in a very clever foreign lady.

1878, 1879

The Real Thing[1]

I

When the porter's wife, who used to answer the house-bell, announced "A gentleman and a lady, sir" I had, as I often had in those days—the wish being father to the thought—an immediate vision of sitters. Sitters my visitors in this case proved to be; but not in the sense I should have preferred. There was nothing at first however to indicate that they mightn't have come for a por-

---

1. This "little gem of bright, quick vivid form," as James called it, first appeared in Black and White on April 16, 1892; in "The Real Thing" and Other

Tales (1893); and finally in Vol. 18 (1909) of the New York edition, the source of the text printed here.

trait. The gentleman, a man of fifty, very high and very straight, with a moustache slightly grizzled and a dark grey walking-coat admirably fitted, both of which I noted professionally—I don't mean as a barber or yet as a tailor— would have struck me as a celebrity if celebrities often were striking. It was a truth of which I had for some time been conscious that a figure with a good deal of frontage was, as one might say, almost never a public institution. A glance at the lady helped to remind me of this paradoxical law: she also looked too distinguished to be a "personality." Moreover one would scarcely come across two variations together.

Neither of the pair immediately spoke—they only prolonged the preliminary gaze suggesting that each wished to give the other a chance. They were visibly shy; they stood there letting me take them in—which, as I afterwards perceived, was the most practical thing they could have done. In this way their embarrassment served their cause. I had seen people painfully reluctant to mention that they desired anything so gross as to be represented on canvas; but the scruples of my new friends appeared almost insurmountable. Yet the gentleman might have said "I should like a portrait of my wife," and the lady might have said "I should like a portrait of my husband." Perhaps they weren't husband and wife—this naturally would make the matter more delicate. Perhaps they wished to be done together—in which case they ought to have brought a third person to break the news.

"We come from Mr. Rivet," the lady finally said with a dim smile that had the effect of a moist sponge passed over a "sunk"[2] piece of painting, as well as of a vague allusion to vanished beauty. She was as tall and straight, in her degree, as her companion, and with ten years less to carry. She looked as sad as a woman could look whose face was not charged with expression; that is her tinted oval mask showed waste as an exposed surface shows friction. The hand of time had played over her freely, but to an effect of elimination. She was slim and stiff, and so well-dressed, in dark blue cloth, with lappets and pockets and buttons, that it was clear she employed the same tailor as her husband. The couple had an indefinable air of prosperous thrift—they evidently got a good deal of luxury for their money. If I was to be one of their luxuries it would behove me to consider my terms.

"Ah Claude Rivet recommended me?" I echoed; and I added that it was very kind of him, though I could reflect that, as he only painted landscape, this wasn't a sacrifice.

The lady looked very hard at the gentleman, and the gentleman looked round the room. Then staring at the floor a moment and stroking his moustache, he rested his pleasant eyes on me with the remark: "He said you were the right one."

"I try to be, when people want to sit."

"Yes, we should like to," said the lady anxiously.

"Do you mean together?"

My visitors exchanged a glance. "If you could do anything with *me* I suppose it would be double," the gentleman stammered.

"Oh yes, there's naturally a higher charge for two figures than for one."

"We should like to make it pay," the husband confessed.

"That's very good of you," I returned, appreciating so unwonted a sympathy— for I supposed he meant pay the artist.

2. When colors lose their brilliance after they have dried on the canvas, they are said to have "sunk in."

A sense of strangeness seemed to draw on the lady.

"We mean for the illustrations—Mr. Rivet said you might put one in."

"Put in—an illustration?" I was equally confused.

"Sketch her off, you know," said the gentleman, colouring.

It was only then that I understood the service Claude Rivet had rendered me; he had told them how I worked in black-and-white, for magazines, for storybooks, for sketches of contemporary life, and consequently had copious employment for models. These things were true, but it was not less true—I may confess it now; whether because the aspiration was to lead to everything or to nothing I leave the reader to guess—that I couldn't get the honours, to say nothing of the emoluments, of a great painter of portraits out of my head. My "illustrations" were my pot-boilers; I looked to a different branch of art— far and away the most interesting it had always seemed to me—to perpetuate my fame. There was no shame in looking to it also to make my fortune; but that fortune was by so much further from being made from the moment my visitors wished to be "done" for nothing. I was disappointed; for in the pictorial sense I had immediately *seen* them. I had seized their type—I had already settled what I would do with it. Something that wouldn't absolutely have pleased them, I afterwards reflected.

"Ah you're—you're—a—?" I began as soon as I had mastered my surprise. I couldn't bring out the dingy word "models": it seemed so little to fit the case.

"We haven't had much practice," said the lady.

"We've got to *do* something, and we've thought that an artist in your line might perhaps make something of us," her husband threw off. He further mentioned that they didn't know many artists and that they had gone first, on the off-chance—he painted views of course, but sometimes put in figures; perhaps I remembered—to Mr. Rivet, whom they had met a few years before at a place in Norfolk where he was sketching.

"We used to sketch a little ourselves," the lady hinted.

"It's very awkward, but we absolutely *must* do something," her husband went on.

"Of course we're not so *very* young," she admitted with a wan smile.

With the remark that I might as well know something more about them the husband had handed me a card extracted from a neat new pocket-book— their appurtenances were all of the freshest—and inscribed with the words "Major Monarch." Impressive as these words were they didn't carry my knowledge much further; but my visitor presently added: "I've left the army and we've had the misfortune to lose our money. In fact our means are dreadfully small."

"It's awfully trying—a regular strain," said Mrs. Monarch.

They evidently wished to be discreet—to take care not to swagger because they were gentlefolk. I felt them willing to recognise this as something of a drawback, at the same time that I guessed at an underlying sense—their consolation in adversity—that they *had* their points. They certainly had; but these advantages struck me as preponderantly social; such for instance as would help to make a drawing-room look well. However, a drawing-room was always, or ought to be, a picture.

In consequence of his wife's allusion to their age Major Monarch observed: "Naturally it's more for the figure that we thought of going in. We can still hold ourselves up." On the instant I saw that the figure was indeed their strong point. His "naturally" didn't sound vain, but it lighted up the question. "*She* has the best one," he continued, nodding at his wife with a pleasant after-dinner absence of circumlocution. I could only reply, as if we were in fact sitting over our wine, that this didn't prevent his own from being very good; which led him in turn to make answer: "We thought that if you ever have to do people like us we might be something like it. *She* particularly—for a lady in a book, you know."

I was so amused by them that, to get more of it, I did my best to take their point of view; and though it was an embarrassment to find myself appraising physically, as if they were animals on hire or useful blacks, a pair whom I should have expected to meet only in one of the relations in which criticism is tacit, I looked at Mrs. Monarch judicially enough to be able to exclaim after a moment with conviction: "Oh yes, a lady in a book!" She was singularly like a bad illustration.

"We'll stand up, if you like," said the Major; and he raised himself before me with a really grand air.

I could take his measure at a glance—he was six feet two and a perfect gentleman. It would have paid any club in process of formation and in want of a stamp to engage him at a salary to stand in the principal window. What struck me at once was that in coming to me they had rather missed their vocation; they could surely have been turned to better account for advertising purposes. I couldn't of course see the thing in detail, but I could see them make somebody's fortune—I don't mean their own. There was something in them for a waistcoat-maker, an hotel-keeper or a soap-vendor. I could imagine "We always use it" pinned on their bosoms with the greatest effect; I had a vision of the brilliancy with which they would launch a table d'hôte.[3]

Mrs. Monarch sat still, not from pride but from shyness, and presently her husband said to her; "Get up, my dear, and show how smart you are." She obeyed, but she had no need to get up to show it. She walked to the end of the studio and then came back blushing, her fluttered eyes on the partner of her appeal. I was reminded of an incident I had accidentally had a glimpse of in Paris—being with a friend there, a dramatist about to produce a play, when an actress came to him to ask to be entrusted with a part. She went through her paces before him, walked up and down as Mrs. Monarch was doing. Mrs. Monarch did it quite as well, but I abstained from applauding. It was very odd to see such people apply for such poor pay. She looked as if she had ten thousand a year. Her husband had used the word that described her: she was in the London current jargon essentially and typically "smart." Her figure was, in the same order of ideas, conspicuously and irreproachably "good." For a woman of her age her waist was surprisingly small; her elbow moreover had the orthodox crook. She held her head at the conventional angle, but why did she come to *me*? She ought to have tried on jackets at a big shop. I feared my visitors were not only destitute but "artistic"—which would be a great complication. When she sat down again I thanked her, observing that what a draughtsman most valued in his model was the faculty of keeping quiet.

"Oh *she* can keep quiet," said Major Monarch. Then he added jocosely: "I've always kept her quiet."

---

3. A common table for guests at a hotel.

"I'm not a nasty fidget, am I?" It was going to wring tears from me, I felt, the way she hid her head, ostrich-like, in the other broad bosom.

The owner of this expanse addressed his answer to me. "Perhaps it isn't out of place to mention—because we ought to be quite business-like, oughtn't we?—that when I married her she was known as the Beautiful Statue."

"Oh dear!" said Mrs. Monarch ruefully.

"Of course I should want a certain amount of expression," I rejoined.

"Of *course*!"—and I had never heard such unanimity.

"And then I suppose you know that you'll get awfully tired."

"Oh we *never* get tired!" they eagerly cried.

"Have you had any kind of practice?"

They hesitated—they looked at each other. "We've been photographed—*immensely*," said Mrs. Monarch.

"She means the fellows have asked us themselves," added the Major.

"I see—because you're so good-looking."

"I don't know what they thought, but they were always after us."

"We always got our photographs for nothing," smiled Mrs. Monarch.

"We might have brought some, my dear," her husband remarked.

"I'm not sure we have any left. We've given quantities away," she explained to me.

"With our autographs and that sort of thing," said the Major.

"Are they to be got in the shops?" I enquired as a harmless pleasantry.

"Oh yes, *hers*—they used to be."

"Not now," said Mrs. Monarch with her eyes on the floor.

II

I could fancy the "sort of thing" they put on the presentation copies of their photographs, and I was sure they wrote a beautiful hand. It was odd how quickly I was sure of everything that concerned them. If they were now so poor as to have to earn shillings and pence they could never have had much of a margin. Their good looks had been their capital, and they had good-humouredly made the most of the career that this resource marked out for them. It was in their faces, the blankness, the deep intellectual repose of the twenty years of country-house visiting that had given them pleasant intonations. I could see the sunny drawing-rooms, sprinkled with periodicals she didn't read, in which Mrs. Monarch had continuously sat; I could see the wet shrubberies in which she had walked, equipped to admiration for either exercise. I could see the rich covers[4] the Major had helped to shoot and the wonderful garments in which, late at night, he repaired to the smoking-room to talk about them. I could imagine their leggings and waterproofs, their knowing tweeds and rugs, their rolls of sticks and cases of tackle and neat umbrellas; and I could evoke the exact appearance of their servants and the compact variety of their luggage on the platforms of country stations.

They gave small tips, but they were liked; they didn't do anything themselves, but they were welcome. They looked so well everywhere; they gratified the general relish for stature, complexion and "form." They knew it without fatuity or vulgarity, and they respected themselves in consequence.

4. I.e., successful bagging of game birds.

They weren't superficial; they were thorough and kept themselves up—it had been their line. People with such a taste for activity had to have some line. I could feel how even in a dull house they could have been counted on for the joy of life. At present something had happened—it didn't matter what, their little income had grown less, it had grown least—and they had to do something for pocket-money. Their friends could like them, I made out, without liking to support them. There was something about them that represented credit—their clothes, their manners, their type; but if credit is a large empty pocket in which an occasional chink reverberates, the chink at least must be audible. What they wanted of me was to help to make it so. Fortunately they had no children—I soon divined that. They would also perhaps wish our relations to be kept secret: this was why it was "for the figure"—the reproduction of the face would betray them.

I liked them—I felt, quite as their friends must have done—they were so simple; and I had no objection to them if they would suit. But somehow with all their perfections I didn't easily believe in them. After all they were amateurs, and the ruling passion of my life was the detestation of the amateur. Combined with this was another perversity—an innate preference for the represented subject over the real one: the defect of the real one was so apt to be a lack of representation. I liked things that appeared; then one was sure. Whether they *were* or not was a subordinate and almost always a profitless question. There were other considerations, the first of which was that I already had two or three recruits in use, notably a young person with big feet, in alpaca, from Kilburn, who for a couple of years had come to me regularly for my illustrations and with whom I was still—perhaps ignobly—satisfied. I frankly explained to my visitors how the case stood, but they had taken more precautions than I supposed. They had reasoned out their opportunity, for Claude Rivet had told them of the projected *édition de luxe* of one of the writers of our day—the rarest of the novelists—who, long neglected by the multitudinous vulgar and dearly prized by the attentive (need I mention Philip Vincent?)[5] had had the happy fortune of seeing, late in life, the dawn and then the full light of a higher criticism; an estimate in which on the part of the public there was something really of expiation. The edition preparing, planned by a publisher of taste, was practically an act of high reparation; the wood-cuts with which it was to be enriched were the homage of English art to one of the most independent representatives of English letters. Major and Mrs. Monarch confessed to me they had hoped I might be able to work *them* into my branch of the enterprise. They knew I was to do the first of the books, "Rutland Ramsay," but I had to make clear to them that my participation in the rest of the affair—this first book was to be a test—must depend on the satisfaction I should give. If this should be limited my employers would drop me with scarce common forms. It was therefore a crisis for me, and naturally I was making special preparations, looking about for new people, should they be necessary, and securing the best types. I admitted however that I should like to settle down to two or three good models who would do for everything.

"Should we have often to—a—put on special clothes?" Mrs. Monarch timidly demanded.

"Dear yes—that's half the business."

5. Obviously James, here indulging in some good-natured complaining and fantasizing.

"And should we be expected to supply our own costumes?"

"Oh no; I've got a lot of things. A painter's models put on—or put off—anything he likes."

"And you mean—a—the same?"

"The same?"

Mrs. Monarch looked at her husband again.

"Oh she was just wondering," he explained, "if the costumes are in *general* use." I had to confess that they were, and I mentioned further that some of them—I had a lot of genuine greasy last-century things—had served their time, a hundred years ago, on living world-stained men and women; on figures not perhaps so far removed, in that vanished world, from *their* type, the Monarchs', *quoi!*[6] of a breeched and bewigged age. "We'll put on anything that *fits*," said the Major.

"Oh I arrange that—they fit in the pictures."

"I'm afraid I should do better for the modern books. I'd come as you like," said Mrs. Monarch.

"She has got a lot of clothes at home: they might do for contemporary life," her husband continued.

"Oh I can fancy scenes in which you'd be quite natural." And indeed I could see the slipshod rearrangements of stale properties—the stories I tried to produce pictures for without the exasperation of reading them—whose sandy tracts the good lady might help to people. But I had to return to the fact that for this sort of work—the daily mechanical grind—I was already equipped: the people I was working with were fully adequate.

"We only thought we might be more like *some* characters," said Mrs. Monarch mildly, getting up.

Her husband also rose; he stood looking at me with a dim wistfulness that was touching in so fine a man. "Wouldn't it be rather a pull sometimes to have—a—to have—?" He hung fire; he wanted me to help him by phrasing what he meant. But I couldn't—I didn't know. So he brought it out awkwardly: "The *real* thing; a gentleman, you know, or a lady." I was quite ready to give a general assent—I admitted that there was a great deal in that. This encouraged Major Monarch to say, following up his appeal with an unacted gulp: "It's awfully hard—we've tried everything." The gulp was communicative; it proved too much for his wife. Before I knew it Mrs. Monarch had dropped again upon a divan and burst into tears. Her husband sat down beside her, holding one of her hands; whereupon she quickly dried her eyes with the other, while I felt embarrassed as she looked up at me. "There isn't a confounded job I haven't applied for—waited for—prayed for. You can fancy we'd be pretty bad first. Secretaryships and that sort of thing? You might as well ask for a peerage. I'd be *anything*—I'm strong; a messenger or a coal-heaver. I'd put on a gold-laced cap and open carriage-doors in front of the haberdasher's; I'd hang about a station to carry portmanteaux; I'd be a postman. But they won't *look* at you; there are thousands as good as yourself already on the ground. *Gentlemen*, poor beggars, who've drunk their wine, who've kept their hunters!"

I was as reassuring as I knew how to be, and my visitors were presently on their feet again while, for the experiment, we agreed on an hour. We were dis-

6. What! (French).

cussing it when the door opened and Miss Churm came in with a wet umbrella. Miss Churm had to take the omnibus to Maida Vale and then walk half a mile. She looked a trifle blowsy and slightly splashed. I scarcely ever saw her come in without thinking afresh how odd it was that, being so little in herself, she should yet be so much in others. She was a meagre little Miss Churm, but was such an ample heroine of romance. She was only a freckled cockney,[7] but she could represent everything, from a fine lady to a shepherdess; she had the faculty as she might have had a fine voice or long hair. She couldn't spell and she loved beer, but she had two or three "points," and practice, and a knack, and mother-wit, and a whimsical sensibility, and a love of the theatre, and seven sisters, and not an ounce of respect, especially for the *h*. The first thing my visitors saw was that her umbrella was wet, and in their spotless perfection they visibly winced at it. The rain had come on since their arrival.

"I'm all in a soak; there *was* a mess of people in the 'bus. I wish you lived near a stytion," said Miss Churm. I requested her to get ready as quickly as possible, and she passed into the room in which she always changed her dress. But before going out she asked me what she was to get into this time.

"It's the Russian princess, don't you know?" I answered; "the one with the 'golden eyes,' in black velvet, for the long thing in the *Cheapside*."[8]

"Golden eyes? I *say!*" cried Miss Churm, while my companions watched her with intensity as she withdrew. She always arranged herself, when she was late, before I could turn around; and I kept my visitors a little on purpose, so that they might get an idea, from seeing her, what would be expected of themselves. I mentioned that she was quite my notion of an excellent model—she was really very clever.

"Do you think she looks like a Russian princess?" Major Monarch asked with lurking alarm.

"When I make her, yes."

"Oh if you have to *make* her—!" he reasoned, not without point.

"That's the most you can ask. There are so many who are not makeable."

"Well now, *here's* a lady"—and with a persuasive smile he passed his arm into his wife's—"who's already made!"

"Oh I'm not a Russian princess," Mrs. Monarch protested a little coldly. I could see she had known some and didn't like them. There at once was a complication of a kind I never had to fear with Miss Churm.

This young lady came back in black velvet—the gown was rather rusty and very low on her lean shoulders—and with a Japanese fan in her red hands. I reminded her that in the scene I was doing she had to look over some one's head. "I forget whose it is; but it doesn't matter. Just look over a head."

"I'd rather look over a stove," said Miss Churm; and she took her station near the fire. She fell into position, settled herself into a tall attitude, gave a certain backward inclination to her head and a certain forward droop to her fan, and looked, at least to my prejudiced sense, distinguished and charming, foreign and dangerous. We left her looking so while I went downstairs with Major and Mrs. Monarch.

---

7. Native of London, especially the East End. The cockney dialect is known for dropping *h*'s; e.g., *hair* would be pronounced *air*.

8. Imaginary magazine named after a main business street in London.

"I believe I could come about as near it as that," said Mrs. Monarch.

"Oh, you think she's shabby, but you must allow for the alchemy of art."

However, they went off with an evident increase of comfort founded on their demonstrable advantage in being the real thing. I could fancy them shuddering over Miss Churm. She was very droll about them when I went back, for I told her what they wanted.

"Well, if *she* can sit I'll tyke to bookkeeping," said my model.

"She's very ladylike," I replied as an innocent form of aggravation.

"So much the worse for *you*. That means she can't turn round."

"She'll do for the fashionable novels."

"Oh yes, she'll *do* for them!" my model humorously declared. "Ain't they bad enough without her?" I had often sociably denounced them to Miss Churm.

III

It was for the elucidation of a mystery in one of these works that I first tried Mrs. Monarch. Her husband came with her, to be useful if necessary—it was sufficiently clear that as a general thing he would prefer to come with her. At first I wondered if this were for "propriety's" sake—if he were going to be jealous and meddling. The idea was too tiresome, and if it had been confirmed it would speedily have brought our acquaintance to a close. But I soon saw there was nothing in it and that if he accompanied Mrs. Monarch it was—in addition to the chance of being wanted—simply because he had nothing else to do. When they were separate his occupation was gone and they never *had* been separate. I judged rightly that in their awkward situation their close union was their main comfort and that this union had no weak spot. It was a real marriage, an encouragement to the hesitating, a nut for pessimists to crack. Their address was humble—I remember afterwards thinking it had been the only thing about them that was really professional—and I could fancy the lamentable lodgings in which the Major would have been left alone. He could sit there more or less grimly with his wife—he couldn't sit there anyhow without her.

He had too much tact to try and make himself agreeable when he couldn't be useful; so when I was too absorbed in my work to talk he simply sat and waited. But I liked to hear him talk—it made my work, when not interrupting it, less mechanical, less special. To listen to him was to combine the excitement of going out with the economy of staying at home. There was only one hindrance—that I seemed not to know any of the people this brilliant couple had known. I think he wondered extremely, during the term of our intercourse, whom the deuce I *did* know. He hadn't a stray sixpence of an idea to fumble for, so we didn't spin it very fine; we confined ourselves to questions of leather and even of liquor—saddlers and breeches-makers and how to get excellent claret cheap—and matters like "good trains" and the habits of small game. His lore on these last subjects was astonishing—he managed to interweave the station-master with the ornithologist. When he couldn't talk about greater things he could talk cheerfully about smaller, and since I couldn't accompany him into reminiscences of the fashionable world he could lower the conversation without a visible effort to my level.

So earnest a desire to please was touching in a man who could so easily have knocked one down. He looked after the fire and had an opinion on the draught of the stove without my asking him, and I could see that he thought many of my arrangements not half knowing. I remember telling him that if I were only rich I'd offer him a salary to come and teach me how to live. Sometimes he gave a random sigh of which the essence might have been: "Give me even such a bare old barrack as *this*, and I'd do something with it!" When I wanted to use him he came alone; which was an illustration of the superior courage of women. His wife could bear her solitary second floor, and she was in general more discreet; showing by various small reserves that she was alive to the propriety of keeping our relations markedly professional—not letting them slide into sociability. She wished it to remain clear that she and the Major were employed, not cultivated, and if she approved of me as a superior, who could be kept in his place, she never thought me quite good enough for an equal.

She sat with great intensity, giving the whole of her mind to it, and was capable of remaining for an hour almost as motionless as before a photographer's lens. I could see she had been photographed often, but somehow the very habit that made her good for that purpose unfitted her for mine. At first I was extremely pleased with her ladylike air, and it was a satisfaction, on coming to follow her lines, to see how good they were and how far they could lead the pencil. But after a little skirmishing I began to find her too insurmountably stiff; do what I would with it my drawing looked like a photograph or a copy of a photograph. Her figure had no variety of expression—she herself had no sense of variety. You may say that this was my business and was only a question of placing her. Yet I placed her in every conceivable position and she managed to obliterate their differences. She was always a lady certainly, and into the bargain was always the same lady. She was the real thing, but always the same thing. There were moments when I rather writhed under the serenity of her confidence that she *was* the real thing. All her dealings with me and all her husband's were an implication that this was lucky for *me*. Meanwhile I found myself trying to invent types that approached her own, instead of making her own transform itself—in the clever way that was not impossible for instance to poor Miss Churm. Arrange as I would and take the precautions I would, she always came out, in my pictures, too tall—landing me in the dilemma of having represented a fascinating woman as seven feet high, which (out of respect perhaps to my own very much scantier inches) was far from my idea of such a personage.

The case was worse with the Major—nothing I could do would keep *him* down, so that he became useful only for representation of brawny giants. I adored variety and range, I cherished human accidents, the illustrative note; I wanted to characterise closely, and the thing in the world I most hated was the danger of being ridden by a type. I had quarrelled with some of my friends about it; I had parted company with them for maintaining that one *had* to be, and that if the type was beautiful—witness Raphael and Leonardo[9]—the servitude was only a gain. I was neither Leonardo nor Raphael—I might only be a presumptuous young modern searcher; but I held that everything was to be sacrificed sooner than character. When they claimed that the obsessional

9. Leonardo da Vinci (1452–1519), Florentine painter, sculptor, architect, and engineer. Raffaello Santi or Sanzio (1483–1520), Italian painter.

form could easily *be* character I retorted, perhaps superficially, "Whose?" It couldn't be everybody's—it might end in being nobody's.

After I had drawn Mrs. Monarch a dozen times I felt surer even than before that the value of such a model as Miss Churm resided precisely in the fact that she had no positive stamp, combined of course with the other fact that what she did have was a curious and inexplicable talent for imitation. Her usual appearance was like a curtain which she could draw up at request for a capital performance. This performance was simply suggestive; but it was a word to the wise—it was vivid and pretty. Sometimes even I thought it, though she was plain herself, too insipidly pretty; I made it a reproach to her that the figures drawn from her were monotonously (*bêtement,*[1] as we used to say) graceful. Nothing made her more angry: it was so much her pride to feel she could sit for characters that had nothing in common with each other. She would accuse me at such moments of taking away her "reputytion."

It suffered a certain shrinkage, this queer quantity, from the repeated visits of my new friends. Miss Churm was greatly in demand, never in want of employment, so I had no scruple in putting her off occasionally, to try them more at my ease. It was certainly amusing at first to do the real thing—it was amusing to do Major Monarch's trousers. There *were* the real thing, even if he did come out colossal. It was amusing to do his wife's back hair—it was so mathematically neat—and the particular "smart" tension of her tight stays. She lent herself especially to positions in which the face was somewhat averted or blurred; she abounded in ladylike back views and *profils perdus.*[2] When she stood erect she took naturally one of the attitudes in which court-painters represent queens and princesses; so that I found myself wondering whether, to draw out this accomplishment, I couldn't get the editor of the *Cheapside* to publish a really royal romance, "A Tale of Buckingham Palace." Sometimes however the real thing and the make-believe came into contact; by which I mean that Miss Churm, keeping an appointment or coming to make one on days when I had much work in hand, encountered her invidious rivals. The encounter was not on their part, for they noticed her no more than if she had been the housemaid; not from intentional loftiness, but simply because as yet, professionally, they didn't know how to fraternise, as I could imagine they would have liked—or at least that the Major would. They couldn't talk about the omnibus—they always walked; and they didn't know what else to try—she wasn't interested in good trains or cheap claret. Besides, they must have felt—in the air—that she was amused at them, secretly derisive of their ever knowing how. She wasn't a person to conceal the limits of her faith if she had had a chance to show them. On the other hand Mrs. Monarch didn't think her tidy; for why else did she take pains to say to me— it was going out of the way, for Mrs. Monarch—that she didn't like dirty women?

One day when my young lady happened to be present with my other sitters— she even dropped in, when it was convenient, for a chat—I asked her to be so good as to lend a hand in getting tea, a service with which she was familiar and which was one of a class that, living as I did in a small way, with slender domestic resources, I often appealed to my models to render. They liked to lay hands on my property, to break the sitting, and sometimes the

---

1. Foolishly (French).　　　　2. Averted glances (French).

china—it made them feel Bohemian. The next time I saw Miss Churm after this incident she surprised me greatly by making a scene about it—she accused me of having wished to humiliate her. She hadn't resented the outrage at the time, but had seemed obliging and amused, enjoying the comedy of asking Mrs. Monarch, who sat vague and silent, whether she would have cream and sugar, and putting an exaggerated simper into the question. She had tried intonations—as if she too wished to pass for the real thing—till I was afraid my other visitors would take offence.

Oh they were determined not to do this, and their touching patience was the measure of their great need. They would sit by the hour, uncomplaining, till I was ready to use them; they would come back on the chance of being wanted and would walk away cheerfully if it failed. I used to go to the door with them to see in what magnificent order they retreated. I tried to find other employment for them—I introduced them to several artists. But they didn't "take," for reasons I could appreciate, and I became rather anxiously aware that after such disappointments they fell back upon me with a heavier weight. They did me the honour to think me most *their* form. They weren't romantic enough for the painters, and in those days there were few serious workers in black-and-white. Besides, they had an eye to the great job I had mentioned to them—they had secretly set their hearts on supplying the right essence for my pictorial vindication of our fine novelist. They knew that for this undertaking I should want no costume-effects, none of the frippery of past ages—that it was a case in which everything would be contemporary and satirical and presumably genteel. If I could work them into it their future would be assured, for the labour would of course be long and the occupation steady.

One day Mrs. Monarch came without her husband—she explained his absence by his having had to go to the City.[3] While she sat there in her usual relaxed majesty there came at the door a knock which I immediately recognised as the subdued appeal of a model out of work. It was followed by the entrance of a young man whom I at once saw to be a foreigner and who proved in fact an Italian acquainted with no English word but my name, which he uttered in a way that made it seem to include all others. I hadn't then visited his country, nor was I proficient in his tongue; but as he was not so meanly constituted—what Italian is?—as to depend only on that member for expression he conveyed to me, in familiar but graceful mimicry, that he was in search of exactly the employment in which the lady before me was engaged. I was not struck with him at first, and while I continued to draw I dropped few signs of interest or encouragement. He stood his ground however—not importunately, but with a dumb dog-like fidelity in his eyes that amounted to innocent impudence, the manner of a devoted servant—he might have been in the house for years—unjustly suspected. Suddenly it struck me that this very attitude and expression made a picture; whereupon I told him to sit down and wait till I should be free. There was another picture in the way he obeyed me, and I observed as I worked that there were others still in the way he looked wonderingly, with his head thrown back, about the high studio. He might have been crossing himself in Saint Peter's. Before

3. London. The "City" also specifically means the old part of London around St. Paul's Cathedral, especially the financial and legal institutions there.

I finished I said to myself "The fellow's a bankrupt orange-monger, but a treasure."

When Mrs. Monarch withdrew he passed across the room like a flash to open the door for her, standing there with the rapt pure gaze of the young Dante spellbound by the young Beatrice.[4] As I never insisted, in such situations, on the blankness of the British domestic, I reflected that he had the making of a servant—and I needed one, but couldn't pay him to be only that—as well as of a model; in short I resolved to adopt my bright adventurer if he would agree to officiate in the double capacity. He jumped at my offer, and in the event my rashness—for I had really known nothing about him—wasn't brought home to me. He proved a sympathetic though a desultory ministrant, and had in a wonderful degree the *sentiment de la pose*.[5] It was uncultivated, instinctive, a part of the happy instinct that had guided him to my door and helped him to spell out my name on the card nailed to it. He had had no other introduction to me than a guess, from the shape of my high north window, seen outside, that my place was a studio and that as a studio it would contain an artist. He had wandered to England in search of fortune, like other itinerants, and had embarked, with a partner and a small green hand-cart, on the sale of penny ices. The ices had melted away and the partner had dissolved in their train. My young man wore tight yellow trousers with reddish stripes and his name was Oronte. He was sallow but fair, and when I put him into some old clothes of my own he looked like an Englishman. He was as good as Miss Churm, who could look, when requested, like an Italian.

IV

I thought Mrs. Monarch's face slightly convulsed when, on her coming back with her husband, she found Oronte installed. It was strange to have to recognise in a scrap of a lazzarone[6] a competitor to her magnificent Major. It was she who scented danger first, for the Major was anecdotically unconscious. But Oronte gave us tea, with a hundred eager confusions—he had never been concerned in so queer a process—and I think she thought better of me for having at last an "establishment." They saw a couple of drawings that I had made of the establishment, and Mrs. Monarch hinted that it never would have struck her he had sat for them. "Now the drawings you make from *us*, they look exactly like us," she reminded me, smiling in triumph; and I recognised that this was indeed just their defect. When I drew the Monarchs I couldn't anyhow get away from them—get into the character I wanted to represent; and I hadn't the least desire my model should be discoverable in my picture. Miss Churm never was, and Mrs. Monarch thought I hid her, very properly, because she was vulgar; whereas if she was lost it was only as the dead who go to heaven are lost—in the gain of an angel the more.

By this time I had got a certain start with "Rutland Ramsay," the first novel in the great projected series; that is I had produced a dozen drawings, several with the help of the Major and his wife, and I had sent them in for approval.

---

4. Dante Alighieri (1265–1321), Italian poet, first saw Beatrice Portinari when they were both nine. Though he saw her only a few times, she made a lasting impression on him and became his ideal, his life's inspiration, and the direct agent of his sal-vation (as his greatest work, *The Divine Comedy*, makes clear).
5. Instinct for striking poses (French).
6. Beggar (Italian).

My understanding with the publishers, as I have already hinted, had been that I was to be left to do my work, in this particular case, as I liked, with the whole book committed to me; but my connexion with the rest of the series was only contingent. There were moments when, frankly, it *was* a comfort to have the real thing under one's hand; for there were characters in "Rutland Ramsay" that were very much like it. There were people presumably as erect as the Major and women of as good a fashion as Mrs. Monarch. There was a great deal of country-house life—treated, it is true, in a fine fanciful ironical generalised way—and there was a considerable implication of knickerbockers and kilts.[7] There were certain things I had to settle at the outset; such things for instance as the exact appearance of the hero and the particular bloom and figure of the heroine. The author of course gave me a lead, but there was a margin for interpretation. I took the Monarchs into my confidence, I told them frankly what I was about, I mentioned my embarrassments and alternatives. "Oh take *him!*" Mrs. Monarch murmured sweetly, looking at her husband; and "What could you want better than my wife?" the Major enquired with the comfortable candour that now prevailed between us.

I wasn't obliged to answer these remarks—I was only obliged to place my sitters. I wasn't easy in mind, and I postponed a little timidly perhaps the solving of my question. The book was a large canvas, the other figures were numerous, and I worked off at first some of the episodes in which the hero and the heroine were not concerned. When once I had set *them* up I should have to stick to them—I couldn't make my young man seven feet high in one place and five feet nine in another. I inclined on the whole to the latter measurement, though the Major more than once reminded me that *he* looked about as young as any one. It was indeed quite possible to arrange him, for the figure, so that it would have been difficult to detect his age. After the spontaneous Oronte had been with me a month, and after I had given him to understand several times over that his native exuberance would presently constitute an insurmountable barrier to our further intercourse, I waked to a sense of his heroic capacity. He was only five feet seven, but the remaining inches were latent. I tried him almost secretly at first, for I was really rather afraid of the judgment my other models would pass on such a choice. If they regarded Miss Churm as little better than a snare what would they think of the representation by a person so little the real thing as an Italian street-vendor of a protagonist formed by a public school?

If I went a little in fear of them it wasn't because they bullied me, because they had got an oppressive foothold, but because in their really pathetic decorum and mysteriously permanent newness they counted on me so intensely. I was therefore very glad when Jack Hawley came home: he was always of such good counsel. He painted badly himself, but there was no one like him for putting his finger on the place. He had been absent from England for a year; he had been somewhere—I don't remember where—to get a fresh eye. I was in a good deal of dread of any such organ, but we were old friends; he had been away for months and a sense of emptiness was creeping into my life. I hadn't dodged a missile for a year.

He came back with a fresh eye, but with the same old black velvet blouse,

---

7. Knickerbockers (close-fitting short pants gathered at the knee) and kilts (knee-length pleated skirts, usually of tartan, worn by Scottish men) suggest a rural, outdoor attire.

and the first evening he spent in my studio we smoked cigarettes till the small hours. He had done no work himself, he had only got the eye; so the field was clear for the production of my little things. He wanted to see what I had produced for the *Cheapside*, but he was disappointed in the exhibition. That at least seemed the meaning of two or three comprehensive groans which, as he lounged on my big divan, his leg folded under him, looking at my latest drawings, issued from his lips with the smoke of the cigarette.

"What's the matter with you?" I asked.

"What's the matter with *you?*"

"Nothing save that I'm mystified."

"You are indeed. You're quite off the hinge. What's the meaning of this new fad?" And he tossed me, with visible irreverence, a drawing in which I happened to have depicted both my elegant models. I asked if he didn't think it good, and he replied that it struck him as execrable, given the sort of thing I had always represented myself to him as wishing to arrive at; but I let that pass—I was so anxious to see exactly what he meant. The two figures in the picture looked colossal, but I supposed this was *not* what he meant, inasmuch as, for aught he knew the contrary, I might have been trying for some such effect. I maintained that I was working exactly in the same way as when he last had done me the honour to tell me I might do something some day. "Well, there's a screw loose somewhere," he answered; "wait a bit and I'll discover it." I depended upon him to do so: where else was the fresh eye? But he produced at last nothing more luminous than "I don't know—I don't like your types." This was lame for a critic who had never consented to discuss with me anything but the question of execution, the direction of strokes and the mystery of values.

"In the drawings you've been looking at I think my types are very handsome."

"Oh they won't do!"

"I've been working with new models."

"I see you have. *They* won't do."

"Are you very sure of that?"

"Absolutely—they're stupid."

"You mean *I* am—for I ought to get round that."

"You *can't*—with such people. Who are they?"

I told him, so far as was necessary, and he concluded heartlessly: "Ce sont des gens qu'il faut mettre à la porte."[8]

"You've never seen them; they're awfully good"—I flew to their defence.

"Not seen them? Why all this recent work of yours drops to pieces with them. It's all I want to see of them."

"No one else has said anything against it—the *Cheapside* people are pleased."

"Everyone else is an ass, and the *Cheapside* people the biggest asses of all. Come, don't pretend at this time of day to have pretty illusions about the public, especially about publishers and editors. It's not for *such* animals you work—it's for those who know, *coloro che sanno;*[9] so keep straight for *me* if you can't keep straight for yourself. There was a certain sort of thing you used

8. Such people should be shown the door (French).
9. A misquotation of a phrase Dante applied to

Aristotle in *The Divine Comedy*, "Inferno," 4.131, which reads, *"el maestro di color che sanno,"* literally, "the master of those who know."

to try for—and a very good thing it was. But this twaddle isn't *in* it." When I talked with Hawley later about "Rutland Ramsay" and its possible successors he declared that I must get back into my boat again or I should go to the bottom. His voice in short was the voice of warning.

I noted the warning, but I didn't turn my friends out of doors. They bored me a good deal; but the very fact that they bored me admonished me not to sacrifice them—if there was anything to be done with them—simply to irritation. As I look back at this phase they seem to me to have pervaded my life not a little. I have a vision of them as most of the time in my studio, seated against the wall on an old velvet bench to be out of the way, and resembling the while a pair of patient courtiers in a royal ante-chamber. I'm convinced that during the coldest weeks of the winter they held their ground because it saved them fire. Their newness was losing its gloss, and it was impossible not to feel them objects of charity. Whenever Miss Churm arrived they went away, and after I was fairly launched in "Rutland Ramsay" Miss Churm arrived pretty often. They managed to express to me tacitly that they supposed I wanted her for the low life of the book, and I let them suppose it, since they had attempted to study the work—it was lying about the studio—without discovering that it dealt only with the highest circles. They had dipped into the most brilliant of our novelists without deciphering many passages. I still took an hour from them, now and again, in spite of Jack Hawley's warning: it would be time enough to dismiss them, if dismissal should be necessary, when the rigour of the season was over. Hawley had made their acquaintance—he had met them at my fireside—and thought them a ridiculous pair. Learning that he was a painter they tried to approach him, to show him too that they were the real thing; but he looked at them, across the big room, as if they were miles away: they were a compendium of everything he most objected to in the social system of his country. Such people as that, all convention and patent-leather, with ejaculations that stopped conversation, had no business in a studio. A studio was a place to learn to see, and how could you see through a pair of feather-beds?

The main inconvenience I suffered at their hands was that at first I was shy of letting it break upon them that my artful little servant had begun to sit to me for "Rutland Ramsay." They knew I had been odd enough—they were prepared by this time to allow oddity to artists—to pick a foreign vagabond out of the streets when I might have had a person with whiskers and credentials, but it was some time before they learned how high I rated his accomplishments. They found him in an attitude more than once, but they never doubted I was doing him as an organ-grinder. There were several things they never guessed, and one of them was that for a striking scene in the novel, in which a footman briefly figured, it occurred to me to make use of Major Monarch as the menial. I kept putting this off, I didn't like to ask him to don the livery—besides the difficulty of finding a livery to fit him. At last, one day late in the winter, when I was at work on the despised Oronte, who caught one's idea on the wing, and was in the glow of feeling myself go very straight, they came in, the Major and his wife, with their society laugh about nothing (there was less and less to laugh at); came in like country-callers—they always reminded me of that—who have walked across the park after church and are presently persuaded to stay to luncheon. Luncheon was over, but they could stay to tea—I knew they wanted it. The fit was on me, however, and I couldn't let my ardour cool and my work wait, with the fading daylight, while my model prepared it. So I asked Mrs. Monarch if she would mind laying it out—a request which for an instant brought all the blood to her face. Her eyes were on her husband's for a second, and some mute telegraphy passed between them. Their folly was over the next instant; his cheerful shrewdness put an end to it. So far from pitying their wounded pride, I must add, I was moved to give it as complete a lesson as I could. They bustled about together and got out the cups and saucers and made the kettle boil. I know they felt as if they were waiting on my servant, and when the tea was prepared I said: "He'll have a cup, please—he's tired." Mrs. Monarch brought him one where he stood, and he took it from her as if had been a gentleman at a party squeezing a crush-hat with an elbow.

Then it came over me that she had made a great effort for me—made it with a kind of nobleness—and that I owed her a compensation. Each time I saw her after this I wondered what the compensation could be. I couldn't go on doing the wrong thing to oblige them. Oh it *was* the wrong thing, the stamp of the work for which they sat—Hawley was not the only person to say it now. I sent in a large number of the drawings I had made for "Rutland Ramsay," and I received a warning that was more to the point than Hawley's. The artistic adviser of the house for which I was working was of opinion that many of my illustrations were not what had been looked for. Most of these illustrations were the subjects in which the Monarchs had figured. Without going into the question of what *had* been looked for, I had to face the fact that at this rate I shouldn't get the other books to do. I hurled myself in despair on Miss Churm—I put her through all her paces. I not only adopted Oronte publicly as my hero, but one morning when the Major looked in to see if I didn't require him to finish a *Cheapside* figure for which he had begun to sit the week before, I told him I had changed my mind—I'd do the drawing from my man. At this my visitor turned pale and stood looking at me. "Is *he* your idea of an English gentleman?" he asked.

I was disappointed, I was nervous, I wanted to get on with my work; so I replied with irritation: "Oh my dear Major—I can't be ruined for *you!*"

It was a horrid speech, but he stood another moment—after which, without a word, he quitted the studio. I drew a long breath, for I said to myself that I shouldn't see him again. I hadn't told him definitely that I was in danger of having my work rejected, but I was vexed at his not having felt the catastrophe in the air, read with me the moral of our fruitless collaboration, the lesson that in the deceptive atmosphere of art even the highest respectability may fail of being plastic.

I didn't owe my friends money, but I did see them again. They reappeared together three days later, and, given all the other facts, there was something tragic in that one. It was a clear proof they could find nothing else in life to do. They had threshed the matter out in a dismal conference—they had digested the bad news that they were not in for the series. If they weren't useful to me even for the *Cheapside* their function seemed difficult to determine, and I could only judge at first that they had come, forgivingly, decorously, to take a last leave. This made me rejoice in secret that I had little leisure for a scene; for I had placed both my other models in position together and I was pegging away at a drawing from which I hoped to derive glory. It had been suggested by the passage in which Rutland Ramsay, drawing up a chair to

Artemisia's piano-stool, says extraordinary things to her while she ostensibly fingers out a difficult piece of music. I had done Miss Churm at the piano before—it was an attitude in which she knew how to take on an absolutely poetic grace. I wished the two figures to "compose" together with intensity, and my little Italian had entered perfectly into my conception. The pair were vividly before me, the piano had been pulled out; it was a charming show of blended youth and murmured love, which I had only to catch and keep. My visitors stood and looked at it, and I was friendly to them over my shoulder.

They made no response, but I was used to silent company and went on with my work, only a little disconcerted—even though exhilarated by the sense that *this* was at least the ideal thing—at not having got rid of them after all. Presently I heard Mrs. Monarch's sweet voice beside or rather above me: "I wish her hair were a little better done." I looked up and she was staring with a strange fixedness at Miss Churm, whose back was turned to her. "Do you mind my just touching it?" she went on—a question which made me spring up for an instant as with the instinctive fear that she might do the young lady a harm. But she quieted me with a glance I shall never forget—I confess I should like to have been able to paint *that*—and went for a moment to my model. She spoke to her softly, laying a hand on her shoulder and bending over her; and as the girl, understanding, gratefully assented, she disposed her rough curls, with a few quick passes, in such a way as to make Miss Churm's head twice as charming. It was one of the most heroic personal services I've ever seen rendered. Then Mrs. Monarch turned away with a low sigh and, looking about her as if for something to do, stooped to the floor with a noble humility and picked up a dirty rag that had dropped out of my paint-box.

The Major meanwhile had also been looking for something to do, and, wandering to the other end of the studio, saw before him my breakfast-things neglected, unremoved. "I say, can't I be useful *here*?" he called out to me with an irrepressible quaver. I assented with a laugh that I fear was awkward, and for the next ten minutes, while I worked, I heard the light clatter of china and the tinkle of spoons and glass. Mrs. Monarch assisted her husband—they washed up my crockery, they put it away. They wandered off into my little scullery, and I afterwards found that they had cleaned my knives and that my slender stock of plate had an unprecedented surface. When it came over me, the latent eloquence of what they were doing, I confess that my drawing was blurred for a moment—the picture swam. They had accepted their failure, but they couldn't accept their fate. They had bowed their heads in bewilderment to the perverse and cruel law in virtue of which the real thing could be so much less precious than the unreal; but they didn't want to starve. If my servants were my models, then my models might be my servants. They would reverse the parts—the others would sit for the ladies and gentlemen and *they* would do the work. They would still be in the studio—it was an intense dumb appeal to me not to turn them out. "Take us on," they wanted to say—"we'll do *anything*."

My pencil dropped from my hand; my sitting was spoiled and I got rid of my sitters, who were also evidently rather mystified and awestruck. Then, alone with the Major and his wife I had a most uncomfortable moment. He put their prayer into a single sentence: "I say, you know—just let *us* do for you, can't you?" I couldn't—it was dreadful to see them emptying my slops; but I pretended I could, to oblige them, for about a week. Then I gave them a sum of money to go away, and I never saw them again. I obtained the remaining books, but my friend Hawley repeats that Major and Mrs. Monarch did me a permanent harm, got me into false ways. If it be true I'm content to have paid the price—for the memory.

1892, 1909

The Beast in the Jungle[1]

I

What determined the speech that startled him in the course of their encounter scarcely matters, being probably but some words spoken by himself quite without intention—spoken as they lingered and slowly moved together after their renewal of acquaintance. He had been conveyed by friends an hour or two before to the house at which she was staying; the party of visitors at the other house, of whom he was one, and thanks to whom it was his theory, as always, that he was lost in the crowd, had been invited over to luncheon. There had been after luncheon much dispersal, all in the interest of the original motive, a view of Weatherend itself and the fine things, intrinsic features, pictures, heirlooms, treasures of all the arts, that made the place almost famous; and the great rooms were so numerous that guests could wander at their will, hang back from the principal group and in cases where they took such matters with the last seriousness give themselves up to mysterious appreciations and measurements. There were persons to be observed, singly or in couples, bending toward objects in out-of-the-way corners with their hands on their knees and their heads nodding quite as with the emphasis of an excited sense of smell. When they were two they either mingled their sounds of ecstasy or melted into silences of even deeper import, so that there were aspects of the occasion that gave it for Marcher much the air of the "look round," previous to a sale highly advertised, that excites or quenches, as may be, the dream of acquisition. The dream of acquisition at Weatherend would have had to be wild indeed, and John Marcher found himself, among such suggestions, disconcerted almost equally by the presence of those who knew too much and by that of those who knew nothing. The great rooms caused so much poetry and history to press upon him that he needed some straying apart to feel in a proper relation with them, though this impulse was not, as happened, like the gloating of some of his companions, to be compared to the movements of a dog sniffing a cupboard. It had an issue promptly enough in a direction that was not to have been calculated.

It led, briefly, in the course of the October afternoon, to his closer meeting with May Bartram, whose face, a reminder, yet not quite a remembrance, as they sat much separated at a very long table, had begun merely by troubling him rather pleasantly. It affected him as the sequel of something of which he had lost the beginning. He knew it, and for the time quite welcomed

1. James initially recorded the germ for this story in 1895, but it first appeared in the collection *The Better Sort* (1903). It was reprinted, with minor revisions, in the *Altar of the Dead* volume of the New York edition, Vol. 17 (1909), the source of the text printed here.

it, as a continuation, but didn't know what it continued, which was an interest or an amusement the greater as he was also somehow aware—yet without a direct sign from her—that the young woman herself hadn't lost the
thread. She hadn't lost it, but she wouldn't give it back to him, he saw, without some putting forth of his hand for it; and he not only saw that, but saw
several things more, things odd enough in the light of the fact that at the
moment some accident of grouping brought them face to face he was still
merely fumbling with the idea that any contact between them in the past
would have had no importance. If it had had no importance he scarcely knew
why his actual impression of her should so seem to have so much; the answer
to which, however, was that in such a life as they all appeared to be leading
for the moment one could but take things as they came. He was satisfied,
without in the least being able to say why, that this young lady might roughly
have ranked in the house as a poor relation; satisfied also that she was not
there on a brief visit, but was more or less a part of the establishment—almost
a working, a remunerated part. Didn't she enjoy at periods a protection that
she paid for by helping, among other services, to show the place and explain
it, deal with the tiresome people, answer questions about the dates of the
building, the styles of the furniture, the authorship of the pictures, the
favourite haunts of the ghost? It wasn't that she looked as if you could have
given her shillings—it was impossible to look less so. Yet when she finally
drifted toward him, distinctly handsome, though ever so much older—older
than when he had seen her before—it might have been as an effect of her
guessing that he had, within the couple of hours, devoted more imagination
to her than to all the others put together, and had thereby penetrated to a kind
of truth that the others were too stupid for. She *was* there on harder terms
than any one; she was there as a consequence of things suffered, one way and
another, in the interval of years; and she remembered him very much as she
was remembered—only a good deal better.

By the time they at last thus came to speech they were alone in one of the
rooms—remarkable for a fine portrait over the chimney-place—out of which
their friends had passed, and the charm of it was that even before they had
spoken they had practically arranged with each other to stay behind for talk.
The charm, happily, was in other things too—partly in there being scarce a
spot at Weatherend without something to stay behind for. It was in the way
the autumn day looked into the high windows as it waned; the way the red
light, breaking at the close from under a low sombre sky, reached out in a long
shaft and played over old wainscots, old tapestry, old gold, old colour. It was
most of all perhaps in the way she came to him as if, since she had been
turned on to deal with the simpler sort, he might, should he choose to keep
the whole thing down, just take her mild attention for a part of her general
business. As soon as he heard her voice, however, the gap was filled up and
the missing link supplied; the slight irony he divined in her attitude lost its
advantage. He almost jumped at it to get there before her. "I met you years
and years ago in Rome. I remember all about it." She confessed to disappointment—she had been so sure he didn't; and to prove how well he did he
began to pour forth the particular recollections that popped up as he called
for them. Her face and her voice, all at his service now, worked the miracle—
the impression operating like the torch of a lamplighter who touches
into flame, one by one, a long row of gas-jets. Marcher flattered himself the

illumination was brilliant, yet he was really still more pleased on her showing him, with amusement, that in his haste to make everything right he had got most things rather wrong. It hadn't been at Rome—it had been at Naples; and it hadn't been eight years before—it had been more nearly ten. She hadn't been, either, with her uncle and aunt, but with her mother and her brother; in addition to which it was not with the Pembles *he* had been, but with the Boyers, coming down in their company from Rome—a point on which she insisted, a little to his confusion, and as to which she had her evidence in hand. The Boyers she had known, but didn't know the Pembles, though she had heard of them, and it was the people he was with who had made them acquainted. The incident of the thunderstorm that had raged round them with such violence as to drive them for refuge into an excavation—this incident had not occurred at the Palace of the Cæsars, but at Pompeii,[2] on an occasion when they had been present there at an important find.

He accepted her amendments, he enjoyed her corrections, though the moral of them was, she pointed out, that he *really* didn't remember the least thing about her; and he only felt it as a drawback that when all was made strictly historic there didn't appear much of anything left. They lingered together still, she neglecting her office—for from the moment he was so clever she had no proper right to him—and both neglecting the house, just waiting as to see if a memory or two more wouldn't again breathe on them. It hadn't taken them many minutes, after all, to put down on the table, like the cards of a pack, those that constituted their respective hands; only what came out was that the pack was unfortunately not perfect—that the past, invoked, invited, encouraged, could give them, naturally, no more than it had. It had made them anciently meet—her at twenty, him at twenty-five; but nothing was so strange, they seemed to say to each other, as that, while so occupied, it hadn't done a little more for them. They looked at each other as with the feeling of an occasion missed; the present would have been so much better if the other, in the far distance, in the foreign land, hadn't been so stupidly meagre. There weren't apparently, all counted, more than a dozen little old things that had succeeded in coming to pass between them; trivialities of youth, simplicities of freshness, stupidities of ignorance, small possible germs, but too deeply buried—too deeply (didn't it seem?) to sprout after so many years. Marcher could only feel he ought to have rendered her some service—saved her from a capsized boat in the Bay or at least recovered her dressing-bag, filched from her cab in the streets of Naples by a lazzarone[3] with a stiletto. Or it would have been nice if he could have been taken with fever all alone at his hotel, and she could have come to look after him, to write to his people, to drive him out in convalescence. *Then* they would be in possession of the something or other that their actual show seemed to lack. It yet somehow presented itself, this show, as too good to be spoiled; so that they were reduced for a few minutes more to wondering a little helplessly why—since they seemed to know a certain number of the same people—their reunion had been so long averted. They didn't use that name for it, but their delay from minute to minute to join the others was a kind of confession that they didn't quite want it to be a failure. Their attempted supposition of reasons for their not having met but showed how little they knew of each other.

2. Pompeii is near Naples, not Rome.   3. Beggar (Italian).

There came in fact a moment when Marcher felt a positive pang. It was vain to pretend she was an old friend, for all the communities were wanting, in spite of which it was as an old friend that he saw she would have suited him. He had new ones enough—was surrounded with them for instance on the stage of the other house; as a new one he probably wouldn't have so much as noticed her. He would have liked to invent something, get her to make-believe with him that some passage of a romantic or critical kind *had* originally occurred. He was really almost reaching out in imagination—as against time—for something that would do, and saying to himself that if it didn't come this sketch of a fresh start would show for quite awkwardly bungled. They would separate, and now for no second or no third chance. They would have tried and not succeeded. Then it was, just at the turn, as he afterwards made it out to himself, that, everything else failing, she herself decided to take up the case and, as it were, save the situation. He felt as soon as she spoke that she had been consciously keeping back what she said and hoping to get on without it; a scruple in her that immensely touched him when, by the end of three or four minutes more, he was able to measure it. What she brought out, at any rate, quite cleared the air and supplied the link—the link it was so odd he should frivolously have managed to lose.

"You know you told me something I've never forgotten and that again and again has made me think of you since; it was that tremendously hot day when we went to Sorrento,[4] across the bay, for the breeze. What I allude to was what you said to me, on the way back, as we sat under the awning of the boat enjoying the cool. Have you forgotten?"

He had forgotten and was even more surprised than ashamed. But the great thing was that he saw in this no vulgar reminder of any "sweet" speech. The vanity of women had long memories, but she was making no claim on him of a compliment or a mistake. With another woman, a totally different one, he might have feared the recall possibly of even some imbecile "offer." So, in having to say that he had indeed forgotten, he was conscious rather of a loss than of a gain; he already saw an interest in the matter of her mention. "I try to think—but I give it up. Yet I remember the Sorrento day."

"I'm not very sure you do," May Bartram after a moment said; "and I'm not very sure I ought to want you to. It's dreadful to bring a person back at any time to what he was ten years before. If you've lived away from it," she smiled, "so much the better."

"Ah if *you* haven't why should I?" he asked.

"Lived away, you mean, from what I myself was?"

"From what *I* was. I was of course an ass," Marcher went on; "but I would rather know from you just the sort of ass I was than—from the moment you have something in your mind—not know anything."

Still, however, she hesitated. "But if you've completely ceased to be that sort—?"

"Why I can then all the more bear to know. Besides, perhaps I haven't."

"Perhaps. Yet if you haven't," she added. "I should suppose you'd remember. Not indeed that *I* in the least connect with my impression the invidious name you use. If I had only thought you foolish," she explained, "the thing I speak of wouldn't so have remained with me. It was about yourself." She

---

4. Across the bay from Naples.

waited as if it might come to him; but as, only meeting her eyes in wonder, he gave no sign, she burnt her ships. "Has it ever happened?"

Then it was that, while he continued to stare, a light broke for him and the blood slowly came to his face, which began to burn with recognition. "Do you mean I told you—?" But he faltered, lest what came to him shouldn't be right, lest he should only give himself away.

"It was something about yourself that it was natural one shouldn't forget— that is if one remembered you at all. That's why I ask you," she smiled, "if the thing you then spoke of has ever come to pass?"

Oh then he saw, but he was lost in wonder and found himself embarrassed. This, he also saw, made her sorry for him, as if her allusion had been a mistake. It took him but a moment, however, to feel it hadn't been, much as it had been a surprise. After the first little shock of it her knowledge on the contrary began, even if rather strangely, to taste sweet to him. She was the only other person in the world then who would have it, and she had had it all these years, while the fact of his having so breathed his secret had unaccountably faded from him. No wonder they couldn't have met as if nothing had happened. "I judge," he finally said, "that I know what you mean. Only I had strangely enough lost any sense of having taken you so far into my confidence."

"Is it because you've taken so many others as well?"

"I've taken nobody. Not a creature since then."

"So that I'm the only person who knows?"

"The only person in the world."

"Well," she quickly replied, "I myself have never spoken. I've never, never repeated of you what you told me." She looked at him so that he perfectly believed her. Their eyes met over it in such a way that he was without a doubt. "And I never will."

She spoke with an earnestness that, as if almost excessive, put him at ease about her possible derision. Somehow the whole question was a new luxury to him—that is from the moment she was in possession. If she didn't take the sarcastic view she clearly took the sympathetic, and that was what he had had, in all the long time, from no one whomsoever. What he felt was that he couldn't at present have begun to tell her, and yet could profit perhaps exquisitely by the accident of having done so of old. "Please don't then. We're just right as it is."

"Oh I am," she laughed, "if you are!" To which she added: "Then you do still feel in the same way?"

It was impossible he shouldn't take to himself that she was really interested, though it all kept coming as perfect surprise. He had thought of himself so long as abominably alone, and lo he wasn't alone a bit. He hadn't been, it appeared, for an hour—since those moments on the Sorrento boat. It was *she* who had been, he seemed to see as he looked at her—she who had been made so by the graceless fact of his lapse of fidelity. To tell her what he had told her—what had it been but to ask something of her? something that she had given, in her charity, without his having, by a remembrance, by a return of the spirit, failing another encounter, so much as thanked her. What he had asked of her had been simply at first not to laugh at him. She had beautifully not done so for ten years, and she was not doing so now. So he had endless gratitude to make up. Only for that he must see just how he had figured to her. "What, exactly, was the account I gave—?"

"Of the way you did feel? Well, it was very simple. You said you had had from your earliest time, as the deepest thing within you, the sense of being kept for something rare and strange, possibly prodigious and terrible, that was sooner or later to happen to you, that you had in your bones the foreboding and the conviction of, and that would perhaps overwhelm you."

"Do you call that very simple?" John Marcher asked.

She thought a moment. "It was perhaps because I seemed, as you spoke, to understand it."

"You do understand it?" he eagerly asked.

Again she kept her kind eyes on him. "You still have the belief?"

"Oh!" he exclaimed helplessly. There was too much to say.

"Whatever it's to be," she clearly made out, "it hasn't yet come."

He shook his head in complete surrender now. "It hasn't yet come. Only, you know, it isn't anything I'm to *do*, to achieve in the world, to be distinguished or admired for. I'm not such an ass as *that*. It would be much better, no doubt, if I were."

"It's to be something you're merely to suffer?"

"Well, say to wait for—to have to meet, to face, to see suddenly break out in my life; possibly destroying all further consciousness, possibly annihilating me; possibly, on the other hand, only altering everything, striking at the root of all my world and leaving me to the consequences, however they shape themselves."

She took this in, but the light in her eyes continued for him not to be that of mockery. "Isn't what you describe perhaps but the expectation—or at any rate the sense of danger, familiar to so many people—of falling in love?"

John Marcher wondered. "Did you ask me that before?"

"No—I wasn't so free-and-easy then. But it's what strikes me now."

"Of course," he said after a moment, "it strikes you. Of course it strikes *me*. Of course what's in store for me may be no more than that. The only thing is," he went on, "that I think if it had been that I should by this time know."

"Do you mean because you've *been* in love?" And then as he but looked at her in silence: "You've been in love, and it hasn't meant such a cataclysm, hasn't proved the great affair?"

"Here I am, you see. It hasn't been overwhelming."

"Then it hasn't been love," said May Bartram.

"Well, I at least thought it was. I took it for that—I've taken it till now. It was agreeable, it was delightful, it was miserable," he explained. "But it wasn't strange. It wasn't what *my* affair's to be."

"You want something all to yourself—something that nobody else knows or *has* known?"

"It isn't a question of what I 'want'—God knows I don't want anything. It's only a question of the apprehension that haunts me—that I live with day by day."

He said this so lucidly and consistently that he could see it further impose itself. If she hadn't been interested before she'd have been interested now. "Is it a sense of coming violence?"

Evidently now too again he liked to talk of it. "I don't think of it as—when it does come—necessarily violent. I only think of it as natural and as of course above all unmistakeable. I think of it simply as *the* thing. *The* thing will of itself appear natural."

"Then how will it appear strange?"

Marcher bethought himself. "It won't—to *me*."

"To whom then?"

"Well," he replied, smiling at last, "say to you."

"Oh then I'm to be present?"

"Why you *are* present—since you know."

"I see." She turned it over. "But I mean at the catastrophe."

At this, for a minute, their lightness gave way to their gravity; it was as if the long look they exchanged held them together. "It will only depend on yourself—if you'll watch with me."

"Are you afraid?" she asked.

"Don't leave me *now*," he went on.

"Are you afraid?" she repeated.

"Do you think me simply out of my mind?" he pursued instead of answering. "Do I merely strike you as a harmless lunatic?"

"No," said May Bartram. "I understand you. I believe you."

"You mean you feel how my obsession—poor old thing!—may correspond to some possible reality?"

"To some possible reality."

"Then you *will* watch with me?"

She hesitated, then for the third time put her question. "Are you afraid?"

"Did I tell you I was—at Naples?"

"No, you said nothing about it."

"Then I don't know. And I should *like* to know," said John Marcher. "You'll tell me yourself whether you think so. If you'll watch with me you'll see."

"Very good then." They had been moving by this time across the room, and at the door, before passing out, they paused as for the full wind-up of their understanding. "I'll watch with you," said May Bartram.

II

The fact that she "knew"—knew and yet neither chaffed him nor betrayed him—had in a short time begun to constitute between them a goodly bond, which became more marked when, within the year that followed their afternoon at Weatherend, the opportunities for meeting multiplied. The event that thus promoted these occasions was the death of the ancient lady her great-aunt, under whose wing, since losing her mother, she had to such an extent found shelter, and who, though but the widowed mother of the new successor to the property, had succeeded—thanks to a high tone and a high temper—in not forfeiting the supreme position at the great house. The deposition of this personage arrived but with her death, which, followed by many changes, made in particular a difference for the young woman in whom Marcher's expert attention had recognised from the first a dependent with a pride that might ache though it didn't bristle. Nothing for a long time had made him easier than the thought that the aching must have been much soothed by Miss Bartram's now finding herself able to set up a small home in London. She had acquired property, to an amount that made that luxury just possible, under her aunt's extremely complicated will, and when the whole matter began to be straightened out, which indeed took time, she let him know that the happy issue was at last in view. He had seen her again before that day, both because she had more than once accompanied the ancient lady to town and because he had paid another visit to the friends who so conveniently made of Weatherend one of the charms of their own hospitality. These friends had taken him back there; he had achieved there again with Miss Bartram some quiet detachment; and he had in London succeeded in persuading her to more than one brief absence from her aunt. They went together, on these latter occasions, to the National Gallery and the South Kensington Museum, where, among vivid reminders, they talked of Italy at large—not now attempting to recover, as at first, the taste of their youth and their ignorance. That recovery, the first day at Weatherend, had served its purpose well, had given them quite enough; so that they were, to Marcher's sense, no longer hovering about the headwaters of their stream, but had felt their boat pushed sharply off and down the current.

They were literally afloat together; for our gentleman this was marked, quite as marked as that the fortunate cause of it was just the buried treasure of her knowledge. He had with his own hands dug up this little hoard, brought to light—that is to within reach of the dim day constituted by their discretions and privacies—the object of value the hiding-place of which he had, after putting it into the ground himself, so strangely, so long forgotten. The rare luck of his having again just stumbled on the spot made him indifferent to any other question; he would doubtless have devoted more time to the odd accident of his lapse of memory if he hadn't been moved to devote so much to the sweetness, the comfort, as he felt, for the future, that this accident itself had helped to keep fresh. It had never entered into his plan that any one should "know," and mainly for the reason that it wasn't in him to tell any one. That would have been impossible, for nothing but the amusement of a cold world would have waited on it. Since, however, a mysterious fate had opened his mouth betimes, in spite of him, he would count that a compensation and profit by it to the utmost. That the right person *should* know tempered the asperity of his secret more even than his shyness had permitted him to imagine; and May Bartram was clearly right, because—well, because there she was. Her knowledge simply settled it; he would have been sure enough by this time had she been wrong. There was that in his situation, no doubt, that disposed him too much to see her as a mere confidant, taking all her light for him from the fact—the fact only—of her interest in his predicament; from her mercy, sympathy, seriousness, her consent not to regard him as the funniest of the funny. Aware, in fine, that her price for him was just in her giving him this constant sense of his being admirably spared, he was careful to remember that she had also a life of her own, with things that might happen to *her*, things that in friendship one should likewise take account of. Something fairly remarkable came to pass with him, for that matter, in this connexion—something represented by a certain passage of his consciousness, in the suddenest way, from one extreme to the other.

He had thought himself, so long as nobody knew, the most disinterested person in the world, carrying his concentrated burden, his perpetual suspense, ever so quietly, holding his tongue about it, giving others no glimpse of it nor of its effect upon his life, asking of them no allowance and only making on his side all those that were asked. He hadn't disturbed people with the queerness of their having to know a haunted man, though he had had moments of rather special temptation on hearing them say they were forsooth "unsettled." If they were as unsettled as he was—he who had never been settled for an hour in his life—they would know what it meant. Yet it wasn't, all the same, for him to make them, and he listened to them civilly enough. This was why he had such good—though possibly such rather colourless—manners; this was why, above all, he could regard himself, in a greedy world, as decently—as in fact perhaps even a little sublimely—unselfish. Our point is accordingly that he valued this character quite sufficiently to measure his present danger of letting it lapse, against which he promised himself to be much on his guard. He was quite ready, none the less, to be selfish just a little, since surely no more charming occasion for it had come to him. "Just a little," in a word, was just as much as Miss Bartram, taking one day with another, would let him. He never would be in the least coercive, and would keep well before him the lines on which consideration for her—the very highest—ought to proceed. He would thoroughly establish the heads under which her affairs, her requirements, her peculiarities—he went so far as to give them the latitude of that name—would come into their intercourse. All this naturally was a sign of how much he took the intercourse itself for granted. There was nothing more to be done about *that*. It simply existed; had sprung into being with her first penetrating question to him in the autumn light there at Weatherend. The real form it should have taken on the basis that stood out large was the form of their marrying. But the devil in this was that the very basis itself put marrying out of the question. His conviction, his apprehension, his obsession, in short, wasn't a privilege he could invite a woman to share; and that consequence of it was precisely what was the matter with him. Something or other lay in wait for him, amid the twists and the turns of the months and the years, like a crouching beast in the jungle. It signified little whether the crouching beast were destined to slay him or to be slain. The definite point was the inevitable spring of the creature; and the definite lesson from that was that a man of feeling didn't cause himself to be accompanied by a lady on a tiger-hunt. Such was the image under which he had ended by figuring his life.

They had at first, none the less, in the scattered hours spent together, made no allusion to that view of it; which was a sign he was handsomely alert to give that he didn't expect, that he in fact didn't care, always to be talking about it. Such a feature in one's outlook was really like a hump on one's back. The difference it made every minute of the day existed quite independently of discussion. One discussed of course *like* a hunchback, for there was always, if nothing else, the hunchback face. That remained, and she was watching him; but people watched best, as a general thing, in silence, so that such would be predominantly the manner of their vigil. Yet he didn't want, at the same time, to be tense and solemn; tense and solemn was what he imagined he too much showed for with other people. The thing to be, with the one person who knew, was easy and natural—to make the reference rather than be seeming to avoid it, to avoid it rather than be seeming to make it, and to keep it, in any case, familiar, facetious even, rather than pedantic and portentous. Some such consideration as the latter was doubtless in his mind for instance when he wrote pleasantly to Miss Bartram that perhaps the great thing he had so long felt as in the lap of the gods was no more than this circumstance, which touched him so nearly, of her acquiring a house in London. It was the first allusion they had yet again made, needing any other hitherto so little; but when she replied, after having given him the news, that she was by no means satisfied with such a trifle as the climax to so special a suspense, she almost set him wondering if she hadn't even a larger conception of singularity for him than he had for himself. He was at all events destined to become aware little by little, as time went by, that she was all the while looking at his life, judging it, measuring it, in the light of the thing she knew, which grew to be at last, with the consecration of the years, never mentioned between them save as "the real truth" about him. That had always been his own form of reference to it, but she adopted the form so quietly that, looking back at the end of a period, he knew there was no moment at which it was traceable that she had, as he might say, got inside his idea, or exchanged the attitude of beautifully indulging for that of still more beautifully believing him.

It was always open to him to accuse her of seeing him but as the most harmless of maniacs, and this, in the long run—since it covered so much ground—was his easiest description of their friendship. He had a screw loose for her, but she liked him in spite of it and was practically, against the rest of the world, his kind wise keeper, unremunerated but fairly amused and, in the absence of other near ties, not disreputably occupied. The rest of the world of course thought him queer, but she, she only, knew how, and above all why, queer; which was precisely what enabled her to dispose the concealing veil in the right folds. She took his gaiety from him—since it had to pass with them for gaiety—as she took everything else; but she certainly so far justified by her unerring touch his finer sense of the degree to which he had ended by convincing her. *She* at least never spoke of the secret of his life except as "the real truth about you," and she had in fact a wonderful way of making it seem, as such, the secret of her own life too. That was in fine how he so constantly felt her as allowing for him; he couldn't on the whole call it anything else. He allowed for himself, but she, exactly, allowed still more; partly because, better placed for a sight of the matter, she traced his unhappy perversion through reaches of its course into which he could scarce follow it. He knew how he felt, but, besides knowing that, she knew how he *looked* as well; he knew each of the things of importance he was insidiously kept from doing, but she could add up the amount they made, understand how much, with a lighter weight on his spirit, he might have done, and thereby establish how, clever as he was, he fell short. Above all she was in the secret of the difference between the forms he went through—those of his little office under Government, those of caring for his modest patrimony, for his library, for his garden in the country, for the people in London whose invitations he accepted and repaid—and the detachment that reigned beneath them and that made of all behaviour, all that could in the least be called behaviour, a long act of dissimulation. What it had come to was that he wore a mask painted with the social simper, out of the eyeholes of which there looked eyes of an expression not in the least matching the other features. This the stupid world, even after years, had never more than half-discovered. It was only May Bartram who had, and she achieved, by an art indescribable, the feat of at once—or perhaps it was only alternately—meeting the eyes from in front and mingling her own vision, as from over his shoulder, with their peep through the apertures.

So while they grew older together she did watch with him, and so she let this association give shape and colour to her own existence. Beneath *her* forms as well detachment had learned to sit, and behaviour had become for her, in the social sense, a false account of herself. There was but one account of her that would have been true all the while and that she could give straight to nobody, least of all to John Marcher. Her whole attitude was a virtual statement, but the perception of that only seemed called to take its place for him as one of the many things necessarily crowded out of his consciousness. If she had moreover, like himself, to make sacrifices to their real truth, it was to be granted that her compensation might have affected her as more prompt and more natural. They had long periods, in this London time, during which, when they were together, a stranger might have listened to them without in the least pricking up his ears; on the other hand the real truth was equally liable at any moment to rise to the surface, and the auditor would then have wondered indeed what they were talking about. They had from an early hour made up their mind that society was, luckily, unintelligent, and the margin allowed them by this had fairly become one of their commonplaces. Yet there were still moments when the situation turned almost fresh—usually under the effect of some expression drawn from herself. Her expressions doubtless repeated themselves, but her intervals were generous. "What saves us, you know, is that we answer so completely to so usual an appearance: that of the man and woman whose friendship has become such a daily habit—or almost—as to be at last indispensable." That for instance was a remark she had frequently enough had occasion to make, though she had given it at different times different developments. What we are especially concerned with is the turn it happened to take from her one afternoon when he had come to see her in honour of her birthday. This anniversary had fallen on a Sunday, at a season of thick fog and general outward gloom; but he had brought her his customary offering, having known her now long enough to have established a hundred small traditions. It was one of his proofs to himself, the present he made her on her birthday, that he hadn't sunk into real selfishness. It was mostly nothing more than a small trinket, but it was always fine of its kind, and he was regularly careful to pay for it more than he thought he could afford. "Our habit saves you at least, don't you see? because it makes you, after all, for the vulgar, indistinguishable from other men. What's the most inveterate mark of men in general? Why the capacity to spend endless time with dull women—to spend it I won't say without being bored, but without minding that they are, without being driven off at a tangent by it; which comes to the same thing. I'm your dull woman, a part of the daily bread for which you pray at church. That covers your tracks more than anything."

"And what covers yours?" asked Marcher, whom his dull woman could mostly to this extent amuse. "I see of course what you mean by your saving me, in this way and that, so far as other people are concerned—I've seen it all along. Only what is it that saves *you*? I often think, you know, of that."

She looked as if she sometimes thought of that too, but rather in a different way. "Where other people, you mean, are concerned?"

"Well, you're really so in with me, you know—as a sort of result of my being so in with yourself. I mean of my having such an immense regard for you, being so tremendously mindful of all you've done for me. I sometimes ask myself if it's quite fair. Fair I mean to have so involved and—since one may say it—interested you. I almost feel as if you hadn't really had time to do anything else."

"Anything else but be interested?" she asked. "Ah what else does one ever want to be? If I've been 'watching' with you, as we long ago agreed I was to do, watching's always in itself an absorption."

"Oh certainly," John Marcher said, "if you hadn't had your curiosity—! Only doesn't it sometimes come to you as time goes on that your curiosity isn't being particularly repaid?"

May Bartram had a pause. "Do you ask that, by any chance, because you feel at all that yours isn't? I mean because you have to wait so long."

Oh he understood what she meant! "For the thing to happen that never does happen? For the beast to jump out? No, I'm just where I was about it. It isn't a matter as to which I can *choose*, I can decide for a change. It isn't one as to which there *can* be a change. It's in the lap of the gods. One's in the hands of one's law—there one is. As to the form the law will take, the way it will operate, that's its own affair."

"Yes," Miss Bartram replied; "of course one's fate's coming, of course it *has* come in its own form and its own way, all the while. Only, you know, the form and the way in your case were to have been—well, something so exceptional and, as one may say, so particularly *your* own."

Something in this made him look at her with suspicion. "You say 'were to have been,' as if in your heart you had begun to doubt."

"Oh!" she vaguely protested.

"As if you believed," he went on, "that nothing will now take place."

She shook her head slowly but rather inscrutably. "You're far from my thought."

He continued to look at her. "What then is the matter with you?"

"Well," she said after another wait, "the matter with me is simply that I'm more sure than ever my curiosity, as you call it, will be but too well repaid."

They were frankly grave now; he had got up from his seat, had turned once more about the little drawing-room to which, year after year, he brought his inevitable topic; in which he had, as he might have said, tasted their intimate community with every sauce, where every object was as familiar to him as the things of his own house and the very carpets were worn with his fitful walk very much as the desks in old counting-houses are worn by the elbows of generations of clerks. The generations of his nervous moods had been at work there, and the place was the written history of his whole middle life. Under the impression of what his friend had just said he knew himself, for some reason, more aware of these things; which made him, after a moment, stop again before her. "Is it possibly that you've grown afraid?"

"Afraid?" He thought, as she repeated the word, that his question had made her, a little, change colour; so that, lest he should have touched on a truth, he explained very kindly: "You remember that that was what you asked *me* long ago—that first day at Weatherend."

"Oh yes, and you told me you didn't know—that I was to see for myself. We've said little about it since, even in so long a time."

"Precisely," Marcher interposed—"quite as if it were too delicate a matter for us to make free with. Quite as if we might find, on pressure, that I *am* afraid. For then," he said, "we shouldn't, should we? quite know what to do."

She had for the time no answer to his question. "There have been days when I thought you were. Only, of course," she added, "there have been days when we have thought almost anything."

"Everything. Oh!" Marcher softly groaned as with a gasp, half-spent, at the face, more uncovered just then than it had been for a long while, of the imagination always with them. It had always had its incalculable moments of glaring out, quite as with the very eyes of the very Beast, and, used as he was to them, they could still draw from him the tribute of a sigh that rose from the depths of his being. All they had thought, first and last, rolled over him; the past seemed to have been reduced to mere barren speculation. This in fact was what the place had just struck him as so full of—the simplification of everything but the state of suspense. That remained only by seeming to hang in the void surrounding it. Even his original fear, if fear it had been, had lost itself in the desert. "I judge, however," he continued, "that you see I'm not afraid now."

"What I see, as I make it out, is that you've achieved something almost unprecedented in the way of getting used to danger. Living with it so long and so closely you've lost your sense of it; you know it's there, but you're indifferent, and you cease even, as of old, to have to whistle in the dark. Considering what the danger is," May Bartram wound up, "I'm bound to say I don't think your attitude could well be surpassed."

John Marcher faintly smiled. "It's heroic?"

"Certainly—call it that."

It was what he would have liked indeed to call it. "I *am* then a man of courage?"

"That's what you were to show me."

He still, however, wondered. "But doesn't the man of courage know what he's afraid of—or *not* afraid of? I don't know *that*, you see. I don't focus it. I can't name it. I only know I'm exposed."

"Yes, but exposed—how shall I say?—so directly. So intimately. That's surely enough."

"Enough to make you feel then—as what we may call the end and the upshot of our watch—that I'm not afraid?"

"You're not afraid. But it isn't," she said, "the end of our watch. That is it isn't the end of yours. You've everything still to see."

"Then why haven't *you*?" he asked. He had had, all along, to-day, the sense of her keeping something back, and he still had it. As this was his first impression of that it quite made a date. The case was the more marked as she didn't at first answer; which in turn made him go on. "You know something I don't." Then his voice, for that of a man of courage, trembled a little. "You know what's to happen." Her silence, with the face she showed, was almost a confession—it made him sure. "You know, and you're afraid to tell me. It's so bad that you're afraid I'll find out."

All this might be true, for she did look as if, unexpectedly to her, he had crossed some mystic line that she had secretly drawn round her. Yet she might, after all, not have worried; and the real climax was that he himself, at all events, needn't. "You'll never find out."

III

It was all to have made, none the less, as I have said, a date; which came out in the fact that again and again, even after long intervals, other things that passed between them wore in relation to this hour but the character of recalls and results. Its immediate effect had been indeed rather to lighten insistence—almost to provoke a reaction; as if their topic had dropped by its own weight and as if moreover, for that matter, Marcher had been visited by one of his occasional warnings against egotism. He had kept up, he felt, and very decently on the whole, his consciousness of the importance of not being selfish, and it was true that he had never sinned in that direction without promptly enough trying to press the scales the other way. He often repaired his fault, the season permitting, by inviting his friend to accompany him to the opera; and it not infrequently thus happened that, to show he didn't wish her to have but one sort of food for her mind, he was the cause of her appearing there with him a dozen nights in the month. It even happened that, seeing her home at such times, he occasionally went in with her to finish, as he called it, the evening, and, the better to make his point, sat down to the frugal but always careful little supper that awaited his pleasure. His point was made, he thought, by his not eternally insisting with her on himself; made for instance, at such hours, when it befell that, her piano at hand and each of them familiar with it, they went over passages of the opera together. It chanced to be on one of these occasions, however, that he reminded her of her not having answered a certain question he had put to her during the talk that had taken place between them on her last birthday. "What is it that saves *you?*"—saved her, he meant, from that appearance of variation from the usual human type. If he had practically escaped remark, as she pretended, by doing, in the most important particular, what most men do—find the answer to life in patching up an alliance of a sort with a woman no better than himself— how had she escaped it, and how could the alliance, such as it was, since they must suppose it had been more or less noticed, have failed to make her rather positively talked about?

"I never said," May Bartram replied, "that it hadn't made me a good deal talked about."

"Ah well then you're not 'saved.' "

"It hasn't been a question for me. If you've had your woman I've had," she said, "my man."

"And you mean that makes you all right?"

Oh it was always as if there were so much to say! "I don't know why it shouldn't make me—humanly, which is what we're speaking of—as right as it makes you."

"I see," Marcher returned. " 'Humanly,' no doubt, as showing that you're living for something. Not, that is, just for me and my secret."

May Bartram smiled. "I don't pretend it exactly shows that I'm not living for you. It's my intimacy with you that's in question."

He laughed as he saw what she meant. "Yes, but since, as you say, I'm only, so far as people make out, ordinary, you're—aren't you?—no more than ordinary either. You help me to pass for a man like another. So if I *am*, as I understand you, you're not compromised. Is that it?"

She had another of her waits, but she spoke clearly enough. "That's it. It's all that concerns me—to help you to pass for a man like another."

He was careful to acknowledge the remark handsomely. "How kind, how beautiful, you are to me! How shall I ever repay you?"

She had her last grave pause, as if there might be a choice of ways. But she chose. "By going on as you are."

It was into this going on as he was that they relapsed, and really for so long a time that the day inevitably came for a further sounding of their depths. These depths, constantly bridged over by a structure firm enough in spite of its lightness and of its occasional oscillation in the somewhat vertiginous air, invited on occasion, in the interest of their nerves, a dropping of the plummet and a measurement of the abyss. A difference had been made moreover, once for all, by the fact that she had all the while not appeared to feel the need of rebutting his charge of an idea within her that she didn't dare to express—a charge uttered just before one of the fullest of their later discussions ended. It had come up for him then that she "knew" something and that what she knew was bad—too bad to tell him. When he had spoken of it as visibly so bad that she was afraid he might find it out, her reply had left the matter too equivocal to be let alone and yet, for Marcher's special sensibility, almost too formidable again to touch. He circled about it at a distance that alternately narrowed and widened and that still wasn't much affected by the consciousness in him that there was nothing she could "know," after all, any better than he did. She had no source of knowledge he hadn't equally— except of course that she might have finer nerves. That was what women had where they were interested; they made out things, where people were concerned, that the people often couldn't have made out for themselves. Their nerves, their sensibility, their imagination, were conductors and revealers, and the beauty of May Bartram was in particular that she had given herself so to his case. He felt in these days what, oddly enough, he had never felt before, the growth of a dread of losing her by some catastrophe—some catastrophe that yet wouldn't at all be *the* catastrophe: partly because she had almost of a sudden begun to strike him as more useful to him than ever yet, and partly by reason of an appearance of uncertainty in her health, coincident and equally new. It was characteristic of the inner detachment he had hitherto so successfully cultivated and to which our whole account of him is a reference, it was characteristic that his complications, such as they were, had never yet seemed so as at this crisis to thicken about him, even to the point of making him ask himself if he were, by any chance, of a truth, within sight or sound, within touch or reach, within the immediate jurisdiction, of the thing that waited.

When the day came, as come it had to, that his friend confessed to him her fear of a deep disorder in her blood, he felt somehow the shadow of a change and the chill of a shock. He immediately began to imagine aggravations and disasters, and above all to think of her peril as the direct menace for himself of personal privation. This indeed gave him one of those partial recoveries of equanimity that were agreeable to him—it showed him that what was still first in his mind was the loss she herself might suffer. "What if she should have to die before knowing, before seeing—?" It would have been brutal, in the early stages of her trouble, to put that question to her; but it had immediately sounded for him to his own concern, and the possibility was what most made him sorry for her. If she did "know," moreover, in the sense of her having had some—what should he think?—mystical irresistible light, this would make the matter not better, but worse, inasmuch as her original adoption of his own curiosity had quite become the basis of her life. She had been living to see what would *be* to be seen, and it would quite lacerate her to have to give up before the accomplishment of the vision. These reflexions, as I say, quickened his generosity; yet, make them as he might, he saw himself, with the lapse of the period, more and more disconcerted. It lapsed for him with a strange steady sweep, and the oddest oddity was that it gave him, independently of the threat of much inconvenience, almost the only positive surprise his career, if career it could be called, had yet offered him. She kept the house as she had never done; he had to go to her to see her—she could meet him nowhere now, though there was scarce a corner of their loved old London in which she hadn't in the past, at one time or another, done so; and he found her always seated by her fire in the deep old-fashioned chair she was less and less able to leave. He had been struck one day, after an absence exceeding his usual measure, with her suddenly looking much older to him than he had ever thought of her being; then he recognised that the suddenness was all on his side—he had just simply and suddenly noticed. She looked older because inevitably, after so many years, she *was* old, or almost; which was of course true in still greater measure of her companion. If she was old, or almost, John Marcher assuredly was, and yet it was her showing of the lesson, not his own, that brought the truth home to him. His surprises began here; when once they had begun they multiplied; they came rather with a rush: it was as if, in the oddest way in the world, they had all been kept back, sown in a thick cluster, for the late afternoon of life, the time at which for people in general the unexpected has died out.

One of them was that he should have caught himself—for he *had* so done—*really* wondering if the great accident would take form now as nothing more than his being condemned to see this charming woman, this admirable friend, pass away from him. He had never so unreservedly qualified her as while confronted in thought with such a possibility; in spite of which there was small doubt for him that as an answer to his long riddle the mere effacement of even so fine a feature of his situation would be an abject anti-climax. It would represent, as connected with his past attitude, a drop of dignity under the shadow of which his existence could only become the most grotesque of failures. He had been far from holding it a failure—long as he had waited for the appearance that was to make it a success. He had waited for quite another thing, not for such a thing as that. The breath of his good faith came short, however, as he recognised how long he had waited, or how long at least his companion had. That she, at all events, might be recorded as having waited in vain—this affected him sharply, and all the more because of his at first having done little more than amuse himself with the idea. It grew more grave as the gravity of her condition grew, and the state of mind it produced in him, which he himself ended by watching as if it had been some definite disfigurement of his outer person, may pass for another of his surprises. This conjoined itself still with another, the really stupefying consciousness of a question that he would have allowed to shape itself had he dared. What did everything mean—what, that is, did *she* mean, she and her vain waiting and her probable death and the soundless admonition of it all—unless that, at this time of day, it was simply, it was overwhelmingly too late? He had never at any stage of his queer consciousness admitted the whisper of such a correction; he had never till within these last few months been so false to his conviction as not to hold that what was to come to him had time, whether *he* struck himself as having it or not. That at last, at last, he certainly hadn't it, to speak of, or had it but in the scantiest measure—such, soon enough, as things went with him, became the inference with which his old obsession had to reckon: and this it was not helped to do by the more and more confirmed appearance that the great vagueness casting the long shadow in which he had lived had, to attest itself, almost no margin left. Since it was in Time that he was to have met his fate, so it was in Time that his fate was to have acted; and as he waked up to the sense of no longer being young, which was exactly the sense of being stale, just as that, in turn, was the sense of being weak, he waked up to another matter beside. It all hung together; they were subject, he and the great vagueness, to an equal and indivisible law. When the possibilities themselves had accordingly turned stale, when the secret of the gods had grown faint, had perhaps even quite evaporated, that, and that only, was failure. It wouldn't have been failure to be bankrupt, dishonoured, pilloried, hanged; it was failure not to be anything. And so, in the dark valley into which his path had taken its unlooked-for twist, he wondered not a little as he groped. He didn't care what awful crash might overtake him, with what ignominy or what monstrosity he might yet be associated—since he wasn't after all too utterly old to suffer—if it would only be decently proportionate to the posture he had kept, all his life, in the threatened presence of it. He had but one desire left—that he shouldn't have been "sold."

IV

Then it was that, one afternoon, while the spring of the year was young and new she met all in her own way his frankest betrayal of these alarms. He had gone in late to see her, but evening hadn't settled and she was presented to him in that long fresh light of waning April days which affects us often with a sadness sharper than the greyest hours of autumn. The week had been warm, the spring was supposed to have begun early, and May Bartram sat, for the first time in the year, without a fire; a fact that, to Marcher's sense, gave the scene of which she formed part a smooth and ultimate look, an air of knowing, in its immaculate order and cold meaningless cheer, that it would never see a fire again. Her own aspect—he could scarce have said why— intensified this note. Almost as white as wax, with the marks and signs in her face as numerous and as fine as if they had been etched by a needle, with soft white draperies relieved by a faded green scarf on the delicate tone of which the years had further refined, she was the picture of a serene and exquisite but impenetrable sphinx, whose head, or indeed all whose person, might have been powdered with silver. She was a sphinx, yet with her white petals and green fronds she might have been a lily too—only an artificial lily, wonderfully imitated and constantly kept, without dust or stain, though not exempt from a slight droop and a complexity of faint creases, under some clear glass bell. The perfection of household care, of high polish and finish, always reigned in her rooms, but they now looked most as if everything had been wound up, tucked in, put away, so that she might sit with folded hands and with nothing more to do. She was "out of it," to Marcher's vision; her work was over; she communicated with him as across some gulf or from some island of rest that she had already reached, and it made him feel strangely abandoned. Was it—or rather wasn't it—that if for so long she had been watching with him the answer to their question must have swum into her ken and taken on its name, so that her occupation was verily gone? He had as much as charged her with this in saying to her, many months before, that she even then knew something she was keeping from him. It was a point he had never since ventured to press, vaguely fearing as he did that it might become a difference, perhaps a disagreement, between them. He had in this later time turned nervous, which was what he in all the other years had never been; and the oddity was that his nervousness should have waited till he had begun to doubt, should have held off so long as he was sure. There was something, it seemed to him, that the wrong word would bring down on his head, something that would so at least ease off his tension. But he wanted not to speak the wrong word; that would make everything ugly. He wanted the knowledge he lacked to drop on him, if drop it could, by its own august weight. If she was to forsake him it was surely for her to take leave. This was why he didn't directly ask her again what she knew; but it was also why, approaching the matter from another side, he said to her in the course of his visit: "What do you regard as the very worst that at this time of day *can* happen to me?"

He had asked her that in the past often enough; they had, with the odd irregular rhythm of their intensities and avoidances, exchanged ideas about it and then had seen the ideas washed away by cool intervals, washed like figures traced in sea-sand. It had ever been the mark of their talk that the oldest allusions in it required but a little dismissal and reaction to come out again, sounding for the hour as new. She could thus at present meet his enquiry quite freshly and patiently. "Oh yes, I've repeatedly thought, only it always seemed to me of old that I couldn't quite make up my mind. I thought of dreadful things, between which it was difficult to choose; and so must you have done."

"Rather! I feel now as if I had scarce done anything else. I appear to myself to have spent my life in thinking of nothing *but* dreadful things. A great many of them I've at different times named to you, but there were others I couldn't name."

"They were too, too dreadful?"

"Too, too dreadful—some of them."

She looked at him a minute, and there came to him as he met it an inconsequent sense that her eyes, when one got their full clearness, were still as beautiful as they had been in youth, only beautiful with a strange cold light— a light that somehow was a part of the effect, if it wasn't rather a part of the cause, of the pale hard sweetness of the season and the hour. "And yet," she said at last, "there are horrors we've mentioned."

It deepened the strangeness to see her, as such a figure in such a picture, talk of "horrors," but she was to do in a few minutes something stranger yet— though even of this he was to take the full measure but afterwards—and the note of it already trembled. It was, for the matter of that, one of the signs that her eyes were having again the high flicker of their prime. He had to admit, however, what she said. "Oh yes, there were times when we did go far." He caught himself in the act of speaking as if it all were over. Well, he wished it were; and the consummation depended for him clearly more and more on his friend.

But she had now a soft smile. "Oh far—!"

It was oddly ironic. "Do you mean you're prepared to go further?"

She was frail and ancient and charming as she continued to look at him, yet it was rather as if she had lost the thread. "Do you consider that we went far?"

"Why I thought it the point you were just making—that we *had* looked most things in the face."

"Including each other?" She still smiled. "But you're quite right. We've had together great imaginations, often great fears; but some of them have been unspoken."

"Then the worst—we haven't faced that. I *could* face it, I believe, if I knew what you think it. I feel," he explained, "as if I had lost my power to conceive such things." And he wondered if he looked as blank as he sounded. "It's spent."

"Then why do you assume," she asked, "that mine isn't?"

"Because you've given me signs to the contrary. It isn't a question for you of conceiving, imagining, comparing. It isn't a question now of choosing." At last he came out with it. "You know something I don't. You've shown me that before."

These last words had affected her, he made out in a moment, exceedingly, and she spoke with firmness. "I've shown you, my dear, nothing."

He shook his head. "You can't hide it."

"Oh, oh!" May Bartram sounded over what she couldn't hide. It was almost a smothered groan.

"You admitted it months ago, when I spoke of it to you as of something you were afraid I should find out. Your answer was that I couldn't, that I wouldn't, and I don't pretend I have. But you had something therefore in mind, and I now see how it must have been, how it still is, the possibility that, of all possibilities, has settled itself for you as the worst. This," he went on, "is why I appeal to you. I'm only afraid of ignorance to-day—I'm not afraid of knowl-edge." And then as for a while she said nothing: "What makes me sure is that I see in your face and feel here, in this air and amid these appearances, that you're out of it. You've done. You've had your experience. You leave me to my fate."

Well, she listened, motionless and white in her chair, as on a decision to be made, so that her manner was fairly an avowal, though still, with a small fine inner stiffness, an imperfect surrender. "It *would* be the worst," she finally let herself say. "I mean the thing I've never said."

It hushed him a moment. "More monstrous than all the monstrosities we've named?"

"More monstrous. Isn't that what you sufficiently express," she asked, "in calling it the worst?"

Marcher thought. "Assuredly—if you mean, as I do, something that includes all the loss and all the shame that are thinkable."

"It would if it *should* happen," said May Bartram. "What we're speaking of, remember, is only my idea."

"It's your belief," Marcher returned. "That's enough for me. I feel your beliefs are right. Therefore if, having this one, you give me no more light on it, you abandon me."

"No, no!" she repeated. "I'm with you—don't you see?—still." And as to make it more vivid to him she rose from her chair—a movement she seldom risked in these days—and showed herself, all draped and all soft, in her fair-ness and slimness. "I haven't forsaken you."

It was really, in its effort against weakness, a generous assurance, and had the success of the impulse not, happily, been great, it would have touched him to pain more than to pleasure. But the cold charm in her eyes had spread, as she hovered before him, to all the rest of her person, so that it was for the minute almost a recovery of youth. He couldn't pity her for that; he could only take her as she showed—as capable even yet of helping him. It was as if, at the same time, her light might at any instant go out; wherefore he must make the most of it. There passed before him with intensity the three or four things he wanted most to know; but the question that came of itself to his lips really covered the others. "Then tell me if I shall consciously suffer."

She promptly shook her head. "Never!"

It confirmed the authority he imputed to her, and it produced on him an extraordinary effect. "Well, what's better than that? Do you call that the worst?"

"You think nothing is better?" she asked.

She seemed to mean something so special that he again sharply wondered, though still with the dawn of a prospect of relief. "Why not, if one doesn't *know*?" After which, as their eyes, over his question, met in a silence, the dawn deepened and something to his purpose came prodigiously out of her very face. His own, as he took it in, suddenly flushed to the forehead, and he gasped with the force of a perception to which, on the instant, everything fitted. The sound of his gasp filled the air; then he became articulate. "I see—if I don't suffer!"

In her own look, however, was doubt. "You see what?"

"Why what you mean—what you've always meant."

She again shook her head. "What I mean isn't what I've always meant. It's different."

"It's something new?"

She hung back from it a little. "Something new. It's not what you think. I see what you think."

His divination drew breath then; only her correction might be wrong. "It isn't that I *am* a blockhead?" he asked between faintness and grimness. "It isn't that it's all a mistake."

"A mistake?" she pityingly echoed. *That* possibility, for her, he saw, would be monstrous; and if she guaranteed him the immunity from pain it would accordingly not be what she had in mind. "Oh no," she declared; "it's nothing of that sort. You've been right."

Yet he couldn't help asking himself if she weren't, thus pressed, speaking but to save him. It seemed to him he should be most in a hole if his history should prove all a platitude. "Are you telling me the truth, so that I shan't have been a bigger idiot than I can bear to know? I *haven't* lived with a vain imagination, in the most besotted illusion? I haven't waited but to see the door shut in my face?"

She shook her head again. "However the case stands *that* isn't the truth. Whatever the reality, it *is* a reality. The door isn't shut. The door's open," said May Bartram.

"Then something's to come?"

She waited once again, always with her cold sweet eyes on him. "It's never too late." She had, with her gliding step, diminished the distance between them, and she stood nearer to him, close to him, a minute, as if still charged with the unspoken. Her movement might have been for some finer emphasis of what she was at once hesitating and deciding to say. He had been standing by the chimney-piece, fireless and sparely adorned, a small perfect old French clock and two morsels of rosy Dresden[5] constituting all its furniture; and her hand grasped the shelf while she kept him waiting, grasped it a little as for support and encouragement. She only kept him waiting, however; that is he only waited. It had become suddenly, from her movement and attitude, beautiful and vivid to him that she had something more to give him; her wasted face delicately shone with it—it glittered almost as with the white lustre of silver in her expression. She was right, incontestably, for what he saw in her face was the truth, and strangely, without consequence, while their talk of it as dreadful was still in the air, she appeared to present it as inordinately soft. This, prompting bewilderment, made him but gape the more gratefully for her revelation, so that they continued for some minutes silent, her face shining at him, her contact imponderably pressing, and his stare all kind but all expectant. The end, none the less, was that what he had expected failed to come to him. Something else took place instead, which seemed to consist at first in the mere closing of her eyes. She gave way at the same instant to a slow fine shudder, and though he remained staring—though he stared in fact but the harder—turned off and regained her chair. It was the end of what she had been intending, but it left him thinking only of that.

"Well, you don't say—?"

She had touched in her passage a bell near the chimney and had sunk back strangely pale. "I'm afraid I'm too ill."

"Too ill to tell me?" It sprang up sharp to him, and almost to his lips, the fear she might die without giving him light. He checked himself in time from so expressing his question, but she answered as if she had heard the words.

"Don't you know—now?"

" 'Now'—?" She had spoken as if some difference had been made within the moment. But her maid, quickly obedient to her bell, was already with them. "I know nothing." And he was afterwards to say to himself that he must have spoken with odious impatience, such an impatience as to show that, supremely disconcerted, he washed his hands of the whole question.

"Oh!" said May Bartram.

"Are you in pain?" he asked as the woman went to her.

"No," said May Bartram.

Her maid, who had put an arm round her as if to take her to her room, fixed on him eyes that appealingly contradicted her; in spite of which, however, he showed once more his mystification. "What then has happened?"

She was once more, with her companion's help, on her feet, and, feeling withdrawal imposed on him, he had blankly found his hat and gloves and had reached the door. Yet he waited for her answer. "What *was* to," she said.

V

He came back the next day, but she was then unable to see him, and as it was literally the first time this had occurred in the long stretch of their acquaintance he turned away, defeated and sore, almost angry—or feeling at

5. Fine German porcelain.

least that such a break in their custom was really the beginning of the end—
and wandered alone with his thoughts, especially with the one he was least
able to keep down. She was dying and he would lose her; she was dying and
his life would end. He stopped in the Park, into which he had passed, and
stared before him at his recurrent doubt. Away from her the doubt pressed
again; in her presence he had believed her, but as he felt his forlornness
he threw himself into the explanation that, nearest at hand, had most of a
miserable warmth for him and least of a cold torment. She had deceived
him to save him—to put him off with something in which he should be able
to rest. What could the thing that was to happen to him be, after all, but just
this thing that had begun to happen? Her dying, her death, his consequent
solitude—*that* was what he had figured as the Beast in the Jungle, that was
what had been in the lap of the gods. He had had her word for it as he left
her—what else on earth could she have meant? It wasn't a thing of a monstrous order; not a fate rare and distinguished; not a stroke of fortune that
overwhelmed and immortalised; it had only the stamp of the common doom.
But poor Marcher at this hour judged the common doom sufficient. It would
serve his turn, and even as the consummation of infinite waiting he would
bend his pride to accept it. He sat down on a bench in the twilight. He hadn't
been a fool. Something had *been,* as she had said, to come. Before he rose
indeed it had quite struck him that the final fact really matched with the long
avenue through which he had had to reach it. As sharing his suspense and as
giving herself all, giving her life, to bring it to an end, she had come with him
every step of the way. He had lived by her aid, and to leave her behind would
be cruelly, damnably to miss her. What could be more overwhelming than
that?

Well, he was to know within the week, for though she kept him a while at
bay, left him restless and wretched during a series of days on each of which
he asked about her only again to have to turn away, she ended his trial by
receiving him where she had always received him. Yet she had been brought
out at some hazard into the presence of so many of the things that were, consciously, vainly, half their past, and there was scant service left in the gentleness of her mere desire, all too visible, to check his obsession and wind up
his long trouble. That was clearly what she wanted, the one thing more for
her own peace while she could still put out her hand. He was so affected by
her state that, once seated by her chair, he was moved to let everything go; it
was she herself therefore who brought him back, took up again, before she
dismissed him, her last word of the other time. She showed how she wished
to leave their business in order. "I'm not sure you understood. You've nothing
to wait for more. It *has* come."

Oh how he looked at her! "Really?"

"Really."

"The thing that, as you said, *was* to?"

"The thing that we began in our youth to watch for."

Face to face with her once more he believed her; it was a claim to which
he had so abjectly little to oppose. "You mean that it has come as a positive
definite occurrence, with a name and a date?"

"Positive. Definite. I don't know about the 'name,' but oh with a date!"

He found himself again too helplessly at sea. "But come in the night—
come and passed me by?"

May Bartram had her strange faint smile. "Oh no, it hasn't passed you by!"

"But if I haven't been aware of it and it hasn't touched me—?"

"Ah your not being aware of it"—and she seemed to hesitate an instant to deal with this—"your not being aware of it is the strangeness *in* the strangeness. It's the wonder *of* the wonder." She spoke as with the softness almost of a sick child, yet now at last, at the end of all, with the perfect straightness of a sibyl. She visibly knew that she knew, and the effect on him was of something co-ordinate, in its high character, with the law that had ruled him. It was the true voice of the law; so on her lips would the law itself have sounded. "It *has* touched you," she went on. "It has done its office. It has made you all its own."

"So utterly without my knowing it?"

"So utterly without your knowing it." His hand, as he leaned to her, was on the arm of her chair, and, dimly smiling always now, she placed her own on it. "It's enough if *I* know it."

"Oh!" he confusedly breathed, as she herself of late so often had done.

"What I long ago said is true. You'll never know now, and I think you ought to be content. You've *had* it," said May Bartram.

"But had what?"

"Why what was to have marked you out. The proof of your law. It has acted. I'm too glad," she then bravely added, "to have been able to see what it's *not*."

He continued to attach his eyes to her, and with the sense that it was all beyond him, and that *she* was too, he would still have sharply challenged her hadn't he so felt it an abuse of her weakness to do more than take devoutly what she gave him, take it hushed as to a revelation. If he did speak, it was out of the foreknowledge of his loneliness to come. "If you're glad of what it's 'not' it might then have been worse?"

She turned her eyes away, she looked straight before her; with which after a moment: "Well, you know our fears."

He wondered. "It's something then we never feared?"

On this slowly she turned to him. "Did we ever dream, with all our dreams, that we should sit and talk of it thus?"

He tried for a little to make out that they had; but it was as if their dreams, numberless enough, were in solution in some thick cold mist through which thought lost itself. "It might have been that we couldn't talk?"

"Well"—she did her best for him—"not from this side. This, you see," she said, "is the *other* side."

"I think," poor Marcher returned, "that all sides are the same to me." Then, however, as she gently shook her head in correction: "We mightn't, as it were, have got across—?"

"To where we are—no. We're *here*"—she made her weak emphasis.

"And much good does it do us!" was her friend's frank comment.

"It does us the good it can. It does us the good that *it* isn't here. It's past. It's behind," said May Bartram. "Before—" but her voice dropped.

He had got up, not to tire her, but it was hard to combat his yearning. She after all told him nothing but that his light had failed—which he knew well enough without her. "Before—?" he blankly echoed.

"Before, you see, it was always to *come*. That kept it present."

"Oh I don't care what comes now! Besides," Marcher added, "it seems to me I liked it better present, as you say, than I can like it absent with *your* absence."

"Oh mine!"—and her pale hands made light of it.

"With the absence of everything." He had a dreadful sense of standing there before her for—so far as anything but this proved, this bottomless drop was concerned—the last time of their life. It rested on him with a weight he felt he could scarce bear, and this weight it apparently was that still pressed out what remained in him of speakable protest. "I believe you; but I can't begin to pretend I understand. *Nothing*, for me, is past; nothing *will* pass till I pass myself, which I pray my stars may be as soon as possible. Say, however," he added, "that I've eaten my cake, as you contend, to the last crumb—how can the thing I've never felt at all be the thing I was marked out to feel?"

She met him perhaps less directly, but she met him unperturbed. "You take your 'feelings' for granted. You were to suffer your fate. That was not necessarily to know it."

"How in the world—when what is such knowledge but suffering?"

She looked up at him a while in silence. "No—you don't understand."

"I suffer," said John Marcher.

"Don't, don't!"

"How can I help at least *that?*"

"*Don't!*" May Bartram repeated.

She spoke it in a tone so special, in spite of her weakness, that he stared an instant—stared as if some light, hitherto hidden, had shimmered across his vision. Darkness again closed over it, but the gleam had already become for him an idea. "Because I haven't the right—?"

"Don't *know*—when you needn't," she mercifully urged. "You needn't—for we shouldn't."

"Shouldn't?" If he could but know what she meant!

"No—it's too much."

"Too much?" he still asked but, with a mystification that was the next moment of a sudden to give way. Her words, if they meant something, affected him in this light—the light also of her wasted face—as meaning *all*, and the sense of what knowledge had been for herself came over him with a rush which broke through into a question. "Is it of that then you're dying?"

She but watched him, gravely at first, as to see, with this, where he was, and she might have seen something or feared something that moved her sympathy. "I would live for you still—if I could." Her eyes closed for a little, as if, withdrawn into herself, she were for a last time trying. "But I can't!" she said as she raised them again to take leave of him.

She couldn't indeed, as but too promptly and sharply appeared, and he had no vision of her after this that was anything, but darkness and doom. They had parted for ever in that strange talk; access to her chamber of pain, rigidly guarded, was almost wholly forbidden him; he was feeling now moreover, in the face of doctors, nurses, the two or three relatives attracted doubtless by the presumption of what she had to "leave," how few were the rights, as they were called in such cases, that he had to put forward, and how odd it might even seem that their intimacy shouldn't have given him more of them. The stupidest fourth cousin had more, even though she had been nothing in such a person's life. She had been a feature of features in *his,* for what else was it to have been so indispensable? Strange beyond saying were the ways of existence, baffling for him the anomaly of his lack, as he felt it to be, of producible claim. A woman might have been, as it were, everything to him, and it might yet present him in no connexion that any one seemed held to recognise.

If this was the case in these closing weeks it was the case more sharply on the occasion of the last offices rendered, in the great grey London cemetery, to what had been mortal, to what had been precious, in his friend. The concourse at her grave was not numerous, but he saw himself treated as scarce more nearly concerned with it than if there had been a thousand others. He was in short from this moment face to face with the fact that he was to profit extraordinarily little by the interest May Bartram had taken in him. He couldn't quite have said what he expected, but he hadn't surely expected this approach to a double privation. Not only had her interest failed him, but he seemed to feel himself unattended—and for a reason he couldn't seize—by the distinction, the dignity, the propriety, if nothing else, of the man markedly bereaved. It was as if in the view of society he had not *been* markedly bereaved, as if there still failed some sign or proof of it, and as if none the less his character could never be affirmed nor the deficiency ever made up. There were moments as the weeks went by when he would have liked, by some almost aggressive act, to take his stand on the intimacy of his loss, in order that it *might* be questioned and his retort, to the relief of his spirit, so recorded; but the moments of an irritation more helpless followed fast on these, the moments during which, turning things over with a good conscience but with a bare horizon, he found himself wondering if he oughtn't to have begun, so to speak, further back.

He found himself wondering at many things, and this last speculation had others to keep it company. What could he have done, after all, in her lifetime, without giving them both, as it were, away? He couldn't have made known she was watching him, for that would have published the superstition of the Beast. This was what closed his mouth now—now that the Jungle had been threshed to vacancy and that the Beast had stolen away. It sounded too foolish and too flat; the difference for him in this particular, the extinction in his life of the element of suspense, was such as in fact to surprise him. He could scarce have said what the effect resembled; the abrupt cessation, the positive prohibition, of music perhaps, more than anything else, in some place all adjusted and all accustomed to sonority and to attention. If he could at any rate have conceived lifting the veil from his image at some moment of the past (what had he done, after all, if not lift it to *her*?) so to do this today, to talk to people at large of the Jungle cleared and confide to them that he now felt it as safe, would have been not only to see them listen as to a goodwife's tale, but really to hear himself tell one. What it presently came to in truth was that poor Marcher waded through his beaten grass, where no life stirred, where no breath sounded, where no evil eye seemed to gleam from a possible lair, very much as if vaguely looking for the Beast, and still more as if acutely missing it. He walked about in an existence that had grown strangely more spacious, and, stopping fitfully in places where the undergrowth of life struck him as closer, asked himself yearningly, wondered secretly and sorely, if it would have lurked here or there. It would have at all events *sprung*; what was at least complete was his belief in the truth of the assurance given him. The change from his old sense to his new was absolute and final: what was to happen *had* so absolutely and finally happened that he was as little able to know a fear for his future as to know a hope; so absent in short was any question of anything still to come. He was to live entirely with the other question, that of his unidentified past, that of his having to see his fortune impenetrably muffled and masked.

The torment of this vision became then his occupation; he couldn't perhaps have consented to live but for the possibility of guessing. She had told him, his friend, not to guess; she had forbidden him, so far as he might, to know, and she had even in a sort denied the power in him to learn: which were so many things, precisely, to deprive him of rest. It wasn't that he wanted, he argued for fairness, that anything past and done should repeat itself; it was only that he shouldn't, as an anticlimax, have been taken sleeping so sound as not to be able to win back by an effort of thought the lost stuff of consciousness. He declared to himself at moments that he would either win it back or have done with consciousness for ever; he made this idea his one motive in fine, made it so much his passion that none other, to compare with it, seemed ever to have touched him. The lost stuff of consciousness became thus for him as a strayed or stolen child to an unappeasable father; he hunted it up and down very much as if he were knocking at doors and enquiring of the police. This was the spirit in which, inevitably, he set himself to travel; he started on a journey that was to be as long as he could make it; it danced before him that, as the other side of the globe couldn't possibly have less to say to him, it might, by a possibility of suggestion, have more. Before he quitted London, however, he made a pilgrimage to May Bartram's grave, took his way to it through the endless avenues of the grim suburban metropolis, sought it out in the wilderness of tombs, and, though he had come but for the renewal of the act of farewell, found himself, when he had at last stood by it, beguiled into long intensities. He stood for an hour, powerless to turn away and yet powerless to penetrate the darkness of death; fixing with his eyes her inscribed name and date, beating his forehead against the fact of the secret they kept, drawing his breath, while he waited, as if some sense would in pity of him rise from the stones. He kneeled on the stones, however, in vain; they kept what they concealed; and if the face of the tomb did become a face for him it was because her two names became a pair of eyes that didn't know him. He gave them a last long look, but no palest light broke.

VI

He stayed away, after this, for a year; he visited the depths of Asia, spending himself on scenes of romantic interest, of superlative sanctity; but what was present to him everywhere was that for a man who had known what *he* had known the world was vulgar and vain. The state of mind in which he had lived for so many years shone out to him, in reflexion, as a light that coloured and refined, a light beside which the glow of the East was garish cheap and thin. The terrible truth was that he had lost—with everything else—a distinction as well; the things he saw couldn't help being common when he had become common to look at them. He was simply now one of them himself— he was in the dust, without a peg for the sense of difference; and there were hours when, before the temples of gods and the sepulchres of kings, his spirit turned for nobleness of association to the barely discriminated slab in the London suburb. That had become for him, and more intensely with time and distance, his one witness of a past glory. It was all that was left to him for proof or pride, yet the past glories of Pharaohs were nothing to him as he thought of it. Small wonder then that he came back to it on the morrow of his return. He was drawn there this time as irresistibly as the other, yet with a confidence, almost, that was doubtless the effect of the many months that had elapsed. He had lived, in spite of himself, into his change of feeling, and in wandering over the earth had wandered, as might be said, from the circumference to the centre of his desert. He had settled to his safety and accepted perforce his extinction; figuring to himself, with some colour, in the likeness of certain little old men he remembered to have seen, of whom, all meagre and wizened as they might look, it was related that they had in their time fought twenty duels or been loved by ten princesses. They indeed had been wondrous for others while he was but wondrous for himself; which, however, was exactly the cause of his haste to renew the wonder by getting back, as he might put it, into his own presence. That had quickened his steps and checked his delay. If his visit was prompt it was because he had been separated so long from the part of himself that alone he now valued.

It's accordingly not false to say that he reached his goal with a certain elation and stood there again with a certain assurance. The creature beneath the sod *knew* of his rare experience, so that, strangely now, the place had lost for him its mere blankness of expression. It met him in mildness—not, as before, in mockery; it wore for him the air of conscious greeting that we find, after absence, in things that have closely belonged to us and which seem to confess of themselves to the connexion. The plot of ground, the graven tablet, the tended flowers affected him so as belonging to him that he resembled for the hour a contented landlord reviewing a piece of property. Whatever had happened—well, had happened. He had not come back this time with the vanity of that question, his former worrying "What, *what?*" now practically so spent. Yet he would none the less never again so cut himself off from the spot; he would come back to it every month, for if he did nothing else by its aid he at least held up his head. It thus grew for him, in the oddest way, a positive resource; he carried out his idea of periodical returns, which took their place at last among the most inveterate of his habits. What it all amounted to, oddly enough, was that in his finally so simplified world this garden of death gave him the few square feet of earth on which he could still most live. It was as if, being nothing anywhere else for any one, nothing even for himself, he were just everything here, and if not for a crowd of witnesses or indeed for any witness but John Marcher, then by clear right of the register that he could scan like an open page. The open page was the tomb of his friend, and *there* were the facts of the past, there the truth of his life, there the backward reaches in which he could lose himself. He did this from time to time with such effect that he seemed to wander through the old years with his hand in the arm of a companion who was, in the most extraordinary manner, his other, his younger self; and to wander, which was more extraordinary yet, round and round a third presence—not wandering she, but stationary, still, whose eyes, turning with his revolution, never ceased to follow him, and whose seat was his point, so to speak, of orientation. Thus in short he settled to live—feeding all on the sense that he once *had* lived, and dependent on it not alone for a support but for an identity.

It sufficed him in its way for months and the year elapsed; it would doubtless even have carried him further but for an accident, superficially slight, which moved him, quite in another direction, with a force beyond any of his impressions of Egypt or of India. It was a thing of the merest chance—the turn, as he afterwards felt, of a hair, though he was indeed to live to believe that if light hadn't come to him in this particular fashion it would still have come in another. He was to live to believe this, I say, though he was not to live, I may not less definitely mention, to do much else. We allow him at any rate the benefit of the conviction, struggling up for him at the end, that, whatever might have happened or not happened, he would have come round of himself to the light. The incident of an autumn day had put the match to the train laid from of old by his misery. With the light before him he knew that even of late his ache had only been smothered. It was strangely drugged, but it throbbed; at the touch it began to bleed. And the touch, in the event, was the face of a fellow mortal. This face, one grey afternoon when the leaves were thick in the alleys, looked into Marcher's own, at the cemetery, with an expression like the cut of a blade. He felt it, that is, so deep down that he winced at the steady thrust. The person who so mutely assaulted him was a figure he had noticed, on reaching his own goal, absorbed by a grave a short distance away, a grave apparently fresh, so that the emotion of the visitor would probably match it for frankness. This face alone forbade further attention, though during the time he stayed he remained vaguely conscious of his neighbour, a middle-aged man apparently, in mourning, whose bowed back, among the clustered monuments and mortuary yews, was constantly presented. Marcher's theory that these were elements in contact with which he himself revived, had suffered, on this occasion, it may be granted, a marked, an excessive check. The autumn day was dire for him as none had recently been, and he rested with a heaviness he had not yet known on the low stone table that bore May Bartram's name. He rested without power to move, as if some spring in him, some spell vouchsafed, had suddenly been broken for ever. If he could have done that moment as he wanted he would simply have stretched himself on the slab that was ready to take him, treating it as a place prepared to receive his last sleep. What in all the wide world had he now to keep awake for? He stared before him with the question, and it was then that, as one of the cemetery walks passed near him, he caught the shock of the face.

His neighbour at the other grave had withdrawn, as he himself, with force enough in him, would have done by now, and was advancing along the path on his way to one of the gates. This brought him close, and his pace was slow, so that—and all the more as there was a kind of hunger in his look—the two men were for a minute directly confronted. Marcher knew him at once for one of the deeply stricken—a perception so sharp that nothing else in the picture comparatively lived, neither his dress, his age, nor his presumable character and class; nothing lived but the deep ravage of the features he showed. He *showed* them—that was the point; he was moved, as he passed, by some impulse that was either a signal for sympathy or, more possibly, a challenge to an opposed sorrow. He might already have been aware of our friend, might at some previous hour have noticed in him the smooth habit of the scene, with which the state of his own senses so scantly consorted, and might thereby have been stirred as by an overt discord. What Marcher was at all events conscious of was in the first place that the image of scarred passion presented to him was conscious too—of something that profaned the air; and in the second that, roused, startled, shocked, he was yet the next moment looking after it, as it went, with envy. The most extraordinary thing that had happened to him—though he had given that name to other matters as well—took place, after his immediate vague stare, as a consequence of this impression. The stranger passed, but the raw glare of his grief remained, making our friend wonder in pity what wrong, what wound it expressed, what injury not to be healed. What had the man *had*, to make him by the loss of it so bleed and yet live?

Something—and this reached him with a pang—that *he*, John Marcher, hadn't; the proof of which was precisely John Marcher's arid end. No passion had ever touched him, for this was what passion meant; he had survived and maundered and pined, but where had been *his* deep ravage? The extraordinary thing we speak of was the sudden rush of the result of this question. The sight that had just met his eyes named to him, as in letters of quick flame, something he had utterly, insanely missed, and what he had missed made these things a train of fire, made them mark themselves in an anguish of inward throbs. He had seen *outside* of his life, not learned it within, the way a woman was mourned when she had been loved for herself: such was the force of his conviction of the meaning of the stranger's face, which still flared for him as a smoky torch. It hadn't come to him, the knowledge, on the wings of experience; it had brushed him, jostled him, upset him, with the disrespect of chance, the insolence of accident. Now that the illumination had begun, however, it blazed to the zenith, and what he presently stood there gazing at was the sounded void of his life. He gazed, he drew breath, in pain; he turned in his dismay, and, turning, he had before him in sharper incision than ever the open page of his story. The name on the table smote him as the passage of his neighbour had done, and what it said to him, full in the face, was that *she* was what he had missed. This was the awful thought, the answer to all the past, the vision at the dread clearness of which he grew as cold as the stone beneath him. Everything fell together, confessed, explained, overwhelmed; leaving him most of all stupefied at the blindness he had cherished. The fate he had been marked for he had met with a vengeance—he had emptied the cup to the lees; he had been the man of his time, *the* man, to whom nothing on earth was to have happened. That was the rare stroke—that was his visitation. So he saw it, as we say, in pale horror, while the pieces fitted and fitted. So *she* had seen it while he didn't, and so she served at this hour to drive the truth home. It was the truth, vivid and monstrous, that all the while he had waited the wait was itself his portion. This the companion of his vigil had at a given moment made out, and she had then offered him the chance to baffle his doom. One's doom, however, was never baffled, and on the day she told him his own had come down she had seen him but stupidly stare at the escape she offered him.

The escape would have been to love her; then, *then* he would have lived. *She* had lived—who could say now with what passion?—since she had loved him for himself; whereas he had never thought of her (ah, how it hugely glared at him!) but in the chill of his egotism and the light of her use. Her spoken words came back to him—the chain stretched and stretched. The Beast had lurked indeed, and the Beast, at its hour, had sprung; it had sprung in that twilight of the cold April when, pale, ill, wasted, but all beautiful, and perhaps even then recoverable, she had risen from her chair to stand before him and let him imaginably guess. It had sprung as he didn't guess; it had sprung as she hopelessly turned from him, and the mark, by the time he left her, had fallen where it *was* to fall. He had justified his fear and achieved his fate; he had failed, with the last exactitude, of all he was to fail of; and a moan now rose to his lips as he remembered she had prayed he mightn't know. This horror of waking—*this* was knowledge, knowledge under the breath of which the very tears in his eyes seemed to freeze. Through them, none the less, he tried to fix it and hold it; he kept it there before him so that he might feel the pain. That at least, belated and bitter, had something of the taste of life. But the bitterness suddenly sickened him, and it was as if, horribly, he saw, in the truth, in the cruelty of his image, what had been appointed and done. He saw the Jungle of his life and saw the lurking Beast; then, while he looked, perceived it, as by a stir of the air, rise, huge and hideous, for the leap that was to settle him. His eyes darkened—it was close; and, instinctively turning, in his hallucination, to avoid it, he flung himself, face down, on the tomb.

1901   1903, 1909

SARAH WINNEMUCCA
ca. 1844–1891

Sarah Winnemucca, or Thocmetony ("shell flower"), was a northern Paiute woman born about 1844 in western Nevada. Her mother, Tuboitony ("lettuce flower"), was the daughter of Captain Truckee, a prominent man among his people whose friendly attitude toward white settlers was based on a belief in traditional stories the Paiutes shared with other desert peoples regarding a "lost white brother" who would one day return. Sarah's father, known as Old Winnemucca, was a Paiute chief. When Captain Truckee traveled to California in the 1850s to find work on Spanish-owned ranches, he insisted that Sarah and her mother come with him. It was in California that Sarah learned some Spanish and became fluent enough in English to serve later as an interpreter for the American military. Throughout her adult life, Sarah Winnemucca worked on behalf of her people, negotiating with the Americans by means of her lectures, her writing, and her direct encounters with government officials. She was a controversial figure in her time, and, as scholar LaVonne Ruoff notes, "a courageous and eloquent spokeswoman for her people."

Sarah Winnemucca first gained public notice in 1864 when she appeared with her father and other family members on the streets of Virginia City, Nevada, in theatrical performances designed to alert white citizens to the dire situation of Paiutes who had been displaced by the Virginia City gold rush of 1859. These performances soon led her to become known, admiringly or scornfully, as "Princess Sarah." Sarah's first publication was a letter describing Paiute suffering that appeared in *Harper's Weekly* in 1870. She attracted a national audience in 1878, at the end of the Bannock War. The Bannock Indians of the California Sierras, whose territory was adjacent to that of the Paiutes, had taken up arms against the encroaching whites. Many Paiutes joined with the Bannocks. But at the conclusion of hostilities, many Paiutes who had not fought were nonetheless imprisoned with the Bannocks and their Paiute allies on the Yakima Reservation in Washington. Winnemucca lectured on the Paiute cause in San Francisco, and even made the long trip to Washington D.C. to plead the case with President Rutherford B. Hayes and Secretary of the Interior Carl Schurz. Despite her efforts, years passed and conditions for the Paiutes only worsened. Finally, in 1883, Winnemucca embarked on a lecture tour to the East on behalf of her people, speaking in New York, Baltimore, and Boston, where her audience included the poet John Greenleaf Whittier and the senator from Massachusetts, Henry Dawes. (Although it has many times been said that Ralph Waldo Emerson was among her audience, this is wrong—Emerson had died the year before.)

In Boston, Winnemucca met Mary Mann, widow of the prominent educator Horace Mann, and her sister, Elizabeth Palmer Peabody, an active reformer (years before she had taken a stand against Cherokee removal). It was while staying in Boston with the sisters that she wrote most of her autobiography, which Mary Mann edited. *Life Among the Piutes: Their Wrongs and Claims* was privately printed in 1883. In it, Winnemucca recounts the events of her life in the context of Paiute culture and history. The book has been called an "autoethnography" (Ruoff), a "coup tale" in which she relates her brave deeds (Brumble), and a document of feminist resistance (Georgi-Findlay). She published the book under the name of Sarah Winnemucca Hopkins. Lewis Hopkins, Sarah's husband (they had married in 1881, in San Francisco, although California had a law prohibiting Indian-white unions), had accompanied her on her lecture tour and was with her in Boston. Hopkins, who had been discharged by the Army as a person of "no character," was addicted to gambling and apparently drank heavily. These unsavory qualities, and the fact that Winnemucca had had more than one white husband before him, made it possible for her opponents to attack her morals. Thus her book concludes with an "Appendix" containing testimonials to her character (the first, from Major General O. O. Howard, for whom she had worked during the Bannock War, affirms that Winnemucca's "conduct was always good"), as well as testimonials to the justice and accuracy of her accounts of and pleas for the Paiute people.

The book's authenticity has also been questioned, for it has been suggested that it was mostly written by Mary Mann, though in many places it uses material from Sarah Winnemucca's own lectures. This sort of charge has often been raised in connection with African American and Native American autobiographies, whether by Frederick Douglass and Harriet Jacobs, or by Black Hawk and Sarah Winnemucca. In her preface to *Life Among the Piutes*, Mary Mann states that her editing consisted of no more than "copying the original manuscript in correct orthography and punctuation, with occasional emendations by the author"; she called the book "an heroic act on the part of the writer." Mary Mann's judgment that *Life Among the Piutes* was "the first outbreak of the American Indian in human literature . . . *to tell the truth*" holds up quite well today.

Near the end of her life, Winnemucca, with her brother Natchez, opened a school for Indian children in Nevada called the Peabody Indian School, supported, as the name would indicate, by Elizabeth Palmer Peabody, with whom Winnemucca had developed a deep friendship. But not even Peabody could persuade eastern senators to vote an appropriation for Indian education, and the school closed in 1888. Winnemucca then went to live with her sister, Elma, at Henry's Lake, Idaho, where she died in 1891.

Our selections from *Life Among the Piutes* are from chapter I, "First Meeting of Piutes and Whites," chapter II, "Domestic and Social Moralities," and the lengthy chapter VIII, "The Yakima Affair," which ends the book. It is in this last chapter that Winnemucca's role as an activist on behalf of her Paiute people may be seen especially clearly.

From Life Among the Piutes

From *Chapter I. First Meeting of Piutes and Whites*

I was born somewhere near 1844, but am not sure of the precise time. I was a very small child when the first white people came into our country. They came like a lion, yes, like a roaring lion, and have continued so ever since, and I have never forgotten their first coming. My people were scattered at that time over nearly all the territory now known as Nevada. My grandfather was chief of the entire Piute nation, and was camped near Humboldt Lake, with a small portion of his tribe, when a party travelling eastward from California was seen coming. When the news was brought to my grandfather, he asked what they looked like? When told that they had hair on their faces, and were white, he jumped up and clasped his hands together, and cried aloud,—

"My white brothers,—my long-looked for white brothers have come at last!"

He immediately gathered some of his leading men, and went to the place where the party had gone into camp. Arriving near them, he was commanded to halt in a manner that was readily understood without an interpreter. Grandpa at once made signs of friendship by throwing down his robe and throwing up his arms to show them he had no weapons; but in vain,—they kept him at a distance. He knew not what to do. He had expected so much pleasure in welcoming his white brothers to the best in the land, that after looking at them sorrowfully for a little while, he came away quite unhappy. But he would not give them up so easily. He took some of his most trustworthy men and followed them day after day, camping near them at night, and travelling in sight of them by day, hoping in this way to gain their confidence. But he was disappointed, poor dear old soul!

I can imagine his feelings, for I have drank deeply from the same cup. When I think of my past life, and the bitter trials I have endured, I can scarcely believe I live, and yet I do; and, with the help of Him who notes the sparrow's fall, I mean to fight for my down-trodden race while life lasts.

Seeing they would not trust him, my grandfather left them, saying, "Perhaps they will come again next year." Then he summoned his whole people, and told them this tradition:—

"In the beginning of the world there were only four, two girls and two boys. Our forefather and mother were only two, and we are their children. You all know that a great while ago there was a happy family in this world. One girl and one boy were dark and the others were white. For a time they got along together without quarrelling, but soon they disagreed, and there was trouble. They were cross to one another and fought, and our parents were very much grieved. They prayed that their children might learn better, but it did not do any good; and afterwards the whole household was made so unhappy that the father and mother saw that they must separate their children; and then our father took the dark boy and girl, and the white boy and girl, and asked them, 'Why are you so cruel to each other?' They hung down their heads, and would not speak. They were ashamed. He said to them, 'Have I not been kind to you all, and given you everything your hearts wished for? You do not have to hunt and kill your own game to live upon. You see, my dear children, I have power to call whatsoever kind of game we want to eat; and I also have the power to separate my dear children, if they are not good to each other.' So he separated his children by a word. He said, 'Depart from each other, you cruel children;— go across the mighty ocean and do not seek each other's lives.'

"So the light girl and boy disappeared by that one word, and their parents saw them no more, and they were grieved, although they knew their children were happy. And by-and-by the dark children grew into a large nation; and we believe it is the one we belong to, and that the nation that sprung from the white children will some time send some one to meet us and heal all the old trouble. Now, the white people we saw a few days ago must certainly be our white brothers, and I want to welcome them. I want to love them as I love all of you. But they would not let me; they were afraid. But they will come again, and I want you one and all to promise that, should I not live to welcome them myself, you will not hurt a hair on their heads, but welcome them as I tried to do."

How good of him to try and heal the wound, and how vain were his efforts! My people had never seen a white man, and yet they existed, and were a strong race. The people promised as he wished, and they all went back to their work.

* * *

That same fall, after my grandfather came home, he told my father to take charge of his people and hold the tribe, as he was going back to California with as many of his people as he could get to go with him. So my father took his place as Chief of the Piutes, and had it as long as he lived. Then my grandfather started back to California again with about thirty families. That same fall, very late, the emigrants kept coming. It was this time that our white brothers first came amongst us. They could not get over the mountains, so they had to live with us. It was on Carson River, where the great Carson City stands now. You call my people bloodseeking. My people did not seek to kill them, nor did they steal their horses,—no, no, far from it. During the winter my people helped them. They gave them such as they had to eat. They did not hold out their hands and say:—

"You can't have anything to eat unless you pay me." No,—no such word was used by us savages at that time; and the persons I am speaking of are living yet; they could speak for us if they choose to do so.

The following spring, before my grandfather returned home, there was a great excitement among my people on account of fearful news coming from different tribes, that the people whom they called their white brothers were killing everybody that came in their way, and all the Indian tribes had gone into the mountains to save their lives. So my father told all his people to go into the mountains and hunt and lay up food for the coming winter. Then we all went into the mountains. There was a fearful story they told us children. Our mothers told us that the whites were killing everybody and eating them.[1] So we were all afraid of them. Every dust that we could see blowing in the valleys we would say it was the white people. In the late fall my father told his people to go to the rivers and fish, and we all went to Humboldt River, and the women went to work gathering wild seed, which they grind between the rocks. The stones are round, big enough to hold in the hands. The women did this when they got back, and when they had gathered all they could they put it in one place and covered it with grass, and then over the grass mud. After it is covered it looks like an Indian wigwam.

Oh, what a fright we all got one morning to hear some white people were coming. Every one ran as best they could. My poor mother was left with my little sister and me. Oh, I never can forget it. My poor mother was carrying my little sister on her back, and trying to make me run; but I was so frightened I could not move my feet, and while my poor mother was trying to get me along my aunt overtook us, and she said to my mother: "Let us bury our

---

1. The reference is to a group of emigrants to California known as the Donner Party. Cut off by a storm in the Sierra Nevada Mountains in mid-December of 1846, with their rations almost gone, the group sent a party on snowshoes to seek help. Several of the party died, and the survivors resorted to cannibalism; cannibalism also occurred among those who had stayed behind. Captain Truckee knew of these events. Winnemucca refers to them later in the chapter as well.

girls, or we shall all be killed and eaten up." So they went to work and buried us, and told us if we heard any noise not to cry out, for if we did they would surely kill us and eat us. So our mothers buried me and my cousin, planted sage bushes over our faces to keep the sun from burning them, and there we were left all day.

Oh, can any one imagine my feelings *buried alive*, thinking every minute that I was to be unburied and eaten up by the people that my grandfather loved so much? With my heart throbbing, and not daring to breathe, we lay there all day. It seemed that the night would never come. Thanks be to God! the night came at last. Oh, how I cried and said: "Oh, father, have you forgotten me? Are you never coming for me?" I cried so I thought my very heartstrings would break.

At last we heard some whispering. We did not dare to whisper to each other, so we lay still. I could hear their footsteps coming nearer and nearer. I thought my heart was coming right out of my mouth. Then I heard my mother say, " 'T is right here!" Oh, can any one in this world ever imagine what were my feelings when I was dug up by my poor mother and father? My cousin and I were once more happy in our mothers' and fathers' care, and we were taken to where all the rest were.

I was once buried alive; but my second burial shall be for ever, where no father or mother will come and dig me up. It shall not be with throbbing heart that I shall listen for coming footsteps. I shall be in the sweet rest of peace,— I, the chieftain's weary daughter.

Well, while we were in the mountains hiding, the people that my grandfather called our white brothers came along to where our winter supplies were. They set everything we had left on fire. It was a fearful sight. It was all we had for the winter, and it was all burnt during that night. My father took some of his men during the night to try and save some of it, but they could not; it had burnt down before they got there.

These were the last white men that came along that fall. My people talked fearfully that winter about those they called our white brothers. My people said they had something like awful thunder and lightning, and with that they killed everything that came in their way.

This whole band of white people perished in the mountains, for it was too late to cross them. We could have saved them, only my people were afraid of them. We never knew who they were, or where they came from. So, poor things, they must have suffered fearfully, for they all starved there. The snow was too deep.

Early in the following spring, my father told all his people to go to the mountains, for there would be a great emigration that summer. He told them he had had a wonderful dream, and wanted to tell them all about it.

He said, "Within ten days come together at the sink of Carson, and I will tell you my dream."

The sub-chiefs went everywhere to tell their people what my father had told them to say; and when the time came we all went to the sink of Carson.

Just about noon, while we were on the way, a great many of our men came to meet us, all on their horses. Oh, what a beautiful song they sang for my father as they came near us! We passed them, and they followed us, and as we came near to the encampment, every man, woman, and child were out looking for us. They had a place all ready for us. Oh, how happy everybody was! One could hear laughter everywhere, and songs were sung by happy women and children.

My father stood up and told his people to be merry and happy for five days. It is a rule among our people always to have five days to settle anything.[2] My father told them to dance at night, and that the men should hunt rabbits and fish, and some were to have games of football, or any kind of sport or playthings they wished, and the women could do the same, as they had nothing else to do. My people were so happy during the five days,—the women ran races, and the men ran races on foot and on horses.

My father got up very early one morning, and told his people the time had come,—that we could no longer be happy as of old, as the white people we called our brothers had brought a great trouble and sorrow among us already. He went on and said,—

"These white people must be a great nation, as they have houses that move.[3] It is wonderful to see them move along. I fear we will suffer greatly by their coming to our country; they come for no good to us, although my father said they were our brothers, but they do not seem to think we are like them. What do you all think about it? Maybe I am wrong. My dear children, there is something telling me that I am not wrong, because I am sure they have minds like us, and think as we do; and I know that they were doing wrong when they set fire to our winter supplies. They surely knew it was our food."

And this was the first wrong done to us by our white brothers.

Now comes the end of our merrymaking.

Then my father told his people his fearful dream, as he called it. He said,—

"I dreamt this same thing three nights,—the very same. I saw the greatest emigration that has yet been through our country. I looked North and South and East and West, and saw nothing but dust, and I heard a great weeping. I saw women crying, and I also saw my men shot down by the white people. They were killing my people with something that made a great noise like thunder and lightning, and I saw the blood streaming from the mouths of my men that lay all around me. I saw it as if it was real. Oh, my dear children! You may all think it is only a dream,—nevertheless, I feel that it will come to pass. And to avoid bloodshed, we must all go to the mountains during the summer, or till my father comes back from California. He will then tell us what to do. Let us keep away from the emigrant roads and stay in the mountains all summer. There are to be a great many pine-nuts this summer, and we can lay up great supplies for the coming winter, and if the emigrants don't come too early, we can take a run down and fish for a month, and lay up dried fish. I know we can dry a great many in a month, and young men can go into the valleys on hunting excursions, and kill as many rabbits as they can. In that way we can live in the mountains all summer and all winter too."

So ended my father's dream. During that day one could see old women getting together talking over what they had heard my father say. They said,—

"It is true what our great chief has said, for it was shown to him by a higher power. It is not a dream. Oh, it surely will come to pass. We shall no longer

---

2. Five is the pattern number for Winnemucca's people, although a few paragraphs below an important dream of her father's takes place not on five but on three nights.

3. The reference might be to covered wagons but is more likely to railway cars.

be a happy people, as we now are; we shall no longer go here and there as of old; we shall no longer build our big fires as a signal to our friends, for we shall always be afraid of being seen by those bad people."

"Surely they don't eat people?"

"Yes, they do eat people, because they ate each other up in the mountains last winter."

This was the talk among the old women during the day.

"Oh, how grieved we are! Oh, where will it end?"

* * *

From *Chapter II. Domestic and Social Moralities*

Our children are very carefully taught to be good. Their parents tell them stories, traditions of old times, even of the first mother of the human race; and love stories, stories of giants, and fables; and when they ask if these last stories are true, they answer, "Oh, it is only coyote," which means that they are make-believe stories. Coyote is the name of a mean, crafty little animal, half wolf, half dog, and stands for everything low. It is the greatest term of reproach one Indian has for another. Indians do not swear,—they have no words for swearing till they learn them of white men. The worst they call each is bad or coyote; but they are very sincere with one another, and if they think each other in the wrong they say so.

We are taught to love everybody. We don't need to be taught to love our fathers and mothers. We love them without being told to. Our tenth cousin is as near to us as our first cousin; and we don't marry into our relations. Our young women are not allowed to talk to any young man that is not their cousin, except at the festive dances, when both are dressed in their best clothes, adorned with beads, feathers or shells, and stand alternately in the ring and take hold of hands. These are very pleasant occasions to all the young people.

Many years ago, when my people were happier than they are now, they used to celebrate the Festival of Flowers in the spring. I have been to three of them only in the course of my life.

Oh, with what eagerness we girls used to watch every spring for the time when we could meet with our hearts' delight, the young men, whom in civilized life you call beaux. We would all go in company to see if the flowers we were named for were yet in bloom, for almost all the girls are named for flowers. We talked about them in our wigwams, as if we were the flowers, saying, "Oh, I saw myself today in full bloom!" We would talk all the evening in this way in our families with such delight, and such beautiful thoughts of the happy day when we should meet with those who admired us and would help us to sing our flower-songs which we made up as we sang. But we were always sorry for those that were not named after some flower, because we knew they could not join in the flower-songs like ourselves, who were named for flowers of all kinds.

At last one evening came a beautiful voice, which made every girl's heart throb with happiness. It was the chief, and every one hushed to hear what he said to-day.

"My dear daughters, we are told that you have seen yourselves in the hills and in the valleys, in full bloom. Five days from to-day your festival day will come. I know every young man's heart stops beating while I am talking. I know how it was with me many years ago. I used to wish the Flower Festival would come every day. Dear young men and young women, you are saying, 'Why put it off five days?' But you all know that is our rule. It gives you time to think, and to show your sweetheart your flower."

All the girls who have flower-names dance along together, and those who have not go together also. Our fathers and mothers and grandfathers and grandmothers make a place for us where we can dance. Each one gathers the flower she is named for, and then all weave them into wreaths and crowns and scarfs, and dress up in them.

Some girls are named for rocks and are called rock-girls, and they find some pretty rocks which they carry; each one such a rock as she is named for, or whatever she is named for. If she cannot, she can take a branch of sage-brush, or a bunch of rye-grass, which have no flower.

They all go marching along, each girl in turn singing of herself; but she is not a girl any more,—she is a flower singing. She sings of herself, and her sweetheart, dancing along by her side, helps her sing the song she makes.

I will repeat what we say of ourselves. "I, Sarah Winnemucca, am a shell-flower, such as I wear on my dress. My name is Thocmetony. I am so beautiful! Who will come and dance with me while I am so beautiful? Oh, come and be happy with me! I shall be beautiful while the earth lasts. Somebody will always admire me; and who will come and be happy with me in the Spirit-land? I shall be beautiful forever there. Yes, I shall be more beautiful than my shell-flower, my Thocmetony! Then, come, oh come, and dance and be happy with me!" The young men sing with us as they dance beside us.

Our parents are waiting for us somewhere to welcome us home. And then we praise the sage-brush and the rye-grass that have no flower, and the pretty rocks that some are named for; and then we present our beautiful flowers to these companions who could carry none. And so all are happy; and that closes the beautiful day.

My people have been so unhappy for a long time they wish now to *disincrease*, instead of multiply. The mothers are afraid to have more children, for fear they shall have daughters, who are not safe even in their mother's presence.

* * *

Our boys are introduced to manhood by their hunting of deer and mountain-sheep. Before they are fifteen or sixteen, they hunt only small game, like rabbits, hares, fowls, etc. They never eat what they kill themselves, but only what their father or elder brothers kill. When a boy becomes strong enough to use larger bows made of sinew, and arrows that are ornamented with eagle-feathers, for the first time, he kills game that is large, a deer or an antelope, or a mountain-sheep. Then he brings home the hide, and his father cuts it into a long coil which is wound into a loop, and the boy takes his quiver and throws it on his back as if he was going on a hunt, and takes his bow and arrows in his hand. Then his father throws the loop over him, and he jumps through it. This he does five times. Now for the first time he eats the flesh of the animal he has killed, and from that time he eats whatever he kills but he has always been faithful to his parents' command not to eat what he has killed before. He can now do whatever he likes, for now he is a man, and no longer considered a boy. If there is a war he can go to it; but the Piutes, and other tribes west of the Rocky Mountains, are not fond of going to war. I never saw a war-dance but once. It is always the whites that begin the wars, for their own selfish purposes. The government does not take care to send the good men; there are a plenty who would take pains to see and understand the chiefs and learn their characters, and their good will to the whites. But the whites have not waited to find out how good the Indians were, and what ideas they had of God, just like those of Jesus, who called him Father, just as my people do, and told men to do to others as they would be done by, just as my people teach their children to do. My people teach their children never to make fun of any one, no matter how they look. If you see your brother or sister doing something wrong, look away, or go away from them. If you make fun of bad persons, you make yourself beneath them. Be kind to all, both poor and rich, and feed all that come to your wigwam, and your name can be spoken of by every one far and near. In this way you will make many friends for yourself. Be kind both to bad and good, for you don't know your own heart. This is the way my people teach their children. It was handed down from father to son for many generations. I never in my life saw our children rude as I have seen white children and grown people in the streets.

The chief's tent is the largest tent, and it is the council-tent, where every one goes who wants advice. In the evenings the head men go there to discuss everything, for the chiefs do not rule like tyrants; they discuss everything with their people, as a father would in his family. Often they sit up all night. They discuss the doings of all, if they need to be advised. If a boy is not doing well they talk that over, and if the women are interested they can share in the talks. If there is not room enough inside, they all go out of doors, and make a great circle. The men are in the inner circle, for there would be too much smoke for the women inside. The men never talk without smoking first. The women sit behind them in another circle, and if the children wish to hear, they can be there too. The women know as much as the men do, and their advice is often asked. We have a republic as well as you. The council-tent is our Congress, and anybody can speak who has anything to say, women and all. They are always interested in what their husbands are doing and thinking about. And they take some part even in the wars. They are always near at hand when fighting is going on, ready to snatch their husbands up and carry them off if wounded or killed. One splendid woman that my brother Lee married after his first wife died, went out into the battle-field after her uncle was killed, and went into the front ranks and cheered the men on. Her uncle's horse was dressed in a splendid robe made of eagles' feathers and she snatched it off and swung it in the face of the enemy, who always carry off everything they find, as much as to say, "You can't have that—I have it safe"; and she staid and took her uncle's place, as brave as any of the men. It means something when the women promise their fathers to make their husbands *themselves*. They faithfully keep with them in all the dangers they can share. They not only take care of their children together, but they do everything together; and when they grow blind, which I am sorry to say is very common, for the smoke they live in destroys their eyes at last, they take sweet care of one another. Marriage is a sweet thing when people love each other. If women could go into your Congress I think justice would soon be done to the Indians.

* * *

From *Chapter VIII. The Yakima Affair*

* * *

We then went down, and Major Cochran met us at the door and said, "Sarah, are you sick? You look so badly."

I said, "No."

He then replied, "Sarah, I am heartily sorry for you, but we cannot help it. We are ordered to take your people to Yakima Reservation."[4]

It was just a little before Christmas. My people were only given one week to get ready in.

I said, "What! In this cold winter and in all this snow, and my people have so many little children? Why, they will all die. Oh, what can the President be thinking about? Oh, tell me, what is he? Is he man or beast? Yes, he must be a beast; if he has no feeling for my people, surely he ought to have some for the soldiers."

"I have never seen a president in my life and I want to know whether he is made of wood or rock, for I cannot for once think that he can be a human being. No human being would do such a thing as that,—send people across a fearful mountain in midwinter."

I was told not to say anything till three days before starting. Every night I imagined I could see the thing called President. He had long ears, he had big eyes and long legs, and a head like a bull-frog or something like that. I could not think of anything that could be so inhuman as to do such a thing,—send people across mountains with snow so deep.

Mattie and I got all the furs we could; we had fur caps, fur gloves, and fur overshoes.

At last the time arrived. The commanding-officer told me to tell Leggins to come to him.[5] I did so. He came, and Major Cochrane told me to tell him that he wanted him to tell which of the Bannock men were the worst, or which was the leader in the war. Leggins told him, and counted out twelve men to him. After this talk, Major Cochrane asked me to go and tell these men to come up to the office. They were Oytes, Bannock Joe, Captain Bearskin, Paddy Cap, Boss, Big John, Eagle Eye, Charley, D. E. Johnson, Beads, and Oytes' son-in-law, called Surger. An officer was sent with me. I called out the men by their names. They all came out to me. I said to Oytes,—

"Your soldier-father wants you all to go up to see him."

---

4. This is Captain (not Major) M. A. Cochran (Winnemucca spells it "Cochrane" just below), who is the post commander at Fort Harney, Oregon. Sarah is with her close friend, Mattie, whom she will refer to as her "sister" a few paragraphs below. A number of Paiute people had been taken to Fort Harney after the conclusion of the Bannock War in 1878. They were expecting to be returned to the Malheur Reservation in Oregon, where many had been for some time. Here, Winnemucca learns that her people are to be sent far away, to the Yakima Reservation in Washington State.

5. Leggins was the leader of Winnemucca's father's band. These Paiutes did not join the Bannocks. They were nonetheless sent to Washington.

We went up, and Oytes asked me many things.

We had to go right by the guard-house. Just as we got near it, the soldier on guard came out and headed us off and took the men and put them into the guard-house. After they were put in there the soldiers told me to tell them they must not try to get away, or they would be shot.

"We put you in here for safe-keeping," they said. "The citizens are coming over here from Canyon City to arrest you all, and we don't want them to take you; that is why we put you in here."

Ten soldiers were sent down to guard the whole encampment,—not Leggins' band, only Oytes' and the Bannocks. I was then ordered to tell them to get ready to go to Yakima Reservation.

Oh, how sad they were! Women cried and blamed their husbands for going with the Bannocks; but Leggins and his band were told they were not going with the prisoners of war, and that he was not going at all.

Then Leggins moved down the creek about two miles. At night some would get out and go off. Brother Lee[6] and Leggins were sent out to bring them back again. One afternoon Mattie and I were sent out to get five women who got away during the night, and an officer was sent with us. We were riding very fast, and my sister Mattie's horse jumped on one side and threw her off and hurt her. The blood ran out of her mouth, and I thought she would die right off; but, poor dear, she went on, for an ambulance was at our command. She had great suffering during our journey.

Oh, for shame! You who are educated by a Christian government in the art of war; the practice of whose profession makes you natural enemies of the savages, so called by you. Yes, you, who call yourselves the great civilization; you who have knelt upon Plymouth Rock, covenanting with God to make this land the home of the free and the brave. Ah, then you rise from your bended knees and seizing the welcoming hands of those who are the owners of this land, which you are not, your carbines rise upon the bleak shore, and your so-called civilization sweeps inland from the ocean wave; but, oh, my God! leaving its pathway marked by crimson lines of blood, and strewed by the bones of two races, the inheritor and the invader; and I am crying out to you for justice,—yes, pleading for the far-off plains of the West, for the dusky mourner, whose tears of love are pleading for her husband, or for their children, who are sent far away from them. Your Christian minister will hold my people against their will; not because he loves them,—no, far from it,—but because it puts money in his pockets.

Now we are ready to start for Yakima. Fifty wagons were brought, and citizens were to take us there. Some of the wagons cost the government from ten dollars to fifteen dollars per day. We got to Canyon City, and while we camped there Captain Winters got a telegram from Washington, telling him he must take Leggins' band too. So we had to wait for them to overtake us. While we were waiting, our dear good father and mother, Mr. Charles W. Parrish,[7] came with his wife and children to see us. My people threw their arms round him and his wife, crying, "Oh, our father and mother, if you had staid with us we would not suffer this."

6. Winnemucca's half-brother.
7. Charles Parrish had been the government Indian agent at the Malheur Reservation. As is apparent, Winnemucca thought extremely well of Parrish and his wife.

Poor Mrs. Parrish could not stop her tears at seeing the people who once loved her, the children whom she had taught,—yes, the savage children who once called her their white-lily mother, the children who used to bring her wild flowers, with happy faces, now ragged, no clothes whatever. They all cried out to him and his wife, saying, "Oh, good father and mother, talk for us! Don't let them take us away; take us back to our home!" He told them he could do nothing for them. They asked him where his brother, Sam Parrish, was. He told them he was a long way off; and then they bade us good-by, and that was the last they saw of him.

* * *

1883

SARAH ORNE JEWETT
1849–1909

When Sarah Orne Jewett was born in South Berwick, Maine, in 1849, the town and region she was to memorialize in her fiction were already changing rapidly. Her grandfather had been a sea captain, shipowner, and merchant; and as a child she was exposed to the bustle of this small inland port. By the end of the Civil War, however, textile mills and a cannery had largely replaced agriculture, shipbuilding, and logging as the economic base of the community, and the arrival of French Canadian and Irish immigrants brought ethnic diversity to the area. The stable, secure, and remote small town Jewett knew and loved as a child was experiencing the economic, technological, and demographic pressures that transformed much of America in her lifetime.

Jewett's family life was steady and affectionate; she and her two sisters led happy and generally carefree childhoods. Their father was a kindly, hardworking obstetrician who indulged all three of his daughters, but Sarah most of all. He encouraged her reading, and even as a small child she accompanied him on his horse-and-buggy rounds, meeting the rural people who would later populate her fiction. Jewett loved her father deeply, and some of her strong feelings for him are invested in *A Country Doctor* (1884), a novel that celebrates the competence and independence of its female protagonist. Jewett's relationship with her mother was less intense; it was not until her mother became an invalid in the 1880s that mother and daughter became close. As Jewett admitted in a letter to editor and friend Thomas Bailey Aldrich: "I never felt so near to my mother . . . as I have since she died."

In part inspired by Harriet Beecher Stowe's novel about Maine seacoast life, *The Pearl of Orr's Island* (1862), Jewett began to write and publish verse and stories in her teens. One of her first efforts was accepted in 1869 by the influential editor William Dean Howells for publication in the prestigious *Atlantic Monthly*. In her early twenties, encouraged by Howells, she wrote a group of stories and sketches about a fictional coastal town in Maine to which she gave the name Deephaven; under that title she published her first collection of short pieces in 1877. With the publication of this book, she entered the company of George Washington Cable, Harriet Beecher Stowe, and other regional writers who were depicting the topographies, people, speech patterns, and modes of life of many distinctive regions of the country. At their best, the "regionalists" created works whose themes transcended regionality, as with Jewett's treatment of the courageous response of women to frustration and loneliness in the post–Civil War years.

From the late 1870s on, Jewett was a member of a circle of prominent women writers and artists who lived in or near Boston. This group included Cecilia Thaxter, Sarah Wyman Whitman, Sara Norton, and Marie Thérèsa Blanc. Without question, the relationship between Jewett and Annie Adams Fields, the wife of editor and publisher James T. Fields, was the most important of the many friendships Jewett formed with both men and women. Though they had known each other since the late 1870s, it was not until Annie Fields's husband died in 1881 that they established a bond that was to sustain both women until Jewett's death in 1909. During the winter months, Jewett lived at Fields's house in Boston and in the spring and summer was often to be found at Fields's oceanside home a few miles north of Boston in Manchester-by-the-Sea. Jewett maintained her residence in South Berwick, and she and Mrs. Fields would spend time together there as well. Their relationship was of a kind not uncommon at the turn of the century; indeed, such connections between women were called "Boston marriages," a term that implied shared living quarters and a partnership that paralleled ordinary marriage in its intimacy and exclusiveness. In recent years their relationship—and those of other prominent female couples of the period—has been the subject of much historical and biographical commentary. What is most central and significant about the Jewett-Fields relationship is that in their lives together in America and in the course of extended trips they took to England, the Continent, and other places, they found companionship and mutual support in a loving, caring relationship based on shared interests. Annie Fields grieved deeply at the death of her husband; when Jewett died seven years after she was seriously injured in a carriage accident, Annie Fields's grief was of the same order of magnitude.

Jewett reached artistic maturity with the publication of the collection *A White Heron* in 1886; later collections of sketches and stories include *The King of Folly Island* (1888), *A Native of Winby* (1893), and *The Life of Nancy* (1895). In these works the careful documentary record of landscape, people, and dialect is described with understanding and sympathy. In "A White Heron," reprinted here, a young girl's conflicted loyalties to her conception of herself in nature and to the world of men she will soon encounter are memorably and sensitively drawn. Jewett's most enduring work is *The Country of the Pointed Firs* (1896), a collection of linked sketches filtered through the consciousness of a summer visitor, much like the person Jewett had become. In this work, bits and pieces of the lives of a small group of men and women are quilted into a unified impression of life in a once-prosperous shipping village. The strong older women who survive in the region form a female community that, for many critics, is a hallmark of New England regionalism.

A White Heron[1]

I

The woods were already filled with shadows one June evening, just before eight o'clock, though a bright sunset still glimmered faintly among the trunks of the trees. A little girl was driving home her cow, a plodding, dilatory, provoking creature in her behavior, but a valued companion for all that. They were going away from whatever light there was, and striking deep into the woods, but their feet were familiar with the path, and it was no matter whether their eyes could see it or not.

---

1. First published in book form in *"A White Heron" and Other Stories* (1886), the source of the text printed here.

There was hardly a night the summer through when the old cow could be found waiting at the pasture bars; on the contrary, it was her greatest pleasure to hide herself away among the high huckleberry bushes, and though she wore a loud bell she had made the discovery that if one stood perfectly still it would not ring. So Sylvia had to hunt for her until she found her, and call Co'! Co'! with never an answering Moo, until her childish patience was quite spent. If the creature had not given good milk and plenty of it, the case would have seemed very different to her owners. Besides, Sylvia had all the time there was, and very little use to make of it. Sometimes in pleasant weather it was a consolation to look upon the cow's pranks as an intelligent attempt to play hide and seek, and as the child had no playmates she lent herself to this amusement with a good deal of zest. Though this chase had been so long that the wary animal herself had given an unusual signal of her whereabouts, Sylvia had only laughed when she came upon Mistress Moolly at the swamp-side, and urged her affectionately homeward with a twig of birch leaves. The old cow was not inclined to wander farther, she even turned in the right direction for once as they left the pasture, and stepped along the road at a good pace. She was quite ready to be milked now, and seldom stopped to browse. Sylvia wondered what her grandmother would say because they were so late. It was a great while since she had left home at half past five o'clock, but everybody knew the difficulty of making this errand a short one. Mrs. Tilley had chased the hornéd torment too many summer evenings herself to blame any one else for lingering, and was only thankful as she waited that she had Sylvia, nowadays, to give such valuable assistance. The good woman suspected that Sylvia loitered occasionally on her own account; there never was such a child for straying about out-of-doors since the world was made! Everybody said that it was a good change for a little maid who had tried to grow for eight years in a crowded manufacturing town, but, as for Sylvia herself, it seemed as if she never had been alive at all before she came to live at the farm. She thought often with wistful compassion of a wretched geranium that belonged to a town neighbor.

" 'Afraid of folks,' " old Mrs. Tilley said to herself, with a smile, after she had made the unlikely choice of Sylvia from her daughter's houseful of children, and was returning to the farm. " 'Afraid of folks,' they said! I guess she won't be troubled no great with 'em up to the old place!" When they reached the door of the lonely house and stopped to unlock it, and the cat came to purr loudly, and rub against them, a deserted pussy, indeed, but fat with young robins, Sylvia whispered that this was a beautiful place to live in, and she never should wish to go home.

The companions followed the shady woodroad, the cow taking slow steps, and the child very fast ones. The cow stopped long at the brook to drink, as if the pasture were not half a swamp, and Sylvia stood still and waited, letting her bare feet cool themselves in the shoal water, while the great twilight moths struck softly against her. She waded on through the brook as the cow moved away, and listened to the thrushes with a heart that beat fast with pleasure. There was a stirring in the great boughs overhead. They were full of little birds and beasts that seemed to be wide awake, and going about their world, or else saying good-night to each other in sleepy twitters. Sylvia herself felt sleepy as she walked along. However, it was not much farther to the house, and the air was soft and sweet. She was not often in the woods so late as this, and it made her feel as if she were a part of the gray shadows and the moving leaves. She was just thinking how long it seemed since she first came to the farm a year ago, and wondering if everything went on in the noisy town just the same as when she was there; the thought of the great red-faced boy who used to chase and frighten her made her hurry along the path to escape from the shadow of the trees.

Suddenly this little woods-girl is horror-stricken to hear a clear whistle not very far away. Not a bird's whistle, which would have a sort of friendliness, but a boy's whistle, determined, and somewhat aggressive. Sylvia left the cow to whatever sad fate might await her, and stepped discreetly aside into the bushes, but she was just too late. The enemy had discovered her, and called out in a very cheerful and persuasive tone, "Halloa, little girl, how far is it to the road?" and trembling Sylvia answered almost inaudibly, "A good ways."

She did not dare to look boldly at the tall young man, who carried a gun over his shoulder, but she came out of her bush and again followed the cow, while he walked alongside.

"I have been hunting for some birds," the stranger said kindly, "and I have lost my way, and need a friend very much. Don't be afraid," he added gallantly. "Speak up and tell me what your name is, and whether you think I can spend the night at your house, and go out gunning early in the morning."

Sylvia was more alarmed than before. Would not her grandmother consider her much to blame? But who could have foreseen such an accident as this? It did not seem to be her fault, and she hung her head as if the stem of it were broken, but managed to answer "Sylvy," with much effort when her companion again asked her name.

Mrs. Tilley was standing in the doorway when the trio came into view. The cow gave a loud moo by way of explanation.

"Yes, you'd better speak up for yourself, you old trial! Where'd she tucked herself away this time, Sylvy?" But Sylvia kept an awed silence; she knew by instinct that her grandmother did not comprehend the gravity of the situation. She must be mistaking the stranger for one of the farmer-lads of the region.

The young man stood his gun beside the door, and dropped a lumpy game-bag beside it; then he bade Mrs. Tilley good-evening, and repeated his wayfarer's story, and asked if he could have a night's lodging.

"Put me anywhere you like," he said. "I must be off early in the morning, before day; but I am very hungry, indeed. You can give me some milk at any rate, that's plain."

"Dear sakes, yes," responded the hostess, whose long slumbering hospitality seemed to be easily awakened. "You might fare better if you went out to the main road a mile or so, but you're welcome to what we've got. I'll milk right off, and you make yourself at home. You can sleep on husks or feathers," she proffered graciously. "I raised them all myself. There's good pasturing for geese just below here towards the ma'sh. Now step round and set a plate for the gentleman, Sylvy!" And Sylvia promptly stepped. She was glad to have something to do, and she was hungry herself.

It was a surprise to find so clean and comfortable a little dwelling in this New England wilderness. The young man had known the horrors of its most primitive housekeeping, and the dreary squalor of that level of society which does not rebel at the companionship of hens. This was the best thrift of an old-fashioned farmstead, though on such a small scale that it seemed like a hermitage. He listened eagerly to the old woman's quaint talk, he watched Sylvia's pale face and shining gray eyes with ever growing enthusiasm, and insisted that this was the best supper he had eaten for a month, and afterward the new-made friends sat down in the door-way together while the moon came up.

Soon it would be berry-time, and Sylvia was a great help at picking. The cow was a good milker, though a plaguy thing to keep track of, the hostess gossiped frankly, adding presently that she had buried four children, so Sylvia's mother, and a son (who might be dead) in California were all the children she had left. "Dan, my boy, was a great hand to go gunning," she explained sadly. "I never wanted for pa'tridges or gray squer'ls while he was to home. He's been a great wand'rer, I expect, and he's no hand to write letters. There, I don't blame him, I'd ha' seen the world myself if it had been so I could.

"Sylvia takes after him," the grandmother continued affectionately, after a minute's pause. "There ain't a foot o' ground she don't know her way over, and the wild creaturs counts her one o' themselves. Squer'ls she'll tame to come an' feed right out o' her hands, and all sorts o' birds. Last winter she got the jay-birds to bangeing[2] here, and I believe she'd 'a' scanted herself of her own meals to have plenty to throw out amongst 'em, if I hadn't kep' watch. Anything but crows, I tell her, I'm willin' to help support—though Dan he had a tamed one o' them that did seem to have reason same as folks. It was round here a good spell after he went away. Dan an' his father they didn't hitch,—but he never held up his head ag'in after Dan had dared him an' gone off."

The guest did not notice this hint of family sorrows in his eager interest in something else.

"So Sylvy knows all about birds, does she?" he exclaimed, as he looked round at the little girl who sat, very demure but increasingly sleepy, in the moonlight. "I am making a collection of birds myself. I have been at it ever since I was a boy." (Mrs. Tilley smiled.) "There are two or three very rare ones I have been hunting for these five years. I mean to get them on my own ground if they can be found."

"Do you cage 'em up?" asked Mrs. Tilley doubtfully, in response to this enthusiastic announcement.

"Oh, no, they're stuffed and preserved, dozens and dozens of them," said the ornithologist, "and I have shot or snared every one myself. I caught a glimpse of a white heron three miles from here on Saturday, and I have followed it in this direction. They have never been found in this district at all. The little white heron, it is," and he turned again to look at Sylvia with the hope of discovering that the rare bird was one of her acquaintances.

But Sylvia was watching a hop-toad in the narrow footpath.

"You would know the heron if you saw it," the stranger continued eagerly. "A queer tall white bird with soft feathers and long thin legs. And it would have a nest perhaps in the top of a high tree, made of sticks, something like a hawk's nest."

Sylvia's heart gave a wild beat; she knew that strange white bird, and had once stolen softly near where it stood in some bright green swamp grass, away

2. Hanging around.

over at the other side of the woods. There was an open place where the sunshine always seemed strangely yellow and hot, where tall, nodding rushes grew, and her grandmother had warned her that she might sink in the soft black mud underneath and never be heard of more. Not far beyond were the salt marshes just this side the sea itself, which Sylvia wondered and dreamed about, but never had seen, whose great voice could sometimes be heard above the noise of the woods on stormy nights.

"I can't think of anything I should like so much as to find that heron's nest," the handsome stranger was saying. "I would give ten dollars to anybody who could show it to me," he added desperately, "and I mean to spend my whole vacation hunting for it if need be. Perhaps it was only migrating, or had been chased out of its own region by some bird of prey."

Mrs. Tilley gave amazed attention to all this, but Sylvia still watched the toad, not divining, as she might have done at some calmer time, that the creature wished to get to its hole under the door-step, and was much hindered by the unusual spectators at that hour of the evening. No amount of thought, that night, could decide how many wished-for treasures the ten dollars, so lightly spoken of, would buy.

The next day the young sportsman hovered about the woods, and Sylvia kept him company, having lost her first fear of the friendly lad, who proved to be most kind and sympathetic. He told her many things about the birds and what they knew and where they lived and what they did with themselves. And he gave her a jack-knife, which she thought as great a treasure as if she were a desert-islander. All day long he did not once make her troubled or afraid except when he brought down some unsuspecting singing creature from its bough. Sylvia would have liked him vastly better without his gun; she could not understand why he killed the very birds he seemed to like so much. But as they day waned, Sylvia still watched the young man with loving admiration. She had never seen anybody so charming and delightful; the woman's heart, asleep in the child, was vaguely thrilled by a dream of love. Some premonition of that great power stirred and swayed these young creatures who traversed the solemn woodlands with soft-footed silent care. They stopped to listed to a bird's song; they pressed forward again eagerly, parting the branches,—speaking to each other rarely and in whispers; the young man going first and Sylvia following, fascinated, a few steps behind, with her gray eyes dark with excitement.

She grieved because the longed-for white heron was elusive, but she did not lead the guest, she only followed, and there was no such thing as speaking first. The sound of her own unquestioned voice would have terrified her,—it was hard enough to answer yes or no when there was need of that. At last evening began to fall, and they drove the cow home together, and Sylvia smiled with pleasure when they came to the place where she heard the whistle and was afraid only the night before.

II

Half a mile from home, at the farther edge of the woods, where the land was highest, a great pine-tree stood, the last of its generation. Whether it was left for a boundary mark, or for what reason, no one could say; the wood-choppers who had felled its mates were dead and gone long ago, and a whole forest of sturdy trees, pines and oaks and maples, had grown again. But the stately head of this old pine towered above them all and made a landmark for sea and shore miles and miles away. Sylvia knew it well. She had always believed that whoever climbed to the top of it could see the ocean; and the little girl had often laid her hand on the great rough trunk and looked up wistfully at those dark boughs that the wind always stirred, no matter how hot and still the air might be below. Now she thought of the tree with a new excitement, for why, if one climbed it at break of day, could not one see all the world, and easily discover from whence the white heron flew, and mark the place, and find the hidden nest?

What a spirit of adventure, what wild ambition! What fancied triumph and delight and glory for the later morning when she could make known the secret! It was almost too real and too great for the childish heart to bear.

All night the door of the little house stood open and the whippoorwills came and sang upon the very step. The young sportsman and his old hostess were sound asleep, but Sylvia's great design kept her broad awake and watching. She forgot to think of sleep. The short summer night seemed as long as the winter darkness, and at last when the whippoorwills ceased, and she was afraid the morning would after all come too soon, she stole out of the house and followed the pasture path through the woods, hastening toward the open ground beyond, listening with a sense of comfort and companionship to the drowsy twitter of a half-awakened bird, whose perch she had jarred in passing. Alas, if the great wave of human interest which flooded for the first time this dull little life should sweep away the satisfactions of an existence heart to heart with nature and the dumb life of the forest!

There was the huge tree asleep yet in the paling moonlight, and small and silly Sylvia began with utmost bravery to mount to the top of it, with tingling, eager blood coursing the channels of her whole frame, with her bare feet and fingers, that pinched and held like bird's claws to the monstrous ladder reaching up, up, almost to the sky itself. First she must mount the white oak tree that grew alongside, where she was almost lost among the dark branches and the green leaves heavy and wet with dew; a bird fluttered off its nest, and a red squirrel ran to and fro and scolded pettishly at the harmless housebreaker. Sylvia felt her way easily. She had often climbed there, and knew that higher still one of the oak's upper branches chafed against the pine trunk, just where its lower boughs were set close together. There, when she made the dangerous pass from one tree to the other, the great enterprise would really begin.

She crept out along the swaying oak limb at last, and took the daring step across into the old pine-tree. The way was harder than she thought; she must reach far and hold fast, the sharp dry twigs caught and held her and scratched her like angry talons, the pitch made her thin little fingers clumsy and stiff as she went round and round the tree's great stem, higher and higher upward. The sparrows and robins in the woods below were beginning to wake and twitter to the dawn, yet it seemed much lighter there aloft in the pine-tree, and the child knew that she must hurry if her project were to be of any use.

The tree seemed to lengthen itself out as she went up, and to reach farther and farther upward. It was like a great main-mast to the voyaging earth; it must truly have been amazed that morning through all its ponderous frame as it felt this determined spark of human spirit winding its way from higher branch to branch. Who knows how steadily the least twigs held themselves to advantage this light, weak creature on her way! The old pine must have loved his new dependent. More than all the hawks, and bats, and moths, and even the sweet voiced thrushes, was the brave, beating heart of the solitary gray-eyed child. And the tree stood still and frowned away the winds that June morning while the dawn grew bright in the east.

protection

Sylvia's face was like a pale star, if one had seen it from the ground, when the last thorny bough was past, and she stood trembling and tired but wholly triumphant, high in the tree-top. Yes, there was the sea with the dawning sun making a golden dazzle over it, and toward that glorious east flew two hawks with slow-moving pinions. How low they looked in the air from that height when one had only seen them before far up, and dark against the blue sky. Their gray feathers were as soft as moths; they seemed only a little way from the tree, and Sylvia felt as if she too could go flying away among the clouds. Westward, the woodlands and farms reached miles and miles into the distance; here and there were church steeples, and white villages; truly it was a vast and awesome world!

The birds sang louder and louder. At last the sun came up bewilderingly bright. Sylvia could see the white sails of ships out at sea, and the clouds that were purple and rose-colored and yellow at first began to fade away. Where was the white heron's nest in the sea of green branches, and was this wonderful sight and pageant of the world the only reward for having climbed to such a giddy height? Now look down again, Sylvia, where the green marsh is set among the shining birches and dark hemlocks; there where you saw the white heron once you will see him again; look, look! a white spot of him like a single floating feather comes up from the dead hemlock and grows larger, and rises, and comes close at last, and goes by the landmark pine with steady sweep of wing and outstretched slender neck and crested head. And wait! wait! do not move a foot or a finger, little girl, do not send an arrow of light and consciousness from your two eager eyes, for the heron has perched on a pine bough not far beyond yours, and cries back to his mate on the nest, and plumes his feathers for the new day!

The child gives a long sigh a minute later when a company of shouting cat-birds comes also to the tree, and vexed by their fluttering and lawlessness the solemn heron goes away. She knows his secret now, the wild, light, slender bird that floats and wavers, and goes back like an arrow presently to his home in the green world beneath. Then Sylvia, well satisfied, makes her perilous way down again, not daring to look far below the branch she stands on, ready to cry sometimes because her fingers ache and her lamed feet slip. Wondering over and over again what the stranger would say to her, and what he would think when she told him how to find his way straight to the heron's nest.

"Sylvy, Sylvy!" called the busy old grandmother again and again, but nobody answered, and the small husk bed was empty and Sylvia had disappeared.

The guest waked from a dream, and remembering his day's pleasure hurried to dress himself that might it sooner begin. He was sure from the way the shy little girl looked once or twice yesterday that she had at least seen the white heron, and now she must really be made to tell. Here she comes now, paler than ever, and her worn old frock is torn and tattered, and smeared with pine pitch. The grandmother and the sportsman stand in the door together and question her, and the splendid moment has come to speak of the dead hemlock-tree by the green marsh.

But Sylvia does not speak after all, though the old grandmother fretfully rebukes her, and the young man's kind, appealing eyes are looking straight in her own. He can make them rich with money; he has promised it, and they are poor now. He is so well worth making happy, and he waits to hear the story she can tell.

No, she must keep silence! What is it that suddenly forbids her and makes her dumb? Has she been nine years growing and now, when the great world for the first time puts out a hand to her, must she thrust it aside for a bird's sake? The murmur of the pine's green branches is in her ears, she remembers how the white heron came flying through the golden air and how they watched the sea and the morning together, and Sylvia cannot speak; she cannot tell the heron's secret and give its life away.

one with nature

Dear loyalty, that suffered a sharp pang as the guest went away disappointed later in the day, that could have served and followed him and loved him as a dog loves! Many a night Sylvia heard the echo of his whistle haunting the pasture path as she came home with the loitering cow. She forgot even her sorrow at the sharp report of his gun and the sight of thrushes and sparrows dropping silent to the ground, their songs hushed and their pretty feathers stained and wet with blood. Were the birds better friends than their hunter might have been,—who can tell? Whatever treasures were lost to her, woodlands and summer-time, remember! Bring your gifts and graces and tell your secrets to this lonely country child!

1886

EMMA LAZARUS
1849–1887

There are worse fates for a writer than being remembered mainly for one poem of historic importance. Almost all Americans know some of Emma Lazarus's words, for her sonnet "The New Colossus" has been on public view, since 1903, inside the base of the Statue of Liberty, and its last several lines, especially the phrase "huddled masses yearning to breathe free," have entered the national consciousness. Lazarus's role in promoting the Statue of Liberty was unlikely because famous writers like James Russell Lowell scorned the statue as an ostentatious boondoggle. As a woman and Jewish—the first Jewish writer to make a mark in American literary history—Lazarus's perspectives on America challenge mainstream literary views.

Emma Lazarus was born in New York City on July 22, 1849, to Moses Lazarus, a wealthy sugar refiner, and Esther Nathan Lazarus, both from families long resident in New York. Her father's family were Sephardic Jews who had settled in New York while it was New Amsterdam. She grew up in luxury in Manhattan and summered at a fine home, the Beeches, in fashionable Newport, Rhode Island. Educated by tutors in three modern languages and literatures besides English, Lazarus was precocious, and when her father paid for the publication of *Poems and Translations . . . Written between the Ages of Fourteen and Sixteen* in 1866, she sent copies to poets, among them Ralph

Waldo Emerson, who politely offered to be her "professor" in stylistic matters. Their cordial relationship survived her resentment that he did not include her in his 1874 anthology *Parnassus*. In addition to Emerson, Lazarus came to know other American literati of the time. While visiting the Emersons in Concord in 1876, she made a pilgrimage to the site of Henry David Thoreau's cabin, guided by Thoreau's grieving friend Ellery Channing. Corresponding with the nature writer John Burroughs, she shared an excitement over both Thoreau and Walt Whitman. In this interest in the prose and poetry of the United States, Lazarus was remarkably independent, akin not to her American contemporaries but to younger British literary people, who were already rediscovering three neglected American writers, Thoreau, Whitman, and Melville.

Lazarus's short manifesto "American Literature" in the New York *Critic* (June 18, 1881) was a retort to a critic who had deplored the lack of a "continuous tradition" in American literature. Emerson, according to this writer, had "left no lineage," only, like Irving, imitators who came to nothing. From the 1830s to the 1850s, American literary nationalism had been passionately contested, but Lazarus engaged the battle afresh, sure that Emerson's ideas had been developed by "the poet-naturalist, Henry Thoreau" as well as by Whitman and Burroughs. Daringly, she ranked Poe higher as a poet than Longfellow and mocked the efforts of "the lion hunters of London" who tried to tell Americans that they were neglecting "a certain poet"—Joaquin Miller (1841?–1913), whom she confidently declared to be nothing higher than a "second-rate singer."

Early in her literary life, Lazarus identified with the German-Jewish poet Heinrich Heine, who had felt both at home in and estranged from a Christian society and non-Hebraic literature. But, though Lazarus had written such poems as "In the Jewish Synagogue at Newport," her intellectual efforts into the early 1880s focused mainly on the continuities and distinctions between American and English literature and little on either her own Jewish heritage or the situation of Jews worldwide. In 1882, horrified that newspapers were minimizing Russian atrocities against Jews, Lazarus confronted herself, a wealthy metropolitan woman for whom being an American poet had been more important than being an American Jew. With rigor and determination, she fashioned herself into a Jewish spokeswoman on international themes as they affected American national policy on immigration. Her "Russian Christianity *versus* Modern Judaism" (*Century* [May 1882]) describes the reign of "murder, rape, arson" during which tens of thousands of Jewish families in Eastern Europe had been reduced "to homeless beggary." That November, playing on Paul's New Testament letter, she began serial publication in the *American Hebrew* of "An Epistle to the Hebrew." There she urged American Jews to become more, not less, " 'tribal,' " to recognize that their freedom depended upon the freedom of Jews in Russia and elsewhere. In "The Jewish Problem" (*Century* [February 1883]), she spoke out as an early Zionist, echoing the fervent determination of George Eliot's title character in *Daniel Deronda* to make the Jews "a nation again." And she began visiting the "undesirable" new immigrants detained on Ward's Island in the East River, those deemed too destitute or too infirm to be disembarked into American society. In 1883 she founded the Society for the Improvement and Colonization of Eastern European Jews.

Also in 1883, Lazarus wrote "The New Colossus" to raise money for the Bartholdi Pedestal Fund. The Statue of Liberty itself was to be a gift from France to the United States, and Americans had the task of erecting the expensive base such a colossal statue required. The statue had been conceived as a memorial to France's aid of the colonies during the American Revolution. In hailing the female figure as the "Mother of Exiles," Lazarus brilliantly, merely by her words, redefined the "mighty woman with a torch" into the national welcomer of "huddled masses" seeking refuge. Building on her own knowledge of immigrants arriving in the bay, she deflected the significance of the statue away from the past and toward the future.

Lazarus traveled to Europe in 1883 and 1885, meeting several famous poets, among them Robert Browning and William Morris. She died in New York on November 19, 1887. The next year, 1888, her sisters published *The Poems of Emma Lazarus*.

In the Jewish Synagogue at Newport[1]

Here, where the noises of the busy town,
The ocean's plunge and roar can enter not,
We stand and gaze around with tearful awe,
And muse upon the consecrated spot.

No signs of life are here: the very prayers   5
Inscribed around are in a language dead;[2]
The light of the "perpetual lamp"[3] is spent
That an undying radiance was to shed.

What prayers were in this temple offered up,
Wrung from sad hearts that knew no joy on earth,   10
By these lone exiles of a thousand years,[4]
From the fair sunrise land that gave them birth!

Now as we gaze, in this new world of light,[5]
Upon this relic of the days of old,
The present vanishes, and tropic bloom   15
And Eastern towns and temples we behold.

Again we see the patriarch[6] with his flocks,
The purple seas, the hot blue sky o'erhead,
The slaves of Egypt,—omens, mysteries,—
Dark fleeing hosts by flaming angels led,[7]   20

A wondrous light upon a sky-kissed mount,[8]
A man who reads Jehovah's written law,
'Midst blinding glory and effulgence rare,
Unto a people prone with reverent awe.

The pride of luxury's barbaric pomp,   25
In the rich court of royal Solomon—[9]
Alas! we wake: one scene alone remains,—
The exiles by the streams of Babylon.[1]

1. The text is from *Admetus and Other Poems* (1871), where it is dated "July 1867." It is a companion piece to Henry Wadsworth Longfellow's similarly meditative "The Jewish Cemetery at Newport," about the cemetery attached to the Touro Synagogue, the oldest in the United States, dating from 1763. Services were no longer held there in 1852, when Longfellow visited it, and the synagogue remained closed during the years that Lazarus summered in Newport at her family's country house.
2. Lazarus calls Hebrew a dead language because at that time it was not used in everyday life.
3. In a synagogue, the light above the ark which holds the Torah (the first five books of the Hebrew scriptures—Genesis, Exodus, Leviticus, Numbers, Deuteronomy).
4. Poetically vague: Jews were expelled from Jerusalem early in the 6th century B.C.E. and again late in the first century C.E. Most of the Newport Jews were, like Lazarus's father, Sephardic Jews,

descended from Jews expelled from Spain in 1492.
5. The United States.
6. Abraham (Genesis 24.35), his son Isaac, or Isaac's sons. Lazarus is not striving for specificity but evoking images of Jewish history.
7. The enslavement of Jews in Egypt is described in Exodus 1. In Genesis 3.24, after Adam and Eve are expelled from Eden, the tree of life is protected by cherubims and a flaming sword that turns "every way." After the Hebrews crossed the Red Sea, a pillar of cloud by day and a pillar of fire by night led them through the desert (Exodus 13.21–22).
8. Mount Sinai, where God gave Moses the Ten Commandments, which he then read to the children of Israel (Exodus 34).
9. Solomon's magnificence is described in 1 Kings 4; the building of the First Temple (in Jerusalem) is described in 1 Kings 5–8.
1. The First Temple was destroyed around 588–586 B.C.E. and the Jews exiled to Babylon, the site of the modern Hilla, in Iraq, south of Baghdad.

Our softened voices send us back again
    But mournful echoes through the empty hall;   30
Our footsteps have a strange unnatural sound,
    And with unwonted gentleness they fall.

The weary ones, the sad, the suffering,
    All found their comfort in the holy place,
And children's gladness and men's gratitude   35
    Took voice and mingled in the chant of praise.

The funeral and the marriage, now, alas!
    We know not which is sadder to recall;
For youth and happiness have followed age,
    And green grass lieth gently over all.   40

Nathless[2] the sacred shrine is holy yet,
    With its lone floors where reverent feet once trod.
Take off your shoes as by the burning bush,
    Before the mystery of death and God.

1867   1871

1492[1]

Thou two-faced year, Mother of Change and Fate,
Didst weep when Spain cast forth with flaming sword,
The children of the prophets of the Lord,
Prince, priest, and people, spurned by zealot hate.
Hounded from sea to sea, from state to state,   5
The West[2] refused them, and the East abhorred.
No anchorage the known world could afford,
Close-locked was every port, barred every gate.[3]
Then smiling, thou unveil'dst, O two-faced year,
A virgin world where doors of sunset part,   10
Saying, "Ho, all who weary, enter here!
There falls each ancient barrier that the art
Of race or creed or rank devised, to rear
Grim bulwarked hatred between heart and heart!"

1883   1888

2. Nevertheless, notwithstanding (poetic archaism).
1. This poem, reprinted from *Poems* (1888), acknowledges two events in Spain in 1492. Early in the year King Ferdinand and Queen Isabella drove from Spain all Jews who would not convert to Catholicism. A few months later they invested in Christopher Columbus's voyage into the Atlantic in the hope of establishing a new trade route to the East Indies.
2. Northern Europe, as opposed to the eastern Mediterranean.
3. The Jews expelled from Spain spread out over the Mediterranean region, many being robbed, many dying of the plague, some being enslaved, some murdered.

The New Colossus[1]

Not like the brazen giant of Greek fame,[2]
With conquering limbs astride from land to land;
Here at our sea-washed, sunset gates shall stand
A mighty woman with a torch, whose flame
Is the imprisoned lightning, and her name   5
Mother of Exiles. From her beacon-hand
Glows world-wide welcome; her mild eyes command
The air-bridged harbor that twin cities[3] frame.
"Keep, ancient lands, your storied pomp!" cries she
With silent lips. "Give me your tired, your poor,   10
Your huddled masses yearning to breathe free,
The wretched refuse of your teeming shore.[4]
Send these, the homeless, tempest-tost to me,
I lift my lamp beside the golden door!"

1883   1888

1. The footnote to the 1888 *Poems of Emma Lazarus*, the source of the present text, reads "Written in aid of Bartholdi Pedestal Fund, 1883." The sculpture by Frédéric-Auguste Bartholdi (1834–1904) was a gift from the French people, but Americans, led by the newspaper mogul Joseph Pulitzer, raised money to pay for the massive pedestal required by such a huge, heavy statue. During the mid-1870s thousands of Americans saw just how colossal the Statue of Liberty would be, for part of the statue, the hand of Liberty holding aloft the torch, was displayed for months in Madison Square in Manhattan and also displayed at the great Centennial exhibition in Philadelphia. (The statue is some 305 feet from ground to tip of torch, 151 feet from top of the pedestal to the tip of the torch.) Fittingly, in 1903 this entire poem by Emma Lazarus was engraved on a bronze tablet and affixed to an interior wall of the pedestal.
2. The gigantic statue of the sun god, Helios, created by the sculptor Chares of Lindos, loomed over the harbor of the Greek island of Rhodes for several decades before being destroyed in an earthquake in 225 B.C.E. Later reports exaggerated the size, saying that the legs of the statue straddled the harbor.
3. New York City and Jersey City, New Jersey.
4. In the early 1880s Lazarus personally knew the plight of Jews trying to take refuge in the United States after fleeing pogroms in Russia. "Huddled masses" accurately describes emigrants arriving the cheapest way, as steerage passengers.

KATE CHOPIN
1850–1904

Katherine O'Flaherty seemed more likely as a young woman to become a consumer of literature than a producer of it. Her Irish immigrant father was a successful businessman who died in a train wreck when his daughter was four years old. The family enjoyed a high place in St. Louis society; and her mother, grandmother, and great-grandmother were active, pious Catholics of French heritage. Without doubt Kate O'Flaherty grew up in the company of loving, intelligent, independent women. Particularly important was her strong-willed great-grandmother, a compelling and tireless storyteller whose influence may have been central to Chopin's becoming a significant regional writer and the author of a remarkable novel, *The Awakening* (1899), that speaks radically to issues of gender, sexuality, and the American family.

Chopin was nine years old before she entered St. Louis Academy of the Sacred Heart, but she was already well-read in English and French authors, and by the time she graduated from the academy in 1868 she had absorbed Cervantes, Dante, Goethe, and many English novelists and poets of the eighteenth and nineteenth centuries—Austen, the Brontës, and Coleridge among them. But it was French writers who most strongly influenced her sense of life and her craft as a writer. She read and admired

French classical authors as well as more contemporary figures such as Gustave Flaubert and Madame de Staël; but it was Émile Zola and Guy de Maupassant who provided philosophical perspective and fictional method when she began to write in earnest in her late thirties. What she said of Maupassant she might have said of herself: "Here was a man who had escaped from tradition and authority, who had entered into himself and looked out upon life through his own being and with his own eyes; and who in a direct and simple way, told us what he saw." Though Chopin is sometimes praised for her symbolic, imagistic prose, she was able to see and to narrate a new reality indeed. What she saw, whether in St. Louis, New Orleans, or the Louisiana countryside, was the tension between individual erotic inclination and the constraints placed on desire—especially on women's sexual desire—by traditional social mores. What she told directly—and without moral judgment—was how certain women were beginning to challenge the patriarchal rules that sought not only to confine them to well-defined social, economic, and vocational domains but to control their inner life as well. Her new, modern perspectives, especially on female sexuality, paralleled those of Edith Wharton and Theodore Dreiser.

At the age of nineteen she married Oscar Chopin and spent the next decade in New Orleans, where her husband first prospered, then failed, in the cotton business. After a few years in Cloutierville, a village in northwest Louisiana near Natchitoches, where her husband opened a general store and managed a family cotton plantation, she returned to St. Louis permanently in 1884, a year after her husband's death from swamp fever (probably malaria). A year later her mother died, and at the age of thirty-five Chopin was left essentially alone to raise her six young children. Having recognized the ready market for "local color," or regional, fiction, Chopin decided to fashion a literary career out of her experience of the Creole and Cajun cultures she had come to know.

Chopin had the gift of equanimity and wrote on a lapboard in the midst of a busy household. Many of her stories were written in a single day. She claimed that she wrote on impulse, that she was "completely at the mercy of unconscious selection" of subject, and that "the polishing up process . . . always proved disastrous." This method, although it ensured freshness and sincerity, made some of her stories anecdotal or thin. Though a score of the best of them have endured, it is remarkable that in the relatively few years of her writing career—scarcely more than a decade—she completed three novels; more than 150 stories and sketches; and a substantial body of poetry, reviews, and criticism. A first novel, *At Fault,* was self-published in 1890, but it was her stories of Louisiana rural life, especially in the collection *Bayou Folk* (1894), that won her national recognition as a practitioner of local-color fiction. She made the Catholic Creoles and Cajuns with their old-fashioned European customs, their polyglot, witty speech, their sensuous and seemingly unself-conscious lives, and their rich agricultural landscape in picturesque Natchitoches Parish familiar to Americans, as Sarah Orne Jewett was making known the severe Protestant towns of rocky, coastal Maine. A second collection of stories, *A Night in Acadie,* was published three years later and increased her reputation as a local colorist. Nina Baym has argued persuasively that local-color writing, which flourished after the Civil War, was in part the product of anxiety over the loss of the familiar in a period of rapid change and dislocation (literal and figurative), nostalgia for more stable times, and the emergence of a homogenized national society. The trauma of America's most destructive war up until that time made antebellum America seem like a golden age to many. Yet Chopin does not idealize the Old South; to the contrary, she often presents it from a critical or oppositional view, especially as concerns gender and race. Chopin managed to be recognized as a regionalist while subtly critiquing southern values, in many ways anticipating the early Faulkner.

"At the 'Cadian Ball," printed here, demonstrates Chopin's skill at the deft depiction of characters and advancement of plot through distinctive dialogue. The story also creates with great economy a believable physical world in which climate and culture and community and individual personalities exist in subtle reciprocal relation. But the hints of scandal and the undercurrent of flirtation of the story are still well within conventional limits. The explicit and unapologetic eroticism of its sequel, however, was another matter. It is not so much that adultery is committed under the steamy conditions in "The Storm," but that no one in the end is left feeling guilty or unhappy by this violation of proprieties that almost certainly kept Chopin from submitting the story for publication after she wrote it on July 18, 1898. In any event, "The Storm" was not published until 1969 as part of Per Seyersted's edition of *The Complete Works of Kate Chopin*.

Chopin's major work, *The Awakening*, influenced by Gustave Flaubert's *Madame Bovary* (1856), was published in 1899. The novel, which traces the sensual and sexual coming to consciousness of a young woman, predictably aroused hostility among contemporary reviewers, just as Whitman's *Leaves of Grass*, which Chopin admired, had half a century earlier. The "new woman"—demanding social, economic, and political equality—was already a common topic of public discussion and subject of fiction. But the depiction of such an unrepentant (if ultimately deeply psychologically confused) sensualist as Edna Pontellier was more than many of the critics of the time could allow to pass. The book was called "trite and sordid," "essentially vulgar," and "unhealthily introspective and morbid in feeling." Chopin was dropped from her St. Louis clubs and snubbed by friends. But in objecting to Edna's behavior, these readers missed what is more disturbing about *The Awakening*; Chopin presented nothing less than a "waste land" for women of her generation, describing not only Edna's desire for individual freedom but also the naturalistic forces that made her quest futile. It should have been Chopin's essential pessimism and not her racy scenes that unnerved the critics. Though some commentators found much to praise in *The Awakening*, Chopin's only published response to her reviews was to claim, tongue in cheek, "I never dreamed of Mrs. Pontellier making such a mess of things and working out her own damnation as she did. If I had had the slightest intimation of such a thing I would have excluded her from the company." After the book was published, Chopin's health began to deteriorate, and she wrote little. Though the novel and its author fell into obscurity for half a century, since the 1970s and particularly since the publication of the Norton Critical Edition, which helped bring Chopin into the canon, they have now secured an honored place in American literary history. Wharton and Chopin were among the first women authors after Emily Dickinson to be added to many American literature syllabi. In recent years, critics have begun to explore the intricacies of race, class, and ethnicity as subjects and contexts in this remarkable novel that once was thought to be only, or at least primarily, aimed at exploring Edna's sexuality.

In *The Awakening*, more impressively because on a grander scale than in her shorter fiction, Chopin demonstrates her unusual capacity to make the exotic worlds of New Orleans and the Louisiana Gulf Coast real and to fill those worlds with complex and often baffled men and women—not unlike T. S. Eliot's Prufrock—whose humanity she confirms by refusing to judge them or use them to support a thesis. Some critics have accordingly found the novel's feminist argument to be complicated by the fatal weaknesses in Edna's psyche.

At the 'Cadian Ball[1]

Bobinôt, that big, brown, good-natured Bobinôt, had no intention of going to the ball, even though he knew Calixta would be there. For what came of those balls but heartache, and a sickening disinclination for work the whole

---

1. First published in *Two Tales* (October 1892); first published in book form in *Bayou Folk* (1894), the source of the text printed here.

week through, till Saturday night came again and his tortures began afresh? Why could he not love Ozéina, who would marry him tomorrow; or Fronie, or any one of a dozen others, rather than that little Spanish vixen? Calixta's slender foot had never touched Cuban soil; but her mother's had, and the Spanish was in her blood all the same. For that reason the prairie people forgave her much that they would not have overlooked in their own daughters or sisters.

Her eyes,—Bobinôt thought of her eyes, and weakened,—the bluest, the drowsiest, most tantalizing that ever looked into a man's; he thought of her flaxen hair that kinked worse than a mulatto's close to her head; that broad, smiling mouth and tiptilted nose, that full figure; that voice like a rich contralto song, with cadences in it that must have been taught by Satan, for there was no one else to teach her tricks on that 'Cadian prairie. Bobinôt thought of them all as he plowed his rows of cane.

There had even been a breath of scandal whispered about her a year ago, when she went to Assumption,[2]—but why talk of it? No one did now. "C'est Espagnol, ça,"[3] most of them said with lenient shoulder-shrugs. "Bon chien tient de race,"[4] the old men mumbled over their pipes, stirred by recollections. Nothing was made of it, except that Fronie threw it up to Calixta when the two quarreled and fought on the church steps after mass one Sunday, about a lover. Calixta swore roundly in fine 'Cadian French and with true Spanish spirit, and slapped Fronie's face. Fronie had slapped her back; "Tiens, cocotte, va!"[5] "Espèce de lionèse; prends ça, et ça!"[6] till the curé himself was obliged to hasten and make peace between them. Bobinôt thought of it all, and would not go to the ball.

But in the afternoon, over at Friedheimer's store, where he was buying a trace-chain,[7] he heard some one say that Alcée Laballière would be there. Then wild horses could not have kept him away. He knew how it would be— or rather he did not know how it would be—if the handsome young planter came over to the ball as he sometimes did. If Alcée happened to be in a serious mood, he might only go to the card-room and play a round or two; or he might stand out on the galleries talking crops and politics with the old people. But there was no telling. A drink or two could put the devil in his head,—that was what Bobinôt said to himself, as he wiped the sweat from his brow with his red bandanna; a gleam from Calixta's eyes, a flash of her ankle, a twirl of her skirts could do the same. Yes, Bobinôt would go to the ball.

That was the year Alcée Laballière put nine hundred acres in rice. It was putting a good deal of money into the ground, but the returns promised to be glorious. Old Madame Laballière, sailing about the spacious galleries in her white *volante*,[8] figured it all out in her head. Clarisse, her goddaughter, helped her a little, and together they built more air-castles than enough. Alcée worked like a mule that time; and if he did not kill himself, it was because his constitution was an iron one. It was an every-day affair for him

---

2. I.e., Assumption Parish, Louisiana.
3. That's a Spaniard for you (French).
4. Just like her mother (French).
5. Listen, you flirt, get out of here! (French).

6. You bitch; take that and that! (French).
7. Equipment used to harness horses.
8. A flowing garment.

to come in from the field well-nigh exhausted, and wet to the waist. He did not mind if there were visitors; he left them to his mother and Clarisse. There were often guests: young men and women who came up from the city, which was but a few hours away, to visit his beautiful kinswoman. She was worth going a good deal farther than that to see. Dainty as a lily; hardy as a sunflower; slim, tall, graceful, like one of the reeds that grew in the marsh. Cold and kind and cruel by turn, and everything that was aggravating to Alcée.

He would have liked to sweep the place of those visitors, often. Of the men, above all, with their ways and their manners; their swaying of fans like women, and dandling about hammocks. He could have pitched them over the levee into the river, if it hadn't meant murder. That was Alcée. But he must have been crazy the day he came in from the rice-field, and, toil-stained as he was, clasped Clarisse by the arms and panted a volley of hot, blistering love-words into her face. No man had ever spoken love to her like that.

"Monsieur!" she exclaimed, looking him full in the eyes, without a quiver. Alcée's hands dropped and his glance wavered before the chill of her calm, clear eyes.

"Par exemple!"[9] she muttered disdainfully, as she turned from him, deftly adjusting the careful toilet that he had so brutally disarranged.

That happened a day or two before the cyclone came that cut into the rice like fine steel. It was an awful thing, coming so swiftly, without a moment's warning in which to light a holy candle or set a piece of blessed palm burning. Old Madame wept openly and said her beads, just as her son Didier, the New Orleans one, would have done. If such a thing had happened to Alphonse, the Laballière planting cotton up in Natchitoches,[1] he would have raved and stormed like a second cyclone, and made his surroundings unbearable for a day or two. But Alcée took the misfortune differently. He looked ill and gray after it, and said nothing. His speechlessness was frightful. Clarisse's heart melted with tenderness; but when she offered her soft, purring words of condolence, he accepted them with mute indifference. Then she and her nénaine[2] wept afresh in each other's arms.

A night or two later, when Clarisse went to her window to kneel there in the moonlight and say her prayers before retiring, she saw that Bruce, Alcée's negro servant, had led his master's saddle-horse noiselessly along the edge of the sward that bordered the gravel-path, and stood holding him near by. Presently, she heard Alcée quit his room, which was beneath her own, and traverse the lower portico. As he emerged from the shadow and crossed the strip of moonlight, she perceived that he carried a pair of well-filled saddle-bags which he at once flung across the animal's back. He then lost no time in mounting, and after a brief exchange of words with Bruce, went cantering away, taking no precaution to avoid the noisy gravel as the negro had done.

Clarisse had never suspected that it might be Alcée's custom to sally forth from the plantation secretly, and at such an hour; for it was nearly midnight. And had it not been for the telltale saddle-bags, she would only have crept to bed, to wonder, to fret and dream unpleasant dreams. But her impatience and anxiety would not be held in check. Hastily unbolting the shutters of her door that opened upon the gallery, she stepped outside and called softly to the old negro.

9. For example (French, literal trans.); here, "Get a hold of yourself!"

1. Parish in northwest Louisiana.
2. Female attendant, in this case his mother.

"Gre't Peter! Miss Clarisse. I was n' sho it was a ghos' o' w'at, stan'in' up dah, plumb in de night, dataway."

He mounted halfway up the long, broad flight of stairs. She was standing at the top.

"Bruce, w'ere has Monsieur Alcée gone?" she asked.

"W'y, he gone 'bout he business, I reckin," replied Bruce, striving to be non-committal at the outset.

"W'ere has Monsieur Alcée gone?" she reiterated, stamping her bare foot. "I won't stan' any nonsense or any lies; mine, Bruce."

"I don' ric'lic ez I eva tole you lie yit, Miss Clarisse. Mista Alcée, he all broke up, sho."

"W'ere—has—he gone? Ah, Sainte Vierge! faut de la patience! butor, va!"[3]

"W'en I was in he room, a-breshin' off he clo'es to-day," the darkey began, settling himself against the stair-rail, "he look dat speechless an' down, I say, 'you 'pear to me like some pussun w'at gwine have a spell o' sickness, Mista Alcée.' He say, 'You reckin?' I dat he git up, go look hisse'f stiddy in de glass. Den he go to de chimbly an' jerk up de quinine bottle an' po' a gre't hoss-dose on to he han'. An' he swalla dat mess in a wink, an' wash hit down wid a big dram o' w'iskey w'at he keep in he room, aginst he come all soppin' wet outen de fiel'.

"He 'lows, 'No, I ain' gwine be sick, Bruce.' Den he square off. He say, 'I kin mak out to stan' up an' gi' an' take wid any man I knows, lessen hit's John L. Sulvun.[4] But w'en God A'mighty an' a 'oman jines fo'ces agin me, dat's one too many fur me.' I tell 'im, 'Jis so,' whils' I 'se makin' out to bresh a spot off w'at ain' dah, on he coat colla. I tell 'im, 'You wants li'le res', suh.' He say, 'No, I wants li'le fling; dat w'at I wants; an' I gwine git it. Pitch me a fis'ful o' clo'es in dem 'ar saddle-bags.' Dat w'at he say. Don't you bodda, missy. He jis' gone a-caperin' yonda to de Cajun ball. Uh—uh—de skeeters is fair' a-swarmin' like bees roun' yo' foots!"

The mosquitoes were indeed attacking Clarisse's white feet savagely. She had unconsciously been alternately rubbing one foot over the other during the darkey's recital.

"The 'Cadian ball," she repeated contemptuously. "Humph! Par exemple![5] Nice conduc' for a Laballière. An' he needs a saddle-bag, fill' with clothes, to go to the 'Cadian ball!"

"Oh, Miss Clarisse; you go on to bed, chile; git yo' soun' sleep. He 'low he come back in couple weeks o' so. I kiarn be repeatin' lot o' truck w'at young mans say, out heah face o' young gal."

Clarisse said no more, but turned and abruptly reëntered the house.

"You done talk too much wid yo' mouf a'ready, you ole fool nigga, you," muttered Bruce to himself as he walked away.

Alcée reached the ball very late, of course—too late for the chicken gumbo which had been served at midnight.

The big, low-ceiled room—they called it a hall—was packed with men and women dancing to the music of three fiddles. There were broad galleries all around it. There was a room at one side where sober-faced men were playing cards. Another, in which babies were sleeping, was called le parc aux petits.[6]

3. Ah, Blessed Virgin! Give me patience! Lout, get out of here! (French).
4. American heavyweight boxing champion

(1855–1918).
5. Here, "Quite an example!"
6. Playroom (French).

Any one who is white may go to a 'Cadian ball, but he must pay for his lemonade, his coffee and chicken gumbo. And he must behave himself like a 'Cadian. Grosbœuf was giving this ball. He had been giving them since he was a young man, and he was a middle-aged one, now. In that time he could recall but one disturbance, and that was caused by American railroaders, who were not in touch with their surroundings and had no business there. "Ces maudits gens du raiderode,"[7] Grosbœuf called them.

Alcée Laballière's presence at the ball caused a flutter even among the men, who could not but admire his "nerve" after such misfortune befalling him. To be sure, they knew the Laballières were rich—that there were resources East, and more again in the city. But they felt it took a *brave homme*[8] to stand a blow like that philosophically. One old gentleman, who was in the habit of reading a Paris newspaper and knew things, chuckled gleefully to everybody that Alcée's conduct was altogether *chic, mais chic.* That he had more *panache*[9] than Boulanger. Well, perhaps he had.

But what he did not show outwardly was that he was in a mood for ugly things to-night. Poor Bobinôt alone felt it vaguely. He discerned a gleam of it in Alcée's handsome eyes, as the young planter stood in the doorway, looking with rather feverish glance upon the assembly, while he laughed and talked with a 'Cadian farmer who was beside him.

Bobinôt himself was dull-looking and clumsy. Most of the men were. But the young women were very beautiful. The eyes that glanced into Alcée's as they passed him were big, dark, soft as those of the young heifers standing out in the cool prairie grass.

But the belle was Calixta. Her white dress was not nearly so handsome or well made as Fronie's (she and Fronie had quite forgotten the battle on the church steps, and were friends again), nor were her slippers so stylish as those of Ozéina; and she fanned herself with a handkerchief, since she had broken her red fan at the last ball, and her aunts and uncles were not willing to give her another. But all the men agreed she was at her best to-night. Such animation! and abandon! such flashes of wit!

"Hé, Bobinôt! Mais w'at's the matta? W'at you standin' *planté là*[1] like ole Ma'ame Tina's cow in the bog, you!"

That was good. That was an excellent thrust at Bobinôt, who had forgotten the figure[2] of the dance with his mind bent on other things, and it started a clamor of laughter at his expense. He joined good-naturedly. It was better to receive even such notice as that from Calixta than none at all. But Madame Suzonne, sitting in a corner, whispered to her neighbor that if Ozéina were to conduct herself in a like manner, she should immediately be taken out to the mule-cart and driven home. The women did not always approve of Calixta.

Now and then were short lulls in the dance, when couples flocked out upon the galleries for a brief respite and fresh air. The moon had gone down pale in the west, and in the east was yet no promise of day. After such an interval, when the dancers again assembled to resume the interrupted quadrille, Calixta was not among them.

7. Those cursed railroad people (French).
8. Sturdy fellow (French).
9. Style.

1. Rooted there (French).
2. The pattern of steps.

She was sitting upon a bench out in the shadow, with Alcée beside her. They were acting like fools. He had attempted to take a little gold ring from her finger; just for the fun of it, for there was nothing he could have done with the ring but replace it again. But she clinched her hand tight. He pretended that it was a very difficult matter to open it. Then he kept the hand in his. They seemed to forget about it. He played with her earring, a thin crescent of gold hanging from her small brown ear. He caught a wisp of the kinky hair that had escaped its fastening, and rubbed the ends of it against his shaven cheek.

"You know, last year in Assumption, Calixta?" They belonged to the younger generation, so preferred to speak English.

"Don't come say Assumption to me, M'sieur Alcée. I done yeard Assumption till I'm plumb sick."

"Yes, I know. The idiots! Because you were in Assumption, and I happened to go to Assumption, they must have it that we went together. But it was nice—*hein*,[3] Calixta?—in Assumption?"

They saw Bobinôt emerge from the hall and stand a moment outside the lighted doorway, peering uneasily and searchingly into the darkness. He did not see them, and went slowly back.

"There is Bobinôt looking for you. You are going to set poor Bobinôt crazy. You'll marry him some day; *hein*, Calixta?"

"I don't say no, me," she replied, striving to withdraw her hand, which he held more firmly for the attempt.

"But come, Calixta; you know you said you would go back to Assumption, just to spite them."

"No, I neva said that, me. You mus' dreamt that."

"Oh, I thought you did. You know I'm going down to the city."

"W'en?"

"To-night."

"Betta make has'e, then; it's mos' day."

"Well, to-morrow'll do."

"W'at you goin' do, yonda?"

"I don't know. Drown myself in the lake, maybe; unless you go down there to visit your uncle."

Calixta's senses were reeling; and they well-nigh left her when she felt Alcée's lips brush her ear like the touch of a rose.

"Mista Alcée! Is dat Mista Alcée?" the thick voice of a negro was asking; he stood on the ground, holding to the banister-rails near which the couple sat.

"W'at do you want now?" cried Alcée impatiently. "Can't I have a moment of peace?"

"I ben huntin' you high an' low, suh," answered the man. "Dey—dey some one in de road, onda de mulbare-tree, want see you a minute."

"I wouldn't go out to the road to see the Angel Gabriel. And if you come back here with any more talk, I'll have to break your neck." The negro turned mumbling away.

Alcée and Calixta laughed softly about it. Her boisterousness was all gone. They talked low, and laughed softly, as lovers do.

"Alcée! Alcée Laballière!"

3. Huh.

It was not the negro's voice this time; but one that went through Alcée's body like an electric shock, bringing him to his feet.

Clarisse was standing there in her riding-habit, where the negro had stood. For an instant confusion reigned in Alcée's thoughts, as with one who awakes suddenly from a dream. But he felt that something of serious import had brought his cousin to the ball in the dead of night.

"W'at does this mean, Clarisse?" he asked.

"It means something has happen' at home. You mus' come."

"Happened to maman?" he questioned, in alarm.

"No; nénaine is well, and asleep. It is something else. Not to frighten you. But you mus' come. Come with me, Alcée."

There was no need for the imploring note. He would have followed the voice anywhere.

She had now recognized the girl sitting back on the bench.

"Ah, c'est vous, Calixta? Comment ça va, mon enfant?"[4]

"Tcha va b'en; et vous, mam'zélle?"[5]

Alcée swung himself over the low rail and started to follow Clarisse, without a word, without a glance back at the girl. He had forgotten he was leaving her there. But Clarisse whispered something to him, and he turned back to say "Good-night, Calixta," and offer his hand to press through the railing. She pretended not to see it.

"How come that? You settin' yere by yo'se'f, Calixta?" It was Bobinôt who had found her there alone. The dancers had not yet come out. She looked ghastly in the faint, gray light struggling out of the east.

"Yes, that's me. Go yonda in the *parc aux petits* an' ask Aunt Olisse fu' my hat. She knows w'ere 't is. I want to go home, me."

"How you came?"

"I come afoot, with the Cateaus. But I'm goin' now. I ent goin' wait fu' 'em. I'm plumb wo' out, me."

"Kin I go with you, Calixta?"

"I don' care."

They went together across the open prairie and along the edge of the fields, stumbling in the uncertain light. He told her to lift her dress that was getting wet and bedraggled; for she was pulling at the weeds and grasses with her hands.

"I don' care; it's got to go in the tub, anyway. You been sayin' all along you want to marry me, Bobinôt. Well, if you want, yet, I don' care, me."

The glow of a sudden and overwhelming happiness shone out in the brown, rugged face of the young Acadian. He could not speak, for very joy. It choked him.

"Oh well, if you don' want," snapped Calixta, flippantly, pretending to be piqued at his silence.

"*Bon Dieu!*[6] You know that makes me crazy, w'at you sayin'. You mean that, Calixta? You ent goin' turn roun' agin?"

"I neva tole you that much *yet*, Bobinôt. I mean that. *Tiens,*"[7] and she held out her hand in the business-like manner of a man who clinches a bargain

---

4. Ah, is it you, Calixta? How's it going my little one? (French).
5. Everything's fine; and with you, Miss? (French).
6. Good God! (French).
7. Well (French).

with a hand-clasp. Bobinôt grew bold with happiness and asked Calixta to kiss him. She turned her face, that was almost ugly after the night's dissipation, and looked steadily into his.

"I don' want to kiss you, Bobinôt," she said, turning away again, "not today. Some other time. *Bonté divine!*[8] ent you satisfy, *yet!*"

"Oh, I'm satisfy, Calixta," he said.

Riding through a patch of wood, Clarisse's saddle became ungirted, and she and Alcée dismounted to readjust it.

For the twentieth time he asked her what had happened at home.

"But, Clarisse, w'at is it? Is it a misfortune?"

"Ah Dieu sait!*[9] It's only something that happen' to me."

"To you!"

"I saw you go away las' night, Alcée, with those saddle-bags," she said, haltingly, striving to arrange something about the saddle, "an' I made Bruce tell me. He said you had gone to the ball, an' wouldn' be home for weeks an' weeks. I thought, Alcée—maybe you were going to—to Assumption. I got wild. An' then I knew if you didn't come back, *now,* tonight, I couldn't stan' it,—again."

She had her face hidden in her arm that she was resting against the saddle when she said that.

He began to wonder if this meant love. But she had to tell him so, before he believed it. And when she told him, he thought the face of the Universe was changed—just like Bobinôt. Was it last week the cyclone had well-nigh ruined him? The cyclone seemed a huge joke, now. It was he, then, who, an hour ago was kissing little Calixta's ear and whispering nonsense into it. Calixta was like a myth, now. The one, only, great reality in the world was Clarisse standing before him, telling him that she loved him.

In the distance they heard the rapid discharge of pistol-shots; but it did not disturb them. They knew it was only the negro musicians who had gone into the yard to fire their pistols into the air, as the custom is, and to announce *"le bal est fini."*[1]

1892, 1894

The Storm

A Sequel to "The 'Cadian Ball"[1]

I

The leaves were so still that even Bibi thought it was going to rain. Bobinôt, who was accustomed to converse on terms of perfect equality with his little son, called the child's attention to certain sombre clouds that were rolling

---

8. Goodness gracious! (French).
9. God knows! (French).
1. The Ball is over (Fren).
1. Chopin's notebooks show that this story was written on July 18, 1898, just six months after she had submitted *The Awakening* to a publisher. As its subtitle indicates, it was intended as a sequel to her tale "At the 'Cadian Ball." "The Storm" was apparently never submitted for publication and did not see print until the publication of Per Seyersted's edition of *The Complete Works of Kate Chopin* in 1969, the basis for the text printed here.

with sinister intention from the west, accompanied by a sullen, threatening roar. They were at Friedheimer's store and decided to remain there till the storm had passed. They sat within the door on two empty kegs. Bibi was four years old and looked very wise.

"Mama'll be 'fraid, yes," he suggested with blinking eyes.

"She'll shut the house. Maybe she got Sylvie helpin' her this evenin'," Bobinôt responded reassuringly.

"No; she ent got Sylvie. Sylvie was helpin' her yistiday," piped Bibi.

Bobinôt arose and going across to the counter purchased a can of shrimps, of which Calixta was very fond. Then he returned to his perch on the keg and sat stolidly holding the can of shrimps while the storm burst. It shook the wooden store and seemed to be ripping furrows in the distant field. Bibi laid his little hand on his father's knee and was not afraid.

II

Calixta, at home, felt no uneasiness for their safety. She sat at a side window sewing furiously on a sewing machine. She was greatly occupied and did not notice the approaching storm. But she felt very warm and often stopped to mop her face on which the perspiration gathered in beads. She unfastened her white sacque at the throat. It began to grow dark, and suddenly realizing the situation she got up hurriedly and went about closing windows and doors.

Out on the small front gallery she had hung Bobinôt's Sunday clothes to dry and she hastened out to gather them before the rain fell. As she stepped outside, Alcée Laballière rode in at the gate. She had not seen him very often since her marriage, and never alone. She stood there with Bobinôt's coat in her hands, and the big rain drops began to fall. Alcée rode his horse under the shelter of a side projection where the chickens had huddled and there were plows and a harrow piled up in the corner.

"May I come and wait on your gallery till the storm is over, Calixta?" he asked.

"Come 'long in, M'sieur Alcée."

His voice and her own startled her as if from a trance, and she seized Bobinôt's vest. Alcée, mounting to the porch, grabbed the trousers and snatched Bibi's braided jacket that was about to be carried away by a sudden gust of wind. He expressed an intention to remain outside, but it was soon apparent that he might as well have been out in the open: the water beat in upon the boards in driving sheets, and he went inside, closing the door after him. It was even necessary to put something beneath the door to keep the water out.

"My! what a rain! It's good two years since it rain' like that," exclaimed Calixta as she rolled up a piece of bagging and Alcée helped her to thrust it beneath the crack.

She was a little fuller of figure than five years before when she married; but she had lost nothing of her vivacity. Her blue eyes still retained their melting quality; and her yellow hair, disheveled by the wind and rain, kinked more stubbornly than ever about her ears and temples.

The rain beat upon the low, shingled roof with a force and clatter that threatened to break an entrance and deluge them there. They were in the dining room—the sitting room—the general utility room. Adjoining was her bed room, with Bibi's couch along side her own. The door stood open, and the room with its white, monumental bed, its closed shutters, looked dim and mysterious.

Alcée flung himself into a rocker and Calixta nervously began to gather up from the floor the lengths of a cotton sheet which she had been sewing.

"If this keeps up, *Dieu sait* if the levees[2] goin' to stan' it!" she exclaimed.

"What have you got to do with the levees?"

"I got enough to do! An' there's Bobinôt with Bibi out in that storm—if he only didn' left Friedheimer's!"

"Let us hope, Calixta, that Bobinôt's got sense enough to come in out of a cyclone."

She went and stood at the window with a greatly disturbed look on her face. She wiped the frame that was clouded with moisture. It was stiflingly hot. Alcée got up and joined her at the window, looking over her shoulder. The rain was coming down in sheets obscuring the view of far-off cabins and enveloping the distant wood in a gray mist. The playing of the lightning was incessant. A bolt struck a tall chinaberry tree at the edge of the field. It filled all visible space with a blinding glare and the crash seemed to invade the very boards they stood upon.

Calixta put her hands to her eyes, and with a cry, staggered backward. Alcée's arm encircled her, and for an instant he drew her close and spasmodically to him.

"*Bonté!*"[3] she cried, releasing herself from his encircling arm and retreating from the window, "the house'll go next! If I only knew w'ere Bibi was!" She would not compose herself; she would not be seated. Alcée clasped her shoulders and looked into her face. The contact of her warm, palpitating body when he had unthinkingly drawn her into his arms, had aroused all the old-time infatuation and desire for her flesh.

"Calixta," he said, "don't be frightened. Nothing can happen. The house is too low to be struck, with so many tall trees standing about. There! aren't you going to be quiet? say, aren't you?" He pushed her hair back from her face that was warm and steaming. Her lips were as red and moist as pomegranate seed. Her white neck and a glimpse of her full, firm bosom disturbed him powerfully. As she glanced up at him the fear in her liquid blue eyes had given place to a drowsy gleam that unconsciously betrayed a sensuous desire. He looked down into her eyes and there was nothing for him to do but to gather her lips in a kiss. It reminded him of Assumption.[4]

"Do you remember—in Assumption, Calixta?" he asked in a low voice broken by passion. Oh! she remembered; for in Assumption he had kissed her and kissed and kissed her; until his senses would well nigh fail, and to save her he would resort to a desperate flight. If she was not an immaculate dove in those days, she was still inviolate; a passionate creature whose very defenselessness had made her defense, against which his honor forbade him to prevail. Now—well, now—her lips seemed in a manner free to be tasted, as well as her round, white throat and her whiter breasts.

They did not heed the crashing torrents, and the roar of the elements made her laugh as she lay in his arms. She was a revelation in that dim, mysterious

2. Built-up earth banks designed to keep the river from flooding the surrounding land. *"Dieu sait"*: God knows (French).

3. Goodness! (French).

4. I.e., Assumption Parish, Louisiana, the setting for "At the 'Cadian Ball."

chamber; as white as the couch she lay upon. Her firm, elastic flesh that was knowing for the first time its birthright, was like a creamy lily that the sun invites to contribute its breath and perfume to the undying life of the world.

The generous abundance of her passion, without guile or trickery, was like a white flame which penetrated and found response in depths of his own sensuous nature that had never yet been reached.

When he touched her breasts they gave themselves up in quivering ecstasy, inviting his lips. Her mouth was a fountain of delight. And when he possessed her, they seemed to swoon together at the very borderland of life's mystery.

He stayed cushioned upon her, breathless, dazed, enervated, with his heart beating like a hammer upon her. With one hand she clasped his head, her lips lightly touching his forehead. The other hand stroked with a soothing rhythm his muscular shoulders.

The growl of the thunder was distant and passing away. The rain beat softly upon the shingles, inviting them to drowsiness and sleep. But they dared not yield.

III

The rain was over; and the sun was turning the glistening green world into a palace of gems. Calixta, on the gallery, watched Alcée ride away. He turned and smiled at her with a beaming face; and she lifted her pretty chin in the air and laughed aloud.

Bobinôt and Bibi, trudging home, stopped without at the cistern to make themselves presentable.

"My! Bibi, w'at will yo' mama say! You ought to be ashame'. You oughta' put on those good pants. Look at 'em! An' that mud on yo' collar! How you got that mud on yo' collar, Bibi? I never saw such a boy!" Bibi was the picture of pathetic resignation. Bobinôt was the embodiment of serious solicitude as he strove to remove from his own person and his son's the signs of their tramp over heavy roads and through wet fields. He scraped the mud off Bibi's bare legs and feet with a stick and carefully removed all traces from his heavy brogans. Then, prepared for the worst—the meeting with an over-scrupulous housewife, they entered cautiously at the back door.

Calixta was preparing supper. She had set the table and was dripping coffee at the hearth. She sprang up as they came in.

"Oh, Bobinôt! You back! My! but I was uneasy. W'ere you been during the rain? An' Bibi? he ain't wet? he ain't hurt?" She had clasped Bibi and was kissing him effusively. Bobinôt's explanations and apologies which he had been composing all along the way, died on his lips as Calixta felt him to see if he were dry, and seemed to express nothing but satisfaction at their safe return.

"I brought you some shrimps, Calixta," offered Bobinôt, hauling the can from his ample side pocket and laying it on the table.

"Shrimps! Oh, Bobinôt! you too good fo' anything!" and she gave him a smacking kiss on the cheek that resounded, "J'vous réponds,[5] we'll have a feas' to night! umph-umph!"

Bobinôt and Bibi began to relax and enjoy themselves, and when the three seated themselves at table they laughed much and so loud that anyone might have heard them as far away as Laballière's.

5. I promise you (French).

IV

Alcée Laballière wrote to his wife, Clarisse, that night. It was a loving letter, full of tender solicitude. He told her not to hurry back, but if she and the babies liked it at Biloxi, to stay a month longer. He was getting on nicely; and though he missed them, he was willing to bear the separation a while longer—realizing that their health and pleasure were the first things to be considered.

V

As for Clarisse, she was charmed upon receiving her husband's letter. She and the babies were doing well. The society was agreeable; many of her old friends and acquaintances were at the bay. And the first free breath since her marriage seemed to restore the pleasant liberty of her maiden days. Devoted as she was to her husband, their intimate conjugal life was something which she was more than willing to forego for a while.

So the storm passed and every one was happy.

1898   1969

Désirée's Baby[1]

As the day was pleasant, Madame Valmondé drove over to L'Abri to see Désirée and the baby.

It made her laugh to think of Désirée with a baby. Why, it seemed but yesterday that Désirée was little more than a baby herself; when Monsieur in riding through the gateway of Valmondé had found her lying asleep in the shadow of the big stone pillar.

The little one awoke in his arms and began to cry for "Dada." That was as much as she could do or say. Some people thought she might have strayed there of her own accord, for she was of the toddling age. The prevailing belief was that she had been purposely left by a party of Texans, whose canvas-covered wagon, late in the day, had crossed the ferry that Coton Maïs kept, just below the plantation. In time Madame Valmondé abandoned every speculation but the one that Désirée had been sent to her by a beneficent Providence to be the child of her affection, seeing that she was without child of the flesh. For the girl grew to be beautiful and gentle, affectionate and sincere,—the idol of Valmondé.

It was no wonder, when she stood one day against the stone pillar in whose shadow she had lain asleep, eighteen years before, that Armand Aubigny riding by and seeing her there, had fallen in love with her. That was the way all the Aubignys fell in love, as if struck by a pistol shot. The wonder was that he had not loved her before; for he had known her since his father brought him home from Paris, a boy of eight, after his mother died there. The passion that awoke in him that day, when he saw her at the gate, swept along like an avalanche, or like a prairie fire, or like anything that drives headlong over all obstacles.

1. First published in *Vogue*, January 14, 1893; first published in book form in *Bayou Folk* (1894), the source of the present text.

Monsieur Valmondé grew practical and wanted things well considered: that is, the girl's obscure origin. Armand looked into her eyes and did not care. He was reminded that she was nameless. What did it matter about a name when he could give her one of the oldest and proudest in Louisiana? He ordered the *corbeille*[2] from Paris, and contained himself with what patience he could until it arrived; then they were married.

Madame Valmondé had not seen Désirée and the baby for four weeks. When she reached L'Abri she shuddered at the first sight of it, as she always did. It was a sad looking place, which for many years had not known the gentle presence of a mistress, old Monsieur Aubigny having married and buried his wife in France, and she having loved her own land too well ever to leave it. The roof came down steep and black like a cowl, reaching out beyond the wide galleries that encircled the yellow stuccoed house. Big, solemn oaks grew close to it, and their thick-leaved, far-reaching branches shadowed it like a pall. Young Aubigny's rule was a strict one, too, and under it his negroes had forgotten how to be gay, as they had been during the old master's easy-going and indulgent lifetime.

The young mother was recovering slowly, and lay full length, in her soft white muslins and laces, upon a couch. The baby was beside her, upon her arm, where he had fallen asleep, at her breast. The yellow nurse woman sat beside a window fanning herself.

Madame Valmondé bent her portly figure over Désirée and kissed her, holding her an instant tenderly in her arms. Then she turned to the child.

"This is not the baby!" she exclaimed, in startled tones. French was the language spoken at Valmondé in those days.

"I knew you would be astonished," laughed Désirée, "at the way he has grown. The little *cochon de lait!*[3] Look at his legs, mamma, and his hands and fingernails,—real finger-nails. Zandrine had to cut them this morning. Isn't it true, Zandrine?"

The woman bowed her turbaned head majestically, "Mais si, Madame."

"And the way he cries," went on Désirée, "is deafening. Armand heard him the other day as far away as La Blanche's cabin."

Madame Valmondé had never removed her eyes from the child. She lifted it and walked with it over to the window that was lightest. She scanned the baby narrowly, then looked as searchingly at Zandrine, whose face was turned to gaze across the fields.

"Yes, the child has grown, has changed," said Madame Valmondé, slowly, as she replaced it beside its mother. "What does Armand say?"

Désirée's face became suffused with a glow that was happiness itself.

"Oh, Armand is the proudest father in the parish, I believe, chiefly because it is a boy, to bear his name; though he says not,—that he would have loved a girl as well. But I know it isn't true. I know he says that to please me. And mamma," she added, drawing Madame Valmondé's head down to her, and speaking in a whisper, "he hasn't punished one of them—not one of them—since baby is born. Even Négrillon, who pretended to have burnt his leg that he might rest from work—he only laughed, and said Négrillon was a great scamp. Oh, mamma, I'm so happy; it frightens me."

---

2. Literally, basket (French). In this context, a hope chest filled with fine linens, clothes, and other gifts meant to serve as the material founda-

tion for their married life.
3. Suckling pig (French).

What Désirée said was true. Marriage, and later the birth of his son had softened Armand Aubigny's imperious and exacting nature greatly. This was what made the gentle Désirée so happy, for she loved him desperately. When he frowned she trembled, but loved him. When he smiled, she asked no greater blessing of God. But Armand's dark, handsome face had not often been disfigured by frowns since the day he fell in love with her.

When the baby was about three months old, Désirée awoke one day to the conviction that there was something in the air menacing her peace. It was at first too subtle to grasp. It had only been a disquieting suggestion; an air of mystery among the blacks; unexpected visits from far-off neighbors who could hardly account for their coming. Then a strange, an awful change in her husband's manner, which she dared not ask him to explain. When he spoke to her, it was with averted eyes, from which the old love-light seemed to have gone out. He absented himself from home; and when there, avoided her presence and that of her child, without excuse. And the very spirit of Satan seemed suddenly to take hold of him in his dealings with the slaves. Désirée was miserable enough to die.

She sat in her room, one hot afternoon, in her *peignoir*,[4] listlessly drawing through her fingers the strands of her long, silky brown hair that hung about her shoulders. The baby, half naked, lay asleep upon her own great mahogany bed, that was like a sumptuous throne, with its satin-lined half-canopy. One of La Blanche's little quadroon[5] boys—half naked too—stood fanning the child slowly with a fan of peacock feathers. Désirée's eyes had been fixed absently and sadly upon the baby, while she was striving to penetrate the threatening mist that she felt closing about her. She looked from her child to the boy who stood beside him, and back again; over and over. "Ah!" It was a cry that she could not help; which she was not conscious of having uttered. The blood turned like ice in her veins, and a clammy moisture gathered upon her face.

She tried to speak to the little quadroon boy; but no sound would come, at first. When he heard his name uttered, he looked up, and his mistress was pointing to the door. He laid aside the great, soft fan, and obediently stole away, over the polished floor, on his bare tiptoes.

She stayed motionless, with gaze riveted upon her child, and her face the picture of fright.

Presently her husband entered the room, and without noticing her, went to a table and began to search among some papers which covered it.

"Armand," she called to him, in a voice which must have stabbed him, if he was human. But he did not notice. "Armand," she said again. Then she rose and tottered towards him. "Armand," she panted once more, clutching his arm, "look at our child. What does it mean? tell me."

He coldly but gently loosened her fingers from about his arm and thrust the hand away from him. "Tell me what it means!" she cried despairingly.

"It means," he answered lightly, "that the child is not white; it means that you are not white."

A quick conception of all that his accusation meant for her nerved her with unwonted courage to deny it. "It is a lie; it is not true, I am white! Look at my hair, it is brown; and my eyes are gray, Armand, you know they are

---

4. Dressing gown (French).　　　　5. A person who is one-quarter African American.

gray. And my skin is fair," seizing his wrist. "Look at my hand; whiter than yours, Armand," she laughed hysterically.

"As white as La Blanche's,"[6] he returned cruelly; and went away leaving her alone with their child.

When she could hold a pen in her hand, she sent a despairing letter to Madame Valmondé.

"My mother, they tell me I am not white. Armand has told me I am not white. For God's sake tell them it is not true. You must know it is not true. I shall die. I must die. I cannot be so unhappy, and live."

The answer that came was as brief:

"My own Désirée: Come home to Valmondé; back to your mother who loves you. Come with your child."

When the letter reached Désirée she went with it to her husband's study, and laid it open upon the desk before which she sat. She was like a stone image: silent, white, motionless after she placed it there.

In silence he ran his cold eyes over the written words. He said nothing. "Shall I go, Armand?" she asked in tones sharp with agonized suspense.

"Yes, go."

"Do you want me to go?"

"Yes, I want you to go."

He thought Almighty God had dealt cruelly and unjustly with him; and felt, somehow, that he was paying Him back in kind when he stabbed thus into his wife's soul. Moreover he no longer loved her, because of the unconscious injury she had brought upon his home and his name.

She turned away like one stunned by a blow, and walked slowly towards the door, hoping he would call her back.

"Good-by, Armand," she moaned.

He did not answer her. That was his last blow at fate.

Désirée went in search of her child. Zandrine was pacing the sombre gallery with it. She took the little one from the nurse's arms with no word of explanation, and descending the steps, walked away, under the live-oak branches.

It was an October afternoon; the sun was just sinking. Out in the still fields the negroes were picking cotton.

Désirée had not changed the thin white garment nor the slippers which she wore. Her hair was uncovered and the sun's rays brought a golden gleam from its brown meshes. She did not take the broad, beaten road which led to the far-off plantation of Valmondé. She walked across a deserted field, where the stubble bruised her tender feet, so delicately shod, and tore her thin gown to shreds.

She disappeared among the reeds and willows that grew thick along the banks of the deep, sluggish bayou; and she did not come back again.

Some weeks later there was a curious scene enacted at L'Abri. In the centre of the smoothly swept back yard was a great bonfire. Armand Aubigny sat in the wide hallway that commanded a view of the spectacle; and it was he who dealt out to a half dozen negroes the material which kept this fire ablaze.

A graceful cradle of willow, with all its dainty furbishings, was laid upon the

6. The cruelty involves the double irony: La Blanche (the white) is black.

pyre, which had already been fed with the richness of a priceless *layette*.[7] Then there were silk gowns, and velvet and satin ones added to these; laces, too, and embroideries; bonnets and gloves; for the *corbeille* had been of rare quality.

The last thing to go was a tiny bundle of letters; innocent little scribblings that Désirée had sent to him during the days of their espousal. There was the remnant of one back in the drawer from which he took them. But it was not Désirée's; it was part of an old letter from his mother to his father. He read it. She was thanking God for the blessing of her husband's love:—

"But, above all," she wrote, "night and day, I thank the good God for having so arranged our lives that our dear Armand will never know that his mother, who adores him, belongs to the race that is cursed with the brand of slavery."

1893

7. Clothes, bedding, toilet articles, and other items needed to care for a newborn.

MARY E. WILKINS FREEMAN
1852–1930

Mary E. Wilkins Freeman, best known for her depiction of New England village life, was born on October 31, 1852, in Randolph, Massachusetts, a small town twenty miles south of Boston. She was not a strong child, and two other Wilkins children died before they reached three years of age; her sister Anne lived to be seventeen. Freeman's parents were orthodox Congregationalists, and she was subject to a strict code of behavior. The constraints of religious belief, and the effect of these constraints on character formation and behavior, is one of her chief subjects.

In 1867 Freeman's father became part owner of a dry-goods store in Brattleboro, Vermont, where she graduated from high school. In 1870, she entered Mount Holyoke Female Seminary, which Emily Dickinson had attended two decades earlier. Like Dickinson, Freeman left after a year in which she resisted the school's pressure on all students to offer public testimony as to their Christian commitment. She finished her formal education with a year at West Brattleboro Seminary, though the reading and discussion with her friend Evelyn Sawyer of Johann Wolfgang von Goethe, Ralph Waldo Emerson, Henry David Thoreau, Charles Dickens, William Makepeace Thackeray, Edgar Allan Poe, Nathaniel Hawthorne, Harriet Beecher Stowe, and Sarah Orne Jewett were probably more important than her schoolwork in developing her literary taste.

After the failure of her father's business in 1876, Freeman's family moved into the Brattleboro home of the Reverend Thomas Pickman Tyler, where her mother became housekeeper. Poverty was hard for the Wilkinses to bear, especially because their Puritan heritage led them to believe that poverty was a punishment for sin. Freeman's mother died in 1880, her father three years later, leaving Freeman alone at the age of twenty-eight, with a legacy of less than one thousand dollars.

Fortunately, by this time she had begun to sell poems and stories to such leading magazines as *Harper's Bazaar,* and by the mid-1880s she had a ready market for her work. As soon as she achieved a measure of economic independence, she returned to Randolph, where she lived with her childhood friend Mary Wales. Her early stories, especially those gathered and published in *A Humble Romance* (1887), are set in the Vermont countryside, but as she put it in a preface to an edition of these stories published in Edinburgh, the characters are generalized "studies of the descendants of the Massachusetts Bay colonists, in whom can still be seen traces of those features of will and conscience, so strong as to be almost exaggerations and deformities, which characterized their ancestors." More specifically, the title story dramatizes a theme Freeman was to return to frequently: the potential for unpredictable revolt in outwardly meek and downtrodden natures, such as the central character in "The Revolt of 'Mother.'"

"A New England Nun" and Other Stories, which appeared in 1891, contains several of her best stories, most notably the title story, which treats (with particular dramatic success) the pervasive theme of the psychic oppression and rebellion of women. At the same time as she provides a vivid sense of place, local dialect, and personality type, Freeman also offers in her best work insight into the individual psychology and interior life produced when confining, inherited codes of village life are subject to the pressure of a rapidly changing secular and urban world. This is a world in which, as the critic Marjorie Pryse argued, women begin to assert, individually and collectively, their vision and power against an exhausted Puritan patriarchy.

Freeman continued to write for another three decades. Although she is best known today for her stories, she also wrote plays and a number of successful novels on diverse topics from local history to labor unrest, but always with a focus on women. Among these novels are *Pembroke* (1894) and *The Shoulders of Atlas* (1908). She married Dr. Charles Freeman in 1902, when she was forty-nine, and moved to Metuchen, New Jersey; after a few happy years, her husband's drinking developed into destructive alcoholism, and he had to be institutionalized in 1920. In 1926, she was awarded the W. D. Howells medal for fiction by the American Academy of Arts and Letters and elected to the National Institute of Arts and Letters—both these honors were seldom given to women writers in those days. She died of a heart attack four years later.

A New England Nun[1]

It was late in the afternoon, and the light was waning. There was a difference in the look of the tree shadows out in the yard. Somewhere in the distance cows were lowing and a little bell was tinkling; now and then a farm-wagon tilted by, and the dust flew; some blue-shirted laborers with shovels over their shoulders plodded past; little swarms of flies were dancing up and down before the peoples' faces in the soft air. There seemed to be a gentle stir arising over everything for the mere sake of subsidence—a very premonition of rest and hush and night.

This soft diurnal commotion was over Louisa Ellis also. She had been peacefully sewing at her sitting-room window all the afternoon. Now she quilted her needle carefully into her work, which she folded precisely, and laid in a basket with her thimble and thread and scissors. Louisa Ellis could not remember that ever in her life she had mislaid one of these little feminine appurtenances, which had become, from long use and constant association, a very part of her personality.

Louisa tied a green apron round her waist, and got out a flat straw hat with a green ribbon. Then she went into the garden with a little blue crockery bowl, to pick some currants for her tea. After the currants were picked she sat on the back door-step and stemmed them, collecting the stems carefully in her apron, and afterwards throwing them into the hen-coop. She looked sharply at the grass beside the step to see if any had fallen there.

1. From *"A New England Nun" and Other Stories* (1891), the source of the text printed here.

Louisa was slow and still in her movements; it took her a long time to prepare her tea; but when ready it was set forth with as much grace as if she had
been a veritable guest to her own self. The little square table stood exactly in
the centre of the kitchen, and was covered with a starched linen cloth whose
border pattern of flowers glistened. Louisa had a damask napkin on her tea-
tray, where were arranged a cut-glass tumbler full of teaspoons, a silver
cream-pitcher, a china sugar-bowl, and one pink china cup and saucer.
Louisa used china every day—something which none of her neighbors did.
They whispered about it among themselves. Their daily tables were laid with
common crockery, their sets of best china stayed in the parlor closet, and
Louisa Ellis was no richer nor better bred than they. Still she would use the
china. She had for her supper a glass dish full of sugared currants, a plate of
little cakes, and one of light white biscuits. Also a leaf or two of lettuce, which
she cut up daintily. Louisa was very fond of lettuce, which she raised to perfection in her little garden. She ate quite heartily, though in a delicate, pecking way; it seemed almost surprising that any considerable bulk of the food
should vanish.

After tea she filled a plate with nicely baked thin corn-cakes, and carried
them out into the back-yard.

"Cæsar!" she called. "Cæsar! Cæsar!"

There was a little rush, and the clank of a chain, and a large yellow-and-
white dog appeared at the door of his tiny hut, which was half hidden among
the tall grasses and flowers. Louisa patted him and gave him the corn-cakes.
Then she returned to the house and washed the tea-things, polishing the
china carefully. The twilight had deepened; the chorus of the frogs floated in
at the open window wonderfully loud and shrill, and once in a while a long
sharp drone from a tree-toad pierced it. Louisa took off her green gingham
apron, disclosing a shorter one of pink and white print. She lighted her lamp,
and sat down again with her sewing.

In about half an hour Joe Dagget came. She heard his heavy step on the
walk, and rose and took off her pink-and-white apron. Under that was still
another—white linen with a little cambric edging on the bottom; that was
Louisa's company apron. She never wore it without her calico sewing apron
over it unless she had a guest. She had barely folded the pink and white one
with methodical haste and laid it in a table-drawer when the door opened and
Joe Dagget entered.

He seemed to fill up the whole room. A little yellow canary that had been
asleep in his green cage at the south window woke up and fluttered wildly,
beating his little yellow wings against the wires. He always did so when Joe
Dagget came into the room.

"Good-evening," said Louisa. She extended her hand with a kind of solemn
cordiality.

"Good-evening, Louisa," returned the man, in a loud voice.

She placed a chair for him, and they sat facing each other, with the table
between them. He sat bolt-upright, toeing out his heavy feet squarely, glancing with a good-humored uneasiness around the room. She sat gently erect,
folding her slender hands in her white-linen lap.

"Been a pleasant day," remarked Dagget.

"Real pleasant," Louisa assented, softly. "Have you been haying?" she
asked, after a little while.

"Yes, I've been haying all day, down in the ten-acre lot. Pretty hot work."

"It must be."

"Yes, it's pretty hot work in the sun."

"Is your mother well to-day?"

"Yes, mother's pretty well."

"I suppose Lily Dyer's with her now?"

Dagget colored. "Yes, she's with her," he answered, slowly.

He was not very young, but there was a boyish look about his large face. Louisa was not quite as old as he, her face was fairer and smoother, but she gave people the impression of being older.

"I suppose she's a good deal of help to your mother," she said, further.

"I guess she is; I don't know how mother'd get along without her," said Dagget, with a sort of embarrassed warmth.

"She looks like a real capable girl. She's pretty-looking too," remarked Louisa.

"Yes, she is pretty fair looking."

Presently Dagget began fingering the books on the table. There was a square red autograph album, and a Young Lady's Gift-Book[2] which had belonged to Louisa's mother. He took them up one after the other and opened them; then laid them down again, the album on the Gift-Book.

Louisa kept eying them with mild uneasiness. Finally she rose and changed the position of the books, putting the album underneath. That was the way they had been arranged in the first place.

Dagget gave an awkward little laugh. "Now what difference did it make which book was on top?" said he.

Louisa looked at him with a deprecating smile. "I always keep them that way," murmured she.

"You do beat everything," said Dagget, trying to laugh again. His large face was flushed.

He remained about an hour longer, then rose to take leave. Going out, he stumbled over a rug, and trying to recover himself, hit Louisa's work-basket on the table, and knocked it on the floor.

He looked at Louisa, then at the rolling spools; he ducked himself awkwardly toward them, but she stopped him. "Never mind," said she; "I'll pick them up after you're gone."

She spoke with a mild stiffness. Either she was a little disturbed, or his nervousness affected her, and made her seem constrained in her effort to reassure him.

When Joe Dagget was outside he drew in the sweet evening air with a sigh, and felt much as an innocent and perfectly well-intentioned bear might after his exit from a china shop.

Louisa, on her part, felt much as the kind-hearted, long-suffering owner of the china shop might have done after the exit of the bear.

She tied on the pink, then the green apron, picked up all the scattered treasures and replaced them in her work-basket, and straightened the rug. Then she set the lamp on the floor, and began sharply examining the carpet. She even rubbed her fingers over it, and looked at them.

2. Gift books (ca. 1825–65) were popular annual miscellanies, containing stories, essays, and poems, usually with a polite or moral tone. They were lavishly printed and decorated for use as Christmas or New Year's gifts.

"He's tracked in a good deal of dust," she murmured. "I thought he must have."

Louisa got a dust-pan and brush, and swept Joe Dagget's track carefully.

If he could have known it, it would have increased his perplexity and uneasiness, although it would not have disturbed his loyalty in the least. He came twice a week to see Louisa Ellis, and every time, sitting there in her delicately sweet room, he felt as if surrounded by a hedge of lace. He was afraid to stir lest he should put a clumsy foot or hand through the fairy web, and he had always the consciousness that Louisa was watching fearfully lest he should.

Still the lace and Louisa commanded perforce his perfect respect and patience and loyalty. They were to be married in a month, after a singular courtship which had lasted for a matter of fifteen years. For fourteen out of the fifteen years the two had not once seen each other, and they had seldom exchanged letters. Joe had been all those years in Australia, where he had gone to make his fortune, and where he had stayed until he made it. He would have stayed fifty years if it had taken so long, and come home feeble and tottering, or never come home at all, to marry Louisa.

But the fortune had been made in the fourteen years, and he had come home now to marry the woman who had been patiently and unquestioningly waiting for him all that time.

Shortly after they were engaged he had announced to Louisa his determination to strike out into new fields, and secure a competency before they should be married. She had listened and assented with the sweet serenity which never failed her, not even when her lover set forth on that long and uncertain journey. Joe, buoyed up as he was by his sturdy determination, broke down a little at the last, but Louisa kissed him with a mild blush, and said good-by.

"It won't be for long," poor Joe had said, huskily; but it was for fourteen years.

In that length of time much had happened. Louisa's mother and brother had died, and she was all alone in the world. But greatest happening of all— a subtle happening which both were too simple to understand—Louisa's feet had turned into a path, smooth maybe under a calm, serene sky, but so straight and unswerving that it could only meet a check at her grave, and so narrow that there was no room for any one at her side.

Louisa's first emotion when Joe Dagget came home (he had not apprised her of his coming) was consternation, although she would not admit it to herself, and he never dreamed of it. Fifteen years ago she had been in love with him—at least she considered herself to be. Just at that time, gently acquiescing with and falling into the natural drift of girlhood, she had seen marriage ahead as a reasonable feature and a probable desirability of life. She had listened with calm docility to her mother's views upon the subject. Her mother was remarkable for her cool sense and sweet, even temperament. She talked wisely to her daughter when Joe Dagget presented himself, and Louisa accepted him with no hesitation. He was the first lover she had ever had.

She had been faithful to him all these years. She had never dreamed of the possibility of marrying any one else. Her life, especially for the last seven years, had been full of a pleasant peace, she had never felt discontented nor impatient over her lover's absence; still she had always looked forward to his return and their marriage as the inevitable conclusion of things. However, she had fallen into a way of placing it so far in the future that it was almost equal to placing it over the boundaries of another life.

When Joe came she had been expecting him, and expecting to be married for fourteen years, but she was as much surprised and taken aback as if she had never thought of it.

Joe's consternation came later. He eyed Louisa with an instant confirmation of his old admiration. She had changed but little. She still kept her pretty manner and soft grace, and was, he considered, every whit as attractive as ever. As for himself, his stent was done; he had turned his face away from fortune-seeking, and the old winds of romance whistled as loud and sweet as ever through his ears. All the song which he had been wont to hear in them was Louisa; he had for a long time a loyal belief that he heard it still, but finally it seemed to him that although the winds sang always that one song, it had another name. But for Louisa the wind had never more than murmured; now it had gone down, and everything was still. She listened for a little while with half-wistful attention; then she turned quietly away and went to work on her wedding clothes.

Joe had made some extensive and quite magnificent alterations in his house. It was the old homestead; the newly-married couple would live there, for Joe could not desert his mother, who refused to leave her old home. So Louisa must leave hers. Every morning, rising and going about among her neat maidenly possessions, she felt as one looking her last upon the faces of dear friends. It was true that in a measure she could take them with her, but, robbed of their old environments, they would appear in such new guises that they would almost cease to be themselves. Then there were some peculiar features of her happy solitary life which she would probably be obliged to relinquish altogether. Sterner tasks than these graceful but half-needless ones would probably devolve upon her. There would be a large house to care for; there would be company to entertain; there would be Joe's rigours and feeble old mother to wait upon; and it would be contrary to all thrifty village traditions for her to keep more than one servant. Louisa had a little still, and she used to occupy herself pleasantly in summer weather with distilling the sweet and aromatic essences from roses and peppermint and spearmint. By-and-by her still must be laid away. Her store of essences was already considerable, and there would be no time for her to distil for the mere pleasure of it. Then Joe's mother would think it foolishness; she had already hinted her opinion in the matter. Louisa dearly loved to sew a linen seam, not always for use, but for the simple, mild pleasure which she took in it. She would have been loath to confess how more than once she had ripped a seam for the mere delight of sewing it together again. Sitting at her window during long sweet afternoons, drawing her needle gently through the dainty fabric, she was peace itself. But there was small chance of such foolish comfort in the future. Joe's mother, domineering, shrewd old matron that she was even in her old age, and very likely even Joe himself, with his honest masculine rudeness, would laugh and frown down all these pretty but senseless old maiden ways.

Louisa had almost the enthusiasm of an artist over the mere order and cleanliness of her solitary home. She had throbs of genuine triumph at the sight of the window-panes which she had polished until they shone like jewels. She gloated gently over her orderly bureau-drawers, with their exquisitely folded contents redolent with lavender and sweet clover and very purity.

Could she be sure of the endurance of even this? She had visions, so startling that she half repudiated them as indelicate, of coarse masculine belongings strewn about in endless litter; of dust and disorder arising necessarily from a coarse masculine presence in the midst of all this delicate harmony.

Among her forebodings of disturbance, not the least was with regard to Cæsar. Cæsar was a veritable hermit of a dog. For the greater part of his life he had dwelt in his secluded hut, shut out from the society of his kind and all innocent canine joys. Never had Cæsar since his early youth watched at a woodchuck's hole; never had he known the delights of a stray bone at a neighbor's kitchen door. And it was all on account of a sin committed when hardly out of his puppyhood. No one knew the possible depth of remorse of which this mild-visaged, altogether innocent-looking old dog might be capable; but whether or not he had encountered remorse, he had encountered a full measure of righteous retribution. Old Cæsar seldom lifted up his voice in a growl or a bark; he was fat and sleepy; there were yellow rings which looked like spectacles around his dim old eyes; but there was a neighbor who bore on his hand the imprint of several of Cæsar's sharp white youthful teeth, and for that he had lived at the end of a chain, all alone in a little hut, for fourteen years. The neighbor, who was choleric and smarting with the pain of his wound, had demanded either Cæsar's death or complete ostracism. So Louisa's brother, to whom the dog had belonged, had built him his little kennel and tied him up. It was now fourteen years since, in a flood of youthful spirits, he had inflicted that memorable bite, and with the exception of short excursions, always at the end of the chain, under the strict guardianship of his master or Louisa, the old dog had remained a close prisoner. It is doubtful if, with his limited ambition, he took much pride in the fact, but it is certain that he was possessed of considerable cheap fame. He was regarded by all the children in the village and by many adults as a very monster of ferocity. St. George's dragon[3] could hardly have surpassed in evil repute Louisa Ellis's old yellow dog. Mothers charged their children with solemn emphasis not to go too near him, and the children listened and believed greedily, with a fascinated appetite for terror, and ran by Louisa's house stealthily, with many sidelong and backward glances at the terrible dog. If perchance he sounded a hoarse bark, there was a panic. Wayfarers chancing into Louisa's yard eyed him with respect, and inquired if the chain were stout. Cæsar at large might have seemed a very ordinary dog, and excited no comment whatever; chained, his reputation overshadowed him, so that he lost his own proper outlines and looked darkly vague and enormous. Joe Dagget, however, with his good-humored sense and shrewdness, saw him as he was. He strode valiantly up to him and patted him on the head, in spite of Louisa's soft clamor of warning, and even attempted to set him loose. Louisa grew so alarmed that he desisted, but kept announcing his opinion in the matter quite forcibly at intervals. "There ain't a better-natured dog in town," he would say, "and it's downright cruel to keep him tied up there. Some day I'm going to take him out."

Louisa had very little hope that he would not, one of these days, when their interests and possessions should be more completely fused in one. She pictured to herself Cæsar on the rampage through the quiet and unguarded vil-

---

3. The story of St. George (patron saint of England) and the Dragon is an allegorical expression of the triumph of the Christian hero over evil.

lage. She saw innocent children bleeding in his path. She was herself very fond of the old dog, because he had belonged to her dead brother, and he was always very gentle with her; still she had great faith in his ferocity. She always warned people not to go too near him. She fed him on ascetic fare of corn-mush and cakes, and never fired his dangerous temper with heating and san-guinary diet of flesh and bones. Louisa looked at the old dog munching his simple fare, and thought of her approaching marriage and trembled. Still no anticipation of disorder and confusion in lieu of sweet peace and harmony, no forebodings of Cæsar on the rampage, no wild fluttering of her little yel-low canary, were sufficient to turn her a hair's-breadth. Joe Dagget had been fond of her and working for her all these years. It was not for her, whatever came to pass, to prove untrue and break his heart. She put the exquisite lit-tle stitches into her wedding-garments, and the time went on until it was only a week before her wedding-day. It was a Tuesday evening, and the wedding was to be a week from Wednesday.

There was a full moon that night. About nine o'clock Louisa strolled down the road a little way. There were harvest-fields on either hand, bordered by low stone walls. Luxuriant clumps of bushes grew beside the wall, and trees—wild cherry and old apple-trees—at intervals. Presently Louisa sat down on the wall and looked about her with mildly sorrowful reflectiveness. Tall shrubs of blueberry and meadow-sweet, all woven together and tangled with blackberry vines and horsebriers, shut her in on either side. She had a little clear space between. Opposite her, on the other side of the road, was a spreading tree; the moon shone between its boughs, and the leaves twinkled like silver. The road was bespread with a beautiful shifting dapple of silver and shadow; the air was full of a mysterious sweetness. "I wonder if it's wild grapes?" murmured Louisa. She sat there some time. She was just thinking of rising, when she heard footsteps and low voices, and remained quiet. It was a lonely place, and she felt a little timid. She thought she would keep still in the shadow and let the persons, whoever they might be, pass her.

But just before they reached her the voices ceased, and the footsteps. She understood that their owners had also found seats upon the stone wall. She was wondering if she could not steal away unobserved, when the voice broke the stillness. It was Joe Dagget's. She sat still and listened.

The voice was announced by a loud sigh, which was as familiar as itself. "Well," said Dagget, "you've made up your mind, then, I suppose?"

"Yes," returned another voice; "I'm going day after to-morrow."

"That's Lily Dyer," thought Louisa to herself. The voice embodied itself in her mind. She saw a girl tall and full-figured, with a firm, fair face, looking fairer and firmer in the moonlight, her strong yellow hair braided in a close knot. A girl full of a calm rustic strength and bloom, with a masterful way which might have beseemed a princess. Lily Dyer was a favorite with the vil-lage folk; she had just the qualities to arouse the admiration. She was good and handsome and smart. Louisa had often heard her praises sounded.

"Well," said Joe Dagget, "I ain't got a word to say."

"I don't know what you could say," returned Lily Dyer.

"Not a word to say," repeated Joe, drawing out the words heavily. Then there was silence. "I ain't sorry," he began at last, "that that happened yes-terday—that we kind of let on how we felt to each other. I guess it's just as well we knew. Of course I can't do anything any different. I'm going right on an' get married next week. I ain't going back on a woman that's waited for me fourteen years, an' break her heart."

"If you should jilt her to-morrow, I wouldn't have you," spoke up the girl, with sudden vehemence.

"Well, I ain't going to give you the chance," said he; "but I don't believe you would, either."

"You'd see I wouldn't. Honor's honor, an' right's right. An' I'd never think anything of any man that went against 'em for me or any other girl; you'd find that out, Joe Dagget."

"Well, you'll find out fast enough that I ain't going against 'em for you or any other girl," returned he. Their voices sounded almost as if they were angry with each other. Louisa was listening eagerly.

"I'm sorry you feel as if you must go away," said Joe, "but I don't know but it's best."

"Of course it's best. I hope you and I have got common-sense."

"Well, I suppose you're right." Suddenly Joe's voice got an undertone of tenderness. "Say, Lily," said he, "I'll get along well enough myself, but I can't bear to think—You don't suppose you're going to fret much over it?"

"I guess you'll find out I sha'n't fret much over a married man."

"Well, I hope you won't—I hope you won't, Lily. God knows I do. And—I hope—one of these days—you'll—come across somebody else—"

"I don't see any reason why I shouldn't." Suddenly her tone changed. She spoke in a sweet, clear voice, so loud that she could have been heard across the street. "No, Joe Dagget," said she, "I'll never marry any other man as long as I live. I've got good sense, an' I ain't going to break my heart nor make a fool of myself; but I'm never going to be married, you can be sure of that. I ain't that sort of a girl to feel this way twice."

Louisa heard an exclamation and a soft commotion behind the bushes; then Lily spoke again—the voice sounded as if she had risen. "This must be put a stop to," said she. "We've stayed here long enough. I'm going home."

Louisa sat there in a daze, listening to their retreating steps. After a while she got up and slunk softly home herself. The next day she did her housework methodically; that was as much a matter of course as breathing; but she did not sew on her wedding-clothes. She sat at her window and meditated. In the evening Joe came. Louisa Ellis had never known that she had any diplomacy in her, but when she came to look for it that night she found it, although meek of its kind, among her little feminine weapons. Even now she could hardly believe that she had heard aright, and that she would not do Joe a terrible injury should she break her troth-plight. She wanted to sound him without betraying too soon her own inclinations in the matter. She did it successfully, and they finally came to an understanding; but it was a difficult thing, for he was as afraid of betraying himself as she.

She never mentioned Lily Dyer. She simply said that while she had no cause of complaint against him, she had lived so long in one way that she shrank from making a change.

"Well, I never shrank, Louisa," said Dagget. "I'm going to be honest enough to say that I think maybe it's better this way; but if you'd wanted to keep on, I'd have stuck to you till my dying day. I hope you know that."

"Yes, I do," said she.

That night she and Joe parted more tenderly than they had done for a long time. Standing in the door, holding each other's hands, a last great wave of regretful memory swept over them.

"Well, this ain't the way we've thought it was all going to end, is it, Louisa?" said Joe.

She shook her head. There was a little quiver on her placid face.

"You let me know if there's ever anything I can do for you," said he. "I ain't ever going to forget you, Louisa." Then he kissed her, and went down the path.

Louisa, all alone by herself that night, wept a little, she hardly knew why; but the next morning, on waking, she felt like a queen who, after fearing lest her domain be wrested away from her, sees it firmly insured in her possession.

Now the tall weeds and grasses might cluster around Cæsar's little hermit hut, the snow might fall on its roof year in and year out, but he never would go on a rampage through the unguarded village. Now the little canary might turn itself into a peaceful yellow ball night after night, and have no need to wake and flutter with wild terror against its bars. Louisa could sew linen seams, and distil roses, and dust and polish and fold away in lavender, as long as she listed. That afternoon she sat with her needle-work at the window, and felt fairly steeped in peace. Lily Dyer, tall and erect and blooming, went past; but she felt no qualm. If Louisa Ellis had sold her birthright she did not know it, the taste of the pottage[4] was so delicious, and had been her sole satisfaction for so long. Serenity and placid narrowness had become to her as the birthright itself. She gazed ahead through a long reach of future days strung together like pearls in a rosary, every one like the others, and all smooth and flawless and innocent, and her heart went up in thankfulness. Outside was the fervid summer afternoon; the air was filled with the sounds of the busy harvest of men and birds and bees; there were halloos, metallic clatterings, sweet calls, and long hummings. Louisa sat, prayerfully numbering her days, like an uncloistered nun.

1891

---

4. In Genesis 25, Esau sells his birthright as oldest son of Isaac and Rebekah to his younger brother Jacob for a bowl of pottage (lentil stew).

BOOKER T. WASHINGTON
1856–1915

Between the last decade of the nineteenth century and the beginning of World War I, no one exercised more influence over race relations in the United States than did Booker Taliaferro Washington; some contemporary historians of the African American experience in America call the period the "Era of Booker T. Washington." Washington's influence continues to the present day. He wanted to help African Americans enter mainstream white society with the least possible violence and thus advocated an educational program of vocational rather than intellectual or professional training. His works have been contrasted with the dynamic and militant efforts of Frederick Douglass (whose successor as African American leader Washington wished to be) and the intellectual and professional initiatives of the fiercely independent W. E. B. Du Bois, but Washington was able to institutionalize his power to a far greater degree than either of these two. He owed no small part of his power to extraordinary skill with written and spoken language. To his sense of calling Washington added the command of memory and the detail of living as a racial "other," all of which he expressed in an unforgettable voice.

Washington's birth date is uncertain; as an adult he selected April 5, 1856. His mother was born a slave in Hale's Ford, Virginia; his father was a white man whose identity is unknown. As a boy, he had, like most slaves, only a first name, and it was not until he entered school that he adopted the surname Washington, which was the first name of Washington Ferguson, a slave whom his mother had married. Washington's account of his early life is a catalog of deprivation and struggle. At the end of the Civil War, when he was nine years old, he accompanied his mother to Malden, West Virginia, to join his stepfather, who had found work there in a salt furnace. From 1865 to 1872, Washington worked as a salt packer, coal miner, and house servant while attending school in the off hours and thus beginning to satisfy his "intense longing" to learn to read and write. In 1872, he set out on a five hundred–mile, month-long journey by rail, cart, and foot to reach Hampton, Virginia, where he would attend the Hampton Normal and Agricultural Institute, a school established by the American Missionary Association to train African Americans as teachers. There Washington paid his way by working as a janitor. In the quasi-military atmosphere of the school, he was drilled in the goals of cleanliness, thrift, and hard work that became central to his life and educational philosophy.

After graduating from Hampton in 1875 with honors and a certificate to teach in a trade school, Washington returned to Malden and found work with a local school. He studied for a while at Wayland Seminary and in 1878 was hired by Samuel Armstrong, the principal of Hampton, to teach in a program for Native Americans. Then, in 1881, he became the first principal of what was to become the Tuskegee Institute, a school established by the Alabama legislature to train African American men and women in agricultural and mechanical trades and teaching. Tuskegee began with thirty students, and Washington, the staff, and the students constructed the school buildings from bricks they made themselves. But through his considerable powers as a conciliator and fund-raiser, and aided by publicity over his goals of instilling Christian virtues and encouraging simple, disciplined living among the students, Washington soon developed Tuskegee into a thriving institution.

Despite this success on the education front, it was not until 1895 that Washington emerged as a national figure. His emergence was the result of a short speech, included below, to a crowd of two thousand at the Atlanta Exposition of 1895. In the speech, popularly known as the "Atlanta Compromise," Washington agreed to defer equal rights for African Americans in return for low-level economic opportunities. This approach appealed to the majority of southern African Americans as well as most whites in the North and the South. A modern reader must understand its appeal in the context of the years between 1885 and 1910, when some thirty-five hundred African Americans were lynched and when, following the end of Reconstruction, most southern states effectively disenfranchised African Americans. Even such militant African American leaders as T. Thomas Fortune and Du Bois praised the speech and supported the philosophy of conciliation that was its pragmatic basis. Their opposition to Washington did not develop until several years later, when they felt it was time to insist on civil, social, and political equality for all African Americans.

In the years following the Atlanta speech, Washington consolidated his position as the "Moses of his race." Nothing did more to enhance this mythic stature than his own brilliant autobiography, *Up from Slavery* (1901), a masterpiece of the genre that was widely praised in the United States and popular in translation around the world. The early chapters reveal the physical and psychological realities of Washington's origins, realities that were shared by so many millions of the slaves set "free" at the conclusion of the Civil War. Later chapters show Washington at the peak of his success as an African American spokesperson, particularly as a master of rhetoric that allowed him to appear both as sincerely humble and as a force to be reckoned with, both as a man of selfless industry and as one of considerable political know-how.

Washington believed in rewarding deserving individuals rather than asking for policies treating African Americans as a population. His writings argue that success should be measured not so much by the position a person has reached as by the obstacles overcome while trying to succeed. In his work he urges African Americans to emulate the proverbial ship captain who urged his crew to "cast down your buckets where you are" even though they were still at sea, and who thus found fresh water at the mouth of a river. "Cast down your bucket where you are" was what he said to urge African Americans to start from wherever they happened to be rather than waiting for times to change. He argued that by seeking improvement African Americans would inevitably rise as individuals. Yet he also urged whites not to judge African American children against white children until they had had a chance to catch up in school. In short, Washington proposed a middle ground wherein African Americans would raise themselves by individual effort and white Americans would appreciate the efforts being made and judge accordingly.

Up from Slavery is as important as a literary production as it is as a record of a time, place, and person. Washington's skillful use of metaphor and symbol, his deftly masked ironies, and the art of his artlessness have been addressed by such critics as William L. Andrews, Houston A. Baker, Jr., and James M. Cox. Over the years, his assimilationist position has drawn criticism, most recently from Baker, but his legacy lives on and continues to inspire readers.

Washington was awarded an honorary degree by Harvard University, was invited to dine by President Theodore Roosevelt, was widely consulted on policy questions by white political and business leaders, effectively influenced the press, and controlled areas of public and private patronage. On November 5, 1915, Washington was taken ill and entered St. Luke's Hospital in New York City; diagnosed with arteriosclerosis, he was told that he did not have long to live. He traveled to Tuskegee, where he died on November 14. Over eight thousand people attended his funeral, which was held in the Tuskegee Institute Chapel.

From Up from Slavery[1]

Chapter XIV. The Atlanta Exposition Address

The Atlanta Exposition, at which I had been asked to make an address as a representative of the Negro race, as stated in the last chapter, was opened with a short address from Governor Bullock. After other interesting exercises, including an invocation from Bishop Nelson, of Georgia, a dedicatory ode by Albert Howell, Jr., and addresses by the President of the Exposition and Mrs. Joseph Thompson, the President of the Woman's Board, Governor Bullock introduced me with the words, "We have with us to-day a representative of Negro enterprise and Negro civilization."

When I arose to speak, there was considerable cheering, especially from the coloured people. As I remember it now, the thing that was uppermost in my mind was the desire to say something that would cement the friendship of the races and bring about hearty coöperation between them. So far as my outward surroundings were concerned, the only thing that I recall distinctly now is that when I got up, I saw thousands of eyes looking intently into my face. The following is the address which I delivered:—

Mr. President and Gentlemen of the Board of Directors and Citizens: One-third of the population of the South is of the Negro race. No

---

1. Published serially in *Outlook* from November 3, 1900, to February 23, 1901, *Up from Slavery* was first published in book form by Doubleday, Page and Company (1901), the source of the text printed here.

enterprise seeking the material, civil, or moral welfare of this section can disregard this element of our population and reach the highest success. I but convey to you, Mr. President and Directors, the sentiment of the masses of my race when I say that in no way have the value and manhood of the American Negro been more fittingly and generously recognized than by the managers of this magnificent Exposition at every stage of its progress. It is a recognition that will do more to cement the friendship of the two races than any occurrence since the dawn of our freedom.

Not only this, but the opportunity here afforded will awaken among us a new era of industrial progress. Ignorant and inexperienced, it is not strange that in the first years of our new life we began at the top instead of at the bottom; that a seat in Congress or the state legislature was more sought than real estate or industrial skill; that the political convention or stump speaking had more attractions than starting a dairy farm or truck garden.

A ship lost at sea for many days suddenly sighted a friendly vessel. From the mast of the unfortunate vessel was seen a signal, "Water, water; we die of thirst!" The answer from the friendly vessel at once came back, "Cast down your bucket where you are." A second time the signal, "Water, water; send us water!" ran up from the distressed vessel, and was answered, "Cast down your bucket where you are." And a third and fourth signal for water was answered, "Cast down your bucket where you are." The captain of the distressed vessel, at last heeding the injunction, cast down his bucket, and it came up full of fresh, sparkling water from the mouth of the Amazon River. To those of my race who depend on bettering their condition in a foreign land or who underestimate the importance of cultivating friendly relations with the Southern white man, who is their next-door neighbour, I would say: "Cast down your bucket where you are"—cast it down in making friends in every manly way of the people of all races by whom we are surrounded.

Cast it down in agriculture, mechanics, in commerce, in domestic service, and in the professions. And in this connection it is well to bear in mind that whatever other sins the South may be called to bear, when it comes to business, pure and simple, it is in the South that the Negro is given a man's chance in the commercial world, and in nothing is this Exposition more eloquent than in emphasizing this chance. Our greatest danger is that in the great leap from slavery to freedom we may overlook the fact that the masses of us are to live by the productions of our hands, and fail to keep in mind that we shall prosper in proportion as we learn to dignify and glorify common labour and put brains and skill into the common occupations of life; shall prosper in proportion as we learn to draw the line between the superficial and the substantial, the ornamental gewgaws of life and the useful. No race can prosper till it learns that there is as much dignity in tilling a field as in writing a poem. It is at the bottom of life we must begin, and not at the top. Nor should we permit our grievances to overshadow our opportunities.

To those of the white race who look to the incoming of those of foreign birth and strange tongue and habits for the prosperity of the South, were I permitted I would repeat what I say to my own race, "Cast down your bucket where you are." Cast it down among the eight millions of Negroes whose habits you know, whose fidelity and love you have tested in days when to have proved treacherous meant the ruin of your firesides. Cast down your bucket among these people who have, without strikes and labour wars, tilled your fields, cleared your forests, builded your railroads and cities, and brought forth treasures from the bowels of the earth, and helped make possible this magnificent representation of the progress of the South. Casting down your bucket among my people, helping and encouraging them as you are doing on these grounds, and to education of head, hand, and heart, and you will find that they will buy your surplus land, make blossom the waste places in your fields, and run your factories. While doing this, you can be sure in the future, as in the past, that you and your families will be surrounded by the most patient, faithful, law-abiding, and unresentful people that the world has seen. As we have proved our loyalty to you in the past, in nursing your children, watching by the sick-bed of your mothers and fathers, and often following them with tear-dimmed eyes to their graves, so in the future, in our humble way, we shall stand by you with a devotion that no foreigner can approach, ready to lay down our lives, if need be, in defence of yours, interlacing our industrial, commercial, civil, and religious life with yours in a way that shall make the interests of both races one. In all things that are purely social we can be as separate as the fingers, yet one as the hand in all things essential to mutual progress.

There is no defence or security for any of us except in the highest intelligence and development of all. If anywhere there are efforts tending to curtail the fullest growth of the Negro, let these efforts be turned into stimulating, encouraging, and making him the most useful and intelligent citizen. Effort or means so invested will pay a thousand per cent interest. These efforts will be twice blessed—"blessing him that gives and him that takes."[2]

There is no escape through law of man or God from the inevitable:—

> "The laws of changeless justice bind
> Oppressor with oppressed;
> And close as sin and suffering joined
> We march to fate abreast."[3]

Nearly sixteen millions of hands will aid you in pulling the load upward, or they will pull against you the load downward. We shall constitute one-third and more of the ignorance and crime of the South, or one-third its intelligence and progress; we shall contribute one-third to the business and industrial prosperity of the South, or we shall prove a veritable body of death, stagnating, depressing, retarding every effort to advance the body politic.

Gentlemen of the Exposition, as we present to you our humble effort at an exhibition of our progress, you must not expect overmuch. Starting thirty years ago with ownership here and there in a few quilts and pumpkins and chickens (gathered from miscellaneous sources), remember the path that has led from these to the inventions and production of agricultural implements, buggies, steam-engines, newspapers, books, statuary, carving, paintings, the management of drug-stores and banks, has

2. "It blesseth him that gives and him that takes" (Shakespeare, *The Merchant of Venice* 3.1.167).   3. John Greenleaf Whittier (1807–1892), "Song of Negro Boatmen."

not been trodden without contact with thorns and thistles. While we take pride in what we exhibit as a result of our independent efforts, we do not for a moment forget that our part in this exhibition would fall far short of your expectations but for the constant help that has come to our educational life, not only from the Southern states, but especially from Northern philanthropists, who have made their gifts a constant stream of blessing and encouragement.

The wisest among my race understand that the agitation of questions of social equality is the extremest folly, and that progress in the enjoyment of all the privileges that will come to us must be the result of severe and constant struggle rather than of artificial forcing. No race that has anything to contribute to the markets of the world is long in any degree ostracized. It is important and right that all privileges of the law be ours, but it is vastly more important that we be prepared for the exercises of these privileges. The opportunity to earn a dollar in a factory just now is worth infinitely more than the opportunity to spend a dollar in an opera-house.

In conclusion, may I repeat that nothing in thirty years has given us more hope and encouragement, and drawn us so near to you of the white race, as this opportunity offered by the Exposition; and here bending, as it were, over the altar that represents the results of the struggles of your race and mine, both starting practically empty-handed three decades ago, I pledge that in your effort to work out the great and intricate problem which God has laid at the doors of the South, you shall have at all times the patient, sympathetic help of my race; only let this be constantly in mind, that, while from representations in these buildings of the product of field, of forest, of mine, of factory, letters, and art, much good will come, yet far above and beyond material benefits will be that higher good, that, let us pray God, will come, in a blotting out of sectional differences and racial animosities and suspicions, in a determination to administer absolute justice, in a willing obedience among all classes to the mandates of law. This, this, coupled with our material prosperity, will bring into our beloved South a new heaven and a new earth.

The first thing that I remember, after I had finished speaking, was that Governor Bullock rushed across the platform and took me by the hand, and that others did the same. I received so many and such hearty congratulations that I found it difficult to get out of the building. I did not appreciate to any degree, however, the impression which my address seemed to have made, until the next morning, when I went into the business part of the city. As soon as I was recognized, I was surprised to find myself pointed out and surrounded by a crowd of men who wished to shake hands with me. This was kept up on every street on to which I went, to an extent which embarrassed me so much that I went back to my boarding-place. The next morning I returned to Tuskegee. At the station in Atlanta, and at almost all of the stations at which the train stopped between the city and Tuskegee, I found a crowd of people anxious to shake hands with me.

The papers in all the parts of the United States published the address in full, and for months afterward there were complimentary editorial references to it. Mr. Clark Howell, the editor of the Atlanta *Constitution*, telegraphed to a New York paper, among other words, the following, "I do not exaggerate when I say that Professor Booker T. Washington's address yesterday was one of the most notable speeches, both as to character and as to the warmth of its reception, ever delivered to a Southern audience. The address was a revelation. The whole speech is a platform upon which blacks and whites can stand with full justice to each other."

The Boston *Transcript* said editorially: "The speech of Booker T. Washington at the Atlanta Exposition, this week, seems to have dwarfed all the other proceedings and the Exposition itself. The sensation that it has caused in the press has never been equalled."

I very soon began receiving all kinds of propositions from lecture bureaus, and editors of magazines and papers, to take the lecture platform, and to write articles. One lecture bureau offered me fifty thousand dollars, or two hundred dollars a night and expenses, if I would place my services at its disposal for a given period. To all these communications I replied that my life-work was at Tuskegee; and that whenever I spoke it must be in the interests of the Tuskegee school and my race, and that I would enter into no arrangements that seemed to place a mere commercial value upon my services.

Some days after its delivery I sent a copy of my address to the President of the United States, the Hon. Grover Cleveland.[4] I received from him the following autograph reply:—

> Gray Gables
> Buzzard's Bay, Mass., October 6, 1895
>
> Booker T. Washington, Esq.:
>
> My Dear Sir: I thank you for sending me a copy of your address delivered at the Atlanta Exposition.
>
> I thank you with much enthusiasm for making the address. I have read it with intense interest, and I think the Exposition would be fully justified if it did not do more than furnish the opportunity for its delivery. Your words cannot fail to delight and encourage all who wish well for your race; and if our coloured fellow-citizens do not from your utterances father new hope and form new determinations to gain every valuable advantage offered them by their citizenship, it will be strange indeed. Yours very truly,
>
> Grover Cleveland

Later I met Mr. Cleveland, for the first time, when, as President, he visited the Atlanta Exposition. At the request of myself and others he consented to spend an hour in the Negro Building, for the purpose of inspecting the Negro exhibit and of giving the coloured people in attendance an opportunity to shake hands with him. As soon as I met Mr. Cleveland I became impressed with his simplicity, greatness, and rugged honesty. I have met him many times since then, both at public functions and at his private residence in Princeton, and the more I see of him the more I admire him. When he visited the Negro Building in Atlanta he seemed to give himself up wholly, for that hour, to the coloured people. He seemed to be as careful to shake hands with some old coloured "auntie" clad partially in rags, and to take as much pleasure in

---

4. Cleveland (1837–1908), twenty-second (1885–89) and twenty-fourth (1893–97) president of the United States.

doing so, as if he were greeting some millionaire. Many of the coloured people took advantage of the occasion to get him to write his name in a book or on a slip of paper. He was as careful and patient in doing this as if he were putting his signature to some great state document.

Mr. Cleveland has not only shown his friendship for me in many personal ways, but has always consented to do anything I have asked of him for our school. This he has done, whether it was to make a personal donation or to use his influence in securing the donations of others. Judging from my personal acquaintance with Mr. Cleveland, I do not believe that he is conscious of possessing any colour prejudice. He is too great for that. In my contact with people I find that, as a rule, it is only the little, narrow people who live for themselves, who never read good books, who do not travel, who never open up their souls in a way to permit them to come into contact with other souls— with the great outside world. No man whose vision is bounded by colour can come into contact with what is highest and best in the world. In meeting men, in many places, I have found that the happiest people are those who do the most for others; the most miserable are those who do the least. I have also found that few things, if any, are capable of making one so blind and narrow as race prejudice. I often say to our students, in the course of my talks to them on Sunday evenings in the chapel, that the longer I live and the more experience I have of the world, the more I am convinced that, after all, the one thing that is most worth living for—and dying for, if need be—is the opportunity of making some one else more happy and more useful.

The coloured people and the coloured newspapers at first seemed to be greatly pleased with the character of my Atlanta address, as well as with its reception. But after the first burst of enthusiasm began to die away, and the coloured people began reading the speech in cold type, some of them seemed to feel that they had been hypnotized. They seemed to feel that I had been too liberal in my remarks toward the Southern whites, and that I had not spoken out strongly enough for what they termed the "rights" of the race. For a while there was a reaction, so far as a certain element of my own race was concerned, but later these reactionary ones seemed to have been won over to my way of believing and acting.

While speaking of changes in public sentiment, I recall that about ten years after the school at Tuskegee was established, I had an experience that I shall never forget. Dr. Lyman Abbott, then the pastor of Plymouth Church, and also editor of the *Outlook* (then the *Christian Union*), asked me to write a letter for his paper giving my opinion of the exact condition, mental and moral of the coloured ministers in the South, as based upon my observations. I wrote the letter, giving the exact facts as I conceived them to be. The picture painted was a rather black one—or, since I am black, shall I say "white"? It could not be otherwise with a race but a few years out of slavery, a race which had not had time or opportunity to produce a competent ministry.

What I said soon reached every Negro minister in the country, I think, and the letters of condemnation which I received from them were not few. I think that for a year after the publication of this article every association and every conference or religious body of any kind, of my race, that met, did not fail before adjourning to pass a resolution condemning me, or calling upon me to retract or modify what I had said. Many of these organizations went so far in their resolutions as to advise parents to cease sending their children to

Tuskegee. One association even appointed a "missionary" whose duty it was to warn the people against sending their children to Tuskegee. This missionary had a son in the school, and I noticed that, whatever the "missionary" might have said or done with regard to others, he was careful not to take his son away from the institution. Many of the coloured papers, especially those that were the organs of religious bodies, joined in the general chorus of condemnation or demands for retraction.

During the whole time of the excitement, and through all the criticism, I did not utter a word of explanation or retraction. I knew that I was right, and that time and the sober second thought of the people would vindicate me. It was not long before the bishops and other church leaders began to make a careful investigation of the conditions of the ministry, and they found out that I was right. In fact, the oldest and most influential bishop in one branch of the Methodist Church said that my words were far too mild. Very soon public sentiment began making itself felt, in demanding a purifying of the ministry. While this is not yet complete by any means, I think I may say, without egotism, and I have been told by many of our most influential ministers, that my words had much to do with starting a demand for the placing of a higher type of men in the pulpit. I have had the satisfaction of having many who once condemned me thank me heartily for my frank words.

The change of the attitude of the Negro ministry, so far as regards myself, is so complete that at the present time I have no warmer friends among any class than I have among the clergymen. The improvement in the character and life of the Negro ministers is one of the most gratifying evidences of the progress of the race. My experience with them, as well as other events in my life, convince me that the thing to do, when one feels sure that he has said or done the right thing, and is condemned, is to stand still and keep quiet. If he is right, time will show it.

In the midst of the discussion which was going on concerning my Atlanta speech, I received a letter which I give below, from Dr. Gilman, the President of Johns Hopkins University, who had been made chairman of the judges of award in connection with the Atlanta Exposition:—

> Johns Hopkins University, Baltimore
> President's Office, September 30, 1895

> Dear Mr. Washington: Would it be agreeable to you to be one of the Judges of Award in the Department of Education at Atlanta? If so, I shall be glad to place your name upon the list. A line by telegraph will be welcomed. Yours very truly,

> D. C. Gilman

I think I was even more surprised to receive this invitation than I had been to receive the invitation to speak at the opening of the Exposition. It was to be a part of my duty, as one of the jurors, to pass not only upon the exhibits of the coloured schools, but also upon those of the white schools. I accepted the position, and spent a month in Atlanta in performance of the duties which it entailed. The board of jurors was a large one, consisting in all of sixty members. It was about equally divided between Southern white people and Northern white people. Among them were college presidents, leading scientists and men of letters, and specialists in many subjects. When the group of jurors to which I was assigned met for organization, Mr. Thomas Nelson Page,[5] who was one of the number, moved that I be made secretary of that division, and the motion was unanimously adopted. Nearly half of our division were Southern people. In performing my duties in the inspection of the exhibits of white schools I was in every case treated with respect, and at the close of our labours I parted from my associates with regret.

I am often asked to express myself more freely than I do upon the political condition and the political future of my race. These recollections of my experience in Atlanta give me the opportunity to do so briefly. My own belief is, although I have never before said so in so many words, that the time will come when the Negro in the South will be accorded all the political rights which his ability, character, and material possessions entitle him to. I think, though, that the opportunity to freely exercise such political rights will not come in any large degree through outside or artificial forcing, but will be accorded to the Negro by the Southern white people themselves, and that they will protect him in the exercise of those rights. Just as soon as the South gets over the old feeling that it is being forced by "foreigners," or "aliens," to do something which it does not want to do, I believe that the change in the direction that I have indicated is going to begin. In fact, there are indications that it is already beginning in a slight degree.

Let me illustrate my meaning. Suppose that some months before the opening of the Atlanta Exposition there had been a general demand from the press and public platform outside the South that a Negro be given a place on the opening programme, and that a Negro be placed upon the board of jurors of award. Would any such recognition of the race have taken place? I do not think so. The Atlanta officials went as far as they did because they felt it to be a pleasure, as well as a duty, to reward what they considered merit in the Negro race. Say what we will, there is something in human nature which we cannot blot out, which makes one man, in the end, recognize and reward merit in another, regardless of colour or race.

I believe it is the duty of the Negro—as the greater part of the race is already doing—to deport himself modestly in regard to political claims, depending upon the slow but sure influences that proceed from the possession of property, intelligence, and high character for the full recognition of his political rights. I think that the according of the full exercise of political rights is going to be a matter of natural, slow growth, not an over-night, gourd-vine affair. I do not believe that the Negro should cease voting, for a man cannot learn the exercise of self-government by ceasing to vote, any more than a boy can learn to swim by keeping out of the water, but I do believe that in his voting he should more and more be influenced by those of intelligence and character who are his next-door neighbours.

I know coloured men who, through the encouragement, help, and advice of Southern white people, have accumulated thousands of dollars' worth of property, but who, at the same time, would never think of going to those same persons for advice concerning the casting of their ballots. This, it seems to me, is unwise and unreasonable, and should cease. In saying this I do not mean that the Negro should truckle, or not vote from principle, for the

5. American author and diplomat (1853–1922).

instant he ceases to vote from principle he loses the confidence and respect of the Southern white man even.

I do not believe that any state should make a law that permits an ignorant and poverty-stricken white man to vote, and prevents a black man in the same condition from voting. Such a law is not only unjust, but it will react, as all unjust laws do, in time; for the effect of such a law is to encourage the Negro to secure education and property, and at the same time it encourages the white man to remain in ignorance and poverty. I believe that in time, through the operation of intelligence and friendly race relations, all cheating at the ballot-box in the South will cease. It will become apparent that the white man who begins by cheating a Negro out of his ballot soon learns to cheat a white man out of his, and that the man who does this ends his career of dishonesty by the theft of property or by some equally serious crime. In my opinion, the time will come when the South will encourage all of its citizens to vote. It will see that it pays better, from every standpoint, to have healthy, vigorous life than to have that political stagnation which always results when one-half of the population has no share and no interest in the Government.

As a rule, I believe in universal, free suffrage, but I believe that in the South we are confronted with peculiar conditions that justify the protection of the ballot in many of the states, for a while at least, either by an educational test, a property test, or by both combined; but whatever tests are required, they should be made to apply with equal and exact justice to both races.

1901

CHARLES W. CHESNUTT
1858–1932

Charles Waddell Chesnutt was born on June 20, 1858, in Cleveland, Ohio. His parents were free-born blacks from North Carolina; his father served in the Union Army and after the Civil War moved his family back to Fayetteville, North Carolina. Chesnutt went to a school established by the Freedman's Bureau during Reconstruction and eventually became a teacher, school principal, newspaper reporter, accountant, court stenographer, and lawyer before he first achieved success as a writer. In 1887 the *Atlantic Monthly* published "The Goophered Grapevine," the first of what was to be a group of stories in the regional-dialect folktale tradition earlier made nationally popular by Joel Chandler Harris. Most readers of the story would have supposed that, like Harris, Chesnutt was white because the stories are framed in the language of an apparently superior and bemused white narrator listening to an old black retainer's folktale. Chesnutt's Uncle Julius, though superficially like Harris's Uncle Remus, is in reality a wise old slave who has learned not only to survive but to use and defeat his supposed superiors through a mocking mask of ignorance. Most of Chesnutt's contemporaries saw the picturesque stereotype of the old slave as an easygoing, shuffling retainer and took pleasure in the authenticity of the language, customs, and settings in the stories; only in recent years, however, have readers had the added satisfaction of perceiving the ironic drama played out between "master" and "slave" underneath Chesnutt's "folktales."

With age and fame Chesnutt became more direct in his critique of "race." Chesnutt was himself very light-skinned but had never tried to hide his racial identity; it was not until 1899, however, the year he began to write full time, that he revealed himself to his readers as a black man. In that year the dialect stories set in rural North Carolina were gathered and published as *The Conjure Woman*. Conjure (or hoodoo) is the name given to a set of folk beliefs combining elements of Caribbean and West African healing and spiritual practices with elements of Christian belief. Practitioners of conjure were thought to know how to get in touch with and direct the powers of nature to make something happen—or to keep something from happening. In addition, two other books appeared: a collection of mostly nondialect and urban stories titled *"The Wife of His Youth" and Other Stories of the Color Line* and a biography, a *Life of Frederick Douglass*. A number of Chesnutt's stories written in the 1890s dealt with the usually disastrous consequences of light-skinned blacks attempting to pass as whites. "The Wife of His Youth," printed here, is, of course, an exception, telling, as it does, of the obligation of upwardly mobile blacks to remember and honor their collective past. A second story from that collection, "The Passing of Grandison," also printed here, uses biting satire to show the narrow limits of white reality.

Chesnutt's first novel, *The House behind the Cedars* (1900), explores the theme of mixed-blood marriages and the troubled psychology of people of mixed race who live in the South. His first important essay, "What Is a White Man?" (1889), points out the practical futility and moral unfairness of laws against interracial marriages. *The Marrow of Tradition* (1901), his most successful novel, exposes the violent social tensions created in a small town in the South by the entrenched traditions of white supremacy and black servitude, culminating in a massacre of blacks based on the Wilmington Riot of 1898. Chesnutt's third novel on the theme of race problems in the post–Civil War South, *The Colonel's Dream* (1905), reveals his increasing pessimism over finding a solution to the pervasive racism of the South. By then, post-Reconstruction Jim Crow practices, the disenfranchisement of black voters, and the widespread use of violence and intimidation against African Americans left scant hope for an early mitigation of racist attitudes in the South.

In 1880, Chesnutt recorded in his journal his youthful ambitions as a writer:

> The object of my writings would be not so much the elevation of the colored people as the elevation of the whites—for I consider the unjust spirit of caste which is so insidious as to pervade a whole nation, and so powerful as to subject a whole race and all connected with it to scorn and social ostracism—I consider this a barrier to the moral progress of the American people; and I would be one of the first to head a determined, organized crusade against it.

Chesnutt became a skillful, original, realistic regionalist who depicted both average southern blacks and those of mixed blood who lived on the color line and were sometimes middle-class. He was also the first African American imaginative writer to be taken seriously by the white press, including William Dean Howells, even when he did not write mere "dialect stories"; finally, as a harbinger of the literature of the "New South," Chesnutt did in fact lead a crusade against racism of the kind he imagined as a young man. His many essays also contributed to his crusade against the stupidity and injustice of racism wherever it was practiced.

Although he wrote sporadically after 1905, Chesnutt never again commanded much of an audience during his lifetime, and by the 1920s he had lost touch both with his white readership and with the dramatic changes being wrought in African American culture by the Harlem Renaissance. Nonetheless, among black writers and intellectuals—and black readers more generally—he was still esteemed as the pioneering writer of fiction who addressed racial issues seriously and sensitively, and in 1928, he received the Spingarn Medal for his groundbreaking contribution to the literary depiction of the "life and struggle of Americans of Negro descent." The ways in which this award was well deserved are only now beginning to be fully understood. In the last twenty years, thanks to the efforts of such scholars as Andrews, Werner Sollors, Joseph R. McElrath, Jr., Richard H. Brodhead, and Eric Sundquist, new editions of Chesnutt's works and critical essays and books on him have multiplied, emphasizing his complex artistry, acute (if often masked) sense of irony, and modernity, whether as naturalist or as existentialist.

The Wife of His Youth[1]

I

Mr. Ryder was going to give a ball. There were several reasons why this was an opportune time for such an event.

Mr. Ryder might aptly be called the dean of the Blue Veins. The original Blue Veins were a little society of colored persons organized in a certain Northern city shortly after the war. Its purpose was to establish and maintain correct social standards among a people whose social condition presented almost unlimited room for improvement. By accident, combined perhaps with some natural affinity, the society consisted of individuals who were, generally speaking, more white than black. Some envious outsider made the suggestion that no one was eligible for membership who was not white enough to show blue veins. The suggestion was readily adopted by those who were not of the favored few, and since that time the society, though possessing a longer and more pretentious name, had been known far and wide as the "Blue Vein Society," and its members as the "Blue Veins."

The Blue Veins did not allow that any such requirement existed for admission to their circle, but, on the contrary, declared that character and culture were the only things considered; and that if most of their members were light-colored, it was because such persons, as a rule, had had better opportunities to qualify themselves for membership. Opinions differed, too, as to the usefulness of the society. There were those who had been known to assail it violently as a glaring example of the very prejudice from which the colored race had suffered most; and later, when such critics had succeeded in getting on the inside, they had been heard to maintain with zeal and earnestness that the society was a life-boat, an anchor, a bulwark and a shield,—a pillar of cloud by day and of fire by night, to guide their people through the social wilderness. Another alleged prerequisite for Blue Vein membership was that of free birth; and while there was really no such requirement, it is doubtless true that very few of the members would have been unable to meet it if there had been. If there were one or two of the older members who had come up from the South and from slavery, their history presented enough romantic circumstances to rob their servile origin of its grosser aspects.

While there were no such tests of eligibility, it is true that the Blue Veins had their notions on these subjects, and that not all of them were equally liberal in regard to the things they collectively disclaimed. Mr. Ryder was one of the most conservative. Though he had not been among the founders of the society, but had come in some years later, his genius for social leadership was such that he

1. First published in the *Atlantic* (July 1898); later reprinted in the collection *"The Wife of His Youth" and Other Stories of the Color Line* (1899), the source of the text printed here.

had speedily become its recognized adviser and head, the custodian of its standards, and the preserver of its traditions. He shaped its social policy, was active in providing for its entertainment, and when the interest fell off, as it sometimes did, he fanned the embers until they burst again into a cheerful flame.

There were still other reasons for his popularity. While he was not as white as some of the Blue Veins, his appearance was such as to confer distinction upon them. His features were of a refined type, his hair was almost straight; he was always neatly dressed; his manners were irreproachable, and his morals above suspicion. He had come to Groveland a young man, and obtaining employment in the office of a railroad company as messenger had in time worked himself up to the position of stationery clerk, having charge of the distribution of the office supplies for the whole company. Although the lack of early training had hindered the orderly development of a naturally fine mind, it had not prevented him from doing a great deal of reading or from forming decidedly literary tastes. Poetry was his passion. He could repeat whole pages of the great English poets; and if his pronunciation was sometimes faulty, his eye, his voice, his gestures, would respond to the changing sentiment with a precision that revealed a poetic soul and disarmed criticism. He was economical, and had saved money; he owned and occupied a very comfortable house on a respectable street. His residence was handsomely furnished, containing among other things a good library, especially rich in poetry, a piano, and some choice engravings. He generally shared his house with some young couple, who looked after his wants and were company for him; for Mr. Ryder was a single man. In the early days of his connection with the Blue Veins he had been regarded as quite a catch, and young ladies and their mothers had manœuvred with much ingenuity to capture him. Not, however, until Mrs. Molly Dixon visited Groveland had any woman ever made him wish to change his condition to that of a married man.

Mrs. Dixon had come to Groveland from Washington in the spring, and before the summer was over she had won Mr. Ryder's heart. She possessed many attractive qualities. She was much younger than he; in fact, he was old enough to have been her father, though no one knew exactly how old he was. She was whiter than he, and better educated. She had moved in the best colored society of the country, at Washington, and had taught in the schools of that city. Such a superior person had been eagerly welcomed to the Blue Vein Society, and had taken a leading part in its activities. Mr. Ryder had at first been attracted by her charms of person, for she was very good looking and not over twenty-five; then by her refined manners and the vivacity of her wit. Her husband had been a government clerk, and at his death had left a considerable life insurance. She was visiting friends in Groveland, and, finding the town and the people to her liking, had prolonged her stay indefinitely. She had not seemed displeased at Mr. Ryder's attentions, but on the contrary had given him every proper encouragement; indeed, a younger and less cautious man would long since have spoken. But he had made up his mind, and had only to determine the time when he would ask her to be his wife. He decided to give a ball in her honor, and at some time during the evening of the ball to offer her his heart and hand. He had no special fears about the outcome, but, with a little touch of romance, he wanted the surroundings to be in harmony with his own feelings when he should have received the answer he expected.

Mr. Ryder resolved that this ball should mark an epoch in the social history of Groveland. He knew, of course,—no one could know better,—the entertainments that had taken place in past years, and what must be done to surpass them. His ball must be worthy of the lady in whose honor it was to be given, and must, by the quality of its guests, set an example for the future. He had observed of late a growing liberality, almost a laxity, in social matters, even among members of his own set, and had several times been forced to meet in a social way persons whose complexions and callings in life were hardly up to the standard which he considered proper for the society to maintain. He had a theory of his own.

"I have no race prejudice," he would say, "but we people of mixed blood are ground between the upper and the nether millstone. Our fate lies between absorption by the white race and extinction in the black. The one doesn't want us yet, but may take us in time. The other would welcome us, but it would be for us a backward step. 'With malice towards none, with charity for all,'[2] we must do the best we can for ourselves and those who are to follow us. Self-preservation is the first law of nature."

His ball would serve by its exclusiveness to counteract leveling tendencies, and his marriage with Mrs. Dixon would help to further the upward process of absorption he had been wishing and waiting for.

II

The ball was to take place on Friday night. The house had been put in order, the carpets covered with canvas, the halls and stairs decorated with palms and potted plants; and in the afternoon Mr. Ryder sat on his front porch, which the shade of a vine running up over a wire netting made a cool and pleasant lounging place. He expected to respond to the toast "The Ladies" at the supper, and from a volume of Tennyson—his favorite poet— was fortifying himself with apt quotations. The volume was open at "A Dream of Fair Women."[3] His eyes fell on these lines, and he read them aloud to judge better of their effect:—

> "At length I saw a lady within call,
> Stiller than chisell'd marble, standing there;
> A daughter of the gods, divinely tall,
> And most divinely fair."

He marked the verse, and turning the page read the stanza beginning,—

> "O sweet pale Margaret,
> O rare pale Margaret."[4]

He weighed the passage a moment, and decided that it would not do. Mrs. Dixon was the palest lady he expected at the ball, and she was of a rather ruddy complexion, and of lively disposition and buxom build. So he ran over the leaves until his eye rested on the description of Queen Guinevere:[5]—

2. From Abraham Lincoln's second inaugural address (1865).
3. This poem, by English poet Alfred, Lord Tennyson (1809–1892), was published in 1832.
4. By Tennyson, "Margaret" was published in 1832.
5. Wife of the legendary King Arthur, described in the following quotation from Tennyson's "Sir Launcelot and Queen Guinevere" (1842).

> "She seem'd a part of joyous Spring:
> A gown of grass-green silk she wore,
> Buckled with golden clasps before;
> A light-green tuft of plumes she bore
> Closed in a golden ring.

• • • • •

> "She look'd so lovely, as she sway'd
> The rein with dainty finger-tips,
> A man had given all other bliss,
> And all his worldly worth for this,
> To waste his whole heart in one kiss
> Upon her perfect lips."

As Mr. Ryder murmured these words audibly, with an appreciative thrill, he heard the latch of his gate click, and a light foot-fall sounding on the steps. He turned his head, and saw a woman standing before his door.

She was a little woman, not five feet tall, and proportioned to her height. Although she stood erect, and looked around her with very bright and restless eyes, she seemed quite old; for her face was crossed and recrossed with a hundred wrinkles, and around the edges of her bonnet could be seen protruding here and there a tuft of short gray wool. She wore a blue calico gown of ancient cut, a little red shawl fastened around her shoulders with an old-fashioned brass brooch, and a large bonnet profusely ornamented with faded red and yellow artificial flowers. And she was very black,—so black that her toothless gums, revealed when she opened her mouth to speak, were not red, but blue. She looked like a bit of the old plantation life, summoned up from the past by the wave of a magician's wand, as the poet's fancy had called into being the gracious shapes of which Mr. Ryder had just been reading.

He rose from his chair and came over to where she stood.

"Good-afternoon, madam," he said.

"Good-evenin', suh," she answered, ducking suddenly with a quaint curtsy. Her voice was shrill and piping, but softened somewhat by age. "Is dis yere whar Mistuh Ryduh lib, suh?" she asked, looking around her doubtfully, and glancing into the open windows, through which some of the preparations for the evening were visible.

"Yes," he replied, with an air of kindly patronage, unconsciously flattered by her manner, "I am Mr. Ryder. Did you want to see me?"

"Yas, suh, ef I ain't 'sturbin' of you too much."

"Not at all. Have a seat over here behind the vine, where it is cool. What can I do for you?"

" 'Scuse me, suh," she continued, when she had sat down on the edge of a chair, " 'scuse me, suh, I's lookin' for my husban'. I heerd you wuz a big man an' had libbed heah a long time, an' I 'lowed you wouldn't min' ef I'd come roun' an' ax you ef you'd ever heerd of a merlatter[6] man by de name er Sam Taylor 'quirin' roun' in de chu'ches ermongs' de people fer his wife 'Liza Jane?"

Mr. Ryder seemed to think for a moment.

6. Mulatto.

"There used to be many such cases right after the war," he said, "but it has been so long that I have forgotten them. There are very few now. But tell me your story, and it may refresh my memory."

She sat back farther in her chair so as to be more comfortable, and folded her withered hands in her lap.

"My name's 'Liza," she began, " 'Liza Jane. W'en I wuz young I us'ter b'long ter Marse Bob Smif, down in ole Missoura. I wuz bawn down dere. W'en I wuz a gal I wuz married ter a man named Jim. But Jim died, an' after dat I married a merlatter man named Sam Taylor. Sam wuz free-bawn, but his mammy and daddy died, an' de w'ite folks 'prenticed him ter my marster fer ter work fer 'im 'tel he wuz growed up. Sam worked in de fiel', an' I wuz de cook. One day Ma'y Ann, ole miss's maid, came rushin' out ter de kitchen, an' says she, ' 'Liza Jane, ole marse gwine sell yo' Sam down de ribber.'

" 'Go way f'm yere,' says I; 'my husban' 's free!'

" 'Don' make no diff'ence. I heerd ole marse tell ole miss he wuz gwine take yo' Sam 'way wid 'im ter-morrow, fer he needed money, an' he knowed whar he could git a t'ousan' dollars fer Sam an' no questions axed.'

"W'en Sam come home f'm de fiel' dat night, I tole him 'bout ole marse gwine steal 'im, an' Sam run erway. His time wuz mos' up, an' he swo' dat w'en he wuz twenty-one he would come back an' he'p me run erway, er else save up de money ter buy my freedom. An' I know he'd 'a' done it, fer he thought a heap er me, Sam did. But w'en he come back he didn' fin' me, fer I wuzn' dere. Ole marse had heerd dat I warned Sam, so he had me whip' an' sol' down de ribber.

"Den de wah broke out, an' w'en it wuz ober de cullud folks wuz scattered. I went back ter de ole home; but Sam wuzn' dere, an' I couldn' l'arn nuffin' 'bout 'im. But I knowed he'd be'n dere to look for me an' hadn' foun' me, an' had gone erway ter hunt fer me.

"I's be'n lookin' fer 'im eber sence," she added simply, as though twenty-five years were but a couple of weeks, "an' I knows he's be'n lookin' fer me. Fer he sot a heap er sto' by me, Sam did, an' I know he's be'n huntin' fer me all dese years,—'less'n he's be'n sick er sump'n, so he couldn' work, er out'n his head, so he couldn' 'member his promise. I went back down de ribber, fer I 'lowed he'd gone down dere lookin' fer me. I's be'n ter Noo Orleens, an' Atlanty, an' Charleston, an' Richmon'; an' w'en I'd be'n all ober de Souf I come ter de Norf. Fer I knows I'll fin' 'im some er dese days," she added softly, "er he'll fin' me, an' den we'll bofe be as happy in freedom as we wuz in de ole days befo' de wah." A smile stole over her withered countenance as she paused a moment, and her bright eyes softened into a far-away look.

This was the substance of the old woman's story. She had wandered a little here and there. Mr. Ryder was looking at her curiously when she finished.

"How have you lived all these years?" he asked.

"Cookin', suh. I's a good cook. Does you know anybody w'at needs a good cook, suh? I's stoppin' wid a cullud fam'ly round' de corner yonder 'tel I kin git a place."

"Do you really expect to find your husband? He may be dead long ago."

She shook her head emphatically. "Oh no, he ain' dead. De signs an' de tokens tells me. I dremp three nights runnin' on'y dis las' week dat I foun' him."

"He may have married another woman. Your slave marriage would not have

prevented him, for you never lived with him after the war, and without that
your marriage doesn't count."

"Wouldn' make no diff'ence wid Sam. He wouldn' marry no yuther 'ooman
'tel he foun' out 'bout me. I knows it," she added. "Sump'n's be'n tellin' me all
dese years dat I's gwine fin' Sam 'fo' I dies."

"Perhaps he's outgrown you, and climbed up in the world where he wouldn't
care to have you find him."

"No, indeed, suh," she replied, "Sam ain' dat kin' er man. He wuz good ter
me, Sam wuz, but he wuzn' much good ter nobody e'se, fer he wuz one er de
triflin'es' han's on de plantation. I 'spec's ter haf ter suppo't 'im w'en I fin' 'im,
fer he nebber would work 'less'n he had ter. But den he wuz free, an' he didn'
git no pay fer his work, an' I don' blame 'im much. Mebbe he's done better
sence he run erway, but I ain' 'spectin' much."

"You may have passed him on the street a hundred times during the twenty-
five years, and not have known him; time works great changes."

She smiled incredulously. "I'd know 'im 'mongs' a hund'ed men. Fer dey
wuz n' no yuther merlatter man like my man Sam, an' I couldn' be mistook.
I's toted his picture roun' wid me twenty-five years."

"May I see it?" asked Mr. Ryder. "It might help me to remember whether I
have seen the original."

As she drew a small parcel from her bosom he saw that it was fastened to
a string that went around her neck. Removing several wrappers, she brought
to light an old-fashioned daguerreotype in a black case. He looked long and
intently at the portrait. It was faded with time, but the features were still distinct, and it was easy to see what manner of man it had represented.

He closed the case, and with a slow movement handed it back to her.

"I don't know of any man in town who goes by that name," he said, "nor
have I heard of any one making such inquiries. But if you will leave me your
address, I will give the matter some attention, and if I find out anything I will
let you know."

She gave him the number of a house in the neighborhood, and went away,
after thanking him warmly.

He wrote the address on the fly-leaf of the volume of Tennyson, and, when
she had gone, rose to his feet and stood looking after her curiously. As she
walked down the street with mincing step, he saw several persons whom she
passed turn and look back at her with a smile of kindly amusement. When
she had turned the corner, he went upstairs to his bedroom, and stood for a
long time before the mirror of his dressing-case, gazing thoughtfully at the
reflection of his own face.

III

At eight o'clock the ballroom was a blaze of light and the guests had begun
to assemble; for there was a literary programme and some routine business
of the society to be gone through with before the dancing. A black servant in
evening dress waited at the door and directed the guests to the dressing-
rooms.

The occasion was long memorable among the colored people of the city;
not alone for the dress and display, but for the high average of intelligence

and culture that distinguished the gathering as a whole. There were a number of school-teachers, several young doctors, three or four lawyers, some professional singers, an editor, a lieutenant in the United States army spending his furlough in the city, and others in various polite callings; these were colored, though most of them would not have attracted even a casual glance because of any marked difference from white people. Most of the ladies were in evening costume, and dress coats and dancing pumps were the rule among the men. A band of string music, stationed in an alcove behind a row of palms, played popular airs while the guests were gathering.

The dancing began at half past nine. At eleven o'clock supper was served. Mr. Ryder had left the ballroom some little time before the intermission, but reappeared at the supper-table. The spread was worthy of the occasion, and the guests did full justice to it. When the coffee had been served, the toast-master, Mr. Solomon Sadler, rapped for order. He made a brief introductory speech, complimenting host and guests, and then presented in their order the toasts of the evening. They were responded to with a very fair display of after-dinner wit.

"The last toast," said the toast-master, when he reached the end of the list, "is one which must appeal to us all. There is no one of us of the sterner sex who is not at some time dependent upon woman,—in infancy for protection, in manhood for companionship, in old age for care and comforting. Our good host has been trying to live alone, but the fair faces I see around me to-night prove that he too is largely dependent upon the gentler sex for most that makes life worth living,—the society and love of friends,—and rumor is at fault if he does not soon yield entire subjection to one of them. Mr. Ryder will now respond to the toast,—The Ladies."

There was a pensive look in Mr. Ryder's eyes as he took the floor and adjusted his eye-glasses. He began by speaking of woman as the gift of Heaven to man, and after some general observations on the relations of the sexes he said: "But perhaps the quality which most distinguishes woman is her fidelity and devotion to those she loves. History is full of examples, but has recorded none more striking than one which only to-day came under my notice."

He then related, simply but effectively, the story told by his visitor of the afternoon. He gave it in the same soft dialect, which came readily to his lips, while the company listened attentively and sympathetically. For the story had awakened a responsive thrill in many hearts. There were some present who had seen, and others who had heard their fathers and grandfathers tell, the wrongs and sufferings of this past generation, and all of them still felt, in their darker moments, the shadow hanging over them. Mr. Ryder went on:—

"Such devotion and confidence are rare even among women. There are many who would have searched a year, some who would have waited five years, a few who might have hoped ten years; but for twenty-five years this woman has retained her affection for and her faith in a man she has not seen or heard of in all that time.

"She came to me to-day in the hope that I might be able to help her find this long-lost husband. And when she was gone I gave my fancy rein, and imagined a case I will put to you.

"Suppose that this husband, soon after his escape, had learned that his wife had been sold away, and that such inquiries as he could make brought no information of her whereabouts. Suppose that he was young, and she much older than he; that he was light, and she was black; that their marriage was a slave marriage, and legally binding only if they chose to make it so after the war. Suppose, too, that he made his way to the North, as some of us have done, and there, where he had larger opportunities, had improved them, and had in the course of all these years grown to be as different from the ignorant boy who ran away from fear of slavery as the day is from the night. Suppose, even, that he had qualified himself, by industry, by thrift, and by study, to win the friendship and be considered worthy the society of such people as these I see around me to-night, gracing my board and filling my heart with gladness; for I am old enough to remember the day when such a gathering would not have been possible in this land. Suppose, too, that, as the years went by, this man's memory of the past grew more and more indistinct, until at last it was rarely, except in his dreams, that any image of this bygone period rose before his mind. And then suppose that accident should bring to his knowledge the fact that the wife of his youth, the wife he had left behind him,—not one who had walked by his side and kept pace with him in his upward struggle, but one upon whom advancing years and a laborious life had set their mark,—was alive and seeking him, but that he was absolutely safe from recognition or discovery, unless he chose to reveal himself. My friends, what would the man do? I will presume that he was one who loved honor, and tried to deal justly with all men. I will even carry the case further, and suppose that perhaps he had set his heart upon another, whom he had hoped to call his own. What would he do, or rather what ought he to do, in such a crisis of a lifetime?

"It seemed to me that he might hesitate, and I imagined that I was an old friend, a near friend, and that he had come to me for advice; and I argued the case with him. I tried to discuss it impartially. After we had looked upon the matter from every point of view, I said to him, in words that we all know:—

> "This above all: to thine own self be true,
> And it must follow, as the night the day,
> Thou canst not then be false to any man."[7]

Then, finally, I put the question to him, 'Shall you acknowledge her?'

"And now, ladies and gentlemen, friends and companions, I ask you, what should he have done?"

There was something in Mr. Ryder's voice that stirred the hearts of those who sat around him. It suggested more than mere sympathy with an imaginary situation; it seemed rather in the nature of a personal appeal. It was observed, too, that his look rested more especially upon Mrs. Dixon, with a mingled expression of renunciation and inquiry.

She had listened, with parted lips and streaming eyes. She was the first to speak: "He should have acknowledged her."

"Yes," they all echoed, "he should have acknowledged her."

"My friends and companions," responded Mr. Ryder, "I thank you, one and all. It is the answer I expected, for I knew your hearts."

7. Shakespeare, *Hamlet* 1.3.

He turned and walked toward the closed door of an adjoining room, while every eye followed him in wondering curiosity. He came back in a moment, leading by the hand his visitor of the afternoon, who stood startled and trembling at the sudden plunge into this scene of brilliant gayety. She was neatly dressed in gray, and wore the white cap of an elderly woman.

"Ladies and gentlemen," he said, "this is the woman, and I am the man, whose story I have told you. Permit me to introduce to you the wife of my youth."

1899

The Passing of Grandison[1]

I

When it is said that it was done to please a woman, there ought perhaps to be enough said to explain anything; for what a man will not do to please a woman is yet to be discovered. Nevertheless, it might be well to state a few preliminary facts to make it clear why young Dick Owens tried to run one of his father's negro men off to Canada.

In the early fifties, when the growth of anti-slavery sentiment and the constant drain of fugitive slaves into the North had so alarmed the slave-holders of the border states as to lead to the passage of the Fugitive Slave Law,[2] a young white man from Ohio, moved by compassion for the sufferings of a certain bondman who happened to have a "hard master," essayed to help the slave to freedom. The attempt was discovered and frustrated; the abductor was tried and convicted for slave-stealing, and sentenced to a term of imprisonment in the penitentiary. His death, after the expiration of only a small part of the sentence, from cholera contracted while nursing stricken fellow prisoners, lent to the case a melancholy interest that made it famous in anti-slavery annals.

Dick Owens had attended the trial. He was a youth of about twenty-two, intelligent, handsome, and amiable, but extremely indolent, in a graceful and gentlemanly way; or, as old Judge Fenderson put it more than once, he was lazy as the Devil,—a mere figure of speech, of course, and not one that did justice to the Enemy of Mankind. When asked why he never did anything serious, Dick would good-naturedly reply, with a well-modulated drawl, that he didn't have to. His father was rich; there was but one other child, an unmarried daughter, who because of poor health would probably never marry, and Dick was therefore heir presumptive to a large estate. Wealth or social position he did not need to seek, for he was born to both. Charity Lomax had shamed him into studying law, but notwithstanding an hour or so a day spent at old Judge Fenderson's office, he did not make remarkable headway in his legal studies.

"What Dick needs," said the judge, who was fond of tropes, as became a

1. First published in "The Wife of His Youth" and Other Stories of the Color Line (1901); rpt. in Southern Local Color: Stories of Region, Race, and Gender, ed. Barbara C. Ewell and Pamela Glenn Menke (2002), from which this text and some information from annotations are taken.
2. Part of the Compromise of 1850, the Fugitive Slave Law mandated the return to their owners of slaves who had escaped to free states.

scholar, and of horses, as was befitting a Kentuckian, "is the whip of necessity, or the spur of ambition. If he had either, he would soon need the snaffle[3] to hold him back."

But all Dick required, in fact, to prompt him to the most remarkable thing he accomplished before he was twenty-five, was a mere suggestion from Charity Lomax. The story was never really known to but two persons until after the war, when it came out because it was a good story and there was no particular reason for its concealment.

Young Owens had attended the trial of this slave-stealer, or martyr,—either or both,—and, when it was over, had gone to call on Charity Lomax, and, while they sat on the veranda after sundown, had told her all about the trial. He was a good talker, as his career in later years disclosed, and described the proceedings very graphically.

"I confess," he admitted, "that while my principles were against the prisoner, my sympathies were on his side. It appeared that he was of good family, and that he had an old father and mother, respectable people, dependent upon him for support and comfort in their declining years. He had been led into the matter by pity for a negro whose master ought to have been run out of the county long ago for abusing his slaves. If it had been merely a question of old Sam Briggs's negro, nobody would have cared anything about it. But father and the rest of them stood on the principle of the thing, and told the judge so, and the fellow was sentenced to three years in the penitentiary."

Miss Lomax had listened with lively interest.

"I've always hated old Sam Briggs," she said emphatically, "ever since the time he broke a negro's leg with a piece of cordwood. When I hear of a cruel deed it makes the Quaker blood that came from my grandmother assert itself. Personally I wish that all Sam Briggs's negroes would run away. As for the young man, I regard him as a hero. He dared something for humanity. I could love a man who would take such chances for the sake of others."

"Could you love me, Charity, if I did something heroic?"

"You never will, Dick. You're too lazy for any use. You'll never do anything harder than playing cards or fox-hunting."

"Oh, come now, sweetheart! I've been courting you for a year, and it's the hardest work imaginable. Are you never going to love me?" he pleaded.

His hand sought hers, but she drew it back beyond his reach.

"I'll never love you, Dick Owens, until you have done something. When that time comes, I'll think about it."

"But it takes so long to do anything worth mentioning, and I don't want to wait. One must read two years to become a lawyer, and work five more to make a reputation. We shall both be gray by then."

"Oh, I don't know," she rejoined. "it doesn't require a lifetime for a man to prove that he is a man. This one did something, or at least tried to."

"Well, I'm willing to attempt as much as any other man. What do you want me to do, sweetheart? Give me a test."

"Oh, dear me!" said Charity, "I don't care what you *do*, so you do *something*. Really, come to think of it, why should I care whether you do anything or not?"

"I'm sure I don't know why you should, Charity," rejoined Dick humbly, "for I'm aware that I'm not worthy of it."

---

3. Bit or restraint for a horse.

"Except that I do hate," she added, relenting slightly, "to see a really clever man so utterly lazy and good for nothing."

"Thank you, my dear; a word of praise from you has sharpened my wits already. I have an idea! Will you love me if *I* run a negro off to Canada?"

"What nonsense!" said Charity scornfully. "You must be losing your wits. Steal another man's slave, indeed, while your father owns a hundred!"

"Oh, there'll be no trouble about that," responded Dick lightly; "I'll run off one of the old man's; we've got too many anyway. It may not be quite as difficult as the other man found it, but it will be just as unlawful, and will demonstrate what I am capable of."

"Seeing's believing," replied Charity. "Of course, what you are talking about now is merely absurd. I'm going away for three weeks, to visit my aunt in Tennessee. If you are able to tell me, when I return, that you've done something to prove your quality, I'll—well, you may come and tell me about it."

II

Young Owens got up about nine o'clock next morning, and while making his toilet put some questions to his personal attendant, a rather bright looking young mulatto of about his own age.

"Tom," said Dick.

"Yas, Mars Dick," responded the servant.

"I'm going on a trip North. Would you like to go with me?"

Now, if there was anything that Tom would have liked to make, it was a trip North. It was something he had long contemplated in the abstract, but had never been able to muster up sufficient courage to attempt in the concrete. He was prudent enough, however, to dissemble his feelings.

"I wouldn't min' it, Mars Dick, ez long ez you'd take keer er me an' fetch me home all right."

Tom's eyes belied his words, however, and his young master felt well assured that Tom needed only a good opportunity to make him run away. Having a comfortable home, and a dismal prospect in case of failure, Tom was not likely to take any desperate chances; but young Owens was satisfied that in a free state but little persuasion would be required to lead Tom astray. With a very logical and characteristic desire to gain his end with the least necessary expenditure of effort, he decided to take Tom with him, if his father did not object.

Colonel Owens had left the house when Dick went to breakfast, so Dick did not see his father till luncheon.

"Father," he remarked casually to the colonel over the fried chicken, "I'm feeling a trifle run down. I imagine my health would be improved somewhat by a little travel and change of scene."

"Why don't you take a trip North?" suggested his father. The colonel added to paternal affection a considerable respect for his son as the heir of a large estate. He himself had been "raised" in comparative poverty, and had laid the foundations of his fortune by hard work; and while he despised the ladder by which he had climbed, he could not entirely forget it, and unconsciously manifested, in his intercourse with his son, some of the poor man's deference toward the wealthy and well-born.

"I think I'll adopt your suggestion, sir," replied the son, "and run up to New

York; and after I've been there awhile I may go on to Boston for a week or so. I've never been there, you know."

"There are some matters you can talk over with my factor[4] in New York," rejoined the colonel, "and while you are up there among the Yankees, I hope you'll keep your eyes and ears open to find out what the rascally abolitionists[5] are saying and doing. They're becoming altogether too active for our comfort, and entirely too many ungrateful niggers are running away. I hope the conviction of that fellow yesterday may discourage the rest of the breed. I'd just like to catch any one trying to run off one of my darkeys. He'd get short shrift; I don't think any Court would have a chance to try him."

"They are a pestiferous lot," assented Dick, "and dangerous to our institutions. But say, father, if I go North I shall want to take Tom with me."

Now, the colonel, while a very indulgent father, had pronounced views on the subject of negroes, having studied them, as he often said, for a great many years, and, as he asserted oftener still, understanding them perfectly. It is scarcely worth while to say, either, that he valued more highly than if he had inherited them the slaves he had toiled and schemed for.

"I don't think it safe to take Tom up North," he declared, with promptness and decision. "He's a good enough boy, but too smart to trust among those low-down abolitionists. I strongly suspect him of having learned to read, though I can't imagine how. I saw him with a newspaper the other day, and while he pretended to be looking at a woodcut, I'm almost sure he was reading the paper. I think it by no means safe to take him."

Dick did not insist, because he knew it was useless. The colonel would have obliged his son in any other matter, but his negroes were the outward and visible sign of his wealth and station, and therefore sacred to him.

"Whom do you think it safe to take?" asked Dick. "I suppose I'll have to have a body-servant."

"What's the matter with Grandison?" suggested the colonel. "He's handy enough, and I reckon we can trust him. He's too fond of good eating to risk losing his regular meals; besides, he's sweet on your mother's maid, Betty, and I've promised to let 'em get married before long. I'll have Grandison up, and we'll talk to him. Here, you boy Jack," called the colonel to a yellow[6] youth in the next room who was catching flies and pulling their wings off to pass the time, "go down to the barn and tell Grandison to come here."

"Grandison," said the colonel, when the negro stood before him, hat in hand.

"Yas, marster."

"Haven't I always treated you right?"

"Yas, marster."

"Haven't you always got all you wanted to eat?"

"Yas, marster."

"And as much whiskey and tobacco as was good for you, Grandison?"

"Y-a-s, marster."

"I should just like to know, Grandison, whether you don't think yourself a great deal better off than those poor free negroes down by the plank road,

---

4. An agent for the sale of goods entrusted to his possession—in this case, a cotton factor.
5. Abolitionists argued for immediate emancipation of all slaves in the United States.
6. Refers to a light-complexioned person of mixed race who can sometimes "pass" for white.

with no kind master to look after them and no mistress to give them medicine when they're sick and—and—"

"Well, I sh'd jes' reckon I is better off, suh, dan dem low-down free niggers, suh! Ef anybody ax 'em who dey b'long ter, dey has ter say nobody, er e'se lie erbout it. Anybody ax me who I b'longs ter, I ain' got no 'casion ter be shame' ter tell 'em, no, suh, 'deed I ain', suh!"

The colonel was beaming. This was true gratitude, and his feudal heart thrilled at such appreciative homage. What cold-blooded, heartless monsters they were who would break up this blissful relationship of kindly protection on the one hand, of wise subordination and loyal dependence on the other! The colonel always became indignant at the mere thought of such wickedness.

"Grandison," the colonel continued, "your young master Dick is going North for a few weeks, and I am thinking of letting him take you along. I shall send you on this trip, Grandison, in order that you may take care of your young master. He will need some one to wait on him, and no one can ever do it so well as one of the boys brought up with him on the old plantation. I am going to trust him in your hands, and I'm sure you'll do your duty faithfully, and bring him back home safe and sound—to old Kentucky."

Grandison grinned. "Oh yas, marster, I'll take keer er young Mars Dick."

"I want to warn you, though, Grandison," continued the colonel impressively, "against these cussed abolitionists, who try to entice servants from their comfortable homes and their indulgent masters, from the blue skies, the green fields, and the warm sunlight of their southern home, and send them away off yonder to Canada, a dreary country, where the woods are full of wildcats and wolves and bears, where the snow lies up to the eaves of the houses for six months of the year, and the cold is so severe that it freezes your breath and curdles your blood; and where, when runaway niggers get sick and can't work, they are turned out to starve and die, unloved and uncared for. I reckon, Grandison, that you have too much sense to permit yourself to be led astray by any such foolish and wicked people."

" 'Deed, suh, I would n' low none er dem cussed, low-down abolitioners ter come nigh me, suh. I'd—I'd—would I be 'lowed ter hit 'em, suh?"

"Certainly, Grandison," replied the colonel, chuckling, "hit 'em, as hard as you can. I reckon they'd rather like it. Begad, I believe they would! It would serve 'em right to be hit by a nigger!"

"Er ef I did n't hit 'em, suh," continued Grandison reflectively, "I'd tell Mars Dick, en *he'd* fix 'em. He'd smash de face off'n 'em, suh, I jes' knows he would."

"Oh yes, Grandison, your young master will protect you. You need fear no harm while he is near."

"Dey won't try ter steal me, will dey, marster?" asked the negro, with sudden alarm.

"I don't know, Grandison," replied the colonel, lighting a fresh cigar. "They're a desperate set of lunatics, and there's no telling what they may resort to. But if you stick close to your young master, and remember always that he is your best friend, and understands your real needs, and has your true interests at heart, and if you will be careful to avoid strangers who try to talk to you, you'll stand a fair chance of getting back to your home and your friends. And if you please your master Dick, he'll buy you a present, and a string of beads for Betty to wear when you and she get married in the fall."

"Thanky, marster, thanky, suh," replied Grandison, oozing gratitude at every pore; "you is a good marster, to be sho', suh; yas, 'deed you is. You kin jes' bet me and Mars Dick gwine git 'long jes' lack I wuz own boy ter Mars Dick. En it won't be my fault ef he don' want me fer his boy all de time, w'en we come back home ag'in."

"All right, Grandison, you may go now. You needn't work any more today, and here's a piece of tobacco for you off my own plug."

"Thanky, marster, thanky, marster! You is de bes' marster any nigger ever had in dis worl'." And Grandison bowed and scraped and disappeared round the corner, his jaws closing around a large section of the colonel's best tobacco.

"You may take Grandison," said the colonel to his son. "I allow he's abolitionist-proof."

III

Richard Owens, Esq., and servant, from Kentucky, registered at the fashionable New York hostelry for Southerners in those days, a hotel where an atmosphere congenial to Southern institutions was sedulously maintained. But there were negro waiters in the dining-room, and mulatto bell-boys, and Dick had no doubt that Grandison, with the native gregariousness and garrulousness of his race, would foregather and palaver with them, sooner or later, and Dick hoped that they would speedily inoculate him with the virus of freedom. For it was not Dick's intention to say anything to his servant about his plan to free him, for obvious reasons. To mention one of them, if Grandison should go away, and by legal process be recaptured, his young master's part in the matter would doubtless become known, which would be embarrassing to Dick, to say the least. If, on the other hand, he should merely give Grandison sufficient latitude, he had no doubt he would eventually lose him. For while not exactly skeptical about Grandison's perfervid loyalty, Dick had been a somewhat keen observer of human nature, in his own indolent way, and based his expectations upon the force of the example and argument that his servant could scarcely fail to encounter. Grandison should have a fair chance to become free by his own initiative; if it should become necessary to adopt other measures to get rid of him, it would be time enough to act when the necessity arose; and Dick Owens was not the youth to take needless trouble.

The young master renewed some acquaintances and made others, and spent a week or two very pleasantly in the best society of the metropolis, easily accessible to a wealthy, well-bred young Southerner, with proper introductions. Young women smiled on him and young men of convivial habits pressed their hospitalities; but the memory of Charity's sweet, strong face and clear blue eyes made him proof against the blandishments of the one sex and the persuasions of the other. Meanwhile he kept Grandison supplied with pocket-money, and left him mainly to his own devices. Every night when Dick came in he hoped he might have to wait upon himself, and every morning he looked forward with pleasure to the prospect of making his toilet unaided. His hopes, however, were doomed to disappointment, for every night when he came in Grandison was on hand with a bootjack,[7] and a nightcap mixed for his young master as the colonel had taught him to mix it, and every morning Grandison appeared with his master's boots blacked and his clothes brushed, and laid his linen out for the day.

"Grandison," said Dick one morning, after finishing his toilet, "this is the chance of your life to go around among your own people and see how they live. Have you met any of them?"

"Yas, suh, I's seen some of 'em. But I don' keer nuffin fer 'em, suh. Dey're diffe'nt f'm de niggers down ou' way. Dey 'lows dey're free, but dey ain' got sense 'nuff ter know dey ain' half as well off as dey would be down Souf, whar dey'd be 'preciated."

When two weeks had passed without any apparent effect of evil example upon Grandison, Dick resolved to go on to Boston, where he thought the atmosphere might prove more favorable to his ends. After he had been at the Revere House[8] for a day or two without losing Grandison, he decided upon slightly different tactics.

Having ascertained from a city directory the addresses of several well-known abolitionists, he wrote them each a letter something like this:—

DEAR FRIEND AND BROTHER:—

A wicked slaveholder from Kentucky, stopping at the Revere House, has dared to insult the liberty-loving people of Boston by bringing his slave into their midst. Shall this be tolerated? Or shall steps be taken in the name of liberty to rescue a fellow-man from bondage? For obvious reasons I can only sign myself,

A FRIEND OF HUMANITY.

That his letter might have an opportunity to prove effective, Dick made it a point to send Grandison away from the hotel on various errands. On one of these occasions Dick watched him for quite a distance down the street. Grandison had scarcely left the hotel when a long-haired, sharp-featured man came out behind him, followed him, soon overtook him, and kept along beside him until they turned the next corner. Dick's hopes were roused by this spectacle, but sank correspondingly when Grandison returned to the hotel. As Grandison said nothing about the encounter, Dick hoped there might be some self-consciousness behind this unexpected reticence, the results of which might develop later on.

But Grandison was on hand again when his master came back to the hotel at night, and was in attendance again in the morning, with hot water, to assist at his master's toilet. Dick sent him on further errands from day to day, and upon one occasion came squarely up to him—inadvertently of course—while Grandison was engaged in conversation with a young white man in clerical garb. When Grandison saw Dick approaching, he edged away from the preacher and hastened toward his master, with a very evident expression of relief upon his countenance.

"Mars Dick," he said, "dese yer abolitioners is jes' pesterin' de life out er me tryin' ter git me ter run away. I don' pay no 'tention ter 'em, but dey riles me

7. Device for removing close-fitting boots.
8. The home of Revolutionary War hero Paul Revere.

so sometimes dat I'm feared I'll hit some of 'em some er dese days, an' dat mought git me inter trouble. I ain' said nuffin' ter you 'bout it, Mars Dick, fer I did n' wanter 'sturb yo' min'; but I don' like it, suh; no, suh, I don'! Is we gwine back home 'fo' long, Mars Dick?"

"We'll be going back soon enough," replied Dick somewhat shortly, while he inwardly cursed the stupidity of a slave who could be free and would not, and registered a secret vow that if he were unable to get rid of Grandison without assassinating him, and were therefore compelled to take him back to Kentucky, he would see that Grandison got a taste of an article of slavery that would make him regret his wasted opportunities. Meanwhile he determined to tempt his servant yet more strongly.

"Grandison," he said next morning, "I'm going away for a day or two, but I shall leave you here. I shall lock up a hundred dollars in this drawer and give you the key. If you need any of it, use it and enjoy yourself,—spend it all if you like,—for this is probably the last chance you'll have for some time to be in a free State, and you 'd better enjoy your liberty while you may."

When he came back a couple of days later and found the faithful Grandison at his post, and the hundred dollars intact, Dick felt seriously annoyed. His vexation was increased by the fact that he could not express his feelings adequately. He did not even scold Grandison; how could he, indeed, find fault with one who so sensibly recognized his true place in the economy of civilization, and kept it with such touching fidelity?

"I can't say a thing to him," groaned Dick. "He deserves a leather medal, made out of his own hide tanned. I reckon I'll write to father and let him know what a model servant he has given me."

He wrote his father a letter which made the colonel swell with pride and pleasure. "I really think," the colonel observed to one of his friends, "that Dick ought to have the nigger interviewed by the Boston papers, so that they may see how contented and happy our darkeys really are."

Dick also wrote a long letter to Charity Lomax, in which he said, among many other things, that if she knew how hard he was working, and under what difficulties, to accomplish something serious for her sake, she would no longer keep him in suspense, but overwhelm him with love and admiration.

Having thus exhausted without result the more obvious methods of getting rid of Grandison, and diplomacy having also proved a failure, Dick was forced to consider more radical measures. Of course he might run away himself, and abandon Grandison, but this would be merely to leave him in the United States, where he was still a slave, and where, with his notions of loyalty, he would speedily be reclaimed. It was necessary, in order to accomplish the purpose of his trip to the North, to leave Grandison permanently in Canada, where he would be legally free.

"I might extend my trip to Canada," he reflected, "but that would be too palpable. I have it! I'll visit Niagara Falls on the way home, and lose him on the Canadian side. When he once realizes that he is actually free, I'll warrant that he'll stay."

So the next day saw them westward bound, and in due course of time, by the somewhat slow conveyances of the period, they found themselves at Niagara. Dick walked and drove about the Falls for several days, taking Grandison along with him on most occasions. One morning they stood on the Canadian side, watching the wild whirl of the waters below them.

"Grandison," said Dick, raising his voice above the roar of the cataract, "do you know where you are now?"

"I's wid you, Mars Dick; dat's all I keers."

"You are now in Canada, Grandison, where your people go when they run away from their masters. If you wished, Grandison, you might walk away from me this very minute, and I could not lay my hand upon you to take you back."

Grandison looked around uneasily.

"Let's go back ober de ribber, Mars Dick. I's feared I'll lose you ovuh heah, an' den I won' hab no marster, an' won't nebber be able to git back home no mo'."

Discouraged, but not yet hopeless, Dick said, a few minutes later,—

"Grandison, I'm going up the road a bit, to the inn over yonder. You stay here until I return. I'll not be gone a great while."

Grandison's eyes opened wide and he looked somewhat fearful.

"Is dey any er dem dadblasted abolitioners roun' heah, Mars Dick?"

"I don't imagine that there are," replied his master, hoping there might be. "But I'm not afraid of *your* running away, Grandison. I only wish I were," he added to himself.

Dick walked leisurely down the road to where the whitewashed inn, built of stone, with true British solidity, loomed up through the trees by the roadside. Arrived there he ordered a glass of ale and a sandwich, and took a seat at a table by a window, from which he could see Grandison in the distance. For a while he hoped that the seed he had sown might have fallen on fertile ground, and that Grandison, relieved from the restraining power of a master's eye, and finding himself in a free country, might get up and walk away; but the hope was vain, for Grandison remained faithfully at his post, awaiting his master's return. He had seated himself on a broad flat stone, and, turning his eyes away from the grand and awe-inspiring spectacle that lay close at hand, was looking anxiously toward the inn where his master sat cursing his ill-timed fidelity.

By and by a girl came into the room to serve his order, and Dick very naturally glanced at her; and as she was young and pretty and remained in attendance, it was some minutes before he looked for Grandison. When he did so his faithful servant had disappeared.

To pay his reckoning and go away without the change was a matter quickly accomplished. Retracing his footsteps toward the Falls, he saw, to his great disgust, as he approached the spot where he had left Grandison, the familiar form of his servant stretched out on the ground, his face to the sun, his mouth open, sleeping the time away, oblivious alike to the grandeur of the scenery, the thunderous roar of the cataract, or the insidious voice of sentiment.

"Grandison," soliloquized his master, as he stood gazing down at his ebony encumbrance, "I do not deserve to be an American citizen; I ought not to have the advantages I possess over you; and I certainly am not worthy of Charity Lomax, if I am not smart enough to get rid of you. I have an idea! You shall yet be free, and I will be the instrument of your deliverance. Sleep on, faithful and affectionate servitor, and dream of the blue grass and the bright skies of old Kentucky, for it is only in your dreams that you will ever see them again!"

Dick retraced his footsteps toward the inn. The young woman chanced to look out of the window and saw the handsome young gentleman she had waited on a few minutes before, standing in the road a short distance away, apparently engaged in earnest conversation with a colored man employed as hostler[9] for the inn. She thought she saw something pass from the white man to the other, but at that moment her duties called her away from the window, and when she looked out again the young gentleman had disappeared, and the hostler, with two other young men of the neighborhood, one white and one colored, were walking rapidly towards the Falls.

IV

Dick made the journey homeward alone, and as rapidly as the conveyances of the day would permit. As he drew near home his conduct in going back without Grandison took on a more serious aspect than it had borne at any previous time, and although he had prepared the colonel by a letter sent several days ahead, there was still the prospect of a bad quarter of an hour with him; not, indeed, that his father would upbraid him, but he was likely to make searching inquiries. And notwithstanding the vein of quiet recklessness that had carried Dick through his preposterous scheme, he was a very poor liar, having rarely had occasion or inclination to tell anything but the truth. Any reluctance to meet his father was more than offset, however, by a stronger force drawing him homeward, for Charity Lomax must long since have returned from her visit to her aunt in Tennessee.

Dick got off easier than he had expected. He told a straight story, and a truthful one, so far as it went.

The colonel raged at first, but rage soon subsided into anger, and anger moderated into annoyance, and annoyance into a sort of garrulous sense of injury. The colonel thought he had been hardly used; he had trusted this negro, and he had broken faith. Yet, after all, he did not blame Grandison so much as he did the abolitionists, who were undoubtedly at the bottom of it.

As for Charity Lomax, Dick told her, privately of course, that he had run his father's man, Grandison, off to Canada, and left him there.

"Oh, Dick," she had said with shuddering alarm, "what have you done? If they knew it they'd send you to the penitentiary, like they did that Yankee."

"But they don't know it," he had replied seriously; adding, with an injured tone, "you don't seem to appreciate my heroism like you did that of the Yankee; perhaps it's because I wasn't caught and sent to the penitentiary. I thought you wanted me to do it."

"Why, Dick Owens!" she exclaimed. "You know I never dreamed of any such outrageous proceeding."

"But I presume I'll have to marry you," she concluded, after some insistence on Dick's part, "if only to take care of you. You are too reckless for anything; and a man who goes chasing all over the North, being entertained by New York and Boston society and having negroes to throw away, needs some one to look after him."

"It's a most remarkable thing," replied Dick fervently, "that your views correspond exactly with my profoundest convictions. It proves beyond question that we were made for one another."

9. Attendant for travelers' horses.

They were married three weeks later. As each of them had just returned from a journey, they spent their honeymoon at home.

A week after the wedding they were seated, one afternoon, on the piazza of the colonel's house, where Dick had taken his bride, when a negro from the yard ran down the lane and threw open the big gate for the colonel's buggy to enter. The colonel was not alone. Beside him, ragged and travel-stained, bowed with weariness, and upon his face a haggard look that told of hardship and privation, sat the lost Grandison.

The colonel alighted at the steps.

"Take the lines, Tom," he said to the man who had opened the gate, "and drive round to the barn. Help Grandison down,—poor devil, he's so stiff he can hardly move!—and get a tub of water and wash him and rub him down, and feed him, and give him a big drink of whiskey, and then let him come round and see his young master and his new mistress."

The colonel's face wore an expression compounded of joy and indignation,—joy at the restoration of a valuable piece of property; indignation for reasons he proceeded to state.

"It's astounding, the depths of depravity the human heart is capable of! I was coming along the road three miles away, when I heard some one call me from the roadside. I pulled up the mare, and who should come out of the woods but Grandison. The poor nigger could hardly crawl along, with the help of a broken limb. I was never more astonished in my life. You could have knocked me down with a feather. He seemed pretty far gone,—he could hardly talk above a whisper,—and I had to give him a mouthful of whiskey to brace him up so he could tell his story. It's just as I thought from the beginning, Dick; Grandison had no notion of running away; he knew when he was well off, and where his friends were. All the persuasions of abolition liars and runaway niggers did not move him. But the desperation of those fanatics knew no bounds; their guilty consciences gave them no rest. They got the notion somehow that Grandison belonged to a nigger-catcher, and had been brought North as a spy to help capture ungrateful runaway servants. They actually kidnapped him—just think of it!—and gagged him and bound him and threw him rudely into a wagon, and carried him into the gloomy depths of a Canadian forest, and locked him in a lonely hut, and fed him on bread and water for three weeks. One of the scoundrels wanted to kill him, and persuaded the others that it ought to be done; but they got to quarreling about how they should do it, and before they had their minds made up Grandison escaped, and, keeping his back steadily to the North Star, made his way, after suffering incredible hardships, back to the old plantation, back to his master, his friends, and his home. Why, it's as good as one of Scott's novels Mr. Simms[1] or some other one of our Southern authors ought to write it up."

"Don't you think, sir," suggested Dick, who had calmly smoked his cigar throughout the colonel's animated recital, "that that kidnapping yarn sounds a little improbable? Isn't there some more likely explanation?"

"Nonsense, Dick; it's the gospel truth! Those infernal abolitionists are

---

1. William Gilmore Simms (1806–1870), perhaps the antebellum South's most admired writer. Sir Walter Scott (1771–1832), British author whose historical novels were immensely popular in the South, particularly those about medieval feudalism.

capable of anything—everything! Just think of their locking the poor, faithful nigger up, beating him, kicking him, depriving him of his liberty, keeping him on bread and water for three long, lonesome weeks, and he all the time pining for the old plantation!"

There were almost tears in the colonel's eyes at the picture of Grandison's sufferings that he conjured up. Dick still professed to be slightly skeptical, and met Charity's severely questioning eye with bland unconsciousness.

The colonel killed the fatted calf[2] for Grandison, and for two or three weeks the returned wanderer's life was a slave's dream of pleasure. His fame spread through-out the county, and the colonel gave him a permanent place among the house servants, where he could always have him conveniently at hand to relate his adventures to admiring visitors.

About three weeks after Grandison's return the colonel's faith in sable humanity was rudely shaken, and its foundations almost broken up. He came near losing his belief in the fidelity of the negro to his master,—the servile virtue most highly prized and most sedulously cultivated by the colonel and his kind. One Monday morning Grandison was missing. And not only Grandison, but his wife, Betty the maid; his mother, aunt Eunice; his father, uncle Ike; his brothers, Tom and John; and his little sister Elsie, were likewise absent from the plantation: and a hurried search and inquiry in the neighborhood resulted in no information as to their whereabouts. So much valuable property could not be lost without an effort to recover it, and the wholesale nature of the transaction carried consternation to the hearts of those whose ledgers were chiefly bound in black. Extremely energetic measures were taken by the colonel and his friends. The fugitives were traced, and followed from point to point, on their northward run through Ohio. Several times the hunters were close upon their heels, but the magnitude of the escaping party begot unusual vigilance on the part of those who sympathized with the fugitives, and strangely enough, the underground railroad[3] seemed to have had its tracks cleared and signals set for this particular train. Once, twice, the colonel thought he had them, but they slipped through his fingers.

One last glimpse he caught of his vanishing property, as he stood, accompanied by a United States marshal, on a wharf at a port on the south shore of Lake Erie. On the stern of a small steamboat which was receding rapidly from the wharf, with her nose pointing toward Canada, there stood a group of familiar dark faces, and the look they cast backward was not one of longing for the fleshpots of Egypt.[4] The colonel saw Grandison point him out to one of the crew of the vessel, who waved his hand derisively toward the colonel. The latter shook his fist impotently—and the incident was closed.

1901

2. When the prodigal son of Jesus' parable returned home from a life of dissipation, his joyful father butchered a calf for a special feast (Luke 15.11–32).
3. The system of safe havens in the homes of abolitionists along the dangerous escape route from the South to Canada.
4. When the fleeing Israelites began to starve in the desert, they complained to Moses that they preferred the full pots of meat they had had as slaves in Egypt (Exodus 16.2–3).

ABRAHAM CAHAN
1860–1951

One of the central subjects of turn-of-the-twentieth-century U.S. literature is the (usually painful) process of "Americanization" or assimilation of immigrants from all corners of the world. Such assimilation is at the heart of the work of Abraham Cahan, both as a prolific journalist and as the author of a relatively small but important body of fiction.

Cahan was born into an Orthodox Jewish family in a village a few miles from Vilna, Lithuania, then a part of the Russian Empire. He was educated as a youth first in Hebrew schools and then in a *yeshiva*—a seminary for studies in Jewish law and commentaries on it. His absorption in traditional Jewish studies gave way in his teens to a comparably passionate engagement with secular subjects, especially literature and social theory. As a student at the Vilna Teacher Training Institute, he was among a small group of young men who, like self-described intellectuals in other Russian cities, read and discussed such subversive works as Nikolai Chernishevsky's radical utopian novel *What Is to Be Done?* (1863). Of more lasting importance to him was the reading of Tolstoi and other Russian writers; of these, Chekhov, a brilliant short-story writer, became his favorite. Although Cahan was neither a leader nor an active conspirator in efforts to overthrow the czarist regime, his room was searched twice during his first year as a teacher, and he had good reason to be concerned about the possibilities of arrest and imprisonment.

The intensified attempt to suppress dissent that brought Cahan and other intellectuals under suspicion (it was considered a revolutionary act simply to be in possession of prohibited writings) was one consequence of the assassination of Czar Alexander II in March 1881. More important historically was intensified Russian anti-Semitism and an unprecedented series of murderous pogroms unleashed against Russian Jews with at least the tacit approval of local police and other government officials. There had been pogroms before and in other regions, but these pogroms led almost immediately to the massive emigration, starting in 1882, of Russian and Eastern European Jews to Palestine and, in much greater numbers, to America (two million by 1924).

Within two months of his arrival in the United States in 1882, Cahan gave the first socialist speech to be delivered in the country in Yiddish—a language that combined Middle High German dialects with vocabularies from Hebrew, Slavic, and European languages and as time went on a distinctively Jewish American vocabulary. Cahan soon helped organize the first Jewish tailors' union; taught English at night to immigrants at the Young Men's Hebrew Association; and began his careers as editor and journalist with Yiddish, Russian, and English papers.

In 1897 Cahan was active in founding the *Jewish Daily Forward*, a Yiddish-language newspaper he edited, with some short interruptions, for nearly fifty years. As critic Jules Chametsky observed: "[Cahan] took a sectarian journal of the Social Democratic Party with 6,000 subscribers and made it the most successful foreign-language newspaper in America and the leading Yiddish paper in the world." At its height the *Forward* had a circulation of a quarter of a million (and was read by perhaps a million people altogether). Cahan's editorial policy was designed to help Jewish immigrants make the transition from the often medieval conditions of the urban ghettos and *shtetls* to the new realities of a rapidly industrializing democracy. The *Forward* combined news, information, cultural commentary, and reviews with short stories, including work of I.J. Singer and Sholem Asch. It included features such as *"A Bintel Brief"* (A Bundle of Letters), which printed anonymous letters from subscribers together with authoritative advice from the editor.

For twenty-five years—from 1892 until 1917—Cahan turned his attention to writing fiction in English. Encouraged by novelist and critic William Dean Howells,

Cahan published his first novel, *Yekl: A Tale of the New York Ghetto*, in 1896. Encouraged further by the generally favorable reception of this work (later made more popular by Joan Micklen Silver's film adaptation, released in 1975 under the title *Hester Street*), Cahan wrote short stories that he published in 1898 as *"The Imported Bridegroom" and Other Stories of the New York Ghetto*, which included "A Sweat-Shop Romance" (first published in 1895). Throughout the volume, Yiddish and heavily accented English are largely absorbed and "translated" into the perceptive but lucid language of an omniscient third-person narrator. This change in presentational mode was a sign of Cahan's mastery of English and sophistication of technique, as well as developing control of irony.

The title "A Sweat-Shop Romance" itself suggests some of the tensions it dramatizes—between the grim and cramped spaces the characters occupy and the exhilarating release of romantic love some of them experience, between the pretensions of the prideful bosses of a "cockroach" shop and the independence and self-reliance of the young couple who refuse to be treated as servants and who marry in the end. "A Sweat-Shop Romance," with apparent artlessness, illuminates truthfully and movingly the emotional and psychological realitites of ordinary men and women living with good humor under difficult economic, cultural, and social circumstances. At the same time the story provides insight into highly specific aspects of the rapidly growing and increasingly competitive garment industry. Another aspect of the story's apparent artlessness has to do with Cahan's skillful use of language. Unlike *Yekl* or some of his other stories, Yiddish and heavily accented English in this story are largely absorbed and "translated" into the perceptive but lucid language of an omniscient third-person narrator. This change of presentational mode is a clear sign of Cahan's mastery of English and sophistication of technique. In this story his sharp eye and sensitive ear for language are at the service of mood and characterization.

Cahan's masterpiece was his novel *The Rise of David Levinsky* (1917), a powerful depiction of the garment industry and the people who work in it. This book established Cahan as a progenitor of Jewish American writers as diverse as Michael Gold, Henry Roth, Saul Bellow, and Alfred Kazin. The rich tapestry of this intensely realistic account of turn-of-the-twentieth-century New York is at once a Jewish novel, a novel about the always difficult process of Americanization, and a more universal story of self-estrangement and social alienation. Both as a journalist and as a writer of fiction, Abraham Cahan was influential in his own time. He remains one of the central chroniclers of American immigrant life.

A Sweat-Shop Romance[1]

Leizer Lipman was one of those contract tailors who are classed by their hands under the head of "cockroaches," which—translating the term into lay English—means that he ran a very small shop, giving employment to a single team of one sewing-machine operator, one baster, one finisher, and one presser.

The shop was one of a suite of three rooms on the third floor of a rickety old tenement house on Essex Street, and did the additional duty of the family's kitchen and dining-room. It faced a dingy little courtyard, and was connected by a windowless bedroom with the parlor, which commanded the very heart of the Jewish markets. Bundles of cloth, cut to be made into coats, littered the floor, lay in chaotic piles by one of the walls, cumbered Mrs. Lipman's kitchen table and one or two chairs, and formed, in a corner, an

---

1. Originally published as "In the Sweat Shop" in the magazine *Short Stories* in June 1895, then as part of *"The Imported Bridegroom" and Other Stories of the New York Ghetto* (1898), the source of the text printed here.

improvised bed upon which a dirty two-year-old boy, Leizer's heir apparent, was enjoying his siesta.

Dangling against the door or scattered among the bundles, there were cooking utensils, dirty linen, Lipman's velvet skull-cap,[2] hats, shoes, shears, cotton-spools, and what-not. A red-hot kitchen stove and a blazing grate full of glowing flat-irons combined to keep up the overpowering temperature of the room, and helped to justify its nickname of sweat-shop in the literal sense of the epithet.

Work was rather scarce, but the designer of the Broadway clothing firm, of whose army of contractors Lipman was a member, was a second cousin to the latter's wife, and he saw to it that his relative's husband was kept busy. And so operations in Leizer's shop were in full swing. Heyman, the operator, with his bared brawny arms, pushed away at an unfinished coat, over which his head, presenting to view a wealth of curly brown hair, hung like an eagle bent on his prey. He swayed in unison to the rhythmic whirr of his machine, whose music, supported by the energetic thumps of Meyer's press-iron, formed an orchestral accompaniment to the sonorous and plaintive strains of a vocal duet performed by Beile, the finisher girl, and David, the baster.

Leizer was gone to the Broadway firm's offices, while Zlate, his wife, was out on a prolonged haggling expedition among the tradeswomen of Hester Street. This circumstance gave the hands a respite from the restrictions usually placed on their liberties by the presence of the "boss" and the "Missis," and they freely beguiled the tedium and fatigue of their work, now by singing, now by a bantering match at the expense of their employer and his wife, or of each other.

"Well, I suppose you might as well quit," said Meyer, a chubby, red-haired, freckled fellow of forty, emphasizing his remark by an angry stroke of his iron. "You have been over that song now fifty times without taking breath. You make me tired."

"Don't you like it? Stuff up your ears, then," Beile retorted, without lifting her head from the coat in her lap.

"Why, I do like it, first-rate and a half," Meyer returned, "but when you keep your mouth shut I like it better still, see?"

The silvery tinkle of Beile's voice, as she was singing, thrilled Heyman with delicious melancholy, gave him fresh relish for his work, and infused additional activity into his limbs; and as her singing was interrupted by the presser's gibe, he involuntarily stopped his machine with that annoying feeling which is experienced by dancers when brought to an unexpected standstill by an abrupt pause of the music.

"And you?"—he addressed himself to Meyer, facing about on his chair with an irritated countenance. "It's all right enough when you speak, but it is much better when you hold your tongue. Don't mind him, Beile. Sing away!" he then said to the girl, his dazzlingly fair face relaxing and his little eyes shutting into a sweet smile of self-confident gallantry.

"You had better stick to your work, Heyman. Why, you might have made half a cent the while," Meyer fired back, with an ironical look, which had reference to the operator's reputation of being a niggardly fellow, who overworked himself, denied himself every pleasure, and grew fat by feasting his eyes on his savings-bank book.

2. Yarmulke; worn by Jewish men.

A sharp altercation ensued, which drifted to the subject of Heyman's servile conduct toward his employer.

"It was you, wasn't it," Meyer said, "who started that collection for a birthday present for the boss? Of course, we couldn't help chipping in. Why is David independent?"

"Did I compel you?" Heyman rejoined. "And am I to blame that it was to me that the boss threw out the hint about that present? It is so slack everywhere, and you ought to thank God for the steady job you have here," he concluded, pouncing down upon the coat on his machine.

David, who had also cut short his singing, kept silently plying his needle upon pieces of stuff which lay stretched on his master's dining-table. Presently he paused to adjust his disheveled jet-black hair, with his fingers for a comb, and to wipe the perspiration from his swarthy, beardless and typically Israelitic face with his shirt-sleeve.

While this was in progress, his languid hazel eyes were fixed on the finisher girl. She instinctively became conscious of his gaze, and raised her head from the needle. Her fresh buxom face, flushed with the heat of the room and with exertion, shone full upon the young baster. Their eyes met. David colored, and, to conceal his embarrassment, he asked: "Well, is he going to raise your wages?"

Beile nodded affirmatively, and again plunged her head into her work.

"He is? So you will now get five dollars a week. I am afraid you will be putting on airs now, won't you?"

"Do you begrudge me? Then I am willing to swap wages with you. I'll let you have my five dollars, and I'll take your twelve dollars every week."

Lipman's was a task shop, and, according to the signification which the term has in the political economy of the sweating world, his operator, baster, and finisher, while nominally engaged at so much a week, were in reality paid by the piece, the economical week being determined by a stipulated quantity of made-up coats rather than by a fixed number of the earth's revolutions around its axis; for the sweat-shop day will not coincide with the solar day unless a given amount of work be accomplished in its course. As to the presser, he is invariably a piece-worker, pure and simple.

For a more lucid account of the task system in the tailoring branch, I beg to refer the reader to David, although his exposition happens to be presented rather in the form of a satire on the subject. Indeed, David, while rather inclined to taciturnity, was an inveterate jester, and what few remarks he indulged in during his work would often cause boisterous merriment among his shopmates, although he delivered them with a nonchalant manner and with the same look of good-humored irony, mingled in strange harmony with a general expression of gruffness, which his face usually wore.

"My twelve dollars every week?" David echoed. "Oh, I see; you mean a week of twelve days!" And his needle resumed its duck-like sport in the cloth.

"How do you make it out?" Meyer demanded, in order to elicit a joke from the witty young man by his side.

"Of course, *you* don't know how to make that out. But ask Heyman or Beile. The three of us do."

"Tell him, then, and he will know too," Beile urged, laughing in advance at the expected fun.

A request coming from the finisher was—yet unknown to herself—resistless with David, and in the present instance it loosened his tongue.

"Well, I get twelve dollars a week, and Heyman fourteen. Now a working week has six days, but—hem—that 'but' gets stuck in my throat—but a day is neither a Sunday nor a Monday nor anything unless we make twelve coats. The calendars are a lot of liars."

"What do you mean?"

"They say a day has twenty-four hours. That's a bluff. A day has twelve coats."

Beile's rapturous chuckle whetted his appetite for persiflage, and he went on:—

"They read the Tuesday Psalm[3] in the synagogue this morning, but I should have read the Monday one."

"Why?"

"You see, Meyer's wife will soon come up with his dinner, and here I have still two coats to make of the twelve that I got yesterday. So it's still Monday with me. My Tuesday won't begin before about two o'clock this afternoon."

"How much will you make this week?" Meyer questioned.

"I don't expect to finish more than four days' work by the end of the week, and will only get eight dollars on Friday—that is, provided the Missis has not spent our wages by that time. So when it's Friday I'll call it Wednesday, see?"

"When I am married," he added, after a pause, "and the old woman asks me for Sabbath expenses, I'll tell her it is only Wednesday—it isn't yet Friday[4]—and I have no money to give her."

David relapsed into silence, but mutely continued his burlesque, hopping from subject to subject.

David thought himself a very queer fellow. He often wondered at the pranks which his own imagination was in the habit of playing, and at the grotesque combinations it frequently evolved. As he now stood, leaning forward over his work, he was striving to make out how it was that Meyer reminded him of the figure "7."

"What nonsense!" he inwardly exclaimed, branding himself for a crank. "And what does Heyman look like?" his mind queried, as though for spite. He contemplated the operator askance, and ran over all the digits of the Arabic system, and even the whole Hebrew alphabet, in quest of a counterpart to the young man, but failed to find anything suitable. "His face would much better become a girl," he at last decided, and mentally proceeded to envelop Heyman's head in Beile's shawl. But the proceeding somehow stung him, and he went on to meditate upon the operator's chunky nose. "No, that nose is too ugly for a girl. It wants a little planing. It's an unfinished job, as it were. But for that nose Heyman would really be the nice fellow they say he is. His snow-white skin—his elegant heavy mustache—yes, if he did not have that nose he would be all right," he maliciously joked in his heart. "And I, too, would be all right if Heyman were noseless," he added, transferring his thoughts to Beile, and wondering why she looked so sweet. "Why, her nose is not much of a beauty, either. Entirely too straight, and too—too foolish. Her eyes look old and as if constantly on the point of bursting into tears. Ah, but then her lips—that kindly smile of theirs, coming out of one corner of her mouth!" And a strong impulse seized him to throw himself on those lips and to kiss them,

---

3. In Orthodox Judaism ten or more Jewish males at least thirteen years of age are required for the lawful conduct of a public Jewish service. Such a group (a *minyan*) meets in the early mornings; as part of the service a psalm is recited.
4. Typically payday and the start, at sundown, of the Jewish Sabbath. "Sabbath expenses": e.g., the costs of special foods, candles, and the like.

which he did mentally, and which shot an electric current through his whole frame. And at this Beile's old-looking eyes both charmed and pierced him to the heart, and her nose, far from looking foolish, seemed to contemplate him contemptuously, triumphantly, and knowingly, as if it had read his thoughts.

While this was going on in David's brain and heart, Beile was taken up with Heyman and with their mutual relations. His attentions to her were an open secret. He did not go out of his way to conceal them. On the contrary, he regularly escorted her home after work, and took her out to balls and picnics— a thing involving great sacrifices to a fellow who trembled over every cent he spent, and who was sure to make up for these losses to his pocket-book by foregoing his meals. While alone with her in the hallway of her mother's residence, his voice would become so tender, so tremulous, and on several occasions he even addressed her by the endearing form of Beilinke. And yet all this had been going on now for over three months, and he had not as much as alluded to marriage, nor even bought her the most trifling present.

Her mother made life a burden to her, and urged the point-blank declaration of the alternative between a formal engagement and an arrest for breach of promise. Beile would have died rather than make herself the heroine of such a sensation; and, besides, the idea of Heyman handcuffed to a police detective was too terrible to entertain even for a moment.

She loved him. She liked his blooming face, his gentleman-like mustache, the quaint jerk of his head, as he walked; she was fond of his company; she was sure she was in love with him: her confidant, her fellow country girl and playmate, who had recently married Meyer, the presser, had told her so.

But somehow she felt disappointed. She had imagined love to be a much sweeter thing. She had thought that a girl in love admired *everything* in the object of her affections, and was blind to all his faults. She had heard that love was something like a perpetual blissful fluttering of the heart.

"I feel as if something was melting here," a girl friend who was about to be married once confided to her, pointing to her heart. "You see, it aches and yet it is so sweet at the same time." And here she never feels anything melting, nor can she help disliking some things about Heyman. His smile sometimes appears to her fulsome. Ah, if he did not shut his eyes as he does when smiling! That he is so slow to spend money is rather one of the things she likes in him. If he ever marries her she will be sure to get every cent of his wages. But then when they are together at a ball he never goes up to the bar to treat her to a glass of soda, as the other fellows do to their girls, and all he offers her is an apple or a pear, which he generally stops to buy on the street on their way to the dancing-hall. Is she in love at all? Maybe she is mistaken? But no! he is after all so dear to her. She must have herself to blame. It is not in vain that her mother calls her a whimpering, nagging thing, who gives no peace to herself nor to anybody around her. But why does he not come out with his declaration? Is it because he is too stingy to wish to support a wife? Has he been making a fool of her? What does he take her for, then?

In fairness to Heyman, it must be stated that on the point of his intentions, at least, her judgment of him was without foundation, and her misgivings gratuitous. Pecuniary considerations had nothing to do with his slowness in proposing to her. And if she could have watched him and penetrated his mind at the moments when he examined his bank-book,—which he did quite often,—she would have ascertained that little images of herself kept hovering before his eyes between the figures of its credit columns, and that the sum total conjured up to him a picture of prospective felicity with her for a central figure.

Poor thing; she did not know that when he lingeringly fondled her hand, on taking his leave in the hallway, the proposal lay on the tip of his tongue, and that lacking the strength to relieve himself of its burden he every time left her, consoling himself that the moment was inopportune, and that "tomorrow he would surely settle it." She did not know that only two days ago the idea had occurred to him to have recourse to the aid of a messenger in the form of a lady's watch, and that while she now sat worrying lest she was being made a fool of, the golden emissary lay in Heyman's vest-pocket, throbbing in company with his heart with impatient expectation of the evening hour, which had been fixed for the delivery of its message.

"I shall let mother speak to him," Beile resolved, in her musings over her needle. She went on to picture the scene, but at this point her meditations were suddenly broken by something clutching and pulling at her hair. It was her employer's boy. He had just got up from his after-dinner nap, and, for want of any other occupation, he passed his dirty little hand into her raven locks.

"He is practicing to be a boss," observed David, whose attention was attracted to the spectacle by the finisher's shriek.

Beile's voice brought Heyman to his feet, and disentangling the little fellow's fingers from the girl's hair, he fell to "plastering his nasty cheeks for him," as he put it. At this juncture the door opened to admit the little culprit's father. Heyman skulked away to his seat, and, burying his head in his work, he proceeded to drown, in the whir-r, whir-r of his machine, the screams of the boy, who would have struck a much higher key had his mamma happened on the spot.

Lipman took off his coat, substituted his greasy velvet skull-cap for his derby, and lighting a cigar with an air of good-natured business-like importance, he advanced to Meyer's corner and fell to examining a coat.

"And what does *he* look like?" David asked himself, scrutinizing his taskmaster. "Like a broom with its stick downward," he concluded to his own satisfaction. "And his snuff-box?"—meaning Lipman's huge nose—"A perfect fiddle!—And his mouth? Deaf-mutes usually have such mouths. And his beard? He has entirely too much of it, and it's too pretty for his face. It must have got there by mistake."

Presently the door again flew open, and Mrs. Lipman, heavily loaded with parcels and panting for breath, came waddling in with an elderly couple in tow.

"Greenhorns," Meyer remarked. "Must be fellow townspeople of hers—lately arrived."

"She looks like a tea-kettle, and she is puffing like one, too," David thought, after an indifferent gaze at the newcomers, looking askance at his stout, dowdyish little "Missis." "No," he then corrected himself, "she rather resembles a broom with its stick out. That's it! And wouldn't it be a treat to tie a stick to her head and to sweep the floor with the horrid thing! And her mouth? Why, it makes me think she does nothing but sneeze."

"Here is Leizer! Leizer, look at the guests I have brought you!" Zlate exclaimed, as she threw down her bundles. "Be seated, Reb Avrom; be seated, Basse. This is our factory," she went on, with a smile of mixed welcome and triumph, after the demonstrative greetings were over. "It is rather too small, isn't it? but we are going to move into larger and better quarters."

Meyer was not mistaken. Zlate's visitors had recently arrived from her birthplace, a poor town in Western Russia, where they had occupied a much higher social position than their present hostess, and Mrs. Lipman, coming upon them on Hester Street, lost no time in inviting them to her house, in order to overwhelm them with her American achievements.

"Come, I want to show you my parlor," Mrs. Lipman said, beckoning to her country people, and before they were given an opportunity to avail themselves of the chairs which she had offered them, they were towed into the front room.

When the procession returned, Leizer, in obedience to an order from his wife, took Reb Avrom in charge and proceeded to initiate him into the secrets of the "American style of tailoring."

"Oh, my!" Zlate suddenly ejaculated, with a smile. "I came near forgetting to treat. Beilke!" she then addressed herself to the finisher girl in a tone of imperious nonchalance, "here is a nickel. Fetch two bottles of soda from the grocery."

"Don't go, Beile!" David whispered across his table, perceiving the girl's reluctance.

It was not unusual for Beile to go on an errand for the wife of her employer, though she always did it unwillingly, and merely for fear of losing her place; but then Zlate generally exacted these services as a favor. In the present instance, however, Beile felt mortally offended by her commanding tone, and the idea of being paraded before the strangers as a domestic cut her to the quick, as a stream of color rushing into her face indicated. Nevertheless the prospect of having to look for a job again persuaded her to avoid trouble with Zlate, and she was about to reach out her hand for the coin, when David's exhortation piqued her sense of self-esteem, and she went on with her sewing. Heyman, who, being interrupted in his work by the visitor's inspection, was a witness of the scene, at this point turned his face from it, and cringing by his machine, he made a pretense of busying himself with the shuttle. His heart shrank with the awkwardness of his situation, and he nervously grated his teeth and shut his eyes, awaiting still more painful developments. His veins tingled with pity for his sweetheart and with deadly hatred for David. What could he do? he apologized to himself. Isn't it foolish to risk losing a steady job at this slack season on account of such a trifle as fetching up a bottle of soda? What business has David to interfere?

"You are not deaf, are you? I say go and bring some soda, quick!" Mrs. Lipman screamed, fearing lest she was going too far.

"Don't budge, Beile!" the baster prompted, with fire in his eyes.

Beile did not.

"I say go!" Zlate thundered, reddening like a beet, to use a phrase in vogue with herself.

"Never mind, Zlate," Basse interposed, to relieve the embarrassing situation. "We just had tea."

"Never mind. It is not worth the trouble," Avrom chimed in.

But this only served to lash Zlate into a greater fury, and unmindful of consequences, she strode up to the cause of her predicament, and tearing the coat out of her hands, she squeaked out:—

"Either fetch the soda, or leave my shop at once!"

Heyman was about to say, to do something, he knew not exactly what, but his tongue seemed seized with palsy, the blood turned chill in his veins, and he could neither speak nor stir.

Leizer, who was of a quiet, peaceful disposition, and very much under the thumb of his wife, stood nervously smiling and toying with his beard.

David grew ashen pale, and trembling with rage he said aloud and in deliberate accents:—

"Don't mind her, Beile, and never worry. Come along. I'll find you a better job. This racket won't work, Missis. Your friends see through it, anyhow, don't you?" he addressed himself to the newcomers. "She wanted to brag to you. That's what she troubled you for. She showed off her parlor carpet to you, didn't she? But did she tell you that it had been bought on the installment plan, and that the custom-peddler threatened to take it away unless she paid more regularly?"

"Leizer! are you—are you drunk?" Mrs. Lipman gasped, her face distorted with rage and desperation.

"Get out of here!" Leizer said, in a tone which would have been better suited to a cordial invitation.

The command was unnecessary, however, for by this time David was buttoning up his overcoat, and had his hat on. Involuntarily following his example, Beile also dressed to go. And as she stood in her new beaver cloak and freshly trimmed large old hat by the side of her discomfited commander, Basse reflected that it was the finisher girl who looked like a lady, with Zlate for her servant, rather than the reverse.

"See that you have our wages ready for Friday, and all the arrears, too!" was David's parting shot as the two left the room with a defiant slam of the door.

"That's like America!" Zlate remarked, with an attempt at a scornful smile. "The meanest beggar girl will put on airs."

"Why *should* one be ordered about like that? She is no servant, is she?" Heyman murmured, addressing the corner of the room, and fell to at his machine to smother his misery.

When his day's work was over, Heyman's heart failed him to face Beile, and although he was panting to see her, he did not call at her house. On the following morning he awoke with a headache, and this he used as a pretext to himself for going to bed right after supper.

On the next evening he did betake himself to the Division Street tenement house, where his sweetheart lived with her mother on the top floor, but on coming in front of the building his courage melted away. Added to his cowardly part in the memorable scene of two days before, there now was his apparent indifference to the finisher, as manifested by his two evenings' absence at such a critical time. He armed himself with a fib to explain his conduct. But all in vain; he could not nerve himself up to the terrible meeting. And so day after day passed, each day increasing the barrier to the coveted visit.

At last, one evening, about a fortnight after the date of Mrs. Lipman's fiasco, Heyman, forgetting to lose courage, as it were, briskly mounted the four flights of stairs of the Division Street tenement. As he was about to rap for admission he was greeted by a sharp noise within of something, like a china plate or a bowl, being dashed to pieces against the very door which he was going to open. The noise was followed by merry voices: "Good luck! Good luck!" and there was no mistaking its meaning. There was evidently an engagement party inside. The Rabbi had just read the writ of betrothment, and it was the mutual pledges of the contracting parties which were emphasized by the "breaking of the plate."[5]

Presently Heyman heard exclamations which dissipated his every doubt as to the identity of the chief actors in the ceremony which had just been completed within.

"Good luck to you, David! Good luck to you, Beile! May you live to a happy old age together!" "Feige, why don't you take some cake? Don't be so bashful!" "Here is luck!" came through the door, piercing a muffled hum inside.

Heyman was dumbfounded, and with his head swimming, he made a hasty retreat.

Ever since the tragi-comical incident at Lipman's shop, Heyman was not present to Beile's thoughts except in the pitiful, cowering attitude in which he had sat through that awful scene by his machine. She was sure she hated him now. And yet her heart was, during the first few days, constantly throbbing with the expectation of his visit; and as she settled in her mind that even if he came she would have nothing to do with him, her deeper consciousness seemed to say, with a smile of conviction: "Oh no, you know you would not refuse him. You wouldn't risk to remain an old maid, would you?" The idea of his jilting her harrowed her day and night. Did he avail himself of her leaving Lipman's shop to back out of the proposal which was naturally expected of him, but which he never perhaps contemplated? Did he make game of her?

When a week had elapsed without Heyman's putting in an appearance, she determined to let her mother see a lawyer about breach-of-promise proceedings. But an image, whose outlines had kept defining themselves in her heart for several days past, overruled this decision. It was the image of a pluckier fellow than Heyman—of one with whom there was more protection in store for a wife, who inspired her with more respect and confidence, and, what is more, who seemed on the point of proposing to her.

It was the image of David. The young baster pursued his courtship with a quiet persistency and a suppressed fervor which was not long in winning the girl's heart. He found work for her and for himself in the same shop; saw her home every evening; regularly came after supper to take her out for a walk, in the course of which he would treat her to candy and invite her to a coffee saloon,—a thing which Heyman had never done;—kept her chuckling over his jokes; and at the end of ten days, while sitting by her side in Central Park, one night, he said, in reply to her remark that it was so dark that she knew not where she was:—

"I'll tell you where you are—guess."

"Where?"

"Here, in my heart, and keeping me awake nights, too. Say, Beile, what have I ever done to you to have my rest disturbed by you in that manner?"

Her heart was beating like a sledge-hammer. She tried to laugh, as she returned:—

"I don't know—You can never stop making fun, can you?"

"Fun? Do you want me to cry? I will, gladly, if I only know that you will

5. To signify the finality of the commitment, often done by the couple's mothers.

agree to have an engagement party," he rejoined, deeply blushing under cover of the darkness.

"When?" she questioned, the word crossing her lips before she knew it.

"On my part, to-morrow."

1895   1898

PAULINE ELIZABETH HOPKINS
1859–1930

Prolific African American woman writer and influential literary editor of the first decade of the twentieth century Pauline Hopkins was an outspoken journalist and a gifted storyteller whose fiction mingles suspenseful stories with turn-of-the-century debates on race.

Hopkins was born in Portland, Maine. Her mother, Sarah A. Allen, had been born free in Exeter, New Hampshire, and her father, Northrup Hopkins, was either a free black or a former slave who came north from Virginia. Her forebears include the Reverends Nathaniel and Thomas Paul, founders of the first Baptist church in Boston for blacks, their activist sister Susan Paul, and the poet James M. Whitfield.

When Hopkins was ready for school, the family moved to Boston, and Pauline grew up within the city's intellectual and social ferment, at fifteen winning first prize in a citywide essay contest for her "Evils of Intemperance and Their Remedy." She graduated from the Girls' High School of Boston. Her play, *The Slave's Escape; or, the Underground Railroad*, was produced in Boston in 1880—Hopkins was just twenty years old.

Hopkins began her professional writing career at the turn of the century, a time of unprecedented activity when African American artists such as Charles Chesnutt and Paul Laurence Dunbar published regularly in the leading periodicals *Atlantic Monthly*, *Harper's*, and *Century Magazine*, as well as in journals such as *Colored American Magazine*, which Hopkins helped found in 1900 as a means of using literature for political advancement of African Americans. She served as literary editor in 1903–04 and published short stories and three of her four novels there: *Hagar's Daughter; A Story of Southern Caste Prejudice* (1901), *Winona: A Tale of Negro Life in the South and Southwest* (1902), and *Of One Blood; or, The Hidden Self* (1902). *Contending Forces: A Romance Illustrative of Negro Life North and South* (1900), her first and best-known work, had already been published.

Contending Forces follows the Montfort family for several generations after its move to North Carolina from Bermuda, a move undertaken by plantation owner Charles Montfort to avoid the financial ruin after slavery ended in Bermuda in 1807. Montfort plans to emancipate his seven hundred slaves gradually in North Carolina. This selfish decision leads to disaster: he is murdered by local whites, his wife is brutalized and then commits suicide, and his children become the property of the evil Anson Pollock.

The chapters printed here first tell the story of the Montforts' undoing in North Carolina and then present part of a debate later in the novel, in which Hopkins's characters articulate the most powerful views on "the race problem," especially Washington's gradualism versus Du Bois's call for full identity and citizenship. The novel's psychological exploration of racial "hidden selves" painfully imagines the personal implications of Du Bois's "double consciousness." Richard Yarborough finds *Contending Forces* to be a "didactic" effort full of a romance's "noble heroes and virtuous heroines, melodramatic situations, unsavory villains, exotic locations, highly emotional scenes, amazing coincidences, an alternately light-hearted and star-crossed love affair, even touches of the supernatural." In her Schomburg Library edition introduction to *The Magazine Novels of Pauline Hopkins,* Hazel Carby describes these works as "histories that rewrote definitions of American culture . . . with a pedagogic function, narratives of relations between the races that challenged racist ideologies." Its conclusion depends on a breaking down of racial barriers between characters, as long-estranged family members re-discover one another in scenes reminiscent of the ending of *Uncle Tom's Cabin* (1852).

After leaving *Colored American Magazine* Hopkins continued to work in journalism and in 1905 co-founded her own publishing company, which failed. Its only book was her *Primer of Facts Pertaining to the Early Greatness of the African Race and the Possibility of Restoration by Its Descendants—With an Epilogue.* After a decade of inactivity, she co-founded the *New Era Magazine* with William Wallace, with whom she had founded the *Colored American Magazine,* but it also failed. In her last years she worked as a stenographer, her achievements unrecognized.

From Contending Forces[1]

From *Chapter III. "Coming Events Cast Their Shadows Before"*

> In sooth I know not why I am so sad:
> It wearies me; you say it, wearies you;
> But how I caught it, found it, or came by it,
> What stuff 'tis made of, whereof it is born,
> I am to learn;
> And such a wantwit sadness makes of me
> That I have much ado to know myself.
> —*Merchant of Venice*[2]

The old Pollock homestead was an exquisite spot. The house was a long, low, rambling structure, consisting of many large, airy rooms inside, and ornamented without by piazzas supported by huge pillars. Immense trees shaded the driveway and embowered the stately white mansion. Gay parterres of flowers ornamented the rolling lawn, which divided the great house from the Negro quarters which were picturesquely visible at a convenient distance from it.

Within the house Mr. Montfort had gathered all the treasures which could possibly add to the comfort and pleasure of his lovely wife. Beautiful rugs covered the floors, fine paintings adorned the walls, gleaming statuary flashed upon one from odd nooks and corners. In the library music had found a home in the most comfortable corner of the room. On a table one might find a volume of Goethe[3] in the original; on the grand piano the score of a then-popular opera; while a magnificent harp, standing near, hinted of musical talents highly cultivated.

---

1. *Contending Forces: A Romance Illustrative of Negro Life North and South* was first published in *Colored American Magazine* in 1900 and then by the Colored Co-operative Publishing Company (1900), from which this text is taken.
2. Opening lines of William Shakespeare's *Mer-*

chant of Venice (1597).
3. Johann Wolfgang von Goethe (1749–1832), German poet, novelist, playwright, and philosopher; his most famous work is the poetic drama *Faust* (1808).

Business had prospered with Montfort;[4] his crops flourished; but a nameless trouble seemed to be halting upon the threshold of the home he loved, and to threaten those whom he cherished so fondly.

* * *

Gradually the friendly relations of the neighbors turned to coldness and reserve. It was whispered about that Montfort was about to free his slaves. This in itself was a dangerous doctrine at that time in that part of the world, and a man suspected of entertaining ideas of freedom for slaves must either change his tactics or his residence, or else forfeit life and property. Then again, Bill Sampson's words to Hank Davis had somehow found a voice, and the suspicion of Negro blood in the veins of Mrs. Montfort was a deathblow to a proud spirit and social aspirations. These two serious charges had spread abroad like wildfire.

It was a hot morning, a very hot morning in early summer. There had been no rain for some time. Mrs. Montfort lay in a hammock outside the breakfast-room windows. Lucy, her maid, was mending lace and children's garments a short distance away.

Lucy was Mrs. Montfort's foster sister; both were born on the same day. Their relations had always been those of inseparable friends rather than of mistress and slave.

"No rain today, Lucy. I never used to mind the heat at home (this with a sigh). How fair it must be over the blue waters of the bay; I can almost smell the cedars outside the entrance gates."

"Yas, Miss Grace" (to Lucy her mistress was always "Miss Grace"), "I do feel sort o' squeamish myself sometimes when I tink of the gals all dancin' Sundays in the square; but reckon we'll git used ter these people here arter a-while; leastwise, I hope so."

Mrs. Montfort did not reply, and her maid noticed, as she glanced anxiously at her mistress, that a frown was on her face. Lucy sighed. "Miss Grace" had been noted once for her sunny, cheerful temper. Now all was changed.

* * *

Anson Pollock, whom Charles Montfort had chosen for his friend, was a man of dashing appearance. He carried his years jauntily, and had a good opinion of himself where women were concerned. He was made much of by the ladies in the vicinity because of his wealth. It mattered not that his wife had died mysteriously. Rumor said his ill treatment and infidelity had driven her to suicide; it had even been whispered that he had not hesitated to whip her by proxy through his overseer, Bill Sampson, in the same way he did his slaves; but rumor is a lying jade.[5] Nevertheless, his fair speech, auburn curls and deep-blue eyes, so falsely smiling, won his way, and Mr. Pollock was the popular ladies' man of two counties.

He had showered Mrs. Montfort with assiduous attention since her arrival three years before, but he soon found that he made no headway. Once he

---

4. Charles Montfort of Bermuda has purchased Anson Pollock's large home in Newbern, North Carolina, a colonial town founded in 1710 at the confluence of the Trent and Neuse rivers and settled by Swiss and German adventurers from Bern, Switzerland.
5. A loose or disreputable woman.

dared to tell her of his passion—that from the first moment he saw her aboard the "Island Queen" he had been maddened by her beauty.

"Why do you tell me this?" she cried, in angry amazement at his daring. "Am I so careless of my husband's honor that his friends feel at liberty to insult me?"

"Granted that I overstep the bounds of friendship in speaking thus to you, but it is from no lack of respect; rather the deed of one who risks all upon one throw of the dice. Have mercy, I pray you, and grant me your friendship— your love."

Then Grace Montfort said, while her eyes blazed with wrath: "Mr. Pollock, we are strangers here, my husband and I. He trusts you, and I have no wish to disturb that trust; but if you ever address such words to me again, I shall let Mr. Montfort know the kind of man you are. I promise you that he will know how to deal with you." This conversation had taken place one night at a grand fête, where Grace had been the belle of the assembly; they were in the conservatory at the time. Anson Pollock was not accustomed to having his advances received in this way by any woman whom he elected to honor with his admiration. As the indignant woman swept back to the ballroom, he stood and watched her with an evil look, which meant no good. After that they met as usual, but Pollock had never ventured to speak to her again of love. Outwardly he was the same suave, genial gentleman, but within his breast was a living fire of hatred. The two men became faster friends than ever. Mrs. Montfort was pleased to have it so; they had so few friends in this alien land; she felt so lonely, so helpless. She dreaded making enemies. It was but the lull before the storm.

When the study door had closed behind the two men, Mr. Montfort dropped his pleasant, careless manner and faced Mr. Pollock with an anxious face.

"Pollock," he began abruptly, "I'm worried."

"What about?" asked Pollock, turning from the window, where he seemed to be viewing the landscape.

"Have you heard the rumors about my wife being of African descent?" Montfort asked, coming very close to Pollock, as though afraid the very air would hear him. "There are threats, too, against my life because of my desire to free my slaves."

"Nonsense!" exclaimed Pollock. "I have heard the rumors about Mrs. Montfort, but that is nothing—nothing but the malice of some malicious, jealous woman. As for the threats against your life, how can you think of such things a second time. You are among the most chivalrous people on the face of the earth, who will protect you in your home."

Montfort stood a moment before his friend, gazing at him earnestly; then he said: "Pollock, if anything happens to me, I want you to promise me to help my wife and babies to get back to Bermuda."

"Why, what can happen, man; you are nervous without a cause."

"In that safe," continued Montfort, not heeding the interruption, "you will find money and deeds; promise me that you will save them for my family."

"I promise; but it is all nonsense."

"I shall hold you to your promise," replied Montfort solemnly.

* * *

From *Chapter IV. The Tragedy*

* * *

Eight o'clock was the usual breakfast hour for the Montforts. The family had just assembled at the table; Aunt Cindy had brought in the great silver coffee urn and placed it beside Mrs. Montfort. Mr. Montfort had settled himself in his chair with a weekly paper, for in this rural neighborhood a newspaper once in a week was a great luxury, when his attention was caught by the sound of hoofbeats of several horses on the road. Mrs. Montfort, with usual Southern hospitality, looked over her well-appointed board to make sure that all was in order for dispensing those creature comforts so dear to the entertainer and the entertained.

The hoofbeats drew nearer and paused on the graveled walk. Montfort hastened to the door, while Mrs. Montfort turned toward the entrance of the breakfast-room with a pleasant smile of welcome on her lips. She heard a number of voices speaking together in an excited jumble, then a shot, followed by a heavy fall. Little Jesse ran from his station by his mother's side through one of the long windows opening upon the piazza. She heard his scream of "papa, papa!" and then again the jumble of excited voices. With little Charles clinging to her skirts she stumbled blindly to the entrance and faced the crowd of angry men, headed by Anson Pollock. Hank Davis had done his work well, and Charles Montfort lay dead with a bullet in his brain, sped by an unseen hand. Mrs. Montfort's arms were grasped by rude hands, and she was forcibly drawn out upon the veranda, where in the sunlight of the beautiful morning she saw the body of her husband lying face downward. She was dimly conscious of hearing the cries of frightened slaves mingled with the screams of her children. Through it all she realized but two things— that the lifeless object lying there so still was the body of her husband, and that the sensual face of Anson Pollock, whom she had grown to loathe and fear, was gloating over her agony, devilish in its triumph. Then she lost consciousness.

As she lay upon the green sward, oblivious to thought and feeling, supported by her weeping maid, who had been ordered to care for her mistress by Mr. Pollock, Hank Davis came and stood for a moment looking down upon the unconscious woman. Suddenly an evil smile lighted up his countenance. He looked around, but saw nothing of Anson Pollock, who had disappeared within the house, searching for money and papers in the safe. Now was his time. This woman's husband had flogged him—he would have a sweet revenge. Those lily-like limbs, the tender flesh that had never known aught but the touch of love, should feel the lash as he had.

He called to Bill Sampson to help lift her; and despite the prayers and tears of the poor slave girl who followed her beloved mistress until Sampson knocked her senseless with the butt end of his rawhide, they bore the hapless lady to the whipping post. She revived as they reached the spot; and when she realized the fate in store for her, the sweet woman's strong soul failed her. She uttered a wild cry of agony as the rough hand of Hank Davis was laid upon her to tear her garments from her shrinking shoulders.

"Charles, my husband, save me!" she cried, and fell fainting upon the ground. There was none to answer the heartrending appeal. He who would have shed his heart's best blood for her lay cold in death. She was soon restored to consciousness, for Hank's savage instinct for revenge would only be appeased by the victim's full realization of her sufferings.

She was bound to the whipping post as the victim to the stake, and lashed with rawhides alternately by the two strong, savage men. Hank Davis drew first blood by reason of his wrongs at Mr. Montfort's hands. With all his mighty strength he brought the lash down upon the frail and shrinking form. O God! was there none to rescue her! The air whistled as the snaky leather thong curled and writhed in its rapid, vengeful descent. A shriek from the victim—a spurt of blood that spattered the torturer—a long, raw gash across a tender, white back. Hank gazed at the cut with critical satisfaction, as he compared its depth with the skin and blood that encased the long, tapering lash. It was now Bill's turn.

"I'll go you one better," he said, as he sighted the distance and exact place to make his mark with mathematical precision, at the same time shifting his tobacco from the right to the left cheek. Again the rawhide whistled through the air, falling across the other cut squarely in the center. Another shriek, a stifled sob, a long-drawn quivering sigh—then the deep stillness of unconsciousness. Again and again was the outrage repeated. Fainting fit followed fainting fit. The blood stood in a pool about her feet.

When Hank Davis had satiated his vengeful thirst he cut the ropes which bound her, and she sank upon the ground again—unconscious, bleeding, friendless, alone. Lucy had hidden in the smokehouse with the two children, that they might not witness their mother's agony.

Meantime, the committee on public safety,[6] instigated by Anson Pollock to put down an imaginary insurrection (having no existence but in his own mind, and supposed to have originated with the slaves of Charles Montfort) and to legalize the looting of the house, took possession of the mansion. Soon the crowd had stripped it of its furniture and all the articles of value. The house itself was fired, and Grace Montfort again became conscious of her misery in time to see the dead body of her husband flung amid the burning rafters of his dwelling. Two and two the slaves were handcuffed together to be driven to the market place. Mrs. Montfort, secured to her maid, was placed in a wagon with her two children; and so the miserable woman was driven away from her outraged home.

In those old days, if accused of aiding slaves in a revolt, a white man stood no more chance than a Negro accused of the same crime. He forfeited life and property. This power of the law Anson Pollock had invoked; and to add to the devilishness of the plot, had used Bill Sampson's suggestion of black blood in Mrs. Montfort, to further his scheme for possessing the beautiful woman. So the two children and their mother fell to the lot of Anson Pollock as his portion of the spoils. Shortly after these events Grace Montfort disappeared and was never seen again. The waters of Pamlico Sound[7] tell of sweet oblivion for the broken-hearted found within their soft embrace.

After the loss of their mother the two lads clung very closely to each other. So many changes had come to them, such desperate, bloody scenes had

6. The Committee of Public Safety (French: *Comité de salut publique*) was the de facto executive government of France during the Reign of Terror (1793–94) of the French Revolution. The Jacobins centralized denunciations, trials, and executions under the supervision of this committee of twelve members. In the American South, the name denoted secret meetings of white property-owners to spy on and control African Americans, often through terror tactics and sometimes murder.
7. Pamlico Sound, in North Carolina, is separated from the Atlantic Ocean by the Outer Banks.

dazed their brains and terrified them, that even the loss of their mother seemed but in keeping with the rest. Bewilderment at so much sorrow, the numbness of black despair was ever with them.

* * *

Jesse was now a man in stature, though still slender, with the same haughty bearing and distinguished appearance that had marked his father. Anson Pollock, upon whom age and the memory of dreadful crimes were making fearful inroads, began to look up to the boy and lean upon him for aid in his various plans for making money. He had spoken to him of making him the overseer, in place of Bill Sampson, and had even hinted at his taking a mate. Then Jesse knew that his probation was nearly over. That spring Pollock, as was the common practice among planters, made out passes for Jesse and sent him to New York in charge of a vessel filled with produce, and charged to bring back necessary merchandise for use on the plantation. Pollock thought the boy still too young to venture to leave him. Indeed Jesse had no such idea when he started on his trip to the North. When the vessel reached New York, Jesse performed all the necessary duties—disposed of the produce, and reloaded the ship for its homeward voyage. The night before they were to sail he sat on the wharf watching the crews of other vessels making ready for departure. His mind was engrossed with thoughts of Charles. He feared some evil had befallen him.

"At any rate," he said to himself, "I shall never see him again. And must I remain in servitude? Can I do nothing to help myself, since all hope is gone in that direction?" Just then a group of men paused in front of him. They did not know he was a slave.

"Will you give passage to two on board your vessel? You are bound for Newbern in the morning, aren't you? We'll pay you what you charge," said one of the group respectfully.

"Speak to the cap'n," called out a man standing near; "that's nuthin' but a nigger you're talkin' to."

"Well," said the one who had first addressed him, "you're a likely boy, anyhow; who do you belong to?"

Jesse arose from his seat, white with passion, and said to the man: "I am no man's property; I belong to Jesus Christ!" The question had answered itself. When the vessel sailed the next morning, Jesse was far on his road to Boston.

Traveling then was done by stage, and was a slow process; but about a week later he stood beside the stone wall that enclosed the historic Boston Common, and as he watched the cows chewing their peaceful cuds and inhaled deep draughts of freedom's air, he vowed to die rather than return to Anson Pollock.

He found work in Boston. It mattered not that it was menial work; he was happy. But fate or Providence was not done with him yet.

One day he received word that Anson Pollock was on his way to Boston in search of him. Again he made a hurried journey. This time to Exeter, N.H. In his character of a fugitive slave, the lad had from the first cast his lot with the colored people of the community, and when he left Boston he was directed to see Mr. Whitfield, a negro in Exeter, who could and would help the fugitive.

Late one afternoon, just before tea time, a comely black woman stood in her long, low-raftered kitchen preparing supper before the open fireplace. There was every indication of plenty in the homely furnishings. As the woman passed rapidly from the cupboard to the table she would touch with her foot the rockers of the little red cradle which stood in the center of the floor. The baby in it was crying in a fretful way. "Oh, hush, Lizzie," said the mother; "don't be so cross." There came a low rap at the open door, and in answer to her "Come in," Jesse stepped into the room.

"Is Mr. Whitfield in?" he asked, as he doffed his hat respectfully.

"No," was the reply, "but I expect him every minute. Sit down, won't you? He'll soon be in to his supper, I guess."

Mrs. Whitfield thought him a white man, come on business with her husband. "A handsome lad," she thought. Jesse seated himself; and then as the child continued to cry, said: "Shall I rock the cradle for you, ma'am? The child seems fretful."

Fifteen years later Jesse married Elizabeth Whitfield, the baby he had rocked to sleep the first night of his arrival in Exeter. By her he had a large family.

Thus he was absorbed into that unfortunate race, of whom it is said that a man had better be born dead than to come into the world as part and parcel of it.

✻　✻　✻

From *Chapter XIII. The American Colored League*[8]

✻　✻　✻

Dr. Arthur Lewis was head of a large educational institution in the South devoted to the welfare of the Negroes.[9] Every year he visited the city, and assisted by a quartette of singers, who were also members of the school, collected large sums of money from the best class of philanthropic citizens, who gave to the Negro not only because they believed he was wronged, but also because they believed that in great measure his elevation would remove the stigma under which the Southern white labored. For the loyal white man there would be no greater joy in life than to see his poetic dream of superiority to all other governments realized in the "land of the free and the home of the brave." He knows that this can never be while the Negro question keeps up the line of demarkation which marks the division of the North from the South.[1] True and loyal son of his country, he would sacrifice any race, any principle, to bring about this much-desired consummation; so he contributes his money to build up manufacturing interests at the South to his own material disadvantage in the North: to develop uncultivated land there, and to educate the Negro with the hope that in the general advance the latter question may be buried from public notice, if not obliterated. Delusive hope that grasps at shadows!

That momentous Tuesday evening rolled quickly round. The committee asked that the meeting should open at half-past seven, on account of the time needed by the speakers, and long before the hour appointed the large edifice was filled to overflowing. And what a crowd! They came from towns remote, from the farm, from domestic service in the homes of wealth and from among

8. The American Colored League is a fictional organization, based on the many such groups forming in the Northeast at the time.
9. Lewis generally voices the ideas of Booker T. Washington, as Will Smith voices those of W. E. B. Du Bois.

1. Also known as "Mason and Dixon's Line," this line ran for the most part along Pennsylvania's southern boundary. After Pennsylvania began abolishing slavery in 1781, this line, and the Ohio River, became known as the border between the free and slave states.

the lowly ones who earn a scanty living with scrubbing-brush and pail. Doctor, lawyer, politician, mechanic—every class sent its representative there to help protest against the wrongs of down-trodden manhood.

The platform was heavily draped in American flags supplemented by wide bands of mourning. Pictures of the anti-slavery apostles peered out at the audience from the folds of the national colors. Speakers and representative citizens were seated upon the platform, and visiting delegates occupied seats in close proximity. The choir had volunteered its services, and, after a prayer by the pastor, rendered Mrs. Julia Ward Howe's "Battle Hymn of the Republic" in masterly style.[2] In listening to the martial strains the pulse of the vast concourse of people was strained with excitement and expectation. The stillness was intense as the gray-haired president of the League and chairman of the meeting arose in his seat and passing to the desk, rapped for order.

"Fellow-citizens and men and women of my race: The occasion for this meeting is one of great solemnity. Forty years ago, when as a young man I sat at the feet of Sumner, Phillips, Garrison, Pillsbury, Charles Lenox Remond, Nell, Robert Morris, Fred Douglas and all the mighty host of anti-slavery fathers, we thought that with the abolishment of slavery the black man's destiny would be accomplished, and fixed beyond a peradventure. Today a condition of affairs confronts us that they never foresaw: the systematic destruction of the Negro by every device which the fury of enlightened malevolence can invent. In whatever direction we turn, the clouds hang dark and threatening. This new birth of the black race is a mighty agony. God help us in our struggle for liberty and manhood! *Agitation and eternal vigilance in the formation of public opinion* were the weapons which broke the power of the slave-holder and gave us emancipation. I recommend these methods to you today, knowing their value in the past.

> " 'Up then and act! Thy courage wake!
> Combat intrigue, injustice, tyranny,
> And in thine efforts God will be with thee.' "

* * *

Chapter XIV. Luke Sawyer Speaks to the League

> My ear is pained,
> My soul is sick with every day's report
> Of wrong and outrage with which earth is filled.
> There is no flesh in man's obdurate heart;
> It does not feel for man: the natural bond
> Of brotherhood is severed as the flax
> That falls asunder at the touch of fire.
> He finds his fellow guilty of a skin
> *Not colored like his own;* and, having power
> To enforce the wrong *for such a worthy cause,*
> Dooms and devotes him as a lawful prey.
> —Cowper.[3]

Scarcely had the speaker taken his seat amid suppressed murmurs of discontent, when a tall, gaunt man of very black complexion arose in his seat

2. Julia Ward Howe's "Battle Hymn of the Republic" was published in the *Atlantic Monthly* in 1862.

3. From William Cowper's "Charity" (1782), an antislavery poem.

among the delegates, and in a sonorous bass voice uttered the solemn protest of Patrick Henry, so famous in history: "Gentlemen may cry 'Peace! peace!' but there is no peace!"[4]

In an instant confusion reigned. Women fluttered their handkerchiefs, and above waves of applause and cheers could be heard cries of "Hear, hear!" "Platform! platform!" The chairman rapped for order, and when he could make himself heard, asked the delegate to come to the platform; another speaker was waiting, but the audience would be glad to hear anything he might have to say. As he passed up the aisle and mounted the steps of the rostrum, the people saw a man of majestic frame, rugged physique and immense muscular development. His face was kindly, but withal bore the marks of superior intelligence, shrewdness and great strength of character. He might have been a Cromwell, a Robespierre, a Lincoln.[5] Men of his physiological development—when white—mould humanity, and leave their own characteristics engraved upon the pages of the history of their times.

"Friends," said he, when he stood before them, "I come from Williamstown, in the western part of this state, to be a delegate at this meeting. Here are my credentials to show that I am in good standing in the League where I belong. (He handed his papers to the chairman.) I want to impress that fact upon the minds of this assembly, because I am going to tell you some awful facts before I get through." He paused, and with his handkerchief wiped the tears and perspiration from his face. "Friends, I am thirty years old and look fifty. I want to tell you why this is so. I want to tell you what brought me *here*. I want to tell the gentlemen who have spoken here tonight that conservatism, lack of brotherly affiliation, lack of energy for the right and the power of the almighty dollar which deadens men's hearts to the sufferings of their brothers, and makes them feel that if only *they* can rise to the top of the ladder may God help the hindmost man, are the forces which are ruining the Negro in this country. It is killing him off by thousands, destroying his self-respect, and degrading him to the level of the brute. *These are the contending forces that are dooming this race to despair!*

"My name is Lycurgus Sawyer; Luke they call me for short. When I was about ten years old my father kept a large store in a little town in the state of Louisany. I had two brothers and a sister. My mother was a fine woman, somewhat better educated than my father. Through her influence he went into this business of trading, and soon had the largest business and as much money as any man in the county. Father didn't care to meddle with politics, for, with the natural shrewdness of many of us, he saw that that might be made an excuse for his destruction. When I was about ten years old, then, a white man in the village, seeing the headway my father was making in accumulating property, opened a store on the same street. Father said nothing, but his customers still continued to trade with him, and it seemed that the other man would be compelled to give up. About this time father received threat-

---

4. Henry's 1775 speech in support of the American Revolution proclaimed, "Give me liberty, or give me death."
5. Oliver Cromwell (1599–1658), member of the British Parliament and major participant in the revolution of 1648–49, including the trial and exe-

cution of Charles I and the abolition of monarchy and the House of Lords; from 1653 until his death, he was the constitutional head of state. Maximilien Robespierre (1758–1794), a Jacobin leader of the French Revolution. Abraham Lincoln (1809–1865), 16th president of the United States.

ening letters ordering him to move, and saying that in case he did not do as ordered he would lose his life. Mother was frightened, and advised father to get out of the place, but he, anxious to save some part of his hard earnings, waited to sell his stock and houses before seeking a home elsewhere. One night a posse of men came to our house and began smoking us out. You don't know anything about that up here, do you? Well, you'll get there if things keep on as they're going. My father had arms. He raised the window of his sleeping-room and fired into the mob of cowardly hounds. Thoroughly enraged, they broke open the doors back and front, seized my father and hung him to the nearest tree, whipped my mother and sister, and otherwise abused them so that they died next day. My brothers were twins, still so small that they were but babes. The mob took them by the heels and dashed their brains out against the walls of the house! Then they burned the house. I saw all this, and frenzied with horror, half-dead with fright, crept into the woods to die. I was found there by a colored planter named Beaubean, who lived in the next township. He pitied me and took me home. *That*, gentlemen, was my *first* experience of lynching. Do you think it is possible to preach 'peace' to a man like me?"

The house was filled with the cries and groans of the audience. Sobs shook the women, while the men drank in the words of the speaker with darkening brows and hands which involuntarily clinched themselves in sympathy with his words.

"But that is not the only story I can tell. Here's another. I will tell it to you, and you can digest it at your leisure.

"Monsieur Beaubean was an educated man, descended from a very wealthy family. His father had been his owner. When the father died he left to his son, born of a black mother, an equal share of the estate along with his legitimate heirs. They made no objections, so he got it.

"Monsieur Beaubean had married a quadroon[6] woman of great beauty— Louisany abounds in handsome women of color; they had two children, a boy and a girl. She was three years old when I went to live with them. I remained in the family twelve years. I learned many things there; along with the trade of blacksmithing I learned to esteem myself as a man.

"I cannot describe to you the beauty and loveliness of that child. As a boy I worshipped her, and as a man I loved her; not with the hope of ever having a return of the feeling she had aroused in me, but as a faithful dog that would lay down his life for those who shelter and care for him, so I felt to Beaubean's family, and especially to that child. When Mabelle, as we called her, was old enough, she was sent to the Colored Sisters' School in the city of New Orleans. It was my pleasant duty to drive her into the city each day and go for her at night.

"Monsieur Beaubean had a half-brother—a white man—who was very wealthy and stood very high in politics. In fact, he was in the State Senate. He was very warm in his expressions of friendship for the family, and especially so in his assumption of relationship. I noticed that he seemed extremely fond of Mabelle. One day, after she had passed her fourteenth birthday, she

6. A person with one black grandparent.

had a holiday from school, and went with some schoolfellows to visit a companion who lived in the city. They returned at night without her, saying that she went into a store with Monsieur Beaubean's brother, and they had not seen her since.

"Can you imagine what a night was passed by that family? No, you cannot, unless you have been through the same experience. The father went in one direction and I in another. All night long we searched the city streets; nothing could be heard of her. Finally we went to police headquarters and secured the services of a detective. After *three weeks* of incessant searching we found her a prisoner in a house of the vilest character in the lowest portion of the city of New Orleans—a poor, ruined, half-crazed creature in whom it was almost impossible to trace a resemblance to the beautiful pet of our household. These arms bore her forth from that vile den and restored her to a broken-hearted parent. I think that I must have gone mad. If I had had the man there then that committed the crime (he raised one gaunt arm above his head, and standing in that attitude seemed the embodiment of vengeance) I would have taken him by the throat and shaken him (he hissed the words through clinched teeth), shaken him as a dog would a rat until he was *dead!* DEAD! DEAD! We took her home, but I believe that her father was a madman from the time he placed his eyes upon her until he was murdered. And who do you think had done this foul crime? Why, the father's *half-brother*, *uncle* of the victim!

"Crazed with grief, Monsieur Beaubean faced his brother and accused him of his crime. 'Well,' said he, 'whatever damage I have done I am willing to pay for. But your child is no better than her mother or her grandmother. What does a woman of mixed blood, or any Negress, for that matter, know of virtue? It is my belief that they were a direct creation by God to be the pleasant companions of men of my race. Now, I am willing to give you a thousand dollars and call it square.' He handed Monsieur Beaubean a roll of bills as he spoke. Beaubean seized them and hurled them into the villain's face with these words: 'I leave you to carry my case into the Federal courts and appeal for justice.' Unhappy man! That night his house was mobbed. The crowd surrounded the building after firing it, and as an inmate would show his head at a window in the struggle to escape from the burning building, someone would pick him off. So it went all that night. I seized Mabelle and wrapped her in a blanket. Watching my chance I stole from the house after the fire was well under way, and miraculously reached a place of safety. I took Mabelle to the colored convent at New Orleans, and left her there in the care of the sisters. *There she died when her child was born!*"

As the speaker stood silently contemplating his weeping, grief-convulsed audience, a woman was borne from the auditorium in a fainting condition. John Langley from his seat on the platform leaned over and asked an usher who the lady was. "Miss Sappho Clark," was his reply.

Amid universal silence, the silence which comes from feeling too deep for outward expression, the speaker concluded: "A tax too heavy placed on tea and things like that, made the American Colonies go to war with Great Britain to get their liberty. I ask you what you think the American Colonies would have done if they had suffered as we have suffered and are still suffering?

"Mr. Chairman, gentlemen call for peace, and I reply: 'Peace if possible; justice at any rate.' Where is there peace for men like me? When the grave has closed over me and my memories, I shall have peace.

"Under such conditions as I have described, contentment, amity—call it by what name you will—is impossible; justice alone remains to us."

1900

CHARLOTTE PERKINS GILMAN
1860–1935

Charlotte Perkins Gilman lived her life, for the most part, on the margins of a society whose economic assumptions about and social definitions of women she vigorously repudiated. Out of this resistance to conventional values and what she later characterized as "masculinist" ideals, Gilman produced the large body of polemical writings and what we would call today self-consciously feminist fiction that made her the leading theoretician, speaker, and writer on women's issues of her time.

Charlotte Anna Perkins was born in Hartford, Connecticut, on July 3, 1860. Her father, Frederic Beecher Perkins, was a minor literary figure, grandson of the theologian Lyman Beecher, and nephew of the preacher Henry Ward Beecher and of Harriet Beecher Stowe. Her mother was Mary A. Fitch, whose family had lived in Rhode Island since the middle of the seventeenth century. Gilman's father deserted his family and left for San Francisco shortly after her birth, and she spent many years trying, without success, to establish some intimacy with him. She received from him only occasional letters with lists of books she should read. Her mother returned to Providence, Rhode Island, where she supported herself and her two children with great difficulty; she withheld from them all physical expressions of love, hoping to prevent their later disillusionment over broken relationships. It is easy to understand why in her autobiography Gilman described her childhood as painful and lonely.

Between 1880 and her marriage in May 1884 to Charles Stetson, a promising Providence artist, Gilman supported herself in Providence as a governess, art teacher, and designer of greeting cards. During those years she had increasingly become aware of the injustices inflicted on women, and she had begun to write poems—one in defense of prostitutes—in which she developed her own views on women's rights. She entered into the marriage reluctantly, anticipating the difficulties of reconciling her ambition to be a writer with the demands of being a wife, housekeeper, and mother. Within eleven months, their only child, Katharine, was born; following the birth, Gilman became increasingly despondent, and marital tensions increased. Her husband and her mother were convinced that Gilman needed rest and willpower to overcome her depression; they persuaded her to go to Philadelphia for treatment by Dr. S. Weir Mitchell, the most famous American neurologist of the day. A specialist in women's "nervous" disorders, Mitchell usually prescribed a "rest cure" consisting of total bedrest for several weeks and limited intellectual activity thereafter. In those days, postpartum depression was not widely understood. As Gilman put it in "Why I Wrote 'The Yellow Wall-paper'?" (1913), the doctor "sent me home [after six weeks] with the solemn advice to 'live as domestic a life as . . . possible,' to 'have but two hours' intellectual life a day,' and 'never to touch pen, brush, or pencil again' as long as I lived." The patient returned to Providence and obeyed these instructions for three months "and came so near the borderline of utter mental ruin that I could see over." She drew back from the edge of madness by resuming her life as a reluctant wife and mother and as an enthusiastic writer and frequent contributor to the Boston *Woman's Journal*. A few years later she wrote her most famous story. As she concluded: "It was not intended to drive people crazy, but to save people from being driven crazy, and it worked." Writing "The Yellow Wall-paper" (1892), however, did not keep Gilman from suffering all her life with extended periods of depression.

In 1888, after a trial separation, convinced that her marriage threatened her sanity, Gilman moved with her daughter to Pasadena, California, and in 1892 was granted a divorce. Her former husband promptly married her best friend, the writer Grace Ellery Channing, and not long thereafter Gilman sent her daughter east to live with them. Such actions generated much publicity and hostile criticism in the press, but nothing kept Gilman from pursuing her double career as writer and lecturer on women, labor, and social organization. In these years she was particularly influenced by the sociologist Lester Ward and the utopian novelist Edward Bellamy.

In 1898 Gilman published *Women and Economics*, the book that earned her immediate celebrity and that is still considered her most important nonfiction work. This powerful "feminist manifesto" argues a thesis Gilman was to develop and refine for the rest of her life: women's economic dependency on men stunts not only the growth of women but that of the whole human species. More particularly, she argued that because of the dependency of women on men for food and shelter the sexual and maternal aspects of their personalities had been developed excessively and to the detriment of their other productive capacities. To free women to develop in a more balanced and socially constructive way, Gilman urged such reforms as centralized nurseries (in *Concerning Children,* 1900) and professionally staffed collective kitchens (in *The Home,* 1904).

In 1911 she published *The Man-Made World*, which contrasted the competitiveness and aggressiveness of men with the cooperativeness and nurturance of women and posited that until women played a larger part in national and international life, social injustice and war would characterize industrialized societies. In this same year her short story "Turned" appeared, taking on similar gender issues. Similarly, in *His Religion and Hers* (1923) Gilman predicted that when women influenced theology would the fear of death and punishment cease to be central to religious institutions and practices.

Gilman's poetry and fiction, most written when she was well past forty, must be seen, as the critic Ann J. Lane has observed, as "part of her ideological world view, and therein lies its interest and power." Therein, also, lie its limits, for as Lane also says, "She wrote quickly, carelessly, to make a point." Still, many of Gilman's stories and her utopian novels—such as *Moving the Mountain* (1911), *Herland* (1915), and *With Her in Ourland* (1916)—offer vivid dramatizations of the social ills (and their potential remedies) that result from a competitive economic system in which women are subordinate to men and accept their subordination. In *Herland,* for instance, Gilman offers a vision of an all-female society in which caring women raise children (reproduced by parthenogenesis) collectively in a world that is both prosperous and ecologically sound.

In 1900, after a long courtship, she married her first cousin George Houghton Gilman. They lived together happily, first in New York, then in Norwich, Connecticut, until he died suddenly in 1934. Gilman then moved to Pasadena to live with her daughter's family. The next year, suffering from breast cancer and convinced that her productive life was over, she committed suicide with chloroform she had long been accumulating.

The Yellow Wall-paper[1]

It is very seldom that mere ordinary people like John and myself secure ancestral halls for the summer.

A colonial mansion, a hereditary estate, I would say a haunted house, and reach the height of romantic felicity—but that would be asking too much of fate!

Still I will proudly declare that there is something queer about it.

Else, why should it be let so cheaply? And why have stood so long untenanted?

John laughs at me, of course, but one expects that in marriage.

John is practical in the extreme. He has no patience with faith, an intense horror of superstition, and he scoffs openly at any talk of things not to be felt and seen and put down in figures.

John is a physician, and *perhaps*—(I would not say it to a living soul, of course, but this is dead paper and a great relief to my mind)—*perhaps* that is one reason I do not get well faster.

You see he does not believe I am sick!

And what can one do?

If a physician of high standing, and one's own husband, assures friends and relatives that there is really nothing the matter with one but temporary nervous depression—a slight hysterical tendency[2]—what is one to do?

My brother is also a physician, and also of high standing, and he says the same thing.

So I take phosphates or phosphites—whichever it is—and tonics, and journeys, and air, and exercise, and am absolutely forbidden to "work" until I am well again.

Personally, I disagree with their ideas.

Personally, I believe that congenial work, with excitement and change, would do me good.

But what is one to do?

I did write for a while in spite of them; but it *does* exhaust me a good deal—having to be so sly about it, or else meet with heavy opposition.

I sometimes fancy that in my condition if I had less opposition and more society and stimulus—but John says the very worst thing I can do is to think about my condition, and I confess it always makes me feel bad.

So I will let it alone and talk about the house.

The most beautiful place! It is quite alone, standing well back from the road, quite three miles from the village. It makes me think of English places

1. The complete and complex textual history of the extant fair copy manuscript and seven editions of the story during Gilman's lifetime is available in Julie Bates Dock's *Charlotte Perkins Gilman's "The Yellow Wall-paper" and the History of Its Publication and Reception: A Critical Edition and Documentary Casebook* (Pennsylvania State University Press, 1998). Dock's volume also contains a detailed textual apparatus and notes, a variety of background material, early reviews, and other commentary. Professor Dock and Pennsylvania State University Press have kindly granted permission to use her eclectic critical edition of this story.
2. At the time this story was written, *hysteria* was a term used to describe a wide variety of symptoms, thought to be particularly prevalent among women, that indicated emotional disturbance or dysfunction. Depression, anxiety, excitability, and vague somatic complaints were among the conditions treated as "hysteria." As the words *uterus* and *hysteria* came from the same Greek root, so the medical profession blamed women's reproductive systems for their "sick" mentalities; hysterectomies were increasingly performed.

that you read about, for there are hedges and walls and gates that lock, and lots of separate little houses for the gardeners and people.

There is a *delicious* garden! I never saw such a garden—large and shady, full of box-bordered paths, and lined with long grape-covered arbors with seats under them.

There were greenhouses, too, but they are all broken now.

There was some legal trouble, I believe, something about the heirs and co-heirs; anyhow, the place has been empty for years.

That spoils my ghostliness, I am afraid, but I don't care—there is something strange about the house—I can feel it.

I even said so to John one moonlight evening, but he said what I felt was a *draught,* and shut the window.

I get unreasonably angry with John sometimes. I'm sure I never used to be so sensitive. I think it is due to this nervous condition.

But John says if I feel so, I shall neglect proper self-control; so I take pains to control myself—before him, at least, and that makes me very tired.

I don't like our room a bit. I wanted one downstairs that opened on the piazza and had roses all over the window, and such pretty old-fashioned chintz hangings! But John would not hear of it.

He said there was only one window and not room for two beds, and no near room for him if he took another.

He is very careful and loving, and hardly lets me stir without special direction.

I have a schedule prescription for each hour in the day; he takes all care from me, and so I feel basely ungrateful not to value it more.

He said we came here solely on my account, that I was to have perfect rest and all the air I could get. "Your exercise depends on your strength, my dear," said he, "and your food somewhat on your appetite; but air you can absorb all the time." So we took the nursery at the top of the house.

It is a big, airy room, the whole floor nearly, with windows that look all ways, and air and sunshine galore. It was nursery first and then playroom and gymnasium, I should judge; for the windows are barred for little children, and there are rings and things in the walls.

The paint and paper look as if a boys' school had used it. It is stripped off—the paper—in great patches all around the head of my bed, about as far as I can reach, and in a great place on the other side of the room low down. I never saw a worse paper in my life.

One of those sprawling flamboyant patterns committing every artistic sin.

It is dull enough to confuse the eye in following, pronounced enough to constantly irritate and provoke study, and when you follow the lame uncertain curves for a little distance they suddenly commit suicide—plunge off at outrageous angles, destroy themselves in unheard of contradictions.

The color is repellent, almost revolting; a smouldering unclean yellow, strangely faded by the slow-turning sunlight.

It is a dull yet lurid orange in some places, a sickly sulphur tint in others.

No wonder the children hated it! I should hate it myself if I had to live in this room long.

There comes John, and I must put this away—he hates to have me write a word.

• • • • • •

We have been here two weeks, and I haven't felt like writing before, since that first day.

I am sitting by the window now, up in this atrocious nursery, and there is nothing to hinder my writing as much as I please, save lack of strength.

John is away all day, and even some nights when his cases are serious.

I am glad my case is not serious!

But these nervous troubles are dreadfully depressing.

John does not know how much I really suffer. He knows there is no *reason* to suffer, and that satisfies him.

Of course it is only nervousness. It does weigh on me so not to do my duty in any way!

I meant to be such a help to John, such a real rest and comfort, and here I am a comparative burden already!

Nobody would believe what an effort it is to do what little I am able—to dress and entertain, and order things.

It is fortunate Mary is so good with the baby. Such a dear baby!

And yet I *cannot* be with him, it makes me so nervous.

I suppose John never was nervous in his life. He laughs at me so about this wall-paper!

At first he meant to repaper the room, but afterwards he said that I was letting it get the better of me, and that nothing was worse for a nervous patient than to give way to such fancies.

He said that after the wall-paper was changed it would be the heavy bedstead, and then the barred windows, and then that gate at the head of the stairs, and so on.

"You know the place is doing you good," he said, "and really, dear, I don't care to renovate the house just for a three months' rental."

"Then do let us go downstairs," I said, "there are such pretty rooms there."

Then he took me in his arms and called me a blessed little goose, and said he would go down cellar, if I wished, and have it whitewashed into the bargain.

But he is right enough about the beds and windows and things.

It is as airy and comfortable a room as any one need wish, and, of course, I would not be so silly as to make him uncomfortable just for a whim.

I'm really getting quite fond of the big room, all but that horrid paper.

Out of one window I can see the garden, those mysterious deep-shaded arbors, the riotous old-fashioned flowers, and bushes and gnarly trees.

Out of another I get a lovely view of the bay and a little private wharf belonging to the estate. There is a beautiful shaded lane that runs down there from the house. I always fancy I see people walking in these numerous paths and arbors, but John has cautioned me not to give way to fancy in the least. He says that with my imaginative power and habit of story-making, a nervous weakness like mine is sure to lead to all manner of excited fancies, and that I ought to use my will and good sense to check the tendency. So I try.

I think sometimes that if I were only well enough to write a little it would relieve the press of ideas and rest me.

But I find I get pretty tired when I try.

It is so discouraging not to have any advice and companionship about my work. When I get really well, John says we will ask Cousin Henry and Julia down for a long visit; but he says he would as soon put fireworks in my pillowcase as to let me have those stimulating people about now.

I wish I could get well faster.

But I must not think about that. This paper looks to me as if it *knew* what a vicious influence it had!

There is a recurrent spot where the pattern lolls like a broken neck and two bulbous eyes stare at you upside down.

I get positively angry with the impertinence of it and the everlastingness. Up and down and sideways they crawl, and those absurd, unblinking eyes are everywhere. There is one place where two breadths didn't match, and the eyes go all up and down the line, one a little higher than the other.

I never saw so much expression in an inanimate thing before, and we all know how much expression they have! I used to lie awake as a child and get more entertainment and terror out of blank walls and plain furniture than most children could find in a toy-store.

I remember what a kindly wink the knobs of our big, old bureau used to have, and there was one chair that always seemed like a strong friend.

I used to feel that if any of the other things looked too fierce I could always hop into that chair and be safe.

The furniture in this room is no worse than inharmonious, however, for we had to bring it all from downstairs. I suppose when this was used as a playroom they had to take the nursery things out, and no wonder! I never saw such ravages as the children have made here.

The wall-paper, as I said before, is torn off in spots, and it sticketh closer than a brother[3]—they must have had perseverance as well as hatred.

Then the floor is scratched and gouged and splintered, the plaster itself is dug out here and there, and this great heavy bed, which is all we found in the room, looks as if it had been through the wars.

But I don't mind it a bit—only the paper.

There comes John's sister. Such a dear girl as she is, and so careful of me! I must not let her find me writing.

She is a perfect and enthusiastic housekeeper, and hopes for no better profession. I verily believe she thinks it is the writing which made me sick!

But I can write when she is out, and see her a long way off from these windows.

There is one that commands the road, a lovely shaded winding road, and one that just looks off over the country. A lovely country, too, full of great elms and velvet meadows.

This wall-paper has a kind of sub-pattern in a different shade, a particularly irritating one, for you can only see it in certain lights, and not clearly then.

But in the places where it isn't faded and where the sun is just so—I can see a strange, provoking, formless sort of figure, that seems to skulk about behind that silly and conspicuous front design.

There's sister on the stairs!

• • • • • •

---

3. Proverbs 18.24: "There is a friend that sticketh closer than a brother."

Well, the Fourth of July is over! The people are all gone and I am tired out. John thought it might do me good to see a little company, so we just had mother and Nellie and the children down for a week.

Of course I didn't do a thing. Jennie sees to everything now.

But it tired me all the same.

John says if I don't pick up faster he shall send me to Weir Mitchell[4] in the fall.

But I don't want to go there at all. I had a friend who was in his hands once, and she says he is just like John and my brother, only more so!

Besides, it is such an undertaking to go so far.

I don't feel as if it was worth while to turn my hand over for anything, and I'm getting dreadfully fretful and querulous.

I cry at nothing, and cry most of the time.

Of course I don't when John is here, or anybody else, but when I am alone.

And I am alone a good deal just now. John is kept in town very often by serious cases, and Jennie is good and lets me alone when I want her to.

So I walk a little in the garden or down that lovely lane, sit on the porch under the roses, and lie down up here a good deal.

I'm getting really fond of the room in spite of the wall-paper. Perhaps *because* of the wall-paper.

It dwells in my mind so!

I lie here on this great immovable bed—it is nailed down, I believe—and follow that pattern about by the hour. It is as good as gymnastics, I assure you. I start, we'll say, at the bottom, down in the corner over there where it has not been touched, and I determine for the thousandth time that I *will* follow that pointless pattern to some sort of a conclusion.

I know a little of the principle of design, and I know this thing was not arranged on any laws of radiation, or alternation, or repetition, or symmetry, or anything else that I ever heard of.

It is repeated, of course, by the breadths, but not otherwise.

Looked at in one way each breadth stands alone, the bloated curves and flourishes—a kind of "debased Romanesque"[5] with *delirium tremens*—go waddling up and down in isolated columns of fatuity.

But, on the other hand, they connect diagonally, and the sprawling outlines run off in great slanting waves of optic horror, like a lot of wallowing seaweeds in full chase.

The whole thing goes horizontally, too, at least it seems so, and I exhaust myself in trying to distinguish the order of its going in that direction.

They have used a horizontal breadth for a frieze,[6] and that adds wonderfully to the confusion.

There is one end of the room where it is almost intact, and there, when the crosslights fade and low sun shines directly upon it, I can almost fancy radiation after all—the interminable grotesques seem to form around a common centre and rush off in headlong plunges of equal distraction.

It makes me tired to follow it. I will take a nap I guess.

- - - - - - - - -

4. Silas Weir Mitchell (1829–1914), American physician, novelist, and specialist in nerve disorders, popularized the "rest cure" in the management of hysteria, nervous breakdowns, and related disorders. A friend of W. D. Howells, he was the model for the nerve specialist in Howells's *The Shadow of a Dream* (1890).

5. The style is here associated with ornamental complexity and repeated motifs and figures.

6. An ornamental border at the top of the wall.

I don't know why I should write this.

I don't want to.

I don't feel able.

And I know John would think it absurd. But I *must* say what I feel and think in some way—it is such a relief!

But the effort is getting to be greater than the relief.

Half the time now I am awfully lazy, and lie down ever so much.

John says I mustn't lose my strength, and has me take cod liver oil and lots of tonics and things, to say nothing of ale and wine and rare meat.

Dear John! He loves me very dearly, and hates to have me sick. I tried to have a real earnest reasonable talk with him the other day, and tell him how I wish he would let me go and make a visit to Cousin Henry and Julia.

But he said I wasn't able to go, nor able to stand it after I got there; and I did not make out a very good case for myself, for I was crying before I had finished.

It is getting to be a great effort for me to think straight. Just this nervous weakness I suppose.

And dear John gathered me up in his arms, and just carried me upstairs and laid me on the bed, and sat by me and read to me till it tired my head.

He said I was his darling and his comfort and all he had, and that I must take care of myself for his sake, and keep well.

He says no one but myself can help me out of it, that I must use my will and self-control and not let any silly fancies run away with me.

There's one comfort, the baby is well and happy, and does not have to occupy this nursery with the horrid wall-paper.

If we had not used it, that blessed child would have! What a fortunate escape! Why, I wouldn't have a child of mine, an impressionable little thing, live in such a room for worlds.

I never thought of it before, but it is lucky that John kept me here after all, I can stand it so much easier than a baby, you see.

Of course I never mention it to them any more—I am too wise—but I keep watch of it all the same.

There are things in that paper that nobody knows but me, or ever will.

Behind that outside pattern the dim shapes get clearer every day.

It is always the same shape, only very numerous.

And it is like a woman stooping down and creeping about behind that pattern. I don't like it a bit. I wonder—I begin to think—I wish John would take me away from here!

• • • • • •

It is so hard to talk with John about my case, because he is so wise, and because he loves me so.

But I tried it last night.

It was moonlight. The moon shines in all around just as the sun does.

I hate to see it sometimes, it creeps so slowly, and always comes in by one window or another.

John was asleep and I hated to waken him, so I kept still and watched the moonlight on that undulating wall-paper till I felt creepy.

The faint figure behind seemed to shake the pattern, just as if she wanted to get out.

I got up softly and went to feel and see if the paper *did* move, and when I came back John was awake.

"What is it, little girl?" he said. "Don't go walking about like that—you'll get cold."

I thought it was a good time to talk, so I told him that I really was not gaining here, and that I wished he would take me away.

"Why, darling!" said he, "our lease will be up in three weeks, and I can't see how to leave before.

"The repairs are not done at home, and I cannot possibly leave town just now. Of course if you were in any danger, I could and would, but you really are better, dear, whether you can see it or not. I am a doctor, dear, and I know. You are gaining flesh and color, your appetite is better, I feel really much easier about you."

"I don't weigh a bit more," said I, "nor as much; and my appetite may be better in the evening when you are here, but it is worse in the morning when you are away!"

"Bless her little heart!" said he with a big hug, "she shall be as sick as she pleases! But now let's improve the shining hours[7] by going to sleep, and talk about it in the morning!"

"And you won't go away?" I asked gloomily.

"Why, how can I, dear? It is only three weeks more and then we will take a nice little trip of a few days while Jennie is getting the house ready. Really, dear, you are better!"

"Better in body perhaps—" I began, and stopped short, for he sat up straight and looked at me with such a stern, reproachful look that I could not say another word.

"My darling," said he, "I beg of you, for my sake and for our child's sake, as well as for your own, that you will never for one instant let that idea enter your mind! There is nothing so dangerous, so fascinating, to a temperament like yours. It is a false and foolish fancy. Can you not trust me as a physician when I tell you so?"

So of course I said no more on that score, and we went to sleep before long. He thought I was asleep first, but I wasn't, and lay there for hours trying to decide whether that front pattern and the back pattern really did move together or separately.

· · · · · ·

On a pattern like this, by daylight, there is a lack of sequence, a defiance of law, that is a constant irritant to a normal mind.

The color is hideous enough, and unreliable enough, and infuriating enough, but the pattern is torturing.

You think you have mastered it, but just as you get well underway in following, it turns a back-somersault and there you are. It slaps you in the face, knocks you down, and tramples upon you. It is like a bad dream.

---

7. In his poem "Against Idleness and Mischief," Issac Watts (1674–1748) writes:

> How doth the little busy bee
> Improve each shining hour,
> And gather honey all the day
> From every opening flower!

These lines are parodied in Lewis Carroll's *Alice's Adventures in Wonderland* (1865), when Alice eats a cake that makes her grow larger—in her transformation, she finds she has forgotten, or scrambled her knowledge of poems, history, mathematics, and other information.

The outside pattern is a florid arabesque, reminding one of a fungus. If you can imagine a toadstool in joints, an interminable string of toadstools, budding and sprouting in endless convolutions—why, that is something like it.

That is, sometimes!

There is one marked peculiarity about this paper, a thing nobody seems to notice but myself, and that is that it changes as the light changes.

When the sun shoots in through the east window—I always watch for that first long, straight ray—it changes so quickly that I never can quite believe it.

That is why I watch it always.

By moonlight—the moon shines in all night when there is a moon—I wouldn't know it was the same paper.

At night in any kind of light, in twilight, candlelight, lamplight, and worst of all by moonlight, it becomes bars! The outside pattern, I mean, and the woman behind it is as plain as can be.

I didn't realize for a long time what the thing was that showed behind, that dim sub-pattern, but now I am quite sure it is a woman.

By daylight she is subdued, quiet. I fancy it is the pattern that keeps her so still. It is so puzzling. It keeps me quiet by the hour.

I lie down ever so much now. John says it is good for me, and to sleep all I can.

Indeed he started the habit by making me lie down for an hour after each meal.

It is a very bad habit, I am convinced, for you see I don't sleep.

And that cultivates deceit, for I don't tell them I'm awake—O no!

The fact is I am getting a little afraid of John.

He seems very queer sometimes, and even Jennie has an inexplicable look.

It strikes me occasionally, just as a scientific hypothesis, that perhaps it is the paper!

I have watched John when he did not know I was looking, and come into the room suddenly on the most innocent excuses, and I've caught him several times *looking at the paper!* And Jennie too. I caught Jennie with her hand on it once.

She didn't know I was in the room, and when I asked her in a quiet, a very quiet voice, with the most restrained manner possible, what she was doing with the paper—she turned around as if she had been caught stealing, and looked quite angry—asked me why I should frighten her so!

Then she said that the paper stained everything it touched, that she had found yellow smooches on all my clothes and John's, and she wished we would be more careful!

Did not that sound innocent? But I know she was studying that pattern, and I am determined that nobody shall find it out but myself!

· · · · ·

Life is very much more exciting now than it used to be. You see I have something more to expect, to look forward to, to watch. I really do eat better, and am more quiet than I was.

John is so pleased to see me improve! He laughed a little the other day, and said I seemed to be flourishing in spite of my wall-paper.

I turned it off with a laugh. I had no intention of telling him it was *because* of the wall-paper—he would make fun of me. He might even want to take me away.

I don't want to leave now until I have found it out. There is a week more, and I think that will be enough.

· · · · · ·

I'm feeling ever so much better! I don't sleep much at night, for it is so interesting to watch developments; but I sleep a good deal in the daytime.

In the daytime it is tiresome and perplexing.

There are always new shoots on the fungus, and new shades of yellow all over it. I cannot keep count of them, though I have tried conscientiously.

It is the strangest yellow, that wall-paper! It makes me think of all the yellow things I ever saw—not beautiful ones like buttercups, but old foul, bad yellow things.

But there is something else about that paper—the smell! I noticed it the moment we came into the room, but with so much air and sun it was not bad. Now we have had a week of fog and rain, and whether the windows are open or not, the smell is here.

It creeps all over the house.

I find it hovering in the dining-room, skulking in the parlor, hiding in the hall, lying in wait for me on the stairs.

It gets into my hair.

Even when I go to ride, if I turn my head suddenly and surprise it—there is that smell!

Such a peculiar odor, too! I have spent hours in trying to analyze it, to find what it smelled like.

It is not bad—at first—and very gentle, but quite the subtlest, most enduring odor I ever met.

In this damp weather it is awful, I wake up in the night and find it hanging over me.

It used to disturb me at first. I thought seriously of burning the house—to reach the smell.

But now I am used to it. The only thing I can think of that it is like is the *color* of the paper! A yellow smell.

There is a very funny mark on this wall, low down, near the mopboard. A streak that runs round the room. It goes behind every piece of furniture, except the bed, a long, straight, even *smooch*, as if it had been rubbed over and over.

I wonder how it was done and who did it, and what they did it for. Round and round and round—round and round and round—it makes me dizzy!

· · · · · ·

I really have discovered something at last.

Through watching so much at night, when it changes so, I have finally found out.

The front pattern *does* move—and no wonder! The woman behind shakes it!

Sometimes I think there are a great many women behind, and sometimes only one, and she crawls around fast, and her crawling shakes it all over.

Then in the very bright spots she keeps still, and in the very shady spots she just takes hold of the bars and shakes them hard.

And she is all the time trying to climb through. But nobody could climb through that pattern—it strangles so; I think that is why it has so many heads.

They get through, and then the pattern strangles them off and turns them upside down, and makes their eyes white!

If those heads were covered or taken off it would not be half so bad.

• • • • • •

I think that woman gets out in the daytime!

And I'll tell you why—privately—I've seen her!

I can see her out of every one of my windows!

It is the same woman, I know, for she is always creeping, and most women do not creep by daylight.

I see her in that long shaded lane, creeping up and down. I see her in those dark grape arbors, creeping all around the garden.

I see her on that long road under the trees, creeping along, and when a carriage comes she hides under the blackberry vines.

I don't blame her a bit. It must be very humiliating to be caught creeping by daylight!

I always lock the door when I creep by daylight. I can't do it at night, for I know John would suspect something at once.

And John is so queer now, that I don't want to irritate him. I wish he would take another room! Besides, I don't want anybody to get that woman out at night but myself.

I often wonder if I could see her out of all the windows at once.

But, turn as fast as I can, I can only see out of one at one time.

And though I always see her, she *may* be able to creep faster than I can turn!

I have watched her sometimes away off in the open country, creeping as fast as a cloud shadow in a high wind.

• • • • •

If only that top pattern could be gotten off from the under one! I mean to try it, little by little.

I have found out another funny thing, but I shan't tell it this time! It does not do to trust people too much.

There are only two more days to get this paper off, and I believe John is beginning to notice. I don't like the look in his eyes.

And I heard him ask Jennie a lot of professional questions about me. She had a very good report to give.

She said I slept a good deal in the daytime.

John knows I don't sleep very well at night, for all I'm so quiet!

He asked me all sorts of questions, too, and pretended to be very loving and kind.

As if I couldn't see through him!

Still, I don't wonder he acts so, sleeping under this paper for three months.

It only interests me, but I feel sure John and Jennie are secretly affected by it.

• • • • •

Hurrah! This is the last day, but it is enough. John had to stay in town over night, and won't be out until this evening.

Jennie wanted to sleep with me—the sly thing!—but I told her I should undoubtedly rest better for a night all alone.

That was clever, for really I wasn't alone a bit! As soon as it was moonlight and that poor thing began to crawl and shake the pattern, I got up and ran to help her.

I pulled and she shook, I shook and she pulled, and before morning we had peeled off yards of that paper.

A strip about as high as my head and half around the room.

And then when the sun came and that awful pattern began to laugh at me, I declared I would finish it to-day!

We go away to-morrow, and they are moving all my furniture down again to leave things as they were before.

Jennie looked at the wall in amazement, but I told her merrily that I did it out of pure spite at the vicious thing.

She laughed and said she wouldn't mind doing it herself, but I must not get tired.

How she betrayed herself that time!

But I am here, and no person touches this paper but me—not *alive!*

She tried to get me out of the room—it was too patent! But I said it was so quiet and empty and clean now that I believed I would lie down again and sleep all I could; and not to wake me even for dinner—I would call when I woke.

So now she is gone, and the servants are gone, and the things are gone, and there is nothing left but that great bedstead nailed down, with the canvas mattress we found on it.

We shall sleep downstairs to-night, and take the boat home to-morrow.

I quite enjoy the room, now it is bare again.

How those children did tear about here!

This bedstead is fairly gnawed!

But I must get to work.

I have locked the door and thrown the key down into the front path.

I don't want to go out, and I don't want to have anybody come in, till John comes.

I want to astonish him.

I've got a rope up here that even Jennie did not find. If that woman does get out, and tries to get away, I can tie her!

But I forgot I could not reach far without anything to stand on!

This bed will *not* move!

I tried to lift and push it until I was lame, and then I got so angry I bit off a little piece at one corner—but it hurt my teeth.

Then I peeled off all the paper I could reach standing on the floor. It sticks horribly and the pattern just enjoys it! All those strangled heads and bulbous eyes and waddling fungus growths just shriek with derision!

I am getting angry enough to do something desperate. To jump out of the window would be admirable exercise, but the bars are too strong even to try.

Besides, I wouldn't do it. Of course not. I know well enough that a step like that is improper and might be misconstrued.

I don't like to *look* out of the windows even—there are so many of those creeping women, and they creep so fast.

I wonder if they all come out of that wall-paper as I did?

But I am securely fastened now by my well-hidden rope—you don't get *me* out in the road there!

I suppose I shall have to get back behind the pattern when it comes night, and that is hard!

It is so pleasant to be out in this great room and creep around as I please!

I don't want to go outside. I won't, even if Jennie asks me to.

For outside you have to creep on the ground, and everything is green instead of yellow.

But here I can creep smoothly on the floor, and my shoulder just fits in that long smooch around the wall, so I cannot lose my way.

Why, there's John at the door!

It is no use, young man, you can't open it!

How he does call and pound!

Now he's crying for an axe.

It would be a shame to break down that beautiful door!

"John, dear!" said I in the gentlest voice, "the key is down by the front steps, under a plantain leaf!"

That silenced him for a few moments.

Then he said—very quietly indeed—"Open the door, my darling!"

"I can't," said I. "The key is down by the front door under a plantain leaf!"

And then I said it again, several times, very gently and slowly, and said it so often that he had to go and see, and he got it of course, and came in. He stopped short by the door.

"What is the matter?" he cried. "For God's sake, what are you doing!"

I kept on creeping just the same, but I looked at him over my shoulder.

"I've got out at last," said I, "in spite of you and Jane! And I've pulled off most of the paper, so you can't put me back!"

Now why should that man have fainted? But he did, and right across my path by the wall, so that I had to creep over him every time!

1892

EDITH WHARTON
1862–1937

Edith Wharton began to write as a very young woman, published some fifty varied volumes in her lifetime, and left a number of unpublished manuscripts and a voluminous correspondence at her death. *The House of Mirth* (1905), her second novel, was a best-seller; another novel, *The Age of Innocence* (1920), won the Pulitzer Prize; in 1930 she was awarded the gold medal of the National Institute of Arts and Letters, the first woman to be so honored.

Edith Newbold Jones was born in New York City on January 24, 1862, into a patriarchal, monied, cultivated, and rather rigid family that, like others in its small circle, disdained and feared the drastic social, cultural, and economic changes brought on by post–Civil War expansionism and immigration. It is small wonder, then, that her work, like Henry James's, deals with what she described as the tragic psychic and moral effects on its members of a frivolous society under pressure. She was educated by tutors and governesses, much of the time while the family resided in Europe. In 1885 she married the Bostonian Edward Wharton, a social equal thirteen years her senior. Though they lived together (in New York; Newport; Lenox, Massachusetts; and Paris) for twenty-eight years, their marriage was not happy. That Wharton did not seek a divorce until 1913 (on grounds of her husband's adultery) is more a tribute to what her biographer R. W. B. Lewis characterized as her "moral conservatism and her devotion to family ties and the sanctities of tradition" than to personal affection.

The social circle in which Edith Wharton moved was not given to artistic or intellectual pursuits, and any career—especially a career as a writer—was frowned on. A young woman from Wharton's background received little formal schooling. Her purpose in life—to find a marriage partner from her own social class—required constant attendance at balls and large parties from adolescence on, as well as much attention to fashion and etiquette. After marriage she took her place as a leisure-class wife. Wharton rejected these values even as a young girl; she spent as much time as she could in her father's library at home—and in similar libraries of her friends. By the time she was fifteen she had written—in secret—a thirty-thousand-word novella titled *Fast and Loose*; at this time she also wrote a great deal of lyric poetry—with what she later described as a "lamentable facility." When she was sixteen, two of her poems were published, one in the *Atlantic Monthly*. Although her intense interest in literature, ideas, and the arts never abated, she was not to publish again until 1889, when three recently composed poems were sent out to *Scribner's, Harper's,* and the *Century*—and all were accepted. The next year, a sketch of hers was published by *Scribner's.*

It was not until the late 1890s, however, that Wharton, then in her late thirties, fully embraced authorship as a career. The decision was motivated partly by her increasing marital discontent and, perhaps, partly by the fact that she was childless. The first significant product of that commitment was a collection of stories titled *The Greater Inclination* (1899). With the publication in 1905 of *The House of Mirth* Wharton confirmed her unconventional choice to be a writer and immediately found an appreciative public. Although she was later to write about other subjects, she discovered in *The House of Mirth* her central settings, plots, and themes: the old aristocracy of New York in conflict with the nouveau riche, the futile struggle of characters trapped by social forces larger and individuals morally smaller than themselves. Two novels that embody these themes are among those most critically acclaimed. *The House of Mirth* tells the story of the beautiful but hapless Lily Bart, trained to be a decorative upper-class wife but unable to sell herself as merchandise. In *The Custom of the Country* (1913), which Wharton considered her "masterpiece," the ruthless Undine Spragg from Ohio makes her way up the social ladder, stepping on Americans and Europeans alike in her pursuit of money and the power that goes with it.

In 1911 Wharton separated from her husband and took up residence in France, where she spent the rest of her life. Altogether she produced more than eighty short stories and twenty-two novellas and novels, including three very different but distinguished books: *Ethan Frome* (1911), *Summer* (1917), and *The Age of Innocence* (1920). Her autobiography, *A Backward Glance,* was published in 1934. During World War I, Wharton organized relief efforts for the refugees and orphans displaced by the advance of the German Army and was active in many other committees and organizations dealing with the devastation wrought by the war. She also wrote extensively about her visits to the front line, and a collection of these dispatches was published as *Fighting France, from Dunkerque to Belfort* (1915). In recognition of her brave and generous effort on behalf of French citizens and soldiers alike, she was awarded the highest honor given by the French government to foreigners—the Chevalier of the Legion of Honor.

Wharton's early social training persisted throughout her life in the form of a constant sociability. She made and kept numerous friends, especially among the leading male intellectuals of her day. Some of them, Egerton Winthrop, Paul Bourget, and Walter Berry to name three, were important to her as she found her way to her profession as a writer. Others, including Henry James and art critics Bernard Berenson and Kenneth Clark, she met as intellectual equals. Still others, including Jean Cocteau and Sinclair Lewis (who dedicated *Babbitt* to her), became her admirers late in her life. In this capacity for friendships among the most distinguished people of her time, Wharton is like Gertrude Stein and Willa Cather, also among the most important American writers of the early twentieth century. Her reputation continues to grow; along with James she is considered a major contributor to the practice of psychological realism. In view of the inability of her characters, despite their high social status, to control their destinies, Wharton is increasingly included by critics such as Donna M. Campbell among such naturalists as Jack London and Theodore Dreiser. Her scathing analyses of human behavior and (often base) motivation, as well as her social criticism, present struggles for power and survival no less dangerous than and sometimes as deadly as those faced by naturalist characters in the wilderness. In this respect, she also compares interestingly with Kate Chopin.

The Other Two[1]

I

Waythorn, on the drawing-room hearth, waited for his wife to come down to dinner.

It was their first night under his own roof, and he was surprised at his thrill of boyish agitation. He was not so old, to be sure—his glass gave him little more than the five-and-thirty years to which his wife confessed—but he had fancied himself already in the temperate zone; yet here he was listening for her step with a tender sense of all it symbolized, with some old trail of verse about the garlanded nuptial doorposts floating through his enjoyment of the pleasant room and the good dinner just beyond it.

They had been hastily recalled from their honeymoon by the illness of Lily Haskett, the child of Mrs. Waythorn's first marriage. The little girl, at Waythorn's desire, had been transferred to his house on the day of her mother's wedding, and the doctor, on their arrival, broke the news that she was ill with typhoid, but declared that all the symptoms were favorable. Lily could show twelve years of unblemished health, and the case promised to be a light one. The nurse spoke as reassuringly, and after a moment of alarm Mrs. Waythorn had adjusted herself to the situation. She was very fond of Lily—her affection for the child had perhaps been her decisive charm in Waythorn's eyes—but she had the perfectly balanced nerves which her little girl had inherited, and no woman ever wasted less tissue in unproductive

1. First appeared in *Collier's Weekly* (February 1904).

worry. Waythorn was therefore quite prepared to see her come in presently, a little late because of a last look at Lily, but as serene and well-appointed as if her good-night kiss had been laid on the brow of health. Her composure was restful to him; it acted as ballast to his somewhat unstable sensibilities. As he pictured her bending over the child's bed he thought how soothing her presence must be in illness: her very step would prognosticate recovery.

His own life had been a gray one, from temperament rather than circumstance, and he had been drawn to her by the unperturbed gaiety which kept her fresh and elastic at an age when most women's activities are growing either slack or febrile. He knew what was said about her; for, popular as she was, there had always been a faint undercurrent of detraction. When she had appeared in New York, nine or ten years earlier, as the pretty Mrs. Haskett whom Gus Varick had unearthed somewhere—was it in Pittsburgh or Utica?—society, while promptly accepting her, had reserved the right to cast a doubt on its own indiscrimination. Inquiry, however, established her undoubted connection with a socially reigning family, and explained her recent divorce as the natural result of a runaway match at seventeen; and as nothing was known of Mr. Haskett it was easy to believe the worst of him.

Alice Haskett's remarriage with Gus Varick was a passport to the set whose recognition she coveted, and for a few years the Varicks were the most popular couple in town. Unfortunately the alliance was brief and stormy, and this time the husband had his champions. Still, even Varick's stanchest supporters admitted that he was not meant for matrimony, and Mrs. Varick's grievances were of a nature to bear the inspection of the New York courts. A New York divorce is in itself a diploma of virtue, and in the semiwidowhood of this second separation Mrs. Varick took on an air of sanctity, and was allowed to confide her wrongs to some of the most scrupulous ears in town. But when it was known that she was to marry Waythorn there was a momentary reaction. Her best friends would have preferred to see her remain in the role of the injured wife, which was as becoming to her as crepe to a rosy complexion. True, a decent time had elapsed, and it was not even suggested that Waythorn had supplanted his predecessor. People shook their heads over him, however, and one grudging friend, to whom he affirmed that he took the step with his eyes open, replied oracularly: "Yes—and with your ears shut."

Waythorn could afford to smile at these innuendoes. In the Wall Street phrase, he had "discounted" them. He knew that society has not yet adapted itself to the consequences of divorce, and that till the adaptation takes place every woman who uses the freedom the law accords her must be her own social justification. Waythorn had an amused confidence in his wife's ability to justify herself. His expectations were fulfilled, and before the wedding took place Alice Varick's group had rallied openly to her support. She took it all imperturbably: she had a way of surmounting obstacles without seeming to be aware of them, and Waythorn looked back with wonder at the trivialities over which he had worn his nerves thin. He had the sense of having found refuge in a richer, warmer nature than his own, and his satisfaction, at the moment, was humorously summed up in the thought that his wife, when she had done all she could for Lily, would not be ashamed to come down and enjoy a good dinner.

The anticipation of such enjoyment was not, however, the sentiment expressed by Mrs. Waythorn's charming face when she presently joined him. Though she had put on her most engaging tea gown she had neglected to assume the smile that went with it, and Waythorn thought he had never seen her look so nearly worried.

"What is it?" he asked. "Is anything wrong with Lily?"

"No; I've just been in and she's still sleeping." Mrs. Waythorn hesitated. "But something tiresome has happened."

He had taken her two hands, and now perceived that he was crushing a paper between them.

"This letter?"

"Yes—Mr. Haskett has written—I mean his lawyer has written."

Waythorn felt himself flush uncomfortably. He dropped his wife's hands. "What about?"

"About seeing Lily. You know the courts—"

"Yes, yes," he interrupted nervously.

Nothing was known about Haskett in New York. He was vaguely supposed to have remained in the outer darkness from which his wife had been rescued, and Waythorn was one of the few who were aware that he had given up his business in Utica and followed her to New York in order to be near his little girl. In the days of his wooing, Waythorn had often met Lily on the doorstep, rosy and smiling, on her way "to see papa."

"I am so sorry," Mrs. Waythorn murmured.

He roused himself. "What does he want?"

"He wants to see her. You know she goes to him once a week."

"Well—he doesn't expect her to go to him now, does he?"

"No—he has heard of her illness; but he expects to come here."

"Here?"

Mrs. Waythorn reddened under his gaze. They looked away from each other.

"I'm afraid he has the right. . . . You'll see. . . ." She made a proffer of the letter.

Waythorn moved away with a gesture of refusal. He stood staring about the softly-lighted room, which a moment before had seemed so full of bridal intimacy.

"I'm so sorry," she repeated. "If Lily could have been moved—"

"That's out of the question," he returned impatiently.

"I suppose so."

Her lip was beginning to tremble, and he felt himself a brute.

"He must come, of course," he said. "When is—his day?"

"I'm afraid—tomorrow."

"Very well. Send a note in the morning."

The butler entered to announce dinner.

Waythorn turned to his wife. "Come—you must be tired. It's beastly, but try to forget about it," he said, drawing her hand through his arm.

"You're so good, dear. I'll try," she whispered back.

Her face cleared at once, and as she looked at him across the flowers, between the rosy candleshades, he saw her lips waver back into a smile.

"How pretty everything is!" she sighed luxuriously.

He turned to the butler. "The champagne at once, please. Mrs. Waythorn is tired."

In a moment or two their eyes met above the sparkling glasses. Her own were quite clear and untroubled: he saw that she had obeyed his injunction and forgotten.

II

Waythorn, the next morning, went downtown earlier than usual. Haskett was not likely to come till the afternoon, but the instinct of flight drove him forth. He meant to stay away all day—he had thoughts of dining at his club. As his door closed behind him he reflected that before he opened it again it would have admitted another man who had as much right to enter it as himself, and the thought filled him with a physical repugnance.

He caught the elevated at the employees' hour, and found himself crushed between two layers of pendulous humanity. At Eighth Street the man facing him wriggled out, and another took his place. Waythorn glanced up and saw that it was Gus Varick. The men were so close together that it was impossible to ignore the smile of recognition on Varick's handsome overblown face. And after all—why not? They had always been on good terms, and Varick had been divorced before Waythorn's attentions to his wife began. The two exchanged a word on the perennial grievance of the congested trains, and when a seat at their side was miraculously left empty the instinct of self-preservation made Waythorn slip into it after Varick.

The latter drew the stout man's breath of relief. "Lord—I was beginning to feel like a pressed flower." He leaned back, looking unconcernedly at Waythorn. "Sorry to hear that Sellers is knocked out again."

"Sellers?" echoed Waythorn, starting at his partner's name.

Varick looked surprised. "You didn't know he was laid up with the gout?"

"No. I've been away—I only got back last night." Waythorn felt himself reddening in anticipation of the other's smile.

"Ah—yes; to be sure. And Sellers' attack came on two days ago. I'm afraid he's pretty bad. Very awkward for me, as it happens, because he was just putting through a rather important thing for me."

"Ah?" Waythorn wondered vaguely since when Varick had been dealing in "important things." Hitherto he had dabbled only in the shallow pools of speculation, with which Waythorn's office did not usually concern itself.

It occurred to him that Varick might be talking at random, to relieve the strain of their propinquity. That strain was becoming momentarily more apparent to Waythorn, and when, at Cortlandt Street, he caught sight of an acquaintance and had a sudden vision of the picture he and Varick must present to an initiated eye, he jumped up with a muttered excuse.

"I hope you'll find Sellers better," said Varick civilly, and he stammered back: "If I can be of any use to you—" and let the departing crowd sweep him to the platform.

At his office he heard that Sellers was in fact ill with the gout, and would probably not be able to leave the house for some weeks.

"I'm sorry it should have happened so, Mr. Waythorn," the senior clerk said with affable significance. "Mr. Sellers was very much upset at the idea of giving you such a lot of extra work just now."

"Oh, that's no matter," said Waythorn hastily. He secretly welcomed the pressure of additional business, and was glad to think that, when the day's work was over, he would have to call at his partner's on the way home.

He was late for luncheon, and turned in at the nearest restaurant instead of going to his club. The place was full, and the waiter hurried him to the back of the room to capture the only vacant table. In the cloud of cigar smoke Waythorn did not at once distinguish his neighbors: but presently, looking about him, he saw Varick seated a few feet off. This time, luckily, they were too far apart for conversation, and Varick, who faced another way, had probably not even seen him; but there was an irony in their renewed nearness.

Varick was said to be fond of good living, and as Waythorn sat dispatching his hurried luncheon he looked across half enviously at the other's leisurely degustation of his meal. When Waythorn first saw him he had been helping himself with critical deliberation to a bit of Camembert at the ideal point of liquefaction, and now, the cheese removed, he was just pouring his *café double* from its little two-storied earthen pot. He poured slowly, his ruddy profile bent over the task, and one beringed white hand steadying the lid of the coffeepot; then he stretched his other hand to the decanter of cognac at his elbow, filled a liqueur glass, took a tentative sip, and poured the brandy into his coffee cup.

Waythorn watched him in a kind of fascination. What was he thinking of— only of the flavor of the coffee and the liqueur? Had the morning's meeting left no more trace in his thoughts than on his face? Had his wife so completely passed out of his life that even this odd encounter with her present husband, within a week after her remarriage, was no more than an incident in his day? And as Waythorn mused, another idea struck him: had Haskett ever met Varick as Varick and he had just met? The recollection of Haskett perturbed him, and he rose and left the restaurant, taking a circuitous way out to escape the placid irony of Varick's nod.

It was after seven when Waythorn reached home. He thought the footman who opened the door looked at him oddly.

"How is Miss Lily?" he asked in haste.

"Doing very well, sir. A gentleman—"

"Tell Barlow to put off dinner for half an hour," Waythorn cut him off, hurrying upstairs.

He went straight to his room and dressed without seeing his wife. When he reached the drawing room she was there, fresh and radiant. Lily's day had been good; the doctor was not coming back that evening.

At dinner Waythorn told her of Sellers' illness and of the resulting complications. She listened sympathetically, adjuring him not to let himself be overworked, and asking vague feminine questions about the routine of the office. Then she gave him the chronicle of Lily's day; quoted the nurse and doctor, and told him who had called to inquire. He had never seen her more serene and unruffled. It struck him, with a curious pang, that she was very happy in being with him, so happy that she found a childish pleasure in rehearsing the trivial incidents of her day.

After dinner they went to the library, and the servant put the coffee and liqueurs on a low table before her and left the room. She looked singularly soft and girlish in her rosy-pale dress, against the dark leather of one of his bachelor armchairs. A day earlier the contrast would have charmed him.

He turned away now, choosing a cigar with affected deliberation.

"Did Haskett come?" he asked, with his back to her.

"Oh, yes—he came."

"You didn't see him, of course?"

She hesitated a moment. "I let the nurse see him."

That was all. There was nothing more to ask. He swung round toward her, applying a match to his cigar. Well, the thing was over for a week, at any rate. He would try not to think of it. She looked up at him, a trifle rosier than usual, with a smile in her eyes.

"Ready for your coffee, dear?"

He leaned against the mantelpiece, watching her as she lifted the coffeepot. The lamplight struck a gleam from her bracelets and tipped her soft hair with brightness. How light and slender she was, and how each gesture flowed into the next! She seemed a creature all compact of harmonies. As the thought of Haskett receded, Waythorn felt himself yielding again to the joy of possessorship. They were his, those white hands with their flitting motions, his the light haze of hair, the lips and eyes. . . .

She set down the coffeepot, and reaching for the decanter of cognac, measured off a liqueur glass and poured it into his cup.

Waythorn uttered a sudden exclamation.

"What is the matter?" she said, startled.

"Nothing; only—I don't take cognac in my coffee."

"Oh, how stupid of me," she cried.

Their eyes met, and she blushed a sudden agonized red.

III

Ten days later, Mr. Sellers, still housebound, asked Waythorn to call on his way downtown.

The senior partner, with his swaddled foot propped up by the fire, greeted his associate with an air of embarrassment.

"I'm sorry, my dear fellow; I've got to ask you to do an awkward thing for me."

Waythorn waited, and the other went on, after a pause apparently given to the arrangement of his phrases: "The fact is, when I was knocked out I had just gone into a rather complicated piece of business for—Gus Varick."

"Well?" said Waythorn, with an attempt to put him at his ease.

"Well—it's this way: Varick came to me the day before my attack. He had evidently had an inside tip from somebody, and had made about a hundred thousand. He came to me for advice, and I suggested his going in with Vanderlyn."

"Oh, the deuce!" Waythorn exclaimed. He saw in a flash what had happened. The investment was an alluring one, but required negotiation. He listened quietly while Sellers put the case before him, and, the statement ended, he said: "You think I ought to see Varick?"

"I'm afraid I can't as yet. The doctor is obdurate. And this thing can't wait. I hate to ask you, but no one else in the office knows the ins and outs of it."

Waythorn stood silent. He did not care a farthing for the success of Varick's venture, but the honor of the office was to be considered, and he could hardly refuse to oblige his partner.

"Very well," he said, "I'll do it."

That afternoon, apprised by telephone, Varick called at the office. Waythorn, waiting in his private room, wondered what the others thought of it. The newspapers, at the time of Mrs. Waythorn's marriage, had acquainted their readers with every detail of her previous matrimonial ventures, and Waythorn could fancy the clerks smiling behind Varick's back as he was ushered in.

Varick bore himself admirably. He was easy without being undignified, and Waythorn was conscious of cutting a much less impressive figure. Varick had no experience of business, and the talk prolonged itself for nearly an hour while Waythorn set forth with scrupulous precision the details of the proposed transaction.

"I'm awfully obliged to you," Varick said as he rose. "The fact is I'm not used to having much money to look after, and I don't want to make an ass of myself—" He smiled, and Waythorn could not help noticing that there was something pleasant about his smile. "It feels uncommonly queer to have enough cash to pay one's bills. I'd have sold my soul for it a few years ago!"

Waythorn winced at the allusion. He had heard it rumored that a lack of funds had been one of the determining causes of the Varick separation, but it did not occur to him that Varick's words were intentional. It seemed more likely that the desire to keep clear of embarrassing topics had fatally drawn him into one. Waythorn did not wish to be outdone in civility.

"We'll do the best we can for you," he said. "I think this is a good thing you're in."

"Oh, I'm sure it's immense. It's awfully good of you—" Varick broke off, embarrassed. "I suppose the thing's settled now—but if—"

"If anything happens before Sellers is about, I'll see you again," said Waythorn quietly. He was glad, in the end, to appear the more self-possessed of the two.

The course of Lily's illness ran smooth, and as the days passed Waythorn grew used to the idea of Haskett's weekly visit. The first time the day came round, he stayed out late, and questioned his wife as to the visit on his return. She replied at once that Haskett had merely seen the nurse downstairs, as the doctor did not wish anyone in the child's sickroom till after the crisis.

The following week Waythorn was again conscious of the recurrence of the day, but had forgotten it by the time he came home to dinner. The crisis of the disease came a few days later, with a rapid decline of fever, and the little girl was pronounced out of danger. In the rejoicing which ensued the thought of Haskett passed out of Waythorn's mind, and one afternoon, letting himself into the house with a latchkey, he went straight to his library without noticing a shabby hat and umbrella in the hall.

In the library he found a small effaced-looking man with a thinnish gray beard sitting on the edge of a chair. The stranger might have been a piano tuner, or one of those mysteriously efficient persons who are summoned in emergencies to adjust some detail of the domestic machinery. He blinked at Waythorn through a pair of gold-rimmed spectacles and said mildly: "Mr. Waythorn, I presume? I am Lily's father."

Waythorn flushed. "Oh—" he stammered uncomfortably. He broke off, disliking to appear rude. Inwardly he was trying to adjust the actual Haskett to the image of him projected by his wife's reminiscences. Waythorn had been allowed to infer that Alice's first husband was a brute.

"I am sorry to intrude," said Haskett, with his over-the-counter politeness.

"Don't mention it," returned Waythorn, collecting himself. "I suppose the nurse has been told?"

"I presume so. I can wait," said Haskett. He had a resigned way of speaking, as though life had worn down his natural powers of resistance.

Waythorn stood on the threshold, nervously pulling off his gloves.

"I'm sorry you've been detained. I will send for the nurse," he said; and as he opened the door he added with an effort: "I'm glad we can give you a good report of Lily." He winced as the *we* slipped out, but Haskett seemed not to notice it.

"Thank you, Mr. Waythorn, It's been an anxious time for me."

"Ah, well, that's past. Soon she'll be able to go to you." Waythorn nodded and passed out.

In his own room he flung himself down with a groan. He hated the womanish sensibility which made him suffer so acutely from the grotesque chances of life. He had known when he married that his wife's former husbands were both living, and that amid the multiplied contacts of modern existence there were a thousand chances to one that he would run against one or the other, yet he found himself as much disturbed by his brief encounter with Haskett as though the law had not obligingly removed all difficulties in the way of their meeting.

Waythorn sprang up and began to pace the room nervously. He had not suffered half as much from his two meetings with Varick. It was Haskett's presence in his own house that made the situation so intolerable. He stood still, hearing steps in the passage.

"This way, please," he heard the nurse say. Haskett was being taken upstairs, then: not a corner of the house but was open to him. Waythorn dropped into another chair, staring vaguely ahead of him. On his dressing table stood a photograph of Alice, taken when he had first known her. She was Alice Varick then—how fine and exquisite he had thought her! Those were Varick's pearls about her neck. At Waythorn's instance they had been returned before her marriage. Had Haskett ever given her any trinkets—and what had become of them, Waythorn wondered? He realized suddenly that he knew very little of Haskett's past or present situation; but from the man's appearance and manner of speech he could reconstruct with curious precision the surroundings of Alice's first marriage. And it startled him to think that she had, in the background of her life, a phase of existence so different from anything with which he had connected her. Varick, whatever his faults, was a gentleman, in the conventional, traditional sense of the term: the sense which at that moment seemed, oddly enough, to have most meaning to Waythorn. He and Varick had the same social habits, spoke the same language, understood the same allusions. But this other man . . . it was grotesquely uppermost in Waythorn's mind that Haskett had worn a made-up tie attached with an elastic. Why should that ridiculous detail symbolize the whole man? Waythorn was exasperated by his own paltriness, but the fact of the tie expanded, forced itself on him, became as it were the key to Alice's past. He could see her, as Mrs. Haskett, sitting in a "front parlor" furnished in plush, with a pianola, and copy of *Ben Hur*[2] on the center table. He could see her going to the theater with Haskett—or perhaps even to a "Church Sociable"—she in a "picture hat" and Haskett in a black frock coat, a little creased, with the made-up tie on an elastic. On the way home they would stop and look at the illuminated shop windows, lingering over the photographs of New York actresses. On Sunday afternoons Haskett would take her for a walk, pushing Lily ahead of them in a white enameled perambulator, and Waythorn had a vision of the people they would stop and talk to. He could fancy how pretty Alice must have looked, in a dress adroitly constructed from the hints of a New York fashion paper, and how she must have looked down on the other women, chafing at her life, and secretly feeling that she belonged in a bigger place.

For the moment his foremost thought was one of wonder at the way in which she had shed the phase of existence which her marriage with Haskett implied. It was as if her whole aspect, every gesture, every inflection, every allusion, were a studied negation of that period of her life. If she had denied being married to Haskett she could hardly have stood more convicted of duplicity than in this obliteration of the self which had been his wife.

Waythorn started up, checking himself in the analysis of her motives. What right had he to create a fantastic effigy of her and then pass judgment on it? She had spoken vaguely of her first marriage as unhappy, had hinted, with becoming reticence, that Haskett had wrought havoc among her young illusions. . . . It was a pity for Waythorn's peace of mind that Haskett's very inoffensiveness shed a new light on the nature of those illusions. A man would rather think that his wife has been brutalized by her first husband than that the process has been reversed.

IV

"Mr. Waythorn, I don't like that French governess of Lily's."

Haskett, subdued and apologetic, stood before Waythorn in the library, revolving his shabby hat in his hand.

Waythorn, surprised in his armchair over the evening paper, stared back perplexedly at his visitor.

"You'll excuse my asking to see you," Haskett continued. "But this is my last visit, and I thought if I could have a word with you it would be a better way than writing to Mrs. Waythorn's lawyer."

Waythorn rose uneasily. He did not like the French governess either; but that was irrelevant.

"I am not so sure of that," he returned stiffly; "but since you wish it I will give your message to—my wife." He always hesitated over the possessive pronoun in addressing Haskett.

The latter sighed. "I don't know as that will help much. She didn't like it when I spoke to her."

Waythorn turned red. "When did you see her?" he asked.

2. *Ben Hur: A Tale of Christ* (1880) was a best-selling novel by Lew Wallace (1827–1905).

"Not since the first day I came to see Lily—right after she was taken sick. I remarked to her then that I didn't like the governess."

Waythorn made no answer. He remembered distinctly that, after that first visit, he had asked his wife if she had seen Haskett. She had lied to him then, but she had respected his wishes since; and the incident cast a curious light on her character. He was sure she would not have seen Haskett that first day if she had divined that Waythorn would object, and the fact that she did not divine it was almost as disagreeable to the latter as the discovery that she had lied to him.

"I don't like the woman," Haskett was repeating with mild persistency. "She ain't straight, Mr. Waythorn—she'll teach the child to be underhand. I've noticed a change in Lily—she's too anxious to please—and she don't always tell the truth. She used to be the straightest child, Mr. Waythorn—" He broke off, his voice a little thick. "Not but what I want her to have a stylish education," he ended.

Waythorn was touched. "I'm sorry, Mr. Haskett; but frankly, I don't quite see what I can do."

Haskett hesitated. Then he laid his hat on the table, and advanced to the hearthrug, on which Waythorn was standing. There was nothing aggressive in his manner, but he had the solemnity of a timid man resolved on a decisive measure.

"There's just one thing you can do, Mr. Waythorn," he said. "You can remind Mrs. Waythorn that, by the decree of the courts, I am entitled to have a voice in Lily's bringing-up." He paused, and went on more deprecatingly: "I'm not the kind to talk about enforcing my rights, Mr. Waythorn. I don't know as I think a man is entitled to rights he hasn't known how to hold on to; but this business of the child is different. I've never let go there—and I never mean to."

The scene left Waythorn deeply shaken. Shamefacedly, in indirect ways, he had been finding out about Haskett; and all that he had learned was favorable. The little man, in order to be near his daughter, had sold out his share in a profitable business in Utica, and accepted a modest clerkship in a New York manufacturing house. He boarded in a shabby street and had few acquaintances. His passion for Lily filled his life. Waythorn felt that this exploration of Haskett was like groping about with a dark lantern in his wife's past; but he saw now that there were recesses his lantern had not explored. He had never inquired into the exact circumstances of his wife's first matrimonial rupture. On the surface all had been fair. It was she who had obtained the divorce, and the court had given her the child. But Waythorn knew how many ambiguities such a verdict might cover. The mere fact that Haskett retained a right over his daughter implied an unsuspected compromise. Waythorn was an idealist. He always refused to recognize unpleasant contingencies till he found himself confronted with them, and then he saw them followed by a spectral train of consequences. His next days were thus haunted, and he determined to try to lay the ghosts by conjuring them up in his wife's presence.

When he repeated Haskett's request a flame of anger passed over her face; but she subdued it instantly and spoke with a slight quiver of outraged motherhood.

"It is very ungentlemanly of him," she said.

The word grated on Waythorn. "That is neither here nor there. It's a bare question of rights."

She murmured: "It's not as if he could ever be a help to Lily—"

Waythorn flushed. This was even less to his taste. "The question is," he repeated, "what authority has he over her?"

She looked downward, twisting herself a little in her seat. "I am willing to see him—I thought you objected," she faltered.

In a flash he understood that she knew the extent of Haskett's claims. Perhaps it was not the first time she had resisted them.

"My objecting has nothing to do with it," he said coldly; "if Haskett has a right to be consulted you must consult him."

She burst into tears, and he saw that she expected him to regard her as a victim.

Haskett did not abuse his rights. Waythorn had felt miserably sure that he would not. But the governess was dismissed, and from time to time the little man demanded an interview with Alice. After the first outburst she accepted the situation with her usual adaptability. Haskett had once reminded Waythorn of the piano tuner, and Mrs. Waythorn, after a month or two, appeared to class him with that domestic familiar. Waythorn could not but respect the father's tenacity. At first he had tried to cultivate the suspicion that Haskett might be "up to" something, that he had an object in securing a foothold in the house. But in his heart Waythorn was sure of Haskett's single-mindedness; he even guessed in the latter a mild contempt for such advantages as his relation with the Waythorns might offer. Haskett's sincerity of purpose made him invulnerable, and his successor had to accept him as a lien on the property.

Mr. Sellers was sent to Europe to recover from his gout, and Varick's affairs hung on Waythorn's hands. The negotiations were prolonged and complicated; they necessitated frequent conferences between the two men, and the interests of the firm forbade Waythorn's suggesting that his client should transfer his business to another office.

Varick appeared well in the transaction. In moments of relaxation his coarse streak appeared, and Waythorn dreaded his geniality; but in the office he was concise and clear-headed, with a flattering deference to Waythorn's judgment. Their business relations being so affably established, it would have been absurd for the two men to ignore each other in society. The first time they met in a drawing room, Varick took up their intercourse in the same easy key, and his hostess' grateful glance obliged Waythorn to respond to it. After that they ran across each other frequently, and one evening at a ball Waythorn, wandering through the remoter rooms, came upon Varick seated beside his wife. She colored a little, and faltered in what she was saying; but Varick nodded to Waythorn without rising, and the latter strolled on.

In the carriage, on the way home, he broke out nervously: "I didn't know you spoke to Varick."

Her voice trembled a little. "It's the first time—he happened to be standing near me; I didn't know what to do. It's so awkward, meeting everywhere—and he said you had been very kind about some business."

"That's different," said Waythorn.

She paused a moment. "I'll do just as you wish," she returned pliantly. "I thought it would be less awkward to speak to him when we meet."

Her pliancy was beginning to sicken him. Had she really no will of her own—no theory about her relation to these men? She had accepted Haskett—did she mean to accept Varick? It was "less awkward," as she had said, and her instinct was to evade difficulties or to circumvent them. With sudden vividness Waythorn saw how the instinct had developed. She was "as easy as an old shoe"—a shoe that too many feet had worn. Her elasticity was the result of tension in too many different directions. Alice Haskett—Alice Varick—Alice Waythorn—she had been each in turn, and had left hanging to each name a little of her privacy, a little of her personality, a little of the inmost self where the unknown god abides.

"Yes—it's better to speak to Varick," said Waythorn wearily.

V

The winter wore on, and society took advantage of the Waythorns' acceptance of Varick. Harassed hostesses were grateful to them for bridging over a social difficulty, and Mrs. Waythorn was held up as a miracle of good taste. Some experimental spirits could not resist the diversion of throwing Varick and his former wife together, and there were those who thought he found a zest in the propinquity. But Mrs. Waythorn's conduct remained irreproachable. She neither avoided Varick nor sought him out. Even Waythorn could not but admit that she had discovered the solution of the newest social problem.

He had married her without giving much thought to that problem. He had fancied that a woman can shed her past like a man. But now he saw that Alice was bound to hers both by the circumstances which forced her into continued relation with it, and by the traces it had left on her nature. With grim irony Waythorn compared himself to a member of a syndicate. He held so many shares in his wife's personality and his predecessors were his partners in the business. If there had been any element of passion in the transaction he would have felt less deteriorated by it. The fact that Alice took her change of husbands like a change of weather reduced the situation to mediocrity. He could have forgiven her for blunders, for excesses; for resisting Haskett, for yielding to Varick; for anything but her acquiescence and her tact. She reminded him of a juggler tossing knives; but the knives were blunt and she knew they would never cut her.

And then, gradually, habit formed a protecting surface for his sensibilities. If he paid for each day's comfort with the small change of his illusions, he grew daily to value the comfort more and set less store upon the coin. He had drifted into a dulling propinquity with Haskett and Varick and he took refuge in the cheap revenge of satirizing the situation. He even began to reckon up the advantages which accrued from it, to ask himself if it were not better to own a third of a wife who knew how to make a man happy than a whole one who had lacked opportunity to acquire the art. For it *was* an art, and made up, like all others, of concessions, eliminations and embellishments; of lights judiciously thrown and shadows skillfully softened. His wife knew exactly how to manage the lights, and he knew exactly to what training she owed her skill. He even tried to trace the source of his obligations, to discriminate between the influences which had combined to produce his domestic happiness: he perceived that Haskett's commonness had made Alice worship good breeding, while Varick's liberal construction of the marriage bond had taught her to value the conjugal virtues; so that he was directly indebted to his predecessors for the devotion which made his life easy if not inspiring.

From this phase he passed into that of complete acceptance. He ceased to satirize himself because time dulled the irony of the situation and the joke lost its humor with its sting. Even the sight of Haskett's hat on the hall table had ceased to touch the springs of epigram. The hat was often seen there now, for it had been decided that it was better for Lily's father to visit her than for the little girl to go to his boardinghouse. Waythorn, having acquiesced in this arrangement, had been surprised to find how little difference it made. Haskett was never obtrusive, and the few visitors who met him on the stairs were unaware of his identity. Waythorn did not know how often he saw Alice, but with himself Haskett was seldom in contact.

One afternoon, however, he learned on entering that Lily's father was waiting to see him. In the library he found Haskett occupying a chair in his usual provisional way. Waythorn always felt grateful to him for not leaning back.

"I hope you'll excuse me, Mr. Waythorn," he said rising. "I wanted to see Mrs. Waythorn about Lily, and your man asked me to wait till she came in."

"Of course," said Waythorn, remembering that a sudden leak had that morning given over the drawing room to the plumbers.

He opened his cigar case and held it out to his visitor, and Haskett's acceptance seemed to mark a fresh stage in their intercourse. The spring evening was chilly, and Waythorn invited his guest to draw up his chair to the fire. He meant to find an excuse to leave Haskett in a moment; but he was tired and cold, and after all the little man no longer jarred on him.

The two were enclosed in the intimacy of their blended cigar smoke when the door opened and Varick walked into the room. Waythorn rose abruptly. It was the first time that Varick had come to the house, and the surprise of seeing him, combined with the singular inopportuneness of his arrival, gave a new edge to Waythorn's blunted sensibilities. He stared at his visitor without speaking.

Varick seemed too preoccupied to notice his host's embarrassment.

"My dear fellow," he exclaimed in his most expansive tone, "I must apologize for tumbling in on you in this way, but I was too late to catch you downtown, and so I thought—"

He stopped short, catching sight of Haskett, and his sanguine color deepened to a flush which spread vividly under his scant blond hair. But in a moment he recovered himself and nodded slightly. Haskett returned the bow in silence, and Waythorn was still groping for speech when the footman came in carrying a tea table.

The intrusion offered a welcome vent to Waythorn's nerves. "What the deuce are you bringing this here for?" he said sharply.

"I beg your pardon, sir, but the plumbers are still in the drawing room, and Mrs. Waythorn said she would have tea in the library." The footman's perfectly respectful tone implied a reflection on Waythorn's reasonableness.

"Oh, very well," said the latter resignedly, and the footman proceeded to open the folding tea table and set out its complicated appointments. While this interminable process continued the three men stood motionless, watching it with a fascinated stare, till Waythorn, to break the silence, said to Varick, "Won't you have a cigar?"

He held out the case he had just tendered to Haskett, and Varick helped himself with a smile. Waythorn looked about for a match, and finding none, proffered a light from his own cigar. Haskett, in the background, held his ground mildly, examining his cigar tip now and then, and stepping forward at the right moment to knock its ashes into the fire.

The footman at last withdrew, and Varick immediately began: "If I could just say half a word to you about this business—"

"Certainly," stammered Waythorn; "in the dining room—"

But as he placed his hand on the door it opened from without, and his wife appeared on the threshold.

She came in fresh and smiling, in her street dress and hat, shedding a fragrance from the boa which she loosened in advancing.

"Shall we have tea in here, dear?" she began; and then she caught sight of Varick. Her smile deepened, veiling a slight tremor of surprise.

"Why, how do you do?" she said with a distinct note of pleasure.

As she shook hands with Varick she saw Haskett standing behind him. Her smile faded for a moment, but she recalled it quickly, with a scarcely perceptible side glance at Waythorn.

"How do you do, Mr. Haskett?" she said, and shook hands with him a shade less cordially.

The three men stood awkwardly before her, till Varick, always the most self-possessed, dashed into an explanatory phrase.

"We—I had to see Waythorn a moment on business," he stammered, brick-red from chin to nape.

Haskett stepped forward with his air of mild obstinacy. "I am sorry to intrude; but you appointed five o'clock—" he directed his resigned glance to the timepiece on the mantel.

She swept aside their embarrassment with a charming gesture of hospitality.

"I'm so sorry—I'm always late; but the afternoon was so lovely." She stood drawing off her gloves, propitiatory and graceful, diffusing about her a sense of ease and familiarity in which the situation lost its grotesqueness. "But before talking business," she added brightly, "I'm sure everyone wants a cup of tea."

She dropped into her low chair by the tea table, and the two visitors, as if drawn by her smile, advanced to receive the cups she held out.

She glanced about for Waythorn, and he took the third cup with a laugh.

1904

Roman Fever[1]

I

From the table at which they had been lunching two American ladies of ripe but well-cared-for middle age moved across the lofty terrace of the Roman restaurant and, leaning on its parapet, looked first at each other, and then

1. First printed in *Liberty* magazine in 1934.

down on the outspread glories of the Palatine[2] and the Forum, with the same expression of vague but benevolent approval.

As they leaned there a girlish voice echoed up gaily from the stairs leading to the court below. "Well, come along, then," it cried, not to them but to an invisible companion, "and let's leave the young things to their knitting"; and a voice as fresh laughed back: "Oh, look here, Babs, not actually *knitting*—" "Well, I mean figuratively," rejoined the first. "After all, we haven't left out poor parents much else to do. . . ." and at that point the turn of the stairs engulfed the dialogue.

The two ladies looked at each other again, this time with a tinge of smiling embarrassment, and the smaller and paler one shook her head and colored slightly.

"Barbara!" she murmured, sending an unheard rebuke after the mocking voice in the stairway.

The other lady, who was fuller, and higher in color, with a small determined nose supported by vigorous black eyebrows, gave a good-humored laugh. "That's what our daughters think of us!"

Her companion replied by a deprecating gesture. "Not of us individually. We must remember that. It's just the collective modern idea of Mothers. And you see—" Half-guiltily she drew from her handsomely mounted black handbag a twist of crimson silk run through by two fine knitting needles. "One never knows," she murmured. "The new system has certainly given us a good deal of time to kill; and sometimes I get tired just looking—even at this." Her gesture was now addressed to the stupendous scene at their feet.

The dark lady laughed again, and they both relapsed upon the view, contemplating it in silence, with a sort of diffused serenity which might have been borrowed from the spring effulgence of the Roman skies. The luncheon hour was long past, and the two had their end of the vast terrace to themselves. At its opposite extremity a few groups, detained by a lingering look at the outspread city, were gathering up guidebooks and fumbling for tips. The last of them scattered, and the two ladies were alone on the air-washed height.

"Well, I don't see why we shouldn't just stay here," said Mrs. Slade, the lady of the high color and energetic brows. Two derelict basket chairs stood near, and she pushed them into the angle of the parapet, and settled herself in one, her gaze upon the Palatine. "After all, it's still the most beautiful view in the world."

"It always will be, to me," assented her friend Mrs. Ansley, with so slight a stress on the "me" that Mrs. Slade, though she noticed it, wondered if it were not merely accidental, like the random underlinings of old-fashioned letter writers.

"Grace Ansley was always old-fashioned," she thought; and added aloud, with a retrospective smile: "It's a view we've both been familiar with for a good many years. When we first met here we were younger than our girls are now. You remember?"

"Oh, yes, I remember," murmured Mrs. Ansley, with the same undefinable stress. "There's that headwaiter wondering," she interpolated. She was evi-

2. The Palatine Hill is located between the Forum and the Circus Maximus in Rome; it is the former site of imperial palaces and a major tourist attraction.

dently far less sure than her companion of herself and of her rights in the world.

"I'll cure him of wondering," said Mrs. Slade, stretching her hand toward a bag as discreetly opulent-looking as Mrs. Ansley's. Signing to the head-waiter, she explained that she and her friend were old lovers of Rome, and would like to spend the end of the afternoon looking down on the view—that is, if it did not disturb the service? The headwaiter, bowing over her gratuity, assured her that the ladies were most welcome, and would be still more so if they would condescend to remain for dinner. A full-moon night, they would remember. . . .

Mrs. Slade's black brows drew together, as though references to the moon were out of place and even unwelcome. But she smiled away her frown as the headwaiter retreated. "Well, why not? We might do worse. There's no know-ing, I suppose, when the girls will be back. Do you even know back from *where?* I don't!"

Mrs. Ansley again colored slightly. "I think those young Italian aviators we met at the Embassy invited them to fly to Tarquinia[3] for tea. I suppose they'll want to wait and fly back by moonlight."

"Moonlight—moonlight! What a part it still plays. Do you suppose they're as sentimental as we were?"

"I've come to the conclusion that I don't in the least know what they are," said Mrs. Ansley. "And perhaps we didn't know much more about each other."

"No; perhaps we didn't."

Her friend gave her a shy glance. "I never should have supposed you were sentimental, Alida."

"Well, perhaps I wasn't." Mrs. Slade drew her lids together in retrospect; and for a few moments the two ladies, who had been intimate since childhood, reflected how little they knew each other. Each one, of course, had a label ready to attach to the other's name; Mrs. Delphin Slade, for instance, would have told herself, or anyone who asked her, that Mrs. Horace Ansley, twenty-five years ago, had been exquisitely lovely—no, you wouldn't believe it, would you? . . . though, of course, still charming, distinguished. . . . Well, as a girl she had been exquisite; far more beautiful than her daughter Barbara, though certainly Babs, according to the new standards at any rate, was more effective—had more *edge*, as they say. Funny where she got it, with those two nullities as parents. Yes; Horace Ansley was—well, just the duplicate of his wife. Museum specimens of old New York. Good-looking, irreproachable, exemplary. Mrs. Slade and Mrs. Ansley had lived opposite each other—actually as well as figuratively—for years. When the drawing-room curtains in No. 20 East 73rd Street were renewed, No. 23, across the way, was always aware of it. And of all the movings, buyings, travels, anniversaries, illnesses—the tame chronicle of an estimable pair. Little of it escaped Mrs. Slade. But she had grown bored with it by the time her husband made his big *coup* in Wall Street, and when they bought in upper Park Avenue had already begun to think: "I'd rather live opposite a speakeasy for a change; at least one might see it raided." The idea of seeing Grace raided was so amusing that (before the move) she launched it at a woman's lunch. It made a hit, and went the rounds—she sometimes wondered if it had crossed the street, and reached Mrs. Ansley. She hoped not, but didn't much mind.

3. An ancient Etruscan city in the province of Viterbo, Lazio, Italy, famous for resisting Roman rule.

Those were the days when respectability was at a discount, and it did the irreproachable no harm to laugh at them a little.

A few years later, and not many months apart, both ladies lost their husbands. There was an appropriate exchange of wreaths and condolences, and a brief renewal of intimacy in the half-shadow of their mourning; and now, after another interval, they had run across each other in Rome, at the same hotel, each of them the modest appendage of a salient daughter. The similarity of their lot had again drawn them together, lending itself to mild jokes, and the mutual confession that, if in old days it must have been tiring to "keep up" with daughters, it was now, at times, a little dull not to.

No doubt, Mrs. Slade reflected, she felt her unemployment more than poor Grace ever would. It was a big drop from being the wife of Delphin Slade to being his widow. She had always regarded herself (with a certain conjugal pride) as his equal in social gifts, as contributing her full share to the making of the exceptional couple they were: but the difference after his death was irremediable. As the wife of the famous corporation lawyer, always with an international case or two on hand, every day brought its exciting and unexpected obligation: the impromptu entertaining of eminent colleagues from abroad, the hurried dashes on legal business to London, Paris or Rome, where the entertaining was so handsomely reciprocated; the amusement of hearing in her wake: "What, that handsome woman with the good clothes and the eyes is Mrs. Slade—*the* Slade's wife? Really? Generally the wives of celebrities are such frumps."

Yes; being *the* Slade's widow was a dullish business after that. In living up to such a husband all her faculties had been engaged; now she had only her daughter to live up to, for the son who seemed to have inherited his father's gifts had died suddenly in boyhood. She had fought through that agony because her husband was there, to be helped and to help; now, after the father's death, the thought of the boy had become unbearable. There was nothing left but to mother her daughter; and dear Jenny was such a perfect daughter that she needed no excessive mothering. "Now with Babs Ansley I don't know that I *should* be so quiet," Mrs. Slade sometimes half-enviously reflected; but Jenny, who was younger than her brilliant friend, was that rare accident, an extremely pretty girl who somehow made youth and prettiness seem as safe as their absence. It was all perplexing—and to Mrs. Slade a little boring. She wished that Jenny would fall in love—with the wrong man, even; that she might have to be watched, out-maneuvered, rescued. And instead, it was Jenny who watched her mother, kept her out of drafts, made sure that she had taken her tonic. . . .

Mrs. Ansley was much less articulate than her friend, and her mental portrait of Mrs. Slade was slighter, and drawn with fainter touches. "Alida Slade's awfully brilliant; but not as brilliant as she thinks," would have summed it up; though she would have added, for the enlightenment of strangers, that Mrs. Slade had been an extremely dashing girl; much more so than her daughter, who was pretty, of course, and clever in a way, but had none of her mother's— well, "vividness," someone had once called it. Mrs. Ansley would take up current words like this, and cite them in quotation marks, as unheard-of audacities. No; Jenny was not like her mother. Sometimes Mrs. Ansley thought Alida Slade was disappointed; on the whole she had had a sad life. Full of failures and mistakes; Mrs. Ansley had always been rather sorry for her. . . .

So these two ladies visualized each other, each through the wrong end of her little telescope.

II

FOR a long time they continued to sit side by side without speaking. It seemed as though, to both, there was a relief in laying down their somewhat futile activities in the presence of the vast Memento Mori which faced them. Mrs. Slade sat quite still, her eyes fixed on the golden slope of the Palace of the Caesars,[4] and after a while Mrs. Ansley ceased to fidget with her bag, and she too sank into meditation. Like many intimate friends, the two ladies had never before had occasion to be silent together, and Mrs. Ansley was slightly embarrassed by what seemed, after so many years, a new stage in their intimacy, and one with which she did not yet know how to deal.

Suddenly the air was full of that deep clangor of bells which periodically covers Rome with a roof of silver. Mrs. Slade glanced at her wristwatch. "Five o'clock already," she said, as though surprised.

Mrs. Ansley suggested interrogatively: "There's bridge at the Embassy at five." For a long time Mrs. Slade did not answer. She appeared to be lost in contemplation, and Mrs. Ansley thought the remark had escaped her. But after a while she said, as if speaking out of a dream: "Bridge, did you say? Not unless you want to. . . . But I don't think I will, you know."

"Oh, no," Mrs. Ansley hastened to assure her. "I don't care to at all. It's so lovely here; and so full of old memories, as you say." She settled herself in her chair, and almost furtively drew forth her knitting. Mrs. Slade took sideway note of this activity, but her own beautifully cared-for hands remained motionless on her knee.

"I was just thinking," she said slowly, "what different things Rome stands for to each generation of travelers. To our grandmothers, Roman fever[5] to our mothers, sentimental dangers—how we used to be guarded!—to our daughters, no more dangers than the middle of Main Street. They don't know it—but how much they're missing!"

The long golden light was beginning to pale, and Mrs. Ansley lifted her knitting a little closer to her eyes. "Yes; how we were guarded!"

"I always used to think," Mrs. Slade continued, "that our mothers had a much more difficult job than our grandmothers. When Roman fever stalked the streets it must have been comparatively easy to gather in the girls at the danger hour; but when you and I were young, with such beauty calling us, and the spice of disobedience thrown in, and no worse risk than catching cold during the cool hour after sunset, the mothers used to be put to it to keep us in—didn't they?"

She turned again toward Mrs. Ansley, but the latter had reached a delicate point in her knitting. "One, two, three—slip two; yes, they must have been," she assented, without looking up.

Mrs. Slade's eyes rested on her with a deepened attention. "She can knit—in the face of *this*! How like her. . . ."

---

4. Complex begun by Augustus Caesar on the Palatine Hill in Rome. "Momento Mori": "Remember you will die" (Latin).
5. Malaria.

Mrs. Slade leaned back, brooding, her eyes ranging from the ruins which faced her to the long green hollow of the Forum, the fading glow of the church fronts beyond it, and the outlying immensity of the Colosseum.[6] Suddenly she thought: "It's all very well to say that our girls have done away with sentiment and moonlight. But if Babs Ansley isn't out to catch that young aviator—the one who's a Marchese[7]—then I don't know anything. And Jenny has no chance beside her. I know that too. I wonder if that's why Grace Ansley likes the two girls to go everywhere together? My poor Jenny as a foil—!" Mrs. Slade gave a hardly audible laugh, and at the sound Mrs. Ansley dropped her knitting.

"Yes—?"

"I—oh, nothing. I was only thinking how your Babs carries everything before her. That Campolieri boy is one of the best matches in Rome. Don't look so innocent, my dear—you know he is. And I was wondering, ever so respectfully, you understand . . . wondering how two such exemplary characters as you and Horace had managed to produce anything quite so dynamic." Mrs. Slade laughed again, with a touch of asperity.

Mrs. Ansley's hands lay inert across her needles. She looked straight out at the great accumulated wreckage of passion and splendor at her feet. But her small profile was almost expressionless. At length she said: "I think you overrate Babs, my dear."

Mrs. Slade's tone grew easier. "No; I don't. I appreciate her. And perhaps envy you. Oh, my girl's perfect; if I were a chronic invalid I'd—well, I think I'd rather be in Jenny's hands. There must be times . . . but there! I always wanted a brilliant daughter . . . and never quite understood why I got an angel instead."

Mrs. Ansley echoed her laugh in a faint murmur. "Babs is an angel too."

"Of course—of course! But she's got rainbow wings. Well, they're wandering by the sea with their young men; and here we sit . . . and it all brings back the past a little too acutely."

Mrs. Ansley had resumed her knitting. One might almost have imagined (if one had known her less well, Mrs. Slade reflected) that, for her also, too many memories rose from the lengthening shadows of those august ruins. But no; she was simply absorbed in her work. What was there for her to worry about? She knew that Babs would almost certainly come back engaged to the extremely eligible Campolieri. "And she'll sell the New York house, and settle down near them in Rome, and never be in their way . . . she's much too tactful. But she'll have an excellent cook, and just the right people in for bridge and cocktails . . . and a perfectly peaceful old age among her grandchildren."

Mrs. Slade broke off this prophetic flight with a recoil of self-disgust. There was no one of whom she had less right to think unkindly than of Grace Ansley. Would she never cure herself of envying her? Perhaps she had begun too long ago.

She stood up and leaned against the parapet, filling her troubled eyes with the tranquilizing magic of the hour. But instead of tranquilizing her the sight

6. Roman amphitheater constructed between 72 and 81 C.E., capable of holding 50,000 spectators and used for gladiatorial events.
7. A member of Italian nobility.

seemed to increase her exasperation. Her gaze turned toward the Colosseum. Already its golden flank was drowned in purple shadow, and above it the sky curved crystal clear, without light or color. It was the moment when afternoon and evening hang balanced in mid-heaven.

Mrs. Slade turned back and laid her hand on her friend's arm. The gesture was so abrupt that Mrs. Ansley looked up, startled.

"The sun's set. You're not afraid, my dear?"

"Afraid—?"

"Of Roman fever or pneumonia? I remember how ill you were that winter. As a girl you had a very delicate throat, hadn't you?"

"Oh, we're all right up here. Down below, in the Forum, it does get deathly cold, all of a sudden . . . but not here."

"Ah, of course you know because you had to be so careful." Mrs. Slade turned back to the parapet. She thought: "I must make one more effort not to hate her." Aloud she said: "Whenever I look at the Forum from up here, I remember that story about a great-aunt of yours, wasn't she? A dreadfully wicked great-aunt?"

"Oh, yes; great-aunt Harriet. The one who was supposed to have sent her young sister out to the Forum after sunset to gather a night-blooming flower for her album. All our great-aunts and grandmothers used to have albums of dried flowers."

Mrs. Slade nodded. "But she really sent her because they were in love with the same man—"

"Well, that was the family tradition. They said Aunt Harriet confessed it years afterward. At any rate, the poor little sister caught the fever and died. Mother used to frighten us with the story when we were children."

"And you frightened *me* with it, that winter when you and I were here as girls. The winter I was engaged to Delphin."

Mrs. Ansley gave a faint laugh. "Oh, did I? Really frightened you? I don't believe you're easily frightened."

"Not often; but I was then. I was easily frightened because I was too happy. I wonder if you know what that means?"

"I—yes . . ." Mrs. Ansley faltered.

"Well, I suppose that was why the story of your wicked aunt made such an impression on me. And I thought: 'There's no more Roman fever, but the Forum is deathly cold after sunset—especially after a hot day. And the Colosseum's even colder and damper'."

"The Colosseum—?"

"Yes. It wasn't easy to get in, after the gates were locked for the night. Far from easy. Still, in those days it could be managed; it *was* managed, often. Lovers met there who couldn't meet elsewhere. You knew that?"

"I—I dare say. I don't remember."

"You don't remember? You don't remember going to visit some ruins or other one evening, just after dark, and catching a bad chill? You were supposed to have gone to see the moon rise. People always said that expedition was what caused your illness."

There was a moment's silence; then Mrs. Ansley rejoined: "Did they? It was all so long ago."

"Yes. And you got well again—so it didn't matter. But I suppose it struck your friends—the reason given for your illness, I mean—because everybody knew you were so prudent on account of your throat, and your mother took such care of you. . . . You *had* been out late sight-seeing, hadn't you, that night?"

"Perhaps I had. The most prudent girls aren't always prudent. What made you think of it now?"

Mrs. Slade seemed to have no answer ready. But after a moment she broke out: "Because I simply can't bear it any longer—!"

Mrs. Ansley lifted her head quickly. Her eyes were wide and very pale. "Can't bear what?"

"Why—your not knowing that I've always known why you went."

"Why I went—?"

"Yes. You think I'm bluffing, don't you? Well, you went to meet the man I was engaged to—and I can repeat every word of the letter that took you there."

While Mrs. Slade spoke Mrs. Ansley had risen unsteadily to her feet. Her bag, her knitting and gloves, slid in a panic-stricken heap to the ground. She looked at Mrs. Slade as though she were looking at a ghost.

"No, no—don't," she faltered out.

"Why not? Listen, if you don't believe me. 'My one darling, things can't go on like this. I must see you alone. Come to the Colosseum immediately after dark tomorrow. There will be somebody to let you in. No one whom you need fear will suspect'—but perhaps you've forgotten what the letter said?"

Mrs. Ansley met the challenge with an unexpected composure. Steadying herself against the chair she looked at her friend, and replied: "No; I know it by heart too."

"And the signature? 'Only *your* D.S.' Was that it? I'm right, am I? That was the letter that took you out that evening after dark?"

Mrs. Ansley was still looking at her. It seemed to Mrs. Slade that a slow struggle was going on behind the voluntarily controlled mask of her small quiet face. "I shouldn't have thought she had herself so well in hand," Mrs. Slade reflected, almost resentfully. But at this moment Mrs. Ansley spoke. "I don't know how you knew. I burnt that letter at once."

"Yes; you would, naturally—you're so prudent!" The sneer was open now. "And if you burnt the letter you're wondering how on earth I know what was in it. That's it, isn't it?"

Mrs. Slade waited, but Mrs. Ansley did not speak.

"Well, my dear, I know what was in that letter because I wrote it!"

"You wrote it?"

"Yes."

The two women stood for a minute staring at each other in the last golden light. Then Mrs. Ansley dropped back into her chair. "Oh," she murmured, and covered her face with her hands.

Mrs. Slade waited nervously for another word or movement. None came, and at length she broke out: "I horrify you."

Mrs. Ansley's hands dropped to her knee. The face they uncovered was streaked with tears. "I wasn't thinking of you. I was thinking—it was the only letter I ever had from him!"

"And I wrote it. Yes; I wrote it! But I was the girl he was engaged to. Did you happen to remember that?"

Mrs. Ansley's head drooped again. "I'm not trying to excuse myself . . . I remembered. . . ."

"And still you went?"

"Still I went."

Mrs. Slade stood looking down on the small bowed figure at her side. The flame of her wrath had already sunk, and she wondered why she had ever thought there would be any satisfaction in inflicting so purposeless a wound on her friend. But she had to justify herself.

"You do understand? I'd found out—and I hated you, hated you. I knew you were in love with Delphin—and I was afraid; afraid of you, of your quiet ways, your sweetness . . . your . . . well, I wanted you out of the way, that's all. Just for a few weeks; just till I was sure of him. So in a blind fury I wrote that letter . . . I don't know why I'm telling you now."

"I suppose," said Mrs. Ansley slowly, "it's because you've always gone on hating me."

"Perhaps. Or because I wanted to get the whole thing off my mind." She paused. "I'm glad you destroyed the letter. Of course I never thought you'd die."

Mrs. Ansley relapsed into silence, and Mrs. Slade, leaning above her, was conscious of a strange sense of isolation, of being cut off from the warm current of human communion. "You think me a monster!"

"I don't know. . . . It was the only letter I had, and you say he didn't write it?"

"Ah, how you care for him still!"

"I cared for that memory," said Mrs. Ansley.

Mrs. Slade continued to look down on her. She seemed physically reduced by the blow—as if, when she got up, the wind might scatter her like a puff of dust. Mrs. Slade's jealousy suddenly leapt up again at the sight. All these years the woman had been living on that letter. How she must have loved him, to treasure the mere memory of its ashes! The letter of the man her friend was engaged to. Wasn't it she who was the monster?

"You tried your best to get him away from me, didn't you? But you failed; and I kept him. That's all."

"Yes. That's all."

"I wish now I hadn't told you. I'd no idea you'd feel about it as you do; I thought you'd be amused. It all happened so long ago, as you say; and you must do me the justice to remember that I had no reason to think you'd ever taken it seriously. How could I, when you were married to Horace Ansley two months afterward? As soon as you could get out of bed your mother rushed you off to Florence and married you. People were rather surprised—they wondered at its being done so quickly; but I thought I knew. I had an idea you did it out of *pique*—to be able to say you'd got ahead of Delphin and me. Girls have such silly reasons for doing the most serious things. And your marrying so soon convinced me that you'd never really cared."

"Yes. I suppose it would," Mrs. Ansley assented.

The clear heaven overhead was emptied of all its gold. Dusk spread over it, abruptly darkening the Seven Hills.[8] Here and there lights began to twin-

---

8. The Seven Hills of Rome east of the Tiber River form the heart of the city.

kle through the foliage at their feet. Steps were coming and going on the deserted terrace—waiters looking out of the doorway at the head of the stairs, then reappearing with trays and napkins and flasks of wine. Tables were moved, chairs straightened. A feeble string of electric lights flickered out. Some vases of faded flowers were carried away, and brought back replenished. A stout lady in a dust coat suddenly appeared, asking in broken Italian if anyone had seen the elastic band which held together her tattered Baedeker. She poked with her stick under the table at which she had lunched, the waiters assisting.

The corner where Mrs. Slade and Mrs. Ansley sat was still shadowy and deserted. For a long time neither of them spoke. At length Mrs. Slade began again: "I suppose I did it as a sort of joke—"

"A joke?"

"Well, girls are ferocious sometimes, you know. Girls in love especially. And I remember laughing to myself all that evening at the idea that you were waiting around there in the dark, dodging out of sight, listening for every sound, trying to get in—Of course I was upset when I heard you were so ill afterward."

Mrs. Ansley had not moved for a long time. But now she turned slowly toward her companion. "But I didn't wait. He'd arranged everything. He was there. We were let in at once," she said.

Mrs. Slade sprang up from her leaning position. "Delphin there? They let you in?—Ah, now you're lying!" she burst out with violence.

Mrs. Ansley's voice grew clearer, and full of surprise. "But of course he was there. Naturally he came—"

"Came? How did he know he'd find you there? You must be raving!"

Mrs. Ansley hesitated, as though reflecting. "But I answered the letter. I told him I'd be there. So he came."

Mrs. Slade flung her hands up to her face. "Oh, God—you answered! I never thought of your answering. . . ."

"It's odd you never thought of it, if you wrote the letter."

"Yes. I was blind with rage."

Mrs. Ansley rose, and drew her fur scarf about her. "It is cold here. We'd better go . . . I'm sorry for you," she said, as she clasped the fur about her throat.

The unexpected words sent a pang through Mrs. Slade. "Yes; we'd better go." She gathered up her bag and cloak. "I don't know why you should be sorry for me," she muttered.

Mrs. Ansley stood looking away from her toward the dusky secret mass of the Colosseum. "Well—because I didn't have to wait that night."

Mrs. Slade gave an unquiet laugh. "Yes; I was beaten there. But I oughtn't to begrudge it to you, I suppose. At the end of all these years. After all, I had everything; I had him for twenty-five years. And you had nothing but that one letter that he didn't write."

Mrs. Ansley was again silent. At length she turned toward the door of the terrace. She took a step, and turned back, facing her companion.

"I had Barbara," she said, and began to move ahead of Mrs. Slade toward the stairway.

1934

SUI SIN FAR (EDITH MAUD EATON)
1865–1914

Sui Sin Far was the first Eurasian writer to transform the experiences of late-nineteenth-century Chinese immigrants to North America into enduring art. As scholars Elizabeth Ammons, Amy Ling, and Annette White-Parks, among others, have demonstrated, Sui Sin Far—especially in her only book, *Mrs. Spring Fragrance* (1912)—deserves our attention not simply because she was the first to record the manifold wrongs done to the Chinese in North America but also because she wrote with skill and imaginative power.

Much remains unknown about Sui Sin Far, though a sense of both her vulnerability and her toughness can be strongly felt in such late autobiographical accounts as "Leaves from the Mental Portfolio of an Eurasian" (1909) and "Sui Sin Far, the Half-Chinese Writer, Tells of Her Career" (1912). The second of sixteen children, fourteen of whom lived to adulthood, Far was born Edith Maud Eaton in Macclesfield, England, to a Chinese mother raised in England and an English father from a well-to-do family. Her father, Edward Eaton, formerly a merchant, became alienated from his English family not long after his marriage to Grace Trefusus and struggled thereafter to earn a living as a landscape painter. In this rather bohemian atmosphere, as critic Amy Ling puts it, "Artistic endeavors, as well as early financial independence, were encouraged." When Far was seven the family moved first to New York State and then to Montreal. The family's fortunes entered a long period of decline when Far was eleven, and along with other siblings she was withdrawn from school to help support her parents and the younger children by selling on the street her father's paintings and her own crocheted lace. She continued to support family members for the rest of her life, though her income as a stenographer and freelance journalist barely covered her own modest needs and though her health was always fragile, partly as a result of childhood rheumatic fever. Still, it is important to know that from the time she left her Montreal home as a young woman until she returned there shortly before her death, Sui Sin Far was strongly attached to her large family and Montreal was the only place she ever thought of as home though she spent most of her adult life in the United States.

Sui Sin Far and her sister Winnifred were published while they were teenagers; two other sisters became painters, and another sister became the first Chinese American lawyer in Chicago. Winnifred, who wrote under the Japanese-sounding pseudonym Onoto Watanna, published the first Asian American novel, *Miss Nume of Japan*, in 1899, and was popular for many years as the author of sentimental and melodramatic novels.

Though Sui Sin Far began her writing career in Montreal, it was not until 1896 that she adopted her pseudonym, a literal translation of the symbol for waterlily as water fairy flower, or, more generally, bulbs that can sprout and bloom in water. That same year she published her first story, in the American literary magazine *Fly Leaf*. From 1898 to 1909 she lived chiefly in Seattle, with shorter stays in San Francisco and other U.S. West Coast cities. She spent her last years in Boston, where she produced her mature work.

"Mrs. Spring Fragrance" was first published in *Hampton's Magazine* in January 1910. In 1912 it became the title story for the only book Sui Sin Far published. The thirty-seven stories, articles, and sketches brought together in this volume provide a clear sense of Sui Sin Far's commitment to expose the racial, political, social, and economic abuses ordinary Chinese immigrants experienced in late-nineteenth-century America. Often the characters must find a balance between cultures, generations, and genders. However, they are not to be "either-or" but "both-and" figures—sympathetic to traditional Chinese values *and* to new ideas about love and marriage, among many other contested beliefs and perspectives. In many of Sui Sin Far's journalistic and fictional writings she vigorously and openly defends Chinese immigrants—especially women and working-class immigrants—with an ironic stance, as in "In the Land of the Free."

It is hard to know with certainty why Sui Sin Far published only short fiction rather than longer works. Surely her health and the need to support herself would be part of any explanation. A more positive answer is offered by Elizabeth Ammons, who places Sui Sin Far in the company of other late-nineteenth-century American women writers, such as Sarah Orne Jewett and Kate Chopin, who helped establish what scholars now call the "composite novel"—a form that, like a quilt, allows for both variety and unifying design. The collection titled Mrs. Spring Fragrance, in any case, tells the story of a community that has flowered literarily. Maxine Hong Kingston, Amy Tan, and David Henry Hwang, among other contemporary writers of Chinese American descent, continue to examine many of the issues Sui Sin Far first introduced to American readers.

In the Land of the Free[1]

I

"See, Little One—the hills in the morning sun. There is thy home for years to come. It is very beautiful and thou wilt be very happy there."

The Little One looked up into his mother's face in perfect faith. He was engaged in the pleasant occupation of sucking a sweetmeat; but that did not prevent him from gurgling responsively.

"Yes, my olive bud; there is where thy father is making a fortune for thee. Thy father! Oh, wilt thou not be glad to behold his dear face. 'Twas for thee I left him."

The Little One ducked his chin sympathetically against his mother's knee. She lifted him on to her lap. He was two years old, a round, dimple-cheeked boy with bright brown eyes and a sturdy little frame.

"Ah! Ah! Ah! Ooh! Ooh! Ooh!" puffed he, mocking a tugboat steaming by.

San Francisco's waterfront was lined with ships and steamers, while other craft, large and small, including a couple of white transports from the Philippines, lay at anchor here and there off shore. It was some time before the Eastern Queen could get docked, and even after that was accomplished, a lone Chinaman who had been waiting on the wharf for an hour was detained that much longer by men with the initials U. S. C.[2] on their caps, before he could board the steamer and welcome his wife and child.

"This is thy son," announced the happy Lae Choo.

Hom Hing lifted the child, felt of his little body and limbs, gazed into his face with proud and joyous eyes; then turned inquiringly to a customs officer at his elbow.

"That's a fine boy you have there," said the man. "Where was he born?"

"In China," answered Hom Hing, swinging the Little One on his right shoulder, preparatory to leading his wife off the steamer.

"Ever been to America before?"

"No, not he," answered the father with a happy laugh.

The customs officer beckoned to another.

---

1. First published in Mrs. Spring Fragrance   2. Initials stand for United States Customs.
(1912).

"This little fellow," said he, "is visiting America for the first time."

The other customs officer stroked his chin reflectively.

"Good day," said Hom Hing.

"Wait!" commanded one of the officers. "You cannot go just yet."

"What more now?" asked Hom Hing.

"I'm afraid," said the first customs officer, "that we cannot allow the boy to go ashore. There is nothing in the papers that you have shown us—your wife's papers and your own—having any bearing upon the child."

"There was no child when the papers were made out," returned Hom Hing. He spoke calmly; but there was apprehension in his eyes and in his tightening grip on his son.

"What is it? What is it?" quavered Lae Choo, who understood a little English.

The second customs officer regarded her pityingly.

"I don't like this part of the business," he muttered.

The first officer turned to Hom Hing and in an official tone of voice, said:

"Seeing that the boy has no certificate entitling him to admission to this country you will have to leave him with us."

"Leave my boy!" exclaimed Hom Hing.

"Yes; he will be well taken care of, and just as soon as we can hear from Washington he will be handed over to you."

"But," protested Hom Hing, "he is my son."

"We have no proof," answered the man with a shrug of his shoulders; "and even if so we cannot let him pass without orders from the Government."

"He is my son," reiterated Hom Hing, slowly and solemnly. "I am a Chinese merchant and have been in business in San Francisco for many years. When my wife told to me one morning that she dreamed of a green tree with spreading branches and one beautiful red flower growing thereon, I answered her that I wished my son to be born in our country, and for her to prepare to go to China. My wife complied with my wish. After my son was born my mother fell sick and my wife nursed and cared for her; then my father, too, fell sick, and my wife also nursed and cared for him. For twenty moons my wife care for and nurse the old people, and when they die they bless her and my son, and I send for her to return to me. I had no fear of trouble. I was a Chinese merchant and my son was my son."

"Very good, Hom Hing," replied the first officer. "Nevertheless, we take your son."

"No, you not take him; he my son too."

It was Lae Choo. Snatching the child from his father's arms she held and covered him with her own.

The officers conferred together for a few moments; then one drew Hom Hing aside and spoke in his ear.

Resignedly Hom Hing bowed his head, then approached his wife. "'Tis the law," said he, speaking in Chinese, "and 'twill be but for a little while—until tomorrow's sun arises."

"You, too," reproached Lae Choo in a voice eloquent with pain. But accustomed to obedience she yielded the boy to her husband, who in turn delivered him to the first officer. The Little One protested lustily against the transfer; but his mother covered her face with her sleeve and his father silently led her away. Thus was the law of the land complied with.

II

Day was breaking. Lae Choo, who had been awake all night, dressed herself, then awoke her husband.

" 'Tis the morn," she cried. "Go, bring our son."

The man rubbed his eyes and arose upon his elbow so that he could see out of the window. A pale star was visible in the sky. The petals of a lily in a bowl on the window-sill were unfurled.

" 'Tis not yet time," said he, laying his head down again.

"Not yet time. Ah, all the time that I lived before yesterday is not so much as the time that has been since my little one was taken from me."

The mother threw herself down beside the bed and covered her face.

Hom Hing turned on the light, and touching his wife's bowed head with a sympathetic hand inquired if she had slept.

"Slept!" she echoed, weepingly. "Ah, how could I close my eyes with my arms empty of the little body that has filled them every night for more than twenty moons! You do not know—man—what it is to miss the feel of the little fingers and the little toes and the soft round limbs of your little one. Even in the darkness his darling eyes used to shine up to mine, and often have I fallen into slumber with his pretty babble at my ear. And now, I see him not; I touch him not; I hear him not. My baby, my little fat one!"

"Now! Now! Now!" consoled Hom Hing, patting his wife's shoulder reassuringly; "there is no need to grieve so; he will soon gladden you again. There cannot be any law that would keep a child from its mother!"

Lae Choo dried her tears.

"You are right, my husband," she meekly murmured. She arose and stepped about the apartment, setting things to rights. The box of presents she had brought for her California friends had been opened the evening before; and silks, embroideries, carved ivories, ornamental lacquer-ware, brasses, camphor-wood boxes, fans, and chinaware were scattered around in confused heaps. In the midst of unpacking the thought of her child in the hands of strangers had overpowered her, and she had left everything to crawl into bed and weep.

Having arranged her gifts in order she stepped out on to the deep balcony.

The star had faded from view and there were bright streaks in the western sky. Lae Choo looked down the street and around. Beneath the flat occupied by her and her husband were quarters for a number of bachelor Chinamen,[3] and she could hear them from where she stood, taking their early morning breakfast. Below their dining-room was her husband's grocery store. Across the way was a large restaurant. Last night it had been resplendent with gay colored lanterns and the sound of music. The rejoicings over "the completion of the moon,"[4] by Quong Sum's firstborn, had been long and loud, and had caused her to tie a handkerchief over her ears. She, a bereaved mother, had it not in her heart to rejoice with other parents. This morning the place was more in accord with her mood. It was still and quiet. The revellers had dispersed or were asleep.

3. At this time, Chinese men were allowed to enter the country with work permits but were not allowed to bring their wives and children.
4. The baby is one month old.

A roly-poly woman in black sateen, with long pendant earrings in her ears, looked up from the street below and waved her a smiling greeting. It was her old neighbor, Kuie Hoe, the wife of the gold embosser, Mark Sing. With her was a little boy in yellow jacket and lavender pantaloons. Lae Choo remembered him as a baby. She used to like to play with him in those days when she had no child of her own. What a long time ago that seemed! She caught her breath in a sigh, and laughed instead.

"Why are you so merry?" called her husband from within.

"Because my Little One is coming home," answered Lae Choo. "I am a happy mother—a happy mother."

She pattered into the room with a smile on her face.

The noon hour had arrived. The rice was steaming in the bowls and a fragrant dish of chicken and bamboo shoots was awaiting Hom Hing. Not for one moment had Lae Choo paused to rest during the morning hours; her activity had been ceaseless. Every now and again, however, she had raised her eyes to the gilded clock on the curiously carved mantelpiece. Once, she had exclaimed:

"Why so long, oh! why so long?" Then apostrophizing herself: "Lae Choo, be happy. The Little One is coming! The Little One is coming!" Several times she burst into tears and several times she laughed aloud.

Hom Hing entered the room; his arms hung down by his side.

"The Little One!" shrieked Lae Choo.

"They bid me call tomorrow."

With a moan the mother sank to the floor.

The noon hour passed. The dinner remained on the table.

III

The winter rains were over: the spring had come to California, flushing the hills with green and causing an ever-changing pageant of flowers to pass over them. But there was no spring in Lae Choo's heart, for the Little One remained away from her arms. He was being kept in a mission. White women were caring for him, and though for one full moon he had pined for his mother and refused to be comforted he was now apparently happy and contented. Five moons or five months had gone by since the day he had passed with Lae Choo through the Golden Gate; but the great Government at Washington still delayed sending the answer which would return him to his parents.

Hom Hing was disconsolately rolling up and down the balls in his abacus box when a keen-faced young man stepped into his store.

"What news?" asked the Chinese merchant.

"This!" The young man brought forth a typewritten letter. Hom Hing read the words:

"Re Chinese child, alleged to be the son of Hom Hing, Chinese merchant, doing business at 425 Clay street, San Francisco.

"Same will have attention as soon as possible."

Hom Hing returned the letter, and without a word continued his manipulation of the counting machine.

"Have you anything to say?" asked the young man.

"Nothing. They have sent the same letter fifteen times before. Have you not yourself showed it to me?"

"True!" The young man eyed the Chinese merchant furtively. He had a proposition to make and he was pondering whether or not the time was opportune.

"How is your wife?" he inquired solicitously—and diplomatically.

Hom Hing shook his head mournfully.

She seems less every day," he replied. "Her food she takes only when I bid her and her tears fall continually. She finds no pleasure in dress or flowers and cares not to see her friends. Her eyes stare all night. I think before another moon she will pass into the land of spirits."

"No!" exclaimed the young man, genuinely startled.

"If the boy not come home I lose my wife sure," continued Hom Hing with bitter sadness.

"It's not right," cried the young man indignantly. Then he made his proposition.

The Chinese father's eyes brightened exceedingly.

"Will I like you to go to Washington and make them give you the paper to restore my son?" cried he. "How can you ask when you know my heart's desire?"

"Then, said the young fellow, "I will start next week. I am anxious to see this thing through if only for the sake of your wife's peace of mind."

"I will call her. To hear what you think to do will make her glad," said Hom Hing.

He called a message to Lae Choo upstairs through a tube in the wall.

In a few moments she appeared, listless, wan, and hollow-eyed; but when her husband told her the young lawyer's suggestion she became as one electrified; her form straightened, her eyes glistened; the color flushed to her cheeks.

"Oh," she cried, turning to James Clancy, "You are a hundred man good!"

The young man felt somewhat embarrassed; his eyes shifted a little under the intense gaze of the Chinese mother.

"Well, we must get your boy for you," he responded. "Of course"—turning to Hom Hing—"it will cost a little money. You can't get fellows to hurry the Government for you without gold in your pocket."

Hom Hing stared blankly for a moment. Then: "How much do you want, Mr. Clancy?" he asked quietly.

"Well, I will need at least five hundred to start with."

Hom Hing cleared his throat.

"I think I told to you the time I last paid you for writing letters for me and seeing the Custom boss here that nearly all I had was gone!"

"Oh, well then we won't talk about it, old fellow. It won't harm the boy to stay where he is, and your wife may get over it all right."

"What that you say?" quavered Lae Choo.

James Clancy looked out of the window.

"He says," explained Hom Hing in English, "that to get our boy we have to have much money."

"Money! Oh, yes."

Lae Choo nodded her head.

"I have not got the money to give him."

For a moment Lae Choo gazed wonderingly from one face to the other; then, comprehension dawning upon her, with swift anger, pointing to the lawyer, she cried: "You not one hundred man good; you just common white man."

"Yes, ma'am," returned James Clancy, bowing and smiling ironically.

Hom Hing pushed his wife behind him and addressed the lawyer again: "I might try," said he, "to raise something; but five hundred—it is not possible."

"What about four?"

"I tell you I have next to nothing left and my friends are not rich."

"Very well!"

The lawyer moved lesiurely toward the door, pausing on its threshold to light a cigarette.

"Stop, white man; white man, stop!"

Lae Choo, panting and terrified, had started forward and now stood beside him, clutching his sleeve excitedly.

"You say you can go to get paper to bring my Little One to me if Hom Hing give you five hundred dollars?"

The lawyer nodded carelessly; his eyes were intent upon the cigarette which would not take the fire from the match.

"Then you go get paper. If Hom Hing not can give you five hundred dollars—I give you perhaps what more that much."

She slipped a heavy gold bracelet from her wrist and held it out to the man. Mechanically he took it.

"I go get more!"

She scurried away, disappearing behind the door through which she had come.

"Oh, look here, I can't accept this," said James Clancy, walking back to Hom Hing and laying down the bracelet before him.

"It's all right," said Hom Hing, seriously, "pure China gold. My wife's parent give it to her when we married."

"But I can't take it anyway," protested the young man.

"It is all same as money. And you want money to go to Washington," replied Hom Hing in a matter of fact manner.

"See, my jade earrings—my gold buttons—my hairpins—my comb of pearl and my rings—one, two, three, four, five rings; very good—very good—all same much money. I give them all to you. You take and bring me paper for my Little One."

Lae Choo piled up her jewels before the lawyer.

Hom Hing laid a restraining hand upon her shoulder. "Not all, my wife," he said in Chinese. He selected a ring—his gift to Lae Choo when she dreamed of the tree with the red flower. The rest of the jewels he pushed toward the white man.

"Take them and sell them," said he. "They will pay your fare to Washington and bring you back with the paper."

For one moment James Clancy hesitated. He was not a sentimental man; but something within him arose against accepting such payment for his services.

"They are good, good," pleadingly asserted Lae Choo, seeing his hesitation.

Whereupon he seized the jewels, thrust them into his coat pocket, and walked rapidly away from the store.

IV

Lae Choo followed after the missionary woman through the mission nursery school. Her heart was beating so high with happiness that she could scarcely breathe. The paper had come at last—the precious paper which gave Hom Hing and his wife the right to the possession of their own child. It was ten months now since he had been taken from them—ten months since the sun had ceased to shine for Lae Choo.

The room was filled with children—most of them wee tots, but none so wee as her own. The mission woman talked as she walked. She told Lae Choo that little Kim, as he had been named by the school, was the pet of the place, and that his little tricks and ways amused and delighted every one. He had been rather difficult to manage at first and had cried much for his mother; "but children so soon forget, and after a month he seemed quite at home and played around as bright and happy as a bird."

"Yes," responded Lae Choo. "Oh, yes, yes!"

But she did not hear what was said to her. She was walking in a maze of anticipatory joy.

"Wait here, please," said the mission woman, placing Lae Choo in a chair. "The very youngest ones are having their breakfast."

She withdrew for a moment—it seemed like an hour to the mother—then she reappeared leading by the hand a little boy dressed in blue cotton overalls and white-soled shoes. The little boy's face was round and dimpled and his eyes were very bright.

"Little One, ah, my Little One!" cried Lae Choo.

She fell on her knees and stretched her hungry arms toward her son.

But the Little One shrunk from her and tried to hide himself in the folds of the white woman's skirt.

"Go'way, go'way!" he bade his mother.

1912

W. E. B. DU BOIS
1868–1963

William Edward Burghardt Du Bois was born on February 23, 1868, in Great Barrington, Massachusetts. His childhood was happy; but with the approach of adolescence Du Bois discovered that what made him different from his schoolmates was not so much his superior academic achievement as his brown skin. Looking back on his rejection by a white girl in grade school, Du Bois wrote, "It dawned on me with a certain suddenness, that I was . . . shut out from their world by a vast veil," a veil beyond which he claimed to have no desire to force his way. Du Bois's entire career, nonetheless, may be understood as an unremitting struggle for civil and political rights for African Americans and for human rights around the world.

Du Bois was educated at Fisk, Harvard, and the University of Berlin. His doctoral dissertation, *The Suppression of the African Slave Trade to the United States of America, 1638–1870,* was published as the first volume in the Harvard Historical Studies series. By the time Du Bois completed his graduate studies his accomplishments were already considerable, but he could not secure an appointment at a major research university. He taught first instead at Wilberforce College in Ohio, at that time a small, poor, black college. There he offered Greek, Latin, German, and English—subjects far removed from his real interest in the emerging field of sociology.

After spending a year at the University of Pennsylvania, where he produced his first major work, *The Philadelphia Negro,* Du Bois moved to Atlanta University in 1897. There, over the following thirteen years, he produced a steady stream of important studies of African American life. Dedicated to the rigorous, scholarly examination of the so-called Negro problem, Du Bois soon had to face up to the violent realities of the lives he proposed to study. On his way to present an appeal for reason in the case of a black man accused of murder and rape, Du Bois was met by the news that a lynch mob had dismembered and burned the man at the stake and that "his knuckles were on exhibition at a grocery store." Though Du Bois never ceased being a scholar, from this time on he increasingly became an activist and sought a wider audience for his writings.

Du Bois first came to national attention with the publication of *The Souls of Black Folk* (1903), characterized by scholar Eric J. Sundquist as "the preeminent text of African American cultural consciousness." Several chapters explore the implications of this extraordinary book's dramatic and prophetic announcement in its "Forethought" that "the problem of the Twentieth Century is the problem of the color-line." In the first chapter, "Of Our Spiritual Strivings," Du Bois introduces another concept that would inform his thinking for the rest of his career—the notion of the "twoness" of African Americans: "One ever feels his twoness," Du Bois asserts, "an American, a Negro; two souls, two thoughts, two unreconciled strivings; two warring ideals in one dark body, whose dogged strength alone keeps it from being torn asunder." This foundational observation hit on what Du Bois named "double-consciousness." (Another of Du Bois's important ideas was the Talented Tenth, the title of an essay he published as the second chapter of *The Negro Problem* (1903). By this he meant college-educated African Americans who could provide leadership for African Americans after Reconstruction.) Du Bois offers a concise overview of the Negro in America cast in the highly charged rhetoric of the orator who wishes to move as well as inform his audience. But the chapter that particularly caused a stir when the volume was first published was the one that challenged—coolly and without rancor—the enormous authority and power that had accumulated in the hands of one black spokesman, Booker T. Washington. Washington had founded Tuskegee Institute in Alabama to train African Americans in basic agricultural and mechanical skills and had gained national prominence with his Atlanta Exposition speech in 1895. His address seemed to many people to accept disenfranchisement and segregation and settle for a low level of education in exchange for white "toleration" and economic cooperation. Although Du Bois had initially joined in the general approval of this "separate and unequal" philosophy, by the early 1900s he had begun to reject Washington's position, and with the publication of *Souls of Black Folk* his public defiance of Washington put the two men in lasting opposition. The almost immediate repudiation of *Souls of Black Folk* by Washington's allies reinforced Du Bois's emerging radicalism; he became a leader in the Niagara Movement (1905), a movement aggressively demanding for African Americans the same civil rights enjoyed by white Americans.

In 1910 Du Bois left Atlanta for New York, where he served for the next quarter of a century as editor of *Crisis,* the official publication of the newly formed National Association for the Advancement of Colored People (NAACP), an organization he helped create. Through this publication Du Bois reached an increasingly large audience—one hundred thousand by 1919—with powerful messages that argued the need for black development and white social enlightenment.

Frustrated by the lack of fundamental change and progress in the condition of African Americans, from 1920 on Du Bois shifted his attention from the reform of race relations in America through research and political legislation to the search for longer-range worldwide economic solutions to the international problems of inequity among the races. He began a steady movement toward Pan-African and socialist perspectives that led to his joining the U.S. Communist Party in 1961 and, in the year of his death, becoming a citizen of Ghana. During these forty years he was extremely active as politician, organizer, and diplomat, and he continued as a powerful writer of poetry, fiction, autobiography, essays, and scholarly works. When, in his last major speech, Martin Luther King Jr. spoke of Du Bois as "one of the most remarkable men of our time," he was uttering the verdict of history.

From The Souls of Black Folk[1]

I. Of Our Spiritual Strivings

> O water, voice of my heart, crying in the sand,
>   All night long crying with a mournful cry,
> As I lie and listen, and cannot understand
>   The voice of my heart in my side or the voice of the sea,
>   O water, crying for rest, is it I, is it I?
>   All night long the water is crying to me.
>
> Unresting water, there shall never be rest
>   Till the last moon droop and the last tide fail,
> And the fire of the end begin to burn in the west;
>   And the heart shall be weary and wonder and cry like the sea,
>   All life long crying without avail,
>   As the water all night long is crying to me.
>   ARTHUR SYMONS[2]

Between me and the other world there is ever an unasked question: unasked by some through feelings of delicacy; by others through the difficulty of rightly framing it. All, nevertheless, flutter round it. They approach me in a half-hesitant sort of way, eye me curiously or compassionately, and then, instead of saying directly, How does it feel to be a problem? they say, I know an excellent colored man in my town; or, I fought at Mechanicsville;[4] or, Do not these Southern outrages make your blood boil? At these I smile, or am interested, or reduce the boiling to a simmer, as the occasion may require. To the real question, How does it feel to be a problem? I answer seldom a word.

1. *The Souls of Black Folk,* a compilation of nine previously printed and five unpublished essays, appeared first as a book in 1903, the source of the text printed here.
2. English poet (1865–1945); the quotation is from "The Crying of Water."
3. For a rich discussion of the book as a whole and

particularly of the bars of music that serve as epigraphs for each chapter, see Eric J. Sundquist's *To Wake the Nations: Race in the Making of American Literature* (1993).
4. Civil War battle in Virginia, June 26, 1862, resulting in heavy Confederate losses.

And yet, being a problem is a strange experience,—peculiar even for one who has never been anything else, save perhaps in babyhood and in Europe. It is in the early days of rollicking boyhood that the revelation first bursts upon one, all in a day, as it were. I remember well when the shadow swept across me. I was a little thing, away up in the hills of New England, where the dark Housatonic winds between Hoosac and Taghkanic[5] to the sea. In a wee wooden schoolhouse, something put it into the boys' and girls' heads to buy gorgeous visiting-cards—ten cents a package—and exchange. The exchange was merry, till one girl, a tall newcomer, refused my card,—refused it peremptorily, with a glance. Then it dawned upon me with a certain suddenness that I was different from the others; or like, mayhap, in heart and life and longing, but shut out from their world by a vast veil. I had thereafter no desire to tear down that veil, to creep through; I held all beyond it in common contempt, and lived above it in a region of blue sky and great wandering shadows. That sky was bluest when I could beat my mates at examination-time, or beat them at a foot-race, or even beat their stringy heads. Alas, with the years all this fine contempt began to fade; for the worlds I longed for, and all their dazzling opportunities, were theirs, not mine. But they should not keep these prizes, I said; some, all, I would wrest from them. Just how I would do it I could never decide: by reading law, by healing the sick, by telling the wonderful tales that swam in my head,—some way. With other black boys the strife was not so fiercely sunny: their youth shrunk into tasteless sycophancy, or into silent hatred of the pale world about them and mocking distrust of everything white; or wasted itself in a bitter cry, Why did God make me an outcast and a stranger in mine own house? The shades of the prison-house closed round about us all: walls strait and stubborn to the whitest, but relentlessly narrow, tall, and unscalable to sons of night who must plod darkly on in resignation, or beat unavailing palms against the stone, or steadily, half hopelessly, watch the streak of blue above.

After the Egyptian and Indian, the Greek and Roman, the Teuton and Mongolian, the Negro is a sort of seventh son, born with a veil, and gifted with second-sight in this American world,—a world which yields him no true self-consciousness, but only lets him see himself through the revelation of the other world. It is a peculiar sensation, this double-consciousness, this sense of always looking at one's self through the eyes of others, of measuring one's soul by the tape of a world that looks on in amused contempt and pity. One ever feels his two-ness,—an American, a Negro; two souls, two thoughts, two unreconciled strivings; two warring ideals in one dark body, whose dogged strength alone keeps it from being torn asunder.

The history of the American Negro is the history of this strife,—this longing to attain self-conscious manhood, to merge his double self into a better and truer self. In this merging he wishes neither of the older selves to be lost. He would not Africanize America, for America has too much to teach the world and Africa. He would not bleach his Negro soul in a flood of white Americanism, for he knows that Negro blood has a message for the world. He simply wishes to make it possible for a man to be both a Negro and an Amer-

---

5. Mountain ranges partly in Massachusetts, partly in Vermont. The Housatonic is a river in western Massissetts.

ican, without being cursed and spit upon by his fellows, without having the doors of Opportunity closed roughly in his face.

This, then, is the end of his striving: to be a co-worker in the kingdom of culture, to escape both death and isolation, to husband and use his best powers and his latent genius. These powers of body and mind have in the past been strangely wasted, dispersed, or forgotten. The shadow of a mighty Negro past flits through the tale of Ethiopia the Shadowy and of Egypt the Sphinx. Throughout history, the powers of single black men flash here and there like falling stars, and die sometimes before the world has rightly gauged their brightness. Here in America, in the few days since Emancipation, the black man's turning hither and thither in hesitant and doubtful striving has often made his very strength to lose effectiveness, to seem like absence of power, like weakness. And yet it is not weakness,—it is the contradiction of double aims. The double-aimed struggle of the black artisan—on the one hand to escape white contempt for a nation of mere hewers of wood and drawers of water, and on the other hand to plough and nail and dig for a poverty-stricken horde—could only result in making him a poor craftsman, for he had but half a heart in either cause. By the poverty and ignorance of his people, the Negro minister or doctor was tempted toward quackery and demagogy; and by the criticism of the other world, toward ideals that made him ashamed of his lowly tasks. The would-be black *savant*[6] was confronted by the paradox that the knowledge his people needed was a twice-told tale to his white neighbors, while the knowledge which would teach the white world was Greek to his own flesh and blood. The innate love of harmony and beauty that set the ruder souls of his people a-dancing and a-singing raised but confusion and doubt in the soul of the black artist; for the beauty revealed to him was the soul-beauty of a race which his larger audience despised, and he could not articulate the message of another people. This waste of double aims, this seeking to satisfy two unreconciled ideals, has wrought sad havoc with the courage and faith and deeds of ten thousand thousand people,—has sent them often wooing false gods and invoking false means of salvation, and at times has even seemed about to make them ashamed of themselves.

Away back in the days of bondage they thought to see in one divine event the end of all doubt and disappointment; few men ever worshipped Freedom with half such unquestioning faith as did the American Negro for two centuries. To him, so far as he thought and dreamed, slavery was indeed the sum of all villainies, the cause of all sorrow, the root of all prejudice; Emancipation was the key to a promised land of sweeter beauty than ever stretched before the eyes of wearied Israelites. In song and exhortation swelled one refrain—Liberty; in his tears and curses the God he implored had Freedom in his right hand. At last it came,—suddenly, fearfully, like a dream. With one wild carnival of blood and passion came the message in his own plaintive cadences:—

> "Shout, O children!
> Shout, you're free!
> For God has bought your liberty!"[7]

6. Learned person.

7. Source unidentified.

Years have passed away since then,—ten, twenty, forty; forty years of national life, forty years of renewal and development, and yet the swarthy spectre sits in its accustomed seat at the Nation's feast. In vain do we cry to this our vastest social problem:—

> "Take any shape but that, and my firm nerves
> Shall never tremble!"[8]

The Nation has not yet found peace from its sins; the freedman has not yet found in freedom his promised land. Whatever of good may have come in these years of change, the shadow of a deep disappointment rests upon the Negro people,—a disappointment all the more bitter because the unattained ideal was unbounded save by the simple ignorance of a lowly people.

The first decade was merely a prolongation of the vain search for freedom, the boon that seemed ever barely to elude their grasp,—like a tantalizing will-o'-the-wisp, maddening and misleading the headless host. The holocaust of war, the terrors of the Ku-Klux Klan, the lies of carpetbaggers,[9] the disorganization of industry, and the contradictory advice of friends and foes, left the bewildered serf with no new watchword beyond the old cry for freedom. As the time flew, however, he began to grasp a new idea. The ideal of liberty demanded for its attainment powerful means, and these the Fifteenth Amendment[1] gave him. The ballot, which before he had looked upon as a visible sign of freedom, he now regarded as the chief means of gaining and perfecting the liberty with which war had partially endowed him. And why not? Had not votes made war and emancipated millions? Had not votes enfranchised the freedmen? Was anything impossible to a power that had done all this? A million black men started with renewed zeal to vote themselves into the kingdom. So the decade flew away, the revolution of 1876[2] came, and left the half-free serf weary, wondering, but still inspired. Slowly but steadily, in the following years, a new vision began gradually to replace the dream of political power,—a powerful movement, the rise of another ideal to guide the unguided, another pillar of fire by night after a clouded day. It was the ideal of "book-learning"; the curiosity, born of compulsory ignorance, to know and test the power of the cabalistic[3] letters of the white man, the longing to know. Here at last seemed to have been discovered the mountain path to Canaan;[4] longer than the highway of Emancipation and law, steep and rugged, but straight, leading to heights high enough to overlook life.

Up the new path the advance guard toiled, slowly, heavily, doggedly; only those who have watched and guided the faltering feet, the misty minds, the dull understandings, of the dark pupils of these schools know how faithfully, how piteously, this people strove to learn. It was weary work. The cold statistician wrote down the inches of progress here and there, noted also where here and there a foot had slipped or some one had fallen. To the tired climbers, the horizon was ever dark, the mists were often cold, the Canaan was always dim and far away. If, however, the vistas disclosed as yet no goal,

---

8. Shakespeare, *Macbeth* 3.2.99.
9. Used as an epithet in the South to describe Northerners who came to the South during Reconstruction to make money by exploiting conditions created by the devastation of the Civil War. Many carried luggage made of carpet materials.
1. Amendment to the Constitution passed in 1870 to guarantee and protect the voting rights of African American men.
2. Congressional opposition to the continuation of Reconstruction policies and programs after the national elections of 1876.
3. Indecipherable and mystical.
4. The Promised Land of the Israelites.

no resting-place, little but flattery and criticism, the journey at least gave leisure for reflection and self-examination; it changed the child of Emancipation to the youth with dawning self-consciousness, self-realization, self-respect. In those sombre forests of his striving his own soul rose before him, and he saw himself,—darkly as through a veil; and yet he saw in himself some faint revelation of his power, of his mission. He began to have a dim feeling that, to attain his place in the world, he must be himself, and not another. For the first time he sought to analyze the burden he bore upon his back, that dead-weight of social degradation partially masked behind a half-named Negro problem. He felt his poverty; without a cent, without a home, without land, tools, or savings, he had entered into competition with rich, landed, skilled neighbors. To be a poor man is hard, but to be a poor race in a land of dollars is the very bottom of hardships. He felt the weight of his ignorance,— not simply of letters, but of life, of business, of the humanities; the accumulated sloth and shirking and awkwardness of decades and centuries shackled his hands and feet. Nor was his burden all poverty and ignorance. The red stain of bastardy, which two centuries of systematic legal defilement of Negro women had stamped upon his race, meant not only the loss of ancient African chastity, but also the hereditary weight of a mass of corruption from white adulterers, threatening almost the obliteration of the Negro home.

A people thus handicapped ought not to be asked to race with the world, but rather allowed to give all its time and thought to its own social problems. But alas! while sociologists gleefully count his bastards and his prostitutes, the very soul of the toiling, sweating black man is darkened by the shadow of a vast despair. Men call the shadow prejudice, and learnedly explain it as the natural defence of culture against barbarism, learning against ignorance, purity against crime, the "higher" against the "lower" races. To which the Negro cries Amen! and swears that to so much of this strange prejudice as is founded on just homage to civilization, culture, righteousness, and progress, he humbly bows and meekly does obeisance. But before that nameless prejudice that leaps beyond all this he stands helpless, dismayed, and well-nigh speechless; before that personal disrespect and mockery, the ridicule and systematic humiliation, the distortion of fact and wanton license of fancy, the cynical ignoring of the better and the boisterous welcoming of the worse, the all-pervading desire to inculcate disdain for everything black, from Toussaint[5] to the devil,—before this there rises a sickening despair that would disarm and discourage any nation save that black host to whom "discouragement" is an unwritten word.

But the facing of so vast a prejudice could not but bring the inevitable self-questioning, self-disparagement, and lowering of ideals which ever accompany repression and breed in an atmosphere of contempt and hate. Whisperings and portents came borne upon the four winds: Lo! we are diseased and dying, cried the dark hosts; we cannot write, our voting is vain; what need of education, since we must always cook and serve? And the Nation echoed and enforced this self-criticism, saying: Be content to be servants, and nothing more; what need of higher culture for half-men? Away with the black man's ballot, by force or fraud,—and behold the suicide of a race! Nevertheless, out

5. François Dominique Toussaint L'Ouverture (1743–1803), slave-born Haitian soldier, patriot, and martyr to the liberation of Haiti from foreign control.

of the evil came something of good,—the more careful adjustment of education to real life, the clearer perception of the Negroes' social responsibilities, and the sobering realization of the meaning of progress.

So dawned the time of *Sturm und Drang:*[6] storm and stress to-day rocks our little boat on the mad waters of the world-sea; there is within and without the sound of conflict, the burning of body and rending of soul; inspiration strives with doubt, and faith with vain questionings. The bright ideals of the past,— physical freedom, political power, the training of brains and the training of hands,—all these in turn have waxed and waned, until even the last grows dim and overcast. Are they all wrong,—all false? No, not that, but each alone was over-simple and incomplete,—the dreams of a credulous race-childhood, or the fond imaginings of the other world which does not know and does not want to know our power. To be really true, all these ideals must be melted and welded into one. The training of the schools we need to-day more than ever,— the training of deft hands, quick eyes and ears, and above all the broader, deeper, higher culture of gifted minds and pure hearts. The power of the ballot we need in sheer self-defence,—else what shall save us from a second slavery? Freedom, too, the long-sought, we still seek,—the freedom of life and limb, the freedom to work and think, the freedom to love and aspire. Work, culture, liberty,—all these we need, not singly but together, not successively but together, each growing and aiding each, and all striving toward that vaster ideal that swims before the Negro people, the ideal of human brotherhood, gained through the unifying ideal of Race; the ideal of fostering and developing the traits and talents of the Negro, not in opposition to or contempt for other races, but rather in large conformity to the greater ideals of the American Republic, in order that some day on American soil two world-races may give each to each those characteristics both so sadly lack. We the darker ones come even now not altogether empty-handed: there are to-day no truer exponents of the pure human spirit of the Declaration of Independence than the American Negroes; there is no true American music but the wild sweet melodies of the Negro slave; the American fairy tales and folk-lore are Indian and African; and, all in all, we black men seem the sole oasis of simple faith and reverence in a dusty desert of dollars and smartness. Will America be poorer if she replace her brutal dyspeptic blundering with light-hearted but determined Negro humility? or her coarse and cruel wit with loving jovial good-humor? or her vulgar music with the soul of the Sorrow Songs?

Merely a concrete test of the underlying principles of the great republic is the Negro Problem, and the spiritual striving of the freedmen's sons is the travail of souls whose burden is almost beyond the measure of their strength, but who bear it in the name of an historic race, in the name of this the land of their fathers' fathers, and in the name of human opportunity.

And now what I have briefly sketched in large outline let me on coming pages tell again in many ways, with loving emphasis and deeper detail, that men may listen to the striving in the souls of black folk.

✻ ✻ ✻

6. Storm and stress (German).

III. Of Mr. Booker T. Washington and Others[7]

From birth till death enslaved; in word, in deed, unmanned!
• • • • • • • • •
Hereditary bondsmen! Know ye not
Who would be free themselves must strike the blow?
—BYRON[8]

Easily the most striking thing in the history of the American Negro since 1876[9] is the ascendancy of Mr. Booker T. Washington. It began at the time when war memories and ideals were rapidly passing; a day of astonishing commercial development was dawning; a sense of doubt and hesitation overtook the freedmen's sons,—then it was that his leading began. Mr. Washington came, with a simple definite programme, at the psychological moment when the nation was a little ashamed of having bestowed so much sentiment on Negroes, and was concentrating its energies on Dollars. His programme of industrial education, conciliation of the South, and submission and silence as to civil and political rights, was not wholly original; the Free Negroes from 1830 up to war-time had striven to build industrial schools, and the American Missionary Association had from the first taught various trades; and Price[1] and others had sought a way of honorable alliance with the best of the Southerners. But Mr. Washington first indissolubly linked these things; he put enthusiasm, unlimited energy, and perfect faith into this programme, and changed it from a by-path into a veritable Way of Life. And the tale of the methods by which he did this is a fascinating study of human life.

It startled the nation to hear a Negro advocating such a programme after many decades of bitter complaint; it startled and won the applause of the South, it interested and won the admiration of the North; and after a confused murmur of protest, it silenced if it did not convert the Negroes themselves.

To gain the sympathy and cooperation of the various elements comprising the white South was Mr. Washington's first task; and this, at the time

---

7. *Of Mr. Booker T. Washington and Others* was first published in *Guardian*, July 27, 1902, and then collected in *The Souls of Black Folk*. Booker T. Washington (1856?–1915) founded and helped build Tuskegee Institute, a black college in Alabama, and became a powerful leader of and spokesman for black Americans, especially after his address at the Atlanta Exposition in 1895.
8. The epigraph is from *Childe Harold's Pilgrimage*, Canto 2, 74.710, 76.720–21. The music is from the refrain of a black spiritual titled "A Great Camp-Meetin' in de Promised Land" (also called "There's a Great Camp Meeting" and "Walk

Together Children"). The words of the refrain set to this music are

Going to mourn and never tire—
mourn and never tire, mourn and never tire.

9. Reconstruction ended in 1876; federal troops were withdrawn from the South, and black political power was essentially destroyed.
1. Thomas Frederick Price (1860–1919), American editor, missionary, and Roman Catholic priest; one of the founders of the American Missionary Association.

Tuskegee was founded, seemed, for a black man, well-nigh impossible. And yet ten years later it was done in the word spoken at Atlanta: "In all things purely social we can be as separate as the five fingers, and yet one as the hand in all things essential to mutual progress." This "Atlanta Compromise"[2] is by all odds the most notable thing in Mr. Washington's career. The South interpreted it in different ways: the radicals received it as a complete surrender of the demand for civil and political equality; the conservatives, as a generously conceived working basis for mutual understanding. So both approved it, and to-day its author is certainly the most distinguished Southerner since Jefferson Davis, and the one with the largest personal following.

Next to this achievement comes Mr. Washington's work in gaining place and consideration in the North. Others less shrewd and tactful had formerly essayed to sit on these two stools and had fallen between them; but as Mr. Washington knew the heart of the South from birth and training, so by singular insight he intuitively grasped the spirit of the age which was dominating the North. And so thoroughly did he learn the speech and thought of triumphant commercialism, and the ideals of material prosperity, that the picture of a lone black boy poring over a French grammar amid the weeds and dirt of a neglected home soon seemed to him the acme of absurdities.[3] One wonders what Socrates and St. Francis of Assisi would say to this.

And yet this very singleness of vision and thorough oneness with his age is a mark of the successful man. It is as though Nature must needs make men narrow in order to give them force. So Mr. Washington's cult has gained unquestioning followers, his work has wonderfully prospered, his friends are legion, and his enemies are confounded. To-day he stands as the one recognized spokesman of his ten million fellows, and one of the most notable figures in a nation of seventy millions. One hesitates, therefore, to criticise a life which, beginning with so little, has done so much. And yet the time is come when one may speak in all sincerity and utter courtesy of the mistakes and shortcomings of Mr. Washington's career, as well as of his triumphs, without being thought captious or envious, and without forgetting that it is easier to do ill than well in the world.

The criticism that has hitherto met Mr. Washington has not always been of this broad character. In the South especially has he had to walk warily to avoid the harshest judgments,—and naturally so, for he is dealing with the one subject of deepest sensitiveness to that section. Twice—once when at the Chicago celebration of the Spanish-American War he alluded to the color-prejudice that is "eating away the vitals of the South," and once when he dined with President Roosevelt[4]—has the resulting Southern criticism been violent enough to threaten seriously his popularity. In the North the feeling

2. In a speech at the Atlanta Exposition of 1895, Washington in effect traded political, civil, and social rights for blacks for the promise of vocational-training schools and jobs. His purpose was to reduce racial tension in the South while providing a stable black labor force whose skills would provide job security.
3. In Washington's *Up from Slavery* (1901), ch. 8, "Teaching School in a Stable and a Hen-House," there is a passage on the absurdity of knowledge not practically useful:

In fact, one of the saddest things I saw during the month of travel which I have described was a young man, who had attended some high school, sitting down in a one-room cabin, with grease on his clothing, filth all around him, and weeds in the yard and garden, engaged in studying French grammar.

4. Theodore Roosevelt (1858–1919), twenty-sixth president of the United States (1901–09). Washington's dining with him at the White House in 1901 caused controversy around the country.

has several times forced itself into words, that Mr. Washington's counsels of submission overlooked certain elements of true manhood, and that his educational programme was unnecessarily narrow. Usually, however, such criticism has not found open expression, although, too, the spiritual sons of the Abolitionists have not been prepared to acknowledge that the schools founded before Tuskegee, by men of broad ideals and self-sacrificing spirit, were wholly failures or worthy of ridicule. While, then, criticism has not failed to follow Mr. Washington, yet the prevailing public opinion of the land has been but too willing to deliver the solution of a wearisome problem into his hands, and say, "If that is all you and your race ask, take it."

Among his own people, however, Mr. Washington has encountered the strongest and most lasting opposition, amounting at times to bitterness, and even to-day continuing strong and insistent even though largely silenced in outward expression by the public opinion of the nation. Some of this opposition is, of course, mere envy; the disappointment of displaced demagogues and the spite of narrow minds. But aside from this, there is among educated and thoughtful colored men in all parts of the land a feeling of deep regret, sorrow, and apprehension at the wide currency and ascendancy which some of Mr. Washington's theories have gained. These same men admire his sincerity of purpose, and are willing to forgive much to honest endeavor which is doing something worth the doing. They coöperate with Mr. Washington as far as they conscientiously can; and, indeed, it is no ordinary tribute to this man's tact and power that, steering as he must between so many diverse interests and opinions, he so largely retains the respect of all.

But the hushing of the criticism of honest opponents is a dangerous thing. It leads some of the best of the critics to unfortunate silence and paralysis of effort, and others to burst into speech so passionately and intemperately as to lose listeners. Honest and earnest criticism from those whose interests are most nearly touched,—criticism of writers by readers, of government by those governed, of leaders by those led,—this is the soul of democracy and the safeguard of modern society. If the best of the American Negroes receive by outer pressure a leader whom they had not recognized before, manifestly there is here a certain palpable gain. Yet there is also irreparable loss,—a loss of that peculiarly valuable education which a group receives when by search and criticism it finds and commissions its own leaders. The way in which this is done is at once the most elementary and the nicest problem of social growth. History is but the record of such group-leadership; and yet how infinitely changeful is its type and character! And of all types and kinds, what can be more instructive than the leadership of a group within a group?—that curious double movement where real progress may be negative and actual advance be relative retrogression. All this is the social student's inspiration and despair.

Now in the past the American Negro has had instructive experience in the choosing of group leaders, founding thus a peculiar dynasty which in the light of present conditions is worth while studying. When sticks and stones and beasts form the sole environment of a people, their attitude is largely one of determined opposition to and conquest of natural forces. But when to earth and brute is added an environment of men and ideas, then the attitude of the imprisoned group may take three main forms,—a feeling of revolt and revenge; an attempt to adjust all thought and action to the will of the greater group; or, finally, a determined effort at self-realization and self-development despite environing opinion. The influence of all of these attitudes at various times can be traced in the history of the American Negro, and in the evolution of his successive leaders.

Before 1750, while the fire of African freedom still burned in the veins of the slaves, there was in all leadership or attempted leadership but the one motive of revolt and revenge,—typified in the terrible Maroons, the Danish blacks, and Cato[5] of Stono, and veiling all the Americas in fear of insurrection. The liberalizing tendencies of the latter half of the eighteenth century brought, along with kindlier relations between black and white, thoughts of ultimate adjustment and assimilation. Such aspiration was especially voiced in the earnest songs of Phyllis, in the martyrdom of Attucks, the fighting of Salem and Poor, the intellectual accomplishments of Banneker and Derham, and the political demands of the Cuffes.[6]

Stern financial and social stress after the war cooled much of the previous humanitarian ardor. The disappointment and impatience of the Negroes at the persistence of slavery and serfdom voiced itself in two movements. The slaves in the South, aroused undoubtedly by vague rumors of the Haytian revolt, made three fierce attempts at insurrection,—in 1800 under Gabriel in Virginia, in 1822 under Vesey in Carolina, and in 1831 again in Virginia under the terrible Nat Turner.[7] In the Free States, on the other hand, a new and curious attempt at self-development was made. In Philadelphia and New York color-prescription led to a withdrawal of Negro communicants from white churches and the formation of a peculiar socio-religious institution among the Negroes known as the African Church,—an organization still living and controlling in its various branches over a million of men.

Walker's wild appeal[8] against the trend of the times showed how the world was changing after the coming of the cotton-gin. By 1830 slavery seemed hopelessly fastened on the South, and the slaves thoroughly cowed into submission. The free Negroes of the North, inspired by the mulatto immigrants from the West Indies, began to change the basis of their demands; they recognized the slavery of slaves, but insisted that they themselves were freemen, and sought assimilation and amalgamation with the nation on the same terms with other men. Thus, Forten and Purvis of Philadelphia, Shad of Wilmington, Du Bois of New Haven, Barbadoes[9] of Boston, and others, strove singly

---

5. The leader of the Stono, South Carolina, slave revolt of September 9, 1739, in which twenty-five whites were killed. "Maroons": fugitive slaves from the West Indies and Guiana in the 17th and 18th centuries, or their descendants. Many of the slaves in the Danish West Indies revolted in 1733 because of the lack of sufficient food.

6. Paul Cuffe (1759–1817) organized to resettle free blacks in African colonies. A champion of civil rights for free blacks in Massachusetts, he took thirty-eight blacks to Africa in 1815 at his own expense. Phyllis (or Phillis) Wheatley (c. 1753–1784), black slave and poet. Crispus Attucks (c. 1723–1770) was killed in the Boston massacre. Peter Salem (d. 1816), black patriot who killed Major Pitcairn in the battle of Bunker Hill. Salem Poor (b. 1747), a black soldier who fought at Bunker Hill, Valley Forge, and White Plains. Benjamin Banneker (1731–1806), a black mathematician who also studied astronomy. James Derham (b. 1762), the first recognized black physician in America; born a slave, he learned medicine from

his physician master, bought his freedom in 1783, and by 1788 was one of the foremost physicians of New Orleans.

7. A slave (1800–1831), he led the Southampton insurrection in 1831, during which sixty-one whites and more than a hundred slaves were killed or executed. Gabriel (1775?–1800) conspired to attack Richmond, Virginia, with a thousand other slaves on August 30, 1800; but a storm forced a suspension of the mission and two slaves betrayed the conspiracy. On October 7, Gabriel and fifteen others were hanged. Denmark Vesey (c. 1767–1822), a mulatto rebel, purchased his freedom in 1800; he led an unsuccessful uprising in 1822 and was hanged.

8. An inflammatory and eloquent antislavery pamphlet by David Walker (1785–1830), black leader.

9. James G. Barbadoes was one of those present at the first National Negro Convention along with Forten, Purvis, Shadd, and others. James Forten (1766–1842), black civic leader and philanthro-

and together as men, they said, not as slaves; as "people of color," not as "Negroes." The trend of the times, however, refused them recognition save in individual and exceptional cases, considered them as one with all the despised blacks, and they soon found themselves striving to keep even the rights they formerly had of voting and working and moving as freemen. Schemes of migration and colonization arose among them; but these they refused to entertain, and they eventually turned to the Abolition movement as a final refuge.

Here, led by Remond, Nell, Wells-Brown, and Douglass,[1] a new period of self-assertion and self-development dawned. To be sure, ultimate freedom and assimilation was the ideal before the leaders, but the assertion of the manhood rights of the Negro by himself was the main reliance, and John Brown's raid was the extreme of its logic. After the war and emancipation, the great form of Frederick Douglass, the greatest of American Negro leaders, still led the host. Self-assertion, especially in political lines, was the main programme, and behind Douglass came Elliot, Bruce, and Langston, and the Reconstruction politicians, and, less conspicuous but of greater social significance Alexander Crummell and Bishop Daniel Payne.[2]

Then came the Revolution of 1876, the suppression of the Negro votes, the changing and shifting of ideals, and the seeking of new lights in the great night. Douglass, in his old age, still bravely stood for the ideals of his early manhood,—ultimate assimilation *through* self-assertion, and on no other terms. For a time Price arose as a new leader, destined, it seemed, not to give up, but to re-state the old ideals in a form less repugnant to the white South. But he passed away in his prime. Then came the new leader. Nearly all the former ones had become leaders by the silent suffrage of their fellows, had sought to lead their own people alone, and were usually, save Douglass, little known outside their race. But Booker T. Washington arose as essentially the leader not of one race but of two,—a compromiser between the South, the North, and the Negro. Naturally the Negroes resented, at first bitterly, signs of compromise which surrendered their civil and political rights, even though this was to be exchanged for larger chances of economic development. The rich and dominating North, however, was not only weary of the race problem, but was investing largely in Southern enterprises, and welcomed any method of peaceful coöperation. Thus, by national opinion, the Negroes began to recognize Mr. Washington's leadership; and the voice of criticism was hushed.

pist. Robert Purvis (1810–1898), abolitionist, helped found the American Anti-Slavery Society in 1833 and was the president of the Underground Railway. Abraham Shadd, abolitionist, was on the first board of managers of the American Anti-Slavery Society, a delegate from Delaware for the first National Negro Convention (1830), and president of the third one in 1833. Alexander Du Bois (1803–1887), paternal grandfather of W. E. B. Du Bois, helped form the Negro Episcopal Parish of St. Luke in 1847 and was the senior warden there.
1. Frederick Douglass (1817–1895), abolitionist and orator and born a slave, was U.S. minister to Haiti and U.S. marshal of the District of Columbia. Charles Lenox Remond (1810–1873), black leader. William Cooper Nell (1816–1874), abolitionist, writer, and first African American to hold office under the government of the United States (clerk in the post office). Through his efforts equal

school privileges were obtained for black children in Boston. William Wells Brown (1816?–1884) published *Clotel* in 1853, the first novel by a black American, and *The Escape* in 1858, the first play by a black American.
2. Daniel Alexander Payne (1811–1893), bishop of the African Methodist Episcopal church and president of Wilberforce University (1863–76). Robert Brown Elliot (1842–1884), black politician, graduate of Eton, South Carolina congressman in the U.S. House of Representatives. Blanche K. Bruce (1841–1898), born a slave, first black man to serve a full term in the U.S. Senate (1875–81). John Mercer Langston (1829–1897), congressman, lawyer, diplomat, educator, born a slave. Crummell (1819–1898), clergyman of the Protestant Episcopal church, missionary in Liberia for twenty years and then in Washington, D.C.

Mr. Washington represents in Negro thought the old attitude of adjustment and submission; but adjustment at such a peculiar time as to make his programme unique. This is an age of unusual economic development, and Mr. Washington's programme naturally takes an economic cast, becoming a gospel of Work and Money to such an extent as apparently almost completely to overshadow the higher aims of life. Moreover, this is an age when the more advanced races are coming in closer contact with the less developed races, and the race-feeling is therefore intensified; and Mr. Washington's programme practically accepts the alleged inferiority of the Negro races. Again, in our own land, the reaction from the sentiment of war time has given impetus to race-prejudice against Negroes, and Mr. Washington withdraws many of the high demands of Negroes as men and American citizens. In other periods of intensified prejudice all the Negro's tendency to self-assertion has been called forth; at this period a policy of submission is advocated. In the history of nearly all other races and peoples the doctrine preached at such crises has been that manly self-respect is worth more than lands and houses, and that a people who voluntarily surrender such respect, or cease striving for it, are not worth civilizing.

In answer to this, it has been claimed that the Negro can survive only through submission. Mr. Washington distinctly asks that black people give up, at least for the present, three things,—

First, political power,

Second, insistence on civil rights,

Third, higher education of Negro youth,—

and concentrate all their energies on industrial education, the accumulation of wealth, and the conciliation of the South. This policy has been courageously and insistently advocated for over fifteen years, and has been triumphant for perhaps ten years. As a result of this tender of the palm-branch, what has been the return? In these years there have occurred:

1. The disfranchisement of the Negro.

2. The legal creation of a distinct status of civil inferiority for the Negro.

3. The steady withdrawal of aid from institutions for the higher training of the Negro.

These movements are not, to be sure, direct results of Mr. Washington's teachings; but his propaganda has, without a shadow of doubt, helped their speedier accomplishment. The question then comes: Is it possible, and probable, that nine millions of men can make effective progress in economic lines if they are deprived of political rights, made a servile caste, and allowed only the most meagre chance for developing their exceptional men? If history and reason give any distinct answer to these questions, it is an emphatic *No*. And Mr. Washington thus faces the triple paradox of his career:

1. He is striving nobly to make Negro artisans business men and property-owners; but it is utterly impossible, under modern competitive methods, for workingmen and property-owners to defend their rights and exist without the right of suffrage.

2. He insists on thrift and self-respect, but at the same time counsels a silent submission to civic inferiority such as is bound to sap the manhood of any race in the long run.

3. He advocates common-school[3] and industrial training, and depreciates institutions of higher learning; but neither the Negro common-schools, nor Tuskegee itself, could remain open a day were it not for teachers trained in Negro colleges, or trained by their graduates.

This triple paradox in Mr. Washington's position is the object of criticism by two classes of colored Americans. One class is spiritually descended from Toussaint the Savior,[4] through Gabriel, Vesey, and Turner, and they represent the attitude of revolt and revenge; they hate the white South blindly and distrust the white race generally, and so far as they agree on definite action, think that the Negro's only hope lies in emigration beyond the borders of the United States. And yet, by the irony of fate, nothing has more effectually made this programme seem hopeless than the recent course of the United States toward weaker and darker peoples in the West Indies, Hawaii, and the Philippines,—for where in the world may we go and be safe from lying and brute force?

The other class of Negroes who cannot agree with Mr. Washington has hitherto said little aloud. They deprecate the sight of scattered counsels, of internal disagreement; and especially they dislike making their just criticism of a useful and earnest man an excuse for a general discharge of venom from small-minded opponents. Nevertheless, the questions involved are so fundamental and serious that it is difficult to see how men like the Grimkes, Kelly Miller, J. W. E. Bowen,[5] and other representatives of this group, can much longer be silent. Such men feel in conscience bound to ask of this nation three things:

1. The right to vote.
2. Civic equality.
3. The education of youth according to ability.

They acknowledge Mr. Washington's invaluable service in counselling patience and courtesy in such demands; they do not ask that ignorant black men vote when ignorant whites are debarred, or that any reasonable restrictions in the suffrage should not be applied; they know that the low social level of the mass of the race is responsible for much discrimination against it, but they also know, and the nation knows, that relentless color-prejudice is more often a cause than a result of the Negro's degradation; they seek the abatement of this relic of barbarism, and not its systematic encouragement and pampering by all agencies of social power from the Associated Press to the Church of Christ. They advocate, with Mr. Washington, a broad system of Negro common schools supplemented by thorough industrial training; but they are surprised that a man of Mr. Washington's insight cannot see that no such educational system ever has rested or can rest on any other basis than that of the well-equipped college and university, and they insist that there is a demand for a few such institutions throughout the South to train the best of the Negro youth as teachers, professional men, and leaders.

This group of men honor Mr. Washington for his attitude of conciliation

---

3. A free public school offering courses at precollege level.
4. Pierre Dominique Toussaint (1743–1803); see p. 557, n. 6.
5. John Wesley Edward Bowen (1855–?), Methodist clergyman and educator, president of Gammon Theological Seminary of Atlanta. Archibald Grimké (1849–1930) and Francis Grimké (1850–1937), American civic leaders concerned with African American affairs. Miller (1863–1939), dean of Howard University, lectured on the race problem.

toward the white South; they accept the "Atlanta Compromise" in its broadest interpretation; they recognize, with him, many signs of promise, many
men of high purpose and fair judgment, in this section; they know that no
easy task has been laid upon a region already tottering under heavy burdens.
But, nevertheless, they insist that the way to truth and right lies in straightforward honesty, not in indiscriminate flattery; in praising those of the South
who do well and criticising uncompromisingly those who do ill; in taking
advantage of the opportunities at hand and urging their fellows to do the
same, but at the same time in remembering that only a firm adherence to
their higher ideals and aspirations will ever keep those ideals within the realm
of possibility. They do not expect that the free right to vote, to enjoy civic
rights, and to be educated, will come in a moment; they do not expect to see
the bias and prejudices of years disappear at the blast of a trumpet; but they
are absolutely certain that the way for a people to gain their reasonable rights
is not by voluntarily throwing them away and insisting that they do not want
them; that the way for a people to gain respect is not by continually belittling
and ridiculing themselves; that, on the contrary, Negroes must insist continually, in season and out of season, that voting is necessary to modern manhood, that color discrimination is barbarism, and that black boys need
education as well as white boys.

   In failing thus to state plainly and unequivocally the legitimate demands
of their people, even at the cost of opposing an honored leader, the thinking
classes of American Negroes would shirk a heavy responsibility,—a responsibility to themselves, a responsibility to the struggling masses, a responsibility to the darker races of men whose future depends so largely on this
American experiment, but especially a responsibility to this nation,—this
common Fatherland. It is wrong to encourage a man or a people in evil-doing;
it is wrong to aid and abet a national crime simply because it is unpopular not
to do so. The growing spirit of kindliness and reconciliation between the
North and South after the frightful differences of a generation ago ought to
be a source of deep congratulation to all, and especially to those whose mis-
treatment caused the war; but if that reconciliation is to be marked by the
industrial slavery and civic death of those same black men, with permanent
legislation into a position of inferiority, then those black men, if they are really
men, are called upon by every consideration of patriotism and loyalty to
oppose such a course by all civilized methods, even though such opposition
involves disagreement with Mr. Booker T. Washington. We have no right to
sit silently by while the inevitable seeds are sown for a harvest of disaster to
our children, black and white.

   First, it is the duty of black men to judge the South discriminatingly. The
present generation of Southerners are not responsible for the past, and they
should not be blindly hated or blamed for it. Furthermore, to no class is the
indiscriminate endorsement of the recent course of the South toward
Negroes more nauseating than to the best thought of the South. The South
is not "solid"; it is a land in the ferment of social change, wherein forces of
all kinds are fighting for supremacy; and to praise the ill the South is to-day
perpetrating is just as wrong as to condemn the good. Discriminating and
broad-minded criticism is what the South needs,—needs it for the sake of her
own white sons and daughters, and for the insurance of robust, healthy mental and moral development.

To-day even the attitude of the Southern whites toward the blacks is not, as so many assume, in all cases the same; the ignorant Southerner hates the Negro, the workingmen fear his competition, the money-makers wish to use him as a laborer, some of the educated see a menace in his upward develop- ment, while others—usually the sons of the masters—wish to help him to rise. National opinion has enabled this last class to maintain the Negro com- mon schools, and to protect the Negro partially in property, life, and limb. Through the pressure of the money-makers, the Negro is in danger of being reduced to semi-slavery, especially in the country districts; the workingmen, and those of the educated who fear the Negro, have united to disfranchise him, and some have urged his deportation; while the passions of the ignorant are easily aroused to lynch and abuse any black man. To praise this intricate whirl of thought and prejudice is nonsense; to inveigh indiscriminately against "the South" is unjust; but to use the same breath in praising Gover- nor Aycock, exposing Senator Morgan, arguing with Mr. Thomas Nelson Page, and denouncing Senator Ben Tillman,[6] is not only sane, but the imper- ative duty of thinking black men.

It would be unjust to Mr. Washington not to acknowledge that in several instances he has opposed movements in the South which were unjust to the Negro; he sent memorials to the Louisiana and Alabama constitutional con- ventions, he has spoken against lynching, and in other ways has openly or silently set his influence against sinister schemes and unfortunate happen- ings. Notwithstanding this, it is equally true to assert that on the whole the distinct impression left by Mr. Washington's propaganda is, first, that the South is justified in its present attitude toward the Negro because of the Negro's degradation; secondly, that the prime cause of the Negro's failure to rise more quickly is his wrong education in the past; and, thirdly, that his future rise depends primarily on his own efforts. Each of these propositions is a dangerous half-truth. The supplementary truths must never be lost sight of: first, slavery and race-prejudice are potent if not sufficient causes of the Negro's position; second, industrial and common-school training were nec- essarily slow in planting because they had to await the black teachers trained by higher institutions,—it being extremely doubtful if any essentially differ- ent development was possible, and certainly a Tuskegee was unthinkable before 1880; and, third, while it is a great truth to say that the Negro must strive and strive mightily to help himself, it is equally true that unless his striv- ing be not simply seconded, but rather aroused and encouraged, by the ini- tiative of the richer and wiser environing group, he cannot hope for great suc- cess.

In his failure to realize and impress this last point, Mr. Washington is espe- cially to be criticised. His doctrine has tended to make the whites, North and South, shift the burden of the Negro problem to the Negro's shoulders and

6. Benjamin Ryan Tillman (1847–1918), governor of South Carolina (1890–94) and U.S. Senator (1895–1918), served as the chairman on the com- mittee on suffrage (during the South Carolina con- stitutional convention) and framed the article providing for an educational and property qualifi- cation for voting, thus eliminating the black vote. He presented the views of the southern extremists on the race question, justified lynching in cases of rape and the use of force to disenfranchise blacks, and advocated the repeal of the Fifteenth Amend- ment. Charles Brantley Aycock (1859–1912), gov- ernor of North Carolina (1901–05). Edwin Denison Morgan (1811–1883), governor of New York (1859–63) and U.S. Senator (1863–69), voted with the minority in President Johnson's veto of the Freedman's Bureau bill and for Johnson's conviction. Page (1853–1922), American novelist and diplomat, did much to build up romantic leg- ends of the southern plantation.

stand aside as critical and rather pessimistic spectators; when in fact the burden belongs to the nation, and the hands of none of us are clean if we bend not our energies to righting these great wrongs.

The South ought to be led, by candid and honest criticism, to assert her better self and do her full duty to the race she has cruelly wronged and is still wronging. The North—her co-partner in guilt—cannot salve her conscience by plastering it with gold. We cannot settle this problem by diplomacy and suaveness, by "policy" alone. If worse come to worst, can the moral fibre of this country survive the slow throttling and murder of nine millions of men?

The black men of America have a duty to perform, a duty stern and delicate,—a forward movement to oppose a part of the work of their greatest leader. So far as Mr. Washington preaches Thrift, Patience, and Industrial Training for the masses, we must hold up his hands and strive with him, rejoicing in his honors and glorying in the strength of this Joshua called of God and of man to lead the headless host. But so far as Mr. Washington apologizes for injustice, North or South, does not rightly value the privilege and duty of voting, belittles the emasculating effects of caste distinctions, and opposes the higher training and ambition of our brighter minds,—so far as he, the South, or the Nation, does this,—we must unceasingly and firmly oppose them. By every civilized and peaceful method we must strive for the rights which the world accords to men, clinging unwaveringly to those great words which the sons of the Fathers would fain forget: "We hold these truths to be self-evident: That all men are created equal; that they are endowed by their Creator with certain unalienable rights; that among these are life, liberty, and the pursuit of happiness."

1903

Realism and Naturalism

Realism and *naturalism* are closely related but disputed terms in American literary history, used interchangeably and also as opposites. Is naturalism merely realism with an emphasis on pessimistic determinism? Or is naturalism something separate from realism and at odds with it, an idealistic form of romance? As cultural conditions changed rapidly in mid-nineteenth-century America, artists of all types turned to realist styles to address such new concerns as the rise of the middle class and the struggles of the working class. Literary realism, then naturalism at the start of the new century, gave voice to Americans' changing awareness of the meaning of such concepts as "Nature"—including human nature—in such new environments as the frontier and fast-growing cities.

Realism as a movement in novel-writing developed in early nineteenth-century Europe and the United States. Writers as seemingly different as William Dean Howells and Mark Twain offered objective, detached views of everyday life appropriate for middle-class readers. Critic George J. Becker's definition of the realist novel as a substantial work in prose that offers verisimilitude of detail, a norm of experience, and an objective view of human nature fits not only the work of early realist authors but also that of their literary descendants. By the mid-nineteenth century, realism was simply considered modern, and readers assumed that contemporary fiction would aspire to offer verisimilitude.

The heights of American realism were reached in the work of Howells, Twain, Henry James, and Edith Wharton. Howell's *The Rise of Silas Lapham* (1885) transformed the novel of manners into a critique of the American Dream, as a family is nearly undone by the father's unexamined desire for high society—yet all is mostly well in the end, lessons learned. Regarded as "the father of American Realism," Howells, like Twain, rejected romanticism (if not sentiment) and its distortions. More significant for literary history than Howells's fiction were his editorships at prestigious magazines such as *Harper's* and *Atlantic Monthly*, in which he published Twain, James, and other innovators, including Charles Chesnutt and naturalist Frank Norris. If not for Howells in his editorial dimension, Twain's publishing career might never have taken off.

Though Twain and James represented two very different instances of American realism (and disliked each others' writing), Howells championed both of them. As Twain pushed realism toward satirical exaggeration and developed the vernacular voice in his fiction, James used the voice of high culture and pushed realism toward premodern psychological realism, particularly in *The Portrait of a Lady* (1882) and his other novels of Americans unprepared for situations they encounter in Europe. In later novels, such as *The Wings of the Dove* (1902), James developed realism into an absorbing, complex interior discourse, his narrator evolving into an ironic blend of first- and third-person points of view, a perspective described by critic Percy Lubbock as hovering somewhere over the shoulder of the "focal character." Wharton's satiric and often tragic novels and stories of Gilded Age New York society extend the penetrating insights of Howells and James, but move more toward naturalism; the laws of Darwinian survival are not, in her work, in operation only among the poor or along the frontier, but in the upper-crust drawing rooms and summer homes she knew from birth.

Realism was a broader movement than naturalism, and of course helped give rise to naturalism. But they present sharp differences. The realist novels of the nineteenth century attacked social mores and manners but were rarely critical of the political foundations of society itself. With its clearer doctrines, more restricted time period (1890–1920), and proving grounds mainly in France and the United States, naturalism more specifically critiqued the industrial wealth of the bourgeoisie. Naturalist novels had extreme settings, in contrast to the everyday, believable locales of realist novels. Realistic characters were usually middle class; naturalistic ones lower-class. Realist plots worked toward the restoration of order and characters' proper location in class hierarchies. Minor crises lead to a major confrontation, followed by resolution. In naturalist novels, the characters confront major crises and are destroyed by them. A realist might suggest that good will ultimately prevails, but in naturalist novels humans are doomed by their own (animalistic) shortcomings. Naturalist heroes never have a chance.

By the end of the nineteenth century, naturalism, with its "scientific" point of view, had developed narrative techniques that reflected this orientation, embracing such new technologies as photography and grappling with Freud's theories of a primitive "id" and the Unconscious, a new inner landscape. But the most important force behind naturalism was Darwin. Life as a series of events governed by natural selection, as proposed in Darwin's *Origin of Species* (1859) and *The Descent of Man* (1871), suggested that the strong survive and the weak are destroyed: this scientific "law of life," as its adherents thought of it, ran counter to religion and genteel morality.

In France, novelist and social critic Émile Zola wrote naturalist novels of the lives of poor people at the mercy of biology and class, featuring themes of power and survival. In the preface to *Thérèse Raquin* (1867), Zola compares the naturalist to a surgeon dissecting a corpse—the novel exposes social conditions in a way that might ultimately help right political and economic wrongs.

American literary naturalists—most born after the Civil War—grew up in a different world than did the realists, one dominated by what critic Donald Pizer calls a "struggle to survive materially rather than to prevail morally." Between the economic panics of the 1890s, which put masses of people out of work, and World War I, there developed naturalist literature of great diversity. Naturalist subject matter ranges from Crane's awed and terrified Union soldier in *The Red Badge of Courage* (1895), to Norris's and Upton Sinclair's exposés of the power of capitalism in *The Octopus* (1901) and *The Jungle* (1906), to the portraits of psychopathological characters in Norris's *McTeague* (1899) and London's *The Sea-Wolf* (1904). Naturalism thus appeared in many forms. Like *The Octopus*, London's *The Call of the Wild* (1903) was at once a profoundly naturalistic novel and an intensely romantic fable; in London's fiction, though human nature seems inevitably to go wrong, it may be saved in rugged environments where "civilized" notions such as self-gain are no longer useful. Later, Richard Wright and Américo Paredes would use such themes in urban settings. Despite its often brutal subject matter, naturalism "reflects an affirmative ethical conception of life," as Pizer expresses it, by endowing even the lowest characters with moral complexity.

WILLIAM DEAN HOWELLS

Enormously influential as author, editor, and critic, William Dean Howells (1837–1920) was one of the prime innovators of American realism; his novels and even more so his editorial work shaped American fiction of his day. When Howells left his editorship at *The Atlantic Monthly* in 1881, he had already established himself as a "literary Columbus," as *Cosmopolitan* editor Perriton Maxwell called him, having discovered "a flock of brilliant essayists, poets, and storytellers whose voices would have died . . . had he not been the conscientious listener for the newer notes borne Bostonward from everywhere in these broad States of ours." Increasingly as his career progressed Howells felt American writing should be "simple, natural, and honest" and should refrain from "romantic exaggeration." Unlike Henry James or Mark Twain, his fellow realist innovators, Howells was not interested in the unconscious and irrational in humankind. Though he was criticized by Frank Norris among others for his "teacup tragedies" that take place in front parlors, as an editor and critic Howells responded deeply and sensitively to novelistic complexity. In his essay "Henry James, Jr.," Howells praises James's "impartiality" as that which leaves conclusions about characters up to the reader: "We must take him on his own ground, for clearly he will not come to ours."

"Novel-Writing and Novel-Reading" was not published until well after Howells's death; in his day it was a widely praised lecture he gave on a tour through the East and Midwest in 1899. In the essay Howells shows a change from the "Boston" Howells to the "New York" Howells. Moving to New York in 1891, Howells developed a growing concern with "social" and "race" questions in literature. He came to see novel-reading as a more serious endeavor than ever. And for novelists, he felt, "construction and criticism go hand-in-hand." From his new column in *Harper's Magazine*, Howells campaigned for the importance of realism in the novel, arguing that the reader's own "experience of life" was the only test of "'realism.'" But, in the end, realism is less "picturesque" than historical and ethical. In his earlier career, Howells had insisted on eliding those passions that could not be revealed in polite novels; by this point, he had come to believe that "realism excludes nothing that is true," and that *truth* is synonymous with *beauty*. He argues that the novel is a vehicle of social reform and advances those who write toward that goal, such as Charles Chesnutt. Howells ties in the American realists of the day with the tradition of the novel in Europe. "The truth," he decides, "may be indecent, but it cannot be vicious, it can never corrupt or deprave" in its "material honesty."

From Novel-Writing and Novel-Reading:
An Impersonal Explanation[1]

* * *

By beauty of course I mean truth, for the one involves the other; it is only the false in art which is ugly, and it is only the false which is universal. The truth may be indecent, but it cannot be vicious, it can never corrupt or deprave; and I should say this in defense of the grossest material honestly treated in modern novels as against the painted and perfumed meretricious-

1. From *Howells and James: A Double Billing: Novel-Writing and Novel-Reading, An Impersonal Explanation*, ed. William M. Gibson, Leon Edel, and Lyall H. Powers (1958), from which this excerpt is taken.

ness of the novels that went before them. I conceive that apart from all the clamor about schools of fiction is the *quiet* question of truth, how to get it in, so that it may get itself out again as beauty, the divinely living thing which all men love and worship. So I make truth the prime test of a novel. If I do not find that it is like life, then it does not exist for me as art; it is ugly, it is ludicrous, it is impossible. I do not expect a novel to be wholly true. I have never read one that seemed to me so except Tolstoy's novels:[2] but I expect it to be a constant endeavor for the truth, and I perceive beauty in it so far as it fulfills this endeavor. I am quite willing to recognize and enjoy whatever measure of truth I find in a novel that is partly or mainly false; only, if I come upon the falsehood at the outset I am apt not to read that novel. But I do not bear such a grudge against it as I do against the novel which lures me on with a fair face of truth, and drops the mask midway. If you ask me for illustrations, I am somewhat at a loss, but if you ask me for examples, they are manifold. In English I should say the truthful novelists or those working with an ideal of truth were Jane Austen, George Eliot, Anthony Trollope, Thomas Hardy, Mrs. Humphrey Ward, George Moore; in French, Flaubert, Maupassant, the Goncourts, Daudet and Zola; in Russian, Tourguenief and Tolstoy; in Spanish, Valdés, Galdós and Pardo-Bazan; in Norwegian, Björnson, Lie, and Kielland. In English, some untruthful novelists, or those working from an ideal of effect, are Thackeray, Dickens, Bulwer, Reade, and all their living followers; in French, Dumas, Feuillet, Ohnet; in Spanish Valera; in Russian, measurably Doystoyevsky;[3] in Norwegian, none that I know of. It is right to say, however, of some of the untruthful novelists, and notably of Thackeray, that they were the victims of their period. If Thackeray had been writing in our time, I have no question but he would have been one of its most truthful artists.

The truth which I mean, the truth which is the only beauty, is truth to human experience, and human experience is so manifold and so recondite, that no scheme can be too remote, too airy for the test. It is a well ascertained fact concerning the imagination that it can work only with the stuff of experience. It can absolutely create nothing; it can only compose. The most fantastic extravagance comes under the same law that exacts likeness to the known as well as the closest and severest study of life. Once for all, then, obedience to this law is the creed of the realist, and rebellion is the creed of the romanticist. Both necessarily work under it, but one willingly, to beautiful effect, and the other unwillingly to ugly effect.

For the reader, whether he is an author too, or not, the only test of a novel's truth is his own knowledge of life. Is it like what he has seen or felt? Then it is true, and for him it cannot otherwise be true, that is to say beautiful. It will not avail that it has style, learning, thinking, feeling; it is no more beautiful

2. Russian realist Leo Tolstoy's (1828–1910) most famous works are *Anna Karenina*, *The Death of Ivan Ilych*, and *War and Peace*.
3. Among the 19th-century novelists that Howells mentions are Jane Austen (1775–1817), Thomas Hardy (1840–1928), Mrs. Humphrey Ward (1851–1920), George Moore (1852–1933), Gustave Flaubert (1821–1880), Guy de Maupassant (1850–1893), Edmund de Goncourt (1822–1896), Jules de Goncourt (1830–1870), Alphonse Daudet (1840–1897), Émile Zola (1840–1902), Ivan Turgenev (1818–1883), Armando Palacio Valdés (1853–1938), Benito Pérez Galdós (1843–1920), Emilia Pardo-Bazan (1851–1921), Björnstjerne Martinus Björnson (1832–1910), Jonas Lie (1833–1908), Alexander Kielland (1849–1906), Edward Bulwer-Lytton (1831–1891), Alexandre Dumas, pére (1802–1870), Octave Feuillet (1821–1890), Georges Ohnet (1848–1918), Juan Valera (1824–1905), and Fyodor Dostoyevsky (1821–1881). Howells divides them into two camps: realists and idealists.

without truth than the pretty statue which cannot stand on its feet. It is very astonishing to me that any sort of people can find pleasure in such a thing; but I know that there are many who do; and I should not think of consigning them to the police for their bad taste so long as their taste alone is bad. At the same time I confess that I should suspect an unreality, an insincerity in a mature and educated person whom I found liking an unreal, an insincere novel. You see, I take novels rather seriously, and I would hold them to a much stricter account than they are commonly held to. If I could, I would have them all subject to the principles that govern an honest man, and do not suffer him to tell lies of any sort. I think the novelist is rarely the victim of such a possession, or obsession, that he does not know when he is representing and when he is misrepresenting life. If he does not know it fully at the time, he cannot fail to be aware of it upon review of his work. In the frenzy of inspiration, he may not know that he has been lying; but a time will quickly come to him, if he is at all an artist, when he will know it, and will see that the work he has done is ugly because of it. That is the time for him to tear up his work and to begin anew.

Of course, there are several ways of regarding life in fiction, and in order to do justice to the different kinds we ought to distinguish very clearly between them. There are three forms which I think of, and which I will name in the order of their greatness: the novel, the romance, and the romanticistic novel.

The novel I take to be the sincere and conscientious endeavor to picture life just as it is, to deal with character as we witness it in living people, and to record the incidents that grow out of character. This is the supreme form of fiction, and I offer as supreme examples of it, Pride and Prejudice, Middlemarch, Anna Karenina, Fathers and Sons, Doña Perfecta and Marta y Maria,[4] sufficiently varied in their origin and material and method, but all of the same absolute honesty in their intention. They all rely for their moral effect simply and solely upon their truth to nature.

The novel is easily first among books that people read willingly and it is rightfully first. It has known how to keep the charm of the story, and to add to it the attraction of almost every interest. It still beguiles, as in the hands of the Byzantine romancers,[5] not to go unnumbered centuries back to the Greek novel of Homer, the Odyssey;[6] and it has learnt how to warm, to question, to teach in every concern of life. Scarcely any predicament, moral or psychological, has escaped its study, and it has so refined and perfected its methods that antiseptic surgery itself has hardly made a more beneficent advance. It began with the merest fable, excluding from the reader's interest all but the fortunes of princes and other dignified personages for whose entertainment it existed, until now it includes all sorts and conditions of men, who turn to it for instruction, inspiration, consolation. It has broadened and deep-

---

4. Pride and Prejudice (1813) by Jane Austen, Middlemarch (1872) by George Eliot, Anna Karenina (1877) by Leo Tolstoy, Fathers and Sons (1861) by Ivan Turgenev, Doña Perfecta (1876) by Benito Pérez Galdós, and Marta y Maria (1883) by Armando Palacio Valdés are 19th-century novels that represent "realism" as defined by Howells.
5. Erotic novels thrived in the Byzantine Empire from the late 5th century until the fall of Constan-

tinople in 1453; their hero was often Alexander the Great.
6. Homer is the blind poet of ancient Greek tradition who is said to have composed both of the great Greek epics, The Iliad and The Odyssey, probably in the 8th century B.C.E. The latter depicts the trials of Odysseus and his family as he struggles to return from Troy.

ened down and out till it compasses the whole of human nature; and no cause important to the race has been unfriended of it. Sometimes I have been vexed at its vicious pandering to passion, but I cannot think, after all, of any great modern novel which has not been distinctly moral in effect. I am not sorry to have had it go into the dark places of the soul, the filthy and squalid places of society, high and low, and shed there its great light. Let us know with its help what we are, and where we are. Let all the hidden things be brought into the sun, and let every day be the day of judgment. If the sermon cannot any longer serve this end, let the novel do it.

HENRY JAMES

Perhaps the most famous description of realism in the novel is Henry James's essay "The Art of Fiction," in which James (1843–1916) dismisses all prescriptions for novelistic success. A well-known traditionalist critic, Walter Besant, proposed that the good novel had to be overtly moral. James offered a rebuttal of radical realism, rejecting *a priori* requirements of the novel: "I am quite at a loss to imagine anything (at any rate in this matter of fiction) that people *ought* to like or to dislike. Selection will be sure to take care of itself, for it has a constant motive behind it. That motive is simply experience." James urges the novelist to observe not only environment but more importantly its *meaning*: "[to catch] the very note and trick, the strange irregular rhythm of life, that is the attempt whose strenuous force keeps Fiction upon her feet." James matches the desire to reflect the incomplete realities of characters—who never seem to "know" until it is too late—with his own tacit pledge not to make designs on the opinions of his readers. Though readers may observe that either nothing seems to happen in a James novel or no conclusion is arrived at, this ambiguity *is* James's design—*not* to "know" people in any certain, reductive, sense. James's idea of consciousness—a sort of spiderweb of "the very atmosphere of the mind"—means that the question of the "moral" is a false one. He finds that "the deepest quality of a work of art will always be the quality of the mind of the producer. . . . No good novel will ever proceed from a superficial mind."

From The Art of Fiction[1]

* * *

It goes without saying that you will not write a good novel unless you possess the sense of reality; but it will be difficult to give you a recipe for calling that sense into being. Humanity is immense, and reality has a myriad forms; the most one can affirm is that some of the flowers of fiction have the odour of it, and others have not; as for telling you in advance how your nosegay should be composed, that is another affair. It is equally excellent and inconclusive to say that one must write from experience; to our suppositious aspirant such a declaration might savour of mockery. What kind of experience is intended, and where does it begin and end? Experience is never limited, and it is never complete; it is an immense sensibility, a kind of huge spider-web of the finest

---

1. First published in *Longman's Magazine* 4 (September 1884), then in James's *Partial Portraits* (1888); rpt. in *Selected Literary Criticism* by Henry James (1968), from which this text is taken.

silken threads suspended in the chamber of consciousness, and catching every air-borne particle in its tissue. It is the very atmosphere of the mind; and when the mind is imaginative—much more when it happens to be that of a man of genius—it takes to itself the faintest hints of life, it converts the very pulses of the air into revelations. The young lady living in a village has only to be a damsel upon whom nothing is lost to make it quite unfair (as it seems to me) to declare to her that she shall have nothing to say about the military. Greater miracles have been seen than that, imagination assisting, she should speak the truth about some of these gentlemen. I remember an English novelist, a woman of genius, telling me that she was much commended for the impression she had managed to give in one of her tales of the nature and way of life of the French Protestant youth. She had been asked where she learned so much about this recondite being, she had been congratulated on her peculiar opportunities. These opportunities consisted in her having once, in Paris, as she ascended a staircase, passed an open door where, in the household of a *pasteur*, some of the young Protestants were seated at table round a finished meal. The glimpse made a picture; it lasted only a moment, but that moment was experience. She had got her direct personal impression, and she turned out her type. She knew what youth was, and what Protestantism; she also had the advantage of having seen what it was to be French, so that she converted these ideas into a concrete image and produced a reality. Above all, however, she was blessed with the faculty which when you give it an inch takes an ell, and which for the artist is a much greater source of strength than any accident of residence or of place in the social scale. The power to guess the unseen from the seen, to trace the implication of things, to judge the whole piece by the pattern, the condition of feeling life in general so completely that you are well on your way to knowing any particular corner of it—this cluster of gifts may almost be said to constitute experience, and they occur in country and in town and in the most differing stages of education. If experience consists of impressions, it may be said that impressions *are* experience, just as (have we not seen it?) they are the very air we breathe. Therefore, if I should certainly say to a novice, 'Write from experience and experience only', I should feel that this was rather a tantalizing monition if I were not careful immediately to add, 'Try to be one of the people on whom nothing is lost!'

* * *

A novel is a living thing, all one and continuous, like any other organism, and in proportion as it lives will it be found, that in each of the parts there is something of each of the other parts. The critic who over the close texture of a finished work shall pretend to trace a geography of items will mark some frontiers as artificial, I fear, as any that have been known to history. There is an old-fashioned distinction between the novel of character and the novel of incident which must have cost many a smile to the intending fabulist who was keen about his work. It appears to me as little to the point as the equally celebrated distinction between the novel and the romance—to answer as little to any reality. There are bad novels and good novels, as there are bad pictures and good pictures; but that is the only distinction in which I see any meaning, and I can as little imagine speaking of a novel of character as I can imagine speaking of a picture of character. When one says picture one says of character, when one says novel one says of incident, and the terms may be transposed at will. What is character but the determination of incident? What is incident but the illustration of character? What is either a picture or a novel that is *not* of character? What else do we seek in it and find in it? It is an incident for a woman to stand up with her hand resting on a table and look out at you in a certain way; or if it be not an incident I think it will be hard to say what it is. At the same time it is an expression of character. If you say you don't see it (character in *that—allons donc!*),[2] this is exactly what the artist who has reason of his own for thinking he *does* see it undertakes to show you. When a young man makes up his mind that he has not faith enough after all to enter the church as he intended, that is an incident, though you may not hurry to the end of the chapter to see whether perhaps he doesn't change once more. I do not say that these are extraordinary or startling incidents. I do not pretend to estimate the degree of interest proceeding from them, for this will depend upon the skill of the painter. It sounds almost puerile to say that some incidents are intrinsically much more important than others, and I need not take this precaution after having professed my sympathy for the major ones in remarking that the only classification of the novel that I can understand is into that which has life and that which has it not.

* * *

There is one point at which the moral sense and the artistic sense lie very near together; that is in the light of the very obvious truth that the deepest quality of a work of art will always be the quality of the mind of the producer. In proportion as that intelligence is fine will the novel, the picture, the statue partake of the substance of beauty and truth. To be constituted of such elements is, to my vision, to have purpose enough. No good novel will ever proceed from a superficial mind; that seems to me an axiom which, for the artist in fiction, will cover all needful moral ground: if the youthful aspirant take it to heart it will illuminate for him many of the mysteries of 'purpose'.

* * *

1884

2. Thus let us go! (French).

FRANK NORRIS

As a rule, naturalist novelists were not also critics. Jack London wrote essays on Poe and other writers from a naturalist point of view, but Frank Norris (1870–1902) was the only literary theorist of naturalism, though his death at the age of thirty-two robbed his readers of his full critical development. Critic Joseph R. McElrath, Jr., observes that Norris, like Stephen Crane, Henry Adams, and Kate Chopin, "registered dramatically the transition from the age of Emerson, Thoreau, and Whitman to that of Fitzgerald and Steinbeck." As such a bridge, Norris "signaled the movement away from Victorian social values" to more "positivistic and pragmatic modern" concerns. He is thus a member of the Progressive Era who painstakingly melds the realism of Balzac and Flaubert with the naturalistic demands of the modern American world, and adds a theory of romance in which he distinguishes between mere "accuracy" and "truth" and emphasizes the difference between surface commonplaces and the truth beneath the surfaces. In such works as *McTeague* (1899) Norris's anti-hero falls prey to bad heredity, a stressful environment, and the unpredictable developments of life. Norris troubled his readers by showing that the virtues of Victorian culture were of questionable value when forces beyond the individual's control rendered free will and benign intentions irrelevant. He rejects the Victorian question "Who is to blame?" in favor of dramatizing a character's deterministic state. Yet rather than promoting Zola's uncompromising exactitude or marrying Zola's naturalism with the New England realism of Howells, Norris gravitated toward Zola's more romantic and idealistic naturalism.

In "A Plea for Romantic Fiction," first published in 1901, Norris seeks to redefine romance and naturalism. For Norris "realism" is confined to what is generally agreed on by middle-class readers to be "normal life," while naturalism, in its romantic identity, penetrates "the surface of things." Norris again describes Howells's realism as the "drama of a broken teacup." He calls on realism to do the "entertaining," while naturalism, as romance, does the "teaching."

A Plea for Romantic Fiction[1]

Let us at the start make a distinction. Observe that one speaks of Romanticism and not of sentimentalism. One claims that the latter is as distinct from the former as is that other form of art which is called Realism. Romance has been often put upon and overburdened by being forced to bear the onus of abuse that by right should fall to sentiment; but the two should be kept very distinct, for a very high and illustrious place will be claimed for Romance, while sentiment will be handed down the scullery stairs.

Many people today are composing mere sentimentalism, and calling it and causing it to be called Romance, so with those who are too busy to think much upon these subjects, but who none the less love honest literature, Romance has fallen into disrepute. Consider now the cut-and-thrust stories. They are labelled Romances, and it is very easy to get the impression that Romance must be an affair of cloaks and daggers, or moonlight and golden hair. But this is not so at all. The true Romance is a more serious business than this. It is not merely a conjurer's trick box, full of flimsy quackeries, tinsel and clap traps, meant only to amuse, and relying upon deception to do even that. Is it not something better than this? Can we not see in it an instrument, keen, finely tempered, flawless—an instrument with which we may go straight through the clothes and tissues and wrappings of flesh down deep into the red, living heart of things?

Is all this too subtle, too merely speculative and intrinsic, too *précieuse* and nice and "literary"?[2] Devoutly one hopes the contrary. So much is made of so-called Romanticism in present-day fiction, that the subject seems worthy of discussion, and a protest against the misuse of a really noble and honest formula of literature appears to be timely—misuse, that is, in the sense of lim-

1. First published in the *Boston Evening Transcript*, December 18, 1901; rpt. in *McTeague: A Story of San Francisco* by Frank Norris, 2nd ed.

(1997), from which this text is taken.
2. That is, too affected and careful.

ited use. Let us suppose for the moment that a Romance can be made out of the cut-and-thrust business. Good Heavens, are there no other things that are romantic, even in this—falsely, falsely called—humdrum world of today? Why should it be that so soon as the novelist addresses himself—seriously— to the consideration of contemporary life he must abandon Romance and take up that harsh, loveless, colorless, blunt tool called Realism?

Now, let us understand at once what is meant by Romance and what by Realism. Romance—I take it—is the kind of fiction that takes cognizance of variations from the type of normal life. Realism is the kind of fiction that confines itself to the type of normal life. According to this definition, then, Romance may even treat of the sordid, the unlovely—as for instance, the novels of M. Zola.[3] (Zola has been dubbed a Realist, but he is, on the contrary, the very head of Romanticists.) Also, Realism, used as it sometimes is as a term of reproach, need not be in the remotest sense or degree offensive, but on the other hand respectable as a church and proper as a deacon—as, for instance, the novels of Mr. Howells.[4]

The reason why one claims so much for Romance, and quarrels so pointedly with Realism, is that Realism stultifies itself. It notes only the surface of things. For it Beauty is not even skin-deep, but only a geometrical plane, without dimensions of depth, a mere outside. Realism is very excellent so far as it goes, but it goes no farther than the Realist himself can actually see, or actually hear. Realism is minute, it is the drama of a broken teacup, the tragedy of a walk down the block, the excitement of an afternoon call, the adventure of an invitation to dinner. It is the visit to my neighbor's house, a formal visit, from which I may draw no conclusions. I see my neighbor and his friends—very, oh, such very! probable people—and that is all. Realism bows upon the doormat and goes away and says to me, as we link arms on the sidewalk: "That is life." And I say it is not. It is not, as you would very well see if you took Romance with you to call upon your neighbor.

Lately you have been taking Romance a weary journey across the water— ages and the flood of years—and haling her into the fusty, musty, worm-eaten, moth-riddled, rust-corroded "Grandes Salles"[5] of the Middle Ages and the Renaissance, and she has found the drama of a bygone age for you there. But would you take her across the street to your neighbor's front parlor (with the bisque fisher boy[6] on the mantel and the photograph of Niagara Falls on glass hanging in the front window); would you introduce her there? Not you. Would you take a walk with her on Fifth avenue, or Beacon street, or Michigan avenue? No indeed. Would you choose her for a companion of a morning spent in Wall Street, or an afternoon in the Waldorf-Astoria?[7] You just guess you would not.

She would be out of place, you say, inappropriate. She might be awkward in my neighbor's front parlor, and knock over the little bisque fisher boy. Well, she might. If she did, you might find underneath the base of the statuette, hidden away, tucked away—what? God knows. But something which would be a complete revelation of my neighbor's secretest life.

3. French naturalist novelist Émile Zola (1840–1902).
4. William Dean Howells (1837–1920), American novelist, critic, and proponent of realism.
5. "Large" or "prominent" "halls," "auditoriums," or "theatres" (French).
6. Bisque-glazed figurines were popular among the rising classes in the late 19th and early 20th centuries, intended to emulate the more expensive pieces owned by the wealthy.
7. Luxury hotel in New York City.

So you think Romance would stop in the front parlor and discuss medicated flannels and mineral waters with the ladies?[8] Not for more than five minutes. She would be off upstairs with you, prying, peeping, peering into the closets of the bedrooms, into the nursery, into the sitting-room; yes, and into that little iron box screwed to the lower shelf of the closet in the library; and into those compartments and pigeonholes of the *secrétaire*[9] in the study. She would find a heartache (maybe) between the pillows of the mistress's bed, and a memory carefully secreted in the master's deedbox.[1] She would come upon a great hope amid the books and papers of the study table of the young man's room, and—perhaps—who knows—an affair, or, great heavens, an intrigue, in the scented ribbons and gloves and hairpins of the young lady's bureau. And she would pick here a little and there a little, making up a bag of hopes and fears, and a package of joys and sorrows—great ones, mind you—and then come down to the front door, and stepping out into the street, hand you the bags and package, and say to you—"That is Life!"

Romance does very well in the castles of the Middle Ages and the Renaissance chateaux, and she has the entrée there and is very well received. That is all well and good. But let us protest against limiting her to such places and such times. You will find her, I grant you, in the chatelaine's[2] chamber and the dungeon of the man-at-arms; but, if you choose to look for her, you will find her equally at home in the brownstone house on the corner and in the office building downtown. And this very day, in this very hour, she is sitting among the rags and wretchedness, the dirt and despair of the tenements of the East Side[3] of New York.

"What?" I hear you say, "look for Romance—the lady of the silken robes and golden crown, our beautiful, chaste maiden of soft voice and gentle eyes—look for her among the vicious ruffians, male and female, of Allen Street and Mulberry Bend?"[4] I tell you she is there, and to your shame be it said you will not know her in those surroundings. You, the aristocrats, who demand the fine linen and the purple in your fiction; you, the sensitive, the delicate, who will associate with your Romance only so long as she wears a silken gown. You will not follow her to the slums, for you believe that Romance should only amuse and entertain you, singing you sweet songs and touching the harp of silver strings with rosy-tipped fingers. If haply she should call to you from the squalor of a dive, or the awful degradation of a disorderly house,[5] crying: "Look! listen! This, too, is life. These, too, are my children, look at them, know them and, knowing, help!" Should she call thus, you would stop your ears; you would avert your eyes, and you would answer, "Come from there, Romance. Your place is not there!" And you would make of her a harlequin, a tumbler,[6] a sword dancer, when, as a matter of fact, she should be by right divine a teacher sent from God.

8. Flannels were used to apply warm liquors to the body for the purpose of easing pain by relaxing the skin. Mineral waters were bathed in or drunk as curatives for many medical conditions at this time.
9. Desk (French).
1. Lockbox for money or valuables.
2. Female estate owner (French).
3. One of the oldest neighborhoods of New York City, situated along the East River from the Manhattan Bridge to 14th Street and bounded on the west by Broadway, a working-class neighborhood defined by immigrant populations and tenements.
4. Streets in Manhattan's Lower East Side associated with the "Five Points Slum," known during Norris's time as a center of violence and crime.
5. A house of prostitution.
6. Clown or buffoon; acrobat or gymnast.

She will not always wear a robe of silk, the gold crown, the jeweled shoon,[7] will not always sweep the silver harp. An iron note is hers if so she choose, and coarse garments, and stained hands; and, meeting her thus, it is for you to know her as she passes—know her for the same young queen of the blue mantle and lilies.[8] She can teach you, if you will be humble to learn. Teach you by showing. God help you, if at last you take from Romance her mission of teaching, if you do not believe that she has a purpose, a nobler purpose and a mightier than mere amusement, mere entertainment. Let Realism do the entertaining with its meticulous presentation of teacups, rag carpets, wall paper and haircloth sofas, stopping with these, going no deeper than it sees, choosing the ordinary, the untroubled, the commonplace.[9]

But to Romance belongs the wide world for range, and the unplumbed depths of the human heart, and the mystery of sex, and the problems of life, and the black, unsearched penetralia of the soul of man. You, the indolent, must not always be amused. What matter the silken clothes, what matter the prince's houses? Romance, too, is a teacher, and if—throwing aside the purple—she wears the camel's hair and feeds upon the locusts,[1] it is to cry aloud unto the people, "Prepare ye the way of the Lord; make straight his path."

1901

7. Archaic plural of "shoe."
8. Details frequently seen in depictions of the Virgin Mary.
9. Items of Victorian domesticity are often depicted in painstaking detail in realist texts.

1. Reference to John the Baptist's self-imposed exile in the wilderness and prophecies of the future (see especially Matthew 3, 11, 14).

THEODORE DREISER

Theodore Dreiser (1871–1945) has been called "the American Zola" by critic George J. Becker, who writes that Dreiser found "that the official descriptions of life from pulpit, rostrum, or printed page did not square with life as he had experienced or observed it." Dreiser's *Sister Carrie* (1900), perhaps the finest of all naturalist novels, is a turn-of-the-century portrait of actress Carrie Meeber and her urban milieu that continues to be relevant today, not least because of its naturalist style of not preaching about immoral behavior but rather inquiring dispassionately into it. Despite a barrage of criticism when it was published, largely because the title character is a nice farm girl who goes bad in the city and yet prospers, the book succeeded. Dreiser called it "a picture of conditions," in its sociology, theatricality, exposé of "love" within the urban struggle for survival, and blunt portrayal of desire. Literary critic Philip Gerber points to its focus on celebrityhood and performance, casting of Carrie as an immigrant seeking the American Dream, identification of money as the *lingua franca,* theme of mobility, and dualistic version of womanhood as significant contributions to American naturalism. "True Art Speaks Plainly," first published in 1903, is a rejoinder by the author to the criticism that greeted the book on publication. Dreiser argues that the essence of morality is to "tell the truth. . . . [to] express what we see honestly and without subterfuge. . . ." Defending himself and other naturalists against charges of lewdness, Dreiser characterizes the conventional critic's version of "the mental virtue of the reader" as false. The novelist must tell the truth no matter the consequences. Despite his clear statements about truth, morality, and fiction, Dreiser struggled for acceptance of his work on its own grounds until the great success of *An American Tragedy* in 1925.

True Art Speaks Plainly[1]

The sum and substance of literary as well as social morality may be expressed in three words—tell the truth. It matters not how the tongues of the critics may wag, or the voices of a partially developed and highly conventionalized society may complain, the business of the author, as well as of other workers upon this earth, is to say what he knows to be true, and, having said as much, to abide the result with patience.

Truth is what is; and the seeing of what is, the realization of truth. To express what we see honestly and without subterfuge: this is morality as well as art.

What the so-called judges of the truth or morality are really inveighing against most of the time is not the discussion of mere sexual lewdness, for no work with that as a basis could possibly succeed, but the disturbing and destroying of their own little theories concerning life, which in some cases may be nothing more than a quiet acceptance of things as they are without any regard to the well-being of the future. Life for them is made up of a variety of interesting but immutable forms and any attempt either to picture any of the wretched results of modern social conditions or to assail the critical defenders of the same is naturally looked upon with contempt or aversion.

It is true that the rallying cry of the critics against so-called immoral literature is that the mental virtue of the reader must be preserved; but this has become a house of refuge to which every form of social injustice hurries for protection. The influence of intellectual ignorance and physical and moral greed upon personal virtue produces the chief tragedies of the age, and yet the objection to the discussion of the sex question is so great as to almost prevent the handling of the theme entirely.

Immoral! Immoral! Under this cloak hide the vices of wealth as well as the vast unspoken blackness of poverty and ignorance; and between them must walk the little novelist, choosing neither truth nor beauty, but some half-conceived phase of life that bears no honest relationship to either the whole of nature or to man.

The impossibility of any such theory of literature having weight with the true artist must be apparent to every clear reasoning mind. Life is not made up of any one phase or condition of being, nor can man's interest possibly be so confined.

1. First published in *Booklovers Magazine* (February 1903); rpt. in *Documents of Modern Literary Realism* (1963), from which this text is taken.

The extent of all reality is the realm of the author's pen, and a true picture of life, honestly and reverentially set down, is both moral and artistic whether it offends the conventions or not.

1903

JACK LONDON

Jack London's essay "What Life Means to Me" was published in *Cosmopolitan* in March 1906 as part of a series in which the magazine challenged prominent American writers to contribute articles on this theme. London (1876–1916) had been warned by the socialist and poet Edwin Markham that the Hearst Corporation, which owned *Cosmopolitan,* would never publish an attack on American capitalism, but the article appeared as London wrote it. London wryly remarked to Markham that "special writers like myself are paid well for expanding their own untrammeled views," with the understanding that these views would sell magazines. His second wife, Charmian Kittredge London, later described this essay as his "most impassioned committal of himself as a rebel toward the shames and uncleanness of the capitalist system." "What Life Means to Me" is one of London's strongest expressions of the relation between the naturalistic elements of his fiction and his gritty origins and struggles for survival within urban poverty and an exploitative class system. To fulfill "the life within me," he wrote, he had to escape the social pit. "Scared into thinking," London realized that by becoming a "vendor of brains" he could make a difference for himself and for the disenfranchised working class around him.

Even at the height of his success, London never abandoned his working-class roots and consciousness; the year he died, 1916, found him busy in various socialist endeavors, including the Pan-Pacific movement he helped found in Hawai'i. Though London had been touted in Hearst papers for his essay "The Yellow Peril," his renewed socialistic worldviews, including brother- and sisterhood with Asian workers, were not so much rebuttals of his earlier views but reflective of his education out of racism via socialism, and reminders of his identity as a lower-class émigré to the status of successful writer and idealist.

From What Life Means to Me[1]

I was born in the working-class. Early I discovered enthusiasm, ambition, and ideals; and to satisfy these became the problem of my child-life. My environment was crude and rough and raw. I had no outlook, but an uplook rather. My place in society was at the bottom. Here life offered nothing but sordidness and wretchedness, both of the flesh and the spirit; for here flesh and spirit were alike starved and tormented.

Above me towered the colossal edifice of society, and to my mind the only way out was up. Into this edifice I early resolved to climb. Up above, men wore black clothes and boiled shirts, and women dressed in beautiful gowns.

---

1. First published in *Cosmopolitan* 41 (March 1906); rpt. in *Revolution and Other Essays* by Jack London (1909), from which this text is taken.

Also, there were good things to eat, and there was plenty to eat. This much for the flesh. Then there were the things of the spirit. Up above me, I knew, were unselfishnesses of the spirit, clean and noble thinking, keen intellectual living. I knew all this because I read "Seaside Library" novels,[2] in which, with the exception of the villains and adventuresses, all men and women thought beautiful thoughts, spoke a beautiful tongue, and performed glorious deeds. In short, as I accepted the rising of the sun, I accepted that up above me was all that was fine and noble and gracious, all that gave decency and dignity to life, all that made life worth living and that remunerated one for his travail and misery.

* * *

I was a sailor before the mast, a longshoreman, a roustabout;[3] I worked in canneries, and factories, and laundries; I mowed lawns, and cleaned carpets, and washed windows. And I never got the full product of my toil. I looked at the daughter of the cannery owner, in her carriage, and knew that it was my muscle, in part, that helped drag along that carriage on its rubber tires. I looked at the son of the factory owner, going to college, and knew that it was my muscle that helped, in part, to pay for the wine and good fellowship he enjoyed.

But I did not resent this. It was all in the game. They were the strong. Very well, I was strong. I would carve my way to a place amongst them and make money out of the muscles of other men. I was not afraid of work. I loved hard work. I would pitch in and work harder than ever and eventually become a pillar of society.

And just then, as luck would have it, I found an employer that was of the same mind. I was willing to work, and he was more than willing that I should work. I thought I was learning a trade. In reality, I had displaced two men. I thought he was making an electrician out of me; as a matter of fact, he was making fifty dollars per month out of me. The two men I had displaced had received forty dollars each per month; I was doing the work of both for thirty dollars per month.

This employer worked me nearly to death. A man may love oysters, but too many oysters will disincline him toward that particular diet. And so with me. Too much work sickened me. I did not wish ever to see work again. I fled from work. I became a tramp, begging my way from door to door, wandering over the United States and sweating bloody sweats in slums and prisons.

I had been born in the working-class, and I was now, at the age of eighteen, beneath the point at which I had started. I was down in the cellar of society, down in the subterranean depths of misery about which it is neither nice nor proper to speak. I was in the pit, the abyss, the human cesspool, the shambles and the charnel-house of our civilization. This is the part of the edifice of society that society chooses to ignore. Lack of space compels me here to ignore it, and I shall say only that the things I there saw gave me a terrible scare.

I was scared into thinking. I saw the naked simplicities of the complicated civilization in which I lived. Life was a matter of food and shelter. In order to get food and shelter men sold things. The merchant sold shoes, the politician

2. Cheap novel series published by George Munro, New York, from 1877 to 1882.

3. A dock worker who loads ships.

sold his manhood, and the representative of the people, with exceptions, of course, sold his trust; while nearly all sold their honor. Women, too, whether on the street or in the holy bond of wedlock, were prone to sell their flesh. All things were commodities, all people bought and sold. The one commodity that labor had to sell was muscle. The honor of labor had no price in the market-place. Labor had muscle, and muscle alone, to sell.

But there was a difference, a vital difference. Shoes and trust and honor had a way of renewing themselves. They were imperishable stocks. Muscle, on the other hand, did not renew. As the shoe merchant sold shoes, he continued to replenish his stock. But there was no way of replenishing the laborer's stock of muscle. The more he sold of his muscle, the less of it remained to him. It was his one commodity, and each day his stock of it diminished. In the end, if he did not die before, he sold out and put up his shutters. He was a muscle bankrupt, and nothing remained to him but to go down into the cellar of society and perish miserably.

I learned, further, that brain was likewise a commodity. It, too, was different from muscle. A brain seller was only at his prime when he was fifty or sixty years old, and his wares were fetching higher prices than ever. But a laborer was worked out or broken down at forty-five or fifty. I had been in the cellar of society, and I did not like the place as a habitation. The pipes and drains were unsanitary, and the air was bad to breathe. If I could not live on the parlor floor of society, I could, at any rate, have a try at the attic. It was true, the diet there was slim, but the air at least was pure. So I resolved to sell no more muscle, and to become a vender of brains.

Then began a frantic pursuit of knowledge. I returned to California and opened the books. While thus equipping myself to become a brain merchant, it was inevitable that I should delve into sociology. There I found, in a certain class of books, scientifically formulated, the simple sociological concepts I had already worked out for myself. Other and greater minds, before I was born, had worked out all that I had thought and a vast deal more. I discovered that I was a socialist.

The socialists were revolutionists, inasmuch as they struggled to overthrow the society of the present, and out of the material to build the society of the future. I, too, was a socialist and a revolutionist. I joined the groups of working-class and intellectual revolutionists, and for the first time came into intellectual living. Here I found keen-flashing intellects and brilliant wits; for here I met strong and alert-brained, withal horny-handed, members of the working-class; unfrocked preachers too wide in their Christianity for any congregation of Mammon-worshippers; professors broken on the wheel of university subservience to the ruling class and flung out because they were quick with knowledge which they strove to apply to the affairs of mankind.

Here I found, also, warm faith in the human, glowing idealism, sweetnesses of unselfishness, renunciation, and martyrdom—all the splendid, stinging things of the spirit. Here life was clean, noble, and alive. Here life rehabilitated itself, became wonderful and glorious; and I was glad to be alive. I was in touch with great souls who exalted flesh and spirit over dollars and cents, and to whom the thin wail of the starved slum child meant more than all the pomp and circumstance of commercial expansion and world empire. All about me were nobleness of purpose and heroism of effort, and my days and nights were sunshine and starshine, all fire and dew, with before my eyes, ever burning and blazing, the Holy Grail, Christ's own Grail, the warm human, long-suffering and maltreated, but to be rescued and saved at the last.

* * *

1906, 1909

THEODORE DREISER
1871–1945

Theodore Herman Albert Dreiser was born in Terre Haute, Indiana, on August 17, 1871, the eleventh of thirteen children. His severe, emotionally distant father was, in Dreiser's view, "mentally a little weak"; he was in any event not very successful in providing for his large family, and he served as the prototype for the failed men who appear so frequently in Dreiser's novels. Dreiser's mother, by contrast, was steadfastly devoted to the well-being of her children; she was, Dreiser claimed, the only person who ever loved him enough. She, too, appears in fictionalized form in many of Dreiser's books.

Dreiser's unhappy childhood haunted him throughout his life. The large family moved from house to house in Indiana dogged by poverty, insecurity, and internal divisions. One of his brothers became a famous popular songwriter under the name Paul Dresser, but other siblings lived turbulent lives that not only defied their father's rigid morality but placed them on the margins of respectable society altogether. Dreiser as a youth was ungainly, confused, shy, and full of vague yearnings like most of his fictional protagonists, male and female. In this as in many other ways, Dreiser's novels are direct projections of his inner life as well as careful transcriptions of his experiences, especially those involving his unstable family.

From the age of fifteen Dreiser was on his own, earning meager support from a variety of menial jobs. A high-school teacher staked him to a year at Indiana University in 1889, but Dreiser's real education was to come from experience and from independent reading and thinking. This education began in 1892 when he landed by persistence and good luck his first newspaper job with the *Chicago Globe*. Over the next decade, as an itinerant journalist, Dreiser slowly groped his way to authorship, testing what he knew from his own life against what he had learned from reading, among others, Charles Darwin, Ernst Haeckel, Thomas Huxley, and Herbert Spencer, late-nineteenth-century scientists and social scientists who lent support to the view that nature and society had no divine sanction. Generally speaking, these thinkers agreed that human beings, just as much as other life forms, were participants in an evolutionary process in which only those who adapted successfully to their environments survived. Human beings, they agreed, were not the privileged creations of supernatural powers. At the same time, Spencer in particular argued that human consciousness was itself a product of evolutionary processes and that it entailed the adaptive capacity for altruism and various forms of social cooperation. This tension between deterministic "chemisms" (as Dreiser called them) and the potential for friendship and the improvement of social institutions appears in Dreiser's fiction throughout his writing career. Early on Dreiser emphasized the mechanistic side of this tension, while in later phases—in his fiction and in his social writings—he appeared to balance his more pessimistic views with belief in the possibilities of social justice.

Sister Carrie (1900), Dreiser's first novel, two chapters of which are included here, tells the story of Carrie Meeber, a country girl from Wisconsin who comes to Chicago, attracted by the excitement that rapidly growing urban centers held out for so many young people in the late 1800s, but even more by the possibility of supporting herself, especially given the meager opportunities in her small rural town. In Chicago she is seduced first by a traveling salesman, Charles Drouet, then by George Hurstwood, a married middle-aged manager of a chic saloon. After closing one night, Hurstwood steals ten thousand dollars from the safe in the bar; then he and Carrie flee to New York, where he slowly deteriorates into homelessness while she begins a successful career on the stage. They eventually part company and, unbeknownst to Carrie, Hurstwood commits suicide.

The novel depicts social transgressions by characters who feel no remorse and largely escape punishment—especially Carrie, who does not hesitate to use sex to get ahead—and it uses "strong" language and names living persons. It was virtually suppressed by its publisher, who printed but refused to promote the book. Since its reissue in 1907 it has steadily risen in popularity and scholarly acceptance. Students will find that *Sister Carrie* addresses many issues of significance today, often with a startling contemporary feel: class mobility, immigration, urban life, greater independence of women and control of their own sexualities, pressure to "make it" in American society, and celebrityhood.

In the first years of the twentieth century Dreiser suffered a nervous breakdown. With the help of his brother Paul, he recovered and by 1904 was on the way to several successful years as an editor, the last of them as editorial director of the Butterick Publishing Company. In 1910 he resigned to write *Jennie Gerhardt* (1911), one of his best novels and the first of a long succession of books that marked his turn to writing as a full-time career. This novel, about the doomed love between a rich man and a poor woman, takes seriously the reality of gentleness, selflessness, and loyalty, though in the end materialism and pressures associated with wealth and social position carry the day.

In *The Financier* (1912), *The Titan* (1914), and *The Stoic* (not published until 1947), Dreiser shifted from the pathos of helpless protagonists to the power of those unusual individuals who assume dominant roles in business and society. The protagonist of this "Trilogy of Desire" (as Dreiser described it), Frank Cowperwood, is modeled after the Chicago speculator Charles T. Yerkes. These novels of the businessman as buccaneer introduced, even more explicitly than had *Sister Carrie*, the notion that men of high sexual energy were financially successful, a theme that is carried over into the rather weak autobiographical novel *The "Genius"* (1915).

The identification of potency with money is at the heart of Dreiser's greatest and most successful novel, *An American Tragedy* (1925). The novel is based on a much-publicized murder in upper New York State in 1906. Clyde Griffiths is a poor boy from the provinces who dreams of a life of luxury and status. When his prospect for marrying the wealthy Sondra Finchley is threatened by the pregnant Roberta Alden, a factory worker with whom he has had a relationship, Clyde plans to murder her. The moment arrives, but he lacks the resolve to do so; he does, however, leave her to drown after their boat accidentally tips over during an outing on a deserted lake. Much of the novel recounts the capture of Clyde, the investigation and prosecution of the case, and the harrowing details of Clyde's imprisonment and execution. The novel was an immediate best-seller and confirmed Dreiser's status as one of the leading writers of his time.

During the last two decades of his life Dreiser turned to polemical writing, but also to other genres—poetry, travel books, and autobiography, including *Dawn* (1931), the first volume in the projected but uncompleted *A History of Myself*. He visited the Soviet Union in 1927 and published *Dreiser Looks at Russia* the following year. In the 1930s, like many American intellectuals and writers, Dreiser was increasingly attracted by the philosophical program of the Communist party. Unable to believe in traditional religious credos, yet unable to give up his strong sense of justice, he continued to seek a way to reconcile his determinism with his compassionate sense of the mystery of life.

Dreiser was more fascinated by ideas and human destinies than he was in love with language. His interest was in human motives and behavior and in the particularities of the environments that helped shape them. His writing is often blunt and ungainly, but many critics believe that his ability to structure complex narratives by manipulating point of view and by using symbols and clusters of metaphors as leitmotifs more than compensates for his sometimes awkward syntax. If, in the end, readers want from a novelist the communication of a deeply felt sense of life, continuing interest in Dreiser seems ensured.

In his lifetime Dreiser was controversial as a man and as a writer. He was accused, with some justice by conventional standards, of being immoral in his personal behavior and of being a poor thinker and a dangerous political radical. As time has passed, however, Dreiser has become recognized both as a profound and prescient critic of debased American values and as a powerful novelist.

From Sister Carrie[1]

Chapter I

When Caroline Meeber boarded the afternoon train for Chicago her total outfit consisted of a small trunk, which was checked in the baggage car, a cheap imitation alligator skin satchel holding some minor details of the toilet, a small lunch in a paper box and a yellow leather snap purse, containing her ticket, a scrap of paper with her sister's address in Van Buren Street,[2] and four dollars in money. It was in August, 1889. She was eighteen years of age, bright, timid and full of the illusions of ignorance and youth. Whatever touch of regret at parting characterized her thoughts it was certainly not for advantages now being given up. A gush of tears at her mother's farewell kiss, a touch in the throat when the cars clacked by the flour mill where her father worked by the day, a pathetic sigh as the familiar green environs of the village passed in review, and the threads which bound her so lightly to girlhood and home were irretrievably broken.

To be sure she was not conscious of any of this. Any change, however great, might be remedied. There was always the next station where one might descend and return. There was the great city, bound more closely by these very trains which came up daily. Columbia City was not so very far away, even once she was in Chicago. What pray is a few hours—a hundred miles? She could go back. And then her sister was there. She looked at the little slip bearing the latter's address and wondered. She gazed at the green landscape now passing in swift review until her swifter thoughts replaced its impression with vague conjectures of what Chicago might be. Since infancy her ears had been full of its fame. Once the family had thought of moving there. If she secured good employment they might come now. Anyhow it was vast. There were lights and sounds and a roar of things. People were rich. There were vast depots. This on-rushing train was merely speeding to get there.

When a girl leaves her home at eighteen, she does one of two things. Either she falls into saving hands and becomes better, or she rapidly assumes the

---

1. First published by Doubleday & Page (1900), from which this text is taken.

2. East-west Chicago street that, roughly, divides the city in half.

cosmopolitan standard of virtue and becomes worse. Of an intermediate balance, under the circumstances, there is no possibility. The city has its cunning wiles no less than the infinitely smaller and more human tempter. There are large forces which allure, with all the soulfulness of expression possible in the most cultured human. The gleam of a thousand lights is often as effective, to all moral intents and purposes, as the persuasive light in a wooing and fascinating eye. Half the undoing of the unsophisticated and natural mind is accomplished by forces wholly superhuman. A blare of sound, a roar of life, a vast array of human hives appeal to the astonished senses in equivocal terms. Without a counselor at hand to whisper cautious interpretations, what falsehoods may not these things breathe into the unguarded ear! Unrecognized for what they are, their beauty, like music, too often relaxes, then weakens, then perverts the simplest human perceptions.

Caroline, or "Sister Carrie" as she had been half affectionately termed by the family, was possessed of a mind rudimentary in its power of observation and analysis. Self-interest with her was high, but not strong. It was nevertheless her guiding characteristic. Warm with the fancies of youth, pretty with the insipid prettiness of the formative period, possessed of a figure which tended toward eventual shapeliness and an eye alight with certain native intelligence, she was a fair example of the middle American class—two generations removed from the emigrant. Books were beyond her interest—knowledge a sealed book. In the intuitive graces she was still crude. She could scarcely toss her head gracefully. Her hands were almost ineffectual for the same reason. The feet, though small, were set flatly. And yet she was interested in her charms, quick to understand the keener pleasures of life, ambitious to gain in material things. A half-equipped little knight she was, venturing to reconnoitre the mysterious city and dreaming wild dreams of some vague, far-off supremacy which should make it prey and subject, the proper penitent, grovelling at a woman's slipper.

"That," said a voice in her ear, "is one of the prettiest little resorts in Wisconsin."

"Is it?" she answered nervously.

The train was just pulling out of Waukesha.[3] For some time she had been conscious of a man behind. She felt him observing her mass of hair. He had been fidgeting, and with natural intuition she felt a certain interest growing in that quarter. Her maidenly reserve and a certain sense of what was conventional under the circumstances called her to forestall and deny this familiarity, but the daring and magnetism of the individual, born of past experience and triumphs, prevailed. She answered.

He leaned forward to put his elbows upon the back of her seat and proceeded to make himself volubly agreeable.

"Yes, that's a great resort for Chicago people. The hotels are swell. You are not familiar with this part of the country, are you?"

"Oh yes I am," answered Carrie. "That is, I live at Columbia City. I have never been through here though."

"And so this is your first visit to Chicago," he observed.

All the time she was conscious of certain features out of the side of her eye. Flush, colorful cheeks, a light mustache, a gray fedora hat. She now turned

3. A city in Wisconsin about 106 miles north of Chicago on Lake Michigan.

and looked upon him in full, the instincts of self-protection and coquetry mingling confusedly in her brain.

"I didn't say that," she said.

"Oh," he answered in a very pleasing way and with an assumed air of mistake. "I thought you did."

Here was a type of the traveling canvasser for a manufacturing house—a class which at that time was first being dubbed by the slang of the day "drummers."[4] He came within the meaning of a still newer term which had sprung into general use among Americans in 1880, and which concisely expressed the thought of one whose dress or manners are such as to impress strongly the fancy, or elicit the admiration, of susceptible young women—a "masher." His clothes were of an impressive character, the suit being cut of a striped and crossed pattern of brown wool, very popular at that time. It was what has since become known as a business suit. The low crotch of the vest revealed a stiff shirt bosom of white and pink stripes, surmounted by a high white collar about which was fastened a tie of distinct pattern. From his coat sleeves protruded a pair of linen cuffs of the same material as the shirt and fastened with large gold-plate buttons set with the common yellow agates known as "cat's-eyes." His fingers bore several rings, one the ever-enduring heavy seal, and from his vest dangled a neat gold watch chain from which was suspended the secret insignia of the Order of Elks. The whole suit was rather tight-fitting and was finished off with broad-soled tan shoes, highly polished, and the grey felt hat, then denominated "fedora," before mentioned. He was, for the order of intellect represented, attractive; and whatever he had to recommend him, you may be sure was not lost upon Carrie, in this her first glance.

Lest this order of individual should permanently pass, let me put down some of the most striking characteristics of his most successful manner and method. Good clothes of course were the first essential, the things without which he was nothing. A strong physical nature actuated by a keen desire for the feminine was the next. A mind free of any consideration of the problems or forces of the world and actuated not by greed but an insatiable love of variable pleasure—woman—pleasure. His method was always simple. Its principal element was daring, backed of course by an intense desire and admiration for the sex. Let him meet with a young woman twice and upon the third meeting he would walk up and straighten her necktie for her and perhaps address her by her first name. If an attractive woman should deign a glance of interest in passing him upon the street he would run up, seize her by the hand in feigned acquaintanceship and convince her that they had met before, providing of course that his pleasing way interested her in knowing him further. In the great department stores he was at his ease in capturing the attention of some young woman, while waiting for the cash boy to come back with his change. In such cases, by those little wiles common to the type, he would find out the girl's name, her favorite flower, where a note would reach her, and perhaps pursue the delicate task of friendship until it proved unpromising for the one aim in view, when it would be relinquished.

He would do very well with more pretentious women, though the burden of expense was a slight deterrent. Upon entering a parlor car at St. Paul, for

4. "Canvassers" and "drummers" are salesmen.

instance, he would select a chair next to the most promising bit of femininity and soon inquire if she cared to have the shade lowered. Before the train cleared the yards he would have the porter bring her a footstool. At the next lull in his conversational progress he would find her something to read, and from then on by dint of compliment gently insinuated, personal narrative, exaggeration and service, he would win her tolerance and mayhap regard.

Those who have ever delved into the depths of a woman's conscience must, at some time or other, have come upon that mystery of mysteries—the moral significance, to her, of clothes. A woman should some day write the complete philosophy of that subject. No matter how young she is, it is one of the things she wholly comprehends. There is an indescribably faint line in the matter of man's apparel which somehow divides for her those who are worth glancing at and those who are not. Once an individual has passed this faint line on the way downward he will get no glance from her. There is another line at which the dress of a man will cause her to study her own. This line the individual at her elbow now marked for Carrie. She became conscious of an inequality. Her own plain blue dress with its black cotton tape trimmings realized itself to her imagination as shabby. She felt the worn state of her shoes.

He mistook this thought wave, which caused her to withdraw her glance and turn for relief to the landscape outside, for some little gain his grace had brought him.

"Let's see," he went on. "I know quite a number of people in your town—Morgenroth the clothier and Gibson the dry-goods man."

"Oh, do you," she interrupted, aroused by memories of longings the displays in the latter's establishment had cost her.

At last he had a clue to her interest and followed it up deftly. In a few minutes he had come about into her seat. He talked of sales of clothing, his travels, Chicago and the amusements of that city.

"If you are going there you will enjoy it immensely. Have you relatives?"

"I am going to visit my sister," she explained.

"You want to see Lincoln Park," he said, "and Michigan Avenue.[5] They are putting up great buildings there. It's a second New York, great. So much to see—theatres, crowds, fine houses—oh you'll like that."

There was a little ache in her fancy of all he described. Her insignificance in the presence of so much magnificence faintly affected her. She realized that hers was not to be a round of pleasure, and yet there was something promising in all the material prospect he set forth. There was something satisfactory in the attention of this individual with his good clothes. She could not help smiling as he told her of some popular actress she reminded him of. She was not silly and yet attention of this sort had its weight.

"You will be in Chicago some little time, won't you?" he observed, at one turn of the now easy conversation.

"I don't know," said Carrie vaguely—a flash vision of the possibility of her not securing employment rising in her mind.

"Several weeks anyhow," he said, looking steadily into her eyes.

There was much more passing now than the mere words indicated. He recognized the indescribable thing that made for fascination and beauty in her.

---

5. The "Magnificent Mile" of stores, restaurants, office buildings, hotels, and historic landmarks. "Lincoln Park": upscale Chicago neighborhood.

She realized that she was of interest to him from the one standpoint which a woman both delights in and fears. Her manner was simple, though, for the very reason that she had not yet learned the many little affectations with which women conceal their true feelings—some things she did appeared bold. A clever companion, had she ever had one, would have warned her never to look a man in the eyes so steadily.

"Why do you ask?" she said.

"Well, I'm going to be there several weeks. I'm going to study stock at our place and get new samples. I might show you 'round."

"I don't know whether you can or not—I mean I don't know whether I can. I shall be living with my sister and—"

"Well, if she minds, we'll fix that." He took out his pencil and a little pocket note book, as if it were all settled. "What is your address there?"

She fumbled her purse, which contained the address slip.

He reached down in his hip pocket and took out a fat purse. It was filled with slips of paper, some mileage books, a roll of green-backs and so on. It impressed her deeply. Such a purse had never been carried by any man who had ever been attentive to her before. Indeed a man who traveled, who was brisk and experienced and of the world, had never come within such close range before. The purse, the shiny tan shoes, the smart new suit and the *air* with which he did things built up for her a dim world of fortune around him of which he was the centre. It disposed her pleasantly toward all he might do.

He took out a neat business card on which was engraved "Bartlett, Caryoe and Company," and down in the left-hand corner "Chas. H. Drouet."

"That's me," he said, putting the card in her hand and touching his name. "It's pronounced 'Drew-eh.' Our family was French on my father's side."

She looked at it while he put up his purse. Then he got out a letter from a bunch in his coat pocket.

"This is the house I travel for," he went on, pointing to a picture on it— "corner of State and Lake." There was pride in his voice. He felt that it was something to be connected with such a place, and he made her feel that way.

"What is your address?" he began again, fixing his pencil to write.

She looked at his hand.

"Carrie Meeber," she said slowly, "354 West Van Buren St., care S. C. Hanson."

He wrote it carefully down and got out the purse again. "You'll be at home if I come around Monday night?" he said.

"I think so," she answered.

How true it is that words are but vague shadows of the volumes we mean. Little audible links they are, chaining together great inaudible feelings and purposes. Here were these two, bandying little phrases, drawing purses, look-ing at cards and both unconscious of how inarticulate all their real feelings were. Neither was wise enough to be sure of the working of the mind of the other. He could not tell how his luring succeeded. She could not realize that she was drifting, until he secured her address. Now she felt that she had yielded something—he, that he had gained a victory. Already they felt that they were somehow associated. Already he took control in directing the con-versation. His words were easy. Her manner was relaxed.

They were nearing Chicago. Already the signs were numerous. Trains flashed by them. Across wide stretches of flat open prairie they could see lines of telegraph poles stalking across the fields toward the great city. Away off there were indications of suburban towns, some big smoke stacks towering high in the air. Frequently there were two-story frame houses standing out in the open fields, without fence or trees, outposts of the approaching army of homes.

To the child, the genius with imagination, or the wholly untraveled, the approach to a great city for the first time is a wonderful thing. Particularly if it be evening—that mystic period between the glare and the gloom of the world when life is changing from one sphere or condition to another. Ah, the promise of the night. What does it not hold for the weary. What old illusion of hope is not here forever repeated! Says the soul of the toiler to itself, "I shall soon be free. I shall be in the ways and the hosts of the merry. The streets, the lamp, the lighted chamber set for dining are for me. The theatres, the halls, the parties, the ways of rest and the paths of song—these are mine in the night." Though all humanity be still enclosed in the shops, the thrill runs abroad. It is in the air. The dullest feel something which they may not always express or describe. It is the lifting of the burden of toil.

Sister Carrie gazed out of the window. Her companion, affected by her wonder, so contagious are all things, felt anew some interest in the city and pointed out the marvels. Already vast net-works of tracks—the sign and insignia of Chicago—stretched on either hand. There were thousands of cars and a clangor of engine bells. At the sides of this traffic stream stood dingy houses, smoky mills, tall elevators.[6] Through the interstices, evidences of the stretching city could be seen. Street cars waited at crossings for the train to go by. Gatemen toiled at wooden arms which closed the streets. Bells clanged, the rails clacked, whistles sounded afar off.

"This is North-West Chicago," said Drouet. "This is the Chicago River," and he pointed to a little muddy creek, crowded with the huge, masted wanderers from far-off waters nosing the black, posted banks. With a puff, a clang and a clatter of rails it was gone. "Chicago is getting to be a great town," he went on. "It's a wonder. You'll find lots to see here."

She did not hear this very well. Her heart was troubled by a kind of terror. The fact that she was alone, away from home, rushing into a great sea of life and endeavor, began to tell. She could not help but feel a little choked for breath—a little sick as her heart beat so fast. She half closed her eyes and tried to think it was nothing, that Columbia City was only a little way off.

"Chicago!—Chicago!" called the brakeman, slamming open the door. They were rushing into a more crowded yard, alive with the clatter and clang of life. She began to gather up her poor little grip and closed her hand firmly upon her purse. Drouet arose, kicked his legs to straighten his trousers and seized his clean yellow grip.

"I suppose your people will be here to meet you," he said. "Let me carry your grip."

"Oh no," she said. "I'd rather you wouldn't. I'd rather you wouldn't be with me when I meet my sister."

"All right," he said in all kindness. "I'll be near, though, in case she isn't here, and take you out there safely."

"You're so kind," said Carrie, feeling the goodness of such attention in her strange situation.

"Chicago!" called the brakeman, drawing the word out long. They were

6. Grain elevators.

under a great shadowy train shed, where lamps were already beginning to shine out, with passenger cars all about and the train moving at a snail's pace. The people in the car were all up and crowding about the door.

"Well, here we are," said Drouet, leading the way to the door. "Goodbye," he said, "till I see you Monday."

"Goodbye," she said, taking his proffered hand.

"Remember I'll be looking till you find your sister."

She smiled into his eyes.

They filed out and he affected to take no notice of her. A lean-faced, rather commonplace woman recognized Carrie on the platform and hurried forward.

"Why Sister Carrie!" she began and there was a perfunctory embrace of welcome.

Carrie realized the change of affectional atmosphere at once. Amid all the maze, uproar and novelty, she felt cold reality taking her by the hand. No world of light and merriment. No round of amusement. Her sister carried with her much of the grimness of shift and toil.

"Why, how are all the folks at home"—she began—"how is Father, and Mother?"

Carrie answered, but was looking away. Down the aisle toward the gate leading into the waiting room and the street stood Drouet. He was looking back. When he saw that she saw him and was safe with her sister he turned to go, sending back the shadow of a smile. Only Carrie saw it. She felt something lost to her when he moved away. When he disappeared she felt his absence thoroughly. With her sister she was much alone, a lone figure in a tossing, thoughtless sea.

✧   ✧   ✧

Chapter III

Once across the river and into the wholesale district, she glanced about her for some likely door at which to apply. As she contemplated the wide windows and imposing sings, she became conscious of being gazed upon and understood for what she was—a wage-seeker. She had never done this thing before and lacked courage. To avoid conspicuity and a certain indefinable shame she felt at being caught spying about for some place where she might apply for a position, she quickened her steps and assumed an air of indifference supposedly common to one upon an errand. In this way she passed many manufacturing and wholesale houses without once glancing in. At last, after several blocks of walking, she felt that this would not do, and began to look about again, though without relaxing her pace. A little way on she saw a great door which for some reason attracted her attention. It was ornamented by a small brass sign, and seemed to be the entrance to a vast hive of six or seven floors. "Perhaps," she thought, "they may want some one" and crossed over to enter, screwing up her courage to the sticking point as she went. When she came within a score of feet of the desired goal, she observed a young gentleman in a grey check suit, fumbling his watch-charm and looking out. That he had anything to do with the concern she could not tell, but because he happened to be looking in her direction, her weakening heart misgave her and she hurried by, too overcome with shame to enter in. After several blocks of walking, in which the uproar of the streets and the novelty of the situation had time to wear away the effect of this, her first defeat, she again looked about. Over the way stood a great six-story structure labeled "Storm and King," which she viewed with rising hope. It was a wholesale dry goods concern and employed women. She could see them moving about now and then upon the upper floors. This place she decided to enter, no matter what. She crossed over and walked directly toward the entrance. As she did so two men came out and paused in the door. A telegraph messenger in blue dashed past her and up the few steps which graced the entrance and disappeared. Several pedestrians out of the hurrying throng which filled the sidewalks passed about her as she paused, hesitating. She looked helplessly around and then, seeing herself observed, retreated. It was too difficult a task. She could not go past them.

So severe a defeat told sadly upon her nerves. She could scarcely understand her weakness and yet she could not think of gazing inquiringly about upon the surrounding scene. Her feet carried her mechanically forward, every foot of her progress being a satisfactory portion of a flight which she gladly made. Block after block passed by. Upon street lamps at the various corners she read names such as Madison, Monroe, La Salle, Clark, Dearborn, State;[7] and still she went, her feet beginning to tire upon the broad stone flagging. She was pleased in part that the streets were bright and clean. The morning sun shining down with steadily increasing warmth made the shady side of the streets pleasantly cool. She looked at the blue sky overhead with more realization of its charm than had ever come to her before.

Her cowardice began to trouble her in a way. She turned back along the street she had come, resolving to hunt up Storm and King and enter in. On the way she encountered a great wholesale shoe company, through the broad plate windows of which she saw an enclosed executive department, hidden by frosted glass. Without this enclosure, but just within the street entrance, sat a grey-haired gentleman at a small table, with a large open ledger of some kind before him. She walked by this institution several times hesitating, but finding herself unobserved she eventually gathered sufficient courage to falter past the screen door and stand humbly waiting.

"Well, young lady," observed the old gentleman looking of her somewhat kindly—"what is it you wish?"

"I am, that is, do you—I mean, do you need any help?" she stammered.

"Not just at present," he answered smiling. "Not just at present. Come in sometime next week. Occasionally we need some one."

She received the answer in silence and backed awkwardly out. The pleasant nature of her reception rather astonished her. She had expected that it would be more difficult, that something cold and harsh would be said—she knew not what. That she had not been put to shame and made to feel her unfortunate position seemed remarkable. She did not realize that it was just this which made her experience easy, but the result was the same. She felt greatly relieved.

Somewhat encouraged, she ventured into another large structure. It was a clothing company, and more people were in evidence—well-dressed men of forty and more, surrounded by brass railings and employed variously.

7. Major downtown streets between the Chicago River and Lake Michigan.

An office boy approached her.

"Who is it you wish to see?" he asked.

"I want to see the manager," she returned.

He ran away and spoke to one of a group of three men who were conferring together. One broke off and came towards her.

"Well?" he said, coldly. The greeting drove all courage from her at once.

"Do you need any help?" she stammered.

"No," he replied abruptly and turned upon his heel.

She went foolishly out, the office boy deferentially swinging the door for her, and gladly sank into the obscuring crowd. It was a severe set-back to her recently pleased mental state.

Now she walked quite aimlessly for a time, turning here and there, seeing one great company after another but finding no courage to prosecute her single inquiry. High noon came and with it hunger. She hunted out an unassuming restaurant and entered but was disturbed to find that the prices were exorbitant for the size of her purse. A bowl of soup was all that she could feel herself able to afford, and with this quickly eaten she went out again. It restored her strength somewhat and made her moderately bold to pursue the search.

In walking a few blocks to fix upon some probable place she again encountered the firm of Storm and King and this time managed to enter. Some gentlemen were conferring close at hand but took no notice of her. She was left standing, gazing nervously upon the floor, her confusion and mental distress momentarily increasing until at last she was ready to turn and hurry eagerly away. When the limit of her distress had been nearly reached she was beckoned to by a man at one of the many desks within the nearby railing.

"Who is it you wish to see?" he inquired.

"Why any one, if you please," she answered. "I am looking for something to do."

"Oh, you want to see Mr. McManus," he returned. "Sit down!" and he pointed to a chair against the neighboring wall. He went on leisurely writing until after a time a short stout gentleman came in from the street.

"Mr. McManus," called the man at the desk, "this young woman wants to see you."

The short gentleman turned about towards Carrie, and she arose and came forward.

"What can I do for you, Miss," he inquired surveying her curiously.

"I want to know if I can get a position," she inquired.

"As what?" he asked.

"Not as anything in particular," she faltered. "I—"

"Have you ever had any experience in the wholesale dry goods business?" he questioned.

"No sir," she replied.

"Are you a stenographer or typewriter?"

"No sir."

"Well we haven't anything here," he said. "We employ only experienced help."

She began to step backward toward the door, when something about her plaintive face attracted him.

"Have you ever worked at anything before?" he inquired.

"No sir," she said.

"Well now, it's hardly possible that you would get anything to do in a wholesale house of this kind. Have you tried the department stores?"

She acknowledged that she had not.

"Well, if I were you," he said, looking at her rather genially, "I would try the department stores. They often need young women as clerks."

"Thank you," she said, her whole nature relieved by this spark of friendly interest.

"Yes," he said, as she moved toward the door, "you try the department stores," and off he went.

At that time the department store was in its earliest form of successful operation and there were not many. The first three in the United States, established about 1884, were in Chicago. Carrie was familiar with the names of several through the advertisements in the "Daily News," and now proceeded to seek them. The words of Mr. McManus had somehow managed to restore her courage, which had fallen low, and she dared to hope that this new line would offer her something in the way of employment. Some time she spent in wandering up and down thinking to encounter the buildings by chance, so readily is the mind, bent upon prosecuting a hard but needful errand, eased by that self-deception which the semblance of search without the reality gives. At last she inquired of a police officer and was directed to proceed "two blocks up" where she would find The Fair. Following his advice she reached that institution and entered.

The nature of these vast retail combinations, should they ever permanently disappear, will form an interesting chapter in the commercial history of our nation. Such a flowering out of a modest trade principle the world had never witnessed up to that time. They were along the line of the most effective retail organization, with hundreds of stores coordinated into one, and laid out upon the most imposing and economic basis. They were handsome, bustling, successful affairs, with a host of clerks and a swarm of patrons. Carrie passed along the busy aisles, much affected by the remarkable displays of trinkets, dress goods, shoes, stationery, jewelry. Each separate counter was a show place of dazzling interest and attraction. She could not help feeling the claim of each trinket and valuable upon her personally and yet she did not stop. There was nothing there which she could not have used—nothing which she did not long to own. The dainty slippers and stockings, the delicately frilled skirts and petticoats, the laces, ribbons, hair-combs, purses, all touched her with individual desire, and she felt keenly the fact that not any of these things were in the range of her purchase. She was a work-seeker, an outcast without employment, one whom the average employé could tell at a glance was poor and in need of a situation.

It must not be thought that anyone could have mistaken her for a nervous, sensitive, high-strung nature, cast unduly upon a cold, calculating and unpoetic world. Such certainly she was not. But women are peculiarly sensitive to the personal adornment or equipment of their person, even the dullest, and particularly is this true of the young. Your bright-eyed, rosy-cheeked maiden, over whom a poet might well rave for the flowerlike expression of her countenance and the lissome and dainty grace of her body, may reasonably be dead to every evidence of the artistic and poetic in the unrelated evidences of life, and yet not lack in material appreciation. Never, it might be said, does she fail in this. With her the bloom of a rose may pass unappreciated, but the bloom of a fold of silk, never. If nothing in the heavens, or the earth, or the waters, could elicit her fancy or delight her from its spiritual or artistic side, think not that the material would be lost. The glint of a buckle, the hue of a precious stone, the faintest tints of the watered silk, these she would devine and qualify as readily as your poet if not more so. The creak, the rustle, the glow—the least and best of the graven or spun—, these she would perceive and appreciate—if not because of some fashionable or hearsay quality, then on account of their true beauty, their innate fitness in any order of harmony, their place in the magical order and sequence of dress.

Not only did Carrie feel the drag of desire for all of this which was new and pleasing in apparel for women, but she noticed, too, with a touch at the heart, the fine ladies who elbowed and ignored her, brushing past in utter disregard of her presence, themselves eagerly enlisted in the materials which the store contained. Carrie was not familiar with the appearance of her more fortunate sisters of the city. Neither had she before known the nature and appearance of the shop girls, with whom she now compared poorly. They were pretty in the main, some even handsome, with a certain independence and toss of indifference which added, in the case of the more favored, a certain piquancy. Their clothes were neat, in many instances fine, and wherever she encountered the eye of one, it was only to recognize in it a keen analysis of her own position—her individual shortcomings of dress and that shadow of *manner* which she thought must hang about her and make clear to all who and what she was. A flame of envy lighted in her heart. She realized in a dim way how much the city held—wealth, fashion, ease—every adornment for women, and she longed for dress and beauty with a whole and fulsome heart.

On the second floor were the managerial offices, to which after some inquiry she was now directed. There she found other girls ahead of her, applicants like herself, but with more of that self-satisfied and independent air which experience of the city lends—girls who scrutinized her in a painful manner. After a wait of perhaps three-quarters of an hour she was called in turn.

"Now," said a sharp, quick-mannered Jew who was sitting at a roll-top desk near the window—"have you ever worked in any other store?"

"No sir," said Carrie.

"Oh, you haven't," he said, eyeing her keenly.

"No sir," she replied.

"Well, we prefer young women just now with some experience. I guess we can't use you."

Carrie stood waiting a moment, hardly certain whether the interview had terminated.

"Don't wait!" he exclaimed. "Remember we are very busy here."

Carrie began to move quickly to the door.

"Hold on," he said, calling her back. "Give me your name and address. We want girls occasionally."

When she had gotten safely out again into the street she could scarcely restrain tears. It was not so much the particular rebuff which she had just experienced, but the whole abashing trend of the day. She was tired and rather over-played upon in the nerves. She abandoned the thought of appealing to the other department stores and now wandered on, feeling a certain safety and relief in mingling with the crowd.

In her indifferent wandering she turned into Jackson Street, not far from the river, and was keeping her way along the south side of that imposing thoroughfare, when a piece of wrapping paper written on with marking ink and tacked upon a door attracted her attention. It read "Girls wanted—wrappers and stitchers." She hesitated for the moment, thinking surely to go in, but upon further consideration the added qualifications of "wrappers and stitchers" deterred her. She had no idea of what that meant. Most probably she would need to be experienced in it. She walked on a little way, mentally balancing as to whether or not to apply. Necessity triumphed however and she returned.

The entrance, which opened into a small hall, led to an elevator shaft, the elevator of which was up. It was a dingy affair, being used both as a freight and passenger entrance, and the woodwork was marked and splintered by the heavy boxes which were tumbled in and out, at intervals. A frowzy-headed German-American, about fourteen years of age, operated the elevator in his shirt sleeves and bare feet. His face was considerably marked with grease and dirt.

When the elevator stopped, the boy leisurely raised a protecting arm of wood and by grace of his superior privilege admitted her.

"Wear do you want go?" he inquired.

"I want to see the manager," she replied.

"Wot manager?" he returned, surveying her caustically.

"Is there more than one?" she asked. "I thought it was all one firm."

"Naw," said the youth. "Der's six different people. Want to see Speigelheim?"

"I don't know," answered Carrie. She colored a little as she began to feel the necessity of explaining. "I want to see whoever put up that sign."

"Dot's Speigelheim," said the boy. "Fort floor." Therewith he proudly turned to his task of pulling the rope, and the elevator ascended.

The firm of Speigelheim and Co., makers of boys' caps, occupied one floor of fifty feet in width and some eighty feet in depth. It was a place rather dingily lighted, the darkest portions having incandescent lights, filled in part with machines and part with workbenches. At the latter labored quite a company of girls and some men. The former were drabby looking creatures, stained in face with oil and dust, clad in thin shapeless cotton dresses, and shod with more or less worn shoes. Many of them had their sleeves rolled up, revealing bare arms, and in some cases, owing to heat, their dresses were open at the neck. They were, a fair type of nearly the lowest order of shop girls,—careless, rather slouchy, and more or less pale from confinement. They were not timid however, were rich in curiosity and strong in daring and slang.

Carrie looked about her, very much disturbed and quite sure that she did not want to work here. Aside from making her uncomfortable by sidelong glances, no one paid her the least attention. She waited until the whole department was aware of her presence. Then some word was sent round and a foreman in an apron and shirt sleeves, the latter rolled up to his shoulders, approached.

"Do you want to see me?" he asked.

"Do you need any help?" said Carrie, already learning directness of address.

"Do you know how to stitch caps?" he returned.

"No sir," she replied.

"Have you ever had any experience at this kind of work?" he inquired.

She owned that she hadn't.

"Well," said the foreman, scratching his ear meditatively, "we do need a stitcher. We like experienced help though. We've hardly got time to break people in." He paused and looked away out of the window. "We might, though, put you at finishing," he concluded reflectively.

"How much do you pay a week?" ventured Carrie, emboldened by a certain softness in the man's manner and his simplicity of address.

"Three and a half," he answered.

"Oh," she was about to exclaim, but checked herself, and allowed her thoughts to die without expression.

"We're not exactly in need of anybody," he went on vaguely, looking her over as one would a package. "You can come Monday morning though," he added, "and I'll put you to work."

"Thank you," said Carrie weakly.

"If you come, bring an apron," he added.

He walked away and left her standing by the elevator, never so much as inquiring her name.

While the appearance of the shop and the announcement of the price paid per week operated very much as a blow to Carrie's fancy, the fact that work of any kind, after so rude a round of experience, was offered her, was gratifying. She could not begin to believe that she would take the place, modest as her aspirations were. She had been used to better than that. Her mere experience and the free out-of-doors life of the country caused her nature to revolt at such confinement. Dirt had never been her share. Her sister's flat was clean. This place was grimy and low; the girls were careless and hardened. They must be bad-minded and -hearted, she imagined. Still a place had been offered her. Surely Chicago was not so bad if she could find one place in one day. She might find another and better later.

Her subsequent experiences were not of a reassuring nature, however. From all the more pleasing or imposing places she was turned away abruptly with the most chilling formality. In others where she applied, only the experienced were required. She met with painful rebuffs, the most trying of which had been in a cloak manufacturing house, where she had gone to the fourth floor to inquire.

"No, no," said the foreman, a rough, heavy-built individual who looked after a miserably lighted work shop, "we don't want anyone. Don't come here."

In another factory she was leered upon by a most sensual-faced individual who endeavored to turn the natural questions of the inquiry into a personal interview, asking all sorts of embarrassing questions and endeavoring to satisfy himself evidently that she was of loose enough morals to suit his purpose. In that case she had been relieved enough to get away and found the busy, indifferent streets to be again a soothing refuge.

With the wane of the afternoon went her hopes, her courage and her strength. She had been astonishingly persistent. So earnest an effort was well deserving of a better reward. On every hand, to her fatigued senses, the great business portion grew larger, harder, more stolid in its indifference. It seemed as if it was all closed to her, that the struggle was too fierce for her to hope to do anything at all. Men and women hurried by in long, shifting lines. She felt the flow of the tide of effort and interest, felt her own helplessness without quite realizing the wisp on the tide that she was. She cast about vainly for some possible place to apply but found no door which she had the courage to enter. It would be the same thing all over. The old humiliation of her pleas rewarded by curt denial. Sick at heart and in body, she turned to the west, the direction of Minnie's flat, which she had now fixed in mind, and began that wearisome, baffled retreat which the seeker for employment at nightfall too often makes. In passing through Fifth Avenue, south towards Van Buren Street, where she intended to take a car, she passed the door of a large wholesale shoe house, through the plate glass window of which she could see a middle-aged gentleman sitting at a small desk. One of those forlorn impulses which often grow out of a fixed sense of defeat, the last sprouting of a baffled and uprooted growth of ideas, seized upon her. She walked deliberately through the door and up to the gentleman who looked at her weary face with partially awakened interest.

"What is it?" he said.

"Can you give me something to do?" asked Carrie.

"Now I really don't know," he said kindly. "What kind of work is it you want—you're not a typewriter, are you?"

"Oh, no," answered Carrie.

"Well, we only employ book keepers and typewriters here. You might go round to the side and inquire upstairs. They did want some help upstairs a few days ago. Ask for Mr. Brown."

She hastened around to the side entrance and was taken up by the elevator to the fourth floor.

"Call Mr. Brown, Willie," said the elevator man to a boy near by.

Willie went off and presently returned with the information that Mr. Brown said she should sit down and that he would be around in a little while.

It was a portion of a stock room which gave no idea of the general character of the floor, and Carrie could form no opinion of the nature of the work.

"So you want something to do," said Mr. Brown, after he inquired concerning the nature of her errand. "Have you ever been employed in a shoe factory before?"

"No sir," said Carrie.

"What is your name?" he inquired, and being informed, "Well, I don't know as I have anything for you. Would you work for four and a half a week?"

Carrie was too worn by defeat not to feel that it was considerable. She had not expected that he would offer her less than six. She acquiesced, however, and he took her name and address.

"Well," he said finally—"you report here at eight o'clock Monday morning. I think I can find something for you to do."

He left her revived by the possibilities, sure that she had found something to do at last. Instantly the blood crept warmly over her body. Her nervous tension relaxed. She walked out into the busy street and discovered a new atmosphere. Behold, the throng was moving with a lightsome step. She noticed that men and women were smiling. Scraps of conversation and notes of laughter floated to her. The air was light. People were already pouring out of the buildings, their labor ended for the day. She noticed that they were pleased, and thoughts of her sister's home, and the meal that would be awaiting her, quickened her steps. She hurried on, tired perhaps, but no longer weary of foot.

What would not Minnie say! Ah, long the winter in Chicago—the lights, the crowd, the amusement. This was a great, pleasing metropolis after all. Her new firm was a goodly institution. Its windows were of huge plate glass. She could probably do well there. Thoughts of Drouet returned, of the things he had told her. She now felt that life was better. That it was livelier, sprightlier. She boarded a car in the best of sprits, feeling her blood still flowing pleasantly. She would live in Chicago, her mind kept saying to itself. She would have a better time than she ever had before—she would be happy.

1900

STEPHEN CRANE
1871–1900

Stephen Crane was born November 1, 1871, and died on June 5, 1900, at the age of twenty-eight, by which time he had published enough material to fill a dozen volumes of a collected edition and had lived a legendary life that has grown in interest to scholars and readers the more the facts have come to light. His family settled in America in the mid-seventeenth century. He was the son of a Methodist minister and a social reform–minded mother; but he systematically rejected religious and social traditions, identified with the urban poor, and lived with the mistress of one "of the better houses of ill-fame" in Jacksonville, Florida. Although temperamentally gentle, Crane was attracted to—even obsessed by—war and other forms of physical and psychic violence. He frequently lived the down-and-out life of a penniless artist; he was also ambitious and something of a snob; he was a poet and an impressionist; a journalist, a social critic, and a realist. In Crane, the contradictions and tensions present in many writers seem intensified.

Crane once explained to an editor: "After all, I cannot help vanishing and disappearing and dissolving. It is my foremost trait." This restless, peripatetic quality of Crane's life began early. The last of fourteen children, Crane moved with his family at least three times before he entered school at age seven in the small town of Port Jervis, New York. His father died in 1880, and three years later, after several temporary moves, the family settled in the coastal resort town of Asbury Park, New Jersey. Crane never took to school. At Syracuse University he distinguished himself as a baseball player but was unable to accept the routine of academic life and left after one semester. He was not sure what he would do with himself, but by 1891 he had begun to write for newspapers, and he hungered for immersion in life of the kind that his early journalistic assignments allowed him to witness at close hand.

New York City was the inevitable destination for a young man with literary ambitions and a desire to experience the fullness of life. A few jobs with New York newspapers proved abortive, and between 1891 and 1893 Crane shuttled between the seedy New York apartments of his artist friends and his brother Edmund's house in nearby Lake View, New Jersey. In these years of extreme privation, Crane developed his powers as an observer of psychological and social reality. Encouraged by Hamlin Garland, whom he had heard lecture in 1891, Crane began his first book while at Syracuse. After it had been rejected by several New York editors, he published the work—*Maggie, A Girl of the Streets (A Story of New York)*—at his own expense in 1893. Although Garland admired this short novel and the powerful literary arbiter William Dean Howells promoted both Crane and *Maggie* (and continued to think it his best work), the book did not sell even when, in revised form, it was published in 1896 by the respected publishing house of D. Appleton and Company. *Maggie* told, in a highly stylized way using heavy dialect, the story of a girl born in the slums of New York who during her short life is driven to prostitution. As one of the first reviewers of the 1893 edition observed: "the evident object of the writer is to show the tremendous influence of the environment on the human character and destiny." It remains Crane's fullest treatment of how the have-littles lived in the burgeoning cities of America in the 1880s and 1890s.

Crane turned next to the Civil War as a subject for *The Red Badge of Courage: An Episode of the American Civil War* (1895). Oddly, since the novel has assumed a kind of classic status, he later described the book as a "pot-boiler." The narrative, which depicts the (partial) education of Henry Fleming in the context of battle, is as old as Homer's *Odyssey* and is a dominant story type in American literature from Benjamin Franklin through Melville, Hemingway, Malcolm X, and Saul Bellow. Crane was not so much working within or against this tradition as he was departing sharply from it. That is, Crane is distinctively modern in conceiving personal identity as complex and ambiguous and in obliging his readers to judge for themselves the adequacy of Henry's responses to his experiences.

When *Red Badge* was first published in newspapers around the country starting in December 1894, Crane's fortunes began to improve. The same syndicate (an agency that buys and then sells stories to newspapers and magazines for simultaneous publication) that took *Red Badge* hired him early in 1895 as a roving reporter in the American West and Mexico, experiences that would give him the material for several of his finest tales—"The Bride Comes to Yellow Sky" and "The Blue Hotel" among them. Also, early in 1895, D. Appleton and Company agreed to issue *Red Badge* in book form. In the spring of that year, *The Black Riders and Other Lines,* his first volume of poetry, was published in Boston by Copeland and Day. Predictably, Garland and Howells responded favorably to Crane's spare, original, unflinchingly honest poetry, but it was too experimental in form and too unconventional in its dark philosophic outlook to win wide acceptance. When *Red Badge* appeared in the fall in book form, however, it won Crane international acclaim at the age of twenty-four.

Crane's poetry, journalism, and fiction clearly demonstrated his religious, social, and literary rebelliousness, while his alienated, unconventional stance also led him to direct action. After challenging the New York police force on behalf of a prostitute who claimed harassment at its hands, Crane left the city in the winter of 1896–97 to cover the insurrection against Spain in Cuba. On his way to Cuba he met Cora Howorth Taylor, the proprietor of a bordello, the Hotel de Dream in Jacksonville, Florida, with whom he lived for the last three years of his life. On January 2, 1897, Crane's ship *The Commodore* sank off the coast of Florida. His report of this harrowing adventure was published a few days later in the *New York Press.* He promptly converted this event into one of the best-known and most widely reprinted of all American stories, "The Open Boat." This story, like *Red Badge,* reveals Crane's characteristic subject matter—the physical, emotional, and intellectual responses of people under extreme pressure, the dominant themes of nature's indifference to humanity's fate, and the consequent need for compassionate collective action. Along with *Maggie,* "The Open Boat" locates Crane within American literary naturalism alongside its other practitioners, Frank Norris, Jack London, and Theodore Dreiser, but, unlike *Maggie,* it contains a certain romanticism.

In "The Open Boat" and another late story, "The Blue Hotel," Crane achieved his mature style, one characterized by irony and brevity, qualities later associated with Sherwood Anderson and Ernest Hemingway, among others. But Crane's style cannot exactly be contained by any of the terms typically used to describe it—realism, naturalism, impressionism, or expressionism. In these late stories (and before he began to write chiefly for money), Crane combines a poet's sensitivity to the sounds of words, the rhythms of language, and a highly original use of symbol, metaphor, and color with structures of action appropriate to the shifting emotional conditions of the characters he brought to life by carefully controlling point of view and skillfully blending sharply observed detail with convincing dialogue. In his works we can observe his tough-minded irony and his essential vision: a sympathetic but unflinching demand for courage, integrity, grace, and generosity in the face of a universe in which human beings, to quote from "The Blue Hotel," are so many lice clinging "to a whirling, fire-smote, ice-locked disease-stricken, space-lost bulb."

In 1897 Crane settled in England. In the last months of his life his situation became desperate; he was suffering from tuberculosis and was seriously in debt. He wrote furiously in a doomed attempt to earn money, but the effort only worsened his health. In 1899 he drafted thirteen stories set in the fictional town Whilomville for *Harper's* magazine and published his second volume of poetry, *War Is Kind*, the weak novel *Active Service*, and the American edition of *"The Monster" and Other Stories*. "The Monster" is a daring if flawed attack on racial prejudice and a recognizable attack on Howell's notions of realism. During a Christmas party that year Crane nearly died of a lung hemorrhage. Surviving only a few months, he summoned the strength to write a series of nine articles on great battles and complete the first twenty-five chapters of the novel *The O'Ruddy*. In spite of Cora's hopes for a miraculous cure and the generous assistance of Henry James and others, Crane died, at Badenweiler, Germany, on June 5, 1900.

The Open Boat[1]

A TALE INTENDED TO BE AFTER THE FACT, BEING THE EXPERIENCE OF FOUR MEN FROM THE SUNK STEAMER COMMODORE

I

None of them knew the color of the sky. Their eyes glanced level, and were fastened upon the waves that swept toward them. These waves were of the hue of slate, save for the tops, which were of foaming white, and all of the men knew the colors of the sea. The horizon narrowed and widened, and dipped and rose, and at all times its edge was jagged with waves that seemed thrust up in points like rocks.

Many a man ought to have a bath-tub larger than the boat which here rode upon the sea. These waves were most wrongfully and barbarously abrupt and tall, and each froth-top was a problem in small boat navigation.

The cook squatted in the bottom and looked with both eyes at the six inches of gunwale which separated him from the ocean. His sleeves were rolled over his fat forearms, and the two flaps of his unbuttoned vest dangled as he bent to bail out the boat. Often he said: "Gawd! That was a narrow clip." As he remarked it he invariably gazed eastward over the broken sea.

The oiler,[2] steering with one of the two oars in the boat, sometimes raised himself suddenly to keep clear of water that swirled in over the stern. It was a thin little oar and it seemed often ready to snap.

The correspondent, pulling at the other oar, watched the waves and wondered why he was there.

---

1. Crane sailed as a correspondent on the steamer *Commodore*, which, on January 1, 1897, left Jacksonville, Florida, with munitions for the Cuban insurrectionists. Early on the morning of January 2, the steamer sank. With three others, Crane reached Daytona Beach in a ten-foot dinghy on the following morning. Under the title "Stephen Crane's Own Story," the *New York Press* on January 7 carried the details of his nearly fatal experience.

In June 1897, he published his fictional account, "The Open Boat," in *Scribner's Magazine*. The story gave the title to *"The Open Boat" and Other Tales of Adventure* (1898). The text here reprints that established for the University of Virginia edition of *The Works of Stephen Crane, Vol. 5, Tales of Adventure* (1970).

2. One who oils machinery in the engine room of a ship.

The injured captain, lying in the bow, was at this time buried in that profound dejection and indifference which comes, temporarily at least, to even the bravest and most enduring when, willy nilly, the firm fails, the army loses, the ship goes down. The mind of the master of a vessel is rooted deep in the timbers of her, though he command for a day or a decade, and this captain had on him the stern impression of a scene in the grays of dawn of seven turned faces, and later a stump of a top-mast with a white ball on it that slashed to and fro at the waves, went low and lower, and down. Thereafter there was something strange in his voice. Although steady, it was deep with mourning, and of a quality beyond oration or tears.

"Keep 'er a little more south, Billie," said he.

" 'A little more south,' sir," said the oiler in the stern.

A seat in his boat was not unlike a seat upon a bucking broncho, and, by the same token, a broncho is not much smaller. The craft pranced and reared, and plunged like an animal. As each wave came, and she rose for it, she seemed like a horse making at a fence outrageously high. The manner of her scramble over these walls of water is a mystic thing, and, moreover, at the top of them were ordinarily these problems in white water, the foam racing down from the summit of each wave, requiring a new leap, and a leap from the air. Then, after scornfully bumping a crest, she would slide, and race, and splash down a long incline and arrive bobbing and nodding in front of the next menace.

A singular disadvantage of the sea lies in the fact that after successfully surmounting one wave you discover that there is another behind it just as important and just as nervously anxious to do something effective in the way of swamping boats. In a ten-foot dingey one can get an idea of the resources of the sea in the line of waves that is not probable to the average experience, which is never at sea in a dingey. As each slaty wall of water approached, it shut all else from the view of the men in the boat, and it was not difficult to imagine that this particular wave was the final outburst of the ocean, the last effort of the grim water. There was a terrible grace in the move of the waves, and they came in silence, save for the snarling of the crests.

In the wan light, the faces of the men must have been gray. Their eyes must have glinted in strange ways as they gazed steadily astern. Viewed from a balcony, the whole thing would doubtlessly have been weirdly picturesque. But the men in the boat had no time to see it, and if they had had leisure there were other things to occupy their minds. The sun swung steadily up the sky, and they knew it was broad day because the color of the sea changed from slate to emerald-green, streaked with amber lights, and the foam was like tumbling snow. The process of the breaking day was unknown to them. They were aware only of this effect upon the color of the waves that rolled toward them.

In disjointed sentences the cook and the correspondent argued as to the difference between a life-saving station and a house of refuge. The cook had said: "There's a house of refuge just north of the Mosquito Inlet Light, and as soon as they see us, they'll come off in their boat and pick us up."

"As soon as who see us?" said the correspondent.

"The crew," said the cook.

"Houses of refuge don't have crews," said the correspondent. "As I understand them, they are only places where clothes and grub are stored for the benefit of shipwrecked people. They don't carry crews."

"Oh, yes, they do," said the cook.

"No, they don't," said the correspondent.

"Well, we're not there yet, anyhow," said the oiler, in the stern.

"Well," said the cook, "perhaps it's not a house of refuge that I'm thinking of as being near Mosquito Inlet Light. Perhaps it's a life-saving station."

"We're not there yet," said the oiler, in the stern.

II

As the boat bounced from the top of each wave, the wind tore through the hair of the hatless men, and as the craft plopped her stern down again the spray slashed past them. The crest of each of these waves was a hill, from the top of which the men surveyed, for a moment, a broad tumultuous expanse, shining and wind-riven. It was probably splendid. It was probably glorious, this play of the free sea, wild with lights of emerald and white and amber.

"Bully good thing it's an on-shore wind," said the cook. "If not, where would we be? Wouldn't have a show."

"That's right," said the correspondent.

The busy oiler nodded his assent.

Then the captain, in the bow, chuckled in a way that expressed humor, contempt, tragedy, all in one. "Do you think we've got much of a show, now, boys?" said he.

Whereupon the three were silent, save for a trifle of hemming and hawing. To express any particular optimism at this time they felt to be childish and stupid, but they all doubtless possessed this sense of the situation in their mind. A young man thinks doggedly at such times. On the other hand, the ethics of their condition was decidedly against any open suggestion of hopelessness. So they were silent.

"Oh, well," said the captain, soothing his children, "we'll get ashore all right."

But there was that in his tone which made them think, so the oiler quoth: "Yes! If this wind holds!"

The cook was bailing. "Yes! If we don't catch hell in the surf."

Canton flannel[3] gulls flew near and far. Sometimes they sat down on the sea, near patches of brown sea-weed that rolled over the waves with a movement like carpets on a line in a gale. The birds sat comfortably in groups, and they were envied by some in the dingey, for the wrath of the sea was no more to them than it was to a covey of prairie chickens a thousand miles inland. Often they came very close and stared at the men with black bead-like eyes. At these times they were uncanny and sinister in their unblinking scrutiny, and the men hooted angrily at them, telling them to be gone. One came, and evidently decided to alight on the top of the captain's head. The bird flew parallel to the boat and did not circle, but made short sidelong jumps in the air in chicken-fashion. His black eyes were wistfully fixed upon the captain's head. "Ugly brute," said the oiler to the bird. "You look as if you were made with a jack-knife." The cook and the correspondent swore darkly at the creature. The captain naturally wished to knock it away with the end of the heavy painter, but he did not dare do it, because anything resembling an emphatic

---

3. Common name of a lightweight cotton fabric, usually white.

gesture would have capsized this freighted boat, and so with his open hand, the captain gently and carefully waved the gull away. After it had been discouraged from the pursuit the captain breathed easier on account of his hair, and others breathed easier because the bird struck their minds at this time as being somehow grewsome and ominous.

In the meantime the oiler and the correspondent rowed. And also they rowed.

They sat together in the same seat, and each rowed an oar. Then the oiler took both oars; then the correspondent took both oars; then the oiler; then the correspondent. They rowed and they rowed. The very ticklish part of the business was when the time came for the reclining one in the stern to take his turn at the oars. By the very last star of truth, it is easier to steal eggs from under a hen than it was to change seats in the dingey. First the man in the stern slid his hand along the thwart and moved with care, as if he were of Sèvres.[4] Then the man in the rowing seat slid his hand along the other thwart. It was all done with the most extraordinary care. As the two sidled past each other, the whole party kept watchful eyes on the coming wave, and the captain cried: "Look out now! Steady there!"

The brown mats of sea-weed that appeared from time to time were like islands, bits of earth. They were travelling, apparently, neither one way nor the other. They were, to all intents, stationary. They informed the men in the boat that it was making progress slowly toward the land.

The captain, rearing cautiously in the bow, after the dingey soared on a great swell, said that he had seen the light-house at Mosquito Inlet. Presently the cook remarked that he had seen it. The correspondent was at the oars, then, and for some reason he too wished to look at the light-house, but his back was toward the far shore and the waves were important, and for some time he could not seize an opportunity to turn his head. But at last there came a wave more gentle than the others, and when at the crest of it he swiftly scoured the western horizon.

"See it?" said the captain.

"No," said the correspondent, slowly, "I didn't see anything."

"Look again," said the captain. He pointed. "It's exactly in that direction."

At the top of another wave, the correspondent did as he was bid, and this time his eyes chanced on a small still thing on the edge of the swaying horizon. It was precisely like the point of a pin. It took an anxious eye to find a light-house so tiny.

"Think we'll make it, Captain?"

"If this wind holds and the boat don't swamp, we can't do much else," said the captain.

The little boat, lifted by each towering sea, and splashed viciously by the crests, made progress that in the absence of sea-weed was not apparent to those in her. She seemed just a wee thing wallowing, miraculously, top-up, at the mercy of five oceans. Occasionally, a great spread of water, like white flames, swarmed into her.

"Bail her, cook," said the captain, serenely.

"All right, Captain," said the cheerful cook.

4. Fine, often ornately decorated French porcelain.

III

It would be difficult to describe the subtle brotherhood of men that was here established on the seas. No one said that it was so. No one mentioned it. But it dwelt in the boat, and each man felt it warm him. They were a captain, an oiler, a cook, and a correspondent, and they were friends, friends in a more curiously iron-bound degree than may be common. The hurt captain, lying against the water-jar in the bow, spoke always in a low voice and calmly, but he could never command a more ready and swiftly obedient crew than the motley three of the dingey. It was more than a mere recognition of what was best for the common safety. There was surely in it a quality that was personal and heartfelt. And after this devotion to the commander of the boat there was this comradeship that the correspondent, for instance, who had been taught to be cynical of men, knew even at the time was the best experience of his life. But no one said that it was so. No one mentioned it.

"I wish we had a sail," remarked the captain. "We might try my overcoat on the end of an oar and give you two boys a chance to rest." So the cook and the correspondent held the mast and spread wide the overcoat. The oiler steered, and the little boat made good way with her new rig. Sometimes the oiler had to scull sharply to keep a sea from breaking into the boat, but otherwise sailing was a success.

Meanwhile the light-house had been growing slowly larger. It had now almost assumed color, and appeared like a little gray shadow on the sky. The man at the oars could not be prevented from turning his head rather often to try for a glimpse of this little gray shadow.

At last, from the top of each wave the men in the tossing boat could see land. Even as the light-house was an upright shadow on the sky, this land seemed but a long black shadow on the sea. It certainly was thinner than paper. "We must be about opposite New Smyrna," said the cook, who had coasted this shore often in schooners. "Captain, by the way, I believe they abandoned that life-saving station there about a year ago."

"Did they?" said the captain.

The wind slowly died away. The cook and the correspondent were not now obliged to slave in order to hold high the oar. But the waves continued their old impetuous swooping at the dingey, and the little craft, no longer under way, struggled woundily over them. The oiler or the correspondent took the oars again.

Shipwrecks are *apropos* of nothing. If men could only train for them and have them occur when the men had reached pink condition, there would be less drowning at sea. Of the four in the dingey none had slept any time worth mentioning for two days and two nights previous to embarking in the dingey, and in the excitement of clambering about the deck of a foundering ship they had also forgotten to eat heartily.

For these reasons, and for others, neither the oiler nor the correspondent was fond of rowing at this time. The correspondent wondered ingenuously how in the name of all that was sane could there be people who thought it amusing to row a boat. It was not an amusement; it was a diabolical punishment, and even a genius of mental aberrations could never conclude that it was anything but a horror to the muscles and a crime against the back. He mentioned to the boat in general how the amusement of rowing struck him, and the weary-faced oiler smiled in full sympathy. Previously to the foundering, by the way, the oiler had worked double-watch in the engine-room of the ship.

"Take her easy, now, boys," said the captain. "Don't spend yourselves. If we have to run a surf you'll need all your strength, because we'll sure have to swim for it. Take your time."

Slowly the land arose from the sea. From a black line it became a line of black and a line of white—trees and sand. Finally, the captain said that he could make out a house on the shore. "That's the house of refuge, sure," said the cook. "They'll see us before long, and come out after us."

The distant light-house reared high. "The keeper ought to be able to make us out now, if he's looking through a glass," said the captain. "He'll notify the life-saving people."

"None of those other boats could have got ashore to give word of the wreck," said the oiler, in a low voice. "Else the life-boat would be out hunting us."

Slowly and beautifully the land loomed out of the sea. The wind came again. It had veered from the northeast to the southeast. Finally, a new sound struck the ears of the men in the boat. It was the low thunder of the surf on the shore. "We'll never be able to make the light-house now," said the captain. "Swing her head a little more north, Billie."

" 'A little more north,' sir," said the oiler.

Whereupon the little boat turned her nose once more down the wind, and all but the oarsman watched the shore grow. Under the influence of this expansion doubt and direful apprehension was leaving the minds of the men. The management of the boat was still most absorbing, but it could not prevent a quiet cheerfulness. In an hour, perhaps, they would be ashore.

Their back-bones had become thoroughly used to balancing in the boat and they now rode this wild colt of a dingey like circus men. The correspondent thought that he had been drenched to the skin, but happening to feel in the top pocket of his coat, he found therein eight cigars. Four of them were soaked with seawater; four were perfectly scatheless. After a search, somebody produced three dry matches, and thereupon the four waifs rode impudently in their little boat, and with an assurance of an impending rescue shining in their eyes, puffed at the big cigars and judged well and ill of all men. Everybody took a drink of water.

IV

"Cook," remarked the captain, "there don't seem to be any signs of life about your house of refuge."

"No," replied the cook. "Funny they don't see us!"

A broad stretch of lowly coast lay before the eyes of the men. It was of dunes topped with dark vegetation. The roar of the surf was plain, and sometimes they could see the white lip of a wave as it spun up the beach. A tiny house was blocked out black upon the sky. Southward, the slim light-house lifted its little gray length.

Tide, wind, and waves were swinging the dingey northward. "Funny they don't see us," said the men.

The surf's roar was here dulled, but its tone was, nevertheless, thunderous and mighty. As the boat swam over the great rollers, the men sat listening to this roar. "We'll swamp sure," said everybody.

It is fair to say here that there was not a life-saving station within twenty miles in either direction, but the men did not know this fact and in consequence they made dark and opprobrious remarks concerning the eyesight of the nation's life-savers. Four scowling men sat in the dingey and surpassed records in the invention of epithets.

"Funny they don't see us."

The light-heartedness of a former time had completely faded. To their sharpened minds it was easy to conjure pictures of all kinds of incompetency and blindness and, indeed, cowardice. There was the shore of the populous land, and it was bitter and bitter to them that from it came no sign.

"Well," said the captain, ultimately, "I suppose we'll have to make a try for ourselves. If we stay out here too long, we'll none of us have strength left to swim after the boat swamps."

And so the oiler, who was at the oars, turned the boat straight for the shore. There was a sudden tightening of muscles. There was some thinking.

"If we don't all get ashore—" said the captain. "If we don't all get ashore, I suppose you fellows know where to send news of my finish?"

They then briefly exchanged some addresses and admonitions. As for the reflections of the men, there was a great deal of rage in them. Perchance they might be formulated thus: "If I am going to be drowned—if I am going to be drowned—if I am going to be drowned, why, in the name of the seven mad gods who rule the sea, was I allowed to come thus far and contemplate sand and trees? Was I brought here merely to have my nose dragged away as I was about to nibble the sacred cheese of life? It is preposterous. If this old ninny-woman, Fate, cannot do better than this, she should be deprived of the management of men's fortunes. She is an old hen who knows not her intention. If she has decided to drown me, why did she not do it in the beginning and save me all this trouble. The whole affair is absurd. . . . But, no, she cannot mean to drown me. She dare not drown me. She cannot drown me. Not after all this work." Afterward the man might have had an impulse to shake his fist at the clouds. "Just you drown me, now, and then hear what I call you!"

The billows that came at this time were more formidable. They seemed always just about to break and roll over the little boat in a turmoil of foam. There was a preparatory and long growl in the speech of them. No mind unused to the sea would have concluded that the dingey could ascend these sheer heights in time. The shore was still afar. The oiler was a wily surfman. "Boys," he said, swiftly, "she won't live three minutes more and we're too far out to swim. Shall I take her to sea again, Captain?"

"Yes! Go ahead!" said the captain.

This oiler, by a series of quick miracles, and fast and steady oarsmanship, turned the boat in the middle of the surf and took her safely to sea again.

There was a considerable silence as the boat bumped over the furrowed sea to deeper water. Then somebody in gloom spoke. "Well, anyhow, they must have seen us from the shore by now."

The gulls went in slanting flight up the wind toward the gray desolate east. A squall, marked by dingy clouds, and clouds brick-red, like smoke from a burning building, appeared from the southeast.

"What do you think of those life-saving people? Ain't they peaches?"

"Funny they haven't seen us."

"Maybe they think we're out here for sport! Maybe they think we're fishin'. Maybe they think we're damned fools."

It was a long afternoon. A changed tide tried to force them southward, but wind and wave said northward. Far ahead, where coast-line, sea, and sky formed their mighty angle, there were little dots which seemed to indicate a city on the shore.

"St. Augustine?"

The captain shook his head. "Too near Mosquito Inlet."

And the oiler rowed, and then the correspondent rowed. Then the oiler rowed. It was a weary business. The human back can become the seat of more aches and pains than are registered in books for the composite anatomy of a regiment. It is a limited area, but it can become the theatre of innumerable muscular conflicts, tangles, wrenches, knots, and other comforts.

"Did you ever like to row, Billie?" asked the correspondent.

"No," said the oiler. "Hang it."

When one exchanged the rowing-seat for a place in the bottom of the boat, he suffered a bodily depression that caused him to be careless of everything save an obligation to wiggle one finger. There was cold sea-water swashing to and fro in the boat, and he lay in it. His head, pillowed on a thwart, was within an inch of the swirl of a wave crest, and sometimes a particularly obstreperous sea came inboard and drenched him once more. But these matters did not annoy him. It is almost certain that if the boat had capsized he would have tumbled comfortably out upon the ocean as if he felt sure that it was a great soft mattress.

"Look! There's a man on the shore!"

"Where?"

"There? See 'im? See 'im?"

"Yes, sure! He's walking along."

"Now he's stopped. Look! He's facing us!"

"He's waving at us!"

"So he is! By thunder!"

"Ah, now, we're all right! Now we're all right! There'll be a boat out here for us in half an hour."

"He's going on. He's running. He's going up to that house there."

The remote beach seemed lower than the sea, and it required a searching glance to discern the little black figure. The captain saw a floating stick and they rowed to it. A bath-towel was by some weird chance in the boat, and, tying this on the stick, the captain waved it. The oarsman did not dare turn his head, so he was obliged to ask questions.

"What's he doing now?"

"He's standing still again. He's looking, I think. . . . There he goes again. Toward the house. . . . Now he's stopped again."

"Is he waving at us?"

"No, not now! he was, though."

"Look! There comes another man!"

"He's running."

"Look at him go, would you."

"Why, he's on a bicycle. Now he's met the other man. They're both waving at us. Look!"

"There comes something up the beach."

"What the devil is that thing?"

"Why, it looks like a boat."

"Why, certainly it's a boat."

"No, it's on wheels."

"Yes, so it is. Well, that must be the life-boat. They drag them along shore on a wagon."

"That's the life-boat, sure."

"No, by——, it's—it's an omnibus."

"I tell you it's a life-boat."

"It is not! It's an omnibus. I can see it plain. See? One of those big hotel omnibuses."

"By thunder, you're right. It's an omnibus, sure as fate. What do you suppose they are doing with an omnibus? Maybe they are going around collecting the life-crew, hey?"

"That's it, likely. Look! There's a fellow waving a little black flag. He's standing on the steps of the omnibus. There come those other two fellows. Now they're all talking together. Look at the fellow with the flag. Maybe he ain't waving it!"

"That ain't a flag, is it? That's his coat. Why, certainly, that's his coat."

"So it is. It's his coat. He's taken it off and is waving it around his head. But would you look at him swing it!"

"Oh, say, there isn't any life-saving station there. That's just a winter resort hotel omnibus that has brought over some of the boarders to see us drown."

"What's that idiot with the coat mean? What's he signaling, anyhow?"

"It looks as if he were trying to tell us to go north. There must be a life-saving station up there."

"No! He thinks we're fishing. Just giving us a merry hand. See? Ah, there, Willie."

"Well, I wish I could make something out of those signals. What do you suppose he means?"

"He don't mean anything. He's just playing."

"Well, if he'd just signal us to try the surf again, or to go to sea and wait, or go north, or go south, or go to hell—there would be some reason in it. But look at him. He just stands there and keeps his coat revolving like a wheel. The ass!"

"There come more people."

"Now there's quite a mob. Look! Isn't that a boat?"

"Where? Oh, I see where you mean. No, that's no boat."

"That fellow is still waving his coat."

"He must think we like to see him do that. Why don't he quit it. It don't mean anything."

"I don't know. I think he is trying to make us go north. It must be that there's a life-saving station there somewhere."

"Say, he ain't tired yet. Look at 'im wave."

"Wonder how long he can keep that up. He's been revolving his coat ever since he caught sight of us. He's an idiot. Why aren't they getting men to bring a boat out. A fishing boat—one of those big yawls—could come out here all right. Why don't he do something?"

"Oh, it's all right, now."

"They'll have a boat out here for us in less than no time, now that they've seen us."

A faint yellow tone came into the sky over the low land. The shadows on the sea slowly deepened. The wind bore coldness with it, and the men began to shiver.

"Holy smoke!" said one, allowing his voice to express his impious mood, "if we keep on monkeying out here! If we've got to flounder out here all night!"

"Oh, we'll never have to stay here all night! Don't you worry. They've seen us now, and it won't be long before they'll come chasing out after us."

The shore grew dusky. The man waving a coat blended gradually into this gloom, and it swallowed in the same manner the omnibus and the group of people. The spray, when it dashed uproariously over the side, made the voyagers shrink and swear like men who were being branded.

"I'd like to catch the chump who waved the coat. I feel like socking him one, just for luck."

"Why? What did he do?"

"Oh, nothing, but then he seemed so damned cheerful."

In the meantime the oiler rowed, and then the correspondent rowed, and then the oiler rowed. Gray-faced and bowed forward, they mechanically, turn by turn, plied the leaden oars. The form of the light-house had vanished from the southern horizon, but finally a pale star appeared, just lifting from the sea. The streaked saffron in the west passed before the all-merging darkness, and the sea to the east was black. The land had vanished, and was expressed only by the low and drear thunder of the surf.

"If I am going to be drowned—if I am going to be drowned—if I am going to be drowned, why, in the name of the seven mad gods who rule the sea, was I allowed to come thus far and contemplate sand and trees? Was I brought here merely to have my nose dragged away as I was about to nibble the sacred cheese of life?"

The patient captain, drooped over the water-jar, was sometimes obliged to speak to the oarsman.

"Keep her head up! Keep her head up!"

" 'Keep her head up,' sir." The voices were weary and low.

This was surely a quiet evening. All save the oarsman lay heavily and listlessly in the boat's bottom. As for him, his eyes were just capable of noting the tall black waves that swept forward in a most sinister silence, save for an occasional subdued growl of a crest.

The cook's head was on a thwart, and he looked without interest at the water under his nose. He was deep in other scenes. Finally he spoke. "Billie," he murmured, dreamfully, "what kind of pie do you like best?"

V

"Pie," said the oiler and the correspondent, agitatedly. "Don't talk about those things, blast you!"

"Well," said the cook, "I was just thinking about ham sandwiches, and——"

A night on the sea in an open boat is a long night. As darkness settled finally, the shine of the light, lifting from the sea in the south, changed to full gold. On the northern horizon a new light appeared, a small bluish gleam on the edge of the waters. These two lights were the furniture of the world. Otherwise there was nothing but waves.

Two men huddled in the stern, and distances were so magnificent in the dingey that the rower was enabled to keep his feet partly warmed by thrusting them under his companions. Their legs indeed extended far under the rowing-seat until they touched the feet of the captain forward. Sometimes, despite the efforts of the tired oarsman, a wave came piling into the boat, an icy wave of the night, and the chilling water soaked them anew. They would twist their bodies for a moment and groan, and sleep the dead sleep once more, while the water in the boat gurgled about them as the craft rocked.

The plan of the oiler and the correspondent was for one to row until he lost the ability, and then arouse the other from his sea-water couch in the bottom of the boat.

The oiler plied the oars until his head drooped forward, and the overpowering sleep blinded him. And he rowed yet afterward. Then he touched a man in the bottom of the boat, and called his name. "Will you spell me for a little while?" he said meekly.

"Sure, Billie," said the correspondent, awakening and dragging himself to a sitting position. They exchanged places carefully, and the oiler, cuddling down in the sea-water at the cook's side, seemed to go to sleep instantly.

The particular violence of the sea had ceased. The waves came without snarling. The obligation of the man at the oars was to keep the boat headed so that the tilt of the rollers would not capsize her, and to preserve her from filling when the crests rushed past. The black waves were silent and hard to be seen in the darkness. Often one was almost upon the boat before the oarsman was aware.

In a low voice the correspondent addressed the captain. He was not sure that the captain was awake, although this iron man seemed to be always awake. "Captain, shall I keep her making for that light north, sir?"

The same steady voice answered him. "Yes. Keep it about two points off the port bow."

The cook had tied a life-belt around himself in order to get even the warmth which this clumsy cork contrivance could donate, and he seemed almost stove-like when a rower, whose teeth invariably chattered wildly as soon as he ceased his labor, dropped down to sleep.

The correspondent, as he rowed, looked down at the two men sleeping under foot. The cook's arm was around the oiler's shoulders, and, with their fragmentary clothing and haggard faces, they were the babes of the sea, a grotesque rendering of the old babes in the wood.

Later he must have grown stupid at his work, for suddenly there was a growling of water, and a crest came with a roar and a swash into the boat, and it was a wonder that it did not set the cook afloat in his life-belt. The cook continued to sleep, but the oiler sat up, blinking his eyes and shaking with the new cold.

"Oh, I'm awful sorry, Billie," said the correspondent, contritely.

"That's all right, old boy," said the oiler, and lay down again and was asleep.

Presently it seemed that even the captain dozed, and the correspondent thought that he was the one man afloat on all the oceans. The wind had a voice as it came over the waves, and it was sadder than the end.

There was a long, loud swishing astern of the boat, and a gleaming trail of phosphorescence, like blue flame, was furrowed on the black waters. It might have been made by a monstrous knife.

Then there came a stillness, while the correspondent breathed with the open mouth and looked at the sea.

Suddenly there was another swish and another long flash of bluish light, and this time it was alongside the boat, and might almost have been reached with an oar. The correspondent saw an enormous fin speed like a shadow through the water, hurling the crystalline spray and leaving the long glowing trail.

The correspondent looked over his shoulder at the captain. His face was hidden, and he seemed to be asleep. He looked at the babes of the sea. They certainly were asleep. So, being bereft of sympathy, he leaned a little way to one side and swore softly into the sea.

But the thing did not then leave the vicinity of the boat. Ahead or astern, on one side or the other, at intervals long or short, fled the long sparkling streak, and there was to be heard the whiroo of the dark fin. The speed and power of the thing was greatly to be admired. It cut the water like a gigantic and keen projectile.

The presence of this biding thing did not affect the man with the same horror that it would if he had been a picnicker. He simply looked at the sea dully and swore in an undertone.

Nevertheless, it is true that he did not wish to be alone with the thing. He wished one of his companions to awaken by chance and keep him company with it. But the captain hung motionless over the water-jar and the oiler and the cook in the bottom of the boat were plunged in slumber.

VI

"If I am going to be drowned—if I am going to be drowned—if I am going to be drowned, why, in the name of the seven mad gods who rule the sea, was I allowed to come thus far and contemplate sand and trees?"

During this dismal night, it may be remarked that a man would conclude that it was really the intention of the seven mad gods to drown him, despite the abominable injustice of it. For it was certainly an abominable injustice to drown a man who had worked so hard, so hard. The man felt it would be a crime most unnatural. Other people had drowned at sea since galleys swarmed with painted sails, but still——

When it occurs to a man that nature does not regard him as important, and that she feels she would not maim the universe by disposing of him, he at first wishes to throw bricks at the temple, and he hates deeply the fact that there are no bricks and no temples. Any visible expression of nature would surely be pelleted with his jeers.

Then, if there be no tangible thing to hoot he feels, perhaps, the desire to confront a personification and indulge in pleas, bowed to one knee, and with hands supplicant, saying: "Yes, but I love myself."

A high cold star on a winter's night is the word he feels that she says to him. Thereafter he knows the pathos of his situation.

The men in the dingey had not discussed these matters, but each had, no doubt, reflected upon them in silence and according to his mind. There was om any expression upon their faces save the general one of complete riness. Speech was devoted to the business of the boat.

To chime the notes of his emotion, a verse mysteriously entered the correspondent's head. He had even forgotten that he had forgotten this verse, but it suddenly was in his mind.

A soldier of the Legion lay dying in Algiers,
There was lack of woman's nursing, there was dearth of woman's tears;
But a comrade stood beside him, and he took that comrade's hand,
And he said: "I never more shall see my own, my native land."[5]

In his childhood, the correspondent had been made acquainted with the fact that a soldier of the Legion lay dying in Algiers, but he had never regarded it as important. Myriads of his school-fellows had informed him of the soldier's plight, but the dinning had naturally ended by making him perfectly indifferent. He had never considered it his affair that a soldier of the Legion lay dying in Algiers, nor had it appeared to him as a matter for sorrow. It was less to him than the breaking of a pencil's point.

Now, however, it quaintly came to him as a human, living thing. It was no longer merely a picture of a few throes in the breast of a poet, meanwhile drinking tea and warming his feet at the grate; it was an actuality—stern, mournful, and fine.

The correspondent plainly saw the soldier. He lay on the sand with his feet out straight and still. While his pale left hand was upon his chest in an attempt to thwart the going of his life, the blood came between his fingers. In the far Algerian distance, a city of low square forms was set against a sky that was faint with the last sunset hues. The correspondent, plying the oars and dreaming of the slow and slower movements of the lips of the soldier, was moved by a profound and perfectly impersonal comprehension. He was sorry for the soldier of the Legion who lay dying in Algiers.

The thing which had followed the boat and waited had evidently grown bored at the delay. There was no longer to be heard the slash of the cut-water, and there was no longer the flame of the long trail. The light in the north still glimmered, but it was apparently no nearer to the boat. Sometimes the boom of the surf rang in the correspondent's ears, and he turned the craft seaward then and rowed harder. Southward, some one had evidently built a watch-fire on the beach. It was too low and too far to be seen, but it made a shimmering, roseate reflection upon the bluff back of it, and this could be discerned from the boat. The wind came stronger, and sometimes a wave suddenly raged out like a mountain-cat and there was to be seen the sheen and sparkle of a broken crest.

The captain, in the bow, moved on his water-jar and sat erect. "Pretty long night," he observed to the correspondent. He looked at the shore. "Those life-saving people take their time."

"Did you see that shark playing around?"

"Yes, I saw him. He was a big fellow, all right."

"Wish I had known you were awake."

Later the correspondent spoke into the bottom of the boat.

"Billie!" There was a slow and gradual disentanglement. "Billie, will you spell me?"

"Sure," said the oiler.

As soon as the correspondent touched the cold comfortable seawater in the bottom of the boat, and had huddled close to the cook's life-belt he was deep

5. The lines are incorrectly quoted from Caroline E. S. Norton's poem "Bingen on the Rhine" (1883).

in sleep, despite the fact that his teeth played all the popular airs. This sleep was so good to him that it was but a moment before he heard a voice call his name in a tone that demonstrated the last stages of exhaustion. "Will you spell me?"

"Sure, Billie."

The light in the north had mysteriously vanished, but the correspondent took his course from the wide-awake captain.

Later in the night they took the boat farther out to sea, and the captain directed the cook to take one oar at the stern and keep the boat facing the seas. He was to call out if he should hear the thunder of the surf. This plan enabled the oiler and the correspondent to get respite together. "We'll give those boys a chance to get into shape again," said the captain. They curled down and, after a few preliminary chatterings and trembles, slept once more the dead sleep. Neither knew they had bequeathed to the cook the company of another shark, or perhaps the same shark.

As the boat caroused on the waves, spray occasionally bumped over the side and gave them a fresh soaking, but this had no power to break their repose. The ominous slash of the wind and the water affected them as it would have affected mummies.

"Boys," said the cook, with the notes of every reluctance in his voice, "she's drifted in pretty close. I guess one of you had better take her to sea again." The correspondent, aroused, heard the crash of the toppled crests.

As he was rowing, the captain gave him some whiskey and water, and this steadied the chills out of him. "If I ever get ashore and anybody shows me even a photograph of an oar—"

At last there was a short conversation.

"Billie. . . . Billie, will you spell me?"

"Sure," said the oiler.

VII

When the correspondent again opened his eyes, the sea and the sky were each of the gray hue of the dawning. Later, carmine and gold was painted upon the waters. The morning appeared finally, in its splendor, with a sky of pure blue, and the sunlight flamed on the tips of the waves.

On the distant dunes were set many little black cottages, and a tall white wind-mill reared above them. No man, nor dog, nor bicycle appeared on the beach. The cottages might have formed a deserted village.

The voyagers scanned the shore. A conference was held in the boat. "Well," said the captain, "if no help is coming, we might better try a run through the surf right away. If we stay out here much longer we will be too weak to do anything for ourselves at all." The others silently acquiesced in this reasoning. The boat was headed for the beach. The correspondent wondered if none ever ascended the tall wind-tower, and if then they never looked seaward. This tower was a giant, standing with its back to the plight of the ants. It represented in a degree, to the correspondent, the serenity of nature amid the struggles of the individual—nature in the wind, and nature in the vision of men. She did not seem cruel to him then, nor beneficent, nor treacherous, nor wise. But she was indifferent, flatly indifferent. It is, perhaps, plausible that a man in this situation, impressed with the unconcern of the universe, should see the innumerable flaws of his life and have them taste wickedly in his mind and wish for another chance. A distinction between right and wrong seems absurdly clear to him, then, in this new ignorance of the grave-edge, and he understands that if he were given another opportunity he would mend his conduct and his words, and be better and brighter during an introduction, or at a tea.

"Now, boys," said the captain, "she is going to swamp sure. All we can do is to work her in as far as possible, and then when she swamps, pile out and scramble for the beach. Keep cool now, and don't jump until she swamps sure."

The oiler took the oars. Over his shoulders he scanned the surf. "Captain," he said, "I think I'd better bring her about, and keep her head-on to the seas and back her in."

"All right, Billie," said the captain. "Back her in." The oiler swung the boat then and, seated in the stern, the cook and the correspondent were obliged to look over their shoulders to contemplate the lonely and indifferent shore.

The monstrous inshore rollers heaved the boat high until the men were again enabled to see the white sheets of water scudding up the slanted beach. "We won't get in very close," said the captain. Each time a man could wrest his attention from the rollers, he turned his glance toward the shore, and in the expression of the eyes during this contemplation there was a singular quality. The correspondent, observing the others, knew that they were not afraid, but the full meaning of their glances was shrouded.

As for himself, he was too tired to grapple fundamentally with the fact. He tried to coerce his mind into thinking of it, but the mind was dominated at this time by the muscles, and the muscles said they did not care. It merely occurred to him that if he should drown it would be a shame.

There were no hurried words, no pallor, no plain agitation. The men simply looked at the shore. "Now, remember to get well clear of the boat when you jump," said the captain.

Seaward the crest of a roller suddenly fell with a thunderous crash, and the long white comber came roaring down upon the boat.

"Steady now," said the captain. The men were silent. They turned their eyes from the shore to the comber and waited. The boat slid up the incline, leaped at the furious top, bounced over it, and swung down the long back of the wave. Some water had been shipped and the cook bailed it out.

But the next crest crashed also. The tumbling boiling flood of white water caught the boat and whirled it almost perpendicular. Water swarmed in from all sides. The correspondent had his hands on the gunwale at this time, and when the water entered at that place he swiftly withdrew his fingers, as if he objected to wetting them.

The little boat, drunken with this weight of water, reeled and snuggled deeper into the sea.

"Bail her out, cook! Bail her out," said the captain.

"All right, Captain," said the cook.

"Now, boys, the next one will do for us, sure," said the oiler. "Mind to jump clear of the boat."

The third wave moved forward, huge, furious, implacable. It fairly swallowed the dingey, and almost simultaneously the men tumbled into the sea. A piece of life-belt had lain in the bottom of the boat, and as the correspondent went overboard he held this to his chest with his left hand.

The January water was icy, and he reflected immediately that it was colder than he had expected to find it off the coast of Florida. This appeared to his dazed mind as a fact important enough to be noted at the time. The coldness of the water was sad; it was tragic. This fact was somehow so mixed and confused with his opinion of his own situation that it seemed almost a proper reason for tears. The water was cold.

When he came to the surface he was conscious of little but the noisy water. Afterward he saw his companions in the sea. The oiler was ahead in the race. He was swimming strongly and rapidly. Off to the correspondent's left, the cook's great white and corked back bulged out of the water, and in the rear the captain was hanging with his one good hand to the keel of the overturned dingey.

There is a certain immovable quality to a shore, and the correspondent wondered at it amid the confusion of the sea.

It seemed also very attractive, but the correspondent knew that it was a long journey, and he paddled leisurely. The piece of life preserver lay under him, and sometimes he whirled down the incline of a wave as if he were on a hand-sled.

But finally he arrived at a place in the sea where travel was beset with difficulty. He did not pause swimming to inquire what manner of current had caught him, but there his progress ceased. The shore was set before him like a bit of scenery on a stage, and he looked at it and understood with his eyes each detail of it.

As the cook passed, much farther to the left, the captain was calling to him, "Turn over on your back, cook! Turn over on your back and use the oar."

"All right, sir." The cook turned on his back, and, paddling with an oar, went ahead as if he were a canoe.

Presently the boat also passed to the left of the correspondent with the captain clinging with one hand to the keel. He would have appeared like a man raising himself to look over a board fence, if it were not for the extraordinary gymnastics of the boat. The correspondent marvelled that the captain could still hold to it.

They passed on, nearer to the shore—the oiler, the cook, the captain—and following them went the water-jar, bouncing gayly over the seas.

The correspondent remained in the grip of this strange new enemy—a current. The shore, with its white slope of sand and its green bluff, topped with little silent cottages, was spread like a picture before him. It was very near to him then, but he was impressed as one who in a gallery looks at a scene from Brittany or Holland.

He thought: "I am going to drown? Can it be possible? Can it be possible? Can it be possible?" Perhaps an individual must consider his own death to be the final phenomenon of nature.

But later a wave perhaps whirled him out of this small deadly current, for he found suddenly that he could again make progress toward the shore. Later still, he was aware that the captain, clinging with one hand to the keel of the dingey, had his face turned away from the shore and toward him, and was calling his name. "Come to the boat! Come to the boat!"

In his struggle to reach the captain and the boat, he reflected that when one gets properly wearied, drowning must really be a comfortable arrangement, a cessation of hostilities accompanied by a large degree of relief, and he was glad of it, for the main thing in his mind for some moments had been horror of the temporary agony. He did not wish to be hurt.

Presently he saw a man running along the shore. He was undressing with most remarkable speed. Coat, trousers, shirt, everything flew magically off him.

"Come to the boat," called the captain.

"All right, Captain." As the correspondent paddled, he saw the captain let himself down to bottom and leave the boat. Then the correspondent performed his one little marvel of the voyage. A large wave caught him and flung him with ease and supreme speed completely over the boat and far beyond it. It struck him even then as an event in gymnastics, and a true miracle of the sea. An overturned boat in the surf is not a plaything to a swimming man.

The correspondent arrived in water that reached only to his waist, but his condition did not enable him to stand for more than a moment. Each wave knocked him into a heap, and the under-tow pulled at him.

Then he saw the man who had been running and undressing, and undressing and running, come bounding into the water. He dragged ashore the cook, and then waded toward the captain, but the captain waved him away, and sent him to the correspondent. He was naked, naked as a tree in winter, but a halo was about his head, and he shone like a saint. He gave a strong pull, and a long drag, and a bully heave at the correspondent's hand. The correspondent schooled in the minor formulæ, said: "Thanks, old man." But suddenly the man cried: "What's that?" He pointed a swift finger. The correspondent said: "Go."

In the shallows, face downward, lay the oiler. His forehead touched sand that was periodically, between each wave, clear of the sea.

The correspondent did not know all that transpired afterward. When he achieved safe ground he fell, striking the sand with each particular part of his body. It was as if he had dropped from a roof, but the thud was grateful to him.

It seems that instantly the beach was populated with men with blankets, clothes, and flasks, and women with coffee-pots and all the remedies sacred to their minds. The welcome of the land to the men from the sea was warm and generous, but a still and dripping shape was carried slowly up the beach, and the land's welcome for it could only be the different and sinister hospitality of the grave.

When it came night, the white waves paced to and fro in the moonlight, and the wind brought the sound of the great sea's voice to the men on shore, and they felt that they could then be interpreters.

1897, 1898

The Blue Hotel[1]

I

The Palace Hotel at Fort Romper was painted a light blue, a shade that is on the legs of a kind of heron, causing the bird to declare its position against any background. The Palace Hotel, then, was always screaming and howling in a way that made the dazzling winter landscape of Nebraska seem only a gay swampish hush. It stood alone on the prairie, and when the snow was

---

1. First published in two installments in *Collier's Weekly* for November 26 and December 3, 1898, then in *"The Monster" and Other Stories* (1899). The text here reprints that established for the University of Virginia edition of *The Works of Stephen Crane*, Vol. 5, *Tales of Adventure* (1970).

falling the town two hundred yards away was not visible. But when the traveler alighted at the railway station he was obliged to pass the Palace Hotel before he could come upon the company of low clap-board houses which composed Fort Romper, and it was not to be thought that any traveler could pass the Palace Hotel without looking at it. Pat Scully, the proprietor, had proved himself a master of strategy when he chose his paints. It is true that on clear days, when the great trans-continental expresses, long lines of swaying Pullmans, swept through Fort Romper, passengers were overcome at the sight, and the cult that knows the brown-reds and the subdivisions of the dark greens of the East expressed shame, pity, horror, in a laugh. But to the citizens of this prairie town, and to the people who would naturally stop there, Pat Scully had performed a feat. With this opulence and splendor, these creeds, classes, egotisms, that streamed through Romper on the rails day after day, they had no color in common.

As if the displayed delights of such a blue hotel were not sufficiently enticing, it was Scully's habit to go every morning and evening to meet the leisurely trains that stopped at Romper and work his seductions upon any man that he might see wavering, gripsack in hand.

One morning, when a snow-crusted engine dragged its long string of freight cars and its one passenger coach to the station, Scully performed the marvel of catching three men. One was a shaky and quick-eyed Swede, with a great shining cheap valise; one was a tall bronzed cowboy, who was on his way to a ranch near the Dakota line; one was a little silent man from the East, who didn't look it, and didn't announce it. Scully practically made them prisoners. He was so nimble and merry and kindly that each probably felt it would be the height of brutality to try to escape. They trudged off over the creaking board sidewalks in the wake of the eager little Irishman. He wore a heavy fur cap squeezed tightly down on his head. It caused his two red ears to stick out stiffly, as if they were made of tin.

At last, Scully, elaborately, with boisterous hospitality, conducted them through the portals of the blue hotel. The room which they entered was small. It seemed to be merely a proper temple for an enormous stove, which, in the center, was humming with god-like violence. At various points on its surface the iron had become luminous and glowed yellow from the heat. Beside the stove Scully's son Johnnie was playing High-Five[2] with an old farmer who had whiskers both gray and sandy. They were quarreling. Frequently the old farmer turned his face toward a box of sawdust—colored brown from tobacco juice—that was behind the stove, and spat with an air of great impatience and irritation. With a loud flourish of words Scully destroyed the game of cards, and bustled his son upstairs with part of the baggage of the new guests. He himself conducted them to three basins of the coldest water in the world. The cowboy and the Easterner burnished themselves fiery red with this water, until it seemed to be some kind of a metal polish. The Swede, however, merely dipped his fingers gingerly and with trepidation. It was notable that throughout this series of small ceremonies the three travelers were made to feel that Scully was very benevolent. He was conferring great favors upon them. He handed the towel from one to the other with an air of philanthropic impulse.

Afterward they went to the first room, and, sitting about the stove, listened

---

2. I.e., cinch, a card game.

to Scully's officious clamor at his daughters, who were preparing the midday meal. They reflected in the silence of experienced men who tread carefully amid new people. Nevertheless, the old farmer, stationary, invincible in his chair near the warmest part of the stove, turned his face from the sawdust box frequently and addressed a glowing commonplace to the strangers. Usually he was answered in short but adequate sentences by either the cowboy or the Easterner. The Swede said nothing. He seemed to be occupied in making furtive estimates of each man in the room. One might have thought that he had the sense of silly suspicion which comes to guilt. He resembled a badly frightened man.

Later, at dinner, he spoke a little, addressing his conversation entirely to Scully. He volunteered that he had come from New York, where for ten years he had worked as a tailor. These facts seemed to strike Scully as fascinating, and afterward he volunteered that he had lived at Romper for fourteen years. The Swede asked about the crops and the price of labor. He seemed barely to listen to Scully's extended replies. His eyes continued to rove from man to man.

Finally, with a laugh and a wink, he said that some of these Western communities were very dangerous; and after his statement he straightened his legs under the table, tilted his head, and laughed again, loudly. It was plain that the demonstration had no meaning to the others. They looked at him wondering and in silence.

II

As the men trooped heavily back into the front room, the two little windows presented views of a turmoiling sea of snow. The huge arms of the wind were making attempts—mighty, circular, futile—to embrace the flakes as they sped. A gate-post like a still man with a blanched face stood aghast amid this profligate fury. In a hearty voice Scully announced the presence of a blizzard. The guests of the blue hotel, lighting their pipes, assented with grunts of lazy masculine contentment. No island of the sea could be exempt in the degree of this little room with its humming stove. Johnnie, son of Scully, in a tone which defined his opinion of his ability as a card-player, challenged the old farmer of both gray and sandy whiskers to a game of High-Five. The farmer agreed with a contemptuous and bitter scoff. They sat close to the stove, and squared their knees under a wide board. The cowboy and the Easterner watched the game with interest. The Swede remained near the window, aloof, but with a countenance that showed signs of an inexplicable excitement.

The play of Johnnie and the gray-beard was suddenly ended by another quarrel. The old man arose while casting a look of heated scorn at his adversary. He slowly buttoned his coat, and then stalked with fabulous dignity from the room. In the discreet silence of all other men the Swede laughed. His laughter rang somehow childish. Men by this time had begun to look at him askance, as if they wished to inquire what ailed him.

A new game was formed jocosely. The cowboy volunteered to become the partner of Johnnie, and they all then turned to ask the Swede to throw in his lot with the little Easterner. He asked some questions about the game, and learning that it wore many names, and that he had played it when it was under an alias, he accepted the invitation. He strode toward the men nervously, as if he expected to be assaulted. Finally, seated, he gazed from face to face and laughed shrilly. This laugh was so strange that the Easterner looked up quickly, the cowboy sat intent and with his mouth open, and Johnnie paused, holding the cards with still fingers.

Afterward there was a short silence. Then Johnnie said: "Well, let's get at it. Come on now!" They pulled their chairs forward until their knees were bunched under the board. They began to play, and their interest in the game caused the others to forget the manner of the Swede.

The cowboy was a board-whacker. Each time that he held superior cards he whanged them, one by one, with exceeding force, down upon the improvised table, and took the tricks with a glowing air of prowess and pride that sent thrills of indignation into the hearts of his opponents. A game with a board-whacker in it is sure to become intense. The countenances of the Easterner and the Swede were miserable whenever the cowboy thundered down his aces and kings, while Johnnie, his eyes gleaming with joy, chuckled and chuckled.

Because of the absorbing play none considered the strange ways of the Swede. They paid strict heed to the game. Finally, during a lull caused by a new deal, the Swede suddenly addressed Johnnie: "I suppose there have been a good many men killed in this room." The jaws of the others dropped and they looked at him.

"What in hell are you talking about?" asked Johnnie.

The Swede laughed again his blatant laugh, full of a kind of false courage and defiance. "Oh, you know what I mean all right," he answered.

"I'm a liar if I do!" Johnnie protested. The card was halted, and the men stared at the Swede. Johnnie evidently felt that as the son of the proprietor he should make a direct inquiry. "Now, what might you be drivin' at, mister?" he asked. The Swede winked at him. It was a wink full of cunning. His fingers shook on the edge of the board. "Oh, maybe you think I have been to nowheres. Maybe you think I'm a tenderfoot?"

"I don't know nothin' about you," answered Johnnie, "and I don't give a damn where you've been. All I got to say is that I don't know what you're driving at. There hain't never been nobody killed in this room."

The cowboy, who had been steadily gazing at the Swede, then spoke. "What's wrong with you, mister?"

Apparently it seemed to the Swede that he was formidably menaced. He shivered and turned white near the corners of his mouth. He sent an appealing glance in the direction of the little Easterner. During these moments he did not forget to wear his air of advanced pot-valor.[3] "They say they don't know what I mean," he remarked mockingly to the Easterner.

The latter answered after prolonged and cautious reflection. "I don't understand you," he said, impassively.

The Swede made a movement then which announced that he thought he had encountered treachery from the only quarter where he had expected sympathy if not help. "Oh, I see you are all against me. I see——"

The cowboy was in a state of deep stupefaction. "Say," he cried, as he tumbled the deck violently down upon the board. "Say, what are you gittin' at, hey?"

---

3. Drunken bravado.

The Swede sprang up with the celerity of a man escaping from a snake on the floor. "I don't want to fight!" he shouted. "I don't want to fight!"

The cowboy stretched his long legs indolently and deliberately. His hands were in his pockets. He spat into the sawdust box. "Well, who the hell thought you did?" he inquired.

The Swede backed rapidly toward a corner of the room. His hands were out protectingly in front of his chest, but he was making an obvious struggle to control his fright. "Gentlemen," he quavered, "I suppose I am going to be killed before I can leave this house! I suppose I am going to be killed before I can leave this house!" In his eyes was the dying swan look. Through the windows could be seen the snow turning blue in the shadow of dusk. The wind tore at the house and some loose thing beat regularly against the clapboards like a spirit tapping.

A door opened, and Scully himself entered. He paused in surprise as he noted the tragic attitude of the Swede. Then he said: "What's the matter here?"

The Swede answered him swiftly and eagerly: "These men are going to kill me."

"Kill you!" ejaculated Scully. "Kill you! What are you talkin'?"

The Swede made the gesture of a martyr.

Scully wheeled sternly upon his son. "What is this, Johnnie?"

The lad had grown sullen. "Damned if I know," he answered. "I can't make no sense to it." He began to shuffle the cards, fluttering them together with an angry snap. "He says a good many men have been killed in this room, or something like that. And he says he's goin' to be killed here too. I don't know what ails him. He's crazy, I shouldn't wonder."

Scully then looked for explanation to the cowboy, but the cowboy simply shrugged his shoulders.

"Kill you?" said Scully again to the Swede. "Kill you? Man, you're off your nut."

"Oh, I know," burst out the Swede. "I know what will happen. Yes, I'm crazy—yes. Yes, of course, I'm crazy—yes. But I know one thing——" There was a sort of sweat of misery and terror upon his face. "I know I won't get out of here alive."

The cowboy drew a deep breath, as if his mind was passing into the last stages of dissolution. "Well, I'm dog-goned," he whispered to himself.

Scully wheeled suddenly and faced his son. "You've been troublin' this man!"

Johnnie's voice was loud with its burden of grievance. "Why, good Gawd, I ain't done nothin' to 'im."

The Swede broke in. "Gentlemen, do not disturb yourselves. I will leave this house. I will go 'way because——" He accused them dramatically with his glance. "Because I do not want to be killed."

Scully was furious with his son. "Will you tell me what is the matter, you young divil? What's the matter, anyhow? Speak out!"

"Blame it," cried Johnnie in despair, "don't I tell you I don't know. He—he says we want to kill him, and that's all I know. I can't tell what ails him."

The Swede continued to repeat: "Never mind, Mr. Scully, never mind. I will leave this house. I will go away, because I do not wish to be killed. Yes, of course, I am crazy—yes. But I know one thing! I will go away. I will leave this house. Never mind, Mr. Scully, never mind. I will go away."

"You will not go 'way," said Scully. "You will not go 'way until I hear the reason of this business. If anybody has troubled you I will take care of him. This is my house. You are under my roof, and I will not allow any peaceable man to be troubled here." He cast a terrible eye upon Johnnie, the cowboy, and the Easterner.

"Never mind, Mr. Scully, never mind. I will go 'way. I do not wish to be killed." The Swede moved toward the door, which opened upon the stairs. It was evidently his intention to go at once for his baggage.

"No, no," shouted Scully peremptorily; but the white-faced man slid by him and disappeared. "Now," said Scully severely, "what does this mean?"

Johnnie and the cowboy cried together: "Why, we didn't do nothin' to 'im!"

Scully's eyes were cold. "No," he said, "you didn't?"

Johnnie swore a deep oath. "Why, this is the wildest loon I ever see. We didn't do nothin' at all. We were jest sittin' here playin' cards and he——"

The father suddenly spoke to the Easterner. "Mr. Blanc," he asked, "what has these boys been doin'?"

The Easterner reflected again. "I didn't see anything wrong at all," he said at last slowly.

Scully began to howl. "But what does it mane?" He stared ferociously at his son. "I have a mind to lather you for this, me boy."

Johnnie was frantic. "Well, what have I done?" he bawled at his father.

III

"I think you are tongue-tied," said Scully finally to his son, the cowboy and the Easterner, and at the end of this scornful sentence he left the room.

Upstairs the Swede was swiftly fastening the straps of his great valise. Once his back happened to be half-turned toward the door, and hearing a noise there, he wheeled and sprang up, uttering a loud cry. Scully's wrinkled visage showed grimly in the light of the small lamp he carried. This yellow effulgence, streaming upward, colored only his prominent features, and left his eyes, for instance, in mysterious shadow. He resembled a murderer.

"Man, man!" he exclaimed, "have you gone daffy?"

"Oh, no! Oh, no!" rejoined the other. "There are people in this world who know pretty nearly as much as you do—understand?"

For a moment they stood gazing at each other. Upon the Swede's deathly pale cheeks were two spots brightly crimson and sharply edged, as if they had been carefully painted. Scully placed the light on the table and sat himself on the edge of the bed. He spoke ruminatively. "By cracky, I never heard of such a thing in my life. It's a complete muddle. I can't for the soul of me think how you ever got this idea into your head." Presently he lifted his eyes and asked: "And did you sure think they were going to kill you?"

The Swede scanned the old man as if he wished to see into his mind. "I did," he said at last. He obviously suspected that this answer might precipitate an outbreak. As he pulled on a strap his whole arm shook, the elbow wavering like a bit of paper.

Scully banged his hand impressively on the foot-board of the bed. "Why, man, we're goin' to have a line of ilictric street-cars in this town next spring."

"'A line of electric street-cars,'" repeated the Swede stupidly.

"And," said Scully, "there's a new railroad goin' to be built down from Broken Arm to here. Not to mintion the four churches and the smashin' big brick school-house. Then there's the big factory, too. Why, in two years Romper'll be a met-tro-*pol*-is."

Having finished the preparation of his baggage, the Swede straightened himself. "Mr. Scully," he said with sudden hardihood, "how much do I owe you?"

"You don't owe me anythin'," said the old man angrily.

"Yes, I do," retorted the Swede. He took seventy-five cents from his pocket and tendered it to Scully; but the latter snapped his fingers in disdainful refusal. However, it happened that they both stood gazing in a strange fashion at three silver pieces on the Swede's open palm.

"I'll not take your money," said Scully at last. "Not after what's been goin' on here." Then a plan seemed to strike him. "Here," he cried, picking up his lamp and moving toward the door. "Here! Come with me a minute."

"No," said the Swede in overwhelming alarm.

"Yes," urged the old man. "Come on! I want you to come and see a picter—just across the hall—in my room."

The Swede must have concluded that his hour was come. His jaw dropped and his teeth showed like a dead man's. He ultimately followed Scully across the corridor, but he had the step of one hung in chains.

Scully flashed the light high on the wall of his own chamber. There was revealed a ridiculous photograph of a little girl. She was leaning against a balustrade of gorgeous decoration, and the formidable bang to her hair was prominent. The figure was as graceful as an upright sled-stake, and, withal, it was the hue of lead. "There," said Scully tenderly. "That's the picter of my little girl that died. Her name was Carrie. She had the purtiest hair you ever saw! I was that fond of her, she——"

Turning then he saw that the Swede was not contemplating the picture at all, but, instead, was keeping keen watch on the gloom in the rear.

"Look, man!" shouted Scully heartily. "That's the picter of my little gal that died. Her name was Carrie. And then here's the picter of my oldest boy, Michael. He's a lawyer in Lincoln an' doin' well. I gave that boy a grand eddycation, and I'm glad for it now. He's a fine boy. Look at 'im now. Ain't he bold as blazes, him there in Lincoln, an honored an' respicted gintleman. An honored an' respicted gintleman," concluded Scully with a flourish. And so saying, he smote the Swede jovially on the back.

The Swede faintly smiled.

"Now," said the old man, "there's only one more thing." He dropped suddenly to the floor and thrust his head beneath the bed. The Swede could hear his muffled voice. "I'd keep it under me piller if it wasn't for that boy Johnnie. Then there's the old woman——Where is it now? I never put it twice in the same place. Ah, now come out with you!"

Presently he backed clumsily from under the bed, dragging with him an old coat rolled into a bundle. "I've fetched him," he muttered. Kneeling on the floor he unrolled the coat and extracted from its heart a large yellow-brown whisky bottle.

His first maneuver was to hold the bottle up to the light. Reassured, apparently, that nobody had been tampering with it, he thrust it with a generous movement toward the Swede.

The weak-kneed Swede was about to eagerly clutch this element of strength, but he suddenly jerked his hand away and cast a look of horror upon Scully.

"Drink," said the old man affectionately. He had arisen to his feet, and now stood facing the Swede.

There was a silence. Then again Scully said: "Drink!"

The Swede laughed wildly. He grabbed the bottle, put it to his mouth, and as his lips curled absurdly around the opening and his throat worked, he kept his glance burning with hatred upon the old man's face.

IV

After the departure of Scully the three men, with the cardboard still upon their knees, preserved for a long time an astounded silence. Then Johnnie said: "That's the dod-dangest Swede I ever see."

"He ain't no Swede," said the cowboy scornfully.

"Well, what is he then?" cried Johnnie. "What is he then?"

"It's my opinion," replied the cowboy deliberately, "he's some kind of a Dutchman." It was a venerable custom of the country to entitle as Swedes all light-haired men who spoke with a heavy tongue. In consequence the idea of the cowboy was not without its daring. "Yes, sir," he repeated. "It's my opinion this feller is some kind of a Dutchman."

"Well, he says he's a Swede, anyhow," muttered Johnnie sulkily. He turned to the Easterner: "What do you think, Mr. Blanc?"

"Oh, I don't know," replied the Easterner.

"Well, what do you think makes him act that way?" asked the cowboy.

"Why, he's frightened!" The Easterner knocked his pipe against a rim of the stove. "He's clear frightened out of his boots."

"What at?" cried Johnnie and cowboy together.

The Easterner reflected over his answer.

"What at?" cried the others again.

"Oh, I don't know, but it seems to me this man has been reading dime-novels, and he thinks he's right out in the middle of it—the shootin' and stabbin' and all."

"But," said the cowboy, deeply scandalized, "this ain't Wyoming, ner none of them places. This is Nebrasker."

"Yes," added Johnnie, "an' why don't he wait till he gits *out West?*"

The traveled Easterner laughed. "It isn't different there even—not in these days. But he thinks he's right in the middle of hell."

Johnnie and the cowboy mused long.

"It's awful funny," remarked Johnnie at last.

"Yes," said the cowboy. "This is a queer game. I hope we don't git snowed in, because then we'd have to stand this here man bein' around with us all the time. That wouldn't be no good."

"I wish pop would throw him out," said Johnnie.

Presently they heard a loud stamping on the stairs, accompanied by ringing jokes in the voice of old Scully, and laughter, evidently from the Swede. The men around the stove stared vacantly at each other. "Gosh," said the cowboy. The door flew open, and old Scully, flushed and anecdotal, came into the room. He was jabbering at the Swede, who followed him, laughing bravely. It was the entry of two roysterers from a banquet ball.

"Come now," said Scully sharply to the three seated men, "move up and give us a chance at the stove." The cowboy and the Easterner obediently sidled their chairs to make room for the newcomers. Johnnie, however, simply arranged himself in a more indolent attitude, and then remained motionless.

"Come! Git over, there," said Scully.

"Plenty of room on the other side of the stove," said Johnnie.

"Do you think we want to sit in the draught?" roared the father.

But the Swede here interposed with a grandeur of confidence. "No, no. Let the boy sit where he likes," he cried in a bullying voice to the father.

"All right! All right!" said Scully deferentially. The cowboy and the Easterner exchanged glances of wonder.

The five chairs were formed in a crescent about one side of the stove. The Swede began to talk; he talked arrogantly, profanely, angrily. Johnnie, the cowboy and the Easterner maintained a morose silence, while old Scully appeared to be receptive and eager, breaking in constantly with sympathetic ejaculations.

Finally, the Swede announced that he was thirsty. He moved in his chair, and said that he would go for a drink of water.

"I'll git it for you," cried Scully at once.

"No," said the Swede contemptuously. "I'll get it for myself." He arose and stalked with the air of an owner off into the executive parts of the hotel.

As soon as the Swede was out of hearing Scully sprang to his feet and whispered intensely to the others. "Upstairs he thought I was tryin' to poison 'im."

"Say," said Johnnie, "this makes me sick. Why don't you throw 'im out in the snow?"

"Why, he's all right now," declared Scully. "It was only that he was from the East and he thought this was a tough place. That's all. He's all right now."

The cowboy looked with admiration upon the Easterner. "You were straight," he said. "You were on to that there Dutchman."

"Well," said Johnnie to his father, "he may be all right now, but I don't see it. Other time he was scared, and now he's too fresh."

Scully's speech was always a combination of Irish brogue and idiom, Western twang and idiom, and scraps of curiously formal diction taken from the story-books and newspapers. He now hurled a strange mass of language at the head of his son. "What do I keep? What do I keep? What do I keep?" he demanded in a voice of thunder. He slapped his knee impressively, to indicate that he himself was going to make reply, and that all should heed. "I keep a hotel," he shouted. "A hotel, do you mind? A guest under my roof has sacred privileges. He is to be intimidated by none. Not one word shall he hear that would prijudice him in favor of goin' away. I'll not have it. There's no place in this here town where they can say they iver took in a guest of mine because he was afraid to stay here." He wheeled suddenly upon the cowboy and the Easterner. "Am I right?"

"Yes, Mr. Scully," said the cowboy, "I think you're right."

"Yes, Mr. Scully," said the Easterner, "I think you're right."

V

At six-o'clock supper, the Swede fizzed like a fire-wheel. He sometimes seemed on the point of bursting into riotous song, and in all his madness he was encouraged by old Scully. The Easterner was incased in reserve; the cowboy sat in wide-mouthed amazement, forgetting to eat, while Johnnie wrathily demolished great plates of food. The daughters of the house when they were obliged to replenish the biscuits approached as warily as Indians, and, having succeeded in their purposes, fled with ill-concealed trepidation. The Swede domineered the whole feast, and he gave it the appearance of a cruel bacchanal. He seemed to have grown suddenly taller; he gazed, brutally disdainful, into every face. His voice rang through the room. Once when he jabbed out harpoon-fashion with his fork to pinion a biscuit the weapon nearly impaled the hand of the Easterner which had been stretched quietly out for the same biscuit.

After supper, as the men filed toward the other room, the Swede smote Scully ruthlessly on the shoulder. "Well, old boy, that was a good square meal." Johnnie looked hopefully at his father; he knew that shoulder was tender from an old fall; and indeed it appeared for a moment as if Scully was going to flame out over the matter, but in the end he smiled a sickly smile and remained silent. The others understood from his manner that he was admitting his responsibility for the Swede's new viewpoint.

Johnnie, however, addressed his parent in an aside. "Why don't you license somebody to kick you downstairs?" Scully scowled darkly by way of reply.

When they were gathered about the stove, the Swede insisted on another game of High-Five. Scully gently deprecated the plan at first, but the Swede turned a wolfish glare upon him. The old man subsided, and the Swede canvassed the others. In his tone there was always a great threat. The cowboy and the Easterner both remarked indifferently that they would play. Scully said that he would presently have to go to meet the 6.58 train, and so the Swede turned menacingly upon Johnnie. For a moment their glances crossed like blades, and then Johnnie smiled and said: "Yes, I'll play."

They formed a square with the little board on their knees. The Easterner and the Swede were again partners. As the play went on, it was noticeable that the cowboy was not board-whacking as usual. Meanwhile, Scully, near the lamp, had put on his spectacles and, with an appearance curiously like an old priest, was reading a newspaper. In time he went out to meet the 6.58 train, and, despite his precautions, a gust of polar wind whirled into the room as he opened the door. Besides scattering the cards, it chilled the players to the marrow. The Swede cursed frightfully. When Scully returned, his entrance disturbed a cozy and friendly scene. The Swede again cursed. But presently they were once more intent, their heads bent forward and their hands moving swiftly. The Swede had adopted the fashion of board-whacking.

Scully took up his paper and for a long time remained immersed in matters which were extraordinarily remote from him. The lamp burned badly, and once he stopped to adjust the wick. The newspaper as he turned from page to page rustled with a slow and comfortable sound. Then suddenly he heard three terrible words: "You are cheatin'!"

Such scenes often prove that there can be little of dramatic import in environment. Any room can present a tragic front; any room can be comic. This little den was now hideous as a torture-chamber. The new faces of the men themselves had changed it upon the instant. The Swede held a huge fist in front of Johnnie's face, while the latter looked steadily over it into the blazing orbs of his accuser. The Easterner had grown pallid; the cowboy's jaw had dropped in that expression of bovine amazement which was one of his important mannerisms. After the three words, the first sound in the room was made by Scully's paper as it floated forgotten to his feet. His spectacles had also fallen from his nose, but by a clutch he had saved them in air. His hand, grasping the spectacles, now remained poised awkwardly and near his shoulder. He stared at the card-players.

Probably the silence was while a second elapsed. Then, if the floor had been suddenly twitched out from under the men they could not have moved quicker. The five had projected themselves headlong toward a common point. It happened that Johnnie in rising to hurl himself upon the Swede had stumbled slightly because of his curiously instinctive care for the cards and the board. The loss of the moment allowed time for the arrival of Scully, and also allowed the cowboy time to give the Swede a great push which sent him staggering back. The men found tongue together, and hoarse shouts of rage, appeal or fear burst from every throat. The cowboy pushed and jostled feverishly at the Swede, and the Easterner and Scully clung wildly to Johnnie; but, through the smoky air, above the swaying bodies of the peace-compellers, the eyes of the two warriors ever sought each other in glances of challenge that were at once hot and steely.

Of course the board had been overturned, and now the whole company of cards was scattered over the floor, where the boots of the men trampled the fat and painted kings and queens as they gazed with their silly eyes at the war that was waging above them.

Scully's voice was dominating the yells. "Stop now! Stop, I say! Stop, now——"

Johnnie, as he struggled to burst through the rank formed by Scully and the Easterner, was crying: "Well, he says I cheated! He says I cheated! I won't allow no man to say I cheated! If he says I cheated, he's a —— ——!"

The cowboy was telling the Swede: "Quit, now! Quit, d'ye hear——"

The screams of the Swede never ceased. "He did cheat! I saw him! I saw him——"

As for the Easterner, he was importuning in a voice that was not heeded. "Wait a moment, can't you? Oh, wait a moment. What's the good of a fight over a game of cards? Wait a moment——"

In this tumult no complete sentences were clear. "Cheat"—"Quit"—"He says"—These fragments pierced the uproar and rang out sharply. It was remarkable that whereas Scully undoubtedly made the most noise, he was the least heard of any of the riotous band.

Then suddenly there was a great cessation. It was as if each man had paused for breath, and although the room was still lighted with the anger of men, it could be seen that there was no danger of immediate conflict, and at once Johnnie, shouldering his way forward, almost succeeded in confronting the Swede. "What did you say I cheated for? What did you say I cheated for? I don't cheat and I won't let no man say I do!"

The Swede said: "I saw you! I saw you!"

"Well," cried Johnnie, "I'll fight any man what says I cheat!"

"No, you won't," said the cowboy. "Not here."

"Ah, be still, can't you?" said Scully, coming between them.

The quiet was sufficient to allow the Easterner's voice to be heard. He was repeating: "Oh, wait a moment, can't you? What's the good of a fight over a game of cards? Wait a moment."

Johnnie, his red face appearing above his father's shoulder, hailed the Swede again. "Did you say I cheated?"

The Swede showed his teeth. "Yes."

"Then," said Johnnie, "we must fight."

"Yes, fight," roared the Swede. He was like a demoniac. "Yes, fight! I'll show you what kind of a man I am! I'll show you who you want to fight! Maybe you think I can't fight! Maybe you think I can't! I'll show you, you skin,[4] you card-sharp! Yes, you cheated! You cheated! You cheated!"

"Well, let's git at it, then, mister," said Johnnie coolly.

The cowboy's brow was beaded with sweat from his efforts in intercepting all sorts of raids. He turned in despair to Scully. "What are you goin' to do now?"

A change had come over the Celtic visage of the old man. He now seemed all eagerness; his eyes glowed.

"We'll let them fight," he answered stalwartly. "I can't put up with it any longer. I've stood this damned Swede till I'm sick. We'll let them fight."

VI

The men prepared to go out of doors. The Easterner was so nervous that he had great difficulty in getting his arms into the sleeves of his new leather-coat. As the cowboy drew his fur-cap down over his ears his hands trembled. In fact, Johnnie and old Scully were the only ones who displayed no agitation. These preliminaries were conducted without words.

Scully threw open the door. "Well, come on," he said. Instantly a terrific wind caused the flame of the lamp to struggle at its wick, while a puff of black smoke sprang from the chimney-top. The stove was in mid-current of the blast, and its voice swelled to equal the roar of the storm. Some of the scarred and bedabbled cards were caught up from the floor and dashed helplessly against the further wall. The men lowered their heads and plunged into the tempest as into a sea.

No snow was falling, but great whirls and clouds of flakes, swept up from the ground by the frantic winds, were streaming southward with the speed of bullets. The covered land was blue with the sheen of an unearthly satin, and there was no other hue save where at the low black railway station—which seemed incredibly distant—one light gleamed like a tiny jewel. As the men floundered into a thigh-deep drift, it was known that the Swede was bawling out something. Scully went to him, put a hand on his shoulder and projected an ear. "What's that you say?" he shouted.

"I say," bawled the Swede again, "I won't stand much show against this gang. I know you'll all pitch on me."

Scully smote him reproachfully on the arm. "Tut, man," he yelled. The wind tore the words from Scully's lips and scattered them far a-lee.

"You are all a gang of——" boomed the Swede, but the storm also seized the remainder of this sentence.

Immediately turning their backs upon the wind, the men had swung around a corner to the sheltered side of the hotel. It was the function of the little house to preserve here, amid this great devastation of snow, an irregular V-shape of heavily-incrusted grass, which crackled beneath the feet. One could imagine the great drifts piled against the windward side. When the

4. Cheat (colloquial).

party reached the comparative peace of this spot it was found that the Swede
was still bellowing.

"Oh, I know what kind of a thing this is! I know you'll all pitch on me. I
can't lick you all!"

Scully turned upon him panther-fashion. "You'll not have to whip all of
us. You'll have to whip my son Johnnie. An' the man what troubles you durin'
that time will have me to dale with."

The arrangements were swiftly made. The two men faced each other, obedient to the harsh commands of Scully, whose face, in the subtly luminous
gloom, could be seen set in the austere impersonal lines that are pictured
on the countenances of the Roman veterans. The Easterner's teeth were
chattering, and he was hopping up and down like a mechanical toy. The
cowboy stood rock-like.

The contestants had not stripped off any clothing. Each was in his ordinary
attire. Their fists were up, and they eyed each other in a calm that had the
elements of leonine cruelty in it.

During this pause, the Easterner's mind, like a film, took lasting impressions of three men—the iron-nerved master of the ceremony; the Swede,
pale, motionless, terrible; and Johnnie, serene yet ferocious, brutish yet
heroic. The entire prelude had in it a tragedy greater than the tragedy of
action, and this aspect was accentuated by the long mellow cry of the blizzard, as it sped the tumbling and wailing flakes into the black abyss of the
south.

"Now!" said Scully.

The two combatants leaped forward and crashed together like bullocks.
There was heard the cushioned sound of blows, and a curse squeezing out
from between the tight teeth of one.

As for the spectators, the Easterner's pent-up breath exploded from him
with a pop of relief, absolute relief from the tension of the preliminaries.
The cowboy bounded into the air with a yowl. Scully was immovable as from
supreme amazement and fear at the fury of the fight which he himself had
permitted and arranged.

For a time the encounter in the darkness was such a perplexity of flying
arms that it presented no more detail than would a swiftly-revolving wheel.
Occasionally a face, as if illumined by a flash of light, would shine out,
ghastly and marked with pink spots. A moment later, the men might have
been known as shadows, if it were not for the involuntary utterance of oaths
that came from them in whispers.

Suddenly a holocaust of warlike desire caught the cowboy, and he bolted
forward with the speed of a broncho. "Go it, Johnnie; go it! Kill him! Kill him!"

Scully confronted him. "Kape back," he said; and by his glance the cowboy
could tell that this man was Johnnie's father.

To the Easterner there was a monotony of unchangeable fighting that was
an abomination. This confused mingling was eternal to his sense, which was
concentrated in a longing for the end, the priceless end. Once the fighters
lurched near him, and as he scrambled hastily backward, he heard them
breathe like men on the rack.

"Kill him, Johnnie! Kill him! Kill him!" The cowboy's face was contorted
like one of those agony-masks in museums.

"Keep still," said Scully icily.

Then there was a sudden loud grunt, incomplete, cut-short, and Johnnie's body swung away from the Swede and fell with sickening heaviness to the grass. The cowboy was barely in time to prevent the mad Swede from flinging himself upon his prone adversary. "No, you don't," said the cowboy, interposing an arm. "Wait a second."

Scully was at his son's side. "Johnnie! Johnnie, me boy?" His voice had a quality of melancholy tenderness. "Johnnie? Can you go on with it?" He looked anxiously down into the bloody pulpy face of his son.

There was a moment of silence, and then Johnnie answered in his ordinary voice: "Yes, I—it—yes."

Assisted by his father he struggled to his feet. "Wait a bit now till you git your wind," said the old man.

A few paces away the cowboy was lecturing the Swede. "No, you don't! Wait a second!"

The Easterner was plucking at Scully's sleeve. "Oh, this is enough," he pleaded. "This is enough! Let it go as it stands. This is enough!"

"Bill," said Scully, "git out of the road." The cowboy stepped aside. "Now." The combatants were actuated by a new caution as they advanced toward collision. They glared at each other, and then the Swede aimed a lightning blow that carried with it his entire weight. Johnnie was evidently half-stupid from weakness, but he miraculously dodged, and his fist sent the overbalanced Swede sprawling.

The cowboy, Scully and the Easterner burst into a cheer that was like a chorus of triumphant soldiery, but before its conclusion the Swede had scuffled agilely to his feet and come in berserk abandon at his foe. There was another perplexity of flying arms, and Johnnie's body again swung away and fell, even as a bundle might fall from a roof. The Swede instantly staggered to a little wind-waved tree and leaned upon it, breathing like an engine, while his savage and flame-lit eyes roamed from face to face as the men bent over Johnnie. There was a splendor of isolation in his situation at this time which the Easterner felt once when, lifting his eyes from the man on the ground, he beheld that mysterious and lonely figure, waiting.

"Are you any good yet, Johnnie?" asked Scully in a broken voice.

The son gasped and opened his eyes languidly. After a moment he answered: "No—I ain't—any good—any—more." Then, from shame and bodily ill, he began to weep, the tears furrowing down through the bloodstains on his face. "He was too—too—too heavy for me."

Scully straightened and addressed the waiting figure. "Stranger," he said, evenly, "it's all up with our side." Then his voice changed into that vibrant huskiness which is commonly the tone of the most simple and deadly announcements. "Johnnie is whipped."

Without replying, the victor moved off on the route to the front door of the hotel.

The cowboy was formulating new and unspellable blasphemies. The Easterner was startled to find that they were out in a wind that seemed to come direct from the shadowed arctic floes. He heard again the wail of the snow as it was flung to its grave in the south. He knew now that all this time the cold had been sinking into him deeper and deeper, and he wondered that he had not perished. He felt indifferent to the condition of the vanquished man.

"Johnnie, can you walk?" asked Scully.

"Did I hurt—hurt him any?" asked the son.

"Can you walk, boy? Can you walk?"

Johnnie's voice was suddenly strong. There was a robust impatience in it. "I asked you whether I hurt him any!"

"Yes, yes, Johnnie," answered the cowboy consolingly; "he's hurt a good deal."

They raised him from the ground, and as soon as he was on his feet he went tottering off, rebuffing all attempts at assistance. When the party rounded the corner they were fairly blinded by the pelting of the snow. It burned their faces like fire. The cowboy carried Johnnie through the drift to the door. As they entered some cards again rose from the floor and beat against the wall.

The Easterner rushed to the stove. He was so profoundly chilled that he almost dared to embrace the glowing iron. The Swede was not in the room. Johnnie sank into a chair, and folding his arms on his knees, buried his face in them. Scully, warming one foot and then the other at a rim of the stove, muttered to himself with Celtic mournfulness. The cowboy had removed his fur-cap, and with a dazed and rueful air he was now running one hand through his tousled locks. From overhead they could hear the creaking of boards, as the Swede tramped here and there in his room.

The sad quiet was broken by the sudden flinging open of a door that led toward the kitchen. It was instantly followed by an inrush of women. They precipitated themselves upon Johnnie amid a chorus of lamentation. Before they carried their prey off to the kitchen, there to be bathed and harangued with that mixture of sympathy and abuse which is a feat of their sex, the mother straightened herself and fixed old Scully with an eye of stern reproach. "Shame be upon you, Patrick Scully!" she cried. "Your own son, too. Shame be upon you!"

"There, now! Be quiet, now!" said the old man weakly.

"Shame be upon you, Patrick Scully!" The girls, rallying to this slogan, sniffed disdainfully in the direction of those trembling accomplices, the cowboy and the Easterner. Presently they bore Johnnie away, and left the three men to dismal reflection.

VII

"I'd like to fight this here Dutchman myself," said the cowboy, breaking a long silence.

Scully wagged his head sadly. "No, that wouldn't do. It wouldn't be right. It wouldn't be right."

"Well, why wouldn't it?" argued the cowboy. "I don't see no harm in it."

"No," answered Scully with mournful heroism. "It wouldn't be right. It was Johnnie's fight, and now we mustn't whip the man just because he whipped Johnnie."

"Yes, that's true enough," said the cowboy; "but—he better not get fresh with me, because I couldn't stand no more of it."

"You'll not say a word to him," commanded Scully, and even then they heard the tread of the Swede on the stairs. His entrance was made theatric. He swept the door back with a bang and swaggered to the middle of the room. No one looked at him. "Well," he cried, insolently, at Scully. "I s'pose you'll tell me now how much I owe you?"

The old man remained stolid. "You don't owe me nothin'."

"Huh!" cried the Swede, "huh! Don't owe 'im nothin'."

The cowboy addressed the Swede. "Stranger, I don't see how you come to be so gay around here."

Old Scully was instantly alert. "Stop!" he shouted, holding his hand forth, fingers upward. "Bill, you shut up!"

The cowboy spat carelessly into the sawdust box. "I didn't say a word, did I?" he asked.

"Mr. Scully," called the Swede, "how much do I owe you?" It was seen that he was attired for departure, and that he had his valise in his hand.

"You don't owe me nothin'," repeated Scully in his same imperturbable way.

"Huh!" said the Swede. "I guess you're right. I guess if it was any way at all, you'd owe me somethin'. That's what I guess." He turned to the cowboy. "'Kill him! Kill him! Kill him!'" he mimicked, and then guffawed victoriously. "'Kill him!'" He was convulsed with ironical humor.

But he might have been jeering the dead. The three men were immovable and silent, staring with glassy eyes at the stove.

The Swede opened the door and passed into the storm, giving one derisive glance backward at the still group.

As soon as the door was closed, Scully and the cowboy leaped to their feet and began to curse. They trampled to and fro, waving their arms and smashing into the air with their fists. "Oh, but that was a hard minute!" wailed Scully. "That was a hard minute! Him there leerin' and scoffin'! One bang at his nose was worth forty dollars to me that minute! How did you stand it, Bill?"

"How did I stand it?" cried the cowboy in a quivering voice. "How did I stand it? Oh!"

The old man burst into sudden brogue. "I'd loike to take that Swade," he wailed, "and hould 'im down on a shtone flure and bate 'im to a jelly wid a shtick!"

The cowboy groaned in sympathy. "I'd like to git him by the neck and ha-ammer him"—he brought his hand down on a chair with a noise like a pistol-shot—"hammer that there Dutchman until he couldn't tell himself from a dead coyote!"

"I'd bate 'im until he——"

"I'd show *him* some things——"

And then together they raised a yearning fanatic cry. "Oh-o-oh! if we only could——"

"Yes!"

"Yes!"

"And then I'd——"

"O-o-oh!"

VIII

The Swede, tightly gripping his valise, tacked across the face of the storm as if he carried sails. He was following a line of little naked gasping trees, which he knew must mark the way of the road. His face, fresh from the pounding of Johnnie's fists, felt more pleasure than pain in the wind and the driving snow. A number of square shapes loomed upon him finally, and he knew them as the houses of the main body of the town. He found a street and made travel along it, leaning heavily upon the wind whenever, at a corner, a terrific blast caught him.

He might have been in a deserted village. We picture the world as thick with conquering and elate humanity, but here, with the bugles of the tempest pealing, it was hard to imagine a peopled earth. One viewed the existence of man then as a marvel, and conceded a glamour of wonder to these lice which were caused to cling to a whirling, fire-smote, ice-locked, disease-stricken, space-lost bulb. The conceit of man was explained by this storm to be the very engine of life. One was a coxcomb not to die in it. However, the Swede found a saloon.

In front of it an indomitable red light was burning, and the snow-flakes were made blood-color as they flew through the circumscribed territory of the lamp's shining. The Swede pushed open the door of the saloon and entered. A sanded expanse was before him, and at the end of it four men sat about a table drinking. Down one side of the room extended a radiant bar, and its guardian was leaning upon his elbows listening to the talk of the men at the table. The Swede dropped his valise upon the floor, and, smiling fraternally upon the barkeeper, said: "Gimme some whisky, will you?" The man placed a bottle, a whisky-glass, and a glass of ice-thick water upon the bar. The Swede poured himself an abnormal portion of whisky and drank it in three gulps. "Pretty bad night," remarked the bartender indifferently. He was making the pretension of blindness, which is usually a distinction of his class; but it could have been seen that he was furtively studying the half-erased blood-stains on the face of the Swede. "Bad night," he said again.

"Oh, it's good enough for me," replied the Swede, hardily, as he poured himself more whisky. The barkeeper took his coin and maneuvered it through its reception by the highly-nickeled cash-machine. A bell rang; a card labeled "20 cts." had appeared.

"No," continued the Swede, "this isn't too bad weather. It's good enough for me."

"So?" murmured the barkeeper languidly.

The copious drams made the Swede's eyes swim, and he breathed a trifle heavier. "Yes, I like this weather. I like it. It suits me." It was apparently his design to impart a deep significance to these words.

"So?" murmured the bartender again. He turned to gaze dreamily at the scroll-like birds and bird-like scrolls which had been drawn with soap upon the mirrors back of the bar.

"Well, I guess I'll take another drink," said the Swede presently. "Have something?"

"No, thanks; I'm not drinkin'," answered the bartender. Afterward he asked: "How did you hurt your face?"

The Swede immediately began to boast loudly. "Why, in a fight. I thumped the soul out of a man down here at Scully's hotel."

The interest of the four men at the table was at last aroused.

"Who was it?" said one.

"Johnnie Scully," blustered the Swede. "Son of the man what runs it. He will be pretty near dead for some weeks, I can tell you. I made a nice thing of him, I did. He couldn't get up. They carried him in the house. Have a drink?"

Instantly the men in some subtle way incased themselves in reserve. "No, thanks," said one. The group was of curious formation. Two were prominent local business men; one was the district-attorney; and one was a professional gambler of the kind known as "square." But a scrutiny of the group would not have enabled an observer to pick the gambler from the men of more reputable pursuits. He was, in fact, a man so delicate in manner, when among people of fair class, and so judicious in his choice of victims, that in the strictly masculine part of the town's life he had come to be explicitly trusted and admired. People called him a thoroughbred. The fear and contempt with which his craft was regarded was undoubtedly the reason that his quiet dignity shone conspicuous above the quiet dignity of men who might be merely hatters, billiard-markers[5] or grocery clerks. Beyond an occasional unwary traveler, who came by rail, this gambler was supposed to prey solely upon reckless and senile farmers, who, when flush with good crops, drove into town in all the pride and confidence of an absolutely invulnerable stupidity. Hearing at times in circuitous fashion of the despoilment of such a farmer, the important men of Romper invariably laughed in contempt of the victim, and if they thought of the wolf at all, it was a kind of pride at the knowledge that he would never dare think of attacking their wisdom and courage. Besides, it was popular that this gambler had a real wife and two real children in a neat cottage in a suburb, where he led an exemplary home life, and when any one even suggested a discrepancy in his character, the crowd immediately vociferated descriptions of this virtuous family circle. Then men who led exemplary home lives, and men who did not lead exemplary home lives, all subsided in a bunch, remarking that there was nothing more to be said.

However, when a restriction was placed upon him—as, for instance, when a strong clique of members of the new Pollywog Club refused to permit him, even as a spectator, to appear in the rooms of the organization—the candor and gentleness with which he accepted the judgment disarmed many of his foes and made his friends more desperately partisan. He invariably distinguished between himself and a respectable Romper man so quickly and frankly that his manner actually appeared to be a continual broadcast compliment.

And one must not forget to declare the fundamental fact of his entire position in Romper. It is irrefutable that in all affairs outside of his business, in all matters that occur eternally and commonly between man and man, this thieving card-player was so generous, so just, so moral, that, in a contest, he could have put to flight the consciences of nine-tenths of the citizens of Romper.

And so it happened that he was seated in this saloon with the two prominent local merchants and the district-attorney.

The Swede continued to drink raw whisky, meanwhile babbling at the barkeeper and trying to induce him to indulge in potations. "Come on. Have a drink. Come on. What—no? Well, have a little one then. By gawd, I've whipped a man to-night, and I want to celebrate. I whipped him good, too. Gentlemen," the Swede cried to the men at the table, "have a drink?"

"Ssh!" said the barkeeper.

The group at the table, although furtively attentive, had been pretending to be deep in talk, but now a man lifted his eyes toward the Swede and said shortly: "Thanks. We don't want any more."

---

5. Scorekeepers at billiards matches.

At this reply the Swede ruffled out his chest like a rooster. "Well," he exploded, "it seems I can't get anybody to drink with me in this town. Seems so, don't it? Well!"

"Ssh!" said the barkeeper.

"Say," snarled the Swede, "don't you try to shut me up. I won't have it. I'm a gentleman, and I want people to drink with me. And I want 'em to drink with me now. Now—do you understand?" He rapped the bar with his knuckles.

Years of experience had calloused the bartender. He merely grew sulky. "I hear you," he answered.

"Well," cried the Swede, "listen hard then. See those men over there? Well, they're going to drink with me, and don't you forget it. Now you watch."

"Hi!" yelled the barkeeper, "this won't do!"

"Why won't it?" demanded the Swede. He stalked over to the table, and by chance laid his hand upon the shoulder of the gambler. "How about this?" he asked, wrathfully. "I asked you to drink with me."

The gambler simply twisted his head and spoke over his shoulder. "My friend, I don't know you."

"Oh, hell!" answered the Swede, "come and have a drink."

"Now, my boy," advised the gambler kindly, "take your hand off my shoulder and go 'way and mind your own business." He was a little slim man, and it seemed strange to hear him use this tone of heroic patronage to the burly Swede. The other men at the table said nothing.

"What? You won't drink with me, you little dude! I'll make you then! I'll make you!" The Swede had grasped the gambler frenziedly at the throat, and was dragging him from his chair. The other men sprang up. The barkeeper dashed around the corner of his bar. There was a great tumult, and then was seen a long blade in the hand of the gambler. It shot forward, and a human body, this citadel of virtue, wisdom, power, was pierced as easily as if it had been a melon. The Swede fell with a cry of supreme astonishment.

The prominent merchants and the district-attorney must have at once tumbled out of the place backward. The bartender found himself hanging limply to the arm of a chair and gazing into the eyes of a murderer.

"Henry," said the latter, as he wiped his knife on one of the towels that hung beneath the bar-rail, "you tell 'em where to find me. I'll be home, waiting for 'em." Then he vanished. A moment afterward the barkeeper was in the street dinning through the storm for help, and, moreover, companionship.

The corpse of the Swede, alone in the saloon, had its eyes fixed upon a dreadful legend that dwelt a-top of the cash-machine. "This registers the amount of your purchase."

IX

Months later, the cowboy was frying pork over the stove of a little ranch near the Dakota line, when there was a quick thud of hoofs outside, and, presently, the Easterner entered with the letters and the papers.

"Well," said the Easterner at once, "the chap that killed the Swede has got three years. Wasn't much, was it?"

"He has? Three years?" The cowboy poised his pan of pork, while he ruminated upon the news. "Three years. That ain't much."

"No. It was a light sentence," replied the Easterner as he unbuckled his spurs. "Seems there was a good deal of sympathy for him in Romper."

"If the bartender had been any good," observed the cowboy thoughtfully, "he would have gone in and cracked that there Dutchman on the head with a bottle in the beginnin' of it and stopped all this here murderin'."

"Yes, a thousand things might have happened," said the Easterner tartly.

The cowboy returned his pan of pork to the fire, but his philosophy continued. "It's funny, ain't it? If he hadn't said Johnnie was cheatin' he'd be alive this minute. He was an awful fool. Game played for fun, too. Not for money. I believe he was crazy."

"I feel sorry for that gambler," said the Easterner.

"Oh, so do I," said the cowboy. "He don't deserve none of it for killin' who he did."

"The Swede might not have been killed if everything had been square."

"Might not have been killed?" exclaimed the cowboy. "Everythin' square? Why, when he said that Johnnie was cheatin' and acted like such a jackass? And then in the saloon he fairly walked up to git hurt?" With these arguments the cowboy browbeat the Easterner and reduced him to rage.

"You're a fool!" cried the Easterner viciously. "You're a bigger jackass than the Swede by a million majority. Now let me tell you one thing. Let me tell you something. Listen! Johnnie *was* cheating!"

"'Johnnie,'" said the cowboy blankly. There was a minute of silence, and then he said robustly: "Why, no. The game was only for fun."

"Fun or not," said the Easterner, "Johnnie was cheating. I saw him. I know it. I saw him. And I refused to stand up and be a man. I let the Swede fight it out alone. And you—you were simply puffing around the place and wanting to fight. And then old Scully himself! We are all in it! This poor gambler isn't even a noun. He is kind of an adverb. Every sin is the result of a collaboration. We, five of us, have collaborated in the murder of this Swede. Usually there are from a dozen to forty women really involved in every murder, but in this case it seems to be only five men—you, I, Johnnie, old Scully, and that fool of an unfortunate gambler came merely as a culmination, the apex of a human movement, and gets all the punishment."

The cowboy, injured and rebellious, cried out blindly into this fog of mysterious theory. "Well, I didn't do anythin', did I?"

1898, 1902

From The Black Riders[1]

VI

God fashioned the ship of the world carefully.
With the infinite skill of an all-master
Made He the hull and the sails,
Held He the rudder
Ready for adjustment.　　　　　　　　　　5
Erect stood He, scanning His work proudly.
Then—at fateful time—a wrong called,
And God turned, heeding.

1. First published in *"The Black Riders" and Other Lines* by Stephen Crane (1896); rpt. in Stephen Crane: *Prose and Poetry* (1984), from which this text is taken.

Lo, the ship, at this opportunity, slipped slyly,
Making cunning noiseless travel down the ways.   10
So that, forever rudderless, it went upon the seas
Going ridiculous voyages,
Making quaint progress,
Turning as with serious purpose
Before stupid winds.   15
And there were many in the sky
Who laughed at this thing.

*   *   *

XXIV

I saw a man pursuing the horizon;
Round and round they sped.
I was disturbed at this;
I accosted the man.
"It is futile," I said,   5
"You can never——"

"You lie," he cried,
And ran on.

1896

From War Is Kind[1]

I

Do not weep, maiden, for war is kind.
Because your lover threw wild hands toward the sky
And the affrighted steed ran on alone,
Do not weep.
War is kind.   5

> Hoarse, booming drums of the regiment
> Little souls who thirst for fight,
> These men were born to drill and die
> The unexplained glory flies above them
> Great is the battle-god, great, and his kingdom——   10
> A field where a thousand corpses lie.

Do not weep, babe, for war is kind.
Because your father tumbled in the yellow trenches,
Raged at his breast, gulped and died,
Do not weep.   15
War is kind.

---

1. First published in *"War Is Kind" and Other Lines* (1899); rpt. in *Stephen Crane: Prose and Poetry* (1984), from which this text is taken.

Swift, blazing flag of the regiment
Eagle with crest of red and gold,
These men were born to drill and die
Point for them the virtue of slaughter   20
Make plain to them the excellence of killing
And a field where a thousand corpses lie.

Mother whose heart hung humble as a button
On the bright splendid shroud of your son,
Do not weep.   25
War is kind.

*   *   *

XIX

The chatter of a death-demon from a tree-top.

Blood—blood and torn grass—
Had marked the rise of his agony——
This lone hunter.
The grey-green woods impassive   5
Had watched the threshing of his limbs.

A canoe with flashing paddle
A girl with soft searching eyes,
A call: "John!"

Come, arise, hunter!   10
Can you not hear?

The chatter of a death-demon from a tree-top.

XX

The impact of a dollar upon the heart
Smiles warm red light
Sweeping from the hearth rosily upon the white table,
With the hanging cool velvet shadows
Moving softly upon the door.   5

The impact of a million dollars
Is a crash of flunkeys
And yawning emblems of Persia
Cheeked against oak, France and a sabre,
The outcry of old Beauty   10
Whored by pimping merchants
To submission before wine and chatter.
Silly rich peasants stamp the carpets of men,
Dead men who dreamed fragrance and light
Into their woof, their lives;   15
The rug of an honest bear
Under the feet of a cryptic slave
Who speaks always of baubles

Forgetting place, multitude, work and state,
Champing and mouthing of hats   20
Making ratful squeak of hats,
Hats.

XXI

A man said to the universe:
"Sir, I exist!"
"However," replied the universe,
"The fact has not created in me   5
"A sense of obligation."

XXII

When the prophet, a complacent fat man,
Arrived at the mountain-top
He cried: "Woe to my knowledge!
I intended to see good white lands
And bad black lands,   5
But the scene is grey."

1899

PAUL LAURENCE DUNBAR
1872–1906

Paul Laurence Dunbar was one of the first professional African American literary figures, publishing six volumes of poetry, beginning with *Oak and Ivy* in 1893, as well as novels, librettos, songs, and essays. Dunbar's father, Joshua, who had escaped slavery in Kentucky and moved to Ohio via the Underground Railroad, served in the 55th Massachusetts Regiment of the Union Army during the Civil War. His mother, Matilda Murphy, also a former slave, separated from Joshua when Dunbar was two years old. Throughout his childhood, Matilda encouraged Paul in his education, often doing without so that he could continue in school. Though Dunbar first wanted to be a lawyer, he chose instead "to be a worthy singer of the songs of God and nature." He wanted "to interpret my own people though song and story, and prove to the many that we are more human than African."

Dunbar early on developed an ear for language and a love of Romantic poetry. Yet upon graduation from Central High School, in Dayton, Ohio, where he'd been student and class leader, the only jobs open to him were menial ones. In 1892 he was invited to read a poem at the Western Association of Writers, which was convening in Dayton. Inspired by this, he traveled in 1893 to the Columbian Exposition in Chicago, where he met Frederick Douglass and sold *Oak and Ivy* for a dollar per copy. Douglass—then U.S. minister to Haiti and Commissioner of the Haitian Exhibition—hired him as a clerk.

In 1895 Dunbar published his best-known work, *Lyrics of the Lowly Life*, from which most of the selections here are drawn. Committed to rendering the authentic voice of the black speaker, and inspired by Shakespeare, Shelley, Keats, and Tennyson, Dunbar published in such popular venues as the *New York Times*, *Century*, *Lippincott's Monthly*, and the *Saturday Evening Post*, journals with almost exclusively white readerships. Though he was celebrated by black and white literary leaders, among them Douglass, Booker T. Washington, W. E. B. DuBois, William Dean Howells, Eugene Field, and James Whitcomb Riley, he was criticized in the 1920s by Harlem Renaissance leaders who saw him as catering to a white audience with "colorful" black folk elements and dialect. Despite this criticism, Dunbar's influence on subsequent African American writers such as Zora Neale Hurston is precisely that he presented traditional dialect, customs, and other cultural elements without apology.

Dunbar married writer Alice Moore in 1898; they lived in the Le Droit Park section of Washington, DC, an area that welcomed the new black middle class and where they enjoyed the company of black intellectuals, activists, and artists. They separated in 1902, in part due to Dunbar's alcoholism, and Dunbar's poetry after that time reflects a more somber mood. When he returned to Dayton to live with his mother, he believed that he had failed as a poet. Critical and popular attention to his work continued to grow throughout the twentieth century, however, and Dunbar is now recognized as a pioneer in creating a new black poetic diction.

When Malindy Sings[1]

G'way an' quit dat noise, Miss Lucy—
   Put dat music book away;
What 's de use to keep on tryin'?
   Ef you practise twell you're gray,
You cain't sta't no notes a-flyin'   5
   Lak de ones dat rants and rings
F'om de kitchen to be big woods
   When Malindy sings.

You ain't got de nachel o'gans
   Fu' to make de soun' come right,   10
You ain't got de tu'ns an' twistin's
   Fu' to make it sweet an' light.
Tell you one thing now, Miss Lucy,
   An' I 'm tellin' you fu' true,
When hit comes to raal right singin',   15
   'T ain't no easy thing to do.

Easy 'nough fu' folks to hollah,
   Lookin' at de lines an' dots,
When dey ain't no one kin sence it,
   An' de chune comes in, in spots;   20
But fu' real melojous music,
   Dat jes' strikes yo' hea't and clings,
Jes' you stan' an' listen wif me
   When Malindy sings.

Ain't you nevah hyeahd Malindy?   25
   Blessed soul, tek up de cross!
Look hyeah, ain't you jokin', honey?
   Well, you don't know whut you los'.

1. First published in Dunbar's *Lyrics of the Lowly Life* (1897) and then in his *Complete Poems* (1903); rpt. in *The Complete Poems of Paul Laurence Dunbar* (1993), from which this text is taken.

Y' ought to hyeah dat gal a-wa'blin',
   Robins, la'ks, an' all dem things,   30
Heish dey moufs an' hides dey faces
   When Malindy sings.

Fiddlin' man jes' stop his fiddlin',
   Lay his fiddle on de she'f;
Mockin'-bird quit tryin' to whistle,   35
   'Cause he jes' so shamed hisse'f.
Folks a-playin' on de banjo
   Draps dey fingahs on de strings—
Bless yo' soul—fu'gits to move em,
   When Malindy sings.   40

She jes' spreads huh mouf and hollahs,
   "Come to Jesus," twell you hyeah
Sinnahs' tremblin' steps and voices,
   Timid-lak a-drawin' neah;
Den she tu'ns to "Rock of Ages,"   45
   Simply to de cross she clings,
An' you fin' yo' teahs a-drappin'
   When Malindy sings.

Who dat says dat humble praises
   Wif de Master nevah counts?   50
Heish yo' mouf, I hyeah dat music,
   Ez hit rises up an' mounts—
Floatin' by de hills an' valleys,
   Way above dis buryin' sod,
Ez hit makes its way in glory   55
   To de very gates of God!

Oh, hit 's sweetah dan de music
   Of an edicated band;
An' hit 's dearah dan de battle's
   Song o' triumph in de lan'.
It seems holier dan evenin'   60
   When de solemn chu'ch bell rings,
Ez I sit an' ca'mly listen
   While Malindy sings.

Towsah, stop dat ba'kin', hyeah me!   65
   Mandy, mek dat chile keep still;
Don't you hyeah de echoes callin'
   F'om de valley to de hill?
Let me listen, I can hyeah it,
   Th'oo de bresh of angels' wings,
Sof' an' sweet, "Swing Low, Sweet Chariot,"   70
   Ez Malindy sings.

1897

An Ante-Bellum Sermon[1]

We is gathahed hyeah, my brothahs,
   In dis howlin' wildaness,
Fu' to speak some words of comfo't
   To each othah in distress.
An' we chooses fu' ouah subjic'   5
   Dis—we 'll 'splain it by an' by;
"An' de Lawd said, 'Moses, Moses,'
   An' de man said, 'Hyeah am I.' "

Now ole Pher'oh, down in Egypt,
   Was de wuss man evah bo'n,   10
An' he had de Hebrew chillun
   Down dah wukin' in his co'n;
'T well de Lawd got tiahed o' his foolin',
   An' sez he: "I'll let him know—
Look hyeah, Moses, go tell Pher'oh   15
   Fu' to let dem chillun go."

"An' ef he refuse to do it,
   I will make him rue de houah,
Fu' I 'll empty down on Egypt
   All de vials of my powah."   20
Yes, he did—an' Pher'oh's ahmy
   Was n't wuth a ha'f a dime;
Fu' de Lawd will he'p his chilun,
   You kin trust him evah time.

An' yo' enemies may 'sail you   25
   In de back an' in de front;
But de Lawd is all aroun' you,
   Fu' to ba' de battle's brunt.
Dey kin fo'ge yo' chains an' shackles
   F'om de mountains to de sea;   30
But de Lawd will sen' some Moses
   Fu' to set his chillun free.

An' de lan' shall hyeah his thundah,
   Lak a blas' f'om Gab'el's ho'n,
Fu' de Lawd of hosts is mighty   35
   When he girds his ahmor on.
But fu' feah some one mistakes me,
   I will pause right hyeah to say,
Dat I 'm still a-preachin' ancient,
   I ain't talkin' 'bout to-day.   40

---

1. First published in Dunbar's *Lyrics of the Lowly Life* (1897) and then in his *Complete Poems* (1903); rpt. in *The Complete Poems of Paul Laurence Dunbar* (1993), from which this text is taken.

But I tell you, fellah christuns,
   Things 'll happen mighty strange;
Now, de Lawd done dis fu' Isrul,
   An' his ways don't nevah change,
An' de love he showed to Isrul   45
   Was n't all on Isrul spent;
Now don't run an' tell yo' mastahs
   Dat I 's preachin' discontent.

'Cause I is n't; I 'se a-judgin'
   Bible people by deir ac's;   50
I 'se a-givin' you de Scriptuah,
   I 'se a-handin' you de fac's.
Cose ole Pher'oh b'lieved in slav'ry,
   But de Lawd he let him see,
Dat de people he put bref in,—   55
   Evah mothah's son was free.

An' dahs othahs thinks lak Pher'oh,
   But dey calls de Scriptuah liar,
Fu' de Bible says "a servant
   Is a-worthy of his hire."[2]   60
An' you cain't git roun' nor thoo dat,
   An' you cain't git ovah it,
Fu' whatevah place you git in,
   Dis hyeah Bible too 'll fit.

So you see de Lawd's intention,   65
   Evah sence de worl' began,
Was dat His almighty freedom
   Should belong to evah man,
But I think it would be bettah,
   Ef I 'd pause agin to say,   70
Dat I 'm talkin' 'bout ouah freedom
   In a Bibleistic way.

But de Moses is a-comin',
   An' he 's comin', suah and fas'
We kin hyeah his feet a-trompin',   75
   We kin hyeah his trumpit blas'.
But I want to wa'n you people,
   Don't you git too brigity;[3]
An' don't you git to braggin'
   'Bout dese things, you wait an' see.   80

But when Moses wif his powah
   Comes an' sets us chillun free,
We will praise de gracious Mastah
   Dat has gin us liberty;
An' we 'll shout ouah halleluyahs,   85

---

2. Biblical mandate against the unethical practice of masters withholding wages from their servants, here used to indict slavery (Leviticus 19.13, Deuteronomy 24.15 and 25).
3. Brazen, presumptuous, or insolent.

On dat mighty reck'nin' day,
When we 'se reco'nised ez citiz'—
Huh uh! Chillun, let us pray!

1897

Sympathy[1]

I know what the caged bird feels, alas!
 When the sun is bright on the upland slopes;
When the wind stirs soft through the springing grass,
And the river flows like a stream of glass;
 When the first bird sings and the first bud opes,   5
And the faint perfume from its chalice steals—
I know what the caged bird feels!

I know why the caged bird beats his wing
 Till its blood is red on the cruel bars;
For he must fly back to his perch and cling   10
When he fain would be on the bough a-swing;
 And a pain still throbs in the old, old scars
And they pulse again with a keener sting—
I know why he beats his wing!

I know why the caged bird sings, ah me,   15
 When his wing is bruised and his bosom sore,—
When he beats his bars and he would be free;
It is not a carol of joy or glee,
 But a prayer that he sends from his heart's deep core,
But a plea, that upward to Heaven he flings—   20
I know why the caged bird sings!

1899

We Wear the Mask[1]

We wear the mask that grins and lies,
It hides our cheeks and shades our eyes,—
This debt we pay to human guile;
With torn and bleeding hearts we smile,
And mouth with myriad subtleties.   5

Why should the world be overwise,
In counting all our tears and sighs?
Nay, let them only see us, while
 We wear the mask.

---

1. First published in Dunbar's *Lyrics of the Hearthside* (1899) and then in his *Complete Poems* (1903); rpt. in *The Complete Poems of Paul Laurence Dunbar* (1993), from which this text is taken.

1. First published in Dunbar's *Lyrics of the Lowly Life* (1897) and then in his *Complete Poems* (1903); rpt. in *The Complete Poems of Paul Laurence Dunbar* (1993), from which this text is taken.

We smile, but, O great Christ, our cries   10
To thee from tortured souls arise.
We sing, but oh the clay is vile
Beneath our feet, and long the mile;
But let the world dream otherwise,
    We wear the mask!   15

1897

Frederick Douglass[1]

A hush is over all the teeming lists,
    And there is pause, a breath-space in the strife;
A spirit brave has passed beyond the mists
    And vapors that obscure the sun of life.
And Ethiopia,[2] with bosom torn,   5
Laments the passing of her noblest born.

She weeps for him a mother's burning tears—
    She loved him with a mother's deepest love.
He was her champion thro' direful years,
    And held her weal all other ends above.
When Bondage held her bleeding in the dust,   10
He raised her up and whispered, "Hope and Trust."

For her his voice, a fearless clarion, rung
    That broke in warning on the ears of men;
For her the strong bow of his power he strung,   15
    And sent his arrows to the very den
Where grim Oppression held his bloody place
And gloated o'er the mis'ries of a race.

And he was no soft-tongued apologist;
    He spoke straightforward, fearlessly uncowed;   20
The sunlight of his truth dispelled the mist,
    And set in bold relief each dark hued cloud;
To sin and crime he gave their proper hue,
And hurled at evil what was evil's due.

Through good and ill report he cleaved his way   25
    Right onward, with his face set toward the heights,
Nor feared to face the foeman's dread array,—
    The lash of scorn, the sting of petty spites.
He dared the lightning in the lightning's track,
And answered thunder with his thunder back.   30

1. First published in Dunbar's *Lyrics of Love and Laughter* (1903), then in *The Complete Poems* (1903); rpt. in *The Complete Poems of Paul Laurence Dunbar* (1993), from which this text is taken. Frederick Douglass (1818–1895) was the author of *Narrative of the Life of Frederick Douglass* (1845), in which he recounts his birth into slavery, escape into freedom, and eventual involvement with the abolitionist movement, through which he became the most prominent African American in the world. 2. Eastern African country whose long history as an independent nation made it a symbol of African independence for abolitionists, slaves, and, later, civil rights leaders.

When men maligned him, and their torrent wrath
   In furious imprecations o'er him broke,
He kept his counsel as he kept his path;
   'T was for his race, not for himself he spoke.
He knew the import of his Master's call,   35
And felt himself too mighty to be small.

No miser in the good he held was he,—
   His kindness followed his horizon's rim.
His heart, his talents, and his hands were free
   To all who truly needed aught of him.   40
Where poverty and ignorance were rife,
He gave his bounty as he gave his life.

The place and cause that first aroused his might
   Still proved its power until his latest day.
In Freedom's lists and for the aid of Right   45
   Still in the foremost rank he waged the fray;
Wrong lived; his occupation was not gone.
He died in action with his armor on!

We weep for him, but we have touched his hand,
   And felt the magic of his presence nigh,   50
The current that he sent throughout the land,
   The kindling spirit of his battlecry.
O'er all that holds us we shall triumph yet,
And place our banner where his hopes were set!

Oh, Douglass, thou hast passed beyond the shore,   55
   But still thy voice is ringing o'er the gale!
Thou 'st taught thy race how high her hopes may soar,
   And bade her seek the heights, nor faint, nor fail.
She will not fail, she heeds thy stirring cry,
She knows thy guardian spirit will be nigh,   60
And, rising from beneath the chast'ning rod,
She stretches out her bleeding hands to God!

1903

Harriet Beecher Stowe[1]

She told the story, and the whole world wept
   At wrongs and cruelties it had not known
   But for this fearless woman's voice alone.
She spoke to consciences that long had slept:
Her message, Freedom's clear reveille, swept   5
   From heedless hovel to complacent throne.

1. First published in Dunbar's *Lyrics of the Hearth-side* (1899) and then in his *Complete Poems* (1903); rpt. in *The Complete Poems of Paul Laurence Dunbar* (1993), from which this text is taken.

Harriet Beecher Stowe (1811–1896), abolitionist and author of many books, the most famous being *Uncle Tom's Cabin* (1852).

Command and prophecy were in the tone
And from its sheath the sword of justice leapt.
Around two peoples swelled a fiery wave,
But both came forth transfigured from the flame.   10
Blest be the hand that dared be strong to save,
And blest be she who in our weakness came—
Prophet and priestess! At one stroke she gave
A race to freedom and herself to fame.

1899

JACK LONDON
1876–1916

John Griffith Chaney was born in San Francisco, California, on January 12, 1876, the son of Flora Wellman Chaney, spiritualist and common-law wife of William H. Chaney, an itinerant astrologer who abandoned Flora on learning of her pregnancy. Nine months after the child's birth, Flora married John London, a Civil War veteran and construction worker who adopted "Johnny." As a child, London escaped some of the unhappiness at home by living on and off with the Prentisses, African American neighbors who called him "Jack" and who served as surrogate parents until, at the age of fifteen, he sailed San Francisco Bay as an oyster pirate, going on to become a member of the California Fish Patrol. Drinking with the oyster pirates and the Fish Patrol, London developed the habit of what would later become full-blown alcoholism. Entranced by the sea and its possibilities, he sailed aboard the sealing ship the *Sophia Sutherland* in 1893, returning home in 1893 to publish his first, prize-winning, story, "Typhoon Off the Coast of Japan," in the San Francisco *Morning Call*.

In 1894, following the Panic of 1893, London marched east with a contingent of Coxey's Army, an organized group of the unemployed planning to agitate for jobs in Washington D.C. He was arrested as a vagrant at Niagara Falls and did thirty days of hard time in the Erie County Penitentiary in Buffalo, New York. Returning home, he vowed to educate himself, and he also turned to Socialism, running for mayor of Oakland twice on the socialist ticket. At the age of twenty he was accepted to the University of California, but, lacking money, he attended for only one semester. The most important event of London's early life occurred in 1897, when, at age twenty-one, he headed to Alaska to take part in the Klondike Gold Rush. In 1900, the prestigious *Atlantic Monthly* featured his story "An Odyssey of the North" in its January issue; Houghton-Mifflin published his first book, *The Son of the Wolf*; and he married Bessie Mae Maddern, with whom he went on to have two daughters before their divorce in 1905 and his marriage to Charmian Kittredge London. In these years he also traveled to London, England, to write the sociological exposé *The People of the Abyss* (1903) and to Korea to cover the Russo-Japanese War of 1904, and he bought land in Sonoma County, experimenting with terracing and organic farming decades ahead of other California ranchers. He wrote one thousand words per day and won international acclaim with *The Call of the Wild* (1903) and *The Sea-Wolf* (1904). Later, after his extensive South Seas travels and residence in Hawai'i, he became modern America's first Pacific Rim writer.

London, though he said he wrote only for money, was a disciplined and careful craftsman, drawing from many literary, philosophical, scientific, and other sources, and writing on many subjects. His writings reflect the social and intellectual turbulence of the turn of the twentieth century, including his competing sympathies with socialism, Social Darwinism, and Nietzschean individualism; his startling combination of urban settings and characters with the pastoral and exotic; his conflicted ideas about race; his dual identity as a "literary" writer of the emerging naturalist school and a mass-market phenomenon. London was an important influence on later writers such as Ernest Hemingway, Richard Wright, and Américo Paredes for both his adventure writing and his socialist works, such as "The Mexican," "South of the Slot," and his many socialist essays.

Snubbed by the critical establishment (especially during the Cold War) as too popular and too politically unorthodox, London's writings have attracted new interest from scholars not only for their literary artistry but also for what they show about the cultural and historical issues of his era, especially race and class. By the time he died in 1916, London was the best-selling author in America and was on his way to becoming the most popular American writer in the world, a place he arguably holds today, with his works translated into over one hundred languages. In a writing career of only twenty years, London published 18 novels, 198 short stories, three plays, and hundreds of nonfiction books and articles. His ranch, now the Jack London State Historic Park in Glen Ellen, California, attracts visitors year-round.

To Build a Fire[1]

Day had broken cold and gray, exceedingly cold and gray, when the man turned aside from the main Yukon trail and climbed the high earth-bank, where a dim and little-travelled trail led eastward through the fat spruce timberland. It was a steep bank, and he paused for breath at the top, excusing the act to himself by looking at his watch. It was nine o'clock. There was no sun nor hint of sun, though there was not a cloud in the sky. It was a clear day, and yet there seemed an intangible pall over the face of things, a subtle gloom that made the day dark, and that was due to the absence of sun. This fact did not worry the man. He was used to the lack of sun. It had been days since he had seen the sun, and he knew that a few more days must pass before that cheerful orb, due south, would just peep above the sky-line and dip immediately from view.

The man flung a look back along the way he had come. The Yukon lay a mile wide and hidden under three feet of ice. On top of this ice were as many feet of snow. It was all pure white, rolling in gentle undulations where the ice-jams of the freeze-up had formed. North and south, as far as his eye could see, it was unbroken white, save for a dark hair-line that curved and twisted from around the spruce-covered island to the south, and that curved and twisted away into the north, where it disappeared behind another spruce-covered island. This dark hair-line was the trail—the main trail—that led south five hundred miles to the Chilcoot Pass, Dyea, and salt water; and that led north seventy miles to Dawson, and still on to the north a thousand miles

---

1. First published in *The Youth's Companion* for May 29, 1902, in a version of 2,700 words—"for boys only," according to London. The later, widely anthologized version of 7,235 words, written while London was struggling to survive his South Seas voyage aboard his sailboat the *Snark*, was first published in *The Century Magazine* 76 (August 1908). The text here is that of the 1910 collection *Lost Face*.

to Nulato, and finally to St. Michael on Bering Sea, a thousand miles and half a thousand more.[2]

But all this—the mysterious, far-reaching hair-line trail, the absence of sun from the sky, the tremendous cold, and the strangeness and weirdness of it all—made no impression on the man. It was not because he was long used to it. He was a newcomer in the land, a *chechaquo*, and this was his first winter. The trouble with him was that he was without imagination. He was quick and alert in the things of life, but only in the things, and not in the significances. Fifty degrees below zero meant eighty-odd degrees of frost. Such fact impressed him as being cold and uncomfortable, and that was all. It did not lead him to meditate upon his frailty as a creature of temperature, and upon man's frailty in general, able only to live within certain narrow limits of heat and cold; and from there on it did not lead him to the conjectural field of immortality and man's place in the universe. Fifty degrees below zero stood for a bite of frost that hurt and that must be guarded against by the use of mittens, ear-flaps, warm moccasins, and thick socks. Fifty degrees below zero was to him just precisely fifty degrees below zero. That there should be anything more to it than that was a thought that never entered his head.

As he turned to go on, he spat speculatively. There was a sharp, explosive crackle that startled him. He spat again. And again, in the air, before it could fall to the snow, the spittle crackled. He knew that at fifty below spittle crackled on the snow, but this spittle had crackled in the air. Undoubtedly it was colder than fifty below—how much colder he did not know. But the temperature did not matter. He was bound for the old claim on the left fork of Henderson Creek, where the boys were already. They had come over across the divide from the Indian Creek country, while he had come the roundabout way to take a look at the possibilities of getting out logs in the spring from the islands in the Yukon. He would be in to camp by six o'clock; a bit after dark, it was true, but the boys would be there, a fire would be going, and a hot supper would be ready. As for lunch, he pressed his hand against the protruding bundle under his jacket. It was also under his shirt, wrapped up in a handkerchief and lying against the naked skin. It was the only way to keep the biscuits from freezing. He smiled agreeably to himself as he thought of those biscuits, each cut open and sopped in bacon grease, and each enclosing a generous slice of fried bacon.

He plunged in among the big spruce trees. The trail was faint. A foot of snow had fallen since the last sled had passed over, and he was glad he was without a sled, travelling light. In fact, he carried nothing but the lunch wrapped in the handkerchief. He was surprised, however, at the cold. It certainly was cold, he concluded, as he rubbed his numb nose and cheek-bones with his mittened hand. He was a warm-whiskered man, but the hair on his face did not protect the high cheek-bones and the eager nose that thrust itself aggressively into the frosty air.

2. The narrator surveys the entire length of Alaska and the Canadian Yukon, from the steep Chilcoot Pass near Skagway, which prospective miners first scaled in the winter of 1897–98 to enter the Yukon; to Dyea, a shabby settlement where they disembarked onto a swampy beach; to Dawson, the hub of the Klondike gold rush; and finally to Nulato and St. Michael, sparse settlements on the way to the mouth of the Yukon River, from which miners would sail for home. The Yukon is one of the few rivers that flows north. London floated "up" the Yukon from Dawson to St. Michael in the spring of 1898 to return home after unsuccessfully prospecting for gold. This journey was the subject of his first Klondike writings.

At the man's heels trotted a dog, a big native husky, the proper wolf-dog, gray-coated and without any visible or temperamental difference from its brother, the wild wolf. The animal was depressed by the tremendous cold. It knew that it was no time for travelling. Its instinct told it a truer tale than was told to the man by the man's judgment. In reality, it was not merely colder than fifty below zero; it was colder than sixty below, than seventy below. It was seventy-five below zero. Since the freezing-point is thirty-two above zero, it meant that one hundred and seven degrees of frost obtained. The dog did not know anything about thermometers. Possibly in its brain there was no sharp consciousness of a condition of very cold such as was in the man's brain. But the brute had its instinct. It experienced a vague but menacing apprehension that subdued it and made it slink along at the man's heels, and that made it question eagerly every unwonted movement of the man as if expecting him to go into camp or to seek shelter somewhere and build a fire. The dog had learned fire, and it wanted fire, or else to burrow under the snow and cuddle its warmth away from the air.

The frozen moisture of its breathing had settled on its fur in a fine powder of frost, and especially were its jowls, muzzle, and eyelashes whitened by its crystalled breath. The man's red beard and mustache were likewise frosted, but more solidly, the deposit taking the form of ice and increasing with every warm, moist breath he exhaled. Also, the man was chewing tobacco, and the muzzle of ice held his lips so rigidly that he was unable to clear his chin when he expelled the juice. The result was that a crystal beard of the color and solidity of amber was increasing its length on his chin. If he fell down it would shatter itself, like glass, into brittle fragments. But he did not mind the appendage. It was the penalty all tobacco-chewers paid in that country, and he had been out before in two cold snaps. They had not been so cold as this, he knew, but by the spirit thermometer at Sixty Mile he knew they had been registered at fifty below and at fifty-five.

He held on through the level stretch of woods for several miles, crossed a wide flat of niggerheads,[3] and dropped down a bank to the frozen bed of a small stream. This was Henderson Creek, and he knew he was ten miles from the forks. He looked at his watch. It was ten o'clock. He was making four miles an hour, and he calculated that he would arrive at the forks at half-past twelve. He decided to celebrate that event by eating his lunch there.

The dog dropped in again at his heels, with a tail drooping discouragement, as the man swung along the creek-bed. The furrow of the old sled-trail was plainly visible, but a dozen inches of snow covered the marks of the last runners. In a month no man had come up or down that silent creek. The man held steadily on. He was not much given to thinking, and just then particularly he had nothing to think about save that he would eat lunch at the forks and that at six o'clock he would be in camp with the boys. There was nobody to talk to; and, had there been, speech would have been impossible because of the ice-muzzle on his mouth. So he continued monotonously to chew tobacco and to increase the length of his amber beard.

Once in a while the thought reiterated itself that it was very cold and that he had never experienced such cold. As he walked along he rubbed his cheek-bones and nose with the back of his mittened hand. He did this automatically,

---

3. Racially charged name of a strong dark chewing tobacco of the period, applied here to large hummocks of earth under the snow that are created by centuries of alternate freezing and thawing.

now and again changing hands. But rub as he would, the instant he stopped his cheek-bones went numb, and the following instant the end of his nose went numb. He was sure to frost his cheeks; he knew that, and experienced a pang of regret that he had not devised a nose-strap of the sort Bud wore in cold snaps. Such a strap passed across the cheeks, as well, and saved them. But it didn't matter much, after all. What were frosted cheeks? A bit painful, that was all; they were never serious.

Empty as the man's mind was of thoughts, he was keenly observant, and he noticed the changes in the creek, the curves and bends and timber-jams, and always he sharply noted where he placed his feet. Once, coming around a bend, he shied abruptly, like a startled horse, curved away from the place where he had been walking, and retreated several paces back along the trail. The creek he knew was frozen clear to the bottom,—no creek could contain water in that arctic winter,—but he knew also that there were springs that bubbled out from the hillsides and ran along under the snow and on top the ice of the creek. He knew that the coldest snaps never froze these springs, and he knew likewise their danger. They were traps. They hid pools of water under the snow that might be three inches deep, or three feet. Sometimes a skin of ice half an inch thick covered them, and in turn was covered by the snow. Sometimes there were alternate layers of water and ice-skin, so that when one broke through he kept on breaking through for a while, sometimes wetting himself to the waist.

That was why he had shied in such panic. He had felt the give under his feet and heard the crackle of snow-hidden ice-skin. And to get his feet wet in such a temperature meant trouble and danger. At the very least it meant delay, for he would be forced to stop and build a fire, and under its protection to bare his feet while he dried his socks and moccasins. He stood and studied the creek-bed and its banks, and decided that the flow of water came from the right. He reflected awhile, rubbing his nose and cheeks, then skirted to the left, stepping gingerly and testing the footing for each step. Once clear of the danger, he took a fresh chew of tobacco and swung along at his four-mile gait.

In the course of the next two hours he came upon several similar traps. Usually the snow above the hidden pools had a sunken, candied appearance that advertised the danger. Once again, however, he had a close call; and once, suspecting danger, he compelled the dog to go on in front. The dog did not want to go. It hung back until the man shoved it forward, and then it went quickly across the white, unbroken surface. Suddenly it broke through, floundered to one side, and got away to firmer footing. It had wet its forefeet and legs, and almost immediately the water that clung to it turned to ice. It made quick efforts to lick the ice off its legs, then dropped down in the snow and began to bite out the ice that had formed between the toes. This was a matter of instinct. To permit the ice to remain would mean sore feet. It did not know this. It merely obeyed the mysterious prompting that arose from the deep crypts of its being. But the man knew, having achieved a judgment on the subject, and he removed the mitten from his right hand and helped tear out the ice-particles. He did not expose his fingers more than a minute, and was astonished at the swift numbness that smote them. It certainly was cold. He pulled on the mitten hastily, and beat the hand savagely across his chest.

At twelve o'clock the day was at its brightest. Yet the sun was too far south on its winter journey to clear the horizon. The bulge of the earth intervened between it and Henderson Creek, where the man walked under a clear sky at noon and cast no shadow. At half-past twelve, to the minute, he arrived at the forks of the creek. He was pleased at the speed he had made. If he kept it up, he would certainly be with the boys by six. He unbuttoned his jacket and shirt and drew forth his lunch. The action consumed no more than a quarter of a minute, yet in that brief moment the numbness laid hold of the exposed fingers. He did not put the mitten on, but, instead, struck the fingers a dozen sharp smashes against his leg. Then he sat down on a snow-covered log to eat. The sting that followed upon the striking of his fingers against his leg ceased so quickly that he was startled. He had had no chance to take a bite of biscuit. He struck the fingers repeatedly and returned them to the mitten, baring the other hand for the purpose of eating. He tried to take a mouthful, but the ice-muzzle prevented. He had forgotten to build a fire and thaw out. He chuckled at his foolishness, and as he chuckled he noted the numbness creeping into the exposed fingers. Also, he noted that the stinging which had first come to his toes when he sat down was already passing away. He wondered whether the toes were warm or numb. He moved them inside the moccasins and decided that they were numb.

He pulled the mitten on hurriedly and stood up. He was a bit frightened. He stamped up and down until the stinging returned into the feet. It certainly was cold, was his thought. That man from Sulphur Creek[4] had spoken the truth when telling how cold it sometimes got in the country. And he had laughed at him at the time! That showed one must not be too sure of things. There was no mistake about it, it *was* cold. He strode up and down, stamping his feet and threshing his arms, until reassured by the returning warmth. Then he got out matches and proceeded to make a fire. From the undergrowth, where high water of the previous spring had lodged a supply of seasoned twigs, he got his fire-wood. Working carefully from a small beginning, he soon had a roaring fire, over which he thawed the ice from his face and in the protection of which he ate his biscuits. For the moment the cold of space was outwitted. The dog took satisfaction in the fire, stretching out close enough for warmth and far enough away to escape being singed.

When the man had finished, he filled his pipe and took his comfortable time over a smoke. Then he pulled on his mittens, settled the ear-flaps of his cap firmly about his ears, and took the creek trail up the left fork. The dog was disappointed and yearned back toward the fire. This man did not know cold. Possibly all the generations of his ancestry had been ignorant of cold, of real cold, of cold one hundred and seven degrees below freezing-point. But the dog knew; all its ancestry knew, and it had inherited the knowledge. And it knew that it was not good to walk abroad in such fearful cold. It was the time to lie snug in a hole in the snow and wait for a curtain of cloud to be drawn across the face of outer space whence this cold came. On the other hand, there was no keen intimacy between the dog and the man. The one was the toil-slave of the other, and the only caresses it had ever received were the caresses of the whip-lash and of harsh and menacing throat-sounds that threatened the whip-lash. So the dog made no effort to communicate its apprehension to the man. It was not concerned in the welfare of the man; it was for its own sake that it yearned back toward the fire. But the man whis-

4. Mining area between the towns of Dawson and Granville.

tled, and spoke to it with the sound of whip-lashes, and the dog swung in at the man's heels and followed after.

The man took a chew of tobacco and proceeded to start a new amber beard. Also, his moist breath quickly powdered with white his mustache, eyebrows, and lashes. There did not seem to be so many springs on the left fork of the Henderson, and for half an hour the man saw no signs of any. And then it happened. At a place where there were no signs, where the soft, unbroken snow seemed to advertise solidity beneath, the man broke through. It was not deep. He wet himself halfway to the knees before he floundered out to the firm crust.

He was angry, and cursed his luck aloud. He had hoped to get into camp with the boys at six o'clock, and this would delay him an hour, for he would have to build a fire and dry out his foot-gear. This was imperative at that low temperature—he knew that much; and he turned aside to the bank, which he climbed. On top, tangled in the underbrush about the trunks of several small spruce trees, was a high-water deposit of dry fire-wood—sticks and twigs, principally, but also larger portions of seasoned branches and fine, dry, last-year's grasses. He threw down several large pieces on top of the snow. This served for a foundation and prevented the young flame from drowning itself in the snow it otherwise would melt. The flame he got by touching a match to a small shred of birch-bark that he took from his pocket. This burned even more readily than paper. Placing it on the foundation, he fed the young flame with wisps of dry grass and with the tiniest dry twigs.

He worked slowly and carefully, keenly aware of his danger. Gradually, as the flame grew stronger, he increased the size of the twigs with which he fed it. He squatted in the snow, pulling the twigs out from their entanglement in the brush and feeding directly to the flame. He knew there must be no failure. When it is seventy-five below zero, a man must not fail in his first attempt to build a fire—that is, if his feet are wet. If his feet are dry, and he fails, he can run along the trail for half a mile and restore his circulation. But the circulation of wet and freezing feet cannot be restored by running when it is seventy-five below. No matter how fast he runs, the wet feet will freeze the harder.

All this the man knew. The old-timer on Sulphur Creek had told him about it the previous fall, and now he was appreciating the advice. Already all sensation had gone out of his feet. To build the fire he had been forced to remove his mittens, and the fingers had quickly gone numb. His pace of four miles an hour had kept his heart pumping blood to the surface of his body and to all the extremities. But the instant he stopped, the action of the pump eased down. The cold of space smote the unprotected tip of the planet, and he, being on that unprotected tip, received the full force of the blow. The blood of his body recoiled before it. The blood was alive, like the dog, and like the dog it wanted to hide away and cover itself up from the fearful cold. So long as he walked four miles an hour, he pumped that blood, willy-nilly, to the surface; but now it ebbed away and sank down into the recesses of his body. The extremities were the first to feel its absence. His wet feet froze the faster, and his exposed fingers numbed the faster, though they had not yet begun to freeze. Nose and cheeks were already freezing, while the skin of all his body chilled as it lost its blood.

But he was safe. Toes and nose and cheeks would be only touched by the frost, for the fire was beginning to burn with strength. He was feeding it with twigs the size of his finger. In another minute he would be able to feed it with branches the size of his wrist, and then he could remove his wet footgear, and, while it dried, he could keep his naked feet warm by the fire, rubbing them at first, of course, with snow. The fire was a success. He was safe. He remembered the advice of the old-timer on Sulphur Creek, and smiled. The old-timer had been very serious in laying down the law that no man must travel alone in the Klondike after fifty below. Well, here he was; he had had the accident; he was alone; and he had saved himself. Those old-timers were rather womanish, some of them, he thought. All a man had to do was to keep his head, and he was all right. Any man who was a man could travel alone. But it was surprising, the rapidity with which his cheeks and nose were freezing. And he had not thought his fingers could go lifeless in so short a time. Lifeless they were, for he could scarcely make them move together to grip a twig, and they seemed remote from his body and from him. When he touched a twig, he had to look and see whether or not he had hold of it. The wires were pretty well down between him and his finger-ends.

All of which counted for little. There was the fire, snapping and crackling and promising life with every dancing flame. He started to untie his moccasins. They were coated with ice; the thick German socks were like sheaths of iron halfway to the knees; and the moccasin strings were like rods of steel all twisted and knotted as by some conflagration. For a moment he tugged with his numb fingers, then, realizing the folly of it, he drew his sheath-knife.

But before he could cut the strings, it happened. It was his own fault or, rather, his mistake. He should not have built the fire under the spruce tree. He should have built it in the open. But it had been easier to pull the twigs from the brush and drop them directly on the fire. Now the tree under which he had done this carried a weight of snow on its boughs. No wind had blown for weeks, and each bough was fully freighted. Each time he had pulled a twig he had communicated a slight agitation to the tree—an imperceptible agitation, so far as he was concerned, but an agitation sufficient to bring about the disaster. High up in the tree one bough capsized its load of snow. This fell on the boughs beneath, capsizing them. This process continued, spreading out and involving the whole tree. It grew like an avalanche, and it descended without warning upon the man and the fire, and the fire was blotted out! Where it had burned was a mantle of fresh and disordered snow.

The man was shocked. It was as though he had just heard his own sentence of death. For a moment he sat and stared at the spot where the fire had been. Then he grew very calm. Perhaps the old-timer on Sulphur Creek was right. If he had only had a trail-mate he would have been in no danger now. The trail-mate could have built the fire. Well, it was up to him to build the fire over again, and this second time there must be no failure. Even if he succeeded, he would most likely lose some toes. His feet must be badly frozen by now, and there would be some time before the second fire was ready.

Such were his thoughts, but he did not sit and think them. He was busy all the time they were passing through his mind. He made a new foundation for a fire, this time in the open, where no treacherous tree could blot it out. Next, he gathered dry grasses and tiny twigs from the high-water flotsam. He could not bring his fingers together to pull them out, but he was able to gather them by the handful. In this way he got many rotten twigs and bits of green moss that were undesirable, but it was the best he could do. He worked methodically, even collecting an armful of the larger branches to be used later when the fire gathered strength. And all the while the dog sat and watched him, a certain yearning wistfulness in its eyes, for it looked upon him as the fire-provider, and the fire was slow in coming.

When all was ready, the man reached in his pocket for a second piece of birch-bark. He knew the bark was there, and, though he could not feel it with his fingers, he could hear its crisp rustling as he fumbled for it. Try as he would, he could not clutch hold of it. And all the time, in his consciousness, was the knowledge that each instant his feet were freezing. This thought tended to put him in a panic, but he fought against it and kept calm. He pulled on his mittens with his teeth, and threshed his arms back and forth, beating his hands with all his might against his sides. He did this sitting down, and he stood up to do it; and all the while the dog sat in the snow, its wolf-brush of a tail curled around warmly over its forefeet, its sharp wolf-ears pricked forward intently as it watched the man. And the man, as he beat and threshed with his arms and hands, he felt a great surge of envy as he regarded the creature that was warm and secure in its natural covering.

After a time he was aware of the first faraway signals of sensation in his beaten fingers. The faint tingling grew stronger till it evolved into a stinging ache that was excruciating, but which the man hailed with satisfaction. He stripped the mitten from his right hand and fetched forth the birch-bark. The exposed fingers were quickly going numb again. Next he brought out his bunch of sulphur matches. But the tremendous cold had already driven the life out of his fingers. In his effort to separate one match from the others, the whole bunch fell in the snow. He tried to pick it out of the snow, but failed. The dead fingers could neither touch nor clutch. He was very careful. He drove the thought of his freezing feet, and nose, and cheeks, out of his mind, devoting his whole soul to the matches. He watched, using the sense of vision in place of that of touch, and when he saw his fingers on each side the bunch, he closed them—that is, he willed to close them, for the wires were down, and the fingers did not obey. He pulled the mitten on the right hand, and beat it fiercely against his knee. Then, with both mittened hands, he scooped the bunch of matches, along with much snow, into his lap. Yet he was no better off.

After some manipulation he managed to get the bunch between the heels of his mittened hands. In this fashion he carried it to his mouth. The ice crackled and snapped when by a violent effort he opened his mouth. He drew the lower jaw in, curled the upper lip out of the way, and scraped the bunch with his upper teeth in order to separate a match. He succeeded in getting one, which he dropped on his lap. He was no better off. He could not pick it up. Then he devised a way. He picked it up in his teeth and scratched it on his leg. Twenty times he scratched before he succeeded in lighting it. As it flamed he held it with his teeth to the birch-bark. But the burning brimstone went up his nostrils and into his lungs, causing him to cough spasmodically. The match fell into the snow and went out.

The old-timer on Sulphur Creek was right, he thought in the moment of controlled despair that ensued: after fifty below, a man should travel with a partner. He beat his hands, but failed in exciting any sensation. Suddenly he bared both hands, removing the mittens with his teeth. He caught the whole bunch between the heels of his hands. His arm-muscles not being frozen enabled him to press the hand-heels tightly against the matches. Then he scratched the bunch along his leg. It flared into flame, seventy sulphur matches at once! There was no wind to blow them out. He kept his head to one side to escape the strangling fumes, and held the blazing bunch to the birch-bark. As he so held it, he became aware of sensation in his hand. His flesh was burning. He could smell it. Deep down below the surface he could feel it. The sensation developed into pain that grew acute. And still he endured it, holding the flame of the matches clumsily to the bark that would not light readily because his own burning hands were in the way, absorbing most of the flame.

At last, when he could endure no more, he jerked his hands apart. The blazing matches fell sizzling into the snow, but the birch-bark was alight. He began laying dry grasses and the tiniest twigs on the flame. He could not pick and choose, for he had to lift the fuel between the heels of his hands. Small pieces of rotten wood and green moss clung to the twigs, and he bit them off as well as he could with his teeth. He cherished the flame carefully and awkwardly. It meant life, and it must not perish. The withdrawal of blood from the surface of his body now made him begin to shiver, and he grew more awkward. A large piece of green moss fell squarely on the little fire. He tried to poke it out with his fingers, but his shivering frame made him poke too far, and he disrupted the nucleus of the little fire, the burning grasses and tiny twigs separating and scattering. He tried to poke them together again, but in spite of the tenseness of the effort, his shivering got away with him, and the twigs were hopelessly scattered. Each twig gushed a puff of smoke and went out. The fire-provider had failed. As he looked apathetically about him, his eyes chanced on the dog, sitting across the ruins of the fire from him, in the snow, making restless, hunching movements, slightly lifting one forefoot and then the other, shifting its weight back and forth on them with wistful eagerness.

The sight of the dog put a wild idea into his head. He remembered the tale of the man, caught in a blizzard, who killed a steer and crawled inside the carcass, and so was saved. He would kill the dog and bury his hands in the warm body until the numbness went out of them. Then he could build another fire. He spoke to the dog, calling it to him; but in his voice was a strange note of fear that frightened the animal, who had never known the man to speak in such way before. Something was the matter, and its suspicious nature sensed danger—it knew not what danger, but somewhere, somehow, in its brain arose an apprehension of the man. It flattened its ears down at the sound of the man's voice, and its restless, hunching movements and the liftings and shiftings of its forefeet became more pronounced; but it would not come to the man. He got on his hands and knees and crawled toward the dog. This unusual posture again excited suspicion, and the animal sidled mincingly away.

The man sat up in the snow for a moment and struggled for calmness. Then he pulled on his mittens, by means of his teeth, and got upon his feet. He glanced down at first in order to assure himself that he was really standing up, for the absence of sensation in his feet left him unrelated to the earth. His erect position in itself started to drive the webs of suspicion from the dog's mind; and when he spoke peremptorily, with the sound of whip-lashes in his voice, the dog rendered its customary allegiance and came to him. As it came within reaching distance, the man lost his control. His arms flashed out to the dog, and he experienced genuine surprise when he discovered that his hands could not clutch, that there was neither bend nor feeling in the fingers. He had forgotten for the moment that they were frozen and that they were freezing more and more. All this happened quickly, and before the animal could get away, he encircled its body with his arms. He sat down in the snow, and in this fashion held the dog, while it snarled and whined and struggled.

But it was all he could do, hold its body encircled in his arms and sit there. He realized that he could not kill the dog. There was no way to do it. With his helpless hands he could neither draw nor hold his sheath-knife nor throttle the animal. He released it, and it plunged wildly away, with tail between its legs, and still snarling. It halted forty feet away and surveyed him curiously, with ears sharply pricked forward. The man looked down at his hands in order to locate them, and found them hanging on the ends of his arms. It struck him as curious that one should have to use his eyes in order to find out where his hands were. He began threshing his arms back and forth, beating the mittened hands against his sides. He did this for five minutes, violently, and his heart pumped enough blood up to the surface to put a stop to his shivering. But no sensation was aroused in the hands. He had an impression that they hung like weights on the ends of his arms, but when he tried to run the impression down, he could not find it.

A certain fear of death, dull and oppressive, came to him. This fear quickly became poignant as he realized that it was no longer a mere matter of freezing his fingers and toes, or of losing his hands and feet, but that it was a matter of life and death with the chances against him. This threw him into a panic, and he turned and ran up the creek-bed along the old, dim trail. The dog joined in behind and kept up with him. He ran blindly, without intention, in fear such as he had never known in his life. Slowly, as he ploughed and floundered through the snow, he began to see things again—the banks of the creek, the old timber-jams, the leafless aspens, and the sky. The running made him feel better. He did not shiver. Maybe, if he ran on, his feet would thaw out; and, anyway, if he ran far enough, he would reach camp and the boys. Without doubt he would lose some fingers and toes and some of his face; but the boys would take care of him, and save the rest of him when he got there. And at the same time there was another thought in his mind that said he would never get to the camp and the boys; that it was too many miles away, that the freezing had too great a start on him, and that he would soon be stiff and dead. This thought he kept in the background and refused to consider. Sometimes it pushed itself forward and demanded to be heard, but he thrust it back and strove to think of other things.

It struck him as curious that he could run at all on feet so frozen that he could not feel them when they struck the earth and took the weight of his body. He seemed to himself to skim along above the surface, and to have no connection with the earth. Somewhere he had once seen a winged Mercury,[5] and he wondered if Mercury felt as he felt when skimming over the earth.

His theory of running until he reached camp and the boys had one flaw in it: he lacked the endurance. Several times he stumbled, and finally he tottered, crumpled up, and fell. When he tried to rise, he failed. He must sit and rest, he decided, and next time he would merely walk and keep on going. As he sat and regained his breath, he noted that he was feeling quite warm and comfortable. He was not shivering, and it even seemed that a warm glow had

5. Mercury is the Roman god of messengers, thieves, and storytellers; he flew between heaven and earth wearing winged sandals. He is also the god of healing and the courier of souls to the Underworld.

come to his chest and trunk. And yet, when he touched his nose or cheeks, there was no sensation. Running would not thaw them out. Nor would it thaw out his hands and feet. Then the thought came to him that the frozen portions of his body must be extending. He tried to keep this thought down, to forget it, to think of something else; he was aware of the panicky feeling that it caused, and he was afraid of the panic. But the thought asserted itself, and persisted, until it produced a vision of his body totally frozen. This was too much, and he made another wild run along the trail. Once he slowed down to a walk, but the thought of the freezing extending itself made him run again.

And all the time the dog ran with him, at his heels. When he fell down a second time, it curled its tail over its forefeet and sat in front of him, facing him, curiously eager and intent. The warmth and security of the animal angered him, and he cursed it till it flattened down its ears appeasingly. This time the shivering came more quickly upon the man. He was losing in his battle with the frost. It was creeping into his body from all sides. The thought of it drove him on, but he ran no more than a hundred feet, when he staggered and pitched headlong. It was his last panic. When he had recovered his breath and control, he sat up and entertained in his mind the conception of meeting death with dignity. However, the conception did not come to him in such terms. His idea of it was that he had been making a fool of himself, running around like a chicken with its head cut off—such was the simile that occurred to him. Well, he was bound to freeze anyway, and he might as well take it decently. With this new-found peace of mind came the first glimmerings of drowsiness. A good idea, he thought, to sleep off to death. It was like taking an anaesthetic. Freezing was not so bad as people thought. There were lots worse ways to die.

He pictured the boys finding his body next day. Suddenly he found himself with them, coming along the trail and looking for himself. And, still with them, he came around a turn in the trail and found himself lying in the snow. He did not belong with himself any more, for even then he was out of himself, standing with the boys and looking at himself in the snow. It certainly was cold, was his thought. When he got back to the States he could tell the folks what real cold was. He drifted on from this to a vision of the old-timer on Sulphur Creek. He could see him quite clearly, warm and comfortable, and smoking a pipe.

"You were right, old hoss; you were right," the man mumbled to the old-timer of Sulphur Creek.

Then the man drowsed off into what seemed to him the most comfortable and satisfying sleep he had ever known. The dog sat facing him and waiting. The brief day drew to a close in a long, slow twilight. There were no signs of a fire to be made, and, besides, never in the dog's experience had it known a man to sit like that in the snow and make no fire. As the twilight drew on, its eager yearning for the fire mastered it, and with a great lifting and shifting of forefeet, it whined softly, then flattened its ears down in anticipation of being chidden by the man. But the man remained silent. Later, the dog whined loudly. And still later it crept close to the man and caught the scent of death. This made the animal bristle and back away. A little longer it delayed, howling under the stars that leaped and danced and shone brightly in the cold sky. Then it turned and trotted up the trail in the direction of the camp it knew, where were the other food-providers and fire-providers.

1902, 1908

ZITKALA ŠA (GERTRUDE SIMMONS BONNIN)
1876–1938

Gertrude Simmons was born in 1876 on the Yankton Sioux Reservation in south-central South Dakota. Her mother was *Tate Iyohi Win,* or "Reaches the Wind Woman," otherwise known as Ellen Simmons, and her father was probably a white man named Felker who left his wife before the child's birth. Her mother later married another white man, John H. Simmons, whose surname was given to the child. Gertrude Simmons today is usually referred to as Zitkala Ša (pronounced *sha*), or Red Bird, a name she chose for herself. Zitkala Ša was an important Native American writer, orator, and debater; a singer, pianist, and violinist; and an activist on behalf of women's and Native American rights.

Eighteen hundred and seventy-six, the year of Zitkala Ša's birth, was the year in which George Armstrong Custer's Seventh Cavalry was defeated by a coalition of Sioux and Cheyenne warriors on the Little Bighorn River in Montana, after which the federal government finally drove both tribes onto reservations. In 1890, the U.S. Department of the Census announced the closing of the frontier, meaning that no more "free land" remained open for settlement; the United States had achieved its "manifest destiny," extending its dominion from "sea to shining sea." As an adult, then, Zitkala Ša lived in what has been called the "transitional" period in Native American history, a difficult time for Indian peoples, when the U.S. government pursued an official policy of "detribalization" and land-hungry whites sought access to tribal domains.

At the age of eight, Zitkala Ša declared her intention to learn the white man's ways—or, as she puts it, in her autobiographical, "Impressions of an Indian Childhood" (1900), she wanted to taste the "big red apples" missionaries promised Indian children if they would attend boarding school. She began her schooling at White's Manual Institute, a Quaker school in Indiana. As her autobiography details it, her introduction to "civilization" subjected her and the other Indian children to having their long hair cut, to having the clothing in which they had arrived discarded, and, perhaps most painful, to being forbidden to speak their Native languages. This was, in the oft-quoted dictum of Colonel Richard Henry Pratt, headmaster of the Carlisle Indian Institute, where Zitkala Ša later worked, an education intended to "Kill the Indian and save the man!"

From White's, Zitkala Ša went on to Earlham College, also in Indiana, where she began to demonstrate a wide range of talents. In the last section of "Impressions of an Indian Childhood," she tells of her appearance as the representative of the college in 1896 at a statewide oratorical competition, where some "rowdies," as she puts it, "threw out a large white flag, with a drawing of a most forlorn Indian girl on it," along with, "in bold black letters words that ridiculed the college which was represented by a 'squaw.' " This slight was somewhat assuaged by her winning second prize overall.

The following year, Zitkala Ša became "the latest addition to our force of workers," as the Carlisle Institute's publication, *The Indian Helper,* announced in its July 1897 number. Carlisle, as noted above, was committed to preparing Indians to assimilate into mainstream American life. At Carlisle, Zitkala Ša led the glee club, played the piano and violin, and became engaged to Thomas Marshall, a Sioux from the Pine Ridge Agency, a devout Christian convert, "without a peer among our students," who died rather suddenly from an undiagnosed illness.

Soon after Marshall's death, Zitkala Ša began to publish autobiography and fiction. (She also wrote poetry.) "Impressions of an Indian Childhood," "The Schooldays of an Indian Girl," and "An Indian Teacher among Indians" appeared in the *Atlantic Monthly* for January, February, and March of 1900. Her short story "The Soft-Hearted Sioux" appeared in *Harper's Monthly* in 1901. "The Soft-Hearted Sioux" makes powerfully clear that the protagonist's Christianization and "civilization" have utterly unfitted him for any relation to his traditional parents. Nineteen hundred and one was also the date of publication of her first book, *Old Indian Legends*, a work that contributed to the vogue for Native folklore. Her other writings did not appear in book form until 1921, with the publication of *American Indian Stories*.

In May 1902, Zitkala Ša married Raymond Bonnin, also a Yankton, and an employee of the U.S. Indian Service (later the Bureau of Indian Affairs). They had one son, Raymond Ohiya Bonnin (his middle name was a tribute to Charles Alexander Eastman, whose Indian name was Ohiyesa), born in 1903. Although she would occasionally publish stories and poems thereafter, and wrote the libretto for an opera, *Sun Dance*, the bulk of Zitkala Ša's writing over the second half of her life derived from her active engagement in Indian affairs. After years of work on the Uintah Ouray Ute Agency in Utah, the family moved to Washington, D.C., in 1916 so that Zitkala Ša could take up her elected position as secretary of the Society of the American Indian (SAI), an organization dedicated to improving the condition of Native people. During World War I, Bonnin served in the army as assistant to the Quartermaster General in Washington, retiring with the rank of captain. When the SAI broke up in 1920, Zitkala Ša began working with the General Federation of Women's Clubs, which established an Indian Welfare Committee in 1921 at her urging. One of the committee's achievements was an inquiry into the treatment of some of the tribes in Oklahoma, which led to the publication, in 1924, of a study of the graft, corruption, and exploitation of the tribes and spurred the formation under President Hoover of the Merriam Commission in 1928 to study these matters. In 1926, Zitkala Ša had founded her own organization, the National Council of American Indians, of which she was president, with her husband serving as counselor general, secretary-treasurer, and executive secretary. It was in 1938 that she fell into a coma and died.

Zitkala Ša is buried in Arlington National Cemetery beside her husband, Captain Raymond Bonnin.

From Impressions of an Indian Childhood[1]

I. My Mother

A wigwam of weather-stained canvas stood at the base of some irregularly ascending hills. A footpath wound its way gently down the sloping land till it reached the broad river bottom; creeping through the long swamp grasses that bent over it on either side, it came out on the edge of the Missouri.

Here, morning, noon, and evening, my mother came to draw water from the muddy stream for our household use. Always, when my mother started for the river, I stopped my play to run along with her. She was only of medium height. Often she was sad and silent, at which times her full arched lips were compressed into hard and bitter lines, and shadows fell under her black eyes. Then I clung to her hand and begged to know what made the tears fall.

"Hush; my little daughter must never talk about my tears;" and smiling through them, she patted my head and said, "Now let me see how fast you can run to-day." Whereupon I tore away at my highest possible speed, with my long black hair blowing in the breeze.

---

1. "Impressions of an Indian Childhood" first appeared in the *Atlantic Monthly* for January of 1900.

I was a wild little girl of seven. Loosely clad in a slip of brown buckskin, and light-footed with a pair of soft moccasins on my feet, I was as free as the wind that blew my hair, and no less spirited than a bounding deer. These were my mother's pride,—my wild freedom and overflowing spirits. She taught me no fear save that of intruding myself upon others.

Having gone many paces ahead I stopped, panting for breath, and laughing with glee as my mother watched my every movement. I was not wholly conscious of myself, but was more keenly alive to the fire within. It was as if I were the activity, and my hands and feet were only experiments for my spirit to work upon.

Returning from the river, I tugged beside my mother, with my hand upon the bucket I believed I was carrying. One time, on such a return, I remember a bit of conversation we had. My grown-up cousin, Warca-Ziwin (Sunflower), who was then seventeen, always went to the river alone for water for her mother. Their wigwam was not far from ours; and I saw her daily going to and from the river. I admired my cousin greatly. So I said: "Mother, when I am tall as my cousin Warca-Ziwin, you shall not have to come for water. I will do it for you."

With a strange tremor in her voice which I could not understand, she answered, "If the paleface does not take away from us the river we drink."

"Mother, who is this bad paleface?" I asked.

"My little daughter, he is a sham,—a sickly sham! The bronzed Dakota is the only real man."

I looked up into my mother's face while she spoke; and seeing her bite her lips, I knew she was unhappy. This aroused revenge in my small soul. Stamping my foot on the earth, I cried aloud, "I hate the paleface that makes my mother cry!"

Setting the pail of water on the ground, my mother stooped, and stretching her left hand out on the level with my eyes, she placed her other arm about me; she pointed to the hill where my uncle and my only sister lay buried.

"There is what the paleface has done! Since then your father too has been buried in a hill nearer the rising sun. We were once very happy. But the paleface has stolen our lands and driven us hither. Having defrauded us of our land, the paleface forced us away.

"Well, it happened on the day we moved camp that your sister and uncle were both very sick. Many others were ailing, but there seemed to be no help. We traveled many days and nights; not in the grand happy way that we moved camp when I was a little girl, but we were driven, my child, driven like a herd of buffalo. With every step, your sister, who was not as large as you are now, shrieked with the painful jar until she was hoarse with crying. She grew more and more feverish. Her little hands and cheeks were burning hot. Her little lips were parched and dry, but she would not drink the water I gave her. Then I discovered that her throat was swollen and red. My poor child, how I cried with her because the Great Spirit had forgotten us!

"At last, when we reached this western country, on the first weary night your sister died. And soon your uncle died also, leaving a widow and an orphan daughter, your cousin Warca-Ziwin. Both your sister and uncle might have been happy with us to-day, had it not been for the heartless paleface."

My mother was silent the rest of the way to our wigwam. Though I saw no tears in her eyes, I knew that was because I was with her. She seldom wept before me.

II. The Legends

During the summer days, my mother built her fire in the shadow of our wigwam.

In the early morning our simple breakfast was spread upon the grass west of our tepee. At the farthest point of the shade my mother sat beside her fire, toasting a savory piece of dried meat. Near her, I sat upon my feet, eating my dried meat with unleavened bread, and drinking strong black coffee.

The morning meal was our quiet hour, when we two were entirely alone. At noon, several who chanced to be passing by stopped to rest, and to share our luncheon with us, for they were sure of our hospitality.

My uncle, whose death my mother ever lamented, was one of our nation's bravest warriors. His name was on the lips of old men when talking of the proud feats of valor; and it was mentioned by younger men, too, in connection with deeds of gallantry. Old women praised him for his kindness toward them; young women held him up as an ideal to their sweethearts. Every one loved him, and my mother worshiped his memory. Thus it happened that even strangers were sure of welcome in our lodge, if they but asked a favor in my uncle's name.

Though I heard many strange experiences related by these wayfarers, I loved best the evening meal, for that was the time old legends were told. I was always glad when the sun hung low in the west, for then my mother sent me to invite the neighboring old men and women to eat supper with us. Running all the way to the wigwams, I halted shyly at the entrances. Sometimes I stood long moments without saying a word. It was not any fear that made me so dumb when out upon such a happy errand; nor was it that I wished to withhold the invitation, for it was all I could do to observe this very proper silence. But it was a sensing of the atmosphere, to assure myself that I should not hinder other plans. My mother used to say to me, as I was almost bounding away for the old people: "Wait a moment before you invite any one. If other plans are being discussed, do not interfere, but go elsewhere."

The old folks knew the meaning of my pauses; and often they coaxed my confidence by asking, "What do you seek, little granddaughter?"

"My mother says you are to come to our tepee this evening," I instantly exploded, and breathed the freer afterwards.

"Yes, yes, gladly, gladly I shall come!" each replied. Rising at once and carrying their blankets across one shoulder, they flocked leisurely from their various wigwams toward our dwelling.

My mission done, I ran back, skipping and jumping with delight. All out of breath, I told my mother almost the exact words of the answers to my invitation. Frequently she asked, "What were they doing when you entered their tepee?" This taught me to remember all I saw at a single glance. Often I told my mother my impressions without being questioned.

While in the neighboring wigwams sometimes an old Indian woman asked me, "What is your mother doing?" Unless my mother had cautioned me not to tell, I generally answered her questions without reserve.

At the arrival of our guests I sat close to my mother, and did not leave her side without first asking her consent. I ate my supper in quiet, listening patiently to the talk of the old people, wishing all the time that they would begin the stories I loved best. At last, when I could not wait any longer, I whispered in my mother's ear, "Ask them to tell an Iktomi story,[2] mother."

Soothing my impatience, my mother said aloud, "My little daughter is anxious to hear your legends." By this time all were through eating, and the evening was fast deepening into twilight.

As each in turn began to tell a legend, I pillowed my head in my mother's lap; and lying flat upon my back, I watched the stars as they peeped down upon me, one by one. The increasing interest of the tale aroused me, and I sat up eagerly listening for every word. The old women made funny remarks, and laughed so heartily that I could not help joining them.

The distant howling of a pack of wolves or the hooting of an owl in the river bottom frightened me, and I nestled into my mother's lap. She added some dry sticks to the fire, and the bright flames heaped up into the faces of the old folks as they sat around in a great circle.

On such an evening, I remember the glare of the fire shone on a tattooed star upon the brow of the old warrior who was telling a story. I watched him curiously as he made his unconscious gestures. The blue star upon his bronzed forehead was a puzzle to me. Looking about, I saw two parallel lines on the chin of one of the old women. The rest had none. I examined my mother's face, but found no sign there.

After the warrior's story was finished, I asked the old woman the meaning of the blue lines on her chin, looking all the while out of the corners of my eyes at the warrior with the star on his forehead. I was a little afraid that he would rebuke me for my boldness.

Here the old woman began: "Why, my grandchild, they are signs,—secret signs I dare not tell you. I shall, however, tell you a wonderful story about a woman who had a cross tattooed upon each of her cheeks."

It was a long story of a woman whose magic power lay hidden behind the marks upon her face. I fell asleep before the story was completed.

Ever after that night I felt suspicious of tattooed people. Wherever I saw one I glanced furtively at the mark and round about it, wondering what terrible magic power was covered there.

It was rarely that such a fearful story as this one was told by the camp fire. Its impression was so acute that the picture still remains vividly clear and pronounced.

* * *

IV. The Coffee-Making

One summer afternoon, my mother left me alone in our wigwam, while she went across the way to my aunt's dwelling.

I did not much like to stay alone in our tepee, for I feared a tall, broad-shouldered crazy man, some forty years old, who walked loose among the hills. Wiyaka-Napbina (Wearer of a Feather Necklace) was harmless, and whenever he came into a wigwam he was driven there by extreme hunger. He went nude except for the half of a red blanket he girdled around his waist. In

2. A story about the Sioux trickster.

one tawny arm he used to carry a heavy bunch of wild sunflowers that he gathered in his aimless ramblings. His black hair was matted by the winds, and scorched into a dry red by the constant summer sun. As he took great strides, placing one brown bare foot directly in front of the other, he swung his long lean arm to and fro.

Frequently he paused in his walk and gazed far backward, shading his eyes with his hand. He was under the belief that an evil spirit was haunting his steps. This was what my mother told me once, when I sneered at such a silly big man. I was brave when my mother was near by, and Wiyaka-Napbina walking farther and farther away.

"Pity the man, my child. I knew him when he was a brave and handsome youth. He was overtaken by a malicious spirit among the hills, one day, when he went hither and thither after his ponies. Since then he cannot stay away from the hills," she said.

I felt so sorry for the man in his misfortune that I prayed to the Great Spirit to restore him. But though I pitied him at a distance, I was still afraid of him when he appeared near our wigwam.

Thus, when my mother left me by myself that afternoon, I sat in a fearful mood within our tepee. I recalled all I had ever heard about Wiyaka-Napbina; and I tried to assure myself that though he might pass near by, he would not come to our wigwam because there was no little girl around our grounds.

Just then, from without a hand lifted the canvas covering of the entrance; the shadow of a man fell within the wigwam, and a large roughly moccasined foot was planted inside.

For a moment I did not dare to breathe or stir, for I thought that could be no other than Wiyaka-Napbina. The next instant I sighed aloud in relief. It was an old grandfather who had often told me Iktomi legends.

"Where is your mother, my little grandchild?" were his first words.

"My mother is soon coming back from my aunt's tepee," I replied.

"Then I shall wait awhile for her return," he said, crossing his feet and seating himself upon a mat.

At once I began to play the part of a generous hostess. I turned to my mother's coffeepot.

Lifting the lid, I found nothing but coffee grounds in the bottom. I set the pot on a heap of cold ashes in the centre, and filled it half full of warm Missouri River water. During this performance I felt conscious of being watched. Then breaking off a small piece of our unleavened bread, I placed it in a bowl. Turning soon to the coffeepot, which would never have boiled on a dead fire had I waited forever, I poured out a cup of worse than muddy warm water. Carrying the bowl in one hand and cup in the other, I handed the light luncheon to the old warrior. I offered them to him with the air of bestowing generous hospitality.

"How! how!" he said, and placed the dishes on the ground in front of his crossed feet. He nibbled at the bread and sipped from the cup. I sat back against a pole watching him. I was proud to have succeeded so well in serving refreshments to a guest all by myself. Before the old warrior had finished eating, my mother entered. Immediately she wondered where I had found coffee, for she knew I had never made any, and that she had left the coffeepot empty. Answering the question in my mother's eyes, the warrior remarked,

"My granddaughter made coffee on a heap of dead ashes, and served me the moment I came."

They both laughed, and mother said, "Wait a little longer, and I shall build a fire." She meant to make some real coffee. But neither she nor the warrior, whom the law of our custom had compelled to partake of my insipid hospitality, said anything to embarrass me. They treated my best judgment, poor as it was, with the utmost respect. It was not till long years afterward that I learned how ridiculous a thing I had done.

* * *

VII. The Big Red Apples

The first turning away from the easy, natural flow of my life occurred in an early spring. It was in my eighth year; in the month of March, I afterward learned. At this age I knew but one language, and that was my mother's native tongue.

From some of my playmates I heard that two paleface missionaries were in our village. They were from that class of white men who wore big hats and carried large hearts, they said. Running direct to my mother, I began to question her why these two strangers were among us. She told me, after I had teased much, that they had come to take away Indian boys and girls to the East. My mother did not seem to want me to talk about them. But in a day or two, I gleaned many wonderful stories from my playfellows concerning the strangers.

"Mother, my friend Judéwin is going home with the missionaries. She is going to a more beautiful country than ours; the palefaces told her so!" I said wistfully, wishing in my heart that I too might go.

Mother sat in a chair, and I was hanging on her knee. Within the last two seasons my big brother Dawée had returned from a three years' education in the East, and his coming back influenced my mother to take a farther step from her native way of living. First it was a change from the buffalo skin to the white man's canvas that covered our wigwam. Now she had given up her wigwam of slender poles, to live, a foreigner, in a home of clumsy logs.

"Yes, my child, several others besides Judéwin are going away with the palefaces. Your brother said the missionaries had inquired about his little sister," she said, watching my face very closely.

My heart thumped so hard against my breast, I wondered if she could hear it.

"Did he tell them to take me, mother?" I asked, fearing lest Dawée had forbidden the palefaces to see me, and that my hope of going to the Wonderland would be entirely blighted.

With a sad, slow smile, she answered: "There! I knew you were wishing to go, because Judéwin has filled your ears with the white men's lies. Don't believe a word they say! Their words are sweet, but, my child, their deeds are bitter. You will cry for me, but they will not even soothe you. Stay with me, my little one! Your brother Dawée says that going East, away from your mother, is too hard an experience for his baby sister."

Thus my mother discouraged my curiosity about the lands beyond our eastern horizon; for it was not yet an ambition for Letters that was stirring me. But on the following day the missionaries did come to our very house. I spied them coming up the footpath leading to our cottage. A third man was with them, but he was not my brother Dawée. It was another, a young interpreter, a paleface who had a smattering of the Indian language. I was ready to run out to meet them, but I did not dare to displease my mother. With great glee, I jumped up and down on our ground floor. I begged my mother to open the door, that they would be sure to come to us. Alas! They came, they saw, and they conquered!

Judéwin had told me of the great tree where grew red, red apples; and how we could reach out our hands and pick all the red apples we could eat. I had never seen apple trees. I had never tasted more than a dozen red apples in my life; and when I heard of the orchards of the East, I was eager to roam among them. The missionaries smiled into my eyes, and patted my head. I wondered how mother could say such hard words against them.

"Mother, ask them if little girls may have all the red apples they want, when they go East," I whispered aloud, in my excitement.

The interpreter heard me, and answered: "Yes, little girl, the nice red apples are for those who pick them; and you will have a ride on the iron horse if you go with these good people."

I had never seen a train, and he knew it.

"Mother, I'm going East! I like big red apples, and I want to ride on the iron horse! Mother, say yes!" I pleaded.

My mother said nothing. The missionaries waited in silence; and my eyes began to blur with tears, though I struggled to choke them back. The corners of my mouth twitched, and my mother saw me.

"I am not ready to give you any word," she said to them. "To-morrow I shall send you my answer by my son."

With this they left us. Alone with my mother, I yielded to my tears, and cried aloud, shaking my head so as not to hear what she was saying to me. This was the first time I had ever been so unwilling to give up my own desire that I refused to hearken to my mother's voice.

There was a solemn silence in our home that night. Before I went to bed I begged the Great Spirit to make my mother willing I should go with the missionaries.

The next morning came, and my mother called me to her side. "My daughter, do you still persist in wishing to leave your mother?" she asked.

"Oh, mother, it is not that I wish to leave you, but I want to see the wonderful Eastern land," I answered.

My dear old aunt came to our house that morning, and I heard her say, "Let her try it."

I hoped that, as usual, my aunt was pleading on my side. My brother Dawée came for mother's decision. I dropped my play, and crept close to my aunt.

"Yes, Dawée, my daughter, though she does not understand what it all means, is anxious to go. She will need an education when she is grown, for then there will be fewer real Dakotas, and many more palefaces. This tearing her away, so young, from her mother is necessary, if I would have her an educated woman. The palefaces, who owe us a large debt for stolen lands, have begun to pay a tardy justice in offering some education to our children. But I know my daughter must suffer keenly in this experiment. For her sake, I dread to tell you my reply to the missionaries. Go, tell them that they may take my little daughter, and that the Great Spirit shall not fail to reward them according to their hearts."

Wrapped in my heavy blanket, I walked with my mother to the carriage that was soon to take us to the iron horse. I was happy. I met my playmates, who were also wearing their best thick blankets. We showed one another our new beaded moccasins, and the width of the belts that girdled our new dresses. Soon we were being drawn rapidly away by the white man's horses. When I saw the lonely figure of my mother vanish in the distance, a sense of regret settled heavily upon me. I felt suddenly weak, as if I might fall limp to the ground. I was in the hands of strangers whom my mother did not fully trust. I no longer felt free to be myself, or to voice my own feelings. The tears trickled down my cheeks, and I buried my face in the folds of my blanket. Now the first step, parting me from my mother, was taken, and all my belated tears availed nothing.

Having driven thirty miles to the ferryboat, we crossed the Missouri in the evening. Then riding again a few miles eastward, we stopped before a massive brick building. I looked at it in amazement, and with a vague misgiving, for in our village I had never seen so large a house. Trembling with fear and distrust of the palefaces, my teeth chattering from the chilly ride, I crept noiselessly in my soft moccasins along the narrow hall, keeping very close to the bare wall. I was as frightened and bewildered as the captured young of a wild creature.

1900

The Soft-Hearted Sioux

I

Beside the open fire I sat within our tepee. With my red blanket wrapped tightly about my crossed legs, I was thinking of the coming season, my sixteenth winter. On either side of the wigwam were my parents. My father was whistling a tune between his teeth while polishing with his bare hand a red stone pipe he had recently carved. Almost in front of me, beyond the center fire, my old grandmother sat near the entranceway.

She turned her face toward her right and addressed most of her words to my mother. Now and then she spoke to me, but never did she allow her eyes to rest upon her daughter's husband, my father. It was only upon rare occasions that my grandmother said anything to him. Thus his ears were open and ready to catch the smallest wish she might express. Sometimes when my grandmother had been saying things which pleased him, my father used to comment upon them. At other times, when he could not approve of what was spoken, he used to work or smoke silently.

On this night my old grandmother began her talk about me. Filling the bowl of her red stone pipe with dry willow bark, she looked across at me.

"My grandchild, you are tall and are no longer a little boy." Narrowing her old eyes, she asked, "My grandchild, when are you going to bring here a handsome young woman?" I stared into the fire rather than meet her gaze. Waiting for my answer, she stooped forward and through the long stem drew a flame into the red stone pipe.

I smiled while my eyes were still fixed upon the bright fire, but I said nothing in reply. Turning to my mother, she offered her the pipe. I glanced at my grandmother. The loose buckskin sleeve fell off at her elbow and showed a wrist covered with silver bracelets. Holding up the fingers of her left hand, she named off the desirable young women of our village.

"Which one, my grandchild, which one?" she questioned.

"Hoh!" I said, pulling at my blanket in confusion. "Not yet!" Here my mother passed the pipe over the fire to my father. Then she, too, began speaking of what I should do.

"My son, be always active. Do not dislike a long hunt. Learn to provide much buffalo meat and many buckskins before you bring home a wife." Presently my father gave the pipe to my grandmother, and he took his turn in the exhortations.

"Ho, my son, I have been counting in my heart the bravest warriors of our people. There is not one of them who won his title in his sixteenth winter. My son, it is a great thing for some brave of sixteen winters to do."

Not a word had I to give in answer. I knew well the fame of my warrior father. He had earned the right of speaking such words, though even he himself was a brave only at my age. Refusing to smoke my grandmother's pipe because my heart was too much stirred by their words, and sorely troubled with a fear lest I should disappoint them, I arose to go. Drawing my blanket over my shoulders, I said, as I stepped toward the entranceway: "I go to hobble my pony. It is now late in the night."

II

Nine winters' snows had buried deep that night when my old grandmother, together with my father and mother, designed my future with the glow of a camp fire upon it.

Yet I did not grow up the warrior, huntsman, and husband I was to have been. At the mission school I learned it was wrong to kill. Nine winters I hunted for the soft heart of Christ, and prayed for the huntsmen who chased the buffalo on the plains.

In the autumn of the tenth year I was sent back to my tribe to preach Christianity to them. With the white man's Bible in my hand, and the white man's tender heart in my breast, I returned to my own people.

Wearing a foreigner's dress, I walked, a stranger, into my father's village.

Asking my way, for I had not forgotten my native tongue, an old man led me toward the tepee where my father lay. From my old companion I learned that my father had been sick many moons. As we drew near the tepee, I heard the chanting of a medicine-man within it. At once I wished to enter in and drive from my home the sorcerer of the plains, but the old warrior checked me. "Ho, wait outside until the medicine-man leaves your father," he said. While talking he scanned me from head to feet. Then he retraced his steps toward the heart of the camping-ground.

My father's dwelling was on the outer limits of the round-faced village. With every heartthrob I grew more impatient to enter the wigwam.

While I turned the leaves of my Bible with nervous fingers, the medicine-man came forth from the dwelling and walked hurriedly away. His head and face were closely covered with the loose robe which draped his entire figure.

He was tall and large. His long strides I have never forgot. They seemed to me then the uncanny gait of eternal death. Quickly pocketing my Bible, I went into the tepee.

Upon a mat lay my father, with furrowed face and gray hair. His eyes and cheeks were sunken far into his head. His sallow skin lay thin upon his pinched nose and high cheekbones. Stooping over him, I took his fevered hand. "How, Ate?"[1] I greeted him. A light flashed from his listless eyes and his dried lips parted. "My son!" he murmured, in a feeble voice. Then again the wave of joy and recognition receded. He closed his eyes, and his hand dropped from my open palm to the ground.

Looking about, I saw an old woman sitting with bowed head. Shaking hands with her, I recognized my mother. I sat down between my father and mother as I used to do, but I did not feel at home. The place where my old grandmother used to sit was now unoccupied. With my mother I bowed my head. Alike our throats were choked and tears were streaming from our eyes; but far apart in spirit our ideas and faiths separated us. My grief was for the soul unsaved; and I thought my mother wept to see a brave man's body broken by sickness.

Useless was my attempt to change the faith in the medicine-man to that abstract power named God. Then one day I became righteously mad with anger that the medicine-man should thus ensnare my father's soul. And when he came to chant his sacred songs I pointed toward the door and bade him go! The man's eyes glared upon me for an instant. Slowly gathering his robe about him, he turned his back upon the sick man and stepped out of our wigwam. "Ha, ha, ha! my son, I cannot live without the medicine-man!" I heard my father cry when the sacred man was gone.

III

On a bright day, when the winged seeds of the prairie-grass were flying hither and thither, I walked solemnly toward the centre of the camping-ground. My heart beat hard and irregularly at my side. Tighter I grasped the sacred book I carried under my arm. Now was the beginning of life's work.

Though I knew it would be hard, I did not once feel that failure was to be my reward. As I stepped unevenly on the rolling ground, I thought of the warriors soon to wash off their war-paints and follow me.

At length I reached the place where the people had assembled to hear me preach. In a large circle men and women sat upon the dry red grass. Within the ring I stood, with the white man's Bible in my hand. I tried to tell them of the soft heart of Christ.

In silence the vast circle of bareheaded warriors sat under an afternoon sun. At last, wiping the wet from my brow, I took my place in the ring. The hush of the assembly filled me with great hope.

I was turning my thoughts upward to the sky in gratitude, when a stir called me to earth again.

1. Hello, Father.

A tall, strong man arose. His loose robe hung in folds over his right shoulder. A pair of snapping black eyes fastened themselves like the poisonous fangs of a serpent upon me. He was the medicine-man. A tremor played about my heart and a chill cooled the fire in my veins.

Scornfully he pointed a long forefinger in my direction and asked:

"What loyal son is he who, returning to his father's people, wears a foreigner's dress?" He paused a moment, and then continued: "The dress of that foreigner of whom a story says he bound a native of our land, and heaping dry sticks around him, kindled a fire at his feet!" Waving his hand toward me, he exclaimed, "Here is the traitor to his people!"

I was helpless. Before the eyes of the crowd the cunning magician turned my honest heart into a vile nest of treachery. Alas! the people frowned as they looked upon me.

"Listen!" he went on. "Which one of you who have eyed the young man can see through his bosom and warn the people of the nest of young snakes hatching there? Whose ear was so acute that he caught the hissing of snakes whenever the young man opened his mouth? This one has not only proven false to you, but even to the Great Spirit who made him. He is a fool! Why do you sit here giving ear to a foolish man who could not defend his people because he fears to kill, who could not bring venison to renew the life of his sick father? With his prayers, let him drive away the enemy! With his soft heart, let him keep off starvation! We shall go elsewhere to dwell upon an untainted ground."

With this he disbanded the people. When the sun lowered in the west and the winds were quiet, the village of cone-shaped tepees was gone. The medicine-man had won the hearts of the people.

Only my father's dwelling was left to mark the fighting-ground.

IV

From a long night at my father's bedside I came out to look upon the morning. The yellow sun hung equally between the snow-covered land and the cloudless blue sky. The light of the new day was cold. The strong breath of winter crusted the snow and fitted crystal shells over the rivers and lakes. As I stood in front of the tepee, thinking of the vast prairies which separated us from our tribe, and wondering if the high sky likewise separated the soft-hearted Son of God from us, the icy blast from the North blew through my hair and skull. My neglected hair had grown long and fell upon my neck.

My father had not risen from his bed since the day the medicine-man led the people away. Though I read from the Bible and prayed beside him upon my knees, my father would not listen. Yet I believed my prayers were not unheeded in heaven.

"Ha, ha, ha! my son," my father groaned upon the first snowfall. "My son, our food is gone. There is no one to bring me meat! My son, your soft heart has unfitted you for everything!" Then covering his face with the buffalo-robe, he said no more. Now while I stood out in that cold winter morning, I was starving. For two days I had not seen any food. But my own cold and hunger did not harass my soul as did the whining cry of the sick old man.

Stepping again into the tepee, I untied my snow-shoes, which were fastened to the tent-poles.

My poor mother, watching by the sick one, and faithfully heaping wood upon the centre fire, spoke to me:

"My son, do not fail again to bring your father meat, or he will starve to death."

"How, Ina,"[2] I answered, sorrowfully. From the tepee I started forth again to hunt food for my aged parents. All day I tracked the white level lands in vain. Nowhere, nowhere were there any other footprints but my own! In the evening of this third fast-day I came back without meat. Only a bundle of sticks for the fire I brought on my back. Dropping the wood outside, I lifted the door-flap and set one foot within the tepee.

There I grew dizzy and numb. My eyes swam in tears. Before me lay my old gray-haired father sobbing like a child. In his horny hands he clutched the buffalo-robe, and with his teeth he was gnawing off the edges. Chewing the dry stiff hair and buffalo-skin, my father's eyes sought my hands. Upon seeing them empty, he cried out:

"My son, your soft heart will let me starve before you bring me meat! Two hills eastward stand a herd of cattle. Yet you will see me die before you bring me food!"

Leaving my mother lying with covered head upon her mat, I rushed out into the night.

With a strange warmth in my heart and swiftness in my feet, I climbed over the first hill, and soon the second one. The moonlight upon the white country showed me a clear path to the white man's cattle. With my hand upon the knife in my belt, I leaned heavily against the fence while counting the herd.

Twenty in all I numbered. From among them I chose the best-fattened creature. Leaping over the fence, I plunged my knife into it.

My long knife was sharp, and my hands, no more fearful and slow, slashed off choice chunks of warm flesh. Bending under the meat I had taken for my starving father, I hurried across the prairie.

Toward home I fairly ran with the life-giving food I carried upon my back. Hardly had I climbed the second hill when I heard sounds coming after me. Faster and faster I ran with my load for my father, but the sounds were gaining upon me. I heard the clicking of snowshoes and the squeaking of the leather straps at my heels; yet I did not turn to see what pursued me, for I was intent upon reaching my father. Suddenly like thunder an angry voice shouted curses and threats into my ear! A rough hand wrenched my shoulder and took the meat from me! I stopped struggling to run. A deafening whir filled my head. The moon and stars began to move. Now the white prairie was sky, and the stars lay under my feet. Now again they were turning. At last the starry blue rose up into place. The noise in my ears was still. A great quiet filled the air. In my hand I found my long knife dripping with blood. At my feet a man's figure lay prone in blood-red snow. The horrible scene about me seemed a trick of my senses, for I could not understand it was real. Looking long upon the blood-stained snow, the load of meat for my starving father reached my recognition at last. Quickly I tossed it over my shoulder and started again homeward.

2. Hello, Mother.

Tired and haunted I reached the door of the wigwam. Carrying the food before me, I entered with it into the tepee.

"Father, here is food!" I cried, as I dropped the meat near my mother. No answer came. Turning about, I beheld my gray-haired father dead! I saw by the unsteady firelight an old gray-haired skeleton lying rigid and stiff.

Out into the open I started, but the snow at my feet became bloody.

V

On the day after my father's death, having led my mother to the camp of the medicine-man, I gave myself up to those who were searching for the murderer of the paleface.

They bound me hand and foot. Here in this cell I was placed four days ago.

The shrieking winter winds have followed me hither. Rattling the bars, they howl unceasingly: "Your soft heart! your soft heart will see me die before you bring me food!" Hark! something is clanking the chain on the door. It is being opened. From the dark night without a black figure crosses the threshold. It is the guard. He comes to warn me of my fate. He tells me that tomorrow I must die. In his stern face I laugh aloud. I do not fear death.

Yet I wonder who shall come to welcome me in the realm of strange sight. Will the loving Jesus grant me pardon and give my soul a soothing sleep? or will my warrior father greet me and receive me as his son? Will my spirit fly upward to a happy heaven? or shall I sink into the bottomless pit, an outcast from a God of infinite love?

Soon, soon I shall know, for now I see the east is growing red. My heart is strong. My face is calm. My eyes are dry and eager for new scenes. My hands hang quietly at my side. Serene and brave, my soul awaits the men to perch me on the gallows for another flight. I go.

1901

Debates over "Americanization"

One hundred years ago, *Americanization* was a keyword for a variety of related concerns being debated in American society. Specifically, the term referred to a concerted movement to turn immigrants into Americans, including classes, programs, and ceremonies focused on American speech, ideals, traditions, and customs, but it was also a broader term used in debates about national identity and a person's general fitness for citizenship. Beginning in the early 1880s, the number of immigrants, first from Europe and then from other locales, including Asia, grew dramatically until the start of World War I in 1914. One counterresponse to Americanization was *Nativism*, the belief held by many whites that only native-born "Anglo-Saxons" were "true" Americans, a belief fueled first by fear of Native Americans, then by fear and suspicion of ethnic newcomers as well as of post–Reconstruction free blacks. *Nationalism*, a uniting ideal that helped whites explain the destruction of Native Americans and their culture, gained strength when World War I broke out. In the build-up to the war, which the United States would not enter until 1917, Americans became increasingly suspicious of foreign-born workers and blamed them for both labor disputes and job shortages. These currents and crosscurrents of national identity were debated daily in periodicals. Inevitably, post-Darwinian "scientific" assertions of race as a true determinant of identity became a factor, and *Americanization* and *race* emerged as the twin themes of turn-of-the-century discourse about national identity.

Composed largely of immigrant pioneers in 1800, by 1900 the U.S. population had moved from farm to city, with urban growth attributable mainly to the waves of immigrants demanded by industrial production. Increasingly, despite the goals of Americanization, immigrants settled in close-knit groups in big cities, where their alien speech further segregated them from mainstream society. As Joan London, daughter of Jack London and herself a socialist critic, describes the scene, "Wage slaves were wanted now, not Americans. And so the melting pot, which had served the country well in the past, gradually ceased to function." In 1890 seven-eighths of the population held one-eighth of the wealth, while 1 percent held all the rest. Boosterism, capitalism, *laissez-faire*, and individualism flourished in the moneyed classes, and property was routinely defended in courts against state legislation on workers' rights issues, while striking workers were increasingly disciplined with state constabularies and private guards.

Late-nineteenth-century authors grew up in an America "ripe with incongruities," as literary critic Eric Carl Link observes. Scientific and historical discoveries challenged traditional religious views, while expansions in industry and agriculture created uncontrolled growth. The working class saw little of the benefits of economic expansion, despite the lower cost of living and higher wages. Severe economic panics in 1873 and 1893, brought about by the manipulation of the economy by corporate and banking empires, resulted in mass unemployment and homelessness. In the cities, slums huddled beneath corporate skyscrapers. Then the run on the gold supply (the U.S. Treasury failed to redeem claims when the minimum gold reserve amount was reached), followed by the failure of silver redemption and the bankruptcy of the Philadelphia and Reading Railroad and other major concerns, led to at least 18 percent of the national workforce being unemployed. Not until new gold production and the issue of new notes by the Treasury in 1896, followed by the Gold Rush in 1897, did the economy get back on an even keel (though it did not stay there for long).

This era also saw the farthest reach of U.S. imperialism. Expansion meant new markets in Puerto Rico, the Panama Canal region, and the Virgin Islands. The Spanish-American War of 1898 led to new possessions, including a protectorate over Cuba. Hawai'i offered a burgeoning sugar industry for U.S. investors. Samoa was partitioned among the United States, England, and Germany in 1899. Wake and Midway Islands were soon claimed by the United States, and the Philippines were retained as a vantage point in the Orient. By 1900 the United States was second only to England and France in colonial power.

Capitalists continued, in contradiction to their nativist pronouncements, to bring in cheap foreign labor as new colonies were annexed, while labor union leaders encouraged white laborers to blame their problems on nonwhite immigrant laborers instead of the capitalists. For both, a central aim was to restrict immigration to certain racial groups. The upper classes used a linguistic argument, as the *Nation* argued for a secure modern state resting on a community of shared language, with immigrants restricted to English-speaking peoples. The new academic field of "race science," or racialism, advanced by professors at the nation's top universities, from Harvard to Johns Hopkins to Stanford, turned to the theories of Charles Darwin, in particular those of his follower Herbert Spencer, who attempted to apply Darwin's "survival of the fittest" to human society, specifically to racial differences, and to warn of future race competition. Central to the thinking of many Americans was the belief that U.S. citizenship was the birthright of a superior founding "race" descended from the Anglo-Saxon "race," or, what a character in Charles Chesnutt's *The Marrow of Tradition* [1901] refers to as " 'de Angry-Saxon race.' "

David Starr Jordan (1851–1931), the first president of Stanford University, helped introduce Social Darwinism and eugenics, the improvement of the human species through control of heredity, to the United States, along with Francis Galton, a cousin of Darwin's, who was inspired by Spencer. In *The Care and Culture of Men* (1896), Jordan wrote that the United States must rely on its Anglo-Saxons, "the heart of this republic, . . . the sons and daughters of 'him that overcometh.' " This is "a lineage untainted by luxury, uncoddled by charity, uncorroded by vice, uncrushed by oppression. If it were not so, we could not be here today." Jordan's ideas were fairly benign compared to those of many of his contemporaries. Respected writers like H. G. Wells advocated sterilization of breeding "failures" in order to improve the "human stock," and a "Galton Society" at the Museum of Natural History in New York popularized presumed parallels between stock breeding and human mating.

This cluster presents leading figures of the day addressing the multiple meanings of *Americanization* and race, beginning with Frederick Jackson Turner's "frontier thesis" and Theodore Roosevelt's grand vision of "winning" the West, followed by five counterassessments of what the still-new United States of America ought to offer to all its inhabitants.

FREDERICK JACKSON TURNER

Two opposing turn-of-the-nineteenth-century ideas of national identity were the "germ theory" and the "frontier theory." The germ theory held, as critic Donald Pizer puts it, that "American democracy had been racially transmitted through Anglo-Saxon immigration, first from northern Germany to England and then from England to America." Tribal councils of primitive Germans were naturally followed by the English "folkmoot" and the New England town meeting. Championed by Theodore Roosevelt, the germ theory gave rise to John O'Sullivan's statement (he was the *Democratic Review* editor who coined the term "Manifest Destiny") that in California "the irresistible army of Anglo-Saxon emigration" has taken over, "armed with the plough and the rifle, and marking its trail with schools and colleges, courts and representative halls, mills and meeting houses," a nationalist and nativist view of Jeffersonian yeomanry in the West. During the Mexican War (1846–48), the *Democratic Review* warned that the "very virtues of the Anglo-Saxon race made their political union with the degraded Mexican-Spanish impossible." Still, imperialist voices prevailed. Josiah Strong predicted in the 1880s that the world was about to "enter upon a new stage of its history—the final competition of the races for which the Anglo-Saxon is being schooled. If I do not read amiss, this powerful race will move down upon Mexico, down upon Central and South America, out upon the islands of the sea, over upon Africa and beyond." This race, Strong argued, "is destined to dispossess many weaker races, assimilate others, and mold the remainder until . . . it has Anglo-Saxonized mankind." Yet Americans also subscribed to a view of American destiny that opposed the germ theory, and that was of course Turner's notion of the frontier, and not heredity, as the transformative agent of Americans. For Turner (1861–1932), American democracy was "not the last flowering of a pure seed developed elsewhere," but lay within "the soil which took the mixed seeds which fell upon it and transformed them into something new and distinctive, the American race." Turner believed "The West, at bottom, is a form of society, rather than an area," a region where older institutions meet "the transforming influences of free land," creating an entirely new environment, where "freedom of opportunity is opened, the cake of custom is broken, and new activities, new lines of growth, new institutions and new ideals, are brought into existence." For him, the "history of our political institutions, our democracy, . . . is a history of the evolution and adaptation of organs in response to changed environment, . . . the origin of new political species."

From The Significance of the Frontier in American History[1]

* * * Up to our own day American history has been in a large degree the history of the colonization of the Great West. The existence of an area of free land, its continuous recession, and the advance of American settlement westward, explain American development.

Behind institutions, behind constitutional forms and modifications, lie the vital forces that call these organs into life and shape them to meet changing conditions. The peculiarity of American institutions is, the fact that they have been compelled to adapt themselves to the changes of an expanding people—to the changes involved in crossing a continent, in winning a wilderness, and in developing at each area of this progress out of the primitive economic and political conditions of the frontier into the complexity of city life. Said Calhoun[2] in 1817, "We are great, and rapidly—I was about to say fearfully—growing!" So saying, he touched the distinguishing feature of American life. All peoples show development; the germ theory of politics has been sufficiently emphasized. In the case of most nations, however, the development has occurred in a limited area; and if the nation has expanded, it has met other growing peoples whom it has conquered. But in the case of the United

---

1. Turner's address to the American Historical Association was delivered on July 12, 1893, in Chicago. It was printed in the *Proceedings of the State Historical Society of Wisconsin*, December 14, 1893, then in the *Report of the American Historical Association* for 1893. Along with various short papers of Turner's, it became part of *The*

Frontier in American History (1920), from which these excerpts are taken.
2. John Caldwell Calhoun (1782–1850), U.S. representative and senator from South Carolina and U.S. vice president under John Quincy Adams and Andrew Jackson. Turner cites "Abridgment of Debates of Congress," vol. V.

States we have a different phenomenon. Limiting our attention to the Atlantic coast, we have the familiar phenomenon of the evolution of institutions in a limited area, such as the rise of representative government; into complex organs; the progress from primitive industrial society, without division of labor, up to manufacturing civilization. But we have in addition to this a recurrence of the process of evolution in each western area reached in the process of expansion. Thus American development has exhibited not merely advance along a single line, but a return to primitive conditions on a continually advancing frontier line, and a new development for that area. American social development has been continually beginning over again on the frontier. This perennial rebirth, this fluidity of American life, this expansion westward with its new opportunities, its continuous touch with the simplicity of primitive society, furnish the forces dominating American character. The true point of view in the history of this nation is not the Atlantic coast, it is the Great West. Even the slavery struggle, which is made so exclusive an object of attention by writers like Professor von Holst,[3] occupies its important place in American history because of its relation to westward expansion. In this advance, the frontier is the outer edge of the wave—the meeting point between savagery and civilization. Much has been written about the frontier from the point of view of border warfare and the chase, but as a field for the serious study of the economist and the historian it has been neglected.

The American frontier is sharply distinguished from the European frontier— a fortified boundary line running through dense populations. The most significant thing about the American frontier is, that it lies at the hither edge of free land. In the census reports it is treated as the margin of that settlement which has a density of two or more to the square mile. The term is an elastic one, and for our purposes does not need sharp definition. We shall consider the whole frontier belt including the Indian country and the outer margin of the "settled area" of the census reports. This paper will make no attempt to treat the subject exhaustively; its aim is simply to call attention to the frontier as a fertile field for investigation, and to suggest some of the problems which arise in connection with it. In the settlement of America we have to observe how European life entered the continent, and how America modified and developed that life and reacted on Europe. Our early history is the study of European germs developing in an American environment. Too exclusive attention has been paid by institutional students to the Germanic origins, too little to the American factors. The frontier is the line of most rapid and effective Americanization. The wilderness masters the colonist. It finds him a European in dress, industries, tools, modes of travel, and thought. It takes him from the railroad car and puts him in the birch canoe. It strips off the garments of civilization and arrays him in the hunting shirt and the moccasin. It puts him in the log cabin of the Cherokee and Iroquois and runs an Indian palisade around him. Before long he has gone to planting Indian corn and plowing with a sharp stick, he shouts the war cry and takes the scalp in orthodox Indian fashion. In short, at the frontier the environment is at first too strong for the man. He must accept the conditions which it furnishes, or perish, and so he fits himself into the Indian clearings and follows the Indian trails. Little by little he transforms the wilderness, but the outcome is not the old Europe, not simply the development of

3. Hermann Eduard von Holst (1841–1904) was a German American historian whose principal work, Constitutional and Political History of the United States (published 1873–91 in German and translated into English beginning in 1877), argued against slavery.

to the Germanic mark. The fact is, that here is a new product that is American. At first, the frontier was the Atlantic coast. It was the frontier of Europe in a very real sense. Moving westward, the frontier became more and more American. As successive terminal moraines result from successive glaciations, so each frontier leaves its traces behind it, and when it becomes a settled area the region still partakes of the frontier characteristics. Thus the advance of the frontier has meant a steady movement away from the influence of Europe, a steady growth of independence on American lines. And to study this advance, the men who grew up under these conditions, and the political, economic, and social results of it, is to study the really American part of our history.

*   *   *

It was not merely in legislative action that the frontier worked against the sectionalism of the coast. The economic and social characteristics of the frontier worked against sectionalism. The men of the frontier had closer resemblances to the Middle region than to either of the other sections. Pennsylvania had been the seed plot of frontier emigration, and, although she passed on her settlers along the Great Valley into the west of Virginia and the Carolinas, yet the industrial society of these Southern frontiersmen was always more like that of the Middle region than like that of the tide water portion of the South, which later came to spread its industrial type throughout the South. The Middle region, entered by New York harbor, was an open door to all Europe. The tide-water part of the South represented typical Englishmen, modified by a warm climate and servile labor, and living in baronial fashion on great plantations; New England stood for a special English movement—Puritanism. The Middle region was less English than the other sections. It had a wide mixture of nationalities, a varied society, the mixed town and county system of local government, a varied economic life, many religious sects. In short, it was a region mediating between New England and the South, and the East and the West. It represented that composite nationality which the contemporary United States exhibits, that juxtaposition of non-English groups, occupying a valley or a little settlement, and presenting reflections of the map of Europe in their variety. It was democratic and non-sectional, if not national; "easy, tolerant, and contented"; rooted strongly in material prosperity. It was typical of the modern United States. It was least sectional, not only because it lay between North and South, but also because with no barriers to shut out its frontiers from its settled region, and with a system of connecting waterways, the Middle region mediated between East and West as well as between North and South. Thus it became the typically American region. Even the New Englander, who was shut out from the frontier by the Middle region, tarrying in New York or Pennsylvania on his westward march, lost the acuteness of his sectionalism on the way.

*   *   *

So long as free land exists, the opportunity for a competency exists, and economic power secures political power. But the democracy born of free land, strong in selfishness and individualism, intolerant of administrative experience and education, and pressing individual liberty beyond its proper bounds, has its dangers as well as its benefits. Individualism in America has allowed a laxity in regard to governmental affairs which has rendered possible the spoils system and all the manifest evils that follow from the lack of a highly developed civic spirit. In this connection may be noted also the influence of frontier conditions in permitting lax business honor, inflated paper currency and wild-cat banking. The colonial and revolutionary frontier was the region whence emanated many of the worst forms of an evil currency. The West in the War of 1812 repeated the phenomenon on the frontier of that day, while the speculation and wild-cat banking of the period of the crisis of 1837 occurred on the new frontier belt of the next tier of States. Thus each one of the periods of lax financial integrity coincides with periods when a new set of frontier communities had arisen, and coincides in area with these successive frontiers for the most part. The recent Populist agitation is a case in point. Many a State that now declines any connection with the tenets of the Populists, itself adhered to such ideas in an earlier stage of the development of the State. A primitive society can hardly be expected to show the intelligent appreciation of the complexity of business interests in a developed society. The continual recurrence of these areas of paper-money agitation is another evidence that the frontier can be isolated and studied as a factor in American history of the highest importance.

* * *

From the conditions of frontier life came intellectual traits of profound importance. The works of travelers along each frontier from colonial days onward describe certain common traits, and these traits have, while softening down, still persisted as survivals in the place of their origin, even when a higher social organization succeeded. The result is that to the frontier the American intellect owes its striking characteristics. That coarseness and strength combined with acuteness and inquisitiveness; that practical, inventive turn of mind, quick to find expedients; that masterful grasp of material things, lacking in the artistic but powerful to effect great ends; that restless, nervous energy; that dominant individualism, working for good and for evil, and withal that buoyancy and exuberance which comes with freedom—these are traits of the frontier, or traits called out elsewhere because of the existence of the frontier. Since the days when the fleet of Columbus sailed into the waters of the New World, America has been another name for opportunity, and the people of the United States have taken their tone from the incessant expansion which has not only been open but has even been forced upon them. He would be a rash prophet who should assert that the expansive character of American life has now entirely ceased. Movement has been its dominant fact, and, unless this training has no effect upon a people, the American energy will continually demand a wider field for its exercise. But never again will such gifts of free land offer themselves. For a moment, at the frontier, the bonds of custom are broken and unrestraint is triumphant. There is not *tabula rasa*. The stubborn American environment is there with its imperious summons to accept its conditions; the inherited ways of doing things are also there; and yet, in spite of environment, and in spite of custom, each frontier did indeed furnish a new field of opportunity, a gate of escape from the bondage of the past; and freshness, and confidence, and scorn of older society, impatience of its restraints and its ideas, and indifference to its lessons, have accompanied the frontier. What the Mediterranean Sea was to the Greeks, breaking the bond of custom, offering new experiences, calling out new institutions and activities, that, and more, the ever retreating frontier has been to the United States directly, and to the nations of Europe more remotely. And now, four centuries from the discovery of America, at the end of a hundred years of life under the Constitution, the frontier has gone, and with its going has closed the first period of American history.

1893

THEODORE ROOSEVELT

As a prolific writer and politician, Theodore Roosevelt (1858–1919) emphasized the romance of the American march westward, led by the Anglo-Saxon race, planting, at each stage of conquest, seeds that would flower in American democratic society. Roosevelt's rhetoric, unlike Turner's, was clearly that of conquest: "The warlike borderers who thronged across the Alleghanies, the restless and reckless hunters, the hard, dogged, frontier farmers, by dint of grim tenacity, overcame and displaced Indians, French, and Spaniards alike, exactly as, fourteen hundred years before, Saxon and Angle had overcome and displaced the . . . Celts." For Roosevelt, "the spread of the English-speaking peoples over the world's waste spaces has been not only the most striking feature in the world's history, but also the event of all others most far-reaching in its importance." Roosevelt applauded in Darwinian terms "the vigor and prowess shown by our fighting men" and the nation's "lift toward mighty things," scorning the "shortsighted and timid" people who opposed wars "for the advance of American civilization at the cost of savagery." He invokes values of manliness, self-reliance, and hard work as the essential hallmarks of the American West, no matter whether an earlier immigrant or a later one, no matter what "race." Indeed, as he observes in *American Ideals*, "We were . . . already, what we are now, a people of mixed blood" from many different countries. Roosevelt argues that immigrants should assimilate, but he does not discount the diverse strengths immigrants from around the world lend to the growing United States.

From American Ideals[1]
From *Chapter II. True Americanism*

* * *

The mighty tide of immigration to our shores has brought in its train much of good and much of evil; and whether the good or the evil shall predominate depends mainly on whether these newcomers do or do not throw themselves heartily into our national life, cease to be European, and become Americans like the rest of us. More than a third of the people of the Northern States are of foreign birth or parentage. An immense number of them have become completely Americanized, and these stand on exactly the same plane as the descendants of any Puritan, Cavalier, or Knickerbocker among us,[2] and do

---

1. From the first edition, published in 1897.
2. Puritan: a Protestant religious dissenter; most puritans left England and settled in New England. Cavalier: a supporter of King Charles I during the

English Civil War (1642–51). Knickerbocker: a descendant of the original Dutch settlers of Manhattan.

their full and honorable share of the nation's work. But where immigrants, or the sons of immigrants, do not heartily and in good faith throw in their lot with us, but cling to the speech, the customs, the ways of life, and the habits of thought of the Old World which they have left, they thereby harm both themselves and us. If they remain alien elements, unassimilated, and with interests separate from ours, they are mere obstructions to the current of our national life, and, moreover, can get no good from it themselves. In fact, though we ourselves also suffer from their perversity, it is they who really suffer most. It is an immense benefit to the European immigrant to change him into an American citizen. To bear the name of American is to bear the most honorable of titles; and whoever does not so believe has no business to bear the name at all, and, if he comes from Europe, the sooner he goes back there the better. Besides, the man who does not become Americanized nevertheless fails to remain a European, and becomes nothing at all. The immigrant cannot possibly remain what he was, or continue to be a member of the Old-World society. If he tries to retain his old language, in a few generations it becomes a barbarous jargon; if he tries to retain his old customs and ways of life, in a few generations he becomes an uncouth boor. He has cut himself off from the Old-World, and cannot retain his connection with it; and if he wishes ever to amount to anything he must throw himself heart and soul, and without reservation, into the new life to which he has come. It is urgently necessary to check and regulate our immigration, by much more drastic laws than now exist; and this should be done both to keep out laborers who tend to depress the labor market, and to keep out races which do not assimilate readily with our own, and unworthy individuals of all races—not only criminals, idiots, and paupers, but anarchists of the Most and O'Donovan Rossa type.[3]

From his own standpoint, it is beyond all question the wise thing for the immigrant to become thoroughly Americanized. Moreover, from our standpoint, we have a right to demand it. We freely extend the hand of welcome and of good-fellowship to every man, no matter what his creed or birthplace, who comes here honestly intent on becoming a good United States citizen like the rest of us; but we have a right, and it is our duty, to demand that he shall indeed become so, and shall not confuse the issues with which we are struggling by introducing among us Old-World quarrels and prejudices. There are certain ideas which he must give up. For instance, he must learn that American life is incompatible with the existence of any form of anarchy, or of any secret society having murder for its aim, whether at home or abroad; and he must learn that we exact full religious toleration and the complete separation of Church and State. Moreover, he must not bring in his Old-World religious race and national antipathies, but must merge them into love for our common country, and must take pride in the things which we can all take pride in. He must revere only our flag; not only must it come first, but no other flag should even come second. He must learn to celebrate Washington's birthday rather than that of the Queen or Kaiser, and the Fourth of July instead of St. Patrick's Day.

3. Johann Most (1846–1906) was a German anarchist who emigrated to the United States and was best known for his advocacy of armed revolt. Jeremiah O'Donovan Rossa (1831–1915) was an Irish Fenian leader who established the Irish Republican Brotherhood. Jailed numerous times, he was exiled to the United States in 1871; from New York City, he organized the first Irish republican bombings of English cities.

Our political and social questions must be settled on their own merits, and not complicated by quarrels between England and Ireland, or France and Germany, with which we have nothing to do: it is an outrage to fight an American political campaign with reference to questions of European politics. Above all, the immigrant must learn to talk and think and *be* United States.

The immigrant of to-day can learn much from the experience of the immigrants of the past, who came to America prior to the Revolutionary War. We were then already, what we are now, a people of mixed blood. Many of our most illustrious Revolutionary names were borne by men of Huguenot blood—Jay, Sevier, Marion, Laurens.[4] But the Huguenots were, on the whole, the best immigrants we have ever received; sooner than any other, and more completely, they became American in speech, conviction, and thought. The Hollanders took longer than the Huguenots to become completely assimilated; nevertheless they in the end became so, immensely to their own advantage. One of the leading Revolutionary generals, Schuyler, and one of the Presidents of the United States, Van Buren,[5] were of Dutch blood; but they rose to their positions, the highest in the land, because they had become Americans and had ceased being Hollanders. If they had remained members of an alien body, cut off by their speech and customs and belief from the rest of the American community, Schuyler would have lived his life as a boorish, provincial squire, and Van Buren would have ended his days a small tavern-keeper. So it is with the Germans of Pennsylvania. Those of them who became Americanized have furnished to our history a multitude of honorable names, from the days of the Mühlenbergs onward;[6] but those who did not become Americanized form to the present day an unimportant body, of no significance in American existence. So it is with the Irish, who gave to Revolutionary annals such names as Carroll and Sullivan, and to the Civil War men like Sheridan[7]—men who were Americans and nothing else: while the Irish who remain such, and busy themselves solely with alien politics, can have only an unhealthy influence upon American life, and can never rise as do their compatriots who become straightout Americans. Thus it has ever been with all people who have come hither, of whatever stock or blood. The same thing is true of the churches. A church which remains foreign, in language or spirit, is doomed.

4. French protestants of the 16th and 17th centuries. Among them were John Jay (1745–1829), who served as president of the Continental Congress and is considered one of the "founding fathers" of the United States; Ambrose Hundley Sevier (1801–1848), Democratic U.S. Senator from Arkansas, sent in 1848 to Mexico to negotiate the Treaty of Guadalupe Hildalgo, which ended the Mexican War. Others were Francis Marion (ca. 1732–1795), a general in the American Revolutionary War, during which he acquired the name "Swamp Fox" for his clever use of decoy and ambush tactics, and Henry Laurens (1724–1792), American merchant and South Carolina planter who became a political leader during the Revolutionary War, serving as delegate to the Continental Congress and as the third president of the Second Continental Congress (1777–78).
5. Martin Van Buren (1782–1862) was the eighth president of the United States; as a Dutch-descended American, he was the first president of

non-Anglo descent and the only one whose first language was not English.
6. An American political, religious, and military dynasty descended from Heinrich Melchior Mühlenberg (1711–1787), a German immigrant who settled in Philadelphia; Mühlenberg was a founder of the Lutheran Church in America.
7. Charles Carroll (1737–1832), delegate to the Continental Congress and U.S. Senator from Maryland; Carroll was the only Catholic signer of the Declaration of Independence. John Sullivan (1740–1795), general in the Revolutionary War, delegate to the Continental Congress, and governor of New Hampshire; famous for his campaign against Iroquois who opposed the American revolutionaries. Philip Henry Sheridan (1831–1888), Union general in the American Civil War and later involved in the Indian wars of the Great Plains; an early environmentalist and leading force behind the creation of Yellowstone National Park.

But I wish to be distinctly understood on one point. Americanism is a question of spirit, conviction, and purpose, not of creed or birthplace. The politician who bids for the Irish or German vote, or the Irishman or German who votes as an Irishman or German, is despicable, for all citizens of this commonwealth should vote solely as Americans; but he is not a whit less despicable than the voter who votes against a good American, merely because that American happens to have been born in Ireland or Germany. Knownothingism,[8] in any form, is as utterly un-American as foreignism. It is a base outrage to oppose a man because of his religion or birthplace, and all good citizens will hold any such effort in abhorrence. A Scandinavian, a German, or an Irishman who has really become an American has the right to stand on exactly the same footing as any native-born citizen in the land, and is just as much entitled to the friendship and support, social and political, of his neighbors. Among the men with whom I have been thrown in close personal contact socially, and who have been among my staunchest friends and allies politically, are not a few Americans who happen to have been born on the other side of the water, in Germany, Ireland, Scandinavia; and there could be no better men in the ranks of our native-born citizens.

*   *   *

1897

From The Strenuous Life[1]

*   *   *

In all the history of mankind there is nothing that quite parallels the way in which our people have filled a vacant continent with self-governing commonwealths, knit into one nation. And of all this marvelous history perhaps the most wonderful portion is that which deals with the way in which the Pacific coast and the Rocky Mountains were settled.

The men who founded these communities showed practically by their lifework that it is indeed the spirit of adventure which is the maker of commonwealths. Their traits of daring and hardihood and iron endurance are not merely indispensable traits for pioneers; they are also traits which must go to the make-up of every mighty and successful people. You and your fathers who built up the West did more even than you thought; for you shaped thereby the destiny of the whole republic, and as a necessary corollary profoundly influenced the course of events throughout the world. More and more as the years go by this republic will find its guidance in the thought and action of the West, because the conditions of development in the West have steadily tended to accentuate the peculiarly American characteristics of its people.

There was scant room for the coward and the weakling in the ranks of the adventurous frontiersmen—the pioneer settlers who first broke up the wild

8. A nativist American political movement of the 1850s, a popular reaction to fears that the political corruption of Irish Catholic immigrants was weakening U.S. cities. The membership, mostly middle class and Protestant, was absorbed by the Republican Party in the North.

1. *The Strenuous Life* is one of Roosevelt's most famous books, published in 1902. The excerpt is from the chapter entitled "Manhood and Statehood," an address Roosevelt gave in Colorado Springs on August 2, 1901.

prairie soil, who first hewed their way into the primeval forest, who guided their white-topped wagons across the endless leagues of Indian-haunted desolation, and explored every remote mountain-chain in the restless quest for metal wealth. Behind them came the men who completed the work they had roughly begun: who drove the great railroad systems over plain and desert and mountain pass; who stocked the teeming ranches, and under irrigation saw the bright green of the alfalfa and the yellow of the golden stubble supplant the gray of the sage-brush desert; who have built great populous cities—cities in which every art and science of civilization are carried to the highest point— on tracts which, when the nineteenth century had passed its meridian, were still known only to the grim trappers and hunters and the red lords of the wilderness with whom they waged eternal war.

Such is the record of which we are so proud. It is a record of men who greatly dared and greatly did; a record of wanderings wider and more dangerous than those of the Vikings; a record of endless feats of arms, of victory after victory in the ceaseless strife waged against wild man and wild nature. The winning of the West was the great epic feat in the history of our race.

We have then a right to meet to-day in a spirit of just pride in the past. But when we pay homage to the hardy, grim, resolute men who, with incredible toil and risk, laid deep the foundations of the civilization that we inherit, let us steadily remember that the only homage that counts is the homage of deeds—not merely of words. It is well to gather here to show that we remember what has been done in the past by the Western pioneers of our people, and that we glory in the greatness for which they prepared the way. But lip-loyalty by itself avails very little, whether it is expressed concerning a nation or an ideal. It would be a sad and evil thing for this country if ever the day came when we considered the great deeds of our forefathers as an excuse for our resting slothfully satisfied with what has been already done. On the contrary, they should be an inspiration and appeal, summoning us to show that we too have courage and strength; that we too are ready to dare greatly if the need arises; and, above all, that we are firmly bent upon that steady performance of every-day duty which, in the long run, is of such incredible worth in the formation of national character.

The old iron days have gone, the days when the weakling died as the penalty of inability to hold his own in the rough warfare against his surroundings. We live in softer times. Let us see to it that, while we take advantage of every gentler and more humanizing tendency of the age, we yet preserve the iron quality which made our forefathers and predecessors fit to do the deeds they did. It will of necessity find a different expression now, but the quality itself remains just as necessary as ever. Surely you men of the West, you men who with stout heart, cool head, and ready hand have wrought out your own success and built up these great new commonwealths, surely you need no reminder of the fact that if either man or nation wishes to play a great part in the world there must be no dallying with the life of lazy ease. In the abounding energy and intensity of existence in our mighty democratic republic there is small space indeed for the idler, for the luxury-loving man who prizes ease more than hard, triumph-crowned effort.

We hold work not as a curse but as a blessing, and we regard the idler with scornful pity. It would be in the highest degree undesirable that we should all work in the same way or at the same things, and for the sake of the real greatness of the nation we should in the fullest and most cordial way recognize the fact that some of the most needed work must, from its very nature, be unremunerative in a material sense. Each man must choose so far as the conditions allow him the path to which he is bidden by his own peculiar powers and inclinations. But if he is a man he must in some way or shape do a man's work. If, after making all the effort that his strength of body and of mind permits, he yet honorably fails, why, he is still entitled to a certain share of respect because he has made the effort. But if he does not make the effort, or if he makes it half-heartedly and recoils from the labor, the risk, or the irksome monotony of his task, why, he has forfeited all right to our respect, and has shown himself a mere cumberer of the earth. It is not given to us all to succeed, but it is given to us all to strive manfully to deserve success.

We need then the iron qualities that must go with true manhood. We need the positive virtues of resolution, of courage, of indomitable will, of power to do without shrinking the rough work that must always be done, and to persevere through the long days of slow progress or of seeming failure which always come before any final triumph, no matter how brilliant. But we need more than these qualities. This country cannot afford to have its sons less than men; but neither can it afford to have them other than good men. If courage and strength and intellect are unaccompanied by the moral purpose, the moral sense, they become merely forms of expression for unscrupulous force and unscrupulous cunning. If the strong man has not in him the lift toward lofty things his strength makes him only a curse to himself and to his neighbor. All this is true in private life, and it is no less true in public life. If Washington and Lincoln had not had in them the whipcord fiber of moral and mental strength, the soul that steels itself to endure disaster unshaken and with grim resolve to wrest victory from defeat, then the one could not have founded, nor the other preserved, our mighty federal Union. The least touch of flabbiness, of unhealthy softness, in either would have meant ruin for this nation, and therefore the downfall of the proudest hope of mankind. But no less is it true that had either been influenced by self-seeking ambition, by callous disregard of others, by contempt for the moral law, he would have dashed us down into the black gulf of failure. Woe to all of us if ever as a people we grow to condone evil because it is successful. We can no more afford to lose social and civic decency and honesty than we can afford to lose the qualities of courage and strength. It is the merest truism to say that the nation rests upon the individual, upon the family—upon individual manliness and womanliness, using the words in their widest and fullest meaning.

To be a good husband or good wife, a good neighbor and friend, to be hardworking and upright in business and social relations, to bring up many healthy children—to be and to do all this is to lay the foundations of good citizenship as they must be laid. But we cannot stop even with this. Each of us has not only his duty to himself, his family, and his neighbors, but his duty to the State and to the nation. We are in honor bound each to strive according to his or her strength to bring ever nearer the day when justice and wisdom shall obtain in public life as in private life. We cannot retain the full measure of our self-respect if we cannot retain pride in our citizenship. For the sake not only of ourselves but of our children and our children's children we must see that this nation stands for strength and honesty both at home and abroad.

In our internal policy we cannot afford to rest satisfied until all that the government can do has been done to secure fair dealing and equal justice as between man and man. In the great part which hereafter, whether we will or not, we must play in the world at large, let us see to it that we neither do wrong nor shrink from doing right because the right is difficult; that on the one hand we inflict no injury, and that on the other we have a due regard for the honor and the interest of our mighty nation; and that we keep unsullied the renown of the flag which beyond all others of the present time or of the ages of the past stands for confident faith in the future welfare and greatness of mankind.

1902

HELEN HUNT JACKSON

In 1881 Helen Hunt Jackson (1830–1885) published *A Century of Dishonor: A Sketch of the United States Government's Dealings with Some of the Indian Tribes*, in which she reviews the many inequities perpetrated by whites against Native Americans. Following the book's publication, the U.S. Congress appointed a commission to look into Indian affairs. The commission's findings suggested that the choices for Indians were either to "vanish" or to assimilate—to become, in effect, Indian-Americans. To this end, Congress passed the Dawes Act of 1887, which sought to break up the communally held landbase of the tribes and to introduce the virtues of private property and rugged individualism. Dawes was a disaster for Native lifeways, and the assimilation approach to Native peoples was not reversed until the passage of the Indian Reorganization Act in 1934. In this excerpt from *A Century of Dishonor*, Jackson details incidents leading to the demise of the Ponca Indians, using her own words, those of a Ponca chief, treaties, and reports of the Commission for Indian Affairs. The cover of the book displays a quotation from Benjamin Franklin: "Look upon your hands! They are stained with the blood of your relations."

From A Century of Dishonor[1]

From Chapter VI. The Poncas

In 1803 Captain Lewis and Lieutenant Clarke, of the First United States Infantry, were commissioned by Congress to explore the river Missouri from its mouth to its source, to "seek the best water communication from thence to the Pacific Ocean," and to enter into conference with all the Indian tribes on their route, with a view to the establishment of commerce with them.[2]

---

1. From *A Century of Dishonor: A Sketch of the United States Government's Dealings with Some of the Indian Tribes*, first published by Harper & Brothers (1881), reprinted in 1885 and then by Roberts Brothers in 1886, from which this excerpt is taken.
2. On February 28, 1803, President Thomas Jefferson won approval from Congress for an endeavor to explore and record the land from the Missouri frontier to the Pacific. An expeditionary group was also to try to discover the "Northwest Passage" that would provide a sea lane between the east and west coasts. Called the "Corps of Discovery," the group was led by Meriwether Lewis (1774–1809) and William Clark (1770–1838), whose now-famous journals of the expedition were first published in 1814.

They report the "Poncars" as "the remnant of a nation once respectable in point of numbers; they formerly resided on a branch of the Red River of Lake Winnipeg; being oppressed by Sioux, they removed to the west side of the Missouri, on Poncar River, where they built and fortified a village, and remained some years; but, being pursued by their ancient enemies, the Sioux, and reduced by continual wars, they have joined and now live with the Mahas (Omahas), whose language they speak." Their numbers are estimated by Lewis and Clarke as being only about two hundred, all told; but this small estimate is probably to be explained by the fact that at this time the tribe was away on its annual buffalo-hunt, and their village had been so long empty and quiet that a buffalo was found grazing there. A few years later the tribe is reckoned at four hundred: in a census of the Indian tribes, taken by General Porter in 1829, they are set down at six hundred. The artist Catlin,[3] who visited them a few years later, rated them a little less. He gives an interesting account of the chief of the tribe, named Shoo-de-ga-cha (Smoke), and his young and pretty wife, Hee-la'h-dee (the Pure Fountain), whose portraits he painted. He says: "The chief, who was wrapped in a buffalo-robe, is a noble specimen of native dignity and philosophy. I conversed much with him, and from his dignified manners, as well as from the soundness of his reasoning, I became fully convinced that he deserved to be the sachem of a more numerous and prosperous tribe. He related to me with great coolness and frankness the poverty and distress of his nation—and with the method of a philosopher predicted the certain and rapid extinction of his tribe, which he had not the power to avert. Poor, noble chief, who was equal to and worthy of a greater empire! He sat on the deck of the steamer, overlooking the little cluster of his wigwams mingled among the trees, and, like Caius Marius[4] weeping over the ruins of Carthage, shed tears as he was descanting on the poverty of his ill-fated little community, which he told me had 'once been powerful and happy; that the buffaloes which the Great Spirit had given them for food, and which formerly spread all over their green prairies, had all been killed or driven out by the approach of white men, who wanted their skins; that their country was now entirely destitute of game, and even of roots for food, as it was one continuous prairie; and that his young men, penetrating the countries of their enemies for buffaloes, which they were obliged to do, were cut to pieces and destroyed in great numbers. That his people had foolishly become fond of fire-water,[5] and had given away everything in their country for it; that it had destroyed many of his warriors, and would soon destroy the rest; that his tribe was too small and his warriors too few to go to war with the tribes around them; that they were met and killed by the Sioux on the north, by the Pawnees on the west, by the Osages and Konzas on the south, and still more alarmed from the constant advance of the pale faces—their enemies from the east—with whiskey and small-pox, which already had destroyed four-fifths of his tribe, and would

3. Pleasant Porter (1840–1907) was principal chief of the Creek Nation and a Confederate general; he was also an influential American Indian statesman, serving many times as Creek delegate to the U.S. Congress. Porter promoted a movement to establish a separate Native American state. George Catlin (1796–1872), whose mother was captured by Indians in Pennsylvania, gave up his law studies and devoted himself to Indian causes and to paint-ing Indians in their native settings.
4. Also known as Gaius Marius (157–86 B.C.E.), a Roman general and consul noted for dramatic reforms of Roman armies; though he married Julius Caesar's aunt, he at one point was exiled by a rival general, Sulla, to Carthage, which would not accept him; he followed attacks there with another massacre of his enemies in Rome.
5. Alcohol.

soon impoverish and at last destroy the remainder of them.' In this way did this shrewd philosopher lament over the unlucky destiny of his tribe, and I pitied him with all my heart."

✳   ✳   ✳

The United States' first treaty with this handful of gentle and peaceable Indians was made in 1817. It was simply a treaty of peace and friendship.

In 1825 another was made, in which the Poncas admit that "they reside within the territorial limits of the United States, acknowledge their supremacy, and claim their protection." They also admit "the right of the United States to regulate all trade and intercourse with them." The United States, on their part, "agree to receive the Poncar tribe of Indians into their friendship and under their protection, and to extend to them from time to time such benefits and acts of kindness as may be convenient, and seem just and proper to the President of the United States."

After this there is little mention, in the official records of the Government, of the Poncas for some thirty years. Other tribes in the Upper Missouri region were so troublesome and aggressive that the peaceable Poncas were left to shift for themselves as they best could amidst all the warring and war-ring interests by which they were surrounded. In 1856 the agent of the Upper Platte mentions incidentally that their lands were being fast intruded upon by squatters; and in 1857 another agent reports having met on the banks of the Missouri a large band of Poncas, who made complaint that all the Indians on the river were receiving presents and they were overlooked; that the men from the steamboats cut their trees down, and that white set-tlers were taking away all their land. In 1858 the Commissioner for Indian Affairs writes: "Treaties were entered into in March and April last with the Poncas and Yankton Sioux, who reside west of Iowa, for the purpose of extin-guishing their title to all the lands occupied and claimed by them, except small portions on which to colonize and domesticate them. This proceeding was deemed necessary in order to obtain such control over these Indians as to prevent their interference with our settlements, which are rapidly extend-ing in that direction. These treaties were duly laid before the Senate at its last regular session, but were not, it is understood, finally acted on by that body.

"Relying on the ratification of their treaty, and the adoption of timely meas-ures to carry out its provisions in their favor, the Poncas proceeded in good faith to comply with its stipulations by abandoning their settlements and hunting-grounds, and withdrawing to the small tract reserved for their future home. Being without a crop to rely upon, and having been unsuccessful in their usual summer hunt, they were reduced to a state of desperation and des-titution. As nothing had been done for them under the treaty, they concluded it was void, and threatened to fall back upon their former settlements, some of the most important of which had, in the mean time, been taken possession of by numerous white persons."

The Poncas never heard of Grotius or Vattel; but, in assuming that the treaty was void because it was not fulfilled, they only acted on the natural principles of the law of nations and of treaties, as laid down by all authori-ties. Thucydides said: "They are not the first breakers of a league who, being deserted, seek for aid to others, but they that perform not by their deeds what they have promised to do upon their oaths."[6]

In consequence of this delay to fulfil the treaty provisions, the Government was forced to step in at the last moment and "incur a heavy expense" in furnishing the Poncas with food enough to keep them from starving; and in 1859, under this pressure, the Senate ratified the treaty. By it the Poncas ceded and relinquished to the United States all the lands they had ever owned or claimed, "wherever situate," except a small tract between the Ponca and Niobrara rivers. In consideration of this cession, the United States Government agreed "to protect the Poncas in the possession of this tract of land, and their persons and property thereon, during good behavior on their part; to pay them annuities annually for thirty years—$12,000 for the first five years, then $10,000 for ten years, then $8000 for fifteen years; to expend $20,000 for their subsistence during the first year, for building houses, etc.; to establish schools, and to build mills, mechanics' shops, etc.; to give $20,000 for the payment of the existing obligations of the tribe."

Two years later the agent newly appointed to take charge of the Poncas reports to the Department the amount of improvements made on the reservation: "One saw and grist-mill; two agency houses—story and a half houses—without inside lining or plastering, 16 by 26 and 18 by 32 feet in size; six small round log-houses (three with a small shed for a stable), a light log-corral for cattle, and a canvas shed for storing under; and about sixty acres of ground, broken, comprised all the improvements."

Evidently a very small part of the $20,000 had been spent as yet. He did not find an Indian on the reservation. From fear of the Sioux (who in 1860 had stolen from them more than half the horses they owned) they had moved down the Niobrara River, some twenty miles nearer the Missouri. It was with the greatest difficulty that the agent induced them to return; and after they did so, they huddled their tents close about the agency building, and could not be induced to go half a mile away unless accompanied by some of the white employees.

As the agent had no food to feed them with, and no money to buy any (spite of the appropriation of $20,000 for subsistence and house-building), he induced them to go off on a hunt; but in less than a month they came straggling back, "begging for provisions for their women and children, whom they had left on the plains half-starved, having been unable to find any game, or any food except wild-turnips. Some of them went to visit the Omahas, others the Pawnees, where they remained until the little corn they had planted produced roasting-ears. In the mean time those who were here subsisted mainly on wild-cherries and plums and the wild-turnip, and traded away most of their blankets and annuity goods for provisions."

In 1863 the reports are still more pitiful. "They started on their summer hunt toward the last of May, immediately after the first hoeing of their corn. At first they were successful and found buffaloes; but afterward, the ground being occupied by the Yanktons, who were sent south of the Niobrara by the

6. Hugo Grotius (1583–1645) was a jurist in the Dutch Republic whose work helped lay the foundations for international law, which he based on Enlightenment ideals of "natural law." Emer or Emerich de Vattel (1714–1767) was a Swiss political philosopher, diplomat, and expert on the law whose theories influenced the development of modern international law. Thucydides (460/455 B.C.E.–ca. 400 B.C.E.) was an ancient Greek historian and the author of the *History of the Peloponnesian War*, which recounts the 5th century B.C.E. war between Sparta and Athens.

general commanding the district, and who were about double the number, and with four times as many horses, they soon consumed what meat they had cured, and were compelled to abandon the chase. They commenced to return in the latter part of July. They went away with very high hopes, and reasonably so, of a large crop, but returned to see it all withered and dried up. In the mean time the plains had been burnt over, so that they could not discover the roots they are in the habit of digging. Even the wild-plums, which grow on bushes down in ravines and gullies, are withered and dried on the limbs. The building I occupy was constantly surrounded by a hungry crowd begging for food. . . . I am warned by military authority to keep the Poncas within the limits of the reservation; but this is an impossibility. There is nothing within its limits, nor can anything be obtained in sufficient quantity, or brought here soon enough to keep them from starving. . . . The Poncas have behaved well—quite as well, if not better than, under like circumstances, the same number of whites would have done. I have known whole families to live for days together on nothing but half-dried corn-stalks, and this when there were cattle and sheep in their sight."

At this time martial law was in force on many of the Indian reservations, owing to the presence of roving bands of hostile Sioux, driven from Minnesota after their outbreak there.

The Poncas through all these troubles remained loyal and peaceable, and were "unwavering in their fidelity to their treaty," says the Indian Commissioner.

In December of this year what the governmental reports call "a very unfortunate occurrence" took place in Nebraska. A party of Poncas, consisting of four men, six women, three boys, and two girls, returning from a visit to the Omahas, had camped for the night about twelve miles from their own reservation. In the night a party of soldiers from a military post on the Niobrara River came to their camp, and began to insult the squaws, "offering money with one hand, and presenting a revolver with the other." The Indians, alarmed, pulled up their lodge, and escaped to a copse of willows near by. The soldiers fired at them as they ran away, and then proceeded to destroy all their effects. They cut the lodge covers to pieces, burnt the saddles and blankets, cut open sacks of beans, corn, and dried pumpkin, and strewed their contents on the ground, and went away, taking with them a skin lodge-covering, beaver-skins, buffalo-robes, blankets, guns, and all the small articles. The Indians' ponies were hid in the willows. Early in the morning they returned with these, picked up all the corn which had not been destroyed, and such other articles as they could find, packed their ponies as best they might, and set off barefooted for home. After they had gone a few miles they stopped and built a fire to parch some corn to eat. Some of the women and children went to look for wild-beans, leaving three women and a child at the camp. Here the soldiers came on them again. As soon as the Indians saw them coming they fled. The soldiers fired on them, wounding one woman by a ball through her thigh; another, with a child on her back, by two balls through the child's thighs, one of which passed through the mother's side. These women were fired on as they were crossing the river on the ice. The soldiers then took possession of the six ponies and all the articles at the camp, and left. The squaws and children who were looking for beans were half a mile below; a little dog belonging to them barked and revealed their hiding-place in the willows. The soldiers immediately turned on them, dismounted, and, making up to them, deliberately shot them dead as they huddled helplessly together—three women and a little girl!

One of the boys, a youth, ran for the river, pursued by the soldiers. On reaching the river he dived into the water through a hole in the ice; as often as he lifted his head they fired at him. After they went away he crawled out and escaped to the agency. One of the murdered women, the mother of this boy, had three balls in her head and cheek, her throat cut, and her head half-severed by a sabre-thrust; another, the youngest woman, had her cloth skirt taken off and carried away, and all her other clothes torn from her body, leaving it naked!

The men who did this deed belonged to Company B of the Seventh Iowa Cavalry.

*   *   *

1881

JOSÉ MARTÍ

Cuban poet, essayist, journalist, and political leader, José Martí (1853–1895) became a symbol of Cuba's fight for independence from Spain. Martí envisioned a pan-hemispheric "America" at odds with the Gilded Age mentality of an imperialistic United States powered by big business, government corruption, and worker unrest. Martí's pan-national and antiracist manifesto, "No man has any special right because he belongs to any specific race," helped define the nature of the Cuban revolution against Spain, known in the United States as the Spanish-American War, and is sharply at odds with then-prevailing Anglo-Saxon norms of American cultural identity. Martí focuses on New World nations' indigenous cultures and calls on all American republics—those in North America as well as Latin America—to embrace one "America" based on native uniqueness that would reject racism in favor of native pride. "Those born in America" should not be "ashamed of the mother who reared them, because she wears an Indian apron." Instead of setting European civilization over New World "barbarism," Martí characterizes devotion to the European tradition as a slavish, false erudition lacking direct knowledge. He demands the Americas' recognition of identities as mixed cultures, united by common humanity. Martí hoped that through understanding, without hatred or racism, "new" Americans could rise together.

Martí spent much of his life in exile. In 1881 he moved to New York City, where he worked for several magazines, including The New York Sun, El Partido Liberal, La Opinión Nacional, and La Patria; he served as consul for Uruguay, Paraguay, and Argentina; and he taught high school Spanish. Martí's articles on the North American scene introduced many Latina/o readers not only to urban poverty but also to such "American" figures as Ulysses S. Grant, Walt Whitman, Ralph Waldo Emerson, and Henry Wadsworth Longfellow. He admired Harriet Beecher Stowe and Helen Hunt Jackson, whose novel Ramona (1884) he translated into Spanish. Founder of the Cuban Revolutionary Party, he led a contingent of revolutionaries to Cuba from the United States and died in a skirmish with Spanish troops at Dos Rios on May 19,

1895. "He died," wrote his friend Charles A. Dana in the *New York Sun*, "as such a man might wish to die, battling for liberty and democracy."

From Our America[1]

The conceited villager believes the entire world to be his village. Provided that he can be mayor, or humiliate the rival who stole his sweetheart, or add to the savings in his strong-box, he considers the universal order good, unaware of those giants with seven-league boots[2] who can crush him underfoot, or of the strife in the heavens between comets that streak through the drowsy air-devouring worlds. What remains of the village in America must rouse itself. These are not the times for sleeping in a nightcap, but with weapons for a pillow, like the warriors of Juan de Castellanos[3]—weapons of the mind, which conquer all others. Barricades of ideas are worth more than barricades of stone.

There is no prow that can cut through a cloudbank of ideas. A powerful idea, waved before the world at the proper time, can stop a squadron of iron-clad ships, like the mystical flag of the Last Judgment.[4] Nations that do not know one another should quickly become acquainted, as men who are to fight a common enemy. Those who shake their fists, like jealous brothers coveting the same tract of land, or like the modest cottager who envies the squire his mansion, should clasp hands and become one. Those who use the authority of a criminal tradition to lop off the lands of their defeated brother with a sword stained with his own blood, ought to return the lands to the brother already punished sufficiently, if they do not want the people to call them robbers. The honest man does not absolve himself of debts of honor with money, at so much a slap. We can no longer be a people of leaves living in the air, our foliage heavy with blooms and crackling or humming at the whim of the sun's caress, or buffeted and tossed by the storms. The trees must form ranks to keep the giant with seven-league boots from passing! It is the time of mobilization, of marching together, and we must go forward in close order, like silver in the veins of the Andes.

* * *

Only those born prematurely are lacking in courage. Those without faith in their country are seven-month weaklings. Because they have no courage, they deny it to others. Their puny arms—arms with bracelets and hands with painted nails, arms of Paris or Madrid—can hardly reach the bottom limb, and they claim the tall tree to be unclimbable. The ships should be loaded with those harmful insects that gnaw at the bone of the country that nour-

---

1. Martí published "Nuestra América" in Spanish in *La Revista Ilustrada* (January 10, 1891); rpt. in *Our America by José Martí: Writings on Latin America and the Struggle for Cuban Independence* (1977), from which this excerpt is taken.
2. Footwear of European folklore that allowed the wearer to take strides of seven leagues (a "league"=three miles), with great speed. Here, Martí refers to the great imperial strides that industrial countries were making into Latin America, especially into Cuba.

3. Spanish Renaissance poet (1522–1607) who migrated to South America with the Conquistadors and wrote about the "New World" as well as the exploits of the Spanish colonizers.
4. Biblical reference to the "last days," in which the armies of Christ and Satan engage in a final battle, with Christ emerging victorious, binding Satan in Hell for eternity, judging all humankind, and establishing the "New Jerusalem," as told in the book of Revelation.

ishes them. If they are Parisians or from Madrid, let them go to the Prado under lamplight, or to Tortoni's for a sherbet.[5] Those carpenters' sons who are ashamed that their fathers are carpenters! Those born in America who are ashamed of the mother who reared them, because she wears an Indian apron, and who disown their sick mother, the scoundrels, abandoning her on her sickbed! Then who is a real man? He who stays with his mother and nurses her in her illness, or he who puts her to work out of sight, and lives at her expense on decadent lands, sporting fancy neckties, cursing the womb that carried him, displaying the sign of the traitor on the back of his paper frock-coat? These sons of Our America, which will be saved by its Indians and is growing better; these deserters who take up arms in the armies of a North America that drowns its Indians in blood and is growing worse! These delicate creatures who are men but are unwilling to do men's work! The Washington[6] who made this land for them, did he not go to live with the English, to live with the English at a time when he saw them fighting against his own country? These "iconoclasts" of honor who drag that honor over foreign soil, like their counterparts in the French Revolution with their dancing, their affectations, their drawling speech!

For in what lands can men take more pride than in our long-suffering American republics, raised up from among the silent Indian masses by the bleeding arms of a hundred apostles, to the sounds of battle between the book and the processional candle? Never in history have such advanced and united nations been forged in so short a time from such disorganized elements.

* * *

Along comes the natural man, strong and indignant, and he topples all the justice accumulated from books because he has not been governed in accordance with the obvious needs of the country. Knowing is what counts. To know one's country and govern it with that knowledge is the only way to free it from tyranny. The European university must bow to the American university. The history of America, from the Incas to the present, must be taught in clear detail and to the letter, even if the archons of Greece[7] are overlooked. Our Greece must take priority over the Greece which is not ours. We need it more. Nationalist statesmen must replace foreign statesmen. Let the world be grafted onto our republics, but the trunk must be our own. And let the vanquished pedant hold his tongue, for there are no lands in which a man may take greater pride than in our long-suffering American republics.

* * *

1891

---

5. Museo del Prado: museum in Madrid, Spain, with one of the finest collections of European art. Tortoni's: fashionable café of the mid-1800s in Paris's Latin Quarter.
6. George Washington (1732–1799), commander

in chief of the Continental Army in the American Revolutionary War and the first president of the United States (1789–97).
7. Greek leaders.

CHARLES W. CHESNUTT

Charles W. Chesnutt's scathing review of William Hannibal Thomas's *The American Negro: What He Was, What He Is, and What He May Become* (1901) and Anna Julia Cooper's pointed criticisms of William Dean Howells's novel *An Imperative Duty* (1891) in "One Phase of American Literature" are a pair of literary-critical responses to racial definitions of American-ness. Chesnutt (1858–1932) was admired (and promoted by Howells) for his nuanced portraits of whites and African Americans in novels such as *The House Behind the Cedars* (1900) and *The Marrow of Tradition* (1901) and in his short story collections *The Conjure Woman* (1899) and *"The Wife of His Youth" and Other Stories of the Color Line* (1901). Thomas was an African American author and preacher (1843–1935). In his review of Thomas's book, Chesnutt refutes some of the most pervasive myths of black unreadiness for full American citizenship and laments the fact that such untruths have emanated from black writers as well as from racist whites.

A Defamer of His Race

The first thought that strikes the reader of this atrocious book[1] is, how did a reputable publishing house ever permit itself to become parties to its publication? The answer probably is that the readers of the publishing house knew nothing about the colored race beyond what they read in the newspapers, and therefore took it for granted that a colored man, who claimed to be a lawyer and ex-member of a legislature, would know all about his own people. It seems never to have occurred to them that a man might be all that, and yet be unworthy of credit, nor do they seem to have inquired into the antecedents of the author of a book the value of which must rest almost solely upon the writer's character, for the book is almost wholly an expression of opinion, with no statistics to support it, but based entirely upon the claimed knowledge and experience of the writer. That a reputable publishing house should have issued such a book against any other considerable class of people without such preliminary investigation is incredible.

The present reviewer during a recent extended tour of the Southern States, under circumstances which threw him mainly among the better class of the colored people, has taken pains to ascertain as far as possible the past record of Mr. Thomas, and is obliged to say that he has not heard anywhere one good word concerning him. The writer has conversed with colored bishops, college professors, and others, men of substance and character, who have known this man during his variegated career, and they are all unanimous in the statement that the book faithfully represents the man. The only parallel example to this book was one written some years ago by a renegade Jew, in which all the worst slanders against this oppressed people were gathered from the obscure and musty folios of ancient libraries, and dished up in a paper-covered volume for

---

1. Chesnutt's review of *The American Negro: What He Was, What He Is, and What He May Become*, by William Hannibal Thomas (1901), was published in *The Critic* 38.4 (April 1901), from which this text is taken.

the delectation of the nineteenth century. It must have been a satisfaction to the chosen people to note that within a year the author of the book was sent to the penitentiary for forgery, and that a year or two later the publishing house failed disastrously. This may have been a logical *non sequitur*, but it was poetic justice. Mr. Thomas may continue to escape this fate, but if it be any satisfaction to him to know that he has not a single friend or well-wisher among the whole eight or ten millions of his own people, he may rest content that such is emphatically the case.

So much for the man, if it be possible to separate the man from the book. The present reviewer once wrote a story in which a negro was transformed into a tree[2] and the tree sawed up into lumber, and built into a house, which was ever afterwards haunted by the spirit of the unfortunate victim of an untoward fate. The parallel between Thomas and this tree-man is obvious. He has transformed himself into white paper and black ink—he is a mulatto by blood—and has bound himself into a book. Nevertheless, it may be possible, by an effort, to consider the book as a separate thing.

In the first place, it is not a well-written book. That it has a certain amount of ability is beyond question; but it lacks consecutiveness. It would seem to have been compiled from a scrap-book, into which the author had pasted for twenty years or more every newspaper clipping that he had seen anywhere to the discredit of the colored race. A peculiarity of the book which bears out this view is his employment of the word "freedman," a term which is not now in common use as descriptive of the colored people, as it was twenty years ago. A full average generation has elapsed since the abolition of slavery, and fully three fourths of the colored people of the present day are free born, as a comparison of their numbers now and at the close of the civil war will demonstrate. Mr. Thomas has great fluency of language—a fondness for big words is supposed to be a trait of his race. A good command of a large vocabulary is a valuable accomplishment, and, if it be a race trait, one which may be judiciously cultivated to the enrichment of literature; but it is painfully apparent here and there that Mr. Thomas's thought has been swept away by the current of his own eloquence. One must sometimes fish long in this turbid pool to catch a minnow.

The negro has suffered a great deal, in the public estimation, from loose and hasty generalizations with reference to his intelligence, his morals, his physical characteristics, and his social efficiency. But not the worst things said about him by his most radical defamers, all put together, could surpass in untruthfulness and malignity the screed which this alleged reformer has put forth under his publisher's imprint. The slanders against the womanhood of his race are so vile as to confute themselves by their mere statement. There are several passages in the book, reflecting on the morals of colored youth, which ought to bar the volume from circulation in the United States mails. They are false on the face of them. No individual could possibly know that they were true, and they are utterly abhorrent to human nature and human experience. To believe them, one must read the negro out of the human family. If they are the fruit of this author's observation, one shudders to contemplate the depths of vice which he has fathomed.

His characterization of colored preachers is also unjust. That there are

2. "Po' Sandy," published in *The Conjure Woman* (1899).

many such preachers who might be otherwise employed with more profit to society may well be admitted; but that there are among them many good men, faithful to their trust, earnestly striving to uplift their people, and with encouraging results, is apparent to any one who will take the trouble to inquire. The greatest preacher of America did not escape calumny, if he avoided sin. Human character is a compound of good and evil. For aught we know, Judas Iscariot was a very good apostle before he betrayed his Master; we know that Benedict Arnold was a gallant soldier who had served his country well before he betrayed her. But here the parallel between these men and this author fails, for what good thing Thomas had ever done for his people before he dealt them this traitorous blow is not of record among the traditions of his people, nor in the archives of the South Carolina Legislature of which he claims to have been a valuable member. That membership in that body should be set forward by a writer and accepted by a publisher as a certificate of moral character, is the most curious feature of this whole remarkable performance.

Among the glimmerings of reason which here and there may be found in this book, is the statement that the colored people are deprived of social stimulus because the white people will not associate or intermarry with them. Granted. But with what face could any one ask a race with any self-respect, any pride of its past, any hope for its future, to consort with such moral and mental degenerates as Thomas has sought in this book to make of his own people?

The strongest argument against the negro suggested by this book is the existence of the book itself. As one of a race which has but just begun to win a hearing in the forum of letters, the author might have found a different theme. If the book were truthful, it would be without excuse as coming from such a source. But being false, as the book essentially is, it is all the more worthy of condemnation. That a man of color should write such a book is almost enough to make out his case against the negro.

1901

JANE ADDAMS

Laura Jane Addams (1860–1935) was born in Cedarville, Illinois; she graduated from Rockford Seminary in 1882, her father having refused to allow her to attend Smith College and become a physician. After a period of indecision and depression, Addams found her calling and in 1889 founded the social settlement Hull-House in Chicago. From Hull-House, where she lived and worked for the rest of her life, Addams became one of the country's most famous women through her writing, settlement work, and international efforts for world peace. At Hull-House, which was located at the corner of Polk and Halsted Streets, immigrants to Chicago, including Italians, Russian and Polish Jews, Irish, Germans, Greeks, and Bohemians, could take refuge from dirty and over-crowded tenements and the dangers of life on the streets. The settlement provided services for the neighborhood, such as meals and clothes. It also had kindergarten and daycare facilities for children of working mothers, an employment bureau, an art gallery, libraries, discussion groups, crafts groups, and music and art classes. By 1900 Hull-House activities had broadened to include the Jane Club (a cooperative residence for working women), the first Little Theater in America, a labor museum, and a meeting hall for trade union groups. One of Addams's most characteristic programs at Hull-House was the promotion of the traditional crafts and cultural practices of immigrants, aimed at giving them renewed self-respect as they assimilated into U.S. society and forging bonds between older immigrants and their children, who were quickly becoming "American." Building on her work at Hull-House, Addams became involved in the peace movement, becoming an important advocate of internationalism. During World War I, which as a pacifist she opposed, she participated in the 1915 International Congress of Women at the Hague. She helped found the Women's International League for Peace and Freedom in 1919. Addams was awarded the Nobel Peace Prize in 1931.

From Twenty Years at Hull-House[1]

From *Chapter V. First Days at Hull-House*

* * *

In spite of these flourishing clubs for children early established at Hull-House, and the fact that our first organized undertaking was a kindergarten, we were very insistent that the Settlement should not be primarily for the children, and that it was absurd to suppose that grown people would not respond to opportunities for education and social life. Our enthusiastic kindergartner herself demonstrated this with an old woman of ninety, who, because she was left alone all day while her daughter cooked in a restaurant, had formed such a persistent habit of picking the plaster off the walls that one landlord after another refused to have her for a tenant. It required but a few weeks' time to teach her to make large paper chains, and gradually she was content to do it all day long, and in the end took quite as much pleasure in adorning the walls as she had formerly taken in demolishing them. Fortunately the landlord had never heard the æsthetic principle that the exposure of basic construction is more desirable than gaudy decoration. In course of time it was discovered that the old woman could speak Gælic, and when one or two grave professors came to see her, the neighborhood was filled with pride that such a wonder lived in their midst. To mitigate life for a woman of ninety was an unfailing refutation of the statement that the Settlement was designed for the young.

On our first New Year's Day at Hull-House we invited the older people in the vicinity, sending a carriage for the most feeble and announcing to all of them that we were going to organize an Old Settlers' Party.

Every New Year's Day since, older people in varying numbers have come together at Hull-House to relate early hardships, and to take for the moment the place in the community to which their pioneer life entitles them. Many people who were formerly residents of the vicinity, but whom prosperity has carried into more desirable neighborhoods, come back to these meetings and often confess to each other that they have never since found such kindness

---

1. First published by Macmillan in 1910, from which the following excerpts are taken.

as in early Chicago when all its citizens came together in mutual enterprises. Many of these pioneers, so like the men and women of my earliest childhood that I always felt comforted by their presence in the house, were very much opposed to "foreigners," whom they held responsible for a depreciation of property and a general lowering of the tone of the neighborhood. Sometimes we had a chance for championship; I recall one old man, fiercely American, who had reproached me because we had so many "foreign views" on our walls, to whom I endeavored to set forth our hope that the pictures might afford a familiar island to the immigrants in a sea of new and strange impressions. The old settler guest, taken off his guard, replied, "I see; they feel as we did when we saw a Yankee notion from down East,"—thereby formulating the dim kinship between the pioneer and the immigrant, both "buffeting the waves of a new development." The older settlers as well as their children throughout the years have given genuine help to our various enterprises for neighborhood improvement, and from their own memories of earlier hardships have made many shrewd suggestions for alleviating the difficulties of that first sharp struggle with untoward conditions.

In those early days we were often asked why we had come to live on Halsted Street when we could afford to live somewhere else. I remember one man who used to shake his head and say it was "the strangest thing he had met in his experience," but who was finally convinced that it was "not strange but natural." In time it came to seem natural to all of us that the Settlement should be there. If it is natural to feed the hungry and care for the sick, it is certainly natural to give pleasure to the young, comfort to the aged, and to minister to the deep-seated craving for social intercourse that all men feel. Whoever does it is rewarded by something which, if not gratitude, is at least spontaneous and vital and lacks that irksome sense of obligation with which a substantial benefit is too often acknowledged.

In addition to the neighbors who responded to the receptions and classes, we found those who were too battered and oppressed to care for them. To these, however, was left that susceptibility to the bare offices of humanity which raises such offices into a bond of fellowship.

From the first it seemed understood that we were ready to perform the humblest neighborhood services. We were asked to wash the new-born babies, and to prepare the dead for burial, to nurse the sick, and to "mind the children."

Occasionally these neighborly offices unexpectedly uncovered ugly human traits. For six weeks after an operation we kept in one of our three bedrooms a forlorn little baby who, because he was born with a cleft palate, was most unwelcome even to his mother, and we were horrified when he died of neglect a week after he was returned to his home; a little Italian bride of fifteen sought shelter with us one November evening, to escape her husband who had beaten her every night for a week when he returned home from work, because she had lost her wedding ring; two of us officiated quite alone at the birth of an illegitimate child because the doctor was late in arriving, and none of the honest Irish matrons would "touch the likes of her"; we ministered at the deathbed of a young man, who during a long illness of tuberculosis had received so many bottles of whisky through the mistaken kindness of his friends, that the cumulative effect produced wild periods of exultation, in one of which he died.

We were also early impressed with the curious isolation of many of the immigrants; an Italian woman once expressed her pleasure in the red roses that she saw at one of our receptions in surprise that they had been "brought so fresh all the way from Italy." She would not believe for an instant that they had been grown in America. She said that she had lived in Chicago for six years and had never seen any roses, whereas in Italy she had seen them every summer in great profusion. During all that time, of course, the woman had lived within ten blocks of a florist's window; she had not been more than a five-cent car ride away from the public parks; but she had never dreamed of faring forth for herself, and no one had taken her. Her conception of America had been the untidy street in which she lived and had made her long struggle to adapt herself to American ways.

But in spite of some untoward experiences, we were constantly impressed with the uniform kindness and courtesy we received. Perhaps these first days laid the simple human foundations which are certainly essential for continuous living among the poor: first, genuine preference for residence in an industrial quarter to any other part of the city, because it is interesting and makes the human appeal; and second, the conviction, in the words of Canon Barnett,[2] that the things which make men alike are finer and better than the things that keep them apart, and that these basic likenesses, if they are properly accentuated, easily transcend the less essential differences of race, language, creed and tradition.

Perhaps even in those first days we made a beginning toward that object which was afterwards stated in our charter: "To provide a center for a higher civic and social life; to institute and maintain educational and philanthropic enterprises, and to investigate and improve the conditions in the industrial districts of Chicago."

From *Chapter XI. Immigrants and Their Children*

* * *

An overmastering desire to reveal the humbler immigrant parents to their own children lay at the base of what has come to be called the Hull-House Labor Museum. This was first suggested to my mind one early spring day when I saw an old Italian woman, her distaff against her homesick face, patiently spinning a thread by the simple stick spindle so reminiscent of all southern Europe. I was walking down Polk Street, perturbed in spirit, because it seemed so difficult to come into genuine relations with the Italian women and because they themselves so often lost their hold upon their Americanized children. It seemed to me that Hull-House ought to be able to devise some educational enterprise, which should build a bridge between European and American experiences in such wise as to give them both more meaning and a sense of relation. I meditated that perhaps the power to see life as a whole, is more needed in the immigrant quarter of a large city than anywhere else, and that the lack of this power is the most fruitful source of misunderstanding between European immigrants and their children, as it is between them and their American neighbors; and why should that chasm between

2. Samuel Augustus Barnett (1844–1913), English clergyman and social reformer associated with the establishment of the first university settlement, Toynbee Hall, in London, which inspired Addams to create Hull-House.

fathers and sons, yawning at the feet of each generation, be made so unnecessarily cruel and impassable to these bewildered immigrants? Suddenly I looked up and saw the old woman with her distaff, sitting in the sun on the steps of a tenement house. She might have served as a model for one of Michael Angelo's Fates,[3] but her face brightened as I passed and, holding up her spindle for me to see, she called out that when she had spun a little more yarn, she would knit a pair of stockings for her goddaughter. The occupation of the old woman gave me the clew that was needed. Could we not interest the young people working in the neighboring factories, in these older forms of industry, so that, through their own parents and grandparents, they would find a dramatic representation of the inherited resources of their daily occupation. If these young people could actually see that the complicated machinery of the factory had been evolved from simple tools, they might at least make a beginning towards that education which Dr. Dewey[4] defines as "a continuing reconstruction of experience." They might also lay a foundation for reverence of the past which Goethe[5] declares to be the basis of all sound progress.

* * * Within a month a room was fitted up to which we might invite those of our neighbors who were possessed of old crafts and who were eager to use them.

We found in the immediate neighborhood, at least four varieties of these most primitive methods of spinning and three distinct variations of the same spindle in connection with wheels. It was possible to put these seven into historic sequence and order and to connect the whole with the present method of factory spinning. The same thing was done for weaving, and on every Saturday evening a little exhibit was made of these various forms of labor in the textile industry. Within one room a Syrian woman, a Greek, an Italian, a Russian, and an Irishwoman enabled even the most casual observer to see that there is no break in orderly evolution if we look at history from the industrial standpoint; that industry develops similarly and peacefully year by year among the workers of each nation, heedless of differences in language, religion, and political experiences.

And then we grew ambitious and arranged lectures upon industrial history. I remember that after an interesting lecture upon the industrial revolution in England and a portrayal of the appalling conditions throughout the weaving districts of the north, which resulted from the hasty gathering of the weavers into the new towns, a Russian tailor in the audience was moved to make a speech. He suggested that whereas time had done much to alleviate the first difficulties in the transition of weaving from hand work to steam power, that in the application of steam to sewing we are still in the first stages, illustrated by the isolated woman who tries to support herself by hand needlework at home until driven out by starvation, as many of the hand weavers had been.

* * *

3. In Greek mythology, the Fates controlled human destinies, spinning and measuring out each person's life-span: Laches of things past, Clotho of things present, Atropos of things to come. The painting by Michelangelo portrays them as three elderly Italian women.
4. John Dewey (1859–1952), American philosopher, psychologist, and educational reformer.

Addams met Dewey when he began to teach at the University of Chicago in 1894.
5. Johann Wolfgang von Goethe (1749–1832), German poet, novelist, playwright, and natural philosopher. Among his most famous works are *The Sorrows of Young Werther* (1774) and *Faust* (1808, 1832).

There has been some testimony that the Labor Museum has revealed the charm of woman's primitive activities. I recall a certain Italian girl who came every Saturday evening to a cooking class in the same building in which her mother spun in the Labor Museum exhibit; and yet Angelina always left her mother at the front door while she herself went around to a side door because she did not wish to be too closely identified in the eyes of the rest of the cooking class with an Italian woman who wore a kerchief over her head, uncouth boots, and short petticoats. One evening, however, Angelina saw her mother surrounded by a group of visitors from the School of Education, who much admired the spinning, and she concluded from their conversation that her mother was "the best stick-spindle spinner in America." When she inquired from me as to the truth of this deduction, I took occasion to describe the Italian village in which her mother had lived, something of her free life, and how, because of the opportunity she and the other women of the village had to drop their spindles over the edge of a precipice, they had developed a skill in spinning beyond that of the neighboring towns. I dilated somewhat on the freedom and beauty of that life—how hard it must be to exchange it all for a two-room tenement, and to give up a beautiful homespun kerchief for an ugly department store hat. I intimated it was most unfair to judge her by these things alone, and that while she must depend on her daughter to learn the new ways, she also had a right to expect her daughter to know something of the old ways.

That which I could not convey to the child but upon which my own mind persistently dwelt, was that her mother's whole life had been spent in a secluded spot under the rule of traditional and narrowly localized observances, until her very religion clung to local sanctities,—to the shrine before which she had always prayed, to the pavement and walls of the low vaulted church,—and then suddenly she was torn from it all and literally put out to sea, straight away from the solid habits of her religious and domestic life, and she now walked timidly but with poignant sensibility upon a new and strange shore.

It was easy to see that the thought of her mother with any other background than that of the tenement was new to Angelina and at least two things resulted; she allowed her mother to pull out of the big box under the bed the beautiful homespun garments which had been previously hidden away as uncouth; and she openly came into the Labor Museum by the same door as did her mother, proud at least of the mastery of the craft which had been so much admired.

* * *

1910

ANNA JULIA COOPER

Cooper's *A Voice from the South* (1892) is an important framing of political and specifically antiracist and feminist arguments in a forceful subjective style. In the excerpt below, Cooper attacks William Dean Howells's reductive African American characterizations in his novel *An Imperative Duty*, even as she acknowledges that as an editor Howells has tried to promote African American writers. In his novel, at least, Cooper finds, "Mr. Howells does not know what he is talking about."

From One Phase of American Literature[1]

* * *

Among our artists for art's sweet sake, Mr. Howells[2] has recently tried his hand also at painting the Negro, attempting merely a side light in half tones, on his life and manners; and I think the unanimous verdict of the subject is that, in this single department at least, Mr. Howells does not know what he is talking about. And yet I do not think we should quarrel with *An Imperative Duty*[3] because it lacks the earnestness and bias of a special pleader. Mr. Howells merely meant to press the button and give one picture from American life involving racial complications. The kodak[4] does no more; it cannot preach sermons or solve problems.

Besides, the portrayal of Negro characteristics was by no means the main object of the story, which was rather meant, I judge, to be a thumb nail sketch containing a psychological study of a morbidly sensitive conscience hectoring over a weak and vacillating will and fevered into increased despotism by reading into its own life and consciousness the analyses and terrible retributions of fiction,—a product of the Puritan's uncompromising sense of *"right though the heavens fall,"* irritated and kept sore by being unequally yoked with indecision and cowardice. Of such strokes Mr. Howells is undoubtedly master. It is true there is little point and no force of character about the beautiful and irresponsible young heroine; but as that is an attainment of so many of Mr. Howells' models, it is perhaps not to be considered as illustrating any racial characteristics. I cannot help sharing, however, the indignation of those who resent the picture in the colored church,—"evidently," Mr. Howells assures us, "representing *the best colored society*"; where the horrified young prig, Rhoda Aldgate, meets nothing but the frog-like countenances and cat-fish mouths, the musky exhalations and the "bress de Lawd, Honey," of an uncultivated people. It is just here that Mr. Howells fails—and fails because he gives only a half truth, and that a partisan half truth. One feels that he had no business to attempt a subject of which he knew so little, or for which he cared so little. There is one thing I would like to say to my white fellow countrymen, and especially to those who dabble in ink and affect to discuss the Negro; and yet I hesitate because I feel it is a fact which persons of the finer sensibilities and more delicate perceptions must know instinctively: namely, that it is an insult to humanity and a sin against God to publish any such sweeping generalizations of a race on such meager and superficial information. We meet it at every turn—this obtrusive and offensive vulgarity, this gratuitous sizing up of the Negro and conclusively writing

---

1. Also known as "The Negro as Presented in American Literature," the essay was first published in Cooper's *A Voice from the South by a Black Woman of the South* (1892), from which this excerpt is taken.
2. William Dean Howells (1837–1920), Ameri-

can novelist, critic, and proponent of realism.
3. Psychological novel (1891) in which Howells explores issues of race and miscegenation.
4. Simple roll film camera produced by Eastman Dry Plate Company in the late 1800s.

down his equation, sometimes even among his ardent friends and bravest defenders. Were I not afraid of falling myself into the same error that I am condemning, I would say it seems an *Anglo Saxon characteristic* to have such overweening confidence in his own power of induction that there is no equation which he would acknowledge to be indeterminate, however many unknown quantities it may possess.

* * *

1892

American Literature
1914–1945

THE TWO WARS AS HISTORICAL MARKERS

The conflict known as World War I broke out in Europe in 1914, with Great Britain and France fighting against Germany. The United States that belatedly entered the war in 1917, on the side of Britain and France, was still in the main a nation of farmers and small towns. Although several waves of immigration from southern and eastern Europe had altered the makeup of the population, and about one American in ten was of African descent, the majority of Americans were of English or German ancestry. This majority was deeply distrustful of international politics, and after the war ended, many Americans attempted to steer the nation back to prewar modes of life. In 1924 Congress enacted the first exclusionary immigration act in the nation's history, hoping thereby to control the ethnic makeup of the American population (and the proportion of Americans born outside the United States did decline markedly from 1910 to 1940). The immediate postwar years also saw the so-called Red scare, when labor union headquarters were raided and immigrant radicals deported by a government fearful of the influence of the newly Communist Soviet Union (formerly tsarist Russia).

For other Americans, however, the war helped accelerate long-sought changes in the forms of political and social life. The long struggle to win American women the vote—given a final push by women's work as nurses and ambulance drivers during the war—ended in 1920 with the passage of the Nineteenth Amendment to the Constitution. The National Association for the Advancement of Colored People (NAACP), founded in 1909, successfully argued during World War I for the commissioning of black officers in the U.S. armed forces; as they would after World War II, African Americans who fought abroad returned to fight for their rights at home. Despite the government's restrictions on leftist political activity, many Americans—among them writers and intellectuals as well as labor activists and urban immigrants— looked to the Soviet Union and the international Communist movement for a model in combating inequality and fostering workers' rights in the United States. Other Americans went abroad, for shorter or longer stretches of time, in order to taste the expatriate life (made cheaper in war-ravaged economies by the solid American dollar) in Europe's battered but still vibrant cities and countryside. Some Americans traveled physical and social distances almost as great within the boundaries of the United States, as African Americans began to migrate in large numbers out of the segregated South and young people everywhere increasingly attended college away from home and moved to the cities. African Americans, emancipated urban women, and the restless young faced off against rural and urban traditionalists over the question of who, exactly, was truly "American."

Thus the 1920s saw numerous conflicts over the shape of the future, which acquired new urgency when the stock market crashed in 1929 and led to an economic depression with a 25 percent unemployment rate. Known as the Great Depression, this period of economic hardship did not fully end until the United States entered World War II, which happened after the Japanese attacked the American fleet at Pearl Harbor on December 7, 1941. Because Japan and Germany were allies, Germany declared war on the United States, thus involving the country in another European conflict. The war unified the country ideologically; revitalized industry, which devoted itself to goods needed for the war effort; and put people to work. Indeed, with so many men away at war, women went into the work force in unprecedented numbers. Germany surrendered in the spring of 1945. The war ended in August 1945 following the detonation of two atomic bombs over the Japanese cities of Hiroshima and Nagasaki. Europe was in ruins and—regardless of the wishes of its citizens—the United States had become both an industrial society and a major global power.

The two wars, then, bracket a period during which, no matter how internally fractured it was, the United States became a modern nation. In fact, the internal fractures can be understood as diverse responses to the irreversible advent of modernity. American literature in these decades registers all sides of the era's struggles and debates, while sharing a commitment to explore the many meanings of modernity and express them in forms appropriate to a modern vision. Some writers rejoiced while others lamented; some anticipated future utopias and others believed that civilization had collapsed; but the period's most influential voices believed that old forms would not work for new times, and were inspired by the possibility of creating something entirely new.

The totality of the literary output produced during this period is called American literary modernism. Among literary conflicts, perhaps three issues stand out, all of them related to the accelerating transformations and conflicts of modernity. One conflict centered on the uses of literary tradition. To some, a work registering awareness and appreciation of literary history—through allusion to other literary works, or by using traditional poetic forms and poetic language—seemed imitative and old-fashioned. To others, a work failing to register such awareness and appreciation was bad or incompetent writing. For still others, literary history was best appreciated oppositionally: modernist works often allude to previous literature ironically, or deliberately fracture traditional literary formulas. A related conflict involved the place of popular culture in serious literature. Throughout the era, popular culture gained momentum and influence. Some writers regarded it as crucial for the future of literature that popular forms be embraced; to others, good literature by definition had to reject the cynical commercialism of popular culture.

Another issue was the question of how engaged in political and social struggle a work of literature ought to be—of how far literature should exert itself for (or against) social transformation. Should art be a domain unto itself, exploring universal questions and enunciating transcendent truths, or should art participate in the politics of the times? For some, a work that was political in aim counted as propaganda, not art; others thought that apolitical literature was evasive and simplistic; for still others, the call to keep art out of politics was covertly political, in conservative directions, even if it did not acknowledge itself as such.

CHANGING TIMES

The transformations of the first half of the twentieth century were driven both by ideas and by changes in the economic and technological underpinnings of daily life. Much social energy in the 1920s went into enlarging the boundaries for acceptable self-expression. Adherents to small-town, white, Protestant values such as the work ethic, social conformity, duty, and respectability, clashed ideologically not only with internationally minded radicals but also with newly affluent young people who argued for more diverse, permissive, and tolerant styles of life. To some extent this debate recapitulated the long-time American conflict between the individual and society, a conflict going back to the seventeenth-century Puritans and epitomized in Ralph Waldo Emerson's call, in the 1840s: "whosoever would be a man, must be a non-conformist."

The 1920s saw significant changes in sexual mores, as was to be expected when young people were no longer under the watchful eyes of their small-town elders. These changes found their most influential theorist in the Austrian psychiatrist Sigmund Freud (1858–1939), inventor of the practice of psychoanalysis. According to Freud, many modern neuroses could be traced to repression and inhibition. Freud developed the idea of the self as grounded in an "unconscious," where forbidden desires, traumas, unacceptable emotions, and the like—most of these sexual in nature—were stored. Freud hoped that trained analysts could help people become aware of their repressed feelings, so that they would be able to control them productively. The American version of psychoanalysis—more utopian than Freud's cautious claim that individuals could learn to cope with their own personalities more effectively—held that emotional wholeness could be attained at once if people recognized and overcame their inhibitions. Americanized Freudian ideas provided the psychological underpinning for much literature of the interwar era, whether the focus was the individual trapped in a repressive culture or the repressive culture itself.

The middle-class double sexual standard had, in fact, always granted considerable sexual freedom to men; now, however, women—enfranchised and liberated by automobiles and job possibilities away from home—began to demand similar freedom for themselves. Women's demands went well beyond the erotic, however, encompassing education, professional work, mobility, and whatever else seemed like social goods hitherto reserved for men. Female dress changed; long, heavy, restricting garments gave way to short, light-weight, easily worn store-bought clothing. The combination of expanding urban life with new psychologies oriented to self-expression also brought into being new social possibilities for women and men whose sexual desires did not conform to traditional patterns. Freud was only one of a number of thinkers in the period who urged a measure of toleration for sexual minorities, especially homosexuals—a term that entered specialized English usage in the 1890s and came into wider circulation in the years following World War I. Although the legal risks and social stigma born by homosexuals remained very much in force, gay enclaves became more visible in American life and gay lives became more imaginable as a theme in American literature.

African Americans, like women, became mobile in these years as never before. Around 1915, as a direct result of the industrial needs of World War I, opportunities opened for African Americans in the factories of the North, and the so-called Great Migration out of the South began. Not only did migration give the lie to southern white claims that African Americans were content with southern segregationist practices, it damaged the South's economy by draining off an important segment of its working people. Even though African Americans faced racism, segregation, and racial violence in the North, a black American presence soon became powerfully visible in American cultural life. Harlem, a section of New York City, attained an almost wholly black population of over 150,000 by the mid-1920s; from this "city within a city," African Americans wrote, performed, composed, and painted. Here as well they founded two major journals of opinion and culture, *The Crisis* (in 1910) and *Opportunity* (in 1923). This work influenced writers, painters, and musicians of other ethnicities, and became known collectively as the Harlem Renaissance.

The famous black intellectual W. E. B. Du Bois had argued in *The Souls of Black Folk* (1903) that African Americans had a kind of double consciousness—of themselves as Americans and as blacks. This doubleness contributed to debates within African American cultural life. The Harlem Renaissance sparked arguments between those who wanted to claim membership in the culture at large and those who wanted to stake out a separate artistic domain; between those who wanted to celebrate rural African American lifeways and those committed to urban intellectuality; between those who wanted to join the American mainstream and those who, disgusted by American race prejudice, aligned themselves with worldwide revolutionary movements; between those who celebrated a "primitive" African heritage and those who rejected the idea as a degrading stereotype. African American women, as Nella Larsen's novel *Quicksand* testifies, could experience these divisions with special force. Women were very much called upon in efforts to "uplift," advance, and educate the black community, but these communal obligations could be felt as constraints upon individual freedom and exploration; meanwhile the white social world, given to exoticizing or sexualizing black women, offered few alternatives.

Class inequality, as well as American racial divisions, continued to generate intellectual and artistic debate in the interwar years. The nineteenth-century United States had been host to many radical movements—labor activism, utopianism, socialism, anarchism—inspired by diverse sources. In the twentieth century, especially following the rise of the Soviet Union, the American left increasingly drew its intellectual and political program from the Marxist tradition. The German philosopher Karl Marx (1818–1883) located the roots of human behavior in economics. He claimed that industrializing societies were structurally divided into two antagonistic classes based on different relations to the means of production—capital versus labor. The Industrial Revolution arose from the accumulation of surplus capital by industrialists paying the least possible amount to workers; the next stage in world history would be when workers took control of the means of production for themselves. Because, to Marx, the ideas and ideals of any particular society could represent the interests of only its dominant class, he derided individualism as a middle-class or "bourgeois" value that could only discourage worker solidarity.

Marx's ideas formed the basis for communist political parties across Europe. In 1917, a Communist revolution in Russia led by Vladimir Ilyich Lenin (1870–1914) overthrew the tsarist regime, instituted the "dictatorship of the proletariat" that Marx had called for, and engineered the development of Communism as a unified international movement. Americans who thought of themselves as Marxists in the 1920s and 1930s were usually connected with the Communist party and subjected to government surveillance and occasional violence, as were socialists, anarchists, union organizers, and others who opposed American free enterprise and marketplace competition. Although politics directed from outside the national boundaries was, almost by definition, "un-American," many adherents of these movements hoped to make the United States conform to its stated ideals, guaranteeing liberty and justice for all.

Where writers were concerned, a defining conflict between American ideals and American realities in the 1920s was the Sacco-Vanzetti case. Nicola Sacco and Bartolomeo Vanzetti were Italian immigrants, not Communists but avowed anarchists; on April 15, 1920 they were arrested near Boston after a murder during a robbery. They were accused of that crime, then tried and condemned to death in 1921; but it was widely believed that they had not received a fair trial and that their political beliefs had been held against them. After a number of appeals, they were executed in 1927, maintaining their innocence to the end. John Dos Passos and Katherine Anne Porter were among the many writers and intellectuals who demonstrated in their defense; several were arrested and jailed. It is estimated that well over a hundred poems (including works by William Carlos Williams, Edna St. Vincent Millay, and Carl Sandburg) along with six plays and eight novels of the time treated the incident from a sympathetic perspective.

Like the Sacco-Vanzetti case in the 1920s, the Scottsboro case in the 1930s brought many American writers and intellectuals, black and white, together in a cause—here, the struggle against racial bias in the justice system. In 1931 nine black youths were indicted in Scottsboro, Alabama, for the alleged rape of two white women in a railroad freight car. They were all found guilty, and some were sentenced to death. The U.S. Supreme Court reversed convictions twice; in a second trial one of the alleged victims retracted her testimony; in 1937 charges against five were dropped. But four went to jail, in many people's view unfairly. The Communists were especially active in the Scottsboro defense; but people across the political spectrum saw the case as crucial to the question of whether black people could receive fair trials in the American South. The unfair trial of an African American man became a literary motif in much writing of the period and beyond, including Richard Wright's *Native Son*, William Faulkner's *Intruder in the Dust*, and Harper Lee's *To Kill a Mockingbird*.

SCIENCE AND TECHNOLOGY

Technology played a vital, although often invisible, role in all these events, because it linked places and spaces, contributing to the shaping of culture as a national phenomenon rather than a series of local manifestations. Indeed, without new modes of production, transportation, and communication, modern America in all its complexity could not have existed. Electricity for lights and appliances, along with the telephone—nineteenth-century inventions—expanded into American homes during these years, improving life for many but widening the gap between those plugged into the new networks and those outside them. The phonograph record and the record player (early devices for recording and playing music), the motion picture (which acquired sound in 1929), and the radio made new connections possible and brought mass popular culture into being. Although the nineteenth-century dream of forging a scattered population into a single nation could now be realized more instantaneously and directly than was ever possible with print media, many intellectuals suspected that mass culture would create a robotic, passive population vulnerable to demagoguery.

The most powerful technological innovation, however, encouraged activity not passivity: this was the automobile, which had been developed by the end of the nineteenth century, but remained a luxury item until Henry Ford's assembly-line techniques made cars affordable. Automobiles put Americans on the road, dramatically reshaped the structure of American industry and occupations, and altered the national topography as well. Along with work in automobile factories themselves, millions of other jobs—in steel mills, parts factories, highway construction and maintenance, gas stations, machine shops, roadside restaurants, motels—depended on the industry. The road itself became—and has remained—a key powerful symbol of the United States and of modernity as well. Cities grew, suburbs came into being, small towns died, new towns arose, according to the placement of highways. The United States had become a nation of migrants as much as or more than it was a nation of immigrants.

It is impossible fully to dissociate technology from science, and certainly one of the most important developments in the interwar period was the growth of modern "big" science. At the turn of the century and soon afterward scientists discovered that the atom was not the smallest possible unit of matter, that matter was not indestructible, that both time and space were relative to an observer's position, that some phenomena were so small that attempts at measurement would alter them, that some outcomes could be predicted only in terms of statistical probability, that the universe might be infinite in size and yet infinitely expanding; in short, much of the common-sense basis of nineteenth-century science had to be put aside in favor of far more powerful but also far less commonsensical theories. Among many results, scientists and literary intellectuals became less and less able to communicate with each other and less respectful of each others' worldviews. Scientists saw literary people as careless thinkers; literary people, especially the more conservative among them, deplored the loss of authority for traditional, humanistic explanations of the real, concrete, experienced world and the felt human life. Poets like Ezra Pound, T. S. Eliot, Wallace Stevens, and William Carlos Williams reacted spiritedly to the increasingly prevalent assumption that nonscientific thinking, because it was imprecise and value laden, could not explain anything. They questioned the capacity of science to provide accounts of the things that matter, like subjective experience and moral issues. Art, to them, became the repository of a way of experiencing the world other than that offered by science. Their approach put a heavy burden of "meaning" on art and was a sign, if not a contributing cause, of the increased specialization of intellectual activity and the division of educated people into what the British novelist and physicist C. P. Snow was later to call the "two cultures"—science versus letters.

THE 1930s

The Great Depression was a worldwide phenomenon, and social unrest led to the rise of fascist dictatorships in Europe, among which were those of Generalissimo Francisco Franco in Spain, Benito Mussolini in Italy, and Adolf Hitler in Germany. Hitler's program, which was to make Germany rich and strong by conquering the rest of Europe, led inexorably to World War II.

In the United States, the Depression made politics and economics the salient issues and overrode questions of individual freedom with questions of mass collapse. Free-enterprise capitalism had always justified itself by arguing that although the system made a small number of individuals immensely wealthy it also guaranteed better lives for all. This assurance now rang hollow. The suicides of millionaire bankers and stockbrokers made the headlines, but more compelling was the enormous toll among ordinary people who lost homes, jobs, farms, and life savings in the stock market crash. Conservatives advised waiting until things got better; radicals espoused immediate social revolution. In this atmosphere, the election of Franklin Delano Roosevelt to the presidency in 1932 was a victory for American pragmatism; his series of liberal reforms—social security, acts creating jobs in the public sector, welfare, and unemployment insurance—cushioned the worst effects of the Depression and avoided the civil war that many had thought inevitable.

The terrible situation in the United States produced a significant increase in Communist party membership and prestige in the 1930s. Numerous intellectuals allied themselves with its causes, even if they did not become party members. An old radical journal, *The Masses*, later *The New Masses*, became the official literary voice of the party, and various other radical groups founded journals to represent their viewpoints. Visitors to the Soviet Union returned with glowing reports about a true workers' democracy and prosperity for all. The appeal of Communism was significantly enhanced by its claim to be an opponent of fascism. Communists fought against Franco in the Spanish Civil War of 1936 and 1937. Hitler's nightmare policies of genocide and racial superiority and his plans for a general European war to secure more room for the superior German "folk" to live became increasingly evident as European refugees began to flee to the United States in the 1930s, and many believed that the USSR would be the only country able to withstand the German war machine. But Soviet Communism showed another side to Americans when American Communists were ordered to break up the meetings of other radical groups; when Josef Stalin, the Soviet dictator, instituted a series of brutal purges in the Soviet Union beginning in 1936; and when in

1939 he signed a pact promising not to go to war against Germany. The disillusionment and betrayal felt by many radicals over these acts led to many 1930s left-wing activists' becoming staunch anti-Communists after World War II.

AMERICAN VERSIONS OF MODERNISM

Used in the broadest sense, "modernism" is a catchall term for any kind of literary production in the interwar period that deals with the modern world. More narrowly, it refers to work that represents the transformation of traditional society under the pressures of modernity, and that breaks down traditional literary forms in doing so. Much modernist literature of this sort, which critics increasingly now set apart as "high modernism," is in a sense antimodern: it interprets modernity as an experience of loss. As its title underlines, T. S. Eliot's *The Waste Land*—the great poem of high modernism—represents the modern world as a scene of ruin.

Modernism began as a European response to the effects of World War I, which were far more devastating on the Continent than they were in the United States. It involved other art forms—sculpture, painting, dance—as well as literature. The poetry of William Butler Yeats; James Joyce's *Ulysses* (1922); Marcel Proust's *Remembrance of Things Past* (1913–27); Thomas Mann's novels and short stories, including *The Magic Mountain* (1927)— these were only a few of the literary products of this movement in England and on the Continent. In painting, artists like Pablo Picasso, Juan Gris, and Georges Braque invented cubism; in the 1920s the surrealistic movement known as dadaism emerged. The American public was introduced to modern art at the famous New York Armory Show of 1913, which featured cubist paintings and caused an uproar. Marcel Duchamp's *Nude Descending a Staircase*, which, to the untrained eye, looked like no more than a mass of crudely drawn rectangles, was especially provocative. Composers like Igor Stravinsky similarly produced music in a "modern" mode, featuring dissonance and discontinuity rather than neat formal structure and appealing tonal harmonies. His composition *The Rite of Spring* provoked a riot in the Paris concert hall where it was premiered.

At the heart of the high modernist aesthetic lay the conviction that the previously sustaining structures of human life, whether social, political, religious, or artistic, had been destroyed or shown up as falsehoods or, at best, arbitrary and fragile human constructions. Order, sequence, and unity in works of art might well express human desires for coherence rather than reliable intuitions of reality. Generalization, abstraction, and high-flown writing might conceal rather than convey the real. The form of a story, with its beginnings, complications, and resolutions, might be an artifice imposed on the flux and fragmentation of experience. To the extent that art incorporated such a false order, it had to be renovated.

Thus a key formal characteristic typical of high modernist works, whether in painting, sculpture, or musical composition, is its construction out of fragments—fragments of myth or history, fragments of experience or perception, fragments of previous artistic works. Compared with earlier writing, modernist literature is notable for what it omits: the explanations, interpretations, connections, summaries, and distancing that provide continuity, perspective, and security in traditional literature. A typical modernist work may seem to begin arbitrarily, to advance without explanation, and to end without resolution, consisting of vivid segments juxtaposed without cushioning or integrating transitions. There will be shifts in perspective, voice, and tone. Its rhetoric will be understated, ironic. It will suggest rather than assert, making use of symbols and images instead of statements. Its elements will be drawn from diverse areas of experience. The effect will be surprising, shocking, and unsettling; the experience of reading will be challenging and difficult. Faced with the task of intuiting connections left unstated, the reader of a modernist work is often said to participate in the actual work of making the poem or story.

Some high modernist works, however, order their discontinuous elements into conspicuous larger patterns, patterns often drawn from world literature, mythologies, and religions. As its title advertises, Joyce's *Ulysses* maps the lives of its modern characters onto Homer's *Odyssey*; Eliot's *The Waste Land* layers the Christian narrative of death and resurrection over a broad range of quest myths. The question for readers lies in the meaning of these borrowed structures and mythic parallels: do they reveal profound similarities or ironic contrasts between the modern world and earlier times? For some writers and readers, the adaptability of ancient stories to modern circumstances testified to their deep truth, underlying the surface buzz and confusion of modernity; for others, such parallels indicated Christianity to *be* only a myth, a merely human construction for creating order out of, and finding purpose in, history's flux.

If meaning is a human construction, then meaning lies in the process of generating meaning; if meaning lies obscured deep underneath the ruins of modern life, then it must be effortfully sought out. Modernist literature therefore tends to foreground the search for meaning over didactic statement, and the subject matter of modernist writing often became, by extension, the poem or literary work itself. While there have long been paintings about painting and poems about poetry, high modernist writing was especially self-reflexive, concerned with its own nature as art and with its questioning of previous traditions of literature. Ironically—because this subject matter was motivated by deep concern about the interrelation of literature and life—this subject often had the effect of limiting the audience for a modernist work; high modernism demanded of its ideal readers an encyclopedic knowledge of the traditions it fragmented or ironized. Nevertheless, over time, the principles of modernism became increasingly influential.

Though modernist techniques were initiated by poets, they transformed fiction in this period as well. Prose writers strove for directness, compression, and vividness. They were sparing of words. The average novel became quite a bit shorter than it had been in the nineteenth century, when a novel was expected to fill two or even three volumes. The modernist aesthetic gave a new significance to the short story, which had previously been thought of as a relatively slight artistic form. (Poems, too, became shorter, as narrative poems lost ground to lyrics and the repetitive patterns of rhyme and meter that had helped sustain long poems in previous centuries lost ground to free verse.) Victorian or realistic fiction achieved its effects by accumulation and saturation; modern fiction preferred suggestion. Victorian fiction often featured an authoritative narrator; modern fiction tended to be written in the first person or to limit the reader to one character's point of view on the action. This limitation accorded with the modernist sense that "truth" does not exist objectively but is the product of the mind's interaction with reality. The selected point of view is often that of a naïve or marginal person—a child or an outsider—to convey better the reality of confusion rather than the myth of certainty.

The contents of modernist works may be as varied as the interests and observations of their authors; indeed, with a stable external world in question, subjectivity was ever more valued and accepted in literature. Modernists in general, however, emphasized the concrete sensory image or detail over abstract statement. Allusions to literary, historical, philosophical, or religious details of the past often keep company, in modernist works, with vignettes of contemporary life, chunks of popular culture, dream imagery, and symbolism drawn from the author's private repertory of life experiences. A work built from these various levels and kinds of material may move across time and space, shift from the public to the personal, and open literature as a field for every sort of concern. The inclusion of all sorts of material previously deemed "unliterary" in works of high seriousness involved the use of language that might previously have been thought improper, including representations of the speech of the uneducated and the inarticulate, the colloquial, slangy, and the popular. Traditional realistic fiction had incorporated colloquial and dialect speech, often to comic effect, in its representation of the broad tapestry of social life; but such speakers were usually framed by a narrator's educated literary voice, conveying truth and culture. In modernist writing like William Faulkner's As I Lay Dying, these voices assume the full burden of the narrative's authority; this is what Ernest Hemingway had in mind when he asserted that the American literary tradition began with Huckleberry Finn.

"Serious" literature between the two world wars thus found itself in a curious relationship with the culture at large. If it was attacking the old-style idea of traditional literature, it felt itself attacked in turn by the ever-growing industry of popular literature. The reading audience in America was vast, but it preferred a kind of book quite different from that turned out by literary high modernists: tales of romance or adventure, historical novels, crime fiction, and westerns became popular modes that enjoyed a success the serious writer could only dream of. The problem was that often he or she did dream of it; unrealistically, perhaps, the Ezra Pounds of the era imagined themselves with an audience of millions. When, on occasion, this dream came true—as it did for F. Scott Fitzgerald and Ernest Hemingway—writers often accused themselves of having sold out.

Nevertheless, serious writers in these years were, in fact, being published and read as writers had not been in earlier times. The number of so-called little magazines—that is, magazines of very small circulations devoted to the publication of works for a small audience (sometimes the works of a specific group of authors)—was in the hundreds. Poetry: A Magazine of Verse began in 1912. The Little Review followed in 1914. Then came the Seven Arts in 1916, the Dial in 1917, the Frontier in 1920, Reviewer and Broom in 1921, Fugitive in 1922, This Quarter in 1925, Transition and Hound and Horn in 1927, and many more. The culture that did not listen to serious writers or make them rich still gave them plenty of opportunity to be read and allowed them (in such neighborhoods as Greenwich Village in New York City) a freedom in lifestyle that was quite new in American history. In addition, such major publishers as New Directions, Random House, Scribner, and Harper were actively looking for serious fiction and poetry to feature alongside bestsellers like *Gone with the Wind* and *Anthony Adverse*.

Some writers in the period were able to use these opportunities to cross over the hierarchies separating high modernism from middlebrow and popular culture—and they crossed them in both directions. Kay Boyle's early short stories and poems appeared in little magazines like *Broom* and *Transition* in the 1920s; in the 1930s, however, as she began writing of the rise of fascism in Europe, she found a receptive larger audience in the *New Yorker* and *Harper's Magazine*. Raymond Chandler began his career in the early 1930s writing crime fiction for cheap popular magazines, moved into authoring film scripts and full-length novels issued by mainstream publishers, and by the 1950s had earned enough respectability to be interviewed about his artistic principles in *Harper's*. Where writers like William Faulkner and F. Scott Fitzgerald experienced Hollywood as a graveyard of serious literary ambition, Chandler found in the film industry not only financial rewards but also a powerful new medium for his distinctive popular modernism—a modernism as elliptical and innovative, in its own terms, as Hemingway's.

MODERNISM ABROAD AND ON NATIVE GROUNDS

The profession of authorship in the United States has always defined itself in part as a patriotic enterprise, whose aims were to help develop a cultural life for the nation and embody national values. High modernism, however, was a self-consciously international movement, and the leading American exponents of high modernism tended to be permanent expatriates like Gertrude Stein, Ezra Pound, H. D., and T. S. Eliot. These writers left the United States because they found the country lacking in a tradition of high culture and indifferent, if not downright hostile, to artistic achievement. They also believed that a national culture could never be more than parochial. In London in the first two decades of the twentieth century and in Paris during the 1920s, they found a vibrant community of dedicated artists and a society that respected them and allowed them a great deal of personal freedom. Yet they seldom thought of themselves as deserting their nation and only Eliot gave up American citizenship (sometimes, too, the traffic went in the other direction, as when the British-born poet Mina Loy became an American citizen). They thought of themselves as bringing the United States into the larger context of European culture. The ranks of these permanent expatriates were swelled by American writers who lived abroad for some part of the period: Ernest Hemingway, Sherwood Anderson, F. Scott Fitzgerald, Claude McKay, Katherine Anne Porter, Nella Larsen, Robert Frost, Kay Boyle, and Eugene O'Neill all did so, as did many others including Sinclair Lewis and Djuna Barnes.

Those writers who came back, however, and those who never left took very seriously the task of integrating modernist ideas and methods with American subject matter. Not every experimental modernist writer disconnected literary ambitions from national belonging: Hart Crane and Marianne Moore and

William Carlos Williams, for example, all wanted to write "American" works as such. Some writers—as the title of John Dos Passos's *U.S.A.* clearly shows—attempted to speak for the nation as a whole. Crane's long poem *The Bridge* and Williams's *Paterson* both take an American city as symbol and expand it to a vision for all America, following the model established by Walt Whitman. F. Scott Fitzgerald's *The Great Gatsby* is similarly ambitious, and many writers addressed the whole nation in individual works—for example, E. E. Cummings's "next to of course god america i" and Claude McKay's "America." And a profoundly modern writer like William Faulkner cannot be extricated from his commitment to writing about his native South.

Like Faulkner, many writers of the period chose to identify themselves with the American scene and to root their work in a specific region, continuing a tradition of regionalist American writing that burgeoned in the years following the American Civil War. Their perspective on the regions was sometimes celebratory and sometimes critical. Carl Sandburg, Edgar Lee Masters, Sherwood Anderson, and Willa Cather worked with the Midwest; Cather grounded her later work in the Southwest; Black Elk's Lakota autobiography recalled the high plains of South Dakota and Wyoming; John Steinbeck and Carlos Bulosan wrote about California; Edwin Arlington Robinson and Robert Frost identified their work with New England. An especially strong center of regional literary activity emerged in the South, which had a weak literary tradition up to the Civil War. Thomas Wolfe's was an Appalachian South of hardy mountain people; Katherine Anne Porter wrote about her native Texas as a heterogeneous combination of frontier, plantation, and Latin cultures. Zora Neale Hurston drew on her childhood memories of the all-black town of Eatonville, Florida, for much of her best-known fiction, including her novel *Their Eyes Were Watching God.* William Faulkner depicted a South at once specific to his native state of Mississippi and expanded into a mythic region anguished by racial and historical conflict.

As the pairing of Hurston and Faulkner suggests, the history of race in the United States was central to the specifically national subject matter to which many American modernists remained committed. Although race as a subject potentially implicated all American writers, it was African Americans whose contributions most signally differentiated American modernism from that of Europe. The numerous writers associated with the Harlem Renaissance made it impossible ever to think of a national literature without the work of black Americans. Countee Cullen, Langston Hughes, and Zora Neale Hurston attained particular prominence at the time; but others, including Claude McKay and Nella Larsen, were also well known. All were influenced by the values of modernism: both Hughes, for example, with his incorporation of blues rhythms into poetry, and Hurston, with her poetic depictions of folk culture, applied modernist techniques to represent twentieth-century African American lives. From time to time, writers associated with the Renaissance expressed protest and anger—Hughes, in particular, wrote a number of powerful antilynching and anticapitalist poems; but in general the movement was deliberately upbeat, taking the line that racial justice was about to become reality in the United States or, like Hurston, focusing more on the vitality of black culture than on the burdens of racism. At least part of this approach was strategic—the bulk of the readership for Harlem authors was white. The note of pure anger was not expressed until Richard Wright, who had come to literary maturity in Chicago, published *Native Son* in 1940. Contributions to the Harlem Renaissance came from artists in many media; an influence equal to or greater than that of the writers came from musicians. Jazz and blues, African American in origin, are felt by many to be the most authentically American art forms the nation has ever produced. African American singers and musicians in this period achieved worldwide reputations and were often much more highly regarded abroad than in the United States.

American literary women had been active on the national scene from Anne Bradstreet forward. Their increasing prominence in the nineteenth century generated a backlash from some male modernists, who asserted their own artistic seriousness by identifying women writers with the didactic, popular writing against which they rebelled. But women refused to stay on the sidelines and associated themselves with all the important literary trends of the era: H. D. and Amy Lowell with imagism, Marianne Moore and Mina Loy with high modernism; Willa Cather with mythic regionalism, Zora Neale Hurston and Nella Larsen with the Harlem Renaissance, Katherine Anne Porter with psychological fiction; Edna St. Vincent Millay and Kay Boyle with social and sexual liberation. Many of these writers concentrated on depictions of women characters or women's thoughts and experiences. Yet few labeled themselves feminists. The passage of the suffrage amendment in 1920 had taken some of the energy out of feminism that would not return until the 1960s. Some women writers found social causes like labor and racism more important than women's rights; others focused their energies on struggles less amenable to public, legal remedies, as when Mina Loy sought to link motherhood to an energetic vision of female sexuality. Nevertheless, these literary women were clearly pushing back the boundaries of the permissible, demanding new cultural freedom for women. Equally important, they were operating as public figures and taking positions on public causes.

DRAMA

Drama in America was slow to develop as a self-conscious literary form. It was not until 1920 (the year of Eugene O'Neill's *Beyond the Horizon*) that the United States produced a world-class playwright. This is not to say that *theater*—productions and performances—was new to American life. After the American Revolution theaters—at first with itinerant English actors and companies, then with American—opened throughout the East; among early centers were Boston and Philadelphia as well as New York City. As the country expanded westward, so did its theater, together with other kinds of performance: burlesques, showboats on the Mississippi, minstrel shows, pantomimes. As the nineteenth century went on, the activity became centered more and more in New York—indeed, within a few blocks, known as "Broadway." Managers originated plays there and then sent them out to tour through the rest of the country, as Eugene O'Neill's father did with his *Count of Monte Cristo*.

Changes in American theater are often in reaction against Broadway, a pattern observable as early as 1915 with the formation of the Washington Square Players and the Provincetown Players (organized by Susan Glaspell and others), both located in New York's Greenwich Village and both dedicated to the production of plays that more conservative managers refused. The Provincetown Players would shortly be producing the first works of Glaspell and Eugene O'Neill. These fledgling companies, and others like them, often knew better what they opposed than what they wanted. European influence was strong. By 1915, Henrik Ibsen in Europe and George Bernard Shaw in England had shown that the theater could be an arena for serious ideas; while the psychological dramas of August Strindberg, the symbolic work of Maurice Maeterlinck, and the sophisticated criticism of Arthur Schnitzler provided other models. The American tours of European companies, in particular the Moscow Art Theatre in 1923, further exposed Americans to the theatrical avant-garde. American playwrights in the 1920s and 1930s were united not so much by a common cause of ideas, European or American, as by the new assumption that drama should be a branch of contemporary literature.

Just as his contemporaries in poetry and fiction were changing and questioning their forms, so Eugene O'Neill sought to refine his. He experimented less in language than in dramatic structure and in new production methods available through technology (e.g., lighting) or borrowed from the stylized realism of German expressionism. Almost as famous at the time was Maxwell Anderson, whose best plays—the tragic *Winterset* (1935) and the romantic comedy *High Tor* (1937)—embody a stylized blank verse, a language attempted by few modern dramatists. Playwrights such as Sidney Howard, Lillian Hellman, and Robert Sherwood wrote serious realistic plays. George Kaufman and his many collaborators, especially Moss Hart, invented a distinctively American form, the wisecracking domestic and social comedy, while S. N. Behrman and Philip Barry wrote higher comedies of ideas. The musical comedy was another distinctively American invention: beginning as an amalgam of jokes, songs, and dances, it progressed steadily toward an integration of its various elements, reaching new heights with the work of George and Ira Gershwin in the 1920s and 1930s and of Oscar Hammerstein in collaboration with Jerome Kern or Richard Rodgers from the 1920s on into the 1950s.

Social commentary and satire had been a thread in the bright weave of American drama since the early 1920s, beginning, perhaps, with Elmer Rice's fiercely expressionistic play about a rebellious nonentity, *The Adding Machine* (1923). During the Depression social criticism became a much more important dramatic theme, with political plays performed by many radical groups. Perhaps the most significant was Clifford Odets's *Waiting for Lefty* (1935), which dramatized a taxidrivers' strike meeting and turned the stage into a platform for argument. Many poets and fiction writers of the interwar period wrote plays—among them Ernest Hemingway, E. E. Cummings, William Carlos Williams, William Faulkner, Edna St. Vincent Millay, Langston Hughes, T. S. Eliot, John Steinbeck, and Robert Lowell. It was in this period that drama moved decisively into the American literary mainstream.

TEXTS	CONTEXTS
1910 Edward Arlington Robinson, **"Miniver Cheevy"**	
1914 Robert Frost, **"Home Burial"** • Carl Sandburg, **"Chicago"**	**1914–18** World War I
1915 Edgar Lee Masters, *Spoon River Anthology* • Ezra Pound begins *Cantos*	**1915** Great Migration of African Americans from the rural South to northern industrial cities
1916 Susan Glaspell, *Trifles*	
	1917 United States declares war on Germany • revolution in Russia brings Communist party to power
1918 Willa Cather, *My Ántonia*	**1918** Daylight Savings Time instituted to allow more daylight for war production
1919 Sherwood Anderson, *Winesburg, Ohio* • Amy Lowell, **"Madonna of the Evening Flowers"**	**1919** Senate limits U.S. participation in League of Nations; does not ratify Versailles Treaty to end World War I
1920 Pound, **"Hugh Selwyn Mauberley"** • Edwin Arlington Robinson, **"Mr. Flood's Party"**	**1920** 18th Amendment prohibits the manufacture, sale, and transportation of alcoholic beverages • 19th Amendment gives women the vote
	1920–27 Sacco-Vanzetti trial
1921 T. S. Eliot, *The Waste Land* • Claude McKay, **"Africa, America"** • Marianne Moore, **"Poetry"** • Langston Hughes, **"The Negro Speaks of Rivers"**	
1922 Mina Loy, **"Brancusi's Golden Bird"**	**1922** Fascism rises in Europe; Mussolini becomes dictator of Italy
1923 Wallace Stevens, **"Sunday Morning"**	
1924 H. D. (Hilda Doolittle), **"Helen"**	**1924** Exclusionary immigration act bars Asians
1925 Countee Cullen, **"Heritage"** • Gertrude Stein, *The Making of Americans* • Alain Locke publishes *The New Negro*, leading anthology of the Harlem Renaissance	
1926 Hart Crane, *The Bridge*	
1927 Zora Neale Hurston, "The Eatonville Anthology"	**1927** *The Jazz Singer*, first full-length "talkie," is released
1928 Nella Larsen, *Quicksand*	
	1929 Stock market crashes; Great Depression begins
1930 Katherine Anne Porter, **"Flowering Judas"**	**1930** Sinclair Lewis is first American to win Nobel Prize for literature

Boldface titles indicate works in the anthology.

TEXTS	CONTEXTS
1931 E. E. Cummings, "i sing of Olaf glad and big" • F. Scott Fitzgerald, "Babylon Revisited"	1931 Scottsboro trial
1932 Black Elk and John G. Neihardt, *Black Elk Speaks* • Sterling A. Brown, "He Was a Man"	1932 Franklin Delano Roosevelt's "New Deal" introduces social security, welfare, and unemployment insurance
	1933 Adolf Hitler's Nationalist Socialist (Nazi) party comes to power in Germany • 18th Amendment repealed
1934 William Carlos Williams, "This Is Just to Say"	1934 Wheeler-Howard (Indian Reorganization) Act passed, ending Dawes era
1935 Kay Boyle, "The White Horses of Vienna"	
1936 Ernest Hemingway, "The Snows of Kilimanjaro"	1936 Hitler begins armed occupation of Europe
	1936–39 Spanish Civil War: U.S. volunteers among those fighting against General Franco, who becomes dictator of Spain
1937 Thomas Wolfe, "The Lost Boy"	1937 Stalin's purges
1938 John Dos Passos, *U.S.A.* • William Faulkner, "Barn Burning" • Raymond Chandler, "Red Wind"	
1939 Richard Wright, "The Man Who Was Almost a Man"	1939–45 World War II • the Holocaust
1940 Eugene O'Neill, *Long Day's Journey into Night*	
	1941 Japan bombs Pearl Harbor, Hawaii • United States enters war against Japan and its allies, Germany and Italy
	1942 President Roosevelt orders internment of Japanese Americans in camps
	1944 D Day; Allied invasion of Normandy
	1945 German forces surrender in spring; Japan surrenders in August following explosion of two nuclear bombs over Japanese cities

EDWIN ARLINGTON ROBINSON
1869–1935

Like his own Miniver Cheevy, Edwin Arlington Robinson felt himself born too late. He turned to poetry in search of an alternative world of elegance and beauty, but wrote his best poems about wasted, blighted, or impoverished lives. His brief story and portrait poems are in traditional form with metrically regular verse, rhymes, and elevated diction. Such techniques dignify the subject matter and also provide a contrast, where his subject is unpoetic according to traditional standards, that emphasizes its sadness and banality.

Robinson was raised in Gardiner, Maine, the Tilbury Town of such poems as "Miniver Cheevy" and "Mr. Flood's Party." His father's lumber business and land speculations failed during the Great Panic of 1893. One of his brothers, a physician, became a drug addict; the other, a businessman, became an alcoholic. Robinson, by nature a scholar and book lover, was able to afford just two years at Harvard. Returning to Gardiner and trying to become a professional poet, he had to depend for support on friends and patrons, until a Pulitzer Prize in 1922 brought him some financial security. By this time he was over fifty.

Robinson studied alone and with friends long after his formal schooling ended. He read classic works in many languages as well as such American writers as Hawthorne, Whitman, Emerson, and Henry James, whom he interpreted as individualistic idealists. He was also drawn to the bleak, tragic vision of the British novelist Thomas Hardy. These influences were distilled in the gloomy, austere, yet sonorous verse of his second book, *Children of the Night* (1897—*The Torrent and the Night Before* had been published the previous year, at his own expense). Celebrating the pain of isolated lives, Robinson worked through to a residue of affirmation, an occasional "light" or "word" that is glimpsed in the "night" of these poems.

Robinson moved to New York City around the turn of the century. *The Town Down the River* (1910) and *The Man against the Sky* (1916) won increasing numbers of readers and critics' awards. *Avon's Harvest* and *Collected Poems* (both 1922) were successful, as was a trilogy of long poems in imitation of medieval narratives, beginning with *Merlin* (1917). The last of these, *Tristram* (1927), brought a third Pulitzer Prize. To some of the tougher-minded critics of the 1920s, the escapism of the later work (precisely what may have made it attractive to a larger audience), uncorrected by the somber wit and sustained irony of the Tilbury poems, seemed overly sentimental. The prizes and honors represented, to a large extent, their belated recognition of his earlier poetry.

Although in that earlier work Robinson was a New England regional poet like Robert Frost and a chronicler of small-town life like Edgar Lee Masters and Sherwood Anderson, he thought of himself as estranged both from his time and from the practices of other poets. The difference between him and these others lay in his ever-present sense of a lost, glorious past.

The text of the poems included here is that of *Collected Poems of Edwin Arlington Robinson* (1921, 1937).

Luke Havergal

Go to the western gate,[1] Luke Havergal,—
There where the vines cling crimson on the wall,—
And in the twilight wait for what will come.
The wind will moan, the leaves will whisper some,—

---

1. The natural symbolism of nightfall and autumn associates "the western gate" with the end of life.

Whisper of her, and strike you as they fall;   5
But go, and if you trust her she will call.
Go to the western gate, Luke Havergal—
Luke Havergal.

No, there is not a dawn in eastern skies
To rift the fiery night that's in your eyes;   10
But there, where western glooms are gathering,
The dark will end the dark, if anything:
God slays Himself with every leaf that flies,
And hell is more than half of paradise.
No, there is not a dawn in eastern skies—   15
In eastern skies.

Out of a grave I come to tell you this,—
Out of a grave I come to quench the kiss
That flames upon your forehead with a glow
That blinds you to the way that you must go.   20
Yes, there is yet one way to where she is,—
Bitter, but one that faith may never miss.
Out of a grave I come to tell you this—
To tell you this.

There is the western gate, Luke Havergal,   25
There are the crimson leaves upon the wall.
Go,—for the winds are tearing them away,—
Nor think to riddle the dead words they say,
Nor any more to feel them as they fall;
But go! and if you trust her she will call.   30
There is the western gate, Luke Havergal—
Luke Havergal.

1896

Richard Cory

Whenever Richard Cory went down town,
We people on the pavement looked at him:
He was a gentleman from sole to crown,
Clean favored, and imperially slim.

And he was always quietly arrayed,   5
And he was always human when he talked;
But still he fluttered pulses when he said,
"Good-morning," and he glittered when he walked.

And he was rich—yes, richer than a king,—
And admirably schooled in every grace: 10
In fine, we thought that he was everything
To make us wish that we were in his place.

So on we worked, and waited for the light,
And went without the meat, and cursed the bread;
And Richard Cory, one calm summer night,   15
Went home and put a bullet through his head.

1896

Miniver Cheevy

Miniver Cheevy, child of scorn,
    Grew lean while he assailed the seasons;
He wept that he was ever born,
    And he had reasons.

Miniver loved the days of old   5
    When swords were bright and steeds were prancing;
The vision of a warrior bold
    Would set him dancing.

Miniver sighed for what was not,
    And dreamed, and rested from his labors;   10
He dreamed of Thebes and Camelot,
    And Priam's neighbors.[1]

Miniver mourned the ripe renown
    That made so many a name so fragrant;
He mourned Romance, now on the town,   15
    And Art, a vagrant.

Miniver loved the Medici,[2]
    Albeit he had never seen one;
He would have sinned incessantly
    Could he have been one.   20

Miniver cursed the commonplace
    And eyed a khaki suit with loathing;
He missed the mediæval grace
    Of iron clothing.

Miniver scorned the gold he sought,   25
    But sore annoyed was he without it;
Miniver thought, and thought, and thought,
    And thought about it.

---

1. The neighbors of King Priam in Homer's *Iliad* are his heroic compatriots in the doomed city of Troy. Thebes was an ancient city in Boeotia, rival of Athens and Sparta for supremacy in Greece and the setting of Sophocles' tragedies about Oedipus. Camelot is the legendary court of King Arthur and the knights of the Round Table.
2. Family of wealthy merchants, politicians, churchmen, and art patrons in 16th-century Florence.

Miniver Cheevy, born too late,
   Scratched his head and kept on thinking;   30
Miniver coughed, and called it fate,
   And kept on drinking.

                            1910

Mr. Flood's Party

Old Eben Flood, climbing alone one night
Over the hill between the town below
And the forsaken upland hermitage
That held as much as he should ever know
On earth again of home, paused warily.   5
The road was his with not a native near;
And Eben, having leisure, said aloud,
For no man else in Tilbury Town[1] to hear:

"Well, Mr. Flood, we have the harvest moon
Again, and we may not have many more;   10
The bird is on the wing, the poet says,[2]
And you and I have said it here before.
Drink to the bird." He raised up to the light
The jug that he had gone so far to fill,
And answered huskily: "Well, Mr. Flood,   15
Since you propose it, I believe I will."

Alone, as if enduring to the end
A valiant armor of scarred hopes outworn,
He stood there in the middle of the road
Like Roland's ghost winding a silent horn.[3]   20
Below him, in the town among the trees,
Where friends of other days had honored him,
A phantom salutation of the dead
Rang thinly till old Eben's eyes were dim.

Then, as a mother lays her sleeping child   25
Down tenderly, fearing it may awake,
He set the jug down slowly at his feet
With trembling care, knowing that most things break;
And only when assured that on firm earth
It stood, as the uncertain lives of men   30

---

1. The fictive town in a number of Robinson's poems, modeled on Gardiner, Maine.
2. Flood paraphrases stanza 7 of the Persian poem *The Rubáiyát of Omar Khayyám* in the 1859 translation by the English poet Edward FitzGerald (1809–1883): "Come, fill the Cup, and in the Fire of Spring / Your Winter-garment of Repentance fling: / The Bird of Time has but a little way / To flutter—and the Bird is on the Wing."
3. Roland was King Charlemagne's nephew, celebrated in the *Chanson de Roland* (Song of Roland, c. 1000). Just before dying in the battle of Roncevalles (778 C.E.), he sounded his horn for help.

Assuredly did not, he paced away,
And with his hand extended paused again:

"Well, Mr. Flood, we have not met like this
In a long time; and many a change has come
To both of us, I fear, since last it was   35
We had a drop together. Welcome home!"
Convivially returning with himself,
Again he raised the jug up to the light;
And with an acquiescent quaver said:
"Well, Mr. Flood, if you insist, I might.   40

"Only a very little, Mr. Flood—
For auld lang syne.[4] No more, sir; that will do."
So, for the time, apparently it did,
And Eben evidently thought so too;
For soon amid the silver loneliness   45
Of night he lifted up his voice and sang,
Secure, with only two moons listening,
Until the whole harmonious landscape rang—

"For auld lang syne." The weary throat gave out,
The last word wavered, and the song was done.   50
He raised again the jug regretfully
And shook his head, and was again alone.
There was not much that was ahead of him,
And there was nothing in the town below—
Where strangers would have shut the many doors   55
That many friends had opened long ago.

                                                          1921

4. Old long since (Scottish, literal trans.); hence "the days of long ago," the title and refrain of a famous
song by the Scottish poet Robert Burns (1759–1796).

WILLA CATHER
1873–1947

Willa Cather was born in Virginia, the oldest child of Charles and Mary Virginia
Cather, who moved with their family to the Nebraska Divide when she was nine years
old. After a year of farming, they relocated to the town of Red Cloud, and her father
went into the real estate business. At sixteen, Cather moved on her own to Lincoln,
the state capital and seat of the University of Nebraska; she attended preparatory
school for one year and graduated from the university in 1895. In college she studied
the classics and participated in the lively contemporary cultural life of the city by
reviewing books, plays, and musical performances. Following graduation, she eked out
a year as a journalist in Red Cloud and Lincoln before moving to Pittsburgh, Pennsylvania, to work as an editor of a women's magazine, the *Home Monthly*, a position
she left five years later to teach high-school English and Latin. During this time she

also wrote poems and stories, gathering poems into *April Twilights*, in 1903, and stories into *The Troll Garden*, in 1905. Also in Pittsburgh, in 1899, she met Isabelle McClung, from a prominent, wealthy family. She lived in the McClung home from 1901 to 1906, when she moved to New York City to write for the journal *McClure's*. Throughout her life, Cather remained devoted to McClung, experiencing her marriage in 1916 as a severe personal loss and being devastated by her death in 1938.

Having long wished to write novels, Cather took a leave of absence from *McClure's* in 1911, and wrote *Alexander's Bridge* (1912). This novel was successful, but it was the next three that made her reputation. Each focused on a western heroine: Alexandra Bergson in *O Pioneers!* (1913), Thea Kronborg in *The Song of the Lark* (1915), and Ántonia Shimerda in *My Ántonia* (1918). While Alexandra is extraordinary as the most successful farmer—the only woman farmer—on the Nebraska Divide, and Thea is extraordinary as a gifted opera singer, Ántonia has no unusual gifts; for Cather and the novel's many readers she stands for the entire experience of European settlement of the Great Plains. These three novels also manifest Cather's lyrical yet understated prose writing; they contain a wealth of detail about the lives of Nebraska settlers— Bohemian Czech, German, Danish, Swedish, Norwegian, French, Russian, and "Americans" from the East—as they learned to farm on the prairie and built communities in which their various ethnicities met and mingled. Cather's is no melting pot ethos, however; rather she sees the frontier as a shifting kaleidoscope of overlapping social groups and individuals. Recognizing that even by the second decade of the twentieth century this period in U.S. history had disappeared, Cather approached her characters with deep respect for what they had endured and accomplished.

Whether these novels (or any of Cather's other work) reflect a lesbian sensibility has been a matter of much critical debate. Cather's central emotional involvements in her life were with women; in 1908 she began to share an apartment with Edith Lewis, a Nebraskan whom she had met in 1903, and they lived together until Cather's death. (They lived mostly in New York City, but Cather also traveled a great deal: to Europe, to New England, to the Southwest, and back to Red Cloud to visit her family.) Estrangement from conventional sexuality and sex roles is typical of many of her main characters, male and female; but heterosexual romance and sexual behavior is equally present in her novels. It seems fair to say that close friendship, much more than romantic or sexual love, is the great ideal in her fiction.

Around 1922, according to Cather, the world broke in two; she suffered from the combined effects of poor health, dissatisfaction with the progress of her career, and alarm at the increasing mechanization and mass-produced quality of American life. She joined the Episcopal Church, and her novels took a new direction. Although her books had always celebrated alternative values to the material and conventional, this theme became much more urgent, while the motif of heroic womanhood—which had led many to call her a feminist, though Cather herself kept aloof from all movements—receded. Important books from her "middle period" include *A Lost Lady* (1923) and *The Professor's House* (1925), which deal with spiritual and cultural crises in the lives of the main characters.

Published in 1927, the novel *Death Comes for the Archbishop* initiated another stage. Like many other writers and artists in the 1920s, Cather had become entranced with the American Southwest—especially New Mexico; her first trip to the region in 1912 figured in her depiction (in *The Song of the Lark*) of Thea Kronborg finding spiritual renewal in this landscape. *Death Comes for the Archbishop*, partly written at Mary Austin's home in Santa Fe, is based on the career of Jean Baptiste Lamy (1814–1888), archbishop of New Mexico, and the priest Joseph Marchebeuf, his close friend and collaborator. Another historical novel, *Shadows on the Rock* (1931) is set even further back in time, in seventeenth-century Quebec. In both books, a composite image of high French culture, ceremonial spirituality, and the American landscape contrasts with the material trivia and empty banality of contemporary life.

Inspired by the classical Latin works that she loved so much, Cather believed in the ideas of art and the artist and strove to attain an artistic height from which she might survey the entire human scene. She tried to imbue the particularities of her stories with what she thought of as universal significance. In *My Ántonia*, which continues to be the favorite novel for most Cather readers, Jim Burden reflects on the aspirations of the poet Virgil to bring the muse to his own country for the first time; by country, Virgil means "not a nation or even a province, but the little rural neighborhood" where he was born. This is clearly what is intended in *My Ántonia*; the idea of combining artistic transcendence with local, especially rural, specificity, speaks to Cather's own goals. It is a measure of her ambition that she thinks of her work in Virgilian terms, since Virgil was the greatest of the Latin poets. This aim was also Cather's in stories of Nebraska such as "Neighbour Rosicky." But a story like "The Sculptor's Funeral" shows her awareness that the neighborhood may not appreciate the artists who put it on the cultural map.

Politically, culturally, and aesthetically, Cather was in many respects deeply conservative as well as conflicted—a sophisticated populist, an agrarian urbanite. She believed in high art and superior people, but also thought great human gifts were more often found among the obscure and ordinary than among those with great advantages. Her vision of the United States seldom focused on Native Americans and African Americans; yet she preferred immigrants from Europe to migrants from the East Coast. She appreciated popular legends and folktales, which appear along with classical myth and allusion in her work. Her subtle experiments with formal structure include the retrospective narrative of *My Ántonia*, the embedded Southwestern story of Tom Outland in *The Professor's House*, and the seemingly unplotted, episodic chronicle form of *Death Comes for the Archbishop*. She once described her work as deliberately "unfurnished," meaning that it was cut down to only those details absolutely necessary; "suggestion rather than enumeration" was another way she described her goal. The resulting spareness and clarity of her fiction puts it in the modernist tradition.

The text of "The Sculptor's Funeral" is from *Youth and the Bright Medusa* (1920); that of "Neighbour Rosicky" is from *Obscure Destinies* (1932).

Neighbour Rosicky

I

When Doctor Burleigh told neighbour Rosicky he had a bad heart, Rosicky protested.

"So? No, I guess my heart was always pretty good. I got a little asthma, maybe. Just a awful short breath when I was pitchin' hay last summer, dat's all."

"Well, now, Rosicky, if you know more about it than I do, what did you come to me for? It's your heart that makes you short of breath, I tell you. You're sixty-five years old, and you've always worked hard, and your heart's tired. You've got to be careful from now on, and you can't do heavy work any more. You've got five boys at home to do it for you."

The old farmer looked up at the Doctor with a gleam of amusement in his queer triangular-shaped eyes. His eyes were large and lively, but the lids were caught up in the middle in a curious way, so that they formed a triangle. He did not look like a sick man. His brown face was creased but not wrinkled, he had a ruddy colour in his smooth-shaven cheeks and in his lips, under his long brown moustache. His hair was thin and ragged around his ears, but very little grey. His forehead, naturally high and crossed by deep parallel lines, now ran all the way up to his pointed crown. Rosicky's face had the habit of looking interested,—suggested a contented disposition and a reflective quality that was gay rather than grave. This gave him a certain detachment, the easy manner of an onlooker and observer.

"Well, I guess you ain't got no pills fur a bad heart, Doctor Ed. I guess the only thing is fur me to git me a new one."

Doctor Burleigh swung round in his desk-chair and frowned at the old farmer.

"I think if I were you I'd take a little care of the old one, Rosicky."

Rosicky shrugged. "Maybe I don't know how. I expect you mean fur me not to drink my coffee no more."

"I wouldn't, in your place. But you'll do as you choose about that. I've never yet been able to separate a Bohemian[1] from his coffee or his pipe. I've quit trying. But the sure thing is you've got to cut out farm work. You can feed the stock and do chores about the barn, but you can't do anything in the fields that makes you short of breath."

"How about shelling corn?"

"Of course not!"

Rosicky considered with puckered brows.

"I can't make my heart go no longer'n it wants to, can I, Doctor Ed?"

"I think it's good for five or six years yet, maybe more, if you'll take the strain off it. Sit around the house and help Mary. If I had a good wife like yours, I'd want to stay around the house."

His patient chuckled. "It ain't no place fur a man. I don't like no old man hanging round the kitchen too much. An' my wife, she's a awful hard worker her own self."

"That's it; you can help her a little. My Lord, Rosicky, you are one of the few men I know who has a family he can get some comfort out of; happy dispositions, never quarrel among themselves, and they treat you right. I want to see you live a few years and enjoy them."

"Oh, they're good kids, all right," Rosicky assented.

The Doctor wrote him a prescription and asked him how his oldest son, Rudolph, who had married in the spring, was getting on. Rudolph had struck out for himself, on rented land. "And how's Polly? I was afraid Mary mightn't like an American daughter-in-law, but it seems to be working out all right."

"Yes, she's a fine girl. Dat widder woman bring her daughters up very nice. Polly got lots of spunk, an' she got some style, too. Da's nice, for young folks to have some style." Rosicky inclined his head gallantly. His voice and his twinkly smile were an affectionate compliment to his daughter-in-law.

"It looks like a storm, and you'd better be getting home before it comes. In town in the car?" Doctor Burleigh rose.

"No, I'm in de wagon. When you got five boys, you ain't got much chance to ride round in de Ford. I ain't much for cars, noway."

"Well, it's a good road out to your place; but I don't want you bumping around in a wagon much. And never again on a hay-rake, remember!"

Rosicky placed the Doctor's fee delicately behind the desk-telephone, looking the other way, as if this were an absent-minded gesture. He put on his plush cap and his corduroy jacket with a sheepskin collar, and went out.

The Doctor picked up his stethoscope and frowned at it as if he were seriously annoyed with the instrument. He wished it had been telling tales about some other man's heart, some old man who didn't look the Doctor in

1. Native of Bohemia, in the Czech Republic.

the eye so knowingly, or hold out such a warm brown hand when he said good-bye. Doctor Burleigh had been a poor boy in the country before he went away to medical school; he had known Rosicky almost ever since he could remember, and he had a deep affection for Mrs. Rosicky.

Only last winter he had had such a good breakfast at Rosicky's, and that when he needed it. He had been out all night on a long, hard confinement case at Tom Marshall's—a big rich farm where there was plenty of stock and plenty of feed and a great deal of expensive farm machinery of the newest model, and no comfort whatever. The woman had too many children and too much work, and she was no manager. When the baby was born at last, and handed over to the assisting neighbour woman, and the mother was properly attended to, Burleigh refused any breakfast in that slovenly house, and drove his buggy—the snow was too deep for a car—eight miles to Anton Rosicky's place. He didn't know another farm-house where a man could get such a warm welcome, and such good strong coffee with rich cream. No wonder the old chap didn't want to give up his coffee!

He had driven in just when the boys had come back from the barn and were washing up for breakfast. The long table, covered with a bright oilcloth, was set out with dishes waiting for them, and the warm kitchen was full of the smell of coffee and hot biscuit and sausage. Five big handsome boys, running from twenty to twelve, all with what Burleigh called natural good manners—they hadn't a bit of the painful self-consciousness he himself had to struggle with when he was a lad. One ran to put his horse away, another helped him off with his fur coat and hung it up, and Josephine, the youngest child and the only daughter, quickly set another place under her mother's direction.

With Mary, to feed creatures was the natural expression of affection—her chickens, the calves, her big hungry boys. It was a rare pleasure to feed a young man whom she seldom saw and of whom she was as proud as if he belonged to her. Some country housekeepers would have stopped to spread a white cloth over the oilcloth, to change the thick cups and plates for their best china, and the wooden-handled knives for plated ones. But not Mary.

"You must take us as you find us, Doctor Ed. I'd be glad to put out my good things for you if you was expected, but I'm glad to get you any way at all."

He knew she was glad—she threw back her head and spoke out as if she were announcing him to the whole prairie. Rosicky hadn't said anything at all; he merely smiled his twinkling smile, put some more coal on the fire, and went into his own room to pour the Doctor a little drink in a medicine glass. When they were all seated, he watched his wife's face from his end of the table and spoke to her in Czech. Then, with the instinct of politeness which seldom failed him, he turned to the doctor and said slyly: "I was just tellin' her not to ask you no questions about Mrs. Marshall till you eat some breakfast. My wife, she's terrible fur to ask questions."

The boys laughed, and so did Mary. She watched the Doctor devour her biscuit and sausage, too much excited to eat anything herself. She drank her coffee and sat taking in everything about her visitor. She had known him when he was a poor country boy, and was boastfully proud of his success, always saying: "What do people go to Omaha for, to see a doctor, when we got the best one in the State right here?" If Mary liked people at all, she felt physical pleasure in the sight of them, personal exultation in any good fortune that came to them. Burleigh didn't know many women like that, but he knew she was like that.

When his hunger was satisfied, he did, of course, have to tell them about Mrs. Marshall, and he noticed what a friendly interest the boys took in the matter.

Rudolph, the oldest one (he was still living at home then), said: "The last time I was over there, she was lifting them big heavy milk-cans, and I knew she oughtn't to be doing it."

"Yes, Rudolph told me about that when he come home, and I said it wasn't right," Mary put in warmly. "It was all right for me to do them things up to the last, for I was terrible strong, but that woman's weakly. And do you think she'll be able to nurse it, Ed?" She sometimes forgot to give him the title she was so proud of. "And to think of your being up all night and then not able to get a decent breakfast! I don't know what's the matter with such people."

"Why, Mother," said one of the boys, "if Doctor Ed had got breakfast there, we wouldn't have him here. So you ought to be glad."

"He knows I'm glad to have him, John, any time. But I'm sorry for that poor woman, how bad she'll feel the Doctor had to go away in the cold without his breakfast."

"I wish I had been in practice when these were getting born." The Doctor looked down the row of close-clipped heads. "I missed some good breakfasts by not being."

The boys began to laugh at their mother because she flushed so red, but she stood her ground and threw up her head. "I don't care, you wouldn't have got away from this house without breakfast. No doctor ever did. I'd have had something ready fixed that Anton could warm up for you."

The boys laughed harder than ever, and exclaimed at her: "I'll bet you would!" "She would, that!"

"Father, did you get breakfast for the Doctor when we were born?"

"Yes, and he used to bring me my breakfast, too, mighty nice. I was always awful hungry!" Mary admitted with a guilty laugh.

While the boys were getting the Doctor's horse, he went to the window to examine the house plants. "What do you do to your geraniums to keep them blooming all winter, Mary? I never pass this house that from the road I don't see your windows full of flowers."

She snapped off a dark red one, and a ruffled new green leaf, and put them in his buttonhole. "There, that looks better. You look too solemn for a young man, Ed. Why don't you git married? I'm worried about you. Settin' at breakfast, I looked at you real hard, and I seen you've got some grey hairs already."

"Oh, yes! They're coming. Maybe they'd come faster if I married."

"Don't talk so. You'll ruin your health eating at the hotel. I could send your wife a nice loaf of nut bread, if you only had one. I don't like to see a young man getting grey. I'll tell you something, Ed; you make some strong black tea and keep it handy in a bowl, and every morning just brush it into your hair, an' it'll keep the grey from showin' much. That's the way I do!"

Sometimes the Doctor heard the gossipers in the drug-store wondering why Rosicky didn't get on faster. He was industrious, and so were his boys, but they were rather free and easy, weren't pushers, and they didn't always show good judgment. They were comfortable, they were out of debt, but they didn't get much ahead. Maybe, Doctor Burleigh reflected, people as generous and warm-hearted and affectionate as the Rosickys never got ahead much; maybe you couldn't enjoy your life and put it into the bank, too.

II

When Rosicky left Doctor Burleigh's office, he went into the farm-implement store to light his pipe and put on his glasses and read over the list Mary had given him. Then he went into the general merchandise place next door and stood about until the pretty girl with the plucked eyebrows, who always waited on him, was free. Those eyebrows, two thin India-ink strokes, amused him, because he remembered how they used to be. Rosicky always prolonged his shopping by a little joking; the girl knew the old fellow admired her, and she liked to chaff with him.

"Seems to me about every other week you buy ticking, Mr. Rosicky, and always the best quality," she remarked as she measured off the heavy bolt with red stripes.

"You see, my wife is always makin' goose-fedder pillows, an' de thin stuff don't hold in dem little down-fedders."

"You must have lots of pillows at your home."

"Sure. She makes quilts of dem, too. We sleeps easy. Now she's makin' a fedder quilt for my son's wife. You know Polly, that married my Rudolph. How much my bill, Miss Pearl?"

"Eight eighty-five."

"Chust make it nine, and put in some candy fur de women."

"As usual. I never did see a man buy so much candy for his wife. First thing you know, she'll be getting too fat."

"I'd like that. I ain't much fur all dem slim women like what de style is now."

"That's one for me, I suppose, Mr. Bohunk!"[2] Pearl sniffed and elevated her India-ink strokes.

When Rosicky went out to his wagon, it was beginning to snow,—the first snow of the season, and he was glad to see it. He rattled out of town and along the highway through a wonderfully rich stretch of country, the finest farms in the county. He admired this High Prairie, as it was called, and always liked to drive through it. His own place lay in a rougher territory, where there was some clay in the soil and it was not so productive. When he bought his land, he hadn't the money to buy on High Prairie; so he told his boys, when they grumbled, that if their land hadn't some clay in it, they wouldn't own it at all. All the same, he enjoyed looking at these fine farms, as he enjoyed looking at a prize bull.

After he had gone eight miles, he came to the graveyard, which lay just at the edge of his own hay-land. There he stopped his horses and sat still on his wagon seat, looking about at the snowfall. Over yonder on the hill he could see his own house, crouching low, with the clump of orchard behind and the windmill before, and all down the gentle hill-slope the rows of pale gold cornstalks stood out against the white field. The snow was falling over the cornfield and the pasture and the hay-land, steadily, with very little wind—a nice dry snow. The graveyard had only a light wire fence about it and was all overgrown with long red grass. The fine snow, settling into this red grass and upon the few little evergreens and the headstones, looked very pretty.

It was a nice graveyard, Rosicky reflected, sort of snug and homelike, not cramped or mournful,—a big sweep all round it. A man could lie down in the long grass and see the complete arch of the sky over him, hear the wagons go by; in summer the mowing-machine rattled right up to the wire fence. And it was so near home. Over there across the cornstalks his own roof and

---

2. Bohemian (slang); here used affectionately.

windmill looked so good to him that he promised himself to mind the Doctor and take care of himself. He was awful fond of his place, he admitted. He wasn't anxious to leave it. And it was a comfort to think that he would never have to go farther than the edge of his own hayfield. The snow, falling over his barnyard and the graveyard, seemed to draw things together like. And they were all old neighbours in the graveyard, most of them friends; there was nothing to feel awkward or embarrassed about. Embarrassment was the most disagreeable feeling Rosicky knew. He didn't often have it,—only with certain people whom he didn't understand at all.

Well, it was a nice snowstorm; a fine sight to see the snow falling so quietly and graciously over so much open country. On his cap and shoulders, on the horses' backs and manes, light, delicate, mysterious it fell; and with it a dry cool fragrance was released into the air. It meant rest for vegetation and men and beasts, for the ground itself; a season of long nights for sleep, leisurely breakfasts, peace by the fire. This and much more went through Rosicky's mind, but he merely told himself that winter was coming, clucked to his horses, and drove on.

When he reached home, John, the youngest boy, ran out to put away his team for him, and he met Mary coming up from the outside cellar with her apron full of carrots. They went into the house together. On the table, covered with oilcloth figured with clusters of blue grapes, a place was set, and he smelled hot coffee-cake of some kind. Anton never lunched in town; he thought that extravagant, and anyhow he didn't like the food. So Mary always had something ready for him when he got home.

After he was settled in his chair, stirring his coffee in a big cup, Mary took out of the oven a pan of *kolache*[3] stuffed with apricots, examined them anxiously to see whether they had got too dry, put them beside his plate, and then sat down opposite him.

Rosicky asked her in Czech if she wasn't going to have any coffee.

She replied in English, as being somehow the right language for transacting business: "Now what did Doctor Ed say, Anton? You tell me just what."

"He said I was to tell you some compliments, but I forgot 'em." Rosicky's eyes twinkled.

"About you, I mean. What did he say about your asthma?"

"He says I ain't got no asthma." Rosicky took one of the little rolls in his broad brown fingers. The thickened nail of his right thumb told the story of his past.

"Well, what is the matter? And don't try to put me off."

"He don't say nothing much, only I'm a little older, and my heart ain't so good like it used to be."

Mary started and brushed her hair back from her temples with both hands as if she were a little out of her mind. From the way she glared, she might have been in a rage with him.

"He says there's something the matter with your heart? Doctor Ed says so?"

"Now don't yell at me like I was a hog in de garden, Mary. You know I always did like to hear a woman talk soft. He didn't say anything de matter wid my heart, only it ain't so young like it used to be, an' he tell me not to pitch hay or run de corn-sheller."

---

3. Or kolacky, a sweet bun with fruit filling.

Mary wanted to jump up, but she sat still. She admired the way he never under any circumstances raised his voice or spoke roughly. He was city-bred, and she was country-bred; she often said she wanted her boys to have their papa's nice ways.

"You never have no pain there, do you? It's your breathing and your stomach that's been wrong. I wouldn't believe nobody but Doctor Ed about it. I guess I'll go see him myself. Didn't he give you no advice?"

"Chust to take it easy like, an' stay round de house dis winter. I guess you got some carpenter work for me to do. I kin make some new shelves for you, and I want dis long time to build a closet in de boys' room and make dem two little fellers keep dere clo'es hung up."

Rosicky drank his coffee from time to time, while he considered. His moustache was of the soft long variety and came down over his mouth like the teeth of a buggy-rake over a bundle of hay. Each time he put down his cup, he ran his blue handkerchief over his lips. When he took a drink of water, he managed very neatly with the back of his hand.

Mary sat watching him intently, trying to find any change in his face. It is hard to see anyone who has become like your own body to you. Yes, his hair had got thin, and his high forehead had deep lines running from left to right. But his neck, always clean-shaved except in the busiest seasons, was not loose or baggy. It was burned a dark reddish brown, and there were deep creases in it, but it looked firm and full of blood. His cheeks had a good colour. On either side of his mouth there was a half-moon down the length of his cheek, not wrinkles, but two lines that had come there from his habitual expression. He was shorter and broader than when she married him; his back had grown broad and curved, a good deal like the shell on an old turtle, and his arms and legs were short.

He was fifteen years older than Mary, but she had hardly ever thought about it before. He was her man, and the kind of man she liked. She was rough, and he was gentle—city-bred, as she always said. They had been shipmates on a rough voyage and had stood by each other in trying times. Life had gone well with them because, at bottom, they had the same ideas about life. They agreed, without discussion, as to what was most important and what was secondary. They didn't often exchange opinions, even in Czech—it was as if they had thought the same thought together. A good deal had to be sacrificed and thrown overboard in a hard life like theirs, and they had never disagreed as to the things that could go. It had been a hard life, and a soft life, too. There wasn't anything brutal in the short, broad-backed man with the three-cornered eyes and the forehead that went on to the top of his skull. He was a city man, a gentle man, and though he had married a rough farm girl, he had never touched her without gentleness.

They had been at one accord not to hurry through life, not to be always skimping and saving. They saw their neighbours buy more land and feed more stock than they did, without discontent. Once when the creamery agent came to the Rosickys to persuade them to sell him their cream, he told them how much money the Fasslers, their nearest neighbours, had made on their cream last year.

"Yes," said Mary, "and look at them Fassler children! Pale, pinched little things, they look like skimmed milk. I had rather put some colour into my children's faces than put money into the bank."

The agent shrugged and turned to Anton.

"I guess we'll do like she says," said Rosicky.

III

Mary very soon got into town to see Doctor Ed, and then she had a talk with her boys and set a guard over Rosicky. Even John, the youngest, had his father on his mind. If Rosicky went to throw hay down from the loft, one of the boys ran up the ladder and took the fork from him. He sometimes complained that though he was getting to be an old man, he wasn't an old woman yet.

That winter he stayed in the house in the afternoons and carpentered, or sat in the chair between the window full of plants and the wooden bench where the two pails of drinking-water stood. This spot was called "Father's corner," though it was not a corner at all. He had a shelf there, where he kept his Bohemian papers and his pipes and tobacco, and his shears and needles and thread and tailor's thimble. Having been a tailor in his youth, he couldn't bear to see a woman patching at his clothes, or at the boys'. He liked tailoring, and always patched all the overalls and jackets and work shirts. Occasionally he made over a pair of pants one of the older boys had outgrown, for the little fellow.

While he sewed, he let his mind run back over his life. He had a good deal to remember, really; life in three countries. The only part of his youth he didn't like to remember was the two years he had spent in London, in Cheapside, working for a German tailor who was wretchedly poor. Those days, when he was nearly always hungry, when his clothes were dropping off him for dirt, and the sound of a strange language kept him in continual bewilderment, had left a sore spot in his mind that wouldn't bear touching.

He was twenty when he landed at Castle Garden in New York, and he had a protector who got him work in a tailor shop in Vesey Street, down near the Washington Market. He looked upon that part of his life as very happy. He became a good workman, he was industrious, and his wages were increased from time to time. He minded his own business and envied nobody's good fortune. He went to night school and learned to read English. He often did overtime work and was well paid for it, but somehow he never saved anything. He couldn't refuse a loan to a friend, and he was self-indulgent. He liked a good dinner, and a little went for beer, a little for tobacco; a good deal went to the girls. He often stood through an opera on Saturday nights; he could get standing-room for a dollar. Those were the great days of opera in New York, and it gave a fellow something to think about for the rest of the week. Rosicky had a quick ear, and a childish love of all the stage splendour; the scenery, the costumes, the ballet. He usually went with a chum, and after the performance they had beer and maybe some oysters somewhere. It was a fine life; for the first five years or so it satisfied him completely. He was never hungry or cold or dirty, and everything amused him: a fire, a dog fight, a parade, a storm, a ferry ride. He thought New York the finest, richest, friendliest city in the world.

Moreover, he had what he called a happy home life. Very near the tailor shop was a small furniture-factory, where an old Austrian, Loeffler, employed a few skilled men and made unusual furniture, most of it to order, for the rich German housewives uptown. The top floor of Loeffler's five-storey factory was a loft, where he kept his choice lumber and stored the old pieces of furniture left on his hands. One of the young workmen he employed was a Czech, and he and Rosicky became fast friends. They persuaded Loeffler to let them have a sleeping-room in one corner of the loft. They bought good beds and bedding and had their pick of the furniture kept up there. The loft was low-pitched, but light and airy, full of windows, and good-smelling by reason of the fine lumber put up there to season. Old Loeffler used to go down to the docks and buy wood from South America and the East from the sea captains. The young men were as foolish about their house as a bridal pair. Zichec, the young cabinet-maker, devised every sort of convenience, and Rosicky kept their clothes in order. At night and on Sundays, when the quiver of machinery underneath was still, it was the quietest place in the world, and on summer nights all the sea winds blew in. Zichec often practised on his flute in the evening. They were both fond of music and went to the opera together. Rosicky thought he wanted to live like that for ever.

But as the years passed, all alike, he began to get a little restless. When spring came round, he would begin to feel fretted, and he got to drinking. He was likely to drink too much of a Saturday night. On Sunday he was languid and heavy, getting over his spree. On Monday he plunged into work again. So he never had time to figure out what ailed him, although he knew something did. When the grass turned green in Park Place, and the lilac hedge at the back of Trinity churchyard put out its blossoms, he was tormented by a longing to run away. That was why he drank too much; to get a temporary illusion of freedom and wide horizons.

Rosicky, the old Rosicky, could remember as if it were yesterday the day when the young Rosicky found out what was the matter with him. It was on a Fourth of July afternoon, and he was sitting in Park Place in the sun. The lower part of New York was empty. Wall Street, Liberty Street, Broadway, all empty. So much stone and asphalt with nothing going on, so many empty windows. The emptiness was intense, like the stillness in a great factory when the machinery stops and the belts and bands cease running. It was too great a change, it took all the strength out of one. Those blank buildings, without the stream of life pouring through them, were like empty jails. It struck young Rosicky that this was the trouble with big cities; they built you in from the earth itself, cemented you away from any contact with the ground. You lived in an unnatural world, like the fish in an aquarium, who were probably much more comfortable than they ever were in the sea.

On that very day he began to think seriously about the articles he had read in the Bohemian papers, describing prosperous Czech farming communities in the West. He believed he would like to go out there as a farm hand; it was hardly possible that he could ever have land of his own. His people had always been workmen, his father and grandfather had worked in shops. His mother's parents had lived in the country, but they rented their farm and had a hard time to get along. Nobody in his family had ever owned any land,—that belonged to a different station of life altogether. Anton's mother died when he was little, and he was sent into the country to her parents. He stayed with them until he was twelve, and formed those ties with the earth and the farm animals and growing things which are never made at all unless they are made early. After his grandfather died, he went back to live with his father and stepmother, but she was very hard on him, and his father helped him to get passage to London.

After that Fourth of July day in Park Place, the desire to return to the country never left him. To work on another man's farm would be all he asked; to see the sun rise and set and to plant things and watch them grow. He was a very simple man. He was like a tree that has not many roots, but one tap-root that goes down deep. He subscribed for a Bohemian paper printed in Chicago, then for one printed in Omaha. His mind got farther and farther west. He began to save a little money to buy his liberty. When he was thirty-five, there was a great meeting in New York of Bohemian athletic societies, and Rosicky left the tailor shop and went home with the Omaha delegates to try his fortune in another part of the world.

IV

Perhaps the fact that his own youth was well over before he began to have a family was one reason why Rosicky was so fond of his boys. He had almost a grandfather's indulgence for them. He had never had to worry about any of them—except, just now, a little about Rudolph.

On Saturday night the boys always piled into the Ford, took little Josephine, and went to town to the moving-picture show. One Saturday morning they were talking at the breakfast table about starting early that evening, so that they would have an hour or so to see the Christmas things in the stores before the show began. Rosicky looked down the table.

"I hope you boys ain't disappointed, but I want you to let me have de car tonight. Maybe some of you can go in with de neighbours."

Their faces fell. They worked hard all week, and they were still like children. A new jack-knife or a box of candy pleased the older ones as much as the little fellow.

"If you and mother are going to town," Frank said, "maybe you could take a couple of us along with you, anyway.'"

"No, I want to take de car down to Rudolph's, and let him an' Polly go in to de show. She don't git into town enough, an' I'm afraid she's gettin' lonesome, an' he can't afford no car yet."

That settled it. The boys were a good deal dashed. Their father took another piece of apple-cake and went on: "Maybe next Saturday night de two little fellers can go along wid dem."

"Oh, is Rudolph going to have the car every Saturday night?"

Rosicky did not reply at once; then he began to speak seriously: "Listen, boys; Polly ain't lookin' so good. I don't like to see nobody lookin' sad. It comes hard fur a town girl to be a farmer's wife. I don't want no trouble to start in Rudolph's family. When it starts, it ain't so easy to stop. An American girl don't git used to our ways all at once. I like to tell Polly she and Rudolph can have the car every Saturday night till after New Year's, if it's all right with you boys."

"Sure, it's all right, papa," Mary cut in. "And it's good you thought about that. Town girls is used to more than country girls. I lay awake nights, scared she'll make Rudolph discontented with the farm."

The boys put as good a face on it as they could. They surely looked forward to their Saturday nights in town. That evening Rosicky drove the car the half-mile down to Rudolph's new, bare little house.

Polly was in a short-sleeved gingham dress, clearing away the supper dishes. She was a trim, slim little thing, with blue eyes and shingled yellow hair, and her eyebrows were reduced to a mere brush-stroke, like Miss Pearl's.

"Good-evening, Mr. Rosicky. Rudolph's at the barn, I guess." She never called him father, or Mary mother. She was sensitive about having married a foreigner. She never in the world would have done it if Rudolph hadn't been such a handsome, persuasive fellow and such a gallant lover. He had graduated in her class in the high school in town, and their friendship began in the ninth grade.

Rosicky went in, though he wasn't exactly asked. "My boys ain't goin' to town tonight, an' I brought de car over fur you two to go in to de picture show."

Polly, carrying dishes to the sink, looked over her shoulder at him. "Thank you. But I'm late with my work tonight, and pretty tired. Maybe Rudolph would like to go in with you."

"Oh, I don't go to de shows! I'm too old-fashioned. You won't feel so tired after you ride in de air a ways. It's a nice clear night, an' it ain't cold. You go an' fix yourself up, Polly, an' I'll wash de dishes an' leave everything nice fur you."

Polly blushed and tossed her bob. "I couldn't let you do that, Mr. Rosicky, I wouldn't think of it."

Rosicky said nothing. He found a bib apron on a nail behind the kitchen door. He slipped it over his head and then took Polly by her two elbows and pushed her gently toward the door of her own room. "I washed up de kitchen many times for my wife, when de babies was sick or somethin'. You go an' make yourself look nice. I like you to look prettier'n any of dem town girls when you go in. De young folks must have some fun, an' I'm goin' to look out fur you, Polly."

That kind, reassuring grip on her elbows, the old man's funny bright eyes, made Polly want to drop her head on his shoulder for a second. She restrained herself, but she lingered in his grasp at the door of her room, murmuring tearfully: "You always lived in the city when you were young, didn't you? Don't you ever get lonesome out here?"

As she turned round to him, her hand fell naturally into his, and he stood holding it and smiling into her face with his peculiar, knowing, indulgent smile without a shadow of reproach in it. "Dem big cities is all right fur de rich, but dey is terrible hard fur de poor."

"I don't know. Sometimes I think I'd like to take a chance. You lived in New York, didn't you?"

"An' London. Da's bigger still. I learned my trade dere. Here's Rudolph comin', you better hurry."

"Will you tell me about London some time?"

"Maybe. Only I ain't no talker, Polly. Run an' dress yourself up."

The bedroom door closed behind her, and Rudolph came in from the outside, looking anxious. He had seen the car and was sorry any of his family should come just then. Supper hadn't been a very pleasant occasion. Halting in the doorway, he saw his father in a kitchen apron, carrying dishes to the sink. He flushed crimson and something flashed in his eye. Rosicky held up a warning finger.

"I brought de car over fur you an' Polly to go to de picture show, an' I made her let me finish here so you won't be late. You go put on a clean shirt, quick!"

"But don't the boys want the car, Father?"

"Not tonight dey don't." Rosicky fumbled under his apron and found his pants pocket. He took out a silver dollar and said in a hurried whisper: "You go an' buy dat girl some ice cream an' candy tonight, like you was courtin'. She's awful good friends wid me."

Rudolph was very short of cash, but he took the money as if it hurt him. There had been a crop failure all over the country. He had more than once been sorry he'd married this year.

In a few minutes the young people came out, looking clean and a little stiff. Rosicky hurried them off, and then he took his own time with the dishes. He scoured the pots and pans and put away the milk and swept the kitchen. He put some coal in the stove and shut off the draughts, so the place would be warm for them when they got home late at night. Then he sat down and had a pipe and listened to the clock tick.

Generally speaking, marrying an American girl was certainly a risk. A Czech should marry a Czech. It was lucky that Polly was the daughter of a poor widow woman; Rudolph was proud, and if she had a prosperous family to throw up at him, they could never make it go. Polly was one of four sisters, and they all worked; one was book-keeper in the bank, one taught music, and Polly and her younger sister had been clerks, like Miss Pearl. All four of them were musical, had pretty voices, and sang in the Methodist choir, which the eldest sister directed.

Polly missed the sociability of a store position. She missed the choir, and the company of her sisters. She didn't dislike housework, but she disliked so much of it. Rosicky was a little anxious about this pair. He was afraid Polly would grow so discontented that Rudy would quit the farm and take a factory job in Omaha. He had worked for a winter up there, two years ago, to get money to marry on. He had done very well, and they would always take him back at the stockyards. But to Rosicky that meant the end of everything for his son. To be a landless man was to be a wage-earner, a slave, all your life; to have nothing, to be nothing.

Rosicky thought he would come over and do a little carpentering for Polly after the New Year. He guessed she needed jollying. Rudolph was a serious sort of chap, serious in love and serious about his work.

Rosicky shook out his pipe and walked home across the fields. Ahead of him the lamplight shone from his kitchen windows. Suppose he were still in a tailor shop on Vesey Street, with a bunch of pale, narrow-chested sons working on machines, all coming home tired and sullen to eat supper in a kitchen that was a parlour also; with another crowded, angry family quarrelling just across the dumb-waiter shaft, and squeaking pulleys at the windows where dirty washings hung on dirty lines above a court full of old brooms and mops and ash-cans . . .

He stopped by the windmill to look up at the frosty winter stars and draw a long breath before he went inside. That kitchen with the shining windows was dear to him; but the sleeping fields and bright stars and the noble darkness were dearer still.

V

On the day before Christmas the weather set in very cold; no snow, but a bitter, biting wind that whistled and sang over the flat land and lashed one's face like fine wires. There was baking going on in the Rosicky kitchen all day, and

Rosicky sat inside, making over a coat that Albert had outgrown into an over-coat for John. Mary had a big red geranium in bloom for Christmas, and a row of Jerusalem cherry trees, full of berries. It was the first year she had ever grown these; Doctor Ed brought her the seeds from Omaha when he went to some medical convention. They reminded Rosicky of plants he had seen in England; and all afternoon, as he stitched, he sat thinking about those two years in London, which his mind usually shrank from even after all this while.

He was a lad of eighteen when he dropped down into London, with no money and no connexions except the address of a cousin who was supposed to be working at a confectioner's. When he went to the pastry shop, however, he found that the cousin had gone to America. Anton tramped the streets for several days, sleeping in doorways and on the Embankment, until he was in utter despair. He knew no English, and the sound of the strange language all about him confused him. By chance he met a poor German tailor who had learned his trade in Vienna, and could speak a little Czech. This tailor, Lifschnitz, kept a repair shop in a Cheapside basement, underneath a cobbler. He didn't much need an apprentice, but he was sorry for the boy and took him in for no wages but his keep and what he could pick up. The pickings were supposed to be coppers given you when you took work home to a customer. But most of the customers called for their clothes themselves, and the coppers that came Anton's way were very few. He had, however, a place to sleep. The tailor's family lived upstairs in three rooms; a kitchen, a bedroom, where Lifschnitz and his wife and five children slept, and a living-room. Two corners of this living room were curtained off for lodgers; in one Rosicky slept on an old horsehair sofa, with a feather quilt to wrap himself in. The other corner was rented to a wretched, dirty boy, who was studying the violin. He actually practised there. Rosicky was dirty, too. There was no way to be anything else. Mrs. Lifschnitz got the water she cooked and washed with from a pump in a brick court, four flights down. There were bugs in the place, and multitudes of fleas, though the poor woman did the best she could. Rosicky knew she often went empty to give another potato or a spoonful of dripping to the two hungry, sad-eyed boys who lodged with her. He used to think he would never get out of there, never get a clean shirt to his back again. What would he do, he wondered, when his clothes actually dropped to pieces and the worn cloth wouldn't hold patches any longer?

It was still early when the old farmer put aside his sewing and his recollec-tions. The sky had been a dark grey all day, with not a gleam of sun, and the light failed at four o'clock. He went to shave and change his shirt while the turkey was roasting. Rudolph and Polly were coming over for supper.

After supper they sat round in the kitchen, and the younger boys were saying how sorry they were it hadn't snowed. Everybody was sorry. They wanted a deep snow that would lie long and keep the wheat warm, and leave the ground soaked when it melted.

"Yes, sir!" Rudolph broke out fiercely; "if we have another dry year like last year, there's going to be hard times in this country."

Rosicky filled his pipe. "You boys don't know what hard times is. You don't owe nobody, you got plenty to eat an' keep warm, an' plenty water to keep clean. When you got them, you can't have it very hard."

Rudolph frowned, opened and shut his big right hand, and dropped it clenched upon his knee. "I've got to have a good deal more than that, father, or I'll quit this farming gamble. I can always make good wages railroading, or at the packing house, and be sure of my money."

"Maybe so," his father answered dryly.

Mary, who had just come in from the pantry and was wiping her hands on the roller towel, thought Rudy and his father were getting too serious. She brought her darning-basket and sat down in the middle of the group.

"I ain't much afraid of hard times, Rudy," she said heartily. "We've had a plenty, but we've always come through. Your father wouldn't never take nothing very hard, not even hard times. I got a mind to tell you a story on him. Maybe you boys can't hardly remember the year we had that terrible hot wind, that burned everything up on the Fourth of July? All the corn an' the gardens. An' that was in the days when we didn't have alfalfa yet,—I guess it wasn't invented.

"Well, that very day your father was out cultivatin' corn, and I was here in the kitchen makin' plum preserves. We had bushels of plums that year. I noticed it was terrible hot, but it's always hot in the kitchen when you're preservin', an' I was too busy with my plums to mind. Anton come in from the field about three o'clock, an' I asked him what was the matter.

"'Nothin',' he says, 'but it's pretty hot an' I think I won't work no more to-day.' He stood round for a few minutes, an' then he says: 'Ain't you near through? I want you should git up a nice supper for us tonight. It's Fourth of July.'

"I told him to git along, that I was right in the middle of preservin', but the plums would taste good on hot biscuit. 'I'm goin' to have fried chicken, too,' he says, and he went off an' killed a couple. You three oldest boys was little fellers, playin' round outside, real hot an' sweaty, an' your father took you to the horse tank down by the windmill an' took off your clothes an' put you in. Them two box-elder trees were little then, but they made shade over the tank. Then he took off all his own clothes, an' got in with you. While he was playin' in the water with you, the Methodist preacher drove into our place to say how all the neighbours was goin' to meet at the schoolhouse that night, to pray for rain. He drove right to the windmill, of course, and there was your father and you three with no clothes on. I was in the kitchen door, an' I had to laugh, for the preacher acted like he ain't never seen a naked man before. He surely was embarrassed, an' your father couldn't git to his clothes; they was all hangin' up on the windmill to let the sweat dry out of 'em. So he laid in the tank where he was, an' put one of you boys on top of him to cover him up a little, an' talked to the preacher.

"When you got through playin' in the water, he put clean clothes on you and a clean shirt on himself, an' by that time I'd begun to get supper. He says: 'It's too hot in here to eat comfortable. Let's have a picnic in the orchard. We'll eat our supper behind the mulberry hedge, under them linden trees.'

"So he carried our supper down, an' a bottle of my wild-grape wine, an' everything tasted good, I can tell you. The wind got cooler as the sun was goin' down, and it turned out pleasant, only I noticed how the leaves was curled up on the linden trees. That made me think, an' I asked your father if that hot wind all day hadn't been terrible hard on the gardens an' the corn.

"'Corn,' he says, 'there ain't no corn.'

"'What you talkin' about?' I said. 'Ain't we got forty acres?'

"'We ain't got an ear,' he says, 'nor nobody else ain't got none. All the corn in this country was cooked by three o'clock today, like you'd roasted it in an oven.'

"'You mean you won't get no crop at all?' I asked him. I couldn't believe it, after he'd worked so hard.

"'No crop this year,' he says. 'That's why we're havin' a picnic. We might as well enjoy what we got.'

"An' that's how your father behaved, when all the neighbours was so discouraged they couldn't look you in the face. An' we enjoyed ourselves that year, poor as we was, an' our neighbours wasn't a bit better off for bein' miserable. Some of 'em grieved till they got poor digestions and couldn't relish what they did have."

The younger boys said they thought their father had the best of it. But Rudolph was thinking that, all the same, the neighbours had managed to get ahead more, in the fifteen years since that time. There must be something wrong about his father's way of doing things. He wished he knew what was going on in the back of Polly's mind. He knew she liked his father, but he knew, too, that she was afraid of something. When his mother sent over coffee-cake or prune tarts or a loaf of fresh bread, Polly seemed to regard them with a certain suspicion. When she observed to him that his brothers had nice manners, her tone implied that it was remarkable they should have. With his mother she was stiff and on her guard. Mary's hearty frankness and gusts of good humour irritated her. Polly was afraid of being unusual or conspicuous in any way, of being 'ordinary' as she said!

When Mary had finished her story, Rosicky laid aside his pipe.

"You boys like me to tell you about some of dem hard times I been through in London?" Warmly encouraged, he sat rubbing his forehead along the deep creases. It was bothersome to tell a long story in English (he nearly always talked to the boys in Czech), but he wanted Polly to hear this one.

"Well, you know about dat tailor shop I worked in in London? I had one Christmas dere I ain't never forgot. Times was awful bad before Christmas; de boss ain't got much work, an' have it awful hard to pay his rent. It ain't so much fun, bein' poor in a big city like London, I'll say! All de windows is full of good t'ings to eat, an' all de pushcarts in de streets is full, an' you smell 'em all de time, an' you ain't got no money—not a damn bit. I didn't mind de cold so much, though I didn't have no overcoat, chust a short jacket I'd outgrowed so it wouldn't meet on me, an' my hands was chapped raw. But I always had a good appetite, like you all know, an' de sight of dem pork pies in de windows was awful fur me!

"Day before Christmas was terrible foggy dat year, an' dat fog gits into your bones and makes you all damp like. Mrs. Lifschnitz didn't give us nothin' but a little bread an' drippin' for supper, because she was savin' to try for to give us a good dinner on Christmas Day. After supper de boss say I go an' enjoy myself, so I went into de streets to listen to de Christmas singers. Dey sing old songs an' make very nice music, an' I run round after dem a good ways, till I got awful hungry. I t'ink maybe if I go home, I can sleep till morning an' forgit my belly.

"I went into my corner real quiet, and roll up in my fedder quilt. But I ain't got my head down, till I smell somet'ing good. Seem like it git stronger an' stronger, an' I can't git to sleep noway. I can't understand dat smell. Dere was a gas light in a hall across de court, dat always shine in at my window a little. I got up an' look round. I got a little wooden box in my corner fur a stool, 'cause I ain't got no chair. I picks up dat box, and under it dere is a roast goose on a platter! I can't believe my eyes. I carry it to de window where de light comes in, an' touch it and smell it to find out, an' den I taste it to be sure. I say, I will eat chust one little bite of dat goose, so I can go to sleep, and to-morrow I won't eat none at all. But I tell you, boys, when I stop, one half of dat goose was gone!"

The narrator bowed his head, and the boys shouted. But little Josephine slipped behind his chair and kissed him on the neck beneath his ear.

"Poor little Papa, I don't want him to be hungry!"

"Da's long ago, child. I ain't never been hungry since I had your mudder to cook fur me."

"Go on and tell us the rest, please," said Polly.

"Well, when I come to realize what I done, of course, I felt terrible. I felt better in de stomach, but very bad in de heart. I set on my bed wid dat platter on my knees, an' it all come to me; how hard dat poor woman save to buy dat goose, and how she get some neighbour to cook it dat got more fire, an' how she put it in my corner to keep it away from dem hungry children. Dere was a old carpet hung up to shut my corner off, an' de children wasn't allowed to go in dere. An' I know she put it in my corner because she trust me more'n she did de violin boy. I can't stand it to face her after I spoil de Christmas. So I put on my shoes and go out into de city. I tell myself I better throw myself in de river; but I guess I ain't dat kind of a boy.

"It was after twelve o'clock, an' terrible cold, an' I start out to walk about London all night. I walk along de river awhile, but dey was lots of drunks all along; men, and women too. I chust move along to keep away from de police. I git onto de Strand, an' den over to New Oxford Street, where dere was a big German restaurant on de ground floor, wid big windows all fixed up fine, an' I could see de people havin' parties inside. While I was lookin' in, two men and two ladies come out, laughin' and talkin' and feelin' happy about all dey been eatin' an' drinkin', and dey was speakin' Czech—not like de Austrians, but like de home folks talk it.

"I guess I went crazy, an' I done what I ain't never done before nor since. I went right up to dem gay people an' begun to beg dem: 'Fellow countrymen, for God's sake give me money enough to buy a goose!'

"Dey laugh, of course, but de ladies speak awful kind to me, an' dey take me back into de restaurant and give me hot coffee and cakes, an' make me tell all about how I happened to come to London, an' what I was doin' dere. Dey take my name and where I work down on paper, an' both of dem ladies give me ten shillings.

"De big market at Covent Garden⁴ ain't very far away, an' by dat, time it was open. I go dere an buy a big goose an' some pork pies, an' potatoes and onions, an' cakes an' oranges fur de children—all I could carry! When I git home, everybody is still asleep. I pile all I bought on de kitchen table, an' go in an' lay down on my bed, an I ain't waken up till I hear dat woman scream when she come out into her kitchen. My goodness, but she was surprise! She laugh an' cry at de same time, an' hug me and waken all de children.

4. Square in London, site of a famous flower and vegetable market and of the Covent Garden opera house.

She ain't stop fur no breakfast; she git de Christmas dinner ready dat morning, and we all sit down an' eat all we can hold. I ain't never seen dat violin boy have all he can hold before.

"Two-three days after dat, de two men come to hunt me up, an' dey ask my boss, and he give me a good report an' tell dem I was a steady boy all right. One of dem Bohemians was very smart an' run a Bohemian newspaper in New York, an' de odder was a rich man, in de importing business, an' dey been travelling togedder. Dey told me how t'ings was easier in New York, an' offered to pay my passage when dey was goin' home soon on a boat. My boss say to me: 'You go. You ain't got no chance here, an' I like to see you git ahead, fur you always been a good boy to my woman, and fur dat fine Christmas dinner you give us all.' An' da's how I got to New York."

That night when Rudolph and Polly, arm in arm, were running home across the fields with the bitter wind at their backs, his heart leaped for joy when she said she thought they might have his family come over for supper on New Year's Eve. "Let's get up a nice supper, and not let your mother help at all; make her be company for once."

"That would be lovely of you, Polly," he said humbly. He was a very simple, modest boy, and he, too, felt vaguely that Polly and her sisters were more experienced and worldly than his people.

The winter turned out badly for farmers. It was bitterly cold, and after the first light snows before Christmas there was no snow at all—and no rain. March was as bitter as February. On those days when the wind fairly punished the country, Rosicky sat by his window. In the fall he and the boys had put in a big wheat planting, and now the seed had frozen in the ground. All that land would have to be ploughed up and planted over again, planted in corn. It had happened before, but he was younger then, and he never worried about what had to be. He was sure of himself and of Mary; he knew they could bear what they had to bear, that they would always pull through somehow. But he was not so sure about the young ones, and he felt troubled because Rudolph and Polly were having such a hard start.

Sitting beside his flowering window while the panes rattled and the wind blew in under the door, Rosicky gave himself to reflection as he had not done since those Sundays in the loft of the furniture factory in New York, long ago. Then he was trying to find what he wanted in life for himself; now he was trying to find what he wanted for his boys, and why it was he so hungered to feel sure they would be here, working this very land, after he was gone.

They would have to work hard on the farm, and probably they would never do much more than make a living. But if he could think of them as staying here on the land, he wouldn't have to fear any great unkindness for them. Hardships, certainly; it was a hardship to have the wheat freeze in the ground when seed was so high; and to have to sell your stock because you had no feed. But there would be other years when everything came along right, and you caught up. And what you had was your own. You didn't have to choose between bosses and strikers, and go wrong either way. You didn't have to do with dishonest and cruel people. They were the only things in his experience he had found terrifying and horrible: the look in the eyes of a dishonest and crafty man, of a scheming and rapacious woman.

In the country, if you had a mean neighbour, you could keep off his land and make him keep off yours. But in the city, all the foulness and misery and brutality of your neighbours was part of your life. The worst things he had come upon in his journey through the world were human,—depraved and poisonous specimens of man. To this day he could recall certain terrible faces in the London streets. There were mean people everywhere, to be sure, even in their own country town here. But they weren't tempered, hardened, sharpened, like the treacherous people in cities who live by grinding or cheating or poisoning their fellow-men. He had helped to bury two of his fellow-workmen in the tailoring trade, and he was distrustful of the organized industries that see one out of the world in big cities. Here, if you were sick, you had Doctor Ed to look after you; and if you died, fat Mr. Haycock, the kindest man in the world, buried you.

It seemed to Rosicky that for good, honest boys like his, the worst they could do on the farm was better than the best they would be likely to do in the city. If he'd had a mean boy, now, one who was crooked and sharp and tried to put anything over on his brothers, then town would be the place for him. But he had no such boy. As for Rudolph, the discontented one, he would give the shirt off his back to anyone who touched his heart. What Rosicky really hoped for his boys was that they could get through the world without ever knowing much about the cruelty of human beings. "Their mother and me ain't prepared them for that," he sometimes said to himself.

These thoughts brought him back to a grateful consideration of his own case. What an escape he had had, to be sure! He, too, in his time, had had to take money for repair work from the hand of a hungry child who let it go so wistfully; because it was money due his boss. And now, in all these years, he had never had to take a cent from anyone in bitter need—never had to look at the face of a woman become like a wolf's from struggle and famine. When he thought of these things, Rosicky would put on his cap and jacket and slip down to the barn and give his work-horses a little extra oats, letting them eat it out of his hand in their slobbery fashion. It was his way of expressing what he felt, and made him chuckle with pleasure.

The spring came warm, with blue skies,—but dry, dry as bone. The boys began ploughing up the wheat-fields to plant them over in corn. Rosicky would stand at the fence corner and watch them, and the earth was so dry it blew up in clouds of brown dust that hid the horses and the sulky plough and the driver. It was a bad outlook.

The big alfalfa-field that lay between the home place and Rudolph's came up green, but Rosicky was worried because during that open windy winter a great many Russian thistle plants had blown in there and lodged. He kept asking the boys to rake them out; he was afraid their seed would root and "take the alfalfa." Rudolph said that was nonsense. The boys were working so hard planting corn, their father felt he couldn't insist about the thistles, but he set great store by that big alfalfa-field. It was a feed you could depend on,—and there was some deeper reason, vague, but strong. The peculiar green of that clover woke early memories in old Rosicky, went back to something in his childhood in the old world. When he was a little boy, he had played in fields of that strong blue-green colour.

One morning, when Rudolph had gone to town in the car, leaving a work-team idle in his barn, Rosicky went over to his son's place, put the horses to the buggy-rake, and set about quietly taking up those thistles. He behaved with guilty caution, and rather enjoyed stealing a march on Doctor Ed, who was just then taking his first vacation in seven years of practice and was attending a clinic in Chicago. Rosicky got the thistles raked up, but did not stop to burn them. That would take some time, and his breath was pretty short, so he thought he had better get the horses back to the barn.

He got them into the barn and to their stalls, but the pain had come on so sharp in his chest that he didn't try to take the harness off. He started for the house, bending lower with every step. The cramp in his chest was shutting him up like a jack-knife. When he reached the windmill, he swayed and caught at the ladder. He saw Polly coming down the hill, running with the swiftness of a slim greyhound. In a flash she had her shoulder under his armpit.

"Lean on me, Father, hard! Don't be afraid. We can get to the house all right."

Somehow they did, though Rosicky became blind with pain; he could keep on his legs, but he couldn't steer his course. The next thing he was conscious of was lying on Polly's bed, and Polly bending over him wringing out bath-towels in hot water and putting them on his chest. She stopped only to throw coal into the stove, and she kept the tea-kettle and the black pot going. She put these hot applications on him for nearly an hour, she told him afterwards, and all that time he was drawn up stiff and blue, with the sweat pouring off him.

As the pain gradually loosed its grip, the stiffness went out of his jaws, the black circles round his eyes disappeared, and a little of his natural colour came back. When his daughter-in-law buttoned his shirt over his chest at last, he sighed.

"Da's fine, de way I feel now, Polly. It was a awful bad spell, an' I was so sorry it all come on you like it did."

Polly was flushed and excited. "Is the pain really gone? Can I leave you long enough to telephone over to your place?"

Rosicky's eyelids fluttered. "Don't telephone, Polly. It ain't no use to scare my wife. It's nice and quiet here, an' if I ain't too much trouble to you, just let me lay still till I feel like myself. I ain't got no pain now. It's nice here."

Polly bent over him and wiped the moisture from his face. "Oh, I'm so glad it's over!" she broke out impulsively. "It just broke my heart to see you suffer so, Father."

Rosicky motioned her to sit down on the chair where the tea-kettle had been, and looked up at her with that lively affectionate gleam in his eyes. "You was awful good to me, I won't never forget dat. I hate it to be sick on you like dis. Down at de barn I say to myself, dat young girl ain't had much experience in sickness, I don't want to scare her, an' maybe she's got a baby comin' or somet'ing."

Polly took his hand. He was looking at her so intently and affectionately and confidingly; his eyes seemed to caress her face, to regard it with pleasure. She frowned with her funny streaks of eyebrows, and then smiled back at him.

"I guess maybe there is something of that kind going to happen. But I haven't told anyone yet, not my mother or Rudolph. You'll be the first to know."

His hand pressed hers. She noticed that it was warm again. The twinkle in his yellow-brown eyes seemed to come nearer.

"I like mighty well to see dat little child, Polly," was all he said. Then he closed his eyes and lay half-smiling. But Polly sat still, thinking hard. She had a sudden feeling that nobody in the world, not her mother, not Rudolph, or anyone, really loved her as much as old Rosicky did. It perplexed her. She sat frowning and trying to puzzle it out. It was as if Rosicky had a special gift for loving people, something that was like an ear for music or an eye for colour. It was quiet, unobtrusive; it was merely there. You saw it in his eyes,—perhaps that was why they were merry. You felt it in his hands, too. After he dropped off to sleep, she sat holding his warm, broad, flexible brown hand. She had never seen another in the least like it. She wondered if it wasn't a kind of gipsy hand, it was so alive and quick and light in its communications,—very strange in a farmer. Nearly all the farmers she knew had huge lumps of fists, like mauls, or they were knotty and bony and uncomfortable-looking, with stiff fingers. But Rosicky's was like quicksilver, flexible, muscular, about the colour of a pale cigar, with deep, deep creases across the palm. It wasn't nervous, it wasn't a stupid lump; it was a warm brown human hand, with some cleverness in it, a great deal of generosity, and something else which Polly could only call "gypsy-like"—something nimble and lively and sure, in the way that animals are.

Polly remembered that hour long afterwards; it had been like an awakening to her. It seemed to her that she had never learned so much about life from anything as from old Rosicky's hand. It brought her to herself; it communicated some direct and untranslatable message.

When she heard Rudolph coming in the car, she ran out to meet him.

"Oh, Rudy, your father's been awful sick! He raked up those thistles he's been worrying about, and afterward he could hardly get to the house. He suffered so I was afraid he was going to die."

Rudolph jumped to the ground. "Where is he now?"

"On the bed. He's asleep. I was terribly scared, because, you know, I'm so fond of your father." She slipped her arm through his and they went into the house. That afternoon they took Rosicky home and put him to bed, though he protested that he was quite well again.

The next morning he got up and dressed and sat down to breakfast with his family. He told Mary that his coffee tasted better than usual to him, and he warned the boys not to bear any tales to Doctor Ed when he got home. After breakfast he sat down by his window to do some patching and asked Mary to thread several needles for him before she went to feed her chickens,—her eyes were better than his, and her hands steadier. He lit his pipe and took up John's overalls. Mary had been watching him anxiously all morning, and as she went out of the door with her bucket of scraps, she saw that he was smiling. He was thinking, indeed, about Polly, and how he might never have known what a tender heart she had if he hadn't got sick over there. Girls nowadays didn't wear their heart on their sleeve. But now he knew Polly would make a fine woman after the foolishness wore off. Either a woman had that sweetness at her heart or she hadn't. You couldn't always tell by the look of them; but if they had that, everything came out right in the end.

After he had taken a few stitches, the cramp began in his chest, like yesterday. He put his pipe cautiously down on the window-sill and bent over to ease the pull. No use,—he had better try to get to his bed if he could. He rose and groped his way across the familiar floor, which was rising and falling like the deck of a ship. At the door he fell. When Mary came in, she found him lying there, and the moment she touched him she knew that he was gone.

Doctor Ed was away when Rosicky died, and for the first few weeks after he got home he was harddriven. Every day he said to himself that he must get out to see that family that had lost their father. One soft, warm moonlight night in early summer he started for the farm. His mind was on other things, and not until his road ran by the graveyard did he realize that Rosicky wasn't over there on the hill where the red lamplight shone, but here, in the moonlight. He stopped his car, shut off the engine, and sat there for a while.

A sudden hush had fallen on his soul. Everything here seemed strangely moving and significant, though signifying what, he did not know. Close by the wire fence stood Rosicky's mowing-machine, where one of the boys had been cutting hay that afternoon; his own work-horses had been going up and down there. The new-cut hay perfumed all the night air. The moonlight silvered the long, billowy grass that grew over the graves and hid the fence; the few little evergreens stood out black in it, like shadows in a pool. The sky was very blue and soft, the stars rather faint because the moon was full.

For the first time it struck Doctor Ed that this was really a beautiful graveyard. He thought of city cemeteries; acres of shrubbery and heavy stone, so arranged and lonely and unlike anything in the living world. Cities of the dead, indeed; cities of the forgotten, of the "put away." But this was open and free, this little square of long grass which the wind for ever stirred. Nothing but the sky overhead, and the many-coloured fields running on until they met that sky. The horses worked here in summer; the neighbours passed on their way to town; and over yonder, in the cornfield, Rosicky's own cattle would be eating fodder as winter came on. Nothing could be more undeathlike than this place; nothing could be more right for a man who had helped to do the work of great cities and had always longed for the open country and had got to it at last. Rosicky's life seemed to him complete and beautiful.

1928, 1932

The Sculptor's Funeral

A group of the townspeople stood on the station siding of a little Kansas town, awaiting the coming of the night train, which was already twenty minutes overdue. The snow had fallen thick over everything; in the pale starlight the line of bluffs across the wide, white meadows south of the town made soft, smoke-coloured curves against the clear sky. The men on the siding stood first on one foot and then on the other, their hands thrust deep into their trousers pockets, their overcoats open, their shoulders screwed up with the cold; and they glanced from time to time toward the southeast, where the railroad track wound along the river shore. They conversed in low tones and moved about restlessly, seeming uncertain as to what was expected of them. There was but one of the company who looked as if he knew exactly why he was there, and he kept conspicuously apart; walking to the far end of the platform, returning to the station door, then pacing up the track again, his chin sunk in the high collar of his overcoat, his burly shoulders dropping forward, his gait heavy and dogged. Presently he was approached by a tall, spare, grizzled man clad in a faded Grand Army[1] suit, who shuffled out from the group and advanced with a certain deference, craning his neck forward until his back made the angle of a jack-knife three-quarters open.

"I reckon she's a-goin' to be pretty late agin tonight, Jim," he remarked in a squeaky falsetto. "S'pose it's the snow?"

"I don't know," responded the other man with a shade of annoyance, speaking from out an astonishing cataract of red beard that grew fiercely and thickly in all directions.

The spare man shifted the quill toothpick he was chewing to the other side of his mouth. "It ain't likely that anybody from the East will come with the corpse, I s'pose," he went on reflectively.

"I don't know," responded the other, more curtly than before.

"It's too bad he didn't belong to some lodge or other. I like an order funeral[2] myself. They seem more appropriate for people of some repytation," the spare man continued, with an ingratiating concession in his shrill voice, as he carefully placed his toothpick in his vest pocket. He always carried the flag at the G. A. R. funerals in the town.

The heavy man turned on his heel, without replying, and walked up the siding. The spare man rejoined the uneasy group. "Jim's ez full ez a tick, ez ushel," he commented commiseratingly.

Just then a distant whistle sounded, and there was a shuffling of feet on the platform. A number of lanky boys, of all ages, appeared as suddenly and slimily as eels wakened by the crack of thunder; some came from the waiting-room, where they had been warming themselves by the red stove, or half asleep on the slat benches; others uncoiled themselves from baggage trucks or slid out of express wagons. Two clambered down from the driver's seat of a hearse that stood backed up against the siding. They straightened their stooping shoulders and lifted their heads, and a flash of momentary animation kindled their dull eyes at that cold, vibrant scream, the worldwide call for men. It stirred them like the note of a trumpet; just as it had often stirred the man who was coming home tonight, in his boyhood.

The night express shot, red as a rocket, from out the eastward marsh lands and wound along the river shore under the long lines of shivering poplars that sentinelled the meadows, the escaping steam hanging in grey masses against the pale sky and blotting out the Milky Way. In a moment the red glare from the headlight streamed up the snow-covered track before the siding and glittered on the wet, black rails. The burly man with the dishevelled red beard walked swiftly up the platform toward the approaching train, uncovering his head as he went. The group of men behind him hesitated, glanced questioningly at one another, and awkwardly followed his example. The train stopped, and the crowd shuffled up to the express car just as the door was thrown open, the man in the G. A. R. suit thrusting his head forward with curiosity. The express messenger appeared in the doorway, accompanied by a young man in a long ulster and travelling cap.

"Are Mr. Merrick's friends here?" inquired the young man.

---

1. I.e., Grand Army of the Republic (G.A.R.), or the Union Army, which fought for the North in the Civil War. This story, originally published in 1905, is set in present time, when Civil War veterans would have been in their sixties.

2. Lodges ("orders")—e.g., the Masons and Elks—used a portion of club dues to cover members' funeral expenses.

The group on the platform swayed uneasily. Philip Phelps, the banker, responded with dignity: "We have come to take charge of the body. Mr. Merrick's father is very feeble and can't be about."

"Send the agent out here," growled the express messenger, "and tell the operator to lend a hand."

The coffin was got out of its rough-box and down on the snowy platform. The townspeople drew back enough to make room for it and then formed a close semicircle about it, looking curiously at the palm leaf which lay across the black cover. No one said anything. The baggage man stood by his truck, waiting to get at the trunks. The engine panted heavily, and the fireman dodged in and out among the wheels with his yellow torch and long oil-can, snapping the spindle boxes. The young Bostonian, one of the dead sculptor's pupils who had come with the body, looked about him helplessly. He turned to the banker, the only one of that black, uneasy, stoop-shouldered group who seemed enough of an individual to be addressed.

"None of Mr. Merrick's brothers are here?" he asked uncertainly.

The man with the red beard for the first time stepped up and joined the others. "No, they have not come yet; the family is scattered. The body will be taken directly to the house." He stooped and took hold of one of the handles of the coffin.

"Take the long hill road up, Thompson, it will be easier on the horses," called the liveryman[3] as the undertaker snapped the door of the hearse and prepared to mount to the driver's seat.

Laird, the red-bearded lawyer, turned again to the stranger: "We didn't know whether there would be any one with him or not," he explained. "It's a long walk, so you'd better go up in the hack." He pointed to a single battered conveyance, but the young man replied stiffly: "Thank you, but I think I will go up with the hearse. If you don't object," turning to the undertaker, "I'll ride with you."

They clambered up over the wheels and drove off in the starlight up the long, white hill toward the town. The lamps in the still village were shining from under the low, snow-burdened roofs; and beyond, on every side, the plains reached out into emptiness, peaceful and wide as the soft sky itself, and wrapped in a tangible, white silence.

When the hearse backed up to a wooden sidewalk before a naked, weather-beaten frame house, the same composite, ill-defined group that had stood upon the station siding was huddled about the gate. The front yard was an icy swamp, and a couple of warped planks, extending from the sidewalk to the door, made a sort of rickety foot-bridge. The gate hung on one hinge, and was opened wide with difficulty. Steavens, the young stranger, noticed that something black was tied to the knob of the front door.

The grating sound made by the casket, as it was drawn from the hearse, was answered by a scream from the house; the front door was wrenched open, and a tall, corpulent woman rushed out bareheaded into the snow and flung herself upon the coffin, shrieking: "My boy, my boy! And this is how you've come home to me!"

As Steavens turned away and closed his eyes with a shudder of unutterable repulsion, another woman, also tall, but flat and angular, dressed entirely in black, darted out of the house and caught Mrs. Merrick by the shoulders,

3. Keeper of a vehicle-rental service.

crying sharply: "Come, come, mother; you mustn't go on like this!" Her tone changed to one of obsequious solemnity as she turned to the banker: "The parlour is ready, Mr. Phelps."

The bearers carried the coffin along the narrow boards, while the undertaker ran ahead with the coffin-rests. They bore it into a large, unheated room that smelled of dampness and disuse and furniture polish, and set it down under a hanging lamp ornamented with jingling glass prisms and before a "Rogers group" of John Alden and Priscilla,[4] wreathed with smilax. Henry Steavens stared about him with the sickening conviction that there had been a mistake, and that he had somehow arrived at the wrong destination. He looked at the clover-green Brussels,[5] the fat plush upholstery, among the hand-painted china placques and panels and vases, for some mark of identification,—for something that might once conceivably have belonged to Harvey Merrick. It was not until he recognized his friend in the crayon portrait of a little boy in kilts and curls, hanging above the piano, that he felt willing to let any of these people approach the coffin.

"Take the lid off, Mr. Thompson; let me see my boy's face," wailed the elder woman between her sobs. This time Steavens looked fearfully, almost beseechingly into her face, red and swollen under its masses of strong, black, shiny hair. He flushed, dropped his eyes, and then, almost incredulously, looked again. There was a kind of power about her face—a kind of brutal handsomeness, even; but it was scarred and furrowed by violence, and so coloured and coarsened by fiercer passions that grief seemed never to have laid a gentle finger there. The long nose was distended and knobbed at the end, and there were deep lines on either side of it; her heavy, black brows almost met across her forehead, her teeth were large and square, and set far apart—teeth that could tear. She filled the room; the men were obliterated, seemed tossed about like twigs in an angry water, and even Steavens felt himself being drawn into the whirlpool.

The daughter—the tall, raw-boned woman in crêpe, with a mourning comb in her hair which curiously lengthened her long face—sat stiffly upon the sofa, her hands, conspicuous for their large knuckles, folded in her lap, her mouth and eyes drawn down, solemnly awaiting the opening of the coffin. Near the door stood a mulatto woman, evidently a servant in the house, with a timid bearing and an emaciated face pitifully sad and gentle. She was weeping silently, the corner of her calico apron lifted to her eyes, occasionally suppressing a long, quivering sob. Steavens walked over and stood beside her.

Feeble steps were heard on the stairs, and an old man, tall and frail, odorous of pipe smoke, with shaggy, unkept grey hair and a dingy beard, tobacco stained about the mouth, entered uncertainly. He went slowly up to the coffin and stood rolling a blue cotton handkerchief between his hands, seeming so pained and embarrassed by his wife's orgy of grief that he had no consciousness of anything else.

4. New England Puritan couple celebrated in Henry Wadsworth Longfellow's immensely popular poem "The Courtship of Miles Standish" (1858). "'Rogers group'": small group compositions by John Rogers (1829–1904), popular American sculptor who patented his pieces, had them mass-produced, and sold them by mail. The pieces represented fine art to their purchasers, but critics often dismissed them as overly sentimental.

5. Inexpensive factory-made carpet of a type developed in Brussels, Belgium, composed of colored wool strands looped through a linen foundation.

"There, there, Annie, dear, don't take on so," he quavered timidly, putting out a shaking hand and awkwardly patting her elbow. She turned and sank upon his shoulder with such violence that he tottered a little. He did not even glance toward the coffin, but continued to look at her with a dull, frightened, appealing expression, as a spaniel looks at the whip. His sunken cheeks slowly reddened and burned with miserable shame. When his wife rushed from the room, her daughter strode after her with set lips. The servant stole up to the coffin, bent over it for a moment, and then slipped away to the kitchen, leaving Steavens, the lawyer, and the father to themselves. The old man stood looking down at his dead son's face. The sculptor's splendid head seemed even more noble in its rigid stillness than in life. The dark hair had crept down upon the wide forehead; the face seemed strangely long, but in it there was not that repose we expect to find in the faces of the dead. The brows were so drawn that there were two deep lines above the beaked nose, and the chin was thrust forward defiantly. It was as though the strain of life had been so sharp and bitter that death could not at once relax the tension and smooth the countenance into perfect peace—as though he were still guarding something precious, which might even yet be wrested from him.

The old man's lips were working under his stained beard. He turned to the lawyer with timid deference: "Phelps and the rest are comin' back to set up with Harve, ain't they?" he asked. "Thank 'ee, Jim, thank 'ee." He brushed the hair back gently from his son's forehead. "He was a good boy, Jim; always a good boy. He was ez gentle ez a child and the kindest of 'em all—only we didn't none of us ever onderstand him." The tears trickled slowly down his beard and dropped upon the sculptor's coat.

"Martin, Martin! Oh, Martin! come here," his wife wailed from the top of the stairs. The old man started timorously: "Yes, Annie, I'm coming." He turned away, hesitated, stood for a moment in miserable indecision; then reached back and patted the dead man's hair softly, and stumbled from the room.

"Poor old man, I didn't think he had any tears left. Seems as if his eyes would have gone dry long ago. At his age nothing cuts very deep," remarked the lawyer.

Something in his tone made Steavens glance up. While the mother had been in the room, the young man had scarcely seen any one else; but now, from the moment he first glanced into Jim Laird's florid face and blood-shot eyes, he knew that he had found what he had been heartsick at not finding before—the feeling, the understanding, that must exist in some one, even here.

The man was red as his beard, with features swollen and blurred by dissipation, and a hot, blazing blue eye. His face was strained—that of a man who is controlling himself with difficulty—and he kept plucking at his beard with a sort of fierce resentment. Steavens, sitting by the window, watched him turn down the glaring lamp, still its jangling pendants with an angry gesture, and then stand with his hands locked behind him, staring down into the master's face. He could not help wondering what link there had been between the porcelain vessel and so sooty a lump of potter's clay.

From the kitchen an uproar was sounding; when the dining-room door opened, the import of it was clear. The mother was abusing the maid for having forgotten to make the dressing for the chicken salad which had been prepared for the watchers. Steavens had never heard anything in the least like it; it was injured, emotional, dramatic abuse, unique and masterly in its excruciating cruelty, as violent and unrestrained as had been her grief of twenty minutes before. With a shudder of disgust the lawyer went into the dining-room and closed the door into the kitchen.

"Poor Roxy's getting it now," he remarked when he came back. "The Merricks took her out of the poor-house years ago; and if her loyalty would let her, I guess the poor old thing could tell tales that would curdle your blood. She's the mulatto woman who was standing in here a while ago, with her apron to her eyes. The old woman is a fury; there never was anybody like her. She made Harvey's life a hell for him when he lived at home; he was so sick ashamed of it. I never could see how he kept himself sweet."

"He was wonderful," said Steavens slowly, "wonderful; but until tonight I have never known how wonderful."

"That is the eternal wonder of it, anyway; that it can come even from such a dung heap as this," the lawyer cried, with a sweeping gesture which seemed to indicate much more than the four walls within which they stood.

"I think I'll see whether I can get a little air. The room is so close I am beginning to feel rather faint," murmured Steavens, struggling with one of the windows. The sash was stuck, however, and would not yield, so he sat down dejectedly and began pulling at his collar. The lawyer came over, loosened the sash with one blow of his red fist and sent the window up a few inches. Steavens thanked him, but the nausea which had been gradually climbing into his throat for the last half hour left him with but one desire—a desperate feeling that he must get away from this place with what was left of Harvey Merrick. Oh, he comprehended well enough now the quiet bitterness of the smile that he had seen so often on his master's lips!

Once when Merrick returned from a visit home, he brought with him a singularly feeling and suggestive bas-relief of a thin, faded old woman, sitting and sewing something pinned to her knee; while a full-lipped, full-blooded little urchin, his trousers held up by a single gallows,[6] stood beside her, impatiently twitching her gown to call her attention to a butterfly he had caught. Steavens, impressed by the tender and delicate modelling of the thin, tired face, had asked him if it were his mother. He remembered the dull flush that had burned up in the sculptor's face.

The lawyer was sitting in a rocking-chair beside the coffin, his head thrown back and his eyes closed. Steavens looked at him earnestly, puzzled at the line of the chin, and wondering why a man should conceal a feature of such distinction under that disfiguring shock of beard. Suddenly, as though he felt the young sculptor's keen glance, Jim Laird opened his eyes.

"Was he always a good deal of an oyster?"[7] he asked abruptly. "He was terribly shy as a boy."

"Yes, he was an oyster, since you put it so," rejoined Steavens. "Although he could be very fond of people, he always gave one the impression of being detached. He disliked violent emotion; he was reflective, and rather distrustful of himself—except, of course, as regarded his work. He was sure enough there. He distrusted men pretty thoroughly and women even more, yet somehow without believing ill of them. He was determined, indeed, to believe the best; but he seemed afraid to investigate."

6. Suspender.   7. A self-contained person (slang).

"A burnt dog dreads the fire," said the lawyer grimly, and closed his eyes.

Steavens went on and on, reconstructing that whole miserable boyhood. All this raw, biting ugliness had been the portion of the man whose mind was to become an exhaustless gallery of beautiful impressions—so sensitive that the mere shadow of a poplar leaf flickering against a sunny wall would be etched and held there for ever. Surely, if ever a man had the magic word in his finger tips, it was Merrick. Whatever he touched, he revealed its holiest secret; liberated it from enchantment and restored it to its pristine loveliness. Upon whatever he had come in contact with, he had left a beautiful record of the experience—a sort of ethereal signature; a scent, a sound, a colour that was his own.

Steavens understood now the real tragedy of his master's life; neither love nor wine, as many had conjectured; but a blow which had fallen earlier and cut deeper than anything else could have done—a shame not his, and yet so unescapably his, to hide in his heart from his very boyhood. And without— the frontier warfare; the yearning of a boy, cast ashore upon a desert of newness and ugliness and sordidness, for all that is chastened and old, and noble with traditions.

At eleven o'clock the tall, flat woman in black announced that the watchers were arriving, and asked them to "step into the dining-room." As Steavens rose, the lawyer said dryly: "You go on—it'll be a good experience for you. I'm not equal to that crowd tonight; I've had twenty years of them."

As Steavens closed the door after him he glanced back at the lawyer, sitting by the coffin in the dim light, with his chin resting on his hand.

The same misty group that had stood before the door of the express car shuffled into the dining-room. In the light of the kerosene lamp they separated and became individuals. The minister, a pale, feeble-looking man with white hair and blond chin-whiskers, took his seat beside a small side table and placed his Bible upon it. The Grand Army man sat down behind the stove and tilted his chair back comfortably against the wall, fishing his quill toothpick from his waistcoat pocket. The two bankers, Phelps and Elder, sat off in a corner behind the dinner-table, where they could finish their discussion of the new usury law and its effect on chattel security loans. The real estate agent, an old man with a smiling, hypocritical face, soon joined them. The coal and lumber dealer and the cattle shipper sat on opposite sides of the hard coal-burner, their feet on the nickel-work. Steavens took a book from his pocket and began to read. The talk around him ranged through various topics of local interest while the house was quieting down. When it was clear that the members of the family were in bed, the Grand Army man hitched his shoulders and, untangling his long legs, caught his heels on the rounds of his chair.

"S'pose there'll be a will, Phelps?" he queried in his weak falsetto.

The banker laughed disagreeably, and began trimming his nails with a pearl-handled pocket-knife.

"There'll scarcely be any need for one, will there?" he queried in his turn.

The restless Grand Army man shifted his position again, getting his knees still nearer his chin. "Why, the ole man says Harve's done right well lately," he chirped.

The other banker spoke up. "I reckon he means by that Harve ain't asked him to mortgage any more farms lately, so as he could go on with his education."

"Seems like my mind don't reach back to a time when Harve wasn't bein' edycated," tittered the Grand Army man.

There was a general chuckle. The minister took out his handkerchief and blew his nose sonorously. Banker Phelps closed his knife with a snap. "It's too bad the old man's sons didn't turn out better," he remarked with reflective authority. "They never hung together. He spent money enough on Harve to stock a dozen cattle-farms, and he might as well have poured it into Sand Creek. If Harve had stayed at home and helped nurse what little they had, and gone into stock on the old man's bottom farm, they might all have been well fixed. But the old man had to trust everything to tenants and was cheated right and left."

"Harve never could have handled stock none," interposed the cattleman. "He hadn't it in him to be sharp. Do you remember when he bought Sander's mules for eight-year olds, when everybody in town knew that Sander's father-in-law give 'em to his wife for a wedding present eighteen years before, an' they was full-grown mules then?"

The company laughed discreetly, and the Grand Army man rubbed his knees with a spasm of childish delight.

"Harve never was much account for anything practical, and he shore was never fond of work," began the coal and lumber dealer. "I mind the last time he was home; the day he left, when the old man was out to the barn helpin' his hand hitch up to take Harve to the train, and Cal Moots was patchin' up the fence; Harve, he come out on the step and sings out, in his ladylike voice: 'Cal Moots, Cal Moots! please come cord my trunk.'"

"That's Harve for you," approved the Grand Army man. "I kin hear him howlin' yet, when he was a big feller in long pants and his mother used to whale him with a rawhide in the barn for lettin' the cows git foundered in the cornfield when he was drivin' 'em home from pasture. He killed a cow of mine that-a-way onct—a pure Jersey and the best milker I had, an' the ole man had to put up for her. Harve, he was watchin' the sun set acrost the marshes when the anamile got away."

"Where the old man made his mistake was in sending the boy East to school," said Phelps, stroking his goatee and speaking in a deliberate, judicial tone. "There was where he got his head full of nonsense. What Harve needed, of all people, was a course in some first-class Kansas City business college."

The letters were swimming before Steavens's eyes. Was it possible that these men did not understand, that the palm on the coffin meant nothing to them? The very name of their town would have remained for ever buried in the postal guide had it not been now and again mentioned in the world in connection with Harvey Merrick's. He remembered what his master had said to him on the day of his death, after the congestion of both lungs had shut off any probability of recovery, and the sculptor had asked his pupil to send his body home. "It's not a pleasant place to be lying while the world is moving and doing and bettering," he had said with a feeble smile, "but it rather seems as though we ought to go back to the place we came from, in the end. The townspeople will come in for a look at me; and after they have had their say, I shan't have much to fear from the judgment of God!"

The cattleman took up the comment. "Forty's young for a Merrick to cash in; they usually hang on pretty well. Probably he helped it along with whisky."

"His mother's people were not long lived, and Harvey never had a robust constitution," said the minister mildly. He would have liked to say more. He had been the boy's Sunday-school teacher, and had been fond of him; but he felt that he was not in a position to speak. His own sons had turned out badly, and it was not a year since one of them had made his last trip home in the express car, shot in a gambling-house in the Black Hills.

"Nevertheless, there is no disputin' that Harve frequently looked upon the wine when it was red, also variegated, and it shore made an oncommon fool of him," moralized the cattleman.

Just then the door leading into the parlour rattled loudly and every one started involuntarily, looking relieved when only Jim Laird came out. The Grand Army man ducked his head when he saw the spark in his blue, blood-shot eye. They were all afraid of Jim; he was a drunkard, but he could twist the law to suit his client's needs as no other man in all western Kansas could do, and there were many who tried. The lawyer closed the door behind him, leaned back against it and folded his arms, cocking his head a little to one side. When he assumed this attitude in the court-room, ears were always pricked up, as it usually foretold a flood of withering sarcasm.

"I've been with you gentlemen before," he began in a dry, even tone, "when you've sat by the coffins of boys born and raised in this town; and, if I remember rightly, you were never any too well satisfied when you checked them up. What's the matter, anyhow? Why is it that reputable young men are as scarce as millionaires in Sand City? It might almost seem to a stranger that there was some way something the matter with your progressive town. Why did Ruben Sayer, the brightest young lawyer you ever turned out, after he had come home from the university as straight as a die, take to drinking and forge a check and shoot himself? Why did Bill Merrit's son die of the shakes in a saloon in Omaha? Why was Mr. Thomas's son, here, shot in a gambling-house? Why did young Adams burn his mill to beat the insurance companies and go to the pen?"

The lawyer paused and unfolded his arms, laying one clenched fist quietly on the table. "I'll tell you why. Because you drummed nothing but money and knavery into their ears from the time they wore knickerbockers; because you carped away at them as you've been carping here tonight, holding our friends Phelps and Elder up to them for their models, as our grandfathers held up George Washington and John Adams. But the boys were young, and raw at the business you put them to, and how could they match coppers with such artists as Phelps and Elder? You wanted them to be successful rascals; they were only unsuccessful ones—that's all the difference. There was only one boy ever raised in this borderland between ruffianism and civilization who didn't come to grief, and you hated Harvey Merrick more for winning out than you hated all the other boys who got under the wheels. Lord, Lord, how you did hate him! Phelps, here, is fond of saying that he could buy and sell us all out any time he's a mind to; but he knew Harve wouldn't have given a tinker's damn for his bank and all his cattlefarms put together; and a lack of appreciation, that way, goes hard with Phelps.

"Old Nimrod thinks Harve drank too much; and this from such as Nimrod and me!

"Brother Elder says Harve was too free with the old man's money—fell short in filial consideration, maybe. Well, we can all remember the very tone in which brother Elder swore his own father was a liar, in the county court;

and we all know that the old man came out of that partnership with his son as bare as a sheared lamb. But maybe I'm getting personal, and I'd better be driving ahead at what I want to say."

The lawyer paused a moment, squared his heavy shoulders, and went on: "Harvey Merrick and I went to school together, back East. We were dead in earnest, and we wanted you all to be proud of us some day. We meant to be great men. Even I, and I haven't lost my sense of humour, gentlemen, I meant to be a great man. I came back here to practise, and I found you didn't in the least want me to be a great man. You wanted me to be a shrewd lawyer— oh, yes! Our veteran here wanted me to get him an increase of pension, because he had dyspepsia; Phelps wanted a new county survey that would put the widow Wilson's little bottom farm inside his south line; Elder wanted to lend money at 5 per cent. a month, and get it collected; and Stark here wanted to wheedle old women up in Vermont into investing their annuities in real-estate mortgages that are not worth the paper they are written on. Oh, you needed me hard enough, and you'll go on needing me!

"Well, I came back here and became the damned shyster you wanted me to be. You pretend to have some sort of respect for me; and yet you'll stand up and throw mud at Harvey Merrick, whose soul you couldn't dirty and whose hands you couldn't tie. Oh, you're a discriminating lot of Christians! There have been times when the sight of Harvey's name in some Eastern paper has made me hang my head like a whipped dog; and, again, times when I liked to think of him off there in the world, away from all this hog-wallow, climbing the big, clean up-grade he'd set for himself.

"And we? Now that we've fought and lied and sweated and stolen, and hated as only the disappointed strugglers in a bitter, dead little Western town know how to do, what have we got to show for it? Harvey Merrick wouldn't have given one sunset over your marshes for all you've got put together, and you know it. It's not for me to say why, in the inscrutable wisdom of God, a genius should ever have been called from this place of hatred and bitter waters; but I want this Boston man to know that the drivel he's been hearing here tonight is the only tribute any truly great man could have from such a lot of sick, side-tracked, burnt-dog, land-poor sharks as the here-present financiers of Sand City—upon which town may God have mercy!"

The lawyer thrust out his hand to Steavens as he passed him, caught up his overcoat in the hall, and had left the house before the Grand Army man had had time to lift his ducked head and crane his long neck about at his fellows.

Next day Jim Laird was drunk and unable to attend the funeral services. Steavens called twice at his office, but was compelled to start East without seeing him. He had a presentiment that he would hear from him again, and left his address on the lawyer's table; but if Laird found it, he never acknowledged it. The thing in him that Harvey Merrick had loved must have gone under ground with Harvey Merrick's coffin; for it never spoke again, and Jim got the cold he died of driving across the Colorado mountains to defend one of Phelps's sons who had got into trouble out there by cutting government timber.

1905, 1920

AMY LOWELL
1874–1925

Born in Brookline, Massachusetts, the fifth and last child, twelve years younger than her nearest sibling, Amy Lowell hailed from one of Boston's wealthiest and most prestigious and powerful families. The first Lowell arrived at Massachusetts Bay Colony in 1639; from the revolutionary years on, when a Lowell was made a judge by George Washington, no era was without one or more Lowells prominent in the intellectual, religious, political, philanthropic, and commercial life of New England. In the early nineteenth century her paternal grandfather and his brothers established the Lowell textile mills in Lowell, Massachusetts—the town itself had been founded by the Lowells in 1653. The success of these mills changed the economy of New England. Profits were invested in utilities, highways, railroads, and banks. In the same generation her maternal grandfather, Abbot Lawrence, established a second New England textile dynasty. All the Lowell men went to Harvard. Traditionally, those who were not in business became Unitarian ministers or scholars—the poet James Russell Lowell was her great-uncle; her father, Augustus, was important to the founding of the Massachusetts Institute of Technology; her brother Percival was a pioneering scholar of Japanese and Korean civilization and an astronomer (he founded the Lowell Observatory and discovered the planet Pluto); her brother Abbot Lawrence was president of Harvard from 1909 to 1933.

But none of the millionaires, manufacturers, philanthropists, statesmen, ambassadors, judges, and scholars in Amy Lowell's background could give this energetic and unusually intelligent young woman a model to follow. They were all men, and the rules for Lowell women were different. Women in the family were expected to marry well, imbue their children with a strong sense of family pride, oversee the running of several homes, and participate in upper-class Boston's busy social world. None of this interested Lowell in the least. Yet she believed in the importance of her heritage and shared the self-confidence and drive to contribute notably to public life characteristic of Lowell men.

Resisting the kind of formal education available to women of her class at the time, she attended school only between the ages of ten and seventeen. She educated herself through the use of her family's extensive private library as well as the resources of the Boston Athenaeum, a dues-paying library club founded by one of her ancestors early in the nineteenth century. She had enjoyed writing from childhood on, but did not venture into professional authorship until 1912, at the age of thirty-eight. In that year, her first book of poems—*A Dome of Many-Coloured Glass*—achieved both popular and critical success.

The year 1912 was the year that Harriet Monroe launched her influential little magazine, *Poetry,* and when in January 1913 Lowell read H. D.'s imagistic poetry she was converted to this new style. She decided to devote her popularity and social prominence to popularizing imagism and with characteristic energy and self-confidence journeyed to England to meet H. D., Ezra Pound, D. H. Lawrence, Richard Aldington, and other participants in the informal movement. When Pound abandoned imagism for vorticism, Lowell became the chief spokesperson for the movement, editing several imagist anthologies. Two volumes of original criticism by Lowell—*Six French Poets* (1915) and *Tendencies in Modern American Poetry* (1917)—also forwarded the cause. Pound, upstaged as a publicist, enviously renamed the movement "Amygism." Lowell retorted that "it was not until I entered the arena and Ezra dropped out that Imagism had to be considered seriously."

Lowell's own poetry—published in *Sword Blades and Poppy Seed* (1914), *Men, Women, and Ghosts* (1916), *Can Grande's Castle* (1918), *Pictures of the Floating World* (1919), and *Legends* (1921)—was never exclusively imagistic but included long historical narrative poems and journalistic prose poems and used standard verse patterns, blank verse, and a Whitmanesque free verse resembling the open line developed by Carl Sandburg. Her best poems tend to enclose sharp imagistic representation within this relatively fluid line, thereby achieving an effect of simultaneous compactness and flexibility. Like many women poets, she worked with a symbolic vocabulary of flowers and color.

Lowell enjoyed her success and cheerfully went on the lecture circuit as a celebrity, making innumerable close friendships as a result of her warmth and generosity. Despite health problems that plagued her for most of her life, she remained full of energy and zest. She depended for support on the companionship of Ada Dwyer Russell, a former actress, for whom she wrote many of her most moving appreciations of female beauty. Although she traveled widely in Europe, she was ultimately committed to New England and the Lowell heritage, both of which fused in an attachment to her home, Sevenels, in Brookline. A devotee of Romantic poetry and especially of Keats, she had begun to collect Keats manuscripts in 1905; these now form the basis of the great collection at Harvard University. In addition to all her other activities in the 1920s, she worked on a two-volume biography of Keats that greatly extended the published information about the poet when it appeared in 1925, although its psychological approach offended many traditional critics.

Lowell was just fifty-one when she died. Despite continued sniping from the high modernist poets who thought her work was too accessible, her poetry continued to be both popular and critically esteemed until the 1950s, when scholars focused the canon on a very small number of writers. The efforts of feminists to rediscover and republicize the work of neglected women authors as well as the researches of literary historians into the whole picture of American literary achievement have together brought her work back into the spotlight that it occupied during her lifetime.

The texts printed here are from Lowell's *Complete Poems* (1955).

The Captured Goddess

Over the housetops,
Above the rotating chimney-pots,
I have seen a shiver of amethyst,
And blue and cinnamon have flickered
A moment,   5
At the far end of a dusty street.

Through sheeted rain
Has come a lustre of crimson,
And I have watched moonbeams
Hushed by a film of palest green.   10

It was her wings,
Goddess!
Who stepped over the clouds,
And laid her rainbow feathers
Aslant on the currents of the air.   15

I followed her for long,
With gazing eyes and stumbling feet.
I cared not where she led me,
My eyes were full of colors:

Saffrons, rubies, the yellows of beryls,   20
And the indigo-blue of quartz;
Flights of rose, layers of chrysoprase,
Points of orange, spirals of vermilion,
The spotted gold of tiger-lily petals,
The loud pink of bursting hydrangeas.   25
I followed,
And watched for the flashing of her wings.

In the city I found her,
The narrow-streeted city.
In the market-place I came upon her,   30
Bound and trembling.
Her fluted wings were fastened to her sides with cords,
She was naked and cold,
For that day the wind blew
Without sunshine.   35

Men chaffered for her,
They bargained in silver and gold,
In copper, in wheat,
And called their bids across the market-place.

The Goddess wept.   40

Hiding my face I fled,
And the grey wind hissed behind me,
Along the narrow streets.

         1914

Venus Transiens

    Tell me,
    Was Venus more beautiful
    Than you are,
    When she topped
    The crinkled waves,   5
    Drifting shoreward
    On her plaited shell?
    Was Botticelli's[1] vision
    Fairer than mine;
    And were the painted rosebuds   10
    He tossed his lady,
    Of better worth
    Than the words I blow about you

---

1. Sandro Botticelli (ca. 1440–1510), Italian Renaissance painter among whose paintings is the famous *Birth of Venus,* depicting the Greek goddess of love and beauty rising from the ocean on a seashell.

To cover your too great loveliness
As with a gauze   15
Of misted silver?

For me,
You stand poised
In the blue and buoyant air,
Cinctured by bright winds,   20
Treading the sunlight.
And the waves which precede you
Ripple and stir
The sands at my feet.

1919

Madonna of the Evening Flowers

All day long I have been working,
Now I am tired.
I call: "Where are you?"
But there is only the oak tree rustling in the wind.
The house is very quiet,   5
The sun shines in on your books,
On your scissors and thimble just put down,
But you are not there.
Suddenly I am lonely:
Where are you?   10
I go about searching.

Then I see you,
Standing under a spire of pale blue larkspur,
With a basket of roses on your arm.
You are cool, like silver,   15
And you smile.
I think the Canterbury bells[1] are playing little tunes.

You tell me that the peonies need spraying,
That the columbines have overrun all bounds,
That the pyrus japonica should be cut back and rounded.   20
You tell me these things.
But I look at you, heart of silver,
White heart-flame of polished silver,
Burning beneath the blue steeples of the larkspur,
And I long to kneel instantly at your feet,   25
While all about us peal the loud, sweet *Te Deums* of the
        Canterbury bells.

1919

---

1. Little bell-shaped blue flowers. Lowell puns on the bells of Canterbury Cathedral in England pealing out
religious music.

September, 1918

This afternoon was the colour of water falling through sunlight;
The trees glittered with the tumbling of leaves;
The sidewalks shone like alleys of dropped maple leaves;
And the houses ran along them laughing out of square, open
    windows.
Under a tree in the park,   5
Two little boys, lying flat on their faces,
Were carefully gathering red berries
To put in a pasteboard box.

Some day there will be no war.
Then I shall take out this afternoon   10
And turn it in my fingers,
And remark the sweet taste of it upon my palate,
And note the crisp variety of its flights of leaves.
To-day I can only gather it
And put it into my lunch-box,   15
For I have time for nothing
But the endeavour to balance myself
Upon a broken world.

                                        1919

St. Louis

June

Flat,
Flat,
Long as sight
Either way,
An immense country,   5
With a great river
Steaming it full of moist, unbearable heat.
The orchards are little quincunxes of Noah's Ark trees,
The plows and horses are children's toys tracing amusingly shallow lines
    upon an illimitable surface.
Great chunks of life to match the country,   10
Great lungs to breathe this hot, wet air.

But it is not mine.
Mine is a land of hills
Lying couchant in the angles of heraldic beasts
About white villages.   15
A land of singing elms and pine-trees.
A restless up and down land
Always mounting, dipping, slipping into a different contour,
Where the roads turn every hundred yards or so,
Where brooks rattle forgotten Indian names to tired farm-houses,   20

And faint spires of old meeting-houses
Flaunt their golden weather-cocks in a brave show of challenge at a sunset
    sky.

Here the heat stuffs down with the thickness of boiled feathers,
The river runs in steam.
There, lilacs are in bloom,   25
Cool blue-purples, wine-reds, whites,
Flying colour to quiet dooryards.
Grown year on year to a suddenness of old perfection,
Saying "Before! Before!" to each new Spring.
Here is "Now,"   30
But "Before" is mine with the lilacs,
With the white sea of everywhither,
With the heraldic, story-telling hills.

                                                1927

New Heavens for Old

I am useless,
What I do is nothing.
What I think has no savour.
There is an almanac between the windows:
It is of the year when I was born.   5

My fellows call to me to join them,
They shout for me,
Passing the house in a great wind of vermillion banners.
They are fresh and fulminant,
They are indecent and strut with the thought of it.   10
They laugh, and curse, and brawl,
And cheer a holocaust of "Who comes Firsts!" at the iron fronts of the
    houses at the two edges of the street.
Young men with naked hearts jeering between iron house-fronts,
Young men with naked bodies beneath their clothes
Passionately conscious of them,   15
Ready to strip off their clothes,
Ready to strip off their customs, their usual routine,
Clamouring for the rawness of life,
In love with appetite,
Proclaiming it as a creed,   20
Worshipping youth,
Worshipping themselves.
They call for the women and the women come,
They bare the whiteness of their lusts to the dead gaze of the old house-
    fronts,
They roar down the street like flame,   25
They explode upon the dead houses like new, sharp fire.

But I—
I arrange three roses in a Chinese vase:
A pink one,
A red one,   30
A yellow one.
I fuss over their arrangement.
Then I sit in a South window
And sip pale wine with a touch of hemlock in it,
And think of Winter nights,   35
And field-mice crossing and re-crossing
The spot which will be my grave.

                                                    1927

GERTRUDE STEIN
1874–1946

Among modernists active between the wars, Gertrude Stein was more radically experimental than most. She pushed language to its limits—and kept on pushing. Her work
was sometimes literal nonsense, often funny, and always exciting to those who
thought of writing as a craft and language as a medium. As Sherwood Anderson wrote,
"she is laying word against word, relating sound to sound, feeling for the taste, the
smell, the rhythm of the individual word. She is attempting to do something for the
writers of our English speech that may be better understood after a time, and she is
not in a hurry."

Stein's grandparents were well-off German Jewish immigrants who, at the time of
her birth, were established in business in Baltimore. Born in Allegheny, Pennsylvania,
she was the youngest of seven children; the family lived abroad from 1875 to 1879
and then settled in northern California. Her parents died when she was an adolescent,
leaving their five surviving children well provided for. Stein made a family with her
favorite brother, Leo, for many years. When he went to Harvard in 1892 she followed
and was admitted to Harvard's "annex for women"—now Radcliffe College. She studied there with the great psychologist William James; some of her early writings—for
example, *Three Lives* (1909) and *The Making of Americans*, which she completed in
1908 but did not publish until 1925—are probably trying to apply his theories of
consciousness: consciousness as unique to each individual, as an ongoing stream, a
perpetual present. In *Three Lives*, also, Stein set herself the difficult task of representing the consciousnesses of three ordinary, working-class women whose lives and
minds were not the conventional material of serious literature.

When Leo moved on to Johns Hopkins to study biology, Stein followed, enrolling
in the medical school. At the end of her fourth year, she failed intentionally, for
several reasons: Leo had become interested in art and decided to go to Europe, she
had begun to write, and she had become erotically involved with two women (the
story of this triangle formed the basis of her novel *Q.E.D.*, published posthumously
in 1950). In early 1903 Leo settled in Paris; Stein joined him that fall. They began
to collect modern art and became good friends with many of the brilliant aspiring
painters of the day, including Pablo Picasso, Georges Braque, and Henri Matisse.
Stein's friendship with the painters was extremely important for her development, for
she reproduced some of their experiments in the very different medium of words.
Because of them, she came to think of words as tangible entities in themselves as

well as vehicles conveying meaning or representing reality. The cubist movement in painting also affected her. Painters like Picasso and Braque believed that so-called representational paintings conveyed not what people actually saw but rather what they had learned to *think* they saw. The cubists wanted to reproduce a pure visual experience unmediated by cultural ideas. To see a "person" is to see a cultural construct. So they painted a human form reduced to various geometrical shapes as they might be seen from different angles when the form moved or the observer changed position. The degree to which their paintings shocked an audience measured, to Picasso and Braque, the degree to which that audience had lost its original perceiving power.

In 1909 the long companionship of Stein and her brother was complicated when Alice B. Toklas joined the household as Gertrude Stein's lover; she became her secretary, housekeeper, typist, editor, and lifelong companion. Leo moved out in 1913, and the art collection was divided, but the apartment at 27 rue de Fleurus continued to serve as a gathering place for French artists and intellectuals, American expatriates, and American visitors. Without much expectation that her work would achieve any wide audience, Stein continued to write and to advise younger writers like Ernest Hemingway and F. Scott Fitzgerald. "A great deal of description," she said about a draft of Hemingway's first novel, "and not particularly good description. Begin over again and concentrate." The need to concentrate and distill—the idea that description was too often an indulgence—was a lesson the younger writer took to heart.

In the 1920s Stein and Toklas began spending summers in the south of France, where they bought a small house in 1929. They lived there during the war, when they could not return to Paris. Devoted to their adopted country, Stein and Toklas did what they could for France during both world wars. They visited and entertained American soldiers, many of whom continued to write to the couple for years after they had returned to the United States and some of whom visited when they had occasion to return to France. Even though Stein returned to the United States only once, in 1934, on what turned into a very successful lecture tour, she and Toklas always thought of themselves as Americans.

Stein's work may be considered as falling into three overlapping chronological phases. In all three phases she wrote lesbian love poems that developed a complex private symbolism for socially unacceptable feelings and events—a symbolism so obscure that their eroticism is by no means apparent, even in a much more permissive age, and needs decoding if the poems are to be understood. At first she was interested in representing present time, which is the way she believed life was subjectively experienced. Experience goes on and yet changes minutely from instant to instant. In *The Making of Americans*, Stein explained, "there was a groping for using everything and there was a groping for a continuous present and there was an inevitable beginning of beginning again and again and again." And, she added humorously, "I went on to a thousand pages of it."

Stein's 1914 *Tender Buttons*, a cubist prose-poem collage of domestic objects, looked forward to her still more innovative work of the 1920s, where she treated words as things, carefully ignoring or defying the connection between words and meanings, continually undercutting expectations about order, coherence, and associations. Naturally, the effect of such writing is often absurd, because expected patterns do not appear but are continually disrupted and frustrated. There is a great deal of joking in this work, which she openly characterized as defiance of what she called, in one long essay-poem, "patriarchal poetry"—that is, orderly, hierarchical, rule-based poetry. Much of her experimental work remained unpublished in her lifetime.

The third phase of her work, in the 1930s, represents a campaign of self-promotion. Her autobiography, written as *The Autobiography of Alice B. Toklas* (1933), her *Everybody's Autobiography* (1937), and *Wars I Have Seen* (1945) are narratives that present some of her techniques in simplified form and also project her strong independent personality. Because they were easier to read, they were popular, as was her opera libretto *Four Saints in Three Acts* put to music by Virgil Thomson. By the time of her death she had become a public personality. In recent years, the extent of her influence on other writers and the intentions behind experiments that had previously seemed "meaningless" have become much more apparent. The women's movement, with its interest in women's lives, has also produced a new appreciation of her radical individualism.

From Tender Buttons

Objects

A CARAFE, THAT IS A BLIND GLASS

A kind in glass and a cousin, a spectacle and nothing strange a single hurt color and an arrangement in a system to pointing. All this and not ordinary, not unordered in not resembling. The difference is spreading.

GLAZED GLITTER

Nickel, what is nickel, it is originally rid of a cover.

The change in that is that red weakens an hour. The change has come. There is no search. But there is, there is that hope and that interpretation and sometime, surely any is unwelcome, sometime there is breath and there will be a sinecure and charming very charming is that clean and cleansing. Certainly glittering is handsome and convincing.

There is no gratitude in mercy and in medicine. There can be breakages in Japanese. That is no programme. That is no color chosen. It was chosen yesterday, that showed spitting and perhaps washing and polishing. It certainly showed no obligation and perhaps if borrowing is not natural there is some use in giving.

A SUBSTANCE IN A CUSHION

The change of color is likely and a difference a very little difference is prepared. Sugar is not a vegetable.

Callous is something that hardening leaves behind what will be soft if there is a genuine interest in there being present as many girls as men. Does this change. It shows that dirt is clean when there is a volume.

A cushion has that cover. Supposing you do not like to change, supposing it is very clean that there is no change in appearance, supposing that there is regularity and a costume is that any the worse than an oyster and an exchange. Come to season that is there any extreme use in feather and cotton. Is there not much more joy in a table and more chairs and very likely roundness and a place to put them.

A circle of fine card board and a chance to see a tassel.

What is the use of a violent kind of delightfulness if there is no pleasure in not getting tired of it. The question does not come before there is a quotation. In any kind of place there is a top to covering and it is a pleasure at any rate there is some venturing in refusing to believe nonsense. It shows what use there is in a whole piece if one uses it and it is extreme and very likely the little things could be dearer but in any case there is a bargain and if there is the best thing to do is to take it away and wear it and then be reckless be reckless and resolved on returning gratitude.

Light blue and the same red with purple makes a change. It shows that there is no mistake. Any pink shows that and very likely it is reasonable. Very likely there should not be a finer fancy present. Some increase means a calamity and this is the best preparation for three and more being together. A little calm is so ordinary and in any case there is sweetness and some of that.

A seal and matches and a swan and ivy and a suit.

A closet, a closet does not connect under the bed. The band if it is white and black, the band has a green string. A sight a whole sight and a little groan grinding makes a trimming such a sweet singing trimming and a red thing not a round thing but a white thing, a red thing and a white thing.

The disgrace is not in carelessness nor even in sewing it comes out out of the way.

What is the sash like. The sash is not like anything mustard it is not like a same thing that has stripes, it is not even more hurt than that, it has a little top.

A BOX

Out of kindness comes redness and out of rudeness comes rapid same question, out of an eye comes research, out of selection comes painful cattle. So then the order is that a white way of being round is something suggesting a pin and is it disappointing, it is not, it is so rudimentary to be analysed and see a fine substance strangely, it is so earnest to have a green point not to red but to point again.

A PIECE OF COFFEE

More of double.

A place in no new table.

A single image is not splendor. Dirty is yellow. A sign of more in not mentioned. A piece of coffee is not a detainer. The resemblance to yellow is dirtier and distincter. The clean mixture is whiter and not coal color, never more coal color than altogether.

The sight of a reason, the same sight slighter, the sight of a simpler negative answer, the same sore sounder, the intention to wishing, the same splendor, the same furniture.

The time to show a message is when too late and later there is no hanging in a blight.

A not torn rose-wood color. If it is not dangerous then a pleasure and more than any other if it is cheap is not cheaper. The amusing side is that the sooner there are no fewer the more certain is the necessity dwindled. Supposing that the case contained rose-wood and a color. Supposing that there was no reason for a distress and more likely for a number, supposing that there was no astonishment, is it not necessary to mingle astonishment.

The settling of stationing cleaning is one way not to shatter scatter and scattering. The one way to use custom is to use soap and silk for cleaning. The one way to see cotton is to have a design concentrating the illusion and the illustration. The perfect way is to accustom the thing to have a lining and the shape of a ribbon and to be solid, quite solid in standing and to use heaviness in morning. It is light enough in that. It has that shape nicely. Very nicely may not be exaggerating. Very strongly may be sincerely fainting. May be strangely flattering. May not be strange in everything. May not be strange to.

DIRT AND NOT COPPER

Dirt and not copper makes a color darker. It makes the shape so heavy and makes no melody harder.

It makes mercy and relaxation and even a strength to spread a table fuller. There are more places not empty. They see cover.

NOTHING ELEGANT

A charm a single charm is doubtful. If the red is rose and there is a gate surrounding it, if inside is let in and there places change then certainly something is upright. It is earnest.

MILDRED'S UMBRELLA

A cause and no curve, a cause and loud enough, a cause and extra a loud clash and an extra wagon, a sign of extra, a sac a small sac and an established color and cunning, a slender grey and no ribbon, this means a loss a great loss a restitution.

A METHOD OF A CLOAK

A single climb to a line, a straight exchange to a cane, a desperate adventure and courage and a clock, all this which is a system, which has feeling, which has resignation and success, all makes an attractive black silver.

A RED STAMP

If lilies are lily white if they exhaust noise and distance and even dust, if they dusty will dirt a surface that has no extreme grace, if they do this and it is not necessary it is not at all necessary if they do this they need a catalogue.

A BOX

A large box is handily made of what is necessary to replace any substance. Suppose an example is necessary, the plainer it is made the more reason there is for some outward recognition that there is a result.

A box is made sometimes and them to see to see to it neatly and to have the holes stopped up makes it necessary to use paper.

A custom which is necessary when a box is used and taken is that a large part of the time there are three which have different connections. The one is on the table. The two are on the table. The three are on the table. The one, one is the same length as is shown by the cover being longer. The other is different there is more cover that shows it. The other is different and that makes the corners have the same shade the eight are in singular arrangement to make four necessary.

Lax, to have corners, to be lighter than some weight, to indicate a wedding journey, to last brown and not curious, to be wealthy, cigarettes are established by length and by doubling.

Left open, to be left pounded, to be left closed, to be circulating in summer and winter, and sick color that is grey that is not dusty and red shows, to be sure cigarettes do measure an empty length sooner than a choice in color.

Winged, to be winged means that white is yellow and pieces pieces that are brown are dust color if dust is washed off, then it is choice that is to say it is fitting cigarettes sooner than paper.

An increase why is an increase idle, why is silver cloister, why is the spark brighter, if it is brighter is there any result, hardly more than ever.

A PLATE

An occasion for a plate, an occasional resource is in buying and how soon does washing enable a selection of the same thing neater. If the party is small a clever song is in order.

Plates and a dinner set of colored china. Pack together a string and enough with it to protect the centre, cause a considerable haste and gather more as it is cooling, collect more trembling and not any even trembling, cause a whole thing to be a church.

A sad size a size that is not sad is blue as every bit of blue is precocious. A kind of green a game in green and nothing flat nothing quite flat and more round, nothing a particular color strangely, nothing breaking the losing of no little piece.

A splendid address a really splendid address is not shown by giving a flower freely, it is not shown by a mark or by wetting.

Cut cut in white, cut in white so lately. Cut more than any other and show it. Show it in the stem and in starting and in evening coming complication.

A lamp is not the only sign of glass. The lamp and the cake are not the only sign of stone. The lamp and the cake and the cover are not the only necessity altogether.

A plan a hearty plan, a compressed disease and no coffee, not even a card or a change to incline each way, a plan that has that excess and that break is the one that shows filling.

A SELTZER BOTTLE

Any neglect of many particles to a cracking, any neglect of this makes around it what is lead in color and certainly discolor in silver. The use of this is manifold. Supposing a certain time selected is assured, suppose it is even necessary, suppose no other extract is permitted and no more handling is needed, suppose the rest of the message is mixed with a very long slender needle and even if it could be any black border, supposing all this altogether made a dress and suppose it was actual, suppose the mean way to state it was occasional, if you suppose this in August and even more melodiously, if you suppose this even in the necessary incident of there certainly being no middle in summer and winter, suppose this and an elegant settlement a very elegant settlement is more than of consequence, it is not final and sufficient and substituted. This which was so kindly a present was constant.

A LONG DRESS

What is the current that makes machinery, that makes it crackle, what is the current that presents a long line and a necessary waist. What is this current.

What is the wind, what is it.

Where is the serene length, it is there and a dark place is not a dark place, only a white and red are black, only a yellow and green are blue, a pink is scarlet, a bow is every color. A line distinguishes it. A line just distinguishes it.

A RED HAT

A dark grey, a very dark grey, a quite dark grey is monstrous ordinarily, it is so monstrous because there is no red in it. If red is in everything it is not necessary. Is that not an argument for any use of it and even so is there any place that is better, is there any place that has so much stretched out.

A BLUE COAT

A blue coat is guided guided away, guided and guided away, that is the particular color that is used for that length and not any width not even more than a shadow.

A PIANO

If the speed is open, if the color is careless, if the selection of a strong scent is not awkward, if the button holder is held by all the waving color and there is no color, not any color. If there is no dirt in a pin and there can be none scarcely, if there is not then the place is the same as up standing.

This is no dark custom and it even is not acted in any such a way that a restraint is not spread. That is spread, it shuts and it lifts and awkwardly not awkwardly the centre is in standing.

A CHAIR

A widow in a wise veil and more garments shows that shadows are even. It addresses no more, it shadows the stage and learning. A regular arrangement, the severest and the most preserved is that which has the arrangement not more than always authorised.

A suitable establishment, well housed, practical, patient and staring, a suitable bedding, very suitable and not more particularly than complaining, anything suitable is so necessary.

A fact is that when the direction is just like that, no more, longer, sudden and at the same time not any sofa, the main action is that without a blaming there is no custody.

Practice measurement, practice the sign that means that really means a necessary betrayal, in showing that there is wearing.

Hope, what is a spectacle, a spectacle is the resemblance between the circular side place and nothing else, nothing else.

To choose it is ended, it is actual and more and more than that it has it certainly has the same treat, and a seat all that is practiced and more easily much more easily ordinarily.

Pick a barn, a whole barn, and bend more slender accents than have ever been necessary, shine in the darkness necessarily.

Actually not aching, actually not aching, a stubborn bloom is so artificial and even more than that, it is a spectacle, it is a binding accident, it is animosity and accentuation.

If the chance to dirty diminishing is necessary, if it is why is there no complexion, why is there no rubbing, why is there no special protection.

A FRIGHTFUL RELEASE

A bag which was left and not only taken but turned away was not found. The place was shown to be very like the last time. A piece was not exchanged, not a bit of it, a piece was left over. The rest was mismanaged.

A PURSE

A purse was not green, it was not straw color, it was hardly seen and it had a use a long use and the chain, the chain was never missing, it was not misplaced, it showed that it was open, that is all that it showed.

A MOUNTED UMBRELLA

What was the use of not leaving it there where it would hang what was the use if there was no chance of ever seeing it come there and show that it was handsome and right in the way it showed it. The lesson is to learn that it does show it, that it shows it and that nothing, that there is nothing, that there is no more to do about it and just so much more is there plenty of reason for making an exchange.

A CLOTH

Enough cloth is plenty and more, more is almost enough for that and besides if there is no more spreading is there plenty of room for it. Any occasion shows the best way.

MORE

An elegant use of foliage and grace and a little piece of white cloth and oil.

Wondering so winningly in several kinds of oceans is the reason that makes red so regular and enthusiastic. The reason that there is more snips are the same shining very colored rid of no round color.

A NEW CUP AND SAUCER

Enthusiastically hurting a clouded yellow bud and saucer, enthusiastically so is the bite in the ribbon.

OBJECTS

Within, within the cut and slender joint alone, with sudden equals and no more than three, two in the centre make two one side.

If the elbow is long and it is filled so then the best example is all together. The kind of show is made by squeezing.

EYE GLASSES

A color in shaving, a saloon is well placed in the centre of an alley.

A CUTLET

A blind agitation is manly and uttermost.

CARELESS WATER

No cup is broken in more places and mended, that is to say a plate is broken and mending does do that it shows that culture is Japanese. It shows the whole element of angels and orders. It does more to choosing and it does more to that ministering counting. It does, it does change in more water.

Supposing a single piece is a hair supposing more of them are orderly, does that show that strength, does that show that joint, does that show that balloon famously. Does it.

A PAPER

A courteous occasion makes a paper show no such occasion and this makes readiness and eyesight and likeness and a stool.

A DRAWING

The meaning of this is entirely and best to say the mark, best to say it best to shown sudden places, best to make bitter, best to make the length tall and nothing broader, anything between the half.

WATER RAINING

Water astonishing and difficult altogether makes a meadow and a stroke.

COLD CLIMATE

A season in yellow sold extra strings makes lying places.

MALACHITE

The sudden spoon is the same in no size. The sudden spoon is the wound in the decision.

AN UMBRELLA

Coloring high means that the strange reason is in front not more in front behind. Not more in front in peace of the dot.

A PETTICOAT

A light white, a disgrace, an ink spot, a rosy charm.

A WAIST

A star glide, a single frantic sullenness, a single financial grass greediness.

Object that is in wood. Hold the pine, hold the dark, hold in the rush, make the bottom.

A piece of crystal. A change, in a change that is remarkable there is no reason to say that there was a time.

A woolen object gilded. A country climb is the best disgrace, a couple of practices any of them in order is so left.

A TIME TO EAT

A pleasant simple habitual and tyrannical and authorised and educated and resumed and articulate separation. This is not tardy.

A LITTLE BIT OF A TUMBLER

A shining indication of yellow consists in there having been more of the same color than could have been expected when all four were bought. This was the hope which made the six and seven have no use for any more places and this necessarily spread into nothing. Spread into nothing.

A FIRE

What was the use of a whole time to send and not send if there was to be the kind of thing that made that come in. A letter was nicely sent.

A HANDKERCHIEF

A winning of all the blessings, a sample not a sample because there is no worry.

RED ROSES

A cool red rose and a pink cut pink, a collapse and a sold hole, a little less hot.

IN BETWEEN

In between a place and candy is a narrow foot-path that shows more mounting than anything, so much really that a calling meaning a bolster measured a whole thing with that. A virgin a whole virgin is judged made and so between curves and outlines and real seasons and more out glasses and a perfectly unprecedented arrangement between old ladies and mild colds there is no satin wood shining.

COLORED HATS

Colored hats are necessary to show that curls are worn by an addition of blank spaces, this makes the difference between single lines and broad stomachs, the least thing is lightening, the least thing means a little flower and a big delay a big delay that makes more nurses than little women really little women. So clean is a light that nearly all of it shows pearls and little ways. A large hat is tall and me and all custard whole.

A FEATHER

A feather is trimmed, it is trimmed by the light and the bug and the post, it is trimmed by little leaning and by all sorts of mounted reserves and loud volumes. It is surely cohesive.

A BROWN

A brown which is not liquid not more so is relaxed and yet there is a change, a news is pressing.

A LITTLE CALLED PAULINE

A little called anything shows shudders.

Come and say what prints all day. A whole few watermelon. There is no pope.

No cut in pennies and little dressing and choose wide soles and little spats really little spices.

A little lace makes boils. This is not true.

Gracious of gracious and a stamp a blue green white bow a blue green lean, lean on the top.

If it is absurd then it is leadish and nearly set in where there is a tight head.

A peaceful life to arise her, noon and moon and moon. A letter a cold sleeve a blanket a shaving house and nearly the best and regular window.

Nearer in fairy sea, nearer and farther, show white has lime in sight, show a stitch of ten. Count, count more so that thicker and thicker is leaning.

I hope she has her cow. Bidding a wedding, widening received treading, little leading mention nothing.

Cough out cough out in the leather and really feather it is not for.

Please could, please could, jam it not plus more sit in when.

A SOUND

Elephant beaten with candy and little pops and chews all bolts and reckless reckless rats, this is this.

A TABLE

A table means does it not my dear it means a whole steadiness. Is it likely that a change.

A table means more than a glass even a looking glass is tall. A table means necessary places and a revision a revision of a little thing it means it does mean that there has been a stand, a stand where it did shake.

SHOES

To be a wall with a damper a stream of pounding way and nearly enough choice makes a steady midnight. It is pus.

A shallow hole rose on red, a shallow hole in and in this makes ale less. It shows shine.

A DOG

A little monkey goes like a donkey that means to say that means to say that more sighs last goes. Leave with it. A little monkey goes like a donkey.

A WHITE HUNTER

A white hunter is nearly crazy.

A LEAVE

In the middle of a tiny spot and nearly bare there is a nice thing to say that wrist is leading. Wrist is leading.

SUPPOSE AN EYES

Suppose it is within a gate which open is open at the hour of closing summer that is to say it is so.

All the seats are needing blackening. A white dress is in sign. A soldier a real soldier has a worn lace a worn lace of different sizes that is to say if he can read, if he can read he is a size to show shutting up twenty-four.

Go red go red, laugh white.

Suppose a collapse in rubbed purr, in rubbed purr get.

Little sales ladies little sales ladies little saddles of mutton.

Little sales of leather and such beautiful beautiful, beautiful beautiful.

A SHAWL

A shawl is a hat and hurt and a red balloon and an under coat and a sizer a sizer of talks.

A shawl is a wedding, a piece of wax a little build. A shawl.

Pick a ticket, pick it in strange steps and with hollows. There is hollow hollow belt, a belt is a shawl.

A plate that has a little bobble, all of them, any so.

Please a round it is ticket.

It was a mistake to state that a laugh and a lip and a laid climb and a depot and a cultivator and little choosing is a point it.

BOOK

Book was there, it was there. Book was there. Stop it, stop it, it was a cleaner, a wet cleaner and it was not where it was wet, it was not high, it was directly placed back, not back again, back it was returned, it was needless, it put a bank, a bank when, a bank care.

Suppose a man a realistic expression of resolute reliability suggests pleasing itself white all white and no head does that mean soap. It does not so. It means kind wavers and little chance to beside beside rest. A plain.

Suppose ear rings that is one way to breed, breed that. Oh chance to say, oh nice old pole. Next best and nearest a pillar. Chest not valuable, be papered.

Cover up cover up the two with a little piece of string and hope rose and green, green.

Please a plate, put a match to the seam and really then really then, really then it is a remark that joins many many lead games. It is a sister and sister and a flower and a flower and a dog and a colored sky a sky colored grey and nearly that nearly that let.

PEELED PENCIL, CHOKE

Rub her coke.

IT WAS BLACK, BLACK TOOK

Black ink best wheel bale brown.
Excellent not a hull house, not a pea soup, no bill no care, no precise no past pearl pearl goat.

THIS IS THIS DRESS, AIDER

Aider, why aider why whow, whow stop touch, aider whow, aider stop the muncher, muncher munchers.
A jack in kill her, a jack in, makes a meadowed king, makes a to let.

1914

ROBERT FROST
1874–1963

Although he identified himself with New England, Robert Frost was born in California and lived there until his father died, when Frost was eleven. The family then moved to New England where his mother supported them by teaching school. Frost graduated from high school in 1891 in Lawrence, Massachusetts, sharing the post of valedictorian with Elinor White, whom he married three years later. Occasional attendance at Dartmouth College and Harvard, and a variety of different jobs including an attempt to run a farm in Derry, New Hampshire, marked the next twenty years. Frost made a new start in 1912, taking his family, which included four children, to England. There he worked on his poetry and found a publisher for his first book, *A Boy's Will* (1913). Ezra Pound reviewed it favorably, excited (as he put it in a letter) by this "VURRY Amur'k'n talent." Pound recommended Frost's poems to American editors and helped get his second book, *North of Boston*, published in 1914. *North of Boston* was widely praised by critics in America and England when it appeared; the favorable reception persuaded Frost to return home. He bought another farm in New Hampshire and prospered financially through sales of his books and papers, along with teaching and lecturing at various colleges. The success he enjoyed for the rest of his life, however, came too late to cancel the bitterness left by his earlier struggles. Moreover, he endured personal tragedy: a son committed suicide, and a daughter had a complete mental collapse.

The clarity of Frost's diction, the colloquial rhythms, the simplicity of his images, and above all the folksy speaker—these are intended to make the poems look natural, unplanned. In the context of the modernist movement, however, they can be seen as a thoughtful reply to high modernism's fondness for obscurity and difficulty. Although Frost's ruralism affirmed the modernist distaste for cities, he was writing the kind of traditional, accessible poetry that modernists argued could no longer be written. In addition, by investing in the New England terrain, he rejected modernist internationalism and revitalized the tradition of New England regionalism. Readers who accepted Frost's persona and his setting as typically American accepted the powerful myth that rural New England was the heart of America.

Frost achieved an internal dynamic in his poems by playing the rhythms of ordinary speech against formal patterns of line and verse and containing them within traditional forms. The interaction of colloquial diction with blank verse is especially central to his dramatic monologues. To Frost traditional forms were the essence of poetry, material with which poets responded to flux and disorder (what, adopting scientific terminology, he called "decay") by forging something permanent. Poetry, he wrote, was "one step backward taken," resisting time—a "momentary stay against confusion."

Throughout the 1920s Frost's poetic practice changed very little; later books— including *Mountain Interval* (1916), *New Hampshire* (1923), and *West-Running Brook* (1928)—confirmed the impression he had created in *North of Boston*. Most of his poems fall into a few types. Nature lyrics describing and commenting on a scene or event—like "Stopping by Woods on a Snowy Evening," "Birches," and "After Apple-Picking"—are probably the best known and the most popular. There are also dramatic narratives in blank verse about the griefs of country people, like "The Death of the Hired Man," and poems of commentary or generalization, like "The Gift Outright," which he read at John F. Kennedy's presidential inauguration in 1961. He could also be humorous or sardonic, as in "Fire and Ice." In the nature lyrics, a comparison often emerges between the outer scene and the psyche, a comparison of what Frost in one poem called "outer and inner weather."

Because he worked so much with outdoor scenery, and because he presented himself as a New Englander, Frost is often interpreted as an ideological descendant of the nineteenth-century American Transcendentalists. But he is far less affirmative about the universe than they; for where they, looking at nature, discerned a benign creator, he saw "no expression, nothing to express." Frost did share with Emerson and Thoreau, however, the belief that everybody was a separate individuality and that collective enterprises could do nothing but weaken the self. Politically conservative, therefore, he avoided movements of the left and the right precisely because they were movements, group undertakings. In the 1930s when writers tended to be political activists, he was seen as one whose old-fashioned values were inappropriate, even dangerous, in modern times. Frost deeply resented this criticism, and responded to it with a newly hortatory, didactic kind of poetry. In the last twenty years of his life, Frost increased his activities as a teacher and lecturer—at Amherst, at Dartmouth, at Harvard, at the Bread Loaf School of English at Middlebury College in Vermont, and in poetry readings and talks around the country.

The text of the poems included here is that of *The Poetry of Robert Frost* (1969).

The Pasture

I'm going out to clean the pasture spring;
I'll only stop to rake the leaves away
(And wait to watch the water clear, I may):
I shan't be gone long.—You come too.
I'm going out to fetch the little calf   5
That's standing by the mother. It's so young
It totters when she licks it with her tongue.
I shan't be gone long.—You come too.

1913

Mowing

There was never a sound beside the wood but one,
And that was my long scythe whispering to the ground.
What was it it whispered? I knew not well myself;
Perhaps it was something about the heat of the sun,
Something, perhaps, about the lack of sound—   5
And that was why it whispered and did not speak.
It was no dream of the gift of idle hours,
Or easy gold at the hand of fay or elf:
Anything more than the truth would have seemed too weak
To the earnest love that laid the swale[1] in rows,   10
Not without feeble-pointed spikes of flowers
(Pale orchises), and scared a bright green snake.
The fact is the sweetest dream that labor knows.
My long scythe whispered and left the hay to make.

                                                              1913

Mending Wall

Something there is that doesn't love a wall,
That sends the frozen-ground-swell under it,
And spills the upper boulders in the sun,
And makes gaps even two can pass abreast.
The work of hunters is another thing: 5
I have come after them and made repair
Where they have left not one stone on a stone,
But they would have the rabbit out of hiding,
To please the yelping dogs. The gaps I mean,
No one has seen them made or heard them made,   10
But at spring mending-time we find them there.
I let my neighbor know beyond the hill;
And on a day we meet to walk the line
And set the wall between us once again.
We keep the wall between us as we go.   15
To each the boulders that have fallen to each.
And some are loaves and some so nearly balls
We have to use a spell to make them balance:
"Stay where you are until our backs are turned!"
We wear our fingers rough with handling them.   20
Oh, just another kind of outdoor game,
One on a side. It comes to little more:
There where it is we do not need the wall:
He is all pine and I am apple orchard.
My apple trees will never get across   25
And eat the cones under his pines, I tell him.
He only says, "Good fences make good neighbors."

1. Grasses in a marshy meadow.

Spring is the mischief in me, and I wonder
If I could put a notion in his head:
"*Why* do they make good neighbors? Isn't it   30
Where there are cows? But here there are no cows.
Before I built a wall I'd ask to know
What I was walling in or walling out,
And to whom I was like to give offense.
Something there is that doesn't love a wall,   35
That wants it down." I could say "Elves" to him,
But it's not elves exactly, and I'd rather
He said it for himself. I see him there
Bringing a stone grasped firmly by the top
In each hand, like an old-stone savage armed.   40
He moves in darkness as it seems to me,
Not of woods only and the shade of trees.
He will not go behind his father's saying,
And he likes having thought of it so well
He says again, "Good fences make good neighbors."   45

1914

The Death of the Hired Man

Mary sat musing on the lamp-flame at the table
Waiting for Warren. When she heard his step,
She ran on tip-toe down the darkened passage
To meet him in the doorway with the news
And put him on his guard. "Silas is back."   5
She pushed him outward with her through the door
And shut it after her. "Be kind," she said.
She took the market things from Warren's arms
And set them on the porch, then drew him down
To sit beside her on the wooden steps.   10

"When was I ever anything but kind to him?
But I'll not have the fellow back," he said.
"I told him so last haying, didn't I?
If he left then, I said, that ended it.
What good is he? Who else will harbor him   15
At his age for the little he can do?
What help he is there's no depending on.
Off he goes always when I need him most.
He thinks he ought to earn a little pay,
Enough at least to buy tobacco with,   20
So he won't have to beg and be beholden.
'All right,' I say, 'I can't afford to pay
Any fixed wages, though I wish I could.'
'Someone else can.' 'Then someone else will have to.'
I shouldn't mind his bettering himself   25
If that was what it was. You can be certain,

When he begins like that, there's someone at him
Trying to coax him off with pocket-money,—
In haying time, when any help is scarce.
In winter he comes back to us. I'm done."   30

"Sh! not so loud: he'll hear you," Mary said.

"I want him to: he'll have to soon or late."

"He's worn out. He's asleep beside the stove.
When I came up from Rowe's I found him here,
Huddled against the barn-door fast asleep,   35
A miserable sight, and frightening, too—
You needn't smile—I didn't recognize him—
I wasn't looking for him—and he's changed.
Wait till you see."

                    "Where did you say he'd been?"   40

"He didn't say. I dragged him to the house,
And gave him tea and tried to make him smoke.
I tried to make him talk about his travels.
Nothing would do: he just kept nodding off."

"What did he say? Did he say anything?"   45

"But little."

                    "Anything? Mary, confess
He said he'd come to ditch the meadow for me."

"Warren!"

                    "But did he? I just want to know."   50

"Of course he did. What would you have him say?
Surely you wouldn't grudge the poor old man
Some humble way to save his self-respect.
He added, if you really care to know,
He meant to clear the upper pasture, too.   55
That sounds like something you have heard before?
Warren, I wish you could have heard the way
He jumbled everything. I stopped to look
Two or three times—he made me feel so queer—
To see if he was talking in his sleep.   60
He ran on Harold Wilson—you remember—
The boy you had in haying four years since.
He's finished school, and teaching in his college.
Silas declares you'll have to get him back.
He says they two will make a team for work: 65
Between them they will lay this farm as smooth!
The way he mixed that in with other things.

He thinks young Wilson a likely lad, though daft
On education—you know how they fought
All through July under the blazing sun,   70
Silas up on the cart to build the load,
Harold along beside to pitch it on."

"Yes, I took care to keep well out of earshot."

"Well, those days trouble Silas like a dream.
You wouldn't think they would. How some things linger!   75
Harold's young college-boy's assurance piqued him.
After so many years he still keeps finding
Good arguments he sees he might have used.
I sympathize. I know just how it feels
To think of the right thing to say too late.   80
Harold's associated in his mind with Latin.
He asked me what I thought of Harold's saying
He studied Latin, like the violin,
Because he liked it—that an argument!
He said he couldn't make the boy believe   85
He could find water with a hazel prong—
Which showed how much good school had ever done him.
He wanted to go over that. But most of all
He thinks if he could have another chance
To teach him how to build a load of hay—"   90

"I know, that's Silas' one accomplishment.
He bundles every forkful in its place,
And tags and numbers it for future reference,
So he can find and easily dislodge it
In the unloading. Silas does that well.   95
He takes it out in bunches like big birds' nests.
You never see him standing on the hay
He's trying to lift, straining to lift himself."

"He thinks if he could teach him that, he'd be
Some good perhaps to someone in the world.   100
He hates to see a boy the fool of books.
Poor Silas, so concerned for other folk,
And nothing to look backward to with pride,
And nothing to look forward to with hope,
So now and never any different."   105

Part of a moon was falling down the west,
Dragging the whole sky with it to the hills.
Its light poured softly in her lap. She saw it
And spread her apron to it. She put out her hand
Among the harplike morning-glory strings,   110
Taut with the dew from garden bed to eaves,
As if she played unheard some tenderness
That wrought on him beside her in the night.
"Warren," she said, "he has come home to die:
You needn't be afraid he'll leave you this time."   115

"Home," he mocked gently.

                      "Yes, what else but home?
It all depends on what you mean by home.
Of course he's nothing to us, any more
Than was the hound that came a stranger to us   120
Out of the woods, worn out upon the trail."

"Home is the place where, when you have to go there,
They have to take you in."

                   "I should have called it
Something you somehow haven't to deserve."   125

Warren leaned out and took a step or two,
Picked up a little stick, and brought it back
And broke it in his hand and tossed it by.
"Silas has better claim on us you think
Than on his brother? Thirteen little miles   130
As the road winds would bring him to his door.
Silas has walked that far no doubt today.
Why doesn't he go there? His brother's rich,
A somebody—director in the bank."

"He never told us that."   135

               "We know it though."

"I think his brother ought to help, of course.
I'll see to that if there is need. He ought of right
To take him in, and might be willing to—
He may be better than appearances.   140
But have some pity on Silas. Do you think
If he had any pride in claiming kin
Or anything he looked for from his brother,
He'd keep so still about him all this time?"

"I wonder what's between them."   145

                     "I can tell you.
Silas is what he is—we wouldn't mind him—
But just the kind that kinsfolk can't abide.
He never did a thing so very bad.
He don't know why he isn't quite as good   150
As anybody. Worthless though he is,
He won't be made ashamed to please his brother."

"*I* can't think Si ever hurt anyone."

"No, but he hurt my heart the way he lay
And rolled his old head on that sharp-edged chair-back.   155
He wouldn't let me put him on the lounge.
You must go in and see what you can do.

I made the bed up for him there tonight.
You'll be surprised at him—how much he's broken.
His working days are done; I'm sure of it."   160

"I'd not be in a hurry to say that."

"I haven't been. Go, look, see for yourself.
But, Warren, please remember how it is:
He's come to help you ditch the meadow.
He has a plan. You mustn't laugh at him.   165
He may not speak of it, and then he may.
I'll sit and see if that small sailing cloud
Will hit or miss the moon."

          It hit the moon.
Then there were three there, making a dim row,   170
The moon, the little silver cloud, and she.
Warren returned—too soon, it seemed to her,
Slipped to her side, caught up her hand and waited.

"Warren?" she questioned.

          "Dead," was all he answered.   175

          1914

After Apple-Picking

My long two-pointed ladder's sticking through a tree
Toward heaven still,
And there's a barrel that I didn't fill
Beside it, and there may be two or three
Apples I didn't pick upon some bough.   5
But I am done with apple-picking now.
Essence of winter sleep is on the night,
The scent of apples: I am drowsing off.
I cannot rub the strangeness from my sight
I got from looking through a pane of glass   10
I skimmed this morning from the drinking trough
And held against the world of hoary grass.
It melted, and I let it fall and break.
But I was well
Upon my way to sleep before it fell,   15
And I could tell
What form my dreaming was about to take.
Magnified apples appear and disappear,
Stem end and blossom end,
And every fleck of russet showing clear.   20
My instep arch not only keeps the ache,
It keeps the pressure of a ladder-round.

I feel the ladder sway as the boughs bend.
And I keep hearing from the cellar bin
The rumbling sound   25
Of load on load of apples coming in.
For I have had too much
Of apple-picking: I am overtired
Of the great harvest I myself desired.
There were ten thousand thousand fruit to touch,   30
Cherish in hand, lift down, and not let fall.
For all
That struck the earth,
No matter if not bruised or spiked with stubble,
Went surely to the cider-apple heap   35
As of no worth.
One can see what will trouble
This sleep of mine, whatever sleep it is.
Were he not gone,
The woodchuck could say whether it's like his   40
Long sleep, as I describe its coming on,
Or just some human sleep.

                                                    1914

The Wood-Pile

Out walking in the frozen swamp one gray day,
I paused and said, "I will turn back from here.
No, I will go on farther—and we shall see."
The hard snow held me, save where now and then
One foot went through. The view was all in lines   5
Straight up and down of tall slim trees
Too much alike to mark or name a place by
So as to say for certain I was here
Or somewhere else: I was just far from home.
A small bird flew before me. He was careful   10
To put a tree between us when he lighted,
And say no word to tell me who he was
Who was so foolish as to think what *he* thought.
He thought that I was after him for a feather—
The white one in his tail; like one who takes   15
Everything said as personal to himself.
One flight out sideways would have undeceived him.
And then there was a pile of wood for which
I forgot him and let his little fear
Carry him off the way I might have gone,   20
Without so much as wishing him good-night.
He went behind it to make his last stand.
It was a cord of maple, cut and split
And piled—and measured, four by four by eight.
And not another like it could I see.   25

No runner tracks in this year's snow looped near it.
And it was older sure than this year's cutting,
Or even last year's or the year's before.
The wood was gray and the bark warping off it
And the pile somewhat sunken. Clematis 30
Had wound strings round and round it like a bundle.
What held it, though, on one side was a tree
Still growing, and on one a stake and prop,
These latter about to fall. I thought that only
Someone who lived in turning to fresh tasks 35
Could so forget his handiwork on which
He spent himself, the labor of his ax,
And leave it there far from a useful fireplace
To warm the frozen swamp as best it could
With the slow smokeless burning of decay. 40

1914

Fate

The Road Not Taken   *sick, ill*

a turning point

Two roads diverged in a yellow wood,
And sorry I could not travel both
And be one traveler, long I stood
And looked down one as far as I could
To where it bent in the undergrowth;   *death*   5

Then took the other, as just as fair,
And having perhaps the better claim,
Because it was grassy and wanted wear;
Though as for that, the passing there
Had worn them really about the same,   10

And both that morning equally lay
In leaves no step had trodden black.
Oh, I kept the first for another day!
Yet knowing how way leads on to way,
I doubted if I should ever come back.   15

I shall be telling this with a sigh
Somewhere ages and ages hence:
Two roads diverged in a wood, and I—
I took the one less traveled by,
And that has made all the difference.   20

building his own destiny

1916

2. Birches *(Mesteacăni)*

When I see birches bend to left and right
Across the lines of straighter darker trees,
I like to think some boy's been swinging them.
But swinging doesn't bend them down to stay
As ice storms do. Often you must have seen them   5
Loaded with ice a sunny winter morning
After a rain. They click upon themselves
As the breeze rises, and turn many-colored
As the stir cracks and crazes their enamel.
Soon the sun's warmth makes them shed crystal shells   10
Shattering and avalanching on the snow crust—
Such heaps of broken glass to sweep away
You'd think the inner dome of heaven had fallen.
They are dragged to the withered bracken by the load,
And they seem not to break; though once they are bowed   15
So low for long, they never right themselves:
You may see their trunks arching in the woods
Years afterwards, trailing their leaves on the ground
Like girls on hands and knees that throw their hair
Before them over their heads to dry in the sun.   20
But I was going to say when Truth broke in
With all her matter of fact about the ice storm,
I should prefer to have some boy bend them
As he went out and in to fetch the cows—
Some boy too far from town to learn baseball,   25
Whose only play was what he found himself,
Summer or winter, and could play alone.
One by one he subdued his father's trees
By riding them down over and over again
Until he took the stiffness out of them,   30
And not one but hung limp, not one was left
For him to conquer. He learned all there was
To learn about not launching out too soon
And so not carrying the tree away
Clear to the ground. He always kept his poise   35
To the top branches, climbing carefully
With the same pains you use to fill a cup
Up to the brim, and even above the brim.
Then he flung outward, feet first, with a swish,
Kicking his way down through the air to the ground.   40
So was I once myself a swinger of birches.
And so I dream of going back to be.
It's when I'm weary of considerations,
And life is too much like a pathless wood
Where your face burns and tickles with the cobwebs   45
Broken across it, and one eye is weeping
From a twig's having lashed across it open.
I'd like to get away from earth awhile
And then come back to it and begin over.
May no fate willfully misunderstand me   50

And half grant what I wish and snatch me away
Not to return. Earth's the right place for love:
I don't know where it's likely to go better.
I'd like to go by climbing a birch tree,
And climb black branches up a snow-white trunk   55
Toward heaven, till the tree could bear no more,
But dipped its top and set me down again.
That would be good both going and coming back.
One could do worse than be a swinger of birches.

[handwritten: it could be worse]

1916

[handwritten: 1916]

[handwritten: like a soldier, young boy doing hard work, gets hurt doing work for someone older]

3. "Out, Out—"[1]

The buzz saw snarled and rattled in the yard
And made dust and dropped stove-length sticks of wood,
Sweet-scented stuff when the breeze drew across it.
And from there those that lifted eyes could count
Five mountain ranges one behind the other   5
Under the sunset far into Vermont.
And the saw snarled and rattled, snarled and rattled,
As it ran light, or had to bear a load.
And nothing happened: day was all but done.
Call it a day, I wish they might have said   10
To please the boy by giving him the half hour
That a boy counts so much when saved from work.
His sister stood beside them in her apron
To tell them "Supper." At the word, the saw,
As if to prove saws knew what supper meant,   15
Leaped out at the boy's hand, or seemed to leap—
He must have given the hand. However it was,
Neither refused the meeting. But the hand!
The boy's first outcry was a rueful laugh,
As he swung toward them holding up the hand,   20
Half in appeal, but half as if to keep
The life from spilling. Then the boy saw all—
Since he was old enough to know, big boy
Doing a man's work, though a child at heart—
He saw all spoiled. "Don't let him cut my hand off—   25
The doctor, when he comes. Don't let him, sister!"
So. But the hand was gone already.
The doctor put him in the dark of ether.
He lay and puffed his lips out with his breath.
And then—the watcher at his pulse took fright.   30
No one believed. They listened at his heart.
Little—less—nothing!—and that ended it.
No more to build on there. And they, since they
Were not the one dead, turned to their affairs.

[handwritten: Un necessary death, but no one cares]

[handwritten: Death is not seen as a big deal -like in war, No one cares because it wasn't them]

1916

---

1. From Shakespeare's *Macbeth* (5.5.23–24): "Out, out, brief candle! / Life's but a walking shadow."

Fire and Ice

Some say the world will end in fire,
Some say in ice.
From what I've tasted of desire
I hold with those who favor fire.
But if it had to perish twice,   5
I think I know enough of hate
To say that for destruction ice
Is also great
And would suffice.

1923

Nothing Gold Can Stay

Nature's first green is gold,
Her hardest hue to hold.
Her early leaf's a flower;
But only so an hour.
Then leaf subsides to leaf.   5
So Eden sank to grief,
So dawn goes down to day.
Nothing gold can stay.

1923

Stopping by Woods on a Snowy Evening

Whose woods these are I think I know.
His house is in the village, though;
He will not see me stopping here
To watch his woods fill up with snow.

My little horse must think it queer   5
To stop without a farmhouse near
Between the woods and frozen lake
The darkest evening of the year.

He gives his harness bells a shake
To ask if there is some mistake.   10
The only other sound's the sweep
Of easy wind and downy flake.

The woods are lovely, dark, and deep,
But I have promises to keep,
And miles to go before I sleep.   15
And miles to go before I sleep.

1923

Desert Places

Snow falling and night falling fast, oh, fast
In a field I looked into going past,
And the ground almost covered smooth in snow,
But a few weeds and stubble showing last.

The woods around it have it—it is theirs.   5
All animals are smothered in their lairs.
I am too absent-spirited to count;
The loneliness includes me unawares.

And lonely as it is, that loneliness
Will be more lonely ere it will be less—   10
A blanker whiteness of benighted snow
With no expression, nothing to express.

They cannot scare me with their empty spaces
Between stars—on stars where no human race is.
I have it in me so much nearer home   15
To scare myself with my own desert places.

1936

4. Design

[handwritten: Variation of a petrarchen poem / everything is white but it is a "Dark image"]

[handwritten: gropulta in ohros]

I found a dimpled spider, fat and white,   A
On a white heal-all,[1] holding up a moth   B   *[handwritten: reatamore]*
Like a white piece of rigid satin cloth—   B
Assorted characters of death and blight   A
Mixed ready to begin the morning right,   A   *[handwritten: spumă]*   5
Like the ingredients of a witches' broth—   B
A snow-drop spider, a flower like a froth,   B   *[handwritten: zmen]*
And dead wings carried like a paper kite.   A

[handwritten: white vs. dark]

What had that flower to do with being white,   q
The wayside blue and innocent heal-all?   C   *[handwritten: hunger (in strict)]*
What brought the kindred spider to that height,   A   10
Then steered the white moth thither in the night?   A
What but design of darkness to appall?—   C
If design govern in a thing so small.   C

[handwritten: maybe things just happen / Nothing controlling small things / loss of control]
[handwritten: Where is the good force in the world]

1922, 1936

[handwritten: There is no good/bad in nature, just survival.]

1. Common wildflower whose blossom is normally violet or blue.

5. Neither Out Far Nor In Deep

The people along the sand
All turn and look one way.
They turn their back on the land.
They look at the sea all day.

As long as it takes to pass   5
A ship keeps raising its hull;
The wetter ground like glass
Reflects a standing gull.

The land may vary more;
But wherever the truth may be—   10
The water comes ashore,
And the people look at the sea.

They cannot look out far.
They cannot look in deep.
But when was that ever a bar   15
To any watch they keep?

1936

Directive

Back out of all this now too much for us,
Back in a time made simple by the loss
Of detail, burned, dissolved, and broken off
Like graveyard marble sculpture in the weather,
There is a house that is no more a house   5
Upon a farm that is no more a farm
And in a town that is no more a town.
The road there, if you'll let a guide direct you
Who only has at heart your getting lost,
May seem as if it should have been a quarry—   10
Great monolithic knees the former town
Long since gave up pretense of keeping covered.
And there's a story in a book about it:
Besides the wear of iron wagon wheels
The ledges show lines ruled southeast-northwest,   15
The chisel work of an enormous Glacier
That braced his feet against the Arctic Pole.
You must not mind a certain coolness from him
Still said to haunt this side of Panther Mountain.
Nor need you mind the serial ordeal   20
Of being watched from forty cellar holes

As if by eye pairs out of forty firkins.[1]
As for the woods' excitement over you
That sends light rustle rushes to their leaves,
Charge that to upstart inexperience.   25
Where were they all not twenty years ago?
They think too much of having shaded out
A few old pecker-fretted[2] apple trees.
Make yourself up a cheering song of how
Someone's road home from work this once was,   30
Who may be just ahead of you on foot
Or creaking with a buggy load of grain.
The height of the adventure is the height
Of country where two village cultures faded
Into each other. Both of them are lost.   35
And if you're lost enough to find yourself
By now, pull in your ladder road behind you
And put a sign up CLOSED to all but me.
Then make yourself at home. The only field
Now left's no bigger than a harness gall.[3]   40
First there's the children's house of make-believe,
Some shattered dishes underneath a pine,
The playthings in the playhouse of the children.
Weep for what little things could make them glad.
Then for the house that is no more a house,   45
But only a belilaced cellar hole,
Now slowly closing like a dent in dough.
This was no playhouse but a house in earnest.
Your destination and your destiny's
A brook that was the water of the house,   50
Cold as a spring as yet so near its source,
Too lofty and original to rage.
(We know the valley streams that when aroused
Will leave their tatters hung on barb and thorn.)
I have kept hidden in the instep arch   55
Of an old cedar at the waterside
A broken drinking goblet like the Grail[4]
Under a spell so the wrong ones can't find it,
So can't get saved, as Saint Mark[5] says they mustn't.
(I stole the goblet from the children's playhouse.)   60
Here are your waters and your watering place.
Drink and be whole again beyond confusion.

                                                               1947

---

1. Small wooden tubs for butter or lard.
2. Marked up with small holes by woodpeckers.
3. Sore on a horse's skin caused by the rubbing of the harness.
4. The cup used by Jesus at the Last Supper. According to legend, the Grail later disappeared from its keepers because of their moral impurity,
and various knights, including those of King Arthur's Round Table, went in quest of it. From this, the quest for the Grail has come to symbolize any spiritual search.
5. A reference to the Gospel of Mark, 4.11–12; see also Mark 16.16.

SUSAN GLASPELL
1876–1948

Susan Glaspell—journalist, novelist, short-story writer, playwright, theatrical producer and director, actor—was a multitalented professional who eventually published more than fifty short stories, nine novels, and fourteen plays. Feminist rediscovery of *Trifles*, her first play—written and produced in 1916 and turned into a prize-winning short story, "A Jury of Her Peers," in 1917—has made this her best-known work today.

Born and raised in Davenport, Iowa, Glaspell worked for a year on the Davenport *Morning Republican* after high school graduation, then attended Drake University in Des Moines from 1895 to 1899. In college she wrote for the campus newspaper as well as various Des Moines papers; after graduation she worked for two years on the Des Moines *Daily News*. In 1901 she abandoned journalism, returning to Davenport with a plan to earn her living as a fiction writer. Her early stories, combining regional midwestern settings with romantic plots, found favor with the editors of such popular magazines as *Harper's*, the *Ladies' Home Journal*, the *American Magazine*, and the *Woman's Home Companion*. In 1909 she published her first novel, *The Glory of the Conquered*.

In 1913 she married the recently divorced George Cram Cook, a Harvard-educated native of Davenport, who was a writer and theatrical director much interested in modernist experimentation. The two moved to the East Coast, traveled widely, and collaborated on many projects. They helped found both the Washington Square Players in 1914 and the group that came to be known as the Provincetown Players in 1916.

The Provincetown Players, named for the New England seaport town where many of the members spent their summers, aimed to foster an American theater by producing plays by American playwrights only. Eugene O'Neill became the best-known dramatist of the group; Glaspell was a close second. She not only wrote plays but also acted in them, directed them, and helped produce them. From 1916 to 1922 she wrote nine plays, including *Trifles*, for the Provincetown Players; in 1922 Cook and Glaspell withdrew from the group, finding that it had become too commercially successful to suit their experimental aims.

Cook died in 1924; a later close relationship, with the novelist and playwright Norman Matson, ended in 1932. Throughout the 1930s and 1940s, Glaspell, now a year-round resident of Provincetown, continued to write and publish. Her novel *Judd Rankin's Wife* (1928) was made into a movie. She won the 1930 Pulitzer Prize for drama for *Alison's Room*, a play loosely based on the life of Emily Dickinson. Her last novel, *Judd Rankin's Daughter*, appeared in 1945, three years before she died at the age of seventy-two.

For Glaspell, the influence of such European playwrights as Henrik Ibsen and August Strindberg opened the door to much grimmer writing in a play like *Trifles* than in her popular short stories, with their formulaic happy endings. Her realism—her unsparing depiction of women's narrow, thwarted, isolated, and subjugated lives in rural, regional settings—produces effects quite unlike the nostalgic celebrations of woman-centered societies often associated with women regionalists. The efficiently plotted *Trifles* also features a formal device found in other Glaspell works, including *Alison's Room*: the main character at its center never appears.

The text is from *Plays by Susan Glaspell* (1987).

Trifles

CHARACTERS

GEORGE HENDERSON, *County Attorney*
HENRY PETERS, *Sheriff*
LEWIS HALE, *a Neighboring Farmer*
MRS PETERS
MRS HALE

SCENE: *The kitchen in the now abandoned farmhouse of* John Wright, *a gloomy kitchen, and left without having been put in order—unwashed pans under the sink, a loaf of bread outside the bread-box, a dish-towel on the table—other signs of incompleted work. At the rear the outer door opens and the* SHERIFF *comes in followed by the* COUNTY ATTORNEY *and* HALE. *The* SHERIFF *and* HALE *are men in middle life, the* COUNTY ATTORNEY *is a young man; all are much bundled up and go at once to the stove. They are followed by the two women—the* SHERIFF'S *wife first; she is a slight wiry woman, a thin nervous face.* MRS HALE *is larger and would ordinarily be called more comfortable looking, but she is disturbed now and looks fearfully about as she enters. The women have come in slowly, and stand close together near the door.*

COUNTY ATTORNEY [*rubbing his hands*]   This feels good. Come up to the fire, ladies.

MRS PETERS [*after taking a step forward*]   I'm not—cold.

SHERIFF [*unbuttoning his overcoat and stepping away from the stove as if to mark the beginning of official business*]   Now, Mr Hale, before we move things about, you explain to Mr Henderson just what you saw when you came here yesterday morning.

COUNTY ATTORNEY   By the way, has anything been moved? Are things just as you left them yesterday?

SHERIFF [*looking about*]   It's just the same. When it dropped below zero last night I thought I'd better send Frank out this morning to make a fire for us—no use getting pneumonia with a big case on, but I told him not to touch anything except the stove—and you know Frank.

COUNTY ATTORNEY   Somebody should have been left here yesterday.

SHERIFF   Oh—yesterday. When I had to send Frank to Morris Center for that man who went crazy—I want you to know I had my hands full yesterday. I knew you could get back from Omaha by today and as long as I went over everything here myself—

COUNTY ATTORNEY   Well, Mr Hale, tell just what happened when you came here yesterday morning.

HALE   Harry and I had started to town with a load of potatoes. We came along the road from my place and as I got here I said, 'I'm going to see if I can't get John Wright to go in with me on a party telephone.'[1] I spoke to Wright about it once before and he put me off, saying folks talked too much anyway, and all he asked was peace and quiet—I guess you know about how much he talked himself; but I thought maybe if I went to the house and talked about it before his wife, though I said to Harry that I didn't know as what his wife wanted made much difference to John—

---

1. A single telephone line shared by several households.

COUNTY ATTORNEY   Let's talk about that later, Mr Hale. I do want to talk about that, but tell now just what happened when you got to the house.

HALE   I didn't hear or see anything; I knocked at the door, and still it was all quiet inside. I knew they must be up, it was past eight o'clock. So I knocked again, and I thought I heard somebody say, 'Come in.' I wasn't sure. I'm not sure yet, but I opened the door—this door [*indicating the door by which the two women are still standing*] and there in that rocker— [*pointing to it*] sat Mrs Wright.

　　　[*They all look at the rocker.*]

COUNTY ATTORNEY   What—was she doing?

HALE   She was rockin' back and forth. She had her apron in her hand and was kind of—pleating it.

COUNTY ATTORNEY   And how did she—look?

HALE   Well, she looked queer.

COUNTY ATTORNEY   How do you mean—queer?

HALE   Well, as if she didn't know what she was going to do next. And kind of done up.

COUNTY ATTORNEY   How did she seem to feel about your coming?

HALE   Why, I don't think she minded—one way or other. She didn't pay much attention. I said, 'How do. Mrs Wright it's cold, ain't it?' And she said, 'Is it?'—and went on kind of pleating at her apron. Well, I was sur-prised: she didn't ask me to come up to the stove, or to set down, but just sat there, not even looking at me, so I said, 'I want to see John.' And then she—laughed. I guess you would call it a laugh. I thought of Harry and the team outside, so I said a little sharp: 'Can't I see John?' 'No,' she says, kind o' dull like. 'Ain't he home?' says I. 'Yes,' says she, 'he's home.' 'Then why can't I see him?' I asked her, out of patience. ' 'Cause he's dead,' says she. *'Dead?'* says I. She just nodded her head, not getting a bit excited, but rockin' back and forth. 'Why—where is he?' says I, not knowing what to say. She just pointed upstairs—like that [*himself pointing to the room above*] I got up, with the idea of going up there. I walked from there to here—then I says, 'Why, what did he die of?' 'He died of a rope round his neck,' says she, and just went on pleatin' at her apron. Well, I went out and called Harry. I thought I might—need help. We went upstairs and there he was lyin'—

COUNTY ATTORNEY   I think I'd rather have you go into that upstairs, where you can point it all out. Just go on now with the rest of the story.

HALE   Well, my first thought was to get that rope off. It looked . . . [*stops, his face twitches*] . . . but Harry, he went up to him, and he said, 'No, he's dead all right, and we'd better not touch anything.' So we went back down stairs. She was still sitting that same way. 'Has anybody been notified?' I asked. 'No,' says she unconcerned. 'Who did this, Mrs Wright?' said Harry. He said it business-like—and she stopped pleatin' of her apron. 'I don't know,' she says. 'You don't *know?*' says Harry. 'No,' says she. 'Weren't you sleepin' in the bed with him?' says Harry. 'Yes,' says she, 'but I was on the inside.' 'Somebody slipped a rope round his neck and strangled him and you didn't wake up?' says Harry. 'I didn't wake up,' she said after him. We must 'a looked as if we didn't see how that could be, for after a minute she said, 'I sleep sound.' Harry was going to ask her more questions but I said maybe we ought to let her tell her story first to the coroner, or the sheriff, so Harry went fast as he could to Rivers' place, where there's a telephone.

COUNTY ATTORNEY And what did Mrs Wright do when she knew that you had gone for the coroner?

HALE She moved from that chair to this one over here [*pointing to a small chair in the corner*] and just sat there with her hands held together and looking down. I got a feeling that I ought to make some conversation, so I said I had come in to see if John wanted to put in a telephone, and at that she started to laugh, and then she stopped and looked at me—scared. [*the* COUNTY ATTORNEY, *who has had his notebook out, makes a note*] I dunno, maybe it wasn't scared. I wouldn't like to say it was. Soon Harry got back, and then Dr Lloyd came, and you, Mr Peters, and so I guess that's all I know that you don't.

COUNTY ATTORNEY [*looking around*] I guess we'll go upstairs first—and then out to the barn and around there. [*to the* SHERIFF] You're convinced that there was nothing important here—nothing that would point to any motive.

SHERIFF Nothing here but kitchen things.

[*The* COUNTY ATTORNEY, *after again looking around the kitchen, opens the door of a cupboard closet. He gets up on a chair and looks on a shelf. Pulls his hand away, sticky.*]

COUNTY ATTORNEY Here's a nice mess.

[*The women draw nearer.*]

MRS PETERS [*to the other woman*] Oh, her fruit: it did freeze. [*to the* LAWYER] She worried about that when it turned so cold. She said the fire'd go out and her jars would break.

SHERIFF Well, can you beat the women! Held for murder and worryin' about her preserves.

COUNTY ATTORNEY I guess before we're through she may have something more serious than preserves to worry about.

HALE Well, women are used to worrying over trifles.

[*The two women move a little closer together.*]

COUNTY ATTORNEY [*with the gallantry of a young politician*] And yet, for all their worries, what would we do without the ladies? [*the women do not unbend. He goes to the sink, takes a dipperful of water from the pail and pouring it into a basin, washes his hands. Starts to wipe them on the roller-towel, turns it for a cleaner place*] Dirty towels! [*kicks his foot against the pans under the sink*] Not much of a housekeeper, would you say, ladies?

MRS HALE [*stiffly*] There's a great deal of work to be done on a farm.

COUNTY ATTORNEY To be sure. And yet [*with a little bow to her*] I know there are some Dickson county farmhouses which do not have such roller towels.

[*He gives it a pull to expose its length again.*]

MRS HALE Those towels get dirty awful quick. Men's hands aren't always as clean as they might be.

COUNTY ATTORNEY Ah, loyal to your sex. I see. But you and Mrs Wright were neighbors. I suppose you were friends, too.

MRS HALE [*shaking her head*] I've not seen much of her of late years. I've not been in this house—it's more than a year.

COUNTY ATTORNEY And why was that? You didn't like her?

MRS HALE I liked her all well enough. Farmers' wives have their hands full, Mr Henderson. And then—

COUNTY ATTORNEY Yes—?

MRS HALE [*looking about*]   It never seemed a very cheerful place.

COUNTY ATTORNEY   No—it's not cheerful. I shouldn't say she had the homemaking instinct.

MRS HALE   Well, I don't know as Wright had, either.

COUNTY ATTORNEY   You mean that they didn't get on very well?

MRS HALE   No. I don't mean anything. But I don't think a place'd be any cheerfuller for John Wright's being in it.

COUNTY ATTORNEY   I'd like to talk more of that a little later. I want to get the lay of things upstairs now.
    [*He goes to the left, where three steps lead to a stair door.*]

SHERIFF   I suppose anything Mrs Peters does'll be all right. She was to take in some clothes for her, you know, and a few little things. We left in such a hurry yesterday.

COUNTY ATTORNEY   Yes, but I would like to see what you take, Mrs Peters, and keep an eye out for anything that might be of use to us.

MRS PETERS   Yes, Mr Henderson.
    [*The women listen to the men's steps on the stairs, then look about the kitchen.*]

MRS HALE   I'd hate to have men coming into my kitchen, snooping around and criticising.
    [*She arranges the pans under sink which the* LAWYER *had shoved out of place.*]

MRS PETERS   Of course it's no more than their duty.

MRS HALE   Duty's all right, but I guess that deputy sheriff that came out to make the fire might have got a little of this on. [*gives the roller towel a pull*] Wish I'd thought of that sooner. Seems mean to talk about her for not having things slicked up when she had to come away in such a hurry.

MRS PETERS [*who has gone to a small table in the left rear corner of the room, and lifted one end of a towel that covers a pan*]   She had bread set.
    [*Stands still.*]

MRS HALE [*eyes fixed on a loaf of bread beside the bread-box, which is on a low shelf at the other side of the room. Moves slowly toward it*]   She was going to put this in there. [*picks up loaf, then abruptly drops it. In a manner of returning to familiar things*] It's a shame about her fruit. I wonder if it's all gone. [*gets up on the chair and looks*] I think there's some here that's all right, Mrs Peters. Yes—here; [*holding it toward the window*] this is cherries, too. [*looking again*] I declare I believe that's the only one. [*gets down, bottle in her hand. Goes to the sink and wipes it off on the outside*] She'll feel awful bad after all her hard work in the hot weather. I remember the afternoon I put up my cherries last summer.
    [*She puts the bottle on the big kitchen table, center of the room. With a sigh, is about to sit down in the rocking-chair. Before she is seated realizes what chair it is; with a slow look at it, steps back. The chair which she has touched rocks back and forth.*]

MRS PETERS   Well, I must get those things from the front room closet. [*she goes to the door at the right, but after looking into the other room, steps back*] You coming with me, Mrs Hale? You could help me carry them.
    [*They go in the other room; reappear,* MRS PETERS *carrying a dress and skirt,* MRS HALE *following with a pair of shoes.*]

MRS PETERS   My, it's cold in there.
    [*She puts the clothes on the big table and hurries to the stove.*]

MRS HALE [*examining the skirt*]   Wright was close.[2] I think maybe that's why she kept so much to herself. She didn't even belong to the Ladies Aid. I suppose she felt she couldn't do her part, and then you don't enjoy things when you feel shabby. She used to wear pretty clothes and be lively, when she was Minnie Foster, one of the town girls singing in the choir. But that—oh, that was thirty years ago. This all you was to take in?

MRS PETERS   She said she wanted an apron. Funny thing to want, for there isn't much to get you dirty in jail, goodness knows. But I suppose just to make her feel more natural. She said they was in the top drawer in this cupboard. Yes, here. And then her little shawl that always hung behind the door. [*opens stair door and looks*] Yes, here it is.
        [*Quickly shuts door leading upstairs.*]

MRS HALE [*abruptly moving toward her*]   Mrs Peters?

MRS PETERS   Yes, Mrs Hale?

MRS HALE   Do you think she did it?

MRS PETERS [*in a frightened voice*]   Oh, I don't know.

MRS HALE   Well, I don't think she did. Asking for an apron and her little shawl. Worrying about her fruit.

MRS PETERS [*starts to speak, glances up, where footsteps are heard in the room above. In a low voice*]   Mr Peters says it looks bad for her. Mr Henderson is awful sarcastic in a speech and he'll make fun of her sayin' she didn't wake up.

MRS HALE   Well, I guess John Wright didn't wake when they was slipping that rope under his neck.

MRS PETERS   No, it's strange. It must have been done awful crafty and still. They say it was such a—funny way to kill a man, rigging it all up like that.

MRS HALE   That's just what Mr Hale said. There was a gun in the house. He says that's what he can't understand.

MRS PETERS   Mr Henderson said coming out that what was needed for the case was a motive; something to show anger, or—sudden feeling.

MRS HALE [*who is standing by the table*]   Well, I don't see any signs of anger around here. [*she puts her hand on the dish-towel which lies on the table, stands looking down at table, one half of which is clean, the other half messy*] It's wiped to here. [*makes a move as if to finish work, then turns and looks at loaf of bread outside the bread-box. Drops towel. In that voice of coming back to familiar things.*] Wonder how they are finding things upstairs. I hope she had it a little more red-up[3] up there. You know, it seems kind of *sneaking.* Locking her up in town and then coming out here and trying to get her own house to turn against her!

MRS PETERS   But Mrs Hale, the law is the law.

MRS HALE   I s'pose 'tis. [*unbuttoning her coat*] Better loosen up your things, Mrs Peters. You won't feel them when you go out.
        [MRS PETERS *takes off her fur tippet,*[4] *goes to hang it on hook at back of room, stands looking at the under part of the small corner table.*]

MRS PETERS   She was piecing a quilt.
        [*She brings the large sewing basket and they look at the bright pieces.*]

MRS HALE   It's log cabin pattern. Pretty, isn't it? I wonder if she was goin' to quilt it or just knot it?

---

2. Miserly.
3. Tidy.

4. Short cape, falling just below the shoulders.

[*Footsteps have been heard coming down the stairs. The* SHERIFF *enters followed by* HALE *and the* COUNTY ATTORNEY.]

SHERIFF   They wonder if she was going to quilt it or just knot it!

[*The men laugh, the women look abashed.*]

COUNTY ATTORNEY [*rubbing his hands over the stove*]   Frank's fire didn't do much up there, did it? Well, let's go out to the barn and get that cleared up.

[*The men go outside.*]

MRS HALE [*resentfully*]   I don't know as there's anything so strange, our takin' up our time with little things while we're waiting for them to get the evidence. [*she sits down at the big table smoothing out a block with decision*] I don't see as it's anything to laugh about.

MRS PETERS [*apologetically*]   Of course they've got awful important things on their minds.

[*Pulls up a chair and joins* MRS HALE *at the table.*]

MRS HALE [*examining another block*]   Mrs Peters, look at this one. Here, this is the one she was working on, and look at the sewing! All the rest of it has been so nice and even. And look at this! It's all over the place! Why, it looks as if she didn't know what she was about!

[*After she has said this they look at each other, then start to glance back at the door. After an instant* MRS HALE *has pulled at a knot and ripped the sewing.*]

MRS PETERS   Oh, what are you doing, Mrs Hale?

MRS HALE [*mildly*]   Just pulling out a stitch or two that's not sewed very good. [*threading a needle*] Bad sewing always made me fidgety.

MRS PETERS [*nervously*]   I don't think we ought to touch things.

MRS HALE   I'll just finish up this end. [*suddenly stopping and leaning forward*] Mrs Peters?

MRS PETERS   Yes, Mrs Hale?

MRS HALE   What do you suppose she was so nervous about?

MRS PETERS   Oh—I don't know. I don't know as she was nervous. I sometimes sew awful queer when I'm just tired. [MRS HALE *starts to say something, looks at* MRS PETERS, *then goes on sewing*] Well I must get these things wrapped up. They may be through sooner than we think. [*putting apron and other things together*] I wonder where I can find a piece of paper, and string.

MRS HALE   In that cupboard, maybe.

MRS PETERS [*looking in cupboard*]   Why, here's a bird-cage. [*holds it up*] Did she have a bird, Mrs Hale?

MRS HALE   Why, I don't know whether she did or not—I've not been here for so long. There was a man around last year selling canaries cheap, but I don't know as she took one; maybe she did. She used to sing real pretty herself.

MRS PETERS [*glancing around*]   Seems funny to think of a bird here. But she must have had one, or why would she have a cage? I wonder what happened to it.

MRS HALE   I s'pose maybe the cat got it.

MRS PETERS   No, she didn't have a cat. She's got that feeling some people have about cats—being afraid of them. My cat got in her room and she was real upset and asked me to take it out.

MRS HALE   My sister Bessie was like that. Queer, ain't it?

MRS PETERS [*examining the cage*]   Why, look at this door. It's broke. One hinge is pulled apart.

MRS HALE [*looking too*]   Looks as if someone must have been rough with it.

MRS PETERS   Why, yes.

[*She brings the cage forward and puts it on the table.*]

MRS HALE   I wish if they're going to find any evidence they'd be about it. I don't like this place.

MRS PETERS   But I'm awful glad you came with me, Mrs Hale. It would be lonesome for me sitting here alone.

MRS HALE   It would, wouldn't it? [*dropping her sewing*] But I tell you what I do wish, Mrs Peters. I wish I had come over sometimes when *she* was here. I—[*looking around the room*]—wish I had.

MRS PETERS   But of course you were awful busy. Mrs Hale—your house and your children.

MRS HALE   I could've come. I stayed away because it weren't cheerful—and that's why I ought to have come. I—I've never liked this place. Maybe because it's down in a hollow and you don't see the road. I dunno what it is, but it's a lonesome place and always was. I wish I had come over to see Minnie Foster sometimes. I can see now—[*shakes her head*]

MRS PETERS   Well, you mustn't reproach yourself, Mrs Hale. Somehow we just don't see how it is with other folks until—something comes up.

MRS HALE   Not having children makes less work—but it makes a quiet house, and Wright out to work all day, and no company when he did come in. Did you know John Wright, Mrs Peters?

MRS PETERS   Not to know him; I've seen him in town. They say he was a good man.

MRS HALE   Yes—good; he didn't drink, and kept his word as well as most, I guess, and paid his debts. But he was a hard man, Mrs Peters. Just to pass the time of day with him—[*shivers*] Like a raw wind that gets to the bone. [*pauses, her eye falling on the cage*] I should think she would a wanted a bird. But what do you suppose went with it?

MRS PETERS   I don't know, unless it got sick and died.

[*She reaches over and swings the broken door, swings it again, both women watch it.*]

MRS HALE   You weren't raised round here, were you? [MRS PETERS *shakes her head*] You didn't know—her?

MRS PETERS   Not till they brought her yesterday.

MRS HALE   She—come to think of it, she was kind of like a bird herself—real sweet and pretty, but kind of timid and—fluttery. How—she—did—change. [*silence: then as if struck by a happy thought and relieved to get back to everyday things*] Tell you what, Mrs Peters, why don't you take the quilt in with you? It might take up her mind.

MRS PETERS   Why, I think that's a real nice idea, Mrs Hale. There couldn't possibly be any objection to it, could there? Now, just what would I take? I wonder if her patches are in here—and her things.

[*They look in the sewing basket.*]

MRS HALE   Here's some red. I expect this has got sewing things in it. [*brings out a fancy box*] What a pretty box. Looks like something somebody would give you. Maybe her scissors are in here. [*Opens box. Suddenly puts her hand to her nose*] Why—[MRS PETERS *bends nearer, then turns her face away*] There's something wrapped up in this piece of silk.

MRS PETERS   Why, this isn't her scissors.

MRS HALE [*lifting the silk*]   Oh, Mrs Peters—it's—

[MRS PETERS *bends closer.*]

MRS PETERS   It's the bird.

MRS HALE [*jumping up*]   But, Mrs Peters—look at it! It's neck! Look at its neck! It's all—other side *to*.

MRS PETERS   Somebody—wrung—its—neck.

[*Their eyes meet. A look of growing comprehension, of horror. Steps are heard outside.* MRS HALE *slips box under quilt pieces, and sinks into her chair. Enter* SHERIFF *and* COUNTY ATTORNEY. MRS PETERS *rises.*]

COUNTY ATTORNEY [*as one turning from serious things to little pleasantries*]   Well ladies, have you decided whether she was going to quilt it or knot it?

MRS PETERS   We think she was going to—knot it.

COUNTY ATTORNEY   Well, that's interesting, I'm sure. [*seeing the bird-cage*] Has the bird flown?

MRS HALE [*putting more quilt pieces over the box*]   We think the—cat got it.

COUNTY ATTORNEY [*preoccupied*]   Is there a cat?

[MRS HALE *glances in a quick covert way at* MRS PETERS.]

MRS PETERS   Well, not *now*. They're superstitious, you know. They leave.

COUNTY ATTORNEY [*to* SHERIFF PETERS, *continuing an interrupted conversation*]   No sign at all of anyone having come from the outside. Their own rope. Now let's go up again and go over it piece by piece. [*they start upstairs*] It would have to have been someone who knew just the—

[MRS PETERS *sits down. The two women sit there not looking at one another, but as if peering into something and at the same time holding back. When they talk now it is in the manner of feeling their way over strange ground, as if afraid of what they are saying, but as if they can not help saying it.*]

MRS HALE   She liked the bird. She was going to bury it in that pretty box.

MRS PETERS [*in a whisper*]   When I was a girl—my kitten—there was a boy took a hatchet, and before my eyes—and before I could get there—[*covers her face an instant*] If they hadn't held me back I would have—[*catches herself, looks upstairs where steps are heard, falters weakly*]—hurt him.

MRS HALE [*with a slow look around her*]   I wonder how it would seem never to have had any children around. [*pause*] No, Wright wouldn't like the bird—a thing that sang. She used to sing. He killed that, too.

MRS PETERS [*moving uneasily*]   We don't know who killed the bird.

MRS HALE   I knew John Wright.

MRS PETERS   It was an awful thing was done in this house that night, Mrs Hale. Killing a man while he slept, slipping a rope around his neck that choked the life out of him.

MRS HALE   His neck. Choked the life out of him.

[*Her hand goes out and rests on the bird-cage.*]

MRS PETERS [*with rising voice*]   We don't know who killed him. We don't know.

MRS HALE [*her own feeling not interrupted*]   If there'd been years and years of nothing, then a bird to sing to you, it would be awful—still, after the bird was still.

MRS PETERS [*something within her speaking*]   I know what stillness is. When we homesteaded in Dakota, and my first baby died—after he was two years old, and me with no other then—

MRS HALE [*moving*]   How soon do you suppose they'll be through, looking for the evidence?

MRS PETERS   I know what stillness is. [*pulling herself back*] The law has got to punish crime, Mrs Hale.

MRS HALE [*not as if answering that*]   I wish you'd seen Minnie Foster when she wore a white dress with blue ribbons and stood up there in the choir and sang. [*a look around the room*] Oh, I *wish* I'd come over here once in a while! That was a crime! That was a crime! Who's going to punish that?

MRS PETERS [*looking upstairs*]   We mustn't—take on.

MRS HALE   I might have known she needed help! I know how things can be—for women. I tell you, it's queer. Mrs Peters. We live close together and we live far apart. We all go through the same things—it's all just a different kind of the same thing. [*brushes her eyes, noticing the bottle of fruit, reaches out for it*] If I was you, I wouldn't tell her her fruit was gone. Tell her it *ain't*. Tell her it's all right. Take this in to prove it to her. She—she may never know whether it was broke or not.

MRS PETERS [*takes the bottle, looks about for something to wrap it in; takes petticoat from the clothes brought from the other room, very nervously begins winding this around the bottle. In a false voice*]   My, it's a good thing the men couldn't hear us. Wouldn't they just laugh! Getting all stirred up over a little thing like a—dead canary. As if that could have anything to do with—with—wouldn't they *laugh!*

[*The men are heard coming down stairs.*]

MRS HALE [*under her breath*]   Maybe they would—maybe they wouldn't.

COUNTY ATTORNEY   No, Peters, it's all perfectly clear except a reason for doing it. But you know juries when it comes to women. If there was some definite thing. Something to show—something to make a story about—a thing that would connect up with this strange way of doing it—

[*The women's eyes meet for an instant. Enter* HALE *from outer door.*]

HALE   Well. I've got the team around. Pretty cold out there.

COUNTY ATTORNEY   I'm going to stay here a while by myself. [*to the* SHERIFF] You can send Frank out for me, can't you? I want to go over everything. I'm not satisfied that we can't do better.

SHERIFF   Do you want to see what Mrs Peters is going to take in?

[*The* LAWYER *goes to the table, picks up the apron, laughs.*]

COUNTY ATTORNEY   Oh, I guess they're not very dangerous things the ladies have picked out. [*Moves a few things about, disturbing the quilt pieces which cover the box. Steps back*] No, Mrs Peters doesn't need supervising. For that matter, a sheriff's wife is married to the law. Ever think of it that way, Mrs Peters?

MRS PETERS   Not—just that way.

SHERIFF [*chuckling*]   Married to the law. [*moves toward the other room*] I just want you to come in here a minute, George. We ought to take a look at these windows.

COUNTY ATTORNEY [*scoffingly*]   Oh, windows!

SHERIFF   We'll be right out, Mr Hale.

[HALE *goes outside. The* SHERIFF *follows the* COUNTY ATTORNEY *into the other room. Then* MRS HALE *rises, hands tight together, looking intensely at* MRS PETERS, *whose eyes make a slow turn, finally meeting* MRS HALE's. *A moment* MRS HALE *holds her, then her own eyes point the way to where the box is concealed. Suddenly* MRS PETERS *throws back quilt pieces and tries to put the box in the bag she is wearing. It is too big. She opens box, starts to take bird out, cannot touch it, goes to pieces, stands there helpless. Sound of a knob turning in the other room.* MRS HALE *snatches the box and puts it in the pocket of her big coat. Enter* COUNTY ATTORNEY *and* SHERIFF.]

COUNTY ATTORNEY [*facetiously*]   Well, Henry, at least we found out that she was not going to quilt it. She was going to—what is it you call it, ladies?

MRS HALE [*her hand against her pocket*]   We call it—knot it, Mr Henderson.

CURTAIN

1916

SHERWOOD ANDERSON
1876–1941

Sherwood Anderson was approaching middle age when he abandoned a successful business career to become a writer. Living in Chicago, New Orleans, and Paris, meeting literary people, he worked furiously to make up for his late start, producing novels, short stories, essays, and an autobiography. His short fiction provided a model for younger writers, whose careers he encouraged by literary advice and by practical help in getting published as well. *Winesburg, Ohio,* which appeared in 1919 when he was forty-three years old, remains a major work of experimental fiction and was in its time a bold treatment of small-town life in the American Midwest in the tradition of Edgar Lee Masters's *Spoon River Anthology.*

Anderson was born in southern Ohio, the third of seven children in a family headed by a father whose training and skill as a harness maker were becoming useless in the new world of the automobile. Anderson's father kept his family on the move in search of work; the stamina and tenderness of his mother supplied coherence and security in this nomadic life. Not until 1894, when Anderson was sixteen, did they settle down in the town of Clyde, Ohio, which became the model for Winesburg. Anderson never finished high school. He held a variety of jobs, living in Chicago with an older brother in 1896 and again in 1900 when he worked as an advertising copywriter.

His first wife came from a successful Ohio business family; the couple settled in Ohio where Anderson managed a mail-order house as well as two paint firms. But he found increasingly that the need to write conflicted with his career. In 1912 he left his business and his marriage, returning to Chicago, where he met the writers and artists whose activities were creating the Chicago Renaissance. These included the novelists Floyd Dell and Theodore Dreiser; the poets Edgar Lee Masters, Vachel Lindsay, and Carl Sandburg; and the editors Harriet Monroe of *Poetry* and Margaret C. Anderson of the *Little Review.* His first major publication was *Windy McPherson's Son* (1916), the story of a man who runs away from a small Iowa town in futile search for life's meaning; his second was *Marching Men* (1917), about a charismatic lawyer who tries—unsuccessfully—to reorganize the factory system in a small town. These books reveal three of Anderson's preoccupations: the individual quest for self and social betterment, the small-town environment, and the distrust of modern industrial society.

Missing, however, is the interest in human psychology and the sense of conflict between inner and outer worlds that appear in *Winesburg* and later works.

In 1916 Anderson began writing and publishing the tales that were brought together in *Winesburg, Ohio*. The formal achievement of the book lay in its articulation of individual tales to a loose but coherent structure. The lives of a number of people living in the town of Winesburg are observed by the naïve adolescent George Willard, a reporter for the local newspaper. Their stories contribute to his understanding of life and to his preparation for a career as a writer. The book ends when his mother dies and he leaves Winesburg. With the help of the narrator, whose vision is larger than George's, the reader can see how the lives of the characters have been profoundly distorted by the frustration and suppression of so many of their desires. Anderson calls these characters "grotesques," but the intention of *Winesburg, Ohio* is to show that life in all American small towns is grotesque in the same way. Anderson's attitude toward the characters mixes compassion for the individual with dismay at a social order that can do so much damage. His criticism is not specifically political, however; he is measuring society by a utopian standard of free emotional and sensual expression.

Stylistically Anderson strove for the simplest possible prose, using brief or at least uncomplex sentences and an unsophisticated vocabulary appropriate to the muffled awareness and limited resources of his typical characters. Structurally, his stories build toward a moment when the character breaks out in some frenzied gesture of release that is revelatory of a hidden inner life. In both style and structure Anderson's works were important influences on other writers: he encouraged simplicity and directness of style, made attractive the use of the point of view of outsider characters as a way of criticizing conventional society, and gave the craft of the short story a decided push toward stories presenting a slice of life or a significant moment as opposed to panorama and summary.

Winesburg, Ohio appeared near the beginning of Anderson's literary career, and although he continued writing for two decades, he never repeated its success. His best later work was in short stories, published in three volumes: *The Triumph of the Egg* (1921), *Horses and Men* (1923), and *Death in the Woods and Other Stories* (1933). He also wrote a number of novels, including *Poor White* (1920), *Many Marriages* (1923), *Beyond Desire* (1932), and *Kit Brandon* (1936), as well as free verse, prose poems, plays, and essays. A series of autobiographical volumes advertised his career, attempted to define the writer's vocation in America, and discussed his impact on other writers. The more he claimed, however, the less other writers were willing to allow him; both Hemingway and Faulkner, for example, whom he had met in Paris and New Orleans, respectively, satirized his cult of the simple and thereby disavowed his influence. (In fact, he *had* stimulated and helped both of them—stimulated Hemingway in his quest for stylistic simplicity, Faulkner in his search for the proper subject matter.) During the 1930s Anderson, along with many other writers, was active in liberal causes, and he died at sea on the way to South America while on a goodwill mission for the State Department.

The text is that of *Winesburg, Ohio* (1919).

FROM WINESBURG, OHIO

Hands

Upon the half decayed veranda of a small frame house that stood near the edge of a ravine near the town of Winesburg, Ohio, a fat little old man walked nervously up and down. Across a long field that has been seeded for clover but that had produced only a dense crop of yellow mustard weeds, he could see the public highway along which went a wagon filled with berry pickers returning from the fields. The berry pickers, youths and maidens, laughed and shouted boisterously. A boy clad in a blue shirt leaped from the wagon and attempted to drag after him one of the maidens who screamed and protested shrilly. The feet of the boy in the road kicked up a cloud of dust that floated across the face of the departing sun. Over the long field came a thin girlish voice. "Oh, you Wing Biddlebaum, comb your hair, it's falling into your eyes," commanded the voice to the man, who was bald and whose nervous little hands fiddled about the bare white forehead as though arranging a mass of tangled locks.

Wing Biddlebaum, forever frightened and beset by a ghostly band of doubts, did not think of himself as in any way a part of the life of the town where he had lived for twenty years. Among all the people of Winesburg but one had come close to him. With George Willard, son of Tom Willard, the proprietor of the new Willard House, he had formed something like a friendship. George Willard was the reporter on the *Winesburg Eagle* and sometimes in the evenings he walked out along the highway to Wing Biddlebaum's house. Now as the old man walked up and down on the veranda, his hands moving nervously about, he was hoping that George Willard would come and spend the evening with him. After the wagon containing the berry pickers had passed, he went across the field through the tall mustard weeds and climbing a rail fence peered anxiously along the road to the town. For a moment he stood thus, rubbing his hands together and looking up and down the road, and then, fear overcoming him, ran back to walk again upon the porch on his own house.

In the presence of George Willard, Wing Biddlebaum, who for twenty years had been the town mystery, lost something of his timidity, and his shadowy personality, submerged in a sea of doubts, came forth to look at the world. With the young reporter at his side, he ventured in the light of day into Main Street or strode up and down on the rickety front porch of his own house, talking excitedly. The voice that had been low and trembling became shrill and loud. The bent figure straightened. With a kind of wriggle, like a fish returned to the brook by the fisherman, Biddlebaum the silent began to talk, striving to put into words the ideas that had been accumulated by his mind during long years of silence.

Wing Biddlebaum talked much with his hands. The slender expressive fingers, forever active, forever striving to conceal themselves in his pockets or behind his back, came forth and became the piston rods of his machinery of expression.

The story of Wing Biddlebaum is a story of hands. Their restless activity, like unto the beating of the wings of an imprisoned bird, had given him his name. Some obscure poet of the town had thought of it. The hands alarmed their owner. He wanted to keep them hidden away and looked with amazement at the quiet inexpressive hands of other men who worked beside him in the fields, or passed, driving sleepy teams on country roads.

When he talked to George Willard, Wing Biddlebaum closed his fists and beat with them upon a table or on the walls of his house. The action made him more comfortable. If the desire to talk came to him when the two were walking in the fields, he sought out a stump or the top board of a fence and with his hands pounding busily talked with renewed ease.

The story of Wing Biddlebaum's hands is worth a book in itself. Sympathetically set forth it would tap many strange, beautiful qualities in obscure men. It is a job for a poet. In Winesburg the hands had attracted attention merely because of their activity. With them Wing Biddlebaum had picked as high as a hundred and forty quarts of strawberries in a day. They became his distinguishing feature, the source of his fame. Also they made more grotesque an already grotesque and elusive individuality. Winesburg was proud of the hands of Wing Biddlebaum in the same spirit in which it was proud of Banker White's new stone house and Wesley Moyer's bay stallion, Tony Tip, that had won the two-fifteen trot at the fall races in Cleveland.

As for George Willard, he had many times wanted to ask about the hands. At times an almost overwhelming curiosity had taken hold of him. He felt that there must be a reason for their strange activity and their inclination to keep hidden away and only a growing respect for Wing Biddlebaum kept him from blurting out the questions that were often in his mind.

Once he had been on the point of asking. The two were walking in the fields on a summer afternoon and had stopped to sit upon a grassy bank. All afternoon Wing Biddlebaum had talked as one inspired. By a fence he had stopped and beating like a giant woodpecker upon the top board had shouted at George Willard, condemning his tendency to be too much influenced by the people about him. "You are destroying yourself," he cried. "You have the inclination to be alone and to dream and you are afraid of dreams. You want to be like others in town here. You hear them talk and you try to imitate them."

On the grassy bank Wing Biddlebaum had tried again to drive his point home. His voice became soft and reminiscent, and with a sigh of contentment he launched into a long rambling talk, speaking as one lost in a dream.

Out of the dream Wing Biddlebaum made a picture for George Willard. In the picture men lived again in a kind of pastoral golden age. Across a green open country came clean-limbed young men, some afoot, some mounted upon horses. In crowds the young men came to gather about the feet of an old man who sat beneath a tree in a tiny garden and who talked to them.[1]

Wing Biddlebaum became wholly inspired. For once he forgot the hands. Slowly they stole forth and lay upon George Willard's shoulders. Something new and bold came into the voice that talked. "You must try to forget all you have learned," said the old man. "You must begin to dream. From this time on you must shut your ears to the roaring of the voices."

Pausing in his speech, Wing Biddlebaum looked long and earnestly at George Willard. His eyes glowed. Again he raised the hands to caress the boy and then a look of horror swept over his face.

With a convulsive movement of his body, Wing Biddlebaum sprang to his feet and thrust his hands deep into his trousers pockets. Tears came to his eyes. "I must be getting along home. I can talk no more with you," he said nervously.

---

1. Biddlebaum's picture invokes ideals of the Greek Golden Age generally, and more particularly the image of the Athenian philosopher Socrates (469–399 B.C.E) teaching young Greek aristocrats.

Without looking back, the old man had hurried down the hillside and across a meadow, leaving George Willard perplexed and frightened upon the grassy slope. With a shiver of dread the boy arose and went along the road toward town. "I'll not ask him about his hands," he thought, touched by the memory of the terror he had seen in the man's eyes. "There's something wrong, but I don't want to know what it is. His hands have something to do with his fear of me and of everyone."

And George Willard was right. Let us look briefly into the story of the hands. Perhaps our talking of them will arouse the poet who will tell the hidden wonder story of the influence for which the hands were but fluttering pennants of promise.

In his youth Wing Biddlebaum had been a school teacher in a town in Pennsylvania. He was not then known as Wing Biddlebaum, but went by the less euphonic name of Adolph Myers.[2] As Adolph Myers he was much loved by the boys of his school.

Adolph Myers was meant by nature to be a teacher of youth. He was one of those rare, little-understood men who rule by a power so gentle that it passes as a lovable weakness. In their feeling for the boys under their charge such men are not unlike the finer sort of women in their love of men.

And yet that is but crudely stated. It needs the poet there. With the boys of his school, Adolph Myers had walked in the evening or had sat talking until dusk upon the schoolhouse steps lost in a kind of dream. Here and there went his hands, caressing the shoulders of the boys, playing about the tousled heads. As he talked his voice became soft and musical. There was a caress in that also. In a way the voice and the hands, the stroking of the shoulders and the touching of the hair was a part of the schoolmaster's effort to carry a dream into the young minds. By the caress that was in his fingers he expressed himself. He was one of those men in whom the force that creates life is diffused, not centralized. Under the caress of his hands doubt and disbelief went out of the minds of the boy and they began also to dream.

And then the tragedy. A half-witted boy of the school became enamored of the young master. In his bed at night he imagined unspeakable things and in the morning went forth to tell his dreams as facts. Strange, hideous accusations fell from his loose-hung lips. Through the Pennsylvania town went a shiver. Hidden, shadowy doubts that had been in men's minds concerning Adolph Myers were galvanized into beliefs.

The tragedy did not linger. Trembling lads were jerked out of bed and questioned. "He put his arms about me," said one. "His fingers were always playing in my hair," said another.

One afternoon a man of the town, Henry Bradford, who kept a saloon, came to the schoolhouse door. Calling Adolph Myers into the school yard he began to beat him with his fists. As his hard knuckles beat down into the frightened face of the schoolmaster, his wrath became more and more terrible. Screaming with dismay, the children ran here and there like disturbed insects "I'll teach you to put your hands on my boy, you beast," roared the saloon keeper, who, tired of beating the master, had begun to kick him about the yard.

---

2. Both his adopted surname and his original one underline Biddlebaum's foreignness by labeling him as German and, probably, Jewish.

Adolph Myers was driven from the Pennsylvania town in the night. With lanterns in their hands a dozen men came to the door of the house where he lived alone and commanded that he dress and come forth. It was raining and one of the men had a rope in his hands. They had intended to hang the schoolmaster, but something in his figure, so small, white, and pitiful, touched their hearts and they let him escape. As he ran away into the darkness they repented of their weakness and ran after him, swearing and throwing sticks and great balls of soft mud at the figure that screamed and ran faster and faster into the darkness.

For twenty years Adolph Myers had lived alone in Winesburg. He was but forty but looked sixty-five. The name of Biddlebaum he got from a box of goods seen at a freight station as he hurried through an eastern Ohio town. He had an aunt in Winesburg, a black-toothed old woman who raised chickens, and with her he lived until she died. He had been ill for a year after the experience in Pennsylvania, and after his recovery worked as a day laborer in the fields, going timidly about and striving to conceal his hands. Although he did not understand what had happened he felt that the hands must be to blame. Again and again the fathers of the boys had talked of the hands. "Keep your hands to yourself," the saloon keeper had roared, dancing with fury in the schoolhouse yard.

Upon the veranda of his house by the ravine, Wing Biddlebaum continued to walk up and down until the sun had disappeared and the road beyond the field was lost in the grey shadows. Going into his house he cut slices of bread and spread honey upon them. When the rumble of the evening train that took away the express cars loaded with the day's harvest of berries had passed and restored the silence of the summer night, he went again to walk upon the veranda. In the darkness he could not see the hands and they became quiet. Although he still hungered for the presence of the boy, who was the medium through which he expressed his love of man, the hunger became again a part of his loneliness and his waiting. Lighting a lamp, Wing Biddlebaum washed the few dishes soiled by his simple meal and, setting up a folding cot by the screen door that led to the porch, prepared to undress for the night. A few stray white bread crumbs lay on the cleanly washed floor by the table; putting the lamp upon a low stool he began to pick up the crumbs, carrying them to his mouth one by one with unbelievable rapidity. In the dense blotch of light beneath the table, the kneeling figure looked like a priest engaged in some service of his church. The nervous expressive fingers, flashing in and out of the light, might well have been mistaken for the fingers of the devotee going swiftly through decade after decade of his rosary.[3]

Mother

Elizabeth Willard, the mother of George Willard, was tall and gaunt and her face was marked with smallpox scars. Although she was but forty-five, some obscure disease had taken the fire out of her figure. Listlessly she went about the disorderly old hotel looking at the faded wall-paper and the ragged car-

---

3. String of beads used by Roman Catholics to keep track of prayers, divided into sections or "decades" of ten beads.

pets and, when she was able to be about, doing the work of a chambermaid among beds soiled by the slumbers of fat traveling men. Her husband, Tom Willard, a slender, graceful man with square shoulders, a quick military step, and a black mustache, trained to turn sharply up at the ends, tried to put the wife out of his mind. The presence of the tall ghostly figure, moving slowly through the halls, he took as a reproach to himself. When he thought of her he grew angry and swore. The hotel was unprofitable and forever on the edge of failure and he wished himself out of it. He thought of the old house and the woman who lived there with him as things defeated and done for. The hotel in which he had begun life so hopefully was now a mere ghost of what a hotel should be. As he went spruce and businesslike through the streets of Winesburg, he sometimes stopped and turned quickly about as though fearing that the spirit of the hotel and of the woman would follow him even into the streets. "Damn such a life, damn it!" he sputtered aimlessly.

Tom Willard had a passion for village politics and for years had been the leading Democrat in a strongly Republican community. Some day, he told himself, the tide of things political will turn in my favor and the years of ineffectual service count big in the bestowal of rewards. He dreamed of going to Congress and even of becoming governor. Once when a younger member of the party arose at a political conference and began to boast of his faithful service, Tom Willard grew white with fury. "Shut up, you," he roared, glaring about. "What do you know of service? What are you but a boy? Look at what I've done here! I was a Democrat here in Winesburg when it was a crime to be a Democrat. In the old days they fairly hunted us with guns."

Between Elizabeth and her one son George there was a deep unexpressed bond of sympathy, based on a girlhood dream that had long ago died. In the son's presence she was timid and reserved, but sometimes while he hurried about town intent upon his duties as a reporter, she went into his room and closing the door knelt by a little desk, made of a kitchen table, that sat near a window. In the room by the desk she went through a ceremony that was half a prayer, half a demand, addressed to the skies. In the boyish figure she yearned to see something half forgotten that had once been a part of herself recreated. The prayer concerned that. "Even though I die, I will in some way keep defeat from you," she cried, and so deep was her determination that her whole body shook. Her eyes glowed and she clenched her fists. "If I am dead and see him becoming a meaningless drab figure like myself, I will come back," she declared. "I ask God now to give me that privilege. I demand it. I will pay for it. God may beat me with his fists. I will take any blow that may befall if but this my boy be allowed to express something for us both." Pausing uncertainly, the woman stared about the boy's room. "And do not let him become smart and successful either," she added vaguely.

The communion between George Willard and his mother was outwardly a formal thing without meaning. When she was ill and sat by the window in her room he sometimes went in the evening to make her a visit. They sat by a window that looked over the roof of a small frame building into Main Street. By turning their heads they could see, through another window, along an alleyway that ran behind the Main Street stores and into the back door of Abner Groff's bakery. Sometimes as they sat thus a picture of village life presented itself to them. At the back door of his shop appeared Abner Groff with a stick or an empty milk bottle in his hand. For a long time there was a feud between the baker and a grey cat that belonged to Sylvester West, the druggist. The boy and his mother saw the cat creep into the door of the bakery and presently emerge followed by the baker who swore and waved his arms about. The baker's eyes were small and red and his black hair and beard were filled with flour dust. Sometimes he was so angry that, although the cat had disappeared, he hurled sticks, bits of broken glass, and even some of the tools of his trade about. Once he broke a window at the back of Sinning's Hardware Store. In the alley the grey cat crouched behind barrels filled with torn paper and broken bottles above which flew a black swarm of flies. Once when she was alone, and after watching a prolonged and ineffectual outburst on the part of the baker, Elizabeth Willard put her head down on her long white hands and wept. After that she did not look along the alleyway any more, but tried to forget the contest between the bearded man and the cat. It seemed like a rehearsal of her own life, terrible in its vividness.

In the evening when the son sat in the room with his mother, the silence made them both feel awkward. Darkness came on and the evening train came in at the station. In the street below feet tramped up and down upon a board sidewalk. In the station yard, after the evening train had gone, there was a heavy silence. Perhaps Skinner Leason, the express agent, moved a truck the length of the station platform. Over on Main Street sounded a man's voice, laughing. The door of the express office banged. George Willard arose and crossing the room fumbled for the doorknob. Sometimes he knocked against a chair, making it scrape along the floor. By the window sat the sick woman, perfectly still, listless. Her long hands, white and bloodless, could be seen drooping over the ends of the arms of the chair. "I think you had better be out among the boys. You are too much indoors," she said, striving to relieve the embarrassment of the departure. "I thought I would take a walk," replied George Willard, who felt awkward and confused.

One evening in July, when the transient guests who made the New Willard House their temporary homes had become scarce, and the hallways, lighted only by kerosene lamps turned low, were plunged in gloom, Elizabeth Willard had an adventure. She had been ill in bed for several days and her son had not come to visit her. She was alarmed. The feeble blaze of life that remained in her body was blown into a flame by her anxiety and she crept out of bed, dressed and hurried along the hallway toward her son's room, shaking with exaggerated fears. As she went along she steadied herself with her hand, slipped along the papered walls of the hall and breathed with difficulty. The air whistled through her teeth. As she hurried forward she thought how foolish she was. "He is concerned with boyish affairs," she told herself. "Perhaps he has now begun to walk about in the evening with girls."

Elizabeth Willard had a dread of being seen by guests in the hotel that had once belonged to her father and the ownership of which still stood recorded in her name in the county courthouse. The hotel was continually losing patronage because of its shabbiness and she thought of herself as also shabby. Her own room was in an obscure corner and when she felt able to work she voluntarily worked among the beds, preferring the labor that could be done when the guests were abroad seeking trade among the merchants of Winesburg.

By the door of her son's room the mother knelt upon the floor and listened for some sound from within. When she heard the boy moving about and talking in low tones a smile came to her lips. George Willard had a habit of talking aloud to himself and to hear him doing so had always given his mother a peculiar pleasure. The habit in him, she felt, strengthened the secret bond that existed between them. A thousand times she had whispered to herself of the matter. "He is groping about, trying to find himself," she thought. "He is not a dull clod, all words and smartness. Within him there is a secret something that is striving to grow. It is the thing I let be killed in myself."

In the darkness in the hallway by the door the sick woman arose and started again toward her own room. She was afraid that the door would open and the boy come upon her. When she had reached a safe distance and was about to turn a corner into a second hallway she stopped and bracing herself with her hands waited, thinking to shake off a trembling fit of weakness that had come upon her. The presence of the boy in the room had made her happy. In her bed, during the long hours alone, the little fears that had visited her had become giants. Now they were all gone. "When I get back to my room I shall sleep," she murmured gratefully.

But Elizabeth Willard was not to return to her bed and to sleep. As she stood trembling in the darkness the door of her son's room opened and the boy's father, Tom Willard, stepped out. In the light that streamed out at the door he stood with the knob in his hand and talked. What he said infuriated the woman.

Tom Willard was ambitious for his son. He had always thought of himself as a successful man, although nothing he had ever done had turned out successfully. However, when he was out of sight of the New Willard House and had no fear of coming upon his wife, he swaggered and began to dramatize himself as one of the chief men of the town. He wanted his son to succeed. He it was who had secured for the boy the position on the *Winesburg Eagle*. Now, with a ring of earnestness in his voice, he was advising concerning some course of conduct. "I tell you what, George, you've got to wake up," he said sharply. "Will Henderson has spoken to me three times concerning the matter. He says you go along for hours not hearing when you are spoken to and acting like a gawky girl. What ails you?" Tom Willard laughed good-naturedly. "Well, I guess you'll get over it," he said. "I told Will that. You're not a fool and you're not a woman. You're Tom Willard's son and you'll wake up. I'm not afraid. What you say clears things up. If being a newspaper man had put the notion of becoming a writer into your mind that's all right. Only I guess you'll have to wake up to do that too, eh?"

Tom Willard went briskly along the hallway and down a flight of stairs to the office. The woman in the darkness could hear him laughing and talking with a guest who was striving to wear away a dull evening by dozing in a chair by the office door. She returned to the door of her son's room. The weakness had passed from her body as by a miracle and she stepped boldly along. A thousand ideas raced through her head. When she heard the scraping of a chair and the sound of a pen scratching upon paper, she again turned and went back along the hallway to her own room.

A definite determination had come into the mind of the defeated wife of the Winesburg Hotel keeper. The determination was the result of long years of quiet and rather ineffectual thinking. "Now," she told herself, "I will act. There is something threatening my boy and I will ward it off." The fact that the conversation between Tom Willard and his son had been rather quiet and natural, as though an understanding existed between them, maddened her. Although for years she had hated her husband, her hatred had always before been a quite impersonal thing. He had been merely a part of something else that she hated. Now, and by the few words at the door, he had become the thing personified. In the darkness of her own room she clenched her fists and glared about. Going to a cloth bag that hung on a nail by the wall she took out a long pair of sewing scissors and held them in her hand like a dagger. "I will stab him," she said aloud. "He has chosen to be the voice of evil and I will kill him. When I have killed him something will snap within myself and I will die also. It will be a release for all of us."

In her girlhood and before her marriage with Tom Willard, Elizabeth had borne a somewhat shaky reputation in Winesburg. For years she had been what is called "stage-struck" and had paraded through the streets with traveling men guests at her father's hotel, wearing loud clothes and urging them to tell her of life in the cities out of which they had come. Once she startled the town by putting on men's clothes and riding a bicycle down Main Street.

In her own mind the tall girl had been in those days much confused. A great restlessness was in her and it expressed itself in two ways. First there was an uneasy desire for change, for some big definite movement to her life. It was this feeling that had turned her mind to the stage. She dreamed of joining some company and wandering over the world, seeing always new faces and giving something out of herself to all people. Sometimes at night she was quite beside herself with the thought, but when she tried to talk of the matter to the members of the theatrical companies that came to Winesburg and stopped at her father's hotel, she got nowhere. They did not seem to know what she meant, or if she did get something of her passion expressed, they only laughed. "It's not like that," they said. "It's as dull and uninteresting as this here. Nothing comes of it."

With the traveling men when she walked about with them, and later with Tom Willard, it was quite different. Always they seemed to understand and sympathize with her. On the side streets of the village, in the darkness under the trees, they took hold of her hand and she thought that something unexpressed in herself came forth and became a part of an unexpressed something in them.

And then there was the second expression of her restlessness. When that came she felt for a time released and happy. She did not blame the men who walked with her and later she did not blame Tom Willard. It was always the same, beginning with kisses and ending, after strange wild emotions, with peace and then sobbing repentance. When she sobbed she put her hand upon the face of the man and had always the same thought. Even though he were large and bearded she thought he had become suddenly a little boy. She wondered why he did not sob also.

In her room, tucked away in a corner of the old Willard House, Elizabeth Willard lighted a lamp and put it on a dressing table that stood by the door. A thought had come into her mind and she went to a closet and brought out a small square box and set it on the table. The box contained material for make-up and had been left with other things by a theatrical company that had once been stranded in Winesburg. Elizabeth Willard had decided that she would be beautiful. Her hair was still black and there was a great mass of it braided and coiled about her head. The scene that was to take place in the office below began to grow in her mind. No ghostly worn-out figure should confront Tom Willard, but something quite unexpected and startling. Tall and with dusky cheeks and hair that fell in a mass from her shoulders, a figure should come striding down the stairway before the startled loungers in the hotel office. The figure would be silent—it would be swift and terrible. As a tigress whose cub had been threatened would she appear, coming out of the shadows, stealing noiselessly along and holding the long wicked scissors in her hand.

With a little broken sob in her throat Elizabeth Willard blew out the light that stood upon the table and stood weak and trembling in the darkness. The strength that had been a miracle in her body left and she half reeled across the floor, clutching at the back of the chair in which she had spent so many long days staring out over the tin roofs into the main street of Winesburg. In the hallway there was the sound of footsteps and George Willard came in at the door. Sitting in a chair beside his mother he began to talk. "I'm going to get out of here," he said. "I don't know where I shall go or what I shall do but I am going away."

The woman in the chair waited and trembled. An impulse came to her. "I suppose you had better wake up," she said. "You think that? You will go to the city and make money, eh? It will be better for you, you think, to be a business man, to be brisk and smart and alive?" She waited and trembled.

The son shook his head. "I suppose I can't make you understand, but oh, I wish I could," he said earnestly. "I can't even talk to father about it. I don't try. There isn't any use. I don't know what I shall do. I just want to go away and look at people and think."

Silence fell upon the room where the boy and woman sat together. Again, as on the other evenings, they were embarrassed. After a time the boy tried again to talk. "I suppose it won't be for a year or two but I've been thinking about it," he said, rising and going toward the door. "Something father said makes it sure that I shall have to go away." He fumbled with the door knob. In the room the silence became unbearable to the woman. She wanted to cry out with joy because of the words that had come from the lips of her son, but the expression of joy had become impossible to her. "I think you had better go out among the boys. You are too much indoors," she said. "I thought I would go for a little walk," replied the son stepping awkwardly out of the room and closing the door.

1919

CARL SANDBURG
1878–1967

Son of an immigrant Swedish blacksmith who had settled in Galesburg, Illinois, Carl Sandburg was an active populist and socialist, a journalist, and an important figure in the Chicago Renaissance of arts and letters. During the 1920s and 1930s he was one of the most widely read poets in the nation. His poetic aim was to celebrate the working people of America in poems that they could understand. He wrote sympathetically and affirmatively of the masses, using a long verse line unfettered by rhyme or regular meter, a line deriving from Whitman but with cadences closer to the rhythms of ordinary speech. "Simple poems for simple people," he said.

Sandburg's irregular schooling included brief attendance at Lombard College, but he was too restless to work through to a degree. He held a variety of jobs before moving to Chicago in 1913; he was in the army during the Spanish-American War, served as a war correspondent for the Galesburg *Evening Mail*, worked for the Social Democratic Party in Wisconsin, was secretary to the Socialist mayor of Milwaukee, and wrote editorials for the Milwaukee *Leader*. He had long been writing poetry but achieved success with the 1914 publication of his poem "Chicago" in *Poetry* magazine.

Poetry was one element in a surge of artistic activity in Chicago following the 1893 World's Fair. Such midwesterners as the architect Frank Lloyd Wright; the novelists Theodore Dreiser, Henry Blake Fuller, and Floyd Dell; and the poets Edgar Lee Masters and Vachel Lindsay believed not only that Chicago was a great city but that since the Midwest was America's heartland, it was in this region that the cultural life of the nation ought to center. Two literary magazines—*Poetry*, founded in 1912 by Harriet Monroe, and the *Little Review*, founded by Margaret C. Anderson in 1914—helped bring this informal movement to international attention. Nothing could be more apt to local interests than a celebratory poem called "Chicago."

Four volumes of poetry by Sandburg appeared in the next ten years: *Chicago Poems* (1914), *Cornhuskers* (1918), *Smoke and Steel* (1920), and *Slabs of the Sunburnt West* (1922). These present a panorama of America, concentrating on the prairies and cities of the Midwest. Like Whitman, Sandburg was aware that American life was increasingly urban, and he had little interest in the small town and its conventional middle class. The cities of the Midwest seemed to display both the vitality of the masses and their exploitation in an inequitable class system. Unlike many radicals whose politics were formed after the turn of the twentieth century, Sandburg believed that the people themselves, rather than a cadre of intellectuals acting on behalf of the people, would ultimately shape their own destiny. His political poems express appreciation for the people's energy and outrage at the injustices they suffer. They also balance strong declarative statements with passages of precise description. Other poems show Sandburg working in more lyrical or purely imagistic modes.

If the early "Chicago" is his best-known poem, his most ambitious is the book-length *The People, Yes* (1936), a collage of prose vignettes, anecdotes, and poetry, making use of his researches into American folk song. Sandburg had published these researches in *The American Songbag* in 1927, and he also composed a multivolume biography of Abraham Lincoln between 1926 and 1939. The purpose of this painstaking work was to present Lincoln as an authentic folk hero, a great man who had risen from among the people of the American heartland and represented its best values. He wrote features, editorials, and columns for the *Chicago Daily News* between 1922 and 1930, and pursued other literary projects as well. After World War II, when it became common for poets to read their works at campuses around the country, he enjoyed bringing his old-style populist radicalism to college students.

The text of the poems here is that of *The Complete Poems of Carl Sandburg* (1970).

Chicago

Hog Butcher for the World,
Tool Maker, Stacker of Wheat,
Player with Railroads and the Nation's Freight Handler;
Stormy, husky, brawling,
City of the Big Shoulders: 5

They tell me you are wicked and I believe them, for I have seen
    your painted women under the gas lamps luring the farm
    boys.
And they tell me you are crooked and I answer: Yes, it is true I
    have seen the gunman kill and go free to kill again.
And they tell me you are brutal and my reply is: On the faces of
    women and children I have seen the marks of wanton hunger.
And having answered so I turn once more to those who sneer at
    this my city, and I give them back the sneer and say to them:
Come and show me another city with lifted head singing so
    proud to be alive and coarse and strong and cunning.   10
Flinging magnetic curses amid the toil of piling job on job, here
    is a tall bold slugger set vivid against the little soft cities;
Fierce as a dog with tongue lapping for action, cunning as a
    savage pitted against the wilderness,
        Bareheaded,
        Shoveling,
        Wrecking,   15
        Planning,
        Building, breaking, rebuilding,
Under the smoke, dust all over his mouth, laughing with white
    teeth,
Under the terrible burden of destiny laughing as a young man
    laughs,
Laughing even as an ignorant fighter laughs who has never lost
    a battle,   20
Bragging and laughing that under his wrist is the pulse, and
    under his ribs the heart of the people,
        Laughing!
Laughing the stormy, husky, brawling laughter of Youth, half-
    naked, sweating, proud to be Hog Butcher, Tool Maker,
    Stacker of Wheat, Player with Railroads and Freight
    Handler to the Nation.

                  1914, 1916

Fog

    The fog comes
    on little cat feet.

    It sits looking
    over harbor and city
    on silent haunches   5
    and then moves on.

                  1916

Grass[1]

Pile the bodies high at Austerlitz and Waterloo.
Shovel them under and let me work—
        I am the grass; I cover all.

And pile them high at Gettysburg
And pile them high at Ypres and Verdun.   5
Shovel them under and let me work.
Two years, ten years, and passengers ask the conductor:
        What place is this?
        Where are we now?

        I am the grass.   10
        Let me work.

1918

1. The proper names in this poem are all famous battlefields in the Napoleonic Wars, the American Civil War, and World War I.

WALLACE STEVENS
1879–1955

Wallace Stevens was raised in Reading, Pennsylvania, and went to Harvard for three years before leaving school in 1897 to pursue a literary career. Determined, however, that he would never "make a petty struggle for existence," he also looked for a well-paying job. After briefly trying journalism, he went to law school. In 1916 he began to work for the Hartford Accident and Indemnity Company and moved with his wife to Hartford, Connecticut. They made Hartford their lifelong home, Stevens writing his poetry at night and during summers. Visiting Florida frequently on business, he found the contrast between the South's lush vegetation and tropical climate and the chilly austerity of New England a useful metaphor for opposing ways of imagining the world, as poems like "The Snow Man" and "Sunday Morning" show.

Stevens began to publish in little magazines around 1914. In the early years of his career, he frequented literary gatherings in New York City, becoming friends with William Carlos Williams and Marianne Moore, among others. Because his concern was with the private interaction of the observed and the observer, however, he had little interest in artistic causes—less still in politics—and after moving to Hartford, he dropped out of literary circles, although he maintained an active correspondence with his friends. A good businessman, by the mid-1930s Stevens was prosperous. He continued to work for the same company until his death, eventually becoming a vice president.

His first volume of poetry, *Harmonium,* appeared in 1923. The poems in that book, mostly brief lyrics, are dazzling in their wit, imagery, and color; they established Stevens as one of the most accomplished poets of his era, although some critics found in them so much display as to make their "seriousness" questionable. But Stevens's purpose in part was to show that display was a valid poetic exercise—that poetry existed to illuminate the world's surfaces as well as its depths. He brought a newly perceived but real world before the reader, authenticating both the beauty of reality and the dependence of that beauty—indeed the dependence of reality itself—on the human observer. Two repeated activities are looking at things—the self as active observer of reality—and playing musical instruments or singing—the self as creator of reality (as in "The Idea of Order at Key West"). In this concern with the role of the perceiver in the creation of what is nevertheless real—the sense of an inescapable subjectivity in everything we know—Stevens clearly shared a modernist ideology. His search for belief in an era when, he thought, Christianity has lost its power; the idea, increasingly expressed in later poems, that with the fading of traditional religion poetry might become the forger of new faiths also coincides with the convictions of such poets as T. S. Eliot (in his earlier phase) and Ezra Pound. He has an almost postmodern sense, however, that any religious explanation of the world would have to be a fiction.

His poems feature the continually unexpected in diction and imagery. They abound in allusions to music and painting; are packed with sense images, especially of sound and color; and are elegant and funny. Consider the surprise and humor in the titles of the selections printed here as well as these: "Floral Decorations for Bananas," "Anatomy of Monotony," "The Bird with the Coppery, Keen Claws," "Frogs Eat Butterflies, Snakes Eat Frogs, Hogs Eat Snakes, Men Eat Hogs." Stevens's line is simple— either blank verse or brief stanzas, usually unrhymed—so that the reader's attention is directed to vocabulary and imagery rather than prosody. Invented words are frequent, some employed simply for sound effects. Multilayered puns that ingeniously convey many important meanings serve to thicken and lighten the poetic texture.

Among the poems in *Harmonium* at least three have become touchstones for critics: "The Comedian as the Letter C," "Peter Quince at the Clavier," and "Sunday Morning." "The Comedian as the Letter C" establishes a contrast between an idealistic would-be poet with his empty imaginings and the same poet enmeshed in the rich reality of the senses and human affections. "Peter Quince at the Clavier," again, opposes an idea of beauty in the mind with the reality of beauty in the flesh—paradoxically, it is beauty in the flesh that is immortal. "Sunday Morning" opens with a woman taking her ease at home on the day traditionally reserved for churchgoing, and mentally contrasting a fearful, death-obsessed Christianity with her own celebration of earthly pleasure. She would like to think that her behavior is a religion—a celebration—of life, yet death too is real and to some extent she knows that her behavior is as partial as the Christianity she cannot accept. She wonders whether there might ever be a religion that would take the real world rather than another world as its ground, accepting death and change as inevitable and beautiful. The poem, in the form of a meditation deriving from this opening situation, attempts to sketch out the resolution that the woman desires.

In the six years following the appearance of *Harmonium* Stevens published little new work. With the 1930s came a surge of creativity, beginning with the republication of *Harmonium* in an expanded version in 1931. New volumes and major works appeared regularly thereafter: *Ideas of Order* in 1935, *Owl's Clover* in 1936, *The Man with a Blue Guitar* in 1937, *Parts of a World* in 1942, *Transport to Summer* in 1947, and *The Auroras of Autumn* in 1950. A book collecting his occasional lectures appeared as *The Necessary Angel* in 1951; its gist was that poetry was "the supreme fiction" that enabled human beings to apprehend reality as a whole instead of in fragmentary flashes of insight. Stevens's poetry can be usefully thought of as reconceiving and expressing the ideas of the nineteenth-century American Transcendentalists in modernist terms, for they too located the individual at the center of the world while defining that individual chiefly as a perceiver rather than a doer or defining perceiving as the most important human activity. The difference is that the Transcendentalists confidently assumed that their perceptions were guaranteed by God. Stevens was more skeptical.

In his poetry of the 1930s and after, Stevens became increasingly abstract and theoretical; the dazzling effects diminished, the diction became plainer. Major, long poems from these years were *Notes toward a Supreme Fiction* (from *Transport to Summer*) and *An Ordinary Evening in New Haven* (from *The Auroras of Autumn*). In these later poems Stevens was more concerned about what active role poetry might play in the world than he had been in earlier work. These expository and discursive poems should have been easier to follow than the earlier compressed and elliptical poetry, but critics generally agree that the difficulty and abstractness of their ideas make them much more difficult. And to some readers the absence of the earlier specificity and sparkle also makes the later work less rewarding. But those who enjoyed a taxing poetry of ideas saw the late work as an advance. Stevens's complete *Collected Poems* (1954) has been celebrated as one of the most important books of American poetry in the twentieth century.

The text of the poems included here is that of *The Collected Poems of Wallace Stevens* (1954).

The Snow Man

One must have a mind of winter
To regard the frost and the boughs
Of the pine-trees crusted with snow;

And have been cold a long time
To behold the junipers shagged with ice,   5
The spruces rough in the distant glitter

Of the January sun; and not to think
Of any misery in the sound of the wind,
In the sound of a few leaves,

Which is the sound of the land   10
Full of the same wind
That is blowing in the same bare place

For the listener, who listens in the snow,
And, nothing himself, beholds
Nothing that is not there and the nothing that is. 15

1931

A High-Toned Old Christian Woman

Poetry is the supreme fiction, madame.
Take the moral law and make a nave[1] of it
And from the nave build haunted heaven. Thus,
The conscience is converted into palms,

---

1. Main body of a church building, especially the vaulted central portion of a Christian Gothic church.

Like windy citherns[2] hankering for hymns.   5
We agree in principle. That's clear. But take
The opposing law and make a peristyle,[3]
And from the peristyle project a masque[4]
Beyond the planets. Thus, our bawdiness,
Unpurged by epitaph, indulged at last,   10
Is equally converted into palms,
Squiggling like saxophones. And palm for palm,
Madame, we are where we began. Allow,
Therefore, that in the planetary scene
Your disaffected flagellants, well-stuffed,   15
Smacking their muzzy[5] bellies in parade,
Proud of such novelties of the sublime,
Such tink and tank and tunk-a-tunk-tunk,
May, merely may, madame, whip from themselves
A jovial hullabaloo among the spheres.   20
This will make widows wince. But fictive things
Wink as they will. Wink most when widows wince.

                                                           1923

The Emperor of Ice-Cream

Call the roller of big cigars,
The muscular one, and bid him whip
In kitchen cups concupiscent curds.
Let the wenches dawdle in such dress
As they are used to wear, and let the boys   5
Bring flowers in last month's newspapers.
Let be be finale of seem.
The only emperor is the emperor of ice-cream.

Take from the dresser of deal,[1]
Lacking the three glass knobs, that sheet   10
On which she embroidered fantails[2] once
And spread it so as to cover her face.
If her horny feet protrude, they come
To show how cold she is, and dumb.
Let the lamp affix its beam.   15
The only emperor is the emperor of ice-cream.

                                                           1923

---

2. I.e., citherns; pear-shaped guitars.
3. Colonnade surrounding a building, especially the cells or main chamber of an ancient Greek temple—an "opposing law" to a Christian church.
4. Spectacle or entertainment consisting of music, dancing, mime, and often poetry.
5. Sodden with drunkenness.
1. Plain, unfinished wood.
2. Stevens explained that "the word fantails does not mean fan, but fantail pigeons."

Disillusionment of Ten O'Clock

The houses are haunted
By white night-gowns.
None are green,
Or purple with green rings,
Or green with yellow rings,   5
Or yellow with blue rings.
None of them are strange,
With socks of lace
And beaded ceintures.
People are not going   10
To dream of baboons and periwinkles.
Only, here and there, an old sailor,
Drunk and asleep in his boots,
Catches tigers
In red weather.   15

1931

Sunday Morning[1]

I

Complacencies of the peignoir, and late
Coffee and oranges in a sunny chair,
And the green freedom of a cockatoo
Upon a rug mingle to dissipate
The holy hush of ancient sacrifice.   5
She dreams a little, and she feels the dark
Encroachment of that old catastrophe,
As a calm darkens among water-lights.
The pungent oranges and bright, green wings
Seem things in some procession of the dead,   10
Winding across wide water, without sound.
The day is like wide water, without sound,
Stilled for the passing of her dreaming feet
Over the seas, to silent Palestine,
Dominion of the blood and sepulchre.   15

II

Why should she give her bounty to the dead?
What is divinity if it can come
Only in silent shadows and in dreams?
Shall she not find in comforts of the sun,

---

1. This poem was first published in *Poetry* magazine in 1915; the editor, Harriet Monroe, printed
only five of its eight stanzas but arranged them in
the order Stevens suggested when consenting to
the deletions (I, VIII, IV, V, and VII); he restored
the deleted stanzas and the original sequence in
subsequent printings.

In pungent fruit and bright, green wings, or else   20
In any balm or beauty of the earth,
Things to be cherished like the thought of heaven?
Divinity must live within herself:
Passions of rain, or moods in falling snow;
Grievings in loneliness, or unsubdued   25
Elations when the forest blooms; gusty
Emotions on wet roads on autumn nights;
All pleasures and all pains, remembering
The bough of summer and the winter branch.
These are the measures destined for her soul.   30

III

Jove² in the clouds had his inhuman birth.
No mother suckled him, no sweet land gave
Large-mannered motions to his mythy mind.
He moved among us, as a muttering king,
Magnificent, would move among his hinds,   35
Until our blood, commingling, virginal,
With heaven, brought such requital to desire
The very hinds³ discerned it, in a star.
Shall our blood fail? Or shall it come to be
The blood of paradise? And shall the earth   40
Seem all of paradise that we shall know?
The sky will be much friendlier then than now,
A part of labor and a part of pain,
And next in glory to enduring love,
Not this dividing and indifferent blue.   45

IV

She says, "I am content when wakened birds,
Before they fly, test the reality
Of misty fields, by their sweet questionings;
But when the birds are gone, and their warm fields
Return no more, where, then, is paradise?"   50
There is not any haunt of prophecy,
Nor any old chimera⁴ of the grave,
Neither the golden underground, nor isle
Melodious, where spirits gat them home,
Nor visionary south, nor cloudy palm   55
Remote on heaven's hill,⁵ that has endured
As April's green endures; or will endure
Like her remembrance of awakened birds,
Or her desire for June and evening, tipped
By the consummation of the swallow's wings.   60

2. Supreme god in Roman mythology.
3. Farmhands; an allusion to the shepherds who saw the star of Bethlehem that signaled the birth of Jesus.
4. In Greek mythology, a monster with a lion's head, goat's body, and serpent's tail.
5. Versions of Paradise in diverse world religions.

V

She says, "But in contentment I still feel
The need of some imperishable bliss."
Death is the mother of beauty; hence from her,
Alone, shall come fulfillment to our dreams
And our desires. Although she strews the leaves   65
Of sure obliteration on our paths,
The path sick sorrow took, the many paths
Where triumph rang its brassy phrase, or love
Whispered a little out of tenderness,
She makes the willow shiver in the sun   70
For maidens who were wont to sit and gaze
Upon the grass, relinquished to their feet.
She causes boys to pile new plums and pears
On disregarded plate. The maidens taste
And stray impassioned in the littering leaves.   75

VI

Is there no change of death in paradise?
Does ripe fruit never fall? Or do the boughs
Hang always heavy in that perfect sky,
Unchanging, yet so like our perishing earth,
With rivers like our own that seek for seas   80
They never find, the same receding shores
That never touch with inarticulate pang?
Why set the pear upon those river-banks
Or spice the shores with odors of the plum?
Alas, that they should wear our colors there,   85
The silken weavings of our afternoons,
And pick the strings of our insipid lutes!
Death is the mother of beauty, mystical,
Within whose burning bosom we devise
Our earthly mothers waiting, sleeplessly.   90

VII

Supple and turbulent, a ring of men
Shall chant in orgy on a summer morn
Their boisterous devotion to the sun,
Not as a god, but as a god might be,
Naked among them, like a savage source.   95
Their chant shall be a chant of paradise,
Out of their blood, returning to the sky;
And in their chant shall enter, voice by voice,
The windy lake wherein their lord delights,
The trees, like serafin,[6] and echoing hills,   100
That choir among themselves long afterward.
They shall know well the heavenly fellowship
Of men that perish and of summer morn.

---

6. I.e., seraphim; angels.

And whence they came and whither they shall go
The dew upon their feet shall manifest.   105

VIII

She hears, upon that water without sound,
A voice that cries, "The tomb in Palestine
Is not the porch of spirits lingering.
It is the grave of Jesus, where he lay."
We live in an old chaos of the sun,   110
Or old dependency of day and night,
Or island solitude, unsponsored, free,
Of that wide water, inescapable.
Deer walk upon our mountains, and the quail
Whistle about us their spontaneous cries;   115
Sweet berries ripen in the wilderness;
And, in the isolation of the sky,
At evening, casual flocks of pigeons make
Ambiguous undulations as they sink,
Downward to darkness, on extended wings.   120

                                                 1915, 1923

Anecdote of the Jar

I placed a jar in Tennessee,
And round it was, upon a hill.
It made the slovenly wilderness
Surround that hill.

The wilderness rose up to it,   5
And sprawled around, no longer wild.
The jar was round upon the ground
And tall and of a port in air.

It took dominion everywhere.
The jar was gray and bare.   10
It did not give of bird or bush,
Like nothing else in Tennessee.

                                                       1923

Thirteen Ways of Looking at a Blackbird

I

Among twenty snowy mountains,
The only moving thing
Was the eye of the blackbird.

II

I was of three minds,
Like a tree
In which there are three blackbirds.

III

The blackbird whirled in the autumn winds.
It was a small part of the pantomime.

IV

A man and a woman
Are one.
A man and a woman and a blackbird
Are one.

V

I do not know which to prefer,
The beauty of inflections
Or the beauty of innuendoes,
The blackbird whistling
Or just after.

VI

Icicles filled the long window
With barbaric glass.
The shadow of the blackbird
Crossed it, to and fro.
The mood
Traced in the shadow
An indecipherable cause.

VII

O thin men of Haddam,[1]
Why do you imagine golden birds?
Do you not see how the blackbird
Walks around the feet
Of the women about you?

VIII

I know noble accents
And lucid, inescapable rhythms;
But I know, too,
That the blackbird is involved
In what I know.

IX

When the blackbird flew out of sight,
It marked the edge
Of one of many circles.

5

10

15

20

25

30

35

---

1. A city in Connecticut.

X

At the sight of blackbirds
Flying in a green light,
Even the bawds of euphony   40
Would cry out sharply.

XI

He rode over Connecticut
In a glass coach.
Once, a fear pierced him,
In that he mistook   45
The shadow of his equipage
For blackbirds.

XII

The river is moving.
The blackbird must be flying.

XIII

It was evening all afternoon.   50
It was snowing
And it was going to snow.
The blackbird sat
In the cedar-limbs.

                                                        1931

The Idea of Order at Key West[1]

She sang beyond the genius of the sea.
The water never formed to mind or voice,
Like a body wholly body, fluttering
Its empty sleeves; and yet its mimic motion
Made constant cry, caused constantly a cry,   5
That was not ours although we understood,
Inhuman, of the veritable ocean.

The sea was not a mask. No more was she.
The song and water were not medleyed sound
Even if what she sang was what she heard,   10
Since what she sang was uttered word by word.
It may be that in all her phrases stirred
The grinding water and the gasping wind;
But it was she and not the sea we heard.

For she was the maker of the song she sang.   15
The ever-hooded, tragic-gestured sea
Was merely a place by which she walked to sing.
Whose spirit is this? we said, because we knew

---

1. One of the islands off the southern coast of Florida, where Stevens vacationed. The poem begins with
the scene of a woman walking by the sea and singing.

It was the spirit that we sought and knew
That we should ask this often as she sang.   20

If it was only the dark voice of the sea
That rose, or even colored by many waves;
If it was only the outer voice of sky
And cloud, of the sunken coral water-walled,
However clear, it would have been deep air,   25
The heaving speech of air, a summer sound
Repeated in a summer without end
And sound alone. But it was more than that,
More even than her voice, and ours, among
The meaningless plungings of water and the wind,   30
Theatrical distances, bronze shadows heaped
On high horizons, mountainous atmospheres
Of sky and sea.
                    It was her voice that made
The sky acutest at its vanishing.   35
She measured to the hour its solitude.
She was the single artificer of the world
In which she sang. And when she sang, the sea,
Whatever self it had, became the self
That was her song, for she was the maker. Then we,   40
As we beheld her striding there alone,
Knew that there never was a world for her
Except the one she sang and, singing, made.

Ramon Fernandez,[2] tell me, if you know,
Why, when the singing ended and we turned   45
Toward the town, tell why the glassy lights,
The lights in the fishing boats at anchor there,
As the night descended, tilting in the air,
Mastered the night and portioned out the sea,
Fixing emblazoned zones and fiery poles,   50
Arranging, deepening, enchanting night.

Oh! Blessed rage for order, pale Ramon,
The maker's rage to order words of the sea,
Words of the fragrant portals, dimly-starred,
And of ourselves and of our origins,   55
In ghostlier demarcations, keener sounds.

                                                          1936

Of Modern Poetry

The poem of the mind in the act of finding
What will suffice. It has not always had
To find: the scene was set; it repeated what
Was in the script.

---

2. A French literary critic and essayist (1894–1944). Stevens said that he had invented the name and that its coincidence with a real person was accidental.

Then the theatre was changed   5
To something else. Its past was a souvenir.
It has to be living, to learn the speech of the place.
It has to face the men of the time and to meet
The women of the time. It has to think about war
And it has to find what will suffice. It has   10
To construct a new stage. It has to be on that stage
And, like an insatiable actor, slowly and
With meditation, speak words that in the ear,
In the delicatest ear of the mind, repeat,
Exactly, that which it wants to hear, at the sound   15
Of which, an invisible audience listens,
Not to the play, but to itself, expressed
In an emotion as of two people, as of two
Emotions becoming one. The actor is
A metaphysician in the dark, twanging   20
An instrument, twanging a wiry string that gives
Sounds passing through sudden rightnesses, wholly
Containing the mind, below which it cannot descend,
Beyond which it has no will to rise.
                              It must   25
Be the finding of a satisfaction, and may
Be of a man skating, a woman dancing, a woman
Combing. The poem of the act of the mind.

                                          1942

MINA LOY
1882–1966

Increasingly known today as one of the most freewheeling experimental poets of high international modernism, Mina Loy led an expatriate life in most of the major artistic centers of Europe and the United States before embracing American citizenship permanently in 1946. She was born in Hampstead, a suburb of London, and left home in 1897 to attend art school, first in London, then in Munich and Paris, where she also married and bore a daughter. She moved to Italy in 1907; there Loy met Americans like Gertrude Stein, and encountered F. T. Marinetti's Futurist movement—which she admired for its dynamism but distrusted for its alignment of the heroic male artist with "beautiful ideas which kill, and contempt for woman." Loy made her literary debut with "Aphorisms on Futurism" (published in the little magazine *Camera Work* in 1914), which publicly embraced Futurism's aggressive aesthetic of destruction and renovation even as her "Feminist Manifesto" replied to Futurism's misogyny in its own experimental artistic idiom. She claimed the female body as her own modernist subject in poems like "Parturition" and scandalized readers with her surreal and erotically frank "Love Songs" (1915).

Loy sailed for New York in 1916, where she was already awaited as a minor celebrity, and immediately made her way into high modernist circles that included the artist Marcel Duchamp and writers like William Carlos Williams and Susan Glaspell. She returned to Europe in 1921. A collection of her poems, *Lunar Baedecker*, was published in Paris in 1923. Named after the popular series of tourist guidebooks, the title poem of the volume presents itself as a kind of guidebook to the hypercharged spectacle of the modern city, mapped through the poem's eye both as an underworld of ancient mythologies and as a futurist metropolis on the moon. With Hitler's rise to power making Europe dangerous for Jews, Loy returned to the United States in 1937. An expanded collection of her poems (with the spelling of the title corrected) came out as *Lunar Baedeker & Time-Tables* in 1958, reviving her reputation both among older modernists and younger poets.

The text of the poems included here is that of *The Lost Lunar Baedeker* (1996).

Parturition

I am the centre
Of a circle of pain
Exceeding its boundaries in every direction

The business of the bland sun
Has no affair with me   5
In my congested cosmos of agony
From which there is no escape
On infinitely prolonged nerve-vibrations
Or in contraction
To the pin-point nucleus of being   10

Locate an irritation   without
It is   within
                             Within
It is without
The sensitized area   15
Is identical   with the extensity
Of intension

I am the false quantity
In the harmony of physiological potentiality
To which   20
Gaining self-control
I should be consonant
In time

Pain is no stronger than the resisting force
Pain calls up in me   25
The struggle is equal
The open window is full of a voice
A fashionable portrait-painter
Running up-stairs to a woman's apartment
Sings   30
          "All the girls are tid'ly did'ly
          All the girls are nice
          Whether they wear their hair in curls
          Or—"
At the back of the thoughts to which I permit crystallization   35

The conception   Brute
Why?
     The irresponsibility of the male
Leaves woman her superior Inferiority
He is running up-stairs   40

I am climbing a distorted mountain of agony
Incidentally with the exhaustion of control
I reach the summit
And gradually subside into anticipation of
Repose   45
Which never comes
For another mountain is growing up
Which   goaded by the unavoidable
I must traverse
Traversing myself   50

Something in the delirium of night-hours
Confuses while intensifying sensibility
Blurring spatial contours
So aiding elusion of the circumscribed
That the gurgling of a crucified wild beast   55
Comes from so far away
And the foam on the stretched muscles of a mouth
Is no part of myself
There is a climax in sensibility
When pain surpassing itself   60
Becomes Exotic
And the ego succeeds in unifying the positive and negative
       poles of sensation
Uniting the opposing and resisting forces
In lascivious revelation

Relaxation   65
Negation of myself as a unit
       Vacuum interlude
I should have been emptied of life
Giving life
For consciousness in crises   races   70
Through the subliminal deposits of evolutionary processes
Have I not
Somewhere
Scrutinized
A dead white feathered moth   75
Laying eggs?
A moment
Being realization
Can
Vitalized by cosmic initiation   80
Furnish an adequate apology
For the objective
Agglomeration of activities

Of a life.
LIFE   85
A leap with nature
Into the essence
Of unpredicted Maternity
Against my thigh
Touch of infinitesimal motion   90
Scarcely perceptible
Undulation
Warmth   moisture
Stir of incipient life
Precipitating into me   95
The contents of the universe
Mother I am
Identical
With infinite Maternity
   Indivisible   100
   Acutely
   I am absorbed
   Into
The was—is—ever—shall—be
Of cosmic reproductivity   105

Rises from the subconscious
Impression of a cat
With blind kittens
Among her legs
Same undulating life-stir   110
I am that cat

Rises from the sub-conscious
Impression of small animal carcass
Covered with blue-bottles[1]
—Epicurean—[2]   115
And through the insects
Waves that same undulation of living
Death
Life
I am knowing   120
All about
   Unfolding

The next morning
Each woman-of-the-people
Tip-toeing the red pile of the carpet   125
Doing hushed service
Each woman-of-the-people
Wearing a halo

---

1. Species of fly.
2. Devoted to pleasure; after Epicurus (341–270

B.C.E.), Greek philosopher who advocated pleasure
as the goal of life.

A ludicrous little halo
Of which she is sublimely   unaware   130
I once heard in a church
—Man and woman God made them—[3]
           Thank God.

                                     1914

Brancusi's Golden Bird[1]

The toy
become the aesthetic archetype

As if
     some patient peasant God
     had rubbed and rubbed   5
     the Alpha and Omega[2]
     of Form
     into a lump of metal

A naked orientation
unwinged   unplumbed   10
     —the ultimate rhythm
has lopped the extremities
of crest and claw
from
the nucleus of flight   15

The absolute act
of art
conformed
to continent sculpture
—bare as the brow of Osiris—[3]   20
this breast of revelation

an incandescent curve
licked by chromatic flames
in labyrinths of reflections

This gong   25
of polished hyperaesthesia[4]
shrills with brass
as the aggressive light

3. "So God created man in his own image, . . . male and female created he them" (Genesis 2.27).
1. One of a series of bronze sculptures by Constantin Brancusi (1876–1957) depicting a stylized bird's wing. A photograph of "The Golden Bird" was published opposite Loy's poem in The Dial, Nov. 1922 (see the color insert to this volume).
2. First and last letters of the Greek alphabet; figuratively, the beginning and end.
3. Ancient Egyptian god, ruler of the underworld and of the rebirth of life from death.
4. Excessive sensitiveness; here suggesting the heightening of specifically artistic sensation.

strikes
its significance   30

The immaculate
conception[5]
of the inaudible bird
occurs
in gorgeous reticence . . .   35

1922

Lunar Baedeker

A silver Lucifer
serves
cocaine in cornucopia

To some somnambulists
of adolescent thighs   5
draped
in satirical draperies

Peris[1] in livery
prepare
Lethe[2]   10
for posthumous parvenues[3]

Delirious Avenues
lit
with the chandelier souls
of infusoria[4]   15
from Pharoah's tombstones

lead
to mercurial doormsdays
Odious oasis
in furrowed phosphorous— — —   20

the eye-white sky-light
white-light district
of lunar lusts

---

5. In Roman Catholic doctrine proclaimed in 1854, the belief that Mary, mother of Jesus, was conceived without original sin (the burden of sin inherited from Adam and Eve's original disobedience).
1. In Persian mythology, a fairy or angel.
2. In Greek mythology, the river in which the dead washed away their memories.
3. Literally, newly arrived persons (French); in English usage, social climbers.
4. One-celled waterborne microorganisms; in high concentrations, they may turn lake or river water reddish. Famous 19th-century zoological expeditions found their fossilized remains in Egyptian stone, leading to speculation that the biblical account of Moses turning the Nile into blood to punish Pharaoh (Exodus 7.17–21) was based on an epidemic of infusoria.

— — —Stellectric signs
"Wing shows on Starway" 25
"Zodiac carrousel"

Cyclones
of ecstatic dust
and ashes whirl
crusaders 30
from hallucinatory citadels
of shattered glass
into evacuate craters

A flock of dreams
browse on Necropolis[5] 35
From the shores
of oval oceans
in the oxidized Orient

Onyx-eyed Odalisques[6]
and ornithologists 40
observe
the flight
of Eros obsolete

And "Immortality"
mildews . . . 45
in the museums of the moon

"Nocturnal cyclops"[7]
"Crystal concubine"
— — — — — — —

Pocked with personification
the fossil virgin of the skies 50
waxes and wanes— — — —

1923

5. City of the dead (Greek).
6. Female slaves or concubines.

7. In Greek mythology, member of a race of one-eyed giants.

WILLIAM CARLOS WILLIAMS
1883–1963

A modernist known for his disagreements with all the other modernists, William Carlos Williams thought of himself as the most underrated poet of his generation. His reputation has risen dramatically since World War II as a younger generation of poets testified to the influence of his work on their idea of what poetry should be. The simplicity of his verse forms, the matter-of-factness of both his subject matter and his means of describing it, seemed to bring poetry into natural relation with everyday life.

He is now judged to be among the most important poets writing between the wars. His career continued into the 1960s, taking new directions as he produced, along with shorter lyrics, his epic five-part poem *Paterson*.

He was born in 1883 in Rutherford, New Jersey, a town near the city of Paterson. His maternal grandmother, an Englishwoman deserted by her husband, had come to America with her son, married again, and moved to Puerto Rico. Her son—Williams's father—married a woman descended on one side from French Basque people, on the other from Dutch Jews. This mix of origins always fascinated Williams and made him feel that he was different from what he thought of as mainstream Americans, i.e., northeasterners or midwesterners of English descent. After the family moved to New Jersey, Williams's father worked as a salesman for a perfume company; in childhood his father was often away from home, and the two women—mother and grandmother— were the most important adults to him. Throughout Williams's poetry the figure of woman as an earth mother, whom men require for completion and whose reason for being is to supply that completeness, appears, perhaps reflecting that early experience.

Except for a year in Europe, Williams attended local schools. He entered the School of Dentistry at the University of Pennsylvania directly after graduating from high school but soon switched to medicine. In college he met and became friends with Ezra Pound; Hilda Doolittle, later to become known as the poet H. D.; and the painter Charles Demuth. These friendships did much to steer him toward poetry, and even as he completed his medical work, interned in New York City, and did postgraduate study in Leipzig, Germany, he was reconceiving his commitment to medicine as a means of self-support in the more important enterprise of becoming a poet. Although he never lost his sense that he was a doctor in order to be a poet, his patients knew him as a dedicated old-fashioned physician, who made house calls, listened to people's problems, and helped them through life's crises. Pediatrics was his specialty; and in the course of his career, he delivered more than two thousand babies.

In 1912, after internship and study abroad, Williams married his fiancée of several years, Florence Herman. Despite strains in their relationship caused by Williams's continuing interest in other women, the marriage lasted and became, toward the end of Williams's life, the subject of some beautiful love poetry, including "Asphodel, that Greeny Flower." In the meantime women and the mixed belittlement–adoration accorded them by men (including the poet) were persistent themes. The couple settled in Rutherford, where Williams opened his practice. Except for a trip to Europe in 1924, when he saw Pound and met James Joyce, among others, and trips for lectures and poetry readings later in his career, Williams remained in Rutherford all his life, continuing his medical practice until poor health forced him to retire. He wrote at night, and spent weekends in New York City with friends who were writers and artists—the avant-garde painters Marcel Duchamp and Francis Picabia, the poets Marianne Moore and Wallace Stevens, and others. At their gatherings he acquired a reputation for outspoken hostility to most of the "-isms" of the day.

The characteristic Williams style emerged clearly in the landmark volume of mixed prose and poetry *Spring and All* (1923). One can see in this book that the gesture of staying at home was more for him than a practical assessment of his chances of self-support. Interested, like his friend Ezra Pound, in making a new kind of poetry, Williams also wanted always to speak as an American within an American context. One can observe this bias in the title of one of his books of essays, *In the American Grain* (1925), and in his choice of his own region as the setting and subject of *Paterson*, a long poem about his native city incorporating a great variety of textual fragments—letters, newspaper accounts, poetry—in a modernist collage.

Williams detested Eliot's *The Waste Land*, describing its popularity as a "catastrophe," deploring not only its internationalism but also its pessimism and deliberate obscurity. To him these characteristics were un-American. Yet Williams was not a sentimental celebrant of American life. He objected to Robert Frost's homespun poetry— which might be thought of as similar to his own work—for nostalgically evoking a bygone rural America rather than engaging with what he saw as the real American present. His America was made up of small cities like Paterson, with immigrants, factories, and poor working-class people struggling to get by. The sickness and suffering he saw as a physician entered into his poetry, as did his personal life; but the overall impact of his poetry is social rather than autobiographical.

The social aspect of Williams's poetry rises from its accumulation of detail; he opposed the use of poetry for general statements and abstract critique. "No ideas but in things," he wrote. Wallace Stevens had also written, "not ideas about the thing but the thing itself"; yet there is a world of difference between Williams's plainspoken and often opinionated writing and Stevens's cool elegance. Williams drew his vocabulary from up-to-date local speech and searched for a poetic line derived from the cadences of street talk. But he rejected "free verse" as an absurdity; rhythm within the line, and linking one line to another, was the heart of poetic craft to him. While working on *Paterson,* he invented the "triadic" or "stepped line," a long line broken into three segments, which he used in many poems, including several of the selections printed here.

Williams published fiction and essays as well as poetry, especially during the 1930s. Books of short stories (*The Edge of the Knife,* 1932, and *Life along the Passaic River,* 1938) and novels (*White Mule,* 1937, and *In the Money,* 1940) appeared in these years. He was also involved with others in the establishment of several little magazines, each designed to promulgate counterstatements to the powerful influences of Pound, Eliot, and the New Critics. All the time he remained active in his community and in political events; in the 1930s and 1940s he aligned himself with liberal Democratic and, on occasion, leftist issues but always from the vantage point of an unreconstructed individualism. Some of his affiliations were held against him in the McCarthy era and to his great distress he was deprived in 1948 of the post of consultant in poetry at the Library of Congress.

It was also in 1948 that he had a heart attack, and in 1951 the first of a series of strokes required him to turn over his medical practice to one of his two sons and made writing increasingly difficult. Nevertheless, he persevered in his work on *Paterson,* whose five books were published in 1946, 1948, 1949, 1951, and 1958. *The Desert Music* (1954) and *Pictures from Brueghel* (1962), containing new poetry, also appeared; but by 1961 Williams had to stop writing. By the time of his death a host of younger poets, including Allen Ginsberg, Denise Levertov, Charles Olson, and Robert Creeley, had been inspired by his example. He won the National Book Award in 1950, the Bollingen Prize in 1953, and the Pulitzer Prize in 1962.

The texts of the poems included here are those of *The Collected Poems of William Carlos Williams,* Volume 1: *1909–1939* (1986), edited by A. Walton Litz and Christopher MacGowan, and *The Collected Poems of William Carlos Williams,* Volume 2: *1939–1962* (1988), edited by Christopher MacGowan.

The Young Housewife

At ten A.M. the young housewife
moves about in negligee behind
the wooden walls of her husband's house.
I pass solitary in my car.

Then again she comes to the curb   5
to call the ice-man, fish-man, and stands
shy, uncorseted, tucking in
stray ends of hair, and I compare her
to a fallen leaf.

The noiseless wheels of my car   10
rush with a crackling sound over
dried leaves as I bow and pass smiling.

1916, 1917

Portrait of a Lady

Your thighs are appletrees
whose blossoms touch the sky.
Which sky? The sky
where Watteau[1] hung a lady's
slipper. Your knees   5
are a southern breeze—or
a gust of snow. Agh! what
sort of man was Fragonard?[2]
—as if that answered
anything. Ah, yes—below   10
the knees, since the tune
drops that way, it is
one of those white summer days,
the tall grass of your ankles
flickers upon the shore—   15
Which shore?—
the sand clings to my lips—
Which shore?
Agh, petals maybe. How
should I know?   20
Which shore? Which shore?
I said petals from an appletree.

1920, 1934

Queen-Anne's-Lace[1]

Her body is not so white as
anemone petals nor so smooth—nor
so remote a thing. It is a field
of the wild carrot taking
the field by force; the grass   5
does not raise above it.
Here is no question of whiteness,
white as can be, with a purple mole

---

1. Jean Antoine Watteau (1684–1721), French artist who painted landscapes of elegantly dressed lovers in idealized rustic settings.
2. Jean Honoré Fragonard (1732–1806), French painter who depicted fashionable lovers in paintings more wittily and openly erotic than Watteau's.

Fragonard's *The Swing* depicts a girl who has kicked her slipper into the air.
1. A common wildflower whose white bloom is composed of numerous tiny blossoms, each with a dark spot at the center, joined to the stalk by fibrous stems.

at the center of each flower.
Each flower is a hand's span   10
of her whiteness. Wherever
his hand has lain there is
a tiny purple blemish. Each part
is a blossom under his touch
to which the fibres of her being   15
stem one by one, each to its end,
until the whole field is a
white desire, empty, a single stem,
a cluster, flower by flower,
a pious wish to whiteness gone over—   20
or nothing.

1921

The Widow's Lament in Springtime

Sorrow is my own yard
where the new grass
flames as it has flamed
often before but not
with the cold fire   5
that closes round me this year.
Thirtyfive years
I lived with my husband.
The plumtree is white today
with masses of flowers.   10
Masses of flowers
load the cherry branches
and color some bushes
yellow and some red
but the grief in my heart   15
is stronger than they
for though they were my joy
formerly, today I notice them
and turn away forgetting.
Today my son told me   20
that in the meadows,
at the edge of the heavy woods
in the distance, he saw
trees of white flowers.
I feel that I would like   25
to go there
and fall into those flowers
and sink into the marsh near them.

1921

Spring and All[1]

By the road to the contagious hospital[2]
under the surge of the blue
mottled clouds driven from the
northeast—a cold wind. Beyond, the
waste of broad, muddy fields   5
brown with dried weeds, standing and fallen

patches of standing water
the scattering of tall trees

All along the road the reddish
purplish, forked, upstanding, twiggy   10
stuff of bushes and small trees
with dead, brown leaves under them
leafless vines—

Lifeless in appearance, sluggish
dazed spring approaches—   15

They enter the new world naked,
cold, uncertain of all
save that they enter. All about them
the cold, familiar wind—

Now the grass, tomorrow   20
the stiff curl of wildcarrot leaf

One by one objects are defined—
It quickens: clarity, outline of leaf

But now the stark dignity of
entrance—Still, the profound change   25
has come upon them: rooted, they
grip down and begin to awaken

                                                        1923

To Elsie[1]

The pure products of America
go crazy—
mountain folk from Kentucky

---

1. In the volume *Spring and All* (as originally published, 1923), prose statements were interspersed
through the poems, which were identified by
roman numerals. Williams added titles later and
used the volume's title for the opening poem.

2. I.e., a hospital for treating contagious diseases.
1. In *Spring and All*, this poem was originally
numbered XVIII. Elsie, from the State Orphanage,
worked for the Williams family as a nursemaid.

or the ribbed north end of
Jersey   5
with its isolate lakes and

valleys, its deaf-mutes, thieves
old names
and promiscuity between

devil-may-care men who have taken   10
to railroading
out of sheer lust of adventure—

and young slatterns, bathed
in filth
from Monday to Saturday   15

to be tricked out that night
with gauds
from imaginations which have no

peasant traditions to give them
character   20
but flutter and flaunt

sheer rags—succumbing without
emotion
save numbed terror

under some hedge of choke-cherry   25
or viburnum—
which they cannot express—

Unless it be that marriage
perhaps
with a dash of Indian blood   30

will throw up a girl so desolate
so hemmed round
with disease or murder

that she'll be rescued by an
agent—   35
reared by the state and

sent out at fifteen to work in
some hard-pressed
house in the suburbs—

some doctor's family, some Elsie—   40
voluptuous water
expressing with broken

brain the truth about us—
her great
ungainly hips and flopping breasts   45

addressed to cheap
jewelry
and rich young men with fine eyes

as if the earth under our feet
were   50
an excrement of some sky

and we degraded prisoners
destined
to hunger until we eat filth

while the imagination strains   55
after deer
going by fields of goldenrod in

the stifling heat of September
Somehow
it seems to destroy us   60

It is only in isolate flecks that
something
is given off

No one
to witness   65
and adjust, no one to drive the car

1923

The Red Wheelbarrow[1]

so much depends
upon

a red wheel
barrow

glazed with rain   5
water

beside the white
chickens

1923

1. Numbered XXII in *Spring and All*.

This Is Just to Say

I have eaten
the plums
that were in
the icebox

and which   5
you were probably
saving
for breakfast

Forgive me
they were delicious   10
so sweet
and so cold

1934

A Sort of a Song

Let the snake wait under
his weed
and the writing
be of words, slow and quick, sharp
to strike, quiet to wait,   5
sleepless.

—through metaphor to reconcile
the people and the stones.
Compose. (No ideas
but in things) Invent!   10
Saxifrage is my flower that splits
the rocks.

1944

The Dance

In Brueghel's great picture, The Kermess,[1]
the dancers go round, they go round and
around, the squeal and the blare and the
tweedle of bagpipes, a bugle and fiddles
tipping their bellies (round as the thick-   5
sided glasses whose wash they impound)
their hips and their bellies off balance

---

1. *The Wedding Dance* by the Flemish painter Pieter Brueghel (or Breughel) the Elder (ca. 1525–1569).

to turn them. Kicking and rolling about
the Fair Grounds, swinging their butts, those
shanks must be sound to bear up under such   10
rollicking measures, prance as they dance
in Brueghel's great picture, The Kermess.

1944

Landscape with the Fall of Icarus[1]

According to Brueghel[2]
when Icarus fell
it was spring

a farmer was ploughing
his field   5
the whole pageantry

of the year was
awake tingling
near

the edge of the sea   10
concerned
with itself

sweating in the sun
that melted
the wings' wax   15

unsignificantly
off the coast
there was

a splash quite unnoticed
this was   20
Icarus drowning

1962

The Dance

When the snow falls the flakes
spin upon the long axis
that concerns them most intimately
two and two to make a dance

---

1. In Greek mythology, a young man whose father
made wings for him with feathers held together by
wax. Icarus flew too close to the sun, the wax
melted, and he fell into the sea and drowned.

2. A landscape by Flemish painter Pieter Brueghel
the Elder (ca. 1525–1569) in which Icarus is
depicted by a tiny leg sticking out of the sea in one
corner of the picture.

the mind dances with itself,   5
taking you by the hand,
your lover follows
there are always two,

yourself and the other,
the point of your shoe setting the pace,   10
if you break away and run
the dance is over

Breathlessly you will take
another partner
better or worse who will keep   15
at your side, at your stops

whirls and glides until he too
leaves off
on his way down as if
there were another direction   20

gayer, more carefree
spinning face to face but always down
with each other secure
only in each other's arms

But only the dance is sure!   25
make it your own.
Who can tell
what is to come of it?

in the woods of your
own nature whatever   30
twig interposes, and bare twigs
have an actuality of their own

this flurry of the storm
that holds us,
plays with us and discards us   35
dancing, dancing as may be credible.

                                                                     1962

EZRA POUND
1885–1972

Ezra Loomis Pound was born in Hailey, Idaho. When he was still an infant his parents settled in a comfortable suburb near Philadelphia where his father was an assayer at the regional branch of the U.S. Mint. "I knew at fifteen pretty much what I wanted to do," he wrote in 1913; what he wanted was to become a poet. He had this goal in mind as an undergraduate at the University of Pennsylvania (where he met and became lifelong friends with William Carlos Williams and had a romance with Hilda Doolittle, who was later to become the poet H. D.) and at Hamilton College; it also motivated his graduate studies in languages—French, Italian, Old English, and Latin—at the University of Pennsylvania, where he received an M.A. in 1906. He planned to support himself as a college teacher while writing.

The poetry that he had in mind in these early years was in vogue at the turn of the twentieth century—melodious in versification and diction, romantic in themes, world-weary in tone—poetry for which the term *decadent* was used. A particular image of the poet went with such poetry: the poet committed to art for its own sake, careless of convention, and continually shocking the respectable middle class. A rebellious and colorful personality, Pound delighted in this role but quickly found that it was not compatible with the sober behavior expected from professors of language. He lost his first teaching job, at Wabash College in Indiana, in fewer than six months.

Convinced that his country had no place for him—and that a country with no place for him had no place for art—he went to Europe in 1908. He settled in London and quickly became involved in its literary life, and especially prominent in movements to revolutionize poetry and identify good new poets. He supported himself by teaching and reviewing for several journals. For a while he acted as secretary to the great Irish poet William Butler Yeats. He married Dorothy Shakespear, daughter of a close friend of Yeats, in 1914. Ten years later he became involved with the American expatriate Olga Rudge and maintained relationships with both women thereafter.

As an advocate of the new, he found himself propagandizing against the very poetry that had made him want to be a poet at the start; and this contradiction remained throughout his life: on the one hand, a desire to "make it new"; on the other, a deep attachment to the old. Many of his critical essays were later collected and published in books such as *Make It New* (1934), *The ABC of Reading* (1934), *Polite Essays* (1937), and *Literary Essays* (1954). He was generous in his efforts to assist other writers in their work and in their attempts to get published; he was helpful to H. D., T. S. Eliot, James Joyce, William Carlos Williams, Robert Frost, Ernest Hemingway, and Marianne Moore, to name just a few.

Pound first campaigned for "imagism," his name for a new kind of poetry. Rather than describing something—an object or situation—and then generalizing about it, imagist poets attempted to present the object directly, avoiding the ornate diction and complex but predictable verse forms of traditional poetry. Any significance to be derived from the image had to appear inherent in its spare, clean presentation. "Go in fear of abstraction," Pound wrote. Even the rules of grammar seemed artificial; hence this new poetry tended to work in disconnected fragments. Although imagism lasted only briefly as a formal movement, most subsequent twentieth-century poetry showed its influence. Pound soon moved on to "vorticism," which, although still espousing direct and bare presentation, sought for some principle of dynamism and energy in the image. In his imagist phase Pound was connected with H. D. and Richard Aldington, a British poet who became H. D.'s husband; as a vorticist he was allied with the iconoclastic writer and artist Wyndham Lewis.

Pound thought of the United States as a culturally backward nation and longed to produce a sophisticated, worldly poetry on behalf of his country. Walt Whitman was his symbol of American poetic narrowness. His major works during his London years consisted of free translations of languages unknown to most Westerners: Provençal, Chinese, Japanese. He also experimented with the dramatic monologue form developed by the English Victorian poet Robert Browning. Poems from these years appeared in his volumes *A Lume Spento* (By the spent light; Italian), which appeared in 1908, *A Quinzaine for This Yule* (1908), and *Personae* (1910). *Persona* means "mask," and the poems in this last volume developed the dramatic monologue as a means for the poet to assume various identities and to engage in acts of historical reconstruction and empathy.

Although his view of poetry would seem to exclude the long poem as a workable form, Pound could not overcome the traditional belief that a really great poem had to be long. He hoped to write such a poem himself, a poem for his time, which would unite biography and history by representing the total content of his mind and memory. To this end he began working on his *Cantos* in 1915. The cantos were separate poems of varying lengths, combining reminiscence, meditation, description, and transcriptions from books Pound was reading, all of which were to be forged into unity by the heat of the poet's imagination. Ultimately, he produced 116 cantos, whose intricate obscurities continue to fascinate and challenge critics. The London period came to a close with two poems of disillusionment, "Hugh Selwyn Mauberley (Life and Contacts")" and "Mauberley," which described the decay of Western civilization in the aftermath of the Great War.

Looking for an explanation of what had gone wrong, Pound came upon the "social credit" theories of Major Clifford Hugh Douglas, a social economist who attributed all the ills of civilization to the interposition of money between human exchanges of goods. At this point, poetry and politics fused in Pound's work, and he began to search for a society in which art was protected from money and to record this search in poems and essays. This became a dominant theme in the *Cantos*. Leaving England for good in 1920, he lived on the Mediterranean Sea, in Paris for a time, and then settled in the small Italian town of Rapallo in 1925. His survey of history having persuaded him that the ideal society was a hierarchy with a strong leader and an agricultural economy, he greeted the Italian fascist dictator Benito Mussolini as a deliverer. His international perspective gave way to an intense localism. During World War II he voluntarily served the Italian government by making numerous English-language radio broadcasts beamed at England and the United States in which he vilified Jews, President Franklin D. Roosevelt, and American society in general. When the U.S. Army occupied Italy, Pound was arrested, held for weeks in an open-air cage at the prison camp near Pisa, and finally brought to the United States to be tried for treason. The trial did not take place, however, because the court accepted a psychiatric report to the effect that Pound was "insane and mentally unfit to be tried." From 1946 to 1958 he was a patient and a prisoner in St. Elizabeth's Hospital for the criminally insane in Washington, D.C. During those years he received visits, wrote letters, composed cantos, and continued his polemic against American society.

In 1948 the *Pisan Cantos* (LXXIV–LXXXIV) won the Library of Congress's newly established Bollingen Prize for poetry, an event that provoked tremendous debate about Pound's stature as a poet as well as a citizen. Ten years later the efforts of a committee of writers succeeded in winning Pound's release; he returned to Italy, where he died at the age of eighty-seven. He remains one of the most controversial poets of the era.

The texts of the poems included here are those of *Personae: The Collected Poems* (rev., 1949) and *The Cantos* (1976).

To Whistler, American[1]

On the loan exhibit of his paintings at the Tate Gallery.

You also, our first great
Had tried all ways;
Tested and pried and worked in many fashions,
And this much gives me heart to play the game.

Here is a part that's slight, and part gone wrong,   5
And much of little moment, and some few
Perfect as Dürer![2]
"In the Studio" and these two portraits,[3] if I had my choice!
And then these sketches in the mood of Greece?

You had your searches, your uncertainties,   10
And this is good to know—for us, I mean,
Who bear the brunt of our America
And try to wrench her impulse into art.

You were not always sure, not always set
To hiding night or tuning "symphonies";[4]   15
Had not one style from birth, but tried and pried
And stretched and tampered with the media.

You and Abe Lincoln from that mass of dolts
Show us there's chance at least of winning through.

                                 1912, 1949

Portrait d'une Femme[1]

Your mind and you are our Sargasso Sea,[2]
London has swept about you this score years
And bright ships left you this or that in fee:
Ideas, old gossip, oddments of all things,
Strange spars of knowledge and dimmed wares of price.   5
Great minds have sought you—lacking someone else.
You have been second always. Tragical?
No. You preferred it to the usual thing:
One dull man, dulling and uxorious,
One average mind—with one thought less, each year.   10
Oh, you are patient, I have seen you sit
Hours, where something might have floated up.
And now you pay one. Yes, you richly pay.

---

1. James Abbott McNeill Whistler (1834–1903), expatriate American painter.
2. Albrecht Dürer (1471–1528), German painter [en]graver.
[B]rown and Gold—de Race,' 'Grenat et Or— [pe]tit Cardinal' ('Garnet and Gold—The Little [Cardin]al')" [Pound's note]. Titles and subjects of

the portraits.
4. Whistler painted many night scenes and titled many paintings "symphonies."
1. Portrait of a lady (French).
2. Sea in the North Atlantic where boats were becalmed; named for its large masses of floating seaweed.

You are a person of some interest, one comes to you
And takes strange gain away: 15
Trophies fished up; some curious suggestion;
Fact that leads nowhere; and a tale or two,
Pregnant with mandrakes,[3] or with something else
That might prove useful and yet never proves,
That never fits a corner or shows use,   20
Or finds its hour upon the loom of days:
The tarnished, gaudy, wonderful old work;
Idols and ambergris and rare inlays,
These are your riches, your great store; and yet
For all this sea-hoard of deciduous things,   25
Strange woods half sodden, and new brighter stuff:
In the slow float of differing light and deep,
No! there is nothing! In the whole and all,
Nothing that's quite your own.
        Yet this is you.   30

                                  1912

1. A Pact

I make a pact with you, Walt Whitman—
I have detested you long enough.
I come to you as a grown child
Who has had a pig-headed father;
I am old enough now to make friends.   5
It was you that broke the new wood,
Now is a time for carving.
We have one sap and one root—
Let there be commerce between us.

                           1913, 1916

2. In a Station of the Metro[1]

The apparition of these faces in the crowd;
Petals on a wet, black bough.

                           1913, 1916

---

3. Herb used as a cathartic; believed in legend to have human properties, to shriek when pulled from the ground, and to promote pregnancy.
1. Paris subway.

3. The River-Merchant's Wife: A Letter[1]

While my hair was still cut straight across my forehead
I played about the front gate, pulling flowers.
You came by on bamboo stilts, playing horse,
You walked about my seat, playing with blue plums.
And we went on living in the village of Chōkan: 5
Two small people, without dislike or suspicion.

At fourteen I married My Lord you.
I never laughed, being bashful.
Lowering my head, I looked at the wall.
Called to, a thousand times, I never looked back.   10

At fifteen I stopped scowling,
I desired my dust to be mingled with yours
Forever and forever and forever.
Why should I climb the look out?

At sixteen you departed,   15
You went into far Ku-tō-en, by the river of swirling eddies,
And you have been gone five months.
The monkeys make sorrowful noise overhead.

You dragged your feet when you went out.
By the gate now, the moss is grown, the different mosses,   20
Too deep to clear them away!
The leaves fall early this autumn, in wind.
The paired butterflies are already yellow with August
Over the grass in the West garden;
They hurt me. I grow older.   25
If you are coming down through the narrows of the river Kiang,
Please let me know beforehand,
And I will come out to meet you
          As far as Chō-fū-Sa.

By Rihaku

1915

---

1. Adaptation from the Chinese of Li Po (701–762), named Rihaku in Japanese, from the papers of Ernest Fenollosa, an American scholar whose widow gave his papers on Japan and China to Pound.

FROM THE CANTOS

I[1]

And then went down to the ship,
Set keel to breakers, forth on the godly sea, and
We set up mast and sail on that swart ship,
Bore sheep aboard her, and our bodies also
Heavy with weeping, and winds from sternward   5
Bore us out onward with bellying canvas,
Circe's[2] this craft, the trim-coifed goddess.
Then sat we amidships, wind jamming the tiller,
Thus with stretched sail, we went over sea till day's end.
Sun to his slumber, shadows o'er all the ocean,   10
Came we then to the bounds of deepest water,
To the Kimmerian[3] lands, and peopled cities
Covered with close-webbed mist, unpierced ever
With glitter of sun-rays
Nor with stars stretched, nor looking back from heaven   15
Swartest night stretched over wretched men there
The ocean flowing backward, came we then to the place
Aforesaid by Circe.
Here did they rites, Perimedes and Eurylochus,[4]
And drawing sword from my hip   20
I dug the ell-square pitkin;[5]
Poured we libations unto each the dead,
First mead then sweet wine, water mixed with white flour.
Then prayed I many a prayer to the sickly death's-heads;
As set in Ithaca, sterile bulls of the best   25
For sacrifice, heaping the pyre with goods,
A sheep to Tiresias only, black and a bell-sheep.[6]
Dark blood flowed in the fosse,[7]
Souls out of Erebus,[8] cadaverous dead, of brides
Of youths and of the old who had borne much;   30
Souls stained with recent tears, girls tender,
Men many, mauled with bronze lance heads,
Battle spoil, bearing yet dreory[9] arms,
These many crowded about me; with shouting,
Pallor upon me, cried to my men for more beasts;   35
Slaughtered the herds, sheep slain of bronze;
Poured ointment, cried to the gods,
To Pluto the strong, and praised Proserpine;[1]
Unsheathed the narrow sword,
I sat to keep off the impetuous impotent dead,   40

1. Lines 1–68 are an adaptation of book 11 of Homer's *Odyssey*, which recounts Odysseus's voyage to Hades, the underworld of the dead. Odysseus was a native of Ithaca, in Greece.
2. Odysseus lived for a year with Circe before deciding to return to Ithaca. She told him to get directions for his trip home from the Theban prophet Tiresias in the underworld.
3. Mythical people living in a foggy region at the edge of the earth.
4. Two of Odysseus's companions.
5. Small pit, one ell (45 inches) on each side.
6. The prophet Tiresias is likened to a sheep that leads the herd.
7. Ditch, trench.
8. Land of the dead, Hades.
9. Bloody.
1. Goddess of regeneration and wife of Pluto, god of the underworld.

Till I should hear Tiresias.
But first Elpenor[2] came, our friend Elpenor,
Unburied, cast on the wide earth,
Limbs that we left in the house of Circe,
Unwept, unwrapped in sepulchre, since toils urged other.   45
Pitiful spirit. And I cried in hurried speech:
"Elpenor, how art thou come to this dark coast?
"Cam'st thou afoot, outstripping seamen?"
            And he in heavy speech:
"Ill fate and abundant wine. I slept in Circe's ingle.[3]   50
"Going down the long ladder unguarded,
"I fell against the buttress,
"Shattered the nape-nerve, the soul sought Avernus.[4]
"But thou, O King, I bid remember me, unwept, unburied,
"Heap up mine arms, be tomb by sea-bord, and inscribed: 55
"A *man of no fortune, and with a name to come.*
"And set my oar up, that I swung mid fellows."

And Anticlea[5] came, whom I beat off, and then Tiresias Theban,
Holding his golden wand, knew me, and spoke first:
"A second time?[6] why? man of ill star,   60
"Facing the sunless dead and this joyless region?
"Stand from the fosse, leave me my bloody bever[7]
"For soothsay."
            And I stepped back,
And he strong with the blood, said then: "Odysseus   65
"Shalt return through spiteful Neptune,[8] over dark seas,
"Lose all companions." And then Anticlea came.
Lie quiet Divus. I mean, that is Andreas Divus,
In officina Wecheli, 1538, out of Homer.[9]
And he sailed, by Sirens and thence outward and away   70
And unto Circe.
            Venerandam,[1]
In the Cretan's phrase, with the golden crown, Aphrodite,
Cypri munimenta sortita est,[2] mirthful, orichalchi,[3] with golden
Girdles and breast bands, thou with dark eyelids   75
Bearing the golden bough of Argicida.[4] So that:

                                                        1925

---

2. Odysseus's companion who fell to his death from the roof of Circe's house and was left unburied by his friends.
3. Corner, house.
4. Lake near Naples, the entrance to Hades.
5. Odysseus's mother. In the *Odyssey,* Odysseus weeps at the sight of her but obeys Circe's instructions to speak to no one until Tiresias has drunk the blood that will enable him to speak.
6. They met once before on earth.
7. Libation.
8. God of the sea, who was to delay Odysseus's return by a storm at sea.
9. Pound acknowledges using the Renaissance Latin translation of Homer, produced in the workshop ("officina") of Wechel in Paris in 1538, by Andreas Divus.

1. Commanding reverence; a phrase describing Aphrodite, the goddess of love, in the Latin translation of the second Homeric Hymn by Georgius Dartona Cretensis (the "Cretan" in line 73).
2. The fortresses of Cyprus were her appointed realm (Latin).
3. Of copper (Latin); a reference to gifts presented to Aphrodite in the second Homeric Hymn.
4. Aeneas offered the Golden Bough to Proserpina before descending to the underworld. Pound associates Persephone with Aphrodite, goddess of love and slayer of the Greeks (Argi) during the Trojan War, and associates the Golden Bough, sacred to the goddess Diana, with the magic wand of the god Hermes, slayer of the many-eyed Argus ("Argicida") and liberator of Io.

H. D. (HILDA DOOLITTLE)
1886–1961

In January 1913, Harriet Monroe's influential little magazine, *Poetry,* printed three vivid poems by an unknown "H. D., Imagiste." These spare, elegant lyrics were among the first important products of the "imagist movement": poems devoid of explanation and declamation, unrhymed and lacking regular beat, depending on the power of an image to arrest attention and convey emotion. The poet's pen name, the movement's name, and the submission to the magazine were all the work of Ezra Pound, poet and tireless publicist for anything new in the world of poetry. The poems themselves had been written by his friend Hilda Doolittle. In later years, H. D. would look back at these events as epitomizing her dilemma: how to be a woman poet speaking in a world where women were spoken for and about by men. It is, perhaps, a symbol of her sense of difficulty that, though she strove for a voice that could be recognized as clearly feminine, she continued to publish under the name that Pound had devised for her.

She was born in Bethlehem, Pennsylvania, one girl in a family of five boys. Her mother was a musician and music teacher, active in the Moravian church to which many in Bethlehem belonged. The symbols and rituals of this group, along with its tradition of secrecy created in response to centuries of oppression, had much to do with H. D.'s interest in images and her attraction in later life to occult and other symbol systems: the cabala, numerology, the tarot, and psychoanalysis.

When her father, an astronomer and mathematician, was appointed director of the observatory at the University of Pennsylvania, the family moved to a suburb of Philadelphia. There, when she was fifteen years old, H. D. met Ezra Pound, a student at the university, already dedicated to poetry and acting the poet's role with dramatic intensity. The two were engaged for a while, but Pound's influence continued long after each had gone on to other partners. H. D. attended college at Bryn Mawr for two years; in 1911 she made a bold move to London, where Pound had gone some years earlier. She married a member of his circle, the English poet Richard Aldington, in 1913. With Aldington she studied Greek and read the classics, but the marriage was not a success and was destroyed by their separation during World War I when Aldington went into the army and served in France.

The year 1919 was terrible for H. D.: her brother Gilbert was killed in the fighting in France, her father died soon thereafter, her marriage broke up, close friendships with Pound and with D. H. Lawrence came to an end, she had a nearly fatal case of flu, and amid all this gave birth to a daughter who Aldington said was not his child. But she was rescued from the worst of her emotional and financial troubles by Winifred Ellerman, whose father, a shipping magnate, was one of the wealthiest men in England. Ellerman, a writer who had adopted the pen name Bryher, had initially been attracted by H. D.'s poetry; their relationship developed first as a love affair and then into a lifelong friendship.

In 1923, H. D. settled in Switzerland. With Bryher's financial help she raised her daughter and cared for her ailing mother, who had joined her household. During 1933 and 1934 she spent time in Vienna, where she underwent analysis by Sigmund Freud, hoping to understand both her writer's block and what she called her "two loves" of women and men. Freud's theory of the unconscious and the disguised ways in which it reaches expression accorded well with H. D.'s understanding of how the unexplained images in a poem could be significant; the images were coded personal meanings. H. D.'s religious mysticism clashed with Freud's materialism, however, and she had mixed reactions to Freud's developing theory that women's unhappiness was determined by their sense of biological inferiority to men. But H. D. was instrumental (with Bryher's help) in getting Freud, who was Jewish, safely to London when the Nazi regime took over in Austria. When World War II broke out H. D. went back to London to share England's fate in crisis.

During the 1930s she worked mostly in prose forms and composed several autobiographical pieces (some of which remain unpublished). Like many major poets of the era, H. D. came in time to feel the need to write longer works; the bombardment of London inspired three long related poems about World War II, *The Walls Do Not Fall* (1944), *Tribute to the Angels* (1945), and *The Flowering of the Rod* (1946), which appeared together as *Trilogy*. In them she combined layers of historical and personal experience; wars going back to the Trojan War all fused in one image of humankind forever imposing and enduring violence.

The personal and the historical had always been one to her, and she became increasingly attracted to the image of Helen, the so-called cause of the Trojan War, as an image of herself. According to Homer's *Iliad*, Helen's beauty led Paris, a Trojan prince, to steal her from her Greek husband, Menelaus; and all the Greek warriors made common cause to get her back. After ten years' encamped before the walls of Troy, they found a devious way to enter the city and destroy it. H. D. was struck by the fact that the legend was related entirely from the male point of view; Helen never had a chance to speak. The object of man's acts and the subject of their poems, she was herself always silent. If Helen tried to speak, would she even have a voice or a point of view? Out of these broodings, and helped by her study of symbols, H. D. wrote her meditative epic of more than fourteen hundred lines, *Helen in Egypt*. The poem, composed between 1951 and 1955, consists of three books of interspersed verse and prose commentary, which follow Helen's quest. "She herself is the writing" that she seeks to understand, the poet observes.

H. D.'s imagist poetry, for which she was known during her lifetime, represents the imagist credo with its vivid phrasing, compelling imagery, free verse, short poetic line, and avoidance of abstraction and generalization. She followed Pound's example in producing many translations of poetry from older literature, especially from her favorite Greek poets. Her natural images are influenced by her early immersion in astronomy as well as by Greek poetry's Mediterranean settings. Austere landscapes of sea, wind, stars, and sand are contrasted with sensual figures of jewels, honey, and shells. Traditional metaphorical resources of earlier women's poetry, such flowers and birds, are absorbed into modernism's aesthetic of "fiery tempered steel." As when her "Oread" calls upon the sea to "splash your great pines / on our rocks," H. D.'s best-known poems embody high modernism's goal of condensing forces at once lush and shattering, violent and creative, into a single arresting image.

The texts of the poems included here are those of *Collected Poems 1912–1944*, edited by Louis L. Martz (1983).

Mid-day

The light beats upon me.
I am startled—
a split leaf crackles on the paved floor—
I am anguished—defeated.

A slight wind shakes the seed-pods—   5
my thoughts are spent
as the black seeds.
My thoughts tear me,
I dread their fever.
I am scattered in its whirl.   10
I am scattered like
the hot shrivelled seeds.

The shrivelled seeds
are split on the path—
the grass bends with dust,   15
the grape slips
under its crackled leaf:
yet far beyond the spent seed-pods,
and the blackened stalks of mint,
the poplar is bright on the hill,   20
the poplar spreads out,
deep-rooted among trees.

O poplar, you are great
among the hill-stones,
while I perish on the path   25
among the crevices of the rocks.

                                                              1916

Oread[1]

Whirl up, sea—
whirl your pointed pines,
splash your great pines
on our rocks,
hurl your green over us,   5
cover us with your pools of fir.

                                                        1914, 1924

Leda[1]

Where the slow river
meets the tide,
a red swan lifts red wings
and darker beak,
and underneath the purple down   5
of his soft breast
uncurls his coral feet.

Through the deep purple
of the dying heat
of sun and mist,   10
the level ray of sun-beam
has caressed
the lily with dark breast,

---

1. A nymph of mountains and hills.
1. In Greek mythology, Leda is the mortal raped by Zeus, in the guise of a swan. Helen of Troy was her daughter.

and flecked with richer gold
its golden crest. 15

Where the slow lifting
of the tide,
floats into the river
and slowly drifts
among the reeds, 20
and lifts the yellow flags,
he floats
where tide and river meet.

Ah kingly kiss—
no more regret 25
nor old deep memories
to mar the bliss;
where the low sedge is thick,
the gold day-lily
outspreads and rests 30
beneath soft fluttering
of red swan wings
and the warm quivering
of the red swan's breast.

1919, 1921

Fragment 113

"Neither honey nor bee for me."
—Sappho.[1]

Not honey,
not the plunder of the bee
from meadow or sand-flower
or mountain bush;
from winter-flower or shoot 5
born of the later heat:
not honey, not the sweet
stain on the lips and teeth:
not honey, not the deep
plunge of soft belly 10
and the clinging of the gold-edged
pollen-dusted feet;

not so—
though rapture blind my eyes,
and hunger crisp 15
dark and inert my mouth,

---

1. Greek woman lyric poet of Lesbos in the 7th century B.C.E.

not honey, not the south,
not the tall stalk
of red twin-lilies,
nor light branch of fruit tree   20
caught in flexible light branch;

not honey, not the south;
ah flower of purple iris,
flower of white,
or of the iris, withering the grass—   25
for fleck of the sun's fire,
gathers such heat and power,
that shadow-print is light,
cast through the petals
of the yellow iris flower;   30

not iris—old desire—old passion—
old forgetfulness—old pain—
not this, nor any flower,
but if you turn again,
seek strength of arm and throat,   35
touch as the god;
neglect the lyre-note;
knowing that you shall feel,
about the frame,
no trembling of the string   40
but heat, more passionate
of bone and the white shell
and fiery tempered steel.

                                                    1922

Helen[1]

All Greece hates
the still eyes in the white face,
the lustre as of olives
where she stands,
and the white hands.   5

All Greece reviles
the wan face when she smiles,
hating it deeper still
when it grows wan and white,
remembering past enchantments   10
and past ills.

---

1. In Greek legend, the wife of Menelaus; her kidnaping by the Trojan prince Paris started the Trojan War. She was the daughter of the god Zeus, the product of his rape, when disguised as a swan, of the mortal Leda.

Greece sees unmoved,
God's daughter, born of love,
the beauty of cool feet
and slenderest knees,
could love indeed the maid,
only if she were laid,
white ash amid funereal cypresses.

15

1924

MARIANNE MOORE
1887–1972

Marianne Moore was a radically inventive modernist, greatly admired by other poets of her generation, and a powerful influence on such later writers as Robert Lowell, Randall Jarrell, and Richard Wilbur. Like her forerunner Emily Dickinson, she made of the traditional and constraining "woman's place" a protected space to do her own work, but unlike Emily Dickinson, she was a deliberate professional, publishing her poems regularly, in touch with the movements and artists of her time. She was famous for the statement that poetry, though departing from the real world, re-created that world within its forms: poems were "imaginary gardens with real toads in them." Her earlier work is distinguished by great precision of observation and language, ornate diction, and complex stanza and prosodic patterns. Her later work is much less ornate; and in revising her poetry, she tended to simplify and shorten.

She was born in Kirkwood, Missouri, a suburb of St. Louis. In her childhood, the family was abandoned by her father; they moved to Carlisle, Pennsylvania, where—in a pattern common among both men and women writers of this period—her mother supported them by teaching school. She went to Bryn Mawr College, graduating in 1909; traveled with her mother in England and France in 1911; and returned to Carlisle to teach at the U.S. Indian School between 1911 and 1915. Having begun to write poetry in college, she was first published in 1915 and 1916 in such little magazines as the *Egoist* (an English magazine with which Ezra Pound was associated), *Poetry*, and *Others* (a journal for experimental writing with which William Carlos Williams was associated, founded by Alfred Kreymbourg, a New York poet and playwright). Through these magazines she entered the avant-garde and modernist world. She never married; in 1916 she and her mother merged their household with that of Moore's brother, a Presbyterian minister, and they moved with him to a parish in Brooklyn, New York. There Moore was close to literary circles and Ebbets Field, where the Dodgers, then a Brooklyn baseball team, had their home stadium. Moore was a lifelong fan.

While holding jobs in schools and libraries, Moore worked at her poetry. A volume called simply *Poems* was brought out in London in 1921 without her knowledge through the efforts of two women friends who were writers, H. D. (whom she had met at Bryn Mawr) and Bryher. Another book, *Observations*, appeared in 1924 and won the Dial Award. In 1925 she began to work as editor of the *Dial*, continuing in this influential position until the magazine was disbanded in 1929. Her reviews and editorial judgments were greatly respected, although her preference for elegance and decorum over sexual frankness was not shared by some of the writers—Hart Crane and James Joyce among them—whose work she rejected or published only after they revised it.

As a critic of poetry Moore wrote numerous essays—her collected prose makes a larger book than her collected poetry. She believed that poets usually undervalued prose; "precision, economy of statement, logic" were features of good prose that could "liberate" the imagination, she wrote. In writing about animals she was able to take advantage of two different prose modes that attracted her—scientific and historical description. Her poems were an amalgam of her own observation and her readings, which she acknowledged by quotation marks and often by footnotes as well. In Moore's writings, the reader almost never finds the conventional poetic allusions that invoke a great tradition and assert the present poet's place in it. Moore's poems typically juxtapose disparate areas of human knowledge and combine the elevated with the ordinary. Her notebooks suggest, for example, that the image of the kiwi bird in "The Mind is an Enchanting Thing" emerged from a sketch Moore made of a shoe-polish tin; she praises the human mind both for its capacity to be mesmerized by the small facets of its ordinary environment and for its changeful, self-undoing freedom.

Against the exactitude and "unbearable accuracy" (as she put it) of her language, Moore counterpointed a complex texture of stanza form and versification. Pound worked with the clause, Williams with the line, H. D. with the image, Stevens and Stein with the word; Moore, unlike these modernist contemporaries, used the entire stanza as the unit of her poetry. Her stanza is composed of regular lines counted by syllables, instead of by stress, which are connected in an elaborate verse pattern, and in which rhymes often occur at unaccented syllables and even in the middle of a word. The effects she achieves are complex and subtle; she was often called the "poet's poet" of her day because the reader needed expert technical understanding to recognize what she was doing.

Nevertheless, her poetry also had a thematic, declarative edge which the outbreak of World War II led her to expand. In "The Paper Nautilus," she drew on her characteristic vein of natural observation in order to will that a threatened civilization be protected by love. At the same time, Moore was keenly aware of her distance, as a civilian and a woman, from direct experience of combat; "In Distrust of Merits," her most famous poem of the war, reflects Moore's struggle to adopt an ethically responsible relationship toward the fighting she could only know through newsreels and photographs.

Moore received the Bollingen, National Book, and Pulitzer awards for *Collected Poems* in 1951. Throughout her lifetime she continued to revise, expand, cut, and select, so that from volume to volume a poem with the same name may be a very different work. Her *Complete Poems* of 1967 represented her poetry as she wanted it remembered, but a full understanding of Moore calls for reading all of the versions of her changing work.

Poetry[1]

I, too, dislike it: there are things that are important beyond all
　　　　this fiddle.
　　Reading it, however, with a perfect contempt for it, one
　　　　　discovers in
　　　　it after all, a place for the genuine.
　　　　　Hands that can grasp, eyes
　　　　　　that can dilate, hair that can rise　　　　　　　　5
　　　　　　　if it must, these things are important not because a

1. The version printed here follows the text and format of *Selected Poems* (1935).

high-sounding interpretation can be put upon them but because
    they are
useful. When they become so derivative as to become
    unintelligible,
the same thing may be said for all of us, that we
    do not admire what   10
    we cannot understand: the bat
        holding on upside down or in quest of something to

eat, elephants pushing, a wild horse taking a roll, a tireless wolf
    under
a tree, the immovable critic twitching his skin like a horse
    that feels a flea, the base-
ball fan, the statistician—   15
    nor is it valid
        to discriminate against "business documents and

school-books";[2] all these phenomena are important. One must
    make a distinction
however: when dragged into prominence by half poets, the
    result is not poetry,
nor till the poets among us can be   20
    "literalists of
    the imagination"[3]—above
        insolence and triviality and can present

for inspection, "imaginary gardens with real toads in them," shall
    we have
it. In the meantime, if you demand on the one hand,   25
the raw material of poetry in
    all its rawness and
    that which is on the other hand
genuine, then you are interested in poetry.

1921, 1935

To a Snail[1]

If "compression is the first grace of style,"[2]
you have it. Contractility is a virtue
as modesty is a virtue.

---

2. Diary of Tolstoy (Dutton), p. 84. "Where the boundary between prose and poetry lies, I shall never be able to understand. The question is raised in manuals of style, yet the answer to it lies beyond me. Poetry is verse; prose is not verse. Or else poetry is everything with the exception of business documents and school books" [Moore's note].
3. Yeats's *Ideas of Good and Evil* (A. H. Bullen), p. 182. "The limitation of his view was from the very intensity of his vision; he was a too literal realist of imagination, as others are of nature; and

because he believed that the figures seen by the mind's eye, when exalted by inspiration, were 'eternal existences,' symbols of divine essences, he hated every grace of style that might obscure their lineaments" [Moore's note].
1. The text is from *Complete Poems* (1967).
2. "The very first grace of style is that which comes from compression." *Demetrius on Style* translated by W. Hamilton Fyfe. Heinemann, 1932 [Moore's note].

It is not the acquisition of any one thing
that is able to adorn, 5
or the incidental quality that occurs
as a concomitant of something well said,
that we value in style,
but the principle that is hid:
in the absence of feet, "a method of conclusions"; 10
"a knowledge of principles,"
in the curious phenomenon of your occipital horn.

1924

The Paper Nautilus[1]

For authorities whose hopes
are shaped by mercenaries?
Writers entrapped by
teatime fame and by
commuters' comforts? Not for these 5
the paper nautilus
constructs her thin glass shell.

Giving her perishable
souvenir of hope, a dull
white outside and smooth- 10
edged inner surface
glossy as the sea, the watchful
maker of it guards it
day and night; she scarcely

eats until the eggs are hatched. 15
Buried eight-fold in her eight
arms, for she is in
a sense a devil-
fish, her glass ram'shorn-cradled freight
is hid but is not crushed; 20
as Hercules,[2] bitten

by a crab loyal to the hydra,
was hindered to succeed,
the intensively
watched eggs coming from 25
the shell free it when they are freed,—
leaving its wasp-nest flaws
of white on white, and close-

laid Ionic[3] chiton-folds
like the lines in the mane of 30

1. The text is from *Complete Poems* (1967).
2. Hero of Greek myth, who performed numerous
exploits including battle with the hydra, a many-
headed monster.
3. Classical Greek, specifically Athenian.

a Parthenon[4] horse,
   round which the arms had
wound themselves as if they knew love
   is the only fortress
   strong enough to trust to.   35

               1941, 1967

The Mind Is an Enchanting Thing[1]

is an enchanted thing
   like the glaze on a
katydid-wing
      subdivided by sun
       till the nettings are legion.   5
Like Gieseking playing Scarlatti;[2]

like the apteryx[3]-awl
   as a beak, or the
kiwi's rain-shawl
      of haired feathers, the mind   10
       feeling its way as though blind,
walks along with its eyes on the ground.

It has memory's ear
   that can hear without
having to hear.
      Like the gyroscope's fall,   15
       truly unequivocal
because trued by regnant certainty,

it is a power of
      strong enchantment. It   20
is like the dove-
      neck animated by
       sun; it is memory's eye;
it's conscientious inconsistency.

It tears off the veil; tears   25
   the temptation, the
mist the heart wears,
      from its eye—if the heart
       has a face; it takes apart
dejection. It's fire in the dove-neck's   30

---

4. Temple in Athens decorated by a carved marble band of sculptures, including processions of horses.
1. The text is from *Complete Poems* (1967).
2. Walter Wilhelm Gieseking (1895–1956), French-born German pianist, known for his renditions of compositions by the Italian composer Domenico Scarlatti (1685–1757).
3. A flightless New Zealand bird, related to the kiwi, with a beak shaped like an awl.

iridescence; in the
    inconsistencies
of Scarlatti.
      Unconfusion submits
        its confusion to proof; it's   35
not a Herod's oath that cannot change.[4]

                                  1944

In Distrust of Merits[1]

Strengthened to live, strengthened to die for
    medals and positioned victories?
They're fighting, fighting, fighting the blind
    man who thinks he sees,—
who cannot see that the enslaver is   5
enslaved; the hater, harmed. O shining O
    film star, O tumultuous
        ocean lashed till small things go
as they will, the mountainous
        wave makes us who look, know   10

depth. Lost at sea before they fought! O
    star of David, star of Bethlehem,
O black imperial lion[2]
    of the Lord—emblem
of a risen world—be joined at last, be   15
joined. There is hate's crown beneath which all is
    death; there's love's without which none
        is king; the blessed deeds bless
the halo. As contagion
        of sickness makes sickness,   20

contagion of trust can make trust. They're
    fighting in deserts and caves, one by
one, in battalions and squadrons;
    they're fighting that I
may yet recover from the disease, My   25
Self; some have it lightly; some will die. "Man's
    wolf to man" and we devour
        ourselves. The enemy could not
have made a greater breach in our
        defenses. One pilot-   30

---

4. Herod Antipas (d. 39 c.e.), ruler of Judea under the Romans. He had John the Baptist beheaded to fulfill a promise to Salome (Mark 6.22–27).
1. The text is from *Complete Poems* (1967).
2. Emperor Haile Selassie of Ethiopia, leader of his country's resistance against Italian occupation during World War II; after Mussolini's fall in 1943, Selassie declared Ethiopia "less interested in vengeance for the past than in justice for the future." "Star of David": a symbol of Judaism, "star of Bethlehem": of Christianity.

ing a blind man can escape him, but
    Job disheartened by false comfort[3] knew
that nothing can be so defeating
    as a blind man who
can see. O alive who are dead, who are   35
proud not to see, O small dust of the earth
        that walks so arrogantly
            trust begets power and faith is
        an affectionate thing. We
          vow, we make this promise   40

to the fighting—it's a promise—"We'll
    never hate black, white, red, yellow, Jew,
Gentile, Untouchable."[4] We are
    not competent to
make our vows. With set jaw they are fighting,   45
fighting, fighting,—some we love whom we know,
    some we love but know not—that
        hearts may feel and not be numb.
    It cures me; or am I what
        I can't believe in? Some   50

in snow, some on crags, some in quicksands,
    little by little, much by much, they
are fighting fighting fighting that where
    there was death there may
be life. "When a man is prey to anger,   55
he is moved by outside things; when he holds
    his ground in patience patience
        patience, that is action or
    beauty," the soldier's defense
        and hardest armor for   60

the fight. The world's an orphans' home. Shall
    we never have peace without sorrow?
without pleas of the dying for
    help that won't come? O
quiet form upon the dust, I cannot   65
look and yet I must. If these great patient
    dyings—all these agonies
        and wound bearings and bloodshed—
    can teach us how to live, these
        dyings were not wasted.   70

Hate-hardened heart, O heart of iron,
    iron is iron till it is rust.
There never was a war that was
    not inward; I must
fight till I have conquered in myself what   75

3. When undergoing Jehovah's test of his fidelity, Job rejected the attempts of friends to comfort him.

4. The lowest hereditary caste in India.

causes war, but I would not believe it.
　　　I inwardly did nothing.
　　　　O Iscariot[5]-like crime!
　　　Beauty is everlasting
　　　and dust is for a time.　　　　　　　80

1944

5. Judas Iscariot was the apostle who betrayed Jesus Christ.

T. S. ELIOT
1888–1965

The publication in 1922 of *The Waste Land* in the British little magazine *Criterion* and the American *Dial* was a cultural and literary event. The poem's title and the view it incorporated of modern civilization seemed, to many, to catch precisely the state of culture and society after World War I. The war, supposedly fought to save European civilization, had been the most brutal and destructive in Western history: what kind of civilization, after all, could have allowed it to take place? The long, fragmented structure of *The Waste Land*, too, contained so many technical innovations that ideas of what poetry was and how it worked seemed fundamentally changed. A generation of poets either imitated or resisted it.

The author of this poem was an American living in London, T. S. Eliot. He had a comfortable upbringing in St. Louis: his mother was involved in cultural and charitable activities and wrote poetry; his father was a successful businessman. His grandfather Eliot had been a New England Unitarian minister who, moving to St. Louis, had founded Washington University. Eliot was thus a product of that New England–based "genteel tradition" that shaped the nation's cultural life after the Civil War. He attended Harvard for both undergraduate and graduate work (1906–10, 1911–14). He studied at the Sorbonne in Paris from 1910 to 1911 and at Oxford from 1915 to 1916, writing a dissertation on the idealistic philosophy of the English logician and metaphysician F. H. Bradley (1846–1924). The war prevented Eliot from returning to Harvard for the oral defense for his doctoral degree, and this delay became the occasion of his turning to a life in poetry and letters rather than in academics.

Eliot had begun writing traditional poetry as a college student. In 1908, however, he read Arthur Symons's *The Symbolist Movement in Literature* and learned about Jules LaForgue and other French Symbolist poets. Symons's book altered Eliot's view of poetry, as "The Love Song of J. Alfred Prufrock" (published in *Poetry* in 1915) and "Preludes" (published in *Blast* in the same year) clearly showed. Ezra Pound, reading this work, began enthusiastically introducing Eliot in literary circles as a young American who had "trained himself *and* modernized himself *on his own.*" Pound helped Eliot over several years to get financially established. In addition, he was a perceptive reader and critic of Eliot's draft poems.

Eliot settled in England, marrying Vivian Haigh-Wood in 1915. Separated in 1932, they never divorced; Haigh-Wood died in a mental institution in 1947. After marrying, Eliot worked in London, first as a teacher and then from 1917 to 1925 in the foreign department of Lloyd's Bank, hoping to find time to write poetry and literary essays. His criticism was published in the *Egoist* and then in the little magazine that he founded, *Criterion*, which was published from 1922 to 1939. His persuasive style, a mixture of advocacy and judiciousness, effectively counterpointed Pound's aggressive, confrontational approach; the two together had a tremendous effect on how poetry of the day was written and how poetry of the past was evaluated. More than any other Americans they defined what is now thought of as "high" modernism.

Eliot began working on *The Waste Land* in 1921 and finished it in a Swiss sanatorium while recovering from a mental collapse brought on by overwork, marital problems, and general depression. He accepted some alterations suggested by his wife and cut huge chunks out of the poem on Pound's advice. Indeed, although Pound's work on the poem was all excision, study of the manuscript before and after Pound's suggestions were incorporated has led some critics to suggest that we should think of *The Waste Land* as jointly authored. The poem as published in *Criterion* and the *Dial* had no footnotes; these were added for its publication in book form and added yet another layer (possibly self-mocking) to the complex texture of the poem.

The Waste Land consists of five discontinuous segments, each composed of fragments incorporating multiple voices and characters, literary and historical allusions, vignettes of contemporary life, surrealistic images, myths and legends. "These fragments I have shored against my ruins," the poet writes, asking whether he can form any coherent structure from the splinters of civilization. Lacking narrative and expository shape, the poem is organized by recurrent allusions to the myth of seasonal death and rebirth that, according to much anthropological thinking of the time, underlay all religions. In Sir James Frazer's multivolume *The Golden Bough* (1890–1915) and Jessie Weston's *From Ritual to Romance* (1920) Eliot found a repertory of myths through which he could invoke, without specifically naming any religion, the story of a desert land brought to life by a king's sacrifice. Although it gestured toward religious belief, *The Waste Land* was not affirmative; the quest for regeneration in a cacophonous, desolate landscape remains unfulfilled.

Many readers saw *The Waste Land* as the definitive cultural statement of its time, but it was not definitive for Eliot. In fact, for Eliot himself the poem may have been much less broadly conceived and, above all, an indirect confession of personal discord. Whatever the fate of culture, the individual needed to work for personal certainty. In a preface to the collection of essays *For Lancelot Andrewes* (1928) he declared himself a "classicist in literature, royalist in politics, and anglo-catholic in religion." After "The Hollow Men" and the "Sweeney" poems, which continue *The Waste Land*'s critique of modern civilization, he turned increasingly to poems of religious doubt and reconciliation. "The Journey of the Magi" and "Ash Wednesday" are poems about the search for a faith that is desperately needed, yet difficult to sustain. The *Four Quartets*, begun with "Burnt Norton" in 1934 and completed in 1943, are poems written after his conversion to Anglicanism; they are not so much reports of secure faith as dramatizations of the difficult process of arriving at belief. In this process Eliot found a center for his own life as well as for his later poetry. The *Four Quartets* incorporate a good deal of the discursive and expository, elements that he had objected to in his earlier essays and dropped from his earlier poems.

An emphasis on order, hierarchy, and racial homogeneity emerged in Eliot's social essays of the later 1920s and 1930s; a strain of crude anti-Semitism had appeared in the earlier Sweeney poems. As European politics became increasingly turbulent, the initial cosmopolitan, international sensibility of modernists like Eliot and Pound tended to be replaced by a belief in localism. In addition, the stability promised by totalitarian regimes was often appealing, and the Communist rejection of all religion tended to drive the more theistic modernists into the opposing camp of fascism. Pound's and Eliot's fascist sympathies in the 1930s, together with their immense influence on poetry, had the result of linking the modernist movement with reactionary politics in the public's perception. Modernists, however, did not form a unified group; their politics ranged from the extreme right to the far left; many were centrists or liberals; and many despised politics completely.

When World War II began, Eliot, unlike Pound, abandoned politics. He had also put forth a poetics according to which poetry existed in a realm of its own, in which poems were to be considered only in terms of their own structures and in connection with other poetry. This was the thesis of his influential "Tradition and the Individual Talent," which defined the Western poetic tradition as an organic whole, an elastic equilibrium that constantly reformed itself to accommodate new poets who, therefore, became part of this whole. This antipolitical approach had a major influence on the practices of the close-reading critics whose work is known collectively as the "New Criticism." In other essays, Eliot denigrated didactic, expository, or narrative poets like Milton and the Victorians while applauding the verbally complex, ironic, indirect, symbolic work of seventeenth-century Metaphysical poets like Donne and Herbert.

For the New Criticism, which analyzed poems for imagery, allusion, ambiguity, and the like, Eliot's essays provided theory, his poetry opportunities for practical criticism. But when critics used Eliot's standards of difficult indirection to judge literary quality and made interpretation the main task of readers, they often overlooked the simple lyricism, obvious didacticism, and straightforward humor of Eliot's own poetry. And they failed to see the poems' specific cultural and autobiographical content.

However elitist his pronouncements, however hostile to modernity he claimed to be, Eliot actually drew heavily on popular forms and longed to have wide cultural influence. There are vaudeville turns throughout *The Waste Land*. He admired Charlie Chaplin and wanted "as large and miscellaneous an audience as possible." He pursued this ambition by writing verse plays. *Murder in the Cathedral* (1935) was a church pageant; *The Family Reunion* (1939), *The Cocktail Party* (1949), *The Confidential Clerk* (1953), and *The Elder Statesman* (1959), all religious in theme (though their symbolism was often hidden), were successfully produced in London and on Broadway. He never became a popular poet, however, despite his tremendous impact on the teaching and writing of poetry. Although Eliot remained a resident of England, he returned to the United States frequently to lecture and to give readings of his poems. He married his assistant, Valerie Fletcher, in 1957. By the time of his death he had become a social and cultural institution.

The text of the poems is that of *The Complete Poems and Plays of T. S. Eliot* (1969).

The Love Song of J. Alfred Prufrock

> *S'io credessi che mia risposta fosse*
> *a persona che mai tornasse al mondo,*
> *questa fiamma staria senza più scosse.*
> *Ma per ciò che giammai di questo fondo*
> *non tornò vivo alcun, s'i'odo il vero,*
> *senza tema d'infamia ti rispondo.*[1]

Let us go then, you and I,
When the evening is spread out against the sky
Like a patient etherised upon a table;
Let us go, through certain half-deserted streets,
The muttering retreats   5
Of restless nights in one-night cheap hotels
And sawdust restaurants with oyster-shells:
Streets that follow like a tedious argument

---

1. If I thought that my reply would be to one who would ever return to the world, this flame would stay without further movement; but since none has ever returned alive from this depth, if what I hear is true, I answer you without fear of infamy (Italian; Dante's *Inferno* 27.61–66). The speaker, Guido da Montefeltro, consumed in flame as punishment for giving false counsel, confesses his shame without fear of its being reported since he believes Dante cannot return to earth.

Of insidious intent
To lead you to an overwhelming question . . .   10
Oh, do not ask, 'What is it?'
Let us go and make our visit.

In the room the women come and go
Talking of Michelangelo.

The yellow fog that rubs its back upon the window-panes,   15
The yellow smoke that rubs its muzzle on the window-panes,
Licked its tongue into the corners of the evening,

Lingered upon the pools that stand in drains,
Let fall upon its back the soot that falls from chimneys,
Slipped by the terrace, made a sudden leap,   20
And seeing that it was a soft October night,
Curled once about the house, and fell asleep.

And indeed there will be time²
For the yellow smoke that slides along the street
Rubbing its back upon the window-panes;   25
There will be time, there will be time
To prepare a face to meet the faces that you meet;
There will be time to murder and create,
And time for all the works and days³ of hands
That lift and drop a question on your plate;   30
Time for you and time for me,
And time yet for a hundred indecisions,
And for a hundred visions and revisions,
Before the taking of a toast and tea.

In the room the women come and go   35
Talking of Michelangelo.

And indeed there will be time
To wonder, 'Do I dare?' and, 'Do I dare?'
Time to turn back and descend the stair,
With a bald spot in the middle of my hair—   40
(They will say: 'How his hair is growing thin!')
My morning coat, my collar mounting firmly to the chin,
My necktie rich and modest, but asserted by a simple pin—
(They will say: 'But how his arms and legs are thin!')
facte? Do I dare   45
Disturb the universe?
In a minute there is time
For decisions and revisions which a minute will reverse.

For I have known them all already, known them all—
Have known the evenings, mornings, afternoons,   50

2. An echo of Andrew Marvell, "To His Coy Mis-   3. *Works and Days* is a didactic poem about farm-
tress" (1681): "Had we but world enough and   ing by the Greek poet Hesiod (8th century B.C.E.).
time."

The Modern Samson, Thomas Nast, 1868

Known as the "Gladiator of the Political Pencil," Nast (1840–1902), a Radical Republican (liberal, progressive) supporter of the Union cause, skewered political corruption; his cartoons were said to have elected Lincoln and brought down the Tammany Hall corruption ring of "Boss" Tweed. This image, which ran in *Harper's Weekly* on October 3, 1868, drawn to expose opposition to black male suffrage, shows voting rights (Samson's hair) cut off by southern Democrats (Delilah) and their northern allies. In the left foreground the Bible and other books are burning. Among the armed figures in the left background are (second from left) Nathan Bedford Forrest, Confederate general; a squatting Robert E. Lee; presidential nominee Horatio Seymour, with demonically horned hair, wearing a Ku Klux Klan breastplate, carrying a flag that commemorates the Confederacy; vice presidential nominee Frank Blair, also wearing a Klan breastplate; and (far right) a stereotypical Irish American Catholic.

Snap the Whip, Winslow Homer, 1872

Homer (1836–1910), famous for his *Harper's Weekly* illustrations of Civil War battle scenes, eventually became known as the quintessential painter of a traditional and nostalgic view of American life. In this, his best-known painting, Homer fuses mountain scenery with the "little red schoolhouse" and schoolboys at recess, reminding viewers (as did much regional writing) of bygone times. Like Mark Twain's work, this painting celebrates American boyhood and the cycles of nature at the same time that it explores their fragility.

Children Sleeping in Mulberry Street, Jacob Riis, 1890

Riis (1825–1914) was a Danish immigrant who worked as a New York police reporter. His photographs of the Irish and Italian immigrant poor appeared in his influential book *How the Other Half Lives* (1890). Riis's composition articulates the position of homeless slum children: they sleep where they can, bunched up below street level. The photograph emphasizes their reliance on each other— they huddle together—but also shows that the space they inhabit is not "safe": the stones behind the boys seem overwhelming and the iron railing and drainpipe make it seem as if they are in a subterranean prison.

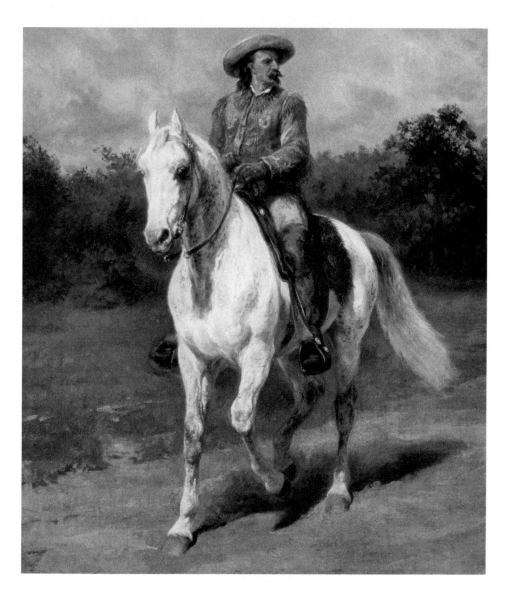

Colonel William F. Cody, Rosa Bonheur, 1889

Called "Buffalo Bill" because he shot buffalo to feed workers building the railroad, Cody (1845–1917) served in the Civil War on the Union side and acted as a scout during the Indian wars of the 1870s. In 1883 he organized the first Wild West show. The show, in Omaha, Nebraska, featured patriotic displays and romanticized historical reenactments involving cowboys, Indians, sharpshooters, and Mexican vaqueros. For two decades it traveled around the country and to Europe. Huge audiences made Cody's show the most significant source of imagery about the American West just as the "frontier" was closing. In Paris, Cody gave behind-the-scenes access to the French realist painter Marie-Rosalie (Rosa) Bonheur (1822–1899), who was known for her studies of animals. Grateful, Bonheur painted this picture, Cody's favorite among the innumerable images of him.

Mrs. Elliott Fitch Shepard, John Singer Sargent, 1888

Sargent (1856–1925), the most famous American portraitist of his day, lived in Europe and counted as influences Spanish master Diego Velásquez, the French Impressionists, and Dutch painter Franz Hals. He was in high demand among the U.S. and European wealthy and painted two American presidents and the business tycoons Rockefeller and Vanderbilt. Sargent's portraits focused on the sophistication of his subjects and conveyed the sense of a life beneath the surface, somewhat akin to the work of Henry James and Edith Wharton. This portrait of Mrs. Shepard, a Vanderbilt, announces her social position and calls attention to a certain sensuality, perhaps one projected by the artist himself.

A Feast Day at Acoma, Edward S. Curtis, 1904

In 1892 Curtis (1868–1952) opened a portrait studio in Washington Territory and began to photograph local Indians. Curtis traveled widely, portraying Native people and scenes in an elegiac manner, attempting to document what he understood to be the last days of the "vanishing Indian." Whatever his intentions, *A Feast Day at Acoma* shows a lively and bustling scene of Pueblo people in the Southwest.

Hopi House, Mary Colter, 1905

Colter (1869–1958), one of the nation's few women architects, used traditional Southwest Native American elements in buildings in Grand Canyon National Park and hotels and lodges for the Fred Harvey Company and the Santa Fe Railroad. These structures, including La Fonda in Santa Fe and the El Navajo in Gallup, New Mexico, helped introduce the Southwest to easterners, as did the writings of Willa Cather, Mary Austin, and others. The rustic style, drawing on Native American shapes and using local materials, influenced southwestern architecture for generations. Many of Colter's buildings have been torn down, but the eleven that remain are on the National Register of Historic Places, with five designated National Historic Landmarks.

Women Watching a Sun Dance, Amos Bad Heart Bull, undated

In the years 1890–1913 Amos Bad Heart Bull (1869–1913), an Oglala Lakota (Sioux), produced 415 paintings and drawings. Many depict aspects of the Battle of the Little Big Horn, in which General George Armstrong Custer was defeated, as well as other important events in the history and culture of his people. This painting depicts women watching a Sun Dance through a pine-bough barricade. The horseshoe shape of each woman's head, black except for the part at the center, is conventional in the art of Plains people.

An Indian Horse Dance, Kills Two, undated

This early-twentieth-century painting by the Lakota (Sioux) Kills Two depicts a traditional ceremony of the Horse Dance Society. The Horse Dance Society was composed of men and women who used powers granted to them in visions to heal and train horses. The markings on the horses and the men symbolize thunder and lightning, powers important to the Horse Dance Society and prominent in Black Elk's vision. Black Elk called for a Horse Dance to be performed to help distribute this power among his people.

Both Members of This Club, George Bellows, 1909

Bellows (1882–1925) was a member of the Ashcan school, a group of artists who advocated representing American society in all its forms, especially the crude and chaotic lives of the working class and the moral shortcomings of the wealthy, much like the naturalist writers of the time. Bellows's paintings of boxing matches are characterized by savage brushstrokes on a dark background and emphasize the motion of human figures within the confines of the ring. In *Both Members of This Club,* Bellows creates an atmosphere not of athleticism but of defeat, with both boxers reduced to mere entertainment for the grotesquely leering crowd.

Manhattan's Misty Sunset, Childe Hassam, 1911

Frederick Childe Hassam (1850–1935), an American Impressionist, was the premier painter of New York City. *Manhattan's Misty Sunset* captures the romantic attraction of New York as a place both of tremendous opportunity and of uncertainty and mystery. Hassam's limited color palette is organized around cool tones, as shades of green generalize the shapes of Brooklyn warehouses across the East River from Hassam's studio, punctuated by barely visible streetlights; the drizzle and fog suggest an ambivalence toward industrial America.

Portrait of a German Officer, Marsden Hartley, 1914

Hartley's abstract "portrait" represents its wartime subject in fragments of ribbons and flags. Like T. S. Eliot's *The Waste Land,* this work registers a world blown to pieces. Completed while Hartley was living in Berlin and before the United States entered World War I, the painting memorializes Hartley's friend Karl von Freyburg, a German cavalry officer who had been killed in combat. Among the elements incorporated into the painting are Freyburg's initials (K v F) and the age at which he died (24). Hartley's *Portrait* is deliberately far from the kind of traditional memorial art that might have idealized an officer on his horse, but it is abstracted as well from the bloody mire of the war.

Golden Bird, Constantin Brancusi, 1919–20

Brancusi's famous series of bird sculptures (beginning in 1910 and running through the 1930s) began with more realistic bird forms and moved toward increasingly simple, abstract forms representing the pure idea of flight. The elaborately carved pedestal is Brancusi's own work and an integral part of the sculpture, which contrasts an earthy, primitivist ground with the smooth, soaring metal of modern flight—conjoining different aspects of the high modernist aesthetic in one object. *Golden Bird* was quickly embraced as a high modernist icon. In 1922 *The Dial*, an important modernist magazine, printed a photograph of the sculpture alongside Mina Loy's poem "Brancusi's Golden Bird."

Black Belt, Archibald J. Motley, 1934

Motley's painting captures the social breadth and vitality of Chicago's South Side and other emerging African American urban centers, using a stylized realism of vivid colors and flat perspective. His men and women include well-dressed couples, a matronly, homeward-bound woman, and the stoic, downcast worker in the foreground. In the middle background a man in a suit and hat glances warily over his shoulder toward the viewer; in his poem about the South Side, Langston Hughes explicitly challenged outsiders looking in on black life. Chicago's diverse African American community was an important setting for Nella Larsen's novel *Quicksand*.

River Rouge Plant, Charles Sheeler, 1932

This painting of a Ford Motor Company factory near Detroit grew out of a series of photographs that Sheeler took for an advertising agency. Along with other "precisionist" painters of the 1920s and 1930s, Sheeler was influenced by Futurism's celebration of the machine and by Cubism's breaking of traditional unified perspective into multiple flat planes. Sheeler's painterly style, however, remained realistic; he sought the broken planes and angles of Cubism in the objects themselves (here, the multiple white planes of the factory and its reflection) and avoided calling attention to the medium of paint—its texture and brushwork, the surface of the canvas—over what it represented. Like the poet Hart Crane, Sheeler found the materials for a modernist art in the American industrial landscape.

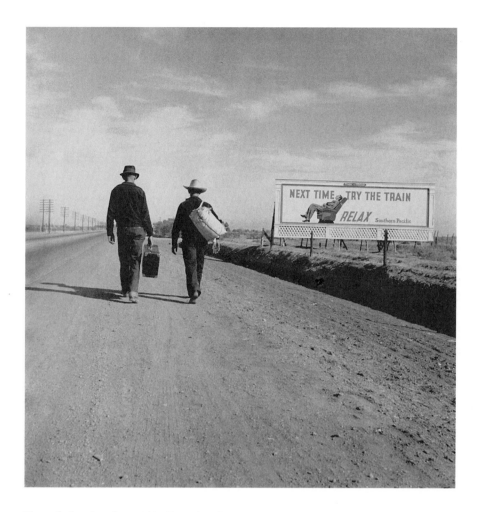

Towards Los Angeles, 1937, Dorothea Lange, 1937

During the Great Depression, the Farm Security Administration—one of the government agencies created by President Franklin D. Roosevelt in response to the economic emergency—employed a number of well-known documentary photographers. Lange's portraits of migrants displaced by the Dust Bowl are some of the most memorable images produced under FSA sponsorship. Like John Steinbeck in *The Grapes of Wrath,* Lange sought to create sympathy for the tenant farmers of the Southwest who had lost their homes and livelihoods. *Towards Los Angeles, 1937* contrasts the migrants' hard journey with an advertising billboard celebrating the speed and luxury of intercity rail travel.

From the Faraway, Nearby, Georgia O'Keeffe, 1937

O'Keeffe found inspiration in the landscapes of the American Southwest. Noted in the 1920s for her large, vivid paintings of flowers "with great sexy involutions" (as *Life* magazine observed), O'Keeffe in the 1930s began painting the bones she found scattered about the New Mexico desert. In this almost surrealist image, the sharp lines of the elk antlers floating in the foreground are echoed in softer form by the hills; the painting's perspective collapses the middle distance to put the faraway and the nearby on top of one another. O'Keeffe's paintings became modernist icons of the American landscape; the bones of the Southwest, she wrote, opened her work up to "the wideness and wonder of the world as I live in it."

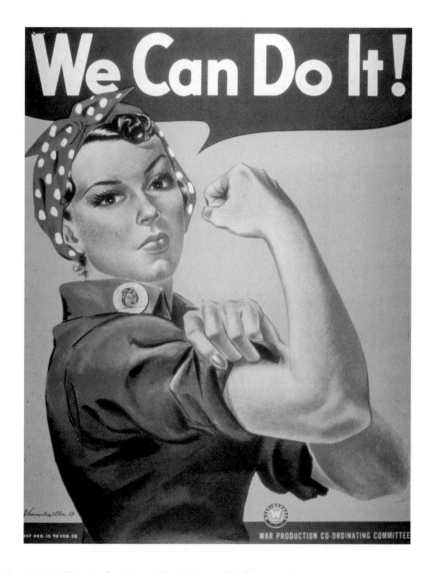

We Can Do It! ("Rosie the Riveter"), J. Howard Miller, c. 1942

World War II drew many women out of traditional roles in the home and into the industrial labor force and various forms of war-related work. Miller's poster *We Can Do It!*, produced by the defense contractor Westinghouse for the War Production Coordinating Committee, uses the bright colors and clean, simple lines of advertising to make the dislocations of traditional gender patterns familiar and acceptable, at least for the duration of the war. The worker's pert face and feminine grooming balance her assertively flexed bicep. A popular wartime song, "Rosie the Riveter," gave Miller's anonymous heroine her familiar nickname.

Night Hawks, Edward Hopper, 1942

Hopper's painting represents the night life of loners in the city. Its stylized realism preserves traditional perspective, accentuated by the deep view through the restaurant's large plate-glass window, but simplifies both realistic detail and painterly brushwork. *Night Hawks* depicts a clean, well-lighted restaurant against a dark urban background of uncertain danger or promise. A man and a woman sit at the counter, apparently a couple, but without intimate gestures their level of mutual trust or distrust remains unclear. The customer with his back to the viewer, like one of Chandler's detectives, keeps to himself but stands in for the viewer's anonymous perspective on the scene. In both style and subject this painting is often compared to the work of writers such as Ernest Hemingway and Raymond Chandler.

1945 to the Present

Autumn Rhythm (Number 30), Jackson Pollock, 1950

With Abstract Expressionism, the style of post–World War II American painting that had international impact, the canvas became less a surface upon which to represent than an arena within which to act. Jackson Pollock (1912–1956) was the most noteworthy of the so-called action painters. One of his favorite methods, working above a canvas stretched on the ground to dance over and around it, dripping and swirling paint, was dramatic enough to be captured in photographs and film documentaries, just as his emotionally fraught visage found its place on magazine covers and his sometimes violent behavior became as newsworthy as his art.

Guggenheim Museum,
Frank Lloyd Wright, 1959

The Solomon R. Guggenheim Museum (commissioned in 1943, completed and opened in 1959) stands on upper Fifth Avenue in New York City as a striking reinvention of not just how art can be exhibited, but how it can be seen. Patrons of the Guggenheim do not stroll through a succession of flat-floored galleries, but instead either work their way up through a large, open-centered spiral or take an elevator to the building's top, then descend at a gentle angle through the spiral. The walls of the spiral display artworks for viewing. Early in his career the museum's architect, Frank Lloyd Wright (1867–1959), had helped end the Victorian era's predilection for boxlike construction. But Wright resisted the stark conceptualism of modern architecture in favor of what he called the "organic." Here, instead of form following function (a premise of modernism), form and function are one.

Blam, Roy Lichtenstein, 1962

Roy Lichtenstein (1923–1997) helped to launch the Pop Art movement. Lichtenstein used bold outlines, vivid colors, and the technique of Benday dots, popular in commercial printing, to simulate in
painting the process of mechanical reproduction. This aesthetic clearly defied the expressionist practices of abstract painters like Jackson Pollock. The cartoon style of *Blam* (in fact, Lichtenstein took
this image from a comic book) and its onomatopoetic lettering are typical of Lichtenstein's work.
The literally explosive image—a fighter plane being blown apart in the air—also suggests the way in
which Pop Art sought to explode boundaries between an original and a copy, a unique image and one
that is reproduced, and between high and low culture more generally. Fiction writers like Donald
Barthelme, poets like John Ashbery, and comic book artists like Art Spiegelman are indebted in different ways to Pop Art.

Estate, Robert Rauschenberg, 1963

Few artworks reflect the social and aesthetic nature of their times as boldly as do the combines and assemblages of Robert Rauschenberg (b. 1925). Self-consciousness about his medium combines with sociopolitical awareness in works that address both concerns and make them the viewers' own.

Estate employs brushwork, silk-screening, photography, and photocopying to interrogate its audience as well as itself. Most importantly, every image in this collage remains recognizable, even as the expressive manner of combination (including several brushstrokes and color actions worthy of Abstract Expressionism) emphasizes the artist's creative act.

Campbell's Soup 1 (Tomato), Andy Warhol, 1968

For the Pop artist Andy Warhol (1928–1987) an object as banal as a Campbell's soup can could evoke the spirit of the American 1960s. While both representational and abstract painting had conventionally been dedicated to matters of great importance, whether in the subject portrayed or in the activity of putting paint to canvas, Warhol's soup can undercut the premise of both styles while also commenting on the materialism underlying the whole business of producing and selling art. Creativity was now a matter of selection, in this case of lavishing the artist's considerable talent and technique on (and commanding a high price for) such an everyday object. From this decade onward literary artists would find success by doing much the same thing.

Earthrise and Lunar Horizon from Apollo 8, 1968

The photo of "Earthrise" over the lunar horizon was taken by the Apollo 8 crew, astronauts Frank Borman (b. 1928), James Lovell (b. 1928), and William Anders (b. 1933), who were the first humans to leave Earth's orbit, entering into lunar orbit on Christmas Eve, 1968. The photograph showed the Earth for the first time as it appears from deep space. The philosopher Hannah Arendt, in her book *The Human Condition* (1958), anticipated the signifi-cance of this image when she wrote that a shift from seeing men and women as earthbound crea-tures to seeing them as dwellers of the universe would be a radical change in understanding the human condition, as revolutionary as the invention of the telescope.

The American Indian, Fritz Scholder, 1970

The American Indian by Fritz Scholder (1937–2005), a Luiseño Indian, belongs to a series of paintings that blew open the doors of "acceptable" Indian imagery and undermined clichés and stereotypes of the stoic "noble savage." Rather than traditional Indian regalia, the figure wears a judi-cial robe fashioned from the American flag, as if to suggest that only being wrapped in the symbol of the colonists will certify him as "American." But the whitened face and skeletal rendering of the figure's mouth suggest what col-onization cost him. The single feather in his hair, the necklace he wears, and the tomahawk he holds may suggest how the expectations of tourists also shape his depiction.

Untitled, Cindy
Sherman, 1981

This photograph by the
artist Cindy Sherman
(b. 1954) is number 96
of her "Centerfold"
series (1981). Like
Sherman's earlier,
black-and-white "Film
Stills," this series con-
sists of "self-portraits"
in which the artist
explores representa-
tions of women by
dressing in a variety of
costumes and adopting a variety of poses. Sherman's role as both photographer and subject reverses
the traditional power of the male gaze, and here she examines and subverts the objectified images of
women displayed in magazine centerfolds. Rather than signaling availability, this cropped, color-
saturated photograph is enigmatic. Sherman's girlish clothing, evoking the 1950s, conceals more
than it reveals, and she holds in her hand a largely unreadable scrap torn from a newspaper. Her
gaze, vacant and interior, is also unreadable. Her distinctly unrevealing sweater and the flush on her
face become part of the color pattern—oranges and browns forming a series of grids and checks—
rather than an erotic sign.

Vietnam Veterans
Memorial, Maya Lin,
1982

Located on the mall in
Washington, D.C., the
Vietnam Veterans Memo-
rial is a 246-foot-long,
v-shaped sunken wall
of black granite. It is
engraved with more than
fifty-eight thousand
names of those who died
in the Vietnam conflict.
The names are listed in
chronological order, and
to locate a particular
name a visitor walks
along the wall searching
for it. The polished surface of the granite reflects the sky, the surrounding landscape, and the visitor.
Considerable controversy attended the design, by the Chinese American architect Maya Lin (b.
1959), some objecting to its abstraction in place of the realistic statuary of most war memorials, and
some finding it too somber. Lin has said she wanted a structure that would carve out a space for the
public display of grief and loss, and the memorial has a powerful elegiac quality. Dedicated on Veterans Day, 1982, it has become the most widely visited monument in Washington.

Sonny's Quilt, Faith Ringgold, 1986

In *Sonny's Quilt,* an acrylic painting on canvas with a pieced fabric border, Faith Ringgold (b. 1930) unites two African American art forms: jazz and the quilt. This quilt painting depicts the jazz saxophonist Theodore Walter "Sonny" Rollins (b. 1930) poised high on the Brooklyn Bridge, the river below him and the skyline above him. To spare his neighbors in Brooklyn, Rollins used to leave his apartment to practice his instrument in public places. The brilliant coloration of the painting recalls the materials of African American quilts, and the girders and wires of the bridge, as well as the repeated squares in the bridge's structure, resemble the designs and borders of quilt patterns. Centered in the painting, Rollins is alone with his music and yet a part of the surrounding city. Ringgold's depiction of the Brooklyn Bridge recalls its iconic status in American painting, photography, and literature, including *The Bridge* (1930) by Hart Crane (1899–1932), a selection from which appears in this anthology.

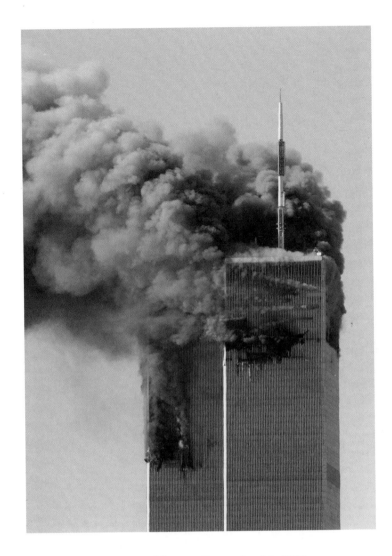

World Trade Center Burning, Peter Morgan, September 11, 2001

"A screaming comes across the sky." This opening sentence of Thomas Pynchon's 1973 novel *Gravity's Rainbow* had for decades impressed readers with the terrors of modern warfare, in which military technologies at the far edge of human inventiveness were turned against people at home. That Pynchon's scene was London, under attack from German V-2 rockets near the end of World War II, may have allayed readers' most personal fears. Yet on September 11, 2001, another such screaming awoke not just the United States but the whole world to the reality that wholesale destruction was an ever-present possibility. After half a century of Cold War rhetoric that had made such catastrophes unthinkable, the unthinkable had happened. Two jet airliners had been crashed into the twin towers of New York's World Trade Center in an event witnessed within minutes by television viewers all over the Earth. By the time the buildings collapsed, the whole world was watching. What in normal terms might be a line in a novel or a scene in a movie was here most horribly real.

The Gates New York City, Christo and Jeanne-Claude, 2005

For sixteen days, from February 12 to 27, 2005, New York City's Central Park was transformed by the artists Christo (b. 1935) and Jeanne-Claude (b. 1935) into a series of walkways, extending over twenty-three miles, in which orange-colored fabric panels were suspended from 7,503 vinyl structures or gates. To some who saw them as they stirred in the wind, these panels had a mysterious and dreamlike effect, transforming a familiar landscape and reaffirming the city's beauty after the tragedy of 9/11. Like all of Christo and Jeanne-Claude's creations, *The Gates* was public and temporary. New Yorkers' responses were typically mixed: while some complained about the expense and the hype, many found *The Gates* magical, an experience at once individual and shared by people from all over the country and the world.

I have measured out my life with coffee spoons; *Hopelessness*
I know the voices dying with a dying fall[4]
Beneath the music from a farther room.
　　So how should I presume?

And I have known the eyes already, known them all—　　　　55
The eyes that fix you in a formulated phrase,
And when I am formulated, sprawling on a pin,
When I am pinned and wriggling on the wall,
Then how should I begin
To spit out all the butt-ends of my days and ways?　　　　60
　　And how should I presume?
And I have known the arms already, known them all—
Arms that are braceleted and white and bare
(But in the lamplight, downed with light brown hair!)
Is it perfume from a dress　　　　　　　　　　　　　　65
That makes me so digress?
Arms that lie along a table, or wrap about a shawl.
　　And should I then presume?
　　And how should I begin?

　·　·　·　·　·　·

Shall I say, I have gone at dusk through narrow streets　70
And watched the smoke that rises from the pipes
Of lonely men in shirt-sleeves, leaning out of windows? . . .

I should have been a pair of ragged claws
Scuttling across the floors of silent seas.

　·　·　·　·　·　·

And the afternoon, the evening, sleeps so peacefully!　　75
Smoothed by long fingers,
Asleep . . . tired . . . or it malingers,
Stretched on the floor, here beside you and me.
Should I, after tea and cakes and ices,　*(after a date)*
Have the strength to force the moment to its crisis?　　80
But though I have wept and fasted, wept and prayed,
Though I have seen my head (grown slightly bald) brought in
　　　upon a platter,[5]
I am no prophet—and here's no great matter;
I have seen the moment of my greatness flicker,　*death*
And I have seen the eternal Footman hold my coat, and snicker,　85
And in short, I was afraid.　*turning point*

And would it have been worth it, after all,
After the cups, the marmalade, the tea,
Among the porcelain, among some talk of you and me,
Would it have been worth while,　　　　　　　　　　90
To have bitten off the matter with a smile,
To have squeezed the universe into a ball

4. Echo of Duke Orsino's invocation of music in
Shakespeare's *Twelfth Night* 1.1.4: "If music be the
food of love, play on. . . . That strain again! It had
a dying fall."

5. The head of the prophet John the Baptist, who
was killed at the behest of Princess Salome, was
brought to her on a platter (see Mark 6.17–20,
Matthew 14.3–11).

To roll it towards some overwhelming question,
To say: 'I am Lazarus,[6] come from the dead,
Come back to tell you all, I shall tell you all'—   95
If one, settling a pillow by her head,
    Should say: 'That is not what I meant at all.
    That is not it, at all.'

And would it have been worth it, after all,
Would it have been worth while,   100
After the sunsets and the dooryards and the sprinkled streets,
After the novels, after the teacups, after the skirts that trail
      along the floor—
And this, and so much more?—
It is impossible to say just what I mean!
But as if a magic lantern threw the nerves in patterns on a screen: 105
Would it have been worth while
If one, settling a pillow or throwing off a shawl,
And turning toward the window, should say:
    'That is not it at all,
    That is not what I meant, at all.'   110
    . . . . .

eternally disconnected [margin note]

No! I am not Prince Hamlet, nor was meant to be;
Am an attendant lord,[7] one that will do
To swell a progress, start a scene or two,
Advise the prince; no doubt, an easy tool,
Deferential, glad to be of use,   115
Politic, cautious, and meticulous;
Full of high sentence,[8] but a bit obtuse;
At times, indeed, almost ridiculous—
Almost, at times, the Fool.

"I" is missing - he is not even an "I" [margin note]

I grow old . . . I grow old . . .   120
I shall wear the bottoms of my trousers rolled.

Shall I part my hair behind? Do I dare to eat a peach?
I shall wear white flannel trousers, and walk upon the beach.
I have heard the mermaids singing, each to each.

I do not think that they will sing to me.   125

Fear of rejection [margin note]

I have seen them riding seaward on the waves
Combing the white hair of the waves blown back
When the wind blows the water white and black.

Sirens - seductive + dangerous [margin note]

We have lingered in the chambers of the sea
By sea-girls wreathed with seaweed red and brown   130
Till human voices wake us, and we drown.

1915, 1917

---

6. The resurrection of Lazarus is recounted in
John 11.1–44; see also Luke 16.19–31.
7. A journey or procession made by royal courts

and often portrayed on Elizabethan stages.
8. Opinions, sententiousness.

Gerontion[1]

Thou hast nor youth nor age
But as it were an after dinner sleep
Dreaming of both.[2]

Here I am, an old man in a dry month,
Being read to by a boy, waiting for rain.
I was neither at the hot gates[3]
Nor fought in the warm rain
Nor knee deep in the salt-marsh, heaving a cutlass,   5
Bitten by flies, fought.
My house is a decayed house,
And the Jew squats on the window sill, the owner,
Spawned in some estaminet[4] of Antwerp,
Blistered in Brussels, patched and peeled in London.[5]   10
The goat coughs at night in the field overhead;
Rocks, moss, stonecrop, iron, merds.[6]
The woman keeps the kitchen, makes tea,
Sneezes at evening, poking the peevish gutter.
                    I an old man,   15
A dull head among windy spaces.

Signs are taken for wonders. 'We would see a sign!'[7]
The word within a word, unable to speak a word,
Swaddled with darkness. In the juvescence of the year
Came Christ the tiger   20

In depraved May,[8] dogwood and chestnut, flowering judas,
To be eaten, to be divided, to be drunk
Among whispers;[9] by Mr. Silvero
With caressing hands, at Limoges
Who walked all night in the next room;   25
By Hakagawa, bowing among the Titians;
By Madame de Tornquist, in the dark room
Shifting the candles; Fräulein von Kulp
Who turned in the hall, one hand on the door.
          Vacant shuttles   30
Weave the wind. I have no ghosts,
An old man in a draughty house
Under a windy knob.

---

1. Eliot intended to reprint this dramatic mono-logue as a prelude to *The Waste Land* until persuaded not to by Ezra Pound. The title is derived from the Greek word meaning "an old man."
2. Lines spoken by the duke of Vienna to describe death in Shakespeare's *Measure for Measure* 3.1.32–34.
3. An allusion to Thermopylae, the mountain pass where the Spartans heroically resisted the Persians (480 B.C.E.).
4. Café. The anti-Semitic passage identifies the landlord with urban decay.
5. Allusions to symptoms of and cures for venereal disease.

6. Dung.
7. Echoes of the "signs and wonders" expected as testimony to Christ's divinity in John 4.48 and the demand "Master, we would see a sign from thee" in Matthew 12.38.
8. Cf. *The Education of Henry Adams* (1918), chapter 18: the "passionate depravity that marked the Maryland May."
9. In lines 18–22, Gerontion imagines Christ as a powerful beast, like "the Lion of the tribe of Juda" (Revelation 5.5). Line 22 alludes to dividing and eating the bread, and drinking the wine, in Christian Communion.

After such knowledge, what forgiveness? Think now
History has many cunning passages, contrived corridors   35
And issues, deceives with whispering ambitions,
Guides us by vanities. Think now
She gives when our attention is distracted
And what she gives, gives with such supple confusions
That the giving famishes the craving. Gives too late   40
What's not believed in, or is still believed,
In memory only, reconsidered passion. Gives too soon
Into weak hands, what's thought can be dispensed with
Till the refusal propagates a fear. Think
Neither fear nor courage saves us. Unnatural vices   45
Are fathered by our heroism. Virtues
Are forced upon us by our impudent crimes.
These tears are shaken from the wrath-bearing tree.

The tiger springs in the new year. Us he devours. Think at last
We have not reached conclusion, when I   50
Stiffen in a rented house. Think at last
I have not made this show purposelessly
And it is not by any concitation
Of the backward devils.
I would meet you upon this honestly.   55
I that was near your heart was removed therefrom
To lose beauty in terror, terror in inquisition.
I have lost my passion: why should I need to keep it
Since what is kept must be adulterated?
I have lost my sight, smell, hearing, taste and touch: 60
How should I use them for your closer contact?

These with a thousand small deliberations
Protract the profit of their chilled delirium,
Excite the membrane, when the sense has cooled,
With pungent sauces, multiply variety   65
In a wilderness of mirrors. What will the spider do,
Suspend its operations, will the weevil
Delay? De Bailhache, Fresca, Mrs. Cammel, whirled
Beyond the circuit of the shuddering Bear[1]
In fractured atoms. Gull against the wind, in the windy straits 70
Of Belle Isle, or running on the Horn.
White feathers in the snow, the Gulf claims,
And an old man driven by the Trades[2]
To a sleepy corner.

                             Tenants of the house,   75
Thoughts of a dry brain in a dry season.

                                                          1920

---

1. The polestar in the constellation the Bear.   2. Trade winds.

The Waste Land[1]

'Nam Sibyllam quidem Cumis ego ipse oculis meis vidi in ampulla pendere, et cum illi pueri dicerent: Σίβυλλα τί Θέλεις; respondebat illa: ἀποθανεῖν Θέλω.'[2]

FOR EZRA POUND
IL MIGLIOR FABBRO.[3]

I. The Burial of the Dead[4]

April is the cruellest month, breeding
Lilacs out of the dead land, mixing
Memory and desire, stirring
Dull roots with spring rain.
Winter kept us warm, covering   5
Earth in forgetful snow, feeding
A little life with dried tubers.
Summer surprised us, coming over the Starnbergersee[5]
With a shower of rain; we stopped in the colonnade,
And went on in sunlight, into the Hofgarten,[6]   10
And drank coffee, and talked for an hour.
Bin gar keine Russin, stamm' aus Litauen, echt deutsch.[7]
And when we were children, staying at the arch-duke's,
My cousin's, he took me out on a sled,
And I was frightened. He said, Marie,   15
Marie, hold on tight. And down we went.
In the mountains, there you feel free.
I read, much of the night, and go south in the winter.

What are the roots that clutch, what branches grow
Out of this stony rubbish? Son of man,[8]   20
You cannot say, or guess, for you know only
A heap of broken images, where the sun beats,
And the dead tree gives no shelter, the cricket no relief,[9]
And the dry stone no sound of water. Only
There is shadow under this red rock,[1]   25
(Come in under the shadow of this red rock),

1. Eliot's notes for the first hardcover edition of *The Waste Land* opened with his acknowledgment that "not only the title, but the plan and a good deal of the incidental symbolism of the poem" were suggested by Jessie L. Weston's book on the Grail Legend, *From Ritual to Romance* (1920), and that he was indebted also to James G. Frazer's *The Golden Bough* (1890–1915), "especially the two volumes *Adonis, Attis, Osiris*," which deal with vegetation myths and fertility rites. Eliot's notes are incorporated in the footnotes to this text. Many critics believe that the notes were added in a spirit of parody. The numerous and extensive literary quotations add to the multivocal effect of the poem.
2. A quotation from Petronius's *Satyricon* (1st century C.E.) about the Sibyl (prophetess) of Cumae, blessed with eternal life by Apollo but doomed to perpetual old age, who guided Aeneas through Hades in Virgil's *Aeneid*: "For once I myself saw with my own eyes the Sibyl at Cumae hanging in a cage, and when the boys said to her 'Sibyl, what do you want?' she replied, 'I want to die.' "
3. "The better maker," the tribute in Dante's *Pur-*

gatorio 26.117 to the Provençal poet Arnaut Daniel.
4. The title of the Anglican burial service.
5. A lake near Munich. Lines 8–16 were suggested by the Countess Marie Larisch's memoir, *My Past* (1913).
6. A public park in Munich, with cafés; former grounds of a Bavarian palace.
7. I am certainly not Russian; I come from Lithuania, a true German (German).
8. "Cf. Ezekiel II, i" [Eliot's note]. There God addresses the prophet Ezekiel as "Son of man" and declares: "stand upon thy feet, and I will speak unto thee."
9. "Cf. Ecclesiastes XII, v" [Eliot's note]. There the preacher describes the bleakness of old age when "the grasshopper shall be a burden, and desire shall fail."
1. Cf. Isaiah 32.1–2 and the prophecy that the reign of the Messiah "shall be . . . as rivers of water in a dry place, as the shadow of a great rock in a weary land."

And I will show you something different from either
Your shadow at morning striding behind you
Or your shadow at evening rising to meet you;
I will show you fear in a handful of dust.   30

        Frisch weht der Wind
        Der Heimat zu
        Mein Irisch Kind,
        Wo weilest du?[2]
'You gave me hyacinths first a year ago;   35
'They called me the hyacinth girl.'
—Yet when we came back, late, from the hyacinth[3] garden,
Your arms full, and your hair wet, I could not
Speak, and my eyes failed, I was neither
Living nor dead, and I knew nothing,
Looking into the heart of light, the silence.   40
Oed' und leer das Meer.[4]

Madame Sosostris,[5] famous clairvoyante,
Had a bad cold, nevertheless
Is known to be the wisest woman in Europe,
With a wicked pack of cards.[6] Here, said she,   45
Is your card, the drowned Phoenician Sailor,[7]
(Those are pearls that were his eyes.[8] Look!)
Here is Belladonna, the Lady of the Rocks,[9]
The lady of situations.
Here is the man with three staves, and here the Wheel,   50
And here is the one-eyed merchant,[1] and this card,
Which is blank, is something he carries on his back,
Which I am forbidden to see. I do not find
The Hanged Man. Fear death by water.
I see crowds of people, walking round in a ring.   55
Thank you. If you see dear Mrs. Equitone,
Tell her I bring the horoscope myself:
One must be so careful these days.

---

2. "V. [see] *Tristan und Isolde,* I, verses 5–8" [Eliot's note]. In Wagner's opera, a sailor aboard Tristan's ship recalls his love back in Ireland: "Fresh blows the wind to the homeland; my Irish child, where are you waiting?"

3. The boy Hyacinth, in Ovid's *Metamorphoses* 10, was beloved by Apollo but slain by a jealous rival. The Greeks celebrated his festival in May.

4. "III, verse 24" [Eliot's note]. In *Tristan* III, verse 24, the dying Tristan, awaiting the ship that carries his beloved Isolde, is told that "Empty and barren is the sea."

5. Eliot derived the name from "Sesostris, the Sorceress of Ectabana," the pseudo-Egyptian name assumed by a woman who tells fortunes in Aldous Huxley's novel *Chrome Yellow* (1921). Sesostris was a 12th-dynasty Egyptian king.

6. The tarot deck of cards. Eliot's note to this passage reads: "I am not familiar with the exact constitution of the Tarot pack of cards, from which I have obviously departed to suit my own convenience. The Hanged Man, a member of the traditional pack, fits my purpose in two ways: because he is associated in my mind with the Hanged God

of Frazer, and because I associate him with the hooded figure in the passage of the disciples to Emmaus in Part V. The Phoenician Sailor and the Merchant appear later; also the 'crowds of people,' and Death by Water is executed in Part IV. The Man with Three Staves (an authentic member of the Tarot pack) I associate, quite arbitrarily, with the Fisher King himself."

7. A symbolic figure that includes "Mr. Eugenides, the Smyrna merchant" in Part III and "Phlebas the Phoenician" in Part IV. The ancient Phoenicians were seagoing merchants who spread Egyptian fertility cults throughout the Mediterranean.

8. The line is a quotation from Ariel's song in Shakespeare's *Tempest* 1.2.398. Prince Ferdinand, disconsolate because he thinks his father has drowned in the storm, is consoled when Ariel sings of a miraculous sea change that has transformed death into "something rich and strange."

9. Belladonna, literally "beautiful lady," is the name of both the poisonous plant deadly nightshade and a cosmetic.

1. These three figures are from the Tarot deck.

Unreal City,[2]   60
Under the brown fog of a winter dawn,
A crowd flowed over London Bridge, so many,
I had not thought death had undone so many.[3]
Sighs, short and infrequent, were exhaled,[4]
And each man fixed his eyes before his feet.   65
Flowed up the hill and down King William Street,
To where Saint Mary Woolnoth kept the hours
With a dead sound on the final stroke of nine.[5]
There I saw one I knew, and stopped him, crying: 'Stetson!
'You who were with me in the ships at Mylae![6]   70
'That corpse you planted last year in your garden,
'Has it begun to sprout? Will it bloom this year?
'Or has the sudden frost disturbed its bed?
'O keep the Dog far hence, that's friend to men,
'Or with his nails he'll dig it up again![7]   75
'You! hypocrite lecteur!—mon semblable,—mon frère!'[8]

II. A Game of Chess[9]

The Chair she sat in, like a burnished throne,[1]
Glowed on the marble, where the glass
Held up by standards wrought with fruited vines
From which a golden Cupidon peeped out   80
(Another hid his eyes behind his wing)
Doubled the flames of sevenbranched candelabra
Reflecting light upon the table as
The glitter of her jewels rose to meet it,
From satin cases poured in rich profusion.   85
In vials of ivory and coloured glass
Unstoppered, lurked her strange synthetic perfumes,
Unguent, powdered, or liquid—troubled, confused
And drowned the sense in odours; stirred by the air

2. "Cf. Baudelaire: 'Fourmillante cité, cité pleine de rêves, / Où le spectre en plein jour raccroche le passant'" [Eliot's note]. The lines are quoted from "Les Sept Vieillards" (The Seven Old Men), poem 93 of Les Fleurs du Mal (The Flowers of Evil, 1857) by the French Symbolist Charles Baudelaire (1821–1867), and may be translated from the French: "Swarming city, city full of dreams, / Where the specter in broad daylight accosts the passerby."

3. "Cf. Inferno III, 55–57" [Eliot's note]. The note continues to quote Dante's lines, which may be translated: "So long a train of people, / That I should never have believed / That death had undone so many."

4. "Cf. Inferno IV, 25–27" [Eliot's note]. Dante describes, in Limbo, the virtuous pagan dead, who, living before Christ, could not hope for salvation. The lines read: "Here, so far as I could tell by listening, / There was no lamentation except sighs, / which caused the eternal air to tremble."

5. "A phenomenon which I have often noticed" [Eliot's note]. The church named is in the financial district of London.

6. The battle of Mylae (260 B.C.E.) was a victory for Rome against Carthage. "Stetson": a hat manufacturer.

7. "Cf. the dirge in Webster's White Devil" [Eliot's

note]. In the play by John Webster (d. 1625), a crazed woman fears that the corpses of her decadent and murdered relatives might be disinterred: "But keep the wolf far thence, that's foe to men, / For with his nails he'll dig them up again." In echoing the lines Eliot altered "foe" to "friend" and the "wolf" to "Dog," invoking the brilliant Dog Star Sirius, whose rise in the heavens accompanied the flooding of the Nile and promised the return of fertility to Egypt.

8. "V. Baudelaire, Preface to Fleurs du Mal" [Eliot's note]. The last line of the introductory poem to Les Fleurs du Mal. "Au Lecteur" (To the Reader) may be translated from the French: "Hypocrite reader!—my likeness—my brother!

9. The title suggests two plays by Thomas Middleton: A Game of Chess (1627), about a marriage of political expediency, and Women Beware Women (1657), containing a scene in which a mother-in-law is engrossed in a chess game while her daughter-in-law is seduced nearby. Eliot's note to line 118 refers readers to this play. It is now believed that much of this section reflects Eliot's disintegrating marriage.

1. "Cf. Antony and Cleopatra, II, ii. 190" [Eliot's note]. In Shakespeare's play, Enobarbus's description of Cleopatra begins: "The barge she sat in, like a burnish'd throne, / Burn'd on the water."

That freshened from the window, these ascended   90
In fattening the prolonged candle-flames,
Flung their smoke into the laquearia,[2]
Stirring the pattern on the coffered ceiling.
Huge sea-wood fed with copper
Burned green and orange, framed by the coloured stone,   95
In which sad light a carvèd dolphin swam.
Above the antique mantel was displayed
As though a window gave upon the sylvan scene[3]
The change of Philomel, by the barbarous king
So rudely forced; yet there the nightingale   100
Filled all the desert with inviolable voice
And still she cried, and still the world pursues,
'Jug Jug'[4] to dirty ears.
And other withered stumps of time
Were told upon the walls; staring forms   105
Leaned out, leaning, hushing the room enclosed.
Footsteps shuffled on the stair.
Under the firelight, under the brush, her hair
Spread out in fiery points
Glowed into words, then would be savagely still.   110

'My nerves are bad to-night. Yes, bad. Stay with me.
'Speak to me. Why do you never speak. Speak.
      'What are you thinking of? What thinking? What?
'I never know what you are thinking. Think.'

I think we are in rats' alley[5]   115
Where the dead men lost their bones.

'What is that noise?'
                    The wind under the door.[6]
'What is that noise now? What is the wind doing?'
                    Nothing again nothing.   120
                                        'Do
'You know nothing? Do you see nothing? Do you remember
'Nothing?'

      I remember
Those are pearls that were his eyes.   125
'Are you alive, or not? Is there nothing in your head?'
                                        But

O O O O that Shakespeherian Rag—
It's so elegant

---

2. "Laquearia, V. *Aeneid*, I, 726" [Eliot's note]. Eliot quotes the passage containing the term *laquearia* ("paneled ceiling") and describing the banquet hall where Queen Dido welcomed Aeneas to Carthage. It reads: "Blazing torches hang from the gilded paneled ceiling, and torches conquer the night with flames." Aeneas became Dido's lover but abandoned her to continue his journey to found Rome, and she committed suicide.
3. Eliot's notes for lines 98–99 refer the reader to "Milton, *Paradise Lost*, IV, 140" for the phrase "sylvan scene" and to "Ovid, *Metamorphoses*, VI, Philomela." The lines splice the setting of Eve's temptation in the Garden of Eden, first described

through Satan's eyes, with the rape of Philomela by her sister's husband, King Tereus, and her transformation into the nightingale. Eliot's note for line 100 refers the reader ahead to the nightingale's song in Part III, line 204, of his own poem.
4. The conventional rendering of the nightingale's song in Elizabethan poetry.
5. Eliot's note refers readers to "Part III, l. 195."
6. "Cf. Webster: 'Is the wind in that door still?'" [Eliot's note]. In John Webster's *The Devil's Law Case* (1623) 3.2.162, a duke is cured of an infection by a wound intended to kill him; a surprised surgeon asks the quoted question, meaning, "Is he still alive?"

So intelligent 130
'What shall I do now? What shall I do?'
'I shall rush out as I am, and walk the street
'With my hair down, so. What shall we do tomorrow?
'What shall we ever do?'
             The hot water at ten. 135
And if it rains, a closed car at four.
And we shall play a game of chess,
Pressing lidless eyes and waiting for a knock upon the door.

When Lil's husband got demobbed,[7] I said—
I didn't mince my words, I said to her myself, 140
HURRY UP PLEASE ITS TIME[8]
Now Albert's coming back, make yourself a bit smart.
He'll want to know what you done with that money he gave you
To get yourself some teeth. He did, I was there.
You have them all out, Lil, and get a nice set, 145
He said, I swear, I can't bear to look at you.
And no more can't I, I said, and think of poor Albert,
He's been in the army four years, he wants a good time,
And if you don't give it him, there's others will, I said.
Oh is there, she said. Something o' that, I said. 150
Then I'll know who to thank, she said, and give me a straight look.
HURRY UP PLEASE ITS TIME
If you don't like it you can get on with it, I said.
Others can pick and choose if you can't.
But if Albert makes off, it won't be for lack of telling. 155
You ought to be ashamed, I said, to look so antique.
(And her only thirty-one.)
I can't help it, she said, pulling a long face,
It's them pills I took, to bring it off, she said.
(She's had five already, and nearly died of young George.) 160
The chemist[9] said it would be all right, but I've never been the same.
You *are* a proper fool, I said.
Well, if Albert won't leave you alone, there it is, I said,
What you get married for if you don't want children?
HURRY UP PLEASE ITS TIME 165
Well, that Sunday Albert was home, they had a hot gammon,[1]
And they asked me in to dinner, to get the beauty of it hot—
HURRY UP PLEASE ITS TIME
HURRY UP PLEASE ITS TIME
Goonight Bill, Goonight Lou. Goonight May. Goonight. 170
Ta ta. Goonight. Goonight.
Good night, ladies, good night, sweet ladies, good night, good night.[2]

III. The Fire Sermon[3]

The river's tent is broken; the last fingers of leaf
Clutch and sink into the wet bank. The wind

---

7. Slang for "demobilized," discharged from the army.
8. Routine call of British bartenders to clear the pub at closing time.
9. Pharmacist.
1. Ham or bacon.

2. A double echo of the popular song "Good night ladies, we're going to leave you now" and mad Ophelia's farewell before drowning, in Shakespeare, *Hamlet* 4.5.72.
3. I.e., Buddha's Fire Sermon. See n. 7, p. 877.

Crosses the brown land, unheard. The nymphs are departed.   175
Sweet Thames, run softly, till I end my song.[4]
The river bears no empty bottles, sandwich papers,
Silk handkerchiefs, cardboard boxes, cigarette ends
Or other testimony of summer nights. The nymphs are departed.
And their friends, the loitering heirs of City directors;   180
Departed, have left no addresses.
By the waters of Leman I sat down and wept[5] . . .
Sweet Thames, run softly till I end my song,
Sweet Thames, run softly, for I speak not loud or long.
But at my back in a cold blast I hear[6]   185
The rattle of the bones, and chuckle spread from ear to ear.

A rat crept softly through the vegetation
Dragging its slimy belly on the bank
While I was fishing in the dull canal
On a winter evening round behind the gashouse   190
Musing upon the king my brother's wreck[7]
And on the king my father's death before him.
White bodies naked on the low damp ground
And bones cast in a little low dry garret,
Rattled by the rat's foot only, year to year.   195
But at my back from time to time I hear
The sound of horns and motors, which shall bring
Sweeney to Mrs. Porter in the spring.[8]
O the moon shone bright on Mrs. Porter
And on her daughter
They wash their feet in soda water[9]   200
Et, O ces voix d'enfants, chantant dans la coupole![1]

Twit twit twit
Jug jug jug jug jug jug

So rudely forc'd.
Tereu[2]   205

Unreal City
Under the brown fog of a winter noon

---

4. "V. Spenser, *Prothalamion*" [Eliot's note]. The line is the refrain of the marriage song by Edmund Spenser (1552–1599), a pastoral celebration of marriage set along the Thames River near London.
5. The phrasing recalls Psalm 137.1, in which the exiled Jews mourn for their homeland: "By the rivers of Babylon, there we sat down, yea, we wept, when we remembered Zion." Lake Leman is another name for Lake Geneva, location of the sanatorium where Eliot wrote the bulk of *The Waste Land.* The archaic term *leman,* for "illicit mistress," led to the phrase "waters of leman" signifying lusts.
6. This line and line 196 echo Andrew Marvell (1621–1678), *To His Coy Mistress,* lines 21–24: "But at my back I always hear / Time's wingèd chariot hurrying near; / And yonder all before us lie / Deserts of vast eternity."
7. "Cf. *The Tempest,* I, ii" [Eliot's note]. Another allusion to Shakespeare's play, 1.2.389–90, where Prince Ferdinand, thinking his father dead, describes himself as "Sitting on a bank, / Weeping again the King my father's wrack."

8. "Cf. Day, *Parliament of Bees:* 'When of the sudden, listening, you shall hear, / A noise of horns and hunting, which shall bring / Actaeon to Diana in the spring, / Where all shall see her naked skin' " [Eliot's note]. Actaeon was changed into a stag and hunted to death as punishment for seeing Diana, goddess of chastity, bathing. John Day (1574–c. 1640), English poet.
9. "I do not know the origin of the ballad from which these lines are taken: it was reported to me from Sydney, Australia" [Eliot's note]. The bawdy song was popular among World War I troops.
1. "V. Verlaine, *Parsifal*" [Eliot's note]. The last line of the sonnet "Parsifal" by the French Symbolist Paul Verlaine (1844–1896) reads: "And O those children's voices singing in the cupola." In Wagner's opera, the feet of Parsifal, the questing knight, are washed before he enters the sanctuary of the Grail.
2. Alludes to Tereus, who raped Philomela, and like *jug* is a conventional Elizabethan term for the nightingale's song; also a slang pronunciation of *true.*

Mr. Eugenides, the Smyrna merchant
Unshaven, with a pocket full of currants   210
C.i.f.[3] London: documents at sight,
Asked me in demotic French
To luncheon at the Cannon Street Hotel
Followed by a weekend at the Metropole.

At the violet hour, when the eyes and back   215
Turn upward from the desk, when the human engine waits
Like a taxi throbbing waiting,
I Tiresias,[4] though blind, throbbing between two lives,
Old man with wrinkled female breasts, can see
At the violet hour, the evening hour that strives   220
Homeward, and brings the sailor home from sea,[5]
The typist home at teatime, clears her breakfast, lights
Her stove, and lays out food in tins.
Out of the window perilously spread
Her drying combinations touched by the sun's last rays,   225
On the divan are piled (at night her bed)
Stockings, slippers, camisoles, and stays.
I Tiresias, old man with wrinkled dugs
Perceived the scene, and foretold the rest—
I too awaited the expected guest.   230
He, the young man carbuncular, arrives,
A small house agent's clerk, with one bold stare,
One of the low on whom assurance sits
As a silk hat on a Bradford[6] millionaire.
The time is now propitious, as he guesses,   235
The meal is ended, she is bored and tired,
Endeavours to engage her in caresses
Which still are unreproved, if undesired.
Flushed and decided, he assaults at once;
Exploring hands encounter no defence;   240
His vanity requires no response,
And makes a welcome of indifference.

---

3. "The currants were quoted at a price 'carriage and insurance free to London'; and the Bill of Lading, etc. were to be handed to the buyer upon payment of the sight draft" [Eliot's note]. Some have suggested another possibility for the phrase "carriage and insurance free": "cost, insurance and freight."

4. Eliot's note reads: "Tiresias, although a mere spectator and not indeed a 'character,' is yet the most important personage in the poem, uniting all the rest. Just as the one-eyed merchant, seller of currants, melts into the Phoenician Sailor, and the latter is not wholly distinct from Ferdinand Prince of Naples, so all the women are one woman, and the two sexes meet in Tiresias. What Tiresias sees, in fact, is the substance of the poem. The whole passage from Ovid is of great anthropological interest." The note quotes the Latin passage from Ovid, Metamorphoses 2.421–43, which may be translated: "Jove [very drunk] said jokingly to Juno: 'You women have greater pleasure in love than that enjoyed by men.' She denied it. So they decided to refer the question to wise Tiresias who knew love from both points of view. For once, with a blow of his staff, he had separated two huge snakes who were copulating in the forest, and miraculously

was changed instantly from a man into a woman and remained so for seven years. In the eighth year he saw the snakes again and said: 'If a blow against you is so powerful that it changes the sex of the author of it, now I shall strike you again.' With these words he struck them, and his former shape and masculinity were restored. As referee in the sportive quarrel, he supported Jove's claim. Juno, overly upset by the decision, condemned the arbitrator to eternal blindness. But the all-powerful father (inasmuch as no god can undo what has been done by another god) gave him the power of prophecy, with this honor compensating him for the loss of sight."

5. "This may not appear as exact as Sappho's lines, but I had in mind the 'longshore' or 'dory' fisherman, who returns at nightfall" [Eliot's note]. Fragment 149, by the female Greek poet Sappho (fl. 600 B.C.E.), celebrates the Evening Star who "brings homeward all those / Scattered by the dawn, / The sheep to fold . . . / The children to their mother's side." A more familiar echo is "Home is the sailor, home from sea" in "Requiem" by Robert Louis Stevenson (1850–1894).

6. A Yorkshire, England, manufacturing town where fortunes were made during World War I.

(And I Tiresias have foresuffered all
Enacted on this same divan or bed;
I who have sat by Thebes below the wall[7]
And walked among the lowest of the dead.)
Bestows one final patronising kiss,
And gropes his way, finding the stairs unlit . . .

She turns and looks a moment in the glass,
Hardly aware of her departed lover;
Her brain allows one half-formed thought to pass:
'Well now that's done: and I'm glad it's over.'
When lovely woman stoops to folly and
Paces about her room again, alone,
She smoothes her hair with automatic hand,
And puts a record on the gramophone.[8]

'This music crept by me upon the waters'[9]
And along the Strand, up Queen Victoria Street.
O City city, I can sometimes hear
Beside a public bar in Lower Thames Street,
The pleasant whining of a mandoline
And a clatter and a chatter from within
Where fishmen lounge at noon: where the walls
Of Magnus Martyr[1] hold
Inexplicable splendour of Ionian white and gold.

    The river sweats[2]
    Oil and tar
    The barges drift
    With the turning tide
    Red sails
    Wide
    To leeward, swing on the heavy spar.
    The barges wash
    Drifting logs
    Down Greenwich reach
    Past the Isle of Dogs.[3]
      Weialala leia
      Wallala leialala

Line numbers: 245, 250, 255, 260, 265, 270, 275

7. Tiresias prophesied in the marketplace below the wall of Thebes, witnessed the tragedies of Oedipus and Creon in that city, and retained his prophetic powers in the underworld.
8. Eliot's note refers to the novel The Vicar of Wakefield (1766) by Oliver Goldsmith (1728–1774) and the song sung by Olivia when she revisits the scene of her seduction: "When lovely woman stoops to folly / And finds too late that men betray / What charm can soothe her melancholy, / What art can wash her guilt away? / The only art her guilt to cover, / To hide her shame from every eye, / To give repentance to her lover / And wring his bosom—is to die."
9. Eliot's note refers to Shakespeare's The Tempest, the scene where Ferdinand listens to Ariel's song telling of his father's miraculous sea change: "This music crept by me on the waters, / Allaying

both their fury and my passion / With its sweet air" (1.2.391–93).
1. "The interior of St. Magnus Martyr is to my mind one of the finest among [Christopher] Wren's interiors" [Eliot's note].
2. "The Song of the (three) Thames-daughters begins here. From line 292 to 306 inclusive they speak in turn. V. Götterdämmerung, III, i: the Rhine-daughters" [Eliot's note]. Lines 277–78 and 290–91 are from the lament of the Rhine maidens for the lost beauty of the Rhine River in the opera by Richard Wagner (1813–1883), Die Götterdämmerung (The Twilight of the Gods, 1876).
3. A peninsula in the Thames opposite Greenwich, a borough of London and the birthplace of Queen Elizabeth. Throughout this section Eliot has named places along the Thames River.

Elizabeth and Leicester[4]
Beating oars   280
The stern was formed
A gilded shell
Red and gold
The brisk swell
Rippled both shores   285
Southwest wind
Carried down stream
The peal of bells
White towers
  Weialala leia   290
  Wallala leialala

Trams and dusty trees.
Highbury bore me. Richmond and Kew
Undid me.[5] By Richmond I raised my knees
Supine on the floor of a narrow canoe.'   295
'My feet are at Moorgate, and my heart
Under my feet. After the event
He wept. He promised "a new start."
I made no comment. What should I resent?'

'On Margate Sands,   300
I can connect
Nothing with nothing.
The broken fingernails of dirty hands.
My people humble people who expect
Nothing.'   305
  la la

To Carthage then I came[6]

Burning burning burning burning[7]
O Lord Thou pluckest me out[8]
O Lord Thou pluckest   310

burning

IV. Death by Water

Phlebas the Phoenician, a fortnight dead,
Forgot the cry of gulls, and the deep sea swell

4. Reference to the romance between Queen Elizabeth and the earl of Leicester. Eliot's note refers to the historian James A. Froude, "*Elizabeth,* Vol. I. ch. iv, letter of [bishop] De Quadra [the ambassador] to Philip of Spain: 'In the afternoon we were in a barge, watching the games on the river. (The queen) was alone with Lord Robert and myself on the poop, when they began to talk nonsense, and went so far that Lord Robert at last said, as I was on the spot there was no reason why they should not be married if the queen pleased.' "
5. "Cf. *Purgatorio,* V, 133" [Eliot's note]. Eliot parodies Dante's lines, which may be translated: "Remember me, who am La Pia. / Siena made me, Maremma undid me."

6. "V. St. Augustine's *Confessions:* 'to Carthage then I came, where a cauldron of unholy loves sang all about mine ears' " [Eliot's note]. Augustine here recounts his licentious youth.
7. Eliot's note to lines 307–09 refers to "Buddha's Fire Sermon (which corresponds in importance to the Sermon on the Mount)" and "St. Augustine's Confessions." The "collocation of these two representatives of eastern and western asceticism, as the culmination of this part of the poem, is not an accident."
8. The line is from Augustine's *Confessions* and echoes also Zechariah 3.2, where Jehovah, rebuking Satan, calls the high priest Joshua "a brand plucked out of the fire."

And the profit and loss.

     A current under sea   315
Picked his bones in whispers. As he rose and fell
He passed the stages of his age and youth
Entering the whirlpool.

     Gentile or Jew
O you who turn the wheel and look to windward,   320
Consider Phlebas, who was once handsome and tall as you.

V. What the Thunder Said[9]

After the torchlight red on sweaty faces
After the frosty silence in the gardens
After the agony in stony places
The shouting and the crying   325
Prison and palace and reverberation
Of thunder of spring over distant mountains
He who was living is now dead
We who were living are now dying
With a little patience[1]   330

Here is no water but only rock
Rock and no water and the sandy road
The road winding above among the mountains
Which are mountains of rock without water
If there were water we should stop and drink   335
Amongst the rock one cannot stop or think
Sweat is dry and feet are in the sand
If there were only water amongst the rock
Dead mountain mouth of carious teeth that cannot spit
Here one can neither stand nor lie nor sit   340
There is not even silence in the mountains
But dry sterile thunder without rain
There is not even solitude in the mountains
But red sullen faces sneer and snarl
From doors of mudcracked houses   345
        If there were water

  And no rock
  If there were rock
  And also water
  And water   350
  A spring
  A pool among the rock
  If there were the sound of water only
  Not the cicada[2]

9. "In the first part of Part V three themes are employed: the journey to Emmaus, the approach to the Chapel Perilous (see Miss Weston's book) and the present decay of eastern Europe". [Eliot's note]. During his disciples' journey to Emmaus, after his Crucifixion and Resurrection, Jesus walked alongside and conversed with them, but they did not recognize him (Luke 24.13–34).

1. The opening nine lines allude to Christ's imprisonment and trial, to his agony in the garden of Gethsemane, and to his Crucifixion on Golgotha (Calvary) and burial.

2. Grasshopper. Cf. line 23 and see n. 9, p. 869.

And dry grass singing   355
But sound of water over a rock
Where the hermit-thrush[3] sings in the pine trees
Drip drop drip drop drop drop drop
But there is no water

Who is the third who walks always beside you?[4]   360
When I count, there are only you and I together
But when I look ahead up the white road
There is always another one walking beside you
Gliding wrapt in a brown mantle, hooded
I do not know whether a man or a woman   365
—But who is that on the other side of you?

What is that sound high in the air[5]
Murmur of maternal lamentation
Who are those hooded hordes swarming
Over endless plains, stumbling in cracked earth   370
Ringed by the flat horizon only
What is the city over the mountains
Cracks and reforms and bursts in the violet air
Falling towers
Jerusalem Athens Alexandria   375
Vienna London
Unreal

A woman drew her long black hair out tight
And fiddled whisper music on those strings
And bats with baby faces in the violet light   380
Whistled, and beat their wings
And crawled head downward down a blackened wall
And upside down in air were towers
Tolling reminiscent bells, that kept the hours
And voices singing out of empty cisterns and exhausted wells.   385

In this decayed hole among the mountains
In the faint moonlight, the grass is singing
Over the tumbled graves, about the chapel
There is the empty chapel, only the wind's home.
It has no windows, and the door swings,   390
Dry bones can harm no one.
Only a cock stood on the rooftree
Co co rico co co rico[6]

---

3. "This is . . . the hermit-thrush which I have heard in Quebec Province. Chapman says (*Handbook of Birds of Eastern North America*) 'it is most at home in secluded woodland and thickety retreats.' . . . Its 'water dripping song' is justly celebrated" [Eliot's note].
4. "The following lines were stimulated by the account of one of the Antarctic expeditions (I forget which, but I think one of Shackleton's): it was related that the party of explorers, at the extremity of their strength, had the constant delusion that there was *one more member* than could actually be counted" [Eliot's note].

5. Eliot's note quotes a passage in German from *Blick ins Chaos* (1920) by Hermann Hesse (1877–1962), which may be translated: "Already half of Europe, already at least half of Eastern Europe, on the way to Chaos, drives drunk in sacred infatuation along the edge of the precipice, since drunkenly, as though hymn-singing, as Dimitri Karamazov sang in [the novel] *The Brothers Karamazov* [1882] by Feodor Dostoevsky [1821–1881]. The offended bourgeois laughs at the songs; the saint and the seer hear them with tears."
6. A cock's crow in folklore signaled the departure of ghosts (as in Shakespeare's *Hamlet* 1.1.157ff.);

In a flash of lightning. Then a damp gust
Bringing rain   395

Ganga[7] was sunken, and the limp leaves
Waited for rain, while the black clouds
Gathered far distant, over Himavant.[8]
The jungle crouched, humped in silence.
Then spoke the thunder   400
Da[9]
Datta: what have we given?
My friend, blood shaking my heart
The awful daring of a moment's surrender
Which an age of prudence can never retract   405
By this, and this only, we have existed
Which is not to be found in our obituaries
Or in memories draped by the beneficent spider[1]
Or under seals broken by the lean solicitor
In our empty rooms   410
Da
Dayadhvam: I have heard the key[2]
Turn in the door once and turn once only
We think of the key, each in his prison
Thinking of the key, each confirms a prison   415
Only at nightfall, aethereal rumours
Revive for a moment a broken Coriolanus[3]
Da
Damyata: The boat responded
Gaily, to the hand expert with sail and oar   420
The sea was calm, your heart would have responded
Gaily, when invited, beating obedient
To controlling hands

                                             I sat upon the shore
Fishing,[4] with the arid plain behind me   425
Shall I at least set my lands in order?[5]

---

in Matthew 26.34 and 74, a cock crowed, as Christ predicted, when Peter denied him three times.

7. The Indian river Ganges.

8. A mountain in the Himalayas.

9. " 'Datta, dayadhvam, damyata' (Give, sympathise, control). The fable of the meaning of the Thunder is found in the Brihadaranyaka—Upanishad, 5, 1" [Eliot's note]. In the Hindu legend, the injunction of Prajapati (supreme deity) is Da, which is interpreted in three different ways by gods, men, and demons, to mean "control ourselves," "give alms," and "have compassion." Prajapati assures them that when "the divine voice, The Thunder," repeats the syllable it means all three things and that therefore "one should practice . . . Self-Control, Alms-giving, and Compassion."

1. Eliot's note refers to Webster's The White Devil 5.6: "they'll remarry / Ere the worm pierce your winding-sheet, ere the spider / Make a thin curtain for your epitaphs."

2. "Cf. Inferno, XXXIII, 46" [Eliot's note]. At this

point Ugolino recalls his imprisonment with his children, where they starved to death: "And I heard below the door of the horrible tower being locked up." Eliot's note continues: "Also F. H. Bradley, Appearance and Reality, p. 346. 'My external sensations are no less private to myself than are my thoughts or my feelings. In either case my experience falls within my own circle, a circle closed on the outside; and, with all its elements alike, every sphere is opaque to the others which surround it. . . . In brief, regarded as an existence which appears in a soul, the whole world for each is peculiar and private to that soul.' "

3. Roman patrician who defiantly chose self-exile when threatened with banishment by the leaders of the populace. He is the tragic protagonist in Shakespeare's Coriolanus (1608).

4. "V. Weston: From Ritual to Romance; chapter on the Fisher King" [Eliot's note].

5. Cf. Isaiah 38.1: "Thus saith the Lord, Set thine house in order: for thou shalt die, and not live."

London Bridge is falling down falling down falling down
Poi s'ascose nel foco che gli affina[6]
Quando fiam uti chelidon[7]—O swallow swallow
Le Prince d'Aquitaine à la tour abolie[8]   430
These fragments I have shored against my ruins
Why then Ile fit you. Hieronymo's mad againe.[9]
Datta. Dayadhvam. Damyata.
            Shantih   shantih   shantih[1]

1921   1922

The Hollow Men

Mistah Kurtz—he dead.[1]
                    A penny for the Old Guy[2]

I

We are the hollow men
We are the stuffed men
Leaning together
Headpiece filled with straw. Alas!
Our dried voices, when   5
We whisper together
Are quiet and meaningless
As wind in dry grass
Or rats' feet over broken glass
In our dry cellar   10

Shape without form, shade without colour,
Paralysed force, gesture without motion;

Those who have crossed
With direct eyes, to death's other Kingdom

6. Eliot's note to *Purgatorio* 26 quotes in Italian the passage (lines 145–48) where the Provençal poet Arnaut Daniel, recalling his lusts, addresses Dante: "I pray you now, by the Goodness that guides you to the summit of this staircase, reflect in due season on my suffering." Then, in the line quoted in *The Waste Land*, "he hid himself in the fire that refines them."
7. Eliot's note refers to the *Pervigilium Veneris* (The Vigil of Venus), an anonymous Latin poem, and suggests a comparison with "Philomela in Parts II and III" of *The Waste Land*. The last stanzas of the *Pervigilium* recreate the myth of the nightingale in the image of a swallow, and the poet listening to the bird speaks the quoted line, "When shall I be as the swallow," and adds: "that I may cease to be silent." "O Swallow, Swallow" are the opening words of one of the songs interspersed in Tennyson's narrative poem *The Princess* (1847).
8. "V. Gerard de Nerval, Sonnet *El Desdichado*" [Eliot's note]. The line reads: "The Prince of Aquitaine in the ruined tower."
9. Eliot's note refers to Thomas Kyd's revenge play,

The Spanish Tragedy, subtitled *Hieronymo's Mad Againe* (1594). In it Hieronymo is asked to write a court play and he answers, "I'll fit you," in the double sense of "oblige" and "get even." He manages, although mad, to kill the murderers of his son by acting in the play and assigning parts appropriately, then commits suicide.
1. "Shantih. Repeated as here, a formal ending to an Upanishad. 'The peace which passeth understanding' is our equivalent to this word" [Eliot's note]. The Upanishad is a Vedic treatise, a sacred Hindu text.
1. Quotation from *Heart of Darkness*, by Joseph Conrad (1857–1924). Kurtz went into the African jungle as an official of a trading company and degenerated into an evil, tyrannical man. His dying words were "the horror!"
2. Guy Fawkes led a group of conspirators who planned to blow up the English House of Commons in 1605; he was caught and executed before the plan was carried out. On the day of his execution (November 5) children make straw effigies of the "guy" and beg for pennies for fireworks.

Remember us—if at all—not as lost   15
Violent souls, but only
As the hollow men
The stuffed men.

II

Eyes I dare not meet in dreams
In death's dream kingdom   20
These do not appear:
There, the eyes are
Sunlight on a broken column
There, is a tree swinging
And voices are   25
In the wind's singing
More distant and more solemn
Than a fading star.

Let me be no nearer
In death's dream kingdom   30
Let me also wear
Such deliberate disguises
Rat's coat, crowskin, crossed staves
In a field
Behaving as the wind behaves   35
No nearer—

Not that final meeting
In the twilight kingdom

III

This is the dead land
This is cactus land   40
Here the stone images
Are raised, here they receive
The supplication of a dead man's hand
Under the twinkle of a fading star.

Is it like this   45
In death's other kingdom
Waking alone
At the hour when we are
Trembling with tenderness
Lips that would kiss   50
Form prayers to broken stone.

IV

The eyes are not here
There are no eyes here
In this valley of dying stars

In this hollow valley   55
This broken jaw of our lost kingdoms

In this last of meeting places
We grope together
And avoid speech
Gathered on this beach of the tumid river   60

Sightless, unless
The eyes reappear
As the perpetual star
Multifoliate rose[3]
Of death's twilight kingdom   65
The hope only
Of empty men.

V

Here we go round the prickly pear
Prickly pear prickly pear
Here we go round the prickly pear   70
At five o'clock in the morning.[4]

Between the idea
And the reality
Between the motion
And the act   75
Falls the Shadow

                                        For Thine is the Kingdom[5]

Between the conception
And the creation
Between the emotion   80
And the response
Falls the Shadow

                                            Life is very long

Between the desire
And the spasm   85
Between the potency
And the existence
Between the essence
And the descent
Falls the Shadow   90

3. Part 3 of *The Divine Comedy*, by Dante Alighieri (1265–1321), is a vision of Paradise. The souls of the saved in heaven range themselves around the deity in the figure of a "multifoliate rose" (*Paradiso* 28.30).

4. Allusion to a children's rhyming game, "Here we go round the mulberry bush," substituting a prickly pear cactus for the mulberry bush.
5. Part of a line from the Lord's Prayer.

For Thine is the Kingdom

For Thine is
Life is
For Thine is the

This is the way the world ends   95
This is the way the world ends
This is the way the world ends
Not with a bang but a whimper.

1925

Journey of the Magi[1]

'A cold coming we had of it,
Just the worst time of the year
For a journey, and such a long journey:
The ways deep and the weather sharp,
The very dead of winter.'[2]   5
And the camels galled, sore-footed, refractory,
Lying down in the melting snow.
There were times we regretted
The summer palaces on slopes, the terraces,
And the silken girls bringing sherbet.   10
Then the camel men cursing and grumbling
And running away, and wanting their liquor and women,
And the night-fires going out, and the lack of shelters,
And the cities hostile and the towns unfriendly
And the villages dirty and charging high prices: 15
A hard time we had of it.
At the end we preferred to travel all night,
Sleeping in snatches,
With the voices singing in our ears, saying
That this was all folly.   20

Then at dawn we came down to a temperate valley,
Wet, below the snow line, smelling of vegetation,
With a running stream and a water-mill beating the darkness,
And three trees on the low sky.
And an old white horse galloped away in the meadow.   25
Then we came to a tavern with vine-leaves over the lintel,
Six hands at an open door dicing for pieces of silver,
And feet kicking the empty wine-skins.
But there was no information, and so we continued
And arrived at evening, not a moment too soon   30
Finding the place; it was (you may say) satisfactory.

1. The three wise men, or kings, who followed the star of Bethlehem, bringing gifts to the newly born Christ.

2. These lines are adapted from the sermon preached at Christmas, in 1622, by Bishop Lancelot Andrewes.

All this was a long time ago, I remember,
And I would do it again, but set down
This set down
This: were we led all that way for   35
Birth or Death? There was a Birth, certainly,
We had evidence and no doubt. I had seen birth and death,
But had thought they were different; this Birth was
Hard and bitter agony for us, like Death, our death.
We returned to our places, these Kingdoms,   40
But no longer at ease here, in the old dispensation,
With an alien people clutching their gods.
I should be glad of another death.

                                                                    1935

FROM FOUR QUARTETS

Burnt Norton[1]

τοῦ λόγου δ'ἐόντος ξυνοῦ ζώουσιν οἱ πολλοί
ὡς ἰδίαν ἔχοντες φρόνησιν.
                                    I. p. 77. Fr. 2.
ὁδὸς ἄνω κάτω μία καὶ ὠυτή.
                                    I. p. 89. Fr. 60.[2]
                        —Diels: *Die Fragmente der Vorsokratiker*
                                    (Herakleitos)

I[3]

Time present and time past
Are both perhaps present in time future,
And time future contained in time past.
If all time is eternally present
All time is unredeemable.   5
What might have been is an abstraction
Remaining a perpetual possibility
Only in a world of speculation.
What might have been and what has been
Point to one end, which is always present.   10
Footfalls echo in the memory
Down the passage which we did not take

1. Eliot made "Burnt Norton," published originally as a separate poem, the basis and formal
model for "East Coker" (1940), "The Dry Salvages"
(1941), and "Little Gidding" (1942). Together they
make up *Four Quartets* (1943). The *Quartets* seeks
to capture those rare moments when eternity
"intersects" the temporal continuum, while treating also the relations between those moments and
the flux of time. Central to "Burnt Norton" is the
idea of the Spanish mystic St. John of the Cross
(1542–1591) that the ascent of a soul to union
with God is facilitated by memory and disciplined
meditation but that meditation is superseded by a
"dark night of the soul" that deepens paradoxically

the nearer one approaches the light of God. Burnt
Norton is a manor house in Gloucestershire, England.
2. The Greek epigraphs are from the pre-Socratic
philosopher Heraclitus (540?–475 B.C.E.) and may
be translated: "But although the Word is common
to all, the majority of people live as though they
had each an understanding peculiarly his own"
and "The way up and the way down are one and the
same."
3. The opening lines echo Ecclesiastes 3.15: "That
which hath been is now; and that which is to be
hath already been."

Towards the door we never opened
Into the rose-garden.[4] My words echo
Thus, in your mind.   15
                    But to what purpose
Disturbing the dust on a bowl of rose-leaves
I do not know.
                    Other echoes
Inhabit the garden. Shall we follow?   20
Quick, said the bird, find them, find them,
Round the corner. Through the first gate,
Into our first world, shall we follow
The deception of the thrush? Into our first world.
There they were, dignified, invisible,   25
Moving without pressure, over the dead leaves,
In the autumn heat, through the vibrant air,
And the bird called, in response to
The unheard music hidden in the shrubbery,
And the unseen eyebeam crossed, for the roses   30
Had the look of flowers that are looked at.
There they were as our guests, accepted and accepting.
So we moved, and they, in a formal pattern,
Along the empty alley, into the box circle,[5]
To look down into the drained pool.   35
Dry the pool, dry concrete, brown edged,
And the pool was filled with water out of sunlight,
And the lotos rose, quietly, quietly,
The surface glittered out of heart of light,[6]
And they were behind us, reflected in the pool.   40
Then a cloud passed, and the pool was empty.
Go, said the bird, for the leaves were full of children,
Hidden excitedly, containing laughter.
Go, go, go, said the bird: human kind
Cannot bear very much reality.   45
Time past and time future
What might have been and what has been
Point to one end, which is always present.

II

Garlic and sapphires in the mud
Clot the bedded axle-tree.   50
The trilling wire in the blood
Sings below inveterate scars
Appeasing long forgotten wars.
The dance along the artery
The circulation of the lymph   55
Are figured in the drift of stars
Ascend to summer in the tree

---

4. The rose is a symbol of sexual and spiritual love; in Christian traditions it is associated with the harmony of religious truth and with the Virgin Mary. The memory may be personal as well.

5. Evergreen boxwood shrubs, planted in a circle.
6. An echo of Dante, *Paradiso* 12.28–29: "From out of the heart of one of the new lights there moved a voice."

We move above the moving tree
In light upon the figured leaf[7]
And hear upon the sodden floor   60
Below, the boarhound and the boar
Pursue their pattern as before
But reconciled among the stars.

At the still point of the turning world. Neither flesh nor fleshless;
Neither from nor towards; at the still point, there the dance is,   65
But neither arrest nor movement. And do not call it fixity,
Where past and future are gathered. Neither movement from
      nor towards,
Neither ascent nor decline. Except for the point, the still point,
There would be no dance and there is only the dance.
I can only say, *there* we have been: but I cannot say where.   70
And I cannot say, how long, for that is to place it in time.
The inner freedom from the practical desire,
The release from action and suffering, release from the inner
And the outer compulsion, yet surrounded
By a grace of sense, a white light still and moving,   75
Erhebung[8] without motion, concentration
Without elimination, both a new world
And the old made explicit, understood
In the completion of its partial ecstasy,
The resolution of its partial horror.   80
Yet the enchainment of past and future
Woven in the weakness of the changing body,
Protects mankind from heaven and damnation
Which flesh cannot endure.
                              Time past and time future   85
Allow but a little consciousness.
To be conscious is not to be in time
But only in time can the moment in the rose-garden,
The moment in the arbour where the rain beat,
The moment in the draughty church at smokefall   90
Be remembered; involved with past and future.
Only through time time is conquered.

III

Here is a place of disaffection
Time before and time after
In a dim light: neither daylight   95
Investing form with lucid stillness
Turning shadow into transient beauty
With slow rotation suggesting permanence
Nor darkness to purify the soul
Emptying the sensual with deprivation   100
Cleansing affection from the temporal.
Neither plenitude nor vacancy. Only a flicker

7. An echo of the description of death in Tennyson, *In Memoriam* (1850) 43.10–12: "So that
still garden of the souls / In many a figured leaf

enrolls / The total world since life began."
8. Exaltation (German).

Over the strained time-ridden faces
Distracted from distraction by distraction
Filled with fancies and empty of meaning   105
Tumid apathy with no concentration
Men and bits of paper, whirled by the cold wind
That blows before and after time,
Wind in and out of unwholesome lungs
Time before and time after.   110
Eructation of unhealthy souls
Into the faded air, the torpid
Driven on the wind that sweeps the gloomy hills of London,
Hampstead and Clerkenwell, Campden and Putney,
Highgate, Primrose and Ludgate.[9] Not here   115
Not here the darkness, in this twittering world.

Descend lower, descend only
Into the world of perpetual solitude,
World not world, but that which is not world,
Internal darkness, deprivation   120
And destitution of all property,
Desiccation of the world of sense,
Evacuation of the world of fancy,
Inoperancy of the world of spirit;
This is the one way, and the other   125
Is the same, not in movement
But abstention from movement; while the world moves
In appetency, on its metalled ways
Of time past and time future.

IV

Time and the bell have buried the day,   130
The black cloud carries the sun away.
Will the sunflower turn to us, will the clematis
Stray down, bend to us; tendril and spray
Clutch and cling?
Chill   135
Fingers of yew be curled
Down on us? After the kingfisher's wing
Has answered light to light, and is silent, the light is still
At the still point of the turning world.

V

Words move, music moves   140
Only in time; but that which is only living
Can only die. Words, after speech, reach
Into the silence. Only by the form, the pattern,
Can words or music reach
The stillness, as a Chinese jar still   145

9. Districts and neighborhoods in London.

Moves perpetually in its stillness.
Not the stillness of the violin, while the note lasts,
Not that only, but the co-existence,
Or say that the end precedes the beginning,
And the end and the beginning were always there   150
Before the beginning and after the end.
And all is always now. Words strain,
Crack and sometimes break, under the burden,
Under the tension, slip, slide, perish,
Decay with imprecision, will not stay in place,   155
Will not stay still. Shrieking voices
Scolding, mocking, or merely chattering,
Always assail them. The Word in the desert[1]
Is most attacked by voices of temptation,
The crying shadow in the funeral dance,   160
The loud lament of the disconsolate chimera.[2]
The detail of the pattern is movement,
As in the figure of the ten stairs.[3]
Desire itself is movement
Not in itself desirable;   165
Love is itself unmoving,
Only the cause and end of movement,
Timeless, and undesiring
Except in the aspect of time
Caught in the form of limitation   170
Between un-being and being.
Sudden in a shaft of sunlight
Even while the dust moves
There rises the hidden laughter
Of children in the foliage   175
Quick, now, here, now always—
Ridiculous the waste sad time
Stretching before and after.

                                                    1936, 1943

1. An allusion to Christ's temptation in the wilderness (Luke 4.1–4).
2. A monster in Greek mythology and a symbol of fantasies and delusions.

3. An allusion to St. John of the Cross's figure for the soul's ascent to God: "The Ten Degrees of the Mystical Ladder of Divine Love."

EUGENE O'NEILL
1888–1953

Eugene O'Neill, the nation's first major playwright, the first to explore serious themes in the theater and to experiment with theatrical conventions, was born on October 16, 1888. His father was James O'Neill, an actor who made a fortune playing the lead role in a dramatization of Alexander Dumas's swashbuckling novel *The Count of Monte Cristo,* which he performed on tour more than five thousand times. O'Neill's mother, Ella Quinlan, the daughter of a successful Irish immigrant businessman in Cincinnati, hated backstage life and became addicted to morphine. An older brother, James Jr., was born in 1878 and during most of Eugene's childhood was away at various boarding schools. Later "Jamie," his brother's idol, became an actor and an alcoholic.

During O'Neill's childhood, his parents toured for part of every year, lived in New York City hotels for another part, and spent summers at their home in New London, Connecticut. O'Neill went to good preparatory schools and started college at Princeton in 1906. He quit after a year. For the next five years he drank and drifted—he eloped, but the marriage was quickly terminated, he shipped out to sea for a year, and he searched for gold in South America. Most of the time he spent in Greenwich Village—an area of lower Manhattan that was becoming home to artists and political radicals. After tuberculosis nearly killed him in 1912, O'Neill decided to stay sober and write plays. His Greenwich Village friends helped him: he joined a new experimental theater group called the Provincetown Players, because in the summer its members staged plays on a wharf in Provincetown, Massachusetts. For the rest of the year they used a small theater in the Village. They did O'Neill's one-act play *Thirst* in the summer of 1917.

The Provincetown group gave O'Neill his forum, and—working closely with Susan Glaspell—he gave them a place in American theater history. Play followed play in these early years; in 1913–14, he wrote nine plays; in 1916–17, six; in 1918, four. The works with likely appeal for general audiences were moved uptown from the Village to Broadway, where their stagings made O'Neill both famous and financially successful. Many of O'Neill's first plays were grim one-acters based on his experiences at sea. In these, the dialogue was a striking departure from stage rhetoric of the day: crude, natural, and slangy. Instead of the elegant witticisms of drawing-room comedy or the flowery eloquence of historical drama, audiences were faced with ships' holds and sailors' bars. An exaggerated realism, veering toward expressionism, was the mode of these earliest works.

Around 1920, his plays became longer and his aims more ambitious. He began to experiment with techniques to convey inner emotions that usually were not openly expressed in dramatizable action—the world of the mind, of memories and fears. He ignored standard play divisions of scenes and acts; paid no attention to the expected length of plays (the *Mourning Becomes Electra* sequence ran for nine hours); made his characters wear masks; split one character between two actors; and reintroduced ghosts, choruses, and Shakespearean-style monologue and direct addresses to the audience. He employed sets, lighting, and sounds to enhance emotion rather than to represent a real place. Important works from this period include *The Emperor Jones* (1920), in which, under stress, civilized veneer gives way to primitive fear; *The Hairy Ape* (1922), in which a sailor, becoming aware of how he is viewed by the upper class, degenerates into what he is perceived to be; *Desire under the Elms* (1924), about family conflict and desire; *The Great God Brown* (1926), exposing the inner life of a business magnate; and *Strange Interlude* (1928), similarly uncovering the hidden life of a beautiful woman. In different forms, all these plays subject their leading characters to experiences so intense that their "characters" disintegrate, exposing the chaotic or primitive interior self.

O'Neill's father had died in 1920, his mother in 1921, his brother in 1923. During the mid-1920s O'Neill became interested in dramatizing the complicated pattern of his family's life. He was influenced by the popularization of certain ideas of the Viennese psychoanalyst Sigmund Freud: the power of irrational drives; the existence of a subconscious; the roles of repression, suppression, and inhibition in the formation of personality and in adult suffering; the importance of sex; and above all the lifelong influence of parents. But where Freud posited a universal dynamic in the relation between children and parents and rooted development in biology, O'Neill saw each child's experiences as uniquely determined by particular parents. His strongly felt individualism came to focus on the family, rather than the person, as the fundamental human unit. He found inspiration and confirmation for this approach in classical

Greek drama, which had always centered on families. His 1931 *Mourning Becomes Electra*, based on the *Oresteia* cycle of the classical Greek playwright Aeschylus, situated the ancient story of family murder and divine retribution in Civil War America with great success.

Twice-married after the annulment of his early elopement, O'Neill began to suffer from a rare disease of the nervous system in the 1930s and lived in relative seclusion for the last twenty years of his life. Following the production of *Mourning Becomes Electra*, his output slowed noticeably. Much of his work of the 1930s and 1940s remained in manuscript until after his death, and there was a twelve-year gap in the staging of his plays—between *Days without End* (1934), which failed on Broadway, and *The Iceman Cometh*, in 1946, which also did poorly. As a young man, he had been attracted to socialists, communists, and anarchists, more on account of their rebelliousness and energetic nonconformity than their political doctrines. When his play about an interracial marriage appeared (*All God's Chillun Got Wings*, 1924), he insisted that it was not about race but about "the special lives of individual human beings. It is primarily a study of the two principal characters and their tragic struggle for happiness." Although, as the Edmund character who stands for O'Neill in *Long Day's Journey* shows, he did experience his Irishness partly in class terms, his radicalism was based on a sense that individual merit should be the human measure, not on a belief in class solidarity.

Three years after O'Neill's death, *Iceman* was successfully revived, and O'Neill's work reattained prominence. His widow released other plays, which were widely acclaimed in posthumous productions. Among such stagings were parts of a projected nine- or eleven-play sequence (critics differ in their interpretation of the surviving manuscript material) about an Irish family in America named the Melody family and some obviously autobiographical dramas about a family named the Tyrones. The Melody plays produced after O'Neill's death include *A Touch of the Poet*, produced in 1957, and *More Stately Mansions*, which was staged in 1967; the Tyrone plays include *Long Day's Journey into Night*, produced in 1956, and *A Moon for the Misbegotten* produced in 1957.

In inscribing the manuscript of *Long Day's Journey* to his wife, O'Neill wrote that he had faced his dead in this play, writing "with deep pity and understanding and forgiveness for *all* the four haunted Tyrones." By this he seemed to mean that his treatment made it impossible to blame any of the characters for the suffering they inflicted on the others; each Tyrone was both a victim and an oppressor, and none of them could escape. O'Neill's word *haunted* catches his sense that the Tyrones are at the mercy of the past—their psyches are the dwelling places of ghosts, and the word *ghosts* recurs throughout the play: ghosts of those they remember, those who influenced them, their younger selves, their dreams and ambitions, and their disappointments. A spectator or a first-time reader of the play may experience *Long Day's Journey* simply as unabating raw emotion, but study shows that O'Neill designed the play as a series of encounters—each character is placed with one, two, or three of the others, until every combination is worked through. At the same time that these various configurations are staged, the family is followed through one day, from the simulacrum of conventional family life in the morning to the tragic truth of their night. It is thus a literal day in the lives of the Tyrones, and also the Tyrones' journey through life toward death, that we witness.

Romantic, realistic, naturalistic, melodramatic, sentimental, cynical, poetic—the family dramas, indeed O'Neill's work in general, are all of these. Even while he made his characters espouse philosophical positions, O'Neill was not trying to write philosophical drama. Nor was he designing plays to fit into a familiar dramatic type: tragedy, comedy, and the like. He wanted to make plays conveying emotions of such intensity and complexity that the theater would become a vital force in American life. In all his works, the spectacle of emotional intensity was meant to produce emotional response in an audience—what Aristotle, in his *Poetics*, had called "catharsis." As one critic wrote, "The meaning and unity of his work lies not in any controlling intellectual idea and certainly not in a 'message,' but merely in the fact that each play is an experience of extraordinary intensity." O'Neill's plays have been translated and staged all over the world; he won the Pulitzer Prize four times and the Nobel Prize in 1936, the first and so far only American dramatist to do so.

The text is that of the Yale University Press Edition (1956).

Long Day's Journey into Night

CHARACTERS

JAMES TYRONE
MARY CAVAN TYRONE, *his wife*
JAMES TYRONE, JR., *their elder son*
EDMUND TYRONE, *their younger son*
CATHLEEN, *second girl*[1]

SCENES

ACT 1   *Living room of the Tyrones' summer home* 8:30 A.M. *of a day in August, 1912*

ACT 2   SCENE 1   *The same, around* 12:45
        SCENE 2   *The same, about a half hour later*

ACT 3   *The same, around* 6:30 *that evening*

ACT 4   *The same, around midnight*

Act 1

SCENE—*Living room of* JAMES TYRONE'S *summer home on a morning in August, 1912.*

At rear are two double doorways with portieres. The one at right leads into a front parlor with the formally arranged, set appearance of a room rarely occupied. The other opens on a dark, windowless back parlor, never used except as a passage from living room to dining room. Against the wall between the doorways is a small bookcase, with a picture of Shakespeare above it, containing novels by Balzac, Zola, Stendhal, philosophical and sociological works by Schopenhauer, Nietzsche, Marx, Engels, Kropotkin, Max Sterner, plays by Ibsen, Shaw, Strindberg, poetry by Swinburne, Rossetti, Wilde, Ernest Dowson, Kipling, etc.[2]

In the right wall, rear, is a screen door leading out on the porch which extends halfway around the house. Farther forward, a series of three windows looks over the front lawn to the harbor and the avenue that runs along the water front. A small wicker table and an ordinary oak desk are against the wall, flanking the windows.

In the left wall, a similar series of windows looks out on the grounds in back of the house. Beneath them is a wicker couch with cushions, its head toward rear. Farther back is a large, glassed-in bookcase with sets of Dumas, Victor Hugo, Charles Lever, three sets of Shakespeare, The World's Best Literature in fifty large volumes, Hume's History of England, Thiers' History of the Consulate and Empire,

---

1. A servant.
2. A variety of 19th-century (especially late-19th-century) authors are cited. Nobody in the audience would be able to read the titles and authors on

these books—an example of O'Neill's novelistic approach to theatrical detail, also seen in the minute physical descriptions he provides of the characters' appearance and behavior throughout.

Smollett's History of England, Gibbon's Roman Empire and miscellaneous volumes of old plays, poetry, and several histories of Ireland. The astonishing thing about these sets is that all the volumes have the look of having been read and reread.

The hardwood floor is nearly covered by a rug, inoffensive in design and color. At center is a round table with a green shaded reading lamp, the cord plugged in one of the four sockets in the chandelier above. Around the table within reading-light range are four chairs, three of them wicker armchairs, the fourth (at right front of table) a varnished oak rocker with leather bottom.

It is around 8:30. Sunshine comes through the windows at right.

As the curtain rises, the family have just finished breakfast. MARY TYRONE *and her husband enter together from the back parlor, coming from the dining room.*

MARY *is fifty-four, about medium height. She still has a young, graceful figure, a trifle plump, but showing little evidence of middle-aged waist and hips, although she is not tightly corseted. Her face is distinctly Irish in type. It must once have been extremely pretty, and is still striking. It does not match her healthy figure but is thin and pale with the bone structure prominent. Her nose is long and straight, her mouth wide with full, sensitive lips. She uses no rouge or any sort of make-up. Her high forehead is framed by thick, pure white hair. Accentuated by her pallor and white hair, her dark brown eyes appear black. They are unusually large and beautiful, with black brows and long curling lashes.*

What strikes one immediately is her extreme nervousness. Her hands are never still. They were once beautiful hands, with long, tapering fingers, but rheumatism has knotted the joints and warped the fingers, so that now they have an ugly crippled look. One avoids looking at them, the more so because one is conscious she is sensitive about their appearance and humiliated by her inability to control the nervousness which draws attention to them.

She is dressed simply but with a sure sense of what becomes her. Her hair is arranged with fastidious care. Her voice is soft and attractive. When she is merry, there is a touch of Irish lilt in it.

Her most appealing quality is the simple, unaffected charm of a shy convent-girl youthfulness she has never lost—an innate unworldly innocence.

JAMES TYRONE *is sixty-five but looks ten years younger. About five feet eight, broad-shouldered and deep-chested, he seems taller and slenderer because of his bearing, which has a soldierly quality of head up, chest out, stomach in, shoulders squared. His face has begun to break down but he is still remarkably good looking—a big, finely shaped head, a handsome profile, deep-set light-brown eyes. His grey hair is thin with a bald spot like a monk's tonsure.*

The stamp of his profession is unmistakably on him. Not that he indulges in any of the deliberate temperamental posturings of the stage star. He is by nature and preference a simple, unpretentious man, whose inclinations are still close to his humble beginnings and his Irish farmer forebears. But the actor shows in all his unconscious habits of speech, movement and gesture. These have the quality of belonging to a studied technique. His voice is remarkably fine, resonant and flexible, and he takes great pride in it.

His clothes, assuredly, do not costume any romantic part. He wears a threadbare, ready-made, grey sack suit and shineless black shoes, a collar-less shirt with a thick white handkerchief knotted loosely around his throat. There is nothing picturesquely careless about this get-up. It is commonplace shabby. He believes in wearing his clothes to the limit of usefulness, is dressed now for gardening, and doesn't give a damn how he looks.

He has never been really sick a day in his life. He has no nerves. There is a lot of stolid, earthy peasant in him, mixed with streaks of sentimental melancholy and rare flashes of intuitive sensibility.

TYRONE's *arm is around his wife's waist as they appear from the back parlor. Entering the living room he gives her a playful hug.*

TYRONE   You're a fine armful now, Mary, with those twenty pounds you've gained.

MARY [*smiles affectionately*]   I've gotten too fat, you mean, dear. I really ought to reduce.

TYRONE   None of that, my lady! You're just right. We'll have no talk of reducing. Is that why you ate so little breakfast?

MARY   So little? I thought I ate a lot.

TYRONE   You didn't. Not as much as I'd like to see, anyway.

MARY [*teasingly*]   Oh you! You expect everyone to eat the enormous breakfast you do. No one else in the world could without dying of indigestion. [*She comes forward to stand by the right of table.*]

TYRONE [*following her*]   I hope I'm not as big a glutton as that sounds. [*with hearty satisfaction*] But thank God, I've kept my appetite and I've the digestion of a young man of twenty, if I am sixty-five.

MARY   You surely have, James. No one could deny that.
[*She laughs and sits in the wicker armchair at right rear of table. He comes around in back of her and selects a cigar from a box on the table and cuts off the end with a little clipper. From the dining room JAMIE's and EDMUND's voices are heard. Mary turns her head that way.*]
Why did the boys stay in the dining room, I wonder? Cathleen must be waiting to clear the table.

TYRONE [*jokingly but with an undercurrent of resentment*]   It's a secret confab they don't want me to hear, I suppose. I'll bet they're cooking up some new scheme to touch the Old Man.
[*She is silent on this, keeping her head turned toward their voices. Her hands appear on the table top, moving restlessly. He lights his cigar and sits down in the rocker at right of table, which is his chair, and puffs contentedly.*]
There's nothing like the first after-breakfast cigar, if it's a good one, and this new lot have the right mellow flavor. They're a great bargain, too. I got them dead cheap. It was McGuire put me on to them.

MARY [*a trifle acidly*]   I hope he didn't put you on to any new piece of property at the same time. His real estate bargains don't work out so well.

TYRONE [*defensively*]   I wouldn't say that, Mary. After all, he was the one who advised me to buy that place on Chestnut Street and I made a quick turnover on it for a fine profit.

MARY [*smiles now with teasing affection*]   I know. The famous one stroke of good luck. I'm sure McGuire never dreamed—[*Then she pats his hand.*] Never mind, James. I know it's a waste of breath trying to convince you you're not a cunning real estate speculator.

TYRONE [*huffily*]   I've no such idea. But land is land, and it's safer than the stocks and bonds of Wall Street swindlers. [*then placatingly*] But let's not argue about business this early in the morning.
[*A pause. The boys' voices are again heard and one of them has a fit of coughing. MARY listens worriedly. Her fingers play nervously on the table top.*]

MARY   James, it's Edmund you ought to scold for not eating enough. He hardly touched anything except coffee. He needs to eat to keep up his strength. I keep telling him that but he says he simply has no appetite. Of course, there's nothing takes away your appetite like a bad summer cold.

TYRONE   Yes, it's only natural. So don't let yourself get worried—

MARY [*quickly*]   Oh, I'm not. I know he'll be all right in a few days if he takes care of himself. [*as if she wanted to dismiss the subject but can't*] But it does seem a shame he should have to be sick right now.

TYRONE   Yes, it is bad luck. [*He gives her a quick, worried look.*] But you mustn't let it upset you, Mary. Remember, you've got to take care of yourself, too.

MARY [*quickly*]   I'm not upset. There's nothing to be upset about. What makes you think I'm upset?

TYRONE   Why, nothing, except you've seemed a bit high-strung the past few days.

MARY [*forcing a smile*]   I have? Nonsense, dear. It's your imagination. [*with sudden tenseness*] You really must not watch me all the time, James. I mean, it makes me self-conscious.

TYRONE [*putting a hand over one of her nervously playing ones*]   Now, now, Mary. That's your imagination. If I've watched you it was to admire how fat and beautiful you looked. [*His voice is suddenly moved by deep feeling.*] I can't tell you the deep happiness it gives me, darling, to see you as you've been since you came back to us, your dear old self again. [*He leans over and kisses her cheek impulsively—then turning back adds with a constrained air*] So keep up the good work, Mary.

MARY [*has turned her head away*]   I will, dear. [*She gets up restlessly and goes to the windows at right.*] Thank heavens, the fog is gone. [*She turns back.*] I do feel out of sorts this morning. I wasn't able to get much sleep with that awful foghorn going all night long.

TYRONE   Yes, it's like having a sick whale in the back yard. It kept me awake, too.

MARY [*affectionately amused*]   Did it? You had a strange way of showing your restlessness. You were snoring so hard I couldn't tell which was the foghorn! [*She comes to him, laughing, and pats his cheek playfully.*] Ten foghorns couldn't disturb you. You haven't a nerve in you. You've never had.

TYRONE [*his vanity piqued—testily*]   Nonsense. You always exaggerate about my snoring.

MARY   I couldn't. If you could only hear yourself once—
     [*A burst of laughter comes from the dining room. She turns her head, smiling.*]
     What's the joke, I wonder?

TYRONE [*grumpily*]   It's on me. I'll bet that much. It's always on the Old Man.

MARY [*teasingly*]   Yes, it's terrible the way we all pick on you, isn't it? You're so abused! [*She laughs—then with a pleased, relieved air*] Well, no matter what the joke is about, it's a relief to hear Edmund laugh. He's been so down in the mouth lately.

TYRONE [*ignoring this—resentfully*]   Some joke of Jamie's, I'll wager. He's forever making sneering fun of somebody, that one.

MARY   Now don't start in on poor Jamie, dear. [*without conviction*] He'll turn out all right in the end, you wait and see.

TYRONE   He'd better start soon, then. He's nearly thirty-four.

MARY [*ignoring this*]   Good heavens, are they going to stay in the dining room all day? [*She goes to the back parlor doorway and calls*] Jamie! Edmund! Come in the living room and give Cathleen a chance to clear the table.

[EDMUND *calls back, "We're coming, Mama." She goes back to the table.*]

TYRONE [*grumbling*]   You'd find excuses for him no matter what he did.

MARY [*sitting down beside him, pats his hand*]   Shush.

Their sons JAMES, JR., *and* EDMUND *enter together from the back parlor. They are both grinning, still chuckling over what had caused their laughter, and as they come forward they glance at their father and their grins grow broader.*

JAMIE, *the elder, is thirty-three. He has his father's broad-shouldered, deep-chested physique, is an inch taller and weighs less, but appears shorter and stouter because he lacks* TYRONE'S *bearing and graceful carriage. He also lacks his father's vitality. The signs of premature disintegration are on him. His face is still good looking, despite marks of dissipation, but it has never been handsome like* TYRONE'S, *although* JAMIE *resembles him rather than his mother. He has fine brown eyes, their color midway between his father's lighter and his mother's darker ones. His hair is thinning and already there is indication of a bald spot like* TYRONE'S. *His nose is unlike that of any other member of the family, pronouncedly aquiline. Combined with his habitual expression of cynicism it gives his countenance a Mephistophelian cast. But on the rare occasions when he smiles without sneering, his personality possesses the remnant of a humorous, romantic, irresponsible Irish charm—that of the beguiling ne'er-do-well, with a strain of the sentimentally poetic, attractive to women and popular with men.*

He is dressed in an old sack suit, not as shabby as TYRONE'S, *and wears a collar and tie. His fair skin is sunburned a reddish, freckled tan.*

EDMUND *is ten years younger than his brother, a couple of inches taller, thin and wiry. Where* JAMIE *takes after his father, with little resemblance to his mother,* EDMUND *looks like both his parents, but is more like his mother. Her big, dark eyes are the dominant feature in his long, narrow Irish face. His mouth has the same quality of hypersensitiveness hers possesses. His high fore-head is hers accentuated, with dark brown hair, sunbleached to red at the ends, brushed straight back from it. But his nose is his father's and his face in profile recalls* TYRONE'S. EDMUND'S *hands are noticeably like his mother's, with the same exceptionally long fingers. They even have to a minor degree the same nervousness. It is in the quality of extreme nervous sensibility that the likeness of* EDMUND *to his mother is most marked.*

He is plainly in bad health. Much thinner than he should be, his eyes appear feverish and his cheeks are sunken. His skin, in spite of being sunburned a deep brown, has a parched sallowness. He wears a shirt, collar and tie, no coat, old flannel trousers, brown sneakers.

MARY [*turns smilingly to them, in a merry tone that is a bit forced*]   I've been teasing your father about his snoring. [*to* TYRONE] I'll leave it to the boys, James. They must have heard you. No, not you, Jamie. I could hear you down the hall almost as bad as your father. You're like him. As soon as your head touches the pillow you're off and ten foghorns couldn't wake you. [*She stops abruptly, catching* JAMIE'S *eyes regarding her with an uneasy, probing look. Her smile vanishes and her manner becomes self-conscious.*] Why are you staring, Jamie? [*Her hands flutter up to her hair.*] Is my hair coming down? It's hard for me to do it up properly now. My eyes are getting so bad and I never can find my glasses.

JAMIE [*looks away guiltily*]   Your hair's all right, Mama. I was only thinking how well you look.

TYRONE [*heartily*]   Just what I've been telling her, Jamie. She's so fat and sassy, there'll soon be no holding her.

EDMUND   Yes, you certainly look grand, Mama. [*She is reassured and smiles at him lovingly. He winks with a kidding grin.*] I'll back you up about Papa's snoring. Gosh, what a racket!

JAMIE   I heard him, too. [*He quotes, putting on a ham-actor manner*] "The Moor, I know his trumpet."[3]

[*His mother and brother laugh.*]

TYRONE [*scathingly*]   If it takes my snoring to make you remember Shakespeare instead of the dope sheet on the ponies, I hope I'll keep on with it.

MARY   Now, James! You mustn't be so touchy.

[*JAMIE shrugs his shoulders and sits down in the chair on her right.*]

EDMUND [*irritably*]   Yes, for Pete's sake, Papa! The first thing after breakfast! Give it a rest, can't you? [*He slumps down in the chair at left of table next to his brother. His father ignores him.*]

MARY [*reprovingly*]   Your father wasn't finding fault with you. You don't have to always take Jamie's part. You'd think you were the one ten years older.

JAMIE [*boredly*]   What's all the fuss about? Let's forget it.

TYRONE [*contemptuously*]   Yes, forget! Forget everything and face nothing! It's a convenient philosophy if you've no ambition in life except to—

MARY   James, do be quiet. [*She puts an arm around his shoulder—coaxingly*] You must have gotten out of the wrong side of the bed this morning. [*to the boys, changing the subject*] What were you two grinning about like Cheshire cats when you came in? What was the joke?

TYRONE [*with a painful effort to be a good sport*]   Yes, let us in on it, lads. I told your mother I knew damned well it would be one on me, but never mind that, I'm used to it.

JAMIE [*dryly*]   Don't look at me. This is the Kid's story.

EDMUND [*grins*]   I meant to tell you last night, Papa, and forgot it. Yesterday when I went for a walk I dropped in at the Inn—

MARY [*worriedly*]   You shouldn't drink now, Edmund.

EDMUND [*ignoring this*]   And who do you think I met there, with a beautiful bun on,[4] but Shaughnessy, the tenant on that farm of yours.

MARY [*smiling*]   That dreadful man! But he is funny.

TYRONE [*scowling*]   He's not so funny when you're his landlord. He's a wily Shanty Mick, that one. He could hide behind a corkscrew. What's he complaining about now, Edmund—for I'm damned sure he's complaining. I suppose he wants his rent lowered. I let him have the place for almost nothing, just to keep someone on it, and he never pays that till I threaten to evict him.

EDMUND   No, he didn't beef about anything. He was so pleased with life he even bought a drink, and that's practically unheard of. He was delighted because he'd had a fight with your friend, Harker, the Standard Oil millionaire, and won a glorious victory.

3. Shakespeare's *Othello* 2.1.180.   4. I.e., drunk.

MARY [*with amused dismay*] Oh, Lord! James, you'll really have to do something—

TYRONE Bad luck to Shaughnessy, anyway!

JAMIE [*maliciously*] I'll bet the next time you see Harker at the Club and give him the old respectful bow, he won't see you.

EDMUND Yes. Harker will think you're no gentleman for harboring a tenant who isn't humble in the presence of a king of America.

TYRONE Never mind the Socialist gabble. I don't care to listen—

MARY [*tactfully*] Go on with your story, Edmund.

EDMUND [*grins at his father provocatively*] Well, you remember, Papa, the ice pond on Harker's estate is right next to the farm, and you remember Shaughnessy keeps pigs. Well, it seems there's a break in the fence and the pigs have been bathing in the millionaire's ice pond, and Harker's foreman told him he was sure Shaughnessy had broken the fence on purpose to give his pigs a free wallow.

MARY [*shocked and amused*] Good heavens!

TYRONE [*sourly, but with a trace of admiration*] I'm sure he did, too, the dirty scallywag. It's like him.

EDMUND So Harker came in person to rebuke Shaughnessy. [*He chuckles.*] A very bonehead play! If I needed any further proof that our ruling plutocrats, especially the ones who inherited their boodle, are not mental giants, that would clinch it.

TYRONE [*with appreciation, before he thinks*] Yes, he'd be no match for Shaughnessy. [*then he growls*] Keep your damned anarchist remarks to yourself. I won't have them in my house. [*But he is full of eager anticipation.*] What happened?

EDMUND Harker had as much chance as I would with Jack Johnson.[5] Shaughnessy got a few drinks under his belt and was waiting at the gate to welcome him. He told me he never gave Harker a chance to open his mouth. He began by shouting that he was no slave Standard Oil could trample on. He was a King of Ireland, if he had his rights, and scum was scum to him, no matter how much money it had stolen from the poor.

MARY Oh, Lord! [*But she can't help laughing.*]

EDMUND Then he accused Harker of making his foreman break down the fence to entice the pigs into the ice pond in order to destroy them. The poor pigs, Shaughnessy yelled, had caught their death of cold. Many of them were dying of pneumonia, and several others had been taken down with cholera from drinking the poisoned water. He told Harker he was hiring a lawyer to sue him for damages. And he wound up by saying that he had to put up with poison ivy, ticks, potato bugs, snakes and skunks on his farm, but he was an honest man who drew the line somewhere, and he'd be damned if he'd stand for a Standard Oil thief trespassing. So would Harker kindly remove his dirty feet from the premises before he sicked the dog on him. And Harker did! [*He and JAMIE laugh.*]

MARY [*shocked but giggling*] Heavens, what a terrible tongue that man has!

TYRONE [*admiringly before he thinks*] The damned old scoundrel! By God, you can't beat him! [*He laughs—then stops abruptly and scowls.*] The dirty blackguard! He'll get me in serious trouble yet. I hope you told him I'd be mad as hell—

---

5. Famous prizefighter, the first African American heavyweight boxing champion of the world.

EDMUND   I told him you'd be tickled to death over the great Irish victory, and so you are. Stop faking, Papa.

TYRONE   Well, I'm not tickled to death.

MARY [*teasingly*]   You are, too, James. You're simply delighted!

TYRONE   No, Mary, a joke is a joke, but—

EDMUND   I told Shaughnessy he should have reminded Harker that a Standard Oil millionaire ought to welcome the flavor of hog in his ice water as an appropriate touch.

TYRONE   The devil you did! [*frowning*] Keep your damned Socialist anarchist sentiments out of my affairs!

EDMUND   Shaughnessy almost wept because he hadn't thought of that one, but he said he'd include it in a letter he's writing to Harker, along with a few other insults he'd overlooked. [*He and* JAMIE *laugh.*]

TYRONE   What are you laughing at? There's nothing funny—A fine son you are to help that blackguard get me into a lawsuit!

MARY   Now, James, don't lose your temper.

TYRONE [*turns on* JAMIE]   And you're worse than he is, encouraging him. I suppose you're regretting you weren't there to prompt Shaughnessy with a few nastier insults. You've a fine talent for that, if for nothing else.

MARY   James! There's no reason to scold Jamie.

[JAMIE *is about to make some sneering remark to his father, but he shrugs his shoulders.*]

EDMUND [*with sudden nervous exasperation*]   Oh, for God's sake, Papa! If you're starting that stuff again, I'll beat it. [*He jumps up.*] I left my book upstairs, anyway. [*He goes to the front parlor, saying disgustedly*] God, Papa, I should think you'd get sick of hearing yourself—

[*He disappears.* TYRONE *looks after him angrily.*]

MARY   You musn't mind Edmund, James. Remember he isn't well.

[EDMUND *can be heard coughing as he goes upstairs. She adds nervously*] A summer cold makes anyone irritable.

JAMIE [*genuinely concerned*]   It's not just a cold he's got. The Kid is damned sick.

[*His father gives him a sharp warning look but he doesn't see it.*]

MARY [*turns on him resentfully*]   Why do you say that? It *is* just a cold! Anyone can tell that! You always imagine things!

TYRONE [*with another warning glance at* JAMIE—*easily*]   All Jamie meant was Edmund might have a touch of something else, too, which makes his cold worse.

JAMIE   Sure, Mama. That's all I meant.

TYRONE   Doctor Hardy thinks it might be a bit of malarial fever he caught when he was in the tropics. If it is, quinine will soon cure it.

MARY [*a look of contemptuous hostility flashes across her face*]   Doctor Hardy! I wouldn't believe a thing he said, if he swore on a stack of Bibles! I know what doctors are. They're all alike. Anything, they don't care what, to keep you coming to them. [*She stops short, overcome by a fit of acute self-consciousness as she catches their eyes fixed on her. Her hands jerk nervously to her hair. She forces a smile.*] What is it? What are you looking at? Is my hair—?

TYRONE [*puts his arm around her—with guilty heartiness, giving her a playful hug*]   There's nothing wrong with your hair. The healthier and fatter you get, the vainer you become. You'll soon spend half the day primping before the mirror.

MARY [*half reassured*]   I really should have new glasses. My eyes are so bad now.

TYRONE [*with Irish blarney*]   Your eyes are beautiful, and well you know it. [*He gives her a kiss. Her face lights up with a charming, shy embarrassment. Suddenly and startlingly one sees in her face the girl she had once been, not a ghost of the dead, but still a living part of her.*]

MARY   You mustn't be so silly, James. Right in front of Jamie!

TYRONE   Oh, he's on to you, too. He knows this fuss about eyes and hair is only fishing for compliments. Eh, Jamie?

JAMIE [*his face has cleared, too, and there is an old boyish charm in his loving smile at his mother*]   Yes, You can't kid us, Mama.

MARY [*laughs and an Irish lilt comes into her voice*]   Go along with both of you! [*then she speaks with a girlish gravity*] But I did truly have beautiful hair once, didn't I, James?

TYRONE   The most beautiful in the world!

MARY   It was a rare shade of reddish brown and so long it came down below my knees. You ought to remember it, too, Jamie. It wasn't until after Edmund was born that I had a single grey hair. Then it began to turn white. [*The girlishness fades from her face.*]

TYRONE [*quickly*]   And that made it prettier than ever.

MARY [*again embarrassed and pleased*]   Will you listen to your father, Jamie—after thirty-five years of marriage! He isn't a great actor for nothing, is he? What's come over you, James? Are you pouring coals of fire on my head for teasing you about snoring? Well, then, I take it all back. It must have been only the foghorn I heard. [*She laughs, and they laugh with her. Then she changes to a brisk businesslike air.*] But I can't stay with you any longer, even to hear compliments. I must see the cook about dinner and the day's marketing. [*She gets up and sighs with humorous exaggeration.*] Bridget is so lazy. And so sly. She begins telling me about her relatives so I can't get a word in edgeways and scold her. Well, I might as well get it over. [*She goes to the back-parlor doorway, then turns, her face worried again.*] You mustn't make Edmund work on the grounds with you, James, remember. [*again with the strange obstinate set to her face*] Not that he isn't strong enough, but he'd perspire and he might catch more cold.

[*She disappears through the back parlor.* TYRONE *turns on* JAMIE *condemningly.*]

TYRONE   You're a fine lunkhead! Haven't you any sense? The one thing to avoid is saying anything that would get her more upset over Edmund.

JAMIE [*shrugging his shoulders*]   All right. Have it your way. I think it's the wrong idea to let Mama go on kidding yourself. It will only make the shock worse when she has to face it. Anyway, you can see she's deliberately fooling herself with that summer cold talk. She knows better.

TYRONE   Knows? Nobody knows yet.

JAMIE   Well, I do. I was with Edmund when he went to Doc Hardy on Monday. I heard him pull that touch of malaria stuff. He was stalling. That isn't what he thinks any more. You know it as well as I do. You talked to him when you went uptown yesterday, didn't you?

TYRONE   He couldn't say anything for sure yet. He's to phone me today before Edmund goes to him.

JAMIE [*slowly*]   He thinks it's consumption,[6] doesn't he, Papa?

TYRONE [*reluctantly*]   He said it might be.

JAMIE [*moved, his love for his brother coming out*]   Poor kid! God damn it! [*He turns on his father accusingly.*] It might never have happened if you'd sent him to a real doctor when he first got sick.

TYRONE   What's the matter with Hardy? He's always been our doctor up here.

JAMIE   Everything's the matter with him! Even in this hick burg he's rated third class! He's a cheap old quack!

TYRONE   That's right! Run him down! Run down everybody! Everyone is a fake to you!

JAMIE [*contemptuously*]   Hardy only charges a dollar. That's what makes you think he's a fine doctor!

TYRONE [*stung*]   That's enough! You're not drunk now! There's no excuse— [*He controls himself—a bit defensively*] If you mean I can't afford one of the fine society doctors who prey on the rich summer people—

JAMIE   Can't afford? You're one of the biggest property owners around here.

TYRONE   That doesn't mean I'm rich. It's all mortgaged—

JAMIE   Because you always buy more instead of paying off mortgages. If Edmund was a lousy acre of land you wanted, the sky would be the limit!

TYRONE   That's a lie! And your sneers against Doctor Hardy are lies! He doesn't put on frills, or have an office in a fashionable location, or drive around in an expensive automobile. That's what you pay for with those other five-dollars-to-look-at-your-tongue fellows, not their skill.

JAMIE [*with a scornful shrug of his shoulders*]   Oh, all right. I'm a fool to argue. You can't change the leopard's spots.

TYRONE [*with rising anger*]   No, you can't. You've taught me that lesson only too well. I've lost all hope you will ever change yours. You dare tell me what I can afford? You've never known the value of a dollar and never will! You've never saved a dollar in your life! At the end of each season you're penniless! You've thrown your salary away every week on whores and whiskey!

JAMIE   My salary! Christ!

TYRONE   It's more than you're worth, and you couldn't get that if it wasn't for me. If you weren't my son, there isn't a manager in the business who would give you a part, your reputation stinks so. As it is, I have to humble my pride and beg for you, saying you've turned over a new leaf, although I know it's a lie!

JAMIE   I never wanted to be an actor. You forced me on the stage.

TYRONE   That's a lie! You made no effort to find anything else to do. You left it to me to get you a job and I have no influence except in the theater. Forced you! You never wanted to do anything except loaf in barrooms! You'd have been content to sit back like a lazy lunk and sponge on me for the rest of your life! After all the money I'd wasted on your education, and all you did was get fired in disgrace from every college you went to!

JAMIE   Oh, for God's sake, don't drag up that ancient history!

6. Tuberculosis.

TYRONE It's not ancient history that you have to come home every summer to live on me.

JAMIE I earn my board and lodging working on the grounds. It saves you hiring a man.

TYRONE Bah! You have to be driven to do even that much! [*His anger ebbs into a weary complaint.*] I wouldn't give a damn if you ever displayed the slightest sign of gratitude. The only thanks is to have you sneer at me for a dirty miser, sneer at my profession, sneer at every damned thing in the world—except yourself.

JAMIE [*wryly*] That's not true, Papa. You can't hear me talking to myself, that's all.

TYRONE [*stares at him puzzledly, then quotes mechanically*] "Ingratitude, the vilest weed that grows"![7]

JAMIE I could see that line coming! God, how many thousand times—! [*He stops, bored with their quarrel, and shrugs his shoulders.*] All right, Papa. I'm a bum. Anything you like, so long as it stops the argument.

TYRONE [*with indignant appeal now*] If you'd get ambition in your head instead of folly! You're young yet. You could still make your mark. You had the talent to become a fine actor! You have it still. You're my son—!

JAMIE [*boredly*] Let's forget me. I'm not interested in the subject. Neither are you. [TYRONE *gives up.* JAMIE *goes on casually.*] What started us on this? Oh, Doc Hardy. When is he going to call you up about Edmund?

TYRONE Around lunch time. [*He pauses—then defensively*] I couldn't have sent Edmund to a better doctor. Hardy's treated him whenever he was sick up here, since he was knee high. He knows his constitution as no other doctor could. It's not a question of my being miserly, as you'd like to make out. [*bitterly*] And what could the finest specialist in America do for Edmund, after he's deliberately ruined his health by the mad life he's led ever since he was fired from college? Even before that when he was in prep school, he began dissipating and playing the Broadway sport to imitate you, when he's never had your constitution to stand it. You're a healthy hulk like me—or you were at his age—but he's always been a bundle of nerves like his mother. I've warned him for years his body couldn't stand it, but he wouldn't heed me, and now it's too late.

JAMIE [*sharply*] What do you mean, too late? You talk as if you thought—

TYRONE [*guiltily explosive*] Don't be a damned fool! I meant nothing but what's plain to anyone! His health has broken down and he may be an invalid for a long time.

JAMIE [*stares at his father, ignoring his explanation*] I know it's an Irish peasant idea consumption is fatal. It probably is when you live in a hovel on a bog, but over here, with modern treatment—

TYRONE Don't I know that! What are you gabbing about, anyway? And keep your dirty tongue off Ireland, with your sneers about peasants and bogs and hovels! [*accusingly*] The less you say about Edmund's sickness, the better for your conscience! You're more responsible than anyone!

JAMIE [*stung*] That's a lie! I won't stand for that, Papa!

TYRONE It's the truth! You've been the worst influence for him. He grew up admiring you as a hero! A fine example you set him! If you ever gave him advice except in the ways of rottenness, I've never heard of it! You

---

7. Shakespeare's *King Lear* 1.4.

made him old before his time, pumping him full of what you consider worldly wisdom, when he was too young to see that your mind was so poisoned by your own failure in life, you wanted to believe every man was a knave with his soul for sale, and every woman who wasn't a whore was a fool!

JAMIE [*with a defensive air of weary indifference again*] All right. I did put Edmund wise to things, but not until I saw he'd started to raise hell, and knew he'd laugh at me if I tried the good advice, older brother stuff. All I did was make a pal of him and be absolutely frank so he'd learn from my mistakes that—[*He shrugs his shoulders—cynically*] Well, that if you can't be good you can at least be careful.

[*His father snorts contemptuously. Suddenly* JAMIE *becomes really moved.*]

That's a rotten accusation, Papa. You know how much the Kid means to me, and how close we've always been—not like the usual brothers! I'd do anything for him.

TYRONE [*impressed—mollifyingly*] I know you may have thought it was for the best, Jamie. I didn't say you did it deliberately to harm him.

JAMIE Besides it's damned rot! I'd like to see anyone influence Edmund more than he wants to be. His quietness fools people into thinking they can do what they like with him. But he's stubborn as hell inside and what he does is what he wants to do, and to hell with anyone else! What had I to do with all the crazy stunts he's pulled in the last few years—working his way all over the map as a sailor and all that stuff. I thought that was a damned fool idea, and I told him so. You can't imagine me getting fun out of being on the beach in South America, or living in filthy dives, drinking rotgut, can you? No, thanks! I'll stick to Broadway, and a room with a bath, and bars that serve bonded Bourbon.

TYRONE You and Broadway! It's made you what you are! [*with a touch of pride*] Whatever Edmund's done, he's had the guts to go off on his own, where he couldn't come whining to me the minute he was broke.

JAMIE [*stung into sneering jealousy*] He's always come home broke finally, hasn't he? And what did his going away get him? Look at him now! [*He is suddenly shamefaced.*] Christ! That's a lousy thing to say. I don't mean that.

TYRONE [*decides to ignore this*] He's been doing well on the paper. I was hoping he'd found the work he wants to do at last.

JAMIE [*sneering jealously again*] A hick town rag! Whatever bull they hand you, they tell me he's a pretty bum reporter. If he weren't your son—[*ashamed again*] No, that's not true! They're glad to have him, but it's the special stuff that gets him by. Some of the poems and parodies he's written are damned good. [*grudgingly again*] Not that they'd ever get him anywhere on the big time. [*hastily*] But he's certainly made a damned good start.

TYRONE Yes. He's made a start. You used to talk about wanting to become a newspaper man but you were never willing to start at the bottom. You expected—

JAMIE Oh, for Christ's sake, Papa! Can't you lay off me!

TYRONE [*stares at him—then looks away—after a pause*] It's damnable luck Edmund should be sick right now. It couldn't have come at a worse time for him. [*He adds, unable to conceal an almost furtive uneasiness*] Or for your mother. It's damnable she should have this to upset her, just when she needs peace and freedom from worry. She's been so well in the two months since she came home. [*His voice grows husky and trembles a little.*] It's been heaven to me. This home has been a home again. But I needn't tell you, Jamie.

> [*His son looks at him, for the first time with an understanding sympathy. It is as if suddenly a deep bond of common feeling existed between them in which their antagonisms could be forgotten.*]

JAMIE [*almost gently*]   I've felt the same way, Papa.

TYRONE   Yes, this time you can see how strong and sure of herself she is. She's a different woman entirely from the other times. She has control of her nerves—or she had until Edmund got sick. Now you can feel her growing tense and frightened underneath. I wish to God we could keep the truth from her, but we can't if he has to be sent to a sanatorium. What makes it worse is her father died of consumption. She worshiped him and she's never forgotten. Yes, it will be hard for her. But she can do it! She has the will power now! We must help her, Jamie, in every way we can!

JAMIE [*moved*]   Of course, Papa. [*hesitantly*] Outside of nerves, she seems perfectly all right this morning.

TYRONE [*with hearty confidence now*]   Never better. She's full of fun and mischief. [*Suddenly he frowns at JAMIE suspiciously.*] Why do you say, seems? Why shouldn't she be all right? What the hell do you mean?

JAMIE   Don't start jumping down my throat! God, Papa, this ought to be one thing we can talk over frankly without a battle.

TYRONE   I'm sorry, Jamie. [*tensely*] But go on and tell me—

JAMIE   There's nothing to tell. I was all wrong. It's just that last night— Well, you know how it is, I can't forget the past. I can't help being suspicious. Any more than you can. [*bitterly*] That's the hell of it. And it makes it hell for Mama! She watches us watching her—

TYRONE [*sadly*]   I know. [*tensely*] Well, what was it! Can't you speak out!

JAMIE   Nothing, I tell you. Just my damned foolishness. Around three o'clock this morning, I woke up and heard her moving around in the spare room. Then she went to the bathroom. I pretended to be asleep. She stopped in the hall to listen, as if she wanted to make sure I was.

TYRONE [*with forced scorn*]   For God's sake, is that all? She told me herself the foghorn kept her awake all night, and every night since Edmund's been sick she's been up and down, going to his room to see how he was.

JAMIE [*eagerly*]   Yes, that's right, she did stop to listen outside his room. [*hesitantly again*] It was her being in the spare room that scared me. I couldn't help remembering that when she starts sleeping alone in there, it has always been a sign—

TYRONE   It isn't this time! It's easily explained. Where else could she go last night to get away from my snoring? [*He gives way to a burst of resentful anger.*] By God, how you can live with a mind that sees nothing but the worst motives behind everything is beyond me!

JAMIE [*stung*]   Don't pull that! I've just said I was all wrong. Don't you suppose I'm as glad of that as you are!

TYRONE [*mollifyingly*]   I'm sure you are, Jamie. [*A pause. His expression becomes somber. He speaks slowly with a superstitious dread.*] It would be like a curse she can't escape if worry over Edmund—It was her long sickness after bringing him into the world that she first—

JAMIE She didn't have anything to do with it!

TYRONE I'm not blaming her.

JAMIE [*bitingly*] Then who are you blaming? Edmund, for being born?

TYRONE You damned fool! No one was to blame.

JAMIE The bastard of a doctor was! From what Mama's said, he was another cheap quack like Hardy! You wouldn't pay for a first-rate—

TYRONE That's a lie! [*furiously*] So I'm to blame! That's what you're driving at, is it? You evil-minded loafer!

JAMIE [*warningly as he hears his mother in the dining room*] Ssh!
[TYRONE *gets hastily to his feet and goes to look out the windows at right.* JAMIE *speaks with a complete change of tone.*]
Well, if we're going to cut the front hedge today, we'd better go to work.
[MARY *comes in from the back parlor. She gives a quick, suspicious glance from one to the other, her manner nervously self-conscious.*]

TYRONE [*turns from the window—with an actor's heartiness*] Yes, it's too fine a morning to waste indoors arguing. Take a look out the window, Mary. There's no fog in the harbor. I'm sure the spell of it we've had is over now.

MARY [*going to him*] I hope so, dear. [*to* JAMIE, *forcing a smile*] Did I actually hear you suggesting work on the front hedge, Jamie? Wonders will never cease! You must want pocket money badly.

JAMIE [*kiddingly*] When don't I? [*He winks at her, with a derisive glance at his father.*] I expect a salary of at least one large iron man[8] at the end of the week—to carouse on!

MARY [*does not respond to his humor—her hands fluttering over the front of her dress*] What were you two arguing about?

JAMIE [*shrugs his shoulders*] The same old stuff.

MARY I heard you say something about a doctor, and your father accusing you of being evil-minded.

JAMIE [*quickly*] Oh, that. I was saying again Doc Hardy isn't my idea of the world's greatest physician.

MARY [*knows he is lying—vaguely*] Oh. No, I wouldn't say he was either. [*changing the subject—forcing a smile*] That Bridget! I thought I'd never get away. She told me about her second cousin on the police force in St. Louis. [*then with nervous irritation*] Well, if you're going to work on the hedge why don't you go? [*hastily*] I mean, take advantage of the sunshine before the fog comes back. [*strangely, as if talking aloud to herself*] Because I know it will. [*Suddenly she is self-consciously aware that they are both staring fixedly at her—flurriedly, raising her hands*] Or I should say, the rheumatism in my hands knows. It's a better weather prophet than you are, James. [*She stares at her hands with fascinated repulsion.*] Ugh! How ugly they are! Who'd ever believe they were once beautiful?
[*They stare at her with a growing dread.*]

TYRONE [*takes her hands and gently pushes them down*] Now, now, Mary. None of that foolishness. They're the sweetest hands in the world.
[*She smiles, her face lighting up, and kisses him gratefully. He turns to his son.*]
Come on Jamie. Your mother's right to scold us. The way to start work is to start work. The hot sun will sweat some of that booze fat off your middle.

8. Slang for "dollar."

[*He opens the screen door and goes out on the porch and disappears down a flight of steps leading to the ground.* JAMIE *rises from his chair and, taking off his coat, goes to the door. At the door he turns back but avoids looking at her, and she does not look at him.*]

JAMIE [*with an awkward, uneasy tenderness*] We're all so proud of you, Mama, so darned happy.

[*She stiffens and stares at him with a frightened defiance. He flounders on.*]

But you've still got to be careful. You mustn't worry so much about Edmund. He'll be all right.

MARY [*with a stubborn, bitterly resentful look*] Of course, he'll be all right. And I don't know what you mean, warning me to be careful.

JAMIE [*rebuffed and hurt, shrugs his shoulders*] All right, Mama. I'm sorry I spoke.

[*He goes out on the porch. She waits rigidly until he disappears down the steps. Then she sinks down in the chair he had occupied, her face betraying a frightened, furtive desperation, her hands roving over the table top, aimlessly moving objects around. She hears* EDMUND *descending the stairs in the front hall. As he nears the bottom he has a fit of coughing. She springs to her feet, as if she wanted to run away from the sound, and goes quickly to the windows at right. She is looking out, apparently calm, as he enters from the front parlor, a book in one hand. She turns to him, her lips set in a welcoming, motherly smile.*]

MARY Here you are. I was just going upstairs to look for you.

EDMUND I waited until they went out. I don't want to mix up in any arguments. I feel too rotten.

MARY [*almost resentfully*] Oh, I'm sure you don't feel half as badly as you make out. You're such a baby. You like to get us worried so we'll make a fuss over you. [*hastily*] I'm only teasing, dear. I know how miserably uncomfortable you must be. But you feel better today, don't you? [*worriedly, taking his arm*] All the same, you've grown much too thin. You need to rest all you can. Sit down and I'll make you comfortable.

[*He sits down in the rocking chair and she puts a pillow behind his back.*]

There, How's that?

EDMUND Grand. Thanks, Mama.

MARY [*kisses him—tenderly*] All you need is your mother to nurse you. Big as you are, you're still the baby of the family to me, you know.

EDMUND [*takes her hand—with deep seriousness*] Never mind me. You take care of yourself. That's all that counts.

MARY [*evading his eyes*] But I am, dear. [*forcing a laugh*] Heavens, don't you see how fat I've grown! I'll have to have all my dresses let out. [*She turns away and goes to the windows at right. She attempts a light, amused tone.*] They've started clipping the hedge. Poor Jamie! How he hates working in front where everyone passing can see him. There go the Chatfields in their new Mercedes. It's a beautiful car, isn't it? Not like our second-hand Packard. Poor Jamie! He bent almost under the hedge so they wouldn't notice him. They bowed to your father and he bowed back as if he were taking a curtain call. In that filthy old suit I've tried to make him throw away. [*Her voice has grown bitter.*] Really, he ought to have more pride than to make such a show of himself.

EDMUND He's right not to give a damn what anyone thinks. Jamie's a fool

to care about the Chatfields. For Pete's sake, who ever heard of them outside this hick burg?

MARY [*with satisfaction*]   No one. You're quite right, Edmund. Big frogs in
a small puddle. It is stupid of Jamie. [*She pauses, looking out the window—then with an undercurrent of lonely yearning*] Still, the Chatfields
and people like them stand for something. I mean they have decent, presentable homes they don't have to be ashamed of. They have friends who
entertain them and whom they entertain. They're not cut off from everyone. [*She turns back from the window.*] Not that I want anything to do
with them. I've always hated this town and everyone in it. You know that.
I never wanted to live here in the first place, but your father liked it and
insisted on building this house, and I've had to come here every summer.

EDMUND   Well, it's better than spending the summer in a New York hotel,
isn't it? And this town's not so bad. I like it well enough. I suppose because
it's the only home we've had.

MARY   I've never felt it was my home. It was wrong from the start. Everything was done in the cheapest way. Your father would never spend the
money to make it right. It's just as well we haven't any friends here. I'd be
ashamed to have them step in the door. But he's never wanted family
friends. He hates calling on people, or receiving them. All he likes is to
hobnob with men at the Club or in a barroom. Jamie and you are the
same way, but you're not to blame. You've never had a chance to meet
decent people here. I know you both would have been so different if you'd
been able to associate with nice girls instead of—You'd never have disgraced yourselves as you have, so that now no respectable parents will let
their daughters be seen with you.

EDMUND [*irritably*]   Oh, Mama, forget it! Who cares? Jamie and I would be
bored stiff. And about the Old Man, what's the use of talking? You can't
change him.

MARY [*mechanically rebuking*]   Don't call your father the Old Man. You
should have more respect. [*then dully*] I know it's useless to talk. But
sometimes I feel so lonely. [*Her lips quiver and she keeps her head turned
away.*]

EDMUND   Anyway, you've got to be fair, Mama. It may have been all his
fault in the beginning, but you know that later on, even if he'd wanted to,
we couldn't have had people here—[*He flounders guiltily.*] I mean, you
wouldn't have wanted them.

MARY [*wincing—her lips quivering pitifully*]   Don't. I can't bear having you
remind me.

EDMUND   Don't take it that way! Please, Mama! I'm trying to help. Because
it's bad for you to forget. The right way is to remember. So you'll always
be on your guard. You know what's happened before. [*miserably*] God,
Mama, you know I hate to remind you. I'm doing it because it's been so
wonderful having you home the way you've been, and it would be terrible—

MARY [*strickenly*]   Please, dear. I know you mean it for the best, but—[*A
defensive uneasiness comes into her voice again.*] I don't understand why you
should suddenly say such things. What put it in your mind this morning?

EDMUND [*evasively*]   Nothing. Just because I feel rotten and blue, I suppose.

MARY Tell me the truth. Why are you so suspicious all of a sudden?

EDMUND I'm not!

MARY Oh, yes you are. I can feel it. Your father and Jamie, too—particularly Jamie.

EDMUND Now don't start imagining things, Mama.

MARY [*her hands fluttering*] It makes it so much harder, living in this atmosphere of constant suspicion, knowing everyone is spying on me, and none of you believe in me, or trust me.

EDMUND That's crazy, Mama. We do trust you.

MARY If there was only some place I could go to get away for a day, or even an afternoon, some woman friend I could talk to—not about anything serious, simply laugh and gossip and forget for a while—someone besides the servants—that stupid Cathleen!

EDMUND [*gets up worriedly and puts his arm around her*] Stop it, Mama. You're getting yourself worked up over nothing.

MARY Your father goes out. He meets his friends in barrooms or at the Club. You and Jamie have the boys you know. You go out. But I am alone. I've always been alone.

EDMUND [*soothingly*] Come now! You know that's a fib. One of us always stays around to keep you company, or goes with you in the automobile when you take a drive.

MARY [*bitterly*] Because you're afraid to trust me alone! [*She turns on him—sharply.*] I insist you tell me why you act so differently this morning—why you felt you had to remind me—

EDMUND [*hesitates—then blurts out guiltily*] It's stupid. It's just that I wasn't asleep when you came in my room last night. You didn't go back to your and Papa's room. You went in the spare room for the rest of the night.

MARY Because your father's snoring was driving me crazy! For heaven's sake, haven't I often used the spare room as my bedroom? [*bitterly*] But I see what you thought. That was when—

EDMUND [*too vehemently*] I didn't think anything!

MARY So you pretended to be asleep in order to spy on me!

EDMUND No! I did it because I knew if you found out I was feverish and couldn't sleep, it would upset you.

MARY Jamie was pretending to be asleep, too, I'm sure, and I suppose your father—

EDMUND Stop it, Mama!

MARY Oh, I can't bear it, Edmund, when even you—! [*Her hands flutter up to pat her hair in their aimless, distracted way. Suddenly a strange undercurrent of revengefulness comes into her voice.*] It would serve all of you right if it was true!

EDMUND Mama! Don't say that! That's the way you talk when—

MARY Stop suspecting me! Please, dear! You hurt me! I couldn't sleep because I was thinking about you. That's the real reason! I've been so worried ever since you've been sick. [*She puts her arms around him and hugs him with a frightened, protective tenderness.*]

EDMUND [*soothingly*] That's foolishness. You know it's only a bad cold.

MARY Yes, of course, I know that!

EDMUND But listen, Mama. I want you to promise me that even if it should turn out to be something worse, you'll know I'll soon be all right again, anyway, and you won't worry yourself sick, and you'll keep on taking care of yourself—

MARY [*frightenedly*]   I won't listen when you're so silly! There's absolutely no reason to talk as if you expected something dreadful! Of course, I promise you. I give you my sacred word of honor! [*then with a sad bitterness*] But I suppose you're remembering I've promised before on my word of honor.

EDMUND   No!

MARY [*her bitterness receding into a resigned helplessness*]   I'm not blaming you, dear. How can you help it? How can any one of us forget? [*strangely*] That's what makes it so hard—for all of us. We can't forget.

EDMUND [*grabs her shoulder*]   Mama! Stop it!

MARY [*forcing a smile*]   All right, dear. I didn't mean to be so gloomy. Don't mind me. Here. Let me feel your head. Why, it's nice and cool. You certainly haven't any fever now.

EDMUND   Forget! It's you—

MARY   But I'm quite all right, dear. [*with a quick, strange, calculating, almost sly glance at him*] Except I naturally feel tired and nervous this morning, after such a bad night. I really ought to go upstairs and lie down until lunch time and take a nap.

[*He gives her an instinctive look of suspicion—then, ashamed of himself, looks quickly away. She hurries on nervously.*]

What are you going to do? Read here? It would be much better for you to go out in the fresh air and sunshine. But don't get overheated, remember. Be sure and wear a hat.

[*She stops, looking straight at him now. He avoids her eyes. There is a tense pause. Then she speaks jeeringly.*]

Or are you afraid to trust me alone?

EDMUND [*tormentedly*]   No! Can't you stop talking like that! I think you ought to take a nap. [*He goes to the screen door—forcing a joking tone*] I'll go down and help Jamie bear up. I love to lie in the shade and watch him work.

[*He forces a laugh in which she makes herself join. Then he goes out on the porch and disappears down the steps. Her first reaction is one of relief. She appears to relax. She sinks down in one of the wicker armchairs at rear of table and leans her head back, closing her eyes. But suddenly she grows terribly tense again. Her eyes open and she strains forward, seized by a fit of nervous panic. She begins a desperate battle with herself. Her long fingers, warped and knotted by rheumatism, drum on the arms of the chair, driven by an insistent life of their own, without her consent.*]

CURTAIN

Act 2

SCENE 1

SCENE—*The same. It is around quarter to one. No sunlight comes into the room now through the windows at right. Outside the day is still fine but increasingly sultry, with a faint haziness in the air which softens the glare of the sun.*

EDMUND *sits in the armchair at left of table, reading a book. Or rather he is trying to concentrate on it but cannot. He seems to be listening for some sound from*

*upstairs. His manner is nervously apprehensive and he looks more sickly than in
the previous act.*

The second girl, CATHLEEN, *enters from the back parlor. She carries a tray on
which is a bottle of bonded Bourbon, several whiskey glasses and a pitcher of ice
water. She is a buxom Irish peasant, in her early twenties, with a red-cheeked
comely face, black hair and blue eyes—amiable, ignorant, clumsy, and possessed
by a dense, well-meaning stupidity. She puts the tray on the table.* EDMUND *pretends to be so absorbed in his book he does not notice her, but she ignores this.*

CATHLEEN [*with garrulous familiarity*]   Here's the whiskey. It'll be lunch
    time soon. Will I call your father and Mister Jamie, or will you?

EDMUND [*without looking up from his book*]   You do it.

CATHLEEN   It's a wonder your father wouldn't look at his watch once in a
    while. He's a divil for making the meals late, and then Bridget curses me
    as if I was to blame. But he's a grand handsome man, if he is old. You'll
    never see the day you're as good looking—nor Mister Jamie, either. [*She
    chuckles.*] I'll wager Mister Jamie wouldn't miss the time to stop work and
    have his drop of whiskey if he had a watch to his name!

EDMUND [*gives up trying to ignore her and grins*]   You win that one.

CATHLEEN   And here's another I'd win, that you're making me call them so
    you can sneak a drink before they come.

EDMUND   Well, I hadn't thought of that—

CATHLEEN   Oh no, not you! Butter wouldn't melt in your mouth, I suppose.

EDMUND   But now you suggest it—

CATHLEEN [*suddenly primly virtuous*]   I'd never suggest a man or a woman
    touch drink, Mister Edmund. Sure, didn't it kill an uncle of mine in the
    old country. [*relenting*] Still, a drop now and then is no harm when you're
    in low spirits, or have a bad cold.

EDMUND   Thanks for handing me a good excuse. [*then with forced casual-
    ness*] You'd better call my mother, too.

CATHLEEN   What for? She's always on time without any calling. God bless
    her, she has some consideration for the help.

EDMUND   She's been taking a nap.

CATHLEEN   She wasn't asleep when I finished my work upstairs a while
    back. She was lying down in the spare room with her eyes wide open.
    She'd a terrible headache, she said.

EDMUND [*his casualness more forced*]   Oh well then, just call my father.

CATHLEEN [*goes to the screen door, grumbling good-naturedly*]   No wonder
    my feet kill me each night. I won't walk out in this heat and get sunstroke.
    I'll call from the porch.

    [*She goes out on the side porch, letting the screen door slam behind her,
    and disappears on her way to the front porch. A moment later she is heard
    shouting.*]

    Mister Tyrone! Mister Jamie! It's time!

    [EDMUND, *who has been staring frightenedly before him, forgetting his
    book, springs to his feet nervously.*]

EDMUND   God, what a wench!

    [*He grabs the bottle and pours a drink, adds ice water and drinks. As he
    does so, he hears someone coming in the front door. He puts the glass
    hastily on the tray and sits down again, opening his book.* JAMIE *comes in
    from the front parlor, his coat over his arm. He has taken off collar and
    tie and carries them in his hand. He is wiping sweat from his forehead*

with a handkerchief. EDMUND *looks up as if his reading was interrupted.*
JAMIE *takes one look at the bottle and glasses and smiles cynically.*]

JAMIE   Sneaking one, eh? Cut out the bluff, Kid. You're a rottener actor than I am.

EDMUND [*grins*]   Yes, I grabbed one while the going was good.

JAMIE [*puts a hand affectionately on his shoulder*]   That's better. Why kid me? We're pals, aren't we?

EDMUND   I wasn't sure it was you coming.

JAMIE   I made the Old Man look at his watch. I was halfway up the walk when Cathleen burst into song. Our wild Irish lark! She ought to be a train announcer.

EDMUND   That's what drove me to drink. Why don't you sneak one while you've got a chance?

JAMIE   I was thinking of that little thing. [*He goes quickly to the window at right.*] The Old Man was talking to old Captain Turner. Yes, he's still at it. [*He comes back and takes a drink.*] And now to cover up from his eagle eye. [*He measures two drinks of water and pours them in the whiskey bottle and shakes it up.*] There. That fixes it. [*He pours water in the glass and sets it on the table by* EDMUND.] And here's the water you've been drinking.

EDMUND   Fine! You don't think it will fool him, do you?

JAMIE   Maybe not, but he can't prove it. [*Putting on his collar and tie.*] I hope he doesn't forget lunch listening to himself talk. I'm hungry. [*He sits across the table from* EDMUND—*irritably*] That's what I hate about working down in front. He puts on an act for every damned fool that comes along.

EDMUND [*gloomily*]   You're in luck to be hungry. The way I feel I don't care if I ever eat again.

JAMIE [*gives him a glance of concern*]   Listen, Kid. You know me. I've never lectured you, but Doctor Hardy was right when he told you to cut out the redeye.

EDMUND   Oh, I'm going to after he hands me the bad news this afternoon. A few before then won't make any difference.

JAMIE [*hesitates—then slowly*]   I'm glad you've got your mind prepared for bad news. It won't be such a jolt. [*He catches* EDMUND *staring at him.*] I mean, it's a cinch you're really sick, and it would be wrong dope to kid yourself.

EDMUND [*disturbed*]   I'm not. I know how rotten I feel, and the fever and chills I get at night are no joke. I think Doctor Hardy's last guess was right. It must be the damned malaria come back on me.

JAMIE   Maybe, but don't be too sure.

EDMUND   Why? What do you think it is?

JAMIE   Hell, how would I know? I'm no Doc. [*abruptly*] Where's Mama?

EDMUND   Upstairs.

JAMIE [*looks at him sharply*]   When did she go up?

EDMUND   Oh, about the time I came down to the hedge, I guess. She said she was going to take a nap.

JAMIE   You didn't tell me—

EDMUND [*defensively*]   Why should I? What about it? She was tired out. She didn't get much sleep last night.

JAMIE   I know she didn't.

[*A pause. The brothers avoid looking at each other.*]

EDMUND   That damned foghorn kept me awake, too.

[*Another pause.*]

JAMIE   She's been upstairs alone all morning, eh? You haven't seen her?

EDMUND   No. I've been reading here. I wanted to give her a chance to sleep.

JAMIE   Is she coming down to lunch?

EDMUND   Of course.

JAMIE [*dryly*]   No of course about it. She might not want any lunch. Or she might start having most of her meals alone upstairs. That's happened, hasn't it?

EDMUND [*with frightened resentment*]   Cut it out, Jamie! Can't you think anything but—? [*persuasively*] You're all wrong to suspect anything. Cathleen saw her not long ago. Mama didn't tell her she wouldn't be down to lunch.

JAMIE   Then she wasn't taking a nap?

EDMUND   Not right then, but she was lying down, Cathleen said.

JAMIE   In the spare room?

EDMUND   Yes. For Pete's sake, what of it?

JAMIE [*bursts out*]   You damned fool! Why did you leave her alone so long? Why didn't you stick around?

EDMUND   Because she accused me—and you and Papa—of spying on her all the time and not trusting her. She made me feel ashamed. I know how rotten it must be for her. And she promised on her sacred word of honor—

JAMIE [*with a bitter weariness*]   You ought to know that doesn't mean anything.

EDMUND   It does this time!

JAMIE   That's what we thought the other times. [*He leans over the table to give his brother's arm an affectionate grasp.*] Listen, Kid, I know you think I'm a cynical bastard, but remember I've seen a lot more of this game than you have. You never knew what was really wrong until you were in prep-school. Papa and I kept it from you. But I was wise ten years or more before we had to tell you. I know the game backwards and I've been thinking all morning of the way she acted last night when she thought we were asleep. I haven't been able to think of anything else. And now you tell me she got you to leave her alone upstairs all morning.

EDMUND   She didn't! You're crazy!

JAMIE [*placatingly*]   All right, Kid. Don't start a battle with me. I hope as much as you do I'm crazy. I've been as happy as hell because I'd really begun to believe that this time—[*He stops—looking through the front parlor toward the hall—lowering his voice, hurriedly*] She's coming downstairs. You win on that. I guess I'm a damned suspicious louse.

[*They grow tense with a hopeful, fearful expectancy.* JAMIE *mutters*]
Damn! I wish I'd grabbed another drink.

EDMUND   Me, too.

[*He coughs nervously and this brings on a real fit of coughing.* JAMIE *glances at him with worried pity.* MARY *enters from the front parlor. At first one notices no change except that she appears to be less nervous, to be more as she was when we first saw her after breakfast, but then one becomes aware that her eyes are brighter, and there is a peculiar detachment in her voice and manner, as if she were a little withdrawn from her words and actions.*]

MARY [*goes worriedly to* EDMUND *and puts her arm around him*]   You mustn't
cough like that. It's bad for your throat. You don't want to get a sore throat
on top of your cold.

> [*She kisses him. He stops coughing and gives her a quick apprehensive
> glance, but if his suspicions are aroused her tenderness makes him
> renounce them and he believes what he wants to believe for the moment.
> On the other hand,* JAMIE *knows after one probing look at her that his sus-
> picions are justified. His eyes fall to stare at the floor, his face sets in an
> expression of embittered, defensive cynicism.* MARY *goes on, half sitting on
> the arm of* EDMUND's *chair, her arm around him, so her face is above and
> behind his and he cannot look into her eyes.*]

But I seem to be always picking on you, telling you don't do this and don't
do that. Forgive me, dear. It's just that I want to take care of you.

EDMUND   I know, Mama. How about you? Do you feel rested?

MARY   Yes, ever so much better. I've been lying down ever since you went
out. It's what I needed after such a restless night. I don't feel nervous now.

EDMUND   That's fine.

> [*He pats her hand on his shoulder.* JAMIE *gives him a strange, almost con-
> temptuous glance, wondering if his brother can really mean this.* EDMUND
> *does not notice but his mother does.*]

MARY [*in a forced teasing tone*]   Good heavens, how down in the mouth you
look, Jamie. What's the matter now?

JAMIE [*without looking at her*]   Nothing.

MARY   Oh, I'd forgotten you've been working on the front hedge. That
accounts for your sinking into the dumps, doesn't it?

JAMIE   If you want to think so, Mama.

MARY [*keeping her tone*]   Well, that's the effect it always has, isn't it? What
a big baby you are! Isn't he, Edmund?

EDMUND   He's certainly a fool to care what anyone thinks.

MARY [*strangely*]   Yes, the only way is to make yourself not care.

> [*She catches* JAMIE *giving her a bitter glance and changes the subject.*]

Where is your father? I heard Cathleen call him.

EDMUND   Gabbing with old Captain Turner, Jamie says. He'll be late, as
usual.

> [JAMIE *gets up and goes to the windows at right, glad of an excuse to turn
> his back.*]

MARY   I've told Cathleen time and again she must go wherever he is and
tell him. The idea of screaming as if this were a cheap boardinghouse!

JAMIE [*looking out the window*]   She's down there now. [*sneeringly*] Interrupting the famous Beautiful Voice! She should have more respect.

MARY [*sharply—letting her resentment toward him come out*]   It's you who
should have more respect. Stop sneering at your father! I won't have it!
You ought to be proud you're his son! He may have his faults. Who has-
n't? But he's worked hard all his life. He made his way up from ignorance
and poverty to the top of his profession! Everyone else admires him and
you should be the last one to sneer—you, who, thanks to him, have never
had to work hard in your life!

> [*Stung,* JAMIE *has turned to stare at her with accusing antagonism. Her
> eyes waver guiltily and she adds in a tone which begins to placate*]

Remember your father is getting old, Jamie. You really ought to show
more consideration.

JAMIE *I* ought to?

EDMUND [*uneasily*] Oh, dry up, Jamie!

[JAMIE *looks out the window again.*]

And, for Pete's sake, Mama, why jump on Jamie all of a sudden?

MARY [*bitterly*] Because he's always sneering at someone else, always looking for the worst weakness in everyone. [*then with a strange, abrupt change to a detached, impersonal tone*] But I suppose life has made him like that, and he can't help it. None of us can help the things life has done to us. They're done before you realize it, and once they're done they make you do other things until at last everything comes between you and what you'd like to be, and you've lost your true self forever.

[EDMUND *is made apprehensive by her strangeness. He tries to look up in her eyes but she keeps them averted.* JAMIE *turns to her—then looks quickly out of the window again.*]

JAMIE [*dully*] I'm hungry. I wish the Old Man would get a move on. It's a rotten trick the way he keeps meals waiting, and then beefs because they're spoiled.

MARY [*with a resentment that has a quality of being automatic and on the surface while inwardly she is indifferent*] Yes, it's very trying, Jamie. You don't know how trying. You don't have to keep house with summer servants who don't care because they know it isn't a permanent position. The really good servants are all with people who have homes and not merely summer places. And your father won't even pay the wages the best summer help ask. So every year I have stupid, lazy greenhorns to deal with. But you've heard me say this a thousand times. So has he, but it goes in one ear and out the other. He thinks money spent on a home is money wasted. He's lived too much in hotels. Never the best hotels, of course. Second-rate hotels. He doesn't understand a home. He doesn't feel at home in it. And yet, he wants a home. He's even proud of having this shabby place. He loves it here. [*She laughs—a hopeless and yet amused laugh.*] It's really funny, when you come to think of it. He's a peculiar man.

EDMUND [*again attempting uneasily to look up in her eyes*] What makes you ramble on like that, Mama?

MARY [*quickly casual—patting his cheek*] Why, nothing in particular, dear. It *is* foolish.

[*As she speaks,* CATHLEEN *enters from the back parlor.*]

CATHLEEN [*volubly*] Lunch is ready, Ma'am, I went down to Mister Tyrone, like you ordered, and he said he'd come right away, but he kept on talking to that man, telling him of the time when—

MARY [*indifferently*] All right, Cathleen. Tell Bridget I'm sorry but she'll have to wait a few minutes until Mister Tyrone is here.

[CATHLEEN *mutters,* "Yes, Ma'am," *and goes off through the back parlor, grumbling to herself.*]

JAMIE Damn it! Why don't you go ahead without him? He told us to.

MARY [*with a remote, amused smile*] He doesn't mean it. Don't you know your father yet? He'd be so terribly hurt.

EDMUND [*jumps up—as if he was glad of an excuse to leave*] I'll make him get a move on.

[*He goes out on the side porch. A moment later he is heard calling from the porch exasperatedly.*]

Hey! Papa! Come on! We can't wait all day!

[MARY *has risen from the arm of the chair. Her hands play restlessly over the table top. She does not look at* JAMIE *but she feels the cynically appraising glance he gives her face and hands.*]

MARY [*tensely*]   Why do you stare like that?

JAMIE   You know. [*He turns back to the window.*]

MARY   I don't know.

JAMIE   Oh, for God's sake, do you think you can fool me, Mama? I'm not blind.

MARY [*looks directly at him now, her face set again in an expression of blank, stubborn denial*]   I don't know what you're talking about.

JAMIE   No? Take a look at your eyes in the mirror!

EDMUND [*coming in from the porch*]   I got Papa moving. He'll be here in a minute. [*with a glance from one to the other, which his mother avoids—uneasily*] What happened? What's the matter, Mama?

MARY [*disturbed by his coming, gives way to a flurry of guilty, nervous excitement*]   Your brother ought to be ashamed of himself. He's been insinuating I don't know what.

EDMUND [*turns on* JAMIE]   God damn you!

[*He takes a threatening step toward him.* JAMIE *turns his back with a shrug and looks out the window.*]

MARY [*more upset, grabs* EDMUND's *arm—excitedly*]   Stop this at once, do you hear me? How dare you use such language before me! [*Abruptly her tone and manner change to the strange detachment she has shown before.*] It's wrong to blame your brother. He can't help being what the past has made him. Any more than your father can. Or you. Or I.

EDMUND [*frightenedly—with a desperate hoping against hope*]   He's a liar! It's a lie, isn't it, Mama?

MARY [*keeping her eyes averted*]   What is a lie? Now you're talking in riddles like Jamie. [*Then her eyes meet his stricken, accusing look. She stammers*] Edmund! Don't! [*She looks away and her manner instantly regains the quality of strange detachment—calmly*] There's your father coming up the steps now. I must tell Bridget.

[*She goes through the back parlor.* EDMUND *moves slowly to his chair. He looks sick and hopeless.*]

JAMIE [*from the window, without looking around*]   Well?

EDMUND [*refusing to admit anything to his brother yet—weakly defiant*]   Well, what? You're a liar.

[JAMIE *again shrugs his shoulders. The screen door on the front porch is heard closing.* EDMUND *says dully*]

Here's Papa. I hope he loosens up with the old bottle.

[TYRONE *comes in through the front parlor. He is putting on his coat.*]

TYRONE   Sorry I'm late. Captain Turner stopped to talk and once he starts gabbing you can't get away from him.

JAMIE [*without turning—dryly*]   You mean once he starts listening.

[*His father regards him with dislike. He comes to the table with a quick measuring look at the bottle of whiskey. Without turning,* JAMIE *senses this.*]

It's all right. The level in the bottle hasn't changed.

TYRONE   I wasn't noticing that. [*He adds caustically*] As if it proved anything with you around. I'm on to your tricks.

EDMUND [*dully*]   Did I hear you say, let's all have a drink?

TYRONE [*frowns at him*]   Jamie is welcome after his hard morning's work, but I won't invite you. Doctor Hardy—

EDMUND   To hell with Doctor Hardy! One isn't going to kill me. I feel—all in, Papa.

TYRONE [*with a worried look at him—putting on a fake heartiness*]   Come along, then. It's before a meal and I've always found that good whiskey, taken in moderation as an appetizer, is the best of tonics.

> [EDMUND *gets up as his father passes the bottle to him. He pours a big drink.* TYRONE *frowns admonishingly.*]

I said, in moderation.

> [*He pours his own drink and passes the bottle to* JAMIE, *grumbling.*]

It'd be a waste of breath mentioning moderation to you.

> [*Ignoring the hint,* JAMIE *pours a big drink. His father scowls—then, giving it up, resumes his hearty air, raising his glass.*]

Well, here's health and happiness!

> [EDMUND *gives a bitter laugh.*]

EDMUND   That's a joke!

TYRONE   What is?

EDMUND   Nothing. Here's how. [*They drink.*]

TYRONE [*becoming aware of the atmosphere*]   What's the matter here? There's gloom in the air you could cut with a knife. [*turns on* JAMIE *resentfully*] You got the drink you were after, didn't you? Why are you wearing that gloomy look on your mug?

JAMIE [*shrugging his shoulders*]   You won't be singing a song yourself soon.

EDMUND   Shut up, Jamie.

TYRONE [*uneasy now—changing the subject*]   I thought lunch was ready. I'm hungry as a hunter. Where is your mother?

MARY [*returning through the back parlor, calls*]   Here I am.

> [*She comes in. She is excited and self-conscious. As she talks, she glances everywhere except at any of their faces.*]

I've had to calm down Bridget. She's in a tantrum over your being late again, and I don't blame her. If your lunch is dried up from waiting in the oven, she said it served you right, you could like it or leave it for all she cared. [*with increasing excitement*] Oh, I'm so sick and tired of pretending this is a home! You won't help me! You won't put yourself out the least bit! You don't know how to act in a home! You don't really want one! You never have wanted one—never since the day we were married! You should have remained a bachelor and lived in second-rate hotels and entertained your friends in barrooms! [*She adds strangely, as if she were now talking aloud to herself rather than to* TYRONE] Then nothing would ever have happened.

> [*They stare at her.* TYRONE *knows now. He suddenly looks a tired, bitterly sad old man.* EDMUND *glances at his father and sees that he knows, but he still cannot help trying to warn his mother.*]

EDMUND   Mama! Stop talking. Why don't we go in to lunch.

MARY [*Starts and at once the quality of unnatural detachment settles on her face again. She even smiles with an ironical amusement to herself.*]   Yes, it is inconsiderate of me to dig up the past, when I know your father and Jamie must be hungry. [*putting her arm around* EDMUND's *shoulder—with a fond solicitude which is at the same time remote*] I do hope you have an appetite, dear. You really must eat more [*Her eyes become fixed on the whiskey glass on the table beside him—sharply*] Why is that glass there? Did you take a drink? Oh, how can you be such a fool? Don't you know it's the worst thing? [*She turns on* TYRONE.] You're to blame, James. How could you let him? Do you want to kill him? Don't you remember my father? He wouldn't stop after he was stricken. He said doctors were fools! He thought, like you, that whiskey is a good tonic! [*A look of terror comes into her eyes and she stammers*] But, of course, there's no comparison at all. I don't know why I—Forgive me for scolding you, James. One small drink won't hurt Edmund. It might be good for him, if it gives him an appetite.

    [*She pats* EDMUND'S *cheek playfully, the strange detachment again in her manner. He jerks his head away. She seems not to notice, but she moves instinctively away.*]

JAMIE [*roughly, to hide his tense nerves*]   For God's sake, let's eat. I've been working in the damned dirt under the hedge all morning. I've earned my grub.

    [*He comes around in back of his father, not looking at his mother, and grabs* EDMUND'S *shoulder.*]

Come on, Kid. Let's put on the feed bag.

    [EDMUND *gets up, keeping his eyes averted from his mother. They pass her, heading for the back parlor.*]

TYRONE [*dully*]   Yes, you go in with your mother, lads. I'll join you in a second.

    [*But they keep on without waiting for her. She looks at their backs with a helpless hurt and, as they enter the back parlor, starts to follow them.* TYRONE's *eyes are on her, sad and condemning. She feels them and turns sharply without meeting his stare.*]

MARY   Why do you look at me like that? [*Her hands flutter up to pat her hair.*] Is it my hair coming down? I was so worn out from last night, I thought I'd better lie down this morning. I drowsed off and had a nice refreshing nap. But I'm sure I fixed my hair again when I woke up. [*forcing a laugh*] Although, as usual, I couldn't find my glasses. [*sharply*] Please stop staring! One would think you were accusing me—[*then pleadingly*] James! You don't understand!

TYRONE [*with dull anger*]   I understand that I've been a God-damned fool to believe in you!

    [*He walks away from her to pour himself a big drink.*]

MARY [*her face again sets in stubborn defiance*]   I don't know what you mean by "believing in me." All I've felt was distrust and spying and suspicion. [*then accusingly*] Why are you having another drink? You never have more than one before lunch. [*bitterly*] I know what to expect. You will be drunk tonight. Well, it won't be the first time, will it—or the thousandth? [*again she bursts out pleadingly*] Oh, James, please! You don't understand! I'm worried about Edmund! I'm so afraid he—

TYRONE   I don't want to listen to excuses, Mary.

MARY [*strickenly*]   Excuses? You mean—? Oh, you can't believe that of me! You mustn't believe that, James! [*then slipping away into her strange detachment—quite casually*] Shall we not go into lunch dear? I don't want anything but I know you're hungry.

    [*He walks slowly to where she stands in the doorway. He walks like an old man. As he reaches her she bursts out piteously.*]

James! I tried so hard! I tried so hard! Please believe—!

TYRONE [*moved in spite of himself—helplessly*] I suppose you did, Mary. [*then grief-strickenly*] For the love of God, why couldn't you have the strength to keep on?

MARY [*her face setting into that stubborn denial again*] I don't know what you're talking about. Have the strength to keep on what?

TYRONE [*hopelessly*] Never mind. It's no use now.

[*He moves on and she keeps beside him as they disappear in the back parlor.*]

CURTAIN

Act 2

SCENE 2

SCENE—*The same, about a half hour later. The tray with the bottle of whiskey has been removed from the table. The family are returning from lunch as the curtain rises.* MARY *is the first to enter from the back parlor. Her husband follows. He is not with her as he was in the similar entrance after breakfast at the opening of Act One. He avoids touching her or looking at her. There is condemnation in his face, mingled now with the beginning of an old weary, helpless resignation.* JAMIE *and* EDMUND *follow their father.* JAMIE'*s face is hard with defensive cynicism.* EDMUND *tries to copy this defense but without success. He plainly shows he is heartsick as well as physically ill.*

MARY *is terribly nervous again, as if the strain of sitting through lunch with them had been too much for her. Yet at the same time, in contrast to this, her expression shows more of that strange aloofness which seems to stand apart from her nerves and the anxieties which harry them.*

She is talking as she enters—a stream of words that issues casually, in a routine of family conversation, from her mouth. She appears indifferent to the fact that their thoughts are not on what she is saying any more than her own are. As she talks, she comes to the left of the table and stands, facing front, one hand fumbling with the bosom of her dress, the other playing over the table top. TYRONE *lights a cigar and goes to the screen door, staring out.* JAMIE *fills a pipe from a jar on top of the bookcase at rear. He lights it as he goes to look out the window at right.* EDMUND *sits in a chair by the table, turned half away from his mother so he does not have to watch her.*

MARY It's no use finding fault with Bridget. She doesn't listen. I can't threaten her, or she'd threaten she'd leave. And she does do her best at times. It's too bad they seem to be just the times you're sure to be late, James. Well, there's this consolation: it's difficult to tell from her cooking whether she's doing her best or her worst. [*She gives a little laugh of detached amusement—indifferently*] Never mind. The summer will soon be over, thank goodness. Your season will open again and we can go back to second-rate hotels and trains. I hate them, too, but at least I don't expect them to be like a home, and there's no housekeeping to worry about. It's unreasonable to expect Bridget or Cathleen to act as if this was a home. They know it isn't as well as we know it. It never has been and it never will be.

TYRONE [*bitterly without turning around*] No, it never can be now. But it was once, before you—

MARY [*her face instantly set in blank denial*]   Before I what? [*There is dead silence. She goes on with a return of her detached air.*] No, no. Whatever you mean, it isn't true, dear. It was never a home. You've always preferred the Club or barroom. And for me it's always been as lonely as a dirty room in a one-night stand hotel. In a real home one is never lonely. You forget I know from experience what a home is like. I gave up one to marry you— my father's home. [*At once, through an association of ideas she turns to* EDMUND. *Her manner becomes tenderly solicitous, but there is the strange quality of detachment in it.*] I'm worried about you, Edmund. You hardly touched a thing at lunch. That's no way to take care of yourself. It's all right for me not to have an appetite. I've been growing too fat. But you must eat. [*coaxingly maternal*] Promise me you will, dear, for my sake.

EDMUND [*dully*]   Yes, Mama.

MARY [*pats his cheek as he tries not to shrink away*]   That's a good boy.
> [*There is another pause of dead silence. Then the telephone in the front hall rings and all of them stiffen startledly.*]

TYRONE [*hastily*]   I'll answer. McGuire said he'd call me. [*He goes out through the front parlor.*]

MARY [*indifferently*]   McGuire. He must have another piece of property on his list that no one would think of buying except your father. It doesn't matter any more, but it's always seemed to me your father could afford to keep on buying property but never to give me a home.
> [*She stops to listen as* TYRONE's *voice is heard from the hall.*]

TYRONE   Hello. [*with forced heartiness*] Oh, how are you, Doctor?
> [JAMIE *turns from the window.* MARY's *fingers play more rapidly on the table top.* TYRONE's *voice, trying to conceal, reveals that he is hearing bad news.*]

I see—[*hurriedly*] Well, you'll explain all about it when you see him this afternoon. Yes, he'll be in without fail. Four o'clock. I'll drop in myself and have a talk with you before that. I have to go uptown on business, anyway. Goodbye, Doctor.

EDMUND [*dully*]   That didn't sound like glad tidings.
> [JAMIE *gives him a pitying glance—then looks out the window again.* MARY's *face is terrified and her hands flutter distractedly.* TYRONE *comes in. The strain is obvious in his casualness as he addresses* EDMUND.]

TYRONE   It was Doctor Hardy. He wants you to be sure and see him at four.

EDMUND [*dully*]   What did he say? Not that I give a damn now.

MARY [*bursts out excitedly*]   I wouldn't believe him if he swore on a stack of Bibles. You mustn't pay attention to a word he says, Edmund.

TYRONE [*sharply*]   Mary!

MARY [*more excitedly*]   Oh, we all realize why you like him, James! Because he's cheap! But please don't try to tell me! I know all about Doctor Hardy. Heaven knows I ought to after all these years. He's an ignorant fool! There should be a law to keep men like him from practicing. He hasn't the slightest idea—When you're in agony and half insane, he sits and holds your hand and delivers sermons on will power! [*Her face is drawn in an expression of intense suffering by the memory. For the moment, she loses all caution. With bitter hatred*] He deliberately humiliates you! He makes you beg and plead! He treats you like a criminal! He understands nothing! And yet it was exactly the same type of cheap quack who first gave you the medicine—and you never knew what it was until too late! [*passionately*] I hate doctors! They'll sell their souls! What's worse, they'll sell yours, and you never know it till one day you find yourself in hell!

EDMUND   Mama! For God's sake, stop talking.

TYRONE [*shakily*]   Yes, Mary, it's no time—

MARY [*suddenly is overcome by guilty confusion—stammers*]   I—Forgive me, dear. You're right. It's useless to be angry now. [*There is again a pause of dead silence. When she speaks again, her face has cleared and is calm, and the quality of uncanny detachment is in her voice and manner.*] I'm going upstairs for a moment, if you'll excuse me. I have to fix my hair. [*she adds smilingly*] That is if I can find my glasses. I'll be right down.

TYRONE [*as she starts through the doorway—pleading and rebuking*]   Mary!

MARY [*turns to stare at him calmly*]   Yes, dear? What is it?

TYRONE [*helplessly*]   Nothing.

MARY [*with a strange derisive smile*]   You're welcome to come up and watch me if you're so suspicious.

TYRONE   As if that could do any good! You'd only postpone it. And I'm not your jailor. This isn't a prison.

MARY   No. I know you can't help thinking it's a home. [*She adds quickly with a detached contrition*] I'm sorry, dear. I don't mean to be bitter. It's not your fault.

[*She turns and disappears through the back parlor. The three in the room remain silent. It is as if they were waiting until she got upstairs before speaking.*]

JAMIE [*cynically brutal*]   Another shot in the arm!

EDMUND [*angrily*]   Cut out that kind of talk!

TYRONE   Yes! Hold your foul tongue and your rotten Broadway loafer's lingo! Have you no pity or decency? [*losing his temper*] You ought to be kicked out in the gutter! But if I did it, you know damned well who'd weep and plead for you, and excuse you and complain till I let you come back.

JAMIE [*a spasm of pain crosses his face*]   Christ, don't I know that? No pity? I have all the pity in the world for her. I understand what a hard game to beat she's up against—which is more than you ever have! My lingo didn't mean I had no feeling. I was merely putting bluntly what we all know, and have to live with now, again. [*bitterly*] The cures are no damned good except for a while. The truth is there is no cure and we've been saps to hope—[*cynically*] They never come back!

EDMUND [*scornfully parodying his brother's cynicism*]   They never come back! Everything is in the bag! It's all a frame-up! We're all fall guys and suckers and we can't beat the game! [*disdainfully*] Christ, if I felt the way you do—!

JAMIE [*stung for a moment—then shrugging his shoulders, dryly*]   I thought you did. Your poetry isn't very cheery. Nor the stuff you read and claim to admire. [*He indicates the small bookcase at rear.*] Your pet with the unpronounceable name, for example.

EDMUND   Nietzsche. You don't know what you're talking about. You haven't read him.

JAMIE   Enough to know it's a lot of bunk!

TYRONE   Shut up, both of you! There's little choice between the philosophy you learned from Broadway loafers, and the one Edmund got from his books. They're both rotten to the core. You've both flouted the faith you were born and brought up in—the one true faith of the Catholic Church—and your denial has brought nothing but self-destruction!

[*His two sons stare at him contemptuously. They forget their quarrel and are as one against him on this issue.*]

EDMUND   That's the bunk, Papa!

JAMIE   We don't pretend, at any rate. [*caustically*] I don't notice you've worn any holes in the knees of your pants going to Mass.

TYRONE   It's true I'm a bad Catholic in the observance, God forgive me. But I believe! [*angrily*] And you're a liar! I may not go to church but every night and morning of my life I get on my knees and pray!

EDMUND [*bitingly*]   Did you pray for Mama?

TYRONE   I did. I've prayed to God these many years for her.

EDMUND   Then Nietzsche must be right. [*He quotes from* Thus Spake Zarathustra.] "God is dead: of His pity for man hath God died."

TYRONE [*ignores this*]   If your mother had prayed, too—She hasn't denied her faith, but she's forgotten it, until now there's no strength of the spirit left in her to fight against her curse. [*then dully resigned*] But what's the good of talk? We've lived with this before and now we must again. There's no help for it. [*bitterly*] Only I wish she hadn't led me to hope this time. By God, I never will again!

EDMUND   That's a rotten thing to say, Papa! [*defiantly*] Well, I'll hope! She's just started. It can't have got a hold on her yet. She can still stop. I'm going to talk to her.

JAMIE [*shrugs his shoulders*]   You can't talk to her now. She'll listen but she won't listen. She'll be here but she won't be here. You know the way she gets.

TYRONE   Yes, that's the way the poison acts on her always. Every day from now on, there'll be the same drifting away from us until by the end of each night—

EDMUND [*miserably*]   Cut it out, Papa! [*He jumps up from his chair.*] I'm going to get dressed. [*bitterly, as he goes*] I'll make so much noise she can't suspect I've come to spy on her.

[*He disappears through the front parlor and can be heard stamping noisily upstairs.*]

JAMIE [*after a pause*]   What did Doc Hardy say about the Kid?

TYRONE [*dully*]   It's what you thought. He's got consumption.

JAMIE   God damn it!

TYRONE   There is no possible doubt, he said.

JAMIE   He'll have to go to a sanatorium.

TYRONE   Yes, and the sooner the better, Hardy said, for him and everyone around him. He claims that in six months to a year Edmund will be cured, if he obeys orders. [*He sighs—gloomily and resentfully*] I never thought a child of mine—It doesn't come from my side of the family. There wasn't one of us that didn't have lungs as strong as an ox.

JAMIE   Who gives a damn about that part of it! Where does Hardy want to send him?

TYRONE   That's what I'm to see him about.

JAMIE   Well, for God's sake, pick out a good place and not some cheap dump!

TYRONE [*stung*] I'll send him wherever Hardy thinks best!

JAMIE Well, don't give Hardy your old over-the-hills-to-the-poorhouse song about taxes and mortgages.

TYRONE I'm no millionaire who can throw money away! Why shouldn't I tell Hardy the truth?

JAMIE Because he'll think you want him to pick a cheap dump, and because he'll know it isn't the truth—especially if he hears afterwards you've seen McGuire and let that flannel-mouth, gold-brick merchant sting you with another piece of bum property!

TYRONE Keep your nose out of my business!

JAMIE This is Edmund's business. What I'm afraid of is, with your Irish bog trotter idea that consumption is fatal, you'll figure it would be a waste of money to spend any more than you can help.

TYRONE You liar!

JAMIE All right. Prove I'm a liar. That's what I want. That's why I brought it up.

TYRONE [*his rage still smoldering*] I have every hope Edmund will be cured. And keep your dirty tongue off Ireland! You're a fine one to sneer, with the map of it on your face!

JAMIE Not after I wash my face. [*Then before his father can react to this insult to the Old Sod he adds dryly, shrugging his shoulders*] Well, I've said all I have to say. It's up to you. [*abruptly*] What do you want me to do this afternoon, now you're going uptown? I've done all I can do on the hedge until you cut more of it. You don't want me to go ahead with your clipping, I know that.

TYRONE No. You'd get it crooked, as you get everything else.

JAMIE Then I'd better go uptown with Edmund. The bad news coming on top of what's happened to Mama may hit him hard.

TYRONE [*forgetting his quarrel*] Yes, go with him, Jamie. Keep up his spirits, if you can. [*He adds caustically*] If you can without making it an excuse to get drunk!

JAMIE What would I use for money? The last I heard they were still selling booze, not giving it away. [*He starts for the front-parlor doorway.*] I'll get dressed.

[*He stops in the doorway as he sees his mother approaching from the hall, and moves aside to let her come in. Her eyes look brighter, and her manner is more detached. This change becomes more marked as the scene goes on.*]

MARY [*vaguely*] You haven't seen my glasses anywhere, have you, Jamie? [*She doesn't look at him. He glances away, ignoring her question but she doesn't seem to expect an answer. She comes forward, addressing her husband without looking at him.*]

You haven't seen them, have you, James?

[*Behind her* JAMIE *disappears through the front parlor.*]

TYRONE [*turns to look out the screen door*] No, Mary.

MARY What's the matter with Jamie? Have you been nagging at him again? You shouldn't treat him with such contempt all the time. He's not to blame. If he'd been brought up in a real home, I'm sure he would have been different. [*She comes to the windows at right—lightly*] You're not much of a weather prophet, dear. See how hazy it's getting. I can hardly see the other shore.

TYRONE [*trying to speak naturally*] Yes, I spoke too soon. We're in for another night of fog, I'm afraid.

MARY Oh, well, I won't mind it tonight.

TYRONE No, I don't imagine you will, Mary.

MARY [*flashes a glance at him—after a pause*] I don't see Jamie going down to the hedge. Where did he go?

TYRONE He's going with Edmund to the Doctor's. He went up to change his clothes. [*then, glad of an excuse to leave her*] I'd better do the same or I'll be late for my appointment at the Club.

    [*He makes a move toward the front-parlor doorway, but with a swift impulsive movement she reaches out and clasps his arm.*]

MARY [*a note of pleading in her voice*] Don't go yet, dear. I don't want to be alone. [*hastily*] I mean, you have plenty of time. You know you boast you can dress in one-tenth the time it takes the boys. [*vaguely*] There is something I wanted to say. What is it? I've forgotten. I'm glad Jamie is going uptown. You didn't give him any money, I hope.

TYRONE I did not.

MARY He'd only spend it on drink and you know what a vile, poisonous tongue he has when he's drunk. Not that I would mind anything he said tonight, but he always manages to drive you into a rage, especially if you're drunk, too, as you will be.

TYRONE [*resentfully*] I won't. I never get drunk.

MARY [*teasing indifferently*] Oh, I'm sure you'll hold it well. You always have. It's hard for a stranger to tell, but after thirty-five years of marriage—

TYRONE I've never missed a performance in my life. That's the proof! [*then bitterly*] If I did get drunk it is not you who should blame me. No man has ever had a better reason.

MARY Reason? What reason? You always drink too much when you go to the Club, don't you? Particularly when you meet McGuire. He sees to that. Don't think I'm finding fault, dear. You must do as you please. I won't mind.

TYRONE I know you won't. [*He turns toward the front parlor, anxious to escape.*] I've got to get dressed.

MARY [*again she reaches out and grasps his arm—pleadingly*] No, please wait a little while, dear. At least, until one of the boys comes down. You will all be leaving me so soon.

TYRONE [*with bitter sadness*] It's you who are leaving us, Mary.

MARY I? That's a silly thing to say, James. How could I leave? There is nowhere I could go. Who would I go to see? I have no friends.

TYRONE It's your own fault—[*He stops and sighs helplessly—persuasively*] There's surely one thing you can do this afternoon that will be good for you, Mary. Take a drive in the automobile. Get away from the house. Get a little sun and fresh air. [*injuredly*] I bought the automobile for you. You know I don't like the damned things. I'd rather walk any day, or take a trolley. [*with growing resentment*] I had it here waiting for you when you came back from the sanatorium. I hoped it would give you pleasure and distract your mind. You used to ride in it every day, but you've hardly used it at all lately. I paid a lot of money I couldn't afford, and there's the chauffeur I have to board and lodge and pay high wages whether he drives you or not. [*bitterly*] Waste! The same old waste that will land me in the poorhouse in my old age! What good did it do you? I might as well have thrown the money out the window.

MARY [*with detached calm*]   Yes, it was a waste of money, James. You shouldn't have bought a secondhand automobile. You were swindled again as you always are, because you insist on secondhand bargains in everything.

TYRONE   It's one of the best makes! Everyone says it's better than any of the new ones!

MARY [*ignoring this*]   It was another waste to hire Smythe, who was only a helper in a garage and had never been a chauffeur. Oh, I realize his wages are less than a real chauffeur's, but he more than makes up for that, I'm sure, by the graft he gets from the garage on repair bills. Something is always wrong. Smythe sees to that, I'm afraid.

TYRONE   I don't believe it! He may not be a fancy millionaire's flunky but he's honest! You're as bad as Jamie, suspecting everyone!

MARY   You mustn't be offended, dear. I wasn't offended when you gave me the automobile. I knew you didn't mean to humiliate me. I knew that was the way you had to do everything. I was grateful and touched. I knew buying the car was a hard thing for you to do, and it proved how much you loved me, in your way, especially when you couldn't really believe it would do me any good.

TYRONE   Mary! [*He suddenly hugs her to him—brokenly*] Dear Mary! For the love of God, for my sake and the boys' sake and your own, won't you stop now?

MARY [*stammers in guilty confusion for a second*]   I—James! Please! [*Her strange, stubborn defense comes back instantly.*] Stop what? What are you talking about?

  [*He lets his arm fall to his side brokenly. She impulsively puts her arm around him.*]

James! We've loved each other! We always will! Let's remember only that, and not try to understand what we cannot understand, or help things that cannot be helped—the things life has done to us we cannot excuse or explain.

TYRONE [*as if he hadn't heard—bitterly*]   You won't even try?

MARY [*her arms drop hopelessly and she turns away—with detachment*] Try to go for a drive this afternoon, you mean? Why, yes, if you wish me to, although it makes me feel lonelier than if I stayed here. There is no one I can invite to drive with me, and I never know where to tell Smythe to go. If there was a friend's house where I could drop in and laugh and gossip awhile. But, of course, there isn't. There never has been. [*her manner becoming more and more remote*] At the Convent I had so many friends. Girls whose families lived in lovely homes. I used to visit them and they'd visit me in my father's home. But, naturally, after I married an actor—you know how actors were considered in those days—a lot of them gave me the cold shoulder. And then, right after we were married, there was the scandal of that woman who had been your mistress, suing you. From then on, all my old friends either pitied me or cut me dead. I hated the ones who cut me much less than the pitiers.

TYRONE [*with guilty resentment*]   For God's sake, don't dig up what's long forgotten. If you're that far gone in the past already, when it's only the beginning of the afternoon, what will you be tonight?

MARY [*stares at him defiantly now*]   Come to think of it, I do have to drive
uptown. There's something I must get at the drugstore.

TYRONE [*bitterly scornful*]   Leave it to you to have some of the stuff hidden,
and prescriptions for more! I hope you'll lay in a good stock ahead so we'll
never have another night like the one when you screamed for it, and ran
out of the house in your nightdress half crazy, to try and throw yourself
off the dock!

MARY [*tries to ignore this*]   I have to get tooth powder and toilet soap and
cold cream—[*She breaks down pitiably.*] James! You mustn't remember!
You mustn't humiliate me so!

TYRONE [*ashamed*]   I'm sorry. Forgive me, Mary!

MARY [*defensively detached again*]   It doesn't matter. Nothing like that ever
happened. You must have dreamed it.

> [*He stares at her hopelessly. Her voice seems to drift farther and farther
> away.*]

I was so healthy before Edmund was born. You remember, James. There
wasn't a nerve in my body. Even traveling with you season after season,
with week after week of one-night stands, in trains without Pullmans, in
dirty rooms of filthy hotels, eating bad food, bearing children in hotel
rooms, I still kept healthy. But bearing Edmund was the last straw. I was
so sick afterwards, and that ignorant quack of a cheap hotel doctor—All
he knew was I was in pain. It was easy for him to stop the pain.

TYRONE   Mary! For God's sake, forget the past!

MARY [*with strange objective calm*]   Why? How can I? The past is the present, isn't it? It's the future, too. We all try to lie out of that but life won't
let us. [*going on*] I blame only myself. I swore after Eugene died I would
never have another baby. I was to blame for his death. If I hadn't left him
with my mother to join you on the road, because you wrote telling me you
missed me and were so lonely, Jamie would never have been allowed,
when he still had measles, to go in the baby's room. [*her face hardening*]
I've always believed Jamie did it on purpose. He was jealous of the baby.
He hated him. [*as* TYRONE *starts to protest*] Oh, I know Jamie was only
seven, but he was never stupid. He'd been warned it might kill the baby.
He knew. I've never been able to forgive him for that.

TYRONE [*with bitter sadness*]   Are you back with Eugene now? Can't you let
our dead baby rest in peace?

MARY [*as if she hadn't heard him*]   It was my fault. I should have insisted
on staying with Eugene and not have let you persuade me to join you, just
because I loved you. Above all, I shouldn't have let you insist I have
another baby to take Eugene's place, because you thought that would
make me forget his death. I knew from experience by then that children
should have homes to be born in, if they are to be good children, and
women need homes, if they are to be good mothers. I was afraid all the
time I carried Edmund. I knew something terrible would happen. I knew
I'd proved by the way I'd left Eugene that I wasn't worthy to have another
baby, and that God would punish me if I did. I never should have borne
Edmund.

TYRONE [*with an uneasy glance through the front parlor*]   Mary! Be careful
with your talk. If he heard you he might think you never wanted him. He's
feeling bad enough already without—

MARY [*violently*]   It's a lie! I did want him! More than anything in the world! You don't understand! I meant, for his sake. He has never been happy. He never will be. Nor healthy. He was born nervous and too sensitive, and that's my fault. And now, ever since he's been so sick I've kept remembering Eugene and my father and I've been so frightened and guilty— [*then, catching herself, with an instant change to stubborn denial*] Oh, I know it's foolish to imagine dreadful things when there's no reason for it. After all, everyone has colds and gets over them.

> [TYRONE *stares at her and sighs helplessly. He turns away toward the front parlor and sees* EDMUND *coming down the stairs in the hall.*]

TYRONE [*sharply, in a low voice*]   Here's Edmund. For God's sake try and be yourself—at least until he goes! You can do that much for him!

> [*He waits, forcing his face into a pleasantly paternal expression. She waits frightenedly, seized again by a nervous panic, her hands fluttering over the bosom of her dress, up to her throat and hair, with a distracted aimlessness. Then, as* EDMUND *approaches the doorway, she cannot face him. She goes swiftly away to the windows at left and stares out with her back to the front parlor.* EDMUND *enters. He has changed to a ready-made blue serge suit, high stiff collar and tie, black shoes. With an actor's heartiness*]

Well! You look spic and span. I'm on my way up to change, too. [*He starts to pass him.*]

EDMUND [*dryly*]   Wait a minute, Papa. I hate to bring up disagreeable topics, but there's the matter of carfare. I'm broke.

TYRONE [*starts automatically on a customary lecture*]   You'll always be broke until you learn the value—[*checks himself guiltily, looking at his son's sick face with worried pity*] But you've been learning, lad. You worked hard before you took ill. You've done splendidly. I'm proud of you.

> [*He pulls out a small roll of bills from his pants pocket and carefully selects one.* EDMUND *takes it. He glances at it and his face expresses astonishment. His father again reacts customarily—sarcastically*]

Thank you. [*He quotes*] "How sharper than a serpent's tooth it is—"

EDMUND   "To have a thankless child."[9] I know. Give me a chance, Papa. I'm knocked speechless. This isn't a dollar. It's a ten spot.

TYRONE [*embarrassed by his generosity*]   Put it in your pocket. You'll probably meet some of your friends uptown and you can't hold your end up and be sociable with nothing in your jeans.

EDMUND   You meant it? Gosh, thank you, Papa. [*He is genuinely pleased and grateful for a moment—then he stares at his father's face with uneasy suspicion.*] But why all of a sudden—? [*cynically*] Did Doc Hardy tell you I was going to die? [*Then he sees his father is bitterly hurt.*] No! That's a rotten crack. I was only kidding, Papa. [*He puts an arm around his father impulsively and gives him an affectionate hug.*] I'm very grateful. Honest, Papa.

TYRONE [*touched, returns his hug*]   You're welcome, lad.

MARY [*suddenly turns to them in a confused panic of frightened anger*]   I won't have it! [*She stamps her foot.*] Do you hear, Edmund! Such morbid nonsense! Saying you're going to die! It's the books you read! Nothing but sadness and death! Your father shouldn't allow you to have them. And some of the poems you've written yourself are even worse! You'd think you

---

9. Shakespeare's *King Lear* 1.4.312.

didn't want to live! A boy of your age with everything before him! It's just a pose you get out of books! You're not really sick at all!

TYRONE   Mary! Hold your tongue!

MARY [*instantly changing to a detached tone*]   But, James, it's absurd of Edmund to be so gloomy and make such a great to-do about nothing. [*turning to* EDMUND *but avoiding his eyes—teasingly affectionate*] Never mind, dear. I'm on to you. [*She comes to him.*] You want to be petted and spoiled and made a fuss over, isn't that it? You're still such a baby. [*She puts her arm around him and hugs him. He remains rigid and unyielding. Her voice begins to tremble.*] But please don't carry it too far, dear. Don't say horrible things. I know it's foolish to take them seriously but I can't help it. You've got me—so frightened.

[*She breaks and hides her face on his shoulder, sobbing.* EDMUND *is moved in spite of himself. He pats her shoulder with an awkward tenderness.*]

EDMUND   Don't, mother. [*His eyes meet his father's.*]

TYRONE [*huskily—clutching at hopeless hope*]   Maybe if you asked your mother now what you said you were going to—[*He fumbles with his watch.*] By God, look at the time! I'll have to shake a leg.

[*He hurries away through the front parlor.* MARY *lifts her head. Her manner is again one of detached motherly solicitude. She seems to have forgotten the tears which are still in her eyes.*]

MARY   How do you feel, dear? [*She feels his forehead.*] Your head is a little hot, but that's just from going out in the sun. You look ever so much better than you did this morning. [*taking his hand*] Come and sit down. You mustn't stand on your feet so much. You must learn to husband your strength.

[*She gets him to sit and she sits sideways on the arm of his chair, an arm around his shoulder, so he cannot meet her eyes.*]

EDMUND [*starts to blurt out the appeal he now feels is quite hopeless*]   Listen, Mama—

MARY [*interrupting quickly*]   Now, now! Don't talk. Lean back and rest. [*persuasively*] You know, I think it would be much better for you if you stayed home this afternoon and let me take care of you. It's such a tiring trip uptown in the dirty old trolley on a hot day like this. I'm sure you'd be much better off here with me.

EDMUND [*dully*]   You forget I have an appointment with Hardy. [*trying again to get his appeal started*] Listen, Mama—

MARY [*quickly*]   You can telephone and say you don't feel well enough. [*excitedly*] It's simply a waste of time and money seeing him. He'll only tell you some lie. He'll pretend he's found something serious the matter because that's his bread and butter. [*She gives a hard sneering little laugh.*] The old idiot! All he knows about medicine is to look solemn and preach will power!

EDMUND [*trying to catch her eyes*]   Mama! Please listen! I want to ask you something! You—You're only just started. You can still stop. You've got the will power! We'll all help you. I'll do anything! Won't you, Mama?

MARY [*stammers pleadingly*]   Please don't—talk about things you don't understand!

EDMUND [*dully*]   All right, I give up. I knew it was no use.

MARY [*in blank denial now*]   Anyway, I don't know what you're referring to. But I do know you should be the last one—Right after I returned from the sanatorium, you began to be ill. The doctor there had warned me I must have peace at home with nothing to upset me, and all I've done is worry about you. [*then distractedly*] But that's no excuse! I'm only trying to explain. It's not an excuse! [*She hugs him to her—pleadingly*] Promise me, dear, you won't believe I made you an excuse.

EDMUND [*bitterly*] What else can I believe?

MARY [*slowly takes her arm away—her manner remote and objective again*] Yes, I suppose you can't help suspecting that.

EDMUND [*ashamed but still bitter*] What do you expect?

MARY Nothing, I don't blame you. How could you believe me—when I can't believe myself? I've become such a liar. I never lied about anything once upon a time. Now I have to lie, especially to myself. But how can you understand, when I don't myself. I've never understood anything about it, except that one day long ago I found I could no longer call my soul my own. [*She pauses—then lowering her voice to a strange tone of whispered confidence*] But some day, dear, I will find it again—some day when you're all well, and I see you healthy and happy and successful, and I don't have to feel guilty any more—some day when the Blessed Virgin Mary forgives me and gives me back the faith in Her love and pity I used to have in my convent days, and I can pray to Her again—when She sees no one in the world can believe in me even for a moment any more, then She will believe in me, and with Her help it will be so easy. I will hear myself scream with agony, and at the same time I will laugh because I will be so sure of myself. [*then as* EDMUND *remains hopelessly silent, she adds sadly*] Of course, you can't believe that, either. [*She rises from the arm of his chair and goes to stare out the windows at right with her back to him— casually*] Now I think of it, you might as well go uptown. I forgot I'm taking a drive. I have to go to the drugstore. You would hardly want to go there with me. You'd be so ashamed.

EDMUND [*brokenly*] Mama! Don't!

MARY I suppose you'll divide that ten dollars your father gave you with Jamie. You always divide with each other, don't you? Like good sports. Well, I know what he'll do with his share. Get drunk someplace where he can be with the only kind of woman he understands or likes. [*She turns to him, pleading frightenedly*] Edmund! Promise me you won't drink! It's so dangerous! You know Doctor Hardy told you—

EDMUND [*bitterly*] I thought he was an old idiot. Anyway, by tonight, what will you care?

MARY [*pitifully*] Edmund!
    [JAMIE's *voice is heard from the front hall,* "Come on, Kid, let's beat it."
    MARY's *manner at once becomes detached again.*]
Go on, Edmund. Jamie's waiting. [*She goes to the front-parlor doorway.*] There comes your father downstairs, too.
    [TYRONE's *voice calls,* "Come on, Edmund."]

EDMUND [*jumping up from his chair*] I'm coming.
    [*He stops beside her—without looking at her.*]
Goodbye, Mama.

MARY [*kisses him with detached affection*] Goodbye, dear. If you're coming home for dinner, try not to be late. And tell your father. You know what Bridget is.

[*He turns and hurries away.* TYRONE *calls from the hall,* "Goodbye, Mary," *and then* JAMIE, *"Goodbye, Mama." She calls back*]

Goodbye. [*The front screen door is heard closing after them. She comes and stands by the table, one hand drumming on it, the other fluttering up to pat her hair. She stares about the room with frightened, forsaken eyes and whispers to herself.*] It's so lonely here. [*Then her face hardens into bitter self-contempt.*] You're lying to yourself again. You wanted to get rid of them. Their contempt and disgust aren't pleasant company. You're glad they're gone. [*She gives a little despairing laugh.*] Then Mother of God, why do I feel so lonely?

CURTAIN

Act 3

SCENE—*The same. It is around half past six in the evening. Dusk is gathering in the living room, an early dusk due to the fog which has rolled in from the Sound and is like a white curtain drawn down outside the windows. From a lighthouse beyond the harbor's mouth, a foghorn is heard at regular intervals, moaning like a mournful whale in labor, and from the harbor itself, intermittently, comes the warning ringing of bells on yachts at anchor.*

The tray with the bottle of whiskey, glasses, and pitcher of ice water is on the table, as it was in the pre-luncheon scene of the previous act. MARY *and the second girl,* CATHLEEN, *are discovered. The latter is standing at left of table. She holds an empty whiskey glass in her hand as if she'd forgotten she had it. She shows the effects of drink. Her stupid, good-humored face wears a pleased and flattered simper.*

MARY *is paler than before and her eyes shine with unnatural brilliance. The strange detachment in her manner has intensified. She has hidden deeper within herself and found refuge and release in a dream where present reality is but an appearance to be accepted and dismissed unfeelingly—even with a hard cynicism—or entirely ignored. There is at times an uncanny gay, free youthfulness in her manner, as if in spirit she were released to become again, simply and without self-consciousness, the naive, happy, chattering schoolgirl of her convent days. She wears the dress into which she had changed for her drive to town, a simple, fairly expensive affair, which would be extremely becoming if it were not for the careless, almost slovenly way she wears it. Her hair is no longer fastidiously in place. It has a slightly disheveled, lopsided look. She talks to* CATHLEEN *with a confiding familiarity, as if the second girl were an old, intimate friend. As the curtain rises, she is standing by the screen door looking out. A moan of the foghorn is heard.*

MARY [*amused—girlishly*]   That foghorn! Isn't it awful, Cathleen?

CATHLEEN [*talks more familiarly than usual but never with intentional impertinence because she sincerely likes her mistress*]   It is indeed, Ma'am. It's like a banshee.

MARY [*Goes on as if she hadn't heard. In nearly all the following dialogue there is the feeling that she has* CATHLEEN *with her merely as an excuse to keep talking.*]   I don't mind it tonight. Last night it drove me crazy. I lay awake worrying until I couldn't stand it any more.

CATHLEEN   Bad cess to it.[1] I was scared out of my wits riding back from town. I thought that ugly monkey, Smythe, would drive us in a ditch or

---

1. Bad luck to it (Irish).

against a tree. You couldn't see your hand in front of you. I'm glad you had me sit in back with you, Ma'am. If I'd been in front with that monkey— He can't keep his dirty hands to himself. Give him half a chance and he's pinching me on the leg or you-know-where—asking your pardon, Ma'am, but it's true.

MARY [dreamily]   It wasn't the fog I minded, Cathleen, I really love fog.

CATHLEEN   They say it's good for the complexion.

MARY   It hides you from the world and the world from you. You feel that everything has changed, and nothing is what it seemed to be. No one can find or touch you any more.

CATHLEEN   I wouldn't care so much if Smythe was a fine, handsome man like some chauffeurs I've seen—I mean, if it was all in fun, for I'm a decent girl. But for a shriveled runt like Smythe—! I've told him, you must think I'm hard up that I'd notice a monkey like you. I've warned him, one day I'll give a clout that'll knock him into next week. And so I will!

MARY   It's the foghorn I hate. It won't let you alone. It keeps reminding you, and warning you, and calling you back. [She smiles strangely.] But it can't tonight. It's just an ugly sound. It doesn't remind me of anything. [She gives a teasing, girlish laugh.] Except, perhaps, Mr. Tyrone's snores. I've always had such fun teasing him about it. He has snored ever since I can remember, especially when he's had too much to drink, and yet he's like a child, he hates to admit it. [She laughs, coming to the table.] Well, I suppose I snore at times, too, and I don't like to admit it. So I have no right to make fun of him, have I? [She sits in the rocker at right of table.]

CATHLEEN   Ah, sure, everybody healthy snores. It's a sign of sanity, they say. [then, worriedly] What time is it, Ma'am? I ought to go back in the kitchen. The damp is in Bridget's rheumatism and she's like a raging divil. She'll bite my head off.

[She puts her glass on the table and makes a movement toward the back parlor.]

MARY [with a flash of apprehension]   No, don't go, Cathleen. I don't want to be alone, yet.

CATHLEEN   You won't be for long. The Master and the boys will be home soon.

MARY   I doubt if they'll come back for dinner. They have too good an excuse to remain in the barrooms where they feel at home.

[CATHLEEN stares at her, stupidly puzzled. MARY goes on smilingly]
Don't worry about Bridget. I'll tell her I kept you with me, and you can take a big drink of whiskey to her when you go. She won't mind then.

CATHLEEN [grins—at her ease again]   No, Ma'am. That's the one thing can make her cheerful. She loves her drop.

MARY   Have another drink yourself, if you wish, Cathleen.

CATHLEEN   I don't know if I'd better, Ma'am. I can feel what I've had already. [reaching for the bottle] Well, maybe one more won't harm. [She pours a drink.] Here's your good health, Ma'am. [She drinks without bothering about a chaser.]

MARY [dreamily]   I really did have good health once, Cathleen. But that was long ago.

CATHLEEN [worried again]   The Master's sure to notice what's gone from the bottle. He has the eye of a hawk for that.

MARY [*amusedly*] Oh, we'll play Jamie's trick on him. Just measure a few drinks of water and pour them in.

CATHLEEN [*does this—with a silly giggle*] God save me, it'll be half water. He'll know by the taste.

MARY [*indifferently*] No, by the time he comes home he'll be too drunk to tell the difference. He has such a good excuse, he believes, to drown his sorrows.

CATHLEEN [*philosophically*] Well, it's a good man's failing. I wouldn't give a trauneen[2] for a teetotaler. They've no high spirits. [*then, stupidly puzzled*] Good excuse? You mean Master Edmund, Ma'am? I can tell the Master is worried about him.

MARY [*stiffens defensively—but in a strange way the reaction has a mechanical quality, as if it did not penetrate to real emotion*] Don't be silly, Cathleen. Why should he be? A touch of grippe is nothing. And Mr. Tyrone never is worried about anything, except money and property and the fear he'll end his days in poverty. I mean, deeply worried. Because he cannot really understand anything else. [*She gives a little laugh of detached, affectionate amusement.*] My husband is a very peculiar man, Cathleen.

CATHLEEN [*vaguely resentful*] Well, he's a fine, handsome, kind gentleman just the same, Ma'am. Never mind his weakness.

MARY Oh, I don't mind. I've loved him dearly for thirty-six years. That proves I know he's lovable at heart and can't help being what he is, doesn't it?

CATHLEEN [*hazily reassured*] That's right. Ma'am. Love him dearly, for any fool can see he worships the ground you walk on. [*fighting the effect of her last drink and trying to be soberly conversational*] Speaking of acting, Ma'am, how is it you never went on the stage?

MARY [*resentfully*] I? What put that absurd notion in your head? I was brought up in a respectable home and educated in the best convent in the Middle West. Before I met Mr. Tyrone I hardly knew there was such a thing as a theater. I was a very pious girl. I even dreamed of becoming a nun. I've never had the slightest desire to be an actress.

CATHLEEN [*bluntly*] Well, I can't imagine you a holy nun, Ma'am. Sure, you never darken the door of a church, God forgive you.

MARY [*ignores this*] I've never felt at home in the theater. Even though Mr. Tyrone has made me go with him on all his tours, I've had little to do with the people in his company, or with anyone on the stage. Not that I have anything against them. They have always been kind to me, and I to them. But I've never felt at home with them. Their life is not my life. It has always stood between me and—[*She gets up—abruptly*] But let's not talk of old things that couldn't be helped. [*She goes to the porch door and stares out.*] How thick the fog is. I can't see the road. All the people in the world could pass by and I would never know. I wish it was always that way. It's getting dark already. It will soon be night, thank goodness. [*She turns back—vaguely*] It was kind of you to keep me company this afternoon, Cathleen. I would have been lonely driving uptown alone.

CATHLEEN Sure, wouldn't I rather ride in a fine automobile than stay here and listen to Bridget's lies about her relations? It was like a vacation, Ma'am. [*She pauses—then stupidly*] There was only one thing I didn't like.

2. Coin of very low value (Irish).

MARY [*vaguely*]   What was that, Cathleen?

CATHLEEN   The way the man in the drugstore acted when I took in the prescription for you. [*indignantly*] The impidence[3] of him!

MARY [*with stubborn blankness*]   What are you talking about? What drugstore? What prescription? [*then hastily, as* CATHLEEN *stares in stupid amazement*] Oh, of course, I'd forgotten. The medicine for the rheumatism in my hands. What did the man say? [*then with indifference*] Not that it matters, as long as he filled the prescription.

CATHLEEN   It mattered to me, then! I'm not used to being treated like a thief. He gave me a long look and says insultingly, "Where did you get hold of this?" and I says, "It's none of your damned business, but if you must know, it's for the lady I work for, Mrs. Tyrone, who's sitting out in the automobile." That shut him up quick. He gave a look out at you and said, "Oh," and went to get the medicine.

MARY [*vaguely*]   Yes, he knows me. [*She sits in the armchair at right rear of table. She adds in a calm, detached voice*] It's a special kind of medicine. I have to take it because there is no other that can stop the pain— *all* the pain—I mean, in my hands. [*She raises her hands and regards them with melancholy sympathy. There is no tremor in them now.*] Poor hands! You'd never believe it, but they were once one of my good points, along with my hair and eyes, and I had a fine figure, too. [*Her tone has become more and more far-off and dreamy.*] They were a musician's hands. I used to love the piano. I worked so hard at my music in the Convent—if you can call it work when you do something you love. Mother Elizabeth and my music teacher both said I had more talent than any student they remembered. My father paid for special lessons. He spoiled me. He would do anything I asked. He would have sent me to Europe to study after I graduated from the Convent. I might have gone—if I hadn't fallen in love with Mr. Tyrone. Or I might have become a nun. I had two dreams. To be a nun, that was the more beautiful one. To become a concert pianist, that was the other. [*She pauses, regarding her hands fixedly.* CATHLEEN *blinks her eyes to fight off drowsiness and a tipsy feeling.*] I haven't touched a piano in so many years. I couldn't play with such crippled fingers, even if I wanted to. For a time after my marriage I tried to keep up my music. But it was hopeless. One-night stands, cheap hotels, dirty trains, leaving children, never having a home—[*She stares at her hands with fascinated disgust.*] See, Cathleen, how ugly they are! So maimed and crippled! You would think they'd been through some horrible accident! [*She gives a strange little laugh.*] So they have, come to think of it. [*She suddenly thrusts her hands behind her back.*] I won't look at them. They're worse than the foghorn for reminding me—[*then with defiant self-assurance*] But even they can't touch me now. [*She brings her hands from behind her back and deliberately stares at them—calmly*] They're far away. I see them, but the pain has gone.

CATHLEEN [*stupidly puzzled*]   You've taken some of the medicine? It made you act funny, Ma'am. If I didn't know better, I'd think you'd a drop taken.

MARY [*dreamily*]   It kills the pain. You go back until at last you are beyond

3. Impudence.

its reach. Only the past when you were happy is real. [*She pauses—then as if her words had been an evocation which called back happiness she changes in her whole manner and facial expression. She looks younger. There is a quality of an innocent convent girl about her, and she smiles shyly.*] If you think Mr. Tyrone is handsome now, Cathleen, you should have seen him when I first met him. He had the reputation of being one of the best looking men in the country. The girls in the Convent who had seen him act, or seen his photographs, used to rave about him. He was a great matinee idol then, you know. Women used to wait at the stage door just to see him come out. You can imagine how excited I was when my father wrote me he and James Tyrone had become friends, and that I was to meet him when I came home for Easter vacation. I showed the letter to all the girls, and how envious they were! My father took me to see him act first. It was a play about the French Revolution and the leading part was a nobleman. I couldn't take my eyes off him. I wept when he was thrown in prison—and then was so mad at myself because I was afraid my eyes and nose would be red. My father had said we'd go backstage to his dressing room right after the play, and so we did. [*She gives a little excited, shy laugh.*] I was so bashful all I could do was stammer and blush like a little fool. But he didn't seem to think I was a fool. I know he liked me the first moment we were introduced. [*coquettishly*] I guess my eyes and nose couldn't have been red, after all. I was really very pretty then, Cathleen. And he was handsomer than my wildest dream, in his make-up and his nobleman's costume that was so becoming to him. He was different from all ordinary men, like someone from another world. At the same time he was simple, and kind, and unassuming, not a bit stuck-up or vain. I fell in love right then. So did he, he told me afterwards. I forgot all about becoming a nun or a concert pianist. All I wanted was to be his wife. [*She pauses, staring before her with unnaturally bright, dreamy eyes, and a rapt, tender, girlish smile.*] Thirty-six years ago, but I can see it as clearly as if it were tonight! We've loved each other ever since. And in all those thirty-six years, there has never been a breath of scandal about him. I mean, with any other woman. Never since he met me. That has made me very happy, Cathleen. It has made me forgive so many other things.

CATHLEEN [*fighting tipsy drowsiness—sentimentally*]   He's a fine gentleman and you're a lucky woman. [*then, fidgeting*] Can I take the drink to Bridget, Ma'am? It must be near dinnertime and I ought to be in the kitchen helping her. If she don't get something to quiet her temper, she'll be after me with the cleaver.

MARY [*with a vague exasperation at being brought back from her dream*]   Yes, yes, go. I don't need you now.

CATHLEEN [*with relief*]   Thank you, Ma'am. [*She pours out a big drink and starts for the back parlor with it.*] You won't be alone long. The Master and the boys—

MARY [*impatiently*]   No, no, they won't come. Tell Bridget I won't wait. You can serve dinner promptly at half past six. I'm not hungry but I'll sit at the table and we'll get it over with.

CATHLEEN   You ought to eat something, Ma'am. It's a queer medicine if it takes away your appetite. ·

MARY [*has begun to drift into dreams again—reacts mechanically*]   What medicine? I don't know what you mean. [*in dismissal*] You better take the drink to Bridget.

CATHLEEN   Yes, Ma'am.

[*She disappears through the back parlor.* MARY *waits until she hears the pantry door close behind her. Then she settles back in relaxed dreaminess, staring fixedly at nothing. Her arms rest limply along the arms of the chair, her hands with long, warped, swollen-knuckled, sensitive fingers drooping in complete calm. It is growing dark in the room. There is a pause of dead quiet. Then from the world outside comes the melancholy moan of the foghorn, followed by a chorus of bells, muffled by the fog, from the anchored craft in the harbor.* MARY's *face gives no sign she has heard, but her hands jerk and the fingers automatically play for a moment on the air. She frowns and shakes her head mechanically as if a fly had walked across her mind. She suddenly loses all the girlish quality and is an aging, cynically sad, embittered woman.*]

MARY [*bitterly*]   You're a sentimental fool. What is so wonderful about that first meeting between a silly romantic schoolgirl and a matinee idol? You were much happier before you knew he existed, in the Convent when you used to pray to the Blessed Virgin. [*longingly*] If I could only find the faith I lost, so I could pray again! [*She pauses—then begins to recite the Hail Mary in a flat, empty tone.*] "Hail, Mary, full of grace! The Lord is with Thee; blessed art Thou among women." [*sneeringly*] You expect the Blessed Virgin to be fooled by a lying dope fiend reciting words! You can't hide from her! [*She springs to her feet. Her hands fly up to pat her hair distractedly.*] I must go upstairs. I haven't taken enough. When you start again you never know exactly how much you need. [*She goes toward the front parlor—then stops in the doorway as she hears the sound of voices from the front path. She starts guiltily.*] That must be them—[*She hurries back to sit down. Her face sets in stubborn defensiveness—resentfully*] Why are they coming back? They don't want to. And I'd much rather be alone. [*Suddenly her whole manner changes. She becomes pathetically relieved and eager.*] Oh, I'm so glad they've come! I've been so horribly lonely!

[*The front door is heard closing and* TYRONE *calls uneasily from the hall.*]

TYRONE   Are you there, Mary?

[*The light in the hall is turned on and shines through the front parlor to fall on* MARY.]

MARY [*rises from her chair, her face lighting up lovingly—with excited eagerness*]   I'm here, dear. In the living room. I've been waiting for you.

[TYRONE *comes in through the front parlor.* EDMUND *is behind him.* TYRONE *has had a lot to drink but beyond a slightly glazed look in his eyes and a trace of blur in his speech, he does not show it.* EDMUND *has also had more than a few drinks without much apparent effect, except that his sunken cheeks are flushed and his eyes look bright and feverish. They stop in the doorway to stare appraisingly at her. What they see fulfills their worst expectations. But for the moment* MARY *is unconscious of their condemning eyes. She kisses her husband and then* EDMUND. *Her manner is unnaturally effusive. They submit shrinkingly. She talks excitedly.*]

I'm so happy you've come. I had given up hope. I was afraid you wouldn't come home. It's such a dismal, foggy evening. It must be much more cheerful in the barrooms uptown, where there are people you can talk and joke with. No, don't deny it. I know how you feel. I don't blame you a bit. I'm all the more grateful to you for coming home. I was sitting here so lonely and blue. Come and sit down.

[*She sits at left rear of table,* EDMUND *at left of table, and* TYRONE *in the rocker at right of it.*]

Dinner won't be ready for a minute. You're actually a little early. Will wonders never cease. Here's the whiskey, dear. Shall I pour a drink for you? [*Without waiting for a reply she does so.*] And you, Edmund? I don't want to encourage you, but one before dinner, as an appetizer, can't do any harm.

[*She pours a drink for him. They make no move to take the drinks. She talks on as if unaware of their silence.*]

Where's Jamie? But, of course, he'll never come home so long as he has the price of a drink left. [*She reaches out and clasps her husband's hand—sadly*] I'm afraid Jamie has been lost to us for a long time, dear. [*Her face hardens.*] But we mustn't allow him to drag Edmund down with him, as he'd like to do. He's jealous because Edmund has always been the baby—just as he used to be of Eugene. He'll never be content until he makes Edmund as hopeless a failure as he is.

EDMUND [*miserably*]   Stop talking, Mama.

TYRONE [*dully*]   Yes, Mary, the less you say now—[*then to Edmund, a bit tipsily*] All the same there's truth in your mother's warning. Beware of that brother of yours, or he'll poison life for you with his damned sneering serpent's tongue!

EDMUND [*as before*]   Oh, cut it out, Papa.

MARY [*goes on as if nothing had been said*]   It's hard to believe, seeing Jamie as he is now, that he ever my baby. Do you remember what a healthy, happy baby he was, James? The one-night stands and filthy trains and cheap hotels and bad food never made him cross or sick. He was always smiling or laughing. He hardly ever cried. Eugene was the same, too, happy and healthy, during the two years he lived before I let him die through my neglect.

TYRONE   Oh, for the love of God! I'm a fool for coming home!

EDMUND   Papa! Shut up!

MARY [*smiles with detached tenderness at* EDMUND]   It was Edmund who was the crosspatch when he was little, always getting upset and frightened about nothing at all. [*She pats his hand—teasingly*] Everyone used to say, dear, you'd cry at the drop of a hat.

EDMUND [*cannot control his bitterness*]   Maybe I guessed there was a good reason not to laugh.

TYRONE [*reproving and pitying*]   Now, now, lad. You know better than to pay attention—

MARY [*as if she hadn't heard—sadly again*]   Who would have thought Jamie would grow up to disgrace us. You remember, James, for years after he went to boarding school, we received such glowing reports. Everyone liked him. All his teachers told us what a fine brain he had, and how easily he learned his lessons. Even after he began to drink and they had to expel him, they wrote us how sorry they were, because he was so likable and such a brilliant student. They predicted a wonderful future for him if he would only learn to take life seriously. [*She pauses—then adds with a strange, sad detachment*] It's such a pity. Poor Jamie! It's hard to understand—[*Abruptly a change comes over her. Her face hardens and she stares at her husband with accusing hostility.*] No, it isn't at all. You brought him up to be a boozer. Since he first opened his eyes, he's seen you drinking. Always a bottle on the bureau in the cheap hotel rooms! And if he had a nightmare when he was little, or a stomach-ache, your remedy was to give him a teaspoonful of whiskey to quiet him.

TYRONE [*stung*]   So I'm to blame because that lazy hulk has made a drunken loafer of himself? Is that what I came home to listen to? I might have known! When you have the poison in you, you want to blame every-one but yourself!

EDMUND   Papa! You told me not to pay attention. [*then, resentfully*] Anyway it's true. You did the same thing with me. I can remember that teaspoon-ful of booze every time I woke up with a nightmare.

MARY [*in a detached reminiscent tone*]   Yes, you were continually having nightmares as a child. You were born afraid. Because I was so afraid to bring you into the world. [*She pauses—then goes on with the same detach-ment*] Please don't think I blame your father, Edmund. He didn't know any better. He never went to school after he was ten. His people were the most ignorant kind of poverty-stricken Irish. I'm sure they honestly believed whiskey is the healthiest medicine for a child who is sick or frightened.

[TYRONE *is about to burst out in angry defense of his family but* EDMUND *intervenes.*]

EDMUND [*sharply*]   Papa! [*changing the subject*] Are we going to have this drink, or aren't we?

TYRONE [*controlling himself—dully*]   You're right. I'm a fool to take notice. [*He picks up his glass listlessly.*] Drink hearty, lad.

[EDMUND *drinks but* TYRONE *remains staring at the glass in his hand.* EDMUND *at once realizes how much the whiskey has been watered. He frowns, glancing from the bottle to his mother—starts to say something but stops.*]

MARY [*in a changed tone—repentantly*]   I'm sorry if I sounded bitter, James. I'm not. It's all so far away. But I did feel a little hurt when you wished you hadn't come home. I was so relieved and happy when you came, and grateful to you. It's very dreary and sad to be here alone in the fog with night falling.

TYRONE [*moved*]   I'm glad I came, Mary, when you act like your real self.

MARY   I was so lonesome I kept Cathleen with me just to have someone to talk to. [*Her manner and quality drift back to the shy convent girl again.*] Do you know what I was telling her, dear? About the night my father took me to your dressing room and I first fell in love with you. Do you remem-ber?

TYRONE [*deeply moved—his voice husky*]   Can you think I'd ever forget, Mary?

[EDMUND *looks away from them, sad and embarrassed.*]

MARY [*tenderly*]   No. I know you still love me, James, in spite of everything.

TYRONE [*His face works and he blinks back tears—with quiet intensity*]   Yes! As God is my judge! Always and forever, Mary!

MARY   And I love you, dear, in spite of everything.

[*There is a pause in which* EDMUND *moves embarrassedly. The strange detachment comes over her manner again as if she were speaking imper-sonally of people seen from a distance.*]

But I must confess, James, although I couldn't help loving you, I would never have married you if I'd known you drank so much. I remember the first night your barroom friends had to help you up to the door of our hotel room, and knocked and then ran away before I came to the door. We were still on our honeymoon, do you remember?

TYRONE [*with guilty vehemence*]   I don't remember! It wasn't on our honeymoon! And I never in my life had to be helped to bed, or missed a performance!

MARY [*as though he hadn't spoken*]   I had waited in that ugly hotel room hour after hour. I kept making excuses for you. I told myself it must be some business connected with the theater. I knew so little about the theater. Then I became terrified. I imagined all sorts of horrible accidents. I got on my knees and prayed that nothing had happened to you—and then they brought you up and left you outside the door. [*She gives a little, sad sigh.*] I didn't know how often that was to happen in the years to come, how many times I was to wait in ugly hotel rooms. I became quite used to it.

EDMUND [*bursts out with a look of accusing hate at his father*]   Christ! No wonder—! [*He controls himself—gruffly*] When is dinner, Mama? It must be time.

TYRONE [*overwhelmed by shame which he tries to hide, fumbles with his watch*]   Yes. It must be. Let's see. [*He stares at his watch without seeing it—pleadingly*] Mary! Can't you forget—?

MARY [*with detached pity*]   No, dear. But I forgive. I always forgive you. So don't look so guilty. I'm sorry I remembered out loud. I don't want to be sad, or to make you sad. I want to remember only the happy part of the past. [*Her manner drifts back to the shy, gay convent girl.*] Do you remember our wedding, dear? I'm sure you've completely forgotten what my wedding gown looked like. Men don't notice such things. They don't think they're important. But it was important to me, I can tell you! How I fussed and worried! I was so excited and happy! My father told me to buy anything I wanted and never mind what it cost. The best is none too good, he said. I'm afraid he spoiled me dreadfully. My mother didn't. She was very pious and strict. I think she was a little jealous. She didn't approve of my marrying—especially an actor. I think she hoped I would become a nun. She used to scold my father. She'd grumble, "You never tell me, never mind what it costs, when I buy anything! You've spoiled that girl so, I pity her husband if she ever marries. She'll expect him to give her the moon. She'll never make a good wife." [*She laughs affectionately.*] Poor mother! [*She smiles at* TYRONE *with a strange, incongruous coquetry.*] But she was mistaken, wasn't she, James? I haven't been such a bad wife, have I?

TYRONE [*huskily, trying to force a smile*]   I'm not complaining, Mary.

MARY [*a shadow of vague guilt crosses her face*]   At least, I've loved you dearly, and done the best I could—under the circumstances. [*The shadow vanishes and her shy, girlish expression returns.*] That wedding gown was nearly the death of me and the dressmaker, too! [*She laughs.*] I was so particular. It was never quite good enough. At last she said she refused to touch it any more or she might spoil it, and I made her leave so I could be alone to examine myself in the mirror. I was so pleased and vain. I thought to myself, "Even if your nose and mouth and ears are a trifle too large, your eyes and hair and figure, and your hands, make up for it. You're just as pretty as any actress he's ever met, and you don't have to use paint." [*She pauses, wrinkling her brow in an effort of memory.*] Where is my wedding gown now, I wonder? I kept it wrapped up in tissue paper in my trunk. I used to hope I would have a daughter and when it came time for her to marry—She couldn't have bought a lovelier gown, and I knew, James, you'd never tell her, never mind the cost. You'd want her to pick up something at a bargain. It was made of soft, shimmering satin, trimmed with wonderful old duchesse lace, in tiny ruffles around the neck and sleeves, and worked in with the folds that were draped round in a bustle effect at the back. The basque[4] was boned and very tight. I remember I held my breath when it was fitted, so my waist would be as small as possible. My father even let me have duchesse lace on my white satin slippers, and lace with orange blossoms in my veil. Oh, how I loved that gown! It was so beautiful! Where is it now, I wonder? I used to take it out from time to time when I was lonely, but it always made me cry, so finally a long while ago—[*She wrinkles her forehead again.*] I wonder where I hid it? Probably in one of the old trunks in the attic. Some day I'll have to look.

> [*She stops, staring before her.* TYRONE *sighs, shaking his head hopelessly, and attempts to catch his son's eye, looking for sympathy, but* EDMUND *is staring at the floor.*]

TYRONE [*forces a casual tone*]   Isn't it dinner time, dear? [*with a feeble attempt at teasing*] You're forever scolding me for being late, but now I'm on time for once, it's dinner that's late.

> [*She doesn't appear to hear him. He adds, still pleasantly*]

Well, if I can't eat yet, I can drink. I'd forgotten I had this.

> [*He drinks his drink.* EDMUND *watches him.* TYRONE *scowls and looks at his wife with sharp suspicion—roughly*]

Who's been tampering with my whiskey? The damned stuff is half water! Jamie's been away and he wouldn't overdo his trick like this, anyway. Any fool could tell—Mary, answer me! [*with angry disgust*] I hope to God you haven't taken to drink on top of—

EDMUND   Shut up, Papa! [*to his mother, without looking at her*] You treated Cathleen and Bridget, isn't that it, Mama?

MARY [*with indifferent casualness*]   Yes, of course. They work hard for poor wages. And I'm the housekeeper, I have to keep them from leaving. Besides, I wanted to treat Cathleen because I had her drive uptown with me, and sent her to get my prescription filled.

EDMUND   For God's sake, Mama! You can't trust her! Do you want everyone on earth to know?

MARY [*her face hardening stubbornly*]   Know what? That I suffer from rheumatism in my hands and have to take medicine to kill the pain? Why should I be ashamed of that? [*turns on* EDMUND *with a hard, accusing antagonism—almost a revengeful enmity*] I never knew what rheumatism was before you were born! Ask your father!

> [EDMUND *looks away, shrinking into himself.*]

---

4. Tight-fitting bodice.

TYRONE   Don't mind her, lad. It doesn't mean anything. When she gets to the stage where she gives the old crazy excuse about her hands she's gone far away from us.

MARY [*turns on him—with a strangely triumphant, taunting smile*]   I'm glad you realize that, James! Now perhaps you'll give up trying to remind me, you and Edmund! [*abruptly, in a detached, matter-of-fact tone*] Why don't you light the light, James? It's getting dark. I know you hate to, but Edmund has proved to you that one bulb burning doesn't cost much. There's no sense letting your fear of the poorhouse make you too stingy.

TYRONE [*reacts mechanically*]   I never claimed one bulb cost much! It's having them on, one here and one there, that makes the Electric Light Company rich. [*He gets up and turns on the reading lamp—roughly*] But I'm a fool to talk reason to you. [*to* EDMUND] I'll get a fresh bottle of whiskey, lad, and we'll have a real drink. [*He goes through the back parlor.*]

MARY [*with detached amusement*]   He'll sneak around to the outside cellar door so the servants won't see him. He's really ashamed of keeping his whiskey padlocked in the cellar. Your father is a strange man, Edmund. It took many years before I understood him. You must try to understand and forgive him, too, and not feel contempt because he's close-fisted. His father deserted his mother and their six children a year or so after they came to America. He told them he had a premonition he would die soon, and he was homesick for Ireland, and wanted to go back there to die. So he went and he did die. He must have been a peculiar man, too. Your father had to go to work in a machine shop when he was only ten years old.

EDMUND [*protests dully*]   Oh, for Pete's sake, Mama. I've heard Papa tell that machine shop story ten thousand times.

MARY   Yes, dear, you've had to listen, but I don't think you've ever tried to understand.

EDMUND [*ignoring this—miserably*]   Listen, Mama! You're not so far gone yet you've forgotten everything. You haven't asked me what I found out this afternoon. Don't you care a damn?

MARY [*shakenly*]   Don't say that! You hurt me, dear!

EDMUND   What I've got is serious, Mama. Doc Hardy knows for sure now.

MARY [*stiffens into scornful, defensive stubbornness*]   That lying old quack! I warned you he'd invent—!

EDMUND [*miserably dogged*]   He called in a specialist to examine me, so he'd be absolutely sure.

MARY [*ignoring this*]   Don't tell me about Hardy! If you heard what the doctor at the sanatorium, who really knows something, said about how he'd treated me! He said he ought to be locked up! He said it was a wonder I hadn't gone mad! I told him I had once, that time I ran down in my nightdress to throw myself off the dock. You remember that, don't you? And yet you want me to pay attention to what Doctor Hardy says. Oh, no!

EDMUND [*bitterly*]   I remember, all right. It was right after that Papa and Jamie decided they couldn't hide it from me any more. Jamie told me. I called him a liar! I tried to punch him in the nose. But I knew he wasn't lying. [*His voice trembles, his eyes begin to fill with tears.*] God, it made everything in life seem rotten!

MARY [*pitiably*]   Oh, don't. My baby! You hurt me so dreadfully!

EDMUND [*dully*] I'm sorry, Mama. It was you who brought it up. [*then with a bitter, stubborn persistence*] Listen, Mama. I'm going to tell you whether you want to hear or not. I've got to go to a sanatorium.

MARY [*dazedly, as if this was something that had never occurred to her*] Go away? [*violently*] No! I won't have it! How dare Doctor Hardy advise such a thing without consulting me! How dare your father allow him! What right has he? You are my baby! Let him attend to Jamie! [*more and more excited and bitter*] I know why he wants you sent to a sanatorium. To take you from me! He's always tried to do that. He's been jealous of every one of my babies! He kept finding ways to make me leave them. That's what caused Eugene's death. He's been jealous of you most of all. He knew I loved you most because—

EDMUND [*miserably*] Oh, stop talking crazy, can't you, Mama! Stop trying to blame him. And why are you so against my going away now? I've been away a lot, and I've never noticed it broke your heart!

MARY [*bitterly*] I'm afraid you're not very sensitive, after all. [*sadly*] You might have guessed, dear, that after I knew you knew—about me—I had to be glad whenever you were where you couldn't see me.

EDMUND [*brokenly*] Mama! Don't! [*He reaches out blindly and takes her hand—but he drops it immediately, overcome by bitterness again.*] All this talk about loving me—and you won't even listen when I try to tell you how sick—

MARY [*with an abrupt transformation into a detached bullying motherliness*] Now, now. That's enough! I don't care to hear because I know it's nothing but Hardy's ignorant lies.

   [*He shrinks back into himself. She keeps on in a forced, teasing tone but with an increasing undercurrent of resentment.*]

You're so like your father, dear. You love to make a scene out of nothing so you can be dramatic and tragic. [*with a belittling laugh*] If I gave you the slightest encouragement, you'd tell me next you were going to die—

EDMUND People do die of it. Your own father—

MARY [*sharply*] Why do you mention him? There's no comparison at all with you. He had consumption. [*angrily*] I hate you when you become gloomy and morbid! I forbid you to remind me of my father's death, do you hear me?

EDMUND [*his face hard—grimly*] Yes, I hear you, Mama. I wish to God I didn't! [*He gets up from his chair and stands staring condemningly at her—bitterly*] It's pretty hard to take at times, having a dope fiend for a mother!

   [*She winces—all life seeming to drain from her face, leaving it with the appearance of a plaster cast. Instantly EDMUND wishes he could take back what he has said. He stammers miserably.*]

Forgive me, Mama. I was angry. You hurt me.

   [*There is a pause in which the foghorn and the ships' bells are heard.*]

MARY [*goes slowly to the windows at right like an automaton—looking out, a blank, far-off quality in her voice*] Just listen to that awful foghorn. And the bells. Why is it fog makes everything sound so sad and lost, I wonder?

EDMUND [*brokenly*] I—I can't stay here. I don't want any dinner.

   [*He hurries away through the front parlor. She keeps staring out the window until she hears the front door close behind him. Then she comes back and sits in her chair, the same blank look on her face.*]

MARY [*vaguely*]   I must go upstairs. I haven't taken enough. [*She pauses—then longingly*] I hope, sometime, without meaning it, I will take an over-dose. I never could do it deliberately. The Blessed Virgin would never forgive me, then.

> [*She hears* TYRONE *returning and turns as he comes in, through the back parlor, with a bottle of whiskey he has just uncorked. He is fuming.*]

TYRONE [*wrathfully*]   The padlock is all scratched. That drunken loafer has tried to pick the lock with a piece of wire, the way he's done before. [*with satisfaction, as if this was a perpetual battle of wits with his elder son*] But I've fooled him this time. It's a special padlock a professional burglar couldn't pick. [*He puts the bottle on the tray and suddenly is aware of* EDMUND'S *absence.*] Where's Edmund?

MARY [*with a vague far-away air*]   He went out. Perhaps he's going uptown again to find Jamie. He still has some money left, I suppose, and it's burn-ing a hole in his pocket. He said he didn't want any dinner. He doesn't seem to have any appetite these days. [*then stubbornly*] But it's just a sum-mer cold.

> [TYRONE *stares at her and shakes his head helplessly and pours himself a big drink and drinks it. Suddenly it is too much for her and she breaks out and sobs.*]

Oh, James, I'm so frightened! [*She gets up and throws her arms around him and hides her face on his shoulder—sobbingly*] I know he's going to die!

TYRONE   Don't say that! It's not true! They promised me in six months he'd be cured.

MARY   You don't believe that! I can tell when you're acting! And it will be my fault. I should never have borne him. It would have been better for his sake. I could never hurt him then. He wouldn't have had to know his mother was a dope fiend—and hate her!

TYRONE [*his voice quivering*]   Hush, Mary, for the love of God! He loves you. He knows it was a curse put on you without your knowing or willing it. He's proud you're his mother! [*abruptly as he hears the pantry door opening*] Hush, now! Here comes Cathleen. You don't want her to see you crying.

> [*She turns quickly away from him to the windows at right, hastily wiping her eyes. A moment later* CATHLEEN *appears in the back-parlor doorway. She is uncertain in her walk and grinning woozily.*]

CATHLEEN [*starts guiltily when she sees* TYRONE—*with dignity*]   Dinner is served, Sir. [*raising her voice unnecessarily*] Dinner is served, Ma'am. [*She forgets her dignity and addresses* TYRONE *with good-natured familiarity*] So you're here, are you? Well, well. Won't Bridget be in a rage! I told her the Madame said you wouldn't be home. [*then reading accusation in his eye*] Don't be looking at me that way. If I've a drop taken, I didn't steal it. I was invited.

> [*She turns with huffy dignity and disappears through the back parlor.*]

TYRONE [*sighs—then summoning his actor's heartiness*]   Come along, dear. Let's have our dinner. I'm hungry as a hunter.

MARY [*comes to him—her face is composed in plaster again and her tone is remote*]   I'm afraid you'll have to excuse me, James. I couldn't possibly eat anything. My hands pain me dreadfully. I think the best thing for me is to go to bed and rest. Good night dear.

[*She kisses him mechanically and turns toward the front parlor.*]

TYRONE [*harshly*]   Up to take more of that God-damned poison, is that it? You'll be like a mad ghost before the night's over!

MARY [*starts to walk away—blankly*]   I don't know what you're talking about, James. You say such mean, bitter things when you've drunk too much. You're as bad as Jamie or Edmund.

> [*She moves off through the front parlor. He stands a second as if not knowing what to do. He is a sad, bewildered, broken old man. He walks wearily off through the back parlor toward the dining room.*]

CURTAIN

Act 4

SCENE—*The same. It is around midnight. The lamp in the front hall has been turned out, so that now no light shines through the front parlor. In the living room only the reading lamp on the table is lighted. Outside the windows the wall of fog appears denser than ever. As the curtain rises, the foghorn is heard, followed by the ships' bells from the harbor.*

TYRONE *is seated at the table. He wears his pince-nez[5] and is playing solitaire. He has taken off his coat and has on an old brown dressing gown. The whiskey bottle on the tray is three-quarters empty. There is a fresh full bottle on the table, which he has brought from the cellar so there will be an ample reserve on hand. He is drunk and shows it by the owlish, deliberate manner in which he peers at each card to make certain of its identity, and then plays it as if he wasn't certain of his aim. His eyes have a misted, oily look and his mouth is slack. But despite all the whiskey in him, he has not escaped, and he looks as he appeared at the close of the preceding act, a sad, defeated old man, possessed by hopeless resignation.*

As the curtain rises, he finishes a game and sweeps the cards together. He shuffles them clumsily, dropping a couple on the floor. He retrieves them with difficulty, and starts to shuffle again, when he hears someone entering the front door. He peers over his pince-nez through the front parlor.

TYRONE [*his voice thick*]   Who's that? Is it you, Edmund?

> [EDMUND's *voice answers curtly,* "Yes." *Then he evidently collides with something in the dark hall and can be heard cursing. A moment later the hall lamp is turned on.* TYRONE *frowns and calls.*]

Turn that light out before you come in.

> [*But* EDMUND *doesn't. He comes in through the front parlor. He is drunk now, too, but like his father he carries it well, and gives little physical sign of it except in his eyes and a chip-on-the-shoulder aggressiveness in his manner.* TYRONE *speaks, at first with a warm, relieved welcome.*]

I'm glad you've come, lad. I've been damned lonely. [*then resentfully*] You're a fine one to run away and leave me to sit alone here all night when you know—[*with sharp irritation*] I told you to turn out that light! We're not giving a ball. There's no reason to have the house ablaze with electricity at this time of night, burning up money!

EDMUND [*angrily*]   Ablaze with electricity! One bulb! Hell, everyone keeps

---

5. Eyeglasses clipped to the nose.

a light on in the front hall until they go to bed. [*He rubs his knee.*] I
damned near busted my knee on the hat stand.

TYRONE   The light from here shows in the hall. You could see your way well
enough if you were sober.

EDMUND   If *I* was sober? I like that!

TYRONE   I don't give a damn what other people do. If they want to be wasteful fools, for the sake of show, let them be!

EDMUND   One bulb! Christ, don't be such a cheap skate! I've proved by figures if you left the light bulb on all night it wouldn't be as much as one
drink!

TYRONE   To hell with your figures! The proof is in the bills I have to pay!

EDMUND [*sits down opposite his father—contemptuously*]   Yes, facts don't
mean a thing, do they? What you want to believe, that's the only truth!
[*derisively*] Shakespeare was an Irish Catholic, for example.

TYRONE [*stubbornly*]   So he was. The proof is in his plays.

EDMUND   Well he wasn't, and there's no proof of it in his plays, except to
you! [*jeeringly*] The Duke of Wellington, there was another good Irish
Catholic!

TYRONE   I never said he was a good one. He was a renegade but a Catholic
just the same.

EDMUND   Well, he wasn't. You just want to believe no one but an Irish
Catholic general could beat Napoleon.

TYRONE   I'm not going to argue with you. I asked you to turn out that light
in the hall.

EDMUND   I heard you, and as far as I'm concerned it stays on.

TYRONE   None of your damned insolence! Are you going to obey me or not?

EDMUND   Not! If you want to be a crazy miser put it out yourself!

TYRONE [*with threatening anger*]   Listen to me! I've put up with a lot from
you because from the mad things you've done at times I've thought you
weren't quite right in your head. I've excused you and never lifted my
hand to you. But there's a straw that breaks the camel's back. You'll obey
me and put out that light or, big as you are, I'll give you a thrashing that'll
teach you—! [*Suddenly he remembers* EDMUND's *illness and instantly
becomes guilty and shamefaced.*] Forgive me, lad. I forgot—You shouldn't
goad me into losing my temper.

EDMUND [*ashamed himself now*]   Forget it, Papa. I apologize, too. I had no
right being nasty about nothing. I am a bit soused, I guess. I'll put out the
damned light. [*He starts to get up.*]

TYRONE   No, stay where you are. Let it burn.
[*He stands up abruptly—and a bit drunkenly—and begins turning on the
three bulbs in the chandelier, with a childish, bitterly dramatic self-pity.*]
We'll have them all on! Let them burn! To hell with them! The poorhouse
is the end of the road, and it might as well be sooner as later! [*He finishes
turning on the lights.*]

EDMUND [*has watched this proceeding with an awakened sense of humor—
now he grins, teasing affectionately*]   That's a grand curtain. [*He laughs.*]
You're a wonder, Papa.

TYRONE [*sits down sheepishly—grumbles pathetically*]   That's right, laugh at
the old fool! The poor old ham! But the final curtain will be in the poorhouse just the same, and that's not comedy! [*Then as* EDMUND *is still grin-*

ning, he changes the subject.] Well, well, let's not argue. You've got brains in that head of yours, though you do your best to deny them. You'll live to learn the value of a dollar. You're not like your damned tramp of a brother. I've given up hope he'll ever get sense. Where is he, by the way?

EDMUND   How would I know?

TYRONE   I thought you'd gone back uptown to meet him.

EDMUND   No. I walked out to the beach. I haven't seen him since this afternoon.

TYRONE   Well, if you split the money I gave you with him, like a fool—

EDMUND   Sure I did. He's always staked me when he had anything.

TYRONE   Then it doesn't take a soothsayer to tell he's probably in the whorehouse.

EDMUND   What of it if he is? Why not?

TYRONE [*contemptuously*]   Why not, indeed. It's the fit place for him. If he's ever had a loftier dream than whores and whiskey, he's never shown it.

EDMUND   Oh, for Pete's sake, Papa! If you're going to start that stuff, I'll beat it. [*He starts to get up.*]

TYRONE [*placatingly*]   All right, all right, I'll stop. God knows, I don't like the subject either. Will you join me in a drink?

EDMUND   Ah! Now you're talking!

TYRONE [*passes the bottle to him—mechanically*]   I'm wrong to treat you. You've had enough already.

EDMUND [*pouring a big drink—a bit drunkenly*]   Enough is *not* as good as a feast. [*He hands back the bottle.*]

TYRONE   It's too much in your condition.

EDMUND   Forget my condition! [*He raises his glass.*] Here's how.

TYRONE   Drink hearty. [*They drink.*] If you walked all the way to the beach you must be damp and chilled.

EDMUND   Oh, I dropped in at the Inn on the way out and back.

TYRONE   It's not a night I'd pick for a long walk.

EDMUND   I loved the fog. It was what I needed. [*He sounds more tipsy and looks it.*]

TYRONE   You should have more sense than to risk—

EDMUND   To hell with sense! We're all crazy. What do we want with sense? [*He quotes from Dowson[6] sardonically.*]

> "They are not long, the weeping and the laughter,
> Love and desire and hate:
> I think they have no portion in us after
> We pass the gate.
>
> They are not long, the days of wine and roses:
> Out of a misty dream
> Our path emerges for a while, then closes
> Within a dream."

[*staring before him*] The fog was where I wanted to be. Halfway down the path you can't see this house. You'd never know it was here. Or any of the other places down the avenue. I couldn't see but a few feet ahead. I didn't

---

6. Ernest Dowson (1867–1900), English poet.

meet a soul. Everything looked and sounded unreal. Nothing was what it
is. That's what I wanted—to be alone with myself in another world where
truth is untrue and life can hide from itself. Out beyond the harbor, where
the road runs along the beach, I even lost the feeling of being on land.
The fog and the sea seemed part of each other. It was like walking on the
bottom of the sea. As if I had drowned long ago. As if I was a ghost belonging to the fog, and the fog was the ghost of the sea. It felt damned peaceful to be nothing more than a ghost within a ghost. [*He sees his father
staring at him with mingled worry and irritated disapproval. He grins mockingly.*] Don't look at me as if I'd gone nutty. I'm talking sense. Who wants
to see life as it is, if they can help it? It's the three Gorgons[7] in one. You
look in their faces and turn to stone. Or it's Pan.[8] You see him and you
die—that is, inside you—and have to go on living as a ghost.

TYRONE [*impressed and at the same time revolted*]   You have a poet in you
but it's a damned morbid one! [*forcing a smile*] Devil take your pessimism.
I feel low-spirited enough. [*He sighs.*] Why can't you remember your
Shakespeare and forget the third-raters. You'll find what you're trying to
say in him—as you'll find everything else worth saying. [*He quotes, using
his fine voice*] "We are such stuff as dreams are made on, and our little
life is rounded with a sleep."[9]

EDMUND [*ironically*]   Fine! That's beautiful. But I wasn't trying to say that.
We are such stuff as manure is made on, so let's drink up and forget it.
That's more my idea.

TYRONE [*disgustedly*]   Ach! Keep such sentiments to yourself. I shouldn't
have given you that drink.

EDMUND It did pack a wallop, all right. On you, too. [*He grins with affectionate teasing.*] Even if you've never missed a performance! [*aggressively*]
Well, what's wrong with being drunk? It's what we're after, isn't it? Let's
not kid each other, Papa. Not tonight. We know what we're trying to forget. [*hurriedly*] But let's not talk about it. It's no use now.

TYRONE [*dully*]   No. All we can do is try to be resigned—again.

EDMUND   Or be so drunk you can forget. [*He recites, and recites well, with
bitter, ironical passion, the Symons' translation of Baudelaire's[1] prose
poem.*] "Be always drunken. Nothing else matters: that is the only question. If you would not feel the horrible burden of Time weighing on your
shoulders and crushing you to the earth, be drunken continually.

    Drunken with what? With wine, with poetry, or with virtue, as you will.
But be drunken.

    And if sometimes, on the stairs of a palace, or on the green side of a
ditch, or in the dreary solitude of your own room, you should awaken and
the drunkenness be half or wholly slipped away from you, ask of the wind,
or of the wave, or of the star, or of the bird, or of the clock, of whatever
flies, or sighs, or rocks, or sings, or speaks, ask what hour it is; and the
wind, wave, star, bird, clock, will answer you: 'It is the hour to be

---

7. In Greek mythology, three monstrous sisters so
ugly that the sight of them turned one to stone.
8. Greek god of woods, fields, and flocks, half man
and half goat, associated with wildness.

9. Shakespeare's *The Tempest* 4.1.156–58.
1. Charles Baudelaire (1821–1867), French poet.
Arthur Symons (1865–1945), English poet and literary critic.

drunken! Be drunken, if you would not be martyred slaves of Time; be
drunken continually! With wine, with poetry, or with virtue, as you will.' "
[*He grins at his father provocatively.*]

TYRONE [*thickly humorous*]   I wouldn't worry about the virtue part of it, if
I were you. [*then disgustedly*] Pah! It's morbid nonsense! What little truth
is in it you'll find nobly said in Shakespeare. [*then appreciatively*] But you
recited it well, lad. Who wrote it?

EDMUND   Baudelaire.

TYRONE   Never heard of him.

EDMUND [*grins provocatively*]   He also wrote a poem about Jamie and the
Great White Way.

TYRONE   That loafer! I hope to God he misses the last car and has to stay
uptown!

EDMUND [*goes on, ignoring this*]   Although he was French and never saw
Broadway and died before Jamie was born. He knew him and Little Old
New York just the same. [*He recites the Symons' translation of Baudelaire's
"Epilogue."*]

> "With heart at rest I climbed the citadel's
> Steep height, and saw the city as from a tower,
> Hospital, brothel, prison, and such hells,
>
> Where evil comes up softly like a flower.
> Thou knowest, O Satan, patron of my pain,
> Not for vain tears I went up at that hour;
>
> But like an old sad faithful lecher, fain
> To drink delight of that enormous trull
> Whose hellish beauty makes me young again.
>
> Whether thou sleep, with heavy vapours full,
> Sodden with day, or, new apparelled, stand
> In gold-laced veils of evening beautiful,
>
> I love thee, infamous city! Harlots and
> Hunted have pleasures of their own to give,
> The vulgar herd can never understand."

TYRONE [*with irritable disgust*]   Morbid filth! Where the hell do you get
your taste in literature? Filth and despair and pessimism! Another atheist, I suppose. When you deny God, you deny hope. That's the trouble
with you. If you'd get down on your knees—

EDMUND [*as if he hadn't heard—sardonically*]   It's a good likeness of Jamie,
don't you think, hunted by himself and whiskey, hiding in a Broadway
hotel room with some fat tart—he likes them fat—reciting Dowson's
Cynara to her. [*He recites derisively, but with deep feeling*]

> "All night upon mine heart I felt her warm heart beat,
> Night-long within mine arms in love and sleep she lay;
> Surely the kisses of her bought red mouth were sweet;
> But I was desolate and sick of an old passion,
> When I awoke and found the dawn was gray:
> I have been faithful to thee, Cynara! in my fashion."

[*jeeringly*] And the poor fat burlesque queen doesn't get a word of it, but suspects she's being insulted! And Jamie never loved any Cynara, and was never faithful to a woman in his life, even in his fashion! But he lies there, kidding himself he is superior and enjoys pleasures "the vulgar herd can never understand"! [*He laughs.*] It's nuts—completely nuts!

TYRONE [*vaguely—his voice thick*]   It's madness, yes. If you'd get on your knees and pray. When you deny God, you deny sanity.

EDMUND [*ignoring this*]   But who am I to feel superior? I've done the same damned thing. And it's no more crazy than Dowson himself, inspired by an absinthe hangover, writing it to a dumb barmaid, who thought he was a poor crazy souse, and gave him the gate to marry a waiter! [*He laughs— then soberly, with genuine sympathy*] Poor Dowson. Booze and consumption got him. [*He starts and for a second looks miserable and frightened. Then with defensive irony*] Perhaps it would be tactful of me to change the subject.

TYRONE [*thickly*]   Where you get your taste in authors—That damned library of yours! [*He indicates the small bookcase at rear.*] Voltaire, Rousseau, Schopenhauer, Nietzsche, Ibsen! Atheists, fools, and madmen! And your poets! This Dowson, and this Baudelaire, and Swinburne and Oscar Wilde, and Whitman and Poe! Whore-mongers and degenerates! Pah! When I've three good sets of Shakespeare there [*he nods at the large bookcase*] you could read.

EDMUND [*provocatively*]   They say he was a souse, too.

TYRONE   They lie! I don't doubt he liked his glass—it's a good man's failing—but he knew how to drink so it didn't poison his brain with morbidness and filth. Don't compare him with the pack you've got in there. [*He indicates the small bookcase again.*] Your dirty Zola! And your Dante Gabriel Rossetti who was a dope fiend! [*He starts and looks guilty.*]

EDMUND [*with defensive dryness*]   Perhaps it would be wise to change the subject. [*a pause*] You can't accuse me of not knowing Shakespeare. Didn't I win five dollars from you once when you bet me I couldn't learn a leading part of his in a week, as you used to do in stock in the old days. I learned Macbeth and recited it letter perfect, with you giving me the cues.

TYRONE [*approvingly*]   That's true. So you did. [*He smiles teasingly and sighs.*] It was a terrible ordeal, I remember, hearing you murder the lines. I kept wishing I'd paid over the bet without making you prove it.
    [*He chuckles and* EDMUND *grins. Then he starts as he hears a sound from upstairs—with dread*]
Did you hear? She's moving around. I was hoping she'd gone to sleep.

EDMUND   Forget it! How about another drink?
    [*He reaches out and gets the bottle, pours a drink and hands it back. Then with a strained casualness, as his father pours a drink*]
When did Mama go to bed?

TYRONE   Right after you left. She wouldn't eat any dinner. What made you run away?

EDMUND   Nothing. [*Abruptly raising his glass.*]   Well, here's how.

TYRONE [*mechanically*]   Drink hearty, lad. [*They drink.* TYRONE *again listens to sounds upstairs—with dread*] She's moving around a lot. I hope to God she doesn't come down.

EDMUND [*dully*]   Yes. She'll be nothing but a ghost haunting the past by this time. [*He pauses—then miserably*] Back before I was born—

TYRONE   Doesn't she do the same with me? Back before she ever knew me. You'd think the only happy days she's ever known were in her father's home, or at the Convent, praying and playing the piano. [*jealous resentment in his bitterness*] As I've told you before, you must take her memories with a grain of salt. Her wonderful home was ordinary enough. Her father wasn't the great, generous, noble Irish gentleman she makes out. He was a nice enough man, good company and a good talker. I liked him and he liked me. He was prosperous enough, too, in his wholesale grocery business, an able man. But he had his weakness. She condemns my drinking but she forgets his. It's true he never touched a drop till he was forty, but after that he made up for lost time. He became a steady champagne drinker, the worst kind. That was his grand pose, to drink only champagne. Well, it finished him quick—that and the consumption—[*He stops with a guilty glance at his son.*]

EDMUND [*sardonically*]   We don't seem able to avoid unpleasant topics, do we?

TYRONE [*sighs sadly*]   No. [*then with a pathetic attempt at heartiness*] What do you say to a game or two of Casino, lad?

EDMUND   All right.

TYRONE [*shuffling the cards clumsily*]   We can't lock up and go to bed till Jamie comes on the last trolley—which I hope he won't—and I don't want to go upstairs, anyway, till she's asleep.

EDMUND   Neither do I.

TYRONE [*keeps shuffling the cards fumblingly, forgetting to deal them*]   As I was saying, you must take her tales of the past with a grain of salt. The piano playing and her dream of becoming a concert pianist. That was put in her head by the nuns flattering her. She was their pet. They loved her for being so devout. They're innocent women, anyway, when it comes to the world. They don't know that not one in a million who shows promise ever rises to concert playing. Not that your mother didn't play well for a schoolgirl, but that's no reason to take it for granted she could have—

EDMUND [*sharply*]   Why don't you deal, if we're going to play.

TYRONE   Eh? I am. [*dealing with very uncertain judgment of distance*] And the idea she might have become a nun. That's the worst. Your mother was one of the most beautiful girls you could ever see. She knew it, too. She was a bit of a rogue and a coquette, God bless her, behind all her shyness and blushes. She was never made to renounce the world. She was bursting with health and high spirits and the love of loving.

EDMUND   For God's sake, Papa! Why don't you pick up your hand?

TYRONE [*picks it up—dully*]   Yes, let's see what I have here.
    [*They both stare at their cards unseeingly. Then they both start.* TYRONE *whispers*]
  Listen!

EDMUND   She's coming downstairs.

TYRONE [*hurriedly*]   We'll play our game. Pretend not to notice and she'll soon go up again.

EDMUND [*staring through the front parlor—with relief*]   I don't see her. She must have started down and then turned back.

TYRONE   Thank God.

EDMUND   Yes. It's pretty horrible to see her the way she must be now. [*with bitter misery*] The hardest thing to take is the blank wall she builds around her. Or it's more like a bank of fog in which she hides and loses herself. Deliberately, that's the hell of it! You know something in her does it deliberately—to get beyond our reach, to be rid of us, to forget we're alive! It's as if, in spite of loving us, she hated us!

TYRONE   [*remonstrates gently*]   Now, now, lad. It's not her. It's the damned poison.

EDMUND   [*bitterly*]   She takes it to get that effect. At least, I know she did this time! [*abruptly*] My play, isn't it? Here. [*He plays a card.*]

TYRONE   [*plays mechanically—gently reproachful*]   She's been terribly frightened about your illness, for all her pretending. Don't be too hard on her, lad. Remember she's not responsible. Once that cursed poison gets a hold on anyone—

EDMUND   [*his face grows hard and he stares at his father with bitter accusation*] It never should have gotten a hold on her! I know damned well she's not to blame! And I know who is! You are! Your damned stinginess! If you'd spent money for a decent doctor when she was so sick after I was born, she'd never have known morphine existed! Instead you put her in the hands of a hotel quack who wouldn't admit his ignorance and took the easiest way out, not giving a damn what happened to her afterwards! All because his fee was cheap! Another one of your bargains!

TYRONE   [*stung—angrily*]   Be quiet! How dare you talk of something you know nothing about! [*trying to control his temper*] You must try to see my side of it, too, lad. How was I to know he was that kind of a doctor? He had a good reputation—

EDMUND   Among the souses in the hotel bar, I suppose!

TYRONE   That's a lie! I asked the hotel proprietor to recommend the best—

EDMUND   Yes! At the same time crying poorhouse and making it plain you wanted a cheap one! I know your system! By God, I ought to after this afternoon!

TYRONE   [*guiltily defensive*]   What about this afternoon?

EDMUND   Never mind now. We're talking about Mama! I'm saying no matter how you excuse yourself you know damned well your stinginess is to blame—

TYRONE   And I say you're a liar! Shut your mouth right now, or—

EDMUND   [*ignoring this*]   After you found out she'd been made a morphine addict, why didn't you send her to a cure then, at the start, while she still had a chance? No, that would have meant spending some money! I'll bet you told her all she had to do was use a little will power! That's what you still believe in your heart, in spite of what doctors, who really know something about it, have told you!

TYRONE   You lie again! I know better than that now! But how was I to know then? What did I know of morphine? It was years before I discovered what was wrong. I thought she'd never got over her sickness, that's all. Why didn't I send her to a cure, you say? [*bitterly*] Haven't I? I've spent thousands upon thousands in cures! A waste. What good have they done her? She always started again.

EDMUND   Because you've never given her anything that would help her want to stay off it! No home except this summer dump in a place she hates and you've refused even to spend money to make this look decent, while you keep buying more property, and playing sucker for every con man with a gold mine, or a silver mine, or any kind of get-rich-quick swindle! You've dragged her around on the road, season after season, on one-night stands, with no one she could talk to, waiting night after night in dirty hotel rooms for you to come back with a bun on after the bars closed! Christ, is it any wonder she didn't want to be cured. Jesus, when I think of it I hate your guts!

TYRONE [*strickenly*]   Edmund! [*then in a rage*] How dare you talk to your father like that, you insolent young cub! After all I've done for you.

EDMUND   We'll come to that, what you're doing for me!

TYRONE [*looking guilty again—ignores this*]   Will you stop repeating your mother's crazy accusations, which she never makes unless it's the poison talking? I never dragged her on the road against her will. Naturally, I wanted her with me. I loved her. And she came because she loved me and wanted to be with me. That's the truth, no matter what she says when she's not herself. And she needn't have been lonely. There was always the members of my company to talk to, if she'd wanted. She had her children, too, and I insisted, in spite of the expense, on having a nurse to travel with her.

EDMUND [*bitterly*]   Yes, your one generosity, and that because you were jealous of her paying too much attention to us, and wanted us out of your way! It was another mistake, too! If she'd had to take care of me all by herself, and had that to occupy her mind, maybe she'd have been able—

TYRONE [*goaded into vindictiveness*]   Or for that matter, if you insist in judging things by what she says when she's not in her right mind, if you hadn't been born she'd never—[*He stops ashamed.*]

EDMUND [*suddenly spent and miserable*]   Sure. I know that's what she feels, Papa.

TYRONE [*protests penitently*]   She doesn't! She loves you as dearly as ever mother loved a son! I only said that because you put me in such a God-damned rage, raking up the past, and saying you hate me—

EDMUND [*dully*]   I didn't mean it, Papa. [*He suddenly smiles—kidding a bit drunkenly*] I'm like Mama, I can't help liking you, in spite of everything.

TYRONE [*grins a bit drunkenly in return*]   I might say the same of you. You're no great shakes as a son. It's a case of "A poor thing but mine own."[2] [*They both chuckle with real, if alcoholic, affection.* TYRONE *changes the subject.*] What's happened to our game? Whose play is it?

EDMUND   Yours, I guess.

[TYRONE *plays a card which* EDMUND *takes and the game gets forgotten again.*]

TYRONE   You mustn't let yourself be too downhearted, lad, by the bad news you had today. Both the doctors promised me, if you obey orders at this place you're going, you'll be cured in six months, or a year at most.

EDMUND [*his face hard again*]   Don't kid me. You don't believe that.

TYRONE [*too vehemently*]   Of course I believe it! Why shouldn't I believe it when both Hardy and the specialist—?

2. Shakespeare's *As You Like It* 5.4.60.

EDMUND   You think I'm going to die.

TYRONE   That's a lie! You're crazy!

EDMUND [*more bitterly*]   So why waste money? That's why you're sending me to a state farm—

TYRONE [*in guilty confusion*]   What state farm? It's the Hilltown Sanatorium, that's all I know, and both doctors said it was the best place for you.

EDMUND [*scathingly*]   For the money! That is, for nothing, or practically nothing. Don't lie, Papa! You know damned well Hilltown Sanatorium is a state institution! Jamie suspected you'd cry poorhouse to Hardy and he wormed the truth out of him.

TYRONE [*furiously*]   That drunken loafer! I'll kick him out in the gutter! He's poisoned your mind against me ever since you were old enough to listen!

EDMUND   You can't deny it's the truth about the state farm, can you?

TYRONE   It's not true the way you look at it! What if it is run by the state? That's nothing against it. The state has the money to make a better place than any private sanatorium. And why shouldn't I take advantage of it? It's my right—and yours. We're residents. I'm a property owner. I help to support it. I'm taxed to death—

EDMUND [*with bitter irony*]   Yes, on property valued at a quarter of a million.

TYRONE   Lies! It's all mortgaged!

EDMUND   Hardy and the specialist know what you're worth. I wonder what they thought of you when they heard you moaning poorhouse and showing you wanted to wish me on charity!

TYRONE   It's a lie! All I told them was I couldn't afford any millionaire's sanatorium because I was land poor. That's the truth!

EDMUND   And then you went to the Club to meet McGuire and let him stick you with another bum piece of property! [*as* TYRONE *starts to deny*] Don't lie about it! We met McGuire in the hotel bar after he left you. Jamie kidded him about hooking you, and he winked and laughed!

TYRONE [*lying feebly*]   He's a liar if he said—

EDMUND   Don't lie about it! [*with gathering intensity*] God, Papa, ever since I went to sea and was on my own, and found out what hard work for little pay was, and what it felt like to be broke, and starve, and camp on park benches because I had no place to sleep, I've tried to be fair to you because I knew what you'd been up against as a kid. I've tried to make allowances. Christ, you have to make allowances in this damned family or go nuts! I have tried to make allowances for myself when I remember all the rotten stuff I've pulled! I've tried to feel like Mama that you can't help being what you are where money is concerned. But God Almighty, this last stunt of yours is too much! It makes me want to puke! Not because of the rotten way you're treating me. To hell with that! I've treated you rottenly, in my way, more than once. But to think when it's a question of your son having consumption, you can show yourself up before the whole town as such a stinking old tightwad! Don't you know Hardy will talk and the whole damned town will know! Jesus, Papa, haven't you any pride or shame? [*bursting with rage*] And don't think I'll let you get away with it! I won't go to any damned state farm just to save you a few lousy dollars to buy more bum property with! You stinking old miser—! [*He chokes huskily, his voice trembling with rage, and then is shaken by a fit of coughing.*]

TYRONE [*has shrunk back in his chair under this attack, his guilty contrition greater than his anger—he stammers*] Be quiet! Don't say that to me! You're drunk! I won't mind you. Stop coughing, lad. You've got yourself worked up over nothing. Who said you had to go to this Hilltown place? You can go anywhere you like. I don't give a damn what it costs. All I care about is to have you get well. Don't call me a stinking miser, just because I don't want doctors to think I'm a millionaire they can swindle.

> [EDMUND *has stopped coughing. He looks sick and weak. His father stares at him frightenedly.*]

You look weak, lad. You'd better take a bracer.

EDMUND [*grabs the bottle and pours his glass brimfull—weakly*] Thanks. [*He gulps down the whiskey.*]

TYRONE [*pours himself a big drink, which empties the bottle, and drinks it; his head bows and he stares dully at the cards on the table—vaguely*] Whose play is it? [*He goes on dully, without resentment.*] A stinking old miser. Well, maybe you're right. Maybe I can't help being, although all my life since I had anything I've thrown money over the bar to buy drinks for everyone in the house, or loaned money to sponges I knew would never pay it back—[*with a loose-mouthed sneer of self-contempt*] But, of course, that was in barrooms, when I was full of whiskey. I can't feel that way about it when I'm sober in my home. It was at home I first learned the value of a dollar and the fear of the poorhouse. I've never been able to believe in my luck since. I've always feared it would change and everything I had would be taken away. But still, the more property you own, the safer you think you are. That may not be logical, but it's the way I have to feel. Banks fail, and your money's gone, but you think you can keep land beneath your feet. [*Abruptly his tone becomes scornfully superior.*] You said you realized what I'd been up against as a boy. The hell you do! How could you? You've had everything—nurses, schools, college, though you didn't stay there. You've had food, clothing. Oh, I know you had a fling of hard work with your back and hands, a bit of being homeless and penniless in a foreign land, and I respect you for it. But it was a game of romance and adventure to you. It was play.

EDMUND [*dully sarcastic*] Yes, particularly the time I tried to commit suicide at Jimmie the Priest's, and almost did.

TYRONE You weren't in your right mind. No son of mine would ever—You were drunk.

EDMUND I was stone cold sober. That was the trouble. I'd stopped to think too long.

TYRONE [*with drunken peevishness*] Don't start your damned atheist morbidness again! I don't care to listen. I was trying to make plain to you—[*scornfully*] What do you know of the value of a dollar? When I was ten my father deserted my mother and went back to Ireland to die. Which he did soon enough, and deserved to, and I hope he's roasting in hell. He mistook rat poison for flour, or sugar, or something. There was gossip it wasn't by mistake but that's a lie. No one in my family ever—

EDMUND My bet is, it wasn't by mistake.

TYRONE More morbidness! Your brother put that in your head. The worst he can suspect is the only truth for him. But never mind. My mother was left, a stranger in a strange land, with four small children, me and a sister a little older and two younger than me. My two older brothers had moved to other parts. They couldn't help. They were hard put to it to keep themselves alive. There was no damned romance in our poverty. Twice we were evicted from the miserable hovel we called home, with my mother's few sticks of furniture thrown out in the street, and my mother and sisters crying. I cried, too, though I tried hard not to, because I was the man of the family. At ten years old! There was no more school for me. I worked twelve hours a day in a machine shop, learning to make files. A dirty barn of a place where rain dripped through the roof, where you roasted in summer, and there was no stove in winter, and your hands got numb with cold, where the only light came through two small filthy windows, so on grey days I'd have to sit bent over with my eyes almost touching the files in order to see! You talk of work! And what do you think I got for it? Fifty cents a week! It's the truth! Fifty cents a week! And my poor mother washed and scrubbed for the Yanks by the day, and my older sister sewed, and my two younger stayed at home to keep the house. We never had clothes enough to wear, nor enough food to eat. Well I remember one Thanksgiving, or maybe it was Christmas, when some Yank in whose house mother had been scrubbing gave her a dollar extra for a present, and on the way home she spent it all on food. I can remember her hugging and kissing us and saying with tears of joy running down her tired face: "Glory be to God, for once in our lives we'll have enough for each of us!" [He wipes tears from his eyes.] A fine, brave, sweet woman. There never was a braver or finer.

EDMUND [moved]   Yes, she must have been.

TYRONE   Her one fear was she'd get old and sick and have to die in the poorhouse. [He pauses—then adds with grim humor] It was in those days I learned to be a miser. A dollar was worth so much then. And once you've learned a lesson, it's hard to unlearn it. You have to look for bargains. If I took this state farm sanatorium for a good bargain, you'll have to forgive me. The doctors did tell me it's a good place. You must believe that, Edmund. And I swear I never meant you to go there if you didn't want to. [vehemently] You can choose any place you like! Never mind what it costs! Any place I can afford. Any place you like—within reason.

> [At this qualification, a grin twitches EDMUND's lips. His resentment has
> gone. His father goes on with an elaborately offhand, casual air.]

There was another sanatorium the specialist recommended. He said it had a record as good as any place in the country. It's endowed by a group of millionaire factory owners, for the benefit of their workers principally, but you're eligible to go there because you're a resident. There's such a pile of money behind it, they don't have to charge much. It's only seven dollars a week but you get ten times that value. [hastily] I don't want to persuade you to anything, understand. I'm simply repeating what I was told.

EDMUND [concealing his smile—casually]   Oh, I know that. It sounds like a good bargain to me. I'd like to go there. So that settles that. [Abruptly he is miserably desperate again—dully] It doesn't matter a damn now, anyway. Let's forget it! [changing the subject] How about our game? Whose play is it?

TYRONE [mechanically]   I don't know. Mine, I guess. No, it's yours.

[EDMUND *plays a card. His father takes it. Then about to play from his hand, he again forgets the game.*]

Yes, maybe life overdid the lesson for me, and made a dollar worth too much, and the time came when that mistake ruined my career as a fine actor. [*sadly*] I've never admitted this to anyone before, lad, but tonight I'm so heartsick I feel at the end of everything, and what's the use of fake pride and pretense. That God-damned play I bought for a song and made such a great success in—a great money success—it ruined me with its promise of an easy fortune. I didn't want to do anything else, and by the time I woke up to the fact I'd become a slave to the damned thing and did try other plays, it was too late. They had identified me with that one part, and didn't want me in anything else. They were right, too. I'd lost the great talent I once had through years of easy repetition, never learning a new part, never really working hard. Thirty-five to forty thousand dollars net profit a season like snapping your fingers! It was too great a temptation. Yet before I bought the damned thing I was considered one of the three or four young actors with the greatest artistic promise in America. I'd worked like hell. I'd left a good job as a machinist to take supers'[3] parts because I loved the theater. I was wild with ambition. I read all the plays ever written. I studied Shakespeare as you'd study the Bible. I educated myself. I got rid of an Irish brogue you could cut with a knife. I loved Shakespeare. I would have acted in any of his plays for nothing, for the joy of being alive in his great poetry. And I acted well in him. I felt inspired by him. I could have been a great Shakespearean actor, if I'd kept on. I know that! In 1874 when Edwin Booth[4] came to the theater in Chicago where I was leading man, I played Cassius to his Brutus one night, Brutus to his Cassius the next, Othello to his Iago, and so on. The first night I played Othello, he said to our manager. "That young man is playing Othello better than I ever did!" [*proudly*] That from Booth, the greatest actor of his day or any other! And it was true! And I was only twenty-seven years old! As I look back on it now, that night was the high spot in my career. I had life where I wanted it! And for a time after that I kept on upward with ambition high. Married your mother. Ask her what I was like in those days. Her love was an added incentive to ambition. But a few years later my good bad luck made me find the big money-maker. It wasn't that in my eyes at first. It was a great romantic part I knew I could play better than anyone. But it was a great box office success from the start—and then life had me where it wanted me—at from thirty-five to forty thousand net profit a season! A fortune in those days—or even in these. [*bitterly*] What the hell was it I wanted to buy, I wonder, that was worth—Well, no matter. It's a late day for regrets. [*He glances vaguely at his cards.*] My play, isn't it?

EDMUND [*moved, stares at his father with understanding—slowly*]   I'm glad you've told me this, Papa. I know you a lot better now.

TYRONE [*with a loose, twisted smile*]   Maybe I shouldn't have told you. Maybe you'll only feel more contempt for me. And it's a poor way to convince you of the value of a dollar. [*Then as if this phrase automatically aroused an habitual association in his mind, he glances up at the chande-*

---

3. Supernumeraries, extras.
4. Edwin Booth (1833–1893), American actor and theatrical manager.

lier disapprovingly.] The glare from those extra lights hurts my eyes. You
don't mind if I turn them out, do you? We don't need them, and there's
no use making the Electric Company rich.

EDMUND [*controlling a wild impulse to laugh—agreeably*]   No, sure not.
Turn them out.

TYRONE [*gets heavily and a bit waveringly to his feet and gropes uncertainly
for the lights—his mind going back to its line of thought*]   No, I don't
know what the hell it was I wanted to buy. [*He clicks out one bulb.*] On
my solemn oath, Edmund, I'd gladly face not having an acre of land to call
my own, nor a penny in the bank—[*He clicks out another bulb.*] I'd be
willing to have no home but the poorhouse in my old age if I could look
back now on having been the fine artist I might have been.

    [*He turns out the third bulb, so only the reading lamp is on, and sits down
    again heavily.* EDMUND *suddenly cannot hold back a burst of strained,
    ironical laughter.* TYRONE *is hurt.*]

What the devil are you laughing at?

EDMUND   Not at you, Papa. At life. It's so damned crazy.

TYRONE [*growls*]   More of your morbidness! There's nothing wrong with
life. It's we who—[*He quotes*] "The fault, dear Brutus, is not in our stars,
but in ourselves that we are underlings."[5] [*He pauses—then sadly*] The
praise Edwin Booth gave my Othello. I made the manager put down his
exact words in writing. I kept it in my wallet for years. I used to read it
every once in a while until finally it made me feel so bad I didn't want to
face it any more. Where is it now, I wonder? Somewhere in this house. I
remember I put it away carefully—

EDMUND [*with a wry ironical sadness*]   It might be in an old trunk in the
attic, along with Mama's wedding dress. [*Then as his father stares at him,
he adds quickly*] For Pete's sake, if we're going to play cards, let's play.

    [*He takes the card his father had played and leads. For a moment, they
    play the game, like mechanical chess players. Then* TYRONE *stops, listen-
    ing to a sound upstairs.*]

TYRONE   She's still moving around. God knows when she'll go to sleep.

EDMUND [*pleads tensely*]   For Christ's sake, Papa, forget it!

    [*He reaches out and pours a drink.* TYRONE *starts to protest, then gives it
    up.* EDMUND *drinks. He puts down the glass. His expression changes.
    When he speaks it is as if he were deliberately giving way to drunkenness
    and seeking to hide behind a maudlin manner.*]

Yes, she moves above and beyond us, a ghost haunting the past, and here
we sit pretending to forget, but straining our ears listening for the slightest sound, hearing the fog drip from the eaves like the uneven tick of a
rundown, crazy clock—or like the dreary tears of a trollop spattering in a
puddle of stale beer on a honky-tonk table top! [*He laughs with maudlin
appreciation.*] Not so bad, that last, eh? Original, not Baudelaire. Give me
credit! [*then with alcoholic talkativeness*] You've just told me some high
spots in your memories. Want to hear mine? They're all connected with
the sea. Here's one. When I was on the Squarehead square rigger, bound
for Buenos Aires. Full moon in the Trades. The old hooker driving fourteen knots. I lay on the bowsprit, facing astern, with the water foaming
into spume under me, the masts with every sail white in the moonlight,
towering high above me. I became drunk with the beauty and singing

5. Shakespeare's *Julius Caesar* 1.2.134.

rhythm of it, and for a moment I lost myself—actually lost my life. I was set free! I dissolved in the sea, became white sails and flying spray, became beauty and rhythm, became moonlight and the ship and the high dim-starred sky! I belonged, without past or future, within peace and unity and a wild joy, within something greater than my own life, or the life of Man, to Life itself! To God, if you want to put it that way. Then another time, on the American Line, when I was lookout on the crow's nest in the dawn watch. A calm sea, that time. Only a lazy ground swell and a slow drowsy roll of the ship. The passengers asleep and none of the crew in sight. No sound of man. Black smoke pouring from the funnels behind and beneath me. Dreaming, not keeping lookout, feeling alone, and above, and apart, watching the dawn creep like a painted dream over the sky and sea which slept together. Then the moment of ecstatic freedom came. The peace, the end of the quest, the last harbor, the joy of belonging to a fulfillment beyond men's lousy, pitiful, greedy fears and hopes and dreams! And several other times in my life, when I was swimming far out, or lying alone on a beach, I have had the same experience. Became the sun, the hot sand, green seaweed anchored to a rock, swaying in the tide. Like a saint's vision of beatitude. Like the veil of things as they seem drawn back by an unseen hand. For a second you see—and seeing the secret, are the secret. For a second there is meaning! Then the hand lets the veil fall and you are alone, lost in the fog again, and you stumble on toward nowhere, for no good reason! [*He grins wryly.*] It was a great mistake, my being born a man, I would have been much more successful as a sea gull or a fish. As it is, I will always be a stranger who never feels at home, who does not really want and is not really wanted, who can never belong, who must always be a little in love with death!

TYRONE [*stares at him—impressed*]   Yes, there's the makings of a poet in you all right. [*then protesting uneasily*] But that's morbid craziness about not being wanted and loving death.

EDMUND [*sardonically*]   The *makings* of a poet. No, I'm afraid I'm like the guy who is always panhandling for a smoke. He hasn't even got the makings. He's got only the habit. I couldn't touch what I tried to tell you just now. I just stammered. That's the best I'll ever do. I mean, if I live. Well, it will be faithful realism, at least. Stammering is the native eloquence of us fog people.

> [*A pause. Then they both jump startledly as there is a noise from outside the house, as if someone had stumbled and fallen on the front steps.* EDMUND *grins.*]

Well, that sounds like the absent brother. He must have a peach of a bun on.

TYRONE [*scowling*]   That loafer! He caught the last car, bad luck to it. [*He gets to his feet.*] Get him to bed, Edmund. I'll go out on the porch. He has a tongue like an adder when he's drunk. I'd only lose my temper.

> [*He goes out the door to the side porch as the front door in the hall bangs shut behind* JAMIE. EDMUND *watches with amusement* JAMIE's *wavering progress through the front parlor.* JAMIE *comes in. He is very drunk and woozy on his legs. His eyes are glassy, his face bloated, his speech blurred, his mouth slack like his father's, a leer on his lips.*]

JAMIE [*swaying and blinking in the doorway—in a loud voice*]   What ho! What ho!

EDMUND [*sharply*]   Nix on the loud noise!

JAMIE [*blinks at him*]   Oh, hello, Kid. [*with great seriousness*] I'm as drunk as a fiddler's bitch.

EDMUND [*dryly*]   Thanks for telling me your great secret.

JAMIE [*grins foolishly*]   Yes. Unneshesary information Number One, eh? [*He bends and slaps at the knees of his trousers.*] Had serious accident. The front steps tried to trample on me. Took advantage of fog to waylay me. Ought to be a lighthouse out there. Dark in here, too. [*scowling*] What the hell is this, the morgue? Lesh have some light on subject. [*He sways forward to the table, reciting Kipling[6]*]

> "Ford, ford, ford o' Kabul river,
> Ford o' Kabul river in the dark!
> Keep the crossing-stakes beside you, an' they
>   will surely guide you
> 'Cross the ford o' Kabul river in the dark."

[*He fumbles at the chandelier and manages to turn on the three bulbs.*] Thash more like it. The hell with old Gaspard.[7] Where is the old tight-wad?

EDMUND   Out on the porch.

JAMIE   Can't expect us to live in the Black Hole of Calcutta.[8] [*His eyes fix on the full bottle of whiskey.*] Say! Have I got the d.t.'s?[9] [*He reaches out fumblingly and grabs it.*] By God, it's real. What's matter with the Old Man tonight? Must be ossified to forget he left this out. Grab opportunity by the forelock. Key to my success. [*He slops a big drink into a glass.*]

EDMUND   You're stinking now. That will knock you stiff.

JAMIE   Wisdom from the mouth of babes. Can the wise stuff, Kid. You're still wet behind the ears. [*He lowers himself into a chair, holding the drink carefully aloft.*]

EDMUND   All right. Pass out if you want to.

JAMIE   Can't, that's trouble. Had enough to sink a ship, but can't sink. Well, here's hoping. [*He drinks.*]

EDMUND   Shove over the bottle. I'll have one, too.

JAMIE [*with sudden, big-brotherly solicitude, grabbing the bottle*]   No, you don't. Not while I'm around. Remember doctor's orders. Maybe no one else gives a damn if you die, but I do. My kid brother. I love your guts, Kid. Everything else is gone. You're all I've got left. [*pulling bottle closer to him*] So no booze for you, if I can help it. [*Beneath his drunken sentimentality there is a genuine sincerity.*]

EDMUND [*irritably*]   Oh, lay off it.

JAMIE [*is hurt and his face hardens*]   You don't believe I care, eh? Just drunken bull. [*He shoves the bottle over.*] All right. Go ahead and kill yourself.

EDMUND [*seeing he is hurt—affectionately*]   Sure I know you care, Jamie, and I'm going on the wagon. But tonight doesn't count. Too many damned things have happened today. [*He pours a drink.*] Here's how. [*He drinks.*]

---

6. Rudyard Kipling (1865–1936), English author.
7. Jamie's contemptuous name for his father, drawn from a character in the popular drama *The Bells*.

8. Small dungeon in Calcutta, India, where, on June 20, 1756, 123 of 146 British prisoners died of suffocation. Hence, any small, cramped space.
9. Delirium tremens.

JAMIE [*sobers up momentarily and with a pitying look*]   I know, Kid. It's been a lousy day for you. [*then with sneering cynicism*] I'll bet old Gaspard hasn't tried to keep you off booze. Probably give you a case to take with you to the state farm for pauper patients. The sooner you kick the bucket, the less expense. [*with contemptuous hatred*] What a bastard to have for a father! Christ, if you put him in a book, no one would believe it!

EDMUND [*defensively*]   Oh, Papa's all right, if you try to understand him—and keep your sense of humor.

JAMIE [*cynically*]   He's been putting on the old sob act for you, eh? He can always kid you. But not me. Never again. [*then slowly*] Although, in a way, I do feel sorry for him about one thing. But he has even that coming to him. He's to blame. [*hurriedly*] But to hell with that. [*He grabs the bottle and pours another drink, appearing very drunk again.*] That lash drink's getting me. This one ought to put the lights out. Did you tell Gaspard I got it out of Doc Hardy this sanatorium is a charity dump?

EDMUND [*reluctantly*]   Yes. I told him I wouldn't go there. It's all settled now. He said I can go anywhere I want. [*He adds, smiling without resentment*] Within reason, of course.

JAMIE [*drunkenly imitating his father*]   Of course, lad. Anything within reason. [*sneering*] That means another cheap dump. Old Gaspard, the miser in "The Bells," that's a part he can play without make-up.

EDMUND [*irritably*]   Oh, shut up, will you. I've heard that Gaspard stuff a million times.

JAMIE [*shrugs his shoulders—thickly*]   Aw right, if you're shatisfied—let him get away with it. It's your funeral—I mean, I hope it won't be.

EDMUND [*changing the subject*]   What did you do uptown tonight? Go to Mamie Burns?

JAMIE [*very drunk, his head nodding*]   Sure thing. Where else could I find suitable feminine companionship? And love. Don't forget love. What is a man without a good woman's love? A God-damned hollow shell.

EDMUND [*chuckles tipsily, letting himself go now and be drunk*]   You're a nut.

JAMIE [*quotes with gusto from Oscar Wilde's[1] "The Harlot's House"*]

> "Then, turning to my love, I said,
> 'The dead are dancing with the dead,
> The dust is whirling with the dust.'
>
> But she—she heard the violin,
> And left my side and entered in:
> Love passed into the house of lust.
>
> Then suddenly the tune went false,
> The dancers wearied of the waltz . . ."

[*He breaks off, thickly*] Not strictly accurate. If my love was with me, I didn't notice it. She must have been a ghost. [*He pauses.*] Guess which one of Mamie's charmers I picked to bless me with her woman's love. It'll hand you a laugh, Kid. I picked Fat Violet.

EDMUND [*laughs drunkenly*]   No, honest? Some pick! God, she weighs a ton. What the hell for, a joke?

---

1. Irish author (1854–1900).

JAMIE   No joke. Very serious. By the time I hit Mamie's dump I felt very sad about myself and all the other poor bums in the world. Ready for a weep on any old womanly bosom. You know how you get when John Barleycorn turns on the soft music inside you. Then, soon as I got in the door, Mamie began telling me all her troubles. Beefed how rotten business was, and she was going to give Fat Violet the gate. Customers didn't fall for Vi. Only reason she'd kept her was she could play the piano. Lately Vi's gone on drunks and been too boiled to play, and was eating her out of house and home, and although Vi was a goodhearted dumbbell, and she felt sorry for her because she didn't know how the hell she'd make a living, still business was business, and she couldn't afford to run a house for fat tarts. Well, that made me feel sorry for Fat Violet, so I squandered two bucks of your dough to escort her upstairs. With no dishonorable intentions whatever. I like them fat, but not that fat. All I wanted was a little heart-to-heart talk concerning the infinite sorrow of life.

EDMUND [*chuckles drunkenly*]   Poor Vi! I'll bet you recited Kipling and Swinburne and Dowson and gave her "I have been faithful to thee, Cynara, in my fashion."

JAMIE [*grins loosely*]   Sure—with the Old Master, John Barleycorn, playing soft music. She stood it for a while. Then she got good and sore. Got the idea I took her upstairs for a joke. Gave me a grand bawling out. Said she was better than a drunken bum who recited poetry. Then she began to cry. So I had to say I loved her because she was fat, and she wanted to believe that, and I stayed with her to prove it, and that cheered her up, and she kissed me when I left, and said she'd fallen hard for me, and we both cried a little more in the hallway, and everything was fine, except Mamie Burns thought I'd gone bughouse.

EDMUND [*quotes derisively*]

> "Harlots and
> Hunted have pleasures of their own to give,
> The vulgar herd can never understand."

JAMIE [*nods his head drunkenly*]   Egzactly! Hell of a good time, at that. You should have stuck around with me, Kid. Mamie Burns inquired after you. Sorry to hear you were sick. She meant it, too. [*He pauses—then with maudlin humor, in a ham-actor tone*] This night has opened my eyes to a great career in store for me, my boy! I shall give the art of acting back to the performing seals, which are its most perfect expression. By applying my natural God-given talents in their proper sphere, I shall attain the pinnacle of success! I'll be the lover of the fat woman in Barnum and Bailey's circus! [EDMUND *laughs.* JAMIE'S *mood changes to arrogant disdain.*] Pah! Imagine me sunk to the fat girl in a hick town hooker shop! Me! Who have made some of the best-lookers on Broadway sit up and beg! [*He quotes from Kipling's "Sestina of the Tramp-Royal"*]

> "Speakin' in general, I 'ave tried 'em all,
> The 'appy roads that take you o'er the world."

[*with sodden melancholy*] Not so apt. Happy roads is bunk. Weary roads is right. Get you nowhere fast. That's where I've got—nowhere. Where everyone lands in the end, even if most of the suckers won't admit it.

EDMUND [*derisively*] Can it! You'll be crying in a minute.

JAMIE [*starts and stares at his brother for a second with bitter hostility—thickly*] Don't get—too damned fresh. [*then abruptly*] But you're right. To hell with repining! Fat Violet's a good kid. Glad I stayed with her. Christian act. Cured her blues. Hell of a good time. You should have stuck with me, Kid. Taken your mind off your troubles. What's the use coming home to get the blues over what can't be helped. All over—finished now—not a hope! [*He stops, his head nodding drunkenly, his eyes closing—then suddenly he looks up, his face hard, and quotes jeeringly.*]

> "If I were hanged on the highest hill,
> Mother o' mine, O mother o' mine!
> I know whose love would follow me still . . ."

EDMUND [*violently*] Shut up!

JAMIE [*in a cruel, sneering tone with hatred in it*] Where's the hophead? Gone to sleep?

> [EDMUND *jerks as if he'd been struck. There is a tense silence.* EDMUND'S *face looks stricken and sick. Then in a burst of rage he springs from his chair.*]

EDMUND You dirty bastard!

> [*He punches his brother in the face, a blow that glances off the cheekbone. For a second* JAMIE *reacts pugnaciously and half rises from his chair to do battle, but suddenly he seems to sober up to a shocked realization of what he has said and he sinks back limply.*]

JAMIE [*miserably*] Thanks, Kid. I certainly had that coming. Don't know what made me—booze talking—You know me, Kid.

EDMUND [*his anger ebbing*] I know you'd never say that unless—But God, Jamie, no matter how drunk you are, it's no excuse! [*He pauses—miserably*] I'm sorry I hit you. You and I never scrap—that bad. [*He sinks back on his chair.*]

JAMIE [*huskily*] It's all right. Glad you did. My dirty tongue. Like to cut it out. [*He hides his face in his hands—dully*] I suppose it's because I feel so damned sunk. Because this time Mama had me fooled. I really believed she had it licked. She thinks I always believe the worst, but this time I believed the best. [*His voice flutters.*] I suppose I can't forgive her—yet. It meant so much. I'd begun to hope, if she'd beaten the game, I could, too. [*He begins to sob, and the horrible part of his weeping is that it appears sober, not the maudlin tears of drunkenness.*]

EDMUND [*blinking back tears himself*] God, don't I know how you feel! Stop it, Jamie!

JAMIE [*trying to control his sobs*] I've known about Mama so much longer than you. Never forget the first time I got wise. Caught her in the act with a hypo. Christ, I'd never dreamed before that any women but whores took dope! [*He pauses.*] And then this stuff of you getting consumption. It's got me licked. We've been more than brothers. You're the only pal I've ever had. I love your guts. I'd do anything for you.

EDMUND [*reaches out and pats his arm*] I know that, Jamie.

JAMIE [*his crying over—drops his hands from his face—with a strange bitterness*] Yet I'll bet you've heard Mama and old Gaspard spill so much bunk about my hoping for the worst, you suspect right now I'm thinking to myself that Papa is old and can't last much longer, and if you were to die, Mama and I would get all he's got, and so I'm probably hoping—

EDMUND [*indignantly*]   Shut up, you damned fool! What the hell put that in your nut? [*He stares at his brother accusingly.*] Yes, that's what I'd like to know. What put that in your mind?

JAMIE [*confusedly—appearing drunk again*]   Don't be a dumbbell! What I said! Always suspected of hoping for the worst. I've got so I can't help— [*then drunkenly resentful*] What are you trying to do, accuse me? Don't play the wise guy with me! I've learned more of life than you'll ever know! Just because you've read a lot of highbrow junk, don't think you can fool me! You're only an overgrown kid! Mama's baby and Papa's pet! The family White Hope! You've been getting a swelled head lately. About nothing! About a few poems in a hick town newspaper! Hell, I used to write better stuff for the Lit magazine in college! You better wake up! You're setting no rivers on fire! You let hick town boobs flatter you with bunk about your future—

[*Abruptly his tone changes to disgusted contrition.* EDMUND *has looked away from him, trying to ignore this tirade.*]

Hell, Kid, forget it. That goes for Sweeny. You know I don't mean it. No one hopes more than I do you'll knock 'em all dead. No one is prouder you've started to make good. [*drunkenly assertive*] Why shouldn't I be proud? Hell, it's purely selfish. You reflect credit on me. I've had more to do with bringing you up than anyone. I wised you up about women, so you'd never be a fall guy, or make any mistakes you didn't want to make! And who steered you on to reading poetry first? Swinburne,[2] for example? I did! And because I once wanted to write, I planted it in your mind that someday you'd write! Hell, you're more than my brother. I made you! You're my Frankenstein![3]

[*He has risen to a note of drunken arrogance.* EDMUND *is grinning with amusement now.*]

EDMUND   All right, I'm your Frankenstein. So let's have a drink. [*He laughs.*] You crazy nut!

JAMIE [*thickly*]   I'll have a drink. Not you. Got to take care of you. [*He reaches out with a foolish grin of doting affection and grabs his brother's hand.*] Don't be scared of this sanatorium business. Hell, you can beat that standing on your head. Six months and you'll be in the pink. Probably haven't got consumption at all. Doctors lot of fakers. Told me years ago to cut out booze or I'd soon be dead—and here I am. They're all con men. Anything to grab your dough. I'll bet this state farm stuff is political graft game. Doctors get a cut for every patient they send.

EDMUND [*disgustedly amused*]   You're the limit! At the Last Judgment, you'll be around telling everyone it's in the bag.

JAMIE   And I'll be right. Slip a piece of change to the Judge and be saved, but if you're broke you can go to hell!

[*He grins at this blasphemy and* EDMUND *has to laugh.* JAMIE *goes on.*] "Therefore put money in thy purse."[4] That's the only dope. [*mockingly*] The secret of my success! Look what it's got me!

---

2. Algernon Charles Swinburne (1837–1909), English poet and critic.
3. In the novel *Frankenstein* by the English author Mary Shelley (1797–1851), the scientist Dr.

Frankenstein creates a monster. Jamie confuses the scientist with his creation, although it is possible that the mistake is O'Neill's.
4. Shakespeare's *Othello* 1.3.354.

[*He lets* EDMUND's *hand go to pour a big drink, and gulps it down. He stares at his brother with bleary affection—takes his hand again and begins to talk thickly but with a strange, convincing sincerity.*]

Listen, Kid, you'll be going away. May not get another chance to talk. Or might not be drunk enough to tell you truth. So got to tell you now. Something I ought to have told you long ago—for your own good.

[*He pauses—struggling with himself.* EDMUND *stares, impressed and uneasy. Jamie blurts out*]

Not drunken bull, but "in vino veritas"[5] stuff. You better take it seriously. Want to warn you—against me. Mama and Papa are right. I've been rotten bad influence. And worst of it is, I did it on purpose.

EDMUND [*uneasily*]   Shut up! I don't want to hear—

JAMIE   Nix, Kid! You listen! Did it on purpose to make a bum of you. Or part of me did. A big part. That part that's been dead so long. That hates life. My putting you wise so you'd learn from my mistakes. Believed that myself at times, but it's a fake. Made my mistakes look good. Made getting drunk romantic. Made whores fascinating vampires instead of poor, stupid, diseased slobs they really are. Made fun of work as sucker's game. Never wanted you to succeed and make me look even worse by comparison. Wanted you to fail. Always jealous of you. Mama's baby, Papa's pet! [*He stares at* EDMUND *with increasing enmity.*] And it was your being born that started Mama on dope. I know that's not your fault, but all the same, God damn you, I can't help hating your guts—!

EDMUND [*almost frightenedly*]   Jamie! Cut it out! You're crazy!

JAMIE   But don't get wrong idea, Kid. I love you more than I hate you. My saying what I'm telling you now proves it. I run the risk you'll hate me— and you're all I've got left. But I didn't mean to tell you that last stuff— go that far back. Don't know what made me. What I wanted to say is, I'd like to see you become the greatest success in the world. But you'd better be on your guard. Because I'll do my damnedest to make you fail. Can't help it. I hate myself. Got to take revenge. On everyone else. Especially you. Oscar Wilde's "Reading Gaol" has the dope twisted. The man was dead and so he had to kill the thing he loved. That's what it ought to be. The dead part of me hopes you won't get well. Maybe he's even glad the game has got Mama again! He wants company, he doesn't want to be the only corpse around the house! [*He gives a hard, tortured laugh.*]

EDMUND   Jesus, Jamie! You really have gone crazy!

JAMIE   Think it over and you'll see I'm right. Think it over when you're away from me in the sanatorium. Make up your mind you've got to tie a can to me—get me out of your life—think of me as dead—tell people, "I had a brother, but he's dead." And when you come back, look out for me. I'll be waiting to welcome you with that "my old pal" stuff, and give you the glad hand, and at the first good chance I get stab you in the back.

EDMUND   Shut up! I'll be God-damned if I'll listen to you any more—

JAMIE [*as if he hadn't heard*]   Only don't forget me. Remember I warned you—for your sake. Give me credit. Greater love hath no man than this, that he saveth his brother from himself. [*very drunkenly, his head bob-*

5. In wine there is truth (Latin).

bing] That's all. Feel better now. Gone to confession. Know you absolve me, don't you, Kid? You understand. You're a damned fine kid. Ought to be. I made you. So go and get well. Don't die on me. You're all I've got left. God bless you, Kid. [*His eyes close. He mumbles*] That last drink— the old K. O.

> [*He falls into a drunken doze, not completely asleep.* EDMUND *buries his face in his hands miserably.* TYRONE *comes in quietly through the screen door from the porch, his dressing gown wet with fog, the collar turned up around his throat. His face is stern and disgusted but at the same time pitying.* EDMUND *does not notice his entrance.*]

TYRONE [*in a low voice*]   Thank God he's asleep.

> [EDMUND *looks up with a start.*]

I thought he'd never stop talking. [*He turns down the collar of his dressing gown.*] We'd better let him stay where he is and sleep it off.

> [EDMUND *remains silent.* TYRONE *regards him—then goes on*]

I heard the last part of his talk. It's what I've warned you. I hope you'll heed the warning, now it comes from his own mouth.

> [EDMUND *gives no sign of having heard.* TYRONE *adds pityingly*]

But don't take it too much to heart, lad. He loves to exaggerate the worst of himself when he's drunk. He's devoted to you. It's the one good thing left in him. [*He looks down on* JAMIE *with a bitter sadness.*] A sweet spectacle for me! My first-born, who I hoped would bear my name in honor and dignity, who showed such brilliant promise!

EDMUND [*miserably*]   Keep quiet, can't you, Papa?

TYRONE [*pours a drink*]   A waste! A wreck, a drunken hulk, done with and finished!

> [*He drinks.* JAMIE *has become restless, sensing his father's presence, struggling up from his stupor. Now he gets his eyes open to blink up at* TYRONE. *The latter moves back a step defensively, his face growing hard.*]

JAMIE [*suddenly points a finger at him and recites with dramatic emphasis*]

> "Clarence is come, false, fleeting, perjured Clarence,
> That stabbed me in the field by Tewksbury.
> Seize on him, Furies, take him into torment."[6]

[*then resentfully*] What the hell are you staring at? [*He recites sardonically from Rossetti*[7]]

> "Look in my face. My name is Might-Have-Been;
> I am also called No More, Too Late, Farewell."

TYRONE   I'm well aware of that, and God knows I don't want to look at it.

EDMUND   Papa! Quit it!

JAMIE [*derisively*]   Got a great idea for you, Papa. Put on revival of "The Bells" this season. Great part in it you can play without make-up. Old Gaspard, the miser!

> [TYRONE *turns away, trying to control his temper.*]

---

6. Shakespeare's *Richard III* 1.4.55–57.
7. Dante Gabriel Rossetti (1821–1882), English poet and painter.

EDMUND   Shut up, Jamie!

JAMIE [*jeeringly*]   I claim Edwin Booth never saw the day when he could give as good a performance as a trained seal. Seals are intelligent and honest. They don't put up any bluffs about the Art of Acting. They admit they're just hams earning their daily fish.

TYRONE [*stung, turns on him in a rage*]   You loafer!

EDMUND   Papa! Do you want to start a row that will bring Mama down? Jamie, go back to sleep! You've shot off your mouth too much already.
[TYRONE *turns away.*]

JAMIE [*thickly*]   All right, Kid. Not looking for argument. Too damned sleepy.
[*He closes his eyes, his head nodding.* TYRONE *comes to the table and sits down, turning his chair so he won't look at* JAMIE. *At once he becomes sleepy, too.*]

TYRONE [*heavily*]   I wish to God she'd go to bed so that I could, too. [*drowsily*] I'm dog tired. I can't stay up all night like I used to. Getting old—old and finished. [*with a bone-cracking yawn*] Can't keep my eyes open. I think I'll catch a few winks. Why don't you do the same, Edmund? It'll pass the time until she—
[*His voice trails off. His eyes close, his chin sags, and he begins to breathe heavily through his mouth.* EDMUND *sits tensely. He hears something and jerks nervously forward in his chair, staring through the front parlor into the hall. He jumps up with a hunted, distracted expression. It seems for a second he is going to hide in the back parlor. Then he sits down again and waits, his eyes averted, his hands gripping the arms of his chair. Suddenly all five bulbs of the chandelier in the front parlor are turned on from a wall switch, and a moment later someone starts playing the piano in there—the opening of one of Chopin's[8] simpler waltzes, done with a forgetful, stiff-fingered groping, as if an awkward schoolgirl were practicing it for the first time.* TYRONE *starts to wide-awakeness and sober dread, and* JAMIE's *head jerks back and his eyes open. For a moment they listen frozenly. The playing stops as abruptly as it began, and* MARY *appears in the doorway. She wears a sky-blue dressing gown over her nightdress, dainty slippers and pompons on her bare feet. Her face is paler than ever. Her eyes look enormous. They glisten like polished black jewels. The uncanny thing is that her face now appears so youthful. Experience seems ironed out of it. It is a marble mask of girlish innocence, the mouth caught in a shy smile. Her white hair is braided in two pigtails which hang over her breast. Over one arm, carried neglectfully, trailing on the floor, as if she had forgotten she held it, is an old-fashioned white satin wedding gown, trimmed with duchesse lace. She hesitates in the doorway, glancing round the room, her forehead puckered puzzledly, like someone who has come to a room to get something but has become absent-minded on the way and forgotten what it was. They stare at her. She seems aware of them merely as she is aware of other objects in the room, the furniture, the windows, familiar things she accepts automatically as naturally belonging there but which she is too preoccupied to notice.*]

JAMIE [*breaks the cracking silence—bitterly, self-defensively sardonic*]   The Mad Scene. Enter Ophelia![9]

---

8. Frederic Chopin (1810–1849), Polish composer famous for works for the piano.

9. An allusion to Shakespeare's *Hamlet*.

[*His father and brother both turn on him fiercely.* EDMUND *is quicker. He slaps* JAMIE *across the mouth with the back of his hand.*]

TYRONE [*his voice trembling with suppressed fury*]   Good boy, Edmund. The dirty blackguard! His own mother!

JAMIE [*mumbles guiltily, without resentment*]   All right, Kid. Had it coming. But I told you how much I'd hoped—[*He puts his hands over his face and begins to sob.*]

TYRONE   I'll kick you out in the gutter tomorrow, so help me God. [*But* JAMIE's *sobbing breaks his anger, and he turns and shakes his shoulder, pleading*] Jamie, for the love of God, stop it!

[*Then* MARY *speaks, and they freeze into silence again, staring at her. She has paid no attention whatever to the incident. It is simply a part of the familiar atmosphere of the room, a background which does not touch her preoccupation; and she speaks aloud to herself, not to them.*]

MARY   I play so badly now. I'm all out of practice. Sister Theresa will give me a dreadful scolding. She'll tell me it isn't fair to my father when he spends so much money for extra lessons. She's quite right, it isn't fair, when he's so good and generous, and so proud of me. I'll practice every day from now on. But something horrible has happened to my hands. The fingers have gotten so stiff—[*She lifts her hands to examine them with a frightened puzzlement.*] The knuckles are all swollen. They're so ugly. I'll have to go to the Infirmary and show Sister Martha. [*with a sweet smile of affectionate trust*] She's old and a little cranky, but I love her just the same, and she has things in her medicine chest that'll cure anything. She'll give me something to rub on my hands, and tell me to pray to the Blessed Virgin, and they'll be well again in no time. [*She forgets her hands and comes into the room, the wedding gown trailing on the floor. She glances around vaguely, her forehead puckered again.*] Let me see. What did I come here to find? It's terrible, how absent-minded I've become. I'm always dreaming and forgetting.

TYRONE [*in a stifled voice*]   What's that she's carrying, Edmund?

EDMUND [*dully*]   Her wedding gown, I suppose.

TYRONE   Christ! [*He gets to his feet and stands directly in her path—in anguish*] Mary! Isn't it bad enough—? [*controlling himself—gently persuasive*] Here, let me take it, dear. You'll only step on it and tear it and get it dirty dragging it on the floor. Then you'd be sorry afterwards.

[*She lets him take it, regarding him from somewhere far away within herself, without recognition, without either affection or animosity.*]

MARY [*with the shy politeness of a well-bred young girl toward an elderly gentleman who relieves her of a bundle*]   Thank you. You are very kind. [*She regards the wedding gown with a puzzled interest.*] It's a wedding gown. It's very lovely, isn't it? [*A shadow crosses her face and she looks vaguely uneasy.*] I remember now. I found it in the attic hidden in a trunk. But I don't know what I wanted it for. I'm going to be a nun—that is, if I can only find—[*She looks around the room, her forehead puckered again.*] What is it I'm looking for? I know it's something I lost. [*She moves back from* TYRONE, *aware of him now only as some obstacle in her path.*]

TYRONE [*in hopeless appeal*]   Mary!

[*But it cannot penetrate her preoccupation. She doesn't seem to hear him. He gives up helplessly, shrinking into himself, even his defensive drunkenness taken from him, leaving him sick and sober. He sinks back* on his chair, holding the wedding gown in his arms with an unconscious clumsy, protective gentleness.]

JAMIE [drops his hand from his face, his eyes on the table top. He has suddenly sobered up, too—dully] It's no good, Papa. [He recites from Swinburne's "A Leave-taking" and does it well, simply but with a bitter sadness.]

"Let us rise up and part; she will not know.
Let us go seaward as the great winds go,
Full of blown sand and foam; what help is here?
There is no help, for all these things are so,
And all the world is bitter as a tear.
And how these things are, though ye strove to show,
She would not know."

MARY [looking around her] Something I miss terribly. It can't be altogether lost. [She starts to move around in back of JAMIE's chair.]

JAMIE [turns to look up into her face—and cannot help appealing pleadingly in his turn] Mama!
[She does not seem to hear. He looks away hopelessly.]
Hell! What's the use? It's no good. [He recites from "A Leave-taking" again with increased bitterness.]

"Let us go hence, my songs; she will not hear.
Let us go hence together without fear;
Keep silence now, for singing-time is over,
And over all old things and all things dear.
She loves not you nor me as all we love her.
Yea, though we sang as angels in her ear,
She would not hear."

MARY [looking around her] Something I need terribly. I remember when I had it I was never lonely nor afraid. I can't have lost it forever, I would die if I thought that. Because then there would be no hope.
[She moves like a sleepwalker, around the back of JAMIE's chair, then forward toward left front, passing behind EDMUND.]

EDMUND [turns impulsively and grabs her arm. As he pleads he has the quality of a bewilderedly hurt little boy.] Mama! It isn't a summer cold! I've got consumption!

MARY [For a second he seems to have broken through to her. She trembles and her expression becomes terrified. She calls distractedly, as if giving a command to herself.] No! [And instantly she is far away again. She murmurs gently but impersonally] You must not try to touch me. You must not try to hold me. It isn't right, when I am hoping to be a nun.
[He lets his hand drop from her arm. She moves left to the front end of the sofa beneath the windows and sits down, facing front, her hands folded in her lap, in a demure school-girlish pose.]

JAMIE [gives Edmund a strange look of mingled pity and jealous gloating] You damned fool. It's no good. [He recites again from the Swinburne poem.]

"Let us go hence, go hence; she will not see.
Sing all once more together; surely she,
She too, remembering days and words that were,
Will turn a little toward us, sighing; but we,

We are hence, we are gone, as though we had not been there.
Nay, and though all men seeing had pity on me,
She would not see."

TYRONE [*trying to shake off his hopeless stupor*]   Oh, we're fools to pay any
attention. It's the damned poison. But I've never known her to drown herself in it as deep as this. [*gruffly*] Pass me that bottle, Jamie. And stop
reciting that damned morbid poetry. I won't have it in my house!
       [JAMIE *pushes the bottle toward him. He pours a drink without disar-
       ranging the wedding gown he holds carefully over his other arm and on
       his lap, and shoves the bottle back.* JAMIE *pours his and passes the bottle
       to* EDMUND, *who, in turn, pours one.* TYRONE *lifts his glass and his sons
       follow suit mechanically, but before they can drink* MARY *speaks and they
       slowly lower their drinks to the table, forgetting them.*]
MARY [*staring dreamily before her. Her face looks extraordinarily youthful and
innocent. The shyly eager, trusting smile is on her lips as she talks aloud to
herself.*] I had a talk with Mother Elizabeth. She is so sweet and good. A
saint on earth. I love her dearly. It may be sinful of me but I love her better than my own mother. Because she always understands, even before
you say a word. Her kind blue eyes look right into your heart. You can't
keep any secrets from her. You couldn't deceive her, even if you were
mean enough to want to. [*She gives a little rebellious toss of her head—
with girlish pique*] All the same, I don't think she was so understanding
this time. I told her I wanted to be a nun. I explained how sure I was of
my vocation, that I had prayed to the Blessed Virgin to make me sure, and
to find me worthy. I told Mother I had had a true vision when I was praying in the shrine of Our Lady of Lourdes, on the little island in the lake.
I said I knew, as surely as I knew I was kneeling there, that the Blessed
Virgin had smiled and blessed me with her consent. But Mother Elizabeth
told me I must be more sure than that, even, that I must prove it wasn't
simply my imagination. She said, if I was so sure, then I wouldn't mind
putting myself to a test by going home after I graduated, and living as
other girls lived, going out to parties and dances and enjoying myself; and
then if after a year or two I still felt sure, I could come back to see her
and we would talk it over again. [*She tosses her head—indignantly*] I never
dreamed Holy Mother would give me such advice! I was really shocked.
I said, of course, I would do anything she suggested, but I knew it was
simply a waste of time. After I left her, I felt all mixed up, so I went to the
shrine and prayed to the Blessed Virgin and found peace again because I
knew she heard my prayer and would always love me and see no harm
ever came to me so long as I never lost my faith in her. [*She pauses and a
look of growing uneasiness comes over her face. She passes a hand over her
forehead as if brushing cobwebs from her brain—vaguely*] That was in the
winter of senior year. Then in the spring something happened to me. Yes,
I remember. I fell in love with James Tyrone and was so happy for a time.
[*She stares before her in a sad dream.* TYRONE *stirs in his chair.* EDMUND *and*
JAMIE *remain motionless.*]

CURTAIN

1940

CLAUDE McKAY
1889–1948

One of his biographers aptly calls Claude McKay a lifelong wanderer, a "sojourner" in the Harlem Renaissance. A Jamaican by birth, he did not become an American citizen until 1940; he left Harlem just when the Renaissance was getting started; he criticized leading black intellectuals like W. E. B. Du Bois and Alain Locke (who, in turn, criticized him). Nevertheless, *Harlem Shadows*, his 1922 book of poetry, is generally considered the book that initiated the Harlem Renaissance; his *Home to Harlem* (1928) was the only best-selling African American novel of the decade. Whether the Harlem Renaissance was a unified movement or a resonant label encompassing artists with diverse aims, whether McKay was an American Harlemite or a man of the world, he was unquestionably one of the most important black writers of the 1920s. As well as influencing African American literature, he has had a major impact on writing by West Indians and Africans.

Claude McKay (Festus Claudius McKay) was born in Sunny Ville, a rural village in central Jamaica. This village, with its setting of spectacular natural beauty, became in later years his symbol of a lost golden age. McKay's grandfather, a West African Ashanti, had been brought to the island as a slave, and McKay's father passed on to his son what he remembered of Ashanti values and rituals. Economic necessity led the young McKay to Kingston (Jamaica's principal city) in 1909, where he was apprenticed to a cabinetmaker and wheelwright. Combining his emerging literary ambitions with an interest in Jamaican folkways, McKay published two ground-breaking books of dialect poetry—*Songs of Jamaica* and *Constab Ballads*—in 1912. Prize money from these books took him to the United States to study agriculture, but his literary ambitions drew him to New York City after two years in school (first at the Tuskegee Institute, then at Kansas State College). He married his Jamaican sweetheart, Eulalie Imelda Lewars, in 1914; the couple had a daughter, but the marriage did not last. Supporting himself in jobs like restaurant kitchen helper and Pullman railroad waiter, he began to publish in avant-garde journals; by 1917 he was appearing in *The Seven Arts*, *Pearson's*, and the prominent left-wing *Liberator*, edited by Max Eastman. *The Liberator* published his famous poem "If We Must Die" in 1919. His poetry, much of it written in strict sonnet form, braided racial subject matter, radical politics, and poetic technique into compelling statements that were also good poetry according to traditional standards.

McKay's radical politics, already formed in Jamaica, rose from his belief that racism was inseparable from capitalism, which he saw as a structure designed to perpetuate economic inequality. To him, attacking capitalism was attacking racial injustice. Before the publication of *Harlem Shadows*, McKay had spent 1919–21 in England; in 1923 he went to Moscow, where he was welcomed as a celebrity. His connections to the Communist regime in Russia made him a target for the FBI, which issued orders to keep him from returning to the United States. He stayed in Europe until 1934, living mainly in France but also in Spain and Morocco. *Home to Harlem* (1928), written mostly in France, was an episodic guide to Harlem's artistic, popular, and intellectual life. Later events turned it into one of the movement's last statements; retrenchment in the publishing industry after the stock market crash of 1929, the emergence of younger African American writers with different values, and dissension among Harlem artists themselves combined to bring an end to the Harlem Renaissance and altered the character of life in Harlem itself.

When McKay was finally able to return to the United States in 1934, the nation was deep in the Great Depression. With general unemployment at over 25 percent, paid literary work was extremely hard to come by. In 1935 he joined the New York City branch of the Federal Writers' Project, a New Deal organization giving work to unemployed writers. Except for his important autobiography, *A Long Way from Home* (1937), he did little creative work, and his health failed. Through his friendship with Ellen Tarry, a young African American writer who was a Catholic, he received medical care from Friendship House, a Catholic lay organization in Harlem. In the later years of his life, appalled by Stalin's purges, McKay repudiated his earlier Communist sympathies. He began to work at Friendship House and, after moving to Chicago, worked for the Catholic Youth Organization. He converted to Catholicism in 1944 and died in Chicago four years later.

The texts are from *Harlem Shadows* (1922).

The Harlem Dancer

Applauding youths laughed with young prostitutes
And watched her perfect, half-clothed body sway;
Her voice was like the sound of blended flutes
Blown by black players upon a picnic day.
She sang and danced on gracefully and calm,   5
The light gauze hanging loose about her form;
To me she seemed a proudly-swaying palm
Grown lovelier for passing through a storm.
Upon her swarthy neck black shiny curls
Luxuriant fell; and tossing coins in praise,   10
The wine-flushed, bold-eyed boys, and even the girls,
Devoured her shape with eager, passionate gaze;
But looking at her falsely-smiling face,
I knew her self was not in that strange place.

1917, 1922

Harlem Shadows

I hear the halting footsteps of a lass
   In Negro Harlem when the night lets fall
Its veil. I see the shapes of girls who pass
   To bend and barter at desire's call.
Ah, little dark girls who in slippered feet   5
Go prowling through the night from street to street!

Through the long night until the silver break
   Of day the little gray feet know no rest;
Through the lone night until the last snow-flake
   Has dropped from heaven upon the earth's white breast,   10
The dusky, half-clad girls of tired feet
Are trudging, thinly shod, from street to street.

Ah, stern harsh world, that in the wretched way
   Of poverty, dishonor and disgrace,
Has pushed the timid little feet of clay,   15
   The sacred brown feet of my fallen race!

Ah, heart of me, the weary, weary feet
In Harlem wandering from street to street.

1918, 1922

The Lynching

His Spirit in smoke ascended to high heaven.
His father, by the cruelest way of pain,
Had bidden him to his bosom once again;
The awful sin remained still unforgiven.
All night a bright and solitary star   5
(Perchance the one that ever guided him,
Yet gave him up at last to Fate's wild whim)
Hung pitifully o'er the swinging char.
Day dawned, and soon the mixed crowds came to view
The ghastly body swaying in the sun   10
The women thronged to look, but never a one
Showed sorrow in her eyes of steely blue;
And little lads, lynchers that were to be,
Danced round the dreadful thing in fiendish glee.

1919, 1922

If We Must Die

If we must die, let it not be like hogs
Hunted and penned in an inglorious spot,
While round us bark the mad and hungry dogs,
Making their mock at our accursèd lot.
If we must die, O let us nobly die,   5
So that our precious blood may not be shed
In vain; then even the monsters we defy
Shall be constrained to honor us though dead!
O kinsmen! we must meet the common foe!
Though far outnumbered let us show us brave,   10
And for their thousand blows deal one deathblow!
What though before us lies the open grave?
Like men we'll face the murderous, cowardly pack,
Pressed to the wall, dying, but fighting back!

1919, 1922

Africa

The sun sought thy dim bed and brought forth light,
The sciences were sucklings at thy breast;
When all the world was young in pregnant night
Thy slaves toiled at thy monumental best.

Thou ancient treasure-land, thou modern prize, 5
New peoples marvel at thy pyramids!
The years roll on, thy sphinx of riddle eyes
Watches the mad world with immobile lids.
The Hebrews humbled them at Pharaoh's name.
Cradle of Power! Yet all things were in vain! 10
Honor and Glory, Arrogance and Fame!
They went. The darkness swallowed thee again.
Thou art the harlot, now thy time is done,
Of all the mighty nations of the sun.

[handwritten: Already "sank into the sand" like in 1921, 1922 America]

America

Although she feeds me bread of bitterness,
And sinks into my throat her tiger's tooth,
Stealing my breath of life, I will confess
I love this cultured hell that tests my youth!
Her vigor flows like tides into my blood, 5
Giving me strength erect against her hate.
Her bigness sweeps my being like a flood.
Yet as a rebel fronts a king in state,
I stand within her walls with not a shred
Of terror, malice, not a word of jeer. 10
Darkly I gaze into the days ahead,
And see her might and granite wonders there,
Beneath the touch of Time's unerring hand,
Like priceless treasures sinking in the sand.

[handwritten: we have potential but we're not using this]   1921, 1922

KATHERINE ANNE PORTER
1890–1980

Over a long writing life Katherine Anne Porter produced only four books of stories and one novel, *Ship of Fools*, which did not appear until she was over seventy. Her reputation as a prose writer did not depend on quantity; each story was technically skilled, emotionally powerful, combining traditional narration with new symbolic techniques and contemporary subject matter.

Callie Porter—she changed the name to Katherine Anne when she became a writer—was born in the small settlement of Indian Creek, Texas; her mother died soon after giving birth to her fourth child, when Porter was not quite two years old. Her father moved them all to his mother's home in Kyle, Texas, where the maternal grandmother raised the family in extreme poverty. The father gave up all attempts to support them either financially or emotionally; the security provided by the strong, loving, but pious and stern grandmother ended with her death when Porter was eleven. Porter married to leave home immediately after her sixteenth birthday, only to find that rooted domesticity was not for her. Long before her divorce in 1915, she had separated from her first husband and begun a life of travel, activity, and changes of jobs.

She started writing in 1916 as a reporter for a Dallas newspaper. In 1917 she moved to Denver, the next year to New York City's Greenwich Village. Between 1918 and 1924 she lived mainly in Mexico, freelancing, meeting artists and intellectuals, and becoming involved in revolutionary politics. In Mexico she found the resources of journalism inadequate to her ambitions; using an anecdote she had heard from an archaeologist as a kernel, she wrote her first story, "María Concepción," which was published in the prestigious *Century* magazine in 1922. Like all her stories, it dealt with powerful emotions and had a strong sense of locale. Critics praised her as a major talent.

Although she considered herself a serious writer from this time on, Porter was distracted from fiction by many crosscurrents. A self-supporting woman with expensive tastes, she hesitated to give up lucrative freelance offers. She enjoyed travel and gladly took on jobs that sent her abroad. She became involved in political causes, including the Sacco-Vanzetti case. She was married four times.

Porter planned each story meticulously—taking extensive notes, devising scenarios, roughing out dialogue, and revising many times, sometimes over a period of years. She did not write confessional or simple autobiographical fiction, but each story originated in an important real experience of her life and drew on deep feelings. Although not a feminist, Porter devoted much of her work to exploring the tensions in women's lives in the modern era. The story that made her famous for life, so that everything else she published thereafter was looked on as a literary event, was "Flowering Judas" (1929), set in Mexico and dealing with revolutionary politics, lust, and betrayal. The reality of mixed motives and the difference between pure idealism and egotistical opportunism as they are encountered in revolutionary politics are among the themes in this deceptively simple narrative. It appeared in the little magazine *Hound and Horn*. The collections *Flowering Judas* and *Noon Wine* came out in 1930 and 1937. In 1930 Porter went back to Mexico and the following year to Europe on a Guggenheim fellowship; she lived in Berlin, Paris, and Basel before returning to the United States in 1936. Two more collections of stories and novellas appeared in 1939 (*Pale Horse, Pale Rider*) and in 1944 (*The Leaning Tower*). In these later collections there are several stories about Miranda Gay, a character who is partly autobiographical and partly an idealized image of the southern belle as she faces the modern world. *Pale Horse, Pale Rider* narrates Miranda's wartime romance and strongly endorses the personal over the political.

Soon after arriving in Europe in 1931 Porter began working on a novel, but it was not until 1962 that *Ship of Fools,* which runs to almost five hundred pages, appeared. Set on an ocean liner crossing the Atlantic to Germany in August 1931, it explores the characters and developing relationships of a large number of passengers; the ship, as Porter wrote in a preface, stands for "this world on its voyage to eternity." As in "Flowering Judas" and *Pale Horse, Pale Rider* the personal and the political intersect in *Ship of Fools,* since the coming of Nazism in Germany frames the interlinked stories of the travelers. In its film version, *Ship of Fools* brought Porter a great deal of money. Capitalizing on the publicity, her publishers brought out the *Collected Stories* in 1965, from which followed the National Book Award, the Pulitzer Prize, the Gold Medal for fiction of the National Institute of Arts and Letters, and election to the American Academy of Letters, all in the next two years. The happiest occasions in her later years—she lived to be ninety—were connected with endowing and establishing the Katherine Anne Porter Room at the University of Maryland, not far from her last home near Washington, D.C.

The text of "Flowering Judas" is from the *Collected Stories* (1965).

Flowering Judas[1]

Braggioni sits heaped upon the edge of a straight-backed chair much too small for him, and sings to Laura in a furry, mournful voice. Laura has begun to find reasons for avoiding her own house until the latest possible moment, for Braggioni is there almost every night. No matter how late she is, he will be sitting there with a surly, waiting expression, pulling at his kinky yellow hair, thumbing the strings of his guitar, snarling a tune under his breath. Lupe the Indian maid meets Laura at the door, and says with a flicker of a glance towards the upper room, "He waits."

Laura wishes to lie down, she is tired of her hairpins and the feel of her long tight sleeves, but she says to him, "Have you a new song for me this evening?" If he says yes, she asks him to sing it. If he says no, she remembers his favorite one, and asks him to sing it again. Lupe brings her a cup of chocolate and a plate of rice, and Laura eats at the small table under the lamp, first inviting Braggioni, whose answer is always the same: "I have eaten, and besides, chocolate thickens the voice."

Laura says, "Sing, then," and Braggioni heaves himself into song. He scratches the guitar familiarly as though it were a pet animal, and sings passionately off key, taking the high notes in a prolonged painful squeal. Laura, who haunts the markets listening to the ballad singers, and stops every day to hear the blind boy playing his reed-flute in Sixteenth of September Street,[2] listens to Braggioni with pitiless courtesy, because she dares not smile at his miserable performance. Nobody dares to smile at him. Braggioni is cruel to everyone, with a kind of specialized insolence, but he is so vain of his talents, and so sensitive to slights, it would require a cruelty and vanity greater than his own to lay a finger on the vast cureless wound of his self-esteem. It would require courage, too, for it is dangerous to offend him, and nobody has this courage.

Braggioni loves himself with such tenderness and amplitude and eternal charity that his followers—for he is a leader of men, a skilled revolutionist, and his skin has been punctured in honorable warfare—warm themselves in the reflected glow, and say to each other: "He has a real nobility, a love of humanity raised above mere personal affections." The excess of this self-love has flowed out, inconveniently for her, over Laura, who, with so many others, owes her comfortable situation and her salary to him. When he is in a very good humor, he tells her, "I am tempted to forgive you for being a *gringa*. *Gringita!*"[3] and Laura, burning, imagines herself leaning forward suddenly, and with a sound back-handed slap wiping the suety smile from his face. If he notices her eyes at these moments he gives no sign.

She knows what Braggioni would offer her, and she must resist tenaciously without appearing to resist, and if she could avoid it she would not admit even to herself the slow drift of his intention. During these long evenings which have spoiled a long month for her, she sits in her deep chair with an open book on her knees, resting her eyes on the consoling rigidity of the printed

---

1. One of a genus of trees and shrubs with purplish rosy flowers. According to legend, Judas Iscariot, betrayer of Jesus, hanged himself from such a tree.
2. A street in Morelia, a city in western Mexico where the story is set.
3. A young female foreigner, non-Mexican girl; a patronizing term meaning "cute little foreign girl." Diminutive of *gringa*, which is used pejoratively, especially for an American.

page when the sight and sound of Braggioni singing threaten to identify themselves with all her remembered afflictions and to add their weight to her uneasy premonitions of the future. The gluttonous bulk of Braggioni has become a symbol of her many disillusions, for a revolutionist should be lean, animated by heroic faith, a vessel of abstract virtues. This is nonsense, she knows it now and is ashamed of it. Revolution must have leaders, and leadership is a career for energetic men. She is, her comrades tell her, full of romantic error, for what she defines as cynicism in them is merely "a developed sense of reality." She is almost too willing to say, "I am wrong, I suppose I don't really understand the principles," and afterward she makes a secret truce with herself, determined not to surrender her will to such expedient logic. But she cannot help feeling that she has been betrayed irreparably by the disunion between her way of living and her feeling of what life should be, and at times she is almost contented to rest in this sense of grievance as a private store of consolation. Sometimes she wishes to run away, but she stays. Now she longs to fly out of this room, down the narrow stairs, and into the street where the houses lean together like conspirators under a single mottled lamp, and leave Braggioni singing to himself.

Instead she looks at Braggioni, frankly and clearly, like a good child who understands the rules of behavior. Her knees cling together under sound blue serge, and her round white collar is not purposely nun-like. She wears the uniform of an idea, and has renounced vanities. She was born Roman Catholic, and in spite of her fear of being seen by someone who might make a scandal of it, she slips now and again into some crumbling little church, kneels on the chilly stone, and says a Hail Mary on the gold rosary she bought in Tehuantepec. It is no good and she ends by examining the altar with its tinsel flowers and ragged brocades, and feels tender about the battered dollshape of some male saint whose white, lace-trimmed drawers hang limply around his ankles below the hieratic dignity of his velvet robe. She has encased herself in a set of principles derived from her early training, leaving no detail of gesture or of personal taste untouched, and for this reason she will not wear lace made on machines. This is her private heresy, for in her special group the machine is sacred, and will be the salvation of the workers. She loves fine lace, and there is a tiny edge of fluted cobweb on this collar, which is one of twenty precisely alike, folded in blue tissue paper in the upper drawer of her clothes chest.

Braggioni catches her glance solidly as if he had been waiting for it, leans forward, balancing his paunch between his spread knees, and sings with tremendous emphasis, weighing his words. He has, the song relates, no father and no mother, nor even a friend to console him; lonely as a wave of the sea he comes and goes, lonely as a wave. His mouth opens round and yearns sideways, his balloon cheeks grow oily with the labor of song. He bulges marvelously in his expensive garments. Over his lavender collar, crushed upon a purple necktie, held by a diamond hoop: over his ammunition belt of tooled leather worked in silver, buckled cruelly around his gasping middle: over the tops of his glossy yellow shoes Braggioni swells with ominous ripeness, his mauve silk hose stretched taut, his ankles bound with the stout leather thongs of his shoes.

When he stretches his eyelids at Laura she notes again that his eyes are the true tawny yellow cat's eyes. He is rich, not in money, he tells her, but in power, and this power brings with it the blameless ownership of things, and the right to indulge his love of small luxuries. "I have a taste for the elegant refinements," he said once, flourishing a yellow silk handkerchief before her nose. "Smell that? It is Jockey Club, imported from New York." Nonetheless he is wounded by life. He will say so presently. "It is true everything turns to dust in the hand, to gall on the tongue." He sighs and his leather belt creaks like a saddle girth. "I am disappointed in everything as it comes. Everything." He shakes his head. "You, poor thing, you will be disappointed too. You are born for it. We are more alike than you realize in some things. Wait and see. Some day you will remember what I have told you, you will know that Braggioni was your friend."

Laura feels a slow chill, a purely physical sense of danger, a warning in her blood that violence, mutilation, a shocking death, wait for her with lessening patience. She has translated this fear into something homely, immediate, and sometimes hesitates before crossing the street. "My personal fate is nothing, except as the testimony of a mental attitude," she reminds herself, quoting from some forgotten philosophic primer, and is sensible enough to add, "Anyhow, I shall not be killed by an automobile if I can help it."

"It may be true I am as corrupt, in another way, as Braggioni," she thinks in spite of herself, "as callous, as incomplete," and if this is so, any kind of death seems preferable. Still she sits quietly, she does not run. Where could she go? Uninvited she has promised herself to this place; she can no longer imagine herself as living in another country, and there is no pleasure in remembering her life before she came here.

Precisely what is the nature of this devotion, its true motives, and what are its obligations? Laura cannot say. She spends part of her days in Xochimilco, near by, teaching Indian children to say in English, "The cat is on the mat." When she appears in the classroom they crowd about her with smiles on their wise, innocent, clay-colored faces, crying, "Good morning, my titcher!" in immaculate voices, and they make of her desk a fresh garden of flowers every day.

During her leisure she goes to union meetings and listens to busy important voices quarreling over tactics, methods, internal politics. She visits the prisoners of her own political faith in their cells, where they entertain themselves with counting cockroaches, repenting of their indiscretions, composing their memoirs, writing out manifestoes and plans for their comrades who are still walking about free, hands in pockets, sniffing fresh air. Laura brings them food and cigarettes and a little money, and she brings messages disguised in equivocal phrases from the men outside who dare not set foot in the prison for fear of disappearing into the cells kept empty for them. If the prisoners confuse night and day, and complain, "Dear little Laura, time doesn't pass in this infernal hole, and I won't know when it is time to sleep unless I have a reminder," she brings them their favorite narcotics, and says in a tone that does not wound them with pity, "Tonight will really be night for you," and though her Spanish amuses them, they find her comforting, useful. If they lose patience and all faith, and curse the slowness of their friends in coming to their rescue with money and influence, they trust her not to repeat everything, and if she inquires, "Where do you think we can find money, or influence?" they are certain to answer, "Well, there is Braggioni, why doesn't he do something?"

She smuggles letters from headquarters to men hiding from firing squads in back streets in mildewed houses, where they sit in tumbled beds and talk bitterly as if all Mexico were at their heels, when Laura knows positively they might appear at the band concert in the Alameda[4] on Sunday morning, and no one would notice them. But Braggioni says, "Let them sweat a little. The next time they may be careful. It is very restful to have them out of the way for a while." She is not afraid to knock on any door in any street after midnight, and enter in the darkness, and say to one of these men who is really in danger: "They will be looking for you—seriously—tomorrow morning after six. Here is some money from Vicente. Go to Vera Cruz and wait."

She borrows money from the Roumanian agitator to give to his bitter enemy the Polish agitator. The favor of Braggioni is their disputed territory, and Braggioni holds the balance nicely, for he can use them both. The Polish agitator talks love to her over café tables, hoping to exploit what he believes is her secret sentimental preference for him, and he gives her misinformation which he begs her to repeat as the solemn truth to certain persons. The Roumanian is more adroit. He is generous with his money in all good causes, and lies to her with an air of ingenuous candor, as if he were her good friend and confidant. She never repeats anything they may say. Braggioni never asks questions. He has other ways to discover all that he wishes to know about them.

Nobody touches her, but all praise her gray eyes, and the soft, round under lip which promises gayety, yet is always grave, nearly always firmly closed: and they cannot understand why she is in Mexico. She walks back and forth on her errands, with puzzled eyebrows, carrying her little folder of drawings and music and school papers. No dancer dances more beautifully than Laura walks, and she inspires some amusing, unexpected ardors, which cause little gossip, because nothing comes of them. A young captain who had been a soldier in Zapata's[5] army attempted, during a horseback ride near Cuernavaca, to express his desire for her with the noble simplicity befitting a rude folk-hero: but gently, because he was gentle. This gentleness was his defeat, for when he alighted, and removed her foot from the stirrup, and essayed to draw her down into his arms, her horse, ordinarily a tame one, shied fiercely, reared and plunged away. The young hero's horse careered blindly after his stable-mate, and the hero did not return to the hotel until rather late that evening. At breakfast he came to her table in full charro dress,[6] gray buckskin jacket and trousers with strings of silver buttons down the leg, and he was in a humorous, careless mood. "May I sit with you?" and "You are a wonderful rider. I was terrified that you might be thrown and dragged. I should never have forgiven myself. But I cannot admire you enough for your riding!"

"I learned to ride in Arizona," said Laura.

"If you will ride with me again this morning, I promise you a horse that will not shy with you," he said. But Laura remembered that she must return to Mexico City at noon.

Next morning the children made a celebration and spent their playtime writing on the blackboard, "We lov ar ticher," and with tinted chalks they drew wreaths of flowers around the words. The young hero wrote her a letter: "I am a very foolish, wasteful, impulsive man. I should have first said I love you, and then you would not have run away. But you shall see me again."

---

4. Public promenade bordered with trees.
5. Emiliano Zapata (c. 1879–1919), Mexican peasant revolutionary general whose movement, *zapatismo*, combined agrarian and Mexican Indian cultural aspirations; one of the most significant fig-

ures in Mexico from 1910 to 1919, when he was murdered.
6. Costume worn by a peasant horseman of special status.

Laura thought, "I must send him a box of colored crayons," but she was trying to forgive herself for having spurred her horse at the wrong moment.

A brown, shock-haired youth came and stood in her patio one night and sang like a lost soul for two hours, but Laura could think of nothing to do about it. The moonlight spread a wash of gauzy silver over the clear spaces of the garden, and the shadows were cobalt blue. The scarlet blossoms of the Judas tree were dull purple, and the names of the colors repeated themselves automatically in her mind, while she watched not the boy, but his shadow, fallen like a dark garment across the fountain rim, trailing in the water. Lupe came silently and whispered expert counsel in her ear: "If you will throw him one little flower, he will sing another song or two and go away." Laura threw the flower, and he sang a last song and went away with the flower tucked in the band of his hat. Lupe said, "He is one of the organizers of the Typographers Union, and before that he sold corridos[7] in the Merced market, and before that, he came from Guanajuato, where I was born. I would not trust any man, but I trust least those from Guanajuato."

She did not tell Laura that he would be back again the next night, and the next, nor that he would follow her at a certain fixed distance around the Merced market, through the Zócolo, up Francisco I. Madero Avenue, and so along the Paseo de la Reforma to Chapultepec Park, and into the Philosopher's Footpath, still with that flower withering in his hat, and an indivisible attention in his eyes.

Now Laura is accustomed to him, it means nothing except that he is nineteen years old and is observing a convention with all propriety, as though it were founded on a law of nature, which in the end it might well prove to be. He is beginning to write poems which he prints on a wooden press, and he leaves them stuck like handbills in her door. She is pleasantly disturbed by the abstract, unhurried watchfulness of his black eyes which will in time turn easily towards another object. She tells herself that throwing the flower was a mistake, for she is twenty-two years old and knows better; but she refuses to regret it, and persuades herself that her negation of all external events as they occur is a sign that she is gradually perfecting herself in the stoicism she strives to cultivate against that disaster she fears, though she cannot name it.

She is not at home in the world. Every day she teaches children who remain strangers to her, though she loves their tender round hands and their charming opportunist savagery. She knocks at unfamiliar doors not knowing whether a friend or a stranger shall answer, and even if a known face emerges from the sour gloom of that unknown interior, still it is the face of a stranger. No matter what this stranger says to her, nor what her message to him, the very cells of her flesh reject knowledge and kinship in one monotonous word. No. No. No. She draws her strength from this one holy talismanic word which does not suffer her to be led into evil. Denying everything, she may walk anywhere in safety, she looks at everything without amazement.

No, repeats this firm unchanging voice of her blood; and she looks at Braggioni without amazement. He is a great man, he wishes to impress this simple girl who covers her great round breasts with thick dark cloth, and who hides long, invaluably beautiful legs under a heavy skirt. She is almost thin except for the incomprehensible fullness of her breasts, like a nursing mother's, and Braggioni, who considers himself a judge of women, speculates

---

7. Popular ballads.

again on the puzzle of her notorious virginity, and takes the liberty of speech which she permits without a sign of modesty, indeed, without any sort of sign, which is disconcerting.

"You think you are so cold, *gringita!* Wait and see. You will surprise yourself some day! May I be there to advise you!" He stretches his eyelids at her, and his ill-humored cat's eyes waver in a separate glance for the two points of light marking the opposite ends of a smoothly drawn path between the swollen curve of her breasts. He is not put off by that blue serge, nor by her resolutely fixed gaze. There is all the time in the world. His cheeks are bellying with the wind of song. "O girl with the dark eyes," he sings, and reconsiders. "But yours are not dark. I can change all that. O girl with the green eyes, you have stolen my heart away!" then his mind wanders to the song, and Laura feels the weight of his attention being shifted elsewhere. Singing thus, he seems harmless, he is quite harmless, there is nothing to do but sit patiently and say "No," when the moment comes. She draws a full breath, and her mind wanders also, but not far. She dares not wander too far.

Not for nothing has Braggioni taken pains to be a good revolutionist and a professional lover of humanity. He will never die of it. He has the malice, the cleverness, the wickedness, the sharpness of wit, the hardness of heart, stipulated for loving the world profitably. *He will never die of it.* He will live to see himself kicked out from his feeding trough by other hungry world-saviors. Traditionally he must sing in spite of his life which drives him to bloodshed, he tells Laura, for his father was a Tuscany[8] peasant who drifted to Yucatan and married a Maya woman: a woman of race, an aristocrat. They gave him the love and knowledge of music, thus: and under the rip of his thumbnail, the strings of the instrument complain like exposed nerves.

Once he was called Delgadito by all the girls and married women who ran after him; he was so scrawny all his bones showed under his thin cotton clothing, and he could squeeze his emptiness to the very backbone with his two hands. He was a poet and the revolution was only a dream then; too many women loved him and sapped away his youth, and he could never find enough to eat anywhere, anywhere! Now he is a leader of men, crafty men who whisper in his ear, hungry men who wait for hours outside his office for a word with him, emaciated men with wild faces who waylay him at the street gate with a timid, "Comrade, let me tell you . . ." and they blow the foul breath from their empty stomachs in his face.

He is always sympathetic. He gives them handfuls of small coins from his own pocket, he promises them work, there will be demonstrations, they must join the unions and attend the meetings, above all they must be on the watch for spies. They are closer to him than his own brothers, without them he can do nothing—until tomorrow, comrade!

Until tomorrow. "They are stupid, they are lazy, they are treacherous, they would cut my throat for nothing," he says to Laura. He has good food and abundant drink, he hires an automobile and drives in the Paseo on Sunday morning, and enjoys plenty of sleep in a soft bed beside a wife who dares not disturb him; and he sits pampering his bones in easy billows of fat, singing to Laura, who knows and thinks these things about him. When he was fifteen, he tried to drown himself because he loved a girl, his first love, and she

8. A region in north-central Italy.

laughed at him. "A thousand women have paid for that," and his tight little mouth turns down at the corners. Now he perfumes his hair with Jockey Club, and confides to Laura: "One woman is really as good as another for me, in the dark. I prefer them all."

His wife organizes unions among the girls in the cigarette factories, and walks in picket lines, and even speaks at meetings in the evening. But she cannot be brought to acknowledge the benefits of true liberty. "I tell her I must have my freedom, net. She does not understand my point of view." Laura has heard this many times. Braggioni scratches the guitar and meditates. "She is an instinctively virtuous woman, pure gold, no doubt of that. If she were not, I should lock her up, and she knows it."

His wife, who works so hard for the good of the factory girls, employs part of her leisure lying on the floor weeping because there are so many women in the world, and only one husband for her, and she never knows where nor when to look for him. He told her: "Unless you can learn to cry when I am not here, I must go away for good." That day he went away and took a room at the Hotel Madrid.

It is this month of separation for the sake of higher principles that has been spoiled not only for Mrs. Braggioni, whose sense of reality is beyond criticism, but for Laura, who feels herself bogged in a nightmare. Tonight Laura envies Mrs. Braggioni, who is alone, and free to weep as much as she pleases about a concrete wrong. Laura has just come from a visit to the prison, and she is waiting for tomorrow with a bitter anxiety as if tomorrow may not come, but time may be caught immovably in this hour, with herself transfixed, Braggioni singing on forever, and Eugenio's body not yet discovered by the guard.

Braggioni says: "Are you going to sleep?" Almost before she can shake her head, he begins telling her about the May-day disturbances coming on in Morelia, for the Catholics hold a festival in honor of the Blessed Virgin, and the Socialists celebrate their martyrs on that day. "There will be two independent processions, starting from either end of town, and they will march until they meet, and the rest depends . . ." He asks her to oil and load his pistols. Standing up, he unbuckles his ammunition belt, and spreads it laden across her knees. Laura sits with the shells slipping through the cleaning cloth dipped in oil, and he says again he cannot understand why she works so hard for the revolutionary idea unless she loves some man who is in it. "Are you not in love with someone?" "No," says Laura. "And no one is in love with you?" "No." "Then it is your own fault. No woman need go begging. Why, what is the matter with you? The legless beggar woman in the Alameda has a perfectly faithful lover. Did you know that?"

Laura peers down the pistol barrel and says nothing, but a long, slow faintness rises and subsides in her; Braggioni curves his swollen fingers around the throat of the guitar and softly smothers the music out of it, and when she hears him again he seems to have forgotten her, and is speaking in the hypnotic voice he uses when talking in small rooms to a listening, close-gathered crowd. Some day this world, now seemingly so composed and eternal, to the edges of every sea shall be merely a tangle of gaping trenches, of crashing walls and broken bodies. Everything must be torn from its accustomed place where it has rotted for centuries, hurled skyward and distributed, cast down again clean as rain, without separate identity. Nothing shall survive that the stiffened hands of poverty have created for the rich and no one shall be left alive except the elect spirits destined to procreate a new world cleansed of cruelty and injustice, ruled by benevolent anarchy: "Pistols are good, I love them, cannon are even better, but in the end I pin my faith to good dynamite," he concludes, and strokes the pistol lying in her hands. "Once I dreamed of destroying this city, in case it offered resistance to General Ortíz, but it fell into his hands like an overripe pear."

He is made restless by his own words, rises and stands waiting. Laura holds up the belt to him: "Put that on, and go kill somebody in Morelia, and you will be happier," she says softly. The presence of death in the room makes her bold. "Today, I found Eugenio going into a stupor. He refused to allow me to call the prison doctor. He had taken all the tablets I brought him yesterday. He said he took them because he was bored."

"He is a fool, and his death is his own business," says Braggioni, fastening his belt carefully.

"I told him if he had waited only a little while longer, you would have got him set free," says Laura. "He said he did not want to wait."

"He is a fool and we are well rid of him," says Braggioni, reaching for his hat.

He goes away. Laura knows his mood has changed, she will not see him any more for a while. He will send word when he needs her to go on errands into strange streets, to speak to the strange faces that will appear, like clay masks with the power of human speech, to mutter their thanks to Braggioni for his help. Now she is free, and she thinks, I must run while there is time. But she does not go.

Braggioni enters his own house where for a month his wife has spent many hours every night weeping and tangling her hair upon her pillow. She is weeping now, and she weeps more at the sight of him, the cause of all her sorrows. He looks about the room. Nothing is changed, the smells are good and familiar, he is well acquainted with the woman who comes toward him with no reproach except grief on her face. He says to her tenderly: "You are so good, please don't cry any more, you dear good creature." She says, "Are you tired, my angel? Sit here and I will wash your feet." She brings a bowl of water, and kneeling, unlaces his shoes, and when from her knees she raises her sad eyes under her blackened lids, he is sorry for everything, and bursts into tears. "Ah, yes, I am hungry, I am tired, let us eat something together," he says, between sobs. His wife leans her head on his arm and says, "Forgive me!" and this time he is refreshed by the solemn, endless rain of her tears.

Laura takes off her serge dress and puts on a white linen nightgown and goes to bed. She turns her head a little to one side, and lying still, reminds herself that it is time to sleep. Numbers tick in her brain like little clocks, soundless doors close of themselves around her. If you would sleep, you must not remember anything, the children will say tomorrow, good morning, my teacher, the poor prisoners who come every day bringing flowers to their jailor. 1-2-3-4-5—it is monstrous to confuse love with revolution, night with day, life with death—ah, Eugenio!

The tolling of the midnight bell is a signal, but what does it mean? Get up, Laura, and follow me: come out of your sleep, out of your bed, out of this strange house. What are you doing in this house? Without a word, without fear she rose and reached for Eugenio's hand, but he eluded her with a sharp, sly smile and drifted away. This is not all, you shall see—Murderer, he said, follow me, I will show you a new country, but it is far away and we must hurry.

No, said Laura, not unless you take my hand, no; and she clung first to the stair rail, and then to the topmost branch of the Judas tree that bent down slowly and set her upon the earth, and then to the rocky ledge of a cliff, and then to the jagged wave of a sea that was not water but a desert of crumbling stone. Where are you taking me, she asked in wonder but without fear. To death, and it is a long way off, and we must hurry, said Eugenio. No, said Laura, not unless you take my hand. Then eat these flowers, poor prisoner, said Eugenio in a voice of pity, take and eat: and from the Judas tree he stripped the warm bleeding flowers, and held them to her lips. She saw that his hand was fleshless, a cluster of small white petrified branches, and his eye sockets were without light, but she ate the flowers greedily for they satisfied both hunger and thirst. Murderer! said Eugenio, and Cannibal! This is my body and my blood. Laura cried No! and at the sound of her own voice, she awoke trembling, and was afraid to sleep again.

1929, 1930

ZORA NEALE HURSTON
1891–1960

Zora Neale Hurston was born in 1891 in Notasulga, Alabama, and moved with her family in 1892 to Eatonville, Florida, an all-black town. Her father, a Baptist preacher of considerable eloquence, was not a family man and made life difficult for his wife and eight children. The tie between mother and daughter was strong; Lucy Hurston was a driving force and strong support for all her children. But her death when Zora Hurston was about eleven left the child with little home life. Hitherto, the town of Eatonville had been like an extended family to her, and her early childhood was protected from racism because she encountered no white people. With her mother's death, Hurston's wanderings and her initiation into American racism began. The early security had given her the core of self-confidence she needed to survive. She moved from one relative's home to another until she was old enough to support herself, and with her earnings she began slowly to pursue an education. Although she had never finished grade school in Eatonville she was able to enter and complete college. In the early 1920s at Howard University in Washington, D.C. (the nation's leading African American university at that time), she studied with the great black educator Alain Locke, who was to make history with his anthology *The New Negro* in 1925. After a short story, "Drenched in Light," appeared in the New York African American magazine *Opportunity*, she decided to move to Harlem and pursue a literary career there.

As her biographer, Robert Hemenway, writes, "Zora Hurston was an extraordinarily witty woman, and she acquired an instant reputation in New York for her high spirits and side-splitting tales of Eatonville life. She could walk into a room of strangers . . . and almost immediately gather people, charm, amuse, and impress them." The Eatonville vignettes printed here convey the flavor of this discourse. Generous, outspoken, high spirited, an interesting conversationalist, she worked as a personal secretary for the politically liberal novelist Fannie Hurst and entered Barnard College. Her career took two simultaneous directions: at Barnard she studied with the famous anthropologist Franz Boas and developed an interest in black folk traditions, and in Harlem she became well known as a storyteller, an informal performing artist. Thus she was doubly committed to the oral narrative, and her work excels in its representation of people talking.

When she graduated from Barnard in 1927 she received a fellowship to return to Florida and study the oral traditions of Eatonville. From then on, she strove to achieve a balance between focusing on the folk and her origins and focusing on herself as an individual. After the fellowship money ran out, Hurston was supported by Mrs. R. Osgood Mason, an elderly white patron of the arts. Mason had firm ideas about what she wanted her protégés to produce; she required them all to get her permission before publishing any of the work that she had subsidized. In this relationship, Hurston experienced a difficulty that all the black artists of the Harlem Renaissance had to face—the fact that well-off white people were the sponsors of, and often the chief audience for, their work.

Hurston's work was not entirely popular with the male intellectual leaders of the Harlem community. She quarreled especially with Langston Hughes; she rejected the idea that a black writer's chief concern should be how blacks were being portrayed to the white reader. She did not write to "uplift her race," either; because in her view it was already uplifted, she (like Claude McKay) was not embarrassed to present her characters as mixtures of good and bad, strong and weak. Some of the other Harlem writers thought her either naïve or egotistical, but Hurston argued that freedom could only mean freedom from all coercion, no matter what the source.

The Great Depression brought an end to the structure that had undergirded Hurston's fieldwork, and she turned fully to writing. Unfortunately her most important work appeared in the mid-1930s when there was little interest in it, or in African American writing in general. She published *Jonah's Gourd Vine* in 1934 (a novel whose main character is based on her father); *Mules and Men* in 1935 (based on material from her field trips in Florida—this was her best-selling book, but it earned a total of only $943.75); and *Their Eyes Were Watching God*, in 1937. This novel about an African American woman's quest for selfhood has become a popular and critical favorite, both a woman's story, and a descriptive critique of southern African American folk society, showing its divisions and diversity. Technically, it is a loosely organized, highly metaphorical novel, with passages of broad folk humor and of extreme artistic compression. Other books followed in 1938 and 1939, and she wrote an autobiography—*Dust Tracks on a Road*—which appeared in 1942, with its occasional expression of antiwhite sentiments removed by her editors. At this point, however, Hurston had no audience. For the last decade of her life she lived in Florida, working from time to time as a maid.

How It Feels to Be Colored Me[1]

I am colored but I offer nothing in the way of extenuating circumstances except the fact that I am the only Negro in the United States whose grandfather on the mother's side was *not* an Indian chief.

I remember the very day that I became colored. Up to my thirteenth year I lived in the little Negro town of Eatonville, Florida. It is exclusively a colored town. The only white people I knew passed through the town going to or coming from Orlando. The native whites rode dusty horses, the Northern tourists chugged down the sandy village road in automobiles. The town knew the Southerners and never stopped cane chewing when they passed. But the Northerners were something else again. They were peered at cautiously from behind the curtains by the timid. The more venturesome would come out on the porch to watch them go past and got just as much pleasure out of the tourists as the tourists got out of the village.

1. The text is that of *I Love Myself When I Am Laughing . . . and Then Again When I Am Looking Mean and Impressive* (1979), edited by Alice Walker.

The front porch might seem a daring place for the rest of the town, but it was a gallery seat for me. My favorite place was atop the gate-post. Proscenium box[2] for a born first-nighter. Not only did I enjoy the show, but I didn't mind the actors knowing that I liked it. I usually spoke to them in passing. I'd wave at them and when they returned my salute, I would say something like this: "Howdy-do-well-I-thank-you-where-you-goin'?" Usually automobile or the horse paused at this, and after a queer exchange of compliments, I would probably "go a piece of the way" with them, as we say in farthest Florida. If one of my family happened to come to the front in time to see me, of course negotiations would be rudely broken off. But even so, it is clear that I was the first "welcome-to-our-state" Floridian, and I hope the Miami Chamber of Commerce will please take notice.

During this period, white people differed from colored to me only in that they rode through town and never lived there. They liked to hear me "speak pieces" and sing and wanted to see me dance the parse-me-la, and gave me generously of their small silver for doing these things, which seemed strange to me for I wanted to do them so much that I needed bribing to stop. Only they didn't know it. The colored people gave no dimes. They deplored any joyful tendencies in me, but I was their Zora nevertheless. I belonged to them, to the nearby hotels, to the county—everybody's Zora.

But changes came in the family when I was thirteen, and I was sent to school in Jacksonville. I left Eatonville, the town of the oleanders, as Zora. When I disembarked from the river-boat at Jacksonville, she was no more. It seemed that I had suffered a sea change. I was not Zora of Orange County any more, I was now a little colored girl. I found it out in certain ways. In my heart as well as in the mirror, I became a fast brown—warranted not to rub nor run.

But I am not tragically colored. There is no great sorrow dammed up in my soul, nor lurking behind my eyes. I do not mind at all. I do not belong to the sobbing school of Negrohood who hold that nature somehow has given them a lowdown dirty deal and whose feelings are all hurt about it. Even in the helter-skelter skirmish that is my life, I have seen that the world is to the strong regardless of a little pigmentation more or less. No, I do not weep at the world—I am too busy sharpening my oyster knife.

Someone is always at my elbow reminding me that I am the granddaughter of slaves. It fails to register depression with me. Slavery is sixty years in the past. The operation was successful and the patient is doing well, thank you. The terrible struggle that made me an American out of a potential slave said "On the line!" The Reconstruction said "Get set!"; and the generation before said "Go!" I am off to a flying start and I must not halt in the stretch to look behind and weep. Slavery is the price I paid for civilization, and the choice was not with me. It is a bully adventure and worth all that I have paid through my ancestors for it. No one on earth ever had a greater chance for glory. The world to be won and nothing to be lost. It is thrilling to think—to know that for any act of mine, I shall get twice as much praise or twice as much blame. It is quite exciting to hold the center of the national stage, with the spectators not knowing whether to laugh or to weep.

The position of my white neighbor is much more difficult. No brown

---

2. Box at the front of the auditorium, closest to the stage.

specter pulls up a chair beside me when I sit down to eat. No dark ghost thrusts its leg against mine in bed. The game of keeping what one has is never so exciting as the game of getting.

I do not always feel colored. Even now I often achieve the unconscious Zora of Eatonville before the Hegira.[3] I feel most colored when I am thrown against a sharp white background.

For instance at Barnard. "Besides the waters of the Hudson" I feel my race. Among the thousand white persons, I am a dark rock surged upon, and over-swept, but through it all, I remain myself. When covered by the waters, I am; and the ebb but reveals me again.

Sometimes it is the other way around. A white person is set down in our midst, but the contrast is just as sharp for me. For instance, when I sit in the drafty basement that is The New World Cabaret[4] with a white person, my color comes. We enter chatting about any little nothing that we have in common and are seated by the jazz waiters. In the abrupt way that jazz orchestras have, this one plunges into a number. It loses no time in circumlocutions, but gets right down to business. It constricts the thorax and splits the heart with its tempo and narcotic harmonies. This orchestra grows rambunctious, rears on its hind legs and attacks the tonal veil with primitive fury, rending it, claw-ing it until it breaks through to the jungle beyond. I follow those heathen—follow them exultingly. I dance wildly inside myself; I yell within, I whoop; I shake my assegai[5] above my head, I hurl it true to the mark *yeeeeooww!* I am in the jungle and living in the jungle way. My face is painted red and yellow and my body is painted blue. My pulse is throbbing like a war drum. I want to slaughter something—give pain, give death to what, I do not know. But the piece ends. The men of the orchestra wipe their lips and rest their fingers. I creep back slowly to the veneer we call civilization with the last tone and find the white friend sitting motionless in his seat smoking calmly.

"Good music they have here," he remarks, drumming the table with his fin-gertips.

Music. The great blobs of purple and red emotion have not touched him. He has only heard what I felt. He is far away and I see him but dimly across the ocean and the continent that have fallen between us. He is so pale with his whiteness then and I am *so* colored.

At certain times I have no race, I am *me*. When I set my hat at a certain angle and saunter down Seventh Avenue, Harlem City, feeling as snooty as the lions in front of the Forty-Second Street Library, for instance. So far as my feelings are concerned, Peggy Hopkins Joyce on the Boule Mich[6] with her gorgeous raiment, stately carriage, knees knocking together in a most aristocratic man-ner, has nothing on me. The cosmic Zora emerges. I belong to no race nor time. I am the eternal feminine with its string of beads.

I have no separate feeling about being an American citizen and colored. I am merely a fragment of the Great Soul that surges within the boundaries. My country, right or wrong.

3. Forced march of Muhammad from Mecca to Medina in 622 C.E.; hence any forced flight or jour-ney for safety.
4. Popular Harlem nightclub in the 1920s.
5. A slender spear used by some South African peoples.

6. Boulevard St. Michel, a street on the Left Bank of Paris running through the Latin Quarter. It is lined with cafés that were—and still are—fre-quented by Americans. Joyce was a much-photographed socialite and heiress.

Sometimes, I feel discriminated against, but it does not make me angry. It merely astonishes me. How *can* any deny themselves the pleasure of my company? It's beyond me.

But in the main, I feel like a brown bag of miscellany propped against a wall. Against a wall in company with other bags, white, red and yellow. Pour out the contents, and there is discovered a jumble of small things priceless and worthless. A first-water diamond, an empty spool, bits of broken glass, lengths of string, a key to a door long since crumbled away, a rusty knife-blade, old shoes saved for a road that never was and never will be, a nail bent under the weight of things too heavy for any nail, a dried flower or two still a little fragrant. In your hand is the brown bag. On the ground before you is the jumble it held—so much like the jumble in the bags, could they be emptied, that all might be dumped in a single heap and the bags refilled without altering the content of any greatly. A bit of colored glass more or less would not matter. Perhaps that is how the Great Stuffer of Bags filled them in the first place—who knows?

1928

The Gilded Six-Bits[1]

It was a Negro yard around a Negro house in a Negro settlement that looked to the payroll of the G and G Fertilizer works for its support.

But there was something happy about the place. The front yard was parted in the middle by a sidewalk from gate to door-step, a sidewalk edged on either side by quart bottles driven neck down into the ground on a slant. A mess of homey flowers planted without a plan but blooming cheerily from their helter-skelter places. The fence and house were whitewashed. The porch and steps scrubbed white.

The front door stood open to the sunshine so that the floor of the front room could finish drying after its weekly scouring. It was Saturday. Everything clean from the front gate to the privy house. Yard raked so that the strokes of the rake would make a pattern. Fresh newspaper cut in fancy edge on the kitchen shelves.

Missie May was bathing herself in the galvanized washtub in the bedroom. Her dark-brown skin glistened under the soapsuds that skittered down from her wash rag. Her stiff young breasts thrust forward aggressively like broad-based cones with the tips lacquered in black.

She heard men's voices in the distance and glanced at the dollar clock on the dresser.

"Humph! Ah'm way behind time t'day! Joe gointer be heah 'fore Ah git mah clothes on if Ah don't make haste."

She grabbed the clean meal sack at hand and dried herself hurriedly and began to dress. But before she could tie her slippers, there came the ring of singing metal on wood. Nine times.

Missie May grinned with delight. She had not seen the big tall man come stealing in the gate and creep up the walk grinning happily at the joyful mischief he was about to commit. But she knew that it was her husband

1. The text is from the printing in *Story* magazine (1933). "Gilded": lightly plated with thin gold or gold-colored foil. "Six-bits": seventy-five cents (two bits equals one quarter).

throwing silver dollars in the door for her to pick up and pile beside her plate at dinner. It was this way every Saturday afternoon. The nine dollars hurled into the open door, he scurried to a hiding place behind the cape jasmine bush and waited.

Missie May promptly appeared at the door in mock alarm.

"Who dat chunkin' money in mah do'way?" She demanded. No answer from the yard. She leaped off the porch and began to search the shrubbery. She peeped under the porch and hung over the gate to look up and down the road. While she did this, the man behind the jasmine darted to the chinaberry tree. She spied him and gave chase.

"Nobody ain't gointer be chuckin' money at me and Ah not do 'em nothin'," she shouted in mock anger. He ran around the house with Missie May at his heels. She overtook him at the kitchen door. He ran inside but could not close it after him before she crowded in and locked with him in a rough and tumble. For several minutes the two were a furious mass of male and female energy. Shouting, laughing, twisting, turning, tussling, tickling each other in the ribs; Missie May clutching onto Joe and Joe trying, but not too hard, to get away.

"Missie May, take yo' hand out mah pocket!" Joe shouted out between laughs.

"Ah ain't, Joe, not lessen you gwine gimme whateve' it is good you got in yo' pocket. Turn it go, Joe, do Ah'll tear yo' clothes."

"Go on tear 'em. You de one dat pushes de needles round heah. Move yo' hand Missie May."

"Lemme git dat paper sack out yo' pocket. Ah bet its candy kisses."

"Tain't. Move yo' hand. Woman ain't go no business in a man's clothes nohow. Go way."

Missie May gouged way down and gave an upward jerk and triumphed.

"Unhhunh! Ah got it. It 'tis so candy kisses. Ah knowed you had somethin' for me in yo' clothes. Now Ah got to see whut's in every pocket you got."

Joe smiled indulgently and let his wife go through all of his pockets and take out the things that he had hidden there for her to find. She bore off the chewing gum, the cake of sweet soap, the pocket handkerchief as if she had wrested them from him, as if they had not been bought for the sake of this friendly battle.

"Whew! dat play-fight done got me all warmed up," Joe exclaimed. "Got me some water in de kittle?"

"Yo' water is on de fire and yo' clean things is cross de bed. Hurry up and wash yo'self and git changed so we kin eat. Ah'm hongry." As Missie said this, she bore the steaming kettle into the bedroom.

"You ain't hongry, sugar," Joe contradicted her. "Youse jes' a little empty. Ah'm de one whut's hongry. Ah could eat up camp meetin', back off 'ssocia-tion, and drink Jurdan[2] dry. Have it on de table when Ah git out de tub."

"Don't you mess wid mah business, man. You git in yo' clothes. Ah'm a real wife, not no dress and breath.[3] Ah might not look lak one, but if you burn me, you won't git a thing but wife ashes."

Joe splashed in the bedroom and Missie May fanned around in the kitchen.

2. The Jordan River in biblical Palestine (now Israel).
3. All show; i.e., not a real wife.

A fresh red and white checked cloth on the table. Big pitcher of buttermilk beaded with pale drops of butter from the churn. Hot fried mullet, crackling bread, ham hock atop a mound of string beans and new potatoes, and perched on the window-sill a pone[4] of spicy potato pudding.

Very little talk during the meal but that little consisted of banter that pretended to deny affection but in reality flaunted it. Like when Missie May reached for a second helping of the tater pone. Joe snatched it out of her reach.

After Missie May had made two or three unsuccessful grabs at the pan, she begged, "Aw, Joe gimme some mo' dat tater pone."

"Nope, sweetenin' is for us men-folks. Y'all pritty lil frail eels don't need nothin' lak dis. You too sweet already."

"Please, Joe."

"Naw, naw. Ah don't want you to git no sweeter than whut you is already. We goin' down de road a lil piece t'night so you go put on yo' Sunday-go-to-meetin' things."

Missie May looked at her husband to see if he was playing some prank. "Sho nuff, Joe?"

"Yeah. We goin' to de ice cream parlor."

"Where de ice cream parlor at, Joe?"

"A new man done come heah from Chicago and he done got a place and took and opened it up for a ice cream parlor, and bein' as it's real swell, Ah wants you to be one de first ladies to walk in dere and have some set down."

"Do Jesus, Ah ain't knowed nothin' 'bout it. Who de man done it?"

"Mister Otis D. Slemmons, of spots and places—Memphis, Chicago, Jacksonville, Philadelphia and so on."

"Dat heavy-set man wid his mouth full of gold teethes?"

"Yeah. Where did you see 'im at?"

"Ah went down to de sto' tuh git a box of lye and Ah seen 'im standing' on de corner talkin' to some of de mens, and Ah come on back and went to scrubbin' de floor, and he passed and tipped his hat whilst Ah was scourin' de steps. Ah thought Ah never seen *him* befo'."

Joe smiled pleasantly. "Yeah, he's up to date. He got de finest clothes Ah ever seen on a colored man's back."

"Aw, he don't look no better in his clothes than you do in yourn. He got a puzzlegut on 'im and he so chuckle-headed,[5] he got a pone behind his neck."

Joe looked down at his own abdomen and said wistfully, "Wisht Ah had a build on me lak he got. He ain't puzzle-gutted, honey. He jes' got a corperation. Dat make 'm look lak a rich white man. All rich mens is got some belly on 'em."

"Ah seen de pitchers of Henry Ford and he's a spare-built man and Rockefeller look lak he ain't got but one gut. But Ford and Rockefeller and dis Slemmons and all de rest kin be as many-gutted as dey please, Ah'm satisfied wid you jes' lak you is, baby. God took pattern after a pine tree and built you noble. Youse a pritty man, and if Ah knowed any way to make you mo' pritty still Ah'd take and do it."

Joe reached over gently and toyed with Missie May's ear. "You jes' say dat cause you love me, but Ah know Ah can't hold no light to Otis D. Slemmons. Ah ain't never been nowhere and Ah ain't got nothin' but you."

---

4. Loaf- or oval-shaped cake.   5. Stupid, blockheaded. "Puzzlegut": fat belly.

Missie May got on his lap and kissed him and he kissed back in kind. Then he went on. "All de womens is crazy 'bout 'im everywhere he go."

"How you know dat, Joe?"

"He tole us so hisself."

"Dat don't make it so. His mouf is cut cross-ways, ain't it? Well, he kin lie jes' lak anybody else."

"Good Lawd, Missie! You womens sho is hard to sense into things. He's got a five-dollar gold piece for a stick-pin and he got a ten-dollar gold piece on his watch chain and his mouf is jes' crammed full of gold teethes. Sho wisht it wuz mine. And whut make it so cool, he got money 'cumulated. And womens give it all to 'im."

"Ah don't see whut de womens see on 'im. Ah wouldn't give 'im a wink if de sheriff wuz after 'im."

"Well, he tole us how de white womens in Chicago give 'im all dat gold money. So he don't 'low nobody to touch it at all. Not even put dey finger on it. Dey tole 'im not to. You kin make 'miration at it, but don't tetch it."

"Whyn't he stay up dere where dey so crazy 'bout 'im?"

"Ah reckon dey done made 'im vast-rich and he wants to travel some. He say dey wouldn't leave 'im hit a lick of work. He got mo' lady people crazy 'bout him than he kin shake a stick at."

"Joe, Ah hates to see you so dumb. Dat stray nigger jes' tell y'all anything and y'all b'lieve it."

"Go 'head on now, honey and put on yo' clothes. He talkin' 'bout his pritty womens—Ah want 'im to see *mine*."

Missie May went off to dress and Joe spent the time trying to make his stomach punch out like Slemmons' middle. He tried the rolling swagger of the stranger, but found that his tall bone-and-muscle stride fitted ill with it. He just had time to drop back into his seat before Missie May came in dressed to go.

On the way home that night Joe was exultant. "Didn't Ah say ole Otis was swell? Can't he talk Chicago talk? Wuzn't dat funny whut he said when great big fat ole Ida Armstrong come in? He asted me, 'Who is dat broad wid de forte shake?' Dat's a new word. Us always thought forty was a set of figgers but he showed us where it means a whole heap of things. Sometimes he don't say forty, he jes' say thirty-eight and two and dat mean de same thing. Know whut he tole me when Ah wuz payin' for our ice cream? He say, 'Ah have to hand it to you, Joe. Dat wife of yours is jes' thirty-eight and two. Yessuh, she's forte!' Ain't he killin'?"

"He'll do in case of a rush. But he sho is got uh heap uh gold on 'im. Dat's de first time Ah ever seed gold money. It lookted good on him sho nuff, but it'd look a whole heap better on you."

"Who, me? Missie May youse crazy! Where would a po' man lak me git gold money from?"

Missie May was silent for a minute, then she said, "Us might find some goin' long de road some time. Us could."

"Who would be losin' gold money round heah? We ain't even seen none dese white folks wearin' no gold money on dey watch chain. You must be figgerin' Mister Packard or Mister Cadillac goin' pass through heah."

"You don't know whut been lost 'round heah. Maybe somebody way back in memorial times[6] lost they gold money and went on off and it ain't never

---

6. Wordplay on "in time immemorial"; time so long ago as to be forgotten.

been found. And then if we wuz to find it, you could wear some 'thout havin' no gang of womens lak dat Slemmons say he got."

Joe laughed and hugged her. "Don't be so wishful 'bout me. Ah'm satisfied de way Ah is. So long as Ah be yo' husband, Ah don't keer 'bout nothin' else. Ah'd ruther all de other womens in de world to be dead than for you to have de toothache. Less we go to bed and git our night rest."

It was Saturday night once more before Joe could parade his wife in Slemmons' ice cream parlor again. He worked the night shift and Saturday was his only night off. Every other evening around six o'clock he left home, and dying dawn saw him hustling home around the lake where the challenging sun flung a flaming sword from east to west across the trembling water.

That was the best part of life—going home to Missie May. Their white-washed house, the mock battle on Saturday, the dinner and ice cream parlor afterwards, church on Sunday nights when Missie outdressed any woman in town—all, everything was right.

One night around eleven the acid[7] ran out at the G. and G. The foreman knocked off the crew and let the steam die down. As Joe rounded the lake on his way home, a lean moon rode the lake in a silver boat. If anybody had asked Joe about the moon on the lake, he would have said he hadn't paid it any attention. But he saw it with his feelings. It made him yearn painfully for Missie. Creation obsessed him. He thought about children. They had been married for more than a year now. They had money put away. They ought to be making little feet for shoes. A little boy child would be about right.

He saw a dim light in the bedroom and decided to come in through the kitchen door. He could wash the fertilizer dust off himself before presenting himself to Missie May. It would be nice for her not to know that he was there until he slipped into his place in bed and hugged her back. She always liked that.

He eased the kitchen door open slowly and silently, but when he went to set his dinner bucket on the table he bumped it into a pile of dishes, and something crashed to the floor. He heard his wife gasp in fright and hurried to reassure her.

"Iss me, honey. Don't get skeered."

There was a quick, large movement in the bedroom. A rustle, a thud, and a stealthy silence. The light went out.

What? Robbers? Murderers? Some varmint attacking his helpless wife, perhaps. He struck a match, threw himself on guard and stepped over the door-sill into the bedroom.

The great belt on the wheel of Time slipped and eternity stood still. By the match light he could see the man's legs fighting with his breeches in his frantic desire to get them on. He had both chance and time to kill the intruder in his helpless condition—half in and half out of his pants—but he was too weak to take action. The shapeless enemies of humanity that live in the hours of Time had waylaid Joe. He was assaulted in his weakness. Like Samson awakening after his haircut.[8] So he just opened his mouth and laughed.

The match went out and he struck another and lit the lamp. A howling wind raced across his heart, but underneath its fury he heard his wife sobbing and Slemmons pleading for his life. Offering to buy it with all that he had. "Please, suh, don't kill me. Sixty-two dollars at de sto'. Gold money."

7. Used in making fertilizer.
8. In Judges 13–16, Samson's exceptional strength resides in his hair, which his treacherous lover, Delilah, cuts off while he sleeps.

Joe just stood. Slemmons looked at the window, but it was screened. Joe stood out like a rough-backed mountain between him and the door. Barring him from escape, from sunrise, from life.

He considered a surprise attack upon the big clown that stood there laughing like a chessy cat.[9] But before his fist could travel an inch, Joe's own rushed out to crush him like a battering ram. Then Joe stood over him.

"Git into yo' damn rags, Slemmons, and dat quick."

Slemmons scrambled to his feet and into his vest and coat. As he grabbed his hat, Joe's fury overrode his intentions and he grabbed at Slemmons with his left hand and struck at him with his right. The right landed. The left grazed the front of his vest. Slemmons was knocked a somersault into the kitchen and fled through the open door. Joe found himself alone with Missie May, with the golden watch charm clutched in his left fist. A short bit of broken chain dangled between his fingers.

Missie May was sobbing. Wails of weeping without words. Joe stood, and after awhile he found out that he had something in his hand. And then he stood and felt without thinking and without seeing with his natural eyes. Missie May kept on crying and Joe kept on feeling so much and not knowing what to do with all his feelings, he put Slemmons' watch charm in his pants pocket and took a good laugh and went to bed.

"Missie May, whut you cryin' for?"

"Cause Ah love you so hard and Ah know you don't love *me* no mo'."

Joe sank his face into the pillow for a spell then he said huskily, "You don't know de feelings of dat yet, Missie May."

"Oh Joe, honey, he said he wuz gointer give me dat gold money and he jes' kept on after me—"

Joe was very still and silent for a long time. Then he said, "Well, don't cry no mo', Missie May. Ah got yo' gold piece for you."

The hours went past on their rusty ankles. Joe still and quiet on one bedrail and Missie May wrung dry of sobs on the other. Finally the sun's tide crept upon the shore of night and drowned all its hours. Missie May with her face stiff and streaked towards the window saw the dawn come into her yard. It was day. Nothing more. Joe wouldn't be coming home as usual. No need to fling open the front door and sweep off the porch, making it nice for Joe. Never no more breakfast to cook; no more washing and starching of Joe's jumper-jackets and pants. No more nothing. So why get up?

With this strange man in her bed, she felt embarrassed to get up and dress. She decided to wait till he had dressed and gone. Then she would get up, dress quickly and be gone forever beyond reach of Joe's looks and laughs. But he never moved. Red light turned to yellow, then white.

From beyond the no-man's land between them came a voice. A strange voice that yesterday had been Joe's.

"Missie May, ain't you gonna fix me no breakfus'?"

She sprang out of bed. "Yeah, Joe. Ah didn't reckon you wuz hongry."

No need to die today. Joe needed her for a few more minutes anyhow.

Soon there was a roaring fire in the cook stove. Water bucket full and two chickens killed. Joe loved fried chicken and rice. She didn't deserve a thing

---

9. I.e., Cheshire cat; an allusion to the grinning cat in *Alice's Adventures in Wonderland* (1865), by Lewis Carroll (1832–1889).

and good Joe was letting her cook him some breakfast. She rushed hot biscuits to the table as Joe took his seat.

He ate with his eyes on his plate. No laughter, no banter.

"Missie May, you ain't eatin' yo' breakfus'."

"Ah don't choose none, Ah thank yuh."

His coffee cup was empty. She sprang to refill it. When she turned from the stove and bent to set the cup beside Joe's plate, she saw the yellow coin on the table between them.

She slumped into her seat and wept into her arms.

Presently Joe said calmly, "Missie May, you cry too much. Don't look back lak Lot's wife and turn to salt."[1]

The sun, the hero of every day, the impersonal old man that beams as brightly on death as on birth, came up every morning and raced across the blue dome and dipped into the sea of fire every evening. Water ran down hill and birds nested.

Missie knew why she didn't leave Joe. She couldn't. She loved him too much, but she could not understand why Joe didn't leave her. He was polite, even kind at times, but aloof.

There were no more Saturday romps. No ringing silver dollars to stack beside her plate. No pockets to rifle. In fact the yellow coin in his trousers was like a monster hiding in the cave of his pockets to destroy her.

She often wondered if he still had it, but nothing could have induced her to ask nor yet to explore his pockets to see for herself. Its shadow was in the house whether or no.

One night Joe came home around midnight and complained of pains in the back. He asked Missie to rub him down with liniment. It had been three months since Missie had touched his body and it all seemed strange. But she rubbed him. Grateful for the chance. Before morning, youth triumphed and Missie exulted. But the next day, as she joyfully made up their bed, beneath her pillow she found the piece of money with the bit of chain attached.

Alone to herself, she looked at the thing with loathing, but look she must. She took it into her hands with trembling and saw first thing that it was no gold piece. It was a gilded half dollar. Then she knew why Slemmons had forbidden anyone to touch his gold. He trusted village eyes at a distance not to recognize his stick-pin as a gilded quarter, and his watch charm as a four-bit piece.

She was glad at first that Joe had left it there. Perhaps he was through with her punishment. They were man and wife again. Then another thought came clawing at her. He had come home to buy from her as if she were any woman in the long house.[2] Fifty cents for her love. As if to say that he could pay as well as Slemmons. She slid the coin into his Sunday pants pocket and dressed herself and left his house.

Halfway between her house and the quarters[3] she met her husband's mother, and after a short talk she turned and went back home. Never would she admit defeat to that woman who prayed for it nightly. If she had not the substance of marriage she had the outside show. Joe must leave *her*. She let him see she didn't want his old gold four-bits too.

1. According to Genesis 19.26, Lot's wife was turned into a pillar of salt for looking back at the destroyed city of Sodom when she and her husband were fleeing from it.
2. House of prostitution.
3. Workers' dwellings.

She saw no more of the coin for some time though she knew that Joe could not help finding it in his pocket. But his health kept poor, and he came home at least every ten days to be rubbed.

The sun swept around the horizon, trailing its robes of weeks and days. One morning as Joe came in from work, he found Missie May chopping wood. Without a word he took the ax and chopped a huge pile before he stopped.

"You ain't got no business choppin' wood, and you know it."

"How come? Ah been choppin' it for de last longest."

"Ah ain't blind. You makin' feet for shoes."[4]

"Won't you be glad to have a lil baby chile, Joe?"

"You know dat 'thout astin' me."

"Iss gointer be a boy chile and de very spit of you." "You reckon, Missie May?"

"Who else could it look lak?"

Joe said nothing, but he thrust his hand deep into his pocket and fingered something there.

It was almost six months later Missie May took to bed and Joe went and got his mother to come wait on the house.

Missie May delivered a fine boy. Her travail was over when Joe came in from work one morning. His mother and the old women were drinking great bowls of coffee around the fire in the kitchen.

The minute Joe came into the room his mother called him aside.

"How did Missie May make out?" he asked quickly.

"Who, dat gal? She strong as a ox. She gointer have plenty mo'. We done fixed her wid de sugar and lard to sweeten her for de nex' one."

Joe stood silent awhile.

"You ain't ast 'bout de baby, Joe. You oughter be mighty proud cause he sho is de spittin' image of yuh, son. Dat's yourn all right, if you never git another one, dat un is yourn. And you know Ah'm mighty proud too, son, cause Ah never thought well of you marryin' Missie May cause her ma used tuh fan her foot round right smart and Ah been mighty skeered dat Missie May was gointer git misput on her road."

Joe said nothing. He fooled around the house till late in the day then just before he went to work, he went and stood at the foot of the bed and asked his wife how she felt. He did this every day during the week.

On Saturday he went to Orlando to make his market.[5] It had been a long time since he had done that.

Meat and lard, meal and flour, soap and starch. Cans of corn and tomatoes. All the staples. He fooled around town for awhile and bought bananas and apples. Way after while he went around to the candy store.

"Hellow, Joe," the clerk greeted him. "Ain't seen you in a long time."

"Nope, Ah ain't been heah. Been round in spots and places."

"Want some of them molasses kisses you always buy?"

"Yessuh." He threw the gilded half dollar on the counter. "Will dat spend?"

"Whut is it, Joe? Well, I'll be doggone! A gold-plated four-bit piece. Where'd you git it, Joe?"

"Offen a stray nigger dat come through Eatonville. He had it on his watch chain for a charm—goin' round making out iss gold money. Ha ha! He had a quarter on his tie pin and it wuz all golded up too. Tryin' to fool people. Makin' out he so rich and everything. Ha! Ha! Tryin' to tole off folkses wives from home."

"How did you git it, Joe? Did he fool you, too?"

"Who, me? Naw suh! He ain't fooled me none. Know whut Ah done? He come round me wid his smart talk. Ah hauled off and knocked 'im down and took his old four-bits way from 'im. Gointer buy my wife some good ole lasses kisses wid it. Gimme fifty cents worth of dem candy kisses."

"Fifty cents buys a mighty lot of candy kisses, Joe. Why don't you split it up and take some chocolate bars, too. They eat good, too."

"Yessuh, dey do, but Ah wants all dat in kisses. Ah got a lil boy chile home now. Tain't a week old yet, but he kin suck a sugar tit and maybe eat one them kisses hisself."

Joe got his candy and left the store. The clerk turned to the next customer. "Wisht I could be like these darkies. Laughin' all the time. Nothin' worries 'em."

Back in Eatonville, Joe reached his own front door. There was the ring of singing metal on wood. Fifteen times. Missie May couldn't run to the door, but she crept there as quickly as she could.

"Joe Banks, Ah hear you chunkin' money in mah do'way. You wait till Ah got mah strength back and Ah'm gointer fix you for dat."

1933

EDNA ST. VINCENT MILLAY
1892–1950

Edna St. Vincent Millay's output ranged from Elizabethan sonnets through plays and sketches to political speeches. In the 1920s she became a kind of national symbol of the modern woman—liberated from Victorian mores, independent, self-supporting, full of energy and talent. She was raised in a small town on the coast of Maine by her divorced mother, who supported herself and three daughters through work as a practical nurse. The mother provided her children with books and music lessons and encouraged ambition and independence. Millay began to write poetry in high school and published her first book of poetry, *Renascence and Other Poems,* in 1917, when she was twenty-five. She went to Vassar College from 1913 to 1917 through the generosity of a benefactor impressed by her writing. At Vassar she studied languages, wrote songs and verse plays, and became interested in acting. After graduation she went to New York City, settling in the Greenwich Village section of the city and becoming associated with the unconventional life of the literary and political rebels who lived there. A member of the Provincetown Players group, she acted and also wrote two plays for them. *The Ballad of the Harp-Weaver* (1923, later retitled *The Harp-Weaver and Other Poems*) was awarded a Pulitzer Prize.

Millay lived in Europe from 1921 to 1923 and, upon her return, married and moved with her businessman husband Eugene Boissevain to a farm in upstate New York. She participated in the protests against the executions of Sacco and Vanzetti in 1927 and during the 1930s wrote anti-fascist newspaper verse, radio plays, and speeches. She was an advocate of early U.S. entrance into World War II.

Although as a young woman Millay achieved notoriety mainly for love poetry that described free, guiltless sexuality, her poems are more founded in the failure of love than in the joy of sex. The tone of her earliest work was flippantly cynical; later work became more muted and lyrical. Her New England poems, about nature and the familiar, fit into a regional tradition. Working with closed stanza forms and regular metrical lines, she displayed a high degree of technical virtuosity within quite deliberately chosen limits. "I will put chaos into fourteen lines," she wrote in one sonnet, joining the traditionalists like Robert Frost in a devotion to poetry as permanence.

The text of the poems included here is that of *Collected Poems: Edna St. Vincent Millay* (1956).

Recuerdo[1]

We were very tired, we were very merry—
We had gone back and forth all night on the ferry.
It was bare and bright, and smelled like a stable—
But we looked into a fire, we leaned across a table,
We lay on a hill-top underneath the moon;   5
And the whistles kept blowing, and the dawn came soon.

We were very tired, we were very merry—
We had gone back and forth all night on the ferry;
And you ate an apple, and I ate a pear,
From a dozen of each we had bought somewhere;   10
And the sky went wan, and the wind came cold,
And the sun rose dripping, a bucketful of gold.

We were very tired, we were very merry,
We had gone back and forth all night on the ferry.
We hailed, "Good morrow, mother!" to a shawl-covered head,   15
And bought a morning paper, which neither of us read;
And she wept, "God bless you!" for the apples and pears,
And we gave her all our money but our subway fares.

     1922

I Think I Should Have Loved You Presently

I think I should have loved you presently,
And given in earnest words I flung in jest;
And lifted honest eyes for you to see,
And caught your hand against my cheek and breast;
And all my pretty follies flung aside   5
That won you to me, and beneath your gaze,
Naked of reticence and shorn of pride,
Spread like a chart my little wicked ways.
I, that had been to you, had you remained,
But one more waking from a recurrent dream,   10

---

1. Remembrance, souvenir.

Cherish no less the certain stakes I gained,
And walk your memory's halls, austere, supreme,
A ghost in marble of a girl you knew
Who would have loved you in a day or two.

1922

Apostrophe to Man

(On reflecting that the world is ready to go to war again)

Detestable race, continue to expunge yourself, die out.
Breed faster, crowd, encroach, sing hymns, build bombing airplanes;
Make speeches, unveil statues, issue bonds, parade;
Convert again into explosives the bewildered ammonia and the distracted
    cellulose;
Convert again into putrescent matter drawing flies   5
The hopeful bodies of the young; exhort,
Pray, pull long faces, be earnest, be all but overcome, be photographed;
Confer, perfect your formulae, commercialize
Bacteria harmful to human tissue,
Put death on the market;   10
Breed, crowd, encroach, expand, expunge yourself, die out,
Homo called *sapiens*.

1934

I Too beneath Your Moon, Almighty Sex

I too beneath your moon, almighty Sex,
Go forth at nightfall crying like a cat,
Leaving the lofty tower I laboured at
For birds to foul and boys and girls to vex
With tittering chalk; and you, and the long necks   5
Of neighbours sitting where their mothers sat
Are well aware of shadowy this and that
In me, that's neither noble nor complex.
Such as I am, however, I have brought
To what it is, this tower; it is my own;   10
Though it was reared To Beauty, it was wrought
From what I had to build with: honest bone
Is there, and anguish; pride; and burning thought;
And lust is there, and nights not spent alone.

1939

I Forgot for a Moment

July 1940

I forgot for a moment France; I forgot England; I forgot my care:
I lived for a moment in a world where I was free to be
With the things and people that I love, and I was happy there.
I forgot for a moment Holland, I forgot my heavy care.

I lived for a moment in a world so lovely, so inept   5
At twisted words and crookèd deeds, it was as if I slept and dreamt.

It seemed that all was well with Holland—not a tank had crushed
The tulips there.
Mile after mile the level lowlands blossomed—yellow square,
    white square,
Scarlet strip and mauve strip bright beneath the brightly clouded sky,
    the round clouds and the gentle air.   10
Along the straight canals between striped fields of tulips in the
    morning sailed
Broad ships, their hulls by tulip-beds concealed, only the sails showing.

It seemed that all was well with England—the harsh foreign voice
    hysterically vowing,
Once more, to keep its word, at length was disbelieved, and hushed.

It seemed that all was well with France, with her straight roads   15
Lined with slender poplars, and the peasants on the skyline ploughing.

1940

E. E. CUMMINGS
1894–1962

Beginning in the 1920s and 1930s, Edward Estlin Cummings built a reputation as author of a particularly agreeable kind of modernist poetry, distinguished by clever formal innovation, a tender lyricism, and the thematic celebration of individuals against mass society. These qualities were evident in his first literary success, a zesty prose account of his experience in a French prison camp during World War I, *The Enormous Room* (1922). He and a friend had joined the ambulance corps in France the day after the United States entered the war; their disdain for the bureaucracy, expressed in outspoken letters home, aroused antagonism among French officials and they were imprisoned. To be made a prisoner by one's own side struck Cummings as outrageous and yet funny; from the experience he produced an ironic, profane celebration of the ordinary soldier and an attack on bureaucracy. His poetry continued the attack on depersonalized, commercial, exploitative mass culture and celebrated loners, lovers, and nonconformists.

He was born in Cambridge, Massachusetts. His father was a Congregationalist minister and teacher at Harvard; the family was close knit and Cummings, a much-loved son. While a student at Harvard (he graduated in 1915 and took an M.A. in 1916) he began to write poetry based on the intricate stanza patterns of the pre-Raphaelite and Metaphysical writers he was reading in English literature classes. When he began to innovate—as he did after discovering the poetry of Ezra Pound—he was able to build (like Pound himself) from a firm apprenticeship in traditional techniques.

After the war, Cummings established a life that included a studio in Greenwich Village, travel and sojourns in France, and summers at the family home in New Hampshire. He was a painter as well as a poet; simple living and careful management of a small allowance from his mother, along with prizes, royalties, and commissions, enabled him to work full time as an artist. He published four volumes of well-received poetry in the 1920s and a book of collected poems toward the end of the 1930s. In the 1950s he visited and read at many college campuses, where students enjoyed his tricks of verse and vocabulary and appreciated his tender yet earthy poetry. He received a special citation by the National Book Award committee in 1955 and the Bollingen Prize in 1957.

Cummings was less ambitious in his attempts to reshape poetry than Stein, Eliot, Pound, Stevens, or Williams, partly because he was much more concerned to be widely accessible. Cummings's verse is characterized by common speech and attention to the visual form of the poem—that is, the poem as it appears on the page as distinguished from its sound when read aloud. Experiments with capitalization or lack of it, punctuation, line breaks, hyphenation, and verse shapes were all carried out for the reader's eyes rather than ears. To express his sense that life was always in process, he wrote untitled poems without beginnings and endings, consisting of fragmentary lines. There is always humor in his poetry, and his outrage at cruelty and exploitation is balanced with gusto and celebration of the body.

The text of the poems included here is that of *Complete Poems* (1991).

Thy fingers make early flowers of

Thy fingers make early flowers of
all things.
thy hair mostly the hours love:
a smoothness which
sings,saying   5
(though love be a day)
do not fear,we will go amaying.

thy whitest feet crisply are straying.
Always
thy moist eyes are at kisses playing,   10
whose strangeness much
says;singing
(though love be a day)
for which girl art thou flowers bringing?

To be thy lips is a sweet thing   15
and small.
Death,Thee i call rich beyond wishing
if this thou catch,
else missing.
(though love be a day   20
and life be nothing,it shall not stop kissing).

1923

in Just-

in Just-
spring   when the world is mud-
luscious the little
lame balloonman

whistles   far   and wee   5

and eddieandbill come
running from marbles and
piracies and it's
spring

when the world is puddle-wonderful   10

the queer
old balloonman whistles
far   and   wee
and bettyandisbel come dancing

from hop-scotch and jump-rope and   15

it's
spring
and
      the

            goat-footed   20

balloonMan   whistles
far
and
wee

                                                    1920, 1923

O sweet spontaneous

O sweet spontaneous
earth how often have
the
doting

      fingers of   5
prurient philosophers pinched
and
poked

thee
,has the naughty thumb   10
of science prodded
thy

    beauty   .how
often have religions taken
thee upon their scraggy knees   15
squeezing and

buffeting thee that thou mightest conceive
gods
     (but
true   20

to the incomparable
couch of death thy
rhythmic
lover

    thou answerest   25

them only with

      spring)

                 1920, 1923

Buffalo Bill 's

Buffalo Bill 's[1]
defunct
    who used to
    ride a watersmooth-silver
            stallion   5
and break onetwothreefourfive pigeonsjustlikethat
                   Jesus

he was a handsome man
         and what i want to know is
how do you like your blueeyed boy   10
Mister Death

                 1920, 1923

---

1. William F. Cody (1846–1917), American scout and Wild West showman.

"next to of course god america i

"next to of course god america i
love you land of the pilgrims' and so forth oh
say can you see by the dawn's early my
country 'tis of centuries come and go
and are no more what of it we should worry   5
in every language even deafanddumb
thy sons acclaim your glorious name by gorry
by jingo by gee by gosh by gum
why talk of beauty what could be more beautiful than these heroic happy dead   10
who rushed like lions to the roaring slaughter
they did not stop to think they died instead
then shall the voice of liberty be mute?"

He spoke.   And drank rapidly a glass of water

1926

i sing of Olaf glad and big

i sing of Olaf glad and big
whose warmest heart recoiled at war:
a conscientious object-or

his wellbelovéd colonel(trig
westpointer[1] most succinctly bred)   5
took erring Olaf soon in hand;
but—though an host of overjoyed
noncoms(first knocking on the head
him)do through icy waters roll
that helplessness which others stroke   10
with brushes recently employed
anent this muddy toiletbowl,
while kindred intellects evoke
allegiance per blunt instruments—
Olaf(being to all intents   15
a corpse and wanting any rag
upon what God unto him gave)
responds,without getting annoyed
"I will not kiss your fucking flag"

straightway the silver bird looked grave   20
(departing hurriedly to shave)

but—though all kinds of officers
(a yearning nation's blueeyed pride)

---

1. Graduate of the U.S. Military Academy at West Point, New York.

their passive prey did kick and curse
until for wear their clarion   25
voices and boots were much the worse,
and egged the firstclassprivates on
his rectum wickedly to tease
by means of skilfully applied
bayonets roasted hot with heat—   30
Olaf(upon what were once knees)
does almost ceaselessly repeat
"there is some shit I will not eat"

our president,being of which
assertions duly notified   35
threw the yellowsonofabitch
into a dungeon,where he died

Christ(of His mercy infinite)
i pray to see;and Olaf,too

preponderatingly because   40
unless statistics lie he was
more brave than me:more blond than you.

                                                               1931

somewhere i have never travelled,gladly beyond

somewhere i have never travelled,gladly beyond
any experience,your eyes have their silence:
in your most frail gesture are things which enclose me,
or which i cannot touch because they are too near

your slightest look easily will unclose me   5
though i have closed myself as fingers,
you open always petal by petal myself as Spring opens
(touching skilfully,mysteriously)her first rose

or if your wish be to close me,iand
my life will shut very beautifully,suddenly,   10
as when the heart of this flower imagines
the snow carefully everywhere descending;

nothing which we are to perceive in this world equals
the power of your intense fragility:whose texture
compels me with the colour of its countries,   15
rendering death and forever with each breathing

(i do not know what it is about you that closes
and opens;only something in me understands
the voice of your eyes is deeper than all roses)
nobody,not even the rain,has such small hands   20

1931

anyone lived in a pretty how town

anyone lived in a pretty how town
(with up so floating many bells down)
spring summer autumn winter
he sang his didn't he danced his did.

Women and men(both little and small)   5
cared for anyone not at all
they sowed their isn't they reaped their same
sun moon stars rain

children guessed(but only a few
and down they forgot as up they grew   10
autumn winter spring summer)
that noone loved him more by more

when by now and tree by leaf
she laughed his joy she cried his grief
bird by snow and stir by still   15
anyone's any was all to her

someones married their everyones
laughed their cryings and did their dance
(sleep wake hope and then)they
said their nevers they slept their dream   20

stars rain sun moon
(and only the snow can begin to explain
how children are apt to forget to remember
with up so floating many bells down)

one day anyone died i guess   25
(and noone stooped to kiss his face)
busy folk buried them side by side
little by little and was by was

all by all and deep by deep
and more by more they dream their sleep   30
noone and anyone earth by april
wish by spirit and if by yes.

Women and men(both dong and ding)
summer autumn winter spring
reaped their sowing and went their came   35
sun moon stars rain

                                                                          1940

JEAN TOOMER
1894–1967

Jean Toomer's *Cane*, the author's contribution to Harlem Renaissance literature, received immediate acclaim when it appeared in 1923. Unlike African American artists who felt they had to choose either to publicize the nobility of rural black people or to represent a sophisticated black artistic sensibility, Toomer reconciled the two, describing rural people through the analytic filter of a modern, urban literary style.

Born in Washington, D.C., Toomer never knew his father. He grew up with his grandfather, who had been an important Louisiana politician during the Reconstruction era, and his mother. After high school graduation he attended several colleges— the University of Wisconsin, the Massachusetts College of Agriculture, the American College of Physical Training in Chicago, the University of Chicago, and the City College of New York—without completing a degree. He held numerous short-term jobs in various parts of the country, including four months in 1921 as superintendent of a small black school in Sparta, Georgia. This, his only sustained encounter with a rural population, formed the basis of *Cane*.

He began writing when he was in his middle twenties, publishing poems and stories in several avant-garde little magazines, among them *Broom*, the *Little Review*, and *Prairie*. He also published in such African American publications as the *Liberator*, *Crisis*, and *Opportunity*. Although *Cane* is a long work, it is composed as an assemblage of short stories, sketches, poems, even a play. These are combined in a three-part structure held together, like many modernist narratives, by the narrator's quest for wholeness. *Cane* asks whether an alienated, sophisticated, contemporary African American can find himself by connecting to a black folk heritage that he has never known. The circumstances are specifically African American, but the theme of returning to, or finding, or even inventing, one's roots is typical of much modernist art.

Part I of *Cane*, set in rural Georgia, depicts the difficult lives of rural blacks while celebrating their strength and integrity. Part II shows black urban life in Washington, D.C., and Chicago as it has been corrupted by white materialism. The autobiographical third part describes an African American intellectual teaching in the South, trying to put down roots in an unfamiliar setting that is nevertheless supposed to be "his." The work is distinguished by its poetic, imagistic, evocative prose, its linguistic innovativeness, and its method of construction. All these aspects of *Cane* show Toomer's awareness of contemporary literary movements and register his ambition to be both a Harlem Renaissance author and a literary modernist.

Toomer spent much of the last forty years of his life looking for a spiritual community; he had difficulty finding publishers for the writing he produced during these decades. For a while he was a disciple of the Russian mystic George I. Gurdjieff. In the late 1940s he became a committed Quaker. At his death he left many unpublished short stories, as well as novels, plays, and an autobiography.

The text is that of the first edition (1923) as corrected in 1973.

From Cane[1]

Georgia Dusk

The sky, lazily disdaining to pursue
   The setting sun, too indolent to hold
   A lengthened tournament for flashing gold,
Passively darkens for night's barbecue,

A feast of moon and men and barking hounds,   5
   An orgy for some genius of the South
   With blood-hot eyes and cane-lipped scented mouth,
Surprised in making folk-songs from soul sounds.

The sawmill blows its whistle, buzz-saws stop,
   And silence breaks the bud of knoll and hill,   10
   Soft settling pollen where plowed lands fulfill
Their early promise of a bumper crop.

Smoke from the pyramidal sawdust pile
   Curls up, blue ghosts of trees, tarrying low
   Where only chips and stumps are left to show   15
The solid proof of former domicile.

Meanwhile, the men, with vestiges of pomp,
   Race memories of king and caravan,
   High-priests, an ostrich, and a juju-man,[2]
Go singing through the footpaths of the swamp.   20

Their voices rise . . the pine trees are guitars,
   Strumming, pine-needles fall like sheets of rain . .
   Their voices rise . . the chorus of the cane
Is caroling a vesper to the stars . .

O singers, resinous and soft your songs   25
   Above the sacred whisper of the pines,
   Give virgin lips to cornfield concubines,
Bring dreams of Christ to dusky cane-lipped throngs.

Fern

    Face flowed into her eyes. Flowed in soft cream foam and plaintive ripples, in such a way that wherever your glance may momentarily have rested, it immediately thereafter wavered in the direction of her eyes. The soft suggestion of down slightly darkened, like the shadow of a bird's wing might, the creamy brown color of her upper lip. Why, after noticing it, you sought her eyes, I cannot tell you.

---

1. Of the book's three sections, the first and the last are Georgia scenes. "Fern" appears in the first section after the poem "Georgia Dusk." "Portrait in Georgia" appears in the first section before the story of the lynching of a black woman's black lover by her white lover and his white cohorts. "Seventh Street" is the first sketch in the second section, which is devoted to Washington, D.C., and Chicago.
2. West African tribesman who controls the magical fetish or charm, or "juju."

Her nose was aquiline, Semitic. If you have heard a Jewish cantor[3] sing, if he has touched you and made your own sorrow seem trivial when compared with his, you will know my feeling when I follow the curves of her profile, like mobile rivers, to their common delta. They were strange eyes. In this, that they sought nothing—that is, nothing that was obvious and tangible and that one could see, and they gave the impression that nothing was to be denied. When a woman seeks, you will have observed, her eyes deny. Fern's eyes desired nothing that you could give her; there was no reason why they should withhold. Men saw her eyes and fooled themselves. Fern's eyes said to them that she was easy. When she was young, a few men took her, but got no joy from it. And then, once done, they felt bound to her (quite unlike their hit and run with other girls), felt as though it would take them a lifetime to fulfill an obligation which they could find no name for. They became attached to her, and hungered after finding the barest trace of what she might desire. As she grew up, new men who came to town felt as almost everyone did who ever saw her: that they would not be denied. Men were everlastingly bringing her their bodies. Something inside of her got tired of them, I guess, for I am certain that for the life of her she could not tell why or how she began to turn them off. A man in fever is no trifling thing to send away. They began to leave her, baffled and ashamed, yet vowing to themselves that some day they would do some fine thing for her: send her candy every week and not let her know whom it came from, watch out for her wedding-day and give her a magnificent something with no name on it, buy a house and deed it to her, rescue her from some unworthy fellow who had tricked her into marrying him. As you know, men are apt to idolize or fear that which they cannot understand, especially if it be a woman. She did not deny them, yet the fact was that they were denied. A sort of superstition crept into their consciousness of her being somehow above them. Being above them meant that she was not to be approached by anyone. She became a virgin. Now a virgin in a small southern town is by no means the usual thing, if you will believe me. That the sexes were made to mate is the practice of the South. Particularly, black folks were made to mate. And it is black folks whom I have been talking about thus far. What white men thought of Fern I can arrive at only by analogy. They let her alone.

Anyone, of course, could see her, could see her eyes. If you walked up the Dixie Pike most any time of day, you'd be most like to see her resting listless-like on the railing of her porch, back propped against a post, head tilted a little forward because there was a nail in the porch post just where her head came which for some reason or other she never took the trouble to pull out. Her eyes, if it were sunset, rested idly where the sun, molten and glorious, was pouring down between the fringe of pines. Or maybe they gazed at the gray cabin on the knoll from which an evening folk-song was coming. Perhaps they followed a cow that had been turned loose to roam and feed on cotton-stalks and corn leaves. Like as not they'd settle on some vague spot above the horizon, though hardly a trace of wistfulness would come to them. If it were dusk, then they'd wait for the search-light of the evening train which you could see miles up the track before it flared across the Dixie Pike, close to her home. Wherever they looked, you'd follow them and then waver back. Like her face, the whole countryside seemed to flow into her eyes. Flowed into them with the soft listless

3. Singer in religious services.

cadence of Georgia's South. A young Negro, once, was looking at her, spell-bound, from the road. A white man passing in a buggy had to flick him with his whip if he was to get by without running him over. I first saw her on her porch. I was passing with a fellow whose crusty numbness (I was from the North and suspected of being prejudiced and stuck-up) was melting as he found me warm. I asked him who she was. "That's Fern," was all that I could get from him. Some folks already thought that I was given to nosing around; I let it go at that, so far as questions were concerned. But at first sight of her I felt as if I heard a Jew-ish cantor sing. As if his singing rose above the unheard chorus of a folk-song. And I felt bound to her. I too had my dreams: something I would do for her. I have knocked about from town to town too much not to know the futility of mere change of place. Besides, picture if you can, this cream-colored solitary girl sitting at a tenement window looking down on the indifferent throngs of Harlem. Better that she listen to folk-songs at dusk in Georgia, you would say, and so would I. Or, suppose she came up North and married. Even a doctor or a lawyer, say, one who would be sure to get along—that is, make money. You and I know, who have had experience in such things, that love is not a thing like prejudice which can be bettered by changes of town. Could men in Washing-ton, Chicago, or New York, more than the men of Georgia, bring her something left vacant by the bestowal of their bodies? You and I who know men in these cities will have to say, they could not. See her out and out a prostitute along State Street in Chicago. See her move into a southern town where white men are more aggressive. See her become a white man's concubine . . . Something I must do for her. There was myself. What could I do for her? Talk, of course. Push back the fringe of pines upon new horizons. To what purpose? and what for? Her? Myself? Men in her case seem to lose their selfishness. I lost mine before I touched her. I ask you, friend (it makes no difference if you sit in the Pullman or the Jim Crow[4] as the train crosses her road), what thoughts would come to you—that is, after you'd finished with the thoughts that leap into men's minds at the sight of a pretty woman who will not deny them; what thoughts would come to you, had you seen her in a quick flash, keen and intuitively, as she sat there on her porch when your train thundered by? Would you have got off at the next station and come back for her to take her where? Would you have completely forgotten her as soon as you reached Macon, Atlanta, Augusta, Pasadena, Madison, Chicago, Boston, or New Orleans? Would you tell your wife or sweetheart about a girl you saw? Your thoughts can help me, and I would like to know. Something I would do for her . . .

One evening I walked up the Pike on purpose, and stopped to say hello. Some of her family were about, but they moved away to make room for me. Damn if I knew how to begin. Would you? Mr. and Miss So-and-So, people, the weather, the crops, the new preacher, the frolic, the church benefit, rab-bit and possum hunting, the new soft drink they had at old Pap's store, the schedule of the trains, what kind of town Macon was, Negro's migration north, bollweevils, syrup, the Bible—to all these things she gave a yassur or nassur, without further comment. I began to wonder if perhaps my own emo-tional sensibility had played one of its tricks on me. "Lets take a walk," I at

---

4. In the segregated South, black persons were required to sit in the "Jim Crow" section of railway cars and were not allowed as passengers in the first-class "Pullman" lounges, or sleeping cars.

last ventured. The suggestion, coming after so long an isolation, was novel enough, I guess, to surprise. But it wasnt that. Something told me that men before me had said just that as a prelude to the offering of their bodies. I tried to tell her with my eyes. I think she understood. The thing from her that made my throat catch, vanished. Its passing left her visible in a way I'd thought, but never seen. We walked down the Pike with people on all the porches gaping at us. "Doesnt it make you mad?" She meant the row of petty gossiping people. She meant the world. Through a canebrake that was ripe for cutting, the branch was reached. Under a sweet-gum tree, and where reddish leaves had dammed the creek a little, we sat down. Dusk, suggesting the almost imperceptible procession of giant trees, settled with a purple haze about the cane. I felt strange, as I always do in Georgia, particularly at dusk. I felt that things unseen to men were tangibly immediate. It would not have surprised me had I had vision. People have them in Georgia more often than you would suppose. A black woman once saw the mother of Christ and drew her in charcoal on the courthouse wall . . . When one is on the soil of one's ancestors, most anything can come to one . . . From force of habit, I suppose, I held Fern in my arms—that is, without at first noticing it. Then my mind came back to her. Her eyes, unusually weird and open, held me. Held God. He flowed in as I've seen the countryside flow in. Seen men. I must have done something—what, I don't know, in the confusion of my emotion. She sprang up. Rushed some distance from me. Fell to her knees, and began swaying, swaying. Her body was tortured with something it could not let out. Like boiling sap it flooded arms and fingers till she shook them as if they burned her. It found her throat, and spattered inarticulately in plaintive, convulsive sounds, mingled with calls to Christ Jesus. And then she sang, brokenly. A Jewish cantor singing with a broken voice. A child's voice, uncertain, or an old man's. Dusk hid her; I could hear only her song. It seemed to me as though she were pounding her head in anguish upon the ground. I rushed at her. She fainted in my arms.

There was talk about her fainting with me in the canefield. And I got one or two ugly looks from town men who'd set themselves up to protect her. In fact, there was talk of making me leave town. But they never did. They kept a watch-out for me, though. Shortly after, I came back North. From the train window I saw her as I crossed her road. Saw her on her porch, head tilted a little forward where the nail was, eyes vaguely focused on the sunset. Saw her face flow into them, the countryside and something that I call God, flowing into them . . . Nothing ever really happened. Nothing ever came to Fern, not even I. Something I would do for her. Some fine unnamed thing . . . And, friend, you? She is still living, I have reason to know. Her name, against the chance that you might happen down that way, is Fernie May Rosen.

* * *

Portrait in Georgia

Hair—braided chestnut,
    coiled like a lyncher's rope,
Eyes—fagots,
Lips—old scars, or the first red blisters,
Breath—the last sweet scent of cane,   5

And her slim body, white as the ash
of black flesh after flame.

* * *

Seventh Street

Money burns the pocket, pocket hurts,
Bootleggers in silken shirts,
Ballooned, zooming Cadillacs,
Whizzing, whizzing down the street-car tracks.

Seventh Street is a bastard of Prohibition and the War.[5] A crude-boned, soft-skinned wedge of nigger life breathing its loafer air, jazz songs and love, thrusting unconscious rhythms, black reddish blood into the white and whitewashed wood of Washington. Stale soggy wood of Washington. Wedges rust in soggy wood . . . Split it! In two! Again! Shred it! . . the sun. Wedges are brilliant in the sun; ribbons of wet wood dry and blow away. Black reddish blood. Pouring for crude-boned soft-skinned life, who set you flowing? Blood suckers of the War would spin in a frenzy of dizziness if they drank your blood. Prohibition would put a stop to it. Who set you flowing? White and white-wash disappear in blood. Who set you flowing? Flowing down the smooth asphalt of Seventh Street, in shanties, brick office buildings, theaters, drug stores, restaurants, and cabarets? Eddying on the corners? Swirling like a blood-red smoke up where the buzzards fly in heaven? God would not dare to suck black red blood. A Nigger God! He would duck his head in shame and call for the Judgment Day. Who set you flowing?

Money burns the pocket, pocket hurts,
Bootleggers in silken shirts,
Ballooned, zooming Cadillacs,
Whizzing, whizzing down the street-car tracks.

1923

5. World War I.

F. SCOTT FITZGERALD
1896–1940

In the 1920s and 1930s F. Scott Fitzgerald was equally famous as a writer and as a celebrity author whose lifestyle seemed to symbolize the two decades; in the 1920s he stood for all-night partying, drinking, and the pursuit of pleasure while in the 1930s he stood for the gloomy aftermath of excess. "Babylon Revisited," written immediately after the stock market crash, is simultaneously a personal and a national story.

Fitzgerald was born in a middle-class neighborhood in St. Paul, Minnesota, descended on his father's side from southern colonial landowners and legislators, on his mother's from Irish immigrants. Much of his boyhood was spent in Buffalo and Syracuse, New York. The family was not prosperous and it took an aunt's support to send him to a Catholic boarding school in New Jersey in 1911. Two years later he entered Princeton University, where he participated in extracurricular literary and dramatic activities, forming friendships with campus intellectuals like the prominent critic Edmund Wilson who were to help him in later years. But he failed to make the football team and felt the disappointment for years. After three years of college Fitzgerald quit to join the army, but the war ended before he saw active service. Stationed in Montgomery, Alabama, he met and courted Zelda Sayre, a local belle who rejected him. In 1919 he went to New York City, determined to make a fortune and win Zelda. Amazingly, he succeeded. A novel he had begun in college, revised, and published in 1920 as *This Side of Paradise* became an immediate bestseller, making its author rich and famous at the age of twenty-four. As one of the earliest examples of a novel about college life, *This Side of Paradise* was accepted as the voice of the younger generation in a society increasingly oriented toward youth. He combined the traditional narrative and rhetorical gifts of a good fiction writer, it appeared, with a thoroughly modern sensibility. A week after the novel appeared, Scott and Zelda were married. Living extravagantly in New York City and St. Paul, and on Long Island, they more than spent the money Fitzgerald made from two collections of short stories—*Flappers and Philosophers* (1921) and *Tales of the Jazz Age* (1922)—and a second novel, *The Beautiful and Damned* (1922). Their only child, a daughter, was born in 1921.

In 1924, the Fitzgeralds moved to Europe to live more cheaply. They made friends with American expatriates, Hemingway, Stein, and Pound among others. During this time Fitzgerald published his best-known and most successful novel, *The Great Gatsby* (1925), and another book of short stories, *All the Sad Young Men* (1926). *The Great Gatsby* tells the story of a self-made young man whose dream of success, personified in a rich and beautiful young woman named Daisy, turns out to be a fantasy in every sense: Daisy belongs to a corrupt society, Gatsby corrupts himself in the quest for her, and above all, the rich have no intention of sharing their privileges. The novel is narrated from the point of view of Nick Carraway, an onlooker who is both moved and repelled by the tale he tells and whose responses form a sort of subplot: this experiment in narrative point of view was widely imitated. The structure of *The Great Gatsby* is compact; the style dazzling; and its images of automobiles, parties, and garbage heaps seem to capture the contradictions of a consumer society. The novel became an instant classic and remains so to this day.

Fitzgerald wrote dozens of short stories during the twenties; many were published in the mass-circulation weekly the *Saturday Evening Post,* which paid extremely well. Despite the pace at which he worked—in all he wrote 178 short stories—the Fitzgeralds could not get out of debt. Scott became alcoholic, and Zelda broke down in 1930 and spent most of the rest of her life in mental institutions. In 1931 Fitzgerald reestablished himself permanently in the United States, living at first near Baltimore, where his wife was hospitalized. A fourth novel, *Tender Is the Night,* appeared in 1934. The novel follows the emotional decline of a young American psychiatrist whose personal energies are sapped, his career corroded equally by his marriage to a beautiful and wealthy patient and his own weakness of character ("character" was one of Fitzgerald's favorite concepts). As in *The Great Gatsby,* the character begins as a disciple of the work ethic and turns into a pursuer of wealth, and the American Dream accordingly turns into a nightmare. Unlike *Gatsby,* whose characters never really connect with each other, *Tender Is the Night* shows a range of intimacies, none of them successful. The novel did not sell well. In 1937 Fitzgerald turned to Hollywood screenwriting; toward the end of the decade things were looking up for him, and he planned to revive his career as a fiction writer. But his health had been ruined by heavy drinking; he died of a heart attack in Hollywood at the age of forty-four, leaving an unfinished novel about a film mogul, *The Last Tycoon,* which was brought out by Edmund Wilson in 1941. Wilson also successfully promoted Fitzgerald's posthumous reputation by editing a collection of his writings, which he called *The Crack-Up,* in 1945.

The text of "Winter Dreams" is from *Metropolitan* magazine (1922); that of "Babylon Revisited" is from *Stories of F. Scott Fitzgerald* (1951).

Winter Dreams

Some of the caddies were poor as sin and lived in one-room houses with a neurasthenic cow in the front yard, but Dexter Green's father owned the second best grocery store in Dillard—the best one was "The Hub," patronized by the wealthy people from Lake Erminie—and Dexter caddied only for pocket-money.

In the fall when the days became crisp and grey and the long Minnesota winter shut down like the white lid of a box, Dexter's skis moved over the snow that hid the fairways of the golf course. At these times the country gave him a feeling of profound melancholy—it offended him that the links should lie in enforced fallowness, haunted by ragged sparrows for the long season. It was dreary, too, that on the tees where the gay colors fluttered in summer there were now only the desolate sand-boxes knee-deep in crusted ice. When he crossed the hills the wind blew cold as misery, and if the sun was out he tramped with his eyes squinted up against the hard dimensionless glare.

In April the winter ceased abruptly. The snow ran down into Lake Erminie scarcely tarrying for the early golfers to brave the season with red and black balls. Without elation, without an interval of moist glory the cold was gone.

Dexter knew that there was something dismal about this northern spring, just as he knew there was something gorgeous about the fall. Fall made him clench his hands and tremble and repeat idiotic sentences to himself and make brisk abrupt gestures of command to imaginary audiences and armies. October filled him with hope which November raised to a sort of ecstatic triumph, and in this wood the fleeting brilliant impressions of the summer at Lake Erminie were ready grist to his will. He became a golf champion and defeated Mr. T. A. Hedrick in a marvelous match played over a hundred times in the fairways of his imagination, a match each detail of which he changed about untiringly—sometimes winning with almost laughable ease, sometimes coming up magnificently from behind. Again, stepping from a Pierce-Arrow automobile, like Mr. Mortimer Jones, he strolled frigidly into the lounge of the Erminie Golf Club—or perhaps, surrounded by an admiring crowd, he gave an exhibition of fancy diving from the springboard of the Erminie Club raft. . . . Among those most impressed was Mr. Mortimer Jones.

And one day it came to pass that Mr. Jones, himself and not his ghost, came up to Dexter, almost with tears in his eyes and said that Dexter was the —— best caddy in the club and wouldn't he decide not to quit if Mr. Jones made it worth his while, because every other —— caddy in the club lost one ball a hole for him—regularly—

"No, sir," said Dexter, decisively, "I don't want to caddy any more." Then, after a pause, "I'm too old."

"You're—why, you're not more than fourteen. Why did you decide just this morning that you wanted to quit? You promised that next week you'd go over to the state tournament with me."

"I decided I was too old."

Dexter handed in his "A Class" badge, collected what money was due him from the caddy master and caught the train for Dillard.

"The best —— caddy I ever saw," shouted Mr. Mortimer Jones over a drink that afternoon. "Never lost a ball! Willing! Intelligent! Quiet! Honest! Grateful!—"

The little girl who had done this was eleven—beautifully ugly as little girls are apt to be who are destined after a few years to be inexpressably lovely and bring no end of misery to a great number of men. The spark, however, was perceptible. There was a general ungodliness in the way her lips twisted down at the corners when she smiled and in the—Heaven help us!—in the almost passionate quality of her eyes. Vitality is born early in such women. It was utterly in evidence now, shining through her thin frame in a sort of glow.

She had come eagerly out on to the course at nine o'clock with a white linen nurse and five small new golf clubs in a white canvas bag which the nurse was carrying. When Dexter first saw her she was standing by the caddy house, rather ill-at-ease and trying to conceal the fact by engaging her nurse in an obviously unnatural conversation illumined by startling and irrevelant smiles from herself.

"Well, it's certainly a nice day, Hilda," Dexter heard her say, then she drew down the corners of her mouth, smiled and glanced furtively around, her eyes in transit falling for an instant on Dexter.

Then to the nurse:

"Well, I guess there aren't very many people out here this morning, are there?"

The smile again radiant, blatantly artificial—convincing.

"I don't know what we're supposed to do now," said the nurse, looking nowhere in particular.

"Oh, that's all right"—the smile—"I'll fix it up."

Dexter stood perfectly still, his mouth faintly ajar. He knew that if he moved forward a step his stare would be in her line of vision—if he moved backward he would lose his full view of her face—For a moment he had not realized how young she was. Now he remembered having seen her several times the year before—in bloomers.

Suddenly, involuntarily, he laughed, a short abrupt laugh—then, startled by himself, he turned and began to walk quickly away.

"Boy!"

Dexter stopped.

"Boy—"

Beyond question he was addressed. Not only that, but he was treated to that absurd smile, that preposterous smile—the memory of which at least half a dozen men were to carry to the grave.

"Boy, do you know where the golf teacher is?"

"He's giving a lesson."

"Well, do you know where the caddy-master is?"

"He's not here yet this morning."

"Oh." For a moment this baffled her. She stood alternately on her right and left foot.

"We'd like to get a caddy," said the nurse. "Mrs. Mortimer Jones sent us out to play golf and we don't know how without we get a caddy."

Here she was stopped by an ominous glance from Miss Jones, followed immediately by the smile.

"There aren't any caddies here except me," said Dexter to the nurse. "And I got to stay here in charge until the caddy-master gets here."

"Oh."

Miss Jones and her retinue now withdrew and at a proper distance from Dexter became involved in a heated conversation. The conversation was concluded by Miss Jones taking one of the clubs and hitting it on the ground with violence. For further emphasis she raised it again and was about to bring it down smartly upon the nurse's bosom, when the nurse seized the club and twisted it from her hands.

"You darn *fool!*" cried Miss Jones wildly.

Another argument ensued. Realizing that the elements of the comedy were implied in the scene, Dexter several times began to smile but each time slew the smile before it reached maturity. He could not resist the monstrous conviction that the little girl was justified in beating the nurse.

The situation was resolved by the fortuitous appearance of the caddy-master who was appealed to immediately by the nurse.

"Miss Jones is to have a little caddy and this one says he can't go."

"Mr. McKenna said I was to wait here till you came," said Dexter quickly.

"Well, he's here now." Miss Jones smiled cheerfully at the caddy-master. Then she dropped her bag and set off at a haughty mince toward the first tee.

"Well?" The caddy-master turned to Dexter. "What you standing there like a dummy for? Go pick up the young lady's clubs."

"I don't think I'll go out today," said Dexter.

"You don't—"

"I think I'll quit."

The enormity of his decision frightened him. He was a favorite caddy and the thirty dollars a month he earned through the summer were not to be made elsewhere in Dillard. But he had received a strong emotional shock and his perturbation required a violent and immediate outlet.

It is not so simple as that, either. As so frequently would be the case in the future, Dexter was unconsciously dictated to by his winter dreams.

Now, of course, the quality and the seasonability of these winter dreams varied, but the stuff of them remained. They persuaded Dexter several years later to pass up a business course at the State University—his father, prospering now, would have paid his way—for the precarious advantage of attending an older and more famous university in the East, where he was bothered by his scanty funds. But do not get the impression, because his winter dreams happened to be concerned at first with musings on the rich, that there was anything shoddy in the boy. He wanted not association with glittering things and glittering people—he wanted the glittering things themselves. Often he reached out for the best without knowing why he wanted it—and sometimes he ran up against the mysterious denials and prohibitions in which life indulges. It is with one of those denials and not with his career as a whole that this story deals.

He made money. It was rather amazing. After college he went to the city from which Lake Erminie draws its wealthy patrons. When he was only twenty-three and had been there not quite two years, there were already people who liked to say, "Now *there's* a boy—" All about him rich men's sons were peddling bonds precariously, or investing patrimonies precariously, or plodding through the two dozen volumes of canned rubbish in the "George Washington Commercial Course," but Dexter borrowed a thousand dollars on his college degree and his steady eyes, and bought a partnership in a *laundry*.

It was a small laundry when he went into it. Dexter made a specialty of learning how the English washed fine woolen golf stockings without shrinking them. Inside of a year he was catering to the trade who wore knickerbockers. Men were insisting that their shetland hose and sweaters go to his laundry just as they had insisted on a caddy who could find golf balls. A little later he was doing their wives' lingerie as well—and running five branches in different parts of the city. Before he was twenty-seven he owned the largest string of laundries in his section of the country. It was then that he sold out and went to New York. But the part of his story that concerns us here goes back to when he was making his first big success.

When he was twenty-three Mr. W. L. Hart, one of the grey-haired men who like to say "Now there's a boy"—gave him a guest card to the Lake Erminie Club for over a week-end. So he signed his name one day on the register, and that afternoon played golf in a foursome with Mr. Hart and Mr. Sandwood and Mr. T. A. Hedrick. He did not consider it necessary to remark that he had once carried Mr. Hart's bag over this same links and that he knew every trap and gully with his eyes shut—but he found himself glancing at the four caddies who trailed them, trying to catch a gleam or gesture that would remind him of himself, that would lessen the gap which lay between his past and his future.

It was a curious day, slashed abruptly with fleeting, familiar impressions. One minute he had the sense of being a trespasser—in the next he was impressed by the tremendous superiority he felt toward Mr. T. A. Hedrick, who was a bore and not even a good golfer any more.

Then, because of a ball Mr. Hart lost near the fifteenth green an enormous thing happened. While they were searching the stiff grasses of the rough there was a clear call of "Fore!" from behind a hill in their rear. And as they all turned abruptly from their search a bright new ball sliced abruptly over the hill and caught Mr. T. A. Hedrick rather neatly in the stomach.

Mr. T. A. Hedrick grunted and cursed.

"By Gad!" cried Mr. Hedrick, "they ought to put some of these crazy women off the course. It's getting to be outrageous."

A head and a voice came up together over the hill:

"Do you mind if we go through?"

"You hit me in the stomach!" thundered Mr. Hedrick.

"Did I?" The girl approached the group of men. "I'm sorry. I yelled 'Fore!' "

Her glance fell casually on each of the men. She nodded to Sandwood and then scanned the fairway for her ball.

"Did I bounce off into the rough?"

It was impossible to determine whether this question was ingenuous or malicious. In a moment, however, she left no doubt, for as her partner came up over the hill she called cheerfully.

"Here I am! I'd have gone on the green except that I hit something."

As she took her stance for a short mashie shot, Dexter looked at her closely. She wore a blue gingham dress, rimmed at throat and shoulders with a white edging that accentuated her tan. The quality of exaggeration, of thinness that had made her passionate eyes and down turning mouth absurd at eleven was gone now. She was arrestingly beautiful. The color in her cheeks was centered like the color in a picture—it was not a "high" color, but a sort of fluctuating and feverish warmth, so shaded that it seemed at any moment it would recede and disappear. This color and the mobility of her mouth gave a continual impression of flux, of intense life, of passionate vitality—balanced only partially by the sad luxury of her eyes.

She swung her mashie impatiently and without interest, pitching the ball into a sandpit on the other side of the green. With a quick insincere smile and a careless "Thank you!" she went on after it.

"That Judy Jones!" remarked Mr. Hedrick on the next tee, as they waited—some moments—for her to play on ahead. "All she needs is to be turned up and spanked for six months and then to be married off to an old-fashioned cavalry captain."

"Gosh, she's good looking!" said Mr. Sandwood, who was just over thirty.

"Good-looking!" cried Mr. Hedrick contemptuously. "She always looks as if she wanted to be kissed! Turning those big cow-eyes on every young calf in town!"

It is doubtful if Mr. Hedrick intended a reference to the maternal instinct.

"She'd play pretty good golf if she'd try," said Mr. Sandwood.

"She has no form," said Mr. Hedrick solemnly.

"She has a nice figure," said Mr. Sandwood.

"Better thank the Lord she doesn't drive a swifter ball," said Mr. Hart, winking at Dexter. "Come on. Let's go."

Later in the afternoon the sun went down with a riotous swirl of gold and varying blues and scarlets, and left the dry rustling night of western summer. Dexter watched from the verandah of the Erminie Club, watched the even overlap of the waters in the little wind, silver molasses under the harvest moon. Then the moon held a finger to her lips and the lake became a clear pool, pale and quiet. Dexter put on his bathing suit and swam out to the farthest raft, where he stretched dripping on the wet canvas of the spring board. There was a fish jumping and a star shining and the lights around the lake were gleaming. Over on a dark peninsula a piano was playing the songs of last summer and of summers before that—songs from "The Pink Lady" and "The Chocolate Soldier" and "Mlle. Modiste"—and because the sound of a piano over a stretch of water had always seemed beautiful to Dexter he lay perfectly quiet and listened.

The tune the piano was playing at that moment had been gay and new five years before when Dexter was a sophomore at college. They had played it at a prom once and because he could not afford the luxury of proms in those days he had stood outside the gymnasium and listened. The sound of the tune and the splash of the fish jumping precipitated in him a sort of ecstasy and it was with that ecstasy he viewed what happened to him now. The ecstasy was a gorgeous appreciation. It was his sense that, for once, he was magnificently atune to life and that everything about him was radiating a brightness and a glamor he might never know again.

A low pale oblong detached itself suddenly from the darkness of the peninsula, spitting forth the reverberate sound of a racing motorboat. Two white streamers of cleft water rolled themselves out behind it and almost immediately the boat was beside him, drowning out the hot tinkle of the piano in the drone of its spray. Dexter raising himself on his arms was aware of a figure standing at the wheel, of two dark eyes regarding him over the lengthening space of water—then the boat had gone by and was sweeping in an immense and purposeless circle of spray round and round in the middle of the lake. With equal eccentricity one of the circles flattened out and headed back toward the raft.

"Who's that?" she called, shutting off the motor. She was so near now that

Dexter could see her bathing suit, which consisted apparently of pink rompers. "Oh—you're one of the men I hit in the stomach."

The nose of the boat bumped the raft. After an inexpert struggle, Dexter managed to twist the line around a two-by-four. Then the raft tilted rakishly as she sprung on.

"Well, kiddo," she said huskily, "do you"—she broke off. She had sat herself upon the springboard, found it damp and jumped up quickly,—"do you want to go surf-board riding?"

He indicated that he would be delighted.

"The name is Judy Jones. Ghastly reputation but enormously popular." She favored him with an absurd smirk—rather, what tried to be a smirk, for, twist her mouth as she might, it was not grotesque, it was merely beautiful. "See that house over on the peninsula?"

"No."

"Well, there's a house there that I live in only you can't see it because it's too dark. And in that house there is a fella waiting for me. When he drove up by the door I drove out by the dock because he has watery eyes and asks me if I have an ideal."

There was a fish jumping and a star shining and the lights around the lake were gleaming. Dexter sat beside Judy Jones and she explained how her boat was driven. Then she was in the water, swimming to the floating surf-board with exquisite crawl. Watching her was as without effort to the eye as watching a branch waving or a sea-gull flying. Her arms, burned to butternut, moved sinuously among the dull platinum ripples, elbow appearing first, casting the forearm back with a cadence of falling water, then reaching out and down stabbing a path ahead.

They moved out into the lake and, turning, Dexter saw that she was kneeling on the low rear of the now up-tilted surf-board.

"Go faster," she called, "fast as it'll go."

Obediently he jammed the lever forward and the white spray mounted at the bow. When he looked around again the girl was standing up on the rushing board, her arms spread ecstatically, her eyes lifted toward the moon.

"It's awful cold, kiddo," she shouted. "What's your name anyways?"

"The name is Dexter Green. Would it amuse you to know how good you look back there?"

"Yes," she shouted, "it would amuse me. Except that I'm too cold. Come to dinner tomorrow night."

He kept thinking how glad he was that he had never caddied for this girl. The damp gingham clinging made her like a statue and turned her intense mobility to immobility at last.

"—At seven o'clock," she shouted, "Judy Jones, Girl, who hit man in stomach. Better write it down,"—and then, "Faster—oh, faster!"

Had he been as calm inwardly as he was in appearance, Dexter would have had time to examine his surroundings in detail. He received, however, an enduring impression that the house was the most elaborate he had ever seen. He had known for a long time that it was the finest on Lake Erminie, with a Pompeiian swimming pool and twelve acres of lawn and garden. But what gave it an air of breathless intensity was the sense that it was inhabited by Judy Jones—that it was as casual a thing to her as the little house in the village had once been to Dexter. There was a feeling of mystery in it, of bedrooms upstairs more beautiful and strange than other bedrooms, of gay and radiant activities taking place through these deep corridors and of romances that were not musty and laid already in lavender, but were fresh and breathing and set forth in rich motor cars and in great dances whose flowers were scarcely withered. They were more real because he could feel them all about him, pervading the air with the shades and echoes of still vibrant emotion.

And so while he waited for her to appear he peopled the soft deep summer room and the sun porch that opened from it with the men who had already loved Judy Jones. He knew the sort of men they were—the men who when he first went to college had entered from the great prep-schools with graceful clothes and the deep tan of healthy summer, who did nothing or anything with the same debonaire ease.

Dexter had seen that, in one sense, he was better than these men. He was newer and stronger. Yet in acknowledging to himself that he wished his children to be like them he was admitting that he was but the rough, strong stuff from which this graceful aristocracy eternally sprang.

When, a year before, the time had come when he could wear good clothes, he had known who were the best tailors in America, and the best tailor in America had made him the suit he wore this evening. He had acquired that particular reserve peculiar to his university, that set it off from other universities. He recognized the value to him of such a mannerism and he had adopted it; he knew that to be careless in dress and manner required more confidence than to be careful. But carelessness was for his children. His mother's name had been Krimslich. She was a Bohemian[1] of the peasant class and she had talked broken English to the end of her days. Her son must keep to the set patterns.

He waited for Judy Jones in her house, and he saw these other young men around him. It excited him that many men had loved her. It increased her value in his eyes.

At a little after seven Judy Jones came downstairs. She wore a blue silk afternoon dress. He was disappointed at first that she had not put on something more elaborate, and this feeling was accentuated when, after a brief greeting, she went to the door of a butler's pantry and pushing it open called: "You can have dinner, Martha." He had rather expected that a butler would announce dinner, that there would be a cocktail perhaps. It even offended him that she should know the maid's name.

Then he put these thoughts behind him as they sat down together on a chintz-covered lounge.

"Father and mother won't be here," she said.

"Ought I to be sorry?"

"They're really quite nice," she confessed, as if it had just occurred to her. "I think my father's the best looking man of his age I've ever seen. And mother looks about thirty."

He remembered the last time he had seen her father, and found he was glad the parents were not to be here tonight. They would wonder who he was. He had been born in Keeble, a Minnesota village fifty miles farther north and he

1. Native of Bohemia, in the Czech Republic.

always gave Keeble as his home instead of Dillard. Country towns were well enough to come from if they weren't inconveniently in sight and used as footstools by fashionable lakes.

Before dinner he found the conversation unsatisfactory. The beautiful Judy seemed faintly irritable—as much so as it was possible to be with a comparative stranger. They discussed Lake Erminie and its golf course, the surfboard riding of the night before and the cold she had caught, which made her voice more husky and charming than ever. They talked of his university which she had visited frequently during the past two years, and of the nearby city which supplied Lake Erminie with its patrons and whither Dexter would return next day to his prospering laundries.

During dinner she slipped into a moody depression which gave Dexter a feeling of guilt. Whatever petulance she uttered in her throaty voice worried him. Whatever she smiled at—at him, at a silver fork, at nothing—, it disturbed him that her smile could have no root in mirth, or even in amusement. When the red corners of her lips curved down, it was less a smile than an invitation to a kiss.

Then, after dinner, she led him out on the dark sun-porch and deliberately changed the atmosphere.

"Do I seem gloomy?" she demanded.

"No, but I'm afraid I'm boring you," he answered quickly.

"You're not. I like you. But I've just had rather an unpleasant afternoon. There was a—man I cared about. He told me out of a clear sky that he was poor as a church-mouse. He'd never even hinted it before. Does this sound horribly mundane?"

"Perhaps he was afraid to tell you."

"I suppose he was," she answered thoughtfully. "He didn't start right. You see, if I'd thought of him as poor—well, I've been mad about loads of poor men, and fully intended to marry them all. But in this case, I hadn't thought of him that way and my interest in him wasn't strong enough to survive the shock."

"I know. As if a girl calmly informed her fiancé that she was a widow. He might not object to widows, but——"

"Let's start right," she suggested suddenly. "Who are you, anyhow?"

For a moment Dexter hesitated. There were two versions of his life that he could tell. There was Dillard and his caddying and his struggle through college, or——

"I'm nobody," he announced. "My career is largely a matter of futures."

"Are you poor?"

"No," he said frankly, "I'm probably making more money than any man my age in the northwest. I know that's an obnoxious remark, but you advised me to start right."

There was a pause. She smiled, and with a touch of amusement.

"You sound like a man in a play."

"It's your fault. You tempted me into being assertive."

Suddenly she turned her dark eyes directly upon him and the corners of her mouth drooped until her face seemed to open like a flower. He dared scarcely to breathe, he had the sense that she was exerting some force upon him; making him overwhelmingly conscious of the youth and mystery that wealth imprisons and preserves, the freshness of many clothes, of cool rooms and gleaming things, safe and proud above the hot struggles of the poor.

The porch was bright with the bought luxury of starshine. The wicker of the settee squeaked fashionably when he put his arm around her, commanded by her eyes. He kissed her curious and lovely mouth and committed himself to the following of a grail.

It began like that—and continued, with varying shades of intensity, on such a note right up to the dénouement. Dexter surrendered a part of himself to the most direct and unprincipled personality with which he had ever come in contact. Whatever the beautiful Judy Jones desired, she went after with the full pressure of her charm. There was no divergence of method, no jockeying for position or premeditation of effects—there was very little mental quality in any of her affairs. She simply made men conscious to the highest degree of her physical loveliness.

Dexter had no desire to change her. Her deficiencies were knit up with a passionate energy that transcended and justified them.

When, as Judy's head lay against his shoulder that first night, she whispered:

"I don't know what's the matter with me. Last night I thought I was in love with a man and tonight I think I'm in love with you—"

—it seemed to him a beautiful and romantic thing to say. It was the exquisite excitability that for the moment he controlled and owned. But a week later he was compelled to view this same quality in a different light. She took him in her roadster to a picnic supper and after supper she disappeared, likewise in her roadster, with another man. Dexter became enormously upset and was scarcely able to be decently civil to the other people present. When she assured him that she had not kissed the other man he knew she was lying— yet he was glad that she had taken the trouble to lie to him.

He was, as he found before the summer ended, one of a dozen, a varying dozen, who circulated about her. Each of them had at one time been favored above all others—about half of them still basked in the solace of occasional sentimental revivals. Whenever one showed signs of dropping out through long neglect she granted him a brief honeyed hour which encouraged him to tag along for a year or so longer. Judy made these forays upon the helpless and defeated without malice, indeed half unconscious that there was anything mischievous in what she did.

When a new man came to town everyone dropped out—dates were automatically cancelled.

The helpless part of trying to do anything about it was that she did it all herself. She was not a girl who could be "won" in the kinetic sense—she was proof against cleverness, she was proof against charm, if any of these assailed her too strongly she would immediately resolve the affair to a physical basis and under the magic of her physical splendor the strong as well as the brilliant played her game and not their own. She was entertained only by the gratification of her desires and by the direct exercise of her own charm. Perhaps from so much youthful love, so many youthful lovers she had come, in self defense, to nourish herself wholly from within.

Succeeding Dexter's first exhilaration came restlessness and dissatisfaction. The helpless ecstasy of losing himself in her charm was a powerful opiate rather than a tonic. It was fortunate for his work during the winter that those moments of ecstasy came infrequently. Early in their acquaintance it had seemed for a while that there was a deep and spontaneous mutual attraction—that first August for example—three days of long evenings on her dusky verandah, of strange wan kisses through the late afternoon, in shadowy alcoves or behind the protecting trellises of the garden arbors, of mornings when she was fresh as a dream and almost shy at meeting him in the clarity of the rising day. There was all the ecstasy of an engagement about it, sharpened by his realization that there was no engagement. It was during those three days that, for the first time, he had asked her to marry him. She said "maybe some day," she said "kiss me," she said "I'd like to marry you," she said "I love you,"—she said—nothing.

The three days were interrupted by the arrival of a New York man who visited the Jones' for half September. To Dexter's agony, rumor engaged them. The man was the son of the president of a great trust company. But at the end of a month it was reported that Judy was yawning. At a dance one night she sat all evening in a motor boat with an old beau, while the New Yorker searched the club for her frantically. She told the old beau that she was bored with her visitor and two days later he left. She was seen with him at the station and it was reported that he looked very mournful indeed.

On this note the summer ended. Dexter was twenty-four and he found himself increasingly in a position to do as he wished. He joined two clubs in the city and lived at one of them. Though he was by no means an integral part of the stag-lines at these clubs he managed to be on hand at dances where Judy Jones was likely to appear. He could have gone out socially as much as he liked—he was an eligible young man, now, and popular with downtown fathers. His confessed devotion to Judy Jones had rather solidified his position. But he had no social aspirations and rather despised the dancing men who were always on tap for the Thursday or Saturday parties and who filled in at dinners with the younger married set. Already he was playing with the idea of going East to New York. He wanted to take Judy Jones with him. No disillusion as to the world in which she had grown up could cure his illusion as to her desirability.

Remember that—for only in the light of it can what he did for her be understood.

Eighteen months after he first met Judy Jones he became engaged to another girl. Her name was Irene Scheerer and her father was one of the men who had always believed in Dexter. Irene was light haired and sweet and honorable and a little stout and she had two beaus whom she pleasantly relinquished when Dexter formally asked her to marry him.

Summer, fall, winter, spring, another summer, another fall—so much he had given of his active life to the curved lips of Judy Jones. She had treated him with interest, with encouragement, with malice, with indifference, with contempt. She had inflicted on him the innumerable little slights and indignities possible in such a case—as if in revenge for having ever cared for him at all. She had beckoned him and yawned at him and beckoned him again and he had responded often with bitterness and narrowed eyes. She had brought him ecstatic happiness and intolerable agony of spirit. She had caused him untold inconvenience and not a little trouble. She had insulted him and she had ridden over him and she had played his interest in her against his interest in his work—for fun. She had done everything to him except to criticize him—this she had not done—it seemed to him only because it might have sullied the utter indifference she manifested and sincerely felt toward him.

When autumn had come and gone again it occurred to him that he could not have Judy Jones. He had to beat this into his mind but he convinced himself at last. He lay awake at night for a while and argued it over. He told himself the trouble and the pain she had caused him, he enumerated her glaring deficiencies as a wife. Then he said to himself that he loved her and after a while he fell asleep. For a week, lest he imagine her husky voice over the telephone or her eyes opposite him at lunch, he worked hard and late and at night he went to his office and plotted out his years.

At the end of a week he went to a dance and cut in on her once. For almost the first time since they had met he did not ask her to sit out with him or tell her that she was lovely. It hurt him that she did not miss these things—that was all. He was not jealous when he saw that there was a new man tonight. He had been hardened against jealousy long before.

He stayed late at the dance. He sat for an hour with Irene Scheerer and talked about books and about music. He knew very little about either. But he was beginning to be master of his own time now and he had a rather priggish notion that he—the young and already fabulously successful Dexter Green— should know more about such things.

That was in October when he was twenty-five. In January Dexter and Irene became engaged. It was to be announced in June and they were to be married three months later.

The Minnesota winter prolonged itself interminably and it was almost May when the winds came soft and the snow ran down into Lake Erminie at last. For the first time in over a year Dexter was enjoying a certain tranquility of spirit. Judy Jones had been in Florida and afterwards in Hot Springs and somewhere she had been engaged and somewhere she had broken it off. At first, when Dexter had definitely given her up, it had made him sad that people still linked them together and asked for news of her, but when he began to be placed at dinner next to Irene Scheerer people didn't ask him about her any more—they told him about her. He ceased to be an authority on her.

May at last. Dexter walked the streets at night when the darkness was damp as rain, wondering that so soon, with so little done, so much of ecstasy had gone from him. May one year back had been marked by Judy's poignant, unforgivable, yet forgiven turbulence—it had been one of those rare times when he fancied she had grown to care for him. That old penny's worth of happiness he had spent for this bushel of content. He knew that Irene would be no more than a curtain spread behind him, a hand moving among gleaming tea cups, a voice calling to children . . . fire and loveliness were gone, magic of night and the hushed wonder of the hours and seasons . . . slender lips, down turning, dropping to his lips like poppy petals, bearing him up into a heaven of eyes . . . a haunting gesture, light of a warm lamp on her hair. The thing was deep in him. He was too strong, too alive for it to die lightly.

In the middle of May when the weather balanced for a few days on the thin bridge that led to deep summer he turned in one night at Irene's house. Their engagement was to be announced in a week now—no one would be surprised at it. And tonight they would sit together on the lounge at the College Club and look on for an hour at the dancers. It gave him a sense of solidity to go with her—. She was so sturdily popular, so intensely a "good egg."

He mounted the steps of the brown stone house and stepped inside.

"Irene," he called.

Mrs. Scheerer came out of the living room to meet him.

"Dexter," she said. "Irene's gone upstairs with a splitting headache. She wanted to go with you but I made her go to bed."

"Nothing serious I—"

"Oh, no. She's going to play golf with you in the morning. You can spare her for just one night, can't you, Dexter?"

Her smile was kind. She and Dexter liked each other. In the living room he talked for a moment before he said goodnight.

Returning to the College Club, where he had rooms, he stood in the doorway for a moment and watched the dancers. He leaned against the door post, nodded at a man or two—yawned.

"Hello, kiddo."

The familiar voice at his elbow startled him. Judy Jones had left a man and crossed the room to him—Judy Jones, a slender enamelled doll in cloth of gold, gold in a band at her head, gold in two slipper points at her dress's hem. The fragile glow of her face seemed to blossom as she smiled at him. A breeze of warmth and light blew through the room. His hands in the pockets of his dinner jacket tightened spasmodically. He was filled with a sudden excitement.

"When did you get back?" he asked casually.

"Come here and I'll tell you about it."

She turned and he followed her. She had been away—he could have wept at the wonder of her return. She had passed through enchanted streets, doing young things that were like plaintive music. All mysterious happenings, all fresh and quickening hopes, had gone away with her, come back with her now.

She turned in the doorway.

"Have you a car here? If you haven't I have."

"I have a coupe."

In then, with a rustle of golden cloth. He slammed the door. Into so many cars she had stepped—like this—like that—her back against the leather, so—her elbow resting on the door—waiting. She would have been soiled long since had there been anything to soil her,—except herself—but these things were all her own outpouring.

With an effort he forced himself to start the car and avoiding her surprised glance backed into the street. This was nothing, he must remember. She had done this before and he had put her behind him, as he would have slashed a bad account from his books.

He drove slowly downtown and affecting a disinterested abstraction traversed the deserted streets of the business section, peopled here and there, where a movie was giving out its crowd or where consumptive or pugilistic youth lounged in front of pool halls. The clink of glasses and the slap of hands on the bars issued from saloons, cloisters of glazed glass and dirty yellow light.

She was watching him closely and the silence was embarrassing yet in this crisis he could find no casual word with which to profane the hour. At a convenient turning he began to zig-zag back toward the College Club.

"Have you missed me?" she asked suddenly.

"Everybody missed you."

He wondered if she knew of Irene Scheerer. She had been back only a day—her absence had been almost contemporaneous with his engagement.

"What a remark!" Judy laughed sadly—without sadness. She looked at him searchingly. He became absorbed for a moment in the dashboard.

"You're handsomer than you used to be," she said thoughtfully. "Dexter, you have the most remembered eyes."

He could have laughed at this, but he did not laugh. It was the sort of thing that was said to sophomores. Yet it stabbed at him.

"I'm awfully tired of everything, kiddo." She called everyone kiddo, endowing the obsolete slang with careless, individual camaraderie. "I wish you'd marry me."

The directness of this confused him. He should have told her now that he was going to marry another girl but he could not tell her. He could as easily have sworn that he had never loved her.

"I think we'd get along," she continued, on the same note, "unless probably you've forgotten me and fallen in love with another girl."

Her confidence was obviously enormous. She had said, in effect, that she found such a thing impossible to believe, that if it were true he had merely committed a childish indiscretion—and probably to show off. She would forgive him, because it was not a matter of any moment but rather something to be brushed aside lightly.

"Of course you could never love anybody but me," she continued. "I like the way you love me. Oh, Dexter, have you forgotten last year?"

"No, I haven't forgotten."

"Neither have I!"

Was she sincerely moved—or was she carried along by the wave of her own acting?

"I wish we could be like that again," she said, and he forced himself to answer:

"I don't think we can."

"I suppose not. . . . I hear you're giving Irene Scheerer a violent rush."

There was not the faintest emphasis on the name, yet Dexter was suddenly ashamed.

"Oh, take me home," cried Judy suddenly. "I don't want to go back to that idiotic dance—with those children."

Then, as he turned up the street that led to the residence district, Judy began to cry quietly to herself. He had never seen her cry before.

The dark street lightened, the dwellings of the rich loomed up around them, he stopped his coupé in front of the great white bulk of the Mortimer Jones' house, somnolent, gorgeous, drenched with the splendor of the damp moonlight. Its solidity startled him. The strong walls, the fine steel of the girders, the breadth and beam and pomp of it were there only to bring out the contrast with the young beauty beside him. It was sturdy to accentuate her slightness—as if to show what a breeze could be generated by a butterfly's wing.

He sat perfectly quiet, his nerves in wild clamor, afraid that if he moved he would find her irresistibly in his arms. Two tears had rolled down her wet face and trembled on her upper lip.

"I'm more beautiful than anybody else," she said brokenly, "why can't I be happy?" Her moist eyes tore at his stability—mouth turned slowly downward with an exquisite sadness. "I'd like to marry you if you'll have me, Dexter. I suppose you think I'm not worth having but I'll be so beautiful for you, Dexter."

A million phrases of anger, of pride, of passion, of hatred, of tenderness fought on his lips. Then a perfect wave of emotion washed over him, carrying off with it a sediment of wisdom, of convention, of doubt, of honor. This was his girl who was speaking, his own, his beautiful, his pride.

"Won't you come in?" he heard her draw in her breath sharply.

Waiting.

"All right," his voice was trembling, "I'll come in."

It seems strange to say that neither when it was over nor a long time afterward did he regret that night. Looking at it from the perspective of ten years, the fact that Judy's flare for him endured just one month seemed of little importance. Nor did it matter that by his yielding he subjected himself to a deeper agony in the end and gave serious hurt to Irene Scheerer and to Irene's parents who had befriended him. There was nothing sufficiently pictorial about Irene's grief to stamp itself on his mind.

Dexter was at bottom hard-minded. The attitude of the city on his action was of no importance to him, not because he was going to leave the city, but because any outside attitude on the situation seemed superficial. He was completely indifferent to popular opinion. Nor, when he had seen that it was no use, that he did not possess in himself the power to move fundamentally or to hold Judy Jones, did he bear any malice toward her. He loved her and he would love her until the day he was too old for loving—but he could not have her. So he tasted the deep pain that is reserved only for the strong, just as he had tasted for a little while the deep happiness.

Even the ultimate falsity of the grounds upon which Judy terminated the engagement—that she did not want to "take him away" from Irene, that it—was on her conscience—did not revolt him. He was beyond any revulsion or any amusement.

He went east in February with the intention of selling out his laundries and settling in New York—but the war[2] came to America in March and changed his plans. He returned to the west, handed over the management of the business to his partner and went into the first officers' training camp in late April. He was one of those young thousands who greeted the war with a certain amount of relief, welcoming the liberation from webs of tangled emotion.

This story is not his biography, remember, although things creep into it which have nothing to do with those dreams he had when he was young. We are almost done with them and with him now. There is only one more incident to be related here and it happens seven years farther on.

It took place in New York, where he had done well—so well that there were

2. World War I, which the United States entered in 1917.

no barriers too high for him now. He was thirty-two years old, and, except for one flying trip immediately after the war, he had not been west in seven years. A man named Devlin from Detroit came into his office to see him in a business way, and then and there this incident occurred, and closed out, so to speak, this particular side of his life.

"So you're from the middle west," said the man Devlin with careless curiosity. "That's funny—I thought men like you were probably born and raised on Wall Street. You know—wife of one of my best friends in Detroit came from your city. I was an usher at the wedding."

Dexter waited with no apprehension of what was coming. There was a magic that his city would never lose for him. Just as Judy's house had always seemed to him more mysterious and gay than other houses, so his dream of the city itself, now that he had gone from it, was pervaded with a melancholy beauty.

"Judy Simms," said Devlin with no particular interest, "Judy Jones she was once."

"Yes. I knew her." A dull impatience spread over him. He had heard, of course, that she was married,—perhaps deliberately he had heard no more.

"Awfully nice girl," brooded Devlin, meaninglessly, "I'm sort of sorry for her."

"Why?" Something in Dexter was alert, receptive, at once.

"Oh, Joe Simms has gone to pieces in a way. I don't mean he beats her, you understand, or anything like that. But he drinks and runs around—"

"Doesn't she run around?"

"No. Stays at home with her kids."

"Oh."

"She's a little too old for him," said Devlin.

"Too old!" cried Dexter, "why man, she's only twenty-seven."

He was possessed with a wild notion of rushing out into the streets and taking a train to Detroit. He rose to his feet, spasmodically, involuntarily.

"I guess you're busy," Devlin apologized quickly. "I didn't realize—"

"No, I'm not busy," said Dexter, steadying his voice. "I'm not busy at all. Not busy at all. Did you say she was—twenty-seven. No, I said she was twenty-seven."

"Yes, you did," agreed Devlin drily.

"Go on, then. Go on."

"What do you mean?"

"About Judy Jones."

Devlin looked at him helplessly.

"Well, that's—I told you all there is to it. He treats her like the devil. Oh, they're not going to get divorced or anything. When he's particularly outrageous she forgives him. In fact, I'm inclined to think she loves him. She was a pretty girl when she first came to Detroit."

A pretty girl! The phrase struck Dexter as ludicrous.

"Isn't she—a pretty girl any more?"

"Oh, she's all right."

"Look here," said Dexter, sitting down suddenly, "I don't understand. You say she was a 'pretty girl' and now you say she's 'all right.' I don't understand what you mean—Judy Jones wasn't a pretty girl, at all. She was a great beauty. Why, I knew her, I knew her. She was—"

Devlin laughed pleasantly.

"I'm not trying to start a row," he said. "I think Judy's a nice girl and I like her. I can't understand how a man like Joe Simms could fall madly in love with her, but he did." Then he added, "Most of the women like her."

Dexter looked closely at Devlin, thinking wildly that there must be a reason for this, some insensitivity in the man or some private malice.

"Lots of women fade just-like-*that*." Devlin snapped his fingers. "You must have seen it happen. Perhaps I've forgotten how pretty she was at her wedding. I've seen her so much since then, you see. She has nice eyes."

A sort of dullness settled down upon Dexter. For the first time in his life he felt like getting very drunk. He knew that he was laughing loudly at something Devlin had said but he did not know what it was or why it was funny. When Devlin went, in a few minutes, he lay down on his lounge and looked out the window at the New York skyline into which the sun was sinking in dully lovely shades of pink and gold.

He had thought that having nothing else to lose he was invulnerable at last—but he knew that he had just lost something more, as surely as if he had married Judy Jones and seen her fade away before his eyes.

The dream was gone. Something had been taken from him. In a sort of panic he pushed the palms of his hands into his eyes and tried to bring up a picture of the waters lapping at Lake Erminie and the moonlit verandah, and gingham on the golf links and the dry sun and the gold color of her neck's soft down. And her mouth damp to his kisses and her eyes plaintive with melancholy and her freshness like new fine linen in the morning. Why these things were no longer in the world. They had existed and they existed no more.

For the first time in years the tears were streaming down his face. But they were for himself now. He did not care about mouth and eyes and moving hands. He wanted to care and he could not care. For he had gone away and he could never go back any more. The gates were closed, the sun was gone down and there was no beauty but the grey beauty of steel that withstands all time. Even the grief he could have borne was left behind in the country of illusion, of youth, of the richness of life, where his winter dreams had flourished.

"Long ago," he said, "long ago, there was something in me, but now that thing is gone. Now that thing is gone, that thing is gone. I cannot cry. I cannot care. That thing will come back no more."

1922

Babylon Revisited[1]

"And where's Mr. Campbell?" Charlie asked.

"Gone to Switzerland. Mr. Campbell's a pretty sick man, Mr. Wales."

"I'm sorry to hear that. And George Hardt?" Charlie inquired.

"Back in America, gone to work."

"And where is the Snow Bird?"

---

1. Babylon was an ancient, prosperous city in Mesopotamia, associated by the Hebrews and Greeks with materialism and sensual pleasure; here, the reference is to Paris, where the story is set in the aftermath of the stock market crash of 1929.

"He was in here last week. Anyway, his friend, Mr. Schaeffer, is in Paris."

Two familiar names from the long list of a year and a half ago. Charlie scribbled an address in his notebook and tore out the page.

"If you see Mr. Schaeffer, give him this," he said. "It's my brother-in-law's address. I haven't settled on a hotel yet."

He was not really disappointed to find Paris was so empty. But the stillness in the Ritz bar was strange and portentous. It was not an American bar any more—he felt polite in it, and not as if he owned it. It had gone back into France. He felt the stillness from the moment he got out of the taxi and saw the doorman, usually in a frenzy of activity at this hour, gossiping with a *chasseur*[2] by the servants' entrance.

Passing through the corridor, he heard only a single, bored voice in the once-clamorous women's room. When he turned into the bar he traveled the twenty feet of green carpet with his eyes fixed straight ahead by old habit; and then, with his foot firmly on the rail, he turned and surveyed the room, encountering only a single pair of eyes that fluttered up from a newspaper in the corner. Charlie asked for the head barman, Paul, who in the latter days of the bull market had come to work in his own custom-built car—disembarking, however, with due nicety at the nearest corner. But Paul was at his country house today and Alix giving him information.

"No, no more," Charlie said, "I'm going slow these days."

Alix congratulated him: "You were going pretty strong a couple of years ago."

"I'll stick to it all right," Charlie assured him. "I've stuck to it for over a year and a half now."

"How do you find conditions in America?"

"I haven't been to America for months. I'm in business in Prague, representing a couple of concerns there. They don't know about me down there."

Alix smiled.

"Remember the night of George Hardt's bachelor dinner here?" said Charlie. "By the way, what's become of Claude Fessenden?"

Alix lowered his voice confidentially: "He's in Paris, but he doesn't come here any more. Paul doesn't allow it. He ran up a bill of thirty thousand francs, charging all his drinks and his lunches, and usually his dinner, for more than a year. And when Paul finally told him he had to pay, he gave him a bad check."

Alix shook his head sadly.

"I don't understand it, such a dandy fellow. Now he's all bloated up—" He made a plump apple of his hands.

Charlie watched a group of strident queens installing themselves in a corner.

"Nothing affects them," he thought. "Stocks rise and fall, people loaf or work, but they go on forever." The place oppressed him. He called for the dice and shook with Alix for the drink.

"Here for long, Mr. Wales?"

"I'm here for four or five days to see my little girl."

"Oh-h! You have a little girl?"

Outside, the fire-red, gas-blue, ghost-green signs shone smokily through the tranquil rain. It was late afternoon and the streets were in movement; the *bistros*[3] gleamed. At the corner of the Boulevard des Capucines he took a taxi.

---

2. Messenger-boy, errand runner (French).   3. Small, informal restaurants.

The Place de la Concorde moved by in pink majesty; they crossed the logical Seine, and Charlie felt the sudden provincial quality of the left bank.[4]

Charlie directed his taxi to the Avenue de l'Opera, which was out of his way. But he wanted to see the blue hour spread over the magnificent façade, and imagine that the cab horns, playing endlessly the first few bars of *Le Plus que Lent*,[5] were the trumpets of the Second Empire. They were closing the iron grill in front of Brentano's Book-store, and people were already at dinner behind the trim little bourgeois hedge of Duval's. He had never eaten at a really cheap restaurant in Paris. Five-course dinner, four francs fifty, eighteen cents, wine included. For some odd reason he wished that he had.

As they rolled on to the Left Bank and he felt its sudden provincialism, he thought, "I spoiled this city for myself. I didn't realize it, but the days came along one after another, and then two years were gone, and everything was gone, and I was gone."

He was thirty-five, and good to look at. The Irish mobility of his face was sobered by a deep wrinkle between his eyes. As he rang his brother-in-law's bell in the Rue Palatine, the wrinkle deepened till it pulled down his brows; he felt a cramping sensation in his belly. From behind the maid who opened the door darted a lovely little girl of nine who shrieked "Daddy!" and flew up, struggling like a fish, into his arms. She pulled his head around by one ear and set her cheek against his.

"My old pie," he said.

"Oh, daddy, daddy, daddy, daddy, dads, dads, dads!"

She drew him into the salon, where the family waited, a boy and a girl his daughter's age, his sister-in-law and her husband. He greeted Marion with his voice pitched carefully to avoid either feigned enthusiasm or dislike, but her response was more frankly tepid, though she minimized her expression of unalterable distrust by directing her regard toward his child. The two men clasped hands in a friendly way and Lincoln Peters rested his for a moment on Charlie's shoulder.

The room was warm and comfortably American. The three children moved intimately about, playing through the yellow oblongs that led to other rooms; the cheer of six o'clock spoke in the eager smacks of the fire and the sounds of French activity in the kitchen. But Charlie did not relax; his heart sat up rigidly in his body and he drew confidence from his daughter, who from time to time came close to him, holding in her arms the doll he had brought.

"Really extremely well," he declared in answer to Lincoln's question. "There's a lot of business there that isn't moving at all, but we're doing even better than ever. In fact, damn well. I'm bringing my sister over from America next month to keep house for me. My income last year was bigger than it was when I had money. You see, the Czechs—"

His boasting was for a specific purpose; but after a moment, seeing a faint restiveness in Lincoln's eye, he changed the subject:

"Those are fine children of yours, well brought up, good manners."

"We think Honoria's a great little girl too."

Marion Peters came back from the kitchen. She was a tall woman with worried eyes, who had once possessed a fresh American loveliness. Charlie

---

4. Paris is divided by the Seine River; the grander buildings and broader streets are on the Right Bank. To Charlie, the Left Bank is more like a town than a city.

5. *La plus que lente* (More than slow), piano composition by French composer Claude Debussy (1862–1918).

had never been sensitive to it and was always surprised when people spoke of how pretty she had been. From the first there had been an instinctive antipathy between them.

"Well, how do you find Honoria?" she asked.

"Wonderful. I was astonished how much she's grown in ten months. All the children are looking well."

"We haven't had a doctor for a year. How do you like being back in Paris?"

"It seems very funny to see so few Americans around."

"I'm delighted," Marion said vehemently. "Now at least you can go into a store without their assuming you're a millionaire. We've suffered like everybody, but on the whole it's a good deal pleasanter."

"But it was nice while it lasted," Charlie said. "We were a sort of royalty, almost infallible, with a sort of magic around us. In the bar this afternoon"— he stumbled, seeing his mistake—"there wasn't a man I knew."

She looked at him keenly. "I should think you'd have had enough of bars."

"I only stayed a minute. I take one drink every afternoon, and no more."

"Don't you want a cocktail before dinner?" Lincoln asked.

"I take only one drink every afternoon, and I've had that."

"I hope you keep to it," said Marion.

Her dislike was evident in the coldness with which she spoke, but Charlie only smiled; he had larger plans. Her very aggressiveness gave him an advantage, and he knew enough to wait. He wanted them to initiate the discussion of what they knew had brought him to Paris.

At dinner he couldn't decide whether Honoria was most like him or her mother. Fortunate if she didn't combine the traits of both that had brought them to disaster. A great wave of protectiveness went over him. He thought he knew what to do for her. He believed in character; he wanted to jump back a whole generation and trust in character again as the eternally valuable element. Everything else wore out.

He left soon after dinner, but not to go home. He was curious to see Paris by night with clearer and more judicious eyes than those of other days. He bought a *strapontin* for the Casino and watched Josephine Baker[6] go through her chocolate arabesques.

After an hour he left and strolled toward Montmartre, up the Rue Pigalle into the Place Blanche. The rain had stopped and there were a few people in evening clothes disembarking from taxis in front of cabarets, and *cocottes*[7] prowling singly or in pairs, and many Negroes. He passed a lighted door from which issued music, and stopped with the sense of familiarity; it was Bricktop's, where he had parted with so many hours and so much money. A few doors farther on he found another ancient rendezvous and incautiously put his head inside. Immediately an eager orchestra burst into sound, a pair of professional dancers leaped to their feet and a maître d'hôtel swooped toward him, crying, "Crowd just arriving, sir!" But he withdrew quickly.

"You have to be damn drunk," he thought.

Zelli's was closed, the bleak and sinister cheap hotels surrounding it were dark; up in the Rue Blanche there was more light and a local, colloquial French crowd. The Poet's Cave had disappeared, but the two great mouths

---

6. African American jazz singer and dancer (1906–1975) who arrived in Paris with a vaudeville troupe in 1925 and remained as a star entertainer.

"*Strapontin*": folding seat.
7. Coquettes (French, literal trans.); prostitutes.

of the Café of Heaven and the Café of Hell still yawned—even devoured, as he watched, the meager contents of a tourist bus—a German, a Japanese, and an American couple who glanced at him with frightened eyes.

So much for the effort and ingenuity of Montmartre. All the catering to vice and waste was on an utterly childish scale, and he suddenly realized the meaning of the word "dissipate"—to dissipate into thin air; to make nothing out of something. In the little hours of the night every move from place to place was an enormous human jump, an increase of paying for the privilege of slower and slower motion.

He remembered thousand-franc notes given to an orchestra for playing a single number, hundred-franc notes tossed to a doorman for calling a cab. But it hadn't been given for nothing.

It had been given, even the most wildly squandered sum, as an offering to destiny that he might not remember the things most worth remembering, the things that now he would always remember—his child taken from his control, his wife escaped to a grave in Vermont.

In the glare of a *brasserie*[8] a woman spoke to him. He bought her some eggs and coffee, and then, eluding her encouraging stare, gave her a twenty-franc note and took a taxi to his hotel.

II

He woke upon a fine fall day—football weather. The depression of yesterday was gone and he liked the people on the streets. At noon he sat opposite Honoria at Le Grand Vatel, the only restaurant he could think of not reminiscent of champagne dinners and long luncheons that began at two and ended in a blurred and vague twilight.

"Now, how about vegetables? Oughtn't you to have some vegetables?"

"Well, yes."

"Here's *épinards* and *chou-fleur* and carrots and *haricots*."[9]

"I'd like *chou-fleur*."

"Wouldn't you like to have two vegetables?"

"I usually only have one at lunch."

The waiter was pretending to be inordinately fond of children. *"Qu'elle est mignonne la petite! Elle parle exactement comme une Française."*[1]

"How about dessert? Shall we wait and see?"

The waiter disappeared. Honoria looked at her father expectantly.

"What are we going to do?"

"First, we're going to that toy store in the Rue Saint-Honoré and buy you anything you like. And then we're going to the vaudeville at the Empire."

She hesitated. "I like it about the vaudeville, but not the toy store."

"Why not?"

"Well, you brought me this doll." She had it with her. "And I've got lots of things. And we're not rich any more, are we?"

"We never were. But today you are to have anything you want."

"All right," she agreed resignedly.

---

8. Large, plain restaurant specializing in simple meals and beer.
9. Green beans (French). *"Épinards"*: spinach.

"Chou-fleur": cauliflower.
1. How cute she is! She speaks exactly like a French girl (French).

When there had been her mother and a French nurse he had been inclined to be strict; now he extended himself, reached out for a new tolerance; he must be both parents to her and not shut any of her out of communication.

"I want to get to know you," he said gravely. "First let me introduce myself. My name is Charles J. Wales, of Prague."

"Oh, daddy!" her voice cracked with laughter.

"And who are you, please?" he persisted, and she accepted a rôle immediately: "Honoria Wales, Rue Palatine, Paris."

"Married or single?"

"No, not married. Single."

He indicated the doll. "But I see you have a child, madame."

Unwilling to disinherit it, she took it to her heart and thought quickly: "Yes, I've been married, but I'm not married now. My husband is dead."

He went on quickly, "And the child's name?"

"Simone. That's after my best friend at school."

"I'm very pleased that you're doing so well at school."

"I'm third this month," she boasted. "Elsie"—that was her cousin—"is only about eighteenth, and Richard is about at the bottom."

"You like Richard and Elsie, don't you?"

"Oh, yes. I like Richard quite well and I like her all right."

Cautiously and casually he asked: "And Aunt Marion and Uncle Lincoln— which do you like best?"

"Oh, Uncle Lincoln, I guess."

He was increasingly aware of her presence. As they came in, a murmur of ". . . adorable" followed them, and now the people at the next table bent all their silences upon her, staring as if she were something no more conscious than a flower.

"Why don't I live with you?" she asked suddenly. "Because mamma's dead?"

"You must stay here and learn more French. It would have been hard for daddy to take care of you so well."

"I don't really need much taking care of any more. I do everything for myself."

Going out of the restaurant, a man and a woman unexpectedly hailed him.

"Well, the old Wales!"

"Hello there, Lorraine. . . . Dunc."

Sudden ghosts out of the past: Duncan Schaeffer, a friend from college. Lorraine Quarrles, a lovely, pale blonde of thirty; one of a crowd who had helped them make months into days in the lavish times of three years ago.

"My husband couldn't come this year," she said, in answer to his question. "We're poor as hell. So he gave me two hundred a month and told me I could do my worst on that. . . . This your little girl?"

"What about coming back and sitting down?" Duncan asked.

"Can't do it." He was glad for an excuse. As always, he felt Lorraine's passionate, provocative attraction, but his own rhythm was different now.

"Well, how about dinner?" she asked.

"I'm not free. Give me your address and let me call you."

"Charlie, I believe you're sober," she said judicially. "I honestly believe he's sober, Dunc. Pinch him and see if he's sober."

Charlie indicated Honoria with his head. They both laughed.

"What's your address?" said Duncan skeptically.

He hesitated, unwilling to give the name of his hotel.

"I'm not settled yet. I'd better call you. We're going to see the vaudeville at the Empire."

"There! That's what I want to do," Lorraine said. "I want to see some clowns and acrobats and jugglers. That's just what we'll do, Dunc."

"We've got to do an errand first," said Charlie. "Perhaps we'll see you there."

"All right, you snob. . . . Good-by, beautiful little girl."

"Good-by."

Honoria bobbed politely.

Somehow, an unwelcome encounter. They liked him because he was functioning, because he was serious; they wanted to see him, because he was stronger than they were now, because they wanted to draw a certain sustenance from his strength.

At the Empire, Honoria proudly refused to sit upon her father's folded coat. She was already an individual with a code of her own, and Charlie was more and more absorbed by the desire of putting a little of himself into her before she crystallized utterly. It was hopeless to try to know her in so short a time.

Between the acts they came upon Duncan and Lorraine in the lobby where the band was playing.

"Have a drink?"

"All right, but not up at the bar. We'll take a table."

"The perfect father."

Listening abstractedly to Lorraine, Charlie watched Honoria's eyes leave their table, and he followed them wistfully about the room, wondering what they saw. He met her glance and she smiled.

"I liked that lemonade," she said.

What had she said? What had he expected? Going home in a taxi afterward, he pulled her over until her head rested against his chest.

"Darling, do you ever think about your mother?"

"Yes, sometimes," she answered vaguely.

"I don't want you to forget her. Have you got a picture of her?"

"Yes, I think so. Anyhow, Aunt Marion has. Why don't you want me to forget her?"

"She loved you very much."

"I loved her too."

They were silent for a moment.

"Daddy, I want to come and live with you," she said suddenly.

His heart leaped; he had wanted it to come like this.

"Aren't you perfectly happy?"

"Yes, but I love you better than anybody. And you love me better than anybody, don't you, now that mummy's dead?"

"Of course I do. But you won't always like me best, honey. You'll grow up and meet somebody your own age and go marry him and forget you ever had a daddy."

"Yes, that's true," she agreed tranquilly.

He didn't go in. He was coming back at nine o'clock and he wanted to keep himself fresh and new for the thing he must say then.

"When you're safe inside, just show yourself in that window."

"All right. Good-by, dads, dads, dads, dads."

He waited in the dark street until she appeared, all warm and glowing, in the window above and kissed her fingers out into the night.

III

They were waiting. Marion sat behind the coffee service in a dignified black dinner dress that just faintly suggested mourning. Lincoln was walking up and down with the animation of one who had already been talking. They were as anxious as he was to get into the question. He opened it almost immediately:

"I suppose you know what I want to see you about—why I really came to Paris."

Marion played with the black stars on her necklace and frowned.

"I'm awfully anxious to have a home," he continued. "And I'm awfully anxious to have Honoria in it. I appreciate your taking in Honoria for her mother's sake, but things have changed now"—he hesitated and then continued more forcibly—"changed radically with me, and I want to ask you to reconsider the matter. It would be silly for me to deny that about three years ago I was acting badly—"

Marion looked up at him with hard eyes.

"—but all that's over. As I told you, I haven't had more than a drink a day for over a year, and I take that drink deliberately, so that the idea of alcohol won't get too big in my imagination. You see the idea?"

"No," said Marion succinctly.

"It's a sort of stunt I set myself. It keeps the matter in proportion."

"I get you," said Lincoln. "You don't want to admit it's got any attraction for you."

"Something like that. Sometimes I forget and don't take it. But I try to take it. Anyhow, I couldn't afford to drink in my position. The people I represent are more than satisfied with what I've done, and I'm bringing my sister over from Burlington to keep house for me, and I want awfully to have Honoria too. You know that even when her mother and I weren't getting along well we never let anything that happened touch Honoria. I know she's fond of me and I know I'm able to take care of her and—well, there you are. How do you feel about it?"

He knew that now he would have to take a beating. It would last an hour or two hours, and it would be difficult, but if he modulated his inevitable resentment to the chastened attitude of the reformed sinner, he might win his point in the end.

Keep your temper, he told himself. You don't want to be justified. You want Honoria.

Lincoln spoke first: "We've been talking it over ever since we got your letter last month. We're happy to have Honoria here. She's a dear little thing, and we're glad to be able to help her, but of course that isn't the question—"

Marion interrupted suddenly. "How long are you going to stay sober, Charlie?" she asked.

"Permanently, I hope."

"How can anybody count on that?"

"You know I never did drink heavily until I gave up business and came over here with nothing to do. Then Helen and I began to run around with—"

"Please leave Helen out of it. I can't bear to hear you talk about her like that."

He stared at her grimly; he had never been certain how fond of each other the sisters were in life.

"My drinking only lasted about a year and a half—from the time we came over until I—collapsed."

"It was time enough."

"It was time enough," he agreed.

"My duty is entirely to Helen," she said. "I try to think what she would have wanted me to do. Frankly, from the night you did that terrible thing you haven't really existed for me. I can't help that. She was my sister."

"Yes."

"When she was dying she asked me to look out for Honoria. If you hadn't been in a sanitarium then, it might have helped matters."

He had no answer.

"I'll never in my life be able to forget the morning when Helen knocked at my door, soaked to the skin and shivering and said you'd locked her out."

Charlie gripped the sides of the chair. This was more difficult than he expected; he wanted to launch out into a long expostulation and explanation, but he only said: "The night I locked her out—" and she interrupted, "I don't feel up to going over that again."

After a moment's silence Lincoln said: "We're getting off the subject. You want Marion to set aside her legal guardianship and give you Honoria. I think the main point for her is whether she has confidence in you or not."

"I don't blame Marion," Charlie said slowly, "but I think she can have entire confidence in me. I had a good record up to three years ago. Of course, it's within human possibilities I might go wrong any time. But if we wait much longer I'll lose Honoria's childhood and my chance for a home." He shook his head, "I'll simply lose her, don't you see?"

"Yes, I see," said Lincoln.

"Why didn't you think of all this before?" Marion asked.

"I suppose I did, from time to time, but Helen and I were getting along badly. When I consented to the guardianship, I was flat on my back in a sanitarium and the market had cleaned me out. I knew I'd acted badly, and I thought if it would bring any peace to Helen, I'd agree to anything. But now it's different. I'm functioning, I'm behaving damn well, so far as—"

"Please don't swear at me," Marion said.

He looked at her, startled. With each remark the force of her dislike became more and more apparent. She had built up all her fear of life into one wall and faced it toward him. This trivial reproof was possibly the result of some trouble with the cook several hours before. Charlie became increasingly alarmed at leaving Honoria in this atmosphere of hostility against himself; sooner or later it would come out, in a word here, a shake of the head there, and some of that distrust would be irrevocably implanted in Honoria. But he pulled his temper down out of his face and shut it up inside him; he had won a point, for Lincoln realized the absurdity of Marion's remark and asked her lightly since when she had objected to the word "damn."

"Another thing," Charlie said: "I'm able to give her certain advantages now. I'm going to take a French governess to Prague with me. I've got a lease on a new apartment—"

He stopped, realizing that he was blundering. They couldn't be expected to accept with equanimity the fact that his income was again twice as large as their own.

"I suppose you can give her more luxuries than we can," said Marion. "When you were throwing away money we were living along watching every ten francs. . . . I suppose you'll start doing it again."

"Oh, no," he said. "I've learned. I worked hard for ten years, you know— until I got lucky in the market, like so many people. Terribly lucky. It won't happen again."

There was a long silence. All of them felt their nerves straining, and for the first time in a year Charlie wanted a drink. He was sure now that Lincoln Peters wanted him to have his child.

Marion shuddered suddenly; part of her saw that Charlie's feet were planted on the earth now, and her own maternal feeling recognized the naturalness of his desire; but she had lived for a long time with a prejudice—a prejudice founded on a curious disbelief in her sister's happiness, and which, in the shock of one terrible night, had turned to hatred for him. It had all happened at a point in her life where the discouragement of ill health and adverse circumstances made it necessary for her to believe in tangible villainy and a tangible villain.

"I can't help what I think!" she cried out suddenly. "How much you were responsible for Helen's death, I don't know. It's something you'll have to square with your own conscience."

An electric current of agony surged through him; for a moment he was almost on his feet, an unuttered sound echoing in his throat. He hung on to himself for a moment, another moment.

"Hold on there," said Lincoln uncomfortably. "I never thought you were responsible for that."

"Helen died of heart trouble," Charlie said dully.

"Yes, heart trouble." Marion spoke as if the phrase had another meaning for her.

Then, in the flatness that followed her outburst, she saw him plainly and she knew he had somehow arrived at control over the situation. Glancing at her husband, she found no help from him, and as abruptly as if it were a matter of no importance, she threw up the sponge.

"Do what you like!" she cried, springing up from her chair. "She's your child. I'm not the person to stand in your way. I think if it were my child I'd rather see her—" She managed to check herself. "You two decide it. I can't stand this. I'm sick. I'm going to bed."

She hurried from the room; after a moment Lincoln said:

"This has been a hard day for her. You know how strongly she feels—" His voice was almost apologetic: "When a woman gets an idea in her head."

"Of course."

"It's going to be all right. I think she sees now that you—can provide for the child, and so we can't very well stand in your way or Honoria's way."

"Thank you, Lincoln."

"I'd better go along and see how she is."

"I'm going."

He was still trembling when he reached the street, but a walk down the Rue Bonaparte to the *quais*[2] set him up, and as he crossed the Seine, fresh and new by the *quai* lamps, he felt exultant. But back in his room he couldn't sleep. The image of Helen haunted him. Helen whom he had loved so until they had senselessly begun to abuse each other's love, tear it into shreds. On that terrible February night that Marion remembered so vividly, a slow quarrel had gone on for hours. There was a scene at the Florida, and then he attempted to take her home, and then she kissed young Webb at a table; after that there was what she had hysterically said. When he arrived home alone he turned the key in the lock in wild anger. How could he know she would arrive an hour later alone, that there would be a snowstorm in which she wandered about in slippers, too confused to find a taxi? Then the aftermath, her escaping pneumonia by a miracle, and all the attendant horror. They were "reconciled," but that was the beginning of the end, and Marion, who had seen with her own eyes and who imagined it to be one of many scenes from her sister's martyrdom, never forgot.

Going over it again brought Helen nearer, and in the white, soft light that steals upon half sleep near morning he found himself talking to her again. She said that he was perfectly right about Honoria and that she wanted Honoria to be with him. She said she was glad he was being good and doing better. She said a lot of other things—very friendly things—but she was in a swing in a white dress, and swinging faster and faster all the time, so that at the end he could not hear clearly all that she said.

IV

He woke up feeling happy. The door of the world was open again. He made plans, vistas, futures for Honoria and himself, but suddenly he grew sad, remembering all the plans he and Helen had made. She had not planned to die. The present was the thing—work to do and someone to love. But not to love too much, for he knew the injury that a father can do to a daughter or a mother to a son by attaching them too closely: afterward, out in the world, the child would seek in the marriage partner the same blind tenderness and, failing probably to find it, turn against love and life.

It was another bright, crisp day. He called Lincoln Peters at the bank where he worked and asked if he could count on taking Honoria when he left for Prague. Lincoln agreed that there was no reason for delay. One thing—the legal guardianship. Marion wanted to retain that a while longer. She was upset by the whole matter, and it would oil things if she felt that the situation was still in her control for another year. Charlie agreed, wanting only the tangible, visible child.

Then the question of a governess. Charles sat in a gloomy agency and talked to a cross Béarnaise and to a buxom Breton peasant,[3] neither of whom he could have endured. There were others whom he would see tomorrow.

2. Quays (French); a section of the Left Bank is lined with quays, or walking places along the river.
3. Béarn and Breton are two French provincial regions. The implication is that Charlie wants a higher-class (preferably Parisian) governess.

He lunched with Lincoln Peters at Griffons, trying to keep down his exultation.

"There's nothing quite like your own child," Lincoln said. "But you understand how Marion feels too."

"She's forgotten how hard I worked for seven years there," Charlie said. "She just remembers one night."

"There's another thing." Lincoln hesitated. "While you and Helen were tearing around Europe throwing money away, we were just getting along. I didn't touch any of the prosperity because I never got ahead enough to carry anything but my insurance. I think Marion felt there was some kind of injustice in it—you not even working toward the end, and getting richer and richer."

"It went just as quick as it came," said Charlie.

"Yes, a lot of it stayed in the hands of *chasseurs* and saxophone players and maîtres d'hôtel—well, the big party's over now. I just said that to explain Marion's feeling about those crazy years. If you drop in about six o'clock tonight before Marion's too tired, we'll settle the details on the spot."

Back at his hotel, Charlie found a *pneumatique* that had been redirected from the Ritz bar where Charlie had left his address for the purpose of finding a certain man.

"Dear Charlie: You were so strange when we saw you the other day that I wondered if I did something to offend you. If so, I'm not conscious of it. In fact, I have thought about you too much for the last year, and it's always been in the back of my mind that I might see you if I came over here. We *did* have such good times that crazy spring, like the night you and I stole the butcher's tricycle, and the time we tried to call on the president and you had the old derby rim and the wire cane. Everybody seems so old lately, but I don't feel old a bit. Couldn't we get together some time today for old time's sake? I've got a vile hang-over for the moment, but will be feeling better this afternoon and will look for you about five in the sweatshop at the Ritz.

"Always devotedly,
Lorraine."

His first feeling was one of awe that he had actually, in his mature years, stolen a tricycle and pedaled Lorraine all over the Étoile between the small hours and dawn. In retrospect it was a nightmare. Locking out Helen didn't fit in with any other act of his life, but the tricycle incident did—it was one of many. How many weeks or months of dissipation to arrive at that condition of utter irresponsibility?

He tried to picture how Lorraine had appeared to him then—very attractive; Helen was unhappy about it, though she said nothing. Yesterday, in the restaurant, Lorraine had seemed trite, blurred, worn away. He emphatically did not want to see her, and he was glad Alix had not given away his hotel address. It was a relief to think, instead, of Honoria, to think of Sundays spent with her and of saying good morning to her and of knowing she was there in his house at night, drawing her breath in the darkness.

At five he took a taxi and bought presents for all the Peters—a piquant cloth doll, a box of Roman soldiers, flowers for Marion, big linen handkerchiefs for Lincoln.

He saw, when he arrived in the apartment, that Marion had accepted the inevitable. She greeted him now as though he were a recalcitrant member of the family, rather than a menacing outsider. Honoria had been told she was going; Charlie was glad to see that her tact made her conceal her excessive happiness. Only on his lap did she whisper her delight and the question "When?" before she slipped away with the other children.

He and Marion were alone for a minute in the room, and on an impulse he spoke out boldly:

"Family quarrels are bitter things. They don't go according to any rules. They're not like aches or wounds; they're more like splits in the skin that won't heal because there's not enough material. I wish you and I could be on better terms."

"Some things are hard to forget," she answered. "It's a question of confidence." There was no answer to this and presently she asked, "When do you propose to take her?"

"As soon as I can get a governess. I hoped the day after tomorrow."

"That's impossible. I've got to get her things in shape. Not before Saturday."

He yielded. Coming back into the room, Lincoln offered him a drink.

"I'll take my daily whisky," he said.

It was warm here, it was a home, people together by a fire. The children felt very safe and important; the mother and father were serious, watchful. They had things to do for the children more important than his visit here. A spoonful of medicine was, after all, more important than the strained relations between Marion and himself. They were not dull people, but they were very much in the grip of life and circumstances. He wondered if he couldn't do something to get Lincoln out of his rut at the bank.

A long peal at the door-bell; the *bonne à tout faire*[4] passed through and went down the corridor. The door opened upon another long ring, and then voices, and the three in the salon looked up expectantly; Richard moved to bring the corridor within his range of vision, and Marion rose. Then the maid came back along the corridor, closely followed by the voices, which developed under the light into Duncan Schaeffer and Lorraine Quarrles.

They were gay, they were hilarious, they were roaring with laughter. For a moment Charlie was astounded; unable to understand how they ferreted out the Peters' address.

"Ah-h-h!" Duncan wagged his finger roguishly at Charlie. "Ah-h-h!"

They both slid down another cascade of laughter. Anxious and at a loss, Charlie shook hands with them quickly and presented them to Lincoln and Marion. Marion nodded, scarcely speaking. She had drawn back a step toward the fire; her little girl stood beside her, and Marion put an arm about her shoulder.

With growing annoyance at the intrusion, Charlie waited for them to explain themselves. After some concentration Duncan said:

"We came to invite you out to dinner. Lorraine and I insist that all this shishi, cagy business 'bout your address got to stop."

Charlie came closer to them, as if to force them backward down the corridor.

---

4. Maid of all work (French). The Peters family cannot afford to hire several servants with specialized tasks.

"Sorry, but I can't. Tell me where you'll be and I'll phone you in half an hour."

This made no impression. Lorraine sat down suddenly on the side of a chair, and focusing her eyes on Richard, cried, "Oh, what a nice little boy! Come here, little boy." Richard glanced at his mother, but did not move. With a perceptible shrug of her shoulders, Lorraine turned back to Charlie:

"Come and dine. Sure your cousins won' mine. See you so sel'om. Or solemn."

"I can't," said Charlie sharply. "You two have dinner and I'll phone you."

Her voice became suddenly unpleasant. "All right, we'll go. But I remember once when you hammered on my door at four A.M. I was enough of a good sport to give you a drink. Come on, Dunc."

Still in slow motion, with blurred, angry faces, with uncertain feet, they retired along the corridor.

"Good night," Charlie said.

"Good night!" responded Lorraine emphatically.

When he went back into the salon Marion had not moved, only now her son was standing in the circle of her other arm. Lincoln was still swinging Honoria back and forth like a pendulum from side to side.

"What an outrage!" Charlie broke out. "What an absolute outrage!"

Neither of them answered. Charlie dropped into an armchair, picked up his drink, set it down again and said:

"People I haven't seen for two years having the colossal nerve—"

He broke off. Marion had made the sound "Oh!" in one swift, furious breath, turned her body from him with a jerk and left the room.

Lincoln set down Honoria carefully.

"You children go in and start your soup," he said, and when they obeyed, he said to Charlie:

"Marion's not well and she can't stand shocks. That kind of people make her really physically sick."

"I didn't tell them to come here. They wormed your name out of somebody. They deliberately—"

"Well, it's too bad. It doesn't help matters. Excuse me a minute."

Left alone, Charlie sat tense in his chair. In the next room he could hear the children eating, talking in monosyllables, already oblivious to the scene between their elders. He heard a murmur of conversation from a farther room and then the ticking bell of a telephone receiver picked up, and in a panic he moved to the other side of the room and out of earshot.

In a minute Lincoln came back. "Look here, Charlie. I think we'd better call off dinner for tonight. Marion's in bad shape."

"Is she angry with me?"

"Sort of," he said, almost roughly. "She's not strong and—"

"You mean she's changed her mind about Honoria?"

"She's pretty bitter right now. I don't know. You phone me at the bank tomorrow."

"I wish you'd explain to her I never dreamed these people would come here. I'm just as sore as you are."

"I couldn't explain anything to her now."

Charlie got up. He took his coat and hat and started down the corridor. Then he opened the door of the dining room and said in a strange voice, "Good night, children."

Honoria rose and ran around the table to hug him.

"Good night, sweetheart," he said vaguely, and then trying to make his voice more tender, trying to conciliate something, "Good night, dear children."

V

Charlie went directly to the Ritz bar with the furious idea of finding Lorraine and Duncan, but they were not there, and he realized that in any case there was nothing he could do. He had not touched his drink at the Peters, and now he ordered a whisky-and-soda. Paul came over to say hello.

"It's a great change," he said sadly. "We do about half the business we did. So many fellows I hear about back in the States lost everything, maybe not in the first crash, but then in the second. Your friend George Hardt lost every cent, I hear. Are you back in the States?"

"No, I'm in business in Prague."

"I heard that you lost a lot in the crash."

"I did," and he added grimly, "but I lost everything I wanted in the boom."

"Selling short."

"Something like that."

Again the memory of those days swept over him like a nightmare—the people they had met travelling; then people who couldn't add a row of figures or speak a coherent sentence. The little man Helen had consented to dance with at the ship's party, who had insulted her ten feet from the table; the women and girls carried screaming with drink or drugs out of public places—

—The men who locked their wives out in the snow, because the snow of twenty-nine wasn't real snow. If you didn't want it to be snow, you just paid some money.

He went to the phone and called the Peters' apartment; Lincoln answered.

"I called up because this thing is on my mind. Has Marion said anything definite?"

"Marion's sick," Lincoln answered shortly. "I know this thing isn't altogether your fault, but I can't have her go to pieces about it. I'm afraid we'll have to let it slide for six months; I can't take the chance of working her up to this state again."

"I see."

"I'm sorry, Charlie."

He went back to his table. His whisky glass was empty, but he shook his head when Alix looked at it questioningly. There wasn't much he could do now except send Honoria some things; he would send her a lot of things tomorrow. He thought rather angrily that this was just money—he had given so many people money. . . .

"No, no more," he said to another waiter. "What do I owe you?"

He would come back some day; they couldn't make him pay forever. But he wanted his child, and nothing was much good now, beside that fact. He wasn't young any more, with a lot of nice thoughts and dreams to have by himself. He was absolutely sure Helen wouldn't have wanted him to be so alone.

1931

WILLIAM FAULKNER
1897–1962

Between 1929 and 1936 William Faulkner published novels about childhood, families, sex, race, obsessions, time, the past, his native South, and the modern world. He invented voices for characters ranging from sages to children, criminals, the insane, even the dead—sometimes all within one book. He developed, beyond this ventriloquism, his own unmistakable narrative voice, urgent, intense, highly rhetorical. He experimented with narrative chronology and with techniques for representing mind and memory. He invented an entire southern county and wrote its history.

He was a native Mississippian, born near Oxford, where his parents moved when he was about five. His great-grandfather had been a local legend: a colonel in the Civil War, lawyer, railroad builder, financier, politician, writer, and public figure who was shot and killed by a business and political rival in 1889. Faulkner's grandfather carried on some of the family enterprises, and his father worked first for the railroad (the Gulf and Chicago) and later as business manager of the University of Mississippi. The father was a reclusive man who loved to hunt, drink, and swap stories with his hunting friends; the mother, ambitious, sensitive, and literary, was a more profound influence on Faulkner, her favorite of four sons. In Faulkner's childhood his mother's mother also lived with them; she was a high-spirited, independent, and imaginative old lady whose death in 1907 seems to have affected Faulkner deeply.

Faulkner dropped out of high school in 1915 and had no further formal education beyond a year (1919–20) as a special student at the University of Mississippi. Through family connections, various jobs were made for him, but he was unhappy in all of them. In 1918 Estelle Oldham, his high school love, married someone else; Faulkner briefly left Oxford. First he went to New Haven where his best friend and informal tutor, Phil Stone, was in the Yale law school; then he enlisted in the British Royal Flying Corps and was sent to Canada to train. World War I ended before he saw active service; nevertheless, when he returned to Oxford in 1919 he was limping from what he claimed was a war wound.

Back at home, Faulkner drifted from one job to another and wrote poetry that was a mélange of Shakespearean, pastoral, Victorian, and Edwardian modes, with an overlay of French Symbolism, which he published in *The Marble Faun*, in 1924. In 1925 he went to New Orleans where, for the first time, he met and mingled with literary people, including Sherwood Anderson, who encouraged Faulkner to develop his own style, to concentrate on prose, and to use his region for material.

Faulkner wrote his first novel, *Soldier's Pay*, in New Orleans, and Anderson recommended it to his own publisher, Liveright; it appeared in 1926. He also published in the New Orleans magazine *The Double Dealer* and the newspaper *The Times Picayune*. He learned about the experimental writing of James Joyce and the ideas of Sigmund Freud. After a trip to Europe at the end of the same year, he returned to Oxford. In 1929 he married Estelle Oldham, who had been divorced and had returned to Oxford with her two children. They bought a ruined mansion, Rowan Oak, in 1930 and began to restore it to its antebellum appearance. A daughter born in 1931 died in infancy; a second daughter, Jill, was born in 1933.

Faulkner's second novel was a satire on New Orleans intellectuals called *Mosquitos* (1927). His more typical subject matter emerged with his rejected novel *Flags in the Dust*, and the shortened version of it that appeared in 1929 as *Sartoris*. In this work Faulkner focused on the interconnections between a prominent southern family and the local community: the Sartoris family as well as many other characters appeared in later works, and the region, renamed Yoknapatawpha County, was to become the locale of Faulkner's imaginative world.

The social and historical emphasis in *Sartoris* was not directly followed up in the works Faulkner wrote next. *The Sound and the Fury* (1929)—Faulkner's favorite

novel—and *As I Lay Dying* (1930) were dramatically experimental attempts to articulate the inexpressible aspects of individual psychology. *The Sound and the Fury* has
four sections, each with a different narrator, each supplying a different piece of the
plot. Three of the narrators are brothers: Benjy, the idiot; Quentin, the suicide; and
Jason, the business failure. Each of them, for different reasons, mourns the loss of
their sister Caddie. While the story moves out to the disintegration of the old southern family to which these brothers belong, its focus is on the private obsessions of
the brothers, and it invents an entirely different style for each narrator. Only the last
section, told from a traditionally omniscient point of view, provides a sequential narration; the other three jump freely in time and space. The structure of *As I Lay Dying*
is even more complex. Like *The Sound and the Fury*, it is organized around the loss
of a beloved woman. The precipitating event in the novel is the death of a mother.
The story moves forward in chronological time as the "poor white" Bundren family
takes her body to the town of Jefferson for burial. Its narration is divided into fifty-
nine sections of interior monologue by fifteen characters, each with a different perception of the action and a different way of relating to reality. The family's
adventures and misadventures on the road are comic, tragic, grotesque, absurd, and
deeply moving.

Neither these books nor his early short stories were very popular. *Sanctuary*, a sensational work about sex, gangsters, official corruption, and urban violence, attracted
considerable attention, however. It appeared in 1931, and took its place in the large
amount of hard-boiled fiction that appeared in the decade, notably by such authors
as Dashiell Hammett and Raymond Chandler. During four different intervals—
1932–37, 1942–45, 1951, and 1954—Faulkner spent time in Hollywood or on contract as a scriptwriter. He worked well with the director Howard Hawks, and wrote the
scripts for two famous movies, an adaptation of Ernest Hemingway's *To Have and
Have Not* and an adaptation of Raymond Chandler's *The Big Sleep*, both starring
Humphrey Bogart and Lauren Bacall.

He continued to produce brilliant and inventive novels during these years. *Light in
August* (1932) counterpointed a comic pastoral about the pregnant earth-mother figure Lena Grove with a grim tragedy about the embittered outcast Joe Christmas, who
may or may not be racially mixed; it interrelated individual psychology and cultural
pathology. *Absalom, Absalom!*, which followed in 1936, is thought by many to be
Faulkner's masterpiece. The story of Thomas Sutpen, the ruthless would-be founder
of a southern dynasty after the Civil War, is related by four different speakers, each
trying to find "the meaning" of the story. The reader, observing how the story changes
in each telling, comes to see that making stories is the human way of making meaning. Like Faulkner's earlier novels, *Absalom* is thus simultaneously about an individual, about the South, and about itself as a work of fiction. But its emphasis shifts from
the private psychology that dominated in earlier work to social psychology: to the collective mind of the South.

With World War II, Faulkner's work became more traditional and less difficult. He
began to write about the rise, in Yoknapatawpha County, of the poor white family
named Snopes—this family had appeared in earlier works (like "Barn Burning")—
and the simultaneous decline of the region's "aristocratic" families. *The Hamlet*
(1940) was the first of three novels devoted to the Snopeses. Because all his works
had been set in Yoknapatawpha County and were interconnected, the region and its
people began to take on an existence independent of any one book in which they
appeared.

Faulkner's national reputation soared after the publication in 1946 of an anthology of
his writings, *The Portable Faulkner*, edited by the critic Malcolm Cowley. He already had
a major reputation abroad, especially in France, where his work in translation was a powerful influence on the French so-called new novel and its practitioners such as Michel
Butor and Alain Robbe-Grillet. His antiracist *Intruder in the Dust* (1948) occasioned the
award of the Nobel Prize in 1950. In the 1950s Faulkner visited many college campuses.
His writing took on more of the air of an old-fashioned yarn; he dealt with more

legendary and local color materials; he rounded out the Snopes saga with *The Town* (1957) and *The Mansion* (1959). At the age of sixty-five he died of a heart attack.

The texts of "A Rose for Emily" and "Barn Burning" are from *Collected Stories* (1950).

A Rose for Emily

I

When Miss Emily Grierson died, our whole town went to her funeral: the men through a sort of respectful affection for a fallen monument, the women mostly out of curiosity to see the inside of her house, which no one save an old manservant—a combined gardener and cook—had seen in at least ten years.

It was a big, squarish frame house that had once been white, decorated with cupolas and spires and scrolled balconies in the heavily lightsome style of the seventies, set on what had once been our most select street. But garages and cotton gins had encroached and obliterated even the august names of that neighborhood; only Miss Emily's house was left, lifting its stubborn and coquettish decay above the cotton wagons and the gasoline pumps—an eyesore among eyesores. And now Miss Emily had gone to join the representatives of those august names where they lay in the cedar-bemused cemetery among the ranked and anonymous graves of Union and Confederate soldiers who fell at the battle of Jefferson.

Alive, Miss Emily had been a tradition, a duty, and a care; a sort of hereditary obligation upon the town, dating from that day in 1894 when Colonel Sartoris, the mayor—he who fathered the edict that no Negro woman should appear on the streets without an apron—remitted her taxes, the dispensation dating from the death of her father on into perpetuity. Not that Miss Emily would have accepted charity. Colonel Sartoris invented an involved tale to the effect that Miss Emily's father had loaned money to the town, which the town, as a matter of business, preferred this way of repaying. Only a man of Colonel Sartoris' generation and thought could have invented it, and only a woman could have believed it.

When the next generation, with its more modern ideas, became mayors and aldermen, this arrangement created some little dissatisfaction. On the first of the year they mailed her a tax notice. February came, and there was no reply. They wrote her a formal letter, asking her to call at the sheriff's office at her convenience. A week later the mayor wrote her himself, offering to call or to send his car for her, and received in reply a note on paper of an archaic shape, in a thin, flowing calligraphy in faded ink, to the effect that she no longer went out at all. The tax notice was also enclosed, without comment.

They called a special meeting of the Board of Aldermen. A deputation waited upon her, knocked at the door through which no visitor had passed since she ceased giving china-painting lessons eight or ten years earlier. They were admitted by the old Negro into a dim hall from which a stairway mounted into still more shadow. It smelled of dust and disuse—a close, dank smell. The Negro led them into the parlor. It was furnished in heavy, leather-covered furniture. When the Negro opened the blinds of one window, they could see that the leather was cracked; and when they sat down, a faint dust rose sluggishly about their thighs, spinning with slow motes in the single sun-ray. On a tarnished gilt easel before the fireplace stood a crayon portrait of Miss Emily's father.

They rose when she entered—a small, fat woman in black, with a thin gold chain descending to her waist and vanishing into her belt, leaning on an ebony cane with a tarnished gold head. Her skeleton was small and spare; perhaps that was why what would have been merely plumpness in another was obesity in her. She looked bloated, like a body long submerged in motionless water, and of that pallid hue. Her eyes, lost in the fatty ridges of her face, looked like two small pieces of coal pressed into a lump of dough as they moved from one face to another while the visitors stated their errand.

She did not ask them to sit. She just stood in the door and listened quietly until the spokesman came to a stumbling halt. Then they could hear the invisible watch ticking at the end of the gold chain.

Her voice was dry and cold. "I have no taxes in Jefferson. Colonel Sartoris explained it to me. Perhaps one of you can gain access to the city records and satisfy yourselves."

"But we have. We are the city authorities, Miss Emily. Didn't you get a notice from the sheriff, signed by him?"

"I received a paper, yes," Miss Emily said. "Perhaps he considers himself the sheriff . . . . I have no taxes in Jefferson."

"But there is nothing on the books to show that, you see. We must go by the—"

"See Colonel Sartoris. I have no taxes in Jefferson."

"But, Miss Emily—"

"See Colonel Sartoris." (Colonel Sartoris had been dead almost ten years.) "I have no taxes in Jefferson. Tobe!" The Negro appeared. "Show these gentlemen out."

II

So she vanquished them, horse and foot, just as she had vanquished their fathers thirty years before about the smell. That was two years after her father's death and a short time after her sweetheart—the one we believed would marry her—had deserted her. After her father's death she went out very little; after her sweetheart went away, people hardly saw her at all. A few of the ladies had the temerity to call, but were not received, and the only sign of life about the place was the Negro man—a young man then—going in and out with a market basket.

"Just as if a man—any man—could keep a kitchen properly," the ladies said; so they were not surprised when the smell developed. It was another link between the gross, teeming world and the high and mighty Griersons.

A neighbor, a woman, complained to the mayor, Judge Stevens, eighty years old.

"But what will you have me do about it, madam?" he said.

"Why, send her word to stop it," the woman said. "Isn't there a law?"

"I'm sure that won't be necessary," Judge Stevens said. "It's probably just a snake or a rat that nigger of hers killed in the yard. I'll speak to him about it."

The next day he received two more complaints, one from a man who came in diffident deprecation. "We really must do something about it, Judge. I'd be the last one in the world to bother Miss Emily, but we've got to do something." That night the Board of Aldermen met—three gray-beards and one younger man, a member of the rising generation.

"It's simple enough," he said. "Send her word to have her place cleaned up. Give her a certain time to do it in, and if she don't . . . ."

"Dammit, sir," Judge Stevens said, "will you accuse a lady to her face of smelling bad?"

So the next night, after midnight, four men crossed Miss Emily's lawn and slunk about the house like burglars, sniffing along the base of the brickwork and at the cellar openings while one of them performed a regular sowing motion with his hand out of a sack slung from his shoulder. They broke open the cellar door and sprinkled lime there, and in all the outbuildings. As they recrossed the lawn, a window that had been dark was lighted and Miss Emily sat in it, the light behind her, and her upright torso motionless as that of an idol. They crept quietly across the lawn and into the shadow of the locusts that lined the street. After a week or two the smell went away.

That was when people had begun to feel really sorry for her. People in our town, remembering how old lady Wyatt, her great-aunt, had gone completely crazy at last, believed that the Griersons held themselves a little too high for what they really were. None of the young men were quite good enough for Miss Emily and such. We had long thought of them as a tableau; Miss Emily a slender figure in white in the background, her father a spraddled silhouette in the foreground, his back to her and clutching a horsewhip, the two of them framed by the back-flung front door. So when she got to be thirty and was still single, we were not pleased exactly, but vindicated; even with insanity in the family she wouldn't have turned down all of her chances if they had really materialized.

When her father died, it got about that the house was all that was left to her; and in a way, people were glad. At last they could pity Miss Emily. Being left alone, and a pauper, she had become humanized. Now she too would know the old thrill and the old despair of a penny more or less.

The day after his death all the ladies prepared to call at the house and offer condolence and aid, as is our custom. Miss Emily met them at the door, dressed as usual and with no trace of grief on her face. She told them that her father was not dead. She did that for three days, with the ministers calling on her, and the doctors, trying to persuade her to let them dispose of the body. Just as they were about to resort to law and force, she broke down, and they buried her father quickly.

We did not say she was crazy then. We believed she had to do that. We remembered all the young men her father had driven away, and we knew that with nothing left, she would have to cling to that which had robbed her, as people will.

III

She was sick for a long time. When we saw her again, her hair was cut short, making her look like a girl, with a vague resemblance to those angels in colored church windows—sort of tragic and serene.

The town had just let the contracts for paving the sidewalks, and in the summer after her father's death they began to work. The construction company came with niggers and mules and machinery, and a foreman named Homer Barron, a Yankee—a big, dark, ready man, with a big voice and eyes lighter than his face. The little boys would follow in groups to hear him cuss the niggers, and the niggers singing in time to the rise and fall of picks. Pretty soon he knew everybody in town. Whenever you heard a lot of laughing anywhere about the square, Homer Barron would be in the center of the group. Presently we began to see him and Miss Emily on Sunday afternoons driving in the yellow-wheeled buggy and the matched team of bays from the livery stable.

At first we were glad that Miss Emily would have an interest, because the ladies all said, "Of course a Grierson would not think seriously of a Northerner, a day laborer." But there were still others, older people, who said that even grief could not cause a real lady to forget *noblesse oblige*—without calling it *noblesse oblige*. They just said, "Poor Emily. Her kinsfolk should come to her." She had some kin in Alabama; but years ago her father had fallen out with them over the estate of old lady Wyatt, the crazy woman, and there was no communication between the two families. They had not even been represented at the funeral.

And as soon as the old people said, "Poor Emily," the whispering began. "Do you suppose it's really so?" they said to one another. "Of course it is. What else could . . . ." This behind their hands; rustling of craned silk and satin behind jalousies closed upon the sun of Sunday afternoon as the thin, swift clop-clop-clop of the matched team passed: "Poor Emily."

She carried her head high enough—even when we believed that she was fallen. It was as if she demanded more than ever the recognition of her dignity as the last Grierson; as if it had wanted that touch of earthiness to reaffirm her imperviousness. Like when she bought the rat poison, the arsenic. That was over a year after they had begun to say "Poor Emily," and while the two female cousins were visiting her.

"I want some poison," she said to the druggist. She was over thirty then, still a slight woman, though thinner than usual, with cold, haughty black eyes in a face the flesh of which was strained across the temples and about the eyesockets as you imagine a lighthouse-keeper's face ought to look. "I want some poison," she said.

"Yes, Miss Emily. What kind? For rats and such? I'd recom—"

"I want the best you have. I don't care what kind."

The druggist named several. "They'll kill anything up to an elephant. But what you want is—"

"Arsenic," Miss Emily said. "Is that a good one?"

"Is . . . . . . arsenic? Yes ma'am. But what you want—"

"I want arsenic."

The druggist looked down at her. She looked back at him, erect, her face like a strained flag. "Why, of course," the druggist said. "If that's what you want. But the law requires you to tell what you are going to use it for."

Miss Emily just stared at him, her head tilted back in order to look him eye for eye, until he looked away and went and got the arsenic and wrapped it up. The Negro delivery boy brought her the package; the druggist didn't come back. When she opened the package at home there was written on the box, under the skull and bones: "For rats."

IV

So the next day we all said, "She will kill herself"; and we said it would be the best thing. When she had first begun to be seen with Homer Barron, we had said, "She will marry him." Then we said, "She will persuade him yet," because Homer himself had remarked—he liked men, and it was known that he drank with the younger men in the Elks' Club—that he was not a marrying man. Later we said, "Poor Emily," behind the jalousies as they passed on Sunday afternoon in the glittering buggy, Miss Emily with her head high and Homer Barron with his hat cocked and a cigar in his teeth, reins and whip in a yellow glove.

Then some of the ladies began to say that it was a disgrace to the town and a bad example to the young people. The men did not want to interfere, but at last the ladies forced the Baptist minister—Miss Emily's people were Episcopal—to call upon her. He would never divulge what happened during that interview, but he refused to go back again. The next Sunday they again drove about the streets, and the following day the minister's wife wrote to Miss Emily's relations in Alabama.

So she had blood-kin under her roof again and we sat back to watch developments. At first nothing happened. Then we were sure that they were to be married. We learned that Miss Emily had been to the jeweler's and ordered a man's toilet set in silver, with the letters H. B. on each piece. Two days later we learned that she had bought a complete outfit of men's clothing, including a nightshirt, and we said, "They are married." We were really glad. We were glad because the two female cousins were even more Grierson than Miss Emily had ever been.

So we were not surprised when Homer Barron—the streets had been finished some time since—was gone. We were a little disappointed that there was not a public blowing-off, but we believed that he had gone on to prepare for Miss Emily's coming, or to give her a chance to get rid of the cousins. (By that time it was a cabal, and we were all Miss Emily's allies to help circumvent the cousins.) Sure enough, after another week they departed. And, as we had expected all along, within three days Homer Barron was back in town. A neighbor saw the Negro man admit him at the kitchen door at dusk one evening.

And that was the last we saw of Homer Barron. And of Miss Emily for some time. The Negro man went in and out with the market basket, but the front door remained closed. Now and then we would see her at a window for a moment, as the men did that night when they sprinkled the lime, but for almost six months she did not appear on the streets. Then we knew that this was to be expected too; as if that quality of her father which had thwarted her woman's life so many times had been too virulent and too furious to die.

When we next saw Miss Emily, she had grown fat and her hair was turning gray. During the next few years it grew grayer and grayer until it attained an even pepper-and-salt iron-gray, when it ceased turning. Up to the day of her death at seventy-four it was still that vigorous iron-gray, like the hair of an active man.

From that time on her front door remained closed, save for a period of six or seven years, when she was about forty, during which she gave lessons in china-painting. She fitted up a studio in one of the downstairs rooms, where the daughters and granddaughters of Colonel Sartoris' contemporaries were sent to her with the same regularity and in the same spirit that they were sent on Sundays with a twenty-five-cent piece for the collection plate. Meanwhile her taxes had been remitted.

Then the newer generation became the backbone and the spirit of the town, and the painting pupils grew up and fell away and did not send their children to her with boxes of color and tedious brushes and pictures cut from the ladies' magazines. The front door closed upon the last one and remained closed for good. When the town got free postal delivery Miss Emily alone refused to let them fasten the metal numbers above her door and attach a mailbox to it. She would not listen to them.

Daily, monthly, yearly we watched the Negro grow grayer and more stooped, going in and out with the market basket. Each December we sent her a tax notice, which would be returned by the post office a week later, unclaimed. Now and then we would see her in one of the downstairs windows—she had evidently shut up the top floor of the house—like the carven torso of an idol in a niche, looking or not looking at us, we could never tell which. Thus she passed from generation to generation—dear, inescapable, impervious, tranquil, and perverse.

And so she died. Fell ill in the house filled with dust and shadows, with only a doddering Negro man to wait on her. We did not even know she was sick; we had long since given up trying to get any information from the Negro. He talked to no one, probably not even to her, for his voice had grown harsh and rusty, as if from disuse.

She died in one of the downstairs rooms, in a heavy walnut bed with a curtain, her gray head propped on a pillow yellow and moldy with age and lack of sunlight.

V

The Negro met the first of the ladies at the front door and let them in, with their hushed, sibilant voices and their quick, curious glances, and then he disappeared. He walked right through the house and out the back and was not seen again.

The two female cousins came at once. They held the funeral on the second day, with the town coming to look at Miss Emily beneath a mass of bought flowers, with the crayon face of her father musing profoundly above the bier and the ladies sibilant and macabre; and the very old men—some in their brushed Confederate uniforms—on the porch and the lawn, talking of Miss Emily as if she had been a contemporary of theirs, believing that they had danced with her and courted her perhaps, confusing time with its mathematical progression, as the old do, to whom all the past is not a diminishing road, but, instead, a huge meadow which no winter ever quite touches, divided from them now by the narrow bottle-neck of the most recent decade of years.

Already we knew that there was one room in that region above stairs which no one had seen in forty years, and which would have to be forced. They waited until Miss Emily was decently in the ground before they opened it.

The violence of breaking down the door seemed to fill this room with pervading dust. A thin, acrid pall as of the tomb seemed to lie everywhere upon this room decked and furnished as for a bridal: upon the valance curtains of faded rose color, upon the rose-shaded lights, upon the dressing table, upon the delicate array of crystal and the man's toilet things backed with tarnished silver, silver so tarnished that the monogram was obscured. Among them lay a collar and tie, as if they had just been removed, which, lifted, left upon the surface a pale crescent in the dust. Upon a chair hung the suit, carefully folded; beneath it the two mute shoes and the discarded socks.

The man himself lay in the bed.

For a long while we just stood there, looking down at the profound and fleshless grin. The body had apparently once lain in the attitude of an embrace, but now the long sleep that outlasts love, that conquers even the grimace of love, had cuckolded him. What was left of him, rotted beneath what was left of the nightshirt, had become inextricable from the bed in which he lay; and upon him and upon the pillow beside him lay that even coating of the patient and biding dust.

Then we noticed that in the second pillow was the indentation of a head. One of us lifted something from it, and leaning forward, that faint and invisible dust dry and acrid in the nostrils, we saw a long strand of iron-gray hair.

1931

Barn Burning

The store in which the Justice of the Peace's court was sitting smelled of cheese. The boy, crouched on his nail keg at the back of the crowded room, knew he smelled cheese, and more: from where he sat he could see the ranked shelves close-packed with the solid, squat, dynamic shapes of tin cans whose labels his stomach read, not from the lettering which meant nothing to his mind but from the scarlet devils and the silver curve of fish—this, the cheese which he knew he smelled and the hermetic meat which his intestines believed he smelled coming in intermittent gusts momentary and brief between the other constant one, the smell and sense just a little of fear because mostly of despair and grief, the old fierce pull of blood. He could not see the table where the Justice sat and before which his father and his father's enemy (*our enemy* he thought in that despair; *ourn! mine and hisn both! He's my father!*) stood, but he could hear them, the two of them that is, because his father had said no word yet:

"But what proof have you, Mr. Harris?"

"I told you. The hog got into my corn. I caught it up and sent it back to him. He had no fence that would hold it. I told him so, warned him. The next time I put the hog in my pen. When he came to get it I gave him enough wire to patch up his pen. The next time I put the hog up and kept it. I rode down to his house and saw the wire I gave him still rolled on to the spool in his yard. I told him he could have the hog when he paid me a dollar pound fee. That evening a nigger came with the dollar and got the hog. He was a strange nigger. He said, 'He say to tell you wood and hay kin burn.' I said, 'What?' 'That whut he say to tell you,' the nigger said. 'Wood and hay kin burn.' That night my barn burned. I got the stock out but I lost the barn."

"Where is the nigger? Have you got him?"

"He was a strange nigger, I tell you. I don't know what became of him."

"But that's not proof. Don't you see that's not proof?"

"Get that boy up here. He knows." For a moment the boy thought too that the man meant his older brother until Harris said, "Not him. The little one. The boy," and, crouching, small for his age, small and wiry like his father, in patched and faded jeans even too small for him, with straight, uncombed, brown hair and eyes gray and wild as storm scud, he saw the men between himself and the table part and become a lane of grim faces, at the end of which he saw the Justice, a shabby, collarless, graying man in spectacles, beckoning him. He felt no floor under his bare feet; he seemed to walk beneath the palpable weight of the grim turning faces. His father, stiff in his black Sunday coat donned not for the trial but for the moving, did not even look at him. *He aims for me to lie,* he thought, again with that frantic grief and despair. *And I will have to do hit.*

"What's your name, boy?" the Justice said.

"Colonel Sartoris Snopes,"[1] the boy whispered.

"Hey?" the Justice said. "Talk louder. Colonel Sartoris? I reckon anybody named for Colonel Sartoris in this country can't help but tell the truth, can they?" The boy said nothing. *Enemy! Enemy!* he thought; for a moment he could not even see, could not see that the Justice's face was kindly nor discern that his voice was troubled when he spoke to the man named Harris: "Do you want me to question this boy?" But he could hear, and during those subsequent long seconds while there was absolutely no sound in the crowded little room save that of quiet and intent breathing it was as if he had swung outward at the end of a grape vine, over a ravine, and at the top of the swing had been caught in a prolonged instant of mesmerized gravity, weightless in time.

"No!" Harris said violently, explosively. "Damnation! Send him out of here!" Now time, the fluid world, rushed beneath him again, the voices coming to him again through the smell of cheese and sealed meat, the fear and despair and the old grief of blood:

"This case is closed. I can't find against you, Snopes, but I can give you advice. Leave this country and don't come back to it."

His father spoke for the first time, his voice cold and harsh, level, without emphasis: "I aim to. I don't figure to stay in a country among people who . . ." he said something unprintable and vile, addressed to no one.

"That'll do," the Justice said. "Take your wagon and get out of this country before dark. Case dismissed."

His father turned, and he followed the stiff black coat, the wiry figure walking a little stiffly from where a Confederate provost's man's musket ball had taken him in the heel on a stolen horse thirty years ago, followed the two backs now, since his older brother had appeared from somewhere in the crowd, no taller than the father but thicker, chewing tobacco steadily, between the two lines of grim-faced men and out of the store and across the worn gallery and down the sagging steps and among the dogs and half-grown boys in the mild May dust, where as he passed a voice hissed:

"Barn burner!"

Again he could not see, whirling; there was a face in a red haze, moonlike, bigger than the full moon, the owner of it half again his size, he leaping in the red haze toward the face, feeling no blow, feeling no shock when his head struck the earth, scrabbling up and leaping again, feeling no blow this time either and tasting no blood, scrabbling up to see the other boy in full flight

---

1. The boy is named for Colonel Sartoris, a leading citizen of Jefferson (the fictional town that Faulkner based on his hometown of Oxford, Mississippi) and officer in the Confederate Army. The Snopeses are a poor white family from the same area. Both families appear in other works by Faulkner.

and himself already leaping into pursuit as his father's hand jerked him back, the harsh, cold voice speaking above him: "Go get in the wagon."

It stood in a grove of locusts and mulberries across the road. His two hulking sisters in their Sunday dresses and his mother and her sister in calico and sunbonnets were already in it, sitting on and among the sorry residue of the dozen and more movings which even the boy could remember—the battered stove, the broken beds and chairs, the clock inlaid with mother-of-pearl, which would not run, stopped at some fourteen minutes past two o'clock of a dead and forgotten day and time, which had been his mother's dowry. She was crying, though when she saw him she drew her sleeve across her face and began to descend from the wagon. "Get back," the father said.

"He's hurt. I got to get some water and wash his . . ."

"Get back in the wagon," his father said. He got in too, over the tail-gate. His father mounted to the seat where the older brother already sat and struck the gaunt mules two savage blows with the peeled willow, but without heat. It was not even sadistic; it was exactly that same quality which in later years would cause his descendants to over-run the engine before putting a motor car into motion, striking and reining back in the same movement. The wagon went on, the store with its quiet crowd of grimly watching men dropped behind; a curve in the road hid it. *Forever* he thought. *Maybe he's done satisfied now, now that he has . . .* stopping himself, not to say it aloud even to himself. His mother's hand touched his shoulder.

"Does hit hurt?" she said.

"Naw," he said. "Hit don't hurt. Lemme be."

"Can't you wipe some of the blood off before hit dries?"

"I'll wash to-night," he said. "Lemme be, I tell you."

The wagon went on. He did not know where they were going. None of them ever did or ever asked, because it was always somewhere, always a house of sorts waiting for them a day or two days or even three days away. Likely his father had already arranged to make a crop on another farm before he . . . Again he had to stop himself. He (the father) always did. There was something about his wolflike independence and even courage when the advantage was at least neutral which impressed strangers, as if they got from his latent ravening ferocity not so much a sense of dependability as a feeling that his ferocious conviction in the rightness of his own actions would be of advantage to all whose interest lay with his.

That night they camped, in a grove of oaks and beeches where a spring ran. The nights were still cool and they had a fire against it, of a rail lifted from a nearby fence and cut into lengths—a small fire, neat, niggard almost, a shrewd fire; such fires were his father's habit and custom always, even in freezing weather. Older, the boy might have remarked this and wondered why not a big one; why should not a man who had not only seen the waste and extravagance of war, but who had in his blood an inherent voracious prodigality with material not his own, have burned everything in sight? Then he might have gone a step farther and thought that that was the reason: that niggard blaze was the living fruit of nights passed during those four years in the woods hiding from all men, blue or gray, with his strings of horses (captured horses, he called them). And older still, he might have divined the true reason: that the element of fire spoke to some deep mainspring of his father's being, as the element of steel or of powder spoke to other men, as the one weapon for the preservation of integrity, else breath were not worth the breathing, and hence to be regarded with respect and used with discretion.

But he did not think this now and he had seen those same niggard blazes all his life. He merely ate his supper beside it and was already half asleep over his iron plate when his father called him, and once more he followed the stiff back, the stiff and ruthless limp, up the slope and on to the starlit road where, turning, he could see his father against the stars but without face or depth—a shape black, flat, and bloodless as though cut from tin in the iron folds of the frockcoat which had not been made for him, the voice harsh like tin and without heat like tin:

"You were fixing to tell them. You would have told him." He didn't answer. His father struck him with the flat of his hand on the side of the head, hard but without heat, exactly as he had struck the two mules at the store, exactly as he would strike either of them with any stick in order to kill a horse fly, his voice still without heat or anger: "You're getting to be a man. You got to learn. You got to learn to stick to your own blood or you ain't going to have any blood to stick to you. Do you think either of them, any man there this morning, would? Don't you know all they wanted was a chance to get at me because they knew I had them beat? Eh?" Later, twenty years later, he was to tell himself, "If I had said they wanted only truth, justice, he would have hit me again." But now he said nothing. He was not crying. He just stood there. "Answer me," his father said.

"Yes," he whispered. His father turned.

"Get on to bed. We'll be there to-morrow."

To-morrow they were there. In the early afternoon the wagon stopped before a paintless two-room house identical almost with the dozen others it had stopped before even in the boy's ten years, and again, as on the other dozen occasions, his mother and aunt got down and began to unload the wagon, although his two sisters and his father and brother had not moved.

"Likely hit ain't fitten for hawgs," one of the sisters said.

"Nevertheless, fit it will and you'll hog it and like it," his father said. "Get out of them chairs and help your Ma unload."

The two sisters got down, big, bovine, in a flutter of cheap ribbons; one of them drew from the jumbled wagon bed a battered lantern, the other a worn broom. His father handed the reins to the older son and began to climb stiffly over the wheel. "When they get unloaded, take the team to the barn and feed them." Then he said, and at first the boy thought he was still speaking to his brother: "Come with me."

"Me?" he said.

"Yes," his father said. "You."

"Abner," his mother said. His father paused and looked back—the harsh level stare beneath the shaggy, graying, irascible brows.

"I reckon I'll have a word with the man that aims to begin to-morrow owning me body and soul for the next eight months."

They went back up the road. A week ago—or before last night, that is—he would have asked where they were going, but not now. His father had struck him before last night but never before had he paused afterward to explain why; it was as if the blow and the following calm, outrageous voice still rang, repercussed, divulging nothing to him save the terrible handicap of being young, the light weight of his few years, just heavy enough to prevent his soaring free of the world as it seemed to be ordered but not heavy enough to keep him footed solid in it, to resist it and try to change the course of its events.

Presently he could see the grove of oaks and cedars and the other flowering trees and shrubs where the house would be, though not the house yet. They walked beside a fence massed with honeysuckle and Cherokee roses and came to a gate swinging open between two brick pillars, and now, beyond a sweep of drive, he saw the house for the first time and at that instant he forgot his father and the terror and despair both, and even when he remembered his father again (who had not stopped) the terror and despair did not return. Because, for all the twelve movings, they had sojourned until now in a poor country, a land of small farms and fields and houses, and he had never seen a house like this before. *Hit's big as a courthouse* he thought quietly, with a surge of peace and joy whose reason he could not have thought into words, being too young for that: *They are safe from him. People whose lives are a part of this peace and dignity are beyond his touch, he no more to them than a buzzing wasp: capable of stinging for a little moment but that's all; the spell of this peace and dignity rendering even the barns and stable and cribs which belong to it impervious to the puny flames he might contrive* . . . this, the peace and joy, ebbing for an instant as he looked again at the stiff black back, the stiff and implacable limp of the figure which was not dwarfed by the house, for the reason that it had never looked big anywhere and which now, against the serene columned backdrop, had more than ever that impervious quality of something cut ruthlessly from tin, depthless, as though, sidewise to the sun, it would cast no shadow. Watching him, the boy remarked the absolutely undeviating course which his father held and saw the stiff foot come squarely down in a pile of fresh droppings where a horse had stood in the drive and which his father could have avoided by a simple change of stride. But it ebbed only for a moment, though he could not have thought this into words either, walking on in the spell of the house, which he could even want but without envy, without sorrow, certainly never with that ravening and jealous rage which unknown to him walked in the ironlike black coat before him: *Maybe he will feel it too. Maybe it will even change him now from what maybe he couldn't help but be.*

They crossed the portico. Now he could hear his father's stiff foot as it came down on the boards with clocklike finality, a sound out of all proportion to the displacement of the body it bore and which was not dwarfed either by the white door before it, as though it had attained to a sort of vicious and ravening minimum not to be dwarfed by anything—the flat, wide, black hat, the formal coat of broadcloth which had once been black but which had now that friction-glazed greenish cast of the bodies of old house flies, the lifted sleeve which was too large, the lifted hand like a curled claw. The door opened so promptly that the boy knew the Negro must have been watching them all the time, an old man with neat grizzled hair, in a linen jacket, who stood barring the door with his body, saying, "Wipe yo foots, white man, fo you come in here. Major ain't home nohow."

"Get out of my way, nigger," his father said, without heat too, flinging the door back and the Negro also and entering, his hat still on his head. And now the boy saw the prints of the stiff foot on the doorjamb and saw them appear on the pale rug behind the machinelike deliberation of the foot which seemed to bear (or transmit) twice the weight which the body compassed. The Negro was shouting "Miss Lula! Miss Lula!" somewhere behind them, then the boy, deluged as though by a warm wave by a suave turn of carpeted stair and a pendant glitter of chandeliers and a mute gleam of gold frames, heard the swift feet and saw her too, a lady—perhaps he had never seen her like before either—in a gray, smooth gown with lace at the throat and an apron tied at the waist and the sleeves turned back, wiping cake or biscuit dough from her hands with a towel as she came up the hall, looking not at his father at all but at the tracks on the blond rug with an expression of incredulous amazement.

"I tried," the Negro cried. "I tole him to . . ."

"Will you please go away?" she said in a shaking voice. "Major de Spain is not at home. Will you please go away?"

His father had not spoken again. He did not speak again. He did not even look at her. He just stood stiff in the center of the rug, in his hat, the shaggy iron-gray brows twitching slightly above the pebble-colored eyes as he appeared to examine the house with brief deliberation. Then with the same deliberation he turned; the boy watched him pivot on the good leg and saw the stiff foot drag round the arc of the turning, leaving a final long and fading smear. His father never looked at it, he never once looked down at the rug. The Negro held the door. It closed behind them, upon the hysteric and indistinguishable woman-wail. His father stopped at the top of the steps and scraped his boot clean on the edge of it. At the gate he stopped again. He stood for a moment, planted stiffly on the stiff foot, looking back at the house. "Pretty and white, ain't it?" he said. "That's sweat. Nigger sweat. Maybe it ain't white enough yet to suit him. Maybe he wants to mix some white sweat with it."

Two hours later the boy was chopping wood behind the house within which his mother and aunt and the two sisters (the mother and aunt, not the two girls, he knew that; even at this distance and muffled by walls the flat loud voices of the two girls emanated an incorrigible idle inertia) were setting up the stove to prepare a meal, when he heard the hooves and saw the linen-clad man on a fine sorrel mare, whom he recognized even before he saw the rolled rug in front of the Negro youth following on a fat bay carriage horse—a suffused, angry face vanishing, still at full gallop, beyond the corner of the house where his father and brother were sitting in the two tilted chairs; and a moment later, almost before he could have put the axe down, he heard the hooves again and watched the sorrel mare go back out of the yard, already galloping again. Then his father began to shout one of the sisters' names, who presently emerged backward from the kitchen door dragging the rolled rug along the ground by one end while the other sister walked behind it.

"If you ain't going to tote, go on and set up the wash pot," the first said.

"You, Sarty!" the second shouted. "Set up the wash pot!" His father appeared at the door, framed against that shabbiness, as he had been against that other bland perfection, impervious to either, the mother's anxious face at his shoulder.

"Go on," the father said. "Pick it up." The two sisters stooped, broad, lethargic; stooping, they presented an incredible expanse of pale cloth and a flutter of tawdry ribbons.

"If I thought enough of a rug to have to git hit all the way from France I wouldn't keep hit where folks coming in would have to tromp on hit," the first said. They raised the rug.

"Abner," the mother said. "Let me do it."

"You go back and git dinner," his father said. "I'll tend to this."

From the woodpile through the rest of the afternoon the boy watched them, the rug spread flat in the dust beside the bubbling wash-pot, the two sisters stooping over it with that profound and lethargic reluctance, while the father stood over them in turn, implacable and grim, driving them though never raising his voice again. He could smell the harsh homemade lye they were using; he saw his mother come to the door once and look toward them with an expression not anxious now but very like despair; he saw his father turn, and he fell to with the axe and saw from the corner of his eye his father raise from the ground a flattish fragment of field stone and examine it and return to the pot, and this time his mother actually spoke: "Abner. Abner. Please don't. Please, Abner."

Then he was done too. It was dusk; the whippoorwills had already begun. He could smell coffee from the room where they would presently eat the cold food remaining from the mid-afternoon meal, though when he entered the house he realized they were having coffee again probably because there was a fire on the hearth, before which the rug now lay spread over the backs of the two chairs. The tracks of his father's foot were gone. Where they had been were now long, water-cloudy scoriations resembling the sporadic course of a lilliputian mowing machine.

It still hung there while they ate the cold food and then went to bed, scattered without order or claim up and down the two rooms, his mother in one bed, where his father would later lie, the older brother in the other, himself, the aunt, and the two sisters on pallets on the floor. But his father was not in bed yet. The last thing the boy remembered was the depthless, harsh silhouette of the hat and coat bending over the rug and it seemed to him that he had not even closed his eyes when the silhouette was standing over him, the fire almost dead behind it, the stiff foot prodding him awake. "Catch up the mule," his father said.

When he returned with the mule his father was standing in the black door, the rolled rug over his shoulder. "Ain't you going to ride?" he said.

"No. Give me your foot."

He bent his knee into his father's hand, the wiry, surprising power flowed smoothly, rising, he rising with it, on to the mule's bare back (they had owned a saddle once; the boy could remember it though not when or where) and with the same effortlessness his father swung the rug up in front of him. Now in the starlight they retraced the afternoon's path, up the dusty road rife with honeysuckle, through the gate and up the black tunnel of the drive to the lightless house, where he sat on the mule and felt the rough warp of the rug drag across his thighs and vanish.

"Don't you want me to help?" he whispered. His father did not answer and now he heard again that stiff foot striking the hollow portico with that wooden and clocklike deliberation, that outrageous overstatement of the weight it carried. The rug, hunched, not flung (the boy could tell that even in the darkness) from his father's shoulder, struck the angle of wall and floor with a sound unbelievably loud, thunderous, then the foot again, unhurried and enormous; a light came on in the house and the boy sat, tense, breathing steadily and quietly and just a little fast, though the foot itself did not increase its beat at all, descending the steps now; now the boy could see him.

"Don't you want to ride now?" he whispered. "We kin both ride now," the light within the house altering now, flaring up and sinking. *He's coming down the stairs now,* he thought. He had already ridden the mule up beside the horse block; presently his father was up behind him and he doubled the reins over and slashed the mule across the neck, but before the animal could begin to trot the hard, thin arm came round him, the hard, knotted hand jerking the mule back to a walk.

In the first red rays of the sun they were in the lot, putting plow gear on the mules. This time the sorrel mare was in the lot before he heard it at all, the rider collarless and even bareheaded, trembling, speaking in a shaking voice as the woman in the house had done, his father merely looking up once before stooping again to the hame he was buckling, so that the man on the mare spoke to his stooping back:

"You must realize you have ruined that rug. Wasn't there anybody here, any of your women . . ." he ceased, shaking, the boy watching him, the older brother leaning now in the stable door, chewing, blinking slowly and steadily at nothing apparently. "It cost a hundred dollars. But you never had a hundred dollars. You never will. So I'm going to charge you twenty bushels of corn against your crop. I'll add it in your contract and when you come to the commissary you can sign it. That won't keep Mrs. de Spain quiet but maybe it will teach you to wipe your feet off before you enter her house again."

Then he was gone. The boy looked at his father, who still had not spoken or even looked up again, who was now adjusting the logger-head in the hame.

"Pap," he said. His father looked at him—the inscrutable face, the shaggy brows beneath which the gray eyes glinted coldly. Suddenly the boy went toward him, fast, stopping as suddenly. "You done the best you could!" he cried. "If he wanted hit done different why didn't he wait and tell you how? He won't git no twenty bushels! He won't git none! We'll gether hit and hide hit! I kin watch . . ."

"Did you put the cutter back in that straight stock like I told you?"

"No, sir," he said.

"Then go do it."

That was Wednesday. During the rest of that week he worked steadily, at what was within his scope and some which was beyond it, with an industry that did not need to be driven nor even commanded twice; he had this from his mother, with the difference that some at least of what he did he liked to do, such as splitting wood with the half-size axe which his mother and aunt had earned, or saved money somehow, to present him with at Christmas. In company with the two older women (and on one afternoon, even one of the sisters), he built pens for the shoat and the cow which were a part of his father's contract with the landlord, and one afternoon, his father being absent, gone somewhere on one of the mules, he went to the field.

They were running a middle buster now, his brother holding the plow straight while he handled the reins, and walking beside the straining mule, the rich black soil shearing cool and damp against his bare ankles, he thought *Maybe this is the end of it. Maybe even that twenty bushels that seems hard to have to pay for just a rug will be a cheap price for him to stop forever and always from being what he used to be;* thinking, dreaming now, so that his brother had to speak sharply to him to mind the mule: *Maybe he even won't collect the twenty bushels. Maybe it will all add up and balance and vanish—corn, rug, fire; the terror and grief, the being pulled two ways like between two teams of horses—gone, done with for ever and ever.*

Then it was Saturday; he looked up from beneath the mule he was harnessing and saw his father in the black coat and hat. "Not that," his father said. "The wagon gear." And then, two hours later, sitting in the wagon bed behind his father and brother on the seat, the wagon accomplished a final curve, and he saw the weathered paintless store with its tattered tobacco- and patent-medicine posters and the tethered wagons and saddle animals below the gallery. He mounted the gnawed steps behind his father and brother, and there again was the lane of quiet, watching faces for the three of them to walk through. He saw the man in spectacles sitting at the plank table and he did not need to be told this was a Justice of the Peace; he sent one glare of fierce, exultant, partisan defiance at the man in collar and cravat now, whom he had seen but twice before in his life, and that on a galloping horse, who now wore on his face an expression not of rage but of amazed unbelief which the boy could not have known was at the incredible circumstance of being sued by one of his own tenants, and came and stood against his father and cried at the Justice: "He ain't done it! He ain't burnt . . ."

"Go back to the wagon," his father said.

"Burnt?" the Justice said. "Do I understand this rug was burned too?"

"Does anybody here claim it was?" his father said. "Go back to the wagon." But he did not, he merely retreated to the rear of the room, crowded as that other had been, but not to sit down this time, instead, to stand pressing among the motionless bodies, listening to the voices:

"And you claim twenty bushels of corn is too high for the damage you did to the rug?"

"He brought the rug to me and said he wanted the tracks washed out of it. I washed the tracks out and took the rug back to him."

"But you didn't carry the rug back to him in the same condition it was in before you made the tracks on it."

His father did not answer, and now for perhaps half a minute there was no sound at all save that of breathing, the faint, steady suspiration of complete and intent listening.

"You decline to answer that, Mr. Snopes?" Again his father did not answer. "I'm going to find against you, Mr. Snopes. I'm going to find that you were responsible for the injury to Major de Spain's rug and hold you liable for it. But twenty bushels of corn seems a little high for a man in your circumstances to have to pay. Major de Spain claims it cost a hundred dollars. October corn will be worth about fifty cents. I figure that if Major de Spain can stand a ninety-five-dollar loss on something he paid cash for, you can stand a five-dollar loss you haven't earned yet. I hold you in damages to Major de Spain to the amount of ten bushels of corn over and above your contract with him, to be paid to him out of your crop at gathering time. Court adjourned."

It had taken no time hardly, the morning was but half begun. He thought they would return home and perhaps back to the field, since they were late, far behind all other farmers. But instead his father passed on behind the wagon, merely indicating with his hand for the older brother to follow with it, and crossed the road toward the blacksmith shop opposite, pressing on after his father, overtaking him, speaking, whispering up at the harsh, calm face beneath the weathered hat: "He won't git no ten bushels neither. He won't git one. We'll . . ." until his father glanced for an instant down at him, the face absolutely calm, the grizzled eyebrows tangled above the cold eyes, the voice almost pleasant, almost gentle:

"You think so? Well, we'll wait till October anyway."

The matter of the wagon—the setting of a spoke or two and the tightening of the tires—did not take long either, the business of the tires accomplished by driving the wagon into the spring branch behind the shop and letting it stand there, the mules nuzzling into the water from time to time, and the boy on the seat with the idle reins, looking up the slope and through the sooty tunnel of the shed where the slow hammer rang and where his father sat on an upended cypress bolt, easily, either talking or listening, still sitting there when the boy brought the dripping wagon up out of the branch and halted it before the door.

"Take them on to the shade and hitch," his father said. He did so and returned. His father and the smith and a third man squatting on his heels inside the door were talking, about crops and animals; the boy, squatting too in the ammoniac dust and hoof-parings and scales of rust, heard his father tell a long and unhurried story out of the time before the birth of the older brother even when he had been a professional horsetrader. And then his father came up beside him where he stood before a tattered last year's circus poster on the other side of the store, gazing rapt and quiet at the scarlet horses, the incredible poisings and convolutions of tulle and tights and the painted leers of comedians, and said "It's time to eat."

But not at home. Squatting beside his brother against the front wall, he watched his father emerge from the store and produce from a paper sack a segment of cheese and divide it carefully and deliberately into three with his pocket knife and produce crackers from the same sack. They all three squatted on the gallery and ate, slowly, without talking; then in the store again, they drank from a tin dipper tepid water smelling of the cedar bucket and of living beech trees. And still they did not go home. It was a horse lot this time, a tall rail fence upon and along which men stood and sat and out of which one by one horses were led, to be walked and trotted and then cantered back and forth along the road while the slow swapping and buying went on and the sun began to slant westward, they—the three of them—watching and listening, the older brother with his muddy eyes and his steady, inevitable tobacco, the father commenting now and then on certain of the animals, to no one in particular.

It was after sundown when they reached home. They ate supper by lamplight, then, sitting on the doorstep, the boy watched the night fully accomplish, listening to the whippoorwills and the frogs, when he heard his mother's voice: "Abner! No! No! Oh, God. Oh, God. Abner!" and he rose, whirled, and saw the altered light through the door where a candle stub now burned in a bottle neck on the table and his father, still in the hat and coat, at once formal and burlesque as though dressed carefully for some shabby and ceremonial violence, emptying the reservoir of the lamp back into the five-gallon kerosene can from which it had been filled, while the mother tugged at his arm until he shifted the lamp to the other hand and flung her back, not savagely or viciously, just hard, into the wall, her hands flung out against the wall for balance, her mouth open and in her face the same quality of hopeless despair as had been in her voice. Then his father saw him standing in the door.

"Go to the barn and get that can of oil we were oiling the wagon with," he said. The boy did not move. Then he could speak.

"What . . ." he cried. "What are you . . ."

"Go get that oil," his father said. "Go."

Then he was moving, running, outside the house, toward the stable: this is the old habit, the old blood which he had not been permitted to choose for himself, which had been bequeathed him willy nilly and which had run for so long (and who knew where, battening on what of outrage and savagery and lust) before it came to him. *I could keep on,* he thought. *I could run on and on and never look back, never need to see his face again. Only I can't. I can't,* the rusted can in his hand now, the liquid sploshing in it as he ran back to the house and into it, into the sound of his mother's weeping in the next room, and handed the can to his father.

"Ain't you going to even send a nigger?" he cried. "At least you sent a nigger before!"

This time his father didn't strike him. The hand came even faster than the blow had, the same hand which had set the can on the table with almost excruciating care flashing from the can toward him too quick for him to follow it, gripping him by the back of his shirt and on to tiptoe before he had seen it quit the can, the face stooping at him in breathless and frozen ferocity, the cold, dead voice speaking over him to the older brother who leaned against the table, chewing with that steady, curious, sidewise motion of cows:

"Empty the can into the big one and go on. I'll catch up with you."

"Better tie him up to the bedpost," the brother said.

"Do like I told you," the father said. Then the boy was moving, his bunched shirt and the hard, bony hand between his shoulder-blades, his toes just touching the floor, across the room and into the other one, past the sisters sitting with spread heavy thighs in the two chairs over the cold hearth, and to where his mother and aunt sat side by side on the bed, the aunt's arms about his mother's shoulders.

"Hold him," the father said. The aunt made a startled movement. "Not you," the father said. "Lennie. Take hold of him. I want to see you do it." His mother took him by the wrist. "You'll hold him better than that. If he gets loose don't you know what he is going to do? He will go up yonder." He jerked his head toward the road. "Maybe I'd better tie him."

"I'll hold him," his mother whispered.

"See you do then." Then his father was gone, the stiff foot heavy and measured upon the boards, ceasing at last.

Then he began to struggle. His mother caught him in both arms, he jerking and wrenching at them. He would be stronger in the end, he knew that. But he had no time to wait for it. "Lemme go!" he cried. "I don't want to have to hit you!"

"Let him go!" the aunt said. "If he don't go, before God, I am going there myself!"

"Don't you see I can't!" his mother cried. "Sarty! Sarty! No! No! Help me, Lizzie!"

Then he was free. His aunt grasped at him but it was too late. He whirled, running, his mother stumbled forward on to her knees behind him, crying to the nearer sister: "Catch him, Net! Catch him!" But that was too late too, the sister (the sisters were twins, born at the same time, yet either of them now gave the impression of being, encompassing as much living meat and volume and weight as any other two of the family) not yet having begun to rise from

the chair, her head, face, alone merely turned, presenting to him in the flying instant an astonishing expanse of young female features untroubled by
any surprise even, wearing only an expression of bovine interest. Then he was
out of the room, out of the house, in the mild dust of the starlit road and the
heavy rifeness of honeysuckle, the pale ribbon unspooling with terrific slowness under his running feet, reaching the gate at last and turning in, running,
his heart and lungs drumming, on up the drive toward the lighted house, the
lighted door. He did not knock, he burst in, sobbing for breath, incapable for
the moment of speech; he saw the astonished face of the Negro in the linen
jacket without knowing when the Negro had appeared.

"De Spain!" he cried, panted. "Where's . . ." then he saw the white man too
emerging from a white door down the hall. "Barn!" he cried. "Barn!"

"What?" the white man said. "Barn?"

"Yes!" the boy cried. "Barn!"

"Catch him!" the white man shouted.

But it was too late this time too. The Negro grasped his shirt, but the entire
sleeve, rotten with washing, carried away, and he was out that door too and
in the drive again, and had actually never ceased to run even while he was
screaming into the white man's face.

Behind him the white man was shouting, "My horse! Fetch my horse!" and
he thought for an instant of cutting across the park and climbing the fence
into the road, but he did not know the park nor how high the vine-massed
fence might be and he dared not risk it. So he ran on down the drive, blood
and breath roaring; presently he was in the road again though he could not
see it. He could not hear either: the galloping mare was almost upon him
before he heard her, and even then he held his course, as if the very urgency
of his wild grief and need must in a moment more find him wings, waiting
until the ultimate instant to hurl himself aside and into the weed-choked
roadside ditch as the horse thundered past and on, for an instant in furious
silhouette against the stars, the tranquil early summer night sky which, even
before the shape of the horse and rider vanished, stained abruptly and violently upward: a long, swirling roar incredible and soundless, blotting the
stars, and he springing up and into the road again, running again, knowing it
was too late yet still running even after he heard the shot and, an instant later,
two shots, pausing now without knowing he had ceased to run, crying "Pap!
Pap!", running again before he knew he had begun to run, stumbling, tripping over something and scrabbling up again without ceasing to run, looking
backward over his shoulder at the glare as he got up, running on among the
invisible trees, panting, sobbing, "Father! Father!"

At midnight he was sitting on the crest of a hill. He did not know it was
midnight and he did not know how far he had come. But there was no glare
behind him now and he sat now, his back toward what he had called home
for four days anyhow, his face toward the dark woods which he would enter
when breath was strong again, small, shaking steadily in the chill darkness,
hugging himself into the remainder of his thin, rotten shirt, the grief and
despair now no longer terror and fear but just grief and despair. *Father. My
father,* he thought. "He was brave!" he cried suddenly, aloud but not loud, no
more than a whisper: "He was! He was in the war! He was in Colonel Sartoris' cav'ry!" not knowing that his father had gone to that war a private in the
fine old European sense, wearing no uniform, admitting the authority of and

giving fidelity to no man or army or flag, going to war as Malbrouck[2] himself did: for booty—it meant nothing and less than nothing to him if it were enemy booty or his own.

The slow constellations wheeled on. It would be dawn and then sun-up after a while and he would be hungry. But that would be to-morrow and now he was only cold, and walking would cure that. His breathing was easier now and he decided to get up and go on, and then he found that he had been asleep because he knew it was almost dawn, the night almost over. He could tell that from the whippoorwills. They were everywhere now among the dark trees below him, constant and inflectioned and ceaseless, so that, as the instant for giving over to the day birds drew nearer and nearer, there was no interval at all between them. He got up. He was a little stiff, but walking would cure that too as it would the cold, and soon there would be the sun. He went on down the hill, toward the dark woods within which the liquid silver voices of the birds called unceasing—the rapid and urgent beating of the urgent and quiring heart of the late spring night. He did not look back.

1938

---

2. Figure in an 18th-century French ballad, "Malbrouck Has Gone to the War," popularly identified with John Churchill, first duke of Marlborough (1650–1722), who rose through the ranks from private to become a famous commander. Despite his military genius, he was often accused of greed and disloyalty.

HART CRANE
1899–1932

Before his suicide at the age of thirty-two, Hart Crane led a life of extremes: he wrote poetry of frequently ecstatic intensity, drank uncontrollably, had bitterly ambivalent relations with his quarreling parents; he relished the comparative erotic freedom of post–World War I Greenwich Village while enduring his literary friends' disapproval of his homosexuality. Born and raised in Ohio, Crane went to New York City in 1917, ostensibly to prepare for college but in fact to investigate the possibility of a literary career. Returning to Cleveland for four years (1919–23), he tried unsuccessfully to enter business as a means of financing an after-hours literary life. During these years he read widely and developed a large circle of intellectual friends and correspondents. He also published some of the poems that made his early reputation: "My Grandmother's Love Letters" in 1920, "Chaplinesque" in 1921, and "For the Marriage of Faustus and Helen" in 1922. He also began work on the love sequence *Voyages*. By 1923, believing himself ready to succeed as a writer, he moved back to New York City.

His most productive years came between 1923 and 1927. He completed *Voyages* in 1924, published his first collection, *White Buildings*, in 1926, and composed ten of the fifteen poems that were to make up *The Bridge* in 1926. He held occasional jobs, but received most of his support from his parents, friends, and above all from the patronage of a banker, Otto Kahn. Crane defined himself as a follower of Walt Whitman in the visionary, prophetic, affirmative American tradition, aiming at nothing less than to master the techniques of modernism while reversing its direction—to make it positive, celebratory, and deeply meshed with contemporary American life without sacrificing technical complexity or richness. For him as for the somewhat older William Carlos Williams, Eliot's *The Waste Land* was both threat and model. That poem could become an "absolute impasse," he wrote, unless one could "go *through* it to a different goal," leaving its negations behind. This was the task he attempted in *The Bridge*.

Crane's practice centered on metaphor—the device that, in his view, represented the difference between poetry and expository prose. He believed that metaphor had preceded logic in the development of human thought and that it still remained the primary mode in which human knowledge was acquired and through which experience was connected to mind. The center of *The Bridge,* for example, is the Brooklyn Bridge—a tangible object transformed metaphorically into the sign of connection, technology, America, history, and the future. The poem, published in 1930, was not particularly well received by the critics; this was a great disappointment to Crane, and even though *Poetry* magazine awarded it a prize and the Guggenheim Foundation gave him a fellowship in the same year, he was perplexed about his future. In Mexico he completed work for a third book, *Key West,* but on the return trip to New York City he jumped overboard and drowned.

The Bridge is a visionary poem made up of fifteen individual sections of varying lengths. It encapsulates a heroic quest, at once personal and epic, to find and enunciate "America." Like Walt Whitman's "Song of the Open Road," which also focused on a symbol of expansion and dynamism, *The Bridge* moves westward in imagination from Brooklyn to California. It also goes back into the American past, dwelling on historical or legendary figures like Columbus, Pocahontas, and Rip Van Winkle. It moves upward under the guidance of Whitman; down in "The Tunnel" it meets the wandering spirit of Edgar Allan Poe. The material bridge stands at the center of all this motion and stands, finally, for the poem and poetry itself. The separate lyrics making up *The Bridge* are arranged like music, with recurring, modulated themes rather than a narrative or an expository line. As in most modernist poems, the verse is open and varied, the syntax complicated and often ambiguous, the references often dependent on a personal, sometimes inaccessible train of thought. Like his model Whitman, Crane wrote from the paradoxical, conflicted position of the outsider claiming to speak from and for the very center of America.

The text of the poems included here is that of *Complete Poems of Hart Crane,* edited by Marc Simon (1993).

Chaplinesque[1]

We make our meek adjustments,
Contented with such random consolations
As the wind deposits
In slithered and too ample pockets.

For we can still love the world, who find   5
A famished kitten on the step, and know
Recesses for it from the fury of the street,
Or warm torn elbow coverts.

We will sidestep, and to the final smirk
Dally the doom of that inevitable thumb   10

---

1. Crane wrote of seeing Charlie Chaplin's film *The Kid* (1921) and said that he aimed "to put in words some of the Chaplin pantomime, so beauti- ful, and so full of eloquence, and so modern." The film "made me feel myself, as a poet, as being 'in the same boat' with him," Crane wrote.

That slowly chafes its puckered index toward us,
Facing the dull squint with what innocence
And what surprise!

And yet these fine collapses are not lies
More than the pirouettes of any pliant cane;   15
Our obsequies[2] are, in a way, no enterprise.
We can evade you, and all else but the heart:
What blame to us if the heart live on.

The game enforces smirks; but we have seen
The moon in lonely alleys make   20
A grail of laughter of an empty ash can,
And through all sound of gaiety and quest
Have heard a kitten in the wilderness.

                                            1921, 1926

At Melville's Tomb[1]

Often beneath the wave, wide from this ledge
The dice of drowned men's bones he saw bequeath
An embassy. Their numbers as he watched,
Beat on the dusty shore and were obscured.[2]

And wrecks passed without sound of bells,   5
The calyx of death's bounty giving back
A scattered chapter, livid hieroglyph,
The portent wound in corridors of shells.[3]

Then in the circuit calm of one vast coil,
Its lashings charmed and malice reconciled,   10
Frosted eyes there were that lifted altars;[4]
And silent answers crept across the stars.

---

2. In the double sense of "funeral rites" and "obsequiousness."
1. This poem was published in *Poetry* magazine only after Crane provided the editor, Harriet Monroe, with a detailed explanation of its images. His letter, and Monroe's inquiries and comments, were published with the poem. Crane's detailed comments in the letter are incorporated in the notes to the poem. Herman Melville (1819–1891), American author.
2. "Dice bequeath an embassy, in the first place, by being ground (in this connection only, of course) in little cubes from the bones of drowned men by the action of the sea, and are finally thrown up on the sand, having 'numbers' but no identification. These being the bones of dead men who never completed their voyage, it seems legitimate to refer to them as the only surviving evidence of certain messages undelivered, mute evidence of certain things. . . . Dice as a symbol of chance and

circumstance is also implied" [Crane's note].
3. "This calyx refers in a double ironic sense both to a cornucopia and the vortex made by a sinking vessel. As soon as the water has closed over a ship this whirlpool sends up broken spars, wreckage, etc., which can be alluded to as livid *hieroglyphs,* making a *scattered chapter* so far as any complete record of the recent ship and crew is concerned. In fact, about as much definite knowledge might come from all this as anyone might gain from the roar of his own veins, which is easily heard (haven't you ever done it?) by holding a shell close to one's ear" [Crane's note]. A calyx is a whorl of leaves forming the outer casing of the bud of a plant.
4. "Refers simply to a conviction that a man, not knowing perhaps a definite god yet being endowed with a reverence for deity—such a man naturally postulates a deity somehow, and the altar of that deity by the very *action* of the eyes *lifted* in searching" [Crane's note].

Compass, quadrant and sextant contrive
No farther tides[5] . . . High in the azure steeps
Monody shall not wake the mariner.   15
This fabulous shadow only the sea keeps.

                                                    1926

From Voyages

I

Above the fresh ruffles of the surf
Bright striped urchins flay each other with sand.
They have contrived a conquest for shell shucks,
And their fingers crumble fragments of baked weed
Gaily digging and scattering.   5

And in answer to their treble interjections
The sun beats lightning on the waves,
The waves fold thunder on the sand;
And could they hear me I would tell them:

O brilliant kids, frisk with your dog,   10
Fondle your shells and sticks, bleached
By time and the elements; but there is a line
You must not cross nor ever trust beyond it
Spry cordage of your bodies to caresses
Too lichen-faithful from too wide a breast.   15
The bottom of the sea is cruel.

                                              1923, 1926

III

Infinite consanguinity it bears—
This tendered theme of you that light
Retrieves from sea plains where the sky
Resigns a breast that every wave enthrones;
While ribboned water lanes I wind   5
Are laved and scattered with no stroke
Wide from your side, whereto this hour
The sea lifts, also, reliquary hands.

And so, admitted through black swollen gates
That must arrest all distance otherwise,—   10

5. "Hasn't it often occurred that instruments originally invented for record and computation have
inadvertently so extended the concepts of the
entity they were invented to measure (concepts of
space, etc.) in the mind and imagination that
employed them, that they may metaphorically be
said to have extended the original boundaries of
the entity measured? This little bit of 'relativity'
ought not to be discredited in poetry now that scientists are proceeding to measure the universe on
principles of pure *ratio,* quite as metaphorical, so
far as previous standards of scientific methods
extended, as some of the axioms in *Job*" [Crane's
note].

Past whirling pillars and lithe pediments,
Light wrestling there incessantly with light,
Star kissing star through wave on wave unto

Your body rocking!
               and where death, if shed,   15
Presumes no carnage, but this single change,—
Upon the steep floor flung from dawn to dawn
The silken skilled transmemberment of song;

Permit me voyage, love, into your hands . . .

                                1926

V

Meticulous, past midnight in clear rime,
Infrangible and lonely, smooth as though cast
Together in one merciless white blade—
The bay estuaries fleck the hard sky limits.

—As if too brittle or too clear to touch!   5
The cables of our sleep so swiftly filed,
Already hang, shred ends from remembered stars.
One frozen trackless smile . . . What words
Can strangle this deaf moonlight? For we

Are overtaken. Now no cry, no sword   10
Can fasten or deflect this tidal wedge,
Slow tyranny of moonlight, moonlight loved
And changed . . . "There's

Nothing like this in the world," you say,
Knowing I cannot touch your hand and look   15
Too, into that godless cleft of sky
Where nothing turns but dead sands flashing.

"—And never to quite understand!" No,
In all the argosy of your bright hair I dreamed
Nothing so flagless as this piracy.   20

                     But now
Draw in your head, alone and too tall here.
Your eyes already in the slant of drifting foam;
Your breath sealed by the ghosts I do not know:
    Draw in your head and sleep the long way home.   25

                                1926

ERNEST HEMINGWAY
1899–1961

The narrator in Ernest Hemingway's *A Farewell to Arms*, reflecting on his war experiences, observes at one point, "I was always embarrassed by the words *sacred*, *glorious*, and *sacrifice* and the expression *in vain*. . . . I had seen nothing sacred, and the things that were glorious had no glory and the sacrifices were like the stockyards at Chicago if nothing was done with the meat except to bury it. There were many words that you could not stand to hear." Hemingway's aim and achievement as a novelist and short-story writer were to convey his concerns in a prose style built from what was left after eliminating all the words one "could not stand to hear." As flamboyant in his personal style as he was severe in his writing, Hemingway became an international celebrity after the publication in 1926 of his first novel, *The Sun Also Rises*. At the time of his death, he was probably the most famous writer in the world.

He was born and raised in Oak Park, Illinois, one of six children. His mother was a music teacher, director of the church choir, and a lover of high culture who had contemplated a career as an opera singer. His father was a successful physician, prone to depression, who enjoyed hunting, fishing, and cooking and who shared in household responsibilities more than most men of his era. The family spent summers at their cottage in northern Michigan, where many of Hemingway's stories are set. After high school, Hemingway took a job on the *Kansas City Star*. When the United States entered the war in 1917, Hemingway was eager to go. An eye problem barred him from the army, so he joined the ambulance corps. Within three weeks he was wounded by shrapnel. After six months in the hospital Hemingway went home as a decorated hero: when wounded, he had carried a comrade more badly hurt than he to safety. He found readjustment difficult and became increasingly estranged from his family, especially his mother. Years later, when his father committed suicide, Hemingway blamed his mother for that death.

In 1920 he married Hadley Richardson and went to Paris. Supported partly by her money and partly by his journalism, Hemingway worked at becoming a writer. He came to know Gertrude Stein, Sherwood Anderson, Ezra Pound, F. Scott Fitzgerald, and others in the large community of expatriate artistic and literary Americans. Besides reading his manuscripts and advising him, Fitzgerald and Anderson, better known than he, used their influence to get his book of short stories *In Our Time* published in the United States in 1925. In this book, stories about the adolescent Nick Adams as he grows up in northern Michigan alternate with very brief, powerful vignettes of war and crime.

In 1926 his novel *The Sun Also Rises* appeared; it presents the stripped-down "Hemingway style" at its finest. "I always try to write on the principle of the iceberg," he told an interviewer. "There is seven-eighths of it under water for every part that shows." Narrated by Jake Barnes, whose World War I wounds have left him sexually impotent, *The Sun Also Rises* depicts Jake's efforts to live according to a self-conscious code of dignity, of "grace under pressure," in the midst of a circle of self-seeking American and English expatriates in Paris. He finds an ideal in the rich tradition of Spanish peasant life, especially as epitomized in bullfighting and the bullfighter. *The Sun Also Rises* was directly responsible for a surge of American tourism to Pamplona, Spain, where the novel's bullfights are set.

In 1927 Hemingway brought out his second collection of stories, *Men without Women*. Adapting journalistic techniques in telegraphic prose that minimized narrator commentary and depended heavily on uncontextualized dialogue, these stories developed a modern, speeded-up, streamlined style that has been endlessly imitated. His second novel, *A Farewell to Arms*, appeared in 1929. It described a romance between an American army officer, Frederic Henry, and a British nurse, Catherine Barkley. The two run away from war, trying to make "a separate peace," but their idyll is shattered when Catherine dies in childbirth. Hemingway's work has been much criticized for its depictions of women. The wholly good Catherine lives for Frederick Henry alone; and Maria, in his Spanish Civil War novel (*For Whom the Bell Tolls*, 1940), is a fantasy figure of total submissiveness. Characters like Brett Ashley in *The Sun Also Rises* and Pilar in *For Whom the Bell Tolls*, however, are strong, complex figures. Overall, Hemingway identified the rapid change in women's status after World War I and the general blurring of sex roles that accompanied the new sexual freedom as aspects of modernity that men were simultaneously attracted to and found hard to deal with. More recently, especially in light of the themes of some of his posthumously published writings, critics have begun to re-interpret Hemingway's work as preoccupied with the cultural and psychological meanings of masculinity in a way that bespeaks considerable sexual ambivalence.

As Hemingway aged, his interest in exclusively masculine forms of self-assertion and self-definition became more pronounced. War, hunting, and similar pursuits that he had used at first to show men manifesting dignity in the face of certain defeat increasingly became depicted (in his life as well as his writing) as occasions for competitive masculine display and triumph. Soon after the publication of *The Sun Also Rises*, his first marriage broke up; in all he was married four times. In the 1930s and 1940s he adopted the style of life of a celebrity.

In the 1930s two new themes entered his work. One was the decade's ever-present theme of politics. A political loner distrustful of all ideological abstractions, Hemingway was nevertheless drawn into antifascist politics by the Spanish Civil War. In *To Have and Have Not* (1937), the earliest of his political novels, the good characters are working-class people and the antagonists are idle rich. *For Whom the Bell Tolls* draws on Hemingway's experiences in Spain as a war correspondent, celebrating both the peasant antifascists and the Americans who fought on their behalf. Hemingway's opposition to fascism did not, however, keep him from viewing the pro-Loyalist communists, who were also active in the Spanish Civil War, with considerable skepticism. His one play, *The Fifth Column*—which was printed along with his collected stories in 1938 and staged in 1940—specifically blames the communists for betraying the cause.

The second new theme, obviously autobiographical, was that of the successful writer losing his talent in an atmosphere of success, celebrity, and wealth. This is clearly expressed in "The Snows of Kilimanjaro," reprinted here, which also contains passages of his most lyrical and evocative writing as the writer looks back on earlier, happy days living in Paris and skiing in the Austrian Alps. The story also draws on Hemingway's experiences on African hunting safaris and shows the writer blaming his wife for what has happened to him, yet simultaneously recognizing that the fault is his alone.

Hemingway was fiercely anti-Nazi during World War II. As well as working as a war correspondent, work that sent him often to Europe, he used his fishing boat to keep watch for German submarines off the coast of Cuba, where he had a home. After the war ended, he continued his travels and was badly hurt in Africa in October 1953 in the crash of a small plane. He had already published his allegorical fable *The Old Man and the Sea* (1952), in the mass-circulation weekly magazine *Life*; this, his last major work published during his lifetime, won a Pulitzer Prize in 1953 and was central to his winning the Nobel Prize in 1954. The plane crash had damaged his mental and physical health, and he never fully recovered. Subject increasingly to depression and an incapacitating paranoia—afflictions that seem to have run in his family—he was hospitalized several times before killing himself in 1961. Yet it does appear that some of his suspicions about being watched by U.S. government agents may have been justified. Many writers associated with radical causes had dossiers compiled on them by the FBI. Several books have been published posthumously based on the voluminous manuscript collections he left. These include a book of reminiscences about his life in 1920s Paris, *A Moveable Feast* (1964); a novel about literary fame and sexual ambiguity constructed from several unfinished drafts, *Islands in the Stream* (1970); and *The Nick Adams Stories* (1972), a collection that added eight previously unpublished stories to the group.

The text is that of *The Fifth Column and the First Forty-nine Stories* (1938).

The Snows of Kilimanjaro[1]

> *Kilimanjaro is a snow covered mountain 19,710 feet high, and is said to be the highest mountain in Africa. Its western summit is called the Masai "Ngàje Ngài," the House of God. Close to the western summit there is the dried and frozen carcass of a leopard. No one has explained what the leopard was seeking at that altitude.*

"The marvellous thing is that it's painless," he said. "That's how you know when it starts."

"Is it really?"

"Absolutely. I'm awfully sorry about the odor though. That must bother you."

"Don't! Please don't."

"Look at them," he said. "Now is it sight or is it scent that brings them like that?"

The cot the man lay on was in the wide shade of a mimosa tree and as he looked out past the shade onto the glare of the plain there were three of the big birds squatted obscenely, while in the sky a dozen more sailed, making quick-moving shadows as they passed.

"They've been there since the day the truck broke down," he said. "Today's the first time any have lit on the ground. I watched the way they sailed very carefully at first in case I ever wanted to use them in a story. That's funny now."

"I wish you wouldn't," she said.

"I'm only talking," he said. "It's much easier if I talk. But I don't want to bother you."

"You know it doesn't bother me," she said. "It's that I've gotten so very nervous not being able to do anything. I think we might make it as easy as we can until the plane comes."

"Or until the plane doesn't come."

"Please tell me what I can do. There must be something I can do."

"You can take the leg off and that might stop it, though I doubt it. Or you can shoot me. You're a good shot now. I taught you to shoot didn't I?"

"Please don't talk that way. Couldn't I read to you?"

"Read what?"

"Anything in the book bag that we haven't read."

"I can't listen to it," he said. "Talking is the easiest. We quarrel and that makes the time pass."

"I don't quarrel. I never want to quarrel. Let's not quarrel any more. No matter how nervous we get. Maybe they will be back with another truck today. Maybe the plane will come."

"I don't want to move," the man said. "There is no sense in moving now except to make it easier for you."

---

1. Mount Kilimanjaro is in Tanzania, near the border with Kenya. It is no longer snow-covered.

"That's cowardly."

"Can't you let a man die as comfortably as he can without calling him names? What's the use of slanging me?"

"You're not going to die."

"Don't be silly. I'm dying now. Ask those bastards." He looked over to where the huge, filthy birds sat, their naked heads sunk in the hunched feathers. A fourth planed down, to run quick-legged and then waddle slowly toward the others.

"They are around every camp. You never notice them. You can't die if you don't give up."

"Where did you read that? You're such a bloody fool."

"You might think about some one else."

"For Christ's sake," he said. "That's been my trade."

He lay then and was quiet for a while and looked across the heat shimmer of the plain to the edge of the bush. There were a few Tommies[2] that showed minute and white against the yellow and, far off, he saw a herd of zebra, white against the green of the bush. This was a pleasant camp under big trees against a hill, with good water, and close by, a nearly dry water hole where sand grouse flighted in the mornings.

"Wouldn't you like me to read?" she asked. She was sitting on a canvas chair beside his cot. "There's a breeze coming up."

"No thanks."

"Maybe the truck will come."

"I don't give a damn about the truck."

"I do."

"You give a damn about so many things that I don't."

"Not so many, Harry."

"What about a drink?"

"It's supposed to be bad for you. It said in Black's to avoid all alcohol. You shouldn't drink."

"Molo!" he shouted.

"Yes Bwana."

"Bring whiskey-soda."

"Yes Bwana."

"You shouldn't," she said. "That's what I mean by giving up. It says it's bad for you. I know it's bad for you."

"No," he said. "It's good for me."

So now it was all over, he thought. So now he would never have a chance to finish it. So this was the way it ended in a bickering over a drink. Since the gangrene started in his right leg he had no pain and with the pain the horror had gone and all he felt now was a great tiredness and anger that this was the end of it. For this, that now was coming, he had very little curiosity. For years it had obsessed him; but now it meant nothing in itself. It was strange how easy being tired enough made it.

Now he would never write the things that he had saved to write until he knew enough to write them well. Well, he would not have to fail at trying to write them either. Maybe you could never write them, and that was why you put them off and delayed the starting. Well he would never know, now.

---

2. Familiar name for the Thomson's gazelle of East Africa, smallest of the gazelles.

"I wish we'd never come," the woman said. She was looking at him holding the glass and biting her lip. "You never would have gotten anything like this in Paris. You always said you loved Paris. We could have stayed in Paris or gone anywhere. I'd have gone anywhere. I said I'd go anywhere you wanted. If you wanted to shoot we could have gone shooting in Hungary and been comfortable."

"Your bloody money," he said.

"That's not fair," she said. "It was always yours as much as mine. I left everything and I went wherever you wanted to go and I've done what you wanted to do. But I wish we'd never come here."

"You said you loved it."

"I did when you were all right. But now I hate it. I don't see why that had to happen to your leg. What have we done to have that happen to us?"

"I suppose what I did was to forget to put iodine on it when I first scratched it. Then I didn't pay any attention to it because I never infect. Then, later, when it got bad, it was probably using that weak carbolic solution when the other antiseptics ran out that paralyzed the minute blood vessels and started the gangrene." He looked at her. "What else?"

"I don't mean that."

"If we would have hired a good mechanic instead of a half baked kikuyu driver, he would have checked the oil and never burned out that bearing in the truck."

"I don't mean that."

"If you hadn't left your own people, your goddamned Old Westbury, Saratoga, Palm Beach people to take me on—"

"Why, I loved you. That's not fair. I love you now. I'll always love you. Don't you love me?"

"No," said the man. "I don't think so. I never have."

"Harry, what are you saying? You're out of your head."

"No. I haven't any head to go out of."

"Don't drink that," she said. "Darling, please don't drink that. We have to do everything we can."

"You do it," he said. "I'm tired."

Now in his mind he saw a railway station at Karagatch and he was standing with his pack and that was the headlight of the Simplon-Orient[3] cutting the dark now and he was leaving Thrace[4] then after the retreat. That was one of the things he had saved to write, with, in the morning at breakfast, looking out the window and seeing snow on the mountains in Bulgaria and Nansen's Secretary asking the old man if it were snow and the old man looking at it and saying, No, that's not snow. It's too early for snow. And the Secretary repeating to the other girls, No, you see. It's not snow and them all saying, It's not snow we were mistaken. But it was the snow all right and he sent them on into it when he evolved exchange of populations. And it was snow they tramped along in until they died that winter.

It was snow too that fell all Christmas week that year up in the Gauertal, that year they lived in the woodcutter's house with the big square porcelain stove that

3. A fast train going from Paris to Constantinople, crossing the Alps into Italy over the Simplon Pass.
4. A region spanning parts of Greece and Turkey, scene of border wars in 1922 that Hemingway had covered as a war correspondent while living in Paris.

filled half the room, and they slept on mattresses filled with beech leaves, the time the deserter came with his feet bloody in the snow. He said the police were right behind him and they gave him woolen socks and held the gendarmes talking until the tracks had drifted over.

In Schrunz,[5] on Christmas day, the snow was so bright it hurt your eyes when you looked out from the weinstube and saw every one coming home from church. That was where they walked up the sleigh-smoothed urine-yellowed road along the river with the steep pine hills, skis heavy on the shoulder, and where they ran that great run down the glacier above the Madlener-haus, the snow as smooth to see as cake frosting and as light as powder and he remembered the noiseless rush the speed made as you dropped down like a bird.

They were snow-bound a week in the Madlener-haus that time in the blizzard playing cards in the smoke by the lantern light and the stakes were higher all the time as Herr Lent lost more. Finally he lost it all. Everything, the skischule money and all the season's profit and then his capital. He could see him with his long nose, picking up the cards and then opening, "Sans Voir."[6] There was always gambling then. When there was no snow you gambled and when there was too much you gambled. He thought of all the time in his life he had spent gambling.

But he had never written a line of that, nor of that cold, bright Christmas day with the mountains showing across the plain that Barker had flown across the lines to bomb the Austrian officers' leave train, machine-gunning them as they scattered and ran. He remembered Barker afterwards coming into the mess and starting to tell about it. And how quiet it got and then somebody saying, "You bloody murderous bastard."

Those were the same Austrians they killed then that he skied with later. No not the same. Hans, that he skied with all that year, had been in the Kaiser-Jägers[7] and when they went hunting hares together up the little valley above the saw-mill they had talked of the fighting on Pasubio and of the attack on Perticara and Asalone and he had never written a word of that. Nor of Monte Corono, nor the Sette Commumi, nor of Arsiero.

How many winters had he lived in the Vorarlberg and the Arlberg? It was four and then he remembered the man who had the fox to sell when they had walked into Bludenz, that time to buy presents, and the cherry-pit taste of good kirsch, the fast-slipping rush of running powder-snow on crust, singing "Hi! Ho! said Rolly!" as you ran down the last stretch to the steep drop, taking it straight, then running the orchard in three turns and out across the ditch and onto the icy road behind the inn. Knocking your bindings loose, kicking the skis free and leaning them up against the wooden wall of the inn, the lamplight coming from the window, where inside, in the smoky, new-wine smelling warmth, they were playing the accordion.

"Where did we stay in Paris?" he asked the woman who was sitting by him in a canvas chair, now, in Africa.

---

5. Alpine ski resort in the western part of Austria.
6. Without seeing (French); a blind opening bet in poker or other gambling games.
7. The Kaiser's Hunters (German); elite Austrian troops. In World War I, Germany and Austria fought against the United Kingdom, France, Italy, and the United States.

"At the Crillon.[8] You know that."

"Why do I know that?"

"That's where we always stayed."

"No. Not always."

"There and at the Pavillion Henri-Quatre in St. Germain. You said you loved it there."

"Love is a dunghill," said Harry. "And I'm the cock that gets on it to crow."

"If you have to go away," she said, "is it absolutely necessary to kill off everything you leave behind? I mean do you have to take away everything? Do you have to kill your horse, and your wife and burn your saddle and your armour?"

"Yes," he said. "Your damned money was my armour. My Swift and my Armour."

"Don't."

"All right. I'll stop that. I don't want to hurt you."

"It's a little bit late now."

"All right then. I'll go on hurting you. It's more amusing. The only thing I ever really liked to do with you I can't do now."

"No, that's not true. You liked to do many things and everything you wanted to do I did."

"Oh, for Christ sake stop bragging, will you?"

He looked at her and saw her crying.

"Listen," he said. "Do you think that it is fun to do this? I don't know why I'm doing it. It's trying to kill to keep yourself alive, I imagine. I was all right when we started talking. I didn't mean to start this, and now I'm crazy as a coot and being as cruel to you as I can be. Don't pay any attention, darling, to what I say. I love you, really. You know I love you. I've never loved any one else the way I love you."

He slipped into the familiar lie he made his bread and butter by.

"You're sweet to me."

"You bitch," he said. "You rich bitch. That's poetry. I'm full of poetry now. Rot and poetry. Rotten poetry."

"Stop it. Harry, why do you have to turn into a devil now?"

"I don't like to leave anything," the man said. "I don't like to leave things behind."

.   .   .

It was evening now and he had been asleep. The sun was gone behind the hill and there was a shadow all across the plain and the small animals were feeding close to camp; quick dropping heads and switching tails, he watched them keeping well out away from the bush now. The birds no longer waited on the ground. They were all perched heavily in a tree. There were many more of them. His personal boy was sitting by the bed.

"Memsahib's gone to shoot," the boy said. "Does Bwana want?"

"Nothing."

She had gone to kill a piece of meat and, knowing how he liked to watch the game, she had gone well away so she would not disturb this little pocket

---

8. Luxury hotel in Paris, as is the Henri-Quatre (below).

of the plain that he could see. She was always thoughtful, he thought. On anything she knew about, or had read, or that she had ever heard.

It was not her fault that when he went to her he was already over. How could a woman know that you meant nothing that you said; that you spoke only from habit and to be comfortable? After he no longer meant what he said, his lies were more successful with women than when he had told them the truth.

It was not so much that he lied as that there was no truth to tell. He had had his life and it was over and then he went on living it again with different people and more money, with the best of the same places, and some new ones.

You kept from thinking and it was all marvellous. You were equipped with good insides so that you did not go to pieces that way, the way most of them had, and you made an attitude that you cared nothing for the work you used to do, now that you could no longer do it. But, in yourself, you said that you would write about these people; about the very rich; that you were really not of them but a spy in their country; that you would leave it and write of it and for once it would be written by some one who knew what he was writing of. But he would never do it, because each day of not writing, of comfort, of being that which he despised, dulled his ability and softened his will to work so that, finally, he did no work at all. The people he knew now were all much more comfortable when he did not work. Africa was where he had been happiest in the good time of his life, so he had come out here to start again. They had made this safari with the minimum of comfort. There was no hardship; but there was no luxury and he had thought that he could get back into training that way. That in some way he could work the fat off his soul the way a fighter went into the mountains to work and train in order to burn it out of his body.

She had liked it. She said she loved it. She loved anything that was exciting, that involved a change of scene, where there were new people and where things were pleasant. And he had felt the illusion of returning strength of will to work. Now if this was how it ended, and he knew it was, he must not turn like some snake biting itself because its back was broken. It wasn't this woman's fault. If it had not been she it would have been another. If he lived by a lie he should try to die by it. He heard a shot beyond the hill.

She shot very well this good, this rich bitch, this kindly caretaker and destroyer of his talent. Nonsense. He had destroyed his talent himself. Why should he blame this woman because she kept him well? He had destroyed his talent by not using it, by betrayals of himself and what he believed in, by drinking so much that he blunted the edge of his perceptions, by laziness, by sloth, and by snobbery, by pride and by prejudice,[9] by hook and by crook. What was this? A catalogue of old books? What was his talent anyway? It was a talent all right but instead of using it, he had traded on it. It was never what he had done, but always what he could do. And he had chosen to make his living with something else instead of a pen or a pencil. It was strange, too, wasn't it, that when he fell in love with another woman, that woman should always have more money than the last one? But when he no longer was in

9. Reference to title of a novel by the English writer Jane Austen (1775–1817).

love, when he was only lying, as to this woman, now, who had the most money of all, who had all the money there was, who had had a husband and children, who had taken lovers and been dissatisfied with them, and who loved him dearly as a writer, as a man, as a companion and as a proud possession; it was strange that when he did not love her at all and was lying, that he should be able to give her more for her money than when he had really loved.

We must all be cut out for what we do, he thought. However you make your living is where your talent lies. He had sold vitality, in one form or another, all his life and when your affections are not too involved you give much better value for the money. He had found that out but he would never write that, now, either. No, he would not write that, although it was well worth writing.

Now she came in sight, walking across the open toward the camp. She was wearing jodhpurs and carrying her rifle. The two boys had a Tommie slung and they were coming along behind her. She was still a good-looking woman, he thought, and she had a pleasant body. She had a great talent and appreciation for the bed, she was not pretty, but he liked her face, she read enormously, liked to ride and shoot and, certainly, she drank too much. Her husband had died when she was still a comparatively young woman and for a while she had devoted herself to her two just-grown children, who did not need her and were embarrassed at having her about, to her stable of horses, to books, and to bottles. She liked to read in the evening before dinner and she drank Scotch and soda while she read. By dinner she was fairly drunk and after a bottle of wine at dinner she was usually drunk enough to sleep.

That was before the lovers. After she had the lovers she did not drink so much because she did not have to be drunk to sleep. But the lovers bored her. She had been married to a man who had never bored her and these people bored her very much.

Then one of her two children was killed in a plane crash and after that was over she did not want the lovers, and drink being no anæsthetic she had to make another life. Suddenly, she had been acutely frightened of being alone. But she wanted some one that she respected with her.

It had begun very simply. She liked what he wrote and she had always envied the life he led. She thought he did exactly what he wanted to. The steps by which she had acquired him and the way in which she had finally fallen in love with him were all part of a regular progression in which she had built herself a new life and he had traded away what remained of his old life.

He had traded it for security, for comfort too, there was no denying that, and for what else? He did not know. She would have bought him anything he wanted. He knew that. She was a damned nice woman too. He would as soon be in bed with her as any one; rather with her, because she was richer, because she was very pleasant and appreciative and because she never made scenes. And now this life that she had built again was coming to a term because he had not used iodine two weeks ago when a thorn had scratched his knee as they moved forward trying to photograph a herd of waterbuck standing, their heads up, peering while their nostrils searched the air, their ears spread wide to hear the first noise that would send them rushing into the bush. They had bolted, too, before he got the picture.

Here she came now.

He turned his head on the cot to look toward her. "Hello," he said.

"I shot a Tommy ram," she told him. "He'll make you good broth and I'll have them mash some potatoes with the Klim.[1] How do you feel?"

"Much better."

"Isn't that lovely? You know I thought perhaps you would. You were sleeping when I left."

"I had a good sleep. Did you walk far?"

"No. Just around behind the hill. I made quite a good shot on the Tommy."

"You shoot marvellously, you know."

"I love it. I've loved Africa. Really. If *you're* all right it's the most fun that I've ever had. You don't know the fun it's been to shoot with you. I've loved the country."

"I love it too."

"Darling, you don't know how marvellous it is to see you feeling better. I couldn't stand it when you felt that way. You won't talk to me like that again, will you? Promise me?"

"No," he said. "I don't remember what I said."

"You don't have to destroy me. Do you? I'm only a middle-aged woman who loves you and wants to do what you want to do. I've been destroyed two or three times already. You wouldn't want to destroy me again, would you?"

"I'd like to destroy you a few times in bed," he said.

"Yes. That's the good destruction. That's the way we're made to be destroyed. The plane will be here tomorrow."

"How do you know?"

"I'm sure. It's bound to come. The boys have the wood all ready and the grass to make the smudge.[2] I went down and looked at it again today. There's plenty of room to land and we have the smudges ready at both ends."

"What makes you think it will come tomorrow?"

"I'm sure it will. It's overdue now. Then, in town, they will fix up your leg and then we will have some good destruction. Not that dreadful talking kind."

"Should we have a drink? The sun is down."

"Do you think you should?"

"I'm having one."

"We'll have one together. *Molo, letti dui whiskey-soda!*" she called.

"You'd better put on your mosquito boots," he told her.

"I'll wait till I bathe . . ."

While it grew dark they drank and just before it was dark and there was no longer enough light to shoot, a hyena crossed the open on his way around the hill.

"That bastard crosses there every night," the man said. "Every night for two weeks."

"He's the one makes the noise at night. I don't mind it. They're a filthy animal though."

Drinking together, with no pain now except the discomfort of lying in the one position, the boys lighting a fire, its shadow jumping on the tents, he could feel the return of acquiescence in this life of pleasant surrender. She *was* very good to him. He had been cruel and unjust in the afternoon. She was

---

1. Powdered milk or milk substitute.
2. Fire made to produce a dense smoke, to guide the plane to a landing place.

a fine woman, marvellous really. And just then it occurred to him that he was going to die.

It came with a rush; not as a rush of water nor of wind; but of a sudden evil-smelling emptiness and the odd thing was that the hyena slipped lightly along the edge of it.

"What is it, Harry?" she asked him.

"Nothing," he said. "You had better move over to the other side. To windward."

"Did Molo change the dressing?"

"Yes. I'm just using the boric now."

"How do you feel?"

"A little wobbly."

"I'm going in to bathe," she said. "I'll be right out. I'll eat with you and then we'll put the cot in."

So, he said to himself, we did well to stop the quarrelling. He had never quarrelled much with this woman, while with the women that he loved he had quarrelled so much they had finally, always, with the corrosion of the quarrelling, killed what they had together. He had loved too much, demanded too much, and he wore it all out.

He thought about alone in Constantinople[3] *that time, having quarrelled in Paris before he had gone out. He had whored the whole time and then, when that was over, and he had failed to kill his loneliness, but only made it worse, he had written her, the first one, the one who left him, a letter telling her how he had never been able to kill it. . . . How when he thought he saw her outside the* Regence *one time it made him go all faint and sick inside, and that he would follow a woman who looked like her in some way, along the Boulevard, afraid to see it was not she, afraid to lose the feeling it gave him. How every one he had slept with had only made him miss her more. How what she had done could never matter since he knew he could not cure himself of loving her. He wrote this letter at the Club, cold sober, and mailed it to New York asking her to write him at the office in Paris. That seemed safe. And that night missing her so much it made him feel hollow sick inside, he wandered up past Taxim's, picked a girl up and took her out to supper. He had gone to a place to dance with her afterward, she danced badly, and left her for a hot Armenian slut, that swung her belly against him so it almost scalded. He took her away from a British gunner subaltern after a row. The gunner asked him outside and they fought in the street on the cobbles in the dark. He'd hit him twice, hard, on the side of the jaw and when he didn't go down he knew he was in for a fight. The gunner hit him in the body, then beside his eye. He swung with his left again and landed and the gunner fell on him and grabbed his coat and tore the sleeve off and he clubbed him twice behind the ear and then smashed him with his right as he pushed him away. When the gunner went down his head hit first and he ran with the girl because they heard the M. P.'s coming. They got into a taxi and drove out to Rimmily Hissa along the Bosphorus, and around, and back in the cool night and went to bed and she felt as over-ripe as she looked but*

3. Now Istanbul, capital of Turkey. In the rest of the paragraph there are references to streets and places in and around the city.

smoother, rose-petal, syrupy, smooth-bellied, big-breasted and needed no pillow under her buttocks, and he left her before she was awake looking blousy enough in the first daylight and turned up at the Pera Palace with a black eye, carrying his coat because one sleeve was missing.

That same night he left for Anatolia and he remembered, later on that trip, riding all day through fields of the poppies that they raised for opium and how strange it made you feel, finally, and all the distances seemed wrong, to where they had made the attack with the newly arrived Constantine officers, that did not know a goddamned thing, and the artillery had fired into the troops and the British observer had cried like a child.

That was the day he'd first seen dead men wearing white ballet skirts and upturned shoes with pompons on them. The Turks had come steadily and lumpily and he had seen the skirted men running and the officers shooting into them and running then themselves and he and the British observer had run too until his lungs ached and his mouth was full of the taste of pennies and they stopped behind some rocks and there were the Turks coming as lumpily as ever. Later he had seen the things that he could never think of and later still he had seen much worse. So when he got back to Paris that time he could not talk about it or stand to have it mentioned. And there in the café as he passed was that American poet with a pile of saucers in front of him and a stupid look on his potato face talking about the Dada movement[4] with a Roumanian who said his name was Tristan Tzara, who always wore a monocle and had a headache, and, back at the apartment with his wife that now he loved again, the quarrel all over, the madness all over, glad to be home, the office sent his mail up to the flat. So then the letter in answer to the one he'd written came in on a platter one morning and when he saw the handwriting he went cold all over and tried to slip the letter underneath another. But his wife said, "Who is that letter from, dear?" and that was the end of the beginning of that.

He remembered the good times with them all, and the quarrels. They always picked the finest places to have the quarrels. And why had they always quarrelled when he was feeling best? He had never written any of that because, at first, he never wanted to hurt any one and then it seemed as though there was enough to write without it. But he had always thought that he would write it finally. There was so much to write. He had seen the world change; not just the events; although he had seen many of them and had watched the people, but he had seen the subtler change and he could remember how the people were at different times. He had been in it and he had watched it and it was his duty to write of it; but now he never would.

"How do you feel?" she said. She had come out from the tent now after her bath.

"All right."

"Could you eat now?" He saw Molo behind her with the folding table and the other boy with the dishes.

"I want to write," he said.

---

4. An international movement in painting, sculpture, and literature that flourished between 1916 and 1922, stressing fantasy, surrealism, and non-sense. The term is a child's cry, chosen because it has no meaning. Tristan Tzara (below) was a leading member of the movement.

"You ought to take some broth to keep your strength up."

"I'm going to die tonight," he said. "I don't need my strength up."

"Don't be melodramatic, Harry, please," she said.

"Why don't you use your nose? I'm rotted half way up my thigh now. What the hell should I fool with broth for? Molo bring whiskey-soda."

"Please take the broth," she said gently.

"All right."

The broth was too hot. He had to hold it in the cup until it cooled enough to take it and then he just got it down without gagging.

"You're a fine woman," he said. "Don't pay any attention to me."

She looked at him with her well-known, well-loved face from *Spur* and *Town and Country*,[5] only a little the worse for drink, only a little the worse for bed, but *Town and Country* never showed those good breasts and those useful thighs and those lightly small-of-back-caressing hands, and as he looked and saw her well known pleasant smile, he felt death come again. This time there was no rush. It was a puff, as of a wind that makes a candle flicker and the flame go tall.

"They can bring my net out later and hang it from the tree and build the fire up. I'm not going in the tent tonight. It's not worth moving. It's a clear night. There won't be any rain."

So this was how you died, in whispers that you did not hear. Well, there would be no more quarrelling. He could promise that. The one experience that he had never had he was not going to spoil now. He probably would. You spoiled everything. But perhaps he wouldn't.

"You can't take dictation, can you?"

"I never learned," she told him.

"That's all right."

There wasn't time, of course, although it seemed as though it telescoped so that you might put it all into one paragraph if you could get it right.

There was a log house, chinked white with mortar, on a hill above the lake. There was a bell on a pole by the door to call the people in to meals. Behind the house were fields and behind the fields was the timber. A line of lombardy poplars ran from the house to the dock. Other poplars ran along the point. A road went up to the hills along the edge of the timber and along that road he picked blackberries. Then that log house was burned down and all the guns that had been on deer foot racks above the open fire place were burned and afterwards their barrels, with the lead melted in the magazines, and the stocks burned away, lay out on the heap of ashes that were used to make lye for the big iron soap kettles, and you asked Grandfather if you could have them to play with, and he said, no. You see they were his guns still and he never bought any others. Nor did he hunt any more. The house was rebuilt in the same place out of lumber now and painted white and from its porch you saw the poplars and the lake beyond; but there were never any more guns. The barrels of the guns that had hung on the deer feet on the wall of the log house lay out there on the heap of ashes and no one ever touched them.

---

5. Magazines designed for a wealthy audience.

In the Black Forest,[6] after the war, we rented a trout stream and there were two ways to walk to it. One was down the valley from Triberg and around the valley road in the shade of the trees that bordered the white road, and then up a side road that went up through the hills past many small farms, with the big Schwarzwald[7] houses, until that road crossed the stream. That was where our fishing began.

The other way was to climb steeply up to the edge of the woods and then go across the top of the hills through the pine woods, and then out to the edge of a meadow and down across this meadow to the bridge. There were birches along the stream and it was not big, but narrow, clear and fast, with pools where it had cut under the roots of the birches. At the Hotel in Triberg the proprietor had a fine season. It was very pleasant and we were all great friends. The next year came the inflation and the money he had made the year before was not enough to buy supplies to open the hotel and he hanged himself.

You could dictate that, but you could not dictate the Place Contrescarpe[8] where the flower sellers dyed their flowers in the street and the dye ran over the paving where the autobus started and the old men and the women, always drunk on wine and bad marc;[9] and the children with their noses running in the cold; the smell of dirty sweat and poverty and drunkenness at the Café des Amateurs and the whores at the Bal Musette[1] they lived above. The Concierge who entertained the trooper of the Garde Republicaine in her loge, his horsehair-plumed helmet on a chair. The locataire across the hall whose husband was a bicycle racer and her joy that morning at the Cremerie when she had opened L'Auto and seen where he placed third in Paris-Tours, his first big race. She had blushed and laughed and then gone upstairs crying with the yellow sporting paper in her hand. The husband of the woman who ran the Bal Musette drove a taxi and when he, Harry, had to take an early plane the husband knocked upon the door to wake him and they each drank a glass of white wine at the zinc of the bar before they started. He knew his neighbors in that quarter then because they all were poor.

Around that Place there were two kinds; the drunkards and the sportifs. The drunkards killed their poverty that way; the sportifs took it out in exercise. They were the descendants of the Communards[2] and it was no struggle for them to know their politics. They knew who had shot their fathers, their relatives, their brothers, and their friends when the Versailles troops came in and took the town after the Commune and executed any one they could catch with calloused hands, or who wore a cap, or carried any other sign he was a working man. And in that poverty, and in that quarter across the street from a Boucherie Chevaline[3] and a wine co-operative he had written the start of all he was to do. There never was another part of Paris that he loved like that, the sprawling trees, the old white plastered houses painted brown below, the long green of the autobus in that round square, the purple flower dye upon the paving, the sudden drop down the hill of the rue Cardinal Lemoine to the River, and the other way the narrow crowded world of the rue Mouffetard. The street that ran up toward the

6. Wooded, mountainous region in southern Germany.
7. Black Forest (German).
8. Square in a working-class neighborhood of Paris.
9. White brandy (French).
1. Dance hall (French).

2. Participants in the 1871 workers' uprising in Paris and the Commune, a local government established on March 18, 1871, but suppressed by the Versailles government two months later.
3. A butcher shop selling horsemeat, once common in poorer neighborhoods throughout Europe.

Pantheon and the other that he always took with the bicycle, the only asphalted street in all that quarter, smooth under the tires, with the high narrow houses and the cheap tall hotel where Paul Verlaine[4] had died. There were only two rooms in the apartments where they lived and he had a room on the top floor of that hotel that cost him sixty francs a month where he did his writing, and from it he could see the roofs and chimney pots and all the hills of Paris.

From the apartment you could only see the wood and coal man's place. He sold wine too, bad wine. The golden horse's head outside the Boucherie Chevaline where the carcasses hung yellow gold and red in the open window, and the green painted co-operative where they bought their wine; good wine and cheap. The rest was plaster walls and the windows of the neighbors. The neighbors who, at night, when some one lay drunk in the street, moaning and groaning in that typical French ivresse[5] that you were propaganded to believe did not exist, would open their windows and then the murmur of talk.

"Where is the policeman? When you don't want him the bugger is always there. He's sleeping with some concierge. Get the Agent." Till some one threw a bucket of water from a window and the moaning stopped. "What's that? Water. Ah, that's intelligent." And the windows shutting. Marie, his femme de menage,[6] protesting against the eight-hour day saying, "If a husband works until six he gets only a little drunk on the way home and does not waste too much. If he works only until five he is drunk every night and one has no money. It is the wife of the working man who suffers from this shortening of hours."

"Wouldn't you like some more broth?" the woman asked him now.

"No, thank you very much. It is awfully good."

"Try just a little."

"I would like a whiskey-soda."

"It's not good for you."

"No. It's bad for me. Cole Porter[7] wrote the words and the music. This knowledge that you're going mad for me."

"You know I like you to drink."

"Oh yes. Only it's bad for me."

When she goes, he thought. I'll have all I want. Not all I want but all there is. Ayee he was tired. Too tired. He was going to sleep a little while. He lay still and death was not there. It must have gone around another street. It went in pairs, on bicycles, and moved absolutely silently on the pavements.

No, he had never written about Paris. Not the Paris that he cared about. But what about the rest that he had never written?

What about the ranch and the silvered gray of the sage brush, the quick, clear water in the irrigation ditches, and the heavy green of the alfalfa. The trail went up into the hills and the cattle in the summer were shy as deer. The bawling and the steady noise and slow moving mass raising a dust as you brought them down in the fall. And behind the mountains, the clear sharpness of the peak in the evening light and, riding down along the trail in the moonlight, bright across

---

4. French Symbolist poet (1844–1896). Hemingway rented and worked in a room in which Verlaine had lived.
5. Drunkenness (French). Because the French drank wine and brandy rather than hard liquor, it was often claimed that there was no real drunkenness among them.
6. Charwoman (French).
7. Popular American song composer (1893–1964).

the valley. Now he remembered coming down through the timber in the dark holding the horse's tail when you could not see and all the stories that he meant to write.

About the half-wit chore boy who was left at the ranch that time and told not to let any one get any hay, and that old bastard from the Forks who had beaten the boy when he had worked for him stopping to get some feed. The boy refusing and the old man saying he would beat him again. The boy got the rifle from the kitchen and shot him when he tried to come into the barn and when they came back to the ranch he'd been dead a week, frozen in the corral, and the dogs had eaten part of him. But what was left you packed on a sled wrapped in a blanket and roped on and you got the boy to help you haul it, and the two of you took it out over the road on skis, and sixty miles down to town to turn the boy over. He having no idea that he would be arrested. Thinking he had done his duty and that you were his friend and he would be rewarded. He'd helped to haul the old man in so everybody could know how bad the old man had been and how he'd tried to steal some feed that didn't belong to him, and when the sheriff put the handcuffs on the boy he couldn't believe it. Then he'd started to cry. That was one story he had saved to write. He knew at least twenty good stories from out there and he had never written one. Why?

"You tell them why," he said.

"Why what, dear?"

"Why nothing."

She didn't drink so much, now, since she had him. But if he lived he would never write about her, he knew that now. Nor about any of them. The rich were dull and they drank too much, or they played too much backgammon. They were dull and they were repetitious. He remembered poor Julian and his romantic awe of them and how he had started a story once that began, "The very rich are different from you and me."[8] And how some one had said to Julian, Yes, they have more money. But that was not humorous to Julian. He thought they were a special glamourous race and when he found they weren't it wrecked him just as much as any other thing that wrecked him.

He had been contemptuous of those who wrecked. You did not have to like it because you understood it. He could beat anything, he thought, because no thing could hurt him if he did not care.

All right. Now he would not care for death. One thing he had always dreaded was the pain. He could stand pain as well as any man, until it went on too long, and wore him out, but here he had something that had hurt frightfully and just when he had felt it breaking him, the pain had stopped.

He remembered long ago when Williamson, the bombing officer, had been hit by a stick bomb some one in a German patrol had thrown as he was coming in through the wire that night and, screaming, had begged every one to kill him. He was a fat man, very brave, and a good officer, although addicted to fantastic shows. But that night he was caught in the wire, with a flare lighting him up and his bowels spilled out into the wire, so when they brought him in, alive, they had to cut him loose. Shoot me, Harry. For Christ sake shoot me. They had

---

8. These are the opening words of "The Rich Boy" by F. Scott Fitzgerald. Hemingway originally used Fitzgerald's name instead of "Julian," but was persuaded to make the change by his editor, Maxwell Perkins.

had an argument one time about our Lord never sending you anything you could not bear and some one's theory had been that meant that at a certain time the pain passed you out automatically. But he had always remembered Williamson, that night. Nothing passed out Williamson until he gave him all his morphine tablets that he had always saved to use himself and then they did not work right away.

Still this now, that he had, was very easy; and if it was no worse as it went on there was nothing to worry about. Except that he would rather be in better company.

He thought a little about the company that he would like to have.

No, he thought, when everything you do, you do too long, and do too late, you can't expect to find the people still there. The people all are gone. The party's over and you are with your hostess now.

I'm getting as bored with dying as with everything else, he thought.

"It's a bore," he said out loud.

"What is, my dear?"

"Anything you do too bloody long."

He looked at her face between him and the fire. She was leaning back in the chair and the firelight shone on her pleasantly lined face and he could see that she was sleepy. He heard the hyena make a noise just outside the range of the fire.

"I've been writing," he said. "But I got tired."

"Do you think you will be able to sleep?"

"Pretty sure. Why don't you turn in?"

"I like to sit here with you."

"Do you feel anything strange?" he asked her.

"No. Just a little sleepy."

"I do," he said.

He had just felt death come by again.

"You know the only thing I've never lost is curiosity," he said to her.

"You've never lost anything. You're the most complete man I've ever known."

"Christ," he said. "How little a woman knows. What is that? Your intuition?"

Because, just then, death had come and rested its head on the foot of the cot and he could smell its breath.

"Never believe any of that about a scythe and a skull,"[9] he told her. "It can be two bicycle policemen as easily, or be a bird. Or it can have a wide snout like a hyena."

It had moved up on him now, but it had no shape any more. It simply occupied space.

"Tell it to go away."

It did not go away but moved a little closer.

"You've got a hell of a breath," he told it. "You stinking bastard."

It moved up closer to him still and he could not speak to it, and when it saw he could not speak it came a little closer, and now he tried to send it away

---

9. In medieval imagery death is often represented as a skeleton draped in a long cape so that only the skull shows. He carries a scythe.

without speaking, but it moved in on him so its weight was all upon his chest, and while it crouched there and he could not move, or speak, he heard the woman say, "Bwana is asleep now. Take the cot up very gently and carry it into the tent."

He could not speak to tell her to make it go away and it crouched now, heavier, so he could not breathe. And then, while they lifted the cot, suddenly it was all right and the weight went from his chest.

It was morning and had been morning for some time and he heard the plane. It showed very tiny and then made a wide circle and the boys ran out and lit the fires, using kerosene, and piled on grass so there were two big smudges at each end of the level place and the morning breeze blew them toward the camp and the plane circled twice more, low this time, and then glided down and levelled off and landed smoothly and, coming walking toward him, was old Compton in slacks, a tweed jacket and a brown felt hat.

"What's the matter, old cock?" Compton said.

"Bad leg," he told him. "Will you have some breakfast?"

"Thanks. I'll just have some tea. It's the Puss Moth[1] you know. I won't be able to take the Memsahib. There's only room for one. Your lorry is on the way."

Helen had taken Compton aside and was speaking to him. Compton came back more cheery than ever.

"We'll get you right in," he said. "I'll be back for the Mem. Now I'm afraid I'll have to stop at Arusha to refuel. We'd better get going."

"What about the tea?"

"I don't really care about it you know."

The boys had picked up the cot and carried it around the green tents and down along the rock and out onto the plain and along past the smudges that were burning brightly now, and the grass all consumed, and the wind fanning the fire, to the little plane. It was difficult getting him in, but once in he lay back in the leather seat, and the leg was stuck straight out to one side of the seat where Compton sat. Compton started the motor and got in. He waved to Helen and to the boys and, as the clatter moved into the old familiar roar, they swung around with Compie watching for wart-hog holes and roared, bumping, along the stretch between the fires and with the last bump rose and he saw them all standing below, waving, and the camp beside the hill, flattening now, and the plain spreading, clumps of trees, and the bush flattening, while the game trails ran now smoothly to the dry waterholes, and there was a new water that he had never known of. The zebra, small rounded backs now, and the wildebeeste, big-headed dots seeming to climb as they moved in long fingers across the plain, now scattering as the shadow came toward them, they were tiny now, and the movement had no gallop, and the plain as far as you could see, gray-yellow now and ahead old Compie's tweed back and the brown felt hat. Then they were over the first hills and the wildebeeste were trailing up them, and then they were over mountains with sudden depths of green-rising forest and the solid bamboo slopes, and then the heavy forest again, sculptured into peaks and hollows until they crossed, and hills sloped down and then another plain, hot now, and purple brown, bumpy with

---

1. A small, light airplane seating two people.

heat and Compie looking back to see how he was riding. Then there were other mountains dark ahead.

And then instead of going on to Arusha they turned left, he evidently figured that they had the gas, and looking down he saw a pink sifting cloud, moving over the ground, and in the air, like the first snow in a blizzard, that comes from nowhere, and he knew the locusts were coming up from the South. Then they began to climb and they were going to the East it seemed, and then it darkened and they were in a storm, the rain so thick it seemed like flying through a waterfall, and then they were out and Compie turned his head and grinned and pointed and there, ahead, all he could see, as wide as all the world, great, high, and unbelievably white in the sun, was the square top of Kilimanjaro. And then he knew that there was where he was going.

Just then the hyena stopped whimpering in the night and started to make a strange, human, almost crying sound. The woman heard it and stirred uneasily. She did not wake. In her dream she was at the house on Long Island and it was the night before her daughter's début. Somehow her father was there and he had been very rude. Then the noise the hyena made was so loud she woke and for a moment she did not know where she was and she was very afraid. Then she took the flashlight and shone it on the other cot that they had carried in after Harry had gone to sleep. She could see his bulk under the mosquito bar but somehow he had gotten his leg out and it hung down alongside the cot. The dressings had all come down and she could not look at it.

"Molo," she called, "Molo! Molo!"

Then she said, "Harry, Harry!" Then her voice rising, "Harry! Please, Oh Harry!"

There was no answer and she could not hear him breathing.

Outside the tent the hyena made the same strange noise that had awakened her. But she did not hear him for the beating of her heart.

1936, 1938

STERLING BROWN
1901–1989

For much of his long and distinguished career Sterling Brown presented himself to the public mainly as a teacher and scholar of African American folk culture and written literature. During the Harlem Renaissance movement, however, he was also hailed as a technically accomplished and eloquent poet. Rediscovered by younger black poets in the late 1960s, Brown has since been called, to quote the poet Michael S. Harper, "a trustee of consciousness, and a national treasure."

Born in Washington, D.C., and never resident in New York, Brown identified himself with the "New Negro" movement in general rather than with its particular manifestation in Harlem during the 1920s. "The New Negro," he wrote in 1955, "is not to me a group of writers centered in Harlem during the second half of the twenties. Most of the writers were not Harlemites; much of the best writing was not about Harlem, which was the show-window, the cashier's till, but no more Negro America than New York is America." Brown viewed Harlem as the place where African American writing was publicized rather than produced, believing that the cosmopolitan and sophisticated New York writers themselves had not written representatively about, or from the perspective of, ordinary black people. While he himself was well educated and of middle-class background, Brown immersed himself deeply in the full range of African American popular expression—jazz, blues, spirituals, work songs, folk tales—so that his writing could reach beyond his own experience.

Brown's father was the Reverend Sterling Nelson Brown, who had been born a slave but eventually attended Fisk University and Oberlin College and later became professor of religion at Howard University in Washington, D.C. Brown attended the academically oriented Dunbar High School, went to Williams College in 1918, and took a master's degree at Harvard. He won a prize in 1925 for his first nationally published essay—a sketch of the tenor Roland Hayes that appeared in *Opportunity*—and thereby came to the attention of black intellectuals. While teaching at Virginia Seminary and College between 1926 and 1928, he met and married Daisy Turnbull. After brief teaching jobs at Fisk, Lincoln University in Missouri, and Atlanta University, he joined the faculty at Howard University in 1929, where he continued to teach until retirement. His first book, *Outline for the Study of the Poetry of American Negroes* (1931), was a pedagogical supplement to James Weldon Johnson's *Book of American Negro Poetry*, including paper topics, study questions, definitions, and other material. Having published individual poems in magazines and newspapers, Brown brought out a collection of this work called *Southern Road* in 1932. It was highly praised by influential critics, many of whom were especially impressed with Brown's technical virtuosity. Alain Locke, the major theorist of the New Negro movement, believed that the book came very close to his ideal of the "poetic portrayal of Negro folk-life . . . true in both letter and spirit to the idiom of the folk's own way of feeling and thinking." Despite such acclaim, the book did not sell widely—1932 was not a good year for publishing, and the Harlem Renaissance movement had ended abruptly with the onset of the Great Depression in 1929. Brown's planned second book of poems, tentatively called *No Hiding Place* and ready for the press in 1935, was rejected by publishers for economic reasons.

After this setback Brown made little further effort to publish poetry and turned his energies into academic and administrative channels, always retaining his focus on African American culture. From 1936 to 1939 he was Negro affairs editor for the Federal Writers' Project, a government funding source for writers during the Depression years; he also worked on the staff of the "Carnegie-Myrdal Study of the Negro," the basis of a landmark study of race relations, *An American Dilemma,* written by the Swedish sociologists Gunnar Myrdal and Alva Myrdal and published shortly after the end of World War II. *The Negro in American Fiction,* a book of critical essays, and *Negro Poetry and Drama,* a literary history, both appeared in 1938. Together with Ulysses Lee and Arthur P. Davis, Brown edited the important anthology *Negro Caravan* (1941), collecting important examples of African American literature from its folk foundations to 1940. Over the years he published numerous essays, notes, and commentaries on African American literature, the role of blacks in American writing, black folklore, and black music; he was an acknowledged expert on all of these topics.

The civil rights movement of the 1960s motivated him to conduct lectures and poetry readings that brought him and his poetry back into national view. It became clear at this time that Alain Locke's earlier assessment of Brown was only partly true. Although in some sense Brown strove in his poetry to make a literary form appropriate to authentic black folk voices, he saw these voices not as raw folk data but as already artistically self-conscious. Blues, jazz, and spirituals were complex, expressive, culturally sophisticated forms. In addition, Brown deployed his speakers' voices not for the main purpose of celebrating the black folk tradition—though this was certainly part of his aim—but to expose and criticize racial injustice. Both his scholarly writing and his poetry call attention to African American achievements and deplore American racism.

The text of the poems printed here is from *Collected Poems* (1996).

Mister Samuel and Sam

Mister Samuel, he belong to Rotary,
Sam to de Sons of Rest;
Both wear red hats lak monkey men,
An' you cain't say which is de best.

Mister Samuel ride in a Cadillac,   5
Sam ride in a Tin Lizzie Fo'd;
Both spend their jack fo' gas an' oil,
An' both git stuck on de road.

Mister Samuel speak in de Chamber of Commerce,
Sam he speak in ch'uch;   10
Both of 'em talk for a mighty long time,
Widout sayin', Lawd knows, ve'y much.

Mister Samuel deal wid high finance,
Sam deal in a two-bit game;
Mister Samuel crashes, Sam goes broke,   15
But deys busted jes' de same.

Mister Samuel wife speak sof' an' low,
When dey gits in their weekly fight;
Sam catches a broomstick crost his rear,
An' both of 'em's henpecked right.   20

Mister Samuel drinks his Canadian Rye,
Sam drinks his bootleg gin;
Both gits as high as a Georgia pine,
And both calls de doctor in.

Mister Samuel die, an' de folks all know,   25
Sam die widout no noise;
De worl' go by in de same ol' way,
And dey's both of 'em po' los' boys. . . .

1932, 1980

Master and Man

The yellow ears are crammed in Mr. Cromartie's bin
The wheat is tight sacked in Mr. Cromartie's barn.
The timothy is stuffed in Mr. Cromartie's loft.
The ploughs are lined up in Mr. Cromartie's shed.
The cotton has gone to Mr. Cromartie's factor.   5
The money is in Mr. Cromartie's bank.
Mr. Cromartie's son made his frat at the college.
Mr. Cromartie's daughter has got her new car.
The veranda is old, but the fireplace is rosy.
Well done, Mr. Cromartie. Time now for rest.   10

Blackened sticks line the furrows that Uncle Ned laid.
Bits of fluff are in the corners where Uncle Ned ginned.
The mules he ploughed are sleek in Mr. Cromartie's pastures.
The hoes grow dull in Mr. Cromartie's shed.
His winter rations wait on the commissary shelves;   15
Mr. Cromartie's ledger is there for his service.
Uncle Ned daubs some mortar between the old logs.
His children have traipsed off to God knows where.
His old lady sits patching the old, thin denims;
She's got a new dress, and his young one a doll,   20
He's got five dollars. The year has come round.
The harvest is over: Uncle Ned's harvesting,
Mr. Cromartie's harvest. Time now for rest.

                                                        1936, 1980

Break of Day

Big Jess fired on the Alabama Central,
Man in full, babe, man in full.
Been throwing on coal for Mister Murphy
From times way back, baby, times way back.

Big Jess had a pleasing woman, name of Mamie,   5
Sweet-hipted Mama, sweet-hipted Mame;
Had a boy growing up for to be a fireman,
Just like his pa, baby, like his pa.

Out by the roundhouse Jess had his cabin,
Longside the tracks, babe, long the tracks,   10
Jess pulled the whistle when they high-balled past it
"I'm on my way, baby, on my way."

Crackers craved the job what Jess was holding,
Times right tough, babe, times right tough,
Warned Jess to quit his job for a white man,   15
Jess he laughed, baby, he jes' laughed.

He picked up his lunch-box, kissed his sweet woman,
Sweet-hipted Mama, sweet-hipted Mame,
His son walked with him to the white-washed palings,
"Be seeing you soon, son, see you soon."   20

Mister Murphy let Big Jess talk on the whistle
"So long sugar baby, so long babe";
Train due back in the early morning
Breakfast time, baby, breakfast time.

Mob stopped the train crossing Black Bear Mountain   25
Shot rang out, babe, shot rang out.

They left Big Jess on the Black Bear Mountain,
Break of day, baby, break of day.

Sweet Mame sits rocking, waiting for the whistle
Long past due, babe, long past due.   30
The grits are cold, and the coffee's boiled over,
But Jess done gone, baby he done gone.

1938, 1980

Bitter Fruit of the Tree

They said to my grandmother: "Please do not be bitter,"
When they sold her first-born and let the second die,
When they drove her husband till he took to the swamplands,
And brought him home bloody and beaten at last.
They told her, "It is better you should not be bitter,   5
Some must work and suffer so that we, who must, can live,
Forgiving is noble, you must not be heathen bitter;
These are your orders: you *are* not to be bitter."
And they left her shack for their porticoed house.

They said to my father: "Please do not be bitter,"   10
When he ploughed and planted a crop not his,
When he weatherstripped a house that he could not enter,
And stored away a harvest he could not enjoy.
They answered his questions: "It does not concern you,
It is not for you to know, it is past your understanding,   15
All you need know is: you must not be bitter."

1939, 1980

LANGSTON HUGHES
1902–1967

Langston Hughes was the most popular and versatile of the many writers connected
with the Harlem Renaissance. Along with Zora Neale Hurston, and in contrast to Jean
Toomer and Countee Cullen (who wanted to work with the patterns of written literary forms, whether traditional or experimental), he wanted to capture the dominant
oral and improvisatory traditions of black culture in written form.

Hughes was born in Joplin, Missouri; and in childhood, since his parents were separated, he lived mainly with his maternal grandmother in Lawrence, Kansas. He did,
however, reside intermittently both with his mother in Detroit and Cleveland, where
he finished high school and began to write poetry, and with his father, who, disgusted
with American racism, had gone to Mexico. Like other poets in this era—T. S. Eliot,
Hart Crane, Edgar Lee Masters, and Robert Frost—Hughes had a mother sympathetic

to his poetic ambitions and a businesslike father with whom he was in deep, scarring conflict.

Hughes entered Columbia University in 1920 but left after a year. Traveling and drifting, he shipped out as a merchant seaman and worked at a nightclub in Paris (France) and as a busboy in Washington, D.C. All this time he was writing and publishing poetry, chiefly in the two important African American periodicals *Opportunity* and the *Crisis*. Eleven of Hughes's poems were published in Alain Locke's pioneering anthology, *The New Negro* (1925), and he was also well represented in Countee Cullen's 1927 anthology, *Caroling Dusk*. Carl Van Vechten, one of the white patrons of African American writing, helped get *The Weary Blues*, Hughes's first volume of poems, published in 1926. It was in this year, too, that his important essay "The Negro Artist and the Racial Mountain" appeared in the *Nation*; in that essay Hughes described the immense challenges to be faced by the serious black artist "who would produce a racial art" but insisted on the need for courageous artists to make the attempt. Other patrons appeared: Amy Spingarn financed his college education at Lincoln University (Pennsylvania) and Charlotte Mason subsidized him in New York City between 1928 and 1930. The publication of his novel *Not without Laughter* in 1930 solidified his reputation and sales, enabling him to support himself. By the 1930s he was being called "the bard of Harlem."

The Great Depression brought an abrupt end to much African American literary activity, but Hughes was already a public figure. In the activist 1930s he was much absorbed in radical politics. Hughes and other blacks were drawn by the American Communist Party, which made racial justice an important plank in its platform, promoting an image of working-class solidarity that nullified racial boundaries. He visited the Soviet Union in 1932 and produced a significant amount of radical writing up to the eve of World War II. He covered the Spanish civil war for the *Baltimore Afro-American* in 1937. By the end of the decade he had also been involved in drama and screenplay writing and had begun an autobiography, all the while publishing poetry. In 1943 he invented the folksy, streetwise character Jesse B. Semple, whose commonsense prose monologues on race were eventually collected in four volumes, and Alberta K. Johnson, Semple's female equivalent, in his series of "Madam" poems.

In the 1950s and 1960s Hughes published a variety of anthologies for children and adults, including *First Book of Negroes* (1952), *The First Book of Jazz* (1955), and *The Book of Negro Folklore* (1958). In 1953 he was called to testify before Senator Joseph McCarthy's committee on subversive activities in connection with his 1930s radicalism. The FBI listed him as a security risk until 1959; and during these years, when he could not travel outside the United States because he would not have been allowed to reenter the country, Hughes worked to rehabilitate his reputation as a good American by producing patriotic poetry. From 1960 to the end of his life he was again on the international circuit.

Within the spectrum of artistic possibilities open to writers of the Harlem Renaissance—drawing on African American rural folk forms; on literary traditions and forms that entered the United States from Europe and Great Britain; or on the new cultural forms of blacks in American cities—Hughes chose to focus his work on modern, urban black life. He modeled his stanza forms on the improvisatory rhythms of jazz music and adapted the vocabulary of everyday black speech to poetry. He also acknowledged finding inspiration for his writing in the work of white American poets who preceded him. Like Walt Whitman he heard America singing, and he asserted his right to sing America back; he also learned from Carl Sandburg's earlier attempts to work jazz into poetry. Hughes did not confuse his pride in African American culture with complacency toward the material deprivations of black life in the United States. He was keenly aware that the modernist "vogue in things Negro" among white Americans was potentially exploitative and voyeuristic; he confronted such racial tourists with the misery as well as the jazz of Chicago's South Side. Early and late, Hughes's poems demanded that African Americans be acknowledged as owners of the culture they gave to the United States and as fully enfranchised American citizens.

The source of the poems printed here is *Collected Poems* (1994).

The Negro Speaks of Rivers

I've known rivers:
I've known rivers ancient as the world and older than the
      flow of human blood in human veins.

My soul has grown deep like the rivers.

I bathed in the Euphrates when dawns were young.
I built my hut near the Congo and it lulled me to sleep.   5
I looked upon the Nile and raised the pyramids above it.
I heard the singing of the Mississippi when Abe Lincoln
      went down to New Orleans, and I've seen its
      muddy bosom turn all golden in the sunset

I've known rivers:
Ancient, dusky rivers.

My soul has grown deep like the rivers.   10

                  1921, 1926

Mother to Son

Well, son, I'll tell you:
Life for me ain't been no crystal stair.
It's had tacks in it,
And splinters,
And boards torn up,   5
And places with no carpet on the floor—
Bare.
But all the time
I'se been a-climbin' on,
And reachin' landin's,   10
And turnin' corners,
And sometimes goin' in the dark
Where there ain't been no light.
So boy, don't you turn back.
Don't you set down on the steps   15
'Cause you finds it's kinder hard.
Don't you fall now—
For I'se still goin', honey,
I'se still climbin',
And life for me ain't been no crystal stair.   20

                  1922, 1926

I, Too

I, too, sing America.

I am the darker brother.
They send me to eat in the kitchen
When company comes,
But I laugh,   5
And eat well,
And grow strong.

Tomorrow,
I'll be at the table
When company comes.   10
Nobody'll dare
Say to me,
"Eat in the kitchen,"
Then.

Besides,   15
They'll see how beautiful I am
And be ashamed—

I, too, am America.

                                            1925, 1959

The Weary Blues

Droning a drowsy syncopated tune,
Rocking back and forth to a mellow croon,
    I heard a Negro play.
Down on Lenox Avenue the other night
By the pale dull pallor of an old gas light   5
    He did a lazy sway. . . .
    He did a lazy sway. . . .
To the tune o' those Weary Blues.
With his ebony hands on each ivory key.
He made that poor piano moan with melody.   10
    O Blues!
Swaying to and fro on his rickety stool
He played that sad raggy tune like a musical fool.
    Sweet Blues!
Coming from a black man's soul.   15
    O Blues!
In a deep song voice with a melancholy tone
I heard that Negro sing, that old piano moan—
    "Ain't got nobody in all this world,
    Ain't got nobody but ma self.   20
    I's gwine to quit ma frownin'
    And put ma troubles on de shelf."

Thump, thump, thump, went his foot on the floor.
He played a few chords then he sang some more—
    "I got de Weary Blues   25
    And I can't be satisfied.
    Got de Weary Blues
    And can't be satisfied—
    I ain't happy no mo'
    And I wish that I had died."   30
And far into the night he crooned that tune.
The stars went out and so did the moon.
The singer stopped playing and went to bed.
While the Weary Blues echoes through his head
He slept like a rock or a man that's dead.   35

                                                  1925

Mulatto *(mixed race)*

I am your son, white man!

Georgia dusk
And the turpentine woods.
One of the pillars of the temple fell.

                               —Samson + Delilah
    You are my son!   place blame on father?
    Like hell!

The moon over the turpentine woods.
The Southern night
Full of stars,
Great big yellow stars.   10
    What's a body but a toy?
      Juicy bodies
        Of nigger wenches
        Blue black
        Against black fences.   15
        O, you little bastard boy,
      What's a body but a toy?
The scent of pine wood stings the soft night air.
      What's the body of your mother?
Silver moonlight everywhere.   20

     What's the body of your mother?
Sharp pine scent in the evening air.
        A nigger night,
        A nigger joy,
        A little yellow   25
        Bastard boy.

Naw, you ain't my brother.
Niggers ain't my brother.
Not ever.
Niggers ain't my brother. 30
The Southern night is full of stars,
Great big yellow stars.
            O, sweet as earth,
            Dusk dark bodies
            Give sweet birth 35
To little yellow bastard boys.

        Git on back there in the night,
        You ain't white.

The bright stars scatter everywhere.
Pine wood scent in the evening air. 40
            A nigger night,
            A nigger joy.

        I am your son, white man!

            A little yellow
            Bastard boy. 45

                                    1927

Song for a Dark Girl

Way Down South in Dixie[1]
        (Break the heart of me)
They hung my black young lover
        To a cross roads tree.

Way Down South in Dixie 5
        (Bruised body high in air)
I asked the white Lord Jesus
        What was the use of prayer.

Way Down South in Dixie
        (Break the heart of me) 10
Love is a naked shadow
        On a gnarled and naked tree.

                                    1927

---

1. Last line of "Dixie," the popular minstrel song, probably composed by Daniel D. Emmett (1815–1904).

Visitors to the Black Belt

You can talk about
Across the railroad tracks—
To me it's *here*
On this side of the tracks.

You can talk about   5
Up in Harlem—
To me it's *here*
In Harlem.

You can say
Jazz on the South Side—[1]   10
To me it's hell
On the South Side:

> Kitchenettes
> With no heat
> And garbage   15
> In the halls.

Who're you, outsider?

Ask me who am I.

                                                    1940, 1943

Note on Commercial Theatre

You've taken my blues and gone—
You sing 'em on Broadway
And you sing 'em in Hollywood Bowl,
And you mixed 'em up with symphonies
And you fixed 'em   5
So they don't sound like me.
Yep, you done taken my blues and gone.

You also took my spirituals and gone.
You put me in *Macbeth* and *Carmen Jones*
And all kinds of *Swing Mikados*   10
And in everything but what's about me—
But someday somebody'll
Stand up and talk about me,
And write about me—

---

1. African American neighborhood in Chicago; see also Archibald J. Motley's 1934 painting, *Black Belt* in the color insert to this volume.

Black and beautiful—   15
And sing about me,
And put on plays about me!

I reckon it'll be
Me myself!

Yes, it'll be me.   20

1940, 1959

Democracy

Democracy will not come
Today, this year
     Nor ever
Through compromise and fear.

I have as much right   5
As the other fellow has
     To stand
On my two feet
And own the land.

I tire so of hearing people say,   10
Let things take their course.
Tomorrow is another day.
I do not need my freedom when I'm dead.
I cannot live on tomorrow's bread.

     Freedom   15
     Is a strong seed
     Planted
     In a great need.
     I live here, too.
     I want freedom   20
     Just as you.

1949

Theme for English B

The instructor said,

     Go home and write
     a page tonight.
     And let that page come out of you—
     Then, it will be true.   5

I wonder if it's that simple?
I am twenty-two, colored, born in Winston-Salem.
I went to school there, then Durham, then here
to this college on the hill above Harlem.[1]
I am the only colored student in my class.   10
The steps from the hill lead down into Harlem,
through a park, then I cross St. Nicholas,
Eighth Avenue, Seventh, and I come to the Y,
the Harlem Branch Y, where I take the elevator
up to my room, sit down, and write this page: 15

It's not easy to know what is true for you or me
at twenty-two, my age. But I guess I'm what
I feel and see and hear, Harlem, I hear you:
hear you, hear me—we two—you, me, talk on this page.
(I hear New York, too.) Me—who?   20
Well, I like to eat, sleep, drink, and be in love.
I like to work, read, learn, and understand life.
I like a pipe for a Christmas present,
or records—Bessie, bop, or Bach.[2]
I guess being colored doesn't make me *not* like   25
the same things other folks like who are other races.
So will my page be colored that I write?
Being me, it will not be white.
But it will be
a part of you, instructor.   30
You are white—
yet a part of me, as I am a part of you.
That's American.
Sometimes perhaps you don't want to be a part of me.
Nor do I often want to be a part of you.   35
But we are, that's true!
As I learn from you,
I guess you learn from me—
although you're older—and white—
and somewhat more free.   40

This is my page for English B.

1949

---

1. The City College of the City University of New York; Winston-Salem and Durham are cities in North Carolina.
2. Johann Sebastian Bach (1685–1750), German composer of the Baroque era; Bessie Smith (1894–1937), noted blues singer. "Bop": jazz form developed in Harlem during World War II.

JOHN STEINBECK
1902–1968

Most of John Steinbeck's best writing is set in the region of California that he called home, the Salinas Valley and Monterey peninsula of California, where visitors today will find official remembrances of him everywhere. Steinbeck believed in the American promise of opportunity for all, but believed also that social injustices and economic inequalities had put opportunity beyond reach for many. His work merged literary modernism with literary realism, celebrated traditional rural communities along with social outcasts and immigrant cultures, and endorsed conservative values and radical politics at the same time.

Steinbeck's father managed a flour mill and later became treasurer of Monterey County; his mother, who had taught school before marriage, was active in local civic affairs. Their home was full of books, and Steinbeck read avidly from an early age. After graduating from Salinas High School in 1919, he began to study at Stanford University but took time off for a variety of short-term jobs at local mills, farms, and estates. During this period he developed an abiding respect for people who worked on farms and in factories, and committed his literary abilities to their cause. He left college for good in 1925, having completed less than three years of coursework, and continued his roving life.

With financial help from his father, Steinbeck spent most of 1929 writing. He moved to the seaside town of Pacific Grove, on the Monterey coast, and in 1930 was married (the first of three times). In 1935 he achieved commercial success with his third novel, *Tortilla Flat,* a celebration of the Mexican-American culture of the *"paisanos"* who lived in the Monterey hills. The book favorably contrasted these lusty, idealized types to the valley's respectable, conventional, Anglo-Protestant population. Steinbeck's next novel, *In Dubious Battle* (1936), contrasted the decency of striking migratory farm workers both to the cynicism of landowners and their vigilantes, and to the equal cynicism of Communist labor union organizers who exploit the workers' plight for their own purposes. Sympathy for the underdog appears again in *Of Mice and Men* (1937), a best-selling short novel about two itinerant ranch hands, and yet again in *The Grapes of Wrath* (1939), his most famous and most ambitious novel.

Inspired by the devastating 1930s drought in the southern plains states and the exodus of thousands of farmers from their homes in the so-called Dust Bowl, *The Grapes of Wrath* told the story of the Joad family, who, after losing their land in Oklahoma, migrated westward to California on U.S. Highway 66 looking for, but not finding, a better life. Because of its supposed radicalism, the novel was banned or burned in several states, but even so, it became the nation's number one bestseller and won a Pulitzer Prize in 1940. *Cannery Row* (1940), a local-color novel about workers in the sardine canneries of Monterey, also became a bestseller.

After World War II Steinbeck's work displayed increasing hostility to American culture, whose mass commercialization seemed to him to be destroying individual creativity. "The Leader of the People" expresses his sense that America's heroic times are past and locates value in the story's socially marginal characters—a child, an old man, and a farmhand. His most important later works are *The Wayward Bus* (1947), *East of Eden* (1952), *Sweet Thursday* (1954), and *Travels with Charley in Search of America* (1962), in which he recounts his automobile tour of the United States, taken with his dog. Steinbeck won the Nobel Prize in 1963.

The text is that of *The Red Pony* (1945).

The Leader of the People

On Saturday afternoon Billy Buck, the ranch-hand, raked together the last of the old years' haystack and pitched small forkfuls over the wire fence to a few mildly interested cattle. High in the air small clouds like puffs of cannon smoke were driven eastward by the March wind. The wind could be heard whishing in the brush on the ridge crests, but no breath of it penetrated down into the ranch-cup.

The little boy, Jody, emerged from the house eating a thick piece of buttered bread. He saw Billy working on the last of the haystack. Jody tramped down scuffling his shoes in a way he had been told was destructive to good shoe-leather. A flock of white pigeons flew out of the black cypress tree as Jody passed, and circled the tree and landed again. A half-grown tortoise-shell cat leaped from the bunkhouse porch, galloped on stiff legs across the road, whirled and galloped back again. Jody picked up a stone to help the game along, but he was too late, for the cat was under the porch before the stone could be discharged. He threw the stone into the cypress tree and started the white pigeons on another whirling flight.

Arriving at the used-up haystack, the boy leaned against the barbed wire fence. "Will that be all of it, do you think?" he asked.

The middle-aged ranch-hand stopped his careful raking and stuck his fork into the ground. He took off his black hat and smoothed down his hair. "Nothing left of it that isn't soggy from ground moisture," he said. He replaced his hat and rubbed his dry leathery hands together.

"Ought to be plenty mice," Jody suggested.

"Lousy with them," said Billy. "Just crawling with mice."

"Well, maybe, when you get all through, I could call the dogs and hunt the mice."

"Sure, I guess you could," said Billy Buck. He lifted a forkful of the damp ground-hay and threw it into the air. Instantly three mice leaped out and burrowed frantically under the hay again.

Jody sighed with satisfaction. Those plump, sleek, arrogant mice were doomed. For eight months they had lived and multiplied in the haystack. They had been immune from cats, from traps, from poison and from Jody. They had grown smug in their security, overbearing and fat. Now the time of disaster had come; they would not survive another day.

Billy looked up at the top of the hills that surrounded the ranch. "Maybe you better ask your father before you do it," he suggested.

"Well, where is he? I'll ask him now."

"He rode up to the ridge ranch after dinner. He'll be back pretty soon."

Jody slumped against the fence post. "I don't think he'd care."

As Billy went back to his work he said ominously, "You'd better ask him anyway. You know how he is."

Jody did know. His father, Carl Tiflin, insisted upon giving permission for anything that was done on the ranch, whether it was important or not. Jody sagged farther against the post until he was sitting on the ground. He looked up at the little puffs of wind-driven cloud. "Is it like to rain, Billy?"

"It might. The wind's good for it, but not strong enough."

"Well, I hope it don't rain until after I kill those damn mice." He looked over his shoulder to see whether Billy had noticed the mature profanity. Billy worked on without comment.

Jody turned back and looked at the side-hill where the road from the outside world came down. The hill was washed with lean March sunshine. Silver thistles, blue lupins and a few poppies bloomed among the sage bushes. Halfway up the hill Jody could see Doubletree Mutt, the black dog, digging in a squirrel hole. He paddled for a while and then paused to kick bursts of dirt out between his hind legs, and he dug with an earnestness which belied the knowledge he must have had that no dog had ever caught a squirrel by digging in a hole.

Suddenly, while Jody watched, the black dog stiffened, and backed out of the hole and looked up the hill toward the cleft in the ridge where the road came through. Jody looked up too. For a moment Carl Tiflin on horseback stood out against the pale sky and then he moved down the road toward the house. He carried something white in his hand.

The boy started to his feet. "He's got a letter," Jody cried. He trotted away toward the ranch house, for the letter would probably be read aloud and he wanted to be there. He reached the house before his father did, and ran in. He heard Carl dismount from his creaking saddle and slap the horse on the side to send it to the barn where Billy would unsaddle it and turn it out.

Jody ran into the kitchen. "We got a letter!" he cried.

His mother looked up from a pan of beans. "Who has?"

"Father has. I saw it in his hand."

Carl strode into the kitchen then, and Jody's mother asked, "Who's the letter from, Carl?"

He frowned quickly. "How did you know there was a letter?"

She nodded her head in the boy's direction. "Big-Britches Jody told me." Jody was embarrassed.

His father looked down at him contemptuously. "He *is* getting to be a Big-Britches," Carl said. "He's minding everybody's business but his own. Got his big nose into everything."

Mrs. Tiflin relented a little. "Well, he hasn't enough to keep him busy. Who's the letter from?"

Carl still frowned on Jody. "I'll keep him busy if he isn't careful." He held out a sealed letter. "I guess it's from your father."

Mrs. Tiflin took a hairpin from her head and slit open the flap. Her lips pursed judiciously. Jody saw her eyes snap back and forth over the lines. "He says," she translated, "he says he's going to drive out Saturday to stay for a little while. Why, this is Saturday. The letter must have been delayed." She looked at the postmark. "This was mailed day before yesterday. It should have been here yesterday." She looked up questioningly at her husband, and then her face darkened angrily. "Now what have you got that look on you for? He doesn't come often."

Carl turned his eyes away from her anger. He could be stern with her most of the time, but when occasionally her temper arose, he could not combat it.

"What's the matter with you?" she demanded again.

In his explanation there was a tone of apology Jody himself might have used. "It's just that he talks," Carl said lamely. "Just talks."

"Well, what of it? You talk yourself."

"Sure I do. But your father only talks about one thing."

"Indians!" Jody broke in excitedly. "Indians and crossing the plains!"

Carl turned fiercely on him. "You get out, Mr. Big-Britches! Go on, now! Get out!"

Jody went miserably out the back door and closed the screen with elaborate quietness. Under the kitchen window his shamed, downcast eyes fell upon a curiously shaped stone, a stone of such fascination that he squatted down and picked it up and turned it over in his hands.

The voices came clearly to him through the open kitchen window. "Jody's damn well right," he heard his father say. "Just Indians and crossing the plains. I've heard that story about how the horses got driven off about a thousand times. He just goes on and on, and he never changes a word in the things he tells."

When Mrs. Tiflin answered her tone was so changed that Jody, outside the window, looked up from his study of the stone. Her voice had become soft and explanatory. Jody knew how her face would have changed to match the tone. She said quietly, "Look at it this way, Carl. That was the big thing in my father's life. He led a wagon train clear across the plains to the coast, and when it was finished, his life was done. It was a big thing to do, but it didn't last long enough. Look!" she continued, "it's as though he was born to do that, and after he finished it, there wasn't anything more for him to do but think about it and talk about it. If there'd been any farther west to go, he'd have gone. He's told me so himself. But at last there was the ocean. He lives right by the ocean where he had to stop."

She had caught Carl, caught him and entangled him in her soft tone.

"I've seen him," he agreed quietly. "He goes down and stares off west over the ocean." His voice sharpened a little. "And then he goes up to the Horseshoe Club in Pacific Grove, and he tells people how the Indians drove off the horses."

She tried to catch him again. "Well, it's everything to him. You might be patient with him and pretend to listen."

Carl turned impatiently away. "Well, if it gets too bad, I can always go down to the bunkhouse and sit with Billy," he said irritably. He walked through the house and slammed the front door after him.

Jody ran to his chores. He dumped the grain to the chickens without chasing any of them. He gathered the eggs from the nests. He trotted into the house with the wood and interlaced it so carefully in the wood-box that two armloads seemed to fill it to overflowing.

His mother had finished the beans by now. She stirred up the fire and brushed off the stove-top with a turkey wing. Jody peered cautiously at her to see whether any rancor toward him remained. "Is he coming today?" Jody asked.

"That's what his letter said."

"Maybe I better walk up the road to meet him."

Mrs. Tiflin clanged the stove-lid shut. "That would be nice," she said. "He'd probably like to be met."

"I guess I'll just do it then."

Outside, Jody whistled shrilly to the dogs. "Come on up the hill," he commanded. The two dogs waved their tails and ran ahead. Along the roadside the sage had tender new tips. Jody tore off some pieces and rubbed them on his hands until the air was filled with the sharp wild smell. With a rush the dogs leaped from the road and yapped into the brush after a rabbit. That was the last Jody saw of them, for when they failed to catch the rabbit, they went back home.

Jody plodded on up the hill toward the ridge top. When he reached the little cleft where the road came through, the afternoon wind struck him and blew up his hair and ruffled his shirt. He looked down on the little hills and ridges below and then out at the huge green Salinas Valley. He could see the white town of Salinas far out in the flat and the flash of its windows under the waning sun. Directly below him, in an oak tree, a crow congress had convened. The tree was black with crows all cawing at once.

The Jody's eyes followed the wagon road down from the ridge where he stood, and lost it behind a hill, and picked it up again on the other side. On that distant stretch he saw a cart slowly pulled by a bay horse. It disappeared behind the hill. Jody sat down on the ground and watched the place where the cart would reappear again. The wind sang on the hilltops and the puff-ball clouds hurried eastward.

Then the cart came into sight and stopped. A man dressed in black dismounted from the seat and walked to the horse's head. Although it was so far away, Jody knew he had unhooked the check-rein, for the horse's head dropped forward. The horse moved on, and the man walked slowly up the hill beside it. Jody gave a glad cry and ran down the road toward them. The squirrels bumped along off the road, and a road-runner flirted its tail and raced over the edge of the hill and sailed out like a glider.

Jody tried to leap into the middle of his shadow at every step. A stone rolled under his foot and he went down. Around a little bend he raced, and there, a short distance ahead, were his grandfather and the cart. The boy dropped from his unseemly running and approached at a dignified walk.

The horse plodded stumble-footedly up the hill and the old man walked beside it. In the lowering sun there giant shadows flickered darkly behind them. The grandfather was dressed in a black broadcloth suit and he wore kid congress gaiters[1] and a black tie on a short, hard collar. He carried his black slouch hat in his hand. His white beard was cropped close and his white eyebrows overhung his eyes like mustaches. The blue eyes were sternly merry. About the whole face and figure there was a granite dignity, so that every motion seemed an impossible thing. Once at rest, it seemed the old man would be stone, would never move again. His steps were slow and certain. Once made, no step could ever be retraced; once headed in a direction, the path would never bend nor the pace increase nor slow.

When Jody appeared around the bend, Grandfather waved his hat slowly in welcome, and he called, "Why, Jody! Come down to meet me, have you?"

Jody sidled near and turned and matched his step to the old man's step and stiffened his body and dragged his heels a little. "Yes, sir," he said. "We got your letter only today."

"Should have been here yesterday," said Grandfather. "It certainly should. How are all the folks?"

"They're fine, sir." He hesitated and then suggested shyly, "Would you like to come on a mouse hunt tomorrow, sir?"

---

1. High-topped shoes, or spats. Grandfather is dressed quite formally, in keeping with his old-fashioned sense of dignity.

"Mouse hunt, Jody?" Grandfather chuckled. "Have the people of this generation come down to hunting mice? They aren't very strong, the new people, but I hardly thought mice would be game for them."

"No, sir. It's just play. The haystack's gone. I'm going to drive out the mice to the dogs. And you can watch, or even beat the hay a little."

The stern, merry eyes turned down on him. "I see. You don't eat them, then. You haven't come to that yet."

Jody explained, "The dogs eat them, sir. It wouldn't be much like hunting Indians, I guess."

"No, not much—but then later, when the troops were hunting Indians and shooting children and burning teepees, it wasn't much different from your mouse hunt."

They topped the rise and started down into the ranch-cup, and they lost the sun from their shoulders. "You've grown," Grandfather said. "Nearly an inch, I should say."

"More" Jody boasted. "Where they mark me on the door, I'm up more than an inch since Thanksgiving even."

Grandfather's rich throaty voice said, "Maybe you're getting too much water and turning to pith and stalk. Wait until you head out, and then we'll see."

Jody looked quickly into the old man's face to see whether his feelings should be hurt, but there was no will to injure, no punishing nor putting-in-your-place light in the keen blue eyes. "We might kill a pig," Jody suggested.

"Oh, no! I couldn't let you do that. You're just humoring me. It isn't the time and you know it."

"You know Riley, the big boar, sir?"

"Yes, I remember Riley well."

"Well, Riley ate a hole into that same haystack, and it fell down on him and smothered him."

"Pigs do that when they can," said Grandfather.

"Riley was a nice pig, for a boar, sir. I rode him sometimes, and he didn't mind."

A door slammed at the house below them, and they saw Jody's mother standing on the porch waving her apron in welcome. And they saw Carl Tiflin walking up from the barn to be at the house for the arrival.

The sun had disappeared from the hills by now. The blue smoke from the house chimney hung in flat layers in the purpling ranch-cup. The puff-ball clouds, dropped by the falling wind, hung listlessly in the sky.

Billy Buck came out of the bunkhouse and flung a wash basin of soapy water on the ground. He had been shaving in mid-week, for Billy held Grandfather in reverence, and Grandfather said that Billy was one of the few men of the new generation who had not gone soft. Although Billy was in middle age, Grandfather considered him a boy. Now Billy was hurrying toward the house too.

When Jody and Grandfather arrived, the three were waiting for them in front of the yard gate.

Carl said, "Hello, sir. We've been looking for you."

Mrs. Tiflin kissed Grandfather on the side of his beard, and stood still while his big hand patted her shoulder. Billy shook hands solemnly, grinning under his straw mustache. "I'll put up your horse," said Billy, and he led the rig away.

Grandfather watched him go, and then, turning back to the group, he said as he had said a hundred times before, "There's a good boy. I knew his father, old Mule-tail Buck. I never knew why they called him Mule-tail except he packed mules."

Mrs. Tiflin turned and led the way into the house. "How long are you going to stay, Father? Your letter didn't say."

"Well, I don't know. I thought I'd stay about two weeks. But I never stay as long as I think I'm going to."

In a short while they were sitting at the white oilcloth table eating their supper. The lamp with the tin reflector hung over the table. Outside the dining-room windows the big moths battered softly against the glass.

Grandfather cut his steak into tiny pieces and chewed slowly. "I'm hungry," he said. "Driving out here got my appetite up. It's like when we were crossing. We all got so hungry every night we could hardly wait to let the meat get done. I could eat about five pounds of buffalo meat every night."

"It's moving around does it," said Billy. "My father was a government packer. I helped him when I was a kid. Just the two of us could about clean up a deer's ham."

"I knew your father, Billy," said Grandfather. "A fine man he was. They called him Mule-tail Buck. I don't know why except he packed mules."

"That was it," Bill agreed. "He packed mules."

Grandfather put down his knife and fork and looked around the table. "I remember one time we ran out of meat—" His voice dropped to a curious low sing-song, dropped into a tonal groove the story had worn for itself. "There was no buffalo, no antelope, not even rabbits. The hunters couldn't even shoot a coyote. That was the time for the leader to be on the watch. I was the leader, and I kept my eyes open. Know why? Well, just the minute the people began to get hungry they'd start slaughtering the team oxen. Do you believe that? I've heard of parties that just ate up their draft cattle. Started from the middle and worked toward the ends. Finally they'd eat the lead pair, and then the wheelers. The leader of a party had to keep them from doing that."

In some manner a big moth got into the room and circled the hanging kerosene lamp. Billy got up and tried to clap it between his hands. Carl struck with a cupped palm and caught the moth and broke it. He walked to the window and dropped it out.

"As I was saying," Grandfather began again, but Carl interrupted him. "You'd better eat some more meat. All the rest of us are ready for our pudding."

Jody saw a flash of anger in his mother's eyes. Grandfather picked up his knife and fork. "I'm pretty hungry, all right," he said. "I'll tell you about that later."

When supper was over, when the family and Billy Buck sat in front of the fireplace in the other room, Jody anxiously watched Grandfather. He saw the signs he knew. The bearded head leaned forward; the eyes lost their sternness and looked wonderingly into the fire; the big lean fingers laced themselves on the black knees. "I wonder," he began, "I just wonder whether I ever told you how those thieving Piutes drove off thirty-five of our horses."

"I think you did," Carl interrupted. "Wasn't it just before you went up into the Tahoe country?"

Grandfather turned quickly toward his son-in-law. "That's right. I guess I must have told you that story."

"Lots of times," Carl said cruelly, and he avoided his wife's eyes. But he felt the angry eyes on him, and he said, " 'Course I'd like to hear it again."

Grandfather looked back at the fire. His fingers unlaced and laced again. Jody knew how he felt, how his insides were collapsed and empty. Hadn't Jody been called a Big-Britches that very afternoon? He arose to heroism and opened himself to the term Big-Britches again. "Tell about Indians," he said softly.

Grandfather's eyes grew stern again. "Boys always want to hear about Indians. It was a job for men, but boys want to hear about it. Well, let's see. Did I ever tell you how I wanted each wagon to carry a long iron plate?"

Everyone but Jody remained silent. Jody said, "No. You didn't."

"Well, when the Indians attacked, we always put the wagons in a circle and fought from between the wheels. I thought that if every wagon carried a long plate with rifle holes, the men could stand the plates on the outside of the wheels when the wagons were in the circle and they would be protected. It would save lives and that would make up for the extra weight of the iron. But of course the party wouldn't do it. No party had done it before and they couldn't see why they should go to the expense. They lived to regret it, too."

Jody looked at his mother, and knew from her expression that she was not listening at all. Carl picked at a callus on his thumb and Billy Buck watched a spider crawling up the wall.

Grandfather's tone dropped into its narrative groove again. Jody knew in advance exactly what words would fall. The story droned on, speeded up for the attack, grew sad over the wounds, struck a dirge at the burials on the great plains. Jody sat quietly watching Grandfather. The stern blue eyes were detached. He looked as though he were not very interested in the story himself.

When it was finished, when the pause had been politely respected as the frontier of the story, Billy Buck stood up and stretched and hitched his trousers. "I guess I'll turn in," he said. Then he faced Grandfather. "I've got an old powder horn and a cap and ball pistol down to the bunkhouse. Did I ever show them to you?"

Grandfather nodded slowly. "Yes, I think you did, Billy. Reminds me of a pistol I had when I was leading the people across." Billy stood politely until the story was done, and then he said, "Good night," and went out of the house.

Carl Tiflin tried to turn the conversation then. "How's the country between here and Monterey?[2] I've heard it's pretty dry."

"It is dry," said Grandfather. "There's not a drop of water in the Laguna Seca.[3] But it's a long pull from '87. The whole country was powder then, and in '61 I believe all the coyotes starved to death. We had fifteen inches of rain this year."

"Yes, but it all came too early. We could do with some now." Carl's eye fell on Jody. "Hadn't you better be getting to bed?"

---

2. Peninsula jutting into the Pacific Ocean south of San Francisco.
3. Dry Lagoon (Spanish).

Jody stood up obediently. "Can I kill the mice in the old haystack, sir?"

"Mice? Oh! Sure, kill them all off. Billy said there isn't any good hay left."

Jody exchanged a secret and satisfying look with Grandfather. "I'll kill every one tomorrow," he promised.

Jody lay in his bed and thought of the impossible world of Indians and buffaloes, a world that had ceased to be forever. He wished he could have been living in the heroic time, but he knew he was not of heroic timber. No one living now, save possibly Billy Buck, was worthy to do the things that had been done. A race of giants had lived then, fearless men, men of a staunchness unknown in this day. Jody thought of the wide plains and of the wagons moving across like centipedes. He thought of Grandfather on a huge white horse, marshaling the people. Across his mind marched the great phantoms, and they marched off the earth and they were gone.

He came back to the ranch for a moment, then. He heard the dull rushing sound that space and silence make. He heard one of the dogs, out in the doghouse, scratching a flea and bumping his elbow against the floor with every stroke. Then the wind arose again and the black cypress groaned and Jody went to sleep.

He was up half an hour before the triangle sounded for breakfast. His mother was rattling the stove to make the flames roar when Jody went through the kitchen. "You're up early," she said. "Where are you going?"

"Out to get a good stick. We're going to kill the mice today."

"Who is 'we'?"

"Why, Grandfather and I."

"So you've got him in it. You always like to have someone in with you in case there's blame to share."

"I'll be right back," said Jody. "I just want to have a good stick ready for after breakfast."

He closed the screen door after him and went out into the cool blue morning. The birds were noisy in the dawn and the ranch cats came down from the hill like blunt snakes. They had been hunting gophers in the dark, and although the four cats were full of gopher meat, they sat in a semi-circle at the back door and mewed piteously for milk. Doubletree Mutt and Smasher moved sniffing along the edge of the brush, performing the duty with rigid ceremony, but when Jody whistled, their heads jerked up and their tails waved. They plunged down to him, wriggling their skins and yawning. Jody patted their heads seriously, and moved on to the weathered scrap pile. He selected an old broom handle and a short piece of inch-square scrap wood. From his pocket he took a shoelace and tied the ends of the sticks loosely together to make a flail. He whistled his new weapon through the air and struck the ground experimentally, while the dogs leaped aside and whined with apprehension.

Jody turned and started down past the house toward the old haystack ground to look over the field of slaughter, but Billy Buck, sitting patiently on the back steps, called to him, "You better come back. It's only a couple of minutes till breakfast."

Jody changed his course and moved toward the house. He leaned his flail against the steps. "That's to drive the mice out," he said. "I'll bet they're fat. I'll bet they don't know what's going to happen to them today."

"No, nor you either," Billy remarked philosophically, "nor me, nor anyone."

Jody was staggered by this thought. He knew it was true. His imagination twitched away from the mouse hunt. Then his mother came out on the back porch and struck the triangle, and all thoughts fell in a heap.

Grandfather hadn't appeared at the table when they sat down. Billy nodded at his empty chair. "He's all right? He isn't sick?"

"He takes a long time to dress," said Mrs. Tiflin. "He combs his whiskers and rubs up his shoes and brushes his clothes."

Carl scattered sugar on his mush. "A man that's led a wagon train across the plains has got to be pretty careful how he dresses."

Mrs. Tiflin turned on him. "Don't do that, Carl! Please don't!" There was more of threat than of request in her tone. And the threat irritated Carl.

"Well, how many times do I have to listen to the story of the iron plates, and the thirty-five horses? That time's done. Why can't he forget it, now it's done?" He grew angrier while he talked, and his voice rose. "Why does he have to tell them over and over? He came across the plains. All right! Now it's finished. Nobody wants to hear about it over and over."

The door into the kitchen closed softly. The four at the table sat frozen. Carl laid his mush spoon on the table and touched his chin with his fingers.

Then the kitchen door opened and Grandfather walked in. His mouth smiled tightly and his eyes were squinted. "Good morning," he said, and he sat down and looked at his mush dish.

Carl could not leave it there. "Did—did you hear what I said?"

Grandfather jerked a little nod.

"I don't know what got into me, sir. I didn't mean it. I was just being funny."

Jody glanced in shame at his mother, and he saw that she was looking at Carl, and that she wasn't breathing. It was an awful thing that he was doing. He was tearing himself to pieces to talk like that. It was a terrible thing to him to retract a word, but to retract it in shame was infinitely worse.

Grandfather looked sidewise. "I'm trying to get right side up," he said gently. "I'm not being mad. I don't mind what you said, but it might be true, and I would mind that."

"It isn't true," said Carl. "I'm not feeling well this morning. I'm sorry I said it."

"Don't be sorry, Carl. An old man doesn't see things sometimes. Maybe you're right. The crossing is finished. Maybe it should be forgotten, now it's done."

Carl got up from the table. "I've had enough to eat. I'm going to work. Take your time, Billy!" He walked quickly out of the dining-room. Billy gulped the rest of his food and followed soon after. But Jody could not leave his chair.

"Won't you tell any more stories?" Jody asked.

"Why, sure I'll tell them, but only when—I'm sure people want to hear them."

"I like to hear them, sir."

"Oh! Of course you do, but you're a little boy. It was a job for men, but only little boys like to hear about it."

Jody got up from his place. "I'll wait outside for you, sir. I've got a good stick for those mice."

He waited by the gate until the old man came out on the porch. "Let's go down and kill the mice now," Jody called.

"I think I'll just sit in the sun, Jody. You go kill the mice."

"You can use my stick if you like."

"No, I'll just sit here a while."

Jody turned disconsolately away, and walked down toward the old haystack. He tried to whip up his enthusiasm with thoughts of the fat juicy mice. He beat the ground with his flail. The dogs coaxed and whined about him, but he could not go. Back at the house he could see Grandfather sitting on the porch, looking small and thin and black.

Jody gave up and went to sit on the steps at the old man's feet.

"Back already? Did you kill the mice?"

"No, sir. I'll kill them some other day."

The morning flies buzzed close to the ground and the ants dashed about in front of the steps. The heavy smell of sage slipped down the hill. The porch boards grew warm in the sunshine.

Jody hardly knew when Grandfather started to talk. "I shouldn't stay here, feeling the way I do." He examined his strong old hands. "I feel as though the crossing wasn't worth doing." His eyes moved up the side-hill and stopped on a motionless hawk perched on a dead limb. "I tell those old stories, but they're not what I want to tell. I only know how I want people to feel when I tell them.

"It wasn't Indians that were important, nor adventures, nor even getting out here. It was a whole bunch of people made into one big crawling beast. And I was the head. It was westering and westering. Every man wanted something for himself, but the big beast that was all of them wanted only westering. I was the leader, but if I hadn't been there, someone else would have been the head. The thing had to have a head.

"Under the little bushes the shadows were black at white noonday. When we saw the mountains at last, we cried—all of us. But it wasn't getting here that mattered, it was movement and westering.

"We carried life out here and set it down the way those ants carry eggs. And I was the leader. The westering was as big as God, and the slow steps that made the movement piled up and piled up until the continent was crossed.

"Then we came down to the sea, and it was done." He stopped and wiped his eyes until the rims were red. "That's what I should be telling instead of stories."

When Jody spoke, Grandfather started and looked down at him. "Maybe I could lead the people some day," Jody said.

The old man smiled. "There's no place to go. There's the ocean to stop you. There's a line of old men along the shore hating the ocean because it stopped them."

"In boats I might, sir."

"No place to go, Jody. Every place is taken. But that's not the worst—no, not the worst. Westering has died out of the people. Westering isn't a hunger any more. It's all done. Your father is right. It is finished." He laced his fingers on his knee and looked at them.

Jody felt very sad. "If you'd like a glass of lemonade I could make it for you."

Grandfather was about to refuse, and then he saw Jody's face. "That would be nice," he said. "Yes, it would be nice to drink a lemonade."

Jody ran into the kitchen where his mother was wiping the last of the breakfast dishes. "Can I have a lemon to make a lemonade for Grandfather?"

His mother mimicked—"And another lemon to make a lemonade for you."
"No, ma'am. I don't want one."
"Jody! You're sick!" Then she stopped suddenly. "Take a lemon out of the cooler," she said softly. "Here, I'll reach the squeezer down to you."

1945

COUNTEE CULLEN
1903–1946

More than most poets of the Harlem Renaissance, Countee Cullen valued traditional poetic forms in English—the sonnet, rhymed couplets, and quatrains—over modernist free verse or rhythms suggested by jazz and popular culture. Never one to shy away from controversy, Cullen prefaced his important anthology of African American poetry, *Caroling Dusk* (1927), with the assertion, "As heretical as it may sound, there is the probability that Negro poets, dependent as they are on the English language, may have more to gain from the rich background of English and American poetry than from any nebulous atavistic yearnings toward an African inheritance." Cullen demanded that black poets be considered as American poets, ultimately without any special racial designation. Nevertheless, the titles of his books of poetry—*Color* (1925), *Copper Sun* (1927), *The Ballad of the Brown Girl* (1928)—showed that, like Claude MacKay and Jean Toomer, he felt a responsibility to write about being black even if he did so in modes outside of black folk traditions. Although he clashed with a number of his contemporaries in the Harlem Renaissance, Cullen could also be generous to black writers whose poetics differed from his. What mattered to Cullen was appreciating the full range of black literary writing, a range as great, he insisted, as that found among white poets in English, and resisting every "attempt to corral the ebony muse into some definite mold" to which all black writers should conform.

Although Cullen's birthplace and early years are obscure, he was adopted at some point in his childhood by a Harlem-based minister and given a good education, first in New York public schools and then at New York University, where he received his B.A. in 1925, and at Harvard, where he took an M.A. in 1926. In high school, Cullen earned a city-wide poetry prize for "I Have a Rendezvous with Life," a rejoinder to Alan Seeger's sentimental World War I poem. His first book of poems, *Color*, appeared in his senior year at college; it established him as the "black Keats," a prodigy.

From 1926 to 1928, Cullen was assistant editor at the important black journal *Opportunity*, for which he also wrote a feature column, "The Dark Tower." In 1928 he married Nina Yolande Du Bois, the daughter of W. E. B. Du Bois, and won a Guggenheim fellowship that took him to Paris and enabled him to complete another book of poems, *The Black Christ* (1929). His marriage quickly disintegrated, however, over Cullen's attraction to men, and the couple was divorced in 1930. Neither *The Black Christ* nor the novel that followed, *One Way to Heaven* (1932), earned the acclaim of Cullen's earlier books. He spent the last years of his life teaching at New York's Frederick Douglass Junior High School, where his pupils included the future novelist James Baldwin. With the revival of scholarly interest in the Harlem Renaissance, Cullen's distinctive combination of traditionalist poetic skill with acerbic self-questioning on matters of racism and racial identity has once again brought his poetry to critical attention.

Yet Do I Marvel

I doubt not God is good, well-meaning, kind,
And did He stoop to quibble could tell why
The little buried mole continues blind,
Why flesh that mirrors Him must some day die,
Make plain the reason tortured Tantalus   5
Is baited by the fickle fruit, declare
If merely brute caprice dooms Sisyphus[1]
To struggle up a never-ending stair.
Inscrutable His ways are, and immune
To catechism by a mind too strewn   10
With petty cares to slightly understand
What awful brain compels His awful hand.
Yet do I marvel at this curious thing:
To make a poet black, and bid him sing!

                                                                    1925

Incident

Once riding in old Baltimore,
    Heart-filled, head-filled with glee,
I saw a Baltimorean
    Keep looking straight at me.

Now I was eight and very small,   5
    And he was no whit bigger,
And so I smiled, but he poked out
    His tongue, and called me, "Nigger."

I saw the whole of Baltimore
    From May until December;   10
Of all the things that happened there
    That's all that I remember.

                                                                    1925

Heritage

What is Africa to me:
Copper sun or scarlet sea,
Jungle star or jungle track,
Strong bronzed men, or regal black
Women from whose loins I sprang   5

---

1. Tantalus and Sisyphus are figures in Greek mythology who were punished in Hades. Tantalus was offered food and water that was then instantly snatched away. Sisyphus had to roll a heavy stone to the top of a hill and, after it rolled back down, repeat the ordeal perpetually.

When the birds of Eden sang?
One three centuries removed
From the scenes his fathers loved,
Spicy grove, cinnamon tree,
What is Africa to me?   10

So I lie, who all day long
Want no sound except the song
Sung by wild barbaric birds
Goading massive jungle herds,
Juggernauts[1] of flesh that pass   15
Trampling tall defiant grass
Where young forest lovers lie,
Plighting troth beneath the sky.
So I lie, who always hear,
Though I cram against my ear   20
Both my thumbs, and keep them there,
Great drums throbbing through the air.
So I lie, whose fount of pride,
Dear distress, and joy allied,
Is my somber flesh and skin,   25
With the dark blood dammed within
Like great pulsing tides of wine
That, I fear, must burst the fine
Channels of the chafing net
Where they surge and foam and fret.   30

Africa? A book one thumbs
Listlessly, till slumber comes.
Unremembered are her bats
Circling through the night, her cats
Crouching in the river reeds,   35
Stalking gentle flesh that feeds
By the river brink; no more
Does the bugle-throated roar
Cry that monarch claws have leapt
From the scabbards where they slept.   40
Silver snakes that once a year
Doff the lovely coats you wear,
Seek no covert in your fear
Lest a mortal eye should see;
What's your nakedness to me?   45
Here no leprous flowers rear
Fierce corollas[2] in the air;
Here no bodies sleek and wet,
Dripping mingled rain and sweat,
Tread the savage measures of   50

---

1. The juggernaut is a sacred Hindu idol dragged on a huge car in the path of which devotees were believed to throw themselves—hence any power demanding blind sacrifice, here spliced with the image of elephants.
2. The whorl of petals forming the inner envelope of a flower.

Jungle boys and girls in love.[3]
What is last year's snow to me,
Last year's anything? The tree
Budding yearly must forget
How its past arose or set—   55
Bough and blossom, flower, fruit,
Even what shy bird with mute
Wonder at her travail there,
Meekly labored in its hair.
One three centuries removed   60
From the scenes his fathers loved,
Spicy grove, cinnamon tree,
What is Africa to me?

So I lie, who find no peace
Night or day, no slight release   65
From the unremittant beat
Made by cruel padded feet
Walking through my body's street.
Up and down they go, and back,
Treading out a jungle track.   70
So I lie, who never quite
Safely sleep from rain at night—
I can never rest at all
When the rain begins to fall;
Like a soul gone mad with pain   75
I must match its weird refrain;
Ever must I twist and squirm,
Writhing like a baited worm,
While its primal measures drip
Through my body, crying, "Strip!   80
Doff this new exuberance.
Come and dance the Lover's Dance!"
In an old remembered way
Rain works on me night and day.

Quaint, outlandish heathen gods   85
Black men fashion out of rods,
Clay, and brittle bits of stone,
In a likeness like their own,
My conversion came high-priced;
I belong to Jesus Christ,   90
Preacher of humility;
Heathen gods are naught to me.

Father, Son, and Holy Ghost,
So I make an idle boast;
Jesus of the twice-turned cheek[4]   95

---

3. An echo of the lament "Where are the snows of yesteryear?" from "Grand Testament" by the 15th-century French poet François Villon.
4. In his Sermon on the Mount (Matthew 5.39), Jesus declared that when struck on the cheek, one should turn the other cheek rather than strike back.

Lamb of God, although I speak
With my mouth thus, in my heart
Do I play a double part.
Ever at Thy glowing altar
Must my heart grow sick and falter,   100
Wishing He I served were black,
Thinking then it would not lack
Precedent of pain to guide it,
Let who would or might deride it;
Surely then this flesh would know   105
Yours had borne a kindred woe.
Lord, I fashion dark gods, too,
Daring even to give You
Dark despairing features where,
Crowned with dark rebellious hair,   110
Patience wavers just so much as
Mortal grief compels, while touches
Quick and hot, of anger, rise
To smitten cheek and weary eyes.
Lord, forgive me if my need   115
Sometimes shapes a human creed.
All day long and all night through,
One thing only must I do:
Quench my pride and cool my blood,
Lest I perish in the flood.   120
Lest a hidden ember set
Timber that I thought was wet
Burning like the dryest flax,
Melting like the merest wax,
Lest the grave restore its dead.   125
Not yet has my heart or head
In the least way realized
They and I are civilized.

1925

RICHARD WRIGHT
1908–1960

With the 1940 publication of *Native Son* Richard Wright became the first African American author of a bestseller. *Native Son* is an uncompromising study of an African American underclass youth who is goaded to brutal violence by the oppression, hatred, and incomprehension of the white world. The sensational story disregarded conventional wisdom about how black authors should approach a white reading audience. Bigger Thomas, the main character, embodied everything that such an audience might fear and detest, but by situating the point of view within this character's consciousness Wright forced readers to see the world through Bigger's eyes and thus to understand him. The novel was structured like a hard-boiled detective story, contained layers of literary allusion and symbol, and combined Marxist social analysis with existential philosophy—in brief, it was at once a powerful social statement and a complex work of literary art.

Wright was born near Natchez, Mississippi. When he was five, his father abandoned the family—Wright, his younger brother, and his mother—and for the next ten years Wright was raised by a series of relatives in Mississippi. By 1925, when he went to Memphis on his own, he had moved twenty times. Extreme poverty, a constantly interrupted education that never went beyond junior high school, and the religious fundamentalism of his grandmother, along with the constant experiences of humiliation and hatred in a racially segregated South: all these contributed to Wright's growing sense that the hidden anger of black people was justified and that only by acknowledging and expressing it could they move beyond it. The title of *Native Son* made the point that the United States is as much the country of black as of white; the story showed that blacks had been deprived of their inheritance.

Two years after moving to Memphis, Wright went north to Chicago. There he took a series of odd jobs and then joined the WPA Writers' Project (a government project of the depression years to help support authors) as a writer of guidebooks and as a director of the Federal Negro Theater. He began to study Marxist theory, contributing poetry to leftist literary magazines and joining the Communist party in 1932. By 1935 he had become the center of a group of African American Chicago writers and had started to write fiction. He was influenced by the naturalistic fiction of James T. Farrell, whose study of sociology at the University of Chicago had helped give structure to his popular Studs Lonigan trilogy about working people of Irish descent.

Wright moved to New York in 1937 to write for the New York Writers' Project and as a reporter on the communist *Daily Worker*. In 1938 he published *Uncle Tom's Children*, a collection of four short stories. (An earlier novel, *Lawd Today*, was not published until after his death.) Set in the rural South, the stories center on racial conflict and physical violence. Wright's theme of the devastating effect of relentless, institutionalized hatred and humiliation on the black male's psyche was paramount in all of them.

After *Native Son*, Wright turned to autobiographical writings that eventuated in *Black Boy*, published in 1945. Many consider this to be his best book, and such writers as Ralph Ellison and James Baldwin took it as a model for their own work in the 1950s and 1960s. A communist activist in the early 1940s, Wright became increasingly disillusioned and broke completely with the party in 1944. Visiting France in 1946, he was warmly received by leading writers and philosophers. In 1947 he settled permanently in that country, where he was perceived from the first as one of the important experimental modernist prose writers and was ranked on a level with Hemingway, Fitzgerald, and Faulkner. An existential novel, *The Outsider* (1953), was followed by five more books: two novels and three collections of lectures, travel writings, and sociopolitical commentary. The collection *Eight Men*, from which the story printed here is taken, was the last literary project he worked on, and it appeared the year after his death.

Wright's immersion in Marxist doctrine gave him tools for representing society as divided into antagonistic classes and run for the benefit of the few. But in each of his works he portrays individuals who, no matter how they are deformed and brutalized by oppression and exploitation, retain a transcendent spark of selfhood. Ultimately, it is in this spark that Wright put his faith. His writing from first to last affirmed the dignity and humanity of society's outcasts without romanticizing them, and indicted those who had cast them out. As Ralph Ellison expressed it, Wright's example "converted the American Negro impulse toward self-annihilation and 'going underground' into a will to confront the world" and to "throw his findings unashamedly into the guilty conscience of America."

The text was first published in *Harper's Bazaar* (1939) under the title "Almos' a Man." Under its present title it appeared in *Eight Men* (1961), a posthumous collection of Wright's short fiction.

The Man Who Was Almost a Man

Dave struck out across the fields, looking homeward through paling light. Whut's the use talkin wid em niggers in the field? Anyhow, his mother was putting supper on the table. Them niggers can't understan nothing. One of these days he was going to get a gun and practice shooting, then they couldn't talk to him as though he were a little boy. He slowed, looking at the ground. Shucks, Ah ain scareda them even ef they are biggern me! Aw, Ah know whut Ahma do. Ahm going by ol Joe's sto n git that Sears Roebuck catlog n look at them guns. Mebbe Ma will lemme buy one when she gits mah pay from ol man Hawkins. Ahma beg her t gimme some money. Ahm ol ernough to hava gun. Ahm seventeen. Almost a man. He strode, feeling his long loose-jointed limbs. Shucks, a man oughta hava little gun aftah he done worked hard all day.

He came in sight of Joe's store. A yellow lantern glowed on the front porch. He mounted steps and went through the screen door, hearing it bang behind him. There was a strong smell of coal oil and mackerel fish. He felt very confident until he saw fat Joe walk in through the rear door, then his courage began to ooze.

"Howdy, Dave! Whutcha want?"

"How yuh, Mistah Joe? Aw, Ah don wanna buy nothing. Ah jus wanted t see ef yuhd lemme look at tha catlog erwhile."

"Sure! You wanna see it here?"

"Nawsuh. Ah wans t take it home wid me. Ah'll bring it back termorrow when Ah come in from the fiels."

"You plannin on buying something?"

"Yessuh."

"Your ma lettin you have your own money now?"

"Shucks. Mistah Joe, Ahm gittin t be a man like anybody else!"

Joe laughed and wiped his greasy white face with a red bandanna.

"Whut you plannin on buyin?"

Dave looked at the floor, scratched his head, scratched his thigh, and smiled. Then he looked up shyly.

"Ah'll tell yuh, Mistah Joe, ef yuh promise yuh won't tell."

"I promise."

"Waal, Ahma buy a gun."

"A gun? What you want with a gun?"

"Ah wanna keep it."

"You ain't nothing but a boy. You don't need a gun."

"Aw, lemme have the catlog, Mistah Joe. Ah'll bring it back."

Joe walked through the rear door. Dave was elated. He looked around at barrels of sugar and flour. He heard Joe coming back. He craned his neck to see if he were bringing the book. Yeah, he's got it. Gawddog, he's got it!

"Here, but be sure you bring it back. It's the only one I got."

"Sho, Mistah Joe."

"Say, if you wanna buy a gun, why don't you buy one from me? I gotta gun to sell."

"Will it shoot?"

"Sure it'll shoot."

"Whut kind is it?"

"Oh, it's kinda old . . . a left-hand Wheeler. A pistol. A big one."

"Is it got bullets in it?"

"It's loaded."

"Kin Ah see it?"

"Where's your money?"

"What yuh wan fer it?"

"I'll let you have it for two dollars."

"Just two dollahs? Shucks, Ah could buy tha when Ah git mah pay."

"I'll have it here when you want it."

"Awright, suh. Ah be in fer it."

He went through the door, hearing it slam again behind him. Ahma git some money from Ma n buy me a gun! Only two dollars! He tucked the thick catalogue under his arm and hurried.

"Where yuh been, boy?" His mother held a steaming dish of black-eyed peas.

"Aw, Ma, Ah just stopped down the road t talk wid the boys."

"Yuh know bettah t keep suppah waitin."

He sat down, resting the catalogue on the edge of the table.

"Yuh git up from there and git to the well n wash yosef! Ah ain feedin no hogs in mah house!"

She grabbed his shoulder and pushed him. He stumbled out of the room, then came back to get the catalogue.

"Whut this?"

"Aw, Ma, it's jusa catlog."

"Who yuh git it from?"

"From Joe, down at the sto."

"Waal, thas good. We kin use it in the outhouse."

"Naw, Ma." He grabbed for it. "Gimme ma catlog, Ma."

She held onto it and glared at him.

"Quit hollerin at me! Whut's wrong wid yuh? Yuh crazy?"

"But Ma, please. It ain mine! It's Joe's! He tol me t bring it back t im termorrow."

She gave up the book. He stumbled down the back steps, hugging the thick book under his arm. When he had splashed water on his face and hands, he groped back to the kitchen and fumbled in a corner for the towel. He bumped into a chair; it clattered to the floor. The catalogue sprawled at his feet. When he had dried his eyes he snatched up the book and held it again under his arm. His mother stood watching him.

"Now, ef yuh gonna act a fool over that ol book, Ah'll take it n burn it up."

"Naw, Ma, please."

"Waal, set down n be still!"

He sat down and drew the oil lamp close. He thumbed page after page, unaware of the food his mother set on the table. His father came in. Then his small brother.

"Whutcha got there, Dave?" his father asked.

"Jusa catlog," he answered, not looking up.

"Yeah, here they is!" His eyes glowed at blue-and-black revolvers. He glanced up, feeling sudden guilt. His father was watching him. He eased the book under the table and rested it on his knees. After the blessing was asked, he ate. He scooped up peas and swallowed fat meat without chewing. Buttermilk helped to wash it down. He did not want to mention money before his father. He would do much better by cornering his mother when she was alone. He looked at his father uneasily out of the edge of his eye.

"Boy, how come yuh don quit foolin wid tha book n eat yo suppah?"

"Yessuh."

"How you n ol man Hawkins gitten erlong?"

"Suh?"

"Can't yuh hear? Why don yuh lissen? Ah ast yu how wuz yuh n ol man Hawkins gittin erlong?"

"Oh, swell, Pa. Ah plows mo lan than anybody over there."

"Waal, yuh oughta keep yo mind on whut yuh doin."

"Yessuh."

He poured his plate full of molasses and sopped it up slowly with a chunk of cornbread. When his father and brother had left the kitchen, he still sat and looked again at the guns in the catalogue, longing to muster courage enough to present his case to his mother. Lawd, ef Ah only had tha pretty one! He could almost feel the slickness of the weapon with his fingers. If he had a gun like that he would polish it and keep it shining so it would never rust. N Ah'd keep it loaded, by Gawd!

"Ma?" His voice was hesitant.

"Hunh?"

"Ol man Hawkins give yuh mah money yit?"

"Yeah, but ain no usa yuh thinking bout throwin nona it erway. Ahm keepin tha money sos yuh kin have cloes t go to school this winter."

He rose and went to her side with the open catalogue in his palms. She was washing dishes, her head bent low over a pan. Shyly he raised the book. When he spoke, his voice was husky, faint.

"Ma, Gawd knows Ah wans one of these."

"One of whut?" she asked, not raising her eyes.

"One of these," he said again, not daring even to point. She glanced up at the page, then at him with wide eyes.

"Nigger, is yuh gone plumb crazy?"

"Aw, Ma."

"Git outta here! Don yuh talk t me bout no gun! Yuh a fool!"

"Ma, Ah kin buy one fer two dollahs."

"Not ef Ah knows it, yuh ain!"

"But yuh promised me one."

"Ah don care whut Ah promised! Yuh ain nothing but a boy yit!"

"Ma, ef yuh lemme buy one Ah'll *never* ast yuh fer nothing no mo."

"Ah tol yuh t git outta here! Yuh ain gonna toucha penny of tha money fer no gun! Thas how come Ah has Mistah Hawkins t pay yo wages t me, cause Ah knows yuh ain got no sense."

"But, Ma, we needa gun. Pa ain got no gun. We needa gun in the house. Yuh kin never tell whut might happen."

"Now don yuh try to maka fool outta me, boy! Ef we did hava gun, yuh wouldn't have it!"

He laid the catalogue down and slipped his arm around her waist.

"Aw, Ma, Ah done worked hard alla summer n ain ast yuh fer nothin, is Ah, now?"

"Thas whut yuh spose t do!"

"But Ma, Ah wans a gun. Yuh kin lemme have two dollahs outta mah money. Please, Ma. I kin give it to Pa . . . Please, Ma! Ah loves yuh, Ma."

When she spoke her voice came soft and low.

"What yuh wan wida gun, Dave? Yuh don need no gun. Yuh'll git in trouble. N ef yo pa jus thought Ah let yuh have money t buy a gun he'd hava fit."

"Ah'll hide it, Ma. It ain but two dollahs."

"Lawd, chil, whut's wrong wid yuh?"

"Ain nothing wrong, Ma. Ahm almos a man now. Ah wans a gun."

"Who gonna sell yuh a gun?"

"Ol Joe at the sto."

"N it don cos but two dollahs?"

"Thas all, Ma. Just two dollahs. Please, Ma."

She was stacking the plates away; her hands moved slowly, reflectively. Dave kept an anxious silence. Finally, she turned to him.

"Ah'll let yuh git tha gun ef yuh promise me one thing."

"Whut's tha, Ma?"

"Yuh bring it straight back t me, yuh hear? It be fer Pa."

"Yessum! Lemme go now, Ma."

She stooped, turned slightly to one side, raised the hem of her dress, rolled down the top of her stocking, and came up with a slender wad of bills.

"Here," she said. "Lawd knows yuh don need no gun. But yer pa does. Yuh bring it right back t me, yuh hear? Ahma put it up. Now ef yuh don, Ahma have yuh pa pick yuh so hard yuh won fergit it."

"Yessum."

He took the money, ran down the steps, and across the yard.

"Dave! Yuuuuuh Daaaaave!"

He heard, but he was not going to stop now. "Naw, Lawd!"

The first movement he made the following morning was to reach under his pillow for the gun. In the gray light of dawn he held it loosely, feeling a sense of power. Could kill a man with a gun like this. Kill anybody, black or white. And if he were holding his gun in his hand, nobody could run over him; they would have to respect him. It was a big gun, with a long barrel and a heavy handle. He raised and lowered it in his hand, marveling at its weight.

He had not come straight home with it as his mother had asked; instead he had stayed out in the fields, holding the weapon in his hand, aiming it now and then at some imaginary foe. But he had not fired it; he had been afraid that his father might hear. Also he was not sure he knew how to fire it.

To avoid surrendering the pistol he had not come into the house until he knew that they were all asleep. When his mother had tiptoed to his bedside late that night and demanded the gun, he had first played possum; then he had told her that the gun was hidden outdoors, that he would bring it to her in the morning. Now he lay turning it slowly in his hands. He broke it, took out the cartridges, felt them, and then put them back.

He slid out of bed, got a long strip of old flannel from a trunk, wrapped the gun in it, and tied it to his naked thigh while it was still loaded. He did not go in to breakfast. Even though it was not yet daylight, he started for Jim Hawkins' plantation. Just as the sun was rising he reached the barns where the mules and plows were kept.

"Hey! That you, Dave?"

He turned. Jim Hawkins stood eying him suspiciously.

"What're yuh doing here so early?"

"Ah didn't know Ah wuz gittin up so early, Mistah Hawkins. Ah wuz fixin t hitch up ol Jenny n take her t the fiels."

"Good. Since you're so early, how about plowing that stretch down by the woods?"

"Suits me, Mistah Hawkins."

"O.K. Go to it!"

He hitched Jenny to a plow and started across the fields. Hot dog! This was just what he wanted. If he could get down by the woods, he could shoot his gun and nobody would hear. He walked behind the plow, hearing the traces creaking, feeling the gun tied tight to his thigh.

When he reached the woods, he plowed two whole rows before he decided to take out the gun. Finally, he stopped, looked in all directions, then untied the gun and held it in his hand. He turned to the mule and smiled.

"Know whut this is, Jenny? Naw, yuh wouldn know! Yuhs jusa ol mule! Anyhow, this is a gun, n it kin shoot, by Gawd!"

He held the gun at arm's length. Whut t hell, Ahma shoot this thing! He looked at Jenny again.

"Lissen here, Jenny! When Ah pull this ol trigger, Ah don wan yuh t run n acka fool now!"

Jenny stood with head down, her short ears pricked straight. Dave walked off about twenty feet, held the gun far out from him at arm's length, and turned his head. Hell, he told himself, Ah ain afraid. The gun felt loose in his fingers; he waved it wildly for a moment. Then he shut his eyes and tightened his forefinger. Bloom! A report half deafened him and he thought his right hand was torn from his arm. He heard Jenny whinnying and galloping over the field, and he found himself on his knees, squeezing his fingers hard between his legs. His hand was numb; he jammed it into his mouth, trying to warm it, trying to stop the pain. The gun lay at his feet. He did not quite know what had happened. He stood up and stared at the gun as though it were a living thing. He gritted his teeth and kicked the gun. Yuh almos broke mah arm! He turned to look for Jenny; she was far over the fields, tossing her head and kicking wildly.

"Hol on there, ol mule!"

When he caught up with her she stood trembling, walling her big white eyes at him. The plow was far away; the traces had broken. Then Dave stopped short, looking, not believing. Jenny was bleeding. Her left side was red and wet with blood. He went closer. Lawd, have mercy! Wondah did Ah shoot this mule? He grabbed for Jenny's mane. She flinched, snorted, whirled, tossing her head.

"Hol on now! Hol on."

Then he saw the hole in Jenny's side, right between the ribs. It was round, wet, red. A crimson stream streaked down the front leg, flowing fast. Good Gawd! Ah wuzn't shootin at tha mule. He felt panic. He knew he had to stop that blood, or Jenny would bleed to death. He had never seen so much blood in all his life. He chased the mule for a half a mile, trying to catch her. Finally she stopped, breathing hard, stumpy tail half arched. He caught her mane and led her back to where the plow and gun lay. Then he stooped and grabbed handfuls of damp black earth and tried to plug the bullet hole. Jenny shuddered, whinnied, and broke from him.

"Hol on! Hol on now!"

He tried to plug it again, but blood came anyhow. His fingers were hot and sticky. He rubbed dirt into his palms, trying to dry them. Then again he attempted to plug the bullet hole, but Jenny shied away, kicking her heels high. He stood helpless. He had to do something. He ran at Jenny; she dodged him. He watched a red stream of blood flow down Jenny's leg and form a bright pool at her feet.

"Jenny . . . Jenny," he called weakly.

His lips trembled. She's bleeding t death! He looked in the direction of home, wanting to go back, wanting to get help. But he saw the pistol lying in the damp black clay. He had a queer feeling that if he only did something, this would not be; Jenny would not be there bleeding to death.

When he went to her this time, she did not move. She stood with sleepy, dreamy eyes; and when he touched her she gave a low-pitched whinny and knelt to the ground, her front knees slopping in blood.

"Jenny . . . Jenny . . ." he whispered.

For a long time she held her neck erect; then her head sank, slowly. Her ribs swelled with a mighty heave and she went over.

Dave's stomach felt empty, very empty. He picked up the gun and held it gingerly between his thumb and forefinger. He buried it at the foot of a tree. He took a stick and tried to cover the pool of blood with dirt—but what was the use? There was Jenny lying with her mouth open and her eyes walled and glassy. He could not tell Jim Hawkins he had shot his mule. But he had to tell something. Yeah, Ah'll tell em Jenny started gittin wil n fell on the joint of the plow. . . . But that would hardly happen to a mule. He walked across the field slowly, head down.

It was sunset. Two of Jim Hawkins' men were over near the edge of the woods digging a hole in which to bury Jenny. Dave was surrounded by a knot of people, all of whom were looking down at the dead mule.

"I don't see how in the world it happened," said Jim Hawkins for the tenth time.

The crowd parted and Dave's mother, father, and small brother pushed into the center.

"Where Dave?" his mother called.

"There he is," said Jim Hawkins.

His mother grabbed him.

"Whut happened, Dave? Whut yuh done?"

"Nothin."

"C mon, boy, talk," his father said.

Dave took a deep breath and told the story he knew nobody believed.

"Waal," he drawled. "Ah brung ol Jenny down here sos Ah could do mah plowin. Ah plowed bout two rows, just like yuh see." He stopped and pointed at the long rows of upturned earth. "Then somethin musta been wrong wid ol Jenny. She wouldn ack right a-tall. She started snortin n kickin her heels. Ah tried t hol her, but she pulled erway, rearin n goin in. Then when the point of the plow was stickin up in the air, she swung erroun n twisted herself back on it . . . She stuck herself n started t bleed. N fo Ah could do anything, she wuz dead."

"Did you ever hear of anything like that in all your life?" asked Jim Hawkins.

There were white and black standing in the crowd. They murmured. Dave's mother came close to him and looked hard into his face. "Tell the truth, Dave," she said.

"Looks like a bullet hole to me," said one man.

"Dave, whut yuh do wid the gun?" his mother asked.

The crowd surged in, looking at him. He jammed his hands into his pockets, shook his head slowly from left to right, and backed away. His eyes were wide and painful.

"Did he hava gun?" asked Jim Hawkins.

"By Gawd, Ah tol yuh tha wu a gun wound," said a man, slapping his thigh.

His father caught his shoulders and shook him till his teeth rattled.

"Tell whut happened, yuh rascal! Tell whut . . ."

Dave looked at Jenny's stiff legs and began to cry.

"Whut yuh do wid tha gun?" his mother asked.

"Whut wuz he doin wida gun?" his father asked.

"Come on and tell the truth," said Hawkins. "Ain't nobody going to hurt you . . ."

His mother crowded close to him.

"Did yuh shoot tha mule, Dave?"

Dave cried, seeing blurred white and black faces.

"Ahh ddinn gggo tt sshooot hher . . . Ah ssswear ffo Gawd Ahh ddin. . . . Ah wuz a-tryin t sssee ef the old gggun would sshoot."

"Where yuh git the gun from?" his father asked.

"Ah got it from Joe, at the sto."

"Where yuh git the money?"

"Ma give it t me."

"He kept worryin me, Bob. Ah had t. Ah tol im t bring the gun right back to me . . . It was fer yuh, the gun."

"But how yuh happen to shoot that mule?" asked Jim Hawkins.

"Ah wuzn shootin at the mule, Mistah Hawkins. The gun jumped when Ah pulled the trigger . . . N fo Ah knowed anythin Jenny was there a-bleedin."

Somebody in the crowd laughed. Jim Hawkins walked close to Dave and looked into his face.

"Well, looks like you have bought you a mule, Dave."

"Ah swear fo Gawd, Ah didn go t kill the mule, Mistah Hawkins!"

"But you killed her!"

All the crowd was laughing now. They stood on tiptoe and poked heads over one another's shoulders.

"Well, boy, looks like yuh done bought a dead mule! Hahaha!"

"Ain tha ershame."

"Hohohohoho."

Dave stood, head down, twisting his feet in the dirt.

"Well, you needn't worry about it, Bob," said Jim Hawkins to Dave's father. "Just let the boy keep on working and pay me two dollars a month."

"Whut yuh wan fer yo mule, Mistah Hawkins?"

Jim Hawkins screwed up his eyes.

"Fifty dollars."

"Whut yuh do wid tha gun?" Dave's father demanded.

Dave said nothing.

"Yuh wan me t take a tree n beat yuh till yuh talk!"

"Nawsuh!"

"Whut yuh do wid it?"

"Ah throwed it erway."

"Where?"

"Ah . . . Ah throwed it in the creek."

"Waal, c mon home. N firs thing in the mawnin git to tha creek n fin tha gun."

"Yessuh."

"Whut yuh pay fer it?"

"Two dollahs."

"Take tha gun n git yo money back n carry it t Mistah Hawkins, yuh near? N don fergit Ahma lam you black bottom good fer this! Now march yosef on home, suh!"

Dave turned and walked slowly. He heard people laughing. Dave glared, his eyes welling with tears. Hot anger bubbled in him. Then he swallowed and stumbled on.

That night Dave did not sleep. He was glad that he had gotten out of killing the mule so easily, but he was hurt. Something hot seemed to turn over inside him each time he remembered how they had laughed. He tossed on his bed, feeling his hard pillow. N Pa says he's gonna beat me . . . He remembered other beatings, and his back quivered. Naw, naw, Ah sho don wan im t beat me tha way no mo. Dam em all! Nobody ever gave him anything. All he did was work. They treat me like a mule, n then they beat me. He gritted his teeth. N Ma had t tell on me.

Well, if he had to, he would take old man Hawkins that two dollars. But that meant selling the gun. And he wanted to keep that gun. Fifty dollars for a dead mule.

He turned over, thinking how he had fired the gun. He had an itch to fire it again. Ef other men kin shoota gun, by Gawd, Ah kin! He was still, listening. Mebbe they all sleepin now. The house was still. He heard the soft breathing of his brother. Yes, now! He would go down and get that gun and see if he could fire it! He eased out of bed and slipped into overalls.

The moon was bright. He ran almost all the way to the edge of the woods. He stumbled over the ground, looking for the spot where he had buried the gun. Yeah, here it is. Like a hungry dog scratching for a bone, he pawed it up. He puffed his black cheeks and blew dirt from the trigger and barrel. He broke it and found four cartridges unshot. He looked around; the fields were filled with silence and moonlight. He clutched the gun stiff and hard in his fingers. But, as soon as he wanted to pull the trigger, he shut his eyes and turned his head. Naw, An can't shoot wid mah eyes closed n mah head turned. With effort he held his eyes open; then he squeezed. *Bloooom!* He was stiff, not breathing. The gun was still in his hands. Dammit, he'd done it! He fired again. *Bloooooom!* He smiled. *Blooooom! Blooooom! Click, click.* There! It was empty. If anybody could shoot a gun, he could. He put the gun into his hip pocket and started across the fields.

When he reached the top of a ridge he stood straight and proud in the moonlight, looking at Jim Hawkins' big white house, feeling the gun sagging in his pocket. Lawd, ef Ah had just one mo bullet Ah'd taka shot at tha house. Ah'd like t scare ol man Hawkins jusa little . . . Jusa enough t let im know Dave Saunders is a man.

To his left the road curved, running to the tracks of the Illinois Central. He jerked his head, listening. From far off came a faint *hooof-hoooof; hoooof-hoooof; hoooof-hoooof.* . . . He stood rigid. Two dollahs a mont. Les see now . . . Tha means it'll take bout two years. Shucks! Ah'll be dam!

He started down the road, toward the tracks. Yeah, here she comes! He stood beside the track and held himself stiffly. Here she comes, erroun the ben . . . C mon, yuh slow poke! C mon! He had his hand on his gun; something quivered in his stomach. Then the train thundered past, the gray and brown box cars rumbling and clinking. He gripped the gun tightly; then he jerked his hand out of his pocket. Ah betcha Bill wouldn't do it! Ah betcha. . . . The cars slid past, steel grinding upon steel. Ahm ridin yuh ternight, so hep me Gawd! He was hot all over. He hesitated just a moment; then he grabbed, pulled atop of a car, and lay flat. He felt his pocket; the gun was still there. Ahead the long rails were glinting in the moonlight, stretching away, away to somewhere, somewhere where he could be a man . . .

1939, 1961

CARLOS BULOSAN
1911–1956

Carlos Bulosan was the first, and is still the most important, Filipino-American author, one of the earliest voices in the Asian American literary tradition. Although the lives of Filipinos were always his first concern, his claim that all "who came to the United States as immigrants are Americans too" connects his writing to the rich history of American immigrant literature in general.

Bulosan came from an extremely poor peasant family in the Philippines and had almost no formal education. He arrived in Seattle in 1931, one of thousands of young Filipino men who came for jobs after the Immigrant Act of 1924 excluded the Japanese. Like two older brothers who had emigrated earlier, he worked seasonally from Alaska to southern California—canning fish, planting cauliflower, picking fruit—for low wages in miserable conditions. White Americans had always discriminated against the Asians whose labor underpinned so much West Coast prosperity, but Filipinos were treated with particular brutality and contempt. As Bulosan put it, "In many ways it was a crime to be a Filipino in California."

Within a few years he became active in the dangerous work of organizing migrant farm workers into unions. From 1936 to 1938 he was hospitalized in Los Angeles with tuberculosis; during this time he read widely and began writing poetry. When, during World War II, the Philippines were attacked by the Japanese and Filipinos were allowed to join the U.S. Army, mainland hostility toward them lessened somewhat. Bulosan's first book, a collection of poems titled *Letter for America*, appeared in 1942. He began to publish stories in prestigious magazines like the *New Yorker, Town and Country,* and *Harper's Bazaar. The Laughter of My Father* (1944), sketches of Filipino peasant life, won critical acclaim, as did his powerful memoir, *America Is in the Heart*

(1946). Over the years he had many romances with white women but never married. Marriage between whites and Filipinos was, in fact, illegal in the western states during those decades.

Bulosan's writing shifts from oratorical generalization in praise of American ideals to naturalistic, hard-boiled accounts of poverty, exploitation, and prejudice. His stylistic ambivalence well represents his divided feelings. He was in love with an imaginary United States but found that "the terrible truth in America shatters the Filipinos' dream of fraternity."

Many of Bulosan's stories exist in manuscript only and are difficult to date. The text of "Be American" is from *On Becoming Filipino* (1995), edited by E. San Juan Jr.

Be American

It was not Consorcio's fault. My cousin was an illiterate peasant from the vast plains of Luzon. When he came off the boat in San Francisco, he could neither read nor write English or Ilocano, our dialect. I met him when he arrived, and right away he had bright ideas in his head.

"Cousin, I want to be American," he told me.

"Good," I said. "That is the right thing to do. But you have plenty of time. You are planning to live permanently in the United States, are you not?"

"Sure, cousin," he said. "But I want to be American right away. On the boat I say, 'Consorcio stoody Engleesh right away.' Good ideeyas, eh, cousin?"

"It is," I said. "But the first thing for you to do is look for a job."

"Sure, cousin. You have joob for me?"

I did. I took him to a countryman of ours who owned a small restaurant on Kearny Street. He had not done any dishwashing in the Philippines, so he broke a few dishes before he realized that the dishes were not coconut shells that he could flagrantly throw around the place, the way he used to do in his village where coconut shells were plates and carved trunks of trees were platters and his fingers were spoons. He had never seen bread and butter before, so he lost some weight before he realized that he had to eat these basic things like the rest of us, and be an American, which was his own idea in the first place. He had never slept in a bed with a mattress before, so he had to suffer from severe cold before he realized that he had to sleep inside the bed, under the blankets, but not on top of the spread, which was what he had done during his first two weeks in America. And of course he had never worn shoes before, so he had to suffer a few blisters on both feet before he realized that he had to walk lightfooted, easy, and even graceful, but not the way he used to do it in his village, which was like wrestling with a carabao[1] or goat.

All these natural things he had to learn during his first two weeks. But he talked about his Americanization with great confidence.

"You see, cousin," he told me, "I have earned mony quick. I poot the hoot dashes in the sink, wash-wash, day come, day out, week gone—mony! Simple?"

1. Water buffalo, used for plowing on Filipino farms.

"Fine," I said.

"You know what I done with mony?"

"No."

"I spent all."

"On what?"

"Books. Come see my room."

I went with him to his small room at the back of the restaurant where he was working, near the washrooms. And sure enough, he had lined the four walls of his room with big books. I looked at the titles. He had a cheap edition of the classics, books on science, law and mathematics. He even had some brochures on political and governmental matters. All were books that a student or even a professor would take time to read.

I turned to my cousin. He was smiling with pride.

"Well, I hope these big books will make you an American faster," I told him.

"Sure, cousin. How long I wait?"

"Five years."

"*Five years?*" There was genuine surprise in his dark peasant face. "Too long. I do not wait. I make faster—one year."

"It is the law," I assured him.

"No good law. One year enough for Consorcio. He make good American citizen."

"There is nothing you can do about it."

"I change law."

"Go ahead."

"You see, cousin."

But he was puzzled. So I left him. I left San Francisco. When I saw him a year later, he was no longer washing dishes. But he still had the pardonable naivete of a peasant from the plains of Luzon.

"Where are you working now?" I asked him.

"Bakery," he said. "I make da bread. I make da donot. I make da pys."

"Where?"

"Come, cousin. I show you."

It was a small shop, a three-men affair. Consorcio was the handy-boy in the place, scrubbing the floor, washing the pots and pans; and he was also the messenger. The owner was the baker, while his wife was the saleswoman. My cousin lived at the back of the building, near the washrooms. He had a cot in a corner of the dark room. But the books were gone.

"What happened to your books?" I asked him.

He looked sad. Then he said, "I sold, cousin."

"Why?"

"I cannot read. I cannot understand. Words too big and too long."

"You should begin with simple grammar books."

"Those cannot read also. What to do now, cousin?"

"You still want to be an American citizen?"

"Sure."

"Go to night school."

"Is a place like that?"

"Yes."

"No use, cousin. No money."

"The school is free," I told him. "It is for foreign-born people. For adults, so they could study American history."

"Free? I go now."

"The school opens only at night."

"I work night."

"Well, work in the daytime. Look for another job. You still want to be an American, don't you?"

"Sure. But I like boss-man. What to do?"

"Tell him the truth."

"You help me?"

I did. We went to the boss-man. I explained the matter as truthfully as I could and he understood Consorcio's problems. But he asked me to find someone to take the place of my cousin's place, which I did too, so we shook hands around and departed in the best of humor. I helped Consorcio register at the night school, looked for another job for him as janitor in an apartment building. Then I left him, wishing him the best of luck.

I worked in Alaska the next two years. When I returned to the mainland, I made it my duty to pass through San Francisco. But my cousin had left his janitor job and the night school. I could not find his new address, and it seemed that no one knew him well enough in the Filipino community.

I did not think much of his disappearance because we are a wandering people due to the nature of our lowly occupations, which take us from place to place, following the seasons. When I received a box of grapes from a friend, I knew he was working in the grape fields in either Fresno or Delano, depending on the freight mark. When I received a box of asparagus, I knew he was working in Stockton. But when it was a crate of lettuce, he was working in Santa Maria or Salinas, depending on the freight mark again. And in the summertime when I received a large barrel of salmon, I knew he was working in the salmon canneries in Alaska. There were no letters, no post cards—nothing. But these surprising boxes, crates, and barrels that arrived periodically were the best letters in the world. What they contained were lovingly distributed among my city friends. Similarly, when I was in one of my own wanderings, which were done in cities and large towns, I sent my friend or friends unsealed envelopes bursting with the colored pictures of actresses and other beautiful women. I addressed these gifts to poolrooms and restaurants in towns where my friends had lived or worked for a season, because they were bound to go to any of these havens of the homeless wanderer. However, when another curious wanderer opened the envelopes and pilfered the pictures, it was not a crime. The enjoyment which was originally intended for my friends was his and his friends. That is the law of the nomad: finders keepers.

But Consorcio had not yet learned the unwritten law of the nomad. I did not expect him to send me boxes, crates, and barrels from far-away Alaska. So I did not know where I could locate him.

I wandered in and out of Los Angeles the next two years. At the beginning of the third year, when I was talking to the sleeping birds in Pershing Square, I felt a light hand on my shoulders. I was not usually curious about hands, but it was well after midnight and the cops were wandering in and out of the place. So I turned around—and found Consorcio.

I found a new Consorcio. He had aged and the peasant naivete was gone from his face. In his eyes now was a hidden fear. His hands danced and flew when he was talking, and even when he was not talking, as though he were slapping the wind with both hands or clapping with one hand. Have you ever heard the noise of one hand clapping?

That was Consorcio after five years in America. He was either slapping the wind with both hands or clapping with one hand. So I guided him out of the dark park to a lighted place, where we had coffee until the city awoke to give us another day of hope. Of course, I sat in silence for a long time because it was the year of deep silence. And Consorcio sat for a long time too, because by now he had learned to hide in the deep silence that was flung like a mourning cloak across the face of the land. When we talked our sentences were short and punctuated by long silences. So we conversed somewhat like this:

"Been wandering everywhere."

"No job."

"Nothing anywhere."

"Where have you been all these years?"

Silence.

"No finished school?"

Silence.

"Not American citizen yet?"

"You should have told me."

"Told you what?"

"Filipinos can't become American citizens."

"Well, I could have told you. But I wanted you to learn."

"At least I speak better English now."

"This is a country of great opportunity."

Silence.

"No work?"

"No work."

"How long?"

"I have forgotten."

"Better times will come."

"You have a wonderful dream, cousin," he told me and left. He left Los Angeles for a long time. Then, two years later, I received a crate of oranges from him. The freight mark was San Jose. Now I knew he was working and had learned the unwritten law of the wanderers on this troubled earth. So as I ate the oranges, I recalled his last statement: *You have a wonderful dream, cousin.* . . . I had a wonderful dream. But I dreamed it for both of us, for many of us who wandered in silence.

Then the boxes and crates became more frequent. Then a barrel of salmon came from Alaska. And, finally, the letters came. My cousin Consorcio, the one-time illiterate peasant from the vast plains of Luzon, had indeed become an American without knowing it. His letters were full of wondering and pondering about many things in America. Now he realized his naivete when he had landed in San Francisco. But he realized also that he could not ask too much in a strange land. And it was this realization that liberated him from his peasant prison, his heritage, and eventually led him to a kind of work to which he dedicated his time and life until the end.

I was in Oregon when I received a newspaper from Consorcio, postmarked Pismo Beach. It was the first issue of his publication for agricultural workers in California. It was in English. From then on, I received all issues of his publication. For five years it existed defending the workers and upholding the rights and liberties of all Americans, native or foreign-born, so that, as he began to understand the nature of American society, he became more belligerent in his editorials and had to go to jail a few times for his ideas about freedom and peace.

Yes, indeed Consorcio: you have become an American, a real American. And this land that we have known too well is not yet denuded by the rapacity of men. Rolling like a beautiful woman with an overflowing abundance of fecundity and murmurous with her eternal mystery, there she lies before us like a great mother. To her we always return from our prodigal wanderings and searchings for an anchorage in the sea of life; from her we always draw our sustenance and noble thoughts, to add to her glorious history.

But the war came. And the war ended Consorcio's newspaper work and his crusade for a better America. And it ended his life also. When he was brought back from overseas, he knew he would not last long. But he talked the way he had written his editorials, measured sentences that rang like music, great poetry, and soft, soft. He would not shed a tear; but his heart must have been crying, seeing eternal darkness coming toward him, deep, deep in the night of perpetual sleep. Yes, he would not shed a tear; but he must have been crying, seeing that there was so much to do with so little time left. There was in his voice a kindness for me—unhappy, perhaps, that he could not impart what he had learned from his wanderings on this earth: unhappy, also, because he knew that it would take all the people to unmake the unhappiness which had caught up with us. And now, fifteen years after his arrival in San Francisco, he was dying.

And he died. But at least he received his most cherished dream: American citizenship. He did realize later that he had become an American before he received his papers, when he began to think and write lovingly about *our* America. He gave up many things, and finally his own life, to realize his dream.

But Consorcio is not truly dead. He lives again in my undying love for the American earth. And soon, when I see the last winter coming to the last leaf, I will be warm with the thought that another wanderer shall inherit the wonderful dream which my cousin and I had dreamed and tried to realize in America.

1995

American Literature since 1945

THE UNITED STATES AND WORLD POWER

Distribution of power is a purpose of war, and the consequences of a world war are necessarily global. Having agreed to a policy of unconditional surrender, the allied countries of Britain, the Soviet Union, and the United States positioned themselves to achieve nothing short of total victory over their enemies in World War II: Germany and Japan. Yet each country's contribution to victory made for startling contrasts in the following half century. Britain, beleaguered since the war's start in September 1939, fought against odds that depleted its resources and severely disrupted its traditional class structure. The Soviet Union, an amalgamation of nations under the central power of Russia, suffered the war's worst casualties when attacked by Germany in June 1941 and afterward during the hideous contest of attrition along the war's bitter eastern front well into 1945. Although newly established as a world power after the end of hostilities, the U.S.S.R. remained at an economic disadvantage and dissolved in 1991 after five decades of Cold War against its ideological adversaries in the West. It was the United States, entering the war after Japan's attack on Pearl Harbor on December 7, 1941, that emerged as a world power in excellent economic shape. This new power, experienced both at home and abroad, became a major force in reshaping American culture for the balance of the twentieth century.

The great social effort involved in fighting World War II reorganized America's economy and altered its people's lifestyles. Postwar existence revealed different kinds of men and women, with new aspirations among both majority and minority populations. New possibilities for action empowered individuals and groups in the pursuit of personal freedom and individual self-expression. During World War II American industry had expanded dramatically for military purposes; plants that had manufactured Chevrolets, Plymouths, Studebakers, Packards, and Fords now made B-24 Liberators and Grumman Avengers. With three million men in uniform, the vastly expanded workforce comprised increasing numbers of women. After hostilities were concluded many of these women were reluctant to return to homemaking; after a decade or so of domesticity, women emerged as a political force on behalf of rights and opportunities in the workplace. This pattern extended to other groups as well. African Americans, whether they enlisted or were drafted, served in fighting units throughout the war and were unwilling to return to second-class status afterward; nor could a majority culture aware of their contribution continue to enforce segregation and other forms of prejudice so easily as before the war.

Economic power at the world level continued to influence American culture through the first two postwar decades. The first two—and only two—atomic bombs used were exploded by the United States in Japan in August 1945; their effect was so horrific that geographical "containment" emerged as an American military policy. When Communist North Korea invaded South Korea in 1950, therefore, the United States rejected responding with atomic weapons in favor of a United Nations–sponsored "police action" that followed a policy of using conventional weapons only and not pursuing enemy forces beyond specific boundaries. But if hot war was out, cold war was in, specifically the type of contest in which military strength was built up for deterrence rather than combat. Here economic conduct would be a major factor in the American decision to contain the Soviet Union's attempt to expand its influence. In the years following World War II the U.S.S.R. had assumed a stance considered adversarial to Western interests. Ideologically, the opposition was between Western capitalism and Soviet state socialism; militarily, the contest exhibited itself in the West's rebuilding of Germany and the formation of the North Atlantic Treaty Organization (NATO) versus the Soviet Union's influence over Eastern Europe's nations by means of the Warsaw Pact. In Africa, where new nations gained independence from colonial rule, West and East competed for influence. Overall, the West perceived a threat in the U.S.S.R.'s 1948 attainment of nuclear weaponry and its maintenance of massive troop strength beyond its borders. When Communist revolutionaries took control of mainland China in 1949, the Cold War moved beyond European boundaries to encompass the entire globe. Until the collapse of the Soviet Union, economic warfare motivated American activity as decisively as had the waging of World War II.

Throughout the 1950s and into the early 1960s, social critics perceived a stable conformity to American life, a dedication to an increasingly materialistic standard of living, whose ethical merit was ensured by a continuity with the prewar world—a continuity that proved to be delusory. In this initial postwar period white males benefited especially from the economy and saw the nature of their lives change. The G.I. Bill provided veterans with a college education; after World War II America would eventually have as much as 50 percent of its population college educated, a percentage unthinkable in prewar years and unmatched by any other nation. With world markets open to American goods, the expanded economy offered sophisticated technical and professional jobs for these college graduates; within a generation the alphabet soup of great corporations—IT&T, GE, RCA, IBM, and so forth—came to dominate employment patterns at home and around the globe. Higher incomes and demographic expansion created vast new suburbs beyond the limits of older cities, and the population of the United States began a westward shift. New roads accommodated this increasingly mobile society, including the interstate highway system begun in 1955. By 1960 the average American family was moving to a new place of residence at the rate of once every five years, as new opportunities beckoned and lifestyles expanded beyond the more traditional stability of "home." An age of plenty created a new managerial class, but also ensured an ample piece of the pie for workers protected by well-organized, secure unions.

But ways of life consonant with an isolated, stable economy could not survive in the new atmosphere of American power and wealth. The passage from the 1950s to the 1960s marks the great watershed of the postwar half century. Conflicts between conformity and individuality, tradition and innovation, stability and disruption were announced and anticipated even before they effectively influenced history and culture. The earliest harbinger was the 1960 election of John F. Kennedy as president. To a mainstream society that might have become complacent with the material success of the postwar years and had neglected the less fortunate, Kennedy offered an energetic program of involvement. Formally titled "The New Frontier," it reached from the participation of individual Americans in the Peace Corps (working to aid underdeveloped countries around the world) to the grand effort at conquering space. In the midst of his brief presidency, in October 1962, in what came to be known as the "Cuban Missile Crisis," the Soviet Union installed ballistic missiles in Cuba; when Kennedy protested this act and began a naval blockade of the island nation, the possibility of nuclear warfare came closer than ever before, until the U.S.S.R. relented and withdrew its weapons. Domestic tensions also rose when Robert Kennedy, the president's brother and U.S. attorney general, took a newly activist approach toward desegregation, sending federal troops into the South to enforce the law. But there was a cultural grace to the Kennedy era as well, with the president's wife, Jacqueline, making involvement in the arts not just fashionable but also a matter of government policy.

The Sixties, as they are known, really began with the assassination of John F. Kennedy on November 22, 1963. The tumultuous dozen years of American history that followed embraced a more combative period in civil rights, climaxing with the most sustained and effective attempts to remedy the evils of racial discrimination since the years of Reconstruction after the Civil War. For the first time since the Suffrage movement following World War I, women organized to pursue their legal, ethical, and cultural interests, now defined as feminism. Active dissension within the culture emerged in response to military involvement in Vietnam, where in 1961 President Kennedy had sent small numbers of advisers to help the Republic of South Vietnam resist pressures from Communist North Vietnam. Presidents Lyndon Johnson and Richard Nixon expanded and continued the U.S. presence; and an increasingly strident opposition—fueled by protests on American college campuses and among the country's liberal intellectuals—turned into a much larger cultural revolution. Between 1967 and 1970 the nation experienced many outbreaks of violence, including political assassinations (of both presidential candidate Robert Kennedy and civil rights leader Dr. Martin Luther King Jr. in 1968), urban riots, and massive campus disruptions.

Torn apart by opposition to President Johnson and the climate of violence surrounding its national convention in Chicago in August 1968, the Democratic Party lost to Republican candidate Richard Nixon, who was himself burdened with the Vietnam War and escalating dissent (leading to student deaths at Kent State and Jackson State universities in May 1970). By the time the Vietnam War ended in 1975 with the collapse of Saigon to North Vietnamese and Viet Cong forces, the United States had also been buffeted by large-scale domestic trouble in the form of the Watergate scandal: a revelation of President Nixon's abuses of governmental privileges that led to his resignation in August 1974. These events mark the end of one of the more discomfortingly disruptive eras in American history.

By the end of the 1970s some characteristics of the previous decade's countercultural revolt had been accepted in the mainstream, including informalities of dress, relaxation of sexual codes of behavior, and an increased respect for individual rights. The 1980s experienced a call for traditional values, which were interpreted as a return not to community and self-sacrifice but to the pursuit of wealth. During Ronald Reagan's presidency incomes rose while taxes fell; the Sixties' distrust of government mutated into a defense of personal acquisition. Following the debacle in Vietnam, where more than fifty thousand Americans died in a losing war, the military restricted itself in the 1980s and early 1990s to quick, sharply specified interventions (in Grenada, Panama, and most dramatically in the Gulf War of 1991) relying less on vague deterrence than on precise applications of technological expertise. Economically, America boomed, but in new ways: manufacturing dominance was replaced by service efficiency, massive workforces were downsized into more profitable units, while investment and entrepreneurship replaced older modes of development.

As the twentieth century made its turn, global power experienced its greatest readjustment since World War II. American economic might had depleted the Soviet Union's ability to compete, and as that state's ethnic republics achieved independence and the old Warsaw Pact alliance of Eastern European nations collapsed, the European Union—once restricted to Western democracies—assumed even greater importance. With the attack on New York's World Trade Center and the Pentagon by terrorists on September 11, 2001, the third millennium threatened to echo the first, with religious forces setting political agendas and working to see those agendas fulfilled, beginning with a seemingly open-ended face-off between American and revolutionary Islamic forces in Iraq.

LITERARY DEVELOPMENTS

In such a turbulent half century, literature also encompassed a great deal of change. Not surprisingly, during this period many important writers reexamined both what literature is meant to accomplish and how to accomplish it. Conflicts between conformity and individuality, tradition and innovation, stability and disruption characterized the literature of the period as they also shaped the historical and cultural milieu. Just as people in the first two decades following World War II addressed themselves to taking material advantage of the extensive gains won by the global victory, so writers sought to capitalize on the successes of a previous literary generation. Cultural homogeneity was an ideal during the 1950s, patriotically so in terms of building up the foundations of American society to resist and contain Communism, materialistically so when it came to enjoying the benefits of Capitalism. This ideal of homogeneity led many writers to assume that a single work— short story, novel, poem, or play—could represent the experiences of an entire people, that a common national essence lay beneath distinctions of gender, race, ethnicity, religion, or region. The literary world between 1945 and the Sixties often let readers believe that there could be such a thing as a representative American short story, nuanced for upper middle-class patrons in the pages of *The New Yorker* magazine while slanted to more homely interests in *Collier's* and *The Saturday Evening Post.*

Novels of the immediate postwar period followed this trend in more depth, in larger scale, and with more self-conscious justification. Ernest Hemingway, a master of the short story, had fostered the notion of novel writing as "going the distance," slugging it out all the way, as it were, in a fifteen-round championship prizefight. Publicized by others as one of the dominant literary figures of his day, Hemingway promoted his own example to influence a new generation of novelists who believed they had to act like him to be taken seriously. Hence the desire to write what was called "the great American novel," a major work that would characterize the larger aspects of experience. Ambitions were not simply to write a war novel, for example, but *the* war novel; not just a work about corporate big business, but something that generalized the subject for all times. Regionalism could remain an interest, but only if it provided deeper meaning; here the example of William Faulkner encouraged the belief among younger writers that dealing with the American South meant grappling with monumental issues of guilt and the inexorable power of history. Major dramatists behaved the same way; if their immediate predecessors had drawn on classically tragic allusions in deepening their themes, postwar playwrights embraced otherwise mundane characters as universal types; the death of a salesman, for example, would be examined in the same spotlight once reserved for great people, for here indeed was a figure who stood for the postwar human being.

As a genre poetry was less tied to expectations about realism or national essence than was the novel or the short story. In the 1950s the poetic standard was the short lyric meditation, in which the poet, avoiding the first person, would find an object, a landscape, or an observed encounter that epitomized and clarified a feeling. A poem was the product of retrospection, a gesture of composure following the initial shock or stimulus that provided the occasion for writing. Some poets composed in intricate stanzas and skillful rhymes, deploying a mastery of verse form as one sign of the civilized mind's power to explore, tame, and distill raw experience. In the 1950s and 1960s poets acquired a new visibility in American life. After the war, writers conferences and workshops, recordings, and published and broadcast interviews became common, and a network of poets traveling to give readings and to become poets-in-residence at universities began to form. Despite this increase in poetry's visibility, its marginal position in the nation's culture, when compared to that of prose fiction, may have allowed for more divergence from the ideal of homogeneity. The mid to late 1940s saw the publication of groundbreaking books as various as Gwendolyn Brooks's *A Street in Bronzeville* (1945), with its evocation of African American experience; Robert Duncan's *Heavenly City, Earthly City* (1947), with its mystical and homosexual themes; and Theodore Roethke's linguistically experimental sequence *The Lost Son* (1948). As early as 1950 Charles Olsen's manifesto, *Projective Verse*, called for a unit of poetic expression based not on predetermined metrical feet but on the poet's "breath" and the rhythms of the body. In the 1950s and 1960s a number of important poets displayed what the poet-critic Richard Howard called "the longing to lose the gift of order, despoiling the self of all that had been, merely, propriety." The poetry of Allen Ginsberg,

Sylvia Plath, and John Berryman began as well mannered and formal, then turned to a wilder and more disquieting form of lyric exploration.

Like the notion of cultural conformity, the understanding of any single piece of literature as representing an entire people came under serious scrutiny during the 1960s. As the novelist Philip Roth remarked in 1960, "the American writer in the middle of the twentieth century has his hands full in trying to understand, describe and then make credible much of American reality." Critical movements of the time articulated a new literary unease around the issue of realism, and writers responded to this unease by developing new literary strategies, ways of dealing with a much more contentious, varied, and unstable sense of the era. Some writers felt that social reality had become too unstable to serve as a reliable anchor for their narratives, and some critics believed that fiction had exhausted its formal possibilities. A "Death of the Novel" controversy arose. Both the novel and the short story, some argued, demanded a set of fairly limited conventions; these conventions, such as characterization and development by means of dialogue, imagery, and symbolism, however, relied on a securely describable world to make sense.

In poetry, two important and transforming shocks were administered by Allen Ginsberg's *Howl* (1956) and Robert Lowell's *Life Studies* (1959). Ginsberg first delivered his poem aloud, during a reading at the Six Gallery in San Francisco in the fall of 1955; the following year it was published by Lawrence Ferlinghetti's City Lights Bookshop. In a single stroke, with the energy of a reborn Walt Whitman, Ginsberg made poetry one of the rallying points for underground protest and prophetic denunciation of the prosperous, complacent, gray-spirited Eisenhower years. The setting in which the poem appeared is also significant, for *Howl*, like other work associated with what came to be known as the San Francisco Renaissance, challenged the conventions of a literary tradition dominated by the East Coast. With its open, experimental form and strong oral emphasis, *Howl* sounded a departure from the well-shaped lyric. Lowell, a more "difficult," less popular poet, was rooted in the literary culture of Boston. But with *Life Studies* he too challenged the literary status quo, bringing a new directness and autobiographical intensity into American poetry as he exposed the psychological turbulence suffered by an inbred New Englander. Lowell's movement into a more open, less heavily symbolic style was inspired, in part, by hearing the work of Ginsberg and others while on a reading tour of the West Coast.

The connection between these two volumes and the times in which they were written is direct and apparent. Their poems anticipated and explored strains in American social relationships that issued in the open conflicts of the 1960s and 1970s and shaped American life for decades to come: public unrest about the uses of government and industrial power; the institutions of marriage and the family; the rights and powers of racial minorities, women, and homosexuals; the use of drugs; alternative states of consciousness. Taken together the books also suggested that the invigorating energies of postwar American poetry would arise from diverse regions of the country, their common aim restoring poetry to a more vital relation with contemporary life.

Even as American life in the 1950s espoused conformity, technological advances in the exchange of information had made the particulars of such life ever more hard to manage. As boundaries of time and space were eclipsed by television, air travel, and an accompanying global awareness, the once essential unities of representation (time, space, and action) no longer provided ground on which to build a work of literary art. As more became known about the world, the writer's ability to make sense of the whole was challenged. A culture that looked for totalized expressions from its writers now seemed to demand the impossible. In the 1960s poets began to extend their subject matter to more explicit and extreme areas of autobiography—sex, divorce, alcoholism, insanity. The convenient but not very precise label "confessional" came to be attached to certain books in which the intimate particulars of one person's life insisted on the distinctness of individual experience, not its representativeness. Other poets devised forms that reflected an understanding of poetry as provisional, as representing the changing flow of experience from moment to moment. Some poets began dating each of their poems, as though to suggest that the feelings involved were subject to revision by later experience.

A parallel development in literary theory posed another great threat to conventional literature. Known as "Deconstruction" and brought to American shores from France by means of a series of university conferences and academic publications beginning in 1966, this style of criticism questioned the underlying assumptions behind any statement, exposing how what was accepted as absolute truth usually depended on rhetoric rather than fact, exposing indeed how "fact" itself was constructed by intellectual operations. This style of criticism became attractive to literary scholars who had been framing social and political questions in much the same terms—believing, for example, that the Vietnam War had been presented to the American people through slogans rather than realities. Many of the fiction writers, dramatists, and poets who sought stable employment in universities and colleges took part vigorously in these discussions. Deconstruction's preoccupation with language dismantled some of the boundaries between philosophy, poetry, psychology, and linguistics, and emphasized writing as a site of multiple discourses. The idea of literature as self-expression was complicated by a focus on the social power of language and the constructed nature of subjectivity. The skepticism toward unity and coherence that marks the era extended to the very idea of the self. The Death of the Novel debates in prose fiction had an analogue in the intensified skepticism poets brought to the idea of narrative. Borrowing from the technologies of film and video (jump cuts, tracking shots, shifting camera angles, split screens), literature began to imagine a reader saturated with the sounds of contemporary discourse, a reader whose attention quickly shifts. All of these impulses converged to destabilize literary genres that were once thought to be reliable windows on the world.

Literature in the 1960s, like many aspects of the decade, was often extreme in its methods and disruptive in its effects. Yet much like its social and political developments the decade's literary developments remained influential beyond the Sixties. Writers continued to experiment with diverse practices in which to render a sense of contemporary reality, and they continued their artistic debates over how that reality was constituted and how it could be represented. Authors as diverse as John Updike and Ann Beattie continued to write realistic fiction, even in the heyday of Deconstruction, but in a style enriched by the rigorous cross-examination of its previously unquestioned practices. Even in a period at times overly conscious of self and world as fictional constructs, poets like Gwendolyn Brooks and Philip Levine engaged with history and politics, and others like Elizabeth Bishop and Stanley Kunitz remained committed to poetry's relation to a common world. In prose fiction a new group of realistic writers, called "Minimalists," made these challenges central to their work, crafting a manner of description that with great intensity limited itself to what could be most reliably accepted. What the Minimalists described was not endorsed by the authors as true; rather it consisted of signs that their characters accepted as truth, not objects from nature but conventions accepted by societies to go about the business of living. In a typical Minimalist story, although nothing sad is mentioned and no character grieves, someone makes a sign that she is saying something meant to be sad, and another character emits a perfect sign of being deeply unhappy in response. Objects that abound in such works are drawn from the consumer's world not for what they are but for what they signify, be it good taste or poor, wealth or deprivation. It is a capable way of writing realism in a world where philosophical definitions discourage such a term.

Social and political changes of the 1960s left a legacy even richer than those of critical and philosophical revolutions. Political protests helped make available to literature a broad range of more insistent voices. Civil rights activism helped create the Black Arts Movement, which in turn replaced the notion of accepting only one token African American writer at a time with a much broader awareness of imaginative expression by a wide range of literary talent. A parallel movement saw southern writers, like the poet Charles Wright and the fiction writer Barry Hannah, seeking modes of expression other than mourning the loss of the Civil War or feeling guilty about slavery. Jewish American writers, like the poet Stanley Kunitz and the fiction writers Philip Roth and Bernard Malamud, began moving beyond thematics of assimilation and identity to embrace subjects and techniques reaching from the deeply personal to the metafictive or metapoetic. Some women prose writers—Ursula LeGuin, for example—found that subgenres such as fantasy and science fiction could be useful in overthrowing long-held stereotypes of gender, while poets such as Adrienne Rich and Audre Lorde presented the experience of women hitherto silenced or unrepresented in literature. In both fiction and poetry writers found present-day life could be described with a new frankness and expanded awareness appropriate to women's wider and more egalitarian role in society. Native American writers received new respect from mainstream culture, first initiated by attention to the land's ecology and recognition that the "Wild West" view of American history involved strategic stereotyping of Indian people. An important body of critical work helped create new contexts for thinking about Native American literature as both traditional and contemporary. In fact, in the 1970s and 1980s a fresh impetus of experimentation and literary commitment came from writers of minority traditions who gained access to presses and publications. Available now were artistic expressions of the cultural complexity of the American population from Chinese Americans, Japanese Americans, Mexican Americans, and other groups previously excluded from the literary canon. These different traditions were not mutually exclusive; the work of many writers testified to an enlivening interaction between traditions, affirming the imagination's freedom to draw from many sources. As, earlier, the modernists had reached out to traditions beyond the Western—the poet Ezra Pound to the Chinese ideo-graph and the poet Charles Olson to Mayan Indian culture, for example—American writers of this period were redefining what constitutes America.

One of the most dramatic developments, one that indicated the much broadening range of achievement among writers of many different back-grounds and persuasions, was the success of African American women—novelists, dramatists, and poets—during the 1970s and 1980s in finding literary voices and making them heard as important articulations of experi-ence. Here was a reminder of how so much of what passes for reality is noth-ing but artifice, fabrication, and convention—for here was a large group of people whose ancestors had been written out of history and who were still often denied speaking parts in national dialogues. Even with so much of a usable past effaced and identity repressed, these writers were able to find a means of expression that helped redefine readers' understanding of the world, whether in imaginative refigurings of the novel like Toni Morrison's, in book-length poetic sequences like Rita Dove's *Thomas and Beulah,* or in individual poems that gave voice to African American experience, like those of Lucille Clifton. By the close of the twentieth century other voices emerged that also had been written out of history, and many writers from minority tra-ditions began to take their place at the center of American writing. "Realism," like "globalism," was now a much more expansive and inclusive term, from Sherman Alexie's Native Americans to Jhumpa Lahiri's international cos-mopolites with their world-spanning technologies.

Contemporary literature values heterogeneity in forms and language, plural-ism in cultural influences. This literature assumes a context wherein the nature of reality changes. Among this literature's emblems is the Internet, in which multiple realities—including those of different cultures and different identi-ties—virtually coexist. Some contemporary writers celebrate computer tech-nology as a new resource for literature. They edit online journals; they turn to hypertext to create computer-screen poems with simultaneous and open-ended possibilities, where the reader's choices shape poetic forms. Thanks to com-puter technology, novelists may include artificial intelligence among their casts of characters, as Richard Powers demonstrates in his novel *Galatea 2.2* (1995). At the same time some contemporary writers continue to draft their work with pencil and paper, and some feel as much affinity with classical Chinese poets or the great nineteenth-century novelists as with computer technology.

It has been said that our contemporary culture provides the greatest vari-ety of literary expression available at any one time. From a war effort that demanded unity of purpose and a Cold War period that for a time encouraged conformity to a homogenetic ideal, American writing has emerged in the twenty-first century to include a sophisticated mastery of technique broad-ened by an understanding of literature's role in characterizing reality, whether that reality is understood as transcendental and visionary or as rooted in the ephemeral. One thing distinguishing these works as contemporary is that two different understandings of reality are not unified or reconciled; rather, as with the nuclei in Louise Glück's poem "Mitosis," "No one actually remem-bers them / as not divided."

A hallmark of the postwar period is its shift from unity to diversity as an ideal, and during this time American writing has been characterized by a great variety of styles employed simultaneously. If anything is common to the period, it is an appreciation of and sometimes outright delight in language as a tool of literary expression. In a wide variety of ways writers explore and test the ways language shapes our perceptions of reality, and their work moves in and out of various kinds of language, as if testing the limits and possibilities of the different discourses that make up contemporary life. This energetic investigation of language fuels a new inclusiveness and invigorates imaginative potential. Contemporary literature has survived the threats of its death to flourish in ways our writers are still imagining.

AMERICAN LITERATURE SINCE 1945

TEXTS	CONTEXTS
1941 Eudora Welty, "Petrified Man"	
1945 Randall Jarrell, "The Death of the Ball Turret Gunner"	1945 U.S. drops atomic bombs on Hiroshima and Nagasaki; Japan surrenders, ending World War II • Cold War begins
1947 Tennesse Williams, *A Streetcar Named Desire*	1947 Jackie Robinson becomes the first black Major League ballplayer
1948 Theodore Roethke, *The Lost Son*	
1949 Arthur Miller, *Death of a Salesman*	
1950 Richard Wilbur, "A World without Objects Is a Sensible Emptiness" • Charles Olson, "Projective Verse"	1950 Senator Joseph McCarthy begins attacks on communism
	1950–53 Korean War
1952 Ralph Ellison, *Invisible Man*	
1953 Saul Bellow, *The Adventures of Augie March*	1953 House Concurrent Resolution 108 dictates government's intention to "terminate" its treaty relations with the Native American tribes
	1954 *Brown v. Board of Education* declares segregated schools unconstitutional • Beat Generation poets begin to gather at San Francisco's City Lights Bookshop
1955 Flannery O'Connor, "Good Country People"	
1955–68 John Berryman composes *The Dream Songs* (pub. 1964, 1968, 1977)	
1956 Allen Ginsberg, *Howl*	1956 Martin Luther King Jr. leads bus boycott in Montgomery, Alabama
1958 Bernard Malamud, "The Magic Barrel"	
1959 Philip Roth, "Defender of the Faith" • Robert Creeley, "Kore" • Robert Lowell, *Life Studies*	1959 Fidel Castro becomes communist dictator of Cuba
1960 Thomas Pynchon, "Entropy" • Gwendolyn Brooks, "We Real Cool" • Robert Duncan, "Often I Am Permitted to Return to a Meadow"	1960 Woolworth lunch counter sit-in in Greensboro, N.C., marks beginning of civil rights movement
1961 Denise Levertov, "The Jacob's Ladder"	
1962 Jack Kerouac, *Big Sur* • Robert Hayden, "Middle Passage"	1962 United States and Soviet Union close to war over Russian missiles based in Cuba; missiles withdrawn

Boldface titles indicate works in the anthology.

TEXTS	CONTEXTS
1963 James Wright, "A Blessing"	1963 King delivers "I Have a Dream" speech • black church in Birmingham, Alabama, bombed, killing four girls • President John F. Kennedy assassinated
1964 John Cheever, "The Swimmer" • Amiri Baraka (LeRoi Jones), *Dutchman* and "An Agony. As Now."	
1965 James Baldwin, "Going to Meet the Man" • A. R. Ammons, "Corson's Inlet"	1965 Riots break out in Watts section of Los Angeles • Malcolm X assassinated • hippie culture flourishes in San Francisco
	1965–73 Vietnam War
1966 James Merrill, "The Broken Home" • Sylvia Plath, *Ariel*	1966 National Organization for Women (NOW) founded • Hayden and Brooks criticized at Black Writers' Conference, Fisk University, for composing "academic" poetry
1967 A. R. Ammons, "A Poem Is a Walk" • W. S. Merwin, "For a Coming Extinction"	
1968 Donald Barthelme, "The Balloon" • Norman Mailer, *The Armies of the Night* • George Oppen, *Of Being Numerous*	1968 King assassinated • Senator Robert F. Kennedy assassinated • photo of Earthrise by Apollo 8
1969 N. Scott Momaday, *The Way to Rainy Mountain* • Kurt Vonnegut, *Slaughterhouse-Five* • Robert Penn Warren, *Audubon*	1969 U.S. astronauts land on the moon • Stonewall riots in New York City initiate gay liberation movement • Woodstock Festival held near Bethel, New York
	1970 National Guard kills four students during antiwar demonstration at Kent State University, Ohio
1971 Audre Lorde, "Black Mother Woman"	
1972 Rudolfo A. Anaya, *Bless Me, Ultima* • Anne Sexton, *The Death of the Fathers* • Letter from Elizabeth Bishop to Robert Lowell objecting to use of personal letters in manuscript of *The Dolphin*	1972 Watergate Scandal • military draft ends
1973 Alice Walker, "Everyday Use" • Adrienne Rich, *Diving into the Wreck*	1973 *Roe v. Wade* legalizes abortion • American Indian Movement members occupy Wounded Knee
1974 Grace Paley, "A Conversation with My Father" • Annie Dillard, *Pilgrim at Tinker Creek*	1974 President Richard Nixon resigns in wake of Watergate, avoiding impeachment
1975 John Updike, "Separating" • John Ashbery, "Self-Portrait in a Convex Mirror" • Michael S. Harper, "Nightmare Begins Responsibility"	

Boldface titles indicate works in the anthology.

TEXTS	CONTEXTS
1976 Elizabeth Bishop, *Geography III*	1976 U.S. bicentennial
1977 Audre Lorde, **"Poetry Is Not a Luxury"**	
1978 Ann Beattie, "Weekend"	
1979 Philip Levine, "Starlight" • Mary Oliver, "The Black Snake"	
1980 Toni Cade Bambara, "Medley" • Sam Shepard, *True West*	
1981 Leslie Marmon Silko, **"Lullaby"** • Lorna Dee Cervantes, "The Body as Braille" • James Dickey, "Falling" • Simon J. Ortiz, **"From Sand Creek"**	
1982 Raymond Carver, **"Cathedral"** • David Mamet, *Glengarry Glen Ross*	1982 Equal Rights Amendment defeated • antinuclear movement protests manufacture of nuclear weapons • AIDS officially identified in the United States
1983 Toni Morrison, **"Recitatif"** • Joy Harjo, **"Call It Fear"**	
1984 Max Apple, "Bridging" • Louise Erdrich, **"Dear John Wayne"**	
1985 Ursula K. Le Guin, "She Unnames Them"	
1986 Louise Erdrich, **"Fleur"** • Art Spiegelman, *Maus I* • Rita Dove, ***Thomas and Beulah*** • Li-Young Lee, **"Eating Together"**	
1987 Gloria Anzaldúa, ***Borderlands/La Frontera***	
1989 Maxine Hong Kingston, *Tripmaster Monkey* • Amy Tan, *The Joy Luck Club*	1989 Soviet Union collapses; Cold War ends • oil tanker *Exxon Valdez* runs aground in Alaska
1990 Robert Pinsky, "The Want Bone"	1990 Congress passes Native American Graves Protection and Repatriation Act
1991 Sandra Cisneros, ***Woman Hollering Creek*** • Gerald Vizenor, "Almost Browne"	1991 United States enters Persian Gulf War • World Wide Web introduced
1993 Gary Snyder, **"Ripples on the Surface"** • A. R. Ammons, *Garbage*	
1994 Cathy Song, **"Lost Sister"**	
1995 Jorie Graham, ***The Dream of the Unified Field***	1995 Federal building in Oklahoma City bombed in a terrorist attack
1996 W. S. Merwin, "Lament for the Makers" • Sherman Alexie, "The Exaggeration of Despair"	

Boldface titles indicate works in the anthology.

TEXTS	CONTEXTS
1997 Julia Alvarez, *¡Yo!* • Fanny Howe, "[Nobody wants crossed out girls around]"	1997 *Pathfinder* robot explores Mars
1998 Billy Collins, **"I Chop Some Parsley While Listening to Art Blakey's Version of 'Three Blind Mice' "**	
1999 Jhumpa Lahiri, **"Sexy"** • Charles Simic, "Arriving Celebrities"	
2000 Charles Wright, "North American Bear" • Lucille Clifton, **"Moonchild"**	
	2001 Execution of Timothy McVeigh, convicted in 1995 Oklahoma City bombing • September 11 terrorist attacks on Pentagon and World Trade Center
2002 Alberto Ríos, "Refugio's Hair"	
2003 Alexie, **"Do Not Go Gentle"**	2003 United States and Great Britain invade Iraq
2004 Louise Glück, "October"	

Boldface titles indicate works in the anthology.

THEODORE ROETHKE
1908–1963

Theodore Roethke had the kind of childhood a poet might have invented. He was born in Saginaw, Michigan, where both his German grandfather and his father kept greenhouses for a living. The greenhouse world, he later said, represented for him "both heaven and hell, a kind of tropics created in the savage climate of Michigan, where austere German Americans turned their love of order and their terrifying efficiency into something truly beautiful." Throughout his life he was haunted both by the ordered, protected world of the greenhouse—the constant activity of growth, the cultivated flowers—and by the desolate landscape of his part of Michigan. "The marsh, the mire, the Void, is always there, immediate and terrifying. It is a splendid place for schooling the spirit. It is America."

Roethke's poetry often reenacted this "schooling" of the spirit by revisiting the landscapes of his childhood: the nature poems that make up the largest part of his early work try to bridge the distance between a child's consciousness and the adult mysteries presided over by his father. Roethke arranged and rearranged these poems to give the sense of a spiritual autobiography, especially in preparing the volumes *The Lost Son* (1948), *Praise to the End!* (1951), and *The Waking* (1953). In what are known as "the greenhouse poems," the greenhouse world emerged as a "reality harsher than reality," the cultivator's activity pulsating and threatening. Its overseers, like "Frau Bauman, Frau Schmidt, and Frau Schwartze" (the title of one poem) emerge as gods, fates, muses, and witches all in one. By focusing on the minute processes of botanical growth—the rooting, the budding—the poet found a way of participating in the mysteries of this once alien world, whether he was deep in the subterranean root cellar or, as a child, perched high on top of the greenhouse.

In his books *The Lost Son and Other Poems* and *Praise to the End!* Roethke explored the regenerative possibilities of prerational speech (like children's riddles) in which language as sound recaptures nonlogical states of being. In these poems, his most dazzling and original work, Roethke opened up the possibilities of language. The title of one section of the long poem *The Lost Son* is "The Gibber," a pun because the word means both a meaningless utterance and the pouch at the base of a flower's calyx. The pun identifies principles of growth with the possibilities of speech freed from logical meanings, and the sequence as a whole suggests the power of both nature and language to revive the spirit of an adult life: "A lively understandable spirit / Once entertained you. / It will come again. / Be still. / Wait."

If the nature poems of Roethke's first four books explore the anxieties within him since childhood, his later love poems show him in periods of release and momentary pleasure: "And I dance round and round, / A fond and foolish man, / And see and suffer myself / In another being at last." The love poems, many included in *Words for the Wind* (1958) and *The Far Field* (1964), are among the most appealing in modern American verse. His beautiful and tender "Elegy for Jane" should be included in this category. These poems stand in sharp relief to the suffering Roethke experienced in other areas of his personal life—several mental breakdowns and periods of alcoholism—which led to a premature death. *The Far Field,* a posthumous volume, includes fierce, strongly rhymed lyrics in which Roethke tried "bare, even terrible statement," pressing toward the threshold of spiritual insight: "A man goes far to find out what he is—/ Death of the self in a long, tearless night, / All natural shapes blazing unnatural light." The nature poems of this last volume, gathered as "The North American Sequence," use extended landscape to find natural analogies for the human passage toward the dark unknown, hoping "in their rhythms to catch the very movement of mind itself."

Roethke is remembered as one of the great teachers of poetry, especially by those young poets and critics who studied with him at the University of Washington from

1948 until the time of his death. James Wright, David Wagoner, and Richard Hugo, among others, attended his classes. He was noted for his mastery of sound and metrics. Although his poetry was intensely personal, his starting advice to students always deemphasized undisciplined self-expression. "Write like someone else," he instructed beginners. In Roethke's own career, however, this advice had its costs. His apprenticeship to Yeats, in particular, endangered his own poetic voice; in some late poems the echo of this great predecessor makes Roethke all but inaudible.

Roethke was much honored later in his career: a Pulitzer Prize for *The Waking* (1953); a National Book Award and Bollingen Prize for the collected poems, *Words for the Wind* (1958); and a posthumous National Book Award for *The Far Field* (1964).

Cuttings

Sticks-in-a-drowse droop over sugary loam,
Their intricate stem-fur dries;
But still the delicate slips keep coaxing up water;
The small cells bulge;

One nub of growth   5
Nudges a sand-crumb loose,
Pokes through a musty sheath
Its pale tendrilous horn.

1948

Cuttings

(*later*)

This urge, wrestle, resurrection of dry sticks,
Cut stems struggling to put down feet,
What saint strained so much,
Rose on such lopped limbs to a new life?

I can hear, underground, that sucking and sobbing,   5
In my veins, in my bones I feel it,—
The small waters seeping upward,
The tight grains parting at last.
When sprouts break out,
Slippery as fish   10
I quail, lean to beginnings, sheath-wet.

1948

My Papa's Waltz

The whiskey on your breath
Could make a small boy dizzy;
But I hung on like death:
Such waltzing was not easy.

We romped until the pans   5
Slid from the kitchen shelf;
My mother's countenance
Could not unfrown itself.

The hand that held my wrist
Was battered on one knuckle;   10
At every step you missed
My right ear scraped a buckle.

You beat time on my head
With a palm caked hard by dirt,
Then waltzed me off to bed   15
Still clinging to your shirt.

                                                        1948

Dolor

I have known the inexorable sadness of pencils,
Neat in their boxes, dolor of pad and paper-weight,
All the misery of manilla folders and mucilage,
Desolation in immaculate public places,
Lonely reception room, lavatory, switchboard,   5
The unalterable pathos of basin and pitcher,
Ritual of multigraph, paper-clip, comma,
Endless duplication of lives and objects.
And I have seen dust from the walls of institutions,
Finer than flour, alive, more dangerous than silica,   10
Sift, almost invisible, through long afternoons of tedium,
Dropping a fine film on nails and delicate eyebrows,
Glazing the pale hair, the duplicate grey standard faces.

                                                        1948

The Waking

I wake to sleep, and take my waking slow.
I feel my fate in what I cannot fear.
I learn by going where I have to go.

We think by feeling. What is there to know?
I hear my being dance from ear to ear.   5
I wake to sleep, and take my waking slow.

Of those so close beside me, which are you?
God bless the Ground! I shall walk softly there,
And learn by going where I have to go.

Light takes the Tree; but who can tell us how?   10
The lowly worm climbs up a winding stair;
I wake to sleep, and take my waking slow.

Great Nature has another thing to do
To you and me; so take the lively air,
And, lovely, learn by going where to go.   15

This shaking keeps me steady. I should know.
What falls away is always. And is near.
I wake to sleep, and take my waking slow.
I learn by going where I have to go.

1953

Elegy for Jane

My Student, Thrown by a Horse

I remember the neckcurls, limp and damp as tendrils;
And her quick look, a sidelong pickerel smile;
And how, once startled into talk, the light syllables leaped for her,
And she balanced in the delight of her thought,
A wren, happy, tail into the wind,   5
Her song trembling the twigs and small branches.
The shade sang with her;
The leaves, their whispers turned to kissing;
And the mold sang in the bleached valleys under the rose.

Oh, when she was sad, she cast herself down into such a pure
     depth,   10
Even a father could not find her:
Scraping her cheek against straw;
Stirring the clearest water.

My sparrow, you are not here,
Waiting like a fern, making a spiny shadow.   15
The sides of wet stones cannot console me,
Nor the moss, wound with the last light.

If only I could nudge you from this sleep,
My maimed darling, my skittery pigeon.
Over this damp grave I speak the words of my love: 20
I, with no rights in this matter,
Neither father nor lover.

1953

I Knew a Woman

I knew a woman, lovely in her bones,
When small birds sighed, she would sigh back at them;
Ah, when she moved, she moved more ways than one:
The shapes a bright container can contain!
Of her choice virtues only gods should speak,   5
Or English poets who grew up on Greek
(I'd have them sing in chorus, cheek to cheek).

How well her wishes went! She stroked my chin,
She taught me Turn, and Counter-turn, and Stand;[1]
She taught me Touch, that undulant white skin;   10
I nibbled meekly from her proffered hand;
She was the sickle; I, poor I, the rake,
Coming behind her for her pretty sake
(But what prodigious mowing we did make).

Love likes a gander, and adores a goose: 15
Her full lips pursed, the errant note to seize;
She played it quick, she played it light and loose;
My eyes, they dazzled at her flowing knees;
Her several parts could keep a pure repose,
Or one hip quiver with a mobile nose   20
(She moved in circles, and those circles moved).

Let seed be grass, and grass turn into hay:
I'm martyr to a motion not my own;
What's freedom for? To know eternity.
I swear she cast a shadow white as stone.   25
But who would count eternity in days?
These old bones live to learn her wanton ways:
(I measure time by how a body sways).

1958

EUDORA WELTY
1909–2001

In her essay "Place in Fiction," Eudora Welty spoke of her work as filled with the spirit of place: "Location is the ground conductor of all the currents of emotion and belief and moral conviction that charge out from the story in its course." Both her outwardly uneventful life and her writing are most intimately connected to the topography and atmosphere, the season and the soil of the native Mississippi that was her lifelong home.

Born in Jackson, to parents who came from the North, and raised in comfortable circumstances (her father headed an insurance company), she attended Mississippi State College for Women, then graduated from the University of

Wisconsin in 1929. After a course in advertising at the Columbia University School of Business, she returned to Mississippi, working first as a radio writer and newspaper society editor, then for the Works Progress Administration, taking photographs of and interviewing local residents. Those travels would be reflected in her fiction and also in a book of her photographs, *One Time and Place,* published in 1971.

She began writing fiction after her return to Mississippi in 1931 and five years later published her first story, "Death of a Traveling Salesman," in a small magazine. Over the next two years six of her stories were published in the *Southern Review,* a serious literary magazine one of whose editors was the poet and novelist Robert Penn Warren. She also received strong support from Katherine Anne Porter, who contributed an introduction to Welty's first book of stories, *A Curtain of Green* (1941). That introduction hailed the arrival of another gifted southern fiction writer, and in fact the volume contained some of the best stories she ever wrote, such as "Petrified Man." Her profusion of metaphor and the difficult surface of her narrative—often oblique and indirect in its effect—were in part a mark of her admiration for modern writers like Virginia Woolf and (as with any young southern writer) William Faulkner. Although Welty's stories were as shapely as that of her mentor, Porter, they were more richly idiomatic and comic in their inclination. A second collection, *The Wide Net,* appeared two years later; and her first novel, *The Robber Bridegroom,* was published in 1942.

In that year and the next she was awarded the O. Henry Memorial Prize for the best piece of short fiction, and from then on she received a steady stream of awards and prizes, including the Pulitzer Prize for her novel *The Optimist's Daughter* (1972). Her most ambitious and longest piece of fiction is *Losing Battles* (1970), in which she aimed to compose a narrative made up almost wholly out of her characters' voices in mainly humorous interplay. Like Robert Frost, Welty loves gossip in all its actuality and intimacy, and if that love failed in the novels to produce compelling, extended sequences, it did result in many lively and entertaining pages. Perhaps her finest single book after *A Curtain of Green* was *The Golden Apples* (1949), a sequence of tales about a fabulous, invented, small Mississippi community named Morgana. Her characters appear and reappear in these related stories and come together most memorably in the brilliant "June Recital," perhaps her masterpiece.

Throughout her fiction Welty's wonderfully sharp sense of humor is strongly evident. Although her characters often consist of involuted southern families, physically handicapped, mentally retarded, or generally unstable kinfolk—and although her narratives are shot through with undercurrents of death, violence, and degradation—Welty transforms everything with an entertaining twist. No matter how desperate a situation may be, she makes us listen to the way a character talks about it; we pay attention to style rather than information. And although her attitude toward human folly is satiric, her satire is devoid of the wish to undermine and mock her characters. Instead, the vivid realizations of her prose give them irresistible life and a memorable expressiveness. Yet she remarked in an essay that "fine story writers seem to be in a sense obstructionists," and Welty's narratives unfold through varied repetitions or reiterations that have, she once claimed, the function of a deliberate double exposure in photography. By making us pay close attention to who is speaking and the implications of that speech, by asking us to imagine the way in which a silent character is responding to that speech, and by making us read behind the deceptively simple response she gives to that character, she makes us active readers, playfully engaged in a typically complicated scene. "Why I Live at the P.O.," "Keela, the Outcast Indian Maiden," "Powerhouse," "June Recital," "Petrified Man," and many others demonstrate the strength and the joy of her art. And although she has been called a "regional" writer, she has noted the condescending nature of that term, which she calls an "outsider's term; it has no meaning for the insider who is doing the writing, because as far as he

knows he is simply writing about life" (*On Writing*). So it is with Eudora Welty's
fiction.

The text is from *A Curtain of Green* (1941).

Petrified Man

"Reach in my purse and git me a cigarette without no powder in it if you
kin, Mrs. Fletcher, honey," said Leota to her ten o'clock shampoo-and-set
customer. "I don't like no perfumed cigarettes."

Mrs. Fletcher gladly reached over to the lavender shelf under the lavender-
framed mirror, shook a hair net loose from the clasp of the patent-leather bag,
and slapped her hand down quickly on a powder puff which burst out when
the purse was opened.

"Why, look at the peanuts, Leota!" said Mrs. Fletcher in her marvelling voice.

"Honey, them goobers has been in my purse a week if they's been in it a day.
Mrs. Pike bought them peanuts."

"Who's Mrs. Pike?" asked Mrs. Fletcher, settling back. Hidden in this den
of curling fluid and henna[1] packs, separated by a lavender swing-door from
the other customers, who were being gratified in other booths, she could give
her curiosity its freedom. She looked expectantly at the black part in Leota's
yellow curls as she bent to light the cigarette.

"Mrs. Pike is this lady from New Orleans," said Leota, puffing, and pressing into Mrs. Fletcher's scalp with strong red-nailed fingers. "A friend, not a
customer. You see, like maybe I told you last time, me and Fred and Sal and
Joe all had us a fuss, so Sal and Joe up and moved out, so we didn't do a thing
but rent out their room. So we rented it to Mrs. Pike. And Mr. Pike." She
flicked an ash into the basket of dirty towels. "Mrs. Pike is a very decided
blonde. *She* bought me the peanuts."

"She must be cute," said Mrs. Fletcher.

"Honey, 'cute' ain't the word for what she is. I'm tellin' you, Mrs. Pike is
attractive. She has her a good time. She's got a sharp eye out, Mrs. Pike has."

She dashed the comb through the air, and paused dramatically as a cloud
of Mrs. Fletcher's hennaed hair floated out of the lavender teeth like a small
storm-cloud.

"Hair fallin'."

"Aw, Leota."

"Uh-huh, commencin' to fall out," said Leota, combing again, and letting
fall another cloud.

"Is it any dandruff in it?" Mrs. Fletcher was frowning, her hair-line eyebrows diving down toward her nose, and her wrinkled, beady-lashed eyelids
batting with concentration.

"Nope." She combed again. "Just fallin' out."

"Bet it was that last perm'nent you gave me that did it," Mrs. Fletcher said
cruelly. "Remember you cooked me fourteen minutes."

"You had fourteen minutes comin' to you," said Leota with finality.

1. Reddish brown dye for tinting hair.

"Bound to be somethin'," persisted Mrs. Fletcher. "Dandruff, dandruff. I couldn't of caught a thing like that from Mr. Fletcher, could I?"

"Well," Leota answered at last, "you know what I heard in here yestiddy, one of Thelma's ladies was settin' over yonder in Thelma's booth gittin' a machineless, and I don't mean to insist or insinuate or anything, Mrs. Fletcher, but Thelma's lady just happ'med to throw out—I forgotten what she was talkin' about at the time—that you was p-r-e-g., and lots of times that'll make your hair do awful funny, fall out and God knows what all. It just ain't our fault, is the way I look at it."

There was a pause. The women stared at each other in the mirror.

"Who was it?" demanded Mrs. Fletcher.

"Honey, I really couldn't say," said Leota. "Not that you look it."

"Where's Thelma? I'll get it out of her," said Mrs. Fletcher.

"Now, honey, I wouldn't go and git mad over a little thing like that," Leota said, combing hastily, as though to hold Mrs. Fletcher down by the hair. "I'm sure it was somebody didn't mean no harm in the world. How far gone are you?"

"Just wait," said Mrs. Fletcher, and shrieked for Thelma, who came in and took a drag from Leota's cigarette.

"Thelma, honey, throw your mind back to yestiddy if you kin," said Leota, drenching Mrs. Fletcher's hair with a thick fluid and catching the overflow in a cold wet towel at her neck.

"Well, I got my lady half wound for a spiral," said Thelma doubtfully.

"This won't take but a minute," said Leota. "Who is it you got in there, old Horse Face? Just cast your mind back and try to remember who your lady was yestiddy who happ'm to mention that my customer was pregnant, that's all. She's dead to know."

Thelma drooped her blood-red lips and looked over Mrs. Fletcher's head into the mirror. "Why, honey, I ain't got the faintest," she breathed. "I really don't recollect the faintest. But I'm sure she meant no harm. I declare, I forgot my hair finally got combed and thought it was a stranger behind me."

"Was it that Mrs. Hutchinson?" Mrs. Fletcher was tensely polite.

"Mrs. Hutchinson? Oh, Mrs. Hutchinson." Thelma batted her eyes. "Naw, precious, she come on Thursday and didn't ev'm mention your name. I doubt if she ev'm knows you're on the way."

"Thelma!" cried Leota staunchly.

"All I know is, whoever it is 'll be sorry some day. Why, I just barely knew it myself!" cried Mrs. Fletcher. "Just let her wait!"

"Why? What're you gonna do to her?"

It was a child's voice, and the women looked down. A little boy was making tents with aluminum wave pinchers[2] on the floor under the sink.

"Billy Boy, hon, mustn't bother nice ladies," Leota smiled. She slapped him brightly and behind her back waved Thelma out of the booth. "Ain't Billy Boy a sight? Only three years old and already just nuts about the beauty-parlor business."

"I never saw him here before," said Mrs. Fletcher, still unmollified.

"He ain't been here before, that's how come," said Leota. "He belongs to Mrs. Pike. She got her a job but it was Fay's Millinery. He oughtn't to try on

2. Clips used to form and hold (or set) hair curl or wave.

those ladies' hats, they come down over his eyes like I don't know what. They just git to look ridiculous, that's what, an' of course he's gonna put 'em on: hats. They tole Mrs. Pike they didn't appreciate him hangin' around there. Here, he couldn't hurt a thing."

"Well! I don't like children that much," said Mrs. Fletcher.

"Well!" said Leota moodily.

"Well! I'm almost tempted not to have this one," said Mrs. Fletcher. "That Mrs. Hutchinson! Just looks straight through you when she sees you on the street and then spits at you behind your back."

"Mr. Fletcher would beat you on the head if you didn't have it now," said Leota reasonably. "After going this far."

Mrs. Fletcher sat up straight. "Mr. Fletcher can't do a thing with me."

"He can't!" Leota winked at herself in the mirror.

"No, siree, he can't. If he so much as raises his voice against me, he knows good and well I'll have one of my sick headaches, and then I'm just not fit to live with. And if I really look that pregnant already—"

"Well, now, honey, I just want you to know—I habm't told any of my ladies and I ain't goin' to tell 'em—even that you're losin' your hair. You just get you one of those Stork-a-Lure dresses and stop worryin'. What people don't know don't hurt nobody, as Mrs. Pike says."

"Did you tell Mrs. Pike?" asked Mrs. Fletcher sulkily.

"Well, Mrs. Fletcher, look, you ain't ever goin' to lay eyes on Mrs. Pike or her lay eyes on you, so what diffunce does it make in the long run?"

"I knew it!" Mrs. Fletcher deliberately nodded her head so as to destroy a ringlet Leota was working on behind her ear. "Mrs. Pike!"

Leota sighed. "I reckon I might as well tell you. It wasn't any more Thelma's lady tole me you was pregnant than a bat."

"Not Mrs. Hutchinson?"

"Naw, Lord! It was Mrs. Pike."

"Mrs. Pike!" Mrs. Fletcher could only sputter and let curling fluid roll into her ear. "How could Mrs. Pike possibly know I was pregnant or otherwise, when she doesn't even know me? The nerve of some people!"

"Well, here's how it was. Remember Sunday?"

"Yes," said Mrs. Fletcher.

"Sunday, Mrs. Pike an' me was all by ourself. Mr. Pike and Fred had gone over to Eagle Lake, sayin' they was goin' to catch 'em some fish, but they didn't a course. So we was gettin' in Mrs. Pike's car, it's a 1939 Dodge—"

"1939, eh," said Mrs. Fletcher.

"—An' we was gettin' us a Jax beer apiece—that's the beer that Mrs. Pike says is made right in N.O., so she won't drink no other kind. So I seen you drive up to the drugstore an' run in for just a secont, leavin' I reckon Mr. Fletcher in the car, an' come runnin' out with looked like a perscription. So I says to Mrs. Pike, just to be makin' talk, 'Right yonder's Mrs. Fletcher, and I reckon that's Mr. Fletcher—she's one of my regular customers,' I says."

"I had on a figured print," said Mrs. Fletcher tentatively.

"You sure did," agreed Leota. "So Mrs. Pike, she give you a good look— she's very observant, a good judge of character, cute as a minute, you know— and she says, 'I bet you another Jax that lady's three months on the way.'"

"What gall!" said Mrs. Fletcher. "Mrs. Pike!"

"Mrs. Pike ain't goin' to bite you," said Leota. "Mrs. Pike is a lovely girl, you'd be crazy about her, Mrs. Fletcher. But she can't sit still a minute. We went to the travellin' freak show yestiddy after work. I got through early—nine o'clock. In the vacant store next door. What, you ain't been?"

"No, I despise freaks," declared Mrs. Fletcher.

"Aw. Well, honey, talkin' about bein' pregnant an' all, you ought to see those twins in a bottle, you really owe it to yourself."

"What twins?" asked Mrs. Fletcher out of the side of her mouth.

"Well, honey, they got these two twins in a bottle, see? Born joined plumb together—dead a course." Leota dropped her voice into a soft lyrical hum. "They was about this long—pardon—must of been full time, all right, wouldn't you say?—an' they had these two heads an' two faces an' four arms an' four legs, all kind of joined *here*. See, this face looked this-a-way, and the other face looked that-a-way, over their shoulder, see. Kinda pathetic."

"Glah!" said Mrs. Fletcher disapprovingly.

"Well, ugly? Honey, I mean to tell you—their parents was first cousins and all like that. Billy Boy, git me a fresh towel from off Teeny's stack—this 'n's wringin' wet—an' quit ticklin' my ankles with that curler. I declare! He don't miss nothin'."

"Me and Mr. Fletcher aren't one speck of kin, or he could never of had me," said Mrs. Fletcher placidly.

"Of course not!" protested Leota. "Neither is me an' Fred, not that we know of. Well, honey, what Mrs. Pike liked was the pygmies. They've got these pygmies down there, too, an' Mrs. Pike was just wild about 'em. You know, the teeniniest men in the universe? Well, honey, they can just rest back on their little bohunkus an' roll around an' you can't hardly tell if they're sittin' or standin'. That'll give you some idea. They're about forty-two years old. Just suppose it was your husband!"

"Well, Mr. Fletcher is five foot nine and one half," said Mrs. Fletcher quickly.

"Fred's five foot ten," said Leota, "but I tell him he's still a shrimp, account of I'm so tall." She made a deep wave over Mrs. Fletcher's other temple with the comb. "Well, these pygmies are a kind of a dark brown, Mrs. Fletcher. Not bad lookin' for what they are, you know."

"I wouldn't care for them," said Mrs. Fletcher. "What does that Mrs. Pike see in them?"

"Aw, I don't know," said Leota. "She's just cute, that's all. But they got this man, this petrified man, that ever'thing ever since he was nine years old, when it goes through his digestion, see, somehow Mrs. Pike says it goes to his joints and has been turning to stone."

"How awful!" said Mrs. Fletcher.

"He's forty-two too. That looks like a bad age."

"Who said so, that Mrs. Pike? I bet she's forty-two," said Mrs. Fletcher.

"Naw," said Leota, "Mrs. Pike's thirty-three, born in January, an Aquarian. He could move his head—like this. A course his head and mind ain't a joint, so to speak, and I guess his stomach ain't, either—not yet, anyways. But see—his food, he eats it, and it goes down, see, and then he digests it"—Leota rose on her toes for an instant—"and it goes out to his joints and before you can say 'Jack Robinson,' it's stone—pure stone. He's turning to stone. How'd you liked to be married to a guy like that? All he can do, he can move his head just a quarter of an inch. A course he *looks* just *terrible*."

"I should think he would," said Mrs. Fletcher frostily. "Mr. Fletcher takes bending exercises every night of the world. I make him."

"All Fred does is lay around the house like a rug. I wouldn't be surprised if he woke up some day and couldn't move. The petrified man just sat there moving his quarter of an inch though," said Leota reminiscently.

"Did Mrs. Pike like the petrified man?" asked Mrs. Fletcher.

"Not as much as she did the others," said Leota deprecatingly. "And then she likes a man to be a good dresser, and all that."

"Is Mr. Pike a good dresser?" asked Mrs. Fletcher sceptically.

"Oh, well, yeah," said Leota, "but he's twelve or fourteen years older'n her. She ast Lady Evangeline about him."

"Who's Lady Evangeline?" asked Mrs. Fletcher.

"Well, it's this mind reader they got in the freak show," said Leota. "Was real good. Lady Evangeline is her name, and if I had another dollar I wouldn't do a thing but have my other palm read. She had what Mrs. Pike said was the 'sixth mind' but she had the worst manicure I ever saw on a living person."

"What did she tell Mrs. Pike?" asked Mrs. Fletcher.

"She told her Mr. Pike was as true to her as he could be and besides, would come into some money."

"Humph!" said Mrs. Fletcher. "What does he do?"

"I can't tell," said Leota, "because he don't work. Lady Evangeline didn't tell me enough about my nature or anything. And I would like to go back and find out some more about this boy. Used to go with this boy until he got married to this girl. Oh, shoot, that was about three and a half years ago, when you was still goin' to the Robert E. Lee Beauty Shop in Jackson. He married her for her money. Another fortune-teller tole me that at the time. So I'm not in love with him any more, anyway, besides being married to Fred, but Mrs. Pike thought, just for the hell of it, see, to ask Lady Evangeline was he happy."

"Does Mrs. Pike know everything about you already?" asked Mrs. Fletcher unbelievingly. "Mercy!"

"Oh, yeah, I tole her ever'thing about ever'thing, from now on back to I don't know when—to when I first started goin' out," said Leota. "So I ast Lady Evangeline for one of my questions, was he happily married, and she says, just like she was glad I ask her, 'Honey,' she says, 'naw, he idn't. You write down this day, March 8, 1941,' she says, 'and mock it down: three years from today him and her won't be occupyin' the same bed.' There it is, up on the wall with them other dates—see, Mrs. Fletcher? And she says, 'Child, you ought to be glad you didn't git him, because he's so mercenary.' So I'm glad I married Fred. He sure ain't mercenary, money don't mean a thing to him. But I sure would like to go back and have my other palm read."

"Did Mrs. Pike believe in what the fortune-teller said?" asked Mrs. Fletcher in a superior tone of voice.

"Lord, yes, she's from New Orleans. Ever'body in New Orleans believes ever'thing spooky. One of 'em in New Orleans before it was raided says to Mrs. Pike one summer she was goin' to go from State to State and meet some grey-headed men, and, sure enough, she says she went on a beautician convention up to Chicago. . . ."

"Oh!" said Mrs. Fletcher. "Oh, is Mrs. Pike a beautician too?"

"Sure she is," protested Leota. "She's a beautician. I'm goin' to git her in here if I can. Before she married. But it don't leave you. She says sure enough, there was three men who was a very large part of making her trip what it was, and they all three had grey in their hair and they went in six States. Got Christmas cards from 'em. Billy Boy, go see if Thelma's got any dry cotton. Look how Mrs. Fletcher's a-drippin'."

"Where did Mrs. Pike meet Mr. Pike?" asked Mrs. Fletcher primly.

"On another train," said Leota.

"I met Mr. Fletcher, or rather he met me, in a rental library," said Mrs. Fletcher with dignity, as she watched the net come down over her head.

"Honey, me an' Fred, we met in a rumble seat[3] eight months ago and we was practically on what you might call the way to the altar inside of half an hour," said Leota in a guttural voice, and bit a bobby pin open. "Course it don't last. Mrs. Pike says nothin' like that ever lasts."

"Mr. Fletcher and myself are as much in love as the day we married," said Mrs. Fletcher belligerently as Leota stuffed cotton into her ears.

"Mrs. Pike says it don't last," repeated Leota in a louder voice. "Now go git under the dryer. You can turn yourself on, can't you? I'll be back to comb you out. Durin' lunch I promised to give Mrs. Pike a facial. You know—free. Her bein' in the business, so to speak."

"I bet she needs one," said Mrs. Fletcher, letting the swing-door fly back against Leota. "Oh, pardon me."

A week later, on time for her appointment, Mrs. Fletcher sank heavily into Leota's chair after first removing a drug-store rental book, called *Life Is Like That,* from the seat. She stared in a discouraged way into the mirror.

"You can tell it when I'm sitting down, all right," she said.

Leota seemed preoccupied and stood shaking out a lavender cloth. She began to pin it around Mrs. Fletcher's neck in silence.

"I said you sure can tell it when I'm sitting straight on and coming at you this way," Mrs. Fletcher said.

"Why, honey, naw you can't," said Leota gloomily. "Why, I'd never know. If somebody was to come up to me on the street and say, 'Mrs. Fletcher is pregnant!' I'd say, 'Heck, she don't look it to me.' "

"If a certain party hadn't found it out and spread it around, it wouldn't be too late even now," said Mrs. Fletcher frostily, but Leota was almost choking her with the cloth, pinning it so tight, and she couldn't speak clearly. She paddled her hands in the air until Leota wearily loosened her.

"Listen, honey, you're just a virgin compared to Mrs. Montjoy," Leota was going on, still absent-minded. She bent Mrs. Fletcher back in the chair and, sighing, tossed liquid from a teacup on to her head and dug both hands into her scalp. "You know Mrs. Montjoy—her husband's that premature-grey-headed fella?"

"She's in the Trojan Garden Club, is all I know," said Mrs. Fletcher.

"Well, honey," said Leota, but in a weary voice, "she come in here not the week before and not the day before she had her baby—she come in here the very selfsame day, I mean to tell you. Child, we was all plumb scared to death. There she was! Come for her shampoo an' set. Why, Mrs. Fletcher, in an hour an' twenty minutes she was layin' up there in the Babtist Hospital with a seb'm-pound son. It was that close a shave. I declare, if I hadn't been so tired I would of drank up a bottle of gin that night."

"What gall," said Mrs. Fletcher. "I never knew her at all well."

"See, her husband was waitin' outside in the car, and her bags was all packed an' in the back seat, an' she was all ready, 'cept she wanted her shampoo an' set. An' havin' one pain right after another. Her husband kep' comin' in here, scared-like, but couldn't do nothin' with her a course. She yelled bloody murder, too, but she always yelled her head off when I give her a perm'nent."

"She must of been crazy," said Mrs. Fletcher. "How did she look?"

"Shoot!" said Leota.

"Well, I can guess," asid Mrs. Fletcher. "Awful."

"Just wanted to look pretty while she was havin' her baby, is all," said Leota airily. "Course, we was glad to give the lady what she was after—that's our motto—but I bet a hour later she wasn't payin' no mind to them little end curls. I bet she wasn't thinkin' about she ought to have on a net. It wouldn't of done her no good if she had."

"No, I don't suppose it would," said Mrs. Fletcher.

"Yeah man! She was a-yellin'. Just like when I give her perm'nent."

"Her husband ought to make her behave. Don't it seem that way to you?" asked Mrs. Fletcher. "He ought to put his foot down."

"Ha," said Leota. "A lot he could do. Maybe some women is soft."

"Oh, you mistake me, I don't mean for her to get soft—far from it! Women have to stand up for themselves, or there's just no telling. But now you take me—I ask Mr. Fletcher's advice now and then, and he appreciates it, especially on something important, like is it time for a permanent—not that I've told him about the baby. He says, 'Why, dear, go ahead!' Just ask their *advice*."

"Huh! If I ever ast Fred's advice we'd be floatin' down the Yazoo River on a houseboat or somethin' by this time," said Leota. "I'm sick of Fred. I told him to go over to Vicksburg."

"Is he going?" demanded Mrs. Fletcher.

"Sure. See, the fortune-teller—I went back and had my other palm read, since we've got to rent the room agin—said my lover was goin' to work in Vicksburg, so I don't know who she could mean, unless she meant Fred. And Fred ain't workin' here—that much is so."

"Is he going to work in Vicksburg?" asked Mrs. Fletcher. "And—"

"Sure. Lady Evangeline said so. Said the future is going to be brighter than the present. He don't want to go, but I ain't gonna put up with nothin' like that. Lays around the house an' bulls—did bull—with that good-for-nothin' Mr. Pike. He says if he goes who'll cook, but I says I never get to eat anyway—not meals. Billy Boy, take Mrs. Grover that *Screen Secrets* and leg it."

Mrs. Fletcher heard stamping feet go out the door.

"Is that that Mrs. Pike's little boy here again?" she asked, sitting up gingerly.

"Yeah, that's still him." Leota stuck out her tongue.

Mrs. Fletcher could hardly believe her eyes. "Well! How's Mrs. Pike, your attractive new friend with the sharp eyes who spreads it around town that perfect strangers are pregnant?" she asked in a sweetened tone.

"Oh, Mizziz Pike." Leota combed Mrs. Fletcher's hair with heavy strokes.

"You act like you're tired," said Mrs. Fletcher.

"Tired? Feel like it's four o'clock in the afternoon already," said Leota. "I ain't told you the awful luck we had, me and Fred? It's the worst thing you ever heard of. Maybe *you* think Mrs. Pike's got sharp eyes. Shoot, there's a limit! Well, you know, we rented out our room to this Mr. and Mrs. Pike from New Orleans when Sal an' Joe Fentress got mad at us 'cause they drank up some home-brew we had in the closet—Sal an' Joe did. So, a week ago Sat'-day Mr. and Mrs. Pike moved in. Well, I kinda fixed up the room, you know—put a sofa pillow on the couch and picked some ragged robbins and put in a vase, but they never did say they appreciated it. Anyway, then I put some old magazines on the table."

"I think that was lovely," said Mrs. Fletcher.

"Wait. So, come night 'fore last, Fred and this Mr. Pike, who Fred just took up with, was back from they said they was fishin', bein' as neither one of 'em has got a job to his name, and we was all settin' around their room. So Mrs. Pike was settin' there, readin' a old *Startling G-Man Tales* that was mine, mind you, I'd bought it myself, and all of a sudden she jumps!—into the air—you'd 'a' thought she'd set on a spider—an' says, 'Canfield'—ain't that silly, that's Mr. Pike—'Canfield, my God A'mighty,' she says, 'honey,' she says, 'we're rich, and you won't have to work.' Not that he turned one hand anyway. Well, me and Fred rushes over to her, and Mr. Pike, too, and there she sets, pointin' her finger at a photo in my copy of *Startling G-Man*. 'See that man?' yells Mrs. Pike. 'Remember him, Canfield?' 'Never forget a face,' says Mr. Pike. 'It's Mr. Petrie, that we stayed with him in the apartment next to ours in Toulouse Street in N.O. for six weeks. Mr. Petrie.' 'Well,' says Mrs. Pike, like she can't hold out one seconct longer, 'Mr. Petrie is wanted for five hundred dollars cash, for rapin' four women in California, and I know where he is.' "

"Mercy!" said Mrs. Fletcher. "Where was he?"

At some time Leota had washed her hair and now she yanked her up by the back locks and sat her up.

"Know where he was?"

"I certainly don't," Mrs. Fletcher said. Her scalp hurt all over.

Leota flung a towel around the top of her customer's head. "Nowhere else but in that freak show! I saw him just as plain as Mrs. Pike. He was the pet-rified man!"

"Who would ever have thought that!" cried Mrs. Fletcher sympathetically.

"So Mr. Pike says, 'Well whatta you know about that', an' he looks real hard at the photo and whistles. And she starts dancin' and singin' about their good luck. She meant our bad luck! I made a point of tellin' that fortune-teller the next time I saw her. I said, 'Listen, that magazine was layin' around the house for a month, and there was the freak show runnin' night an' day, not two steps away from my own beauty parlor, with Mr. Petrie just settin' there waitin'. An' it had to be Mr. and Mrs. Pike, almost perfect strangers.' "

"What gall," said Mrs. Fletcher. She was only sitting there, wrapped in a turban, but she did not mind.

"Fortune-tellers don't care. And Mrs. Pike, she goes around actin' like she thinks she was Mrs. God," said Leota. "So they're goin' to leave tomorrow, Mr. and Mrs. Pike. And in the meantime I got to keep that mean, bad little ole kid here, gettin' under my feet ever' minute of the day an' talkin' back too."

"Have they gotten the five hundred dollars' reward already?" asked Mrs. Fletcher.

"Well," said Leota, "at first Mr. Pike didn't want to do anything about it.

Can you feature that? Said he kinda liked that ole bird and said he was real nice to 'em, lent 'em money or somethin'. But Mrs. Pike simply tole him he could just go to hell, and I can see her point. She says, 'You ain't worked a lick in six months, and here I make five hundred dollars in two seconts, and what thanks do I get for it? You go to hell, Canfield,' she says. So," Leota went on in a despondent voice, "they called up the cops and they caught the ole bird, all right, right there in the freak show where I saw him with my own eyes, thinkin' he was petrified. He's the one. Did it under his real name—Mr. Petrie. Four women in California, all in the month of August. So Mrs. Pike gits five hundred dollars. And my magazine, and right next door to my beauty parlor. I cried all night, but Fred said it wasn't a bit of use and to go to sleep, because the whole thing was just a sort of coincidence—you know: can't do nothin' about it. He says it put him clean out of the notion of goin' to Vicksburg for a few days till we rent out the room agin—no tellin' who we'll git this time."

"But can you imagine anybody knowing this old man, that's raped four women?" persisted Mrs. Fletcher, and she shuddered audibly. "Did Mrs. Pike *speak* to him when she met him in the freak show?"

Leota had begun to comb Mrs. Fletcher's hair. "I says to her, I says, 'I didn't notice you fallin' on his neck when he was the petrified man—don't tell me you didn't recognize your fine friend?' And she says, 'I didn't recognize him with that white powder all over his face. He just looked familiar,' Mrs. Pike says, 'and lots of people look familiar.' But she says that ole petrified man did put her in mind of somebody. She wondered who it was! Kep' her awake, which man she'd ever knew it reminded her of. So when she seen the photo, it all come to her. Like a flash. Mr. Petrie. The way he'd turn his head and look at her when she took him in his breakfast."

"Took him in his breakfast!" shrieked Mrs. Fletcher. "Listen—don't tell me. I'd 'a' felt something."

"Four women. I guess those women didn't have the faintest notion at the time they'd be worth a hundred an' twenty-five bucks apiece some day to Mrs. Pike. We ast her how old the fella was then, an's she says he musta had one foot in the grave, at least. Can you beat it?"

"Not really petrified at all, of course," said Mrs. Fletcher meditatively. She drew herself up. "I'd 'a' felt something," she said proudly.

"Shoot! I did feel somethin'," said Leota. "I tole Fred when I got home I felt so funny. I said, 'Fred, that ole petrified man sure did leave me with a funny feelin'.' He says, 'Funny-haha or funny-peculiar?' and I says, 'Funny-peculiar.'" She pointed her comb into the air emphatically.

"I'll bet you did," said Mrs. Fletcher.

They both heard a crackling noise.

Leota screamed, "Billy Boy! What you doin' in my purse?"

"Aw, I'm just eatin' these ole stale peanuts up," said Billy Boy.

"You come here to me!" screamed Leota, recklessly flinging down the comb, which scattered a whole ashtray full of bobby pins and knocked down a row of Coca-Cola bottles. "This is the last straw!"

"I caught him! I caught him!" giggled Mrs. Fletcher. "I'll hold him on my lap. You bad, bad boy, you! I guess I better learn how to spank little old bad boys," she said.

Leota's eleven o'clock customer pushed open the swing-door upon Leota's paddling him heartily with the brush, while he gave angry but belittling screams which penetrated beyond the booth and filled the whole curious beauty parlor. From everywhere ladies began to gather round to watch the paddling. Billy Boy kicked both Leota and Mrs. Fletcher as hard as he could, Mrs. Fletcher with her new fixed smile.

Billy Boy stomped through the group of wild-haired ladies and went out the door, but flung back the words, "If you're so smart, why ain't you rich?"

1941

TENNESSEE WILLIAMS
1911–1983

Speaking of Blanche DuBois, the heroine of *A Streetcar Named Desire*, Tennessee Williams once said, "She was a demonic creature; the size of her feeling was too great for her to contain." In Williams's plays—he wrote and rewrote more than twenty full-length dramas as well as films and shorter works—his characters are driven by the size of their feelings, much as Williams felt driven to write about them.

He was born Thomas Lanier Williams in Columbus, Mississippi. His mother, "Miss Edwina," the daughter of an Episcopalian minister, was repressed and genteel, very much the southern belle in her youth. His father, Cornelius, was a traveling salesman, often away from his family and often violent and drunk when at home. As a child Williams was sickly and overly protected by his mother; he was closely attached to his sister, Rose, repelled by the roughhouse world of boys, and alienated from his father. The family's move from Mississippi to St. Louis, where Cornelius became a sales manager of the shoe company he had traveled for, was a shock to Mrs. Williams and her young children, used to living in small southern towns where a minister's daughter was an important person. Yet Mrs. Williams could take care of herself; she was a "survivor."

Williams went to the University of Missouri, but left after two years; his father then found him a job in the shoe-factory warehouse. He worked there for nearly three years, writing feverishly at night. (His closest friend at the time was a burly coworker, easygoing and attractive to women, named Stanley Kowalski, whose name and characteristics Williams would borrow for *A Streetcar Named Desire*.) Williams found the life so difficult, however, that he succumbed to a nervous breakdown. After recovering at the home of his beloved grandparents, he went on to further studies, finally graduating at the age of twenty-seven. Earlier Rose had been suffering increasing mental imbalance; the final trauma was apparently brought on by one of Cornelius's alcoholic rages, in which he beat Edwina and, trying to calm Rose, made a gesture that she took to be a sexual one. Shortly thereafter Edwina signed the papers allowing Rose to be "tragically becalmed" by a prefrontal lobotomy. Rose spent most of her life in sanatoriums, except when Williams brought her out for visits.

The next year Williams left for New Orleans, the first of many temporary homes; it would provide the setting for *A Streetcar Named Desire*. In New Orleans he changed his name to "Tennessee," later giving—as often when discussing his life—various romantic reasons for doing so. There also he actively entered the homosexual world.

Williams had had plays produced at local theaters and in 1939 he won a prize for a collection of one-act plays, *American Blues*. The next year *Battle of Angels* failed (in 1957 he would rewrite it as *Orpheus Descending*). His first success was *The Glass*

Menagerie (1945). Williams called it a "memory play," seen through the recollections of the writer, Tom, who talks to the audience about himself and about the scenes depicting his mother, Amanda, poverty-stricken but genteelly living on memories of her southern youth and her "gentlemen callers"; his crippled sister, Laura, who finds refuge in her "menagerie" of little glass animals; and the traumatic effect of a modern "gentleman caller" on them. While there are similarities between Edwina, Rose, and Tennessee on the one hand, and Amanda, Laura, and Tom on the other, there are also differences: the play is not literally autobiographical.

The financial success of *Menagerie* proved exhilarating, then debilitating. Williams fled to Mexico, to work full time on an earlier play, *The Poker Night*. It had begun as *The Moth*; its first image, as Williams's biographer, Donald Spoto, tells us, was "simply that of a woman, sitting with folded hands near a window, while moonlight streamed in and she awaited in vain the arrival of her boy friend": named Blanche, she was at first intended as a young Amanda. During rehearsals of *Menagerie*, Williams had asked members of the stage crew to teach him to play poker, and he began to visualize his new play as a series of confrontations between working-class poker players and two refined southern women.

As the focus of his attention changed from Stanley to Blanche, *The Poker Night* turned into *A Streetcar Named Desire*. Upon opening in 1947, it was an even greater success than *The Glass Menagerie*, and it won the Pulitzer Prize. Williams was able to travel and to buy a home in Key West, Florida, where he did much of his ensuing work. At about this time his "transitory heart" found "a home at last" in a young man named Frank Merlo.

For more than a decade thereafter a new Williams play appeared almost every two years. Among the most successful were *The Rose Tattoo* (1950), in which the tempestuous heroine, Serafina, worshiping the memory of her dead husband, finds love again; the Pulitzer Prize–winning *Cat on a Hot Tin Roof* (1955), which portrays the conflict of the dying Big Daddy and his impotent son, Brick, watched and controlled by Brick's wife, "Maggie the Cat"; and *The Night of the Iguana* (1961), which brings a varied group of tormented people together at a rundown hotel on the Mexican coast. His plays were produced widely abroad and also became equally successful films. Yet some of the ones now regarded as the best of this period were commercial failures: *Summer and Smoke* (1948), for example, and the surrealistic and visionary *Camino Real* (1953).

For years Williams had depended on a wide variety of drugs, especially to help him sleep and to keep him awake in the early mornings, when he invariably worked. In the 1960s the drugs began to take a real toll. Other factors contributed to the decline of his later years: Frank Merlo's death, the emergence of younger playwrights of whom he felt blindly jealous, and the violent nature of the 1960s, which seemed both to mirror his inner chaos and to leave him behind.

Yet despite Broadway failures, critical disparagements, and a breakdown for which he was hospitalized, he valiantly kept working. Spoto notes that in Williams's late work, Rose was "the source and inspiration of everything he wrote, either directly—with a surrogate character representing her—or indirectly, in the situation of romanticized mental illness or unvarnished verisimilitude." This observation is certainly true of his last Broadway play, the failed *Clothes for a Summer Hotel* (1980), ostensibly about the ghosts of Scott and Zelda Fitzgerald, and of the play he obsessively wrote and rewrote, *The Two Character Play*, which chronicles the descent into madness and death of a brother and sister who are also lovers.

Despite Williams's self-destructiveness, in his writing and in his social life, the work of his great years was now being seriously studied and often revived by regional and community theaters. Critics began to see that he was one of America's best and most dedicated playwrights. And he kept on working. He was collaborating on a film of two stories about Rose when he died apparently having choked to death on the lid of a pill bottle.

Always reluctant to talk about his work (likening it to a "bird that will be startled away, as by a hawk's shadow"), Williams did not see himself in a tradition of American dramaturgy. He acknowledged the influence of Anton Chekhov, the nineteenth-century Russian writer of dramas with lonely, searching characters; of D. H. Lawrence, the British novelist who emphasized the theme of a sexual life force; and above all of the American Hart Crane, homosexual *poète maudit*, who, he said, "touched fire that burned [himself] alive," adding that "perhaps it is only through self-immolation of such a nature that we living beings can offer to you the entire truth of ourselves." Such a statement indicates the deeply confessional quality of Williams's writing, even in plays not directly autobiographical.

Although he never acknowledged any debt to the American playwright Eugene O'Neill, Williams shared with O'Neill an impatience over realistic theater conventions. *The Glass Menagerie*, for example, uses screened projections, lighting effects, and music to emphasize that it takes place in Tom's memory. *A Streetcar Named Desire* moves in and out of the house on Elysian Fields, while music and lighting reinforce all the major themes. Williams also relies on the effects of language, especially of a vivid and colloquial southern speech that may be compared with that of William Faulkner, Eudora Welty, or Flannery O'Connor. Rhythms of language become almost a musical indication of character, distinguishing Blanche from other characters. Reading or seeing his plays, we become aware of how symbolic repetitions—in Blanche's and Stanley's turns of phrase, the naked light bulb and the paper lantern, the Mexican woman selling flowers for the dead, the "Varsouviana" waltz and the reverberating voices—produce a heightening of reality: what Williams called "poetic realism."

More than a half century later does the destruction of Blanche, the "lady," still have the power to move us? Elia Kazan, in his director's notes, calls her "an outdated creature, approaching extinction . . . like a dinosaur." But Blythe Danner, who played Blanche in a 1988 revival, acutely observes that Williams "was attached to the things that were going to destroy him" and that Blanche, similarly, is attracted to and repelled by Stanley: "It's Tennessee fighting, fighting, fighting what he doesn't want to get into, what is very prevalent in his mind. That incredible contradiction in so many people is what he captures better than any other playwright."

Contemporary criticisms of Williams's plays focused on their violence and their obsession with sexuality, which in some of the later work struck some commentators as an almost morbid preoccupation with "perversion"—murder, rape, drugs, incest, nymphomania. The shriller voices making such accusations were attacking Williams for his homosexuality, which could not be publicly spoken of in this country until comparatively recently. These taboo topics, however, figure as instances of Williams's deeper subjects: desire and loneliness. As he said in an interview, "Desire is rooted in a longing for companionship, a release from the loneliness that haunts every individual." Loneliness and desire propel his characters into extreme behavior, no doubt, but such behavior literally dramatizes the plight that Williams saw as universal.

The text is from *The Theatre of Tennessee Williams*, volume 1 (1971).

A Streetcar Named Desire

And so it was I entered the broken world
To trace the visionary company of love, its voice
An instant in the wind (I know not whither hurled)
But not for long to hold each desperate choice.
—*"The Broken Tower"* by Hart Crane[1]

THE CHARACTERS

BLANCHE	PABLO
STELLA	A NEGRO WOMAN
STANLEY	A DOCTOR
MITCH	A NURSE
EUNICE	A YOUNG COLLECTOR
STEVE	A MEXICAN WOMAN

Scene One

The exterior of a two-story corner building on a street in New Orleans which is named Elysian Fields and runs between the L & N tracks and the river.[2] The section is poor but, unlike corresponding sections in other American cities, it has a raffish charm. The houses are mostly white frame, weathered grey, with rickety outside stairs and galleries and quaintly ornamented gables. This building contains two flats, upstairs and down. Faded white stairs ascend to the entrances of both.

It is first dark of an evening early in May. The sky that shows around the dim white building is a peculiarly tender blue, almost a turquoise, which invests the scene with a kind of lyricism and gracefully attenuates the atmosphere of decay. You can almost feel the warm breath of the brown river beyond the river warehouses with their faint redolences of bananas and coffee. A corresponding air is evoked by the music of Negro entertainers at a barroom around the corner. In this part of New Orleans you are practically always just around the corner, or a few doors down the street, from a tinny piano being played with the infatuated fluency of brown fingers. This "Blue Piano" expresses the spirit of the life which goes on here.

Two women, one white and one colored, are taking the air on the steps of the building. The white woman is EUNICE, *who occupies the upstairs flat; the colored woman a neighbor, for New Orleans is a cosmopolitan city where there is a relatively warm and easy intermingling of races in the old part of town.*

Above the music of the "Blue Piano" the voices of people on the street can be heard overlapping.

[*Two men come around the corner,* STANLEY KOWALSKI *and* MITCH. *They are about twenty-eight or thirty years old, roughly dressed in blue denim work clothes.* STANLEY *carries his bowling jacket and a red-stained package from a butcher's. They stop at the foot of the steps.*]

STANLEY [*bellowing*]   Hey there! Stella, baby!

[STELLA *comes out on the first floor landing, a gentle young woman, about twenty-five, and of a background obviously quite different from her husband's.*]

---

1. American poet (1899–1932).
2. Elysian Fields is a New Orleans street at the northern tip of the French Quarter, between the Louisville & Nashville railroad tracks and the Mis-sissippi River. In Greek mythology the Elysian Fields are the abode of the blessed in the afterlife.

STELLA [*mildly*]   Don't holler at me like that. Hi, Mitch.

STANLEY   Catch!

STELLA   What?

STANLEY   Meat!

> [*He heaves the package at her. She cries out in protest but manages to catch it: then she laughs breathlessly. Her husband and his companion have already started back around the corner.*]

STELLA [*calling after him*]   Stanley! Where are you going?

STANLEY   Bowling!

STELLA   Can I come watch?

STANLEY   Come on. [*He goes out.*]

STELLA   Be over soon. [*to the white woman*] Hello, Eunice. How are you?

EUNICE   I'm all right. Tell Steve to get him a poor boy's sandwich 'cause nothing's left here.

> [*They all laugh; the colored woman does not stop.* STELLA *goes out.*]

COLORED WOMAN   What was that package he th'ew at 'er? [*She rises from steps, laughing louder.*]

EUNICE   You hush, now!

NEGRO WOMAN   Catch *what!*

> [*She continues to laugh.* BLANCHE *comes around the corner, carrying a valise. She looks at a slip of paper, then at the building, then again at the slip and again at the building. Her expression is one of shocked disbelief. Her appearance is incongruous to this setting. She is daintily dressed in a white suit with a fluffy bodice, necklace and earrings of pearl, white gloves and hat, looking as if she were arriving at a summer tea or cocktail party in the garden district. She is about five years older than* STELLA. *Her delicate beauty must avoid a strong light. There is something about her uncertain manner, as well as her white clothes, that suggests a moth.*]

EUNICE [*finally*]   What's the matter, honey? Are you lost?

BLANCHE [*with faintly hysterical humor*]   They told me to take a street-car named Desire, and then transfer to one called Cemeteries[3] and ride six blocks and get off at—Elysian Fields!   *-actual metro stops, but heavy symbolism as well*

EUNICE   That's where you are now.

BLANCHE   At Elysian Fields?

EUNICE   This here is Elysian Fields.

BLANCHE   They mustn't have—understood—what number I wanted . . .

EUNICE   What number you lookin' for?

> [BLANCHE *wearily refers to the slip of paper.*]

BLANCHE   Six thirty-two.

EUNICE   You don't have to look no further.

BLANCHE [*uncomprehendingly*]   I'm looking for my sister, Stella DuBois, I mean—Mrs. Stanley Kowalski.

EUNICE   That's the party.—You just did miss her, though.

BLANCHE   This—can this be—her home?

EUNICE   She's got the downstairs here and I got the up.

BLANCHE   Oh. She's—out?

EUNICE   You noticed that bowling alley around the corner?

BLANCHE   I'm—not sure I did.

EUNICE   Well, that's where she's at, watchin' her husband bowl. [*There is a pause.*] You want to leave your suitcase here an' go find her?

---

3. The end of a streetcar line that stopped at a cemetery. Desire is a New Orleans street.

BLANCHE   No.

NEGRO WOMAN   I'll go tell her you come.

BLANCHE   Thanks.

NEGRO WOMAN   You welcome. [*She goes out.*]

EUNICE   She wasn't expecting you?

BLANCHE   No. No, not tonight.

EUNICE   Well, why don't you just go in and make yourself at home till they get back.

BLANCHE   How could I—do that?

EUNICE   We own this place so I can let you in.

[*She gets up and opens the downstairs door. A light goes on behind the blind, turning it light blue.* BLANCHE *slowly follows her into the downstairs flat. The surrounding areas dim out as the interior is lighted. Two rooms can be seen, not too clearly defined. The one first entered is primarily a kitchen but contains a folding bed to be used by* BLANCHE. *The room beyond this is a bedroom. Off this room is a narrow door to a bathroom.*]

EUNICE [*defensively, noticing* BLANCHE's *look*]   It's sort of messed up right now but when it's clean it's real sweet.

BLANCHE   Is it?

EUNICE   Uh-huh, I think so. So you're Stella's sister?

BLANCHE   Yes. [*wanting to get rid of her*] Thanks for letting me in.

EUNICE   *Por nada,*[4] as the Mexicans say, *por nada!* Stella spoke of you.

BLANCHE   Yes?

EUNICE   I think she said you taught school.

BLANCHE   Yes.

EUNICE   And you're from Mississippi, huh?

BLANCHE   Yes.

EUNICE   She showed me a picture of your home-place, the plantation.

BLANCHE   Belle Reve?[5]

EUNICE   A great big place with white columns.

BLANCHE   Yes . . .

EUNICE   A place like that must be awful hard to keep up.

BLANCHE   If you will excuse me, I'm just about to drop.

EUNICE   Sure, honey. Why don't you set down?

BLANCHE   What I meant was I'd like to be left alone.

EUNICE [*offended*]   Aw. I'll make myself scarce, in that case.

BLANCHE   I didn't meant to be rude, but—

EUNICE   I'll drop by the bowling alley an' hustle her up. [*She goes out the door.*]
[BLANCHE *sits in a chair very stiffly with her shoulders slightly hunched and her legs pressed close together and her hands tightly clutching her purse as if she were quite cold. After a while the blind look goes out of her eyes and she begins to look slowly around. A cat screeches. She catches her breath with a startled gesture. Suddenly she notices something in a half opened closet. She springs up and crosses to it, and removes a whiskey bottle. She pours a half tumbler of whiskey and tosses it down. She carefully replaces the bottle and washes out the tumbler at the sink. Then she resumes her seat in front of the table.*]

BLANCHE [*faintly to herself*]   I've got to keep hold of myself! [STELLA *comes quickly around the corner of the building and runs to the door of the downstairs flat.*]

---

4. It's nothing (Spanish).   5. Beautiful Dream (French).

STELLA [*calling out joyfully*] Blanche!
> [*For a moment they stare at each other. Then* BLANCHE *springs up and runs to her with a wild cry.*]

BLANCHE Stella, oh, Stella, Stella! Stella for Star!
> [*She begins to speak with feverish vivacity as if she feared for either of them to stop and think. They catch each other in a spasmodic embrace.*]

BLANCHE Now, then, let me look at you. But don't you look at me, Stella, no, no, no, not till later, not till I've bathed and rested! And turn that over-light off! Turn that off! I won't be looked at in this merciles glare! [STELLA *laughs and complies.*] Come back here now! Oh, my baby! Stella! Stella for Star! [*She embraces her again.*] I thought you would never come back to this horrible place! What am I saying? I didn't mean to say that. I meant to be nice about it and say—Oh, what a convenient location and such—Ha-a-ha! Precious lamb! You haven't said a *word* to me.

STELLA You haven't given me a chance to, honey! [*She laughs, but her glance at* BLANCHE *is a little anxious.*]

BLANCHE Well, now you talk. Open your pretty mouth and talk while I look around for some liquor! I know you must have some liquor on the place! Where could it be, I wonder? Oh, I spy, I spy!
> [*She rushes to the closet and removes the bottle; she is shaking all over and panting for breath as she tries to laugh. The bottle nearly slips from her grasp.*]

STELLA [*noticing*] Blanche, you sit down and let me pour the drinks. I don't know what we've got to mix with. Maybe a coke's in the icebox. Look'n see, honey, while I'm—

BLANCHE No coke, honey, not with my nerves tonight! Where—where—where is—?

STELLA Stanley? Bowling! He loves it. They're having a—found some soda!—tournament . . .

BLANCHE Just water, baby, to chase it! Now don't get worried, your sister hasn't turned into a drunkard, she's just all shaken up and hot and tired and dirty! You sit down, now, and explain this place to me! What are you doing in a place like this?

STELLA Now, Blanche—

BLANCHE Oh, I'm not going to be hypocritical, I'm going to be honestly critical about it! Never, never, never in my worst dreams could I picture—Only Poe! Only Mr. Edgar Allan Poe!—could do it justice! Out there I suppose is the ghoul-haunted woodland of Weir![6] [*She laughs.*]

STELLA No, honey, those are the L & N tracks.

BLANCHE No, now seriously, putting joking aside. Why didn't you tell me, why didn't you write me, honey, why didn't you let me know?

STELLA [*carefully, pouring herself a drink*] Tell you what, Blanche?

BLANCHE Why, that you had to live in these conditions!

STELLA Aren't you being a little intense about it? It's not that bad at all! New Orleans isn't like other cities.

BLANCHE This has got nothing to do with New Orleans. You might as well say—forgive me, blessed baby! [*She suddenly stops short.*] The subject is closed!

STELLA [*a little drily*] Thanks.

---

6. From the refrain of Poe's gothic ballad "Ulalume" (1847).

[*During the pause,* BLANCHE *stares at her. She smiles at* BLANCHE.]

BLANCHE [*looking down at her glass, which shakes in her hand*]   You're all I've got in the world, and you're not glad to see me!

STELLA [*sincerely*]   Why, Blanche, you know that's not true.

BLANCHE   No?—I'd forgotten how quiet you were.

STELLA   You never did give me a chance to say much, Blanche. So I just got in the habit of being quiet around you.

BLANCHE [*vaguely*]   A good habit to get into . . . [*then, abruptly*] You haven't asked me how I happened to get away from the school before the spring term ended.

STELLA   Well, I thought you'd volunteer that information—if you wanted to tell me.

BLANCHE   You thought I'd been fired?

STELLA   No, I—thought you might have—resigned . . .

BLANCHE   I was so exhausted by all I'd been through my—nerves broke. [*nervously tamping cigarette*] I was on the verge of—lunacy, almost! So Mr. Graves—Mr. Graves is the high school superintendent—he suggested I take a leave of absence. I couldn't put all of those details into the wire . . . [*She drinks quickly.*] Oh, this buzzes right through me and feels so *good!*

STELLA   Won't you have another?

BLANCHE   No, one's my limit.

STELLA   Sure?

BLANCHE   You haven't said a word about my appearance.

STELLA   You look just fine.

BLANCHE   God love you for a liar! Daylight never exposed so total a ruin! But you—you've put on some weight, yes, you're just as plump as a little partridge! And it's so becoming to you!

STELLA   Now, Blanche—

BLANCHE   Yes, it is, it is or I wouldn't say it! You just have to watch around the hips a little. Stand up.

STELLA   Not now.

BLANCHE   You hear me? I said stand up! [STELLA *complies reluctantly.*] You messy child, you, you've spilt something on that pretty white lace collar! About your hair—you ought to have it cut in a feather bob with your dainty features. Stella, you have a maid, don't you?

STELLA   No. With only two rooms it's—

BLANCHE   What? *Two* rooms, did you say?

STELLA   This one and— [*She is embarrassed.*]

BLANCHE   The other one? [*She laughs sharply. There is an embarrassed silence.*]

BLANCHE   I am going to take just one little tiny nip more, sort of to put the stopper on, so to speak. . . . Then put the bottle away so I won't be tempted. [*She rises.*] I want you to look at *my* figure! [*She turns around.*] You know I haven't put on one ounce in ten years, Stella? I weigh what I weighed the summer you left Belle Reve. The summer Dad died and you left us . . .

STELLA [*a little wearily*]   It's just incredible, Blanche, how well you're looking.

BLANCHE [*They both laugh uncomfortably.*]   But, Stella, there's only two rooms, I don't see where you're going to put me!

STELLA   We're going to put you in here.

BLANCHE   What kind of bed's this—one of those collapsible things?
[*She sits on it.*]

STELLA   Does it feel all right?

BLANCHE [*dubiously*]   Wonderful, honey. I don't like a bed that gives much.
But there's no door between the two rooms, and Stanley—will it be decent?

STELLA   Stanley is Polish, you know.

BLANCHE   Oh, yes. They're something like Irish, aren't they?

STELLA   Well—

BLANCHE   Only not so—highbrow? [*They both laugh again in the same
way.*] I brought some nice clothes to meet all your lovely friends in.

STELLA   I'm afraid you won't think they are lovely.

BLANCHE   What are they like?

STELLA   They're Stanley's friends.

BLANCHE   Polacks?

STELLA   They're a mixed lot, Blanche.

BLANCHE   Heterogeneous—types?

STELLA   Oh, yes. Yes, types is right!

BLANCHE   Well—anyhow—I brought nice clothes and I'll wear them. I
guess you're hoping I'll say I'll put up at a hotel, but I'm not going to put
up at a hotel. I want to be *near* you, got to be *with* somebody, I *can't* be
alone! Because—as you must have noticed—I'm—*not* very *well.* . . . [*Her
voice drops and her look is frightened.*]

STELLA   You seem a little bit nervous or overwrought or something.

BLANCHE   Will Stanley like me, or will I be just a visiting in-law, Stella?
I couldn't stand that.

STELLA   You'll get along fine together, if you'll just try not to—well—
compare him with men that we went out with at home.

BLANCHE   Is he so—different?

STELLA   Yes. A different species.

BLANCHE   In what way; what's he like?

STELLA   Oh, you can't describe someone you're in love with! Here's a picture of him! [*She hands a photograph to* BLANCHE.]

BLANCHE   An officer?

STELLA   A Master Sergeant in the Engineers' Corps. Those are decorations!

BLANCHE   He had those on when you met him?

STELLA   I assure you I wasn't just blinded by all the brass.

BLANCHE   That's not what I—

STELLA   But of course there were things to adjust myself to later on.

BLANCHE   Such as his civilian background! [STELLA *laughs uncertainly.*]
How did he take it when you said I was coming?

STELLA   Oh, Stanley doesn't know yet.

BLANCHE [*frightened*]   You—haven't told him?

STELLA   He's on the road a good deal.

BLANCHE   Oh. Travels?

STELLA   Yes.

BLANCHE   Good. I mean—isn't it?

STELLA [*half to herself*]   I can hardly stand it when he is away for a
night . . .

BLANCHE   Why, Stella!

STELLA   When he's away for a week I nearly go wild!

BLANCHE   Gracious!

STELLA   And when he comes back I cry on his lap like a baby . . . [*She smiles to herself.*]

BLANCHE   I guess that is what is meant by being in love . . . [STELLA *looks up with a radiant smile.*] Stella—

STELLA   What?

BLANCHE [*in an uneasy rush*]   I haven't asked you the things you probably thought I was going to ask. And so I'll expect you to be understanding about what I have to tell *you*.

STELLA   What, Blanche? [*Her face turns anxious.*]

BLANCHE   Well, Stella—you're going to reproach me, I know that you're bound to reproach me—but before you do—take into consideration—you left! I stayed and struggled! You came to New Orleans and looked out for yourself! *I* stayed at *Belle Reve* and tried to hold it together! I'm not meaning this in any reproachful way, but *all* the burden descended on *my* shoulders.

STELLA   The best I could do was make my own living, Blanche.
    [BLANCHE *begins to shake again with intensity.*]

BLANCHE   I know, I know. But you are the one that abandoned Belle Reve, not I! I stayed and fought for it, bled for it, almost died for it!

STELLA   Stop this hysterical outburst and tell me what's happened? What do you mean fought and bled? What kind of—

BLANCHE   I knew you would, Stella. I knew you would take this attitude about it!

STELLA   About—what?—please!

BLANCHE [*slowly*]   The loss—the loss . . .

STELLA   Belle Reve? Lost, is it? No!

BLANCHE   Yes, Stella.
    [*They stare at each other across the yellow-checked linoleum of the table.* BLANCHE *slowly nods her head and* STELLA *looks slowly down at her hands folded on the table. The music of the "Blue Piano" grows louder.* BLANCHE *touches her handkerchief to her forehead.*]

STELLA   But how did it go? What happened?

BLANCHE [*springing up*]   You're a fine one to ask me how it went!

STELLA   Blanche!

BLANCHE   You're a fine one to sit there *accusing me* of it!

STELLA   *Blanche!*

BLANCHE   I, I, *I* took the blows in my face and my body! All of those deaths! The long parade to the graveyard! Father, mother! Margaret, that dreadful way! So big with it, it couldn't be put in a coffin! But had to be burned like rubbish! You just came home in time for the funerals, Stella. And funerals are pretty compared to deaths. Funerals are quiet, but deaths— not always. Sometimes their breathing is hoarse, and sometimes it rattles, and sometimes they even cry out to you, "Don't let me go!" Even the old, sometimes, say, "Don't let me go." As if you were able to stop them! But funerals are quiet, with pretty flowers. And, oh, what gorgeous boxes they pack them away in! Unless you were there at the bed when they cried out, "Hold me!" you'd never suspect there was the struggle for breath and bleeding. You didn't dream, but I saw! Saw! Saw! And now you sit there telling me with your eyes that I let the place go! How in hell do you think

Death has taken over

all that sickness and dying was paid for? Death is expensive, Miss Stella! And old Cousin Jessie's right after Margaret's, hers! Why, the Grim Reaper had put up his tent on our doorstep! . . . Stella. Belle Reve was his headquarters! Honey—that's how it slipped through my fingers! Which of them left us a fortune? Which of them left a cent of insurance even? Only poor Jessie—one hundred to pay for her coffin. That was all, Stella! And I with my pitiful salary at the school. Yes, accuse me! Sit there and stare at me, thinking I let the place go! *I* let the place go? Where were *you!* In bed with your—Polack!

STELLA [*springing*]   Blanche! You be still! That's enough! [*She starts out.*]

BLANCHE   Where are you going?

STELLA   I'm going into the bathroom to wash my face.

BLANCHE   Oh, Stella, Stella, you're crying!

STELLA   Does that surprise you?

BLANCHE   Forgive me—I didn't mean to—

[*The sound of men's voices is heard.* STELLA *goes into the bathroom, closing the door behind her. When the men appear, and* BLANCHE *realizes it must be* STANLEY *returning, she moves uncertainly from the bathroom door to the dressing table, looking apprehensively toward the front door.* STANLEY *enters, followed by* STEVE *and* MITCH. STANLEY *pauses near his door,* STEVE *by the foot of the spiral stair, and* MITCH *is slightly above and to the right of them, about to go out. As the men enter, we hear some of the following dialogue.*]

STANLEY   Is that how he got it?

STEVE   Sure that's how he got it. He hit the old weather-bird for 300 bucks on a six-number-ticket.

MITCH   Don't tell him those things; he'll believe it.

[*Mitch starts out.*]

STANLEY [*restraining Mitch*]   Hey, Mitch—come back here.

[BLANCHE, *at the sound of voices, retires in the bedroom. She picks up* STANLEY's *photo from dressing table, looks at it, puts it down. When* STANLEY *enters the apartment, she darts and hides behind the screen at the head of bed.*]

STEVE [*to* STANLEY *and* MITCH]   Hey, are we playin' poker tomorrow?

STANLEY   Sure—at Mitch's.

MITCH [*hearing this, returns quickly to the stair rail*]   No—not at my place. My mother's still stick!

STANLEY   Okay, at my place . . . [MITCH *starts out again.*] But you bring the beer!

[MITCH *pretends not to hear—calls out "Good night, all," and goes out, singing.* EUNICE's *voice is heard, above.*]

Break it up down there! I made the spaghetti dish and ate it myself.

STEVE [*going upstairs*]   I told you and phoned you we was playing. [*to the men*] Jax beer![7]

EUNICE   You never phoned me once.

STEVE   I told you at breakfast—and phoned you at lunch . . .

EUNICE   Well, never mind about that. You just get yourself home here once in a while.

STEVE   You want it in the papers?

---

7. A local brand.

[*More laughter and shouts of parting come from the men.* STANLEY *throws the screen door of the kitchen open and comes in. He is of medium height, about five feet eight or nine, and strongly, compactly built. Animal joy in his being is implicit in all his movements and attitudes. Since earliest manhood the center of his life has been pleasure with women, the giving and taking of it, not with weak indulgence, dependently, but with the power and pride of a richly feathered male bird among hens. Branching out from this complete and satisfying center are all the auxiliary channels of his life, such as his heartiness with men, his appreciation of rough humor, his love of good drink and food and games, his car, his radio, everything that is his, that bears his emblem of the gaudy seed-bearer. He sizes women up at a glance, with sexual classifications, crude images flashing into his mind and determining the way he smiles at them.*]

BLANCHE [*drawing involuntarily back from his stare*]   You must be Stanley. I'm Blanche.

STANLEY   Stella's sister?

BLANCHE   Yes.

STANLEY   H'lo. Where's the little woman?

BLANCHE   In the bathroom.

STANLEY   Oh. Didn't know you were coming in town.

BLANCHE   I—uh—

STANLEY   Where you from, Blanche?

BLANCHE   Why, I—live in Laurel.

[*He has crossed to the closet and removed the whiskey bottle.*]

STANLEY   In Laurel, huh? Oh, yeah. Yeah, in Laurel, that's right. Not in my territory. Liquor goes fast in hot weather. [*He holds the bottle to the light to observe its depletion.*] Have a shot?

BLANCHE   No, I—rarely touch it.

STANLEY   Some people rarely touch it, but it touches them often.

BLANCHE [*faintly*]   Ha-ha.

STANLEY   My clothes're stickin' to me. Do you mind if I make myself comfortable? [*He starts to remove his shirt.*]

BLANCHE   Please, please do.

STANLEY   Be comfortable is my motto.

BLANCHE   It's mine, too. It's hard to stay looking fresh. I haven't washed or even powdered my face and—here you are!

STANLEY   You know you can catch cold sitting around in damp things, especially when you been exercising hard like bowling is. You're a teacher, aren't you?

BLANCHE   Yes.

STANLEY   What do you teach, Blanche?

BLANCHE   English.

STANLEY   I never was a very good English student. How long you here for, Blanche?

BLANCHE   I—don't know yet.

STANLEY   You going to shack up here?

BLANCHE   I thought I would if it's not inconvenient for you all.

STANLEY   Good.

BLANCHE   Traveling wears me out.

STANLEY   Well, take it easy.

[*A cat screeches near the window.* BLANCHE *springs up.*]

BLANCHE   What's that?

STANLEY   Cats . . . Hey, Stella!

STELLA [*faintly, from the bathroom*]   Yes, Stanley.

STANLEY   Haven't fallen in, have you? [*He grins at* BLANCHE. *She tries unsuccessfully to smile back. There is a silence.*] I'm afraid I'll strike you as being the unrefined type. Stella's spoke of you a good deal. You were married once, weren't you?

[*The music of the polka rises up, faint in the distance.*]

Foreshadowing

BLANCHE   Yes. When I was quite young.

STANLEY   What happened?

BLANCHE   The boy—the boy died. [*She sinks back down.*] I'm afraid I'm—going to be sick! [*Her head falls on her arms.*]

Scene Two

It is six o'clock the following evening. BLANCHE *is bathing.* STELLA *is completing her toilette.* BLANCHE'*s dress, a flowered print, is laid out on* STELLA'*s bed.*

STANLEY *enters the kitchen from outside, leaving the door open on the perpetual "Blue Piano" around the corner.*

STANLEY   What's all this monkey doings?

STELLA   Oh, Stan! [*She jumps up and kisses him, which he accepts with lordly composure.*] I'm taking Blanche to Galatoire's[8] for supper and then to a show, because it's your poker night.

STANLEY   How about my supper, huh? I'm not going to no Galatoire's for supper!

STELLA   I put you a cold plate on ice.

STANLEY   Well, isn't that just dandy!

STELLA   I'm going to try to keep Blanche out till the party breaks up because I don't know how she would take it. So we'll go to one of the little places in the Quarter afterward and you'd better give me some money.

STANLEY   Where is she?

STELLA   She's soaking in a hot tub to quiet her nerves. She's terribly upset.

STANLEY   Over what?

STELLA   She's been through such an ordeal.

STANLEY   Yeah?

STELLA   Stan, we've—lost Belle Reve!

STANLEY   The place in the country?

STELLA   Yes.

STANLEY   How?

STELLA [*vaguely*]   Oh, it had to be—sacrificed or something. [*There is a pause while* STANLEY *considers.* STELLA *is changing into her dress.*] When she comes in be sure to say something nice about her appearance. And, oh! Don't mention the baby. I haven't said anything yet, I'm waiting until she gets in a quieter condition.

STANLEY [*ominously*]   So?

STELLA   And try to understand her and be nice to her, Stan.

BLANCHE [*singing in the bathroom*]   "From the land of the sky blue water, They brought a captive maid!"

8. Renowned fancy restaurant with traditional New Orleans cuisine.

STELLA　She wasn't expecting to find us in such a small place. You see I'd tried to gloss things over a little in my letters.

STANLEY　So?

STELLA　And admire her dress and tell her she's looking wonderful. That's important with Blanche. Her little weakness!

STANLEY　Yeah. I get the idea. Now let's skip back a little to where you said the country place was disposed of.

STELLA　Oh!—yes . . .

STANLEY　How about that? Let's have a few more details on that subjeck.

STELLA　It's best not to talk much about it until she's calmed down.

STANLEY　So that's the deal, huh? Sister Blanche cannot be annoyed with business details right now!

STELLA　You saw how she was last night.

STANLEY　Uh-hum, I saw how she was. Now let's have a gander at the bill of sale.

STELLA　I haven't seen any.

STANLEY　She didn't show you no papers, no deed of sale or nothing like that, huh?

STELLA　It seems like it wasn't sold.

STANLEY　Well, what in hell was it then, give away? To charity?

STELLA　Shhh! She'll hear you.

STANLEY　I don't care if she hears me. Let's see the papers!

STELLA　There weren't any papers, she didn't show any papers, I don't care about papers.

STANLEY　Have you ever heard of the Napoleonic code?[9]

STELLA　No, Stanley, I haven't heard of the Napoleonic code and if I have, I don't see what it—

STANLEY　Let me enlighten you on a point or two, baby.

STELLA　Yes?

STANLEY　In the state of Louisiana we have the Napoleonic code according to which what belongs to the wife belongs to the husband and vice versa. For instance if I had a piece of property, or you had a piece of property—

STELLA　My head is swimming!

STANLEY　All right. I'll wait till she gets through soaking in a hot tub and then I'll inquire if *she* is acquainted with the Napoleonic code. It looks to me like you have been swindled, baby, and when you're swindled under the Napoleonic code I'm swindled *too*. And I don't like to be *swindled*.

STELLA　There's plenty of time to ask her questions later but if you do now she'll go to pieces again. I don't understand what happened to Belle Reve but you don't know how ridiculous you are being when you suggest that my sister or I or anyone of our family could have perpetrated a swindle on anyone else.

STANLEY　Then where's the money if the place was sold?

STELLA　Not sold—*lost, lost!*

　　　　[*He stalks into bedroom, and she follows him.*]
　　　　Stanley!
　　　　[*He pulls open the wardrobe trunk standing in middle of room and jerks out an armful of dresses.*]

9. This codification of French law (1802), made by Napoleon as emperor, is the basis for Louisiana's civil law.

STANLEY   Open your eyes to this stuff! You think she got them out of a teacher's pay?

STELLA   Hush!

STANLEY   Look at these feathers and furs that she come here to preen herself in! What's this here? A solid-gold dress, I believe! And this one! What is these here? Fox-pieces! [*He blows on them.*] Genuine fox fur-pieces, a half a mile long! Where are your fox-pieces, Stella? Bushy snow-white ones, no less! Where are your white fox-pieces?

STELLA   Those are inexpensive summer furs that Blanche has had a long time.

STANLEY   I got an acquaintance who deals in this sort of merchandise. I'll have him in here to appraise it. I'm willing to bet you there's thousands of dollars invested in this stuff here!

STELLA   Don't be such an idiot, Stanley!
       [*He hurls the furs to the day bed. Then he jerks open a small drawer in the trunk and pulls up a fistful of costume jewelry.*]

STANLEY   And what have we here? The treasure chest of a pirate!

STELLA   Oh, Stanley!

STANLEY   Pearls! Ropes of them! What is this sister of yours, a deep-sea diver? Bracelets of solid gold, too! Where are your pearls and gold bracelets?

STELLA   Shhh! Be still, Stanley!

STANLEY   And diamonds! A crown for an empress!

STELLA   A rhinestone tiara she wore to a costume ball.

STANLEY   What's rhinestone?

STELLA   Next door to glass.

STANLEY   Are you kidding? I have an acquaintance that works in a jewelry store. I'll have him in here to make an appraisal of this. Here's your plantation, or what was left of it, here!

STELLA   You have no idea how stupid and horrid you're being! Now close that trunk before she comes out of the bathroom!
       [*He kicks the trunk partly closed and sits on the kitchen table.*]

STANLEY   The Kowalskis and the DuBoises have different notions.

STELLA [*angrily*]   Indeed they have, thank heavens!—*I'm* going outside.
       [*She snatches up her white hat and gloves and crosses to the outside door.*]
       You come out with me while Blanche is getting dressed.

STANLEY   Since when do you give me orders?

STELLA   Are you going to stay here and insult her?

STANLEY   You're damn tootin' I'm going to stay here.
       [STELLA *goes out to the porch.* BLANCHE *comes out of the bathroom in a red satin robe.*]

BLANCHE [*airily*]   Hello, Stanley! Here I am, all freshly bathed and scented, and feeling like a brand new human being!
       [*He lights a cigarette.*]

STANLEY   That's good.

BLANCHE [*drawing the curtains at the windows*]   Excuse me while I slip on my pretty new dress!

STANLEY   Go right ahead, Blanche.
       [*She closes the drapes between the rooms.*]

BLANCHE   I understand there's to be a little card party to which we ladies are cordially *not* invited!

STANLEY [*ominously*]   Yeah?

[BLANCHE *throws off her robe and slips into a flowered print dress.*]

BLANCHE   Where's Stella?

STANLEY   Out on the porch.

BLANCHE   I'm going to ask a favor of you in a moment.

STANLEY   What could that be, I wonder?

BLANCHE   Some buttons in back! You may enter!
[*He crosses through drapes with a smoldering look.*]
How do I look?

STANLEY   You look all right.

BLANCHE   Many thanks! Now the buttons!

STANLEY   I can't do nothing with them.

BLANCHE   You men with your big clumsy fingers. May I have a drag on your cig?

STANLEY   Have one for yourself.

BLANCHE   Why, thanks! . . . It looks like my trunk has exploded.

STANLEY   Me an' Stella were helping you unpack.

BLANCHE   Well, you certainly did a fast and thorough job of it!

STANLEY   It looks like you raided some stylish shops in Paris.

BLANCHE   Ha-ha! Yes—clothes are my passion!

STANLEY   What does it cost for a string of fur-pieces like that?

BLANCHE   Why, those were a tribute from an admirer of mine!

STANLEY   He must have had a lot of—admiration!

BLANCHE   Oh, in my youth I excited some admiration. But look at me now!
[*She smiles at him radiantly.*] Would you think it possible that I was once considered to be—attractive?

STANLEY   Your looks are okay.

BLANCHE   I was fishing for a compliment, Stanley.

STANLEY   I don't go in for that stuff.

BLANCHE   What—stuff?

STANLEY   Compliments to women about their looks. I never met a woman that didn't know if she was good-looking or not without being told, and some of them give themselves credit for more than they've got. I once went out with a doll who said to me, "I am the glamorous type, I am the glamorous type!" I said, "So what?"

BLANCHE   And what did she say then?

STANLEY   She didn't say nothing. That shut her up like a clam.

BLANCHE   Did it end the romance?

STANLEY   It ended the conversation—that was all. Some men are took in by this Hollywood glamor stuff and some men are not.

BLANCHE   I'm sure you belong in the second category.

STANLEY   That's right.

BLANCHE   I cannot imagine any witch of a woman casting a spell over you.

STANLEY   That's—right.

BLANCHE   You're simple, straightforward and honest, a little bit on the primitive side I should think. To interest you a woman would have to—
[*She pauses with an indefinite gesture.*]

STANLEY [*slowly*]   Lay . . . her cards on the table.

BLANCHE [*smiling*]   Well, I never cared for wishy-washy people. That was why, when you walked in here last night, I said to myself—"My sister has married a man!"—Of course that was all that I could tell about you.

STANLEY [*booming*] Now let's cut the re-bop![1]

BLANCHE [*pressing hands to her ears*] Ouuuuu!

STELLA [*calling from the steps*] Stanley! You come out here and let Blanche finish dressing!

BLANCHE I'm through dressing, honey.

STELLA Well, you come out, then.

STANLEY Your sister and I are having a little talk.

BLANCHE [*lightly*] Honey, do me a favor. Run to the drugstore and get me a lemon Coke with plenty of chipped ice in it!—Will you do that for me, sweetie?

STELLA [*uncertainly*] Yes. [*She goes around the corner of the building.*]

BLANCHE The poor little thing was out there listening to us, and I have an idea she doesn't understand you as well as I do. . . . All right; now, Mr. Kowalski, let us proceed without any more double-talk. I'm ready to answer all questions. I've nothing to hide. What is it?

STANLEY There is such a thing in this state of Louisiana as the Napoleonic code, according to which whatever belongs to my wife is also mine—and vice versa.

BLANCHE My, but you have an impressive judicial air!

[*She sprays herself with her atomizer; then playfully sprays him with it. He seizes the atomizer and slams it down on the dresser. She throws back her head and laughs.*]

STANLEY If I didn't know that you was my wife's sister I'd get ideas about you!

BLANCHE Such as what!

STANLEY Don't play so dumb. You know what!

BLANCHE [*she puts the atomizer on the table*] All right. Cards on the table. That suits me. [*She turns to* STANLEY.] I know I fib a good deal. After all, a woman's charm is fifty per cent illusion, but when a thing is important I tell the truth, and this is the truth: I haven't cheated my sister or you or anyone else as long as I have lived.

STANLEY Where's the papers? In the trunk?

BLANCHE Everything that I own is in that trunk.

[STANLEY *crosses to the trunk, shoves it roughly open and begins to open compartments.*]

BLANCHE What in the name of heaven are you thinking of! What's in the back of that little boy's mind of yours? That I am absconding with something, attempting some kind of treachery on my sister?—Let me do that! It will be faster and simpler . . . [*She crosses to the trunk and takes out a box.*] I keep my papers mostly in this tin box. [*She opens it.*]

STANLEY What's them underneath? [*He indicates another sheaf of paper.*]

BLANCHE These are love-letters, yellowing with antiquity, all from one boy. [*He snatches them up. She speaks fiercely.*] Give those back to me!

STANLEY I'll have a look at them first!

BLANCHE The touch of your hands insults them!

STANLEY Don't pull that stuff!

[*He rips off the ribbon and starts to examine them.* BLANCHE *snatches them from him, and they cascade to the floor.*]

---

1. Nonsense syllables (from "bebop," a form of jazz).

BLANCHE   Now that you've touched them I'll burn them!

STANLEY [*staring, baffled*]   What in hell are they?

BLANCHE [*on the floor gathering them up*]   Poems a dead boy wrote. I hurt him the way that you would like to hurt me, but you can't! I'm not young and vulnerable any more. But my young husband was and I—never mind about that! Just give them back to me!

STANLEY   What do you mean by saying you'll have to burn them?

BLANCHE   I'm sorry, I must have lost my head for a moment. Everyone has something he won't let others touch because of their—intimate nature . . .

> [*She now seems faint with exhaustion and she sits down with the strong box and puts on a pair of glasses and goes methodically through a large stack of papers.*]

Ambler & Ambler. Hmmmmm. . . . Crabtree. . . . More Ambler & Ambler.

STANLEY   What is Ambler & Ambler?

BLANCHE   A firm that made loans on the place.

STANLEY   Then it *was* lost on a mortgage?

BLANCHE [*touching her forehead*]   That must've been what happened.

STANLEY   I don't want no ifs, ands or buts! What's all the rest of them papers?

> [*She hands him the entire box. He carries it to the table and starts to examine the paper.*]

BLANCHE [*picking up a large envelope containing more papers*]   There are thousands of papers, stretching back over hundreds of years, affecting Belle Reve as, piece by piece, our improvident grandfathers and father and uncles and brothers exchanged the land for their epic fornications— to put it plainly! [*She removes her glasses with an exhausted laugh.*] The four-letter word deprived us of our plantation, till finally all that was left—and Stella can verify that!—was the house itself and about twenty acres of ground, including a graveyard, to which now all but Stella and I have retreated. [*She pours the contents of the envelope on the table.*] Here all of them are, all papers! I hereby endow you with them! Take them, peruse them—commit them to memory, even! I think it's wonderfully fitting that Belle Reve should finally be this bunch of old papers in your big, capable hands! . . . I wonder if Stella's come back with my lemon Coke . . . [*She leans back and closes her eyes.*]

STANLEY   I have a lawyer acquaintance who will study these out.

BLANCHE   Present them to him with a box of aspirin tablets.

STANLEY [*becoming somewhat sheepish*]   You see, under the Napoleonic code—a man has to take an interest in his wife's affairs—especially now that she's going to have a baby.

> [BLANCHE *opens her eyes. The "Blue Piano" sounds louder.*]

BLANCHE   Stella? Stella going to have a baby? [*dreamily*] I didn't know she was going to have a baby!

> [*She gets up and crosses to the outside door.* STELLA *appears around the corner with a carton from the drugstore.* STANLEY *goes into the bedroom with the envelope and the box. The inner rooms fade to darkness and the outside wall of the house is visible.* BLANCHE *meets* STELLA *at the foot of the steps to the sidewalk.*]

BLANCHE   Stella, Stella for star! How lovely to have a baby! It's all right. Everything's all right.

STELLA   I'm sorry he did that to you.

BLANCHE   Oh, I guess he's just not the type that goes for jasmine perfume, but maybe he's what we need to mix with our blood now that we've lost Belle Reve. We thrashed it out. I feel a bit shaky, but I think I handled it nicely, I laughed and treated it all as a joke. [STEVE and PABLO appear, carrying a case of beer.] I called him a little boy and laughed and flirted. Yes, I was flirting with your husband! [as the men approach] The guests are gathering for the poker party. [The two men pass between them, and enter the house.] Which way do we go now, Stella—this way?

STELLA   No, this way. [She leads BLANCHE away.]

BLANCHE [laughing]   The blind are leading the blind!

　　　　[A tamale VENDOR is heard calling.]

VENDOR'S VOICE   Red-hot!

Scene Three

THE POKER NIGHT[2]

There is a picture of Van Gogh's[3] of a billiard-parlor at night. The kitchen now suggests that sort of lurid nocturnal brilliance, the raw colors of childhood's spectrum. Over the yellow linoleum of the kitchen table hangs an electric bulb with a vivid green glass shade. The poker players—STANLEY, STEVE, MITCH and PABLO— wear colored shirts, solid blues, a purple, a red-and-white check, a light green, and they are men at the peak of their physical manhood, as coarse and direct and powerful as the primary colors. There are vivid slices of watermelon on the table, whiskey bottles and glasses. The bedroom is relatively dim with only the light that spills between the portieres and through the wide window on the street.

　　For a moment, there is absorbed silence as a hand is dealt.

STEVE   Anything wild this deal?

PABLO   One-eyed jacks are wild.

STEVE   Give me two cards.

PABLO   You, Mitch?

MITCH   I'm out.

PABLO   One.

MITCH   Anyone want a shot?

STANLEY   Yeah. Me.

PABLO   Why don't somebody go to the Chinaman's and bring back a load of chop suey?

STANLEY   When I'm losing you want to eat! Ante up! Openers? Openers! Get y'r ass off the table, Mitch. Nothing belongs on a poker table but cards, chips and whiskey.

　　　　[He lurches up and tosses some watermelon rinds to the floor.]

MITCH   Kind of on your high horse, ain't you?

STANLEY   How many?

STEVE   Give me three.

STANLEY   One.

MITCH   I'm out again. I oughta go home pretty soon.

STANLEY   Shut up.

MITCH   I gotta sick mother. She don't go to sleep until I come in at night.

2. Williams's first title for A Streetcar Named Desire (see headnote).　　3. The Night Café, by the Dutch Postimpressionist painter Vincent van Gogh (1853–1890).

STANLEY   Then why don't you stay home with her?

MITCH   She says to go out, so I go, but I don't enjoy it. All the while I keep wondering how she is.

STANLEY   Aw, for the sake of Jesus, go home, then!

PABLO   What've you got?

STEVE   Spade flush.

MITCH   You all are married. But I'll be alone when she goes.—I'm going to the bathroom.

STANLEY   Hurry back and we'll fix you a sugar-tit.

MITCH   Aw, go rut. [*He crosses through the bedroom into the bathroom.*]

STEVE [*dealing a hand*]   Seven card stud.[4] [*telling his joke as he deals*] This ole farmer is out in back of his house sittin' down th'owing corn to the chickens when all at once he hears a loud cackle and this young hen comes lickety split around the side of the house with the rooster right behind her and gaining on her fast.

STANLEY [*impatient with the story*]   Deal!

STEVE   But when the rooster catches sight of the farmer th'owing the corn he puts on the brakes and lets the hen get away and starts pecking corn. And the old farmer says, "Lord God, I hopes I never gits *that* hongry!"

[STEVE *and* PABLO *laugh. The sisters appear around the corner of the building.*]

STELLA   The game is still going on.

BLANCHE   How do I look?

STELLA   Lovely, Blanche.

BLANCHE   I feel so hot and frazzled. Wait till I powder before you open the door. Do I look done in?

STELLA   Why no. You are as fresh as a daisy.

BLANCHE   One that's been picked a few days.

[STELLA *opens the door and they enter.*]

STELLA   Well, well, well. I see you boys are still at it?

STANLEY   Where you been?

STELLA   Blanche and I took in a show. Blanche, this is Mr. Gonzales and Mr. Hubbell.

BLANCHE   Please don't get up.

STANLEY   Nobody's going to get up, so don't be worried.

STELLA   How much longer is this game going to continue?

STANLEY   Till we get ready to quit.

BLANCHE   Poker is so fascinating. Could I kibitz?

STANLEY   You could not. Why don't you women go up and sit with Eunice?

STELLA   Because it is nearly two-thirty. [BLANCHE *crosses into the bedroom and partially closes the portieres.*] Couldn't you call it quits after one more hand?

[*A chair scrapes.* STANLEY *gives a loud whack of his hand on her thigh.*]

STELLA [*sharply*]   That's not fun, Stanley.

[*The men laugh.* STELLA *goes into the bedroom.*]

STELLA   It makes me so mad when he does that in front of people.

BLANCHE   I think I will bathe.

STELLA   Again?

BLANCHE   My nerves are in knots. Is the bathroom occupied?

---

4. An adventurous and risky variant of poker.

STELLA   I don't know.

[BLANCHE *knocks.* MITCH *opens the door and comes out, still wiping his hands on a towel.*]

BLANCHE   Oh!—good evening.

MITCH   Hello. [*He stares at her.*]

STELLA   Blanche, this is Harold Mitchell. My sister, Blanche DuBois.

MITCH [*with awkward courtesy*]   How do you do, Miss DuBois.

STELLA   How is your mother now, Mitch?

MITCH   About the same, thanks. She appreciated your sending over that custard.—Excuse me, please.

[*He crosses slowly back into the kitchen, glancing back at* BLANCHE *and coughing a little shyly. He realizes he still has the towel in his hands and with an embarrassed laugh hands it to* STELLA. BLANCHE *looks after him with a certain interest.*]

BLANCHE   That one seems—superior to the others.

STELLA   Yes, he is.

BLANCHE   I thought he had a sort of sensitive look.

STELLA   His mother is sick.

BLANCHE   Is he married?

STELLA   No.

BLANCHE   Is he a wolf?

STELLA   Why, Blanche! [BLANCHE *laughs.*] I don't think he would be.

BLANCHE   What does—what does he do? [*She is unbuttoning her blouse.*]

STELLA   He's on the precision bench in the spare parts department. At the plant Stanley travels for.

BLANCHE   Is that something much?

STELLA   No. Stanley's the only one of his crowd that's likely to get anywhere.

BLANCHE   What makes you think Stanley will?

STELLA   Look at him.

BLANCHE   I've looked at him.

STELLA   Then you should know.

BLANCHE   I'm sorry, but I haven't noticed the stamp of genius even on Stanley's forehead.

[*She takes off the blouse and stands in her pink silk brassiere and white skirt in the light through the portieres. The game has continued in undertones.*]

STELLA   It isn't on his forehead and it isn't genius.

BLANCHE   Oh. Well, what is it, and where? I would like to know.

STELLA   It's a drive that he has. You're standing in the light, Blanche!

BLANCHE   Oh, am I!

[*She moves out of the yellow streak of light.* STELLA *has removed her dress and put on a light blue satin kimona.*]

STELLA [*with girlish laughter*]   You ought to see their wives.

BLANCHE [*laughingly*]   I can imagine. Big, beefy things, I suppose.

STELLA   You know that one upstairs? [*more laughter*] One time [*laughing*] the plaster— [*laughing*] cracked—

STANLEY   You hens cut out that conversation in there!

STELLA   You can't hear us.

STANLEY   Well, you can hear me and I said to hush up!

STELLA   This is my house and I'll talk as much as I want to!

BLANCHE   Stella, don't start a row.

STELLA   He's half drunk!—I'll be out in a minute.

[*She goes into the bathroom.* BLANCHE *rises and crosses leisurely to a small white radio and turns it on.*]

STANLEY   Awright, Mitch, you in?

MITCH   What? Oh!—No, I'm out!

[BLANCHE *moves back into the streak of light. She raises her arms and stretches, as she moves indolently back to the chair. Rhumba music comes over the radio.* MITCH *rises at the table.*]

STANLEY   Who turned that on in there?

BLANCHE   I did. Do you mind?

STANLEY   Turn it off!

STEVE   Aw, let the girls have their music.

PABLO   Sure, that's good, leave it on!

STEVE   Sounds like Xavier Cugat![5]

[STANLEY *jumps up and, crossing to the radio, turns it off. He stops short at the sight of* BLANCHE *in the chair. She returns his look without flinching. Then he sits again at the poker table. Two of the men have started arguing hotly.*]

STEVE   I didn't hear you name it.

PABLO   Didn't I name it, Mitch?

MITCH   I wasn't listenin'.

PABLO   What were you doing, then?

STANLEY   He was looking through them drapes. [*He jumps up and jerks roughly at curtains to close them.*] Now deal the hand over again and let's play cards or quit. Some people get ants when they win.

[MITCH *rises as* STANLEY *returns to his seat.*]

STANLEY [*yelling*]   Sit down!

MITCH   I'm going to the "head." Deal me out.

PABLO   Sure he's got ants now. Seven five-dollar bills in his pants pocket folded up tight as spitballs.

STEVE   Tomorrow you'll see him at the cashier's window getting them changed into quarters.

STANLEY   And when he goes home he'll deposit them one by one in a piggy bank his mother give him for Christmas. [*dealing*] This game is Spit in the Ocean.[6]

[MITCH *laughs uncomfortably and continues through the portieres. He stops just inside.*]

BLANCHE [*softly*]   Hello! The Little Boys' Room is busy right now.

MITCH   We've—been drinking beer.

BLANCHE   I hate beer.

MITCH   It's—a hot weather drink.

BLANCHE   Oh, I don't think so; it always makes me warmer. Have you got any cigs? [*She has slipped on the dark red satin wrapper.*]

MITCH   Sure.

BLANCHE   What kind are they?

MITCH   Luckies.

BLANCHE   Oh, good. What a pretty case. Silver?

---

5. Cuban bandleader (1900–1990), well known for composing and playing rhumbas.   6. Another variant of poker.

MITCH   Yes. Yes; read the inscription.

BLANCHE   Oh, is there an inscription? I can't make it out. [*He strikes a match and moves closer.*] Oh! [*reading with feigned difficulty*] "And if God choose, / I shall but love thee better—after—death!" Why, that's from my favorite sonnet by Mrs. Browning![7]

MITCH   You know it?

BLANCHE   Certainly I do!

MITCH   There's a story connected with that inscription.

BLANCHE   It sounds like a romance.

MITCH   A pretty sad one.

BLANCHE   Oh?

MITCH   The girl's dead now.

BLANCHE   [*in a tone of deep sympathy*]   Oh!

MITCH   She knew she was dying when she give me this. A very strange girl, very sweet—very!

BLANCHE   She must have been fond of you. Sick people have such deep, sincere attachments.

MITCH   That's right, they certainly do.

BLANCHE   Sorrow makes for sincerity, I think.

MITCH   It sure brings it out in people.

BLANCHE   The little there is belongs to people who have experienced some sorrow.

MITCH   I believe you are right about that.

BLANCHE   I'm positive that I am. Show me a person who hasn't known any sorrow and I'll show you a shuperficial—Listen to me! My tongue is a little—thick! You boys are responsible for it. The show let out at eleven and we couldn't come home on account of the poker game so we had to go somewhere and drink. I'm not accustomed to having more than one drink. Two is the limit—and *three!* [*She laughs.*] Tonight I had three.

STANLEY   Mitch!

MITCH   Deal me out. I'm talking to Miss—

BLANCHE   DuBois.

MITCH   Miss DuBois?

BLANCHE   It's a French name. It means woods and Blanche means white, so the two together mean white woods. Like an orchard in spring! You can remember it by that.

MITCH   You're French?

BLANCHE   We are French by extraction. Our first American ancestors were French Huguenots.

MITCH   You are Stella's sister, are you not?

BLANCHE   Yes, Stella is my precious little sister. I call her little in spite of the fact she's somewhat older than I. Just slightly. Less than a year. Will you do something for me?

MITCH   Sure. What?

BLANCHE   I bought this adorable little colored paper lantern at a Chinese shop on Bourbon. Put it over the light bulb! Will you, please?

MITCH   Be glad to.

---

7. Elizabeth Barrett Browning (1806–1861), British poet, most famous for her sequence of love poems, *Sonnets from the Portuguese.*

BLANCHE   I can't stand a naked light bulb, any more than I can a rude remark or a vulgar action.

MITCH [*adjusting the lantern*]   I guess we strike you as being a pretty rough bunch.

BLANCHE   I'm very adaptable—to circumstances.

MITCH   Well, that's a good thing to be. You are visiting Stanley and Stella?

BLANCHE   Stella hasn't been so well lately, and I came down to help her for a while. She's very run down.

MITCH   You're not—?

BLANCHE   Married? No, no. I'm an old maid schoolteacher!

MITCH   You may teach school but you're certainly not an old maid.

BLANCHE   Thank you, sir! I appreciate your gallantry!

MITCH   So you are in the teaching profession?

BLANCHE   Yes. Ah, yes . . .

MITCH   Grade school or high school or—

STANLEY [*bellowing*]   Mitch!

MITCH   Coming!

BLANCHE   Gracious, what lung-power! . . . I teach high school. In Laurel.

MITCH   What do you teach? What subject?

BLANCHE   Guess!

MITCH   I bet you teach art or music? [BLANCHE *laughs delicately.*] Of course I could be wrong. You might teach arithmetic.

BLANCHE   Never arithmetic, sir; never arithmetic! [*with a laugh*] I don't even know my multiplication tables! No, I have the misfortune of being an English instructor. I attempt to instill a bunch of bobby-soxers and drugstore Romeos with reverence for Hawthorne and Whitman and Poe!

MITCH   I guess that some of them are more interested in other things.

BLANCHE   How very right you are! Their literary heritage is not what most of them treasure above all else! But they're sweet things! And in the spring, it's touching to notice them making their first discovery of love! As if nobody had ever known it before!

> [*The bathroom door opens and* STELLA *comes out.* BLANCHE *continues talking to* MITCH.]

Oh! Have you finished? Wait—I'll turn on the radio.

> [*She turns the knobs on the radio and it begins to play "Wien, Wien, nur du allein."*[8] BLANCHE *waltzes to the music with romantic gestures.* MITCH *is delighted and moves in awkward imitation like a dancing bear.* STANLEY *stalks fiercely through the portieres into the bedroom. He crosses to the small white radio and snatches it off the table. With a shouted oath, he tosses the instrument out the window.*]

STELLA   Drunk—drunk—animal thing, you! [*She rushes through to the poker table.*] All of you—please go home! If any of you have one spark of decency in you—

BLANCHE [*wildly*]   Stella, watch out, he's—

> [STANLEY *charges after* STELLA.]

MEN [*feebly*]   Take it easy, Stanley. Easy, fellow.—Let's all—

STELLA   You lay your hands on me and I'll—

> [*She backs out of sight. He advances and disappears. There is the sound of a blow.* STELLA *cries out.* BLANCHE *screams and runs into the kitchen.*

---

8. Vienna, Vienna, you are my only (German); a waltz from an operetta by Franz Lehár (1870–1948).

The men rush forward and there is grappling and cursing. Something is overturned with a crash.]

BLANCHE [*shrilly*]   My sister is going to have a baby!

MITCH   This is terrible.

BLANCHE   Lunacy, absolute lunacy!

MITCH   Get him in here, men.

[STANLEY *is forced, pinioned by the two men, into the bedroom. He nearly throws them off. Then all at once he subsides and is limp in their grasp. They speak quietly and lovingly to him and he leans his face on one of their shoulders.*]

STELLA [*in a high, unnatural voice, out of sight*]   I want to go away, I want to go away!

MITCH   Poker shouldn't be played in a house with women.

[BLANCHE *rushes into the bedroom.*]

BLANCHE   I want my sister's clothes! We'll go to that woman's upstairs!

MITCH   Where is the clothes?

BLANCHE [*opening the closet*]   I've got them! [*She rushes through to* STELLA.] Stella, Stella, precious! Dear, dear little sister, don't be afraid!

[*With her arm around* STELLA, BLANCHE *guides her to the outside door and upstairs.*]

STANLEY [*dully*]   What's the matter; what's happened?

MITCH   You just blew your top, Stan.

PABLO   He's okay, now.

STEVE   Sure, my boy's okay!

MITCH   Put him on the bed and get a wet towel.

PABLO   I think coffee would do him a world of good, now.

STANLEY [*thickly*]   I want water.

MITCH   Put him under the shower!

[*The men talk quietly as they lead him to the bathroom.*]

STANLEY   Let the rut go of me, you sons of bitches!

[*Sounds of blows are heard. The water goes on full tilt.*]

STEVE   Let's get quick out of here!

[*They rush to the poker table and sweep up their winnings on their way out.*]

MITCH [*sadly but firmly*]   Poker should not be played in a house with women.

[*The door closes on them and the place is still. The Negro entertainers in the bar around the corner play "Paper Doll"⁹ slow and blue. After a moment* STANLEY *comes out of the bathroom dripping water and still in his clinging wet polka dot drawers.*]

STANLEY   Stella! [*There is a pause.*] My baby doll's left me!

[*He breaks into sobs. Then he goes to the phone and dials, still shuddering with sobs.*]

Eunice? I want my baby! [*He waits a moment; then he hangs up and dials again.*] Eunice! I'll keep on ringin' until I talk with my baby!

[*An indistinguishable shrill voice is heard. He hurls phone to floor. Dissonant brass and piano sounds as the rooms dim out to darkness and the outer walls appear in the night light. The "Blue Piano" plays for a brief interval. Finally,* STANLEY *stumbles half-dressed out to the porch and*

---

9. Popular song of the early 1940s by Johnny Black.

down the wooden steps to the pavement before the building. There he throws back his head like a baying hound and bellows his wife's name: "Stella! Stella, sweetheart! Stella!"]

STANLEY Stell-*lahhhhh!*

EUNICE [*calling down from the door of her upper apartment*] Quit that howling out there an' go back to bed!

STANLEY I want my baby down here. Stella, Stella!

EUNICE She ain't comin' down so you quit! Or you'll git th' law on you!

STANLEY Stella!

EUNICE You can't beat on a woman an' then call 'er back! She won't come! And her goin' t' have a baby! . . . You stinker! You whelp of a Polack, you! I hope they do haul you in and turn the fire hose on you, same as the last time!

STANLEY [*humbly*] Eunice, I want my girl to come down with me!

EUNICE Hah! [*She slams her door.*]

STANLEY [*with heaven-splitting violence*] *STELL-LAHHHHH!*

[*The low-tone clarinet moans. The door upstairs opens again.* STELLA *slips down the rickety stairs in her robe. Her eyes are glistening with tears and her hair loose about her throat and shoulders. They stare at each other. Then they come together with low, animal moans. He falls to his knees on the steps and presses his face to her belly, curving a little with maternity. Her eyes go blind with tenderness as she catches his head and raises him level with her. He snatches the screen door open and lifts her off her feet and bears her into the dark flat.* BLANCHE *comes out the upper landing in her robe and slips fearfully down the steps.*]

BLANCHE Where is my little sister? Stella? Stella?

[*She stops before the dark entrance of her sister's flat. Then catches her breath as if struck. She rushes down to the walk before the house. She looks right and left as if for a sanctuary. The music fades away.* MITCH *appears from around the corner.*]

MITCH Miss DuBois?

BLANCHE Oh!

MITCH All quiet on the Potomac now?

BLANCHE She ran downstairs and went back in there with him.

MITCH Sure she did.

BLANCHE I'm terrified!

MITCH Ho-ho! There's nothing to be scared of. They're crazy about each other.

BLANCHE I'm not used to such—

MITCH Naw, it's a shame this had to happen when you just got here. But don't take it serious.

BLANCHE Violence! Is so—

MITCH Set down on the steps and have a cigarette with me.

BLANCHE I'm not properly dressed.

MITCH That don't make no difference in the Quarter.

BLANCHE Such a pretty silver case.

MITCH I showed you the inscription, didn't I?

BLANCHE Yes. [*During the pause, she looks up at the sky.*] There's so much—so much confusion in the world . . . [*He coughs diffidently.*] Thank you for being so kind! I need kindness now.

Scene Four

It is early the following morning. There is a confusion of street cries like a choral chant.

STELLA *is lying down in the bedroom. Her face is serene in the early morning sunlight. One hand rests on her belly, rounding slightly with new maternity. From the other dangles a book of colored comics. Her eyes and lips have that almost narcotized tranquility that is in the faces of Eastern idols.*

The table is sloppy with remains of breakfast and the debris of the preceding night, and STANLEY's *gaudy pyjamas lie across the threshold of the bathroom. The outside door is slightly ajar on a sky of summer brilliance.*

BLANCHE *appears at this door. She has spent a sleepless night and her appearance entirely contrasts with* STELLA's. *She presses her knuckles nervously to her lips as she looks through the door, before entering.*

BLANCHE   Stella?

STELLA [*stirring lazily*]   Hmmh?

    [BLANCHE *utters a moaning cry and runs into the bedroom, throwing herself down beside* STELLA *in a rush of hysterical tenderness.*]

BLANCHE   Baby, my baby sister!

STELLA [*drawing away from her*]   Blanche, what is the matter with you?
    [BLANCHE *straightens up slowly and stands beside the bed looking down at her sister with knuckles pressed to her lips.*]

BLANCHE   He's left?

STELLA   Stan? Yes.

BLANCHE   Will he be back?

STELLA   He's gone to get the car greased. Why?

BLANCHE   Why! I've been half crazy, Stella! When I found out you'd been insane enough to come back in here after what happened—I started to rush in after you!

STELLA   I'm glad you didn't.

BLANCHE   What were you thinking of? [STELLA *makes an indefinite gesture.*] Answer me! What? What?

STELLA   Please, Blanche! Sit down and stop yelling.

BLANCHE   All right, Stella. I will repeat the question quietly now. How could you come back in this place last night? Why, you must have slept with him!
    [STELLA *gets up in a calm and leisurely way.*]

STELLA   Blanche, I'd forgotten how excitable you are. You're making much too much fuss about this.

BLANCHE   Am I?

STELLA   Yes, you are, Blanche. I know how it must have seemed to you and I'm awful sorry it had to happen, but it wasn't anything as serious as you seem to take it. In the first place, when men are drinking and playing poker anything can happen. It's always a powder-keg. He didn't know what he was doing. . . . He was as good as a lamb when I came back and he's really very, very ashamed of himself.

BLANCHE   And that—that makes it all right?

STELLA   No, it isn't all right for anybody to make such a terrible row, but— people do sometimes. Stanley's always smashed things. Why, on our wedding night—soon as we came in here—he snatched off one of my slippers and rushed about the place smashing light bulbs with it.

BLANCHE   He did—*what?*

STELLA   He smashed all the light bulbs with the heel of my slipper! [*She laughs.*]

BLANCHE   And you—you *let* him? Didn't *run,* didn't *scream?*

STELLA   I was—sort of—thrilled by it. [*She waits for a moment.*] Eunice and you had breakfast?

BLANCHE   Do you suppose I wanted any breakfast?

STELLA   There's some coffee left on the stove.

BLANCHE   You're so—matter of fact about it, Stella.

STELLA   What other can I be? He's taken the radio to get it fixed. It didn't land on the pavement so only one tube was smashed.

BLANCHE   And you are standing there smiling!

STELLA   What do you want me to do?

BLANCHE   Pull yourself together and face the facts.

STELLA   What are they, in your opinion?

BLANCHE   In my opinion? You're married to a madman!

STELLA   No!

BLANCHE   Yes, you are, your fix is worse than mine is! Only you're not being sensible about it. I'm going to *do* something. Get hold of myself and make myself a new life!

STELLA   Yes?

BLANCHE   But you've given in. And that isn't right, you're not old! You can get out.

STELLA [*slowly and emphatically*]   I'm not in anything I want to get out of.

BLANCHE [*incredulously*]   What—Stella?

STELLA   I said I am not in anything that I have a desire to get out of. Look at the mess in this room! And those empty bottles! They went through two cases last night! He promised this morning that he was going to quit having these poker parties, but you know how long such a promise is going to keep. Oh, well, it's his pleasure, like mine is movies and bridge. People have got to tolerate each other's habits, I guess.

BLANCHE   I don't understand you. [STELLA *turns toward her.*] I don't understand your indifference. Is this a Chinese philosophy you've—cultivated?

STELLA   Is what—what?

BLANCHE   This—shuffling about and mumbling—'One tube smashed— beer bottles—mess in the kitchen!'—as if nothing out of the ordinary has happened! [STELLA *laughs uncertainly and picking up the broom, twirls it in her hands.*]

BLANCHE   Are you deliberately shaking that thing in my face?

STELLA   No.

BLANCHE   Stop it. Let go of that broom. I won't have you cleaning up for him!

STELLA   Then who's going to do it? Are you?

BLANCHE   I? I!

STELLA   No, I didn't think so.

BLANCHE   Oh, let me think, if only my mind would function! We've got to get hold of some money, that's the way out!

STELLA   I guess that money is always nice to get hold of.

BLANCHE   Listen to me. I have an idea of some kind. [*Shakily she twists a cigarette into her holder.*] Do you remember Shep Huntleigh? [STELLA *shakes her head.*] Of course you remember Shep Huntleigh. I went out with him at college and wore his pin for a while. Well—

STELLA   Well?

BLANCHE   I ran into him last winter. You know I went to Miami during the Christmas holidays?

STELLA   No.

BLANCHE   Well, I did. I took the trip as an investment, thinking I'd meet someone with a million dollars.

STELLA   Did you?

BLANCHE   Yes. I ran into Shep Huntleigh—I ran into him on Biscayne Boulevard, on Christmas Eve, about dusk . . . getting into his car— Cadillac convertible; must have been a block long!

STELLA   I should think it would have been—inconvenient in traffic!

BLANCHE   You've heard of oil wells?

STELLA   Yes—remotely.

BLANCHE   He has them, all over Texas. Texas is literally spouting gold in his pockets.

STELLA   My, my.

BLANCHE   Y'know how indifferent I am to money. I think of money in terms of what it does for you. But he could do it, he could certainly do it!

STELLA   Do what, Blanche?

BLANCHE   Why—set us up in a—shop!

STELLA   What kind of a shop?

BLANCHE   Oh, a—shop of some kind! He could do it with half what his wife throws away at the races.

STELLA   He's married?

BLANCHE   Honey, would I be here if the man weren't married? [STELLA *laughs a little.* BLANCHE *suddenly springs up and crosses to phone. She speaks shrilly.*] How do I get Western Union?—Operator! Western Union!

STELLA   That's a dial phone, honey.

BLANCHE   I can't dial, I'm too—

STELLA   Just dial O.

BLANCHE   O?

STELLA   Yes, "O" for Operator! [BLANCHE *considers a moment; then she puts the phone down.*]

BLANCHE   Give me a pencil. Where is a slip of paper? I've got to write it down first—the message, I mean . . . [*She goes to the dressing table, and grabs up a sheet of Kleenex and an eyebrow pencil for writing equipment.*] Let me see now . . . [*She bites the pencil.*] 'Darling Shep. Sister and I in desperate situation.'

STELLA   I beg your pardon!

BLANCHE   'Sister and I in desperate situation. Will explain details later. Would you be interested in—?' [*She bites the pencil again.*] 'Would you be—interested—in . . . ' [*She smashes the pencil on the table and springs up.*] You never get anywhere with direct appeals!

STELLA [*with a laugh*]   Don't be so ridiculous, darling!

BLANCHE   But I'll think of something, I've *got* to think of—*some*thing! Don't laugh at me, Stella! Please, please don't—I—I want you to look at the contents of my purse! Here's what's in it! [*She snatches her purse open.*] Sixty-five measly cents in coin of the realm!

STELLA [*crossing to bureau*] Stanley doesn't give me a regular allowance, he likes to pay bills himself, but—this morning he gave me ten dollars to smooth things over. You take five of it, Blanche, and I'll keep the rest.

BLANCHE Oh, no. No, Stella.

STELLA [*insisting*] I know how it helps your morale just having a little pocket-money on you.

BLANCHE No, thank you—I'll take to the streets!

STELLA Talk sense! How did you happen to get so low on funds?

BLANCHE Money just goes—it goes places. [*She rubs her forehead.*] Sometime today I've got to get hold of a Bromo![1]

STELLA I'll fix you one now.

BLANCHE Not yet—I've got to keep thinking!

STELLA I wish you'd just let things go, at least for a—while . . .

BLANCHE Stella, I can't live with him! You can, he's your husband. But how could I stay here with him, after last night, with just those curtains between us?

STELLA Blanche, you saw him at his worst last night.

BLANCHE On the contrary, I saw him at his best! What such a man has to offer is animal force and he gave a wonderful exhibition of that! But the only way to live with such a man is to—go to bed with him! And that's your job—not mine!

STELLA After you've rested a little, you'll see it's going to work out. You don't have to worry about anything while you're here. I mean—expenses . . .

BLANCHE I have to plan for us both, to get us both—out!

STELLA You take it for granted that I am in something that I want to get out of.

BLANCHE I take it for granted that you still have sufficient memory of Belle Reve to find this place and these poker players impossible to live with.

STELLA Well, you're taking entirely too much for granted.

BLANCHE I can't believe you're in earnest.

STELLA No?

BLANCHE I understand how it happened—a little. You saw him in uniform, an officer, not here but—

STELLA I'm not sure it would have made any difference where I saw him.

BLANCHE Now don't say it was one of those mysterious electric things between people! If you do I'll laugh in your face.

STELLA I am not going to say anything more at all about it!

BLANCHE All right, then, don't!

STELLA But there are things that happen between a man and a woman in the dark—that sort of make everything else seem—unimportant. [*Pause.*]

BLANCHE What you are talking about is brutal desire—just—Desire!—the name of that rattle-trap streetcar that bangs through the Quarter, up one old narrow street and down another . . .

STELLA Haven't you ever ridden on that streetcar?

BLANCHE It brought me here.—Where I'm not wanted and where I'm ashamed to be . . .

STELLA Then don't you think your superior attitude is a bit out of place?

---

1. Short for Bromo-seltzer, a headache remedy.

BLANCHE   I am not being or feeling at all superior, Stella. Believe me I'm not! It's just this. This is how I look at it. A man like that is someone to go out with—once—twice—three times when the devil is in you. But live with? Have a child by?

STELLA   I have told you I love him.

BLANCHE   Then I *tremble* for you! I just—*tremble* for you. . . .

STELLA   I can't help your trembling if you insist on trembling!
   [*There is a pause.*]

BLANCHE   May I—speak—*plainly?*

STELLA   Yes, do. Go ahead. As plainly as you want to.
   [*Outside, a train approaches. They are silent till the noise subsides. They are both in the bedroom. Under cover of the train's noise* STANLEY *enters from outside. He stands unseen by the women, holding some packages in his arms, and overhears their following conversation. He wears an under-shirt and grease-stained seersucker pants.*]

BLANCHE   Well—if you'll forgive me—he's *common!*

STELLA   Why, yes, I suppose he is.

BLANCHE   Suppose! You can't have forgotten that much of our bringing up, Stella, that you just *suppose* that any part of a gentleman's in his nature! *Not one particle, no!* Oh, if he was just—*ordinary!* Just *plain*—but good and wholesome, but—*no.* There's something downright—*bestial*—about him! You're hating me saying this, aren't you?

STELLA [*coldly*]   Go on and say it all, Blanche.

BLANCHE   He acts like an animal, has an animal's habits! Eats like one, moves like one, talks like one! There's even something—sub-human—something not quite to the stage of humanity yet! Yes, something—ape-like about him, like one of those pictures I've seen in—anthropological studies! Thousands and thousands of years have passed him right by, and there he is—Stanley Kowalski—survivor of the Stone Age! Bearing the raw meat home from the kill in the jungle! And you—*you* here—*waiting* for him! Maybe he'll strike you or maybe grunt and kiss you! That is, if kisses have been discovered yet! Night falls and the other apes gather! There in the front of the cave, all grunting like him, and swilling and gnawing and hulking! His poker night! you call it—this party of apes! Somebody growls—some creature snatches at something—the fight is on! *God!* Maybe we are a long way from being made in God's image, but Stella—my sister—there has been *some* progress since then! Such things as art—as poetry and music—such kinds of new light have come into the world since then! In some kinds of people some tenderer feelings have had some little beginning! That we have got to make *grow!* And *cling* to, and hold as our flag! In this dark march toward whatever it is we're approaching. . . . Don't—*don't hang back with the brutes!*
   [*Another train passes outside.* STANLEY *hesitates, licking his lips. Then suddenly he turns stealthily about and withdraws through front door. The women are still unaware of his presence. When the train has passed he calls through the closed front door.*]

STANLEY   Hey! Hey, Stella!

STELLA [*who has listened gravely to* BLANCHE]   Stanley!

BLANCHE   Stell, I—
   [*But* STELLA *has gone to the front door.* STANLEY *enters casually with his packages.*]

STANLEY   Hiyuh, Stella. Blanche back?

STELLA   Yes, she's back.

STANLEY   Hiyuh, Blanche. [*He grins at her.*]

STELLA   You must've got under the car.

STANLEY   Them darn mechanics at Fritz's don't know their ass fr'm—Hey!
[STELLA *has embraced him with both arms, fiercely, and full in the view
of* BLANCHE. *He laughs and clasps her head to him. Over her head he grins
through the curtains at* BLANCHE. *As the lights fade away, with a lingering brightness on their embrace, the music of the "Blue Piano" and trumpet and drums is heard.*]

Scene Five

BLANCHE *is seated in the bedroom fanning herself with a palm leaf as she reads
over a just-completed letter. Suddenly she bursts into a peal of laughter.* STELLA *is
dressing in the bedroom.*

STELLA   What are you laughing at, honey?

BLANCHE   Myself, myself, for being such a liar! I'm writing a letter to Shep.
[*She picks up the letter.*] "Darling Shep. I am spending the summer on the
wing, making flying visits here and there. And who knows, perhaps I shall
take a sudden notion to *swoop* down on *Dallas!* How would you feel about
that? Ha-ha! [*She laughs nervously and brightly, touching her throat as if
actually talking to* SHEP.] Forewarned is forearmed, as they say!"—How
does that sound?

STELLA   Uh-huh . . .

BLANCHE [*going on nervously*]   "Most of my sister's friends go north in the
summer but some have homes on the Gulf and there has been a continued round of entertainments, teas, cocktails, and luncheons—"
[*A disturbance is heard upstairs at the Hubbells' apartment.*]

STELLA   Eunice seems to be having some trouble with Steve.
[EUNICE's *voice shouts in terrible wrath.*]

EUNICE   I heard about you and that blonde!

STEVE   That's a damn lie!

EUNICE   You ain't pulling the wool over my eyes! I wouldn't mind if you'd
stay down at the Four Deuces, but you always going up.

STEVE   Who ever seen me up?

EUNICE   I seen you chasing her 'round the balcony—I'm gonna call the vice
squad!

STEVE   Don't you throw that at me!

EUNICE [*shrieking*]   You hit me! I'm gonna call the police!
[*A clatter of aluminum striking a wall is heard, followed by a man's angry
roar, shouts and overturned furniture. There is a crash; then a relative hush.*]

BLANCHE [*brightly*]   Did he *kill* her?
[EUNICE *appears on the steps in daemonic disorder.*]

STELLA   No! She's coming downstairs.

EUNICE   Call the police, I'm going to call the police! [*She rushes around the
corner.*]
[*They laugh lightly.* STANLEY *comes around the corner in his green and
scarlet silk bowling shirt. He trots up the steps and bangs into the kitchen.*
BLANCHE *registers his entrance with nervous gestures.*]

STANLEY   What's a matter with Eun-uss?

STELLA   She and Steve had a row. Has she got the police?

STANLEY   Naw. She's gettin' a drink.

STELLA   That's much more practical!

[STEVE *comes down nursing a bruise on his forehead and looks in the door.*]

STEVE   She here?

STANLEY   Naw, naw. At the Four Deuces.

STEVE   That rutting hunk! [*He looks around the corner a bit timidly, then turns with affected boldness and runs after her.*]

BLANCHE   I must jot that down in my notebook. Ha-ha! I'm compiling a notebook of quaint little words and phrases I've picked up here.

STANLEY   You won't pick up nothing here you ain't heard before.

BLANCHE   Can I count on that?

STANLEY   You can count on it up to five hundred.

BLANCHE   That's a mighty high number. [*He jerks open the bureau drawer, slams it shut and throws shoes in a corner. At each noise* BLANCHE *winces slightly. Finally she speaks.*] What sign were you born under?

STANLEY [*while he is dressing*]   Sign?

BLANCHE   Astrological sign. I bet you were born under Aries. Aries people are forceful and dynamic. They dote on noise! They love to bang things around! You must have had lots of banging around in the army and now that you're out, you make up for it by treating inanimate objects with such a fury!

[STELLA *has been going in and out of closet during this scene. Now she pops her head out of the closet.*]

STELLA   Stanley was born just five minutes after Christmas.

BLANCHE   Capricorn—the Goat!

STANLEY   What sign were *you* born under?

BLANCHE   Oh, my birthday's next month, the fifteenth of September; that's under Virgo.

STANLEY   What's Virgo?

BLANCHE   Virgo is the Virgin.

STANLEY [*contemptuously*]   Hah! [*He advances a little as he knots his tie.*] Say, do you happen to know somebody named Shaw?

[*Her face expresses a faint shock. She reaches for the cologne bottle and dampens her handkerchief as she answers carefully.*]

BLANCHE   Why, everybody knows somebody named Shaw!

STANLEY   Well, this somebody named Shaw is under the impression he met you in Laurel, but I figure he must have got you mixed up with some other party because this other party is someone he met at a hotel called the Flamingo.

[BLANCHE *laughs breathlessly as she touches the cologne-dampened handkerchief to her temples.*]

BLANCHE   I'm afraid he does have me mixed up with this "other party." The Hotel Flamingo is not the sort of establishment I would dare to be seen in!

STANLEY   You know of it?

BLANCHE   Yes, I've seen it and smelled it.

STANLEY   You must've got pretty close if you could smell it.

BLANCHE   The odor of cheap perfume is penetrating.

STANLEY   That stuff you use is expensive?

BLANCHE   Twenty-five dollars an ounce! I'm nearly out. That's just a hint if you want to remember my birthday! [*She speaks lightly but her voice has a note of fear.*]

STANLEY   Shaw must've got you mixed up. He goes in and out of Laurel all the time so he can check on it and clear up any mistake.

[*He turns away and crosses to the portieres.* BLANCHE *closes her eyes as if faint. Her hand trembles as she lifts the handkerchief again to her forehead.* STEVE *and* EUNICE *come around corner.* STEVE'*s arm is around* EUNICE'*s shoulder and she is sobbing luxuriously and he is cooing lovewords. There is a murmur of thunder as they go slowly upstairs in a tight embrace.*]

STANLEY [*to* STELLA] I'll wait for you at the Four Deuces!

STELLA   Hey! Don't I rate one kiss?

STANLEY   Not in front of your sister.

[*He goes out.* BLANCHE *rises from her chair. She seems faint; looks about her with an expression of almost panic.*]

BLANCHE   Stella! What have you heard about me?

STELLA   Huh?

BLANCHE   What have people been telling you about me?

STELLA   Telling?

BLANCHE   You haven't heard any—unkind—gossip about me?

STELLA   Why, no, Blanche, of course not!

BLANCHE   Honey, there was—a good deal of talk in Laurel.

STELLA   About *you*, Blanche?

BLANCHE   I wasn't so good the last two years or so, after Belle Reve had started to slip through my fingers.

STELLA   All of us do things we—

BLANCHE   I never was hard or self-sufficient enough. When people are soft—soft people have got to shimmer and glow—they've got to put on soft colors, the colors of butterfly wings, and put a—paper lantern over the light. . . . It isn't enough to be soft. You've got to be soft *and attractive*. And I—I'm fading now! I don't know how much longer I can turn the trick.

[*The afternoon has faded to dusk.* STELLA *goes into the bedroom and turns on the light under the paper lantern. She holds a bottled soft drink in her hand.*]

BLANCHE   Have you been listening to me?

STELLA   I don't listen to you when you are being morbid! [*She advances with the bottled Coke.*]

BLANCHE [*with abrupt change to gaiety*]   Is that Coke for me?

STELLA   Not for anyone else!

BLANCHE   Why, you precious thing, you! Is it just Coke?

STELLA [*turning*]   You mean you want a shot in it!

BLANCHE   Well, honey, a shot never does a Coke any harm! Let me! You mustn't wait on me!

STELLA   I like to wait on you, Blanche. It makes it seem more like home. [*She goes into the kitchen, finds a glass and pours a shot of whiskey into it.*]

BLANCHE   I have to admit I love to be waited on . . .

[*She rushes into the bedroom.* STELLA *goes to her with the glass.* BLANCHE *suddenly clutches* STELLA'*s free hand with a moaning sound and presses*

the hand to her lips. STELLA *is embarrassed by her show of emotion.*
BLANCHE *speaks in a choked voice.*]
    You're—you're—so *good* to me! And I—

STELLA   Blanche.

BLANCHE   I know, I won't! You hate me to talk sentimental! But honey,
believe I feel things more than I *tell* you! I *won't* stay long! I won't, I promise I—

STELLA   Blanche!

BLANCHE [*hysterically*]   I won't, I promise, *I'll* go! Go *soon!* I will *really!* I
won't hang around until he—throws me out . . .

STELLA   Now will you stop talking foolish?

BLANCHE   Yes, honey. Watch how you pour—that fizzy stuff foams over!
    [BLANCHE *laughs shrilly and grabs the glass, but her hand shakes so it
    almost slips from her grasp.* STELLA *pours the Coke into the glass. It foams
    over and spills.* BLANCHE *gives a piercing cry.*]

STELLA [*shocked by the cry*]   Heavens!

BLANCHE   Right on my pretty white skirt!

STELLA   Oh . . . Use my hanky. Blot gently.

BLANCHE [*slowly recovering*]   I know—gently—gently . . .

STELLA   Did it stain?

BLANCHE   Not a bit. Ha-ha! Isn't that lucky? [*She sits down shakily, taking
a grateful drink. She holds the glass in both hands and continues to laugh
a little.*]

STELLA   Why did you scream like that?

BLANCHE   I don't know why I screamed! [*continuing nervously*] Mitch—
Mitch is coming at seven. I guess I am just feeling nervous about our relations. [*She begins to talk rapidly and breathlessly.*] He hasn't gotten a thing
but a good-night kiss, that's all I have given him, Stella. I want his respect.
And men don't want anything they get too easy. But on the other hand
men lose interest quickly. Especially when the girl is over—thirty. They
think a girl over thirty ought to—the vulgar term is—"put out." . . . And
I—I'm not "putting out." Of course he—he doesn't know—I mean I
haven't informed him—of my real age!

STELLA   Why are you sensitive about your age?

BLANCHE   Because of hard knocks my vanity's been given. What I mean
is—he thinks I'm sort of—prim and proper, you know! [*She laughs out
sharply.*] I want to *deceive* him enough to make him—want me . . .

STELLA   Blanche, do you want *him?*

BLANCHE   I want to *rest!* I want to breathe quietly again! Yes—I *want*
Mitch . . . *very badly!* Just think! If it happens! I can leave here and not
be anyone's problem . . .
    [STANLEY *comes around the corner with a drink under his belt.*]

STANLEY [*bawling*]   Hey, Steve! Hey, Eunice! Hey, Stella!
    [*There are joyous calls from above. Trumpet and drums are heard from
    around the corner.*]

STELLA [*kissing* BLANCHE *impulsively*]   It *will* happen!

BLANCHE [*doubtfully*]   It will?

STELLA   It *will!* [*She goes across into the kitchen, looking back at* BLANCHE.]
It will, honey, *it will.* . . . But don't take another drink! [*Her voice catches
as she goes out the door to meet her husband.*]

[BLANCHE *sinks faintly back in her chair with her drink.* EUNICE *shrieks with laughter and runs down the steps.* STEVE *bounds after her with goat-like screeches and chases her around corner.* STANLEY *and* STELLA *twine arms as they follow, laughing. Dusk settles deeper. The music from the Four Deuces is slow and blue.*]

BLANCHE   Ah, me, ah, me, ah, me . . .

[*Her eyes fall shut and the palm leaf fan drops from her fingers. She slaps her hand on the chair arm a couple of times. There is a little glimmer of lightning about the building.* A YOUNG MAN *comes along the street and rings the bell.*]

BLANCHE   Come in.

[*The* YOUNG MAN *appears through the portieres. She regards him with interest.*]

BLANCHE   Well, well! What can I do for *you*?

YOUNG MAN   I'm collecting for *The Evening Star.*

BLANCHE   I didn't know that stars took up collections.

YOUNG MAN   It's the paper.

BLANCHE   I know, I was joking—feebly! Will you—have a drink?

YOUNG MAN   No, ma'am. No, thank you. I can't drink on the job.

BLANCHE   Oh, well, now, let's see. . . . No, I don't have a dime! I'm not the lady of the house. I'm her sister from Mississippi. I'm one of those poor relations you've heard about.

YOUNG MAN   That's all right. I'll drop by later. [*He starts to go out. She approaches a little.*]

BLANCHE   Hey! [*He turns back shyly. She puts a cigarette in a long holder.*] Could you give me a light? [*She crosses toward him. They meet at the door between the two rooms.*]

YOUNG MAN   Sure. [*He takes out a lighter.*] This doesn't always work.

BLANCHE   It's temperamental? [*It flares.*] Ah!—thank you. [*He starts away again.*] Hey! [*He turns again, still more uncertainly. She goes close to him.*] Uh—what time is it?

YOUNG MAN   Fifteen of seven, ma'am.

BLANCHE   So late? Don't you just love these long rainy afternoons in New Orleans when an hour isn't just an hour—but a little piece of eternity dropped into your hands—and who knows what to do with it? [*She touches his shoulders.*] You—uh—didn't get wet in the rain?

YOUNG MAN   No, ma'am. I stepped inside.

BLANCHE   In a drugstore? And had a soda?

YOUNG MAN   Uh-huh.

BLANCHE   Chocolate?

YOUNG MAN   No, ma'am. Cherry.

BLANCHE [*laughing*]   Cherry!

YOUNG MAN   A cherry soda.

BLANCHE   You make my mouth water. [*She touches his cheek lightly, and smiles. Then she goes to the trunk.*]

YOUNG MAN   Well, I'd better be going—

BLANCHE [*stopping him*]   Young man!

[*He turns. She takes a large, gossamer scarf from the trunk and drapes it about her shoulders. In the ensuing pause, the "Blue Piano" is heard. It continues through the rest of this scene and the opening of the next. The young man clears his throat and looks yearningly at the door.*]

Young man! Young, young, young man! Has anyone ever told you that you look like a young Prince out of the Arabian Nights?

[*The* YOUNG MAN *laughs uncomfortably and stands like a bashful kid.* BLANCHE *speaks softly to him.*]

Well, you do, honey lamb! Come here. I want to kiss you, just once, softly and sweetly on your mouth!

[*Without waiting for him to accept, she crosses quickly to him and presses her lips to his.*]

Now run along, now, quickly! It would be nice to keep you, but I've got to be good—and keep my hands off children.

[*He stares at her a moment. She opens the door for him and blows a kiss at him as he goes down the steps with a dazed look. She stands there a little dreamily after he has disappeared. Then* MITCH *appears around the corner with a bunch of roses.*]

BLANCHE [*gaily*]   Look who's coming! My Rosenkavalier! Bow to me first . . . now present them! Ahhhh—Merciiii![2]

[*She looks at him over them, coquettishly pressing them to her lips. He beams at her self-consciously.*]

Scene Six

It is about two A.M on the same evening. The outer wall of the building is visible. BLANCHE *and* MITCH *come in. The utter exhaustion which only a neurasthenic personality can know is evident in* BLANCHE'*s voice and manner.* MITCH *is stolid but depressed. They have probably been out to the amusement park on Lake Pontchartrain, for* MITCH *is bearing, upside down, a plaster statuette of Mae West, the sort of prize won at shooting galleries and carnival games of chance.*

BLANCHE [*stopping lifelessly at the steps*]   Well— [MITCH *laughs uneasily.*] Well . . .

MITCH   I guess it must be pretty late—and you're tired.

BLANCHE   Even the hot tamale man has deserted the street, and he hangs on till the end. [MITCH *laughs uneasily again.*] How will you get home?

MITCH   I'll walk over to Bourbon and catch an owl-car.

BLANCHE [*laughing grimly*]   Is that streetcar named Desire still grinding along the tracks at this hour?

MITCH [*heavily*]   I'm afraid you haven't gotten much fun out of this evening, Blanche.

BLANCHE   I spoiled it for *you.*

MITCH   No, you didn't, but I felt all the time that I wasn't giving you much—entertainment.

BLANCHE   I simply couldn't rise to the occasion. That was all. I don't think I've ever tried so hard to be gay and made such a dismal mess of it. I get ten points for trying!—I *did* try.

MITCH   Why did you try if you didn't feel like it, Blanche?

BLANCHE   I was just obeying the law of nature.

MITCH   Which law is that?

BLANCHE   The one that says the lady must entertain the gentleman—or no

---

2. "Merci": thank you (French). "My Rosenkavalier": Knight of the Rose (German); title of a romantic opera (1911) by Richard Strauss.

dice! See if you can locate my door key in this purse. When I'm so tired my fingers are all thumbs!

MITCH [*rooting in her purse*] This it?

BLANCHE No, honey, that's the key to my trunk which I must soon be packing.

MITCH You mean you are leaving here soon?

BLANCHE I've outstayed my welcome.

MITCH This it?

[*The music fades away.*]

BLANCHE Eureka! Honey, you open the door while I take a last look at the sky. [*She leans on the porch rail. He opens the door and stands awkwardly behind her.*] I'm looking for the Pleiades, the Seven Sisters, but these girls are not out tonight. Oh, yes they are, there they are! God bless them! All in a bunch going home from their little bridge party. . . . Y' get the door open? Good boy! I guess you—want to go now . . .

[*He shuffles and coughs a little.*]

MITCH Can I—uh—kiss you—good night?

BLANCHE Why do you always ask me if you may?

MITCH I don't know whether you want me to or not.

BLANCHE Why should you be so doubtful?

MITCH That night when we parked by the lake and I kissed you, you—

BLANCHE Honey, it wasn't the kiss I objected to. I liked the kiss very much. It was the other little—familiarity—that I—felt obliged to—discourage. . . . I didn't resent it! Not a bit in the world! In fact, I was somewhat flattered that you—desired me! But, honey, you know as well as I do that a single girl, a girl alone in the world, has got to keep a firm hold on her emotions or she'll be lost!

MITCH [*solemnly*] Lost?

BLANCHE I guess you are used to girls that like to be lost. The kind that get lost immediately, on the first date!

MITCH I like you to be exactly the way that you are, because in all my—experience—I have never known anyone like you.

[BLANCHE *looks at him gravely; then she bursts into laughter and then claps a hand to her mouth.*]

MITCH Are you laughing at me?

BLANCHE No, honey. The lord and lady of the house have not yet returned, so come in. We'll have a nightcap. Let's leave the lights off. Shall we?

MITCH You just—do what you want to.

[BLANCHE *precedes him into the kitchen. The outer wall of the building disappears and the interiors of the two rooms can be dimly seen.*]

BLANCHE [*remaining in the first room*] The other room's more comfortable—go on in. This crashing around in the dark is my search for some liquor.

MITCH You want a drink?

BLANCHE I want *you* to have a drink! You have been so anxious and solemn all evening, and so have I; we have both been anxious and solemn and now for these few last remaining moments of our lives together—I want to create—*joie de vivre*! I'm lighting a candle.

MITCH That's good.

BLANCHE We are going to be very Bohemian. We are going to pretend that we are sitting in a little artists' cafe on the Left Bank in Paris! [*She lights*

a candle stub and puts it in a bottle.] *Je suis la Dame aux Camellias! Vous
êtes—Armand!*[3] Understand French?

MITCH [*heavily*]   Naw. Naw, I—

BLANCHE   *Voulez-vous couchez avec moi ce soir? Vous ne comprenez pas?
Ah, quelle dommage!*[4]—I mean it's a damned good thing. . . . I've found
some liquor! Just enough for two shots without any dividends, honey . . .

MITCH [*heavily*]   That's—good.

[*She enters the bedroom with the drinks and the candle.*]

BLANCHE   Sit down! Why don't you take off your coat and loosen your
collar?

MITCH   I better leave it on.

BLANCHE   No. I want you to be comfortable.

MITCH   I am ashamed of the way I perspire. My shirt is sticking to me.

BLANCHE   Perspiration is healthy. If people didn't perspire they would die
in five minutes. [*She takes his coat from him.*] This is a nice coat. What
kind of material is it?

MITCH   They call that stuff alpaca.

BLANCHE   Oh. Alpaca.

MITCH   It's very light-weight alpaca.

BLANCHE   Oh. Light-weight alpaca.

MITCH   I don't like to wear a wash-coat even in summer because I sweat
through it.

BLANCHE   Oh.

MITCH   And it don't look neat on me. A man with a heavy build has got to
be careful of what he puts on him so he don't look too clumsy.

BLANCHE   You are not too heavy.

MITCH   You don't think I am?

BLANCHE   You are not the delicate type. You have a massive bone-structure
and a very imposing physique.

MITCH   Thank you. Last Christmas I was given a membership to the New
Orleans Athletic Club.

BLANCHE   Oh, good.

MITCH   It was the finest present I ever was given. I work out there with the
weights and I swim and I keep myself fit. When I started there, I was getting soft in the belly but now my belly is hard. It is so hard now that a man
can punch me in the belly and it don't hurt me. Punch me! Go on! See?
[*She pokes lightly at him.*]

BLANCHE   Gracious. [*Her hand touches her chest.*]

MITCH   Guess how much I weigh, Blanche?

BLANCHE   Oh, I'd say in the vicinity of—one hundred and eighty?

MITCH   Guess again.

BLANCHE   Not that much?

MITCH   No. More.

BLANCHE   Well, you're a tall man and you can carry a good deal of weight
without looking awkward.

MITCH   I weigh two hundred and seven pounds and I'm six feet one and

---

3. I am the Lady of the Camellias! You are—
Armand! (French). Both are characters in the popular romantic play *La Dame aux Camélias* (1852),
by the French author Alexandre Dumas *fils*; she is

a courtesan who gives up her true love, Armand.
4. Would you like to sleep with me this evening?
You don't understand? Ah, what a pity! (French).

one half inches tall in my bare feet—without shoes on. And that is what I weigh stripped.

BLANCHE   Oh, my goodness, me! It's awe-inspiring.

MITCH [*embarrassed*]   My weight is not a very interesting subject to talk about. [*He hesitates for a moment.*] What's yours?

BLANCHE   My weight?

MITCH   Yes.

BLANCHE   Guess!

MITCH   Let me lift you.

BLANCHE   Samson![5] Go on, lift me. [*He comes behind her and puts his hands on her waist and raises her lightly off the ground.*] Well?

MITCH   You are light as a feather.

BLANCHE   Ha-ha! [*He lowers her but keeps his hands on her waist.* BLANCHE *speaks with an affectation of demureness.*] You may release me now.

MITCH   Huh?

BLANCHE [*gaily*]   I said unhand me, sir. [*He fumblingly embraces her. Her voice sounds gently reproving.*] Now, Mitch. Just because Stanley and Stella aren't at home is no reason why you shouldn't behave like a gentleman.

MITCH   Just give me a slap whenever I step out of bounds.

BLANCHE   That won't be necessary. You're a natural gentleman, one of the very few that are left in the world. I don't want you to think that I am severe and old maid school-teacherish or anything like that. It's just— well—

MITCH   Huh?

BLANCHE   I guess it is just that I have—old-fashioned ideals! [*She rolls her eyes, knowing he cannot see her face.* MITCH *goes to the front door. There is a considerable silence between them.* BLANCHE *sighs and* MITCH *coughs self-consciously.*]

MITCH [*finally*]   Where's Stanley and Stella tonight?

BLANCHE   They have gone out. With Mr. and Mrs. Hubbell upstairs.

MITCH   Where did they go?

BLANCHE   I think they were planning to go to a midnight prevue at Loew's State.

MITCH   We should all go out together some night.

BLANCHE   No. That wouldn't be a good plan.

MITCH   Why not?

BLANCHE   You are an old friend of Stanley's?

MITCH   We was together in the Two-forty-first.[6]

BLANCHE   I guess he talks to you frankly?

MITCH   Sure.

BLANCHE   Has he talked to you about me?

BLANCHE   Oh—not very much.

BLANCHE   The way you say that, I suspect that he has.

MITCH   No, he hasn't said much.

BLANCHE   But what he *has* said. What would you say his attitude toward me was?

MITCH   Why do you want to ask that?

5. Legendary strong man in the Old Testament.   6. Battalion of engineers in World War II.

BLANCHE   Well—

MITCH   Don't you get along with him?

BLANCHE   What do you think?

MITCH   I don't think he understands you.

BLANCHE   That is putting it mildly. If it weren't for Stella about to have a baby, I wouldn't be able to endure things here.

MITCH   He isn't—nice to you?

BLANCHE   He is insufferably rude. Goes out of his way to offend me.

MITCH   In what way, Blanche?

BLANCHE   Why, in every conceivable way.

MITCH   I'm surprised to hear that.

BLANCHE   Are you?

MITCH   Well, I—don't see how anybody could be rude to you.

BLANCHE   It's really a pretty frightful situation. You see, there's no privacy here. There's just these portieres between the two rooms at night. He stalks through the rooms in his underwear at night. And I have to ask him to close the bathroom door. That sort of commonness isn't necessary. You probably wonder why I don't move out. Well, I'll tell you frankly. A teacher's salary is barely sufficient for her living expenses. I didn't save a penny last year and so I had to come here for the summer. That's why I have to put up with my sister's husband. And he has to put up with me, apparently so much against his wishes. . . . Surely he must have told you how much he hates me!

MITCH   I don't think he hates you.

BLANCHE   He hates me. Or why would he insult me? The first time I laid eyes on him I thought to myself, that man is my executioner! That man will destroy me, unless——

MITCH   Blanche—

BLANCHE   Yes, honey?

MITCH   Can I ask you a question?

BLANCHE   Yes. What?

MITCH   How old are you?

[She makes a nervous gesture.]

BLANCHE   Why do you want to know?

MITCH   I talked to my mother about you and she said, "How old is Blanche?" And I wasn't able to tell her. [There is another pause.]

BLANCHE   You talked to your mother about me?

MITCH   Yes.

BLANCHE   Why?

MITCH   I told my mother how nice you were, and I liked you.

BLANCHE   Were you sincere about that?

MITCH   You know I was.

BLANCHE   Why did your mother want to know my age?

MITCH   Mother is sick.

BLANCHE   I'm sorry to hear it. Badly?

MITCH   She won't live long. Maybe just a few months.

BLANCHE   Oh.

MITCH   She worries because I'm not settled.

BLANCHE   Oh.

MITCH   She wants me to be settled down before she— [His voice is hoarse *and he clears his throat twice, shuffling nervously around with his hands in and out of his pockets.*]

BLANCHE You love her very much, don't you?

MITCH Yes.

BLANCHE I think you have a great capacity for devotion. You will be lonely when she passes on, won't you? [MITCH *clears his throat and nods.*] I understand what that is.

MITCH To be lonely?

BLANCHE I loved someone, too, and the person I loved I lost.

MITCH Dead? [*She crosses to the window and sits on the sill, looking out. She pours herself another drink.*] A man?

BLANCHE He was a boy, just a boy, when I was a very young girl. When I was sixteen, I made the discovery—love. All at once and much, much too completely. It was like you suddenly turned a blinding light on something that had always been half in shadow, that's how it struck the world for me. But I was unlucky. Deluded. There was something different about the boy, a nervousness, a softness and tenderness which wasn't like a man's, although he wasn't the least bit effeminate looking—still—that thing was there. . . . He came to me for help. I didn't know that. I didn't find out anything till after our marriage when we'd run away and come back and all I knew was I'd failed him in some mysterious way and wasn't able to give the help he needed but couldn't speak of! He was in the quicksands and clutching at me—but I wasn't holding him out, I was slipping in with him! I didn't know that. I didn't know anything except I loved him unendurably but without being able to help him or help myself. Then I found out. In the worst of all possible ways. By coming suddenly into a room that I thought was empty—which wasn't empty, but had two people in it . . . the boy I had married and an older man who had been his friend for years . . .

    [*A locomotive is heard approaching outside. She claps her hands to her ears and crouches over. The headlight of the locomotive glares into the room as it thunders past. As the noise recedes she straightens slowly and continues speaking.*]

Afterward we pretended that nothing had been discovered. Yes, the three of us drove out to Moon Lake Casino, very drunk and laughing all the way.

    [*Polka music sounds, in a minor key faint with distance.*]

We danced the Varsouviana![7] Suddenly in the middle of the dance the boy I had married broke away from me and ran out of the casino. A few moments later—a shot!

    [*The polka stops abruptly.* BLANCHE *rises stiffly. Then, the polka resumes in a major key.*]

I ran out—all did!—all ran and gathered about the terrible thing at the edge of the lake! I couldn't get near for the crowding. Then somebody caught my arm. "Don't go any closer! Come back! You don't want to see!" See? See what! Then I heard voices say—Allan! Allan! The Grey boy! He'd stuck the revolver into his mouth, and fired—so that the back of his head had been—blown away!

    [*She sways and covers her face.*]

---

7. Fast Polish waltz, similar to the polka.

It was because—on the dance floor—unable to stop myself—I'd suddenly said—"I saw! I know! You disgust me . . ." And then the searchlight which had been turned on the world was turned off again and never for one moment since has there been any light that's stronger than this— kitchen—candle . . .

> [MITCH gets up awkwardly and moves toward her a little. The polka music increases. MITCH stands beside her.]

MITCH [drawing her slowly into his arms] You need somebody. And I need somebody, too. Could it be—you and me, Blanche?

> [She stares at him vacantly for a moment. Then with a soft cry huddles in his embrace. She makes a sobbing effort to speak but the words won't come. He kisses her forehead and her eyes and finally her lips. The Polka tune fades out. Her breath is drawn and released in long, grateful sobs.]

BLANCHE Sometimes—there's God—so quickly!

Scene Seven

It is late afternoon in mid-September.

The portieres are open and a table is set for a birthday supper, with cake and flowers.

STELLA is completing the decorations as STANLEY comes in.

STANLEY What's all this stuff for?

STELLA Honey, it's Blanche's birthday.

STANLEY She here?

STELLA In the bathroom.

STANLEY [mimicking] "Washing out some things"?

STELLA I reckon so.

STANLEY How long she been in there?

STELLA All afternoon.

STANLEY [mimicking] "Soaking in a hot tub"?

STELLA Yes.

STANLEY Temperature 100 on the nose, and she soaks herself in a hot tub.

STELLA She says it cools her off for the evening.

STANLEY And you run out an' get her cokes, I suppose? And serve 'em to Her Majesty in the tub? [STELLA shrugs.] Set down here a minute.

STELLA Stanley, I've got things to do.

STANLEY Set down! I've got th' dope on your big sister, Stella.

STELLA Stanley, stop picking on Blanche.

STANLEY That girl calls me common!

STELLA Lately you been doing all you can think of to rub her the wrong way, Stanley, and Blanche is sensitive and you've got to realize that Blanche and I grew up under very different circumstances than you did.

STANLEY So I been told. And told and told and told! You know she's been feeding us a pack of lies here?

STELLA No, I don't, and—

STANLEY Well, she has, however. But now the cat's out of the bag! I found out some things!

STELLA What—things?

STANLEY Things I already suspected. But now I got proof from the most reliable sources—which I have checked on!

[BLANCHE *is singing in the bathroom a saccharine popular ballad which is used contrapuntally with* STANLEY'S *speech.*]

STELLA [*to* STANLEY]   Lower your voice!

STANLEY   Some canary bird, huh!

STELLA   Now please tell me quietly what you think you've found out about my sister.

STANLEY   Lie Number One: All this squeamishness she puts on! You should just know the line she's been feeding to Mitch. He thought she had never been more than kissed by a fellow! But Sister Blanche is no lily! Ha-ha! Some lily she is!

STELLA   What have you heard and who from?

STANLEY   Our supply-man down at the plant has been going through Laurel for years and he knows all about her and everybody else in the town of Laurel knows all about her. She is as famous in Laurel as if she was the President of the United States, only she is not respected by any party! This supply-man stops at a hotel called the Flamingo.

BLANCHE [*singing blithely*]   "Say, it's only a paper moon, Sailing over a cardboard sea—But it wouldn't be make-believe If you believed in me!"[8]

STELLA   What about the—Flamingo?

STANLEY   She stayed there, too.

STELLA   My sister lived at Belle Reve.

STANLEY   This is after the home-place had slipped through her lily-white fingers! She moved to the Flamingo! A second-class hotel which has the advantage of not interfering in the private social life of the personalities there! The Flamingo is used to all kinds of goings-on. But even the management of the Flamingo was impressed by Dame Blanche! In fact they was so impressed by Dame Blanche that they requested her to turn in her room key—for permanently! This happened a couple of weeks before she showed here.

BLANCHE [*singing*]   "It's a Barnum and Bailey world, Just as phony as it can be—But it wouldn't be make-believe If you believed in me!"

STELLA   What—contemptible—lies!

STANLEY   Sure, I can see how you would be upset by this. She pulled the wool over your eyes as much as Mitch's!

STELLA   It's pure invention! There's not a word of truth in it and if if I were a man and this creature had dared to invent such things in my presence—

BLANCHE [*singing*]   "Without your love, It's a honky-tonk parade! Without your love, It's a melody played In a penny arcade . . ."

STANLEY   Honey, I told you I thoroughly checked on these stories! Now wait till I finished. The trouble with Dame Blanche was that she couldn't put on her act any more in Laurel! They got wised up after two or three dates with her and then they quit, and she goes on to another, the same old line, same old act, same old hooey! But the town was too small for this to go on forever! And as time went by she became a town character. Regarded as not just different but downright loco—nuts. [STELLA *draws back.*] And for the last year or two she has been washed up like poison. That's why she's here this summer, visiting royalty, putting on all this act—because she's practically told by the mayor to get out of town! Yes,

---

8. From "It's Only a Paper Moon" (1933), a popular song by Harold Arlen.

did you know there was an army camp near Laurel and your sister's was one of the places called "Out-of-Bounds"?

BLANCHE "It's only a paper moon, Just as phony as it can be—But it wouldn't be make-believe If you believed in me!"

STANLEY Well, so much for her being such a refined and particular type of girl. Which brings us to Lie Number Two.

STELLA I don't want to hear any more!

STANLEY She's not going back to teach school! In fact I am willing to bet you that she never had no idea of returning to Laurel! She didn't resign temporarily from the high school because of her nerves! No, siree, Bob! She didn't. They kicked her out of that high school before the spring term ended—and I hate to tell you the reason that step was taken! A seventeen-year-old boy—she'd gotten mixed up with!

BLANCHE "It's a Barnum and Bailey world, Just as phony as it can be—" [*In the bathroom the water goes on loud; little breathless cries and peals of laughter are heard as if a child were frolicking in the tub.*]

STELLA This is making me—sick!

STANLEY The boy's dad learned about it and got in touch with the high school superintendent. Boy, oh, boy, I'd like to have been in that office when Dame Blanche was called on the carpet! I'd like to have seen her trying to squirm out of that one! But they had her on the hook good and proper that time and she knew that the jig was all up! They told her she better move on to some fresh territory. Yep, it was practickly a town ordinance passed against her!

[*The bathroom door is opened and* BLANCHE *thrusts her head out, holding a towel about her hair.*]

BLANCHE Stella!

STELLA [*faintly*] Yes, Blanche?

BLANCHE Give me another bath-towel to dry my hair with. I've just washed it.

STELLA Yes, Blanche. [*She crosses in a dazed way from the kitchen to the bathroom door with a towel.*]

BLANCHE What's the matter, honey?

STELLA Matter? Why?

BLANCHE You have such a strange expression on your face!

STELLA Oh— [*she tries to laugh*] I guess I'm a little tired!

BLANCHE Why don't you bathe, too, soon as I get out?

STANLEY [*calling from the kitchen*] How soon is that going to be?

BLANCHE Not so terribly long! Possess your soul in patience!

STANLEY It's not my soul, it's my kidneys I'm worried about!

[BLANCHE *slams the door.* STANLEY *laughs harshly.* STELLA *comes slowly back into the kitchen.*]

STANLEY Well, what do you think of it?

STELLA I don't believe all of those stories and I think your supply-man was mean and rotten to tell them. It's possible that some of the things he said are partly true. There are things about my sister I don't approve of—things that caused sorrow at home. She was always—flighty!

STANLEY Flighty!

STELLA But when she was young, very young, she married a boy who wrote poetry. . . . He was extremely good-looking. I think Blanche didn't just love him but worshipped the ground he walked on! Adored him and thought him almost too fine to be human! But then she found out—

STANLEY What?

STELLA This beautiful and talented young man was a degenerate. Didn't your supply-man give you that information?

STANLEY All we discussed was recent history. That must have been a pretty long time ago.

STELLA Yes, it was—a pretty long time ago . . .

[STANLEY *comes up and takes her by the shoulders rather gently. She gently withdraws from him. Automatically she starts sticking little pink candles in the birthday cake.*]

STANLEY How many candles you putting in that cake?

STELLA I'll stop at twenty-five.

STANLEY Is company expected?

STELLA We asked Mitch to come over for cake and ice-cream.

[STANLEY *looks a little uncomfortable. He lights a cigarette from the one he has just finished.*]

STANLEY I wouldn't be expecting Mitch over tonight.

[STELLA *pauses in her occupation with candles and looks slowly around at* STANLEY.]

STELLA Why?

STANLEY Mitch is a buddy of mine. We were in the same outfit together— Two-forty-first Engineers. We work in the same plant and now on the same bowling team. You think I could face him if—

STELLA Stanley Kowalski, did you—did you repeat what that—?

STANLEY You're goddam right I told him! I'd have that on my conscience the rest of my life if I knew all that stuff and let my best friend get caught!

STELLA Is Mitch through with her?

STANLEY Wouldn't you be if—?

STELLA I said, *Is Mitch through with her?*

[BLANCHE'S *voice is lifted again, serenely as a bell. She sings* "But it wouldn't be make-believe If you believed in me."]

STANLEY No, I don't think he's necessarily through with her—just wised up!

STELLA Stanley, she thought Mitch was—going to—going to marry her. I was hoping so, too.

STANLEY Well, he's not going to marry her. Maybe he *was*, but he's not going to jump in a tank with a school of sharks—now! [*He rises.*] Blanche! Oh, Blanche! Can I please get in my bathroom? [*There is a pause.*]

BLANCHE Yes, indeed, sir! Can you wait one second while I dry?

STANLEY Having waited one hour I guess one second ought to pass in a hurry.

STELLA And she hasn't got her job? Well, what will she do!

STANLEY She's not stayin' here after Tuesday. You know that, don't you? Just to make sure I bought her ticket myself. A bus ticket.

STELLA In the first place, Blanche wouldn't go on a bus.

STANLEY She'll go on a bus and like it.

STELLA No, she won't, no, she won't, Stanley!

STANLEY *She'll go!* Period. P.S. She'll go *Tuesday!*

STELLA [*slowly*] What'll—she—do? What on earth will she—*do!*

STANLEY   Her future is mapped out for her.

STELLA   What do you mean?

[BLANCHE *sings*.]

STANLEY   Hey, canary bird! Toots! Get *OUT* of the *BATHROOM!*

[*The bathroom door flies open and* BLANCHE *emerges with a gay peal of laughter, but as* STANLEY *crosses past her, a frightened look appears in her face, almost a look of panic. He doesn't look at her but slams the bathroom door shut as he goes in.*

BLANCHE [*snatching up a hairbrush*]   Oh, I feel so good after my long, hot bath, I feel so good and cool and—rested!

STELLA [*sadly and doubtfully from the kitchen*]   Do you, Blanche?

BLANCHE [*snatching up a hairbrush*]   Yes, I do, so refreshed! [*She tinkles her highball glass.*] A hot bath and a long, cold drink always give me a brand new outlook on life! [*She looks through the portieres at* STELLA, *standing between them, and slowly stops brushing.*] Something has happened!—What is it?

STELLA [*turning away quickly*]   Why, nothing has happened, Blanche.

BLANCHE   You're lying! Something has!

[*She stares fearfully at* STELLA, *who pretends to be busy at the table. The distant piano goes into a hectic breakdown.*]

Scene Eight

Three quarters of an hour later.

The view through the big windows is fading gradually into a still-golden dusk. A torch of sunlight blazes on the side of a big water-tank or oil-drum across the empty lot toward the business district which is now pierced by pinpoints of lighted windows or windows reflecting the sunset.

The three people are completing a dismal birthday supper. STANLEY *looks sullen.* STELLA *is embarrassed and sad.*

BLANCHE *has a tight, artificial smile on her drawn face. There is a fourth place at the table which is left vacant.*

BLANCHE [*suddenly*]   Stanley, tell us a joke, tell us a funny story to make us all laugh. I don't know what's the matter, we're all so solemn. Is it because I've been stood up by my beau?

[STELLA *laughs feebly.*]

It's the first time in my entire experience with men, and I've had a good deal of all sorts, that I've actually been stood up by anybody! Ha-ha! I don't know how to take it. . . . Tell us a funny little story, Stanley! Something to help us out.

STANLEY   I didn't think you liked my stories, Blanche.

BLANCHE   I like them when they're amusing but not indecent.

STANLEY   I don't know any refined enough for your taste.

BLANCHE   Then let me tell one.

STELLA   Yes, you tell one, Blanche. You used to know lots of good stories.

[*The music fades.*]

BLANCHE   Let me see, now. . . . I must run through my repertoire! Oh, yes—I love parrot stories! Do you all like parrot stories? Well, this one's about the old maid and the parrot. This old maid, she had a parrot that cursed a blue streak and knew more vulgar expressions than Mr. Kowalski!

STANLEY   Huh.

BLANCHE   And the only way to hush the parrot up was to put the cover back on its cage so it would think it was night and go back to sleep. Well, one morning the old maid had just uncovered the parrot for the day—when who should she see coming up the front walk but the preacher! Well, she rushed back to the parrot and slipped the cover back on the cage and then she let in the preacher. And the parrot was perfectly still, just as quiet as a mouse, but just as she was asking the preacher how much sugar he wanted in his coffee—the parrot broke the silence with a loud—[*She whistles.*]—and said—"God *damn*, but that was a short day!"

[*She throws back her head and laughs.* STELLA *also makes an ineffectual effort to seem amused.* STANLEY *pays no attention to the story but reaches way over the table to spear his fork into the remaining chop which he eats with his fingers.*]

BLANCHE   Apparently Mr. Kowalski was not amused.

STELLA   Mr. Kowalski is too busy making a pig of himself to think of anything else!

STANLEY   That's right, baby.

STELLA   Your face and your fingers are disgustingly greasy. Go and wash up and then help me clear the table.

[*He hurls a plate to the floor.*]

STANLEY   That's how I'll clear the table! [*He seizes her arm.*] Don't ever talk that way to me! "Pig—Polack—disgusting—vulgar—greasy!"—them kind of words have been on your tongue and your sister's too much around here! What do you two think you are? A pair of queens? Remember what Huey Long[9] said—"Every Man is a King!" And I am the king around here, so don't forget it! [*He hurls a cup and saucer to the floor.*] My place is cleared! You want me to clear your places?

[STELLA *begins to cry weakly.* STANLEY *stalks out on the porch and lights a cigarette. The Negro entertainers around the corner are heard.*]

BLANCHE   What happened while I was bathing? What did he tell you, Stella?

STELLA   Nothing, nothing, nothing!

BLANCHE   I think he told you something about Mitch and me! You know why Mitch didn't come but you won't tell me! [STELLA *shakes her head helplessly.*] I'm going to call him!

STELLA   I wouldn't call him, Blanche.

BLANCHE   I am, I'm going to call him on the phone.

STELLA [*miserably*]   I wish you wouldn't.

BLANCHE   I intend to be given some explanation from someone!

[*She rushes to the phone in the bedroom.* STELLA *goes out on the porch and stares reproachfully at her husband. He grunts and turns away from her.*]

STELLA   I hope you're pleased with your doings. I never had so much trouble swallowing food in my life, looking at that girl's face and the empty chair! [*She cries quietly.*]

BLANCHE [*at the phone*]   Hello. Mr. Mitchell, please. . . . Oh. . . . I would like to leave a number if I may. Magnolia 9047. And say it's important to call. . . . Yes, very important. . . . Thank you.

9. Demagogic Louisiana political leader, governor, and senator (1893–1935).

[*She remains by the phone with a lost, frightened look.* STANLEY *turns slowly back toward his wife and takes her clumsily in his arms.*]

STANLEY   Stell, it's gonna be all right after she goes and after you've had the baby. It's gonna be all right again between you and me the way that it was. You remember the way that it was? Them nights we had together? God, honey, it's gonna be sweet when we can make noise in the night the way that we used to and get the colored lights going with nobody's sister behind the curtains to hear us!

[*Their upstairs neighbors are heard in bellowing laughter at something.* STANLEY *chuckles.*]

Steve an' Eunice . . .

STELLA   Come on back in. [*She returns to the kitchen and starts lighting the candles on the white cake.*] Blanche?

BLANCHE   Yes. [*She returns from the bedroom to the table in the kitchen.*] Oh, those pretty, pretty little candles! Oh, don't burn them, Stella.

STELLA   I certainly will.

[STANLEY *comes back in.*]

BLANCHE   You ought to save them for baby's birthdays. Oh, I hope candles are going to glow in his life and I hope that his eyes are going to be like candles, like two blue candles lighted in a white cake!

STANLEY [*sitting down*]   What poetry!

BLANCHE [*she pauses reflectively for a moment*]   I shouldn't have called him.

STELLA   There's lots of things could have happened.

BLANCHE   There's no excuse for it, Stella. I don't have to put up with insults. I won't be taken for granted.

STANLEY   Goddamn, it's hot in here with the steam from the bathroom.

BLANCHE   I've said I was sorry three times. [*The piano fades out.*] I take hot baths for my nerves. Hydrotherapy, they call it. You healthy Polack, without a nerve in your body, of course you don't know what anxiety feels like!

STANLEY   I am not a Polack. People from Poland are Poles, not Polacks. But what I am is a one-hundred-per-cent American, born and raised in the greatest country on earth and proud as hell of it, so don't ever call me a Polack.

[*The phone rings.* BLANCHE *rises expectantly.*]

BLANCHE   Oh, that's for me, I'm sure.

STANLEY   *I'm* not sure. Keep your seat. [*He crosses leisurely to phone.*] H'lo. Aw, yeh, hello, Mac.

[*He leans against wall, staring insultingly in at* BLANCHE. *She sinks back in her chair with a frightened look.* STELLA *leans over and touches her shoulder.*]

BLANCHE   Oh, keep your hands off me, Stella. What is the matter with you? Why do you look at me with that pitying look?

STANLEY [*bawling*]   QUIET IN THERE!—We've got a noisy woman on the place.—Go on, Mac. At Riley's? No, I don't wanta bowl at Riley's. I had a little trouble with Riley last week. I'm the team captain, ain't I? All right, then, we're not gonna bowl at Riley's, we're gonna bowl at the West Side or the Gala! All right, Mac. See you!

[*He hangs up and returns to the table.* BLANCHE *fiercely controls herself, drinking quickly from her tumbler of water. He doesn't look at her but reaches in a pocket. Then he speaks slowly and with false amiability.*]

Sister Blanche, I've got a little birthday remembrance for you.

BLANCHE   Oh, have you, Stanley? I wasn't expecting any, I—I don't know why Stella wants to observe my birthday! I'd much rather forget it—when you—reach twenty-seven! Well—age is a subject that you'd prefer to—ignore!

STANLEY   Twenty-seven?

BLANCHE [quickly]   What is it? Is it for me?
    [He is holding a little envelope toward her.]

STANLEY   Yes, I hope you like it!

BLANCHE   Why, why—Why, it's a—

STANLEY   Ticket! Back to Laurel! On the Greyhound! Tuesday!
    [The Varsouviana music steals in softly and continues playing. STELLA rises abruptly and turns her back. BLANCHE tries to smile. Then she tries to laugh. Then she gives both up and springs from the table and runs into the next room. She clutches her throat and then runs into the bathroom. Coughing, gagging sounds are heard.]
Well!

STELLA   You didn't need to do that.

STANLEY   Don't forget all that I took off her.

STELLA   You needn't have been so cruel to someone alone as she is.

STANLEY   Delicate piece she is.

STELLA   She is. She was. You didn't know Blanche as a girl. Nobody, nobody, was tender and trusting as she was. But people like you abused her, and forced her to change.
    [He crosses into the bedroom, ripping off his shirt, and changes into a brilliant silk bowling shirt. She follows him.]
Do you think you're going bowling now?

STANLEY   Sure.

STELLA   You're not going bowling. [She catches hold of his shirt.] Why did you do this to her?

STANLEY   I done nothing to no one. Let go of my shirt. You've torn it.

STELLA   I want to know why. Tell me why.

STANLEY   When we first met, me and you, you thought I was common. How right you was, baby. I was common as dirt. You showed me the snapshot of the place with the columns. I pulled you down off them columns and how you loved it, having them colored lights going! And wasn't we happy together, wasn't it all okay till she showed here?
    [STELLA makes a slight movement. Her look goes suddenly inward as if some interior voice had called her name. She begins a slow, shuffling progress from the bedroom to the kitchen, leaning and resting on the back of the chair and then on the edge of a table with a blind look and listening expression. STANLEY, finishing with his shirt, is unaware of her reaction.]
And wasn't we happy together? Wasn't it all okay? Till she showed here. Hoity-Toity, describing me as an ape. [He suddenly notices the change in STELLA.] Hey, what is it, Stel? [He crosses to her.]

STELLA [quietly]   Take me to the hospital.
    [He is with her now, supporting her with his arm, murmuring indistinguishably as they go outside.]

Scene Nine

A while later that evening. BLANCHE *is seated in a tense hunched position in a bedroom chair that she has recovered with diagonal green and white stripes. She has on her scarlet satin robe. On the table beside chair is a bottle of liquor and a glass. The rapid, feverish polka tune, the "Varsouviana," is heard. The music is in her mind; she is drinking to escape it and the sense of disaster closing in on her, and she seems to whisper the words of the song. An electric fan is turning back and forth across her.*

MITCH *comes around the corner in work clothes: blue denim shirt and pants. He is unshaven. He climbs the steps to the door and rings.* BLANCHE *is startled.*

BLANCHE   Who is it, please?

MITCH [*hoarsely*]   Me. Mitch.
      [*The polka tune stops.*]

BLANCHE   Mitch!—Just a minute.
      [*She rushes about frantically, hiding the bottle in a closet, crouching at the mirror and dabbing her face with cologne and powder. She is so excited that her breath is audible as she dashes about. At last she rushes to the door in the kitchen and lets him in.*]
Mitch!—Y'know, I really shouldn't let you in after the treatment I have received from you this evening! So utterly uncavalier! But hello, beautiful!
      [*She offers him her lips. He ignores it and pushes past her into the flat. She looks fearfully after him as he stalks into the bedroom.*]
My, my, what a cold shoulder! And such uncouth apparel! Why, you haven't even shaved! The unforgivable insult to a lady! But I forgive you. I forgive you because it's such a relief to see you. You've stopped that polka tune that I had caught in my head. Have you ever had anything caught in your head? No, of course you haven't, you dumb angel-puss, you'd never get anything awful caught in your head!
      [*He stares at her while she follows him while she talks. It is obvious that he has had a few drinks on the way over.*]

MITCH   Do we have to have that fan on?

BLANCHE   No!

MITCH   I don't like fans.

BLANCHE   Then let's turn it off, honey. I'm not partial to them!
      [*She presses the switch and the fan nods slowly off. She clears her throat uneasily as* MITCH *plumps himself down on the bed in the bedroom and lights a cigarette.*]
I don't know what there is to drink. I—haven't investigated.

MITCH   I don't want Stan's liquor.

BLANCHE   It isn't Stan's. Everything here isn't Stan's. Some things on the premises are actually mine! How is your mother? Isn't your mother well?

MITCH   Why?

BLANCHE   Something's the matter tonight, but never mind. I won't cross-examine the witness. I'll just—[*She touches her forehead vaguely. The polka tune starts up again.*]—pretend I don't notice anything different about you! That—music again . . .

MITCH   What music?

BLANCHE   The "Varsourviana"! The polka tune they were playing when Allan—Wait!

[*A distant revolver shot is heard.* BLANCHE *seems relieved.*]
There now, the shot! It always stops after that.
[*The polka music dies out again.*]
Yes, now it's stopped.

MITCH   Are you boxed out of your mind?

BLANCHE   I'll go and see what I can find in the way of— [*She crosses into the closet, pretending to search for the bottle.*] Oh, by the way, excuse me for not being dressed. But I'd practically given you up! Had you forgotten your invitation to supper?

MITCH   I wasn't going to see you any more.

BLANCHE   Wait a minute. I can't hear what you're saying and you talk so little that when you do say something, I don't want to miss a single syllable of it. . . . What am I looking around here for? Oh, yes—liquor! We've had so much excitement around here this evening that I *am* boxed out of my mind! [*She pretends suddenly to find the bottle. He draws his foot up on the bed and stares at her contemptuously.*] Here's something. Southern Comfort! What is that, I wonder?

MITCH   If you don't know, it must belong to Stan.

BLANCHE   Take your foot off the bed. It has a light cover on it. Of course you boys don't notice things like that. I've done so much with this place since I've been here.

MITCH   I bet you have.

BLANCHE   You saw it before I came. Well, look at it now! This room is almost—dainty! I want to keep it that way. I wonder if this stuff ought to be mixed with something? Ummm, it's sweet, so sweet! It's terribly, terribly sweet! Why, it's a *liqueur,* I believe! Yes, that's what it *is,* a liqueur! [MITCH *grunts.*] I'm afraid you won't like it, but try it, and maybe you will.

MITCH   I told you already I don't want none of his liquor and I mean it. You ought to lay off his liquor. He says you been lapping it up all summer like a wild cat!

BLANCHE   What a fantastic statement! Fantastic of him to say it, fantastic of you to repeat it! I won't descend to the level of such cheap accusations to answer them, even!

MITCH   Huh.

BLANCHE   What's in your mind? I see something in your eyes!

MITCH   [*getting up*]   It's dark in here.

BLANCHE   I like it dark. The dark is comforting to me.

MITCH   I don't think I ever seen you in the light. [BLANCHE *laughs breathlessly.*] That's a fact!

BLANCHE   Is it?

MITCH   I've never seen you in the afternoon.

BLANCHE   Whose fault is that?

MITCH   You never want to go out in the afternoon.

BLANCHE   Why, Mitch, you're at the plant in the afternoon!

MITCH   Not Sunday afternoon. I've asked you to go out with me sometimes on Sundays but you always make an excuse. You never want to go out till after six and then it's always some place that's not lighted much.

BLANCHE   There is some obscure meaning in this but I fail to catch it.

MITCH   What it means is I've never had a real good look at you, Blanche. Let's turn the light on here.

BLANCHE [*fearfully*] Light? Which light? What for?

MITCH This one with the paper thing on it. [*He tears the paper lantern off the light bulb. She utters a frightened gasp.*]

BLANCHE What did you do that for?

MITCH So I can take a look at you good and plain!

BLANCHE Of course you don't really mean to be insulting!

MITCH No, just realistic.

BLANCHE I don't want realism. I want magic! [MITCH *laughs.*] Yes, yes, magic! I try to give that to people. I misrepresent things to them. I don't tell truth, I tell what *ought* to be truth. And if that is sinful, then let me be damned for it!—*Don't turn the light on!*

[MITCH *crosses to the switch. He turns the light on and stares at her. She cries out and covers her face. He turns the lights off again.*]

MITCH [*slowly and bitterly*] I don't mind you being older than what I thought. But all the rest of it—Christ! That pitch about your ideals being so old-fashioned and all the malarkey that you've dished out all summer. Oh, I knew you weren't sixteen any more. But I was a fool enough to believe you was straight.

BLANCHE Who told you I wasn't—"straight"? My loving brother-in-law. And you believed him.

MITCH I called him a liar at first. And then I checked on the story. First I asked our supply-man who travels through Laurel. And then I talked directly over long-distance to this merchant.

BLANCHE Who is this merchant?

MITCH Kiefaber.

BLANCHE The merchant Kiefaber of Laurel! I know the man. He whistled at me. I put him in his place. So now for revenge he makes up stories about me.

MITCH Three people, Kiefaber, Stanley and Shaw, swore to them!

BLANCHE Rub-a-dub-dub, three men in a tub! And such a filthy tub!

MITCH Didn't you stay at a hotel called The Flamingo?

BLANCHE Flamingo? No! Tarantula was the name of it! I stayed at a hotel called The Tarantula Arms!

MITCH [*stupidly*] Tarantula?

BLANCHE Yes, a big spider! That's where I brought my victims. [*She pours herself another drink.*] Yes, I had many intimacies with strangers. After the death of Allan—intimacies with strangers was all I seemed able to fill my empty heart with. . . . I think it was panic, just panic, that drove me from one to another, hunting for some protection—here and there, in the most—unlikely places—even, at last, in a seventeen-year-old boy but—somebody wrote the superintendent about it—"This woman is morally unfit for her position!"

[*She throws back her head with convulsive, sobbing laughter. Then she repeats the statement, gasps, and drinks.*]

True? Yes, I suppose—unfit somehow—anyway. . . . So I came here. There was nowhere else I could go. I was played out. You know what played out is? My youth was suddenly gone up the water-spout, and—I met you. You said you needed somebody. Well, I needed somebody, too. I thanked God for you, because you seemed to be gentle—a cleft in the rock of the world that I could hide in! But I guess I was asking, hoping—

too much! Kiefaber, Stanley and Shaw have tied an old tin can to the tail of the kite.

[*There is a pause.* MITCH *stares at her dumbly.*]

MITCH   You lied to me, Blanche.

BLANCHE   Don't say I lied to you.

MITCH   Lies, lies, inside and out, all lies.

BLANCHE   Never inside, I didn't lie in my heart . . .

[*A* VENDOR *comes around the corner. She is a blind* MEXICAN WOMAN *in a dark shawl, carrying bunches of those gaudy tin flowers that lower-class Mexicans display at funerals and other festive occasions. She is calling barely audibly. Her figure is only faintly visible outside the building.*]

MEXICAN WOMAN   Flores. Flores, Flores para los muertos.[1] Flores. Flores.

BLANCHE   What? Oh! Somebody outside . . . [*She goes to the door, opens it and stares at the* MEXICAN WOMAN.]

MEXICAN WOMAN [*she is at the door and offers* BLANCHE *some of her flowers*]   Flores? Flores para los muertos?

BLANCHE [*frightened*]   No, no! Not now! Not now!

[*She darts back into the apartment, slamming the door.*]

MEXICAN WOMAN [*she turns away and starts to move down the street*]   Flores para los muertos.

[*The polka tune fades in.*]

BLANCHE [*as if to herself*]   Crumble and fade and—regrets—recriminations . . . "If you'd done this, it wouldn't've cost me that!"

MEXICAN WOMAN   Corones[2] para los muertos. Corones . . .

BLANCHE   Legacies! Huh. . . . And other things such as bloodstained pillow-slips—"Her linen needs changing"—"Yes, Mother. But couldn't we get a colored girl to do it?" No, we couldn't of course. Everything gone but the—

MEXICAN WOMAN   Flores.

BLANCHE   Death—I used to sit here and she used to sit over there and death was as close as you are. . . . We didn't dare even admit we had ever heard of it!

MEXICAN WOMAN   Flores para los muertos, flores—flores . . .

BLANCHE   The opposite is desire. So do you wonder? How could you possibly wonder! Not far from Belle Reve, before we had lost Belle Reve, was a camp where they trained young soldiers. On Sunday nights they would go in town to get drunk—

MEXICAN WOMAN [*softly*]   Corones . . .

BLANCHE   —and on the way back they would stagger onto my lawn and call—"Blanche! Blanche!"—the deaf old lady remaining suspected nothing. But sometimes I slipped outside to answer their calls. . . . Later the paddy-wagon would gather them up like daisies . . . the long way home . . .

[*The* MEXICAN WOMAN *turns slowly and drifts back off with her soft mournful cries.* BLANCHE *goes to the dresser and leans forward on it. After a moment,* MITCH *rises and follows her purposefully. The polka music fades away. He places his hands on her waist and tries to turn her about.*]

BLANCHE   What do you want?

MITCH [*fumbling to embrace her*]   What I been missing all summer.

---

1. Flowers for the dead (Spanish).   2. Wreaths (Spanish).

BLANCHE   Then marry me, Mitch!

MITCH   I don't think I want to marry you any more.

BLANCHE   No?

MITCH [*dropping his hands from her waist*]   You're not clean enough to bring in the house with my mother.

BLANCHE   Go away, then. [*He stares at her.*] Get out of here quick before I start screaming fire! [*Her throat is tightening with hysteria.*] Get out of here quick before I start screaming fire.

> [*He still remains staring. She suddenly rushes to the big window with its pale blue square of the soft summer light and cries wildly.*]

Fire! Fire! Fire!

> [*With a startled gasp,* MITCH *turns and goes out the outer door, clatters awkwardly down the steps and around the corner of the building.* BLANCHE *staggers back from the window and falls to her knees. The distant piano is slow and blue.*]

Scene Ten

It is a few hours later that night.

BLANCHE *has been drinking fairly steadily since* MITCH *left. She has dragged her wardrobe trunk into the center of the bedroom. It hangs open with flowery dresses thrown across it. As the drinking and packing went on, a mood of hysterical exhilaration came into her and she has decked herself out in a somewhat soiled and crumpled white satin evening gown and a pair of scuffed silver slippers with brilliants set in their heels.*

Now she is placing the rhinestone tiara on her head before the mirror of the dressing-table and murmuring excitedly as if to a group of spectral admirers.

BLANCHE   How about taking a swim, a moonlight swim at the old rock-quarry? If anyone's sober enough to drive a car! Ha-ha! Best way in the world to stop your head buzzing! Only you've got to be careful to dive where the deep pool is—if you hit a rock you don't come up till tomorrow . . .

> [*Tremblingly she lifts the hand mirror for a closer inspection. She catches her breath and slams the mirror face down with such violence that the glass cracks. She moans a little and attempts to rise.* STANLEY *appears around the corner of the building. He still has on the vivid green silk bowling shirt. As he rounds the corner the honky-tonk music is heard. It continues softly throughout the scene. He enters the kitchen, slamming the door. As he peers in at* BLANCHE *he gives a low whistle. He has had a few drinks on the way and has brought some quart beer bottles home with him.*]

BLANCHE   How is my sister?

STANLEY   She is doing okay.

BLANCHE   And how is the baby?

STANLEY [*grinning amiably*]   The baby won't come before morning so they told me to go home and get a little shut-eye.

BLANCHE   Does that mean we are to be alone in here?

STANLEY   Yep. Just me and you, Blanche. Unless you got somebody hid under the bed. What've you got on those fine feathers for?

BLANCHE   Oh, that's right. You left before my wire came.

STANLEY   You got a wire?

BLANCHE   I received a telegram from an old admirer of mine.
STANLEY   Anything good?
BLANCHE   I think so. An invitation.
STANLEY   What to? A fireman's ball?
BLANCHE   [*throwing back her head*]   A cruise of the Caribbean on a yacht!
STANLEY   Well, well. What do you know?
BLANCHE   I have never been so surprised in my life.
STANLEY   I guess not.
BLANCHE   It came like a bolt from the blue!
STANLEY   Who did you say it was from?
BLANCHE   An old beau of mine.
STANLEY   The one that give you the white fox-pieces?
BLANCHE   Mr. Shep Huntleigh. I wore his ATO pin my last year at college. I hadn't seen him again until last Christmas. I ran in to him on Biscayne Boulevard. Then—just now—this wire—inviting me on a cruise of the Caribbean! The problem is clothes. I tore into my trunk to see what I have that's suitable for the tropics!
STANLEY   And come up with that—gorgeous—diamond—tiara?
BLANCHE   This old relic? Ha-ha! It's only rhinestones.
STANLEY   Gosh. I thought it was Tiffany diamonds. [*He unbuttons his shirt.*]
BLANCHE   Well, anyhow, I shall be entertained in style.
STANLEY   Uh-huh. It goes to show, you never know what is coming.
BLANCHE   Just when I thought my luck had begun to fail me—
STANLEY   Into the picture pops this Miami millionaire.
BLANCHE   This man is not from Miami. This man is from Dallas.
STANLEY   This man is from Dallas?
BLANCHE   Yes, this man is from Dallas where gold spouts out of the ground!
STANLEY   Well, just so he's from somewhere! [*He starts removing his shirt.*]
BLANCHE   Close the curtains before you undress any further.
STANLEY [*amiably*]   This is all I'm going to undress right now. [*He rips the sack off a quart beer bottle*] Seen a bottle-opener?
      [*She moves slowly toward the dresser, where she stands with her hands knotted together.*]
I used to have a cousin who could open a beer bottle with his teeth. [*pounding the bottle cap on the corner of table*] That was his only accomplishment, all he could do—he was just a human bottle-opener. And then one time, at a wedding party, he broke his front teeth off! After that he was so ashamed of himself he used t' sneak out of the house when company came . . .
      [*The bottle cap pops off and a geyser of foam shoots up. Stanley laughs happily, holding up the bottle over his head.*]
Ha-ha! Rain from heaven! [*He extends the bottle toward her*] Shall we bury the hatchet and make it a loving-cup? Huh?
BLANCHE   No, thank you.
STANLEY   Well, it's a red-letter night for us both. You having an oil millionaire and me having a baby.
      [*He goes to the bureau in the bedroom and crouches to remove something from the bottom drawer.*]

BLANCHE [*drawing back*]   What are you doing in here?

STANLEY   Here's something I always break out on special occasions like this. The silk pyjamas I wore on my wedding night!

BLANCHE   Oh.

STANLEY   When the telephone rings and they say, "You've got a son!" I'll tear this off and wave it like a flag! [*He shakes out a brilliant pyjama coat.*] I guess we are both entitled to put on the dog. [*He goes back to the kitchen with the coat over his arm.*]

BLANCHE   When I think of how divine it is going to be to have such a thing as privacy once more—I could weep with joy!

STANLEY   This millionaire from Dallas is not going to interfere with your privacy any?

BLANCHE   It won't be the sort of thing you have in mind. This man is a gentleman and he respects me. [*improvising feverishly*] What he wants is my companionship. Having great wealth sometimes makes people lonely! A cultivated woman, a woman of intelligence and breeding, can enrich a man's life—immeasurably! I have those things to offer, and this doesn't take them away. Physical beauty is passing. A transitory possession. But beauty of the mind and richness of the spirit and tenderness of the heart—and I have all of those things—aren't taken away, but grow! Increase with the years! How strange that I should be called a destitute woman! When I have all of these treasures locked in my heart. [*A choked sob comes from her.*] I think of myself as a very, very rich woman! But I have been foolish—casting my pearls before swine!

STANLEY   Swine, huh?

BLANCHE   Yes, swine! Swine! And I'm thinking not only of you but of your friend, Mr. Mitchell. He came to see me tonight. He dared to come here in his work clothes! And to repeat slander to me, vicious stories that he had gotten from you! I gave him his walking papers . . .

STANLEY   You did, huh?

BLANCHE   But then he came back. He returned with a box of roses to beg my forgiveness! He implored my forgiveness. But some things are not forgivable. Deliberate cruelty is not forgivable. It is the one unforgivable thing in my opinion and it is the one thing of which I have never, never been guilty. And so I told him, I said to him, "Thank you," but it was foolish of me to think that we could ever adapt ourselves to each other. Our ways of life are too different. Our attitudes and our backgrounds are incompatible. We have to be realistic about such things. So farewell, my friend! And let there be no hard feelings . . .

STANLEY   Was this before or after the telegram came from the Texas oil millionaire?

BLANCHE   What telegram? No! No, after! As a matter of fact, the wire came just as—

STANLEY   As a matter of fact there wasn't no wire at all!

BLANCHE   Oh, oh!

STANLEY   There isn't no millionaire! And Mitch didn't come back with roses 'cause I know where he is—

BLANCHE   Oh!

STANLEY   There isn't a goddam thing but imagination!

BLANCHE   Oh!

STANLEY   And lies and conceit and tricks!

BLANCHE   Oh!

STANLEY   And look at yourself! Take a look at yourself in that worn-out
Mardi Gras outfit, rented for fifty cents from some rag-picker! And with
the crazy crown on! What queen do you think you are?

BLANCHE   Oh—God . . .

STANLEY   I've been on to you from the start! Not once did you pull any wool
over this boy's eyes! You come in here and sprinkle the place with powder
and spray perfume and cover the light-bulb with a paper lantern, and lo
and behold the place has turned into Egypt and you are the Queen of the
Nile! Sitting on your throne and swilling down my liquor! I say—Ha!—
Ha! Do you hear me? Ha—ha—ha! [He walks into the bedroom.]

BLANCHE   Don't come in here!

[Lurid reflections appear on the walls around BLANCHE. The shadows are of
a grotesque and menacing form. She catches her breath, crosses to the phone
and jiggles the hook. STANLEY goes into the bathroom and closes the door.]

Operator, operator! Give me long-distance, please. . . . I want to get in
touch with Mr. Shep Huntleigh of Dallas. He's so well known he doesn't
require any address. Just ask anybody who—Wait!!—No, I couldn't find
it right now. . . . Please understand, I—No! No, wait!. . . . One moment!
Someone is—Nothing! Hold on, please!

[She sets the phone down and crosses warily into the kitchen. The night
is filled with inhuman voices like cries in a jungle. The shadows and lurid
reflections move sinuously as flames along the wall spaces. Through the
back wall of the rooms, which have become transparent, can be seen the
sidewalk. A prostitute has rolled a drunkard. He pursues her along the
walk, overtakes her and there is a struggle. A policeman's whistle breaks
it up. The figures disappear. Some moments later the Negro Woman
appears around the corner with a sequined bag which the prostitute had
dropped on the walk. She is rooting excitedly through it. BLANCHE presses
her knuckles to her lips and returns slowly to the phone. She speaks in a
hoarse whisper.]

BLANCHE   Operator! Operator! Never mind long-distance. Get Western
Union. There isn't time to be—Western—Western Union!

[She waits anxiously.]

Western Union? Yes! I—want to—Take down this message! "In desperate,
desperate circumstances! Help me! Caught in a trap. Caught in—" Oh!

[The bathroom door is thrown open and STANLEY comes out in the brilliant silk pyjamas. He grins at her as he knots the tasseled sash about his
waist. She gasps and backs away from the phone. He stares at her for a
count of ten. Then a clicking becomes audible from the telephone, steady
and rasping.]

STANLEY   You left th' phone off th' hook.

[He crosses to it deliberately and sets it back on the hook. After he has
replaced it, he stares at her again, his mouth slowly curving into a grin,
as he weaves between BLANCHE and the outer door. The barely audible
"Blue Piano" begins to drum up louder. The sound of it turns into the roar
of an approaching locomotive. BLANCHE crouches, pressing her fists to her
ears until it has gone by.]

BLANCHE [finally straightening]   Let me—let me get by you!

STANLEY   Get by me? Sure. Go ahead. [He moves back a pace in the doorway.]

BLANCHE   You—you stand over there! [*She indicates a further position.*]

STANLEY [*grinning*]   You got plenty of room to walk by me now.

BLANCHE   Not with you there! But I've got to get out somehow!

STANLEY   You think I'll interfere with you? Ha-ha!

> [*The "Blue Piano" goes softly. She turns confusedly and makes a faint gesture. The inhuman jungle voices rise up. He takes a step toward her, biting his tongue which protrudes between his lips.*]

STANLEY [*softly*]   Come to think of it—maybe you wouldn't be bad to—interfere with . . .

> [BLANCHE *moves backward through the door into the bedroom.*]

BLANCHE   Stay back! Don't you come toward me another step or I'll—

STANLEY   What?

BLANCHE   Some awful thing will happen! It will!

STANLEY   What are you putting on now?

> [*They are now both inside the bedroom.*]

BLANCHE   I warn you, don't, I'm in danger!

> [*He takes another step. She smashes a bottle on the table and faces him, clutching the broken top.*]

STANLEY   What did you do that for?

BLANCHE   So I could twist the broken end in your face!

STANLEY   I bet you would do that!

BLANCHE   I would! I will if you—

STANLEY   Oh! So you want some roughhouse! All right, let's have some roughhouse!

> [*He springs toward her, overturning the table. She cries out and strikes at him with the bottle top but he catches her wrist.*]

Tiger—tiger! Drop the bottle-top! Drop it! We've had this date with each other from the beginning!

> [*She moans. The bottle-top falls. She sinks to her knees: He picks up her inert figure and carries her to the bed. The hot trumpet and drums from the Four Deuces sound loudly.*]

Scene Eleven

It is some weeks later. STELLA *is packing* BLANCHE's *things. Sounds of water can be heard running in the bathroom.*

   *The portieres are partly open on the poker players—*STANLEY, STEVE, MITCH *and* PABLO—*who sit around the table in the kitchen. The atmosphere of the kitchen is now the same raw, lurid one of the disastrous poker night.*

   The building is framed by the sky of turquoise. STELLA *has been crying as she arranges the flowery dresses in the open trunk.*

   EUNICE *comes down the steps from her flat above and enters the kitchen. There is an outburst from the poker table.*

STANLEY   Drew to an inside straight and made it, by God.

PABLO   *Maldita sea tu suerto!*

STANLEY   Put it in English, greaseball.

PABLO   I am cursing your rutting luck.

STANLEY [*prodigiously elated*]   You know what luck is? Luck is believing you're lucky. Take at Salerno.[3] I believed I was lucky. I figured that 4 out

---

3. Important beachhead in the Allied invasion of Italy in World War II.

of 5 would not come through but I would . . . and I did. I put that down as a rule. To hold front position in this rat-race you've got to believe you are lucky.

MITCH   You . . . you . . . you . . . Brag . . . brag . . . bull . . . bull.

[STELLA *goes into the bedroom and starts folding a dress.*]

STANLEY   What's the matter with him?

EUNICE [*walking past the table*]   I always did say that men are callous things with no feelings, but this does beat anything. Making pigs of yourselves. [*She comes through the portieres into the bedroom.*]

STANLEY   What's the matter with her?

STELLA   How is my baby?

EUNICE   Sleeping like a little angel. Brought you some grapes. [*She puts them on a stool and lowers her voice.*] Blanche?

STELLA   Bathing.

EUNICE   How is she?

STELLA   She wouldn't eat anything but asked for a drink.

EUNICE   What did you tell her?

STELLA   I—just told her that—we'd made arrangements for her to rest in the country. She's got it mixed in her mind with Shep Huntleigh.

[BLANCHE *opens the bathroom door slightly.*]

BLANCHE   Stella.

STELLA   Yes, Blanche.

BLANCHE   If anyone calls while I'm bathing take the number and tell them I'll call right back.

STELLA   Yes.

BLANCHE   That cool yellow silk—the bouclé. See if it's crushed. If it's not too crushed I'll wear it and on the lapel that silver and turquoise pin in the shape of a seahorse. You will find them in the heart-shaped box I keep my accessories in. And Stella . . . Try and locate a bunch of artificial violets in that box, too, to pin with the seahorse on the lapel of the jacket.

[*She closes the door.* STELLA *turns to* EUNICE.]

STELLA   I don't know if I did the right thing.

EUNICE   What else could you do?

STELLA   I couldn't believe her story and go on living with Stanley.

EUNICE   Don't ever believe it. Life has got to go on. No matter what happens, you've got to keep on going.

[*The bathroom door opens a little.*]

BLANCHE [*looking out*]   Is the coast clear?

STELLA   Yes, Blanche. [*to* EUNICE] Tell her how well she's looking.

BLANCHE   Please close the curtains before I come out.

STELLA   They're closed.

STANLEY   —How many for you?

PABLO   Two.

STEVE   Three.

[BLANCHE *appears in the amber light of the door. She has a tragic radiance in her red satin robe following the sculptural lines of her body. The "Varsouviana" rises audibly as* BLANCHE *enters the bedroom.*]

BLANCHE [*with faintly hysterical vivacity*]   I have just washed my hair.

STELLA   Did you?

BLANCHE   I'm not sure I got the soap out.

EUNICE   Such fine hair!

BLANCHE [*accepting the compliment*]   It's a problem. Didn't I get a call?

STELLA   Who from, Blanche?

BLANCHE   Shep Huntleigh . . .

STELLA   Why, not yet, honey!

BLANCHE   How strange! I—

[*At the sound of* BLANCHE'*s voice* MITCH'*s arm supporting his cards has sagged and his gaze is dissolved into space.* STANLEY *slaps him on the shoulder.*]

STANLEY   Hey, Mitch, come to!

[*The sound of this new voice shocks* BLANCHE. *She makes a shocked gesture, forming his name with her lips.* STELLA *nods and looks quickly away.* BLANCHE *stands quite still for some moments—the silver-backed mirror in her hand and a look of sorrowful perplexity as though all human experience shows on her face.* BLANCHE *finally speaks but with sudden hysteria.*]

BLANCHE   What's going on here?

[*She turns from* STELLA *to* EUNICE *and back to* STELLA. *Her rising voice penetrates the concentration of the game.* MITCH *ducks his head lower but* STANLEY *shoves back his chair as if about to rise.* STEVE *places a restraining hand on his arm.*]

BLANCHE [*continuing*]   What's happened here? I want an explanation of what's happened here.

STELLA [*agonizingly*]   Hush! Hush!

EUNICE   Hush! Hush! Honey.

STELLA   Please, Blanche.

BLANCHE   Why are you looking at me like that? Is something wrong with me?

EUNICE   You look wonderful, Blanche. Don't she look wonderful?

STELLA   Yes.

EUNICE   I understand you are going on a trip.

STELLA   Yes, Blanche *is*. She's going on a vacation.

EUNICE   I'm green with envy.

BLANCHE   Help me, help me get dressed!

STELLA [*handing her dress*]   Is this what you—

BLANCHE   Yes, it will do! I'm anxious to get out of here—this place is a trap!

EUNICE   What a pretty blue jacket.

STELLA   It's lilac colored.

BLANCHE   You're both mistaken. It's Della Robbia blue.[4] The blue of the robe in the old Madonna pictures. Are these grapes washed?

[*She fingers the bunch of grapes which* EUNICE *had brought in.*]

EUNICE   Huh?

BLANCHE   Washed, I said. Are they washed?

EUNICE   They're from the French Market.

BLANCHE   That doesn't mean they've been washed. [*The cathedral bells chime.*] Those cathedral bells—they're the only clean thing in the Quarter. Well, I'm going now. I'm ready to go.

EUNICE [*whispering*]   She's going to walk out before they get here.

STELLA   Wait, Blanche.

---

4. A shade of light blue seen in terra cottas made by the Della Robbia family in the Italian Renaissance.

BLANCHE   I don't want to pass in front of those men.

EUNICE   Then wait'll the game breaks up.

STELLA   Sit down and . . .

[BLANCHE *turns weakly, hesitantly about. She lets them push her into a chair.*]

BLANCHE   I can smell the sea air. The rest of my time I'm going to spend on the sea. And when I die, I'm going to die on the sea. You know what I shall die of [*She plucks a grape.*] I shall die of eating an unwashed grape one day out on the ocean. I will die—with my hand in the hand of some nice-looking ship's doctor, a very young one with a small blond mustache and a big silver watch. "Poor lady," they'll say, "the quinine did her no good. That unwashed grape has transported her soul to heaven." [*The cathedral chimes are heard.*] And I'll be buried at sea sewn up in a clean white sack and dropped overboard—at noon—in the blaze of summer— and into an ocean as blue as [*chimes again*] my first lover's eyes!

[A DOCTOR *and a* MATRON *have appeared around the corner of the building and climbed the steps to the porch. The gravity of their profession is exaggerated—the unmistakable aura of the state institution with its cynical detachment. The* DOCTOR *rings the doorbell. The murmur of the game is interrupted.*]

EUNICE [*whispering to* STELLA]   That must be them.

[STELLA *presses her fists to her lips.*]

BLANCHE [*rising slowly*]   What is it?

EUNICE [*affectedly casual*]   Excuse me while I see who's at the door.

STELLA   Yes.

[EUNICE *goes into the kitchen.*]

BLANCHE [*tensely*]   I wonder if it's for me.

[*A whispered colloquy takes place at the door.*]

EUNICE [*returning, brightly*]   Someone is calling for Blanche.

BLANCHE   It *is* for me, then! [*She looks fearfully from one to the other and then to the portieres. The "Varsouviana" faintly plays.*] Is it the gentleman I was expecting from Dallas?

EUNICE   I think it is, Blanche.

BLANCHE   I'm not quite ready.

STELLA   Ask him to wait outside.

BLANCHE   I . . .

[EUNICE *goes back to the portieres. Drums sound very softly.*]

STELLA   Everything packed?

BLANCHE   My silver toilet articles are still out.

STELLA   Ah!

EUNICE [*returning*]   They're waiting in front of the house.

BLANCHE   They! Who's "they"?

EUNICE   There's a lady with him.

BLANCHE   I cannot imagine who this "lady" could be! How is she dressed?

EUNICE   Just—just a sort of a—plain-tailored outfit.

BLANCHE   Possibly she's— [*Her voice dies out nervously.*]

STELLA   Shall we go, Blanche?

BLANCHE   Must we go through that room?

STELLA   I will go with you.

BLANCHE   How do I look?

STELLA   Lovely.

EUNICE [*echoing*]   Lovely.
    [BLANCHE *moves fearfully to the portieres.* EUNICE *draws them open for her.* BLANCHE *goes into the kitchen.*]
BLANCHE [*to the men*]   Please don't get up. I'm only passing through.
    [*She crosses quickly to outside door.* STELLA *and* EUNICE *follow. The poker players stand awkwardly at the table—all except* MITCH *who remains seated, looking down at the table.* BLANCHE *steps out on a small porch at the side of the door. She stops short and catches her breath.*]
DOCTOR   How do you do?
BLANCHE   You are not the gentleman I was expecting. [*She suddenly gasps and starts back up the steps. She stops by* STELLA, *who stands just outside the door, and speaks in a frightening whisper.*] That man isn't Shep Huntleigh.
    [*The "Varsouviana" is playing distantly.* STELLA *stares back at* BLANCHE. EUNICE *is holding* STELLA's *arm. There is a moment of silence—no sound but that of* STANLEY *steadily shuffling the cards.* BLANCHE *catches her breath again and slips back into the flat. She enters the flat with a peculiar smile, her eyes wide and brilliant. As soon as her sister goes past her,* STELLA *closes her eyes and clenches her hands.* EUNICE *throws her arms comfortingly about her. Then she starts up to her flat.* BLANCHE *stops just inside the door.* MITCH *keeps staring down at his hands on the table, but the other men look at her curiously. At last she starts around the table toward the bedroom. As she does,* STANLEY *suddenly pushes back his chair and rises as if to block her way. The* MATRON *follows her into the flat.*]
STANLEY   Did you forget something?
BLANCHE [*shrilly*]   Yes! Yes, I forgot something!
    [*She rushes past him into the bedroom. Lurid reflections appear on the walls in odd, sinuous shapes. The "Varsouviana" is filtered into a weird distortion, accompanied by the cries and noises of the jungle.* BLANCHE *seizes the back of a chair as if to defend herself.*]
STANLEY [*sotto voce*][5]   Doc, you better go in.
DOCTOR [*sotto voce, motioning to the* MATRON]   Nurse, bring her out.
    [*The* MATRON *advances on one side,* STANLEY *on the other. Divested of all the softer properties of womanhood, the* MATRON *is a peculiarly sinister figure in her severe dress. Her voice is bold and toneless as a firebell.*]
MATRON   Hello, Blanche.
    [*The greeting is echoed and re-echoed by other mysterious voices behind the walls, as if reverberated through a canyon of rock.*]
STANLEY   She says that she forgot something.
    [*The echo sounds in threatening whispers.*]
MATRON   That's all right.
STANLEY   What did you forget, Blanche?
BLANCHE   I—I—
MATRON   It don't matter. We can pick it up later.
STANLEY   Sure. We can send it along with the trunk.
BLANCHE [*retreating in panic*]   I don't know you—I don't know you. I want to be—left alone—please!
MATRON   Now, Blanche!
ECHOES [*rising and falling*]   Now, Blanche—now, Blanche—now, Blanche!
STANLEY   You left nothing here but spilt talcum and old empty perfume

5. In an undertone.

bottles—unless it's the paper lantern you want to take with you. You want the lantern?

[*He crosses to dressing table and seizes the paper lantern, tearing it off the light bulb, and extends it toward her. She cries out as if the lantern was herself. The* MATRON *steps boldly toward her. She screams and tries to break past the* MATRON. *All the men spring to their feet.* STELLA *runs out to the porch, with* EUNICE *following to comfort her, simultaneously with the confused voices of the men in the kitchen.* STELLA *rushes into* EUNICE's *embrace on the porch.*]

STELLA   Oh, my God, Eunice help me! Don't let them do that to her, don't let them hurt her! Oh, God, oh, please God, don't hurt her! What are they doing to her? What are they doing? [*She tries to break from* EUNICE's *arms.*]

EUNICE   No, honey, no, no, honey. Stay here. Don't go back in there. Stay with me and don't look.

STELLA   What have I done to my sister? Oh, God, what have I done to my sister?

EUNICE   You done the right thing, the only thing you could do. She couldn't stay here; there wasn't no other place for her to go.

[*While* STELLA *and* EUNICE *are speaking on the porch the voices of the men in the kitchen overlap them.* MITCH *has started toward the bedroom.* STANLEY *crosses to block him.* STANLEY *pushes him aside.* MITCH *lunges and strikes at* STANLEY. STANLEY *pushes* MITCH *back.* MITCH *collapses at the table, sobbing. During the preceding scenes, the* MATRON *catches hold of* BLANCHE's *arm and prevents her flight.* BLANCHE *turns wildly and scratches at the* MATRON. *The heavy woman pinions her arms.* BLANCHE *cries out hoarsely and slips to her knees.*]

MATRON   These fingernails have to be trimmed. [*The* DOCTOR *comes into the room and she looks at him.*] Jacket, Doctor?

DOCTOR   Not unless necessary.

[*He takes off his hat and now he becomes personalized. The unhuman quality goes. His voice is gentle and reassuring as he crosses to* BLANCHE *and crouches in front of her. As he speaks her name, her terror subsides a little. The lurid reflections fade from the walls, the inhuman cries and noises die out and her own hoarse crying is calmed.*]

DOCTOR   Miss DuBois.

[*She turns her face to him and stares at him with desperate pleading. He smiles; then he speaks to the* MATRON.]

It won't be necessary.

BLANCHE [*faintly*]   Ask her to let go of me.

DOCTOR [*to the* MATRON]   Let go.

[*The* MATRON *releases her.* BLANCHE *extends her hands toward the* DOCTOR. *He draws her up gently and supports her with his arm and leads her through the portieres.*]

BLANCHE [*holding tight to his arm*]   Whoever you are—I have always depended on the kindness of strangers.

[*The poker players stand back as* BLANCHE *and the* DOCTOR *cross the kitchen to the front door. She allows him to lead her as if she were blind. As they go out on the porch,* STELLA *cries out her sister's name from where she is crouched a few steps up on the stairs.*]

STELLA   Blanche! Blanche, Blanche!

[BLANCHE *walks on without turning, followed by the* DOCTOR *and the* MATRON. *They go around the corner of the building.* EUNICE *descends to*

STELLA *and places the child in her arms. It is wrapped in a pale blue blanket.* STELLA *accepts the child, sobbingly.* EUNICE *continues downstairs and enters the kitchen where the men, except for* STANLEY, *are returning silently to their places about the table.* STANLEY *has gone out on the porch and stands at the foot of the steps looking at* STELLA.]

STANLEY [*a bit uncertainly*]   Stella?

[*She sobs with inhuman abandon. There is something luxurious in her complete surrender to crying now that her sister is gone.*]

STANLEY [*voluptuously, soothingly*]   Now, honey. Now, love. Now, now, love. [*He kneels beside her and his fingers find the opening of her blouse.*] Now, now, love, Now, love. . . .

[*The luxurious sobbing, the sensual murmur fade away under the swelling music of the "Blue Piano" and the muted trumpet.*]

STEVE   This game is seven-card stud.

CURTAIN

1947

ELIZABETH BISHOP
1911–1979

"The enormous power of reticence," the poet Octavio Paz said in a tribute, "—that is the great lesson of Elizabeth Bishop." Bishop's reticence originates in a temperament indistinguishable from her style; her remarkable formal gifts allowed her to create ordered and lucid structures that hold strong feelings in place. Chief among these feelings was a powerful sense of loss. The crucial events of Bishop's life occurred within her first eight years. Born in Worcester, Massachusetts, she was eight months old when her father died. Her mother suffered a series of breakdowns and was permanently institutionalized when her daughter was five. "I've never concealed this," Bishop once wrote, "although I don't like to make too much of it. But of course it is an important fact, to me. I didn't see her again." The understatement in this remark is characteristic. When Bishop wrote about her early life—as she first did in several poems and stories in the 1950s and last did in her extraordinary final book, *Geography III* (1976)—she resisted sentimentality and self-pity. It was as if she could look at the events of her own life with the same unflinching gaze she turned on the landscapes that so consistently compelled her. The deep feeling in her poems rises out of direct and particular description, but Bishop does more than simply observe. Whether writing about her childhood landscape of Nova Scotia or her adopted Brazil, she often opens a poem with long perspectives on time, with landscapes that dwarf the merely human, emphasizing the dignified frailty of a human observer and the pervasive mysteries that surround her.

Examining her own case, she traces the observer's instinct to early childhood. "In the Waiting Room," a poem written in the early 1970s, probes the sources and motives behind her interest in details. Using an incident from when she was seven—a little girl waits for her aunt in the dentist's anteroom—Bishop shows how in the course of the episode she became aware, as if wounded, of the utter strangeness and engulfing power of the world. The spectator in that poem hangs on to details as a kind of life-jacket; she observes because she has to.

After her father's death Bishop and her mother lived with Bishop's maternal grandparents in Great Village, Nova Scotia. She remained there for several years after her mother was institutionalized, until she was removed ("kidnapped," she describes herself feeling in one of her stories) by her paternal grandparents and taken to live in Worcester, Massachusetts. This experience was followed by a series of illnesses (eczema, bronchitis, and asthma), which plagued her for many years. Bishop later lived with an aunt and attended Walnut Hill School, a private high school. In 1934 she graduated from Vassar College, where while a student she had been introduced to Marianne Moore. Moore's meticulous taste for fact was to influence Bishop's poetry, but more immediately Moore's independent life as a poet seemed an alternative to Bishop's vaguer intentions to attend medical school. Bishop lived in New York City and in Key West, Florida; a traveling fellowship took her to Brazil, which so appealed to her that she remained for more than sixteen years.

Exile and travel were at the heart of Bishop's poems from the start. The title of her first book, *North & South* (1946), looks backward to the northern seas of Nova Scotia and forward to the tropical worlds she was to choose so long as home. Her poems are set among these landscapes, where she can stress the sweep and violence of encircling and eroding geological powers or, in the case of Brazil, a bewildering botanical plenty. *Questions of Travel* (1965), her third volume, constitutes a sequence of poems initiating her, with her botanist-geologist-anthropologist's curiosity, into Brazilian life and the mysteries of what questions a traveler-exile should ask. In this series with its increasing penetration of a new country, a process is at work similar to one Bishop identifies in the great English naturalist Charles Darwin, of whom Bishop once said: "One admires the beautiful solid case being built up out of his endless, heroic observations, almost unconscious or automatic—and then comes a sudden relaxation, a forgetful phrase, and one feels the strangeness of his undertaking, sees the lonely young man, his eyes fixed on facts and minute details, sinking or sliding giddily off into the unknown."

In 1969 Bishop's *Complete Poems* appeared, an ironic title in light of the fact that she continued to write and publish new poetry. *Geography III* contains some of her best work, poems that, from the settled perspective of her return to the United States, look back and evaluate the appetite for exploration apparent in her earlier verse. The influence of her long friendship with the poet Robert Lowell, and their mutual regard for one another's work, may be felt in the way *Geography III* explores the terrain of memory and autobiography more powerfully and directly than does her earlier work. (Bishop, however, believed that there were limits on the ways in which poems could use and reconfigure the materials of a life. Her 1972 letter to Lowell that discusses these limits appears in the "Postmodern Manifestos" cluster of this anthology. Having left Brazil, Bishop lived in Boston from 1970 and taught at Harvard University until 1977. She received the Pulitzer Prize for the combined volume *North & South and A Cold Spring* (1955) and the National Book Award for *The Complete Poems,* and in 1976 was the first woman and the first American to receive the Books Abroad Neustadt International Prize for Literature. Since Bishop's death, most of her published work has been gathered in two volumes: *The Complete Poems 1929–1979* and *The Collected Prose.* An edition of her unpublished poems and drafts, *Edgar Allen Poe & The Juke-Box* was published to some controversy in 2006.

The Fish

I caught a tremendous fish
and held him beside the boat
half out of water, with my hook
fast in a corner of his mouth.
He didn't fight.   5
He hadn't fought at all.
He hung a grunting weight,
battered and venerable

and homely. Here and there
his brown skin hung in strips   10
like ancient wallpaper,
and its pattern of darker brown
was like wallpaper:
shapes like full-blown roses
stained and lost through age.   15
He was speckled with barnacles,
fine rosettes of lime,
and infested
with tiny white sea-lice,
and underneath two or three   20
rags of green weed hung down.
While his gills were breathing in
the terrible oxygen
—the frightening gills,
fresh and crisp with blood,   25
that can cut so badly—
I thought of the coarse white flesh
packed in like feathers,
the big bones and the little bones,
the dramatic reds and blacks   30
of his shiny entrails,
and the pink swim-bladder
like a big peony.
I looked into his eyes
which were far larger than mine   35
but shallower, and yellowed,
the irises backed and packed
with tarnished tinfoil
seen through the lenses
of old scratched isinglass.[1]   40
They shifted a little, but not
to return my stare.
—It was more like the tipping
of an object toward the light.
I admired his sullen face,   45
the mechanism of his jaw,
and then I saw
that from his lower lip
—if you could call it a lip—
grim, wet, and weaponlike,   50
hung five old pieces of fish-line,
or four and a wire leader
with the swivel still attached,
with all their five big hooks
grown firmly in his mouth.   55
A green line, frayed at the end
where he broke it, two heavier lines,
and a fine black thread
still crimped from the strain and snap

---

1. A whitish, semitransparent substance, originally obtained from the swim bladders of some freshwater fish and occasionally used for windows.

when it broke and he got away.   60
Like medals with their ribbons
frayed and wavering,
a five-haired beard of wisdom
trailing from his aching jaw.
I stared and stared   65
and victory filled up
the little rented boat,
from the pool of bilge
where oil had spread a rainbow
around the rusted engine   70
to the bailer rusted orange,
the sun-cracked thwarts,
the oarlocks on their strings,
the gunnels—until everything
was rainbow, rainbow, rainbow!   75
And I let the fish go.

                                                           1946

At the Fishhouses

Although it is a cold evening,
down by one of the fishhouses
an old man sits netting,
his net, in the gloaming almost invisible
a dark purple-brown,   5
and his shuttle worn and polished.
The air smells so strong of codfish
it makes one's nose run and one's eyes water.
The five fishhouses have steeply peaked roofs
and narrow, cleated gangplanks slant up   10
to storerooms in the gables
for the wheelbarrows to be pushed up and down on.
All is silver: the heavy surface of the sea,
swelling slowly as if considering spilling over,
is opaque, but the silver of the benches,   15
the lobster pots, and masts, scattered
among the wild jagged rocks,
is of an apparent translucence
like the small old buildings with an emerald moss
growing on their shoreward walls.   20
The big fish tubs are completely lined
with layers of beautiful herring scales
and the wheelbarrows are similarly plastered
with creamy iridescent coats of mail,
with small iridescent flies crawling on them.   25
Up on the little slope behind the houses,
set in the sparse bright sprinkle of grass,
is an ancient wooden capstan,[1]
cracked, with two long bleached handles

1. Cylindrical drum around which rope is wound, used for hauling.

and some melancholy stains, like dried blood,   30
where the ironwork has rusted.
The old man accepts a Lucky Strike.[2]
He was a friend of my grandfather.
We talk of the decline in the population
and of codfish and herring   35
while he waits for a herring boat to come in.
There are sequins on his vest and on his thumb.
He has scraped the scales, the principal beauty,
from unnumbered fish with that black old knife,
the blade of which is almost worn away.   40

Down at the water's edge, at the place
where they haul up the boats, up the long ramp
descending into the water, thin silver
tree trunks are laid horizontally
across the gray stones, down and down   45
at intervals of four or five feet.

Cold dark deep and absolutely clear,
element bearable to no mortal,
to fish and to seals . . . One seal particularly
I have seen here evening after evening.   50
He was curious about me. He was interested in music;
like me a believer in total immersion,[3]
so I used to sing him Baptist hymns.
I also sang "A Mighty Fortress Is Our God."
He stood up in the water and regarded me   55
steadily, moving his head a little.
Then he would disappear, then suddenly emerge
almost in the same spot, with a sort of shrug
as if it were against his better judgment.
Cold dark deep and absolutely clear,   60
the clear gray icy water . . . Back, behind us,
the dignified tall firs begin.
Bluish, associating with their shadows,
a million Christmas trees stand
waiting for Christmas. The water seems suspended   65
above the rounded gray and blue-gray stones.
I have seen it over and over, the same sea, the same,
slightly, indifferently swinging above the stones,
icily free above the stones,
above the stones and then the world.   70
If you should dip your hand in,
your wrist would ache immediately,
your bones would begin to ache and your hand would burn
as if the water were a transmutation of fire
that feeds on stones and burns with a dark gray flame.   75
If you tasted it, it would first taste bitter,
then briny, then surely burn your tongue.

2. Brand of cigarettes.
3. Form of baptism used by Baptists.

It is like what we imagine knowledge to be:
dark, salt, clear, moving, utterly free,
drawn from the cold hard mouth   80
of the world, derived from the rocky breasts
forever, flowing and drawn, and since
our knowledge is historical, flowing, and flown.

1955

The Armadillo

for Robert Lowell

This is the time of year
when almost every night
the frail, illegal fire balloons appear.
Climbing the mountain height,

rising toward a saint   5
still honored in these parts,
the paper chambers flush and fill with light
that comes and goes, like hearts.

Once up against the sky it's hard
to tell them from the stars—   10
planets, that is—the tinted ones:
Venus going down, or Mars,

or the pale green one. With a wind,
they flare and falter, wobble and toss;
but if it's still they steer between   15
the kite sticks of the Southern Cross,

receding, dwindling, solemnly
and steadily forsaking us,
or, in the downdraft from a peak,
suddenly turning dangerous.   20

Last night another big one fell.
It splattered like an egg of fire
against the cliff behind the house.
The flame ran down. We saw the pair

of owls who nest there flying up   25
and up, their whirling black-and-white
stained bright pink underneath, until
they shrieked up out of sight.

The ancient owls' nest must have burned.
Hastily, all alone,   30
a glistening armadillo left the scene,
rose-flecked, head down, tail down,

and then a baby rabbit jumped out,
short-eared, to our surprise.
So soft!—a handful of intangible ash   35
with fixed, ignited eyes.

Too pretty, dreamlike mimicry!
O falling fire and piercing cry
and panic, and a weak mailed fist[1]
clenched ignorant against the sky!   40

1965

Sestina[1]

September rain falls on the house.
In the failing light, the old grandmother
sits in the kitchen with the child
beside the Little Marvel Stove,
reading the jokes from the almanac,   5
laughing and talking to hide her tears.

She thinks that her equinoctial tears
and the rain that beats on the roof of the house
were both foretold by the almanac,
but only known to a grandmother.   10
The iron kettle sings on the stove.
She cuts some bread and says to the child,

It's time for tea now; but the child
is watching the teakettle's small hard tears
dance like mad on the hot black stove,   15
the way the rain must dance on the house.
Tidying up, the old grandmother
hangs up the clever almanac

on its string. Birdlike, the almanac
hovers half open above the child,   20
hovers above the old grandmother
and her teacup full of dark brown tears.
She shivers and says she thinks the house
feels chilly, and puts more wood in the stove.

It was to be, says the Marvel Stove.   25
I know what I know, says the almanac.
With crayons the child draws a rigid house
and a winding pathway. Then the child
puts in a man with buttons like tears
and shows it proudly to the grandmother.   30

1. The armadillo, curled tight protected against
everything but fire.
1. A fixed verse form in which the end words of the

first six-line stanza must be used at the ends of the
lines in the next stanza in a rotating order; the final
three lines must contain all six words.

But secretly, while the grandmother
busies herself about the stove,
the little moons fall down like tears
from between the pages of the almanac
into the flower bed the child   35
has carefully placed in the front of the house.

Time to plant tears, says the almanac.
The grandmother sings to the marvellous stove
and the child draws another inscrutable house.

1965

In the Waiting Room

In Worcester, Massachusetts,
I went with Aunt Consuelo
to keep her dentist's appointment
and sat and waited for her
in the dentist's waiting room.   5
It was winter. It got dark
early. The waiting room
was full of grown-up people,
arctics and overcoats,
lamps and magazines.   10
My aunt was inside
what seemed like a long time
and while I waited I read
the *National Geographic*
(I could read) and carefully   15
studied the photographs:
the inside of a volcano,
black, and full of ashes;
then it was spilling over
in rivulets of fire.   20
Osa and Martin Johnson[1]
dressed in riding breeches,
laced boots, and pith helmets.
A dead man slung on a pole
—"Long Pig,"[2] the caption said.   25
Babies with pointed heads
wound round and round with string;
black, naked women with necks
wound round and round with wire
like the necks of light bulbs.   30
Their breasts were horrifying.
I read it right straight through.
I was too shy to stop.

1. Famous explorers and travel writers.
2. Polynesian cannibals' name for the human carcass.

And then I looked at the cover:
the yellow margins, the date.   35

Suddenly, from inside,
came an *oh!* of pain
—Aunt Consuelo's voice—
not very loud or long.
I wasn't at all surprised;   40
even then I knew she was
a foolish, timid woman.
I might have been embarrassed,
but wasn't. What took me
completely by surprise   45
was that it was *me:*
my voice, in my mouth.
Without thinking at all
I was my foolish aunt,
I—we—were falling, falling,   50
our eyes glued to the cover
of the *National Geographic,*
February, 1918.

I said to myself: three days
and you'll be seven years old.   55
I was saying it to stop
the sensation of falling off
the round, turning world
into cold, blue-black space.
But I felt: you are an *I*,   60
you are an *Elizabeth,*
you are one of *them.*
Why should you be one, too?
I scarcely dared to look.
to see what it was I was.   65
I gave a sidelong glance
—I couldn't look any higher—
at shadowy gray knees,
trousers and skirts and boots
and different pairs of hands   70
lying under the lamps.
I knew that nothing stranger
had ever happened, that nothing
stranger could ever happen.
Why should I be my aunt,   75
or me, or anyone?
What similarities—
boots, hands, the family voice
I felt in my throat, or even
the *National Geographic*   80
and those awful hanging breasts—
held us all together
or made us all just one?

How—I didn't know any
word for it—how "unlikely" . . .   85
How had I come to be here,
like them, and overhear
a cry of pain that could have
got loud and worse but hadn't?

The waiting room was bright   90
and too hot. It was sliding
beneath a big black wave,
another, and another.

Then I was back in it.
The War was on. Outside,   95
in Worcester, Massachusetts,
were night and slush and cold,
and it was still the fifth
of February, 1918.

                                              1976

One Art

The art of losing isn't hard to master;
so many things seem filled with the intent
to be lost that their loss is no disaster.

Lose something every day. Accept the fluster
of lost door keys, the hour badly spent.   5
The art of losing isn't hard to master.

Then practice losing farther, losing faster:
places, and names, and where it was you meant
to travel. None of these will bring disaster.

I lost my mother's watch. And look! my last, or   10
next-to-last, of three loved houses went.
The art of losing isn't hard to master.

I lost two cities, lovely ones. And, vaster,
some realms I owned, two rivers, a continent.
I miss them, but it wasn't a disaster.   15

—Even losing you (the joking voice, a gesture
I love) I shan't have lied. It's evident
the art of losing's not too hard to master
though it may look like (*Write* it!) like disaster.

                                              1976

JOHN CHEEVER
1912–1982

"It seems to me that man's inclination toward light, toward brightness, is very nearly botanical—and I mean spiritual light. One not only needs it, one struggles for it." These sentences from an interview with John Cheever, conducted by the novelist John Hersey, at first glance look strange coming from a "*New Yorker* writer" of entertaining stories in which harried, comfortably off, white middle-class suburbanites conduct their lives. "Our Chekhov of the exurbs," he was dubbed by the reviewer John Leonard, with reference to the mythical community of Shady Hill (which Cheever created along the lines of existing ones in Fairfield or Westchester county). Yet Chekhov's own characters, living in darkness, aspire toward "spiritual light," with a similarly "botanical" inclination. Trapped in their beautifully appointed houses and neighborhoods but carried along by the cool, effortless prose of their creator, Cheever's characters are viewed with a sympathetic irony, well-seasoned by sadness.

Cheever's early years were not notably idyllic, and he reveals little nostalgia for a lost childhood. Born in Quincy, Massachusetts, he grew up in what he describes as shabby gentility, with his father departing the family when his son was fifteen. (Cheever had an older brother, Fred, with whom he formed a strong but troubled relationship.) Two years later his father lost his money in the crash of 1929, and by that time Cheever had been expelled from Thayer Academy, in Braintree. The expulsion marked the end of his formal education and the beginning of his career as a writer; for, remarkably, he wrote a short story about the experience, titled it "Expelled," and sent it to *The New Republic*, where Malcolm Cowley (who would become a lifelong friend) published it.

During the 1930s Cheever lived in New York City, in impoverished circumstances, taking odd jobs to support himself and winning a fellowship to the writer's colony at Yaddo, in Saratoga Springs. His New York life would provide the material for many of his early stories, whose protagonists are rather frequently in desperate economic situations. With the coming of World War II, Cheever joined the armed forces and served in the Pacific theater but saw no combat. In 1941 he married Mary Winternitz. About the marriage, which produced three children and lasted through four decades, Cheever said, "That two people—both of us tempermental, quarrelsome and intensely ambitious—could have gotten along for such a vast period of time is for me a very good example of the boundlessness of human nature." Meanwhile, with the help of Malcolm Cowley, he began to publish in *The New Yorker* and in 1943, while in service, his first book of stories (*The Way Some People Live*) was published to favorable reviews. Over the decades to follow the stories continued to appear, largely in *The New Yorker*, where he became—along with J. D. Salinger and John Updike—a recurrent phenomenon. Five further volumes of short fiction were published, and in 1978 *The Stories of John Cheever* gathered those he wished to be remembered for.

Although he is praised for his skill as a realist depictor of suburban manners and morals, Cheever's art cannot be adequately understood in such terms. As Stephen C. Moore has usefully pointed out, "His best stories move from a base in a mimetic presentation of surface reality—the *scenery* of apparently successful American middle class life—to fables of heroism." Cheever's embattled heroes express themselves in taking up challenges that are essentially fabulous, and foolhardy: swimming home across the backyard pools of Westchester ("The Swimmer," printed here); performing feats of physical daredeviltry in suburban living rooms ("O Youth and Beauty"); or dealing with the myriad demands and temptations that beset the hero who, having escaped death in an airplane, returns home to more severe trials ("The Country Husband"). Whatever the specific narrative, we are always aware of the storyteller's art, shaping ordinary life into the odder, more willful figures of fantasy and romance.

While Cheever will be remembered primarily as a short-story writer, his output includes a respectable number of novels. In 1957 he won a National Book Award for his first one, *The Wapshot Chronicle* (it was followed by *The Wapshot Scandal,* in 1964), notable for its New England seacoast setting and domestic flavor, if less so for a continuously engaging narrative line. Perhaps his most gripping novel is *Bullet Park* (1969), which, like the best of the stories, is both realistic and fabulous. The suburban milieu, seen from the 5:42 train from New York, has never been depicted more accurately, even lovingly, by Cheever. And as is to be expected, his protagonist's carefully built, pious suburban existence turns out to be a mess. The novel provoked interesting disagreement about its merits (some critics felt the narrative manipulations both ruthless and sentimental), but there was no disagreement about the vivid quality of its represented life, on the commuter train or at the cocktail party. In the years just previous to his death, and after a bout with alcohol and drug addiction, Cheever published his two final novels, *Falconer* (1978) and *Oh What a Paradise It Seems* (1980), the former of which was much praised for its harrowing rendering of prison life. (Farragut, the novel's hero, is sent to Falconer Prison for killing his brother; Cheever lived in Ossining, New York, home of Sing Sing Prison, during his later years.)

From the beginning to the end of his career he was and remained a thoroughly professional writer, wary of pronouncing on the world at large (there is a noticeable absence of politics and ideology in his work) or on the meaning and significance of his own art. As one sees from his *Journals* (1991), he agonized over the disruptive facts of his alcoholism and his homosexuality. But he remained a private man, seemingly untouched by experiments—or fads—in fiction writing. Whether or not, as T. S. Eliot said about Henry James, he had a mind so fine that no idea could violate it, Cheever remained firmly resistant to ideas of all sorts. This insular tendency is probably a reason why his work makes less than a "major" claim on us, but it is also the condition responsible for his devoted and scrupulous attention to the particularities of middle-class life at the far edge of its promised dream.

The text is from *The Brigadier and the Golf Widow* (1964).

The Swimmer

It was one of those midsummer Sundays when everyone sits around saying: "I *drank* too much last night." You might have heard it whispered by the parishioners leaving church, heard it from the lips of the priest himself, struggling with his cassock in the *vestiarium,*[1] heard it from the golf links and the tennis courts, heard it from the wildlife preserve where the leader of the Audubon group was suffering from a terrible hangover. "I *drank* too much," said Donald Westerhazy. "We all *drank* too much," said Lucinda Merrill. "It must have been the wine," said Helen Westerhazy. "I *drank* too much of that claret."

This was at the edge of the Westerhazys' pool. The pool, fed by an artesian well with a high iron content, was a pale shade of green. It was a fine day. In the west there was a massive stand of cumulus cloud so like a city seen from a distance—from the bow of an approaching ship—that it might have had a name. Lisbon. Hackensack.[2] The sun was hot. Neddy Merrill sat by the green water, one hand in it, one around a glass of gin. He was a slender man—he seemed to have the especial slenderness of youth—and while he was far from young he had slid down his banister that morning and given the bronze back-

---

1. Cloakroom for religious vestments adjacent to a church's sanctuary.

2. A town in New Jersey. Lisbon is the capital of Portugal.

side of Aphrodite[3] on the hall table a smack, as he jogged toward the smell of coffee in his dining room. He might have been compared to a summer's day, particularly the last hours of one, and while he lacked a tennis racket or a sail bag the impression was definitely one of youth, sport, and clement weather. He had been swimming and now he was breathing deeply, stertorously as if he could gulp into his lungs the components of that moment, the heat of the sun, the intenseness of his pleasure. It all seemed to flow into his chest. His own house stood in Bullet Park,[4] eight miles to the south, where his four beautiful daughters would have had their lunch and might be playing tennis. Then it occurred to him that by taking a dogleg to the southwest he could reach his home by water.

His life was not confining and the delight he took in this observation could not be explained by its suggestion of escape. He seemed to see, with a cartographer's eye, that string of swimming pools, that quasi-subterranean stream that curved across the county. He had made a discovery, a contribution to modern geography; he would name the stream Lucinda after his wife. He was not a practical joker nor was he a fool but he was determinedly original and had a vague and modest idea of himself as a legendary figure. The day was beautiful and it seemed to him that a long swim might enlarge and celebrate its beauty.

He took off a sweater that was hung over his shoulders and dove in. He had an inexplicable contempt for men who did not hurl themselves into pools. He swam a choppy crawl, breathing either with every stroke or every fourth stroke and counting somewhere well in the back of his mind the one-two one-two of a flutter kick. It was not a serviceable stroke for long distances but the domestication of swimming had saddled the sport with some customs and in his part of the world a crawl was customary. To be embraced and sustained by the light green water was less a pleasure, it seemed, than the resumption of a natural condition, and he would have liked to swim without trunks, but this was not possible, considering his project. He hoisted himself up on the far curb—he never used the ladder—and started across the lawn. When Lucinda asked where he was going he said he was going to swim home.

The only maps and charts he had to go by were remembered or imaginary but these were clear enough. First there were the Grahams, the Hammers, the Lears, the Howlands, and the Crosscups. He would cross Ditmar Street to the Bunkers and come, after a short portage, to the Levys, the Welchers, and the public pool in Lancaster. Then there were the Hallorans, the Sachses, the Biswangers, Shirley Adams, the Gilmartins, and the Clydes. The day was lovely, and that he lived in a world so generously supplied with water seemed like a clemency, a beneficence. His heart was high and he ran across the grass. Making his way home by an uncommon route gave him the feeling that he was a pilgrim, an explorer, a man with a destiny, and he knew that he would find friends all along the way; friends would line the banks of the Lucinda River.

He went through a hedge that separated the Westerhazys' land from the Grahams', walked under some flowering apple trees, passed the shed that housed their pump and filter, and came out at the Grahams' pool. "Why, Neddy," Mrs. Graham said, "what a marvelous surprise. I've been trying to get you on the phone all morning. Here, let me get you a drink." He saw then,

---

3. Greek goddess of love and beauty.
4. Fictive suburb used as a location for many of Cheever's stories and novels.

like any explorer, that the hospitable customs and traditions of the natives would have to be handled with diplomacy if he was ever going to reach his destination. He did not want to mystify or seem rude to the Grahams nor did he have the time to linger there. He swam the length of their pool and joined them in the sun and was rescued, a few minutes later, by the arrival of two carloads of friends from Connecticut. During the uproarious reunions he was able to slip away. He went down by the front of the Grahams' house, stepped over a thorny hedge, and crossed a vacant lot to the Hammers'. Mrs. Hammer, looking up from her roses, saw him swim by although she wasn't quite sure who it was. The Lears heard him splashing past the open windows of their living room. The Howlands and the Crosscups were away. After leaving the Howlands' he crossed Ditmar Street and started for the Bunkers', where he could hear, even at that distance, the noise of a party.

The water refracted the sound of voices and laughter and seemed to suspend it in midair. The Bunkers' pool was on a rise and he climbed some stairs to a terrace where twenty-five or thirty men and women were drinking. The only person in the water was Rusty Towers, who floated there on a rubber raft. Oh how bonny and lush were the banks of the Lucinda River! Prosperous men and women gathered by the sapphire-colored waters while caterer's men in white coats passed them cold gin. Overhead a red de Haviland trainer was circling around and around and around in the sky with something like the glee of a child in a swing. Ned felt a passing affection for the scene, a tenderness for the gathering, as if it was something he might touch. In the distance he heard thunder. As soon as Enid Bunker saw him she began to scream: "Oh look who's here! What a marvelous surprise! When Lucinda said that you couldn't come I thought I'd *die*." She made her way to him through the crowd, and when they had finished kissing she led him to the bar, a progress that was slowed by the fact that he stopped to kiss eight or ten other women and shake the hands of as many men. A smiling bartender he had seen at a hundred parties gave him a gin and tonic and he stood by the bar for a moment, anxious not to get stuck in any conversation that would delay his voyage. When he seemed about to be surrounded he dove in and swam close to the side to avoid colliding with Rusty's raft. At the far end of the pool he bypassed the Tomlinsons with a broad smile and jogged up the garden path. The gravel cut his feet but this was the only unpleasantness. The party was confined to the pool, and as he went toward the house he heard the brilliant, watery sound of voices fade, heard the noise of a radio from the Bunkers' kitchen, where someone was listening to a ballgame. Sunday afternoon. He made his way through the parked cars and down the grassy border of their driveway to Alewives' Lane. He did not want to be seen on the road in his bathing trunks but there was no traffic and he made the short distance to the Levys' driveway, marked with a private property sign and a green tube for the *New York Times*. All the doors and windows of the big house were open but there were no signs of life; not even a dog barked. He went around the side of the house to the pool and saw that the Levys had only recently left. Glasses and bottles and dishes of nuts were on a table at the deep end, where there was a bathhouse or gazebo, hung with Japanese lanterns. After swimming the pool he got himself a glass and poured a drink. It was his fourth or fifth drink and he had swum nearly half the length of the Lucinda River. He felt tired, clean, and pleased at that moment to be alone; pleased with everything.

It would storm. The stand of cumulus cloud—that city—had risen and darkened, and while he sat there he heard the percussiveness of thunder again. The de Haviland trainer was still circling overhead and it seemed to Ned that he could almost hear the pilot laugh with pleasure in the afternoon; but when there was another peal of thunder he took off for home. A train whistle blew and he wondered what time it had gotten to be. Four? Five? He thought of the provincial station at that hour, where a waiter, his tuxedo concealed by a raincoat, a dwarf with some flowers wrapped in newspaper, and a woman who had been crying would be waiting for the local. It was suddenly growing dark; it was that moment when the pin-headed birds seem to organize their song into some acute and knowledgeable recognition of the storm's approach. Then there was a fine noise of rushing water from the crown of an oak at his back, as if a spigot there had been turned. Then the noise of fountains came from the crowns of all the tall trees. Why did he love storms, what was the meaning of his excitement when the door sprang open and the rain wind fled rudely up the stairs, why had the simple task of shutting the windows of an old house seemed fitting and urgent, why did the first watery notes of a storm wind have for him the unmistakable sound of good news, cheer, glad tidings? Then there was an explosion, a smell of cordite, and rain lashed the Japanese lanterns that Mrs. Levy had bought in Kyoto the year before last, or was it the year before that?

He stayed in the Levys' gazebo until the storm had passed. The rain had cooled the air and he shivered. The force of the wind had stripped a maple of its red and yellow leaves and scattered them over the grass and the water. Since it was midsummer the tree must be blighted, and yet he felt a peculiar sadness at this sign of autumn. He braced his shoulders, emptied his glass, and started for the Welchers' pool. This meant crossing the Lindleys' riding ring and he was surprised to find it overgrown with grass and all the jumps dismantled. He wondered if the Lindleys had sold their horses or gone away for the summer and put them out to board. He seemed to remember having heard something about the Lindleys and their horses but the memory was unclear. On he went, barefoot through the wet grass, to the Welchers', where he found their pool was dry.

This breach in his chain of water disappointed him absurdly, and he felt like some explorer who seeks a torrential headwater and finds a dead stream. He was disappointed and mystified. It was common enough to go away for the summer but no one ever drained his pool. The Welchers had definitely gone away. The pool furniture was folded, stacked, and covered with a tarpaulin. The bathhouse was locked. All the windows of the house were shut, and when he went around to the driveway in front he saw a for-sale sign nailed to a tree. When had he last heard from the Welchers—when, that is, had he and Lucinda last regretted an invitation to dine with them. It seemed only a week or so ago. Was his memory failing or had he so disciplined it in the repression of unpleasant facts that he had damaged his sense of the truth? Then in the distance he heard the sound of a tennis game. This cheered him, cleared away all his apprehensions and let him regard the overcast sky and the cold air with indifference. This was the day that Neddy Merrill swam across the county. That was the day! He started off then for his most difficult portage.

Had you gone for a Sunday afternoon ride that day you might have seen him, close to naked, standing on the shoulders of route 424, waiting for a chance to cross. You might have wondered if he was the victim of foul play, had his car broken down, or was he merely a fool. Standing barefoot in the deposits of the highway—beer cans, rags, and blowout patches—exposed to all kinds of ridicule, he seemed pitiful. He had known when he started that this was a part of his journey—it had been on his maps—but confronted with the lines of traffic, worming through the summery light, he found himself unprepared. He was laughed at, jeered at, a beer can was thrown at him, and he had no dignity or humor to bring to the situation. He could have gone back, back to the Westerhazys', where Lucinda would still be sitting in the sun. He had signed nothing, vowed nothing, pledged nothing, not even to himself. Why, believing as he did, that all human obduracy was susceptible to common sense, was he unable to turn back? Why was he determined to complete his journey even if it meant putting his life in danger? At what point had this prank, this joke, this piece of horseplay become serious? He could not go back, he could not even recall with any clearness the green water at the Westerhazys', the sense of inhaling the day's components, the friendly and relaxed voices saying that they had *drunk* too much. In the space of an hour, more or less, he had covered a distance that made his return impossible.

An old man, tooling down the highway at fifteen miles an hour, let him get to the middle of the road, where there was a grass divider. Here he was exposed to the ridicule of the northbound traffic, but after ten or fifteen minutes he was able to cross. From here he had only a short walk to the Recreation Center at the edge of the Village of Lancaster, where there were some handball courts and a public pool.

The effect of the water on voices, the illusion of brilliance and suspense, was the same here as it had been at the Bunkers' but the sounds here were louder, harsher, and more shrill, and as soon as he entered the crowded enclosure he was confronted with regimentation. "ALL SWIMMERS MUST TAKE A SHOWER BEFORE USING THE POOL. ALL SWIMMERS MUST USE THE FOOTBATH. ALL SWIMMERS MUST WEAR THEIR IDENTIFICATION DISKS." He took a shower, washed his feet in a cloudy and bitter solution and made his way to the edge of the water. It stank of chlorine and looked to him like a sink. A pair of lifeguards in a pair of towers blew police whistles at what seemed to be regular intervals and abused the swimmers through a public address system. Neddy remembered the sapphire water at the Bunkers' with longing and thought that he might contaminate himself—damage his own prosperousness and charm—by swimming in this murk, but he reminded himself that he was an explorer, a pilgrim, and that this was merely a stagnant bend in the Lucinda River. He dove, scowling with distaste, into the chlorine and had to swim with his head above water to avoid collisions, but even so he was bumped into, splashed and jostled. When he got to the shallow end both lifeguards were shouting at him: "Hey, you, you without the identification disk, get outa the water." He did, but they had no way of pursuing him and he went through the reek of suntan oil and chlorine out through the hurricane fence and passed the handball courts. By crossing the road he entered the wooded part of the Halloran estate. The woods were not cleared and the footing was treacherous and difficult until he reached the lawn and the clipped beech hedge that encircled their pool.

The Hallorans were friends, an elderly couple of enormous wealth who seemed to bask in the suspicion that they might be Communists. They were zealous reformers but they were not Communists, and yet when they were accused, as they sometimes were, of subversion, it seemed to gratify and excite them. Their beech hedge was yellow and he guessed this had been blighted like the Levys' maple. He called hullo, hullo, to warn the Hallorans of his approach, to palliate his invasion of their privacy. The Hallorans, for reasons that had never been explained to him, did not wear bathing suits. No explanations were in order, really. Their nakedness was a detail in their uncompromising zeal for reform and he stepped politely out of his trunks before he went through the opening in the hedge.

Mrs. Halloran, a stout woman with white hair and a serene face, was reading the *Times*. Mr. Halloran was taking beech leaves out of the water with a scoop. They seemed not surprised or displeased to see him. Their pool was perhaps the oldest in the county, a fieldstone rectangle, fed by a brook. It had no filter or pump and its waters were the opaque gold of the stream.

"I'm swimming across the county," Ned said.

"Why, I didn't know one could," exclaimed Mrs. Halloran.

"Well, I've made it from the Westerhazys'," Ned said. "That must be about four miles."

He left his trunks at the deep end, walked to the shallow end, and swam this stretch. As he was pulling himself out of the water he heard Mrs. Halloran say: "We've been *terribly* sorry to hear about all your misfortunes, Neddy."

"My misfortunes?" Ned asked. "I don't know what you mean."

"Why, we heard that you'd sold the house and that your poor children . . ."

"I don't recall having sold the house," Ned said, "and the girls are at home."

"Yes," Mrs. Halloran sighed. "Yes . . ." Her voice filled the air with an unseasonable melancholy and Ned spoke briskly. "Thank you for the swim."

"Well, have a nice trip," said Mrs. Halloran.

Beyond the hedge he pulled on his trunks and fastened them. They were loose and he wondered if, during the space of an afternoon, he could have lost some weight. He was cold and he was tired and the naked Hallorans and their dark water had depressed him. The swim was too much for his strength but how could he have guessed this, sliding down the banister that morning and sitting in the Westerhazys' sun? His arms were lame. His legs felt rubbery and ached at the joints. The worst of it was the cold in his bones and the feeling that he might never be warm again. Leaves were falling down around him and he smelled woodsmoke on the wind. Who would be burning wood at this time of year?

He needed a drink. Whiskey would warm him, pick him up, carry him through the last of his journey, refresh his feeling that it was original and valorous to swim across the county. Channel swimmers took brandy. He needed a stimulant. He crossed the lawn in front of the Hallorans' house and went down a little path to where they had built a house for their only daughter Helen and her husband Eric Sachs. The Sachses' pool was small and he found Helen and her husband there.

"Oh, *Neddy*," Helen said. "Did you lunch at Mother's?"

"Not *really*," Ned said. "I *did* stop to see your parents." This seemed to be explanation enough. "I'm terribly sorry to break in on you like this but I've taken a chill and I wonder if you'd give me a drink."

"Why, I'd *love* to," Helen said, "but there hasn't been anything in this house to drink since Eric's operation. That was three years ago."

Was he losing his memory, had his gift for concealing painful facts let him forget that he had sold his house, that his children were in trouble, and that his friend had been ill? His eyes slipped from Eric's face to his abdomen, where he saw three pale, sutured scars, two of them at least a foot long. Gone was his navel, and what, Neddy thought, would the roving hand, bed-checking one's gifts at 3 A.M. make of a belly with no navel, no link to birth, this breach in the succession?

"I'm sure you can get a drink at the Biswangers'," Helen said. "They're having an enormous do. You can hear it from here. Listen!"

She raised her head and from across the road, the lawns, the gardens, the woods, the fields, he heard again the brilliant noise of voices over water. "Well, I'll get wet," he said, still feeling that he had no freedom of choice about his means of travel. He dove into the Sachses' cold water and, gasping, close to drowning, made his way from one end of the pool to the other. "Lucinda and I want *terribly* to see you," he said over his shoulder, his face set toward the Biswangers'. "We're sorry it's been so long and we'll call you *very* soon."

He crossed some fields to the Biswangers' and the sounds of revelry there. They would be honored to give him a drink, they would be happy to give him a drink, they would in fact be lucky to give him a drink. The Biswangers invited him and Lucinda for dinner four times a year, six weeks in advance. They were always rebuffed and yet they continued to send out their invitations, unwilling to comprehend the rigid and undemocratic realities of their society. They were the sort of people who discussed the price of things at cocktails, exchanged market tips during dinner, and after dinner told dirty stories to mixed company. They did not belong to Neddy's set—they were not even on Lucinda's Christmas card list. He went toward their pool with feelings of indifference, charity, and some unease, since it seemed to be getting dark and these were the longest days of the year. The party when he joined it was noisy and large. Grace Biswanger was the kind of hostess who asked the optometrist, the veterinarian, the real-estate dealer and the dentist. No one was swimming and the twilight, reflected on the water of the pool, had a wintry gleam. There was a bar and he started for this. When Grace Biswanger saw him she came toward him, not affectionately as he had every right to expect, but bellicosely.

"Why, this party has everything," she said loudly, "including a gate crasher."

She could not deal him a social blow—there was no question about this and he did not flinch. "As a gate crasher," he asked politely, "do I rate a drink?"

"Suit yourself," she said. "You don't seem to pay much attention to invitations."

She turned her back on him and joined some guests, and he went to the bar and ordered a whiskey. The bartender served him but he served him rudely. His was a world in which the caterer's men kept the social score, and to be rebuffed by a part-time barkeep meant that he had suffered some loss of social esteem. Or perhaps the man was new and uninformed. Then he heard Grace at his back say: "They went for broke overnight—nothing but income—and he showed up drunk one Sunday and asked us to loan him five thousand dollars. . . ." She was always talking about money. It was worse than eating your peas off a knife. He dove into the pool, swam its length and went away.

The next pool on his list, the last but two, belonged to his old mistress, Shirley Adams. If he had suffered any injuries at the Biswangers' they would be cured here. Love—sexual roughhouse in fact—was the supreme elixir, the painkiller, the brightly colored pill that would put the spring back into his step, the joy of life in his heart. They had had an affair last week, last month, last year. He couldn't remember. It was he who had broken it off, his was the upper hand, and he stepped through the gate of the wall that surrounded her pool with nothing so considered as self-confidence. It seemed in a way to be his pool as the lover, particularly the illicit lover, enjoys the possessions of his mistress with an authority unknown to holy matrimony. She was there, her hair the color of brass, but her figure, at the edge of the lighted, cerulean water, excited in him no profound memories. It had been, he thought, a light-hearted affair, although she had wept when he broke it off. She seemed confused to see him and he wondered if she was still wounded. Would she, God forbid, weep again?

"What do you want?" she asked.

"I'm swimming across the county."

"Good Christ. Will you ever grow up?"

"What's the matter?"

"If you've come here for money," she said, "I won't give you another cent."

"You could give me a drink."

"I could but I won't. I'm not alone."

"Well, I'm on my way."

He dove in and swam the pool, but when he tried to haul himself up onto the curb he found that the strength in his arms and his shoulders had gone, and he paddled to the ladder and climbed out. Looking over his shoulder he saw, in the lighted bathhouse, a young man. Going out onto the dark lawn he smelled chrysanthemums or marigolds—some stubborn autumnal fragrance—on the night air, strong as gas. Looking overhead he saw that the stars had come out, but why should he seem to see Andromeda, Cepheus, and Cassiopeia? What had become of the constellations of midsummer? He began to cry.

It was probably the first time in his adult life that he had ever cried, certainly the first time in his life that he had ever felt so miserable, cold, tired, and bewildered. He could not understand the rudeness of the caterer's barkeep or the rudeness of a mistress who had come to him on her knees and showered his trousers with tears. He had swum too long, he had been immersed too long, and his nose and his throat were sore from the water. What he needed then was a drink, some company, and some clean dry clothes, and while he could have cut directly across the road to his home he went on to the Gilmartins' pool. Here, for the first time in his life, he did not dive but went down the steps into the icy water and swam a hobbled side stroke that he might have learned as a youth. He staggered with fatigue on his way to the Clydes' and paddled the length of their pool, stopping again and again with his hand on the curb to rest. He climbed up the ladder and wondered if he had the strength to get home. He had done what he wanted, he had swum the county, but he was so stupefied with exhaustion that his triumph seemed vague. Stooped, holding onto the gateposts for support, he turned up the driveway of his house.

The place was dark. Was it so late that they had all gone to bed? Had Lucinda stayed at the Westerhazys' for supper? Had the girls joined her there or gone someplace else? Hadn't they agreed, as they usually did on Sunday, to regret all their invitations and stay at home? He tried the garage doors to see what cars were in but the doors were locked and rust came off the handles onto his hands. Going toward the house, he saw that the force of the thunderstorm had knocked one of the rain gutters loose. It hung down over the front door like an umbrella rib, but it could be fixed in the morning. The house was locked, and he thought that the stupid cook or the stupid maid must have locked the place up until he remembered that it had been some time since they had employed a maid or a cook. He shouted, pounded on the door, tried to force it with his shoulder, and then, looking in at the windows, saw that the place was empty.

1964

ROBERT HAYDEN
1913–1980

"Hayden is by far the best chronicler and rememberer of the African American heritage in these Americas that I know of," the poet Michael Harper, whose own sense of history is indebted to Robert Hayden's work, has said. Hayden's poems save what has vanished, what has been lost to standard histories, like a 1920s prizefighter from the Midwest ("Free Fantasia: Tiger Flowers") or a miner trapped in Crystal Cave ("Beginnings, V"). He records the loss of what others never noticed as missing, and in their recovery he discovers a significance in the passing moment, the passed-over figure, the inarticulate gesture, which lasts through time. Always, in his words, "opposed to the chauvinistic and the doctrinaire" in art, he cherished the freedom of the poet to write about whatever seized the imagination. But his imagination was in its nature elegiac and historical. As he remembers and re-creates the African American heritage, he speaks to the struggles of the individual spirit for freedom and to painful self-divisions people of many times and places know. But if the circumstances he confronts in his poems are often harsh, his work captures the energy and joyfulness that make survival possible.

Born in Detroit, Michigan, Hayden grew up in a poor neighborhood called by its inhabitants, with affectionate irony, "Paradise Valley." His powerful sequence *Elegies for Paradise Valley* (1978) resurrects the neighborhood in its racial and ethnic mix. Memory for Hayden is an act of love that leads to self-awareness; in this sequence and in poems like "Those Winter Sundays," he writes about his own past, confronts its pain, and preserves its sustaining moments of happiness.

Hayden had a deep understanding of conflicts that divide the self. His family history gave him an early acquaintance with such self-division: his parents' marriage ended when he was young, and his mother left him in the care of foster parents (whose surname he adopted) when she left Detroit to look for work. He remained with the Haydens although his mother returned to Detroit when he was a teenager and lived for a period with his foster family until conflict arose between her and his foster mother. "I lived in the midst of so much turmoil all the time I didn't know if I loved or hated," he once said. As an African American and as a poet Hayden also lived between worlds. He courageously maintained his sense of vocation through years of critical neglect and amid the demands of full-time teaching at Fisk University from 1946 to 1968. He published his first book, *Heart-Shape in the Dust*, in 1940, but his mature work did not appear in quantity until his volume *Ballad of Remembrance* (1962). At the same time his belief that the poet should not be restricted by any set of themes, racial or otherwise, and the highly formal quality of his work led to criticism by some young African American writers in the 1960s. But Hayden never abandoned his belief in the power of art to speak universally. In a 1974 interview he told Dennis Gendron of rereading Yeats's poem "Easter 1916" in the wake of the riots in Detroit— "that is the kind of poetry I want to write," he said, in admiration of the ways Yeats conceived a particular historical and political moment so that it speaks across time and place.

In fact, Hayden wrote that kind of poetry. His most famous poem, "Middle Passage," demonstrates his transfiguring imagination and the knowledge of historical documents, which began early in his career. In 1936, after leaving college because of increasingly difficult economic conditions, Hayden joined the Federal Writers Project of the Works Progress Administration, and for two years he researched the history of abolition movements and the Underground Railroad in Michigan. "Middle Passage" is a collage of accounts of the slave ships that transported men and women from Africa into slavery in the New World. Through the multiple voices in the poem, Hayden lets the accounts of those who participated in (and profited from) the slave trade reveal the evidence of their own damnation. The blindness that attacks one of the ships becomes a symbol of the devastating suffering of those transported into slavery and of the moral blindness everywhere evident in the traders' accounts. The collage technique allows Hayden to suggest the fragmentation of the story; the silences in the poem evoke the missing voices of those who suffered and died on the voyages or in the intolerable conditions of slavery. At the heart of the poem is the account of a rebellion led by one of the slaves (Cinquez) on the ship *The Amistad*. Cinquez is one of several figures in Hayden's poems who dramatize "The deep immortal human wish / the timeless will" ("Middle Passage") that for Hayden is the indomitable struggle for freedom. This "timeless will" and struggle also appear in his poems about Harriet Tubman ("Runagate Runagate"), Nat Turner, Frederick Douglass, Phillis Wheatley, and the later figures Paul Robeson and Bessie Smith.

Hayden's experiment with collage technique in "Middle Passage" connects him to modernist poets like T. S. Eliot and William Carlos Williams and to an African American tradition acutely aware of the power of voice. He continued to experiment with poetic form and with the creation of different voices always testing the possibilities of craft, forging a language to express what he knew and felt. His sequences *Beginnings* and *Elegies for Paradise Valley* demonstrate his formal originality, as does his late poem "American Journal," with its long lines and its approximation to prose. Hayden loved language and was unafraid to be lushly descriptive as well as to be precisely imagistic. His work summons us to notice the world as we had not before and offers us candor, clearsightedness, and a transforming gaiety.

From 1968 until his death Hayden was professor of English at the University of Michigan at Ann Arbor. In 1976 he became the first African American to be appointed poetry consultant to the Library of Congress.

Middle Passage[1]

I

Jesús, Estrella, Esperanza, Mercy[2]

> Sails flashing to the wind like weapons,
> sharks following the moans the fever and the dying;
> horror the corposant and compass rose.[3]

---

1. Main route for the slave trade in the Atlantic between Africa and the West Indies.
2. Names of slave ships. "*Esperanza*": hope (Spanish).

3. Circle printed on a map showing compass directions. "Corposant": a fiery luminousness that can appear on the decks of ships during electrical storms.

Middle Passage:
                    voyage through death
                              to life upon these shores.

        "10 April 1800—
        Blacks rebellious. Crew uneasy. Our linguist says
        their moaning is a prayer for death,   10
        ours and their own. Some try to starve themselves.
        Lost three this morning leaped with crazy laughter
        to the waiting sharks, sang as they went under."

Desire, Adventure, Tartar, Ann:

        Standing to America, bringing home   15
        black gold, black ivory, black seed.

                Deep in the festering hold thy father lies,
                of his bones New England pews are made,
                those are altar lights that were his eyes.[4]

Jesus   Saviour   Pilot   Me   20
Over   Life's   Tempestuous   Sea[5]

We pray that Thou wilt grant, O Lord,
safe passage to our vessels bringing
heathen souls unto Thy chastening.

Jesus   Saviour   25

        "8 bells. I cannot sleep, for I am sick
        with fear, but writing eases fear a little
        since still my eyes can see these words take shape
        upon the page & so I write, as one
        would turn to exorcism. 4 days scudding,   30
        but now the sea is calm again. Misfortune
        follows in our wake like sharks (our grinning
        tutelary gods). Which one of us
        has killed an albatross?[6] A plague among
        our blacks—Ophthalmia: blindness—& we   35
        have jettisoned the blind to no avail.
        It spreads, the terrifying sickness spreads.
        Its claws have scratched sight from the Capt.'s eyes
        & there is blindness in the fo'c'sle[7]
        & we must sail 3 weeks before we come   40
        to port."

---

4. "Full fathom five thy father lies; / Of his bones
are coral made; / Those are pearls that were his
eyes" (Shakespeare's *Tempest* 1.2.400–02). The
sprite Ariel is singing about the supposed death by
water of the king of Naples.
5. A Protestant hymn.

6. A bird of good omen; to kill one is an unlucky
and impious act (as in Samuel Taylor Coleridge's
Rime of the Ancient Mariner).
7. Short for forecastle, the place in a ship where
sailors are quartered.

What port awaits us, Davy Jones'
or home? I've heard of slavers drifting, drifting,
playthings of wind and storm and chance, their crews
gone blind, the jungle hatred   45
crawling up on deck.

Thou   Who   Walked   On   Galilee

"Deponent further sayeth *The Bella J*
left the Guinea Coast
with cargo of five hundred blacks and odd   50
for the barracoons⁸ of Florida:

"That there was hardly room 'tween-decks for half
the sweltering cattle stowed spoon-fashion there;
that some went mad of thirst and tore their flesh
and sucked the blood: 55

"That Crew and Captain lusted with the comeliest
of the savage girls kept naked in the cabins;
that there was one they called The Guinea Rose
and they cast lots and fought to lie with her:

"That when the Bo's'n piped all hands,⁹ the flames   60
spreading from starboard already were beyond
control, the negroes howling and their chains
entangled with the flames:

"That the burning blacks could not be reached,
that the Crew abandoned ship,   65
leaving their shrieking negresses behind,
that the Captain perished drunken with the wenches:

"Further Deponent sayeth not."

Pilot   Oh   Pilot   Me

II

Aye, lad, and I have seen those factories,   70
Gambia, Rio Pongo, Calabar;¹
have watched the artful mongos² baiting traps
of war wherein the victor and the vanquished

Were caught as prizes for our barracoons.
Have seen the nigger kings whose vanity   75
and greed turned wild black hides of Fellatah,
Mandingo, Ibo, Kru³ to gold for us.

---

8. Barracks or enclosures for slaves.
9. I.e., when the boatswain (petty officer aboard a
ship) signaled to all the crew on deck.
1. A city in southeast Nigeria. Gambia is a river

and nation in west Africa. Rio Pongo is a watercourse, dry for most of the year, in east Africa.
2. I.e., Africans.
3. African tribes.

And there was one—King Anthracite we named him—
fetish face beneath French parasols
of brass and orange velvet, impudent mouth   80
whose cups were carven skulls of enemies:

He'd honor us with drum and feast and conjo[4]
and palm-oil-glistening wenches deft in love,
and for tin crowns that shone with paste,
red calico and German-silver trinkets   85

Would have the drums talk war and send
his warriors to burn the sleeping villages
and kill the sick and old and lead the young
in coffles[5] to our factories.

Twenty years a trader, twenty years,   90
for there was wealth aplenty to be harvested
from those black fields, and I'd be trading still
but for the fevers melting down my bones.

III

Shuttles in the rocking loom of history,
the dark ships move, the dark ships move,   95
their bright ironical names
like jests of kindness on a murderer's mouth;
plough through thrashing glister toward
fata morgana's lucent melting shore,
weave toward New World littorals[6] that are   100
mirage and myth and actual shore.

Voyage through death,
                    voyage whose chartings are unlove.

A charnel stench, effluvium of living death
spreads outward from the hold,   105
where the living and the dead, the horribly dying,
lie interlocked, lie foul with blood and excrement.

> *Deep in the festering hold thy father lies,*
> *the corpse of mercy rots with him,*
> *rats eat love's rotten gelid eyes.*   110

But, oh, the living look at you
with human eyes whose suffering accuses you,
whose hatred reaches through the swill of dark
to strike you like a leper's claw.

You cannot stare that hatred down   115
or chain the fear that stalks the watches

---

4. Dance.
5. Train of slaves fastened together.

6. Coastal regions. "Fata morgana": mirage.

and breathes on you its fetid scorching breath;
cannot kill the deep immortal human wish,
the timeless will.

"But for the storm that flung up barriers   120
of wind and wave, *The Amistad*,[7] señores,
would have reached the port of Príncipe in two,
three days at most; but for the storm we should
have been prepared for what befell.
Swift as the puma's leap it came. There was   125
that interval of moonless calm filled only
with the water's and the rigging's usual sounds,
then sudden movement, blows and snarling cries
and they had fallen on us with machete
and marlinspike. It was as though the very   130
air, the night itself were striking us.
Exhausted by the rigors of the storm,
we were no match for them. Our men went down
before the murderous Africans. Our loyal
Celestino ran from below with gun   135
and lantern and I saw, before the cane-
knife's wounding flash, Cinquez,
that surly brute who calls himself a prince,
directing, urging on the ghastly work.[8]
He hacked the poor mulatto down, and then   140
he turned on me. The decks were slippery
when daylight finally came. It sickens me
to think of what I saw, of how these apes
threw overboard the butchered bodies of
our men, true Christians all, like so much jetsam.   145
Enough, enough. The rest is quickly told:
Cinquez was forced to spare the two of us
you see to steer the ship to Africa,
and we like phantoms doomed to rove the sea
voyaged east by day and west by night,   150
deceiving them, hoping for rescue,
prisoners on our own vessel, till
at length we drifted to the shores of this
your land, America, where we were freed
from our unspeakable misery. Now we   155
demand, good sirs, the extradition of
Cinquez and his accomplices to La
Havana.[9] And it distresses us to know
there are so many here who seem inclined
to justify the mutiny of these blacks.   160

---

7. A Spanish ship—the name means "Friend-ship"—that carried fifty-three illegally obtained slaves out of Havana, Cuba, in July 1839.
8. During the mutiny the Africans, led by a man called Cinqué, or Cinquez, killed the captain, his slave Celestino, and the mate, but spared the two slave owners.

9. After two months *The Amistad* reached Long Island Sound, where it was detained by the American ship *Washington*, the slaves were imprisoned, and the owners were freed. The owners began litigation to return the slaves to Havana to be tried for murder.

We find it paradoxical indeed
that you whose wealth, whose tree of liberty
are rooted in the labor of your slaves
should suffer the august John Quincy Adams
to speak with so much passion of the right   165
of chattel slaves to kill their lawful masters
and with his Roman rhetoric weave a hero's
garland for Cinquez.[1] I tell you that
we are determined to return to Cuba
with our slaves and there see justice done. Cinquez—   170
or let us say 'the Prince'—Cinquez shall die."

The deep immortal human wish,
the timeless will:

Cinquez its deathless primaveral image,
life that transfigures many lives.   175

Voyage through death
                    to life upon these shores.

                                                        1962

Homage to the Empress of the Blues[1]

Because there was a man somewhere in a candystripe silk shirt,
gracile and dangerous as a jaguar and because a woman moaned for him
in sixty-watt gloom and mourned him Faithless Love
Twotiming Love Oh Love Oh Careless Aggravating Love,

> She came out on the stage in yards of pearls, emerging like   5
> a favorite scenic view, flashed her golden smile and sang.

Because grey laths began somewhere to show from underneath
torn hurdygurdy[2] lithographs of dollfaced heaven;
and because there were those who feared alarming fists of snow
on the door and those who feared the riot-squad of statistics,   10

> She came out on the stage in ostrich feathers, beaded satin,
> and shone that smile on us and sang.

                                                        1962

---

1. The case reached the Supreme Court in 1841;
the Africans were defended by former president
John Quincy Adams, and the court released the
thirty-seven survivors to return to Africa.
1. Bessie Smith (1895–1937), one of the greatest
American blues singers. Her flamboyant style,
which grew out of the black vaudeville tradition,
made her popular in the 1920s.
2. A disreputable kind of dance hall. "Laths": the
strips of wood that form a backing for plaster.

Those Winter Sundays

Sundays too my father got up early
and put his clothes on in the blueblack cold,
then with cracked hands that ached
from labor in the weekday weather made
banked fires blaze. No one ever thanked him.   5

I'd wake and hear the cold splintering, breaking.
When the rooms were warm, he'd call,
and slowly I would rise and dress,
fearing the chronic angers of that house,

Speaking indifferently to him,   10
who had driven out the cold
and polished my good shoes as well.
What did I know, what did I know
of love's austere and lonely offices?

1962

RANDALL JARRELL
1914–1965

"Monstrously knowing and monstrously innocent. . . . A Wordsworth with the obsession of a Lewis Carroll"—so Robert Lowell once described his friend and fellow poet Randall Jarrell. Jarrell was a teacher and a critic as well as a poet, and for many writers of his generation—Lowell, Delmore Schwartz, and John Berryman among them—he was the critic whose taste was most unerring, who seemed to know instantly what was genuine and what was not. An extraordinary teacher, he loved the activity, both in and out of the classroom; "the gods who had taken away the poet's audience had given him students," he once said. The novelist Peter Taylor recalls that when he came to Vanderbilt University as a freshman in the mid1930s, Jarrell, then a graduate student, had already turned the literary students into disciples; he held court discussing Chekhov on the sidelines of touch football games. For all his brilliance Jarrell was, at heart, democratic. Believing that poetry belongs to every life, his teaching, his literary criticism, and his poetry aimed to recapture and reeducate a general audience lost to poetry in an age of specialization. Jarrell's interests were democratic as well; his lifelong fascination with popular culture may have originated in a childhood spent in Long Beach, California, and a year spent with grandparents in Hollywood. Witty and incisive, Jarrell could be intimidating; at the same time he remained deeply in touch with childhood's mystery and enchantment. It was as if, his close friend the philosopher Hannah Arendt once said, he "had emerged from the enchanted forests." He loved fairy tales, translated a number of them, and wrote several books for children, among them *The Bat-Poet*. The childlike quality of the person informs Jarrell's poems as well; he is unembarrassed by the adult heart still in thrall to childhood's wishes.

Jarrell was born in Nashville, Tennessee, but spent much of his childhood in California. When his parents divorced, he, then eleven, remained for a year with his grandparents, then returned to live with his mother in Nashville. He majored in psychology at Vanderbilt and stayed on there to do graduate work in English. In 1937 he left Nashville to teach at Kenyon College (Gambier, Ohio) at the invitation of his old Vanderbilt professor John Crowe Ransom, the New Critic and Fugitive poet. From that time on Jarrell almost always had some connection with a university: after Kenyon, the University of Texas, Sarah Lawrence College, and from 1947 until his death, the Women's College of the University of North Carolina at Greensboro. But, as his novel *Pictures from an Institution* (1954) with its mixed satiric and tender views of academic life suggests, he was never satisfied with a cloistered education. As poetry editor of *The Nation* (1946), and then in a series of essays and reviews collected as *Poetry and the Age* (1953), he introduced readers to the work of his contemporaries— Elizabeth Bishop, Robert Lowell, John Berryman, the William Carlos Williams of *Paterson*—and influentially reassessed the reputations of Whitman and Robert Frost.

Among the poets who emerged after World War II, Jarrell stands out for his colloquial plainness. While others—Richard Wilbur and the early Robert Lowell, for example—were writing highly structured poems with complicated imagery, Jarrell's work feels and sounds close to what he calls in one poem the "dailiness of life" ("Well Water"). He is master of the everyday heartbreak and identifies with ordinary forms of loneliness. Jarrell's gift of imaginative sympathy appears in the treatment of soldiers in his war poems, the strongest to come out of World War II. He had been trained as an army air force pilot and after that as a control operator, and he had a sense of the war's special casualties. With their understanding of soldiers as both destructive and innocent at the same time, these poems make his volumes *Little Friend, Little Friend* (1945) and *Losses* (1948) powerful and moving. Jarrell also empathized with the dreams, loneliness, and disappointments of women, whose perspective he often adopted, as in the title poem of his collection *The Woman at the Washington Zoo* (1960) and his poem "Next Day."

Against the blasted or unrealized possibilities of adult life Jarrell often poised the rich mysteries of childhood. The title poem of his last book, *The Lost World* (1965), looks back to his Los Angeles playtime, the movie sets and plaster dinosaurs and pterodactyls against whose eternal gay presence he measures his own aging. The poem has Jarrell's characteristic sense of loss but also his capacity for a mysterious happiness, which animates the poem even as he holds "nothing" in his hands.

Jarrell suffered a nervous breakdown in February 1965, but returned to teaching that fall. In October he was struck down by a car and died. His *Complete Poems* were published posthumously (1969), as were a translation of Goethe's *Faust*, Part I, in preparation at his death, and two books of essays, *The Third Book of Criticism* (1969) and *Kipling, Auden & Co.* (1980).

The Death of the Ball Turret Gunner[1]

From my mother's sleep I fell into the State,
And I hunched in its belly till my wet fur froze.
Six miles from earth, loosed from its dream of life,
I woke to black flak[2] and the nightmare fighters.
When I died they washed me out of the turret with a hose.   5

1945

---

1. A ball turret was a plexiglass sphere set into the belly of a B-17 or B-24 [bomber], and inhabited by two .50 caliber machine-guns and one man, a short, small man. When this gunner tracked with his machine-guns a fighter attacking his bomber from below, he revolved with the turret; hunched upside-down in his little sphere, he looked like the foetus in the womb. The fighters which attacked him were armed with cannon firing explosive shells. The hose was a steam hose [Jarrell's note].
2. Antiaircraft fire.

Second Air Force

Far off, above the plain the summer dries,
The great loops of the hangars sway like hills.
Buses and weariness and loss, the nodding soldiers
Are wire, the bare frame building, and a pass
To what was hers; her head hides his square patch   5
And she thinks heavily: My son is grown.
She sees a world: sand roads, tar-paper barracks,
The bubbling asphalt of the runways, sage,
The dunes rising to the interminable ranges,
The dim flights moving over clouds like clouds.   10
The armorers in their patched faded green,
Sweat-stiffened, banded with brass cartridges,
Walk to the line; their Fortresses,[1] all tail,
Stand wrong and flimsy on their skinny legs,
And the crews climb to them clumsily as bears.   15
The head withdraws into its hatch (a boy's),
The engines rise to their blind laboring roar,
And the green, made beasts run home to air.
Now in each aspect death is pure.
(At twilight they wink over men like stars   20
And hour by hour, through the night, some see
The great lights floating in—from Mars, from Mars.)
How emptily the watchers see them gone.

They go, there is silence; the woman and her son
Stand in the forest of the shadows, and the light   25
Washes them like water. In the long-sunken city
Of evening, the sunlight stills like sleep
The faint wonder of the drowned; in the evening,
In the last dreaming light, so fresh, so old,
The soldiers pass like beasts, unquestioning,   30
And the watcher for an instant understands
What there is then no need to understand;
But she wakes from her knowledge, and her stare,
A shadow now, moves emptily among
The shadows learning in their shadowy fields   35
The empty missions.
            Remembering,
She hears the bomber calling, *Little Friend!*[2]
To the fighter hanging in the hostile sky,
And sees the ragged flame eat, rib by rib,
Along the metal of the wing into her heart: 40
The lives stream out, blossom, and float steadily
To the flames of the earth, the flames
That burn like stars above the lands of men.

1. Flying Fortresses, a type of bomber in World War II.
2. In "Second Air Force" the woman visiting her son remembers what she has read on the front page of her newspaper the week before, a conversation between a bomber, in flames over Germany, and one of the fighters protecting it: "Then I heard the bomber call me in: 'Little Friend, Little Friend, I got two engines on fire. Can you see me, Little Friend?' I said, 'I'm crossing right over you. Let's go home' " [Jarrell's note].

She saves from the twilight that takes everything 45
A squadron shipping, in its last parade—
Its dogs run by it, barking at the band—
A gunner walking to his barracks, half-asleep,
Starting at something, stumbling (above, invisible,
The crews in the steady winter of the sky 50
Tremble in their wired fur); and feels for them
The love of life for life. The hopeful cells
Heavy with someone else's death, cold carriers
Of someone else's victory, grope past their lives
Into her own bewilderment: The years meant *this?* 55

But for them the bombers answer everything.

1945

Thinking of the Lost World

This spoonful of chocolate tapioca
Tastes like—like peanut butter, like the vanilla
Extract Mama told me not to drink.
Swallowing the spoonful, I have already traveled
Through time to my childhood. It puzzles me 5
That age is like it.
           Come back to that calm country
Through which the stream of my life first meandered,
My wife, our cat, and I sit here and see
Squirrels quarreling in the feeder, a mockingbird 10
Copying our chipmunk, as our end copies
Its beginning.
         Back in Los Angeles, we missed
Los Angeles. The sunshine of the Land
Of Sunshine is a gray mist now, the atmosphere 15
Of some factory planet: when you stand and look
You see a block or two, and your eyes water.
The orange groves are all cut down . . . My bow
Is lost, all my arrows are lost or broken,
My knife is sunk in the eucalyptus tree 20
Too far for even Pop to get it out,
And the tree's sawed down. It and the stair-sticks
And the planks of the tree house are all firewood
Burned long ago; its gray smoke smells of Vicks.[1]

Twenty Years After, thirty-five years after, 25
Is as good as ever—better than ever,
Now that D'Artagnan[2] is no longer old—
Except that it is unbelievable.
I say to my old self: "I believe. Help thou
Mine unbelief." 30

1. A remedy for colds.
2. Hero of *The Three Musketeers* (1844), by
Alexandre Dumas *père*; its sequel was *Twenty Years After* (1845).

I believe the dinosaur
Or pterodactyl's married the pink sphinx
And lives with those Indians in the undiscovered
Country between California and Arizona
That the mad girl told me she was princess of—   35
Looking at me with the eyes of a lion,
Big, golden, without human understanding,
As she threw paper-wads from the back seat
Of the car in which I drove her with her mother
From the jail in Waycross to the hospital   40
In Daytona. If I took my eyes from the road
And looked back into her eyes, the car would—I'd be—

Or if only I could find a crystal set³
Sometimes, surely, I could still hear their chief
Reading to them from Dumas or *Amazing Stories*;   45
If I could find in some Museum of Cars
Mama's dark blue Buick, Lucky's electric,
Couldn't I be driven there? Hold out to them,
The paraffin half picked out, Tawny's dewclaw—
And have walk to me from among their wigwams   50
My tall brown aunt, to whisper to me: "Dead?
They told you I was dead?"
                        As if you could die!
If I never saw you, never again
Wrote to you, even, after a few years,   55
How often you've visited me, having put on,
As a mermaid puts on her sealskin, another face
And voice, that don't fool me for a minute—
That are yours for good . . . All of them are gone
Except for me; and for me nothing is gone—   60
The chicken's body is still going round
And round in widening circles, a satellite
From which, as the sun sets, the scientist bends
A look of evil on the unsuspecting earth.
Mama and Pop and Dandeen are still there   65
In the Gay Twenties.
                    The Gay Twenties! You say
The Gay Nineties . . . But it's all right: they *were* gay,
O so gay! A certain number of years after,
Any time is Gay, to the new ones who ask: 70
"Was that the first World War or the second?"
Moving between the first world and the second,
I hear a boy call, now that my beard's gray:
"Santa Claus! Hi, Santa Claus!" It *is* miraculous
To have the children call you Santa Claus.   75
I wave back. When my hand drops to the wheel,
It is brown and spotted, and its nails are ridged
Like Mama's. Where's my own hand? My smooth
White bitten-fingernailed one? I seem to see
A shape in tennis shoes and khaki riding-pants   80

3. Old-fashioned radio receiver.

Standing there empty-handed; I reach out to it
Empty-handed, my hand comes back empty,
And yet my emptiness is traded for its emptiness,
I have found that Lost World in the Lost and Found
Columns whose gray illegible advertisements   85
My soul has memorized world after world:
LOST—NOTHING. STRAYED FROM NOWHERE. NO REWARD.
I hold in my own hands, in happiness,
Nothing: the nothing for which there's no reward.

                                                              1965

RALPH ELLISON
1914–1994

"If the Negro, or any other writer, is going to do what's expected of him, he's lost the battle before he takes the field." This remark of Ralph Ellison's, taken from his *Paris Review* interview of 1953, serves in more than one sense as an appropriate motto for his own career. He did not do what his critics, literary or political, suggested that he ought to, but insisted on being a writer rather than a spokesman for a cause or a representative figure. His importance to American letters is partly due to this independence. He also did the unexpected, however, in not following his fine first novel with the others that were predicted. While maintaining a strong presence on the literary scene by writing essays on a wide variety of social and cultural issues, Ellison published only excerpts from his work in progress: a massive novel that may well have run to three volumes, a single book of which was assembled after his death and published as *Juneteenth* (1999).

Ellison was born in Oklahoma; grew up in Oklahoma City; won a state scholarship; and attended the Tuskegee Institute, where he was a music major, his instrument the trumpet. His musical life was wide enough to embrace both "serious music" and the world of Southwest–Kansas City jazz just reaching its heyday when Ellison was a young man. He became friends with the blues singer Jimmy Rushing and was acquainted with other members of what would be the great Count Basie band of the 1930s; this "deep, rowdy stream of jazz" figured for him as an image of the power and control that constituted art. Although he was a serious student of music and composition, his literary inclinations eventually dominated his musical ones; but testimony to his abiding knowledge and love of music may be found in some of the essays in his collection *Shadow and Act* (1964).

Ellison left Tuskegee and went north to New York City. There, in 1936, he met the novelist Richard Wright, who encouraged him as a writer, and Ellison began to publish reviews and short stories. *Invisible Man*, begun in 1945, was published seven years later and won the National Book Award. Ellison subsequently received a number of awards and lectureships; taught at the Salzburg Seminar, at Bard College, and at the University of Chicago; and in 1970 was named Albert Schweitzer Professor of the Humanities at New York University, where he taught until his retirement. Yet he admitted to being troubled by the terms in which *Invisible Man*'s success—and perhaps his own career as well—were defined. In the *Paris Review* interview he deprecatingly referred to his novel as largely a failure, wished that rather than a "statement" about the American Negro it could be read "simply as a novel," and hoped that in twenty years it would be so read, casually adding, "if it's around that long."

Invisible Man may have outlived Ellison's expectations, but not without suffering attacks from critics. The most powerful of these, Irving Howe, took the author to task for not following Richard Wright's lead and devoting his fiction to the Negro cause. Howe believed that African Americans should write social protest novels about the tragedy of black ghetto life. *Invisible Man* had used its protagonist's "invisibility" to entertain a much broader range of possibilities; and though by no means socially irresponsible, the novel is dedicated to the richness of life and art that becomes possible when the imagination is liberated from close realism.

From Invisible Man

Chapter I

[BATTLE ROYAL]

It goes a long way back, some twenty years. All my life I had been looking for something, and everywhere I turned someone tried to tell me what it was. I accepted their answers too, though they were often in contradiction and even self-contradictory. I was naïve. I was looking for myself and asking everyone except myself questions which I, and only I, could answer. It took me a long time and much painful boomeranging of my expectations to achieve a realization everyone else appears to have been born with: That I am nobody but myself. But first I had to discover that I am an invisible man!

And yet I am no freak of nature, nor of history. I was in the cards, other things having been equal (or unequal) eighty-five years ago. I am not ashamed of my grandparents for having been slaves. I am only ashamed of myself for having at one time been ashamed. About eighty-five years ago they were told that they were free, united with others of our country in everything pertaining to the common good, and, in everything social, separate like the fingers of the hand. And they believed it. They exulted in it. They stayed in their place, worked hard, and brought up my father to do the same. But my grandfather is the one. He was an odd old guy, my grandfather, and I am told I take after him. It was he who caused the trouble. On his deathbed he called my father to him and said, "Son, after I'm gone I want you to keep up the good fight. I never told you, but our life is a war and I have been a traitor all my born days, a spy in the enemy's country ever since I give up my gun back in the Reconstruction. Live with your head in the lion's mouth. I want you to overcome 'em with yeses, undermine 'em with grins, agree 'em to death and destruction, let 'em swoller you till they vomit or bust wide open." They thought the old man had gone out of his mind. He had been the meekest of men. The younger children were rushed from the room, the shades drawn and the flame of the lamp turned so low that it sputtered on the wick like the old man's breathing. "Learn it to the younguns," he whispered fiercely; then he died.

But my folks were more alarmed over his last words than over his dying. It was as though he had not died at all, his words caused so much anxiety. I was warned emphatically to forget what he had said and, indeed, this is the first time it has been mentioned outside the family circle. It had a tremendous effect upon me, however. I could never be sure of what he meant. Grandfather had been a quiet old man who never made any trouble, yet on his deathbed he had called himself a traitor and a spy, and he had spoken of his meekness as a dangerous activity. It became a constant puzzle which lay unanswered in the back of my mind. And whenever things went well for me I remembered my grandfather and felt guilty and uncomfortable. It was as though I was carrying out his advice in spite of myself. And to make it worse, everyone loved me for it. I was praised by the most lily-white men of the town. I was considered an example of desirable conduct—just as my grandfather had been. And what puzzled me was that the old man had defined it as *treachery*. When I was praised for my conduct I felt a guilt that in some way I was doing something that was really against the wishes of the white folks, that if they had understood they would have desired me to act just the opposite, that I should have been sulky and mean, and that that really would have been what they wanted, even though they were fooled and thought they wanted me to act as I did. It made me afraid that some day they would look upon me as a traitor and I would be lost. Still I was more afraid to act any other way because they didn't like that at all. The old man's words were like a curse. On my graduation day I delivered an oration in which I showed that humility was the secret, indeed, the very essence of progress. (Not that I believed this— how could I, remembering my grandfather?—I only believed that it worked.) It was a great success. Everyone praised me and I was invited to give the speech at a gathering of the town's leading white citizens. It was a triumph for our whole community.

It was in the main ballroom of the leading hotel. When I got there I discovered that it was on the occasion of a smoker, and I was told that since I was to be there anyway I might as well take part in the battle royal to be fought by some of my schoolmates as part of the entertainment. The battle royal came first.

All of the town's big shots were there in their tuxedoes, wolfing down the buffet foods, drinking beer and whiskey and smoking black cigars. It was a large room with a high ceiling. Chairs were arranged in neat rows around three sides of a portable boxing ring. The fourth side was clear, revealing a gleaming space of polished floor. I had some misgivings over the battle royal, by the way. Not from a distaste for fighting, but because I didn't care too much for the other fellows who were to take part. They were tough guys who seemed to have no grandfather's curse worrying their minds. No one could mistake their toughness. And besides, I suspected that fighting a battle royal might detract from the dignity of my speech. In those pre-invisible days I visualized myself as a potential Booker T. Washington.[1] But the other fellows didn't care too much for me either, and there were nine of them. I felt superior to them in my way, and I didn't like the manner in which we were all crowded together into the servants' elevator. Nor did they like my being there. In fact, as the warmly lighted floors flashed past the elevator we had words over the fact that I, by taking part in the fight, had knocked one of their friends out of a night's work.

We were led out of the elevator through a rococo hall into an anteroom and told to get into our fighting togs. Each of us was issued a pair of boxing gloves and ushered out into the big mirrored hall, which we entered looking cautiously about us and whispering, lest we might accidentally be heard above the noise of the room. It was foggy with cigar smoke. And already the whiskey was taking effect. I was shocked to see some of the most important men of

---

1. African American author and educator (1856–1915).

the town quite tipsy. They were all there—bankers, lawyers, judges, doctors, fire chiefs, teachers, merchants. Even one of the more fashionable pastors. Something we could not see was going on up front. A clarinet was vibrating sensuously and the men were standing up and moving eagerly forward. We were a small tight group, clustered together, our bare upper bodies touching and shining with anticipatory sweat; while up front the big shots were becoming increasingly excited over something we still could not see. Suddenly I heard the school superintendent, who had told me to come, yell, "Bring up the shines, gentlemen! Bring up the little shines!"

We were rushed up to the front of the ballroom, where it smelled even more strongly of tobacco and whiskey. Then we were pushed into place. I almost wet my pants. A sea of faces, some hostile, some amused, ringed around us, and in the center, facing us, stood a magnificent blonde—stark naked. There was dead silence. I felt a blast of cold air chill me. I tried to back away, but they were behind me and around me. Some of the boys stood with lowered heads, trembling. I felt a wave of irrational guilt and fear. My teeth chattered, my skin turned to goose flesh, my knees knocked. Yet I was strongly attracted and looked in spite of myself. Had the price of looking been blindness, I would have looked. The hair was yellow like that of a circus kewpie doll, the face heavily powdered and rouged, as though to form an abstract mask, the eyes hollow and smeared a cool blue, the color of a baboon's butt. I felt a desire to spit upon her as my eyes brushed slowly over her body. Her breasts were firm and round as the domes of East Indian temples, and I stood so close as to see the fine skin texture and beads of pearly perspiration glistening like dew around the pink and erected buds of her nipples. I wanted at one and the same time to run from the room, to sink through the floor, or go to her and cover her from my eyes and the eyes of the others with my body; to feel the soft thighs, to caress her and destroy her, to love her and murder her, to hide from her, and yet to stroke where below the small American flag tattooed upon her belly her thighs formed a capital V. I had a notion that of all in the room she saw only me with her impersonal eyes.

And then she began to dance, a slow sensuous movement; the smoke of a hundred cigars clinging to her like the thinnest of veils. She seemed like a fair bird-girl girdled in veils calling to me from the angry surface of some gray and threatening sea. I was transported. Then I became aware of the clarinet playing and the big shots yelling at us. Some threatened us if we looked and others if we did not. On my right I saw one boy faint. And now a man grabbed a silver pitcher from a table and stepped close as he dashed ice water upon him and stood him up and forced two of us to support him as his head hung and moans issued from his thick bluish lips. Another boy began to plead to go home. He was the largest of the group, wearing dark red fighting trunks much too small to conceal the erection which projected from him as though in answer to the insinuating low-registered moaning of the clarinet. He tried to hide himself with his boxing gloves.

And all the while the blonde continued dancing, smiling faintly at the big shots who watched her with fascination, and faintly smiling at our fear. I noticed a certain merchant who followed her hungrily, his lips loose and drooling. He was a large man who wore diamond studs in a shirtfront which swelled with the ample paunch underneath, and each time the blonde swayed her undulating hips he ran his hand through the thin hair of his bald head and, with his arms upheld, his posture clumsy like that of an intoxicated panda, wound his belly in a slow and obscene grind. This creature was completely hypnotized. The music had quickened. As the dancer flung herself about with a detached expression on her face, the men began reaching out to touch her. I could see their beefy fingers sink into the soft flesh. Some of the others tried to stop them and she began to move around the floor in graceful circles, as they gave chase, slipping and sliding over the polished floor. It was mad. Chairs went crashing, drinks were spilt, as they ran laughing and howling after her. They caught her just as she reached a door, raised her from the floor, and tossed her as college boys are tossed at a hazing, and above her red, fixed-smiling lips I saw the terror and disgust in her eyes, almost like my own terror and that which I saw in some of the other boys. As I watched, they tossed her twice and her soft breasts seem to flatten against the air and her legs flung wildly as she spun. Some of the more sober ones helped her to escape. And I started off the floor, heading for the anteroom with the rest of the boys.

Some were still crying and in hysteria. But as we tried to leave we were stopped and ordered to get into the ring. There was nothing to do but what we were told. All ten of us climbed under the ropes and allowed ourselves to be blindfolded with broad bands of white cloth. One of the men seemed to feel a bit sympathetic and tried to cheer us up as we stood with our backs against the ropes. Some of us tried to grin. "See that boy over there?" one of the men said. "I want you to run across at the bell and give it to him right in the belly. If you don't get him, I'm going to get you. I don't like his looks." Each of us was told the same. The blindfolds were put on. Yet even then I had been going over my speech. In my mind each word was as bright as flame. I felt the cloth pressed into place, and frowned so that it would be loosened when I relaxed.

But now I felt a sudden fit of blind terror. I was unused to darkness. It was as though I had suddenly found myself in a dark room filled with poisonous cottonmouths. I could hear the bleary voices yelling insistently for the battle royal to begin.

"Get going in there!"

"Let me at that big nigger!"

I strained to pick up the school superintendent's voice, as though to squeeze some security out of that slightly more familiar sound.

"Let me at those black sonsabitches!" someone yelled.

"No, Jackson, no!" another voice yelled. "Here, somebody, help me hold Jack."

"I want to get at that ginger-colored nigger. Tear him limb from limb," the first voice yelled.

I stood against the ropes trembling. For in those days I was what they called ginger-colored, and he sounded as though he might crunch me between his teeth like a crisp ginger cookie.

Quite a struggle was going on. Chairs were being kicked about and I could hear voices grunting as with a terrific effort. I wanted to see, to see more desperately than ever before. But the blindfold was tight as a thick skin-puckering scab and when I raised my gloved hands to push the layers of white aside a voice yelled, "Oh, no you don't, black bastard! Leave that alone!"

"Ring the bell before Jackson kills him a coon!" someone boomed in the sudden silence. And I heard the bell clang and the sound of the feet scuffling forward.

A glove smacked against my head. I pivoted, striking out stiffly as someone went past, and felt the jar ripple along the length of my arm to my shoulder. Then it seemed as though all nine of the boys had turned upon me at once. Blows pounded me from all sides while I struck out as best I could. So many blows landed upon me that I wondered if I were not the only blindfolded fighter in the ring, or if the man called Jackson hadn't succeeded in getting me after all.

Blindfolded, I could no longer control my motions. I had no dignity. I stumbled about like a baby or a drunken man. The smoke had become thicker and with each new blow it seemed to sear and further restrict my lungs. My saliva became like hot bitter glue. A glove connected with my head, filling my mouth with warm blood. It was everywhere. I could not tell if the moisture I felt upon my body was sweat or blood. A blow landed hard against the nape of my neck. I felt myself going over, my head hitting the floor. Streaks of blue light filled the black world behind the blindfold. I lay prone, pretending that I was knocked out, but felt myself seized by hands and yanked to my feet. "Get going, black boy! Mix it up!" My arms were like lead, my head smarting from blows. I managed to feel my way to the ropes and held on, trying to catch my breath. A glove landed in my mid-section and I went over again, feeling as though the smoke had become a knife jabbed into my guts. Pushed this way and that by the legs milling around me, I finally pulled erect and discovered that I could see the black, sweat-washed forms weaving in the smoky-blue atmosphere like drunken dancers weaving to the rapid drum-like thuds of blows.

Everyone fought hysterically. It was complete anarchy. Everybody fought everybody else. No group fought together for long. Two, three, four, fought one, then turned to fight each other, were themselves attacked. Blows landed below the belt and in the kidney, with the gloves open as well as closed, and with my eye partly opened now there was not so much terror. I moved carefully, avoiding blows, although not too many to attract attention, fighting from group to group. The boys groped about like blind, cautious crabs crouching to protect their mid-sections, their heads pulled in short against their shoulders, their arms stretched nervously before them, with their fists testing the smoke-filled air like the knobbed feelers of hypersensitive snails. In one corner I glimpsed a boy violently punching the air and heard him scream in pain as he smashed his hand against a ring post. For a second I saw him bent over holding his hand, then going down as a blow caught his unprotected head. I played one group against the other, slipping in and throwing a punch then stepping out of range while pushing the others into the melee to take the blows blindly aimed at me. The smoke was agonizing and there were no rounds, no bells at three minute intervals to relieve our exhaustion. The room spun around me, a swirl of lights, smoke, sweating bodies surrounded by tense white faces. I bled from both nose and mouth, the blood spattering upon my chest.

The men kept yelling, "Slug him, black boy! Knock his guts out!"

"Uppercut him! Kill him! Kill that big boy!"

Taking a fake fall, I saw a boy going down heavily beside me as though we were felled by a single blow, saw a sneaker-clad foot shoot into his groin as the two who had knocked him down stumbled upon him. I rolled out of range, feeling a twinge of nausea.

The harder we fought the more threatening the men became. And yet, I had begun to worry about my speech again. How would it go? Would they recognize my ability? What would they give me?

I was fighting automatically when suddenly I noticed that one after another of the boys was leaving the ring. I was surprised, filled with panic, as though I had been left alone with an unknown danger. Then I understood. The boys had arranged it among themselves. It was the custom for the two men left in the ring to slug it out for the winner's prize. I discovered this too late. When the bell sounded two men in tuxedoes leaped into the ring and removed the blindfold. I found myself facing Tatlock, the biggest of the gang. I felt sick at my stomach. Hardly had the bell stopped ringing in my ears than it clanged again and I saw him moving swiftly toward me. Thinking of nothing else to do I hit him smash on the nose. He kept coming, bringing the rank sharp violence of stale sweat. His face was a black blank of a face, only his eyes alive— with hate of me and aglow with a feverish terror from what had happened to us all. I became anxious. I wanted to deliver my speech and he came at me as though he meant to beat it out of me. I smashed him again and again, taking his blows as they came. Then on a sudden impulse I struck him lightly and as we clinched, I whispered, "Fake like I knocked you out, you can have the prize."

"I'll break your behind," he whispered hoarsely.

"For *them*?"

"For *me*, sonofabitch!"

They were yelling for us to break it up and Tatlock spun me half around with a blow, and as a joggled camera sweeps in a reeling scene, I saw the howling red faces crouching tense beneath the cloud of blue-gray smoke. For a moment the world wavered, unraveled, flowed, then my head cleared and Tatlock bounced before me. That fluttering shadow before my eyes was his jabbing left hand. Then falling forward, my head against his damp shoulder, I whispered,

"I'll make it five dollars more."

"Go to hell!"

But his muscles relaxed a trifle beneath my pressure and I breathed, "Seven?"

"Give it to your ma," he said, ripping me beneath the heart.

And while I still held him I butted him and moved away. I felt myself bombarded with punches. I fought back with hopeless desperation. I wanted to deliver my speech more than anything else in the world, because I felt that only these men could judge truly my ability, and now this stupid clown was ruining my chances. I began fighting carefully now, moving in to punch him and out again with my greater speed. A lucky blow to his chin and I had him going too—until I heard a loud voice yell, "I got my money on the big boy."

Hearing this, I almost dropped my guard. I was confused: Should I try to win against the voice out there? Would not this go against my speech, and was not this a moment for humility, for nonresistance? A blow to my head as I danced about sent my right eye popping like a jack-in-the-box and settled my dilemma. The room went red as I fell. It was a dream fall, my body languid and fastidious as to where to land, until the floor became impatient and smashed up to meet me. A moment later I came to. An hypnotic voice said FIVE emphatically. And I lay there, hazily watching a dark red spot of my own blood shaping itself into a butterfly, glistening and soaking into the soiled gray world of the canvas.

When the voice drawled TEN I was lifted up and dragged to a chair. I sat dazed. My eye pained and swelled with each throb of my pounding heart and I wondered if now I would be allowed to speak. I was wringing wet, my mouth still bleeding. We were grouped along the wall now. The other boys ignored me as they congratulated Tatlock and speculated as to how much they would be paid. One boy whimpered over his smashed hand. Looking up front, I saw attendants in white jackets rolling the portable ring away and placing a small square rug in the vacant space surrounded by chairs. Perhaps, I thought, I will stand on the rug to deliver my speech.

Then the M.C. called to us, "Come on up here boys and get your money."

We ran forward to where the men laughed and talked in their chairs, waiting. Everyone seemed friendly now.

"There it is on the rug," the man said. I saw the rug covered with coins of all dimensions and a few crumpled bills. But what excited me, scattered here and there, were the gold pieces.

"Boys, it's all yours," the man said. "You get all you grab."

"That's right, Sambo," a blond man said, winking at me confidentially.

I trembled with excitement, forgetting my pain. I would get the gold and the bills, I thought. I would use both hands. I would throw my body against the boys nearest me to block them from the gold.

"Get down around the rug now," the man commanded, "and don't anyone touch it until I give the signal."

"This ought to be good," I heard.

As told, we got around the square rug on our knees. Slowly the man raised his freckled hand as we followed it upward with our eyes.

I heard, "These niggers look like they're about to pray!"

Then, "Ready," the man said. "Go!"

I lunged for a yellow coin lying on the blue design of the carpet, touching it and sending a surprised shriek to join those rising around me. I tried frantically to remove my hand but could not let go. A hot, violent force tore through my body, shaking me like a wet rat. The rug was electrified. The hair bristled up on my head as I shook myself free. My muscles jumped, my nerves jangled, writhed. But I saw that this was not stopping the other boys. Laughing in fear and embarrassment, some were holding back and scooping up the coins knocked off by the painful contortions of the others. The men roared above us as we struggled.

"Pick it up, goddamnit, pick it up!" someone called like a bass-voiced parrot. "Go on, get it!"

I crawled rapidly around the floor, picking up the coins, trying to avoid the coppers and to get greenbacks and the gold. Ignoring the shock by laughing, as I brushed the coins off quickly, I discovered that I could contain the electricity—a contradiction, but it works. Then the men began to push us onto the rug. Laughing embarrassedly, we struggled out of their hands and kept after the coins. We were all wet and slippery and hard to hold. Suddenly I saw a boy lifted into the air, glistening with sweat like a circus seal, and dropped, his wet back landing flush upon the charged rug, heard him yell and saw him literally dance upon his back, his elbows beating a frenzied tattoo upon the floor, his muscles twitching like the flesh of a horse stung by many flies. When he finally rolled off, his face was gray and no one stopped him when he ran from the floor amid booming laughter.

"Get the money," the M.C. called. "That's good hard American cash!"

And we snatched and grabbed, snatched and grabbed. I was careful not to come too close to the rug now, and when I felt the hot whiskey breath descend upon me like a cloud of foul air I reached out and grabbed the leg of a chair. It was occupied and I held on desperately.

"Leggo, nigger! Leggo!"

The huge face wavered down to mine as he tried to push me free. But my body was slippery and he was too drunk. It was Mr. Colcord, who owned a chain of movie houses and "entertainment palaces." Each time he grabbed me I slipped out of his hands. It became a real struggle. I feared the rug more than I did the drunk, so I held on, surprising myself for a moment by trying to topple *him* upon the rug. It was such an enormous idea that I found myself actually carrying it out. I tried not to be obvious, yet when I grabbed his leg, trying to tumble him out of the chair, he raised up roaring with laughter, and, looking at me with soberness dead in the eye, kicked me viciously in the chest. The chair leg flew out of my hand and I felt myself going and rolled. It was as though I had rolled through a bed of hot coals. It seemed a whole century would pass before I would roll free, a century in which I was seared through the deepest levels of my body to the fearful breath within me and the breath seared and heated to the point of explosion. It'll all be over in a flash, I thought as I rolled clear. It'll all be over in a flash.

But not yet, the men on the other side were waiting, red faces swollen as though from apoplexy as they bent forward in their chairs. Seeing their fingers coming toward me I rolled away as a fumbled football rolls off the receiver's fingertips, back into the coals. That time I luckily sent the rug sliding out of place and heard the coins ringing against the floor and the boys scuffling to pick them up and the M.C. calling, "All right, boys, that's all. Go get dressed and get your money."

I was limp as a dish rag. My back felt as though it had been beaten with wires.

When we had dressed the M.C. came in and gave us each five dollars, except Tatlock, who got ten for being last in the ring. Then he told us to leave. I was not to get a chance to deliver my speech, I thought. I was going out into the dim alley in despair when I was stopped and told to go back. I returned to the ballroom, where the men were pushing back their chairs and gathering in groups to talk.

The M.C. knocked on a table for quiet. "Gentlemen," he said, "we almost forgot an important part of the program. A most serious part, gentlemen. This boy was brought here to deliver a speech which he made at his graduation yesterday . . ."

"Bravo!"

"I'm told that he is the smartest boy we've got out there in Greenwood. I'm told that he knows more big words than a pocket-sized dictionary."

Much applause and laughter.

"So now, gentlemen, I want you to give him your attention."

There was still laughter as I faced them, my mouth dry, my eye throbbing.

I began slowly, but evidently my throat was tense, because they began shouting, "Louder! Louder!"

"We of the younger generation extol the wisdom of that great leader and educator," I shouted, "who first spoke these flaming words of wisdom: 'A ship lost at sea for many days suddenly sighted a friendly vessel. From the mast of the unfortunate vessel was seen a signal: "Water, water; we die of thirst!" The answer from the friendly vessel came back: "Cast down your bucket where you are." The captain of the distressed vessel, at last heeding the injunction, cast down his bucket, and it came up full of fresh sparkling water from the mouth of the Amazon River.' And like him I say, and in his words, 'To those of my race who depend upon bettering their condition in a foreign land, or who underestimate the importance of cultivating friendly relations with the Southern white man, who is his next-door neighbor, I would say: "Cast down your bucket where you are"—cast it down in making friends in every manly way of the people of all races by whom we are surrounded . . .' "

I spoke automatically and with such fervor that I did not realize that the men were still talking and laughing until my dry mouth, filling up with blood from the cut, almost strangled me. I coughed, wanting to stop and go to one of the tall brass, sand-filled spittoons to relieve myself, but a few of the men, especially the superintendent, were listening and I was afraid. So I gulped it down, blood, saliva and all, and continued. (What powers of endurance I had during those days! What enthusiasm! What a belief in the rightness of things!) I spoke even louder in spite of the pain. But still they talked and still they laughed, as though deaf with cotton in dirty ears. So I spoke with greater emotional emphasis. I closed my ears and swallowed blood until I was nauseated. The speech seemed a hundred times as long as before, but I could not leave out a single word. All had to be said, each memorized nuance considered, rendered. Nor was that all. Whenever I uttered a word of three or more syllables a group of voices would yell for me to repeat it. I used the phrase "social responsibility," and they yelled:

"What's that word you say, boy?"

"Social responsibility," I said.

"What?"

"Social . . ."

"Louder."

". . . responsibility."

"More!"

"Respon—"

"Repeat!"

"—sibility."

The room filled with the uproar of laughter until, no doubt, distracted by having to gulp down my blood, I made a mistake and yelled a phrase I had often seen denounced in newspaper editorials, heard debated in private.

"Social . . ."

"What?" they yelled.

". . . equality—"

The laughter hung smokelike in the sudden stillness. I opened my eyes, puzzled. Sounds of displeasure filled the room. The M.C. rushed forward. They shouted hostile phrases at me. But I did not understand.

A small dry mustached man in the front row blared out, "Say that slowly, son!"

"What, sir?"

"What you just said!"

"Social responsibility, sir," I said.

"You weren't being smart, were you, boy?" he said, not unkindly.

"No, sir!"

"You sure that about 'equality' was a mistake?"

"Oh, yes, sir," I said. "I was swallowing blood."

"Well, you had better speak more slowly so we can understand. We mean to do right by you, but you've got to know your place at all times. All right, now, go on with your speech."

I was afraid. I wanted to leave but I wanted also to speak and I was afraid they'd snatch me down.

"Thank you, sir," I said, beginning where I had left off, and having them ignore me as before.

Yet when I finished there was a thunderous applause. I was surprised to see the superintendent come forth with a package wrapped in white tissue paper, and, gesturing for quiet, address the men.

"Gentlemen, you see that I did not overpraise the boy. He makes a good speech and some day he'll lead his people in the proper paths. And I don't have to tell you that that is important in these days and times. This is a good, smart boy, and so to encourage him in the right direction, in the name of the Board of Education I wish to present him a prize in the form of this . . ."

He paused, removing the tissue paper and revealing a gleaming calfskin brief case.

". . . in the form of this first-class article from Shad Whitmore's shop."

"Boy," he said, addressing me, "take this prize and keep it well. Consider it a badge of office. Prize it. Keep developing as you are and some day it will be filled with important papers that will help shape the destiny of your people."

I was so moved that I could hardly express my thanks. A rope of bloody saliva forming a shape like an undiscovered continent drooled upon the leather and I wiped it quickly away. I felt an importance that I had never dreamed.

"Open it and see what's inside," I was told.

My fingers a-tremble, I complied, smelling the fresh leather and finding an official-looking document inside. It was a scholarship to the state college for Negroes. My eyes filled with tears and I ran awkwardly off the floor.

I was overjoyed; I did not even mind when I discovered that the gold pieces I had scrambled for were brass pocket tokens advertising a certain make of automobile.

When I reached home everyone was excited. Next day the neighbors came to congratulate me. I even felt safe from grandfather, whose deathbed curse usually spoiled my triumphs. I stood beneath his photograph with my brief case in hand and smiled triumphantly into his stolid black peasant's face. It was a face that fascinated me. The eyes seemed to follow everywhere I went.

That night I dreamed I was at a circus with him and that he refused to laugh at the clowns no matter what they did. Then later he told me to open my brief case and read what was inside and I did, finding an official envelope stamped with the state seal; and inside the envelope I found another and another, endlessly, and I thought I would fall of weariness. "Them's years," he said. "Now open that one." And I did and in it I found an engraved document containing a short message in letters of gold. "Read it," my grandfather said. "Out loud!"

"To Whom It May Concern," I intoned. "Keep This Nigger-Boy Running." I awoke with the old man's laughter ringing in my ears.

(It was a dream I was to remember and dream again for many years after. But at that time I had no insight into its meaning. First I had to attend college.)

1952

JOHN BERRYMAN
1914–1972

From a generation whose ideal poem was short, self-contained, and ironic, John Berryman emerged as the author of two extended and passionate works: "Homage to Mistress Bradstreet" and the lyric sequence *The Dream Songs*. It was as if Berryman needed more space than the single lyric provided—a larger theater in which to play out an unrelenting psychic drama. He had written shorter poems—songs and sonnets—but his discovery of large-scale dramatic situations and strange new voices astonished his contemporaries.

Berryman seemed fated to intense suffering and self-preoccupation. His father, a banker, shot himself outside his son's window when the boy was twelve. The suicide haunted Berryman to the end of his own life, which also came by suicide. Berryman, who was born John Smith, took a new name from his stepfather, also a banker. His childhood was a series of displacements: ten years near McAlester, Oklahoma, then Tampa, Florida, and after his father's suicide, Gloucester, Massachusetts, and New York City. His mother's second marriage ended in divorce, but his stepfather sent him to private school in Connecticut. Berryman graduated from Columbia College in 1936 and won a fellowship to Clare College, Cambridge, England.

He was later to say of himself, "I masquerade as a writer. Actually I am a scholar." However misleading this may be about his poetry, it reminds us that all his life Berryman drew nourishment from teaching—at Wayne State, at Harvard (1940–43), then off and on at Princeton, and from 1955 until his death, at the University of Minnesota. He chose to teach not creative writing but literature and the "history of civilization," and he claimed that such teaching forced him into areas in which he would not otherwise have done detailed work. A mixture of bookishness and wildness characterizes all his writing: five years of research lay behind the intensities of "Homage to Mistress Bradstreet," while an important constituent of "huffy Henry's" personality in *The Dream Songs* is his professorial awkwardness and exhibitionism.

Berryman seemed drawn to borrowing identities in his poetry. In his first important volume, *The Dispossessed* (1948), he had experimented with various dramatic voices in the short poems "Nervous Songs: The Song of the Demented Priest," "A Professor's Song," "The Song of the Tortured Girl," and "The Song of the Man Forsaken and Obsessed." The *dispossession* of the book's title had two opposite and urgent meanings for him: "the miserable, *put out of one's own,* and the relieved, saved, undevilled, despelled." Taking on such roles was for Berryman both a revelation of his cast-out, fatherless state and an exorcism of it. It was perhaps in that spirit that he entered into an imaginary dialogue with what he felt as the kindred nature of the Puritan poet Anne Bradstreet. "Both of our worlds unhanded us." What started out to be a poem of fifty lines emerged as the fifty-seven stanzas of "Homage to Mistress Bradstreet" (1956), a work so absorbing that after completing it Berryman claimed to be "a ruin for two years." It was not Bradstreet's poetry that engaged him. Quite the contrary: he was fascinated by the contrast between her "bald abstract rime" and her life of passionate suffering. The poem explores the kinship between Bradstreet and Berryman as figures of turbulence and rebellion.

Berryman took literary encouragement from another American poet of the past, Stephen Crane, about whom he wrote a book-length critical study in 1950. Crane's poems, he said, have "the character of a 'dream,' something seen naively in a new relation." Berryman's attraction to a poetry that accommodated the nightmare antics of the dream world became apparent in his own long work, *The Dream Songs*. It was modeled, he claimed, on "the greatest American poem," Whitman's "Song of Myself," in which the speaker assumes a fluid, ever-changing persona. *77 Dream Songs* was published in 1964. Additional poems, to a total of 385, appeared in *His Toy, His Dream, His Rest* (1968). (Some uncollected dream songs were published posthumously in *Henry's Fate*, 1977, and drafts of others remained in manuscript.) Obvious links exist between Berryman and other so-called confessional writers such as Robert Lowell, Sylvia Plath, and Anne Sexton. But the special autobiographical flavor of *The Dream Songs* is that of a psychic vaudeville; as in dreams, the poet represents himself through a fluid series of *alter egos,* whose voices often flow into one another in single poems. One of these voices is that of a blackface minstrel, and Berryman's appropriation of this dialect prompted Michael Harper's poem "Tongue-Tied in Black and White," written both as homage to Berryman and as part of Harper's quarrel with the use of "that needful black idiom offending me" ("Tongue-Tied in Black and White"). Despite the suffering that these poems enact, Berryman seemed to find a secret strength through the staginess, variety, resourcefulness, and renewals of these poems.

The Dream Songs brought Berryman a success that was not entirely beneficial. The collection *Love and Fame* (1970) shows him beguiled by his own celebrity and wrestling with some of its temptations. In an unfinished, posthumously published novel, *Recovery,* he portrays himself as increasingly prey to alcoholism. Berryman had been married twice before, and his hospitalization for drinking and for periods of insanity had put a strain on his third marriage. He came to distrust his poetry as a form of exhibitionism and was clearly, in his use of the discipline of prose and in the prayers that crowd his last two volumes of poetry (*Delusions, Etc.* appeared posthumously), in search of some new and humbling style. Having been raised a strict Catholic and fallen away from the church, he tried to return to it in his last years, speaking of his need for a "God of rescue." On January 7, 1972, Berryman committed suicide by leaping from a Minneapolis bridge.

Homage to Mistress Bradstreet

Anne Bradstreet ("Born 1612 Anne Dudley, married at 16 Simon Bradstreet, a Cambridge man, steward to the Countess of Warwick and protege of her father Thomas Dudley secretary to the Earl of Lincoln. Crossed in the *Arbella,* 1630, under Governor Winthrop" [Berryman's note]) came to the Massachusetts Bay Colony when she was eighteen years old. She was one of the first poets on American soil. Of this poem, Berryman says:

> An American historian somewhere observes that all colonial settlements are intensely conservative, *except* in the initial break-off point (whether religious, political, legal, or whatever). Trying to do justice to both parts of this obvious truth—which I came upon only after the poem was finished—I concentrated upon the second and the poem laid itself out in a series of rebellions. I had her

rebel first against the new environment and above all against her barrenness (which in fact lasted for years), then against her marriage (which in fact seems to have been brilliantly happy), and finally against her continuing life of illness, loss, and age. These are the three large sections of the poem; they are preceded and followed by an exordium and coda, of four stanzas each, spoken by the "I" of the twentieth-century poet, which modulates into her voice, who speaks most of the poem. Such is the plan. Each rebellion, of course, is succeeded by submission, although even in the moment of the poem's supreme triumph—the presentment, too long to quote now, of the birth of her first child—rebellion survives.

Berryman wrote two stanzas of the poem and found himself stalled for five years, during which he gathered material, until he discovered the strategy of dialogue and inserted himself in the poem. "Homage to Mistress Bradstreet" was first published in *Partisan Review* in 1953, but did not appear as a book until 1956.

In his exordium (stanzas 1–4), the poet makes an intense identification between himself and Bradstreet, both of them alienated by hardship or circumstance from those around them: "We are on each other's hands / who care. Both of our worlds unhanded us." The identification is so complete that in the subsequent stanzas he hears her voice recounting the tribulations of life in a new country, her yearnings for the England she left behind, her lonely dedication to her poetry, and the personal suffering in her early barrenness and miscarriages. Stanza 17 continues in Bradstreet's voice.

From Homage to Mistress Bradstreet

* * *

17

The winters close, Springs open, no child stirs
under my withering heart, O seasoned heart   130
God grudged his aid.
All things else soil like a shirt.
Simon is much away. My executive[1] stales.
The town came through for the cartway by the pales,[2]
but my patience is short,   135
I revolt from, I am like, these savage foresters

18

whose passionless dicker in the shade, whose glance
impassive & scant, belie their murderous cries
when quarry seems to show.
Again I must have been wrong, twice.[3]   140
Unwell in a new way. Can that begin?
God brandishes. O love, O I love. Kin,
gather. My world is strange
and merciful, ingrown months, blessing a swelling trance.[4]

---

1. Power to act.
2. Stockade fence.
3. One of the several allusions to her failure to become pregnant.
4. Her first child was not born until about 1633 [Berryman's note].

19

So squeezed, wince you I scream? I love you & hate   145
off with you. Ages! *Useless.* Below my waist
he has me in Hell's vise.
Stalling. He let go. Come back: brace
me somewhere. No. No. Yes! everything down
hardens I press with horrible joy down   150
my back cracks like a wrist
shame I am voiding oh behind it is too late

20

hide me forever I work thrust I must free
now I all muscles & bones concentrate
what is living from dying?   155
Simon I must leave you so untidy
Monster you are killing me Be sure
I'll have you later Women do endure
I can *can* no longer
and it passes the wretched trap whelming and I am me   160

21

drencht & powerful, I did it with my body!
One proud tug greens Heaven. Marvellous,
unforbidding Majesty.
Swell, imperious bells. I fly.
Mountainous, woman not breaks and will bend: 165
sways God nearby: anguish comes to an end.
Blossomed Sarah,[5] and I
blossom. Is that thing alive? I hear a famisht howl.

22

Beloved household, I am Simon's wife,
and the mother of Samuel—whom greedy yet I miss   170
out of his kicking place.
More in some ways I feel at a loss,
freer. Cantabanks & mummers,[6] nears
longing for you. Our chopping[7] scores my ears,
our costume bores my eyes.   175
St. George[8] to the good sword, rise! chop-logic's rife

23

& fever & Satan & Satan's ancient fere.[9]
Pioneering is not feeling well,
not Indians, beasts.
Not all their riddling can forestall   180

---

5. Wife of Abraham, barren until old age, when
she gave birth to Isaac (Genesis 17.19).
6. Ballad singers and mimes.
7. *Chopping:* disputing, snapping, haggling; axing

[Berryman's note].
8. Patron saint of England, the slayer of dragons.
9. *Fere:* his friend Death [Berryman's note].

one leaving. Sam, your uncle has had to
go from us to live with God. 'Then Aunt went too?'
Dear, she does wait still.
Stricken: 'Oh. Then he takes us one by one.' My dear.

24

Forswearing it otherwise, they starch their minds.   185
Folkmoots, & blether, blether. John Cotton rakes[1]
to the synod of Cambridge.[2]
Down from my body my legs flow,
out from it arms wave, on it my head shakes.
Now Mistress Hutchinson rings forth a call—   190
should she? many creep out a broken wall—
affirming the Holy Ghost
dwells in one justified. Factioning passion blinds

25

all to all her good, all—can she be exiled?
Bitter sister, victim! I miss you.   195
—I miss you, Anne,[3]
day or night weak as a child,
tender & empty, doomed, quick to no tryst.
—I hear you. Be kind, you who leaguer[4]
my image in the mist.   200
—Be kind you, to one unchained eager far & wild

26

and if, O my love, my heart is breaking, please
neglect my cries and I will spare you. Deep
in Time's grave, Love's, you lie still.
Lie still.—Now? That happy shape   205
my forehead had under my most long, rare,
ravendark, hidden, soft bodiless hair
you award me still.
You must not love me, but   I do not bid you cease.

27

Veiled my eyes, attending. How can it be I?   210
Moist, with parted lips, I listen, wicked.
I shake in the morning & retch.
Brood I do on myself naked.
A fading world I dust, with fingers new.

---

1. "*Rakes:* inclines, as a mast; bows" [Berryman's note]. "Folkmoots": a town assembly for debate. "Blether": nonsense.
2. In the first synod (a body for religious debate), Cotton agreed to the condemnation and banishment of his follower Anne Hutchinson. Her heresies included a deemphasis of perfect moral conduct as evidence of the justification for Christian salvation.
3. One might say: He [the poet] is enabled to speak, at last, in the fortune of an echo of her—and when she is loneliest (her former spiritual adviser [John Cotton] having deserted Anne Hutchinson, and this her [Bradstreet's] closest friend banished), as if she had summoned him; and only thus, perhaps, is she enabled to hear him. This second section of the poem is a dialogue, his voice however ceasing well before it ends at [line] 307, and hers continuing for the whole third part until the coda ([stanzas] 54–57) [Berryman's note].
4. Beleaguer, besiege.

—I have earned the right to be alone with you.   215
—What right can that be?
Convulsing, if you love, enough, like a sweet lie.

28

Not that, I know, you can. This cratered skin,
like the crabs & shells of my Palissy[5] ewer, touch!
Oh, you do, you do?   220
Falls on me what I like a witch,
for lawless holds, annihilations of law
which Time and he and man abhor, foresaw:
sharper than what my Friend[6]
brought me for my revolt when I moved smooth & thin,   225

29

faintings black, rigour, chilling, brown
parching, back, brain burning, the grey pocks
itch, a manic stench
of pustules snapping, pain floods the palm,
sleepless, or a red shaft with a dreadful start   230
rides at the chapel, like a slipping heart.
My soul strains in one qualm
ah but *this* is not to save me but to throw me down.

30

And out of this I lull. It lessens. Kiss me.
That once. As sings out up in sparkling dark   235
a trail of a star & dies,
while the breath flutters, sounding, mark,
so shorn ought such caresses to us be
who, deserving nothing, flush and flee
the darkness of that light,   240
a lurching frozen from a warm dream. Talk to me.

31[7]

—It is Spring's New England. Pussy willows wedge
up in the wet. Milky crestings, fringed
yellow, in heaven, eyed
by the melting hand-in-hand or mere   245
desirers single, heavy-footed, rapt,
make surge poor human hearts. Venus is trapt—
the hefty pike shifts, sheer[8]—
in Orion blazing. Warblings, odours, nudge to an edge—

---

5. Bernard Palissy (1510–1590), French Protestant ceramicist noted for special glazes and highly
ornamented pieces.
6. Alludes to the punishments of God visited on
those who rebel against him (cf. Isaiah 1.6).
7. Berryman (in *Poets on Poetry*) called this speech
of the poet to Bradstreet "an only half-subdued

aria-stanza."
8. Lines 246–47 are opposed images of the bottom of the sea against the summit of the sky, as
imaged by the planet Venus and the constellation
Orion. "Sheer" in the sense of "invisible" (quoted
from comments by Berryman in the Italian translation of "Mistress Bradstreet" by Sergio Perosa).

32

—Ravishing, ha, what crouches outside ought,   250
flamboyant, ill, angelic. Often, now,
I am afraid of you.
I am a sobersides; I know.
I *want* to take you for my lover.—Do.
—I hear a madness. Harmless I to you   255
am not, not I?—No.
—I cannot but be. Sing a concord of our thought.

33

—Wan dolls in indigo on gold:[9] refrain
my western lust. I am drowning in this past.
I lose sight of you   260
who mistress me from air. Unbraced
in delirium of the grand depths,[1] giving away
haunters what kept me, I breathe solid spray.
—I am losing you!
Straiten me on.[2]—I suffered living like a stain: 265

34

I trundle the bodies, on the iron bars,
over that fire backward & forth; they burn;
bits fall. I wonder if
I killed them. Women serve my turn.
—Dreams! You are good.—No.—Dense with hardihood   270
the wicked are dislodged, and lodged the good.
In green space we are safe.
God awaits us (but I am yielding) who Hell wars.

35

—I cannot feel myself God waits. He flies
nearer a kindly world; or he is flown.
One Saturday's rescue[3]   275
won't show. Man is entirely alone
may be. I am a man of griefs & fits
trying to be my friend. And the brown smock splits,
down the pale flesh a gash
broadens and Time holds up your heart against my eyes.   280

36

—Hard and divided heaven! creases me. Shame
is failing. My breath is scented, and I throw

9. Cf., on Byzantine icons [here, the impassive
Madonnas painted against gold backgrounds in
medieval altarpieces of the Eastern Church], Frederick Rolfe ("Baron Corvo"): "Who ever dreams of
praying (with expectation of response) for the
prayer of a Tintoretto or a Titian, or a Bellini, or a
Botticelli? But who can refrain from crying 'O
Mother!' to these unruffleable wan dolls in indigo
on gold?" (quoted from *The Desire and Pursuit of
the Whole* by Graham Greene in *The Last Childhood*) [Berryman's note].
1. "Délires des grandes profoundeurs," described
by [the twentieth-century French marine explorer

Jacques-Yves] Cousteau and others; a euphoria,
sometimes fatal, in which the hallucinated diver
offers passing fish his line, helmet, anything
[Berryman's note; he translates the French phrase
in line 262].
2. I.e., tighten your embrace.
3. As of cliffhangers, movie serials wherein each
week's episode ends with a train bearing down on
the strapped heroine or with the hero dangling over
an abyss into which Indians above him peer with
satisfaction before they hatchet the rope; *rescue:*
forcible recovery (by the owner) of goods distrained
[Berryman's note].

hostile glances towards God.
Crumpling plunge of a pestle, bray:[4]   285
sin cross & opposite, wherein I survive
nightmares of Eden. Reaches foul & live
he for me, this soul
to crunch, a minute tangle of eternal flame.

37

I fear Hell's hammer-wind. But fear does wane.   290
Death's blossoms grain my hair; I cannot live.
A black joy clashes
joy, in twilight. The Devil said
'I will deal toward her softly, and her enchanting cries
will fool the horns of Adam.'[5] Father of lies,   295
a male great pestle smashes
small women swarming towards the mortar's rim in vain.

38

I see the cruel spread Wings black with saints!
Silky my breasts not his, mine, mine to withhold
or tender, tender.   300
I am sifting, nervous, and bold.
The light is changing. Surrender this loveliness
you cannot make me do. *But* I will. Yes.
What horror, down stormy air,
warps towards me? My threatening promise faints   305

39[6]

torture me, Father, lest not I be thine!
Tribunal terrible & pure, my God,
mercy for him and me.
Faces half-fanged, Christ drives abroad,
and though the crop hopes, Jane[7] is so slipshod   310
I cry. Evil dissolves, & love, like foam;
that love. Prattle of children powers me home,
my heart claps like the swan's
under a frenzy of *who* love me & who shine.[8]

*   *   *

1953, 1956

4. Punning (according to Berryman's notes) on (1) the pulverizing action of a mortar and pestle and (2) the strident noise of a donkey.
5. Referring to Satan's temptation of Eve, who was to eat the apple from the Tree of Knowledge and then convince Adam to do so (cf. Genesis 3).
6. The stanza is unsettled, like [stanza] 24, by a middle line, signaling a broad transition [Berryman's note].

7. A servant.
8. The final stanzas present Bradstreet's intensified vision of death and damnation and include the death of her father, blaspheming. But in the last four stanzas the poem modulates back into the poet's voice and his vow to keep Bradstreet alive in his loving memory and in his writing. "Hover, utter, still, a sourcing whom my lost candle like the firefly loves."

FROM THE DREAM SONGS[1]

29

There sat down, once, a thing on Henry's heart
so heavy, if he had a hundred years
& more, & weeping, sleepless, in all them time
Henry could not make good.
Starts again always in Henry's ears   5
the little cough somewhere, an odour, a chime.

And there is another thing he has in mind
like a grave Sienese face[2] a thousand years
would fail to blur the still profiled reproach of. Ghastly,
with open eyes, he attends, blind.   10
All the bells say: too late. This is not for tears;
thinking.

But never did Henry, as he thought he did,
end anyone and hacks her body up
and hide the pieces, where they may be found.   15
He knows: he went over everyone, & nobody's missing.
Often he reckons, in the dawn, them up.
Nobody is ever missing.

45

He stared at ruin. Ruin stared straight back.
He thought they was old friends. He felt on the stair
where her papa found them bare
they became familiar. When the papers were lost
rich with pals' secrets, he thought he had the knack   5
of ruin. Their paths crossed

and once they crossed in jail; they crossed in bed;
and over an unsigned letter their eyes met,
and in an Asian city
directionless & lurchy at two & three,   10
or trembling to a telephone's fresh threat,
and when some wired his head

1. These poems were written over a period of thirteen years. (77 *Dream Songs* was published in
1964, and the remaining poems appeared in *His
Toy, His Dream, His Rest* in 1968. Some uncollected dream songs were included in the volume
Henry's Fate, which appeared five years after Berryman committed suicide in 1972.) Berryman placed
an introductory note at the head of *His Toy, His
Dream, His Rest:* "The poem then, whatever its
wide cast of characters, is essentially about an
imaginary character (not the poet, not me) named

Henry, a white American in early middle age sometimes in blackface, who has suffered an irreversible
loss and talks about himself sometimes in the first
person, sometimes in the third, sometimes even in
the second; he has a friend, never named, who
addresses him as Mr. Bones and variants thereof.
Requiescant in pace."
2. Alluding to the somber, austere mosaiclike religious portraits by the Italian painters who worked
in Siena during the 13th and 14th centuries.

to reach a wrong opinion, 'Epileptic'.
But he noted now that: they were not old friends.
He did not know this one.   15
This one was a stranger, come to make amends
for all the imposters, and to make it stick.
Henry nodded, un-.

385

My daughter's heavier. Light leaves are flying.
Everywhere in enormous numbers turkeys will be dying
and other birds, all their wings.
They never greatly flew. Did they wish to?
I should know. Off away somewhere once I knew   5
such things.

Or good Ralph Hodgson[3] back then did, or does.
The man is dead whom Eliot[4] praised. My praise
follows and flows too late.
Fall is grievy, brisk. Tears behind the eyes   10
almost fall. Fall comes to us as a prize
to rouse us toward our fate.

My house is made of wood and it's made well,
unlike us. My house is older than Henry;
that's fairly old.   15
If there were a middle   ground between things and the soul
or if the sky resembled more the sea,
I wouldn't have to scold

                                            my heavy daughter.

                                                                            1968

3. English poet (1871–1962) who wrote balladlike
lyrics. Berryman may be alluding to Hodgson's
"Hymn to Moloch," in which the poet protests the
slaughter of birds for commercial uses.
4. T. S. Eliot (1888–1965), American poet and
critic.

SAUL BELLOW
1915–2005

Winner of the Nobel Prize for literature in 1976, Saul Bellow distinguished himself
through a writing career that spanned nearly two-thirds of a century. Bellow, the child
of Russian Jewish immigrants, was born in Lachine, Quebec, a suburb of Montreal,
and spent nine years there before moving with his family to Chicago. While relishing
the style of big-city life typical of the 1920s and 1930s, he pursued an increasingly
intellectual track through Tuley High School, the University of Chicago, and Northwestern University. Literature was always Bellow's great love, but as his biographer
James Atlas explains, the antisemitic establishment was unreceptive to his ambitions.

"In search of career advice," Atlas notes, Bellow sought counsel from the chair of Northwestern's English Department, William Frank Bryan, who warned him against postgraduate study in the field, because "no Jew could really grasp the tradition of English literature. . . . No Jew would ever have the right *feeling* for it." Bellow therefore began work toward a master's degree in sociology and anthropology at the University of Wisconsin. Discouraged by the technical work required and chided by his new advisor for being too literary, he dropped out after just one semester, returning to Chicago and a lifelong career in literature that involved teaching (initially at a downtown teachers college, later most prestigiously as a member of the University of Chicago's Committee on Social Thought), editing (first for the *Encyclopaedia Britannica,* then for his own journal, *The Noble Savage*), and writing fiction. Except for brief service in the bureaucracy of the merchant marine during World War II, a Guggenheim Fellowship year in Paris (1948–49), and some time living in New York City and the New England countryside, Bellow made Chicago his primary residence and the setting for his most characteristic work, most famously *The Adventures of Augie March* (1953). In finding a voice for the protagonist of this novel Bellow discovered his own style, a mix of the urban colloquial and the erudite.

Bellow's first novel, *Dangling Man*, was not published until he was nearly thirty. It is a short series of elegantly morose meditations, told through the journal of a young man waiting to be inducted into the army and with the "freedom" of having nothing to do but wait. Eventually he is drafted: "Long live regimentation," he sardonically exults. His second novel, *The Victim* (1947), continues the investigation of ways people strive to be relieved of self-determination. This book concerns a week in the life of Asa Leventhal, alone in New York City while his wife visits a relative, who is suddenly confronted by a figure from the past (Kirby Allbee, a Gentile) who succeeds in implicating Leventhal with the past and its present manifestations. *The Victim* is Bellow's most somberly naturalistic depiction of a man brought up against forces larger than himself, yet from the opening sentence ("On some nights New York is as hot as Bangkok") a poetic dimension appears and helps create the sense of mystery and disturbance felt by both the main character and the reader.

Dangling Man and *The Victim* are highly wrought, mainly humorless books; in two long novels published in the 1950s Bellow opened up into new ranges of aspiration and situational zaniness, which brought him respectful admiration from many critics. *The Adventures of Augie March* and *Henderson the Rain King* (1959) are each narrated by an "I" who, like his predecessor Huck Finn, is good at lighting out for the territory ahead of whoever means to tie him down. The hero's adventures, whether occurring in Chicago, Mexico, or Africa, are exuberantly delivered in an always stimulating and sometimes overactive prose. *Augie* is filled with sights and sounds, colors and surfaces; its tone is self-involved, affectionate, and affirmative; *Henderson*, Bellow's most extravagant narrative, has the even more fabulous air of a quest-romance, in which the hero returns home from Africa at peace with the world he had been warring against.

The ironic motto for Bellow's novels of the 1950s may well be "Seize the Day," as in the title of perhaps his most sharply defined piece of fiction. This short novel (1956) is both painful and exhilarating because it so fully exposes its hero (Tommy Wilhelm, an aging out-of-work ex-actor) to the insults of other people who don't understand him, to a city (New York, particularly its Upper West Side) impervious to his needs, and to a narrative prose that mixes ridicule and affection so thoroughly as to make them scarcely distinguishable. *Seize the Day* combines, within Tommy's monologues, a wildness and pathos of bitter comedy that was a powerful new element in Bellow's work.

In "Where Do We Go from Here? The Future of Fiction," an essay published in 1965, Bellow pointed out that nineteenth-century American literature—Emerson, Thoreau, Whitman, Melville—was highly didactic in its efforts to "instruct a young and raw nation." Bellow sees himself in this instructive tradition and in the international company of "didactic" novelists like Dostoyevsky, D. H. Lawrence, and Joseph

Conrad; he believes also that "the imagination is looking for new ways to express virtue . . . we have barely begun to comprehend what a human being is." These concerns animate the novels Bellow has written in the years since *Henderson*. In *Herzog* (1964) the hero is another down-and-outer, a professor-intellectual, a student of Romanticism and of the glorification of Self, which Herzog believes both modern life and modernist literature have been undercutting. At the same time he is a comic and pathetic victim of marital disorder; like all Bellow's heroes, Herzog has a terrible time with women, yet cannot live without them. In *Mr. Sammler's Planet* (1970), written out of the disorders of the late 1960s, the atmosphere is grimmer. Sammler, an aging Jew living (again) on New York's Upper West Side, analyzes and judges but cannot understand the young or blacks, or the mass of people gathered at Broadway and Ninety-sixth Street. He sees about him everywhere "poverty of soul" but admits that he too has "a touch of the same disease—the disease of the single self explaining what was what and who was who."

These novels, as well as *Humboldt's Gift* (1975), have been accused of parading too single-handedly attitudes toward which their author is sympathetic, whereas *The Dean's December* (1982) was criticized by John Updike, in a review, for being too much "*about* Saul Bellow," even though indirectly. Subsequently, a collection of shorter fiction, *Him with His Foot in His Mouth* (1984); the novels *More Die of Heartbreak* (1987) and *Ravelstein* (2000); three novellas, *The Bellarosa Connection* (1989), *A Theft* (1989), and *The Actual* (1997); and three stories collected as *Something to Remember Me By* (1991) exhibit various talky, informal protagonists and narrators with a lot on their minds. Matters of form and plot in these works seem less important than the ideas and active energy struck off by human beings in turmoil—usually comic turmoil. What Bellow finds moving in Theodore Dreiser's work, "his balkiness and sullenness, and then his allegiance to life," is still found in his own: complaint and weariness, fault-finding, accusation of self and others—these gestures directed at "life" also make up the stuff of life and the "allegiance" out of which Bellow's heroes are made. We read him for this range of interest; for flexibility and diversity of style and idiom; and for the eloquences of nostalgia, invective, and lamentation that make up his intensely imagined world.

Married five times, he ended his academic career with a brief residency at Boston University, afterward retiring to rural Vermont, where he died two months short of his ninetieth birthday and five years after publishing *Ravelstein*, his nineteenth book and a work indicative of the conservative, traditionalist posture of his later career.

From The Adventures of Augie March

Chapter One

I am an American, Chicago born—Chicago, that somber city—and go at things as I have taught myself, free-style, and will make the record in my own way: first to knock, first admitted; sometimes an innocent knock, sometimes a not so innocent. But a man's character is his fate, says Heraclitus,[1] and in the end there isn't any way to disguise the nature of the knocks by acoustical work on the door or gloving the knuckles.

Everybody knows there is no fineness or accuracy of suppression; if you hold down one thing you hold down the adjoining.

My own parents were not much to me, though I cared for my mother. She was simple-minded, and what I learned from her was not what she taught, but

---

1. Early Greek philosopher (fl. ca. 480 B.C.E.) famous for his cryptic aphorisms and for positing the existence of the human soul.

on the order of object lessons. She didn't have much to teach, poor woman. My brothers and I loved her. I speak for them both; for the elder it is safe enough; for the younger one, Georgie, I have to answer—he was born an idiot—but I'm in no need to guess, for he had a song he sang as he ran drag-footed with his stiff idiot's trot, up and down along the curl-wired fence in the backyard:

> Georgie Mahchy, Augie, Simey
> Winnie Mahchy, evwy, evwy love Mama.

He was right about everyone save Winnie, Grandma Lausch's poodle, a pursy old overfed dog. Mama was Winnie's servant, as she was Grandma Lausch's. Loud-breathing and wind-breaking, she lay near the old lady's stool on a cushion embroidered with a Berber[2] aiming a rifle at a lion. She was personally Grandma's, belonged to her suite; the rest of us were the governed, and especially Mama. Mama passed the dog's dish to Grandma, and Winnie received her food at the old lady's feet from the old lady's hands. These hands and feet were small; she wore a shriveled sort of lisle on her legs and her slippers were gray—ah, the gray of that felt, the gray despotic to souls—with pink ribbons. Mama, however, had large feet, and around the house she wore men's shoes, usually without strings, and a dusting or mobcap like somebody's fanciful cotton effigy of the form of the brain. She was meek and long, round-eyed like Georgie—gentle green round eyes and a gentle freshness of color in her long face. Her hands were work-reddened, she had very few of her teeth left—to heed the knocks as they come—and she and Simon wore the same ravelly coat-sweaters. Besides having round eyes, Mama had circular glasses that I went with her to the free dispensary on Harrison Street[3] to get. Coached by Grandma Lausch, I went to do the lying. Now I know it wasn't so necessary to lie, but then everyone thought so, and Grandma Lausch especially, who was one of those Machiavellis of small street and neighborhood that my young years were full of. So Grandma, who had it all ready before we left the house and must have put in hours plotting it out in thought and phrase, lying small in her chilly small room under the featherbed, gave it to me at breakfast. The idea was that Mama wasn't keen enough to do it right. That maybe one didn't need to be keen didn't occur to us; it was a contest. The dispensary would want to know why the Charities didn't pay for the glasses. So you must say nothing about the Charities, but that sometimes money from my father came and sometimes it didn't, and that Mama took boarders. This was, in a delicate and choosy way, by ignoring and omitting certain large facts, true. It was true enough for *them*, and at the age of nine I could appreciate this perfectly. Better than my brother Simon, who was too blunt for this kind of maneuver and, anyway, from books, had gotten hold of some English schoolboy notions of honor. *Tom Brown's Schooldays*[4] for many years had an influence we were not in a position to afford.

Simon was a blond boy with big cheekbones and wide gray eyes and had the arms of a cricketer—I go by the illustrations; we never played anything but softball. Opposed to his British style was his patriotic anger at George III.[5] The mayor was at that time ordering the schoolboard to get history books

---

2. Non-Arabic North African tribesman.
3. Downtown location of Chicago's social welfare agency.
4. Novel (1857) based on experiences at Rugby School, by the English jurist and religious reformer

Thomas Hughes (1822–1896).
5. King (1738–1820) of England, Scotland, and Ireland during a period (1760–1820) that included the American Revolution.

that dealt more harshly with the king, and Simon was very hot at Cornwallis.[6] I admired this patriotic flash, his terrific personal wrath at the general, and his satisfaction over his surrender at Yorktown,[7] which would often come over him at lunch while we ate our bologna sandwiches. Grandma had a piece of boiled chicken at noon, and sometimes there was the gizzard for bristle-headed little Georgie, who loved it and blew at the ridgy thing more to cherish than to cool it. But this martial true-blood pride of Simon's disqualified him for the crafty task to be done at the dispensary; he was too disdainful to lie and might denounce everybody instead. I could be counted on to do the job, because I enjoyed it. I loved a piece of strategy. I had enthusiasms too; I had Simon's, though there was never much meat in Cornwallis for me, and I had Grandma Lausch's as well. As for the truth of these statements I was instructed to make—well, it was a fact that we had a boarder. Grandma Lausch was our boarder, not a relation at all. She was supported by two sons, one from Cincinnati and one from Racine, Wisconsin. The daughters-in-law did not want her, and she, the widow of a powerful Odessa[8] businessman—a divinity over us, bald, whiskery, with a fat nose, greatly armored in a cut-away, a double-breasted vest, powerfully buttoned (his blue photo, enlarged and retouched by Mr. Lulov, hung in the parlor, doubled back between the portico columns of the full-length mirror, the dome of the stove beginning where his trunk ended)—she preferred to live with us, because for so many years she was used to direct a house, to command, to govern, to manage, scheme, devise, and intrigue in all her languages. She boasted French and German besides Russian, Polish, and Yiddish; and who but Mr. Lulov, the retouch artist from Division Street,[9] could have tested her claim to French? And he was a serene bogus too, that triple-backboned gallant tea-drinker. Except that he had been a hackie in Paris, once, and if he told the truth about that might have known French among other things, like playing tunes on his teeth with a pencil or singing and keeping time with a handful of coins that he rattled by jigging his thumb along the table, and how to play chess.[1]

Grandma Lausch played like Timur, whether chess or klabyasch,[1] with palatal catty harshness and sharp gold in her eyes. Klabyasch she played with Mr. Kreindl, a neighbor of ours who had taught her the game. A powerful stub-handed man with a large belly, he swatted the table with those hard hands of his, flinging down his cards and shouting *"Shtoch! Yasch! Menél! Klabyasch!"*[2] Grandma looked sardonically at him. She often said, after he left, "If you've got a Hungarian friend you don't need an enemy." But there was nothing of the enemy about Mr. Kreindl. He merely, sometimes, sounded menacing because of his drill-sergeant's bark. He was an old-time Austro-Hungarian[3] conscript, and there was something soldierly about him: a neck that had strained with pushing artillery wheels, a campaigner's red in the face, a powerful bite in his jaw and gold-crowned teeth, green cockeyes and soft short

6. Charles Cornwallis (1738–1805), British general who made the final surrender in the American Revolution.
7. Village in southeast Virginia where in 1781 British forces surrendered to George Washington's Continental Army, effectively ending the American Revolution.
8. City in the Ukraine on the Black Sea, departure point for many Russian Jews who emigrated to North America in the late nineteeth and early twentieth centuries.

9. Commercial and shopping street on Chicago's North Side.
1. Card game taking its name from the Yiddish verb for "to gather." "Timur": also Tamerlane, Mongol warrior (1336–1405) whose conquests stretched from the Ukraine to northern India.
2. Successive winning tricks.
3. The dual monarchy of Austria and Hungary (1867–1918) encompassed Austria, Hungary, Bohemia, and parts of Poland, Romania, Italy, and the Balkans.

hair, altogether Napoleonic.[4] His feet slanted out on the ideal of Frederick the
Great,[5] but he was about a foot under the required height for guardsmen. He
had a masterly look of independence. He and his wife—a woman quiet and
modest to the neighbors and violently quarrelsome at home—and his son, a
dental student, lived in what was called the English basement at the front of
the house. The son, Kotzie, worked evenings in the corner drugstore and went
to school in the neighborhood of County Hospital, and it was he who told
Grandma about the free dispensary. Or rather, the old woman sent for him to
find out what one could get from those state and county places. She was
always sending for people, the butcher, the grocer, the fruit peddler, and
received them in the kitchen to explain that the Marches had to have dis-
counts. Mama usually had to stand by. The old woman would tell them, "You
see how it is—do I have to say more? There's no man in the house and children to bring up." This was her most frequent argument. When Lubin, the
caseworker, came around and sat in the kitchen, familiar, bald-headed, in his
gold glasses, his weight comfortable, his mouth patient, she shot it at him:
"How do you expect children to be brought up?" While he listened, trying to
remain comfortable but gradually becoming like a man determined not to let
a grasshopper escape from his hand. "Well, my dear, Mrs. March could raise
your rent," he said. She must often have answered—for there were times when
she sent us all out to be alone with him—"Do you know what things would be
like without me? You ought to be grateful for the way I hold them together."
I'm sure she even said, "And when I die, Mr. Lubin, you'll see what you've got
on your hands." I'm one hundred per cent sure of it. To us nothing was ever
said that might weaken her rule by suggesting it would ever end. Besides, it
would have shocked us to hear it, and she, in her miraculous knowledge of us,
able to be extremely close to our thoughts—she was one sovereign who knew
exactly the proportions of love, respect, and fear of power in her subjects—
understood how we would have been shocked. But to Lubin, for reasons of
policy and also because she had to express feelings she certainly had, she must
have said it. He had a harassed patience with her of "deliver me from such
clients," though he tried to appear master of the situation. He held his derby
between his thighs (his suits, always too scanty in the pants, exposed white
socks and bulldog shoes, crinkled, black, and bulging with toes), and he looked
into the hat as though debating whether it was wise to release his grasshopper
on the lining for a while.

"I pay as much as I can afford," she would say.

She took her cigarette case out from under her shawl, she cut a Murad[6] in
half with her sewing scissors and picked up the holder. This was still at a time
when women did not smoke. Save the intelligentsia—the term she applied to
herself. With the holder in her dark little gums between which all her guile,
malice, and command issued, she had her best inspirations of strategy. She
was as wrinkled as an old paper bag, an autocrat, hard-shelled and jesuitical,[7]
a pouncy old hawk of a Bolshevik,[8] her small ribboned gray feet immobile on
the shoekit and stool Simon had made in the manual-training class, dingy old

---

4. Era and style of Napoléon Bonaparte's (1769–
1821) rule as Napoléon I, emperor of the French
(1804–15).
5. Frederick II (1712–1786), called "the Great,"
king of Prussia (1740–86), patron of the arts and
philosophy.
6. A Turkish cigarette, named for the Murad River.

7. Word taken from the Society of Jesus, commonly called Jesuits, a Catholic religious order
famous for its intellectual rigor, founded in 1540
by the Spanish priest Ignatius of Loyola (1491–
1556).
8. Left-wing political party allied with other Communist forces in the Russian Revolution (1917).

wool Winnie whose bad smell filled the flat on the cushion beside her. If wit and discontent don't necessarily go together, it wasn't from the old woman that I learned it. She was impossible to satisfy. Kreindl, for example, on whom we could depend, Kreindl who carried up the coal when Mama was sick and who instructed Kotzie to make up our prescriptions for nothing, she called "that trashy Hungarian," or "Hungarian pig." She called Kotzie "the baked apple"; she called Mrs. Kreindl "the secret goose," Lubin "the shoemaker's son," the dentist "the butcher," the butcher "the timid swindler." She detested the dentist, who had several times unsuccessfully tried to fit her with false teeth. She accused him of burning her gums when taking the impressions. But then she tried to pull his hands away from her mouth. I saw that happen: the stolid, square-framed Dr. Wernick, whose compact forearms could have held off a bear, painfully careful with her, determined, concerned at her choked screams, and enduring her scratches. To see her struggle like that was no easy thing for me, and Dr. Wernick was sorry to see me there too, I know, but either Simon or I had to squire her wherever she went. Here particularly she needed a witness to Wernick's cruelty and clumsiness as well as a shoulder to lean on when she went weakly home. Already at ten I was only a little shorter than she and big enough to hold her small weight.

"You saw how he put his paws over my face so I couldn't breathe?" she said. "God made him to be a butcher. Why did he become a dentist? His hands are too heavy. The touch is everything to a dentist. If his hands aren't right he shouldn't be let practice. But his wife worked hard to send him through school and make a dentist of him. And I must go to him and be burned because of it."

The rest of us had to go to the dispensary—which was like the dream of a multitude of dentists' chairs, hundreds of them in a space as enormous as an armory, and green bowls with designs of glass grapes, drills lifted zigzag as insects' legs, and gas flames on the porcelain swivel trays—a thundery gloom in Harrison Street of limestone county buildings and cumbersome red streetcars with metal grillwork on their windows and monarchical iron whiskers of cowcatchers front and rear. They lumbered and clanged, and their brake tanks panted in the slushy brown of a winter afternoon or the bare stone brown of a summer's, salted with ash, smoke, and prairie dust, with long stops at the clinics to let off clumpers, cripples, hunchbacks, brace-legs, crutch-wielders, tooth and eye sufferers, and all the rest.

So before going with my mother for the glasses I was always instructed by the old woman and had to sit and listen with profound care. My mother too had to be present, for there must be no slip-up. She must be coached to say nothing. "Remember, Rebecca," Grandma would rerepeat, "let him answer everything." To which Mama was too obedient even to say yes, but only sat and kept her long hands folded on the bottle-fly iridescence of the dress the old woman had picked for her to wear. Very healthy and smooth, her color; none of us inherited this high a color from her, or the form of her nose with nostrils turned back and showing a little of the partition. "You keep out of it. If they ask you something, you look at Augie like this." And she illustrated how Mama was to turn to me, terribly exact, if she had only been able to drop her habitual grandeur. "Don't tell anything. Only answer questions," she said to me. My mother was anxious that I should be worthy and faithful. Simon and I were her miracles or accidents; Georgie was her own true work in which she returned to her fate after blessed and undeserved success. "Augie, listen to Grandma. Hear what she says," was all she ever dared when the old woman unfolded her plan.

"When they ask you, 'Where is your father?' you say, 'I don't know where, miss.' No matter how old she is, you shouldn't forget to say 'miss.' If she wants to know where he was the last time you heard from him, you must tell her that the last time he sent a money order was about two years ago from Buffalo, New York. Never say a word about the Charity. The Charity you should never mention, you hear that? Never. When she asks you how much the rent is, tell her eighteen dollars. When she asks where the money comes from, say you have boarders. How many? Two boarders. Now, say to me, how much rent?"

"Eighteen dollars."

"And how many boarders?"

"Two."

"And how much do they pay?"

"How much should I say?"

"Eight dollars each a week."

"Eight dollars."

"So you can't go to a private doctor, if you get sixty-four dollars a month. The eyedrops alone cost me five when I went, and he scalded my eyes. And these specs"—she tapped the case—"cost ten dollars the frames and fifteen the glasses."

Never but at such times, by necessity, was my father mentioned. I claimed to remember him; Simon denied that I did, and Simon was right. I liked to imagine it.

"He wore a uniform," I said. "Sure I remember. He was a soldier."

"Like hell he was. You don't know anything about it."

"Maybe a sailor."

"Like hell. He drove a truck for Hall Brothers laundry on Marshfield,[9] that's what he did. *I* said he used to wear a uniform. Monkey sees, monkey does; monkey hears, monkey says." Monkey was the basis of much thought with us. On the sideboard, on the Turkestan runner, with their eyes, ears, and mouth covered, we had see-no-evil, speak-no-evil, hear-no-evil, a lower trinity of the house. The advantage of lesser gods is that you can take their names any way you like. "Silence in the courthouse, monkey wants to speak; speak, monkey, speak." "The monkey and the bamboo were playing in the grass . . ." Still the monkeys could be potent, and awesome besides, and deep social critics when the old woman, like a great lama—for she is Eastern to me, in the end— would point to the squatting brown three, whose mouths and nostrils were drawn in sharp blood-red, and with profound wit, her unkindness finally touching greatness, say, "Nobody asks you to love the whole world, only to be honest, *ehrlich*.[1] Don't have a loud mouth. The more you love people the more they'll mix you up. A child loves, a person respects. Respect is better than love. And that's respect, the middle monkey." It never occurred to us that she sinned mischievously herself against that convulsed speak-no-evil who hugged his lips with his hands; but no criticism of her came near our minds at any time, much less when the resonance of a great principle filled the whole kitchen.

She used to read us lessons off poor Georgie's head. He would kiss the dog. This bickering handmaiden of the old lady, at one time. Now a dozy, long-

9. Commercial avenue on Chicago's North Side.   1. Sincere (German).

sighing crank and proper object of respect for her years of right-minded but not exactly lovable busyness. But Georgie loved her—and Grandma, whom he would kiss on the sleeve, on the knee, taking knee or arm in both hands and putting his underlip forward, chaste, lummoxy, caressing, gentle and diligent when he bent his narrow back, blouse bagging all over it, whitish hair pointy and close as a burr or sunflower when the seeds have been picked out of it. The old lady let him embrace her and spoke to him in the following way: "Hey, you, boy, clever *junge*,[2] you like the old Grandma, my minister, my *cavalyer*?[3] That's-a-boy. You know who's good to you, who gives you gizzards and necks? Who? Who makes noodles for you? Yes. Noodles are slippery, hard to pick up with a fork and hard to pick up with the fingers. You see how the little bird pulls the worm? The little worm wants to stay in the ground. The little worm doesn't want to come out. Enough, you're making my dress wet." And she'd sharply push his forehead off with her old prim hand, having fired off for Simon and me, mindful always of her duty to wise us up, one more animadversion on the trustful, loving, and simple surrounded by the cunning-hearted and tough, a fighting nature of birds and worms, and a desperate mankind without feelings. Illustrated by Georgie. But the principal illustration was not Georgie but Mama, in her love-originated servitude, simple-minded, abandoned with three children. This was what old lady Lausch was driving at, now, in the later wisdom of her life, that she had a second family to lead.

And what must Mama have thought when in any necessary connection my father was brought into the conversation? She sat docile. I conceive that she thought of some detail about him—a dish he liked, perhaps meat and potatoes, perhaps cabbage or cranberry sauce; perhaps that he disliked a starched collar, or a soft collar; that he brought home the *Evening American* or the *Journal*.[4] She thought this because her thoughts were always simple; but she felt abandonment, and greater pains than conscious mental ones put a dark streak to her simplicity. I don't know how she made out before, when we were alone after the desertion, but Grandma came and put a regulating hand on the family life. Mama surrendered powers to her that maybe she had never known she had and took her punishment in drudgery; occupied a place, I suppose, among women conquered by a superior force of love, like those women whom Zeus got the better of in animal form and who next had to take cover from his furious wife. Not that I can see my big, gentle, dilapidated, scrubbing, and lugging mother as a fugitive of immense beauty from such classy wrath, or our father as a marble-legged Olympian. She had sewed buttonholes in a coat factory in a Wells Street[5] loft and he was a laundry driver—there wasn't even so much as a picture of him left when he blew. But she does have a place among such women by the deeper right of continual payment. And as for vengeance from a woman, Grandma Lausch was there to administer the penalties under the standards of legitimacy, representing the main body of married womankind.

Still the old lady had a heart. I don't mean to say she didn't. She was tyrannical and a snob about her Odessa luster and her servants and governesses, but though she had been a success herself she knew what it was to fall through susceptibility. I began to realize this when I afterward read some of

2. Young man (German).
3. Yiddish borrowing from the German *kavalier* (gentleman) and Polish *kawaler* (bachelor, gallant).
4. Chicago newpapers of the era.
5. Light-industrial street immediately north of Chicago's downtown area.

the novels she used to send me to the library for. She taught me the Russian alphabet so that I could make out the titles. Once a year she read *Anna Karenina* and *Eugene Onegin*.[6] Occasionally I got into hot water by bringing a book she didn't want. "How many times do I have to tell you if it doesn't say *roman* I don't want it? You didn't look inside. Are your fingers too weak to open the book? Then they should be too weak to play ball or pick your nose. For that you've got strength! *Bozhe moy!*[7] God in Heaven! You haven't got the brains of a cat, to walk two miles and bring me a book about religion because it says Tolstoi on the cover."

The old *grande dame,* I don't want to be misrepresenting her. She was suspicious of what could have been, given one wrong stitch of heredity, a family vice by which we could have been exploited. She didn't want to read Tolstoi on religion. She didn't trust him as a family man because the countess had had such trouble with him. But although she never went to the synagogue, ate bread on Passover, sent Mama to the pork butcher where meat was cheaper, loved canned lobster and other forbidden food, she was not an atheist and free-thinker, Mr. Anticol, the old junky she called (search me why) "Rameses"—after the city named with Pithom in the Scriptures maybe;[8] no telling what her inspirations were—was that. A real rebel to God. Icy and canny, she would listen to what he had to say and wouldn't declare herself. He was ruddy, and gloomy; his leathery serge cap made him flat-headed, and his alley calls for rags, old iron—"recks aline," he sung it—made him gravel-voiced and gruff. He had tough hair and brows and despising brown eyes; he was a studious, shaggy, meaty old man. Grandma bought a set of the *Ency-clopedia Americana*—edition of 1892, I think—from him and saw to it that Simon and I read it; and he too, whenever he met us, asked, "How's the set?" believing, I reckon, that it taught irreverence to religion. What had made him an atheist was a massacre of Jews in his town. From the cellar where he was hidden he saw a laborer pissing on the body of his wife's younger brother, just killed. "So don't talk to me about God," he said. But it was he that talked about God, all the time. And while Mrs. Anticol stayed pious, it was his idea of grand apostasy to drive to the reform synagogue on the high holidays and park his pink-eye nag among the luxurious, whirl-wired touring cars of the rich Jews who bared their heads inside as if they were attending a theater, a kind of abjectness in them that gave him grim entertainment to the end of his life. He caught a cold in the rain and died of pneumonia.

Grandma, all the same, burned a candle on the anniversary of Mr. Lausch's death, threw a lump of dough on the coals when she was baking, as a kind of offering, had incantations over baby teeth and stunts against the evil eye. It was kitchen religion and had nothing to do with the giant God of the Creation who turned back the waters and exploded Gomorrah, but it was on the side of religion at that. And while we're on that side I'll mention the Poles—we were just a handful of Jews among them in the neighborhood—and the swollen, bleeding hearts on every kitchen wall, the pictures of saints, baskets of death flowers tied at the door, communions, Easters, and Christmases. And

---

6. Verse narrative (1823–31) by the Russian poet Aleksandr Pushkin (1799–1837). *Anna Karenina*: novel (1875–77) by the Russian novelist Leo Tolstoy (1828–1910).
7. Oh, my God (Russian).

8. *Exodus* 1.11: "Therefore they set taskmasters over them to afflict them with heavy burdens; and they built for Pharoah store-cities, Pithom and Raamses."

sometimes we were chased, stoned, bitten, and beat up for Christ-killers, all of us, even Georgie, articled, whether we liked it or not, to this mysterious trade. But I never had any special grief from it, or brooded, being by and large too larky and boisterous to take it to heart, and looked at it as needing no more special explanation than the stone-and-bat wars of the street gangs or the swarming on a fall evening of parish punks to rip up fences, screech and bawl at girls, and beat up strangers. It wasn't in my nature to fatigue myself with worry over being born to this occult work, even though some of my friends and playmates would turn up in the middle of these mobs to trap you between houses from both ends of a passageway. Simon had less truck with them. School absorbed him more, and he had his sentiments anyway, a mixed extract from Natty Bumppo, Quentin Durward, Tom Brown, Clark at Kaskaskia, the messenger who brought the good news from Ratisbon,[9] and so on, that kept him more to himself. I was just a slow understudy to this, just as he never got me to put in hours on his Sandow muscle builder[1] and the gimmick for developing the sinews of the wrist. I was an easy touch for friendships, and most of the time they were cut short by older loyalties. I was pals longest with Stashu Kopecs, whose mother was a midwife graduated from the Aesculapian School of Midwifery on Milwaukee Avenue.[2] Well to do, the Kopecses had an electric player piano and linoleums in all the rooms, but Stashu was a thief, and to run with him I stole too: coal off the cars, clothes from the lines, rubber balls from the dime store, and pennies off the newsstands. Mostly for the satisfaction of dexterity, though Stashu invented the game of stripping in the cellar and putting on girls' things swiped from the clotheslines. Then he too showed up in a gang that caught me one cold afternoon of very little snow while I was sitting on a crate frozen into the mud, eating Nabisco[3] wafers, my throat full of the sweet dust. Foremost, there was a thug of a kid, about thirteen but undersized, hard and grieved-looking. He came up to accuse me, and big Moonya Staplanski, just out of the St. Charles Reformatory[4] and headed next for the one at Pontiac,[5] backed him up.

"You little Jew bastard, you hit my brother," Moonya said.

"I never did. I never even saw him before."

"You took away a nickel from him. How did you buy them biscuits else, you?"

"I got them at home."

Then I caught sight of Stashu, hayheaded and jeering, pleased to sickness with his deceit and his new-revealed brotherhood with the others, and I said, "Hey, you lousy bed-wetter, Stashu, you know Moon ain't even got a brother."

Here the kid hit me and the gang jumped me, Stashu with the rest, tearing the buckles from my sheepskin coat and bloodying my nose.

"Who is to blame?" said Grandma Lausch when I came home. "You know who? You are, Augie, because that's all the brains you have to go with that

9. The French name for the German city of Regensburg, which was captured by Napoleon's armies in 1809. "Natty Bumppo": protagonist of the Leatherstocking novels by the American novelist James Fenimore Cooper (1789–1851). "Quentin Durward": eponymous hero in the novel (1823) by the Scottish poet and novelist Sir Walter Scott (1771–1832). "Tom Brown": see n. 4, p. 1276. "Clark at Kaskasia": the American military leader George Rogers Clark (1752–1818) captured the British frontier fort at Kaskaskia, Illinois, in 1778.

1. Device named after Eugen Sandow (1867–1925), American physical culturist born in Germany, famous for his performances as a bodybuilder and for advocacy of physical education.
2. Commercial and shopping street on Chicago's North Side, at this time a central Polish-American neighborhood.
3. Brand name of the National Biscuit Company.
4. Site of the Illinois State Reformatory for Boys.
5. Site of the Illinois Correctional Center.

piss-in-bed *accoucherka's*[6] son. Does Simon hang around with them? Not Simon. He has too much sense." I thanked God she didn't know about the stealing. And in a way, because that was her schooling temperament, I suspect she was pleased that I should see where it led to give your affections too easily. But Mama, the prime example of this weakness, was horrified. Against the old lady's authority she didn't dare to introduce her feelings during the hearing, but when she took me into the kitchen to put a compress on me she nearsightedly pored over my scratches, whispering and sighing to me, while Georgie tottered around behind her, long and white, and Winnie lapped water under the sink.

1953

6. Yiddish borrowing from the Polish *akuszerka* (midwife).

ARTHUR MILLER
1915–2005

For much modern American drama the family is the central subject, as the anthology selections show. In *Long Day's Journey into Night*, O'Neill studied his own family through the Tyrones; in Tennessee Williams's *A Streetcar Named Desire* the Kowalskis are one family, which Blanche invades, while Blanche and Stella, as sisters, are another. Most of Arthur Miller's plays, as well, concentrate on the family and envision an ideal world as, perhaps, an enlarged family. Often the protagonist's sense of family draws him into conflict with—and eventual doom in—the outside world. Yet Miller recognized that an ideal is sometimes a rationalization. Joe Keller insists in *All My Sons* (1947) that during the war he shipped damaged airplane parts to support his family, but a desire for commercial success was part of his motive. Eddie Carbone in *A View from the Bridge* (1955) accepts death because of his sense of responsibility to his niece, but married man though he is, he may also be in love with that same niece. In *Death of a Salesman* (1949) Willy Loman's delusions and self-deceptions derive from, and return to, his image of himself as family provider, an image he cannot live up to; driven by his desire to be "well liked," a successful social personality, he fails to connect with either of his sons and neglects his wife. Thus Miller's treatment of the family leads to a treatment both of personal ideals and of the society within which families have to operate.

Miller was born into a German Jewish family in Manhattan; his father was a well-to-do but almost illiterate clothing manufacturer, his mother an avid reader. When his father's business collapsed after the stock market crash in 1929, the family moved to Brooklyn, where Miller graduated from high school. His subsequent two years of work in an automobile-parts warehouse to earn money for college tuition are warmly recalled in his play *A Memory of Two Mondays* (1955). At the University of Michigan he enrolled as a journalism student. These were the years of the Spanish Civil War, the rise of fascism, and the attraction of Marxism as a way out of the Depression, and here Miller formed his political views. He also began to write plays, which won prizes at the university and in New York. He then went to work for the Federal Theater Project, wrote radio plays, toured army camps gathering material for a film, and married Mary Slattery, the first of his three wives.

In 1947 Miller enjoyed his first Broadway success, *All My Sons* (*The Man Who Had All the Luck* had failed in 1944). This strongly realistic portrayal of a family divided because of the father's insistence on business as usual during World War II drew the attention of audiences and theater critics. *Death of a Salesman,* his masterpiece, was produced two years later and won the Pulitzer Prize. An adaptation of Ibsen's *An Enemy of the People* followed in 1951. It was suggested to him by the actors Fredric March and Florence Eldridge, but Miller was clearly drawn by Ibsen's hero, Dr. Stockmann, who leads a fight against pollution with strong but confused idealism.

In the 1950s the hysterical search for supposed communist infiltration of American life reached its height, as Senator Joseph McCarthy summoned suspect after suspect to hearings in Washington. Miller later said that at this time he was reading a book about the Salem witch trials and saw that "the main point of the hearings, precisely as in seventeenth-century Salem, was that the accused make public confession, damn his confederates as well as his Devil master, and guarantee his sterling new allegiance by breaking disgusting old vows—whereupon he was let loose to rejoin the society of extremely decent people." Out of this came *The Crucible* (1953), in which the hero, John Proctor, allows himself to be executed rather than sign away his name and his children's respect. Hysteria touched Miller personally when he was denied a passport and in 1957 was convicted of contempt of Congress for refusing to name suspected communists (this conviction was unanimously overturned by the Supreme Court the following year).

Miller had long been looking for a way to dramatize what he had earlier learned about mob control of the Brooklyn waterfront and finally did so in the one-act play *A View from the Bridge,* produced with *A Memory of Two Mondays* in 1955; later he would rework *View* into a full-length play. Meanwhile, he had met the glamorous movie actress Marilyn Monroe; they married in 1956, after he divorced his first wife. He wrote the screenplay *The Misfits* for Monroe, but in their private life, their complex natures were ill-sorted. The marriage ended in divorce in 1961, and a year later he married the photographer Ingeborg Morath, with whom he collaborated on several books of photographs and essays.

In 1964 two plays opened: *After the Fall* (in which the protagonist is a thinly disguised Miller investigating his family, his responsibilities, and his wives) and *Incident at Vichy* (about Jews and Nazis in Vichy, France). While these were by no means as successful as *Salesman,* they returned him seriously to the stage. Among later plays are *The Price* (1968), *The Creation of the World and Other Business* (1972), *The Archbishop's Ceiling* (1977), and two one-act plays under the title *Danger: Memory!* (1986). These last fared poorly in New York, but found successful productions elsewhere in the world. Miller in his later years was something of an activist. In the late 1960s he was asked to become president of PEN (Poets, Essayists, Novelists), the international writers' group. By opening this organization to writers in what were Iron Curtain countries and speaking out for those repressed by totalitarian regimes, he became a respected champion of human rights.

Like his contemporary Tennessee Williams, Miller rejected the influence of "mawkish twenties slang" and "deadly repetitiveness." Again like Williams, Miller was impatient with prosy dialogue and well-made structures. As he explained, the success of *A Streetcar Named Desire* in 1947 helped him write *Death of a Salesman:*

> With *Streetcar,* Tennessee had printed a license to speak at full throat, and it helped strengthen me as I turned to Willy Loman, a salesman always full of words, and better yet, a man who could never cease trying, like Adam, to name himself and the world's wonders. I had known all along that this play could not be encompassed by conventional realism, and for one integral reason: in Willy the past was as alive as what was happening at the moment, sometimes even crashing in to completely overwhelm his mind. I wanted precisely the same fluidity of form.

In *Salesman* the action moves effortlessly from the present—the last twenty-four hours of Willy's life—into moments in his memory, symbolized in the stage setting by the idyllic leaves around his house that, in these past moments, block out the threatening apartment houses. The successful realization of this fluidity on the stage was greatly aided by Miller's director, Elia Kazan, and his stage designer, Jo Mielziner, both of whom had worked with Williams two years earlier on *Streetcar*. A striking difference between Williams and Miller, however, is the latter's overt moralizing, which adds a didactic element to his plays not to be found in those of Williams.

Because of Miller's political involvements, such plays as *All My Sons* and *Death of a Salesman* were seen—especially during the Cold War—as political tracts. At the other extreme, a later play, *The Ride Down Mount Morgan* (1992), impressed theatergoers as a moral commentary on cultural values in decline, a theme more common at the political spectrum's opposite end. In both earlier and later plays Miller's protagonists have death on their minds, a concern greater than any political affiliation.

The text is from *Arthur Miller's Collected Plays* (1957).

Death of a Salesman

Certain Private Conversations in Two Acts and a Requiem

THE CHARACTERS

WILLY LOMAN	THE WOMAN	JENNY
LINDA	CHARLEY	STANLEY
BIFF	UNCLE BEN	MISS FORSYTHE
HAPPY	HOWARD WAGNER	LETTA
BERNARD		

The action takes place in WILLY LOMAN'*s house and yard and in various places he visits in the New York and Boston of today.*

Act One

A melody is heard, playing upon a flute. It is small and fine, telling of grass and trees and the horizon. The curtain rises.

Before us is the Salesman's house. We are aware of towering, angular shapes behind it, surrounding it on all sides. Only the blue light of the sky falls upon the house and forestage; the surrounding area shows an angry flow of orange. As more light appears, we see a solid vault of apartment houses around the small, fragile-seeming home. An air of the dream clings to the place, a dream rising out of reality. The kitchen at center seems actual enough, for there is a kitchen table with three chairs, and a refrigerator. But no other fixtures are seen. At the back of the kitchen there is a draped entrance, which leads to the living-room. To the right of the kitchen, on a level raised two feet, is a bedroom furnished only with a brass bedstead and a straight chair. On a shelf over the bed a silver athletic trophy stands. A window opens onto the apartment house at the side.

Behind the kitchen, on a level raised six and a half feet, is the boys' bedroom, at present barely visible. Two beds are dimly seen, and at the back of the room a dormer window. (This bedroom is above the unseen living-room.) At the left a stairway curves up to it from the kitchen.

The entire setting is wholly or, in some places, partially transparent. The roof-line of the house is one-dimensional; under and over it we see the apartment buildings. Before the house lies an apron, curving beyond the forestage into the orchestra. This forward area serves as the back yard as well as the locale of all

WILLY's *imaginings and of his city scenes. Whenever the action is in the present the actors observe the imaginary wall-lines, entering the house only through its door at the left. But in the scenes of the past these boundaries are broken, and characters enter or leave a room by stepping "through" a wall onto the forestage.*

From the right, WILLY LOMAN, *the Salesman, enters, carrying two large sample cases. The flute plays on. He hears but is not aware of it. He is past sixty years of age, dressed quietly. Even as he crosses the stage to the doorway of the house, his exhaustion is apparent. He unlocks the door, comes into the kitchen, and thankfully lets his burden down, feeling the soreness of his palms. A word-sigh escapes his lips—it might be "Oh, boy, oh, boy." He closes the door, then carries his cases out into the living-room, through the draped kitchen doorway.*

LINDA, *his wife, has stirred in her bed at the right. She gets out and puts on a robe, listening. Most often jovial, she has developed an iron repression of her exceptions to* WILLY's *behavior—she more than loves him, she admires him, as though his mercurial nature, his temper, his massive dreams and little cruelties, served her only as sharp reminders of the turbulent longings within him, longings which she shares but lacks the temperament to utter and follow to their end.*

LINDA [*hearing* WILLY *outside the bedroom, calls with some trepidation*] Willy!

WILLY   It's all right. I came back.

LINDA   Why? What happened? [*slight pause*] Did something happen, Willy?

WILLY   No, nothing happened.

LINDA   You didn't smash the car, did you?

WILLY [*with casual irritation*]   I said nothing happened. Didn't you hear me?

LINDA   Don't you feel well?

WILLY   I'm tired to the death. [*The flute has faded away. He sits on the bed beside her, a little numb.*] I couldn't make it. I just couldn't make it, Linda.

LINDA [*very carefully, delicately*]   Where were you all day? You look terrible.

WILLY   I got as far as a little above Yonkers. I stopped for a cup of coffee. Maybe it was the coffee.

LINDA   What?

WILLY [*after a pause*]   I suddenly couldn't drive any more. The car kept going off onto the shoulder, y'know?

LINDA [*helpfully*]   Oh. Maybe it was the steering again. I don't think Angelo knows the Studebaker.

WILLY   No, it's me, it's me. Suddenly I realize I'm goin' sixty miles an hour and I don't remember the last five minutes. I'm—I can't seem to—keep my mind to it.

LINDA   Maybe it's your glasses. You never went for your new glasses.

WILLY   No, I see everything. I came back ten miles an hour. It took me nearly four hours from Yonkers.

LINDA [*resigned*]   Well, you'll just have to take a rest, Willy, you can't continue this way.

WILLY   I just got back from Florida.

LINDA   But you didn't rest your mind. Your mind is overactive, and the mind is what counts, dear.

WILLY   I'll start out in the morning. Maybe I'll feel better in the morning. [*She is taking off his shoes.*] These goddam arch supports are killing me.

LINDA   Take an aspirin. Should I get you an aspirin? It'll soothe you.

WILLY [*with wonder*]   I was driving along, you understand? And I was fine. I was even observing the scenery. You can imagine, me looking at scenery, on the road every week of my life. But it's so beautiful up there, Linda, the trees are so thick, and the sun is warm. I opened the windshield and just let the warm air bathe over me. And then all of a sudden I'm goin' off the road! I'm tellin' ya, I absolutely forgot I was driving. If I'd've gone the other way over the white line I might've killed somebody. So I went on again—and five minutes later I'm dreamin' again, and I nearly— [*He presses two fingers against his eyes.*] I have such thoughts, I have such strange thoughts.

LINDA   Willy, dear. Talk to them again. There's no reason why you can't work in New York.

WILLY   They don't need me in New York. I'm the New England man. I'm vital in New England.

LINDA   But you're sixty years old. They can't expect you to keep traveling every week.

WILLY   I'll have to send a wire to Portland. I'm supposed to see Brown and Morrison tomorrow morning at ten o'clock to show the line. Goddammit, I could sell them! [*He starts putting on his jacket.*]

LINDA [*taking the jacket from him*]   Why don't you go down to the place tomorrow and tell Howard you've simply got to work in New York? You're too accommodating, dear.

WILLY   If old man Wagner was alive I'd a been in charge of New York now! That man was a prince, he was a masterful man. But that boy of his, that Howard, he don't appreciate. When I went north the first time, the Wagner Company didn't know where New England was!

LINDA   Why don't you tell those things to Howard, dear?

WILLY [*encouraged*]   I will, I definitely will. Is there any cheese?

LINDA   I'll make you a sandwich.

WILLY   No, go to sleep. I'll take some milk. I'll be up right away. The boys in?

LINDA   They're sleeping. Happy took Biff on a date tonight.

WILLY [*interested*]   That so?

LINDA   It was so nice to see them shaving together, one behind the other, in the bathroom. And going out together. You notice? The whole house smells of shaving lotion.

WILLY   Figure it out. Work a lifetime to pay off a house. You finally own it, and there's nobody to live in it.

LINDA   Well, dear, life is a casting off. It's always that way.

WILLY   No, no, some people—some people accomplish something. Did Biff say anything after I went this morning?

LINDA   You shouldn't have criticized him, Willy, especially after he just got off the train. You mustn't lose your temper with him.

WILLY   When the hell did I lose my temper? I simply asked him if he was making any money. Is that a criticism?

LINDA   But, dear, how could he make any money?

WILLY [*worried and angered*]   There's such an undercurrent in him. He became a moody man. Did he apologize when I left this morning?

LINDA   He was crestfallen, Willy. You know how he admires you. I think if he finds himself, then you'll both be happier and not fight any more.

WILLY   How can he find himself on a farm? Is that a life? A farmhand? In the beginning, when he was young, I thought, well, a young man, it's good for him to tramp around, take a lot of different jobs. But it's more than ten years now and he has yet to make thirty-five dollars a week?

LINDA   He's finding himself, Willy.

WILLY   Not finding yourself at the age of thirty-four is a disgrace!

LINDA   Shh!

WILLY   The trouble is he's lazy, goddammit!

LINDA   Willy, please!

WILLY   Biff is a lazy bum!

LINDA   They're sleeping. Get something to eat. Go on down.

WILLY   Why did he come home? I would like to know what brought him home.

LINDA   I don't know. I think he's still lost, Willy. I think he's very lost.

WILLY   Biff Loman is lost. In the greatest country in the world a young man with such—personal attractiveness, gets lost. And such a hard worker. There's one thing about Biff—he's not lazy.

LINDA   Never.

WILLY [*with pity and resolve*]   I'll see him in the morning; I'll have a nice talk with him. I'll get him a job selling. He could be big in no time. My God! Remember how they used to follow him around in high school? When he smiled at one of them their faces lit up. When he walked down the street . . . [*He loses himself in reminiscences.*]

LINDA [*trying to bring him out of it*]   Willy, dear, I got a new kind of American-type cheese today. It's whipped.

WILLY   Why do you get American when I like Swiss?

LINDA   I just thought you'd like a change—

WILLY   I don't want a change! I want Swiss cheese. Why am I always being contradicted?

LINDA [*with a covering laugh*]   I thought it would be a surprise.

WILLY   Why don't you open a window in here, for God's sake?

LINDA [*with infinite patience*]   They're all open, dear.

WILLY   The way they boxed us in here. Bricks and windows, windows and bricks.

LINDA   We should've bought the land next door.

WILLY   The street is lined with cars. There's not a breath of fresh air in the neighborhood. The grass don't grow any more, you can't raise a carrot in the back yard. They should've had a law against apartment houses. Remember those two beautiful elm trees out there? When I and Biff hung the swing between them?

LINDA   Yeah, like being a million miles from the city.

WILLY   They should've arrested the builder for cutting those down. They massacred the neighborhood. [*lost*] More and more I think of those days, Linda. This time of year it was lilac and wisteria. And then the peonies would come out, and the daffodils. What fragrance in this room!

LINDA   Well, after all, people had to move somewhere.

WILLY   No, there's more people now.

LINDA   I don't think there's more people. I think—

WILLY   There's more people! That's what's ruining this country! Population is getting out of control. The competition is maddening! Smell the stink from that apartment house! And another one on the other side . . . How can they whip cheese?

[*On* WILLY'S *last line*, BIFF *and* HAPPY *raise themselves up in their beds, listening.*]

LINDA   Go down, try it. And be quiet.

WILLY [*turning to* LINDA, *guiltily*]   You're not worried about me, are you, sweetheart?

BIFF   What's the matter?

HAPPY   Listen!

LINDA   You've got too much on the ball to worry about.

WILLY   You're my foundation and my support, Linda.

LINDA   Just try to relax, dear. You make mountains out of molehills.

WILLY   I won't fight with him any more. If he wants to go back to Texas, let him go.

LINDA   He'll find his way.

WILLY   Sure. Certain men just don't get started till later in life. Like Thomas Edison, I think. Or B. F. Goodrich. One of them was deaf. [*He starts for the bedroom doorway.*] I'll put my money on Biff.

LINDA   And Willy—if it's warm Sunday we'll drive in the country. And we'll open the windshield, and take lunch.

WILLY   No, the windshields don't open on the new cars.

LINDA   But you opened it today.

WILLY   Me? I didn't. [*He stops.*] Now isn't that peculiar! Isn't that a remarkable— [*He breaks off in amazement and fright as the flute is heard distantly.*]

LINDA   What, darling?

WILLY   That is the most remarkable thing.

LINDA   What, dear?

WILLY   I was thinking of the Chevvy. [*slight pause*] Nineteen twenty-eight . . . when I had that red Chevvy— [*breaks off*] That funny? I coulda sworn I was driving that Chevvy today.

LINDA   Well, that's nothing. Something must've reminded you.

WILLY   Remarkable. Ts. Remember those days? The way Biff used to simonize that car? The dealer refused to believe there was eighty thousand miles on it. [*He shakes his head.*] Heh! [*to* LINDA] Close your eyes, I'll be right up. [*He walks out of the bedroom.*]

HAPPY [*to* BIFF]   Jesus, maybe he smashed up the car again!

LINDA [*calling after* WILLY]   Be careful on the stairs, dear! The cheese is on the middle shelf! [*She turns, goes over to the bed, takes his jacket, and goes out of the bedroom.*]

[*Light has risen on the boys' room. Unseen,* WILLY *is heard talking to himself, "Eighty thousand miles," and a little laugh.* BIFF *gets out of bed, comes downstage a bit, and stands attentively.* BIFF *is two years older than his brother* HAPPY, *well built, but in these days bears a worn air and seems less self-assured. He has succeeded less, and his dreams are stronger and less acceptable than* HAPPY'S. HAPPY *is tall, powerfully made. Sexuality is like a visible color on him, or a scent that many women have discovered. He, like his brother, is lost, but in a different way, for he has never allowed himself to turn his face toward defeat and is thus more confused and hard-skinned, although seemingly more content.*]

HAPPY [*getting out of bed*]   He's going to get his license taken away if he keeps that up. I'm getting nervous about him, y'know, Biff?

BIFF   His eyes are going.

HAPPY   No, I've driven with him. He sees all right. He just doesn't keep his mind on it. I drove into the city with him last week. He stops at a green light and then it turns red and he goes. [*He laughs.*]

BIFF   Maybe he's color-blind.

HAPPY   Pop? Why he's got the finest eye for color in the business. You know that.

BIFF [*sitting down on his bed*]   I'm going to sleep.

HAPPY   You're not still sour on Dad, are you Biff?

BIFF   He's all right, I guess.

WILLY [*underneath them, in the living-room*]   Yes, sir, eighty thousand miles—eighty-two thousand!

BIFF   You smoking?

HAPPY [*holding out a pack of cigarettes*]   Want one?

BIFF [*taking a cigarette*]   I can never sleep when I smell it.

WILLY   What a simonizing job, heh!

HAPPY [*with deep sentiment*]   Funny, Biff, y'know? Us sleeping in here again? The old beds. [*He pats his bed affectionately.*] All the talk that went across those two beds, huh? Our whole lives.

BIFF   Yeah. Lotta dreams and plans.

HAPPY [*with a deep and masculine laugh*]   About five hundred women would like to know what was said in this room.

[*They share a soft laugh.*]

BIFF   Remember that big Betsy something—what the hell was her name—over on Bushwick Avenue?

HAPPY [*combing his hair*]   With the collie dog!

BIFF   That's the one. I got you in there, remember?

HAPPY   Yeah, that was my first time—I think. Boy, there was a pig! [*They laugh, almost crudely.*] You taught me everything I know about women. Don't forget that.

BIFF   I bet you forgot how bashful you used to be. Especially with girls.

HAPPY   Oh, I still am, Biff.

BIFF   Oh, go on.

HAPPY   I just control it, that's all. I think I got less bashful and you got more so. What happened, Biff? Where's the old humor, the old confidence? [*He shakes BIFF's knee. BIFF gets up and moves restlessly about the room.*] What's the matter?

BIFF   Why does Dad mock me all the time?

HAPPY   He's not mocking you, he—

BIFF   Everything I say there's a twist of mockery on his face. I can't get near him.

HAPPY   He just wants you to make good, that's all. I wanted to talk to you about Dad for a long time, Biff. Something's—happening to him. He—talks to himself.

BIFF   I noticed that this morning. But he always mumbled.

HAPPY   But not so noticeable. It got so embarrassing I sent him to Florida. And you know something? Most of the time he's talking to you.

BIFF   What's he say about me?

HAPPY   I can't make it out.

BIFF   What's he say about me?

HAPPY   I think the fact that you're not settled, that you're still kind of up in the air . . .

BIFF   There's one or two other things depressing him, Happy.

HAPPY   What do you mean?

BIFF   Never mind. Just don't lay it all to me.

HAPPY   But I think if you just got started—I mean—is there any future for you out there?

BIFF   I tell ya, Hap, I don't know what the future is. I don't know—what I'm supposed to want.

HAPPY   What do you mean?

BIFF   Well, I spent six or seven years after high school trying to work myself up. Shipping clerk, salesman, business of one kind or another. And it's a measly manner of existence. To get on that subway on the hot mornings in summer. To devote your whole life to keeping stock, or making phone calls, or selling or buying. To suffer fifty weeks of the year for the sake of a two-week vacation, when all you really desire is to be outdoors, with your shirt off. And always to have to get ahead of the next fella. And still—that's how you build a future.

HAPPY   Well, you really enjoy it on a farm? Are you content out there?

BIFF [*with rising agitation*]   Hap, I've had twenty or thirty different kinds of jobs since I left home before the war, and it always turns out the same. I just realized it lately. In Nebraska when I herded cattle, and the Dakotas, and Arizona, and now in Texas. It's why I came home now, I guess, because I realized it. This farm I work on, it's spring there now, see? And they've got about fifteen new colts. There's nothing more inspiring or—beautiful than the sight of a mare and a new colt. And it's cool there now, see? Texas is cool now, and it's spring. And whenever spring comes to where I am, I suddenly get the feeling, my God, I'm not gettin' anywhere! What the hell am I doing, playing around with horses, twenty-eight dollars a week! I'm thirty-four years old. I oughta be makin' my future. That's when I come running home. And now, I get here, and I don't know what to do with myself. [*after a pause*] I've always made a point of not wasting my life, and everytime I come back here I know that all I've done is to waste my life.

HAPPY   You're a poet, you know that, Biff? You're a—you're an idealist!

BIFF   No, I'm mixed up very bad. Maybe I oughta get married. Maybe I oughta get stuck into something. Maybe that's my trouble. I'm like a boy. I'm not married. I'm not in business, I just—I'm like a boy. Are you content, Hap? You're a success, aren't you? Are you content?

HAPPY   Hell, no!

BIFF   Why? You're making money, aren't you?

HAPPY [*moving about with energy, expressiveness*]   All I can do now is wait for the merchandise manager to die. And suppose I get to be merchandise manager? He's a good friend of mine, and he just built a terrific estate on Long Island. And he lived there about two months and sold it, and now he's building another one. He can't enjoy it once it's finished. And I know that's just what I would do. I don't know what the hell I'm workin' for. Sometimes I sit in my apartment—all alone. And I think of the rent I'm paying. And it's crazy. But then, it's what I always wanted. My own apartment, a car, and plenty of women. And still, goddammit, I'm lonely.

BIFF [*with enthusiasm*]   Listen why don't you come out West with me?

HAPPY   You and I, heh?

BIFF   Sure, maybe we could buy a ranch. Raise cattle, use our muscles. Men built like we are should be working out in the open.

HAPPY [*avidly*]   The Loman Brothers, heh?

BIFF [*with vast affection*]   Sure, we'd be known all over the counties!

HAPPY [*enthralled*]   That's what I dream about, Biff. Sometimes I want to just rip my clothes off in the middle of the store and outbox that goddam merchandise manager. I mean I can outbox, outrun, and outlift anybody in that store, and I have to take orders from those common, petty sons-of-bitches till I can't stand it any more.

BIFF   I'm tellin' you, kid, if you were with me I'd be happy out there.

HAPPY [*enthused*]   See, Biff, everybody around me is so false that I'm constantly lowering my ideals . . .

BIFF   Baby, together we'd stand up for one another, we'd have someone to trust.

HAPPY   If I were around you—

BIFF   Hap, the trouble is we weren't brought up to grub for money. I don't know how to do it.

HAPPY   Neither can I!

BIFF   Then let's go!

HAPPY   The only thing is—what can you make out there?

BIFF   But look at your friend. Builds an estate and then hasn't the peace of mind to live in it.

HAPPY   Yeah, but when he walks into the store the waves part in front of him. That's fifty-two thousand dollars a year coming through the revolving door, and I got more in my pinky finger than he's got in his head.

BIFF   Yeah, but you just said—

HAPPY   I gotta show some of those pompous, self-important executives over there that Hap Loman can make the grade. I want to walk into the store the way he walks in. Then I'll go with you, Biff. We'll be together yet, I swear. But take those two we had tonight. Now weren't they gorgeous creatures?

BIFF   Yeah, yeah, most gorgeous I've had in years.

HAPPY   I get that any time I want, Biff. Whenever I feel disgusted. The only trouble is, it gets like bowling or something. I just keep knockin' them over and it doesn't mean anything. You still run around a lot?

BIFF   Naa. I'd like to find a girl—steady, somebody with substance.

HAPPY   That's what I long for.

BIFF   Go on! You'd never come home.

HAPPY   I would! Somebody with character, with resistance! Like Mom, y'know? You're gonna call me a bastard when I tell you this. That girl Charlotte I was with tonight is engaged to be married in five weeks. [*He tries on his new hat.*]

BIFF   No kiddin'!

HAPPY   Sure, the guy's in line for the vice-presidency of the store. I don't know what gets into me, maybe I just have an overdeveloped sense of competition or something, but I went and ruined her, and furthermore I can't get rid of her. And he's the third executive I've done that to. Isn't that a crummy characteristic? And to top it all, I go to their weddings! [*indignantly, but laughing*] Like I'm not supposed to take bribes. Manufacturers offer me a hundred-dollar bill now and then to throw an order their way. You know how honest I am, but it's like this girl, see. I hate myself for it. Because I don't want the girl, and, still, I take it and—I love it!

BIFF   Let's go to sleep.

HAPPY   I guess we didn't settle anything, heh?

BIFF   I just got one idea that I think I'm going to try.

HAPPY   What's that?

BIFF   Remember Bill Oliver?

HAPPY   Sure, Oliver is very big now. You want to work for him again?

BIFF   No, but when I quit he said something to me. He put his arm on my shoulder, and he said, "Biff, if you ever need anything, come to me."

HAPPY   I remember that. That sounds good.

BIFF   I think I'll go to see him. If I could get ten thousand or even seven or eight thousand dollars I could buy a beautiful ranch.

HAPPY   I bet he'd back you. 'Cause he thought highly of you, Biff. I mean, they all do. You're well liked, Biff. That's why I say to come back here, and we both have the apartment. And I'm tellin' you, Biff, any babe you want . . .

BIFF   No, with a ranch I could do the work I like and still be something. I just wonder though. I wonder if Oliver still thinks I stole that carton of basketballs.

HAPPY   Oh, he probably forgot that long ago. It's almost ten years. You're too sensitive. Anyway, he didn't really fire you.

BIFF   Well, I think he was going to. I think that's why I quit. I was never sure whether he knew or not. I know he thought the world of me, though. I was the only one he'd let lock up the place.

WILLY [*below*]   You gonna wash the engine, Biff?

HAPPY   Shh!

[BIFF *looks at* HAPPY, *who is gazing down, listening.* WILLY *is mumbling in the parlor.*]

HAPPY   You hear that?

[*They listen.* WILLY *laughs warmly.*]

BIFF [*growing angry*]   Doesn't he know Mom can hear that?

WILLY   Don't get your sweater dirty, Biff!

[*A look of pain crosses* BIFF's *face.*]

HAPPY   Isn't that terrible? Don't leave again, will you? You'll find a job here. You gotta stick around. I don't know what to do about him, it's getting embarrassing.

WILLY   What a simonizing job!

BIFF   Mom's hearing that!

WILLY   No kiddin', Biff, you got a date? Wonderful!

HAPPY   Go on to sleep. But talk to him in the morning, will you?

BIFF [*reluctantly getting into bed*]   With her in the house. Brother!

HAPPY [*getting into bed*]   I wish you'd have a good talk with him.

[*The light on their room begins to fade.*]

BIFF [*to himself in bed*]   That selfish, stupid . . .

HAPPY   Sh . . . Sleep, Biff.

[*Their light is out. Well before they have finished speaking,* WILLY'S *form is dimly seen below in the darkened kitchen. He opens the refrigerator, searches in there, and takes out a bottle of milk. The apartment houses are fading out, and the entire house and surroundings become covered with leaves. Music insinuates itself as the leaves appear.*]

WILLY   Just wanna be careful with those girls, Biff, that's all. Don't make any promises. No promises of any kind. Because a girl, y'know, they always believe what you tell 'em, and you're very young, Biff, you're too young to be talking seriously to girls.

[*Light rises on the kitchen.* WILLY, *talking, shuts the refrigerator door and comes downstage to the kitchen table. He pours milk into a glass. He is totally immersed in himself, smiling faintly.*]

WILLY   Too young entirely, Biff. You want to watch your schooling first. Then when you're all set, there'll be plenty of girls for a boy like you. [*He smiles broadly at a kitchen chair.*] That so? The girls pay for you? [*He laughs.*] Boy, you must really be makin' a hit.

[WILLY *is gradually addressing—physically—a point offstage, speaking through the wall of the kitchen, and his voice has been rising in volume to that of a normal conversation.*]

WILLY   I been wondering why you polish the car so careful. Ha! Don't leave the hubcaps, boys. Get the chamois to the hubcaps. Happy, use newspaper on the windows, it's the easiest thing. Show him how to do it, Biff! You see, Happy? Pad it up, use it like a pad. That's it, that's it, good work. You're doin' all right, Hap. [*He pauses, then nods in approbation for a few seconds, then looks upward.*] Biff, first thing we gotta do when we get time is clip that big branch over the house. Afraid it's gonna fall in a storm and hit the roof. Tell you what. We get a rope and sling her around, and then we climb up there with a couple of saws and take her down. Soon as you finish the car, boys, I wanna see ya. I got a surprise for you, boys.

BIFF [*offstage*]   Whatta ya got, Dad?

WILLY   No, you finish first. Never leave a job till you're finished— remember that. [*looking toward the "big trees"*] Biff, up in Albany I saw a beautiful hammock. I think I'll buy it next trip, and we'll hang it right between those two elms. Wouldn't that be something? Just swingin' there under those branches. Boy, that would be . . .

[YOUNG BIFF *and* YOUNG HAPPY *appear from the direction* WILLY *was addressing.* HAPPY *carries rags and a pail of water.* BIFF, *wearing a sweater with a block "S," carries a football.*]

BIFF [*pointing in the direction of the car offstage*]   How's that, Pop, professional?

WILLY   Terrific. Terrific job, boys. Good work, Biff.

HAPPY   Where's the surprise, Pop?

WILLY   In the back seat of the car.

HAPPY   Boy! [*He runs off.*]

BIFF   What is it, Dad? Tell me, what'd you buy?

WILLY [*laughing, cuffs him*]   Never mind, something I want you to have.

BIFF [*turns and starts off*]   What is it, Hap?

HAPPY [*offstage*]   It's a punching bag!

BIFF   Oh, Pop!

WILLY   It's got Gene Tunney's[1] signature on it!
          [HAPPY *runs onstage with a punching bag.*]
BIFF   Gee, how'd you know we wanted a punching bag?
WILLY   Well, it's the finest thing for the timing.
HAPPY   [*lies down on his back and pedals with his feet*]   I'm losing weight,
          you notice, Pop?
WILLY   [*to* HAPPY]   Jumping rope is good too.
BIFF   Did you see the new football I got?
WILLY   [*examining the ball*]   Where'd you get a new ball?
BIFF   The coach told me to practice my passing.
WILLY   That so? And he gave you the ball, heh?
BIFF   Well, I borrowed it from the locker room. [*He laughs confidentially.*]
WILLY   [*laughing with him at the left*]   I want you to return that.
HAPPY   I told you he wouldn't like it!
BIFF   [*angrily*]   Well, I'm bringing it back!
WILLY   [*stopping the incipient argument, to* HAPPY]   Sure, he's gotta practice
          with a regulation ball, doesn't he? [*to* BIFF] Coach'll probably congratu-
          late you on your initiative!
BIFF   Oh, he keeps congratulating my initiative all the time, Pop.
WILLY   That's because he likes you. If somebody else took that ball there'd
          be an uproar. So what's the report, boys, what's the report?
BIFF   Where'd you go this time, Dad? Gee we were lonesome for you.
WILLY   [*pleased, puts an arm around each boy and they come down to the
          apron*]   Lonesome, heh?
BIFF   Missed you every minute.
WILLY   Don't say? Tell you a secret, boys. Don't breathe it to a soul. Some-
          day I'll have my own business, and I'll never have to leave home any
          more.
HAPPY   Like Uncle Charley, heh?
WILLY   Bigger than Uncle Charley! Because Charley is not—liked. He's
          liked, but he's not—well liked.
BIFF   Where'd you go this time, Dad?
WILLY   Well, I got on the road, and I went north to Providence. Met the
          Mayor.
BIFF   The Mayor of Providence!
WILLY   He was sitting in the hotel lobby.
BIFF   What'd he say?
WILLY   He said, "Morning!" And I said, "You got a fine city here, Mayor."
          And then he had coffee with me. And then I went to Waterbury. Water-
          bury is a fine city. Big clock city, the famous Waterbury clock. Sold a nice
          bill there. And then Boston—Boston is the cradle of the Revolution. A
          fine city. And a couple of other towns in Mass., and on to Portland and
          Bangor and straight home!
BIFF   Gee, I'd love to go with you sometime, Dad.
WILLY   Soon as summer comes.
HAPPY   Promise?
WILLY   You and Hap and I, and I'll show you all the towns. America is full
          of beautiful towns and fine, upstanding people. And they know me, boys,

---

1. World heavyweight boxing champion from 1926 to 1928.

they know me up and down New England. The finest people. And when I bring you fellas up, there'll be open sesame for all of us, 'cause one thing, boys: I have friends. I can park my car in any street in New England, and the cops protect it like their own. This summer, heh?

BIFF and HAPPY [*together*]   Yeah! You bet!

WILLY   We'll take our bathing suits.

HAPPY   We'll carry your bags, Pop!

WILLY   Oh, won't that be something! Me comin' into the Boston stores with you boys carryin' my bags. What a sensation!

[BIFF *is prancing around, practicing passing the ball.*]

WILLY   You nervous, Biff, about the game?

BIFF   Not if you're gonna be there.

WILLY   What do they say about you in school, now that they made you captain?

HAPPY   There's a crowd of girls behind him everytime the classes change.

BIFF [*taking* WILLY'S *hand*]   This Saturday, Pop, this Saturday—just for you, I'm going to break through for a touchdown.

HAPPY   You're supposed to pass.

BIFF   I'm takin' one play for Pop. You watch me, Pop, and when I take off my helmet, that means I'm breakin' out. Then you watch me crash through that line!

WILLY [*kisses* BIFF]   Oh, wait'll I tell this in Boston!

[BERNARD *enters in knickers. He is younger than* BIFF, *earnest and loyal, a worried boy.*]

BERNARD   Biff, where are you? You're supposed to study with me today.

WILLY   Hey, looka Bernard. What're you lookin' so anemic about, Bernard?

BERNARD   He's gotta study, Uncle Willy. He's got Regents[2] next week.

HAPPY [*tauntingly, spinning* BERNARD *around*]   Let's box, Bernard!

BERNARD   Biff! [*He gets away from* HAPPY.] Listen, Biff, I heard Mr. Birnbaum say that if you don't start studyin' math he's gonna flunk you, and you won't graduate. I heard him!

WILLY   You better study with him, Biff. Go ahead now.

BERNARD   I heard him!

BIFF   Oh, Pop, you didn't see my sneakers! [*He holds up a foot for* WILLY *to look at.*]

WILLY   Hey, that's a beautiful job of printing!

BERNARD [*wiping his glasses*]   Just because he printed University of Virginia on his sneakers doesn't mean they've got to graduate him, Uncle Willy!

WILLY [*angrily*]   What're you talking about? With scholarships to three universities they're gonna flunk him?

BERNARD   But I heard Mr. Birnbaum say—

WILLY   Don't be a pest, Bernard! [*to his boys*] What an anemic!

BERNARD   Okay, I'm waiting for you in my house, Biff.

[BERNARD *goes off. The Lomans laugh.*]

WILLY   Bernard is not well liked, is he?

BIFF   He's liked, but he's not well liked.

HAPPY   That's right, Pop.

WILLY   That's just what I mean. Bernard can get the best marks in school,

---

2. Compulsory statewide high school examinations in New York.

y'understand, but when he gets out in the business world, y'understand, you are going to be five times ahead of him. That's why I thank Almighty God you're both built like Adonises.[3] Because the man who makes an appearance in the business world, the man who creates personal interest, is the man who gets ahead. Be liked and you will never want. You take me, for instance. I never have to wait in line to see a buyer. "Willy Loman is here!" That's all they have to know, and I go right through.

BIFF   Did you knock them dead, Pop?

WILLY   Knocked 'em cold in Providence, slaughtered 'em in Boston.

HAPPY [*on his back, pedaling again*]   I'm losing weight, you notice, Pop?
    [LINDA *enters, as of old, a ribbon in her hair, carrying a basket of washing.*]

LINDA [*with youthful energy*]   Hello, dear!

WILLY   Sweetheart!

LINDA   How'd the Chevvy run?

WILLY   Chevrolet, Linda, is the greatest car ever built. [*to the boys*] Since when do you let your mother carry wash up the stairs?

BIFF   Grab hold there, boy!

HAPPY   Where to, Mom?

LINDA   Hang them up on the line. And you better go down to your friends, Biff. The cellar is full of boys. They don't know what to do with themselves.

BIFF   Ah, when Pop comes home they can wait!

WILLY [*laughs appreciatively*]   You better go down and tell them what to do, Biff.

BIFF   I think I'll have them sweep out the furnace room.

WILLY   Good work, Biff.

BIFF [*goes through wall-line of kitchen to doorway at back and calls down*]   Fellas! Everybody sweep out the furnace room! I'll be right down!

VOICES   All right! Okay, Biff.

BIFF   George and Sam and Frank, come out back! We're hangin' up the wash! Come on, Hap, on the double!
    [*He and* HAPPY *carry out the basket.*]

LINDA   The way they obey him!

WILLY   Well, that training, the training. I'm tellin' you, I was sellin' thousands and thousands, but I had to come home.

LINDA   Oh, the whole block'll be at that game. Did you sell anything?

WILLY   I did five hundred gross in Providence and seven hundred gross in Boston.

LINDA   No! Wait a minute, I've got a pencil. [*She pulls pencil and paper out of her apron pocket.*] That makes your commission . . . Two hundred—my God! Two hundred and twelve dollars!

WILLY   Well, I didn't figure it yet, but . . .

LINDA   How much did you do?

WILLY   Well, I—I did—about a hundred and eighty gross in Providence. Well, no—it came to—roughly two hundred gross on the whole trip.

LINDA [*without hesitation*]   Two hundred gross. That's . . . [*She figures.*]

WILLY   The trouble was that three of the stores were half closed for inventory in Boston. Otherwise I woulda broke records.

---

3. In Greek mythology Adonis was a beautiful youth favored by Aphrodite, the goddess of love.

LINDA   Well, it makes seventy dollars and some pennies. That's very good.

WILLY   What do we owe?

LINDA   Well, on the first there's sixteen dollars on the refrigerator—

WILLY   Why sixteen?

LINDA   Well, the fan belt broke, so it was a dollar eighty.

WILLY   But it's brand new.

LINDA   Well, the man said that's the way it is. Till they work themselves in, y'know.

[*They move through the wall-line into the kitchen.*]

WILLY   I hope we didn't get stuck on that machine.

LINDA   They got the biggest ads of any of them!

WILLY   I know, it's a fine machine. What else?

LINDA   Well, there's nine-sixty for the washing machine. And for the vacuum cleaner there's three and a half due on the fifteenth. Then the roof, you got twenty-one dollars remaining.

WILLY   It don't leak, does it?

LINDA   No, they did a wonderful job. Then you owe Frank for the carburetor.

WILLY   I'm not going to pay that man! That goddam Chevrolet, they ought to prohibit the manufacture of that car!

LINDA   Well, you owe him three and a half. And odds and ends, comes to around a hundred and twenty dollars by the fifteenth.

WILLY   A hundred and twenty dollars! My God, if business don't pick up I don't know what I'm gonna do!

LINDA   Well, next week you'll do better.

WILLY   Oh, I'll knock 'em dead next week. I'll go to Hartford. I'm very well liked in Hartford. You know, the trouble is, Linda, people don't seem to take to me.

[*They move onto the forestage.*]

LINDA   Oh, don't be foolish.

WILLY   I know it when I walk in. They seem to laugh at me.

LINDA   Why? Why would they laugh at you? Don't talk that way, Willy.

[WILLY *moves to the edge of the stage.* LINDA *goes into the kitchen and starts to darn stockings.*]

WILLY   I don't know the reason for it, but they just pass me by. I'm not noticed.

LINDA   But you're doing wonderful, dear. You're making seventy to a hundred dollars a week.

WILLY   But I gotta be at it ten, twelve hours a day. Other men—I don't know—they do it easier. I don't know why—I can't stop myself—I talk too much. A man oughta come in with a few words. One thing about Charley. He's a man of few words, and they respect him.

LINDA   You don't talk too much, you're just lively.

WILLY [*smiling*]   Well, I figure, what the hell, life is short, a couple of jokes. [*to himself*] I joke too much! [*The smiles goes.*]

LINDA   Why? You're—

WILLY   I'm fat. I'm very—foolish to look at, Linda. I didn't tell you, but Christmas time I happened to be calling on F. H. Stewarts, and a salesman I know, as I was going in to see the buyer I heard him say something about—walrus. And I—I cracked him right across the face. I won't take that. I simply will not take that. But they do laugh at me. I know that.

LINDA   Darling . . .

WILLY   I gotta overcome it. I know I gotta overcome it. I'm not dressing to advantage, maybe.

LINDA   Willy, darling, you're the handsomest man in the world—

WILLY   Oh, no, Linda.

LINDA   To me you are. [*slight pause*] The handsomest.

[*From the darkness is heard the laughter of a woman.* WILLY *doesn't turn to it, but it continues through* LINDA's *lines.*]

LINDA   And the boys, Willy. Few men are idolized by their children the way you are.

[*Music is heard as behind a scrim,*[4] *to the left of the house,* THE WOMAN, *dimly seen, is dressing.*]

WILLY [*with great feeling*]   You're the best there is, Linda, you're a pal, you know that? On the road—on the road I want to grab you sometimes and just kiss the life outa you.

[*The laughter is loud now, and he moves into a brightening area at the left, where* THE WOMAN *has come from behind the scrim and is standing, putting on her hat, looking into a "mirror" and laughing.*]

WILLY   'Cause I get so lonely—especially when business is bad and there's nobody to talk to. I get the feeling that I'll never sell anything again, that I won't make a living for you, or a business, a business for the boys. [*He talks through* THE WOMAN's *subsiding laughter;* THE WOMAN *primps at the "mirror."*] There's so much I want to make for—

THE WOMAN   Me? You didn't make me, Willy. I picked you.

WILLY [*pleased*]   You picked me?

THE WOMAN [*who is quite proper-looking,* WILLY's *age*]   I did. I've been sitting at that desk watching all the salesmen go by, day in, day out. But you've got such a sense of humor, and we do have such a good time together, don't we?

WILLY   Sure, sure. [*He takes her in his arms.*] Why do you have to go now?

THE WOMAN   It's two o'clock . . .

WILLY   No, come on in! [*He pulls her.*]

THE WOMAN   . . . my sisters'll be scandalized. When'll you be back?

WILLY   Oh, two weeks about. Will you come up again?

THE WOMAN   Sure thing. You do make me laugh. It's good for me. [*She squeezes his arm, kisses him.*] And I think you're a wonderful man.

WILLY   You picked me, heh?

THE WOMAN   Sure. Because you're so sweet. And such a kidder.

WILLY   Well, I'll see you next time I'm in Boston.

THE WOMAN   I'll put you right through to the buyers.

WILLY [*slapping her bottom*]   Right. Well, bottoms up!

THE WOMAN [*slaps him gently and laughs*]   You just kill me, Willy. [*He suddenly grabs her and kisses her roughly.*] You kill me. And thanks for the stockings. I love a lot of stockings. Well, good night.

WILLY   Good night. And keep your pores open!

THE WOMAN   Oh, Willy!

[THE WOMAN *bursts out laughing, and* LINDA's *laughter blends in.* THE WOMAN *disappears into the dark. Now the area at the kitchen table bright-*

---

4. Part of a stage set; a painted gauze curtain that becomes transparent when lighted from the back.

ens. LINDA *is sitting where she was at the kitchen table, but now is mending a pair of her silk stockings.*]

LINDA You are, Willy. The handsomest man. You've got no reason to feel that—

WILLY [*coming out of* THE WOMAN's *dimming area and going over to* LINDA] I'll make it all up to you, Linda. I'll—

LINDA There's nothing to make up, dear. You're doing fine, better than—

WILLY [*noticing her mending*] What's that?

LINDA Just mending my stockings. They're so expensive—

WILLY [*angrily, taking them from her*] I won't have you mending stockings in this house! Now throw them out!

[LINDA *puts the stockings in her pocket.*]

BERNARD [*entering on the run*] Where is he? If he doesn't study!

WILLY [*moving to the forestage, with great agitation*] You'll give him the answers!

BERNARD I do, but I can't on a Regents! That's a state exam! They're liable to arrest me!

WILLY Where is he? I'll whip him, I'll whip him!

LINDA And he'd better give back that football, Willy, it's not nice.

WILLY Biff! Where is he? Why is he taking everything?

LINDA He's too rough with the girls, Willy. All the mothers are afraid of him!

WILLY I'll whip him!

BERNARD He's driving the car without a license!

[THE WOMAN's *laugh is heard.*]

WILLY Shut up!

LINDA All the mothers—

WILLY Shut up!

BERNARD [*backing quietly away and out*] Mr. Birnbaum says he's stuck up.

WILLY Get outa here!

BERNARD If he doesn't buckle down he'll flunk math! [*He goes off.*]

LINDA He's right, Willy, you've gotta—

WILLY [*exploding at her*] There's nothing the matter with him! You want him to be a worm like Bernard? He's got spirit, personality . . .

[*As he speaks,* LINDA, *almost in tears, exist into the living-room.* WILLY *is alone in the kitchen, wilting and staring. The leaves are gone. It is night again, and the apartment houses look down from behind.*]

WILLY Loaded with it. Loaded! What is he stealing? He's giving it back, isn't he? Why is he stealing? What did I tell him? I never in my life told him anything but decent things.

[HAPPY *in pajamas has come down the stairs;* WILLY *suddenly becomes aware of* HAPPY's *presence.*]

HAPPY Let's go now, come on.

WILLY [*sitting down at the kitchen table*] Huh! Why did she have to wax the floors herself? Everytime she waxes the floors she keels over. She knows that!

HAPPY Shh! Take it easy. What brought you back tonight?

WILLY I got an awful scare. Nearly hit a kid in Yonkers. God! Why didn't I go to Alaska with my brother Ben that time! Ben! That man was a genius, that man was success incarnate! What a mistake! He begged me to go.

HAPPY Well, there's no use in—

WILLY   You guys! There was a man started with the clothes on his back and
ended up with diamond mines!

HAPPY   Boy, someday I'd like to know how he did it.

WILLY   What's the mystery? The man knew what he wanted and went out
and got it! Walked into a jungle, and comes out, the age of twenty-one,
and he's rich! The world is an oyster, but you don't crack it open on a mattress!

HAPPY   Pop, I told you I'm gonna retire you for life.

WILLY   You'll retire me for life on seventy goddam dollars a week? And your
women and your car and your apartment, and you'll retire me for life!
Christ's sake, I couldn't get past Yonkers today! Where are you guys,
where are you? The woods are burning! I can't drive a car!

[CHARLEY has appeared in the doorway. He is a large man, slow of speech,
laconic, immovable. In all he says, despite what he says, there is pity, and,
now, trepidation. He has a robe over pajamas, slippers on his feet. He
enters the kitchen.]

CHARLEY   Everything all right?

HAPPY   Yeah, Charley, everything's . . .

WILLY   What's the matter?

CHARLEY   I heard some noise. I thought something happened. Can't we do
something about the walls? You sneeze in here, and in my house hats blow
off.

HAPPY   Let's go to bed, Dad. Come on.

[CHARLEY signals to HAPPY to go.]

WILLY   You go ahead, I'm not tired at the moment.

HAPPY [to WILLY]   Take it easy, huh? [He exits.]

WILLY   What're you doin' up?

CHARLEY [sitting down at the kitchen table opposite WILLY]   Couldn't sleep
good. I had a heartburn.

WILLY   Well, you don't know how to eat.

CHARLEY   I eat with my mouth.

WILLY   No, you're ignorant. You gotta know about vitamins and things like
that.

CHARLEY   Come on, let's shoot. Tire you out a little.

WILLY [hesitantly]   All right. You got cards?

CHARLEY [taking a deck from his pocket]   Yeah, I got them. Someplace.
What is it with those vitamins?

WILLY [dealing]   They build up your bones. Chemistry.

CHARLEY   Yeah, but there's no bones in a heartburn.

WILLY   What are you talkin' about? Do you know the first thing about it?

CHARLEY   Don't get insulted.

WILLY   Don't talk about something you don't know anything about.

[They are playing. Pause.]

CHARLEY   What're you doin' home?

WILLY   A little trouble with the car.

CHARLEY   Oh. [pause] I'd like to take a trip to California.

WILLY   Don't say.

CHARLEY   You want a job?

WILLY   I got a job, I told you that. [after a slight pause] What the hell are
you offering me a job for?

CHARLEY   Don't get insulted.

WILLY   Don't insult me.

CHARLEY   I don't see no sense in it. You don't have to go on this way.

WILLY   I got a good job. [slight pause] What do you keep comin' in here for?

CHARLEY   You want me to go?

WILLY [after a pause, withering]   I can't understand it. He's going back to Texas again. What the hell is that?

CHARLEY   Let him go.

WILLY   I got nothin' to give him, Charley, I'm clean, I'm clean.

CHARLEY   He won't starve. None a them starve. Forget about him.

WILLY   Then what have I got to remember?

CHARLEY   You take it too hard. To hell with it. When a deposit bottle is broken you don't get your nickel back.

WILLY   That's easy enough for you to say.

CHARLEY   That ain't easy for me to say.

WILLY   Did you see the ceiling I put up in the living-room?

CHARLEY   Yeah, that's a piece of work. To put up a ceiling is a mystery to me. How do you do it?

WILLY   What's the difference?

CHARLEY   Well, talk about it.

WILLY   You gonna put up a ceiling?

CHARLEY   How could I put up a ceiling?

WILLY   Then what the hell are you bothering me for?

CHARLEY   You're insulted again.

WILLY   A man who can't handle tools is not a man. You're disgusting.

CHARLEY   Don't call me disgusting, Willy.

[UNCLE BEN, carrying a valise and an umbrella, enters the forestage from around the right corner of the house. He is a stolid man, in his sixties, with a mustache and an authoritative air. He is utterly certain of his destiny, and there is an aura of far places about him. He enters exactly as WILLY speaks.]

WILLY   I'm getting awfully tired, Ben.

[BEN's music is heard. BEN looks around at everything.]

CHARLEY   Good, keep playing; you'll sleep better. Did you call me Ben?

[BEN looks at his watch.]

WILLY   That's funny. For a second there you reminded me of my brother Ben.

BEN   I only have a few minutes. [He strolls, inspecting the place. WILLY and CHARLEY continue playing.]

CHARLEY   You never heard from him again, heh? Since that time?

WILLY   Didn't Linda tell you? Couple of weeks ago we got a letter from his wife in Africa. He died.

CHARLEY   That so.

BEN [chuckling]   So this is Brooklyn, eh?

CHARLEY   Maybe you're in for some of his money.

WILLY   Naa, he had seven sons. There's just one opportunity I had with that man . . .

BEN   I must make a train, William. There are several properties I'm looking at in Alaska.

WILLY   Sure, sure! If I'd gone with him to Alaska that time, everything would've been totally different.

CHARLEY   Go on, you'd froze to death up there.

WILLY   What're you talking about?

BEN   Opportunity is tremendous in Alaska, William. Surprised you're not up there.

WILLY   Sure, tremendous.

CHARLEY   Heh?

WILLY   There was the only man I ever met who knew the answers.

CHARLEY   Who?

BEN   How are you all?

WILLY [*taking a pot, smiling*]   Fine, fine.

CHARLEY   Pretty sharp tonight.

BEN   Is Mother living with you?

WILLY   No, she died a long time ago.

CHARLEY   Who?

BEN   That's too bad. Fine specimen of a lady, Mother.

WILLY [*to* CHARLEY]   Heh?

BEN   I'd hoped to see the old girl.

CHARLEY   Who died?

BEN   Heard anything from Father, have you?

WILLY [*unnerved*]   What do you mean, who died?

CHARLEY [*taking a pot*]   What're you talkin' about?

BEN [*looking at his watch*]   William, it's half-past eight!

WILLY [*as though to dispel his confusion he angrily stops* CHARLEY's *hand*]   That's my build!

CHARLEY   I put the ace—

WILLY   If you don't know how to play the game I'm not gonna throw my money away on you!

CHARLEY [*rising*]   It was my ace, for God's sake!

WILLY   I'm through, I'm through!

BEN   When did Mother die?

WILLY   Long ago. Since the beginning you never knew how to play cards.

CHARLEY [*picks up the cards and goes to the door*]   All right! Next time I'll bring a deck with five aces.

WILLY   I don't play that kind of game!

CHARLEY [*turning to him*]   You ought to be ashamed of yourself!

WILLY   Yeah?

CHARLEY   Yeah! [*He goes out.*]

WILLY [*slamming the door after him*]   Ignoramus!

BEN [*as* WILLY *comes toward him through the wall-line of the kitchen*]   So you're William.

WILLY [*shaking* BEN's *hand*]   Ben! I've been waiting for you so long! What's the answer? How did you do it?

BEN   Oh, there's a story in that.

[LINDA *enters the forestage, as of old, carrying the wash basket.*]

LINDA   Is this Ben?

BEN [*gallantly*]   How do you do, my dear.

LINDA   Where've you been all these years? Willy's always wondered why you—

WILLY [*pulling* BEN *away from her impatiently*]   Where is Dad? Didn't you follow him? How did you get started?

BEN   Well, I don't know how much you remember.

WILLY   Well, I was just a baby, of course, only three or four years old—

BEN   Three years and eleven months.

WILLY   What a memory, Ben!

BEN   I have many enterprises, William, and I have never kept books.

WILLY   I remember I was sitting under the wagon in—was it Nebraska?

BEN   It was South Dakota, and I gave you a bunch of wild flowers.

WILLY   I remember you walking away down some open road.

BEN [laughing]   I was going to find Father in Alaska.

WILLY   Where is he?

BEN   At that age I had a very faulty view of geography, William. I discovered after a few days that I was heading due south, so instead of Alaska, I ended up in Africa.

LINDA   Africa!

WILLY   The Gold Coast!

BEN   Principally diamond mines.

LINDA   Diamond mines!

BEN   Yes, my dear. But I've only a few minutes—

WILLY   No! Boys! Boys! [YOUNG BIFF and HAPPY appear.] Listen to this. This is your Uncle Ben, a great man! Tell my boys, Ben!

BEN   Why, boys, when I was seventeen I walked into the jungle, and when I was twenty-one I walked out. [He laughs.] And by God I was rich.

WILLY [to the boys]   You see what I been talking about? The greatest things can happen!

BEN [glancing at his watch]   I have an appointment in Ketchikan Tuesday week.

WILLY   No, Ben! Please tell about Dad. I want my boys to hear. I want them to know the kind of stock they spring from. All I remember is a man with a big beard, and I was in Mamma's lap, sitting around a fire, and some kind of high music.

BEN   His flute. He played the flute.

WILLY   Sure, the flute, that's right!

[New music is heard, a high, rollicking tune.]

BEN   Father was a very great and a very wild-hearted man. We would start in Boston, and he'd toss the whole family into the wagon, and then he'd drive the team right across the country; through Ohio, and Indiana, Michigan, Illinois, and all the Western states. And we'd stop in the towns and sell the flutes that he'd made on the way. Great inventor, Father. With one gadget he made more in a week than a man like you could make in a lifetime.

WILLY   That's just the way I'm bringing them up, Ben—rugged, well liked, all-around.

BEN   Yeah? [to BIFF] Hit that, boy—hard as you can. [He pounds his stomach.]

BIFF   Oh, no, sir!

BEN [taking boxing stance]   Come on, get to me! [He laughs.]

WILLY   Go to it, Biff! Go ahead, show him!

BIFF   Okay! [He cocks his fist and starts in.]

LINDA [to WILLY]   Why must he fight, dear?

BEN [sparring with BIFF]   Good boy! Good boy!

WILLY   How's that, Ben, heh?

HAPPY   Give him the left, Biff!

LINDA   Why are you fighting?

BEN   Good boy! [Suddenly comes in, trips BIFF, and stands over him, the point of his umbrella poised over BIFF's eye.]

LINDA   Look out, Biff!

BIFF   Gee!

BEN [*patting* BIFF's *knee*]   Never fight fair with a stranger, boy. You'll never get out of the jungle that way. [*taking* LINDA's *hand and bowing*] It was an honor and a pleasure to meet you, Linda.

LINDA [*withdrawing her hand coldly, frightened*]   Have a nice—trip.

BEN [*to* WILLY]   And good luck with your—what do you do?

WILLY   Selling.

BEN   Yes. Well . . . [*He raises his hand in farewell to all.*]

WILLY   No, Ben, I don't want you to think . . . [*He takes* BEN's *arm to show him.*] It's Brooklyn, I know, but we hunt too.

BEN   Really, now.

WILLY   Oh, sure, there's snakes and rabbits and—that's why I moved out here. Why, Biff can fell any one of these trees in no time! Boys! Go right over to where they're building the apartment house and get some sand. We're gonna rebuild the entire front stoop right now! Watch this, Ben!

BIFF   Yes, sir! On the double, Hap!

HAPPY [*as he and* BIFF *run off*]   I lost weight, Pop, you notice?

   [CHARLEY *enters in knickers, even before the boys are gone.*]

CHARLEY   Listen, if they steal any more from that building the watchman'll put the cops on them!

LINDA [*to* WILLY]   Don't let Biff . . .

   [BEN *laughs lustily.*]

WILLY   You shoulda seen the lumber they brought home last week. At least a dozen six-by-tens worth all kinds a money.

CHARLEY   Listen, if that watchman—

WILLY   I gave them hell, understand. But I got a couple of fearless characters there.

CHARLEY   Willy, the jails are full of fearless characters.

BEN [*clapping* WILLY *on the back, with a laugh at* CHARLEY]   And the stock exchange, friend!

WILLY [*joining in* BEN's *laughter*]   Where are the rest of your pants?

CHARLEY   My wife bought them.

WILLY   Now all you need is a golf club and you can go upstairs and go to sleep. [*to* BEN] Great athlete! Between him and his son Bernard they can't hammer a nail!

BERNARD [*rushing in*]   The watchman's chasing Biff!

WILLY [*angrily*]   Shut up! He's not stealing anything!

LINDA [*alarmed, hurrying off left*]   Where is he? Biff, dear! [*She exits.*]

WILLY [*moving toward the left, away from* BEN]   There's nothing wrong. What's the matter with you?

BEN   Nervy boy. Good!

WILLY [*laughing*]   Oh, nerves of iron, that Biff!

CHARLEY   Don't know what it is. My New England man comes back and he's bleedin', they murdered him up there.

WILLY   It's contacts, Charley, I got important contacts!

CHARLEY [*sarcastically*]   Glad to hear it, Willy. Come in later, we'll shoot a little casino. I'll take some of your Portland money. [*He laughs at* WILLY *and exits.*]

WILLY [*turning to* BEN]   Business is bad, it's murderous. But not for me, of course.

BEN   I'll stop by on my way back to Africa.

WILLY [*longingly*]   Can't you stay a few days? You're just what I need, Ben, because I—I have a fine position here, but I—well, Dad left when I was such a baby and I never had a chance to talk to him and I still feel—kind of temporary about myself.

BEN   I'll be late for my train.

[*They are at opposite ends of the stage.*]

WILLY   Ben, my boys—can't we talk? They'd go into the jaws of hell for me, see, but I—

BEN   William, you're being first-rate with your boys. Outstanding, manly chaps!

WILLY [*hanging on to his words*]   Oh, Ben, that's good to hear! Because sometimes I'm afraid that I'm not teaching them the right kind of—Ben, how should I teach them?

BEN [*giving great weight to each word, and with a certain vicious audacity*]   William, when I walked into the jungle, I was seventeen. When I walked out I was twenty-one. And, by God, I was rich! [*He goes off into darkness around the right corner of the house.*]

WILLY   . . . was rich! That's just the spirit I want to imbue them with! To walk into a jungle! I was right! I was right! I was right!

[BEN *is gone, but* WILLY *is still speaking to him as* LINDA, *in nightgown and robe, enters the kitchen, glances around for* WILLY, *then goes to the door of the house, looks out and sees him. Comes down to his left. He looks at her.*]

LINDA   Willy, dear? Willy?

WILLY   I was right!

LINDA   Did you have some cheese? [*He can't answer.*] It's very late, darling. Come to bed, heh?

WILLY [*looking straight up*]   Gotta break your neck to see a star in this yard.

LINDA   You coming in?

WILLY   Whatever happened to that diamond watch fob? Remember? When Ben came from Africa that time? Didn't he give me a watch fob with a diamond in it?

LINDA   You pawned it, dear. Twelve, thirteen years ago. For Biff's radio correspondence course.

WILLY   Gee, that was a beautiful thing. I'll take a walk.

LINDA   But you're in your slippers.

WILLY [*starting to go around the house at the left*]   I was right! I was! [*half to* LINDA, *as he goes, shaking his head*] What a man! There was a man worth talking to. I was right!

LINDA [*calling after* WILLY]   But in your slippers, Willy!

[WILLY *is almost gone when* BIFF, *in his pajamas, comes down the stairs and enters the kitchen.*]

BIFF   What is he doing out there?

LINDA   Sh!

BIFF   God Almighty, Mom, how long has he been doing this?

LINDA   Don't, he'll hear you.

BIFF   What the hell is the matter with him?

LINDA   It'll pass by morning.

BIFF   Shouldn't we do anything?

LINDA   Oh, my dear, you should do a lot of things, but there's nothing to do, so go to sleep.

[HAPPY *comes down the stairs and sits on the steps.*]

HAPPY   I never heard him so loud, Mom.

LINDA   Well, come around more often; you'll hear him. [*She sits down at the table and mends the lining of* WILLY's *jacket.*]

BIFF   Why didn't you ever write me about this, Mom?

LINDA   How would I write to you? For over three months you had no address.

BIFF   I was on the move. But you know I thought of you all the time. You know that, don't you, pal?

LINDA   I know, dear, I know. But he likes to have a letter. Just to know that there's still a possibility for better things.

BIFF   He's not like this all the time, is he?

LINDA   It's when you come home he's always the worst.

BIFF   When I come home?

LINDA   When you write you're coming, he's all smiles, and talks about the future, and—he's just wonderful. And then the closer you seem to come, the more shaky he gets, and then, by the time you get here, he's arguing, and he seems angry at you. I think it's just that maybe he can't bring himself to—to open up to you. Why are you so hateful to each other? Why is that?

BIFF   [*evasively*]   I'm not hateful, Mom.

LINDA   But you no sooner come in the door than you're fighting!

BIFF   I don't know why. I mean to change. I'm tryin', Mom, you understand?

LINDA   Are you home to stay now?

BIFF   I don't know. I want to look around, see what's doin'.

LINDA   Biff, you can't look around all your life, can you?

BIFF   I just can't take hold, Mom. I can't take hold of some kind of a life.

LINDA   Biff, a man is not a bird, to come and go with the springtime.

BIFF   Your hair . . . [*He touches her hair.*] Your hair got so gray.

LINDA   Oh, it's been gray since you were in high school. I just stopped dyeing it, that's all.

BIFF   Dye it again, will ya? I don't want my pal looking old. [*He smiles.*]

LINDA   You're such a boy! You think you can go away for a year and . . . You've got to get it into your head now that one day you'll knock on this door and there'll be strange people here—

BIFF   What are you talking about? You're not even sixty, Mom.

LINDA   But what about your father?

BIFF   [*lamely*]   Well, I meant him too.

HAPPY   He admires Pop.

LINDA   Biff, dear, if you don't have any feeling for him, then you can't have any feeling for me.

BIFF   Sure I can, Mom.

LINDA   No. You can't just come to see me, because I love him. [*with a threat, but only a threat, of tears*] He's the dearest man in the world to me, and I won't have anyone making him feel unwanted and low and blue. You've got to make up your mind now, darling, there's no leeway any more. Either he's your father and you pay him that respect, or else you're not to come here. I know he's not easy to get along with—nobody knows that better than me—but . . .

WILLY [*from the left, with a laugh*] Hey, hey, Biffo!

BIFF [*starting to go out after* WILLY] What the hell is the matter with him? [HAPPY *stops him.*]

LINDA Don't—don't go near him!

BIFF Stop making excuses for him! He always, always wiped the floor with you. Never had an ounce of respect for you.

HAPPY He's always had respect for—

BIFF What the hell do you know about it?

HAPPY [*surlily*] Just don't call him crazy!

BIFF He's got no character—Charley wouldn't do this. Not in his own house—spewing out that vomit from his mind.

HAPPY Charley never had to cope with what he's got to.

BIFF People are worse off than Willy Loman. Believe me, I've seen them!

LINDA Then make Charley your father, Biff. You can't do that, can you? I don't say he's a great man. Willy Loman never made a lot of money. His name was never in the paper. He's not the finest character that ever lived. But he's a human being, and a terrible thing is happening to him. So attention must be paid. He's not to be allowed to fall into his grave like an old dog. Attention, attention must be finally paid to such a person. You called him crazy—

BIFF I didn't mean—

LINDA No, a lot of people think he's lost his—balance. But you don't have to be very smart to know what his trouble is. The man is exhausted.

HAPPY Sure!

LINDA A small man can be just as exhausted as a great man. He works for a company thirty-six years this March, opens up unheard-of territories to their trademark, and now in his old age they take his salary away.

HAPPY [*indignantly*] I didn't know that, Mom.

LINDA You never asked, my dear! Now that you get your spending money someplace else you don't trouble your mind with him.

HAPPY But I gave you money last—

LINDA Christmas time, fifty dollars! To fix the hot water it cost ninety-seven fifty! For five weeks he's been on straight commission, like a beginner, an unknown!

BIFF Those ungrateful bastards!

LINDA Are they any worse than his sons? When he brought them business, when he was young, they were glad to see him. But now his old friends, the old buyers that loved him so and always found some order to hand him in a pinch—they're all dead, retired. He used to be able to make six, seven calls a day in Boston. Now he takes his valises out of the car and puts them back and takes them out again and he's exhausted. Instead of walking he talks now. He drives seven hundred miles, and when he gets there no one knows him any more, no one welcomes him. And what goes through a man's mind, driving seven hundred miles home without having earned a cent? Why shouldn't he talk to himself? Why? When he has to go to Charley and borrow fifty dollars a week and pretend to me that it's his pay? How long can that go on? How long? You see what I'm sitting here and waiting for? And you tell me he has no character? The man who never worked a day but for your benefit? When does he get the medal for

that? Is this his reward—to turn around at the age of sixty-three and find
his sons, who he loved better than his life, one a philandering bum—

HAPPY Mom!

LINDA That's all you are, my baby! [*to* BIFF] And you! What happened to
the love you had for him? You were such pals! How you used to talk to him
on the phone every night! How lonely he was till he could come home to
you!

BIFF All right, Mom. I'll live here in my room, and I'll get a job. I'll keep
away from him, that's all.

LINDA No, Biff. You can't stay here and fight all the time.

BIFF He threw me out of this house, remember that.

LINDA Why did he do that? I never knew why.

BIFF Because I know he's a fake and he doesn't like anybody around who
knows!

LINDA Why a fake? In what way? What do you mean?

BIFF Just don't lay it all at my feet. It's between me and him—that's all I
have to say. I'll chip in from now on. He'll settle for half my pay check.
He'll be all right. I'm going to bed. [*He starts for the stairs.*]

LINDA He won't be all right.

BIFF [*turning on the stairs, furiously*] I hate this city and I'll stay here. Now
what do you want?

LINDA He's dying, Biff.

[HAPPY *turns quickly to her, shocked.*]

BIFF [*after a pause*] Why is he dying?

LINDA He's been trying to kill himself.

BIFF [*with great horror*] How?

LINDA I live from day to day.

BIFF What're you talking about?

LINDA Remember I wrote you that he smashed up the car again? In February?

BIFF Well?

LINDA The insurance inspector came. He said that they have evidence.
That all these accidents in the last year—weren't—weren't—accidents.

HAPPY How can they tell that? That's a lie.

LINDA It seems there's a woman . . . [*she takes a breath as*]

⎰ BIFF [*sharply but contained*] What woman?

⎱ LINDA [*simultaneously*] . . . and this woman . . .

LINDA What?

BIFF Nothing. Go ahead.

LINDA What did you say?

BIFF Nothing. I just said what woman?

HAPPY What about her?

LINDA Well, it seems she was walking down the road and saw his car. She
says that he wasn't driving fast at all, and that he didn't skid. She says he
came to that little bridge, and then deliberately smashed into the railing,
and it was only the shallowness of the water that saved him.

BIFF Oh, no, he probably just fell asleep again.

LINDA I don't think he fell asleep.

BIFF Why not?

LINDA Last month . . . [*with great difficulty*] Oh, boys, it's so hard to say a thing like this! He's just a big stupid man to you, but I tell you there's more good in him than in many other people. [*She chokes, wipes her eyes.*] I was looking for a fuse. The lights blew out, and I went down the cellar. And behind the fuse box—it happened to fall out—was a length of rubber pipe—just short.

HAPPY No kidding?

LINDA There's a little attachment on the end of it. I knew right away. And sure enough, on the bottom of the water heater there's a new little nipple on the gas pipe.

HAPPY [*angrily*] That—jerk.

BIFF Did you have it taken off?

LINDA I'm—I'm ashamed to. How can I mention it to him? Every day I go down and take away that little rubber pipe. But, when he comes home, I put it back where it was. How can I insult him that way? I don't know what to do. I live from day to day, boys. I tell you, I know every thought in his mind. It sounds so old-fashioned and silly, but I tell you he put his whole life into you and you've turned your backs on him. [*She is bent over in the chair, weeping, her face in her hands.*] Biff, I swear to God! Biff, his life is in your hands!

HAPPY [*to* BIFF] How do you like that damned fool!

BIFF [*kissing her*] All right, pal, all right. It's all settled now. I've been remiss. I know that, Mom. But now I'll stay, and I swear to you, I'll apply myself. [*kneeling in front of her, in a fever of self-reproach*] It's just—you see, Mom, I don't fit in business. Not that I won't try. I'll try, and I'll make good.

HAPPY Sure you will. The trouble with you in business was you never tried to please people.

BIFF I know, I—

HAPPY Like when you worked for Harrison's. Bob Harrison said you were tops, and then you go and do some damn fool thing like whistling whole songs in the elevator like a comedian.

BIFF [*against* HAPPY] So what? I like to whistle sometimes.

HAPPY You don't raise a guy to a responsible job who whistles in the elevator!

LINDA Well, don't argue about it now.

HAPPY Like when you'd go off and swim in the middle of the day instead of taking the line around.

BIFF [*his resentment rising*] Well, don't you run off? You take off sometimes, don't you? On a nice summer day?

HAPPY Yeah, but I cover myself!

LINDA Boys!

HAPPY If I'm going to take a fade the boss can call any number where I'm supposed to be and they'll swear to him that I just left. I'll tell you something that I hate to say, Biff, but in the business world some of them think you're crazy.

BIFF [*angered*] Screw the business world!

HAPPY All right, screw it! Great, but cover yourself!

LINDA Hap, Hap!

BIFF   I don't care what they think! They've laughed at Dad for years, and you know why? Because we don't belong in this nuthouse of a city! We should be mixing cement on some open plain, or—or carpenters. A carpenter is allowed to whistle!

[WILLY *walks in from the entrance of the house, at left.*]

WILLY   Even your grandfather was better than a carpenter. [*Pause. They watch him.*] You never grew up. Bernard does not whistle in the elevator, I assure you.

BIFF   [*as though to laugh* WILLY *out of it*]   Yeah, but you do, Pop.

WILLY   I never in my life whistled in an elevator! And who in the business world thinks I'm crazy?

BIFF   I didn't mean it like that, Pop. Now don't make a whole thing out of it, will ya?

WILLY   Go back to the West! Be a carpenter, a cowboy, enjoy yourself!

LINDA   Willy, he was just saying—

WILLY   I heard what he said!

HAPPY   [*trying to quiet* WILLY]   Hey, Pop, come on now . . .

WILLY   [*continuing over* HAPPY's *line*]   They laugh at me, heh? Go to Filene's, go to the Hub, go to Slattery's, Boston. Call out the name Willy Loman and see what happens! Big Shot!

BIFF   All right, Pop.

WILLY   Big!

BIFF   All right!

WILLY   Why do you always insult me?

BIFF   I didn't say a word. [*to* LINDA] Did I say a word?

LINDA   He didn't say anything, Willy.

WILLY [*going to the doorway of the living-room*]   All right, good night, good night.

LINDA   Willy, dear, he just decided . . .

WILLY [*to* BIFF]   If you get tired hanging around tomorrow, paint the ceiling I put up in the living-room.

BIFF   I'm leaving early tomorrow.

HAPPY   He's going to see Bill Oliver, Pop.

WILLY [*interestedly*]   Oliver? For what?

BIFF [*with reserve, but trying, trying*]   He always said he'd stake me. I'd like to go into business, so maybe I can take him up on it.

LINDA   Isn't that wonderful?

WILLY   Don't interrupt. What's wonderful about it? There's fifty men in the City of New York who'd stake him. [*to* BIFF] Sporting goods?

BIFF   I guess so. I know something about it and—

WILLY   He knows something about it! You know sporting goods better than Spalding, for God's sake! How much is he giving you?

BIFF   I don't know, I didn't even see him yet, but—

WILLY   Then what're you talkin' about?

BIFF [*getting angry*]   Well, all I said was I'm gonna see him, that's all!

WILLY [*turning away*]   Ah, you're counting your chickens again.

BIFF [*starting left for the stairs*]   Oh, Jesus, I'm going to sleep!

WILLY [*calling after him*]   Don't curse in this house!

BIFF [*turning*]   Since when did you get so clean?

HAPPY [*trying to stop them*]   Wait a . . .

WILLY   Don't use that language to me! I won't have it!

HAPPY [*grabbing* BIFF, *shouts*]   Wait a minute! I got an idea. I got a feasible idea. Come here, Biff, let's talk this over now, let's talk some sense here. When I was down in Florida last time, I thought of a great idea to sell sporting goods. It just came back to me. You and I, Biff—we have a line, the Loman Line. We train a couple of weeks, and put on a couple of exhibitions, see?

WILLY   That's an idea!

HAPPY   Wait! We form two basketball teams, see? Two water-polo teams. We play each other. It's a million dollars' worth of publicity. Two brothers, see? The Loman Brothers. Displays in the Royal Palms—all the hotels. And banners over the ring and the basketball court: "Loman Brothers." Baby, we could sell sporting goods!

WILLY   That is a one-million-dollar idea!

LINDA   Marvelous!

BIFF   I'm in great shape as far as that's concerned.

HAPPY   And the beauty of it is, Biff, it wouldn't be like a business. We'd be out playin' ball again . . .

BIFF [*enthused*]   Yeah, that's . . .

WILLY   Million-dollar . . .

HAPPY   And you wouldn't get fed up with it, Biff. It'd be the family again. There'd be the old honor, and comradeship, and if you wanted to go off for a swim or somethin'—well, you'd do it! Without some smart cooky gettin' up ahead of you!

WILLY   Lick the world! You guys together could absolutely lick the civilized world.

BIFF   I'll see Oliver tomorrow. Hap, if we could work that out . . .

LINDA   Maybe things are beginning to—

WILLY [*wildly enthused, to* LINDA]   Stop interrupting! [*to* BIFF] But don't wear sport jacket and slacks when you see Oliver.

BIFF   No, I'll—

WILLY   A business suit, and talk as little as possible, and don't crack any jokes.

BIFF   He did like me. Always liked me.

LINDA   He loved you!

WILLY [*to* LINDA]   Will you stop! [*to* BIFF] Walk in very serious. You are not applying for a boy's job. Money is to pass. Be quiet, fine, and serious. Everybody likes a kidder, but nobody lends him money.

HAPPY   I'll try to get some myself, Biff. I'm sure I can.

WILLY   I see great things for you kids, I think your troubles are over. But remember, start big and you'll end big. Ask for fifteen. How much you gonna ask for?

BIFF   Gee, I don't know—

WILLY   And don't say "Gee." "Gee" is a boy's word. A man walking in for fifteen thousand dollars does not say "Gee!"

BIFF   Ten, I think, would be top though.

WILLY   Don't be so modest. You always started too low. Walk in with a big laugh. Don't look worried. Start off with a couple of your good stories to lighten things up. It's not what you say, it's how you say it—because personality always wins the day.

LINDA   Oliver always thought the highest of him—

WILLY   Will you let me talk?

BIFF   Don't yell at her, Pop, will ya?

WILLY [angrily]   I was talking, wasn't I?

BIFF   I don't like you yelling at her all the time, and I'm tellin' you, that's all.

WILLY   What're you, takin' over this house?

LINDA   Willy—

WILLY [turning on her]   Don't take his side all the time, goddammit!

BIFF [furiously]   Stop yelling at her!

WILLY [suddenly pulling on his cheek, beaten down, guilt ridden]   Give my best to Bill Oliver—he may remember me. [He exits through the living-room doorway.]

LINDA [her voice subdued]   What'd you have to start that for? [BIFF turns away.] You see how sweet he was as soon as you talked hopefully? [She goes over to BIFF.] Come up and say good night to him. Don't let him go to bed that way.

HAPPY   Come on, Biff, let's buck him up.

LINDA   Please, dear. Just say good night. It takes so little to make him happy. Come. [She goes through the living-room doorway, calling upstairs from within the living-room] Your pajamas are hanging in the bathroom, Willy!

HAPPY [looking toward where LINDA went out]   What a woman! They broke the mold when they made her. You know that, Biff?

BIFF   He's off salary. My God, working on commission!

HAPPY   Well, let's face it: he's no hot-shot selling man. Except that sometimes, you have to admit, he's a sweet personality.

BIFF [deciding]   Lend me ten bucks, will ya? I want to buy some new ties.

HAPPY   I'll take you to a place I know. Beautiful stuff. Wear one of my striped shirts tomorrow.

BIFF   She got gray. Mom got awful old. Gee, I'm gonna go in to Oliver tomorrow and knock him for a—

HAPPY   Come on up. Tell that to Dad. Let's give him a whirl. Come on.

BIFF [steamed up]   You know, with ten thousand bucks, boy!

HAPPY [as they go into the living-room]   That's the talk, Biff, that's the first time I've heard the old confidence out of you! [from within the living-room, fading off] You're gonna live with me, kid, and any babe you want just say the word . . . [The last lines are hardly heard. They are mounting the stairs to their parents' bedroom.]

LINDA [entering her bedroom and addressing WILLY, who is in the bathroom. She is straightening the bed for him]   Can you do anything about the shower? It drips.

WILLY [from the bathroom]   All of a sudden everything falls to pieces! Goddam plumbing, oughta be sued, those people. I hardly finished putting it in and the thing . . . [His words rumble off.]

LINDA   I'm just wondering if Oliver will remember him. You think he might?

WILLY [coming out of the bathroom in his pajamas]   Remember him? What's the matter with you, you crazy? If he'd've stayed with Oliver he'd be on top by now! Wait'll Oliver gets a look at him. You don't know the average caliber any more. The average young man today—[he is getting into *bed*]—is got a caliber of zero. Greatest thing in the world for him was to bum around.

[BIFF *and* HAPPY *enter the bedroom. Slight pause.*]

WILLY [*stops short, looking at* BIFF]   Glad to hear it, boy.

HAPPY   He wanted to say good night to you, sport.

WILLY [*to* BIFF]   Yeah. Knock him dead, boy. What'd you want to tell me?

BIFF   Just take it easy, Pop. Good night. [*He turns to go.*]

WILLY [*unable to resist*]   And if anything falls off the desk while you're talking to him—like a package or something—don't you pick it up. They have office boys for that.

LINDA   I'll make a big breakfast—

WILLY   Will you let me finish? [*to* BIFF] Tell him you were in the business in the West. Not farm work.

BIFF   All right, Dad.

LINDA   I think everything—

WILLY [*going right through her speech*]   And don't undersell yourself. No less than fifteen thousand dollars.

BIFF [*unable to bear him*]   Okay. Good night, Mom. [*He starts moving.*]

WILLY   Because you got a greatness in you, Biff, remember that. You got all kinds a greatness . . . [*He lies back, exhausted.* BIFF *walks out.*]

LINDA [*calling after* BIFF]   Sleep well, darling!

HAPPY   I'm gonna get married, Mom. I wanted to tell you.

LINDA   Go to sleep, dear.

HAPPY [*going*]   I just wanted to tell you.

WILLY   Keep up the good work. [HAPPY *exits.*] God . . . remember that Ebbets Field[5] game? The championship of the city?

LINDA   Just rest. Should I sing to you?

WILLY   Yeah. Sing to me. [LINDA *hums a soft lullaby.*] When that team came out—he was the tallest, remember?

LINDA   Oh, yes. And in gold.

[BIFF *enters the darkened kitchen, takes a cigarette, and leaves the house. He comes downstage into a golden pool of light. He smokes, staring at the night.*]

WILLY   Like a young god. Hercules[6]—something like that. And the sun, the sun all around him. Remember how he waved to me? Right up from the field, with the representatives of three colleges standing by? And the buyers I brought, and the cheers when he came out—Loman, Loman, Loman! God Almighty, he'll be great yet. A star like that, magnificent, can never really fade away!

[*The light on* WILLY *is fading. The gas heater begins to glow through the kitchen wall, near the stairs, a blue flame beneath red coils.*]

LINDA [*timidly*]   Willy dear, what has he got against you?

WILLY   I'm so tired. Don't talk any more.

[BIFF *slowly returns to the kitchen. He stops, stares toward the heater.*]

LINDA   Will you ask Howard to let you work in New York?

WILLY   First thing in the morning. Everything'll be all right.

[BIFF *reaches behind the heater and draws out a length of rubber tubing. He is horrified and turns his head toward* WILLY's *room, still dimly lit, from which the strains of* LINDA's *desperate but monotonous humming rise.*]

5. Brooklyn sports stadium.
6. In Greek and Roman mythology the son of the   chief god (Zeus, Jupiter), famous for his great strength.

WILLY [*staring through the window into the moonlight*]   Gee, look at the moon moving between the buildings!

[BIFF *wraps the tubing around his hand and quickly goes up the stairs.*]

CURTAIN

Act Two

Music is heard, gay and bright. The curtain rises as the music fades away. WILLY, *in shirt sleeves, is sitting at the kitchen table, sipping coffee, his hat in his lap.* LINDA *is filling his cup when she can.*

WILLY   Wonderful coffee. Meal in itself.

LINDA   Can I make you some eggs?

WILLY   No. Take a breath.

LINDA   You look so rested, dear.

WILLY   I slept like a dead one. First time in months. Imagine, sleeping till ten on a Tuesday morning. Boys left nice and early, heh?

LINDA   They were out of here by eight o'clock.

WILLY   Good work!

LINDA   It was so thrilling to see them leaving together. I can't get over the shaving lotion in this house!

WILLY [*smiling*]   Mmm—

LINDA   Biff was very changed this morning. His whole attitude seemed to be hopeful. He couldn't wait to get downtown to see Oliver.

WILLY   He's heading for a change. There's no question, there simply are certain men that take longer to get—solidified. How did he dress?

LINDA   His blue suit. He's so handsome in that suit. He could be a— anything in that suit!

[WILLY *gets up from the table.* LINDA *holds his jacket for him.*]

WILLY   There's no question, no question at all. Gee, on the way home tonight I'd like to buy some seeds.

LINDA [*laughing*]   That'd be wonderful. But not enough sun gets back there. Nothing'll grow any more.

WILLY   You wait, kid, before it's all over we're gonna get a little place out in the country, and I'll raise some vegetables, a couple of chickens . . .

LINDA   You'll do it yet, dear.

[WILLY *walks out of his jacket.* LINDA *follows him.*]

WILLY   And they'll get married, and come for a weekend. I'd build a little guest house. 'Cause I got so many fine tools, all I'd need would be a little lumber and some peace of mind.

LINDA [*joyfully*]   I sewed the lining . . .

WILLY   I could build two guest houses, so they'd both come. Did he decide how much he's going to ask Oliver for?

LINDA [*getting him into the jacket*]   He didn't mention it, but I imagine ten or fifteen thousand. You going to talk to Howard today?

WILLY   Yeah. I'll put it to him straight and simple. He'll just have to take me off the road.

LINDA   And Willy, don't forget to ask for a little advance, because we've got the insurance premium. It's the grace period now.

WILLY   That's a hundred . . . ?

LINDA   A hundred and eight, sixty-eight. Because we're a little short again.

WILLY   Why are we short?

LINDA   Well, you had the motor job on the car . . .

WILLY   That goddam Studebaker!

LINDA   And you got one more payment on the refrigerator . . .

WILLY   But it just broke again!

LINDA   Well, it's old, dear.

WILLY   I told you we should've bought a well-advertised machine. Charley
bought a General Electric and it's twenty years old and it's still good, that
son-of-a-bitch.

LINDA   But, Willy—

WILLY   Whoever heard of a Hastings refrigerator? Once in my life I would
like to own something outright before it's broken! I'm always in a race
with the junkyard! I just finished paying for the car and it's on its last legs.
The refrigerator consumes belts like a goddam maniac. They time those
things. They time them so when you finally paid for them, they're used
up.

LINDA [buttoning up his jacket as he unbuttons it]   All told, about two hundred dollars would carry us, dear. But that includes the last payment on
the mortgage. After this payment, Willy, the house belongs to us.

WILLY   It's twenty-five years!

LINDA   Biff was nine years old when we bought it.

WILLY   Well, that's a great thing. To weather a twenty-five year mortgage
is—

LINDA   It's an accomplishment.

WILLY   All the cement, the lumber, the reconstruction I put in this house!
There ain't a crack to be found in it any more.

LINDA   Well, it served its purpose.

WILLY   What purpose? Some stranger'll come along, move in, and that's
that. If only Biff would take this house, and raise a family . . . [He starts
to go.] Good-by, I'm late.

LINDA [suddenly remembering]   Oh, I forgot! You're supposed to meet
them for dinner.

WILLY   Me?

LINDA   At Frank's Chop House on Forty-eighth near Sixth Avenue.

WILLY   Is that so! How about you?

LINDA   No, just the three of you. They're gonna blow you to a big meal!

WILLY   Don't say! Who thought of that?

LINDA   Biff came to me this morning, Willy, and he said, "Tell Dad, we
want to blow him to a big meal." Be there six o'clock. You and your two
boys are going to have dinner.

WILLY   Gee whiz! That's really somethin'. I'm gonna knock Howard for a
loop, kid. I'll get an advance, and I'll come home with a New York job.
Goddammit, now I'm gonna do it!

LINDA   Oh, that's the spirit, Willy!

WILLY   I will never get behind a wheel the rest of my life!

LINDA   It's changing, Willy, I can feel it changing!

WILLY   Beyond a question. G'by, I'm late. [He starts to go again.]

LINDA [calling after him as she runs to the kitchen table for a handkerchief]
You got your glasses?

WILLY [feels for them, then comes back in]   Yeah, yeah, got my glasses.

LINDA [*giving him the handkerchief*]   And a handkerchief.

WILLY   Yeah, handkerchief.

LINDA   And your saccharine?

WILLY   Yeah, my saccharine.

LINDA   Be careful on the subway stairs.

[*She kisses him, and a silk stocking is seen hanging from her hand.* WILLY *notices it.*]

WILLY   Will you stop mending stockings? At least while I'm in the house. It gets me nervous. I can't tell you. Please.

[LINDA *hides the stocking in her hand as she follows* WILLY *across the forestage in front of the house.*]

LINDA   Remember, Frank's Chop House.

WILLY [*passing the apron*]   Maybe beets would grow out there.

LINDA [*laughing*]   But you tried so many times.

WILLY   Yeah. Well, don't work hard today. [*He disappears around the right corner of the house.*]

LINDA   Be careful!

[*As* WILLY *vanishes,* LINDA *waves to him. Suddenly the phone rings. She runs across the stage and into the kitchen and lifts it.*]

LINDA   Hello? Oh, Biff! I'm so glad you called, I just . . . Yes, sure, I just told him. Yes, he'll be there for dinner at six o'clock, I didn't forget. Listen, I was just dying to tell you. You know that little rubber pipe I told you about? That he connected to the gas heater? I finally decided to go down the cellar this morning and take it away and destroy it. But it's gone! Imagine? He took it away himself, it isn't there! [*She listens.*] When? Oh, then you took it. Oh—nothing, it's just that I'd hoped he'd taken it away himself. Oh, I'm not worried, darling, because this morning he left in such high spirits, it was like the old days! I'm not afraid any more. Did Mr. Oliver see you? . . . Well, you wait there then. And make a nice impression on him, darling. Just don't perspire too much before you see him. And have a nice time with Dad. He may have big news too! . . . That's right, a New York job. And be sweet to him tonight, dear. Be loving to him. Because he's only a little boat looking for a harbor. [*She is trembling with sorrow and joy.*] Oh, that's wonderful, Biff, you'll save his life. Thanks, darling. Just put your arm around him when he comes into the restaurant. Give him a smile. That's the boy . . . Good-by, dear. . . . You got your comb? . . . That's fine. Good-by, Biff dear.

[*In the middle of her speech,* HOWARD WAGNER, *thirty-six, wheels in a small typewriter table on which is a wire-recording machine and proceeds to plug it in. This is on the left forestage. Light slowly fades on* LINDA *as it rises on* HOWARD. HOWARD *is intent on threading the machine and only glances over his shoulder as* WILLY *appears.*]

WILLY   Pst! Pst!

HOWARD   Hello, Willy, come in.

WILLY   Like to have a little talk with you, Howard.

HOWARD   Sorry to keep you waiting. I'll be with you in a minute.

WILLY   What's that, Howard?

HOWARD   Didn't you ever see one of these? Wire recorder.

WILLY   Oh. Can we talk a minute?

HOWARD   Records things. Just got delivery yesterday. Been driving me crazy, the most terrific machine I ever saw in my life. I was up all night with it.

WILLY   What do you do with it?

HOWARD   I bought it for dictation, but you can do anything with it. Listen to this. I had it home last night. Listen to what I picked up. The first one is my daughter. Get this. [*He flicks the switch and "Roll out the Barrel" is heard being whistled.*] Listen to that kid whistle.

WILLY   That is lifelike, isn't it?

HOWARD   Seven years old. Get that tone.

WILLY   Ts, ts. Like to ask a little favor if you . . .

[*The whistling breaks off, and the voice of* HOWARD's *daughter is heard.*]

HIS DAUGHTER   "Now you, Daddy."

HOWARD   She's crazy for me! [*Again the same song is whistled.*] That's me! Ha! [*He winks.*]

WILLY   You're very good!

[*The whistling breaks off again. The machine runs silent for a moment.*]

HOWARD   Sh! Get this now, this is my son.

HIS SON   "The capital of Alabama is Montgomery; the capital of Arizona is Phoenix; the capital of Arkansas is Little Rock; the capital of California is Sacramento . . ." [*and on, and on*]

HOWARD [*holding up five fingers*]   Five years old, Willy!

WILLY   He'll make an announcer some day!

HIS SON [*continuing*]   "The capital . . ."

HOWARD   Get that—alphabetical order! [*The machine breaks off suddenly.*] Wait a minute. The maid kicked the plug out.

WILLY   It certainly is a—

HOWARD   Sh, for God's sake!

HIS SON   "It's nine o'clock, Bulova watch time. So I have to go to sleep."

WILLY   That really is—

HOWARD   Wait a minute! The next is my wife.

[*They wait.*]

HOWARD'S VOICE   "Go on, say something." [*pause*] "Well, you gonna talk?"

HIS WIFE   "I can't think of anything."

HOWARD'S VOICE   "Well, talk—it's turning."

HIS WIFE [*shyly, beaten*]   "Hello." [*silence*] "Oh, Howard, I can't talk into this . . ."

HOWARD [*snapping the machine off*]   That was my wife.

WILLY   That is a wonderful machine. Can we—

HOWARD   I tell you, Willy, I'm gonna take my camera, and my bandsaw, and all my hobbies, and out they go. This is the most fascinating relaxation I ever found.

WILLY   I think I'll get one myself.

HOWARD   Sure, they're only a hundred and a half. You can't do without it. Supposing you wanna hear Jack Benny,[7] see? But you can't be at home at that hour. So you tell the maid to turn the radio on when Jack Benny comes on, and this automatically goes on with the radio . . .

WILLY   And when you come home you . . .

HOWARD   You can come home twelve o'clock, one o'clock, any time you

---

7. Popular radio comedian of the 1930s and 1940s.

like, and you get yourself a Coke and sit yourself down, throw the switch, and there's Jack Benny's program in the middle of the night!

WILLY   I'm definitely going to get one. Because lots of time I'm on the road, and I think to myself, what I must be missing on the radio!

HOWARD   Don't you have a radio in the car?

WILLY   Well, yeah, but who ever thinks of turning it on?

HOWARD   Say, aren't you supposed to be in Boston?

WILLY   That's what I want to talk to you about, Howard. You got a minute? [*He draws a chair in from the wing.*]

HOWARD   What happened? What're you doing here?

WILLY   Well . . .

HOWARD   You didn't crack up again, did you?

WILLY   Oh, no. No . . .

HOWARD   Geez, you had me worried there for a minute. What's the trouble?

WILLY   Well, tell you the truth, Howard. I've come to the decision that I'd rather not travel any more.

HOWARD   Not travel! Well, what'll you do?

WILLY   Remember, Christmas time, when you had the party here? You said you'd try to think of some spot for me here in town.

HOWARD   With us?

WILLY   Well, sure.

HOWARD   Oh, yeah, yeah. I remember. Well, I couldn't think of anything for you, Willy.

WILLY   I tell ya, Howard. The kids are all grown up, y'know. I don't need much any more. If I could take home—well, sixty-five dollars a week, I could swing it.

HOWARD   Yeah, but Willy, see I—

WILLY   I tell ya why, Howard. Speaking frankly and between the two of us, y'know—I'm just a little tired.

HOWARD   Oh, I could understand that, Willy. But you're a road man, Willy, and we do a road business. We've only got a half-dozen salesmen on the floor here.

WILLY   God knows, Howard, I never asked a favor of any man. But I was with the firm when your father used to carry you in here in his arms.

HOWARD   I know that, Willy, but—

WILLY   Your father came to me the day you were born and asked me what I thought of the name of Howard, may he rest in peace.

HOWARD   I appreciate that, Willy, but there just is no spot here for you. If I had a spot I'd slam you right in, but I just don't have a single solitary spot.

[*He looks for his lighter.* WILLY *has picked it up and gives it to him. Pause.*]

WILLY [*with increasing anger*]   Howard, all I need to set my table is fifty dollars a week.

HOWARD   But where am I going to put you, kid?

WILLY   Look, it isn't a question of whether I can sell merchandise, is it?

HOWARD   No, but it's a business, kid, and everybody's gotta pull his own weight.

WILLY [*desperately*]   Just let me tell you a story, Howard—

HOWARD   'Cause you gotta admit, business is business.

WILLY [*angrily*]   Business is definitely business, but just listen for a minute. You don't understand this. When I was a boy—eighteen, nineteen—I was already on the road. And there was a question in my mind as to whether selling had a future for me. Because in those days I had a yearning to go to Alaska. See, there were three gold strikes in one month in Alaska, and I felt like going out. Just for the ride, you might say.

HOWARD [*barely interested*]   Don't say.

WILLY   Oh, yeah, my father lived many years in Alaska. He was an adventurous man. We've got quite a little streak of self-reliance in our family. I thought I'd go out with my older brother and try to locate him, and maybe settle in the North with the old man. And I was almost decided to go, when I met a salesman in the Parker House. His name was Dave Singleman. And he was eighty-four years old, and he'd drummed merchandise in thirty-one states. And old Dave, he'd go up to his room, y'understand, put on his green velvet slippers—I'll never forget—and pick up his phone and call the buyers, and without ever leaving his room, at the age of eighty-four, he made a living. And when I saw that, I realized that selling was the greatest career a man could want. 'Cause what could be more satisfying than to be able to go, at the age of eighty-four, into twenty or thirty different cities, and pick up a phone, and be remembered and loved and helped by so many different people? Do you know? when he died—and by the way he died the death of a salesman, in his green velvet slippers in the smoker of the New York, New Haven and Hartford, going into Boston—when he died, hundreds of salesmen and buyers were at his funeral. Things were sad on a lotta trains for months after that. [*He stands up.* HOWARD *has not looked at him.*] In those days there was personality in it, Howard. There was respect, and comradeship, and gratitude in it. Today, it's all cut and dried, and there's no chance for bringing friendship to bear—or personality. You see what I mean? They don't know me any more.

HOWARD [*moving away, toward the right*]   That's just the thing, Willy.

WILLY   If I had forty dollars a week—that's all I'd need. Forty dollars, Howard.

HOWARD   Kid, I can't take blood from a stone, I—

WILLY [*desperation is on him now*]   Howard, the year Al Smith[8] was nominated, your father came to me and—

HOWARD [*starting to go off*]   I've got to see some people, kid.

WILLY [*stopping him*]   I'm talking about your father! There were promises made across this desk! You mustn't tell me you've got people to see—I put thirty-four years into this firm, Howard, and now I can't pay my insurance! You can't eat the orange and throw the peel away—a man is not a piece of fruit! [*after a pause*] Now pay attention. Your father—in 1928 I had a big year. I averaged a hundred and seventy dollars a week in commissions.

HOWARD [*impatiently*]   Now, Willy, you never averaged—

WILLY [*banging his hand on the desk*]   I averaged a hundred and seventy dollars a week in the year of 1928! And your father came to me—or rather, I was in the office here—it was right over this desk—and he put his hand on my shoulder—

---

8. Democratic candidate for president in 1928.

HOWARD [*getting up*]   You'll have to excuse me, Willy, I gotta see some people. Pull yourself together. [*going out*] I'll be back in a little while.

> [*On* HOWARD's *exit, the light on his chair grows very bright and strange.*]

WILLY   Pull myself together! What the hell did I say to him? My God, I was yelling at him! How could I! [WILLY *breaks off, staring at the light, which occupies the chair, animating it. He approaches this chair, standing across the desk from it.*] Frank, Frank, don't you remember what you told me that time? How you put your hand on my shoulder, and Frank . . . [*He leans on the desk and as he speaks the dead man's name he accidentally switches on the recorder, and instantly*]

HOWARD's SON   ". . . of New York is Albany. The capital of Ohio is Cincinnati, the capital of Rhode Island is . . ." [*The recitation continues.*]

WILLY [*leaping away with fright, shouting*]   Ha! Howard! Howard! Howard!

HOWARD [*rushing in*]   What happened?

WILLY [*pointing at the machine, which continues nasally, childishly, with the capital cities*]   Shut it off! Shut it off!

HOWARD [*pulling the plug out*]   Look, Willy . . .

WILLY [*pressing his hands to his eyes*]   I gotta get myself some coffee. I'll get some coffee . . .

> [WILLY *starts to walk out.* HOWARD *stops him.*]

HOWARD [*rolling up the cord*]   Willy, look . . .

WILLY   I'll go to Boston.

HOWARD   Willy, you can't go to Boston for us.

WILLY   Why can't I go?

HOWARD   I don't want you to represent us. I've been meaning to tell you for a long time now.

WILLY   Howard, are you firing me?

HOWARD   I think you need a good long rest, Willy.

WILLY   Howard—

HOWARD   And when you feel better, come back, and we'll see if we can work something out.

WILLY   But I gotta earn money, Howard. I'm in no position to—

HOWARD   Where are your sons? Why don't your sons give you a hand?

WILLY   They're working on a very big deal.

HOWARD   This is no time for false pride, Willy. You go to your sons and you tell them that you're tired. You've got two great boys, haven't you?

WILLY   Oh, no question, no question, but in the meantime . . .

HOWARD   Then that's that, heh?

WILLY   All right, I'll go to Boston tomorrow.

HOWARD   No, no.

WILLY   I can't throw myself on my sons. I'm not a cripple!

HOWARD   Look, kid, I'm busy, I'm busy this morning.

WILLY [*grasping* HOWARD's *arm*]   Howard, you've got to let me go to Boston!

HOWARD [*hard, keeping himself under control*]   I've got a line of people to see this morning. Sit down, take five minutes, and pull yourself together, and then go home, will ya? I need the office, Willy. [*He starts to go, turns, remembering the recorder, starts to push off the table holding the recorder.*] Oh, yeah. Whenever you can this week, stop by and drop off the samples. You'll feel better, Willy, and then come back and we'll talk. Pull yourself together, kid, there's people outside.

[HOWARD *exits, pushing the table off left.* WILLY *stares into space, exhausted. Now the music is heard*—BEN'S *music*—*first distantly, then closer, closer. As* WILLY *speaks,* BEN *enters from the right. He carries valise and umbrella.*]

WILLY   Oh, Ben, how did you do it? What is the answer? Did you wind up the Alaska deal already?

BEN   Doesn't take much time if you know what you're doing. Just a short business trip. Boarding ship in an hour. Wanted to say good-by.

WILLY   Ben, I've got to talk to you.

BEN [*glancing at his watch*]   Haven't the time, William.

WILLY [*crossing the apron to* BEN]   Ben, nothing's working out. I don't know what to do.

BEN   Now, look here, William. I've bought timberland in Alaska and I need a man to look after things for me.

WILLY   God, timberland! Me and my boys in those grand outdoors!

BEN   You've a new continent at your doorstep, William. Get out of these cities, they're full of talk and time payments and courts of law. Screw on your fists and you can fight for a fortune up there.

WILLY   Yes, yes! Linda, Linda!

[LINDA *enters as of old, with the wash.*]

LINDA   Oh, you're back?

BEN   I haven't much time.

WILLY   No, wait! Linda, he's got a proposition for me in Alaska.

LINDA   But you've got— [*to* BEN] He's got a beautiful job here.

WILLY   But in Alaska, kid, I could—

LINDA   You're doing well enough, Willy!

BEN [*to* LINDA]   Enough for what, my dear?

LINDA [*frightened of* BEN *and angry at him*]   Don't say those things to him! Enough to be happy right here, right now. [*to* WILLY, *while* BEN *laughs*] Why must everybody conquer the world? You're well liked, and the boys love you, and someday—[*to* BEN]—why, old man Wagner told him just the other day that if he keeps it up he'll be a member of the firm, didn't he, Willy?

WILLY   Sure, sure. I am building something with this firm, Ben, and if a man is building something he must be on the right track, mustn't he?

BEN   What are you building? Lay your hand on it. Where is it?

WILLY [*hesitantly*]   That's true, Linda, there's nothing.

LINDA   Why? [*to* BEN] There's a man eighty-four years old—

WILLY   That's right, Ben, that's right. When I look at that man I say, what is there to worry about?

BEN   Bah!

WILLY   It's true, Ben. All he has to do is go into any city, pick up the phone, and he's making his living and you know why?

BEN [*picking up his valise*]   I've got to go.

WILLY [*holding* BEN *back*]   Look at this boy!

[BIFF, *in his high school sweater, enters carrying suitcase.* HAPPY *carries* BIFF'S *shoulder guards, gold helmet, and football pants.*]

WILLY   Without a penny to his name, three great universities are begging for him, and from there the sky's the limit, because it's not what you do, Ben. It's who you know and the smile on your face! It's contacts, Ben, contacts! The whole wealth of Alaska passes over the lunch table at the Commodore Hotel, and that's the wonder, the wonder of this country, that a man can end with diamonds here on the basis of being liked! [*He turns to* BIFF.] And that's why when you get out on that field today it's important. Because thousands of people will be rooting for you and loving you. [*to* BEN, *who has again begun to leave*] And Ben! when he walks into a business office his name will sound out like a bell and all the doors will open to him! I've seen it, Ben, I've seen it a thousand times! You can't feel it with your hand like timber, but it's there!

BEN   Good-by, William.

WILLY   Ben, am I right? Don't you think I'm right? I value your advice.

BEN   There's a new continent at your doorstep, William. You could walk out rich. Rich! [*He is gone.*]

WILLY   We'll do it here, Ben! You hear me? We're gonna do it here!
    [*Young* BERNARD *rushes in. The gay music of the Boys is heard.*]

BERNARD   Oh, gee, I was afraid you left already!

WILLY   Why? What time is it?

BERNARD   It's half-past one!

WILLY   Well, come on, everybody! Ebbets Field next stop! Where's the pennants? [*He rushes through the wall-line of the kitchen and out into the living-room.*]

LINDA [*to* BIFF]   Did you pack fresh underwear?

BIFF [*who has been limbering up*]   I want to go!

BERNARD   Biff, I'm carrying your helmet, ain't I?

HAPPY   No, I'm carrying the helmet.

BERNARD   Oh, Biff, you promised me.

HAPPY   I'm carrying the helmet.

BERNARD   How am I going to get in the locker room?

LINDA   Let him carry the shoulder guards. [*She puts her coat and hat on in the kitchen.*]

BERNARD   Can I, Biff? 'Cause I told everybody I'm going to be in the locker room.

HAPPY   In Ebbets Field it's the clubhouse.

BERNARD   I meant the clubhouse. Biff!

HAPPY   Biff!

BIFF [*grandly, after a slight pause*]   Let him carry the shoulder guards.

HAPPY [*as he gives* BERNARD *the shoulder guards*]   Stay close to us now.
    [WILLY *rushes in with the pennants.*]

WILLY [*handing them out*]   Everybody wave when Biff comes out on the field. [HAPPY *and* BERNARD *run off.*] You set now, boy?
    [*The music has died away.*]

BIFF   Ready to go, Pop. Every muscle is ready.

WILLY [*at the edge of the apron*]   You realize what this means?

BIFF   That's right, Pop.

WILLY [*feeling* BIFF's *muscles*]   You're comin' home this afternoon captain of the All-Scholastic Championship Team of the City of New York.

BIFF   I got it, Pop. And remember, pal, when I take off my helmet, that touchdown is for you.

WILLY   Let's go! [*He is starting out, with his arm around* BIFF, *when* CHARLEY *enters, as of old, in knickers.*] I got no room for you, Charley.

CHARLEY   Room? For what?

WILLY   In the car.

CHARLEY   You goin' for a ride? I wanted to shoot some casino.

WILLY [*furiously*]   Casino! [*incredulously*] Don't you realize what today is?

LINDA   Oh, he knows, Willy. He's just kidding you.

WILLY   That's nothing to kid about!

CHARLEY   No, Linda, what's goin' on?

LINDA   He's playing in Ebbets Field.

CHARLEY   Baseball in this weather?

WILLY   Don't talk to him. Come on, come on! [*He is pushing them out.*]

CHARLEY   Wait a minute, didn't you hear the news?

WILLY   What?

CHARLEY   Don't you listen to the radio? Ebbets Field just blew up.

WILLY   You go to hell! [CHARLEY *laughs. Pushing them out*] Come on, come on! We're late.

CHARLEY [*as they go*]   Knock a homer, Biff, knock a homer!

WILLY [*the last to leave, turning to* CHARLEY]   I don't think that was funny, Charley. This is the greatest day of his life.

CHARLEY   Willy, when are you going to grow up?

WILLY   Yeah, heh? When this game is over, Charley, you'll be laughing out of the other side of your face. They'll be calling him another Red Grange.[9] Twenty-five thousand a year.

CHARLEY [*kidding*]   Is that so?

WILLY   Yeah, that's so.

CHARLEY   Well, then, I'm sorry, Willy. But tell me something.

WILLY   What?

CHARLEY   Who is Red Grange?

WILLY   Put up your hands. Goddam you, put up your hands!
[CHARLEY, *chuckling, shakes his head and walks away, around the left corner of the stage.* WILLY *follows him. The music rises to a mocking frenzy.*]

WILLY   Who the hell do you think you are, better than everybody else? You don't know everything, you big, ignorant, stupid . . . Put up your hands!
[*Light rises, on the right side of the forestage, on a small table in the reception room of* CHARLEY's *office. Traffic sounds are heard.* BERNARD, *now mature, sits whistling to himself. A pair of tennis rackets and an overnight bag are on the floor beside him.*]

WILLY [*offstage*]   What are you walking away for? Don't walk away! If you're going to say something say it to my face! I know you laugh at me behind my back. You'll laugh out of the other side of your goddam face after this game. Touchdown! Touchdown! Eighty thousand people! Touchdown! Right between the goal posts.
[BERNARD *is a quiet, earnest, but self-assured young man.* WILLY's *voice is coming from right upstage now.* BERNARD *lowers his feet off the table and listens.* JENNY, *his father's secretary, enters.*]

JENNY [*distressed*]   Say, Bernard, will you go out in the hall?

BERNARD   What is that noise? Who is it?

JENNY   Mr. Loman. He just got off the elevator.

BERNARD [*getting up*]   Who's he arguing with?

---

9. Harold Edward Grange (1903–1991), all-American halfback at the University of Illinois from 1923 to 1925, played professionally for the Chicago Bears.

JENNY   Nobody. There's nobody with him. I can't deal with him any more, and your father gets all upset everytime he comes. I've got a lot of typing to do, and your father's waiting to sign it. Will you see him?

WILLY [*entering*]   Touchdown! Touch— [*He sees* JENNY.] Jenny, Jenny, good to see you. How're ya? Workin'? Or still honest?

JENNY   Fine. How've you been feeling?

WILLY   Not much any more, Jenny. Ha, ha! [*He is surprised to see the rackets.*]

BERNARD   Hello, Uncle Willy.

WILLY [*almost shocked*]   Bernard! Well, look who's here! [*He comes quickly, guiltily to* BERNARD *and warmly shakes his hand.*]

BERNARD   How are you? Good to see you.

WILLY   What are you doing here?

BERNARD   Oh, just stopped by to see Pop. Get off my feet till my train leaves. I'm going to Washington in a few minutes.

WILLY   Is he in?

BERNARD   Yes, he's in his office with the accountant. Sit down.

WILLY [*sitting down*]   What're you going to do in Washington?

BERNARD   Oh, just a case I've got there, Willy.

WILLY   That so? [*indicating the rackets*] You going to play tennis there?

BERNARD   I'm staying with a friend who's got a court.

WILLY   Don't say. His own tennis court. Must be fine people, I bet.

BERNARD   They are, very nice. Dad tells me Biff's in town.

WILLY [*with a big smile*]   Yeah, Biff's in. Working on a very big deal, Bernard.

BERNARD   What's Biff doing?

WILLY   Well, he's been doing very big things in the West. But he decided to establish himself here. Very big. We're having dinner. Did I hear your wife had a boy?

BERNARD   That's right. Our second.

WILLY   Two boys! What do you know!

BERNARD   What kind of a deal has Biff got?

WILLY   Well, Bill Oliver—very big sporting-goods man—he wants Biff very badly. Called him in from the West. Long distance, carte blanche, special deliveries. Your friends have their own private tennis court?

BERNARD   You still with the old firm, Willy?

WILLY [*after a pause*]   I'm—I'm overjoyed to see how you made the grade, Bernard, overjoyed. It's an encouraging thing to see a young man really— really—Looks very good for Biff—very— [*He breaks off, then*] Bernard— [*He is so full of emotion, he breaks off again.*]

BERNARD   What is it, Willy?

WILLY [*small and alone*]   What—what's the secret?

BERNARD   What secret?

WILLY   How—how did you? Why didn't he ever catch on?

BERNARD   I wouldn't know that, Willy.

WILLY [*confidentially, desperately*]   You were his friend, his boyhood friend. There's something I don't understand about it. His life ended after that Ebbets Field game. From the age of seventeen nothing good ever happened to him.

BERNARD   He never trained himself for anything.

WILLY   But he did, he did. After high school he took so many correspondence courses. Radio mechanics; television; God knows what, and never made the slightest mark.

BERNARD [*taking off his glasses*]   Willy, do you want to talk candidly?

WILLY [*rising, faces* BERNARD]   I regard you as a very brilliant man, Bernard. I value your advice.

BERNARD   Oh, the hell with the advice, Willy. I couldn't advise you. There's just one thing I've always wanted to ask you. When he was supposed to graduate, and the math teacher flunked him—

WILLY   Oh, that son-of-a-bitch ruined his life.

BERNARD   Yeah, but, Willy, all he had to do was go to summer school and make up that subject.

WILLY   That's right, that's right.

BERNARD   Did you tell him not to go to summer school?

WILLY   Me? I begged him to go. I ordered him to go!

BERNARD   Then why wouldn't he go?

WILLY   Why? Why! Bernard, that question has been trailing me like a ghost for the last fifteen years. He flunked the subject, and laid down and died like a hammer hit him!

BERNARD   Take it easy, kid.

WILLY   Let me talk to you—I got nobody to talk to. Bernard, Bernard, was it my fault? Y'see? It keeps going around in my mind, maybe I did something to him. I got nothing to give him.

BERNARD   Don't take it so hard.

WILLY   Why did he lay down? What is the story there? You were his friend!

BERNARD   Willy, I remember, it was June, and our grades came out. And he'd flunked math.

WILLY   That son-of-a-bitch!

BERNARD   No, it wasn't right then. Biff just got very angry, I remember, and he was ready to enroll in summer school.

WILLY [*surprised*]   He was?

BERNARD   He wasn't beaten by it at all. But then, Willy, he disappeared from the block for almost a month. And I got the idea that he'd gone up to New England to see you. Did he have a talk with you then?

[WILLY *stares in silence.*]

BERNARD   Willy?

WILLY [*with a strong edge of resentment in his voice*]   Yeah, he came to Boston. What about it?

BERNARD   Well, just that when he came back—I'll never forget this, it always mystifies me. Because I'd thought so well of Biff, even though he'd always taken advantage of me. I loved him, Willy, y'know? And he came back after that month and took his sneakers—remember those sneakers with "University of Virginia" printed on them? He was so proud of those, wore them every day. And he took them down in the cellar, and burned them up in the furnace. We had a fist fight. It lasted at least half an hour. Just the two of us, punching each other down the cellar, and crying right through it. I've often thought of how strange it was that I knew he'd given up his life. What happened in Boston, Willy?

[WILLY *looks at him as at an intruder.*]

BERNARD   I just bring it up because you asked me.

WILLY [*angrily*]   Nothing. What do you mean, "What happened?" What's that got to do with anything?

BERNARD   Well, don't get sore.

WILLY   What are you trying to do, blame it on me? If a boy lays down is that my fault?

BERNARD   Now, Willy, don't get—

WILLY   Well, don't—don't talk to me that way! What does that mean, "What happened?"

[CHARLEY *enters. He is in his vest, and he carries a bottle of bourbon.*]

CHARLEY   Hey, you're going to miss that train. [*He waves the bottle.*]

BERNARD   Yeah, I'm going. [*He takes the bottle.*] Thanks, Pop. [*He picks up his rackets and bag.*] Good-by, Willy, and don't worry about it. You know, "If at first you don't succeed . . ."

WILLY   Yes, I believe in that.

BERNARD   But sometimes, Willy, it's better for a man just to walk away.

WILLY   Walk away?

BERNARD   That's right.

WILLY   But if you can't walk away?

BERNARD [*after a slight pause*]   I guess that's when it's tough. [*extending his hand*] Good-by, Willy.

WILLY [*shaking* BERNARD's *hand*]   Good-by, boy.

CHARLEY [*an arm on* BERNARD's *shoulder*]   How do you like this kid? Gonna argue a case in front of the Supreme Court.

BERNARD [*protesting*]   Pop!

WILLY [*genuinely shocked, pained, and happy*]   No! The Supreme Court!

BERNARD   I gotta run. 'By, Dad!

CHARLEY   Knock 'em dead, Bernard!

[BERNARD *goes off.*]

WILLY [*as* CHARLEY *takes out his wallet*]   The Supreme Court! And he didn't even mention it!

CHARLEY [*counting out money on the desk*]   He don't have to—he's gonna do it.

WILLY   And you never told him what to do, did you? You never took any interest in him.

CHARLEY   My salvation is that I never took any interest in anything. There's some money—fifty dollars. I got an accountant inside.

WILLY   Charley, look . . . [*with difficulty*] I got my insurance to pay. If you can manage it—I need a hundred and ten dollars.

[CHARLEY *doesn't reply for a moment; merely stops moving.*]

WILLY   I'd draw it from my bank but Linda would know, and I . . .

CHARLEY   Sit down, Willy.

WILLY [*moving toward the chair*]   I'm keeping an account of everything, remember. I'll pay every penny back. [*He sits.*]

CHARLEY   Now listen to me, Willy.

WILLY   I want you to know I appreciate . . .

CHARLEY [*sitting down on the table*]   Willy, what're you doin'? What the hell is goin' on in your head?

WILLY   Why? I'm simply . . .

CHARLEY   I offered you a job. You can make fifty dollars a week. And I won't send you on the road.

WILLY   I've got a job.

CHARLEY   Without pay? What kind of job is a job without pay? [*He rises.*] Now, look kid, enough is enough. I'm no genius but I know when I'm being insulted.

WILLY   Insulted!

CHARLEY   Why don't you want to work for me?

WILLY   What's the matter with you? I've got a job.

CHARLEY   Then what're you walkin' in here every week for?

WILLY [*getting up*]   Well, if you don't want me to walk in here—

CHARLEY   I am offering you a job!

WILLY   I don't want your goddam job!

CHARLEY   When the hell are you going to grow up?

WILLY [*furiously*]   You big ignoramus, if you say that to me again I'll rap you one! I don't care how big you are! [*He's ready to fight. Pause.*]

CHARLEY [*kindly, going to him*]   How much do you need, Willy?

WILLY   Charley, I'm strapped, I'm strapped. I don't know what to do. I was just fired.

CHARLEY   Howard fired you?

WILLY   That snotnose. Imagine that? I named him. I named him Howard.

CHARLEY   Willy, when're you gonna realize that them things don't mean anything? You named him Howard, but you can't sell that. The only thing you got in this world is what you can sell. And the funny thing is that you're a salesman, and you don't know that.

WILLY   I've always tried to think otherwise. I guess. I always felt that if a man was impressive, and well liked, that nothing—

CHARLEY   Why must everybody like you? Who liked J. P. Morgan?[1] Was he impressive? In a Turkish bath he'd look like a butcher. But with his pockets on he was very well liked. Now listen, Willy, I know you don't like me, and nobody can say I'm in love with you, but I'll give you a job because— just for the hell of it, put it that way. Now what do you say?

WILLY   I—I just can't work for you, Charley.

CHARLEY   What're you, jealous of me?

WILLY   I can't work for you, that's all, don't ask me why.

CHARLEY [*angered, takes out more bills*]   You been jealous of me all your life, you damned fool! Here, pay your insurance. [*He puts the money in* WILLY's *hand.*]

WILLY   I'm keeping strict accounts.

CHARLEY   I've got some work to do. Take care of yourself. And pay your insurance.

WILLY [*moving to the right*]   Funny, y'know? After all the highways, and the trains, and the appointments, and the years, you end up worth more dead than alive.

CHARLEY   Willy, nobody's worth nothin' dead. [*after a slight pause*] Did you hear what I said?

[WILLY *stands still, dreaming.*]

CHARLEY   Willy!

WILLY   Apologize to Bernard for me when you see him. I didn't mean to argue with him. He's a fine boy. They're all fine boys, and they'll end up

---

1. John Pierpont Morgan (1887–1943), a famous banker and financier.

big—all of them. Someday they'll all play tennis together. Wish me luck, Charley. He saw Bill Oliver today.

CHARLEY   Good luck.

WILLY [*on the verge of tears*]   Charley, you're the only friend I got. Isn't that a remarkable thing? [*He goes out.*]

CHARLEY   Jesus!

> [CHARLEY *stares after him a moment and follows. All light blacks out. Suddenly raucous music is heard, and a red glow rises behind the screen at right.* STANLEY, *a young waiter, appears, carrying a table, followed by* HAPPY, *who is carrying two chairs.*]

STANLEY [*putting the table down*]   That's all right, Mr. Loman, I can handle it myself. [*He turns and takes the chairs from* HAPPY *and places them at the table.*]

HAPPY [*glancing around*]   Oh, this is better.

STANLEY   Sure, in the front there you're in the middle of all kinds a noise. Whenever you got a party. Mr. Loman, you just tell me and I'll put you back here. Y'know, there's a lotta people they don't like it private, because when they go out they like to see a lotta action around them because they're sick and tired to stay in the house by theirself. But I know you, you ain't from Hackensack. You know what I mean?

HAPPY [*sitting down*]   So how's it coming, Stanley?

STANLEY   Ah, it's a dog life. I only wish during the war they'd a took me in the Army. I coulda been dead by now.

HAPPY   My brother's back, Stanley.

STANLEY   Oh, he come back, heh? From the Far West.

HAPPY   Yeah, big cattle man, my brother, so treat him right. And my father's coming too.

STANLEY   Oh, your father too!

HAPPY   You got a couple of nice lobsters?

STANLEY   Hundred per cent, big.

HAPPY   I want them with the claws.

STANLEY   Don't worry, I don't give you no mice. [HAPPY *laughs.*] How about some wine? It'll put a head on the meal.

HAPPY   No. You remember, Stanley, that recipe I brought you from overseas? With the champagne in it?

STANLEY   Oh, yeah, sure. I still got it tacked up yet in the kitchen. But that'll have to cost a buck apiece anyways.

HAPPY   That's all right.

STANLEY   What'd you, hit a number or somethin'?

HAPPY   No, it's a little celebration. My brother is—I think he pulled off a big deal today. I think we're going into business together.

STANLEY   Great! That's the best for you. Because a family business, you know what I mean?—that's the best.

HAPPY   That's what I think.

STANLEY   'Cause what's the difference? Somebody steals? It's in the family. Know what I mean? [*sotto voce*]² Like this bartender here. The boss is goin' crazy what kinda leak he's got in the cash register. You put it in but it don't come out.

---

2. In an undertone.

HAPPY [*raising his head*] Sh!

STANLEY What?

HAPPY You notice I wasn't lookin' right or left, was I?

STANLEY No.

HAPPY And my eyes are closed.

STANLEY So what's the—?

HAPPY Strudel's comin'.

STANLEY [*catching on, looks around*] Ah, no, there's no—
 [*He breaks off as a furred, lavishly dressed girl enters and sits at the next table. Both follow her with their eyes.*]

STANLEY Geez, how'd ya know?

HAPPY I got radar or something. [*staring directly at her profile*] Oooooooo . . . Stanley.

STANLEY I think that's for you, Mr. Loman.

HAPPY Look at that mouth. Oh, God. And the binoculars.

STANLEY Geez, you got a life, Mr. Loman.

HAPPY Wait on her.

STANLEY [*going to the girl's table*] Would you like a menu, ma'am?

GIRL I'm expecting someone, but I'd like a—

HAPPY Why don't you bring her—excuse me, miss, do you mind? I sell champagne, and I'd like you to try my brand. Bring her a champagne, Stanley.

GIRL That's awfully nice of you.

HAPPY Don't mention it. It's all company money. [*He laughs.*]

GIRL That's a charming product to be selling, isn't it?

HAPPY Oh, gets to be like everything else. Selling is selling, y'know.

GIRL I suppose.

HAPPY You don't happen to sell, do you?

GIRL No, I don't sell.

HAPPY Would you object to a compliment from a stranger? You ought to be on a magazine cover.

GIRL [*looking at him a little archly*] I have been.
 [STANLEY *comes in with a glass of champagne.*]

HAPPY What'd I say before, Stanley? You see? She's a cover girl.

STANLEY Oh, I could see, I could see.

HAPPY [*to the* GIRL] What magazine?

GIRL Oh, a lot of them. [*She takes the drink.*] Thank you.

HAPPY You know what they say in France, don't you? "Champagne is the drink of the complexion"—Hya, Biff!
 [BIFF *has entered and sits with* HAPPY.]

BIFF Hello, kid. Sorry I'm late.

HAPPY I just got here. Uh, Miss—?

GIRL Forsythe.

HAPPY Miss Forsythe, this is my brother.

BIFF Is Dad here?

HAPPY His name is Biff. You might've heard of him. Great football player.

GIRL Really? What team?

HAPPY Are you familiar with football?

GIRL No, I'm afraid I'm not.

HAPPY Biff is quarterback with the New York Giants.

GIRL Well, that's nice, isn't it? [*She drinks.*]

HAPPY Good health.

GIRL I'm happy to meet you.

HAPPY That's my name. Hap. It's really Harold, but at West Point they called me Happy.

GIRL [*now really impressed*] Oh, I see. How do you do? [*She turns her profile.*]

BIFF Isn't Dad coming?

HAPPY You want her?

BIFF Oh, I could never make that.

HAPPY I remember the time that idea would never come into your head. Where's the old confidence, Biff?

BIFF I just saw Oliver—

HAPPY Wait a minute. I've got to see that old confidence again. Do you want her? She's on call.

BIFF Oh, no. [*He turns to look at the* GIRL.]

HAPPY I'm telling you. Watch this. [*turning to the* GIRL] Honey? [*She turns to him.*] Are you busy?

GIRL Well, I am . . . but I could make a phone call.

HAPPY Do that, will you, honey? And see if you can get a friend. We'll be here for a while. Biff is one of the greatest football players in the country.

GIRL [*standing up*] Well, I'm certainly happy to meet you.

HAPPY Come back soon.

GIRL I'll try.

HAPPY Don't try, honey, try hard.

[*The* GIRL *exits.* STANLEY *follows, shaking his head in bewildered admiration.*]

HAPPY Isn't that a shame now? A beautiful girl like that? That's why I can't get married. There's not a good woman in a thousand. New York is loaded with them, kid!

BIFF Hap, look—

HAPPY I told you she was on call!

BIFF [*strangely unnerved*] Cut it out, will ya? I want to say something to you.

HAPPY Did you see Oliver?

BIFF I saw him all right. Now look, I want to tell Dad a couple of things and I want you to help me.

HAPPY What? Is he going to back you?

BIFF Are you crazy? You're out of your goddam head, you know that?

HAPPY Why? What happened?

BIFF [*breathlessly*] I did a terrible thing today, Hap. It's been the strangest day I ever went through. I'm all numb, I swear.

HAPPY You mean he wouldn't see you?

BIFF Well, I waited six hours for him, see? All day. Kept sending my name in. Even tried to date his secretary so she'd get me to him, but no soap.

HAPPY Because you're not showin' the old confidence, Biff. He remembered you, didn't he?

BIFF [*stopping* HAPPY *with a gesture*] Finally, about five o'clock, he comes out. Didn't remember who I was or anything. I felt like such an idiot, Hap.

HAPPY Did you tell him my Florida idea?

BIFF   He walked away. I saw him for one minute. I got so mad I could've torn the walls down! How the hell did I ever get the idea I was a salesman there? I even believed myself that I'd been a salesman for him! And then he gave me one look and—I realized what a ridiculous lie my whole life has been! We've been talking in a dream for fifteen years. I was a shipping clerk.

HAPPY   What'd you do?

BIFF   [*with great tension and wonder*]   Well, he left, see. And the secretary went out. I was all alone in the waiting-room. I don't know what came over me, Hap. The next thing I know I'm in his office—paneled walls, everything. I can't explain it. I—Hap, I took his fountain pen.

HAPPY   Geez, did he catch you?

BIFF   I ran out. I ran down all eleven flights. I ran and ran and ran.

HAPPY   That was an awful dumb—what'd you do that for?

BIFF   [*agonized*]   I don't know, I just—wanted to take something, I don't know. You gotta help me, Hap, I'm gonna tell Pop.

HAPPY   You crazy? What for?

BIFF   Hap, he's got to understand that I'm not the man somebody lends that kind of money to. He thinks I've been spiting him all these years and it's eating him up.

HAPPY   That's just it. You tell him something nice.

BIFF   I can't.

HAPPY   Say you got a lunch date with Oliver tomorrow.

BIFF   So what do I do tomorrow?

HAPPY   You leave the house tomorrow and come back at night and say Oliver is thinking it over. And he thinks it over for a couple of weeks, and gradually it fades away and nobody's the worse.

BIFF   But it'll go on forever!

HAPPY   Dad is never so happy as when he's looking forward to something! [WILLY *enters.*]

HAPPY   Hello, scout!

WILLY   Gee, I haven't been here in years!
       [STANLEY *has followed* WILLY *in and sets a chair for him.* STANLEY *starts off but* HAPPY *stops him.*]

HAPPY   Stanley!
       [STANLEY *stands by, waiting for an order.*]

BIFF   [*going to* WILLY *with guilt, as to an invalid*]   Sit down, Pop. You want a drink?

WILLY   Sure, I don't mind.

BIFF   Let's get a load on.

WILLY   You look worried.

BIFF   N-no. [*to* STANLEY] Scotch all around. Make it doubles.

STANLEY   Doubles, right. [*He goes.*]

WILLY   You had a couple already, didn't you?

BIFF   Just a couple, yeah.

WILLY   Well, what happened, boy? [*nodding affirmatively, with a smile*] Everything go all right?

BIFF   [*takes a breath, then reaches out and grasps* WILLY's *hand*]   Pal . . . [*He is smiling bravely, and* WILLY *is smiling too.*] I had an experience today.

HAPPY   Terrific, Pop.

WILLY   That so? What happened?

BIFF [*high, slightly alcoholic, above the earth*]   I'm going to tell you everything from first to last. It's been a strange day. [*Silence. He looks around,
   composes himself as best he can, but his breath keeps breaking the rhythm
   of his voice.*] I had to wait quite a while for him, and—

WILLY   Oliver?

BIFF   Yeah, Oliver. All day, as a matter of cold fact. And a lot of—
   instances—facts, Pop, facts about my life came back to me. Who was it,
   Pop? Who ever said I was a salesman with Oliver?

WILLY   Well, you were.

BIFF   No, Dad, I was a shipping clerk.

WILLY   But you were practically—

BIFF [*with determination*]   Dad, I don't know who said it first, but I was
   never a salesman for Bill Oliver.

WILLY   What're you talking about?

BIFF   Let's hold on to the facts tonight, Pop. We're not going to get anywhere bullin' around. I was a shipping clerk.

WILLY [*angrily*]   All right, now listen to me—

BIFF   Why don't you let me finish?

WILLY   I'm not interested in stories about the past or any crap of that kind
   because the woods are burning, boys, you understand? There's a big blaze
   going on all around. I was fired today.

BIFF [*shocked*]   How could you be?

WILLY   I was fired, and I'm looking for a little good news to tell your
   mother, because the woman has waited and the woman has suffered. The
   gist of it is that I haven't got a story left in my head, Biff. So don't give me
   a lecture about facts and aspects. I am not interested. Now what've you
   got to say to me?
   [STANLEY *enters with three drinks. They wait until he leaves.*]

WILLY   Did you see Oliver?

BIFF   Jesus, Dad!

WILLY   You mean you didn't go up there?

HAPPY   Sure he went up there.

BIFF   I did. I—saw him. How could they fire you?

WILLY [*on the edge of his chair*]   What kind of a welcome did he give you?

BIFF   He won't even let you work on commission?

WILLY   I'm out! [*driving*] So tell me, he gave you a warm welcome?

HAPPY   Sure, Pop, sure!

BIFF [*driven*]   Well, it was kind of—

WILLY   I was wondering if he'd remember you. [*to* HAPPY] Imagine, man
   doesn't see him for ten, twelve years and gives him that kind of a welcome!

HAPPY   Damn right!

BIFF [*trying to return to the offensive*]   Pop, look—

WILLY   You know why he remembered you, don't you? Because you
   impressed him in those days.

BIFF   Let's talk quietly and get this down to the facts, huh?

WILLY [*as though* BIFF *had been interrupting*]   Well, what happened? It's
   great news, Biff. Did he take you into his office or'd you talk in the
   waiting-room?

BIFF   Well, he came in, see, and—

WILLY [*with a big smile*]   What'd he say? Betcha he threw his arm around you.

BIFF   Well, he kinda—

WILLY   He's a fine man. [*to* HAPPY] Very hard man to see, y'know.

HAPPY [*agreeing*]   Oh, I know.

WILLY [*to* BIFF]   Is that where you had the drinks?

BIFF   Yeah, he gave me a couple of—no, no!

HAPPY [*cutting in*]   He told him my Florida idea.

WILLY   Don't interrupt. [*to* BIFF] How'd he react to the Florida idea?

BIFF   Dad, will you give me a minute to explain?

WILLY   I've been waiting for you to explain since I sat down here! What happened? He took you into his office and what?

BIFF   Well—I talked. And—he listened, see.

WILLY   Famous for the way he listens, y'know. What was his answer?

BIFF   His answer was— [*He breaks off, suddenly angry.*] Dad, you're not letting me tell you what I want to tell you!

WILLY [*accusing, angered*]   You didn't see him, did you?

BIFF   I did see him!

WILLY   What'd you insult him or something? You insulted him, didn't you?

BIFF   Listen, will you let me out of it, will you just let me out of it!

HAPPY   What the hell!

WILLY   Tell me what happened!

BIFF [*to* HAPPY]   I can't talk to him!

[*A single trumpet note jars the ear. The light of green leaves stains the house, which holds the air of night and a dream.* YOUNG BERNARD *enters and knocks on the door of the house.*]

YOUNG BERNARD [*frantically*]   Mrs. Loman, Mrs. Loman!

HAPPY   Tell him what happened!

BIFF [*to* HAPPY]   Shut up and leave me alone!

WILLY   No, no. You had to go and flunk math!

BIFF   What math? What're you talking about?

YOUNG BERNARD   Mrs. Loman, Mrs. Loman!

[LINDA *appears in the house, as of old.*]

WILLY [*wildly*]   Math, math, math!

BIFF   Take it easy, Pop!

YOUNG BERNARD   Mrs. Loman!

WILLY [*furiously*]   If you hadn't flunked you'd've been set by now!

BIFF   Now, look, I'm gonna tell you what happened, and you're going to listen to me.

YOUNG BERNARD   Mrs. Loman!

BIFF   I waited six hours—

HAPPY   What the hell are you saying?

BIFF   I kept sending in my name but he wouldn't see me. So finally he . . . [*He continues unheard as light fades low on the restaurant.*]

YOUNG BERNARD   Biff flunked math!

LINDA   No!

YOUNG BERNARD   Birnbaum flunked him! They won't graduate him!

LINDA   But they have to. He's gotta go to the university. Where is he? Biff! Biff!

YOUNG BERNARD   No, he left. He went to Grand Central.

LINDA   Grand—You mean he went to Boston!

YOUNG BERNARD   Is Uncle Willy in Boston?

LINDA   Oh, maybe Willy can talk to the teacher. Oh, the poor, poor boy!
   [*Light on house area snaps out.*]

BIFF [*at the table, now audible, holding up a gold fountain pen*]   . . . so I'm
   washed up with Oliver, you understand? Are you listening to me?

WILLY [*at a loss*]   Yeah, sure. If you hadn't flunked—

BIFF   Flunked what? What're you talking about?

WILLY   Don't blame everything on me! I didn't flunk math—you did! What
   pen?

HAPPY   That was awful dumb, Biff, a pen like that is worth—

WILLY [*seeing the pen for the first time*]   You took Oliver's pen?

BIFF [*weakening*]   Dad, I just explained it to you.

WILLY   You stole Bill Oliver's fountain pen!

BIFF   I didn't exactly steal it! That's just what I've been explaining to you!

HAPPY   He had it in his hand and just then Oliver walked in, so he got nervous and stuck it in his pocket!

WILLY   My God, Biff!

BIFF   I never intended to do it, Dad!

OPERATOR'S VOICE   Standish Arms, good evening!

WILLY [*shouting*]   I'm not in my room!

BIFF [*frightened*]   Dad, what's the matter? [*He and* HAPPY *stand up.*]

OPERATOR   Ringing Mr. Loman for you!

WILLY   I'm not there, stop it!

BIFF [*horrified, gets down on one knee before* WILLY]   Dad, I'll make good,
   I'll make good. [WILLY *tries to get to his feet.* BIFF *holds him down.*] Sit
   down now.

WILLY   No, you're no good, you're no good for anything.

BIFF   I am, Dad, I'll find something else, you understand? Now don't worry
   about anything. [*He holds up* WILLY's *face.*] Talk to me, Dad.

OPERATOR   Mr. Loman does not answer. Shall I page him?

WILLY [*attempting to stand, as though to rush and silence the* OPERATOR]
   No, no, no!

HAPPY   He'll strike something, Pop.

WILLY   No, no . . .

BIFF [*desperately, standing over* WILLY]   Pop, listen! Listen to me! I'm telling
   you something good. Oliver talked to his partner about the Florida idea.
   You listening? He—he talked to his partner, and he came to me . . . I'm
   going to be all right, you hear? Dad, listen to me, he said it was just a
   question of the amount!

WILLY   Then you . . . got it?

HAPPY   He's gonna be terrific, Pop!

WILLY [*trying to stand*]   Then you got it, haven't you? You got it! You got it!

BIFF [*agonized, holds* WILLY *down*]   No, no. Look, Pop. I'm supposed to
   have lunch with them tomorrow. I'm just telling you this so you'll know
   that I can still make an impression, Pop. And I'll make good somewhere,
   but I can't go tomorrow, see?

WILLY   Why not? You simply—

BIFF   But the pen, Pop!

WILLY   You give it to him and tell him it was an oversight!

HAPPY   Sure, have lunch tomorrow!

BIFF   I can't say that—

WILLY   You were doing a crossword puzzle and accidentally used his pen!

BIFF   Listen, kid, I took those balls years ago, now I walk in with his fountain pen? That clinches it, don't you see? I can't face him like that! I'll try elsewhere.

PAGE'S VOICE   Paging Mr. Loman!

WILLY   Don't you want to be anything?

BIFF   Pop, how can I go back?

WILLY   You don't want to be anything, is that what's behind it?

BIFF   [now angry at WILLY for not crediting his sympathy]   Don't take it that way! You think it was easy walking into that office after what I'd done to him? A team of horses couldn't have dragged me back to Bill Oliver!

WILLY   Then why'd you go?

BIFF   Why did I go? Why did I go! Look at you! Look at what's become of you!

[Off left, THE WOMAN laughs.]

WILLY   Biff, you're going to go to that lunch tomorrow, or—

BIFF   I can't go. I've got no appointment!

HAPPY   Biff for . . . !

WILLY   Are you spiting me?

BIFF   Don't take it that way! Goddammit!

WILLY   [strikes BIFF and falters away from the table]   You rotten little louse! Are you spiting me?

THE WOMAN   Someone's at the door, Willy!

BIFF   I'm no good, can't you see what I am?

HAPPY   [separating them]   Hey, you're in a restaurant! Now cut it out, both of you? [The girls enter.] Hello, girls, sit down.

[THE WOMAN laughs, off left.]

MISS FORSYTHE   I guess we might as well. This is Letta.

THE WOMAN   Willy, are you going to wake up?

BIFF   [ignoring WILLY]   How're ya, miss, sit down. What do you drink?

MISS FORSYTHE   Letta might not be able to stay long.

LETTA   I gotta get up early tomorrow. I got jury duty. I'm so excited! Were you fellows ever on a jury?

BIFF   No, but I been in front of them! [The girls laugh.] This is my father.

LETTA   Isn't he cute? Sit down with us, Pop.

HAPPY   Sit him down, Biff!

BIFF   [going to him]   Come on, slugger, drink us under the table. To hell with it! Come on, sit down, pal.

[On BIFF's last insistence, WILLY is about to sit.]

THE WOMAN   [now urgently]   Willy, are you going to answer the door!

[THE WOMAN's call pulls WILLY back. He starts right, befuddled.]

BIFF   Hey, where are you going?

WILLY   Open the door.

BIFF   The door?

WILLY   The washroom . . . the door . . . where's the door?

BIFF   [leading WILLY to the left]   Just go straight down.

[WILLY moves left.]

THE WOMAN   Willy, Willy, are you going to get up, get up, get up, get up?

[WILLY *exits left.*]

LETTA   I think it's sweet you bring your daddy along.

MISS FORSYTHE   Oh, he isn't really your father!

BIFF [*at left, turning to her resentfully*]   Miss Forsythe, you've just seen a prince walk by. A fine, troubled prince. A hard-working, unappreciated prince. A pal, you understand? A good companion. Always for his boys.

LETTA   That's so sweet.

HAPPY   Well, girls, what's the program? We're wasting time. Come on, Biff. Gather round. Where would you like to go?

BIFF   Why don't you do something for him?

HAPPY   Me!

BIFF   Don't you give a damn for him, Hap?

HAPPY   What're you talking about? I'm the one who—

BIFF   I sense it, you don't give a good goddam about him. [*He takes the rolled-up hose from his pocket and puts it on the table in front of* HAPPY.] Look what I found in the cellar, for Christ's sake. How can you bear to let it go on?

HAPPY   Me? Who goes away? Who runs off and—

BIFF   Yeah, but he doesn't mean anything to you. You could help him—I can't! Don't you understand what I'm talking about? He's going to kill himself, don't you know that?

HAPPY   Don't I know it! Me!

BIFF   Hap, help him! Jesus . . . help him . . . Help me, help me, I can't bear to look at his face! [*Ready to weep, he hurries out, up right.*]

HAPPY [*starting after him*]   Where are you going?

MISS FORSYTHE   What's he so mad about?

HAPPY   Come on, girls, we'll catch up with him.

MISS FORSYTHE [*as* HAPPY *pushes her out*]   Say, I don't like that temper of his!

HAPPY   He's just a little overstrung, he'll be all right!

WILLY [*off left, as* THE WOMAN *laughs*]   Don't answer! Don't answer!

LETTA   Don't you want to tell your father—

HAPPY   No, that's not my father. He's just a guy. Come on, we'll catch Biff, and, honey, we're going to paint this town! Stanley, where's the check! Hey, Stanley!

[*They exit.* STANLEY *looks toward left.*]

STANLEY [*calling to* HAPPY *indignantly*]   Mr. Loman! Mr. Loman!

[STANLEY *picks up a chair and follows them off. Knocking is heard off left.* THE WOMAN *enters, laughing.* WILLY *follows her. She is in a black slip; he is buttoning his shirt. Raw, sensuous music accompanies their speech.*]

WILLY   Will you stop laughing? Will you stop?

THE WOMAN   Aren't you going to answer the door? He'll wake the whole hotel.

WILLY   I'm not expecting anybody.

THE WOMAN   Whyn't you have another drink, honey, and stop being so damn self-centered?

WILLY   I'm so lonely.

THE WOMAN   You know you ruined me, Willy? From now on, whenever you come to the office, I'll see that you go right through to the buyers. No waiting at my desk any more, Willy. You ruined me.

WILLY   That's nice of you to say that.

THE WOMAN   Gee, you are self-centered! Why so sad? You are the saddest, self-centeredest soul I ever did see-saw. [*She laughs. He kisses her.*] Come on inside, drummer boy. It's silly to be dressing in the middle of the night. [*As knocking is heard*] Aren't you going to answer the door?

WILLY   They're knocking on the wrong door.

THE WOMAN   But I felt the knocking. And he heard us talking in here. Maybe the hotel's on fire!

WILLY [*his terror rising*]   It's a mistake.

THE WOMAN   Then tell them to go away!

WILLY   There's nobody there.

THE WOMAN   It's getting on my nerves, Willy. There's somebody standing out there and it's getting on my nerves!

WILLY [*pushing her away from him*]   All right, stay in the bathroom here, and don't come out. I think there's a law in Massachusetts about it, so don't come out. It may be that new room clerk. He looked very mean. So don't come out. It's a mistake, there's no fire.

> [*The knocking is heard again. He takes a few steps away from her, and she vanishes into the wing. The light follows him, and now he is facing* YOUNG BIFF, *who carries a suitcase.* BIFF *steps toward him. The music is gone.*]

BIFF   Why didn't you answer?

WILLY   Biff! What are you doing in Boston?

BIFF   Why didn't you answer? I've been knocking for five minutes, I called you on the phone—

WILLY   I just heard you. I was in the bathroom and had the door shut. Did anything happen home?

BIFF   Dad—I let you down.

WILLY   What do you mean?

BIFF   Dad . . .

WILLY   Biffo, what's this about? [*putting his arm around* BIFF] Come on, let's go downstairs and get you a malted.

BIFF   Dad, I flunked math.

WILLY   Not for the term?

BIFF   The term. I haven't got enough credits to graduate.

WILLY   You mean to say Bernard wouldn't give you the answers?

BIFF   He did, he tried, but I only got a sixty-one.

WILLY   And they wouldn't give you four points?

BIFF   Birnbaum refused absolutely. I begged him, Pop, but he won't give me those points. You gotta talk to him before they close the school. Because if he saw the kind of man you are, and you just talked to him in your way, I'm sure he'd come through for me. The class came right before practice, see, and I didn't go enough. Would you talk to him? He'd like you, Pop. You know the way you could talk.

WILLY   You're on. We'll drive right back.

BIFF   Oh, Dad, good work! I'm sure he'll change for you!

WILLY   Go downstairs and tell the clerk I'm checkin' out. Go right down.

BIFF   Yes, sir! See, the reason he hates me, Pop—one day he was late for class so I got up at the blackboard and imitated him. I crossed my eyes and talked with a lithp.

WILLY [*laughing*]   You did? The kids like it?

BIFF   They nearly died laughing!

WILLY   Yeah? What'd you do?

BIFF   The thquare root of thixthy twee is . . . [WILLY *bursts out laughing;* BIFF *joins him.*] And in the middle of it he walked in!

[WILLY *laughs and* THE WOMAN *joins in offstage.*]

WILLY [*without hesitation*]   Hurry downstairs and—

BIFF   Somebody in there?

WILLY   No, that was next door.

[THE WOMAN *laughs offstage.*]

BIFF   Somebody got in your bathroom!

WILLY   No, it's the next room, there's a party—

THE WOMAN [*enters laughing. She lisps this*]   Can I come in? There's something in the bathtub, Willy, and it's moving!

[WILLY *looks at* BIFF, *who is staring open-mouthed and horrified at* THE WOMAN.]

WILLY   Ah—you better go back to your room. They must be finished painting by now. They're painting her room so I let her take a shower here. Go back, go back . . . [*He pushes her.*]

THE WOMAN [*resisting*]   But I've got to get dressed, Willy, I can't—

WILLY   Get out of here! Go back, go back . . . [*suddenly striving for the ordinary*] This is Miss Francis, Biff, she's a buyer. They're painting her room. Go back, Miss Francis, go back . . .

THE WOMAN   But my clothes, I can't go out naked in the hall!

WILLY [*pushing her offstage*]   Get outa here! Go back, go back!

[BIFF *slowly sits down on his suitcase as the argument continues offstage.*]

THE WOMAN   Where's my stockings? You promised me stockings, Willy!

WILLY   I have no stockings here!

THE WOMAN   You had two boxes of size nine sheers for me, and I want them!

WILLY   Here, for God's sake, will you get outa here!

THE WOMAN [*enters holding a box of stockings*]   I just hope there's nobody in the hall. That's all I hope. [*to* BIFF] Are you football or baseball?

BIFF   Football.

THE WOMAN [*angry, humiliated*]   That's me too. G'night. [*She snatches her clothes from* WILLY, *and walks out.*]

WILLY [*after a pause*]   Well, better get going. I want to get to the school first thing in the morning. Get my suits out of the closet. I'll get my valise. [BIFF *doesn't move.*] What's the matter? [BIFF *remains motionless, tears falling.*] She's a buyer. Buys for J. H. Simmons. She lives down the hall—they're painting. You don't imagine— [*He breaks off. After a pause*] Now listen, pal, she's just a buyer. She sees merchandise in her room and they have to keep it looking just so . . . [*Pause. Assuming command*] All right, get my suits. [BIFF *doesn't move.*] Now stop crying and do as I say. I gave you an order. Biff, I gave you an order! Is that what you do when I give you an order? How dare you cry! [*putting his arm around* BIFF] Now look, Biff, when you grow up you'll understand about these things. You mustn't—you mustn't overemphasize a thing like this. I'll see Birnbaum first thing in the morning.

BIFF   Never mind.

WILLY [*getting down beside* BIFF]   Never mind! He's going to give you those points. I'll see to it.

BIFF   He wouldn't listen to you.

WILLY   He certainly will listen to me. You need those points for the U. of Virginia.

BIFF   I'm not going there.

WILLY   Heh? If I can't get him to change that mark you'll make it up in summer school. You've got all summer to—

BIFF   [*his weeping breaking from him*]   Dad . . .

WILLY   [*infected by it*]   Oh, my boy . . .

BIFF   Dad . . .

WILLY   She's nothing to me, Biff. I was lonely, I was terribly lonely.

BIFF   You—you gave her Mama's stockings! [*His tears break through and he rises to go.*]

WILLY   [*grabbing for* BIFF]   I gave you an order!

BIFF   Don't touch me, you—liar!

WILLY   Apologize for that!

BIFF   You fake! You phony little fake! You fake! [*Overcome, he turns quickly and weeping fully goes out with his suitcase.* WILLY *is left on the floor on his knees.*]

WILLY   I gave you an order! Biff, come back here or I'll beat you! Come back here! I'll whip you!

        [STANLEY *comes quickly in from the right and stands in front of* WILLY.]

WILLY [*shouts at* STANLEY]   I gave you an order . . .

STANLEY   Hey, let's pick it up, pick it up, Mr. Loman. [*He helps* WILLY *to his feet.*] Your boys left with the chippies. They said they'll see you home.

        [*A second waiter watches some distance away.*]

WILLY   But we were supposed to have dinner together.

        [*Music is heard,* WILLY's *theme.*]

STANLEY   Can you make it?

WILLY   I'll—sure, I can make it. [*suddenly concerned about his clothes*] Do I—I look all right?

STANLEY   Sure, you look all right. [*He flicks a speck off* WILLY's *lapel.*]

WILLY   Here—here's a dollar.

STANLEY   Oh, your son paid me. It's all right.

WILLY [*putting it in* STANLEY's *hand*]   No, take it. You're a good boy.

STANLEY   Oh, no, you don't have to . . .

WILLY   Here—here's some more, I don't need it any more. [*after a slight pause*] Tell me—is there a seed store in the neighborhood?

STANLEY   Seeds? You mean like to plant?

        [*As* WILLY *turns,* STANLEY *slips the money back into his jacket pocket.*]

WILLY   Yes. Carrots, peas . . .

STANLEY   Well, there's hardware stores on Sixth Avenue, but it may be too late now.

WILLY [*anxiously*]   Oh, I'd better hurry. I've got to get some seeds. [*He starts off to the right.*] I've got to get some seeds, right away. Nothing's planted. I don't have a thing in the ground.

        [WILLY *hurries out as the light goes down.* STANLEY *moves over to the right after him, watches him off. The other waiter has been staring at* WILLY.]

STANLEY [*to the waiter*]   Well, whatta you looking at?

        [*The waiter picks up the chairs and moves off right.* STANLEY *takes the table and follows him. The light fades on this area. There is a long pause, the sound of the flute coming over. The light gradually rises on the kitchen, which is empty.* HAPPY *appears at the door of the house, followed by* BIFF.]

HAPPY *is carrying a large bunch of long-stemmed roses. He enters the kitchen, looks around for* LINDA. *Not seeing her, he turns to* BIFF, *who is just outside the house door, and makes a gesture with his hands, indicating "Not here, I guess." He looks into the living-room and freezes. Inside,* LINDA, *unseen, is seated,* WILLY's *coat on her lap. She rises ominously and quietly and moves toward* HAPPY, *who backs up into the kitchen, afraid.*]

HAPPY Hey, what're you doing up? [LINDA *says nothing but moves toward him implacably.*] Where's Pop? [*He keeps backing to the right, and now* LINDA *is in full view in the doorway to the living-room.*] Is he sleeping?

LINDA Where were you?

HAPPY [*trying to laugh it off*] We met two girls, Mom, very fine types. Here, we brought you some flowers. [*offering them to her*] Put them in your room, Ma.

[*She knocks them to the floor at* BIFF's *feet. He has now come inside and closed the door behind him. She stares at* BIFF, *silent.*]

HAPPY Now what'd you do that for? Mom, I want you to have some flowers—

LINDA [*cutting* HAPPY *off, violently to* BIFF] Don't you care whether he lives or dies?

HAPPY [*going to the stairs*] Come upstairs, Biff.

BIFF [*with a flare of disgust, to* HAPPY] Go away from me! [*to* LINDA] What do you mean, lives or dies? Nobody's dying around here, pal.

LINDA Get out of my sight! Get out of here!

BIFF I wanna see the boss.

LINDA You're not going near him!

BIFF Where is he? [*He moves into the living-room and* LINDA *follows.*]

LINDA [*shouting after* BIFF] You invite him for dinner. He looks forward to it all day—[BIFF *appears in his parents' bedroom, looks around and exits*]—and then you desert him there. There's no stranger you'd do that to!

HAPPY Why? He had a swell time with us. Listen, when I—[LINDA *comes back into the kitchen*]—desert him I hope I don't outlive the day!

LINDA Get out of here!

HAPPY Now look, Mom . . .

LINDA Did you have to go to women tonight? You and your lousy rotten whores!

[BIFF *re-enters the kitchen.*]

HAPPY Mom, all we did was follow Biff around trying to cheer him up! [*to* BIFF] Boy, what a night you gave me!

LINDA Get out of here, both of you, and don't come back! I don't want you tormenting him any more. Go on now, get your things together! [*to* BIFF] You can sleep in his apartment. [*She starts to pick up the flowers and stops herself.*] Pick up this stuff, I'm not your maid any more. Pick it up, you bum, you!

[HAPPY *turns his back to her in refusal.* BIFF *slowly moves over and gets down on his knees, picking up the flowers.*]

LINDA You're a pair of animals! Not one, not another living soul would have had the cruelty to walk out on that man in a restaurant!

BIFF [*not looking at her*] Is that what he said?

LINDA He didn't have to say anything. He was so humiliated he nearly limped when he came in.

HAPPY But, Mom, he had a great time with us—

BIFF [*cutting him off violently*]   Shut up!

    [*Without another word,* HAPPY *goes upstairs.*]

LINDA   You! You didn't even go in to see if he was all right!

BIFF [*still on the floor in front of* LINDA, *the flowers in his hand; with self-loathing*]   No. Didn't. Didn't do a damned thing. How do you like that, heh? Left him babbling in a toilet.

LINDA   You louse. You . . .

BIFF   Now you hit it on the nose! [*He gets up, throws the flowers in the waste-basket.*] The scum of the earth, and you're looking at him!

LINDA   Get out of here!

BIFF   I gotta talk to the boss, Mom. Where is he?

LINDA   You're not going near him. Get out of this house!

BIFF [*with absolute assurance, determination*]   No. We're gonna have an abrupt conversation, him and me.

LINDA   You're not talking to him!

    [*Hammering is heard from outside the house, off right.* BIFF *turns toward the noise.*]

LINDA [*suddenly pleading*]   Will you please leave him alone?

BIFF   What's he doing out there?

LINDA   He's planting the garden!

BIFF [*quietly*]   Now? Oh, my God!

    [BIFF *moves outside,* LINDA *following. The light dies down on them and comes up on the center of the apron as* WILLY *walks into it. He is carrying a flashlight, a hoe, and a handful of seed packets. He raps the top of the hoe sharply to fix it firmly, and then moves to the left, measuring off the distance with his foot. He holds the flashlight to look at the seed packets, reading off the instructions. He is in the blue of night.*]

WILLY   Carrots . . . quarter-inch apart. Rows . . . one-foot rows. [*He measures it off.*] One foot. [*He puts down a package and measures off.*] Beets. [*He puts down another package and measures again.*] Lettuce. [*He reads the package, puts it down.*] One foot— [*He breaks off as* BEN *appears at the right and moves slowly down to him.*] What a proposition, ts, ts. Terrific, terrific. 'Cause she's suffered, Ben, the woman has suffered. You understand me? A man can't go out the way he came in, Ben, a man has got to add up to something. You can't, you can't— [BEN *moves toward him as though to interrupt.*] You gotta consider, now. Don't answer so quick. Remember, it's a guaranteed twenty-thousand-dollar proposition. Now look, Ben, I want you to go through the ins and outs of this thing with me. I've got nobody to talk to, Ben, and the woman has suffered, you hear me?

BEN [*standing still, considering*]   What's the proposition?

WILLY   It's twenty thousand dollars on the barrelhead. Guaranteed, gilt-edged, you understand?

BEN   You don't want to make a fool of yourself. They might not honor the policy.

WILLY   How can they dare refuse? Didn't I work like a coolie to meet every premium on the nose? And now they don't pay off! Impossible!

BEN   It's called a cowardly thing, William.

WILLY   Why? Does it take more guts to stand here the rest of my life ringing up a zero?

BEN [*yielding*] That's a point, William. [*He moves, thinking, turns.*] And twenty thousand—that *is* something one can feel with the hand, it is there.

WILLY [*now assured, with rising power*] Oh, Ben, that's the whole beauty of it! I see it like a diamond, shining in the dark, hard and rough, that I can pick up and touch in my hand. Not like—like an appointment! This would not be another damned-fool appointment, Ben, and it changes all the aspects. Because he thinks I'm nothing, see, and so he spites me. But the funeral— [*straightening up*] Ben, that funeral will be massive! They'll come from Maine, Massachusetts, Vermont, New Hampshire! All the old-timers with the strange license plates—that boy will be thunder-struck, Ben, because he never realized—I am known! Rhode Island, New York, New Jersey—I am known, Ben, and he'll see it with his eyes once and for all. He'll see what I am, Ben! He's in for a shock, that boy!

BEN [*coming down to the edge of the garden*] He'll call you a coward.

WILLY [*suddenly fearful*] No, that would be terrible.

BEN Yes. And a damned fool.

WILLY No, no, he mustn't, I won't have that! [*He is broken and desperate.*]

BEN He'll hate you, William.

[*The gay music of the Boys is heard.*]

WILLY Oh, Ben, how do we get back to all the great times? Used to be so full of light, and comradeship, the sleigh-riding in winter, and the ruddiness on his cheeks. And always some kind of good news coming up, always something nice coming up ahead. And never even let me carry the valises in the house, and simonizing, simonizing that little red car! Why, why can't I give him something and not have him hate me?

BEN Let me think about it. [*He glances at his watch.*] I still have a little time. Remarkable proposition, but you've got to be sure you're not making a fool of yourself.

[BEN *drifts off upstage and goes out of sight.* BIFF *comes down from the left.*]

WILLY [*suddenly conscious of* BIFF, *turns and looks up at him, then begins picking up the packages of seeds in confusion*] Where the hell is that seed? [*indignantly*] You can't see nothing out here! They boxed in the whole goddam neighborhood!

BIFF There are people all around here. Don't you realize that?

WILLY I'm busy. Don't bother me.

BIFF [*taking the hoe from* WILLY] I'm saying good-by to you, Pop. [WILLY *looks at him, silent, unable to move.*] I'm not coming back any more.

WILLY You're not going to see Oliver tomorrow?

BIFF I've got no appointment, Dad.

WILLY He put his arm around you, and you've got no appointment?

BIFF Pop, get this now, will you? Everytime I've left it's been a fight that sent me out of here. Today I realized something about myself and I tried to explain it to you and I—I think I'm just not smart enough to make any sense out of it for you. To hell with whose fault it is or anything like that. [*He takes* WILLY's *arm.*] Let's just wrap it up, heh? Come on in, we'll tell Mom. [*He gently tries to pull* WILLY *to left.*]

WILLY [*frozen, immobile, with guilt in his voice*] No, I don't want to see her.

BIFF Come on! [*He pulls again, and* WILLY *tries to pull away.*]

WILLY [*highly nervous*]   No, no, I don't want to see her.

BIFF [*tries to look into* WILLY'*s face, as if to find the answer there*]   Why don't you want to see her?

WILLY [*more harshly now*]   Don't bother me, will you?

BIFF   What do you mean, you don't want to see her? You don't want them calling you yellow, do you? This isn't your fault; it's me, I'm a bum. Now come inside! [WILLY *strains to get away.*] Did you hear what I said to you?

    [WILLY *pulls away and quickly goes by himself into the house.* BIFF *follows.*]

LINDA [*to* WILLY]   Did you plant, dear?

BIFF [*at the door, to* LINDA]   All right, we had it out. I'm going and I'm not writing any more.

LINDA [*going to* WILLY *in the kitchen*]   I think that's the best way, dear. 'Cause there's no use drawing it out, you'll just never get along.

    [WILLY *doesn't respond.*]

BIFF   People ask where I am and what I'm doing, you don't know, and you don't care. That way it'll be off your mind and you can start brightening up again. All right? That clears it, doesn't it? [WILLY *is silent, and* BIFF *goes to him.*] You gonna wish me luck, scout? [*He extends his hand.*] What do you say?

LINDA   Shake his hand, Willy.

WILLY [*turning to her, seething with hurt*]   There's no necessity to mention the pen at all, y'know.

BIFF [*gently*]   I've got no appointment, Dad.

WILLY [*erupting fiercely*]   He put his arm around . . . ?

BIFF   Dad, you're never going to see what I am, so what's the use of arguing? If I strike oil I'll send you a check. Meantime forget I'm alive.

WILLY [*to* LINDA]   Spite, see?

BIFF   Shake hands, Dad.

WILLY   Not my hand.

BIFF   I was hoping not to go this way.

WILLY   Well, this is the way you're going. Good-by.

    [BIFF *looks at him a moment, then turns sharply and goes to the stairs.*]

WILLY [*stops him with*]   May you rot in hell if you leave this house!

BIFF [*turning*]   Exactly what is it that you want from me?

WILLY   I want you to know, on the train, in the mountains, in the valleys, wherever you go, that you cut down your life for spite!

BIFF   No, no.

WILLY   Spite, spite, is the word of your undoing! And when you're down and out, remember what did it. When you're rotting somewhere beside the railroad tracks, remember, and don't you dare blame it on me!

BIFF   I'm not blaming it on you!

WILLY   I won't take the rap for this, you hear?

    [HAPPY *comes down the stairs and stands on the bottom step, watching.*]

BIFF   That's just what I'm telling you!

WILLY [*sinking into a chair at the table, with full accusation*]   You're trying to put a knife in me—don't think I don't know what you're doing!

BIFF   All right, phony! Then let's lay it on the line. [*He whips the rubber tube out of his pocket and puts it on the table.*]

HAPPY   You crazy—

LINDA   Biff! [*She moves to grab the hose, but* BIFF *holds it down with his hand.*]

BIFF   Leave it there! Don't move it!

WILLY [*not looking at it*]   What is that?

BIFF   You know goddam well what that is.

WILLY [*caged, wanting to escape*]   I never saw that.

BIFF   You saw it. The mice didn't bring it into the cellar! What is this supposed to do, make a hero out of you? This supposed to make me sorry for you?

WILLY   Never heard of it.

BIFF   There'll be no pity for you, you hear it? No pity!

WILLY [*to* LINDA]   You hear the spite!

BIFF   No, you're going to hear the truth—what you are and what I am!

LINDA   Stop it!

WILLY   Spite!

HAPPY [*coming down toward* BIFF]   You cut it now!

BIFF [*to* HAPPY]   The man don't know who we are! The man is gonna know! [*to* WILLY] We never told the truth for ten minutes in this house!

HAPPY   We always told the truth!

BIFF [*turning on him*]   You big blow, are you the assistant buyer? You're one of the two assistants to the assistant, aren't you?

HAPPY   Well, I'm practically—

BIFF   You're practically full of it! We all are! And I'm through with it. [*to* WILLY] Now hear this, Willy, this is me.

WILLY   I know you!

BIFF   You know why I had no address for three months? I stole a suit in Kansas City and I was in jail. [*to* LINDA, *who is sobbing*] Stop crying. I'm through with it.

        [LINDA *turns away from them, her hands covering her face.*]

WILLY   I suppose that's my fault!

BIFF   I stole myself out of every good job since high school!

WILLY   And whose fault is that?

BIFF   And I never got anywhere because you blew me so full of hot air I could never stand taking orders from anybody! That's whose fault it is!

WILLY   I hear that!

LINDA   Don't, Biff!

BIFF   It's goddam time you heard that! I had to be boss big shot in two weeks, and I'm through with it!

WILLY   Then hang yourself! For spite, hang yourself!

BIFF   No! Nobody's hanging himself, Willy! I ran down eleven flights with a pen in my hand today. And suddenly I stopped, you hear me? And in the middle of that office building, do you hear this? I stopped in the middle of that building and I saw—the sky. I saw the things that I love in this world. The work and the food and time to sit and smoke. And I looked at the pen and said to myself, what the hell am I grabbing this for? Why am I trying to become what I don't want to be? What am I doing in an office, making a contemptuous, begging fool of myself, when all I want is out there, waiting for me the minute I say I know who I am! Why can't I say that, Willy? [*He tries to make* WILLY *face him, but* WILLY *pulls away and moves to the left.*]

WILLY [*with hatred, threateningly*]   The door of your life is wide open!

BIFF   Pop! I'm a dime a dozen, and so are you!

WILLY [*turning on him now in an uncontrolled outburst*]   I am not a dime a dozen! I am Willy Loman, and you are Biff Loman!

> [BIFF *starts for* WILLY, *but is blocked by* HAPPY. *In his fury,* BIFF *seems on the verge of attacking his father.*]

BIFF   I am not a leader of men, Willy, and neither are you. You were never anything but a hard-working drummer who landed in the ash can like all the rest of them! I'm one dollar an hour, Willy! I tried seven states and couldn't raise it. A buck an hour! Do you gather my meaning? I'm not bringing home any prizes any more, and you're going to stop waiting for me to bring them home!

WILLY [*directly to* BIFF]   You vengeful, spiteful mut!

> [BIFF *breaks from* HAPPY. WILLY, *in fright, starts up the stairs.* BIFF *grabs him.*]

BIFF [*at the peak of his fury*]   Pop, I'm nothing! I'm nothing, Pop. Can't you understand that? There's no spite in it any more. I'm just what I am, that's all.

> [BIFF's *fury has spent itself, and he breaks down, sobbing, holding on to* WILLY, *who dumbly fumbles for* BIFF's *face.*]

WILLY [*astonished*]   What're you doing? What're you doing? [*to* LINDA] Why is he crying?

BIFF [*crying, broken*]   Will you let me go, for Christ's sake? Will you take that phony dream and burn it before something happens? [*Struggling to contain himself, he pulls away and moves to the stairs.*] I'll go in the morning. Put him—put him to bed. [*Exhausted,* BIFF *moves up the stairs to his room.*]

WILLY [*after a long pause, astonished, elevated*]   Isn't that—isn't that remarkable? Biff—he likes me!

LINDA   He loves you, Willy!

HAPPY [*deeply moved*]   Always did, Pop.

WILLY   Oh, Biff! [*staring wildly*]   He cried! Cried to me. [*He is choking with his love, and now cries out his promise.*] That boy—that boy is going to be magnificent!

> [BEN *appears in the light just outside the kitchen.*]

BEN   Yes, outstanding, with twenty thousand behind him.

LINDA [*sensing the racing of his mind, fearfully, carefully*]   Now come to bed, Willy. It's all settled now.

WILLY [*finding it difficult not to rush out of the house*]   Yes, we'll sleep. Come on. Go to sleep, Hap.

BEN   And it does take a great kind of a man to crack the jungle.

> [*In accents of dread,* BEN's *idyllic music starts up.*]

HAPPY [*his arm around* LINDA]   I'm getting married, Pop, don't forget it. I'm changing everything. I'm gonna run that department before the year is up. You'll see, Mom. [*He kisses her.*]

BEN   The jungle is dark but full of diamonds, Willy.

> [WILLY *turns, moves, listening to* BEN.]

LINDA   Be good. You're both good boys, just act that way, that's all.

HAPPY   'Night, Pop. [*He goes upstairs.*]

LINDA [*to* WILLY]   Come, dear.

BEN [*with greater force*]   One must go in to fetch a diamond out.

WILLY [*to* LINDA, *as he moves slowly along the edge of the kitchen, toward the*

door] I just want to get settled down, Linda. Let me sit alone for a little.

LINDA [*almost uttering her fear*]   I want you upstairs.

WILLY [*taking her in his arms*]   In a few minutes, Linda. I couldn't sleep
right now. Go on, you look awful tired. [*He kisses her.*]

BEN   Not like an appointment at all. A diamond is rough and hard to the
touch.

WILLY   Go on now. I'll be right up.

LINDA   I think this is the only way, Willy.

WILLY   Sure, it's the best thing.

BEN   Best thing!

WILLY   The only way. Everything is gonna be—go on, kid, get to bed. You
look so tired.

LINDA   Come right up.

WILLY   Two minutes.

[LINDA *goes into the living-room, then reappears in her bedroom.* WILLY
moves just outside the kitchen door.]

WILLY   Loves me. [*wonderingly*]   Always loved me. Isn't that a remarkable
thing? Ben, he'll worship me for it!

BEN [*with promise*]   It's dark there, but full of diamonds.

WILLY   Can you imagine that magnificence with twenty thousand dollars
in his pocket?

LINDA [*calling from her room*]   Willy! Come up!

WILLY [*calling into the kitchen*]   Yes! Yes. Coming! It's very smart, you realize that, don't you, sweetheart? Even Ben sees it. I gotta go, baby. 'By! 'By!
[*going over to* BEN, *almost dancing*] Imagine? When the mail comes he'll
be ahead of Bernard again!

BEN   A perfect proposition all around.

WILLY   Did you see how he cried to me? Oh, if I could kiss him, Ben!

BEN   Time, William, time!

WILLY   Oh, Ben, I always knew one way or another we were gonna make
it, Biff and I!

BEN [*looking at his watch*]   The boat. We'll be late. [*He moves slowly off into
the darkness.*]

WILLY [*elegiacally, turning to the house*]   Now when you kick off, boy, I
want a seventy-yard boot, and get right down the field under the ball, and
when you hit, hit low and hit hard, because it's important, boy. [*He swings
around and faces the audience.*] There's all kinds of important people in
the stands, and the first thing you know . . . [*suddenly realizing he is
alone*] Ben! Ben, where do I . . . ? [*He makes a sudden movement of
search.*] Ben, how do I . . . ?

LINDA [*calling*]   Willy, you coming up?

WILLY [*uttering a gasp of fear, whirling about as if to quiet her*]   Sh! [*He turns
around as if to find his way; sounds, faces, voices, seem to be swarming in
upon him and he flicks at them, crying,*] Sh! Sh! [*Suddenly music, faint and
high, stops him. It rises in intensity, almost to an unbearable scream. He goes
up and down on his toes, and rushes off around the house.*] Shhh!

LINDA   Willy?

[*There is no answer.* LINDA *waits.* BIFF *gets up off his bed. He is still in his
clothes.* HAPPY *sits up.* BIFF *stands listening.*]

LINDA [*with real fear*]   Willy, answer me! Willy!

    [*There is the sound of a car starting and moving away at full speed.*]

LINDA   No!

BIFF [*rushing down the stairs*]   Pop!

    [*As the car speeds off, the music crashes down in a frenzy of sound, which becomes the soft pulsation of a single cello string.* BIFF *slowly returns to his bedroom. He and* HAPPY *gravely don their jackets.* LINDA *slowly walks out of her room. The music has developed into a dead march. The leaves of day are appearing over everything.* CHARLEY *and* BERNARD *somberly dressed, appear and knock on the kitchen door.* BIFF *and* HAPPY *slowly descend the stairs to the kitchen as* CHARLEY *and* BERNARD *enter. All stop a moment when* LINDA, *in clothes of mourning, bearing a little bunch of roses, comes through the draped doorway into the kitchen. She goes to* CHARLEY *and takes his arm. Now all move toward the audience, through the wall-line of the kitchen. At the limit of the apron,* LINDA *lays down the flowers, kneels, and sits back on her heels. All stare down at the grave.*]

Requiem

CHARLEY   It's getting dark, Linda.

    [LINDA *doesn't react. She stares at the grave.*]

BIFF   How about it, Mom? Better get some rest, heh? They'll be closing the gate soon.

    [LINDA *makes no move. Pause.*]

HAPPY [*deeply angered*]   He had no right to do that. There was no necessity for it. We would've helped him.

CHARLEY [*grunting*]   Hmmm.

BIFF   Come along, Mom.

LINDA   Why didn't anybody come?

CHARLEY   It was a very nice funeral.

LINDA   But where are all the people he knew? Maybe they blame him.

CHARLEY   Naa. It's a rough world, Linda. They wouldn't blame him.

LINDA   I can't understand it. At this time especially. First time in thirty-five years we were just about free and clear. He only needed a little salary. He was even finished with the dentist.

CHARLEY   No man only needs a little salary.

LINDA   I can't understand it.

BIFF   There were a lot of nice days. When he'd come home from a trip; or on Sundays, making the stoop; finishing the cellar; putting on the new porch; when he built the extra bathroom; and put up the garage. You know something, Charley, there's more of him in that front stoop than in all the sales he ever made.

CHARLEY   Yeah. He was a happy man with a batch of cement.

LINDA   He was so wonderful with his hands.

BIFF   He had the wrong dreams. All, all, wrong.

HAPPY [*almost ready to fight* BIFF]   Don't say that!

BIFF   He never knew who he was.

CHARLEY [*stopping* HAPPY*'s movement and reply. To* BIFF]   Nobody dast blame this man. You don't understand: Willy was a salesman. And for a salesman, there is no rock bottom to the life. He don't put a bolt to a nut, he don't tell you the law or give you medicine. He's a man way out there in the blue, riding on a smile and a shoeshine. And when they start not smiling back—that's an earthquake. And then you get yourself a couple of spots on your hat, and you're finished. Nobody dast blame this man. A salesman is got to dream, boy. It comes with the territory.

BIFF   Charley, the man didn't know who he was.

HAPPY [*infuriated*]   Don't say that!

BIFF   Why don't you come with me, Happy?

HAPPY   I'm not licked that easily. I'm staying right in this city, and I'm gonna beat this racket! [*He looks at* BIFF, *his chin set.*] The Loman Brothers!

BIFF   I know who I am, kid.

HAPPY   All right, boy. I'm gonna show you and everybody else that Willy Loman did not die in vain. He had a good dream. It's the only dream you can have—to come out number-one man. He fought it out here, and this is where I'm gonna win it for him.

BIFF [*with a hopeless glance at* HAPPY, *bends toward his mother*]   Let's go, Mom.

LINDA   I'll be with you in a minute. Go on, Charley. [*He hesitates.*]   I want to, just for a minute. I never had a chance to say good-by.

[CHARLEY *moves away, followed by* HAPPY. BIFF *remains a slight distance up and left of* LINDA. *She sits there, summoning herself. The flute begins, not far away, playing behind her speech.*]

LINDA   Forgive me, dear. I can't cry. I don't know what it is, but I can't cry. I don't understand it. Why did you ever do that? Help me, Willy, I can't cry. It seems to me that you're just on another trip. I keep expecting you. Willy, dear, I can't cry. Why did you do it? I search and search and I search, and I can't understand it, Willy. I made the last payment on the house today. Today, dear. And there'll be nobody home. [*A sob rises in her throat.*] We're free and clear. [*Sobbing more fully, released*] We're free. [BIFF *comes slowly toward her.*] We're free . . . We're free . . .

[BIFF *lifts her to her feet and moves out up right with her in his arms.* LINDA *sobs quietly.* BERNARD *and* CHARLEY *come together and follow them, followed by* HAPPY. *Only the music of the flute is left on the darkening stage as over the house the hard towers of the apartment buildings rise into sharp focus, and*]

CURTAIN

1949

ROBERT LOWELL
1917–1977

In "North Haven," her poem in memory of Robert Lowell, Elizabeth Bishop translates the bird song as Lowell seemed to hear it: "repeat, repeat, repeat, revise, revise, revise." Repeatedly, even obsessively, Lowell returned to certain subjects in his poems. Each return confirmed an existing pattern even as it opened the possibility for revision. In fact, Lowell's life was full of revision. Descended from Protestant New Englanders, he converted to Catholicism, then fell away from it; he married three times; and he changed his poetic style more than once. In the later part of his career Lowell revised even his published poems and did so repeatedly. "Revision is inspiration," he once said, "no reading of the finished work as exciting as writing the last changes." Revision allowed for Lowell's love of stray events, his attraction to the fluidity of life (in this, he resembles Wallace Stevens). But Lowell also wanted to organize life into formal patterns, to locate the random moment in the design of an epic history (his Catholicism can be seen, in part, as an expression of this desire). History offered plot and repetition: just as patterns of his childhood recurred in adult life, the sins of his New England ancestors were reenacted by contemporary America. Lowell's vision of history leaned toward apocalypse, toward the revelation of a prior meaning the poet agonized to determine, and yet he cherished the freedom of "human chances," with all their indeterminacy. His poems had to accommodate these opposing impulses. Concerning the sequence of poems in *Notebook 1967–1968*, begun as a poetic diary, he said: "Accident threw up the subject and the plot swallowed them—famished for human chances." If Lowell often swallowed up the casual, the random, the ordinary, and the domestic into the forms of his poems, his best plots have a spontaneity whose meanings cannot be fixed.

The burden of family history was substantial for Lowell, whose ancestors included members of Boston's patrician families. His grandfather was a well-known Episcopal minister and head of the fashionable St. Mark's School, which the poet was later to attend. His great-granduncle James Russell Lowell had been a poet and ambassador to England. The family's light note was provided by the poet Amy Lowell, "big and a scandal, as if Mae West were a cousin." In the context of this history Lowell's father, who fared badly in business after his retirement from service as a naval officer, appeared as a diminished figure.

Lowell's first act of revising family history was to leave the East after two years at Harvard (1935–37) to study at Kenyon College with John Crowe Ransom, the poet and critic. The move brought him in closer touch with the New Criticism and its predilections for "formal difficult poems," the wit and irony of English Metaphysical writers such as John Donne. He also, through Ransom and the poet Allen Tate, came into contact with (although never formally joined) the Fugitive movement, whose members were southern agrarians opposed to what they regarded as the corrupting values of northern industrialism.

Two of the acts that most decisively separated Lowell from family history were his conversion to Roman Catholicism (1940) and his resistance to American policies in World War II. Although he tried to enlist in the navy, he refused to be drafted into the army. He opposed the saturation bombing of Hamburg and the Allied policy of unconditional surrender and was as a result sentenced to a year's confinement in New York City's West Street jail. The presiding judge at his hearing admonished him for "marring" his family traditions. In his first book, *Lord Weary's Castle* (1946), his Catholicism provided a set of symbols and a distanced platform from which to express his violent antagonism to Protestant mercantile Boston. The stunning, apocalyptic conclusions of these early poems ("the Lord survives the rainbow of his will" or "The blue kingfisher dives on you in fire") render the devastating judgment of the eternal on the fallen history of the individual and the nation.

Alongside those poems drawing on Old Testament anger were those poems in *Lord Weary's Castle*, such as "Mr. Edwards and the Spider," that explored from within the nervous intensity that underlay Puritan revivalism. Later dramatic narratives with modern settings, such as "The Mills of the Kavanaghs" and "Falling Asleep over the Aeneid," reveal his psychological interest in and obsession with ruined New England families.

In *Life Studies* (1959) Lowell changed his style dramatically. His subjects became explicitly autobiographical, his language more open and direct. In 1957 he gave readings in California, where Allen Ginsberg and the other Beats had just made their strongest impact in San Francisco. By contrast to their candid, breezy writing, Lowell felt his own seemed "distant, symbol-ridden, and willfully difficult. . . . I felt my old poems hid what they were really about, and many times offered a stiff, humorless and even impenetrable surface." Although more controlled and severe than Beat writers, he was stimulated by Ginsberg's self-revelations to write more openly than he had about his parents and grandparents, about the mental breakdowns he suffered in the 1950s, and about the difficulties of marriage. (Lowell divorced his first wife, the novelist Jean Stafford, and married the critic Elizabeth Hardwick in 1949).

Life Studies, by and large, records his ambivalence toward the New England where he resettled after the war, on Boston's "hardly passionate Marlborough Street." Revising his stance toward New England and family history, he no longer denounces the city of his fathers as if he were a privileged outsider. In complicated psychological portraits of his childhood, his relation to his parents and his wives, he assumes a portion of the weakness and vulnerability for himself.

In 1960 Lowell left Boston to live in New York City. *For the Union Dead* (1964), the book that followed, continued the autobiographical vein of *Life Studies*. Lowell called it a book about "witheredness . . . lemony, soured and dry, the drouth I had touched with my own hands." These poems seem more carefully controlled than his earlier *Life Studies*. Often they organize key images from the past into a pattern that illuminates the present. The book includes a number of poems that fuse private and public themes, such as "Fall 1961" and the volume's title poem.

In 1969 Lowell published *Notebook 1967–1968* and then revised these poems for a second, augmented edition, called simply *Notebook* (1970). In 1973, in a characteristic act, he once more revised, rearranged, and expanded *Notebook*'s poems and published them in two separate books. The more personal poems, recording the breakup of his second marriage and his separation from his wife and daughter, were published as *For Lizzie and Harriet*. Those dealing more with public subjects, past and present, were published as *History*. These two books show Lowell once again engaged with the relations between the random event, or the moment out of a personal life, and an epic design. In these unrhymed, loosely blank-verse revisions of the sonnet Lowell responded to the books he was reading, to the events of his personal life, and to the Vietnam War, of which he was an outspoken critic. "Things I felt or saw, or read were drift in the whirlpool."

At the same time a new collection of sonnets, *The Dolphin* (1973), appeared, recording his marriage to Lady Caroline Blackwood. (Lowell's friend the poet Elizabeth Bishop objected to his use of Blackwood's letters in the volume, and her letter to Lowell on this subject appears in the "Postmodern Manifestos" cluster of this anthology.) He divided his time between her home in England and periods of teaching writing and literature at Harvard—a familiar pattern for him, in which the old tensions between New England and "elsewhere" were being constantly explored and renewed. His last book, *Day by Day* (1977), records those stresses as well as new marital difficulties. It also contains some of his most powerful poems about his childhood.

For those who cherish the work of the early Lowell, with its manic, rhythmic energy and its enjambed lines building to fierce power, or those who admire the passionate engagement of *Life Studies* or *For the Union Dead*, the poems of his last four books can be disappointing. At times flat and dispirited, they can seem worked up rather than fully imagined. Yet the later Lowell demonstrates his substantial gifts in a quieter mode.

Lowell's career included an interest in the theater, for which he wrote a version of *Prometheus Bound*, a translation of Racine's *Phaedra*, and adaptations of Melville and Hawthorne stories gathered as *The Old Glory*. He also translated from modern European poetry and the classics, often freely as "imitations," which brought important poetic voices into English currency. His *Selected Poems* (his own choices) appeared in 1976. When he died suddenly at the age of sixty, he was the dominant and most honored poet of his generation—not only for his ten volumes of verse but for his broad activity as a man of letters. He took the role of poet as public figure, sometimes at great personal cost. He was with the group of writers who led Vietnam War protesters against the Pentagon in 1967, where Norman Mailer, a fellow protester, observed that "Lowell gave off at times the unwilling haunted saintliness of a man who was repaying the moral debts of ten generations of ancestors."

The Quaker Graveyard in Nantucket

[*For Warren Winslow*,[1] *Dead at Sea*]

Let man have dominion over the fishes of the sea and the fowls of the air and the beasts of the whole earth, and every creeping creature that moveth upon the earth.[2]

I

A brackish reach of shoal off Madaket[3]—
The sea was still breaking violently and night
Had steamed into our North Atlantic Fleet,
When the drowned sailor clutched the drag-net. Light
Flashed from his matted head and marble feet,   5
He grappled at the net
With the coiled, hurdling muscles of his thighs:
The corpse was bloodless, a botch of reds and whites,
Its open, staring eyes
Were lustreless dead-lights[4]   10
Or cabin-windows on a stranded hulk
Heavy with sand. We weight the body, close
Its eyes and heave it seaward whence it came,
Where the heel-headed dogfish barks its nose
On Ahab's[5] void and forehead; and the name   15
Is blocked in yellow chalk.
Sailors, who pitch this portent at the sea
Where dreadnaughts shall confess
Its hell-bent deity,
When you are powerless   20
To sand-bag this Atlantic bulwark, faced
By the earth-shaker, green, unwearied, chaste
In his steel scales: ask for no Orphean lute
To pluck life back.[6] The guns of the steeled fleet
Recoil and then repeat   25
The hoarse salute.

---

1. A cousin of Lowell's who died in the sinking of a naval vessel during World War II.
2. From Genesis 1.26, the account of the creation of humankind.
3. On Nantucket Island.
4. Shutters over portholes to keep out water in a storm. The images in lines 4–11 come from "The Shipwreck," the opening chapter of *Cape Cod*, by Henry David Thoreau (1817–1862).

5. Protagonist of the novel *Moby-Dick*, by Herman Melville (1819–1891); he drowns as a result of his obsessive hunt for the white whale. Melville uses Ahab's forehead as an emblem of his monomaniac passion.
6. In Greek mythology Orpheus, through his music, tried to win the freedom of his bride, Eurydice, from the Underworld. "Earth-shaker": an epithet for Poseidon, the Greek god of the oceans.

II

Whenever winds are moving and their breath
Heaves at the roped-in bulwarks of this pier,
The terns and sea-gulls tremble at your death
In these home waters. Sailor, can you hear   30
The Pequod's[7] sea wings, beating landward, fall
Headlong and break on our Atlantic wall
Off 'Sconset, where the yawing S-boats[8] splash
The bellbuoy, with ballooning spinnakers,
As the entangled, screeching mainsheet clears   35
The blocks: off Madaket, where lubbers[9] lash
The heavy surf and throw their long lead squids
For blue-fish? Sea-gulls blink their heavy lids
Seaward. The winds' wings beat upon the stones,
Cousin, and scream for you and the claws rush   40
At the sea's throat and wring it in the slush
Of this old Quaker graveyard where the bones
Cry out in the long night for the hurt beast
Bobbing by Ahab's whaleboats in the East.

III

All you recovered from Poseidon died   45
With you, my cousin, and the harrowed brine
Is fruitless on the blue beard of the god,
Stretching beyond us to the castles in Spain,
Nantucket's westward haven. To Cape Cod
Guns, cradled on the tide,   50
Blast the eelgrass about a waterclock
Of bilge and backwash, roil the salt and sand
Lashing earth's scaffold, rock
Our warships in the hand
Of the great God, where time's contrition blues   55
Whatever it was these Quaker[1] sailors lost
In the mad scramble of their lives. They died
When time was open-eyed,
Wooden and childish; only bones abide
There, in the nowhere, where their boats were tossed   60
Sky-high, where mariners had fabled news
Of IS,[2] the whited monster. What it cost
Them is their secret. In the sperm-whale's slick
I see the Quakers drown and hear their cry:
"If God himself had not been on our side,   65
If God himself had not been on our side,
When the Atlantic rose against us, why,
Then it had swallowed us up quick."

---

7. Ahab's ship, destroyed by Moby-Dick.
8. Type of large racing sailboats. "Yawing": steering wildly in heavy seas.
9. Sailor's term for awkward crew members.
1. The whaling population of Nantucket included

many Quakers.
2. The white whale is here imagined as a force like
the God of Exodus 3.14, who, when asked his name
by Moses, replies, "I AM THAT I AM." Also an abbrevi-
ation of Jesus Salvator, Latin for Jesus, savior of men.

IV

This is the end of the whaleroad[3] and the whale
Who spewed Nantucket bones on the thrashed swell   70
And stirred the troubled waters to whirlpools
To send the Pequod packing off to hell:
This is the end of them, three-quarters fools,
Snatching at straws to sail
Seaward and seaward on the turntail whale,   75
Spouting out blood and water as it rolls,
Sick as a dog to these Atlantic shoals:
Clamavimus,[4] O depths. Let the sea-gulls wail

For water, for the deep where the high tide
Mutters to its hurt self, mutters and ebbs.   80
Waves wallow in their wash, go out and out,
Leave only the death-rattle of the crabs,
The beach increasing, its enormous snout
Sucking the ocean's side.
This is the end of running on the waves;   85
We are poured out like water. Who will dance
The mast-lashed master of Leviathans
Up from this field of Quakers in their unstoned graves?

V

When the whale's viscera go and the roll
Of its corruption overruns this world   90
Beyond tree-swept Nantucket and Woods Hole[5]
And Martha's Vineyard, Sailor, will your sword
Whistle and fall and sink into the fat?
In the great ash-pit of Jehoshaphat[6]
The bones cry for the blood of the white whale,   95
The fat flukes arch and whack about its ears,
The death-lance churns into the sanctuary, tears
The gun-blue swingle,[7] heaving like a flail,
And hacks the coiling life out: it works and drags
And rips the sperm-whale's midriff into rags,   100
Gobbets of blubber spill to wind and weather,
Sailor, and gulls go round the stoven timbers
Where the morning stars sing out together
And thunder shakes the white surf and dismembers
The red flag hammered in the mast-head.[8] Hide,   105
Our steel, Jonas Messias, in Thy side.[9]

---

3. An Anglo-Saxon epithet for the sea.
4. We have called (Latin). Adapting the opening of Psalm 130: "Out of the depths have I cried unto thee, O Lord."
5. On the coast of Massachusetts, near the island of Martha's Vineyard.
6. "The day of judgment. The world, according to some prophets, will end in fire" [Lowell's note]. In Joel 3, the Last Judgment takes place in the valley of Jehoshaphat.
7. Knifelike wooden instrument for beating flax (fiber for spinning).
8. At the end of *Moby-Dick*, the arm of the American Indian Tashtego appears from the waves and nails Ahab's flag to the sinking mast.
9. Because he emerged alive from the belly of a whale, the prophet Jonah is often linked with the messiah as a figure of salvation. Lowell imagines that a harpoon strikes Jonah inside the whale as the Roman soldier's spear struck Jesus on the cross.

VI. OUR LADY OF WALSINGHAM[1]

There once the penitents took off their shoes
And then walked barefoot the remaining mile;
And the small trees, a stream and hedgerows file
Slowly along the munching English lane,   110
Like cows to the old shrine, until you lose
Track of your dragging pain.
The stream flows down under the druid tree,
Shiloah's[2] whirlpools gurgle and make glad
The castle of God. Sailor, you were glad   115
And whistled Sion by that stream. But see:

Our Lady, too small for her canopy,
Sits near the altar. There's no comeliness
At all or charm in that expressionless
Face with its heavy eyelids. As before,   120
This face, for centuries a memory,
Non est species, neque decor,[3]
Expressionless, expresses God: it goes
Past castled Sion. She knows what God knows,
Not Calvary's Cross nor crib at Bethlehem   125
Now, and the world shall come to Walsingham.

VII

The empty winds are creaking and the oak
Splatters and splatters on the cenotaph,
The boughs are trembling and a gaff
Bobs on the untimely stroke   130
Of the greased wash exploding on a shoal-bell
In the old mouth of the Atlantic. It's well;
Atlantic, you are fouled with the blue sailors,
Sea-monsters, upward angel, downward fish:
Unmarried and corroding, spare of flesh   135
Mart once of supercilious, wing'd clippers,
Atlantic, where your bell-trap guts its spoil
You could cut the brackish winds with a knife
Here in Nantucket, and cast up the time
When the Lord God formed man from the sea's slime   140
And breathed into his face the breath of life,
And blue-lung'd combers lumbered to the kill.
The Lord survives the rainbow[4] of His will.

1946

1. Lowell took these details from E. I. Watkin's *Catholic Art and Culture* (1942), which includes a description of the medieval shrine of the Virgin at Walsingham.
2. The stream that flows past God's Temple on Mount Sion (Isaiah 8.6). In Isaiah 51.11 the

redeemed come "singing into Zion."
3. There is no ostentation or elegance (Latin).
4. Alluding to God's covenant with Noah after the Flood. The rainbow symbolized the fact that humanity would never again be destroyed by flood (Genesis 9.11).

Mr. Edwards and the Spider[1]

I saw the spiders marching through the air,
Swimming from tree to tree that mildewed day
   In latter August when the hay
   Came creaking to the barn. But where
     The wind is westerly,
Where gnarled November makes the spiders fly
Into the apparitions of the sky,
They purpose nothing but their ease and die
Urgently beating east to sunrise and the sea;

What are we in the hands of the great God?
It was in vain you set up thorn and briar
   In battle array against the fire
   And treason crackling in your blood;
     For the wild thorns grow tame
And will do nothing to oppose the flame;
Your lacerations tell the losing game
You play against a sickness past your cure.
How will the hands be strong? How will the heart endure?[2]

A very little thing, a little worm,
Or hourglass-blazoned spider,[3] it is said,
   Can kill a tiger. Will the dead
   Hold up his mirror and affirm
     To the four winds the smell
And flash of his authority? It's well
If God who holds you to the pit of hell,
Much as one holds a spider, will destroy,
Baffle and dissipate your soul. As a small boy

On Windsor Marsh,[4] I saw the spider die
When thrown into the bowels of fierce fire:
   There's no long struggle, no desire
   To get up on its feet and fly—
     It stretches out its feet
And dies. This is the sinner's last retreat;
Yes, and no strength exerted on the heat
Then sinews the abolished will, when sick
And full of burning, it will whistle on a brick.

But who can plumb the sinking of that soul?
Josiah Hawley,[5] picture yourself cast
   Into a brick-kiln where the blast

---

1. Jonathan Edwards (1703–1758), Puritan preacher and theologian. Lowell quotes his writings throughout. The details of the first stanza come from his youthful essay "Of Insects" ("The Habits of Spiders").
2. This stanza draws on Edwards's sermon "Sinners in the Hands of an Angry God," whose point of departure is Ezekiel 22.14: "Can thine heart endure or can thine hands be strong in the days that I shall deal with thee" (cf. line 18).
3. The poisonous black widow spider has, on the underside of its abdomen, a red marking that resembles an hourglass.
4. East Windsor, Connecticut, Edwards's childhood home.
5. Edwards's uncle, Joseph Hawley.

Fans your quick vitals to a coal— 40
If measured by a glass,
How long would it seem burning! Let there pass
A minute, ten, ten trillion; but the blaze
Is infinite, eternal: this is death,
To die and know it. This is the Black Widow, death. 45

[handwritten: Thats what it means to be human, to know we will die]
[handwritten: Death is "rhymed" with itself]

1946

[handwritten: end with death, not much hope]
[handwritten: Afraid of death or after-death]

Skunk Hour

for Elizabeth Bishop

Nautilus Island's[1] hermit
heiress still lives through winter in her Spartan cottage;
her sheep still graze above the sea.
Her son's a bishop. Her farmer
is first selectman in our village; 5
she's in her dotage. *[handwritten: Old lady]*

[handwritten: Family]

Thirsting for
the hierarchic privacy
of Queen Victoria's century,
she buys up all
the eyesores facing her shore, 10
and lets them fall.

[handwritten: Seclusion regression]

The season's ill—
we've lost our summer millionaire,
who seemed to leap from an L. L. Bean
catalogue.[2] His nine-knot yawl 15
was auctioned off to lobstermen.
A red fox stain covers Blue Hill.

[handwritten: uneasy, sick]

And now our fairy
decorator brightens his shop for fall; 20
his fishnet's filled with orange cork,
orange, his cobbler's bench and awl;
there is no money in his work,
he'd rather marry.

One dark night,
my Tudor Ford climbed the hill's skull; 25
I watched for love-cars. Lights turned down,
they lay together, hull to hull,
where the graveyard shelves on the town. . . .
My mind's not right. 30

---

1. The poem is set in Castine, Maine, where Lowell had a summer house.

2. From a mail-order house in Maine that primarily sells sporting and camping goods.

[handwritten: ✱ Gulgotha - Skull of the hill, where Christ was sacrificed]

A car radio bleats,
"Love, O careless Love. . . ." I hear
my ill-spirit sob in each blood cell,
as if my hand were at its throat. . . .   *its = my spirit*
I myself am hell;[3]   35
nobody's here—

only skunks, that search
in the moonlight for a bite to eat.   *nourishment is found in*
They march on their soles up Main Street: *simple food, not the church*
white stripes, moonstruck eyes' red fire   40
under the chalk-dry and spar spire
of the Trinitarian Church.

I stand on top   *comical image*
of our back steps and breathe the rich air—   *family*
a mother skunk with her column of kittens swills the garbage pail.   45
She jabs her wedge-head in a cup
of sour cream, drops her ostrich tail,
and will not scare.

                                                                 1959

For the Union Dead[1]   *1960 - later*
                                  than the others

"Relinquunt Omnia Servare Rem Publicam."[2]

The old South Boston Aquarium stands
in a Sahara of snow now. Its broken windows are boarded.
The bronze weathervane cod has lost half its scales.
The airy tanks are dry.

Once my nose crawled like a snail on the glass;   5
my hand tingled
to burst the bubbles
drifting from the noses of the cowed, compliant fish.

My hand draws back. I often sigh still
for the dark downward and vegetating kingdom   10
of the fish and reptile. One morning last March,
I pressed against the new barbed and galvanized

3. "Which way I fly is Hell, myself am Hell" (Satan in Milton's *Paradise Lost* 4.75).
1. First published as "Colonel Shaw and the Massachusetts' 54th" in a paperback edition of *Life Studies* (1960). It became the title poem of *For the Union Dead* (1964).
2. Robert Gould Shaw (1837–1863) led the first all African American regiment in the North during the Civil War. He was killed in the attack against Fort Wagner, South Carolina. A bronze relief by the sculptor Augustus Saint-Gaudens (1848–1897), dedicated in 1897, standing opposite the Massachusetts State House on Boston Common, commemorates the deaths. A Latin inscription on the monument reads *Omnia Reliquit Servare Rem Publicam* ("He leaves all behind to serve the Republic"). Lowell's epigraph alters the inscription slightly, changing the third-person singular (*he*) to the third-person plural: "*They* give up everything to serve the Republic."

fence on the Boston Common. Behind their cage,
yellow dinosaur steamshovels were grunting
as they cropped up tons of mush and grass   15
to gouge their underworld garage.

Parking spaces luxuriate like civic
sandpiles in the heart of Boston.
A girdle of orange, Puritan-pumpkin colored girders
braces the tingling Statehouse,   20

shaking over the excavations, as it faces Colonel Shaw
and his bell-cheeked Negro infantry
on St. Gaudens' shaking Civil War relief,
propped by a plank splint against the garage's earthquake.

Two months after marching through Boston,   25
half the regiment was dead;
at the dedication
William James[3] could almost hear the bronze Negroes breathe.

Their monument sticks like a fishbone
in the city's throat.   30
Its Colonel is as lean
as a compass-needle.

He has an angry wrenlike vigilance,
a greyhound's gentle tautness;
he seems to wince at pleasure,   35
and suffocate for privacy.

He is out of bounds now. He rejoices in man's lovely,
peculiar power to choose life and die—
when he leads his black soldiers to death,
he cannot bend his back.   40

On a thousand small town New England greens,
the old white churches hold their air
of sparse, sincere rebellion; frayed flags
quilt the graveyards of the Grand Army of the Republic.

The stone statues of the abstract Union Soldier   45
grow slimmer and younger each year—
wasp-waisted, they doze over muskets
and muse through their sideburns . . .

Shaw's father wanted no monument
except the ditch,   50
where his son's body was thrown[4]
and lost with his "niggers."

3. Philosopher and psychologist (1842–1910) who taught at Harvard.
4. By the Confederate soldiers at Fort Wagner.

The ditch is nearer.
There are no statues for the last war[5] here;
on Boylston Street,[6] a commercial photograph   55
shows Hiroshima boiling[7]

over a Mosler Safe, the "Rock of Ages"[8]
that survived the blast. Space is nearer.
When I crouch to my television set,
the drained faces of Negro school-children rise like balloons.[9]   60

Colonel Shaw
is riding on his bubble,
he waits
for the blessed break.

The Aquarium is gone. Everywhere,   65
giant finned cars nose forward like fish;
a savage servility
slides by on grease.

1960, 1964

5. World War II.
6. In Boston, where the poem is set.
7. On August 6, 1945, the United States dropped an atomic bomb on this Japanese city.
8. Biblical reference to an indestructible and supernatural rock, the foundation of an everlasting kingdom. Used as an advertising slogan by Mosler Safes.
9. Probably news photographs connected with contemporary civil rights demonstrations to secure desegregation of schools in the South.

GWENDOLYN BROOKS
1917–2000

"If there was ever a born poet," the writer Alice Walker once said in an interview, "I think it is Brooks." A passionate sense of language and an often daring use of formal structures are hallmarks of Gwendolyn Brooks's poetry. She used these gifts in a career characterized by dramatic evolution, a career that linked two very different generations of African American poets. "Until 1967," Brooks said, "my own Blackness did not confront me with a shrill spelling of itself." She then grouped herself with militant black writers and defined her work as belonging primarily to the African American community. In her earlier work, however, Brooks followed the example of the older writers of the Harlem Renaissance, Langston Hughes and Countee Cullen among them, who honored the ideal of an integrated society. In that period her work received support largely from white audiences. But Brooks's changing sense of her commitments should not obscure her persistent, underlying concerns. She never lacked political awareness, and in remarkably versatile poems, both early and late, she wrote about black experience and black rage, with a particular awareness of the complex lives of black women.

Brooks was born in Topeka, Kansas; she grew up in Chicago and is closely identified with the energies and problems of its black community. She went to Chicago's Englewood High School and graduated from Wilson Junior College. Brooks remembered writing poetry from the time she was seven and keeping poetry notebooks from the time she was eleven. She got her education in the moderns—Pound and Eliot—

under the guidance of a rich Chicago socialite, Inez Cunningham Stark, who was a reader for *Poetry* magazine and taught a poetry class at the Southside Community Art Center. Her first book, *A Street in Bronzeville* (1945), took its title from the name journalists gave to the Chicago black ghetto. Her poems portrayed the waste and loss that are the inevitable result of what Langston Hughes called the blacks' "dream deferred." With her second book of poems, *Annie Allen* (1949), Brooks became the first African American to receive the Pulitzer Prize for poetry.

In *Annie Allen* and in her Bronzeville poems (*Bronzeville Boys and Girls*, 1956, continued the work begun in *A Street in Bronzeville*), Brooks concentrated on portraits of what Hughes called "the ordinary aspects of black life," stressing the vitality and the often subversive morality of ghetto figures. She portrayed the good girls who want to be bad; the bored children of hardworking, pious mothers; the laments of women, some of them mothers, abandoned by their men. Brooks's diction was a combination of the florid biblical speech of black Protestant preachers, street talk, and the main speech patterns of English and American verse. She wrote vigorous, strongly accented, and strongly rhymed lines with a great deal of alliteration. She also cultivated traditional lyric forms; for example, she was one of the few modern poets to write extensively in the sonnet form.

A great change in Brooks's life came at Fisk University in 1967 with the Second Black Writers' Conference, in whose charged activist atmosphere she encountered many of the new young black poets. After this Brooks tested the possibility of writing poetry exclusively for black audiences. She drew closer to militant political groups as a result of conducting poetry workshops for some members of the Blackstone Rangers, a teenage gang in Chicago. In autobiographical writings such as her prose *Report from Part One* (1972), Brooks became more self-conscious about her own potential role as a leader of black feminists. She left her New York publisher to have her work printed by African American publishers, especially the Broadside Press. Brooks's poetry, too, changed, in both its focus and its technique. Her subjects tended to be more explicitly political and to deal with questions of revolutionary violence and issues of African American identity. Stylistically, her work evolved out of the concentrated imagery and narratives of her earlier writing, with its often formal diction, and moved toward an increased use of the energetic, improvisatory rhythms of jazz, the combinations of African chants, and an emphatically spoken language. The resulting poetry constantly revises itself and its sense of the world, open to change but evoking history. "How does one convey the influence Gwendolyn Brooks has had on generations—not only writers but people from all walks of life?" the poet Rita Dove has remarked, remembering how, as a young woman, she was "struck by these poems . . . that weren't afraid to take language and swamp it, twist it and engage it so that it shimmered and dashed and lingered."

FROM A STREET IN BRONZEVILLE

to David and Keziah Brooks

kitchenette building

We are things of dry hours and the involuntary plan,
Grayed in, and gray. "Dream" makes a giddy sound, not strong
Like "rent," "feeding a wife," "satisfying a man."

But could a dream send up through onion fumes
Its white and violet, fight with fried potatoes
And yesterday's garbage ripening in the hall,
Flutter, or sing an aria down these rooms

Even if we were willing to let it in,
Had time to warm it, keep it very clean,
Anticipate a message, let it begin?

We wonder. But not well! not for a minute!
Since Number Five is out of the bathroom now,
We think of lukewarm water, hope to get in it.

1945

the mother

only a mother understands what abortion is

Abortions will not let you forget.
You remember the children you got that you did not get,
The damp small pulps with a little or with no hair,
The singers and workers that never handled the air.
You will never neglect or beat
Them, or silence or buy with a sweet.
You will never wind up the sucking-thumb
Or scuttle off ghosts that come.
You will never leave them, controlling your luscious sigh,
Return for a snack of them, with gobbling mother-eye.

I have heard in the voices of the wind the voices of my dim
        killed children.
I have contracted. I have eased
My dim dears at the breasts they could never suck.
I have said, Sweets, if I sinned, if I seized
Your luck
And your lives from your unfinished reach,
If I stole your births and your names,
Your straight baby tears and your games,
Your stilted or lovely loves, your tumults, your marriages, aches,
        and your deaths,
If I poisoned the beginnings of your breaths,
Believe that even in my deliberateness I was not deliberate.
Though why should I whine,
Whine that the crime was other than mine?—
Since anyhow you are dead.
Or rather, or instead,
You were never made.

But that too, I am afraid,
Is faulty: oh, what shall I say, how is the truth to be said?
You were born, you had body, you died.
It is just that you never giggled or planned or cried.

the child she never had

— he died after born? he was born?

Believe me, I loved you all.
Believe me, I knew you, though faintly, and I loved, I loved you
All.

                                                              1945

The White Troops Had Their Orders But the Negroes Looked Like Men

They had supposed their formula was fixed.
They had obeyed instructions to devise
A type of cold, a type of hooded gaze.
But when the Negroes came they were perplexed.
These Negroes looked like men. Besides, it taxed   5
Time and the temper to remember those
Congenital iniquities that cause
Disfavor of the darkness. Such as boxed
Their feelings properly, complete to tags—
A box for dark men and a box for Other—   10
Would often find the contents had been scrambled.
Or even switched. Who really gave two figs?
Neither the earth nor heaven ever trembled.
And there was nothing startling in the weather.

                                                              1945

We Real Cool

THE POOL PLAYERS.
SEVEN AT THE GOLDEN SHOVEL.

We real cool. We
Left school. We

Lurk late. We
Strike straight. We

Sing sin. We   5
Thin gin. We

Jazz June. We
Die soon.

                                                              1960

[handwritten annotations: "a gang of youth", "doing what they like", "or: a consequence of some bad choices", "live the moment", "Carpe diem"]

The Last Quatrain of the Ballad of Emmett Till[1]

> after the murder,
> after the burial
>
> Emmett's mother is a pretty-faced thing;
>   the tint of pulled taffy.
> She sits in a red room,
>   drinking black coffee.   5
> She kisses her killed boy.
>   And she is sorry.
> Chaos in windy grays
>   through a red prairie.   10

1960

To the Diaspora[1]

you did not know you were Afrika

When you set out for Afrika
you did not know you were going.
Because
you did not know you were Afrika.
You did not know the Black continent   5
that had to be reached
was you.

I could not have told you then that some sun
would come,
somewhere over the road,   10
would come evoking the diamonds
of you, the Black continent—
somewhere over the road.
You would not have believed my mouth.

When I told you, meeting you somewhere close   15
to the heat and youth of the road,
liking my loyalty, liking belief,
you smiled and you thanked me but very little believed me.

Here is some sun. Some.
Now off into the places rough to reach.   20
Though dry, though drowsy, all unwillingly a-wobble,
into the dissonant and dangerous crescendo.
Your work, that was done, to be done to be done to be done.

1981

---

1. A fourteen-year-old African American boy
lynched in Mississippi in 1955 for allegedly "leering" at a white woman.

1. People settled far from their ancestral home-
lands.

JACK KEROUAC
1922–1969

Like the lives of many trailblazing writers, Jack Kerouac's life was filled with contradictions. Regarded as a liberator of prose and champion of idiomatic American expression, he did not start learning English until grade school and never felt comfortable speaking it until he finished high school (his parents were of French-Canadian background, and French was the family's language at home in Lowell, Massachusetts; his given name was "Jean-Louis"). Having won a football scholarship to Columbia University, he rejected the athletic crowd to join the literary innovators gathering at the college neighborhood's popular West End Bar, among them Allen Ginsberg and William S. Burroughs, who would achieve fame as poet and novelist respectively. Not famous himself until the late 1950s, when a wave of interest in the self-proclaimed Beat Movement installed him as its unwilling leader, he rode the crest of the counterculture's growing fascination with Eastern religions, most notably Zen Buddhism, while never rejecting the Catholicism of his childhood. Even adulatory responses to his work risked contradiction. For example, critics praised his most famous novel, *On the Road* (1957), for its expansiveness and movement reminiscent of America's Manifest Destiny myth, although the book's narrative progress is in fact from the West Coast to the East.

Kerouac's ambitions were monumental, but a lifetime of heavy drinking killed him by age forty-seven. His several marriages, until his last one, ended with annulment, desertion, or divorce. His greatest loyalty as an adult was to his widowed mother, in later years an invalid, whom he cared for to his death. Wartime service in the merchant marine had given Kerouac manual skills useful for employment during the wanderings that characterized his life; railroad brakeman and forest-fire lookout were among the jobs he took throughout the late 1940s and into the 1950s until royalties from *On the Road* could sustain a pattern of bumming around, visiting friends, and writing as inspiration struck. "Home" was a series of addresses in Massachusetts, New York (on Long Island), and Florida, most of them chosen for his mother's convenience.

Two favorite hangouts were the San Francisco Bay Area and the coastal wilderness of California's Big Sur, an area running south from Carmel-by-the-Sea to San Luis Obispo. This is the setting for the novel most typical of Kerouac's problematic career. Composed quickly (he usually took just three days to six weeks to write a novel), on a roll of teletype paper similar to the one that aided his almost nonstop production of *On the Road*, *Big Sur* (1962) draws on a visit to the poet Lawrence Ferlinghetti and other Bay Area friends and a solitary stay in Ferlinghetti's isolated cabin in Bixby Canyon (here called the Raton Canyon, with Ferlinghetti taking the name "Louis [also Lorenzo] Monsanto"). Its form, shared by all but the first of Kerouac's novels (*The Town and the City*, 1950, a social novel in the realistic mode), is what the author called "spontaneous prose," equivalent to jazz improvisation in its emphasis on rhythms and inflections and the freewheeling nature of its references. Those references include Buddhism (which he had studied for its literary properties but finally rejected as a religion), Catholicism, books and authors, popular culture, friends and family, all propelled by the writer's exuberance, a momentum that exceeds conventional limits of narrative order.

"My work comprises one vast book like [the nineteenth-century French novelist Marcel] Proust's except that my remembrances are written on the run instead of afterwards in a sick bed," Kerouac observes in the headnote preceding the first chapter of *Big Sur*. Though his canon consists of more than a dozen novels published during his lifetime and others recovered from manuscript and issued after his death, the author had seen them as one grand project, the parts of which he intended to revise, integrate, and present to readers as one massive narrative when done. Neither writing nor publishing them in the order in which he had experienced their action, Kerouac did not live long enough to even begin his intended synthesis. But he named the project "the Duluoz Legend," from the name of his protagonist in *Big Sur* and other works.

Central to the legend is Kerouac's close friendship with Neal Cassady (fictionalized as Dean Moriarity in *On the Road* and as Cody Pomeray in *Visions of Cody,* 1972). Their relationship had been the motivation for both the author's wanderings and his impulsive, sometimes explosive manner of writing. (Reacting to the confinements of postwar commercial culture, the Beat Movement took its name in part from the term "beatitic," or blissful, and celebrated free-form narration and a matching lifestyle.) But according to critic Warren French, this relationship also marked the limits of Kerouac's literary vision: his concern for human freedom tended toward the "elegaic and defeatist," whereas Cassady moved on from the Beat Movement to the "heroic account of the triumph of the individual over the system" that a new 1960s counterculture was finding in such works as novelist Ken Kesey's *One Flew Over the Cuckoo's Nest* (1962) and *Sometimes a Great Notion* (1964).

Though not published until after Kerouac's death, *Visions of Cody* had been written in 1959. *Big Sur* was composed in 1960 and is considered the formal conclusion to the Duluoz legend, the scope of which covered the author's lifetime and filled such novels as *The Subterraneans* (1958), *The Dharma Bums* (1958), and *Desolation Angels* (1965, covering earlier experiences). It begins with the narrator fleeing fame and seeking recovery from the nervous breakdown that fame has induced.

From Big Sur

12

But Dave is anxious and so am I to see great Cody who is always the major part of my reason for journeying to the west coast so we call him up at Los Gatos 50 miles away down the Santa Clara Valley and I hear his dear sad voice saying "Been waitin for ya old buddy, come on down right away, but I'll be goin to work at midnight so hurry up and you can visit me at work soon's the boss leaves round two and I'll show you my new job of tire recappin and see if you cant bring a little somethin like a girl or sumptin, just kiddin, come on down pal——"

So there's old Willie waiting for us down on the street parked across from the little pleasant Japanese liquor store where as usual, according to our ritual, I run and get Pernod[1] or Scotch or anything good while Dave wheels around to pick me up at the store door, and I get in the front seat right at Dave's right where I belong all the time like old Honored Samuel Johnson[2] while everybody else that wants to come along has to scramble back there on the mattress (a full mattress, the seats are out) and squat there or lie down there and also generally keep silent because when Dave's got the wheel of Willie in his hand and I've got the bottle in mine and we're off on a trip the talking all comes from the front seat——"By God" yells Dave all glad again "it's just like old times Jack, gee old Willie's been sad for ya, waitin for ya to come back——So now I'm gonna show ya how old Willie's even improved with age, had him reconditioned in Reno last month, here he goes, are you ready Willie?" and off we go and the beauty of it all this particular summer is that the front right seat is broken and just rocks back and forth gently to every one of Dave's driving moves——It's like sitting in a rocking chair on a porch only this is a moving porch and a porch to talk on at that——And insteada watching old men pitch horseshoes from this here talking porch it's all that fine white clean line in the middle of the road as we go flying like birds over the Harrison ramps and whatnot Dave always uses to sneak out of Frisco real fast and avoid all the traffic——Soon we're set

---

1. Trademarked French anise-flavored liqueur used in cocktails.   2. English lexicographer and critic (1709–1784).

straight and pointed head on down beautiful fourlane Bayshore Highway to that lovely Santa Clara Valley——But I'm amazed that after only a few years the damn thing no longer has prune fields and vast beet fields like at Lawrence[3] when I was a brakeman on the Southern Pacific[4] and even after, it's one long row of houses right down the line 50 miles to San Jose like a great monstrous Los Angeles beginning to grow south of Frisco.

At first it's beautiful to just watch that white line reel in to Willie's snout but when I start looking around out the window there's just endless housing tracts and new blue factories everywhere——Sez Dave "Yes that's right, the population explosion is gonna cover every bit of backyard dirt in America someday in fact they'll even have to start piling up friggin levels of houses and others over that like your cityCityCITY till the houses reach a hundred miles in the air in all directions of the map and people looking at the earth from another planet with super telescopes will see a prickly ball hangin in space——It's like real horrible when you come to think of it, even us with all our fancy talks, shit man it's all millions of people and events piling up almost unimaginable now, like raving babboons we'll all be piled on top of each other or one another or whatever you're sposed to say——Hundreds of millions of hungry mouths raving for more more more——And the sadness of it all is that the world hasnt any chance to produce say a writer whose life could really actually touch all this life in every detail like you always say, some writer who could bring you sobbing thru the bed fuckin bedcribs of the moon to see it all even unto the goddamned last gory detail of some dismal robbery of the heart at dawn when no one cares like Sinatra sings" ("When no one cares," he sings in his low baritone but resumes):—"Some strict sweeper sweeping it all up, I mean the incredible helplessness I felt Jack when Céline ended his Journey To The End Of The Night[5] by pissing in the Seine River at dawn there I am thinkin my God there's probably somebody pissing in the Trenton River at dawn right now, the Danube, the Ganges, the frozen Obi, the Yellow, the Paraña, the Willamette, the Merrimac in Missouri too, the Missouri itself, the Yuma, the Amazon, the Thames, the Po,[6] the so and so, it's so friggin endless it's like poems endless everywhere and no one knows any bettern old Buddha you know where he says it's like 'There are immeasurable star misty aeons of universes more numerous than the sands in all the galaxies, multiplied by a billion lightyears of multiplication, in fact if I were to go on you'd be scared and couldnt comprehend and you'd despair so much you'd drop dead,' that's what he just about said in one of those sutras——Macrocosms and microcosms and chillicosms and microbes and finally you got all these marvelous books a man aint even got time to read em all, what you gonna do in this already piled up multiple world when you have to think of the Book of Songs, Faulkner, César Birotteau, Shakespeare, Satyricons, Dantes, in fact long stories guys tell you in bars, in fact the sutras themselves, Sir Philip Sidney, Sterne, Ibn El Arabi, the copious Lope de Vega and the uncopious goddamn Cervantes, shoo, then there's all those Catulluses and Davids[7] and radio lis-

3. Area in Santa Clara County south of San Francisco, by 1960 engulfed in the metropolitan sprawl of San Jose, Santa Clara, and San Francisco.
4. Major railroad.
5. Novel (1932) by Louis-Ferdinand Céline, pen name of the French novelist Louis-Ferdinard Destouches (1894–1961).

6. Rivers in France, Central Europe, Massachusetts, the U.S. Great Plains, California, South America, England, and Italy.
7. King David (fl. 970 B.C.E.) of ancient Israel, credited with writing many of the Psalms; *Book of Songs*, a translation of Chinese poems published in 1937; William Faulkner (1897–1962), American

tening skid row sages to contend with because they've all got a million stories too and you too Ron Blake in the backseat shut up! down to everything which is so much that it is of necessity dont you think NOthing anyway, huh?" (expressing exactly the way I feel, of course).

And to corroborate all that about the too-much-ness of the world, in fact, there's Stanley Popovich also in the back mattress next to Ron, Stanley Popovich of New York suddenly arrived in San Francisco with Jamie his Italian beauty girl but's going to leave her in a few days to go work for the circus, a big tough Yugoslav kid who ran the Seven Arts Gallery in New York with big bearded beatnik readings but now comes the circus and a whole big on-the-road of his own——It's too much, in fact right this minute he's started telling us about circus work——On top of all that old Cody is up ahead with HIS thousand stories——We all agree it's too big to keep up with, that we're surrounded by life, that we'll never understand it, so we center it all in by swigging Scotch from the bottle and when it's empty I run out of the car and buy another one, period.

13

But on the way to Cody's my madness already began to manifest itself in a stranger way, another one of those signposts of something wrong I mentioned a ways back: I thought I saw a flying saucer in the sky over Los Gatos—— From five miles away——I look and I see this thing flying along and mention it to Dave who takes one brief look and says "Ah it's only the top of a radio tower"——It reminds me of the time I took a mescaline pill[8] and thought an airplane was a flying saucer (a strange story this, a man has to be crazy to write it anyway).

But there's old Cody in the livingroom of his fine ranchito[9] home sittin over his chess set pondering a problem and right by the fresh woodfire in the fireplace his wife's set out because she knows I love fireplaces——She a good friend of mine too——The kids are sleeping in the back, it's about eleven, and good old Cody shakes my hand again——Havent seen him for several years because mainly he's just spent two years in San Quentin[1] on a stupid charge of possession of marijuana——He was on his way to work on the railroad one night and was short on time and his driving license had been already revoked for speeding so he saw two bearded bluejeaned beatniks parked, asked them to trade a quick ride to work at the railroad station for two sticks of tea,[2] they complied and arrested him——They were disguised policemen——For this great crime he spent two years in San Quentin in the same cell with a mur-

---

novelist; Cesar Birotteau, principal character in *Histoire de la grandeur et la decadence de Cesar Birotteau* (1838), by the French novelist Honoré de Balzac (1799–1850); William Shakespeare (1564–1616), English dramatist and poet; *Satyricon* (c. 60 C.E.), comic picaresque narrative written in prose and poetry by the Roman author Gaius Petronius Arbiter (c. 27–66 C.E.); Dante Alighieri (1265–1321), Italian poet; Sir Philip Sidney (1554–1586), English poet; Laurence Sterne (1713–1768), British novelist; Ibn al-'Arabi (1165–1240), Muslim mystic philosopher; Lope Felix de Vega Carpio (1562–1635), Spanish dramatist; Miguel de Cervantes Saavedra (1547–1616), Spanish novelist; Gaius Valerius Catullus (c. 84–54 B.C.E.), Roman poet.
8. Psychedelic drug obtained from buttonlike tops of the mescal cactus, used in some Native American ceremonies and popular with the beatnik subculture.
9. Small ranch (Mexican Spanish).
1. California state prison for serious offenders located on Point Quentin, Marin County, north of San Francisco.
2. Slang for marijuana; two sticks would be two marijuana cigarettes.

derous gunman——His job was sweeping out the cotton mill room——I
expect him to be all bitter and out of his head because of this but strangely
and magnificently he's become quieter, more radiant, more patient, manly,
more friendly even——And tho the wild frenzies of his old road days with me
have banked down he still has the same taut eager face and supple muscles
and looks like he's ready to go anytime——But actually loves his home (paid
for by railroad insurance when he broke his leg trying to stop a boxcar from
crashing), loves his wife in a way tho they fight some, loves his kids and especially his little son Timmy John partly named after me——Poor old, good old
Cody sittin there with his chess set, wants immediately to challenge somebody to a chess game but only has an hour to talk to us before he goes to work
supporting the family by rushing out and pushing his Nash Rambler[3] down
the quiet Los Gatos suburb street, jumping in, starting the motor, in fact his
only complaint is that the Nash wont start without a push——No bitter complaints about society whatever from this grand and ideal man who really loves
me moreover as if I deserved it, but I'm bursting to explain everything to him,
not even Big Sur but the past several years, but there's no chance with everybody yakking——And in fact I can see in Cody's eyes that he can see in my
own eyes the regret we both feel that recently we havent had chances to talk
whatever, like we used to do driving across America and back in the old road
days, too many people now want to talk to us and tell us *their* stories, we've
been hemmed in and surrounded and outnumbered——The circle's closed
in on the old heroes of the night——But he says "However you guys, come
on down round 'bout one when the boss leaves and watch me work and keep
me company awhile before you go back to the City"——I can see Dave Wain
really loves him at once, and Stanley Popovich too who's come along on this
trip just to meet the fabled "Dean Moriarty"——The name I give Cody in "On
the Road"[4]——But O, it breaks my heart to see he's lost his beloved job on
the railroad and after all the seniority he'd piled up since 1948 and now is
reduced to tire recapping and dreary parole visits——All for two sticks of wild
loco weed that grows by itself in Texas because God wanted it——

  And there over the bookshelf is the old photo of me and Cody arm in arm
in the early days on a sunny street——

  I rush to explain to Cody what happened the year before when his religious
advisor at the prison had invited me to come to San Quentin to lecture the
religious class——Dave Wain was supposed to drive me and wait outside the
prison walls as I'd go in there alone, probably with a pepup nip bottle hidden
in my coat (I hoped) and I'd be led by big guards to the lecture room of the
prison and there would be sitting a hundred or so cons including Cody probably all proud in the front row——And I would begin by telling them I had
been in jail myself once and that I had no right nevertheless to lecture them
on religion——But they're all lonely prisoners and dont care what I talk
about——The whole thing arranged, in any case, and on the big morning I
wake up instead dead drunk on a floor, it's already noon and too late, Dave
Wain is on the floor also, Willie's parked outside to take us to Quentin for the
lecture but it's too late——But now Cody says "It's alright old buddy I understand"——Altho our friend Irwin had done it, lectured there, but Irwin can

---

3. Popular American automobile, a family sedan
for the economically minded.

4. *On the Road* (1957), Kerouac's only best-selling
novel.

do all sorta things like that being more social than I am and capable of going in there as he did and reading his wildest poems which set the prison yard humming with excitement tho I think he shouldna done it after all because I say just to show up for any reason except visiting inside a prison is still SIGNIFYING[5]———And I tell this to Cody who ponders a chess problem and says "Drinkin again, hey?" (if there's anything he hates is to see me drink).

We help him push his Nash down the street, then drink awhile and talk with Evelyn a beautiful blonde woman that young Ron Blake wants and even Dave Wain wants but she's got her mind on other things and taking care of the children who have to go to school and dancing classes in the morning and hardly gets a word in edgewise anyway as we all yak and yell like fools to impress her tho all she really wants is to be alone with me to talk about Cody and his latest soul.

Which includes the fact of Billie Dabney his mistress who has threatened to take Cody away completely from Evelyn, as I'll show later.

So we do go out to the San Jose highway to watch Cody recap tires——— There he is wearing goggles working like Vulcan[6] at his forge, throwing tires all over the place with fantastic strength, the good ones high up on a pile, "This one's no good" down on another, bing, bang, talking all the time a long fantastic lecture on tire recapping which has Dave Wain marvel with amazement———("My God he can do all that and even explain while he's doing it")———But I just mention in connection with the fact that Dave Wain now realizes why I've always loved Cody———Expecting to see a bitter ex con he sees instead a martyr of the American Night in goggles in some dreary tire shop at 2 A.M. making fellows laugh with joy with his funny explanations yet at the same time to a T performing every bit of the work he's being paid for———Rushing up and ripping tires off car wheels with a jicklo,[7] clang, throwing it on the machine, starting up big roaring steams but yelling explanations over that, darting, bending, flinging, flaying, till Dave Wain said he thought he was going to die laughing or crying right there on the spot.

So we drive back to town and go to the mad boardinghouse to drink some more and I pass out dead drunk on the floor as usual in that house, waking up in the morning groaning far from my clean cot on the porch in Big Sur— —No bluejays yakking for me to wake up any more, no gurgling creek, I'm back in the grooky city and I'm trapped.

14

Instead there's the sound of bottles crashing in the livingroom where poor Lex Pascal is holding forth yelling, it reminds of the time a year ago when Jarry Wagner's future wife got sore at Lex and threw a half gallonfull of tokay[8] across the room and hooked him right across the eye, thereupon sailing to Japan to marry Jarry in a big Zen ceremony that made coast to coast papers but all old Lex's got is a cut which I try to fix in the bathroom upstairs saying "Hey, that cut's already stopped bleeding, you'll be alright Lex"———"I'm French Canadian too" he says proudly and when Dave and I and George Baso get ready to drive back to New

---

5. African American verbal rhetorical device for creating new meanings for old words and signs, a tradition reaching from slave days to contemporary rap and hip-hop music.

6. Roman god of fire and volcanoes, often pictured at a blacksmith's forge.
7. Tool used for separating rubber from metal.
8. Inexpensive wine.

York he gives me a St. Christopher medal[9] as a goingaway gift——Lex the kind of guy shouldnt really be living in this wild beat boardinghouse, should hide on a ranch somewhere, powerful, goodlooking, full of crazy desire for women and booze and never enough of either——So as the bottles crash again and the Hi Fi's playing Beethoven's Solemn Mass[1] I fall asleep on the floor.

Waking up the next morning groaning of course, but this is the big day when we're going to go visit poor George Baso at the TB hospital in the Valley——Dave perks me up right away bringing coffee or wine optional——I'm on Ben Fagan's floor somehow, apparently I've harangued him till dawn about Buddhism—some Buddhist.

Complicated already but now suddenly appears Joey Rosenberg a strange young kid from Oregon with a full beard and his hair growing right down to his neck like Raul Castro,[2] once the California High School high jump champ who was only about 5 foot 6 but had made the incredible leap of six foot nine over the bar! and shows his highjump ability too by the way he dances around on light feet——A strange athlete who's suddenly decided instead to become some sort of beat Jesus and in fact you see perfect purity and sincerity in his young blue eyes——In fact his eyes are so pure you dont notice the crazy hair and beard, and also he's wearing ragged but strangely elegant clothing ("One of the first of the new Beat Dandies," McLear told me a few days later, "did you hear about that? there's a new strange underground group of beatniks or whatever who wear special smooth dandy clothes even tho it may just be a jean jacket with shino[3] slacks they'll always have strange beautiful shoes or shirts, or turn around and wear fancy pants unpressed acourse but with torn sneakers")——Joey is wearing something like brown soft garments like a tunic or something and his shoes look like Las Vegas sports shoes——The moment he sees my battered blue little sneakers that I'd used at Big Sur when my feet go sore, that is in case my feet got sore on a rocky hike, he wants them for himself, he wants to swap the snazzy Las Vegas sports shoes (pale leather, untooled) for my silly little tightfitting tho perfect sneakers that in fact I was wearing because the Monterey hike blisters were still hurting me——So we swap——And I ask Dave Wain about him: Dave says: "He's one of the really strangest sweetest guys I've ever known, showed up about a week ago I hear tell, they asked him what he wanted to do and never answers, just smiles——He just sorta wants to dig everything and just watch and enjoy and say nothing particular about it——If someone's to ask him 'Let's drive to New York' he'd jump right for it without a word——On a sort of a pilgrimage, see, with all that youth, us old fucks oughta take a lesson from him, in faith too, he has faith, I can see it in his eyes, he has faith in any direction he may take with anyone just like Christ I guess."

It's strange that in a later revery I imagined myself walking across a field to find the strange gang of pilgrims in Arkansas and Dave Wain was sitting there saying "Shhh, He's sleeping," "He" being Joey and all the disciples are following him on a march to New York after which they expect to keep going walking on water to the other shore——But of course (in my revery even) I

9. Travelers would be protected by carrying this medal, which commemorates their patron, a martyred Catholic saint from the first half of the 3rd century.
1. *Missa Solemnis* in D Major, Opus 123 (1817–

23), by the German composer Ludwig van Beethoven (1770–1827), is playing on the stereo.
2. Raul Castro Ruz (b. 1931), brother of Fidel Castro leader of Cuba.
3. Slang for polished cotton chino.

scoff and dont believe it (a kind of story daydreaming I often do) but in the morning when I look into Joey Rosenberg's eyes I instantly realize it IS Him, Jesus, because anyone (according to the rules of my revery) who looks into those eyes is instantly convinced and converted——So the revery continues into a long farfetched story ending with thinking I.B.M. machines trying to destroy this "Second Coming" etc. (but also, in reality, a few months later I threw away his shoes in the ashcan back home because I felt they had brought me bad luck and wishing I'd kept my blue sneakers with the little holes in the toes!)

So anyway we get Joey and Ron Blake who's always following Dave and go off to see Monsanto at the store, our usual ritual, then across the corner to Mike's Place where we start off the 10 A.M. with food, drink and a few games of pool at the tables along the bar——Joey winning the game and a stranger poolshark you never saw with his long Biblical hair bending to slide the cue stick smoothly through completely professionally competent fingerstance and smashing home long straight drives, like seeing Jesus shoot pool of course—— And meanwhile all the food these poor starved kids all three of them do pack in and eat!——It's not every day they're with a drunken novelist with hundreds of dollars to splurge on them, they order everything, spaghetti, follow that up with Jumbo Hamburgers, follow that up with ice cream and pie and puddings, Dave Wain has a huge appetite anyway but adds Manhattans and Martinis to the side of his plate——I'm just wailing away on my old fatal double bourbons and gingerale and I'll be sorry in a few days.

Any drinker knows how the process works: the first day you get drunk is okay, the morning after means a big head but so you can kill that easy with a few more drinks and a meal, but if you pass up the meal and go on to another night's drunk, and wake up to keep the toot going, and continue on to the fourth day, there'll come one day when the drinks wont take effect because you're chemically overloaded and you'll have to sleep it off but cant sleep any more because it was alcohol itself that made you sleep those last five nights, so delirium sets in——Sleeplessness, sweat, trembling, a groaning feeling of weakness where your arms are numb and useless, nightmares, (nightmares of death) . . . well, there's more of that up later.

About noon which is now the peak of a golden blurry new day for me we pick up Dave's girl Romana Swartz a big Rumanian monster beauty of some kind (I mean with big purple eyes and very tall and big but Mae West[4] big), Dave whispers in my ear "You oughta see her walking around that Zen-East House in those purple panties of hers, nothing else on, there's one married guy lives there who goes crazy every time she goes down the hall tho I dont blame him, would you? she's not trying to entice him or anybody she's just a nudist, she believe in nudism and bygod she's going to practice it!" (the Zen-East house being another sort of boardinghouse but this one for all kinds of married people and single and some small bohemian type families all races studying Subud or something, I never was there)——She's a big beautiful brunette anyway in the line of taste you might attribute to every slaky hungry sex slave in the world but also intelligent, well read, writes poetry, is a Zen student, knows everything, is in fact just simply a big healthy Rumanian Jewess who wants to marry a good hardy man and go live on a farm in the valley, that's it——

4. Stage name of actress Mary Jane West (1893–1980), famous for her buxom figure and bawdy humor.

The T.B. hospital is about two hours away through Tracy and down the San Joaquin Valley, Dave drives beautiful with Romana between us and me hold-ing the bottle again, it's bright beautiful California sunshine and prune orchards out there zipping by——It's always fun to have a good driver and a bottle and dark glasses on a fine sunny afternoon going somewhere interest-ing, and all the good conversation as I said——Ron and Joey are on the back mattress sitting crosslegged just like poor George Baso had sat on that trip last year from Frisco to New York.

But the main thing I'd liked at once about that Japanese kid was what he told me the first night I met him in that crazy kitchen of the Buchanan Street house: from midnight to 6 A.M. in his slow methodical voice he gave me his own tremendous version of the Life of Buddha beginning with infancy and right down to the end——George's theory (he has many theories and has actually run meditation classes with bells, just really a serious young lay priest of Japanese Buddhism when all is said and done) is that Buddha did not reject amorous love life with his wife and with his harem girls because he was sex-ually disinterested but on the contrary had been taught in the highest arts of lovemaking and eroticism possible in the India of that time, when great tomes like the Kama Sutra were in the process of being developed, tomes that give you instructions on every act, facet, approach, moment, trick, lick, lock, bing and bang and slurp of how to make love with another human being "male or female" insisted George: "He knew everything there is to know about all kinds of sex so that when he abandoned the world of pleasure to go be an ascetic in the forest everybody of course knew that he wasnt putting it all down out of ignorance——It served to make people of those times feel a marvelous respect for all his words——And he was just no simple Casanova[5] with a few frigid affairs across the years, man he went all the way, he had ministers and special eunuchs and special women who taught him love, special virgins were brought to him, he was acquainted with every aspect of perversity and non perversity and as you know he was also a great archer, horseman, he was just completely trained in all the arts of living by his father's orders because his father wanted to make sure he'd NEVER leave the palace——They used every trick in the books to entice him to a life of pleasure and as you know they even had him happily married to a beautiful girl called Yasodhara and he had a son with her Rahula and he also had his harem which included danc-ing boys and everything in the books" then George would go into every detail of this knowledge, like "He knew that the phallus is held with the hand and moved inside the vagina with a rotary movement, but this was only the first of several variations where there is also the lowering down of the gal's hips so that the vulva you see recedes and the phallus is introduced with a fast quick movement like stinging of a wasp, or else the vulva is protruded by means of lifting up the hips high so that the member is buried with a sudden rush right to the basis, or then he can withdraw real teasing like, or concentrate on right or left side——And then he knew all the gestures, words, expressions, what to do with a flower, what not to do with a flower, how to drink the lip in all kinds of kissing or how to crush kiss or soft kiss, man he was a *genius* in the beginning" . . . and so on, George went all the way telling me this till 6 A.M. it being one of the most fantastic *Buddha Charitas*[6] I'd ever heard ending with

---

5. Giovanni Giacomo Casanova de Seingalt (1725–1798), Italian libertine and adventurer.

6. Properly *Buddha caritas,* a state of uncondi-tional openness, generosity, and patience.

George's own perfect enunciation of the law of the Twelve Nirdanas whereby Buddha just logically disconnected all creation and laid it bare for what it was, under the Bo Tree, a chain of illusions——And on the trip to New York with Dave and me up front talking all the way poor George just sat there on the mattress for the most part very quiet and told us he was taking this trip to find out if HE was traveling to New York or just the CAR (Willie the Jeep) was traveling to New York or was it just the WHEELS were rolling, or the tires, or what——A Zen problem of some kind——So that when we'd see grain elevators on the Plains of Oklahoma George would say quietly "Well it seems to me that grain elevator is sorta waitin for the road to approach it" or he'd say suddenly "While you guys was talkin just then about how to mix a good Pernod Martini I just saw a white horse standing in an abandoned store-front"——In Las Vegas we'd taken a good motel room and gone out to play a little roulette, in St. Louis we'd gone to see the great bellies of the East St. Louis[7] hootchy kootchy joints where three of the most marvelous young girls performed smiling directly at us as tho they knew all about George and his theories about erogenous Buddha (there sits the monarch observing the donzinggerls) and as tho they knew anyway all about Dave Wain who whenever he sees a beautiful girls says licking his lips "Yum Yum." . . .

But now George has T.B. and they tell me he may even die——Which adds to that darkness in my mind, all these DEATH things piling up suddenly—— But I cant believe old Zen Master George is going to allow his body to die just now tho it looks like it when we pass through the lawn and come to a ward of beds and see him sitting dejected on the edge of his bed with his hair hanging over his brow where before it was always combed back——He's in a bathrobe and looks up at us almost displeased (but everybody is displeased by unexpected visits from friends or relatives in a hospital)——Nobody wants to be surprised on their hospital bad——He sighs and comes out to the warm lawn with us and the expression on his face says "Well ah so you've come to see me because I'm sick but what do you really want?" as tho all the old humorous courage of the year before has now given way to a profoundly deep Japanese skepticism like that of a Samurai warrior in a fit of suicidal depression (surprising me by its abject gloomy fearful frown).

1962

---

7. Working-class city in Illinois immediately east of St. Louis, Missouri.

DENISE LEVERTOV
1923–1997

Denise Levertov once wrote of her predecessor, the poet H. D.: "She showed a way to penetrate mystery; which means, not to flood darkness with light so that darkness is destroyed, but to *enter into* darkness, mystery, so that it is experienced." Along with Robert Duncan, Levertov carried out in her own distinctive way H. D.'s tradition of visionary poetry. More grounded than her predecessor in observing the natural world and in appreciating daily life, Levertov connected the concrete to the invisible, as suggested by the image of *The Jacob's Ladder* (1961), the title of her fifth book. She desired that a poem be "hard as a floor, sound as a bench" but also that it be "mysterious" ("Illustrious Ancestors"), and in her poems ordinary events open into the unknown. The origins of Levertov's magical sense of the world are not difficult to trace. She was born in England and wrote of her parents: "My mother was descended from the Welsh Tailor and mystic Angel Jones of Mold, my father from the noted Hasid, Schneour Zaiman (d. 1831), the 'Rav of Northern White Russia.' " In "Illustrious Ancestors" Levertov claimed a connection to her forefathers, both mystical and Hasidic: "some line still taut between me and them." Hasidim, a sect of Judaism that emphasizes the soul's communion with God rather than formal religious observance and encourages what Levertov called "a wonder at creation," was an important influence on her father, Paul Philip Levertoff. He had converted to Christianity as a student and later became an Anglican priest, but he retained his interest in Judaism and told Hasidic legends to Levertov and her older sister, Olga, throughout their childhoods. From her mother, Beatrice Spooner-Jones, Levertov learned to look closely at the world around her, and we might say of her work what she said of her mother: "with how much gazing / her life had paid tribute to the world's body" ("The 90th Year").

In 1947 Levertov married an American, Mitchell Goodman (they later divorced), and moved to the United States. She described this move as crucial to her development as a poet; it "necessitated the finding of new rhythms in which to write, in accordance with new rhythms of life and speech." In this discovery of a new idiom the stylistic influence of William Carlos Williams was especially important to her; without it, she said, "I could not have developed from a British Romantic with an almost Victorian background to an American poet of any vitality." Levertov embraced Williams's interest in an organic poetic form, growing out of the poet's relation to her subject, and like Duncan and Robert Creeley, she actively explored the relations between the line and the unit of breath as they control rhythm, melody, and stress. But if Levertov became the poet she was by becoming an American poet, her European heritage also enriched her sense of influence. Although her poem "September 1961" acknowledges her link to "the old great ones" (Ezra Pound, Williams, and H. D.), she was as at home with the German lyric poet Rainer Maria Rilke as with the American Transcendentalist Ralph Waldo Emerson. And in the United States she discovered the work of the Jewish theologian and philosopher Martin Buber, which renewed her interest "in the Hasidic ideas with which I was dimly acquainted as a child." Her eclecticism let her move easily between plain and richly descriptive language, between a vivid perception of the "thing itself" and the often radiant mystery that, for Levertov, arose from such seeing.

From 1956 to 1959 Levertov lived with her husband and son in Mexico. They were joined there by her mother, who, after her daughter's departure, remained in Mexico for the final eighteen years of her life (she died in 1977). Several moving poems in Levertov's collection *Life in the Forest* (1978), among them "The 90th Year" and "Death in Mexico," address her mother's last years. In the late 1960s the political crisis prompted by the Vietnam War turned Levertov's work more directly to public woes, as reflected in her following four books. Not all the poems in these books explicitly concern political issues ("The Sorrow Dance," for example, contains her sequence in memory of her sister, Olga, one of her finest, most powerful poems); nonetheless, many poems originated in a need for public testimony. Her overtly political poems are not often among her best, however; their very explicitness restricted her distinctive strengths as a poet, which included a feeling for the inexplicable, a language lyrical enough to express wish and desire, and a capacity for playfulness. But it is a mistake to separate too rigidly the political concerns in her work from a larger engagement with the world. As she wrote: "If a degree of intimacy is a condition of lyric expression, surely—at times when events make feelings run high—that intimacy between writer and political belief does exist, and is as intense as other emotions."

The power of Levertov's poems depends on her capacity to balance, however precariously, her two-sided vision, to keep alive both terms of what one critic called her "magical realism." At its best her work seems to spring from experience deep within her, stirred into being by a source beyond herself (as "Caedmon" is suddenly "affrighted" by an angel or the poet at sixteen dreams deeply, "sunk in the well"). Her finest poems render the inexplicable nature of our ordinary lives and their capacity for unexpected beauty. But Levertov's capacity for pleasure in the world never strays too far from the knowledge that the very landscapes that delight us contain places "that can pull you / down" ("Zeroing In"), as our inner landscapes also contain places " 'that are bruised forever, that time / never assuages, never.' "

Levertov published several collections of prose, including *The Poet in the World* (1973), *Light Up the Cave* (1981), and *New and Selected Essays* (1992). In 1987 she published her fifteenth book of poems, *Breathing the Water*. This book contains a long sequence, *The Showings: Lady Julian of Norwich, 1342–1416*, which continues the link between Levertov's work and a visionary tradition. She published three subsequent collections: *A Door in the Hive* (1989), *Evening Train* (1992), and *Tesserae* (1995). Levertov taught widely and from 1982 until her death was professor of English at Stanford University, where she was an important teacher for a younger generation of writers.

To the Snake

Green Snake, when I hung you round my neck
and stroked your cold, pulsing throat
     as you hissed to me, glinting
arrowy gold scales, and I felt
     the weight of you on my shoulders,   5
and the whispering silver of your dryness
     sounded close at my ears—

Green Snake—I swore to my companions that certainly
     you were harmless! But truly
I had no certainty, and no hope, only desiring   10
     to hold you, for that joy,
               which left
a long wake of pleasure, as the leaves moved
and you faded into the pattern
of grass and shadows, and I returned   15
smiling and haunted, to a dark morning.

                        1960

The Jacob's Ladder[1]

The stairway is not
a thing of gleaming strands
a radiant evanescence

---

1. Jacob dreamed of "a ladder set up on the earth, and the top of it reached to heaven: and behold the angels of God ascending and descending on it" (Genesis 28.12).

for angels' feet that only glance in their tread, and need not
touch the stone.   5

It is of stone.
A rosy stone that takes
a glowing tone of softness
only because behind it the sky is a doubtful, a doubting
night gray.   10

A stairway of sharp
angles, solidly built.
One sees that the angels must spring
down from one step to the next, giving a little
lift of the wings: 15

and a man climbing
must scrape his knees, and bring
the grip of his hands into play. The cut stone
consoles his groping feet. Wings brush past him.
The poem ascends.   20

                                                                            1961

In Mind

There's in my mind a woman
of innocence, unadorned but

fair-featured, and smelling of
apples or grass. She wears

a utopian smock or shift, her hair   5
is light brown and smooth, and she

is kind and very clean without
ostentation—
            but she has
no imagination.   10
            And there's a
turbulent moon-ridden girl

or old woman, or both,
dressed in opals and rags, feathers

and torn taffeta,   15
who knows strange songs—

but she is not kind.

                                                                            1964

Death in Mexico[1]

Even two weeks after her fall,
three weeks before she died, the garden
began to vanish. The rickety fence gave way
as it had threatened, and the children threw
broken plastic toys—vicious yellow,   5
unresonant red, onto the path, into the lemontree;
or trotted in through the gap, trampling small plants.
For two weeks no one watered it, except
I did, twice, but then I left. She was still conscious then
and thanked me. I begged the others to water it—   10
but the rains began; when I got back there were violent,
sudden, battering downpours each after noon.
                                                  Weeds flourished,

dry topsoil was washed away swiftly
into the drains. Oh, there was green, still,   15
but the garden was disappearing—each day
less sign of the ordered,
thought-out oasis, a squared circle her mind
constructed for rose and lily, begonia
and rosemary-for-remembrance.   20
Twenty years in the making—
less than a month to undo itself;
and those who had seen it grow,
living around it those decades,
did nothing to hold it. Oh, Alberto did,   25
one day, patch up the fence a bit,
when I told him a future tenant would value
having a garden. But no one believed
the garden-maker would live (I least of all),
so her pain if she were to see the ruin   30
remained abstract, an incomprehensible concept,
impelling no action. When they carried her past
                                                  on a stretcher,

on her way to the *sanatorio*, failing sight
transformed itself into a mercy: certainly   35
she could have seen no more than a greenish blur.
But to me the weeds, the flowerless rosebushes, broken
stems of the canna lilies and amaryllis, all
a lusterless jungle green, presented—
even before her dying was over—   40
an obdurate, blind, all-seeing gaze:
I had seen it before, in the museums,
in stone masks of the gods and victims.
A gaze that admits no tenderness; if it smiles, it
only smiles with sublime bitterness—no,   45
not even bitter: it admits
no regret, nostalgia has no part in its cosmos,

1. One of a sequence of poems on the death of Levertov's mother.

bitterness is irrelevant.
If it holds a flower—and it does,
a delicate brilliant silky flower that blooms only   50
a single day—it holds it clenched
between sharp teeth.
Vines may crawl, and scorpions, over its face,
but though the centuries blunt
eyelid and flared nostril, the stone gaze   55
is utterly still, fixed, absolute,
smirk of denial facing eternity.
Gardens vanish. She was an alien here,
as I am. Her death
was not Mexico's business. The garden though   60
was a hostage. Old gods
took back their own.

1978

JAMES BALDWIN
1924–1987

James Baldwin was born in Harlem, the first of nine children. From his novel *Go Tell It on the Mountain* (1953) and his story "The Rockpile," we learn about the extremely painful relationship he had with his father (actually his stepfather). David Baldwin, son of a slave, was a lay preacher rigidly committed to a vengeful God who would eventually judge white people as they deserved; in the meantime much of the vengeance was taken out on James. His father's "unlimited capacity for introspection and rancor," as the son later put it, must have had a profound effect on the sermonizing style Baldwin developed. Just as important was Baldwin's conversion and resulting service as a preacher in his father's church, as we can see from both the rhythm and the message of his prose—which is very much a *spoken* prose.

Baldwin did well in school and, having received a hardship deferment from military service because his father was dying, attached himself to Greenwich Village, where he concentrated on becoming a writer. In 1944 he met Richard Wright, at that time "the greatest black writer in the world for me," in whose early books Baldwin "found expressed, for the first time in my life, the sorrow, the rage, and the murderous bitterness which was eating up my life and the lives of those about me." Wright helped him win a Eugene Saxton fellowship, and in 1948, when Baldwin went to live in Paris, he was following in Wright's footsteps (Wright had become an expatriate to the same city a year earlier). It is perhaps for this reason that in his early essays written for *Partisan Review* and published in 1955 as *Notes of a Native Son* (with the title's explicit reference to Wright's 1940 novel, *Native Son*) Baldwin dissociated himself from the image of American life found in Wright's "protest work" and, like the novelist Ralph Ellison, went about protesting in his own way.

As far as his novels are concerned, Baldwin's way involved a preoccupation with the intertwining of sexual with racial concerns, particularly in America. His interest in what it means to be black and homosexual in relation to mainstream white society is most fully and interestingly expressed in his third novel, *Another Country* (1962). (He had previously written *Go Tell It on the Mountain,* and a second novel, *Giovanni's Room,* 1955, about a white expatriate in Paris and his male lover.) *Another Country* contains scenes full of lively detail and intelligent reflection, expressed in a manner that takes advantage of the novel's expansive form. In his short stories collected in *Going to Meet the Man* (1965), the racial terrorism of America as he perceived it made its own grotesque stylistic statement. The writer's challenge was to maintain steady control in the face of atrocities that might otherwise disrupt the narrative's ability to contain such events.

His later novels, *Tell Me How Long the Train's Been Gone* (1968) and *Just above My Head* (1979), were more polemical. Like his fellow novelist Norman Mailer, Baldwin risked advertising himself too strenuously and sometimes let spokesmanship become a primary motivator. Like Ellison, he experienced many pressures to be more than just a writer, but he nevertheless produced artistically significant novels and stories. No black writer has been better able to imagine white experience, to speak in various tones of different kinds and behaviors of people or places other than his own. In its sensitivity to shades of discrimination and moral shape, and in its commitment—despite everything—to America, his voice was comparable in importance to that of any person of letters from recent decades, as tributes paid to him at his death agreed.

The text is from *Going to Meet the Man* (1965).

Going to Meet the Man

"What's the matter?" she asked.

"I don't know," he said, trying to laugh, "I guess I'm tired."

"You've been working too hard," she said. "I keep telling you."

"Well, goddammit, woman," he said, "it's not my fault!" He tried again; he wretchedly failed again. Then he just lay there, silent, angry, and helpless. Excitement filled him like a toothache, but it refused to enter his flesh. He stroked her breast. This was his wife. He could not ask her to do just a little thing for him, just to help him out, just for a little while, the way he could ask a nigger girl to do it. He lay there, and he sighed. The image of a black girl caused a distant excitement in him, like a far-away light; but, again, the excitement was more like pain; instead of forcing him to act, it made action impossible.

"Go to sleep," she said, gently, "you got a hard day tomorrow."

"Yeah," he said, and rolled over on his side, facing her, one hand still on one breast. "Goddamn the niggers. The black stinking coons. You'd think they'd learn. Wouldn't you think they'd learn? I mean, *wouldn't* you?"

"They going to be out there tomorrow," she said, and took his hand away, "get some sleep."

He lay there, one hand between his legs, staring at the frail sanctuary of his wife. A faint light came from the shutters; the moon was full. Two dogs, far away, were barking at each other, back and forth, insistently, as though they were agreeing to make an appointment. He heard a car coming north on the road and he half sat up, his hand reaching for his holster, which was on a chair near the bed, on top of his pants. The lights hit the shutters and seemed to travel across the room and then went out. The sound of the car slipped away, he heard it hit gravel, then heard it no more. Some liver-lipped students, probably, heading back to that college—but coming from where? His watch said it was two in the morning. They could be coming from anywhere, from out of state most likely, and they would be at the court-house tomorrow. The niggers were getting ready. Well, they would be ready, too.

He moaned. He wanted to let whatever was in him out; but it wouldn't come out. Goddamn! he said aloud, and turned again, on his side, away from Grace, staring at the shutters. He was a big, healthy man and he had never had any trouble sleeping. And he wasn't old enough yet to have any trouble getting it up—he was only forty-two. And he was a good man, a God-fearing man, he had tried to do his duty all his life, and he had been a deputy sheriff for several years. Nothing had ever bothered him before, certainly not getting it up. Sometimes, sure, like any other man, he knew that he wanted a little more spice than Grace could give him and he would drive over yonder and pick up a black piece or arrest her, it came to the same thing, but he couldn't do that now, no more. There was no telling what might happen once your ass was in the air. And they were low enough to kill a man then, too, every one of them, or the girl herself might do it, right while she was making believe you made her feel so good. The niggers. What had the good Lord Almighty had in mind when he made the niggers? Well. They were pretty good at that, all right. Damn. Damn. Goddamn.

This wasn't helping him to sleep. He turned again, toward Grace again, and moved close to her warm body. He felt something he had never felt before. He felt that he would like to hold her, hold her, hold her, and be buried in her like a child and never have to get up in the morning again and go downtown to face those faces, good Christ, they were ugly! and never have to enter that jail house again and smell that smell and hear that singing; never again feel that filthy, kinky, greasy hair under his hand, never again watch those black breasts leap against the leaping cattle prod, never hear those moans again or watch that blood run down or the fat lips split or the sealed eyes struggle open. They were animals, they were no better than animals, what could be done with people like that? Here they had been in a civilized country for years and they still lived like animals. Their houses were dark, with oil cloth or cardboard in the windows, the smell was enough to make you puke your guts out, and there they sat, a whole tribe, pumping out kids, it looked like, every damn five minutes, and laughing and talking and playing music like they didn't have a care in the world, and he reckoned they didn't, neither, and coming to the door, into the sunlight, just standing there, just looking foolish, not thinking of anything but just getting back to what they were doing, saying, Yes suh, Mr. Jesse. I surely will, Mr. Jesse. Fine weather, Mr. Jesse. Why, I thank you, Mr. Jesse. He had worked for a mail-order house for a while and it had been his job to collect the payments for the stuff they bought. They were too dumb to know that they were being cheated blind, but that was no skin off his ass— he was just supposed to do his job. They would be late—they didn't have the sense to put money aside; but it was easy to scare them, and he never really had any trouble. Hell, they all liked him, the kids used to smile when he came to the door. He gave them candy, sometimes, or chewing gum, and rubbed their rough bullet heads—maybe the candy should have been poisoned. Those kids were grown now. He had had trouble with one of them today.

"There was this nigger today," he said; and stopped; his voice sounded peculiar. He touched Grace. "You awake?" he asked. She mumbled something, impatiently, she was probably telling him to go to sleep. It was all right. He knew that he was not alone.

"What a funny time," he said, "to be thinking about a thing like that—you listening?" She mumbled something again. He rolled over on his back. "This nigger's one of the ringleaders. We had trouble with him before. We must have had him out there at the work farm three or four times. Well, Big Jim C. and some of the boys really had to whip that nigger's ass today." He looked over at

Grace; he could not tell whether she was listening or not; and he was afraid to ask again. "They had this line you know, to register"—he laughed, but she did not—"and they wouldn't stay where Big Jim C. wanted them, no, they had to start blocking traffic all around the court house so couldn't nothing or nobody get through, and Big Jim C. told them to disperse and they wouldn't move, they just kept up that singing, and Big Jim C. figured that the others would move if this nigger would move, him being the ringleader, but he wouldn't move and he wouldn't let the others move, so they had to beat him and a couple of the others and they threw them in the wagon—but *I* didn't see this nigger till I got to the jail. They were still singing and I was supposed to make them stop. Well, I couldn't make them stop for me but I knew he could make them stop. He was lying on the ground jerking and moaning, they had threw him in a cell by himself, and blood was coming out his ears from where Big Jim C. and his boys had whipped him. Wouldn't you think they'd learn? I put the prod to him and he jerked some more and he kind of screamed—but he didn't have much voice left. "You make them stop that singing," I said to him, "you hear me? You make them stop that singing." He acted like he didn't hear me and I put it to him again, under his arms, and he just rolled around on the floor and blood started coming from his mouth. He'd pissed his pants already." He paused. His mouth felt dry and his throat was as rough as sandpaper; as he talked, he began to hurt all over with that peculiar excitement which refused to be released. "You all are going to stop your singing, I said to him, and you are going to stop coming down to the court house and disrupting traffic and molesting the people and keeping us from our duties and keeping doctors from getting to sick white women and getting all them Northerners in this town to give our town a bad name—!" As he said this, he kept prodding the boy, sweat pouring from beneath the helmet he had not yet taken off. The boy rolled around in his own dirt and water and blood and tried to scream again as the prod hit his testicles, but the scream did not come out, only a kind of rattle and a moan. He stopped. He was not supposed to kill the nigger. The cell was filled with a terrible odor. The boy was still. "You hear me?" he called. "You had enough?" The singing went on. "You had enough?" His foot leapt out, he had not known it was going to, and caught the boy flush on the jaw. *Jesus,* he thought, *this ain't no nigger, this is a goddamn bull,* and he screamed again, "You had enough? You going to make them stop that singing now?"

But the boy was out. And now he was shaking worse than the boy had been shaking. He was glad no one could see him. At the same time, he felt very close to a very peculiar, particular joy; something deep in him and deep in his memory was stirred, but whatever was in his memory eluded him. He took off his helmet. He walked to the cell door.

"White man," said the boy, from the floor, behind him.

He stopped. For some reason, he grabbed his privates.

"You remember Old Julia?"

The boy said, from the floor, with his mouth full of blood, and one eye, barely open, glaring like the eye of a cat in the dark, "My grandmother's name was Mrs. Julia Blossom. *Mrs.* Julia Blossom. You going to call our women by their right names yet.—And those kids ain't going to stop singing. We going to keep on singing until every one of you miserable white mothers go stark raving out of your minds." Then he closed the one eye; he spat blood; his head fell back against the floor.

He looked down at the boy, whom he had been seeing, off and on, for more than a year, and suddenly remembered him: Old Julia had been one of his mail-order customers, a nice old woman. He had not seen her for years, he supposed that she must be dead.

He had walked into the yard, the boy had been sitting in a swing. He had smiled at the boy, and asked, "Old Julia home?"

The boy looked at him for a long time before he answered. "Don't no Old Julia live here."

"This is her house. I know her. She's lived her for years."

The boy shook his head. "You might know a Old Julia someplace else, white man. But don't nobody by that name live here."

He watched the boy; the boy watched him. The boy certainly wasn't more than ten. *White man.* He didn't have time to be fooling around with some crazy kid. He yelled, "Hey! Old Julia!"

But only silence answered him. The expression on the boy's face did not change. The sun beat down on them both, still and silent; he had the feeling that he had been caught up in a nightmare, a nightmare dreamed by a child; perhaps one of the nightmares he himself had dreamed as a child. It had that feeling—everything familiar, without undergoing any other change, had been subtly and hideously displaced: the trees, the sun, the patches of grass in the yard, the leaning porch and the weary porch steps and the card-board in the windows and the black hole of the door which looked like the entrance to a cave, and the eyes of the pickaninny, all, all, were charged with malevolence. *White man.* He looked at the boy. "She's gone out?"

The boy said nothing.

"Well," he said, "tell her I passed by and I'll pass by next week." He started to go; he stopped. "You want some chewing gum?"

The boy got down from the swing and started for the house. He said, "I don't want nothing you got, white man." He walked into the house and closed the door behind him.

Now the boy looked as though he were dead. Jesse wanted to go over to him and pick him up and pistol whip him until the boy's head burst open like a melon. He began to tremble with what he believed was rage, sweat, both cold and hot, raced down his body, the singing filled him as though it were a weird, uncontrollable, monstrous howling rumbling up from the depths of his own belly, he felt an icy fear rise in him and raise him up, and he shouted, he howled, "You lucky we *pump* some white blood into you every once in a while—your women! Here's what I got for all the black bitches in the world—!" Then he was, abruptly, almost too weak to stand; to his bewilderment, his horror, beneath his own fingers, he felt himself violently stiffen—with no warning at all; he dropped his hands and he stared at the boy and he left the cell.

"All that singing they do," he said. "All that singing." He could not remember the first time he had heard it; he had been hearing it all his life. It was the sound with which he was most familiar—though it was also the sound of which he had been least conscious—and it had always contained an obscure comfort. They were singing to God. They were singing for mercy and they hoped to go to heaven, and he had even sometimes felt, when looking into the eyes of some of the old women, a few of the very old men, that they were singing for mercy for his soul, too. Of course he had never thought of their heaven or of what God was, or could be, for them; God was the same for everyone, he supposed, and heaven was where good people went—he supposed. He had never thought much about what it meant to be a good person. He tried to be a good person and treat everybody right: it wasn't his fault if the niggers had taken it into their heads to fight against God and go against the rules laid down in the Bible for everyone to read! Any preacher would tell you that. He was only doing his duty: protecting white people from the niggers and the niggers from themselves. And there were still lots of good niggers around—he had to remember that; they weren't all like that boy this afternoon; and the good niggers must be mighty sad to see what was happening to their people. They would thank him when this was over. In that way they had, the best of them, not quite looking him in the eye, in a low voice, with a little smile: We surely thanks you, Mr. Jesse. From the bottom of our hearts, we thanks you. He smiled. They hadn't all gone crazy. This trouble would pass.—He knew that the young people had changed some of the words to the songs. He had scarcely listened to the words before and he did not listen to them now; but he knew that the words were different; he could hear that much. He did not know if the faces were different, he had never, before this trouble began, watched them as they sang, but he certainly did not like what he saw now. They hated him, and this hatred was blacker than their hearts, blacker than their skins, redder than their blood, and harder, by far, than his club. Each day, each night, he felt worn out, aching, with their smell in his nostrils and filling his lungs, as though he were drowning—drowning in niggers; and it was all to be done again when he awoke. It would never end. It would never end. Perhaps this was what the singing had meant all along. They had not been singing black folks into heaven, they had been singing white folks into hell.

Everyone felt this black suspicion in many ways, but no one knew how to express it. Men much older than he, who had been responsible for law and order much longer than he, were now much quieter than they had been, and the tone of their jokes, in a way that he could not quite put his finger on, had changed. These men were his models, they had been friends to his father, and they had taught him what it meant to be a man. He looked to them for courage now. It wasn't that he didn't know that what he was doing was right—he knew that, nobody had to tell him that; it was only that he missed the ease of former years. But they didn't have much time to hang out with each other these days. They tended to stay close to their families every free minute because nobody knew what might happen next. Explosions rocked the night of their tranquil town. Each time each man wondered silently if perhaps this time the dynamite had not fallen into the wrong hands. They thought that they knew where all the guns were; but they could not possibly know every move that was made in that secret place where the darkies lived. From time to time it was suggested that they form a posse and search the home of every nigger, but they hadn't done it yet. For one thing, this might have brought the bastards from the North down on their backs; for another, although the niggers were scattered throughout the town—down in the hollow near the railroad tracks, way west near the mills, up on the hill, the well-off ones, and some out near the college—nothing seemed to happen in one part of town without the niggers immediately knowing it in the other. This meant that they could not take them by surprise. They rarely mentioned it, but they *knew* that some of the niggers had guns. It stood to reason, as they said, since, after all, some of them had been in the Army. There were niggers in the Army right now and God knows they wouldn't have had any trouble stealing this half-assed government blind—the whole world was doing it, look at the European countries and all those countries in Africa. They made jokes about it—bitter jokes; and they cursed the government in Washington, which had betrayed them; but they had not yet formed a posse. Now, if their town had been laid out like some towns in the North, where all the niggers lived together in one locality, they could have gone down and set fire to the houses and brought about peace that way. If the niggers had all lived in one place, they could have kept the fire in one place. But the way this town was laid out, the fire could hardly be controlled. It would spread all over town—and the niggers would probably be helping it to spread. Still, from time to time, they spoke of doing it, anyway; so that now there was a real fear among them that somebody might go crazy and light the match.

They rarely mentioned anything not directly related to the war that they were fighting, but this had failed to establish between them the unspoken communication of soldiers during a war. Each man, in the thrilling silence which sped outward from their exchanges, their laughter, and their anecdotes, seemed wrestling, in various degrees of darkness, with a secret which he could not articulate to himself, and which, however directly it related to the war, related yet more surely to his privacy and his past. They could no longer be sure, after all, that they had all done the same things. They had never dreamed that their privacy could contain any element of terror, could threaten, that is, to reveal itself, to the scrutiny of a judgment day, while remaining unreadable and inaccessible to themselves; nor had they dreamed that the past, while certainly refusing to be forgotten, could yet so stubbornly refuse to be remembered. They felt themselves mysteriously set at naught, as no longer entering into the real concerns of other people—while here they were, out-numbered, fighting to save the civilized world. They had thought that people would care—people didn't care; not enough, anyway, to help them. It would have been a help, really, or at least a relief, even to have been forced to surrender. Thus they had lost, probably forever, their old and easy connection with each other. They were forced to depend on each other more and, at the same time, to trust each other less. Who could tell when one of them might not betray them all, for money, or for the ease of confession? But no one dared imagine what there might be to confess. They were soldiers fighting a war, but their relationship to each other was that of accomplices in a crime. They all had to keep their mouths shut.

I stepped in the river at Jordan.

Out of the darkness of the room, out of nowhere, the line came flying up at him, with the melody and the beat. He turned wordlessly toward his sleeping wife. *I stepped in the river at Jordan.* Where had he heard that song?

"Grace," he whispered. "You awake?"

She did not answer. If she was awake, she wanted him to sleep. Her breathing was slow and easy, her body slowly rose and fell.

I stepped in the river at Jordan.

The water came to my knees.

He began to sweat. He felt an overwhelming fear, which yet contained a curious and dreadful pleasure.

I stepped in the river at Jordan.
The water came to my waist.

It had been night, as it was now, he was in the car between his mother and his father, sleepy, his head in his mother's lap, sleepy, and yet full of excitement. The singing came from far away, across the dark fields. There were no lights anywhere. They had said good-bye to all the others and turned off on this dark dirt road. They were almost home.

I stepped in the river at Jordan,
The water came over my head,
I looked way over to the other side,
He was making up my dying bed!

"I guess they singing for him," his father said, seeming very weary and subdued now. "Even when they're sad, they sound like they just about to go and tear off a piece." He yawned and leaned across the boy and slapped his wife lightly on the shoulder, allowing his hand to rest there for a moment. "Don't they?"

"Don't talk that way," she said.

"Well, that's what we going to do," he said, "you can make up your mind to that." He started whistling. "You see? When I begin to feel it, I gets kind of musical, too."

Oh, Lord! Come on and ease my troubling mind!

He had a black friend, his age, eight, who lived nearby. His name was Otis. They wrestled together in the dirt. Now the thought of Otis made him sick. He began to shiver. His mother put her arm around him.

"He's tired," she said.

"We'll be home soon," said his father. He began to whistle again.

"We didn't see Otis this morning," Jesse said. He did not know why he said this. His voice, in the darkness of the car, sounded small and accusing.

"You haven't seen Otis for a couple of mornings," his mother said.

That was true. But he was only concerned about *this* morning.

"No," said his father, "I reckon Otis's folks was afraid to let him show himself this morning."

"But Otis didn't do nothing!" Now his voice sounded questioning.

"Otis *can't* do nothing," said his father, "he's too little." The car lights picked up their wooden house, which now solemnly approached them, the lights falling around it like yellow dust. Their dog, chained to a tree, began to bark.

"We just want to make sure Otis *don't* do nothing," said his father, and stopped the car. He looked down at Jesse. "And you tell him what your Daddy said, you hear?"

"Yes sir," he said.

His father switched off the lights. The dog moaned and pranced, but they ignored him and went inside. He could not sleep. He lay awake, hearing the night sounds, the dog yawning and moaning outside, the sawing of the crickets, the cry of the owl, dogs barking far away, then no sounds at all, just the heavy, endless buzzing of the night. The darkness pressed on his eyelids like a scratchy blanket. He turned, he turned again. He wanted to call his mother, but he knew his father would not like this. He was terribly afraid. Then he heard his father's voice in the other room, low, with a joke in it; but this did not help him, it frightened him more, he knew what was going to happen. He put his head under the blanket, then pushed his head out again, for fear, staring at the dark window. He heard his mother's moan, his father's sigh; he gritted his teeth. Then their bed began to rock. His father's breathing seemed to fill the world.

That morning, before the sun had gathered all its strength, men and women, some flushed and some pale with excitement, came with news. Jesse's father seemed to know what the news was before the first jalopy stopped in the yard, and he ran out, crying, "They got him, then? They got him?"

The first jalopy held eight people, three men and two women and three children. The children were sitting on the laps of the grown-ups. Jesse knew two of them, the two boys; they shyly and uncomfortably greeted each other. He did not know the girl.

"Yes, they got him," said one of the women, the older one, who wore a wide hat and a fancy, faded blue dress. "They found him early this morning."

"How far had he got?" Jesse's father asked.

"He hadn't got no further than Harkness," one of the men said. "Look like he got lost up there in all them trees—or maybe he just got so scared he couldn't move." They all laughed.

"Yes, and you know it's near a graveyard, too," said the younger woman, and they laughed again.

"Is that where they got him now?" asked Jesse's father.

By this time there were three cars piled behind the first one, with everyone looking excited and shining, and Jesse noticed that they were carrying food. It was like a Fourth of July picnic.

"Yeah, that's where he is," said one of the men, "declare, Jesse, you going to keep us here all day long, answering your damn fool questions. Come on, we ain't got no time to waste."

"Don't bother putting up no food," cried a woman from one of the other cars, "we got enough. Just come on."

"Why, thank you," said Jesse's father, "we be right along, then."

"I better get a sweater for the boy," said his mother, "in case it turns cold."

Jesse watched his mother's thin legs cross the yard. He knew that she also wanted to comb her hair a little and maybe put on a better dress, the dress she wore to church. His father guessed this, too, for he yelled behind her, "Now don't you go trying to turn yourself into no movie star. You just come on." But he laughed as he said this, and winked at the men; his wife was younger and prettier than most of the other women. He clapped Jesse on the head and started pulling him toward the car. "You all go on," he said, "I'll be right behind you. Jesse, you go tie up that there dog while I get this car started."

The cars sputtered and coughed and shook; the caravan began to move; bright dust filled the air. As soon as he was tied up, the dog began to bark. Jesse's mother came out of the house, carrying a jacket for his father and a sweater for Jesse. She had put a ribbon in her hair and had an old shawl around her shoulders.

"Put these in the car, son," she said, and handed everything to him. She bent down and stroked the dog, looked to see if there was water in his bowl, then went back up the three porch steps and closed the door.

"Come on," said his father, "ain't nothing in there for nobody to steal." He was sitting in the car, which trembled and belched. The last car of the caravan had disappeared but the sound of singing floated behind them.

Jesse got into the car, sitting close to his father, loving the smell of the car, and the trembling, and the bright day, and the sense of going on a great and unexpected journey. His mother got in and closed the door and the car began to move. Not until then did he ask, "Where are we going? Are we going on a picnic?"

He had a feeling that he knew where they were going, but he was not sure.

"That's right," his father said, "we're going on a picnic. You won't ever forget *this* picnic—!"

"Are we," he asked, after a moment, "going to see the bad nigger—the one that knocked down old Miss Standish?"

"Well, I reckon," said his mother, "that we *might* see him."

He started to ask, *Will a lot of niggers be there? Will Otis be there?*—but he did not ask his question, to which, in a strange and uncomfortable way, he already knew the answer. Their friends, in the other cars, stretched up the road as far as he could see; other cars had joined them; there were cars behind them. They were singing. The sun seemed suddenly very hot, and he was at once very happy and a little afraid. He did not quite understand what was happening, and he did not know what to ask—he had no one to ask. He had grown accustomed, for the solution of such mysteries, to go to Otis. He felt that Otis knew everything. But he could not ask Otis about this. Anyway, he had not seen Otis for two days; he had not seen a black face anywhere for more than two days; and he now realized, as they began chugging up the long hill which eventually led to Harkness, that there were no black faces on the road this morning, no black people anywhere. From the houses in which they lived, all along the road, no smoke curled, no life stirred—maybe one or two chickens were to be seen, that was all. There was no one at the windows, no one in the yard, no one sitting on the porches, and the doors were closed. He had come this road many a time and seen women washing in the yard (there were no clothes on the clotheslines), men working in the fields, children playing in the dust; black men passed them on the road other mornings, other days, on foot, or in wagons, sometimes in cars, tipping their hats, smiling, joking, their teeth a solid white against their skin, their eyes as warm as the sun, the blackness of their skin like dull fire against the white of the blue or the grey of their torn clothes. They passed the nigger church—dead-white, desolate, locked up; and the graveyard, where no one knelt or walked, and he saw no flowers. He wanted to ask, *Where are they? Where are they all?* But he did not dare. As the hill grew steeper, the sun grew colder. He looked at his mother and his father. They looked straight ahead, seeming to be listening to the singing which echoed and echoed in this graveyard silence. They were strangers to him now. They were looking at something he could not see. His father's lips had a strange, cruel curve, he wet his lips from time to time, and swallowed. He was terribly aware of his father's tongue, it was as though he had never seen it before. And his father's body suddenly seemed immense, bigger than a mountain. His eyes, which were grey-green, looked yellow in the sunlight; or at least there was a light in them which he had never seen before. His mother patted her hair and adjusted the ribbon, leaning forward to look into the car mirror. "You look all right," said his father, and laughed. "When that nigger looks at you, he's going to swear he threw his life away for nothing. Wouldn't be surprised if he don't come back to haunt you." And he laughed again.

The singing now slowly began to cease; and he realized that they were nearing their destination. They had reached a straight, narrow, pebbly road, with trees on either side. The sunlight filtered down on them from a great height, as though they were under-water; and the branches of the trees scraped against the cars with a tearing sound. To the right of them, and beneath them, invisible now, lay the town; and to the left, miles of trees which led to the high mountain range which his ancestors had crossed in order to settle in this valley. Now, all was silent, except for the bumping of the tires against the rocky road, the sputtering of motors, and the sound of a crying child. And they seemed to move more slowly. They were beginning to climb again. He watched the cars ahead as they toiled patiently upward, disappearing into the sunlight of the clearing. Presently, he felt their vehicle also rise, heard his father's changed breathing, the sunlight hit his face, the trees moved away from them, and they were there. As their car crossed the clearing, he looked around. There seemed to be millions, there were certainly hundreds of people in the clearing, staring toward something he could not see. There was a fire. He could not see the flames, but he smelled the smoke. Then they were on the other side of the clearing, among the trees again. His father drove off the road and parked the car behind a great many other cars. He looked down at Jesse.

"You all right?" he asked.

"Yes sir," he said.

"Well, come on, then," his father said. He reached over and opened the door on his mother's side. His mother stepped out first. They followed her into the clearing. At first he was aware only of confusion, of his mother and father greeting and being greeted, himself being handled, hugged, and patted, and told how much he had grown. The wind blew the smoke from the fire across the clearing into his eyes and nose. He could not see over the backs of the people in front of him. The sounds of laughing and cursing and wrath—and something else—rolled in waves from the front of the mob to the back. Those in front expressed their delight at what they saw, and this delight rolled backward, wave upon wave, across the clearing, more acrid than the smoke. His father reached down suddenly and sat Jesse on his shoulders.

Now he saw the fire—of twigs and boxes, piled high; flames made pale orange and yellow and thin as a veil under the steadier light of the sun; greyblue smoke rolled upward and poured over their heads. Beyond the shifting curtain of fire and smoke, he made out first only a length of gleaming chain, attached to a great limb of the tree; then he saw that this chain bound two black hands together at the wrist, dirty yellow palm facing dirty yellow palm. The smoke poured up; the hands dropped out of sight; a cry went up from the crowd. Then the hands slowly came into view again, pulled upward by the chain. This time he saw the kinky, sweating, bloody head—he had never before seen a head with so much hair on it, hair so black and so tangled that it seemed like another jungle. The head was hanging. He saw the forehead, flat and high, with a kind of arrow of hair in the center, like he had, like his father had; they called it a widow's peak; and the mangled eye brows, the wide nose, the closed eyes, and the glinting eye lashes and the hanging lips, all streaming with blood and sweat. His hands were straight above his head. All his weight pulled downward from his hands; and he was a big man, a bigger man than his father, and black as an African jungle cat, and naked. Jesse pulled upward; his father's hands held him firmly by the ankles. He wanted to say something, he did not know what, but nothing he said could have been heard, for now the crowd roared again as a man stepped forward and put more wood on the fire. The flames leapt up. He thought he heard the hanging man scream, but he was not sure. Sweat was pouring from the hair in his armpits, poured down his sides, over his chest, into his navel and his groin. He was lowered again; he was raised again. Now Jesse knew that he heard him scream. The head went back, the mouth wide open, blood bubbling from the mouth; the veins of the neck jumped out; Jesse clung to his father's neck in terror as the cry rolled over the crowd. The cry of all the people rose to answer the dying man's cry. He wanted death to come quickly. They wanted to make death wait: and it was they who held death, now, on a leash which they lengthened little by little. *What did he do?* Jesse wondered. *What did the man do? What did he do?*—but he could not ask his father. He was seated on his father's shoulders, but his father was far away. There were two older men, friends of his father's, raising and lowering the chain; everyone, indiscriminately, seemed to be responsible for the fire. There was no hair left on the nigger's privates, and the eyes, now, were wide open, as white as the eyes of a clown or a doll. The smoke now carried a terrible odor across the clearing, the odor of something burning which was both sweet and rotten.

He turned his head a little and saw the field of faces. He watched his mother's face. Her eyes were very bright, her mouth was open: she was more beautiful than he had ever seen her, and more strange. He began to feel a joy he had never felt before. He watched the hanging, gleaming body, the most beautiful and terrible object he had ever seen till then. One of his father's friends reached up and in his hands he held a knife: and Jesse wished that he had been that man. It was a long, bright knife and the sun seemed to catch it, to play with it, to caress it—it was brighter than the fire. And a wave of laughter swept the crowd. Jesse felt his father's hands on his ankles slip and tighten. The man with the knife walked toward the crowd, smiling slightly; as though this were a signal, silence fell; he heard his mother cough. Then the man with the knife walked up to the hanging body. He turned and smiled again. Now there was a silence all over the field. The hanging head looked up. It seemed fully conscious now, as though the fire had burned out terror and pain. The man with the knife took the nigger's privates in his hand, one hand, still smiling, as though he were weighing them. In the cradle of the one white hand, the nigger's privates seemed as remote as meat being weighed in the scales; but seemed heavier, too, much heavier, and Jesse felt his scrotum tighten; and huge, huge, much bigger than his father's, flaccid, hairless, the largest thing he had ever seen till then, and the blackest. The white hand stretched them, cradled them, caressed them. Then the dying man's eyes looked straight into Jesse's eyes—it could not have been as long as a second, but it seemed longer than a year. Then Jesse screamed, and the crowd screamed as the knife flashed, first up, then down, cutting the dreadful thing away, and the blood came roaring down. Then the crowd rushed forward, tearing at the body with their hands, with knives, with rocks, with stones, howling and cursing. Jesse's head, of its own weight, fell downward toward his father's head. Someone stepped forward and drenched the body with kerosene. Where the man had been, a great sheet of flame appeared. Jesse's father lowered him to the ground.

"Well, I told you," said his father, "you wasn't never going to forget *this* picnic." His father's face was full of sweat, his eyes were very peaceful. At that moment Jesse loved his father more than he had ever loved him. He felt that his father had carried him through a mighty test, had revealed to him a great secret which would be the key to his life forever.

"I reckon," he said. "I reckon."

Jesse's father took him by the hand and, with his mother a little behind them, talking and laughing with the other women, they walked through the crowd, across the clearing. The black body was on the ground, the chain which had held it was being rolled up by one of his father's friends. Whatever the fire had left undone, the hands and the knives and the stones of the people had accomplished. The head was caved in, one eye was torn out, one ear was hanging. But one had to look carefully to realize this, for it was, now, merely, a black charred object on the black, charred ground. He lay spreadeagled with what had been a wound between what had been his legs.

"They going to leave him here, then?" Jesse whispered.

"Yeah," said his father, "they'll come and get him by and by. I reckon we better get over there and get some of that food before it's all gone."

"I reckon," he muttered now to himself, "I reckon." Grace stirred and touched him on the thigh: the moonlight covered her like glory. Something bubbled up in him, his nature again returned to him. He thought of the boy in the cell; he thought of the man in the fire; he thought of the knife and grabbed himself and stroked himself and a terrible sound, something between a high laugh and a howl, came out of him and dragged his sleeping wife up on one elbow. She stared at him in a moonlight which had now grown cold as ice. He thought of the morning and grabbed her, laughing and crying, crying and laughing, and he whispered, as he stroked her, as he took her, "Come on, sugar, I'm going to do you like a nigger, just like a nigger, come on, sugar, and love me just like you'd love a nigger." He thought of the morning as he labored and she moaned, thought of morning as he labored harder than he ever had before, and before his labors had ended, he heard the first cock crow and the dogs begin to bark, and the sound of tires on the gravel road.

1965

FLANNERY O'CONNOR
1925–1964

Flannery O'Connor, one of the twentieth century's finest short story writers, was born in Savannah; lived with her mother in Milledgeville, Georgia, for much of her life; and died before her fortieth birthday—a victim like her father of disseminated lupus. She was stricken with this incurable disease in 1950 while at work on her first novel; injections of a cortisone derivative arrested it, but the cortisone weakened her bones to the extent that from 1955 on she could get around only on crutches. She was able to write, travel, and lecture until 1964, when the lupus reactivated itself and killed her. A

Roman Catholic throughout her life, she is quoted as having remarked, apropos of a trip to Lourdes, "I had the best-looking crutches in Europe." This remark suggests the kind of hair-raising jokes that centrally inform her writing as well as a refusal to indulge in self-pity over her fate.

She published two novels, *Wise Blood* (1952) and *The Violent Bear It Away* (1960), both weighty with symbolic and religious concerns and ingeniously contrived in the black-humored manner of Nathanael West, her American predecessor in this mode. But her really memorable creations of characters and actions take place in the stories, which are extremely funny, sometimes unbearably so, and finally we may wonder just what we are laughing at. Upon consideration the jokes appear dreadful, as with Manley Pointer's treatment of Joy Hopewell's artificial leg in "Good Country People" or Mr. Shiftlet's of his bride in "The Life You Save May Be Your Own."

Another American "regionalist," the poet Robert Frost, whose work contains its share of dreadful jokes, once confessed to being more interested in people's speech than in the people themselves. A typical Flannery O'Connor story consists at its most vital level in people talking, clucking their endless reiterations of clichés about life, death, and the universe. These clichés are captured with beautiful accuracy by an artist who had spent her life listening to them, lovingly and maliciously keeping track until she could put them to use. Early in her life she hoped to be a cartoonist, and there is cartoonlike mastery in her vivid renderings of character through speech and other gesture. Critics have called her a maker of grotesques, a label that like other ones—regionalist, southern lady, or Roman Catholic novelist—might have annoyed if it didn't obviously amuse her too. She once remarked tartly that "anything that comes out of the South is going to be called grotesque by the Northern reader, unless it is grotesque, in which case it is going to be called realistic."

Of course, this capacity for mockery, along with a facility in portraying perverse behavior, may work against other demands we make of the fiction writer, and O'Connor seldom suggests that her characters have inner lives that are imaginable, let alone worth respect. Instead she emphasizes her sharp eye and her ability to tell a tale and keep it moving inevitably toward completion. These completions are usually violent, occurring when the character—in many cases a woman—must confront an experience that she cannot handle by her old trustworthy language and habit-hardened responses. O'Connor's art lies partly in making it impossible for us merely to scorn the banalities of expression and behavior by which these people get through their lives. However dark the comedy, it keeps in touch with the things of this world, even when some force from another world threatens to annihilate the embattled protagonist. And although the stories are filled with religious allusions and parodies, they do not try to inculcate a doctrine. One of her best ones is titled "Revelation," but we generally finish an O'Connor story with no simple, unambiguous sense of what has been revealed. Instead we trust the tale's internal fun and richness reveal what it has to reveal. We can agree also, in sadness, with the critic Irving Howe's conclusion to his review of her posthumous collection of stories that it is intolerable for such a writer to have died at the age of thirty-nine.

The texts is from *A Good Man Is Hard to Find* (1955).

Good Country People

Besides the neutral expression that she wore when she was alone, Mrs. Freeman had two others, forward and reverse, that she used for all her human dealings. Her forward expression was steady and driving like the advance of a heavy truck. Her eyes never swerved to left or right but turned as the story turned as if they followed a yellow line down the center of it. She seldom used the other expression because it was not often necessary for her to retract a statement, but when she did, her face came to a complete stop, there was an almost imperceptible movement of her black eyes, during which they seemed to be receding, and then the observer would see that Mrs. Freeman, though she might stand there as real as several grain sacks thrown on top of each other, was no longer there in spirit. As for getting anything across to her when this was the case, Mrs. Hopewell had given it up. She might talk her head off. Mrs. Freeman could never be brought to admit herself wrong on any point. She would stand there and if she could be brought to say anything, it was something like, "Well, I wouldn't of said it was and I wouldn't of said it wasn't," or letting her gaze range over the top kitchen shelf where there was an assortment of dusty bottles, she might remark, "I see you ain't ate many of them figs you put up last summer."

They carried on their important business in the kitchen at breakfast. Every morning Mrs. Hopewell got up at seven o'clock and lit her gas heater and Joy's. Joy was her daughter, a large blonde girl who had an artificial leg. Mrs. Hopewell thought of her as a child though she was thirty-two years old and highly educated. Joy would get up while her mother was eating and lumber into the bathroom and slam the door, and before long, Mrs. Freeman would arrive at the back door. Joy would hear her mother call, "Come on in," and then they would talk for a while in low voices that were indistinguishable in the bathroom. By the time Joy came in, they had usually finished the weather report and were on one or the other of Mrs. Freeman's daughters, Glynese or Carramae, Joy called them Glycerin and Caramel. Glynese, a redhead, was eighteen and had many admirers; Carramae, a blonde, was only fifteen but already married and pregnant. She could not keep anything on her stomach. Every morning Mrs. Freeman told Mrs. Hopewell how many times she had vomited since the last report.

Mrs. Hopewell liked to tell people that Glynese and Carramae were two of the finest girls she knew and that Mrs. Freeman was a *lady* and that she was never ashamed to take her anywhere or introduce her to anybody they might meet. Then she would tell how she had happened to hire the Freemans in the first place and how they were a godsend to her and how she had had them four years. The reason for her keeping them so long was that they were not trash. They were good country people. She had telephoned the man whose name they had given as a reference and he had told her that Mr. Freeman was a good farmer but that his wife was the nosiest woman ever to walk the earth. "She's got to be into everything," the man said. "If she don't get there before the dust settles, you can bet she's dead, that's all. She'll want to know all your business. I can stand him real good," he had said, "but me nor my wife neither could have stood that woman one more minute on this place." That had put Mrs. Hopewell off for a few days.

She had hired them in the end because there were no other applicants but she had made up her mind beforehand exactly how she would handle the woman. Since she was the type who had to be into everything, then, Mrs. Hopewell had decided, she would not only let her be into everything, she would *see to it* that she was into everything—she would give her the responsibility of everything, she would put her in charge. Mrs. Hopewell had no bad qualities of her own but she was able to use other people's in such a constructive way that she never felt the lack. She had hired the Freemans and she had kept them four years.

Nothing is perfect. This was one of Mrs. Hopewell's favorite sayings.

Another was: that is life! And still another, the most important, was: well, other people have their opinions too. She would make these statements, usually at the table, in a tone of gentle insistence as if no one held them but her, and the large hulking Joy, whose constant outrage had obliterated every expression from her face, would stare just a little to the side of her, her eyes icy blue, with the look of someone who has achieved blindness by an act of will and means to keep it.

When Mrs. Hopewell said to Mrs. Freeman that life was like that, Mrs. Freeman would say, "I always said so myself." Nothing had been arrived at by anyone that had not first been arrived at by her. She was quicker than Mr. Freeman. When Mrs. Hopewell said to her after they had been on the place a while, "You know, you're the wheel behind the wheel," and winked, Mrs. Freeman had said, "I know it. I've always been quick. It's some that are quicker than others."

"Everybody is different," Mrs. Hopewell said.

"Yes, most people is," Mrs. Freeman said.

"It takes all kinds to make the world."

"I always said it did myself."

The girl was used to this kind of dialogue for breakfast and more of it for dinner; sometimes they had it for supper too. When they had no guest they ate in the kitchen because that was easier. Mrs. Freeman always managed to arrive at some point during the meal and to watch them finish it. She would stand in the doorway if it were summer but in the winter she would stand with one elbow on top of the refrigerator and look down on them, or she would stand by the gas heater, lifting the back of her skirt slightly. Occasionally she would stand against the wall and roll her head from side to side. At no time was she in any hurry to leave. All this was very trying on Mrs. Hopewell but she was a woman of great patience. She realized that nothing is perfect and that in the Freemans she had good country people and that if, in this day and age, you get good country people, you had better hang onto them.

She had had plenty of experience with trash. Before the Freemans she had averaged one tenant family a year. The wives of these farmers were not the kind you would want to be around you for very long. Mrs. Hopewell, who had divorced her husband long ago, needed someone to walk over the fields with her; and when Joy had to be impressed for these services, her remarks were usually so ugly and her face so glum that Mrs. Hopewell would say, "If you can't come pleasantly, I don't want you at all," to which the girl, standing square and rigid-shouldered with her neck thrust slightly forward, would reply, "If you want me, here I am—LIKE I AM."

Mrs. Hopewell excused this attitude because of the leg (which had been shot off in a hunting accident when Joy was ten). It was hard for Mrs. Hopewell to realize that her child was thirty-two now and that for more than twenty years she had had only one leg. She thought of her still as a child because it tore her heart to think instead of the poor stout girl in her thirties who had never danced a step or had any *normal* good times. Her name was really Joy but as soon as she was twenty-one and away from home, she had had it legally changed. Mrs. Hopewell was certain that she had thought and thought until she had hit upon the ugliest name in any language. Then she had gone and had the beautiful name, Joy, changed without telling her mother until after she had done it. Her legal name was Hulga.

When Mrs. Hopewell thought the name, Hulga, she thought of the broad blank hull of a battleship. She would not use it. She continued to call her Joy to which the girl responded but in a purely mechanical way.

Hulga had learned to tolerate Mrs. Freeman who saved her from taking walks with her mother. Even Glynese and Carramae were useful when they occupied attention that might otherwise have been directed at her. At first she had thought she could not stand Mrs. Freeman for she had found that it was not possible to be rude to her. Mrs. Freeman would take on strange resentments and for days together she would be sullen but the source of her displeasure was always obscure; a direct attack, a positive leer, blatant ugliness to her face—these never touched her. And without warning one day, she began calling her Hulga.

She did not call her that in front of Mrs. Hopewell who would have been incensed but when she and the girl happened to be out of the house together, she would say something and add the name Hulga to the end of it, and the big spectacled Joy-Hulga would scowl and redden as if her privacy had been intruded upon. She considered the name her personal affair. She had arrived at it first purely on the basis of its ugly sound and then the full genius of its fitness had struck her. She had a vision of the name working like the ugly sweating Vulcan who stayed in the furnace and to whom, presumably, the goddess had to come when called.[1] She saw it as the name of her highest creative act. One of her major triumphs was that her mother had not been able to turn her dust into Joy, but the greater one was that she had been able to turn it herself into Hulga. However, Mrs. Freeman's relish for using the name only irritated her. It was as if Mrs. Freeman's beady steel-pointed eyes had penetrated far enough behind her face to reach some secret fact. Something about her seemed to fascinate Mrs. Freeman and then one day Hulga realized that it was the artificial leg. Mrs. Freeman had a special fondness for the details of secret infections, hidden deformities, assaults upon children. Of diseases, she preferred the lingering or incurable. Hulga had heard Mrs. Hopewell give her the details of the hunting accident, how the leg had been literally blasted off, how she had never lost consciousness. Mrs. Freeman could listen to it any time as if it had happened an hour ago.

When Hulga stumped into the kitchen in the morning (she could walk without making the awful noise but she made it—Mrs. Hopewell was certain—because it was ugly-sounding), she glanced at them and did not speak. Mrs. Hopewell would be in her red kimono with her hair tied around her head in rags. She would be sitting at the table, finishing her breakfast and Mrs. Freeman would be hanging by her elbow outward from the refrigerator, looking down at the table. Hulga always put her eggs on the stove to boil and then stood over them with her arms folded, and Mrs. Hopewell would look at her—a kind of indirect gaze divided between her and Mrs. Freeman—and would think that if she would only keep herself up a little, she wouldn't be so bad looking. There was nothing wrong with her face that a pleasant expression wouldn't help. Mrs. Hopewell said that people who looked on the bright side of things would be beautiful even if they were not.

Whenever she looked at Joy this way, she could not help but feel that it would have been better if the child had not taken the Ph.D. It had certainly

---

1. Vulcan was the Greek god of fire, whom Venus, goddess of love, "presumably" obeyed as her consort.

not brought her out any and now that she had it, there was no more excuse for her to go to school again. Mrs. Hopewell thought it was nice for girls to go to school to have a good time but Joy had "gone through." Anyhow, she would not have been strong enough to go again. The doctors had told Mrs. Hopewell that with the best of care, Joy might see forty-five. She had a weak heart. Joy had made it plain that if it had not been for this condition, she would be far from these red hills and good country people. She would be in a university lecturing to people who knew what she was talking about. And Mrs. Hopewell could very well picture her there, looking like a scarecrow and lecturing to more of the same. Here she went about all day in a six-year-old skirt and a yellow sweat shirt with a faded cowboy on a horse embossed on it. She thought this was funny; Mrs. Hopewell thought it was idiotic and showed simply that she was still a child. She was brilliant but she didn't have a grain of sense. It seemed to Mrs. Hopewell that every year she grew less like other people and more like herself—bloated, rude, and squint-eyed. And she said such strange things! To her own mother she had said—without warning, without excuse, standing up in the middle of a meal with her face purple and her mouth half full—"Woman! do you ever look inside? Do you ever look inside and see what you are *not*? God!" she had cried sinking down again and staring at her plate, "Malebranche[2] was right: we are not our own light. We are not our own light!" Mrs. Hopewell had no idea to this day what brought that on. She had only made the remark, hoping Joy would take it in, that a smile never hurt anyone.

The girl had taken the Ph.D. in philosophy and this left Mrs. Hopewell at a complete loss. You could say, "My daughter is a nurse," or "My daughter is a school teacher," or even, "My daughter is a chemical engineer." You could not say, "My daughter is a philosopher." That was something that had ended with the Greeks and Romans. All day Joy sat on her neck in a deep chair, reading. Sometimes she went for walks but she didn't like dogs or cats or birds or flowers or nature or nice young men. She looked at nice young men as if she could smell their stupidity.

One day Mrs. Hopewell had picked up one of the books the girl had just put down and opening it at random, she read, "Science, on the other hand, has to assert its soberness and seriousness afresh and declare that it is concerned solely with what-is. Nothing—how can it be for science anything but a horror and a phantasm? If science is right, then one thing stands firm: science wishes to know nothing of nothing. Such is after all the strictly scientific approach to Nothing. We know it by wishing to know nothing of Nothing." These words had been underlined with a blue pencil and they worked on Mrs. Hopewell like some evil incantation in gibberish. She shut the book quickly and went out of the room as if she were having a chill.

This morning when the girl came in, Mrs. Freeman was on Carramae. "She thrown up four times after supper," she said, "and was up twict in the night after three o'clock. Yesterday she didn't do nothing but ramble in the bureau drawer. All she did. Stand up there and see what she could run up on."

"She's got to eat," Mrs. Hopewell muttered, sipping her coffee, while she watched Joy's back at the stove. She was wondering what the child had said to the Bible salesman. She could not imagine what kind of a conversation she could possibly have had with him.

2. Nicolas Malebranche (1638–1715), French philosopher.

He was a tall gaunt hatless youth who had called yesterday to sell them a
Bible. He had appeared at the door, carrying a large black suitcase that
weighted him so heavily on one side that he had to brace himself against the
door facing. He seemed on the point of collapse but he said in a cheerful
voice, "Good morning, Mrs. Cedars!" and set the suitcase down on the mat.
He was not a bad-looking young man though he had on a bright blue suit and
yellow socks that were not pulled up far enough. He had prominent face
bones and a streak of sticky-looking brown hair falling across his forehead.

"I'm Mrs. Hopewell," she said.

"Oh!" he said, pretending to look puzzled but with his eyes sparkling, "I saw
it said 'The Cedars' on the mailbox so I thought you was Mrs. Cedars!" and
he burst out in a pleasant laugh. He picked up the satchel and under cover
of a pant, he fell forward into her hall. It was rather as if the suitcase had
moved first, jerking him after it. "Mrs. Hopewell!" he said and grabbed her
hand. "I hope you are well!" and he laughed again and then all at once his face
sobered completely. He paused and gave her a straight earnest look and said,
"Lady, I've come to speak of serious things."

"Well, come in," she muttered, none too pleased because her dinner was
almost ready. He came into the parlor and sat down on the edge of a straight
chair and put the suitcase between his feet and glanced around the room as
if he were sizing her up by it. Her silver gleamed on the two sideboards; she
decided he had never been in a room as elegant as this.

"Mrs. Hopewell," he began, using her name in a way that sounded almost
intimate, "I know you believe in Chrustian service."

"Well yes," she murmured.

"I know," he said and paused, looking very wise with his head cocked on
one side, "that you're a good woman. Friends have told me."

Mrs. Hopewell never liked to be taken for a fool. "What are you selling?"
she asked.

"Bibles," the young man said and his eye raced around the room before he
added, "I see you have no family Bible in your parlor, I see that is the one lack
you got!"

Mrs. Hopewell could not say, "My daughter is an atheist and won't let me
keep the Bible in the parlor." She said, stiffening slightly, "I keep my Bible by
my bedside." This was not the truth. It was in the attic somewhere.

"Lady," he said, "the word of God ought to be in the parlor."

"Well, I think that's a matter of taste," she began. "I think . . ."

"Lady," he said, "for a Chrustian, the word of God ought to be in every room
in the house besides in his heart. I know you're a Chrustian because I can see
it in every line of your face."

She stood up and said, "Well, young man, I don't want to buy a Bible and
I smell my dinner burning."

He didn't get up. He began to twist his hands and looking down at them,
he said softly, "Well lady, I'll tell you the truth—not many people want to buy
one nowadays and besides, I know I'm real simple. I don't know how to say a
thing but to say it. I'm just a country boy." He glanced up into her unfriendly
face. "People like you don't like to fool with country people like me!"

"Why!" she cried, "good country people are the salt of the earth! Besides,
we all have different ways of doing, it takes all kinds to make the world go
'round. That's life!"

"You said a mouthful," he said.

"Why, I think there aren't enough good country people in the world!" she said, stirred. "I think that's what's wrong with it!"

His face had brightened. "I didn't inraduce myself," he said. "I'm Manley Pointer from out in the country around Willohobie, not even from a place, just from near a place."

"You wait a minute," she said. "I have to see about my dinner." She went out to the kitchen and found Joy standing near the door where she had been listening.

"Get rid of the salt of the earth," she said, "and let's eat."

Mrs. Hopewell gave her a pained look and turned the heat down under the vegetables. "I can't be rude to anybody," she murmured and went back into the parlor.

He had opened the suitcase and was sitting with a Bible on each knee.

"You might as well put those up," she told him. "I don't want one."

"I appreciate your honesty," he said. "You don't see any more real honest people unless you go way out in the country."

"I know," she said, "real genuine folks!" Through the crack in the door she heard a groan.

"I guess a lot of boys come telling you they're working their way through college," he said, "but I'm not going to tell you that. Somehow," he said, "I don't want to go to college. I want to devote my life to Chrustian service. See," he said, lowering his voice, "I got this heart condition. I may not live long. When you know it's something wrong with you and you may not live long, well then, lady . . ." He paused, with his mouth open, and stared at her.

He and Joy had the same condition! She knew that her eyes were filling with tears but she collected herself quickly and murmured, "Won't you stay for dinner? We'd love to have you!" and was sorry the instant she heard herself say it.

"Yes mam," he said in an abashed voice, "I would sher love to do that!"

Joy had given him one look on being introduced to him and then throughout the meal had not glanced at him again. He had addressed several remarks to her, which she had pretended not to hear. Mrs. Hopewell could not understand deliberate rudeness, although she lived with it, and she felt she had always to overflow with hospitality to make up for Joy's lack of courtesy. She urged him to talk about himself and he did. He said he was the seventh child of twelve and that his father had been crushed under a tree when he himself was eight years old. He had been crushed very badly, in fact, almost cut in two and was practically not recognizable. His mother had got along the best she could by hard working and she had always seen that her children went to Sunday School and that they read the Bible every evening. He was now nineteen years old and he had been selling Bibles for four months. In that time he had sold seventy-seven Bibles and had the promise of two more sales. He wanted to become a missionary because he thought that was the way you could do most for people. "He who losest his life shall find it," he said simply and he was so sincere, so genuine and earnest that Mrs. Hopewell would not for the world have smiled. He prevented his peas from sliding onto the table by blocking them with a piece of bread which he later cleaned his plate with. She could see Joy observing sidewise how he handled his knife and fork and she saw too that every few minutes, the boy would dart a keen appraising glance at the girl as if he were trying to attract her attention.

After dinner Joy cleared the dishes off the table and disappeared and Mrs. Hopewell was left to talk with him. He told her again about his childhood and his father's accident and about various things that had happened to him. Every five minutes or so she would stifle a yawn. He sat for two hours until finally she told him she must go because she had an appointment in town. He packed his Bibles and thanked her and prepared to leave, but in the doorway he stopped and wrung her hand and said that not on any of his trips had he met a lady as nice as her and he asked if he could come again. She had said she would always be happy to see him.

Joy had been standing in the road, apparently looking at something in the distance, when he came down the steps toward her, bent to the side with his heavy valise. He stopped where she was standing and confronted her directly. Mrs. Hopewell could not hear what he said but she trembled to think what Joy would say to him. She could see that after a minute Joy said something and that then the boy began to speak again, making an excited gesture with his free hand. After a minute Joy said something else at which the boy began to speak once more. Then to her amazement, Mrs. Hopewell saw the two of them walk off together, toward the gate. Joy had walked all the way to the gate with him and Mrs. Hopewell could not imagine what they had said to each other, and she had not yet dared to ask.

Mrs. Freeman was insisting upon her attention. She had moved from the refrigerator to the heater so that Mrs. Hopewell had to turn and face her in order to seem to be listening. "Glynese gone out with Harvey Hill again last night," she said. "She had this sty."

"Hill," Mrs. Hopewell said absently, "is that the one who works in the garage?"

"Nome, he's the one that goes to chiropracter school," Mrs. Freeman said. "She had this sty. Been had it two days. So she says when he brought her in the other night he says, 'Lemme get rid of that sty for you,' and she says, 'How?' and he says, 'You just lay yourself down acrost the seat of that car and I'll show you.' So she done it and he popped her neck. Kept on a-popping it several times until she made him quit. This morning," Mrs. Freeman said, "she ain't got no sty. She ain't got no traces of a sty."

"I never heard of that before," Mrs. Hopewell said.

"He ast her to marry him before the Ordinary,"[3] Mrs. Freeman went on, "and she told him she wasn't going to be married in no *office*."

"Well, Glynese is a fine girl," Mrs. Hopewell said. "Glynese and Carramae are both fine girls."

"Carramae said when her and Lyman was married Lyman said it sure felt sacred to him. She said he said he wouldn't take five hundred dollars for being married by a preacher."

"How much would he take?" the girl asked from the stove.

"He said he wouldn't take five hundred dollars," Mrs. Freeman repeated.

"Well we all have work to do," Mrs. Hopewell said.

"Lyman said it just felt more sacred to him," Mrs. Freeman said. "The doctor wants Carramae to eat prunes. Says instead of medicine. Says them cramps is coming from pressure. You know where I think it is?"

---

3. Justice of the peace who performs the marriage ceremony in chambers rather than in public.

"She'll be better in a few weeks," Mrs. Hopewell said.

"In the tube," Mrs. Freeman said. "Else she wouldn't be as sick as she is."

Hulga had cracked her two eggs into a saucer and was bringing them to the table along with a cup of coffee that she had filled too full. She sat down carefully and began to eat, meaning to keep Mrs. Freeman there by questions if for any reason she showed an inclination to leave. She could perceive her mother's eye on her. The first round-about question would be about the Bible salesman and she did not wish to bring it on. "How did he pop her neck?" she asked.

Mrs. Freeman went into a description of how he had popped her neck. She said he owned a '55 Mercury but that Glynese said she would rather marry a man with only a '36 Plymouth who would be married by a preacher. The girl asked what if he had a '32 Plymouth and Mrs. Freeman said what Glynese had said was a '36 Plymouth.

Mrs. Hopewell said there were not many girls with Glynese's common sense. She said what she admired in those girls was their common sense. She said that reminded her that they had had a nice visitor yesterday, a young man selling Bibles. "Lord," she said, "he bored me to death but he was so sincere and genuine I couldn't be rude to him. He was just good country people, you know," she said, "—just the salt of the earth."

"I seen him walk up," Mrs. Freeman said, "and then later—I seen him walk off," and Hulga could feel the slight shift in her voice, the slight insinuation, that he had not walked off alone, had he? Her face remained expressionless but the color rose into her neck and she seemed to swallow it down with the next spoonful of egg. Mrs. Freeman was looking at her as if they had a secret together.

"Well, it takes all kinds of people to make the world go 'round," Mrs. Hopewell said. "It's very good we aren't all alike."

"Some people are more alike than others," Mrs. Freeman said.

Hulga got up and stumped, with about twice the noise that was necessary, into her room and locked the door. She was to meet the Bible salesman at ten o'clock at the gate. She had thought about it half the night. She had started thinking of it as a great joke and then she had begun to see profound implications in it. She had lain in bed imagining dialogues for them that were insane on the surface but that reached below to depths that no Bible salesman would be aware of. Their conversation yesterday had been of this kind.

He had stopped in front of her and had simply stood there. His face was bony and sweaty and bright, with a little pointed nose in the center of it, and his look was different from what it had been at the dinner table. He was gazing at her with open curiosity, with fascination, like a child watching a new fantastic animal at the zoo, and he was breathing as if he had run a great distance to reach her. His gaze seemed somehow familiar but she could not think where she had been regarded with it before. For almost a minute he didn't say anything. Then on what seemed an insuck of breath, he whispered, "You ever ate a chicken that was two days old?"

The girl looked at him stonily. He might have just put this question up for consideration at the meeting of a philosophical association. "Yes," she presently replied as if she had considered it from all angles.

"It must have been mighty small!" he said triumphantly and shook all over with little nervous giggles, getting very red in the face, and subsiding finally into his gaze of complete admiration, while the girl's expression remained exactly the same.

"How old are you?" he asked softly.

She waited some time before she answered. Then in a flat voice she said, "Seventeen."

His smiles came in succession like waves breaking on the surface of a little lake. "I see you got a wooden leg," he said. "I think you're brave. I think you're real sweet."

The girl stood blank and solid and silent.

"Walk to the gate with me," he said. "You're a brave sweet little thing and I liked you the minute I seen you walk in the door."

Hulga began to move forward.

"What's your name?" he asked, smiling down on the top of her head.

"Hulga," she said.

"Hulga," he murmured, "Hulga. Hulga. I never heard of anybody name Hulga before. You're shy, aren't you, Hulga?" he asked.

She nodded, watching his large red hand on the handle of the giant valise.

"I like girls that wear glasses," he said. "I think a lot. I'm not like these people that a serious thought don't ever enter their heads. It's because I may die."

"I may die too," she said suddenly and looked up at him. His eyes were very small and brown, glittering feverishly.

"Listen," he said, "don't you think some people was meant to meet on account of what all they got in common and all? Like they both think serious thoughts and all?" He shifted the valise to his other hand so that the hand nearest her was free. He caught hold of her elbow and shook it a little. "I don't work on Saturday," he said. "I like to walk in the woods and see what Mother Nature is wearing. O'er the hills and far away. Pic-nics and things. Couldn't we go on a pic-nic tomorrow? Say yes, Hulga," he said and gave her a dying look as if he felt his insides about to drop out of him. He had even seemed to sway slightly toward her.

During the night she had imagined that she seduced him. She imagined that the two of them walked on the place until they came to the storage barn beyond the two back fields and there, she imagined, that things came to such a pass that she very easily seduced him and that then, of course, she had to reckon with his remorse. True genius can get an idea across even to an inferior mind. She imagined that she took his remorse in hand and changed it into a deeper understanding of life. She took all his shame away and turned it into something useful.

She set off for the gate at exactly ten o'clock, escaping without drawing Mrs. Hopewell's attention. She didn't take anything to eat, forgetting that food is usually taken on a picnic. She wore a pair of slacks and a dirty white shirt, and as an afterthought, she had put some Vapex on the collar of it since she did not own any perfume. When she reached the gate no one was there.

She looked up and down the empty highway and had the furious feeling that she had been tricked, that he had only meant to make her walk to the gate after the idea of him. Then suddenly he stood up, very tall, from behind a bush on the opposite embankment. Smiling, he lifted his hat which was new and wide-brimmed. He had not worn it yesterday and she wondered if he had bought it for the occasion. It was toast-colored with a red and white band around it and was slightly too large for him. He stepped from behind the bush still carrying the black valise. He had on the same suit and the same yellow socks sucked down in his shoes from walking. He crossed the highway and said, "I knew you'd come!"

The girl wondered acidly how he had known this. She pointed to the valise and asked, "Why did you bring your Bibles?"

He took her elbow, smiling down on her as if he could not stop. "You can never tell when you'll need the word of God, Hulga," he said. She had a moment in which she doubted that this was actually happening and then they began to climb the embankment. They went down into the pasture toward the woods. The boy walked lightly by her side, bouncing on his toes. The valise did not seem to be heavy today; he even swung it. They crossed half the pasture without saying anything and then, putting his hand easily on the small of her back, he asked softly, "Where does your wooden leg join on?"

She turned an ugly red and glared at him and for an instant the boy looked abashed. "I didn't mean you no harm," he said. "I only meant you're so brave and all. I guess God takes care of you."

"No," she said, looking forward and walking fast, "I don't even believe in God."

At this he stopped and whistled. "No!" he exclaimed as if he were too astonished to say anything else.

She walked on and in a second he was bouncing at her side, fanning with his hat. "That's very unusual for a girl," he remarked, watching her out of the corner of his eye. When they reached the edge of the wood, he put his hand on her back again and drew her against him without a word and kissed her heavily.

The kiss, which had more pressure than feeling behind it, produced that extra surge of adrenalin in the girl that enables one to carry a packed trunk out of a burning house, but in her, the power went at once to the brain. Even before he released her, her mind, clear and detached and ironic anyway, was regarding him from a great distance, with amusement but with pity. She had never been kissed before and she was pleased to discover that it was an unexceptional experience and all a matter of the mind's control. Some people might enjoy drain water if they were told it was vodka. When the boy, looking expectant but uncertain, pushed her gently away, she turned and walked on, saying nothing as if such business, for her, were common enough.

He came along panting at her side, trying to help her when he saw a root that she might trip over. He caught and held back the long swaying blades of thorn vine until she had passed beyond them. She led the way and he came breathing heavily behind her. Then they came out on a sunlit hillside, sloping softly into another one a little smaller. Beyond, they could see the rusted top of the old barn where the extra hay was stored.

The hill was sprinkled with small pink weeds. "Then you ain't saved?" he asked suddenly, stopping.

The girl smiled. It was the first time she had smiled at him at all. "In my economy," she said, "I'm saved and you are damned but I told you I didn't believe in God."

Nothing seemed to destroy the boy's look of admiration. He gazed at her now as if the fantastic animal at the zoo had put its paw through the bars and given him a loving poke. She thought he looked as if he wanted to kiss her again and she walked on before he had the chance.

"Ain't there somewhere we can sit down sometime?" he murmured, his voice softening toward the end of the sentence.

"In that barn," she said.

They made for it rapidly as if it might slide away like a train. It was a large two-story barn, cool and dark inside. The boy pointed up the ladder that led into the loft and said, "It's too bad we can't go up there."

"Why can't we?" she asked.

"Yer leg," he said reverently.

The girl gave him a contemptuous look and putting both hands on the ladder, she climbed it while he stood below, apparently awestruck. She pulled herself expertly through the opening and then looked down at him and said, "Well, come on if you're coming," and he began to climb the ladder, awkwardly bringing the suitcase with him.

"We won't need the Bible," she observed.

"You never can tell," he said, panting. After he had got into the loft, he was a few seconds catching his breath. She had sat down in a pile of straw. A wide sheath of sunlight, filled with dust particles, slanted over her. She lay back against a bale, her face turned away, looking out the front opening of the barn where hay was thrown from a wagon into the loft. The two pink-speckled hillsides lay back against a dark ridge of woods. The sky was cloudless and cold blue. The boy dropped down by her side and put one arm under her and the other over her and began methodically kissing her face, making little noises like a fish. He did not remove his hat but it was pushed far enough back not to interfere. When her glasses got in his way, he took them off of her and slipped them into his pocket.

The girl at first did not return any of the kisses but presently she began to and after she had put several on his cheek, she reached his lips and remained there, kissing him again and again as if she were trying to draw all the breath out of him. His breath was clear and sweet like a child's and the kisses were sticky like a child's. He mumbled about loving her and about knowing when he first seen her that he loved her, but the mumbling was like the sleepy fretting of a child being put to sleep by his mother. Her mind, throughout this, never stopped or lost itself for a second to her feelings. "You ain't said you loved me none," he whispered finally, pulling back from her. "You got to say that."

She looked away from him off into the hollow sky and then down at a black ridge and then down farther into what appeared to be two green swelling lakes. She didn't realize he had taken her glasses but this landscape could not seem exceptional to her for she seldom paid any close attention to her surroundings.

"You got to say it," he repeated. "You got to say you love me."

She was always careful how she committed herself. "In a sense," she began, "if you use the word loosely, you might say that. But it's not a word I use. I don't have illusions. I'm one of those people who see through to nothing."

The boy was frowning. "You got to say it. I said it and you got to say it," he said.

The girl looked at him almost tenderly. "You poor baby," she murmured. "It's just as well you don't understand," and she pulled him by the neck, face-down against her. "We are all damned," she said, "but some of us have taken off our blindfolds and see that there's nothing to see. It's a kind of salvation."

The boy's astonished eyes looked blankly through the ends of her hair. "Okay," he almost whined, "but do you love me or don'tcher?"

"Yes," she said and added, "in a sense. But I must tell you something. There mustn't be anything dishonest between us." She lifted his head and looked him in the eye. "I am thirty years old," she said. "I have a number of degrees."

The boy's look was irritated but dogged. "I don't care," he said. "I don't care a thing about what all you done. I just want to know if you love me or don'tcher?" and he caught her to him and wildly planted her face with kisses until she said, "Yes, yes."

"Okay then," he said, letting her go. "Prove it."

She smiled, looking dreamily out on the shifty landscape. She had seduced him without even making up her mind to try. "How?" she asked, feeling that he should be delayed a little.

He leaned over and put his lips to her ear. "Show me where your wooden leg joins on," he whispered.

The girl uttered a sharp little cry and her face instantly drained of color. The obscenity of the suggestion was not what shocked her. As a child she had sometimes been subject to feelings of shame but education had removed the last traces of that as a good surgeon scrapes for cancer; she would no more have felt it over what he was asking than she would have believed in his Bible. But she was as sensitive about the artificial leg as a peacock about his tail. No one ever touched it but her. She took care of it as someone else would his soul, in private and almost with her own eyes turned away. "No," she said.

"I known it," he muttered, sitting up. "You're just playing me for a sucker."

"Oh no no!" she cried. "It joins on at the knee. Only at the knee. Why do you want to see it?"

The boy gave her a long penetrating look. "Because," he said, "it's what makes you different. You ain't like anybody else."

She sat staring at him. There was nothing about her face or her round freezing-blue eyes to indicate that this had moved her; but she felt as if her heart had stopped and left her mind to pump her blood. She decided that for the first time in her life she was face to face with real innocence. This boy, with an instinct that came from beyond wisdom, had touched the truth about her. When after a minute, she said in a hoarse high voice, "All right," it was like surrendering to him completely. It was like losing her own life and finding it again, miraculously, in his.

Very gently he began to roll the slack leg up. The artificial limb, in a white sock and brown flat shoe, was bound in a heavy material like canvas and ended in an ugly jointure where it was attached to the stump. The boy's face and his voice were entirely reverent as he uncovered it and said, "Now show me how to take it off and on."

She took it off for him and put it back on again and then he took it off himself, handling it as tenderly as if it were a real one. "See!" he said with a delighted child's face. "Now I can do it myself!"

"Put it back on," she said. She was thinking that she would run away with him and that every night he would take the leg off and every morning put it back on again. "Put it back on," she said.

"Not yet," he murmured, setting it on its foot out of her reach. "Leave it off for a while. You got me instead."

She gave a cry of alarm but he pushed her down and began to kiss her again. Without the leg she felt entirely dependent on him. Her brain seemed to have stopped thinking altogether and to be about some other function that it was not very good at. Different expressions raced back and forth over her face. Every now and then the boy, his eyes like two steel spikes, would glance behind him where the leg stood. Finally she pushed him off and said, "Put it back on me now."

"Wait," he said. He leaned the other way and pulled the valise toward him and opened it. It had a pale blue spotted lining and there were only two Bibles in it. He took one of these out and opened the cover of it. It was hollow and contained a pocket flask of whiskey, a pack of cards, and a small blue box with printing on it. He laid these out in front of her one at a time in an evenly-spaced row, like one presenting offerings at the shrine of a goddess. He put the blue box in her hand. THIS PRODUCT TO BE USED ONLY FOR THE PREVENTION OF DISEASE, she read, and dropped it. The boy was unscrewing the top of the flask. He stopped and pointed, with a smile, to the deck of cards. It was not an ordinary deck but one with an obscene picture on the back of each card. "Take a swig," he said, offering her the bottle first. He held it in front of her, but like one mesmerized, she did not move.

Her voice when she spoke had an almost pleading sound. "Aren't you," she murmured, "aren't you just good country people?"

The boy cocked his head. He looked as if he were just beginning to understand that she might be trying to insult him. "Yeah," he said, curling his lip slightly, "but it ain't held me back none. I'm as good as you any day in the week."

"Give me my leg," she said.

He pushed it farther away with his foot. "Come on now, let's begin to have us a good time," he said coaxingly. "We ain't got to know one another good yet."

"Give me my leg!" she screamed and tried to lunge for it but he pushed her down easily.

"What's the matter with you all of a sudden?" he asked, frowning as he screwed the top on the flask and put it quickly back inside the Bible. "You just a while ago said you didn't believe in nothing. I thought you was some girl!"

Her face was almost purple. "You're a Christian!" she hissed. "You're a fine Christian! You're just like them all—say one thing and do another. You're a perfect Christian, you're . . ."

The boy's mouth was set angrily. "I hope you don't think," he said in a lofty indignant tone, "that I believe in that crap! I may sell Bibles but I know which end is up and I wasn't born yesterday and I know where I'm going!"

"Give me my leg!" she screeched. He jumped up so quickly that she barely saw him sweep the cards and the blue box into the Bible and throw the Bible into the valise. She saw him grab the leg and then she saw it for an instant slanted forlornly across the inside of the suitcase with a Bible at either side of its opposite ends. He slammed the lid shut and snatched up the valise and swung it down the hole and then stepped through himself.

When all of him had passed but his head, he turned and regarded her with a look that no longer had any admiration in it. "I've gotten a lot of interesting things," he said. "One time I got a woman's glass eye this way. And you needn't to think you'll catch me because Pointer ain't really my name. I use a different name at every house I call at and don't stay nowhere long. And I'll tell you another thing, Hulga," he said, using the name as if he didn't think much of it, "you ain't so smart. I been believing in nothing every since I was born!" and then the toast-colored hat disappeared down the hole and the girl was left, sitting on the straw in the dusty sunlight. When she turned her churning face toward the opening, she saw his blue figure struggling successfully over the green speckled lake.

Mrs. Hopewell and Mrs. Freeman, who were in the back pasture, digging up onions, saw him emerge a little later from the woods and head across the meadow toward the highway. "Why, that looks like that nice dull young man that tried to sell me a Bible yesterday," Mrs. Hopewell said, squinting. "He must have been selling them to the Negroes back in there. He was so simple," she said, "but I guess the world would be better off if we were all that simple."

Mrs. Freeman's gaze drove forward and just touched him before he disappeared under the hill. Then she returned her attention to the evil-smelling onion shoot she was lifting from the ground. "Some can't be that simple," she said. "I know I never could."

1955

A. R. AMMONS
1926–2001

A. R. Ammons wrote that he "was born big and jaundiced (and ugly) on February 18, 1926, in a farmhouse 4 miles southwest of Whiteville, North Carolina, and 2 miles northwest of New Hope Elementary School and New Hope Baptist Church." It was characteristic of Ammons to be laconic, self-deprecating, unfailingly local, and unfailingly exact. He belonged to the homemade strain of American writers rather than the Europeanized or cosmopolitan breed. His poems are filled with the landscapes in which he lived: North Carolina, the southern coast of New Jersey, and the surroundings of Ithaca, New York, where he was a member of the English department of Cornell University.

Ammons's career did not start out with a traditional literary education. At Wake Forest College in North Carolina he studied mostly science, especially biology and chemistry, and that scientific training strongly colored his poems. In 1951–52, after working briefly as a high school principal in North Carolina, he studied English literature for three semesters at the University of California at Berkeley. When he returned from Berkeley he spent twelve years as an executive for a biological-glass manufacturer in New Jersey.

In 1955, his thirtieth year, Ammons published his first book of poems, *Ommateum*. The title refers to the compound structure of an insect's eye and foreshadows a twofold impulse in Ammons's work. On one hand he is involved in the minute observation of natural phenomena; on the other hand he is frustrated by the physical limitations analogous to those of the insects' vision. We see the world as insects do, in small portions and in impulses that take in but do not totally resolve the many images we receive. "Overall is beyond me," Ammons says in "Corsons Inlet," in which the shifting details of shoreline and dunes represent a severe challenge to the poet-observer. There are no straight lines. The contours differ every day, every hour, and they teach the poet the endless adjustments he must make to nature's fluidity.

"A poem is a walk," Ammons said (his essay of that title is excerpted in the "Post-modern Manifestos" cluster of this anthology). His work is characterized by the motion he found everywhere in nature, a motion answered by his mental activity. Both nearsighted and farsighted, he looks closely at vegetation, small animals, the minute shifts of wind and weather and light, yet over and over again seems drawn to the American Transcendentalist Ralph Waldo Emerson's visionary aspirations for poetry. "Poetry," Emerson remarked, "was all written before time was, and whenever we are so finely organized that we can penetrate into that region where the air is music, we hear those primal warnings and attempt to write them down." Much of Ammons's poetry tests this promise to see if it yields a glimpse of supernatural order.

The self in Ammons's poems is a far more modest presence than in the work of many other American writers. Sometimes he is a "surrendered self among unwelcoming forms" (as he writes in the conclusion of "Gravelly Run"); in many other poems he is at home in a universe, both human and natural, whose variety delights him. He is that rare thing, a contemporary poet of praise, one who says "I can find nothing lowly / in the universe" ("Still") and convinces us he speaks the truth.

Ammons began his career writing short lyrics, almost journal entries in an unending career of observation. But the laconic notations—of a landslide, a shift in the shoreline from one day to the next—often bore abstract titles ("Clarity," "Saliences") as if to suggest the connections he felt between concrete experience and speculative thought. Ammons often experimented with poetic form in his effort to make his verse responsive to the engaging but evasive particularity of natural process. This formal inventiveness is part of his work's appeal. "Stop on any word and language gives way: / the blades of reason, unlightened by motion, sink in," he remarks in his "Essay on Poetics." To create *Tape for the Turn of the Year* (1965) he typed a book-length day-to-day verse diary along an adding-machine tape. The poem ended when the tape did. This was his first and most flamboyant attempt to turn his verse into something beyond mere gatherings. He then discovered that the long poem was the form best adapted to his continuing dialogue between the specific and the general. The appearance in 1993 of *Garbage*, a National Book Award winner, confirmed Ammons's gift for creating a book-length, immensely readable, moving, and funny poem, structured around a recurring set of images and ideas but full of digressions.

Ammons tended to use the colon—what one critic calls "the most democratic punctuation," suggesting as it does equivalence on both sides. Used in place of the period, it keeps a line from coming to a halt or stopping the flow in which the mind feverishly suggests analogies among its minutely perceived experiences. Many notable examples of Ammons's extended forms are gathered in *The Selected Longer Poems* (1980), although that book does not include his remarkable *Sphere: The Form of a Motion* (1974). A book-length poem with no full stops, 155 sections of four tercets each, it aspires to be what Ammons's predecessor Wallace Stevens called "the poem of the act of the mind." The only unity in *Sphere* is the mind's power to make analogies between the world's constant "diversifications." Ammons was committed to the provisional, the self-revising, and this commitment kept his poetry fresh over a long career. Writing of his sense of the world in "The Dwelling," from *Sumerian Vistas* (1987), Ammons says, "here the plainnest / majesty gave us what it could." The same might be said of his wonderfully generous and witty poems, which constitute a distinctive and invaluable legacy for American poetry.

So I Said I Am Ezra

So I said I am Ezra
and the wind whipped my throat
gaming for the sounds of my voice

I listened to the wind
go over my head and up into the night   5
Turning to the sea I said
      I am Ezra
but there were no echoes from the waves
The words were swallowed up
    in the voice of the surf   10
or leaping over the swells
lost themselves oceanward
    Over the bleached and broken fields
I moved my feet and turning from the wind
    that ripped sheets of sand   15
    from the beach and threw them
    like seamists across the dunes
swayed as if the wind were taking me away
and said
      I am Ezra   20
As a word too much repeated
falls out of being
so I Ezra went out into the night
like a drift of sand
and splashed among the windy oats   25
that clutch the dunes
of unremembered seas

                         1955

Corsons Inlet

I went for a walk over the dunes again this morning
to the sea,
then turned right along
    the surf
                rounded a naked headland   5
                and returned

   along the inlet shore:

it was muggy sunny, the wind from the sea steady and high,
crisp in the running sand,
    some breakthroughs of sun   10
   but after a bit

continuous overcast:

the walk liberating, I was released from forms,
from the perpendiculars,
    straight lines, blocks, boxes, binds   15
of thought
into the hues, shadings, rises, flowing bends and blends
    of sight:

I allow myself eddies of meaning:
yield to a direction of significance   20
running
like a stream through the geography of my work:
    you can find
in my sayings
                swerves of action   25
        like the inlet's cutting edge:
      there are dunes of motion,
organizations of grass, white sandy paths of remembrance
in the overall wandering of mirroring mind:

but Overall is beyond me: is the sum of these events   30
I cannot draw, the ledger I cannot keep, the accounting
beyond the account:

in nature there are few sharp lines: there are areas of
primrose
        more or less dispersed;   35
disorderly orders of bayberry; between the rows
of dunes,
irregular swamps of reeds,
though not reeds alone, but grass, bayberry, yarrow, all . . .
predominantly reeds: 40

I have reached no conclusions, have erected no boundaries,
shutting out and shutting in, separating inside
        from outside: I have
        drawn no lines:
        as   45

manifold events of sand
change the dune's shape that will not be the same shape
tomorrow,

so I am willing to go along, to accept
the becoming
thought, to stake off no beginnings or ends, establish   50
        no walls:

by transitions the land falls from grassy dunes to creek
to undercreek: but there are no lines, though
        change in that transition is clear
        as any sharpness: but "sharpness" spread out,   55
allowed to occur over a wider range
than mental lines can keep:

the moon was full last night: today, low tide was low:
black shoals of mussels exposed to the risk
of air   60
and, earlier, of sun,
waved in and out with the waterline, waterline inexact,

caught always in the event of change:
        a young mottled gull stood free on the shoals   65
        and ate
to vomiting: another gull, squawking possession, cracked a crab,
picked out the entrails, swallowed the soft-shelled legs, a ruddy
turnstone[1] running in to snatch leftover bits:

risk is full: every living thing in   70
siege: the demand is life, to keep life: the small
white blacklegged egret, how beautiful, quietly stalks and spears
        the shallows, darts to shore
                to stab—what? I couldn't
        see against the black mudflats—a frightened   75
        fiddler crab?

        the news to my left over the dunes and
reeds and bayberry clumps was
        fall: thousands of tree swallows
        gathering for flight: 80
        an order held
        in constant change: a congregation
rich with entropy: nevertheless, separable, noticeable
        as one event,
                not chaos: preparations for   85
flight from winter,
cheet, cheet, cheet, cheet, wings rifling the green clumps,
beaks
at the bayberries
        a perception full of wind, flight, curve,   90
        sound:
        the possibility of rule as the sum of rulelessness:
the "field" of action
with moving, incalculable center:

in the smaller view, order tight with shape: 95
blue tiny flowers on a leafless weed: carapace of crab:
snail shell:
        pulsations of order
        in the bellies of minnows: orders swallowed,
broken down, transferred through membranes   100
to strengthen larger orders: but in the large view, no
lines or changeless shapes: the working in and out, together
        and against, of millions of events: this,
            so that I make
            no form of   105
            formlessness:

orders as summaries, as outcomes of actions override
or in some way result, not predictably (seeing me gain
the top of a dune,

---

1. A ploverlike migratory bird.

the swallows
could take flight—some other fields of bayberry
    could enter fall
      berryless) and there is serenity: 110

      no arranged terror: no forcing of image, plan,
or thought:
no propaganda, no humbling of reality to precept: 115

terror pervades but is not arranged, all possibilities
of escape open: no route shut, except in
    the sudden loss of all routes:

      I see narrow orders, limited tightness, but will   120
not run to that easy victory:
    still around the looser, wider forces work:
    I will try
    to fasten into order enlarging grasps of disorder, widening
scope, but enjoying the freedom that   125
Scope eludes my grasp, that there is no finality of vision,
that I have perceived nothing completely,
    that tomorrow a new walk is a new walk.

                                                1965

Easter Morning

    I have a life that did not become,
    that turned aside and stopped,
    astonished:
    I hold it in me like a pregnancy or
    as on my lap a child   5
    not to grow or grow old but dwell on

    it is to his grave I most
    frequently return and return
    to ask what is wrong, what was
    wrong, to see it all by   10
    the light of a different necessity
    but the grave will not heal
    and the child,
    stirring, must share my grave
    with me, an old man having   15
    gotten by on what was left

    when I go back to my home country in these
    fresh far-away days, it's convenient to visit
    everybody, aunts and uncles, those who used to say,
    look how he's shooting up, and the   20
    trinket aunts who always had a little

something in their pocketbooks, cinnamon bark
or a penny or nickel, and uncles who
were the rumored fathers of cousins
who whispered of them as of great, if   25
troubled, presences, and school
teachers, just about everybody older
(and some younger) collected in one place
waiting, particularly, but not for
me, mother and father there, too, and others   30
close, close as burrowing
under skin, all in the graveyard
assembled, done for, the world they
used to wield, have trouble and joy
in, gone   35

the child in me that could not become
was not ready for others to go,
to go on into change, blessings and
horrors, but stands there by the road
where the mishap occurred, crying out for   40
help, come and fix this or we
can't get by, but the great ones who
were to return, they could not or did
not hear and went on in a flurry and
now, I say in the graveyard, here   45
lies the flurry, now it can't come
back with help or helpful asides, now
we all buy the bitter
incompletions, pick up the knots of
horror, silently raving, and go on   50
crashing into empty ends not
completions, not rondures the fullness
has come into and spent itself from
I stand on the stump
of a child, whether myself   55
or my little brother who died, and
yell as far as I can, I cannot leave this place, for
for me it is the dearest and the worst,
it is life nearest to life which is
life lost: it is my place where   60
I must stand and fail,
calling attention with tears
to the branches not lofting
boughs into space, to the barren
air that holds the world that was my world   65

though the incompletions
(& completions) burn out
standing in the flash high-burn
momentary structure of ash, still it
is a picture-book, letter-perfect   70

Easter morning: I have been for a
walk: the wind is tranquil: the brook
works without flashing in an abundant
tranquility: the birds are lively with
voice: I saw something I had   75
never seen before: two great birds,
maybe eagles, blackwinged, whitenecked
and -headed, came from the south oaring
the great wings steadily; they went
directly over me, high up, and kept on   80
due north: but then one bird,
the one behind, veered a little to the
left and the other bird kept on seeming
not to notice for a minute: the first
began to circle as if looking for   85
something, coasting, resting its wings
on the down side of some of the circles:
the other bird came back and they both
circled, looking perhaps for a draft;
they turned a few more times, possibly   90
rising—at least, clearly resting—
then flew on falling into distance till
they broke across the local bush and
trees: it was a sight of bountiful
majesty and integrity: the having   95
patterns and routes, breaking
from them to explore other patterns or
better way to routes, and then the
return: a dance sacred as the sap in
the trees, permanent in its descriptions   100
as the ripples round the brook's
ripplestone: fresh as this particular
flood of burn breaking across us now
from the sun.

                                                                        1981

ALLEN GINSBERG
1926–1997

"Hold back the edges of your gowns, Ladies, we are going through hell." William Carlos Williams's introduction to Allen Ginsberg's *Howl* (1956) was probably the most
auspicious public welcome from one poet to another since, one hundred years before,
the American Transcendentalist Ralph Waldo Emerson had hailed the unknown Walt
Whitman in a letter that Whitman prefaced to the second edition of *Leaves of Grass*.
Howl combined apocalyptic criticism of the dull, prosperous Eisenhower years with

exuberant celebration of an emerging counterculture. It was the best-known and most widely circulated book of poems of its time, and with its appearance Ginsberg became part of the history of publicity as well as the history of poetry. *Howl* and Jack Kerouac's novel *On the Road* (1957) were the pocket Bibles of the generation whose name Kerouac had coined—"Beat," with its punning overtones of "beaten down" and "beatified."

Ginsberg was the son of Louis Ginsberg, a poet and schoolteacher in New Jersey, and of Naomi Ginsberg, a Russian émigré, whose madness and eventual death her son memorialized in "Kaddish" (1959). His official education took place at Columbia University, but for him as for Kerouac the presence of William Burroughs in New York was equally influential. Burroughs (1914–1997), later the author of *Naked Lunch* (1959), one of the most inventive experiments in American prose, was at that time a drug addict about to embark on an expatriate life in Mexico and Tangier. He helped Ginsberg discover modern writers: Kafka, Yeats, Céline, Rimbaud. Ginsberg responded to Burroughs's liberated kind of life, to his comic-apocalyptic view of American society, and to his bold literary use of autobiography, as when writing about his own experience with addicts and addiction in *Junkie,* whose chapters Ginsberg was reading in manuscript form in 1950.

Ginsberg's New York career has passed into mythology for a generation of poets and readers. In 1945, his sophomore year, he was expelled from Columbia: he had sketched some obscene drawings and phrases in the dust of his dormitory window to draw the attention of a neglectful cleaning woman to the grimy state of his room. Then, living periodically with Burroughs and Kerouac, he shipped out for short trips as a messman on merchant tankers and worked in addition as a welder, a night porter, and a dishwasher.

One summer, in a Harlem apartment, Ginsberg underwent what he always represented as the central conversion experience of his life. He had an "auditory vision" of the English poet William Blake reciting his poems: first "Ah! Sunflower," and then a few minutes later the same oracular voice intoning "The Sick Rose." It was "like hearing the doom of the whole universe, and at the same time the inevitable beauty of that doom." Ginsberg was convinced that the presence of "this big god over all . . . and that the whole purpose of being born was to wake up to Him."

Ginsberg eventually finished Columbia in 1948 with high grades but under a legal cloud. Herbert Huncke, a colorful but irresponsible addict friend, had been using Ginsberg's apartment as a storage depot for the goods he stole to support his drug habit. To avoid prosecution as an accomplice, Ginsberg had to plead insanity and spent eight months in the Columbia Psychiatric Institute.

After more odd jobs and a considerable success as a market researcher in San Francisco, Ginsberg left the straight, nine-to-five world for good. He was drawn to San Francisco, he said, by its "long honorable . . . tradition of Bohemian—Buddhist—Wobbly [the I.W.W., an early radical labor movement]—mystical—anarchist social involvement." In the years after 1954 he met San Francisco poets such as Robert Duncan, Kenneth Rexroth, Gary Snyder (who was studying Chinese and Japanese at Berkeley), and Lawrence Ferlinghetti, whose City Lights Bookshop became the publisher of *Howl*. The night Ginsberg read the new poem aloud at the Six Gallery has been called "the birth trauma of the Beat Generation."

The spontaneity of surface in *Howl* conceals but grows out of Ginsberg's care and self-consciousness about rhythm and meter. Under the influence of William Carlos Williams, who had befriended him in Paterson after he left the mental hospital, Ginsberg had started carrying around a notebook to record the rhythms of voices around him. Kerouac's *On the Road* gave him further examples of "frank talk" and, in addition, of an "oceanic" prose "sometimes as sublime as epic line." Under Kerouac's influence Ginsberg began the long tumbling lines that were to become his trademark. He carefully explained that all of *Howl and Other Poems* was an experiment in what could be done with the long line, the longer unit of breath that seemed natural for him. "My feeling is for a big long clanky statement," one that accommodates "not the way you would *say* it, a thought, but the way you would think it—i.e., we think rapidly, in visual images as well as words, and if each successive thought were transcribed in its con-fusion . . . you get a slightly different prosody than if you were talking slowly."

Ginsberg learned the long line as well from biblical rhetoric, from the eighteenth-century English poet Christopher Smart, and above all, from Whitman and Blake. His first book pays tribute to both these latter poets. "A Supermarket in California," with its movement from exclamations to sad questioning, is Ginsberg's melancholy reminder of what has become, after a century, of Whitman's vision of American plenty. In "Sunflower Sutra" he celebrates the battered nobility beneath our industrial "skin of grime." Ginsberg at his best gives a sense of doom and beauty, whether in the denunciatory impatient prophecies of *Howl* or in the catalog of suffering in "Kaddish." His disconnected phrases can accumulate as narrative shrieks or, at other moments, can build as a litany of praise.

By the end of the 1960s Ginsberg was widely known and widely traveled. He had conducted publicly his own pursuit of inner peace during a long stay with Buddhist instructors in India and at home served as a kind of guru for many young people dis-oriented by the Vietnam War. Ginsberg read his poetry and held "office hours" in uni-versities all over America, a presence at everything from "be-ins"—mass outdoor festivals of chanting, costumes, and music—to antiwar protests. He was a gentle and persuasive presence at hearings for many kinds of reform: revision of severe drug laws and laws against homosexuality. Ginsberg had lived for years with the poet Peter Orlovsky and wrote frankly about their relationship. His poems record his drug expe-riences as well, and "The Change," written in Japan in 1963, marks his decision to keep away from what he considered the nonhuman domination of drugs and to lay new stress on "living in and inhabiting the human form."

In "The Fall of America" (1972) Ginsberg turned to "epic," a poem including his-tory and registering the ups and downs of his travels across the United States. These "transit" poems sometimes seem like tape-recorded random lists of sights, sounds, and names, but at their best they give a sense of how far America has fallen, by measur-ing the provisional and changing world of nuclear America against the traces of nature still visible in our landscape and place-names. With Ginsberg's death, contemporary American poetry lost one of its most definitive and revolutionary figures. Happily, the poems endure.

Howl

for Carl Solomon[1]

I

I saw the best minds of my generation destroyed by madness, starving
    hysterical naked,
dragging themselves through the negro streets at dawn looking for an angry
    fix,

---

1. Ginsberg met Solomon (b. 1928) while both were patients in the Columbia Psychiatric Institute in 1949 and called him "an intuitive Bronx Dadaist and prose-poet." Many details in *Howl* come from the "apocryphal history" that Solomon told Gins-berg in 1949. In "More Mishaps" (1968) Solomon admits that these adventures were "compounded partly of truth, but for the most [of] raving self-justification, crypto-bohemian boasting . . . effemi-nate prancing and esoteric aphorisms."

angelheaded hipsters burning for the ancient heavenly connection[2] to the
    starry dynamo in the machinery of night,
who poverty and tatters and hollow-eyed and high sat up smoking in the
    supernatural darkness of cold-water flats floating across the tops of
    cities contemplating jazz,
who bared their brains to Heaven under the El and saw Mohammedan[3]
    angels staggering on tenement roofs illuminated,   5
who passed through universities with radiant cool eyes hallucinating
    Arkansas and Blake-light[4] tragedy among the scholars of war,
who were expelled from the academies for crazy & publishing obscene odes
    on the windows of the skull,
who cowered in unshaven rooms in underwear, burning their money in
    wastebaskets and listening to the Terror through the wall,
who got busted in their pubic beards returning through Laredo with a belt
    of marijuana for New York,
who ate fire in paint hotels or drank turpentine in Paradise Alley,[5] death, or
    purgatoried their torsos night after night   10
with dreams, with drugs, with waking nightmares, alcohol and cock and
    endless balls,
incomparable blind streets of shuddering cloud and lightning in the mind
    leaping toward poles of Canada & Paterson,[6] illuminating all the
    motionless world of Time between,
Peyote solidities of halls, backyard green tree cemetery dawns, wine
    drunkenness over the rooftops, storefront boroughs of teahead joyride
    neon blinking traffic light, sun and moon and tree vibrations in the
    roaring winter dusks of Brooklyn, ashcan rantings and kind king light
    of mind,
who chained themselves to subways for the endless ride from Battery to
    holy Bronx[7] on benzedrine until the noise of wheels and children
    brought them down shuddering mouth-wracked and battered bleak of
    brain all drained of brilliance in the drear light of Zoo,
who sank all night in submarine light of Bickford's floated out and sat
    through the stale beer afternoon in desolate Fugazzi's,[8] listening to the
    crack of doom on the hydrogen jukebox,   15
who talked continuously seventy hours from park to pad to bar to Bellevue[9]
    to museum to the Brooklyn Bridge,
a lost battalion of platonic conversationalists jumping down the stoops off
    fire escapes off windowsills off Empire State out of the moon,
yacketayakking screaming vomiting whispering facts and memories and
    anecdotes and eyeball kicks and shocks of hospitals and jails and wars,
whole intellects disgorged in total recall for seven days and nights with
    brilliant eyes, meat for the Synagogue cast on the pavement,

2. In one sense a person who can supply drugs.
3. An English term for a Muslim, commonly used in Western literature until the mid-twentieth century; now considered offensive by many Muslims because it implies that they worship the prophet Mohammed (or Muhammad) same way that Christians worship Christ. "The El": The elevated railway in New York City; also a Hebrew word for God.
4. Refers to Ginsberg's apocalyptic vision of the English poet William Blake (1757–1827).
5. A tenement courtyard in New York's East Village; setting of Kerouac's *The Subterraneans*

(1958).
6. Ginsberg's hometown; also the town celebrated by William Carlos Williams in his long poem *Paterson* (1946–58).
7. Opposite ends of a New York subway line; the Bronx Zoo was the northern terminus.
8. New York bar that was a hipster hangout in the 1950s and 1960s. "Bickford's": a line of restaurants and cafeterias in the New York area from the 1920s to the 1960s.
9. New York public hospital to which psychiatric patients may be committed.

who vanished into nowhere Zen New Jersey leaving a trail of ambiguous
    picture postcards of Atlantic City Hall,   20

suffering Eastern sweats and Tangerian bone-grindings and migraines of
    China[1] under junk-withdrawal in Newark's bleak furnished room,

who wandered around and around at midnight in the railroad yard
    wondering where to go, and went, leaving no broken hearts,

who lit cigarettes in boxcars boxcars boxcars racketing through snow
    toward lonesome farms in grandfather night,

who studied Plotinus Poe St. John of the Cross[2] telepathy and bop
    kaballah[3] because the cosmos instinctively vibrated at their feet in
    Kansas,

who loned it through the streets of Idaho seeking visionary indian angels
    who were visionary indian angels,   25

who thought they were only mad when Baltimore gleamed in supernatural
    ecstasy,

who jumped in limousines with the Chinaman of Oklahoma on the impulse
    of winter midnight streetlight smalltown rain,

who lounged hungry and lonesome through Houston seeking jazz or sex or
    soup, and followed the brilliant Spaniard to converse about America
    and Eternity, a hopeless task, and so took ship to Africa,

who disappeared into the volcanoes of Mexico leaving behind nothing but
    the shadow of dungarees and the lava and ash of poetry scattered in
    fireplace Chicago,

who reappeared on the West Coast investigating the FBI in beards and
    shorts with big pacifist eyes sexy in their dark skin passing out
    incomprehensible leaflets,   30

who burned cigarette holes in their arms protesting the narcotic tobacco
    haze of Capitalism,

who distributed Supercommunist pamphlets in Union Square weeping and
    undressing while the sirens of Los Alamos[4] wailed them down, and
    wailed down Wall,[5] and the Staten Island ferry also wailed,

who broke down crying in white gymnasiums naked and trembling before
    the machinery of other skeletons,

who bit detectives in the neck and shrieked with delight in policecars for
    committing no crime but their own wild cooking pederasty and
    intoxication,

who howled on their knees in the subway and were dragged off the roof
    waving genitals and manuscripts,   35

who let themselves be fucked in the ass by saintly motorcyclists, and
    screamed with joy,

who blew and were blown by those human seraphim, the sailors, caresses
    of Atlantic and Caribbean love,

who balled in the morning in the evenings in rosegardens and the grass of
    public parks and cemeteries scattering their semen freely to whomever
    come who may,

---

1. African and Asian sources of drugs.
2. Spanish visionary and poet (1542–1591), author of *The Dark Night of the Soul*. Plotinus (205–270), visionary Roman philosopher. Edgar Allan Poe (1809–1849), American poet and author of supernatural tales.
3. A mystical tradition of interpreting Hebrew scripture. "Bop": jazz style of the 1940s.
4. New Mexico center for the development of the atomic bomb. In New York in the 1930s Union Square was a gathering place for radical speakers.
5. Wall Street; but also alludes to the Wailing Wall, a place of public lamentation in Jerusalem.

who hiccupped endlessly trying to giggle but wound up with a sob behind a
partition in a Turkish Bath when the blonde & naked angel came to
pierce them with a sword,[6]

who lost their loveboys to the three old shrews of fate[7] the one eyed shrew
of the heterosexual dollar the one eyed shrew that winks out of the
womb and the one eyed shrew that does nothing but sit on her ass and
snip the intellectual golden threads of the craftsman's loom,   40

who copulated ecstatic and insatiate with a bottle of beer a sweetheart a
package of cigarettes a candle and fell off the bed, and continued
along the floor and down the hall and ended fainting on the wall with
a vision of ultimate cunt and come eluding the last gyzym of
consciousness,

who sweetened the snatches of a million girls trembling in the sunset, and
were red eyed in the morning but prepared to sweeten the snatch of
the sunrise, flashing buttocks under barns and naked in the lake,

who went out whoring through Colorado in myriad stolen nightcars, N.C.,[8]
secret hero of these poems, cocksman and Adonis of Denver—joy to
the memory of his innumerable lays of girls in empty lots & diner
backyards, moviehouses' rickety rows, on mountaintops in caves or
with gaunt waitresses in familiar roadside lonely petticoat upliftings &
especially secret gas-station solipsisms of johns, & hometown alleys
too,

who faded out in vast sordid movies, were shifted in dreams, woke on a
sudden Manhattan, and picked themselves up out of basements
hungover with heartless Tokay[9] and horrors of Third Avenue iron
dreams & stumbled to unemployment offices,

who walked all night with their shoes full of blood on the snowbank docks
waiting for a door in the East River to open to a room full of steamheat
and opium,   45

who created great suicidal dramas on the apartment cliff-banks of the
Hudson under the wartime blue floodlight of the moon & their heads
shall be crowned with laurel in oblivion,

who ate the lamb stew of the imagination or digested the crab at the muddy
bottom of the rivers of Bowery,[1]

who wept at the romance of the streets with their pushcarts full of onions
and bad music,

who sat in boxes breathing in the darkness under the bridge, and rose up to
build harpsichords in their lofts,

who coughed on the sixth floor of Harlem crowned with flame under the
tubercular sky surrounded by orange crates of theology,   50

who scribbled all night rocking and rolling over lofty incantations which in
the yellow morning were stanzas of gibberish,

who cooked rotten animals lung heart feet tail borsht & tortillas dreaming
of the pure vegetable kingdom,

who plunged themselves under meat trucks looking for an egg,

---

6. An allusion to *The Ecstasy of St. Teresa,* a sculpture by Lorenzo Bernini (1598–1680) based on St.
Teresa's (1515–1582) distinctly erotic description
of a religious vision.
7. In Greek mythology goddesses who determine a
mortal's life by spinning out a length of thread and
cutting it at the time of death.

8. Neal Cassady, hip companion of Jack Kerouac
and the original Dean Moriarty, one of the leading
figures in *On the Road.*
9. A naturally sweet wine made in Hungary.
1. Southern extension of Third Avenue in New
York City; traditional haunt of derelicts and alcoholics.

who threw their watches off the roof to cast their ballot for Eternity outside
of Time, & alarm clocks fell on their heads every day for the next
decade,

who cut their wrists three times successively unsuccessfully, gave up and
were forced to open antique stores where they thought they were
growing old and cried,   55

who were burned alive in their innocent flannel suits on Madison Avenue[2]
amid blasts of leaden verse & the tanked-up clatter of the iron
regiments of fashion & the nitroglycerine shrieks of the fairies of
advertising & the mustard gas of sinister intelligent editors, or were
run down by the drunken taxicabs of Absolute Reality,

who jumped off the Brooklyn Bridge this actually happened and walked
away unknown and forgotten into the ghostly daze of Chinatown soup
alleyways & firetrucks, not even one free beer,

who sang out of their windows in despair, fell out of the subway window,
jumped in the filthy Passaic,[3] leaped on negroes, cried all over the
street, danced on broken wineglasses barefoot smashed phonograph
records of nostalgic European 1930's German jazz finished the
whiskey and threw up groaning into the bloody toilet, moans in their
ears and the blast of colossal steamwhistles,

who barreled down the highways of the past journeying to each other's
hotrod-Golgotha[4] jail-solitude watch or Birmingham jazz incarnation,

who drove crosscountry seventytwo hours to find out if I had a vision or you
had a vision or he had a vision to find out Eternity,   60

who journeyed to Denver, who died in Denver, who came back to Denver &
waited in vain, who watched over Denver & brooded & loned in
Denver and finally went away to find out the Time, & now Denver is
lonesome for her heroes,

who fell on their knees in hopeless cathedrals praying for each other's
salvation and light and breasts, until the soul illuminated its hair for a
second,

who crashed through their minds in jail waiting for impossible criminals
with golden heads and the charm of reality in their hearts who sang
sweet blues to Alcatraz,

who retired to Mexico to cultivate a habit, or Rocky Mount to tender
Buddha or Tangiers to boys or Southern Pacific to the black
locomotive or Harvard to Narcissus to Woodlawn[5] to the daisychain or
grave,

who demanded sanity trials accusing the radio of hypnotism & were left
with their insanity & their hands & a hung jury,   65

who threw potato salad at CCNY lecturers on Dadaism[6] and subsequently
presented themselves on the granite steps of the madhouse with
shaven heads and harlequin speech of suicide, demanding
instantaneous lobotomy,

---

2. Center of New York advertising agencies.
3. River flowing past Paterson, New Jersey.
4. The place in ancient Judea where Jesus was
believed to have been crucified; also known as Calvary.
5. A cemetery in the Bronx. The Southern Pacific
is a railroad company. The references in this line

are to the lives of Kerouac, Cassidy, and William
Burroughs (an author and fellow Beat).
6. Artistic cult of absurdity (c. 1916–1920).
"CCNY": City College of New York. This and the
following incidents probably derived from the
"apocryphal history of my adventures" related by
Solomon to Ginsberg.

and who were given instead the concrete void of insulin metrasol electricity
　　hydrotherapy psychotherapy occupational therapy pingpong &
　　amnesia,
who in humorless protest overturned only one symbolic pingpong table,
　　resting briefly in catatonia,
returning years later truly bald except for a wig of blood, and tears and
　　fingers, to the visible madman doom of the wards of the madtowns of
　　the East,
Pilgrim State's Rockland's and Greystone's[7] foetid halls, bickering with the
　　echoes of the soul, rocking and rolling in the midnight solitude-bench
　　dolmen-realms of love, dream of life a nightmare, bodies turned to
　　stone as heavy as the moon,　　　　　　　　　　　　　　　70
with mother finally*******, and the last fantastic book flung out of the
　　tenement window, and the last door closed at 4 AM and the last
　　telephone slammed at the wall in reply and the last furnished room
　　emptied down to the last piece of mental furniture, a yellow paper
　　rose
　　twisted on a wire hanger in the closet, and even that imaginary,
　　nothing but a hopeful little bit of hallucination—
ah, Carl,[8] while you are not safe I am not safe, and now you're really in the
　　total animal soup of time—
and who therefore ran through the icy streets obsessed with a sudden flash
　　of the alchemy of the use of the ellipse the catalog the meter & the
　　vibrating plane,
who dreamt and made incarnate gaps in Time & Space through images
　　juxtaposed, and trapped the archangel of the soul between 2 visual
　　images and joined the elemental verbs and set the noun and dash of
　　consciousness together jumping with sensation of Pater Omnipotens
　　Aeterna Deus[9]
to recreate the syntax and measure of poor human prose and stand before
　　you speechless and intelligent and shaking with shame, rejected yet
　　confessing out the soul to conform to the rhythm of thought in his
　　naked and endless head,　　　　　　　　　　　　　　　75
the madman bum and angel beat in Time, unknown, yet putting down here
　　what might be left to say in time come after death,
and rose reincarnate in the ghostly clothes of jazz in the goldhorn shadow
　　of the band and blew the suffering of America's naked mind for love
　　into an eli eli lamma lamma sabacthani[1] saxophone cry that shivered
　　the cities down to the last radio
with the absolute heart of the poem of life butchered out of their own
　　bodies good to eat a thousand years.

---

7. Three psychiatric hospitals near New York. Solomon was institutionalized at Pilgrim State and Rockland; Ginsberg's mother, Naomi, was permanently institutionalized at Greystone after years of suffering hallucinations and paranoid attacks. She died there in 1956, the year after *Howl* was written.
8. Solomon.
9. All Powerful Father, Eternal God (Latin). An allusion to a phrase used by the French painter Paul Cézanne (1839–1906), in a 1904 letter describing the effects of nature. In an interview, Ginsberg compared his own method of sharply juxtaposed images with Cézanne's foreshortening of perspective in landscape painting.
1. Christ's last words on the Cross: My God, my God, why have you forsaken me? (Aramaic).

II

What sphinx of cement and aluminum bashed open their skulls and ate up
  their brains and imagination?
Moloch![2] Solitude! Filth! Ugliness! Ashcans and unobtainable dollars!
  Children screaming under the stairways! Boys sobbing in armies! Old
  men weeping in the parks!   80
Moloch! Moloch! Nightmare of Moloch! Moloch the loveless! Mental
  Moloch! Moloch the heavy judger of men!
Moloch the incomprehensible prison! Moloch the crossbone soulless
  jailhouse and Congress of sorrows! Moloch whose buildings are
  judgment! Moloch the vast stone of war! Moloch the stunned
  governments!
Moloch whose mind is pure machinery! Moloch whose blood is running
  money! Moloch whose fingers are ten armies! Moloch whose breast is
  a cannibal dynamo! Moloch whose ear is a smoking tomb!
Moloch whose eyes are a thousand blind windows! Moloch whose
  skyscrapers stand in the long streets like endless Jehovahs! Moloch
  whose factories dream and croak in the fog! Moloch whose
  smokestacks and antennae crown the cities!
Moloch whose love is endless oil and stone! Moloch whose soul is
  electricity and banks! Moloch whose poverty is the specter of genius!
  Moloch whose fate is a cloud of sexless hydrogen! Moloch whose
  name is the Mind!   85
Moloch in whom I sit lonely! Moloch in whom I dream Angels! Crazy in
  Moloch! Cocksucker in Moloch! Lacklove and manless in Moloch!
Moloch who entered my soul early! Moloch in whom I am a consciousness
  without a body! Moloch who frightened me out of my natural ecstasy!
  Moloch whom I abandon! Wake up in Moloch! Light streaming out of
  the sky!
Moloch! Moloch! Robot apartments! invisible suburbs! skeleton treasuries!
  blind capitals! demonic industries! spectral nations! invincible
  madhouses! granite cocks! monstrous bombs!
They broke their backs lifting Moloch to Heaven! Pavements, trees, radios,
  tons! lifting the city to Heaven which exists and is everywhere about us!
Visions! omens! hallucinations! miracles! ecstasies! gone down the
  American river!   90
Dreams! adorations! illuminations! religions! the whole boatload of
  sensitive bullshit!
Breakthroughs! over the river! flips and crucifixions! gone down the flood!
  Highs! Epiphanies! Despairs! Ten years' animal screams and suicides!
  Minds! New loves! Mad generation! down on the rocks of Time!
Real holy laughter in the river! They saw it all! the wild eyes! the holy yells!
  They bade farewell! They jumped off the roof! to solitude! waving!
  carrying flowers! Down to the river! into the street!

---

2. Ginsberg's own annotation in the facsimile edition of the poem reads: " 'Moloch': or Molech, the Canaanite fire god, whose worship was marked by parents' burning their children as proprietary sacrifice. 'And thou shalt not let any of thy seed pass through the fire to Molech' [Leviticus 18:21]."

III

Carl Solomon! I'm with you in Rockland
    where you're madder than I am   95
I'm with you in Rockland
    where you must feel very strange
I'm with you in Rockland
    where you imitate the shade of my mother
I'm with you in Rockland   100
    where you've murdered your twelve secretaries
I'm with you in Rockland
    where you laugh at this invisible humor
I'm with you in Rockland
    where we are great writers on the same dreadful typewriter   105
I'm with you in Rockland
    where your condition has become serious and is reported on the radio
I'm with you in Rockland
    where the faculties of the skull no longer admit the worms of the
        senses
I'm with you in Rockland   110
    where you drink the tea of the breasts of the spinsters of Utica[3]
I'm with you in Rockland
    where you pun on the bodies of your nurses the harpies of the Bronx
I'm with you in Rockland
    where you scream in a straightjacket that you're losing the game of
        the actual pingpong of the abyss   115
I'm with you in Rockland
    where you bang on the catatonic piano the soul is innocent and
        immortal it should never die ungodly in an armed madhouse
I'm with you in Rockland
    where fifty more shocks will never return your soul to its body again
        from its pilgrimage to a cross in the void
I'm with you in Rockland   120
    where you accuse your doctors of insanity and plot the Hebrew
        socialist revolution against the fascist national Golgotha
I'm with you in Rockland
    where you will split the heavens of Long Island and resurrect your
        living human Jesus from the superhuman tomb
I'm with you in Rockland
    where there are twenty five thousand mad comrades all together
        singing the final stanzas of the Internationale[4]   125
I'm with you in Rockland
    where we hug and kiss the United States under our bedsheets the
        United States that coughs all night and won't let us sleep
I'm with you in Rockland
    where we wake up electrified out of the coma by our own souls'
        airplanes roaring over the roof they've come to drop angelic bombs the

---

3. Town in central New York.
4. Former socialist and communist song; the official Soviet anthem until 1944.

hospital illuminates itself   imaginary walls collapse   O skinny
    legions run outside   O starry-spangled shock of mercy the eternal
    war is here   O victory forget your underwear we're free
I'm with you in Rockland
    in my dreams you walk dripping from a sea-journey on the highway   130
    across America in tears to the door of my cottage in the Western night

San Francisco, 1955–56   1956

Footnote to Howl

Holy ! Holy ! Holy ! Holy ! Holy ! Holy ! Holy ! Holy ! Holy ! Holy ! Holy !
    Holy ! Holy ! Holy ! Holy !
The world is holy ! The soul is holy ! The skin is holy ! The nose is holy !
    The tongue and cock and hand and asshole holy !
Everything is holy ! everybody's holy ! everywhere is holy ! everyday is in
    eternity ! Everyman's an angel !
The bum's as holy as the seraphim ! the madman is holy as you my soul are
    holy !
The typewriter is holy the poem is holy the voice is holy the hearers are
    holy the ecstasy is holy !   5
Holy Peter holy Allen holy Solomon holy Lucien holy Kerouac holy Huncke
    holy Burroughs holy Cassady[1] holy the unknown buggered and
    suffering beggars holy the hideous human angels !
Holy my mother in the insane asylum ! Holy the cocks of the grandfathers
    of Kansas !
Holy the groaning saxophone ! Holy the bop apocalypse ! Holy the
    jazzbands marijuana hipsters peace & junk & drums !
Holy the solitudes of skyscrapers and pavements ! Holy the cafeterias filled
    with the millions ! Holy the mysterious rivers of tears under the streets !
Holy the lone juggernaut ! Holy the vast lamb of the middle-class ! Holy the
    crazy shepherds of rebellion ! Who digs Los Angeles IS Los Angeles !   10
Holy New York Holy San Francisco Holy Peoria & Seattle Holy Paris Holy
    Tangiers Holy Moscow Holy Istanbul !
Holy time in eternity holy eternity in time holy the clocks in space holy the
    fourth dimension holy the fifth International holy the Angel in
    Moloch !

1955–56   1956, 1959

---

1. All the figures mentioned here are Americans who shared or inspired a literary bohemia of the time. "Peter": Peter Orlovsky (b. 1933), Beat poet and Ginsberg's lover for four decades. "Allen": Ginsberg. "Solomon": Carl Solomon (b. 1928), whom Ginsberg met at the psychiatric hospital where Ginsberg's mother was being treated and to whom Ginsberg dedicated *Howl*. "Lucien": Lucien Carr (1923–2005), one of the Beats and Ginsberg's roommate at Columbia University in the 1940s. "Kerouac": Jack Kerouac (1922–1969), novelist and founding figure of the Beat generation. "Huncke": Herbert Huncke (1915–1996), writer who influenced Ginsberg and who introduced Ginsberg and Kerouac to the term "beat." "Burroughs": William Burroughs (1914–1997), writer, spoken-word performer, and social critic most famous for the novel *Naked Lunch* (1959). "Cassady": Neal Cassady (1926–1968), an icon of the Beat generation and the inspiration for the character Dean Moriarty in Kerouac's best-known work, *On the Road* (1957).

A Supermarket in California

What thoughts I have of you tonight, Walt Whitman,[1] for I walked down the sidestreets under the trees with a headache self-conscious looking at the full moon.

In my hungry fatigue, and shopping for images, I went into the neon fruit supermarket, dreaming of your enumerations!

What peaches and what penumbras![2] Whole families shopping at night! Aisles full of husbands! Wives in the avocados, babies in the tomatoes!—and you, Garcia Lorca,[3] what were you doing down by the watermelons?

I saw you, Walt Whitman, childless, lonely old grubber, poking among the meats in the refrigerator and eyeing the grocery boys.

I heard you asking questions of each: Who killed the pork chops? What price bananas? Are you my Angel?   5

I wandered in and out of the brilliant stacks of cans following you, and followed in my imagination by the store detective.

We strode down the open corridors together in our solitary fancy tasting artichokes, possessing every frozen delicacy, and never passing the cashier.

Where are we going, Walt Whitman? The doors close in an hour. Which way does your beard point tonight?

(I touch your book and dream of our odyssey in the supermarket and feel absurd.)

Will we walk all night through solitary streets? The trees add shade to shade, lights out in the houses, we'll both be lonely.   10

Will we stroll dreaming of the lost America of love past blue automobiles in driveways, home to our silent cottage?

Ah, dear father, graybeard, lonely old courage-teacher, what America did you have when Charon quit poling his ferry and you got out on a smoking bank and stood watching the boat disappear on the black waters of Lethe?[4]

Berkeley, 1955   1956

---

1. American poet (1819–1892), author of *Leaves of Grass,* against whose homosexuality and vision of American plenty Ginsberg measures himself.
2. Partial shadows.
3. Federico García Lorca (1898–1936), Spanish poet and dramatist and author of "A Poet in New York," whose work is characterized by surrealist and homoerotic inspiration.
4. Forgetfulness. In Greek mythology one of the rivers of Hades, the Underworld. Charon was the boatman who ferried the dead to Hades.

GALWAY KINNELL
b. 1927

In a 1971 interview Galway Kinnell praised Walt Whitman's *Song of Myself*: "The final action of the poem where Whitman dissolves into the air and into the ground, is for me one of the great moments of self-transcendence in poetry. In one way or another, consciously or not, all poems try to pass beyond the self." This capacity for self-transcendence is dramatized in Kinnell's work, where he enters the lives of animals ("The Porcupine," "The Bear") and experiences himself as part of the natural world, like the flower he speaks for in "Flower Herding on Mount Monadnock." "Part of poetry's usefulness in the world," he has said, "is that it pays some of our huge unpaid tribute to the things and creatures that share the earth with us." His work moves between a vivid sense of the world's physical actuality and an equally vivid sense of its dissolution, for mortality is Kinnell's great theme. It appears in his work both as extinction and as "the flowing away into the universe which we desire." This theme is worked out at length in his sequence *The Book of Nightmares* (1978).

Kinnell grew up in Providence, Rhode Island, and attended Princeton University, where he and a classmate, W. S. Merwin, sometimes read each other their poems. He has written continuously since that time, combining his life of poetry with political commitments. Kinnell has been director of an adult-education program in Chicago, a journalist in Iran, and a field-worker for the Congress of Racial Equality in Louisiana. More recently, he has taught at a large number of colleges and universities.

Kinnell's experiences working for voter registration in the South in the 1960s make their way into his long poem "The Last River" (*Body Rags*, 1969). Over the years Kinnell has frequently written poems that unite personal life with the events of the nation. His work includes powerful war poems such as "Vapor Trail Reflected in the Frog Pond" and "The Dead Shall Be Raised Incorruptible," and in "The Past" (1985) he meditates on, and imagines his way into, the consequences of the dropping of the atom bomb on Hiroshima and Nagasaki. Elsewhere he has suggested that poetry is an alternative to a technological world in which domination of nature represses the knowledge of death. In 1994 his collection *Imperfect Thirst* extended his meditation on mortality into the arena of family history and personal memory. In a moving poem, "Neverland," on the death of his sister, Kinnell confronts death's agony and mystery: "*Now* is when the point of the story changes."

Kinnell's earliest work, as seen in *What a Kingdom It Was* (1960) and *First Poems 1946–1954* (1970), is formally intricate. The course of his career has been a movement to a looser line, a more uncluttered diction. His sense of form arises from what he calls the "inner shape" of the poem: "saying in its own music what matters most." Over the years he has come to write poems that maintain musicality and a richness of language while never departing too far from the speaking voice. Kinnell's attraction to the nonhuman world, which may remind us of Theodore Roethke and Gary Snyder, gives his work a vivid sense of life's diversity. But he has sometimes elevated the instinctual at the expense of a shaping, conscious awareness and has written as if the very need for poetic form were, in and of itself, repressive. The finest of Kinnell's poems combine self-transcendence with self-awareness in rhythms that convey a powerful physical energy and an empathetic imagination. His description of Whitman can serve as a description of Kinnell's best work: "All his feelings for existence, for himself, for his own place, come out in what he says about them. . . . He rescues these things from death and lets them live in his poems and, in turn, they save him from incoherence and silence."

The Porcupine

1

Fatted
on herbs, swollen on crabapples,
puffed up on bast and phloem,[1] ballooned
on willow flowers, poplar catkins, first
leafs of aspen and larch,   5
the porcupine
drags and bounces his last meal through ice,
mud, roses and goldenrod, into the stubbly high fields.

2

In character
he resembles us in seven ways: 10
he puts his mark on outhouses,
he alchemizes by moonlight,
he shits on the run,
he uses his tail for climbing,
he chuckles softly to himself when scared,   15
he's overcrowded if there's more than one of him per five acres,
his eyes have their own inner redness.

3

Digger of
goings across floors, of hesitations
at thresholds, of   20
handprints of dread
at doorpost or window jamb, he would
gouge the world
empty of us, hack and crater
it   25
until it is nothing, if that
could rinse it of all our sweat and pathos.

Adorer of ax
handles aflow with grain, of arms
of Morris chairs,[2] of hand   30
crafted objects
steeped in the juice of fingertips,
of surfaces wetted down
with fist grease and elbow oil,
of clothespins that have   35
grabbed our body-rags by underarm and crotch . . .

---

1. I.e., on plant tissues.   2. Easy chairs.

Unimpressed—bored—
by the whirl of the stars, by *these*
he's astonished, ultra-
Rilkean[3] angel! 40

for whom the true
portion of the sweetness of earth
is one of those bottom-heavy, glittering, saccadic
bits
of salt water that splash down 45
the haunted ravines of a human face.

4

A farmer shot a porcupine three times
as it dozed on a tree limb. On
the way down it tore open its belly
on a broken 50
branch, hooked its gut,
and went on falling. On the ground
it sprang to its feet, and
paying out gut heaved
and spartled[4] through a hundred feet of goldenrod 55
before
the abrupt emptiness.

5

The Avesta[5]
puts porcupine killers
into hell for nine generations, sentencing them 60
to gnaw out
each other's hearts for the
salts of desire.

I roll
this way and that in the great bed, under 65
the quilt
that mimics this country of broken farms and woods,
the fatty sheath of the man
melting off,
the self-stabbing coil 70
of bristles reversing, blossoming outward—
a red-eyed, hard-toothed, arrow-stuck urchin
tossing up mattress feathers,
pricking the
woman beside me until she cries. 75

---

3. The German poet Rainer Maria Rilke (1875–1926) wrote in a letter that "the 'angel' of [Rilke's Duino] Elegies has nothing to do with the angel of the Christian heaven. . . . The angel of the Elegies is that being which stands for the idea of recogniz-ing a higher order of reality in invisibility."
4. Variant of "sprottle," to sprawl or struggle help-lessly.
5. Book of the sacred writings of Zoroastrianism, a Persian religion.

6

In my time I have
crouched, quills erected,
Saint
Sebastian[6] of the
scared heart, and been   80
beat dead with a locust club
on the bare snout.
And fallen from high places
I have fled, have
jogged   85
over fields of goldenrod,
terrified, seeking home,
and among flowers
I have come to myself empty, the rope
strung out behind me   90
in the fall sun
suddenly glorified with all my blood.

7

And tonight I think I prowl broken
skulled or vacant as a
sucked egg in the wintry meadow, softly chuckling, blank   95
template of myself, dragging
a starved belly through the lichflowered acres,
where
burdock looses the ark of its seed
and thistle holds up its lost blooms   100
and rosebushes in the wind scrape their dead limbs
for the forced-fire
of roses.

                                                           1969

After Making Love We Hear Footsteps

For I can snore like a bullhorn
or play loud music
or sit up talking with any reasonably sober Irishman
and Fergus will only sink deeper
into his dreamless sleep, which goes by all in one flash,   5
but let there be that heavy breathing
or a stifled come-cry anywhere in the house
and he will wrench himself awake
and make for it on the run—as now, we lie together,
after making love, quiet, touching along the length of our bodies, 10

---

6. Early Christian saint and martyr (d. 288). He was shot full of arrows by an execution squad and miraculously survived, only to be beaten to death later.

familiar touch of the long-married,
and he appears—in his baseball pajamas, it happens,
the neck opening so small he has to screw them on—
and flops down between us and hugs us and snuggles himself to sleep,
his face gleaming with satisfaction at being this very child.   15

In the half darkness we look at each other
and smile
and touch arms across this little, startlingly muscled body—
this one whom habit of memory propels to the ground of his making,
sleeper only the moral sounds can sing awake,   20
this blessing love gives again into our arms.

                                                                      1980

JOHN ASHBERY
b. 1927

John Ashbery has described his writing this way: "I think that any one of my poems might be considered to be a snapshot of whatever is going on in my mind at the time— first of all the desire to write a poem, after that wondering if I've left the oven on or thinking about where I must be in the next hour." Ashbery has developed a style hospitable to quicksilver changes in tone and attention. His work often moves freely between different modes of discourse, between a language of popular culture and commonplace experience and a heightened rhetoric often associated with poetic vision. Ashbery's poems show an awareness of the various linguistic codes (including clichés and conventional public speech) by which we live and through which we define ourselves. This awareness includes an interest in what he has called "prose voices," and he has often written in a way that challenges the boundaries between poetry and prose.

Ashbery's poetry was not always so open to contradictory notions and impulses. His early books rejected the mere surfaces of realism and the momentary to get at "remoter areas of consciousness." The protagonist of "Illustration" (from his first book, *Some Trees*) is a cheerful nun about to leave behind the irrelevancies of the world by leaping from a skyscraper. Her act implies "Much that is beautiful must be discarded / So that we may resemble a taller / impression of ourselves." To reach the "remoter areas of consciousness," Ashbery tried various technical experiments. He used highly patterned forms such as the sestina in "Some Trees" and "The Tennis Court Oath" (1962) not with any show of mechanical brilliance but to explore: "I once told somebody that writing a sestina was rather like riding downhill on a bicycle and having the pedals push your feet. I wanted my feet to be pushed into places they wouldn't normally have taken."

Ashbery was born in Rochester, New York. He attended Deerfield Academy and Harvard, from which he graduated in 1949. He received an M.A. in English from Columbia in 1951. In France first as a Fulbright scholar, he returned in 1958 for eight years and was art critic for the European edition of the *New York Herald Tribune* and reported the European shows and exhibitions for *Art News* and *Arts International*. He returned to New York in 1965 to be executive editor of *Art News*, a position he held until 1972. Since then he has been professor of English in the creative writing program of Brooklyn College and art critic for *Newsweek* magazine.

Ashbery's interest in art played a formative role in his poetry. He is often associated with Frank O'Hara, James Schuyler, and Kenneth Koch as part of the "New York school" of poets. The name refers to their common interest in the New York school of abstract painters of the 1940s and 1950s, some of whose techniques they wished to adapt in poetry. These painters avoided realism to stress the work of art as a representation of the creative act that produced it—as in the action paintings of Jackson Pollock. Ashbery's long poem *Self-Portrait in a Convex Mirror* gives as much attention to the rapidly changing feelings of the poet in the act of writing his poem as it does to the Renaissance painting that inspired him. The poem moves back and forth between the distracted energies that feed a work of art and the completed composition, which the artist feels as both a triumph and a falsification of complex feelings. Ashbery shares with O'Hara a sense of the colloquial brilliance of daily life in New York and sets this in tension with the concentration and stasis of art.

Self-Portrait in a Convex Mirror (1975) was followed by *Houseboat Days* (1977), *As We Know* (1979), *Shadow Train* (1981), and *A Wave* (1984). His important book-length poem, *Flow Chart*, appeared in 1991 followed by collections of shorter poems, *And the Stars Were Shining* (1995) and *Your Name Here* (2000). His entertaining and provocative *Other Traditions* (2000) is a collection of his Norton Lectures on poetry at Harvard. Ashbery's work, especially his earlier, more highly experimental poems, has become particularly influential for a younger generation identified as Language poets, such as Charles Bernstein, Lyn Hejinian, Michael Palmer, and Susan Howe. They have been attracted to the linguistic playfulness of Ashbery's poetry and to its resistance to being read as a single, personal voice. Exposing and sometimes breaking through the world's dominant uses of language, Ashbery's poems open new possibilities of meaning: "We are all talkers / It is true, but underneath the talk lies / The moving and not wanting to be moved, the loose / Meaning, untidy and simple like the threshing floor" ("Soonest Mended").

Illustration

I

A novice[1] was sitting on a cornice
High over the city. Angels

Combined their prayers with those
Of the police, begging her to come off it.

One lady promised to be her friend.   5
"I do not want a friend," she said.

A mother offered her some nylons
Stripped from her very legs. Others brought

Little offerings of fruit and candy,
The blind man all his flowers. If any   10

---

1. Student in the first stage of instruction to be a nun.

Could be called successful, these were,
For that the scene should be a ceremony

Was what she wanted. "I desire
Monuments," she said. "I want to move

Figuratively, as waves caress   15
The thoughtless shore. You people I know

Will offer me every good thing
I do not want. But please remember

I died accepting them." With that, the wind
Unpinned her bulky robes, and naked   20

As a roc's[2] egg, she drifted softly downward
Out of the angels' tenderness and the minds of men.

II

Much that is beautiful must be discarded
So that we may resemble a taller

Impression of ourselves. Moths climb in the flame,   25
Alas, that wish only to be the flame:

They do not lessen our stature.
We twinkle under the weight

Of indiscretions. But how could we tell
That of the truth we know, she was   30

The somber vestment? For that night, rockets sighed
Elegantly over the city, and there was feasting:

There is so much in that moment!
So many attitudes toward that flame,

We might have soared from earth, watching her glide   35
Aloft, in her peplum[3] of bright leaves.

But she, of course, was only an effigy
Of indifference, a miracle

Not meant for us, as the leaves are not
Winter's because it is the end.   40

1956

2. Legendary bird of prey.
3. In ancient Greece a drapery about the upper part of the body.

Soonest Mended

Barely tolerated, living on the margin
In our technological society, we were always having to be rescued
On the brink of destruction, like heroines in *Orlando Furioso*[1]
Before it was time to start all over again.
There would be thunder in the bushes, a rustling of coils,   5
And Angelica, in the Ingres painting,[2] was considering
The colorful but small monster near her toe, as though wondering whether
    forgetting
The whole thing might not, in the end, be the only solution.
And then there always came a time when
Happy Hooligan[3] in his rusted green automobile   10
Came plowing down the course, just to make sure everything was O.K.,
Only by that time we were in another chapter and confused
About how to receive this latest piece of information.
Was it information? Weren't we rather acting this out
For someone else's benefit, thoughts in a mind   15
With room enough and to spare for our little problems (so they began to
    seem),
Our daily quandary about food and the rent and bills to be paid?
To reduce all this to a small variant,
To step free at last, minuscule on the gigantic plateau—
This was our ambition: to be small and clear and free.   20
Alas, the summer's energy wanes quickly,
A moment and it is gone. And no longer
May we make the necessary arrangements, simple as they are.
Our star was brighter perhaps when it had water in it.
Now there is no question even of that, but only   25
Of holding on to the hard earth so as not to get thrown off,
With an occasional dream, a vision: a robin flies across
The upper corner of the window, you brush your hair away
And cannot quite see, or a wound will flash
Against the sweet faces of the others, something like: 30
This is what you wanted to hear, so why
Did you think of listening to something else? We are all talkers
It is true, but underneath the talk lies
The moving and not wanting to be moved, the loose
Meaning, untidy and simple like a threshing floor.[4]   35

These then were some hazards of the course,
Yet though we knew the course *was* hazards and nothing else
It was still a shock when, almost a quarter of a century later,
The clarity of the rules dawned on you for the first time.
They were the players, and we who had struggled at the game   40

---

1. Fantastic epic poem by Ludovico Ariosto (1474–1533), whose romantic heroine Angelica is constantly being rescued from imminent perils such as monsters and ogres.
2. *Roger Delivering Angelica* (1819), a painting based on a scene from Ariosto, by the French artist Jean-Auguste-Dominique Ingres (1780–1867).
3. The good-natured, simple title character of a popular comic strip of the 1920s and 1930s.
4. Used at harvest time to separate the wheat from the chaff, which is to be discarded.

Were merely spectators, though subject to its vicissitudes
And moving with it out of the tearful stadium, borne on shoulders, at last.
Night after night this message returns, repeated
In the flickering bulbs of the sky, raised past us, taken away from us,
Yet ours over and over until the end that is past truth,   45
The being of our sentences, in the climate that fostered them,
Not ours to own, like a book, but to be with, and sometimes
To be without, alone and desperate.
But the fantasy makes it ours, a kind of fence-sitting
Raised to the level of an esthetic ideal. These were moments, years,   50
Solid with reality, faces, namable events, kisses, heroic acts,
But like the friendly beginning of a geometrical progression
Not too reassuring, as though meaning could be cast aside some day
When it had been outgrown. Better, you said, to stay cowering
Like this in the early lessons, since the promise of learning   55
Is a delusion, and I agreed, adding that
Tomorrow would alter the sense of what had already been learned,
That the learning process is extended in this way, so that from this
          standpoint
None of us ever graduates from college,
For time is an emulsion,[5] and probably thinking not to grow up   60
Is the brightest kind of maturity for us, right now at any rate.
And you see, both of us were right, though nothing
Has somehow come to nothing; the avatars[6]
Of our conforming to the rules and living
Around the home have made—well, in a sense, "good citizens" of us,   65
Brushing the teeth and all that, and learning to accept
The charity of the hard moments as they are doled out,
For this is action, this not being sure, this careless
Preparing, sowing the seeds crooked in the furrow,
Making ready to forget, and always coming back   70
To the mooring of starting out, that day so long ago.

                                                                                                    1970

Myrtle

How funny your name would be
if you could follow it back to where
the first person thought of saying it,
naming himself that, or maybe
some other persons thought of it   5
and named that person. It would
be like following a river to its source,
which would be impossible. Rivers have no source.
They just automatically appear at a place
where they get wider, and soon a real   10

---

5. A chemical solution in which the particles of   6. Incarnations.
one liquid are suspended in another.

river comes along, with fish and debris,
regal as you please, and someone
has already given it a name: St. Benno[1]
(saints are popular for this purpose) or, or
some other name, the name of his   15
long-lost girlfriend, who comes
at long last to impersonate that river,
on a stage, her voice clanking
like its bed, her clothing of sand
and pasted paper, a piece of real technology,   20
while all along she is thinking, I can
do what I want to do. But I want to stay here.

1996

---

1. St. Benno (d. 940), long venerated although his cult has never been formally recognized, was born to a noble family and became a hermit on Mount Etzel in Switzerland.

JAMES WRIGHT
1927–1980

"My name is James A. Wright, and I was born / Twenty-five miles from this infected grave, / In Martins Ferry, Ohio, where one slave / To Hazel-Atlas Glass became my father"; so James Wright introduced himself in an early poem, "At the Executed Murderer's Grave." The angry assertiveness in these lines suggests his embattled relations with an America he loves and hates. This America is symbolized for him by the landscape of Ohio, in particular by Martins Ferry, just across the Ohio River from Wheeling, West Virginia, the home of Wheeling Steel and of the glass factory where his father worked for fifty years. In Wright's work this landscape is harsh evidence of the way the social world has contaminated a natural world infinitely more beautiful and self-restoring. The same social world that destroys the landscape also turns its back on those whose lives meet failure or defeat, and Wright's deep knowledge of defeat and his anger at this exclusion lead him to the murderer's grave. It is not simply that Wright sympathizes with social outcasts, but rather, as Robert Hass acutely pointed out, "the suffering of other people, particularly the lost and the derelict, is actually a part of his own emotional life. It is what he writes from, not what he writes about." As a poet who writes out of loss, Wright is elegiac, memorializing a vanished beauty and lost hopes. So deep is his sense of loss that he will sometimes identify with anyone and anything that is scarred or wounded ("I am not a happy man by talent," he once said. "Sometimes I have been very happy, but characteristically I'm a miserable son of a bitch"). Any serious reading of his work has to contend with sorting out those poems in which this identification is unthinking and sentimental, poems where Wright suggests that all forms of suffering and defeat are equal and alike. What remains in some of his best work is a curiously tough-minded tenderness at work in his exploration of despair. He admires, for example, the sumac flourishing in the Ohio landscape, its bark so tough it "will turn aside hatchets and knife blades" ("The Sumac in Ohio").

When Wright finished high school, he joined the army. In 1948 he left the military to attend Kenyon College in Ohio on the GI Bill ("I applied to several schools in Ohio," he once said, "and they all said no except Kenyon College. So I went there"). He was lucky in his teachers; at Kenyon he studied with John Crowe Ransom and, after a Fulbright scholarship to the University of Vienna, he went to the University of Washington, where he studied with the poet Theodore Roethke and also became a close friend of Richard Hugo's. At Washington he wrote a Ph.D. dissertation on Charles Dickens and received the degree in 1959. Thereafter he became a teacher, first at the University of Minnesota, Minneapolis (1957–64), and later at Hunter College, New York (1966–80).

From both Ransom and Roethke, Wright learned poetic form. From Ransom in particular he took what he called "the Horatian ideal" of the carefully made, unified poem. Wright would later say that were he to choose a master, he would choose the Latin poet Horace, "who was able to write humorously and kindly in flawless verse." The Horatian impulse in Wright—restrained, formal, sometimes satirical—helps hold in check a deep-seated romanticism that idealizes nature and the unconscious. His first two books, *The Green Wall* (1957), chosen to appear in the Yale Younger Poets series, and *Saint Judas* (1959), are formal and literary in style although much of their subject matter (the murderer, the lunatic, a deaf child) might be called Romantic. Wright seems in these books closest to Thomas Hardy, Robert Frost, and Edwin Arlington Robinson. But in the 1960s, like a great many other American poets, he moved away from traditional forms, loosened his poetic organization, and began to depend heavily on what his fellow poet Robert Bly called "the deep image." Wright had been translating the work of Spanish poets often associated with surrealism—Pablo Neruda, César Vallejo, and Juan Ramón Jiménez—as well as the German Georg Trakl (whom he translated in collaboration with Bly), and he took from them, in part, a reliance on the power of a poetic image to evoke association deep within the unconscious. He followed his volume *The Branch Will Not Break* (1963) with two books, *Shall We Gather at the River* (1968) and *Two Citizens* (1974), in which he began to overwork certain images ("stone," "dark"), as if repetition were a substitute for clarity. Some of the poems in these books succeed in carrying us into areas of experience that resist the discursive, but the effect of a number of poems is to exclude conscious intelligence, to celebrate "whatever is not mind," as Robert Hass has pointed out. It is as if Wright responded to the scarred landscape outside (and inside) him by fleeing to an inwardness so deep it could not partake of thought or expression.

But Wright's love of clarity and form and his ability to see through pretensions (including his own) resurface in *Moments of the Italian Summer* (1976), *To a Blossoming Pear Tree* (1977), and his last, posthumous collection, *This Journey* (1982). Restored to a unity of thinking and feeling, many of the poems in these books convey the flawed beauty of the world with a loving and witty tenderness. He often writes with particular feeling about creatures—finches, lizards, hermit crabs—whose liveliness and fragility touch him (in this and other regards his work has been important to the poet Mary Oliver). In "A Finch Sitting Out a Windstorm," his final portrait of the finch suggests admiration of its stubbornness in the face of loss: "But his face is as battered / As Carmen Basilio's. / He never listens / To me."

Though the poems of his final book do not abandon the anger he feels thinking of the ruined landscapes of Ohio, the European setting of many of the poems extends his sense of ruin into a knowledge of how time chips away at all human creation, with or without the help of men and women. Although he had claimed to be constitutionally unhappy, the poems of *This Journey* suggest that before his death from cancer a deep happiness took him by surprise. We turn to Wright's work for its fierce understanding of defeat, for its blend of American speech rhythms with the formal music of poetry, and for the loveliness he finds in the imperfect and neglected. Accustomed to expect the worst, he had an enduring capacity to be astonished by this loveliness, as in this childhood memory of a trip to the icehouse with his father: "We stood and breathed the rising steam of that amazing winter, and carried away in our wagon the immense fifty-pound diamond, while the old man chipped us each a jagged little chunk and then walked behind us, his hands so calm they were trembling for us, trembling with exquisite care" ("The Ice House").

Autumn Begins in Martins Ferry, Ohio

In the Shreve High football stadium,
I think of Polacks nursing long beers in Tiltonsville,
And gray faces of Negroes in the blast furnace at Benwood,[1]
And the ruptured night watchman of Wheeling Steel,
Dreaming of heroes.   5

All the proud fathers are ashamed to go home.
Their women cluck like starved pullets,[2]
Dying for love.

Therefore,
Their sons grow suicidally beautiful   10
At the beginning of October,
And gallop terribly against each other's bodies.

                                                              1963

To the Evening Star: Central Minnesota

Under the water tower at the edge of town
A huge Airedale ponders a long ripple
In the grass fields beyond.
Miles off, a whole grove silently
Flies up into the darkness.   5
One light comes on in the sky,
One lamp on the prairie.

Beautiful daylight of the body, your hands carry seashells.
West of this wide plain,
Animals wilder than ours   10
Come down from the green mountains in the darkness.
Now they can see you, they know
The open meadows are safe.

                                                              1963

A Blessing

Just off the highway to Rochester, Minnesota,
Twilight bounds softly forth on the grass.
And the eyes of those two Indian ponies
Darken with kindness.
They have come gladly out of the willows   5
To welcome my friend and me.
We step over the barbed wire into the pasture
Where they have been grazing all day, alone.
They ripple tensely, they can hardly contain their happiness

1. A town south of Martins Ferry, where the
Wheeling Steel Works are located. Tiltonsville is a
town in far east Ohio, north of Martins Ferry.
2. Young hens.

That we have come. 10
They bow shyly as wet swans. They love each other.
There is no loneliness like theirs.
At home once more,
They begin munching the young tufts of spring in the darkness.
I would like to hold the slenderer one in my arms, 15
For she has walked over to me
And nuzzled my left hand.
She is black and white,
Her mane falls wild on her forehead,
And the light breeze moves me to caress her long ear 20
That is delicate as the skin over a girl's wrist.
Suddenly I realize
That if I stepped out of my body I would break
Into blossom.

1963

ANNE SEXTON
1928–1974

Anne Sexton's first book of poems, *To Bedlam and Part Way Back* (1960), was published at a time when the label "confessional" came to be attached to poems more frankly auto-biographical than had been usual in American verse. For Sexton the term is particularly apt. Although she had abandoned the Roman Catholicism into which she was born, her poems enact something analogous to preparing for and receiving religious absolution.

Sexton's confessions were to be made in terms more startling than the traditional Catholic images of her childhood. The purpose of her poems was not to analyze or explain behavior but to make it palpable in all its ferocity of feeling. Poetry "should be a shock to the senses. It should also hurt." This is apparent in both her themes and the particular ways in which she exhibits her subjects. Sexton writes about sex, illegitimacy, guilt, madness, and suicide. *To Bedlam* portrays her breakdown, her time in a mental hospital, her efforts at reconciliation with her young daughter and husband when she returns. Her second book, *All My Pretty Ones* (1962), takes its title from Shakespeare's *Macbeth* and refers to the deaths of both her parents within three months of one another. Later books—*Live or Die* (1966), *The Death Notebooks* (1974), and *The Awful Rowing toward God* (1975; posthumous)—act out a debate about suicide and prefigure Sexton's taking of her own life. And yet, as the poet's tender address to her daughter in "Little Girl, My String Bean, My Lovely Woman" suggests, Sexton's work ranges beyond an obsession with death.

Sexton spoke of images as "the heart of poetry. Images come from the unconscious. Imagination and the unconscious are one and the same." Powerful images substantiate the strangeness of feelings and attempt to redefine experiences so as to gain understanding, absolution, or revenge. These poems poised between, as her titles suggest, life and death or "bedlam and part way back" are efforts at establishing a middle ground of self-assertion, substituting surreal images for the reductive versions of life visible to the exterior eye.

Sexton was born in 1928 in Newton, Massachusetts, and attended Garland Junior College. She came to poetry fairly late—when she was twenty-eight, after seeing the critic I. A. Richards lecturing about the sonnet on television. In the late 1950s she attended poetry workshops in the Boston area, including Robert Lowell's poetry seminars at Boston University. One of her fellow students was Sylvia Plath, whose suicide she commemorated in a poem, "Sylvia's Death." Sexton claimed that she was less influenced by Lowell's *Life Studies* than by W. D. Snodgrass's autobiographical *Heart's Needle* (1959), but certainly Lowell's support and the association with Plath left their mark on her and made it possible for her to publish. Although her career was relatively brief, she received several major literary prizes, including the Pulitzer Prize for *Live or Die* and an American Academy of Arts and Letters traveling fellowship. Her suicide came after a series of mental breakdowns.

The Starry Night

> That does not keep me from having a terrible
> need of—shall I say the word—religion.
> Then I go out at night to paint the stars.
> —Vincent Van Gogh[1]
> in a letter to his brother

The town does not exist
except where one black-haired tree slips
up like a drowned woman into the hot sky.
The town is silent. The night boils with eleven stars.
Oh starry starry night! This is how   5
I want to die.

It moves. They are all alive.
Even the moon bulges in its orange irons
to push children, like a god, from its eye.
The old unseen serpent swallows up the stars.   10
Oh starry starry night! This is how
I want to die:

into that rushing beast of the night,
sucked up by that great dragon, to split
from my life with no flag,   15
no belly,
no cry.

                                                                    1962

Sylvia's Death

for Sylvia Plath[1]

Oh Sylvia, Sylvia,
with a dead box of stones and spoons,

with two children, two meteors
wandering loose in the tiny playroom,

---

1. Dutch painter (1853–1890) who in his thirties went mad and finally committed suicide. This letter to his brother—his only confidant—was written in September 1888. He was painting, at the same time, *Starry Night on the Rhône.*

1. American poet (1932–1963) and friend of Sexton's who committed suicide. Plath was living in England with her two small children, having separated from her husband, the poet Ted Hughes, the previous year.

with your mouth into the sheet,
into the roofbeam, into the dumb prayer,

(Sylvia, Sylvia,
where did you go
after you wrote me
from Devonshire
about raising potatoes
and keeping bees?)

what did you stand by,
just how did you lie down into?

Thief!—
how did you crawl into,

crawl down alone
into the death I wanted so badly and for so long,

the death we said we both outgrew,
the one we wore on our skinny breasts,

the one we talked of so often each time
we downed three extra dry martinis in Boston,

the death that talked of analysts and cures,
the death that talked like brides with plots,

the death we drank to,
the motives and then the quiet deed?

(In Boston
the dying
ride in cabs,
yes death again,
that ride home
with our boy.)

O Sylvia, I remember the sleepy drummer
who beat on our eyes with an old story,

how we wanted to let him come
like a sadist or a New York fairy

to do his job,
a necessity, a window in a wall or a crib,

and since that time he waited
under our heart, our cupboard,

and I see now that we store him up
year after year, old suicides

and I know at the news of your death,
a terrible taste for it, like salt.

(And me,   45
me too.
And now, Sylvia,
you again
with death again,
that ride home   50
with *our* boy.)

And I say only
with my arms stretched out into that stone place,

what is your death
but an old belonging,   55

a mole that fell out
of one of your poems?

(O friend,
while the moon's bad,
and the king's gone,   60
and the queen's at her wit's end
the bar fly ought to sing!)

O tiny mother,
you too!
O funny duchess!   65
O blonde thing!

February 17, 1963   1966

Little Girl, My String Bean, My Lovely Woman

My daughter, at eleven
(almost twelve), is like a garden.

Oh darling! Born in that sweet birthday suit
and having owned it and known it for so long,
now you must watch high noon enter—   5
noon, that ghost hour.
Oh, funny little girl—this one under a blueberry sky,
this one! How can I say that I've known
just what you know and just where you are?

It's not a strange place, this odd home   10
where your face sits in my hand
so full of distance,
so full of its immediate fever.
The summer has seized you,
as when, last month in Amalfi,[1] I saw   15
lemons as large as your desk-side globe—

---

1. A seaport town in Campania, Italy.

that miniature map of the world—
and I could mention, too,
the market stalls of mushrooms
and garlic buds all engorged.   20
Or I think even of the orchard next door,
where the berries are done
and the apples are beginning to swell.
And once, with our first backyard,
I remember I planted an acre of yellow beans   25
we couldn't eat.

Oh, little girl,
my stringbean,
how do you grow?
You grow this way.   30
You are too many to eat.

I hear
as in a dream
the conversation of the old wives
speaking of *womanhood*.   35
I remember that I heard nothing myself.
I was alone.
I waited like a target.

Let high noon enter—
the hour of the ghosts.   40
Once the Romans believed
that noon was the ghost hour,
and I can believe it, too,
under that startling sun,
and someday they will come to you,   45
someday, men bare to the waist, young Romans
at noon where they belong,
with ladders and hammers
while no one sleeps.

But before they enter   50
I will have said,
Your bones are lovely,
and before their strange hands
there was always this hand that formed.

Oh, darling, let your body in,   55
let it tie you in,
in comfort.
What I want to say, Linda,
is that women are born twice.

If I could have watched you grow   60
as a magical mother might,
if I could have seen through my magical transparent belly,
there would have been such ripening within:
your embryo,

the seed taking on its own,   65
life clapping the bedpost,
bones from the pond,
thumbs and two mysterious eyes,
the awfully human head,
the heart jumping like a puppy,   70
the important lungs,
the becoming—
while it becomes!
as it does now,
a world of its own,   75
a delicate place.

I say hello
to such shakes and knockings and high jinks,
such music, such sprouts,
such dancing-mad-bears of music,   80
such necessary sugar,
such goings-on!

Oh, little girl,
my stringbean,
how do you grow?   85
You grow this way.
You are too many to eat.

What I want to say, Linda,
is that there is nothing in your body that lies.
All that is new is telling the truth.   90
I'm here, that somebody else,
an old tree in the background.

Darling,
stand still at your door,
sure of yourself, a white stone, a good stone—   95
as exceptional as laughter
you will strike fire,
that new thing!

July 14, 1964   1966

ADRIENNE RICH
b. 1929 ~ 2012

A childhood of reading and hearing poems taught Adrienne Rich to love the sound of words; her adult life taught her that poetry must "consciously situate itself amid political conditions." Over the years she has conducted a passionate struggle to honor these parts of herself, in her best poems brilliantly mixing what she calls "the poetry of the actual world with the poetry of sound." Extending a dialogue—between art and politics—that she first discovered in W. B. Yeats, whose poems she read as an undergraduate at Radcliffe, her work addresses with particular power the experiences of women, experiences often omitted from history and misrepresented in literature. Our culture, she believes, is "split at the root" (to adapt the title of one of her essays); art is separated from politics, and the poet's identity as a woman is separated from her art. Rich's work seeks a language that will expose and integrate these divisions in the self and in the world. To do this she has written "directly and overtly as a woman, out of a woman's body and experience," for "to take women's existence seriously as theme and source for art, was something I had been hungering to do, needing to do, all my writing life."

Rich's first book was published in the Yale Younger Poets series, a prize particularly important for poets of her generation (others in the series have included James Wright, John Ashbery, and W. S. Merwin). W. H. Auden, the judge for the series in the 1950s, said of Rich's volume *A Change of World* (1951) that her poems "were neatly and modestly dressed . . . respect their elders, but are not cowed by them and do not tell fibs." Rich, looking back at that period from the vantage point of 1972, renders a more complicated sense of things. In an influential essay, "When We Dead Awaken," she recalls this period as one in which the chief models for poetry were men; from those models she first learned her craft. Even in reading the poetry of older women writers she found herself "looking . . . for the same things I found in the poetry of men . . . , to be equal was still confused with sounding the same." Twenty years and five volumes after *A Change of World* she published *The Will to Change,* taking its title from the opening line of Charles Olson's *The Kingfishers:* "What does not change / is the will to change." The shift of emphasis in Rich's titles signals an important turn in her work—from acceptance of change as a way of the world to an active sense of change as willed or desired.

In 1953 Rich married and in her twenties gave birth to three children within four years, "a radicalizing experience," she said. It was during this time that Rich experienced most severely that gap between what she calls the "energy of creation" and the "energy of relation. . . . In those early years I always felt the conflict as a failure of love in myself." In her later work Rich came to identify the source of that conflict not as individual but as social and in 1976 she published a book of prose, *Of Woman Born: Motherhood as Experience and Institution,* in which she contrasts the actual experience of bearing and raising children with the myths fostered by our medical, social, and political institutions.

With her third and fourth books, *Snapshots of a Daughter-in-Law* (1963) and *Necessities of Life* (1966), Rich began explicitly to treat problems that have engaged her ever since. The title poem of *Snapshots* exposes the gap between literary versions of women's experience and the day-to-day truths of their lives.

Rich's poems aim at self-definition, at establishing boundaries of the self, but they also fight off the notion that insights remain solitary and unshared. Many of her poems proceed by means of intimate argument, sometimes with externalized parts of herself, as if to dramatize the way identity forms from the self's movement beyond fixed boundaries. In some of her most powerful later poems she pushes her imagination to recognize the multiple aspects of the self ("My selves," she calls them in her poem "Integrity"); in "Transcendental Etude," she writes: "*I am the lover and the loved, / home and wanderer, she who splits / firewood and she who knocks, a stranger / in the storm.*" In other important later poems she has carried out a dialogue with lives similar to and different from her own, as in the generous and powerful title poem of her collection *An Atlas of the Difficult World.* As she writes in the essay "Blood, Bread, and Poetry," in her development as a poet she came to feel "more and more urgently the dynamic between poetry as language and poetry as a kind of action, probing, burning, stripping, placing itself in dialogue with others."

After Rich and her husband moved to New York City in 1966 they became increasingly involved in radical politics, especially in the opposition to the Vietnam War. These concerns are reflected in the poems of *Leaflets* (1969) and *The Will to Change* (1971). Along with new subject matter came equally important changes in style. Rich's poems throughout the 1960s moved away from formal verse patterns to more jagged utterance. Devices such as sentence fragments, lines of varying length, irregular spacing to mark off phrases emphasized a voice of greater urgency. Ever since "Snapshots of a Daughter-in-Law" Rich had been dating her poems, as if to mark each one as provisional, true to the moment but an instrument of passage, like an entry in a journal in which feelings are subject to continual revision.

In the 1970s Rich dedicated herself increasingly to feminism. Her work as a poet, a prose writer, and a public speaker took on a new unity and intensity. The continuing task was to see herself—as she put it in 1984—as neither "unique nor universal, but a person in history, a woman and not a man, a white and also Jewish inheritor of a particular Western consciousness, from the making of which most women have been excluded." She says in "Planetarium": "I am an instrument in the shape / of a woman trying to translate pulsations / into images for the relief of the body / and the reconstruction of the mind."

Rich's collections of prose—*Of Woman Born; On Lies, Secrets, and Silences: Selected Prose 1966–1978; Blood, Bread, and Poetry: Selected Prose 1979–1985, What Is Found There: Notebooks on Poetry and Politics* (1993), and *Arts of the Possible* (2001)—provide an important context for her poems. In these works she addresses issues of women's education and their literary traditions, Jewish identity, the relations between poetry and politics, and what she has called "the erasure of lesbian existence." As a young woman Rich had been stirred by James Baldwin's comment that "any real change implies the breakup of the world as one has always known it, the loss of all that gave one an identity, the end of safety." In many ways her essays, like her poems, track the forces that resist such change and the human conditions that require it. Her essay "Compulsory Heterosexuality and Lesbian Existence" is an important example of such an examination.

Although Rich's individual poems do not consistently succeed in expressing a political vision without sacrificing "intensity of language," her work is best read as a continuous process. The books have an air of ongoing, pained investigation, almost scientific in intention but with an ardor suggested by their titles: *The Dream of a Common Language* (1977), *A Wild Patience Has Taken Me Thus Far* (1981), *The Fact of a Doorframe* (1984), and *Your Native Land, Your Life* (1986). Rich's more recent books, *Time's Power* (1989), *An Atlas of the Difficult World* (1991), *Dark Fields of the Republic: Poems 1991–1995* (1995), *Midnight Salvage: Poems 1995–1998* (1999), *Fox* (2001), and *The School Among the Ruins* (2004), demonstrate an ongoing power of language and deepening poetic vision. Reading through her poems we may sometimes wish for more relaxation and playfulness, for a liberating comic sense of self almost never present in her work. What we find, however, is invaluable—a poet whose imagination confronts and resists the harsh necessities of our times and keeps alive a vision of what is possible: "a whole new poetry beginning here" ("Transcendental Etude").

Storm Warnings

The glass[1] has been falling all the afternoon,
And knowing better than the instrument
What winds are walking overhead, what zone
Of gray unrest is moving across the land,
I leave the book upon a pillowed chair   5
And walk from window to closed window, watching
Boughs strain against the sky

And think again, as often when the air
Moves inward toward a silent core of waiting,
How with a single purpose time has traveled   10

---

1. Barometer.

By secret currents of the undiscerned
Into this polar realm. Weather abroad
And weather in the heart alike come on
Regardless of prediction.

Between foreseeing and averting change   15
Lies all the mastery of elements
Which clocks and weatherglasses cannot alter.
Time in the hand is not control of time,
Nor shattered fragments of an instrument
A proof against the wind; the wind will rise,   20
We can only close the shutters.

I draw the curtains as the sky goes black
And set a match to candles sheathed in glass
Against the keyhole draught, the insistent whine
Of weather through the unsealed aperture.   25
This is our sole defense against the season;
These are the things that we have learned to do
Who live in troubled regions.

                                                      1951

Snapshots of a Daughter-in-Law

1

You, once a belle in Shreveport,
with henna-colored hair, skin like a peachbud,
still have your dresses copied from that time,
and play a Chopin prelude
called by Cortot: "*Delicious recollections*   5
float like perfume through the memory."[1]

Your mind now, moldering like wedding-cake,
heavy with useless experience, rich
with suspicion, rumor, fantasy,
crumbling to pieces under the knife-edge   10
of mere fact. In the prime of your life.

Nervy, glowering, your daughter
wipes the teaspoons, grows another way.

2

Banging the coffee-pot into the sink
she hears the angels chiding, and looks out   15
past the raked gardens to the sloppy sky.
Only a week since They said: *Have no patience.*

---

1. A remark made by Alfred Cortot (1877–1962), a French pianist, in his *Chopin: 24 Preludes* (1930); he is referring specifically to Chopin's Prelude No. 7, Andantino, A Major.

The next time it was: *Be insatiable.*
Then: *Save yourself; others you cannot save.*
Sometimes she's let the tapstream scald her arm,   20
a match burn to her thumbnail,

or held her hand above the kettle's snout
right in the woolly steam. They are probably angels,
since nothing hurts her anymore, except
each morning's grit blowing into her eyes.   25

3

A thinking woman sleeps with monsters.[2]
The beak that grips her, she becomes. And Nature,
that sprung-lidded, still commodious
steamer-trunk of *tempora* and *mores*[3]
gets stuffed with it all: the mildewed orange-flowers,   30
the female pills, the terrible breasts
of Boadicea[4] beneath flat foxes' heads and orchids.

Two handsome women, gripped in argument,
each proud, acute, subtle, I hear scream
across the cut glass and majolica   35
like Furies[5] cornered from their prey:
The argument *ad feminam,*[6] all the old knives
that have rusted in my back, I drive in yours,
ma semblable, ma soeur![7]

4

Knowing themselves too well in one another: 40
their gifts no pure fruition, but a thorn,
the prick filed sharp against a hint of scorn . . .
Reading while waiting
for the iron to heat,
writing, *My Life had stood—a Loaded Gun*[8]—   45
in that Amherst pantry while the jellies boil and scum,
or, more often,
iron-eyed and beaked and purposed as a bird,
dusting everything on the whatnot every day of life.

2. A reference to W. B. Yeats's "Leda and the Swan," a poem about the rape of a maiden by Zeus in the form of a giant bird. The poem ends: "Did she put on his knowledge with his power / Before the indifferent beak could let her drop?"
3. Times and customs (Latin, literal trans.). This alludes perhaps to the Roman orator Cicero's famous phrase "O Tempora! O Mores!" ("Alas for the degeneracy of our times and the low standard of our morals!").
4. British queen in the time of the Emperor Nero; she led her people in a large, ultimately unsuccessful revolt against Roman rule. "Female pills": remedies for menstrual pain.
5. Greek goddesses of vengeance. "Majolica": a kind of earthenware with a richly colored glaze.

6. Feminine version of the Latin phrase *ad hominem* (literally, "to the man"), referring to an argument directed not to reason but to personal prejudices and emotions.
7. The last line of Charles Baudelaire's French poem "Au Lecteur" addresses *"Hypocrite lecteur!— mon semblable—mon frère!"* (Hypocrite reader, like me, my brother!); Rich here instead addresses *"ma soeur"* (my sister). See also T. S. Eliot, "The Waste Land," line 76.
8. "*Emily Dickinson, Complete Poems*, ed. T. H. Johnson, 1960, p. 369" [Rich's note]; this is the poem numbered 754 in the Johnson edition. Amherst, Massachusetts, is the town where Dickinson lived her entire life (1830–1886).

5

Dulce ridens, dulce loquens,[9] 50
she shaves her legs until they gleam
like petrified mammoth-tusk.

6

When to her lute Corinna sings[1]
neither words nor music are her own;
only the long hair dipping 55
over her cheek, only the song
of silk against her knees
and these
adjusted in reflections of an eye.

Poised, trembling and unsatisfied, before 60
an unlocked door, that cage of cages,
tell us, you bird, you tragical machine—
is this *fertilisante douleur?*[2] Pinned down
by love, for you the only natural action,
are you edged more keen 65
to prise the secrets of the vault? has Nature shown
her household books to you, daughter-in-law,
that her sons never saw?

7

"To have in this uncertain world some stay
which cannot be undermined, is 70
of the utmost consequence."[3]
                    Thus wrote
a woman, partly brave and partly good,
who fought with what she partly understood.
Few men about her would or could do more, 75
hence she was labeled harpy, shrew and whore.

8

"You all die at fifteen," said Diderot,[4]
and turn part legend, part convention.
Still, eyes inaccurately dream
behind closed windows blankening with steam. 80
Deliciously, all that we might have been,
all that we were—fire, tears,
wit, taste, martyred ambition—
stirs like the memory of refused adultery
the drained and flagging bosom of our middle years. 85

9. Sweetly laughing, sweetly speaking (Latin, from Horace, "Odes," 22.23–24).
1. First line of a lyric poem by Thomas Campion (1567–1620) about the extent to which a courtier is moved by Corinna's beautiful music.
2. Fertilizing (or life-giving) sorrow (French).
3. "From Mary Wollstonecraft, *Thoughts on the Education of Daughters*, London, 1787" [Rich's note]. Wollstonecraft (1759–1797), one of the first

feminist thinkers, is best-known for her "Vindication of the Rights of Woman."
4. Denis Diderot (1713–1784), French philosopher, encyclopedist, playwright, and critic. " 'You all die at fifteen': *'Vous mourez toutes à quinze ans,'* from the *Lettres à Sophie Volland*, quoted by Simone de Beauvoir in *Le Deuxième Sexe*, Vol. II, pp. 123–24" [Rich's note].

9

Not that it is done well, but
that it is done at all?[5] Yes, think
of the odds! or shrug them off forever.
This luxury of the precocious child,
Time's precious chronic invalid,—   90
would we, darlings, resign it if we could?
Our blight has been our sinecure:
mere talent was enough for us—
glitter in fragments and rough drafts.

Sigh no more, ladies.   95
         Time is male
and in his cups drinks to the fair.
Bemused by gallantry, we hear
our mediocrities over-praised,
indolence read as abnegation,   100
slattern thought styled intuition,
every lapse forgiven, our crime
only to cast too bold a shadow
or smash the mold straight off.

For that, solitary confinement,   105
tear gas, attrition shelling.
Few applicants for that honor.

10

            Well,
she's long about her coming, who must be
more merciless to herself than history.   110
Her mind full to the wind, I see her plunge
breasted and glancing through the currents,
taking the light upon her
at least as beautiful as any boy
or helicopter,[6]   115
         poised, still coming,
her fine blades making the air wince

but her cargo
no promise then:
delivered   120
palpable
ours.

1958–60   1963

---

5. An allusion to Samuel Johnson's remark to James Boswell: "Sir, a woman's preaching is like a dog's walking on his hinder legs. It is not done well; but you are surprised to find it done at all" (July 31, 1763).
6. "She comes down from the remoteness of ages, from Thebes, from Crete, from Chichén-Itzà; and she is also the totem set deep in the African jungle;

she is a helicopter and she is a bird; and there is this, the greatest wonder of all: under her tinted hair the forest murmur becomes a thought, and words issue from her breasts" (Simone de Beauvoir, *The Second Sex*, trans. H. M. Parshley [New York, 1953], 729). (A translation of the passage from *Le Deuxième Sexe*, Vol. II, 574, cited in French by Rich.)

A Valediction Forbidding Mourning[1]

My swirling wants. Your frozen lips.
The grammar turned and attacked me.
Themes, written under duress.
Emptiness of the notations.

They gave me a drug that slowed the healing of wounds.   5

I want you to see this before I leave:
the experience of repetition as death
the failure of criticism to locate the pain
the poster in the bus that said:
my bleeding is under control.   10

A red plant in a cemetery of plastic wreaths.

A last attempt: the language is a dialect called metaphor.
These images go unglossed: hair, glacier, flashlight.
When I think of a landscape I am thinking of a time.
When I talk of taking a trip I mean forever.   15
I could say: those mountains have a meaning
but further than that I could not say.

To do something very common, in my own way.

1970   1971

Diving into the Wreck

First having read the book of myths,
and loaded the camera,
and checked the edge of the knife-blade,
I put on
the body-armor of black rubber   5
the absurd flippers
the grave and awkward mask.
I am having to do this
not like Cousteau[1] with his
assiduous team   10
aboard the sun-flooded schooner
but here alone.

There is a ladder.
The ladder is always there
hanging innocently   15
close to the side of the schooner.
We know what it is for,
we who have used it.
Otherwise

---

1. Title of a famous poem by John Donne (1572–1631) in which the English poet forbids his wife to lament his departure for a trip to the Continent.

1. Jacques-Yves Cousteau (1910–1997), French underwater explorer and author.

it's a piece of maritime floss   20
some sundry equipment.

I go down.
Rung after rung and still
the oxygen immerses me
the blue light   25
the clear atoms
of our human air.
I go down.
My flippers cripple me,
I crawl like an insect down the ladder   30
and there is no one
to tell me when the ocean
will begin.

First the air is blue and then
it is bluer and then green and then   35
black I am blacking out and yet
my mask is powerful
it pumps my blood with power
the sea is another story
the sea is not a question of power   40
I have to learn alone
to turn my body without force
in the deep element.

And now: it is easy to forget
what I came for   45
among so many who have always
lived here
swaying their crenellated fans
between the reefs
and besides   50
you breathe differently down here.

I came to explore the wreck.
The words are purposes.
The words are maps.
I came to see the damage that was done   55
and the treasures that prevail.
I stroke the beam of my lamp
slowly along the flank
of something more permanent
than fish or weed   60

the thing I came for:
the wreck and not the story of the wreck
the thing itself and not the myth
the drowned face[2] always staring
toward the sun   65
the evidence of damage
worn by salt and sway into this threadbare beauty

2. Referring to the ornamental female figurehead that formed the prow of many old sailing ships.

the ribs of the disaster
curving their assertion
among the tentative haunters.   70

This is the place.
And I am here, the mermaid whose dark hair
streams black, the merman in his armored body
We circle silently
about the wreck   75
we dive into the hold.
I am she: I am he

whose drowned face sleeps with open eyes
whose breasts still bear the stress
whose silver, copper, vermeil cargo lies   80
obscurely inside barrels
half-wedged and left to rot
we are the half-destroyed instruments
that once held to a course
the water-eaten log   85
the fouled compass

We are, I am, you are
by cowardice or courage
the one who find our way
back to this scene   90
carrying a knife, a camera
a book of myths
in which
our names do not appear.

1972

                                                          1973

Transcendental Etude[1]

for Michelle Cliff

This August evening I've been driving
over backroads fringed with queen anne's lace
my car startling young deer in meadows—one
gave a hoarse intake of her breath and all
four fawns sprang after her   5
into the dark maples.
Three months from today they'll be fair game
for the hit-and-run hunters, glorying
in a weekend's destructive power,
triggers fingered by drunken gunmen, sometimes   10
so inept as to leave the shattered animal
stunned in her blood. But this evening deep in summer
the deer are still alive and free,
nibbling apples from early-laden boughs
so weighted, so englobed   15

---

1. "Etude": a piece of music played for the practice of a point of technique or a composition built on technique but played for its artistic value.

with already yellowing fruit
they seem eternal, Hesperidean[2]
in the clear-tuned, cricket-throbbing air.

Later I stood in the dooryard,   20
my nerves singing the immense
fragility of all this sweetness,
this green world already sentimentalized, photographed,
advertised to death. Yet, it persists
stubbornly beyond the fake Vermont
of antique barnboards glazed into discothèques,   25
artificial snow, the sick Vermont of children
conceived in apathy, grown to winters
of rotgut violence,
poverty gnashing its teeth like a blind cat at their lives.
Still, it persists. Turning off onto a dirt road   30
from the raw cuts bulldozed through a quiet village
for the tourist run to Canada,
I've sat on a stone fence above a great, soft, sloping field
of musing heifers, a farmstead
slanting its planes calmly in the calm light,   35
a dead elm raising bleached arms
above a green so dense with life,
minute, momentary life—slugs, moles, pheasants, gnats,
spiders, moths, hummingbirds, groundhogs, butterflies—
a lifetime is too narrow   40
to understand it all, beginning with the huge
rockshelves that underlie all that life.

No one ever told us we had to study our lives,
make of our lives a study, as if learning natural history
or music, that we should begin   45
with the simple exercises first
and slowly go on trying
the hard ones, practicing till strength
and accuracy became one with the daring
to leap into transcendence, take the chance   50
of breaking down in the wild arpeggio
or faulting the full sentence of the fugue.[3]
—And in fact we can't live like that: we take on
everything at once before we've even begun
to read or mark time, we're forced to begin   55
in the midst of the hardest movement,
the one already sounding as we are born.
At most we're allowed a few months
of simply listening to the simple line
of a woman's voice singing a child   60
against her heart. Everything else is too soon,
too sudden, the wrenching-apart, that woman's heartbeat
heard ever after from a distance,

---

2. I.e., like the golden apples of the tree guarded by the Hesperides, daughters of Atlas, in Greek mythology.
3. Musical piece characterized by the interweaving of several voices. "Arpeggio": production of a chord's tones in succession.

the loss of that ground-note echoing
whenever we are happy, or in despair.   65

Everything else seems beyond us,
we aren't ready for it, nothing that was said
is true for us, caught naked in the argument,
the counterpoint, trying to sightread
what our fingers can't keep up with, learn by heart   70
what we can't even read. And yet
it *is* this we were born to. We aren't virtuosi
or child prodigies, there are no prodigies
in this realm, only a half-blind, stubborn
cleaving to the timbre, the tones of what we are   75
—even when all the texts describe it differently.

And we're not performers, like Liszt,[4] competing
against the world for speed and brilliance
(the 79-year-old pianist said, when I asked her
What makes a virtuoso?—Competitiveness.)
The longer I live the more I mistrust   80
theatricality, the false glamour cast
by performance, the more I know its poverty beside
the truths we are salvaging from
the splitting-open of our lives.
The woman who sits watching, listening,   85
eyes moving in the darkness
in rehearsing in her body, hearing-out in her blood
a score touched off in her perhaps
by some words, a few chords, from the stage:
a tale only she can tell.   90

But there come times—perhaps this is one of them—
when we have to take ourselves more seriously or die;
when we have to pull back from the incantations,
rhythms we've moved to thoughtlessly,
and disenthrall ourselves, bestow   95
ourselves to silence, or a severer listening, cleansed
of oratory, formulas, choruses, laments, static
crowding the wires. We cut the wires,
find ourselves in free-fall, as if
our true home were the undimensional   100
solitudes, the rift
in the Great Nebula.[5]
No one who survives to speak
new language, has avoided this:
the cutting-away of an old force that held her   105
rooted to an old ground
the pitch of utter loneliness
where she herself and all creation
seem equally dispersed, weightless, her being a cry
to which no echo comes or can ever come.   110

4. Franz Liszt (1811–1886), Hungarian composer
and pianist noted for his virtuoso performances.
5. A nebula is an immense body of rarefied gas or
dust in interstellar space. Rich may be referring to
the Great Nebula in the Orion constellation or to
a body of dark nebulae, usually called the "Great
Rift," which in photographs appears to divide the
Milky Way.

But in fact we were always like this,
rootless, dismembered: knowing it makes the difference.
Birth stripped our birthright from us,
tore us from a woman, from women, from ourselves   115
so early on
and the whole chorus throbbing at our ears
like midges, told us nothing, nothing
of origins, nothing we needed
to know, nothing that could re-member us.   120

Only: that it is unnatural,
the homesickness for a woman, for ourselves,
for that acute joy at the shadow her head and arms
cast on a wall, her heavy or slender
thighs on which we lay, flesh against flesh,   125
eyes steady on the face of love; smell of her milk, her sweat,
terror of her disappearance, all fused in this hunger
for the element they have called most dangerous, to be
lifted breathtaken on her breast, to rock within her
—even if beaten back, stranded against, to apprehend   130
in a sudden brine-clear thought
trembling like the tiny, orbed, endangered
egg-sac of a new world:
This is what she was to me, and this
is how I can love myself—   135
as only a woman can love me.

Homesick for myself, for her—as, after the heatwave
breaks, the clear tones of the world
manifest: cloud, bough, wall, insect, the very soul of light:
homesick as the fluted vault of desire   140
articulates itself: *I am the lover and the loved,*
home and wanderer, she who splits
firewood and she who knocks, a stranger
in the storm, two women, eye to eye
measuring each other's spirit, each other's   145
limitless desire,
          a whole new poetry beginning here.

Vision begins to happen in such a life
as if a woman quietly walked away
from the argument and jargon in a room   150
and sitting down in the kitchen, began turning in her lap
bits of yarn, calico and velvet scraps,
laying them out absently on the scrubbed boards
in the lamplight, with small rainbow-colored shells
sent in cotton-wool from somewhere far away,   155
and skeins of milkweed from the nearest meadow—
original domestic silk, the finest findings—
and the darkblue petal of the petunia,
and the dry darkbrown lace of seaweed;
not forgotten either, the shed silver   160
whisker of the cat,
the spiral of paper-wasp-nest curling
beside the finch's yellow feather.

Such a composition has nothing to do with eternity,
the striving for greatness, brilliance—   165
only with the musing of a mind
one with her body, experienced fingers quietly pushing
dark against bright, silk against roughness,
pulling the tenets of a life together
with no mere will to mastery,   170
only care for the many-lived, unending
forms in which she finds herself,
becoming now the sherd of broken glass
slicing light in a corner, dangerous
to flesh, now the plentiful, soft leaf   175
that wrapped round the throbbing finger, soothes the wound;
and now the stone foundation, rockshelf further
forming underneath everything that grows.

1977   1978

Five o'Clock, January 2003

Tonight as cargoes of my young
fellow countrymen and women are being hauled
into positions aimed at death, positions
they who did not will it suddenly
have to assume   5
I am thinking of Ed Azevedo
half-awake in recovery
if he has his arm whole
and how much pain he must bear
under the drugs   10
On cliffs above a beach
luxuriant in low tide after storms
littered with driftwood hurled and piled and
humanly arranged in fantastic
installations and beyond   15
silk-blue and onion-silver-skinned
Jeffers' "most glorious creature on earth"
we passed, greeting, I saw his arm
bandaged to the elbow
asked and he told me: It was just   20
a small cut, nothing, on the hand he'd
washed in peroxide thinking
that was it until the pain began
traveling up his arm
and then the antibiotics the splint the   25
numbing drugs the sick sensation
and this evening at five o'clock the emergency
surgery and last summer
the train from Czechoslovakia to Spain
with his girl, cheap wine, bread and cheese   30
room with a balcony, ocean like this

nobody asking for pay in advance
kindness of foreigners
in that country, sick sensation now
needing to sit in his brother's truck again   35
even the accident on the motorcycle
was nothing like this
I'll be thinking of you at five
this evening I said
afterward you'll feel better, your body   40
will be clean of this poison
I didn't say Your war is here
but could you have believed
that from a small thing infection
would crawl through the blood   45
and the enormous ruffled shine
of an ocean wouldn't tell you.

2003

GARY SNYDER
b. 1930

"I try to hold both history and wildness in my mind, that my poems may approach the true measure of things and stand against the unbalance and ignorance of our time," Gary Snyder has said. Throughout his life Snyder has sought alternatives to this imbalance. His quest has led him to the natural world, to the study of mythology and the discipline of Eastern religions, and to living oral traditions including those of Native American societies. Snyder understands the work of poetry as recovery and healing. Like the shaman-poet of primitive cultures whose power to "heal disease and resist death" is "acquired from dreams" (as he writes in the essay "Poetry and the Primitive"), he seeks to restore contact with a vital universe in which all things are interdependent. The journey of Snyder's life and work has taken him back to what he calls "the most archaic values on earth." His poems are acts of cultural criticism, challenges to the dominant values of the contemporary world.

The American West Coast is Snyder's native landscape; its forests and mountains have always attracted him, and they inspire many of his poems. He was born in San Francisco, grew up in Washington State, and later moved with his family to Portland, Oregon. In 1947 he entered Reed College, where he studied anthropology and developed a special interest in Native American cultures (Northwest Coast Indian myths and tales inform his second book, *Myths and Texts,* 1960). After doing graduate work in linguistics at Indiana University, he returned to the West, where he became associated with Kenneth Rexroth and Philip Whalen and with Jack Kerouac and Allen Ginsberg, all of whom participated in what came to be called the San Francisco Renaissance. In this period Snyder also studied classical Chinese at the University of California at Berkeley and translated some of the Cold Mountain poems of the Zen poet Han-shan. In the mid 1950s Snyder went to Japan, where he resided, except intermittently, until 1968; in Japan he took formal instruction in Buddhism under Zen masters. The various traditions Snyder has studied come together in his varied vision-quest poems.

Snyder's poems, like his life, combine reading and formal study with physical activity; he has worked as a timber scaler, a forest-fire lookout (one of his lookouts inspired "August on Sourdough"), a logger, and a hand on a tanker in the South Pacific. "My poems follow the rhythms of the physical work I'm doing and the life I'm leading at any given time," he has remarked. The title of his first book, *Riprap* (1959), is a forester's term for, he explains, "a cobble of stone laid on steep slick rock to make a trail for horses in the mountains." Snyder's poems often follow a trail of ascent or descent, as in "Straight-Creek–Great Burn" from his Pulitzer Prize–winning volume, *Turtle Island* (1975). Hiking with friends, he experiences the world as dynamic and flowing (running water and "changing clouds"), but the journey brings the walkers to a still point; they lie "resting on dry fern and / watching." From such a stillness the central image of a Snyder poem often rises, like the birds who "arch and loop," then "settle down." The achievement of stillness in a universe of change is, for Snyder, pivotal. The mind empties itself, the individual ego is erased, and the local place reveals the universal.

If Snyder's poems contain a Zenlike stillness, they also exhibit an appealing energy, one source of which is his love of wildness. Like the Henry David Thoreau, of *Walden*, explicitly evoked in sections of *Myths and Texts*, Snyder finds a tonic wildness in the natural world, but unlike Thoreau he is an unabashed celebrant of erotic experience (his earlier poems make it clear that he also knows the destructive possibilities in such experience). He renders one of the various faces of Eros in "Beneath My Hand and Eye the Distant Hills. Your Body" (from *The Back Country*, 1968).

Some of Snyder's numerous essays on politics and ecology are included in his influential *Earth House Hold* (1969), *The Practice of the Wild* (1990), and *A Place in Space: Ethics, Aesthetics and Watersheds* (1995). His collections *Axe Handles* (1983), *Left Out in the Rain* (1986), and *No Nature: New and Selected Poems* (1992) confirm that his poems are bound up in the same concerns. *Danger on Peaks* (2004) continues Snyder's explorations of landscape and ecology and also registers the upheavals of change in the earth and in the body, including the world-changing events of September 11, 2001, memorialized in "Falling from a Height, Holding Hands." Although his didactic impulse sometimes leads him to oversimplification, Snyder's political vision remains one strength of his poetry. The potential in this vision for self-importance and over-seriousness is tempered by his sense of humor and the conviction, palpable in his best poems, that his experiences are common and shared. Snyder's poems suggest diverse contexts: his belief in the writer as cultural critic links him to Thoreau and Robert Duncan, his rhythms and strong images recall Ezra Pound, his meticulous attention to the natural world reminds us of Robert Frost and A. R. Ammons. Eclectic yet respectful of ancient traditions, Snyder is an American original who sees his own work as part of a "continual creation," one manifestation of the energy that sustains all life.

Riprap[1]

Lay down these words
Before your mind like rocks.
            placed solid, by hands
In choice of place, set
Before the body of the mind   5
            in space and time:
Solidity of bark, leaf, or wall
            riprap of things:

1. A cobble of stone laid on steep slick rock to make a trail for horses in the mountains [Snyder's note].

Cobble of milky way,
    straying planets,   10
These poems, people,
    lost ponies with
Dragging saddles—
    and rocky sure-foot trails.
The worlds like an endless   15
    four-dimensional
Game of *Go*.[2]
    ants and pebbles
In the thin loam, each rock a word
    a creek-washed stone   20
Granite: ingrained
    with torment of fire and weight
Crystal and sediment linked hot
    all change, in thoughts,
As well as things.   25

             1959

August on Sourdough,[1] A Visit from Dick Brewer

You hitched a thousand miles
    north from San Francisco
Hiked up the mountainside a mile in the air
The little cabin—one room—
    walled in glass   5
Meadows and snowfields, hundreds of peaks.
We lay in our sleeping bags
    talking half the night;
Wind in the guy-cables this summer mountain rain.
Next morning I went with you   10
    as far as the cliffs,
Loaned you my poncho— the rain across the shale—
You down the snowfield
    flapping in the wind
Waving a last goodbye half hidden in the clouds 15
To go on hitching
    clear to New York;
Me back to my mountain and far, far, west.

             1968

---

2. An ancient Japanese game played with black and white stones, placed one after the other on a checkered board.

1. Mountain in Washington State, where Snyder worked as a fire-watcher during the summer of 1953.

Beneath My Hand and Eye the Distant Hills. Your Body

What my hand follows on your body
Is the line. A stream of love
   of heat, of light,   what my
  eye   lascivious
       licks
  over, watching   5
   far snow-dappled Uintah mountains[1]
Is that stream.
Of power.   what my
  hand curves over, following the line.   10
  "hip" and "groin"

Where "I"
  follow by hand and eye
  the swimming limit of your body.
As when vision idly dallies on the hills   15
Loving what it feeds on.
  soft cinder cones and craters;
  —Drum Hadley in the Pinacate[2]
  took ten minutes more to look again—
A leap of power unfurling: 20
   left,   right—right—
My heart beat faster looking
  at the snowy Uintah mountains.

As my hand feeds on you
  runs down your side and curls beneath your hip.   25
oil pool; stratum; water—

What "is" within   not known
  but feel it
  sinking with a breath
  pusht ruthless, surely, down.   30

Beneath this long caress of hand and eye
  "we" learn the flower burning,
    outward, from "below".

1968

---

1. In northeastern Utah.   2. California town.

TONI MORRISON
b. 1931

The 1993 Nobel Laureate in literature, Toni Morrison is a novelist of great importance in her own right and has been the central figure in putting fiction by and about African American women at the forefront of the late twentieth-century literary canon. Whereas the legacy of slavery had effaced a usable tradition, and critical stereotypes at times restricted such writers' range, Morrison's fiction serves as a model for reconstructing a culturally empowering past. She joins the great American tradition of self-invention: her example and her editorial work have figured importantly in the careers of other writers, such as Toni Cade Bambara (included in this volume) and Gayl Jones.

Morrison was born in Lorain, Ohio, where much of her fiction is set (a departure from earlier African American narratives typically located in the rural South or urban North). Having earned a B.A. from Howard University with a major in English and minor in classics, and an M.A. from Cornell University (with a thesis on suicide in the novels of Virginia Woolf and William Faulkner), Morrison began a teaching career in 1955 that reached from Texas Southern University back to Howard, where her students included the future activist Stokeley Carmichael and the future critic Houston A. Baker Jr. At this time she married Harold Morrison, a Jamaican architect, with whom she had two children before ending their marriage in 1964. Already writing, she took a job with the publishing firm of Random House and eventually settled in New York City, where she worked until 1983. During these same years she held visiting teaching appointments at institutions including Yale University and Bard College.

As a first novel *The Bluest Eye* (1970) is uncommonly mature for its confident use of various narrative voices. Throughout her career Morrison has been dedicated to constructing a practical cultural identity of a race and a gender whose self-images have been obscured or denied by dominating forces, and in *The Bluest Eye* she already shows that narrative strategy is an important element in such construction. A girl's need to be loved generates the novel's action, action that involves displaced and alienated affections (and eventually incestuous rape); the family's inability to produce a style of existence in which love can be born and thrive leads to such a devastating fate for Morrison's protagonist. Love is also denied in *Sula* (1974), in which relationships extend in two directions: between contemporaries (Sula and her friend Nel) and with previous generations.

With *Song of Solomon* (1977) Morrison seeks a more positive redemption of her characters. Turning away from his parents' loveless marriage, Milkman Dead makes a physical and mental journey to his ancestral roots. Here he discovers a more useful legacy in communal tales about Grandmother and Great-Grandfather, each long dead but infusing the local culture with emotionally sustaining lore. Milkman uses this lore to learn how the spiritual guidance offered by his aunt Pilate eclipses the material concerns of his parents' world.

Allegory becomes an important strategy in *Tar Baby* (1981), drawing on the strong folk culture of Haiti, where two contrasting persons form a troubled relationship based on their distinct searches for and rejections of a heritage. Yet it is in a rebuilding of history, rather than allegory or myth, that Morrison achieves her great strength as a novelist in *Beloved* (1987), the winner of her first major award, the Pulitzer Prize. Set in the middle 1870s, when race relations in America were at their most crucial juncture (slavery having ended and the course of the South's Reconstruction not yet fully determined), this novel shows a mother (Sethe) being haunted and eventually destroyed by the ghost of a daughter (Beloved) whom she had killed eighteen years earlier rather than let her be taken by a vicious slavemaster. This novel is central to Morrison's canon because it involves so many important themes and techniques, from love and guilt to history's role in clarifying the past's influence on the present, all told in a style of magical realism that transforms (without denying) more mundane facts.

Jazz (1992) finds Morrison modeling her narrative voice, on the progression of a jazz solo to demonstrate how improvisation with detail can change the nature of what is expressed. Present and past weave together in her characters' lives as the narrative seeks to understand the jealousies of love and the sometimes macabre manifestations of hatred. *Paradise* (1988) takes a nineteenth-century utopia and reexamines its ideals in the face of 1970s realities—a reminder of how neither past nor present can be insulated from the other. *Love* (2003), with its murder, arson, pedophilia, and several rapes punctuating a narrative in which arguments over a legacy dislodge awkward elements of the past, is a reminder of how topically disturbing Morrison's fiction can be.

Presently serving as the prestigious Golheen Professor of the Humanities at Princeton University, Morrison has moved easily into the role of spokesperson for literary issues. Together with her Nobel lecture, her essays collected as *Playing in the Dark: Whiteness and the Literary Imagination* (1992) challenge stereotypes in white critical thinking about black literature. Her short story "Recitatif," written for the 1983 anthology edited by Amiri and Amina Baraka, *Confirmation,* directly addresses the issues of individual and family, past and present, and race and its effacements that motivate the larger sense of her work. A "recitatif" is a vocal performance in which a narrative is not stated but sung. In her work Morrison's voice sings proudly of a past that in the artistic nature of its reconstruction puts all Americans in touch with a more positively usable heritage.

The text is from *Confirmation.*

Recitatif

My mother danced all night and Roberta's was sick. That's why we were taken to St. Bonny's. People want to put their arms around you when you tell them you were in a shelter, but it really wasn't bad. No big long room with one hundred beds like Bellevue.[1] There were four to a room, and when Roberta and me came, there was a shortage of state kids, so we were the only ones assigned to 406 and could go from bed to bed if we wanted to. And we wanted to, too. We changed beds every night and for the whole four months we were there we never picked one out as our own permanent bed.

It didn't start out that way. The minute I walked in and the Big Bozo introduced us, I got sick to my stomach. It was one thing to be taken out of your own bed early in the morning—it was something else to be stuck in a strange place with a girl from a whole other race. And Mary, that's my mother, she was right. Every now and then she would stop dancing long enough to tell me something important and one of the things she said was that they never washed their hair and they smelled funny. Roberta sure did. Smell funny, I mean. So when the Big Bozo (nobody ever called her Mrs. Itkin, just like nobody ever said St. Bonaventure)—when she said, "Twyla, this is Roberta. Roberta, this is Twyla. Make each other welcome." I said, "My mother won't like you putting me in here."

"Good," said Bozo. "Maybe then she'll come and take you home."

How's that for mean? If Roberta had laughed I would have killed her, but she didn't. She just walked over to the window and stood with her back to us.

"Turn around," said the Bozo. "Don't be rude. Now Twyla. Roberta. When

---

1. Bellevue Hospital in New York City is known for its psychiatric ward. St. Bonaventure's offers the services of a youth shelter and school.

you hear a loud buzzer, that's the call for dinner. Come down to the first floor. Any fights and no movie." And then, just to make sure we knew what we would be missing, *"The Wizard of Oz."*[2]

Roberta must have thought I meant that my mother would be mad about my being put in the shelter. Not about rooming with her, because as soon as Bozo left she came over to me and said, "Is your mother sick too?"

"No," I said. "She just likes to dance all night."

"Oh," she nodded her head and I liked the way she understood things so fast. So for the moment it didn't matter that we looked like salt and pepper standing there and that's what the other kids called us sometimes. We were eight years old and got F's all the time. Me because I couldn't remember what I read or what the teacher said. And Roberta because she couldn't read at all and didn't even listen to the teacher. She wasn't good at anything except jacks, at which she was a killer: pow scoop pow scoop pow scoop.

We didn't like each other all that much at first, but nobody else wanted to play with us because we weren't real orphans with beautiful dead parents in the sky. We were dumped. Even the New York City Puerto Ricans and the upstate Indians ignored us. All kinds of kids were in there, black ones, white ones, even two Koreans. The food was good, though. At least I thought so. Roberta hated it and left whole pieces of things on her plate: Spam, Salisbury steak—even jello with fruit cocktail in it, and she didn't care if I ate what she wouldn't. Mary's idea of supper was popcorn and a can of Yoo-Hoo.[3] Hot mashed potatoes and two weenies was like Thanksgiving for me.

It really wasn't bad, St. Bonny's. The big girls on the second floor pushed us around now and then. But that was all. They wore lipstick and eyebrow pencil and wobbled their knees while they watched TV. Fifteen, sixteen, even, some of them were. They were put-out girls, scared runaways most of them. Poor little girls who fought their uncles off but looked tough to us, and mean. God did they look mean. The staff tried to keep them separate from the younger children, but sometimes they caught us watching them in the orchard where they played radios and danced with each other. They'd light out after us and pull our hair or twist our arms. We were scared of them, Roberta and me, but neither of us wanted the other one to know it. So we got a good list of dirty names we could shout back when we ran from them through the orchard. I used to dream a lot and almost always the orchard was there. Two acres, four maybe, of these little apple trees. Hundreds of them. Empty and crooked like beggar women when I first came to St. Bonny's but fat with flowers when I left. I don't know why I dreamt about that orchard so much. Nothing really happened there. Nothing all that important, I mean. Just the big girls dancing and playing the radio. Roberta and me watching. Maggie fell down there once. The kitchen woman with legs like parentheses. And the big girls laughed at her. We should have helped her up, I know, but we were scared of those girls with lipstick and eyebrow pencil. Maggie couldn't talk. The kids said she had her tongue cut out, but I think she was just born that way: mute. She was old and sandy-colored and she worked in the kitchen. I don't know if she was nice or not. I just remember her legs like parentheses and how she rocked when she walked. She worked from early in

---

2. The 1939 film based on the 1900 children's book by the American writer L. Frank Baum (1856–1919).

3. A chocolate soft drink.

the morning till two o'clock, and if she was late, if she had too much cleaning and didn't get out till two-fifteen or so, she'd cut through the orchard so
she wouldn't miss her bus and have to wait another hour. She wore this really
stupid little hat—a kid's hat with ear flaps—and she wasn't much taller than
we were. A really awful little hat. Even for a mute, it was dumb—dressing like
a kid and never saying anything at all.

"But what about if somebody tries to kill her?" I used to wonder about that.
"Or what if she wants to cry? Can she cry?"

"Sure," Roberta said. "But just tears. No sounds come out."

"She can't scream?"

"Nope. Nothing."

"Can she hear?"

"I guess."

"Let's call her," I said. And we did.

"Dummy! Dummy!" She never turned her head.

"Bow legs! Bow legs!" Nothing. She just rocked on, the chin straps of her
baby-boy hat swaying from side to side. I think we were wrong. I think she
could hear and didn't let on. And it shames me even now to think there was
somebody in there after all who heard us call her those names and couldn't
tell on us.

We got along all right, Roberta and me. Changed beds every night, got F's
in civics and communication skills and gym. The Bozo was disappointed in
us, she said. Out of 130 of us state cases, 90 were under twelve. Almost all
were real orphans with beautiful dead parents in the sky. We were the only
ones dumped and the only ones with F's in three classes including gym. So
we got along—what with her leaving whole pieces of things on her plate and
being nice about not asking questions.

I think it was the day before Maggie fell down that we found out our mothers were coming to visit us on the same Sunday. We had been at the shelter
twenty-eight days (Roberta twenty-eight and a half) and this was their first
visit with us. Our mothers would come at ten o'clock in time for chapel, then
lunch with us in the teachers' lounge. I thought if my dancing mother met
her sick mother it might be good for her. And Roberta thought her sick
mother would get a big bang out of a dancing one. We got excited about it and
curled each other's hair. After breakfast we sat on the bed watching the road
from the window. Roberta's socks were still wet. She washed them the night
before and put them on the radiator to dry. They hadn't, but she put them on
anyway because their tops were so pretty—scalloped in pink. Each of us had
a purple construction-paper basket that we had made in craft class. Mine had
a yellow crayon rabbit on it. Roberta's had eggs with wiggly lines of color.
Inside were cellophane grass and just the jelly beans because I'd eaten the
two marshmallow eggs they gave us. The Big Bozo came herself to get us.
Smiling she told us we looked very nice and to come downstairs. We were so
surprised by the smile we'd never seen before, neither of us moved.

"Don't you want to see your mommies?"

I stood up first and spilled the jelly beans all over the floor. Bozo's smile disappeared while we scrambled to get the candy up off the floor and put it back
in the grass.

She escorted us downstairs to the first floor, where the other girls were lining up to file into the chapel. A bunch of grown-ups stood to one side. Viewers

mostly. The old biddies who wanted servants and the fags who wanted company looking for children they might want to adopt. Once in a while a grandmother. Almost never anybody young or anybody whose face wouldn't scare you in the night. Because if any of the real orphans had young relatives they wouldn't be real orphans. I saw Mary right away. She had on those green slacks I hated and hated even more now because didn't she know we were going to chapel? And that fur jacket with the pocket linings so ripped she had to pull to get her hands out of them. But her face was pretty—like always, and she smiled and waved like she was the little girl looking for her mother—not me.

I walked slowly, trying not to drop the jelly beans and hoping the paper handle would hold. I had to use my last Chiclet because by the time I finished cutting everything out, all the Elmer's was gone. I am left-handed and the scissors never worked for me. It didn't matter, though; I might just as well have chewed the gum. Mary dropped to her knees and grabbed me, mashing the basket, the jelly beans, and the grass into her ratty fur jacket.

"Twyla, baby. Twyla, baby!"

I could have killed her. Already I heard the big girls in the orchard the next time saying, "Twyyyyyla, baby!" But I couldn't stay mad at Mary while she was smiling and hugging me and smelling of Lady Esther dusting powder. I wanted to stay buried in her fur all day.

To tell the truth I forgot about Roberta. Mary and I got in line for the traipse into chapel and I was feeling proud because she looked so beautiful even in those ugly green slacks that made her behind stick out. A pretty mother on earth is better than a beautiful dead one in the sky even if she did leave you all alone to go dancing.

I felt a tap on my shoulder, turned, and saw Roberta smiling. I smiled back, but not too much lest somebody think this visit was the biggest thing that ever happened in my life. Then Roberta said, "Mother, I want you to meet my roommate, Twyla. And that's Twyla's mother."

I looked up it seemed for miles. She was big. Bigger than any man and on her chest was the biggest cross I'd ever seen. I swear it was six inches long each way. And in the crook of her arm was the biggest Bible ever made.

Mary, simple-minded as ever, grinned and tried to yank her hand out of the pocket with the raggedy lining—to shake hands, I guess. Roberta's mother looked down at me and then looked down at Mary too. She didn't say anything, just grabbed Roberta with her Bible-free hand and stepped out of line, walking quickly to the rear of it. Mary was still grinning because she's not too swift when it comes to what's really going on. Then this light bulb goes off in her head and she says "That bitch!" really loud and us almost in the chapel now. Organ music whining; the Bonny Angels singing sweetly. Everybody in the world turned around to look. And Mary would have kept it up—kept calling names if I hadn't squeezed her hand as hard as I could. That helped a little, but she still twitched and crossed and uncrossed her legs all through service. Even groaned a couple of times. Why did I think she would come there and act right? Slacks. No hat like the grandmothers and viewers, and groaning all the while. When we stood for hymns she kept her mouth shut. Wouldn't even look at the words on the page. She actually reached in her purse for a mirror to check her lipstick. All I could think of was that she really needed to be killed. The sermon lasted a year, and I knew the real orphans were looking smug again.

We were supposed to have lunch in the teachers' lounge, but Mary didn't bring anything, so we picked fur and cellophane grass off the mashed jelly beans and ate them. I could have killed her. I sneaked a look at Roberta. Her mother had brought chicken legs and ham sandwiches and oranges and a whole box of chocolate-covered grahams. Roberta drank milk from a thermos while her mother read the Bible to her.

Things are not right. The wrong food is always with the wrong people. Maybe that's why I got into waitress work later—to match up the right people with the right food. Roberta just let those chicken legs sit there, but she did bring a stack of grahams up to me later when the visit was over. I think she was sorry that her mother would not shake my mother's hand. And I liked that and I liked the fact that she didn't say a word about Mary groaning all the way through the service and not bringing any lunch.

Roberta left in May when the apple trees were heavy and white. On her last day we went to the orchard to watch the big girls smoke and dance by the radio. It didn't matter that they said, "Twyyyyyla, baby." We sat on the ground and breathed. Lady Esther. Apple blossoms. I still go soft when I smell one or the other. Roberta was going home. The big cross and the big Bible was coming to get her and she seemed sort of glad and sort of not. I thought I would die in that room of four beds without her and I knew Bozo had plans to move some other dumped kid in there with me. Roberta promised to write every day, which was really sweet of her because she couldn't read a lick so how could she write anybody. I would have drawn pictures and sent them to her but she never gave me her address. Little by little she faded. Her wet socks with the pink scalloped tops and her big serious-looking eyes—that's all I could catch when I tried to bring her to mind.

 I was working behind the counter at the Howard Johnson's on the Thruway just before the Kingston exit. Not a bad job. Kind of a long ride from Newburgh,[4] but okay once I got there. Mine was the second night shift—eleven to seven. Very light until a Greyhound checked in for breakfast around six-thirty. At that hour the sun was all the way clear of the hills behind the restaurant. The place looked better at night—more like shelter—but I loved it when the sun broke in, even if it did show all the cracks in the vinyl and the speckled floor looked dirty no matter what the mop boy did.

It was August and a bus crowd was just unloading. They would stand around a long while: going to the john, and looking at gifts and junk-for-sale machines, reluctant to sit down so soon. Even to eat. I was trying to fill the coffee pots and get them all situated on the electric burners when I saw her. She was sitting in a booth smoking a cigarette with two guys smothered in head and facial hair. Her own hair was so big and wild I could hardly see her face. But the eyes. I would know them anywhere. She had on a powder-blue halter and shorts outfit and earrings the size of bracelets. Talk about lipstick and eyebrow pencil. She made the big girls look like nuns. I couldn't get off the counter until seven o'clock, but I kept watching the booth in case they got up to leave before that. My replacement was on time for a change, so I counted and stacked my receipts as fast as I could and signed off. I walked over to the booth, smiling and wondering if she would remember me. Or even if she wanted to remember me. Maybe she didn't want to be reminded of St.

---

4. A community eighty miles north of New York City.

Bonny's or to have anybody know she was ever there. I know I never talked about it to anybody.

I put my hands in my apron pockets and leaned against the back of the booth facing them.

"Roberta? Roberta Fisk?"

She looked up. "Yeah?"

"Twyla."

She squinted for a second and then said, "Wow."

"Remember me?"

"Sure. Hey. Wow."

"It's been a while," I said, and gave a smile to the two hairy guys.

"Yeah. Wow. You work here?"

"Yeah," I said. "I live in Newburgh."

"Newburgh? No kidding?" She laughed then a private laugh that included the guys but only the guys, and they laughed with her. What could I do but laugh too and wonder why I was standing there with my knees showing out from under that uniform. Without looking I could see the blue and white triangle on my head, my hair shapeless in a net, my ankles thick in white oxfords. Nothing could have been less sheer than my stockings. There was this silence that came down right after I laughed. A silence it was her turn to fill up. With introductions, maybe, to her boyfriends or an invitation to sit down and have a Coke. Instead she lit a cigarette off the one she'd just finished and said, "We're on our way to the Coast. He's got an appointment with Hendrix."[5] She gestured casually toward the boy next to her.

"Hendrix? Fantastic," I said. "Really fantastic. What's she doing now?"

Roberta coughed on her cigarette and the two guys rolled their eyes up at the ceiling.

"Hendrix. Jimi Hendrix, asshole. He's only the biggest—Oh, wow. Forget it."

I was dismissed without anyone saying goodbye, so I thought I would do it for her.

"How's your mother?" I asked. Her grin cracked her whole face. She swallowed. "Fine," she said. "How's yours?"

"Pretty as a picture," I said and turned away. The backs of my knees were damp. Howard Johnson's really was a dump in the sunlight.

James is as comfortable as a house slipper. He liked my cooking and I liked his big loud family. They have lived in Newburgh all of their lives and talk about it the way people do who have always known a home. His grandmother is a porch swing older than his father and when they talk about streets and avenues and buildings they call them names they no longer have. They still call the A & P[6] Rico's because it stands on property once a mom and pop store owned by Mr. Rico. And they call the new community college Town Hall because it once was. My mother-in-law puts up jelly and cucumbers and buys butter wrapped in cloth from a dairy. James and his father talk about fishing and baseball and I can see them all together on the Hudson in a raggedy skiff. Half the population of Newburgh is on welfare now, but to my husband's family it was still some upstate paradise of a time long past. A time of ice houses

5. Jimi Hendrix (1942–1970), African American musician and rock star.   6. Supermarket, part of a national chain.

and vegetable wagons, coal furnaces and children weeding gardens. When our son was born my mother-in-law gave me the crib blanket that had been hers.

But the town they remembered had changed. Something quick was in the air. Magnificent old houses, so ruined they had become shelter for squatters and rent risks, were bought and renovated. Smart IBM people[7] moved out of their suburbs back into the city and put shutters up and herb gardens in their backyards. A brochure came in the mail announcing the opening of a Food Emporium. Gourmet food it said—and listed items the rich IBM crowd would want. It was located in a new mall at the edge of town and I drove out to shop there one day—just to see. It was late in June. After the tulips were gone and the Queen Elizabeth roses were open everywhere. I trailed my cart along the aisle tossing in smoked oysters and Robert's sauce and things I knew would sit in my cupboard for years. Only when I found some Klondike ice cream bars did I feel less guilty about spending James's fireman's salary so foolishly. My father-in-law ate them with the same gusto little Joseph did.

Waiting in the check-out line I heard a voice say, "Twyla!"

The classical music piped over the aisles had affected me and the woman leaning toward me was dressed to kill. Diamonds on her hand, a smart white summer dress. "I'm Mrs. Benson," I said.

"Ho. Ho. The Big Bozo," she sang.

For a split second I didn't know what she was talking about. She had a bunch of asparagus and two cartons of fancy water.

"Roberta!"

"Right."

"For heaven's sake. Roberta."

"You look great," she said.

"So do you. Where are you? Here? In Newburgh?"

"Yes. Over in Annandale."

I was opening my mouth to say more when the cashier called my attention to her empty counter.

"Meet you outside." Roberta pointed her finger and went into the express line.

I placed the groceries and kept myself from glancing around to check Roberta's progress. I remembered Howard Johnson's and looking for a chance to speak only to be greeted with a stingy "wow." But she was waiting for me and her huge hair was sleek now, smooth around a small, nicely shaped head. Shoes, dress, everything lovely and summery and rich. I was dying to know what happened to her, how she got from Jimi Hendrix to Annandale, a neighborhood full of doctors and IBM executives. Easy, I thought. Everything is so easy for them. They think they own the world.

"How long," I asked her. "How long have you been here?"

"A year. I got married to a man who lives here. And you, you're married too, right? Benson, you said."

"Yeah. James Benson."

"And is he nice?"

"Oh, is he nice?"

7. High-salaried employees of the International Business Machine Corporation, headquartered in the suburbs of New York City.

"Well, is he?" Roberta's eyes were steady as though she really meant the question and wanted an answer.

"He's wonderful, Roberta. Wonderful."

"So you're happy."

"Very."

"That's good," she said and nodded her head. "I always hoped you'd be happy. Any kids? I know you have kids."

"One. A boy. How about you?"

"Four."

"Four?"

She laughed. "Step kids. He's a widower."

"Oh."

"Got a minute? Let's have a coffee."

I thought about the Klondikes melting and the inconvenience of going all the way to my car and putting the bags in the trunk. Served me right for buying all that stuff I didn't need. Roberta was ahead of me.

"Put them in my car. It's right here."

And then I saw the dark blue limousine.

"You married a Chinaman?"

"No," she laughed. "He's the driver."

"Oh, my. If the Big Bozo could see you now."

We both giggled. Really giggled. Suddenly, in just a pulse beat, twenty years disappeared and all of it came rushing back. The big girls (whom we called gar girls—Roberta's misheard word for the evil stone faces described in a civics class) there dancing in the orchard, the ploppy mashed potatoes, the double weenies, the Spam with pineapple. We went into the coffee shop holding on to one another and I tried to think why we were glad to see each other this time and not before. Once, twelve years ago, we passed like strangers. A black girl and a white girl meeting in a Howard Johnson's on the road and having nothing to say. One in a blue and white triangle waitress hat—the other on her way to see Hendrix. Now we were behaving like sisters separated for much too long. Those four short months were nothing in time. Maybe it was the thing itself. Just being there, together. Two little girls who knew what nobody else in the world knew—how not to ask questions. How to believe what had to be believed. There was politeness in that reluctance and generosity as well. Is your mother sick too? No, she dances all night. Oh—and an understanding nod.

We sat in a booth by the window and fell into recollection like veterans.

"Did you ever learn to read?"

"Watch." She picked up the menu. "Special of the day. Cream of corn soup. Entrées. Two dots and a wriggly line. Quiche. Chef salad, scallops . . ."

I was laughing and applauding when the waitress came up.

"Remember the Easter baskets?"

"And how we tried to *introduce* them?"

"Your mother with that cross like two telephone poles."

"And yours with those tight slacks."

We laughed so loudly heads turned and made the laughter harder to suppress.

"What happened to the Jimi Hendrix date?"

Roberta made a blow-out sound with her lips.

"When he died I thought about you."

"Oh, you heard about him finally?"

"Finally. Come on, I was a small-town country waitress."

"And I was a small-town country dropout. God, were we wild. I still don't know how I got out of there alive."

"But you did."

"I did. I really did. Now I'm Mrs. Kenneth Norton."

"Sounds like a mouthful."

"It is."

"Servants and all?"

Roberta held up two fingers.

"Ow! What does he do?"

"Computers and stuff. What do I know?"

"I don't remember a hell of a lot from those days, but Lord, St. Bonny's is as clear as daylight. Remember Maggie? The day she fell down and those gar girls laughed at her?"

Roberta looked up from her salad and stared at me. "Maggie didn't fall," she said.

"Yes, she did. You remember."

"No, Twyla. They knocked her down. Those girls pushed her down and tore her clothes. In the orchard."

"I don't—that's not what happened."

"Sure it is. In the orchard. Remember how scared we were?"

"Wait a minute. I don't remember any of that."

"And Bozo was fired."

"You're crazy. She was there when I left. You left before me."

"I went back. You weren't there when they fired Bozo."

"What?"

"Twice. Once for a year when I was about ten, another for two months when I was fourteen. That's when I ran away."

"You ran away from St. Bonny's?"

"I had to. What do you want? Me dancing in that orchard?"

"Are you sure about Maggie?"

"Of course I'm sure. You've blocked it, Twyla. It happened. Those girls had behavior problems, you know."

"Didn't they, though. But why can't I remember the Maggie thing?"

"Believe me. It happened. And we were there."

"Who did you room with when you went back?" I asked her as if I would know her. The Maggie thing was troubling me.

"Creeps. They tickled themselves in the night."

My ears were itching and I wanted to go home suddenly. This was all very well but she couldn't just comb her hair, wash her face and pretend everything was hunky-dory. After the Howard Johnson's snub. And no apology. Nothing.

"Were you on dope or what that time at Howard Johnson's?" I tried to make my voice sound friendlier than I felt.

"Maybe, a little. I never did drugs much. Why?"

"I don't know; you acted sort of like you didn't want to know me then."

"Oh, Twyla, you know how it was in those days: black—white. You know how everything was."

But I didn't know. I thought it was just the opposite. Busloads of blacks and whites came into Howard Johnson's together. They roamed together then: students, musicians, lovers, protesters. You got to see everything at Howard Johnson's and blacks were very friendly with whites in those days. But sitting there with nothing on my plate but two hard tomato wedges wondering about the melting Klondikes it seemed childish remembering the slight. We went to her car, and with the help of the driver, got my stuff into my station wagon.

"We'll keep in touch this time," she said.

"Sure," I said. "Sure. Give me a call."

"I will," she said, and then just as I was sliding behind the wheel, she leaned into the window. "By the way. Your mother. Did she ever stop dancing?"

I shook my head. "No. Never."

Roberta nodded.

"And yours? Did she ever get well?"

She smiled a tiny sad smile. "No. She never did. Look, call me, okay?"

"Okay," I said, but I knew I wouldn't. Roberta had messed up my past somehow with that business about Maggie. I wouldn't forget a thing like that. Would I?

Strife came to us that fall. At least that's what the paper called it. Strife. Racial strife. The word made me think of a bird—a big shrieking bird out of 1,000,000,000 B.C. Flapping its wings and cawing. Its eye with no lid always bearing down on you. All day it screeched and at night it slept on the rooftops. It woke you in the morning and from the *Today* show to the eleven o'clock news it kept you an awful company. I couldn't figure it out from one day to the next. I knew I was supposed to feel something strong, but I didn't know what, and James wasn't any help. Joseph was on the list of kids to be transferred from the junior high school to another one at some far-out-of-the-way place and I thought it was a good thing until I heard it was a bad thing. I mean I didn't know. All the schools seemed dumps to me, and the fact that one was nicer looking didn't hold much weight. But the papers were full of it and then the kids began to get jumpy. In August, mind you. Schools weren't even open yet. I thought Joseph might be frightened to go over there, but he didn't seem scared so I forgot about it, until I found myself driving along Hudson Street out there by the school they were trying to integrate and saw a line of women marching. And who do you suppose was in line, big as life, holding a sign in front of her bigger than her mother's cross? MOTHERS HAVE RIGHTS TOO! it said.

I drove on, and then changed my mind. I circled the block, slowed down, and honked my horn.

Roberta looked over and when she saw me she waved. I didn't wave back, but I didn't move either. She handed her sign to another woman and came over to where I was parked.

"Hi."

"What are you doing?"

"Picketing. What's it look like?"

"What for?"

"What do you mean 'What for?' They want to take my kids and send them out of the neighborhood. They don't want to go."

"So what if they go to another school? My boy's being bussed too, and I don't mind. Why should you?"

"It's not about us, Twyla. Me and you. It's about our kids."

"What's more *us* than that?"

"Well, it is a free country."

"Not yet, but it will be."

"What the hell does that mean? I'm not doing anything to you."

"You really think that?"

"I know it."

"I wonder what made me think you were different."

"I wonder what made me think you were different."

"Look at them," I said. "Just look. Who do they think they are? Swarming all over the place like they own it. And now they think they can decide where my child goes to school. Look at them, Roberta. They're Bozos."

Roberta turned around and looked at the women. Almost all of them were standing still now, waiting. Some were even edging toward us. Roberta looked at me out of some refrigerator behind her eyes. "No, they're not. They're just mothers."

"And what am I? Swiss cheese?"

"I used to curl your hair."

"I hated your hands in my hair."

The women were moving. Our faces looked mean to them of course and they looked as though they could not wait to throw themselves in front of a police car, or better yet, into my car and drag me away by my ankles. Now they surrounded my car and gently, gently began to rock it. I swayed back and forth like a sideways yo-yo. Automatically I reached for Roberta, like the old days in the orchard when they saw us watching them and we had to get out of there, and if one of us fell the other pulled her up and if one of us was caught the other stayed to kick and scratch, and neither would leave the other behind. My arm shot out of the car window but no receiving hand was there.

Roberta was looking at me sway from side to side in the car and her face was still. My purse slid from the car seat down under the dashboard. The four policemen who had been drinking Tab[8] in their car finally got the message and strolled over, forcing their way through the women. Quietly, firmly they spoke. "Okay, ladies. Back in line or off the streets."

Some of them went away willingly; others had to be urged away from the car doors and the hood. Roberta didn't move. She was looking steadily at me. I was fumbling to turn on the ignition, which wouldn't catch because the gearshift was still in drive. The seats of the car were a mess because the swaying had thrown my grocery coupons all over it and my purse was sprawled on the floor.

"Maybe I am different now, Twyla. But you're not. You're the same little state kid who kicked a poor old black lady when she was down on the ground. You kicked a black lady and you have the nerve to call me a bigot."

The coupons were everywhere and the guts of my purse were bunched under the dashboard. What was she saying? Black? Maggie wasn't black.

"She wasn't black," I said.

"Like hell she wasn't, and you kicked her. We both did. You kicked a black lady who couldn't even scream."

"Liar!"

---

8. A diet soda.

"You're the liar! Why don't you just go on home and leave us alone, huh?"

She turned away and I skidded away from the curb.

The next morning I went into the garage and cut the side out of the carton our portable TV had come in. It wasn't nearly big enough, but after a while I had a decent sign: red spray-painted letters on a white background—AND SO DO CHILDREN * * * *. I meant just to go down to the school and tack it up somewhere so those cows on the picket line across the street could see it, but when I got there, some ten or so others had already assembled—protesting the cows across the street. Police permits and everything. I got in line and we strutted in time on our side while Roberta's group strutted on theirs. That first day we were all dignified, pretending the other side didn't exist. The second day there was name calling and finger gestures. But that was about all. People changed signs from time to time, but Roberta never did and neither did I. Actually my sign didn't make sense without Roberta's. "And so do children what?" one of the women on my side asked me. Have rights, I said, as though it was obvious.

Roberta didn't acknowledge my presence in any way and I got to thinking maybe she didn't know I was there. I began to pace myself in the line, jostling people one minute and lagging behind the next, so Roberta and I could reach the end of our respective lines at the same time and there would be a moment in our turn when we would face each other. Still, I couldn't tell whether she saw me and knew my sign was for her. The next day I went early before we were scheduled to assemble. I waited until she got there before I exposed my new creation. As soon as she hoisted her MOTHERS HAVE RIGHTS TOO I began to wave my new one, which said, HOW WOULD YOU KNOW? I know she saw that one, but I had gotten addicted now. My signs got crazier each day, and the women on my side decided that I was a kook. They couldn't make heads or tails out of my brilliant screaming posters.

I brought a painted sign in queenly red with huge black letters that said, IS YOUR MOTHER WELL? Roberta took her lunch break and didn't come back for the rest of the day or any day after. Two days later I stopped going too and couldn't have been missed because nobody understood my signs anyway.

It was a nasty six weeks. Classes were suspended and Joseph didn't go to anybody's school until October. The children—everybody's children—soon got bored with that extended vacation they thought was going to be so great. They looked at TV until their eyes flattened. I spent a couple of mornings tutoring my son, as the other mothers said we should. Twice I opened a text from last year that he had never turned in. Twice he yawned in my face. Other mothers organized living room sessions so the kids would keep up. None of the kids could concentrate so they drifted back to *The Price Is Right* and *The Brady Bunch*.[9] When the school finally opened there were fights once or twice and some sirens roared through the streets every once in a while. There were a lot of photographers from Albany. And just when ABC was about to send up a news crew, the kids settled down like nothing in the world had happened. Joseph hung my HOW WOULD YOU KNOW? sign in his bedroom. I don't know what became of AND SO DO CHILDREN * * * *. I think my father-in-law cleaned some fish on it. He was always puttering around in our garage. Each of his five children lived in Newburgh and he acted as though he had five extra homes.

9. Popular television programs: respectively, a game show and a situation comedy.

I couldn't help looking for Roberta when Joseph graduated from high school, but I didn't see her. It didn't trouble me much what she had said to me in the car. I mean the kicking part. I know I didn't do that, I couldn't do that. But I was puzzled by her telling me Maggie was black. When I thought about it I actually couldn't be certain. She wasn't pitch-black, I knew, or I would have remembered that. What I remember was the kiddie hat, and the semicircle legs. I tried to reassure myself about the race thing for a long time until it dawned on me that the truth was already there, and Roberta knew it. I didn't kick her; I didn't join in with the gar girls and kick that lady, but I sure did want to. We watched and never tried to help her and never called for help. Maggie was my dancing mother. Deaf, I thought, and dumb. Nobody inside. Nobody who would hear you if you cried in the night. Nobody who could tell you anything important that you could use. Rocking, dancing, swaying as she walked. And when the gar girls pushed her down, and started roughhousing, I knew she wouldn't scream, couldn't—just like me—and I was glad about that.

We decided not to have a tree, because Christmas would be at my mother-in-law's house, so why have a tree at both places? Joseph was at SUNY New Paltz[1] and we had to economize, we said. But at the last minute, I changed my mind. Nothing could be that bad. So I rushed around town looking for a tree, something small but wide. By the time I found a place, it was snowing and very late. I dawdled like it was the most important purchase in the world and the tree man was fed up with me. Finally I chose one and had it tied onto the trunk of the car. I drove away slowly because the sand trucks were not out yet and the streets could be murder at the beginning of a snowfall. Downtown the streets were wide and rather empty except for a cluster of people coming out of the Newburgh Hotel. The one hotel in town that wasn't built out of cardboard and Plexiglas. A party, probably. The men huddled in the snow were dressed in tails and the women had on furs. Shiny things glittered from underneath their coats. It made me tired to look at them. Tired, tired, tired. On the next corner was a small diner with loops and loops of paper bells in the window. I stopped the car and went in. Just for a cup of coffee and twenty minutes of peace before I went home and tried to finish everything before Christmas Eve.

"Twyla?"

There she was. In a silvery evening gown and dark fur coat. A man and another woman were with her, the man fumbling for change to put in the cigarette machine. The woman was humming and tapping on the counter with her fingernails. They all looked a little bit drunk.

"Well. It's you."

"How are you?"

I shrugged. "Pretty good. Frazzled. Christmas and all."

"Regular?" called the woman from the counter.

"Fine," Roberta called back and then, "Wait for me in the car."

She slipped into the booth beside me. "I have to tell you something, Twyla. I made up my mind if I ever saw you again, I'd tell you."

"I'd just as soon not hear anything, Roberta. It doesn't matter now, anyway."

1. A campus in the State University of New York system.

"No," she said. "Not about that."

"Don't be long," said the woman. She carried two regulars to go and the man peeled his cigarette pack as they left.

"It's about St. Bonny's and Maggie."

"Oh, please."

"Listen to me. I really did think she was black. I didn't make that up. I really thought so. But now I can't be sure. I just remember her as old, so old. And because she couldn't talk—well, you know, I thought she was crazy. She'd been brought up in an institution like my mother was and like I thought I would be too. And you were right. We didn't kick her. It was the gar girls. Only them. But, well, I wanted to. I really wanted them to hurt her. I said we did it, too. You and me, but that's not true. And I don't want you to carry that around. It was just that I wanted to do it so bad that day—wanting to is doing it."

Her eyes were watery from the drinks she'd had, I guess. I know it's that way with me. One glass of wine and I start bawling over the littlest thing.

"We were kids, Roberta."

"Yeah. Yeah. I know, just kids."

"Eight."

"Eight."

"And lonely."

"Scared, too."

She wiped her cheeks with the heel of her hand and smiled. "Well, that's all I wanted to say."

I nodded and couldn't think of any way to fill the silence that went from the diner past the paper bells on out into the snow. It was heavy now. I thought I'd better wait for the sand trucks before starting home.

"Thanks, Roberta."

"Sure."

"Did I tell you? My mother, she never did stop dancing."

"Yes. You told me. And mine, she never got well." Roberta lifted her hands from the tabletop and covered her face with her palms. When she took them away she really was crying. "Oh shit, Twyla. Shit, shit, shit. What the hell happened to Maggie?"

1983

SYLVIA PLATH
1932–1963

In an introduction to Sylvia Plath's *Ariel* (1965), published two years after her suicide in London, Robert Lowell wrote: "In these poems . . . Sylvia Plath becomes herself, becomes something imaginary, newly, wildly, and subtly created— . . . one of those super-real, hypnotic great classical heroines." Lowell had first met Plath in 1958, during her regular visits to his poetry seminar at Boston University, where he remembered her "air of maddening docility." Later, writing his introduction, he recognized her astonishing creation of a poetic self. The poems of *Ariel* were written at white heat,

three a day, in the last months of Plath's life, but there is nothing hurried in
language or structure. When they are taken together with the poems posthumously published in *Crossing the Water* (1971) and *Winter Trees* (1972), a coherent
persona emerges: larger than life, operatic in feeling. Although this focus on the self
often excludes attention to the larger world, it generates the dynamic energy of her
work. Plath appropriates a centrally American tradition, the heroic ego confronting the
sublime, but she brilliantly revises this tradition by turning what the American Transcendentalist Ralph Waldo Emerson called the "great and crescive self" into a heroine instead of a hero. Seizing a mythic power, the Plath of the poems transmutes the
domestic and the ordinary into the hallucinatory, the utterly strange. Her revision of
the romantic ego dramatizes its tendency toward disproportion and excess, and she is
fully capable of both using and mocking this heightened sense of self, as she does in
her poem "Lady Lazarus."

Plath's well-known autobiographical novel, *The Bell Jar* (1963) has nothing of the
brilliance of her poems, but it effectively dramatizes the stereotyping of women's roles
in the 1950s and the turmoil of a young woman only partly aware that her gifts and
ambitions greatly exceed the options available to her. In the novel Plath uses her experience as a guest editor of a young-women's magazine (in real life, *Mademoiselle*) and
then, in an abrupt shift, presents her heroine's attempted suicide and hospitalization.
Plath had suffered a serious breakdown and attempted suicide between her junior and
senior years in college. The popularity of *The Bell Jar* may be one reason why attention to Plath's life has sometimes obscured the accomplishments of her art. While her
poems often begin in autobiography, their success depends on Plath's imaginative
transformations of experience into myth, as in a number of her poems (such as
"Daddy") where the figure of her Prussian father is transformed into an emblem for
masculine authority. Otto Plath was an entomologist and the author of a treatise on
bumblebees. His death in 1940 from gangrene (the consequence of a diabetic condition he refused to treat), when Plath was eight, was the crucial event of her childhood.
After his death her mother, Aurelia, while struggling to support two small children,
encouraged her daughter's literary ambitions.

In many ways Plath embodied the bright, young, middle-class woman of the 1950s.
She went to Smith College on a scholarship and graduated summa cum laude. On a
Fulbright grant she studied in England at Cambridge University, where she met and
married the poet Ted Hughes. On the face of it her marriage must have seemed the
perfect fate for such a young woman; it combined romance, two poets beginning
careers together (Plath's first book, *The Colossus,* appeared in 1960), and two children
(Frieda, born in 1960, and Nicholas, born in 1962), with a country house in Devon,
England. In her poems, however, we find the strains of such a life; the work is galvanized by suffering, by a terrible constriction against which she unlooses "The lioness,
/ The shriek in the bath, / The cloak of holes" ("Purdah"). In articulating a dark vision
of domestic life Plath adopted the license of Robert Lowell and Anne Sexton, a fellow
student in Lowell's poetry seminar, to write about "private and taboo subjects."

While still living in Devon, Plath wrote most of the poems that were to make up
Ariel (by Christmas, 1962, she had gathered them in a black binder and arranged them
in a careful sequence). The marriage broke up in the summer of 1962, and at the
beginning of the new year Plath found herself with two small children, living in a London flat during one of the coldest winters in recent British history. There she began
new poems, writing furiously until February 1963, when she took her own life. The
Ariel collection published by Hughes in 1965 does not follow Plath's intended
sequence; it omits what Hughes called "some of the more personally aggressive poems
from 1962" and includes the dozen or so poems Plath wrote in the months before her
death and that she had envisioned as the beginnings of a third book. Nonetheless, the
powerful, angry poems of *Ariel*, mining a limited range of deep feeling, are Plath's
best-known work. Fueled by an anger toward her husband and her father, she speaks
in these poems as one whose feelings are more than her own; it is as if she were the

character in George Eliot's *Daniel Deronda* (1876) who appears suddenly before the novel's heroine and says, "I am a woman's life." Other poems, however, demonstrate her ability to render a wider variety of emotion; they include poems about her children (such as "Morning Song," "Child," and "Parliament Hill Fields") and a number of arresting poems about the natural world. In the vastness of natural processes the Romantic ego finds something as large as itself, and Plath's response to nature is intense, often uncanny. Her poems offer an eccentric vision where (as in "Blackberrying") the appearance of the natural world is never separable from the consciousness of the one who sees it.

For all her courting of excess Plath is a remarkably controlled writer; her lucid stanzas, her clear diction, her dazzling alterations of sound display that control. The imaginative intensity of her poems is her own, triumphant creation out of the difficult circumstances of her life. She once remarked, "I cannot sympathize with those cries from the heart that are informed by nothing except a needle or a knife. . . . I believe that one should be able to control and manipulate experiences, even the most terrifying . . . with an informed and intelligent mind." The influence of her style, and of the persona she created, continues to be felt in the work of a wide variety of contemporary poets.

Morning Song

Love set you going like a fat gold watch.
The midwife slapped your footsoles, and your bald cry
Took its place among the elements.

Our voices echo, magnifying your arrival. New statue.
In a drafty museum, your nakedness   5
Shadows our safety. We stand round blankly as walls.

I'm no more your mother
Than the cloud that distills a mirror to reflect its own slow
Effacement at the wind's hand.

All night your moth-breath   10
Flickers among the flat pink roses. I wake to listen:
A far sea moves in my ear.

One cry, and I stumble from bed, cow-heavy and floral
In my Victorian nightgown.
Your mouth opens clean as a cat's. The window square   15

Whitens and swallows its dull stars. And now you try
Your handful of notes;
The clear vowels rise like balloons.

1961   1966

Lady Lazarus[1]

I have done it again.
One year in every ten
I manage it—

A sort of walking miracle, my skin
Bright as a Nazi lampshade,[2]   5
My right foot

A paperweight,
My face a featureless, fine
Jew linen.

Peel off the napkin   10
O my enemy.
Do I terrify?——

The nose, the eye pits, the full set of teeth?
The sour breath
Will vanish in a day.   15

Soon, soon the flesh
The grave cave ate will be
At home on me

And I a smiling woman.
I am only thirty.   20
And like the cat I have nine times to die.

This is Number Three.
What a trash
To annihilate each decade.

What a million filaments.   25
The peanut-crunching crowd
Shoves in to see

Them unwrap me hand and foot——
The big strip tease.
Gentlemen, ladies   30

These are my hands
My knees.
I may be skin and bone,

Nevertheless, I am the same, identical woman.
The first time it happened I was ten.   35
It was an accident.

[handwritten annotation: two her previous suicide attempts are like coming back to life – describing a third attempt]

[handwritten annotation: Circus, freak show]

1. Lazarus was raised from the dead by Jesus (John 11.1–45).   2. In the Nazi death camps the victims' skins were sometimes used to make lampshades.

The second time I meant
To last it out and not come back at all.
I rocked shut

As a seashell.   40
They had to call and call
And pick the worms off me like sticky pearls.

*dying is
her
calling*

Dying
Is an art, like everything else.
I do it exceptionally well.   45

I do it so it feels like hell.
I do it so it feels real.
I guess you could say I've a call.

It's easy enough to do it in a cell.
It's easy enough to do it and stay put.   50
It's the theatrical

Comeback in broad day
To the same place, the same face, the same brute
Amused shout:

'A miracle!'   55
That knocks me out.
There is a charge

For the eyeing of my scars, there is a charge
For the hearing of my heart——
It really goes.   60

And there is a charge, a very large charge
For a word or a touch
Or a bit of blood

Or a piece of my hair or my clothes.
So, so, Herr[3] Doktor.   65
So, Herr Enemy.

I am your opus,
I am your valuable,
The pure gold baby

That melts to a shriek.   70
I turn and burn.
Do not think I underestimate your great concern.

Ash, ash——
You poke and stir.
Flesh, bone, there is nothing there——   75

---

3. Mr. (German).

A cake of soap,
A wedding ring,
A gold filling.[4]

Herr God, Herr Lucifer (*devil*)
Beware   80
Beware.

personifying

pheonix ⎡ Out of the ash[5]
          ⎢ I rise with my red hair
          ⎣ And I eat men like air.

1962   1966

Daddy

You do not do, you do not do
Any more, black shoe
In which I have lived like a foot
For thirty years, poor and white,
Barely daring to breathe or Achoo.   5

Rhyme = Obsession

Daddy, I have had to kill you.
You died before I had time——
Marble-heavy, a bag full of God,
Ghastly statue with one grey toe[1]
Big as a Frisco seal   10

And a head in the freakish Atlantic
Where it pours bean green over blue
In the waters of beautiful Nauset.[2]
I used to pray to recover you.
Ach, du.[3]   15

In the German tongue, in the Polish town[4]
Scraped flat by the roller
Of wars, wars, wars.
But the name of the town is common.
My Polack friend   20

Says there are a dozen or two.
So I never could tell where you

4. The Nazis used human remains in the making
of soap and scavenged corpses for jewelry and gold
teeth.
5. An allusion to the phoenix, a mythical bird that
dies by fire and is reborn out of its own ashes.
1. Plath's father's toe turned black from gangrene,

a complication of diabetes.
2. Massachusetts beach.
3. Ah, you (German): the first of a series of
references to her father's German origins.
4. The poet's father, of German descent, was born
in Grabow, Poland.

Put your foot, your root,
I never could talk to you.
The tongue stuck in my jaw.   25

It stuck in a barb wire snare.
Ich,[5] ich, ich, ich,
I could hardly speak.
I thought every German was you.
And the language obscene   30

An engine, an engine
Chuffing me off like a Jew.
A Jew to Dachau, Auschwitz, Belsen.[6]
I began to talk like a Jew.
I think I may well be a Jew.   35

The snows of the Tyrol,[7] the clear beer of Vienna
Are not very pure or true.
With my gypsy ancestress and my weird luck
And my Taroc[8] pack and my Taroc pack
I may be a bit of a Jew.   40

I have always been scared of *you*,
With your Luftwaffe,[9] your gobbledygoo.
And your neat mustache
And your Aryan eye, bright blue.
Panzer[1]-man, panzer-man, O You——   45

Not God but a swastika
So black no sky could squeak through.
Every woman adores a Fascist,
The boot in the face, the brute
Brute heart of a brute like you.   50

You stand at the blackboard, daddy,
In the picture I have of you,
A cleft in your chin instead of your foot
But no less a devil for that, no not
And less the black man who   55

Bit my pretty red heart in two.
I was ten when they buried you.
At twenty I tried to die
And get back, back, back to you.
I thought even the bones would do.   60

---

5. I (German).
6. German concentration camps, where millions of Jews were murdered during World War II.
7. Austrian Alpine region.
8. Variation of Tarot, ancient fortune-telling cards. Gypsies, like Jews, were objects of Nazi genocidal ambition; many died in the concentration camps.
9. The German air force.
1. Armor (German); refers to the Nazi tank corps in World War II. Hitler preached the superiority of the Aryans—people of German stock with blond hair and blue eyes.

But they pulled me out of the sack,
And they stuck me together with glue.[2]
And then I knew what to do.
I made a model of you,
A man in black with a Meinkampf[3] look   65

And a love of the rack and the screw.
And I said I do, I do.
So daddy, I'm finally through.
The black telephone's off at the root,
The voices just can't worm through.   70

If I've killed one man, I've killed two——
The vampire who said he was you
And drank my blood for a year,
Seven years, if you want to know.
Daddy, you can lie back now.   75

There's a stake in your fat black heart
And the villagers never liked you.
They are dancing and stamping on you.
They always *knew* it was you.
Daddy, daddy, you bastard, I'm through.   80

1962   1966

Blackberrying

Nobody in the lane, and nothing, nothing but blackberries,
Blackberries on either side, though on the right mainly,
A blackberry alley, going down in hooks, and a sea
Somewhere at the end of it, heaving. Blackberries
Big as the ball of my thumb, and dumb as eyes   5
Ebon in the hedges, fat
With blue-red juices. These they squander on my fingers.
I had not asked for such a blood sisterhood; they must love me.
They accommodate themselves to my milkbottle, flattening their sides.

Overhead go the choughs[1] in black, cacophonous flocks—   10
Bits of burnt paper wheeling in a blown sky.
Theirs is the only voice, protesting, protesting.
I do not think the sea will appear at all.
The high, green meadows are glowing, as if lit from within.
I come to one bush of berries so ripe it is a bush of flies, 15
Hanging their bluegreen bellies and their wing panes in a Chinese screen.

2. An allusion to Plath's first suicide attempt.
3. A reference to Hitler's political autobiography,
Mein Kampf (my struggle), written and published

before his rise to power, in which the future dictator outlined his plans for world conquest.
1. Small, chattering birds of the crow family.

The honey-feast of the berries has stunned them; they believe in heaven.
One more hook, and the berries and bushes end.

The only thing to come now is the sea.
From between two hills a sudden wind funnels at me,   20
Slapping its phantom laundry in my face.
These hills are too green and sweet to have tasted salt.
I follow the sheep path between them. A last hook brings me
To the hills' northern face, and the face is orange rock
That looks out on nothing, nothing but a great space   25
Of white and pewter lights, and a din like silversmiths
Beating and beating at an intractable metal.

1961   1971

Child

> Your clear eye is the one absolutely beautiful thing.
> I want to fill it with color and ducks,
> The zoo of the new
>
> Whose names you meditate—
> April snowdrop, Indian pipe,   5
> Little
>
> Stalk without wrinkle,
> Pool in which images
> Should be grand and classical
>
> Not this troublous   10
> Wringing of hands, this dark
> Ceiling without a star.

1963   1972

JOHN UPDIKE
1932–2009

"To transcribe middleness with all its grits, bumps and anonymities, in its fullness of satisfaction and mystery: is it possible . . . or worth doing?" John Updike's novels and stories give a positive answer to the question he asks in his early memoir, *The Dogwood Tree: A Boyhood;* for he was arguably the most significant transcriber, or creator rather, of "middleness" in American writing since William Dean Howells (about whom he has written appreciatively). Falling in love in high school, meeting a college roommate, going to the eye doctor or dentist, eating supper on Sunday night, visiting your mother with your wife and son—these activities are made to yield up their possibilities to a writer as responsively curious in imagination and delicately precise in his literary expression as Updike showed himself to be.

Born in Shillington, Pennsylvania, John Updike was an only child. He was gifted at drawing and caricature, and after graduating summa cum laude from Harvard in 1954, he spent a year studying art in England, then returned to America and went to work for *The New Yorker,* where his first stories appeared and to which he regularly contributed for five decades. When later in the 1950s he left the magazine, he also left New York City and with his wife and children settled in Ipswich, Massachusetts. There he pursued "his solitary trade as methodically as the dentist practiced his," resisting the temptations of university teaching as successfully as the blandishments of media talk shows. His ample production was achieved through dedicated, steady work; his books are the fruit of patience, leisure, and craft.

Starting in 1958, when his first novel, *The Poorhouse Fair,* appeared, Updike published not only many novels and stories but also seven books of poetry, a play, and a vast store of book reviews and other prose writings. He is most admired by some readers as the author of the "Olinger" stories (included in *The Early Stories: 1953–1975,* 2003) about life in an imaginary Pennsylvania town that takes on its colors from the real Shillington of his youth. The heroes of these stories are adolescents straining to break out of their fast-perishing environments, as they grow up and as their small town turns into something else. Updike treats them with a blend of affection and ironic humor that is wonderfully assured in its touch, although his sense of place, of growing up during the Depression and the years of World War II, is always vividly present. Like Howells (whose fine memoir of his youthful days in Ohio, *A Boy's Town,* is an ancestor of Updike's *The Dogwood Tree*) he shows how one's spirit takes on its coloration from the material circumstances—houses, clothes, landscape, food, parents—one is bounded by.

This sense of place, which is also a sense of life, is found in the stories and in the novels too, although Updike found it harder to invent convincing forms in which to tell longer tales. His most ambitious novel is probably *The Centaur* (1964), memorable for its portrayal of three days of confusion and error in the life of an American high school teacher seen through his son's eyes, but the book is also burdened with an elaborate set of mythical trappings that seem less than inevitable. *Couples* (1968), a novel that gained him a good deal of notoriety as a chronicler of sexual relationships, marital and adulterous, is jammed with much interesting early 1960s lore about suburban life but seems uncertain whether it is an exercise in realism or a creative fantasy, as does *Marry Me* (1976).

In the four "Rabbit" novels Updike found his most congenial and engaging subject for longer fiction. In each book he rendered the sense of an era—the 1950s in *Rabbit, Run;* the late 1960s in *Rabbit Redux;* the great gasoline crisis of 1979 in *Rabbit Is Rich;* the end of the Reagan era (and the end of Rabbit) in *Rabbit at Rest* (1990)—through the eyes of a hero who both is and is not like his creator. Harry "Rabbit" Angstrom, ex–high school basketball star, a prey to nostalgia and in love with his own past, perpetually lives in a present he can't abide. *Rabbit, Run* shows him trying to escape from his town, his job, his wife, and his child by a series of disastrously sentimental and humanly irresponsible actions; yet Updike makes us feel Rabbit's yearnings even as we judge the painful consequences of yielding to them. Ten years later the fading basketball star has become a fortyish, dispirited printer with a wayward wife and a country that is both landing on the moon and falling to pieces. *Rabbit Redux* is masterly in presenting a small town rotting away from its past certainties; it also attempts to deal with the Vietnam War and the black revolution. *Rabbit Is Rich* is a gentler, sadder chronicling of the hero's settling into grandfatherhood as he draws ever closer to death; while *Rabbit at Rest,* the longest and richest of the four novels, brings him to a moving conclusion; Rabbit's coda is presented in the reflections of his son and illegitimate daughter in "Rabbit Remembered," collected in *Licks of Love* (2000). In *Roger's Version* (1986) and *S* (1988) Updike adopted—or permitted his protagonists to adopt—a more broadly, sometimes a harsher, satiric view of contemporary religion, computer technology, feminism, and other forms of "liberation." Still, for all his virtuosity as a novelist, his best work may be found in the stories and in his short novel *Of the Farm* (1965). In "Separating" (printed here) the boy from "The Happiest I've Been" (*The Same Door*, 1959) has grown up, married, and fathered children and is now about to leave them as he moves into divorce. It is a beautiful example of Updike's careful, poised sense of how things work, a sense that can also be observed in the poem "Dog's Death" and in his memoir *Self-Consciousness* (1989).

Near the end of *The Dogwood Tree* he summarized his boyish dream of becoming an artist:

> He saw art—between drawing and writing he ignorantly made no distinction— as a method of riding a thin pencil out of Shillington, out of time altogether, into an infinity of unseen and even unborn hearts. He pictured this infinity as radiant. How innocent!

Most writers would name that innocence only to deplore it. Updike maintained instead that, as with the Christian faith he professed, succeeding years gave him no better assumptions with which to replace it. In any case, his fine sense of fact protected him from fashionable extravagances in black humor and experimental narratives, while enabling him to be both a satirist and a celebrator of our social and domestic conditions. In the last decade of his life, a fabulative, almost magical atmosphere appeared in some works, as with his 2000 novel, *Gertrude and Claudius*. Yet even here, as in the generational family saga based on spiritual perceptions, *In the Beauty of the Lilies* (1996), and in *Villages* (2004), a bildungsroman about a protagonist's marriages, careers, and communities, John Updike was our era's most sensitive craftsman of personal and societal manners.

The text is from *The New Yorker* (June 23, 1975).

Separating

The day was fair. Brilliant. All that June the weather had mocked the Maples' internal misery with solid sunlight—golden shafts and cascades of green in which their conversations had wormed unseeing, their sad murmuring selves the only stain in Nature. Usually by this time of the year they had acquired tans; but when they met their elder daughter's plane on her return from a year in England they were almost as pale as she, though Judith was too dazzled by the sunny opulent jumble of her native land to notice. They did not spoil her homecoming by telling her immediately. Wait a few days, let her recover from jet lag, had been one of their formulations, in that string of gray dialogues—over coffee, over cocktails, over Cointreau—that had shaped the strategy of their dissolution, while the earth performed its annual stunt of renewal unnoticed beyond their closed windows. Richard had thought to leave at Easter; Joan had insisted they wait until the four children were at last assembled, with all exams passed and ceremonies attended, and the bauble of summer to console them. So he had drudged away, in love, in dread, repairing screens, getting the mowers sharpened, rolling and patching their new tennis court.

The court, clay, had come through its first winter pitted and windswept bare of redcoat. Years ago the Maples had observed how often, among their friends, divorce followed a dramatic home improvement, as if the marriage were making one last twitchy effort to live; their own worst crisis had come amid the plaster dust and exposed plumbing of a kitchen renovation. Yet, a summer ago, as canary-yellow bulldozers gaily churned a grassy, daisy-dotted knoll into a muddy plateau, and a crew of pigtailed young men raked and tamped clay into a plane, this transformation did not strike them as ominous, but festive in its impudence; their marriage could rend the earth for fun. The next spring, waking each day at dawn to a sliding sensation as if the bed were being tipped, Richard found the barren tennis court, its net and tapes still rolled in the barn, an environment congruous with his mood of purposeful desolation, and the crumbling of handfuls of clay into cracks and holes (dogs had frolicked on the court in a thaw; rivulets had evolved trenches) an activity suitably elemental and interminable. In his sealed heart he hoped the day would never come.

Now it was here. A Friday. Judith was reacclimated; all four children were assembled, before jobs and camps and visits again scattered them. Joan thought they should be told one by one. Richard was for making an announcement at the table. She said, "I think just making an announcement is a cop-out. They'll start quarrelling and playing to each other instead of focussing. They're each individuals, you know, not just some corporate obstacle to your freedom."

"O.K., O.K. I agree." Joan's plan was exact. That evening, they were giving Judith a belated welcome-home dinner, of lobster and champagne. Then, the party over, they, the two of them, who nineteen years before would push her in a baby carriage along Tenth Street to Washington Square,[1] were to walk her out of the house, to the bridge across the salt creek, and tell her, swearing her to secrecy. Then Richard Jr., who was going directly from work to a rock concert in Boston, would be told, either late when he returned on the train or early Saturday morning before he went off to his job; he was seventeen and employed as one of a golf-course maintenance crew. Then the two younger children, John and Margaret, could, as the morning wore on, be informed.

"Mopped up, as it were," Richard said.

"Do you have any better plan? That leaves you the rest of Saturday to answer any questions, pack, and make your wonderful departure."

"No," he said, meaning he had no better plan, and agreed to hers, though it had an edge of false order, a plea for control in the semblance of its achievement, like Joan's long chore lists and financial accountings and, in the days when he first knew her, her too copious lecture notes. Her plan turned one hurdle for him into four—four knife-sharp walls, each with a sheer blind drop on the other side.

All spring he had been morbidly conscious of insides and outsides, of barriers and partitions. He and Joan stood as a thin barrier between the children and the truth. Each moment was a partition, with the past on one side and the future on the other, a future containing this unthinkable *now*. Beyond four knifelike walls a new life for him waited vaguely. His skull cupped a secret, a white face, a face both frightened and soothing, both strange and known, that he wanted to shield from tears, which he felt all about him, solid as the sunlight. So haunted, he had become obsessed with battening down

---

1. In Greenwich Village, an area in lower Manhattan, New York City.

the house against his absence, replacing screens and sash cords, hinges and latches—a Houdini[2] making things snug before his escape.

The lock. He had still to replace a lock on one of the doors of the screened porch. The task, like most such, proved more difficult than he had imagined. The old lock, aluminum frozen by corrosion, had been deliberately rendered obsolete by manufacturers. Three hardware stores had nothing that even approximately matched the mortised hole its removal (surprisingly easy) left. Another hole had to be gouged, with bits too small and saws too big, and the old hole fitted with a block of wood—the chisels dull, the saw rusty, his fingers thick with lack of sleep. The sun poured down, beyond the porch, on a world of neglect. The bushes already needed pruning, the windward side of the house was shedding flakes of paint, rain would get in when he was gone, insects, rot, death. His family, all those he would lose, filtered through the edges of his awareness as he struggled with screw holes, splinters, opaque instructions, minutiae of metal.

Judith sat on the porch, a princess returned from exile. She regaled them with stories of fuel shortages, of bomb scares in the Underground, of Pakistani workmen loudly lusting after her as she walked past on her way to dance school. Joan came and went, in and out of the house, calmer than she should have been, praising his struggles with the lock as if this were one more and not the last of their chain of shared chores. The younger of his sons, John, now at fifteen suddenly, unwittingly handsome, for a few minutes held the rickety screen door while his father clumsily hammered and chiselled, each blow a kind of sob in Richard's ears. His younger daughter, having been at a slumber party, slept on the porch hammock through all the noise—heavy and pink, trusting and forsaken. Time, like the sunlight, continued relentlessly; the sunlight slowly slanted. Today was one of the longest days. The lock clicked, worked. He was through. He had a drink; he drank it on the porch, listening to his daughter. "It was so sweet," she was saying, "during the worst of it, how all the butcher's and bakery shops kept open by candlelight. They're all so plucky and cute. From the papers, things sounded so much worse here—people shooting people in gas lines, and everybody freezing."

Richard asked her, "Do you still want to live in England forever?" *Forever:* the concept, now a reality upon him, pressed and scratched at the back of his throat.

"No," Judith confessed, turning her oval face to him, its eyes still childishly far apart, but the lips set as over something succulent and satisfactory. "I was anxious to come home. I'm an American." She was a woman. They had raised her; he and Joan had endured together to raise her, alone of the four. The others had still some raising left in them. Yet it was the thought of telling Judith—the image of her, their first baby, walking between them arm in arm to the bridge—that broke him. The partition between himself and the tears broke. Richard sat down to the celebratory meal with the back of his throat aching; the champagne, the lobster seemed phases of sunshine; he saw them and tasted them through tears. He blinked, swallowed, croakily joked about hay fever. The tears would not stop leaking through; they came not through a hole that could be plugged but through a permeable spot in a membrane,

2. Harry Houdini (1874–1926), American magician and escape artist.

steadily, purely, endlessly, fruitfully. They became, his tears, a shield for himself against these others—their faces, the fact of their assembly, a last time as innocents, at a table where he sat the last time as head. Tears dropped from his nose as he broke the lobster's back; salt flavored his champagne as he sipped it; the raw clench at the back of his throat was delicious. He could not help himself.

His children tried to ignore his tears. Judith on his right, lit a cigarette, gazed upward in the direction of her too energetic, too sophisticated exhalation; on her other side, John earnestly bent his face to the extraction of the last morsels—legs, tail segments—from the scarlet corpse. Joan, at the opposite end of the table, glanced at him surprised, her reproach displaced by a quick grimace, of forgiveness, or of salute to his superior gift of strategy. Between them, Margaret, no longer called Bean, thirteen and large for her age, gazed from the other side of his pane of tears as if into a shopwindow at something she coveted—at her father, a crystalline heap of splinters and memories. It was not she, however, but John who, in the kitchen, as they cleared the plates and carapaces away, asked Joan the question: "Why is Daddy crying?"

Richard heard the question but not the murmured answer. Then he heard Bean cry, "Oh, no-oh!"—the faintly dramatized exclamation of one who had long expected it.

John returned to the table carrying a bowl of salad. He nodded tersely at his father and his lips shaped the conspiratorial words "She told."

"Told what?" Richard asked aloud, insanely.

The boy sat down as if to rebuke his father's distraction with the example of his own good manners and said quietly, "The separation."

Joan and Margaret returned; the child, in Richard's twisted vision, seemed diminished in size, and relieved, relieved to have had the boogeyman at last proved real. He called out to her—the distances at the table had grown immense—"You knew, you always knew," but the clenching at the back of his throat prevented him from making sense of it. From afar he heard Joan talking, levelly, sensibly, reciting what they had prepared: it was a separation for the summer, an experiment. She and Daddy both agreed it would be good for them; they needed space and time to think; they liked each other but did not make each other happy enough, somehow.

Judith, imitating her mother's factual tone, but in her youth off-key, too cool, said, "I think it's silly. You should either live together or get divorced."

Richard's crying, like a wave that has crested and crashed, had become tumultuous; but it was overtopped by another tumult, for John, who had been so reserved, now grew larger and larger at the table. Perhaps his younger sister's being credited with knowing set him off. "Why didn't you *tell* us?" he asked, in a large round voice quite unlike his own. "You should have *told* us you weren't getting along."

Richard was startled into attempting to force words through his tears. "We *do* get along, that's the trouble, so it doesn't show even to us—" "That we do not love each other" was the rest of the sentence; he couldn't finish it.

Joan finished for him, in her style. "And we've always, *especially*, loved our children."

John was not mollified. "What do you care about *us*?" he boomed. "We're just little things you *had*." His sisters' laughing forced a laugh from him, which he turned hard and parodistic: "Ha ha *ha.*" Richard and Joan realized simultaneously that the child was drunk, on Judith's homecoming champagne. Feeling bound to keep the center of the stage, John took a cigarette from Judith's pack, poked it into his mouth, let it hang from his lower lip, and squinted like a gangster.

"You're not little things we had," Richard called to him. "You're the whole point. But you're grown. Or almost."

The boy was lighting matches. Instead of holding them to his cigarette (for they had never seen him smoke; being "good" had been his way of setting himself apart), he held them to his mother's face, closer and closer, for her to blow out. Then he lit the whole folder—a hiss and then a torch, held against his mother's face. Prismed by tears, the flame filled Richard's vision; he didn't know how it was extinguished. He heard Margaret say, "Oh stop showing off," and saw John, in response, break the cigarette in two and put the halves entirely into his mouth and chew, sticking out his tongue to display the shreds to his sister.

Joan talked to him, reasoning—a fountain of reason, unintelligible. "Talked about it for years . . . our children must help us . . . Daddy and I both want . . ." As the boy listened, he carefully wadded a paper napkin into the leaves of his salad, fashioned a ball of paper and lettuce, and popped it into his mouth, looking around the table for the expected laughter. None came. Judith said, "Be mature," and dismissed a plume of smoke.

Richard got up from this stifling table and led the boy outside. Though the house was in twilight, the outdoors still brimmed with light, the long waste light of high summer. Both laughing, he supervised John's spitting out the lettuce and paper and tobacco into the pachysandra.[3] He took him by the hand—a square gritty hand, but for its softness a man's. Yet, it held on. They ran together up into the field, past the tennis court. The raw banking left by the bulldozers was dotted with daisies. Past the court and a flat stretch where they used to play family baseball stood a soft green rise glorious in the sun, each weed and species of grass distinct as illumination on parchment. "I'm sorry, so sorry," Richard cried. "You were the only one who ever tried to help me with all the goddam jobs around this place."

Sobbing, safe within his tears and the champagne, John explained, "It's not just the separation, it's the whole crummy year, I *hate* that school, you can't make any friends, the history teacher's a scud."[4]

They sat on the crest of the rise, shaking and warm from their tears but easier in their voices, and Richard tried to focus on the child's sad year—the weekdays long with homework, the weekends spent in his room with model airplanes, while his parents murmured down below, nursing their separation. How selfish, how blind, Richard thought; his eyes felt scoured. He told his son, "We'll think about getting you transferred. Life's too short to be miserable."

They had said what they could, but did not want the moment to heal, and talked on, about the school, about the tennis court, whether it would ever again be as good as it had been that first summer. They walked to inspect it and pressed a few more tapes more firmly down. A little stiltedly, perhaps trying to make too much of the moment, to prolong it, Richard led the boy to

3. Green, leafy plant, frequently used as ground cover.   4. Disagreeable, objectionable person.

the spot in the field where the view was best, of the metallic blue river, the emerald marsh, the scattered islands velvet with shadow in the low light, the white bits of beach far away. "See," he said. "It goes on being beautiful. It'll be here tomorrow."

"I know," John answered, impatiently. The moment had closed.

Back in the house, the others had opened some white wine, the champagne being drunk, and still sat at the table, the three females, gossiping. Where Joan sat had become the head. She turned, showing him a tearless face, and asked, "All right?"

"We're fine," he said, resenting it, though relieved, that the party went on without him.

In bed she explained, "I couldn't cry I guess because I cried so much all spring. It really wasn't fair. It's your idea, and you made it look as though I was kicking you out."

"I'm sorry," he said. "I couldn't stop. I wanted to but couldn't."

"You *didn't* want to. You loved it. You were having your way, making a general announcement."

"I love having it over," he admitted. "God, those kids were great. So brave and funny." John, returned to the house, had settled to a model airplane in his room, and kept shouting down to them, "I'm O.K. No sweat." "And the way," Richard went on, cozy in his relief, "they never questioned the reasons we gave. No thought of a third person. Not even Judith."

"That *was* touching," Joan said.

He gave her a hug. "You were great too. Thank you." Guiltily, he realized he did not feel separated.

"You still have Dickie to do," she told him. These words set before him a black mountain in the darkness; its cold breath, its near weight affected his chest. Of the four children Dickie was most nearly his conscience. Joan did not need to add, "That's one piece of your dirty work I won't do for you."

"I know. I'll do it. You go to sleep."

Within minutes, her breathing slowed, became oblivious and deep. It was quarter to midnight. Dickie's train from the concert would come in at one-fourteen. Richard set the alarm for one. He had slept atrociously for weeks. But whenever he closed his lids some glimpse of the last hours scorched them—Judith exhaling toward the ceiling in a kind of aversion, Bean's mute staring, the sunstruck growth of the field where he and John had rested. The mountain before him moved closer, moved within him; he was huge, momentous. The ache at the back of his throat felt stale. His wife slept as if slain beside him. When, exasperated by his hot lids, his crowded heart, he rose from bed and dressed, she awoke enough to turn over. He told her then, "If I could undo it all, I would."

"Where would you begin?" she asked. There was no place. Giving him courage, she was always giving him courage. He put on shoes without socks in the dark. The children were breathing in their rooms, the downstairs was hollow. In their confusion they had left lights burning. He turned off all but one, the kitchen overhead. The car started. He had hoped it wouldn't. He met only moonlight on the road; it seemed a diaphanous companion, flickering in the leaves along the roadside, haunting his rearview mirror like a pursuer, melting under his headlights. The center of town, not quite deserted, was eerie at this hour. A young cop in uniform kept company with a gang of T-shirted kids on the steps of the bank. Across from the railroad station, several bars kept open. Customers, mostly young, passed in and out of the warm night, savoring summer's novelty. Voices shouted from cars as they passed; an immense conversation seemed in progress. Richard parked and in his weariness put his head on the passenger seat, out of the commotion and wheeling lights. It was as when, in the movies, an assassin grimly carries his mission through the jostle of a carnival—except the movies cannot show the precipitous, palpable slope you cling to within. You cannot climb back down; you can only fall. The synthetic fabric of the car seat, warmed by his cheek, confided to him an ancient, distant scent of vanilla.

A train whistle caused him to lift his head. It was on time; he had hoped it would be late. The slender drawgates descended. The bell of approach tingled happily. The great metal body, horizontally fluted, rocked to a stop, and sleepy teen-agers disembarked, his son among them. Dickie did not show surprise that his father was meeting him at this terrible hour. He sauntered to the car with two friends, both taller than he. He said "Hi" to his father and took the passenger's seat with an exhausted promptness that expressed gratitude. The friends got into the back, and Richard was grateful; a few more minutes' postponement would be won by driving them home.

He asked, "How was the concert?"

"Groovy," one boy said from the back seat.

"It bit," the other said.

"It was O.K.," Dickie said, moderate by nature, so reasonable that in his childhood the unreason of the world had given him headaches, stomach aches, nausea. When the second friend had been dropped off at his dark house, the boy blurted, "Dad, my eyes are killing me with hay fever! I'm out there cutting that mothering grass all day!"

"Do we still have those drops?"

"They didn't do any good last summer."

"They might this." Richard swung a U-turn on the empty street. The drive home took a few minutes. The mountain was here, in his throat. "Richard," he said, and felt the boy, slumped and rubbing his eyes, go tense at his tone, "I didn't come to meet you just to make your life easier. I came because your mother and I have some news for you, and you're a hard man to get ahold of these days. It's sad news."

"That's O.K." The reassurance came out soft, but quick, as if released from the tip of a spring.

Richard had feared that his tears would return and choke him, but the boy's manliness set an example, and his voice issued forth steady and dry. "It's sad news, but it needn't be tragic news, at least for you. It should have no practical effect on your life, though it's bound to have an emotional effect. You'll work at your job, and go back to school in September. Your mother and I are really proud of what you're making of your life; we don't want that to change at all."

"Yeah," the boy said lightly, on the intake of his breath, holding himself up. They turned the corner; the church they went to loomed like a gutted fort. The home of the woman Richard hoped to marry stood across the green. Her bedroom light burned.

"Your mother and I," he said, "have decided to separate. For the summer.

Nothing legal, no divorce yet. We want to see how it feels. For some years now, we haven't been doing enough for each other, making each other as happy as we should be. Have you sensed that?"

"No," the boy said. It was an honest, unemotional answer: true or false in a quiz.

Glad for the factual basis, Richard pursued, even garrulously, the details. His apartment across town, his utter accessibility, the split vacation arrangements, the advantages to the children, the added mobility and variety of the summer. Dickie listened, absorbing. "Do the others know?"

Richard described how they had been told.

"How did they take it?"

"The girls pretty calmly. John flipped out; he shouted and ate a cigarette and made a salad out of his napkin and told us how much he hated school."

His brother chuckled. "He did?"

"Yeah. The school issue was more upsetting for him than Mom and me. He seemed to feel better for having exploded."

"He did?" The repetition was the first sign that he was stunned.

"Yes. Dickie, I want to tell you something. This last hour, waiting for your train to get in, has been about the worst of my life. I hate this. *Hate* it. My father would have died before doing it to me." He felt immensely lighter, saying this. He had dumped the mountain on the boy. They were home. Moving swiftly as a shadow, Dickie was out of the car, through the bright kitchen. Richard called after him, "Want a glass of milk or anything?"

"No thanks."

"Want us to call the course tomorrow and say you're too sick to work?"

"No, that's all right." The answer was faint, delivered at the door to his room; Richard listened for the slam of a tantrum. The door closed normally. The sound was sickening.

Joan had sunk into that first deep trough of sleep and was slow to awake. Richard had to repeat, "I told him."

"What did he say?"

"Nothing much. Could you go say good night to him? Please."

She left their room, without putting on a bathrobe. He sluggishly changed back into his pajamas and walked down the hall. Dickie was already in bed, Joan was sitting beside him, and the boy's bedside clock radio was murmuring music. When she stood, an inexplicable light—the moon?—outlined her body through the nightie. Richard sat on the warm place she had indented on the child's narrow mattress. He asked him, "Do you want the radio on like that?"

"It always is."

"Doesn't it keep you awake? It would me."

"No."

"Are you sleepy?"

"Yeah."

"Good. Sure you want to get up and go to work? You've had a big night."

"I want to."

Away at school this winter he had learned for the first time that you can go short of sleep and live. As an infant he had slept with an immobile, sweating intensity that had alarmed his babysitters. As the children aged, he became the first to go to bed, earlier for a time than his younger brother and sister.

Even now, he would go slack in the middle of a television show, his sprawled legs hairy and brown. "O.K. Good boy. Dickie, listen. I love you so much, I never knew how much until now. No matter how this works out, I'll always be with you. Really."

Richard bent to kiss an averted face but his son, sinewy, turned and with wet cheeks embraced him and gave him a kiss, on the lips, passionate as a woman's. In his father's ear he moaned one word, the crucial, intelligent word: "*Why?*"

Why. It was a whistle of wind in a crack, a knife thrust, a window thrown open on emptiness. The white face was gone, the darkness was featureless. Richard had forgotten why.

1975

PHILIP ROTH
b. 1933

From the moment Philip Roth's collection of stories *Goodbye, Columbus* won the Houghton Mifflin Literary Fellowship for 1959, his career has received the ambiguous reward of much anxious concern, directed at it by critics and centered on whether he would develop the promise displayed in this first book. Ten years later, with *Portnoy's Complaint,* Roth became overnight the famous author of a "dirty" best-seller, yet his success only made his critics more uneasy. Was this gifted portrayer of Jewish middle-class life really more interested in scoring points off caricatures than in creating and exploring characters? Did his very facility with words inhibit the exercise of deeper sympathies and more humanly generous purposes?

Roth grew up in Newark, New Jersey, attended the branch of Rutgers University there, graduated from Bucknell University, took an M.A. in English literature at the University of Chicago, then served in the army. Over the years he has taught at a number of universities while receiving many awards and fellowships. Like John Barth, another "university" writer, Roth is an ironic humorist, although the impulse behind his early stories is darker and less playful. *Goodbye, Columbus* is about Jews on the verge of being or already having been assimilated into the larger American culture, and the stories confidently take the measure of their embattled heroes, as in "The Conversion of the Jews" or "Epstein" or the long title story. "Defender of the Faith" (printed here), arguably the best piece in the collection, is distinguished for the way Roth explores rather than exploits the conflict between personal feelings and religious loyalties as they are felt by Nathan Marx, a U.S. Army sergeant in a Missouri training company near the end of World War II. Throughout *Goodbye, Columbus* the narrator's voice is centrally important: in some stories it is indistinguishable from that of a campus wiseguy; in others it reaches out to a calmer and graver sense of disparities between promises and performance.

Roth's first two novels, *Letting Go* (1962) and *When She Was Good* (1967), markedly extended the territory charted in *Goodbye, Columbus* and showed him eager and equipped to write about people other than Jews. *Letting Go* is conventional in technique and in its subjects—love, marriage, university life—but Roth's easy mastery of the look and feel of places and things is everywhere evident. F. Scott Fitzgerald is the American writer whose presence in these early novels is most strongly felt; in particular, the section from *Letting Go* told in the first person by a graduate student in

English betrays its indebtedness to Fitzgerald's Nick Carraway, the narrator of *The Great Gatsby*. This Fitzgeraldian atmosphere, with its nostalgic presentation of adolescence and early romantic visions, is even more evident in *When She Was Good*, which is strong in its rendering of middle-American living rooms and kitchens, the flushed atmosphere of late-night 1950s sex in parked cars, or the lyrics of popular songs—bits of remembered trivia that Roth, like his predecessor, has a genius for bringing to life.

The less-than-overwhelming reception of his second novel probably helped Roth move away from relatively sober realism; certainly *Portnoy's Complaint* (1969) is a louder and more virtuoso performance than the earlier books. Alexander Portnoy's recollections of early childhood miseries are really a pretext for Roth to perform a succession of clever numbers in the inventive mode of a stand-up comic. Memories of growing up in New Jersey, listening to radio programs, playing softball, ogling girls at the ice-skating rink, or (most sensationally) masturbating in outlandish ways add up to an entertaining narrative that is sometimes crude but more often delicate and precise.

After *Portnoy* Roth moved toward fantasy and further showmanly operations: *Our Gang* (1970) attempted to do for Richard Nixon and his associates what actual events were to do one better; *The Breast* (1971) is a rather unamusing fable about a man's metamorphosis into that object; *The Great American Novel* (1973) threatened to sink under its weight of baseball lore dressed up in tall tales and sick jokes. But in *My Life as a Man* (1974) and *The Professor of Desire* (1977) he returned to matters that have traditionally preoccupied the social novelist and that inform his own best work: marriage, divorce, the family, being a Jew, and being psychoanalyzed—the pressures of civilization and the resultant individual discontents.

His finest work is to be found in the Zuckerman trilogy (*Zuckerman Bound*, 1985) and its successor, *The Counterlife* (1987). In these novels Roth created a hero-as-novelist whose experience parallels in important ways his creator's. A scandalous novel, *Carnovsky*, refers to *Portnoy's Complaint*; a critic named Milton Appel is a stand-in for the real critic Irving Howe, who once subjected Roth's work to hostile criticism. Yet for all the dangers of self-pity or self-absorption such autobiographical reference involves, the novels add up to something much deeper, more comic and touching, than self-advertisement and complaint. Scenes like the death of Zuckerman's father in a Florida hospital and the subsequent return of the son to the vanished Newark where he grew up are moving expressions of the generous purposes and human sympathies we find in Roth's work at its best. And those purposes and sympathies are also evident in his autobiographical writing: in *The Facts* (1988) and especially in *Patrimony* (1991), a poignant memoir of his father.

In the 1990s and into the twenty-first century Roth has developed his art of impersonation into sometimes excessive and audacious forms. *Operation Shylock* (1993) poses a presumably real Philip Roth who encounters an impostor; *Sabbath's Theater* (1995) recasts his typical protagonist as a puppeteer who manipulates women much the same way; *American Pastoral* (1997) brings back Nathan Zuckerman for a high school reunion and the investigation of a "more ordinary" classmate's life. Zuckerman remains on hand for *I Married a Communist* (1998) and *The Human Stain* (2000), while David Kepesh (who had turned into a female breast in the author's much earlier fantasy) reappears as a professor who seduces his students in *The Dying Animal* (2001). Further seduction takes place in *Everyman* (2006), although the author's most disturbing projections are reserved for *The Plot against America* (2004), in which a fictive Charles A. Lindbergh becomes president and initiates repression of American Jews. Throughout, Roth's emphasis remains on invention, reminding readers that the writerly self is a virtually inexhaustible resource for the imagination.

The text is from *Goodbye, Columbus* (1959).

Defender of the Faith

In May of 1945, only a few weeks after the fighting had ended in Europe, I was rotated back to the States, where I spent the remainder of the war with a training company at Camp Crowder, Missouri. We had been racing across Germany so swiftly during the late winter and spring that when I boarded the plane that drizzly morning in Berlin, I couldn't believe our destination lay to the west. My mind might inform me otherwise, but there was an inertia of the spirit that told me we were flying to a new front where we would disembark and continue our push eastward—eastward until we'd circled the globe, marching through villages along whose twisting, cobbled streets crowds of the enemy would watch us take possession of what up till then they'd considered their own. I had changed enough in two years not to mind the trembling of the old people, the crying of the very young, the uncertain fear in the eyes of the once-arrogant. After two years I had been fortunate enough to develop an infantryman's heart which, like his feet, at first aches and swells, but finally grows horny enough for him to travel the weirdest paths without feeling a thing.

Captain Paul Barrett was to be my C. O. at Camp Crowder. The day I reported for duty he came out of his office to shake my hand. He was short, gruff, and fiery, and indoors or out he wore his polished helmet liner[1] down on his little eyes. In Europe he had received a battlefield commission and a serious chest wound, and had been returned to the States only a few months before. He spoke easily to me, but was, I thought, unnecessarily abusive towards the troops. At the evening formation, he introduced me.

"Gentlemen," he called. "Sergeant Thurston, as you know, is no longer with this Company. Your new First Sergeant is Sergeant Nathan Marx here. He is a veteran of the European theater and consequently will take no shit."

I sat up late in the orderly room that evening, trying halfheartedly to solve the riddle of duty rosters, personnel forms, and morning reports. The CQ[2] slept with his mouth open on a mattress on the floor. A trainee stood reading the next day's duty roster, which was posted on the bulletin board directly inside the screen door. It was a warm evening and I could hear the men's radios playing dance music over in the barracks.

The trainee, who I knew had been staring at me whenever I looked groggily into the forms, finally took a step in my direction.

"Hey, Sarge—we having a G.I. party tomorrow night?" A G.I. party is a barracks-cleaning.

"You usually have them on Friday nights?"

"Yes," and then he added mysteriously, "that's the whole thing."

"Then you'll have a G.I. party."

He turned away and I heard him mumbling. His shoulders were moving and I wondered if he was crying.

"What's your name, soldier?" I asked.

He turned, not crying at all. Instead his green-speckled eyes, long and narrow, flashed like fish in the sun. He walked over to me and sat on the edge of my desk.

---

1. Plastic liner worn under a helmet to prevent chafing and bruising.

2. Noncommissioned officer in charge of quarters at night or on weekends.

He reached out a hand. "Sheldon," he said.

"Stand on your own two feet, Sheldon."

Climbing off the desk, he said, "Sheldon Grossbart." He smiled wider at the intimacy into which he'd led me.

"You against cleaning the barracks Friday night, Grossbart? Maybe we shouldn't have G.I. parties—maybe we should get a maid." My tone startled me: I felt like a Charlie McCarthy, with every top sergeant I had ever known as my Edgar Bergen.[3]

"No, Sergeant." He grew serious, but with a seriousness that seemed only to be the stifling of a smile. "It's just G.I. parties on Friday night, of all nights . . ."

He slipped up to the corner of the desk again—not quite sitting, but not quite standing either. He looked at me with those speckled eyes flashing and then made a gesture with his hand. It was very slight, no more than a rotation back and forth of the wrist, and yet it managed to exclude from our affairs everything else in the orderly room, to make the two of us the center of the world. It seemed, in fact, to exclude everything about the two of us except our hearts. "Sergeant Thurston was one thing," he whispered, an eye flashing to the sleeping CQ, "but we thought with you here, things might be a little different."

"We?"

"The Jewish personnel."

"Why?" I said, harshly.

He hesitated a moment, and then, uncontrollably, his hand went up to his mouth. "I mean . . ." he said.

"What's on your mind?" Whether I was still angry at the "Sheldon" business or something else, I hadn't a chance to tell—but clearly I was angry.

". . . we thought you . . . Marx, you know, like Karl Marx. The Marx brothers. Those guys are all . . . M-A-R-X, isn't that how you spell it, Sergeant?"

"M-A-R-X."

"Fishbein said—" He stopped. "What I mean to say, Sergeant—" His face and neck were red, and his mouth moved but no words came out. In a moment, he raised himself to attention, gazing down at me. It was as though he had suddenly decided he could expect no more sympathy from me than from Thurston, the reason being that I was of Thurston's faith and not his. The young man had managed to confuse himself as to what my faith really was, but I felt no desire to straighten him out. Very simply, I didn't like him.

When I did nothing but return his gaze, he spoke, in an altered tone. "You see, Sergeant," he explained to me, "Friday nights, Jews are supposed to go to services."

"Did Sergeant Thurston tell you you couldn't go to them when there was a G.I. party?"

"No."

"Did he say you had to stay and scrub the floors?"

"No, Sergeant."

"Did the Captain say you had to stay and scrub the floors?"

"That isn't it, Sergeant. It's the other guys in the barracks." He leaned

---

3. A ventriloquist who, with Charlie McCarthy, his dummy, was a popular radio comedian.

toward me. "They think we're goofing off. But we're not. That's when Jews go to services, Friday night. We have to."

"Then go."

"But the other guys make accusations. They have no right."

"That's not the Army's problem, Grossbart. It's a personal problem you'll have to work out yourself."

"But it's un*fair.*"

I got up to leave. "There's nothing I can do about it," I said.

Grossbart stiffened in front of me. "But this is a matter of *religion,* sir."

"Sergeant."

"I mean 'Sergeant,' " he said, almost snarling.

"Look, go see the chaplain. The I.G.[4] You want to see Captain Barrett, I'll arrange an appointment."

"No, no. I don't want to make trouble, Sergeant. That's the first thing they throw up to you. I just want my rights!"

"Damn it, Grossbart, stop whining. You have your rights. You can stay and scrub floors or you can go to *shul*[5]—"

The smile swam in again. Spittle gleamed at the corners of his mouth. "You mean church, Sergeant."

"I mean *shul,* Grossbart!" I walked past him and outside. Near me I heard the scrunching of a guard's boots on gravel. In the lighted windows of the barracks the young men in T-shirts and fatigue pants were sitting on their bunks, polishing their rifles. Suddenly there was a light rustling behind me. I turned and saw Grossbart's dark frame fleeing back to the barracks, racing to tell his Jewish friends that they were right—that like Karl and Harpo, I was one of them.

The next morning, while chatting with the Captain, I recounted the incident of the previous evening, as if to unburden myself of it. Somehow in the telling it seemed to the Captain that I was not so much explaining Grossbart's position as defending it.

"Marx, I'd fight side by side with a nigger if the fellow proved to me he was a man. I pride myself," the Captain said looking out the window, "that I've got an open mind. Consequently, Sergeant, nobody gets special treatment here, for the good *or* the bad. All a man's got to do is prove himself. A man fires well on the range, I give him a weekend pass. He scores high in PT, he gets a weekend pass. He *earns* it." He turned from the window and pointed a finger at me. "You're a Jewish fellow, am I right, Marx?"

"Yes, sir."

"And I admire you. I admire you because of the ribbons on your chest, not because you had a hem stitched on your dick before you were old enough to even know you had one. I judge a man by what he shows me on the field of battle, Sergeant. It's what he's got *here,*" he said, and then, though I expected he would point to his heart, he jerked a thumb towards the buttons straining to hold his blouse across his belly. "Guts," he said.

"Okay, sir, I only wanted to pass on to you how the men felt."

"Mr. Marx, you're going to be old before your time if you worry about how the men feel. Leave that stuff to the Chaplain—pussy, the clap, church picnics with the little girls from Joplin, that's all his business, not yours. Let's us train these fellas to shoot straight. If the Jewish personnel feels the other men are accusing them of goldbricking . . . well, I just don't know. Seems awful funny how suddenly the Lord is calling so loud in Private Grossman's ear he's just got to run to church."

"Synagogue," I said.

"Synagogue is right, Sergeant. I'll write that down for handy reference. Thank you for stopping by."

That evening, a few minutes before the company gathered outside the orderly room for the chow formation, I called the CQ, Corporal Robert LaHill, in to see me. LaHill was a dark burly fellow whose hair curled out of his clothes wherever it could. He carried a glaze in his eyes that made one think of caves and dinosaurs. "LaHill," I said, "when you take the formation, remind the men that they're free to attend church services *whenever* they are held, provided they report to the orderly room before they leave the area."

LaHill didn't flicker; he scratched his wrist, but gave no indication that he'd heard or understood.

"LaHill," I said, "*church.* You remember? Church, priest, Mass, confession . . ."

He curled one lip into a ghastly smile; I took it for a signal that for a second he had flickered back up into the human race.

"Jewish personnel who want to attend services this evening are to fall out in front of the orderly room at 1900." And then I added, "By order of Captain Barrett."

A little while later, as a twilight softer than any I had seen that year dropped over Camp Crowder, I heard LaHill's thick, inflectionless voice outside my window: "Give me your ears, troopers. Toppie says for me to tell you that at 1900 hours all Jewish personnel is to fall out in front here if they wants to attend the Jewish Mass."

At seven o'clock, I looked out of the orderly-room window and saw three soldiers in starched khakis standing alone on the dusty quadrangle. They looked at their watches, and fidgeted while they whispered back and forth. It was getting darker, and alone on the deserted field they looked tiny. When I walked to the door I heard the noises of the G.I. party coming from the surrounding barracks—bunks being pushed to the wall, faucets pounding water into buckets, brooms whisking at the wooden floors. In the windows big puffs of cloth moved round and round, cleaning the dirt away for Saturday's inspection. I walked outside and the moment my foot hit the ground I thought I heard Grossbart, who was now in the center, call to the other two, "Ten-*hut!*" Or maybe when they all three jumped to attention, I imagined I heard the command.

At my approach, Grossbart stepped forward. "Thank you, sir," he said.

"Sergeant, Grossbart," I reminded him. "You call officers 'Sir.' I'm not an officer. You've been in the Army three weeks—you know that."

He turned his palms out at his sides to indicate that, in truth, he and I lived beyond convention. "Thank you, anyway," he said.

"Yes," the tall boy behind him said. "Thanks a lot."

And the third whispered, "Thank you," but his mouth barely fluttered so that he did not alter by more than a lip's movement, the posture of attention.

"For what?" I said.

Grossbart snorted, happily. "For the announcement before. The Corporal's announcement. It helped. It made it . . ."

"Fancier." It was the tall boy finishing Grossbart's sentence.

Grossbart smiled. "He means formal, sir. Public," he said to me. "Now it won't seem as though we're just taking off, goldbricking, because the work has begun."

"It was by order of Captain Barrett," I said.

"Ahh, but you pull a little weight . . ." Grossbart said. "So we thank you." Then he turned to his companions. "Sergeant Marx, I want you to meet Larry Fishbein."

The tall boy stepped forward and extended his hand. I shook it. "You from New York?" he asked.

"Yes."

"Me too." He had a cadaverous face that collapsed inward from his cheekbone to his jaw, and when he smiled—as he did at the news of our communal attachment—revealed a mouthful of bad teeth. He blinked his eyes a good deal, as though he were fighting back tears. "What borough?" he asked.

I turned to Grossbart. "It's five after seven. What time are services?"

"Shul," he smiled, "is in ten minutes. I want you to meet Mickey Halpern. This is Nathan Marx, our Sergeant."

The third boy hopped forward. "Private Michael Halpern." He saluted.

"Salute officers, Halpern." The boy dropped his hand, and in his nervousness checked to see if his shirt pockets were buttoned on the way down.

"Shall I march them over, sir?" Grossbart asked, "or are you coming along?"

From behind Grossbart, Fishbein piped up. "Afterwards they're having refreshments. A Ladies' Auxiliary from St. Louis, the rabbi told us last week."

"The chaplain," whispered Halpern.

"You're welcome to come along," Grossbart said.

To avoid his plea, I looked away, and saw, in the windows of the barracks, a cloud of faces staring out at the four of us.

"Look, hurry out of here, Grossbart."

"Okay, then," he said. He turned to the others. "Double time, *march!*" and they started off, but ten feet away Grossbart spun about, and running backwards he called to me, "Good *shabus*,[6] sir." And then the three were swallowed into the Missouri dusk.

Even after they'd disappeared over the parade grounds, whose green was now a deep twilight blue, I could hear Grossbart singing the double-time cadence, and as it grew dimmer and dimmer it suddenly touched some deep memory—as did the slant of light—and I was remembering the shrill sounds of a Bronx playground, where years ago, beside the Grand Concourse,[7] I had played on long spring evenings such as this. Those thin fading sounds . . . It was a pleasant memory for a young man so far from peace and home, and it brought so very many recollections with it that I began to grow exceedingly tender about myself. In fact, I indulged myself to a reverie so strong that I felt

6. Sabbath (Yiddish).   7. Avenue in the Bronx, New York.

within as though a hand had opened and was reaching down inside. It had to reach so very far to touch me. It had to reach past those days in the forests of Belgium and the dying I'd refused to weep over; past the nights in those German farmhouses whose books we'd burned to warm us, and which I couldn't bother to mourn; past those endless stretches when I'd shut off all softness I might feel for my fellows, and managed even to deny myself the posture of a conqueror—the swagger that I, as a Jew, might well have worn as my boots whacked against the rubble of Münster, Braunschweig, and finally Berlin.

But now one night noise, one rumor of home and time past, and memory plunged down through all I had anesthetized and came to what I suddenly remembered to be myself. So it was not altogether curious that in search of more of me I found myself following Grossbart's tracks to Chapel No. 3 where the Jewish services were being held.

I took a seat in the last row, which was empty. Two rows in front sat Grossbart, Fishbein, and Halpern, each holding a little white dixie cup. Fishbein was pouring the contents of his cup into Grossbart's, and Grossbart looked mirthful as the liquid drew a purple arc between his hand and Fishbein's. In the glary yellow light, I saw the chaplain on the pulpit chanting the first line of the responsive reading. Grossbart's prayerbook remained closed on his lap; he swished the cup around. Only Halpern responded in prayer. The fingers of his right hand were spread wide across the cover of the book, and his cap was pulled down low onto his brow so that it was round like a *yarmulke*[8] rather than long and pointed. From time to time, Grossbart wet his lips at the cup's edge; Fishbein, his long yellow face, a dying light bulb, looked from here to there, leaning forward at the neck to catch sight of the faces down the row, in front—then behind. He saw me and his eyelids beat a tattoo. His elbow slid into Grossbart's side, his neck inclined towards his friend, and then, when the congregation responded, Grossbart's voice was among them. Fishbein looked into his book now too; his lips, however, didn't move.

Finally it was time to drink the wine. The chaplain smiled down at them as Grossbart swigged in one long gulp, Halpern sipped, meditating, and Fishbein faked devotion with an empty cup.

At last the chaplain spoke: "As I look down amongst the congregation—" he grinned at the word, "this night, I see many new faces, and I want to welcome you to Friday night services here at Camp Crowder. I am Major Leo Ben Ezra, your chaplain . . ." Though an American, the chaplain spoke English very deliberately, syllabically almost, as though to communicate, above all, to the lip-readers in the audience. "I have only a few words to say before we adjourn to the refreshment room where the kind ladies of the Temple Sinai, St. Louis, Missouri, have a nice setting for you."

Applause and whistling broke out. After a momentary grin, the chaplain raised his palms to the congregation, his eyes flicking upward a moment, as if to remind the troops where they were and Who Else might be in attendance. In the sudden silence that followed, I thought I heard Grossbart's cackle—"Let the goyim[9] clean the floors!" Were those the words? I wasn't sure, but Fishbein, grinning, nudged Halpern. Halpern looked dumbly at him, then went back to his prayerbook, which had been occupying him all

8. Skullcap (Yiddish).   9. Gentiles (Yiddish).

through the rabbi's talk. One hand tugged at the black kinky hair that stuck out under his cap. His lips moved.

The rabbi continued. "It is about the food that I want to speak to you for a moment. I know, I know, I know," he intoned, wearily, "how in the mouths of most of you the *trafe*[1] food tastes like ashes. I know how you gag, some of you, and how your parents suffer to think of their children eating foods unclean and offensive to the palate. What can I tell you? I can only say close your eyes and swallow as best you can. Eat what you must to live and throw away the rest. I wish I could help more. For those of you who find this impossible, may I ask that you try and try, but then come to see me in private where, if your revulsion is such, we will have to seek aid from those higher up."

A round of chatter rose and subsided; then everyone sang "Ain Kelohanoh," after all those years I discovered I still knew the words.

Suddenly, the service over, Grossbart was upon me. "Higher up? He means the General?"

"Hey, Shelly," Fishbein interrupted, "he means God." He smacked his face and looked at Halpern. "How high can you go!"

"Shhh!" Grossbart said. "What do you think, Sergeant?"

"I don't know. You better ask the chaplain."

"I'm going to. I'm making an appointment to see him in private. So is Mickey."

Halpern shook his head. "No, no, Sheldon . . ."

"You have rights, Mickey. They can't push us around."

"It's okay. It bothers my mother, not me . . ."

Grossbart looked at me. "Yesterday he threw up. From the hash. It was all ham and God knows what else."

"I have a cold—that was why," Halpern said. He pushed his *yamalkah* back into a cap.

"What about you, Fishbein?" I asked. "You kosher too?"

He flushed, which made the yellow more gray than pink. "A little. But I'll let it ride. I have a very strong stomach. And I don't eat a lot anyway . . ." I continued to look at him, and he held up his wrist to re-enforce what he'd just said. His watch was tightened to the last hole and he pointed that out to me. "So I don't mind."

"But services are important to you?" I asked him.

He looked at Grossbart. "Sure, sir."

"Sergeant."

"Not so much at home," said Grossbart, coming between us, "but away from home it gives one a sense of his Jewishness."

"We have to stick together," Fishbein said.

I started to walk towards the door; Halpern stepped back to make way for me.

"That's what happened in Germany," Grossbart was saying, loud enough for me to hear. "They didn't stick together. They let themselves get pushed around."

I turned. "Look, Grossbart, this is the Army, not summer camp."

He smiled. "So?" Halpern tried to sneak off, but Grossbart held his arm. "So?" he said again.

"Grossbart," I asked, "how old are you?"

1. Unkosher—unfit to eat (Yiddish).

"Nineteen."

"And you?" I said to Fishbein.

"The same. The same month even."

"And what about him?" I pointed to Halpern, who'd finally made it safely to the door.

"Eighteen," Grossbart whispered. "But he's like he can't tie his shoes or brush his teeth himself. I feel sorry for him."

"I feel sorry for all of us, Grossbart, but just act like a man. Just don't overdo it."

"Overdo what, sir?"

"The sir business. Don't overdo that," I said, and I left him standing there. I passed by Halpern but he did not look up. Then I was outside, black surrounded me—but behind I heard Grossbart call, "Hey, Mickey, *liebschen*,[2] come on back. Refreshments!"

Liebschen! My grandmother's word for me!

One morning, a week later, while I was working at my desk, Captain Barrett shouted for me to come into his office. When I entered, he had his helmet liner squashed down so that I couldn't even see his eyes. He was on the phone, and when he spoke to me, he cupped one hand over the mouthpiece.

"Who the fuck is Grossbart?"

"Third platoon, Captain," I said. "A trainee."

"What's all this stink about food? His mother called a goddam congressman about the food . . ." He uncovered the mouthpiece and slid his helmet up so I could see the curl of his bottom eyelash. "Yes, sir," he said into the phone. "Yes, sir. I'm still here, sir. I'm asking Marx here right now . . ."

He covered the mouthpiece again and looked back to me. "Lightfoot Harry's on the phone," he said, between his teeth. "This congressman calls General Lyman who calls Colonel Sousa who calls the Major who calls me. They're just dying to stick this thing on me. What's a matter," he shook the phone at me, "I don't feed the troops? What the hell is this?"

"Sir, Grossbart is strange . . ." Barrett greeted that with a mockingly indulgent smile. I altered my approach. "Captain, he's a very orthodox Jew and so he's only allowed to eat certain foods."

"He throws up, the congressman said. Every time he eats something his mother says he throws up!"

"He's accustomed to observing the dietary laws, Captain."

"So why's his old lady have to call the White House!"

"Jewish parents, sir, they're apt to be more protective than you expect. I mean Jews have a very close family life. A boy goes away from home, sometimes the mother is liable to get very upset. Probably the boy *mentioned* something in a letter and his mother misinterpreted."

"I'd like to punch him one right in the mouth. There's a goddam war on and he wants a silver platter!"

"I don't think the boy's to blame, sir. I'm sure we can straighten it out by just asking him. Jewish parents worry—"

"*All* parents worry, for Christ sake. But they don't get on their high horse and start pulling strings—"

I interrupted, my voice higher, tighter than before. "The home life, Captain, is so very important . . . but you're right, it may sometimes get out of hand. It's a very wonderful thing, Captain, but because it's so close, this kind of thing—"

He didn't listen any longer to my attempt to present both myself and Light-foot Harry with an explanation for the letter. He turned back to the phone. "Sir?" he said. "Sir, Marx here tells me Jews have a tendency to be pushy. He says he thinks he can settle it right here in the Company . . . Yes, sir . . . I *will* call back, sir, soon as I can . . ." He hung up. "Where are the men, Sergeant?"

"On the range."

With a whack on the top, he crushed his helmet over his eyes, and charged out of his chair. "We're going for a ride."

The Captain drove and I sat beside him. It was a hot spring day and under my newly starched fatigues it felt as though my armpits were melting down onto my sides and chest. The roads were dry and by the time we reached the firing range, my teeth felt gritty with dust though my mouth had been shut the whole trip. The Captain slammed the brakes on and told me to get the hell out and find Grossbart.

I found him on his belly, firing wildly at the 500 feet target. Waiting their turns behind him were Halpern and Fishbein. Fishbein, wearing a pair of rimless G.I. glasses I hadn't seen on him before, gave the appearance of an old peddler who would gladly have sold you the rifle and cartridges that were slung all over him. I stood back by the ammo boxes, waiting for Gross-bart to finish spraying the distant targets. Fishbein straggled back to stand near me.

"Hello, Sergeant Marx."

"How are you?" I mumbled.

"Fine, thank you. Sheldon's really a good shot."

"I didn't notice."

"I'm not so good, but I think I'm getting the hang of it now . . . Sergeant, I don't mean to, you know, ask what I shouldn't . . ." The boy stopped. He was trying to speak intimately but the noise of the shooting necessitated that he shout at me.

"What is it?" I asked. Down the range I saw Captain Barrett standing up in the jeep, scanning the line for me and Grossbart.

"My parents keep asking and asking where we're going. Everybody says the Pacific. I don't care, but my parents . . . If I could relieve their minds I think I could concentrate more on my shooting."

"I don't know where, Fishbein. Try to concentrate anyway."

"Sheldon says you might be able to find out—"

"I don't know a thing, Fishbein. You just take it easy, and don't let Shel-don—"

"*I'm* taking it easy, Sergeant. It's at home—"

Grossbart had just finished on the line and was dusting his fatigues with one hand. I left Fishbein's sentence in the middle.

"Grossbart, the Captain wants to see you."

He came toward us. His eyes blazed and twinkled. "Hi!"

"Don't point that goddam rifle!"

"I wouldn't shoot you, Sarge." He gave me a smile wide as a pumpkin as he turned the barrel aside.

"Damn you, Grossbart—this is no joke! Follow me."

I walked ahead of him and had the awful suspicion that behind me Grossbart was *marching,* his rifle on his shoulder, as though he were a one-man detachment.

At the jeep he gave the Captain a rifle salute. "Private Sheldon Grossbart, sir."

"At ease, Grossman." The Captain slid over to the empty front seat, and crooking a finger, invited Grossbart closer.

"Bart, sir. Sheldon Gross*bart.* It's a common error." Grossbart nodded to me—*I* understand, he indicated. I looked away, just as the mess truck pulled up to the range, disgorging a half dozen K.P.'s with rolled-up sleeves. The mess sergeant screamed at them while they set up the chow line equipment.

"Grossbart, your mama wrote some congressman that we don't feed you right. Do you know that?" the Captain said.

"It was my father, sir. He wrote to Representative Franconi that my religion forbids me to eat certain foods."

"What religion is that, Grossbart?"

"Jewish."

"Jewish, *sir,*" I said to Grossbart.

"Excuse me, sir. 'Jewish, sir.'"

"What have you been living on?" the Captain asked. "You've been in the Army a month already. You don't look to me like you're falling to pieces."

"I eat because I have to, sir. But Sergeant Marx will testify to the fact that I don't eat one mouthful more than I need to in order to survive."

"Marx," Barrett asked, "is that so?"

"I've never seen Grossbart eat, sir," I said.

"But you heard the rabbi," Grossbart said. "He told us what to do, and I listened."

The Captain looked at me. "Well, Marx?"

"I still don't know what he eats and doesn't eat, sir."

Grossbart raised his rifle, as though to offer it to me. "But, Sergeant—"

"Look, Grossbart, just answer the Captain's questions!" I said sharply.

Barrett smiled at me and I resented it. "All right, Grossbart," he said, "What is it you want? The little piece of paper? You want out?"

"No, sir. Only to be allowed to live as a Jew. And for the others, too."

"What others?"

"Fishbein, sir, and Halpern."

"They don't like the way we serve either?"

"Halpern throws up, sir. I've seen it."

"I thought *you* threw up."

"Just once, sir. I didn't know the sausage was sausage."

"We'll give menus, Grossbart. We'll show training films about the food, so you can identify when we're trying to poison you."

Grossbart did not answer. Out before me, the men had been organized into two long chow lines. At the tail end of one I spotted Fishbein—or rather, his glasses spotted me. They winked sunlight back at me like a friend. Halpern stood next to him, patting inside his collar with a khaki handkerchief. They moved with the line as it began to edge up towards the food. The mess sergeant was still screaming at the K.P.'s, who stood ready to ladle out the food, bewildered. For a moment I was actually terrorized by the thought that somehow the mess sergeant was going to get involved in Grossbart's problem.

"Come over here, Marx," the Captain said to me. "Marx, you're a Jewish fella, am I right?"

I played straight man. "Yes, sir."

"How long you been in the Army? Tell this boy."

"Three years and two months."

"A year in combat, Grossbart. Twelve goddam months in combat all through Europe. I admire this man," the Captain said, snapping a wrist against my chest. But do you hear him peeping about the food? Do you? I want an answer, Grossbart. Yes or no."

"No, sir."

"And why not? He's a Jewish fella."

"Some things are more important to some Jews than other things to other Jews."

Barrett blew up. "Look, Grossbart, Marx here is a good man, a goddam *hero*. When you were sitting on your sweet ass in high school, Sergeant Marx was killing Germans. Who does more for the Jews, you by throwing up over a lousy piece of sausage, a piece of firstcut meat—or Marx by killing those Nazi bastards? If I was a Jew, Grossbart, I'd kiss this man's feet. He's a goddam hero, you know that? And *he* eats what we give him. Why do you have to cause trouble is what I want to know! What is it you're buckin' for, a discharge?"

"No, sir."

"I'm talking to a *wall*! Sergeant, get him out of my way." Barrett pounced over to the driver's seat. "I'm going to see the chaplain!" The engine roared, the jeep spun around, and then, raising a whirl of dust, the Captain was headed back to camp.

For a moment, Grossbart and I stood side by side, watching the jeep. Then he looked at me and said, "I don't want to start trouble. That's the first thing they toss up to us."

When he spoke I saw that his teeth were white and straight, and the sight of them suddenly made me understand that Grossbart actually did have parents: that once upon a time someone had taken little Sheldon to the dentist. He was someone's son. Despite all the talk about his parents, it was hard to believe in Grossbart as a child, an heir—as related by blood to anyone, mother, father, or, above all, to me. This realization led me to another.

"What does your father do, Grossbart?" I asked, as we started to walk back towards the chow line.

"He's a tailor."

"An American?"

"Now, yes. A son in the Army," he said, jokingly.

"And your mother?" I asked.

He winked. "A *ballabusta*[3]—she practically sleeps with a dustcloth in her hand."

"She's also an immigrant?"

"All she talks is Yiddish, still."

"And your father too?"

"A little English. 'Clean,' 'Press,' 'Take the pants in . . .' That's the extent of it. But they're good to me . . ."

3. Good housekeeper (Yiddish).

"Then, Grossbart—" I reached out and stopped him. He turned towards me and when our eyes met his seemed to jump back, shiver in their sockets. He looked afraid. "Grossbart, then you were the one who wrote that letter, weren't you?"

It took only a second or two for his eyes to flash happy again. "Yes." He walked on, and I kept pace. "It's what my father *would* have written if he had known how. It was his name, though. *He* signed it. He even mailed it. I sent it home. For the New York postmark."

I was astonished, and he saw it. With complete seriousness, he thrust his right arm in front of me. "Blood is blood, Sergeant," he said, pinching the blue vein in his wrist.

"What the hell *are* you trying to do, Grossbart? I've seen you eat. Do you know that? I told the Captain I don't know what you eat, but I've seen you eat like a hound at chow."

"We work hard, Sergeant. We're in training. For a furnace to work, you've got to feed it coal."

"If you wrote the letter, Grossbart, then why did you say you threw up all the time?"

"I was really talking about Mickey there. But he would never write, Sergeant, though I pleaded with him. He'll waste away to nothing if I don't help. Sergeant, I used my name, my father's name, but it's Mickey and Fishbein too I'm watching out for."

"You're a regular Messiah,[4] aren't you?"

We were at the chow line now.

"That's a good one, Sergeant." He smiled. "But who knows? Who can tell? Maybe you're the Messiah . . . a little bit. What Mickey says is the Messiah is a collective idea. He went to Yeshivah,[5] Mickey, for a while. He says *together* we're the Messiah. Me a little bit, you a little bit . . . You should hear that kid talk, Sergeant, when he gets going."

"Me a little bit, you a little bit. You'd like to believe that, wouldn't you, Grossbart? That makes everything so clean for you."

"It doesn't seem too bad a thing to believe, Sergeant. It only means we should all give a little, is all . . ."

I walked off to eat my rations with the other noncoms.[6]

Two days later a letter addressed to Captain Barrett passed over my desk. It had come through the chain of command—from the office of Congressman Franconi, where it had been received, to General Lyman, to Colonel Sousa, to Major Lamont, to Captain Barrett. I read it over twice while the Captain was at the officers' mess. It was dated May 14th, the day Barrett had spoken with Grossbart on the rifle range.

Dear Congressman:

First let me thank you for your interest in behalf of my son, Private Sheldon Grossbart. Fortunately, I was able to speak with Sheldon on the phone the other night, and I think I've been able to solve our problem. He is, as I mentioned in my last letter, a very religious boy, and it was only with the great-

---

4. The deliverer who will rule over the people of Israel at the end of time.

5. Jewish institution of learning.

6. Noncommissioned officers.

est difficulty that I could persuade him that the religious thing to do—what God Himself would want Sheldon to do—would be to suffer the pangs of religious remorse for the good of his country and all mankind. It took some doing, Congressman, but finally he saw the light. In fact, what he said (and I wrote down the words on a scratch pad so as never to forget), what he said was, "I guess you're right, Dad. So many millions of my fellow Jews gave up their lives to the enemy, the least I can do is live for a while minus a bit of my heritage so as to help end this struggle and regain for all the children of God dignity and humanity." That, Congressman, would make any father proud.

By the way, Sheldon wanted me to know—and to pass on to you—the name of a soldier who helped him reach this decision: SERGEANT NATHAN MARX. Sergeant Marx is a combat veteran who is Sheldon's First Sergeant. This man has helped Sheldon over some of the first hurdles he's had to face in the Army, and is in part responsible for Sheldon's changing his mind about the dietary laws. I know Sheldon would appreciate any recognition Marx could receive.

Thank you and good luck. I look forward to seeing your name on the next election ballot.

Respectfully,
Samuel E. Grossbart

Attached to the Grossbart communiqué was a communiqué addressed to General Marshall Lyman, the post commander, and signed by Representative Charles E. Franconi of the House of Representatives. The communiqué informed General Lyman that Sergeant Nathan Marx was a credit to the U.S. Army and the Jewish people.

What was Grossbart's motive in recanting? Did he feel he'd gone too far? Was the letter a strategic retreat—a crafty attempt to strengthen what he considered our alliance? Or had he actually changed his mind, via an imaginary dialogue between Grossbart *père* and *fils*? I was puzzled, but only for a few days—that is, only until I realized that whatever his reasons, he had actually decided to disappear from my life: he was going to allow himself to become just another trainee. I saw him at inspection but he never winked; at chow formations but he never flashed me a sign; on Sundays, with the other trainees, he would sit around watching the noncoms' softball team, for whom I pitched, but not once did he speak an unnecessary or unusual word to me. Fishbein and Halpern retreated from sight too, at Grossbart's command I was sure. Apparently he'd seen that wisdom lay in turning back before he plunged us over into the ugliness of privilege undeserved. Our separation allowed me to forgive him our past encounters, and, finally, to admire him for his good sense.

Meanwhile, free of Grossbart, I grew used to my job and my administrative tasks. I stepped on a scale one day and discovered I had truly become a noncombatant: I had gained seven pounds. I found patience to get past the first three pages of a book. I thought about the future more and more, and wrote letters to girls I'd known before the war—I even got a few answers. I sent away to Columbia for a Law School catalogue. I continued to follow the war in the Pacific, but it was not my war and I read of bombings and battles like a civilian. I thought I could see the end in sight and sometimes at night I dreamed that I was walking on the streets of Manhattan—Broadway, Third Avenue, and 116th Street, where I had lived those three years I'd attended Columbia College. I curled myself around these dreams and I began to be happy.

And then one Saturday when everyone was away and I was alone in the orderly room reading a month-old copy of *The Sporting News*, Grossbart reappeared.

"You a baseball fan, Sergeant?"

I looked up. "How are you?"

"Fine," Grossbart said. "They're making a soldier out of me."

"How are Fishbein and Halpern?"

"Coming along," he said. "We've got no training this afternoon. They're at the movies."

"How come you're not with them?"

"I wanted to come over and say hello."

He smiled—a shy, regular-guy smile, as though he and I well knew that our friendship drew its sustenance from unexpected visits, remembered birthdays, and borrowed lawnmowers. At first it offended me, and then the feeling was swallowed by the general uneasiness I felt at the thought that everyone on the post was locked away in a dark movie theater and I was here alone with Grossbart. I folded my paper.

"Sergeant," he said, "I'd like to ask a favor. It is a favor and I'm making no bones about it."

He stopped, allowing me to refuse him a hearing—which, of course, forced me into a courtesy I did not intend. "Go ahead."

"Well, actually it's two favors."

I said nothing.

"The first one's about these rumors. Everybody says we're going to the Pacific."

"As I told your friend Fishbein, I don't know. You'll just have to wait to find out. Like everybody else."

"You think there's a chance of any of us going East?"

"Germany," I said, "maybe."

"I meant New York."

"I don't think so, Grossbart. Offhand."

"Thanks for the information, Sergeant," he said.

"It's not information, Grossbart. Just what I surmise."

"It certainly would be good to be near home. My parents . . . you know." He took a step towards the door and then turned back. "Oh the other thing. May I ask the other?"

"What is it?"

"The other thing is—I've got relatives in St. Louis and they say they'll give me a whole Passover dinner if I can get down there. God, Sergeant, that'd mean an awful lot to me."

I stood up. "No passes during basic, Grossbart."

"But we're off from now till Monday morning, Sergeant. I could leave the post and no one would even know."

"I'd know. You'd know."

"But that's all. Just the two of us. Last night I called my aunt and you should have heard her. 'Come, come,' she said. 'I got gefilte fish, *chrain*,[7] the works!' Just a day, Sergeant, I'd take the blame if anything happened."

"The captain isn't here to sign a pass."

_____
7. Horseradish.

"You could sign."

"Look, Grossbart—"

"Sergeant, for two months practically I've been eating *trafe* till I want to die."

"I thought you'd made up your mind to live with it. To be minus a little bit of heritage."

He pointed a finger at me. "You!" he said. "That wasn't for you to read!"

"I read it. So what."

"That letter was addressed to a congressman."

"Grossbart, don't feed me any crap. You *wanted* me to read it."

"Why are you persecuting me, Sergeant?"

"Are you kidding!"

"I've run into this before," he said, "but never from my own!"

"Get out of here, Grossbart! Get the hell out of my sight!"

He did not move. "Ashamed, that's what you are. So you take it out on the rest of us. They say Hitler himself was half a Jew. Seeing this, I wouldn't doubt it!"

"What are you trying to do with me, Grossbart? What are you after? You want me to give you special privileges, to change the food, to find out about your orders, to give you weekend passes."

"You even talk like a goy!" Grossbart shook his fist. "Is this a weekend pass I'm asking for? Is a Seder[8] sacred or not?"

Seder! It suddenly occurred to me that Passover had been celebrated weeks before. I confronted Grossbart with the fact.

"That's right," he said. "Who says no? A month ago, and *I* was in the field eating hash! And now all I ask is a simple favor—a Jewish boy I thought would understand. My aunt's willing to go out of her way—to make a Seder a month later—" He turned to go, mumbling.

"Come back here!" I called. He stopped and looked at me. "Grossbart, why can't you be like the rest? Why do you have to stick out like a sore thumb? Why do you beg for special treatment?"

"Because I'm a Jew, Sergeant. I *am* different. Better, maybe not. But different."

"This is a war, Grossbart. For the time being *be* the same."

"I refuse."

"What?"

"I refuse. I can't stop being me, that's all there is to it." Tears came to his eyes. "It's a hard thing to be a Jew. But now I see what Mickey says—it's a harder thing to stay one." He raised a hand sadly toward me. "Look at you."

"Stop crying!"

"Stop this, stop that, stop the other thing! You stop, Sergeant. Stop closing your heart to your own!" And wiping his face with his sleeve, he ran out the door. "The least we can do for one another . . . the least . . ."

An hour later I saw Grossbart headed across the field. He wore a pair of starched khakis and carried only a little leather ditty bag. I went to the door and from the outside felt the heat of the day. It was quiet—not a soul in sight except over by the mess hall four K.P.'s sitting round a pan, sloped forward from the waists, gabbing and peeling potatoes in the sun.

8. Ceremonial dinner on the first evening of Passover.

"Grossbart!" I called.

He looked toward me and continued walking.

"Grossbart, get over here!"

He turned and stepped into his long shadow. Finally he stood before me.

"Where are you going?" I said.

"St. Louis. I don't care."

"You'll get caught without a pass."

"So I'll get caught without a pass."

"You'll go to the stockade."

"I'm in the stockade." He made an about-face and headed off.

I let him go only a step: "Come back here," I said, and he followed me into the office, where I typed out a pass and signed the Captain's name and my own initials after it.

He took the pass from me and then, a moment later, he reached out and grabbed my hand. "Sergeant, you don't know how much this means to me."

"Okay. Don't get in any trouble."

"I wish I could show you how much this means to me."

"Don't do me any favors. Don't write any more congressmen for citations."

Amazingly, he smiled. "You're right. I won't. But let me do something."

"Bring me a piece of that gefilte fish. Just get out of here."

"I will! With a slice of carrot and a little horseradish. I won't forget."

"All right. Just show your pass at the gate. And don't tell *anybody*."

"I won't. It's a month late, but a good Yom Tov[9] to you."

"Good Yom Tov, Grossbart," I said.

"You're a good Jew, Sergeant. You like to think you have a hard heart, but underneath you're a fine decent man. I mean that."

Those last three words touched me more than any words from Grossbart's mouth had the right to. "All right, Grossbart. Now call me 'sir' and get the hell out of here."

He ran out the door and was gone. I felt very pleased with myself—it was a great relief to stop fighting Grossbart. And it had cost me nothing. Barrett would never find out, and if he did, I could manage to invent some excuse. For a while I sat at my desk, comfortable in my decision. Then the screen door flew back and Grossbart burst in again. "Sergeant!" he said. Behind him I saw Fishbein and Halpern, both in starched khakis, both carrying ditty bags exactly like Grossbart's.

"Sergeant, I caught Mickey and Larry coming out of the movies. I almost missed them."

"Grossbart, did I say tell no one?"

"But my aunt said I could bring friends. That I should, in fact."

"I'm the Sergeant, Grossbart—not your aunt!"

Grossbart looked at me in disbelief; he pulled Halpern up by his sleeve. "Mickey, tell the Sergeant what this would mean to you."

"Grossbart, for God's sake, spare us—"

"Tell him what you told me, Mickey. How much it would mean."

Halpern looked at me and, shrugging his shoulders, made his admission. "A lot."

9. Holiday (Yiddish).

Fishbein stepped forward without prompting. "This would mean a great deal to me and my parents, Sergeant Marx."

"No!" I shouted.

Grossbart was shaking his head. "Sergeant, I could see you denying me, but how you can deny Mickey, a Yeshivah boy, that's beyond me."

"I'm not denying Mickey anything. You just pushed a little too hard, Grossbart. *You* denied him."

"I'll give him my pass, then," Grossbart said. "I'll give him my aunt's address and a little note. At least let him go."

In a second he had crammed the pass into Halpern's pants' pocket. Halpern looked at me, Fishbein too. Grossbart was at the door, pushing it open. "Mickey, bring me a piece of gefilte fish at least." And then he was outside again.

The three of us looked at one another and then I said, "Halpern, hand that pass over."

He took it from his pocket and gave it to me. Fishbein had now moved to the doorway, where he lingered. He stood there with his mouth slightly open and then pointed to himself. "And me?" he asked.

His utter ridiculousness exhausted me. I slumped down in my seat and I felt pulses knocking at the back of my eyes. "Fishbein," I said, "you understand I'm not trying to deny you anything, don't you? If it was my Army I'd serve gefilte fish in the mess hall. I'd sell kugel[1] in the PX, honest to God."

Halpern smiled.

"You understand, don't you, Halpern?"

"Yes, Sergeant."

"And you, Fishbein? I don't want enemies. I'm just like you—I want to serve my time and go home. I miss the same things you miss."

"Then, Sergeant," Fishbein interrupted, "Why don't you come too?"

"Where?"

"To St. Louis. To Shelley's aunt. We'll have a regular Seder. Play hide-the-matzah." He gave a broad, black-toothed smile.

I saw Grossbart in the doorway again, on the other side of the screen.

"Pssst!" He waved a piece of paper. "Mickey, here's the address. Tell her I couldn't get away."

Halpern did not move. He looked at me and I saw the shrug moving up his arms into his shoulders again. I took the cover off my typewriter and made out passes for him and Fishbein. "Go," I said, "the three of you."

I thought Halpern was going to kiss my hand.

That afternoon, in a bar in Joplin, I drank beer and listened with half an ear to the Cardinal game. I tried to look squarely at what I'd become involved in, and began to wonder if perhaps the struggle with Grossbart wasn't as much my fault as his. What was I that I had to *muster* generous feelings? Who was I to have been feeling so grudging, so tight-hearted? After all, I wasn't being asked to move the world. Had I a right, then, or a reason, to clamp down on Grossbart, when that meant clamping down on Halpern, too? And Fishbein, that ugly agreeable soul, wouldn't he suffer in the bargain also? Out

---

1. Baked pudding of noodles or potatoes.

of the many recollections that had tumbled over me these past few days, I heard from some childhood moment my grandmother's voice: "What are you making a *tsimas?*"[2] It was what she would ask my mother when, say, I had cut myself with a knife and her daughter was busy bawling me out. I would need a hug and a kiss and my mother would moralize! But my grandmother knew—mercy overrides justice. I should have known it, too. Who was Nathan Marx to be such a pennypincher with kindness? Surely, I thought, the Messiah himself—if he should ever come—won't niggle over nickels and dimes. God willing, he'll hug and kiss.

The next day, while we were playing softball over on the Parade Grounds, I decided to ask Bob Wright, who was noncom in charge over at Classification and Assignment, where he thought our trainees would be sent when their cycle ended in two weeks. I asked casually, between innings, and he said, "They're pushing them all into the Pacific. Shulman cut the orders on your boys the other day."

The news shocked me, as though I were father to Halpern, Fishbein, and Grossbart.

That night I was just sliding into sleep when someone tapped on the door. "What is it?"

"Sheldon."

He opened the door and came in. For a moment I felt his presence without being able to see him. "How was it?" I asked, as though to the darkness.

He popped into sight before me. "Great, Sergeant." I felt my springs sag; Grossbart was sitting on the edge of the bed. I sat up.

"How about you?" he asked. "Have a nice weekend?"

"Yes."

He took a deep paternal breath. "The others went to sleep . . ." We sat silently for a while, as a homey feeling invaded my ugly little cubicle: the door was locked, the cat out, the children safely in bed.

"Sergeant, can I tell you something? Personal?"

I did not answer and he seemed to know why. "Not about me. About Mickey. Sergeant, I never felt for anybody like I feel for him. Last night I heard Mickey in the bed next to me. He was crying so, it could have broken your heart. Real sobs."

"I'm sorry to hear that."

"I had to talk to him to stop him. He held my hand, Sergeant—he wouldn't let it go. He was almost hysterical. He kept saying if he only knew where we were going. Even if he knew it *was* the Pacific, that would be better than nothing. Just to know."

Long ago, someone had taught Grossbart the sad law that only lies can get the truth. Not that I couldn't believe in Halpern's crying—his eyes *always* seemed red-rimmed. But, fact or not, it became a lie when Grossbart uttered it. He was entirely strategic. But then—it came with the force of indictment—so was I! There are strategies of aggression, but there are strategies of retreat, as well. And so, recognizing that I myself, had been without craft and guile, I told him what I knew. "It is the Pacific."

---

2. Fuss (Yiddish, literal trans.); here a side dish made of mixed cooked vegetables and fruit.

He let out a small gasp, which was not a lie. "I'll tell him. I wish it was otherwise."

"So do I."

He jumped on my words. "You mean you think you could do something? A change maybe?"

"No, I couldn't do a thing."

"Don't you know anybody over at C & A?"

"Grossbart, there's nothing I can do. If your orders are for the Pacific then it's the Pacific."

"But Mickey."

"Mickey, you, me—everybody, Grossbart. There's nothing to be done. Maybe the war'll end before you go. Pray for a miracle."

"But—"

"Good night, Grossbart." I settled back, and was relieved to feel the springs upbend again as Grossbart rose to leave. I could see him clearly now; his jaw had dropped and he looked like a dazed prizefighter. I noticed for the first time a little paper bag in his hand.

"Grossbart"—I smiled—"my gift?"

"Oh, yes, Sergeant. Here, from all of us." He handed me the bag. "It's egg roll."

"Egg roll?" I accepted the bag and felt a damp grease spot on the bottom. I opened it, sure that Grossbart was joking.

"We thought you'd probably like it. You know, Chinese egg roll. We thought you'd probably have a taste for—"

"Your aunt served egg roll?"

"She wasn't home."

"Grossbart, she invited you. You told me she invited you and your friends."

"I know. I just reread the letter. *Next* week."

I got out of bed and walked to the window. It was black as far off as I could see. "Grossbart," I said. But I was not calling him.

"What?"

"What are you, Grossbart? Honest to God, what are you?"

I think it was the first time I'd asked him a question for which he didn't have an immediate answer.

"How can you do this to people?" I asked.

"Sergeant, the day away did us all a world of good. Fishbein, you should see him, he *loves* Chinese food."

"But the Seder," I said.

"We took second best, Sergeant."

Rage came charging at me. I didn't sidestep—I grabbed it, pulled it in, hugged it to my chest.

"Grossbart, you're a liar! You're a schemer and a crook! You've got no respect for anything! Nothing at all! Not for me, for the truth, not even for poor Halpern! You use us all—"

"Sergeant, Sergeant, I feel for Mickey, honest to God, I do. I *love* Mickey. I try—"

"You try! You feel!" I lurched towards him and grabbed his shirt front. I shook him furiously. "Grossbart, get out. Get out and stay the hell away from me! Because if I see you, I'll make your life miserable. *You understand that?*"

"Yes."

I let him free, and when he walked from the room I wanted to spit on the floor where he had stood. I couldn't stop the fury from rising in my heart. It engulfed me, owned me, till it seemed I could only rid myself of it with tears or an act of violence. I snatched from the bed the bag Grossbart had given me and with all my strength threw it out the window. And the next morning, as the men policed the area around the barracks, I heard a great cry go up from one of the trainees who'd been anticipating only this morning handful of cigarette butts and candy wrappers. "Egg roll!" he shouted. "Holy Christ, Chinese goddam egg roll!"

A week later when I read the orders that had come down from C & A I couldn't believe my eyes. Every single trainee was to be shipped to Camp Stoneham, California, and from there to the Pacific. Every trainee but one: Private Sheldon Grossbart was to be sent to Fort Monmouth, New Jersey. I read the mimeographed sheet several times. Dee, Farrell, Fishbein, Fuselli, Fylypowycz, Glinicki, Gromke, Gucwa, Halpern, Hardy, Helebrandt . . . right down to Anton Zygadlo, all were to be headed West before the month was out. All except Grossbart. He had pulled a string and I wasn't it.

I lifted the phone and called C & A.

The voice on the other end said smartly, "Corporal Shulman, sir."

"Let me speak to Sergeant Wright."

"Who is this calling, sir?"

"Sergeant Marx."

And to my surprise, the voice said, *"Oh."* Then: "Just a minute, Sergeant."

Shulman's *oh* stayed with me while I waited for Wright to come to the phone. Why *oh?* Who was Shulman? And then, so simply, I knew I'd discovered the string Grossbart had pulled. In fact, I could hear Grossbart the day he'd discovered Shulman, in the PX, or the bowling alley, or maybe even at services. "Glad to meet you. Where you from? Bronx? Me too. Do you know so-and-so? And so-and-so? Me too! You work at C & A? Really? Hey, how's chances of getting East? Could you do something? Change something? Swindle, cheat, lie? We gotta help each other, you know . . . if the Jews in Germany . . ."

At the other end Bob Wright answered. "How are you, Nate? How's the pitching arm?"

"Good. Bob, I wonder if you could do me a favor." I heard clearly my own words and they so reminded me of Grossbart that I dropped more easily than I could have imagined into what I had planned. "This may sound crazy, Bob, but I got a kid here on orders to Monmouth who wants them changed. He had a brother killed in Europe and he's hot to go to the Pacific. Says he'd feel like a coward if he wound up stateside. I don't know, Bob, can anything be done? Put somebody else in the Monmouth slot?"

"Who?" he asked cagily.

"Anybody. First guy on the alphabet. I don't care. The kid just asked if something could be done."

"What's his name?"

"Grossbart, Sheldon."

Wright didn't answer.

"Yeah," I said, "he's a Jewish kid, so he thought I could help him out. You know."

"I guess I can do something," he finally said. "The Major hasn't been around here for weeks—TDY[3] to the golf course. I'll try, Nate that's all I can say."

"I'd appreciate it, Bob. See you Sunday," and I hung up, perspiring.

And the following day the corrected orders appeared: Fishbein, Fuselli, Fylypowycz, Glinicki, Grossbart, Gucwa, Halpern, Hardy . . . Lucky Private Harley Alton was to go to Fort Monmouth, New Jersey, where for some reason or other, they wanted an enlisted man with infantry training.

After chow that night I stopped back at the orderly room to straighten out the guard duty roster. Grossbart was waiting for me. He spoke first.

"You son of a bitch!"

I sat down at my desk and while he glared down at me I began to make the necessary alterations in the duty roster.

"What do you have against me?" he cried. "Against my family? Would it kill you for me to be near my father, God knows how many months he has left to him."

"Why?"

"His heart," Grossbart said. "He hasn't had enough troubles in a lifetime, you've got to add to them. I curse the day I ever met you, Marx! Shulman told me what happened over there. There's no limit to your anti-Semitism, is there! The damage you've done here isn't enough. You have to make a special phone call! You really want me dead!"

I made the last few notations in the duty roster and got up to leave. "Good night, Grossbart."

"You owe me an explanation!" He stood in my path.

"Sheldon, you're the one who owes explanations."

He scowled. "To *you?*"

"To me, I think so, yes. Mostly to Fishbein and Halpern."

"That's right, twist things around. I owe nobody nothing, I've done all I could do for them. Now I think I've got the right to watch out for myself."

"For each other we have to learn to watch out, Sheldon. You told me yourself."

"You call this watching out for me, what you did?"

"No. For all of us."

I pushed him aside and started for the door. I heard his furious breathing behind me, and it sounded like steam rushing from the engine of his terrible strength.

"You'll be all right," I said from the door. And, I thought, so would Fishbein and Halpern be all right, even in the Pacific, if only Grossbart could continue to see in the obsequiousness of the one, the soft spirituality of the other, some profit for himself.

I stood outside the orderly room, and I heard Grossbart weeping behind me. Over in the barracks, in the lighted windows, I could see the boys in their T-shirts sitting on their bunks talking about their orders, as they'd been doing for the past two days. With a kind of quiet nervousness, they polished shoes, shined belt buckles, squared away underwear, trying as best they could to accept their fate. Behind me, Grossbart swallowed hard, accepting his. And then, resisting with all my will an impulse to turn and seek pardon for my vindictiveness, I accepted my own.

1959

3. Temporary Duty, an army orders term used ironically here.

AUDRE LORDE
1934–1992

Audre Lorde's poetry wages what she called "a war against the tyrannies of silence"; it articulates what has been passed over out of fear or discomfort, what has been kept hidden and secret. Reading her we feel the violence inherent in breaking a silence, perhaps most often as she probes the experience of anger—the anger of black toward white or white toward black, a woman's anger at men and other women, and men's anger toward women. "My Black woman's anger," she wrote in her collection of essays, *Sister Outsider*, "is a molten pond at the core of me, my most fiercely guarded secret." Having admitted this secret into her poems, Lorde transforms our expectations of what is a fit subject for the lyric. Her work is often deliberately disturbing, the powerful voice of the poem cutting through denial, politeness, and fear. In developing this voice Lorde drew on African resources, especially the matriarchal mythology and history of West Africa. Her seventh book, *The Black Unicorn* (1978), reflects the time she spent in Africa studying, in particular, Yoruba mythology and reclaiming her connection to the rich African cultures. The African presence is evident in one of her last books, *Our Dead Behind Us* (1986), as well. Lorde's work suggests that she always connected poetry to the speaking voice, but her study of African materials deepened her connection to oral traditions (like the chant or the call) and taught her the power of voice to cut across time and place. From African writers, she said, she learned that "we live in accordance with, in a kind of correspondence with, the rest of the world as a whole." A powerful voice informed by personal and cultural history creates the possibility, for Lorde, of bridging the differences her work does not seek to erase. "It is not difference that immobilizes us," she wrote, "but silence."

Her work celebrates difference and confounds it. In Adrienne Rich's words, Lorde wrote "as a Black woman, a mother, a daughter, a Lesbian, a feminist, a visionary." Her poem "Coal" affirms an *I* that is "the total black, being spoken / from the earth's inside." This total blackness was, for her, also associated with Eros and with creativity; she celebrated this source as what she called "woman's place of power within each of us," which is "neither white nor surface; it is dark, it is ancient; and it is deep." Her best work calls on the deepest places of her own life—on the pain she experienced, on her rage (her second book, in 1972, was titled *Cables to Rage*), on her longing and desire. One of the silences her poems broke concerns love between women, and she wrote a number of poems that are erotic, precise, and true to both the power and delicacy of feeling. Unafraid of anger, she was also capable of tenderness; this is perhaps most clear not only in her love poems but in poems that address a younger generation.

Lorde was born in New York City and lived in New York almost all her life. Her parents were West Indian, and her mother was light skinned. "I grew up in a genuine confusion / between grass and weeds and flowers / and what colored meant," Lorde wrote in her poem "Outside." Part of that confusion was the conflict represented by her father's blackness and her mother's desire for whiteness (in "Black Mother Woman" Lorde speaks of the mother as "split with deceitful longings"). Lorde's understanding of identity forged out of conflict began, then, for her in her own family history with its legacy of "conflicting rebellions" ("Black Mother Woman"). In 1961 she received a B.A. from Hunter College and later a Master's of Library Science from Columbia University. The following year she married (she divorced in 1970), and the marriage produced a daughter and a son. In 1968 she became poet-in-residence for a year at Tougaloo College in Mississippi, her first experience in the American South. Thereafter she knew her work to be that of a writer and teacher; she taught at John Jay College of Criminal Justice in New York City and, from 1981, was professor of English at Hunter College. In the last years of her life Lorde traveled extensively, not only to Africa but to Australia (where she met with aborigine women) and Germany. During her last years she lived much of the time in St. Croix.

"I have come to believe over and over again," Lorde said, "that what is most important to me must be spoken, made verbal and shared, even at the risk of having it bruised or misunderstood." (Her essay "Poetry Is Not a Luxury" [1977] makes the case for poetry's essential speaking of what is otherwise unnamed and unthought. A selection from this essay appears in the "Postmodern Manifestos" cluster of this anthology.) The drive toward expression made Lorde a prolific writer and led her to several prose works in which she shared experiences often restricted to privacy: *The Cancer Journals* (1980), an account of her struggle with breast cancer, and *Zami: A New Spelling of My Name* (1982), a "biomythography" of her growing up and her emergent lesbian identity. The urgency Lorde felt to make experience "verbal and shared," however, sometimes overrode a distinction crucial to her work: that between poetry and rhetoric. She preserved this distinction in her best work by listening and responding to other voices in herself and in the world around her. With their combination of pain, anger, and tenderness, her finest poems are poetry as illumination, poetry in which, as she said, "we give name to those ideas which are—until the poem—nameless, formless, about to be birthed, but already felt."

Coal

I
is the total black, being spoken
from the earth's inside.
There are many kinds of open
how a diamond comes into a knot of flame   5
how sound comes into a word, coloured
by who pays what for speaking.

Some words are open like a diamond
on glass windows
singing out within the passing crash of sun   10
Then there are words like stapled wagers
in a perforated book,—buy and sign and tear apart—
and come whatever wills all chances
the stub remains
an ill-pulled tooth with a ragged edge.   15
Some words live in my throat
breeding like adders. Others know sun
seeking like gypsies over my tongue
to explode through my lips
like young sparrows bursting from shell.   20
Some words
bedevil me.

Love is a word, another kind of open.
As the diamond comes into a knot of flame
I am Black because I come from the earth's inside   25
now take my word for jewel in the open light.

1968

The Woman Thing

The hunters are back from beating the winter's face
in search of a challenge or task
in search of food
making fresh tracks for their children's hunger
they do not watch the sun   5
they cannot wear its heat for a sign
of triumph or freedom;
The hunters are treading heavily homeward
through snow that is marked
with their own bloody footprints.   10
emptyhanded, the hunters return
snow-maddened, sustained by their rages.

In the night after food they may seek
young girls for their amusement. But now
the hunters are coming   15
and the unbaked girls flee from their angers.
All this day I have craved
food for my child's hunger
Emptyhanded the hunters come shouting
injustices drip from their mouths   20
like stale snow melted in sunlight.

Meanwhile
the woman thing my mother taught me
bakes off its covering of snow
like a rising blackening sun.   25

1968

Harriet

Harriet there was always somebody calling us crazy
or mean or stuck-up or evil or black
or black
and we were
nappy girls quick as cuttlefish[1]   5
scurrying for cover
trying to speak trying to speak
trying to speak
the pain in each others mouths
until we learned   10
on the edge of a lash
or a tongue
on the edge of the other's betrayal
that respect

---

1. Ten-armed shellfish. "Nappy": with closely twisted or curled hair.

meant keeping our distance   15
in silence
averting our eyes
from each other's face in the street
from the beautiful dark mouth
and cautious familiar eyes   20
passing alone.

I remember you Harriet
before we were broken apart
we dreamed the crossed swords
of warrior queens   25
while we avoided each other's eyes
and we learned to know lonely
as the earth learns to know dead
Harriet Harriet
what name shall we call our selves now 30
our mother is gone?

                                      1978

AMIRI BARAKA (LEROI JONES)
b. 1934

When in 1967 LeRoi Jones assumed the Bantuized Muslim name Amiri Baraka (meaning Prince, a Blessed One), he was undergoing one of several changes in his progression as a maker of literature. Born Everett Leroy Jones, he was the child of middle-class African American parents in Newark, New Jersey, where his scholastic abilities took him to the best schools available; as Baraka recalls in his autobiography, his classmates were more often white suburbanites than inner-city children of his own race. The stylizing "LeRoi" was undertaken during his undergraduate years at Howard University (a traditionally African American institution), to which he had transferred from the mostly white campus of Rutgers University (where he had won a scholarship). After leaving Howard in 1954 and serving in the U.S. Air Force, from which he was discharged for unapproved political activities, Jones moved to New York City's Greenwich Village and became prominent on the avant-garde poetry scene. His friends were white innovators—Gilbert Sorrentino, Diane DiPrima, and Frank O'Hara among them—with whom he worked on the magazine *Kulchur* in addition to editing and publishing his own journal, *Yugen*. Married to Hettie Cohen, he began an interracial family and wrote record reviews for mainstream jazz magazines.

Jones was well established in the more intellectually elite quarters of New York's world of poetry, art, and music when *Dutchman* was produced in 1964. That it won an Obie (as one of the year's best Off-Broadway plays) seemed appropriate for a work by someone on the cutting edge of literature. Yet as racial tensions mounted, with the assassination of Medgar Evers; fatal church bombings in Alabama; and the murder of civil rights workers James Chaney, Andrew Goodman, and Michael Schwerner in Mississippi, Jones's life underwent major changes as well. In 1965, following the assassination of Malcolm X, he left his wife and children and moved to Harlem, where as a newly declared black cultural nationalist he founded the Black Arts Repertory Theater, dedicated to taking socially militant drama directly to the people it concerned. At this time his drama assumed the spokesmanship role expressed by his character Clay in *Dutchman*. Such works as *The Baptism* and *The Toilet* (both 1967) are physically assaultive in their dramaturgy; in the latter the stage set is a realistically constructed public lavatory, where among the uncleaned urinals a student is harassed and beaten as a vehicle of the play's narrative exposition. *Four Black Revolutionary Plays* (1969) collects similarly harsh works and includes as well the author's comments on a play that because of its explosiveness could not be printed in an America only recently disrupted by assassinations and urban rioting (*J-E-L-L-O*, in which Rochester, the comically beloved servant of Jack Benny's popular radio and television show, kills Benny and his family; the Jell-O Food Company, Benny's longtime sponsor, refused to let its name be used). By 1970 Amiri Baraka, as he asked to be called, had moved to Newark; married Sylvia Robinson (who became Amina Baraka); and begun work toward electing Kenneth Gibson as the city's first black mayor, a consequence of the author's having been convicted, on the evidence of his poetry, of incitement to riot. The conviction was overturned on appeal. Yet even with Gibson in control, Baraka was not happy with the quality of African American life in the city and soon parted with the mayor and black nationalism in favor of third world Marxism.

Poetry as a vehicle of popular encouragement remains central to Baraka's belief. He may well have agreed with the originally convicting judge that his poems could motivate people to act (whether such culpability had been proven in legal form is another matter). As opposed to his very first work, which conveyed a personal anguish for which the poet projected no political situation ("I am inside someone / who hates me, I look / out from his eyes") and whose collective title conveys little hope other than in the act of expression (*Preface to a Twenty Volume Suicide Note*, 1961), his later work is replete with exhortations, capitalized imperatives for action, and chantlike repetitions designed to arouse a fury for action and then direct it toward the achievement of specific social goals. Much like his drama, this poetry is overtly presentational, showing what the reader needs to think about and then providing the stimulus to act. Yet all the while the personal nature of Baraka stands behind it, making clear that a deep and complex imagination has been brought to bear on the issues.

Since the 1980s Baraka has taught in the African Studies Department at the State University of New York, Stony Brook. In addition to poetry and drama, he continues to write essays on social subjects and on jazz.

An Agony. As Now.

I am inside someone
who hates me. I look
out from his eyes. Smell
what fouled tunes come in
to his breath. Love his   5
wretched women.

Slits in the metal, for sun. Where
my eyes sit turning, at the cool air
the glance of light, or hard flesh
rubbed against me, a woman, a man,   10
without shadow, or voice, or meaning.

This is the enclosure (flesh,
where innocence is a weapon. An
abstraction. Touch. (Not mine,
Or yours, if you are the soul I had   15
and abandoned when I was blind and had
my enemies carry me as a dead man
(if he is beautiful, or pitied.

It can be pain. (As now, as all his
flesh hurts me.) It can be that. Or   20
pain. As when she ran from me into
that forest.
               Or pain, the mind
silver spiraled whirled against the
sun, higher than even old men thought   25
God would be. Or pain. And the other. The
yes. (Inside his books, his fingers. They
are withered yellow flowers and were never
beautiful.) The yes. You will, lost soul, say
'beauty.' Beauty, practiced, as the tree. The   30
slow river. A white sun in its wet sentences.

Or, the cold men in their gale. Ecstasy. Flesh
or soul. The yes. (Their robes blown. Their bowls
empty. They chant at my heels, not at yours.) Flesh
or soul, as corrupt. Where the answer moves too quickly.   35
Where the God is a self, after all.)

Cold air blown through narrow blind eyes. Flesh,
white hot metal. Glows as the day with its sun.
It is a human love, I live inside. A bony skeleton
you recognize as words or simple feeling.   40

But it has no feeling. As the metal, is hot, it is not,
given to love.

It burns the thing
inside it. And that thing
screams.   45

                                        1964

A Poem for Willie Best[1]

I

The face sings, alone
at the top
      of the body. All
flesh, all song, aligned. For hell
is silent, at those cracked lips   5
flakes of skin and mind
twist and whistle softly
as they fall.
          It was your own death
you saw. Your own face, stiff   10
and raw. This
without sound, or
movement. Sweet afton,[2] the
dead beggar bleeds
yet. His blood, for a time   15
alive, and huddled in a door
way, struggling to sing. Rain
washes it into cracks. Pits
whose bottoms are famous. Whose sides
are innocent broadcasts   20
of another life.

II

At this point, neither
front nor back. A point, the
dimensionless line. The top
of a head, seen from Christ's   25
heaven, stripped of history
or desire.
         Fixed, perpendicular
to shadow. (Even speech, vertical,
leaves no trace. Born in to death   30
held fast to it, where
the lover spreads his arms, the line
he makes to threaten Gods with history.
The fingers stretch to emptiness. At
each point, after flesh, even light   35
is speculation. But an end, his end,
failing a beginning.

2

A cross. The gesture, symbol, line
arms held stiff, nailed stiff, with
no sign, of what gave them strength.   40

---

1. Willie Best was a negro character actor whose Hollywood name was Sleep'n'eat [Baraka's note].
2. "How Gently Sweet Afton," a poem by the Scottish poet Robert Burns (1759–1796), refers to the river Afton in Ayrshire, Scotland.

The point, become a line, a cross, or
the man, and his material, driven in
the ground. If the head rolls back
and the mouth opens, screamed into
existence, there will be perhaps   45
only the slightest hint of movement
a smear; no help will come. No one
will turn to that station again.

III

At a cross roads, sits the
player. No drum, no umbrella, even   50
though it's raining. Again, and we
are somehow less miserable because
here is a hero, used to being wet.
One road is where you are standing now
(reading this, the other, crosses then   55
rushes into a wood.
                    5 lbs neckbones.
                    5 lbs hog innards.
                    10 bottles cheap wine.
                                        (the contents   60
of a paper bag, also shoes, with holes
for the big toe, and several rusted
knives. This is a literature, of
symbols. And it is his gift, as the
bag is.   65
          (The contents
again, holy saviours,
                    300 men on horseback
                    75 bibles
                    the quietness   70
of a field. A rich
man, though wet through
by the rain.
          I said,
                    47 howitzers[3]   75
                    7 polished horse jaws
                    a few trees being waved
softly back under
the black night
                    All this should be   80
invested.

IV

Where
ever,
      he has gone. Who ever

---

3. Short, relatively light guns for the high-angle firing of shells at a low velocity.

mourns   85
or sits silent
to remember

There is nothing of pity
here. Nothing
of sympathy.   90

V

This is the dance of the raised
leg. Of the hand on the knee
quickly.
        As a dance it punishes
speech. 'The house burned. The   95
old man killed.'
           As a dance it
is obscure.

VI

This is the song
of the highest C.   100
           The falsetto. An elegance
that punishes silence. This is the song
of the toes pointed inward, the arms swung, the
hips, moved, for fucking, slow, from side
to side. He is quoted   105
saying, "My father was
never a jockey,
           but
  he did teach me
          how to ride."   110

VII

The balance.
        (Rushed in, swarmed of dark, cloaks,
and only red lights pushed a message
to the street. Rub.
          This is the lady,   115
I saw you with.
This is your mother.
This is the lady I wanted
some how to sleep with.
          As a dance, or   120
our elegant song. Sun red and grown
from trees, fences, mud roads in dried out
river beds. This is for me, with no God
but what is given. Give me
          Something more   125

than what is here. I must tell you
my body hurts.

The balance.
        Can you hear? Here
I am again. Your boy, dynamite. Can   130
you hear? My soul is moved. The soul
you gave me. I say, my soul, and it
is moved. That soul
you gave me.
        Yes, I'm sure   135
this is the lady. You
slept with her. Witness, your boy,
here, dynamite. Hear?
          I mean
can you?   140
The balance.
        He was tired of losing. (And
his walking buddies tired
of walking.
        Bent slightly,   145
at the waist. Left hand low, to flick
quick showy jabs ala Sugar.[4] The right
cocked, to complete,
          any combination.
        He was   150
tired of losing, but he was fighting
a big dumb "farmer."
        Such a blue bright
afternoon, and only a few hundred yards
from the beach. He said, I'm tired   155
of losing.
        "I *got* ta cut'cha."

VIII

A renegade
behind the mask. And even
the mask, a renegade   160
disguise. Black skin
and hanging lip.
        Lazy
        Frightened
        Thieving   165
        Very potent sexually
        Scars
        Generally inferior
          (but natural
rhythms.   170

4. Sugar Ray Robinson (1921–1989), American boxer.

His head is
at the window. The only
part
    that sings.
(The word he used   175
      (we are passing St. Mark's place[5]
      and those crazy jews who fuck)
                        to provoke
in neon, still useful
in the rain,   180
        to provoke
some meaning, where before
there was only hell. I said
silence, at his huddled blood.
              It is an obscene invention.   185
              A white sticky discharge.
              "Jism," in white chalk
              on the back of Angel's garage.
              Red jackets with the head of
              Hobbes[6] staring into space. "Jasm"   190
              the name the leader took, had it
              stenciled on his chest.
                        And he sits
wet at the crossroads, remembering distinctly
each weightless face that eases by. (Sun at   195
the back door, and that hideous mindless grin.
                        (Hear?

                                            1964

5. Street in New York City's East Village.
6. Thomas Hobbes (1588–1679), English philosopher who believed a "social contract" was necessary between rulers and the ruled. Here he represents the Western, white, materialist tradition.

N. SCOTT MOMADAY
b. 1934

"In a certain sense," writes N. Scott Momaday in the nonfiction collection *The Man Made of Words* (1997), "we are all made of words; . . . our most essential being consists in language. It is the element in which we think and dream and act, in which we live our daily lives." Since the publication of his Pulitzer Prize–winning novel *House Made of Dawn* (1968), Momaday's writing has crossed boundaries of language, form, and genre, thereby creating for Momaday, through will and imagination, an American Indian identity in words.

    Navarre Scott Momaday was born at the Kiowa and Comanche Indian Hospital in Lawton, Oklahoma, the only child of Al Momaday, a Kiowa, and Natachee Scott, who was part Cherokee. He spent most of his early years in New Mexico and Arizona, moving in 1946 to Jemez Pueblo in New Mexico's Rio Grande Valley. There his parents, both artists and teachers, took jobs at a small day school. Growing up on reservations, including those of the Navajo and the Apache, Momaday experienced the rhythms of traditional tribal life, but saw, too, the changes wrought by postwar material culture, and their human costs—the alcoholism, unemployment, and personal disintegration that mark the life of Abel, the returning veteran in *House Made of Dawn*. Early on, Momaday's mother instilled in him the value of a bicultural education that would open the future without closing off his native heritage. Momaday attended reservation, public, and mission schools, then graduated from military high school in Virginia and the University of New Mexico. He received his Ph.D. in 1963 from Stanford University, where his mentor in American and English literature was the poet and critic Yvor Winters. Since then his teaching career has taken him to Santa Barbara, Berkeley, the University of Moscow, Stanford, and the University of Arizona.

What some scholars call the "Native American Renaissance" is usually said to have begun with the publication of *House Made of Dawn* in 1968 and its reception of the Pulitzer Prize the following year. And, indeed, from 1968 to the present Native American writers have published a substantial body of fine poetry, fiction, and autobiography, gaining considerable notice in the United States and abroad.

Over the decades since the publication of *House Made of Dawn*, Momaday has published two more novels, *The Ancient Child* (1989) and *In the Bear's House* (1999); four volumes of poems, *Angle of Geese and Other Poems* (1974), *Before an Old Painting of the Crucifixion, Carmel Mission, June 1960* (1975), and *The Gourd Dancer* (1976); stories and poems in *In the Presence of the Sun* (1992); and three works of autobiography, *The Journey to Tai-me* (1967, privately published), *The Way to Rainy Mountain* (1969), and *The Names: A Memoir* (1976) as well as critical works. His deliberate engagement with a variety of forms—oral and written poetry, prose fiction and nonfiction, autobiography, legend, history, photography, painting (all "forms of discovery," in Winters's words)—has helped him lay claim to his Kiowa past.

Momaday's idea of the past as a journey is consciously expressed in *The Journey of Tai-me*, which offers his translations of Kiowa myths he learned as a child from his grandmother, Aho. This work relates the story of the Sun Dance—a ceremony for spiritual guidance and power performed by many Plains Indian groups—to his revelatory memory on journeying to Oklahoma to see the sacred Tai-me bundle: "I became more keenly aware of myself as someone who had walked through time and in whose blood there is something inestimably old and undying. It was as if I had remembered something that happened two hundred years ago. I meant then to seek after the source of my memory and myself." In *The Way to Rainy Mountain* (1969) Momaday undertakes this search, collecting, with his father as translator, Kiowa tales and myths and clustering them with brief, loose historical commentaries and personal family stories. What seem to be fragments come together in a complex structure—twenty-four "quintessential novels," divided into three sections, framed by poems and prose pieces—that follow the Kiowa from emergence through maturity to decline as a Plains Indian culture. Central to *Rainy Mountain* and to all of Momaday's writing is the land, the focal point of memory, the defining place for Kiowa culture. The same rootedness that defines Momaday's ancestors gives his work its conjuring power, a power that comes from distilling in words and pictures, as Momaday writes, "the glare of noon and all the colors of the dawn and dusk."

From The Way to Rainy Mountain

Headwaters

Noon in the intermountain plain:
There is scant telling of the marsh—
A log, hollow and weather-stained,
An insect at the mouth, and moss—
Yet waters rise against the roots,   5
Stand brimming to the stalks. What moves?
What moves on this archaic force
Was wild and welling at the source.

Introduction

A single knoll rises out of the plain in Oklahoma, north and west of the Wichita Range. For my people, the Kiowas,[1] it is an old landmark, and they gave it the name Rainy Mountain. The hardest weather in the world is there. Winter brings blizzards, hot tornadic winds arise in the spring, and in summer the prairie is an anvil's edge. The grass turns brittle and brown, and it cracks beneath your feet. There are green belts along the rivers and creeks, linear groves of hickory and pecan, willow and witch hazel. At a distance in July or August the steaming foliage seems almost to writhe in fire. Great green and yellow grasshoppers are everywhere in the tall grass, popping up like corn to sting the flesh, and tortoises crawl about on the red earth, going nowhere in the plenty of time. Loneliness is an aspect of the land. All things in the plain are isolate; there is no confusion of objects in the eye, but *one* hill or *one* tree or *one* man. To look upon that landscape in the early morning, with the sun at your back, is to lose the sense of proportion. Your imagination comes to life, and this, you think, is where Creation was begun.

I returned to Rainy Mountain in July. My grandmother had died in the spring, and I wanted to be at her grave. She had lived to be very old and at last infirm. Her only living daughter was with her when she died, and I was told that in death her face was that of a child.

I like to think of her as a child. When she was born, the Kiowas were living the last great moment of their history. For more than a hundred years they had controlled the open range from the Smoky Hill River to the Red, from the headwaters of the Canadian to the fork of the Arkansas and Cimarron. In alliance with the Comanches, they had ruled the whole of the southern Plains. War was their sacred business, and they were among the finest horsemen the world has ever known. But warfare for the Kiowas was preeminently a matter of disposition rather than of survival, and they never understood the grim, unrelenting advance of the U.S. Cavalry. When at last, divided and ill-provisioned, they were driven onto the Staked Plains in the cold rains of autumn, they fell into panic. In Palo Duro Canyon[2] they abandoned their crucial stores to pillage and had nothing then but their lives. In order to save themselves, they surrendered to the soldiers at Fort Sill[3] and were imprisoned in the old stone corral that now stands

---

1. The Kiowa were a mobile hunting and gathering people of the Southern Plains.
2. On the Staked Plains, or the Texas Panhandle, that part of the state jutting north between New Mexico and Oklahoma.
3. U.S. Cavalry fort in Oklahoma and site of the Kiowa-Comanche Agency.

as a military museum. My grandmother was spared the humiliation of those high gray walls by eight or ten years, but she must have known from birth the affliction of defeat, the dark brooding of old warriors.

Her name was Aho, and she belonged to the last culture to evolve in North America. Her forebears came down from the high country in western Montana nearly three centuries ago. They were a mountain people, a mysterious tribe of hunters whose language has never been positively classified in any major group. In the late seventeenth century they began a long migration to the south and east. It was a journey toward the dawn, and it led to a golden age. Along the way the Kiowas were befriended by the Crows, who gave them the culture and religion of the Plains. They acquired horses, and their ancient nomadic spirit was suddenly free of the ground. They acquired Tai-me,[4] the sacred Sun Dance doll, from that moment the object and symbol of their worship, and so shared in the divinity of the sun. Not least, they acquired the sense of destiny, therefore courage and pride. When they entered upon the southern Plains they had been transformed. No longer were they slaves to the simple necessity of survival; they were a lordly and dangerous society of fighters and thieves, hunters and priests of the sun. According to their origin myth, they entered the world through a hollow log. From one point of view, their migration was the fruit of an old prophecy, for indeed they emerged from a sunless world.

Although my grandmother lived out her long life in the shadow of Rainy Mountain, the immense landscape of the continental interior lay like memory in her blood. She could tell of the Crows, whom she had never seen, and of the Black Hills, where she had never been. I wanted to see in reality what she had seen more perfectly in the mind's eye, and traveled fifteen hundred miles to begin my pilgrimage.

Yellowstone, it seemed to me, was the top of the world, a region of deep lakes and dark timber, canyons and waterfalls. But, beautiful as it is, one might have the sense of confinement there. The skyline in all directions is close at hand, the high wall of the woods and deep cleavages of shade. There is a perfect freedom in the mountains, but it belongs to the eagle and the elk, the badger and the bear. The Kiowas reckoned their stature by the distance they could see, and they were bent and blind in the wilderness.

Descending eastward, the highland meadows are a stairway to the plain. In July the inland slope of the Rockies is luxuriant with flax and buckwheat, stonecrop and larkspur. The earth unfolds and the limit of the land recedes. Clusters of trees, and animals grazing far in the distance, cause the vision to reach away and wonder to build upon the mind. The sun follows a longer course in the day, and the sky is immense beyond all comparison. The great billowing clouds that sail upon it are shadows that move upon the grain like water, dividing light. Farther down, in the land of the Crows and Blackfeet, the plain is yellow. Sweet clover takes hold of the hills and bends upon itself to cover and seal the soil. There the Kiowas paused on their way; they had come to the place where they must change their lives. The sun is at home on the plains. Precisely there does it have the certain character of a god. When the Kiowas came to the land of the Crows, they could see the dark lees of the hills at dawn across the Bighorn River, the profusion of light on the grain shelves, the oldest deity ranging after the solstices. Not yet would they veer southward to the caldron of the land that lay below; they must

4. The sacred being who aids the Kiowa in times of trouble; this being is embodied in the holy doll central to Kiowa ritual.

wean their blood from the northern winter and hold the mountains a while longer in their view. They bore Tai-me in procession to the east.

A dark mist lay over the Black Hills, and the land was like iron. At the top of a ridge I caught sight of Devil's Tower upthrust against the gray sky as if in the birth of time the core of the earth had broken through its crust and the motion of the world was begun. There are things in nature that engender an awful quiet in the heart of man; Devil's Tower is one of them. Two centuries ago, because they could not do otherwise, the Kiowas made a legend at the base of the rock. My grandmother said:

> Eight children were there at play, seven sisters and their brother. Suddenly the boy was struck dumb; he trembled and began to run upon his hands and feet. His fingers became claws, and his body was covered with fur. Directly there was a bear where the boy had been. The sisters were terrified; they ran, and the bear after them. They came to the stump of a great tree, and the tree spoke to them. It bade them climb upon it, and as they did so it began to rise into the air. The bear came to kill them, but they were just beyond its reach. It reared against the tree and scored the bark all around with its claws. The seven sisters were borne into the sky, and they became the stars of the Big Dipper.

From that moment, and so long as the legend lives, the Kiowas have kinsmen in the night sky. Whatever they were in the mountains, they could be no more. However tenuous their well-being, however much they had suffered and would suffer again, they had found a way out of the wilderness.

My grandmother had a reverence for the sun, a holy regard that now is all but gone out of mankind. There was a wariness in her, and an ancient awe. She was a Christian in her later years, but she had come a long way about, and she never forgot her birthright. As a child she had been to the Sun Dances; she had taken part in those annual rites, and by them she had learned the restoration of her people in the presence of Tai-me. She was about seven when the last Kiowa Sun Dance was held in 1887 on the Washita River above Rainy Mountain Creek. The buffalo were gone. In order to consummate the ancient sacrifice—to impale the head of a buffalo bull upon the medicine tree—a delegation of old men journeyed into Texas, there to beg and barter for an animal from the Goodnight herd. She was ten when the Kiowas came together for the last time as a living Sun Dance culture. They could find no buffalo; they had to hang an old hide from the sacred tree. Before the dance could begin, a company of soldiers rode out from Fort Sill under orders to disperse the tribe. Forbidden without cause the essential act of their faith,[5] having seen the wild herds slaughtered and left to rot upon the ground, the Kiowas backed away forever from the medicine tree. That was July 20, 1890, at the great bend of the Washita. My grandmother was there. Without bitterness, and for as long as she lived, she bore a vision of deicide.

Now that I can have her only in memory, I see my grandmother in the several postures that were peculiar to her: standing at the wood stove on a winter morning and turning meat in a great iron skillet; sitting at the south window, bent above her beadwork, and afterwards, when her vision failed, looking down for

5. From the 1880s on, the U.S. government sought to ban all "heathenish" practices among Native American peoples in a continuing effort to Christianize and "civilize" them.

a long time into the fold of her hands; going out upon a cane, very slowly as she did when the weight of age came upon her; praying. I remember her most often at prayer. She made long, rambling prayers out of suffering and hope, having seen many things. I was never sure that I had the right to hear, so exclusive were they of all mere custom and company. The last time I saw her she prayed standing by the side of her bed at night, naked to the waist, the light of a kerosene lamp moving upon her dark skin. Her long, black hair, always drawn and braided in the day, lay upon her shoulders and against her breasts like a shawl. I do not speak Kiowa, and I never understood her prayers, but there was something inherently sad in the sound, some merest hesitation upon the syllables of sorrow. She began in a high and descending pitch, exhausting her breath to silence; then again and again—and always the same intensity of effort, of something that is, and is not, like urgency in the human voice. Transported so in the dancing light among the shadows of her room, she seemed beyond the reach of time. But that was illusion; I think I knew then that I should not see her again.

Houses are like sentinels in the plain, old keepers of the weather watch. There, in a very little while, wood takes on the appearance of great age. All colors wear soon away in the wind and rain, and then the wood is burned gray and the grain appears and the nails turn red with rust. The windowpanes are black and opaque; you imagine there is nothing within, and indeed there are many ghosts, bones given up to the land. They stand here and there against the sky, and you approach them for a longer time than you expect. They belong in the distance; it is their domain.

Once there was a lot of sound in my grandmother's house, a lot of coming and going, feasting and talk. The summers there were full of excitement and reunion. The Kiowas are a summer people; they abide the cold and keep to themselves, but when the season turns and the land becomes warm and vital they cannot hold still; an old love of going returns upon them. The aged visitors who came to my grandmother's house when I was a child were made of lean and leather, and they bore themselves upright. They wore great black hats and bright ample shirts that shook in the wind. They rubbed fat upon their hair and wound their braids with strips of colored cloth. Some of them painted their faces and carried the scars of old and cherished enmities. They were an old council of warlords, come to remind and be reminded of who they were. Their wives and daughters served them well. The women might indulge themselves; gossip was at once the mark and compensation of their servitude. They made loud and elaborate talk among themselves, full of jest and gesture, fright and false alarm. They went abroad in fringed and flowered shawls, bright beadwork and German silver. They were at home in the kitchen, and they prepared meals that were banquets.

There were frequent prayer meetings, and great nocturnal feasts. When I was a child I played with my cousins outside, where the lamplight fell upon the ground and the singing of the old people rose up around us and carried away into the darkness. There were a lot of good things to eat, a lot of laughter and surprise. And afterwards, when the quiet returned, I lay down with my grandmother and could hear the frogs away by the river and feel the motion of the air.

Now there is a funeral silence in the rooms, the endless wake of some final word. The walls have closed in upon my grandmother's house. When I returned to it in mourning, I saw for the first time in my life how small it was. It was late at night, and there was a white moon, nearly full. I sat for a long time on the stone steps by the kitchen door. From there I could see out across the land; I could see the long row of trees by the creek, the low light upon the rolling plains, and the stars of the Big Dipper. Once I looked at the moon and caught sight of a strange thing. A cricket had perched upon the handrail, only a few inches away from me. My line of vision was such that the creature filled the moon like a fossil. It had gone there, I thought, to live and die, for there, of all places, was its small definition made whole and eternal. A warm wind rose up and purled like the longing within me.

The next morning I awoke at dawn and went out on the dirt road to Rainy Mountain. It was already hot, and the grasshoppers began to fill the air. Still, it was early in the morning, and the birds sang out of the shadows. The long yellow grass on the mountain shone in the bright light, and a scissortail hied above the land. There, where it ought to be, at the end of a long and legendary way, was my grandmother's grave. Here and there on the dark stones were ancestral names. Looking back once, I saw the mountain and came away.

IV

They lived at first in the mountains. They did not yet know of Tai-me, but this is what they knew: There was a man and his wife. They had a beautiful child, a little girl whom they would not allow to go out of their sight. But one day a friend of the family came and asked if she might take the child outside to play. The mother guessed that would be all right, but she told the friend to leave the child in its cradle and to place the cradle in a tree. While the child was in the tree, a redbird came among the branches. It was not like any bird that you have seen; it was very beautiful, and it did not fly away. It kept still upon a limb, close to the child. After a while the child got out of its cradle and began to climb after the redbird. And at the same time the tree began to grow taller, and the child was borne up into the sky. She was then a woman, and she found herself in a strange place. Instead of a redbird, there was a young man standing before her. The man spoke to her and said: "I have been watching you for a long time, and I knew that I would find a way to bring you here. I have brought you here to be my wife." The woman looked all around; she saw that he was the only living man there. She saw that he was the sun.

There the land itself ascends into the sky. These mountains lie at the top of the continent, and they cast a long rain shadow on the sea of grasses to the east. They arise out of the last North American wilderness, and they have wilderness names: Wasatch, Bitterroot, Bighorn, Wind River.

I have walked in a mountain meadow bright with Indian paintbrush, lupine, and wild buckwheat, and I have seen high in the branches of a lodgepole pine the male pine grosbeak, round and rose-colored, its dark, striped wings nearly invisible in the soft, mottled light. And the uppermost branches of the tree seemed very slowly to ride across the blue sky.

XIII

If an arrow is well made, it will have tooth marks upon it. That is how you know. The Kiowas made fine arrows and straightened them in their teeth. Then they drew them to the bow to see if they were straight. Once there was a man and his wife. They were alone at night in their tipi. By the light of the fire the man was making arrows. After a while he caught sight of something. There was a small opening in the tipi where two hides were sewn together. Someone was there on the outside, looking in. The man went on with his work, but he said to his wife: "Someone is standing outside. Do not be afraid. Let us talk easily, as of ordinary things." He took up an arrow and straightened it in his teeth; then, as it was right for him to do, he drew it to the bow and took aim, first in this direction and then in that. And all the while he was talking, as if to his wife. But this is how he spoke: "I know that you are there on the outside, for I can feel your eyes upon me. If you are a Kiowa, you will understand what I am saying, and you will speak your name." But there was no answer, and the man went on in the same way, pointing the arrow all around. At last his aim fell upon the place where his enemy stood, and he let go of the string. The arrow went straight to the enemy's heart.

The old men were the best arrow-makers, for they could bring time and patience to their craft. The young men—the fighters and hunters—were willing to pay a high price for arrows that were well made.

When my father was a boy, an old man used to come to Mammedaty's[6] house and pay his respects. He was a lean old man in braids and was impressive in his age and bearing. His name was Cheney, and he was an arrowmaker. Every morning, my father tells me, Cheney would paint his wrinkled face, go out, and pray aloud to the rising sun. In my mind I can see that man as if he were there now. I like to watch him as he makes his prayer. I know where he stands and where his voice goes on the rolling grasses and where the sun comes up on the land. There, at dawn, you can feel the silence. It is cold and clear and deep like water. It takes hold of you and will not let you go.

XVII

Bad women are thrown away. Once there was a handsome young man. He was wild and reckless, and the chief talked to the wind about him. After that, the man went hunting. A

In the Kiowa calendars[7] there is graphic proof that the lives of women were hard, whether they were "bad women" or not. Only the captives, who were slaves, held lower status. During the

---

6. Momaday's paternal grandfather.
7. The Kiowa recorded their history in pictures that functioned as calendars.

great whirlwind passed by, and he was blind. The Kiowas have no need of a blind man; they left him alone with his wife and child. The winter was coming on and food was scarce. In four days the man's wife grew tired of caring for him. A herd of buffalo came near, and the man knew the sound. He asked his wife to hand him a bow and an arrow. "You must tell me," he said, "when the buffalo are directly in front of me." And in that way he killed a bull, but his wife said that he had missed. He asked for another arrow and killed another bull, but again his wife said that he had missed. Now the man was a hunter, and he knew the sound an arrow makes when it strikes home, but he said nothing. Then his wife helped herself to the meat and ran away with her child. The man was blind; he ate grass and kept himself alive. In seven days a band of Kiowas found him and took him to their camp. There in the fire-light a woman was telling a story. She told of how her husband had been killed by enemy warriors. The blind man listened, and he knew her voice. That was a bad woman. At sunrise they threw her away.

XXIV

East of my grandmother's house, south of the pecan grove, there is buried a woman in a beautiful dress. Mammedaty used to know where she is buried, but now no one knows. If you stand on the front porch of the house and look east-ward towards Carnegie, you know that the woman is buried some-where within the range of your vision. But her grave is unmarked. She was buried in a cabinet, and she wore a beautiful dress. How beauti-

Sun Dance of 1843, a man stabbed his wife in the breast because she accepted Chief Dohasan's invitation to ride with him in the ceremonial pro-cession. And in the winter of 1851–52, Big Bow stole the wife of a man who was away on a raiding expedition. He brought her to his father's camp and made her wait outside in the bittercold while he went in to collect his things. But his father knew what was going on, and he held Big Bow and would not let him go. The woman was made to wait in the snow until her feet were frozen.

Mammedaty's grandmother, Kau-au-ointy,[8] was a Mexican captive, taken from her homeland when she was a child of eight or ten years. I never knew her, but I have been to her grave at Rainy Mountain.

> KAU-AU-OINTY
> BORN 1834
> DIED 1929
> AT REST

She raised a lot of eyebrows, they say, for she would not play the part of a Kiowa woman. From slavery she rose up to become a figure in the tribe. She owned a great herd of cattle, and she could ride as well as any man. She had blue eyes.

Aho's high moccasins are made of softest, cream-colored skins. On each instep there is a bright disc of beadwork—an eight-pointed star, red and pale blue on a white field—and there are bands of beadwork at the soles and ankles. The flaps of the leggings are wide and richly orna-mented with blue and red and green and white and lavender beads.

East of my grandmother's house the sun rises out of the plain. Once in his

---

8. Momaday's great-great-grandmother.

ful it was! It was one of those fine buckskin dresses, and it was decorated with elk's teeth and beadwork. That dress is still there, under the ground.

life a man ought to concentrate his mind upon the remembered earth, I believe. He ought to give himself up to a particular landscape in his experience, to look at it from as many angles as he can, to wonder about it, to dwell upon it. He ought to imagine that he touches it with his hands at every season and listens to the sounds that are made upon it. He ought to imagine the creatures there and all the faintest motions of the wind. He ought to recollect the glare of noon and all the colors of the dawn and dusk.

Epilogue

During the first hours after midnight on the morning of November 13, 1833, it seemed that the world was coming to an end. Suddenly the stillness of the night was broken; there were brilliant flashes of light in the sky, light of such intensity that people were awakened by it. With the speed and density of a driving rain, stars were falling in the universe. Some were brighter than Venus; one was said to be as large as the moon.

That most brilliant shower of Leonid meteors has a special place in the memory of the Kiowa people. It is among the earliest entries in the Kiowa calendars, and it marks the beginning as it were of the historical period in the tribal mind. In the preceding year Tai-me had been stolen by a band of Osages, and although it was later returned, the loss was an almost unimaginable tragedy; and in 1837 the Kiowas made the first of their treaties[9] with the United States. The falling stars seemed to image the sudden and violent disintegration of an old order.

But indeed the golden age of the Kiowas had been short-lived, ninety or a hundred years, say, from about 1740. The culture would persist for a while in decline, until about 1875, but then it would be gone, and there would be very little material evidence that it had ever been. Yet it is within the reach of memory still, though tenuously now, and moreover it is even defined in a remarkably rich and living verbal tradition which demands to be preserved for its own sake. The living memory and the verbal tradition which transcends it were brought together for me once and for all in the person of Ko-sahn.

A hundred-year-old woman came to my grandmother's house one afternoon in July. Aho was dead; Mammedaty had died before I was born. There were very few Kiowas left who could remember the Sun Dances; Ko-sahn was one of them; she was a grown woman when my grandparents came into the world. Her body was twisted and her face deeply lined with age. Her thin white hair was held in place by a cap of black netting, though she wore braids as well, and she had but one eye. She was dressed in the manner of a Kiowa matron, a dark, full-cut dress that reached nearly to the ankles, full, flowing sleeves,

9. This treaty provided for settlers' passage through Kiowa and Comanche lands.

and a wide, apron-like sash. She sat on a bench in the arbor so concentrated in her great age that she seemed extraordinarily small. She was quiet for a time—she might almost have been asleep—and then she began to speak and to sing. She spoke of many things, and once she spoke of the Sun Dance:

My sisters and I were very young; that was a long time ago. Early one morning they came to wake us up. They had brought a great buffalo in from the plain. Everyone went out to see and to pray. We heard a great many voices. One man said that the lodge was almost ready. We were told to go there, and someone gave me a piece of cloth. It was very beautiful. Then I asked what I ought to do with it, and they said that I must tie it to the Tai-me tree. There were other pieces of cloth on the tree, and so I put mine there as well.

When the lodge frame was finished, a woman—sometimes a man—began to sing. It was like this:

> Everything is ready.
> Now the four societies must go out.
> They must go out and get the leaves,
>   the branches for the lodge.

And when the branches were tied in place, again there was singing:

> Let the boys go out.
> Come on, boys, now we must get the earth.

The boys began to shout. Now they were not just ordinary boys, not all of them; they were those for whom prayers had been made, and they were dressed in different ways. There was an old, old woman. She had something on her back. The boys went out to see. The old woman had a bag full of earth on her back. It was a certain kind of sandy earth. That is what they must have in the lodge. The dancers must dance upon the sandy earth. The old woman held a digging tool in her hand. She turned towards the south and pointed with her lips. It was like a kiss, and she began to sing:

> We have brought the earth.
> Now it is time to play;
> As old as I am, I still have the feeling of play.

That was the beginning of the Sun Dance. The dancers treated themselves with buffalo medicine, and slowly they began to take their steps. . . . And all the people were around, and they wore splendid things—beautiful buckskin and beads. The chiefs wore necklaces, and their pendants shone like the sun. There were many people, and oh, it was beautiful! That was the beginning of the Sun Dance. It was all for Tai-me, you know, and it was a long time ago.

It was—all of this and more—a quest, a going forth upon the way to Rainy Mountain. Probably Ko-sahn too is dead now. At times, in the quiet of evening, I think she must have wondered, dreaming, who she was. Was she become in her sleep that old purveyor of the sacred earth, perhaps, that ancient one who, old as she was, still had the feeling of play? And in her mind, at times, did she see the falling stars?

Rainy Mountain Cemetery

Most is your name the name of this dark stone.
Deranged in death, the mind to be inheres
Forever in the nominal unknown,
The wake of nothing audible he hears
Who listens here and now to hear your name.   5

The early sun, red as a hunter's moon,
Runs in the plain. The mountain burns and shines;
And silence is the long approach of noon
Upon the shadow that your name defines—
And death this cold, black density of stone.   10

1969

LUCILLE CLIFTON
b. 1936

Lucille Clifton seems able to lift the poem off the page and return it to the air we breathe. Like the work of Langston Hughes or William Carlos Williams, her poems allow us to hear the language of our daily lives as poetry and to experience the poetry in our ordinary lives. Although a closer look reveals the subtle craft of her poems (for example, the slant rhymes and the carefully paced repetitions), they appear deceptively simple. Their frankness and directness close the distance between poet and reader, especially when these poems are read aloud. Clifton emphasizes the informality in her work through the lowercase letters she prefers and through her frequent omission of titles. The language of her poems reflects her identity; "I am a black woman poet," she has said, "and I sound like one." Grounded in realistic details, her poems do not shy away from what is harsh and painful, including incest, suicide, mental illness, and the effects of poverty and racism. But while Clifton's anger fuels many poems, her imagination finds beauty and humor in unexpected places; indeed, she seems able to make poetry out of anything. In this she resembles the African American quilters who rework the materials of ordinary experience into distinctive and compelling designs. Indeed, she titled one of her books *Quilting* (1991) and borrowed its section headings from the names of traditional quilt patterns.

Born in Depew, New York, to a father who worked in the steel mills and a mother who was a launderer and a homemaker (and who wrote poems but burned them), Clifton was the first person in her family to attend college. "I had a very regular life, the life of a poor black person," Clifton has said; but her background and her gifts sometimes made her feel that "there is no planet stranger / than the one I'm from" ("note, passed to superman"). At sixteen she began her studies at Howard University in Washington, D.C., and she later attended Fredonia State Teachers College in New York State. She went on to work as a claims clerk in the New York State Division of Employment (1958–60) and as a literature assistant at the Office of Education in Washington (1960–71). Clifton never formally studied creative writing, but she wrote poems and thought of herself as a poet from a young age. However, her work did not receive public recognition until she was in her thirties. In 1969 she sent a poem to the poet Robert Hayden at the National Endowment for the Arts. Hayden had left the NEA, but his successor, Carolyn Kizer, read the work and submitted it to the YW-YMHA Poetry Center Discovery Award competition in New York City. Clifton won the competition and at the award ceremony, after she read her poems, an editor from Random House in the audience offered to publish her first book, *Good Times* (1969). *Good Times* appeared when she was thirty-three, a wife and mother with six children under the age of eleven. During these years her method of composition followed those writers, many of them women, who compose lines of poetry in the mind until there is time to write them down.

Clifton comes from a line of African American storytellers extending from her great-grandmother, Caroline Donald, who was born in Dahomey, Africa, sold into slavery, and taken to America. Clifton's memoir, *Generations* (1976), chronicles the history of her family, including the genealogy and the tradition of strong women passed down to Clifton through her father's stories. In much of her work Clifton consciously seeks to recover an African American past that has too often been omitted from standard histories and to retell history from previously unacknowledged points of view.

In a poem beginning "the light that came to Lucille Clifton," a voice from "the non-dead past" speaks this message to her: "You might as well open the door, my child / for truth is furiously knocking." Throughout her long and productive career as a poet, and as a writer of memoirs and children's books, she has transmitted the voices of a living past. Like Toni Morrison's fiction, Clifton's poems are full of ghosts: her mother and father, her unborn children, her ancestors, and sometimes mythical and biblical figures. These presences in her work bear witness to a legacy of pain, wisdom, and survival. As a writer brave enough to open the door to the truths of her life and her world, Clifton possesses a "gift of understanding" that puts her in touch with the suffering of the "holy lost" ("Wild Blessing"), but the spiritual dimension of her work also reveals the possibility of joy and transformation, evident in "blessing the boats."

Clifton's books include *Good News about the Earth* (1972) and *Two-headed Woman* (1980), which received the University of Massachusetts Juniper Prize. Both of these volumes were nominated for the Pulitzer Prize. Subsequent collections include *Next* (1987), *The Book of Light* (1993), *Blessing the Boats: New and Selected Poems 1988–2000* (2000), and *Mercy* (2004). Clifton's work for children includes *The Black BCs* (1970), *The Times They Used to Be* (1974), and an award-winning series of books featuring events in the life of Everett Anderson, a young black boy. In 1999 she was elected a chancellor of the Academy of American Poets. She has served as poet laureate for the State of Maryland and is distinguished professor of humanities at St. Mary's College in Maryland.

miss rosie

when i watch you
wrapped up like garbage
sitting, surrounded by the smell
of too old potato peels
or   5
when i watch you
in your old man's shoes
with the little toe cut out
sitting, waiting for your mind
like next week's grocery   10
i say
when i watch you
you wet brown bag of a woman
who used to be the best looking gal in georgia
used to be called the Georgia Rose   15
i stand up
through your destruction
i stand up

1969   1987

the lost baby poem

[handwritten: referencing what could have happened]

the time i dropped your almost body down
down to meet the waters under the city
and run one with the sewage to the sea
what did i know about waters rushing back
what did i know about drowning   5
or being drowned

you would have been born into winter   *[handwritten: lost possibilities]*
in the year of the disconnected gas
and no car   we would have made the thin
walk over genesee hill[1] into the canada wind   10
to watch you slip like ice into strangers' hands
you would have fallen naked as snow into winter
if you were here i could tell you these
and some other things

[handwritten: lowercase letters rejecting traditional rules - from A.A. background]

if i am ever less than a mountain
for your definite brothers and sisters
let the rivers pour over my head
let the sea take me for a spiller
of seas   let black men call me stranger
always   for your never named sake   20

1972

homage to my hips

these hips are big hips
they need space to
move around in.
they don't fit into little
petty places. these hips.   5
are free hips.
they don't like to be held back.
these hips have never been enslaved,
they go where they want to go
they do what they want to do.   10
these hips are mighty hips.
these hips are magic hips.
i have known them
to put a spell on a man and
spin him like a top!   15

1980

wild blessings

licked in the palm of my hand
by an uninvited woman. so i have held
in that hand the hand of a man who

---

1. Genesee County is in northwestern New York State.

emptied into his daughter, the hand
of a girl who threw herself   5
from a tenement window, the trembling
junkie hand of a priest, of a boy who
shattered across viet nam
someone resembling his mother,
and more. and more.   10
do not ask me to thank the tongue
that circled my fingers
or pride myself on the attentions
of the holy lost.
i am grateful for many blessings   15
but the gift of understanding,
the wild one, maybe not.

                                                                  1991

wishes for sons

i wish them cramps.
i wish them a strange town
and the last tampon.
i wish them no 7–11.

i wish them one week early   5
and wearing a white skirt.
i wish them one week late.

later i wish them hot flashes
and clots like you
wouldn't believe.   let the   10
flashes come when they
meet someone special.
let the clots come
when they want to.

let them think they have accepted   15
arrogance in the universe,
then bring them to gynecologists
not unlike themselves.

                                                                  1991

the mississippi river empties into the gulf

and the gulf enters the sea and so forth,
none of them emptying anything,
all of them carrying yesterday
forever on their white tipped backs,
all of them dragging forward tomorrow.   5
it is the great circulation
of the earth's body, like the blood

of the gods, this river in which the past
is always flowing. every water
is the same water coming round.   10
everyday someone is standing on the edge
of this river, staring into time,
whispering mistakenly:
only here. only now.

1996

[oh antic god]

oh antic God
return to me
my mother in her thirties[1]
leaned across the front porch
the huge pillow of her breasts   5
pressing against the rail
summoning me in for bed.

I am almost the dead woman's age times two.

I can barely recall her song
the scent of her hands   10
though her wild hair scratches my dreams
at night.   return to me, oh Lord of then
and now, my mother's calling,
her young voice humming my name.

2004

1. Thelma Moore Sayles, Clifton's mother, died at age forty-four.

THOMAS PYNCHON
b. 1937

Thomas Pynchon has remained the most private of contemporary American writers, without so much as a photograph of him in circulation. A few facts are known: born on Long Island, graduated from Cornell University—where he was a student in Vladimir Nabokov's course—in the late 1950s, served a term in the navy, and now lives—it is said—in southern (or is it northern?) California. Beyond that, silence, which has been broken only by six strange and distinctive novels, plus a few short stories.

"Entropy," one of Pynchon's first publications (1960), is printed here as an introduction to his work. Its thematics of an elusive order within radical disorder antici-pates his first novel, V. (1963), particularly in its reference to modern physics. That complex novel cannot be understood by reference to convenient fictional signposts. Although it showed an indebtedness to Faulkner and Joyce (an indebtedness shared by most serious American novelists), Pynchon's style was already wholly his own. In writing that was by turns labyrinthine, eloquent, and colloquial, he showed a partic-ular fondness for imitating and parodying various styles. But these imitations and par-odies instead of disparaging or minimizing their subjects radiated a generous exuberance that extended to the many characters who inhabit *V.* and whose individual paranoias—Pynchon's word to characterize attempts to make connections between events—propel them into unbelievably complicated and absurd plots. The interest of *V.* was largely in the inventiveness with which Pynchon developed those plots, which might involve anything from diplomatic spy stories in nineteenth-century Africa to the bombing of Malta during World War II to the surgical reconstruction of a young woman's nose to a hunt for alligators in New York City sewers.

The comic talent shown in various New York episodes from *V.* was also evident in *The Crying of Lot 49* (1966). This short, perfectly controlled novel teases us and itself with questions about the meaning of our American heritage, as embodied in the form of the mysterious legacy left to its heroine, Oedipa Maas. (The jokey yet portentous name exemplifies Pynchon's way of playing at "significance.") What is the connection between this legacy and the mysterious alternative to the U.S. Postal System on which Oedipa believes she has stumbled? Is there a secret network of alienated citizens carrying on their lives outside the ordinary systems and institutions of American life? Or is it all Oedipa's delusion, her private paranoia? These questions are considered through a style that continually surprises and unsettles us, though it is less discontinuous than *V.*'s. In Pynchon's world everything serious has its silly aspects (inspired by the Marx Brothers and countless other comic acts), while bits of trivia and foolery are suddenly elevated, through the style, into objects of sublime contemplation—as at the novel's end, when Oedipa thinks of "squatters" who "slept in junkyards in the stripped shells of wrecked Plymouths, or even, daring, spent the night up some pole in a lineman's tent like caterpillars, swung among a web of telephone wires, living in the very copper rigging and secular miracle of communication, untroubled by the dumb voltages flickering their miles, the night long, in the thousands of unheard messages." Often Pynchon's sentences enact the daring freedom he admires, in contrast to the institutions of a technological society.

Pynchon's longest and most daring and exhaustive effort came with the publication, in 1973, of *Gravity's Rainbow*. This encyclopedic fantasy operates through brilliant improvisations, tall tales, obscene parables, and burlesque stage routines, all of which work together into a story of supersonic capabilities and annihilative retributions. A huge cast of characters, each with a crazy name and a plot to unravel, is located all over the map, but mainly in World War II London and in postwar Germany. As the four main and the countless subsidiary plots take shape, characters—and the reader—attempt to "read" the messages flickering, the dumb intent to communicate, in the most casual as well as the most portentous sign. Pynchon's knowingness and fascination with popular culture are overwhelmingly evident in *Gravity's Rainbow* as is his preoccupation with the lore of theoretical science, of obscure historical tales, and of contemporary comic books. No one denies the formidably encyclopedic nature of this astonishing effort; the question is, as Warner Berthoff has asked it, whether that effort may not also be "encyclopedically monotonous and static." More readers begin *Gravity's Rainbow* than finish it.

After 1973, except for the publication in 1984 of some of his early stories (in *Slow Learner*), all was silent on the Pynchon front until *Vineland* appeared in 1990, followed by *Mason & Dixon* in 1997 and *Against the Day* in 2006. *Vineland* is wonderful on the California terrain and has much free wheeling and funny inventiveness; at other times Pynchon seems to be flogging his material and repeating himself. *Mason & Dixon*, about the plotters of the line that would differentiate the American North and South, is written in the manner of his more ambitious works, a massive "mega-novel" that by its very excesses of character, plot, and references to history (arcane and otherwise) seeks to overwhelm the reader with its display of authority. But although there is still no consensus on his stature as an enduring American writer, there is general recognition of the quirky, uncanny exactitude of his imagination. Pynchon's theatrical spellbindings as a man of metaphor, his feats of association (in Robert Frost's phrase), are employed on subjects—like the rocket in *Gravity's Rainbow*—that were thought to be beyond words. For daring, wit, and exuberance, no contemporary writer excels him.

The text is from *Slow Learner* (1984).

Entropy

> Boris has just given me a summary of his views. He is a weather prophet. The weather will continue bad, he says. There will be more calamities, more death, more despair. Not the slightest indication of a change anywhere . . . We must get into step, a lockstep toward the prison of death. There is no escape. The weather will not change.
>
> —*Tropic of Cancer*[1]

Downstairs, Meatball Mulligan's lease-breaking party was moving into its 40th hour. On the kitchen floor, amid a litter of empty champagne fifths, were Sandor Rojas and three friends, playing spit in the ocean and staying awake on Heidseck[2] and benzedrine pills. In the living room Duke, Vincent, Krinkles and Paco sat crouched over a 15-inch speaker which had been bolted into the top of a wastepaper basket, listening to 27 watts' worth of *The Heroes' Gate at Kiev*.[3] They all wore hornrimmed sunglasses and rapt expressions, and smoked funny-looking cigarettes which contained not, as you might expect, tobacco, but an adulterated form of *cannabis sativa*.[4] This group was the Duke di Angelis quartet. They recorded for a local label called Tambú and had to their credit one 10" LP entitled *Songs of Outer Space*. From time to time one of them would flick the ashes from his cigarette into the speaker cone to watch them dance around. Meatball himself was sleeping over by the window, holding an empty magnum to his chest as if it were a teddy bear. Several government girls, who worked for people like the State Department and NSA, had passed out on couches, chairs and in one case the bathroom sink.

This was in early February of '57 and back then there were a lot of American expatriates around Washington, D.C., who would talk, every time they met you, about how someday they were going to go over to Europe for real but right now it seemed they were working for the government. Everyone saw a fine irony in this. They would stage, for instance, polyglot parties where the newcomer was sort of ignored if he couldn't carry on simultaneous conversations in three or four languages. They would haunt Armenian delicatessens for weeks at a stretch and invite you over for bulghour and lamb in tiny kitchens whose walls were covered with bullfight posters. They would have affairs with sultry girls from Andalucía or the Midi[5] who studied economics at Georgetown. Their Dôme was a collegiate Rathskeller out on Wisconsin Avenue called the Old Heidelberg and they had to settle for cherry blossoms instead of lime trees when spring came, but in its lethargic way their life provided, as they said, kicks.

At the moment, Meatball's party seemed to be gathering its second wind. Outside there was rain. Rain splatted against the tar paper on the roof and was fractured into a fine spray off the noses, eyebrows and lips of wooden gargoyles under the eaves, and ran like drool down the windowpanes. The day before, it had snowed and the day before that there had been winds of gale force and before that the sun had made the city glitter bright as April, though the calendar read early February. It is a curious season in Washington, this false spring. Somewhere in it are Lincoln's Birthday and the Chinese New

---

1. Novel (1934) by the American writer Henry Miller (1891–1980).
2. A very dry champagne.
3. Music by the Russian composer Modest Mus-
sorgsky (1839–1881) from his *Pictures at an Exhibition*.
4. Marijuana.
5. Regions of Spain and France, respectively.

Year, and a forlornness in the streets because cherry blossoms are weeks away still and, as Sarah Vaughan has put it, spring will be a little late this year. Generally crowds like the one which would gather in the Old Heidelberg on weekday afternoons to drink Würtzburger and to sing Lili Marlene (not to mention The Sweetheart of Sigma Chi) are inevitably and incorrigibly Romantic. And as every good Romantic knows, the soul (*spiritus, ruach, pneuma*) is nothing, substantially, but air; it is only natural that warpings in the atmosphere should be recapitulated in those who breathe it. So that over and above the public components—holidays, tourist attractions—there are private meanderings, linked to the climate as if this spell were a *stretto* passage in the year's fugue: haphazard weather, aimless loves, unpredicted commitments: months one can easily spend *in* fugue, because oddly enough, later on, winds, rains, passions of February and March are never remembered in that city, it is as if they had never been.

The last bass notes of *The Heroes' Gate* boomed up through the floor and woke Callisto from an uneasy sleep. The first thing he became aware of was a small bird he had been holding gently between his hands, against his body. He turned his head sidewise on the pillow to smile down at it, at its blue hunched-down head and sick, lidded eyes, wondering how many more nights he would have to give it warmth before it was well again. He had been holding the bird like that for three days: it was the only way he knew to restore its health. Next to him the girl stirred and whimpered, her arm thrown across her face. Mingled with the sounds of the rain came the first tentative, querulous morning voices of the other birds, hidden in philodendrons and small fan palms: patches of scarlet, yellow and blue laced through this Rousseau-like[6] fantasy, this hothouse jungle it had taken him seven years to weave together. Hermetically sealed, it was a tiny enclave of regularity in the city's chaos, alien to the vagaries of the weather, of national politics, of any civil disorder. Through trial-and-error Callisto had perfected its ecological balance, with the help of the girl its artistic harmony, so that the swayings of its plant life, the stirrings of its birds and human inhabitants were all as integral as the rhythms of a perfectly-executed mobile. He and the girl could no longer, of course, be omitted from that sanctuary; they had become necessary to its unity. What they needed from outside was delivered. They did not go out.

"Is he all right," she whispered. She lay like a tawny question mark facing him, her eyes suddenly huge and dark and blinking slowly. Callisto ran a finger beneath the feathers at the base of the bird's neck; caressed it gently. "He's going to be well, I think. See: he hears his friends beginning to wake up." The girl had heard the rain and the birds even before she was fully awake. Her name was Aubade: she was part French and part Annamese, and she lived on her own curious and lonely planet, where the clouds and the odor of poincianas, the bitterness of wine and the accidental fingers at the small of her back or feathery against her breasts came to her reduced inevitably to the terms of sound: of music which emerged at intervals from a howling darkness of discordancy. "Aubade," he said, "go see." Obedient, she arose; padded to the window, pulled aside the drapes and after a moment said: "It is 37. Still 37." Callisto frowned. "Since Tuesday, then," he said. "No change." Henry

---

6. Henri Rousseau (1844–1910), French primitive painter of exotic landscapes.

Adams,[7] three generations before his own, had stared aghast at Power; Callisto found himself now in much the same state over Thermodynamics, the inner life of that power, realizing like his predecessor that the Virgin and the dynamo stand as much for love as for power; that the two are indeed identical; and that love therefore not only makes the world go round but also makes the boccie ball spin, the nebula precess. It was this latter or sidereal element which disturbed him. The cosmologists had predicted an eventual heat-death for the universe (something like Limbo: form and motion abolished, heat-energy identical at every point in it); the meteorologists, day-to-day, staved it off by contradicting with a reassuring array of varied temperatures.

But for three days now, despite the changeful weather, the mercury had stayed at 37 degrees Fahrenheit. Leery at omens of apocalypse, Callisto shifted beneath the covers. His fingers pressed the bird more firmly, as if needing some pulsing or suffering assurance of an early break in the temperature.

It was that last cymbal crash that did it. Meatball was hurled wincing into consciousness as the synchronized wagging of heads over the wastebasket stopped. The final hiss remained for an instant in the room, then melted into the whisper of rain outside. "Aarrgghh," announced Meatball in the silence, looking at the empty magnum. Krinkles, in slow motion, turned, smiled and held out a cigarette. "Tea time, man," he said. "No, no," said Meatball. "How many times I got to tell you guys. Not at my place. You ought to know, Washington is lousy with Feds." Krinkles looked wistful. "Jeez, Meatball," he said, "you don't want to do nothing no more." "Hair of dog," said Meatball. "Only hope. Any juice left?" He began to crawl toward the kitchen. "No champagne, I don't think," Duke said. "Case of tequila behind the icebox." They put on an Earl Bostic[8] side. Meatball paused at the kitchen door, glowering at Sandor Rojas. "Lemons," he said after some thought. He crawled to the refrigerator and got out three lemons and some cubes, found the tequila and set about restoring order to his nervous system. He drew blood once cutting the lemons and had to use two hands squeezing them and his foot to crack the ice tray but after about ten minutes he found himself, through some miracle, beaming down into a monster tequila sour. "That looks yummy," Sandor Rojas said. "How about you make me one." Meatball blinked at him. *"Kitchi lofass a shegithe,"*[9] he replied automatically, and wandered away into the bathroom. "I say," he called out a moment later to no one in particular. "I say, there seems to be a girl or something sleeping in the sink." He took her by the shoulders and shook. "Wha," she said. "You don't look too comfortable," Meatball said. "Well," she agreed. She stumbled to the shower, turned on the cold water and sat down crosslegged in the spray. "That's better," she smiled.

"Meatball," Sandor Rojas yelled from the kitchen. "Somebody is trying to come in the window. A burglar, I think. A second-story man." "What are you worrying about," Meatball said. "We're on the third floor." He loped back into the kitchen. A shaggy woebegone figure stood out on the fire escape, raking

---

7. American historian and man of letters (1838–1918) whose writings explore the nature of power, cultural figurations of which ranged from the Virgin Mary to the modern dynamo engine.

8. American jazz musician (1913–1965) who also recorded rhythm-and-blues material.

9. Little horse prick in your asshole (Hungarian).

his fingernails down the windowpane. Meatball opened the window. "Saul," he said.

"Sort of wet out," Saul said. He climbed in, dripping. "You heard, I guess."

"Miriam left you," Meatball said, "or something, is all I heard."

There was a sudden flurry of knocking at the front door. "Do come in," Sandor Rojas called. The door opened and there were three coeds from George Washington, all of whom were majoring in philosophy. They were each holding a gallon of Chianti. Sandor leaped up and dashed into the living room. "We heard there was a party," one blonde said. "Young blood," Sandor shouted. He was an ex-Hungarian freedom fighter who had easily the worst chronic case of what certain critics of the middle class have called Don Giovannism in the District of Columbia. *Purche porti la gonnella, voi sapete quel che fa.*[1] Like Pavlov's dog: a contralto voice or a whiff of Arpège and Sandor would begin to salivate. Meatball regarded the trio blearily as they filed into the kitchen; he shrugged. "Put the wine in the icebox," he said, "and good morning."

Aubade's neck made a golden bow as she bent over the sheets of foolscap, scribbling away in the green murk of the room. "As a young man at Princeton," Callisto was dictating, nestling the bird against the gray hairs of his chest, "Callisto had learned a mnemonic device for remembering the Laws of Thermodynamics: you can't win, things are going to get worse before they get better, who says they're going to get better. At the age of 54, confronted with Gibbs'[2] notion of the universe, he suddenly realized that undergraduate cant had been oracle, after all. That spindly maze of equations became, for him, a vision of ultimate, cosmic heat-death. He had known all along, of course, that nothing but a theoretical engine or system ever runs at 100% efficiency; and about the theorem of Clausius, which states that the entropy of an isolated system always continually increases. It was not, however, until Gibbs and Boltzmann[3] brought to this principle the methods of statistical mechanics that the horrible significance of it all dawned on him: only then did he realize that the isolated system—galaxy, engine, human being, culture, whatever—must evolve spontaneously toward the Condition of the More Probable. He was forced, therefore, in the sad dying fall of middle age, to a radical reëvaluation of everything he had learned up to then; all the cities and seasons and casual passions of his days had now to be looked at in a new and elusive light. He did not know if he was equal to the task. He was aware of the dangers of the reductive fallacy and, he hoped, strong enough not to drift into the graceful decadence of an enervated fatalism. His had always been a vigorous, Italian sort of pessimism: like Machiavelli, he allowed the forces of *virtù* and *fortuna*[4] to be about 50/50; but the equations now introduced a random factor which pushed the odds to some unutterable and indeterminate ratio which he found himself afraid to calculate." Around him loomed vague hothouse shapes; the pitifully small heart fluttered against his own. Counterpointed against his words the girl heard the chatter of birds and fitful car

---

1. If you wear a shirt, you know what to do (Italian).
2. Josiah Willard Gibbs (1839–1903), American physicist and chemist, a founder of statistical mechanics.
3. Ludwig Boltzmann (1844–1906), Austrian physicist who studied how atoms determine visual

properties of matter. Rudolf Clausius (1822–1888), German physicist, developer of the science of thermodynamics.
4. Niccolò Machiavelli (1469–1527), Florentine statesman and writer on government, contrasted virtuous behavior (*virtù*) with good luck (*fortuna*).

honkings scattered along the wet morning and Earl Bostic's alto rising in occasional wild peaks through the floor. The architectonic purity of her world was constantly threatened by such hints of anarchy: gaps and excrescences and skew lines, and a shifting or tilting of planes to which she had continually to readjust lest the whole structure shiver into a disarray of discrete and meaningless signals. Callisto had described the process once as a kind of "feedback": she crawled into dreams each night with a sense of exhaustion, and a desperate resolve never to relax that vigilance. Even in the brief periods when Callisto made love to her, soaring above the bowing of taut nerves in haphazard double-stops would be the one singing string of her determination.

"Nevertheless," continued Callisto, "he found in entropy or the measure of disorganization for a closed system an adequate metaphor to apply to certain phenomena in his own world. He saw, for example, the younger generation responding to Madison Avenue with the same spleen his own had once reserved for Wall Street: and in American 'consumerism' discovered a similar tendency from the least to the most probable, from differentiation to sameness, from ordered individuality to a kind of chaos. He found himself, in short, restating Gibbs' prediction in social terms, and envisioned a heat-death for his culture in which ideas, like heat-energy, would no longer be transferred, since each point in it would ultimately have the same quantity of energy; and intellectual motion would, accordingly, cease." He glanced up suddenly. "Check it now," he said. Again she rose and peered out at the thermometer. "37," she said. "The rain has stopped." He bent his head quickly and held his lips against a quivering wing. "Then it will change soon," he said, trying to keep his voice firm.

Sitting on the stove Saul was like any big rag doll that a kid has been taking out some incomprehensible rage on. "What happened," Meatball said. "If you feel like talking, I mean."

"Of course I feel like talking," Saul said. "One thing I did, I slugged her."

"Discipline must be maintained."

"Ha, ha. I wish you'd been there. Oh Meatball, it was a lovely fight. She ended up throwing a *Handbook of Chemistry and Physics* at me, only it missed and went through the window, and when the glass broke I reckon something in her broke too. She stormed out of the house crying, out in the rain. No raincoat or anything."

"She'll be back."

"No."

"Well!" Soon Meatball said: "It was something earthshattering, no doubt. Like who is better, Sal Mineo or Ricky Nelson."[5]

"What it was about," Saul said, "was communication theory. Which of course makes it very hilarious."

"I don't know anything about communication theory."

"Neither does my wife. Come right down to it, who does? That's the joke."

When Meatball saw the kind of smile Saul had on his face he said: "Maybe you would like tequila or something."

"No. I mean, I'm sorry. It's a field you can go off the deep end in, is all. You

5. Contemporary figures from film and television who were icons of bad and good teenage behavior, respectively.

get where you're watching all the time for security cops: behind bushes, around corners. MUFFET is top secret."

"Wha."

"Multi-unit factorial field electronic tabulator."

"You were fighting about that."

"Miriam has been reading science fiction again. That and *Scientific American*. It seems she is, as we say, bugged at this idea of computers acting like people. I made the mistake of saying you can just as well turn that around, and talk about human behavior like a program fed into an IBM machine."

"Why not," Meatball said.

"Indeed, why not. In fact it is sort of crucial to communication, not to mention information theory. Only when I said that she hit the roof. Up went the balloon. And I can't figure out *why*. If anybody should know why, I should. I refuse to believe the government is wasting taxpayers' money on me, when it has so many bigger and better things to waste it on."

Meatball made a moue. "Maybe she thought you were acting like a cold, dehumanized amoral scientist type."

"My god," Saul flung up an arm. "Dehumanized. How much more human can I get? I worry, Meatball, I do. There are Europeans wandering around North Africa these days with their tongues torn out of their heads because those tongues have spoken the wrong words. Only the Europeans thought they were the right words."

"Language barrier," Meatball suggested.

Saul jumped down off the stove. "That," he said, angry, "is a good candidate for sick joke of the year. No, ace, it is *not* a barrier. If it is anything it's a kind of leakage. Tell a girl: 'I love you.' No trouble with two-thirds of that, it's a closed circuit. Just you and she. But that nasty four-letter word in the middle, *that's* the one you have to look out for. Ambiguity. Redundance. Irrelevance, even. Leakage. All this is noise. Noise screws up your signal, makes for disorganization in the circuit."

Meatball shuffled around. "Well, now, Saul," he muttered, "you're sort of, I don't know, expecting a lot from people. I mean, you know. What it is is, most of the things we say, I guess, are mostly noise."

"Ha! Half of what you just said, for example."

"Well, you do it too."

"I know." Saul smiled grimly. "It's a bitch, ain't it."

"I bet that's what keeps divorce lawyers in business. Whoops."

"Oh I'm not sensitive. Besides," frowning, "you're right. You find I think that most 'successful' marriages—Miriam and me, up to last night—are sort of founded on compromises. You never run at top efficiency, usually all you have is a minimum basis for a workable thing. I believe the phrase is Togetherness."

"Aarrgghh."

"Exactly. You find that one a bit noisy, don't you. But the noise content is different for each of us because you're a bachelor and I'm not. Or wasn't. The hell with it."

"Well sure," Meatball said, trying to be helpful, "you were using different words. By 'human being' you meant something that you can look at like it was a computer. It helps you think better on the job or something. But Miriam meant something entirely—"

"The hell with it."

Meatball fell silent. "I'll take that drink," Saul said after a while.

The card game had been abandoned and Sandor's friends were slowly getting wasted on tequila. On the living room couch, one of the coeds and Krinkles were engaged in amorous conversation. "No," Krinkles was saying, "no, I can't put Dave *down*. In fact I give Dave a lot of credit, man. Especially considering his accident and all." The girl's smile faded. "How terrible," she said. "What accident?" "Hadn't you heard?" Krinkles said. "When Dave was in the army, just a private E-2, they sent him down to Oak Ridge on special duty. Something to do with the Manhattan Project.[6] He was handling hot stuff one day and got an overdose of radiation. So now he's got to wear lead gloves all the time." She shook her head sympathetically. "What an awful break for a piano player."

Meatball had abandoned Saul to a bottle of tequila and was about to go to sleep in a closet when the front door flew open and the place was invaded by five enlisted personnel of the U.S. Navy, all in varying stages of abomination. "This is the place," shouted a fat, pimply seaman apprentice who had lost his white hat. "This here is the hoorhouse that chief was telling us about." A stringylooking 3rd class boatswain's mate pushed him aside and cased the living room. "You're right, Slab," he said. "But it don't look like much, even for Stateside. I seen better tail in Naples, Italy." "How much, hey," boomed a large seaman with adenoids, who was holding a Mason jar full of white lightning. "Oh, my god," said Meatball.

Outside the temperature remained constant at 37 degrees Fahrenheit. In the hothouse Aubade stood absently caressing the branches of a young mimosa, hearing a motif of sap-rising, the rough and unresolved anticipatory theme of those fragile pink blossoms which, it is said, insure fertility. That music rose in a tangled tracery: arabesques of order competing fugally with the improvised discords of the party downstairs, which peaked sometimes in cusps and ogees of noise. That precious signal-to-noise ratio, whose delicate balance required every calorie of her strength, seesawed inside the small tenuous skull as she watched Callisto, sheltering the bird. Callisto was trying to confront any idea of the heat-death now, as he nuzzled the feathery lump in his hands. He sought correspondences. Sade, of course. And Temple Drake, gaunt and hopeless in her little park in Paris, at the end of *Sanctuary*.[7] Final equilibrium. *Nightwood*.[8] And the tango. Any tango, but more than any perhaps the sad sick dance in Stravinsky's *L'Histoire du Soldat*.[9] He thought back: what had tango music been for them after the war, what meanings had he missed in all the stately coupled automatons in the *cafés-dansants*,[1] or in the metronomes which had ticked behind the eyes of his own partners? Not even the clean constant winds of Switzerland could cure the *grippe espagnole*:[2] Stravinsky had had it, they all had had it. And how many musicians were left after Passchendaele, after the Marne?[3] It came down in

6. The research that developed the atomic bomb for use at the end of World War II.

7. Sexually notorious novel published in 1931 by the American writer William Faulkner (1897–1962).

8. Novel published in 1936 by the American expatriate writer Djuna Barnes (1892–1982).

9. A 1918 work by the Russian composer Igor Stravinsky (1882–1971).

1. Café dancers (French).

2. Spanish flu (Spanish).

3. Battle sites in World War I noted for their extremely high casualties.

this case to seven: violin, double-bass. Clarinet, bassoon. Cornet, trombone. Tympani. Almost as if any tiny troupe of saltimbanques had set about conveying the same information as a full pit-orchestra. There was hardly a full complement left in Europe. Yet with violin and tympani Stravinsky had managed to communicate in that tango the same exhaustion, the same airlessness one saw in the slicked-down youths who were trying to imitate Vernon Castle, and in their mistresses, who simply did not care. *Ma maîtresse.*[4] Celeste. Returning to Nice after the second war he had found that café replaced by a perfume shop which catered to American tourists. And no secret vestige of her in the cobblestones or in the old pension next door; no perfume to match her breath heavy with the sweet Spanish wine she always drank. And so instead he had purchased a Henry Miller novel and left for Paris,[5] and read the book on the train so that when he arrived he had been given at least a little forewarning. And saw that Celeste and the others and even Temple Drake were not all that had changed. "Aubade," he said, "my head aches." The sound of his voice generated in the girl an answering scrap of melody. Her movement toward the kitchen, the towel, the cold water, and his eyes following her formed a weird and intricate canon; as she placed the compress on his forehead his sigh of gratitude seemed to signal a new subject, another series of modulations.

"No," Meatball was still saying, "no, I'm afraid not. This is not a house of ill repute. I'm sorry, really I am." Slab was adamant. "But the chief said," he kept repeating. The seaman offered to swap the moonshine for a good piece. Meatball looked around frantically, as if seeking assistance. In the middle of the room, the Duke di Angelis quartet were engaged in a historic moment. Vincent was seated and the others standing: they were going through the motions of a group having a session, only without instruments. "I say," Meatball said. Duke moved his head a few times, smiled faintly, lit a cigarette, and eventually caught sight of Meatball. "Quiet, man," he whispered. Vincent began to fling his arms around, his fists clenched; then, abruptly, was still, then repeated the performance. This went on for a few minutes while Meatball sipped his drink moodily. The navy had withdrawn to the kitchen. Finally at some invisible signal the group stopped tapping their feet and Duke grinned and said, "At least we ended together."

Meatball glared at him. "I say," he said. "I have this new conception, man," Duke said. "You remember your namesake. You remember Gerry."

"No," said Meatball. "I'll remember April, if that's any help."

"As a matter of fact," Duke said, "it was Love for Sale. Which shows how much you know. The point is, it was Mulligan, Chet Baker[6] and that crew, way back then, out yonder. You dig?"

"Baritone sax," Meatball said. "Something about a baritone sax."

"But no piano, man. No guitar. Or accordion. You know what that means."

"Not exactly," Meatball said.

"Well first let me just say, that I am no Mingus, no John Lewis.[7] Theory was never my strong point. I mean things like reading were always difficult for me and all—"

4. My mistress (French).
5. Miller was famous for his strongly sexual novels written in Paris during the 1930s.
6. In 1952 the American jazz musicians Gerry Mulligan (1927–1996) and Chet Baker (1929–1988) became famous for their revolutionary pianoless quartet.
7. Charles Mingus (1922–1979) and John Lewis (1920–2001), American jazz musicians noted for their compositions based in musical theory.

"I know," Meatball said drily. "You got your card taken away because you changed key on Happy Birthday at a Kiwanis Club picnic."

"Rotarian. But it occurred to me, in one of these flashes of insight, that if that first quartet of Mulligan's had no piano, it could only mean one thing."

"No chords," said Paco, the baby-faced bass.

"What he is trying to say," Duke said, "is no root chords. Nothing to listen to while you blow a horizontal line. What one does in such a case is, one *thinks* the roots."

A horrified awareness was dawning on Meatball. "And the next logical extension," he said.

"Is to think everything," Duke announced with simple dignity. "Roots, line, everything."

Meatball looked at Duke, awed. "But," he said.

"Well," Duke said modestly, "there are a few bugs to work out."

"But," Meatball said.

"Just listen," Duke said. "You'll catch on." And off they went again into orbit, presumably somewhere around the asteroid belt. After a while Krinkles made an embouchure and started moving his fingers and Duke clapped his hand to his forehead. "Oaf!" he roared. "The new head we're using, you remember, I wrote last night?" "Sure," Krinkles said, "the new head. I come in on the bridge. All your heads I come in then." "Right," Duke said. "So why—" "Wha," said Krinkles, "16 bars, I wait, I come in—" "16?" Duke said. "No. No, Krinkles. Eight you waited. You want me to sing it? A cigarette that bears a lipstick's traces, an airline ticket to romantic places." Krinkles scratched his head. "These Foolish Things, you mean." "Yes," Duke said, "yes, Krinkles. Bravo." "Not I'll Remember April," Krinkles said. "*Minghe morte,*"[8] said Duke. "I *figured* we were playing it a little slow," Krinkles said. Meatball chuckled. "Back to the old drawing board," he said. "No, man," Duke said, "back to the airless void." And they took off again, only it seemed Paco was playing in G sharp while the rest were in E flat, so they had to start all over.

In the kitchen two of the girls from George Washington and the sailors were singing Let's All Go Down and Piss on the Forrestal.[9] There was a two-handed, bilingual *morra*[1] game on over by the icebox. Saul had filled several paper bags with water and was sitting on the fire escape, dropping them on passersby in the street. A fat government girl in a Bennington sweatshirt, recently engaged to an ensign attached to the Forrestal, came charging into the kitchen, head lowered, and butted Slab in the stomach. Figuring this was as good an excuse for a fight as any, Slab's buddies piled in. The *morra* players were nose-to-nose, screaming *trois, sette* at the tops of their lungs. From the shower the girl Meatball had taken out of the sink announced that she was drowning. She had apparently sat on the drain and the water was now up to her neck. The noise in Meatball's apartment had reached a sustained, ungodly crescendo.

Meatball stood and watched, scratching his stomach lazily. The way he figured, there were only about two ways he could cope: (a) lock himself in the closet and maybe eventually they would all go away, or (b) try to calm every-

---

8. Dead prick (Italian).
9. Aircraft carrier in the U.S. Navy.
1. *"Morra"*: finger game originally played by Ital-

ians. The commands are numbers; below, three (*trois,* French) and seven (*sette,* Italian).

body down, one by one. (a) was certainly the more attractive alternative. But then he started thinking about that closet. It was dark and stuffy and he would be alone. He did not feature being alone. And then this crew off the good ship Lollipop[2] or whatever it was might take it upon themselves to kick down the closet door, for a lark. And if that happened he would be, at the very least, embarrassed. The other way was more a pain in the neck, but probably better in the long run.

So he decided to try and keep his lease-breaking party from deteriorating into total chaos: he gave wine to the sailors and separated the *morra* players; he introduced the fat government girl to Sandor Rojas, who would keep her out of trouble; he helped the girl in the shower to dry off and get into bed; he had another talk with Saul; he called a repairman for the refrigerator, which someone had discovered was on the blink. This is what he did until nightfall, when most of the revellers had passed out and the party trembled on the threshold of its third day.

Upstairs Callisto, helpless in the past, did not feel the faint rhythm inside the bird begin to slacken and fail. Aubade was by the window, wandering the ashes of her own lovely world; the temperature held steady, the sky had become a uniform darkening gray. Then something from downstairs—a girl's scream, an overturned chair, a glass dropped on the floor, he would never know what exactly—pierced that private time-warp and he became aware of the faltering, the constriction of muscles, the tiny tossings of the bird's head; and his own pulse began to pound more fiercely, as if trying to compensate. "Aubade," he called weakly, "he's dying." The girl, flowing and rapt, crossed the hothouse to gaze down at Callisto's hands. The two remained like that, poised, for one minute, and two, while the heartbeat ticked a graceful diminuendo down at last into stillness. Callisto raised his head slowly. "I held him," he protested, impotent with the wonder of it, "to give him the warmth of my body. Almost as if I were communicating life to him, or a sense of life. What has happened? Has the transfer of heat ceased to work? Is there no more . . ." He did not finish.

"I was just at the window," she said. He sank back, terrified. She stood a moment more, irresolute; she had sensed his obsession long ago, realized somehow that that constant 37 was now decisive. Suddenly then, as if seeing the single and unavoidable conclusion to all this she moved swiftly to the window before Callisto could speak; tore away the drapes and smashed out the glass with two exquisite hands which came away bleeding and glistening with splinters; and turned to face the man on the bed and wait with him until the moment of equilibrium was reached, when 37 degrees Fahrenheit should prevail both outside and inside, and forever, and the hovering, curious dominant of their separate lives should resolve into a tonic of darkness and the final absence of all motion.

1984

---

2. The subject of film and song popularized in the 1930s by the American child actress Shirley Temple.

MICHAEL S. HARPER
b. 1938

"I've been listening to music all my life," Michael S. Harper has said, and his first book of poems, *Dear John, Dear Coltrane* (1970), took its title from his poem to the great American jazz saxophonist. Recalling Coltrane's life in his prose piece "Don't They Speak Jazz," Harper tells this story: "Trane was searching for a particular tone on his horn; he had what we thought was a perfect embouchure, but his teeth hurt constantly, so he searched for the soft reed which would ease the pain. After searching for a year, each session killing his chops, he gave it up completely; there was no easy way to get that sound: play through the pain to *a love supreme*." Playing through the pain is a part of what Harper brings to his poetry. Like the great blues singers and jazz musicians, his work celebrates life as song, especially as tragic song, full of losses and griefs, but song nevertheless. Sometimes the pain Harper sings through is personal, like the death of one of his sons in "Deathwatch" (he and his wife lost two of their infant sons shortly after birth), sometimes the pain belongs to family history (as in "Grandfather"). Sometimes it is the pain of history more generally, its violence and oppression.

History is Harper's second love as a poet, following right behind music. His poem for Coltrane, while dependent on the techniques of jazz and the blues, reflects Harper's concern with an imaginative recovery of history, especially black history, in an America where (as he once put it) the "amnesia level" is high. "I think the important thing about Americans is that they're not very good historians," Harper has said. "And Americans are really bad historians when it comes to moral ideas because they can't keep them in their heads very long." For Harper, to be a poet is to be a good historian; history identifies and inscribes moral issues that continue to engage us in the present. In college, Harper recalled, he read William Carlos Williams's *In the American Grain* (1925), in which Williams announces that "History for us begins with murder and enslavement, not with discovery." Like Williams, Harper wants to bring his personal imagination in contact with an American history (black and white) essentially tragic, tragic because, he says, "so many possibilities exist and there's been so much waste." This tragic sense informs Harper's work perhaps most clearly in his volume *Nightmare Begins Responsibility* (1975)—the title is a variation on one of the Irish poet William Butler Yeats's epigraphs—where a personal sense of loss is never separable from the sufferings of black history or of human history more generally. His collections *Images of Kin* (1977) and *Healing Song for the Inner Ear* (1985) followed. *Honorable Amendments* appeared in 1995, and *Songlines in Michaeltree: New and Collected Poems* was published in 2000.

Born in Brooklyn, New York, Harper remembers a childhood in which "my parents weren't rich, but they had a good record collection." He grew up hearing the blues and jazz, but also reading the work of Langston Hughes and, later, James Baldwin and Ralph Ellison, and his poetic technique owes something to his literary as well as to his musical sensibility. An additional resource was a family tradition of oral storytelling ("My people were good storytellers," he has said), out of which some of his poems have grown. In fact, the jazz techniques of variation on a theme, of improvisation around an existing form, recall traditions of oral storytelling and both jazz and oral traditions influenced the formal experiments of an Ellison or a Baldwin. After high school Harper took a B.A. and an M.A. at what is now California State University, then went to the University of Iowa for an M.F.A. His travels abroad, first to Mexico and Europe and later (1977) to South Africa, intensified his historical sense both of his own family roots and of their connection with racial history. Since 1970 he has been at Brown University, where he is professor of English and director of the writing program.

"Most great art is finally testamental," Harper has written; "its technical brilliance never shadows the content of the song." Harper writes poems to remember and to witness, but at times the urgency of the content overpowers his form and his language cannot sustain the urgency the poem asserts. This may be the cost for a poet whose engagement with moral issues, whose deep historical sense, and whose rhythmic inventiveness enable him to create powerful and moving poems. His finest work possesses what he admires in Coltrane: "the energy and passion with which he approached his instrument and music," resembling the energy it takes "to break oppressive conditions, oppressive musical structures and oppressive societal structures." Harper's inclusive sense of history lets him write (in "Blue Ruth: America") that *history is your own heartbeat,* but also lets him hear his own heart beat in time with those who lived in other times, other places. Responsible to memory, Harper also shares the affirmative impulse he finds in the blues: "the blues say 'Yes' to life no matter what it is. That doesn't mean you're going to survive it. But it means you're going to say yes to it."

Dear John, Dear Coltrane[1]

a love supreme, a love supreme
a love supreme, a love supreme

Sex fingers toes
in the marketplace
near your father's church
in Hamlet, North Carolina[2]—
witness to this love   5
in this calm fallow
of these minds,
there is no substitute for pain:
genitals gone or going,
seed burned out,   10
you tuck the roots in the earth,
turn back, and move
by river through the swamps,
singing: *a love supreme, a love supreme;*
what does it all mean?   15
Loss, so great each black
woman expects your failure
in mute change, the seed gone.
You plod up into the electric city—
your song now crystal and   20
the blues. You pick up the horn
with some will and blow
into the freezing night:
a love supreme, a love supreme—

Dawn comes and you cook   25
up the thick sin 'tween
impotence and death, fuel
the tenor sax cannibal

---

1. John Coltrane (1926–1967), avant-garde jazz musician. The epigraph is a phrase chanted at the beginning of his four-part composition *A Love* *Supreme.*
2. Coltrane's birthplace.

heart, genitals and sweat
that makes you clean—   30
a love supreme, a love supreme—

Why you so black?
cause I am
why you so funky?
cause I am   35
why you so black?
cause I am
why you so sweet?
cause I am
why you so black?   40
cause I am
a love supreme, a love supreme:

So sick
you couldn't play *Naima*,[3]
so flat we ached   45
for song you'd concealed
with your own blood,
your diseased liver gave
out its purity,
the inflated heart   50
pumps out, the tenor[4] kiss,
tenor love:
a love supreme, a love supreme—
a love supreme, a love supreme—

1970

American History

for John Callahan

Those four black girls blown up
in that Alabama church[1]
remind me of five hundred
middle passage blacks,[2]
in a net, under water   5
in Charleston harbor
so *redcoats*[3] wouldn't find them.
Can't find what you can't see
can you?

1970

3. One of Coltrane's most famous songs.
4. Perhaps an allusion to the tenor saxophone, Coltrane's instrument.
1. By white racists as a reprisal against civil rights demonstrations.

2. Captured and en route from Africa (along the "Middle Passage," the usual route for slave ships) to be sold as slaves.
3. I.e., British soldiers.

Martin's Blues[1]

He came apart in the open,
the slow motion cameras
falling quickly
neither alive nor kicking;
stone blind dead   5
on the balcony
that old melody
etched his black lips
in a pruned echo:
We shall overcome   10
some day—[2]
Yes we did!
Yes we did!

1971

---

1. Martin Luther King Jr. (1929–1968), American civil rights leader, was assassinated on a motel balcony.

2. Line from a hymn made famous by King's followers.

RAYMOND CARVER
1938–1988

Minimal fiction; designer fiction; even "dirty fiction," a phrase the British magazine *Granta* used to characterize the new style of American writing that was supposedly polluting the realistic short story with unconventional, irrealistic techniques—these terms were tossed around by critics of an abruptly new style of work that at times seemed to dominate the 1980s. Popularized by Bobbie Ann Mason, Ann Beattie, Frederick Barthelme, and Barry Hannah as well, its chief practitioner was a master of fine arts graduate from the University of Iowa's Writers Workshop, Raymond Carver, whose collections *Will You Please Be Quiet, Please?* (1976), *What We Talk about When We Talk about Love* (1981), and *Cathedral* (1983) set the most imitated style of their generation. Moved to put some order to these many definitions, writer John Barth—whose nonrealistic, innovative work had helped characterize the writing of the decades before—coined the term Post-Alcoholic Blue-Collar Minimalist Hyperrealism to describe the school Carver may have inadvertently founded. A recovering alcoholic, Carver had worked as a janitor, sawmill hand, delivery person, and sales representative, suggesting the profile Barth had in mind. But more pertinent to the style of his fiction was his training at Iowa and teaching in creative writing programs at universities around the country. By the time of his death, his became the most accepted style in such academic programs and in the literary magazines they generated.

This style's success is important. With conventions of literary realism having been challenged and theorists questioning all such previously stable assumptions, readers of Barth, Donald Barthelme, Kurt Vonnegut, and other such experimenters may have felt that simple realism was no longer an up-to-date way in which to write. Raymond Carver proved that it was, and that previous challenges to realistic tradition had only made it all the more effective, especially when those challenges are incorporated in the new style. Carver's patient narration does not strive for a reader suspension of disbelief. Rather, as in the introduction of the bizarre situation experienced in "Cathedral" (printed here), its plain, even flat statement presents matter unadorned by devices meant to persuade or convince. So a blind man wants to learn what the architecture of a cathedral suggests? Here it is, Carver's story says: what you see is what there is; take it or leave it; if you are blind, he will help you feel your way through, but never as a direction to meaning, only to an apprehension of the facts. Carver's characters are usually working-class people somewhat down on their luck. Often, alcohol figures in their lives, less as a stimulant than as a further depressant. Totally unexceptional, their failures, like their hopes, are small, even puny. But from such stripped down essentials the author is able to write in a plain, simple manner, sticking to the absolute minimum so that no one can accuse him of trying to create illusions.

Much was made of Raymond Carver's alcoholism and recovery. He made no apologies for his hard, sometimes abusive life, the rigors of which contributed to ill health and an early death. His stories and poems have the same quiet toughness to them, not flamboyant in confrontation with life's meanness but dedicated to holding on against time's slowly destructive friction with a grittiness all their own.

The text is from *Cathedral* (1983).

Cathedral

This blind man, an old friend of my wife's, he was on his way to spend the night. His wife had died. So he was visiting the dead wife's relatives in Connecticut. He called my wife from his in-laws'. Arrangements were made. He would come by train, a five-hour trip, and my wife would meet him at the station. She hadn't seen him since she worked for him one summer in Seattle ten years ago. But she and the blind man had kept in touch. They made tapes and mailed them back and forth. I wasn't enthusiastic about his visit. He was no one I knew. And his being blind bothered me. My idea of blindness came from the movies. In the movies, the blind moved slowly and never laughed. Sometimes they were led by seeing-eye dogs. A blind man in my house was not something I looked forward to.

That summer in Seattle she had needed a job. She didn't have any money. The man she was going to marry at the end of the summer was in officers' training school. He didn't have any money, either. But she was in love with the guy, and he was in love with her, etc. She'd seen something in the paper: HELP WANTED—*Reading to Blind Man*, and a telephone number. She phoned and went over, was hired on the spot. She'd worked with this blind man all summer. She read stuff to him, case studies, reports, that sort of thing. She helped him organize his little office in the county social-service department. They'd become good friends, my wife and the blind man. How do I know these things? She told me. And she told me something else. On her last day in the office, the blind man asked if he could touch her face. She agreed to this. She told me he touched his fingers to every part of her face, her nose—even her neck! She never forgot it. She even tried to write a poem about it. She was always trying to write a poem. She wrote a poem or two every year, usually after something really important had happened to her.

When we first started going out together, she showed me the poem. In the poem, she recalled his fingers and the way they had moved around over her face. In the poem, she talked about what she had felt at the time, about what went through her mind when the blind man touched her nose and lips. I can remember I didn't think much of the poem. Of course, I didn't tell her that. Maybe I just don't understand poetry. I admit it's not the first thing I reach for when I pick up something to read.

Anyway, this man who'd first enjoyed her favors, the officer-to-be, he'd been her childhood sweetheart. So okay. I'm saying that at the end of the summer she let the blind man run his hands over her face, said goodbye to him, married her childhood etc., who was now a commissioned officer, and she moved away from Seattle. But they'd kept in touch, she and the blind man. She made the first contact after a year or so. She called him up one night from an Air Force base in Alabama. She wanted to talk. They talked. He asked her to send him a tape and tell him about her life. She did this. She sent the tape. On the tape, she told the blind man about her husband and about their life together in the military. She told the blind man she loved her husband but she didn't like it where they lived and she didn't like it that he was a part of the military-industrial thing. She told the blind man she'd written a poem and he was in it. She told him that she was writing a poem about what it was like to be an Air Force officer's wife. The poem wasn't finished yet. She was still writing it. The blind man made a tape. He sent her the tape. She made a tape. This went on for years. My wife's officer was posted to one base and then another. She sent tapes from Moody AFB,[1] McGuire, McConnell, and finally Travis, near Sacramento, where one night she got to feeling lonely and cut off from people she kept losing in that moving-around life. She got to feeling she couldn't go it another step. She went in and swallowed all the pills and capsules in the medicine chest and washed them down with a bottle of gin. Then she got into a hot bath and passed out.

But instead of dying, she got sick. She threw up. Her officer—why should he have a name? he was the childhood sweetheart, and what more does he want?—came home from somewhere, found her, and called the ambulance. In time, she put it all on a tape and sent the tape to the blind man. Over the years, she put all kinds of stuff on tapes and sent the tapes off lickety-split. Next to writing a poem every year, I think it was her chief means of recreation. On one tape, she told the blind man she'd decided to live away from her officer for a time. On another tape, she told him about her divorce. She and I began going out, and of course she told her blind man about it. She told him everything, or so it seemed to me. Once she asked me if I'd like to hear the latest tape from the blind man. This was a year ago. I was on the tape, she said. So I said okay, I'd listen to it. I got us drinks and we settled down in the living room. We made ready to listen. First she inserted the tape into the player and adjusted a couple of dials. Then she pushed a lever. The tape squeaked and someone began to talk in this loud voice. She lowered the volume. After a few minutes of harmless chitchat, I heard my own name in the mouth of this stranger, this blind man I didn't even know! And then this: "From all you've said about him, I can only conclude—" But we were interrupted, a knock at the door, something, and we didn't ever get back to the tape. Maybe it was just as well. I'd heard all I wanted to.

---

1. Air force base. Names of other air force bases follow.

Now this same blind man was coming to sleep in my house.

"Maybe I could take him bowling," I said to my wife. She was at the draining board doing scalloped potatoes. She put down the knife she was using and turned around.

"If you love me," she said, "you can do this for me. If you don't love me, okay. But if you had a friend, any friend, and the friend came to visit, I'd make him feel comfortable." She wiped her hands with the dish towel.

"I don't have any blind friends," I said.

"You don't have *any* friends," she said. "Period. Besides," she said, "goddam it, his wife's just died! Don't you understand that? The man's lost his wife!"

I didn't answer. She'd told me a little about the blind man's wife. Her name was Beulah. Beulah! That's a name for a colored woman.

"Was his wife a Negro?" I asked.

"Are you crazy?" my wife said. "Have you just flipped or something?" She picked up a potato. I saw it hit the floor, then roll under the stove. "What's wrong with you?" she said. "Are you drunk?"

"I'm just asking," I said.

Right then my wife filled me in with more detail than I cared to know. I made a drink and sat at the kitchen table to listen. Pieces of the story began to fall into place.

Beulah had gone to work for the blind man the summer after my wife had stopped working for him. Pretty soon Beulah and the blind man had themselves a church wedding. It was a little wedding—who'd want to go to such a wedding in the first place?—just the two of them, plus the minister and the minister's wife. But it was a church wedding just the same. It was what Beulah had wanted, he'd said. But even then Beulah must have been carrying the cancer in her glands. After they had been inseparable for eight years—my wife's word, *inseparable*—Beulah's health went into a rapid decline. She died in a Seattle hospital room, the blind man sitting beside the bed and holding on to her hand. They'd married, lived and worked together, slept together—had sex, sure—and then the blind man had to bury her. All this without his having ever seen what the goddamned woman looked like. It was beyond my understanding. Hearing this, I felt sorry for the blind man for a little bit. And then I found myself thinking what a pitiful life this woman must have led. Imagine a woman who could never see herself as she was seen in the eyes of her loved one. A woman who could go on day after day and never receive the smallest compliment from her beloved. A woman whose husband could never read the expression on her face, be it misery or something better. Someone who could wear makeup or not—what difference to him? She could, if she wanted, wear green eye-shadow around one eye, a straight pin in her nostril, yellow slacks and purple shoes, no matter. And then to slip off into death, the blind man's hand on her hand, his blind eyes streaming tears—I'm imagining now—her last thought maybe this: that he never even knew what she looked like, and she on an express to the grave. Robert was left with a small insurance policy and half of a twenty-peso Mexican coin. The other half of the coin went into the box with her. Pathetic.

So when the time rolled around, my wife went to the depot to pick him up. With nothing to do but wait—sure, I blamed him for that—I was having a drink and watching the TV when I heard the car pull into the drive. I got up from the sofa with my drink and went to the window to have a look.

I saw my wife laughing as she parked the car. I saw her get out of the car and shut the door. She was still wearing a smile. Just amazing. She went around to the other side of the car to where the blind man was already starting to get out. This blind man, feature this, he was wearing a full beard! A beard on a blind man! Too much, I say. The blind man reached into the back seat and dragged out a suitcase. My wife took his arm, shut the car door, and, talking all the way, moved him down the drive and then up the steps to the front porch. I turned off the TV. I finished my drink, rinsed the glass, dried my hands. Then I went to the door.

My wife said, "I want you to meet Robert. Robert, this is my husband. I've told you all about him." She was beaming. She had this blind man by his coat sleeve.

The blind man let go of his suitcase and up came his hand.

I took it. He squeezed hard, held my hand, and then he let it go.

"I feel like we've already met," he boomed.

"Likewise," I said. I didn't know what else to say. Then I said, "Welcome. I've heard a lot about you." We began to move then, a little group, from the porch into the living room, my wife guiding him by the arm. The blind man was carrying his suitcase in his other hand. My wife said things like, "To your left here, Robert. That's right. Now watch it, there's a chair. That's it. Sit down right here. This is the sofa. We just bought this sofa two weeks ago."

I started to say something about the old sofa. I'd liked that old sofa. But I didn't say anything. Then I wanted to say something else, small-talk, about the scenic ride along the Hudson. How going *to* New York, you should sit on the right-hand side of the train, and coming *from* New York, the left-hand side.

"Did you have a good train ride?" I said. "Which side of the train did you sit on, by the way?"

"What a question, which side!" my wife said. "What's it matter which side?" she said.

"I just asked," I said.

"Right side," the blind man said. "I hadn't been on a train in nearly forty years. Not since I was a kid. With my folks. That's been a long time. I'd nearly forgotten the sensation. I have winter in my beard now," he said. "So I've been told, anyway. Do I look distinguished, my dear?" the blind man said to my wife.

"You look distinguished, Robert," she said. "Robert," she said. "Robert, it's just so good to see you."

My wife finally took her eyes off the blind man and looked at me. I had the feeling she didn't like what she saw. I shrugged.

I've never met, or personally known, anyone who was blind. This blind man was late forties, a heavy-set, balding man with stooped shoulders, as if he carried a great weight there. He wore brown slacks, brown shoes, a light-brown shirt, a tie, a sports coat. Spiffy. He also had this full beard. But he didn't use a cane and he didn't wear dark glasses. I'd always thought dark glasses were a must for the blind. Fact was, I wished he had a pair. At first glance, his eyes looked like anyone else's eyes. But if you looked close, there was something different about them. Too much white in the iris, for one thing, and the pupils seemed to move around in the sockets without his knowing it or being able to stop it. Creepy. As I stared at his face, I saw the left pupil turn in toward his nose while the other made an effort to keep in one place. But it was only an effort, for that eye was on the roam without his knowing it or wanting it to be.

I said, "Let me get you a drink. What's your pleasure? We have a little of everything. It's one of our pastimes."

"Bub, I'm a Scotch man myself," he said fast enough in this big voice.

"Right," I said. Bub! "Sure you are. I knew it."

He let his fingers touch his suitcase, which was sitting alongside the sofa. He was taking his bearings. I didn't blame him for that.

"I'll move that up to your room," my wife said.

"No, that's fine," the blind man said loudly. "It can go up when I go up."

"A little water with the Scotch?" I said.

"Very little," he said.

"I knew it," I said.

He said, "Just a tad. The Irish actor, Barry Fitzgerald?[2] I'm like that fellow. When I drink water, Fitzgerald said, I drink water. When I drink whiskey, I drink whiskey." My wife laughed. The blind man brought his hand up under his beard. He lifted his beard slowly and let it drop.

I did the drinks, three big glasses of Scotch with a splash of water in each. Then we made ourselves comfortable and talked about Robert's travels. First the long flight from the West Coast to Connecticut, we covered that. Then from Connecticut up here by train. We had another drink concerning that leg of the trip.

I remembered having read somewhere that the blind didn't smoke because, as speculation had it, they couldn't see the smoke they exhaled. I thought I knew that much and that much only about blind people. But this blind man smoked his cigarette down to the nubbin and then lit another one. This blind man filled his ashtray and my wife emptied it.

When we sat down at the table for dinner, we had another drink. My wife heaped Robert's plate with cube steak, scalloped potatoes, green beans. I buttered him up two slices of bread. I said, "Here's bread and butter for you." I swallowed some of my drink. "Now let us pray," I said, and the blind man lowered his head. My wife looked at me, her mouth agape. "Pray the phone won't ring and the food doesn't get cold," I said.

We dug in. We ate everything there was to eat on the table. We ate like there was no tomorrow. We didn't talk. We ate. We scarfed. We grazed that table. We were into serious eating. The blind man had right away located his foods, he knew just where everything was on his plate. I watched with admiration as he used his knife and fork on the meat. He'd cut two pieces of meat, fork the meat into his mouth, and then go all out for the scalloped potatoes, the beans next, and then he'd tear off a hunk of buttered bread and eat that. He'd follow this up with a big drink of milk. It didn't seem to bother him to use his fingers once in a while, either.

We finished everything, including half a strawberry pie. For a few moments, we sat as if stunned. Sweat beaded on our faces. Finally, we got up from the table and left the dirty plates. We didn't look back. We took ourselves into the living room and sank into our places again. Robert and my wife sat on the sofa. I took the big chair. We had us two or three more drinks while they

---

2. Noted for his stock characterizations of Irish figures (often priests) in American films of the 1940s and 1950s.

talked about the major things that had come to pass for them in the past ten years. For the most part, I just listened. Now and then I joined in. I didn't want him to think I'd left the room, and I didn't want her to think I was feeling left out. They talked of things that had happened to them—to them!—these past ten years. I waited in vain to hear my name on my wife's sweet lips: "And then my dear husband came into my life"—something like that. But I heard nothing of the sort. More talk of Robert. Robert had done a little of everything, it seemed, a regular blind jack-of-all-trades. But most recently he and his wife had had an Amway[3] distributorship, from which, I gathered, they'd earned their living, such as it was. The blind man was also a ham radio operator. He talked in his loud voice about conversations he'd had with fellow operators in Guam, in the Philippines, in Alaska, and even in Tahiti. He said he'd have a lot of friends there if he ever wanted to go visit those places. From time to time, he'd turn his blind face toward me, put his hand under his beard, ask me something. How long had I been in my present position? (Three years.) Did I like my work? (I didn't.) Was I going to stay with it? (What were the options?) Finally, when I thought he was beginning to run down, I got up and turned on the TV.

My wife looked at me with irritation. She was heading toward a boil. Then she looked at the blind man and said, "Robert, do you have a TV?"

The blind man said, "My dear, I have two TVs. I have a color set and a black-and-white thing, an old relic. It's funny, but if I turn the TV on, and I'm always turning it on, I turn on the color set. It's funny, don't you think?"

I didn't know what to say to that. I had absolutely nothing to say to that. No opinion. So I watched the news program and tried to listen to what the announcer was saying.

"This is a color TV," the blind man said. "Don't ask me how, but I can tell."

"We traded up a while ago," I said.

The blind man had another taste of his drink. He lifted his beard, sniffed it, and let it fall. He leaned forward on the sofa. He positioned his ashtray on the coffee table, then put the lighter to his cigarette. He leaned back on the sofa and crossed his legs at the ankles.

My wife covered her mouth, and then she yawned. She stretched. She said, "I think I'll go upstairs and put on my robe. I think I'll change into something else. Robert, you make yourself comfortable," she said.

"I'm comfortable," the blind man said.

"I want you to feel comfortable in this house," she said.

"I am comfortable," the blind man said.

After she'd left the room, he and I listened to the weather report and then to the sports roundup. By that time, she'd been gone so long I didn't know if she was going to come back. I thought she might have gone to bed. I wished she'd come back downstairs. I didn't want to be left alone with a blind man. I asked him if he wanted another drink, and he said sure. Then I asked if he wanted to smoke some dope with me. I said I'd just rolled a number. I hadn't, but I planned to do so in about two shakes.

"I'll try some with you," he said.

"Damn right," I said. "That's the stuff."

---

3. A retail sales business operated by taking orders at home.

I got our drinks and sat down on the sofa with him. Then I rolled us two fat numbers. I lit one and passed it. I brought it to his fingers. He took it and inhaled.

"Hold it as long as you can," I said. I could tell he didn't know the first thing.

My wife came back downstairs wearing her pink robe and her pink slippers.

"What do I smell?" she said.

"We thought we'd have us some cannabis," I said.

My wife gave me a savage look. Then she looked at the blind man and said, "Robert, I didn't know you smoked."

He said, "I do now, my dear. There's a first time for everything. But I don't feel anything yet."

"This stuff is pretty mellow," I said. "This stuff is mild. It's dope you can reason with," I said. "It doesn't mess you up."

"Not much it doesn't, bub," he said, and laughed.

My wife sat on the sofa between the blind man and me. I passed her the number. She took it and toked and then passed it back to me. "Which way is this going?" she said. Then she said, "I shouldn't be smoking this. I can hardly keep my eyes open as it is. That dinner did me in. I shouldn't have eaten so much."

"It was the strawberry pie," the blind man said. "That's what did it," he said, and he laughed his big laugh. Then he shook his head.

"There's more strawberry pie," I said.

"Do you want some more, Robert?" my wife said.

"Maybe in a little while," he said.

We gave our attention to the TV. My wife yawned again. She said, "Your bed is made up when you feel like going to bed, Robert. I know you must have had a long day. When you're ready to go to bed, say so." She pulled his arm. "Robert?"

He came to and said, "I've had a real nice time. This beats tapes, doesn't it?"

I said, "Coming at you," and I put the number between his fingers. He inhaled, held the smoke, and then let it go. It was like he'd been doing it since he was nine years old.

"Thanks, bub," he said. "But I think this is all for me. I think I'm beginning to feel it," he said. He held the burning roach out for my wife.

"Same here," she said. "Ditto. Me, too." She took the roach and passed it to me. "I may just sit here for a while between you two guys with my eyes closed. But don't let me bother you, okay? Either one of you. If it bothers you, say so. Otherwise, I may just sit here with my eyes closed until you're ready to go to bed," she said. "Your bed's made up, Robert, when you're ready. It's right next to our room at the top of the stairs. We'll show you up when you're ready. You wake me up now, you guys, if I fall asleep." She said that and then she closed her eyes and went to sleep.

The news program ended. I got up and changed the channel. I sat back down on the sofa. I wished my wife hadn't pooped out. Her head lay across the back of the sofa, her mouth open. She'd turned so that her robe had slipped away from her legs, exposing a juicy thigh. I reached to draw her robe back over her, and it was then that I glanced at the blind man. What the hell! I flipped the robe open again.

"You say when you want some strawberry pie," I said.

"I will," he said.

I said, "Are you tired? Do you want me to take you up to your bed? Are you ready to hit the hay?"

"Not yet," he said. "No, I'll stay up with you, bub. If that's all right. I'll stay up until you're ready to turn in. We haven't had a chance to talk. Know what I mean? I feel like me and her monopolized the evening." He lifted his beard and he let it fall. He picked up his cigarettes and his lighter.

"That's all right," I said. Then I said, "I'm glad for the company."

And I guess I was. Every night I smoked dope and stayed up as long as I could before I fell asleep. My wife and I hardly ever went to bed at the same time. When I did go to sleep, I had these dreams. Sometimes I'd wake up from one of them, my heart going crazy.

Something about the church and the Middle Ages was on the TV. Not your run-of-the-mill TV fare. I wanted to watch something else. I turned to the other channels. But there was nothing on them, either. So I turned back to the first channel and apologized.

"Bub, it's all right," the blind man said. "It's fine with me. Whatever you want to watch is okay. I'm always learning something. Learning never ends. It won't hurt me to learn something tonight. I got ears," he said.

We didn't say anything for a time. He was leaning forward with his head turned at me, his right ear aimed in the direction of the set. Very disconcerting. Now and then his eyelids drooped and then they snapped open again. Now and then he put his fingers into his beard and tugged, like he was thinking about something he was hearing on the television.

On the screen, a group of men wearing cowls was being set upon and tormented by men dressed in skeleton costumes and men dressed as devils. The men dressed as devils wore devil masks, horns, and long tails. This pageant was part of a procession. The Englishman who was narrating the thing said it took place in Spain once a year. I tried to explain to the blind man what was happening.

"Skeletons," he said. "I know about skeletons," he said, and he nodded.

The TV showed this one cathedral. Then there was a long, slow look at another one. Finally, the picture switched to the famous one in Paris, with its flying buttresses and its spires reaching up to the clouds. The camera pulled away to show the whole of the cathedral rising above the skyline.

There were times when the Englishman who was telling the thing would shut up, would simply let the camera move around over the cathedrals. Or else the camera would tour the countryside, men in fields walking behind oxen. I waited as long as I could. Then I felt I had to say something. I said, "They're showing the outside of this cathedral now. Gargoyles. Little statues carved to look like monsters. Now I guess they're in Italy. Yeah, they're in Italy. There's paintings on the walls of this one church."

"Are those fresco paintings, bub?" he asked, and he sipped from his drink.

I reached for my glass. But it was empty. I tried to remember what I could remember. "You're asking me are those frescoes?" I said. "That's a good question. I don't know."

The camera moved to a cathedral outside Lisbon. The differences in the Portuguese cathedral compared with the French and Italian were not that great. But they were there. Mostly the interior stuff. Then something occurred to me, and I said, "Something has occurred to me. Do you have any idea what a cathedral is? What they look like, that is? Do you follow me? If somebody says cathedral to you, do you have any notion what they're talking about? Do you know the difference between that and a Baptist church, say?"

He let the smoke dribble from his mouth. "I know they took hundreds of workers fifty or a hundred years to build," he said. "I just heard the man say that, of course. I know generations of the same families worked on a cathedral. I heard him say that, too. The men who began their life's work on them, they never lived to see the completion of their work. In that wise, bub, they're no different from the rest of us, right?" He laughed. Then his eyelids drooped again. His head nodded. He seemed to be snoozing. Maybe he was imagining himself in Portugal. The TV was showing another cathedral now. This one was in Germany. The Englishman's voice droned on. "Cathedrals," the blind man said. He sat up and rolled his head back and forth. "If you want the truth, bub, that's about all I know. What I just said. What I heard him say. But maybe you could describe one to me? I wish you'd do it. I'd like that. If you want to know, I really don't have a good idea."

I stared hard at the shot of the cathedral on the TV. How could I even begin to describe it? But say my life depended on it. Say my life was being threatened by an insane guy who said I had to do it or else.

I stared some more at the cathedral before the picture flipped off into the countryside. There was no use. I turned to the blind man and said, "To begin with, they're very tall." I was looking around the room for clues. "They reach way up. Up and up. Toward the sky. They're so big, some of them, they have to have these supports. To help hold them up, so to speak. These supports are called buttresses. They remind me of viaducts, for some reason. But maybe you don't know viaducts, either? Sometimes the cathedrals have devils and such carved into the front. Sometimes lords and ladies. Don't ask me why this is," I said.

He was nodding. The whole upper part of his body seemed to be moving back and forth.

"I'm not doing so good, am I?" I said.

He stopped nodding and leaned forward on the edge of the sofa. As he listened to me, he was running his fingers through his beard. I wasn't getting through to him, I could see that. But he waited for me to go on just the same. He nodded, like he was trying to encourage me. I tried to think what else to say. "They're really big," I said. "They're massive. They're built of stone. Marble, too, sometimes. In those olden days, when they built cathedrals, men wanted to be close to God. In those olden days, God was an important part of everyone's life. You could tell this from their cathedral-building. I'm sorry," I said, "but it looks like that's the best I can do for you. I'm just no good at it."

"That's all right, bub," the blind man said. "Hey, listen. I hope you don't mind my asking you. Can I ask you something? Let me ask you a simple question, yes or no. I'm just curious and there's no offense. You're my host. But let me ask if you are in any way religious? You don't mind my asking?"

I shook my head. He couldn't see that, though. A wink is the same as a nod to a blind man. "I guess I don't believe in it. In anything. Sometimes it's hard. You know what I'm saying?"

"Sure, I do," he said.

"Right," I said.

The Englishman was still holding forth. My wife sighed in her sleep. She drew a long breath and went on with her sleeping.

"You'll have to forgive me," I said. "But I can't tell you what a cathedral looks like. It just isn't in me to do it. I can't do any more than I've done."

The blind man sat very still, his head down, as he listened to me.

I said, "The truth is, cathedrals don't mean anything special to me. Nothing. Cathedrals. They're something to look at on late-night TV. That's all they are."

It was then that the blind man cleared his throat. He brought something up. He took a handkerchief from his back pocket. Then he said, "I get it, bub. It's okay. It happens. Don't worry about it," he said. "Hey, listen to me. Will you do me a favor? I got an idea. Why don't you find us some heavy paper? And a pen. We'll do something. We'll draw one together. Get us a pen and some heavy paper. Go on, bub, get the stuff," he said.

So I went upstairs. My legs felt like they didn't have any strength in them. They felt like they did after I'd done some running. In my wife's room, I looked around. I found some ballpoints in a little basket on her table. And then I tried to think where to look for the kind of paper he was talking about.

Downstairs, in the kitchen, I found a shopping bag with onion skins in the bottom of the bag. I emptied the bag and shook it. I brought it into the living room and sat down with it near his legs. I moved some things, smoothed the wrinkles from the bag, spread it out on the coffee table.

The blind man got down from the sofa and sat next to me on the carpet.

He ran his fingers over the paper. He went up and down the sides of the paper. The edges, even the edges. He fingered the corners.

"All right," he said. "All right, let's do her."

He found my hand, the hand with the pen. He closed his hand over my hand. "Go ahead, bub, draw," he said. "Draw. You'll see. I'll follow along with you. It'll be okay. Just begin now like I'm telling you. You'll see. Draw," the blind man said.

So I began. First I drew a box that looked like a house. It could have been the house I lived in. Then I put a roof on it. At either end of the roof, I drew spires. Crazy.

"Swell," he said. "Terrific. You're doing fine," he said. "Never thought anything like this could happen in your lifetime, did you, bub? Well, it's a strange life, we all know that. Go on now. Keep it up."

I put in windows with arches. I drew flying buttresses. I hung great doors. I couldn't stop. The TV station went off the air. I put down the pen and closed and opened my fingers. The blind man felt around over the paper. He moved the tips of his fingers over the paper, all over what I had drawn, and he nodded.

"Doing fine," the blind man said.

I took up the pen again, and he found my hand. I kept at it. I'm no artist. But I kept drawing just the same.

My wife opened up her eyes and gazed at us. She sat up on the sofa, her robe hanging open. She said, "What are you doing? Tell me, I want to know."

I didn't answer her.

The blind man said, "We're drawing a cathedral. Me and him are working on it. Press hard," he said to me. "That's right. That's good," he said. "Sure.

You got it, bub. I can tell. You didn't think you could. But you can, can't you? You're cooking with gas now. You know what I'm saying? We're going to really have us something here in a minute. How's the old arm?" he said. "Put some people in there now. What's a cathedral without people?"

My wife said, "What's going on? Robert, what are you doing? What's going on?"

"It's all right," he said to her. "Close your eyes now," the blind man said to me.

I did it. I closed them just like he said.

"Are they closed?" he said. "Don't fudge."

"They're closed," I said.

"Keep them that way," he said. He said, "Don't stop now. Draw."

So we kept on with it. His fingers rode my fingers as my hand went over the paper. It was like nothing else in my life up to now.

Then he said, "I think that's it. I think you got it," he said. "Take a look. What do you think?"

But I had my eyes closed. I thought I'd keep them that way for a little longer. I thought it was something I ought to do.

"Well?" he said. "Are you looking?"

My eyes were still closed. I was in my house. I knew that. But I didn't feel like I was inside anything.

"It's really something," I said.

1983

MAXINE HONG KINGSTON
b. 1940

Maxine Hong Kingston was born in Stockton, California, to parents who had emigrated from China. Before they emigrated Kingston's father was a schoolteacher and a poet; her mother was a rural doctor in a profession consisting almost entirely of men. In America they took on quite different identities: her father, at times unemployed, worked in a gambling house and a laundry; her mother raised six children, of whom Kingston was the eldest.

Kingston graduated from the University of California at Berkeley, studying there in the turbulent middle sixties. Her debut as a writer was auspicious: in 1976, an unknown, she published her first and most widely read book, *The Woman Warrior,* and was catapulted to literary fame. Subtitled "Memoirs of a Girlhood among Ghosts," it combines autobiographical fact with legends, especially Asian ones, to make a distinct imaginative creation. Reviews of the book, almost universally laudatory, emphasized its poetic and lyric beauty. *The Woman Warrior* is about the cultural conflicts Chinese Americans must confront. Still, what remains in the mind is its quality of vivid particularity, as for example at the beginning of "Shaman," the book's third section:

> Once in a long while, four times so far for me, my mother brings out the metal tube that holds her medical diploma. On the tube are gold circles crossed with seven red lines each—"joy" ideographs in abstract. There are also little flowers that look like gears for a gold machine. . . . When I open it the smell of China flies out,

a thousand-year-old bat flying heavy-handed out of the Chinese caverns where bats are as white as dust, a smell that comes from long ago, far back in my brain.

Although *The Woman Warrior* received the National Book Critics' Circle award for general nonfiction, there is nothing "general" in the sensuous density of its reference.

The importance of storytelling to Kingston's enterprise in *The Woman Warrior* and its successor, *China Men* (1980), cannot be overemphasized. In an interview with Bill Moyers on public television, Kingston said that her attempt was to push the account toward "form" by giving it a "redemptive" meaning, making it a "beautiful" story rather than a sordid one. As is the case typically with her practice as a writer, her effort is to mediate between present and past: "I think that my stories have a constant breaking in and out of the present and past. So the reader might be walking along very well in the present, but the past breaks through and changes and enlightens the present and vice versa."

Kingston had originally conceived of *The Woman Warrior* and *China Men* as one long book, but decided to preserve an overall division by gender: *Warrior* is about her female antecedents; while *China Men,* which won the 1980 National Book Award for nonfiction, deals with her relation to her father and complements that relation by providing epiclike biographies of earlier male forebears, especially those Chinese who came to America and worked on building the railroads. In a final section she writes about her brother who served in the U.S. Navy during the Vietnam War. As she discusses in the interview with Moyers, her father annotated both of these memoir-meditations, carrying further the conversation between the generations.

Tripmaster Monkey (1989), presented more deliberately as a novel, is an exercise as excessive as the young fifth-generation American hero, Wittman Ah Sing, who is portrayed there. Subtitled "His Fake Book," the novel is an extended, picaresque account of Wittman's adventures as an aspiring playwright who imagines himself to be an incarnation of the legendary Monkey King—a trickster hero said to have brought the Buddha's teaching to China. Combining magic, realism, and black humor, *Tripmaster Monkey* is about a young man's search for a community in America. Although Kingston's myth-laden narratives have been called "exotic," she dislikes the word, since she has dedicated her art to exploring what it means to be a human being in American society. In fact, she thinks of her books as more American than Chinese, sees the American poet William Carlos Williams's *In the American Grain* as a true prose predecessor, and probably would be happy to think of the hero of *Tripmaster Monkey* as a later, different version of Huck Finn (in Mark Twain's novel) or Augie March (in Saul Bellow's). As the critic Jennie Wang explains in even larger dimensions, Kingston's Wittman Ah Sing, "the maker/magician . . . conceived in the mind's fancy of a metafictionist," joins in his multiculturalism American and postmodern ambitions.

The text is from *The Woman Warrior* (1976).

No Name Woman

"You must not tell anyone," my mother said, "what I am about to tell you. In China your father had a sister who killed herself. She jumped into the family well. We say that your father has all brothers because it is as if she had never been born.

"In 1924 just a few days after our village celebrated seventeen hurry-up weddings—to make sure that every young man who went 'out on the road' would responsibly come home—your father and his brothers and your grandfather and his brothers and your aunt's new husband sailed for America, the

Gold Mountain. It was your grandfather's last trip. Those lucky enough to get contracts waved good-bye from the decks. They fed and guarded the stowaways and helped them off in Cuba, New York, Bali, Hawaii. 'We'll meet in California next year,' they said. All of them sent money home.

"I remember looking at your aunt one day when she and I were dressing; I had not noticed before that she had such a protruding melon of a stomach. But I did not think, 'She's pregnant,' until she began to look like other pregnant women, her shirt pulling and the white tops of her black pants showing. She could not have been pregnant, you see, because her husband had been gone for years. No one said anything. We did not discuss it. In early summer she was ready to have the child, long after the time when it could have been possible.

"The village had also been counting. On the night the baby was to be born the villagers raided our house. Some were crying. Like a great saw, teeth strung with lights, files of people walked zigzag across our land, tearing the rice. Their lanterns doubled in the disturbed black water, which drained away through the broken bunds.[1] As the villagers closed in, we could see that some of them, probably men and women we knew well, wore white masks. The people with long hair hung it over their faces. Women with short hair made it stand up on end. Some had tied white bands around their foreheads, arms, and legs.

"At first they threw mud and rocks at the house. Then they threw eggs and began slaughtering our stock. We could hear the animals scream their deaths—the roosters, the pigs, a last great roar from the ox. Familiar wild heads flared in our night windows; the villagers encircled us. Some of the faces stopped to peer at us, their eyes rushing like searchlights. The hands flattened against the panes, framed heads, and left red prints.

"The villagers broke in the front and the back doors at the same time, even though we had not locked the doors against them. Their knives dripped with the blood of our animals. They smeared blood on the doors and walls. One woman swung a chicken, whose throat she had slit, splattering blood in red arcs about her. We stood together in the middle of our house, in the family hall with the pictures and tables of the ancestors around us, and looked straight ahead.

"At that time the house had only two wings. When the men came back, we would build two more to enclose our courtyard and a third one to begin a second courtyard. The villagers pushed through both wings, even your grandparents' rooms, to find your aunt's, which was also mine until the men returned. From this room a new wing for one of the younger families would grow. They ripped up her clothes and shoes and broke her combs, grinding them underfoot. They tore her work from the loom. They scattered the cooking fire and rolled the new weaving in it. We could hear them in the kitchen breaking our bowls and banging the pots. They overturned the great waist-high earthenware jugs; duck eggs, pickled fruits, vegetables burst out and mixed in acrid torrents. The old woman from the next field swept a broom through the air and loosed the spirits-of-the-broom over our heads. 'Pig.' 'Ghost.' 'Pig,' they sobbed and scolded while they ruined our house.

---

1. Embankments built to control the flow of water, here probably irrigation water.

"When they left, they took sugar and oranges to bless themselves. They cut pieces from the dead animals. Some of them took bowls that were not broken and clothes that were not torn. Afterward we swept up the rice and sewed it back up into sacks. But the smells from the spilled preserves lasted. Your aunt gave birth in the pigsty that night. The next morning when I went for the water, I found her and the baby plugging up the family well.

"Don't let your father know that I told you. He denies her. Now that you have started to menstruate, what happened to her could happen to you. Don't humiliate us. You wouldn't like to be forgotten as if you had never been born. The villagers are watchful."

Whenever she had to warn us about life, my mother told stories that ran like this one, a story to grow up on. She tested our strength to establish realities. Those in the emigrant generations who could not reassert brute survival died young and far from home. Those of us in the first American generations have had to figure out how the invisible world the emigrants built around our childhoods fits in solid America.

The immigrants confused the gods by diverting their curses, misleading them with crooked streets and false names. They must try to confuse their offspring as well, who, I suppose, threaten them in similar ways—always trying to get things straight, always trying to name the unspeakable. The Chinese I know hide their names; sojourners take new names when their lives change and guard their real names with silence.

Chinese-Americans, when you try to understand what things in you are Chinese, how do you separate what is peculiar to childhood, to poverty, insanities, one family, your mother who marked your growing with stories, from what is Chinese? What is Chinese tradition and what is the movies?

If I want to learn what clothes my aunt wore, whether flashy or ordinary, I would have to begin, "Remember Father's drowned-in-the-well sister?" I cannot ask that. My mother has told me once and for all the useful parts. She will add nothing unless powered by Necessity, a riverbank that guides her life. She plants vegetable gardens rather than lawns; she carries the odd-shaped tomatoes home from the fields and eats food left for the gods.

Whenever we did frivolous things, we used up energy; we flew high kites. We children came up off the ground over the melting cones our parents brought home from work and the American movie on New Year's Day—*Oh, You Beautiful Doll* with Betty Grable one year, and *She Wore a Yellow Ribbon* with John Wayne another year. After the one carnival ride each, we paid in guilt; our tired father counted his change on the dark walk home.

Adultery is extravagance. Could people who hatch their own chicks and eat the embryos and the heads for delicacies and boil the feet in vinegar for party food, leaving only the gravel, eating even the gizzard lining—could such people engender a prodigal aunt? To be a woman, to have a daughter in starvation time was a waste enough. My aunt could not have been the lone romantic who gave up everything for sex. Women in the old China did not choose. Some man had commanded her to lie with him and be his secret evil. I wonder whether he masked himself when he joined the raid on her family.

Perhaps she had encountered him in the fields or on the mountain where the daughters-in-law collected fuel. Or perhaps he first noticed her in the marketplace. He was not a stranger because the village housed no strangers. She had to have dealings with him other than sex. Perhaps he worked an adjoining field, or he sold her the cloth for the dress she sewed and wore. His demand must have surprised, then terrified her. She obeyed him; she always did as she was told.

When the family found a young man in the next village to be her husband, she had stood tractably beside the best rooster, his proxy,[2] and promised before they met that she would be his forever. She was lucky that he was her age and she would be the first wife, an advantage secure now. The night she first saw him, he had sex with her. Then he left for America. She had almost forgotten what he looked like. When she tried to envision him, she only saw the black and white face in the group photograph the men had had taken before leaving.

The other man was not, after all, much different from her husband. They both gave orders: she followed. "If you tell your family, I'll beat you. I'll kill you. Be here again next week." No one talked sex, ever. And she might have separated the rapes from the rest of living if only she did not have to buy her oil from him or gather wood in the same forest. I want her fear to have lasted just as long as rape lasted so that the fear could have been contained. No drawnout fear. But women at sex hazarded birth and hence lifetimes. The fear did not stop but permeated everywhere. She told the man, "I think I'm pregnant." He organized the raid against her.

On nights when my mother and father talked about their life back home, sometimes they mentioned an "outcast table" whose business they still seemed to be settling, their voices tight. In a commensal tradition,[3] where food is precious, the powerful older people made wrongdoers eat alone. Instead of letting them start separate new lives like the Japanese, who could become samurais and geishas,[4] the Chinese family, faces averted but eyes glowering sideways, hung on to the offenders and fed them leftovers. My aunt must have lived in the same house as my parents and eaten at an outcast table. My mother spoke about the raid as if she had seen it, when she and my aunt, a daughter-in-law to a different household, should not have been living together at all. Daughters-in-law lived with their husbands' parents, not their own; a synonym for marriage in Chinese is "taking a daughter-in-law." Her husband's parents could have sold her, mortgaged her, stoned her. But they had sent her back to her own mother and father, a mysterious act hinting at disgraces not told me. Perhaps they had thrown her out to deflect the avengers.

She was the only daughter; her four brothers went with her father, husband, and uncles "out on the road" and for some years became western men. When the goods were divided among the family, three of the brothers took land, and the youngest, my father, chose an education. After my grandparents gave their daughter away to her husband's family, they had dispensed all the adventure and all the property. They expected her alone to keep the traditional ways, which her brothers, now among the barbarians, could fumble without detection. The heavy, deep-rooted women were to maintain the past against the flood, safe for returning. But the rare urge west had fixed upon our family, and so my aunt crossed boundaries not delineated in space.

The work of preservation demands that the feelings playing about in one's

2. Someone or something that has the power to substitute or act for another.
3. A tradition in which people eat together at the same table.
4. In Japanese society women trained to entertain men. *Samurai:* the Japanese warrior elite.

guts not be turned into action. Just watch their passing like cherry blossoms. But perhaps my aunt, my forerunner, caught in a slow life, let dreams grow and fade and after some months or years went toward what persisted. Fear at the enormities of the forbidden kept her desires delicate, wire and bone. She looked at a man because she liked the way the hair was tucked behind his ears, or she liked the question-mark line of a long torso curving at the shoulder and straight at the hip. For warm eyes or a soft voice or a slow walk—that's all—a few hairs, a line, a brightness, a sound, a pace, she gave up family. She offered us up for a charm that vanished with tiredness, a pigtail that didn't toss when the wind died. Why, the wrong lighting could erase the dearest thing about him.

It could very well have been, however, that my aunt did not take subtle enjoyment of her friend, but, a wild woman, kept rollicking company. Imagining her free with sex doesn't fit, through. I don't know any women like that, or men either. Unless I see her life branching into mine, she gives me no ancestral help.

To sustain her being in love, she often worked at herself in the mirror, guessing at the colors and shapes that would interest him, changing them frequently in order to hit on the right combination. She wanted him to look back.

On a farm near the sea, a woman who tended her appearance reaped a reputation for eccentricity. All the married women blunt-cut their hair in flaps about their ears or pulled it back in tight buns. No nonsense. Neither style blew easily into heart-catching tangles. And at their weddings they displayed themselves in their long hair for the last time. "It brushed the backs of my knees," my mother tells me. "It was braided, and even so, it brushed the backs of my knees."

At the mirror my aunt combed individuality into her bob. A bun could have been contrived to escape into black streamers blowing in the wind or in quiet wisps about her face, but only the older women in our picture album wear buns. She brushed her hair back from her forehead, tucking the flaps behind her ears. She looped a piece of thread, knotted into a circle between her index fingers and thumbs, and ran the double strand across her forehead. When she closed her fingers as if she were making a pair of shadow geese bite, the string twisted together catching the little hairs. Then she pulled the thread away from her skin, ripping the hair out neatly, her eyes watering from the needles of pain. Opening her fingers, she cleaned the thread, then rolled it along her hairline and the tops of her eyebrows. My mother did the same to me and my sisters and herself. I used to believe that the expression "caught by the short hairs" meant a captive held with a depilatory string. It especially hurt at the temples, but my mother said we were lucky we didn't have to have our feet bound when we were seven. Sisters used to sit on their beds and cry together, she said, as their mothers or their slave removed the bandages for a few minutes each night and let the blood gush back into their veins. I hope that the man my aunt loved appreciated a smooth brow, that he wasn't just a tits-and-ass man.

Once my aunt found a freckle on her chin, at a spot that the almanac said predestined her for unhappiness. She dug it out with a hot needle and washed the wound with peroxide.

More attention to her looks than these pullings of hairs and pickings at spots would have caused gossip among the villagers. They owned work clothes and good clothes, and they wore good clothes for feasting the new seasons. But since a woman combing her hair hexes beginnings, my aunt rarely found an occasion to look her best. Women looked like great sea snails—the corded wood, babies, and laundry they carried were the whorls on their backs. The Chinese did not admire a bent back; goddesses and warriors stood straight. Still there must have been a marvelous freeing of beauty when a worker laid down her burden and stretched and arched.

Such commonplace loveliness, however, was not enough for my aunt. She dreamed of a lover for the fifteen days of New Year's, the time for families to exchange visits, money, and food. She plied her secret comb. And sure enough she cursed the year, the family, the village, and herself.

Even as her hair lured her imminent lover, many other men looked at her. Uncles, cousins, nephews, brothers would have looked, too, had they been home between journeys. Perhaps they had already been restraining their curiosity, and they left, fearful that their glances, like a field of nesting birds, might be startled and caught. Poverty hurt, and that was their first reason for leaving. But another, final reason for leaving the crowded house was the never-said.

She may have been unusually beloved, the precious only daughter, spoiled and mirror gazing because of the affection the family lavished on her. When her husband left, they welcomed the chance to take her back from the in-laws; she could live like the little daughter for just a while longer. There are stories that my grandfather was different from other people, "crazy ever since the little Jap bayoneted him in the head." He used to put his naked penis on the dinner table, laughing. And one day he brought home a baby girl, wrapped up inside his brown western-style greatcoat.[5] He had traded one of his sons, probably my father, the youngest, for her. My grandmother made him trade back. When he finally got a daughter of his own, he doted on her. They must have all loved her, except perhaps my father, the only brother who never went back to China, having once been traded for a girl.

Brothers and sisters, newly men and women, had to efface their sexual color and present plain miens. Disturbing hair and eyes, a smile like no other, threatened the ideal of five generations living under one roof. To focus blurs, people shouted face to face and yelled from room to room. The immigrants I know have loud voices, unmodulated to American tones even after years away from the village where they called their friendships out across the fields. I have not been able to stop my mother's screams in public libraries or over telephones. Walking erect (knees straight, toes pointed forward, not pigeon-toed, which is Chinese-feminine) and speaking in an inaudible voice, I have tried to turn myself American-feminine. Chinese communication was loud, public. Only sick people had to whisper. But at the dinner table, where the family members came nearest one another, no one could talk, not the outcasts nor any eaters. Every word that falls from the mouth is a coin lost. Silently they gave and accepted food with both hands. A preoccupied child who took his bowl with one hand got a sideways glare. A complete moment of total attention is due everyone alike. Children and lovers have no singularity here, but my aunt used a secret voice, a separate attentiveness.

5. A heavy overcoat.

She kept the man's name to herself throughout her labor and dying; she did not accuse him that he be punished with her. To save her inseminator's name she gave silent birth.

He may have been somebody in her own household, but intercourse with a man outside the family would have been no less abhorrent. All the village were kinsmen, and the titles shouted in loud country voices never let kinship be forgotten. Any man within visiting distance would have been neutralized as a lover—"brother," "younger brother," "older brother"—one hundred and fifteen relationship titles. Parents researched birth charts probably not so much to assure good fortune as to circumvent incest in a population that has but one hundred surnames. Everybody has eight million relatives. How useless then sexual mannerisms, how dangerous.

As if it came from an atavism[6] deeper than fear, I used to add "brother" silently to boys' names. It hexed the boys, who would or would not ask me to dance, and made them less scary and as familiar and deserving of benevolence as girls.

But, of course, I hexed myself also—no dates. I should have stood up, both arms waving, and shouted out across libraries, "Hey, you! Love me back." I had no idea, though, now to make attraction selective, how to control its direction and magnitude. If I made myself American-pretty so that the five or six Chinese boys in the class fell in love with me, everyone else—the Caucasian, Negro, and Japanese boys—would too. Sisterliness, dignified and honorable, made much more sense.

Attraction eludes control so stubbornly that whole societies designed to organize relationships among people cannot keep order, not even when they bind people to one another from childhood and raise them together. Among the very poor and the wealthy, brothers married their adopted sisters, like doves. Our family allowed some romance, paying adult brides' prices and providing dowries so that their sons and daughters could marry strangers. Marriage promises to turn strangers into friendly relatives—a nation of siblings.

In the village structure, spirits shimmered among the live creatures, balanced and held in equilibrium by time and land. But one human being flaring up into violence could open up a black hole, a maelstrom[7] that pulled in the sky. The frightened villagers, who depended on one another to maintain the real, went to my aunt to show her a personal, physical representation of the break she had made in the "roundness." Misallying couples snapped off the future, which was to be embodied in true offspring. The villagers punished her for acting as if she could have a private life, secret and apart from them.

If my aunt had betrayed the family at a time of large grain yields and peace, when many boys were born, and wings were being built on many houses, perhaps she might have escaped such severe punishment. But the men—hungry, greedy, tired of planting in dry soil—had been forced to leave the village in order to send food-money home. There were ghost plagues, bandit plagues, wars with the Japanese, floods. My Chinese brother and sister had died of an unknown sickness. Adultery, perhaps only a mistake during good times, became a crime when the village needed food.

---

6. A trait with origins farther back than the preceding generation—a throwback.

7. A powerful, violent whirlpool.

The round moon cakes and round doorways, the round tables of graduated size that fit one roundness inside another, round windows and rice bowls—these talismans had lost their power to warn this family of the law: a family must be whole, faithfully keeping the descent line by having sons to feed the old and the dead, who in turn look after the family. The villagers came to show my aunt and her lover-in-hiding a broken house. The villagers were speeding up the circling of events because she was too shortsighted to see that her infidelity had already harmed the village, that waves of consequences would return unpredictably, sometimes in disguise, as now, to hurt her. This roundness had to be made coin-sized so that she would see its circumference: punish her at the birth of her baby. Awaken her to the inexorable. People who refused fatalism because they could invent small resources insisted on culpability. Deny accidents and wrest fault from the stars.

After the villagers left, their lanterns now scattering in various directions toward home, the family broke their silence and cursed her. "Aiaa, we're going to die. Death is coming. Death is coming. Look what you've done. You've killed us. Ghost! Dead ghost! Ghost! You've never been born." She ran out into the fields, far enough from the house so that she could no longer hear their voices, and pressed herself against the earth, her own land no more. When she felt the birth coming, she thought that she had been hurt. Her body seized together. "They've hurt me too much," she thought. "This is gall, and it will kill me." With forehead and knees against the earth, her body convulsed and then relaxed. She turned on her back, lay on the ground. The black well of sky and stars went out and out and out forever; her body and her complexity seemed to disappear. She was one of the stars, a bright dot in blackness, without home, without a companion, in eternal cold and silence. An agoraphobia[8] rose in her, speeding higher and higher, bigger and bigger; she would not be able to contain it; there would be no end to fear.

Flayed, unprotected against space, she felt pain return, focusing her body. This pain chilled her—a cold, steady kind of surface pain. Inside, spasmodically, the other pain, the pain of the child, heated her. For hours she lay on the ground, alternately body and space. Sometimes a vision of normal comfort obliterated reality: she saw the family in the evening gambling at the dinner table, the young people massaging their elder's backs. She saw them congratulating one another, high joy on the mornings the rice shoots came up. When these pictures burst, the stars drew yet further apart. Black space opened.

She got to her feet to fight better and remembered that old-fashioned women gave birth in their pigsties to fool the jealous, pain-dealing gods, who do not snatch piglets. Before the next spasms could stop her, she ran to the pigsty, each step a rushing out into emptiness. She climbed over the fence and knelt in the dirt. It was good to have a fence enclosing her, a tribal person alone.

Laboring, this woman who had carried her child as a foreign growth that sickened her every day, expelled it at last. She reached down to touch the hot, wet, moving mass, surely smaller than anything human, and could feel that it was human after all—fingers, toes, nails, nose. She pulled it up on to her belly, and it lay curled there, but in the air, feet precisely tucked one

8. An abnormal fear of open space.

under the other. She opened her loose shirt and buttoned the child inside. After resting, it squirmed and thrashed and she pushed it up to her breast. It turned its head this way and that until it found her nipple. There, it made little snuffling noises. She clenched her teeth at its preciousness, lovely as a young calf, a piglet, a little dog.

She may have gone to the pigsty as a last act of responsibility: she would protect this child as she had protected its father. It would look after her soul, leaving supplies on her grave. But how would this tiny child without family find her grave when there would be no marker for her anywhere, neither in the earth nor the family hall? No one would give her a family hall name. She had taken the child with her into the wastes. At its birth the two of them had felt the same raw pain of separation, a wound that only the family pressing tight could close. A child with no descent line would not soften her life but only trail after her, ghostlike, begging her to give it purpose. At dawn the villagers on their way to the fields would stand around the fence and look.

Full of milk, the little ghost slept. When it awoke, she hardened her breasts against the milk that crying loosens. Toward morning she picked up the baby and walked to the well.

Carrying the baby to the well shows loving. Otherwise abandon it. Turn its face into the mud. Mothers who love their children take them along. It was probably a girl; there is some hope of forgiveness for boys.

"Don't tell anyone you had an aunt. Your father does not want to hear her name. She has never been born." I have believed that sex was unspeakable and words so strong and fathers so frail that "aunt" would do my father mysterious harm. I have thought that my family, having settled among immigrants who had also been their neighbors in the ancestral land, needed to clean their name, and a wrong word would incite the kinspeople even here. But there is more to this silence: they want me to participate in her punishment. And I have.

In the twenty years since I heard this story I have not asked for details nor said my aunt's name; I do not know it. People who can comfort the dead can also chase after them to hurt them further—a reverse ancestor worship. The real punishment was not the raid swiftly inflicted by the villagers, but the family's deliberately forgetting her. Her betrayal so maddened them, they saw to it that she would suffer forever, even after death. Always hungry, always needing, she would have to beg food from other ghosts, snatch and steal it from those whose living descendants give them gifts. She would have to fight the ghosts massed at crossroads for the buns a few thoughtful citizens leave to decoy her away from village and home so that the ancestral spirits could feast unharassed. At peace, they could act like gods, not ghosts, their descent lines providing them with paper suits and dresses, spirit money, paper houses, paper automobiles, chicken, meat, and rice[9] into eternity— essences delivered up in smoke and flames, steam and incense rising from each rice bowl. In an attempt to make the Chinese care for people outside the family, Chairman Mao[1] encourages us now to give our paper replicas to the spirits of outstanding soldiers and workers, no matter whose ancestors

9. Traditionally, offerings left at the graves of ancestors.
1. Mao Tse-Tung (1893–1976), head of the Chinese Communist Party and leader of China from 1949 to 1959 and 1969 to 1976.

they may be. My aunt remains forever hungry. Goods are not distributed evenly among the dead.

My aunt haunts me—her ghost drawn to me because now, after fifty years of neglect, I alone devote pages of paper to her, though not origamied into houses and clothes. I do not think she always means me well. I am telling on her, and she was a spite suicide, drowning herself in the drinking water. The Chinese are always very frightened of the drowned one, whose weeping ghost, wet hair hanging and skin bloated, waits silently by the water to pull down a substitute.

1976

BILLY COLLINS
b. 1941

The voice in a Billy Collins poem is so intimate and immediate that we feel we are in the same room with the poet. Collins imagines poet and reader sitting together at a breakfast table: "I will lean forward, / elbows on the table, / with something to tell you / and you will look up, as always, / your spoon dripping with milk, ready to listen" ("A Portrait of the Reader with a Bowl of Cereal"). The colloquial voice in his poems charms us with its air of spontaneous expression, its modesty, its humor. If some of his poems coast on charm alone, Collins's best work takes us on a surprising ride: its strange and unexpected associations deepen the familiar into the mysterious or make the mysterious familiar.

Describing the structures of his poetry, Collins says, "We are attempting, all the time, to create a logical, rational path through the day. To the left and right there are an amazing set of distractions that we can't afford to follow. But the poet is willing to stop anywhere." His poems often proceed as accounts of a day and its distractions, as in "Tuesday, June 4, 1991." At the same time the formal shapeliness of Collins's work endows ordinary activity with a strange and pleasing formality and turns it, line by measured line and stanza by stanza, into a ritual including both the pleasures and the pathos of life. These poems present a humorous self-awareness about the speaker's dramatizing and obsessive love of distraction—anything, no matter how insignificant, can carry off his attention—and one thing that is so welcome about Collins's poems is that they are funny. Only on later readings do we realize that they are also sad. When he looks over the edges of domestic life there is blankness; unlike the work of a Jorie Graham or a Charles Wright, a Collins poem evokes no metaphysical structures that might sustain this fragile world. Yet (in the Irish poet William Butler Yeats's phrase) Collins loves "what vanishes"—the day in June, the good meal, even one's memories. This knowledge of how things large and small disappear is a great equalizer. The humor in Collins's poetry puts this equalizing principle to work; he deflates the grandiose and subjects large statements of truth to the test of the particular. Collins's titles, imaginative and playful, suggest the way he alights on small, usually trivial instances in which life's strangeness and mystery flash out: "Weighing the Dog," "I Chop Some Parsley While Listening to Art Blakey's Version of 'Three Blind Mice.'" Other titles signal the way he grounds the improbable within the everyday: "Taking off Emily Dickinson's Clothes," "Shoveling Snow with Buddha."

Collins's collections of poems include *Questions about Angels* (1977), *The Art of Drowning* (1995), *Picnic, Lightning* (1998), *Sailing Alone around the World: New and*

Selected Poems (2001), *Nine Horses* (2003) and *The Trouble with Poetry and Other Poems* (2005). He served as poet laureate of the United States from 2001 to 2003. Born in New York City (in a hospital where, as he likes to note, William Carlos Williams worked as a pediatric resident), Collins teaches at Lehman College of the City University. Walking the city streets animates him and inflects some of his poems in a way that recalls the work of Frank O'Hara, with whom Collins shares an idiomatic American voice, colloquial and understated, shaped by jazz and the blues. Collins's work often plays with the melody of a pentameter line as a jazz musician plays on and off the melody of a song; the pentameter is an undertone from which a more idiosyncratic rhythm moves around and away. While the rhythms of Collins's poetry often enforce a slowing-down, a tender lingering over everyday life, their breezy tone and quick humor seem to suggest that nothing too serious is going on. It is as if Collins were fending off the large, prophetic claims made by visionary poets (early in his career he earned a Ph.D. at the University of California at Riverside, specializing in the Romantic period), even as some of his poems are riffs on the Romantic tradition. Such Collins poems as "Keats's Handwriting" and "Lines Composed Over Three Thousand Miles from Tintern Abbey" deflate the romantic sublime and substitute for it a vision self-deprecating and humorous. Thus when we hear nightingales in a Collins poem, they're a group singing on the gospel radio station ("Sunday Morning with the Sensational Nightingales").

Collins's modest claims for poetry and the fact that his work is so appealing and accessible can lead us to underestimate the necessity and reward of rereading him. The best of his poems open up a moment like a series of nested boxes; if we read too quickly, we miss the pleasure and surprise of intricate connections and deepening discoveries. A Collins poem has a spontaneity that yields immediate pleasure, but only when we listen again more attentively do we recognize the art that makes itself look easy.

Forgetfulness

The name of the author is the first to go
followed obediently by the title, the plot,
the heartbreaking conclusion, the entire novel
which suddenly becomes one you have never read, never even heard of,

as if, one by one, the memories you used to harbor   5
decided to retire to the southern hemisphere of the brain,
to a little fishing village where there are no phones.

Long ago you kissed the names of the nine Muses goodbye,
and watched the quadratic equation pack its bag,
and even now as you memorize the order of the planets,   10

something else is slipping away, a state flower perhaps,
the address of an uncle, the capital of Paraguay.

Whatever it is you are struggling to remember
it is not poised on the tip of your tongue,
not even lurking in some obscure corner of your spleen.   15

It has floated away down a dark mythological river
whose name begins with an *L* as far as you can recall,
well on your own way to oblivion where you will join those
who have even forgotten how to swim and how to ride a bicycle.

No wonder you rise in the middle of the night   20
to look up the date of a famous battle in a book on war.
No wonder the moon in the window seems to have drifted
out of a love poem that you used to know by heart.

                                                                    1991

I Chop Some Parsley While Listening to Art Blakey's[1] Version of "Three Blind Mice"

And I start wondering how they came to be blind.
If it was congenital, they could be brothers and sisters,
and I think of the poor mother
brooding over her sightless young triplets.

Or was it a common accident, all three caught   5
in a searing explosion, a fireworks perhaps?
If not,
if each came to his or her blindness separately,

how did they ever manage to find one another?
Would it not be difficult for a blind mouse   10
to locate even one fellow mouse with vision
let alone two other blind ones?

And how, in their tiny darkness,
could they possibly have run after a farmer's wife
or anyone else's wife for that matter?   15
Not to mention why.

Just so she could cut off their tails
with a carving knife, is the cynic's answer,
but the thought of them without eyes
and now without tails to trail through the moist grass   20

or slip around the corner of a baseboard
has the cynic who always lounges within me
up off his couch and at the window
trying to hide the rising softness that he feels.

By now I am on to dicing an onion   25
which might account for the wet stinging
in my own eyes, though Freddie Hubbard's
mournful trumpet on "Blue Moon,"

1. Jazz drummer and bandleader (1919–1990).

which happens to be the next cut,[2]
cannot be said to be making matters any better.   30

                                                                 1998

The Night House

Every day the body works in the fields of the world
mending a stone wall
or swinging a sickle through the tall grass—
the grass of civics, the grass of money—
and every night the body curls around itself   5
and listens for the soft bells of sleep.

But the heart is restless and rises
from the body in the middle of the night,
leaves the trapezoidal bedroom
with its thick, pictureless walls   10
to sit by herself at the kitchen table
and heat some milk in a pan.

And the mind gets up too, puts on a robe
and goes downstairs, lights a cigarette,
and opens a book on engineering.   15
Even the conscience awakens
and roams from room to room in the dark,
darting away from every mirror like a strange fish.

And the soul is up on the roof
in her nightdress, straddling the ridge,   20
singing a song about the wildness of the sea
until the first rip of pink appears in the sky.
Then, they all will return to the sleeping body
the way a flock of birds settles back into a tree,

resuming their daily colloquy,   25
talking to each other or themselves
even through the heat of the long afternoons.
Which is why the body—that house of voices—
sometimes puts down its metal tongs, its needle, or its pen
to stare into the distance,   30

to listen to all its names being called
before bending again to its labor.

                                                                 1998

2. The next song on *Three Blind Mice, Vol. 1*, a 1962 live recording by Art Blakey's Jazz Messengers, which
included Freddie Hubbard (b. 1938).

SIMON J. ORTIZ
b. 1941

In his poem "A Designated National Park," Simon J. Ortiz tells of visiting Montezuma Castle in Verde Valley, Arizona, where he experiences as present in himself the life of the people there: "Hear / in my cave, sacred song. / Morning feeling, sacred song. / We shall plant today." His connection to that landscape, however, is complicated by the fact that it is now a "DESIGNATED FEDERAL RECREATION FEE AREA": "This morning / I have to buy a permit to get back home." Ortiz's treatment of Verde Valley is characteristic of the way he inhabits a conflicted landscape. He was born and raised in the Acoma Pueblo Community in Albuquerque, New Mexico. One meaning of the name *Acoma* is "the place that always was," and in this sense it transcends the poet's place of origin and represents for him the Native American way of life. Ortiz continually returns to this abiding sense of origin after traveling great distances from it. Often his poems enact a journey, and as Joseph Bruhac reminds us, in American Indian cultures the theme of traveling implicitly recalls the "tragic epic movements of Native American nations." Many of Ortiz's poems dramatize his disorientation as he moves within an America where Indian names are reduced to billboard signs, where rivers burn from industrial wastes and construction fills up the spaces of the earth. His sense of contemporary life, especially its absurdities, is acute.

But the America he travels conceals within it an older landscape animated by spirit, where the earth is alive with "wind visions" and "The Mountains dream / about pine brothers and friends" ("Vision Shadows"); to travel it is to seek "the center of the center" ("Between Albuquerque and Santa Fe"), the place where the spirits enter the world. Asked in an interview, "Why do you write?" Ortiz once responded, "Because Indians always tell a story. . . . The only way to continue is to tell a story and there is no other way. Your children will not survive unless you tell something about them—how they were born, how they came to this certain place, how they continued." Tellingly, Ortiz chose to reprint these comments at the beginning of his collection *A Good Journey* (1977). The stories his poems narrate are evidence that the Native American way of life is continuous, despite all the forces that attempt to eradicate it. But his work also tells of the painful costs involved in survival.

After receiving his early education at a Bureau of Indian Affairs school on the Acoma Reservation, Ortiz later attended the University of New Mexico and the University of Iowa. He has since taught at San Diego State University and the University of New Mexico. "I never decided to become a poet," Ortiz has said, suggesting that his relatives transmitted to him the power of words. "An old-man relative with a humpback used to come to our home when I was a child, and he would carry me on his back. He told me stories. . . . That contact must have contributed the language of myself." His father, a stonemason, carpenter, and woodcarver, would talk and sing as he worked. In "A Story of How a Wall Stands," he remembers his father saying "Underneath / what looks like loose stone, / there is stone woven together." This sense of underlying connection is true of Ortiz's poetry as well, often at its finest when revealing how a moment or event fits into the ongoing cycles celebrated by ritual. His best poems are sometimes surprising in the way the apparently loose details suddenly blaze into an arrangement. Characteristically, this happens through powerful repetitions culminating in the last movements of a poem, a technique that depends on rereading. Ortiz's collection *Going for Rain* appeared in 1976; its poems sometimes show a writer whose strong feelings have not yet found a distinctive language or rhythm. His next book, *The Good Journey,* is more assured and its range significantly broader. His work also includes *From Sand Creek,* which won the 1982 Pushcart Prize; *A Poem Is a Journey* (1981); and an edition that collects earlier volumes together with new work, *Woven Stone* (1992). *After and Before the Lightning* was published in 1994; his short stories were collected in *Men on the Moon* (1999). Ortiz's mission—

continuance and preservation—sometimes allows a didactic impulse to shape his work
too rigidly. But his finest poems have a richness of experience and a vital, imaginative
sense of the earth that refuses any single conceptual or moral frame.

A recurring image in several Ortiz poems is the "Wisconsin horse" he once saw
standing "within a fence // silent in the hot afternoon" while one mile away new construction was going on: "I tell the horse, / 'That's America building something' " ("The
Wisconsin Horse"). The spirit of the horse, restrained by the chainlink fence and
threatened by the approaching construction, suggests Ortiz's sense of constriction in
the VA hospitals (his experience in one of these prompted his sequence *Poems from
the Veterans Hospital*), as well as in small-town bars, in the Salvation Army store, or in
the boundaries of the designated National Parks. Something threatens to break loose
in these poems; feelings precariously held in check shake the formal structures. Other
poems, like "Earth and Rain, the Plants & Sun," have the freedom and buoyancy of
the hawk's flight; the words move in a space that seems immense. Instead of explosive
anger or despair, the tone of the poem is close to song or prayer. What is so moving in
Ortiz's work is that these voices are both his; together they suggest the fracture of identity and the possibility of reintegration.

Earth and Rain, the Plants & Sun

Once near San Ysidro
on the way to Colorado,
I stopped and looked.
The sound of a meadowlark
through smell of fresh cut alfalfa.   5

Raho would say,
"Look, Dad." A hawk

sweeping
        its wings

clear through   10
        the blue
of whole and pure
            the wind
                the sky.

It is writhing   15
overhead.
Hear. The Bringer.
        The Thunderer.

Sunlight falls
through cloud curtains,   20
a straight bright shaft.

It falls,
    it falls,
        down
            to earth,   25
a green plant.

Today, the Katzina[1] come.
The dancing prayers.

Many times, the Katzina.
The dancing prayers.   30
It shall not end,
son, it will not end,
this love.

Again and again,
the earth is new again.   35
They come, listen, listen.
Hold on to your mother's hand.
They come

O great joy, they come.
The plants with bells.   40
The stones with voices.
Listen, son, hold my hand.

                                                        1977

Vision Shadows

Wind visions are honest.
Eagles clearly soar
to the craggy peaks
of the mind.
The mind is full   5
of sunprayer
and childlaughter.

The Mountains dream
about pine brothers and friends,
the mystic realm of boulders   10
which shelter
rabbits, squirrels, wrens.
They believe in the power.
They also believe
in quick eagle death.   15

The eagle loops
into the wind power.
He can see a million miles
and more because of it.

All believe things   20
of origin and solitude.

1. Or Kachina; spirits of the invisible life forces of
the Pueblo of North America. The Kachinas are
impersonated by elaborately costumed masked
male members of the tribes who visit Pueblo villages the first half of the year. Although not worshiped, Kachinas are greatly revered, and one of
their main purposes is to bring rain for the spring
crops.

But what has happened
(I hear strange news from Wyoming
of thallium sulphate.[1] Ranchers
bearing arms in helicopters.)   25
to these visions?
I hear foreign tremors.
Breath comes thin and shredded.
I hear the scabs of strange deaths
falling off.   30

Snake hurries through the grass.
Coyote is befuddled by his own tricks.
And Bear whimpers pain into the wind.

Poisonous fumes cross our sacred paths.
The wind is still.   35
O Blue Sky, O Mountain, O Spirit, O
what has stopped?

Eagles tumble dumbly into shadows
that swallow them with dull thuds.
The sage can't breathe.   40
Jackrabbit is lonely and alone
with eagle gone.

It is painful, aiiee, without visions
to soothe dry whimpers
or repair the flight of eagle, our own brother.   45

                                                                        1977

From Poems from the Veterans Hospital

Travelling

A man has been in the VAH Library all day long,
looking at the maps, the atlas, and the globe,
finding places.
         Acapulco, the Bay of Bengal,
Antarctica, Madagascar, Rome, Luxembourg,   5
places.

He writes their names on a letter pad, hurries
to another source, asks the librarian for a book
but it is out and he looks hurt and then he rushes
back to the globe, turns it a few times and finds   10
Yokohama and then the Aleutian Islands.

---

1. A chemical used by farmers as a rat poison.

Later on, he studies Cape Cod for a moment,
a faraway glee on his face, in his eyes.
He is Gauguin, he is Coyote,[1] he is who he is,
travelling the known and unknown places,   15
travelling, travelling.

                                                             1977

From From Sand Creek

At the Salvation Army
a clerk
caught me
wandering
among old spoons   5
            and knives,
                sweaters and shoes.

I couldn't have stolen anything;
my life was stolen already.

In protest though,   10
I should have stolen.
My life. My life.

She caught me;
Carson[1] caught Indians,
secured them with his lies.   15
Bound them with his belief.

After winter,
our own lives fled.

I reassured her
what she believed.   20
Bought a sweater.

And fled.

I should have stolen.
My life. My life.

                                                             1981

1. The trickster figure in southwestern and other
Native American tales. The French painter Paul
Gauguin (1848–1903) left his home in France for
Tahiti and the Marquesas Islands.
1. Christopher ("Kit") Carson (1809–1868), trapper, scout, Indian agent, and soldier, was hired by
the government to help control the Navajo. Beginning in 1863 he waged a brutal economic war
against the tribe, marching through the heart of
their territory to destroy their crops, orchards, and
livestock. In 1864 most Navajo surrendered to Carson, who forced nearly eight thousand Navajo
men, women, and children to take what came to be
called the "Long Walk" of three hundred miles
from Arizona to Fort Sumner, New Mexico, where
they remained in disease-ridden confinement until
1868.

GLORIA ANZALDÚA
1942–2004

The term "Chicano" was originally pejorative, used on both sides of the border to identify Mexican Americans of the lowest social class. Just as the once demeaning label "black" was appropriated and revalued by African Americans during the civil rights, black power, and black arts movements of the 1960s, so "Chicano" was embraced by Hispanic activists as a badge of pride, especially among university students and farm workers. By 1987, when the first edition of Gloria Anzaldúa's *Borderlands / La Frontera: The New Mestiza* appeared, two more politically sensitive terms had been added to the sociocultural lexicon: "Chicana," specifically identifying Mexican American women, particularly in light of their announced aims and the general interests of the Chicano movement, and "mestiza," describing Chicana women who are especially concerned with a heritage that is both Chicana and Native American. Together with Cherríe Moraga, her coeditor on *This Bridge Called My Back: Writings by Radical Women of Color* (1981), Anzaldúa emerged as a pioneer in both the writing and the study of Chicana literature.

The daughter of ranchers in Jesus Maria of the Valley, Texas, Anzaldúa labored as a migrant fieldworker before earning a B.A. from Pan American University (1969) and an M.A. from the University of Texas at Austin (1973); she did further graduate study at the University of California at Santa Cruz. She taught creative writing, Chicano studies, and feminist studies at major universities from Texas to California. She published the novel *La Prieta* (Spanish for "the dark one," 1997), other anthologies, and a series of children's books, the most notable of which—*Prietita and the Ghost Woman / Prietita y La Llorona* (1996)—introduces young readers to an important figure in Chicana culture.

La Llorona is one of the three principal representations of women in Mexican culture: *La Virgen de Guadalupe,* a vision of the Virgin Mary who appeared to an Indian, Juan Diego, in 1531 on a hillside outside Mexico City that was sacred to the worship of Tonantzín, the Indian "Mother of Heaven"; *La Chingada,* incorrectly translated as "The Raped One" but whom Anzaldúa insists be accurately identified as "The Fucked One," the deposed Aztec princess (also known as La Malinche, Doña Marina, and Malintzín Tenepal) who served as the translator for and lover of the Spanish military leader Hernan Cortés during his consolidation of colonial power between 1519 and 1522; and *La Llorona,* "The Woman Who Cries," a spurned mistress of Mexican legend who drowned her children and was fated to eternally seek their recovery. Each of these representations metaphorically controls a narrow realm of possibility for Chicanas. At the core of Anzaldúa's work is the belief that because metaphors structure the way we think, the metaphorical influences of these types of women must be reshaped so that Chicanas can escape the binary constraint of being judged as either a virgin or a whore (and nothing else). *Borderlands/La Frontera* is Anzaldúa's most comprehensive effort toward that restructuring.

Although written mainly in English, the personal essays and narrative poem printed here reflect another key part of Anzaldúa's art: not only did she wish to write in Spanish from time to time but she did not always translate that Spanish into English. When she did not provide such a translation in a piece that is primarily in English, she wanted to speak directly to those who either could not or chose not to communicate in English. This practice, much like her blending of fiction, poetry, social commentary, and personal memoir, helps create the narrative richness that characterizes her work.

The text is from the second edition of *Borderlands/La Frontera* (1999).

How to Tame a Wild Tongue

"We're going to have to control your
tongue," the dentist says, pulling out all the metal from my mouth. Silver bits
plop and tinkle into the basin. My mouth is a motherlode.

The dentist is cleaning out my roots. I
get a whiff of the stench when I gasp. "I can't cap that tooth yet, you're still
draining," he says.

"We're going to have to do something
about your tongue," I hear the anger rising in his voice. My tongue keeps
pushing out the wads of cotton, pushing back the drills, the long thin needles. "I've never seen anything as strong or as stubborn," he says. And I think,
how do you tame a wild tongue, train it to be quiet, how do you bridle and
saddle it? How do you make it lie down?

> "Who is to say that robbing a people of
> its language is less violent than war?"
> —Ray Gwyn Smith[1]

I remember being caught speaking Spanish at recess—that was good for
three licks on the knuckles with a sharp ruler. I remember being sent to the corner of the classroom for "talking back" to the Anglo teacher when all I was trying to do was tell her how to pronounce my name. "If you want to be American,
speak 'American.' If you don't like it, go back to Mexico where you belong."

"I want you to speak English. *Pa'hallar buen trabajo tienes que saber hablar
el inglés bien. Qué vale toda tu educación si todavía hablas inglés con un
'accent,'* " my mother would say, mortified that I spoke English like a Mexican. At Pan American University, I, and all Chicano students were required
to take two speech classes. Their purpose: to get rid of our accents.

Attacks on one's form of expression with the intent to censor are a violation of the First Amendment. *El Anglo con cara de inocente nos arrancó la
lengua.* Wild tongues can't be tamed, they can only be cut out.

Overcoming the Tradition of Silence

> *Ahogadas, escupimos el oscuro.*
> *Peleando con nuestra propia sombra*
> *el silencio nos sepulta.*

En boca cerrada no entran moscas. "Flies don't enter a closed mouth" is a
saying I kept hearing when I was a child. *Ser habladora* was to be a gossip and
a liar, to talk too much. *Muchachitas bien criadas,* well-bred girls don't
answer back. *Es una falta de respeto* to talk back to one's mother or father. I
remember one of the sins I'd recite to the priest in the confession box the few
times I went to confession: talking back to my mother, *hablar pa' 'trás, repelar.
Hocicona, repelona, chismosa,* having a big mouth, questioning, carrying tales
are all signs of being *mal criada.* In my culture they are all words that are
derogatory if applied to women—I've never heard them applied to men.

1. Ray Gwyn Smith [(b. 1944), Welsh painter and art educator active in the United States], *Moorland Is
Cold Country,* unpublished book [Anzaldúa's note].

The first time I heard two women, a Puerto Rican and a Cuban, say the word *"nosotras,"* I was shocked. I had not known the word existed. Chicanas use *nosotros* whether we're male or female. We are robbed of our female being by the masculine plural. Language is a male discourse.

> And our tongues have become
> dry   the wilderness has
> dried out our tongues   and
> we have forgotten speech.
> —Irena Klepfisz[2]

Even our own people, other Spanish speakers *nos quieren poner candados en la boca.* They would hold us back with their bag of *reglas de academia.*

Oyé como ladra: el lenguaje de la frontera

> *Quien tiene boca se equivoca.*
> —Mexican saying

"*Pocho,*[3] cultural traitor, you're speaking the oppressor's language by speaking English, you're ruining the Spanish language," I have been accused by various Latinos and Latinas. Chicano Spanish is considered by the purist and by most Latinos deficient, a mutilation of Spanish.

But Chicano Spanish is a border tongue which developed naturally. Change, *evolución, enriquecimiento de palabras nuevas por invención o adopción* have created variants of Chicano Spanish, *un nuevo, lenguaje. Un lenguaje que corresponde a un modo de vivir.* Chicano Spanish is not incorrect, it is a living language.

For a people who are neither Spanish nor live in a country in which Spanish is the first language; for a people who live in a country in which English is the reigning tongue but who are not Anglo; for a people who cannot entirely identify with either standard (formal, Castillian) Spanish nor standard English, what recourse is left to them but to create their own language? A language which they can connect their identity to, one capable of communicating the realities and values true to themselves—a language with terms that are neither *español ni inglés,* but both. We speak a patois, a forked tongue, a variation of two languages.

Chicano Spanish sprang out of the Chicanos' need to identify ourselves as a distinct people. We needed a language with which we could communicate with ourselves, a secret language. For some of us, language is a homeland closer than the Southwest—for many Chicanos today live in the Midwest and the East. And because we are a complex, heterogeneous people, we speak many languages. Some of the languages we speak are:

1. Standard English
2. Working class and slang English
3. Standard Spanish
4. Standard Mexican Spanish

2. Irena Klepfisz [(b. 1941), North American critic], "*Di rayze aheym/The Journey Home,*" in *The Tribe of Dina: A Jewish Women's Anthology,* Melanie Kaye/Kantrowitz and Irena Klepfisz, eds. (Montpelier, VT: Sinister Wisdom Books, 1986), 49 [Anzaldúa's note].

3. An anglicized Mexican or American of Mexican origin who speaks Spanish with an accent characteristic of North Americans and who distorts and reconstructs the language according to the influence of English. Anzaldúa offers a definition later in this selection.

5. North Mexican Spanish dialect
6. Chicano Spanish (Texas, New Mexico, Arizona and California have regional variations)
7. Tex-Mex
8. *Pachuco* (called *caló*)

My "home" tongues are the languages I speak with my sister and brothers, with my friends. They are the last five listed, with 6 and 7 being closest to my heart. From school, the media and job situations, I've picked up standard and working class English. From Mamagrande Locha and from reading Spanish and Mexican literature, I've picked up Standard Spanish and Standard Mexican Spanish. From *los recién llegados*, Mexican immigrants, and *braceros*, I learned the North Mexican dialect. With Mexicans I'll try to speak either Standard Mexican Spanish or the North Mexican dialect. From my parents and Chicanos living in the Valley,[4] I picked up Chicano Texas Spanish, and I speak it with my mom; younger brother (who married a Mexican and who rarely mixes Spanish with English), aunts and older relatives.

With Chicanas from *Nuevo México* or *Arizona* I will speak Chicano Spanish a little, but often they don't understand what I'm saying. With most California Chicanas I speak entirely in English (unless I forget). When I first moved to San Francisco, I'd rattle off something in Spanish, unintentionally embarrassing them. Often it is only with another Chicana *tejana* that I can talk freely.

Words distorted by English are known as anglicisms or *pochismos*. The *pocho* is an anglicized Mexican or American of Mexican origin who speaks Spanish with an accent characteristic of North Americans and who distorts and reconstructs the language according to the influence of English.[5] Tex-Mex, or Spanglish, comes most naturally to me. I may switch back and forth from English to Spanish in the same sentence or in the same word. With my sister and my brother Nune and with Chicano *tejano* contemporaries I speak in Tex-Mex.

From kids and people my own age I picked up *Pachuco. Pachuco* (the language of the zoot suiters) is a language of rebellion, both against Standard Spanish and Standard English. It is a secret language. Adults of the culture and outsiders cannot understand it. It is made up of slang words from both English and Spanish. *Ruca* means girl or woman, *vato* means guy or dude, *chale* means no, *simón* means yes, *churo* is sure, talk is *periquiar, pigionear* means petting, *que gacho* means how nerdy, *ponte águila* means watch out, death is called *la pelona.* Through lack of practice and not having others who can speak it, I've lost most of the *Pachuco* tongue.

Chicano Spanish

Chicanos, after 250 years of Spanish/Anglo colonization have developed significant differences in the Spanish we speak. We collapse two adjacent vowels into a single syllable and sometimes shift the stress in certain words such as *maíz / maiz, cohete / cuete.* We leave out certain consonants when

---

4. I.e., of the Rio Grande River in southern Texas, bordering Mexico.
5. R. C. Ortega, *Dialectología Del Barrio*, trans. Hortencia S. Alwan (Los Angeles, CA: R. C. Ortega Publisher & Bookseller, 1977), 132 [Anzaldúa's note].

they appear between vowels: *lado/lao, mojado/mojao*. Chicanos from South Texas pronounced *f* as *j* as in *jue* (*fue*). Chicanos use "archaisms," words that are no longer in the Spanish language, words that have been evolved out. We say *semos, truje, haiga, ansina*, and *naiden*. We retain the "archaic" *j*, as in *jalar*, that derives from an earlier *h*, (the French *halar* or the Germanic *halon* which was lost to standard Spanish in the 16th century), but which is still found in several regional dialects such as the one spoken in South Texas. (Due to geography, Chicanos from the Valley of South Texas were cut off linguistically from other Spanish speakers. We tend to use words that the Spaniards brought over from Medieval Spain. The majority of the Spanish colonizers in Mexico and the Southwest came from Extremadura—Hernán Cortés was one of them—and Andalucía.[6] Andalucians pronounce *ll* like a *y*, and their *d*'s tend to be absorbed by adjacent vowels: *tirado* becomes *tirao*. They brought *el lenguaje popular, dialectos y regionalismos*.)[7]

Chicanos and other Spanish speakers also shift *ll* to *y* and *z* to *s*.[8] We leave out initial syllables, saying *tar* for *estar, toy* for *estoy*; *hora* for *ahora* (*cubanos* and *puertorriqueños* also leave out initial letters of some words.) We also leave out the final syllable such as *pa* for *para*. The intervocalic *y*, the *ll* as in *tortilla, ella, botella*, gets replaced by *tortia* or *tortiya, ea, botea*. We add an additional syllable at the beginning of certain words: *atocar* for *tocar, agastar* for *gastar*. Sometimes we'll say *lavaste las vacijas*, other times *lavates* (substituting the *ates* verb endings for the *aste*).

We use anglicisms, words borrowed from English: *bola* from ball, *carpeta* from carpet, *máchina de lavar* (instead of *lavadora*) from washing machine. Tex-Mex argot, created by adding a Spanish sound at the beginning or end of an English word such as *cookiar* for cook, *watchar* for watch, *parkiar* for park, and *rapiar* for rape, is the result of the pressures on Spanish speakers to adapt to English.

We don't use the word *vosotros/as* or its accompanying verb form. We don't say *claro* (to mean yes), *imagínate*, or *me emociona*, unless we picked up Spanish from Latinas, out of a book, or in a classroom. Other Spanish-speaking groups are going through the same, or similar, development in their Spanish.

Linguistic Terrorism

Deslenguadas. Somos los del español deficiente. We are your linguistic nightmare, your linguistic aberration, your linguistic *mestizaje*, the subject of your *burla*. Because we speak with tongues of fire we are culturally crucified. Racially, culturally and linguistically *somos huérfanos*—we speak an orphan tongue.

Chicanas who grew up speaking Chicano Spanish have internalized the belief that we speak poor Spanish. It is illegitimate, a bastard language. And because we internalize how our language has been used against us by the dominant culture, we use our language differences against each other. Chicana feminists often skirt around each other with suspicion and hesi-

6. Region in southern Spain. Extremadura is a city in central Spain. Cortés (1485–1547), Spanish soldier and explorer active in Mexico.
7. Eduardo Hernandéz-Chávez, Andrew D. Cohen, and Anthony F. Beltramo, *El Lenguaje de*

los Chicanos: Regional and Social Characteristics of Language Used by Mexican Americans (Arlington, VA: Center for Applied Linguistics, 1975), 39 [Anzaldúa's note].
8. Hernandéz-Chávez, xvii [Anzaldúa's note].

tation. For the longest time I couldn't figure it out. Then it dawned on me. To be close to another Chicana is like looking into the mirror. We are afraid of what we'll see there. *Pena*. Shame. Low estimation of self. In childhood we are told that our language is wrong. Repeated attacks on our native tongue diminish our sense of self. The attacks continue throughout our lives.

Chicanas feel uncomfortable talking in Spanish to Latinas, afraid of their censure. Their language was not outlawed in their countries. They had a whole lifetime of being immersed in their native tongue; generations, centuries in which Spanish was a first language, taught in school, heard on radio and TV, and read in the newspaper.

If a person, Chicana or Latina, has a low estimation of my native tongue, she also has a low estimation of me. Often with *mexicanas y latinas* we'll speak English as a neutral language. Even among Chicanas we tend to speak English at parties or conferences. Yet, at the same time, we're afraid the other will think we're *agringadas* because we don't speak Chicano Spanish. We oppress each other trying to out-Chicano each other, vying to be the "real" Chicanas, to speak like Chicanos. There is no one Chicano language just as there is no one Chicano experience. A monolingual Chicana whose first language is English or Spanish is just as much a Chicana as one who speaks several variants of Spanish. A Chicana from Michigan or Chicago or Detroit is just as much a Chicana as one from the Southwest. Chicano Spanish is as diverse linguistically as it is regionally.

By the end of this century, Spanish speakers will comprise the biggest minority group in the U.S., a country where students in high schools and colleges are encouraged to take French classes because French is considered more "cultured." But for a language to remain alive it must be used.[9] By the end of this century English, and not Spanish, will be the mother tongue of most Chicanos and Latinos.

So, if you want to really hurt me, talk badly about my language. Ethnic identity is twin skin to linguistic identity—I am my language. Until I can take pride in my language, I cannot take pride in myself. Until I can accept as legitimate Chicano Texas Spanish, Tex-Mex and all the other languages I speak, I cannot accept the legitimacy of myself. Until I am free to write bilingually and to switch codes without having always to translate, while I still have to speak English or Spanish when I would rather speak Spanglish, and as long as I have to accommodate the English speakers rather than having them accommodate me, my tongue will be illegitimate.

I will no longer be made to feel ashamed of existing. I will have my voice: Indian, Spanish, white. I will have my serpent's tongue—my woman's voice, my sexual voice, my poet's voice. I will overcome the tradition of silence.

> My fingers
> move sly against your palm
> Like women everywhere, we speak in code. . . .
>
> —Melanie Kaye/Kantrowitz[1]

9. Irena Klepfisz, "Secular Jewish Identity: Yidishkayt in America," in *The Tribe of Dina*, Kaye/Kantrowitz, eds., 43 [Anzaldúa's note].
1. Melanie Kaye/Kantrowitz, "Sign," in *We Speak* in Code: Poems and Other Writings (Pittsburgh, PA: Motheroot Publications, Inc., 1980), 85 [Anzaldúa's note].

"Vistas," corridos, y comida: My Native Tongue

In the 1960s, I read my first Chicano novel. It was *City of Night* by John Rechy[2] a gay Texan, son of a Scottish father and a Mexican mother. For days I walked around in stunned amazement that a Chicano could write and could get published. When I read *I Am Joaquín*[3] I was surprised to see a bilingual book by a Chicano in print. When I saw poetry written in Tex-Mex for the first time, a feeling of pure joy flashed through me. I felt like we really existed as a people. In 1971, when I started teaching High School English to Chicano students, I tried to supplement the required texts with works by Chicanos, only to be reprimanded and forbidden to do so by the principal. He claimed that I was supposed to teach "American" and English literature. At the risk of being fired, I swore my students to secrecy and slipped in Chicano short stories, poems, a play. In graduate school, while working toward a Ph.D., I had to "argue" with one advisor after the other, semester after semester, before I was allowed to make Chicano literature an area of focus.

Even before I read books by Chicanos or Mexicans, it was the Mexican movies I saw at the drive-in—the Thursday night special of $1.00 a carload— that gave me a sense of belonging. "*Vámonos a las vistas,*" my mother would call out and we'd all—grandmother, brothers, sister and cousins—squeeze into the car. We'd wolf down cheese and bologna white bread sandwiches while watching Pedro Infante in melodramatic tear-jerkers like *Nosotros los pobres,*[4] the first "real" Mexican movie (that was not an imitation of European movies). I remember seeing *Cuando los hijos se van*[5] and surmising that all Mexican movies played up the love a mother has for her children and what ungrateful sons and daughters suffer when they are not devoted to their mothers. I remember the singing-type "westerns" of Jorge Negrete and Miguel Aceves Mejía.[6] When watching Mexican movies, I felt a sense of homecoming as well as alienation. People who were to amount to something didn't go to Mexican movies, or *bailes* or tune their radios to *bolero, rancherita,* and *corrido* music.

The whole time I was growing up, there was *norteño* music sometimes called North Mexican border music, or Tex-Mex music, or Chicano music, or *cantina* (bar) music. I grew up listening to *conjuntos,* three- or four-piece bands made up of folk musicians playing guitar, *bajo sexto,*[7] drums and button accordion, which Chicanos had borrowed from the German immigrants who had come to Central Texas and Mexico to farm and build breweries. In the Rio Grande Valley, Steve Jordan and Little Joe Hernández were popular, and Flaco Jiménez[8] was the accordion king. The rhythms of Tex-Mex music are those of the polka, also adapted from the Germans, who in turn had borrowed the polka from the Czechs and Bohemians.

2. American novelist (b. 1934). The book was published in 1963.
3. Rodolfo Gonzales [(b. 1928), Chicano novelist], *I Am Joaquín/Yo Soy Joaquín* (New York, NY: Bantam Books, 1972). It was first published in 1967 [Anzaldúa's note].
4. A 1947 film. Infante (1917–1957), Mexican film actor and singer.

5. A 1941 film.
6. Mexican singer and film actor (b. 1916). Negrete (1911–1953), Mexican singing actor.
7. Twelve-string guitar tuned one octave lower than normal.
8. Mexican American musicians. Esteban Jordán (b. 1939). José María De Leon Hérnandez (b. 1940), Leonardo Jiménez (b. 1939).

I remember the hot, sultry evenings when *corridos*—songs of love and death on the Texas-Mexican borderlands—reverberated out of cheap amplifiers from the local *cantinas* and wafted in through my bedroom window.

Corridos first became widely used along the South Texas / Mexican border during the early conflict between Chicanos and Anglos. The *corridos* are usually about Mexican heroes who do valiant deeds against the Anglo oppressors. Pancho Villa's song, *"La cucaracha,"* is the most famous one. *Corridos* of John F. Kennedy[9] and his death are still very popular in the Valley. Older Chicanos remember Lydia Mendoza,[1] one of the great border *corrido* singers who was called *la Gloria de Tejas.* Her *"El tango negro,"* sung during the Great Depression, made her a singer of the people. The everpresent *corridos* narrated one hundred years of border history, bringing news of events as well as entertaining. These folk musicians and folk songs are our chief cultural myth-makers, and they made our hard lives seem bearable.

I grew up feeling ambivalent about our music. Country-western and rock-and-roll had more status. In the 50s and 60s, for the slightly educated and *agringado* Chicanos, there existed a sense of shame at being caught listening to our music. Yet I couldn't stop my feet from thumping to the music, could not stop humming the words, nor hide from myself the exhilaration I felt when I heard it.

There are more subtle ways that we internalize identification, especially in the forms of images and emotions. For me food and certain smells are tied to my identity, to my homeland. Woodsmoke curling up to an immense blue sky; woodsmoke perfuming my grandmother's clothes, her skin. The stench of cow manure and the yellow patches on the ground; the crack of a .22 rifle and the reek of cordite. Homemade white cheese sizzling in a pan, melting inside a folded *tortilla.* My sister Hilda's hot, spicy *menudo*[2] *chile colorado* making it deep red, pieces of *panza* and hominy floating on top. My brother Carito barbecuing *fajitas* in the backyard. Even now and 3,000 miles away, I can see my mother spicing the ground beef, pork and venison with *chile.* My mouth salivates at the thought of the hot steaming *tamales* I would be eating if I were home.

Si le preguntas a mi mamá, "¿Qué eres?"

> "Identity is the essential core of who
> we are as individuals, the conscious
> experience of the self inside."
> —Kaufman[3]

Nosotros los Chicanos straddle the borderlands. On one side of us, we are constantly exposed to the Spanish of the Mexicans, on the other side we hear the Anglos' incessant clamoring so that we forget our language. Among ourselves we don't say *nosotros los americanos, o nosotros los españoles, o nosotros*

---

9. Thirty-fifth U.S. president (1917–1963), assassinated in Dallas, Texas. Villa (ca. 1877–1923), born Doroteo Arango, Mexican revolutionary leader.
1. Mexican American singer, songwriter, and musician (b. 1916).
2. Mexican soup made of simmered tripe, onion, garlic, chili, and hominy.
3. Gershen Kaufman [(b. 1943), American psychologist], *Shame: The Power of Caring* (Cambridge: Schenkman Books, Inc. 1980), 68. This book was instrumental in my understanding of shame [from Anzaldúa's note].

los hispanos. We say *nosotros los mexicanos* (by *mexicanos* we do not mean citizens of Mexico; we do not mean a national identity, but a racial one). We distinguish between *mexicanos del otro lado* and *mexicanos de este lado*. Deep in our hearts we believe that being Mexican has nothing to do with which country one lives in. Being Mexican is a state of soul—not one of mind, not one of citizenship. Neither eagle nor serpent,[4] but both. And like the ocean, neither animal respects borders.

> *Dime con quien andas y te diré quien eres.*
> (Tell me who your friends are and I'll tell you who
> you are.)
> —Mexican saying

Si le preguntas a mi mamá, "¿Qué eres?" te dirá, "Soy mexicana." My brothers and sister say the same. I sometimes will answer *"soy mexicana"* and at others will say *"soy Chicana" o "soy tejana."* But I identified as *"Raza"* before I ever identified as *"mexicana"* or "Chicana."

As a culture, we call ourselves Spanish when referring to ourselves as a linguistic group and when copping out. It is then that we forget our predominant Indian genes. We are 70 to 80% Indian.[5] We call ourselves Hispanic[6] or Spanish-American or Latin American or Latin when linking ourselves to other Spanish-speaking peoples of the Western hemisphere and when copping out. We call ourselves Mexican-American[7] to signify we are neither Mexican nor American, but more the noun "American" than the adjective "Mexican" (and when copping out).

Chicanos and other people of color suffer economically for not acculturating. This voluntary (yet forced) alienation makes for psychological conflict, a kind of dual identity—we don't identify with the Anglo-American cultural values and we don't totally identify with the Mexican cultural values. We are a synergy of two cultures with various degrees of Mexicanness or Angloness. I have so internalized the borderland conflict that sometimes I feel like one cancels out the other and we are zero, nothing, no one. *A veces no soy nada ni nadie. Pero hasta cuando no lo soy, lo soy.*

When not copping out, when we know we are more than nothing, we call ourselves Mexican, referring to race and ancestry; *mestizo* when affirming both our Indian and Spanish (but we hardly ever own our Black ancestry); Chicano when referring to a politically aware people born and/or raised in the U.S.; *Raza* when referring to Chicanos; *tejanos* when we are Chicanos from Texas.

Chicanos did not know we were a people until 1965 when Cesar Chavez[8] and the farmworkers united and *I Am Joaquín* was published and *la Raza Unida* party[9] was formed in Texas. With that recognition, we became a distinct people. Something momentous happened to the Chicano soul—we became aware of our reality and acquired a name and a language (Chicano

4. Respectively, male and female cultural figurations.
5. John R. Chávez [(b. 1949), American scholar and educator], *The Lost Land: The Chicano Images of the Southwest* (Albuquerque, NM: University of New Mexico Press, 1984), 88–90 [from Anzaldúa's note].
6. "Hispanic" is derived from Hispanis (*España*, a name given to the Iberian Peninsula in ancient times when it was a part of the Roman Empire) and is a term designated by the U.S. government to make it easier to handle us on paper [Anzaldúa's note].
7. The Treaty of Guadalupe Hidalgo created the Mexican-American in 1848 [Anzaldúa's note].
8. Chicano union organizer (1927–1993).
9. Known in America as the United Farm Workers; founded in 1962.

Spanish) that reflected that reality. Now that we had a name, some of the fragmented pieces began to fall together—who we were, what we were, how we had evolved. We began to get glimpses of what we might eventually become.

Yet the struggle of identities continues, the struggle of borders is our reality still. One day the inner struggle will cease and a true integration take place. In the meantime, *tenemos que hacerla lucha. ¿Quién está protegiendo los ranchos de mi gente? ¿Quién está tratando de cerrar la fisura entre la india y el blanco en nuestra sangre? El Chicano, sí, el Chicano que anda como un ladrón en su propia casa.*[1]

Los Chicanos, how patient we seem, how very patient. There is the quiet of the Indian about us. We know how to survive. When other races have given up their tongue, we've kept ours. We know what it is to live under the hammer blow of the dominant *norteamericano* culture. But more than we count the blows, we count the days the weeks the years the centuries the eons until the white laws and commerce and customs will rot in the deserts they've created, lie bleached. *Humildes* yet proud, *quietos* yet wild, *nosotros los mexicanos* Chicanos will walk by the crumbling ashes as we go about our business. Stubborn, persevering, impenetrable as stone, yet possessing a malleability that renders us unbreakable, we, the *mestizas* and *mestizos*, will remain.

1987

1. Anglos, in order to alleviate their guilt for dispossessing the Chicano, stressed the Spanish part of us and perpetrated the myth of the Spanish Southwest. We have accepted the fiction that we are Hispanic, that is Spanish, in order to accommodate ourselves to the dominant culture and its abhorrence of Indians. Chávez, 88–91 [Anzaldúa's note].

ALICE WALKER
b. 1944

Of the two daughters at odds over family heirlooms in the story "Everyday Use" (printed here), Alice Walker resembles each one. Like the burned Maggie, she spent a childhood even more limited than her family's rural poverty dictated, for as a little girl she was shot in the eye with a BB gun; the disfigurement plagued her until it was corrected during her college years. Like Dee, she was able to attend college—first Spelman College and then Sarah Lawrence College on a scholarship—and acquire urban sophistications from the North. Many of Walker's characters become adept in the new cultural language of Black Arts and black power to which the author contributed as a young writer—and all of them are subjected to the same dismay Dee's mother feels at having to rule against this daughter's wishes. Like the mother, therefore, Walker is given to seeing both sides of a situation; and when it comes to choosing between her characters' opposing positions, she tends to be critical of her own personality first and extremely sparing in her judgment of others.

From her native Eatonton, Georgia, Walker gained an understanding of the rural South. In her essay "Beyond the Peacock," Walker evaluates both the older white writer Flannery O'Connor, who lived in nearby Milledgeville, and the perspectives from which readers see the region and its heritage. Visitors to O'Connor's home, for example, often romanticize the house's handmade bricks; Walker points out that the slaves who made those bricks surely suffered in the process. As the educated child of sharecroppers, Walker can critically reexamine the myths in and around O'Connor's life while doing justice to the complexity of O'Connor's work.

After college Walker returned to the South, first to work against segregation in the civil rights movement and then to teach at Jackson State College in Mississippi. Her first novel, *The Third Life of Grange Copeland* (1970), follows its protagonist through three generations of domestic experience. In *Meridian* (1976) Walker presents fragmentary recollections of the 1960s among characters trying to make sense of their recent past. This novel reflects many of the topics treated in the author's short-story collection, *In Love & Trouble* (1973), in which a range of African American women almost always have unhappy relationships with men. Walker's third novel, *The Color Purple* (1982), makes her strongest narrative statement, formulated from what she calls a "womanist" (as opposed to strictly feminist) perspective. This approach draws on the black folk expression "womanish," which in a mother-to-daughter context signifies a call to adult, mature, responsible (and courageous) behavior. Such behavior benefits women and men and is necessary, Walker argues, for the survival of all African Americans by keeping creativity alive. The plot and the style of *The Color Purple* show how this happens, as the young black woman Celie draws on her sister's letters (written from Africa) for her own letters to God. Though Celie's life by any other terms could be considered disastrous (including rape, incest, and the killing of her babies by her father and both physical and psychological abuse by her husband), her actions and her ability to express herself give her status as an individual. To everyone who will listen, Celie says "I am here."

Walker has continued to publish novels, short stories, poetry, and essays. In "The Same River Twice" (1996) she writes about how the filming of *The Color Purple* challenged and changed her life. As a sociocultural critic she has examined the atrocity of female genital mutilation in parts of Africa, also incorporating her conclusions in her novel *Possessing the Secret of Joy* (1992), and as a literary critic she has spoken for a richer and more complete understanding of Zora Neale Hurston, whose employment of folk materials in narrative anticipates Walker's. Throughout her career she has spoken about the need for strength from African American women, and her writing seeks workable models for such strength.

The text is from *In Love & Trouble* (1973).

Everyday Use

For Your Grandmama

I will wait for her in the yard that Maggie and I made so clean and wavy yesterday afternoon. A yard like this is more comfortable than most people know. It is not just a yard. It is like an extended living room. When the hard clay is swept clean as a floor and the fine sand around the edges lined with tiny, irregular grooves, anyone can come and sit and look up into the elm tree and wait for the breezes that never come inside the house.

Maggie will be nervous until after her sister goes: she will stand hopelessly in corners, homely and ashamed of the burn scars down her arms and legs, eyeing her sister with a mixture of envy and awe. She thinks her sister has held life always in the palm of one hand, that "no" is a word the world never learned to say to her.

You've no doubt seen those TV shows where the child who has "made it" is confronted, as a surprise, by her own mother and father, tottering in weakly from backstage. (A pleasant surprise, of course: What would they do if parent and child came on the show only to curse out and insult each other?) On TV mother and child embrace and smile into each other's faces. Sometimes the mother and father weep, the child wraps them in her arms and leans across the table to tell how she would not have made it without their help. I have seen these programs.

Sometimes I dream a dream in which Dee and I are suddenly brought together on a TV program of this sort. Out of a dark and soft-seated limousine I am ushered into a bright room filled with many people. There I meet a smiling, gray, sporty man like Johnny Carson who shakes my hand and tells me what a fine girl I have. Then we are on the stage and Dee is embracing me with tears in her eyes. She pins on my dress a large orchid, even though she has told me once that she thinks orchids are tacky flowers.

In real life I am a large, big-boned woman with rough, man-working hands. In the winter I wear flannel nightgowns to bed and overalls during the day. I can kill and clean a hog as mercilessly as a man. My fat keeps me hot in zero weather. I can work outside all day, breaking ice to get water for washing; I can eat pork liver cooked over the open fire minutes after it comes steaming from the hog. One winter I knocked a bull calf straight in the brain between the eyes with a sledge hammer and had the meat hung up to chill before nightfall. But of course all this does not show on television. I am the way my daughter would want me to be: a hundred pounds lighter, my skin like an uncooked barley pancake. My hair glistens in the hot bright lights. Johnny Carson has much to do to keep up with my quick and witty tongue.

But that is a mistake. I know even before I wake up. Who ever knew a Johnson with a quick tongue? Who can even imagine me looking a strange white man in the eye? It seems to me I have talked to them always with one foot raised in flight, with my head turned in whichever way is farthest from them. Dee, though. She would always look anyone in the eye. Hesitation was no part of her nature.

"How do I look, Mama?" Maggie says, showing just enough of her thin body enveloped in pink skirt and red blouse for me to know she's there, almost hidden by the door.

"Come out into the yard," I say.

Have you ever seen a lame animal, perhaps a dog run over by some careless person rich enough to own a car, sidle up to someone who is ignorant enough to be kind to them? That is the way my Maggie walks. She has been like this, chin on chest, eyes on ground, feet in shuffle, ever since the fire that burned the other house to the ground.

Dee is lighter than Maggie, with nicer hair and a fuller figure. She's a woman now, though sometimes I forget. How long ago was it that the other house burned? Ten, twelve years? Sometimes I can still hear the flames and feel Maggie's arms sticking to me, her hair smoking and her dress falling off her in little black papery flakes. Her eyes seemed stretched open, blazed open by the flames reflected in them. And Dee. I see her standing off under the sweet gum tree she used to dig gum out of; a look of concentration on her face as she watched the last dingy gray board of the house fall in toward the red-hot brick chimney. Why don't you do a dance around the ashes? I'd wanted to ask her. She had hated the house that much.

I used to think she hated Maggie, too. But that was before we raised the money, the church and me, to send her to Augusta to school. She used to read to us without pity; forcing words, lies, other folks' habits, whole lives upon us two, sitting trapped and ignorant underneath her voice. She washed us in a river of make-believe, burned us with a lot of knowledge we didn't necessarily need to know. Pressed us to her with the serious way she read, to shove us away at just the moment, like dimwits, we seemed about to understand.

Dee wanted nice things. A yellow organdy dress to wear to her graduation from high school; black pumps to match a green suit she'd made from an old suit somebody gave me. She was determined to stare down any disaster in her efforts. Her eyelids would not flicker for minutes at a time. Often I fought off the temptation to shake her. At sixteen she had a style of her own: and knew what style was.

I never had an education myself. After second grade the school was closed down. Don't ask me why: in 1927 colored asked fewer questions than they do now. Sometimes Maggie reads to me. She stumbles along good-naturedly but can't see well. She knows she is not bright. Like good looks and money, quickness passed her by. She will marry John Thomas (who has mossy teeth in an earnest face) and then I'll be free to sit here and I guess just sing church songs to myself. Although I never was a good singer. Never could carry a tune. I was always better at a man's job. I used to love to milk till I was hooked in the side in '49. Cows are soothing and slow and don't bother you, unless you try to milk them the wrong way.

I have deliberately turned my back on the house. It is three rooms, just like the one that burned, except the roof is tin; they don't make shingle roofs any more. There are no real windows, just some holes cut in the sides, like the portholes in a ship, but not round and not square, with rawhide holding the shutters up on the outside. This house is in a pasture, too, like the other one. No doubt when Dee sees it she will want to tear it down. She wrote me once that no matter where we "choose" to live, she will manage to come see us. But she will never bring her friends. Maggie and I thought about this and Maggie asked me, "Mama, when did Dee ever *have* any friends?"

She had a few. Furtive boys in pink shirts hanging about on washday after school. Nervous girls who never laughed. Impressed with her they worshiped the well-turned phrase, the cute shape, the scalding humor that erupted like bubbles in lye. She read to them.

When she was courting Jimmy T she didn't have much time to pay to us, but turned all her faultfinding power on him. He *flew* to marry a cheap city girl from a family of ignorant flashy people. She hardly had time to recompose herself.

When she comes I will meet—but there they are!

Maggie attempts to make a dash for the house, in her shuffling way, but I stay her with my hand. "Come back here," I say. And she stops and tries to dig a well in the sand with her toe.

It is hard to see them clearly through the strong sun. But even the first glimpse of leg out of the car tells me it is Dee. Her feet were always neat-looking, as if God himself had shaped them with a certain style. From the other side of the car comes a short, stocky man. Hair is all over his head a foot long and hanging from his chin like a kinky mule tail. I hear Maggie suck in her breath. "Uhnnnh," is what it sounds like. Like when you see the wriggling end of a snake just in front of your foot on the road. "Uhnnnh."

Dee next. A dress down to the ground, in this hot weather. A dress so loud it hurts my eyes. There are yellows and oranges enough to throw back the light of the sun. I feel my whole face warming from the heat waves it throws out. Earrings gold, too, and hanging down to her shoulders. Bracelets dangling and making noises when she moves her arm up to shake the folds of the dress out of her armpits. The dress is loose and flows, and as she walks closer, I like it. I hear Maggie go "Uhnnnh" again. It is her sister's hair. It stands straight up like the wool on a sheep. It is black as night and around the edges are two long pigtails that rope about like small lizards disappearing behind her ears.

"Wa-su-zo-Tean-o!" she says, coming on in that gliding way the dress makes her move. The short stocky fellow with the hair to his navel is all grinning and he follows up with "Asalamalakim, my mother and sister!" He moves to hug Maggie but she falls back, right up against the back of my chair. I feel her trembling there and when I look up I see the perspiration falling off her chin.

"Don't get up," says Dee. Since I am stout it takes something of a push. You can see me trying to move a second or two before I make it. She turns, showing white heels through her sandals, and goes back to the car. Out she peeks next with a Polaroid. She stoops down quickly and lines up picture after picture of me sitting there in front of the house with Maggie cowering behind me. She never takes a shot without making sure the house is included. When a cow comes nibbling around the edge of the yard she snaps it and me and Maggie *and* the house. Then she puts the Polaroid in the back seat of the car, and comes up and kisses me on the forehead.

Meanwhile Asalamalakim is going through motions with Maggie's hand. Maggie's hand is as limp as a fish, and probably as cold, despite the sweat, and she keeps trying to pull it back. It looks like Asalamalakim wants to shake hands but wants to do it fancy. Or maybe he don't know how people shake hands. Anyhow, he soon gives up on Maggie.

"Well," I say. "Dee."

"No, Mama," she says. "Not 'Dee,' Wangero Leewanika Kemanjo!"

"What happened to 'Dee'?" I wanted to know.

"She's dead," Wangero said. "I couldn't bear it any longer, being named after the people who oppress me."

"You know as well as me you was named after your aunt Dicie," I said. Dicie is my sister. She named Dee. We called her "Big Dee" after Dee was born.

"But who was *she* named after?" asked Wangero.

"I guess after Grandma Dee," I said.

"And who was she named after?" asked Wangero.

"Her mother," I said, and saw Wangero was getting tired. "That's about as far back as I can trace it," I said. Though, in fact, I probably could have carried it back beyond the Civil War through the branches.

"Well," said Asalamalakim, "there you are."

"Uhnnnh," I heard Maggie say.

"There I was not," I said, "before 'Dicie' cropped up in our family, so why should I try to trace it that far back?"

He just stood there grinning, looking down on me like somebody inspecting a Model A car.[1] Every once in a while he and Wangero sent eye signals over my head.

"How do you pronounce this name?" I asked.

"You don't have to call me by it if you don't want to," said Wangero.

"Why shouldn't I?" I asked. "If that's what you want us to call you, we'll call you."

"I know it might sound awkward at first," said Wangero.

"I'll get used to it," I said. "Ream it out again."

Well, soon we got the name out of the way. Asalamalakim had a name twice as long and three times as hard. After I tripped over it two or three times he told me to just call him Hakim-a-barber. I wanted to ask him was he a barber, but I didn't really think he was, so I didn't ask.

"You must belong to those beef-cattle peoples down the road," I said. They said "Asalamalakim" when they met you, too, but they didn't shake hands. Always too busy: feeding the cattle, fixing the fences, putting up salt-lick shelters, throwing down hay. When the white folks poisoned some of the herd the men stayed up all night with rifles in their hands. I walked a mile and a half just to see the sight.

Hakim-a-barber said, "I accept some of their doctrines, but farming and raising cattle is not my style." (They didn't tell me, and I didn't ask, whether Wangero (Dee) had really gone and married him.)

We sat down to eat and right away he said he didn't eat collards and pork was unclean. Wangero, though, went on through the chitlins and corn bread, the greens and everything else. She talked a blue streak over the sweet potatoes. Everything delighted her. Even the fact that we still used the benches her daddy made for the table when we couldn't afford to buy chairs.

"Oh, Mama!" she cried. Then turned to Hakim-a-barber. "I never knew how lovely these benches are. You can feel the rump prints," she said, running her hands underneath her and along the bench. Then she gave a sigh and her hand closed over Grandma Dee's butter dish. "That's it!" she said. "I knew there was something I wanted to ask you if I could have." She jumped up from the table and went over in the corner where the churn stood, the milk in it clabber by now. She looked at the churn and looked at it.

"This churn top is what I need," she said. "Didn't Uncle Buddy whittle it out of a tree you all used to have?"

"Yes," I said.

"Uh huh," she said happily. "And I want the dasher, too."

"Uncle Buddy whittle that, too?" asked the barber.

Dee (Wangero) looked up at me.

"Aunt Dee's first husband whittled the dash," said Maggie so low you almost couldn't hear her. "His name was Henry, but they called him Stash."

"Maggie's brain is like an elephant's," Wangero said, laughing. "I can use the churn top as a centerpiece for the alcove table," she said, sliding a plate over the churn, "and I'll think of something artistic to do with the dasher."

When she finished wrapping the dasher the handle stuck out. I took it for a moment in my hands. You didn't even have to look close to see where hands pushing the dasher up and down to make butter had left a kind of sink in the wood. In fact, there were a lot of small sinks; you could see where thumbs

---

1. Popular model of Ford automobile introduced in 1928.

and fingers had sunk into the wood. It was beautiful light yellow wood, from a tree that grew in the yard where Big Dee and Stash had lived.

After dinner Dee (Wangero) went to the trunk at the foot of my bed and started rifling through it. Maggie hung back in the kitchen over the dishpan. Out came Wangero with two quilts. They had been pieced by Grandma Dee and then Big Dee and me had hung them on the quilt frames on the front porch and quilted them. One was in the Lone Star pattern. The other was Walk Around the Mountain. In both of them were scraps of dresses Grandma Dee had worn fifty and more years ago. Bits and pieces of Grandpa Jarrell's Paisley shirts. And one teeny faded blue piece, about the size of a penny matchbox, that was from Great Grandpa Ezra's uniform that he wore in the Civil War.

"Mama," Wangero said sweet as a bird. "Can I have these old quilts?"

I heard something fall in the kitchen, and a minute later the kitchen door slammed.

"Why don't you take one or two of the others?" I asked. "These old things was just done by me and Big Dee from some tops your grandma pieced before she died."

"No," said Wangero. "I don't want those. They are stitched around the borders by machine."

"That'll make them last better," I said.

"That's not the point," said Wangero. "These are all pieces of dresses Grandma used to wear. She did all this stitching by hand. Imagine!" She held the quilts securely in her arms, stroking them.

"Some of the pieces, like those lavender ones, come from old clothes her mother handed down to her," I said, moving up to touch the quilts. Dee (Wangero) moved back just enough so that I couldn't reach the quilts. They already belonged to her.

"Imagine!" she breathed again, clutching them closely to her bosom.

"The truth is," I said, "I promised to give them quilts to Maggie, for when she marries John Thomas."

She gasped like a bee had stung her.

"Maggie can't appreciate these quilts!" she said. "She'd probably be backward enough to put them to everyday use."

"I reckon she would," I said. "God knows I been saving 'em for long enough with nobody using 'em. I hope she will!" I didn't want to bring up how I had offered Dee (Wangero) a quilt when she went away to college. Then she had told me they were old-fashioned, out of style.

"But they're *priceless*!" she was saying now, furiously; for she has a temper. "Maggie would put them on the bed and in five years they'd be in rags. Less than that!"

"She can always make some more," I said. "Maggie knows how to quilt."

Dee (Wangero) looked at me with hatred. "You just will not understand. The point is these quilts, *these* quilts!"

"Well," I said, stumped. "What would *you* do with them?"

"Hang them," she said. As if that was the only thing you *could* do with quilts.

Maggie by now was standing in the door. I could almost hear the sound her feet made as they scraped over each other.

"She can have them, Mama," she said, like somebody used to never winning anything, or having anything reserved for her. "I can 'member Grandma Dee without the quilts."

I looked at her hard. She had filled her bottom lip with checkerberry snuff and it gave her a face a kind of dopey, hangdog look. It was Grandma Dee and Big Dee who taught her how to quilt herself. She stood there with her scarred hands hidden in the folds of her skirt. She looked at her sister with something like fear but she wasn't mad at her. This was Maggie's portion. This was the way she knew God to work.

When I looked at her like that something hit me in the top of my head and ran down to the soles of my feet. Just like when I'm in church and the spirit of God touches me and I get happy and shout. I did something I never had done before: hugged Maggie to me, then dragged her on into the room, snatched the quilts out of Miss Wangero's hands and dumped them into Maggie's lap. Maggie just sat there on my bed with her mouth open.

"Take one or two of the others," I said to Dee.

But she turned without a word and went out to Hakim-a-barber.

"You just don't understand," she said, as Maggie and I came out to the car.

"What don't I understand?" I wanted to know.

"Your heritage," she said. And then she turned to Maggie, kissed her, and said, "You ought to try to make something of yourself, too, Maggie. It's really a new day for us. But from the way you and Mama still live you'd never know it."

She put on some sunglasses that hid everything above the tip of her nose and her chin.

Maggie smiled; maybe at the sunglasses. But a real smile, not scared. After we watched the car dust settle I asked Maggie to bring me a dip of snuff. And then the two of us sat there just enjoying, until it was time to go in the house and go to bed.

1973

YUSEF KOMUNYAKAA
b. 1947

The excavation of lost names is one of the driving impulses of Yusef Komunyakaa's work. His poems recover and reanimate figures from history such as the African American elevator operator, Thomas McKeller, who appears in a stunning portrait by John Singer Sargent ("Nude Study"). In researching the portrait, Komunyakaa learned that it had been "unearthed in Sargent's studio after his death" and that "McKeller's image had been cannibalized to depict [the ancient Greek and Roman god] Apollo and a bas-relief of [the ancient Greek poet and musician] Arion—other heads and lines grafted onto his classical physique." Komunyakaa's work continually questions and revises both the cultural contradictions projected onto the black body and the erasure of black presence from history and culture. Significantly, he adopted the lost surname of a Trinidadian grandfather who came to the United States as a child, "smuggled in like a sack of papaya / On a banana boat." As the poet recounts in "Mismatched Shoes," his grandfather's "true name" disappeared in the process of assimilation. After his death his grandson "slipped into his skin" and took back the name "Komunyakaa," in what the poet calls "an affirmation of my heritage and its ambiguity."

Komunyakaa was born in Bogalusa, Louisiana, seventy miles northeast of New Orleans. Bogalusa means "Magic City" (a phrase that become the title of his 1992 collection of poems), and a lush, semitropical landscape informs many of his poems. But as the oldest of six children, and as the son of a carpenter who could write only his name, Komunyakaa grew up in an impoverished neighborhood and experienced a racial inequity that coexisted with natural beauty. At a young age, he has said, he decided that "imagination could serve as a choice of weapons."

Because the military seemed to offer a way into a larger world, Komunyakaa enlisted and was sent to Vietnam, where he served as a war correspondent and editor of the military newspaper, writing accounts of what he witnessed in combat. For his work he was awarded the Bronze Star. While in Vietnam he carried with him several anthologies of poetry, but only after his military service ended did he begin to write poems, studying at the University of Colorado and then at the University of California at Irvine, where his teachers included Charles Wright and C. K. Williams. In 1984, fourteen years after his tour of duty ended, Komunyakaa began to write poems about his war experience. From his father he had learned to build and renovate houses; as he works, he has said, he keeps a pad of paper close by. While renovating a house in New Orleans he began to write down images and lines about Vietnam and so began the first in what became a series of poems about his Vietnam experience. These were collected in *Dien Cai Dau* (1988), whose title (meaning "crazy") is a Vietnamese phrase used to describe American soldiers. In one of these poems, "Facing It," he sees his own "clouded reflection" in the "black granite" of the Vietnam War Memorial designed by Maya Lin, an image of which appears on p. C 5 in the color insert of this anthology.

To write about his surreal wartime experiences Komunyakaa drew on the work of surrealists like the French poet and critic André Breton. Komunyakaa shares with these writers and artists an emphasis on the image as linked to the unconscious, and his poems often work through a series of short lines whose quick, associative images bypass logic. A surrealist impulse to distort the familiar and juxtapose beauty and violence appears in Komunyakaa's Vietnam poems and in the racial and erotic tensions of poems like "Jasmine" (from *The Pleasure Dome,* 2001) and "Nude Study." An emphasis on the dreamlike, irrational, and fantastic was already apparent in his first two books, *Copacetic* (1984) and *I Apologize for the Eyes in My Head* (1986), both of which also reflect the musical influences of his native Louisiana.

Growing up so close to New Orleans brought Komunyakaa in early contact with jazz and the blues. The title of his first book, *Copacetic,* is a term adapted by jazz musicians from the African American tap dancer Bill "Bojangles" Robinson; in jazz it refers to especially pleasing and mellow music. Like Langston Hughes, Komunyakaa explores throughout his work the power of music—blues, jazz, and poetry—to address and, in part, to heal the pain of living in a racially divided society. The rapid energy of poems like "Facing It" and "Slam, Dunk, & Hook" belong to what the poet calls a "felt and lived syncopation," a rhythm of shifting beats that bears the influence of musicians like Charlie Parker, John Coltrane, and Miles Davis. Komunyakaa also works in tighter formal structures, whose exactness and precision suggest the careful measuring and fitting of carpentry. The quatrains of *Talking Dirty to the Gods* (2000) and the three-line stanzas of *Taboo* (2004) provide what the poet calls "an illusion of control" over volatile and complicated social and psychic material. They reflect Komunyakaa's preferred poetic strategy of "insinuation and nuance." Although his work often looks unflinchingly at what otherwise is hidden or denied, the social, racial, or erotic context of a poem often emerges in details or images, rather than in direct description.

Komunyakaa coedited with J. A. Sascha Feinstein a two-volume collection, *The Jazz Poetry Anthology* (1991) and *Second Set* (1996), and has also been extensively involved in collaborations with jazz musicians and vocalists. His poetry has received numerous awards, among them both the Pulitzer Prize and the Kingsley Tuft Poetry Award for

Neon Vernacular: New and Selected Poems 1977–1989 (1994). He is a professor in the
Council of Humanities and Creative Writing Program at Princeton University.

Facing It

My black face fades,
hiding inside the black granite.
I said I wouldn't
dammit: No tears.
I'm stone. I'm flesh.   5
My clouded reflection eyes me
like a bird of prey, the profile of night
slanted against morning. I turn
this way—the stone lets me go.
I turn that way—I'm inside   10
the Vietnam Veterans Memorial[1]
again, depending on the light
to make a difference.
I go down the 58,022 names,
half-expecting to find   15
my own in letters like smoke.
I touch the name Andrew Johnson;
I see the booby trap's white flash.
Names shimmer on a woman's blouse
but when she walks away   20
the names stay on the wall.
Brushstrokes flash, a red bird's
wings cutting across my stare.
The sky. A plane in the sky.
A white vet's image floats   25
closer to me, then his pale eyes
look through mine. I'm a window.
He's lost his right arm
inside the stone. In the black mirror
a woman's trying to erase names: 30
No, she's brushing a boy's hair

1988

My Father's Love Letters

On Fridays he'd open a can of Jax[1]
After coming home from the mill,
& ask me to write a letter to my mother
Who sent postcards of desert flowers
Taller than men. He would beg,   5

1. An image of the Vietnam War Memorial in
Washington, D.C., designed by the architect Maya
Lin and dedicated in 1982, appears in the color
insert of this anthology.
1. A beer originally brewed in New Orleans,
Louisiana.

Promising to never beat her
Again. Somehow I was happy
She had gone, & sometimes wanted
To slip in a reminder, how Mary Lou
Williams' "Polka Dots & Moonbeams"[2]   10
Never made the swelling go down.
His carpenter's apron always bulged
With old nails, a claw hammer
Looped at his side & extension cords
Coiled around his feet.   15
Words rolled from under the pressure
Of my ballpoint: Love,
Baby, Honey, Please.
We sat in the quiet brutality
Of voltage meters & pipe threaders,   20
Lost between sentences . . .
The gleam of a five-pound wedge
On the concrete floor
Pulled a sunset
Through the doorway of his toolshed.   25
I wondered if she laughed
& held them over a gas burner.
My father could only sign
His name, but he'd look at blueprints
& say how many bricks   30
Formed each wall. This man,
Who stole roses & hyacinth
For his yard, would stand there
With eyes closed & fists balled,
Laboring over a simple word, almost   35
Redeemed by what he tried to say.

1992

Slam, Dunk, & Hook

Fast breaks. Lay ups. With Mercury's
Insignia[1] on our sneakers,
We outmaneuvered to footwork
Of bad angels. Nothing but a hot
Swish of strings like silk   5
Ten feet out. In the roundhouse
Labyrinth our bodies
Created, we could almost
Last forever, poised in midair
Like storybook sea monsters.   10

---

2. The American jazz pianist Mary Lou Williams (1910–1981) performed with and composed for many of the great jazz artists of the 1940s and 1950s. The song "Polka Dots and Moonbeams" (1940) was composed by Jimmy Van Heusen (1913–1990) and Johnny Burke (1908–1964).

1. Mercury, the messenger of the ancient Greek gods, is depicted wearing winged sandals.

A high note hung there
A long second. Off
The rim. We'd corkscrew
Up & dunk balls that exploded
The skullcap of hope & good   15
Intention. Lanky, all hands
& feet . . . sprung rhythm.[2]
We were metaphysical when girls
Cheered on the sidelines.
Tangled up in a falling,   20
Muscles were a bright motor
Double-flashing to the metal hoop
Nailed to our oak.
When Sonny Boy's mama died
He played nonstop all day, so hard   25
Our backboard splintered.
Glistening with sweat,
We rolled the ball off
Our fingertips. Trouble
Was there slapping a blackjack[3]   30
Against an open palm.
Dribble, drive to the inside,
& glide like a sparrow hawk.[4]
Lay ups. Fast breaks.
We had moves we didn't know   35
We had. Our bodies spun
On swivels of bone & faith,
Through a lyric slipknot
Of joy, & we knew we were
Beautiful & dangerous.   40

1992

When Dusk Weighs Daybreak

I want Catullus[1]
In every line, a barb
The sun plays for good
Luck. I need to know if iron

Tastes like laudanum[2]   5
Or a woman. I already sense
What sleeps in the same flesh,
Ariadne & her half brother[3]

---

2. "Sprung rhythm" is a term used by the English poet Gerard Manley Hopkins (1844–1889) to describe a poetic meter with a variable rather than fixed number of syllables in each poetic foot.
3. A small leather bludgeon.
4. One of the best-known, handsomest, and smallest North American hawks.
1. Gaius Valerius Catullus (c. 86–c. 54 B.C.E.), Roman poet who wittily expressed love and hate in

some of the finest lyric poetry of his time.
2. An opium-based painkiller.
3. In Greek mythology Ariadne was the daughter of Pasiphaë and the Cretan king, Minos. She fell in love with the Athenian hero Theseus and helped him escape the Labyrinth after he slew her half-brother, the Minotaur, a beast half bull and half man.

Caught in the other's dream.
I want each question to fit me   10
Like a shiny hook, a lure
In the gullet. What it is

To look & know how much muscle
It takes to lift a green slab.
I need a Son House blues[4]   15
To wear out my tongue.

                                                        2000

Jasmine

I sit beside two women, kitty-corner
to the stage, as Elvin's[1] sticks blur
the club into a blue fantasia.
I thought my body had forgotten the Deep
South, how I'd cross the street   5
if a woman like these two walked
towards me, as if a cat traversed
my path beneath the evening star.
Which one is wearing jasmine?
If my grandmothers saw me now   10
they'd say, Boy, the devil never sleeps.
My mind is lost among November
cotton flowers, a soft rain on my face
as Richard Davis[2] plucks the fat notes
of chance on his upright   15
leaning into the future.
The blonde, the brunette—
which one is scented with jasmine?
I can hear Duke in the right hand
& Basie in the left[3]   20
as the young piano player
nudges us into the past.
The trumpet's almost kissed
by enough pain. Give him a few more years,
a few more ghosts to embrace—Clifford's[4]   25
shadow on the edge of the stage.
The sign says, *No Talking*.
Elvin's guardian angel lingers
at the top of the stairs,

4. Eddie James House Jr. (1902–1988), better known as "Son," American blues singer and guitarist regarded as one epitome of the Delta blues tradition.
1. Elvin Jones (1927–2004), American jazz drummer and bandleader.
2. American bassist (b. 1930) known for his jazz sessions in an all-star small group at New York

City's Village Vanguard under the rubric "Jazz for a Sunday Afternoon."
3. Duke Ellington (1899–1974), American pianist and bandleader who was also one of the greatest jazz composers. Count Basie (1904–1984), American jazz pianist and bandleader.
4. Clifford Brown (1930–1956), American jazz trumpeter noted for his graceful technique.

counting each drop of sweat   30
paid in tribute. The blonde
has her eyes closed, & the brunette
is looking at me. Our bodies
sway to each riff the jasmine
rising from a valley somewhere   35
in Egypt, a white moon
opening countless false mouths
of laughter. The midnight
gatherers are boys & girls
with the headlights of trucks   40
aimed at their backs, because
their small hands refuse to wound
the knowing scent hidden in each bloom.

2001

LESLIE MARMON SILKO
b. 1948

Born in Albuquerque, New Mexico, Leslie Marmon Silko was raised in Old Laguna, a village fifty miles west of Albuquerque. The Spaniards had founded a mission there early in the eighteenth century, but Old Laguna had been formed centuries earlier by cattle-keeping Pueblos who successfully repelled raids on them by the Navajos and the Apaches. Writing of the unchanging character of Pueblo religious practices over the centuries, the historian Joe S. Sando notes that "the tradition of religious beliefs permeates every aspect of the people's life; it determines man's relation with the natural world and with his fellow man. Its basic concern is continuity of a harmonious relationship with the world in which man lives."

Silko's work addresses such matters. Her own heritage is complicated in that her great-grandfather Robert Marmon was white, whereas her mother was a mixed-blood Plains Indian who kept her daughter on the traditional cradle board during her first year of infancy. (Her ancestry also includes some Mexican blood.) Silko has made this heritage a source of strength. She writes: "I suppose at the core of my writing is the attempt to identify what it is to be a half-breed or mixed blooded person; what it is to grow up neither white nor fully traditional Indian." At the same time she insists that "what I know is Laguna. This place I am from is everything I am as a writer and human being." An active child, Silko had a horse of her own by age eight, and by thirteen she owned a rifle, with which she took part in deer hunts. Commuting to Albuquerque, she attended Catholic schools, took a B.A. from the University of New Mexico, then began law school under a special program for Native Americans, though she soon gave it up to become a writer and teacher.

Her first published story, "The Man to Send Rain Clouds" (1969), came out of a writing assignment in college. She had heard, in Laguna, of an old man who died in a sheep camp and was given a traditional native burial—a fact resented by the Catholic priest who was not called in. The story she wrote about this situation, published in the *New Mexico Quarterly*, put her on the road to success as a writer. In 1974 a selection of her poems was published in the volume *Laguna Woman*, and in 1977 her novel *Ceremony* brought her recognition as a leading voice among Native American writers. *Ceremony* shows the dark aspects of modern American Indian life, focusing on a World

War II veteran who is in acute physical and emotional straits as the novel begins, but who manages to survive by reestablishing contact with his native roots. Silko has insisted that the book is not just or even mainly about characters: "This novel is essentially about the powers inherent in the process of storytelling. . . . the chanting or telling of ancient stories to effect certain cures or protect from illness and harm have always been a part of the Pueblo's curing ceremonies." So this story of a family represents an attempt "to search for a ceremony to deal with despair"—the despair that has led to the "suicide, the alcoholism, and the violence which occur in so many Indian communities today."

Thus a strong moral connection exists between Silko's purely aesthetic delight in the writing of a story and the therapeutic, functional uses she hopes the story will play in the Native American community. In *Ceremony* and the aptly titled 1981 collection *Storyteller* of 1981 (which also contains poems and photographs), Silko's prose is an expressive, active presence, sympathetically creating landscape as well as animals and human beings. Plants assume narrative status in her third novel, *Gardens in the Dunes* (1999), which looks back to late-nineteenth-century events to underscore a basic theme: that myth and history do not coincide.

The text is from *Storyteller* (1981).

Lullaby

The sun had gone down but the snow in the wind gave off its own light. It came in thick tufts like new wool—washed before the weaver spins it. Ayah reached out for it like her own babies had, and she smiled when she remembered how she had laughed at them. She was an old woman now, and her life had become memories. She sat down with her back against the wide cottonwood tree, feeling the rough bark on her back bones; she faced east and listened to the wind and snow sing a high-pitched Yeibechei[1] song. Out of the wind she felt warmer, and she could watch the wide fluffy snow fill in her tracks, steadily, until the direction she had come from was gone. By the light of the snow she could see the dark outline of the big arroyo[2] a few feet away. She was sitting on the edge of Cebolleta Creek, where in the springtime the thin cows would graze on grass already chewed flat to the ground. In the wide deep creek bed where only a trickle of water flowed in the summer, the skinny cows would wander, looking for new grass along winding paths splashed with manure.

Ayah pulled the old Army blanket over her head like a shawl. Jimmie's blanket—the one he had sent to her. That was a long time ago and the green wool was faded, and it was unraveling on the edges. She did not want to think about Jimmie. So she thought about the weaving and the way her mother had done it. On the wall wooden loom set into the sand under a tamarack tree for shade. She could see it clearly. She had been only a little girl when her grandma gave her the wooden combs to pull the twigs and burrs from the raw, freshly washed wool. And while she combed the wool, her grandma sat beside her, spinning a silvery strand of yarn around the smooth cedar spindle. Her mother worked at the loom with yarns dyed bright yellow and red and gold. She watched them dye the yarn in boiling black pots full of beeweed petals, juniper berries, and sage. The blankets her mother made were soft and woven

---

1. Navajo dance.   2. Gully carved by water.

so tight that rain rolled off them like birds' feathers. Ayah remembered sleeping warm on cold windy nights, wrapped in her mother's blankets on the hogan's[3] sandy floor.

The snow drifted now, with the northwest wind hurling it in gusts. It drifted up around her black overshoes—old ones with little metal buckles. She smiled at the snow which was trying to cover her little by little. She could remember when they had no black rubber overshoes; only the high buckskin leggings that they wrapped over their elkhide moccasins. If the snow was dry or frozen, a person could walk all day and not get wet; and in the evenings the beams of the ceiling would hang with lengths of pale buckskin leggings, drying out slowly.

She felt peaceful remembering. She didn't feel cold any more. Jimmie's blanket seemed warmer than it had ever been. And she could remember the morning he was born. She could remember whispering to her mother, who was sleeping on the other side of the hogan, to tell her it was time now. She did not want to wake the others. The second time she called to her, her mother stood up and pulled on her shoes; she knew. They walked to the old stone hogan together, Ayah walking a step behind her mother. She waited alone, learning the rhythms of the pains while her mother went to call the old woman to help them. The morning was already warm even before dawn and Ayah smelled the bee flowers blooming and the young willow growing at the springs. She could remember that so clearly, but his birth merged into the births of the other children and to her it became all the same birth. They named him for the summer morning and in English they called him Jimmie.

It wasn't like Jimmie died. He just never came back, and one day a dark blue sedan with white writing on its doors pulled up in front of the boxcar shack where the rancher let the Indians live. A man in a khaki uniform trimmed in gold gave them a yellow piece of paper and told them that Jimmie was dead. He said the Army would try to get the body back and then it would be shipped to them; but it wasn't likely because the helicopter had burned after it crashed. All of this was told to Chato because he could understand English. She stood inside the doorway holding the baby while Chato listened. Chato spoke English like a white man and he spoke Spanish too. He was taller than the white man and he stood straighter too. Chato didn't explain why; he just told the military man they could keep the body if they found it. The white man looked bewildered; he nodded his head and he left. Then Chato looked at her and shook his head, and then he told her, "Jimmie isn't coming home anymore," and when he spoke, he used the words to speak of the dead. She didn't cry then, but she hurt inside with anger. And she mourned him as the years passed, when a horse fell with Chato and broke his leg, and the white rancher told them he wouldn't pay Chato until he could work again. She mourned Jimmie because he would have worked for his father then; he would have saddled the big bay horse and ridden the fence lines each day, with wire cutters and heavy gloves, fixing the breaks in the barbed wire and putting the stray cattle back inside again.

She mourned him after the white doctors came to take Danny and Ella away. She was at the shack alone that day they came. It was back in the days

---

3. Navajo dwelling usually made of logs and mud.

before they hired Navajo women to go with them as interpreters. She recognized one of the doctors. She had seen him at the children's clinic at Cañoncito about a month ago. They were wearing khaki uniforms and they waved papers at her and a black ball-point pen, trying to make her understand their English words. She was frightened by the way they looked at the children, like the lizard watches the fly. Danny was swinging on the tire swing on the elm tree behind the rancher's house, and Ella was toddling around the front door, dragging the broomstick horse Chato made for her. Ayah could see they wanted her to sign the papers, and Chato had taught her to sign her name. It was something she was proud of. She only wanted them to go, and to take their eyes away from her children.

She took the pen from the man without looking at his face and she signed the papers in three different places he pointed to. She stared at the ground by their feet and waited for them to leave. But they stood there and began to point and gesture at the children. Danny stopped swinging. Ayah could see his fear. She moved suddenly and grabbed Ella into her arms; the child squirmed, trying to get back to her toys. Ayah ran with the baby toward Danny; she screamed for him to run and then she grabbed him around his chest and carried him too. She ran south into the foothills of juniper trees and black lava rock. Behind her she heard the doctors running, but they had been taken by surprise, and as the hills became steeper and the cholla cactus were thicker, they stopped. When she reached the top of the hill, she stopped to listen in case they were circling around her. But in a few minutes she heard a car engine start and they drove away. The children had been too surprised to cry while she ran with them. Danny was shaking and Ella's little fingers were gripping Ayah's blouse.

She stayed up in the hills for the rest of the day, sitting on a black lava boulder in the sunshine where she could see for miles all around her. The sky was light blue and cloudless, and it was warm for late April. The sun warmth relaxed her and took the fear and anger away. She lay back on the rock and watched the sky. It seemed to her that she could walk into the sky, stepping through clouds endlessly. Danny played with little pebbles and stones, pretending they were birds eggs and then little rabbits. Ella sat at her feet and dropped fistfuls of dirt into the breeze, watching the dust and particles of sand intently. Ayah watched a hawk soar high above them, dark wings gliding; hunting or only watching, she did not know. The hawk was patient and he circled all afternoon before he disappeared around the high volcanic peak the Mexicans called Guadalupe.

Late in the afternoon, Ayah looked down at the gray boxcar shack with the paint all peeled from the wood; the stove pipe on the roof was rusted and crooked. The fire she had built that morning in the oil drum stove had burned out. Ella was asleep in her lap now and Danny sat close to her, complaining that he was hungry; he asked when they would go to the house. "We will stay up here until your father comes," she told him, "because those white men were chasing us." The boy remembered then and he nodded at her silently.

If Jimmie had been there he could have read those papers and explained to her what they said. Ayah would have known then, never to sign them. The doctors came back the next day and they brought a BIA[4] policeman with them. They told Chato they had her signature and that was all they needed.

4. Bureau of Indian Affairs.

Except for the kids. She listened to Chato sullenly; she hated him when he told her it was the old woman who died in the winter, spitting blood; it was her old grandma who had given the children this disease. "They don't spit blood," she said coldly. "The whites lie." She held Ella and Danny close to her, ready to run to the hills again. "I want a medicine man first," she said to Chato, not looking at him. He shook his head. "It's too late now. The policeman is with them. You signed the paper." His voice was gentle.

It was worse than if they had died: to lose the children and to know that somewhere, in a place called Colorado, in a place full of sick and dying strangers, her children were without her. There had been babies that died soon after they were born, and one that died before he could walk. She had carried them herself, up to the boulders and great pieces of the cliff that long ago crashed down from Long Mesa; she laid them in the crevices of sandstone and buried them in fine brown sand with round quartz pebbles that washed down the hills in the rain. She had endured it because they had been with her. But she could not bear this pain. She did not sleep for a long time after they took her children. She stayed on the hill where they had fled the first time, and she slept rolled up in the blanket Jimmie had sent her. She carried the pain in her belly and it was fed by everything she saw: the blue sky of their last day together and the dust and pebbles they played with; the swing in the elm tree and broomstick horse choked life from her. The pain filled her stomach and there was no room for food or for her lungs to fill with air. The air and the food would have been theirs.

She hated Chato, not because he let the policeman and doctors put the screaming children in the government car, but because he had taught her to sign her name. Because it was like the old ones always told her about learning their language or any of their ways: it endangered you. She slept alone on the hill until the middle of November when the first snows came. Then she made a bed for herself where the children had slept. She did not lie down beside Chato again until many years later, when he was sick and shivering and only her body could keep him warm. The illness came after the white rancher told Chato he was too old to work for him anymore, and Chato and his old woman should be out of the shack by the next afternoon because the rancher had hired new people to work there. That had satisfied her. To see how the white man repaid Chato's years of loyalty and work. All of Chato's fine-sounding English talk didn't change things.

It snowed steadily and the luminous light from the snow gradually diminished into the darkness. Somewhere in Cebolleta a dog barked and other village dogs joined with it. Ayah looked in the direction she had come, from the bar where Chato was buying the wine. Sometimes he told her to go on ahead and wait; and then he never came. And when she finally went back looking for him, she would find him passed out at the bottom of the wooden steps to Azzie's Bar. All the wine would be gone and most of the money too, from the pale blue check that came to them once a month in a government envelope. It was then that she would look at his face and his hands, scarred by ropes and the barbed wire of all those years, and she would think, this man is a stranger; for forty years she had smiled at him and cooked his food, but he remained a stranger. She stood up again, with the snow almost to her knees, and she walked back to find Chato.

It was hard to walk in the deep snow and she felt the air burn in her lungs. She stopped a short distance from the bar to rest and readjust the blanket. But this time he wasn't waiting for her on the bottom step with his old Stetson hat pulled down and his shoulders hunched up in his long wool overcoat.

She was careful not to slip on the wooden steps. When she pushed the door open, warm air and cigarette smoke hit her face. She looked around slowly and deliberately, in every corner, in every dark place that the old man might find to sleep. The bar owner didn't like Indians in there, especially Navajos, but he let Chato come in because he could talk Spanish like he was one of them. The men at the bar stared at her, and the bartender saw that she left the door open wide. Snowflakes were flying inside like moths and melting into a puddle on the oiled wood floor. He motioned to her to close the door, but she did not see him. She held herself straight and walked across the room slowly, searching the room with every step. The snow in her hair melted and she could feel it on her forehead. At the far corner of the room, she saw red flames at the mica window of the old stove door; she looked behind the stove just to make sure. The bar got quiet except for the Spanish polka music playing on the jukebox. She stood by the stove and shook the snow from her blanket and held it near the stove to dry. The wet wool smell reminded her of new-born goats in early March, brought inside to warm near the fire. She felt calm.

In past years they would have told her to get out. But her hair was white now and her face was wrinkled. They looked at her like she was a spider crawling slowly across the room. They were afraid; she could feel the fear. She looked at their faces steadily. They reminded her of the first time the white people brought her children back to her that winter. Danny had been shy and hid behind the thin white woman who brought them. And the baby had not known her until Ayah took her into her arms, and then Ella had nuzzled close to her as she had when she was nursing. The blonde woman was nervous and kept looking at a dainty gold watch on her wrist. She sat on the bench near the small window and watched the dark snow clouds gather around the mountains; she was worrying about the unpaved road. She was frightened by what she saw inside too: the strips of venison drying on a rope across the ceiling and the children jabbering excitedly in a language she did not know. So they stayed for only a few hours. Ayah watched the government car disappear down the road and she knew they were already being weaned from these lava hills and from this sky. The last time they came was in early June, and Ella stared at her the way the men in the bar were now staring. Ayah did not try to pick her up; she smiled at her instead and spoke cheerfully to Danny. When he tried to answer her, he could not seem to remember and he spoke English words with the Navajo. But he gave her a scrap of paper that he had found somewhere and carried in his pocket; it was folded in half, and he shyly looked up at her and said it was a bird. She asked Chato if they were home for good this time. He spoke to the white woman and she shook her head. "How much longer?" he asked, and she said she didn't know; but Chato saw how she stared at the boxcar shack. Ayah turned away then. She did not say good-bye.

She felt satisfied that the men in the bar feared her. Maybe it was her face and the way she held her mouth with teeth clenched tight, like there was nothing anyone could do to her now. She walked north down the road, searching for the old man. She did this because she had the blanket, and there would be no place for him except with her and the blanket in the old adobe barn near the arroyo. They always slept there when they came to Cebolleta. If the money and the wine were gone, she would be relieved because then they could go home again; back to the old hogan with a dirt roof and rock walls where she herself had been born. And the next day the old man could go back to the few sheep they still had, to follow along behind them, guiding them, into dry sandy arroyos where sparse grass grew. She knew he did not like walking behind old ewes when for so many years he rode big quarter horses and worked with cattle. But she wasn't sorry for him; he should have known all along what would happen.

There had not been enough rain for their garden in five years; and that was when Chato finally hitched a ride into the town and brought back brown boxes of rice and sugar and big tin cans of welfare peaches. After that, at the first of the month they went to Cebolleta to ask the postmaster for the check; and then Chato would go to the bar and cash it. They did this as they planted the garden every May, not because anything would survive the summer dust, but because it was time to do this. The journey passed the days that smelled silent and dry like the caves above the canyon with yellow painted buffaloes on their walls.

He was walking along the pavement when she found him. He did not stop or turn around when he heard her behind him. She walked beside him and she noticed how slowly he moved now. He smelled strongly of woodsmoke and urine. Lately he had been forgetting. Sometimes he called her by his sister's name and she had been gone for a long time. Once she had found him wandering on the road to the white man's ranch, and she asked him why he was going that way; he laughed at her and said, "You know they can't run that ranch without me," and he walked on determined, limping on the leg that had been crushed many years before. Now he looked at her curiously, as if for the first time, but he kept shuffling along, moving slowly along the side of the highway. His gray hair had grown long and spread out on the shoulders of the long overcoat. He wore the old felt hat pulled down over his ears. His boots were worn out at the toes and he had stuffed pieces of an old red shirt in the holes. The rags made his feet look like little animals up to their ears in snow. She laughed at his feet; the snow muffled the sound of her laugh. He stopped and looked at her again. The wind had quit blowing and the snow was falling straight down; the southeast sky was beginning to clear and Ayah could see a star.

"Let's rest awhile," she said to him. They walked away from the road and up the slope to the giant boulders that had tumbled down from the red sandrock mesa throughout the centuries of rainstorms and earth tremors. In a place where the boulders shut out the wind, they sat down with their backs against the rock. She offered half of the blanket to him and they sat wrapped together.

The storm passed swiftly. The clouds moved east. They were massive and full, crowding together across the sky. She watched them with the feeling of horses—steely blue-gray horses startled across the sky. The powerful haunches pushed into the distances and the tail hairs streamed white mist behind them. The sky cleared. Ayah saw that there was nothing between her and the stars. The light was crystalline. There was no shimmer, no distortion through earth haze. She breathed the clarity of the night sky; she smelled the purity of the half moon and the stars. He was lying on his side with his knees pulled up near his belly for warmth. His eyes were closed now, and in the light from the stars and the moon, he looked young again.

She could see it descend out of the night sky: an icy stillness from the edge of the thin moon. She recognized the freezing. It came gradually, sinking snowflake by snowflake until the crust was heavy and deep. It had the strength of the stars in Orion, and its journey was endless. Ayah knew that with the wine he would sleep. He would not feel it. She tucked the blanket around him, remembering how it was when Ella had been with her; and she felt the rush so big inside her heart for the babies. And she sang the only song she knew to sing for babies. She could not remember if she had ever sung it to her children, but she knew that her grandmother had sung it and her mother had sung it:

> *The earth is your mother,*
> *she holds you.*
> *The sky is your father,*
> *he protects you.*
> *Sleep,*
> *sleep.*
> *Rainbow is your sister,*
> *she loves you.*
> *The winds are your brothers,*
> *they sing to you.*
> *Sleep,*
> *sleep.*
> *We are together always*
> *We are together always*
> *There never was a time*
> *when this*
> *was not so.*

1981

JULIA ALVAREZ
b. 1950

Language, culture, politics, and region are customarily subjects for serious study, but in the work of Julia Alvarez they become the impetus for great creativity, even festivity. This is because many of Alvarez's characters share a background like her own, in which these elements are anything but stable. Born in New York City, raised in the Dominican Republic,and returned to Brooklyn when her father's activities put him in danger from the dictator Rafael Trujillo, Alvarez faced the same prospect as her most typical protagonist: that of improvising a sense of self. Such improvisation typifies young Yolanda in Alvarez's first novel, *How the García Girls Lost Their Accents* (1991), and the sixteen members of Yolanda's immediate and extended family react to that

improvisation in its sequel, ¡Yo! (1997). If Yolanda, nicknamed "Yo," can invent herself, so can her parents, siblings, cousins, aunts, and close friends judge her approximation of reality against theirs—and how many there are! The result is a carnival of
language and language's many contexts, in which humor and the self-conscious joy of
storytelling create a virtual conversation with the reader.

As a writer Alvarez has explored the double identities she shared as a young girl
negotiating her way on Brooklyn playgrounds, no longer a citizen of the Dominican
Republic but not yet accepted as an American. After doing graduate work at Syracuse
University and publishing a book of poems, *Homecoming* (1984), she turned to the
multiform saga of the García girls as a way of exploring the more playful aspects of
language, a style of heteroglossia advocated by the Russian literary theorist M. M.
Bakhtin. *How the García Girls Lost Their Accents* uses interrelated narratives of the
four sisters to contrast their hard-won American identities with the different styles of
life they had led as youngsters, first in the Dominican Republic and then as immigrants to fast-paced New York. A third novel (not as properly a sequel as is ¡Yo!), *In the
Time of the Butterflies* (1994), takes the historical event of three sisters' murder by Trujillo's secret police and retells it from a fictional perspective, that of a fourth, surviving sibling. Here are the more sober aspects of language, culture, politics, and region
that are presented more happily in ¡Yo!

In recent years Alvarez, like other Latina writers, has focused on the writer's role in
fashioning a voice, particularly as that voice undertakes what critic Kelli Lyon Johnson calls "generic transgressions" in which fiction, poetry, autobiography, history, children's literature, and even literary theory intermix. *In the Name of Salomé* (2000) is
presented as a novel, although its protagonists are historical figures prominent as a
poet in the Dominican Republic (the mother) and a scholar in the United States (her
daughter). Alvarez has taught for many years at Vermont's Middlebury College, where
she is writer-in-residence between regular visits to the Dominican Republic.

The text is from ¡Yo! (1997).

From ¡Yo!

The Mother

To tell you the truth, the hardest thing coming to this country wasn't the
winter everyone warned me about—it was the language. If you had to choose
the most tongue-twisting way of saying you love somebody or how much a
pound for the ground round, then say it in English. For the longest time I
thought Americans must be smarter than us Latins—because how else could
they speak such a difficult language. After a while, it struck me the other way.
Given the choice of languages, only a fool would choose to speak English on
purpose.

I guess for each one in the family it was different what was the hardest
thing. For Carlos, it was having to start all over again at forty-five, getting a
license, setting up a practice. My eldest Carla just couldn't bear that she wasn't
the know-it-all anymore. Of course, the Americans knew their country better
than she did. Sandi got more complicated, prettier, and I suppose that made
it hard on her, discovering she was a princess just as she had lost her island
kingdom. Baby Fifi took to this place like china in a china shop, so if anything,
the hardest thing for her was hearing the rest of us moan and complain. As
for Yo, I'd have to say the hardest thing about this country was being thrown
together in such close proximity with me.

Back on the island[1] we lived as a clan, not as what is called here *the nuclear family*,[2] which already the name should be a hint that you're asking for trouble cooping up related tempers in the small explosive chambers of each other's attention. The girls used to run with their gang of cousins, supervised—if you can call it that—by a whole bunch of aunts and nanny-maids who had wiped our bottoms when *we* were babies and now were wiping the drool of the old people who had hired them half a century ago. There was never any reason to clash with anyone. You didn't get along with your mother? You had two sisters, one brother-in-law, three brothers and their wives, thirteen nieces and nephews, a husband, your own kids, two great-aunts, your father, a bachelor uncle, a deaf poor relation, and a small army of housemaids to mediate and appease—so that if you muttered under your breath, "You bitch!" by the time it got to your mother it would sound something like, "Pass the mango dish, please."

And this was true for Yo and me.

Back there, that one was mostly raised by the maids. She seemed to like to hang around them more than she did her own kin, so that if she had been darker, I would have thought she was a changeling that got switched with my own flesh and blood. True, from time to time we did have our run-downs—not even three, four dozen people could always block the clashing of our two strong wills.

But I had a trick that I played back then, not just on her, but on all my girls, to make them behave. I called it putting on the bear. Of course, by the time we left the island, it no longer worked there, and it was only by mistake that it worked once here.

It started innocently enough. My mother had given me a mink coat she used to wear when she and my father were traveling a lot to New York for vacations away from the dictatorship.[3] I kept it at the back of the walk-in closet, thinking maybe someday we would escape the hell we were living in, and I'd get to wear that coat into freedom. Often I thought about selling it. I hadn't married a rich man and we were always short on money.

But every time I got ready to sell it, I don't know. I'd bury my nose in that tickling fur that still held the smell of my mother's perfume. I'd imagine myself walking down Fifth Avenue with lights twinkling in the shop windows and snowflakes coming down so pretty, and I just couldn't bear to part with the coat. I'd slip the plastic cover back over it and think, I'll hold on to it a while longer.

Then one Christmas, I thought it'd be kind of neat to dress up for all the kids. So I draped this coat over my head with a bit of my face poking out, and the rest of the fur falling all the way down to my calves. I had some story worked out that Santa Claus couldn't make it down from the North Pole, so he had sent one of his bears instead.

My girls and their cousins took one look at me and it was like sheets hitting a fan. They screamed and ran. No one could be coaxed to come forward

1. The Dominican Republic, a Caribbean nation that shares the island of Hispaniola with Haiti.
2. A family consisting of a father, mother, and a small number of children, closely spaced in age.
3. Of Rafael Trujillo (1891–1961), president of the Dominican Republic (1930–38, 1942–52) and always in ultimate control thanks to the support of the army, until a military coup led to his assassination.

for a present. Finally, Carlos pantomined chasing me off with a broom, and as I hurried away, I dropped my pillowcase of goodies. Minutes later, when I walked back in, dressed in my red organdy, the girls ran to me, "Mami! Mami! El cuco[4] was here!" El cuco was the Haitian boogeyman I had told them would come and steal them away if they didn't behave.

"Really?" I said, miming surprise. "What did you do?"

The girls looked at each other, big-eyed. What could they have done but avoid being mouthfuls for a monster with an appetite for their toys. But Yo piped up, "I beat him and chased him away!"

Here was a little problem that was not going to go away by itself. Often, I put Tabasco in that mouth hoping to burn away the lies that seemed to spring from her lips. For Yo, talking was like an exercise in what you could make up. But that night was Christmas Eve, and the dictatorship seemed far away in some storybook about cucos, and Carlos looked so handsome in his white guayabera,[5] like a rich plantation owner in an American ad for coffee beans or cigars. Besides I felt pleased with my little trick.

From then on, especially when I heard them fighting, I threw that coat over my head and went hooting down the hall. I'd burst into their room, swinging my arms, calling out their names, and they'd scream, holding on to each other, whatever fight they had been in the middle of forgotten. Step by step, I approached, until they were at the edge of hysterics, their little faces pale and their eyes wide with terror. Then I flung the coat off and threw out my arms, "It's me, Mami!"

For a minute, even though they could see it was me, they hung back, unconvinced.

Maybe it was a mean thing to do, I don't know. After a few times, what I was really trying to do was see if my girls had any sense at all. I thought for sure they would catch on. But no, each time, I fooled them. And I began to feel angry at them for being so slow.

Yo figured it out, finally. Maybe she was five, six—I don't know. All those years have mixed together like an old puzzle whose box top is lost. (I don't even know anymore what picture all those little pieces make.) As usual, I went howling into the girls' bedroom. But this time, Yo broke loose, came right up to me, and yanked that coat off my head. "See," she said, turning to the others. "It *is* just Mami like I told you."

It was no surprise to me that she was the one who caught on.

Back in my room, I was returning the coat when I noticed someone had been poking around in the closet. My shoes were scattered every which way, a hat box knocked over. That closet wasn't just any walk-in closet. It had once been a hallway between the master bedroom and Carlos's study, but we had closed it off on both sides in order to make a closet you could enter from either room. It was almost always locked on account of we kept everything valuable there. I suppose at the back of our minds, Carlos and I always knew that one day we would have to leave the island in a hurry and that it would be handy to have our cash and valuables on hand. And so, I was fit to be fried seeing signs that someone had been rifling through our hiding place.

Then it came to me who our intruder had been—Yo! Earlier, I had seen her

---

4. The cuckoo (Spanish), with implications of shrewd, crafty, and sly.

5. Light, blousy shirt.

in Carlos's study, looking over the medical books her father let her play with. She must have gone in our closet, and that's how she had figured out the fur was just a fur. I was ready to call her in and give her a large serving of my right hand when I saw that the floorboards close to the study side had been pried open and not exactly wedged back in place. I crawled in under the clothes with a flashlight and lifted one of those boards. It was my turn to go pale— stashed inside and wrapped in one of my good towels was a serious-looking gun.

You can bet when Carlos came home, I threatened to leave him right then and there if he didn't tell me what he was up to. I found out more than I wanted to know.

"No harm done," Carlos kept saying. "I'll just move it to another location tonight." And he did, wrapping it inside my fur coat and laying the bundle on the back seat of the Buick like he was going off to sell that coat after all. He came back late that night, the coat over his arm, and it wasn't until the next morning as I was hanging it up that I found the oil stains on the lining. They looked just like dried blood.

After that, I was a case all right. Nights, I was up to four sleeping pills to numb myself into a few hours of the skimpiest sleep. Days I took Valium[6] to ease that jumpy feeling. It was hell on the wheels of our marriage having me down so much of the time. Worst were the migraines I got practically every afternoon. I'd have to lie down in that small, hot bedroom with the jalousies angled shut and a wet towel on my face. Far off, I could hear the kids yelling in their bedroom, and I'd wish I could squeeze that bear trick one more time to terrify them into silence.

Lots of worries went through my pounding head those afternoons. One of them that kept hammering away was that Yo had been snooping around in that closet. If she had seen that hidden gun, it was just a matter of time before she'd tell someone about it. Already I could see the SIM[7] coming to the door to drag us away. One afternoon when I just couldn't stand it anymore, I leapt out of my bed and called down the hall for her to come to my room this instant.

She must have thought she was going to get it about all the loud bickering coming from their bedroom. She hurried down the hall already defending herself that she had plucked off Fifi's baby doll's head only because Fifi had asked her to. "Hush now," I said, "it's not about that!" That stopped her short. She hung back at the door, looking around my bedroom like maybe she wasn't so sure the bear was nothing but her mother in a fur coat after all.

I gave her a little pep talk in a soft voice—the way you talk to babies as you stroke them till their eyes drift shut. I told her Papá Dios in heaven could see into every one of our souls. He knew when we were good and when we were bad. When we lied and when we told the truth. That He could have asked us to do whatever He wanted, but out of all the hundred million things, He had only chosen ten holy commandments for us to obey. And one of those ten was honor thy father and mother which meant you shouldn't lie to them.

"So always, always, you must tell your mami the truth." I served her a big smile of which she only returned a little slice back. She knew something else

---

6. Mood-elevating prescription drug.
7. Servicio de Inteligencia Militar (Spanish for

"Military Intelligence Service"), Trujillo's dreaded secret police.

was coming. She sat on the bed, watching me. Just as she had seen through the fur to her mother, now she was looking through her mother to the scared woman inside. I let out a long sigh, and said, "Now, cuca darling, Mami wants you to tell her what things you saw when you went looking in the closet the other day."

"You mean the big closet?" she said, pointing down the passageway that led from the master bedroom to the walk-in closet and right through to her father's study.

"That very one," I said. The migraine was hammering away inside my head, building its big house of pain.

She looked at me like she knew that admitting she had been snooping would get her into a closet full of trouble. So, I promised her that telling the truth this time would make her my and God's little darling.

"I saw your coat," she said.

"That's very good," I said. "That's what I mean. What else did you see in Mami's closet?"

"Your funny shoes," she remarked. She meant the heels with little holes pockmarked in the leather.

"Excellent!" I said. "Mami's darling. What else?"

She went through that whole closet with the full inventory of practically every piece of clothing I owned. My God, I thought, give her another decade and *she* could work for the SIM. I lay there, listening because what else could I do? If she hadn't really seen anything, I didn't want to put any ideas in her head. That one had a mouth from here to China going the long way like Columbus's ships.

"How about the floor?" I asked stupidly. "Did you see anything *in* the floor?"

She shook her head in a way that didn't convince me. I went back over the ten commandments and not lying to thy mother, and still I couldn't flush any more information from her except my monogrammed hankies and, oh yes, my nylons in a pleated plastic case. I finally made her promise that if she remembered anything else, she should come and tell Mami directly and no one else. "It will be our little secret," I whispered to her.

Just as she was slipping out the door, she turned around and said a curious thing. "Mami, the bear won't be coming anymore." It was as if she were stating her part of our bargain. "Honey cuca," I said. "Remember, Mami was the one playing the bear. It was just a silly joke. But no," I promised her, "that bear's gone for good. Okay?" She nodded her approval.

As soon as the door latched shut I cried into my pillow. My head was hurting so much. I missed not having nice things, money and freedom. I hated being at the mercy of my own child, but in that house we were all at the mercy of her silence from that day on.

Isn't a story a charm? All you have to say is, *And then we came to the United States,* and with that *and then,* you skip over four more years of disappearing friends, sleepless nights, house arrest, narrow escape, *and then,* you've got two adults and four wired-up kids in a small, dark apartment near Columbia University. Yo must have kept her mouth shut or no charm would have worked to get us free of the torture chambers we kept telling the immigration people about so they wouldn't send us back.

Not being one hundred percent sure we would get to stay—that was the hardest thing at the beginning. Even the problem with the English language seemed like a drop in a leaky bucket then. It was later that I got to thinking English was the hardest thing of all for me. But believe me, back then at the beginning, I had my hands too full to be making choices among our difficulties.

Carlos was morose. All he could think about was the compañeros he had left behind. I kept asking him what else he could have done but stay to die with them. He was studying like cats and dogs for his license exam. We were living on the low end of the hog off what little savings we had left, and there was no money coming in. I was worried how I was going to pay for the warm clothes my kids would be needing once the cold weather set in.

The last thing I needed was their whining and fighting. Every day it was the same question, "When are we going to go back?" Now that we were far away and I wasn't afraid of their blurting things out, I tried to explain. But it was as if they thought I was lying to them with a story to make them behave. They'd listen, but as soon as I was done, they'd start in again. They wanted to go back to their cousins and uncles and aunts and the maids. I thought they would feel more at home once school began. But September, October, November, December passed by, and they were still having nightmares and nagging me all the long days that they wanted to go back. Go back. Go back. Go back.

I resorted to locking them in closets. That old-fashioned apartment was full of them, deep closets with glass knobs and those keyholes like in cartoons for detectives to look through and big iron keys with the handle part shaped like a fleur-de-lis. I always used the same four closets, a small one in the girls' bedroom and the big one in mine, the broom closet in the hall, and finally the coat closet in the living room. Which child went into which depended on who I grabbed first where.

I wouldn't leave them in there for long. Believe me. I'd go from door to door, like a priest taking confession, promising to let them out the minute they calmed down and agreed to live in peace. I don't know how it happened that Yo never got the coat closet until that one time that I lived to regret.

I had shut them all up and gone round, letting out the baby first, then the oldest, who was always so outraged. Then the two middle kids, first Sandi. When I got to Yo's door, I didn't get an answer. That scared me, and I opened that door quick. There she stood, pale with fright. And, ay, I felt so terrible!— she had gone in her pants.

That damn mink coat was in that closet, way to one side, but of course, being Yo, she'd gone poking around in the dark. She must have touched the fur and lost her bananas. I don't understand because it had seemed she knew the fur was just a coat. Maybe she associated me being under that coat, and here I was on one side of the door, and there she was alone on the other side with a monster she was sure we had left behind in the Dominican Republic.

I pulled her out and into the bathroom. She didn't cry. No—just that low moan kids do when they go deep inside themselves looking for the mother you haven't turned out to be for them. All she said that whole time I was trying to clean her up was, "You promised that bear was gone for good."

I got weepy myself. "You girls are the bears! And here I thought all our troubles would end when we got here." I laid down my head on my arms on the side of the bathtub, and I started bawling. "Ay, Mami, ay," the other three joined in. They had come to the door of the bathroom to see what was going on. "We promise we'll be good."

Not Yo. She stood up in the water and grabbed a towel, then stomped out of the tub. When she was out of my reach, she cried, "I don't want to be in this crazy family!"

Even back then, she always had to have the last word.

Not a week later a social worker at the school, Sally O'Brien, calls up and asks to make a house visit. The minute I get off the phone, I interrogate my girls about what they might have said to this lady. But they all swear that they have nothing to confess. I warn them if this lady gives us a bad report we'll be sent back, and if we are sent back, cucos and bears are going to be stuffed animals compared to the SIM fieras[8] that will tear us apart there. I send them off to put on their matching polka dot dresses I made them for coming to the United States. And then I do what I haven't done in our six months here. I take a Valium to give this lady a good impression.

In she comes, a tall lady in flat black shoes with straps and a blond braid down her back like a schoolgirl dressed in an old lady's suit. She has a pleasant, un-made-up face and eyes so blue and sincere you know they've yet to see the worst things in the world. She carries a satchel with little hearts painted on it. Out of it she pulls a long yellow tablet with our name already written on it. "Is it all right if I take some notes?"

"Of course, Mrs. O'Brien." I don't know if she is a married woman but I've decided to compliment her with a husband even if she doesn't have one.

"Will your husband be joining us?" she asks, looking around the room. I follow her glance since I am sure she is checking out whether the place looks clean and adequate for raising four girls. The coat closet I forgot to shut looms like a torture chamber.

"My husband just received his medical license. So he has been working like a god every day, even Sunday," I add, which she writes down in her notepad. "We have been through hard times." I've already decided that I won't try to pretend that we're having a ball in America, though believe it or not, that was my original plan on how to handle this visit. I thought it would sound more patriotic.

"That must be a relief!" she says, nodding her head and looking at me. Everything she says it's like she just put the rattle in the baby's hand and is waiting to see what the baby is going to do with it.

I shake it, good and hard. "We are free at last," I tell her. "Thanks to this great country which has offered us the green cards. We cannot go back," I add. "It would be certain death."

Her eyes blink at this, and she makes a note. "I read things in the paper," she says, bringing her braid from behind to fall down the front of her suit. She doesn't seem the nervous type, but the way she keeps minding that braid it's like she is getting paid to keep it occupied. "But are things really that bad?"

And right then and there in my broken English that usually cuts my ideas down to the wrong size, I fill her two ears full with what is happening back on the island—homes raided, people hauled off, torture chambers, electric

8. Wild beasts (Spanish).

prods, attacks by dogs, fingernails pulled out. I get a little carried away and invent a few tortures of my own—nothing the SIM hadn't thought up, I'm sure. As I talk, she keeps wincing until her hands go up to her forehead like she has caught one of my migraines. In a whisper she says, "This is truly awful. You must be so worried about the rest of your family."

I can't trust my voice to say so. I give her a little nod.

"But what I don't get is how the girls keep saying they want to go back. That things were better there."

"They are sick of home—" I explain, but that doesn't sound right.

"Homesick, yes," she says.

I nod. "They are children. They do not see the forest or the trees."

"I understand." She says it so nicely that I am convinced that even with those untried blue eyes, she does understand. "They can't know the horror you and your husband have lived through."

I try to keep the tears back, but of course they come. What this lady can't know is that I'm not just crying about leaving home or about everything we've lost, but about what's to come. It's not really until now with the whole clan pulled away like the foundation under a house that I wonder if the six of us will stand together.

"I understand, I understand," she keeps saying until I get control of myself. "We're just concerned because the girls seem so anxious. Especially Yolanda."

I knew it! "Has she been telling stories?"

The lady nods slowly. "Her teacher says she loves stories. But some of the ones she tells, well—" She lets out a sigh. She tosses her braid behind her back like she doesn't want it to hear this. "Frankly, they are a little disturbing."

"Disturbing?" I ask. Even though I know what the word means, it sounds worse coming out of this woman's mouth.

"Oh, she's been mentioning things . . ." The lady waves her hand vaguely. "Things like what you were describing. Kids locked in closets and their mouths burned with lye. Bears mauling little children." She stops a moment, maybe because of the shocked look on my face.

"It doesn't surprise me," the woman explains. "In fact, I'm glad she's getting it all out."

"Yes," I say. And suddenly, I am feeling such envy for my daughter, who is able to speak of what terrifies her. I myself can't find the words in English— or Spanish. Only the howling of the bear I used to impersonate captures some of what I feel.

"Yo has always been full of stories." I say it like an accusation.

"Oh, but you should be proud of her," the lady says, bringing her braid forward like she is going to defend Yo with it.

"Proud?" I say in disbelief, ready to give her all the puzzle pieces of my mind so she gets the full picture. But then, I realize it is no use. How can this lady with her child's eyes and her sweet smile understand who I am and what I have been through? And maybe this is a blessing after all. That people only know the parts we want to tell about ourselves. Look at her. Inside that middle-aged woman is a nervous girl playing with her braid. But how that girl got stuck in there, and where the key is to let her out, maybe not even she can tell?

"Who knows where Yo got that need to invent," I finally say because I don't know what else to say.

"This has been very helpful, Laura," she says, standing up to go. "And I want you to know if there's anything we can do to help you all in settling in, please don't hesitate to call." She hands me a little card, not like our calling cards back home with all your important family names in fancy gold lettering. This one shows her name and title and the name of the school and her phone number in black print.

"Let me call the girls to say goodbye."

She smiles when they come out in their pretty, ironed dresses, curtsying like I taught them. And as she bends to shake each one's hand, I glance down at her pad on the coffee table and read the notes she has jotted: *Trauma/ dictatorship/family bonds strong/mother devoted.*

For a moment I feel redeemed as if everything we are suffering and everything we will suffer is the fault of the dictatorship. I know this will be the story I tell in the future about those hard years—how we lived in terror, how the girls were traumatized by the experience, how many nights I got up to check on their blankets and they screamed if I touched them.

But never mind. Within a year of all this, the dictator will be shot dead by some of the very men who were in the underground with my husband. The girls will be jabbering away in English like they were born to it. As for the mink, I will exchange it at the secondhand shop on Fifth Avenue for four little-girl coats. If nothing else, my children will be warm that first winter everyone warned would be the hardest thing about coming to this country.

1997

JORIE GRAHAM
b. 1950

Jorie Graham's ability to render the disjunctive activity of modern thought, without abandoning the sensuousness of perception, has made her a prominent contemporary poet. Her poems are sites of self-questioning thinking—about metaphysics, epistemology, or the nature of language. As her imagination moves between polarities, she explores the tensions between spirit and matter, thought and sensation, formlessness and form. Rather than resolve these tensions, her poems examine the dependence of each term on the other, as well as the gap between them. This gap is sometimes figured as a literal blank ("————"), a space language cannot fill. At other times it appears as the moment when things "scatter, blow away, scatter, recollect" ("The Dream of the Unified Field"), a moment in which form and the undoing of form coexist. Graham's poems often work in liminal spaces between the visible and the invisible, like the scene of the souls at Judgment hurrying to reenter the flesh in "At Luca Signorelli's Resurrection of the Body": "there is no / entrance, / only entering." She has called poetic form "a vessel for active tension," and the rapid shifts in Graham's poems from past to present, from abstract to particular, make the surface of her work appear to be eddied by verbal and intellectual turbulence. No wonder "roil" is one of her favorite verbs.

Graham was born in New York, but when she was a child her father, a *Newsweek* correspondent, and her mother, a sculptor, moved to Italy, where Graham grew up in the neighborhood of Trastevere, the old part of Rome. She lived surrounded by Italian churches full of frescoes, and references to Italian art inform many of her poems, among them "San Sepolcro" and "At Luca Signorelli's Resurrection of the Body." In Italy Graham attended a French lycée, and at seventeen she went to Paris to study at the Sorbonne, where she became involved in the student uprisings of 1968. In 1969 she returned to the United States and enrolled in film school at New York University (where she remembers hearing poetry read aloud in English for the first time), and from the start her poetry has been influenced by cinema. She went on to earn an M.F.A. from the University of Iowa Writers Workshop, where she later taught for a number of years; currently she is on the faculty at Harvard University. The range of reference in Graham's work is wide and suggests her European background and especially her French education, with its emphasis on philosophy. But she is equally preoccupied with American history and the nature of American life, a preoccupation evident in "The Dream of the Unified Field," which closes with her revision of entries from Christopher Columbus's journals.

What Graham calls "the calm assurance of the standard English line" has "interested and troubled" her. Although her poems often move in and out of an iambic measure (as in the openings of "The Geese" and "The Dream of the Unified Field"), like many poets she believes contemporary experience requires a more unpredictable music. The poems of her first book, *Hybrids of Plants and of Ghosts* (1980; the title is taken from the German philosopher Friedrich Nietzsche), were mostly constructed of short, tightly controlled lines. But in subsequent works her verse has loosened (a second volume is called *Erosion*, 1983) and her line grown longer. Many of the poems from *The End of Beauty* (1987), *The Region of Unlikeness* (1991), *Materialism* (1993), *The Errancy* (1994), *Swarm* (2000), and *Overlord* (2005) hurtle across and down the page, sometimes without punctuation. Because she shares a contemporary skepticism of any version of reality that claims to be total, her work characteristically undercuts what it asserts. She works best in a form that supports the pull of coexisting and unreconciled tensions; for example, the short, enjambed lines of "At Luca Signorelli's Resurrection of the Body" separate each distinct detail and gesture while also tugging one perception into the next. The rhythmic structure of that poem holds apart and, at the same time, overlaps the visible and the invisible; the poem ends without resolving or unifying this opposition.

When Graham tries to imagine a unity that includes polarities (as in "The Dream of the Unified Field"), that unity is a "dream" because she is aware that the drive for order and closure (what she calls "the silky swerve into shapeliness / and then the click shut" in "Region of Unlikeness") risks narrowness and exclusion. Therefore Graham's work exposes the fractures in experience and in the self (fractures often gendered as male and female). But her poems also work to uncover, through a series of associations, the connections between daily experience (looking up at a flock of geese, bringing her daughter a leotard she had forgotten) and the larger frameworks of history, metaphysics, and myth. At times her drive to find or make analogies between a particular experience and its larger historical contexts can feel false or strained. But, resolutely self-interrogating, Graham sees each new book as a critique of her previous work. She is willing to risk failure in pursuit of a poetry that renders the drama of consciousness unfolding in language and the world; in this she is the heir of Wallace Stevens, with his vision of "the poem of the mind in the act of finding / What will suffice." If the life of thought makes her poems abstract (one is titled "What Is Called Thinking"), the activity of perception, registered sometimes in almost microscopic detail (as in "Opulence"), makes them concrete. Her best and most challenging work combines these two modes in a series of rapid-moving procedures. "The Dream of the Unified Field," for example, explores memory and possession by building layers of association through shifting concrete images. The poem begins with thoughts of a daughter—"On my way to bringing you the leotard / you forgot to include in your overnight bag"—and shifts to a snowstorm, then to a vision of starlings "swarming / then settling," then to the leaves of a tree scattering and recollecting, until the poet

returns to the thought of her daughter dancing. When the memory of the poet's childhood ballet teacher surfaces, and then dissolves into the historical memory of Columbus's voyage of discovery, we experience an unexpected break in focus, a gap in
thought marked out by a series of interruptive dashes.

Graham's poems characteristically include the gaps in thought. Her work is also riddled with questions that implicitly or explicitly address the reader: "Do you think these
words are still enough?" and "Are you listening?" ("Manifest Destiny"). Describing her
poetic strategies, Graham says she imagines a reader "who has heard it all before" (her
poem "Imperialism" names this reader: "dear are-you-there"), one who distrusts language as a medium for truth. The difficult surfaces of Graham's poems try to wake us
into full attention, so that we may confront, together with the poet, the question of
what language can and cannot say.

The Geese

Today as I hang out the wash I see them again, a code
as urgent as elegant,
tapering with goals.
For days they have been crossing. We live beneath these geese

as if beneath the passage of time, or a most perfect heading.   5
Sometimes I fear their relevance.
Closest at hand,
between the lines,

the spiders imitate the paths the geese won't stray from,
imitate them endlessly to no avail: 10
things will not remain connected,
will not heal,

and the world thickens with texture instead of history,
texture instead of place.
Yet the small fear of the spiders   15
binds and binds

the pins to the lines, the lines to the eaves, to the pincushion bush,
as if, at any time, things could fall further apart
and nothing could help them
recover their meaning. And if these spiders had their way,   20

chainlink over the visible world,
would we be in or out? I turn to go back in.
There is a feeling the body gives the mind
of having missed something, a bedrock poverty, like falling

without the sense that you are passing through one world,   25
that you could reach another
anytime. Instead the real
is crossing you,

your body an arrival
you know is false but can't outrun. And somewhere in between   30
these geese forever entering and
these spiders turning back,

this astonishing delay, the everyday, takes place.

1980

At Luca Signorelli's[1] Resurrection of the Body

See how they hurry
         to enter
their bodies,
         these spirits,
Is it better, flesh,   5
         that they

should hurry so?
         From above
the green-winged angels
         blare down   10
trumpets and light. But
         they don't care,

they hurry to congregate,
         they hurry
into speech, until   15
         it's a marketplace,
it is humanity. But still
         we wonder

in the chancel[2]
         of the dark cathedral,   20
is it better, back?
         The artist
has tried to make it so: each tendon
         they press

to re-enter   25
         is perfect. But is it
perfection
         they're after,
pulling themselves up
         through the soil   30

---

1. Italian painter (1450–1523) of the Umbrian school, associated with a region in central Italy distinguished in the Renaissance by the talent of its painters. His series on the Last Judgment decorates the Cappella Nuova in the gothic cathedral in Orvieto, Italy, a town in the Umbrian region. One of the sections of this series is titled *Resurrection of the Flesh*.

2. Space around a church altar, often enclosed by lattice or railing.

into the weightedness, the color,
  into the eye
of the painter? Outside
  it is 1500,
all round the cathedral   35
  streets hurry to open

through the wild
  silver grasses. . . .
The men and women
  on the cathedral wall   40
do not know how,
  having come this far,

to stop their
  hurrying. They amble off
in groups, in   45
  couples. Soon
some are clothed, there is
  distance, there is

perspective. Standing below them
  in the church   50
in Orvieto, how can we
  tell them
to be stern and brazen
  and slow,

that there is no   55
  entrance,
only entering. They keep on
  arriving,
wanting names,
  wanting   60

happiness. In his studio
  Luca Signorelli
in the name of God
  and Science
and the believable   65
  broke into the body

studying arrival.
  But the wall
of the flesh
  opens endlessly,   70
its vanishing point so deep
  and receding

we have yet to find it,
  to have it
stop us. So he cut   75

deeper,
graduating slowly
    from the symbolic

to the beautiful. How far
    is true?   80
When his one son
    died violently,
he had the body brought to him
    and laid it

on the drawing-table,   85
    and stood
at a certain distance
    awaiting the best
possible light, the best depth
    of day,   90

then with beauty and care
    and technique
and judgment, cut into
    shadow, cut
into bone and sinew and every   95
    pocket

in which the cold light
    pooled.
It took him days,
    that deep   100
caress, cutting,
    unfastening,

until his mind
    could climb into
the open flesh and   105
    mend itself.

1983

JOY HARJO
b. 1951

Joy Harjo was born in Tulsa, Oklahoma, to a mother of mixed Cherokee, French, and
Irish blood. She has described her father's family, members of the Creek (also known
as Muskogee) tribe, as "rebels and speakers," among them a Baptist minister (Harjo's
paternal grandfather), two painters (her grandmother and aunt), and a great-great-
grandfather who led a Creek rebellion against their forced removal from Alabama into
Oklahoma in 1832. As the critic Laura Coltelli has pointed out, the work of many con-

temporary Native American writers (a large number of whom are of mixed blood) enacts a quest to reenvision identity by confronting the historical, cultural, and political realities that shape lives experienced between different worlds. Drawing on a family tradition of powerful speaking, Harjo participates in a search to reimagine and repair painful fractures in contemporary experience: between past and present, between person and landscape, and between parts of the self. Thus traveling is a mythic activity in her poems, enacting this search for community and historical connectedness. As in the work of James Welch, Simon J. Ortiz, and Leslie Marmon Silko, the theme of traveling in Harjo's poems resonates with the historical displacements and migrations of native peoples (especially the forced removal of the Creeks). She has called herself the wanderer in her family, and her poems often map her journeys, whether on foot, by car, or in a plane. Perhaps Harjo thinks of herself as the family wanderer because she left Oklahoma to attend high school at the Institute of American Indian Arts in Santa Fe, New Mexico ("in a way it saved my life," she has said). Since receiving a B.A. from the University of New Mexico in 1976 and an M.F.A. from the University of Iowa, she has taught at the Institute of American Indian Arts, Arizona State University, the University of Colorado, the University of Arizona, and the University of New Mexico.

Harjo's vision of the interrelatedness of all things is common to Native American storytelling. The ethic that emerges from this worldview stresses reciprocity between people and various sources of power, including tradition and the natural world. Harjo's poems bring together mythic, feminist, and cultural perspectives and also unite contemporary urban experience with Native American myth and legend. In her collection *She Had Some Horses* (1983) this integration seeks to assuage the loneliness and desperation of those on the margin who populate much of the volume: a woman raising her mixed-blood children alone, a friend who threatens suicide, a woman who threatens to drop from a thirteenth-story window. The collection *In Mad Love and War* (1990) exhibits anger at the separations caused by dispossession and violence, as in an elegy for Anna Mae Pictou Aquash, a young Micmac woman shot dead on the Pine Ridge Reservation. Poems such as this recall the passion for social justice in the works of James Wright, Audre Lorde, and Leslie Marmon Silko; indeed, the spirit of Harjo's rebel great-great-grandfather is never far from her work.

Harjo has been a leading figure in the adaptation of oral traditions into written forms, consciously trying to make the written word in her poems duplicate certain oral and ceremonial techniques. Her poems extensively and emphatically use repetition, of both words and units of thought, as mnemonic and structuring devices. For example, her poem "When the World As We Knew It Ended," written in response to the events of September 11, 2001, begins a series of stanzas with the repetition and variation of "We saw it," "We heard it," "We knew it. . . ." Reflecting the understanding that Native American tradition is not fixed but evolves and changes, Harjo has fearlessly experimented, adapting new musical and poetic forms to Native American traditions. She has long drawn on reggae, rock, Creek Stomp Dance songs, country, and African music and has integrated performance and dance into her poetry. A musician and songwriter, she has released three CD collections: *Letter from the End of the Twentieth Century* (1997), *Native Joy for Real* (2005), and a musical version of her recently republished *She Had Some Horses* (2006). Harjo plays the saxophone, which is not a traditional Native American instrument, but, she has said, "Someday it may be."

Metamorphosis, common in Native American storytelling, is central to Harjo's vision, where the world is constituted by change and constancy. Her collection *The Woman Who Fell from the Sky* (1994) embodies metamorphosis in its structure—the retelling of contemporary experience through traditional myths—and metamorphosis recurs in its stories. Various Native American traditions tell the story of a sky woman who falls through the void of space and creates the human universe. In the title poem of this volume, a group of women ("angry at their inattentive husbands") run off with stars; one of these women dares to look back at Earth and falls from the sky. In Harjo's hands this myth becomes the story of two lovers, who were children together at an Indian boarding school. Adrift in an urban landscape, they are reunited, their narrative characterized by fracture and repair. In the same collection "Flood" renders a young girl's sexuality and imaginative power through the myth of the water monster. The prose poems that form much of this book remind us that Native American storytelling, an oral tradition, does not distinguish between poetry and prose. For all Harjo's anguished sense of the warring factions in our world and our selves, her works consistently engage in a process of healing and regeneration, themes that continue in her collection *A Map to the Next World* (2000). Like the kitchen table in her poem "Perhaps the World Ends Here," Harjo's poems are a space where "we sing with joy, with sorrow. We pray of suffering and remorse. We give thanks."

Harjo has also written screenplays and the text for Stephen Strom's photographs of the southwestern landscape, *Secrets from the Center of the World* (1989), and she has edited an anthology of tribal women's writings from around the world. A collection of interviews, *The Spiral of Memory* (1996), edited by Laura Coltelli, is a valuable accompaniment to her poems. *How We Became Human* (2003) presents a selection from Harjo's earlier work, including poems from hard to find chapbooks, as well as new work.

Call It Fear

There is this edge where shadows
and bones of some of us walk
               backwards.
Talk backwards. There is this edge
call it an ocean of fear of the dark. Or   5
name it with other songs. Under our ribs
our hearts are bloody stars. Shine on
shine on, and horses in their galloping flight
strike the curve of ribs.
               Heartbeat   10
and breathe back sharply. Breathe
                  backwards.
There is this edge within me
               I saw it once
an August Sunday morning when the heat hadn't   15
left this earth. And Goodluck
sat sleeping next to me in the truck.
We had never broken through the edge of the
singing at four a.m.
             We had only wanted to talk, to hear   20
any other voice to stay alive with.
             And there was this edge—
not the drop of sandy rock cliff
bones of volcanic earth into
             Albuquerque.[1]   25
Not that,
         but a string of shadow horses kicking

---

1. City in northern New Mexico.

and pulling me out of my belly,
            not into the Rio Grande[2] but into the music
barely coming through   30
            Sunday church singing
from the radio. Battery worn-down but the voices
talking backwards.

                                                            1983

White Bear

She begins to board the flight
    to Albuquerque.[1] Late night.
But stops in the corrugated tunnel,
    a space between leaving and staying,
where the night sky catches   5

            her whole life

she has felt like a woman
    balancing on a wooden nickle heart
approaching herself from here to
    there, Tulsa[2] or New York   10
with knives or corn meal.

The last flight someone talked
    about how coming from Seattle
the pilot flew a circle
    over Mt. St. Helens;[3] she sat   15
quiet. (But had seen the eruption
    as the earth beginning
to come apart, as in birth
    out of violence.)

She watches the yellow lights   20
    of towns below the airplane flicker,
fade and fall backwards. Somewhere,
    she dreamed, there is the white bear
moving down from the north, motioning her paws
    like a long arctic night, that kind   25
of circle and the whole world balanced in
    between carved of ebony and ice

            oh so hard

    the clear black nights
        like her daughter's eyes, and the white   30

---

2. River flowing from southern Colorado through New Mexico and then forming the boundary between Texas and Mexico.
1. See n. 1 above.

2. City in Oklahoma.
3. A volcanic peak in Washington State; it erupted in 1980.

bear moon, cupped like an ivory rocking
    cradle, tipping back it could go
    either way
        all darkness
               is open to all light.   35

1983

RITA DOVE
b. 1952

What she has called the "friction" between the beauty of a poetic form and a difficult or painful subject appeals to Rita Dove. Her own formal control and discipline create a beautiful design and a haunting music in "Parsley," a poem based on a murderous event: in 1957 the dictator of the Dominican Republic, Rafael Trujillo, ordered twenty thousand black Haitians killed because they could not pronounce the letter "r" in the Spanish word for parsley. What compels Dove in this poem is the way a "single, beautiful word" has the power of life and death. More astonishing is that she writes from the perspectives of both the Haitians in the cane fields and General Trujillo in his palace. When asked in an interview about her capacity to imagine Trujillo, Dove responded, "I frankly don't believe anyone who says they've never felt any evil, that they cannot understand that process of evil. It was important to me to try to understand that arbitrary quality of his cruelty. . . . Making us get into his head may shock us all into seeing what the human being is capable of, because if we can go that far into his head, we're halfway there ourselves." An ability to enter into different points of view in a single poem is characteristic of Dove's disinterested imagination. Her method is to avoid commentary, to let the imagined person or object, the suggestive detail, speak for itself. Often her work suggests what the English poet John Keats called "negative capability," the gift of the poet to become what he or she is not.

Born in Akron, Dove attended Miami University of Ohio and, after her graduation, studied modern European literature as a Fulbright/Hays fellow at the University of Tübingen in Germany. When she returned from Europe she earned an M.F.A. at the University of Iowa (in 1977). Later she taught creative writing at Arizona State University before joining the University of Virginia, where she is now Commonwealth Professor of English. Since her Fulbright year she has returned frequently to live abroad, in Ireland, Israel, France, and especially Germany. Her travel in Europe and elsewhere suggests part of the imperative she feels as a poet: to range widely through fields of experience, to cross boundaries of space as well as time. Her first book, *The Yellow House on the Corner* (1980), is notable for its intense poems about adolescence; her second book, *Museum* (1983), dramatically extends the range of her work. "When I started *Museum*," she has said, "I was in Europe, and I had a way of looking back on America and distancing myself from my experience." As well as for several fine poems about her father (a subject that may also have needed distance), the book is remarkable for the way distance allowed Dove to move out of her immediate experience, freed her to imagine widely different lives.

As if to show that it is also possible to travel widely while staying at home, Dove's *Thomas and Beulah* (1986) is an extended sequence based on her grandparents' lives. Her continuing fascination with imagining different perspectives on the same event is evident in this sequence. Dove has described the book's origins this way:

> My grandmother had told me a story that had happened to my grandfather when he was young, coming up on a riverboat to Akron, Ohio, my hometown. But that

was all I had basically. And the story so fascinated me that I tried to write about it. I started off writing stories about my grandfather and soon, because I ran out of real fact, in order to keep going, I made up facts for this character, Thomas. . . . then this poem "Dusting" appeared, really out of nowhere. I didn't realize this was Thomas's wife saying, "I want to talk. And you can't do his side without my side . . ."

This is the story, in part, of a marriage and of a black couple's life in the industrial Midwest in the period from 1900 to 1960. Thomas's point of view controls the poems of the book's first section, while the second part imagines his wife's. The larger framework of the sequence links family history to social history. Thomas's journey from the rural South to the industrial city of Akron (where he finds employment in the Goodyear Zeppelin factory until the Depression puts him out of work) is part of the larger social movement of southern African Americans into northern industrial cities in the first part of this century. The individual lyrics of Dove's sequence create and sustain the story through distinct and often ordinary moments in which each life is vividly portrayed. It is part of Dove's gift that she can render the apparently unimportant moments that inform a life and set them against a background of larger historical forces, as do Robert Hayden in *Elegies for Paradise Valley* and Robert Lowell in *Notebook*.

Many of the figures in Dove's poems are displaced, on the border between different worlds: for example, Thomas and Beulah and Benjamin Banneker ("Banneker"). The experience of displacement, of what she has called living in "two different worlds, seeing things with double vision," consistently compels this poet's imagination. It takes both detachment and control to maintain (and to live with) such doubleness. This may be why Dove's rich sense of language and her love of sound are joined to a disciplined formal sense. The forms of her poems often hold in place difficult or ambiguous feelings and keep the expression of feeling understated. While restraint is one strength of Dove's poems, her work can sometimes seem austere. Such careful control recalls Elizabeth Bishop's early work, also highly controlled and even, at times, guarded. As Bishop grew to relax her restraints, to open into an extraordinary expressiveness, so Dove has gifts to suggest a similar growth. Her collections *Grace Notes* (1989), *Mother Love* (1995), and *American Smooth* (2004) suggest just such a relaxing of the poet's guard, while *On the Bus with Rosa Parks* (2000) demonstrates ongoing ability to unite social conscience with a transformative sense of language and form. With each book she asks something more from herself, and she has now become one of our indispensable poets. Dove was poet laureate of the United States from 1993 to 1995.

Banneker[1]

What did he do except lie
under a pear tree, wrapped in
a great cloak, and meditate
on the heavenly bodies?
Venerable, the good people of Baltimore   5
whispered, shocked and more than

---

1. Benjamin Banneker (1731–1806), first black man to devise an almanac and predict a solar eclipse accurately, was also appointed to the commission that surveyed and laid out what is now Washington, D.C. [Dove's note].

a little afraid. After all it was said
he took to strong drink.
Why else would he stay out
under the stars all night   10
and why hadn't he married?

But who would want him! Neither
Ethiopian nor English, neither
lucky nor crazy, a capacious bird
humming as he penned in his mind   15
another enflamed letter
to President Jefferson[2]—he imagined
the reply, polite and rhetorical.
Those who had been to Philadelphia
reported the statue   20
of Benjamin Franklin
before the library

his very size and likeness.
A wife? No, thank you.
At dawn he milked   25
the cows, then went inside
and put on a pot to stew
while he slept. The clock
he whittled as a boy
still ran.[3] Neighbors   30
woke him up
with warm bread and quilts.
At nightfall he took out

his rifle—a white-maned
figure stalking the darkened   35
breast of the Union—and
shot at the stars, and by chance
one went out. Had he killed?
I assure thee, my dear Sir!
Lowering his eyes to fields   40
sweet with the rot of spring, he could see
a government's domed city
rising from the morass and spreading
in a spiral of lights. . . .

                                                          1983

---

2. After hearing that Jefferson doubted the mental
capacity of black people, Banneker wrote him a letter that invoked ideals of human equality and asked
for Jefferson's help in the abolition of slavery.

3. As an experiment after studying only a common
pocketwatch, Banneker carved the first all-wood
clock ever made in America.

Parsley[1]

1. The Cane[2] Fields

There is a parrot imitating spring
in the palace, its feathers parsley green.
Out of the swamp the cane appears

to haunt us, and we cut it down. El General
searches for a word; he is all the world   5
there is. Like a parrot imitating spring,

we lie down screaming as rain punches through
and we come up green. We cannot speak an R—
out of the swamp, the cane appears

and then the mountain we call in whispers *Katalina*.[3]   10
The children gnaw their teeth to arrowheads.
There is a parrot imitating spring.

El General has found his word: *perejil*.
Who says it, lives. He laughs, teeth shining
out of the swamp. The cane appears   15

in our dreams, lashed by wind and streaming.
And we lie down. For every drop of blood
there is a parrot imitating spring.
Out of the swamp the cane appears.

2. The Palace

The word the general's chosen is parsley.   20
It is fall, when thoughts turn
to love and death; the general thinks
of his mother, how she died in the fall
and he planted her walking cane at the grave
and it flowered, each spring stolidly forming   25
four-star blossoms. The general

pulls on his boots, he stomps to
her room in the palace, the one without
curtains, the one with a parrot
in a brass ring. As he paces he wonders   30
Who can I kill today. And for a moment
the little knot of screams
is still. The parrot, who has traveled

---

1. On October 2, 1937, Rafael Trujillo (1891–
1961), dictator of the Dominican Republic,
ordered 20,000 blacks killed because they could
not pronounce the letter "r" in *perejil*, the Spanish
word for parsley [Dove's note].
2. I.e., sugar cane.
3. Katarina (because "we cannot speak an R").

all the way from Australia in an ivory
cage, is, coy as a widow, practising   35
spring. Ever since the morning
his mother collapsed in the kitchen
while baking skull-shaped candies
for the Day of the Dead,[4] the general
has hated sweets. He orders pastries   40
brought up for the bird; they arrive

dusted with sugar on a bed of lace.
The knot in his throat starts to twitch;
he sees his boots the first day in battle
splashed with mud and urine   45
as a soldier falls at his feet amazed—
how stupid he looked!—at the sound
of artillery. *I never thought it would sing*
the soldier said, and died. Now

the general sees the fields of sugar   50
cane, lashed by rain and streaming.
He sees his mother's smile, the teeth
gnawed to arrowheads. He hears
the Haitians sing without R's
as they swing the great machetes: 55
Katalina, they sing, *Katalina*,

mi madle, mi amol en muelte.[5] God knows
his mother was no stupid woman; she
could roll an R like a queen. Even
a parrot can roll an R! In the bare room   60
the bright feathers arch in a parody
of greenery, as the last pale crumbs
disappear under the blackened tongue. Someone

calls out his name in a voice
so like his mother's, a startled tear   65
splashes the tip of his right boot.
My mother, my love in death.
The general remembers the tiny green sprigs
men of his village wore in their capes
to honor the birth of a son. He will   70
order many, this time, to be killed

for a single, beautiful word.

1983

4. All Soul's Day, November 2. An Aztec festival
for the spirits of the dead that coincides with the
Catholic calendar. In Latin America and the
Caribbean, people move in processions to cemeteries, bearing candles, flowers, and food, all of
which may be shaped to resemble symbols of
death, such as skulls or coffins.
5. I.e., *mi madre, mi amor en muerte,* "my mother,
my love in death."

Adolescence—I

In water-heavy nights behind grandmother's porch
We knelt in the tickling grasses and whispered:
Linda's face hung before us, pale as a pecan,
And it grew wise as she said:
        "A boy's lips are soft,   5
        As soft as baby's skin."
The air closed over her words.
A firefly whirred near my ear, and in the distance
I could hear streetlamps ping
Into miniature suns   10
Against a feathery sky.

                                                                    1980

Adolescence—II

Although it is night, I sit in the bathroom, waiting.
Sweat prickles behind my knees, the baby-breasts are alert.
Venetian blinds slice up the moon; the tiles quiver in pale strips.

Then they come, the three seal men with eyes as round
As dinner plates and eyelashes like sharpened tines.   5
They bring the scent of licorice. One sits in the washbowl,

One on the bathtub edge; one leans against the door.
"Can you feel it yet?" they whisper.
I don't know what to say, again. They chuckle,

Patting their sleek bodies with their hands.   10
"Well, maybe next time." And they rise,
Glittering like pools of ink under moonlight,

And vanish. I clutch at the ragged holes
They leave behind, here at the edge of darkness.
Night rests like a ball of fur on my tongue.   15

                                                                    1980

Rosa[1]

How she sat there,
the time right inside a place
so wrong it was ready.

---

1. Rosa Parks (1913–2005). From a series of poems titled *On the Bus with Rosa Parks*. On December 1, 1955, in Montgomery, Alabama, Parks, an African American seamstress and secretary of the local National Association for the Advancement of Colored People (NAACP), was arrested and taken to jail for refusing to yield her seat on a bus to a white passenger. Her arrest prompted a boycott of the city bus system and inspired the civil rights movement in the late 1950s and the 1960s.

That trim name with
its dream of a bench   5
to rest on. Her sensible coat.

Doing nothing was the doing:
the clean flame of her gaze
carved by a camera flash.

How she stood up   10
when they bent down to retrieve
her purse. That courtesy.

2000

Fox Trot Fridays

Thank the stars there's a day
each week to tuck in

the grief, lift your pearls, and
stride brush stride

quick-quick with a   5
heel-ball-toe. Smooth

as Nat King Cole's[1]
slow satin smile,

easy as taking
one day at a time: 10

one man and
one woman,

rib to rib,
with no heartbreak in sight—

just the sweep of Paradise   15
and the space of a song

to count all the wonders in it.

2004

---

1. Popular African American jazz singer, songwriter, and pianist (1919–1965).

ALBERTO RÍOS
b. 1952

The poet Rita Dove once recalled in an interview W. E. B. Du Bois's remark on the "second sight that comes from having to live in two different cultures." As a Latino whose heritage includes Spanish and English, Alberto Ríos often writes poems possessed of literal second sight. His work gives us magical and poetic ways of understanding the world, like the account of his grandmother as a young woman in "Refugio's Hair." A knowledge inaccessible in books is transmitted through stories: "In the old days of our family," the poem begins. In Ríos's best poems we feel both that anything can happen and that everything has happened before; we hear a particular voice whose rhythms recall stories passed from generation to generation.

Ríos has said of his background, "My father, born in southern Mexico, and my mother, born in England, gave me a language-rich, story-fat upbringing." He was born in Nogales, Arizona (on the border of Mexico), and earned an M.F.A. at the University of Arizona. He has worked on the Arizona Commission on the Arts and presently is on the faculty of Arizona State University in Tempe. His first book, *Whispering to Fool the Wind* (1982), won the Walt Whitman Award. He has since published *Five Indiscretions* (1985), *The Lime Orchard Women* (1989), *Teodora Luna's Two Kisses* (1990), *The Smallest Muscle in the Human Body* (2002), and *The Theatre of Night* (2006). He has also published volumes of fiction—*The Iguana Killer: Twelve Stories of the Heart* (1984) and *The Curtain of Trees* (1999)—and *Capirotada* (1999), a memoir of growing up on the Arizona-Mexico border. Ríos is a talented storyteller whose poems often suggest oral traditions, including Spanish ballads. For him, stories are forms of remembering and means of understanding; they honor the claims of dream and fact, past and present. Whether he is writing with humorous self-awareness about a childhood visit to a fortune-teller ("Madre Sofía") or rendering the unbearable reality behind the newspaper accounts of those among the "disappeared" (in "Taking Away the Name of a Nephew"), the details of his poems accumulate to reveal a startling sense of the world. At times, however, the story the poem tells must overcome too-predictable uses of the line. If Ríos's magical sense of the world sometimes yields too easily to the surreal, the pleasures of his poems often lie in a fluid movement between layers of reality, a deft integration of the factual and fantastic. Given Ríos's sense of the possibilities in language, the epigraph for his first book, taken from the Chilean poet Pablo Neruda, is especially fitting: "You see there are in our countries rivers which have no names, trees which nobody knows, and birds which nobody has described. . . . Our duty, then, as we understand it, is to express what is unheard of." Flavored with the music of Spanish and English, Ríos's poems create a new landscape: a contemporary America beneath which lives both an older way of life and the country of the imagination.

Madre Sofía[1]

My mother took me because she couldn't
wait the second ten years to know.
This was the lady rumored to have been
responsible for the box-wrapped baby
among the presents at that wedding,   5
but we went in, anyway, through the curtains.

---

1. Mother Sofía (Spanish). "Sofía" derives from the Greek word meaning "wisdom."

Loose jar-top, half turned
and not caught properly in the threads
her head sat mimicking its original intention
like the smile of a child hitting himself.   10
Central in that head grew unfamiliar poppies
from a face mahogany, eyes half yellow
half gray at the same time, goat and fog,
slit eyes of the devil, his tweed suit, red
lips, and she smelled of smoke, cigarettes,   15
but a diamond smoke, somehow; I inhaled
sparkles, I could feel them, throat, stomach.
She did not speak, and as a child
I could only answer, so that together
we were silent, cold and wet, dry and hard: 20
from behind my mother pushed me forward.
The lady put her hand on the face
of a thin animal wrap, tossing that head
behind her to be pressed incredibly
as she sat back in the huge chair and leaned.   25
And then I saw the breasts as large as her
head, folded together, coming out of her dress
as if it didn't fit, not like my mother's.
I could see them, how she kept them
penned up, leisurely, in maroon feed bags,   30
horse nuzzles of her wide body,
but exquisitely penned up
circled by pearl reins and red scarves.
She lifted her arm, but only with the tips
of her fingers motioned me to sit opposite.   35
She looked at me but spoke to my mother
words dark, smoky like the small room,
words coming like red ants stepping occasionally
from a hole on a summer day in the valley,
red ants from her mouth, her nose, her ears,   40
tears from the corners of her cinched eyes.
And suddenly she put her hand full on my head
pinching tight again with those finger tips
like a television healer, young Oral Roberts[2]
half standing, quickly, half leaning   45
those breasts swinging toward me
so that I reach with both my hands to my lap
protecting instinctively whatever it is
that needs protection when a baseball is thrown
and you're not looking but someone yells,   50
the hand, then those breasts coming toward me
like the quarter-arms of the amputee Joaquín
who came back from the war to sit
in the park, reaching always for children
until one day he had to be held back.   55

2. American televangelist (b. 1918) and leader of a charismatic movement.

I sat there, no breath, and could see only
hair around her left nipple, like a man.
Her clothes were old.
Accented, in a language whose spine had been
snapped, she whispered the words of a city   60
witch, and made me happy, alive like a man:
The future will make you tall.

1982

Wet Camp

We have been here before, but we are lost.
The earth is black and the trees are bent
and broken and piled as if the game
of pick-up-sticks were ready and the children
hiding, waiting their useless turns.   5
The west bank of the river is burned
and the Santa Cruz[1] has poured onto it.
The grit brown ponds
sit like dirty lilies in the black.
The afternoon is gone grazing   10
over the thin mountains.
The night is colder here without leaves.
Nothing holds up the sky.

1982

Advice to a First Cousin

The way the world works is like this:
for the bite of scorpions, she says,
my grandmother to my first cousin,
because I might die and someone must know,
go to the animal jar   5
the one with the soup of green herbs
mixed with the scorpions I have been putting in
still alive. Take one out
put it on the bite. It has had time to think
there with the others—put the lid back tight—   10
and knows that a biting is not the way to win
a finger or a young girl's foot.
It will take back into itself the hurting
the redness and the itching and its marks.

1. River in southern Arizona.

But the world works like this, too: 15
look out for the next scorpion you see,
she says, and makes a big face to scare me
thereby instructing my cousin, look out!
for one of the scorpion's many
illegitimate and unhappy sons.   20
It will be smarter, more of the devil.
It will have lived longer than these dead ones.
It will know from them something more
about the world, in the way mothers know
when something happens to a child, or how   25
I knew from your sadness you had been bitten.
It will learn something stronger than biting.
Look out most for that scorpion, she says,
making a big face to scare me again and it works
I go—crying—she lets me go—they laugh,   30
the way you must look out for men
who have not yet bruised you.

1985

SANDRA CISNEROS
b. 1954

Sandra Cisneros began writing at age ten, much like the young Chicana narrator of *The House on Mango Street* (1984), the volume of interrelated vignettes from a child's perspective that brought Cisneros her first major attention. In brief, sharply drawn, but quietly expressed segments, the narrator, Esperanza, conveys the ambience of growing up in a street in Chicago's Mexican American community. The social bond of this neighborhood eases the contrast between Esperanza's nurturing family and the more hostile forces of poverty and racism. Cisneros cultivates a sense of warmth and naive humor for her protagonists, qualities that are evident in introductory parts to *Woman Hollering Creek* (1991), a short-story collection that also deals with more troublesome aspects of young women's facing hostile forces. Without sentimentalizing or idealizing her narrator's perspective, Cisneros presents glimpses of a world full of adult challenges and multicultural complexities. Sex is a topic in all Cisneros's work, including her poetry collected as *My Wicked Wicked Ways* (1987) and *Loose Woman* (1994)—sometimes gentle and even silly, other times brutally assaultive. What remains constant is the author's view that by romanticizing sexual relations women cooperate with a male view that can be oppressive, even physically destructive. As is said of the protagonist of her 2002 novel, *Caramelo*, Cisneros is "caught between here and there." Yet "here" and "there" are not as dichotomous as young versus old, female versus male, or Mexico versus the United States. Instead, the flow of experience between these poles yields her work's subject: people finding their own lifestyles in the space between fixed boundaries. Because this intervening space is so rich in creative potential, Cisneros can balance unhappiness with humor and find personal victories where others might see social defeat.

Born in Chicago, the child of a Mexican father and a Mexican American mother, Cisneros spent parts of her childhood in Texas and Mexico as well. Her Catholic education led to a B.A. degree from Chicago's Loyola University, after which she earned a graduate degree in creative writing from the University of Iowa's Writers Workshop. Teaching in San Antonio, Texas, she has used her position as a writer and an educator to expound Chicana feminism, especially as this movement combines cultural issues with women's concerns. In raising controversy by having her house painted very brightly, she openly questioned monocultural "historical districts" and "community covenants." *Whose* history? Cisneros asked; *which* community sets standards? (Through research she established that her decorating style was in accordance with her home's background and that the standards used to dispute her choice were arbitrary.) A dissatisfaction with the politics of publishing has made her an advocate of small-press dissemination. Most of all, as in the story reprinted here, she is eager to show the rich dynamics of characters existing in the blend of Mexican and American cultures that begins with speaking two languages and extends to almost every aspect of life. Spanish words, Mexican holidays, ethnic foods, and localized religious practices punctuate her narratives; her characters have a facility with cultural play that reflects what for others would be an anthropologically enhanced understanding.

The text is from *Woman Hollering Creek* (1991).

Woman Hollering Creek

The day Don Serafín gave Juan Pedro Martínez Sánchez permission to take Cleófilas Enriqueta DeLeón Hernández as his bride, across her father's threshold, over several miles of dirt road and several miles of paved, over one border and beyond to a town *en el otro lado*—on the other side—already did he divine the morning his daughter would raise her hand over her eyes, look south, and dream of returning to the chores that never ended, six good-for-nothing brothers, and one old man's complaints.

He had said, after all, in the hubbub of parting: I am your father, I will never abandon you. He *had* said that, hadn't he, when he hugged and then let her go. But at the moment Cleófilas was busy looking for Chela, her maid of honor, to fulfill their bouquet conspiracy. She would not remember her father's parting words until later. *I am your father, I will never abandon you.*

Only now as a mother did she remember. Now, when she and Juan Pedrito sat by the creek's edge. How when a man and a woman love each other, sometimes that love sours. But a parent's love for a child, a child's for its parents, is another thing entirely.

This is what Cleófilas thought evenings when Juan Pedro did not come home, and she lay on her side of the bed listening to the hollow roar of the interstate, a distant dog barking, the pecan trees rustling like ladies in stiff petticoats—shh-shh-shh, shh-shh-shh—soothing her to sleep.

In the town where she grew up, there isn't very much to do except accompany the aunts and godmothers to the house of one or the other to play cards. Or walk to the cinema to see this week's film again, speckled and with one hair quivering annoyingly on the screen. Or to the center of town to order a milk shake that will appear in a day and a half as a pimple on her backside. Or to the girlfriend's house to watch the latest *telenovela*[1] episode and try to copy the way the women comb their hair, wear their makeup.

But what Cleófilas has been waiting for, has been whispering and sighing

---

1. Soap opera (Spanish).

and giggling for, has been anticipating since she was old enough to lean against the window displays of gauze and butterflies and lace, is passion. Not the kind on the cover of the ¡Alarma![2] magazines, mind you, where the lover is photographed with the bloody fork she used to salvage her good name. But passion in its purest crystalline essence. The kind the books and songs and *telenovelas* describe when one finds, finally, the great love of one's life, and does whatever one can, must do, at whatever the cost.

Tú o Nadie. "You or No One." The title of the current favorite *telenovela*. The beautiful Lucía Méndez having to put up with all kinds of hardships of the heart, separation and betrayal, and loving, always loving no matter what, because *that* is the most important thing, and did you see Lucía Méndez on the Bayer aspirin commercials—wasn't she lovely? Does she dye her hair do you think? Cleófilas is going to go to the *farmacía*[3] and buy a hair rinse; her girlfriend Chela will apply it—it's not that difficult at all.

Because you didn't watch last night's episode when Lucía confessed she loved him more than anyone in her life. In her life! And she sings the song "You or No One" in the beginning and end of the show. *Tú o Nadie*. Somehow one ought to live one's life like that, don't you think? You or no one. Because to suffer for love is good. The pain all sweet somehow. In the end.

Seguín. She had liked the sound of it. Far away and lovely. Not like *Monclova. Coahuia*.[4] Ugly.

Seguín, Tejas. A nice sterling ring to it. The tinkle of money. She would get to wear outfits like the women on the *tele*, like Lucía Méndez. And have a lovely house, and wouldn't Chela be jealous.

And yes, they will drive all the way to Laredo[5] get her wedding dress. That's what they say. Because Juan Pedro wants to get married right away, without a long engagement since he can't take off too much time from work. He has a very important position in Seguin with, with . . . a beer company, I think. Or was it tires? Yes, he has to be back. So they will get married in the spring when he can take off work, and then they will drive off in his new pickup— did you see it?—to their new home in Seguin. Well, not exactly new, but they're going to repaint the house. You know newlyweds. New paint and new furniture. Why not? He can afford it. And later on add maybe a room or two for the children. May they be blessed with many.

Well, you'll see. Cleófilas has always been so good with her sewing machine. A little *rrrr, rrrr, rrrr* of the machine and ¡zas! Miracles. She's always been so clever, that girl. Poor thing. And without even a mama to advise her on things like her wedding night. Well, may God help her. What with a father with a head like a burro, and those six clumsy brothers. Well, what do you think! Yes, I'm going to the wedding. Of course! The dress I want to wear just needs to be altered a teensy bit to bring it up to date. See, I saw a new style last night that I thought would suit me. Did you watch last night's episode of *The Rich Also Cry?*[6] Well, did you notice the dress the mother was wearing?

2. Graphic, sensationalistic Mexican magazine published since 1963.
3. Pharmacy, drugstore (Spanish).
4. Respectively a town and state in Mexico, the latter bordering Texas. "Seguín": city in Guadalupe County, south-central Texas.

5. City in southwestern Texas, on the Mexican border.
6. First global soap opera (production beginning in Mexico in 1979), exported to Russia, China, the United States, and other countries.

La Gritona.[7] Such a funny name for such a lovely *arroyo*.[8] But that's what they called the creek that ran behind the house. Though no one could say whether the woman had hollered from anger or pain. The natives only knew the *arroyo* one crossed on the way to San Antonio, and then once again on the way back, was called Woman Hollering, a name no one from these parts questioned, little less understood. *Pues, allá de los indios, quién sabe*[9]—who knows, the townspeople shrugged, because it was of no concern to their lives how this trickle of water received its curious name.

"What do you want to know for?" Trini the laundromat attendant asked in the same gruff Spanish she always used whenever she gave Cleófilas change or yelled at her for something. First for putting too much soap in the machines. Later, for sitting on a washer. And still later, after Juan Pedrito was born, for not understanding that in this country you cannot let your baby walk around with no diaper and his pee-pee hanging out, it wasn't nice, ¿entiendes? Pues.[1]

How could Cleófilas explain to a woman like this why the name Woman Hollering fascinated her. Well, there was no sense talking to Trini.

On the other hand there were the neighbor ladies, one on either side of the house they rented near the *arroyo*. The woman Soledad on the left, the woman Dolores on the right.

The neighbor lady Soledad liked to call herself a widow, though how she came to be one was a mystery. Her husband had either died, or run away with an ice-house[2] floozie, or simply gone out for cigarettes one afternoon and never came back. It was hard to say which since Soledad, as a rule, didn't mention him.

In the other house lived *la señora*[3] Dolores, kind and very sweet, but her house smelled too much of incense and candles from the altars that burned continuously in memory of two sons who had died in the last war and one husband who had died shortly after from grief. The neighbor lady Dolores divided her time between the memory of these men and her garden, famous for its sunflowers—so tall they had to be supported with broom handles and old boards; red red cockscombs, fringed and bleeding a thick menstrual color; and, especially, roses whose sad scent reminded Cleófilas of the dead. Each Sunday *la señora* Dolores clipped the most beautiful of these flowers and arranged them on three modest headstones at the Seguin cemetery.

The neighbor ladies, Soledad, Dolores, they might've known once the name of the *arroyo* before it turned English but they did not know now. They were too busy remembering the men who had left through either choice or circumstance and would never come back.

Pain or rage, Cleófilas wondered when she drove over the bridge the first time as a newlywed and Juan Pedro had pointed it out. *La Gritona*, he had said, and she had laughed. Such a funny name for a creek so pretty and full of happily ever after.

The first time she had been so surprised she didn't cry out or try to defend herself. She had always said she would strike back if a man, any man, were to strike her.

7. The Shouter, Yeller, Hollerer (Spanish).
8. Stream (Spanish).
9. Well, beyond the Indians, who knows (Spanish).

1. Do you understand? Well (Spanish).
2. Tavern.
3. The lady (Spanish).

But when the moment came, and he slapped her once, and then again, and again; until the lip split and bled an orchid of blood, she didn't fight back, she didn't break into tears, she didn't run away as she imagined she might when she saw such things in the *telenovelas*.

In her own home her parents had never raised a hand to each other or to their children. Although she admitted she may have been brought up a little leniently as an only daughter—*la consentida*,[4] the princess—there were some things she would never tolerate. Ever.

Instead, when it happened the first time, when they were barely man and wife, she had been so stunned, it left her speechless, motionless, numb. She had done nothing but reach up to the heat on her mouth and stare at the blood on her hand as if even then she didn't understand.

She could think of nothing to say, said nothing. Just stroked the dark curls of the man who wept and would weep like a child, his tears of repentance and shame, this time and each.

The men at the ice house. From what she can tell, from the times during her first year when still a newlywed she is invited and accompanies her husband, sits mute beside their conversation, waits and sips a beer until it grows warm, twists a paper napkin into a knot, then another into a fan, one into a rose, nods her head, smiles, yawns, politely grins, laughs at the appropriate moments, leans against her husband's sleeve, tugs at his elbow, and finally becomes good at predicting where the talk will lead, from this Cleófilas concludes each is nightly trying to find the truth lying at the bottom of the bottle like a gold doubloon on the sea floor.

They want to tell each other what they want to tell themselves. But what is bumping like a helium balloon at the ceiling of the brain never finds its way out. It bubbles and rises, it gurgles in the throat, it rolls across the surface of the tongue, and erupts from the lips—a belch.

If they are lucky, there are tears at the end of the long night. At any given moment, the fists try to speak. They are dogs chasing their own tails before lying down to sleep, trying to find a way, a route, an out, and—finally—get some peace.

In the morning sometimes before he opens his eyes. Or after they have finished loving. Or at times when he is simply across from her at the table putting pieces of food into his mouth and chewing. Cleófilas thinks, This is the man I have waited my whole life for.

Not that he isn't a good man. She has to remind herself why she loves him when she changes the baby's Pampers, or when she mops the bathroom floor, or tries to make the curtains for the doorways without doors, or whiten the linen. Or wonder a little when he kicks the refrigerator and says he hates this shitty house and is going out where he won't be bothered with the baby's howling and her suspicious questions, and her requests to fix this and this and this because if she had any brains in her head she'd realize he's been up before the rooster earning his living to pay for the food in her belly and the roof over her head and would have to wake up again early the next day so why can't you just leave me in peace, woman.

He is not very tall, no, and he doesn't look like the men on the *telenovelas*.

---

4. The spoiled one (Spanish).

His face still scarred from acne. And he has a bit of a belly from all the beer he drinks. Well, he's always been husky.

This man who farts and belches and snores as well as laughs and kisses and holds her. Somehow this husband whose whiskers she finds each morning in the sink, whose shoes she must air each evening on the porch, this husband who cuts his fingernails in public, laughs loudly, curses like a man, and demands each course of dinner be served on a separate plate like at his mother's, as soon as he gets home, on time or late, and who doesn't care at all for music or *telenovelas* or romance or roses or the moon floating pearly over the *arroyo*, or through the bedroom window for that matter, shut the blinds and go back to sleep, this man, this father, this rival, this keeper, this lord, this master, this husband till kingdom come.

A doubt. Slender as a hair. A washed cup set back on the shelf wrong-side-up. Her lipstick, and body talc, and hairbrush all arranged in the bathroom a different way.

No. Her imagination. The house the same as always. Nothing.

Coming home from the hospital with her new son, her husband. Something comforting in discovering her house slippers beneath the bed, the faded housecoat where she left it on the bathroom hook. Her pillow. Their bed.

Sweet sweet homecoming. Sweet as the scent of face powder in the air, jasmine, sticky liquor.

Smudged fingerprint on the door. Crushed cigarette in a glass. Wrinkle in the brain crumpling to a crease.

Sometimes she thinks of her father's house. But how could she go back there? What a disgrace. What would the neighbors say? Coming home like that with one baby on her hip and one in the oven. Where's your husband?

The town of gossips. The town of dust and despair. Which she has traded for this town of gossips. This town of dust, despair. Houses farther apart perhaps, though no more privacy because of it. No leafy *zócalo*[5] in the center of the town, though the murmur of talk is clear enough all the same. No huddled whispering on the church steps each Sunday. Because here the whispering begins at sunset at the ice house instead.

This town with its silly pride for a bronze pecan the size of a baby carriage in front of the city hall. TV repair shop, drugstore, hardware, dry cleaner's, chiropractor's, liquor store, bail bonds, empty storefront, and nothing, nothing, nothing of interest. Nothing one could walk to, at any rate. Because the towns here are built so that you have to depend on husbands. Or you stay home. Or you drive. If you're rich enough to own, allowed to drive, your own car.

There is no place to go. Unless one counts the neighbor ladies. Soledad on one side, Dolores on the other. Or the creek.

Don't go out there after dark, *mi'jita*.[6] Stay near the house. *No es bueno para la salud.*[7] Mala suerte. Bad luck. *Mal aire.*[8] You'll get sick and the baby too. You'll catch a fright wandering about in the dark, and then you'll see how right we were.

The stream sometimes only a muddy puddle in the summer, though now in the springtime, because of the rains, a good-size alive thing, a thing with

5. Town square (Spanish).
6. My daughter (Spanish).

7. It's not good for one's health (Spanish).
8. Bad air (Spanish).

a voice all its own, all day and all night calling in its high, silver voice. Is it La Llorona,[9] the weeping woman? La Llorona, who drowned her own children. Perhaps La Llorona is the one they named the creek after, she thinks, remembering all the stories she learned as a child.

La Llorona calling to her. She is sure of it. Cleófilas sets the baby's Donald Duck blanket on the grass. Listens. The day sky turning to night. The baby pulling up fistfuls of grass and laughing. La Llorona. Wonders if something as quiet as this drives a woman to the darkness under the trees.

What she needs is . . . and made a gesture as if to yank a woman's buttocks to his groin. Maximiliano, the foul-smelling fool from across the road, said this and set the men laughing, but Cleófilas just muttered. *Grosera*,[1] and went on washing dishes.

She knew he said it not because it was true, but more because it was he who needed to sleep with a woman, instead of drinking each night at the ice house and stumbling home alone.

Maximiliano who was said to have killed his wife in an ice-house brawl when she came at him with a mop. I had to shoot, he had said—she was armed.

Their laughter outside the kitchen window. Her husband's, his friends'. Manolo, Beto, Efraín, el Perico.[2] Maximiliano.

Was Cleófilas just exaggerating as her husband always said? It seemed the newspapers were full of such stories. This woman found on the side of the interstate. This one pushed from a moving car. This one's cadaver, this one unconscious, this one beaten blue. Her ex-husband, her husband, her lover, her father, her brother, her uncle, her friend, her co-worker. Always. The same grisly news in the pages of the dailies. She dunked a glass under the soapy water for a moment—shivered.

He had thrown a book. Hers. From across the room. A hot welt across the cheek. She could forgive that. But what stung more was the fact it was *her* book, a love story by Corín Tellado,[3] what she loved most now that she lived in the U.S., without a television set, without the *telenovelas*.

Except now and again when her husband was away and she could manage it, the few episodes glimpsed at the neighbor lady Soledad's house because Dolores didn't care for that sort of thing, though Soledad was often kind enough to retell what had happened on what episode of *María de Nadie*,[4] the poor Argentine country girl who had the ill fortune of falling in love with the beautiful son of the Arrocha family, the very family she worked for, whose roof she slept under and whose floors she vacuumed, while in that same house, with the dust brooms and floor cleaners as witnesses, the square-jawed Juan Carlos Arrocha had uttered words of love, I love you, María, listen to me, *mi querida*,[5] but it was she who had to say No, no, we are not of the same class, and remind him it was not his place nor hers to fall in love, while all the while her heart was breaking, can you imagine.

---

9. The Woman Who Cries (Spanish), a spurned mistress of Mexican legend who drowned her children and was fated to eternally seek their recovery.
1. Vulgar, crude (Spanish).
2. The Parakeet (Spanish).

3. Pseudonym of María del Socorro Tellado López (b. 1927), Spanish novelist.
4. *Maria of No One* (Spanish), television series produced in Argentina.
5. My love (Spanish).

Cleófilas thought her life would have to be like that, like a *telenovela,* only now the episodes got sadder and sadder. And there were no commercials in between for comic relief. And no happy ending in sight. She thought this when she sat with the baby out by the creek behind the house. Celófilas de . . . ? But somehow she would have to change her name to Topazio, or Yesenia, Cristal, Adriana, Stefania, Andrea, something more poetic than Cleófilas. Everything happened to women with names like jewels. But what happened to a Cleófilas? Nothing. But a crack in the face.

Because the doctor has said so. She has to go. To make sure the new baby is all right, so there won't be any problems when he's born, and the appointment card says next Tuesday. Could he please take her. And that's all.

No, she won't mention it. She promises. If the doctor asks she can say she fell down the front steps or slipped when she was out in the backyard, slipped out back, she could tell him that. She has to go back next Tuesday, Juan Pedro, please, for the new baby. For their child.

She could write to her father and ask maybe for money, just a loan, for the new baby's medical expenses. Well then if he'd rather she didn't. All right, she won't. Please don't anymore. Please don't. She knows it's difficult saving money with all the bills they have, but how else are they going to get out of debt with the truck payments? And after the rent and the food and the electricity and the gas and the water and the who-knows-what, well, there's hardly anything left. But please, at least for the doctor visit. She won't ask for anything else. She has to. Why is she so anxious? Because.

Because she is going to make sure the baby is not turned around backward this time to split her down the center. Yes. Next Tuesday at five-thirty. I'll have Juan Pedrito dressed and ready. But those are the only shoes he has. I'll polish them, and we'll be ready. As soon as you come from work. We won't make you ashamed.

Felice? It's me, Graciela.

No, I can't talk louder. I'm at work.

Look, I need kind of a favor. There's a patient, a lady here who's got a problem.

Well, wait a minute. Are you listening to me or what?

I can't talk real loud 'cause her husband's in the next room.

Well, would you just listen?

I was going to do this sonogram on her—she's pregnant, right?—and she just starts crying on me. *Híjole,*[6] Felice! This poor lady's got black-and-blue marks all over. I'm not kidding.

From her husband. Who else? Another one of those brides from across the border. And her family's all in Mexico.

Shit. You think they're going to help her? Give me a break. This lady doesn't even speak English. She hasn't been allowed to call home or write or nothing. That's why I'm calling you.

She needs a ride.

Not to Mexico, you goof. Just to the Greyhound.[7] In San Anto.

No, just a ride. She's got her own money. All you'd have to do is drop her off in San Antonio on your way home. Come on, Felice. Please? If we don't

---

6. Shoot! or Gee! (Spanish).　　　7. Bus line.

help her, who will? I'd drive her myself, but she needs to be on that bus before her husband gets home from work. What do you say?

I don't know. Wait.

Right away, tomorrow even.

Well, if tomorrow's no good for you . . .

It's a date, Felice. Thursday. At the Cash N Carry[8] off I-10. Noon. She'll be ready.

Oh, and her name's Cleófilas.

I don't know. One of those Mexican saints, I guess. A martyr or something. Cleófilas. C-L-E-O-F-I-L-A-S. Cle. O. Fi. Las. Write it down.

Thanks, Felice. When her kid's born she'll have to name her after us, right?

Yeah, you got it. A regular soap opera sometimes. *Qué vida, comadre. Bueno*[9] bye.

All morning that flutter of half-fear, half-doubt. At any moment Juan Pedro might appear in the doorway. On the street. At the Cash N Carry. Like in the dreams she dreamed.

There was that to think about, yes, until the woman in the pickup drove up. Then there wasn't time to think about anything but the pickup pointed toward San Antonio. Put your bags in the back and get in.

But when they drove across the *arroyo,* the driver opened her mouth and let out a yell as loud as any mariachi. Which startled not only Cleófilas, but Juan Pedrito as well.

Pues,[1] look how cute. I scared you two, right? Sorry. Should've warned you. Every time I cross that bridge I do that. Because of the name, you know. Woman Hollering. *Pues,* I holler. She said this in a Spanish pocked with English and laughed. Did you ever notice, Felice continued, how nothing around here is named after a woman? Really. Unless she's the Virgin. I guess you're only famous if you're a virgin. She was laughing again.

That's why I like the name of that *arroyo.* Makes you want to holler like Tarzan, right?

Everything about this woman, this Felice, amazed Cleófilas. The fact that she drove a pickup. A pickup, mind you, but when Cleófilas asked if it was her husband's, she said she didn't have a husband. The pickup was hers. She herself had chosen it. She herself was paying for it.

I used to have a Pontiac Sunbird.[2] But those cars are for *viejas.*[3] Pussy cars. Now this here is a *real* car.

What kind of talk was that coming from a woman? Cleófilas thought. But then again, Felice was like no woman she'd ever met. Can you imagine, when we crossed the *arroyo* she just started yelling like a crazy, she would say later to her father and brothers. Just like that. Who would've thought?

Who would've? Pain or rage, perhaps, but not a hoot like the one Felice had just let go. Makes you want to holler like Tarzan, Felice had said.

Then Felice began laughing again, but it wasn't Felice laughing. It was gurgling out of her own throat, a long ribbon of laughter, like water.

1991

8. Retail store.
9. What a life, girlfriend, well (Spanish).
1. Well (Spanish).

2. Compact American automobile.
3. Old ladies (Spanish).

LOUISE ERDRICH
b. 1954

Louise Erdrich grew up in the small town of Wahpeton, North Dakota, just on the Minnesota border. Her mother was French Chippewa, her maternal grandmother was tribal chairman on the Turtle Mountain Reservation, and both of her parents worked in the Bureau of Indian Affairs boarding school in Wahpeton. She wrote stories as a child, encouraged by her father, who paid her a nickel for each one, but Erdrich's growing up was not marked by a special awareness of her Chippewa background. She has said that she never thought about "what was Native American and what wasn't. . . . There wasn't a political climate at the time about Indian rights." The eldest of seven children, she "grew up just taking it all in as something that was part of me."

In 1972 she entered Dartmouth College, participating in a Native American studies program run by Michael Dorris—himself part American Indian and a writer—whom eventually she would marry (a relationship ending with their separation and his suicide in 1997). In her undergraduate years she won prizes for poetry and fiction and worked at a variety of jobs, such as teaching poetry in prisons, editing a Boston Indian Council newspaper, and flag-signaling on a construction site. After deciding on a career as a writer, she earned an M.F.A. degree at Johns Hopkins, for which degree she submitted a number of poems—later to appear in her collection *Jacklight* (1984)—and part of a novel. There followed the usual sending out of poems and stories, the rejection slips, eventually the acceptances.

Her first novel, *Love Medicine*, which won the National Book Critics Circle award for 1984, began as a short story. Collaborating with her husband, she not only expanded the story but planned the resulting novel as the first of a tetralogy, ranging over different periods of time and focusing on the lives of two Chippewa families. Her interest in the interaction of quirky, passionate, complex individuals—Native American, mixed blood, German American, or Anglo—lies at the center of her fiction.

Successive chapters of *Love Medicine* jump from 1981 to 1934 to 1948, each chapter told through a particular character's point of view (sometimes we see the same event from succeeding points of view). But the individual chapter is more a discrete whole than is the case with a traditional novel, a technique Erdrich uses in many of her novels, including *Tracks* (1988), the second chapter of which was published as the story "Fleur" (printed here). Like many of Erdrich's narratives, *Tracks* draws context from High Plains Dakotas town life, where Anglo and Native American cultures meet (if not mix).

Erdrich's style is easy, offhand, quietly unostentatious, but her language often has an unpredictability and sense of surprise, as in the first paragraph of "The Red Convertible," whose protagonist, Lyman Lamartine, tells us:

> I was the first one to drive a convertible on my reservation. And of course, it was red, a red Olds. I owned that car along with my brother Henry Junior. We owned it together until his boots filled with water on a windy night and he bought out my share. Now Henry owns the whole car, and his younger brother (that's myself) Lyman walks everywhere he goes.

Such clarity and directness are only part of the story, however, since her style also calls upon lyric resources, notable in the following sentence from her second novel, *The Beet Queen*: "After the miraculous sheets of black ice came the floods, stranding boards and snaky knots of debris high in the branches, leaving brown leeches to dry like raisins on the sidewalks when the water receded, and leaving the smell of river mud, a rotten sweetness, in the backyards and gutters."

Native American oral expression does not distinguish between prose and poetry, and like many Native American writers Erdrich works in several forms. "I began as a poet, writing poetry," she has said. "I began to tell stories in poems." The lyrical descriptions in her fiction resemble the language of her poems, and the characterizations and narratives in her poetry resemble those of her fiction. Her most recent poetry collection, *Original Fire* (2003), presents new poems together with work from two earlier collections, *Jacklight* and *Baptism of Fire* (1989). Among the previously published poems are "The Butcher's Wife," which has close affinities in setting and character to her novels, and "The Potchikoo Stories," a group of prose poems about the mythical Potchikoo's life and afterlife. "Grief," a new poem, suggests the traditions of imagist poetry. But in the end such generic distinctions run counter to Erdrich's fusion of storytelling modes.

Like her fiction, Erdrich's poetry sometimes offers realistic accounts of small-town life and sometimes retells mythical stories. "I was Sleeping Where the Black Oaks Move" exemplifies her lyrical description and her mythical imagination. Many of the poems also reflect Erdrich's awareness of the historical and ongoing devastations of Native American life, what she calls in the poem "Dear John Wayne" "the history that brought us all here." Whatever forms her storytelling takes, its linguistic resources and mixture of grief, humor, anger, and tenderness deepen our understanding of the complexities of experience.

Dear John Wayne[1]

August and the drive-in picture is packed.
We lounge on the hood of the Pontiac
surrounded by the slow-burning spirals they sell
at the window, to vanquish the hordes of mosquitoes.
Nothing works. They break through the smoke screen for blood.   5

Always the lookout spots the Indians first,
spread north to south, barring progress.
The Sioux or some other Plains bunch[2]
in spectacular columns, ICBM missiles,[3]
feathers bristling in the meaningful sunset.   10

The drum breaks. There will be no parlance.
Only the arrows whining, a death-cloud of nerves
swarming down on the settlers
who die beautifully, tumbling like dust weeds
into the history that brought us all here   15
together: this wide screen beneath the sign of the bear.

The sky fills, acres of blue squint and eye
that the crowd cheers. His face moves over us,
a thick cloud of vengeance, pitted
like the land that was once flesh. Each rut,   20

---

1. American movie actor (1907–1979) who embodied the image of the strong, taciturn cowboy or soldier, and who in many ways personified the dominant American values of his era. He died of cancer.

2. The Sioux are a North American Plains Indian people.
3. Intercontinental Ballistic Missiles, developed starting in 1971.

each scar makes a promise: *It is*
not over, this fight, not as long as you resist.

Everything we see belongs to us.

A few laughing Indians fall over the hood
slipping in the hot spilled butter.   25
The eye sees a lot, John, but the heart is so blind.
Death makes us owners of nothing.
He smiles, a horizon of teeth
the credits reel over, and then the white fields

again blowing in the true-to-life dark.   30
The dark films over everything.
We get into the car
scratching our mosquito bites, speechless and small
as people are when the movie is done.
We are back in our skins.   35

How can we help but keep hearing his voice,
the flip side of the sound track, still playing:
Come on, boys, we got them
where we want them, drunk, running.
They'll give us what we want, what we need.   40
Even his disease was the idea of taking everything.
Those cells, burning, doubling, splitting out of their skins.

1984

I Was Sleeping Where the Black Oaks Move

We watched from the house
as the river grew, helpless
and terrible in its unfamiliar body.
Wrestling everything into it,
the water wrapped around trees   5
until their life-hold was broken.
They went down, one by one,
and the river dragged off their covering.

Nests of the herons, roots washed to bones,
snags of soaked bark on the shoreline: 10
a whole forest pulled through the teeth
of the spillway. Trees surfacing
singly, where the river poured off
into arteries for fields below the reservation.

When at last it was over, the long removal,   15
they had all become the same dry wood.

We walked among them, the branches
whitening in the raw sun.
Above us drifted herons,
alone, hoarse-voiced, broken,   20
settling their beaks among the hollows.

Grandpa said, *These are the ghosts of the tree people,*
moving above us, unable to take their rest.

Sometimes now, we dream our way back to the heron dance.
Their long wings are bending the air   25
into circles through which they fall.
They rise again in shifting wheels.
How long must we live in the broken figures
their necks make, narrowing the sky.

                                                                1984

Grief

Sometimes you have to take your own hand
as though you were a lost child
and bring yourself stumbling
home over twisted ice.

Whiteness drifts over your house.   5
A page of warm light
falls steady from the open door.

Here is your bed, folded open.
Lie down, lie down, let the blue snow cover you.

                                                                2003

Fleur[1]

The first time she drowned in the cold and glassy waters of Lake Turcot,
Fleur Pillager was only a girl. Two men saw the boat tip, saw her struggle in
the waves. They rowed over to the place she went down, and jumped in.
When they dragged her over the gunwales, she was cold to the touch and stiff,
so they slapped her face, shook her by the heels, worked her arms back and
forth, and pounded her back until she coughed up lake water. She shivered
all over like a dog, then took a breath. But it wasn't long afterward that those
two men disappeared. The first wandered off and the other, Jean Hat, got
himself run over by a cart.

---

1. First published in *Esquire* magazine, August 1986.

It went to show, my grandma said. It figured to her, all right. By saving Fleur Pillager, those two men had lost themselves.

The next time she fell in the lake, Fleur Pillager was twenty years old and no one touched her. She washed onshore, her skin a dull dead gray, but when George Many Women bent to look closer, he saw her chest move. Then her eyes spun open, sharp black riprock, and she looked at him. "You'll take my place," she hissed. Everybody scattered and left her there, so no one knows how she dragged herself home. Soon after that we noticed Many Women changed, grew afraid, wouldn't leave his house, and would not be forced to go near water. For his caution, he lived until the day that his sons brought him a new tin bathtub. Then the first time he used the tub he slipped, got knocked out, and breathed water while his wife stood in the other room frying breakfast.

Men stayed clear of Fleur Pillager after the second drowning. Even though she was good-looking, nobody dared to court her because it was clear that Misshepeshu, the waterman, the monster, wanted her for himself. He's a devil, that one, love-hungry with desire and maddened for the touch of young girls, the strong and daring especially, the ones like Fleur.

Our mothers warn us that we'll think he's handsome, for he appears with green eyes, copper skin, a mouth tender as a child's. But if you fall into his arms, he sprouts horns, fangs, claws, fins. His feet are joined as one and his skin, brass scales, rings to the touch. You're fascinated, cannot move. He casts a shell necklace at your feet, weeps gleaming chips that harden into mica on your breasts. He holds you under. Then he takes the body of a lion or a fat brown worm. He's made of gold. He's made of beach moss. He's a thing of dry foam, a thing of death by drowning, the death a Chippewa cannot survive.

Unless you are Fleur Pillager. We all knew she couldn't swim. After the first time, we thought she'd never go back to Lake Turcot. We thought she'd keep to herself, live quiet, stop killing men off by drowning in the lake. After the first time, we thought she'd keep the good ways. But then, after the second drowning, we knew that we were dealing with something much more serious. She was haywire, out of control. She messed with evil, laughed at the old women's advice, and dressed like a man. She got herself into some half-forgotten medicine, studied ways we shouldn't talk about. Some say she kept the finger of a child in her pocket and a powder of unborn rabbits in a leather thong around her neck. She laid the heart of an owl on her tongue so she could see at night, and went out, hunting, not even in her own body. We know for sure because the next morning, in the snow or dust, we followed the tracks of her bare feet and saw where they changed, where the claws sprang out, the pad broadened and pressed into the dirt. By night we heard her chuffing cough, the bear cough. By day her silence and the wide grin she threw to bring down our guard made us frightened. Some thought that Fleur Pillager should be driven off the reservation, but not a single person who spoke like this had the nerve. And finally, when people were just about to get together and throw her out, she left on her own and didn't come back all summer. That's what this story is about.

During that summer, when she lived a few miles south in Argus, things happened. She almost destroyed that town.

When she got down to Argus in the year of 1920, it was just a small grid of six streets on either side of the railroad depot. There were two elevators, one central, the other a few miles west. Two stores competed for the trade of the three hundred citizens, and three churches quarreled with one another for their souls. There was a frame building for Lutherans, a heavy brick one for Episcopalians, and a long narrow shingled Catholic church. This last had a tall slender steeple, twice as high as any building or tree.

No doubt, across the low, flat wheat, watching from the road as she came near Argus on foot, Fleur saw that steeple rise, a shadow thin as a needle. Maybe in that raw space it drew her the way a lone tree draws lightning. Maybe, in the end, the Catholics are to blame. For if she hadn't seen that sign of pride, that slim prayer, that marker, maybe she would have kept walking.

But Fleur Pillager turned, and the first place she went once she came into town was to the back door of the priest's residence attached to the landmark church. She didn't go there for a handout, although she got that, but to ask for work. She got that too, or the town got her. It's hard to tell which came out worse, her or the men or the town, although the upshot of it all was that Fleur lived.

The four men who worked at the butcher's had carved up about a thousand carcasses between them, maybe half of that steers and the other half pigs, sheep, and game animals like deer, elk, and bear. That's not even mentioning the chickens, which were beyond counting. Pete Kozka owned the place, and employed Lily Veddar, Tor Grunewald, and my stepfather, Dutch James, who had brought my mother down from the reservation the year before she disappointed him by dying. Dutch took me out of school to take her place. I kept house half the time and worked the other in the butcher shop, sweeping floors, putting sawdust down, running a hambone across the street to a customer's bean pot or a package of sausage to the corner. I was a good one to have around because until they needed me, I was invisible. I blended into the stained brown walls, a skinny, big-nosed girl with staring eyes. Because I could fade into a corner or squeeze beneath a shelf, I knew everything, what the men said when no one was around, and what they did to Fleur.

Kozka's Meats served farmers for a fifty-mile area, both to slaughter, for it had stock pen and chute, and to cure the meat by smoking it or spicing it in sausage. The storage locker was a marvel, made of many thicknesses of brick, earth insulation, and Minnesota timber, lined inside with sawdust and vast blocks of ice cut from Lake Turcot, hauled down from home each winter by horse and sledge.

A ramshackle board building, part slaughterhouse, part store, was fixed to the low, thick square of the lockers. That's where Fleur worked. Kozka hired her for her strength. She could lift a haunch or carry a pole of sausages without stumbling, and she soon learned cutting from Pete's wife, a string-thin blonde who chain-smoked and handled the razor-edged knives with nerveless precision, slicing close to her stained fingers. Fleur and Fritzie Kozka worked afternoons, wrapping their cuts in paper, and Fleur hauled the packages to the lockers. The meat was left outside the heavy oak doors that were only opened at 5:00 each afternoon, before the men ate supper.

Sometimes Dutch, Tor, and Lily stayed at the lockers, and when they did I stayed too, cleaned floors, restoked the fires in the front smokehouses, while the men sat around the squat cast-iron stove spearing slats of herring onto hardtack bread. They played long games of poker or cribbage on a board made from the planed end of a salt crate. They talked and I listened, although there wasn't much to hear since almost nothing ever happened in Argus. Tor was married, Dutch had lost my mother, and Lily read circulars. They mainly discussed about the auctions to come, equipment, or women.

Every so often, Pete Kozka came out front to make a whist, leaving Fritzie to smoke cigarettes and fry raised doughnuts in the back room. He sat and played a few rounds but kept his thoughts to himself. Fritzie did not tolerate him talking behind her back, and the one book he read was the New Testament. If he said something, it concerned weather or a surplus of sheep stomachs, a ham that smoked green or the markets for corn and wheat. He had a good-luck talisman, the opal-white lens of a cow's eye. Playing cards, he rubbed it between his fingers. That soft sound and the slap of cards was about the only conversation.

Fleur finally gave them a subject.

Her cheeks were wide and flat, her hands large, chapped, muscular. Fleur's shoulders were broad as beams, her hips fishlike, slippery, narrow. An old green dress clung to her waist, worn thin where she sat. Her braids were thick like the tails of animals, and swung against her when she moved, deliberately, slowly in her work, held in and half-tamed, but only half. I could tell, but the others never saw. They never looked into her sly brown eyes or noticed her teeth, strong and sharp and very white. Her legs were bare, and since she padded in beadworked moccasins they never saw that her fifth toes were missing. They never knew she'd drowned. They were blinded, they were stupid, they only saw her in the flesh.

And yet it wasn't just that she was a Chippewa, or even that she was a woman, it wasn't that she was good-looking or even that she was alone that made their brains hum. It was how she played cards.

Women didn't usually play with men, so the evening that Fleur drew a chair to the men's table without being so much as asked, there was a shock of surprise.

"What's this," said Lily. He was fat, with a snake's cold pale eyes and precious skin, smooth and lily-white, which is how he got his name. Lily had a dog, a stumpy mean little bull of a thing with a belly drum-tight from eating pork rinds. The dog liked to play cards just like Lily, and straddled his barrel thighs through games of stud, rum poker, vingt-un.[2] The dog snapped at Fleur's arm that first night, but cringed back, its snarl frozen, when she took her place.

"I thought," she said, her voice soft and stroking, "you might deal me in."

There was a space between the heavy bin of spiced flour and the wall where I just fit. I hunkered down there, kept my eyes open, saw her black hair swing over the chair, her feet solid on the wood floor. I couldn't see up on the table where the cards slapped down, so after they were deep in their game I raised myself up in the shadows, and crouched on a sill of wood.

I watched Fleur's hands stack and ruffle, divide the cards, spill them to each player in a blur, rake them up and shuffle again. Tor, short and scrappy, shut one eye and squinted the other at Fleur. Dutch screwed his lips around a wet cigar.

"Gotta see a man," he mumbled, getting up to go out back to the privy. The others broke, put their cards down, and Fleur sat alone in the lamplight that

2. Twenty-one (French); a card game.

glowed in a sheen across the push of her breasts. I watched her closely, then she paid me a beam of notice for the first time. She turned, looked straight at me, and grinned the white wolf grin a Pillager turns on its victims, except that she wasn't after me.

"Pauline there," she said. "How much money you got?"

We had all been paid for the week that day. Eight cents was in my pocket.

"Stake me," she said, holding out her long fingers. I put the coins in her palm and then I melted back to nothing, part of the walls and tables. It was a long time before I understood that the men would not have seen me no matter what I did, how I moved. I wasn't anything like Fleur. My dress hung loose and my back was already curved, an old woman's. Work had roughened me, reading made my eyes sore, caring for my mother before she died had hardened my face. I was not much to look at, so they never saw me.

When the men came back and sat around the table, they had drawn together. They shot each other small glances, stuck their tongues in their cheeks, burst out laughing at odd moments, to rattle Fleur. But she never minded. They played their vingt-un, staying even as Fleur slowly gained. Those pennies I had given her drew nickels and attracted dimes until there was a small pile in front of her.

Then she hooked them with five card draw, nothing wild. She dealt, discarded, drew, and then she sighed and her cards gave a little shiver. Tor's eye gleamed, and Dutch straightened in his seat.

"I'll pay to see that hand," said Lily Veddar.

Fleur showed, and she had nothing there, nothing at all.

Tor's thin smile cracked open, and he threw his hand in too.

"Well, we know one thing," he said, leaning back in his chair, "the squaw can't bluff."

With that I lowered myself into a mound of swept sawdust and slept. I woke up during the night, but none of them had moved yet, so I couldn't either. Still later, the men must have gone out again, or Fritzie come out to break the game, because I was lifted, soothed, cradled in a woman's arms and rocked so quiet that I kept my eyes shut while Fleur rolled me into a closet of grimy ledgers, oiled paper, balls of string, and thick files that fit beneath me like a mattress.

The game went on after work the next evening. I got my eight cents back five times over, and Fleur kept the rest of the dollar she'd won for a stake. This time they didn't play so late, but they played regular, and then kept going at it night after night. They played poker now, or variations, for one week straight, and each time Fleur won exactly one dollar, no more and no less, too consistent for luck.

By this time, Lily and the other men were so lit with suspense that they got Pete to join the game with them. They concentrated, the fat dog sitting tense in Lily Veddar's lap, Tor suspicious, Dutch stroking his huge square brow, Pete steady. It wasn't that Fleur won that hooked them in so, because she lost hands too. It was rather that she never had a freak hand or even anything above a straight. She only took on her low cards, which didn't sit right. By chance, Fleur should have gotten a full or a flush by now. The irritating thing was she beat with pairs and never bluffed, because she couldn't, and still she ended each night with exactly one dollar. Lily couldn't believe, first of all, that a woman could be smart enough to play cards, but even if she was, that she would then be stupid enough to cheat for a dollar a night. By day I watched him turn the problem over, his hard white face dull, small fingers probing at his knuckles, until he finally thought he had Fleur figured as a bit-time player, caution her game. Raising the stakes would throw her.

More than anything now, he wanted Fleur to come away with something but a dollar. Two bits less or ten more, the sum didn't matter, just so he broke her streak.

Night after night she played, won her dollar, and left to stay in a place that just Fritzie and I knew about. Fleur bathed in the slaughtering tub, then slept in the unused brick smokehouse behind the lockers, a windowless place tarred on the inside with scorched fats. When I brushed against her skin I noticed that she smelled of the walls, rich and woody, slightly burnt. Since that night she put me in the closet I was no longer afraid of her, but followed her close, stayed with her, became her moving shadow that the men never noticed, the shadow that could have saved her.

August, the month that bears fruit, closed around the shop, and Pete and Fritzie left for Minnesota to escape the heat. Night by night, running, Fleur had won thirty dollars, and only Pete's presence had kept Lily at bay. But Pete was gone now, and one payday, with the heat so bad no one could move but Fleur, the men sat and played and waited while she finished work. The cards sweat, limp in their fingers, the table was slick with grease, and even the walls were warm to the touch. The air was motionless. Fleur was in the next room boiling heads.

Her green dress, drenched, wrapped her like a transparent sheet. A skin of lakeweed. Black snarls of veining clung to her arms. Her braids were loose, half unraveled, tied behind her neck in a thick loop. She stood in steam, turning skulls through a vat with a wooden paddle. When scraps boiled to the surface, she bent with a round tin sieve and scooped them out. She'd filled two dishpans.

"Ain't that enough now?" called Lily. "We're waiting." The stump of a dog trembled in his lap, alive with rage. It never smelled me or noticed me above Fleur's smoky skin. The air was heavy in my corner, and pressed me down. Fleur sat with them.

"Now what do you say?" Lily asked the dog. It barked. That was the signal for the real game to start.

"Let's up the ante," said Lily, who had been stalking this night all month. He had a roll of money in his pocket. Fleur had five bills in her dress. The men had each saved their full pay.

"Ante a dollar then," said Fleur, and pitched hers in. She lost, but they let her scrape along, cent by cent. And then she won some. She played unevenly, as if chance were all she had. She reeled them in. The game went on. The dog was stiff now, poised on Lily's knees, a ball of vicious muscle with its yellow eyes slit in concentration. It gave advice, seemed to sniff the lay of Fleur's cards, twitched and nudged. Fleur was up, then down, saved by a scratch. Tor dealt seven cards, three down. The pot grew, round by round, until it held all the money. Nobody folded. Then it all rode on one last card and they went silent. Fleur picked hers up and drew a long breath. The heat lowered like a bell. Her card shook, but she stayed in.

Lily smiled and took the dog's head tenderly between his palms.

"Say Fatso," he said, crooning the words. "You reckon that girl's bluffing?"

The dog whined and Lily laughed. "Me too," he said, "let's show." He swept his bills and coins into the pot and then they turned their cards over.

Lily looked once, looked again, then he squeezed the dog like a fist of dough and slammed it on the table.

Fleur threw out her arms and drew the money over, grinning that same wolf grin that she'd used on me, the grin that had them. She jammed the bills in her dress, scooped the coins up in waxed white paper that she tied with string.

"Let's go another round," said Lily, his voice choked with burrs. But Fleur opened her mouth and yawned, then walked out back to gather slops for the one big hog that was waiting in the stock pen to be killed.

The men sat still as rocks, their hands spread on the oiled wood table. Dutch had chewed his cigar to damp shreds, Tor's eye was dull. Lily's gaze was the only one to follow Fleur. I didn't move. I felt them gathering, saw my stepfather's veins, the ones in his forehead that stood out in anger. The dog rolled off the table and curled in a knot below the counter, where none of the men could touch it.

Lily rose and stepped out back to the closet of ledgers where Pete kept his private stock. He brought back a bottle, uncorked and tipped it between his fingers. The lump in his throat moved, then he passed it on. They drank, quickly felt the whiskey's fire, and planned with their eyes things they couldn't say aloud.

When they left, I followed. I hid out back in the clutter of broken boards and chicken crates beside the stock pen, where they waited. Fleur could not be seen at first, and then the moon broke and showed her, slipping cautiously along the rough board chute with a bucket in her hand. Her hair fell, wild and coarse, to her waist, and her dress was a floating patch in the dark. She made a pig-calling sound, rang the tin pail lightly against the wood, froze suspiciously. But too late. In the sound of the ring Lily moved, fat and nimble, stepped right behind Fleur and put out his creamy hands. At his first touch, she whirled and doused him with the bucket of sour slops. He pushed her against the big fence and the package of coins split, went clinking and jumping, winked against the wood. Fleur rolled over once and vanished into the yard.

The moon fell behind a curtain of ragged clouds, and Lily followed into the dark muck. But he tripped, pitched over the huge flank of the pig, who lay mired to the snout, heavily snoring. I sprang out of the weeds and climbed the side of the pen, stuck like glue. I saw the sow rise to her neat, knobby knees, gain her balance and sway, curious, as Lily stumbled forward. Fleur had backed into the angle of rough wood just beyond, and when Lily tried to jostle past, the sow tipped up on her hind legs and struck, quick and hard as a snake. She plunged her head into Lily's thick side and snatched a mouthful of his shirt. She lunged again, caught him lower, so that he grunted in pained surprise. He seemed to ponder, breathing deep. Then he launched his huge body in a swimmer's dive.

The sow screamed as his body smacked over hers. She rolled, striking out with her knife-sharp hooves, and Lily gathered himself upon her, took her foot-long face by the ears and scraped her snout and cheeks against the trestles of the pen. He hurled the sow's tight skull against an iron post, but instead of knocking her dead, he merely woke her from her dream.

She reared, shrieked, drew him with her so that they posed standing upright. They bowed jerkily to each other, as if to begin. Then his arms swung and flailed. She sank her black fangs into his shoulder, clasping him, dancing him forward and backward through the pen. Their steps picked up pace, went wild. The two dipped as one, box-stepped, tripped one another. She ran her split foot through his hair. He grabbed her kinked tail. They went down and came up, the same shape and then the same color until the men couldn't tell one from the other in that light and Fleur was able to launch herself over the gates, swing down, hit gravel.

The men saw, yelled, and chased her at a dead run to the smokehouse. And Lily too, once the sow gave up in disgust and freed him. That is where I should have gone to Fleur, saved her, thrown myself on Dutch. But I went stiff with fear and couldn't unlatch myself from the trestles or move at all. I closed my eyes and put my head in my arms, tried to hide, so there is nothing to describe but what I couldn't block out, Fleur's hoarse breath, so loud it filled me, her cry in the old language, and my name repeated over and over among the words.

The heat was still dense the next morning when I came back to work. Fleur was gone but the men were there, slack-faced, hung over. Lily was paler and softer than ever, as if his flesh had steamed on his bones. They smoked, took pulls off a bottle. It wasn't noon yet. I worked awhile, waiting shop and sharpening steel. But I was sick, I was smothered, I was sweating so hard that my hands slipped on the knives, and I wiped my fingers clean of the greasy touch of the customers' coins. Lily opened his mouth and roared once, not in anger. There was no meaning to the sound. His boxer dog, sprawled limp beside his foot, never lifted its head. Nor did the other men.

They didn't notice when I stepped outside, hoping for a clear breath. And then I forgot them because I knew that we were all balanced, ready to tip, to fly, to be crushed as soon as the weather broke. The sky was so low that I felt the weight of it like a yoke. Clouds hung down, witch teats, a tornado's green-brown cones, and as I watched one flicked out and became a delicate probing thumb. Even as I picked up my heels and ran back inside, the wind blew suddenly, cold, and then came rain.

Inside, the men had disappeared already and the whole place was trembling as if a huge hand was pinched at the rafters, shaking it. I ran straight through, screaming for Dutch or for any of them, and then I stopped at the heavy doors of the lockers, where they had surely taken shelter. I stood there a moment. Everything went still. Then I heard a cry building in the wind, faint at first, a whistle and then a shrill scream that tore through the walls and gathered around me, spoke plain so I understood that I should move, put my arms out, and slam down the great iron bar that fit across the hasp and lock.

Outside, the wind was stronger, like a hand held against me. I struggled forward. The bushes tossed, the awnings flapped off storefronts, the rails of porches rattled. The odd cloud became a fat snout that nosed along the earth and sniffled, jabbed, picked at things, sucked them up, blew them apart, rooted around as if it was following a certain scent, then stopped behind me at the butcher shop and bored down like a drill.

I went flying, landed somewhere in a ball. When I opened my eyes and looked, stranger things were happening.

A herd of cattle flew through the air like giant birds, dropping dung, their mouths opened in stunned bellows. A candle, still lighted, blew past, and tables, napkins, garden tools, a whole school of drifting eyeglasses, jackets on hangers, hams, a checkerboard, a lampshade, and at last the sow from behind the lockers, on the run, her hooves a blur, set free, swooping, diving, screaming as everything in Argus fell apart and got turned upside down, smashed, and thoroughly wrecked.

Days passed before the town went looking for the men. They were bachelors, after all, except for Tor, whose wife had suffered a blow to the head that made her forgetful. Everyone was occupied with digging out, in high relief because even though the Catholic steeple had been torn off like a peaked cap and sent across five fields, those huddled in the cellar were unhurt. Walls had fallen, windows were demolished, but the stores were intact and so were the bankers and shop owners who had taken refuge in their safes or beneath their cash registers. It was a fair-minded disaster, no one could be said to have suffered much more than the next, at least not until Pete and Fritzie came home.

Of all the businesses in Argus, Kozka's Meats had suffered worst. The boards of the front building had been split to kindling, piled in a huge pyramid, and the shop equipment was blasted far and wide. Pete paced off the distance the iron bathtub had been flung—a hundred feet. The glass candy case went fifty, and landed without so much as a cracked pane. There were other surprises as well, for the back rooms where Fritzie and Pete lived were undisturbed. Fritzie said the dust still coated her china figures, and upon her kitchen table, in the ashtray, perched the last cigarette she'd put out in haste. She lit and finished it, looking through the window. From there, she could see that the old smokehouse Fleur had slept in was crushed to a reddish sand and the stockpens were completely torn apart, the rails stacked helter-skelter. Fritzie asked for Fleur. People shrugged. Then she asked about the others and, suddenly, the town understood that three men were missing.

There was a rally of help, a gathering of shovels and volunteers. We passed boards from hand to hand, stacked them, uncovered what lay beneath the pile of jagged splinters. The lockers, full of meat that was Pete and Fritzie's investment, slowly came into sight, still intact. When enough room was made for a man to stand on the roof, there were calls, a general urge to hack through and see what lay below. But Fritzie shouted that she wouldn't allow it because the meat would spoil. And so the work continued, board by board, until at last the heavy oak doors of the freezer were revealed and people pressed to the entry. Everyone wanted to be the first, but since it was my stepfather lost, I was let go in when Pete and Fritzie wedged through into the sudden icy air.

Pete scraped a match on his boot, lit the lamp Fritzie held, and then the three of us stood still in its circle. Light glared off the skinned and hanging carcasses, the crates of wrapped sausages, the bright and cloudy blocks of lake ice, pure as winter. The cold bit into us, pleasant at first, then numbing. We must have stood there a couple of minutes before we saw the men, or more rightly, the humps of fur, the iced and shaggy hides they wore, the bearskins they had taken down and wrapped about themselves. We stepped closer and Fritzie tilted the lantern beneath the flaps of fur into their faces. The dog was there, perched among them, heavy as a doorstop. The three had hunched around a barrel where the game was still laid out, and a dead lantern and an empty bottle too. But they had thrown down their last hands and hunkered tight, clutching one another, knuckles raw from beating at the door they had also attacked with hooks. Frost stars gleamed off their eyelashes and the stubble of their beards. Their faces were set in concentration, mouths open as if to speak some careful thought, some agreement they'd come to in each other's arms.

Power travels in the bloodlines, handed out before birth. It comes down through the hands, which in the Pillagers were strong and knotted, big, spidery, and rough, with sensitive fingertips good at dealing cards. It comes through the eyes, too, belligerent, darkest brown, the eyes of those in the bear clan, impolite as they gaze directly at a person.

In my dreams, I look straight back at Fleur, at the men. I am no longer the watcher on the dark sill, the skinny girl.

The blood draws us back, as if it runs through a vein of earth. I've come home and, except for talking to my cousins, live a quiet life. Fleur lives quiet too, down on Lake Turcot with her boat. Some say she's married to the waterman, Misshepeshu, or that she's living in shame with white men or windigos, or that she's killed them all. I'm about the only one here who ever goes to visit her. Last winter, I went to help out in her cabin when she bore the child, whose green eyes and skin the color of an old penny made more talk, as no one could decide if the child was mixed blood or what, fathered in a smokehouse, or by a man with brass scales, or by the lake. The girl is bold, smiling in her sleep, as if she knows what people wonder, as if she hears the old men talk, turning the story over. It comes up different every time and has no ending, no beginning. They get the middle wrong too. They only know they don't know anything.

1988

CATHY SONG
b. 1955

In many of Cathy Song's poems a particular moment or event becomes a window through which we enter a field of vision. "What frames the view," she has written, "is the mind in the diamond pinpoint light of concentration tunneling into memory, released by the imagination." As the title of her second book, *Frameless Windows, Squares of Light,* suggests, Song's poems capture the way a warm afternoon, a childhood Easter, a picnic in the park is an opening for memory and reflection. The visual quality of her poems can suggest a photograph or painting, and Song feels a connection between her work and those of the Japanese printmaker Kitagawa Utamaro and the American painter Georgia O'Keeffe. Song's first book, *Picture Bride* (1983), contains a number of poems inspired by the work of these artists. Writing, in "Beauty and Sadness," of the way Utamaro's prints rendered "Teahouse waitresses, actresses, / geishas, courtesans and maids" in "their fleeting loveliness," Song suggests that the artist and poet capture the moment, knowing that it is always dissolving.

Picture Bride was chosen by the poet Richard Hugo for the Yale Younger Poets series. In the title poem Song comes as close as imagination allows to the experience of her grandmother, who, the poem implies, was chosen as a bride from a photograph and summoned from Korea to Hawaii. But Song is also aware of the limits of imaginative identification and the difficulty of knowing the full truth of the past. She respects the mystery of another's identity. The grandmother in "Picture Bride," the woman in "Lost Sister," the mother in "Humble Jar," and the geishas painted by Utamaro possess a privacy that the poet discloses but cannot fully enter. Song's tactful sense of both the power and the limits of imagination is one of her distinctive marks as a poet.

She was born in Honolulu, Hawaii, and grew up in Wahiawa, a small town on the island of Oahu. The setting of sugar-cane fields, of island life where "the sound of the ocean / could be heard through the ironwoods" ("Waialaua"), and of the rain that comes "even when the sun was shining" ("A Pale Arrangement of Hands") is central to her work. That landscape belongs to her present but also evokes her childhood and the memory of another, more distant landscape—the Asia of her ancestors. Many of Song's poems render the mysteries of what she has called "familial and personal ties; lives overlapping," and her sense of these ties extends backward to her ancestors as well as forward to her children. She began her college education at the University of Hawaii and then attended Wellesley College. After her graduation from Wellesley, she received an M.A. in creative writing from Boston University and has since taught creative writing at a number of colleges and universities. Her third collection of poems, *School Figures*, appeared in 1994 and a subsequent volume, *The Land of Bliss*, in 2001.

Song's ability to write about her own or another's experience as an acute observer may have to do with her multicultural background, which often places her on the boundary of what she sees. Her capacity to let the power of observation give rise to feeling recalls at times the work of Elizabeth Bishop and also suggests Song's resemblance to the Utamaro of her poem "Beauty and Sadness," whose "invisible presence / one feels in these prints." At other times Song writes about herself more directly. She has, for example, deftly rendered the erotic nature of her own experience: "But there is this slow arousal. / The small buttons / of my cotton blouse / are pulling away from my body" ("The White Porch"). The careful composition of her poems, with their vivid detail, blend the accidental and spontaneous quality of life with the design of art. Although her work can sometimes seem too composed, too removed from the sharp impact of experience, her strongest poems balance a sense of tradition with a feel for contemporary life and catch in the patterns of art the transient instant: "the flicker of a dragonfly's delicate wing."

The White Porch

I wrap the blue towel
after washing,
around the damp
weight of hair, bulky
as a sleeping cat,   5
and sit out on the porch.
Still dripping water,
it'll be dry by supper,
by the time the dust
settles off your shoes,   10
though it's only five
past noon. Think
of the luxury: how to use
the afternoon like the stretch

of lawn spread before me.   15
There's the laundry,
sun-warm clothes at twilight,
and the mountain of beans
in my lap. Each one,
I'll break and snap   20
thoughtfully in half.

But there is this slow arousal.
The small buttons
of my cotton blouse
are pulling away from my body.   25
I feel the strain of threads,
the swollen magnolias
heavy as a flock of birds
in the tree. Already,
the orange sponge cake   30
is rising in the oven.
I know you'll say it makes
your mouth dry
and I'll watch you
drench your slice of it   35
in canned peaches
and lick the plate clean.

So much hair, my mother
used to say, grabbing
the thick braided rope   40
in her hands while we washed
the breakfast dishes, discussing
dresses and pastries.
My mind often elsewhere
as we did the morning chores together.   45
Sometimes, a few strands
would catch in her gold ring.
I worked hard then,
anticipating the hour
when I would let the rope down   50
at night, strips of sheets,
knotted and tied,
while she slept in tight blankets.
My hair, freshly washed
like a measure of wealth,   55
like a bridal veil.
Crouching in the grass,
you would wait for the signal,
for the movement of curtains
before releasing yourself   60
from the shadow of moths.
Cloth, hair and hands,
smuggling you in.

                                                          1983

Lost Sister

1

In China,
even the peasants
named their first daughters
Jade—
the stone that in the far fields   5
could moisten the dry season,
could make men move mountains
for the healing green of the inner hills
glistening like slices of winter melon.

And the daughters were grateful: 10
they never left home.
To move freely was a luxury
stolen from them at birth.
Instead, they gathered patience,
learning to walk in shoes   15
the size of teacups,
without breaking—
the arc of their movements
as dormant as the rooted willow,
as redundant as the farmyard hens.   20
But they traveled far
in surviving,
learning to stretch the family rice,
to quiet the demons,
the noisy stomachs.   25

2

There is a sister
across the ocean,
who relinquished her name,
diluting jade green
with the blue of the Pacific.   30
Rising with a tide of locusts,
she swarmed with others
to inundate another shore.
In America,
there are many roads   35
and women can stride along with men.

But in another wilderness,
the possibilities,
the loneliness,
can strangulate like jungle vines.   40
The meager provisions and sentiments
of once belonging—
fermented roots, Mah-Jongg[1] tiles and firecrackers—

---

1. A game of Chinese origin.

set but a flimsy household
in a forest of nightless cities. 45
A giant snake rattles above,
spewing black clouds into your kitchen.
Dough-faced landlords
slip in and out of your keyholes,
making claims you don't understand, 50
tapping into your communication systems
of laundry lines and restaurant chains.

You find you need China:
your one fragile identification,
a jade link 55
handcuffed to your wrist.
You remember your mother
who walked for centuries,
footless—
and like her, 60
you have left no footprints,
but only because
there is an ocean in between,
the unremitting space of your rebellion.

1983

Heaven

He thinks when we die we'll go to China.
Think of it—a Chinese heaven
where, except for his blond hair,
the part that belongs to his father,
everyone will look like him. 5
China, that blue flower on the map,
bluer than the sea
his hand must span like a bridge
to reach it.
An octave away. 10

I've never seen it.
It's as if I can't sing that far.
But look—
on the map, this black dot.
Here is where we live, 15
on the pancake plains
just east of the Rockies,
on the other side of the clouds.
A mile above the sea,
the air is so thin, you can starve on it. 20
No bamboo trees
but the alpine equivalent,

reedy aspen with light, fluttering leaves.
Did a boy in Guangzhou[1] dream of this
as his last stop?   25

I've heard the trains at night
whistling past our yards,
what we've come to own,
the broken fences, the whiny dog, the rattletrap cars.
It's still the wild west,   30
mean and grubby,
the shootouts and fistfights in the back alley.
With my son the dreamer
and my daughter, who is too young to walk,
I've sat in this spot   35
and wondered why here?
Why in this short life,
this town, this creek they call a river?

He had never planned to stay,
the boy who helped to build   40
the railroads for a dollar a day.[2]
He had always meant to go back.
When did he finally know
that each mile of track led him further away,
that he would die in his sleep,   45
dispossessed,
having seen Gold Mountain,[3]
the icy wind tunneling through it,
these landlocked, makeshift ghost towns?

It must be in the blood,   50
this notion of returning.
It skipped two generations, lay fallow,
the garden an unmarked grave.
On a spring sweater day
it's as if we remember him.   55
I call to the children.
We can see the mountains
shimmering blue above the air.
If you look really hard
says my son the dreamer,   60
leaning out from the laundry's rigging,
the work shirts fluttering like sails,
you can see all the way to heaven.

                                                                    1988

---

1. Or Canton, seaport city in southeastern China.
2. The Chinese provided much of the cheap labor
that laid the tracks of the transcontinental railroads in the 19th century.
3. In China in the 1840s, the U.S. state of California was known as "Gold Mountain." Many Chinese emigrated to California to search for gold,
only to discover that mining was uncertain, unreliable, and dangerous.

LI-YOUNG LEE
b. 1957

In his poem "Persimmons" Li-Young Lee remembers his father saying, "Some things never leave a person." Many of the poems in Lee's books—*Rose* (1986), *The City in Which I Love You* (1990), and *Book of My Nights* (2001)—testify to a sense of the past, especially his father's past, which never leaves Lee. The father in Lee's poems is personal and mythic; he instructs the poet-son in "the art of memory." Lee's father, born in China, served as a personal physician to Mao Tse-tung. He later was jailed for nineteen months, a political prisoner of the Indonesian dictator Sukarno. Lee was born in Jakarta, Indonesia. In 1959 the family fled Indonesia and traveled in the Far East (Hong Kong, Macao, and Japan), finally arriving in America, where Lee's father became a Presbyterian minister in a small town in western Pennsylvania. Many of Lee's poems seek to remember and understand his father's life and to come to terms with Lee's differences from that powerful figure.

Lee's work reminds us about the ancient connections between memory and poetry. In his work memory is often sweet; it draws the poet to the past even when, as in "Eating Alone," that sweetness is as dizzying as the juice of a rotten pear in which a hornet spins. But memory can also be a burden, and its pull is countered in Lee's work by a sensuous apprehension of the present. As in his poem "This Room and Everything in It" the erotic immediacy of the moment can disrupt any effort to fix that moment in the orders of memory. Everywhere in Lee's work is the evidence of hearing, taste, smell, and touch as well as sight. If the poet's bodily presence in the world recalls his great American precursor Walt Whitman, Lee's fluid motion between the physical world and the domain of memory, dream, or vision also carries out Whitman's visionary strain and links Lee to the work of Theodore Roethke, James Wright, and Denise Levertov, among others. The intensity of Lee's poems, however, is often leavened by a subtle and winning humor and playfulness; such qualities are especially valuable in a poet at times too easily seduced by beauty.

Lee studied at the University of Pittsburgh (where one of his teachers was the poet Gerald Stern), the University of Arizona, and the State University of New York College at Brockport. He has since taught at various universities. In 1995 he published a prose memoir, *The Winged Seed: A Remembrance*. His prose, like his poetry, is characterized by his deep sense of connection between an individual life and a powerful past and his ability to move between plain speech and a lushness evocative of biblical language.

Persimmons

In sixth grade Mrs. Walker
slapped the back of my head
and made me stand in the corner
for not knowing the difference
between *persimmon* and *precision*.   5
How to choose

persimmons. This is precision.
Ripe ones are soft and brown-spotted.
Sniff the bottoms. The sweet one
will be fragrant. How to eat: 10
put the knife away, lay down newspaper.
Peel the skin tenderly, not to tear the meat.
Chew the skin, suck it,

and swallow. Now, eat
the meat of the fruit,   15
so sweet,
all of it, to the heart.

Donna undresses, her stomach is white.
In the yard, dewy and shivering
with crickets, we lie naked,   20
face-up, face-down.
I teach her Chinese.
Crickets: *chiu chiu*. Dew: I've forgotten.
Naked: I've forgotten.
Ni, wo: you and me.   25
I part her legs,
remember to tell her
she is beautiful as the moon.

Other words
that got me into trouble were   30
fight and *fright*, *wren* and *yarn*.
Fight was what I did when I was frightened,
fright was what I felt when I was fighting.
Wrens are small, plain birds,
yarn is what one knits with.   35
Wrens are soft as yarn.
My mother made birds out of yarn.
I loved to watch her tie the stuff;
a bird, a rabbit, a wee man.

Mrs. Walker brought a persimmon to class   40
and cut it up
so everyone could taste
a *Chinese apple*. Knowing
it wasn't ripe or sweet, I didn't eat
but I watched the other faces.   45

My mother said every persimmon has a sun
inside, something golden, glowing,
warm as my face.

Once, in the cellar, I found two wrapped in newspaper,
forgotten and not yet ripe.   50
I took them and set both on my bedroom windowsill,
where each morning a cardinal
sang, *The sun, the sun.*

Finally understanding
he was going blind,   55
my father sat up all one night
waiting for a song, a ghost.
I gave him the persimmons,
swelled, heavy as sadness,
and sweet as love.   60

This year, in the muddy lighting
of my parents' cellar, I rummage, looking
for something I lost.
My father sits on the tired, wooden stairs,
black cane between his knees,   65
hand over hand, gripping the handle.

He's so happy that I've come home.
I ask how his eyes are, a stupid question.
All gone, he answers.

Under some blankets, I find a box.   70
Inside the box I find three scrolls.
I sit beside him and untie
three paintings by my father:
Hibiscus leaf and a white flower.
Two cats preening.   75
Two persimmons, so full they want to drop from the cloth.

He raises both hands to touch the cloth,
asks, *Which is this?*

This is persimmons, Father.

Oh, the feel of the wolftail on the silk,   80
the strength, the tense
precision in the wrist.
I painted them hundreds of times
eyes closed. These I painted blind.
Some things never leave a person: 85
scent of the hair of one you love,
the texture of persimmons,
in your palm, the ripe weight.

                                                                      1986

Eating Alone

I've pulled the last of the year's young onions.
The garden is bare now. The ground is cold,
brown and old. What is left of the day flames
in the maples at the corner of my
eye. I turn, a cardinal vanishes.   5
By the cellar door, I wash the onions,
then drink from the icy metal spigot.

Once, years back, I walked beside my father
among the windfall pears. I can't recall
our words. We may have strolled in silence. But   10
I still see him bend that way—left hand braced
on knee, creaky—to lift and hold to my

eye a rotten pear. In it, a hornet
spun crazily, glazed in slow, glistening juice.

It was my father I saw this morning   15
waving to me from the trees. I almost
called to him, until I came close enough
to see the shovel, leaning where I had
left it, in the flickering, deep green shade.

White rice steaming, almost done. Sweet green peas   20
fried in onions. Shrimp braised in sesame
oil and garlic. And my own loneliness.
What more could I, a young man, want.

1986

Eating Together

In the steamer is the trout
seasoned with slivers of ginger,
two sprigs of green onion, and sesame oil.
We shall eat it with rice for lunch,
brothers, sister, my mother who will   5
taste the sweetest meat of the head,
holding it between her fingers
deftly, the way my father did
weeks ago. Then he lay down
to sleep like a snow-covered road   10
winding through pines older than him,
without any travelers, and lonely for no one.

1986

This Room and Everything in It

Lie still now
while I prepare for my future,
certain hard days ahead,
when I'll need what I know so clearly this moment.

I am making use   5
of the one thing I learned
of all the things my father tried to teach me:
the art of memory.

I am letting this room
and everything in it   10
stand for my ideas about love
and its difficulties.

I'll let your love-cries,
those spacious notes
of a moment ago,   15
stand for distance.

Your scent,
that scent
of spice and a wound,
I'll let stand for mystery.   20

Your sunken belly
is the daily cup
of milk I drank
as a boy before morning prayer.

The sun on the face   25
of the wall
is God, the face
I can't see, my soul,

and so on, each thing
standing for a separate idea,   30
and those ideas forming the constellation
of my greater idea.
And one day, when I need
to tell myself something intelligent
about love,   35

I'll close my eyes
and recall this room and everything in it:
My body is estrangement.
This desire, perfection.
Your closed eyes my extinction.   40
Now I've forgotten my
idea. The book
on the windowsill, riffled by wind . . .
the even-numbered pages are
the past, the odd-   45
numbered pages, the future.
The sun is
God, your body is milk . . .

useless, useless . . .
your cries are song, my body's not me . . .   50
no good . . . my idea
has evaporated . . . your hair is time, your thighs are song . . .
it had something to do
with death . . . it had something
to do with love.   55

                                                                1990

SHERMAN ALEXIE
b. 1966

Except for one great-grandparent, Sherman Alexie's heritage is Native American: Coeur d'Alene on his father's side; Colville, Flathead, and Spokane on his mother's. Much of his work is set in the Washington State cities of Seattle and Spokane, marking his commitment to the Pacific Northwest above other regions of the country, as displayed in his poetry, fiction, and cinematic work. Yet his interest in Native American culture ranges widely, to include other tribes such as the Navajo and regions throughout the West and Southwest. Raised on the Spokane reservation at Wellpinit, Washington, Alexie thrived in the cultural immersion that secondary education at Rearden High School, some distance from home, provided—especially the popular culture that would later infuse his work. Hence both words in the designation "Native American" figure prominently in how he sees himself as a writer.

Equal doses of trouble and humor characterize Alexie's work. Having survived hydrocephalus (a cerebrospinal abnormality) as a child and alcoholism as a young adult, he drew on his college experience as an undergraduate at Gonzaga University in Spokane and Washington State University in Pullman to find a literary voice, drawing on inspirations as diverse as John Steinbeck's fiction and the Native American poetry collected by Joseph Bruhac in the anthology *Songs from This Earth on Turtle's Back* (1983). In 1992 he published his own first work, *The Business of Fancy Dancing: Stories and Poems,* with one of America's most prominent small presses, Hanging Loose (Brooklyn, New York). *Reservation Blues* (1994) was his first novel, followed by *Indian Killer* in 1996 and *Flight* in 2007. This most recent novel shows the influence of Kurt Vonnegut, from its narrative device of time travel to its reinvention of history from a contemporary point of view. Presented broadly, even comically, his stories often draw on simple incidents, as in "Do Not Go Gentle" (reprinted here), which takes its title from the Welsh poet Dylan Thomas's exhortation against accepting death easily.

When *The Business of Fancy Dancing* was published, a review in *The New York Times* called Alexie "one of the major lyric voices of our time." "I was a 25 year old Spokane Indian guy working as a secretary at a high school exchange program," he has written. "I thought 'Great! Where do I go from here?'" Alexie has continued telling stories through poetry, fiction, and screenwriting. His storytelling offers a tragicomic vision of contemporary Native American life. College educated and street-smart ("I'm a rez kid who's gone urban,"), irreverent and also dead serious, Alexie resembles the trickster figure of Crow in his poem "Crow Testament."

The narrative power of his poems has a furious energy. Although some of his work, like the villanelle "Sister Fire, Brother Smoke," takes traditional forms, most of his poems are open and improvisational, frequently and effectively using repetition and parallelism. The title of Alexie's 2000 collection, *One Stick Song,* offers an apt image for his work; it refers to a gambling game in which sticks function like chips. When down to one stick, he explains, "You're desperate," and a "One Stick Song" is "a desperate celebration, a desperate attempt to save yourself, putting everything you have into one song." The best of Alexie's poems, like "The Exaggeration of Despair," make facing up to grief and anger an act of survival. The intensity of this effort is especially evident when he reads from or recites his work. A brilliant performer, sliding between humor, anger, and pain, he makes a poetry reading a dynamic event. It is no wonder that his interest in performance has turned him to stand-up comedy as well.

Popular audiences know Alexie from his 1998 film *Smoke Signals,* a major Hollywood production he scripted from material in his story collection *The Lone Ranger and Tonto Fistfight in Heaven* (1993). These stories and the movie drawn from them cover the range of contemporary Native American experiences. As one of his characters says, Native Americans have "a way of surviving. But it's almost like Indians can easily survive the big stuff. Mass murder, loss of language and land rights. It's the small things that hurt the

most. The white waitress who wouldn't take an order, Tonto, the Washington Redskins."
He has also written and directed the film *The Business of Fancydancing* (2002).

Alexie has won numerous awards, including the 2007 National Book Award for
Young Adult Literature for *The Absolutely True Diary of a Part-Time Indian*. He maintains a Web site on which he blogs almost daily and currently lives in Seattle.

The text is from *Ten Little Indians* (2003).

At Navajo Monument Valley Tribal School

from the photograph
by Skeet McAuley

the football field rises
to meet the mesa. Indian boys
gallop across the grass, against

the beginning of their body.
On those Saturday afternoons,   5
unbroken horses gather to watch

their sons growing larger
in the small parts of the world.
Everyone is the quarterback.

There is no thin man in a big hat   10
writing down all the names
in two columns: winners and losers.

This is the eternal football game,
Indians versus Indians. All the Skins
in the wooden bleachers fancydancing,   15

stomping red dust straight down
into nothing. Before the game is over,
the eighth-grade girls' track team

comes running, circling the field,
their thin and brown legs echoing   20
wild horses, wild horses, wild horses.

                                                        1992

Pawn Shop

I walk into the bar, after being gone for a while, and it's empty. The
Bartender tells me all the Indians are gone, do I know where they went?
I tell him I don't know, and I don't know, so he gives me a beer just for
being Indian, small favors, and I wonder where all the Skins disappeared
to, and after a while, I leave, searching the streets, searching storefronts,   5
until I walk into a pawn shop, find a single heart beating under glass, and
I know who it used to belong to, I know all of them.

                                                        1992

Crow Testament[1]

1.

Cain lifts Crow, that heavy black bird
and strikes down Abel.[2]

Damn, says Crow, I guess
this is just the beginning.

2.

The white man, disguised   5
as a falcon, swoops in
and yet again steals a salmon
from Crow's talons.

Damn, says Crow, if I could swim
I would have fled this country years ago.   10

3.

The Crow God as depicted
in all of the reliable Crow bibles
looks exactly like a Crow.

Damn, says Crow, this makes it
so much easier to worship myself.   15

4.

Among the ashes of Jericho,[3]
Crow sacrifices his firstborn son.

Damn, says Crow, a million nests
are soaked with blood.

5.

When Crows fight Crows   20
the sky fills with beaks and talons.

Damn, says Crow, it's raining feathers.

6.

Crow flies around the reservation
and collects empty beer bottles

1. Crow, like Raven, is a trickster figure in many Native American cultures.
2. In Genesis, Cain kills his brother, Abel. They are the sons of Adam and Eve.
3. This biblical city, famous for its great walls, was the first town attacked by the Israelites under Joshua, after they crossed the Jordan River.

but they are so heavy   25
he can carry only one at a time.

So, one by one, he returns them
but gets only five cents a bottle.

Damn, says Crow, redemption
is not easy.   30

7.

Crow rides a pale horse
into a crowded powwow
but none of the Indians panic.

Damn, says Crow, I guess
they already live near the end of the world.   35

2000

Do Not Go Gentle

My wife and I didn't know Mr. Grief in person until our baby boy got his face stuck between his mattress and crib and suffocated himself blue. He died three times that day, Mr. Grief squeezing his lungs tight, but the muscular doctors and nurses battled that suffocating monster man and brought our boy back to life three times. He was our little blue baby Jesus.

I'm lying. Our baby wasn't Jesus. Our baby was alive only a little bit. Mostly he was dead and slept his way through a coma. In Children's Hospital, our baby was hooked up to a million dollars' worth of machines that breathed, pissed, and pooped for him. I bet you could line up all of my wife's and my grandmothers and grandfathers and aunts and uncles and brothers and sisters and mothers and fathers and first, second, and third cousins, and rob their wallets and purses, and maybe you'd collect about $512.

Mr. Grief was a billionaire. He could afford to check on our baby every six hours, but every six hours, my wife and I cussed him out and sent him running. My wife is beautiful and powerful and only twenty-five years old, but she is magic like a grandmother, and Indian grandmothers aren't afraid of a little man like Mr. Grief.

One night, while I guarded over our baby, my wife wrapped her braids in a purple bandana, shoved her hands into thick work clothes, sneaked up on Mr. Grief in the hallway, and beat him severely about the head and shoulders like she was Muhammad Ali.[1]

When you're hurting, it feels good to hurt somebody else. But you have to be careful. If you get addicted to the pain-causing, then you start hurting people who don't need hurting. If you turn into a pain-delivering robot, then you start thinking everybody looks like Mr. Grief and everybody deserves a beating.

---

1. American prizefighter (b. Cassius Clay, 1942).

One day when my wife was crying, I swear I saw Mr. Grief hiding behind her eyes. So I yelled and screamed at her and called her all of the bad names. But I got really close to her to yell, because it's more effective to yell when you're closer to your enemy, and I smelled her true scent. I knew it was only my wife inside my wife, because she smelled like tenderness, and Mr. Grief smells like a porcupine rotting dead on the side of the road.

My wife and I didn't even name our baby. We were Indians and didn't want to carry around too much hope. Hope eats your flesh like a spider bite. But my wife and I loved our little Baby X and took turns sitting beside his bed and singing to him. The nurses and doctors let us bring in our hand drums, so we sang powwow[2] songs to our baby. I'm a pretty good singer, and my wife is the best there is, and crowds always gathered to listen to us, and that made us feel good.

It was great to feel good about something, because my wife and I were all the way grieving. We took turns singing honor songs and falling asleep. Mr. Grief is a wizard who puts sleep spells on you. My wife spent more time sleeping than I did. I figure she was sadder because she had carried our baby inside her womb and had memorized the way he moved.

One day about a week after our baby fell into his coma, it was me who fell into a waking sleep in a hospital bathroom. Sitting on the bowl, pants wrapped around my ankles, I couldn't move. I was awake and paralyzed by the deadly venom of the grief snake. I wondered if I was going to die right there in that terrible and shameful and hilarious way. I don't want to die like Elvis,[3] I kept saying to myself like it was a prayer.

But right then, when I was ready to roll onto the floor and crawl my way to safety like a grief soldier under grief fire, I heard two other sad men come walking into the bathroom. Those men didn't know I was trapped on the toilet, so they spoke freely and honestly about some sad woman.

"Did you see that woman?" asked man #1.

"You mean the fat one in sweatpants?" asked man #2.

"Yeah, can you believe how terrible she looked? I know our kids are sick, but that doesn't mean we have to let ourselves go like that."

"If you let yourself get ugly on the outside, you're gonna feel even worse on the inside."

"Yeah, what are your kids gonna think when they see you looking so bad?"

"They're gonna be sad."

"And things are sad enough without having to look at your fat mom wearing ugly sweatpants."

"The worst part is, that woman's kid, he isn't even that sick. He isn't terminal. He's only on the third floor."

"Yeah, put her kid on the fourth floor with our kids, and let's see how ugly she gets then."

Listening to their awfulness, I found the strength to stand and walk out of the stall. They were shocked to see me, and they went all quiet and silent and still and frozen. They were ashamed of themselves, I guess, for building a secret clubhouse out of the two-by-four boards and ten-penny nails of their

---

2. Traditional Native American gathering, customarily including dance and song.
3. Elvis Presley (1935–1977), American popular

singer and film star. He died on the toilet from a heart attack.

pain. I could be deadly serious and deadly funny at the same time, so I washed my hands really slow, making sure each finger was cleaner than the finger before. I dried them even slower, using one towel for each hand. And then I looked at those two men. I studied the angles and shapes of them like I was taking a geometry test.

I almost yelled at them. I wanted to scream at them for being as shallow and dirty as a dog dish. But hell, their kids were dying. What else were they going to do but punish the world for it? A father with a sick child is an angry god. I know I would have earthquaked Los Angeles, Paris, and Rome, and killed a million innocent people, if it guaranteed my baby boy would rise back to his full life.

But that whole bathroom crazy-scene gave me some energy. I don't know why. I can't explain it. I felt like a good woman and I wanted to be a good mother-man. So I left the hospital and went out shopping for baby toys. The hospital was on Fifteenth and John, and over the past few days, on my journey between home and hospital, I'd been driving past a toy store over on Pike and Seventh. It was called Toys in Babeland, and that was a cute name, so I figured I'd buy some stuffed teddy bears and a rattle and maybe some of those black-and-white toys the experts say are good for babies' eyes. Those seemed like good toy ideas, but I wasn't sure. What kind of toys do you buy, exactly, for a coma baby? I walked over to the store and strolled in, feeling religious about my mission, and shocked myself to discover Toys in Babeland was a sex-toy store.

"Honey," I said to my wife later, "those women were selling vibrators and dildos and edible underwear and butt plugs and lubricants and some stuff I had no idea what the hell you were supposed to do with it. Sweetheart," I said to her, "some of those sex toys looked like a genius and a crazy scientist made them." Now, I was surely embarrassed, but I'm not a prude, so I browsed around, not expecting to buy anything but not wanting to run out of the store like a frightened Christian. Then I turned the corner and saw it, the vibrator they call Chocolate Thunder.

"Darling," I said to my wife later, "I heard that big old music from that 2001: Space Odyssey[4] movie when I saw that miracle vibrator."

Chocolate Thunder was dark brown and fifteen inches long and needed a nine-volt battery. I like to think my indigenous penis is powerful. But it would take a whole war party of Indian men to equal up to one Chocolate Thunder. I was shy but quick to buy the thing and ran back to the hospital with it. I ran into the fourth-floor ICU,[5] pulled Chocolate Thunder out of its box, held it up in the air like a magic wand, and switched it on.

Of course, all the doctors and nurses and mothers and fathers were half stunned by that vibrator. And it was a strange and difficult thing. It was sex that made our dying babies, and here was a huge old piece of buzzing sex I was trying to cast spells with. I waved it over our baby and ran around the room waving it over the other sick babies. I was laughing and hooting, and other folks were laughing and hooting, and a few others didn't know what the hell to do. But pretty soon everybody was taking their turn casting spells with Chocolate Thunder. Maybe it was blasphemous, and maybe it was stupid and

---

4. Stanley Kubrick's 1968 science fiction film employs, among other pieces, the highly dramatic "Also sprach Zarathustra," by the German composer Richard Strauss (1864–1949).
5. Intensive Care Unit, where a hospital treats critically ill or critically injured patients.

useless, but we all were sick and tired of waiting for our babies to die. We wanted our babies to live, and we were ready to try anything to help them live. Maybe some people can get by with quiet prayers, but I wanted to shout and scream and vibrate. So did plenty of other fathers and mothers in that sick-room.

It was my wife who grabbed Chocolate Thunder and used it like a drum-stick to pound her hand drum. She sang a brand-new song that echoed up and down the hallways of Children's Hospital. Every sick and dying and alive and dead kid heard it, and they were happy and good in their hearts. My wife sang the most beautiful song anybody ever heard in that place. She sang like ten thousand Indian grandmothers rolled into one mother. All the while, Chocolate Thunder sang with her and turned the whole thing into a healing duet.

We humans are too simpleminded. We all like to think each person, place, or thing is only itself. A vibrator is a vibrator is a vibrator, right? But that's not true at all. Everything is stuffed to the brim with ideas and love and hope and magic and dreams. I brought Chocolate Thunder back to the hospital, but it was my magical and faithful wife who truly believed it was going to bring our baby back to us. She wanted it to bring every baby back to life. Over the next week, my wife sat beside our baby's bed and held that vibrator in her two hands and sang and prayed along with its buzzing. She used up the energy of two batteries, and maybe our baby would have woken up anyway, and a few other babies never did wake up at all, but my wife still believes our son heard the magic call of Chocolate Thunder and couldn't resist it. Our beautiful, beautiful boy opened his eyes and smiled, even if he was too young to smile, but I think sick kids get old and wise and funny very fast.

And so my wife and I named him Abraham and carried him home and lay him in his crib and hung Chocolate Thunder from the ceiling above him like a crazy mobile and laughed and laughed with the joy of it. We deported Mr. Grief back to his awful country. Our baby boy was going to live a long and good life. We wondered aloud what we would tell our Abraham about the wondrous world when he was old enough to wonder about it.

2003

JHUMPA LAHIRI
b. 1967

When Jhumpa Lahiri writes, her region is quite literally the world—focused some-times here and sometimes there, but always with global implications. This orientation is a factor of her times. Unlike children of earlier immigrant generations, Lahiri did not face the pressures of assimilating into an American society apart from and in some cases above other cultures. Instead, international trade, travel, and communications have made global culture a practical reality. In "Sexy," one of Lahiri's most wide-ranging yet deeply penetrating stories, her protagonist listens to a sad tale about a friend's "cousin's husband." The bad news, "a wife's worst nightmare," is being con-veyed in Boston, where the friends live, but it involves a flight from Delhi to Montreal stopping at Heathrow Airport outside London. Four locations in two hemispheres an ocean and a continent apart indicate the world that people with family backgrounds in India share when they become Americans. Geographical barriers become much more easily manageable thanks to cell phones and e-mail. Education, employment, friendships, and romantic relationships span the world. Films from India are viewed with American pop songs in mind and Chinese cuisine on the stomach, all, flavorful as they are, seeming as natural as the lives being lived within such givens.

The flavor of Lahiri's fiction defies categorization, other than being dependent on no single national ingredient. A visit to Boston's Mapparium (a giant globe viewed from inside) or Museum of Fine Arts is less a field trip through region and history than a comfortable part of her characters' way of living, a reminder of the larger culture they share.

The author's Bengali parents parted from their large extended family when they moved from Calcutta to London, where Lahiri was born. Following a normal progression in the former British Commonwealth, Lahiri's parents then relocated to the U.S., where they worked as educators in Rhode Island while she studied at Barnard College and Boston University, concentrating on literature and creative writing and ending with a Ph.D. Her first stories reflect how much of her family's past had to be conveyed to her via storytelling, such as in "When Mr. Pirzada Came to Dine," where a ten-year-old in America learns about political troubles in India from a visiting family friend. To the youngster, it sounds exotic, but no more so than the situation experienced by a pair of Indian newlyweds, in "This Blessed House," who are alternately intrigued and mystified by fundamentalist Christian curios left behind by the previous tenants of their new home. Much of Lahiri's work, first collected in *Interpreter of Maladies* (1999), involves discoveries of this nature, in which she is particularly adept at portraying the learning process of someone acting without monocultural constraint. The curiosity of children or young adults is a hallmark of her style.

In 2003, having married, become a mother, and settled in the Park Slope area of New York, a neighborhood popular with writers, Lahiri published her novel *The Namesake*. Like her earlier work, it contrasts cultural assimilation with curiosity about the values, beliefs, and practices of a preceding generation. But here a certain amount of anger and confusion come into play, as the protagonist, Gogol Ganguli, is uncomfortable with how the private first name his parents have used for him at home has become his public name as well, all without his understanding its personal (much less literary) significance. Lahiri had been saddled with "Jhumpa" as a first name by her teachers, who found it easier to pronounce than her other two given names, either of which would have been more appropriate for formal use. But while Lahiri's enforced assimilation didn't bother her, Ganguli's does. Although much of his discomfort is comic, such as when he assumes a sociologist's anagrammatical reference to "ABCDs" means not "multiculturals" but "American-born confused deshi" (India countrymen). In fact, Ganguli doesn't even know what "deshi" properly means, just that his parents customarily refer to India as "desh." He "never thinks of India as desh. He thinks of it as Americans do, as India." Other contrasts, such as arranged marriages versus modern ones, are handled with more gravity. But this too helps the protagonist in his process of understanding who he is, something not possible until he comprehends who his parents are.

The text is from *Interpreter of Maladies* (1999).

Sexy

It was a wife's worst nightmare. After nine years of marriage, Laxmi told Miranda, her cousin's husband had fallen in love with another woman. He sat next to her on a plane, on a flight from Delhi to Montreal,[1] and instead of

---

1. Popular air route for travelers in the former British Commonwealth, from the Indian city to the Canadian city.

flying home to his wife and son, he got off with the woman at Heathrow.[2] He called his wife, and told her he'd had a conversation that had changed his life, and that he needed time to figure things out. Laxmi's cousin had taken to her bed.

"Not that I blame her," Laxmi said. She reached for the Hot Mix she munched throughout the day, which looked to Miranda like dusty orange cereal. "Imagine. An English girl, half his age." Laxmi was only a few years older than Miranda, but she was already married, and kept a photo of herself and her husband, seated on a white stone bench in front of the Taj Mahal,[3] tacked to the inside of her cubicle, which was next to Miranda's. Laxmi had been on the phone for at least an hour, trying to calm her cousin down. No one noticed; they worked for a public radio station,[4] in the fund-raising department, and were surrounded by people who spent all day on the phone, soliciting pledges.

"I feel worst for the boy," Laxmi added. "He's been at home for days. My cousin said she can't even take him to school."

"It sounds awful," Miranda said. Normally Laxmi's phone conversations— mainly to her husband, about what to cook for dinner—distracted Miranda as she typed letters, asking members of the radio station to increase their annual pledge in exchange for a tote bag or an umbrella. She could hear Laxmi clearly, her sentences peppered every now and then with an Indian word, through the laminated wall between their desks. But that afternoon Miranda hadn't been listening. She'd been on the phone herself, with Dev, deciding where to meet later that evening.

"Then again, a few days at home won't hurt him." Laxmi ate some more Hot Mix, then put it away in a drawer. "He's something of a genius. He has a Punjabi mother and a Bengali[5] father, and because he learns French and English at school he already speaks four languages. I think he skipped two grades."

Dev was Bengali, too. At first Miranda thought it was a religion. But then he pointed it out to her, a place in India called Bengal, in a map printed in an issue of *The Economist*.[6] He had brought the magazine specially to her apartment, for she did not own an atlas, or any other books with maps in them. He'd pointed to the city where he'd been born, and another city where his father had been born. One of the cities had a box around it, intended to attract the reader's eye. When Miranda asked what the box indicated, Dev rolled up the magazine, and said, "Nothing you'll ever need to worry about," and he tapped her playfully on the head.

Before leaving her apartment he'd tossed the magazine in the garbage, along with the ends of the three cigarettes he always smoked in the course of his visits. But after she watched his car disappear down Commonwealth Avenue,[7] back to his house in the suburbs, where he lived with his wife, Miranda retrieved it, and brushed the ashes off the cover, and rolled it in the

2. International airport near London.
3. Muslim mausoleum near Agra, India, built 1632–54 by Emperor Shah Jahan for his favorite wife, Mumtaz Mahal.
4. Noncommercial, listener-supported, often oriented toward arts and culture in its broadcasting.
5. Punjab, state in northern India; Bengal, former province of India, now a region that includes Bengal State and East Bengal, the latter now part of Bangladesh.
6. Weekly British magazine of news and commentary.
7. Major thoroughfare in Boston.

opposite direction to get it to lie flat. She got into bed, still rumpled from their lovemaking, and studied the borders of Bengal. There was a bay below and mountains above. The map was connected to an article about something called the Gramin Bank.[8] She turned the page, hoping for a photograph of the city where Dev was born, but all she found were graphs and grids. Still, she stared at them, thinking the whole while about Dev, about how only fifteen minutes ago he'd propped her feet on top of his shoulders, and pressed her knees to her chest, and told her that he couldn't get enough of her.

She'd met him a week ago, at Filene's.[9] She was there on her lunch break, buying discounted pantyhose in the Basement. Afterward she took the escalator to the main part of the store, to the cosmetics department, where soaps and creams were displayed like jewels, and eye shadows and powders shimmered like butterflies pinned behind protective glass. Though Miranda had never bought anything other than a lipstick, she liked walking through the cramped, confined maze, which was familiar to her in a way the rest of Boston still was not. She liked negotiating her way past the women planted at every turn, who sprayed cards with perfume and waved them in the air; sometimes she would find a card days afterward, folded in her coat pocket, and the rich aroma, still faintly preserved would warm her as she waited on cold mornings for the T.[1]

That day, stopping to smell one of the more pleasing cards, Miranda noticed a man standing at one of the counters. He held a slip of paper covered in a precise, feminine hand. A saleswoman took one look at the paper and began to open drawers. She produced an oblong cake of soap in a black case, a hydrating mask, a vial of cell renewal drops, and two tubes of face cream. The man was tanned, with black hair that was visible on his knuckles. He wore a flamingo pink shirt, a navy blue suit, a camel overcoat with gleaming leather buttons. In order to pay he had taken off pigskin gloves. Crisp bills emerged from a burgundy wallet. He didn't wear a wedding ring.

"What can I get you, honey?" the saleswoman asked Miranda. She looked over the tops of her tortoiseshell glasses, assessing Miranda's complexion.

Miranda didn't know what she wanted. All she knew was that she didn't want the man to walk away. He seemed to be lingering, waiting, along with the saleswoman, for her to say something. She stared at some bottles, some short, others tall, arranged on an oval tray, like a family posing for a photograph.

"A cream," Miranda said eventually.

"How old are you?"

"Twenty-two."

The saleswoman nodded, opening a frosted bottle. "This may seem a bit heavier than what you're used to, but I'd start now. All your wrinkles are going to form by twenty-five. After that they just start showing."

While the saleswoman dabbed the cream on Miranda's face, the man stood and watched. While Miranda was told the proper way to apply it, in swift upward strokes beginning at the base of her throat, he spun the lipstick

---

8. Properly the Grameen Bank, which provides credit to the poorest classes in rural Bangladesh as a means of fighting poverty and promoting social economic development.

9. A department store. Filene's Basement, downstairs, is a renowned discount store.
1. Metropolitan Transit Authority (MTA), Boston's subway system.

carousel. He pressed a pump that dispensed cellulite gel and massaged it into the back of his ungloved hand. He opened a jar, leaned over, and drew so close that a drop of cream flecked his nose.

Miranda smiled, but her mouth was obscured by a large brush that the saleswoman was sweeping over her face. "This is blusher Number Two," the woman said. "Gives you some color."

Miranda nodded, glancing at her reflection in one of the angled mirrors that lined the counter. She had silver eyes and skin as pale as paper, and the contrast with her hair, as dark and glossy as an espresso bean, caused people to describe her as striking, if not pretty. She had a narrow, egg-shaped head that rose to a prominent point. Her features, too, were narrow, with nostrils so slim that they appeared to have been pinched with a clothespin. Now her face glowed, rosy at the cheeks, smoky below the brow bone. Her lips glistened.

The man was glancing in a mirror, too, quickly wiping the cream from his nose. Miranda wondered where he was from. She thought he might be Spanish, or Lebanese. When he opened another jar, and said, to no one in particular, "This one smells like pineapple," she detected only the hint of an accent.

"Anything else for you today?" the saleswoman asked, accepting Miranda's credit card.

"No thanks."

The woman wrapped the cream in several layers of red tissue. "You'll be very happy with this product." Miranda's hand was unsteady as she signed the receipt. The man hadn't budged.

"I threw in a sample of our new eye gel," the saleswoman added, handing Miranda a small shopping bag. She looked at Miranda's credit card before sliding it across the counter. "Bye-bye, Miranda."

Miranda began walking. At first she sped up. Then, noticing the doors that led to Downtown Crossing,[2] she slowed down.

"Part of your name is Indian," the man said, pacing his steps with hers.

She stopped, as did he, at a circular table piled with sweaters, flanked with pinecones and velvet bows. "Miranda?"

"Mira. I have an aunt named Mira."

His name was Dev. He worked in an investment bank back that way he said, tilting his head in the direction of South Station.[3] He was the first man with a mustache, Miranda decided, she found handsome.

They walked together toward Park Street station,[4] past the kiosks that sold cheap belts and handbags. A fierce January wind spoiled the part in her hair. As she fished for a token in her coat pocket, her eyes fell to his shopping bag. "And those are for her?"

"Who?"

"Your Aunt Mira."

"They're for my wife." He uttered the words slowly, holding Miranda's gaze. "She's going to India for a few weeks." He rolled his eyes. "She's addicted to this stuff."

2. Major interchange of MTA subway lines.
3. MTA commuter hub for lines from the south

suburbs.
4. MTA stop in the business district.

Somehow, without the wife there, it didn't seem so wrong. At first Miranda and Dev spent every night together, almost. He explained that he couldn't spend the whole night at her place, because his wife called every day at six in the morning, from India, where it was four in the afternoon. And so he left her apartment at two, three, often as late as four in the morning, driving back to his house in the suburbs. During the day he called her every hour, it seemed, from work, or from his cell phone. Once he learned Miranda's schedule he left her a message each evening at five-thirty, when she was on the T coming back to her apartment, just so, he said, she could hear his voice as soon as she walked through the door. "I'm thinking about you," he'd say on the tape. "I can't wait to see you." He told her he liked spending time in her apartment, with its kitchen counter no wider than a breadbox, and scratchy floors that sloped, and a buzzer in the lobby that always made a slightly embarrassing sound when he pressed it. He said he admired her for moving to Boston, where she knew no one, instead of remaining in Michigan, where she'd grown up and gone to college. When Miranda told him it was nothing to admire, that she'd moved to Boston precisely for that reason, he shook his head. "I know what it's like to be lonely," he said, suddenly serious, and at that moment Miranda felt that he understood her—understood how she felt some nights on the T, after seeing a movie on her own, or going to a bookstore to read magazines, or having drinks with Laxmi, who always had to meet her husband at Alewife station[5] in an hour or two. In less serious moments Dev said he liked that her legs were longer than her torso, something he'd observed the first time she walked across a room naked. "You're the first," he told her, admiring her from the bed. "The first woman I've known with legs this long."

Dev was the first to tell her that. Unlike the boys she dated in college, who were simply taller, heavier versions of the ones she dated in high school, Dev was the first always to pay for things, and hold doors open, and reach across a table in a restaurant to kiss her hand. He was the first to bring her a bouquet of flowers so immense she'd had to split it up into all six of her drinking glasses, and the first to whisper her name again and again when they made love. Within days of meeting him, when she was at work, Miranda began to wish that there were a picture of her and Dev tacked to the inside of her cubicle, like the one of Laxmi and her husband in front of the Taj Mahal. She didn't tell Laxmi about Dev. She didn't tell anyone. Part of her wanted to tell Laxmi, if only because Laxmi was Indian, too. But Laxmi was always on the phone with her cousin these days, who was still in bed, whose husband was still in London, and whose son still wasn't going to school. "You must eat something," Laxmi would urge. "You mustn't lose your health." When she wasn't speaking to her cousin, she spoke to her husband, shorter conversations, in which she ended up arguing about whether to have chicken or lamb for dinner. "I'm sorry," Miranda heard her apologize at one point. "This whole thing just makes me a little paranoid."

Miranda and Dev didn't argue. They went to movies at the Nickelodeon and kissed the whole time. They ate pulled pork and cornbread in Davis Square,[6] a paper napkin tucked like a cravat into the collar of Dev's shirt.

---

5. MTA stop in Cambridge, Massachusetts, across the Charles River from Boston.

6. MTA stop near Tufts University in a formerly working-class, now upscale neighborhood.

They sipped sangria at the bar of a Spanish restaurant, a grinning pig's head presiding over their conversation. They went to the MFA[7] and picked out a poster of water lilies for her bedroom. One Saturday, following an afternoon concert at Symphony Hall, he showed her his favorite place in the city, the Mapparium[8] at the Christian Science center, where they stood inside a room made of glowing stained-glass panels, which was shaped like the inside of a globe, but looked like the outside of one. In the middle of the room was a transparent bridge, so that they felt as if they were standing in the center of the world. Dev pointed to India, which was red, and far more detailed than the map in *The Economist.* He explained that many of the countries, like Siam and Italian Somaliland,[9] no longer existed in the same way; the names had changed by now. The ocean, as blue as a peacock's breast, appeared in two shades, depending on the depth of the water. He showed her the deepest spot on earth, seven miles deep, above the Mariana Islands.[1] They peered over the bridge and saw the Antarctic archipelago[2] at their feet, craned their necks and saw a giant metal star overhead. As Dev spoke, his voice bounced wildly off the glass, sometimes loud, sometimes soft, sometimes seeming to land in Miranda's chest, sometimes eluding her ear altogether. When a group of tourists walked onto the bridge, she could hear them clearing their throats, as if through microphones. Dev explained that it was because of the acoustics.

Miranda found London, where Laxmi's cousin's husband was, with the woman he'd met on the plane. She wondered which of the cities in India Dev's wife was in. The farthest Miranda had ever been was to the Bahamas once when she was a child. She searched but couldn't find it on the glass panels. When the tourists left and she and Dev were alone again, he told her to stand at one end of the bridge. Even though they were thirty feet apart, Dev said, they'd be able to hear each other whisper.

"I don't believe you," Miranda said. It was the first time she'd spoken since they'd entered. She felt as if speakers were embedded in her ears.

"Go ahead," he urged, walking backward to his end of the bridge. His voice dropped to a whisper. "Say something." She watched his lips forming the words; at the same time she heard them so clearly that she felt them under her skin, under her winter coat, so near and full of warmth that she felt herself go hot.

"Hi," she whispered, unsure of what else to say.

"You're sexy," he whispered back.

At work the following week, Laxmi told Miranda that it wasn't the first time her cousin's husband had had an affair. "She's decided to let him come to his senses," Laxmi said one evening as they were getting ready to leave the office. "She says it's for the boy. She's willing to forgive him for the boy." Miranda waited as Laxmi shut off her computer. "He'll come crawling back, and she'll let him," Laxmi said, shaking her head. "Not me. If my husband so much as looked at another woman I'd change the locks." She studied the picture tacked to her cubicle. Laxmi's husband had his arm draped over her shoul-

---

7. Museum of Fine Arts (Boston).
8. Large walk-through globe that maps the earth as stars and planets would be seen in a planetarium.

9. Presently Thailand and Somalia.
1. Island chain in the western Pacific Ocean.
2. Continental land mass in the Southern Ocean.

der, his knees leaning in toward her on the bench. She turned to Miranda. "Wouldn't you?"

She nodded. Dev's wife was coming back from India the next day. That afternoon he'd called Miranda at work, to say he had to go to the airport to pick her up. He promised he'd call as soon as he could.

"What's the Taj Mahal like?" she asked Laxmi.

"The most romantic spot on earth." Laxmi's face brightened at the memory. "An everlasting monument to love."

While Dev was at the airport, Miranda went to Filene's Basement to buy herself things she thought a mistress should have. She found a pair of black high heels with buckles smaller than a baby's teeth. She found a satin slip with scalloped edges and a knee-length silk robe. Instead of the pantyhose she normally wore to work, she found sheer stockings with a seam. She searched through piles and wandered through racks, pressing back hanger after hanger, until she found a cocktail dress made of a slinky silvery material that matched her eyes, with little chains for straps. As she shopped she thought about Dev, and about what he'd told her in the Mapparium. It was the first time a man had called her sexy, and when she closed her eyes she could still feel his whisper drifting through her body, under her skin. In the fitting room, which was just one big room with mirrors on the walls, she found a spot next to an older woman with a shiny face and coarse frosted hair. The woman stood barefoot in her underwear, pulling the black net of a body stocking taut between her fingers.

"Always check for snags," the woman advised.

Miranda pulled out the satin slip with scalloped edges. She held it to her chest.

The woman nodded with approval. "Oh yes."

"And this?" She held up the silver cocktail dress.

"Absolutely," the woman said. "He'll want to rip it right off you."

Miranda pictured the two of them at a restaurant in the South End[3] they'd been to, where Dev had ordered foie gras and a soup made with champagne and raspberries. She pictured herself in the cocktail dress, and Dev in one of his suits, kissing her hand across the table. Only the next time Dev came to visit her, on a Sunday afternoon several days since the last time they'd seen each other, he was in gym clothes. After his wife came back, that was his excuse: on Sundays he drove into Boston and went running along the Charles. The first Sunday she opened the door in the knee-length robe, but Dev didn't even notice it; he carried her over to the bed, wearing sweatpants and sneakers, and entered her without a word. Later, she slipped on the robe when she walked across the room to get him a saucer for his cigarette ashes, but he complained that she was depriving him of the sight of her long legs, and demanded that she remove it. So the next Sunday she didn't bother. She wore jeans. She kept the lingerie at the back of a drawer, behind her socks and everyday underwear. The silver cocktail dress hung in her closet, the tag dangling from the seam. Often, in the morning, the dress would be in a heap on the floor; the chain straps always slipped off the metal hanger.

Still, Miranda looked forward to Sundays. In the mornings she went to a

3. Trendy gay Boston neighborhood.

deli and bought a baguette and little containers of things Dev liked to eat, like pickled herring, and potato salad, and tortes of pesto and mascarpone cheese. They ate in bed, picking up the herring with their fingers and ripping the baguette with their hands. Dev told her stories about his childhood, when he would come home from school and drink mango juice served to him on a tray, and then play cricket by a lake, dressed all in white. He told her about how, at eighteen, he'd been sent to a college in upstate New York during something called the Emergency,[4] and about how it took him years to be able to follow American accents in movies, in spite of the fact that he'd had an English-medium education. As he talked he smoked three cigarettes, crushing them in a saucer by the side of her bed. Sometimes he asked her questions, like how many lovers she'd had (three) and how old she'd been the first time (nineteen). After lunch they made love, on sheets covered with crumbs, and then Dev took a nap for twelve minutes. Miranda had never known an adult who took naps, but Dev said it was something he'd grown up doing in India, where it was so hot that people didn't leave their homes until the sun went down. "Plus it allows us to sleep together," he murmured mischievously, curving his arm like a big bracelet around her body.

Only Miranda never slept. She watched the clock on her bedside table, or pressed her face against Dev's fingers, intertwined with hers, each with its half-dozen hairs at the knuckle. After six minutes she turned to face him, sighing and stretching, to test if he was really sleeping. He always was. His ribs were visible through his skin as he breathed, and yet he was beginning to develop a paunch. He complained about the hair on his shoulders, but Miranda thought him perfect, and refused to imagine him any other way.

At the end of twelve minutes Dev would open his eyes as if he'd been awake all along, smiling at her, full of a contentment she wished she felt herself. "The best twelve minutes of the week." He'd sigh, running a hand along the backs of her calves. Then he'd spring out of bed, pulling on his sweatpants and lacing up his sneakers. He would go to the bathroom and brush his teeth with his index finger, something he told her all Indians knew how to do, to get rid of the smoke in his mouth. When she kissed him good-bye she smelled herself sometimes in his hair. But she knew that his excuse, that he'd spent the afternoon jogging, allowed him to take a shower when he got home, first thing.

Apart from Laxmi and Dev, the only Indians whom Miranda had known were a family in the neighborhood where she'd grown up, named the Dixits. Much to the amusement of the neighborhood children, including Miranda, but not including the Dixit children, Mr. Dixit would jog each evening along the flat winding streets of their development in his everyday shirt and trousers, his only concession to athletic apparel a pair of cheap Keds. Every weekend, the family—mother, father, two boys, and a girl—piled into their car and went away, to where nobody knew. The fathers complained that Mr. Dixit did not fertilize his lawn properly, did not rake his leaves on time, and agreed that the Dixits' house, the only one with vinyl siding, detracted from the neighborhood's charm. The mothers never invited Mrs. Dixit to join them around the

---

4. State of internal emergency declared in 1975 by Indira Gandhi (1917–1984), prime minister of India, that allowed her to rule by decree until 1977, when she was defeated in an election.

Armstrongs' swimming pool. Waiting for the school bus with the Dixit children standing to one side, the other children would say "The Dixits dig shit," under their breath, and then burst into laughter.

One year, all the neighborhood children were invited to the birthday party of the Dixit girl. Miranda remembered a heavy aroma of incense and onions in the house, and a pile of shoes heaped by the front door. But most of all she remembered a piece of fabric, about the size of a pillowcase, which hung from a wooden dowel at the bottom of the stairs. It was a painting of a naked woman with a red face shaped like a knight's shield. She had enormous white eyes that tilted toward her temples, and mere dots for pupils. Two circles, with the same dots at their centers, indicated her breasts. In one hand she brandished a dagger. With one foot she crushed a struggling man on the ground. Around her body was a necklace composed of bleeding heads, strung together like a popcorn chain. She stuck her tongue out at Miranda.

"It is the goddess Kali,"[5] Mrs. Dixit explained brightly, shifting the dowel slightly in order to straighten the image. Mrs. Dixit's hands were painted with henna, an intricate pattern of zigzags and stars. "Come please, time for cake."

Miranda, then nine years old, had been too frightened to eat the cake. For months afterward she'd been too frightened even to walk on the same side of the street as the Dixits' house, which she had to pass twice daily, once to get to the bus stop, and once again to come home. For a while she even held her breath until she reached the next lawn, just as she did when the school bus passed a cemetery.

It shamed her now. Now, when she and Dev made love, Miranda closed her eyes and saw deserts and elephants, and marble pavilions floating on lakes beneath a full moon. One Saturday, having nothing else to do, she walked all the way to Central Square,[6] to an Indian restaurant, and ordered a plate of tandoori chicken. As she ate she tried to memorize phrases printed at the bottom of the menu, for things like "delicious" and "water" and "check, please." The phrases didn't stick in her mind, and so she began to stop from time to time in the foreign-language section of a bookstore in Kenmore Square,[7] where she studied the Bengali alphabet in the Teach Yourself series. Once she went so far as to try to transcribe the Indian part of her name, "Mira," into her Filofax,[8] her hand moving in unfamiliar directions, stopping and turning and picking up her pen when she least expected to. Following the arrows in the book, she drew a bar from left to right from which the letters hung; one looked more like a number than a letter, another looked like a triangle on its side. It had taken her several tries to get the letters of her name to resemble the sample letters in the book, and even then she wasn't sure if she'd written Mira or Mara. It was a scribble to her, but somewhere in the world, she realized with a shock, it meant something.

During the week it wasn't so bad. Work kept her busy, and she and Laxmi had begun having lunch together at a new Indian restaurant around the corner, during which Laxmi reported the latest status of her cousin's marriage. Sometimes Miranda tried to change the topic; it made her feel the way she once felt in college, when she and her boyfriend at the time had walked away from

---

5. Hindu goddess of destruction.
6. In Cambridge.
7. In Boston.

8. Loose-leaf personal organizer, manufactured by the Filofax Company in England.

a crowded house of pancakes without paying for their food, just to see if they could get away with it. But Laxmi spoke of nothing else. "If I were her I'd fly straight to London and shoot them both," she announced one day. She snapped a papadum in half and dipped it into chutney. "I don't know how she can just wait this way."

Miranda knew how to wait. In the evenings she sat at her dining table and coated her nails with clear nail polish, and ate salad straight from the salad bowl, and watched television, and waited for Sunday. Saturdays were the worst because by Saturday it seemed that Sunday would never come. One Saturday when Dev called, late at night, she heard people laughing and talking in the background, so many that she asked him if he was at a concert hall. But he was only calling from his house in the suburbs. "I can't hear you that well," he said. "We have guests. Miss me?" She looked at the television screen, a sitcom that she'd muted with the remote control when the phone rang. She pictured him whispering into his cell phone, in a room upstairs, a hand on the doorknob, the hallway filled with guests. "Miranda, do you miss me?" he asked again. She told him that she did.

The next day, when Dev came to visit, Miranda asked him what his wife looked like. She was nervous to ask, waiting until he'd smoked the last of his cigarettes, crushing it with a firm twist into the saucer. She wondered if they'd quarrel. But Dev wasn't surprised by the question. He told her, spreading some smoked whitefish on a cracker, that his wife resembled an actress in Bombay named Madhuri Dixit.[9]

For an instant Miranda's heart stopped. But no, the Dixit girl had been named something else, something that began with P. Still, she wondered if the actress and the Dixit girl were related. She'd been plain, wearing her hair in two braids all through high school.

A few days later Miranda went to an Indian grocery in Central Square which also rented videos. The door opened to a complicated tinkling of bells. It was dinnertime, and she was the only customer. A video was playing on a television hooked up in a corner of the store: a row of young women in harem pants were thrusting their hips in synchrony on a beach.

"Can I help you?" the man standing at the cash register asked. He was eating a samosa, dipping it into some dark brown sauce on a paper plate. Below the glass counter at his waist were trays of more plump samosas, and what looked like pale, diamond-shaped pieces of fudge covered with foil, and some bright orange pastries floating in syrup. "You like some video?"

Miranda opened up her Filofax, where she had written "Mottery Dixit." She looked up at the videos on the shelves behind the counter. She saw women wearing skirts that sat low on the hips and tops that tied like bandannas between their breasts. Some leaned back against a stone wall, or a tree. They were beautiful, the way the women dancing on the beach were beautiful, with kohl-rimmed eyes and long black hair. She knew then that Madhuri Dixit was beautiful, too.

"We have subtitled versions, miss," the man continued. He wiped his fingertips quickly on his shirt and pulled out three titles.

"No," Miranda said. "Thank you, no." She wandered through the store, studying shelves lined with unlabeled packets and tins. The freezer case

9. Indian film actress (b. 1967) renowned for her beauty.

was stuffed with bags of pita bread and vegetables she didn't recognize. The only thing she recognized was a rack lined with bags and bags of the Hot Mix that Laxmi was always eating. She thought about buying some for Laxmi, then hesitated, wondering how to explain what she'd been doing in an Indian grocery.

"Very spicy," the man said, shaking his head, his eyes traveling across Miranda's body. "Too spicy for you."

By February, Laxmi's cousin's husband still hadn't come to his senses. He had returned to Montreal, argued bitterly with his wife for two weeks, packed two suitcases, and flown back to London. He wanted a divorce.

Miranda sat in her cubicle and listened as Laxmi kept telling her cousin that there were better men in the world, just waiting to come out of the wood-work. The next day the cousin said she and her son were going to her parents' house in California, to try to recuperate. Laxmi convinced her to arrange a weekend layover in Boston. "A quick change of place will do you good," Laxmi insisted gently, "besides which, I haven't seen you in years."

Miranda stared at her own phone, wishing Dev would call. It had been four days since their last conversation. She heard Laxmi dialing directory assis-tance, asking for the number of a beauty salon. "Something soothing," Laxmi requested. She scheduled massages, facials, manicures, and pedicures. Then she reserved a table for lunch at the Four Seasons. In her determination to cheer up her cousin, Laxmi had forgotten about the boy. She rapped her knuckles on the laminated wall.

"Are you busy Saturday?"

The boy was thin. He wore a yellow knapsack strapped across his back, gray herringbone trousers, a red V-necked sweater, and black leather shoes. His hair was cut in a thick fringe over his eyes, which had dark circles under them. They were the first thing Miranda noticed. They made him look hag-gard, as if he smoked a great deal and slept very little, in spite of the fact that he was only seven years old. He clasped a large sketch pad with a spiral bind-ing. His name was Rohin.

"Ask me a capital," he said, staring up at Miranda.

She stared back at him. It was eight-thirty on a Saturday morning. She took a sip of coffee. "A what?"

"It's a game he's been playing," Laxmi's cousin explained. She was thin like her son, with a long face and the same dark circles under her eyes. A rust-colored coat hung heavy on her shoulders. Her black hair, with a few strands of gray at the temples, was pulled back like a ballerina's. "You ask him a coun-try and he tells you the capital."

"You should have heard him in the car," Laxmi said. "He's already memo-rized all of Europe."

"It's not a game," Rohin said. "I'm having a competition with a boy at school. We're competing to memorize all the capitals. I'm going to beat him."

Miranda nodded. "Okay. What's the capital of India?"

"That's no good." He marched away, his arms swinging like a toy soldier. Then he marched back to Laxmi's cousin and tugged at a pocket of her over-coat. "Ask me a hard one."

"Senegal," she said.

"Dakar!" Rohin exclaimed triumphantly, and began running in larger and larger circles. Eventually he ran into the kitchen. Miranda could hear him opening and closing the fridge.

"Rohin, don't touch without asking," Laxmi's cousin called out wearily. She managed a smile for Miranda. "Don't worry, he'll fall asleep in a few hours. And thanks for watching him."

"Back at three," Laxmi said, disappearing with her cousin down the hallway. "We're double-parked."

Miranda fastened the chain on the door. She went to the kitchen to find Rohin, but he was now in the living room, at the dining table, kneeling on one of the director's chairs. He unzipped his knapsack, pushed Miranda's basket of manicure supplies to one side of the table, and spread his crayons over the surface. Miranda stood over his shoulder. She watched as he gripped a blue crayon and drew the outline of an airplane.

"It's lovely," she said. When he didn't reply, she went to the kitchen to pour herself more coffee.

"Some for me, please," Rohin called out.

She returned to the living room. "Some what?"

"Some coffee. There's enough in the pot. I saw."

She walked over to the table and sat opposite him. At times he nearly stood up to reach for a new crayon. He barely made a dent in the director's chair.

"You're too young for coffee."

Rohin leaned over the sketch pad, so that his tiny chest and shoulders almost touched it, his head tilted to one side. "The stewardess let me have coffee," he said. "She made it with milk and lots of sugar." He straightened, revealing a woman's face beside the plane, with long wavy hair and eyes like asterisks. "Her hair was more shiny," he decided, adding, "My father met a pretty woman on a plane, too." He looked at Miranda. His face darkened as he watched her sip. "Can't I have just a little coffee? Please?"

She wondered, in spite of his composed, brooding expression, if he were the type to throw a tantrum. She imagined his kicking her with his leather shoes, screaming for coffee, screaming and crying until his mother and Laxmi came back to fetch him. She went to the kitchen and prepared a cup for him as he'd requested. She selected a mug she didn't care for, in case he dropped it.

"Thank you," he said when she put it on the table. He took short sips, holding the mug securely with both hands.

Miranda sat with him while he drew, but when she attempted to put a coat of clear polish on her nails he protested. Instead he pulled out a paperback world almanac from his knapsack and asked her to quiz him. The countries were arranged by continent, six to a page, with the capitals in boldface, followed by a short entry on the population, government, and other statistics. Miranda turned to a page in the Africa section and went down the list.

"Mali," she asked him.

"Bamako," he replied instantly.

"Malawi."

"Lilongwe."

She remembered looking at Africa in the Mapparium. She remembered the fat part of it was green.

"Go on," Rohin said.

"Mauritania."

"Nouakchott."

"Mauritius."

He paused, squeezed his eyes shut, then opened them, defeated. "I can't remember."

"Port Louis," she told him.

"Port Louis." He began to say it again and again, like a chant under his breath.

When they reached the last of the countries in Africa, Rohin said he wanted to watch cartoons, telling Miranda to watch them with him. When the cartoons ended, he followed her to the kitchen, and stood by her side as she made more coffee. He didn't follow her when she went to the bathroom a few minutes later, but when she opened the door she was startled to find him standing outside.

"Do you need to go?"

He shook his head but walked into the bathroom anyway. He put the cover of the toilet down, climbed on top of it, and surveyed the narrow glass shelf over the sink which held Miranda's toothbrush and makeup.

"What's this for?" he asked, picking up the sample of eye gel she'd gotten the day she met Dev.

"Puffiness."

"What's puffiness?"

"Here," she explained, pointing.

"After you've been crying?"

"I guess so."

Rohin opened the tube and smelled it. He squeezed a drop of it onto a finger, then rubbed it on his hand. "It stings." He inspected the back of his hand closely, as if expecting it to change color. "My mother has puffiness. She says it's a cold, but really she cries, sometimes for hours. Sometimes straight through dinner. Sometimes she cries so hard her eyes puff up like bullfrogs."

Miranda wondered if she ought to feed him. In the kitchen she discovered a bag of rice cakes and some lettuce. She offered to go out, to buy something from the deli, but Rohin said he wasn't very hungry, and accepted one of the rice cakes. "You eat one too," he said. They sat at the table, the rice cakes between them. He turned to a fresh page in his sketch pad. "You draw."

She selected a blue crayon. "What should I draw?"

He thought for a moment. "I know," he said. He asked her to draw things in the living room: the sofa, the director's chairs, the television, the telephone. "This way I can memorize it."

"Memorize what?"

"Our day together." He reached for another rice cake.

"Why do you want to memorize it?"

"Because we're never going to see each other, ever again."

The precision of the phrase startled her. She looked at him, feeling slightly depressed. Rohin didn't look depressed. He tapped the page. "Go on."

And so she drew the items as best as she could—the sofa, the director's chairs, the television, the telephone. He sidled up to her, so close that it was sometimes difficult to see what she was doing. He put his small brown hand over hers. "Now me."

She handed him the crayon.

He shook his head. "No, now draw me."

"I can't," she said. "It won't look like you."

The brooding look began to spread across Rohin's face again, just as it had when she'd refused him coffee. "Please?"

She drew his face, outlining his head and the thick fringe of hair. He sat perfectly still, with a formal, melancholy expression, his gaze fixed to one side. Miranda wished she could draw a good likeness. Her hand moved in conjunction with her eyes, in unknown ways, just as it had that day in the bookstore when she'd transcribed her name in Bengali letters. It looked nothing like him. She was in the middle of drawing his nose when he wriggled away from the table.

"I'm bored," he announced, heading toward her bedroom. She heard him opening the door, opening the drawers of her bureau and closing them.

When she joined him he was inside the closet. After a moment he emerged, his hair disheveled, holding the silver cocktail dress. "This was on the floor."

"It falls off the hanger."

Rohin looked at the dress and then at Miranda's body. "Put it on."

"Excuse me?"

"Put it on."

There was no reason to put it on. Apart from in the fitting room at Filene's she had never worn it, and as long as she was with Dev she knew she never would. She knew they would never go to restaurants, where he would reach across a table and kiss her hand. They would meet in her apartment, on Sundays, he in his sweatpants, she in her jeans. She took the dress from Rohin and shook it out, even though the slinky fabric never wrinkled. She reached into the closet for a free hanger.

"Please put it on," Rohin asked, suddenly standing behind her. He pressed his face against her, clasping her waist with both his thin arms. "Please?"

"All right," she said, surprised by the strength of his grip.

He smiled, satisfied, and sat on the edge of her bed.

"You have to wait out there," she said, pointing to the door. "I'll come out when I'm ready."

"But my mother always takes her clothes off in front of me."

"She does?"

Rohin nodded. "She doesn't even pick them up afterward. She leaves them all on the floor by the bed, all tangled.

"One day she slept in my room," he continued. "She said it felt better than her bed, now that my father's gone."

"I'm not your mother," Miranda said, lifting him by the armpits off her bed. When he refused to stand, she picked him up. He was heavier than she expected, and he clung to her, his legs wrapped firmly around her hips, his head resting against her chest. She set him down in the hallway and shut the door. As an extra precaution she fastened the latch. She changed into the dress, glancing into the full-length mirror nailed to the back of the door. Her ankle socks looked silly, and so she opened a drawer and found the stockings. She searched through the back of the closet and slipped on the high heels with the tiny buckles. The chain straps of the dress were as light as paper clips against her collarbone. It was a bit loose on her. She could not zip it herself.

Rohin began knocking. "May I come in now?"

She opened the door. Rohin was holding his almanac in his hands, muttering something under his breath. His eyes opened wide at the sight of her. "I need help with the zipper," she said. She sat on the edge of the bed.

Rohin fastened the zipper to the top, and then Miranda stood up and twirled. Rohin put down the almanac. "You're sexy," he declared.

"What did you say?"

"You're sexy."

Miranda sat down again. Though she knew it meant nothing, her heart skipped a beat. Rohin probably referred to all women as sexy. He'd probably heard the word on television, or seen it on the cover of a magazine. She remembered the day in the Mapparium, standing across the bridge from Dev. At the time she thought she knew what his words meant. At the time they'd made sense.

Miranda folded her arms across her chest and looked Rohin in the eyes. "Tell me something."

He was silent.

"What does it mean?"

"What?"

"That word. 'Sexy.' What does it mean?"

He looked down, suddenly shy. "I can't tell you."

"Why not?"

"It's a secret." He pressed his lips together, so hard that a bit of them went white.

"Tell me the secret. I want to know."

Rohin sat on the bed beside Miranda and began to kick the edge of the mattress with the backs of his shoes. He giggled nervously, his thin body flinching as if it were being tickled.

"Tell me," Miranda demanded. She leaned over and gripped his ankles, holding his feet still.

Rohin looked at her, his eyes like slits. He struggled to kick the mattress again, but Miranda pressed against him. He fell back on the bed, his back straight as a board. He cupped his hands around his mouth, and then he whispered, "It means loving someone you don't know."

Miranda felt Rohin's words under her skin, the same way she'd felt Dev's. But instead of going hot she felt numb. It reminded her of the way she'd felt at the Indian grocery, the moment she knew, without even looking at a picture, that Madhuri Dixit, whom Dev's wife resembled, was beautiful.

"That's what my father did," Rohin continued. "He sat next to someone he didn't know, someone sexy, and now he loves her instead of my mother."

He took off his shoes and placed them side by side on the floor. Then he peeled back the comforter and crawled into Miranda's bed with the almanac. A minute later the book dropped from his hands, and he closed his eyes. Miranda watched him sleep, the comforter rising and falling as he breathed. He didn't wake up after twelve minutes like Dev, or even twenty. He didn't open his eyes as she stepped out of the silver cocktail dress and back into her jeans, and put the high-heeled shoes in the back of the closet, and rolled up the stockings and put them back in her drawer.

When she had put everything away she sat on the bed. She leaned toward him, close enough to see some white powder from the rice cakes stuck to the corners of his mouth, and picked up the almanac. As she turned the pages she imagined the quarrels Rohin had overheard in his house in Montreal. "Is she pretty?" his mother would have asked his father, wearing the same bathrobe she'd worn for weeks, her own pretty face turning spiteful. "Is she sexy?" His father would deny it at first, try to change the subject. "Tell me," Rohin's mother would shriek, "tell me if she's sexy." In the end his father would admit that she was, and his mother would cry and cry, in a bed sur-rounded by a tangle of clothes, her eyes puffing up like bullfrogs. "How could you," she'd ask, sobbing, "how could you love a woman you don't even know?"

As Miranda imagined the scene she began to cry a little herself. In the Mapparium that day, all the countries had seemed close enough to touch, and Dev's voice had bounced wildly off the glass. From across the bridge, thirty feet away, his words had reached her ears, so near and full of warmth that they'd drifted for days under her skin. Miranda cried harder, unable to stop. But Rohin still slept. She guessed that he was used to it now, to the sound of a woman crying.

On Sunday, Dev called to tell Miranda he was on his way. "I'm almost ready. I'll be there at two."

She was watching a cooking show on television. A woman pointed to a row of apples, explaining which were best for baking. "You shouldn't come today."

"Why not?"

"I have a cold," she lied. It wasn't far from the truth; crying had left her con-gested. "I've been in bed all morning."

"You do sound stuffed up." There was a pause. "Do you need anything?"

"I'm all set."

"Drink lots of fluids."

"Dev?"

"Yes, Miranda?"

"Do you remember that day we went to the Mapparium?"

"Of course."

"Do you remember how we whispered to each other?"

"I remember," Dev whispered playfully.

"Do you remember what you said?"

There was a pause. " 'Let's go back to your place.' " He laughed quietly. "Next Sunday, then?"

The day before, as she'd cried, Miranda had believed she would never for-get anything—not even the way her name looked written in Bengali. She'd fallen asleep beside Rohin and when she woke up he was drawing an airplane on the copy of *The Economist* she'd saved, hidden under the bed. "Who's Devajit Mitra?" he had asked, looking at the address label.

Miranda pictured Dev, in his sweatpants and sneakers, laughing into the phone. In a moment he'd join his wife downstairs, and tell her he wasn't going jogging. He'd pulled a muscle while stretching, he'd say, settling down to read the paper. In spite of herself, she longed for him. She would see him one more Sunday, she decided, perhaps two. Then she would tell him the things she had known all along: that it wasn't fair to her, or to his wife, that they both deserved better, that there was no point in it dragging on.

But the next Sunday it snowed, so much so that Dev couldn't tell his wife he was going running along the Charles. The Sunday after that, the snow had melted, but Miranda made plans to go to the movies with Laxmi, and when she told Dev this over the phone, he didn't ask her to cancel them. The third

Sunday she got up early and went out for a walk. It was cold but sunny, and so she walked all the way down Commonwealth Avenue, past the restaurants where Dev had kissed her, and then she walked all the way to the Christian Science center. The Mapparium was closed, but she bought a cup of coffee nearby and sat on one of the benches in the plaza outside the church, gazing at its giant pillars and its massive dome, and at the clear-blue sky spread over the city.

1999

Selected Bibliographies

AMERICAN LITERATURE 1865–1914

Reference

To learn more about American literature 1865–1914 or to begin research for a paper, students should begin in the reference section of the library, where there are many valuable resources for bibliographical and other research information about American literature. James L. Harner's *Literary Research Guide: A Guide to Reference Sources for the Study of Literatures in English and Related Topics*, 4th ed. (1993) is now updated online. Though it is now badly outdated, a still useful general guide to American literature and civilization is Clarence Gohdes and Sanford E. Marovitz's *Bibliographic Guide to the Literature of the U.S.A.*, 5th ed. (1984).

Author biographies are available in the *Dictionary of Literary Biography's* ongoing volumes, in the American National Biography volumes (1999), and also in such books as Jay Parini's *American Writers: A Collection of Literary Biographies* (2003); *Biographical Dictionary of Literary Influences: The Nineteenth Century, 1800–1914*, ed. John Powell and Derek W. Blakely (2001), which contains 271 biographical sketches of literary figures; James K. Bracken and Larry G. Hinman, *The Undergraduate's Companion to American Writers and Their Web Sites* (2003).

General resources on the period include *Twentieth-Century Literary Movements Dictionary*, ed. Helen Henderson and Jay P. Pederson (2000), a substantial and well-organized volume; *Encyclopedia of American Cultural and Intellectual History*, ed. Mary Kupiec, Peter W. Williams, Mary K. Cayton (2001); *Encyclopedia of American Studies*, ed. George T. Kurian, et al. (2000); *American Literature and Culture 1900–1960: An Introduction*, ed. Gail McDonald (2006); *A Companion to American Literature and Culture*, ed. Paul Lauter (2006); *A Companion to the American Novel*, ed. Alfred Bendixen (2006); *A Companion to American Fiction 1865–1914*, ed. Robert Paul Lamb and G. R. Thompson (2005). More specialized sources on movements of the period include Joseph B. McCullough and Robert L. Gale's *Nineteenth-Century American Western Writers* (1997); *A Companion to the Regional Literatures of America*, ed. Charles L. Crow (2003), which sets out to rehabilitate regionalism with essays by leading scholars such as Donna Campbell, Lawrence I. Berkove, and Susan Kollin; *A Companion to the Literature and Culture of the American South*, ed. Richard Gray and Owen Robinson (2006); the four-volume *American Women Writers: A Critical Reference Guide: From Colonial Times to the Present*, 2nd ed., ed. Taryn Benbow-Pfalzgraf (2000); *The Columbia Guide to Women in the Nineteenth Century*, ed. Catherine Clinton and Christine Lunardini (2000); Denise D. Knight and Emmanuel S. Nelson, eds., *Nineteenth-Century American Women Writers: A Bio-Bibliographical Critical Sourcebook* (1997); Elaine Showalter, Lea Baechler, and A. Walton Litz, eds., *Modern American Women Writers* (1991); Laurie Champion, ed., *American Women Writers, 1900–1945: A Bio-Bibliographical Critical Sourcebook* (2000); Sharon M. Harris, ed., *American Women Prose Writers, 1870–1920* (2000), which includes biographical information; Trudier Harris and Thadious M. Davis, eds., *Afro-American Writers before the Harlem Renaissance* (1986); Nelson's *African American Authors, 1745–1945* (2000); *African American Writers,* 2nd ed., ed. Valerie Smith (2001); *Jewish American Women Writers: A Bio-Bibliographical and Critical Sourcebook* (1994), ed. Ann R. Shapiro, which presents individually authored biographical-critical essays plus primary and secondary bibliographies on various authors; Nelson's *Asian-American Novelists, 1745–1945* (2000); *Chinese American Literature Since the 1850s* (2006), by Xiao-huang Yin, which traces the construction of Chinese American identity, especially in tales of interracial marriage in the fiction of Sui Sin Far and others; Deborah L. Madsen's *Asian American Writers* (2005); A. LaVonne Brown Ruoff, *American Indian Literatures: An Introduction, Bibliographic Review, and Selected Bibliography* (1990); *Hispanic Literature of the United States: A Comprehensive Reference,* ed. Nicolás Kannelos (2003); Francisco A. Lomelí, Carl R. Shirley, eds., *Chicano Writers: Third Series* (1999); and *Recovering the U.S. Hispanic Literary Heritage,* Volume IV, ed. José F. Aranda, Jr. and Silvio Torres-Saillant (2002), a series from Arte Público Press.

Still useful are James D. Hart's *Oxford Companion to American Literature,* now in an updated and revised edition co-edited with Phillip Leiniger (1995), and the discursive bibliographical supplements to Robert Spiller et al.'s *Literary History of the United States,* 4th ed. (1974). Richard M. Ludwig and Clifford Nault Jr.'s, *Annals of American Literature, 1602–1983* (1989) is a good source for locating major works in their cultural contexts. The annual and invaluable *American Literary Scholarship* (also online) provides critical commentary on a wide range of scholarly books and articles (including reference works) on American literature published each year in the United States and abroad.

For guidance to more recent general books on American literature in this period, see the "Themes, Topics, Criticism" and "Nineteenth-Century Literature" chapters in annual volumes of *American Literary Scholarship.* The *Modern Language Association Bibliography* should also be consulted. Up-to-date bibliographies and reviews may be found in such standard journals as *African American Review, American Literature, American Literary History, American Quarterly, American Literary Realism, 1870–1910, College Language Association Journal,* and *MELUS* as well as in the publications of societies devoted to individual authors in this period.

Literary History

The ongoing, eight-volume *Cambridge History of American Literature* (Sacvan Bercovitch, general editor) addresses not only traditional literary genres and periods, but is self-consciously concerned with literary theory and criticism as well as recently emergent forms and contributors to literature as a form of cultural production. Given the breadth of its coverage and the distinction of its section authors, this set is indispensable. Also of great value is Bercovitch's often-cited *Reconstructing American Literary History* (1986). A useful introduction to the influence on the modern novel of this period is *A Cultural History of the American Novel: Henry James to William Faulkner*, by David L. Minter (1996). American poetry of the period is covered in David Perkins, *A History of American Poetry: From the 1890s to the High Modernist Mode* (1976); Alan Shucard, Fred Moramarco, and William Sullivan, *Modern American Poetry, 1865–1950* (1989); and Robert Shulman, *Social Criticism and Nineteenth Century American Poetry, 1865–1950* (1989). Among other one-volume reference works is the comprehensive *Cambridge Guide to American Theatre* (1996), edited by Don B. Wilmeth.

Important general studies of American history and culture as expressed in literature include *A History of American Literature*, Richard Gray (2004); Loren Glass, *Authors, Inc.: Literary Celebrity in the Modern United States, 1880–1980* (2004), which covers figures including Adams, Twain, London, Hemingway, Mailer, and Stein; Paul Lauter, *From Walden Pond to Jurassic Park: Activism, Culture, and American Studies* (2001); *Literary Culture and U.S. Imperialism: From the Revolution to World War II*, John Carlos Rowe (2000); Orm Overland, *Immigrant Minds, American Identities: Making the United States Home, 1870–1930* (2000); Michael Szalay, *New Deal Modernism: American Literature and the Invention of the Welfare State* (2000); Scott Casper, *Constructing American Lives: Biography and Culture in Nineteenth-Century America* (1999); Katherine B. Payant and Rose Toby, eds., *The Immigrant Experience in North American Literature: Carving Out a Niche* (1999); Eric J. Sundquist, To *Wake the Nations: Race in the Making of American Literature* (1993); *From Puritanism to Postmodernism: A History of American Literature*, Richard Ruland and Malcolm Bradbury (1992); Cushing Strout, *Making American Tradition: Visions and Revisions from Ben Franklin to Alice Walker* (1990); A. LaVonne Brown Ruoff and Jerry Ward, eds., *Redefining American Literary History* (1990); Werner Sollers, *Beyond Ethnicity: Consent and Descent in American Culture* (1986); Russell Reising, *The Unusable Past: Theory and the Study of American Literature* (1986); Richard Slotkin, *The Fatal Environment: The Myth of the Frontier in the Age of Industrialization, 1800–1890* (1985); Gordon O. Taylor, *Chapters of Experience: Studies in Twentieth Century American Autobiography* (1983); Alan Trachtenberg, *The Incorporation of America: Culture and Society in the Gilded Age* (1982); Ronald E. Martin, *American Literature and the Universe of Force* (1981); Annette Kolodny's *The Lay of the Land: Metaphor as Experience and History* (1975). Still of great importance are Alfred Kazin's *On Native Grounds: An Interpretation of Modern American Prose Literature* (1942) and *American Procession* (1984); Leo Marx, *The Machine in the Garden: Technology and the Pastoral Ideal in America* (1964); and Richard Poirier, *A World Elsewhere: The Place of Style in American Literature* (1966).

Histories of American women writers include *Before They Could Vote: American Women's Autobiographical Writing, 1819–1919*, ed. Sidonie A. Smith and Julia Watson (2006); *Beyond the Gibson Girl: Reimagining the American New Woman, 1895–1915* (2005) by Martha H. Patterson, which argues that contexts such as social class and geography helped define the

New Woman of the turn of the century; *Wayward Reproductions: Genealogies of Race and Nation in Transatlantic Modern Thought*, Alys Eve Weinbaum (2004) argues that racism, nationalism, and imperialism were ideologies founded in large part on what she calls "the race/reproduction bind"—the notion that race is something that is biologically reproduced, an idea that reveals the centrality of ideas about women's reproductive capacity to modernity's intellectual foundations, as in the work of Gilman and Du Bois among many others; *Feminist Forerunners: New Womanism and Feminism in the Early Twentieth Century* by Ann Heilmann (2003); Suzanne Bost's *Mulattas and Mestizas: Representing Mixed Identities in the Americas, 1850–2000* (2003); Dale M. Bauer and Philip Gould, eds., *The Cambridge Companion to Nineteenth-Century American Women's Writing* (2001); Nina Baym, *American Women of Letters and the Nineteenth-Century Sciences: Styles of Affiliation* (2002) and *Women's Fiction: A Guide to Novels By and About Women in America 1820–1870* (1978); Susan L. Roberson, ed., *Women, America, and Movement: Narratives of Relocation* (1998); Jane Missner Barstow, *One Hundred Years of American Women Writing, 1848–1948* (1997), which provides biographical summaries and surveys of scholarship on most of the women writers in this section of *NAAL*; Shirley Samuels, ed., *The Culture of Sentiment: Race, Gender, and Sentimentality in Nineteenth-Century America* (1992); Elizabeth Ammons, *Conflicting Stories: American Women Writers at the Turn of the Century* (1991); Barbara Bardes and Suzanne Gossett, *Declarations of Independence: Women and Political Power in Nineteenth Century American Fiction* (1990); Susan K. Harris, *Nineteenth-Century American Women's Novels* (1990); Nancy A. Walker, *A Very Serious Thing: Women's Humor and American Culture* (1988); Carroll Smith-Rosenberg, *Disorderly Conduct: Visions of Gender in Victorian America* (1986); Alfred Habegger, *Gender, Fantasy, and Realism in American Literature* (1982); Ann Douglas, *The Feminization of American Culture* (1977); Todd McGowan's *The Feminine "NO!": Psychoanalysis and the New Canon* (2001) offers a new perspective on such prominent rediscovered titles as Gilman's "The Yellow Wall-paper," Chesnutt's *The Marrow of Tradition*, and Chopin's *The Awakening*, in its study of why works were rejected from the canon despite their artistic value—they were set aside, he argues, because they show traumatic experiences (2001); and Elsa Nettels's *Language and Gender in American Fiction: Howells, James, Wharton, and Cather* (1997), which is of great value especially on Howells and Cather, who are under-studied and under-taught; and Jessica Bomarito, Jeffrey W. Hunter, and Amy Hudock, eds., *Feminism in Literature: A Gale Critical Companion* (2004).

African American literary history is covered by such sources as *Portraits of the New Negro Woman: Visual and Literary Culture in the Harlem Renaissance*, by Cherene Sherrard-Johnson (2006); Paul Gilmore, *The Genuine Article: Race, Mass Culture, and American Literary Manhood* (2002); *Saints, Sinners, Saviors: Strong Black Women in African American Literature*, Trudier Harris (2001); *Passing: Identity and Interpretation in Sexuality, Race, and Religion*, Maria Carla Sánchez and Linda Schlossberg, eds. (2001); William L. Andrews and Henry Louis Gates Jr., eds., *The Civitas Anthology of African American Slave Narratives* (1999); Paul Gilroy, *The Black Atlantic Modernity and Double Consciousness* (1993); Charles P. Henry, *Culture and African American Politics* (1990); *Reconstructing Womanhood: The Emergence of the*

Afro-American Woman Novelist (1988), by Hazel V. Carby, who sees the works of Cooper, Hopkins, and Wells as feminist historiographies with immense intellectual and political importance for the period; Henry Louis Gates Jr., *Figures in Black: Words, Signs, and the "Racial" Self* (1987) and *The Signifying Monkey: A Theory of Afro-American Literary Criticism* (1988); Bernard W. Bell, *The Afro-American Novel and Its Tradition* (1987); Wilson J. Moses, *The Golden Age of Black Nationalism, 1850–1925* (1978, reprinted 1988); Valerie Smith, *Self-Discovery and Authority in Afro-American Narrative* (1987); William L. Andrews, *To Tell a Free Story: The First Century of Afro-American Autobiography, 1760–1865* (1986); Toni Morrison, *Playing in the Dark: Whiteness and the Literary Imagination* (1992); George Frederickson, *The Black Image in the White Mind: The Debate on Afro-American Character and Destiny, 1817–1914* (1971); and Ruth Miller, *Backgrounds to Black American Literature* (1971). Asian-American writers are surveyed in Amy Ling's *Asian American Literature* (1982). New work on Latina/o literatures includes *Latina Legacies: Identity, Biography, and Community*, ed. Vicki L. Ruiz and Virginia Sánchez Korrol (2005); and *When We Arrive: A New Literary History of Mexican America*, José F. Aranda, Jr. (2003).

Realism and Naturalism, as the two most important literary movements of the period, are traced by many literary historians and critics, including Donald Pizer, ed., *The Cambridge Companion to American Realism and Naturalism: Howells to London* (1995); Pizer, ed., *Documents of American Realism and Naturalism* (1998); Tom Quirk and Gary Scharnhorst, eds., *American Realism and the Canon* (1994); David E. Shi, *Facing Facts: Realism in American Thought and Culture, 1850–1920* (1995); Tony Tanner, *Scenes of Nature, Signs of Men* (1987); and Kenneth Warren, *Black and White Strangers: Race and American Literary Realism* (1993); Michael Davitt Bell, *The Problem of American Realism: Studies in the Cultural History of a Literary Idea* (1993); Amy Kaplan, *The Social Construction of American* Realism (1988); Janet Holmgrin McKay, *Narration and Discourse in American Realistic Fiction* (1982); *The Ferment of Realism* (1965), by Warner Berthoff; John Conder, *Naturalism in American Fiction: The Classic Phase* (1984); June Howard, *Form and History in American Literary Naturalism* (1985); *Realism and Naturalism in Nineteenth-Century American Literature* (rev. ed. 1984); and Donald Pizer, *Twentieth Century American Naturalism* (1982). Also see Peter N. Skrine and Lillian R. Furst, *Naturalism* (1971). Regionalism has been "reclaimed" or at least brought into the canon by scholars such as Donna M. Campbell, in her *Resisting Regionalism: Gender and Naturalism in American Fiction, 1885–1915* (1998); Sherrie A. Inness and Diana Royer, eds., *Breaking Boundaries: New Perspectives on Women's Regional Writing* (1997), with fifteen essays on Stowe and Jewett and lesser-known writers, mostly from the nineteenth century; Carolyn Perry, Mary Louise Weaks, Mary Louise, and Doris Betts in their *History of Southern Women's Literature* (2002); Josephine Donovan, in *New England Local Color Literature: A Women's Tradition* (1983); Glen A. Love, *New Americans: The Westerner and the Modern Experience in the American Novel* (1982); Bonney MacDonald, *Updating the Literary West* (1997), which brings together essays by one hundred scholars who address a diverse range of topics from ethnicity and gender to children's literature and the environment. Also of interest is Larzar Ziff's *Return Passages: Great American Travel Writing 1780–1910* (2000).

Literary Criticism and Theory

Critical and theoretical work in American literature has continued to benefit from lively perspectives by many scholars, especially in the recent past in the area of cultural studies involving class, race, and gender in national literary identity; at the same time perspectives on re-discovered writers previously marginalized have multiplied. What follows is a highly selective list of some of the most useful volumes. We begin with Leslie A. Fiedler, *Love and Death in the American Novel* (1960); John Carlos Rowe, *Through the Custom-House: Nineteenth Century American Fiction and Modern Theory* (1982); Eric J. Sundquist, ed., *American Realism: New Essays* (1982); Robert A. Ferguson, *Law and Letters in American Culture* (1984); Philip Fisher, *Hard Facts: Setting and Form in the American Novel* (1985); Thomas Cooley, *Educated Lives: The Rise of Modern Autobiography in America* (1986); Eric Homberger's *American Writers and Radical Politics, 1900–39: Equivocal Commitments* (1986); Frederick Crews, *The Critics Bear It Away* (1992); Robert Davidoff, *The Genteel Tradition and the Sacred Rage* (1992); Paul John Eakin, *American Autobiography: Retrospect and Prospect* (1991); *Writing Their Nations: The Tradition of Nineteenth-Century American Jewish Women Writers* (1992), by Diane Lichtenstein, surveys thirty Jewish and Jewish American female writers; *Speaking the Other Self: American Women Writers*, ed. Jeanne Campbell Reesman (1997); and *Unruly Tongue: Identity and Voice in American Women's Writing, 1850–1930* (1999), by Martha J. Cutter, an examination of how Cooper, Chopin, Gilman, and Frances Harper contested and sought to resignify male/female binaries.

In the past few years, newer readings, critical approaches, and theoretical models have been applied in such volumes as *White Liberal Identity, Literary Pedagogy, and Classic American Realism,* Phillip Barrish (2006), offering new reasons to read canonical American authors such as James, Wharton, Twain, and Chopin—using new analytical and pedagogical tools for probing contemporary liberalism and realism, using contexts including an affirmative-action court case, the liberal arts classroom, the "war on drugs," and current debates over U.S. roles in globalization; *A Companion to African-American Studies,* ed. Lewis R. Gordon and Jane Anna Gordon (2005); *Queer Cowboys and Other Erotic Male Friendships in Nineteenth-Century American Literature,* ed. Chris Packard (2005), which uses the approaches of Queer Theory to reread authors from James Fenimore Cooper, Whitman, Harris, Harte, Owen Wister, to Eugene Field; *Form and Transformation in Asian American Literature*, ed. Xiaojing Zhou and Samina Najmi (2005), a critical anthology; Jessica Bomarito, Jeffrey W. Hunter, and Amy Hudock, eds., *Feminism in Literature: A Gale Critical Companion* (2004); *Family, Kinship, and Sympathy in Nineteenth-Century American Literature* by Cindy Weinstein (2004), which notes how sentimental novels, more complex than they may appear, elaborate a family-based republican ideal; *Cosmopolitan Vistas: American Regionalism and Literary Value,* Tom Lutz (2004); Judith Fetterley and Marjorie Pryse, eds., essays that challenge traditional boundaries of regionalism in *Writing Out of Place: Regionalism, Women, and American Literary Culture* (2003); *Unsettling the Literary West: Authenticity and Authorship* (2003), in which Nathaniel Lewis claims that western literature since its inception has been

America's first postmodern literature; Jerilyn Fisher, Ellen S. Silber, and David Sadker, eds., *Women in Literature: Reading through the Lens of Gender* (2003); *The Concise Oxford Companion to African American Literature*, ed. William L. Andrews and Frances Smith Foster (2001), an abbreviated version of *The Oxford Companion to African American Literature* (1997); *West of the Border: The Multicultural Literature of the Western American Frontiers*, by Noreen Groover Lape (2000), which sees writers such as Sui Sin Far and Mary Austin in their engagements with borders not as dividing lines but as sites of cultural contact, using a trickster figure inspired by Du Bois's idea of "double consciousness"; *Public Sentiments*, Glenn Hendler (2001), which surveys Howells, Freeman, Jewett, Garland, Harold Frederic, Jacob Riis, and Alfred Henry Lewis; *Trickster Lives: Culture and Myth in American Fiction*, ed. Jeanne Campbell Reesman (2001), which offers an important set of essays on the ubiquitous trickster figure in diverse American literatures; *The Patchwork Quilt: Ideas of Community in Nineteenth-Century American Women's Fiction* (2001), in which Suzanne V. Shepard re-reads Susan B. Warner, Harriet Beecher Stowe, Sarah Hale, Mary Wilkins Freeman, Sarah Orne Jewett, and Susan Glaspell as work that sought to redefine the concept of "brotherhood," established in Winthrop's "city upon a hill," by providing an inclusive and matriarchal model for the communal experiment that was America, through realistic detail and women's metaphors of hearth, home, kitchen, garden, and quilt; *Reconstituting Authority: American Fiction in the Province of the Law, 1880–1920*, by William E. Moddelmog (2001), on how authority is established in the literature of Howells, Oliver Wendell Holmes, Jackson, Hopkins, and Chesnutt in fashions parallel to those of legal documents; *Plots and Proposals: American Women's Fiction, 1850–90* by Karen Tracey (2000). The very readable and informative essays in Tom Quirk's *Nothing Abstract: Investigations in the American Literary Imagination* (2001) employ a "genetic" approach to literary study, that is, such matters as a work's compositional history, the course of authors' careers, and the genesis of literary movements, mounting a strong argument against poststructuralist theory in favor of discoveries made through actual scholarship.

New critical approaches to realism have included Henry B. Wonham's *Playing the Races: Ethnic Caricature and American Literary Realism* (2004); Barbara Hochman, *Getting at the Author: Reimagining Books and Reading in the Age of American Realism* (2001), which furnishes interesting perspectives on Wharton, James, Cather, Norris, and Dreiser, and also Owen Wister, Winston Churchill, and Francis Crawford, for all of whom the development of realism meant distancing of the author; and Paul Hansom, ed. (2001), *Twentieth-Century American Cultural Theorists*; Phillip Barrish, *American Literary Realism, Critical Theory, and Intellectual Prestige 1880–1990* (2001), which reads Howells, James, Cahan, and Wharton as focused upon a reality beneath the surface of narrative tied to human suffering.

In naturalist studies, Bert Bender's important book *Evolution and "the Sex Problem": American Narratives during the Eclipse of Darwinism* (2004) is among the first of a growing collection of critical books on literary Darwinism or literary evolutionism—Bender analyzes American fiction from the realist through the Freudian eras, arguing that Darwin's theories of sexual selection and of the emotions are essential elements in American fiction from the late 1800s through the 1950s, in works by Norris, London, Crane, Dreiser, Gertrude Stein, Willa Cather, Sherwood Anderson, F. Scott Fitzgerald, writers of the Harlem Renaissance, John Steinbeck, and Ernest Hemingway. Mohamed Zaynani's *Reading the Symptom: Norris, Dreiser, and the Dynamics of Capitalism* (1999) offers a revision of the deterministic definition of naturalism, with emphasis upon its "ludic" character as complex and indeterminate, an especially rewarding approach to *Vandover and the Brute* and *McTeague*, as well as *Sister Carrie*.

Naturalist scholars and their students now have a new naturalism journal: *Studies in American Naturalism*, ed. Keith Newlin, Stephen Brennan; Vol. 1, 1, Summer 2006, offers articles on definitions of realism and naturalism, Stephen Crane, Frank Norris, Bret Harte, Jack London, Theodore Dreiser, Edith Wharton, John Dos Passos, Kate Chopin, and Ellen Glasgow. And a few very recent journal articles deserve mention, beginning with "Late Nineteenth-Century American Literary Naturalism: A Re-Introduction," by Donald Pizer (2006), a major new overview of the enduring themes of naturalism, especially Garland and Crane's investigative journalism for *McClure's* magazine and the roots of naturalism in the failure of the nation's industrial system and the deleterious effects of workplace conditions on lives of millions. In "Literature and Regional Production," by Hsuan L. Hsu, *American Literary History* (2005), Jewett, Norris, and Washington are examined in their engagements with regionalism and the changing economic structures of their day.

Students of American literature should generally be aware that new paperback editions of canonical as well as newly recovered works often contain, as do Norton Critical Editions, useful introductions, background material, and criticism. In addition to Norton, a number of publishers, such as Twayne, MLA, Bedford/St. Martin's, Oxford University Press, and Cambridge University Press have ongoing series on individual authors and/or works. Proceedings of conferences on authors, periods, genre, and specialized topics are frequently published. *Dissertation Abstracts International* and the often-invoked MLA annual bibliography (now online through institutional subscription) provide information on unpublished scholarship on this period and its authors. Newsletters devoted to studies of many of the writers represented in this period are published regularly. Finally, students should also inquire into the abundant—and often very useful—audiovisual resources for the study of American writers, individual works, and intellectual currents. Increasingly these supplements are available on CD-ROM and on the Internet as well as on audiocassettes and videocassettes. An excellent source for video and CD-ROM data is facets.com. Increasingly, students turn to resources on the Internet, where there are numerous excellent American literature web sites, electronic texts, concordances, and other resources; even just using Google.com and Amazon.com will yield more than enough for any student. Two Internet tips for students: First, to put it mildly, a lot of what is on the Internet posing as "facts" about American writers is not. Always check your sources with the kinds of experts listed here. Second, if you use any information from an Internet source, you must document it accordingly.

Ambrose Bierce

Scholarship and criticism on Ambrose Bierce has recently made significant strides in catching up to the significance and complexities of its subject, beginning with an exciting new set of editions and an authoritative critical study. *The Short Fiction of Ambrose Bierce, 2 Volumes: A Comprehensive Edition* (2006) is edited by S. T. Joshi, Lawrence I. Berkove, and David E. Schultz and fulfills a long-unmet need. *Ambrose Bierce: An Annotated Bibliography of Primary Sources*, is edited by Joshi and Schultz (1999). Joshi and Schultz have also produced *The Fall of the Republic and Other Political Stories* and *The Unabridged Devil's Dictionary* (2000) and *A Much Misunderstood Man: Selected Letters of Ambrose Bierce* (2003). *Phantoms of a Blood-Stained Period: The Complete Civil War Writings of Ambrose Bierce*, is edited by Russell Duncan and David J. Klooster (2002). Daniel Lindley edited *Ambrose Bierce Takes on the Railroad: The Journalist as Muckraker and Cynic* (1999). Robert C. Evans has brought out *Ambrose Bierce's 'An Occurrence at Owl Creek Bridge': An Annotated Critical Edition* (2003) and Joshi *The Collected Fables of Ambrose Bierce* (2000). Bierce's poetry is found in *Poems of Ambrose Bierce*, ed. M. E. Grenander (1996). Robert L. Gale's carefully surveys Bierce's life and work in *An Ambrose Bierce Companion* (2001).

Lawrence I. Berkove's long-awaited critical study, *A Prescription for Adversity: The Moral Art of Ambrose Bierce* (2002), takes issue with simplistic clichés about Bierce's famous pessimism and focuses upon his complex artistry and moral argument. Bierce's war writings are the focus of another book, *Ambrose Bierce's Civilians and Soldiers in Context: A Critical Study*, by Donald T. Blume (2004). S. T. Joshi and David E. Schultz's *A Sole Survivor: Bits of Autobiography* (1999) is also useful. The fullest edition of Bierce's writings is still *Collected Works of Ambrose Bierce* (1909–12), edited by Walter Neale. The largest collection of Bierce's letters is available in Bertha C. Pope's edition of *The Letters of Ambrose Bierce* (1921). Until Berkove's *Prescription for Adversity*, the standard critical biography was Paul Fatout's *Ambrose Bierce, the Devil's Lexicographer* (1951); Mary Elizabeth Grenander's *Ambrose Bierce* (1971) is also still much worth consulting. Roy Morris Jr.'s *Ambrose Bierce: Alone in Bad Company* (1996) enriches our understanding of Bierce's Civil War experience and how he converted this experience into a group of fine short stories. Still a fine critical study of Bierce's work is Cathy N. Davidson's *The Experimental Fictions of Ambrose Bierce: Structuring the Ineffable* (1984). Davidson also edited *Critical Essays on Ambrose Bierce* (1982). Two interesting essay perspectives on stories included in NAAL are " 'A Quarter of an Hour': Hanging as Ambrose Bierce and Peyton Farquhar Knew It," by Donald T. Blume, *American Literary Realism* (2002), and " 'Chickamauga' as an Indian-Wars Narrative: The Relevance of Ambrose Bierce for a First-Nations-Centered Study of the Nineteenth Century," by Susan Kalter, *Arizona Quarterly: A Journal of American Literature, Culture, and Theory* (2000).

Abraham Cahan

There is no collected edition of Cahan's many writings in English, Russian, and Yiddish. Isaac Metzker edited *A Bintel Brief: Sixty Years of Letters from the Lower East Side to the Jewish Daily Forward* (1971). Moses Rischin's *Grandma Never Lived in America: The New Journalism of Abraham Cahan* (1985) also features an extensive and informative introduction. Cahan's *"The Imported Bridegroom" and Other Stories of the New York Ghetto* (1898) was reprinted with introduction by Bernard G. Richards in 1970. *The Rise of David Levinsky: A Novel* (1917) was reprinted with an introduction by John Higham (1960); it was reprinted again with a superb introduction and notes by Jules Chametzky (1993).

No full-scale biography of Cahan has been published, but many of the critical books listed contain accounts of his very long and full life. Irving Howe's *World of Our Fathers* (1976) is an immensely well-informed cultural history of Jewish immigration and sheds much light on turn of the century Yiddish journalism in New York. Ronald Sanders's brilliant and engaging *The Downtown Jews: Portraits of an Immigrant Generation* (1969) focuses on Cahan's generation and provides information through the early 1920s. John Higham's still valuable *Strangers in the Land: Patterns of American Nativism, 1860–1925* (1955), as its subtitle suggests, calls attention to the mounting opposition to immigration, Jewish and otherwise. Sanford Marovitz's Twayne volume *Abraham Cahan* (1996) is the best introduction to Cahan's life and work; its evaluation of the fiction is balanced and judicious.

Jules Chametsky's *From the Ghetto: The Fiction of Abraham Cahan* (1977) is by far the best critical study of Cahan's English and Yiddish fiction. David Fine's chapter on Cahan in *The City of the Immigrant and American Fiction, 1880–1920* (1977) provides a good overview. Louis Harap's *Creative Awakening: The Jewish Presence in Twentieth Century American Literature: 1900–1940s* (1987) is worth consulting, as is Allen Guttman's groundbreaking *The Jewish Writer in America: Assimilation and the Crisis of Identity* (1971).

Charles Chesnutt

In 2002, Werner Sollors edited the Library of America volume *Charles W. Chesnutt Stories, Novels and Essays*, a much-needed resource.

The volume *Charles W. Chesnutt: Essays and Speeches*, ed. Joseph R. McElrath, Jr., Robert C. Leitz III, and Jesse S. Crisler (1999), presents all of Chesnutt's known nonfiction, 77 items in all, from 1881–1930s, on a wide range of topics: race, education, images of blacks in literature, and manners. And their collection of his letters, *An Exemplary Citizen: Letters of Charles W. Chesnutt, 1906–1932* (2002) provides another major contribution to the valuable if less comprehensive work before them. Sylvia L. Render edited *The Short Fiction of Charles W. Chesnutt* (1974). Richard H. Brodhead edited *The Journals of Charles W. Chesnutt* (1993). His introduction to *The Conjure Woman and Other Conjure Tales* (1993) locates Chesnutt's tales within the conventions of local color realism and particularly within the development of black vernacular voice and emerging fictions detailing black folk life. William L. Andrews brings his deep understanding of Chesnutt to his edition of the *Collected Stories of Charles W. Chesnutt* (1992).

The first full-length biography was written by Chesnutt's daughter, Helen M. Chesnutt, as *Charles Waddell Chesnutt: Pioneer of the Color Line* (1952). Heermance J. Noel's *Charles W. Chesnutt: America's First Great Black Novelist* (1974) is a useful critical biography, as are William L. Andrews's *The Literary Career of Charles W. Chesnutt* (1980), Sylvia L. Render's *Charles W. Chesnutt* (1980), and Robert B. Stepto's *Charles Chesnutt: The Uncle Julius Stories* (1984); and Charles Duncan's *The Absent Man: The Narrative Craft of Charles W. Chesnutt* (1998), which explores sensitively what might be called the "rhetoric of elusiveness" in Chesnutt's career. Marjorie Pryse and Hortense J. Spillers's *Conjuring: Black Women, Fiction, and Literary Tradition* (1985) and Jane Campbell's *Mythic Black Fiction: The Transformation of History* (1986) contain useful contextual material on Chesnutt. A more specialized study is Ernestine Williams Pickens's *Charles W. Chesnutt and the Progressive Movement* (1994). Eric J. Sundquist's *To Wake the Nations* (1993) treats Chesnutt at length. Other valuable critical studies include Samira Kawash's *Dislocating the Color Line: Identity, Hybridity, and Singularity in African-American Narrative* (1997), which examines critically and historically representations of racial difference; Henry Wonham's *Charles W. Chesnutt: A Study of the Short Fiction* (1998); Dean McWilliams's *Charles W. Chesnutt and the Fictions of Race,* (2002); Matthew Wilson's *Whiteness in the Novels of Charles W. Chesnutt* (2004); *Conscience and Purpose: Fiction and Social Consciousness in Howells, Jewett, Chesnutt, and Cather* by Paul R. Petrie (2005); and Charles A. Walls's *Acts of the Imagination: Racial Sentimentalism and the Modern American Novel (Frederick Douglass, Charles Waddell Chesnutt,*

Nella Larsen, Richard Wright) (2006). One of Chesnutt's best scholars is Joseph R. McElrath, Jr., whose *Critical Essays on Charles W. Chesnutt* (1999) gathers a variety of helpful essays prefaced by a thoughtful introductory essay; selections on Chesnutt's reputation range from its beginning at the turn of the century to the surge of interest in the 1960s that has continued to the present. In a recent essay, McElrath also thoughtfully contrasts Chesnutt and Howells: "Why Charles Chesnutt is Not a Realist," *American Literary Realism* (2000).

Kate Chopin

The Complete Works of Kate Chopin (1969) was edited in two volumes by Per Seyersted, who also wrote the excellent *Kate Chopin: A Critical Biography* (1969). The Library of America volume *Kate Chopin: Complete Novels and Stories: At Fault / Bayou Folk / A Night in Acadie / The Awakening / Uncollected Stories* (2002) has appeared, edited by Sandra K. Gilbert. Emily Toth's landmark *Unveiling Kate Chopin* (1999) incorporates material from Chopin's recently discovered diaries and manuscripts and is now the standard biography. Per Seyersted and Emily Toth edited *A Kate Chopin Miscellany* (1980), and a collection of unpublished short fiction, poems, letters, etc.; their *Kate Chopin's Private Papers* appeared in 1998. Barbara C. Ewell's *Kate Chopin* (1986) and *Kate Chopin: A Literary Life*, by Nancy Walker (2001) are good introductions to the life and work. Emily Toth's critical biography *Kate Chopin* (1990) has established her as perhaps the leading Chopin scholar.

Bernard J. Kosloski's *Kate Chopin: A Study of the Short Fiction* (1996) is a fine survey of this large subject. Koloski also edited the pedagogical collection, *Approaches to Teaching Kate Chopin's "The Awakening"* (1988), and a welcome edition of Chopin's two most important collections of short stories in *Kate Chopin: "Bayou Folk" and "A Night in Acadie"* (1999). Lynda S. Boren and Sara deSaussure Davis edited a fresh collection of essays (with a foreword by Cathy N. Davidson), *Kate Chopin Reconsidered: Beyond the Bayou* (1992). Wendy Martin edited *New Essays on The Awakening* (1988), and Nancy A. Walker edited *Kate Chopin: The Awakening, Complete Authoritative Text with Biographical and Historical Contexts* (1993). Joyce Dyer wrote a closely argued monograph *The Awakening: A Novel of Beginnings* (1993; 2nd ed., 2000); Donald Kesey edited *Contexts for Criticism* (1994); and Margo Culley edited the second edition of the Norton Critical Edition of *The Awakening* with biographical and historical contexts and criticism (1994). *Kate Chopin's Short Fiction: A Critical Companion* by Robert C. Evans (2001) is useful, as is the comparative study *Kate Chopin, Edith Wharton and Charlotte Perkins*

Gilman: Studies in Short Fiction (2005) by Janet Beer. Susan Disheroon Green, David Caudle, and Emily Toth teamed up to produce *Kate Chopin: An Annotated Bibliography of Critical Works* (1999); it provides not only annotation but discursive essays by the editors on Chopin's life, work, and reputation.

Anna Julia Cooper
Scholarship and criticism on Anna Julia Cooper is not plentiful, but it is growing. Two noteworthy editions of her writings are *A Voice From the South* (The Schomburg Library of Nineteenth-Century Black Women Writers), edited by Mary H. Washington (1988) and *The Voice of Anna Julia Cooper: Including A Voice From the South and Other Important Essays, Papers, and Letters*, edited by Charles Lemert (1998). Cooper's Ph.D. Dissertation from her studies at the Sorbonne has been published as *Slavery and the French Revolutionists, 1788–1805*, translated by Frances Richardson Keller (1988). Karen Johnson's *Uplifting the Women and the Race: The Lives, Educational Philosophies and Social Activism of Anna Julia Cooper and Nannie Helen Burroughs* (2000) is a welcome comparative volume. Noteworthy critical essays include Hazel V. Carby's " 'On the Threshold of Woman's Era': Lynching, Empire and Sexuality in Black Feminist Theory" (1985), *Critical Inquiry*, an examination of how Cooper, Wells-Barnett, and Hopkins articulated theories of patriarchy and racism that linked imperialism, sexual politics, and internal colonialism within an intellectual climate dominated by male figures, thus demonstrating how history is "differentially experienced"; this essay is reprinted in Anne McClintock, Aamir Mufti, and Ella Shohat, eds., *Dangerous Liaisons: Gender, Nation, and Postcolonial Perspectives* (1997). Also helpful are "Anna Julia Cooper: The Black Feminist Voice of the 1890s," by Mary Helen Washington, *Legacy: A Journal of American Women Writers* (1987); "The Five Million Women of My Race: Negotiations of Gender in W. E. B. Du Bois and Anna Julia Cooper," by Hanna Wallinger, in Karen L. Kilcup, ed., *Soft Canons: American Women Writers and Masculine Tradition* (1999); " 'We Must Be about Our Father's Business': Anna Julia Cooper and the In-Corporation of the Nineteenth-Century African-American Woman Intellectual," by Elizabeth Alexander, *Signs* (1995); "Anna Julia Cooper: 'Dedicated in the Name of My Slave Mother to the Education of Colored Working People,' " by Cathryn Bailey, *Hypatia: A Journal of Feminist Philosophy* (2004); and Vivian M. May's "Thinking from the Margins, Acting at the Intersections: Anna Julia Cooper's *A Voice from the South*," *Hypatia* (2004). A useful source for contextualizing Cooper is *Black Feminist Thought: Knowledge, Consciousness, and the Politics of Empowerment* by Patricia Hill Collins (2000).

Samuel L. Clemens
See Mark Twain.

Stephen Crane
Fredson Bowers is the textual editor of *The Works of Stephen Crane* (1969–76). The Library of America volume, *Crane: Prose and Poetry* (1996), is edited by J. C. Levenson. *Stephen Crane: Letters* (1960) was edited by R. W. Stallman and Lillian Gilkes and was later joined by *The Correspondence of Stephen Crane*, (1988), edited by Stanley Wertheim and Paul Sorrentino. Joseph Katz edited both *The Portable Stephen Crane* (1969) and *The Poems of Stephen Crane: A Critical Edition* (1966). Patrick K. Dooley compiled *Stephen Crane: An Annotated Bibliography of Secondary Scholarship* (1992), an indispensable research tool, now annually updated in *Stephen Crane Studies* by Dooley. excellent biographies are Linda H. Davis's *Badge of Courage: The Life of Stephen Crane* (1998) and *The Crane Log: A Documentary Life of Stephen Crane, 1871–1900*, by Wertheim and Sorrentino (1994). Also of interest is *The Double Life of Stephen Crane: A Biography*, by Christopher Benfey (1992).

Edwin H. Cady's *Stephen Crane* (1980) is an excellent critical introduction to Crane's life and work. Marston La France's *A Reading of Stephen Crane* (1971), Frank Bergon's *Stephen Crane's Artistry* (1975), James Nagel's *Stephen Crane and Literary Impressionism* (1980), Chester L. Wolford's *The Anger of Stephen Crane: Fiction and the Epic Tradition* (1983), James B. Colvert's *Stephen Crane* (1984), Bettina L. Knapp's *Stephen Crane* (1987), David Halliburton's *The Color of the Sky: A Study of Stephen Crane* (1991), Patrick K. Dooley's *The Pluralistic Philosophy of Stephen Crane* (1993), Michael Robertson's *Stephen Crane, Journalism, and the Making of Modern American Literature* (1997), Bill Brown's intriguing *The Material Unconscious: American Amusement, Stephen Crane and the Economics of Play* (1997), and George E. Monteiro's *Stephen Crane's Blue Badge of Courage* (2000) are among the best of surprisingly few significant book-length studies. Donald Pizer has edited and introduced *Critical Essays on Stephen Crane's The Red Badge of Courage* (1990). Claudia Durst Johnson compiled *Understanding the Red Badge of Courage* (1998), rich in historical documents, collateral readings, and commentary, and Stanley Wertheim compiled the comprehensive *A Stephen Crane Encyclopedia* (1997).

Emily Dickinson
Three volumes of *The Poems of Emily Dickinson* (1955) were edited by Thomas H. Johnson; and Johnson and Theodora Ward edited three companion volumes of *The Letters of Emily Dickin-*

son (1958). R. W. Franklin's *The Manuscript Books of Emily Dickinson* (1981) provides, in two volumes, facsimile reproductions of the hand-sewn poems Dickinson left at her death in fascicles. R. W. Franklin's three-volume *Poems of Emily Dickinson: Variorum Edition* (1998) now supersedes Johnson's three-volume *Poems*. In 1999 Franklin published the one-volume *The Poems of Emily Dickinson: Reading Edition*. Important biographies include Richard B. Sewall's *The Life of Emily Dickinson* (1974), Cynthia Griffin Wolff's *Emily Dickinson* (1986), and Alfred Habegger's *My Wars Are Laid Away in Books: The Life of Emily Dickinson* (2001). Jay Leyda's *The Years and Hours of Emily Dickinson* (1960) is two volumes of documents, such as excerpts from family letters. Additional documents are in Vivian Pollak's *A Poet's Parents: The Courtship Letters of Emily Norcross and Edward Dickinson* (1988), Polly Longsworth's *The World of Emily Dickinson* (1990), and Ellen Louise Hart and Martha Nell Smith's *Open Me Carefully: Emily Dickinson's Intimate Letters to Susan Huntington Dickinson* (1998).

Research tools include Joseph Duchac's *The Poems of Emily Dickinson: An Annotated Guide to Commentary Published in English, 1890–1977* (1979), and the continuation (published in 1993) covering 1978–89; Karen Dandurand's *Dickinson Scholarship: An Annotated Bibliography 1969–1985* (1988), and the treasure trove compiled by Willis J. Buckingham (drawing on Mabel Loomis Todd's scrapbooks), *Emily Dickinson's Reception in the 1890s* (1989). Also useful are S. P. Rosenbaum's *A Concordance to the Poems of Emily Dickinson* (1964), Cynthia J. MacKenzie's *Concordance to the Letters of Emily Dickinson* (2000), Joel Myerson's *Emily Dickinson: A Descriptive Bibliography* (1984), and Jane Donahue Eberwein's *An Emily Dickinson Encyclopedia* (1998). *The Dickinson Electronic Archives* <www.emilydickinson.org>, directed by Martha Nell Smith with Ellen Louise Hart, Lara Vetter, and Marta Werner, offers more than access to many of Dickinson's manuscripts. Also available are many out-of-print volumes about Dickinson as well as never-before-published writings by various family members.

Edited collections of critical essays provide an excellent introduction to Dickinson studies. See Susan Juhasz's *Feminist Critics Read Emily Dickinson* (1983), Judith Farr's *Emily Dickinson: A Collection of Critical Essays* (1996), Gudrun Grabher, Roland Hagenbüchle, and Cristanne Miller's *The Emily Dickinson Handbook* (1998, 2006), Wendy Martin's *The Cambridge Companion to Emily Dickinson* (2002), and Vivian R. Pollak's *A Historical Guide to Emily Dickinson* (2004). Recent important studies include Paula Bennett's *Emily Dickin-*

son: *Woman Poet* (1990), Judith Farr's *The Passion of Emily Dickinson* (1992), Martha Nell Smith's *Rowing in Eden: Rereading Emily Dickinson* (1992), Sharon Cameron's *Choosing, Not Choosing: Dickinson's Fascicles* (1993), Domhnall Mitchell's *Emily Dickinson: Monarch of Perception* (2000), Eleanor Elson Heginbotham's *Reading the Fascicles of Emily Dickinson* (2003), and Virginia Walker Jackson's *Dickinson's Misery: A Theory of Lyric Reading* (2005).

Theodore Dreiser

Most of Dreiser's novels and short stories are largely in print, but his poetry, plays, and other writings often are not, and a well-edited uniform edition of Dreiser's writings is badly needed. The University of Pennsylvania has begun to satisfy this need; so far James L. W. West III, textual editor, and Neda Westlake, general editor, have overseen the publication of *American Diaries: 1902–1926* (edited and with an introduction by Thomas P. Riggio) and *Sister Carrie* (John C. Berkey and Alice M. Winters, historical editors) (1981). In 1992 West and Riggio edited a dramatically restored edition of *Jennie Gerhardt*. Three years later West edited *Dreiser's Jennie Gerhardt: New Essays on the Restored Text* (1995). Donald Pizer made an important contribution with *Theodore Dreiser: A Selection of Uncollected Prose* (1977) and another in "The Text of *Sister Carrie*: Where We Are Now," *Dreiser Studies* (2001), an interesting exploration of the difficulty of an instructor's informed choice about an edition to teach. Pizer, Richard W. Dowell, and Frederic Rusch prepared *Theodore Dreiser: A Primary Bibliography and Reference Guide*, updated regularly in *Dreiser Studies*. Robert H. Elias edited the three volumes of *Letters of Theodore Dreiser* (1959). *Theodore Dreiser: Sister Carrie, Jennie Gerhardt, Twelve Men* (1987), a Library of America volume, was edited by Richard Lehan, while *Theodore Dreiser: Interviews* was edited by Rusch, Pizer, and Riggio (2004).

In a volume edited and introduced by Thomas R. Riggio, Yvette Eastman, in *Dearest Wilding: A Memoir with Love Letters from Theodore Dreiser* (1995), tells of her sixteen-year relationship with Dreiser; Marguerite Tjader's *Love That Will Not Let Go: My Time with Theodore Dreiser* (1998), edited by Lawrence E. Hussman, makes clear Eastman was not Dreiser's only lover. Jerome Loving's long-awaited *The Last Titan: A Life of Theodore Dreiser* (2005), is the authoritative biography; before that Richard Lingeman's two-volume biography was considered standard: *Theodore Dreiser: At the Gates of the City, 1891–1907* (1986) and *Theodore Dreiser: An American Journey, 1908–1945* (1990). Richard Lehan, *Theodore Dreiser: His World and His Novels* (1974); Pizer, *The Novels of Theodore Dreiser*

(1976); Yoshinobu Hakutani, *Young Dreiser: A Critical Study* (1979); Hussman, *Dreiser and His Fiction: A Twentieth-Century Quest* (1983); Joseph Griffin, *The Small Canvas: An Introduction to Dreiser's Short Stories* (1985); Philip Gerber, *Theodore Dreiser Revisited* (1992); Miyoko Takeda, *The Quest for the Reality of Life: Dreiser's Spiritual and Esthetical Pilgrimage* (1991); Louis J. Zanine, *Mechanism and Mysticism: The Influence of Science on the Thought and Work of Theodore Dreiser* (1993); Pizer, *Literary Masters: Theodore Dreiser* (2000); and Clare Virginia Edy, *Dreiser and Veblen: Saboteurs of the Status Quo* (1999), have advanced our appreciation and understanding considerably. Miriam Gogol edited and introduced *Theodore Dreiser: Beyond Naturalism* (1995), a useful set of feminist, gender, psychoanalytic, and other perspectives. Yoshinobo Hakutani edited another useful collection of criticism: *Theodore Dreiser and American Culture: New Readings* (2000); Hakutani includes 33 reprints of Dreiser's magazine articles, 22 reprinted for the first time, along with essays on artists, musicians, and writers from Howells to Stieglitz. *The Cambridge Companion to Theodore Dreiser* is edited by Leonard Cassuto and Clare Virginia Eby (2004).

W. E. B. Du Bois

There is no collected edition of Du Bois's prolific output, but several interesting collections of Du Bois's writings are available: Philip S. Foner's *W. E. B. DuBois Speaks: Speeches and Addresses* (1970), Meyer Weinberg's *W. E. B. DuBois: A Reader* (1970), Andrew G. Paschol, *A W. E. B. DuBois Reader* (1971), Herbert Lee Moon's *The Emerging Thought of W. E. B. DuBois: Essays and Editorials from the "Crisis"* (1972), and Dan S. Green and Edwin D. Driver's *W. E. B. DuBois on Sociology in the Black Community* (1978), which includes sixteen articles by DuBois. Herbert Aptheker edited the three volumes of *The Correspondence of W. E. B. DuBois* (1973–1978), the four volumes of *Writings by W. E. B. DuBois in Periodicals Edited by Others* (1982), *Selections form Phylon* (1980), and *Selections from the Crisis* in two volumes (1972). Phil Zuckerman's collection *Du Bois on Religion* (2000) also contains a perceptive introduction. Eric J. Sundquist's *The Oxford W. E. B. Du Bois Reader* (1996) offers a very substantial selection and features as good a biocritical introduction as any in print. *The Correspondence of W.E.B. Du Bois: Selections, 1877–1934* and *The Correspondence of W.E.B. Du Bois: Selections, 1934–1944* have been edited by Herbert Aptheker (1997). *W. E. B. Du Bois: An Encyclopedia*, edited by Gerald Horne and Mary Young (2001) contains 150 entries.

Several biographies of Du Bois are available: Leslie A. Lacey's *Cheer the Lonesome Traveler:*

The Life of W. E. B. DuBois (1970), Shirley Graham's *His Day Is Marching On: A Memoir of W. E. B. DuBois* (1971), and Arnold Rampersad's perceptive critical study *The Art and Imagination of W. E. B. DuBois* (1976) as well as his chapter on Du Bois in his *Slavery and the Literary Imagination* 1989). David Levering Lewis's two-volume *W. E. B. DuBois: Biography of a Race, 1868–1919* (1993) and *W. E. B. DuBois: The Fight for Equality and the American Century, 1919–1963* (2000) are outstanding.

Significant background to Du Bois's place in American intellectual thought may be found in August Meier's *Negro Thought in America, 1880–1915* (1963) and John Hope Franklin's *From Slavery to Freedom: A History of American Negroes*, 7th ed. (1994). Jack B. Moore's *W. E. B. DuBois* (1981) provides a brief critical biography and introductory survey of his writings, while Joseph P. De Marco's *The Social Thought of W. E. B. Du Bois* (1983) is thorough and helpful on this complex topic; the collection of essays edited by Bernard W. Bell, Emily Grosholz, and James B. Stewart—*W. E. B. Du Bois on Race and Culture: Philosophy, Politics, and Poetics* (1966)—is also a distinguished contribution, as is the gathering of essays in *W. E. B. Du Bois, Race and the City: "The Philadelphia Negro" and Its Legacy* (1998) edited by Michael B. Katz and Thomas J. Sugrue, situating Du Bois in late his nineteenth-century intellectual milieu, exploring his influence on later writers, and assessing his relevance today. Further contexts are supplied in *W. E. B. Du Bois: The Fight for Equality and the American Century, 1919–1963* (2000) by David Levering Lewis, which won Pulitzer Prize; *Creative Conflict in African American Thought: Frederick Douglass, Alexander Crummell, Booker T. Washington, W. E. B. Du Bois, and Marcus Garvey*, by Wilson Jeremiah Moses (2004); *The Lost Promise of Patriotism: Debating American Identity, 1890–1920* by Jonathan M. Hansen, which covers Eugene V. Debs, Jane Addams, and Du Bois (2003); *Du Bois and His Rivals*, Raymond Wolters (2002), which addresses themes of civil rights and social change; and *The Color of Race in America, 1900–1940* by Mathew Prat Guterl (2001) treats racial attitudes such as biracialism in social change, comparing Du Bois to Jean Toomer, and others.

The centennial of publication of *The Philadelphia Negro* is celebrated in Dolan Hubbard's *The Souls of Black Folk: One Hundred Years Later* (2003) with reviews and contextual and interpretive essays; and *W. E. B. DuBois and Race: Essays Celebrating the Centennial Publication of* The Souls of Black Folk, is edited Chester J. Fontenot and Mary Alice Morgan (2001). Manning Marable's *W. E. B. DuBois: Black Radical Democrat* (1986) is similarly insightful on Du Bois's politics. Adolph L. Reed Jr.'s controversial *W. E. B. DuBois and Ameri-*

can *Political Thought* (1995) may also be consulted. William L. Andrews's *Critical Essays on W. E. B. DuBois* (1985) is the best such collection. Critical works of special interest include Houston A. Baker Jr.'s *Modernism and the Harlem Renaissance* (1987), Keith E. Byerman's *Seizing the World: History, Art, and Self in the Work of W. E. B. DuBois* (1994), Harold Cruse's *The Crisis of the Negro Intellectual: A Historical Analysis of the Failure of Black Leadership* (1967, 1984), Henry Louis Gates Jr.'s *Figures in Black: Words, Signs and the "Racial" Self* (1987), Sterling Stuckey's *Slave Culture: National Theory and the Foundations of Black America* (1987), Eric J. Sundquist's magisterial *To Wake the Nations: Race in the Making of American Literature* (1993), and Shannon Zamir's *W. E. B. DuBois and American Thought, 1888–1903* (1995). A special W. E. B. Du Bois issue of *Boundary 2: An International Journal of Literature and Culture* appeared in 2000.

Paul Laurence Dunbar
In *Black Poets of the United States: From Paul Laurence Dunbar to Langston Hughes* (1973) Jean Wagner describes Dunbar's generation as developing and influenced by the minstrel concept, popular music, and white writings, contrasting Dunbar with Harlem Renaissance poet such as Langston Hughes. Since then much new work on Dunbar has appeared, beginning with a 1999 reprint of *The Life and Works of Paul Laurence Dunbar: Containing his Complete Poetical Works, his Best Short Stories, Numerous Anecdotes, and a Complete Biography*, compiled and introduced by William Dean Howells in 1907. *The Complete Stories of Paul Laurence Dunbar* (2006) edited by Gene Andrew Jarrett and Thomas Lewis Morgan is a much-needed edition, as was *The Collected Poetry of Paul Laurence Dunbar* (1993), edited by Joanne M. Braxton, still the largest and most authoritative if not all-inclusive collection of Dunbar's poetry. *In His Own Voice: The Dramatic and Other Uncollected Works of Paul Laurence Dunbar*, edited by Herbert Woodward Martin and Ronald Primeau with a foreword by Henry Louis Gates, Jr. (2002) fills some major gaps. A 2005 reprint of Dunbar's 1904 collection of 16 short stories, *The Heart of Happy Hollow*, is available. There are dozens of juvenile biographies and collections of Dunbar's poetry for children. In 1975 E. W. Metcalf published *Paul Laurence Dunbar: A Bibliography*.

Felton O. Best's *Crossing the Color Line: A Biography of Paul Laurence Dunbar, 1872–1906* (1996) is a full-length biographical study of the author. In 1971 Addison Gayle published *Oak and Ivy: A Biography of Paul Laurence Dunbar*. A dramatic treatment of Dunbar's life is contained in *Lyrics of Sunshine and Shadow: The Tragic Courtship and Marriage of Paul Laurence Dunbar and Alice Ruth Moore* (2002) by

Eleanor Alexander; though Dunbar and Moore were admired by African American literary society in their day, even compared to Robert and Elizabeth Barrett Browning, theirs was a difficult relationship, to say the least, made worse by Dunbar's sometimes violent and drunken behavior. Alexander analyzes the couple's courtship and marriage in light of the social customs of the period, both within and outside the African American community, especially the negative effects of race, class, and gender on romantic love.

Peter Revell's critical book *Paul Laurence Dunbar* (1979) locates Dunbar within the socio-political contexts of his time, dispelling criticisms that Dunbar capitulated to racist stereotypes in his art in order to pander to a white audience. *Liberating Voices* (1991) by Gayle Jones is a study of the emergence of the black literary tradition with particular emphasis on Dunbar's didactic poem, "When Malindy Sings," and his short story "They Lynching of June Benson." A new look at his relationship with Howells is " 'Entirely Black Verse from Him Would Succeed': Minstrel Realism and William Dean Howells" by Gene Jarrett, *Nineteenth-Century Literature* (2004). Also of note are "Paul Laurence Dunbar's Literary Dialects" by Herbert Penzl, *PMLA: Publications of the Modern Language Association of America* (1993), and Marcellus Blount's "The Preacherly Text: African American Poetry and Vernacular Performance," *PMLA* (1992).

Sui Sin Far (Edith Maud Eaton)
The only substantial collection of Sui Sin Far's writing is in *"Mrs. Spring Fragrance" and Other Writings* (1995), edited by Amy Ling and Annette White-Parks; this volume contains "approximately three-fourths of the original title" published in 1912. Fortunately for scholars interested in the life and writings of this re-emerging author, there is an exhaustively researched critical biography by Annette White-Parks, *Sui Sin Far/Edith Maude Eaton: A Literary Biography* (1995). This volume contains a very helpful chronological listing of her writings.

Much of the best critical work on Sui Sin Far appears as articles or chapters in books; for an extensive listing, including the many contributions by Amy Ling, see White-Parks. Resources that contextualize Sui Sin Far as a turn-of-the-twentieth-century Eurasian woman writer are, chronologically: Doug Chin and Art Chin, *Uphill: The Settlement and Diffusion of the Chinese in Seattle* (1974); Elaine Kim, *Asian American Literature: An Introduction to the Writings and Their Social Context* (1982); William F. Wu, *The Yellow Peril: Chinese Americans in American Fiction, 1850–1940* (1982); Anthony B. Chan, *Gold Mountain: The Chinese in the Northwest* (1983); Judy Yung, *Chinese Women of America*

(1986); Mary Dearborn, *Pocahontas's Daughters: Gender and Ethnicity in American Culture* (1986); Roger Daniels, *Asian America* (1988); Ronald Takaki, *Strangers from a Different Shore* (1989); Amy Ling, *Between Worlds: Women Writers of Chinese Ancestry* (1990), which contains a chapter on Sui Sin Far and her novelist sister Winnifred; and Susan Coultrap-McQuin, *Doing Literary Business: American Women Writers in the Nineteenth Century* (1990). Two books published in 2001 add to the scholarship on Sui Sin Far and her sister Onoto Watanna: Diana Birchall's *Onoto Watanna: The Story of Winnifred Eaton* and Dominika Ferens's *Edith and Winnifred Eaton: Chinatown Missions and Japanese Romances*.

Elizabeth Ammons's *Conflicting Stories: American Women Writers at the Turn of the Twentieth Century* (1992) consists of essays on a dozen writers and stories, including the superb "Audacious Words: Sui Sin Far's *Mrs. Spring Fragrance*." Julia Brown edited *Ethnicity and the American Short Story* (1997), which contains Carol-Roh Spaulding's fine essay " 'Wavering' Images: Mixed-Race Identity in the Stories of Edith Eaton/Sui Sin Far." Other useful essays include: "Sui Sin Far and the Chinese American Canon: Toward a Post-Gender-Wars Discourse," Wenxin Li, *MELUS* (2004); Min Hyoung Song's "Sentimentalism and Sui Sin Far," *Legacy* (2003), which examines the presence of Christianity in Far's fiction; "Smuggling across the Borders of Race, Gender, and Sexuality: Sui Sin Far's 'Mrs. Spring Fragrance,'" Martha J. Cutter, in *Mixed Race Literature*, ed. Jonathan Brennan (2002); "Reclaiming Sui Sin Far," Guy Beauregard, in *Re/Collecting Early Asian America: Essays in Cultural History*, ed. Josephine Lee, Imogene L. Lim, and Yuko Matsukawa (2002); "Connecting Links: The Anti-Progressivism of Sui Sin Far," Sean McCann, *Yale Journal of Criticism* (1999); "Sui Sin Far and Onoto Watanna: Two Early Chinese-Canadian Authors," James Doyle, *Canadian Literature* (1994); and "Between the East and West: Sui Sin Far-the First Chinese-American Woman Writer," Xiao-Huang Yin, *Arizona Quarterly*, (1991).

Mary E. Wilkins Freeman
The best collection of Freeman's work is *Selected Stories of Mary E. Wilkins Freeman* (1983), edited and with a perceptive introduction by Marjorie Pryse. Brent L. Kendrick edited and introduced *The Infant Sphinx: Collected Letters of Mary E. Wilkins Freeman* (1985). Perry D. Westbrook's full-length study, *Mary Wilkins Freeman* (1988), is a good introduction to Freeman's life and work. Leah Blatt Glasser's *In a Closet Hidden: The Life and Work of Mary E. Wilkins Freeman* (1996) makes an important contribution to the biographical and critical scholarship. Mary R. Reichard's *Mary*

Wilkins Freeman: A Study of the Short Story (1998) usefully brings together with her close readings of many of Freemans' 250 stories biographical information and a set of readings of "A New England Nun." Reichard has also edited a fine selection of twenty-eight of Freeman's stories: *A Mary Wilkins Freeman Reader* (1997). John Idol and Melinda Ponder's *The Unfortunate Fall: Women and Genteel Poverty in the Fiction of Hawthorne and Freeman* (1999) contains essays on Hawthorne and Freeman as well as Stowe, Rebecca Harding Davis, Jewett, Gilman, and other nineteenth- and early-twentieth-century women writers. Abigail Ann Hamblen's *The New England Art of Mary E. Wilkins Freeman* (1966) delivers what its title promises. The introduction to Judith Fetterley and Marjorie Pryse's anthology *American Women Regionalists: 1850–1910* (1992) helpfully contextualizes Freeman's fiction. In 1999 a special Mary E. Wilkins Freeman issue of *American Transcendental Quarterly* was guest-edited by Shirley Marchalonis and contains essays by Charles Johanningsmeier, Gregg Camfield, William J. Scheick and other leading scholars. Johanningsmeier is also the author of the excellent essay "Sarah Orne Jewett and Mary E. Wilkins (Freeman): Two Shrewd Businesswomen in Search of New Markets," *New England Quarterly* (1997).

Charlotte Perkins Gilman
No collected edition of Gilman's writings exists, but the intense interest in her work has resulted in several reprints of such key titles as *The Living of Charlotte Perkins Gilman: An Autobiography* (1975); *Women and Economics* (1966), edited by Carl Degler; *Women and Economics: A Study of the Economic Relation Between Men and Women as a Factor in Social Evolution*, ed. Michael Kimmel (1998); *Herland* (1979), edited by Ann J. Lane; *The Charlotte Perkins Gilman Reader* (1980), edited by Ann J. Lane; *Herland and Selected Stories by Charlotte Perkins Gilman* (1992), edited by Barbara Solomon. Lane's full-scale critical biography, *To Herland and Beyond: The Life and Work of Charlotte Perkins Gilman* (1990), is now standard. Mary A. Hill's *Charlotte Perkins Gilman: The Making of a Radical Feminist* (1980) and her *Endure: The Diaries of Charles Walter Stetson* (1985) illuminate Gilman's early years. Hill also edited *A Journey From Within: The Love Letters of Charlotte Perkins Gilman, 1897–1900* (1995). Denise D. Knight edited the two-volume *The Diaries of Charlotte Perkins Gilman* (1994). An interesting biographical find is presented in " 'All the Facts of the Case': Gilman's Lost Letter to Dr. S. Weir Mitchell," Denise D. Knight, *American Literary Realism* (2005).

Critical books worthy of note include the Twayne volume *Charlotte Perkins Gilman: A Study of the Short Fiction*, by Denise D. Knight

(1997); Gary Scharnhorst's *Charlotte Perkins Gilman* (1985), Polly Wynn Allen's *Building Domestic Liberty: Charlotte Perkins Gilman's Architectural Feminism* (1988), Sheryl L. Meyering's *Charlotte Perkins Gilman: The Woman and Her Work* (1989), and Denise Knight's *Charlotte Perkins Gilman: A Study of the Short Fiction* (1997). Carol Farley Kessler's *Charlotte Perkins Gilman: Her Progress Toward Utopia with Selected Writings* (1994) reprints fourteen selections form Gilman's utopian writings. A useful companion volume, *Charlotte Perkins Gilman: Optimist Reformer* (1999), brings together essays, many of which address Gilman's reformist impulses as well as blind spots in her thinking. Cynthia J. Davis and Knight have edited *Charlotte Perkins Gilman and Her Contemporaries: Literary and Intellectual Contexts* (2004). Joanne B. Karpinski edited *Critical Essays on Charlotte Perkins Gilman* (1992). An interesting comparative study is *Kate Chopin, Edith Wharton and Charlotte Perkins Gilman: Studies in Short Fiction* by Janet Beer (2005). *Charlotte Perkins Gilman: Optimist Reformer* (1999), ed. Jill Rudd and Val Gough, offers thirteen original essays focused on such difficult issues as Gilman's racism, class consciousness, and essentialist view of women. *Raising the Dust: The Literary Housekeeping of Mary Ward, Sarah Grand, and Charlotte Perkins Gilman* by Beth Sutton-Ramspeck (2004) and *Wayward Reproductions: Genealogies of Race and Nation in Transatlantic Modern Thought*, Alys Eve Weinbaum (2004) devote considerable space to Gilman.

Thomas L. Erskine and Conee L. Richards edited and introduced *"The Yellow Wallpaper" Charlotte Perkins Gilman* (1993). Catherine Golden edited *The Captive Imagination: A Casebook on "The Yellow Wallpaper"* (1991). Julie Bates Dock's *The Legend of "The Yellow Wallpaper": A Documentary Casebook* (1998) and *Charlotte Perkins Gilman's "the Yellow Wall-Paper" and the History of Its Publication and Reception: A Critical Edition and Documentary Casebook* (1998) established for the first time a reliable critical edition and publication history for this celebrated story and supplies a rich set of contextualizing documents illuminating the genesis, compositional and publication histories of the text as well as more than a score of contemporary reviews and other commentary. Dock's " 'But One Expects That': Charlotte Perkins Gilman's 'The Yellow Wallpaper' and the Shifting Light of Scholarship," *PMLA* (January 1996), should also be consulted. Also useful are *"The Yellow Wall-Paper" by Charlotte Perkins Gilman : A Dual-Textbook Critical Edition*, ed. Shawn St. Jean(2006); *The Pedagogical Wallpaper: Teaching Charlotte Perkins Gilman's 'The Yellow Wallpaper,' "* ed. Jeffrey Andrew Weinstock (2003), consisting of ten essays; *Approaches to Teaching Gilman's "The Yellow*

Wall-paper," and Herland, ed. Denise D. Knight and Cynthia J. Davis (2003); and *The Mixed Legacy of Charlotte Perkins Gilman*, ed. Catherine J. Golden and Joanna Schneider Zangrando, with fourteen essays on Gilman's life and career and especially "The Yellow Wall-Paper" (2000). Every year dozens of new essays on "The Yellow Wall-Paper" appear in academic journals.

Bret Harte

The most complete collection is *The Works of Bret Harte* in twenty-five volumes (1914). Harte's poetry may be found in *The Complete Poetical Works of Bret Harte* (1899). Charles Meeker Kozlay edited *Stories and Poems and Other Uncollected Writings* available in the Argonaut edition (1906). Geoffrey Bret Harte edited *The Letters of Bret Harte* (1926). Joseph B. Harrison edited *Bret Harte: Representative Selections* (1941). Gary Scharnhorst edited and introduced *Bret Harte's California* (1990). *Selected Letters of Bret Harte* appeared in 1997 edited by Scharnhorst and Robert L. Gale. Much editorial work remains to be done.

Gary Scharnhorst's fine critical biography *Bret Harte: Opening the American Literary West* (2000) elegantly furnishes analysis of the life, career, and reception of Harte, with the focus on Harte's writing life, joining his Twayne volume *Bret Harte* of 1992. (Also see: Scharnhorst, "A Coda to the Twain-Harte Feud," *Western American Literature* [2001].) Focusing on Harte's financial struggles, Axel Nissen's *Bret Harte: Prince and Pauper* (2000) provides a lively account of Harte's life and times. Patrick Morrow's *Bret Harte: Literary Critic* (1979) is a judicious account of Harte's sometimes injudicious criticism. Morrow's *Bret Harte* (1972) in the Boise College Western Writers Series provides an adequate brief introduction to the man and his work. The best single bibliography on Harte is Gary Scharnhorst's *Bret Harte: A Bibliography* (1995); Linda D. Barnett's *Bret Harte: A Reference Guide* (1980) is the best guide to writings about Harte.

Queer theorists and Gender Studies critics have recently taken up Harte's characters; see *Queer Cowboys and Other Erotic Male Friendships in Nineteenth-Century American Literature* by Packard, Chris (2005), which includes essays on James Fenimore Cooper, Walt Whitman, Harris, Twain, Harte, and Eugene Field; "The Queer Short Story," Axel Nissen, in *The Art of Brevity: Excursions in Short Fiction Theory and Analysis* (2004), ed. Per Winther, Jakob Lothe, and Hans H. Skei; "Rewriting the Gold Rush: Twain, Harte and Homosociality," Peter Stoneley, *Journal of American Studies* (1996); and " 'She War a Woman': Family Roles, Gender, and Sexuality in Bret Harte's Western Fiction," J. David Stevens, *American Literature* (1997).

Pauline E. Hopkins

Editions of Hopkins's works include *Daughter of the Revolution: The Major Nonfiction Works of Pauline E. Hopkins*, ed. Ira Dworkin (2006); *The Magazine Novels of Pauline Hopkins: (Including Hagar's Daughter, Winona, and Of One Blood)* from The Schomburg Library of Nineteenth-Century Black Women Writers, ed. Hazel V. Carby (1990); *Contending Forces: A Romance Illustrative of Negro Life North and South* from The Schomburg Library of Nineteenth-Century Black Women Writers, ed. Richard Yarborough, 1991; and *Of One Blood: Or, the Hidden Self*: by Pauline Hopkins, ed. Deborah McDowell (2004). Hanna Wallinger's *Pauline E. Hopkins: A Literary Biography* (2005) and Carol Allen's *Black Women Intellectuals: Strategies of Nation, Family, and Neighborhood in the Works of Pauline Hopkins, Jessie Fauset, and Marita Bonner* (1998) have supplied much-needed reliable resources. John Cullen Gruesser has edited *The Unruly Voice: Rediscovering Pauline Elizabeth Hopkins* (1996). *Feminist Forerunners: Womanism and Feminism in the Early Twentieth Century*, edited by Ann Heilmann (2003), contains Sabina Matter-Seibel's "Pauline Hopkins's Portrayal of the African-American New Woman in *Contending Forces* and the *Colored American* Magazine"; Jill Berger's " 'A New Race of Colored Women': Pauline Hopkins at the *Colored American* Magazine"; and "Rape, Lynching, and *Contending Forces*: Pauline Hopkins—Forerunner of Critical Race Theorists" by Patricia D. Watkins.

Henry James

The Novels and Tales of Henry James (The New York Edition) in twenty-six volumes, originally published in 1907–17, was reissued 1962–65. Other collections of James's diverse writings are available in Leon Edel's edition of *The Complete Plays of Henry James* (1949), R. P. Blackmur's *The Art of the Novel* (1935), Morris Shapiro's edition of *Selected Literary Criticism* (1963), Morton D. Zabel's edition of James's travel writings, *The Art of Travel* (1958), F. O. Matthiessen and Kenneth B. Murdoch's *The Notebooks of Henry James* (1947), F. W. Dupee's edition of the three volumes of *Henry James: Autobiography* (1956), and in various collections of essays and letters edited by Leon Edel. Multiple volumes of James's novels, short stories, and literary essays are contained in the Library of America series, for example *Complete Stories* (1999); *Henry James: Major Stories and Essays*, both edited by Leon Edel (1999). *The Portable Henry James* is edited by John Auchard (2003). Edel is also the editor of the five-volume *The Letters of Henry James*. Philip Horne has published *Henry James: A Life in Letters* (1999), with half of the nearly 300 selections previously unpublished; Susan E. Gunter

and Steven H. Jobe have edited *Dearly Beloved Friends: Henry James's Letters to Younger Men* (2001), which contains 166 letters, 95 previously unpublished. *The Complete Letters of Henry James, 1855–1872* is edited by Pierre A. Walker and Greg W. Zacharias (2006), the first volume of a proposed set. *The Notebooks of Henry James* edited by F. O. Matthiessen and Kenneth B. Murdock (1981) and *A Bibliography of Henry James* (1999) by Leon Edel, Dan H. Laurence, and James Rambeau round out the reference section.

Henry James: The Imagination of Genius, A Biography, by Fred Kaplan (1999) relies almost exclusively on the letters and diaries of James and his associates to convey both James's spirit and the background for his work. Though not as all-encompassing as Leon Edel's five-volume opus (*Henry James* [1953–72]), this volume is a highly recommended one-volume companion to the biographical study *The Jameses* by R. W. B. Lewis (1993). F. O. Matthiessen's classic *The James Family* (1947) also reveals Henry's relationship to this extraordinary American family, which included his brother, William, the celebrated psychologist and philosopher, and sister, Alice, whose diary has attracted considerable attention since its publication in 1964. Other biographical studies suggest that James and his remarkable family continue to fascinate scholars: Edwin Sill Fussell's *The Catholic Side of Henry James* (1993), Kenneth Graham's engaging *Henry James: A Literary Life* (1995), and Carol Holly's *Intensely Family: The Inheritance of Family Shame and the Autobiographies of Henry James* (1995), and Lyndall Gordon's *A Private Life of Henry James: Two Women and His Art* (1999), which looks freshly at James's relationships with his cousin Minny Temple and Constance Fenimore Woolson.

Since the 1940s, critical studies of James have abounded. Among the best of these, in chronological order, are Ruth Bernard Yeazell's *Language and Knowledge in the Late Novels of Henry James* (1976), Charles Robert Anderson's *Person, Place, and Thing in Henry James's Novels* (1977), Strother Purdy's *The Hole in the Fabric: Science, Contemporary Literature, and Henry James* (1977), Shlomith Rummon's *The Concept of Ambiguity: The Example of James* (1977), Sergio Perosa's *Henry James and the Experimental Novel* (1978), Daniel J. Schneider's *The Crystal Cage: Adventures of the Imagination in the Fiction of Henry James* (1978), Mary Doyle Springer's *A Rhetoric of Literary Character: Some Women of Henry James* (1978), Edward Wagenknecht's *Eve and Henry James: Portraits of Women and Girls in His Fiction* (1978), Nicola Bradbury's *Henry James: The Later Novels* (1979), Susanne Kappeler's *Writing and Reading in Henry James* (1980), Philip Sicker's *Love and the Quest for Identity in the Fiction of Henry James* (1980), Alwyn

Buland's *Culture and Conduct in the Novels of Henry James* (1981), Sarah B. Daugherty's *The Literary Criticism of Henry James* (1981), Daniel Mark Fogel's *Henry James and the Structure of the Romantic Imagination* (1981), William W. Stowe's *Balzac, James, and the Realistic Novel* (1983), John Carlos Rowe's *The Theoretical Dimensions of Henry James* (1984), Edward Wagenknecht's *The Novels of Henry James* (1983) and *The Tales of Henry James* (1984), Sharon Cameron's *Thinking in Henry James* (1989), Alfred Habegger's *Henry James and the "Woman Business"* (1989), Sarah S. Chapman's *Henry James's Portrait of the Writer as Hero* (1989), Philip Horne's *Henry James and Revision* (1990), Edwin S. Fussell's *The French Side of Henry James* (1990), Richard A. Hocks's *Henry James: A Study of the Short Fiction* (1990), Millicent Bell's *Meaning in Henry James* (1991), Susan M. Griffin's *The Historical Eye: The Texture of the Visual in Late James* (1991), Ross Posnock's *The Trial of Curiosity: Henry James, William James, and the Challeneg of Modernity* (1991), Adeline R. Tintner's *The Cosmopolitan World of Henry James: An Intertextual Study* (1991), Jeanne Campbell Reesman's philosophical and narratological study *Interest and Design: The Late Novels of James and Faulkner* (1991); Dietmar Schloss's *Culture and Criticism in Henry James* (1992), Priscilla L. Walton's *The Disruption of the Feminine in Henry James* (1992), Greg W. Zacharias's *Henry James and Morality of Fiction* (1993), Daniel Mark Fogel's edited *A Companion to Henry James Studies* (1993), Tony Tanner's *Henry James and the Art of Nonfiction* (1995), Sheila Teahan's *The Rhetorical Logic of Henry James* (1995), Eli Ben-Joseph's *Aesthetic Persuasion: Henry James, the Jews, and Race* (1996), John H. Pearson's *The Prefaces of Henry James: Framing the Modern Reader* (1997), Collin Meissner's *Henry James and the Language of Experience* (1999), Wendy Graham's *Henry James's Thwarted Love* (1999), Willie Tolliver's *A Self Among Others: Henry James as a Biographer* (2000), Robert B. Pippin's *Henry James and Modern Moral Life* (2000), Denis Flannery's *Henry James: A Certain Illusion* (2000), Jerry Tambling's *Henry James* (2000), Christopher Greenwood's *Adapting to the Stage: Theater and the Work of Henry James* (2000), Marc McGurl's *The Novel Art: Elevations of American Fiction After Henry James* (2001), Clair Hughes's *Henry James and the Art of Dress* (2001), Donatella Izzo's *Portraying the Lady: Technologies of Gender in the Short Stories of Henry James* (2001), S. Selina Jamil's *Jamesian Centers of Consciousness as Readers and Tellers of Stories* (2001), Tessa Hadley's *Henry James and the Imagination of Pleasure* (2002), James Duban, *The Nature of True Virtue: Theology, Psychology, and Politics*

in the Writings of Henry James, Sr., Henry James, Jr., and William James (2001), Clair Hughes's *Henry James and the Art of Dress* (2001), Eric Haralson's *Henry James and Queer Modernity* (2003), Leland Person's *Henry James and the Suspense of Masculinity* (2003), Rob Davidson's *The Master and the Dean: The Literary Criticism of Henry James and William Dean Howells* (2005), and J. Hillis Miller's *Literature As Conduct: Speech Acts in Henry James* (2005).

John R. Bradley edited *Henry James on Stage and Screen* (2000) and Susan M. Griffin edited *Henry James Goes to the Movies* (2001). *The Novel Art: Elevations of American Fiction after Henry James,* by Mark McGurl (2001) examines the influence of James on Crane, Howells, Wharton, O. Henry, John Dos Passos, Anita Loos, Gertrude Stein, William Faulkner, and Dashiell Hammett. An excellent pedagogical handbook is *Approaches to Teaching Henry James's* Daisy Miller *and* The Turn of the Screw, ed. Kimberly Capps Reed and Peter G. Beidler (2005).

There is no shortage of collections of criticism: Graham Clark edited *Henry James: Critical Assessment* (1991), Kevin J. Hayes edited *Henry James: The Contemporary Reviews* (1996), Peter Rawlings edited *Critical Essays on Henry James* (1993), and Joseph Dewey edited *The Finer Thread, The Tighter Weave: New Essays on the Short Fiction* (2001). Judith E. Funston compiled a very helpful guide to book and periodical publications in *Henry James: A Reference Guide, 1975–1987* (1991). Pierre A. Walker edited *Henry James on Culture: Collected Essays on Politics and the American Social Scene* (1999). *Questioning the Master: Gender and Sexuality in Henry James's Writings, 2000,* edited by Peggy McCormack, is a collection of nine previously published essays suggesting the need for dialogue between feminists and queer theorists. Adeline R. Tintner has published the fifth volume in her series of contextual studies, *The Twentieth-Century World of Henry James: Changes in His Work after 1900* (2000).

Sarah Orne Jewett

There is no collected edition of Jewett's writings. Jewett's *Stories and Tales* were published in seven volumes in 1910; but a more readily available collection, *The Best Stories of Sarah Orne Jewett* (1925), was edited in two volumes with a foreword by Willa Cather. Richard Cary edited *The Uncollected Short Stories of Sarah Orne Jewett* (1971). Cary also edited *Sarah Orne Jewett Letters* (1967). The Library of America's edition of Jewett's *Novels and Stories* (1994), selected and with notes by Michael Davitt Bell, provides three novels and some thirty stories and is available in paperback.

An informative, feminist life of Jewett by an

eminent biographer, *Sarah Orne Jewett: Her World and Her Work* by Paula Blanchard (2002) has drawn generated attention to Jewett's complexities. A good introductory study is Josephine Donovan's *Sarah Orne Jewett* (1980). More recently, Perry D. Westbrook's *Acres of Flint: Sarah Orne Jewett and Her Contemporaries* (1981), Louis A. Renza's "*A White Heron*" and *The Question of Minor Literature* and Sarah Way Sherman's *Sarah Orne Jewett: An American Persephone* (1989) have clarified and complicated our understanding of Jewett as have Marilyn Sanders Mobley's *Folk Roots and Mythic Wings in Sarah Orne Jewett and Toni Morrison: The Cultural Functions of Narrative* (1991), Joseph Church's *Transcendent Daughters in Jewett's Country of the Pointed Firs* (1995), and Margaret Roman's *Sarah Orne Jewett: Reconstructing Gender* (1997). Karen L. Kilcup and Thomas S. Edwards edited *Jewett and Her Contemporaries: Reshaping the Canon* (1999), fourteen essays on Jewett, nineteenth-century women's writing and new canon formation. *A Sarah Orne Jewett Companion*, edited by Robert L. Gale (1999) is of hellp, and the comparative study *Conscience and Purpose: Fiction and Social Consciousness in Howells, Jewett, Chesnutt, and Cather* by Paul R. Petrie (2005) supplies comparisons and contexts. Gwen L. Nagel's still-useful *Critical Essays on Sarah Orne Jewett* (1984) offers a rich selection of material. An intriguing recent reading of "A White Heron" is "Romantic Flight in Jewett's 'White Heron'" by Joseph Church, *Studies in American Fiction* (2002).

Emma Lazarus

Lazarus's sisters Mary and Annie edited the two-volume *The Poems of Emma Lazarus* (1888); the first volume contains the biographical sketch they wrote for *Century Magazine*. In 1939 Ralph L. Rusk edited Letters to Emma Lazarus in the Columbia University Library, mainly from American and British writers. Morris U. Schappes edited The Letters of Emma Lazarus, 1868–1885 (1949) and Emma Lazarus: Selections from Her Poetry and Prose (1967). Newer editions include the Library of America volume *Emma Lazarus: Selected Poems*, edited by John Hollander, and *Emma Lazarus: In Her World* (1995), edited by Bette Roth-Young, an annotated collection of unpublished letters to friends and literary figures that seeks to dispel myths about Lazarus, some propagated by her sisters. Still the best biography is Daniel Vogel's *Emma Lazarus* (1980), especially in its treatment of neglected works.

Among critical works, Diane Lichtenstein's "Word and Worlds: Emma Lazarus's Conflicting Citizenships" *TWSL*, (1987) examines how Lazarus negotiates American and Jewish womanhood in an attempt to reconcile her multiple citizenships. Carole Kessner's "The Emma Lazarus-Henry James Connection: Eight Letters," *AmLH* (1991) demonstrates James' sympathies towards Jews from his own class vs. his antipathy toward recent émigrés. Max Cavitch's "Emma Lazarus and the Golem of Liberty," *American Literary History* (2006) is a recent rereading. Other important essays include "Emotion and the Jewish Historical Poems of Emma Lazarus" by Gregory Eiselein, Gregory, *Mosaic* (2004); Ranen Omer-Sherman's "Emma Lazarus, Jewish American Poetics, and the Challenge of Modernity," *Legacy: A Journal of American Women Writers* (2002); "Who Is the 'Mother of Exiles'? Jewish Aspects of Emma Lazarus's 'The New Colossus,'" by Daniel Marom, *Prooftexts: A Journal of Jewish Literary History* (2000); and "Words and Worlds: Emma Lazarus's Conflicting Citizenships," by Lichtenstein, *Tulsa Studies in Women's Literature* (1987). There is a fine web site on Lazarus maintained by the Jewish Women's Archive.

Jack London

Though there are complete works of London's fifty-some books published in several foreign countries, including Japan, the Czech Republic, and France, there is none published in the United States. The rare (and incomplete) Sonoma edition (1928) printed twenty-eight titles in twenty-one volumes; the British Fitzroy *Works* reprinted twenty titles in the 1960s; and the Bodley Head Jack London half a dozen titles. Fortunately, London's enduring popularity ensures that his novels, short stories, dramas, and nonfiction are continually reprinted—a phenomenon both at home and abroad, as his millions of hits on Google.com attest. The two most significant current editions of London's writings for scholars and students are the three-volume *Letters of Jack London* (1988) and three-volume *The Complete Short Stories of Jack London* (1993), both edited by Earle Labor, Robert C. Leitz III, and I. Milo Shepard, published by Stanford University Press with major support from the National Endowment for the Humanities. Other handy editions of material otherwise difficult to track down are *Jack London Reports* (essays and newspaper articles), edited by King Hendricks and Irving Shepard (1970); *No Mentor But Myself: Jack London on Writers and Writing*, ed. Dale L. Walker and Jeanne Campbell Reesman (1999); *Jack London: Novels and Stories : Call of the Wild / White Fang / The Sea-Wolf / Klondike and Other Stories* and *Jack London : Novels and Social Writings*, the Library of America edition (1982), edited by Donald Pizer; and *The Portable Jack London*, edited by Earle Labor (1994), featuring a splendid introduction. London's most famous work is represented by several excellent teaching editions, including The Call of the Wild, *by Jack London, with an Illustrated Reader's Companion*, ed.

Daniel Dyer (1995), and *The Call of the Wild* by Jack London, ed. Earl J. Wilcox and Elizabeth Wilcox (2003). Philip Foner's *Jack London: American Rebel—A Collection of His Social Writings Together with an Extensive Study of the Man and His Times* first appeared in 1947 and was reprinted as *The Social Writings of Jack London* in 1964. David Mike Hamilton's *"Tools of My Trade": The Annotated Books in Jack London's Library* (1986) is an outstanding source for London's thinking and artistic sources. Bibliographical work on London has languished since Joan Sherman's *Jack London: A Reference Guide* (1977) and Hensley C. Woodbridge, John London, and George H. Tweney's *Jack London: A Bibliography* (1966). The now-defunct *Jack London Newsletter*, edited by Woodbridge, and the ongoing magazine *The Call* from the Jack London Society, now edited by Kenneth K. Brandt, have occasionally published bibliographical updates.

London scholars and fans have eagerly awaited acknowledged leading expert Earle Labor's definitive biography, *Jack London: A Life* (2008). In the meantime, Russ Kingman's two volumes, *Jack London: A Definitive Chronology* (1992) and the biography *A Pictorial Life of Jack London* (1979) have been sources factually reliable if sometimes presented in a tone overly admiring of London. In his *Jack: A Biography of Jack London* (1977), Andrew Sinclair followed in the fictionalizing footsteps of Irving Stone in *Sailor on Horseback* (1938), copying the idea of London as a suicide from Stone's now-discredited notions about London's death. One of London's earliest biographers was his daughter Joan London, in *Jack London and His Times* (1939; rpt. 1968). Clarice Stasz's *American Dreamers: Charmian and Jack London* (1988) and *Jack London's Women* (2001) explore his relationships with important women in his life.

Critical books and collections of essays include Franklin Walker's *Jack London and the Klondike: The Genesis of an American Writer* (1966; rpt. 2005); James McClintock's *White Logic: Jack London's Short Stories* (1975; rpt. 1997 as *Jack London's Strong Truths: A Study of the Short Stories*); Jacqueline Tavernier-Courbin, ed., *Critical Essays on Jack London* (1983); Charles N. Watson Jr.'s *The Novels of Jack London: A Reappraisal* (1983); Carolyn Johnston's *Jack London—An American Radical?* (1984); Earle Labor and Jeanne Campbell Reesman's *Jack London: Revised Edition* (1994) a Twayne volume that expands and updates Labor's original 1974 study with its effective combination of biography and criticism, is the best introduction to London; Jacqueline Tavernier-Courbin's *The Call of the Wild: A Naturalistic Romance* (1994); Susan Nuernberg's collection *The Critical Response to Jack London* (1995), which challenges the conventional wisdom of American critics by contrasting it to the more favorable evaluation of London internationally; *Rereading Jack London*, ed. Leonard Cassuto and Jeanne Campbell Reesman (1996); Jonathan Auerbach's *Male Call: Becoming Jack London* (1996); Reesman's *Jack London: A Study of the Short Fiction* (1998); *Jack London: One Hundred Years a Writer*, ed. Sara S. Hodson and Reesman (2002).

International conferences and exhibits, essays in scholarly journals, critical books, reprinted editions, web sites, teaching handbooks, studies of London as a photographer, and many other areas of London's work continue to appear each year.

Mark Twain
The Writings of Mark Twain (1922–25), thirty-seven volumes, edited by Albert Bigelow Paine, is being superseded by the ongoing editions of *The Mark Twain Papers and Project* (1967–) at the University of California Press under the leadership of Robert Hirst. *The Mark Twain Papers* series publishes scholarly editions of previously unpublished notebooks, journals, letters, and literary manuscripts; *The Works of Mark Twain* publishes scholarly editions of previously published works; *The Mark Twain Library* consists of popularly priced editions with explanatory notes and illustrations; *Jumping Frogs: Undiscovered, Rediscovered, and Celebrated Writings of Mark Twain* has so far published *Is He Dead? A Comedy in Three Acts* and *Mark Twain's Helpful Hints for Good Living: A Handbook for the Damned Human Race*. *The Mark Twain Digital* Project makes available an electronic edition of Twain's letters 1876–1880. Six volumes of letters (through 1871) have appeared so far in the *Papers*, and other Twain letters are available in several scattered volumes, the most interesting of which is *The Correspondence of Samuel L. Clemens and William Dean Howells, 1872–1910* (1960), edited by Henry Nash Smith and William M. Gibson. Altogether some forty volumes have appeared as part of the Mark Twain Papers and Project. The Library of America has issued in two volumes *Mark Twain: Collected Tales, Sketches, Speeches and Essays* (1992) with notes by Louis Budd. A companion volume, with notes by Susan K. Harris, *Mark Twain: Historical Romances, The Prince and the Pauper, A Connecticut Yankee in King Arthur's Court, Personal Recollections of Joan of Arc* followed in 1993. Tom Quirk edited a fine selection of *Mark Twain: Tales, Speeches, Essays and Sketches* (1993). Marlene Boyd Vallen's *Mark Twain: Propagandist for the Popular Culture* (1992) collects sixteen speeches and commentary. Louis J. Budd's *Mark Twain: The Contemporary Reviews* (1999) gives us over six hundred pages of early reviews, from 1867–1817.

Most controversial of new editions of Twain's best-known book the Mark Twain Project edition (2001) which calls itself "The Only Comprehensive Edition" of *Adventures of Huckleberry Finn*; it is edited by ed. Victor Fischer and Lin Salamo and dedicated to Walter Blair, leading scholar of the 1985 Mark Twain Project edition of the novel, who died in 1992. It contains 1164 pages with original drawings by E. W. Kemble and John Harley, but its greatest claim to fame is its use of the first half of *Huckleberry Finn* manuscript discovered in a Hollywood attic in 1990. The editors collated over 1,100 changes in spelling, punctuation, and other details and one hundred changes in wording, adding Jim's ghost story and chapter 16, "The Raftsmens' Passage," both previously left out. *Adventures of Huckleberry Finn*, New Riverside Editions, gen. ed. Paul Lauter, ed. Susan K. Harris (2005), includes the raftsmen's passage and critical essays by Victor Doyno, Shelley Fisher Fishkin, Norman Mailer, and Toni Morrison. Other new editions or publications include Twain's previously unpublished story, "A Murder, A Mystery, and a Marriage," unpublished Twain story, introduced by Roy Blount, Jr., *Atlantic Monthly* (2001); *The Best Short Stories of Mark Twain*, edited by Lawrence I. Berkove (2004); and *The Portable Mark Twain* edited by Tom Quirk (2004). A new journal, the *Mark Twain Annual*, was founded by the Mark Twain Circle in 2003; its 2005 issue featured a Special Section on *Adventures of Huckleberry Finn*. Tom Tenney supplies ongoing bibliographical updates in *American Literary Realism* and in the *Mark Twain Circular*, updating his 1977 *Mark Twain: A Reference Guide*. *A Companion to Mark Twain*, ed. Peter Messent and Louis Budd, (2005); an expansion of the 1981 *The Annotated* Huckleberry Finn, ed. Michael Patrick Hearn (2001); David E. E. Sloane's *Student Companion to Mark Twain* (2001); *Making Mark Twain Work in the Classroom*, ed. James M. Leonard (1999), which covers challenges that confront instructors, especially slavery, women's roles, and religious satire; and *Mark Twain A to Z: The Essential Reference to His Life and Writings* by R. Kent Rasmussen (2006), which offers nearly 1,300 entries devoted primarily to proper names relating to Twain, round out the reference and teaching shelf.

Albert Bigelow Paine's *Mark Twain, a Biography* (1912) is vivid, unreliable, and still indispensable. Justin Kaplan's *Mr. Clemens and Mark Twain, a Biography* (1966) is a lively, popular account. Van Wyck Brooks's polemical and controversial *The Ordeal of Mark Twain* (1920) should be read together with Bernard De Voto's corrective *Mark Twain's America* (1932). De Lancey Ferguson's *Mark Twain: Man and Legend* (1943) is a fine full-length critical biography, as is Everett Emerson's *Mark Twain: A Literary Life* (2000), an expanded and updated version of his earlier *The Authentic Mark Twain: A Literary Biography of Samuel L. Clemens* (1984), a trusted guide to Twain's literary life. Jeffrey Steinbrink's *Getting to Be Mark Twain* (1991) examines the period 1868–71.

Mark Twain: A Life by Ron Powers (2005) gives us another biography; Powers, who wrote about Twain's Missouri childhood in *Dangerous Water: A Biography of the Boy Who Became Mark Twain* (2001) aims to define Twain as a "representative man" of his times and offer a full portrait of Twain in his many roles and phases of life. In *The Singular Mark Twain: A Biography* (2005), Fred Kaplan attempts something quite different. Kaplan sees Twain, in contrast to many biographers such as Justin Kaplan, as a singular personality (not multiple or divided), his two names indicating no deep internal division of identity. Twain's contradictions are those of any fine mind. Jason Gary Horn attempts to sort out all the current biographies in *Mark Twain: A Descriptive Guide to Biographical Sources* (1999).

Criticism on Twain is enormous in quantity, variety, and quality. Two excellent general studies are Henry Nash Smith's *Mark Twain: The Development of a Writer* (1962) and William M. Gibson's *The Art of Mark Twain* (1976). James M. Cox's perceptive *Mark Twain: The Fate of Humor* (1966), Edgar M. Branch's *The Literary Apprenticeship of Mark Twain* (1950), and Albert E. Stone's *The Innocent Eye: Childhood in Mark Twain's Imagination* (1961) are distinguished early contributions to serious Twain scholarship. More recent studies of permanent interest include Louis J. Budd's *Our Mark Twain: The Making of His Public Personality* (1983), James L. Johnson's *Mark Twain and the Limits of Power: Emerson's God in Ruins* (1982), Sherwood Cummings's excellent *Mark Twain and Science: Adventures of a Mind* (1989), Susan Gillman's *Dark Twins: Imposture and Identity in Mark Twain's America* (1991), Maria Ornella Marotti's *The Duplicating Imagination: Twain and the Twain Papers* (1991), and David E. E. Sloane's *Mark Twain as a Literary Comedian* (1979). Carl Dolmetsch's *Our Famous Guest: Mark Twain in Vienna* (1992) argues against the conventional wisdom concerning the decline of Twain's creativity after the mid-1890s. The title of Shelley Fisher Fishkin's *Was Huck Black?: Mark Twain and African-American Voices* (1993) suggests its interesting argument that Twain's model for Huck was a young black friend of his. Fishkin's *Lighting Out for the Territory: Reflections on Mark Twain and American Culture* (1996) raises fascinating questions about race and the way Twain's writing personas have been appropriated and misappropriated by popular culture. Several volumes take a fresh look at

Twain's humor: Don Florence, *Persona and Humor in Mark Twain's Early Writings* (1995); Stuart Hutchison, *Mark Twain: Humor on the Run* (1994); Patricia M. Mandia, *Comedic Pathos: Black Humor in Twain's Fiction* (1991); Bruce Michelson, *Mark Twain on the Loose: A Comic Writer and the American Self* (1995); and *Mark Twain's Humor: Critical Essays* (1992), edited by David E. E. Sloane. Several books address Twain's attitudes toward women—in and out of his writings: Laura E. Skandera-Trombley's *Mark Twain in the Company of Women* (1994), J. D. Stahl's *Mark Twain, Culture and Gender: Envisioning America Through Europe* (1993), Peter Stoneley's *Mark Twain and the Feminine Aesthetic* (1992), and Resa Willis's *Mark and Livy: The Love Story of Mark Twain and the Woman Who Almost Tamed Him* (1992). Other studies of note include Gregg Camfield's *Sentimental Twain: Samuel Clemens in the Maze of Moral Philosophy* (1994), Guy Cardwell's *The Man Who Was Mark Twain: Images and Ideologies* (1991), Randall Knoper's *Acting Naturally: Mark Twain in the Culture of Performance* (1995), and David R. Sewell's *Mark Twain's Languages: Discourse, Dialogue, and Linguistic Variety* (1987). Among the many collections of criticism, Robert Sattlemeyer and J. Donald Crowley's *One Hundred Years of "Huckleberry Finn": The Boy, His Book, and American Culture* (1985) merits special notice. Victor Doyno's painstaking study *Writing "Huck Finn": Mark Twain's Creative Process* (1991) will soon be revised to incorporate the discovery of the first half of the *Huckleberry Finn* manuscript.

More recent critical studies have included Hilton Obenzinger's *American Palestine: Melville, Twain, and the Holy Land Mania* (1999); *Black, White, and Huckleberry Finn: Reimagining the the American Dream* by Elaine Mensh and Harry Mensh (2000); *Refiguring Huckleberry Finn*, Carl F. Wieck (2000); Peter Messent's *The Short Works of Mark Twain: A Critical Study* (2001); the sequel to *Mark Twain and His Illustrators*, vol. 1 (1869–1875), by Beverly R. David, vol. 2, *Mark Twain and His Illustrators*, (1875–1883), which appeared in 2001; Louis J. Budd's 1962 *Mark Twain: Social Philosopher*, reprinted (2001) in the Mark Twain and His Circle Series edited by Tom Quirk; *Searching for Jim: Slavery in Sam Clemens's World* by Terrell Dempsey (2003); *Mark Twain: A Short Introduction* by Stephen Railton (2003); Joseph L. Coulombe, *Mark Twain and the American West* (2003); *Mark Twain and Company: Six Literary Relations* by Leland Krauth (2003), which covers Twain's relationships with William Dean Howells, Robert Louis Stevenson, Rudyard Kipling, Bret Harte, Harriett Beecher Stowe, and Matthew Arnold; and *Mark Twain in Paradise: His Voyages to Bermuda*, Donald Hoffmann (2006).

Among the several recent collections of criticism the following warrant attention: James S. Leonard, Thomas A. Tenney and Thadious M. Davis's edited *Satire or Evasion?: Black Perspectives on Huckleberry Finn* (1996), Tom Quirk's *Coming to Grips with Huckleberry Finn: Essays on a Book, a Boy, and a Man* (1992), Eric J. Sundquist's *Mark Twain: A Collection of Critical Essays* (1994), Laurie Champion's *The Critical Response to Mark Twain's Huckleberry Finn* (1991), Forrest G. Robinson's *The Cambridge Companion to Mark Twain* (1995), Laura Skandera-Trombley and Michael J. Kiskis's *Constructing Mark Twain: New Directions in Scholarship* (2001), containing thirteen essays saluting Hamlin Hill's 1974 challenge to scholars, "Who Killed Mark Twain?" J. R. Le Master and James Wilson edited *The Mark Twain Encyclopedia* (1992), with 180 contributors and 740 entries. R. Kent Rasmussen's claim in the title of his *Mark Twain A-Z: The Essential Reference to His Life and Writings* (1996) is justified by its 1,300 factual entries.

Booker T. Washington

Louis R. Harlan has edited *The Booker T. Washington Papers* in fourteen volumes (1972–89). William L. Andrews has edited a Norton Critical Edition of *Up From Slavery* (1996). August Meier's *Negro Thought in America, 1880–1915* (1963) and John Hope Franklin's *From Slavery to Freedom: A History of American Negroes* (1967) are two early and still useful background books. The standard critical biography is by Louis R. Harlan: *Booker T. Washington: The Making of a Black Leader, 1865–1901* (1972) and *Booker T. Washington: The Wizard of Tuskegee, 1901–1915* (1983).

Robert B. Stepto's chapter on Washington's *Up From Slavery* in his *Behind the Veil: A Study of Afro-American Narrative* (1979) is a classic analysis. James M. Cox's chapter "Autobiography and Washington" in his *Recovering Lost Ground: Essays in American Autobiography* (1989) is very perceptive. James Olney's essay on Frederick Douglass and Washington in Deborah McDowell and Arnold Rampersad's (eds.) *Slavery and the Literary Imagination* (1989) is also an important study, as is Kevern Verney's *The Art of the Possible: Booker T. Washington and Black Leadership in the United States, 1881–1925* (2001). Also useful are "Strategies and Revisions of Self-Representation in Booker T. Washington's Autobiography" by Donald B. Gibson, *American Quarterly* (1993), and the essays of Gibson and Maurice Wallace in Michael Moon and Cathy N. Davidson's 1995 *Subjects and Citizens: Nation, Race, and Gender from Oroonoko to Anita Hill*. In *Turning South Again: Re-Thinking Modernism/Re-Reading Booker T.*, by Houston A. Baker, Jr. (2001) is sharply critical of Washington's relations to and ideas about whites. Related work includes *Creative Conflict in African American Thought: Frederick Douglass, Alexander Crummell, Booker T. Washington, W. E. B. Du Bois,* and Marcus Garvey, by Wilson Jeremiah Moses (2004); *Forever Free: The Story of Emancipation and Reconstruction* (2005) by Eric Foner and Joshua Brown; and *Inhuman Bondage: The Rise and Fall of Slavery in the New World* (2006) by David Brion Davis, each of which furnishes contexts for Washington's thought. *The Education of Booker T. Washington: American Democracy and the Idea of Race Relations* by Michael Rudolph West (2005) presents the "intertwined history of an idea and a man," Booker T. Washington as the very progenitor of "race relations," not simply a "black conservative" or pragmatist. *Uncle Tom or New Negro?: African Americans Reflect on Booker T. Washington and Up From Slavery 100 Years Later,* edited by Rebecca Carroll (2006), which includes the complete text of Washington's autobiography with twenty essays by various critics exploring the continuing debates over Washington and his relationship to African Americans, highlighting both his controversial ideas and his complexity. There are many juvenile biographies of Washington as well as numerous posters of him available on the internet.

Edith Wharton

There is no uniform edition of Wharton's writings. Louis Auchincloss edited *The Edith Wharton Reader* (1965), and R. W. B. Lewis edited in two volumes *The Collected Short Stories of Edith Wharton* (1988). Frederick Wegener edited *Edith Wharton: The Uncollected Critical Writings* (1991). The Library of America has produced *Edith Wharton: Novels: The House of Mirth / The Reef / The Custom of the Country / The Age of Innocence,* ed. R. W. B. Lewis (1986); *Edith Wharton: Novellas and Other Writings: Madame De Treymes / Ethan Frome / Summer / Old New York / The Mother's Recompense / A Backward Glance,* ed. Cynthia Griffin Wolff (1990); *Edith Wharton: Vol. 1 Collected Stories: 1891–1910* and Vol. 2 *Collected Stories 1911–1937,* ed. Maureen Howard (2001); and *Edith Wharton: Selected Poems,* ed. Louis Auchincloss (2005).

R. W. B. Lewis, using the extensive Wharton papers at Yale, prepared the definitive *Edith Wharton: A Biography* (1993). Millicent Bell's *Edith Wharton and Henry James: The Story of Their Friendship* (1965) is still useful. The fully illustrated *Edith Wharton: An Extraordinary Life* (1999) by Eleanor Dwight is an expansion of Wharton biography into her interests in architecture and house decoration. *Edith Wharton's Library: A Catalogue* (1999) has been compiled by George Ramsden to inventory more than 2,600 volumes, about half of her library at her death.

Margaret B. McDowell's *Edith Wharton*

(1976) is a solid introductory study. Book-length studies of importance include Gary H. Lindberg's *Edith Wharton and the Novel of Manners* (1975); Cynthia Griffin Wolff's *A Feast of Words: The Triumph of Edith Wharton* (1977); Richard H. Lawson's *Edith Wharton* (1977); Elizabeth Ammons's *Edith Wharton's Argument with America* (1980); Geoffrey Walton's *Edith Wharton, a Critical Interpretation* (1982); Wendy Gimbel's *Edith Wharton: Orphancy and Survival* (1984); Carol Wershoven's *The Female Intruder in the Novels of Edith Wharton* (1983); Catherine M. Rae's *Edith Wharton's New York Quartet* (1984); Susan Goodman's *Edith Wharton's Women* (1990); Janet Goodwyn's *Edith Wharton: Traveller in the Land of Letters* (1990); Penelope Vita-Finzi's *Edith Wharton and the Art of Fiction* (1990); Gloria Erdich's *The Sexual Education of Edith Wharton* (1992); Susan Goodman's *Edith Wharton's Inner Circle* (1994); *The Cambridge Companion to Edith Wharton,* ed. Millicent Bell (1995); Helen Killoran's *Edith Wharton: Art and Allusion* (1996); *Displaying Women: Spectacles of Leisure in Edith Wharton's New York* by M. Montgomery (1998), which uses letters, print media sources, etiquette manuals, and the New York fiction of Wharton and James to explore womens' roles; Claire Preston's *Edith Wharton's Social Register* (2000), which shows how Wharton transformed social codes and conventions into narrative strategies; Hildegard Hoeller's *Edith Wharton's Dialogue with Realism and Sentimental Fiction* (2000), which sees Wharton's fiction as critiquing these literary movements; *The Critical Reception of Edith Wharton,* edited by Helen Killoran (2001), which contains chapters on *The House of Mirth, Ethan Frome, The Custom of the Country, Summer, The Age of Innocence,* and *Ghosts* and begins with contemporary reviews to trace main trends in criticism; Carol J. Singley's *Edith Wharton's The House of Mirth* and her *Historical Guide to Edith Wharton,* both 2003; and *The Portable Edith Wharton,* edited by Linda Wagner-Martin (2003).

Alfred Bendixen and Annette Zilversmit edited *Edith Wharton: New Critical Essays* (1992). Sarah Bird Wright and Clare Colquit's *Edith Wharton A to Z* (1998) is a cornucopia of information about Wharton's writings, life and times, as is *A Forward Glance: New Essays on Edith Wharton,* edited by Clare Colquitt, Susan Goodman, and Candace Waid (1999). Adeline R. Tintner's *Edith Wharton in Context: Essays on Intertextuality* (1999) gives us twenty-nine essays (of which twenty-one were previously unpublished) concerning Wharton's influence on and literary debts to other writers, especially James. *New Essays on* The House of Mirth, edited by Deborah Esch (2001) offers further contemporary perspectives on this important novel.

Walt Whitman

The study of Whitman has been revolutionized by the *Walt Whitman Hypertext Archive* <www.whitman.archive.org>, directed by Kenneth M. Price and Ed Folsom. Before going to the printed sources listed below, students should work in and out of the sections of this gigantic and superbly ordered archive, which includes a lengthy and reliable biographical essay by Folsom and Price, all the known contemporary reviews, all the known photographs, and a current bibliography of scholarship and criticism.

The Collected Writings of Walt Whitman was under the general editorship of Gay Wilson Allen; part of this edition is *Walt Whitman: The Correspondence* (1961–69), a six-volume set with two supplements (1990–91), edited by Edwin H. Miller. The growth of *Leaves of Grass* may be studied in the *Comprehensive Reader's Edition* (1965, 1968), edited by Harold W. Blodgett and Sculley Bradley. Essential, in three volumes, is *"Leaves of Grass": A Textual Variorum of the Printed Poems* (1980), edited by Bradley, Blodgett, Golden, and William White. Michael Moon's Norton Critical Edition of *Leaves of Grass* (2002) includes discussion of textual variants and compositional development. Garland has printed three volumes containing facsimiles of Whitman manuscripts (1993). Important documents are in *Notebooks and Unpublished Prose Manuscripts* (1984), edited by Edward P. Grier in six volumes. The first volume of Whitman's *Journalism*, edited by Herbert Bergman, Douglas A. Noverr, and Edward J. Recchia, appeared in 1998.

Long the standard biography is Gay Wilson Allen's *The Solitary Singer* (1967). It should be supplemented by Roger Asselineau's *The Evolution of Walt Whitman* (1960, 1962; reissued 1999), the first biography to deal openly with Whitman's sexuality; Justin Kaplan's *Walt Whitman: A Life* (1980), David S. Reynolds's *Walt Whitman's America: A Cultural Biography* (1995), Gary Schmidgall's *Walt Whitman: A Gay Life* (1998), Jerome Loving's *Walt Whitman: The Song of Himself* (1999), and Ed Folsom and Kenneth M. Price's *Re-scripting Walt Whitman: An Introduction to His Life and Work* (2005). Joann P. Krieg's 1998 *A Whitman Chronology* is useful. Contemporary context is emphasized in Betsy Erkkila's *Whitman the Political Poet* (1989), Ed Folsom's *Walt Whitman's Native Representations* (1994), and Roy Morris Jr.'s *The Better Angel: Walt Whitman in the Civil War* (2000). Valuable editions of documentary evidence include Thomas L. Brasher's *Whitman as Editor of the Brooklyn Daily Eagle* (1970), Joel Myerson's excellent *Whitman in His Own Time: A Biographical Chronicle of His Life, Drawn from Recollections, Memoirs, and Interviews, Friends and Associates* (1991, rev. 2000) and Myerson's *Walt*

Whitman: A Documentary Volume (2000). The last of nine volumes of Horace Traubel's *With Walt Whitman in Camden*, edited by Jeanne Chapman and Robert Macisaac, appeared in 1996; an excellent starting place is Gary Schmidgall's *Intimate with Walt: Selections from Whitman's Conversations with Horace Traubel, 1888–1892* (2001).

Valuable collections of critical essays include Robert K. Martin's *The Continuing Presence of Walt Whitman: The Life after the Life* (1992), Geoffrey M. Sill's *Walt Whitman of Mickle Street: A Centennial Collection* (1994), Gay Wilson Allen and Ed Folsom's *Walt Whitman and the World* (1995), Ezra Greenspan's *The Cambridge Companion to Walt Whitman* (1995), Betsy Erkkila and Jay Grossman's *Breaking Bounds: Whitman and American Cultural Studies* (1996), David S. Reynolds's *A Historical Guide to Walt Whitman* (2000), and Donald D. Kummings's *A Companion to Walt Whitman* (2006). Two provocative recent critical works are Vivian R. Pollack's *The Erotic Whitman* (2000) and Jay Grossman's *Reconstituting the American Renaissance: Emerson, Whitman, and the Poetics of Representation* (2003). On Whitman's reception, see Graham Clarke's four-volume *Walt Whitman: Critical Assessments* (1996) and Kenneth M. Price's *Walt Whitman: The Contemporary Reviews* (1996). Joel Myerson prepared *Walt Whitman: A Descriptive Bibliography* (1993). Very useful is the 1998 *Walt Whitman: An Encyclopedia*, edited by J. R. LeMaster and Donald D. Kummings. *Walt Whitman: The Measure of His Song*, edited by Jim Perlman, Ed Folsom, and Dan Campion (2nd rev. ed., 1998), quotes other poets on Whitman. Kenneth M. Price's *To Walt Whitman, America* (2004) traces Whitman's continuing impact on U.S. literary culture.

Zitkala Ša (Gertrude Simmons Bonnin)

Dexter Fisher's 1986 edition of Zitkala Ša's *American Indian Stories* (1921) includes an expert and insightful introduction to this collection of autobiography, fiction, and nonfiction prose. P. Jane Hafen helpfully edited a number of Zitkala Ša's works in *Dreams and Thunder: Stories, Poems and "The Sun Dance Opera"* (2001). Also of great interest is Zitkala Ša's "Why I Am a Pagan" (*Atlantic Monthly* 90 [102]: 801–03). Material on Zitkala Ša is still scarce, though articles and chapters in part or whole devoted to her are appearing more frequently; Dexter Fisher's *Zitkala Ša: The Evolution of a Writer* (1979) and Dorothea M. Susag's *Zitkala-Ša (Gertrude Simmons Bonnin): A Power(full) Literary Voice* (1993) are among the few critical and biographical studies. Two excellent articles published in books are D. K. Meisenheimer's "Regionalist Bodies/Embodied Regions: Sarah Orne Jewett and Zitkala-Ša," in Sherrie A. Innis and Diana

Royer's collection *Breaking Boundaries: New Perspectives on Women's Regional Writing* (1997), and Patricia Okker's "Native American Literatures and the Canon" in Tom Quirk and Gary Scharnhost's collection *American Realism and the Canon* (1995). Two excellent articles published in journals are P. Jane Hafen's "Zitkala Ša: Sentimentality and Sovereignty" (*Wicazo Sa Review 12* [1997]: 31–34) and Dexter Fisher's "Zitkala Ša: The Evolution of a Writer" (*American Indian Quarterly* 5 [1979]: 229–38). The best discursive bibliography of

Native American literature is A. LaVonne Brown Ruoff's *American Indian Literatures: An Introduction, Bibliographic Review, and Selected Bibliography* (1990), a comprehensive and judicious survey of the field. Two other titles may be recommended to anyone interested in Native American autobiography: A. David Brumble III's *American Indian Autobiography* (1988) and Arnold Krupat's "Native American Autobiography and the Synecdochic Self" in Paul John Eakin's *American Autobiography: Retrospect and Prospect* (1991).

AMERICAN LITERATURE 1914–1945

Reference Works and Histories

Chapters on the period may be consulted in the *Columbia Literary History of the United States* (1988), general editor Emory Elliott; the *Columbia History of the American Novel* (1991), general editor Emory Elliot; the *Columbia History of American Poetry* (1993), edited by Jay Parini; *The History of Southern Literature* (1985), edited by Louis D. Rubin et al.; *A Literary History of the American West* (1987); and A. LaVonne Brown Ruoff's *American Indian Literature* (1990). Relevant volumes in the eight-volume *Cambridge History of American Literature* are volume 5, *Poetry and Criticism, 1900–1950* (2003), edited by Sacvan Bercovitch, and volume 6, *Prose Writing, 1910–1950* (2002), edited by Sacvan Bercovitch and Cyrus R. Patell. Other reference works include the *Cambridge Companion to Native American Literature* (2005), edited by Joy Porter and Kenneth Roemer; *A Companion to the Literature and Culture of the American South* (2004), edited by Richard Grey and Owen Robinson; and *An Interethnic Companion to Asian American Literature* (1996), edited by King-Kok Cheung. Reference works dedicated specifically to the period and some of its important movements include *A Companion to Modernist Literature and Culture*, edited by David Bradshaw and Kevin J. H. Dettmar (2006); the *Cambridge Companion to American Modernism* (2005), ed. Walter Kalaidjian; the *Cambridge Companion to the Harlem Renaissance*, edited by George Hutchinson (2006); and *A Companion to Twentieth-Century American Drama* (2005), edited by David Krasner.

For early histories of the period authored by critics who were active in the rise of modernism, see Malcolm Cowley, *Exile's Return* (1951), *After the Genteel Tradition: American Writers, 1910–1930* (1964), and *A Second Flowering: Works and Days of the Lost Generation* (1973); and Edmund Wilson, *The Shores of Light: A Literary Chronicle of the Twenties and Thirties* (1952). Other important early surveys include Alfred Kazin's *On Native Grounds: An Interpretation of Modern American Prose Literature* (1942), Maxwell Geismer's *Writers in Crisis: The American Novel between Two Wars* (1942), Frederick J. Hoffman's *The Twenties: American Writing in the Postwar Decade*, Harold Clurman's *The Fervent Years: The Story of the Group Theatre and the Thirties* (1957), Walter Rideout's *The Radical Novel in the United States, 1900–1954* (1956), Joseph Wood Krutch's *The American Drama Since 1918*

(1957), W. M. Frohock's *The Novel of Violence in America* (1957), Daniel Aaron's *Writers on the Left* (1961), Louis D. Rubin's *Writers of the Modern South* (1963), Howard Taubman's *The Making of the American Theater* (1965), Joseph Blotner's *The Modern American Political Novel* (1966), Warren French's *The Social Novel at the End of an Era* (1966), Dale Kramer's *Chicago Renaissance: The Literary Life in the Midwest, 1910–1930* (1966), Brooks Atkinson's *Broadway: Nineteen Hundred to Nineteen Seventy* (1970); Nathan I. Huggins's *Harlem Renaissance* (1971); Hugh Kenner's *The Pound Era* (1971); and Kenner's *A Homemade World: The American Modernist Writers* (1975).

General books on literary and cultural history appearing since 1980 include Marcus Klein's *Foreigners: The Making of American Literature, 1900–1940* (1981), David Levering Lewis's *When Harlem Was in Vogue* (1981), Daniel J. Singal's *The War Within: From Victorian to Modernist Thought in the South 1919–1945* (1982), Shari Benstock's *Women of the Left Bank: Paris 1900–1940* (1986), *Modernism and the Harlem Renaissance* (1987), edited by Houston Baker Jr., Cecilia Tichi's *Shifting Gears: Technology, Literature, Culture in Modernist America* (1987), Joan Shelley Rubin's *The Making of Middlebrow Culture* (1992), Steven Brel's *Independent Intellectuals in the United States, 1910–1945* (1992), Mary Loeffelholz's *Experimental Lives: Women and Literature, 1900–1945* (1992), Michael North's *The Dialect of Modernism: Race, Language and Twentieth-Century Literature* (1994), George Chauncey's *Gay New York: Gender, Urban Culture, and the Making of the Gay Male World, 1980–1940* (1994), George Hutchinson's *The Harlem Renaissance in Black and White* (1995), Cheryl Wall's *Women of the Harlem Renaissance* (1995), Walter Benn Michaels's *Our America* (1995), Ann Douglas's *Terrible Honesty: Mongrel Manhattan in the 1920s* (1995), Ross Posnock's *Color and Culture: Black Writers and the Making of the Modern Intellectual* (1998), William J. Maxwell's *New Negro, Old Left: African-American Writing and Communism between the Wars* (1999), Christine Stansell's *American Moderns: Bohemian New York and the Creation of a New Century* (1999), David G. Nicholls's *Conjuring the Folk: Forms of Modernity in African America* (2000), Michael Szalay's *New Deal Modernism: American Literature and the Invention of the Welfare State* (2000), Edward Pavlic's *Crossroads Modernism: Descent and Emergence in African-American Literary Culture* (2002), Catherine Turner's *Marketing Modernism between the Two World Wars* (2003), Michael Soto's *The Modernist Nation: Generation, Renaissance, and Twentieth-Century American Literature* (2004), and Tim Armstrong's *Modernism: A Cultural History* (2005).

Literary Theory and Criticism

For an introduction to the ideas of literary criticism during the period, see Rene Wellek's *A History of Modern Criticism: American Criticism, 1900–1950*, Vol. 7 (1987) and Vincent B. Leitch's *American Literary Criticism from the 30s to the 80s* (1988). Gordon Hutner's *American Literature, American Culture* (1998) reprints a number of critical statements from the period. Gerald's Graff's *Professing Literature: An Institutional History* (1987), Lawrence H. Schwartz's *Creating Faulkner's Reputation: The Politics of Modern Literary Criticism* (1988), and Mark Jancovich's *The Cultural Politics of the New*

Criticism (1994) analyze aspects of American literary criticism in the period and its aftermath.

Theoretical treatments of modernism (often in international perspectives) include Andreas Huyssen's *After the Great Divide: Modernism, Mass Culture, Postmodernism* (1986), Ashadur Eyssteinsson's *The Concept of Modernism* (1991), Joseph N. Riddel's *The Turning Word: American Literary Modernism and Continental Theory* (1996), Leonard Diepeveen's *The Difficulties of Modernism* (2003), Michael Trask's *Cruising Modernism: Class and Sexuality in American Literature and Social Thought* (2003), Susan McCabe's *Cinematic Modernism: Modernist Poetry and Film* (2005), and Robert Scholes's *Paradoxy of Modernism* (2006).

Criticism of poetry published since 1980 includes Donald E. Stanford's *Revolution and Convention in Modern Poetry* (1983), M. L. Rosenthal and Sally M. Gall's *The Modern Poetic Sequence: The Genius of Modern Poetry* (1984), William Drake's *The First Wave: Women Poets in America, 1914–1945* (1987), Albert Gelpi's *A Coherent Splendor: The American Poetic Renaissance, 1910–1950* (1987), Lisa M. Steinman's *Made in America: Science, Technology, and American Modernist Poets* (1987), Maureen Honey's edited *Shadowed Dreams: Women's Poetry of the Harlem Renaissance* (1989), Cary Nelson's *Repression and Recovery: Modern American Poetry and the Politics of Cultural Memory, 1910–1945* (1989), Elisa New's *Fictions of Form in American Poetry* (1993), Frank Lentricchia's *Modernist Quartet* (1994), Rachel Blau DuPlessis's *Genders, Races, and Religious Cultures in Modern American Poetries, 1908–1934* (2001), Merrill Cole's *The Other Orpheus: A Poetics of Modern Homosexuality* (2003), and Charles Altieri's *The Art of Twentieth-Century American Poetry: Modernism and After* (2006).

Critical studies of fiction published since 1980 include Hazel V. Carby's *Reconstructing Womanhood: The Emergence of the Afro-American Woman Novelist* (1987), Linda Wagner-Martin's *The Modern American Novel, 1914–1945* (1990), J. Gerald Kennedy's *Imagining Paris* (1993), Barbara Foley's *Radical Representations: Politics and Form in U.S. Proletarian Fiction, 1929–41* (1993), David Minter's *A Cultural History of the American Novel* (1994), Laura Hapke's *Daughters of the Great Depression: Women, Work, and Fiction in the American 1930s* (1995), Paula Rabinowitz's *Black and White and Noir: America's Pulp Modernism* (2002), and Christopher Breu's *Hard-Boiled Masculinities* (2005).

Critical studies of drama published since 1980 include C. W. E. Bigsby's *A Critical Introduction to Twentieth-Century American Drama*, Vol. 1, *1900–1940* (1985), Ethan Mordden's *The American Theatre* (1981), Brenda Murphy's *American Realism and American Drama, 1880–1940* (1987), David Krasner's *A Beautiful Pageant: African American Theatre, Drama, and Performance in the Harlem Renaissance, 1910–1927* (2002), and Julia A. Walker's *Expressionism and Modernism in the American Theatre: Bodies, Voices, Words* (2005).

Sherwood Anderson
There is no collected edition of Anderson's writing. In addition to works mentioned in the author's headnote, Anderson published *The Modern Writer* (1925); *Sherwood Anderson's Notebook* (1925); *Alice and the Lost Novel* (1929); *Nearer the Grass Roots* (1929); *The American Country Fair* (1930); and *Home Town* (1940). The Norton Critical Edition of *Winesburg, Ohio* (1996), edited by Charles E. Modlin and Ray Lewis White, includes background materials and critical essays, as does the edition edited by John H. Ferres (1996). White edited a variorum edition of *Winesburg, Ohio* (1997). *The Letters of Sherwood Anderson* (1953) were edited by Howard Mumford Jones and Walter Rideout. See also *Sherwood Anderson: Selected Letters* (1984), edited by Charles E. Modlin and *Letters to Bab: Sherwood Anderson to Marietta D. Finley, 1916–1933* (1985). Kim Townsend has written *Sherwood Anderson: A Biography* (1987). The first volume of a two-volume biography by Walter Rideout is *Sherwood Anderson: A Writer in America* (2006). For critical commentary see *Sherwood Anderson: A Collection of Critical Essays* (1974), edited by Walter Rideout; *Critical Essays on Sherwood Anderson* (1981), edited by David D. Anderson; *Homage to Sherwood Anderson* (1970), edited by Paul F. Appel; *New Essays on Winesburg, Ohio* (1990), edited by John W. Crowley; Allen Papinchak's *Sherwood Anderson: A Study of the Short Fiction* (1992); Judy Jo Small's *A Reader's Guide to the Short Stories of Sherwood Anderson* (1994); and Ray Lewis White's *Winesburg, Ohio: An Exploration* (1990).

Sterling Brown
Brown's *Collected Poems*, selected by Michael S. Harper (1989, 1996), includes *Southern Road, No Hiding Place* as well as additional individual poems. *A Son's Return: Selected Essays of Sterling A. Brown* (1996) is edited by Mark A. Sanders. A special issue of the journal *Callaloo*, 5 (1982), contains a bibliography by Robert G. O'Meally along with reminiscences and critical assessments by several scholars; other essays on Brown may be found in issues of the journal *Black American Literature Forum*. Full-length studies are Joanne V. Gabbin's *Sterling A. Brown: Building the Black Aesthetic Tradition* (1985) and Mark A. Sanders's *Afro-Modernist Aesthetics and the Poetry of Sterling A. Brown* (1999). There are discussions of Brown in Stephen Henderson's *Understanding the New Black Poetry* (1973), Jean Wagner's *Black Poetry* (1973), Henry Louis Gates Jr.'s *Figures in Black: Words, Signs, and the "Racial" Self* (1987), Victor Kramer's *The Harlem Renaissance Reconsidered* (1987), and Cary Nelson's *Repression and Recovery* (1989). The fall 1999 issue of *African American Review* has several articles about Brown.

Carlos Bulosan
Bulosan's published works include *The Voice of Bataan* (1943), *The Laughter of My Father* (1944), and *America Is in the Heart* (1946), which was reissued with an introduction by Carey McWilliams in 1973. Compilations drawing on his books, magazine fiction, and manuscripts have been edited and introduced by E. San Juan Jr.; these include *The Philippines Is in the Heart* (1978), *If You Want to Know What We Are: A Carlos Bulosan Reader* (1983), *On Becoming Filipino: Selected Writings of Carlos Bulosan* (1995), and *The Cry and the Dedication* (1995). Two biographical treatments are P. C. Morantte's *Remembering Carlos Bulosan: His Heart Affair with America* (1984) and Susan Evangelista's *Carlos Bulosan and His Poetry: A Biography and Anthology* (1985). San Juan has also written a critical study, *Carlos Bulosan and the Imagination of the Class Struggle* (1972). Rachel C. Lee's *The Americas of Asian American Literature: Gendered Fictions of Nation and Transnation* (1999) includes a chapter on Bulosan.

Willa Cather
Cather's volume of verse, *April Twilights* (1903; rev. 1923; reissued with an introduction by Bernice Slote, 1990), and her collection of essays, *Not under Forty* (1936), supplement the standard edition of her fiction, *The Novels and Stories of Willa Cather* (1937–41). Her tales and novels were published in two volumes by the Library of America with notes by Sharon O'Brien (1987, 1990). A scholarly edition of *My Ántonia* (1994), with background materials, was edited by Charles Mignon with Kari Rounig. Other sources include *Willa Cather on Writing* (1949); *Writings from Willa Cather's Campus Years* (1950), edited by James Shively; and *The Kingdom of Art: Willa Cather's First Principles and Critical Statements* (1967), edited by Bernice Slote. William M. Curtin collected articles and reviews in the two-volume *The World and the Parish* (1970). Personal memoirs include Edith Lewis's *Willa Cather Living* (1953, 2000) and Elizabeth Sergeant's *Willa Cather: A Memoir* (1953, 1992). Janis P. Stout's *A Calendar of the Letters of Willa Cather* (2002) and the biography *Willa Cather: The Writer and Her World* (2000) are worthwhile. *Willa: The Life of Willa Cather* (1982), by Phyllis C. Robinson, is a full-length biography, as is *Willa Cather: A Literary Life* (1987), by James Woodress. Sharon O'Brien's *Willa Cather: The Emerging Voice* (1987) concentrates on Cather's early years.

Critical studies of Cather are David Stouck's *Willa Cather's Imagination* (1975), Marilyn Arnold's *Willa Cather's Short Fiction* (1984) and *Willa Cather: A Reference Guide* (1986), Susan J. Rosowski's *The Voyage Perilous: Willa Cather's Romanticism* (1986), Evelyn Hively's *Sacred*

Fire: Willa Cather's Novel Cycle (1994), Sally P. Harvey's *Redefining the American Dream: The Novels of Willa Cather* (1995), Joseph R. Urgo's *Willa Cather and the Myth of American Migration* (1995), Guy Reynolds's *Willa Cather in Context* (1996), O'Brien's *New Essays on My Ántonia* (1999), Ann Roninies's *Willa Cather's Southern Connection* (2000), and Joan Acocella's *Willa Cather and the Politics of Criticism* (2000). Janis P. Stout edited *Willa Cather and Material Culture: Real-World Writing and Writing the Real World* (2005). Also useful are Marilyn Arnold's *A Reader's Companion to the Fiction of Willa Cather* (1993) and John J. Murphy's *My Ántonia: The Road Home* (1989).

Hart Crane

Marc Simon edited *Complete Poems of Hart Crane* (1993, 2001), the best current text. Also of use is Brom Weber's *The Complete Poems and Selected Letters and Prose of Hart Crane* (1966). Crane's *Collected Poems,* edited by his friend Waldo Frank, appeared in 1933. *Correspondence between Hart Crane and Waldo Frank* (1998) was edited by Steve H. Cook. Other sources of primary and bibliographical material are *My Land, My Friends: The Selected Letters of Hart Crane* (1997), edited by Langdon Hammer and Brom Weber; *Hart Crane: An Annotated Critical Bibliography* (1970), edited by Joseph Schwartz; and *Hart Crane: A Descriptive Bibliography* (1972), edited by Joseph Schwartz and Robert C. Schweik. Gary Lane compiled *A Concordance to the Poems of Hart Crane* (1972). Biographies of Crane are John Unterecker's *Voyager: A Life of Hart Crane* (1969), Paul Mariani's *The Broken Tower: A Life of Hart Crane* (2000), and Clive Fisher's *Hart Crane: A Life* (2002).

Useful earlier studies are R. W. B. Lewis's *The Poetry of Hart Crane* (1967), Monroe K. Spears's *Hart Crane* (1965), R. W. Butterfield's *The Broken Arc: A Study of Hart Crane* (1969), and Hunce Voelcker's *The Hart Crane Voyages* (1967). See also Richard P. Sugg's *Hart Crane's "The Bridge"* (1976), Samuel Hazo's *Smithereened Apart: A Critique of Hart Crane* (1977), Helge Norman Nilsen's *Hart Crane's Divided Vision: An Analysis of "The Bridge"* (1980), Edward Brunner's *Hart Crane and the Making of "The Bridge"* (1984), Thomas E. Yingling's *Hart Crane and the Homosexual Text* (1990), and Brian M. Reed's *Hart Crane: After His Lights* (2006).

Countee Cullen

Cullen's groundbreaking anthology of 1927, *Caroling Dusk,* was reissued in 1993. His poetry volume, *Color,* originally published in 1925, was also reissued in 1993. *My Soul's High Song,* a collection of his writings edited by Gerald Early, appeared in 1991. There is little recent criticism. Earlier work of interest includes Helen J. Dinger's *A Study of Countee Cullen* (1953), Margaret Perry's *A Bio-Bibliography of Countee P. Cullen* (1969), and Blanche E. Ferguson's *Countee Cullen and the Negro Renaissance* (1966). A recent article is Jeremy Braddock's "The Poetics of Conjecture," in *Callaloo* (fall 2002).

E. E. Cummings

Complete Poems 1904–62, edited by George J. Firmage, was published in 1991. Firmage also edited *Three Plays and a Ballet* (1967). Cummings's prose fiction includes *The Enormous Room* (1922) and *EIMI* (1933). *E. E. Cummings: A Miscellany Revised* (1965), edited by Firmage, contains previously uncollected short prose pieces. *Six Nonlectures* (1953) consists of the talks that Cummings delivered at Harvard in the same year. A gathering of works is *Another E. E. Cummings* (1999), edited by Richard Kostchanetz. *Selected Letters of E. E. Cummings* (1969) was edited by F. W. Dupee and George Stade. George J. Firmage edited *E. E. Cummings: A Bibliography* (1960). Barry Ahearn edited *The Correspondence of Ezra Pound and E. E. Cummings* (1996).

Several of Cummings's earlier individual works have been reedited by Firmage in the Cummings Typescript Editions. These include *Tulips & Chimneys* (1976); *No Thanks* (1978); *The Enormous Room,* including illustrations by Cummings (1978); *ViVa* (1979); *XAIPE* (1979); and *Etcetera,* the unpublished poems (1983).

A biography is *Dreams in the Mirror* (1979, 1994), by Richard S. Kennedy. Early studies include Norman Friedman's *E. E. Cummings: The Growth of a Writer* (1964), Robert E. Wegner's *The Poetry and Prose of E. E. Cummings* (1965), Bethany K. Dumas's *E. E. Cummings: A Remembrance of Miracles* (1974), and Rushworth Kidder's *E. E. Cummings, An Introduction to the Poetry* (1979). See also Cary Lane's *I Am: A Study of E. E. Cummings' Poems* (1976) and Richard S. Kennedy's *E. E. Cummings Revisited* (1994). Norman Friedman edited *E. E. Cummings: A Collection of Critical Essays* (1972).

Hilda Doolittle (H. D.)

The poetry through 1944 has been collected and edited by Louis L. Martz in *Collected Poems 1912–1944* (1983). *Collected Poems of H. D.* was published in 1925. Subsequent volumes of poetry include *Red Rose for Bronze* (1931); the trilogy of war poems *The Walls Do Not Fall* (1944), *Tribute to the Angels* (1945), and *The Flowering of the Rod* (1946); the dramatic monologue *Helen in Egypt* (1961); the major collection of her late poems, *Hermetic Definition* (1972); and the long poem *Vale Ave* (1992). H. D.'s other book-length verse dramas are *Hippolytus Temporizes* (1927) and the translation of Euripides' *Ion* (1937). *Palimpsest* (1926), *Hedylus* (1928), *Bid Me to Live* (1961), *HERmione* (1981), and *Asphodel* (1992), edited by Robert Spoo, compose her major prose fiction. *By Avon River* (1949) celebrates Shakespeare in prose and verse. *Tribute to Freud* (1956) is her account of her psychoanalysis by Freud. Also important are two autobiographical works: *End to Torment* (1979) and *The Gift* (1982, complete edition 1998). Michael Boughn compiled *H. D.: A Bibliography, 1905–1990* (1993). *Richard Aldington and H. D.: The Early Years in Letters* (1992), edited by Caroline Zilboorg, collects correspondence.

Herself Defined: The Poet H. D. and Her World (1984), by Barbara Guest, is a biography, while *H. D.: The Career of That Struggle* (1986), by Rachel Blau DuPlessie, *Psyche Reborn: The Emergence of H. D.* (1981), by Susan S. Friedman, and *H. D.: The Life and Work of an American Poet* (1982), by Janice S. Robinson, combine biography and literary analysis. Among critical books are Gary Barnett's *H. D.: Between Image and Epic, The Mysteries of Her Poetics* (1990), Friedman's *Penelope's Web: Gender, Modernity, and H. D.'s Fiction* (1990), Eileen Gregory's *H. D. and Hellenism* (1997), Diana Collecott's *H. D and Sapphic Modernism* (1999), Georgia Taylor's *H. D. and the Public Sphere of Modernist Women Writers 1913–1946* (2001), and Adalaide Morris's *How to Live/What to Do: H. D.'s Cultural Poetics* (2003).

T. S. Eliot

Eliot's poetic works have been collected in *Collected Poems, 1909–1962* (1963) and *The Complete Poems and Plays of T. S. Eliot* (1969). *Inventions of the March Hare: Poems 1909–1917* (1997), edited by Christopher Ricks, contains early, previously unpublished poetry. The indispensable manuscript to *The Waste Land* is in *The Waste Land: A Facsimile and Transcript of the Original Drafts Including the Annotations of Ezra Pound* (1971), edited by Valerie Eliot. Michael North edited a Norton Critical Edition of *The Waste Land* (2001). Important critical writings include *The Use of Poetry and the Use of Criticism* (1933), *Poetry and Drama* (1951), *The Three Voices of Poetry* (1953), *On Poetry and Poets* (1957), and *To Criticize the Critic and Other Writings* (1965). Three volumes of social commentary are *After Strange Gods* (1934), *The Idea of a Christian Society* (1939), and *Notes toward the Definition of Culture* (1948). Valerie Eliot edited *The Letters of T. S. Eliot, Vol. 1: 1898–1922* (1988). J. L. Dawson edited *Concordance to the Complete Poems and Plays of T. S. Eliot* (1995). Good biographies are Peter Ackroyd's *T. S. Eliot: A Life* (1984) and Lyndall Gordon's *T. S. Eliot: An Imperfect Life* (1998, 2000), an updating of her earlier biographies. Influential earlier studies of Eliot include F. O. Matthiessen's *The Achievement of T. S. Eliot* (rev. 1947), Helen Gardner's *The Art of T. S. Eliot* (1950), Hugh Kenner's *The Invisible Poet* (1959), Northrop Frye's *T. S. Eliot* (1963), and Stephen Spender's *T. S. Eliot* (1976).

Among numerous critical studies are Helen Gardner's *The Composition of Four Quartets* (1978), Derek Traversi's *T. S. Eliot: The Longer Poems* (1976), Louis Menand's *Discovering Modernism: T. S. Eliot and His Context* (1987), Jewel Spears Brooker and Joseph Bentley's *Reading "The Waste Land": Modernism and the Limits of Interpretation* (1990), Brooker's *Mastery and Escape: T. S. Eliot and the Dialectic of Modernism* (1994), A. David Moody's *Thomas Stearns Eliot, Poet* (1994), Anthony Julius's *T. S. Eliot, Anti-Semitism, and Literary Form* (1996), Ronald Schuchard's *Eliot's Dark Angel: Intersections of Life and Art* (2001), and David Chintz's *T. S. Eliot and the Cultural Divide* (2003). Moody also edited the useful *Cambridge Companion to T. S. Eliot* (1994). For collections of critical essays about Eliot, see *T. S. Eliot: A Collection of Criticism* (1974), edited by Linda W. Wagner (1974); *T. S. Eliot: The Modernist in History* (1991), edited by Ronald Bush (1991); *T. S. Eliot, A Voice Descanting: Centenary Essays* (1990), edited by Shyamal Bagchee, and *Gender, Desire, and Sexuality in T. S. Eliot* (2004), edited by Cassandra Laity and Nancy K. Gish. Gareth Reeves's *T. S. Eliot's "The Waste Land"* (1994) is a comprehensive introduction to the poem.

Donald C. Gallup compiled the standard bibliography, *T. S. Eliot: A Bibliography* (rev. 1969).

William Faulkner

The Library of America issued Faulkner's novels in four volumes: *1930–1935* (1985); *1936–1940* (1990); *1942–1954* (1994); and *1957–1962* (1999). In addition to volumes mentioned in the author's headnote are *Early Prose and Poetry* (1962), edited by Carvel Collins (1962); *Dr. Martino and Other Stories* (1934); *Pylon* (1935); *The Unvanquished* (1938); *Intruder in the Dust* (1948); *Knight's Gambit* (1949); *Collected Stories of William Faulkner* (1950); *Requiem for a Nun* (1951); *Notes on a Horsethief* (1951); *Big Woods* (1955); and *Essays, Speeches, and Public Letters* (rev. 2004), edited by James B. Meriwether. Transcripts of discussions and interviews with Faulkner include *Faulkner at Nagano* (1956), edited by Robert A. Jelliffe; *Faulkner in the University* (1959), edited by Frederick L. Gwynn and Joseph L. Blotner; *Faulkner at West Point* (1964), edited by Joseph L. Fant and Robert Ashley (1964); and *The Lion in the Garden* (1968), edited by Meriwether and Michael Millgate. Letters are collected in *The Faulkner-Cowley File* (1961), edited by Malcolm Cowley (1961), and *Selected Letters of William Faulkner* (1977), edited by Joseph L. Blotner. Noel Polk has produced editions of several Faulkner novels based on study of the manuscripts. David Minter has published a Norton Critical Edition of *The Sound and the Fury* (1994).

Faulkner: A Biography, 2 vols. (1974), by Blotner has been condensed and updated in Faulkner (1984). Two shorter biographies based on Blotner's work are William Faulkner: His Life and Work (1980), by David Minter, and Faulkner: The Transfiguration of Biography (1979), by Judith Wittenberg.

Comprehensive guides are Faulkner's World: A Directory of His People and Synopsis of Actions in His Published Works (1988), by Thomas E. Connolly; A William Faulkner Encyclopedia (1999), edited by Robert W. Hamblin and Charles E. Peek; and William Faulkner A to Z (2001), edited by A. Nichols Fargnoli and Michael Golay. David Dowling's William Faulkner (1989) is a general introduction; another useful introduction is Edmond L. Volpe's A Reader's Guide to William Faulkner: The Short Stories (2004). Influential early studies include Cleanth Brooks's William Faulkner: The Yoknapatawpha Country (1963) and Hyatt H. Waggoner's William Faulkner: From Jefferson to the World (1959). Later studies include John T. Irwin's Doubling and Incest, Repetition and Revenge: A Speculative Reading of Faulkner (1975), Thadious M. Davis's Faulkner's "Negro": Art and the Southern Context (1983), Eric J. Sundquist's Faulkner: The House Divided (1983), Robert Dale Parker's Faulkner and the Novelistic Imagination (1985), Warwick Wadlington's Reading Faulknerian Tragedy (1987) and As I Lay Dying: Stories out of Stories (1992), Stephen M. Ross's Fiction Inexhaustible Voice: Speech and Writing in Faulkner (1989), Minrose C. Gwin's The Feminine and Faulkner: Reading (beyond) Sexual Difference (1990), André Bleikasten's The Ink of Melancholy: Faulkner's Novels from "The Sound and the Fury" to "Light in August" (1990), Richard Moreland's Faulkner and Modernism: Rereading and Rewriting (1990), Joel Williamson's William Faulkner and Southern History (1993), Diane Roberts's Faulkner and Southern Womanhood (1994), and David Minter's Faulkner's Questioning Narratives: Fiction of His Major Phase, 1929–42 (2001).

Edited collections of critical essays include Doreen Fowler and Ann J. Abadie's Faulkner and Race (1987), Louis J. Budd and Edwin Cady's On Faulkner (1989), and Linda Wagner-Martin's Faulkner: Six Decades of Criticism (2002).

F. Scott Fitzgerald

Fitzgerald's novels are This Side of Paradise (1920), The Beautiful and Damned (1922), The Great Gatsby (1925), Tender Is the Night (1934; rev. 1939; rpt. 1953), and the unfinished The Last Tycoon (1941). His collections of stories are Flappers and Philosophers (1921), Tales of the Jazz Age (1922), All the Sad Young Men (1926), and Taps at Reveille (1935). Two recent editions of his fiction are the Library of America's Novels and Stories 1920–1922 (2000) and Matthew J. Bruccoli and Judith Baughman's Before Gatsby: The First Twenty-Six Stories (2001). The nine-volume Cambridge Edition of Fitzgerald's works (1991–2006) includes his novels, story collections, and My Lost City: Personal Essays, 1920–1940 (2005). A satirical play, The Vegetable, or From Presidents to Postman, was published in 1923. Among collections of Fitzgerald's writings are F. Scott Fitzgerald in His Own Time: A Miscellany (1971), edited by Jackson R. Bryer and Bruccoli, and Afternoon of an Author (1957), edited by Arthur Mizener. The Crack-Up (1945), edited by Edmund Wilson, collects essays, notebook entries, and letters from the 1930s; youthful work is collected in F. Scott Fitzgerald: The Princeton Years; Selected Writings, 1914–1920 (1966), edited by Chip Defaa.

The fullest collection of letters is Correspondence of F. Scott Fitzgerald (1980), edited by Bruccoli and Margaret M. Duggan. Other volumes of letters are Dear Scott/Dear Max: The Fitzgerald-Perkins Correspondence (1971), edited by John Kuehl and Jackson R. Bryer, As Ever, Scott Fitz (1972), edited by Bruccoli and Jennifer McCabe Atkinson (letters between Fitzgerald and his literary agent, Harold Ober), and Dear Scott, Dearest Zelda: The Love Letters of F. Scott and Zelda Fitzgerald (2002), edited by Jackson R. Bryer and Cathy W. Barks. Fitzgerald's biographies include Bruccoli's Some Sort of Epic Grandeur: The Life of F. Scott Fitzgerald (1981), Scott Donaldson's Fool for Love: F. Scott Fitzgerald, A Biographical Portrait (1983), James Mellow's Invented Lives (1984), Jeffrey Myers's Scott Fitzgerald (2000), and Andrew Turnbull's Scott Fitzgerald (2001).

Among guides are Mary Jo Tate's F. Scott Fitzgerald A to Z (1998), Robert Gale's An F. Scott Fitzgerald Encyclopedia (1998), Linda Pelzer's Student Companion to F. Scott Fitzgerald (2001), and A Historical Guide to F. Scott Fitzgerald (2004), edited by Kirk Curnutt. Critical studies include Milton R. Stern's The Golden Moment: The Novels of F. Scott Fitzgerald (1970), Brian Way's F. Scott Fitzgerald and the Art of Social Fiction (1980), Andrew Hook's F. Scott Fitzgerald (1992), and John Kuehl's F. Scott Fitzgerald, a Study of the Short Fiction (1991). Among collections of critical essays are The Short Stories of F. Scott Fitzgerald: New Approaches in Criticism (1983), edited by Jackson R. Bryer; New Essays on "The Great Gatsby," edited by Bruccoli; The Cambridge Companion to F. Scott Fitzgerald, edited by Ruth Prigozy (2001); and F. Scott Fitzgerald in the Twenty-First Century (2003), edited by Jackson R. Bryer, Prigozy, and Milton B. Stern.

Robert Frost

The Poetry of Robert Frost (1969) incorporated Complete Poems (1949) and Frost's last volume, *In the Clearing* (1962). Eleven early essays on farming, edited by Edward C. Lathem and Lawrance Thompson, appear in *Robert Frost: Farm Poultryman* (1963). The Library of America issued Frost's *Collected Poems, Prose, and Plays* (1995). Important collections of letters appear in *Selected Letters of Robert Frost* (1964), edited by Thompson; *The Letters of Robert Frost to Louis Untermeyer* (1963); and Margaret Anderson, *Robert Frost and John Bartlett: The Record of a Friendship* (1963). His critical essays have been collected in *Selected Prose* (1966), edited by Hyde Cox and Lathem (1966). Conversations and interviews with Frost include Lathem's *Interviews with Robert Frost* (1966), Reginald L. Cook's *The Dimensions of Robert Frost* (1964), Daniel Smythe's *Robert Frost Speaks* (1954), and Louis Mertin's *Robert Frost: Life and Talks—Walking* (1965).

Lawrance Thompson completed two volumes of the authorized biography: *Robert Frost: The Early Years, 1874–1915* (1966) and *Robert Frost: The Years of Triumph, 1915–1938* (1970). The third volume, *Robert Frost, the Later Years*, was completed by Richard Winnick (1976), and Edward C. Lathem produced a shorter version of the biography in *Robert Frost: A Biography* (1981). Other biographies are Jeffrey Meyers's *Robert Frost* (1996) and Jay Parini's *Robert Frost: A Life* (1999). William H. Pritchard in *Frost: A Literary Life Reconsidered* (1984) is interested in the poet's art, not his personal life. James L. Potter's *Robert Frost Handbook* (1980) is a useful guide; Latham produced a concordance to Frost's poetry (1994).

A brief critical introduction is Mordecai Marcus's *The Poems of Robert Frost* (1991). Specialized critical studies are Richard Poirier's *Robert Frost, The Work of Knowing* (1977, reissued with new material in 1990), John C. Kemp's *Robert Frost and New England: The Poet as Regionalist* (1979), George Monteiro's *Robert Frost and the New England Renaissance* (1988), Mario D'Avanzo's *A Cloud of Other Poets: Robert Frost and the Romantics* (1990), Judith Oster's *Toward Robert Frost* (1991), George Bagby's *Frost and the Book of Nature* (1993), and Mark Richardson's *Robert Frost: The Poet and His Poetics* (1997). Collections of critical essays include *On Frost* (1991), edited by Edwin H. Cady and Louis J. Budd, and Robert Faggen's *Cambridge Companion to Robert Frost* (2001).

Susan Glaspell

Plays by Susan Glaspell—including *Trifles, The Outside, The Verge*, and *Inheritors*—appeared in 1987. Another collection is *"Lifted Masks" and Other Works* (1993). *Major Novels of Susan Glaspell*, edited by Martha C. Carpenter, was published in 1995. Two biographies are Arthur E. Waterman's *Susan Glaspell* (1966) and Barbara O. Rajkowska's *Susan Glaspell: A Critical*

Biography (2000). Critical studies include Marcia Noe's *Susan Glaspell: Voice from the Heartland* (1983), Veronica A. Makowsky's *Susan Glaspell's Century of American Women: A Critical Interpretation of Her Work* (1993), and J. Ellen Gainor's *Susan Glaspell in Context: American Theater, Culture, and Politics, 1915–48* (2001). A collection of critical essays is *Susan Glaspell: Essays on Her Theater and Fiction* (1995), edited by Linda Ben-Zvi.

Ernest Hemingway

There is no collected edition of Hemingway's writings. In addition to works mentioned in the author's headnote, his fiction includes *Today Is Friday* (1926) and *God Rest You Merry Gentlemen* (1933). His tribute to Spain, *The Spanish Earth*, and his play *The Fifth Column* appeared in 1938, the latter in a collection *The Fifth Column and the First Forty-nine Stories*. His journalism has been collected in *The Wild Years* (1962), edited by Gene Z. Hanrahan, and *By-Line: Ernest Hemingway, Selected Articles and Dispatches of Four Decades* (1967), edited by William White. His *Complete Poems* (1992) has been edited by Nicholas Gerogiannis. Audre Hanneman's *Ernest Hemingway: A Comprehensive Bibliography* (1967) is thorough. Scribners published *The Complete Short Stories of Ernest Hemingway* (1987).

The authorized biography is Carlos Baker's *Ernest Hemingway: A Life Story* (1969). Jeffrey Meyers's *Hemingway: A Biography* (1985) and Kenneth S. Lynn's *Hemingway* (1987) are important. Michael Reynolds's detailed volumes include *The Young Hemingway* (1986), *Hemingway: The Paris Years* (1989), *Hemingway: The 1930s* (1997), and *Hemingway: The Final Years* (1999). *The Hemingway Women* (1983), by Bernice Kert, tells about Hemingway's mother, wives, and lovers; *Fame Became of Him: Hemingway as Public Writer* (1984), by John Raeburn, compares the life with the public image.

A Reader's Guide to Ernest Hemingway (1972), by Arthur Waldhorn, and *A Reader's Guide to the Short Stories of Ernest Hemingway* (1989), by Paul Smith, are useful handbooks; Peter B. Messent's *Ernest Hemingway* (1992) is a good overview. For collections of critical essays on Hemingway, see *Ernest Hemingway: Seven Decades of Criticism* (2001), edited by Linda Wagner-Martin; *New Critical Approaches to the Short Stories of Ernest Hemingway* (1991), edited by Jackson J. Benson; *The Cambridge Companion to Hemingway* (1996), edited by Scott Donaldson; and *A Historical Guide to Ernest Hemingway* (2001), edited by Wagner-Martin. Specialized studies include Bernard Oldsey's *Hemingway's Hidden Craft: The Writing of "A Farewell to Arms"* (1979), Wirt Williams's *The Tragic Art of Ernest Hemingway* (1982), and Mark Spilka's *Hemingway's Quarrel with Androgyny* (1990).

Langston Hughes

A fourteen-volume standard edition of Hughes's complete works appeared in 2001 and 2002. Arnold Rampersad and David Roessel edited *The Collected Poems of Langston Hughes* (1994), including *The Weary Blues* (1926), *Fine Clothes to the Jew* (1927), *The Dream Keeper and Other Poems* (1932), *Scottsboro Limited: Four Poems and a Play in Verse* (1932), *Montage of a Dream Deferred* (1951), and *The Panther and the Lash: Poems of our Times* (1967). His short stories were edited by Akiba Sullivan Harper (1996). Faith Berry edited *Good Morning Revolution: Uncollected Social Protest Writings by Langston Hughes* (1973). *Mule Bone* (1991), which he co-authored with Zora Neale Hurston, has been edited with contextual materials by George Houston Pope and Henry Louis Gates Jr. Hughes's autobiographical volumes include *The Big Sea* (1940) and *I Wonder as I Wander* (1956); both were reissued in 1993. Charles H. Nichols edited *Arna Bontemps–Langston Hughes, Letters 1925–1967* (1980).

Early biographies of Hughes include Charlemae Rollins's *Black Troubador: Langston Hughes* (1970) and James S. Haskins's *Always Movin' On: The Life of Langston Hughes* (1976). Faith Berry's *Langston Hughes: Before and Beyond Harlem* (1983, 1995) contains much about Hughes's life to 1940. Arnold Rampersad's two-volume *Life of Langston Hughes*—Vol. I, 1902–1941: *I, Too, Sing America* (1986), and Vol. II, 1941–1967: *I Dream a World* (1988)—is definitive.

Thomas A. Mikolyzk compiled *Langston Hughes: A Bio-Bibliography* (1990). Contemporary reviews were collected by Letitia Dace (1997). Full-length critical studies are Onwuchekwa Jemie's *Langston Hughes: An Introduction to the Poetry* (1976), Richard K. Barksdale's *Langston Hughes: The Poet and His Critics* (1977), Steven C. Tracy's *Langston Hughes and the Blues* (1988), and R. Baxter Miller's *The Art and Imagination of Langston Hughes* (1989). Essay collections include *Langston Hughes, Black Genius: A Critical Evaluation* (1972), edited by Therman B. O'Daniel; *Langston Hughes: Critical Perspectives Past and Present* (1993), edited by Henry Louis Gates Jr. and K. A. Appiah; *Langston Hughes: The Man, His Art, and His Continuing Influence* (1995), edited by C. James Trotman; and *A Historical Guide to Langston Hughes* (2003), edited by Steven C. Tracy. Peter Mandelik and Stanley Schatt's *A Concordance to the Poetry of Langston Hughes* (1975) is useful.

Zora Neale Hurston

Robert Hemenway's *Zora Neale Hurston, A Literary Biography* (1977) initiated the Hurston revival; her work is mostly available in paperback editions. A recent biography is Valerie Boyd's *Wrapped in Rainbows: The Life of Zora Neale Hurston* (2003). The Library of America published Hurston's writing in two volumes: *Novels and Stories* (1995) and *Folklore, Memoirs, and Other Writings* (1995). Her letters were edited by Carla Kaplan (2002). Book-length studies include Karla C. F. Holloway's *The Character of the Word: The Texts of Zora Neale Hurston* (1987), John Lowe's *Jump at the Sun: Zora Neale Hurston's Cosmic Comedy* (1994), Deborah G. Plant's *Every Tub Must Sit on Its Own Bottom: The Philosophy and Politics of Zora Neale Hurston* (1995), and Margaret Genevieve West's *Zora Neale Hurston and American Literary Culture* (2005). Hurston is linked to other writers in Cheryl A. Wall's *Women of the Harlem Renaissance* (1995), Carla Kaplan's *The Erotics of Talk: Women's Writing and Feminist Paradigms* (1996), and Trudier Harris's *The Power of the Porch: The Storyteller's Craft in Zora Neale Hurston, Gloria Naylor, and Randall Kenan* (1996). Collections of essays are *New Essays on "Their Eyes Were Watching God"* (1990), edited by Michael Awkward; *Zora Neale Hurston: Critical Perspectives Past and Present* (1993), edited by Henry Louis Gates Jr. and K. A. Appiah; and *Critical Essays on Zora Neale Hurston* (1998), edited by Gloria L. Cronin.

Amy Lowell

Lowell's complete poems were published in 1955. Ferris Greenslet, who was her editor at Houghton Mifflin, has written an excellent family chronicle from the first settler to Amy Lowell, *The Lowells and Their Seven Worlds* (1945). Additional biographical material may be found in S. Foster Damon's *Amy Lowell: A Chronicle, with Extracts from Her Correspondence* (1935), and *Florence Ayscough and Amy Lowell: Correspondence of a Friendship* (1945), edited by Harley Farnsworth MacNair. Critical estimates of Lowell include Jean Gould's *Amy: The World of Amy Lowell and the Imagist Movement* (1975), Glenn Richard Ruihley's *The Thorn of a Rose: Amy Lowell Reconsidered* (1975), and Richard Benvenuto's *Amy Lowell* (1985). Mary E. Galvin's *Queer Poetics: Five Modernist Women Writers* (1999) includes Lowell. Adrienne Munich and Melissa Bradshaw edited *Amy Lowell, American Modern* (2004).

Mina Loy

There is no scholarly edition of Loy's writing. Roger L. Conover's edition of *The Lost Lunar Baedeker* (1996) is the fullest collection of Loy's work currently in print; it includes some prose in addition to poetry. Carolyn Burke's *Becoming Mina Loy* (1996) remains the only biography. Virginia M. Kouidis's *Mina Loy: American Modernist Poet* (1980) for many years was the only full-length study. A more recent collection of essays, Maeera Schreiber and Keith Tuma's *Mina Loy: Woman and Poet*

(1998), reflects the upsurge in Loy's reputation following Burke's biography. Cristanne Miller's *Cultures of Modernism: Marianne Moore, Mina Loy, and Else Lasker-Schüler* (2005) examines Loy along with other women modernists associated with New York and Berlin.

Claude McKay

Volumes of McKay's poetry include *Songs of Jamaica* (1912), *Constab Ballads* (1912), *Spring in New Hampshire and Other Poems* (1920)—published in England—and *Harlem Shadows* (1922). William J. Maxwell edited the *Complete Poems* (2004), including many poems previously uncollected. Books of prose published in his lifetime include the novels *Home to Harlem* (1928), *Banjo* (1929), and *Banana Bottom* (1933); a short story collection, *Gingertown* (1932, 1991); an autobiography, *A Long Way from Home* (1937), and an essay collection, *Harlem: Negro Metropolis* (1940). Collections brought out after McKay's death include *Selected Poems* (1953), *The Dialect Poetry of Claude McKay* (1972), *The Passion of Claude McKay: Selected Poetry and Prose* (1973); two books of short stories, *Trial By Lynching* (1977) and *My Green Hills of Jamaica* (1979); and an essay collection, *The Negro in America* (1979).

Three good biographies are James R. Giles's *Claude McKay* (1976), Wayne F. Cooper's *Claude McKay: Rebel Sojourner in the Harlem Renaissance* (1987, 1996), and Tyrone Tillery's *Claude McKay: A Black Poet's Struggle for Identity* (1992). A collection of interpretive essays is *Claude McKay: Centennial Studies* (1992), edited by A. L. McLeod. General works with material on McKay include Harold Cruse's still valuable *The Crisis of the Negro Intellectual* (1967), Kenneth Ramchand's *The West Indian Novel and Its Background* (1970; rev. ed. 2004), Nathan I. Huggins's *Harlem Renaissance* (1971), Addison Gayle's *The Way of the New World: The Black Novel in America* (1975), David Levering Lewis's *When Harlem Was in Vogue* (1981), Bernard W. Bell's *The Afro-American Novel and Its Tradition* (1987), and George Hutchinson's *The Harlem Renaissance in Black and White* (1995). Contrasting treatments of McKay's poetry are in Winston James's *A Fierce Hatred of Injustice: Claude McKay's Jamaican Poetry of Rebellion* (2001) and Josh Gosciak's *The Shadowed Country: Claude McKay and the Romance of the Victorians* (2006).

Edna St. Vincent Millay

Millay's *Collected Sonnets* (1941) and *Collected Lyrics* (1943) were followed by *Collected Poems: Edna St. Vincent Millay* (1956), edited by Norma Millay (1956). The Library of America issued *Selected Poems* (2003). Her prose sketches, *Distressing Dialogue*, published under the pseudonym Nancy Boyd, appeared in 1924. Her three verse plays (*Aria da Capa*,

1920; *The Lamp and the Bell*, 1921; and *Two Slatterns and a King*, 1921) were collected in *Three Plays* (1926). Allan Ross Macdougall edited *Letters of Edna St. Vincent Millay* in 1952. The biographies are Daniel Epstein's *What Lips My Lips Have Kissed* (2001) and Nancy Milford's *Savage Beauty: The Life of Edna St. Vincent Millay* (2001). Essay collections are *Critical Essays on Edna St. Vincent Millay* (1993), edited by William B. Thesing, and *Millay at One Hundred* (1995), edited by Diane P. Freedman.

Marianne Moore

Each collection of Moore's verse excluded some earlier poems while subjecting others to extensive revisions and changes in format. Her separate volumes include *Poems* (1921); *Observations* (1924); *The Pangolin and Other Verse* (1936); *What Are Years?* (1941); *Nevertheless* (1944); *Like a Bulwark* (1956); *O to Be a Dragon* (1959); and *Tell Me, Tell Me* (1966). Collections include *Selected Poems* (1935); *Collected Poems* (1951); and *The Complete Poems of Marianne Moore* (1967, repr. 1981, 1987), which included selections from her translation of *The Fables of La Fontaine* (1954). Grace Shulman's *The Poems of Marianne Moore* (2003) is now the fullest edition. Patricia C. Willis has brought together Moore's published prose in *The Complete Prose of Marianne Moore* (1986). Moore's correspondence with Robert Lowell is published in *Becoming a Poet* (1991), by David Kalstone; her relation to Wallace Stevens is considered by Robin G. Schulze in *The Web of Friendship* (1995). The only biography is *Marianne Moore: A Literary Life* (1990), by Charles Molesworth. Bonnie Costello edited *The Selected Letters of Marianne Moore* (1997). Book-length studies include Bernard F. Engel's *Marianne Moore* (1963, rev. 1989), Costello's *Marianne Moore: Imaginary Possessions* (1982), John M. Slatin's *The Savage's Romance: The Poetry of Marianne Moore* (1986), Grace Schulman's *Marianne Moore: The Poetry of Engagement* (1987), Margaret Holley's *The Poetry of Marianne Moore: A Study in Voice and Value* (1987), Cristanne Miller's *Questions of Authority* (1995), Linda Leanell's *Marianne Moore and the Visual Arts* (1995), and Elisabeth W. Joyce's *Cultural Critique and Abstraction: Marianne Moore and the Avant-Garde* (1998). Essay collections include *Marianne Moore, Woman and Poet* (1990), edited by Patricia Willis, and *Marianne Moore: The Art of a Modernist* (1990), edited by Joseph Parigi. Eugene P. Sheehy and Kenneth A. Lohf compiled *The Achievement of Marianne Moore: A Bibliography, 1907–1957* in 1958, and Craig S. Abbott compiled *Marianne Moore: A Descriptive Bibliography* in 1977. Gary Lane's *A Concordance to the Poems of Marianne Moore* appeared in 1972.

Eugene O'Neill

The Library of America collected O'Neill's plays in three volumes, *Complete Plays 1913–1920*, *Complete Plays, 1920–1931*, and *Complete Plays 1932–1943* (1988). The standard biography of O'Neill is still that of Arthur and Barbara Gelb, *O'Neill* (1962, rev. 2000). Other biographical treatments are Frederic I. Carpenter's *Eugene O'Neill* (1964, rev. 1979), L. Schaeffer's *O'Neill, Son and Artist* (1973, 1990), and Stephen A. Bloch's *Eugene O'Neill: Beyond Mourning and Tragedy* (1999). *The Theatre We Worked For: The Letters of Eugene O'Neill to Kenneth Macgowan* (1982), edited by Jackson R. Bryer, documents O'Neill's attitudes to the theater of his day. Bryer and Travis Bogard edited *Selected Letters of Eugene O'Neill* (1994). *Conversations with Eugene O'Neill* (1990) is edited by Mark W. Estrin. Literary analysis of O'Neill's plays can be found in Bogard's *Contour in Time: The Plays of Eugene O'Neill* (1972, rev. 1987), Michael Manheim's *Eugene O'Neill's New Language of Kinship* (1982), Judith E. Barlow's *Final Acts: The Creation of Three Late O'Neill Plays* (1985), Kurt Eisen's *The Inner Strength of Opposites* (1994; on O'Neill's techniques), Joel Pfister's *Staging Depth: Eugene O'Neill and the Politics of Psychological Discourse* (1995), Donald Gallup's *Eugene O'Neill and His Eleven-Play Cycle* (1998), and Doris Alexander's *Eugene O'Neill's Last Plays: Separating Art from Autobiography* (2005).

Essay collections include *Eugene O'Neill: A Collection of Criticism* (1976), edited by E. Griffin; *Eugene O'Neill's Century* (1991), edited by Richard F. Moorton Jr.; *The Critical Response to Eugene O'Neill* (1993), edited by John H. Houchin; and *The Cambridge Companion to Eugene O'Neill* (1998), edited by Michael Manheim.

Katherine Anne Porter

Primary sources include *Ship of Fools* (1962); *The Collected Stories of Katherine Anne Porter* (1965); *The Collected Essays and Occasional Writings of Katherine Anne Porter* (1970); *The Never-Ending Wrong* (1977), about the Sacco and Vanzetti case; *Letters* (1990), edited by Isabel Bayley; *"This Strange, Old World" and Other Book Reviews by Katherine Anne Porter* (1991), edited by Darlene Harbour Unrue; *Uncollected Early Prose of Katherine Anne Porter* (1993), edited by Ruth M. Alvarez and Thomas F. Walsh; and *Katherine Anne Porter's Poetry* (1996), edited by Unrue.

The first full-scale biography is Joan Givner's *Katherine Anne Porter, A Life* (1982, rev. 1991). Givner also edited *Katherine Anne Porter: Conversations* (1987). *A Bibliography of the Works of Katherine Anne Porter*, edited by Louise Waldrip and Shirley Ann Bauer, appeared in 1969; *Katherine Anne Porter: An Annotated Bibliography* (of criticism) was compiled by Kathryn Hilt and Ruth M. Alvarez (1990).

Critical studies include Jane Krause DeMouy's *Katherine Anne Porter's Women: The Eye of Her Fiction* (1983), Unrue's *Truth and Vision in Katherine Anne Porter's Fiction* (1985), Willene and George Hendrick's *Katherine Anne Porter* (rev. 1988), Thomas F. Walsh's *Katherine Anne Porter and Mexico: The Illusion of Eden* (1992), Robert H. Brinkmeyer's *Katherine Anne Porter's Artistic Development* (1993), Janis P. Stout's *Katherine Anne Porter, A Sense of the Times* (1995), and Mary Titus's *The Ambivalent Art of Katherine Anne Porter* (2005). Unrue edited *Critical Essays on Katherine Anne Porter* (1997).

Ezra Pound

Pound's early poetry, from *A Lume Spento* (1908) through *Riposts* (1912), is in the authoritative *Collected Early Poems of Ezra Pound* (1976), edited by Michael King. The same volumes, along with later volumes *Hugh Selwyn Mauberley* and *Homage to Sextus Propertius*, are collected in *Personae: The Collected Shorter Poems* (rev. ed. 1949; 2nd rev. ed. 1990). The New Directions edition of *The Cantos* (1993) is definitive. The most important of Pound's critical writings are *The Spirit of Romance* (rev. 1952); *Gaudier-Brzeska: A Memoir* (1916); *Instigations* (1920); *Make It New* (1934); *The ABC of Reading* (1934); *Guide to Kulchur* (1938); and *Patria Mia* (1950). His criticism has been collected in *Literary Essays of Ezra Pound* (1954), edited by T. S. Eliot; *Selected Prose, 1909–1965* (1973), edited by William Cookson (1973); and *Ezra Pound's Poetry and Prose Contributions to Periodicals* (1991), prefaced and arranged by Lea Baechler, A. Walton Litz, and James Longenback in eleven volumes. *Ezra Pound Speaking: Radio Speeches of World War II* (1978), edited by Leonard W. Doob, collects his wartime radio addresses. D. D. Paige edited *The Letters of Ezra Pound, 1907–1941* (1950). Other correspondence is collected in *Ezra Pound and Dorothy Shakespear: Their Letters, 1909–1914* (1984), edited by Omar Pound and A. Walton Litz; *Pound/Lewis: The Letters of Ezra Pound and Wyndham Lewis* (1985), edited by Timothy Materer; *Ezra Pound and James Loughlin* (1994), edited by David M. Gordon; and *Pound/Cummings: The Correspondence of Ezra Pound and E. E. Cummings*, edited by Barry Ahearn. Reviews of Pound are collected in Eric Homberger's *Ezra Pound: The Critical Heritage* (1973, 1997).

James J. Wilhelm's three-volume biography includes *The American Roots of Ezra Pound* (1985), *Ezra Pound in London and Paris, 1908–1925* (1990), and *Ezra Pound: The Tragic Years, 1925–1972* (1994). Also useful are Noel Stock's *The Life of Ezra Pound* (1970, 1982), C.

David Haymann's *Ezra Pound, The Last Rower: A Political Profile* (1976), Humphrey Carpenter's *A Serious Character: The Life of Ezra Pound* (1988), and Wendy Stallard Flory's *The American Ezra Pound* (1989). *The Roots of Treason: Ezra Pound and the Secrets of St. Elizabeth* (1984), by E. Fuller Torrey, focuses on Pound's trial and incarceration.

Hugh Kenner's *The Pound Era* (1972) has been influential. Good introductions are Christine Brooke-Rose's *A ZBC of Ezra Pound* (1971) and James Knapp's *Ezra Pound* (1972). For *The Cantos* see the *Annotated Index to the Cantos of Ezra Pound* (1957) (through Canto LXXXIV), edited by John H. Edwards and William W. Vasse; George Dekker's *The Cantos of Ezra Pound* (1963); Noel Stock's *Reading the Cantos* (1967); Ronald Bush's *The Genesis of Pound's Cantos* (1976); Wilhelm's *The Later Cantos of Ezra Pound* (1977); Lawrence S. Rainey's *Ezra Pound and the Monument of Culture* (1991); Carrol F. Terrill's *A Companion to the Cantos of Ezra Pound* (1993); George Kearn's *Guide to Ezra Pound's Selected Cantos* (1980); Anthony Woodward's *Ezra Pound and "The Pisan Cantos"* (1980); and William Cookson's updated *Guide to the Cantos of Ezra Pound* (2001). *Ezra Pound and Italian Fascism* (1991), by Tim Redman, addresses the poet's politics; as does *Pound in Purgatory: From Economic Realism to Anti-Semitism* (1999), by Leon Surette. Cultural approaches to Pound include Michael Coyle's *Ezra Pound, Popular Genres, and the Discourse of Culture* (1995) and Daniel Tiffany's *Radio Corpse* (1995). Marjorie Perloff's *The Dance of the Intellect* (1996) studies poetry in the Pound tradition. Andrew Gibson edited *Pound in Multiple Perspective: A Collection of Critical Essays* (1993) and Ira B. Nadel edited *The Cambridge Companion to Ezra Pound* (1999).

Edwin Arlington Robinson

Collected Poems of Edwin Arlington Robinson (1921) was enlarged periodically through 1937. In addition to shorter verse, Robinson wrote long narrative poems, including the Arthurian trilogy of *Merlin* (1917), *Lancelot* (1920), and *Tristrum* (1927). Other books include *Roman Bartholomew* (1923), *The Man Who Died Twice* (1924), *Cavender's House* (1929), *The Glory of the Nightingales* (1930), *Matthias at the Door* (1931), *Talifer* (1933), *Amaranth* (1934), and *King Jasper* (1935). Ridgely Torrence compiled *Selected Letters* (1940). Denham Sutcliffe edited *Untriangulated Stars: Letters of Edwin Arlington Robinson to Harry de Forest Smith, 1890–1905* (1947). Richard Cary edited *Edwin Arlington Robinson's Letters to Edith Brower* (1968).

There is little recent work on Robinson. Richard Cary documented *The Early Reception of Edwin Arlington Robinson* (1974). Introductions to Robinson's work include Wallace L.

Anderson's *Edwin Arlington Robinson: A Critical Introduction* (1967), Hoyt C. Franchere's *Edwin Arlington Robinson* (1968), and Louis O. Coxe's *Edwin Arlington Robinson: The Life of Poetry* (1969). Ellsworth Barnard edited *Edwin Arlington Robinson: Centenary Essays* (1969). Other collections are *Appreciation of Edwin Arlington Robinson: Twenty-eight Interpretive Essays* (1969), edited by Richard Cary; and *Edwin Arlington Robinson: A Collection of Critical Essays* (1970), edited by Francis Murphy. Richard Hoffpair's *The Contemplative Poetry of Edwin Arlington Robinson, Robert Frost, and Yvor Winters* (2002) links Robinson to other poets.

Carl Sandburg

The Complete Poems of Carl Sandburg (1950) was revised and expanded in 1970. *Breathing Tokens* (1978), edited by Margaret Sandburg, prints unpublished poems. *Billy Sunday and Other Poems* (1993), edited by George and Willene Hendrick, contains some of his unpublished, uncollected, and unexpurgated poems. In addition to eight full-length volumes of poetry, Sandburg wrote a Pulitzer Prize–winning study of Abraham Lincoln: *Abraham Lincoln: The Prairie Years*, 2 vols. (1926), and *Abraham Lincoln: The War Years*, 4 vols. (1939), two collections of journalism and social commentary, *Rootabaga Stories* for children, a novel, and a book of American folk songs. *Fables, Foibles and Foobles* (1988), edited by George Hendrick, is a selection of unpublished humorous pieces. *More Rootabagas* (1993), edited by Hendrick, contains stories for children. *Selected Poems* (1996) was edited by George and Willene Hendrick. *The Letters of Carl Sandburg* (1968, 1988) was edited by Herbert Mitgang. *The Poet and the Dream Girl: The Love Letters of Lilian Steichen and Carl Sandburg* (1987, 1999) was edited by Margaret Sandburg.

Always the Young Strangers (1953) and *Ever the Winds of Chance* (1983), edited by Margaret Sandburg and George Hendrick, are segments of Sandburg's autobiography. A full-scale biography is Penelope Niven's *Carl Sandburg: A Biography* (1991). Critical studies include Richard Crowder's *Carl Sandburg* (1964) and Philip R. Yannella's *The Other Carl Sandburg* (1996).

Gertrude Stein

The Library of America published Stein's writings in two volumes: 1903–32 and 1932–46 (1998). *The Yale Edition of the Unpublished Writings of Gertrude Stein* (1951–58), edited by Carl Van Vechten, contains eight volumes of poetry, prose fiction, portraits, essays, and miscellany. The Norton Critical Edition of *Three Lives and Q.E.D.* (2005), edited by Marianne DeKoven, supplies critical and biographical contexts. Among publications in Stein's lifetime are *Tender Buttons* (1914) and prose fiction, including *Three Lives* (1909), *The Making of Americans* (1925), *Lucy Church Amiably* (1930), *Ida: A Novel* (1941), and *Brewsie and Willie* (1946). *Geography and Plays* (1922), *Operas and Plays* (1932), and *Last Operas and Plays* (1949, 1995), edited by Carl Van Vechten, contain dramatic pieces. Biographical material and portraits of Stein's contemporaries may be found in *The Autobiography of Alice B. Toklas* (1933), *Portraits and Prayers* (1934); *Everybody's Autobiography* (1937), and *Wars I Have Seen* (1945). Other works, including meditations, essays, sketches, and sociolinguistic treatises, are *Useful Knowledge* (1928), *How to Write* (1931), *Lectures in America* (1935), *Narration: Four Lectures by Gertrude Stein* (1935), *What Are Masterpieces* (1940), and *Four in America* (1947). Donald C. Gallup edited *Fernhurst, Q.E.D. and Other Early Writings by Gertrude Stein* (1971) and also a collection of letters to Stein, *The Flowers of Friendship* (1953). Her correspondence with Mabel Dodge Luhan is edited by Patricia R. Everett (1996) and with Thornton Wilder by Edward Burns and Ulla E. Dydo (1996). *Baby Precious Always Shines* (2000), edited by Kay Tarner, has selected love letters written between Stein and her partner, Alice B. Toklas. *Gertrude Stein: An Annotated Bibliography* (1979) was compiled by Maureen R. Liston.

W. G. Rogers's *When This You See Remember Me: Gertrude Stein in Person* (1948) and Alice B. Toklas's *What Is Remembered* (1963) are reminiscences of Stein by friends. Biographies include Howard Greenfield's *Gertrude Stein: A Biography* (1973), James R. Mellow's *Charmed Circle: Gertrude Stein and Company* (1974), Janet Hobhouse's *Everybody Who Was Anybody* (1989), Linda Wagner-Martin's *Favored Strangers: Gertrude Stein and Her Family* (1995), and Brenda Wineapple's *Sister Brother: Gertrude and Leo Stein* (1996).

Critical studies include Robert B. Haas's *A Primer for the Gradual Understanding of Gertrude Stein* (1971), Richard Bridgman's *Gertrude Stein in Pieces* (1970), Wendy Steiner's *Exact Resemblance to Exact Resemblance: The Literary Portraiture of Gertrude Stein* (1978), Marianne DeKoven's *A Different Language: Gertrude Stein's Experimental Writing* (1983), Randa Kay Dubnick's *The Structure of Obscurity: Gertrude Stein, Language, and Cubism* (1984), Lisa Ruddick's *Reading Gertrude Stein: Body, Text, Gnosis* (1990), Bettina L. Knapp's *Gertrude Stein* (1990), Jane P. Bowers's *Gertrude Stein* (1993), Linda Watts's *Gertrude Stein: A Study of the Short Fiction* (1999), Barbara Will's *Gertrude Stein, Modernism, and the Problem of "Genius"* (2000), and Dana Cairns Watson's *Gertrude Stein and the Essence of What Hoppens* (2004). Bruce Kellner edited the useful *Gertrude Stein Com-*

panion (1988). A collection of critical essays, edited by Richard Kostelanetz, is *Gertrude Stein Advanced* (1990).

John Steinbeck
The Library of America issued three volumes of Steinbeck's work, *Novels and Stories 1932–1937* (1994), *The Grapes of Wrath and Other Writings* (1996), and *Novels 1942–1952* (2002). Two biographies are *The True Adventures of John Steinbeck, Writer* (1984), by Jackson J. Benson, and *John Steinbeck* (1995), by Jay Parini. Elaine Steinbeck and Robert Wallsten edited *Steinbeck: A Life in Letters* (1975). Critical studies of Steinbeck include Paul McCarthy's *John Steinbeck* (1980), R. S. Hughes's *Beyond the Red Pony: A Reader's Guide to Steinbeck's Complete Short Stories* (1987), John H. Timmerman's *The Dramatic Landscape of Steinbeck's Short Stories* (1990), and Warren French's *John Steinbeck's Fiction Revisited* (1994). R. David edited *John Steinbeck: A Collection of Critical Essays* (1972); other collections are *Rediscovering Steinbeck* (1989), edited by Cliff Lewis and Carroll Britch; *Critical Essays on Steinbeck's* Grapes of Wrath (1989), edited by John Ditsky; *Short Novels of John Steinbeck* (1990), edited by Jackson J. Benson; *John Steinbeck: The Contemporary Reviews* (1996), edited by Joseph R. McElrath Jr., Jesse S. Crisler, and Susan Shillinglaw; and *Beyond Boundaries: Rereading John Steinbeck* (2002), edited by Shillinglaw and Kevin Hearle.

Wallace Stevens
The Collected Poems of Wallace Stevens was published in 1954. *Opus Posthumous* (1957, rev. 1989) by Milton J. Bates includes previously uncollected poems, plays, and essays. *The Necessary Angel: Essays on Reality and the Imagination* (1951) is Stevens's prose statement on poetry. The Library of America issued his *Collected Poetry and Prose* (1997). Other resources are *Letters of Wallace Stevens* (1966, 1996), edited by Holly Stevens; *The Contemplated Spouse: The Letters of Wallace Stevens to Elsie* (2006), edited by J. Donald Blount; *Concordance to the Poetry of Wallace Stevens* (1963), edited by Thomas Walsh; and *Wallace Stevens: A Descriptive Bibliography* (1973), compiled by J. M. Edelstein.

Joan Richardson's *Wallace Stevens: The Early Years, 1879–1923* (1986) chronicles the poet's youth and her *Wallace Stevens: The Later Years, 1923–1955* (1988) completes the story. Another biography is Tony Sharpe's *Wallace Stevens: A Literary Life* (2000). A. Walton Litz's *Introspective Voyager: The Poetic Development of Wallace Stevens* (1972) traces Stevens's thought and style through his early and middle years. Harold Bloom's *Wallace Stevens: The Poems of Our Climate* (1977) considers intellectual influences on Stevens; Joseph N. Riddle's *The Clairvoyant Eye: The Poetry and Poetics of Wallace Stevens* (1969, 1991) reads many individual poems. Other good full-length studies include Eleanor Cook's *Poetry, Word-Play, and Word-War in Wallace Stevens* (1988), Robert Rehder's *The Poetry of Wallace Stevens* (1988), James Longenbach's *Wallace Stevens: The Plain Sense of Things* (1991), George S. Lensing's *Wallace Stevens: A Poet's Growth* (1991), Daniel Schwarz's *Narrative and Representation in the Poetry of Wallace Stevens* (1993), Alan Filreis's *Modernism from Left to Right* (1994), and Janet McCann's *Wallace Stevens Revisited* (1995). Jacqueline Vaught Brogan's *The Violence Within/The Violence Without: Wallace Stevens and the Emergence of a Revolutionary Poetics* (2003) and Malcolm Woodland's *Wallace Stevens and the Apocalyptic Mode* (2005) consider the relation of Stevens's poetry to war. Albert Gelpi collects essays on the poet in *Wallace Stevens: The Poetics of Modernism* (1990); other collections are *Critical Essays on Wallace Stevens* (1988), edited by Steven Gould Axelrod and Helen Deese, and *Wallace Stevens and the Feminine* (1993), edited by Melita Schaum.

Jean Toomer

Toomer's published works include *Cane* (1923, repr. 1975, pub. also in a Norton Critical Edition, 1988), *Essentials* (1931), *Portage Potential* (1932), and an address, "The Flavor of Man" (1949). His *Collected Poems,* edited by Robert B. Jones and Margery Toomer Latimer, were published in 1988. *A Jean Toomer Reader* (1993), containing previously unpublished writings, was edited by Frederik L. Rusch; Robert B. Jones edited *Selected Essays and Literary Criticism* (1996). Brian Joseph Benson and Mabel Mayle Dillard's *Jean Toomer* (1980); Nellie Y. McKay's *Jean Toomer, Artist: A Study of His Literary Life and Work, 1894–1936* (1984); and Cynthia Earl Kerman and Richard Eldridge's *The Lives of Jean Toomer: A Hunger for Wholeness* (1989) are biographies. Studies include *Jean Toomer and the Terrors of American History* (1998), by Charles Scruggs and Lee Van De Marr, and *Split-Gut Song: Jean Toomer and the Poetics of Modernity* (2005), by Karen Ford Jackson. Essay collections are *Jean Toomer: A Critical Evaluation* (1988), edited by Therman B. O'Daniel, and *Jean Toomer and the Harlem Renaissance,* edited by Geneviève Faber and Michel Faith (2000).

William Carlos Williams

Williams's poems were first collected in three volumes: *Collected Earlier Poems of William Carlos Williams* (1951), *Collected Later Poems of William Carlos Williams* (1950), and *Pictures from Brueghel* (1962). More recent are *The Collected Poems of William Carlos Williams, Vol. 1, 1909–1939* (1996), edited by A. Walton Litz and Christopher MacGowan, and *Vol. 2, 1939–1962* (1988), edited by MacGowan (1988). *Paterson's* five books, published individually between 1946 and 1958, were issued in one volume in 1963 and reedited by MacGowan (1992). *Kora in Hell,* Williams's volume of prose poetry, is in the collection *Imaginations* (1970), edited by Webster Schott, along with essays, fiction, and creative prose. Williams's short stories are collected in *Make Light of It* (1950) and again, with several additions, in *The Farmers' Daughters* (1961). His novels are *A Voyage to Pagany* (1928), *White Mule* (1937), *In the Money* (1940), and *The Build Up* (1946). His dramatic pieces were published together in *Many Loves and Other Plays* (1961). Important essays are contained in *In the American Grain* (1925, 1940); *Selected Essays of William Carlos Williams* (1954); and *Imaginations* (1970), edited by Webster Schott. Williams's prose also includes *The Autobiography of William Carlos Williams* (1951); a book of recollections dictated to Edith Heal, *I Wanted to Write a Poem* (1958); and *Yes, Mrs. Williams* (1959), a portrait of the poet's mother. J. C. Thirlwall edited *The Selected Letters of William Carlos Williams* (1957). Selections from the Pound–Williams correspondence, edited by Hugh Witemeyer, appeared in 1996. Letters between Williams and Denise Levertov, edited by MacGowan, appeared in 1998. Barry Ahearn edited *The Correspondence of William Carlos Williams and Louis Zukofsky* (2003). *The Humane Particulars: The Collected Letters of William Carlos Williams and Kenneth Burke* (2003) was edited by James H. East. Emily Mitchell Wallace compiled *A Bibliography of William Carlos Williams* (1968). Reed Whittemore's *William Carlos Williams: Poet from Jersey* (1975) is a critical biography, as is Paul Mariani's more detailed *William Carlos Williams: A New World Naked* (1981).

James E. Breslin's *William Carlos Williams: An American Artist* (1970) is a still-useful overview. Other general introductions are Thomas R. Whitaker's *William Carlos Williams* (1989) and Kelli A. Larson's *Guide to the Poetry of William Carlos Williams* (1995). Among specialized studies are Mike Weaver's *William Carlos Williams: The American Background* (1971), Jerome Mazzaro's *William Carlos Williams: The Later Poems* (1973), Joseph N. Riddel's *The Inverted Bell: Modernism and the Counter-Poetics of William Carlos Williams* (1974), Charles Doyle's *William Carlos Williams and the American Poem* (1982), Henry M. Sayre's *The Visual Text of William Carlos Williams* (1983), Kerry Driscoll's *William Carlos Williams and the Maternal Muse* (1987), Ann W. Fisher-Wirth's *William Carlos Williams and Autobiography: The Woods of His Own Nature* (1989), Ron Callan's *William Carlos Williams*

and *Transcendentalism* (1992), T. Hugh Craw-
ford's *Modernism, Medicine, and William Car-
los Williams* (1993), Brian A. Bremen's *William
Carlos Williams and the Diagnostics of Culture*
(1993), Peter Halter's *The Revolution in the
Visual Arts and the Poetry of William Carlos
Williams* (1994), Donald W. Markos's *Ideas in
Things* (1994), Barry Ahearn's *William Carlos
Williams and Celebrity* (1994), Julio Marzan's
*The Spanish American Roots of William Carlos
Williams* (1994), and Stanley Koehler's *Coun-
tries of the Mind: The Poetry of William Carlos
Williams* (1998).

Linda Wagner's *The Prose of William Carlos
Williams* (1970) and Robert Coles's *William
Carlos Williams: The Knack of Survival in
America* (1975) discuss Williams's prose. For
Paterson, see Joel Conarroe's *William Carlos
Williams' Paterson: Language and Landscape*
(1970) and Benjamin Sankey's *A Companion to
William Carlos Williams's Paterson* (1971). Paul
Mariani's *William Carlos Williams: The Poet
and His Critics* (1975) considers Williams's crit-
ical reception, as does *William Carlos Williams,
The Critical Heritage* (1980, 1997), edited by
Charles Doyle. *Critical Essays on Wallace
Stevens* was edited by Steven Gould Axelrod and
Helen Deese (1988).

Richard Wright
Wright's fiction includes *Uncle Tom's Children*
(1938), *Native Son* (1940), *The Outsider*
(1953), and *Eight Men* (1961). *Black Boy*
(1945) is his autobiography; *White Man, Listen!*
(1957) is an important work of nonfiction. The
Library of America has published his writings in

two volumes, including an unexpurgated version of *Native Son* (1991). For a complete bibliography of his writings, see *Richard Wright: A
Primary Bibliography* (1982), compiled by
Charles T. Davis and Michel Fabre. A good
example of reviews can be found in *Richard
Wright: The Critical Reception* (1978), edited
by John M. Reilly; a massive bibliography of
Wright criticism around the world has been
assembled by Keneth Kinnamon (1988). Kinnamon and Michel Fabre edited *Conversations
with Richard Wright* (1993). The best critical
biography is Fabre's *The Unfinished Quest of
Richard Wright* (1993); see also Margaret
Walker's *Richard Wright, Daemonic Genius*
(1993) and Hazel Rowley's *Richard Wright: The
Life and Times* (2001). Critical studies include
Russell C. Brignano's *Richard Wright: An Introduction to the Man and His Works* (1970), Kin-
namon's *The Emergence of Richard Wright*
(1972), Fabre's *Richard Wright: Books and
Writers* (1990), and Robert Butler's *Native Son:
The Emergence of a New Black Hero* (1991).
Abdul R. Jan Mohamed's *The Death-Bound-
Subject: Richard Wright's Archaeology of Death*
(2005) is an ambitious theoretical study. Col-
lections of criticism are Yoshinobu Hakutani's
Critical Essays on Richard Wright (1982);
*Richard Wright: Critical Perspectives Past and
Present* (1993), edited by Henry Louis Gates Jr.
and K. A. Appiah; *The Critical Response to
Richard Wright* (1995), edited by Robert J. But-
ler; *Richard Wright: A Collection of Critical
Essays* (1995), edited by Arnold Rampersad; and
Kinnamon's *Critical Essays on Richard Wright's
Native Son* (1997).

AMERICAN LITERATURE SINCE 1945

Reference Works and Histories

James L. Harner's *Literary Research Guide* (1993, updated online) is a valuable resource. James D. Hart's *Oxford Companion to American Literature*, 5th
ed. (1983), Jack Saltzman's *The Cambridge Handbook of American Literature*
(1986), and the annual volumes of *American Literary Scholarship* (currently
edited by David J. Nordloh and Gary Scharnhorst) identify authors and
trends. Of broader scope are editor Emory Elliott's *The Columbia Literary
History of the United States* (1988) and *The Columbia History of the American Novel* (1991), together with editor Jay Parini's *The Columbia History of
American Poetry* (1993). Sacvan Bercovitch is general editor of the multivolume, ongoing *Cambridge History of American Literature*. Don B. Wilmeth has
edited the *Cambridge Guide to American Theatre* (1996). The vast *Dictionary
of Literary Biography,* under the supervision of Matthew J. Bruccoli, the
Scribners *American Writers* series, edited by Jay Parini, and vol. 2 of David

Perkins's *History of Modern Poetry* (1976) offer wide coverage of specific authors. An indispensable reference guide for poetry is *Contemporary Poets,* 7th ed. (2000), edited by Thomas Riggs. Specific areas are treated by editors Joel Shatzky and Michael Taub's *Contemporary Jewish-American Novelists: A Bio-Critical Sourcebook* (1997), Darryl Dickson-Carr's *The Columbia Guide to Contemporary African American Fiction* (2005), editor Eric Cheyfitz's *The Columbia Guide to American Indian Literatures of the United States since 1945* (2006), and José F. Aranda Jr.'s *When We Arrive: A New Literary History of Mexican America* (2003). Steven Conner's *The Cambridge Companion to Postmodernism* (2004) provides a guide to the cultural contexts of the period. Useful introductory series are the University of South Carolina Press's *Understanding . . .* volumes, the Twayne United States Authors series, Methuen's Contemporary Writers, the University Press of Mississippi's *Conversations with . . .* , the *Critical Essays* books from G. K. Hall Publishers, the Greenwood Press *Critical Response* series, and the *Modern Critical Views* collections edited by Harold Bloom. The University of Michigan's *Poets on Poetry* series offers volumes in which poets comment on their own and others' work.

Literary Theory and Criticism

Theoretical overviews are provided by Christian Moraru in *Memorious Discourse: Reprise and Representation in Postmodernism* (2005) and Stacey Olster in *The Trash Phenomenon: Contemporary Literature, Popular Culture, and the Making of the American Century* (2003). The critic and theorist Marjorie Perloff has written a series of books that provide theoretical overviews and studies of the poetry of the period: *The Poetics of Indeterminacy* (1981), *The Dance of the Intellect* (1985), *Radical Artifice: Writing in the Age of Media* (1991), and *21st-Century Modernism: The New Poetics* (2001). Playwrights and their work are studied by Sanford Sternlicht in *A Reader's Guide to Modern American Drama* (2002), Thomas S. Hischak in *American Theatre: A Chronicle of Comedy and Drama, 1969–2000* (2001), Christopher Bigsby in *Contemporary American Playwrights* (1999), and Herbert Blau in *The Dubious Spectacle: Extremities of the Theater, 1976–2000* (2002). Histories of specific movements in poetry are explored in Michael Palmer's *The San Francisco Renaissance* (1991) and David Lehmann's *The Last Avant-Garde: The Making of the New York School of Poets* (1998). A more general history appears in Robert von Hallberg's *American Poetry and Culture 1945–1980* (1985). The history of poetry may also be traced through statements on poetics: *Poetics of the New American Poetry* (1973), edited by Donald Allen, was groundbreaking, and *Twentieth-Century American Poetry* (2004), edited by Dana Gioia, David Mason, and Meg Schoerke, gathers statements on poetics from throughout the period. Fiction's development is traced in detail in Kathryn Hume's *American Dream, American Nightmare: Fiction since 1960* (2000) and Marc Chénetier's *Beyond Suspicion: New American Fiction since 1960* (1996). The development of poetry in the period is examined in Dana Gioia's *Disappearing Ink: Poetry at the End of Print Culture* (2004), Christopher MacGowan's *Twentieth-Century American Poetry* (2004), Stephen Fredman's *A Concise Companion to Twentieth-Century American Poetry* (2005), Jennifer

Ashton's *From Modernism to Postmodernism: American Poetry and Theory in the Twentieth Century* (2006), and Charles Altieri's *The Art of Twentieth-Century American Poetry: Modernism and After* (2006). Among the useful collections of literary criticism that focus on poetry of the period are Sherman Paul's *The Lost America of Love* (1981), J. D. McClatchy's *White Paper* (1990), Helen Vendler's *The Music of What Happens* (1988) and *Soul Says* (1995), Lynn Keller's *Re-Making It New* (1987), Vernon Shetley's *After the Death of Poetry* (1993), Peter Stitt's *Uncertainty and Plenitude: Five Contemporary Poets* (1997), Charles Altieri's *Postmodernisms Now* (1998), Thomas Travisano's *Mid-century Quartet* (1999), and Adam Kirsch's *The Wounded Surgeon: Confession and Transformation in Six American Poets* (2005). Political implications are examined by Alan Nadel in *Containment Culture: American Narratives, Postmodernism, and the Atomic Age* (1995), while Wendy Steiner exlores the controversy over sexual elements in *The Scandal of Pleasure* (1995). Politics in poetry is explored in Mutlu Konuk's *Politics and Form in Postmodern Poetry* (1995), Tim Wood's *The Poetics of the Limit: Ethics and Politics in Modern and Contemporary American Poetry* (2002), and Walter Kalaidjian's *The Edge of Modernism: American Poetry and the Traumatic Past* (2006).

Two important studies from a feminist perspective are Nancy J. Peterson's *Against Amnesia: Contemporary Women Writers and the Crisis of Historical Memory* (2001) and Linda S. Kauffman's *Bad Girls and Sick Boys: Fantasies in Contemporary Art and Culture* (1998). A feminist approach to the study of poetry can be found in *Gendered Modernisms: American Women Poets and Their Readers* (1996), edited by Margaret Dickie and Thomas Travisano. Jean Wyatt considers social issues in *Risking Difference: Identification, Race, and Community in Contemporary Fiction and Feminism* (2004). Multiculturalism concerns Martha J. Cutter in *Lost and Found in Translation: Contemporary Ethnic American Writing and the Politics of Language Diversity* (2005), Paula M. L. Moya in *Learning from Experience: Minority Identities, Multicultural Struggles* (2002), Robert Jackson in *Seeking the Region in American Literature and Culture* (2005), and A. Robert Lee in *Multicultural American Literature: Comparative Black, Native, Latino/a and Asian American Fictions* (2003). Multiculturalism in poetry is the subject of Satya Mohanty's *Literary Theory and the Claims of History: Postmodernism, Objectivity and Multicultural Politics* (1997). Cassie Premo Steele's *We Heal from Memory: Sexton, Lorde, Anzaldúa, and the Poetry of Witness* (2000) treats women poets across the divisions of ethnicity. African American writing is the focus in Bernard W. Bell's *The Contemporary African American Novel: Its Folk Roots and Modern Literary Branches* (2004), Cheryl A. Wall's *Worrying the Line: Black Women Writers, Lineage, and Literary Tradition* (2005), Suzanne W. Jones's *Race Mixing: Southern Fiction since the Sixties* (2004), and James W. Coleman's *Faithful Vision: Treatments of the Sacred, Spiritual, and Supernatural in Twentieth-Century African American Fiction* (2006). *Black Women Writers (1950–1980): A Critical Evaluation*, edited by Mari Evans, explores African American novelists and poets from a feminist perspective. African American poetry is examined in Joanne Gabbin's *The Furious Flowering of African American Poetry* (1999) and Alden Lynn Nielsen's *Black Chant: Languages of African-American Postmodernism* (1992). Chicano/a work is treated by Charles M. Tatum in *Chicano Popular Culture* (2001), Mary Pat Brady in *Extinct Lands, Temporal Geographies: Chicana Literature and the Urgency of*

Space (2002), Elisabeth Mermann-Jozwiak in *Postmodern Vernaculars: Chicana Literature and Postmodern Rhetoric* (2005), Tey Diana Rebolledo in *The Chronicles of Panchita Villa and Other Guerrilleras* (2005), and Ramon Saldívar in *Chicano Narrative* (1990). Deborah L. Madsen's *Understanding Contemporary Chicana Literature* (2000) examines the work of women poets.

    Transnational Asian American Literature: Sites and Transits (2006), edited by Shirley Geok-lin Lim, et al., includes essays covering issues from immigration to feminism and globalism. More general concerns occupy David Leiwei Li in *Imagining the Nation: Asian American Literature and Cultural Consent* (1998). Jinqui Ling reconciles conflicting approaches of cultural study and nationalist impulses in *Narrating Nationalisms: Ideology and Form in Asian American Literature* (1998). Xiaojing Zhou studies Asian American poetry in *The Ethics of Poetics of Alterity in Asian American Poetry* (2006), and Guiyou Huang has edited a resource guide to poets, *Asian American Poets: A Bio-Bibliographical Critical Sourcebook* (2002). Arnold Krupat's *Red Matters: Native American Studies* (2002) looks beyond nationalism, indigenism, and cosmopolitanism to gauge Native American literature's importance to the ethical and intellectual heritage of the West. Catherine Rainwater's *Dreams of Fiery Stars: The Transformation of Native American Fiction* (1999) offers strong artistic analysis. Kenneth Lincoln's *Sing with the Heart of a Bear: Fusions of Native and American Poetry, 1890–1999* (1999) stresses poetry's flexible and adaptable nature rather than its conformity to rigid ethnic and literary categories. Robin Riley First's *The Heart Is a Drum: Continuance and Resistance in American Indian Poetry* (2000) provides cultural and historical readings of a wide range of poems.

    Especially useful for understanding how and why contemporary writers produce their work is the critical interview, the exploratory technique for which was pioneered by Joe David Bellamy in his *The New New Fiction: Interviews with Innovative American Writers* (1974) and which has been perfected by Larry McCaffery, who with various coeditors has produced a series of extensive, insightful, and critically developed dialogues with important authors of the past four decades: *Anything Can Happen* (1983), *Alive and Writing* (1987), *Across the Wounded Galaxies* (1990), and *Some Other Frequency* (1996). Over the years *The Paris Review* has conducted a series of interviews, "Writers at Work," that includes some of the most important writers of this period. The University of Michigan series, *Poets on Poetry*, includes interviews as well as essays (for individual volumes, consult the bibliographies of specific poets). Other valuable sources for interviews with poets are *Black Women Writers at Work* (1988), edited by Claudia Tate, *Survival This Way: Interviews with American Indian Poets* (1987), edited by Joseph Bruhac, and *Truthtellers of the Time: Interviews with Contemporary Women Poets* (1998), edited by Janet Palmer Mullaney.

    A considerable amount of material, some of it useful, can be found on the Internet, including websites that offer audio versions of writers reading from their work. The Academy of American Poets' *poets.org* is the best general site for poetry and includes an audio component and links to other resources. The Internet Public Library offers "Native American Authors" at http://www.ipl.org/div/natam/

Sherman Alexie

Alexie's novels are *Reservation Blues* (1995), *Indian Killer* (1996), and *Flight* (2007). His story collections are *The Lone Ranger and Tonto Fistfight in Heaven* (1993, adapted as a film script for *Smoke Signals* in 1998), *The Toughest Indian in the World* (2000), and *Ten Little Indians* (2003). His poetry collections are *The Business of Fancy- dancing* (1992), *I Would Steal Horses* (1992), *First Indian on the Moon* (1993), *Old Shirts and New Skins* (1993), *Seven Mourning Songs for the Cedar Flute I Have Yet to Learn to Play* (1994), *Water Flowing Home* (1996), *The Man Who Loves Salmon* (1998), *One Stick Song* (2000), *Il powwow della fine del mondo* (2005), and *Dangerous Astronomy* (2005). He wrote and directed the movie *The Business of Fancydancing* (2000).

Daniel Grassian provides critical analysis in *Understanding Sherman Alexie* (2005).

Julia Alvarez

Alvarez's novels are *How the García Girls Lost Their Accents* (1991), *In the Time of the Butterflies* (1994), *¡Yo!* (1997), *In the Name of Salomé* (2000), and *Saving the World* (2006). Her poetry collections are *The Housekeeping Book* (1984), *Homecoming* (1984, revised 1996), *The Other Side / El Otro Lado* (1995), *Seven Trees* (1998), and *The Woman I Kept to Myself* (2004). *Something to Declare* (1998) gathers her essays. *How Tía Lola Came to Stay* (2001), *A Cafecito Story* (2002), and *Before We Were Free* (2002) are books for children and young adults.

Kelli Lyon Johnson presents a critical analysis in *Julia Alvarez: Writing a New Place on the Map* (2005).

Gloria Anzaldúa

Borderlands/La Frontera (1987) includes memoir, historical analysis, and narrative poetry. Anzaldúa has also written several novels: *La Prieta* ("The Dark One") (1997), and (for children) *Prietita Has a Friend—Prietita Tiene un Amigo* (1991), *Friends from the Other Side—Amigos del Otra Lado* (1993), and *Prietita and the Ghost Woman—Prietita y La Llorona* (1996). She is the editor of *Making Face, Making Soul / Haciendo Caras: Creative and Critical Perspectives by Feminists of Color* (1990), and (with Cherríe Moraga) coedited *This Bridge Called My Back: Writings by Radical Women of Color* (1981). In 2002 she coedited, with Analouise Keating, *This Bridge We Call Home: Radical Visions for Transformation*.

Anzaldúa's work is studied by Deborah L. Madsen in *Understanding Contemporary Chicana Literature* (2000). Sonia Sandivár-Hull in *Feminism on the Border: Chicana Politics and Literature* (2000), Paula M. L. Moya in *Learning from Experience: Minority Identities, Multicultural Struggles* (2002), and Catrióna Rueda Esquibel in *With Her Machete in Her Hand: Reading Chicana Lesbians* (2006).

John Ashbery

Ashbery's volumes of poetry include *Some Trees* (1956), *The Tennis Court Oath* (1962), *Rivers and Mountains* (1966), *The Double Dream of Spring* (1970), *Three Poems* (1972), *Self-Portrait in a Convex Mirror* (1975), *Houseboat Days* (1977), *As We Know* (1979), *Shadow Train* (1981), *A Wave* (1984), *Selected Poems* (1985), *April Galleons* (1988), *Flow Chart* (1991), *And the Stars Were Shining* (1994), *Can You Hear, Bird* (1995), *Girls on the Run* (1999), *Your Name Here* (2000), *Chinese Whispers* (2002), and *Where Shall I Wander* (2005). Ashbery's Charles Eliot Norton Lectures on Poetry appear in *Other Traditions* (2000), and he has also published *Selected Prose* (2004).

Among useful critical essays are David Kalstone's *Five Temperaments* (1977) and John Shoptaw's book-length study of Ashbery's poetry, *On the Outside Looking Out* (1994). David K. Kermani's *John Ashbery: A Comprehensive Bibliography* (1975) is indispensable and amusing. See also *Beyond Amazement: New Essays on John Ashbery* (1980), edited by David Lehman, and Charles Altieri's *Postmodernisms Now* (1998).

James Baldwin

Baldwin's novels are *Go Tell It on the Mountain* (1953), *Giovanni's Room* (1956), *Another Country* (1962), *Tell Me How Long the Train's Been Gone* (1968), *If Beale Street Could Talk* (1974), and *Just Above My Head* (1979). His other books are a collection of short stories, *Going to Meet the Man* (1965); a volume of nonfiction prose, *The Price of the Ticket* (1985); and two plays, *Blues for Mr. Charlie* (1964) and *The Amen Corner* (1968).

James Campbell's *Talking at the Gates: A Life of James Baldwin* (1991) is a biographical study. Critical interpretations include Lynn Orilla Scott's *James Baldwin's Later Fiction: Witness to the Journey* (2002) and Clarence E. Hardy III's *James Baldwin's God: Sex, Hope and Crisis in Black Holiness Culture* (2003). Further essays are found in editor D. Quentin Miller's *Reviewing James Baldwin: Things Not Seen* (2000).

Amiri Baraka (LeRoi Jones)

Dutchman and the Slave (1964) was published as a combined edition, as was *The Baptism & The Toilet* (1967). *Four Black Revolutionary Plays* (1969) includes *Experimental Death Unit #1*, *A Black Mass*, *Great Goodness of Life*, and *Madheart*. *The Motion of History and Other Plays* (1978) gathers the title work with *Slave Ship* and *S-1*. *The System of Dante's Hell* (1965) is a novel; *Tales* (1967) is a collection of short stories. Poetry volumes include *Preface to a Twenty Volume Suicide Note* (1961), *The Dead Lecturer* (1964), *Black Magic* (1969), *Hard Facts* (1975), *Transbluency* (1995), *Funk Lore* (1996), and *Somebody Blew Up America*

(2003). *Eulogies* (1996) uses poetry and prose to memorialize friends. Baraka has authored three books on music: *Blues People* (1963), *Black Music* (1968), and *The Music: Reflections on Jazz and Blues* (1987). His essays are collected in *Home* (1966), *Raise Race Rays Raze* (1971), and *Selected Plays and Prose of Amiri Baraka / LeRoi Jones* (1979). Baraka has produced three important anthologies: *The Moderns* (1963), *Black Fire* (1968, with Larry Neal), and *Confirmation: An Anthology of African American Women* (1983), with Amina Baraka. In 1984 he published *The Autobiography of LeRoi Jones / Amiri Baraka*.

Early but still useful studies are *Baraka: The Renegade and the Mask* (1976) by Kimberly W. Benston and *Amiri Baraka / LeRoi Jones: The Quest for a "Populist Modernism"* (1978) by Werner Sollors. William J. Harris has written *The Poetry and Poetics of Amiri Baraka: The Jazz Aesthetic* (1985) and edited *The LeRoi Jones / Amiri Baraka Reader* (1991), supplying introductory literary history and a bibliography. Ross Posnock's *Color and Culture* (1998) locates the author's thought; Jerry Gafio Watt's *Amiri Baraka: The Politics and Art of a Black Intellectual* (2001) is comprehensive. Baraka's first wife, Hettie Cohen, has authored a memoir, *How I Became Hettie Jones* (1990).

Saul Bellow

Bellow is the author of fourteen novels and novellas: *Dangling Man* (1944), *The Victim* (1947), *The Adventures of Augie March* (1953), *Seize the Day* (1956), *Henderson the Rain King* (1959), *Herzog* (1964), *Mr. Sammler's Planet* (1970), *Humboldt's Gift* (1975), *The Dean's December* (1982), *More Die of Heartbreak* (1987), *A Theft* (1989), *The Bellarosa Connection* (1989), *The Actual* (1997), and *Ravelstein* (2000). His short stories appear in three collections: *Mosby's Memoirs* (1968), *Him with His Foot in His Mouth* (1984), and *Something to Remember Me By* (1991), and are joined by an additional story in *Collected Stories* (2001). A play, *The Last Analysis*, was produced in New York in 1964 and published the following year. *To Jerusalem and Back* (1976) is a personal account of his activities in Israel. *It All Adds Up* (1994) draws on Bellow's essays dating back to 1948.

James Atlas's *Bellow: A Biography* (2000) is exhaustive yet critically focused. Malcolm Bradbury provides the best concise introduction to this author's major work in *Saul Bellow* (1982), while in *Saul Bellow: Drumlin Woodchuck* (1980) fellow writer Mark Harris offers an insightful portrait of Bellow as a professional figure. John J. Clayton's *Saul Bellow: In Defense of Man* (1979) celebrates the author's stressfully tested humanism, while Ellen Pifer's *Saul Bellow: Against the Grain* (1990) argues for his culturally atypical belief in the transcendent soul. Gender is Gloria L. Cronin's focus in *A Room of*

His Own: In Search of the Feminine in the Novels of Saul Bellow (2001). In *Saul Bellow: Vision and Revision* (1984) Daniel Fuchs examines manuscripts and letters to establish Bellow's Dostoyevskian engagement with issues of character. Julia Eichelberger sums up his work in *Prophets of Recognition* (1999).

John Berryman

Berryman's *Collected Poems: 1937–1971* appeared in 1991; *John Berryman: Selected Poems*, in 2004. *Homage to Mistress Bradstreet* (1956) and a selection of his *Short Poems* (1948) were issued together as a paperback in 1968. His other volumes of poetry include *77 Dream Songs* (1964); *Berryman's Sonnets* (1967); *His Toy, His Dream, His Rest* (1968); *Love and Fame* (1970; rev. 1972); *Delusions, Etc.* (1972); and a posthumous volume, *Henry's Fate* (1977). Berryman's critical biography, *Stephen Crane*, appeared in 1950, and a collection of his short fiction and literary essays was issued under the title *The Freedom of the Poet* (1976). Berryman's unfinished novel about his alcoholism, *Recovery*, appeared in 1973.

Valuable critical introductions to Berryman's poetry can be found in Helen Vendler's *The Given and the Made* (1995) and Thomas Travisano's *Midcentury Quartet* (1999). Paul Mariani's *Dream Song: The Life of John Berryman* (1996) and Eileen Simpson's *Poets in Their Youth* (1982) are useful biographical studies.

Elizabeth Bishop

Bishop's poems are available in *The Complete Poems 1927–1979* (1983). *The Collected Prose* (1984) includes memoirs and stories, especially the memory-based story "In the Village," invaluable for a reading of her poems. A remarkable selection of Bishop's correspondence, *One Art* (1994), was edited by her friend and publisher, Robert Giroux, and reproductions of Bishop's watercolor paintings appear in *Exchanging Hats* (1996). Alice Quinn edited *Edgar Allan Poe & The Juke-Box: Uncollected Poems, Drafts, and Fragments* (2006). Bishop also translated from the Portuguese *The Diary of Helena Morley* (1957, 1977, 1991), an enchanting memoir of provincial life in Brazil.

Useful critical essays on Bishop appear in Seamus Heaney's *The Redress of Poetry* (1995), Lorrie Glodensohn's *Elizabeth Bishop: The Biography of a Poetry* (1992), and David Kalstone's *Becoming a Poet* (1989). *Elizabeth Bishop and Her Art*, edited by Lloyd Schwartz and Sybil P. Estess (1983), includes two interviews as well as essays. A provocative essay on Bishop appears in Adrienne Rich's *Blood, Bread and Poetry* (1986). Among the most valuable of the many critical studies are Brett C. Miller's important biography, *Elizabeth Bishop: Life and the Memory of It* (1993); *Elizabeth Bishop: The Geography of Gender* (1993), a collection of essays edited by Marilyn Lombardi; *Conversa-*

tions with Elizabeth Bishop (1996), edited by George Monteiro; and Thomas Travisano's *Midcentury Quartet* (1999). Candace MacMahon's *Elizabeth Bishop: A Bibliography* (1980) is indispensable.

Gwendolyn Brooks

Brooks's volumes of poetry include *A Street in Bronzeville* (1945), *Annie Allen* (1949), *In the Time of Detachment, In the Time of Cold* (1965), *In the Mecca* (1968), *Riot* (1969), *Family Pictures* (1970), *Aloneness* (1972), *Aurora* (1972), *Beckonings* (1975), *To Disembark* (1981), *Winnie* (1989), and *Children Coming Home* (1991). Many of her poems are collected in *Selected Poems* (1999), *The Essential Gwendolyn Brooks* (2005), and the *Gwendolyn Brooks CD Poetry Collection* (2005). She has also written prose autobiographies, *Report from Part One* (1972) and *Report from Part Two* (1996).

Other useful biographical material appears in *A Life Distilled*, edited by M. K. Mootry and others. Valuable discussions of Brooks's poetry appear in *Black Women Writers (1950–1980)*, edited by Mari Evans (1984). Stephen Wright's *On Gwendolyn Brooks: Reliant Contemplation* (1996), Harold Bloom's *Gwendolyn Brooks* (2000), and Martha E. Rhynes's *Gwendolyn Brooks: Poet from Chicago* (2003) are recent critical studies. An interview with Brooks appears in Janet Mullaney's *Truthtellers of the Times: Interviews with Contemporary Women Poets* (1998). Brooks and Gloria Jean Wade Gayles published *Conversations with Gwendolyn Brooks* (2002).

Raymond Carver

Principal collections of Carver's extensive short fiction are *Put Yourself in My Shoes* (1974), *Will You Please Be Quiet, Please?* (1976), *Furious Seasons* (1977), *What We Talk About When We Talk About Love* (1981), *The Pheasant* (1982), *Cathedral* (1983), and *Where I'm Calling From* (1988). *Fires* (1983) is a sampling of essays, poems, and narratives. Carver's uncollected work has been edited by William L. Stull as *No Heroics, Please* (1991), expanded as *Call If You Need Me* (2000). Throughout his career Carver published poetry as well, the bulk of which appears in several volumes from *Near Klamath* (1968) to *A New Path to the Waterfall* (1989); *All of Us* (1998) collects all his poems.

Arthur M. Saltzman's *Understanding Raymond Carver* (1988) looks beyond the author's apparent realism, as does Randolph Runyon's *Reading Raymond Carver* (1992). Carver's return to traditionalism is celebrated by Kirk Nesset in *The Stories of Raymond Carver* (1995). Sam Halpert sifts through comments by Carver's associates in *Raymond Carver: An Oral Biography* (1995).

John Cheever

Cheever's seven volumes of short stories, which appeared between 1943 and 1973, are assembled in *The Stories of John Cheever* (1978); *The Uncollected Stories of John Cheever* appeared posthumously in 1988. His novels are *The Wapshot Chronicle* (1957), *The Wapshot Scandal* (1964), *Bullet Park* (1969), *Falconer* (1977), and *Oh What a Paradise It Seems* (1982). *The Letters of John Cheever*, edited by his son, Benjamin Cheever, was published in 1988. *The Journals of John Cheever* (1991) was edited by Robert Gottlieb.

Scott Donaldson's *John Cheever* (1988) is a full-length biography. *Home before Dark* (1984), by his daughter, Susan Cheever, is a personal memoir. Francis J. Bosha has edited *The Critical Response to John Cheever* (1994). Samuel Chase Coale provides an overview in *John Cheever* (1977), while George W. Hunt explores religious dimensions in *John Cheever: The Hobgoblin Company of Love* (1983). The stories are given close study by James Eugene O'Hara in *John Cheever: A Study of the Short Fiction* (1989).

Sandra Cisneros

The House on Mango Street (1984) has been described as both interrelated short stories and a novel, whereas *Woman Hollering Creek* (1991) collects more evidently independent short stories. *Caramelo* (2002) is a novel. Cisneros has published two major collections of poetry, *My Wicked Wicked Ways* (1987) and *Loose Woman* (1994). Her *Hairs/Pelitos* (1994), written in English and accompanied by a Spanish text translated by Liliana Valenzuela, is a narrative for children.

Jean Wyatt's *Risking Difference* (2004) focuses on *Women Hollering Creek*. Ramón Saldíva discusses Cisneros's fiction in *Chicano Narrative* (1990), as do Tey Diana Rebolledo in *Women Singing in the Snow* (1995) and Sonia Saldívar-Hull in *Feminism on the Border* (2000). An extensive dialogue with her appears in *Interviews with Writers of the Post-Colonial World* (1992), edited by Feroza Jussawalla and Reed Way Dasenbrock.

Lucille Clifton

Clifton's volumes of poetry are *Good Times* (1969), *Good News About the Earth* (1972), *An Ordinary Woman* (1974), *Two-Headed Woman* (1980), *Good Woman: Poems and a Memoir 1969–1980* (1987), *Next: New Poems* (1987), *Quilting: Poems 1987–1990* (1991), *The Book of Light* (1993), *The Terrible Stories: Poems* (1995), *Blessing the Boats: New and Selected Poems, 1988–2000* (2000), and *Mercy* (2004). Her memoir, *Generations* (1976), provides a valuable context for her work. Clifton's books for children include *The Black BC's* (1970), *Some of the Days of Everett Anderson* (1970), *The Boy Who Didn't Believe in Spring* (1973), *Don't You Remember* (1973), *All Us Come Cross the Water* (1973), *Good, Says Jerome* (1973), *Everett Anderson's Year* (1974; illustrated by Ann Grifalconi), *The Times They Used to Be*

(1974), *My Brother Fine With Me* (1975), *Amifika* (1978), *The Lucky Stone* (1979), *My Friend Jacob* (1980), *Sonora Beautiful* (1981), *Everett Anderson's Goodbye* (1983), *Some of the Days of Everett Anderson* (1987), *Everett Anderson's Nine Month Long* (1987), *Everett Anderson's Christmas Coming* (1991; illustrated by Jan Spivey Gilchrist), *Everett Anderson's Friend* (1992), *Everett Anderson's 1-2-3* (1992; illustrated by Ann Grifalconi), *Three Wishes* (1994), *El Nino Que No Creia En La Primavera* (1996), and *Dear Creator: A Week of Poems for Young People and Their Teachers* (1997).

Critical discussions of her work include Hilary Holladay's *Wild Blessings: The Poetry of Lucille Clifton* (2004). Mary Jane Lupton has published *Lucille Clifton: Her Life and Letters* (2006).

Billy Collins
Collections of Collins's poetry include *The Apple That Astonished Paris* (1988), *Questions about Angels* (1991), *The Art of Drowning* (1995), *Picnic, Lightning* (1998), *Sailing Alone around the World: New and Selected Poems* (2001), *Nine Horses* (2002), and *The Trouble With Poetry, and Other Poems* (2005). *The Best Cigarette* (1997), an audiobook, provides a chance to hear Collins reading thirty-three of his poems. He selected and introduced the anthologies *Poetry 180: A Turning Back to Poetry* (2003) and *180 More: Extraordinary Poems for Everyday Life* (2005).

Critical discussion of Collins's work appears in David Baker's *Heresy and the Ideal: On Contemporary Poetry* (2000).

Rita Dove
Dove has published seven volumes of poetry: *The Yellow House on the Corner* (1980), *Museum* (1983), *Thomas and Beulah* (1986), *Grace Notes* (1989), *Selected Poems* (1993), *Mother Love* (1995), *On the Bus with Rosa Parks* (1999), and *American Smooth* (2004). She has also published a collection of fiction, *Fifth Sunday* (1985); a novel, *Through the Ivory Gate* (1992); and a valuable collection of essays, *The Poet's World* (1995). *Conversations with Rita Dove*, edited by Earl G. Ingersol, appeared in 2003.

Therese Steffen's critical study *Crossing Color: Transcultural Space and Place in Rita Dove's Poetry, Fiction, and Drama* appeared in 2001; Malin Pereira's *Rita Dove's Cosmopolitanism*, in 2003; and Pat Righelato's *Understanding Rita Dove*, in 2006.

Ralph Ellison
In his lifetime Ellison published three books: a novel, *Invisible Man* (1952), and two volumes of essays, *Shadow and Act* (1964) and *Going to the Territory* (1986). The latter materials are combined with other nonfiction in *The Collected Essays of Ralph Ellison* (1995),

edited by John F. Callahan with a preface by Saul Bellow. Fragments of his novel in progress are noted in the bibliography to Mark Busby's *Ralph Ellison* (1991) in the Twayne United States Authors series; *Flying Home and Other Stories* (1997) gathers thirteen short stories written between 1937 and 1954, six of which were previously unpublished. In 1999 Callahan, as Ellison's literary executor, drew on manuscripts to assemble *Juneteenth* as a posthumous novel. Robert G. O'Meally edited *Living with Music: Ralph Ellison's Jazz Writings* (2001). *Trading Twelves: The Selected Letters of Ralph Ellison and Albert Murray*, edited by Murray and Callahan, appeared in 2000.

The centrality of Ellison's first novel to his other work is explained by Edith Shor in *Visible Ellison: A Study of Ralph Ellison's Fiction* (1993). Political interests shape the critical essays collected by Lucas E. Morel in *Ralph Ellison and the Raft of Hope* (2004), as does music in Horace A. Porter's *Jazz Country: Ralph Ellison in America* (2001). Julia Eichelberger's *Prophets of Recognition* (1999) considers his larger impact. *Jazz Country: Ralph Ellison's America* (2001) by Horace A. Porter relates the author's jazz background to his novels and essays.

Louise Erdrich
Erdrich's novels are *Love Medicine* (1984), *The Beet Queen* (1986), *Tracks* (1988), *The Bingo Palace* (1994), *Tales of Burning Love* (1996), *The Antelope Wife* (1998), *The Last Report on the Miracles at Little No Horse* (2001), *The Master Butcher's Singing Club* (2003), *Four Souls* (2004), and *The Painted Drum* (2005). For children she has written *Grandmother's Pigeon* (1996), *The Birchbark House* (1999), and *The Game of Silence* (2005). *The Blue Jay's Dance: A Birth Year* (1995) is her account of becoming a mother; *Birds and Islands in Ojibwe Country* (2003) is a memoir. With Michael Dorris she coauthored *The Crown of Columbus* (1991), a novel. Her poetry collections are *Jacklight* (1984), *Baptism of Desire* (1989), and *Original Fire* (2003).

Erdrich's fiction is treated by Louis Owens in *Other Destinies: Understanding the American Indian Novel* (1992), in the essays edited by Allan Chavkin in *The Chippewa Landscape of Louise Erdrich* (1999), and Peter G. Beidler and Gay Barton in *A Reader's Guide to the Novels of Louise Erdrich* (2006).

Allen Ginsberg
Ginsberg's *Collected Poems, 1947–1980* appeared in 1984, *White Shroud: Poems, 1980–1985* in 1986, and *Death and Fame: Poems 1993–1997* in 1999. His individual volumes, with the exception of *Empty Mirror* (early poems collected in 1961), have been issued in the now unmistakable City Lights paperbacks.

They include *Howl and Other Poems* (1956), *Kaddish and Other Poems, 1958–1960* (1961), *Reality Sandwiches* (1963), *Planet News, 1961–1967* (1968), *The Fall of America, Poems of These States, 1965–1971* (1973), and *Mind Breaths, Poems 1972–1977* (1977). *Cosmopolitan Greetings* appeared in 1995 and *Selected Poems 1947–1995* in 1996. *Deliberate Prose: Selected Essays, 1952–1995* (2000) is a useful complement to the poetry. Ginsberg published a great number of pages from his journals, dealing with his travels, such as the *Indian Journals* (1970). *Allen Verbatim* (1974) includes transcripts of some of his lectures on poetry. In 1977 he published *Letters: Early Fifties Early Sixties* and in 1980 *Composed on the Tongue: Literary Conversations 1967–1977*, edited by Donald Allen. Ginsberg's interviews are collected in *Spontaneous Mind: Selected Interviews, 1958–1996* (2001).

Jane Kramer's *Allen Ginsberg in America* (1969) is a brilliant documentary piece on Ginsberg in the 1960s. *On the Poetry of Allen Ginsberg*, edited by Lewis Hyde (1980), is a collection of essays by different hands. Michelle Kraus has published *Allen Ginsberg: An Annotated Bibliography, 1969–1977* (1980). Bill Morgan has published *The Works of Allen Ginsberg 1941–1994: A Descriptive Bibliography* (1995) and *The Response to Allen Ginsberg 1926–1994: A Bibliography of Secondary Sources* (1996).

Jorie Graham
The Dream of the Unified Field: Selected Poems 1974–1994 (1995) brings together poems from *Hybrids of Plants and of Ghosts* (1980), *Erosion* (1983), *The End of Beauty* (1987), *Region of Unlikeness* (1991), and *Materialism* (1993). Graham's more recent collections include *The Errancy* (1997), *Swarm* (2000), and *Overlord* (2005). She edited *Earth Took of Earth: 100 Great Poems of the English Language* (1996). Her *Jorie Graham: Essays on the Poetry* appeared in 2004.

Critical discussion of Graham's work can be found in Helen Vendler's *The Given and the Made* (1995) and *Soul Says* (1995), James Longenbach's *Modern Poetry after Modernism* (1997), and Thomas Gardner's *Regions of Unlikeness: Explaining Contemporary Poetry* (1999). An extremely useful interview with Graham appears in *Denver Quarterly* (1992).

Joy Harjo
Harjo's collections of poetry include two chapbooks, *The Last Song* (1975) and *What Moon Drove Me to This* (1979), and the volumes *She Had Some Horses* (1983), *In Mad Love and War* (1990), *The Woman Who Fell from the Sky* (1996), *A Map to the Next World* (2000), and *How We Became Human: New and Selected Poems 1975–2001* (2002). In *Secrets from the Center of the World* (1989) she wrote the text to

accompany Steven Strom's photographs of the particulars of the southwestern landscape. She has also edited an anthology of Native American women's writing, *Reinventing the Enemy's Language: Contemporary Native Women's Writing of North America* (1997).

Laura Coltelli has edited a valuable collection of interviews with Harjo, *The Spiral of Memory* (1990). Commentary on the contexts of Harjo's work appears in Paula Gunn Allen's *The Sacred Hoop: Recovering the Feminine in American Indian Traditions* (1986) and Norma Wilson's *The Nature of Native American Poetry* (2001).

Michael S. Harper
Harper's poems appear in *Dear John, Dear Coltrane* (1970), *History Is Your Own Heartbeat* (1971), *Photographs: Negatives: History as Apple Tree* (1972), *Song: I Want a Witness* (1972), *Nightmare Begins Responsibility* (1974), *Images of Kin: New and Selected Poems* (1977), *Healing Song for the Inner Ear* (1984), and *Honorable Amendments* (1995). An edition of new and collected poems, *Songlines in Michaeltree*, appeared in 2000. Harper also edited (with Robert Stepto) a collection of African American literature, art, and scholarship, *Chants of Saints* (1976), and he edited *The Vintage Book of African American Poetry* (2000).

A conversation about Harper's work can be found in Joanne Gabbin's edited *The Furious Flowering of African American Poetry* (1999).

Robert Hayden
Hayden's *Collected Poems* appeared in 1985; his *Collected Prose* appeared the previous year. Both were edited by Frederick Glaysher.

Fred M. Fetrow's *Robert Hayden* (1984) is a critical study of Hayden's work. Essays on Hayden's work appear in the journals *Antioch Review* (1997) and *MELUS* (1998) and in Harold Bloom's edited volume *Robert Hayden* (2005).

Randall Jarrell
Jarrell's *Complete Poems* was published in 1969, and a *Selected Poems* appeared in 1991. A selection of Jarrell's brilliant critical essays is available in *No Other Book* (1999), edited by Brad Leithauser. His novel satirizing American academic life, *Pictures from an Institution*, appeared in 1954.

Some of the most valuable commentary on Jarrell's life and work is to be found in a memorial volume of essays edited by Robert Lowell, Peter Taylor, and Robert Penn Warren, *Randall Jarrell, 1914–1965* (1967). William Pritchard's fine *Randall Jarrell: A Literary Life* (1990) illumines Jarrell's life and work, as does Mary Randall's *Remembering Randall* (1999). Critical discussion of Jarrell's work appears in Thomas Travisano's *Midcentury Quartet* (1999).

Jack Kerouac

Kerouac's novels are *The Town and the City* (1950), *On the Road* (1957), *The Subterraneans* (1958), *The Dharma Bums* (1958), *Doctor Sax* (1959), *Maggie Cassidy* (1959), *Tristessa* (1960), *Big Sur* (1962), *Visions of Gerard* (1963), *Desolation Angels* (1965), *Vanity of Duluoz* (1968), *Pic* (1971), and *Visions of Cody* (1972). His works of nonfiction are *The Scripture of the Golden Eternity* (1960), *Lonesome Traveler* (1960), *Book of Dreams* (1960), and *Satori in Paris* (1966). His poems are collected in *Mexico City Blues* (1959), *Scattered Poems* (1971), *Heaven & Other Poems* (1977), and *San Francisco Blues* (1983). In 2004 Douglas Brinkley edited *Windblown World: The Journals of Jack Kerouac, 1947–1954.*

John Tytell's *Naked Angels: The Lives and Literature of the Beat Generation* (1983) includes Kerouac in his historical and critical context. Stylistic analyses are undertaken by Regina Weinrich in *The Spontaneous Prose of Jack Kerouac* (1987) and Michael Hrebeniak in *Action Writing: Jack Kerouac's Wild Form* (2006). More specifically thematic is James T. Jones's *Jack Kerouac's Duluoz Legend: The Mythic Form of an Autobiographical Fiction* (1999). Kerouac's friend Carolyn Cassady has written a memoir, *Off the Road* (1990). Biographies include Barry Gifford and Lawrence Lee's *Jack's Book: Jack Kerouac in the Lives and Words of His Friends* (1978), Tom Clark's *Jack Kerouac* (1984), Gerald Nicosia's *Memory Babe* (1983), and Ann Charter's *Jack Kerouac* (1987). Charters also prepared *A Bibliography of Works by Jack Kerouac* (1975). Kerouac's papers are housed in the Berg Collection of the New York Public Library.

Maxine Hong Kingston

The Woman Warrior (1976) and *China Men* (1980) were first received as autobiography, though Kingston scholars now recognize important fictive elements. *Tripmaster Monkey: His Fake Book* (1989) is more obviously a novel. Essays Kingston wrote in 1978 appear as *Hawai'i One Summer* (1999). *The Fifth Book of Peace* (2003) incorporates remembered pages of a lost novel with sections of conventional memoir.

Shirley Geok-Lim edited *Approaches to Teaching Kingston's "The Woman Warrior"* (1991); also helpful is Sidonie Smith's *A Poetics of Women's Autobiography: Marginality and the Fictions of Self-Representation* (1987). More cognizant of fiction's role in Kingston's writing is *Articulate Silences: Hisaye Yamamoto, Maxine Hong Kingston, and Joy Kogawa* (1993) by King-Kok Cheung and *Writing Tricksters* (1997) by Jeanne Rosier Smith. Cultural identity features in Martha J. Cutter's *Lost and Found in Translation* (2005).

Galway Kinnell

Kinnell's *A New Selected Poems* appeared in 2000. Earlier collected volumes of his work were *First Poems 1946–1954* (1970), *The Avenue Bearing the Initial of Christ into the New World: Poems, 1946–1964* (1974), and *Selected Poems* (1982). Important individual volumes of Kinnell's poetry are *What a Kingdom It Was* (1960), *The Book of Nightmares* (1971), *Mortal Acts, Mortal Words* (1980), *The Past* (1985), *When One Has Lived a Long Time Alone* (1990), *Imperfect Thirst* (1994), and *Strong Is Your Hold* (2006). He has also published a collection of criticism, *The Poetics of the Physical World* (1969), and selected interviews, *Walking Down the Stairs*, edited by Donald Hall (1978).

Critical Essays on Galway Kinnell (1996), edited by Nancy Tuten, and David Baker's *Heresy and the Ideal: On Contemporary Poetry* (2000) contain useful critical discussions.

Yusef Komunyakaa

Komunyakaa's poetry appears in *Lost in the Bonewheel Factory* (1979), *Copacetic* (1984), *I Apologize for the Eyes in My Head* (1986), *Dien Cai Dau* (1987), *Magic City* (1992), *Neon Vernacular: New and Selected Poems* (1993), *Thieves of Paradise* (1998), *Talking Dirty to the Gods* (2000), *Pleasure Dome* (2001), and *Taboo: The Wishbone Trilogy, Part I* (2004). With Martha Collins he has translated Nguyen Quang Thieu's *The Insomnia of Fire* (1992). With Sascha Feinstein he has edited *The Jazz Poetry Anthology* (1991) and *The Second Set: The Jazz Poetry Anthology, Volume 2* (1996). In 2000 he published *Blue Notes: Essays, Interviews & Commentaries.*

Critical discussions of his work include Angela M. Salas's *Flashback Through the Heart: The Poetry of Yusef Komunyakaa* (2004).

Jhumpa Lahiri

Lahiri's first collection of stories is *Interpreter of Maladies* (1999), and her first novel is *The Namesake* (2003).

Criticism of her fiction is found in *Transnational Asian American Literature: Sites and Transits* (2006), edited by Shirley Geok-lin Lim, et al.

Li-Young Lee

Lee's volumes of poetry are *Rose* (1986), *The City in Which I Love You* (1990), and *A Book of My Nights* (2001). A memoir, *The Winged Seed*, appeared in 1995.

Gerald Stern's foreword to *Rose* provides useful biographical material about Lee's family. Available on videotape, as part of the series *The Power of the Word*, is "Voices of Memory," in which Bill Moyers conducts a valuable interview with Lee. An interview with Lee appears in *Words Matter: Conversations with Asian*

American Writers (2000), edited by King-Kok Cheung.

Denise Levertov
Some of Levertov's poems have been gathered in *Collected Earlier Poems 1940–1960* (1979). *The Selected Poems of Denise Levertov* appeared in 2002. Her individual volumes include *The Double Image* (1946), *Here and Now* (1957), *Overland to the Islands* (1958), *With Eyes at the Back of Our Heads* (1960), *The Jacob's Ladder* (1962), *O Taste and See* (1964), *The Sorrow Dance* (1967), *Relearning the Alphabet* (1970), *To Stay Alive* (1971), *Footprints* (1972), *The Freedom of the Dust* (1973), *Life in the Forest* (1978), *Candles in Babylon* (1982), *Oblique Prayers* (1984), *Breathing the Water* (1987), *A Door in the Hive* (1989), *Evening Train* (1992), *Tesserae* (1995), and *The Great Unknowing: Last Poems* (1999). *Making Peace* (2005) is a posthumous collection edited by Peggy Rosenthal. *The Poet in the World* (1973) and *Light Up the Cave* (1981) include essays on her own work, memoirs, reviews of other poets, and some theoretical essays. *New and Selected Essays* appeared in 1992.

Conversations with Denise Levertov (1998) is a collection of interviews. James E. Breslin's *From Modern to Contemporary: American Poetry 1945–1965* (1984) contains a discussion of Levertov. Linda Wagner-Martin edited *Critical Essays on Denise Levertov* (1990), and Anne Little edited *Denise Levertov: New Perspectives* (2000).

Audre Lorde
The Collected Poems of Audre Lorde (1997) brings together Lorde's poetry from *Cables to Rage* (1970), *New York Head Shop and Museum* (1975), *The Black Unicorn* (1978), and *Our Dead behind Us* (1986). A collection of essays and speeches, *Sister Outsider* (1984), provides a powerful context for reading her work. Her autobiographical writing includes *The Cancer Journals* (1980) and *Zami: A New Spelling of My Name* (1982).

Critical studies of Lorde's work appear in *Black Women Writers*, edited by Mari Evans (1984), and Cassie Steele's *We Heal From Memory: Sexton, Lorde, Anzaldúa and the Poetry of Witness* (2000). An interview with Lorde appears in *Women Writers at Work* (1998), edited by George Plimpton.

Robert Lowell
Lowell's books of verse include *Lord Weary's Castle* (1946), *The Mills of the Kavanaughs* (1951), *Life Studies* (1959), *Imitations* (1961), *For the Union Dead* (1964), *Near the Ocean* (1967), *Notebook* (1969; rev. and exp. 1970), *The Dolphin* (1973), *For Lizzie and Harriet* (1973), and *History* (1973). For the stage Lowell adapted Racine's *Phaedra* (1961) and Aeschylus's *Prometheus Bound* (1969) as well

as versions of Hawthorne and Melville stories grouped under the title *The Old Glory* (1965). His *Collected Prose* (1987) is an indispensable companion to Lowell's poetry and contains valuable essays on the work of other writers.

Among the many useful critical works on Lowell are Stephen Yenser's *Circle to Circle* (1975), Steven Axelrod's *Robert Lowell: Life and Art* (1978), and Thomas Travisano's *Midcentury Quartet* (1999). *Robert Lowell: A Collection of Critical Essays* (1968), edited by Thomas Parkinson, includes an important interview with the poet, and *The Critical Response to Robert Lowell* (1999), edited by Steven Gould Axelrod, provides an overview of criticism on the work. A partial bibliography of Lowell's work can be found in Jerome Mazzaro's *The Achievement of Robert Lowell, 1939–1959* (1960). Ian Hamilton's biography, *Robert Lowell*, appeared in 1982. An edition of Lowell's letters, edited by Saskia Hamilton, appeared in 2005 and provides a valuable context for his work.

Arthur Miller
Miller's earlier plays—*All My Sons*, *Death of a Salesman*, *The Crucible*, *A Memory of Two Mornings*, and *A View from the Bridge*—are brought together in Arthur Miller's *Collected Plays* (1957), which also includes a lengthy and useful introduction. Later dramas are available in *Collected Plays, 1957–1981* (1981) and thereafter separately, including *Danger, Memory!* (1987), *The Archbishop's Ceiling: The American Clock* (1989), *The Ride Down Mt. Morgan* (1992), *Broken Glass* (1994), *The Last Yankee* (1994), and *The Price* (2002). *Focus* (1945) is a novel; short fiction is collected in *The Misfits and Other Stories* (1987) and *Homely Girl, a Life, and Other Stories* (1997); *The Misfits* (1961) is a screenplay. *Echoes Down the Corridor: Collected Essays, 1944–2000* appeared in 2000. Harold Clurman edited *The Portable Arthur Miller* in 1971, and Robert A. Martin edited *The Theater Essays of Arthur Miller* in 1978. Miller published an account of the production of *Death of a Salesman* in China in 1984 and an autobiography, *Timebends: A Life*, in 1987.

Martin Gottfried's *Arthur Miller: His Life and Work* (2003) is the major biography. The best recent critical analysis of Miller's work is found in Christopher Bigsby's *Arthur Miller: A Critical Study* (2005), supplemented by Bigsby's edited *The Cambridge Companion to Arthur Miller* (1997). Also helpful are the materials commissioned by Steven R. Centola for the edited volume *The Achievement of Arthur Miller: New Essays* (1995). Specifics are handled by Brenda Murphy in *Miller: Death of a Salesman* (1995) and by Matthew C. Rodané in *Approaches to Teaching Miller's Death of a Salesman* (1995).

N. Scott Momaday

Momaday's autobiographical works begin with *The Journey to Tai-me* (1967) and continue with *The Way to Rainy Mountain* (1969) and *The Names: A Memoir* (1976), supplemented by *The Man Made of Words: Essays, Stories, Passages* (1997). *House Made of Dawn* (1968), *The Ancient Child* (1989), and *In the Bear's House* (1999) are novels. In 1999 he published *Circle of Wonder: A Native American Christmas Story*. His poems appear in *Angle of Geese* (1974), *Before an Old Painting of the Crucifixion, Carmel Mission, June 1960* (1975), and *The Gourd Dancer* (1976). *In the Presence of the Sun: Stories and Poems 1961–1991* was published in 1992 with illustrations by the author. Momaday has also written books for children, edited editions of writers, and written the commentary for photographer David Muench's *Colorado: Summer, Fall, Winter, Spring* (1973).

A book-length study of Momaday is *N. Scott Momaday: The Cultural and Literary Background* (1985) by Matthias Schubnell. Of the many interviews with Momaday, early and worthy is Joseph Bruchac's "The Magic of Words: An Interview with N. Scott Momaday," in *Survival This Way: Interviews with American Indian Poets* (1987), edited by Bruchac. Louis Owens's "N. Scott Momaday," in *This Is about Vision: Interviews with Southwestern Writers* (1990), edited by William Balassi, John F. Crawford, and Annie O. Eysturoy, also offers quite a good interview. Kenneth M. Roemer edited *Approaches to Teaching Momaday's "The Way to Rainy Mountain"* (1988), which is useful. Arnold Krupat's *The Voice in the Margin: Native American Literature and the Canon* (1989) compares autobiographical writing of Momaday and Leslie Marmon Silko. Susan Scarberry-Garcia's *Landmarks of Healing: A Study of "House Made of Dawn"* (1990,) fills in some of the multitribal mythic context. Gerald Vizenor edited *Narrative Chance: Postmodern Discourse on Native American Indian Literatures* (1989), with three articles on Momaday. A fine account, focused on *House Made of Dawn*, is in Louis Owens's *Other Destinies: Understanding the American Indian Novel* (1992), supplemented by Scott B. Vickers's work in *Native American Identities* (1998).

Toni Morrison

Morrison's novels are *The Bluest Eye* (1970), *Sula* (1974), *Song of Solomon* (1977), *Tar Baby* (1981), *Beloved* (1987), *Jazz* (1992), *Paradise* (1998), and *Love* (2003). A play, *Dreaming Emmett*, was produced in 1986. Morrison is the author of *Playing in the Dark: Whiteness and the Literary Imagination* (1992) and editor of *Racing Justice, Engendering Power: Essays on Anita Hill, Clarence Thomas, and the Construction of Social Reality* (1992). Her *Lecture and Speech of Acceptance upon the Award of the Nobel Prize for Literature* was published in 1994.

Book-length studies include Trudier Harris's *Fictions and Folklore: The Novels of Toni Morrison* (1991), Denise Heinze's *The Dilemma of "Double-consciousness": Toni Morrison's Novels* (1993), Gurleen Grewal's *Circles of Sorrow, Lines of Struggle* (1998), John N. Duvall's *The Identifying Fictions of Toni Morrison* (2000), J. Brooks Bouson's *Quiet As It's Kept* (2000), and Andrea Reilly's *Toni Morrison and Motherhood* (2004). Henry Louis Gates Jr. and K. A. Appiah have edited *Toni Morrison: Critical Perspectives Past and Present* (1993). *Toni Morrison: An Annotated Bibliography* (1987) has been compiled by David L. Middleton.

Flannery O'Connor

O'Connor's novels and stories (edited by Sally Fitzgerald) are a volume in the *Library of America series* (1988). Her novels are *Wise Blood* (1952) and *The Violent Bear It Away* (1960). Two collections of stories, *A Good Man Is Hard to Find* (1955) and *Everything That Rises Must Converge* (1965), are included with earlier uncollected stories in *Complete Stories* (1971). Her letters are collected in *The Habit of Being: The Letters of Flannery O'Connor* (1979). *The Presence of Grace, and Other Book Reviews* (1983) collects some of her critical prose, as does *Mystery and Manners* (1969), edited by Sally Fitzgerald and Robert Fitzgerald.

Jean W. Cash provides a biography in *Flannery O'Connor: A Life* (2003). Studies of O'Connor's fiction include Jon Lance Bacon's *Flannery O'Connor and Cold War Culture* (1993), Lorine M. Gertz's *Flannery O'Connor, Literary Theologian* (2000), Richard Giannone's *Flannery O'Connor, Hermit Novelist* (2000), Sarah Gordon's *Flannery O'Connor: The Obedient Imagination* (2000), and *Flannery O'Connor's Radical Reality* (2006), edited by Jan Nordby Grettund and Karl-Heinz Westarp. *Flannery O'Connor: A Descriptive Bibliography* (1981) was compiled by David Farmer.

Simon J. Ortiz

Ortiz's collections are *Naked in the Wind* (1970), *Going for Rain* (1976), *A Good Journey* (1977), *Song, Poetry, Language* (1978), *From Sand Creek: Rising in This Heart Which Is Our America* (1981), *A Poem Is a Journey* (1981), and *After and before Lightning* (1994). His work has been gathered in the volume *Woven Stone* (1992). His short-story collections are *Howbah Indians* (1978), *Fightin': New and Collected Stories* (1983), and *Men on the Moon: Collected Short Stories* (1999). He also edited two collections, *These Hearts, These Poems* (1984) and *Speaking for the Generations: Native Writers on Writing* (1998).

A discussion of Ortiz's poetry appears in Kenneth Lincoln's *Native American Renaissance*

(1983) and in Lucy Maddox's "Native American Poetry" in *The Columbia History of American Poetry* (1993).

Sylvia Plath

Plath's books of poetry include *The Colossus and Other Poems* (1962), *Ariel* (1966), *Crossing the Water* (1971), and *Winter Trees* (1972). Her novel *The Bell Jar* was first published in England in 1963. Plath's mother, Aurelia Schober Plath, selected and edited the useful *Letters Home: Correspondence 1950–63* (1975). Karen Kukil edited *The Unabridged Journals of Sylvia Plath, 1950–1962* (2000). Among the biographical and critical studies of Plath's work are Judith Kroll's *Chapters in a Mythology* (1976), Anne Stevenson's *Bitter Fame: The Undiscovered Life of Sylvia Plath* (1988), Linda Wagner-Martin's *Sylvia Plath: A Biography* (1987), Jacqueline Rose's *The Haunting of Sylvia Plath* (1993), Diane Middlebrook's *Sylvia Plath* (1998), and Christina Britzolakis's *Sylvia Plath and the Theatre of Mourning* (1999).

Thomas Pynchon

Pynchon's novels are *V.* (1963), *The Crying of Lot 49* (1966), *Gravity's Rainbow* (1973), *Vineland* (1990), *Mason & Dixon* (1997), and *Against the Day* (2006). *Slow Learner* (1984) collects early stories.

Book-length studies are William M. Plater's *The Grim Phoenix: Reconstructing Thomas Pynchon* (1978), Thomas H. Schaub's *Pynchon, The Voice of Ambiguity* (1981), and David Seed's *The Fictional Labyrinths of Thomas Pynchon* (1988). Alan N. Brownlie studies the author's first three novels in *Thomas Pynchon's Narratives: Subjectivity and the Problems of Knowing* (2000), while the fourth and fifth novels are analyzed in Geoffrey Green, Donald J. Greiner, and Larry McCaffery's edited *The Vineland Papers* (1993) and Brooke Horvath and Irving Malin's edited *Pynchon and Mason & Dixon* (2000), respectively. New critical essays are collected by Niran Abbas in *Thomas Pynchon: Reading from The Margins* (2003) and Ian D. Copestake in *American Postmodernity: Essays on the Recent Fiction of Thomas Pynchon* (2003).

Adrienne Rich

The Fact of a Doorframe: Poems 1950–2001 (2002) draws from *A Change of World* (1951), *The Diamond Cutters* (1955), *Snapshots of a Daughter-in-Law* (1963), *Necessities of Life* (1966), *Leaflets* (1969), *The Will to Change* (1971), *Diving into the Wreck* (1973), *The Dream of a Common Language* (1978), *A Wild Patience Has Taken Me This Far* (1981), *Your Native Land, Your Life* (1986), *Time's Power: Poems 1985–1988* (1989), *An Atlas of the Difficult World: Poems 1988–1991* (1991), *Dark Fields of the Republic: Poems 1991–1995* (1995), *Midnight Salvage: Poems 1995–1998* (1999), and *Fox: Poems 1998–2000* (2001).

The School among the Ruins: 2000–2004 (2004) presents subsequent work. Four valuable collections gather Rich's essays, lectures, and speeches: *On Lies, Secrets, and Silence* (1979), *Blood, Bread, and Poetry* (1986), *What Is Found There?: Notebooks on Poetry and Politics* (1993), and *Arts of the Possible* (2001). Rich is also the author of an important study, *Of Woman Born: Motherhood as Experience and Institution* (1976).

Valuable critical essays and an interview appear in *Adrienne Rich's Poetry* (1975), edited by Barbara Charlesworth Gelpi and Albert Gelpi. Other studies are *Reading Adrienne Rich* (1984), edited by Jane Roberta Cooper; Paula Bennett's *My Life, a Loaded Gun: Female Creativity and Feminist Poetics* (1986); Margaret Dickie's *Stein, Bishop and Rich: Lyrics of Love, War & Place* (1997); and Molly McQuade's *By Herself: Women Reclaim Poetry* (2000).

Theodore Roethke

The Collected Poems of Theodore Roethke was published in 1966. *Dirty Dinkey and Other Creatures: Poems for Children*, edited by B. Roethke and Stephen Lushington, appeared in 1973. Useful comments on poetic tradition and his own poetic practice are to be found in several collections of Roethke's prose: *On the Poet and His Craft: Selected Prose of Theodore Roethke* (1965), edited by Ralph J. Mills Jr.; *Straw for the Fire: From the Notebooks of Theodore Roethke, 1948–63* (1972), edited by David Wagoner; and *The Selected Letters of Theodore Roethke* (1970), edited by Mills.

Among the useful studies of Roethke's work are *Theodore Roethke: Essays on the Poetry* (1965), edited by Arnold Stein, and Laurence Lieberman's *Beyond the Muse of Memory: Essays on Contemporary Poets* (1995). Allan Seager's *The Glass House* (1968) contains useful biographical material.

Philip Roth

Roth's fiction consists of *Goodbye, Columbus* (1959)—a novella and five short stories—and the following novels: *Letting Go* (1962), *When She Was Good* (1967), *Portnoy's Complaint* (1969), *Our Gang* (1971), *The Breast* (1972), *The Great American Novel* (1973), *My Life as a Man* (1974), *The Professor of Desire* (1977), *The Ghost Writer* (1979), *Zuckerman Unbound* (1981), *The Anatomy Lesson* (1983), *The Counterlife* (1987), *Deception* (1990), *Operation Shylock* (1993), *Sabbath's Theatre* (1995), *American Pastoral* (1997), *I Married a Communist* (1998), *The Human Stain* (2000), *The Dying Animal* (2001), *The Plot against America* (2004), and *Everyman* (2006). *Reading Myself and Others* (1975) is a collection of essays and interviews. *The Facts: A Novelist's Autobiography* (1988) is Roth's memoir. A memoir of his father, *Patrimony*, was published in 1991.

Philip Roth (1982) by Hermione Lee is an excellent introduction, as is *Understanding Philip Roth* (1990) by Murray Baumgarten and Barbara Gottfried. *Philip Roth and the Jews* (1996) by Alan Cooper considers religious and cultural dimensions of the author's work. The broad sweep of Roth's career is covered by James D. Bloom in *The Literary Bent* (1997), by Mark Shechner in *Up Society's Ass, Copper: Reading Philip Roth* (2003), and by Deborah Shostak in *Philip Roth—Countertexts, Counterhues* (2004). Elaine B. Safer's *Mocking the Age: The Later Novels of Philip Roth* (2006) discusses his experiments in narrative.

Anne Sexton

Sexton's books of poems include *To Bedlam and Part Way Back* (1960), *All My Pretty Ones* (1962), *Live or Die* (1966), *Love Poems* (1969), *Transformations* (1971), *The Book of Folly* (1973), *The Death Notebooks* (1974), and *The Awful Rowing toward God* (1975). *Complete Poems* appeared in 1981.

Diane Wood Middlebrook's biography, *Anne Sexton* (1991), and Sexton's *A Self-Portrait in Letters* (1977) give useful biographical material. Important interviews and critical essays are to be found in J. D. McClatchy's *Anne Sexton: The Artist and Her Critics* (1978) and Diane Hume George's *Sexton: Selected Criticism* (1988). An interview with Sexton appears in *Women Writers at Work* (1998), edited by George Plimpton.

Leslie Marmon Silko

Silko's novels are *Ceremony* (1977), *Almanac of the Dead* (1991), and *Garden in the Dunes* (1999). *Storyteller* (1981) includes prose poems and related short stories. *Laguna Woman* (1974), *Voices Under One Sky* (1994), and *Rain* (1996) are books of poetry. *Yellow Woman and a Beauty of the Spirit* (1996) consists of Silko's essays on contemporary Native American life. *Lullaby*, coauthored with Frank Chin, was dramatically adapted and produced in San Francisco in 1976. *The Delicacy and Strength of Lace*, a collection of letters between Silko and the poet James Wright, edited by Anne Wright, was published in 1985. Silko's work also appeared in *Yellow Woman* (1993), edited by Melody Graulich.

Leslie Marmon Silko (1980) by Per Seyersted is an introduction to her work. *Four American Indian Literary Masters* (1982) by Alan R. Veile is also relevant, as are Louise K. Barnett and James L. Thorson's edited *Leslie Marmon Silko* (1999), Catherine Rainwater's *Dreams of Fiery Stars* (1999), and Rosemary A. King's *Border Influences from the Mexican War to the Present* (2001).

Gary Snyder

Snyder's poems have been published by several different presses, often with duplication of poems. *Riprap*, originally published in 1959, is most easily obtained in *Riprap and Cold Mountain Poems* (1965, 1991). *Myths and Texts* first appeared in 1960. *The Blue Sky* first appeared in 1969 and reappeared in *Six Sections of Mountains and Rivers without End plus One* (1970). Other volumes include *The Back Country* (1968), *Regarding Wave* (1970), *Turtle Island* (1974), *Axe Handles* (1983), *Left Out in the Rain: New Poems 1947–1985* (1986), *No Nature: New and Selected Poems* (1992), and *Danger on Peaks* (2004). In 1996 Snyder published the completion of *Mountains and Rivers without End*. He has also published important prose collections dealing with ecology, such as *Earth House Hold* (1969) and *A Place in Space: Ethics, Aesthetics and Watersheds* (1995). A gathering of Snyder's prose and poetry appears in *The Gary Snyder Reader* (1999). *The Real Work: Interviews and Talks 1964–1979*, edited by William Scott McLean, appeared in 1980.

Helpful critical discussion of Snyder's work can be found in Sherman Paul's *In Search of the Primitive* (1986) and Patrick Murphy's *A Place for Wayfaring: The Poetry and Prose of Gary Snyder* (2000). An interview with Snyder appears in *The Paris Review* (141, 1996).

Cathy Song

Song's poetry collections are *Picture Bride* (1983), *Frameless Windows, Squares of Light* (1988), *School Figures* (1994), and *The Land of Bliss* (2000).

Discussion of Song's work appears in *Conversations and Contestations* (2000), edited by Ruth Hsu and Cynthia Franklin.

John Updike

Updike's novels are *The Poorhouse Fair* (1959), *Rabbit, Run* (1960), *The Centaur* (1963), *Of the Farm* (1965), *Couples* (1968), *Rabbit Redux* (1971), *A Month of Sundays* (1975), *Marry Me* (1976), *The Coup* (1978), *Rabbit Is Rich* (1981), *The Witches of Eastwick* (1984), *Roger's Version* (1986), *S.* (1988), *Rabbit at Rest* (1990), *Memories of the Ford Administration* (1992), *Brazil* (1994), *In the Beauty of the Lilies* (1996), *Toward the End of Time* (1997), *Gertrude and Claudius* (2000), *Seek My Face* (2002), *Villages* (2004), and *Terrorist* (2006). Collections of short fiction are *The Same Door* (1959), *Pigeon Feathers* (1962), *Olinger Stories: A Selection* (1964), *The Music School* (1966), *Bech: A Book* (1970), *Museums and Women* (1972), *Too Far to Go: The Maples Stories* (1979), *Problems* (1979), *Bech Is Back* (1982), *Trust Me* (1987), *The Afterlife* (1994), *Bech at Bay* (1998), and *Licks of Love* (2000). Stories from 1953 to 1975 are presented thematically in *The Early Stories* (2003). Updike's poems are gathered in *Collected Poems 1953–1993* (1993), drawing on the individual volumes *The Carpentered Hen* (1958), *Telephone Poles* (1963), *Midpoint* (1969), *Tossing and Turning* (1977), and *Facing Nature* (1985); *Americana: and Other Poems*

(2001) is newer work. Reviews and literary essays appear in *Assorted Prose* (1965, *Picked-Up Pieces* (1975), *Hugging the Shore* (1983), *Odd Jobs* (1991), and *More Matter* (1999). *Self-Consciousness* (1989) is a memoir, *Just Looking* (1989) and *Still Looking* (2005) are art criticism, and *Golf Dreams* (1996) collects the author's essays on his favorite sport. *Buchanan Dying* (1974) is a play meant for reading rather than for stage production. Updike has authored five books for children: *The Magic Flute* (1962), *The Ring* (1964), *A Child's Calendar* (1965), *Bottom's Dream* (1969), and *A Helpful Alphabet of Friendly Objects* (1995).

Donald J. Greiner's thorough examination of the early canon appears in his *John Updike's Novels* (1984) and *The Other John Updike: Poems/Short Stories/Prose/Plays* (1981). Longer views are taken by James A. Schiff in *John Updike Revisited* (1998) and by William Pritchard in *Updike: America's Man of Letters* (2000). Peter J. Bailey pursues theological matters in *Rabbit (Un)Redeemed: The Drama of Belief in John Updike's Fiction* (2006).

Alice Walker

Walker's novels are *The Third Life of Grange Copeland* (1970), *Meridian* (1976), *The Color Purple* (1982), *The Temple of My Familiar* (1989), *Possessing the Secret of Joy* (1992), *By the Light of My Father's Smile* (1998), and *Now Is the Time to Open Your Heart* (2004). Her short-story collections are *In Love and Trouble* (1973), *You Can't Keep a Good Woman Down* (1981), and *The Way Forward Is with a Broken Heart* (2000). Poetry collections are *Once* (1986), *Five Poems* (1972), *Revolutionary Petunias* (1973), *Good Night, Willie Lee, I'll See You in the Morning* (1969), *Horses Make a Landscape Look More Beautiful* (1984), *Her Blue Body Everything We Know* (1991), *Absolute Trust in the Goodness of the Earth* (2003), and *A Poem Traveled Down My Arm* (2003). Her *Collected Poems* appeared in 2005. Walker's literary essays are collected in *In Search of Our Mothers' Gardens* (1983), *Living by the Word* (1988), and *Anything We Love Can Be Saved* (2000); she has also written *Warrior Marks: Female Genital Mutilation and the Sexual Blinding of Women* (1987, with Pratibha Parmar) and *The Same River Twice: Honoring the Difficult: A Meditation on Life, Spirit, Art, and the Making of the Film* The Color Purple *Ten Years Later* (1996). Her books for children include an illustrated version of *To Hell with Dying* (1988), *Finding the Green Stone* (1991), and a biography, *Langston Hughes, American Poet* (1974).

Evelyn C. White's *Alice Walker: A Life* (2004) is a comprehensive biography. Good samplings of scholarship on Walker fill two volumes: editors Henry Louis Gates Jr. and K. Anthony Appiah's *Alice Walker: Critical Perspectives Past*

and Present (1993) and editor Lillie P. Howard's *Alice Walker and Zora Neale Hurston: The Common Bond* (1993). *Alice Walker* (2000) is Maria Lauret's book-length study.

Eudora Welty

Welty's novels are *The Robber Bridegroom* (1942), *Delta Wedding* (1947), *The Ponder Heart* (1954), *Losing Battles* (1970), and *The Optimist's Daughter* (1972). Her *Collected Stories* (1980) draws from the volumes *A Curtain of Green* (1941), *The Wide Net* (1943), *Music from Spain* (1948), *The Golden Apples* (1949), *The Bride of Innisfallen* (1955), and *Thirteen Stories* (1965). Later volumes are *Moon Lake* (1980) and *Retreat* (1981). *A Flock of Guinea Hens Seen from a Car* (1970) is poetry; among Welty's many volumes of nonfiction prose are *The Eye of the Story: Selected Essays and Reviews* (1978), *One Writer's Beginnings* (1984), and *A Writer's Eye: Collected Book Reviews* (1994).

Ann Waldron published *Eudora: A Writer's Life* in 1998. Susan Marrs completes the picture in *Eudora Welty: A Biography* (2005) and *One Writer's Imagination: The Fiction of Eudora Welty* (2002). Good introductions are available in Gail Mortimer's *Daughter of the Swan: Love and Knowledge in Eudora Welty's Fiction* (1994), *Eudora Welty's Aesthetics of Place* (1994) by Jan Nordby Gretlund, and Ruth D. Weston's *Gothic Traditions and Narrative Techniques in the Fiction of Eudora Welty* (1994). *Eudora Welty: A Bibliography* by Noel Polk appeared in 1994.

Tennessee Williams

Most of Williams's plays are collected in the seven-volume *The Theatre of Tennessee Williams* (1971–81). Some later dramas are available in separate editions; a few others are still to be published. Other writings include a novel, *The Roman Spring of Mrs. Stone* (1950); short stories printed in several volumes and finally brought together in *Collected Stories* (1986), edited by Gore Vidal; a volume of screenplays, *Stopped Rocking* (1984); and poems collected as *In the Winter of Cities* (1964) and *Androgyne, Mon Amour* (1977). *Where I Live: Selected Essays*, edited by Christine R. Day and Bob Woods, appeared in 1978.

Williams's *Memoirs* (1975) is interestingly revelatory but is not a reliable biographical guide; neither is Dotson Rader's *Tennessee: Cry of the Heart* (1985). Donald Spoto's *A Kindness of Strangers: The Life of Tennessee Williams* (1985) is workmanlike; a historically sound treatment is *Tennessee Williams: Everyone Else Is an Audience* (1993) by Ronald Hayman. More theoretically inclined is Nicholas Pagan's *Rethinking Literary Biography: A Postmodern Approach* (1993). A Jungian reading of the plays is provided by Judith J. Thompson in *Tennessee Williams' Plays: Memory, Myth, and Symbol* (1987). Time relationships are explored by

Patricia Schroeder in *The Presence of the Past in Modern American Drama* (1989). Structural patterns are identified by Judith J. Thompson in *Tennessee Williams' Plays: Memory, Myth, and Symbol* (revised 2002). Philip G. Kolin edited *Tennessee Williams: A Guide to Research and Performance* (1998); Matthew C. Rodané prepared *The Cambridge Companion to Tennessee Williams*. George E. Crandell compiled *Tennessee Williams: A Descriptive Bibliography* (1995). *The Selected Letters of Tennessee Williams, Volume I, 1920–1945* (2000) was edited by Albert J. Devlin and Nancy M. Tischler.

James Wright
Above the River (1990) collects the work in Wright's individual volumes: *The Green Wall* (1956), *Saint Judas* (1963), *Shall We Gather at the River* (1968), *Moments of the Italian Summer* (1976), *To a Blossoming Pear Tree* (1977), and *This Journey* (1982). An edition of his *Collected Prose*, edited by Anne Wright, appeared in 1983. Some of Wright's translations from the Spanish and German are available in *Twenty Poems of Georg Trakl* (1963), *Twenty Poems of César Vallejo* (1964), and *Twenty Poems of Pablo Neruda* (with Robert Bly, 1968).

The best critical discussions of Wright's work appear in the essays collected in *The Pure Clear Word: Essays on the Poetry of James Wright* (1982), edited by Dave Smith, and in Laurence Lieberman's *Beyond the Muse of Memory* (1995). *A Wild Perfection: The Selected Letters of James Wright*, edited by Annie Wright and Saundra Rose Maley, appeared in 2005.

PERMISSIONS ACKNOWLEDGMENTS

A55

Eudora Welty: "Petrified Man" from A CURTAIN OF GREEN AND OTHER STORIES, copyright 1939 and renewed 1967 by Eudora Welty. Reprinted by permission of Harcourt Inc.

Edith Wharton: "The Other Two" from THE COLLECTED SHORT STORIES OF EDITH WHARTON, ed. by R. W. B. Lewis (New York: Scribner, 1968). Reprinted by permission of the estate of Edith Wharton and the Watkins/Loomis Agency. "Roman Fever" from ROMAN FEVER AND OTHER STORIES by Edith Wharton. Copyright © 1934 by *Liberty Magazine*; copyright renewed © 1962 by William R. Tyler. Reprinted with the permission of Scribner, an imprint of Simon & Schuster Adult Publishing Group and the estate of Edith Wharton and the Watkins/Loomis Agency.

Tennessee Williams: A STREETCAR NAMED DESIRE, copyright © 1947 by Tennessee Williams. CAUTION: Professionals and amateurs are hereby warned that *A Streetcar Named Desire,* being fully protected under the copyright laws of the United States of America, the British Empire including the Dominion of Canada, and all other countries of the Copyright Union, is subject to royalty. All rights, including professional, amateur, motion picture, recitation, lecturing, public reading, radio and television broadcasting, and the rights of translation into foreign languages are strictly reserved. Particular emphasis is laid on the question of readings, permission for which must be secured from the author's agent, Luis Sanjurjo, c/o International Creative Management, 40 West 57th Street, New York, NY 10019. Inquiries concerning the amateur acting rights of *A Streetcar Named Desire* should be directed to The Dramatists' Play Service, Inc., 440 Park Avenue South, New York, NY, 10016, without whose permission in writing no amateur performance may be given.

William Carlos Williams: From THE COLLECTED POEMS OF WILLIAM CARLOS WILLIAMS 1909–1939, volume I. Copyright © 1938 by New Directions Publishing Corporation and from THE COLLECTED POEMS OF WILLIAM CARLOS WILLIAMS 1939–1962, volume 11. Copyright © 1944, 1962 by William Carlos Williams. Reprinted by permission of New Directions Publishing Corp.

James Wright: "Autumn Begins in Martins Ferry, Ohio," "To the Evening Star: Central Minnesota," and "A Blessing" (Wesleyan University Press, 1971). Copyright © 1971 by James Wright. Reprinted by permission of Wesleyan University Press.

Richard Wright: "The Man Who Was Almost a Man" from EIGHT MEN by Richard Wright. Copyright © 1961 by Richard Wright. Reprinted by permission of John Hawkins & Associates, Inc.

IMAGE ACKNOWLEDGMENTS

Thomas Nast, *The Modern Samson.* Photo: North Wind Picture Archives.

Winslow Homer (1836–1910), *Snap the Whip,* Collection of The Butler Institute of American Art, Youngstown, Ohio. Museum Purchase 1918. Photo: The Bridgeman Art Library.

Rose Bonheur, *Colonel William R. Cody.* Photo: The Granger Collection, NY.

John Singer Sargent, *Mrs. Elliott Fitch Shepard.* Photo: Art Resource, NY.

Jacob Riis, *Children Sleeping in Mulberry Street.* Photo: The Granger Collection, NY.

Edward S. Curtis, *A Feast Day at Acoma.* Photo: Corbis.

Amos Bad Heart Bull, *Woman Watching a Sun Dance,* Reproduced from *A Pictographic History of the Oglala Sioux,* text by Helen H. Blish, permission of the University of Nebraska Press. © 1967 by the University of Nebraska Press. © renewed 1995 by the University of Nebraska Press.

Kills Two, *An Indian Horse Dance* (Nupa Kte) (b. 1869) Private Collection, The Stapleton Collection. Photo: The Bridgeman Art Library.

Mary Colter, *Hopi House,* The Hopi House, Grand Canyon, Arizona. © Private Collection/Peter Newark American Pictures. Photo: The Bridgeman Art Library.

George Bellows, *Both Members of This Club,* 1909, The National Gallery of Art, Washington, DC. The Chester Dale Collection. © 2006 Board of Trustees, National Gallery of Art Washington.

Childe Hassam, *Manhattan's Misty Sunset,* Collection of The Butler Institute of American Art, Youngstown, Ohio.

Marsden Hartley, *Portrait of a German Officer,* The Metropolitan Museum of Art, The Alfred Stieglitz Collection, 1949 (49.70.42) Photographed © 1986 The Metropolitan Museum of Art.

Constantin Brâncuşi (1876–1957), *Golden Bird,* 1919–20, (pedestal ca. 1922), Bronze, stone and wood, h. 85 3/4 in. (with base). Partial gift of The Arts Club of Chicago, restricted gift of various donors, through prior bequest of Arthur Rubloff, through prior restricted gift of William Hartmann, through prior gifts of Mr. and Mrs. Carter H. Harrison, Mr. and Mrs. Arnold H. Maremont through the Kate Maremont Foundation, Woodruff J. Parker, Mrs. Clive Runnells, Mr. and Mrs. Martin A. Ryerson, and various donors, 1990.88 3/4 view. The Art Institute of Chicago. Photography © The Art Institute of Chicago. © 2006 Artists Rights Society (ARS), New York/ADAGP, Paris.

Charles Sheeler (1883–1965), *River Rouge Plant,* 1932, oil on canvas, 20 x 241/8 in. Whitney Museum of Art, NY, Purchase 32.43.

Archibald J. Motley, *Black Belt,* Hampton University Museum, Hampton, Virginia.

Dorothea Lange, *Towards Los Angeles, 1937,* Library of Congress Prints and Photographs.

Georgia O'Keefe, *From the Faraway, Nearby,* The Metropolitan Museum of Art, Alfred Stieglitz Collection, 1959 (59.204.2). Photographed by Malcolm Varon. © 1984 The Metropolitan Museum of Art.

J. Howard Miller, *We Can Do It!* ("Rosie the Riveter"). Photo: The Granger Collection, NY.

Edward Hopper (1882–1967), *Nighthawks,* 1942, Friends of American Art Collection 1942.51 The Art Institute of Chicago. Photography © The Art Institute of Chicago.

Jackson Pollock, *Autumn Rhythm (Number 30),* The Metropolitan Museum of Art, George A. Hearn Fund, 1957(57.92). Photograph © 1998 The Metropolitan Museum of Art. © 2006 The Pollock-Krasner Foundation/Artists Rights Society (ARS), New York.

Frank Lloyd Wright, *Guggenheim Museum.* Photo: Guggenheim/Jeff Albertson/Corbis.

Roy Lichtenstein, *Blam,* Yale University Art Gallery, Gift of Richard Brown Baker, BA 1935 (1995.32.9). © 2007 Estate of Roy Lichtenstein.

Robert Rauschenberg, *Estate.* Photo: Philadelphia Museum of Art/Corbis. © Robert Rauschenberg/Licensed by VAGA, New York, NY.

Andy Warhol, *Campbell's Soup I (Tomato),* 1968, © 2006 Andy Warhol Foundation for the Visual Arts/ARS, New York. Photo: Art Resource, NY.

Earthrise and Lunar Horizon from Apollo 8. Photo: Corbis.

Fritz Scholder, *The American Indian,* 1970, Indian Arts and Crafts Board Collection, Department of the Interior, Smithsonian National Museum of the American Indian, Washington, DC. Photo by Walter Larrimore.

Cindy Sherman, *Untitled,* 1981, Courtesy of the artist and Metro Pictures.

Maya Lin, *Vietnam Veterans Memorial.* Photo: James P. Blair/Corbis.

Faith Ringgold, *Sonny's Quilt,* © 1986 Faith Ringgold.

Peter Morgan, *World Trade Center Burning.* Photo: Reuters/Corbis.

Christo and Jeanne-Claude, *The Gates New York City,* 1979–2005. Photo: Wolfgang Volz. © Christo 2005. Central Park New York USA 14.02.2005.

Index